THE VANISHED SERIES

BOOKS 1-3

B. B. GRIFFITH

Griffith Publishing
Denver

Publication Information

The Vanished Series: Books 1-3

Ebook ISBN: 978-0-9963726-5-7

Paperback ISBN: 978-1-7353058-7-5

Written by B. B. Griffith

Cover design by Damonza

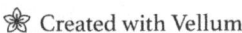 Created with Vellum

FOLLOW THE CROW

B. B. GRIFFITH

To Mom.
For everything.

Strange—is it not?—that of the myriads who
Before us passed the door of Darkness through,
  Not one returns to tell us of the road
Which to discover we must travel too.

- Omar Khayyám
Rubaiyat
(Edward Fitzgerald, trans.)

1

BEN DEJOOLI

I f you drive due west from the city of Albuquerque, New Mexico, for two hours and then cut north before you hit the city of Gallup, you'll see a big stretch of glass—flat nothing dusted with sand, slightly lighter in color than the rest of the Red Rock Country to the north. It's called the Chaco Flats, and it'll go wavy on you in the distance, give you an unsettled feeling in your gut and make your eyes water to look at it if you catch it at mid-day. If you were tempted to turn back at this point, to get yourself back to humanity in Albuquerque or to cut northeast to Santa Fe, you wouldn't be the first. You might even be tempted to keep going west, straight on to what passes for civilization at the shithole Nevada border towns, and if you did, I wouldn't exactly blame you. But if you have enough gas in the tank and want to see one of the greatest feats of social engineering the United States ever attempted, head north through the flats and keep driving until you hit the Chaco Navajo Reservation.

You can't miss it. Drive far enough north and all roads eventually lead to Chaco. Whether or not you'll be happy you came is another matter entirely. I promise you'll find the rez. But that's all I can promise. You'll know it by the dented sign that says Welcome to the Navajo Nation. The dents come from buckshot fired by drunk kids with nothing better to do. For years we kept replacing it only to find it shot up again the next morning. Nothing says "shoot me" like a pristine white tribal sign leering at you along a seven-mile straightaway. I'm a tribal cop, and even I know that. But don't let some shot-up sign scare you away. There's plenty that'll scare you, mind. Just not that.

So say you drive from Albuquerque, and say you got the gas and the morbid curiosity once you hit the flats, and say you head north and pass the buckshot welcome sign, then you'd hit the welcome center. It's nice. Renovated just last year. Come on in and take a seat, and we'll show you a pretty video and an entire wall full of educational pamphlets about what it means to be Navajo, from patent (proud nation of warriors and statesmen) to present (it's complicated). There's a gift shop there too, and directions to our popular stopovers, including the Tribal Museum, Old Town, and the Wapati Casino.

The employees at the welcome center won't tell you this, because it's one of the cushiest jobs in the rez and they don't want to lose it, but we *really* hope that you hit the highlights and bounce out of here, hopefully a few bucks lighter. Maybe with a nice arrowhead collection or a little plastic tomahawk for the kids. Stick to the main road. Because if you don't, you'll start to notice things.

For instance, if you were to turn left off the main road about a quarter mile past the welcome center but before the turnoff to Wapati, you'd see that the cleaner houses and apartments sort of disappear on you. You duck your head to check the car radio then look up, and all of a sudden you're at a row of tract homes. This is the Painted Sand development, and it's not that bad, actually. What's bad is another quarter mile south, where there aren't even homes. Just metal boxes. Like a bunch of semi-trucks dropped their freight containers off the side of the road and left them there to slowly rust out but before that happened about six people moved into each one. This place doesn't have a name. At the station we call it Boxes. You go there with your partner, and you keep your gun hand free.

Today, if you were to drive past Boxes where the concrete turns to packed gravel and the gravel turns to dirt and the dirt turns to mud, you'd find a bootleg bar called Sancho's. And today, if you were stupid enough to walk inside, you'd find me, Ben Dejooli, officer of the Navajo Nation Police, and my partner Danny Ninepoint. And if I saw you, I'd usually tell you to get the hell out for your own good, especially if you were white. But today I've got worse problems, and it looks like you're along for the ride anyway. Maybe you're a stubborn one, like me. Like most of us here at Chaco. Don't get me wrong, we have a lot of nice places on the rez. Places that are beautiful and peaceful and welcoming. It's just that the cops don't go to any of them.

Today, some poor Navajo ended up dead in the storeroom of Sancho's, strewn out on the floor amid empty bottles, the sick still damp on his face, and a needle still stuck in his arm. His rubber tie-off dangles loosely from around his bicep. He's purpled and stiff.

"Found him when I opened up," says Sancho, a ruddy-faced Navajo with a round, bearish head and a banded tail of black hair halfway down his back. I check my watch. Bootleg joints open early in Chaco, and the sun is already high in the sky.

"That was almost two hours ago, Sancho," I say. Danny gives me a quick, wary look from under the flat brim of his hat. Danny thinks I talk too much. Or maybe it's that I just say the wrong things. He's usually right. Danny was an NNPD veteran back when I started, and that's going on six years now. He doesn't like to let me forget it. But when things go south, there is no better Navajo to have your back. He usually finishes things before they start. They call him Ninepoint because he was already as big as a nine-point buck back when you're that age when kids start giving you nicknames. So you can imagine how big he is now. He carries around a scalp knife with a bone hilt and a beaded leather wrist strap. He keeps it where his gun should be and his gun where his stick should be. It's a clear enough warning: mess with Danny Ninepoint and he's going straight for the knife.

Sancho glares at me for a half second longer than a civilian should rightly glare at a cop. And a couple seconds longer than he'd ever glare at Ninepoint.

"We didn't find him 'til later. We called you boys as soon as we stumbled 'cross him." He sounds like he's talking about a raccoon that got stuck in the ducts. I squat down to get a better look at the dead guy. He's puffy and mottled, but I recognize him as one of the old regulars who works the Wapati penny slots. He's even got a Wapati Casino jacket on, muddy and frayed. Probably a comp. You sit for five years pumping coins into a box, and they'll be happy to give you a buffet voucher and a jacket. The jacket looks well- worn. The guy's old. Well-traveled. He doesn't strike me as the type to overdose on heroin like some teenaged tweeker, but I keep that to myself for now.

"You normally let your customers shoot up in your back room, Sancho?" I ask. Sancho doesn't answer me. One of the barflies shifts forward in his chair. He doesn't get up, exactly, but he's letting me know he could get up and over real quick if he wanted to. He's staring at me through the mirror behind the bar and rolling an empty shot glass. Danny sees it too and steps in.

"Now just hold on here. Nobody is saying anyone did anything." He points at the barfly. "And you, big fella, if I see you get up from that seat, I'll paste you to it. You hear me? Mean mug the mirror all you want, but you stay set."

"Sorry, Ninepoint," Sancho says on behalf of the bar, but he's looking right at me. "It's just that your partner's been known to run his mouth, and I like my bar and my life here just fine." His eyes glitter. He knows what he's saying.

See, Sancho doesn't like me. Neither do any of Sancho's regulars. Or most people on the rez, for that matter. Your average Navajo isn't exactly buddy-buddy with Navajo Police, no different from the US cops and the civvies on the outside, but they'll abide a steady presence like Danny. They know Danny. They trust Danny. Also, Danny doesn't give them much of a choice. With me it's different. There are two things a Navajo cop gets known for. The first is killing another

Navajo. That's bad, but people know that sometimes bad things happen. Hell, sometimes they'll even allow that the other guy deserved it. The other is banishing a Navajo. That's worse. Danny never did that. As far as I know, nobody on the Force has done that. Nobody but me.

Technically NNPD can't banish anyone ourselves. Only the tribal court can do that. When you're banished it means you are no longer Navajo. It means you've been thrown from the Navajo Way. Our path is no longer yours to walk. Your soul has been untethered from the souls of the People, and you are now a wanderer. It's a heavy hand. The heaviest. The only time it's been used in Chaco in recent memory was in a case I helped build against Joseph Flatwood. A case that didn't make me any friends, and that took away the best friend I had.

This isn't the first time someone's jabbed me about the banishment like this. It won't be the last. Still, it gets to me. It's not like I don't think about it every day already. That case ripped my family apart. It ripped my life apart. Flatwood and I ran together. He was my best friend right up until the second I decided to banish him. Now he's dead to me, but sometimes, when I dream about the old days, we're still raising hell together.

I know I should back down from Sancho, but I can't. I've never been very good at letting things be. "I cut Joey Flatwood loose, and he and I were friends. Imagine what I'd do to a shitbreath old pusher like you."

"Now Ben—" Danny says, but stops when the big fella and the man to his left, both of them built like fire-hydrants, get up from their seats. We're trained to defuse situations, but I never liked Sancho, and I never liked his bar. And right now, I just don't feel like defusing.

"You're what's wrong with this rez, Sancho," I say. "If it was up to me I'd dump you and your drunk fuck friends out in the middle of the flats then come back here and burn this place to the ground."

When I get in Sancho's face he backs down, even though he's a good foot taller than me. He wasn't lying when he said he cared about his business, such as it is. But the big fella and his friend don't back down. They're the type to get liquored up at ten in the morning hoping for something like this to go down. The type who think Navajo cops aren't real cops. The type who think Indians shouldn't police other Indians. There are a lot of people that think like these two, and for them, this is payday.

The quiet one decks me first. I shoulda known. It's always the quiet one. To my credit, I do stay on my feet. I'm small, but I'm wiry. I can bend. He damn near knocks me to the floor, but I pop back up like a toy and jack him once in the throat while I reach for my stick. He clutches his neck, and I flip my baton from its holster. Sancho is screaming something in Navajo that I know I should understand, but everything starts to spin and I don't recognize this type of spin. I've been hit plenty of times, even knocked out a time or two, and I know that spin. That's a suck-the-world-out-from-under-you spin where one second you're on your feet and the next you're on your face. This time it's sort of like when you stand up too fast, but worse. Like if you stood up too fast with a hangover and a sack of sand around your neck. There's a high-pitched ringing in my head. It's so loud I feel like it's coming from my face where he popped me. In my daze I think that maybe if I cover my face it'll mute the sound, so I do. I almost fall over, but I steady myself on a bar stool.

Under normal circumstances I'd probably be in for an ass kicking, hitching up like that in the middle of a fight like I need a tap out and a glass of water, but I've got Danny Ninepoint with me. By the time I shake the spins from my head, Joe and his quiet, sucker-punching friend are sprawled out on the floor, and Danny is pulsing one fist like it's just warming up and pulling his long black hair back around with the other.

"You alright, Dejooli?" he asks, and I can tell he's none too happy with me either.

"Yeah, just...wasn't expecting that."

"Maybe you should have," he says, and it's a reprimand and it stings, still, even after six years. But the good thing about Danny is that's where it ends. I try to straighten up, but the buzzing lingers and Danny must see it on my face.

"Watch the door," he says. "I'll write all this up."

I nod, grateful for some air. I hadn't noticed it before, but Sancho's smells like sulfur. Which is fitting, I suppose.

Outside I wave away a few of the rig monkeys fresh off the night shift looking for a drink, and they grumble but leave all the same and wait in the shadows for us to finish up. For some reason the smell is slow in going away, and maybe it's the adrenaline, or the knock to the head, but everything around me is intensely bright. The ruts in the dirt are sharp and clean, the rust on the cars looks like rich mud. The dirt-spackled yellow of the tenement houses seems saturated, almost like it's glowing. When the fall sun breaks from the clouds, I can barely feel the heat it gives, but it flashes like a bomb of light. I cover my eyes and I turn away until it's cloudy again. When I turn back, a crow sits on top of our squad car, on the light array, and it's staring right at me.

The Navajo have a rhyme and reason for every living thing under the sun, and I'm going to be honest with you, I forget most of them. And if you were to point out a crow on any given day and ask me what it *means* I'd look at you like you're a lunatic. But this crow is different. This thing is massive, almost as tall as the driver's side window, and the flashing hazard lights don't faze it at all. Its eyes glisten black, then yellow, black then yellow, in time with the lights, and as it shifts in the light I see a peculiar coloring, almost like it's striped in dark red underneath the ink black of its outer feathers. I realize I'm expecting it to do something, like talk to me, or point the way to an ancient secret with its bony beak. Instead it takes a huge shit on the squad car, then squawks once and flies away just as Danny walks out of the door. He walks out alone. The fire behind his eyes is calmed. His face is wide and smooth and unknowable once more. Sort of like the Chaco flats.

"Can't help but notice you didn't arrest anyone," I say, resisting the urge to massage my temples.

"If we arrested every drunk Navajo we came across we'd have paperwork out the ass. You know this."

"How about every drunk Navajo who assaults a cop? How 'bout that, Danny? In a sane world that guy is in jail."

Danny Ninepoint gives me that flat gaze that says I still don't understand. I'm not sure how I still can't understand after six years, but I somehow don't. I'm trying, but I keep not understanding.

"Sancho's run that bootleg shack for almost twenty years now."

"So?"

"So you tell me what happens to guys like the big fella and all his drunk friends when they get their stipends and show up at Sancho's only to find we've shut it down because some boozebag swung at a cop. I booked the big guy once before on a disturbance call because he was hopped up on paint thinner. I let him out of the tank the next morning, and he asks for a ride right here. These are the type of guys who ask cops for rides to bars, Ben. I'd rather they be Sancho's problem."

I see his point, but I'm not willing to concede it yet. "And the dead man? We just gonna let that one slide too?"

Danny looks away, and for a split second I think he's gonna say yes. But then he shakes his head.

"Of course not. I reported him to IHS. They'll give us the autopsy. I know what you're thinking, but Sancho isn't a pusher. He's an asshole, but he's not a pusher. He's not lying when he says he wants to keep his business. He's not stupid. This place is his life."

I know Danny doesn't mean to bring up Flatwood. Danny doesn't hold it over me like the rest of the rez. It was Danny who told me to stick to my guns in the whole mess, to see it through, to take the stand against Joey. But it still stings.

"Look, the point is this is just what it looks like. That old gambler probably lost a bit too much at Wapati, went to a place he knows, Sancho or one of these guys forgot to check the back, and he settled in for one last kick. That's it. No need to get anybody arrested."

I still don't feel right about the whole thing, but my head is killing me and the place smells like a million matches, so I nod. Danny claps me on the back with his bowl of a hand. In the car, the radio buzzes from dispatch, crackles a code, and waits for a response.

"C'mon, we got shit to do," Danny says.

On the drive out I look for the crow. I see a lot of crows, but I don't see the one from before. I think I'd recognize that one if I saw it again, even at a glance.

2

BEN DEJOOLI

The rest of the day I'm thinking about Sancho's and that dead gambler. Danny and I go on a few more calls after lunch—routine stuff, a minor wreck outside of Wapati between an uninsured beater and some poor family in a minivan who cut through Chaco on their way to Farmington up north. We drove down along the floodplain to make sure it was all clear, meaning no tweekers or squatters. Sometimes people think the rains are done by this time in the fall, but we usually get one or two more big ones before the end of October, and they'll sweep that entire flood channel clean in a second. Dirt, debris, animals, people, all of it.

The whole time we're making rounds I want to bring up Sancho's, but I know Danny is done with it. He's old school. After he files a thing away in his mind, it's over. He's also seen a lot more dead Navajo than me. But it's more than just the OD. It's the whole scene back there. It was bad all around. The drunk and the dead and the smell of burning. Nobody should spend their last seconds on this earth holed up on the floor of Sancho's back room. And then there was the crow. And how I almost pitched over. On my drive home after our shift, some guy catches me spacing out at a stoplight and honks. I'm thinking about how palsied the gambler looked, like he was clawing at the needle with his last breath, and how sad it was that all the guy had to his name was a Wapati jacket, dull gold and dirty. Nothing at all in his pockets, no rings, no necklaces. Not even a shitty bead bracelet. Nothing.

I can feel my eye swelling up where the quiet one sucker-punched me. That'll be a fun little reminder of how I punked out when it counted, staring at me in the mirror for a few weeks. This is one of those days you should try to put behind you as soon as you clock out, but it just won't leave me.

The way I've been talking about the run-down tenements and shacks on the fringe of Chaco, you may think that where I live is a world away. You'd be wrong. My home is one half of a split duplex a quarter mile north of the police station. I live there with my father and my grandmother, which is pretty standard around here. People live with their families under one roof their entire lives. Believe it or not, with just the three of us there's a lot of space. We each have our own room, and there's a small kitchen and a yard out back that we share with the neighbors. Just one bathroom, but by now we all know the routine and nobody bumps into anybody else. In fact, it's down-right spacious considering that when we first moved in, back before I joined NNPD, there were five of us. Back then it was my sister Ana and me in my room, and Mom and Dad in theirs, and my grand-mother content in the small storage room off of the kitchen. But then I lost my sister, and because I lost my sister I lost my mom, although in a different way. She still stops by every now and then, but for the most part she's long gone. She lives in a studio apartment in Albu-querque now and has a job as a caretaker there. You could say that she banished herself.

It's late by now, and since the night quickens even earlier in the fall, it's nearly full on dark by the time I get home. But it's a false dark. You can't trust the early dark of fall. You want to think the day is over, but it's not.

As soon as I get in, I get a beer from the icebox. I'm not even going to try to hide it. Gam would know anyway, because she always knows. Dad's different. I could eat dinner with an icepack plastered to my face and my father wouldn't notice until it was brought to his attention.

I'm sitting in the kitchen eating a reheated mole stew and holding a cold beer to my puffy eye when Gam comes in. She mostly cooks and knits these days, and the kitchen is her domain. She seems to know any time anyone crosses the small threshold she's carved out for herself there. When she sees me with the beer pressed to my face, she pauses. Her face darkens, then she sees that I'm eating lukewarm mole on rice and takes it from me, shooing me out of her space. She gestures for me to sit at the small table across from the refrigerator while she puts the stew on the stove top and takes a smoked chicken breast from the refrigerator. She shreds the breast with two forks while the sauce heats and then adds the chicken. All the while, she's quiet, waiting for me to talk, but I don't feel like talking, not least of all because she makes me do it in Navajo, and despite her best efforts, my Navajo has always sucked. She refuses to speak English. I have a hunch that she's fluent, but if you don't speak Navajo to her, she won't answer you. She stirs the stew and stares at me with that benign, blank expression her generation has. The look that says they've got all the time in the world to sit right there waiting for you. She's small —the top half of her body barely clears the counter—and her long black hair has gone entirely grey, but that look is still strong.

I sigh and set the can down, then I crack it open and take a big swig.

"*Bad day at work,*" I say, in Navajo. She nods and plates the stew and sets it in front of me.

"*Did you catch them?*" she asks. I don't know how to explain the Sancho's situation in English, much less in Navajo, so I just grunt and give a weak nod. She watches me placidly, and I know she can see right through me, but just then Dad comes home and she stands again, ready to dish up another plate.

"*I'm going to bed,*" he says in Navajo, waving her off. He slurs just a bit, and I can see Gam's slight frown.

"*You should eat dinner,*" Gam shouts.

"*I'm not hungry right now,*" he says quietly, and softly closes the door behind him. Gam covers the stew and sets it back in the refrigerator. Dad will eat it later tonight when he pads around the house, usually from one in the morning to three or four. He's up every night at the witching hours. Has been ever since Ana disappeared. Most of the time he just watches television, but every now and then I catch him out back where Ana used to play. There's a pile of rocks in a little sandbox there that she loved to stack and arrange. Mostly he just sits and stares at that, too, like it was the television, although a couple times I've seen him talking to it like it's a shrine of some sort and not a six-year-old pile of rocks. He looks hunched these days, and since he's as short as I am it doesn't do him any favors. He's been drinking more, too. Gam and I know it, even though we haven't said anything yet. He only works part time at the hardware store south of the welcome center, but he's gone the whole work day. He's not the type to go to Sancho's, but he's probably at some place just a step up. Which isn't saying much.

Gam looks down at the ground and says everything without speaking a word. Oren Dejooli is her son, and she is embarrassed by him. She never forgave my mother for leaving him and still refuses to be in the same room with her on the rare occasions she comes through the reservation. Gam's generation took everything on the cheek and kept plodding, especially as it concerned their husbands. The idea of leaving everything and running away to the city like Mom did is foreign to her, but more and more I think she's beginning to understand how strange Dad has become.

I made a conscious decision not to dwell on Ana. Every day I tell myself to file it away. Do like Ninepoint does. You can see how well that's worked. Like talking to Gam in English. You can say whatever you want, but you're not gonna get any results. Over the six years since she went missing her name has become an all-encompassing thing that hangs over the house and follows us around every day. Our lives have been shattered and then rearranged into pre-Ana and post-Ana. The line that separates them is Ana, too. She's everywhere you look around here, but nowhere to be found.

I want to keep Gam around. The thought of her shuffling back into her room to pick up her knitting strikes me as unbearably sad just now.

"*You know Sancho's?*" I ask her. She frowns and makes a spitting motion. She knows it all right. Gam knows just about everywhere on the rez and just about everyone. And their parents. She speaks of people in terms of 'the kid of so-and-so," or, more likely, "the no-good kid of so-and-so."

"*A guy died there last night. An old Navajo. He was always at Wapati, or walking along the roads by Wapati in a gold jacket. He was a...*" I struggle to find the words, but Gam finds them for me.

"*Alone,*" she says, and a brief flash of genuine sadness bows her face. It throws me for a second. She says something in Navajo that I don't catch completely, but I think it's an old prayer. Something about a last visit and the end of a journey.

"*You knew him?*" I ask. Already she's composed herself again, and she waves her bony hand dismissively.

"*He was old, like me. Old people know each other in small towns. That's all. How did he die?*"

"Drugs," I say, in English. I don't know the Navajo word for drugs. I'm not sure there is a Navajo word for drugs. Gam pauses in her stirring of the pot. She furrows her brow, then shakes her head.

"*No,*" she says, simply.

"No?" I ask, incredulous. Gam shakes her head once, sharply. I laugh. I can't help it. I'd spent this whole day trying to convince myself that there was nothing wrong with an old timer overdosing in the backroom at Sancho's, and I'd basically done it, too, by the time I walked in the house, so it annoys me that she throws open that door in my mind again. Especially when there's nothing I can do about it. My laugh sounds harsh and hollow. Gam frowns at me.

"I guess you're pretty sure of that," I say in English, not expecting a response, not wanting one.

"*Die at Sancho's?*" she says, stirring the pot again. "*No. Not him.*"

"Oh yeah?" I ask, fully switched to English now. "And where was he 'supposed' to die, then?"

Gam watches me calmly.

"Where is a man supposed to die?" I ask.

"At home."

"He lived out of his camper, Gam. He had no home."

Gam shakes her small, round head in soft rebuke. Her bun flops.

"The gambler's home is the Arroyo," she says.

The Arroyo is just like it's advertised. It's a wash at the far end of the floodplain, due south of where Danny and I swept through today. It's also the prime car camping spot on the reservation. If you live out of your car in this country, there's a good chance you'll get robbed if you're on your own. A sleeping man in a car is a prime target. Lock your doors and they'll smash your windows. If the tweekers and the drunks see something valuable inside, it doesn't matter if you're in it or not. If you're a camper, it's best to stick together. 'Course, it's best not to sleep in your car at all, but for most of these folks that's not a choice, so they park in a half-circle around the top of the Arroyo. It's gotten to the point where it's become a neighborhood in its own right.

Danny said when he first started that Sani, the chief of police, wanted them gone. Said they were unsightly, and ramshackle neighborhoods often come with ramshackle "businesses," most of which aren't remotely legal. When an old camper blew up and took a pair of Navajo with it, two more casualties of the meth businesses, Sani told Danny and his partner at the time to clear them all out. The two of them blew into the Arroyo like a whirlwind and screamed and thumped cars (and a few people) with their sticks. The cars left for a day and then pulled back in the next night. That's the thing about neighborhoods on wheels. They're tough to catch.

"The Arroyo is nobody's home," I tell Gam.

"The Arroyo," she says again, nodding. End of discussion. She picks up her bowl of stew, goes to her corner chair and sets it carefully down on a pull-out tray. She takes a bite, then she picks up her knitting. It's the beginning of a blanket, and it's gonna be a beautiful one, too. As I watch her, I see her hands shaking, and not for the first time I wonder if that blanket is ever going to get finished.

That night I don't sleep. I sort of fade in and out of consciousness, but I wouldn't call it sleeping. When I'm alone in my bed I realize that the ringing in my head that started at Sancho's never really left me. It was perched behind my forehead and murmuring to me the whole time; it just took complete quiet to notice. Every time I start to drift, the sulfur smell comes back to me and I blink myself awake, scrunching my nose. My eye feels tight and puffy, and my head throbs in time with my heartbeat. I already know I'm getting the brawler's wink.

I'm not sure exactly what makes me shoot out of bed, but some time near midnight I come around and find I'm already standing by the window, panting, with my heart in my throat. After my blood slows and my eyes adjust, I see my dad standing outside in the moonlight, staring at Ana's shrine. There's also a skittering on the roof. My first thought is it's a squirrel my dad somehow disturbed on his nightly excursions about the house, but on second listen this thing sounds too big. There's a sharp tap, and then I hear the explosive fluttering of wings. Big wings. Crow wings. I look up and out the window and strain my eyes to scan the sky, but the moon has thrown everything above ground into inky black relief. It's as if the bird, or whatever it is, is absorbed into the fabric of the night as soon as it leaves the roof. I turn back to Dad. He doesn't seem to notice anything but the rocks in front of him.

I sit back down on the bed, take some deep breaths, and listen hard for the ringing. I think it's gone, which is a relief, but in its place is a strange quiet. And the quiet is made worse by the fact that my dad is in the back yard sitting on the dry grass and staring at a cairn my sister made six years ago like it's a totem pole rooted to the secrets of her vanishing. I remember when Ana built that thing. She attached no significance to it. She was messing around in the back yard, digging up weeds looking for "fossils." She plopped some rocks on top of each other on her way to the next door of her imagination, the way nine-year-old girls do. Dad has made them far heavier than they were ever meant to be. After another fifteen minutes of listening to this silence, I give up, throw on an undershirt, and go downstairs. I move by the light of the muted television, not wanting to wake Gam, and I sit at the table again, drink an entire glass of water, and stare at my father, trying to make sense of him. The stew pot is empty and meticulously washed. Dad is a fastidious man. He doesn't want to disturb anyone with what he's dealing with at midnight on the back lawn. He doesn't want to disturb us with Ana. He knows each of us has our own Ana to deal with, and he's a hardline Navajo in that. His problems are his own.

Gam and I know he goes outside like this. Gam thinks it's far more normal than I do, and she thinks the fact that I find this type of ritualistic meditation strange is proof of a creeping white influence. Usually I just let him alone with his grief. But tonight I'm not getting back to sleep, I already know it, so I slide open the door and step outside. The porch light catches my motion and flicks on, and Dad is startled. He jumps up and backs away from the light. He doesn't meet my eye.

"The rocks saying anything to you tonight?" I ask.

I think my dad was expecting some sort of scolding, so when he hears the soft tone of my voice, he steps forward and looks up at me.

"Stranger things have happened," he says. "But no. They are quiet."

"Rocks can't tell you where Ana is," I say, and then, because I think the day still has its fingers in me, and because somewhere I feel that fucking crow still watching me, I say, "Flatwood might have been able to, but he's gone now. Is that why you're out here? Is it because of me? Because I got rid of him? Because he was never going to help us, Dad. Whatever he knew he took with him when he was banished."

Dad seems to snap out of his fog, and he shakes his head, his face imploring. "Is that what you think? That I'm out here blaming you?"

"The thought has crossed my mind, yeah. Everyone else blames me for Flatwood. And I've had a shitty day. Another day in which people who have no idea what happened that night somehow hate me for agreeing to testify against the guy who abducted my sister. Like I'm the bad guy."

Dad steps forward into the full flush of the floodlight, and I can see just how pitted and hollow his eyes are. "Not me, Ben. Never me. Do you understand me?" His eyes still have a touch of liquor to them.

He grabs me by the shoulders for a moment, and I'm struck by how much we look alike. He has the same sharp features that I do and the same softly sloping eyes. It's just that he looks hollowed out, and he's shrinking. It's hard to watch. Some part of me thinks a son should never grow taller than his father.

Dad turns his head back to the cairn and drops his hands from my shoulders. "I was the one who left him alone with her. I was the one who stepped out for a quick drink. I was the one who thought I needed a drink because she'd been in the hospital for nearly a month and it was draining on me. I was the one who dropped my guard."

"Dad—"

"—and I was her father, Ben. You did your duty. In front of the court and the elders, you stood like a man. All you did was tell them the truth. I was the one who failed her."

"Nobody failed anybody, Dad. Joey was practically a member of the family. Things that bad don't happen because you step out for a drink. Things that bad happen whether you step out or not."

Dad walks back to the cairn and moves out of the way so the light washes over it. He cocks his head at it like an old dog.

"I think I see her, sometimes," he says.

"So do I. Every day."

"But only when I watch a thing until my eyes stop watching. Only when I drift. That's why I come out here. Because I can drift."

I understand where he's coming from, but I also think the whisky I can still smell on his breath might be helping with his "drifting." It's not that I'm not sympathetic. It's just that if I kept hanging on to Ana the way he does, I'd have driven myself insane by now. Sometimes I wonder if that's not the route Dad's heading down, and sometimes I wonder if he's not doing it on purpose.

"Are you gonna come inside?" I ask.

"No, you go in. This is my time."

So I leave him. But I don't go back to bed either. I spend the next hour listening for a bird on my roof, and at one in the morning I feel more awake and restless than I did outside talking to Dad. Whenever I don't know exactly what's bothering me, I tackle the first thing that I think of, and the first thing I can think of is Gam saying the word *Arroyo* like it was the answer to everything.

I get up, splash some water on my face, throw on another layer of deodorant, and button myself back into my uniform. I strap on my belt and holster my gun and grab my keys and my flat-brimmed hat. Danny Ninepoint would hate me going to the Arroyo alone, but Danny would also hate me waking his ass up at the birth of the morning to chase after a dead man he was over and done with the second we left the bar. So I don't call him.

The road to the Arroyo is winding and barren. It's past Main Street, and past the tenements, and past the fringe, and past the stretch of desert beyond. After a good dust storm, the tracks can sometimes be hard to follow, but I've been here more times than I can count, and I know my way. It's only when I get into the velvet black of the desert at night—when the headlights of my old truck get swallowed up five feet in front of me—that a small part of me wonders if this was a smart thing to do at all, much less alone. And the buzzing begins again. But it's not so bad, and I've come this far already, and I don't think I can stand turning around and finding my dad still staring at a pile of rocks, so I kick into low gear and creep my way out into the desert.

The Arroyo appears in front of me like a shelf on the ocean floor. The drop-off beyond the campers that ring the ledge is steep, and at this hour looks a shade darker than black. In the daylight it's a trash pit, but right now it seems like a swirling door to the worst Chaco has to offer. Almost all of the cars sit silent and cold like boulders, but a handful are lit from within, and I can see shapes shifting about like genies in lamps. Danny and I have been here in the dead hours before. Usually this group knows enough to let a patrolling cop be, but then again, I thought that about the men at Sancho's up until today too.

Already I see blinking eyes peeking out of makeshift curtains like coyotes caught in my headlights. A van nearby starts its engine. That's to warn those still awake that a cop is here. In the daytime they aren't so subtle. It's three honks. Nice that they're considerate to the sleeping vagrants, I suppose.

I'm looking for a memorial of some sort. If the gambler was really a part of the Arroyo, they'll know he's dead by now and will have set up something to mark his passing. They're addicts and drunks here for the most part, but they are a tight community and they watch their own. It's been that way since Gam's time. The Navajo don't like death. Old school Navajo, like many of the folks at the Arroyo, still think death is a thing that's catching, so they'll have cleaned and purified his camping spot and gathered anything he may have left about for burial. It takes me nearly a full pass before I find it.

In the darkness it just looks like an empty spot between camps, but it stands out like a lost tooth and I slow down. When my headlights glint off the small pile in the center of the space, I know I've found the right place. I throw my truck into park and check the perimeter. There's a rusted out camper to the right that's as dark as a cellar closet. To my left is a flatbed truck with a tarp stretched over it. A one man job. But that one man is out in the night leaning against his truck and smoking a cigarette. The cherry burns like a demon's eye in the blackness. He stares me down as I hop out. I can't tell if he's being surly or if he's bored. Around here it's most likely both.

I close the door to my truck gently, keeping one eye on the smoker. He's dressed in a faded Cleveland Indians baseball jersey and tear-off gym slacks, and he's swimming in them. He's not wearing shoes, and his head lolls a bit toward the ground, like he's watching me out of the top of his eyes.

"Officer," he says. He doesn't sound condescending, but he doesn't sound happy to see me, either. "Funny seeing your kind at this hour."

Guys like this don't worry me. What worries me is if he causes a scene and brings the whole shithole camp down on me. I'm hoping he knows the drill and doesn't want anything more than a late night smoke.

"A man showed up dead today," I say. "He was an Arroyo man. In fact, unless I'm way off, I'd say he lived right here. People knew him as the gambler."

The smoker is silent, but that tells me as much as I need to know. "You're holding vigil," I say.

"I am. Not that it would matter to an apple like you."

The Navajo who live at the Arroyo are probably the worst off of any of us, but they're fierce nationalists. You get some of the most hardline Navajos living out of vans on the edge of the desert out here, and they stick to the old ways. They respect the purification periods and observe the holy days and practice the chant ways, and they look down on anyone who doesn't and still calls themselves a Navajo. I try not to take it personally when he calls me an apple. I think he'd call any Indian who didn't live hand-to-mouth right next to him an apple. It means red on the outside, white on the inside.

"His name was Oka Chalk," he says. "He'd been here longer than any of us. He only became the gambler because of fuckers like you and the shit you bring into our land."

A lot of people lump NNPD in with tribal politics and the dealings of the council and the elders. Never mind that we have nothing to do with Wapati or the finances of this rez. We're just tasked with trying to keep it together.

"Easy," I say. "I'm just trying to figure out what happened to the man.""Seems clear. He died," says the smoker, staring blackly at me.

"Yeah, I got that." I stare right back at him. "Thing is, what's a veteran Arroyo man doing dying like a common smackhead?"

This throws him. His glower cracks just a bit. "Smack?" he asks.

"Yeah. Smack. The gamb...Oka Chalk died in his own puke propped against the backroom of a dive bar near the fringe. So I'ma ask you something, seeing as you're on vigil and all and that probably means you and him were friends. Does that sound like the guy you knew?"

The smoker takes a big drag, and it washes over his head in the white of the moon.

"Smack?" he asks again, and I know he's speaking to himself. And I already know that's not how the gambler died. I also know I'll never get a straight answer from this guy. They have a code around here, and it doesn't include working with "apple" cops like me. Instead, I take a look at Chalk's camp site.

It looks like the gambler lived his life out in a fifteen-foot square of dirt where he parked his car. I look out beyond the Arroyo drop-off and try to give the dead man the benefit of the doubt. I say to myself that there was probably some beauty here, in the unfiltered sunsets and the endless plains, but I can't sell it to myself. Right now this patch of dirt reminds me a lot of the prison cells we have down at the station. And at least there you have plumbing.

There are tokens in the center of his spot, left by the Arroyo community. Herbs and flowers mostly, and piñon and juniper branches. Things meant to purify the space. There are also other gifts with no Navajo significance at all. A carved wooden whistle and a tattered stuffed rabbit. There are folded notes, as well, and a collection of coins. The tokens form a big pile, about a foot high, in the dead center of the spot. I get the feeling that the gambler was well liked here. I turn back to the smoker with a new appreciation. I see now that the man looks bereaved. And here I was about to come out swinging. I decide to come clean to the guy.

"Look. Something about this doesn't sit well with me. About this whole thing. I don't know what yet, but I'm trying to figure it out. All I know is he shouldn't have died that way."

The smoker watches me for a good fifteen seconds in silence. Then he speaks.

"He used to give me a spare can of beer every now and then. That's all. But around here, that's enough. I said I'd hold vigil because I think he was a man worth it. I don't know nothing about him more than that."

I nod. Sounds about right. Sounds like the end of a poorly placed hunch.

"But I do know this," the smoker says, and it sounds like he was debating telling me this thing, this one thing, from the second I said I was out here trying to place the gambler on the right side of the books. "He started this token pile," the smoker says.

This throws me.

"What? You mean he knew he was gonna die?"

"Don't know nothin' bout that. Just know the last time I saw him, after he pulled out of his spot in that van of his, he got out, walked back over here, and set down the first token. Then he left."

I cross my arms and turn to the token pile. I walk over to it and kneel down. I gently move pieces of the pile, and the smoker doesn't seem to mind, so I go digging. I set each piece in a row to the left of the pile, flowers, beaded jewelry, bits of pounded leather, coins, braided strips of hair, until I get to the very bottom, and there I find a totem.

A totem is a powerful thing for an Indian, especially an old-timer, for whom these things generally mean more than for your average young buck. The Navajo believe that a person and an animal can be connected and that connection is unique and powerful. We don't carve any totem poles or anything like that, but if a Navajo believes strongly enough that they are connected to an animal, sometimes they carve it out of rock or stone and make it into a totem that they keep on them, usually in a pouch by their side. Different animals mean different things, but the connection is always personal and symbolic. I feel like I used to see more totem pouches on people when I was young. I even thought of making a totem myself when I was a kid. I wanted a bear. The bear is popular because it stands for power and courage and great strength, all things a little boy wants. The problem is, you don't choose your animal. Your animal chooses you. I've never seen a bear in my life, and I don't much care to, and I'll be the first to tell you I don't exactly have "great strength," so there went that.

If a Navajo has a totem, he never parts from it, which makes it strange that the gambler would leave his behind. And the gambler's totem is a crow. A solid turquoise crow, about the size of a walnut, and beautifully detailed. The marbling of the turquoise makes it look like it's in mid-flight even as it sits in the dirt in front of me.

The crow is a strange animal in Navajo lore. It's not that the crow has negative connotations or anything, but it's not exactly the type of animal you see carved into totems. In fact, I'd never seen a crow totem in my life. The crow stands for spiritual strength, but it's also a symbol of change. In Navajo stories, the crow is often tricky, and sometimes he's actually a shape-shifter. You never quite know where he's coming from. And if we count the tapping on the roof, which I do, this is the third encounter with our tricky friend I've had in the past twenty-four hours. I'm not exactly a spiritual man, but I'm not blind, either. I look up at the smoker, who watches me calmly. The buzzing in my head gets louder.

"It's a crow," I say, lamely. He nods.

"Don't touch it," he says, but he doesn't need to worry. You don't touch another man's totem. It's wrong. Even I know that.

I carefully bury it once more and then stand, too quickly. I stagger for a few steps until I right myself on my truck. The smoker is still watching me, and an image of him peering, cigarette limp in his mouth, spins around my head. The smell is back again, but it's stronger, almost like plastic burning. I gag with the intensity of it.

The smoker says something to me, but I'm holding on to my truck for dear life and I'm not listening anyway because all of a sudden I see thousands of crows and I realize that the night sky has been a patchwork of oil-black feathers all along. They seem to wave gently like heat coming up from tar on the road. The leather and bones and coins in the pile seem to dance, like the crow totem is trying to work its way out. I look up at the smoker to see what he thinks of all this, and he's still trying to talk to me. His brow is furrowed, but his words sound like gibberish. I have an irrational urge to grab the crow and steal it for my own, an abhorrent thing for a Navajo to do to another Navajo, especially one who has just left this world, but right at this moment it doesn't seem strange at all. It seems right. My vision is constricting, but still the crow calls to me, like light shining through the holes in a black button.

And in a brief moment of clarity I realize I'm going to pass out, and this is about the last place in the world a guy should pass out, especially a cop. I try to get into my truck, but my body is floating away from me bit by bit. I paw at the com on my shoulder, click it on, and mutter into it.

"Danny. Danny, I'm at the Arroyo. Danny, I need..." What do I need? Whatever is coming from my mouth is distant and muffled and certainly doesn't sound like my voice. I drop my hand from the com. The white noise that comes back from it floods over me, and I drop to the ground. My head bounces off the runner of my truck, but I'm too far gone to care.

Then everything is black.

3

CAROLINE ADAMS

I always get slammed with work at the end of a night shift. Like, half an hour before I'm supposed to go home. And it takes all of the Nurse-Fu I've accumulated over the past two years working here not to rip my hair out. It's not even the late admission itself, or that it's an ER overflow. We get overflow admissions all the time here on the oncology floor. Albuquerque General is constantly overflowing, and it's usually the same people spilling in and out. No, what gets to me most is the cutesy way my nurse manager says it: *Car-o-line, we got one more for ya!* As if she was out looking for four leaf clovers on my behalf. I try very hard not to express disappointment. I know better than that. I feel like she watches me for it. Mary Ellen is the kind of manager who swears by the power of a positive attitude even as she pisses everyone off. Or maybe it's just me. Although I don't think so, because I've seen other nurses scowl after her, some doctors, too, although they're doctors and they can get away with it. I tried to bring it up once in the break room, but I didn't have the words to explain what bothers me so much, and I felt like the other girls there were waiting expectantly for some ammo to use against me. So I talked about how I felt like I'd gained ten pounds since starting night shift, which set off a round of the usual *Oh my God I know*s and brought us back to safe ground. Sometimes I don't know about this floor. For nurses, a lot of my co-workers can be quite uncaring. Exhibit A is that I have no friends here. But again, maybe that's just me.

If our ER gets a late-night rush, it's usually because of the Navajo. I'm not being racist here or anything—nurses don't have time to be racist. It's just a fact. And if we get an overflow case and it's a Navajo, they usually give it to me. Maybe they think I'm better with Navajo patients because I spend one day a week working at the Chaco Health Center inside Chaco Rez and should therefore have some sort of connection with the Navajo. I have no such thing. I've tried, but the Navajo are a close people. Or maybe I'm a bad nurse. I waste a lot of time obsessing over things like this, in case you can't tell. And since we're being honest, I think I might as well tell you that the reason I work one day a week at CHC is because it's a condition of the government grant that put me through nursing school. I find it rewarding, don't get me wrong, but it's not like I came out of school on some crusade to help the Navajo. That's just what ended up happening.

When Mary Ellen tells me about the new admission, I'm already taking care of one Navajo who happens to be detoxing from alcohol, and it's not going well for either of us. Alcohol withdrawal is a mess. Detoxing from opiates or stimulants can be bad, but going cold turkey won't kill a drug addict. Detoxing from alcohol can kill you, so we have this step-down system that tapers the patient over a long period of time in which they tend to threaten your life and spit in your face.

I don't blame patients for what they say when they're detoxing. I know they're not in their right minds. I try not to take it personally when grizzled old men with purple noses call me a cunt or tell me I'm a waste of time and to get the fucking doctor. I'm getting better about it, but for a while I stayed up late wondering if I *was* a waste of time. Or, more specifically, If I'd wasted my time becoming a nurse. Those were early jitters. I hardly have those any more. Still, when you have to have the CNAs restrain the patient and strap a face-mask on the guy to keep him from spitting at you while you take his vitals, you

do wonder. And this guy is taking it to such extremes I feel like I
might start laughing.

"Any tingling in the hands or feet?" I ask.

"Cunt."

"How about your stomach? Do you still feel nauseous?"

"You cunt!"

"If you have any appetite at all it'd be really good if we could get
something in your stomach."

"Yoouuuuuuuuuu..." he winds up, puffing his chest out like a
mangy goose. "Cuuuuunnnnnnnnnnnntttt!" he finishes, whooshing out
like a whoopee cushion. The CNA in there with me, a big Mexican
woman named Inez, smiles kindly at me.

"Well," she says, "at least we know there's no shortness of breath."

I let out a sharp laugh before I can cover my mouth, which sets
him off in a string of babbling. This is the kind of laugh that
threatens to go manic, so I have to excuse myself from the room and
take some deep breaths. Naturally that's when the attending doctor
walks by. I have a moment of panic when I see the long white coat
and here I am leaning against the wall trying to keep it together,
either about to laugh or about to cry. But then I realize it's Doctor
Bennet and I relax again, but only a little. He's a floor favorite, but
he's still a doctor.

Doctor Bennet is a tall, thin redhead. I'm a small girl myself, and
I'm pretty sure we have the same waist size. He's a foot taller than me,
too, so I think I have him beat in the thigh and calf muscle mass as
well. He wears well-fitted slacks when he's attending, and trim white
shirts with thin ties of every color. I'm not sure I've ever seen him
repeat a tie, which is impressive, and every one of them is as thin as a
ruler. A thick tie would look like a dinner napkin on him. He's
holding a medication cup between his thumb and forefinger, and he
holds it out to me.

"Caroline," Bennet says, in his formal way, although he does
smile. "I was glad to see you on the schedule tonight. This is from the
pharmacy. Benzos for your detox patient."

I take the cup and thank him, bobbing my head wearily.

"How's the night been?" he asks.

"Cuuunnnnnnnnnnt!" comes a throaty reply from inside the room. I blush and reach over to close the door softly. I look about and see that two nurses at the nearby charting desk are staring at us.

"About like that," I say.

Doctor Bennet doesn't laugh, but his eyes do. "I see," he says, putting his hands on his flat hips.

"And I have another admission," I say. "I don't think I'll be leaving any time soon."

Bennet checks his watch. He knows night shift switches over soon and that if I haven't admitted my last patient I haven't done any of my charting. And that means I'll be here well into the morning.

"Tell you what," he says, and he gently plucks the medication cup back from me. "I'll take care of our friend here. You get to your admission."

I could hug him. Then I blush again because of how totally out of line that would be. Wouldn't the girls at the charting desk like that? God knows what kind of firestorm that would set off. Thankfully I'm already sweaty and red from the general work day, so the blush blends right in. I give him a breathy thanks, and if he sees how desperately relieved I am, he doesn't let on. He glances briefly at the pills, nods at me, and just walks right into the room.

"Now that's quite enough of that," he says, and his voice is hard and final, and it works. The patient shuts up. Another thing about Doctor Bennet. He may look like a reed, but he's got an incredible bedside manner. He sets patients right. Sometimes that means he cracks down on them and sometimes that means he's gentle, but either way it's always what they need.

But I'm already gone, down the hall, into the next room and to my admit. And not a second too soon, either, because when I knock and open the door he's already sitting up and probing his IV line, looking to pull. It's a miracle the bed alarm didn't go off. That might just have been the straw that broke the nurse's back.

"Whoa, whoa! What are you doing?" I ask, a little too desperately. "Let's just sit still for a second, shall we?"

I skid over and grab his arm and check that the line is secure, and
I'm so flustered that it takes me a minute to realize that he hasn't said
anything at all. I look up at him and realize he's as surprised to find
me holding his arm as I am to find him trying to pull his IV line. I can
tell he's a Navajo, and what with the late hour and all the nastiness
with my last patient, I brace myself for more trouble, but it never
comes.

"Sorry," he says, and he takes his fingers off of his line. His face is
smooth and dark, not ravaged or ruddy like some of the Navajo that I
come across, and his eyes are clear and deeply brown. The kind of
brown that is at the bottom of a jar of honey. I suppose *eye* is more
appropriate, since one is wide and alert and the other looks like it
caught a baseball. He's also young. My age. Maybe younger. And
short. Shorter than me. But cut in that stringy, athletic way. And by
now I realize I'm staring.

"...It's just, I don't think I need to be here," he says. "I didn't want
to bother anyone. Thought I might just slip out."

He has a touch of the Navajo accent, the careful emphasis on each
word, and I can't help but smile. This smile is nowhere near the
manic smile I was fighting down in the hallway outside. This one
relaxes my face.

"Slip out? You can't really 'slip out' of a hospital, I'm afraid. We
have to sign you in and out. Plus, you just got here."

"I feel fine, now, really," he says. And now that he's not going
anywhere, I pick up his chart from the foot of the bed.

"Ben Dejooli," I say. "Navajo?" Whenever I see a patient uncomfortable, I start talking. Sometimes they don't even answer me, but it
does settle them more often than not. If anything, it's simply better
than the sterile white noise of a hospital. "What's Dejooli mean, if
you don't mind me asking? I work at the Chaco Health Clinic once a
week. I like to hear about Navajo names."

This stills him, and he looks at me with a newfound interest.

"It means 'gone.'"

"Gone?"

"Well, it means 'went upward.' But things in Navajo have a lot of different meanings. I think it's more like 'gone.'"

He seems distant all of a sudden, and I wonder if I screwed up by going down this line of conversation, so I bring it back to the task at hand.

"Says here you lost consciousness on the reservation. A Daniel Ninepoint called in the ambulance, and when you were non-responsive they bypassed the clinic and brought you straight here."

Ben looks down, and I can see that he's ashamed. A lot of Navajo men are ashamed of illness. They associate it with weakness.

"I woke up in the ambulance. Tried to get them to turn around. They wouldn't listen. I'm fine. I don't need to be here. I just passed out is all. Haven't you ever passed out?"

"Not that I can remember," I say. But the answer is no. I would remember. I remember everything. And I would be such a hypochondriac about it that I'd probably check myself into the hospital as soon as I woke up. "It's most likely nothing, but we still need to check some things. See if you concussed yourself. I see you have a black eye."

"That's from before. So Danny found me?" he asks, grimacing.

"Don't know about that, but he called the ambulance."

"Great," he says, shaking his head.

"I take it he's not a friend of yours."

"He's my partner."

Wonderful, I think. *He's gay. Naturally.*

"I'm a cop. He won't be too happy with me. I wasn't supposed to be where I was when I passed out."

I blink. *A cop.* Why am I so relieved he has that kind of partner? What is going on here?

"Where was that?" I ask, to keep him talking.

"The Arroyo." He rubs gently at his face and taps softly around his eye. "Never mind. Look, I really need to go. I gotta straighten this out."

I've found that when a patient tries to derail an admit—which happens often because there are a whole litany of questions I'm supposed to ask—it's best just to power through.

"The black eye is from earlier? Before you passed out at the Arroyo?"

"Yeah."

"Is it from a fall?"

"Yeah. I fell into a fist." He says this looking down at his lap, but I laugh. Then it strikes me that he might be offended, so I cut it off with a cough. I'm still working on Navajo humor.

"Well, sometimes concussion symptoms show up late. Did you feel nausea, or light headedness after you were hit?"

"He didn't knock me out," Ben says, a little defensively. "He only got in one punch."

"Sometimes people can lose consciousness for only a second and don't even realize it. Usually there's disorientation and nausea afterwards. "

Ben pauses, and I can tell he's not telling me something. It's very hard to fool a nurse. We may miss things on our own, but we can usually tell if you keep things from us.

"No nausea," he says softly. "But..."

I wait.

"But I was...I don't know. Things got blurry and I couldn't talk, so I sat down for a second. But it cleared."

"And this was before the Arroyo?"

"Yeah. Yesterday morning. It was a rough day." He eyes his uniform, folded, with his belt and badge hanging neatly from the chair nearby. His gun he'll have to get from the checkout desk at the front entrance. He looks uncomfortable, more than just embarrassed. He's swallowing and brushing at nothing on his forehead. He looks up at the hanging bag he's connected to and then down at the bed. He crinkles the sheets, and he starts breathing faster. I've seen this before too. White Coat Syndrome. I think some part of him is terrified of the hospital.

"Listen, Ben, we'll get you out of here as soon as we can, but—"

"Do you smell that?" he asks.

"What?"

"That smell, it's like a...a burning smell. Is something on fire?"

I look around myself and even try a subtle sniff of my armpits while he's ghosting his head back and forth.

"Nothing's burning, Ben. It's okay. You're okay."

I do something I rarely do uninvited, which is step forward and lay a hand on his shoulder. He reaches up and tries to wrap his fingers around my wrist. I'm expecting him to throw my hand away, but when he grips me he just holds on. All the while he's sniffing, moving his head a fraction of an inch and sniffing again. He looks out of the small window as if he's expecting to see someone there, then he blinks several times, and all of a sudden he's under control again. Or at least faking it well. He looks up at me and even manages a shaky smile. He plucks his fingers away and sets his hands in his lap.

"Like I said. Tough day, that's all."

I unclip a small pen-light from my breast pocket and look into his pupils, and he allows it. There is no delayed dilation, no trouble tracking. None of the symptoms of a concussion. But rather than make me feel better, this gives me a cold, clammy feeling. Like water is dripping down my back. I'm an oncology nurse, and two things here raise huge red flags for me. One: he smells a smell that is not there. Two: when he tried to grab my hand, he missed by a good six inches on his first attempt. Like he was swiping at a missing ladder rung.

"Ben, was that time after you got hit the first time you smelled something burning?"

"I think so. Near enough, anyway."

"How many times have you had to sit down to get your bearings?"

Ben shrugs. "A few. I don't drink as much water as I should, and I think I'm kind of dehydrated—"

"Think with me here. More than twice?"

Ben nods.

"More than five times?"

Ben nods.

"More than ten times?"

Ben thinks, then shrugs. Which might as well be a nod. I swallow.

"It always goes away," he says, but he's eyeing the equipment again and picking lightly at the skin on the back of his hand. He's trying to look around me and out the door.

"Ben...are you alright?" I ask.

His face finds mine and softens. "Yeah, really, I am. I just...I don't like hospitals."

"Not many people do," I say, by way of reassurance, but it comes out sounding condescending, and I shake my head. I'm not normally like this around patients. I keep the second-guessing and endless over-analysis out of the patient rooms. Usually it hits me around three in the morning. Or three in the afternoon. Whenever I'm supposed to be sleeping.

"Sorry. What I mean is that it's normal to feel stressed out in a hospital. It's a proven effect. It's called White Coat Syndrome. It skews a lot of our blood pressure readings."

Ben nods and manages a half smile. I can tell he knows about White Coat and that he also knows what he has is worse, but I don't want to press him. He's eyeing me with this soft, tired, lopsided wink, and it's ludicrously endearing. Probably because he doesn't mean it to be.

"I don't even know your name," he says.

"Caroline."

"Caroline," he says, nodding. "I know you're just doing your job. But I'm fine, and I really want to go. No offense."

When you work on a cancer floor, you see cancer everywhere. Melanoma on arms and backs at the gym, liver cancer in the pallid, red-nosed strangers you pass on the street, lung cancer in the chronic, wet cough of someone next to you in line. You learn to dampen down the desire to smack some medical sense into these people, but the urge never really leaves you once you've worked on an oncology floor. Right now I really, really want to grasp Ben Dejooli by the shoulders and tell him to hell with what he wants. What he needs is to get an MRI immediately, and if he's lucky, it'll say that all he's having are cluster migraines or that it's vertigo or something.

But that's me running away with myself again. That's three a.m. Caroline. If I let her loose, it's all over.

"How would you even get home?"

"I'd take a cab."

"A cab from here to Chaco? You know how expensive that is?"

He taps his teeth together and nods.

"There's nobody you can call?"

"There are people I can call. But I'd rather take a cab."

I shake my head at the stubbornness of men in general.

"Well, if you really want to go, you and the attending physician have to sign an AMA form."

"What's that?"

"It's a form that says you're leaving against medical advice."

"Whose?"

"Mine."

He ponders this, and me, for another moment before nodding. I take a big breath and throw up my hands.

"All right. I'll get the doctor."

I leave the room before I can say anything else. I don't know why this guy is affecting me like this. I'm acting like a nursing student, not an experienced RN. Actually, I'm acting more like a pining teenager, if I'm completely honest with myself.

I find Doctor Bennet at the computers drinking a large, black coffee. He's both hunched over and tucked under the desk, and he makes the chair he's sitting in look like it belongs in a kindergarten class. He looks up at me and presses his lips together. No doubt I look like a flustered hen. Except sweaty. It's amazing how working nights throws off your internal temperature. I'm freezing one second, then I'm clammy the next.

"What's up?" he asks.

"The patient is nine seventeen wants an AMA."

"That was quick."

"He's insistent. I think he has a problem with hospitals."

"And what do you think? Should we let him go?"

This is another reason why all the nurses love Doctor Bennet. He asks us what we think. Yeah, I know, it doesn't take much. But you would be absolutely flabbergasted at the number of doctors who treat us like hospital accessories about on par with the vending machines.

"They brought him in because he blacked out, but I can't find any evidence of a concussion. He's responsive and alert, aside from the paranoia. He's not complaining of any pain."

"Well, if he wants to go and he can go, we gotta let him go."

I deflate a little at this, and Doctor Bennet sees it.

"What's the problem? I'd have thought you'd be relieved." He checks his plastic Timex watch. "You're already here past shift change."

"It's just...he's complaining of a burning smell. And I think he may have some visual impairment. Depth judgment issues."

"Is he driving?"

"No."

Bennet creaks back in his chair and crosses his long arms over his white coat.

"And this isn't his first episode. He said he's had at least five of these incidents in the past."

"You think he may have a brain tumor," Bennet says.

I don't answer him, but that's answer enough. It's always a strange thing when you pull out the word 'tumor' in a diagnosis. It's such a heavy word. Nobody wants to say it. We get as used to it on the oncology floor as I think anyone can, but it's still heavy, even to us.

The other reason I stay quiet is because technically nurses aren't supposed to diagnose anything. That's what the white coats are for. I know a lot of doctors who would laugh my concerns off as the nervous ramblings of a young nurse, but like I said, Bennet is different.

"You're serious about this, aren't you." It's not a question, it's an observation.

"I know it's not really my place to say—"

"Of course it's your place," he says, stopping me as he gets a call on his phone. He snaps it from the table and answers it with a gruff "Bennet." He's quiet for a moment, and I look elsewhere. There are about a million things that I should be doing, but none of them seem all that important at the moment. Bennet says, "Can they wait?" and then he waits for a moment. "Then they'll have to wait," he says. He clicks the phone off and looks up at me, and his brow softens again. As he unfolds himself and stands tall, he grabs his stethoscope and drapes it around his shoulders.

"Let me get a look at him," he says.

When we walk in to Ben Dejooli's room, Bennet has the AMA clipped to the board in his hand.

"Hi, Ben," he says, pulling the low stool out with his foot and sitting down in front of the bed. He grabs Ben's charts and flips through them, and there is a silence that would have been awkward if I was the only one here with Ben. But Bennet makes it seem like an expectant silence. Like a conductor about to take the stage.

"So you passed out," he says.

Ben nods. I can tell that he is weary. He doesn't want to go through all of this again.

"Did Caroline tell you that she wants to count out a brain tumor?"

Ben widens his eyes. Which is an amazingly restrained response. I have to lean back on the door frame, but Bennet moves on. His delivery is so straightforward it's as if he's told Ben that he might be allergic to cats. And because Bennet doesn't treat the elephant in the room like an elephant, it doesn't become an elephant.

"No," Ben says, looking up at me. I can't hold his gaze. This is the first time I can ever remember turning away from a patient like this.

"And I have to say, Ben, after reading her admission, I agree that it's a concern. Something is giving you trouble."

I never gave him an admission, but that hardly matters now.

"So I'm gonna do a couple of things here. First, I'm going to sign this AMA. You're free to go. We aren't liable for anything that happens to you." Bennet wipes his hands across the air as if to shoo the legalese away.

"Second, I'm going to write up a referral to the CT clinic. Indian Health Services will take care of your costs." So Bennet knows he's Navajo too. It shouldn't surprise me. The doctors at Albuquerque

General have a program where they rotate at the Chaco Health Clinic. I've seen him there once or twice. He's smiled at me.

"What's a CT?" Ben asks.

"It's a brain scan," Bennet says, grabbing for the pen and pad in his front pocket. "We just want to rule out the worst, that's all."

He rips a page from his pad and hands it to Ben, who looks at it like it's written in a foreign language.

"Just take that to the clinic, second floor."

"I really can't today," Ben says, and I can see he's gone a little pallid, but it's more than that. His general color seems to be fading. "Maybe in a couple of days," he says, half-heartedly.

"The referral is good for a month, but I really would encourage you to go as soon as you can. Just get it over with, and then we'll go from there."

"So I can leave?" he asks.

Bennet signs the AMA form on his clipboard and then hands it to Ben. "This certifies that you are leaving under your own power and against medical advice. Sign here."

Bennet's tone is strong, but Ben doesn't flinch. He takes the clipboard, signs his name as a little scribble and then holds out his arm with the line in it. "Can you help me out of this?"

Bennet's phone rings again, and he snaps it from his hip, glancing at the readout.

"I have to move," he says.

"I'll unhook him," I say. Bennet nods. At the door, he gives one last, unreadable look to Ben and is gone.

"He wasn't very happy with me," Ben says, smiling sadly as I pull the line from his arm and push the rig aside.

"I'm not very happy with you either," I say, not daring to meet his eyes again. "Promise me you'll get that scan."

He laughs and looks at me strangely. "Promise you?"

"Yes. Promise me."

"I can't promise you, I hardly know you."

"Fine," I say, curtly, before attempting to bring down my trusty curtain of separation. Well, trusty until now, anyway. "Your clothes are on the dresser there. Have a good night." I turn to go.

"Caroline..."

I stop at the door and glance over my shoulder. He's still sitting on the bed. His feet dangle above the floor. His coloring is strange. I can tell that he wants to say something, but he doesn't know how. I don't know how I know this, exactly, except to say that it's almost like it's coming off of him in waves. I feel like I can sense the exact moment when he gives up and resigns himself.

"Look, I'll try to get the scan, okay?" he says. I've heard this tone before. It's the same tone people use when in polite company as an alternative to a flat no.

"Well, *really* try," I say, after another long moment where I feel like I'm staring at him like he's a mirage. It's almost like his skin is smoking. It strikes me that perhaps I need to get more sleep. Either that or maybe I have something wrong with my own head.

Then my phone buzzes and I can hear a bed alarm going off somewhere in the back, and I'm off running. It's almost forty minutes later when I finally clock out, and by then Ben's room has been empty for about thirty-nine of them.

4

BEN DEJOOLI

I'd planned on calling a cab from outside the hospital, slinking back to the rez and never talking about this little episode again, but when I get outside I see that Dad and Gam are already in the lobby. Gam is nested in a chair, puffed up in her old down jacket, and she's looking right at me when the elevator doors open. She hops down from her chair and shuffles my way, shaking her head at me. My father is at the help desk, and he looks white as a sheet. He might be the only person on earth who hates hospitals more than I do. That he even got this far past the front doors speaks volumes about how worried he must have been about me. I'm touched, actually.

Gam is now nodding her head and patting me on the side of the arm and muttering in Navajo, too low for me to understand. I grasp her bony hand, its skin paper thin.

"I'm okay, Gam," I say. She keeps nodding and shaking her head at the same time.

"Ben!" Dad says, striding over to me. "I came as soon as I heard. Danny told us. What happened? What happened to you?" I haven't seen him this worked up in years. He's borderline frantic, and I think it's best to get all three of us out of the hospital. We have bad memories of this place.

"Come on," I say, shepherding Gam in front of me. Dad follows and soon we're outside and in the car. I said I could drive, but Dad insists. He's treating me like I'm some flower, which is exactly what I didn't want, and exactly why I was hoping to sneak my way back home. It takes until we're cruising down the highway, the sun cracking over the horizon behind, before his free hand stops trembling. Gam is sitting in the back seat, nearly buried in her coat and scarf. Her eyes are closed, but I know she's listening.

"I'd been feeling off all day. I just blacked out for a bit, that's all."

"That's all? Ben. Danny scared us to death. Said they found you at the Arroyo. And I kept thinking if it was something I said, or what, and I was having these flashbacks of Ana—"

"This isn't like that, Dad. I'm not sick, I don't feel weak, it's totally different."

Gam says something in the back to the tune of *Ana said the same thing*, but I cut her off right there. Ana was anemic. She didn't know what it was like to feel well. She was always tired, but she refused to sit still. She wanted to be a normal nine-year-old girl. I just had a bad day on the job. Totally different.

"Gam, this isn't what Ana had," I say, and it feels weird even to equate the two. Neither of them is that reassured, but eventually I think they sense that I haven't had much sleep and so when I lay my head back and close my eyes they leave it be for the rest of the ride back to Chaco. I wish I could say I did get some sleep, but in my mind I keep seeing the black curtain of feathers that seemed to fall over me right before I lost it at the Arroyo. Gam starts humming something. An old Navajo song I remember her singing to Ana and me when we were little and couldn't fall asleep, our beds side by side. It was always me that worried about the dark. Ana wasn't afraid of anything. Not even of dying. She just liked to hear Gam sing. I roll my head and open my eyes to look at Gam, but she's not looking back at me. She's looking out the front window, and her eyes are small slits in the shadow of her face. I follow her gaze, and I see nothing but flat road and rolling desert hills. I'm about to close my eyes again when I catch movement in the far distance, high in the sky. A whole mess of crows streaks ahead of us, like pepper strewn across a table. I try to blink them away. I've had enough of crows. But when I open my eyes again, they're still there, and it's like they're leading our car back home. One in particular. A huge one at the head of the flock.

When we get home, the crows wheel off and away, but I still watch the sky out of the kitchen window while I manage to eat some cereal and calm my gut. I sit with Gam while she knits. Dad is off at the hardware store. Danny calls, and I pick up, and he tells me to sit out the day to recover, everything will keep 'til then.

"You know what I'mma say, don't you?" he asks.

"That I'm an idiot."

"No, you're no idiot, Ben. But sometimes you do dumb things. Can you imagine if I had to explain to your grandmother that you disappeared at the Arroyo while I was sleeping?"

"I know, Danny."

"Did you run into trouble out there?" he asks. "Tell me true."

"No trouble. I think maybe that sucker punch at Sancho's hit me harder than I thought."

Danny grunts in agreement.

"Did you find anything, at least? Was it worth it?"

Danny Ninepoint has one tone when he speaks. It's slow and methodical, like he's reading a speech. It's hard to tell if he's angry or if he's disappointed, although if I was to guess I'd say he's almost always just a little bit of both.

"No," I say, sighing. "Just a vigil and a token pile for burial."

Danny grunts again.

"Don't ever do that again, Ben. Go off without me like that."

"I know. I won't."

And just like that I know he's done talking about it. Just like I know he was done talking about the gambler, but I couldn't let it go. Danny could have said that's what I get for picking at things when they're settled, but he doesn't. He doesn't have to. He knows I get it.

"Get some sleep. Tomorrow we got some work to do."

"All right. And Danny. Thanks for looking out for me."

"Yep."

"And for dropping it now that it's done."

"Yep."

And that's that. Right now I've never been more grateful for the single-track mind of Danny Ninepoint. I take his advice and get to bed early. I sleep for twelve straight hours, and when I wake up again it's just past four in the morning. I think I have maybe another hour in me, and I flip my pillow and try to sink back to sleep again. But I think I was dreaming of the hospital because I'm in mid-thought when I wake up, and I'm thinking about the way Caroline looked when she asked me to promise to get that scan. She looked afraid. There's really no other word for it. And I wonder if I should be afraid too, but I feel better than I have in weeks. I just can't fathom that I have anything seriously wrong with me. Still, that look of hers lingers.

My brain is a funny thing. It's that look of hers that's on my mind when I wake up, but it's the way she held my shoulder, and the feeling I got when I held on to her hand for a moment, that ends up lulling me away and back into another solid hour of dreamless sleep.

The next morning Dad takes me to get my truck at the Arroyo. Dad drops me off but refuses to leave without me. Says he wants to follow me out. He's still handling me with care, but I see no way around it for a little while, at least until the sour taste of the whole event washes out.

I walk up to my truck with my tail between my legs. I don't want to see the smoker again, or anyone, for that matter. Thankfully, it looks like the vigil is over. In fact, it looks like the campers moved away from this edge of the Arroyo entirely. There's nobody here at all. If it weren't for the fact that my truck was still parked where I left it (and still locked, and intact, which is a blessing), I might have thought I had the site wrong. But no, this was it. In the light of early morning, the big black pit beyond the lip looks about as ominous as a sledding hill. The vigil pile is long gone too. It takes me until I walk over to where the pile was to realize I'm looking for the crow totem. I sigh, not really knowing why I'm disappointed. It's not my crow, after all. It feels right that it should be buried. Decommissioned. Given back to the earth, just like the gambler himself.

Dad honks. He doesn't like it here, and I know I'm lingering. I take one last look around the site, and it looks almost like it's been swept. Like someone took a big, wide- framed straw broom and flattened the whole place. There aren't even any footprints. That's why I stop on the walk back to my truck when I see the tire tracks. They stand out like huge fingerprints, especially to someone like me, who is trained to see them. Uneven weight—the front tread is clean but the back has displaced dirt around it. Medium width but long from front to rear. I'd say a rear-wheel drive, four-door sedan. There aren't a lot of those around here. Mostly trucks and vans and campers. If I had to guess, I'd say this tread looks a lot like an official vehicle. A town car or maybe a standard cop cruiser.

Could Danny have come by? Maybe. He thought I might have run into trouble when we talked on the phone. Maybe he came to check out the scene before I did. But he smacked my hand for coming here alone at night. He's a big bastard, but even he wouldn't be keen on jumping in his car and racing down here in the dead of night. Especially once he got confirmation that the ambulance picked me up.

I follow the tracks from where I pick them up coming out of the loose rubble, crossing over into the finer dust near the ring of the slope. They look to stop in front of the gambler's old camp site, and then there's a clear sprayback of dust and two divots. Whoever they were, they came here looking for something, either found it or didn't, and then peeled out.

I know I should file away this whole thing. Should have long ago, like Danny, but something about it won't let me close the drawer. I have this crazy desire to look for turned earth, and a creeping suspicion that even if I could find the gambler's burial pile, it would be missing one crow.

But I'm late, and I'm making Dad late for his day by wasting time, and Danny said we had work to do, so I get in my truck, start her up, and pull out. I wave at Dad on the way by, and he nods. He pulls out after me, and we leave the Arroyo behind. I check the rear mirror for crows out of instinct, but there are no black specks on the horizon. Nothing but the sharp, cold blue of a fall morning.

DANNY WASN'T LYING when he said we had work to do. Turns out it was more work than usual, it's just Danny didn't want to lay it on me the day before. As soon as I get into the station I can tell that something is up. We have this rotating group of young kids that work the front desk, another cush job staffed by the council, and usually all they want to do is talk, but today they're all business. At first I think it's me and my episode, but Danny's not a talker, and he wouldn't throw me under the bus like that. When I get to my desk I can see that it's not just me. Our district is big; we have nearly a hundred cops who work the streets and desks here, and usually the patrol guys are in the kitchen, shooting the shit, while the higher-ups gossip in their offices. The central desks generally serve more as places to sit than to work, but not today. Today everyone is glued to their seats. Today you could hear a pin drop in the kitchen. There's still a full pot of coffee. That means things are serious.

It doesn't take me long to see why the station has flipped a switch. It has something to do with the two men in black off-the-rack suits who are talking to the chief behind closed doors. I can see through the window of his office, and so can everyone else.

Danny sits down with a steaming cup of joe.

"What's all this?" I ask. "They don't look Navajo."

"They're not," Danny says, keeping his voice low.

New Mexico state patrol has come into our jurisdiction a handful of times, but never dressed like they were attending a funeral. Only one type of law dresses like that.

"FBI," I say. Danny nods.

The Feds have no jurisdiction here. The US Government checks its people and its power at the welcome sign, usually, so this is strange.

"What do they want?"

Danny looks up at me. "Rumor is they're asking about Flatwood."

Danny says this like he was reading a grocery list. Same way he says anything. But he watches me carefully because he knows what's going through my head right now. It's not enough that people like Sancho have to throw Flatwood in my face, as if I didn't already think of the man every day of my life. It's not enough for people to quiet down every now and then when I walk into the station kitchen. Now the Feds have come to remind me, and all of us, of the man I banished. I take a deep breath, and I think I smell a tinge of sulfur.

"Ben, they're not here for you. Not as far as I can see. They haven't talked about anything to me."

"I wasn't even a cop when that happened," I say. I became a cop right after that happened. Because that happened.

Danny holds his hands out low and nods as if to say *you don't have to explain anything to me.*

"Just lay low and see what it is that they want. Hopefully just a file of some sort, then they're gone. No reason to think they're here to dig up old bones."

I appreciate the sentiment, but I know in real life things don't work like that. There are no coincidences. That's why I'm not surprised when the phone at our desk lights up. Danny watches me. I know it's not for him. I pick up.

"Dejooli," I say.

"Ben, its Sani. You have a minute?"

As if I wouldn't have a minute for the captain. I look up at Danny and then over at the closed office, behind glass. The agents are looking my way. Danny nods slowly to tell me it's okay. One step at a time.

"'Course, Cap," I say. "Be right in."

I hang up and look down at my desk, nodding to myself. Makes sense that the guy I banished would haunt me every day since. Seems quite Navajo of him. I get up without another word and make my way to the big office.

Sani Yokana is a veteran of the Chaco rez. I say veteran because he's more than just an experienced cop. He worked the streets like me for ten years, then made detective, then lieutenant, now captain. He's savvy. Nobody becomes head of the Chaco district of NNPD without knowing their way around tribal politics. Thankfully, Sani has a no-nonsense reputation and seems to have reached his position without owing too many favors, at least that I've heard of. I think it helps that he's not a member of the council and has no intention of ever being a member of the council, and has, in fact, come as close as anyone I've ever met to telling the council to fuck off while still keeping his job. He likes to run our department his way. He's a heavyset man, wide bodied, with long, grey hair that he never bands. When I walk in the office, all three men watch me. The suits are blank, but Sani gives me a pinched nod. He looks a bit piqued. I can tell that he's not exactly itching to drudge up the Flatwood case again either.

"Ben, this is Agent Parsons and Agent Douglas. They're with the FBI."

I shake their hands. Some Indians say that all white men look the same. I never held with that until now. Both are medium height, medium build. Brown hair, neatly parted. Pale complexion, not a hint of facial hair. No smile to speak of. All business. These are men whose profession it is to get in, get out, and get forgotten. They are wearing different colored ties, at least. I can give them that.

"They have a few questions to ask you about Joseph Flatwood," Sani says, furrowing his weathered brow. He's not happy having these agents in his station. I can tell before they even open their mouths that they have an air of blank-check entitlement to them. No doubt they've been trained extensively about Indian affairs, but I'd be surprised if either of them had ever set foot on a reservation before.

"Mr. Dejooli—" Parsons begins.

"Call me Ben."

"...Ben. We have an open investigation regarding Joseph Flatwood, whom we know to have been an acquaintance of yours. It's progressed to a point where we feel you might be able to help us."

I look at Sani for a long moment. He barely holds a scowl at bay. The dimple in his chin turns into a pothole.

"Council has given them free run of whatever resources Public Safety can provide," he says, strained.

Now that's interesting. For the council to buddy up with the Feds, Flatwood must really be raising hell.

"All right," I say, slowly.

"But first you need to understand that this is a classified case, and no details about what we will tell you should leave this room. It's standard protocol for an ongoing investigation."

I feel a twinge of pain behind my forehead. It's like Agent Parsons is reading from cue cards behind me.

"Okay...but listen, I haven't seen Joey Flatwood in almost six years. Not since he was banished. I haven't heard from him either, if that's what you're getting at. That's kind of the whole point."

Agent Douglas nods his head. "We know. We've been tracking Flatwood for years now. He's been all over the southwestern United States, but just about the only place he hasn't popped up is anywhere near Chaco Reservation."

Banished means banished. Flatwood respected the council, and our laws. That was one of the worst parts of watching him go: I knew he would be gone forever. I was glad of it, and I hated it at the same time. I still remember the way he turned back and nodded at me after he passed the welcome sign going the other way. It was a reassuring nod, as if he wanted to say *It's okay, Ben.* That's what made it so terrible. Nothing was okay. My sister was gone. We'd decided it was my best friend's fault, and now he was going, too. He should have fought it, but it was like he gave up. That, more than anything, is what I keep coming back to in the middle of the night when I wonder for the millionth time if Joey Flatwood is really the reason Ana is gone. Why didn't he deny it? I scrunch up my nose to try and cut off the subtle burning smell, but it's getting stronger.

"I thought he might be dead," I say. "The way he just...disappeared like that. No word of him at all."

"Oh, he's not dead," Parsons says. "At least, not yet. He's come close to killing himself several times, though."

Parsons' textbook delivery makes me want to smack him. If Joey tried to kill himself, it's probably because of me. There was a long stretch of time, right afterwards, when I wanted to kill him myself.

But the idea of him wandering the southwest, drifting in and out of depression, makes me feel wretched. I'm almost positive that he knows what happened to Ana, and I hate him for refusing to tell me, but it's been six years now and sometimes I think if I knew then how hard friends are to come by, I might have been a little slower to take the stand. I swallow down the distaste and try to match the agents' flair for deadpan.

"In fact," Douglas says, "that's what we wanted to talk to you about."

"What, Flatwood trying to kill himself?"

"And failing...when he shouldn't."

"I don't follow you."

"We have reason to believe that Joseph Flatwood should be dead, but he's not."

"You mean he's bad at killing himself?"

"No, he's quite good. He's just...still here."

I cross my hands over my chest and look at Sani, who gives me a small eyebrow shrug. "Why do you guys care if he kills himself?"

Parsons clears his throat. "Between suicide attempts he has a penchant for robbing hospitals. We started following Flatwood after security cameras in three separate states picked him up lifting pills from the medicine cabinets."

Joey Flatwood, a drug addict? That's even less believable to me than the gambler as a drug addict. Joey's grandpa used to lecture us about drugs, and Joey got a firsthand education of the mess they can turn a man into living out at the Arroyo. He never touched the stuff. We made a pact back in the day. Cut our palms with Joey's grandpa's old buck knife.

"He robs hospitals?"

"Yes. We have him on security footage taking enough to drop a man twice his size. He looked right at the camera. He's quite brazen. We also believe he may be selling what he doesn't take, to keep himself liquid and able to move."

"And this is Joseph Flatwood? Joey Flatwood? About my height, bit bigger in the chest. He's got a split lip—"

"That was repaired, but poorly. Bowlegged. Grew up in your *Arroyo*," Parsons says the word with mild distaste. "Has the tattoos on his knuckles to prove it."

"It's him, Ben," Sani says. "I've seen the tapes."

I shake my head in disbelief. "Can I see these tapes?"

Douglas looks at Parsons, who doesn't move a muscle, but some agreement is passed between them.

"If you'll help us build a file on him, yes. We'll give you access to the tapes."

"Ben, I've told them we'll give them what we have, but you don't have to work with them further. These gentlemen know where their jurisdiction lies."

My first instinct is to turn around and walk right out the door. I'd already helped the council build a case against Joey once, and I've been paying for it ever since. Now the US government wants me to help build another case, and I'm thinking how it is that it falls to me to damn a man twice. I think maybe the gods are giving me the retribution I asked for six years ago in spades, only right now I'm not so sure I want it anymore. It won't make Ana any less gone. I oughta take a page out of the Danny Ninepoint playbook and throw out the playbook. But I can't. I'm not like Danny. I just don't know why, but my book is bolted open. As surely as Dad wanders the back yard. As surely as Sancho and his ilk talk circles around Flatwood to let me know they remember. For some reason, Joey Flatwood can't be forgotten. Not yet.

"What are you gonna do with him, when you catch him?" I wasn't naive enough to think Joey could run forever. Not from the Feds.

"We're going to prosecute him on narcotics charges, breaking and entering, trafficking, and theft, and then, quite frankly, we're going to breathe a sigh of relief," says Parsons.

"Why's that?"

"Because his behavior fits certain profiles. We have reason to believe that Joseph Flatwood is on his way to hurting a lot of people."

Just then a huge crow clatters to a landing on the sill of the high window in Sani's office, and it startles all four of us. It grapples with the stubby awning for a moment, its long black claws scraping at the metal. I step closer to it, looking for a flash of red and terrified that I'll find it.

"They're all over the place these days. It's that time of the fall," Sani says.

The crow watches us sidelong, its arrowed head nearly pressed up against the glass. In profile I can see that its beak is like a six-inch shard of obsidian. It only lingers for a moment, then it drops from the sill. I can hear the beating of its wings. Still staring at the empty sky where it was, I know my answer.

"All right. I'll help. Give me the tapes and a few days to run it down. I'll tell you what I can."

"How about two days. We'd need a full character profile. What he was like growing up. How you knew him. What he was like in school. Any warning signs you might think of. And, of course, a full account of the banishment. We want your personal opinions, Ben. You knew him best."

I nod. "Two days," I say. Something about how eager these men are doesn't sit well with me. The whole story is off. Suddenly I remember the Arroyo. The tracks. The Feds roll around in just the type of town car that would leave those marks. I saw a Lincoln town car parked out front, in the handicapped spot, coming in. That would have done it. They wouldn't have any care for the gambler, of course, but there were strange similarities: the drugs, the Arroyo...the crows. Pieces of a bigger story all butting up against each other like tumbleweeds. If the Feds knew Joey grew up in the Arroyo, what else did they know? And what weren't they telling me?

5

CAROLINE ADAMS

I've been thinking a lot about Ben Dejooli, and it's kind of annoying me. I'll be working along, giving meds or helping a patient to the bathroom, and then out of nowhere he pops into my mind. I have four patients today, and one of them is a really large Navajo. Morbidly obese. She requires our specialized bed and the new hoisting system to get her on her feet so she can get to the restroom. She's also extremely rude to me and to every other person assigned to her. And a lot of people have been assigned to her. This is her sixth time gracing us with her presence in my tenure here. She's been bumped from the ER and onto the Oncology overflow. She is what we call a frequent flyer. She doesn't have cancer, but she has just about everything else. That's what happens when you're two hundred and fifty pounds overweight. You get everything.

I have no problem with fat people, but I do have a problem with mean people. Especially when we are understaffed and one of my patients who actually has cancer looks ready to code on me at the drop of a hat, and instead of tending to him like I should I have to deal with this woman and her whining for more pain meds and accusations of abuse from the staff. It's all I can do not to file her away, and just when I'm about to give up on everything—her, the Navajo, Chaco

Reservation, the whole day—Ben Dejooli pops into my mind. He's looking at me with that haunted gaze, and his eyes are like dime-sized windows into the rich-clay bottom of a lake. And it gets me through the rotation and keeps me moving until I can get a half a minute in the break room to eat my granola bar.

But then, when I'm two bites in to my "dinner," my phone rings and the code alarm goes off at the same time. That means it's my patient dying, and I drop the bar and start running, along with everyone else. Mary Ellen grabs the crash cart from the manager's station and is a half-step behind me. When I get there, the CNA is already doing chest compressions, and there is more blood than I have ever seen at once pouring from the patient's mouth. This is one of those horrible times when a nurse is faced with a crossroads, and this is the longest I've ever stood frozen in one spot during a code. It feels like half a minute, but in reality it's just a few seconds. Then Mary Ellen is behind me with the crash cart and in full-blown battle-manager mode, and I can see why she's the boss.

"Get him on his side," she says, firm and cold as winter stone, as she's rolling out the defibrillator pads. All hesitation gone, I wade into the blood, jam both hands under the patient fireman style, and roll him halfway around while Mary Ellen slaps one pad to his back.

"Front," she says, and I ease him back as Mary Ellen slaps the second to his chest. He is completely non-responsive. It's like moving a bag of dirt. I place the Ambu oxygen bag over his face, but he's still breathing blood and it smears against the inner plastic like melted lipstick. It's already collecting in a pool.

"We're gonna need suction," I say. My voice is distant and small, but another nurse hears me and preps the vacuum.

"Clear!" snaps Mary Ellen, and we all step away. I take the Ambu bag with me, and blood drips from the mouthpiece in a steady line. We wait for a horrible eternity for the readout. It says "No shock advised. Continue CPR." We all move in. Mary Ellen revs the panel again while a doctor injects the IV with epinephrine. The second nurse sucks the blood from in and around his mouth then steps back, and I pump oxygen. The CNA is sweating profusely but hasn't given up on the CPR. God bless him. We're supposed to do this for three minutes before we can shock him again. That's what the book says. It feels like an hour.

"Clear!"

We step back. In the movies the patients jolt. In real life it's more of a sad shudder.

We wait for the readout. "No shock advised. Continue CPR."

We move back in.

Suck, squeeze, suck, squeeze. The Ambu mouthpiece leaves red rings around his nose and lips. They dry black just in time for another suction and then another squeeze of the bag. They're lurid on his ghost-pale skin. There is no movement under his eyelids, and all of a sudden I notice I'm quietly crying. Some detached part of me wonders when that started. How long have I been here? Minutes? Hours?

"I'm calling it," I hear, and Bennet's voice is like a bucket of cold water. He's looking at the readouts. His face is grim, but his voice is strong.

"He's dead. There's nothing else we can do. He had lung cancer. Once the tumor bursts into the great vessels there's nothing that's going to stop the bleeding. It was only a matter of time. We knew it. He knew it."

And now that he says it, I see the blood is everywhere. It's on the patient. On the bed. On the floor. Up and down my sleeves and on the CNA's face. It's on Bennet, too. Tears roll down my cheeks, but I don't want to touch my face. Bennet looks at me, and his eyes soften. I think if he says anything to me I'm going to break down, but he just nods, thank God.

"Everyone give your roles to the nurse at the door. Time of death, three twenty-seven."

It takes ten minutes to sort out the roles for the log, and by then everyone is shaking, including me. The CNA most of all. I make a mental note to buy him coffee, or lunch. Then I almost laugh out loud at how tiny that gesture would be, all things considered, and it occurs to me that I am in a minor state of shock.

The line limps along. I step up.

"Caroline Adams. I'm the primary nurse."

Then I shuffle out. We all shuffle out in different directions like we're lost in the place we've worked for years. I just cross the hall. I'll need to clean him up and present the body to the family.

"Anybody willing to help me do post-mortem?" I ask, and it feels like I haven't talked for days. I have to clear my throat. I'm pretty sure I squeak.

The CNA nods at me, and Bennet says, "I will." I want to hug both of them then go to sleep for a week. And all of a sudden I'm thinking about Ben Dejooli again. Would he bleed like that? Probably not. If my worst fears are true and he has a brain tumor, he'd probably go out like a candle. There'd be no blood at all. Just the cancer pushing down on the nerve system until he stopped breathing. Bennet brings me back from the brink of breakdown again when he hands me a stack of wet towels. Then he and the CNA roll the patient and strip the bed. I've never seen a doctor do anything like this before, and it's the next thing that makes me want to cry. I viciously clear my throat and dab my face with the hot towel. I'm supposed to be one of the strong ones here.

I busy myself cleaning the floor and swallow down the ball in my throat. Eventually I'm under control. The repetitive swabbing movement helps. But then a strange thing happens. I don't usually go in for supernatural stuff. I believe that there's something bigger than me out there, and I guess I call that thing God. But when you've seen death like I have, you recognize it less as a scary passage or sacred departing and more as just the flipside of life. It's what's at the bottom of the sack of time all of us is handed when we come in to this world. I suppose this makes me disillusioned, but if it does, I'd challenge you to find a nurse out there who isn't. A lot of people prefer to keep the guts and gristle of life behind the skin, like our bodies are bags of magic. Doctors take the opposite extreme. Nurses, for whatever reason, are wired differently. We get in this game for the people, but we also see the guts for what they are: guts. This patient is gone. That's why it gives me pause when I feel something brush past my back while I'm cleaning the patient's face and mouth. I actually step aside.

"Sorry," I say, thinking it's Bennet or the CNA trying to get around me, even though I know it felt different. More subtle. Like a whisper. The brush of a blade of grass.

Bennet looks up at me from across the room. "It wasn't your fault, Caroline. It was stage four lung cancer." The CNA looks up at me and nods in silent agreement. He's by the far closet pulling out new sheets. Neither of them is anywhere near me. I blink at them until I realize that Bennet mistook my meaning, then go back to gently swabbing the side of the dead man's face. Then it happens again, and this time it's like I can hear the crinkle of the bed, like he's sitting up, even though he's just as still and rigid as when I started cleaning him. This time I step back, and I can feel the hairs on my forearms standing on end. Which would be understandable if I were the type to get creeped out by a dead body, but I'm not, which makes it all the stranger.

Then I swear I feel the movement of air on the damp at the back of my neck, and I find myself turning and staring at a spot in the middle of the room. My eyes tell me nothing is standing there, but there is just a hint of color to the air. Like that same strange smoke I saw on Ben's skin, but this is a different color, and it takes me a minute to recognize that it was the unique color of my patient. It snuffed out when he died, I realize this now, yet here it is again, like an echo of cologne passing by me for just a moment. And then it's gone. And, naturally, the two men I asked to help me clean and dress the room catch me staring into space like a cat.

Later, after it's all over and I've changed into my second pair of scrubs and convinced myself that the strange smoke and the soft touch of air were the result of shock, when I'm sitting back down at the table where nobody's touched my granola bar and it lies there like a sad relic of the time when my patient was still alive, Bennet comes in and sits down across from me. He's not wearing his coat anymore, and he's changed his shirt. His tie is a different color too, although it's just as skinny. It almost makes me smile.

"That was a bad one, Caroline. They're gonna do a debrief. I think you should go."

I nod. I pick up the bar, look at it, then set it down again. "Do you remember Ben Dejooli? The patient I had last week? He's Navajo. He passed out on the reservation."

Bennet nods.

"Did he ever fulfill that CT scan?"

"Not yet," Bennet says, and he seems confident in his answer. I wonder if Ben hasn't crossed his mind a time or two since that early morning as well.

I'm not surprised he hasn't gotten the scan. Not in the least. For one, he's a young Navajo man. And he's in a macho line of work on top of that, one that doesn't give him a lot of free time, from what I've seen of Chaco. And top it all off with that terrified look in his eyes— that look that practically begged me to get him out of the hospital— and you have a textbook recipe for negligence.

"He's not going to," I say, and I know it's true. That ball in my throat makes a grand re-entrance. I have to look away and scrunch up my face, so I'm sure it looks like I'm disgusted and not oddly heartbroken. It's probably better that I look disgusted. It's easier to explain away.

Bennet picks at his tie, brushes it flat. He rests his elbows on the table and lets out a deep breath.

"I wouldn't be so sure," he says.

"You work at the CHC same as I do. It's hard...with the Indians...and cancer." It's so much more than that, and my words come out sounding pathetic, but Bennet seems to understand.

"I've found that some of the Navajo need reminding. It's not their way to work on our schedule. They have their own schedule. It's been theirs for thousands of years."

"I'll never see him again," I say.

Bennet looks at me head-on, and I know that his bright-blue eyes, sharp and alive and refreshing after the horrible stillness behind the lids of the man I just saw die, can see damn near right through me.

"You're really worried about this guy," he says, but it's not accusatory. It's soft, and it's appreciative.

I nod. "I see a lot of crap out there at CHC, a lot of things that can't be helped, and I don't want to count him in that number. Somehow I think it's really important that I help him if I can."

Bennet nods again, and I notice that the sharp, aquiline blue is more than just in his eyes. It's all over him. I rub at my own eyes. The color's still there, rolling in soft wisps off of his skin.

"How about this. When are you next at the CHC?" he asks, clearly unaware that he's suddenly glowing blue. It occurs to me that I'm having a breakdown of some sort in the break room. I stare at the table and pretend to be figuring.

"Next Tuesday," I say.

"Why don't I do a little switching around and take the attending shift that day, and after we wrap up we can go find him? Nudge him along a bit."

I look at him head on. Smoke or no, that is an incredibly gracious thing to offer.

"You would do that?" I ask.

"Why not? He's a cop, right? I've been to the Chaco station tons of times working with patients who come to the clinic. I'll make an excuse to get over there at the end of the day when most of the cops are doing their own paperwork. With any luck we'll find him."

"And then what?" I ask, but I feel better than I have in weeks at just the thought of being able to address this Ben thing, this nagging fear, instead of sitting and waiting for bad things to happen.

"Well, that's up to you, but I'm sure you'll think of something," he says, and he smiles. And then I smile, and I can't help but notice that his smoke dances a bit. It makes me smile all over again, and I wonder if this is what a lunatic feels before a giggling fit.

"Okay," I say, perhaps a little too quickly.

"So it's a date?"

"It's a date."

It's only afterwards, in that night's three a.m. wonderings, that it occurs to me that maybe Bennet meant 'date' as in *date*. I actually blush, as if I was still talking to him and not alone in my bed. Probably he meant it just as a turn of phrase. Ninety-nine percent chance he meant it that way. Although doctors rarely mince words. Okay, maybe a ninety-five percent chance. And the other thing is that I could tell he was dancing without him ever moving his feet. He was dancing on the inside. I don't know what is happening to me, but if I'm going blind or nuts or having a breakdown, at least I got to see Owen Bennet dance first.

6

OWEN BENNET

I f you asked me why I proposed the idea of finding this Ben Dejooli, I'd say ostensibly because I have a responsibility as a doctor to help my patients however I can, and then I'd probably add that I, Owen Bennet, personally have an additional responsibility to the Navajo people of Chaco Reservation. It's in keeping with a long line of Bennet doctors who find their practice and then find their cause. My grandfather's practice was a small pediatric clinic in Essex County; his cause was the underserved communities of upstate Massachusetts. Granddad in particular, with his black bag and his racks upon racks of black suits, would find the idea of a site visit like the one I proposed for Ben Dejooli completely normal. My father's practice was in South Boston. He did general medicine. His cause was the Southie Irish-Americans. Working class men and women who might go twenty years at a time without a checkup were it not for him.

I don't have a practice, per se, since I'm an attending at ABQ General. That didn't go over well in the family, so I doubled up on the cause. The Navajo. I work full time for the hospital and then volunteer another full day at least once a week for the Chaco Health Clinic. The sixty-hour work week is brutal, quite frankly, but it didn't kill my grandfather (although Alzheimer's did) and it didn't kill my father (he just loved whisky), and it's damn well not going to kill me.

It's for a good cause. That's what I'd tell you if you were to ask why I'm going out of my way here. But the reality is that I think I'm in love with Caroline Adams. I also think I'm terrible at hiding it.

I wish I could tell you that I'm no stranger to love. That I've had my heart broken a time or two then pieced myself back together again. That I'm stronger for it and all that. But if I told you that I would be lying. I feel that physicians are hobbled in love to begin with. My grandfather used to say that the only thing more powerful than the knowledge a doctor has is the illusion that he has even more. There has to be distance, he would say. He was remarkably cold for a pediatrician, but he was fabulous at what he did. Dad was a bit warmer, but even he told me that people don't like to look behind the curtain. They don't like to know that their physician is also a man. He is a physician first, and then a man. We may be the only profession in the world where those two are switched around. Interesting men, Dad and Granddad. You can imagine where father and husband fell on their lists.

Distance. Curtain. Practice. Cause. Is it any wonder that I have no idea what I'm doing when these feelings for Caroline slap me in the face?

Thankfully, I know what I'm doing when I make my rounds, even when I'm at the Chaco Health Clinic, where every new hire (or volunteer, as the case may be) walks around the cramped hallways with this look about them like they've stepped onto another planet. I don't blame them. I was that way, too, when I first came here nearly seven years ago. And in a lot of ways, when you step onto the Chaco Reservation you are stepping onto another planet.

Caroline was that way, too. But it's been almost five years for her, and she's leveled out. Once she hits her five-year mark she's fulfilled her grant stipulations with the US Government. She won't have to work at the CHC anymore if she doesn't want to. I've spent an embarrassing number of hours wondering if she'll leave Chaco, and then ABQ General, too. It's a decent enough place, but if you feel no obligation to stay in Albuquerque, it would certainly be easy enough to leave, too.

Sometimes I have these drawn-out fantasies where she tells me she is going to leave and it forces me to make some sort of move on her. But like I said: That's not me. It took nearly everything I had to ask her to go after Ben Dejooli with me. I felt like my heart was beating so hard it was vibrating my tie like a base string. The trick to not looking like a lovelorn sop is to keep it professional. Thankfully, that is my zone. That is where I am king. Call me Doctor Professional. That is why I've been able to work with Caroline at the CHC for nearly five years without seeming untoward or awkward. But time is ticking, and I don't want to back myself into a corner with all the rest of the kids who are too afraid to ask the girls to dance. I have to leave my zone.

The CHC isn't a MASH unit, but it's no Mayo Clinic either. It's a repurposed office building, four stories, and it has that cubicle claustrophobia about it still. We have two old conference rooms that we use for revolving-door office hours for six hours a day on the main floor. I try to get there when I can, but mostly we stock it with the resident docs. It's good practice for them. Other than that there's a small waiting room that is almost always at capacity, and then three other floors' worth of patient rooms. Just over seventy-five beds. We get about two hundred thousand outpatient encounters a year. We cram 'em in, as they say, but it's better than nothing. I like to think we do all right.

The day of our trip passes like a blur. I see Caroline occasionally, but most of the time I'm in and out of patient rooms one after another, like I've misplaced my keys and am popping in to have a look around. Here at the CHC we are strongly urged to keep patient visits to five minutes and under. That kind of thing drives me crazy, and my grandfather would most likely have spoken to every administrator there is, face-to-face, about the travesty of rushing a physician. My father knew how to work within the system better. He would have written a strongly worded letter. I simply endure. The one time I do get a free minute and Caroline is nearby, it is she who brings up our impending outing. As if it could have slipped my mind.

"Doctor Bennet," she says. "How are your rounds?"

"Never-ending. But that comes with the territory," I say, and inwardly cringe. Territory? Who am I, Meriwether Lewis?

"We're still on for this afternoon, right?" she asks, and she raises a hopeful eyebrow. She could have asked for just about anything right then, and I would have done it.

We're still getting tattoos, right?

Sure are!

We're still running away to Bali, right?

Got my bags right here!

What actually comes out is, "If you're able, yes."

"Oh good!" she says. "Yeah, I think I'll be ready at shift change. Three p.m.? Meet you outside?"

"I'll be there," I say, and she's off. She's one of the most senior staff we have now at this place, where the turnover is, quite frankly, pretty ridiculous. I try not to think what it would be like if she left. I throw myself headlong into the next patient, an emphysematous male, forty-seven, mild tachycardia, moderate diabetes risk. Suffering from light-headedness, like our friend Ben Dejooli was, but the culprit here is obvious, whereas Ben doesn't smoke and he's not overweight. I go on like this, room after room, and soon enough, work blurs my emotions, and I can pull the curtain across once more.

Before I know it, I'm waiting out in my old SUV for Caroline, and I'm putting my palms in front of the vents to try and dry them off. It's a balmy fifty-eight degrees according to the readout on the dash. A textbook New Mexico fall day. I see her walk out of the front doors of the Center, and when I tap the horn, she waves. I turn off the blasting air. I can see that she walks with a bit of tenderness, and I think it's from having to single- handedly roll that stage four lung cancer patient over during that code last week. I've been there before. You can throw your back out in those types of situations and have no idea it happened until you're in the shower that night and all of a sudden you can't reach the shampoo. My heart goes out to her. It's tough enough having to deal with a bloody code without also having it sit in the small of your back for the next two weeks.

"All right," she says, smiling and huffing slightly. "That's over."

I wonder if I should bring up the fact that her contract is up in about a month. It doesn't seem the thing to open with.

"Are you ready?"

"Ready? You act like this is some sort of war zone we're going into."

I laugh, and it sounds cavernous. I clip it short. "It's no war zone. It's a nice community. Parts of it, anyway."

"Do you know your way around Chaco?"

"I've been all over Chaco. I know it well enough."

"I've never been past the CHC."

"There's no reason for you to, unless you like to gamble. Also there's a great Mexican food place off the main drive, if you're willing to look past the tracked up floors." I scratch at my collar. I'm nervous talking now. The words keep coming. "And a bar that's pretty friendly if you go left at the welcome center and drive for a few blocks. Dirt cheap. Called the Chaco Pourhouse."

She looks at me with this barely veiled expression of amazement, and it occurs to me that I've pushed the curtain pretty far back at this point. But that was the whole idea, wasn't it? Time to move forward with my head up? Power through?

"What, you don't think doctors drink?"

"Oh, I know doctors drink. I just wasn't sure about you."

"Well," I say, and I have no follow-up, so I shrug. She's already looking out the window. I'm dreading the silence, so I turn on tour guide mode.

"The rez has parts that people are supposed to see and take pictures of and experience, and then it has parts that are best left alone."

We're driving on the main drag, north, skirting the welcome center and cutting through the nicer neighborhoods to get to the council buildings, where the police station is.

"What's best left alone?" she asks, watching a huge murder of crows that is cutting a wide circle in the sky in sync, like a flock of homing pigeons. They seem to be scanning the ground like bomber pilots and calling out landing spots.

"You don't want to go too far north. You hit some of the track bars and the row houses, and then beyond that is a place called the Arroyo. Sort of a gypsy camp for the poorest of the poor Navajo out by this big depression in the desert. I've had a handful of calls come from there, working at the CHC. It's pretty hairy." I puff up a bit here. She seems like she's interested in the rez, and I want to show her that I know it better than most white boys.

She throws me a curveball. "I'd like to go there some day," she says.

"The Arroyo?"

"Yeah. The Navajo...they're tough, but they're also, I dunno. Kinda...wonderful." She's blushing now.

"I know what you mean," I say, and I say it sincerely. "I have this bracelet."

"What?"

"I wear a bracelet. A young Navajo girl gave it to me. She was a patient of mine, back when I was a resident working at CHC. She had a goiter, very treatable but something that was literally ruining her life. It was a simple thyroid issue. That's all. But it was big and ugly, and it ostracized her. Had for years."

I still remember the day that girl gave me the bracelet. She hardly smiled. She walked up to me, set it in my hand, then she turned around and walked away, and I stared at it until my eyes started to water. That's what is running through my head, but that's a little too much, I think, for the moment, so I say, "She gave me a bracelet. I wear it under my cuff."

I take one hand from the wheel and wiggle the cuff up a bit to show her, and I suddenly feel like a child holding up a piece of noodle art, so I tuck it back in and clear my throat. I've worn it for years. It probably looks like a matted piece of string to her anyway.

"That's incredible," she says. "I had a woman come back with some food she'd cooked for me. I remember how good that felt. Also I had a grandmother cry once and shake both of my hands pretty vigorously after I discharged her. I'm hoping they were tears of gratitude. I'm almost a hundred percent sure that they were."

I look at her sidelong and can see that in her mind she's actually revisiting those tears and reaffirming her diagnosis. I laugh. I can't help it. She looks at me and smiles. She knows I'm laughing with her.

"That's pretty amazing," I say. "Nobody ever cooked for me before."

"You really care about them."

I nod. "I don't think I meant to. But it happened. Still, places like the Arroyo, or the strip out by the tracks, those places I don't care for."

Before I know it, and before I want it to happen, the Chaco Police Station is around the corner. It's hard to miss. A big, long barn structure built out of salmon-pink adobe composite. A big, chrome disk stands out front, like a quarter balanced on edge. A memorial to those officers who have lost their lives in the line of duty over the years. As we pull in to park I can see that she's nervous. She's staring blankly at the front entrance.

"Ready? Remember, it's no big deal. I'm just checking on some files, and you came along. We'll see what we can see." I shrug.

She nods.

7

BEN DEJOOLI

W hen I agreed to write up a report on Joey Flatwood for the Feds I knew it would be like raking over a scar that still aches. I don't do well remembering how Ana disappeared. I've tried very hard to remember my little sister as she was, running around the house, handing me odds and ends that she thought were little pieces of treasure, singing or humming to herself. The Division of Public Safety already has a formal report on the night in question, but it was written by another officer. I wasn't a part of the force yet. Essentially, what those agents asked me to do was write up a report as if I was the officer who answered my own emergency call.

I'm not a good writer. I'm good at listing facts and observations. I can pick apart a crime scene better than anyone I know, but when it comes to telling people *why* I think a thing, or *why* I did what I did, I'm at a loss for words. I'm the type of cop who acts on instincts, for better or for worse. Most of the time it does me good. Sometimes it ends up with me passed out solo at the Arroyo in the dead of night. What can I say? I've had more than my fair share of misreads, but it's the only way I know how to work. Maybe this is the reason I've essentially been running the same beat route for years. Danny passed on the chance to become a detective. He hates the desk. Says the beat is in his blood. They never even asked me, and I don't think they intend to, all things considered. I'm reminded of that every now and then when the kitchen quiets.

I have a picture of Ana on my half of the desk. Two pictures, actually. One is a five-by-nine of her sitting on Gam's lap when she was seven. Dad took it. I can see Mom smiling at them just in the corner. Ana is just about to start wriggling free, but Gam's holding her close with just a hint of a smile on her face that says she knows Ana's about to make a run for it. Ana has this gleam in her eye. She was always wanting to run. But I suppose all kids are like that.

The other picture is her fourth-grade school photo. Wallet sized. The last one she ever took. It was the picture we gave the cops. It sits in the corner of the same frame. She fooled Gam that day and convinced her to let her dress herself. She's wearing a shiny purple windbreaker with three bows in her hair, and her smile runs ear to ear.

I turn back to the blinking cursor. I start with dates. That's easy enough. I could be dead asleep and if you told me to name a date, any date, I'd say Tuesday, August 1, 2006. When I'm dead and gone you can ask my grave the same thing, and the wind'll whip the desert dust up and you'll hear it speak: Tuesday, August 1, 2006.

I start writing a bullet point list of the worst series of events in my life.

- *3 p.m., I come home for a late lunch and find Ana on the floor of the living room. Grandmother is asleep in her room. Mother and Father are out. Ana does not move when I walk into the house. I know something is wrong because Ana has a congenital heart defect.*

Had. Ana *had* a congenital heart defect. I could write how all of her life I had half an eye on her. Worried sick about that tiny cough and about the breathless way she would come in from playing out back, wondering if she might be dying where she stood. We'd been in and out of the hospital countless times. Each time she cried, and each time another dime's worth of dread of the place dropped into my pocket as well. But I don't know how to write these things. So I don't.

- *Ana was non-responsive when I shook her, but she was breathing.*

Barely. I had to lick the back of my hand and put it on her lips to make sure it wasn't just wishful thinking. But we had prepared for this. We had plans. We ran practice drills. I called 911. First responders took Ana to the CHC, where she was admitted in critical condition. The doctors were able to stabilize her, and after eight hours she was upgraded to stable condition. Eight hours in which I sat in a tiny waiting room with Mom, Dad, and Gam, convinced that the last time I would ever see Ana alive was when she was shooting away on a rolling bed surrounded by medical staff, the double doors swinging shut behind her, in and out of phase. I didn't know then that later on I would actually wish it had worked out that way. Opened and closed. Like those doors. I don't know how the doctors saved her. Shocked her or shot her full of something that got her heart back in sync and going again. I didn't care. All I cared about was that she was okay.

We moved Ana to ABQ General as soon as she was able to be moved. There they ran her through a battery of tests, again and again while we waited and watched from behind glass. An eternity later, an old, fat white man who we were told was head of pediatric medicine came out into the waiting room, stood with his hands behind his back, and told us that she needed a heart transplant. Like we could pick it up at the supermarket. Without a transplant, she would not survive the year. Until a transplant became available, she would need to stay at the hospital.

And so we waited.

Ana was a high profile candidate. Young. All of her life in front of her. Otherwise perfectly healthy. She had the whole dwindling Navajo Nation angle too, and the government likes to trumpet how much they care about us. We were told there was a very good chance she'd find a donor.

Ana was weak and slept a lot, but she understood what was happening. She was willing to climb any mountain if it meant she could have her run of the backyard again. What she didn't understand was why it was taking so long, and why she couldn't leave her bed. It was tough on all of us. At first all four of us stayed at her side, all day and all night. But when days dragged to weeks, dragged to months, we started doing shifts. One at a time. People did a lot for us. For the Navajo, blood runs deep. Gam's friends, the real old school Navajo, came to pray and perform a modified Blessingway. Our neighbors cleaned our house and took care of some of the bills. IHS insurance covered everything at the hospital, thank God, but we weren't working as much, so people organized fundraisers to help us cover daily costs. The hardware store paid Dad time and a half for every hour he worked. We were inundated with food. And throughout all of it, Joey Flatwood was there for me. He cooked me food (which was not good) and snuck in beer (which was delicious). He brought me books for when he couldn't be there, and conversation and games for Ana when he could be there.

And then, eventually, he offered to sit with Ana when one of us needed a break. For any time at all. Thirty minutes to go smoke a cigarette. An hour to go take a drive. Even a whole night if we just wanted to take a breather. He was happy to.

Ana knew Joey. He was my best friend. He'd been around her since before she could remember. She trusted him as much as any of us did. And the hospital drags on you after a while. It's like the fluorescent lights suck the moisture from your skin. So we let him in.

Joey sat in Ana's room while Dad went outside for air. And there it was. That's all I know. I wasn't there that night. I was at home applying for jobs. Thinking about if I should go to college. Thinking what it would mean if I did go to college, off the rez. How I wouldn't be looked at the same way again around here. Just like my mother. It's strange to think of now, on this side of things. I chose not to go to college, and I was still cast out anyway.

How do I put this in a police report? I can't, so the next gap in the report is about a mile wide.

- *Father returned from his shift at Chaco Hardware to find Ana gone, and Joseph Flatwood non-responsive on a chair near her empty bed.*

But he wasn't non-responsive like Ana was non-responsive when I found her. He looked like the floor had shifted under him. His eyes were open and staring at the wall across Ana's empty bed. Dad shook the hell out of him. Said he slapped him. Joey wouldn't be brought back from wherever he was. He just kept staring. Never blinking. When I got there, after Dad called me out-of-his-mind with panic, I slapped Joey too. More than a slap, to be honest. It was a full-bore knockout-button uppercut, straight to that shutdown switch to the right of the chin. When he dropped to the floor, it was the first time he shut his eyes in over an hour. Before then the nurses had been giving him drops.

He was never the same after that day. He sat in the Chaco jail for a month without speaking a word. As the chances we'd find Ana grew slimmer by the day, he sat. The police told me all he did was stare at the wall during the day and sleep at night. If you could call it sleep. They said he did a lot of screaming at night. They said if you didn't put his food in front of his face, he wouldn't eat it. It took them nearly four days to figure that out. In those first four days he didn't eat anything.

- *Subsequent examination of the security camera footage over the time frame in which Ana went missing showed nothing out of the ordinary.*

There was no recording of what happened in the room, but there didn't need to be. Her room was on the ninth floor of ABQ General, and it had one window and one door. The window was intact. The

camera in the hallway showed that the door never opened. Yet Ana
was gone.

- *An anomaly in the footage provided us with the only plausible*
  explanation.

It was weak. I knew that much, even then. It was basically what
they call a "break line." It's when the camera misses some frames. It
looks like a stutter step. Like the camera blinked. The Chaco detectives told me that there was a chance that Ana was snatched in that
blink. I know. I didn't believe it either.

They dusted the room. They talked to every single worker on the
floor at that time. They pored over every piece of camera footage,
from that hallway on floor nine to every other floor in the place.
Elevators too. They questioned state police outside of the Chaco
border about crossings that day. They did everything. All we had was
that stutter step. Either she'd been taken in that second, or she'd
disappeared into thin air. 'Disappeared into thin air' doesn't look
good on a police report.

- *It was determined that Ana had been abducted from her*
  hospital room at 3:28 in the afternoon.

The nowhere hour. The forgotten slice of the day. Nobody ever
asks what you're doing at three in the afternoon.

- *Subsequent analysis of her monitoring systems showed a*
  malfunction in the machinery.

Malfunction is a bad word for it. The machine didn't work at all.
According to the beeping box, she was stable, then erratic, then gone.
It seemed to have reset itself. Nobody reported any bed alarm or
crash alarm. It was as if at 3:28 in the afternoon the machine had
never been attached to Ana in the first place. Her IV line hung limply
from a saline bag, the needle and tape still attached.

- *Nobody reported seeing anyone other than Joseph Flatwood enter the room, and once he was there, he never left.*

When I got to the room and found Joey blank, there was no trace of my sister. It was so undisturbed, without even a scent of her, that I was convinced they'd moved Joey into another room. Maybe if I'd sat with him right afterwards. Worked with him somehow instead of snapping and popping him in the face. Maybe if I'd convinced him to tell me what he'd done while it was still fresh, maybe I could have gotten something out of him. It's Triage 101. Every Chaco cop takes the course. The quicker you stitch a wound up, the less chance there is of a scar. I think the Chaco cops left everything split open too long. It's part of the reason I joined up afterwards. I didn't want it happening to anyone else. I'm not one to puff myself up, but I guarantee you if I had been behind a badge that day, I would know exactly what had happened to Ana.

Instead I was a terrified eighteen-year-old boy. I remember I kept running places. Up and down the halls. In and out of the front door. Around the parking lot. I yelled for her like she was a lost puppy. I screamed her name until my voice was hoarse and the police threw a blanket over me in the dead heat of August and sat me in the back of a cruiser. I didn't have a chance to look clearly at anything. And even if I'd had the sanity, I didn't have the ability. I wouldn't have known what to look for. But knowing that doesn't make it any easier. I felt like a kid who can't reach the phone when his mom is choking. When time is of the essence.

- *That day I start to see crows.*

I actually write this. I write this in the report before I know what I'm doing, and after I write it I stare at the letters for a moment as if they'd been spelled out on a Ouija board. I sniff. There's a tingling in the back of my throat. Like a drip. It smells like sulfur. My head throbs once, expands and then compresses back. I look out of the skylights above, and it's almost like I'm expecting to see the crow.

The big crow with the red shine to him. The one on the car. The one in the sky on the drive back from the hospital. The one that lives in the corner of my sight. But there's nothing but broken blue sky. I can't look away. It's like I can feel the big thing, right out of sight, perched on a branch and staring at me through the wall with unblinking eyes. There's a pressure in my head, a slow-building whistling. I grip the edge of my desk as I delete the words. Nobody needs to know that.

"Hey." Danny Ninepoint kicks me under the desk. "What's wrong with you these days?"

I blink. The bubble pops. Only the soft throb of a headache remains, but I've lived with that for months now.

"It's just this report." I flick my hand at the computer. "I don't like going back to this."

"Well, pull it together. It looks like you're the hot buck at the dance this week," he says, nodding his head to the door.

Two white people are at the front desk, and I recognize both of them. It's the doctor from the hospital and Caroline, and they're looking right at me. It takes all I've got not to swear under my breath or flinch like a spooked dog. Last thing I need is to give any one of the fifteen bored cops within earshot more ammo to use against me.

"You want me to go talk to 'em?" Danny mutters.

"Nah," I say. "Maybe..." Maybe what? Maybe they're here on business? The doctor has been round before. He's conferred with the detectives once or twice on hard cases where a Navajo ended up in the hospital. But Caroline? It's funny how her name comes to me like a letter dropping through a mail slot and plunking on the floor. Her name, and her hand on my shoulder. I remember them both quite clearly.

Like it or not, the doctor is coming towards me, walking like a stork. Out of the corner of my eye I see Danny shake his head in exasperation. I think he's tired of the parade too.

"Officer Dejooli?" the doctor asks, all business. Five or six cops turn to watch.

"Yeah," I say, defeated.

"I found a nurse who's willing to make a statement," he says, evenly.

"What?"

"The drunk driver. He came in to the ER a little over a week ago under police escort. Sorry it took so long. I want to nail that bastard as much as anybody, but it's been crazy at the hospital all week."

It takes me way longer than it should to realize that he's making all of this up to get me to talk to Caroline. He's so steady that for a good five seconds I actually think I may have processed a drunk driving case and forgotten about it.

"Right," I say.

"She's right over there. I have some other business with Sani, and I thought I'd bring her down. You know. Two birds and all that."

The cops all go back to their work. This guy is good.

"All right. Thanks."

And just like that he turns and lopes off towards the big offices. I clear my throat, smooth my uniform, and take a step towards reception before Danny hands me a notepad.

"Might want this. If you're taking a statement and all."

"Oh. Thanks."

He nods, his head already back to the reports.

Caroline smiles at me as I walk up to her, and it's not the smile of a girl who is supposed to be meeting someone for the first time.

"Hi," I say, glancing at the front desk. "I'm Ben Dejooli. I'll take your statement, if you're ready."

"I am," she says, and she clasps her hands demurely behind her back, but not before she brushes them on her pants. That's a telltale sign of clammy palms. She's nervous as hell.

"Right this way," I say, and I lead her to one of the empty conference rooms on the main level. She follows a half step behind. I flick on the lights and shut the door behind us, then I turn and just watch her.

At first she tries to be nonchalant, but she can only meet my eyes for about five seconds at a time. Then she screws up one side of her face, and for a horrible moment I think she's about to cry. When she looks up at me again I can see that she is almost as surprised as I am to find herself where she is. She looks around the room like she's lost.

"Is this about me?" I ask, quietly.

"No," she says, shaking her head vigorously. "Doctor Bennet had some files to give one of your people." She pauses and her eyes widen, as if she's insulted me. "I just thought I'd come with him to..."

"To..."

She looks up at the ceiling, giving up.

"To see if you'd ever gone to get that scan, except I know that you haven't because I could see that the order was never fulfilled. So what I really came to ask was why the hell you didn't go. There. There it is."

She's trying to stare bullets at me now. Her hands are on her hips. She's still wearing scrubs from work. Black pants that fit her like a tarp and a blue top that looks like it was cut from paper. I think she's wearing clogs, too, and I know that sounds bad, but it's not like that. If anything it was sort of cute. Maybe more than cute.

"You came all this way to tell me to do what the doctor said?"

"Yes," she says, point blank. And that's when it finally hits me: maybe there's really something wrong with me. My whole life nobody has done anything like this on my behalf. Something as good as a girl like her coming out here to see me has to have a flipside. Everything has a balance.

"You think I'm really sick? I...I've been fine. I haven't passed out or anything since."

But as soon as the words come out of my mouth I know I haven't been fine. My head has been hurting. Now that I think about it, I don't think it ever stopped hurting. I can't remember when it didn't hurt, even just a little. It's become background noise, that's all.

"Yes," she says, softly this time, and her eyes sweep over me, over my head and arms and the skin of my hands. "I do think you're sick," she says.

"What do you think I have?" It almost doesn't come out because it feels like I have a fistful of sand in my mouth.

"I don't know. Could be a lot of things."

"The doctor said you thought it was a tumor back at the hospital—"

"I don't know," she says again, but I can tell that's exactly what she's thinking. I'm not gonna lie, the more I think about it, the more it seems possible. When you pass out and come to in an ambulance, your brain automatically leaps to the worst of the worst. You're dying. You have something fundamentally wrong with you. But when Caroline and Doctor Bennet told me to get the scan, something in me rebelled. It's more than just how hospitals mess with me; I refused to believe it could happen to me. Cancer is so huge, so faceless. Something that you assume attacks without mercy. A dark spot inside you that sucks you away. It's not a headache. Not a momentary spate of dizziness. And yet, here Caroline is, trying not to look like she's pleading with me.

"Look, I'm right in the middle of a big case here. When it's over, I'll try to get to that scan. I promise this time."

It sounds weak, I know. To promise to try? This is exactly what she doesn't want to hear, and I can tell that her mind is tumbling over itself. But just when she looks about to come back at me there's a knock at the door, and it stills her. It's Bennet. I open the door, and he looks briefly between Caroline and me.

"I'm all set," he says. "Did you get what you needed?"

Caroline scowls, then frowns. Then she sort of deflates and shrugs, and that hits me. Bennet looks at me plainly and then nods.

"Well, you did what you could," he says.

Caroline brushes past me, and the two of them are gone in a blink. I stand in the empty conference room for another full minute, staring at nothing, trying to probe my own brain for parts of it that might be killing me. Like I said, I know I'm not *fine*. But am I *dying*? There seems like there should be a lot of ground between those two.

I end up staying at the station long after Danny and most everyone else on the day shift goes home. The night shift is half as strong, personnel-wise. On the rez there are basically two hotspots of activity. One is around ten in the evening, which the night shift takes on with fresh eyes and ears, and the other is at rush hour, about five in the afternoon. There's an old tongue-in-cheek saying around here. All of your calls essentially come from the same type of Indian: he's pissed off after work and starting shit and then drunk after dinner and starting shit.

Nobody around Danny's and my desk is scheduled for night shift, so I have a bit of space. Since nobody talks to me, I don't have any distractions, either. The shift change just sort of happens around me while I'm writing up the profile part of the report for the Feds. This is the part I've been dreading the most. Here is where I'm supposed to talk about Joey himself. I rub at my face. The only way to get through this is to just write whatever comes to my mind.

Joey was no saint, I write. *He was the only man I ever met who gave me the guts to go places that scared me and to do things I was afraid to do. He used to say that we were clipped at the knees in life just having to live at Chaco, so we owed it to ourselves to own the place. He said we'd be the rat kings. Joey never would admit it, but outside of Danny Ninepoint, I never met a man more proud to be a Navajo.*

I met Joey when we were thirteen years old, in those first days of middle school when kids hammer out the pecking order, and we decided to stick together. He lived at the Arroyo with his grandfather on his mother's side. His mother died when he was young. He didn't know his father. But his grandfather was a good man. A Navajo of the old ways. He hunted and trapped for food. He had a small herb garden in the window of his camper. He would capture water from rain, which he prayed for, and he would eat rabbit and prairie dog, which he also prayed for. He butchered them in the old way, too. Giving thanks. Never taking anything for granted. When we could, my family would pass cuts of beef and cans of food to Joey, for the both of them. His grandfather was too proud to take handouts, but Joey was more practical, and he had a soft spot for Dinty Moore stew. We ran together all throughout our teenaged years.

Looking at that last sentence, it hardly seems a fitting way to describe seven years of raising hell, chasing after cars and girls, drinking when we shouldn't and smoking when we shouldn't and what we shouldn't, usually on Joey's lead. Cigarettes that made us sick, and a couple of times peyote, that made us sicker. Swearing to watch each other's backs. Swearing in blood, smeared on our hands, dark like mud, cut with Joey's grandfather's knife, which had seemed like a sword then, and, in all honesty, probably would seem like a sword now, too. It was a huge goddamn knife. I wonder if Joey took it with him. The only one I've ever seen like it is Danny's scalp knife, which makes sense, since he has a lot of the old ways in him too.

I write, *Joey's grandfather died right around the time Ana's heart condition took a turn for the worse.* Looking back on it now, it was a subtle turn, but it was a turn nonetheless. She wasn't gaining any weight, she wasn't growing, she seemed to be shrinking, if anything. While the rest of her classmates and her friends were pushing their way up the hill into puberty, it was like she tripped and slowly began rolling backwards. But her eyes were always bright and winking, if a little softer than usual, and she laughed and ran, if a touch slower. I worried myself sick over her, playing out terrible scenarios in my mind, trying to imagine a Ben Dejooli who had no sister. I know now that I didn't give Joey what he needed then, as a friend, as a blood brother. I was selfish. His family was all gone. I still had mine, but it was going, and I wallowed in it. I don't even remember his grandfather's burial. That's how muddled I was.

We offered to take him in, have him live with us in our house, but he politely declined. He was seventeen, after all. His grandfather's camper and all that came with it, sparse as it was, was his now. Knife and all. And he knew his way around the Arroyo. He was a man now.

Still, that was the beginning of the change in him.

Joey became obsessed with death. Our conversations, whenever we met up, eventually turned to death and dying. Which I suppose is normal for a kid who has just lost his only family. Still, this went on for an entire year. Joey was there when his grandfather died. Their camper wasn't big enough for him to have been anywhere else. He said he went in his sleep, but I often wonder if his passing wasn't...uglier somehow.

I believe that this was part of the reason he offered to start watching over Ana.

The main reason he offered was because he could see the toll the wait was taking on me and on my family. But I've always felt that he was unnaturally comfortable there. In the hospital, around Ana, who was dying by degrees. I don't mean to seem like he was eager or creepy about it, not like that, but he did settle in quickly. He took one shift a week at first, just a couple of hours. He did construction day-work that started early, so he would come hang out with Ana in the mid-afternoon to give one of us a break. At night he'd go back to the Arroyo.

And there's another thing that's been bothering me, although I'm not quite sure why. Before he was banished, Joey lived in the spot where the smoker had parked for his vigil. Joey and the gambler would have been neighbors. The gambler probably had that spot for decades. He would have seen Joey grow up. There's a good chance Joey and the gambler were friends.

Something about finding these connections where they shouldn't be bothers me. The gambler and Joey should have nothing to do with each other, but they do. I just don't know how yet. I feel like I'm just outside of understanding, like I'm jumping up to get a peek through a window in my mind, looking for a glimpse of Joey or Ana, and instead I find the gambler watching me. In my mind's eye he's not dead, though. He's just silent. And staring at me dressed in dull gold and holding a turquoise crow tightly in his hand. And he thumps his fist to his heart...

I jump in my seat as a gust of wind kicks up and bits of desert sand pepper the outside of the station. The windows themselves seem to pop and settle, and the old fan that circles slowly above the main floor squeals angrily. The handful of other cops at their desks look up as well, brought out of their work, or their dozing. There is a feeling of resignation in the main room; the late night storms of autumn always signal that winter is close behind. Fall is the best season in New Mexico. It's warm and colorful, and it stretches itself like a cat, lingering in the sunny spots as long as it can. Winter is the worst. It's not cold, not exactly, but it's not warm either. It's some-where in the damp between. The colors fall flat. The desert trees and bushes seem confused, like they don't know if they should shed their leaves or gut it out until spring.

Profiling Joey has put me in a bad frame of mind. I'm feeling twinges of the same sort of sick helplessness that tinges this entire series of events a drained sepia color in my memory. It's time to wrap it up.

The last time I saw Joseph Flatwood was the day he was banished. At the reading of his sentence.

We were on the south edge of the reservation. He had his camper on the 'out' side of the Chaco line, and representatives from the tribal council and tribal court stood on the inside. I insisted that I go, too. I wanted to see him break down. I held out hope that he might finally give me something, some precious grain of information that would let me know what had happened in the room during that camera blip when Ana disappeared, but he said nothing.

He remained silent as the court read its decision. He looked at the ground the entire time. Although I did notice that he was crying.

I feel it's important to note this in the report. He looked at me, too. I stood off of the road with Gam, who also insisted on coming. He looked right at me and his eyes were screaming something that I couldn't quite understand, but his mouth was an unwavering frown, like a horseshoe. I almost called out to him. I was either going to scream at him or plead with him, but my grandmother sensed it first and gripped my shoulder like a vice, stilling me.

And then it was over. Joey Flatwood was no longer a Navajo in the eyes of the council. The voice of the people had spoken. He was cast out. There was no great clap of thunder. No driving sheet of rain or swelling of wind, but it did feel like a cord had been cut. A musical chord in my heart, like the string of a guitar. It twanged and thumped in my mind, and then it was still. Joey never stopped watching me, even when the cops led him across the threshold, even when each man and woman turned their back upon him, one by one. I was the last. Gam had to physically turn me. I'm not sure I could have done it otherwise.

Eventually I heard him shuffle away. Heard him get into his camper, and the engine roll over slowly, struggling to life. And then he pulled away. There was no peel out. No skittering of the desert dust underneath his wheels. It was a slow, quiet rolling away. When I turned around again, his camper was a dot on the horizon, but his eyes, silently screaming at me, brimming with tears, they stuck with me long afterwards.

You could say that they never really left me.

I have to wipe at my own eyes, which I do quickly and brusquely with the sleeve of my jacket. For the first time since it happened, I find words coming to me that I never turned to before, either out of fear, or out of anger, or sadness, or all three. For years I had assumed he knew something but wouldn't tell me. Surely he knew. He was there, for God's sake.

But what if he knew something but *couldn't* tell me?

The thought triggers a massive wave of pressure in my head, and I'm forced to lay down on my arms on my desk. I sit like this for several minutes, breathing deeply, trying to get my eyes to focus correctly again. Watching my breath fog the desk. I'm not sure if I black out again, but if I did it was only for a short time, and, thankfully, I'm not the only cop sleeping at his desk at this hour. When I sit up I do it slowly, blinking heavily. There is a sour taste in my mouth and a whiff of matches in my nose.

By the time I pull myself together enough to finish my statement, it's nearly one in the morning, and by then I'm sure of two things.

The first is that Joey Flatwood saw something terrible that day in Ana's room.

The second is that Caroline was right. I need to go get that goddamn brain scan.

8

CAROLINE ADAMS

Well. That was a complete disaster.

I've been going over the trip to Chaco in my mind frame by frame; stopping and rewinding, slow motion, pausing here and there. It's three in the morning now, and I'm more convinced than ever that not only did I not convince Ben to get scanned, but I also made a complete ass of myself in front of him, and later in front of Doctor Bennet, and in general in front of God and everybody. It would be good if I just ran away. I could probably get to Arizona before my car gave out. I haven't changed the oil in a year. I haven't done anything in a year, really. And just like that, bits of my anxiety snowball into each other until I find myself in the bathroom thinking I'm going to throw up. I don't, of course, but I do stare at myself in the mirror until my nose bumps the glass, trying to find any trace of color like I saw on Ben and on Doctor Bennet. But whatever I can see on other people I can't see on me, so I pee, then get some water and get back in bed. I listen to the storm blow against the wall and let my regrets wash over me like weak little lake waves.

I think it's time I was honest with myself. I think it's time I call this what it is. I have a stupid little juvenile twelve-year-old girl crush on Ben Dejooli, and it's infuriating. I want to be rid of it. I think that's why I went to the station, to purge myself of this. This isn't normal for me, I promise. I don't want to give you the wrong impression. I don't pine. I'm not a piner.

Ben has every right to think I'm a lunatic. He should have called the cops on me. Except he is a cop. He should have called himself on me. That would have been great. But not in any sort of sexual way. Just in a sort of escort-the-crazy-cat-lady-off-the-premises type of way. And I don't even have any cats. I've often thought I should get a cat. My apartment is pretty small, but I think a lazy cat would be fine. Or an indoor/outdoor cat. Although an outdoor cat on the Albuquerque outskirts would stand a one-in-five chance of getting destroyed by a coyote every time it left the apartment. If I got a cat only to have it eaten I would need therapy. I probably need therapy already.

These are the things I think about at three in the morning.

I really hope he gets that scan. I hope because I want him to start fighting the cancer that I somehow already know is in him. Just like I know that something was in that room after that horrible code. I just know it. I want him to get the ball rolling. He's dying, and it's time to get to work.

How do I know? I can see it. I can see what is wrong with him. That's what the colors are, some sort of visual representation of what is going on inside of people. It's like how you can see when a patient is yellowed by jaundice; he has a color to him. Actually, it would be like if a patient turned yellow from jaundice and I was the only person in the world who could see it. That's a bit more accurate. Just to make sure, I asked Doctor Bennet on the drive home if Ben looked darker, kind of reddish, and he looked at me like I was joking with him.

"He looked okay to me," he said. And then out of nowhere I started sobbing.

I haven't cried since my first year on the floor. I didn't cry when my mom called and told me that my dog died. I didn't cry when a tiny dove flew into my window and I could see it flop dead to the ground two floors below on the sidewalk. I didn't cry when I had to work Christmas last year and couldn't go home and I sat in my apartment and drank out of a jug of Carlo Rossi wine watching the Hallmark channel with nothing but a ficus with a droopy star for decoration, like something straight out of *A Charlie Brown Christmas*. That was a cryable moment if there ever was one. But I didn't then. And I did today. God in heaven. And in front of Doctor Bennet, too.

Of course, he played it off perfectly. He was so kind. He patted my knee and said it's okay and let me wheeze it out while I stared out of the window and wished the radio was on a little louder. When I said I was sorry he said there's no reason to be. He's had his fair share of these days too. He didn't even call it a breakdown, which is what I'm pretty sure it was. And the fact that he was so kind to me made it even worse, of course.

I have to get ahold of myself. In general. I have to allow for the fact that some people just want to die. And there's nothing I can do about it. If they want to die, they want to die. And I think Ben maybe wants to die. He was red. He was this blackish red that was just *wrong*.

While we're on the subject of my mental breakdown, I might as well come clean with you and say that I think I've been seeing these colors in some form for much of my life. I know this now. I've been *seeing* but not *noticing*. Now I'm noticing. It's kind of like how I *saw* wedding bands on people's ring fingers all of my life, but only really started *noticing* them once I hit my mid-twenties. The colors have always been there. In a way, this is a good thing. One of the first tests we give people who think they have an abnormal growth is the longevity test. Is this new? How long have you felt the lump? How long have you had that mole? Has it always been that size? If the answer is "for a while," we can relax. If the answer is "I don't know," we nod and tell them to keep an eye on it. What we don't want is changes. And this strange color filter I have is no change. What is a change is that the colors are stronger now. By the day. And they are trying to tell me something about the person who shows them.

I do a lot of internet research over the next couple of days. Especially late at night when I can't sleep. I pride myself on my internet diagnosis skills. I'm an RN by degree, but I'm a full-blown wizard-status doctor on the internet. The closest I can come to diagnosing what I have is a condition called "synesthesia" where people associate colors with things like letters. Each letter has its own unique color. Except that's not really what I have. I see colors around people, and they don't define the people, they help describe the person at that moment in time.

One piece of information pretty much hits the nail on the head. I stumble across it around four in the morning, right about when I usually berate myself for still being awake and make myself lie down and stare at the dark ceiling, stubbornly willing sleep to come like I've put myself in time out. That's when I find this thing called 'aura sight' at the bottom of the internet.

I know. I agree. I had a good laugh about it too, even at four in the morning. Telling someone who works in healthcare that they have a psychic ability is liable to get you laughed out of the room. We don't have time for this nonsense. We're big people doing big people things. There's a "joke" that goes around the cancer floor. What do you call a cancer patient who uses a "healer" instead of a doctor?

Dead.

Not really a *ha ha* joke, but you get the point. We barely sniff at homeopathy. You can imagine what we think of this psychic crap. But that doesn't change the fact that aura sight comes pretty damn close to whatever I have. The good news is I think I've ruled out that I'm dying. The bad news is that I've ruled in that I may be a kook.

Thankfully I wasn't scheduled to work the floor on the same day as Doctor Bennet until four days after our little excursion. By then I'd gone through all the phases of over-analysis, and my internal pendulum had settled firmly into a depressed resignation that at best I'm just abnormal. When I next saw him on the floor, it was during another hectic night shift and I'd forgotten completely about Chaco and everything else in favor of trying to remember which meds I'd given to a particularly challenging bone marrow transplant patient and at which hours. In that respect my work can be a blessing. You don't get time to mope.

"Are you feeling better?" he asks me, speaking softly in the break room. He sat down next to me during my granola bar supper. Or breakfast. Or whatever you call a meal you eat at four a.m. I look up at him and see that he's still blue. I blink and rub at my eyes. Still blue. A faint, soft halo of blue smoke that seems to puff off of his shoulders and head. It's his blue. I know that now. It's genuine and caring and a little sad. I don't know how I know that, but I do. You'll just have to trust me.

"I'm fine," I say, and I'm sure it comes out sounding snippy because I'm exhausted and working when normal people are in deep REM sleep. His smoke twitches a little and darkens a shade. I have an irresistible urge to lighten it up again. Get it back to the color of his eyes.

"I never got a chance to really thank you for what you did," I say. "For taking me. Making excuses for me to be a nosy little snot. For not freaking out when I was...freaking out. In the car."

He smiles. It's like a crack in the clouds. It's working.

"No worries," he says. "I know what it's like to want to see a patient make it. Especially a Navajo. There are some real train wrecks on that reservation. You and I both know that. This Ben guy, he strikes me as a good man. I can see why you like him." He smiles again, but it's a little forced this time and his color twitches. Then his phone buzzes, and he lets out a big breath as he pops it from his side and eyes it.

"Work calls. See you around?"

"You know it."

He taps the table, looks desperately likes he want to say something, taps the table again, and pops up and out of the door.

I don't see him the rest of the week. I don't see anyone outside of the nurses who are scheduled to work my side of the unit, my patients, and my pillow. That's the way night shift is. Weeks when I work nights I'm like a vampire. When I'm not at work, I'm shut in my apartment in a pharmaceutically induced black hole of sleep with the shades drawn against the harsh late-fall sun and my noise machine humming. There's a little note on the front door of my apartment that says "Do not disturb. Night shift in progress." The landlord and even my neighbors' little kids know what it means. I am a zombie if awoken. I slept through a fire alarm once. And one other time I woke up during a fire alarm, and I'm told I actually shuffled out to the main foyer with the rest of the complex, though I don't remember it. I came to in the shower with my underwear on. I must have thought it was time to get ready for work.

At any rate, the point is that the few people I do know, know better than to try and get ahold of me when I'm on nights, because I'm a groggy mess. That's why when my buzzing phone wakes me up I know it's not a good thing, since in my state it would have to have been buzzing a long time. Multiple tries. I paw at it, grab it, and bring it close to my face. I see two screens. Both of them say I've missed five calls. It's from the hospital. This cannot be good. I steady myself and click answer.

"Hello?"

"Caroline! Thank God. It's Owen."

It takes me about ten seconds to put together that Owen is Doctor Bennet. He's Doctor Owen Bennet. I wonder if I'm dreaming.

"Are you there?"

"Yeah. Yeah, sorry, I..."

"You're sleeping, I know. And I feel like an ass, but I don't work with you for a week and I had to try and call you."

"What? Why?"

He pauses, then says, "It's about Ben Dejooli. I've had some news..."

9

OWEN BENNET

I'm sitting in my apartment, and I'm cursing my tenacity, cursing Navajo stubbornness, and drinking bourbon.

I'm not sure *where* I went wrong, but I know I went wrong. I know it because Caroline ended up crying in my car, and since then the one time I saw her she looked at me like she was in a daze, or seeing me for the first time, or something. I don't know if it was me or Ben Dejooli or what, but it was something, and now everything is ruined.

I take another swig. Who am I kidding. It was me. A doctor who has worked out here for the better part of a decade should know better than to try and push the Navajo into anything. That's rule number one. There's white man time, and there's Indian time. Indians work on Indian time. If you want to work with them, you'd better work on Indian time too. It was a rookie mistake, thinking I could make her feel better out at Chaco.

What on God's green earth am I thinking here, anyway? What is my end game? What, in my wildest fantasies, do I want to happen? Somehow I sweep Caroline off of her feet? Convince her to stay here with me in my two bedroom apartment in Albuquerque? Maybe we clean out the second room of all of the useless gadgets I jam in there and we have babies and they grow up with Navajo kids and everyone dances the rain dance and we all live happily ever after? Is what I'm looking for basically the first Thanksgiving? I thought I was past all this. I have my practice, more or less, and I have my cause. The problem is now I have a girl. Or a dream of a girl.

I'm suddenly disgusted by the way I live. This happens sometimes. It's like a bout of nausea or a wave of vertigo. It passes, but when it happens I hate everything I surround myself with. I have no idea how to spend money. Or save money. I stuff it places or put it into stupid projects. I open investment accounts and play the markets like I know what I'm doing. I buy ridiculous gadgets like massage chairs and hydroponic vegetable gardens and memory foam pillows and microwaveable slippers. I use them for a day or a week or a month. I invest in things no sane man would invest in. Small pink slip companies from Australia that are getting into uranium mining. Drug companies that I pick at random from the complimentary pens one of their reps drops off on the floor. I have a jar full. All of these things I do. Some of them make me money. Some of them don't. I don't care. I have plenty of money. I'd have plenty of money if everything went tits up. We used to say that you could earn like a prince and live like a king in Boston. It was better than New York that way, where you had to earn like a god just to live like a man. Well, in ABQ you can earn like a man and live like a king. Especially if you have nobody to spend on except yourself.

I take another swig of bourbon. It tastes terrible. Now, you see? This is something I could legitimately upgrade. There is no reason why I should be making a quarter million a year and be swilling plastic bottle bourbon at three a.m. in my apartment. I shouldn't be swilling any bourbon at three a.m., actually, but if I'm gonna swill, it should at least be something decent. In a house.

I don't want to give you the wrong impression. I'm not a drinker. Not a *drinker* drinker, anyway. Dad was a *drinker* drinker. Not abusive or anything, just a booze hound. That is possible, believe it or not. I only allow myself late night drinks when I have the next day off, which, if you knew my colleagues, shows a remarkable level of restraint, comparatively.

I'm going through stacks of charts. I go through a record review for every patient I have. After that I usually go to bed, but this Caroline thing has me a little off. So I go through more bourbon. Sometimes when I can't sleep I do what's called a 'dead review,' where I whip through past records in our system and pull out everyone who has died and move their files into inactive status. I get the morgue records and cross-reference them with our hospital system. There are generally a lot of overlaps. This is the definition of busywork. I am fully aware that I am doing this so I don't have to think about Caroline crying in my car because she's most likely in love with Ben Dejooli.

It's interesting when you flip through the Chaco Health Center files. I find myself lingering on pictures of the Navajo. One of the first things they teach residents that are going to CHC is that your bedside manner with the Navajo needs to be different. Clear and direct doesn't always go over so well. You have to be much more reactive; let them take the lead. Especially with the old guard. And the old guard is mostly what shows up at the Center. I'm struck by how flat their expressions are. Flat like a lake. Calm. Expansive.

There's one man in particular who gives me pause. His name is Oka Chalk. He looks haunted. He has the kind of lined, tanned face that you would instantly associate with an elder Navajo, but his eyes look like the eyes of a young man. Of a young warrior. I remember seeing him off and on at CHC for blood pressure issues related to drinking. His chart says he asphyxiated on his own vomit. The report notes drug paraphernalia on his person at the time of death, but the toxicology came back inconclusive. Positive on alcohol in the system. Well above the legal limit, but nothing that would kill a seasoned drinker. Curious. But with no living relatives and nobody to follow up, his case was open and shut. Like far too many of the Chaco cases.

I pull him from the active files and mark him deceased. On to the next. I do this for an hour until I grow weary and slightly depressed. The bourbon is swimming in my head. The night has whispered by me, and the sky is opening up to the sun. In the distance, a flock of crows stirs as the first rays hit the bare tree where they rest. They shuffle and stretch their wings like a single organism, twitchy and black. One of them caws loudly. A sharp, brief sound, like the scratching of a record. I should really be in bed. This is bad, even for a day off. I know I'll never be able to sleep long enough through the day to make up for this the rest of the week. But something in the call of the crow sobers me and draws me back to my computer.

I flip to the active files and pull up Ben Dejooli for the tenth time. I reload his chart. The scan fulfillment status goes from *N/A* to *processed*. I take the last swig of my bourbon and cough a little. I pull out my phone and call the hospital.

"Radiology, how can I help you?"

"This is Doctor Owen Bennet. I was hoping to get the results of a scan that went through."

"One moment."

The hold music sounds particularly ridiculous to me. The bourbon still burns my throat. I find I'm tapping the hem of my jeans rapidly and standing in front of the window, staring at the crows.

"This is Diagnostics. What's your patient number, Doctor Bennet?"

I recite Ben's number from memory, forcing myself to slow down. I'm not quite sure why I'm acting like a student waiting for his board results. I've done this countless times before. But in all those other times there was no Caroline involved.

"Doctor Bennet?"

"Yes."

"I'm loading the file now. You should have access momentarily."

"Thank you."

I hang up and squeeze my phone. I make myself wait for an entire minute, then I refresh my log-in on the system. Ben's file is there. And it's bad.

I see two separate causes for outright concern. The first is in the front left lobe. Three inches in diameter. The second is in the rear left lobe, one and a half inches in diameter.

I am speechless.

Multiple instances almost always indicate metastatic activity. This is not benign. The tissue surrounding the sites are in necrosis. These look like late-stage glioblastoma multiforme tumors. We'd need to radiate the sites to reduce their size before we even thought about operating.

Caroline was right. Ben Dejooli is dying.

A sound tears me away from the scan. It is the crows. They've all taken flight at once in a massive black cloak and are sweeping towards me. Right towards the window, all of them shrieking at once. They look as though they will collide with the window, and I find myself backing away, into the kitchen. I even throw up my hands before they swoop up and over the building, their calls dropping away as they gain altitude. I sit down again, my heart racing. I take out the phone once more, and this time I dial the contact number for Ben Dejooli. It's barely five in the morning, but he picks up.

"Hello?" he asks.

This is always the worst part. The part before you bring a man's entire world down around him.

"Ben?"

"Who is this?" he asks, wary.

"Ben, this is Doctor Owen Bennet, with ABQ General. I have the results of your scan."

He pauses.

"It's bad, isn't it," he says, very clearly. No one has ever said this to me before. It throws me for a loop.

"Yes. I'm afraid it is. We're going to want to get you on a treatment plan immediately."

"Like radiation?"

"Yes. And chemotherapy. In preparation for surgery. But first let's schedule a consult. I'll be there to explain everything."

He is quiet. I can only wait.

"I can't do that," he says.

"Ben, I don't think you understand..."

"I understand. I'm a dead man."

"No. Not if you choose to fight."

"And if I don't?"

"If you don't, it's my opinion you have at most a couple of months. Maybe weeks."

"Shit."

"Yes. Shit. But there are options."

"Chemotherapy? Like, the chemical kind?"

"Yes. We would radiate the tumors initially, here, at the hospital, then put you on an aggressive chemotherapy regimen with the aim of shrinking the tumors before surgery."

"Tumors? Like, more than one?"

"Yes, I believe there is clear evidence of two, and maybe one more potential site."

"Shit."

I'm standing at the kitchen counter and I hang my head. I feel like whatever buzz the bourbon gave me left with the crows and now my head weighs a hundred pounds. "I wish...I really, *really* wish I had better news, Ben."

"I can't go back to that hospital. I don't do well in that hospital."

"Well, you're gonna have to, if you want to give yourself a chance."

"No, you don't understand. I can't. And not just because of...it's also because cancer here, at Chaco, it doesn't go over well. I...it just...for the Navajo it's a mark of death."

"Not if I can help it, it's not."

"Can anything be done here? At home? At my home? In private?"

Now this is an interesting question. I rub at my face and try to get my brain working the way I know it should. We do have off-site programs for chemotherapy. And the hospital likes to appear to bend over backward for the Navajo community. I bet I could get a request for offsite delivery pushed through, given Ben's position as a police-man. I am aware of more about the stigma of cancer among the Navajo than Ben would think.

"I could probably get the chemotherapy off-site. But the initial radiation has to be done in a lab. Can you give me that? If I can get you the treatment at home?"

He pauses. "Yes. I can do that. I suppose. It's either that or die in a couple weeks."

He says this with such a cavalier tone that it chills me. It occurs to me that he has exhibited none of the usual traumatic overtones. His voice is calm and clear. No tears. No wavering. He is responsive, and not in shock. It's not unlike the discussions I have with other doctors about swapping shifts. Straightforward. Practical. I jump at the opening.

"I'll call you back within the hour, okay? Stay by your phone."

"All right."

I move to hang up, but he speaks again.

"Hey, doc?"

"Yes?"

"Who would give me the chemotherapy? At home?"

"One of our oncology nurses."

"Can I request one?"

I already know where this is going. I can't help but laugh. It's a strange, desperate laugh. Thankfully I cover the mouthpiece first.

"Caroline Adams?" I ask.

"Y...yeah."

I shake my head, but I say, "Yes. I think I can make that happen."

"Thanks."

"Ben, we can beat this. I've seen people with stage four diagnoses beat it before."

He pauses again, and I think that maybe I've finally gotten through to him. I picture him holding his head, or covering the receiver while he gathers himself, steels himself for the battle. But after a minute he speaks again, and his voice is as even as glass.

"Yeah. I guess we'll see."

I get this uncanny feeling he's trying to let me down easy.

As soon as I hang up, I call the hospital on the off chance I can catch Caroline, but they tell me she was released early and went home from night shift two hours ago. I nearly curse out loud at the poor charge nurse, but I catch myself, thank her, and hang up. Then I stare at my phone for another ten full minutes as the sunbeams creep into my living room. Dust motes swirl about my table and my head. This is insanity. I had plenty of chances to disassociate myself from this. Let Ben be Ben and Caroline be Caroline. I know they want each other. It's like they reach towards each other when they are together. Even an analytical robot like myself can see that. Where along the line did I think it would *help* my chances with Caroline to throw her into close quarters with Ben? A terrible thought creeps into my brain, and the more I try to shut it out the stronger it becomes.

Don't worry. He'll be dead soon anyway.

And the sickness that washes over me immediately afterwards tells me something else: I do not want that. I desperately want this man to live. I want this man to live because keeping people alive is what I was born to do, but mostly because I know it would make Caroline happy. And we come back to the common denominator. And me, staring at my phone. I know she's sleeping by now, but every minute that passes is another minute of wiggle room for Ben Dejooli to back out. With the Navajo, you better strike while the iron is hot. God knows when you'll get another chance.

I pick up the phone and dial her number. Again, and again, and again. By the time she answers I'm so far beyond embarrassed that it's become a battle of wills between me and the ring tone. When she picks up, I let out a little hoot. "Caroline! Thank God. It's Owen."

She's groggy. For a second I think she's hung up on me, but she hasn't. I apologize profusely.

"I've had some news..." I say, and in the excitement it comes back to me that I'm about to tell her that Ben has late stage brain cancer. I pull the curtain across, and my face slackens. I take a breath.

"Ben got the scan. His results just came in."

She clears her throat. "You wouldn't be calling me at home if it was all clear, would you," she says, and her voice is thick.

"No. You were right. I would diagnose it as late stage GBM. Maybe stage four."

She exhales slowly, and I picture her in her bed slumping over like a deflating balloon. I think she's gearing up to shed the tears Ben wouldn't, so I jump in again.

"He wants to fight it," I say, and as soon as I do, I know that isn't entirely true. But he's willing to give it a shot, at least.

"Really?" she asks, echoing my doubt.

"I'm going to order off-site chemotherapy. Given his circumstances, I'm sure it will be approved."

"That's good of you," she says, and she means it.

"The reason I called you is that he requested you administer the regimen. You personally."

She makes a series of glottal sounds then says, "Are you fucking kidding me right now?"

I've never heard her swear before. For some reason, it makes me smile. It is in no way emphatic, more like someone cussing in their sleep.

"No. But he needs an answer right now, and I need to get him in the books or he could run. You know what I mean?"

"Yes."

"Yes you know or yes you'll do it?"

"Yes and yes. Just yes all around."

"Okay then. I'll get it ordered up. We'll start as soon as possible. I'll get the schedule to you when you wake up."

"Let's do it," she says, and I have the strange feeling that she's looking at herself in the mirror. Self-affirming.

"Talk to you soon then."

"Doctor Bennet."

"Owen. Please."

"Owen. Thank you. All of this, it's been a mess up and down, and I've totally overextended my welcome on basically every facet of it to the point where I'm even starting to annoy myself these days."

"Caroline. I wanted to do it. I'm with you. Do you understand?"

"Yes," she says softly. "Thank you. So much."

"Let's get him healthy, then we can thank each other. Sleep tight."

I hang up the phone and stare at it for a minute, wondering what just happened to me, to Ben, to Caroline, to all of us. Then I move over to my couch and collapse into a sleep that lasts until the sun starts to set again.

10

BEN DEJOOLI

I'm a mess after the scan. If you want to know what my darkness looks like, my own personal hell, imagine an hour-long brain scan with the specter of death hanging over you, and you'll come pretty damn close. I thought it was bad coming to in an ambulance on its way to the hospital. I thought it was bad sitting and waiting to be discharged. None of those discomforts held a candle to this.

I used to feel sorry for the Navajo who balked at modern medicine. I understood why they might not feel comfortable visiting a hospital, of course, but to throw the whole thing out the window was just reckless. I still have a healthy respect for modern medicine, even after everything that happened with Ana. I saw how the doctors helped her, relieved her suffering during the bad times. But the machines and the implements and the sounds; it's not hard at all to see why a Navajo would distrust these things. They are sterile and plastic and metal. Basically anti-Navajo. And, let's be honest, they can be terrifying.

Take the CT scanner, for instance. It's a big white tube, like the mouth of an enormous bloated fish. The techs slide its tongue out and strap you on it, and then the fish eats you in slow motion while its guts churn and rotate and clank and beep and motors spin around your head in the murky light inside. Faceless voices tell you to be still. Sometimes they tell you to close your eyes. It feels like you're hiding in a closet while something terrible stalks the room outside. They give you a stick with a button on it and tell you to push it if you panic, but then caution you not to push it unless you *really* panic because it'll screw up the whole scan and you'll have to do it again.

I think I *really* panicked in the parking lot. But I gritted my teeth during the scan. I was there. I would finish.

When it was all over, I practically ran outside. I took the stairs, not the elevator. I never wanted to be boxed in in anything again. In the parking lot the sky was robin's egg blue, and I just breathed for a full minute, staring up and blinking. I thought I'd never seen anything so beautiful in my entire life. Then I moved quickly to my car. NNPD move in and out of ABQ General all the time, and I didn't want to be recognized.

I think I get an inkling of what's happening at my house before I even pull into my usual spot on the side of our street. I'd noticed a thin stream of white smoke from a little ways off that gave me goose bumps, but I was still shaken up and focusing on driving. The smoke is like a thin pole the color of a cloud. It's streaming into the sky, and it looks to be coming from my side of the duplex. I throw my truck in park and run into the house, but inside all is quiet. I push through the living room and kitchen and out to the backyard, where I see Dad staring at Ana's pyre while a small wood fire is crackling in our old outdoor pit. He turns when the screen door slams after me. He is wearing leather breeches and is shirtless. His eyes are red, either from the smoke or from the liquor he holds in his hand. I know that in his own way he is trying to purify himself. For what is what worries me.

Dad says, "Your grandmother..."

For a terrible moment I think she's dead. It would be in line with the path that seems set out for me these days.

But then he says, "She is at the Arroyo. She has told me to bring you there."

Rather than put me at ease, this whispers along my back, and I shiver. Dad walks up to me in big, uneven steps and looks at me questioningly. He smells of campfire and whisky. It is not altogether unpleasant.

"Is she okay?" I ask.

He takes my hand the way Mom did when I was young.

"Yes," he says. "But are you?"

My spine pricks again. This is about me, not about Gam.

"We should get to the Arroyo," he says, and he walks, bare chested, to the passenger's side of my truck. He opens the door and plops himself inside, waiting.

Gam used to go to the Arroyo often when she was young. She told me she lived there for a time when she was learning the Navajo Way, which I took to mean a polite way of saying when my great-grandparents were on hard times. But she hasn't been back there in years. In fact, a couple of times she's gone off on the Arroyo as the dregs of Chaco. Once she even spat when I said Danny and I had the Arroyo rounds that week. I don't know why she would be there now, but I don't like anything about it. I hop up behind the wheel and fire up the truck.

The entire way there, Dad never speaks. As the Arroyo comes into view, the sun is setting. A bowl of heavy red light spills just over the edges and into the pit, but the light is retreating and night is moving in. I pull in where my memory tells me to, where Joey Flatwood used to live, and next to where the gambler lived and was mourned. But before I can stop, my dad taps me with his hand and shakes his head. He points beyond the Arroyo, into the rolling desert left of the setting sun. I turn to him, but he doesn't look at me. I know what's out there. That is where the hogans are.

"The hogans?" I ask. Dad nods.

"Why is Gam at the hogans?" I ask, but I know why. There is only one reason you go to the hogans these days. My palms start sweating. I flip the truck in reverse and pull back out along the main path, but where it curves towards the west I cut out along a sparse, rutted trail.

The truck bounces and creaks. I slow to a crawl and keep moving forward out into the desert.

There were six hogans when I was young, evenly spaced in a long line, each separated by a good distance. Now perhaps four are usable. They are squat, rounded structures made of wood and mud, just tall enough to walk in and big enough for four or five people. Each has one door cut into it, facing the east, where blessings come from. In the center of every roof is a smoke hole where evil is expelled. Even the Arroyo kids don't mess around with the hogans. There is something about these things; they forbid it. Years ago, the six most prominent families in Chaco each had a hogan and used them regularly for ceremonies. Blessingways and chants, or just a place to gather and sweat together. As the families fell apart or mixed with others, or just got lazy, some of the hogans went the way of the dust and mud of their build. These days, the big ceremonies, the Nightway dance with all the fire and the whooping that the tourists love and things like that, all of those are performed at the cultural center in a makeshift hogan. But these: these are the real deal. Or they were, at least, once.

The hogans blink onto the horizon like beads on a table. The sun cuts across the tops of them and lays there like a red blanket. I can see that the one farthest along the line to the left is leaning haphazardly, slumped and drunken. Abandoned for a generation. But there are crows there. Lots of them. They stir with the noise of my truck and then settle again. All of them are facing me. I turn to Dad. I have this childish need to point them out to my father, like that will make them go away. I wonder when they began to frighten me. I steel myself. It's easy to lose your head when you go beyond the rez, into the deep rez, and then into the desert.

Dad points at the hogan dead center, where I see more white smoke, a single, continuous string, like the trunk of an aspen tree, pouring from the smoke hole and spreading into the sky. That's where Gam is.

When I pull up, Gam is waiting for me. She is staring at me, dressed in a heavy, poncho-like dressing gown, and she wears a beaded kerchief on her head that gathers her long gray hair. At her waist is a buckskin bag. It's the bag that seals the deal for me. If it weren't for the bag, I'd say she was out here to teach me something about my ancestors. But that's an old buckskin bag. One of a handful of things in her room she told us never to touch. That's a Singer's Bag. Gam is here to do work, and I think she's here to do work on me.

When I walk up to her, she is quiet and watchful. She looks at me like I stumbled out of the desert behind the hogans. Like she didn't instruct Dad to bring me here.

"Hello, Dejooli," she says, in Navajo. She's not using my first name on purpose. Ben is a white man's name.

"What is this, Grandmother?" I ask.

"Evil is upon you. We must treat with the Holy People to expel it. Find alignment once more."

"Evil? Name the evil."

"You are sick. In your brain."

I straighten at this, come up from where I was talking at her eye level. Gam knew I passed out. She knew I ended up at the hospital. But the way she says this to me makes me think she knows more. Out of the corner of my eye, I see the crows at the abandoned hogan shuffle themselves about and then settle once more. Before I can question her, she speaks again.

"You have been marked by the white man's medicine," she says.

"Grandmother, I went because I gave my word that I would go. That is no reason to call a Blessingway."

I see two others making their way around the hogan, blessing it with pollen. One of them is big and square. His long black hair reaches the middle of his back, and his dark arms are like cable cords. He wears leather chaps over a breechcloth, and the beaded strap of his scalp knife swings about his knees. It's Danny Ninepoint.

Gam waves away my words. *"This is no Blessingway,"* she says, and her voice chills me more than the setting sun. *"There is another mark on you. A mark that runs deeper than the white man's poison."* She reaches into her buckskin bag and pulls out a handful of black ash.

"Come," she says.

In a Blessingway, the Singer essentially calls upon the Holy

People to pay a visit to the hogan and bless the patient, but as far as I know it doesn't involve black ash. Another of the Holyway ceremonies does, though: the Evilway.

This is an exorcism.

Gam turns away, and I follow her toward the hogan openmouthed. It's like I can't turn away. Dad and Gam enter the Hogan, Dad at a stoop. Gam barely needs to duck her head.

"Wait, Gam, hold on just a second," I say, in English. My Navajo deserts me when I panic. Gam doesn't hold on. Gam doesn't stop. She enters the hogan and begins preparing. I stare at the mouth of the hogan, a faint glow now visible from the small fire that will mark its center, until Danny comes around my way and stops in front of me.

"You want to wear your shirt?" he asks, so matter of fact that at first I have no idea what he's talking about. It's like he's asking me to pass the salt.

"Danny, what is this all about?"

"Your family says you're sick. And that something is coming for you. I think so too." Now that he's up close, I see fine scratches around his eyes and bigger scabs raking down his cheeks.

"What the hell happened to your face?"

He waves off my question, but his hand is marked too, like it was peppered with buckshot.

"Domestic dispute by the Boxes. The guy was hopped up on amphetamines. Fought like a bear. Bardo and I took him down."

Without his customary NNPD polish, I can see that he's weary. He looks like he's been chasing ghosts of his own. Bardo's partner retired last year. I wonder, not for the first time, if he's been picking up my slack and covering for me when I've had to make these hospital trips.

"You should have called me, Danny. I'm your fucking partner."

He waves it off again.

"If I'm sick, I need a doctor. Not a chant. This is a waste of time."

"You don't believe in the power of the Chantway?" he asks. He's not accusing, just curious.

Of course Danny believes. Danny believes as much as Gam believes. They're both from the same deep end of the Navajo pool.

"No, I mean, I do, I guess...I don't know. But this is ridiculous. How much money did this cost?" Calling a Chantway is not cheap. They require certain officiates and certain sacred objects and preparation time.

"She brought in two Arroyo men for the sandpainting. Nobody else knows. She has prepared all day."

"An Evilway? I mean, *really*?"

Danny nods.

I shake my head in disbelief. "That takes what, a day and a half?"

"Two full nights."

"This shit isn't fair to you. I know you've been working twice as hard on my account."

"I took care of it. Got Bardo and Yuska to cover our beat. Said we needed to work some things out. No big deal. It happens all the time with partners. Don't worry about me. This is about you."

My hands drop to my sides.

"Now. You want to wear your shirt?" he asks again.

I unbutton my shirt. "No, I don't want to wear my fuckin' shirt," I say, but the words have no fire behind them.

Danny takes a pinch of pollen from the buckskin sack at his waist and holds it up to my mouth. I open, like a toddler. He tosses it in and mutters a prayer I can't quite make out. Then he takes a second pinch, bigger this time, and plumes it on the top of my head. I hold back a sneeze. He nods, then continues around the hogan, consecrating. I go through the door and inside. I barely have to bend, either, but if Danny's coming in, he's coming in on hands and knees.

The hogan is hot and already hazy. A small fire made of new wood is burning in the center. It's not much bigger than a dinner plate, but it gives off a lot of smoke and not all of it escapes through the smokehole. Two old men I vaguely recognize are pouring thin streams of fine, colored sand into a mural that stretches in a rainbow around the far side of the fire. When I walk in, they look up briefly and nod. One is so old I can't tell if his eyes are open or not.

There are five figures in the mural, each drawn in a subtly different combination of simple, angled shapes and alternating patterns. Their bodies are long ovals in three colors and their arms are represented by patterned white lines and dots like Morse code. Each character stands on a thick, charcoal black line. I've been to a handful of Chantways in my time, both for the tourists and for the Navajo, and I can tell you that trying to decipher the sand paintings is like trying to learn another language; I can get the general sense, but the specifics are beyond me. Here, it's a good bet that at least four of the figures are the Holy Family: the Sun, the Slayer Twins (those were always my favorite as a kid), and, of course, Changing Woman. I think she's the biggest one. But this fifth one on the far right that stands apart from the Family, I can't say I've ever seen anything like it before. It's a figure all in black, made entirely of charcoal grains. Its eyes aren't sand, though; they're lumps of turquoise rock. I can't say why, exactly, but I don't like it.

The basic idea of a Navajo chant is that you want to call attention to yourself. You want the Holy People to notice you. To come on over and bless you or your family or business, or, with the Evilway, to set things right in you. I'd be lying if I said I hold by all of this. But all the same, I'd rather not call the attention of that last fella on the right if I can help it.

Gam throws me a breechcloth. I stare at it, then at her. She sighs and turns around. I strip down to nothing and affix the breechcloth over myself. When she turns around again, I hold out my hands.

"Now what?" I ask, in Navajo.

"Now we wait for the end of the sand painting. In the smoke."

She flops to sitting in a heap and carefully arrays her Singer's Bag in front of her. She pulls a plastic baggie full of twigs, herbs, and blackened wood from within it and empties it into a nearby pestle. She begins to slowly grind the concoction together. When it's a rough powder, she takes a handful and tosses it into the fire. There is no hiss or bang or colored fire, just more smoke. She adds water from an old quart jug to what remains in the mortar and keeps grinding. The sulfur smell comes on strong, but I can't tell if it's because of whatever she tossed on the fire or if it's just me. I blink rapidly, and my eyes begin to water. Neither the sand painters nor Gam take any notice of me.

I feel movement in the smoke and see Dad. He carries a crude mask made of sewn buckskin, like a leather ski mask with tiny slits for the eyes. Feathers have been sewn in at the sides and hang heavy with beads. I think I recognize it from home. As a kid I stumbled across it in the closet looking for where Mom might have hidden my slingshot from me. At the time, it scared the shit out of me. Still sort of does. Dad sits next to me and begins mixing a bucketful of ash with water and earth. Another movement of smoke, and Danny Nine-point appears. His eyes are hard and determined. Almost manic. I can tell he's sort of getting off on all of this. Danny always loved this stuff. In his hand he carries another mask, like Dad's, but his is adorned with horsehair and woven brush around the neck. Neither of them look at me. Both stare heavily into the fire, unblinking.

"The fifth painting..." I say to Gam, if for no other reason than to break the heavy silence. She nods, still grinding. "Who is it? Turquoise Man?"

Turquoise Man is a strong Navajo figure. He stands with a Navajo for life. Makes him invincible. Gam sucks at her teeth. It's her way of saying yes and no. Gam starts to remove things from her bag. Some of them I recognize. I see the miniature bow and two ornate chant arrows. I see the bull roarer and a bunch of unravelers made of string and feathers and herbs wrapped over themselves into rough balls. There's an old bison-hoof rattle and a smooth, curved stick. But then there are other things: a wooden contraption that looks sort of like ancient brass knuckles that sprouted crow feathers. A big bone, maybe the shoulder blade of a bison, grooved and dyed dark black. A shard of obsidian the size of my hand, and then, finally, and I sense most importantly, a box made of bone, about the size of a deck of cards. This she holds with two hands and carefully sets at her feet, closest to her. Then she presses her balled fist to her chest, right at her sternum, and grimaces. I've been to an Evilway before, once, years ago. But I don't recall seeing the box. In fact, I've never seen the box before, not at any Chantway, or at any ceremony.

"Is this an Evilway, Grandmother?" I ask.

Gam sucks at her teeth.

I try to ask more, but the smoke is making my head spin a bit, and before I can speak Gam gets up. She reaches into one of her pockets and pulls out a fistful of cornmeal. She moves to each of the four cardinal beams of the hogan and rubs the cornmeal along it with a single, deliberate stroke. She holds up an oak twig in her other hand and begins a prayer song that I partly recognize and partly don't. It's beautiful, rhythmic and crooning and insistent at the same time. This is the opener. The call that lets the Holy People know we are here. It could be the smoke, or it could be just my imagination, but somewhere in the back of my head I get this strange, creeping sensation, and I picture the fifth figure, the one in black, sitting on some other plane and opening one bright turquoise eye.

The smoke is heavy now, but I feel like I'm the only one affected by it. I look around, and the two old sand painters are chanting along with Gam, putting the final touches on their work. Dad and Danny are sitting on either side of Gam, who has returned to her mortar and pestle. Dad is focused on the ashes, and Danny stares into the coals with wide eyes that are shot through with red. The smoke is as white as bone, and it's pouring through the roof like it's the spout of a kettle. Things are wavy for me. I've never had a high tolerance for anything, really. Not alcohol, not weed back when Joey and I used to smoke whatever shit hash we could buy off people in the tracts, none of it. It never stopped me back then, but it was just the way it was. Joey used to give me a lot of grief for it, even as he'd carry me home.

Both of the old men stand as one and survey their work like two regulars gossiping at the bar. They point at certain parts, nodding. They both turn to the black figure and nod silently. They move behind Gam and sit next to each other and pick up her chant in soft echoes, like the walls of a canyon. Gam nods at Dad and at Danny, and they both rise, Dad with the bucket. He sets it in front of me, and both men grab globs of ash paste and begin coating me with it.

I stand with my arms out at my sides as they coat me with black. This is in keeping with the Evilway, but even my smoke-addled brain can see differences. Gam takes the obsidian and brushes it the length of her left arm before pricking her palm. A bead of blood rises, and she moves over to the black figure and presses it upon its chest. Her hand comes away grainy with charcoal, and she touches her chest again with that same grimace, like something burns there. When I am covered head to toe in ash, Gam, still chanting, comes to me with a palmful of feathery ash. She steps up to me, then away, and blows the ash over me. Then she asks me to lie down by the fire. It's just as well. I realize that Danny Ninepoint has basically been propping me up for the past five minutes. I look at him and see that he seems addled, too. His eyes are glassy and red, but his grip is as sure as stone. He looks eagerly from me to Gam and back to me. Dad is bobbing with the chant. He is not with us, I can tell. It's like he's staring at Ana's cairn again in the backyard.

When I lie down, Gam gives me her bowl. I look in and see a black, watery mixture. I'm not really sure at this point when I stopped humoring everybody and dove into this headlong, but I'm still not about to drink something that looks like pond water without knowing what's in it. Gam lifts it up to me, and I take it and lift it back up to her and try to ask what it is, but my mouth isn't working right. My words sound mealy and thick. Still, she gets it.

"Struck wood and struck ground."

By which she means it's wood from a tree hit by lightning, and the ground around it. Lighting is bad news for Navajo. Powerful, and bad news. In some corner of my brain I know that whatever that lightning hit must have some psychoactive effect, since Gam threw some of it on the fire and now I'm feeling like I'm sinking into the pine mat they set me on. The rational part of me, the cop part, tells me to knock that poison onto the ground. But the other part of me, the grandson, the son, the brother....tells me to grab it and to drink it. So I do. It tastes like mouthwash. The rest of the ceremony I experience in flashes.

It seems like I've only blinked, but I can feel things on me now. I look down at myself, and I can see that they are several of the items in Gam's Singer's Bag. The unravelers have already been partly unraveled at my feet and shins. There are black feathers at my knees. The hoof rattle sits over my groin, and the carved bone on my chest. Altogether they couldn't weigh more than five pounds, but I could no more move them right now than fly into the night sky. The chanting is still ongoing. Always ongoing. I recognize certain words like *path* and *sky* and *wing*, but the rest is too much for me to make out. I fade again.

The next time I come to is horrifying. If I could move, I would run. I see the Slayer Twins as soon as I open my eyes. They are leaning over me, like some bizarre doctors mid-operation. A quiet part of my mind whispers that these are the masks I saw earlier, that this is Danny and my father, but the rest of me refuses to believe it. The rest of me sees the twins for who they are: *Naayee Neizghani*, Monster Slayer, and *To Bajishchini*, Born for Water. It is them. I know it as surely as I know that I am truly ill. I know it as surely as I know that the white man's scan will come back with a death sentence. These things hit me with such force and clarity that they are impossible to deny.

I watch as they shoot the chant arrows over my body. They travel slowly, but I can feel the air moving around them. Their fletching parts the smoke. The chanting gets louder. I fade again.

The third time I come around, it's like I've left the hogan altogether. The singing might as well be the sound of the wind or the rain. It isn't so much a thing being done as it is a thing that has always been, like air. I can't see the Slayer Twins anymore, nor can I see the old sand painters. All I see is my grandmother. Her eyes are closed, and she is finishing the unraveling. I can't see what she is removing from the unraveling, but at intervals she tosses things into the fire and each pops like a nut. The motion is one with the chant: the singing, the pop. I feel as though I have sweat and dried, and sweat again. Like I've broken a string of fevers.

Gam takes my hands and places a pair of painted sticks in them, presenting each to me, all while singing. Each time she looks in my eyes, I can see the concern there, the sadness. In the quiet corner of my mind I know that she knows I have cancer, even before I know. Even before the doctors know, or the scan shows it. Does she really believe she can chant cancer away? Something in her eyes tells me no. Something in her eyes tells me what this Chantway is truly about: it's about opening a path for the fifth figure.

In the thick, roiling smoke of the hogan I sense the chant reaching a climax. It's a slow build, but Gam's pitch is rising and the intervals are shortening. This is when I see her pull out the small bone box that she kept close to her. There is a tightening in the air, a pressurizing, and I know that this is the reason she chanted in the first place. To present whatever is in this box to whatever Holy People have been called to this hogan, and to present me with it, to link me to it. She shows the box to me and looks me in the eye very clearly. She is making sure I am grounded for this, not floating away on whatever smoke and potion is coursing through me. I manage a nod. The sulfur smell is stronger than ever. I get this morbid thought that maybe the smell is my brain burning, or dying, or freezing, or whatever the hell a tumor does to you, but these thoughts don't bother me like they should. They've been muted. It's like they are being whispered to me.

Gam lifts the bone box up in the center of the hogan, and she flips it open. She reaches inside and pulls out a crow. A turquoise crow. It looks exactly like the turquoise crow that the gambler had at his vigil. She brings it down to my level, flying it over my body from toe to head. She presses it briefly against my dry lips and then over my eyes. The cut, the size, the style of the crow in flight, all of these are the same as the gambler's, but there is a thick vein of white marbling in the right wing of Gam's, and the coloring is so pure it's almost blue. This is a different crow, and yet it is not.

I try to speak to her. Try to ask her how it can be that she has the same totem as the gambler, what it means, why crows haunt me at every turn, but nothing comes out.

Gam places the crow totem on my forehead. It rests there like it was nesting. It's almost like it burrows down an inch into my brain. Everything on me feels so heavy. I just want to sleep. I want to let the crow carry me down and leave me buried miles below the earth. Just when I think I'm sunk, the pressure pops. The chanting, which was feverish a moment ago, is quieted. Like wind over the mouth of a cave. And that's when I see her.

It's Ana.

She is at the door to the hogan. The moonlight pours in from behind her. Then the sunlight. Then the moonlight again. She ducks inside, which I think is a very strange thing for a vision to do, because I know that this is a vision. A stray thought brought forth from my brain, borne from smoke and herbs and sweat, that's all. It has to be.

But it's still Ana. I call her name, but my voice only roars in my mind. I can see her turning from me, and it's like she's embarrassed. Like when I caught her drawing on the walls once with her crayons, and she turned away from me and hid them under her shirt. *Ana, I said then. Ana, what did you do?* And she turned away. I walked around her, and she turned back the other way. *Ana, did you draw on the walls?* A shrug. A small smile forming in the corner of her mouth. She turns like this now, in the hogan.

Ana? Why won't you look at me? You're my Ana. You're in my head. I just want to see your face.

There's that small smile, and then she turns to me. But it's not Ana anymore.

It starts as Ana, but then her warm brown eyes melt. They turn to black, and their color melts downward in two long triangles. Her soft brown coloring bleaches, fades to white in front of me like it's been baked in the sun for millennia, until what I see is a small girl with the face of eternity on her. Of Black and White. Of Absolutes.

And then whatever she is speaks to me.

Do not be afraid, my brother. All things pass.

This Ana that is not Ana, this creature, it passes from my toes to my head, and it grasps the crow totem on my forehead and yanks it out like a root.

Then all is black.

When I wake again, it is because Danny Ninepoint has poured a bucket of cold water on me. I take a huge breath, like it is my first, and then I sneeze three times. I roll and pop my neck and blink water from my eyes. Ash is running all down my face and into pools around my head.

"Welcome back," Danny says. Then he walks out of the hogan.

I sit up, calming my heart, placing myself. Everyone is gone. The sand paintings are gone. The men are gone. Grandmother is gone. There is a stale smoke smell coming from everywhere. The early morning sun creeps through the eastern door, lighting dust motes like flakes of floating ash. I sit up, and my head feels like it's twice the size.

"Take your time," Danny says from outside.

I have to crawl out of the hogan. When I do, I collapse onto the desert floor and start shivering like a dog. Danny sweeps down with a blanket.

"What day is it?" I ask.

"Dawn of the third day. Monday."

"Shit. We gotta get to work."

"Why do you think I'm here, honcho?" Danny looks at me with a straight face, but his eyes are smiling.

"What the fuck happened in there?"

"A lot."

"Danny, did you see Ana?"

"Your sister? No. But I saw other things." His eyes turn glassy for a minute, manic. That and the scratches on his face combine to make him look a bit like a junkie. It looks out of place on a man like Danny.

"Did you see Ana?" he asks.

"Sort of," I say. Danny nods. He's the only man I know who would take this as a reasonable answer. He helps me up and into my truck. He takes my keys and drives me home, where I take a five-minute shower and slam a cup of black coffee. As I'm getting into my uniform, I get a call from Doctor Owen Bennet. He tells me I'm dying.

I can't even act surprised.

11

CAROLINE ADAMS

I'm ripping down the highway with a bag of chemical poison in the back seat of my car. The pump and pole rigging sits next to me in the passenger's seat. It's secured with the seatbelt and shifts about awkwardly as I change lanes. There's no good way to move rigging. It only breaks down so much. It's like trying to pack a lamp.

The chemo itself is a sack of clear liquid, like a bag of water, but the plastic is thick and heavy. It's wrapped in a protective sheaf and secured in a bright red cooler with yellow biohazard symbols all over it. The cooler is locked in three separate places with plastic ties. I am terrified of it. You'd think after four years of chemo certification I'd get over it. You'd be wrong. The second I start to take it for granted is the day I drop a bag on the floor and rupture it and clear out the entire wing and have to go through a flushing regimen that I've heard is not fun *at all*.

Under normal circumstances I'd be going five under the speed limit, hugging the right lane, hands at ten and two, no radio on. Mom would certainly be proud. But normal has pretty much gone out the window here in the past couple of weeks. I've never given a chemo regimen off-site. I don't even like giving chemo at the hospital. But when Owen told me that Ben asked for me personally, I was all over it. I can't stop thinking about Ben, and what scares me even more than carrying a quart of cell-destroying liquid is the thought that Ben might change his mind. So instead of my usual careful driving, I'm going fifteen over the limit on my way to Chaco and praying I don't see a cop. Then I laugh out loud, because I am going to see a cop. And you can forget ten and two: my palms are so sweaty that I'm alternating them in front of the vents. As for the radio, I'm listening to a Top Forty station blaring pop music, because if it's quiet I start to think too much about what I'm doing and what it means that he asked for me personally. I need to save that for three a.m. Right now I need to do my fricking job.

Once I pass the welcome center and the CHC I'm totally lost. Owen seemed to know his way around here by heart. You'd think that after five years of shifts at the CHC that I would know my way about too. Guess not. I'm in over my head, but I don't care. I bust out my phone, but the GPS coverage isn't so good. Doesn't surprise me that these backstreets might be among the last to get digitized, but eventually I hone in on Ben's place.

Ben wanted to start treatment at his house, on his day off. He was fairly short on the phone. It took some time to figure out a schedule that worked. Where he could be alone. Apparently his grandmother is around the house most of the time, but she has a card game on Tuesday afternoons. He thought it best that nobody else was around. I said whatever he could do I would make work for me, and here I am. Before he hung up, he said thank you, and he sounded so genuine, and even a little scared, that I knew I'd make Tuesdays work.

His place is one half of a split duplex that doesn't look much bigger than my apartment. Still, outside of the main strip to Wapati Casino with its manicured desert foliage and squared landscaping and quaint houses of adobe and Spanish tiling, which even I know is for show, his place is one of the nicer I see within blocks. It's clean and simple and tended.

Ben is on the lookout for me. I can see him at the window. The curtains ruffle, and he opens the door even before I can park my car.

When he walks out to me, he checks both ways down the street. I feel a bit like the ugly stepsister, and I think he knows it as soon as he comes up to me because he pauses and looks down for a second. I can see him make a conscious decision to stop being embarrassed.

"Hi, Ben," I say.

"Thanks for...for coming."

"It sucks," I say. He laughs, thank God. His coloring is better, less angry red and more like the red of a sunrise, but there's still a touch of black to him, a representation of what's frightening him. It's not a natural color. If I was to hazard a guess, I'd say it was a visual representation of the cancer. There's something else, too, about the way his coloring shows itself. It's simmering, like a heavy soup about to boil. He's putting on a good show, but he's pretty freaked out. About the cancer, sure, but it's more than that. Something has happened to him that has rattled him deeply.

"You knew the whole time," he says.

I shake my head. "Nah, I just...I get these feelings sometimes, and I...It's just hard to unsee them once I see them."

"It's funny. You and my grandmother. Between the two of you I don't know why I even needed to get that damn scan." He looks up at the sky overhead and then around at the sky behind him. I follow his gaze. Nothing but blue. Not even a cloud.

"We should get inside," he says.

He carries in the rig while I shoulder my tote bag and then carefully pull the chemo crate out of the back seat. He eyes it warily as we walk up the front steps. I wish I could tell him it's not as bad as it looks, but it is.

The front room of the house doubles as a living room and dining room, actually probably triples as a living room, dining room, and TV room. It's neat and clean and uncluttered. He's moved a well-used recliner, the green seat cushion worn to white, to an opening in front of the mantel. I set the crate down like it's full of eggs, and he tries not to stare at it while I set up the rig. Meanwhile I try not to stare at everything that makes this place his home, starting with the pictures. I see the grandmother and father in one. The three of them and what looks to be his mother in another. There's one picture in the center where he looks like a teenager and he's with a young girl. They have the same color eyes. They practically beam out of the picture frame. I look over at him as he ponders the crate and see that his eyes are soft now, no such smile behind them anymore. He sees me looking, and I panic a little and my fingers slip on the screw that tightens the neck of the rigging. To cover it up I ask him about her.

"Is that your sister?"

"Yeah," he says. "Ana. But she's been gone almost six years now."

My face flushes, and I'm sure I look as red as a baboon.

"I'm so sorry," I say, which is such a stupid thing to say, that phrase, because even if you are sorry, so very sorry, even if you're genuine, you sound canned. Just looking at a picture of that little girl, I know I would have fallen a little in love with her if she were around and smiled at me like that.

"Me too," he says, and he looks from the picture to me. "It's all right, Caroline. I'm the one that's supposed to be nervous here." He gently takes the pieces of the rig from my fingers, which feel like sausages. "I can set the rig up. I've seen a lot of them in my day. You can...do whatever needs to be done with that thing." He nods over at the chemo crate.

"You have any scissors?" I ask.

"Down the hall in the kitchen. In the big drawer."

I walk into the kitchen. It's spotless, but it has a well-used feel, a subtle layered smell of spices and oils that makes my stomach growl. I slide open the big drawer under the microwave and find the scissors, then turn to go. But I pause when I see a second room, off to the right. It looks like it was a small sitting room, but it's been converted into a tiny bedroom. I crane my neck, making sure to keep behind the refrigerator enough so Ben won't see how rude I'm being, and I see that the room is almost monastic. The floor has nothing on it. There is nothing on the walls. The bed would only accommodate two-thirds of me and is pulled hospital-tight. There's a beautiful Navajo blanket folded lengthways across it, but that's about all of the color there is to see, except for something on a small shelf above the bed: two painted sticks crossed over a worn leather pouch. The pouch is open, and the opening is facing me. Something is glinting there. It's a cold, white glint. A box of some kind. I feel myself take a step towards it, and as soon as I do a shadow drops down over the window, and I have to stifle a scream. I stumble back into the open drawer, and my butt slams it shut with a loud bang.

It's a crow, on the windowsill. And not just any crow. It's the biggest crow I have ever seen. It looks prehistoric. As it settles, its coloring seems to blur and change in the dull light of the fall sun. At first it's black as night, and then it looks shot through with red, then black again. For one terrible minute I think it's in the room, but it flaps its wings and they brush against the outside of the window with a raspy raking sound.

A cold, whispered dread falls over me, the same type of feeling I had after that lung cancer patient bled out on us, when I was cleaning his room. There's a subtle movement in the air where there shouldn't be. I almost scream again, but this time it's no jump scare. It's because the crow is looking at me. Looking right at me with an eye the size of a golf ball and as black as marble. The fact that it doesn't make a sound, not even a squawk, makes it somehow even worse. It's just perched there, on the ledge, taking up the whole sill, its head turned flush right against the window. I can see a flat, sticky disk where its eye is pushing against the glass. Its beak taps once against it with the sound of a cracking knuckle.

Then Ben is there beside me.

"Caroline? Everything okay?"

The spell is broken. I take my first breath in what feels like minutes. I look from him back to the window, but the crow is gone.

"I'm sorry, I...I thought I saw something."

He looks through the window himself, and his coloring darkens to a deep clay. It's not fear that he is feeling, but it's close, something like a mixture of dread and inevitability.

"What did you see?" he asks, but I can tell he already knows.

"It was a bird. A big bird."

He nods. "I've been having something of a bird problem lately."

I cock my eyebrow at him.

"Kinda hard to explain. C'mon, let's get this over with." He nods back towards the front room. When we get back there I notice he's held my hand for the short walk. I'd like to think it's not because he thinks I'm a snoop that he has to keep tabs on. I file it away. Prime three a.m. material, right there.

Back in the front room, I open my tote and pull out my yellow chemo gown. It crinkles like a bag of chips as I pull it on. It has matching gloves, too. High fashion in the nursing world.

"What the hell?" Ben says.

"It's standard, don't worry."

"Is that to protect you?"

"Yeah, in case something happens when I start your line."

"To protect you from getting it on your skin?"

"Exactly."

"To protect you from what you're about to put in my bloodstream?"

"That's right." I nod, then realize he's incredulous. I pause before saying, "Look, this is strong stuff. But you need strong stuff. Know what I'm saying?"

After a second he nods.

"Plus, I think hazard yellow is a pretty good color on me. No?"

He cracks a smile that is a shadow of the one in the picture, but even a shadow works for me.

"All right," I say, "let's get this show on the road."

I snip the four protective ties and open the crate. The hood bag is inside another bag labeled Cytotoxic, which I pull out like a lunch pail.

"This is Avastana. You know what it does, right?"

"Yeah. They told me it'll wipe me out. I'll puke my guts out in the short term and lose my hair in the long term." His tone is as dry as bone. I can't tell if he's joking. I never know what the doctors tell these guys, and although Owen is the best of them, docs by nature are dorks who often have a hard time not explaining things like they're a textbook. I figure I should run it down for him in plain English.

"Basically cancer is just cells that are changing way too fast. This stuff kills those cells. It also kills any cells that look like those cells. Other fast moving cells, things like hair cells that grow fast, or mucous membranes that are naturally active. That's why your hair will most likely fall out. You'll also probably get abrasions and sores in your mouth and lower GI."

"My ass?"

"Yeah. Your ass."

"So this is the red button."

"What?"

"The nuclear option."

"Yeah. You could say that."

He sits down in the old chair and deflates for a second before pulling himself together. He is getting quite dark. And not just in the coloring that only I can see. "That's pretty much what the doctor said."

"Doctor Bennet?"

"Yeah."

I nod and pull up a fold-out chair that was propped against the couch. I pop it open next to his armrest and sit down by the hanging bag next to him. It's like a big chemical sprig of mistletoe. I grab his hand, and I'm not ashamed to admit that the spark of pure, rich clay coloring that I see float from him makes me feel good. It makes me feel like a nurse.

"I'll be right here, Ben. You and me. All right?"

He squeezes my hand and looks into my eyes.

"You and me," he says. "Okay. Hit me."

I prep his vein. Every nurse judges a man by his veins. It sounds weird, but when you spend as much time fretting over hitting veins for lines as we do, and studying how best to hit veins, and reading about where we have to start lines on people when we can't find their veins, you learn to appreciate a nice, fat, dark vein. Ben's veins are crazy prominent on his arms. They look like earthworms. A blind nurse could start a chemo line on this guy. I hit his forearm vein on the first try and have to stop myself from whooping. He doesn't even flinch. I flush the IV, tape it down, and turn to the pump. I program a drip level and pull the clamp. That's that. I turn back to him and find he's been watching me the whole time.

"Now what?" he asks.

"Now we wait. It's a two-hour infusion."

"Two hours?"

"Yeah. You want a book?"

"Nah."

"I brought some cards, too. Or I could turn on the TV for you if you want."

"Nah," he says again, but he's tapping his foot. He looks a shade yellow. Nervous.

"When do I start feeling like shit?" he asks.

"With most people it's an hour or two after the infusion."

He nods, and his foot tapping intensifies. He follows the line from his arm up to the bag, and he's fixated on the pump drip like it's an hourglass. Without even meaning to, I rest my hand on his bobbing knee. The pallid mist fades away from him like vapor in the sun. Part of me feels guilty at knowing how I affect him. A small part. The rest of me is elated.

"Talk to me," he says.

"Talk to you?"

"Yeah, I...whenever Ana or I had to do hospital things, we would talk to each other. Whenever she had tests. We'd talk nonstop."

"Okay," I say, nodding. "Okay, uh. What would you like to talk about?"

"I dunno. Anything."

"What's your favorite color?"

"Red," he says, with a slight smirk.

"I knew it. All right, now you."

"Okay. What are you doing here?" he asks.

"Sorry?"

"I mean on the shithole outskirts of New Mexico. You have family in Albuquerque?" He traces the line from his arm back up the bag, his eyes wide.

"No, no family in Albuquerque, or anywhere near it. My family is from Iowa."

"So why here?" he asks, turning back to me.

"I got a grant from the government. They gave me money to go to nursing school. In return I gave them five years—twelve hours a week at the Chaco Health Center."

"Like the army," he says and starts to laugh. He nods to himself. "Dealing with the Navajo *is* kinda like a war."

"It's not like that. I had a specified term in an underserved community. It could have been anywhere. HUD areas. Inner city hospitals. Rural clinics. Anything."

"And are you glad you were sent to Chaco?"

I nod. I don't even have to think. "I knew it was the right decision the day I got a tupperware full of food from this old Navajo woman. She was a patient of mine during one of my rotations. She took the bus out to ABQ General. I don't even know where she got on."

"Had to have been in Grants City, just south. No bus system in Chaco."

"That's what I figured. She hitched her way out of the rez and then took the bus into Albuquerque just to give me food."

"I bet it was awesome."

"Oh my God. You have no idea. Best chicken I've ever had in my life. And I was new then, too. I hadn't had a home-cooked meal in months. I didn't even have pots in my apartment yet. I literally cried while I ate it all."

We're quiet for a moment, but it's a comfortable quiet. The house settles around us in the late afternoon cool.

"And then you came," I say. I don't really know why. I have this dangerous and peculiar tendency to panic around men I like, but when I do, I also have this liberating side effect of throwing caution to the wind. I think I've been in a low-grade panic since I got that call from Owen telling me Ben wanted off-site chemo and wanted it from me.

"Me?" Ben says.

"Yeah. You. You take the good with the bad when you work at the CHC. There's plenty of both, I think, but the good is quiet while the bad is loud. The bad shows up on my patient rounds late at night half-dead or detoxing. That's loud. That has a loud color. But you, you're good. And you're a quiet good. And you have a nice color, and I bet it'd be nicer if you didn't have such a mountain on your shoulders. I can see it weighing you down. I'm rambling now. I'll shut up."

For a second I think he's going to make me explain myself and my weird Technicolor Dream Vision, and then he'll laugh me out of his house and straight into therapy. But he says nothing. It's wonderful. It's wonderfully Navajo.

"All right. Your turn," he says.

"What's the deal with the crow?" I ask. I don't even skip a beat. Neither does he.

"I wish I knew," he says. Then he looks up at the ceiling like he could see through it to the sky. "All I know is that recently I've been seeing a lot of crows. But I think they've been around longer than that. You know? I think it's kind of a thing I've had for a long time around me but I'm only now coming to see it."

"Tell me about it."

"What?"

"Nothing. Keep going."

"I mean, it's late fall. This is when the crows gather. It should be normal. But it's not. "

"Because of the big guy?"

"Yeah. The big guy. And I sort of feel like they're always gathering around me. Does that sound crazy?"

I think for a second. A couple of weeks ago maybe it would have sounded crazy. Not anymore.

"No."

He lets out a breath. "That's good."

"But why? Why are they following you?"

"I think it has something to do with a gambler. And this place on the desert boundary called the Arroyo. And Ana."

"Your sister?"

"Yeah. I don't know how. But it does. And..." He squints and drops his head and then blinks rapidly. I lean in closer to him.

"Ben? You all right? What are you feeling?"

"I just feel...I feel like I'm running out of time. I had this Evilway. It's a Navajo chant ceremony. I saw things. I'm not sure if it was good for me. I think it's speeding things up."

He's rambling now. Pouring forth. Like I've lanced a blister.

"I saw Ana. I saw her."

"What, like a vision?"

"Yes. But no. It was more. It was...terrible. She came in the hogan when..." He drops his head again, straining to remember. Then he pops up, his eyes bright with recognition.

"The crow. The totem. Or was that a vision too?" His eyes shoot back towards the kitchen, towards where the back room is. He makes a move to get up, and I have to settle him.

"You have to wait the infusion out."

He sits down again and swallows hard. "I feel strange," he says.

"I know. So do I. Let's keep talking."

So we do. Until every last drip of Avastana is coursing through his veins. We talk about our parents, his estranged but nearby, mine together but far away. We talk about paying bills and working late. We talk about night shifts and groggy mornings and old friends. He talks about a guy named Joey like a good friend, but in past tense. I don't want to make the same mistake I did with his sister, so I don't pursue it.

He looks weary when I eventually pull his line. I press a cotton ball to his vein, and he takes a huge, shuddering breath and closes his eyes.

"Weird to think of that stuff inside me."

"It's going to work," I say.

"I don't feel all that bad," he says. "Just tired."

"Give it a few hours."

"I thought you were supposed to make me feel better," he says, smiling up at me.

"I'm here to help you, not pat your head." But I pat his head anyway. Then the doorbell rings.

His color muddies. His smoke had been strengthening despite the chemo, moving to a stronger red, but it yellows with the knocking. His eyes snap to the door, then he looks at me. His eyes tell me all I need to know. Nobody was supposed to bother us. We're both silent, thinking the same thing: maybe they'll just go away.

The doorbell rings again, then someone pounds on the door. I wince at the sound.

"Want me to get it?" I whisper.

He shakes his head. "Help me up."

I take his outstretched hand with both of mine and pull him to his feet. He steadies himself and eyes the door with narrow lids. He sets his shoulders and moves over to the door. There's no window in the door—it's just a slab of wood—but there's a chain catch, and he slides it to before opening the door a crack. I hear a man's voice outside.

"Mr. Dejooli?"

"Yes," Ben says.

"It's Agent Parsons, with the FBI. I'm here with Agent Douglas as well. May we speak with you?"

"It's not a good time," Ben says.

"I'm afraid we must insist," the other, Douglas, says from behind the door. His voice is lower, just above a growl.

"Insist all you want," Ben says. "I can't talk to you today. If it's about the report, it can wait until tomorrow." Ben moves to close the door, but it thuds against a shoe.

"We found Joseph Flatwood," says Parsons.

Ben freezes.

"We need to talk with you," says Douglas, more forcefully this time.

Ben rests his head against the back of the door for a moment, then slides the catch free. He swings open the door and two men in drab suits and bad ties step inside. They have the instantly forgettable faces of government lackeys. They eye me with a clinical unease. They take in the rig and the bag without comment. There can be no mistaking what's going on here, though. I'm still dressed like a chicken, after all.

"All right," Ben says. "What is it?"

The agents look at me, and then something unsaid passes between them.

"She's with me," Ben says. "Now out with it."

I flush. I staunch a smile. Agent Parsons gives me a pitying look before turning to Ben. "Flatwood hit another hospital. In Flagstaff."

"And you got him?"

"No. He got away. Again."

I try to see Ben's color. It's hard. He's hiding it well, something I suspect he is doing without thinking. The Navajo are very good at affecting a passive face when they want to.

"How?" he asks.

"We don't know. From the looks of it, he just...disappears."

"What?"

"He shoots up now, right on site. Right where he steals the drugs. He should be in a coma, but instead, he gets away."

"But you said you know where he is?"

"He drives an old motorcycle. We've had our eye out for it ever since a traffic camera picked him up in Portland. We found it outside of the hospital in Flagstaff, and we bugged it in case he eluded us again."

"Good thing," Ben says. Neither of the agents moves a muscle. "So where's he going?"

"East. Fast. His movements are erratic. He would be hard to catch, even if we wanted to."

"But you don't."

"No. We don't want to tip him off."

Ben puts his hands on his hips, and I can see that he wants to scratch at his stomach. His nausea would be knocking at the door right about now.

"I don't understand. What do you want from me?" Ben asks, and it breaks my heart to hear the hint of desperation in his voice.

"We know where he's going, Ben. There's only one major hospital on his route that's big enough for him to slip in and out unnoticed."

I go cold. "ABQ General," I say, before I can stop myself.

The agents turn to me briefly, then nod as if they were approving of the pictures on the mantel. "And he's almost there. We're just ahead of him."

"Well, catch him then. What are you standing here for?" Ben says.

Parsons smooths at his tie. Douglas scratches at his neck. Their coloring is hard to describe. It's flat brown. Almost dead. There's been very little movement until now, but at Ben's insistence a muted flash of mottled black speckles around both men. They're embarrassed. And angry about it.

"We have tried. Twice our people had him dead to rights. Twice he got away."

"You don't think you can catch him," Ben says, and I hear a hint of a smile in his voice.

"We think you might have a better shot," Parsons says.

"Me? You're kidding. What makes you think I could do anything?" He sounds incredulous, but I know otherwise. I can see it in how he sharpens, like a camera snapping to focus. He wants to see this Joey character. This friend I thought was dead. He wants it badly.

I jump in, before anyone can say anything. "Ben, you're going to be very sick soon. We don't know how you're going to react, but odds are it's not going to be good. You shouldn't leave this house."

The agents seem totally disinterested in me. Disinterested in everything but getting Ben to go with them. They're so *flat*. Like they're cutouts of men.

"I don't like them," I say. I cover my mouth for a second, then drop my hand before I look too much like a little girl. "I mean...what I mean is that if they have a tracker on him, you can get him tomorrow. Or the next day."

Or never, and you can just stay with me. And I'll talk to you. And hold your hand.

"He's getting violent," Parsons says evenly. "He assaulted two orderlies at Flagstaff Presbyterian Hospital. Hurt one of them fairly badly. He is extremely hard to take down. His strength is...outsized. We read your report. You can get in his head. Talk to him. Slow him down or distract him enough for our guys to take him down."

"Ben—" I begin, pleading.

"We don't have a lot of time, Mr. Dejooli. A matter of hours. And it's a little over an hour to get there."

I drop my hands to my sides, and my gown crinkles loudly. I already know I've lost.

"Okay," Ben says. "I'll go. Just give me five minutes."

The agents nod, then turn to leave. One of them, Douglas, turns to me and stares at me with the blank malice of a guard dog. Then he follows Parsons out. Ben and I are alone again.

"I have to go. You don't know about things between Joey and me. I... just have to go, that's all."

"You're gonna get sick."

"I'll bring a bag."

"Dammit, Ben," I say, quietly.

"I'm sorry. I wouldn't go if it was anything else. You gotta believe me."

I rummage around roughly in my tote until I find the anti-nausea medication I brought along with me.

"Here," I say, throwing it a little harder than I had intended. He catches it out of midair, and it rattles. "Take two. Then take two more in two hours. So on and so forth. It'll help, but it won't take care of everything. You're gonna feel like garbage."

He looks so grateful and relieved that I can't stay mad at him. I'm not sure it's my place to keep him anywhere if he wants to go. I can only say what I can say. I take off my gown and start packing things away while he dashes to the back. I hear him pour a glass of water and gulp the pills down, then I hear him cut left to his room. When he comes back out, he's in uniform. Hat and all. He pauses in the kitchen and looks back at the side room where I saw the crow at the window. He takes a tentative step forward and seems to be thinking. I try to fade into the wall while still watching him. He takes a few slow steps and reaches up where the bag is with the sticks. He sets them aside and slowly reaches in the bag. His back is to me so I can't see what he's doing, but he stays like this for several moments, long enough to where I'm afraid the agents might ring the doorbell again.

When he turns around from the bag, he looks spooked. He tucks his shirt in and pats at his belt, but his mind is elsewhere. He takes his hat off and scratches at his head, then plunks it back on and walks back to the front room. By then I'm all packed up.

"Thank you, Caroline," he says, but he's dazed. His color is flashing faintly, like lights underwater. He wants to tell me something, but he can't. "I'll see you...when?"

"Next week. But call me if you feel weird. Or if anything. For anything, I mean."

He nods and holds the door open for me. He follows me out, and I watch as he gets into a big black Suburban. It turns around and takes off like a rocket, and I'm left outside alone, holding the rig and the cooler.

I almost drop everything on the street when a flock of crows that had stood silent watch in the tree nearby suddenly explodes into flight in a firework of black. They take off after the Suburban, and I can still hear their keening and squawking even when they look like a floating black ribbon in the distance against the sky.

12

OWEN BENNET

We've had our fair share of bad apples visit the oncology floor. Cancer doesn't go away just because the person who has it is in prison. Cancer doesn't make a distinction between the girl next door and a violent offender. Cancer is cancer. You can debate the ethics of it from a taxpayer's perspective all you want, but the law, my oath, and my beliefs tell me that if a person needs treatment, they should get it. No matter what.

Usually you can tell a dangerous patient is on their way because the hospital beefs up security at the entrances and exits to the floor, and two guards are assigned to prep a room, do sweeps, and remove anything that could be used as a weapon. In other words, it's pretty obvious, and it sets the staff abuzz and generally creates a heightened tension that everyone could do without. It's tense enough on the onc floor as it is.

This time is different. Very different. But different because everything looks exactly the same. When I get to the hospital, it looks like business as usual. I'm the attending. I relieve the night attending. I get report. I review any material changes from the cases I prepped overnight. I get my schedule, I drink my coffee, and I start making rounds. Then I'm charting in the on-call room when the CEO, Dick

Schwartz, walks in flanked by what looks like two accountants. Schwartz seems like he's about to keel over. In fact, he looks so peaked that I think he's come to check himself in.

"Hello, Doctor Bennet," Schwartz says. "Can I speak with you?"

Outside of the one day around Thanksgiving when he and the other C-level administrators hand out turkeys to everyone and shake their hands, I have never spoken with Dick Schwartz in my life. He has no reason to know my name. There are hundreds and hundreds of doctors in his employ. Now all of a sudden I'm the one feeling peaked.

"Mr. Schwartz," I say, watching as the other two check the hallway outside and close the door to the on-call room. I see a black shoulder holster under the arm of one of them. Not accountants after all. Schwartz pulls out a chair and positions himself so that his jacket doesn't rumple under him.

"We have a situation here," he says, and he clasps his hands together on the table. "Things are moving rather fast. I've only just been appraised of the situation myself by the agents here, but the gist of it is that we have a violent criminal on his way to ABQ General."

"All right. You want me to handle the transfer personally?"

Schwartz swallows.

"He's not being transferred. In fact, he's not in custody at all. Yet."

I furrow my brow. "I'm not sure I follow."

"This man, he targets hospitals for their drugs. He prefers oncology floors, for whatever reason." Schwartz looks at one of the agents, who nods. "Maybe because onc floors stock high levels of pain killers, but either way, we think he's going to end up here."

"And what do you want me to do?"

"That's just it. Nothing."

"What?"

The agent by the door steps in. "We need things to appear completely normal here. The suspect must not be tipped off in any way."

I clear my throat. "So...what, just let him roam the halls? I have a responsibility for the safety of my nurses and staff as well as the patients."

"If his other hits are any indication, you won't even see him. He's...very good. And to date he hasn't harmed anyone unless approached first, although we believe he may start to attack indiscriminately if he isn't stopped. He does occasionally go into patient rooms."

"My God."

"The sickest patients, it would seem," says the other agent, with chagrin. "He likes the ones who are dying."

"What's he do to them?" I ask.

A nurse tries to come into the break room, but is blocked by the agent, who waves her off like a fly before turning back to me. "To date he's just stared at them," he says.

"He is a severe addict, doctor," says the first agent. "If what he steals is any indication, he will not be in his right mind."

"So are we supposed to keep him here for you?"

"No," he says, and he pulls a security camera still from the breast pocket of his jacket and hands it to me. It's of a young Navajo man, squat, with that peculiar, faded look of an addict. He looks like a man who was once strong and is now retreating from that strength, as if his skin doesn't quite fit right. He wears a black leather jacket and has wild black hair down to his lower back. His eyes flash vacantly in the camera exposure.

"This is him. If you see him, stay away. If you see any of your staff approaching him, intervene. But like I said, I don't think you'll see him. That is why we won't be notifying the rest of the floor. We think it would do more harm than good."

"How are you going to catch him? You are catching him, right? Not just escorting him from hospital to hospital?"

Neither agent bats an eye.

"Let us take care of that. All you need to do is stay alert and act normal. And if either Agent Douglas or I tells you to do something, do it."

I look at Dick Schwartz for help. I don't like the tone or the demeanor of either of these agents, but I get no help from Schwartz, who looks as harrowed as I feel. Something tells me this isn't the time to get into a discussion of liability. Something tells me nothing I can say will change a damn thing. This guy is coming no matter what. But I make a mental note to step into Schwartz's office with a vengeance if we all survive this thing.

"How long do I have?"

"About fifteen minutes," Parsons says, as he reaches over and plucks the photograph from my hands.

"Thank you, Doctor Bennet," Schwartz says, but his eyes are saying *I'm sorry. These men will not be put off.*

Then all three of them sweep out of the room, and I'm left alone with the approaching storm.

I can only thank God that Caroline isn't working today.

13

BEN DEJOOLI

The agents point out the motorcycle as it approaches. We're parked in the general lot, right next to a whole host of trucks and SUVs. We look just like everyone else, and there's no way that Joey could notice us or hear us in the car, but still we talk in whispers.

It's a beautiful vintage Honda 650. Round body. Black and gold coloring. It's the bike we'd dreamed of buying and restoring as kids, even down to the offset striping on the gas tank.

"That son of a bitch," I say. The agents nod, unaware.

First thing: that Honda doesn't look like the kind of thing a drug addict would be zipping around on. Drug addicts don't restore classic motorcycles. They scrap 'em and hock 'em.

As he pops over the hill and comes to a stop at the light before the turn off, I get my first good look at him. Sort of. He's in riding leathers and boots, and he wears a red kerchief over his face. It's pinned to him above the nose by a big pair of reflective aviator goggles. It's him though. He doesn't wear a helmet, and it looks like he hasn't cut his hair in the six years since I last saw him. It nearly settles down to his seat and is as black as night.

That's the second thing. He doesn't exactly look inconspicuous.

I have to take my eyes from him because I'm going to vomit again, but otherwise I'd be mesmerized.

I've nearly filled a second grocery bag with vomit. We tossed the first one out of the window on the highway. I think next time I'll tell Caroline I need to take the anti-nausea stuff before she pricks me. I'm pretty sure the two capsules I took with water before I left are intact in that bag on the side of the highway. Still, it's not all bad. I kind of like how disgusted the agents are. These guys grate on me. They have less than zero concern about any of the human aspects of this sting, or whatever you'd call what's going on here. It's like they're getting orders beamed to their heads at the same time. Like rats on a mission through a maze, they're that focused. I feel like they'd eat through the walls if that's what it took.

Joey pulls into the general lot and coasts right up to the motor-cycle parking at the front, maybe twenty feet from the double door entrance. He throws the kickstand out and steps off. He pulls down his bandana, and I get a good look at the face of a man I made sure was kicked out of Chaco forever. The man I threw from the Navajo Way. He looks terrible. He always had a squat body, but he doesn't fill it out anymore. His eyes are wide and bulging. His mouth is set, clenched, and his face is gaunt and angled to the bone. He doesn't look thin, not exactly. He looks worse than thin. He looks diminished. He looks like he's fading.

But he doesn't act like it. And that's the third thing I notice. Joey walks right into the hospital without even blinking. Not a care for the security cameras at every door. Not even a glance in either direction. This is not a man who is worried about the twenty-five-to-life he's facing if and when these suits pull him in.

The agents are on their earpieces, muttering. Parsons nods and turns to me.

"Ninth floor. Oncology. He's going up. It's showtime, Mr. Dejooli." He pops open the door.

"Remember," Douglas says, "if you can hold him, hold him. Shoot him if you have to. Just don't kill him."

Those are some pretty open orders right there. Back at the station Danny would call that "permission to start shit."

I nod. Then I'm off. I pull my hat down low, and I have to grin at the thought that I'm doing more to disguise myself than Joey did. When I reach the elevators he's already gone up. I push the button a bunch of times and wait for an interminable thirty seconds as his elevator hits nine then comes back down. When it opens, it's empty.

When I reach the ninth floor, I don't see him anywhere. I stutter step onto the floor and look around. No Joey. I go up to the receptionist, who is nervously tapping a pack of cigarettes and checking her watch.

"Did you see a guy come up here? Biker guy? Dressed in leather?"

"When?" she asks.

"Just now. Like right now."

She looks at me sideways. "Nope. You're the only visitor in the last couple of minutes."

I stare at her long enough to make her nervous. "Anything else?" she asks sharply.

I turn around and go back out to the elevators. It makes no sense. He had to have walked by the front desk. I finger the com on my shoulder. "You sure he went up the main elevator?"

"Yes," comes the reply. I can imagine Parsons grinding his teeth.

"The front desk says—"

"He went in. He's on the floor. Now you see what we mean when we say he's tricky."

Tricky my ass. Something else is at work here. He's nearby. It's like I can feel him. The sulfur has been picking up in intensity, packing deeper in my nostrils. I have to go near the corner and hold the crook of my elbow over my mouth to keep from retching. When I stand up again, I waver a bit before snapping to focus. This chemo is nasty, but then again, I was warned.

I walk back towards the desk. Then right past the desk.

"Can I *help* you?" the receptionist asks again.

"I'm here to prep a room for an inmate transfer," I say over my shoulder. I can tell she wants to stop me, but I think she wants her cigarette break more. I pass through to the main hall.

The floor is laid out like a horseshoe, the front desk at the bow and patient rooms at intervals down either rung. In the middle are a slew of computers and cubicles and lockers and whatnot for the staff. I shoot a glance down one side and don't see him. I cut across the middle to the other side, and I still don't see him. There's a fire exit at the far back, but it's alarmed. And anyway, I know he's still here somewhere. Ever since the Evilway, like it or not, I've been feeling more, seeing more, smelling more than I should be. Could be that I sweat out toxins for two straight days. Could be that I have a quart of cell-bleach in my system. Could also be that I'm dying. Whatever it is, if it helps me get this shit straight, I'll take what I can get.

I start down the near hallway, noting which doors are closed on my left and swinging my head right to clear the computer area. I don't see him, but when I turn around, the doors I thought were closed are open, and some of the ones that were open are closed. It's a funhouse from hell. I really don't want to start knocking on doors. At the end of the hallway, I find the pill case, right where the agents said it would be.

I also find Doctor Bennet, staring at it with wide eyes because it's swinging open like a rusty gate and with a circle the size of a fist cut out of it.

"Shit," I mutter, and Bennet looks up at me. His eyes get wider.

"Are you here for him?" Bennet whispers.

"Yeah. When did this happen?"

"Now. I mean just now."

"Did you see where he went?"

"No. I didn't see anything." He steps up and in front of the case as a pair of nurses walk by. He nods weakly at their passing greeting.

"What are you talking about? Which way did he go, Bennet?"

"You don't get it. I was watching the case. I've been watching it for twenty minutes. Nothing happened. I blinked and then this."

My eyes start to water. My face feels like it's burning. I try to hold my guts in, but I have to grab a trashcan quick, turn away, and puke.

Thankfully I have nothing left in me now. It just sounds like I'm spitting. I turn back to Bennet, and he's softened.

"You shouldn't be out like you are. You must be in a good deal of pain."

"I'll be in worse pain if I can't catch Joey—"

And then there he is. I see him out of the corner of my eye, clear as day. Dressed in black with the red bandana pulled down around his neck. He's right there, twenty feet down the hall, staring at me. Except when I turn to look at him, he's gone.

"What? Do you see him?" Bennet asks.

"Sort of..." I say, turning back to Bennet, and then there he is again. Same spot. This time I stay still and don't turn to look. It could be that my eyes are dripping water, could be that I feel like I have a hotpot on my head, but he looks like a nightmare. His eyes are way too big, and his mouth is the same black circle shape as his eyes. The rest of his face has been smudged. Pasty skin coloring extends beyond the borders of where his face should be. And it's moving. All by itself. He looks like he's screaming, but he's not. He's standing still with his hands balled in fists at his side, and he's staring right at me. And now it's my turn to feel scared. Whatever this is, it's not Joey Flatwood. Not the Joey I knew.

Then something grabs Joey's attention, and he darts off sideways across the horseshoe to the other side of the floor. He's gone in a blink. It's like he steps through the walls. A second later, the bells and whistles go off. It's a code. I know that from the old days. Someone is dying. The Navajo people don't believe in coincidences. But even if I did, I sure as hell wouldn't believe this was a coincidence. Bennet looks at me. I nod. He straightens and rolls up his sleeves. I respect that. I respect a guy who owns up to what's coming.

"Follow the running," he says, and he takes off down the hall. We're joined by a bunch of other people in scrubs, and soon five or six of us whip around the bend and towards the blinking blue light above the room at the far end of the corridor. I put my hand on my gun. I feel like I'm gonna throw up again, but this time I'm not sure if it's all about the chemo. I strain forward and pull ahead of the wave, and I'm the first one into the room. There he is. He's leaning over the patient, his face inches from the old man's. His black hair forms a waving tent over the small figure in the bed. He's speaking. Chanting something, but it's muddled. It's not unlike what Gam was singing in the Evilway, but it sounds like it's coming from a tinny speaker underwater.

"Joey, get away from the bed!" I say, and I pull my gun. He looks up at me with a jerk, and I'm expecting the vacant black holes and the dripping oil face I saw in the corridor, but it's just Joey. A rail-thin, walking-dead-man version of Joey, but Joey.

And then he's gone.

And I have people yelling at me. I'm spinning in a circle in the room, but he's nowhere. And then I'm being pushed away, and I see Bennet calming people down and pushing me out of the room, and calming some more. People are giving orders, and I hear the whining sound of that shocker pad revving. The nurses are crowded around the unconscious old man on the bed, and I'm just outside, looking in.

No Joey.

"I think I'm losing my mind," I say out loud, just to hear my voice, just to make sure I'm still here and not dreaming. I wipe sweat from my clammy brow, and Bennet comes over to me.

"I...I think I'm worse than I thought I was. I'm seeing things," I say. I feel like I want to cry. This must be what it's like to go insane: visual hallucinations so strong you swear on your family that they're true. I get this loopy thought that maybe I died during the Evilway and this is where I ended up, doomed to chase the man I banished forever. I feel at the wall, only half sure it exists. Then I collapse against it.

"I saw him too," Bennet says quietly. I look up at him, reach for him with my eyes like a drowning man would a raft.

"You saw him?"

Bennet nods. "Ben. Can you tell me what is going on here?" He speaks very slowly, as if he's walking a thin line of sanity himself.

"Wish I could. Holy hell do I wish I could. He's still here somewhere. I can feel it."

Alarms are still blaring in the room. Bennet pops back into the chaos and then out again to check on me. He shakes his head. No Joey. Then he steps on something with a loud crunch. He looks down. He's crushed a white pill to powder under his shoe.

"He must have gotten by in all the shoving," Bennet says.

"Can you go across to the other wing?" I ask. "I'll start at the back end of this one. We work our way forward. If you see or hear anything, or think you see or hear anything, you call out. You hear me?"

Bennet nods, takes one more look at the code to assure himself it's being taken care of, then trots across the horseshoe again.

I walk down my hallway towards the back fire exit. I walk slowly, with my palms held out and my hands open, like I'm trying to catch the air. If I can't see him, maybe I can feel him.

It's difficult to focus on your periphery. Impossible, actually. So my mind's eye watches my side view while I try my best to keep staring at the fire door straight ahead of me. Every time I hear a door open or close, I look toward it in a snap, but it's just the hospital moving around me, doctors and nurses and staff going about the day. I reach the far door. No sign of him. I spin around and curse under my breath.

I listen for Bennet on the opposite side, but nothing is out of the ordinary. A small cheer comes from the code room, and nurses and staff start to file out. Guess the little old man made it after all. At least somebody is getting a happy ending here. I slump and walk back towards the front bend. My mind tells me Joey is long gone, but I still sense something in my heart. I still sense that burning darkness that came from his eyes, but it's weaker now. I pause by the door to the little old man's room, still open. His little old wife is crying tears of joy at his side, her head not far from where Joey's had been, but this time he's looking back at her with rheumy eyes. They clasp hands, thin and frail like dried flowers, but there is life there still. They have another minute with each other. And another. His wife has this sort of delirious pitch to her voice, like when you're on the tables at Wapati and you're playing on house money. It draws me a little closer to the room. It makes me smile. They don't have a care for anything but each other.

Maybe that's why they don't see Joey.

Because he's right there. In the corner of the room. And he's not some side-seen apparition this time either. No melting flesh, no dark pits for eyes. He's a flesh and blood man that I can see straight on. And he can see me straight on too. He sees me before I see him. Every cop instinct they drill into you for a time like this, when you get blind-sided by something, goes right out the window. I don't react. I can't react. If he wanted to tackle me or bum rush me, he could have, right then and there. Joey was always bigger than me, and even down fifty pounds like he is right now, his eyes still have this fire to them. They aren't the eyes of a dying man. If he wanted to, he could give me a run for my money. But he doesn't. What he does do is lift a gloved finger to his lips and then move his gaze out of the doorway, beckoning.

He wants to talk.

I cock my head and squint. *You're fucking kidding me, right?*

He holds out his hands wide and bobs his head. *You know I could run if I want. You know you'd never catch me.*

It's funny how after all these years I can still read him like a book. No words required. I take a breath and purse my lips. *Fine.* Joey always got what he wanted when we were kids, why should things change now? I back out of the door and into the hallway. He follows me. We both stare at each other until we stop just a few rooms back from the far corner by the exit.

"I knew it was you," he says. And he's smiling. He looks like he wants to hug me, but he holds back. Instead he just takes me in. "It's good to see you, Big B."

His voice triggers an avalanche of memories I don't want to feel right now. Things like us screaming down the flood plain on our bicycles with the warm New Mexico night air whipping past our bare chests. I push back against them by focusing on the pack of morphine nodules I see hanging out of his bulging pockets. The audacity of this fucking guy.

"I gotta bring you in, Joey."

"You can't bring me in," he says. "I'm not Navajo, remember?" He smiles a hollow smile that reminds me of the holes in his face I saw minutes ago.

"I'm not working for NNPD here," I say.

His smile drops. "Those bastard suits?"

"They're the FBI. They don't fuck around. They want you alive, but I think there's a big gap between 'moving' and 'alive' for these guys."

"Tell me about it," he says. "You can't trust them, Ben. You don't know what their motives are."

"Shut up, Joey. Just shut up and come with me. I don't want to hash out everything again. I really don't. I want to get you behind bars and then go home."

"They don't want me," he says. "Nobody wants me. You of all people should know that."

"Fuck you. Don't start with that shit. You brought this on yourself." I find myself gripping his jacket, balling the leather in my fist. "All you had to do was talk, you miserable piece of shit. That's all you had to do. If you didn't take her yourself, then tell us what you saw. You were in the goddamn room with her!"

He lets me grab him. He moves with my trembling arms. His face is sallow, his jaw slack, and I can see just how much weight he's lost. "Look at you," I say, and I push him back a step. "Instead of facing yourself, you've decided to wipe yourself out. You're a fucking coward, Joey. You're a coward, and I don't have room for this shit in my life anymore because it's destroying me too."

For a second, he looks like I struck him across the face, but he rallies. "You're a good man, Ben," he says. "A better man than I am. But you're such a cop. You see two points and work your ass off to draw a straight line between them. But this story is no straight line. I think you're coming to see that now."

"You're fucked up, Joey. Something fucked you up. You need help. You're an addict, man. You're knocking off hospitals and getting crazy.

You've crossed state lines. That's why the FBI is here. And they don't give up."

Joey shakes his head. "Yeah, well, neither do I," he mutters.

"Let's just walk out of these doors and nobody gets shot, okay? That's what they want. That's what I want, too."

"Like I said, they don't want me."

"Well, what do they want?"

He reaches in his pocket with one gloved hand and grips something. He has it out and in his palm before I can blink, never mind draw my gun.

"They want this," he says.

It's a turquoise crow. Same as the gambler's. Same as Gam's. I can only stare at it.

"You've seen this before?" he asks. "Doesn't surprise me. Not with the path you've walked. Not with the path you have to walk still."

"Where did you get that?" I ask, my mind numb.

"I pulled it from the hands of a dead man in Colorado. Don't worry. I didn't kill him. But your friends in the suits did. I snatched it before they could find it." He smiles. "They were pretty pissed off when it wasn't where they thought it would be."

Part of my mind is telling me not to listen to the words of an addict on the run, but over the past weeks I seem to have put some distance between that part and the rest of me. A rift has opened, a rip in my fabric that started as an unraveling when Ana left me but that has been getting bigger every day and finally split down the seam in that hogan. I don't understand what Joey is saying, but I know he's telling me the truth.

"I don't know how many of these totems there are, Ben, but they want them all. Bad. And I think they'll stop at nothing to get them."

"But why? It's just a crow," I say, but I don't believe that, and he knows it.

"No such thing as *just a crow*, my brother. And they want it for the same reason I want it. Because they want to find Ana."

I step back. His words hit me like rocks. I feel bruised. I feel bile rise in my throat. The sulfur smell hits me with the force of a wildfire. My vision wavers and I hitch to the side, but Joey grabs me.

"You think I've been running this whole time—I know it. But I'm not running. I'm *looking* for her. The suits think they understand everything. That the more crows they get the closer they'll be. But they don't get it." His face is manic. His eyes glassy. "I don't either, but I'm getting closer. This shit?" He taps the vials in his pocket. "I hate this shit. But it gets me closer. The drugs, and the crow, and...and these places"—he holds out his hands to the hospital around him—" where people are battling death. Each gets me a little closer to finding her, Ben! They're all pieces of a puzzle, and they're coming together. But I'm running out of time."

"Ana?" I whisper. "Ana?" I say her name like a ward. I say it like I used to say it in my sleep before Gam would wake me and sing to me. An eighteen-year-old man weeping in his grandmother's arms.

My com crackles. It's subtle, but we both hear it. The agents are coming. I grab him by the jacket again, but my grip is weak. He pulls one leather glove off with his teeth and pries my fingers from him.

"I have to keep you here," I say, but there's nothing behind it. There's nothing in me anymore. Nothing but a rising sickness and the unsettling feeling of empty burning in my veins. He takes my fingers in his.

"I'm sorry, Ben. I'm so sorry," he says, and I have a series of flashbacks of him walking away across the rez boundary, him looking at me and weeping, but still walking away. "But time is short."

Then he takes the crow from his gloved hand and grips it with his bare hand, and he blinks out of sight. I look left and right for him, and I see him in flashes, like a man glimpsed through the crack of a door.

"Goodbye," he whispers. I feel the air part as he moves away. He's gone, and it's just me, sobbing against a wall. The fire alarm goes off. I turn my head towards the front, waiting for the agents, but instead I see Bennet, and he rushes to me as I slide down the wall. He saw the whole thing. Or enough of it anyway. It's written on his face. He's like a man who just woke up in a strange place and is looking for anything familiar to grab onto. I think I'm the same way because when he kneels down to me we grab each other, and that's when the cavalry comes in. The two agents, sure, but another three as well, and a handful of state police for good measure, guns out, scaring the shit out of everybody.

Bennet does what I can't do. He stands up in the bedlam and screams like a foghorn, "He's gone! He ran! The fire exit! Quickly!" Then he throws an arm around my back. "Come on, man," he whispers. "With me."

Bennet parts the sea of agents and cops that runs around us, and he half-carries me into a darkened patient room. He helps me onto the bed, grabs a bucket, and slides it in front of me, and I lose my guts again. I puke red, and I see red. Then I see black spots, and then I'm out.

WHEN I WAKE UP, it's like my life is on repeat. I'm strapped to another damn machine, with another damn baggie dripping itself into my veins. Except this time I don't even have my comfy lounger, and the nurse in my room isn't Caroline. She's older, and when she hears me stir, she dials a number on her phone and bustles over to my bed.

"How are you feeling?" she asks.

"Like hell. What's in the bag?"

"You're dehydrated. We're just giving you some fluids, that's all."

Then everything comes back to me, and I try to sit up. But this nurse is big, and she pushes a beefy hand down on my sternum.

"Easy there."

My head is pounding. Watching things hurts. Blinking hurts. I close my eyes and focus on not moving them under my lids, and that helps stave off another wave of nausea.

"What time is it?"

"It's just after six," says another voice, and this one I recognize. Bennet. I open my eyes a smidge and watch him through my eyelashes. "Same day. You've only been out for about two hours. Thank you, Mary Ellen. I'll take it from here."

Mary Ellen shuffles out, and Bennet closes the door behind her before sliding a small stool next to the bed. I shuffle a bit in a sad attempt to sit up, but he shakes his head and stills me with a single touch.

"Rest, Ben. Your body has no idea what's going on."

"Neither does the rest of me," I mutter.

Bennet glances at the door and nods. "He got away," he says, his voice low. "The agents and the rest of them canvassed the place for an hour before that Parsons guy called them all off. He and Douglas left without a word. Kind of a pissy couple, those two."

I let out a breath that rattles my throat, but I say nothing.

"Now why do I get the feeling that you aren't all that torn up about the dangerous drug addict's daring escape?"

"He said some things to me. Some things that rang true."

"About that rock he held in his hand? That made him invisible?" Bennet finishes with a sad laugh and creaks back in his seat. He runs his hands up and down his face a couple of times. "I can't believe I'm saying this. I can't believe I just said that without tacking on 'here's a referral to a counselor' or 'that's a side effect of the medication'."

"The crow is real. I don't know what it does, exactly, but whatever it is, it's real. It happened. But it wasn't just that. We have a history, him and me, and now I'm starting to rethink it."

"Is that good, or bad?"

"Neither. It just is. But he told me to watch out for the Feds."

"Sounds like something a criminal on the run would say."

"Nah. I get it. I get what he's saying. I never liked those two stiffs. They always rubbed me the wrong way."

Bennet is quiet, but I know he won't disagree. I know they chafe him too. The way they have blinders on. They're too cold. Too calculating. It's unnatural.

"He said the Feds weren't after him. They were after the crow."

"If it can do what I think I saw it do, it could be very valuable. It's...miraculous."

"He told me it wasn't the only one. That the Feds are on a tear to find all of them."

And then it hits me: *and I know exactly where one is.*

"Where did they go?" I ask, my voice froggy. "The Feds. Where did they go?"

"I don't know. Like I said, they just tore off. Not a word."

If they knew about Joey's crow, they could know about Gam's crow too. Joey said they'd stop at nothing. Said they wanted all the crows, and something about Ana, but that was flushed from my mind. I had to get to Gam. I grit my teeth and push to a sitting position. I see an explosion of colors, and my head feels like a sack of sand is resting on it.

"What are you doing? You have to rest, Ben."

"No. I have to go. I have to get to my grandmother. I think she's in trouble."

"You aren't going anywhere tonight, man. Even if I let you, you wouldn't make it out that door."

My eyes water with pain and frustration, and fear. Magic crows, shadow-walking people, none of these things particularly scare me, but the thought of those two men knocking on our door and Gam opening it up to them terrifies me.

"Here," Bennet says, pulling his cell phone from his pocket. "Call her. Warn her."

We don't have a landline and Gam hasn't picked up a phone in years, but I give Dad a shot. The phone rings. And rings. And rings. His voicemail picks up and says his mailbox is full. Like it's been for years. I hang up. The look I give Bennet must be so pathetically terrified that it's catching. His eyes go wide, and his pale face blanches a whiter shade.

"Isn't there anyone? Anyone at all?" he asks.

My mind races, and somehow, like it's done for the past few days, it settles on Caroline. What was she doing after my chemo? She said she was going back to the CHC to log a couple more hours. If she's still there, she'd be minutes away from my house.

Bennet peers at me and nods slowly. He takes his phone back and flips through his contacts.

"I'll call her," he says. "But you gotta explain all this."

14

CAROLINE ADAMS

I'm basically worthless at the CHC after the chemo session with Ben. I'm making my rounds, but I'm not really there. With the Navajo you really have to work sometimes to get them to open up, and I pride myself on working hard to do that, but not today. Today I'm like the dead-weight guy in the group project. Of the five of us from ABQ General who are scheduled here, I'm by far the most worthless. One of the nurses even ends up cleaning up after me when I forget a patient on one of my rounds. A nurse's worst nightmare. Don't worry, they were fine. Sleeping. Thank God, but still...

The day can't end soon enough. I feel drained. I'm not sure what to make of what happened at Ben's house, with him storming off like that with those weird men. To say nothing of the crows. I think it speaks to my mental state that I'm more worried about Ben getting into that Suburban than I am about the staring contest I had with a monster crow, or his thousand crow buddies that scared the hell out of me when I was getting into my car. The human mind is a strange thing. When something that out of whack happens, I think my mind flat refuses to let me dwell on it. Instead it pushes it to the back. I don't forget it. It's still there, sort of waving at me, but in its place my mind swaps in other things, stupid things. Like how Ben held my hand when the chemo was first dripping into him. How he looked at me. Monster crows from hell could be swarming all around us, ending the world, and I would still be awake at three a.m. thinking about what it meant that Ben held my hand.

Naturally the days you want to end the fastest last the longest, and soon enough I'm regretting my decision to log a few more hours. I get a late admit: a young woman with severe cramping. She's been in before, around this time of the month, by the looks of her chart. A targeted birth control prescription would fix all this up, even I know that. But no, she's been prescribed a series of catch-all intrauterine devices to which she's reacting badly. Owen would have figured this out before she sat down on the exam table. I wish he was here. I don't feel comfortable talking to the attending on rotation here today, an older man. He means well, but he's from the school of physicians that believes nurses should be seen, not heard.

Anyway, the poor girl is in a lot of pain, and it's around six in the evening when we finally get her comfortable. By then I've let my charting pile up, and I'm late on my final rounds. I stop in the quiet end of the hallway and take a few seconds. I do this sometimes when I know I'm being a shitty nurse. I just stop it all and stand where there are relatively few people and roll my neck for a second. With this job, it's so easy to run and run and run, but you just can't do that because you burn out. And when you burn out, you stop being a nurse and become just another employee. And there is a difference.

On top of all of this I also have my grant fulfillment to think about. I'm weeks away from a clean slate. No loans. No debt. Nothing. Pretty soon the CHC administration will sign off on my contract and hand me my receipt, and if I want to I can get in my car and leave everything behind me. I can't quite imagine the freedom I'd have. It gives me a strange sense of vertigo to think about it, like I'm standing at the edge of a cliff. I have to admit, it's kind of intriguing. On the other hand, it would make me a tourist. I know this place doesn't need tourists. It takes five years at Chaco just to get your foot in the door with a lot of the Navajo. I've put in a lot of work. I don't want to admit it, even to myself, but my decision on whether to stay or go is going to rest on whether Ben lives or dies.

My phone rings. I don't like to answer my phone at work because my hands are gross, and I don't want to touch it. It's usually solicitors anyway, but I'm still taking my thirty seconds, and I don't mind taking another thirty. I'm already gonna be here until seven in any case. Maybe it's my mom calling to say hi. Or that something terrible has happened. I pull my phone out of my front pocket. It's Owen. My pulse drops like a lead ball then bounces to racing. I get that feeling that you get when someone calls you at two in the morning: this isn't good, but I have to answer it.

"Hello?"

"Caroline! Thank you. Thank you."

It doesn't sound like Owen. It sounds like...but no. It can't be.

"Caroline, it's Ben. I need your help."

"Ben? Why are you...but what..."

"Please," he says, and that stops me. I can hear pain in his voice. I can almost see the black wisping off of him, coming over the line, and smoking out of my end of the phone.

"What do you need?"

"I need you to go back to my house. I'll explain everything along the way."

It takes five minutes and the promise of a double latte to one of the other nurses to get her to take care of the rest of my charting, and I'm out the door.

I PULL BACK onto Ben's street, but this time the crows are gone. There isn't a bird in the sky, but somehow it feels worse for their absence. The street is deserted. No cars out front. There aren't even any porch lights on.

"Are you there?" asks Ben, still on the line with me. He's told me about Joey Flatwood and what happened at the hospital. Owen is with him and chimed in occasionally, and I think that's why I finally believed his story about the crow totem. I don't believe in magic, never have, never will. Nor does Owen, I don't think. But I'm not going to sit here and tell you that I think death snuffs out a person forever. Who am I to say ours is the only plane of existence? Maybe this Joey guy, maybe he exists in a different way than we do. A way with its own rules and science and medicine. It's a stretch, I know, but I'm still secretly applauding myself for not writing both of them off as insane right off the bat. After all, I'm the one seeing colors. I'm the one that can see people's thoughts in their mist. For better or for worse, the three of us are thick as thieves in the nut house.

"Yeah," I answer him. "It's really quiet here. No sign of anybody. Wait..." I peer at the front door. It looks splintered at the lock. Uh oh. "Ben, I think the door's been forced."

I get out of my car and close the car door as quietly as I can. In the past ten minutes, it's dropped fifteen degrees. The sun has left this side of the street. I can hear both men speaking with each other on the other end. "I'm going in," I say.

"Wait, Caroline. Are you sure? They could still be there. Bennet is calling the cops. You should wait." He's a bad liar. Even over the phone. He wants somebody in there as soon as possible, and I'm the closest to hand. My mind is made up.

"If she's in there, she could be hurt," I say.

"Keep your guard up."

I put the phone in my pocket, still on the line, and push open the front door. It slides easily out, and then easily back when I make no move to go inside. Pieces of the jamb are strewn across the floor inside. I listen for any movement. There is nothing. I decide against announcing myself and slide inside, licking my lips and trying to work saliva back into my mouth. It's so still inside that a passing airplane rings loudly in my ears. A dog barks somewhere far away. Dust swirls in the low light where I'd set up the chemo rig hours before.

The place has been ransacked. A quick job. Upended drawers, flipped couch cushions. The picture of Ana and Ben sticks out from its shattered frame on the floor. I bend to pick it up, and that's when I hear a sound from the back. It's not much, but it's definitely something.

I switch tack. Time to be brave. "Hello?" I ask, and it comes out in a weak squeak. The sound stops immediately. I right the picture on the mantle again and walk slowly around the glass and debris towards the kitchen.

"Caroline? What is it?"

I jump, but it's just Ben, over the phone. I reach in my pocket and end the call. There's that shuffling again. I round the corner into the kitchen proper, and that's when I see the blood. A trail of it in a dark red line, almost black, like smeared tar on the tiles. It goes from the little side room through a corner of the kitchen and then out the back door. I look out the back door and see a man there, face down, by a small pile of rocks in the back yard. He isn't moving, and he has no color at all coming off of him. I know he's dead. I move towards him, but as I'm about to push the screen open, I hear the shuffling again and snap my head right, towards where I saw the crow through the window earlier.

And I see the crow again. Only it's inside this time, and it's in tatters on the ground, next to an old woman who can only be Ben's grandmother. She isn't moving, but the crow is. Barely. Its wings have both been broken, and its head is at an awkward angle. But it's trying to move closer to the old woman. When I step into the doorframe, it appraises me with one cloudy black eye and pauses. It blinks once, then goes back to its sad, flopping shuffle. It's terrifying, but it's in pain, and all malice that it may once have possessed has fled it. It manages to bump its sleek crown against the woman's side, and there it rests, like an old dog with its master.

The window in the room is shattered, and I see bits of feathers stuck to the jagged ends of the glass there. More feathers float lazily about in the breeze coming in. The bird still watches me, and then it squawks feebly. That's when the old woman stirs.

I step forward and pause again as the crow snaps at me and sort of gurgles. It hits me that this crow is protecting the woman. That it will die protecting the woman. And then I see the painfully slow rise and fall of both the crow's streaked chest and Ben's grandmother's chest, and I know that when the one dies, the other will die too. It's their coloring. They share it. It's a beautiful, sparkling strand of silver, like a heartstring, but it's weak and gossamer and looks like it could be snapped with the ease of brushing away a spider web.

I kneel down next to the old woman, and I can hear that she's struggling to breathe. Her neck is mottled and bruised and crumpled. Her windpipe is crushed. Blood runs from her nose. Her eyelids flutter and creep open, and she sees me. She focuses slowly, but if she is surprised to find a strange woman in her room, she doesn't show it. She mutters something softly in Navajo that I can't understand. My phone is buzzing like mad in my pocket. I fish it out and answer Ben's call.

"Ben, she's been attacked," I say, the panic wavering my voice. "Talk to her." I put the phone by her head, and I can hear Ben speaking on the other line in a near wail, but she seems to take no notice of him or of the phone. She's looking plainly at me.

"Help is coming," I say. "Just hold on," and I grip her bony hand.

"Police," she says. Then she says a name that sounds like Dejooli.

"Ben? Yes, he is coming. He will come soon. You can talk to him here, see?"

"Police," she says again. Then something that sounds like *nine-pin* or *nine-point*, and I am reminded of Ben's partner. The man who called the ambulance for him at the Arroyo.

"Yes. The police are coming. Just hold on."

The bird rests its head on her hip, unblinking, barely breathing, but watching keenly. Watching and understanding. It's such an alien feeling coming from a bird that I want to apologize to it too and tell it to hold on, help is on the way, but I stop myself. I've allowed a lot of stuff today, but speaking to a bird like it can understand me, even if it can, might be the straw that sends the camel to the nuthouse.

I pull down the collar of the woman's sweater, and I'm thinking how maybe I can open up that airway to buy her a little more time. The damage is severe. Her neck looks like a crumpled piece of tin. Still, I could get a knife and a pen. It might give us another ten minutes. Or it might kill her. I start looking around the room, and that's when I see the leather bag and the painted sticks from before, only the sticks have both been snapped in half and the leather bag has been ripped open. Next to it is a beautiful box that looks like it's made of ivory or bone. It's been snapped in two as well. The top half is upside down next to the bottom half, and inside is nothing but a handful of fine black sand. Some of it is scattered around the floor. I get the feeling that whatever was there is gone.

"I'm going to try to do something to your neck, to help you breathe," I say. I make a move to get up, but she holds me and eyes me with the same frank assessment as the bird. She shakes her head and squeezes my hand, and I realize that she is going to die here with me. The thought hits me with such force that I sit down on my rump next to her and sort of slump like an old doll. She pats me on the knee, her breath crackling like paper. She still watches me like she knows me. She is remarkably unafraid. Ben's pleading is softer, more diminished. There is a stretch of silence. He is listening, too.

"Who did this to you?" I ask.

"Police," she says, then she waves it off with a tiny brushing motion of her finger. I understand. It no longer matters. It is a thing that was done. What matters now is what happens next.

"The crow," she says. "Stone crow. He takes." I look back at the bone box. So there was a stone crow in there. Already I'm linking it to what Ben told me about Joey Flatwood. I know it was more precious, and far more dangerous, than any mere ornament or jewel. She pulls weakly at my hand, and I lean closer. She closes her eyes and speaks in lilting Navajo. It sounds like wind whistling through trees.

"God, I wish I understood you," I say, helplessly. "Maybe Ben can —" but she quiets me with the barest hint of a squeeze of my hand.

"Wrong thinking," she says.

"What's wrong thinking?"

"The stone crow. Is important. But only guardians."

"Guardians? Guarding what?"

She drops my hand and snakes her own back up to her neck, and I think for a moment that she is looking for the source of her pain, for the source of her death. But then she slips her hands into her collar and grasps something on her chest. She carefully pulls it out, and in her hand I see a small silver bell hung around her neck with a simple leather strap. It is no bigger than my thumb. In a way it's no different from something you might see hanging on a Christmas tree, but there is a powerful weight to it that I can see with the same sight that shows me the colors. It is a weight so heavy that it is warping the faint silver strands that are what remains of her life, bowing them out and away like a powerful magnet. If we exist in one place, and Joey Flatwood another, and those that have passed from us exist on a third, then this thing that is a bell and not a bell cuts through all of those places like a hot knife through butter. I can see this just by looking at it.

Ben's grandmother sees what I see. She sees it in my eyes, and she sighs with a smile that says to me *I have chosen correctly.*

"The stone guards the silver," she says, and she hands it to me. I reach out for it. I am drawn to it, but before I can take it, she stills me with a look.

"No ring," she says, and her eyes focus to pins. I see that she has her thumb firmly on the tongue of the bell. The crow titters, and its broken wings twitch. They don't have much time left.

"No ring," she says again. "Never ring."

"No ring," I say, nodding.

She looks at me for a moment longer, and I get this feeling that she knows all about me. Knows everything I think and feel as surely as if I had lived with her in this room all of my life. She gives one final nod.

"Take," she says.

Very carefully, she transfers the bell to me. I slip the leather over her head. She lets up on the tongue last, and I clamp my own thumb over it. I feel like silencing that bell is, in all likelihood, the most important thing I have ever done in my life. I take it, and it doesn't make a sound. Physically it's actually quite light, but only because I expect it to be so heavy. It gleams a thick, milky silver color, creamier than normal silver, richer and more pure. It's also cold. Very cold.

Tin-mug-in-the-freezer cold. It almost burns, but I'll be damned if I'm gonna take my thumb away from that clapper.

She nods appreciatively. Then she puts her thin lips together and shushes me.

"Secret," she says. "You, and Ben."

I nod.

She starts singing. Ben is still quiet on his end of the line, listening.

I don't know what it is she is saying, but I do know that it is a final song. A song of endings. I don't need to know the words to know that she is giving thanks. It is not sad, not particularly. It simply is, in the Navajo way. She closes her eyes, and I know she is seeing beyond herself now, bidding farewell to the path she has walked and welcoming the path ahead. It sounds like she is greeting an old friend, and when I see tears fall from the corners of her eyes, I feel that they aren't tears of pain or sorrow, but tears of joy. And I feel the same soft brush that I felt in the hospital after my patient died. The crow feels it too, because it twitches its silky black head and tracks the unseen movement of something terrible and beautiful walking through the door and over to this woman dying in front of me. The thing that walks in is the thing she sings for. The rhythm of her song slows. I press the bell tighter, holding it still with every fiber of my being, because it's burning in earnest now. It's calling out to whatever has walked into this room. It wants to be with this new thing, not with me. Perhaps it is even one and the same with this new thing. It wants to ring, but I won't let it.

I am not afraid, because I know in my heart that this thing, which I can only call Death, isn't here for me, isn't concerned with me, may not even see me. But it is here for the grandmother. There is a soft breath of air, and the silver strands of color that are the woman's and the crow's break and float away. The song is over. Both are dead. There is another movement in the air, barely a flutter, and then Death is gone too, and I am alone.

I let up on my grip and look down at the bell. I lift my thumb, but there is no longer any tongue there. The clapper is gone. Now the bell looks more like a candlesnuffer. But I know I felt the clapper when the grandmother was dying. I know it was there. I think it's still there, where I can't see it. It's just waiting.

I slip the necklace and bell that isn't a bell over my head and tuck it close to my chest. It is still ice cold but not burning cold anymore. I would say goodbye to the grandmother, but I know that she is long gone. What is left on the floor is more one with the shattered glass and splintered wood around it than the flesh and blood she was. Ben heard the final song as well as I did, but he is talking now. Quietly. His voice sadly diminished through the tiny speaker of my phone. He is saying his own goodbye, and I leave him to it.

I hear sirens. They are close. I stand and gather myself, and that's when I remember the other body, the one that trailed the blood out of the back door. I follow it out into the back yard and come upon the man. I am expecting the intruder, but I know I'm wrong. This man has been stabbed. He has died clutching his stomach and trailing his heart's blood, but he is otherwise unscathed. He was not the one the crow died defending the grandmother from. As I bend down closer to his face, I see an instant resemblance. He has the same soft slope of the forehead and boxy cheekbones, the same soft brown skin.

Ben's father.

Did he come home and stumble upon the intruders? Did he try to defend the grandmother too? Whatever happened, when he was stabbed, he wanted to be here, out here in the back. I follow his path, the one cut short when he bled out, and I see that he is reaching for a pyre of rocks just outside of the lawn. To further confuse things, he is smiling. It's plain on his face. Not a grimace, either, or a death snarl. It is a genuine smile.

When death came for Ben's father, he was happy about it.

15

BEN DEJOOLI

The Navajo are not sentimentalists in death. My mother seems to have forgotten this. She has been away too long. She wants a fresh cut pine box for both Gam and Dad and a ceremony with speakers and eulogies and suits and ties and tears. She fights with the people of the Arroyo, with whom Gam and Dad shared their final wishes for burial in the old style. She screams at them until I have to hold her back. I see reappearing shades of the blank horror that wiped her mind when Ana vanished. She is all too used to this type of thing.

In the end, she exhausts herself and sleeps for many hours, and the people of the Arroyo take my father and my grandmother away. I help. When they are laid on the cliff, the men who carried them along with me strip and burn our clothes and sweat in a hogan for some time. I think I pass out. I find myself in a small circle of campers later, by a fire, underneath a blanket with a diamond weave of stars above me. Nobody bothers me. Nobody speaks as I dress in the clothes that were left out for me, and I find my truck and drive back to my house. On the drive out, I see a flickering fire in the distance, and I know that the Arroyo men have burned the hogan where Gam held my Evilway.

There is nothing for me here anymore. I appreciate the purification rituals that the men of the Arroyo gave me. I know that they are simply trying to wash death off of me, but the truth is, I don't care if death finds me anymore. I would welcome death, now. A clean Navajo would never set foot in a house of the dead, which is what my house has become. But I am not clean. No matter how much I sweat, I am marked. I know this now. I know this because the crows follow me.

The crows are bolder by the day. They hop from tree to tree as I walk. They soar high above me, cutting on the currents and then doubling back again to hover just behind me. They sit on the lawn of my boarded-up house with blood still staining the floor. They coat the roof like ink. They make the barren winter trees sway again with dark life. And they are completely silent. Even when I go to shoo them, they never squawk or titter. They are mourning, I think, much like I am. They are mourning the big one. The big red crow that Caroline found dead by my grandmother.

Or perhaps they are simply waiting. The way that their hundreds of black-tar eyes glisten in the hollow sun gives me a feeling like a pressure drop before a storm. Perhaps they are waiting for the thundercloud to break. Perhaps they are waiting for me.

My mom won't go near the house. She holes up at a motel off the highway while I survey the scene of the crime. By now the cops are long gone. Danny called me himself to take my statement. I asked if he wanted to walk the house with me, but he said he'd already been there and didn't want to see it again. That tells me it's bad. I asked him if there was conclusive evidence pinning it on the Feds. He was quiet for a moment, and I knew he was contemplating letting me down easy, but that's just not Danny's way.

"No," he said, simply.

Of course not. They would be pros. Still, I want to check it out. Danny tries to dissuade me, but ultimately he lets it be. He knows I have to close that door myself.

I step over the police tape and walk up to the front door as the sun is setting. It's been nearly three days since it happened, and this is the first time I've come home, although I can't rightly call it home anymore. I fish around in my pocket for my keys, and I'm surprised to find that my hand swims in my pocket now. This is a fitted uniform I'm wearing. Or it used to be. I pull out my hand and study it like it's foreign to me. Bony, thin. My fingers remind me of my grandmother's. I can loop my thumb and pinkie around my wrist. I touch my neck and find bones there too, bones everywhere. I run my hands through my hair, and it comes away in feathered clumps. I clamp my hat down on my head like it's the only thing keeping the top of me from blowing away. Behind me the crows shuffle their wings.

I step through the doorway and flick on the lights. I see what Caroline described. The place was ransacked as they searched for the crow totem. There are evidence markers strewn about the living room: little tents with numbers on them that lead me through the house like some nightmare museum exhibit. Everything is shattered and strewn except one picture of me and Ana. The frame is broken, but standing. I step over to it and pick it up. Pieces of glass fall to the ground. I barely recognize myself. I remember when this was taken. It was after I graduated from high school. We had a party in the back yard. The picture was supposed to be just of me, but Ana was messing around and shouldered her way into the frame, pushing her face next to mine. The photo has been damaged. It looks like it was scratched up during the fall, because now there are two long gashes under Ana's eyes and her face is warped. She looks a lot like she looked when I hallucinated seeing her in the hogan during the Evilway.

I almost drop the picture in my hurry to set it down. It wobbles and falls flat on the mantle with a clatter that makes me jump. I stare at it a moment longer, half expecting it to move, but it doesn't. I chide myself. The world isn't falling apart, it's just me. The only bogeyman here is the one in my head.

I follow the evidence markers down the hall, into the kitchen, flicking on all the lights as I go, just like I would if I was coming home from work and getting ready to sit at the table and eat some of Gam's leftovers or maybe try to coax Dad into a conversation and have a beer or two before watching TV until I fall asleep. But not anymore.

The blood is like a painted track. Like a dragged brush that leads out the back door. It's strange to see a thing that was inside my father on such lurid display here. It makes the murder doubly obscene. My father, for all intents and purposes, died when Ana left us. The spark that made him my dad went with her. The rest was just going through the motions. This blood would have embarrassed him. He wanted the perfect Navajo death: to leave like an old wolf, to walk out on everything and everyone without a word and sit down away from the world and die alone. Maybe underneath a tree or by a creek. His body left to nature. Burdening no one.

Sorry, Dad. Guess things didn't really work out for either of us.

Gam's room paints a picture. The shattered window, the broken bone box. There are black feathers everywhere, like little shadows. It looks like the forensics group tried to number them but gave up. Gam's quilt, ancient even when I was born, is strewn across the floor. I pick it up and fold it, evidence be damned. The medicine sticks that were used in the Evilway are broken and strewn about. There was a struggle here on more than one level. There is a dried pool of blood by the door and a spattering along the wall above it. A telltale sign of a flicked knife. So Dad was stabbed here. In this room. Somehow that brings me a measure of comfort. He was coming to help Gam.

The far side of the bedroom tells another story. There are individual droplets everywhere, and most of them are on the floor. Caroline said she found the big crow in here. If I were to guess, I'd say the blood pattern follows something that might drip from a beak.

A smudge of blood mars the linoleum where Gam's body had been. It has a Rorschach symmetry to it, as if it's been pressed, perhaps by a knee. I picture a man kneeling down here and strangling my grandmother. I trace the ground and find another mark, a streaking like dragged fingers that leads to where the bone box lies. I picture that same man, still bleeding, having finished the killing, resting his hand upon the floor not far from where I listened to Gam's final song.

There is blood on the bone box, too. It looks like there were clear fingerprints on the top of the box that were then smudged. In fact, much of the blood evidence is smudged. Now that I look for it, it's clear as day. Almost methodical: a wiped mark on the window, and on the doorframe, and on the doorknob. A smeared streak by the door and again on the screen leading out back. A big smudge in the hallway, this probably a footprint with a tread that would have helped identify the killer, now just a dirty grease smear on old wood. Danny wasn't kidding when he said the evidence was scant.

When I step out onto the lawn, the motion sensors kick on, and I'm flooded in bright porch light. I cover my eyes, and I hear crows move like the rustling of a heavy curtain. I step under the tape marking off the back porch and try to get a sense of my father's final crawl.

He came out here alone. After the killers left. You can see the gripping, ripping tracks of his progress: small scratches in the dust of the brick porch where he pulled himself with his left hand, his right hand no doubt staunching his gut wound. There is a level sweep mark there, most likely from his right arm, its elbow jutting out.

There is still so much blood. It's like a railroad track. He knew he was going to die. He knew he had minutes left, and yet some deep ember inside him, not yet snuffed, called him outside to where he was always most comfortable after Ana disappeared. He came out here for a reason. I follow his ghost out to the lawn. The blood isn't as clear here. The dry winter grass sucked it up same as water, but there is a square marker where he died, right by the edge of the lawn, where Ana's cairn is.

Or was.

It's gone now. Knocked down. All the stones strewn about the ground. Where once there was a careful stack there is now a haphazard pile.

From an outsider's perspective, it would look like nothing but a pile of rocks among a dead winter garden. Easily overlooked. But to my father this was a holy place. He tended it from the day Ana left us. Building that tiny tower from the flat rocks in the backyard was one of the last things she did, and Dad was determined to keep it as it was. I'd seen him out there in storms and in snow. In wind and in rain, checking on it, making sure it still stood. In the rare times when a few stones fell or moved, he was inconsolable. He drank heavily and repositioned it exactly as it was. That pile, a plaything to Ana, became her gravestone to him. And here it was destroyed, and not by any killer or evidence team or detective or cop. I think it was destroyed by him.

As if they hear my thoughts, a group of crows hops from the fence to the ground. They bow quickly to the grass and cock their heads, listening. But they watch me.

"What are you?" I ask.

No answer. They bow and listen.

"Help me," I say.

They start to step quickly on the grass like they're dancing. Then they stop and bow to listen. They do this several times, and then one dashes its beak into the earth, rips half of a worm from the ground, and swallows it as it watches me. Never blinking.

"Well, fuck you then," I say. It snaps its beak with the final bite and burrows into the earth again, flipping a small clump of grass away.

I turn back to the rocks. Now that I stare at them, they don't look strewn out of anger or sorrow. They look broken down and then piled again, like they're meant to fill a hole. I reach down and pick up a rock, and the crows freeze in their dance. One has a night crawler wriggling in its mouth, but still it doesn't move. I toss the stone away and grab the next in the pile, and the crows go back to work with me. I toss this stone too, and then I start digging, flipping stones away to get to the heart of the pile. That's where I find it.

It's a strip of beaded leather. The leather is worn almost to white and the beads are rubbed lumpy.

I know this strip of leather. I've known it for years. And I know the scalp knife it hung from before my father ripped it off the weapon and stashed it as his final gift to me.

I know who killed Dad and Gam, and it kills me too.

16

OWEN BENNET

We kept Ben at ABQ General for as long as we could that night. Longer than he wanted, because he didn't have a ride until his mother was able to make the trip from Santa Fe. That was maybe the worst part of the entire ordeal for me. Worse than the insanity with Joey Flatwood—that's something you deal with in your own mind, and it makes it or breaks it. Worse than watching Ben hold the phone while his grandmother died—I've seen a lot of messy deaths. But watching him sit there in the waiting room, staring at the floor, for five hours like a forgotten child—that ripped me to pieces. Just the fact that he couldn't catch a ride. Such a stupid thing that hit home like a sledgehammer. Caroline was at the police station making a statement. I tried to give him money for a cab, but he looked at me like his mind was breaking, so I just let him sit. Maybe it was best that he went with his mom. No man should go home alone to that hell.

I didn't get much sleep that night. I started drinking bourbon again. When I met the sunrise I was no more settled than I was when I tried to hand Ben cab money. And then I had to go to work again.

It's funny when you go through something like that. Something big and shattering and life-distorting, and then after it happens you wake up the next morning the same as always. You put your pants on and eat your breakfast and get in your car and take the same route to work and you log in to the same system, and all the while you want to just scream at everyone, *How can you go on like this? The world is different now!* But nobody knows. Nobody cares. People have their own problems. And who's to say a few of these people haven't come across some Joey Flatwoods of their own?

I spoke with Caroline that day, the day after Ben's life shattered to pieces, and she told me about what she'd found. About the crow and the two bodies and the robbery and the bone box. She told me that Ben's grandmother had a crow of her own. I asked Caroline what she said to her, if she knew who attacked her, or what. She said Ben's grandmother was too far gone. That she just sang her way out.

She's a terrible liar, Caroline. I think it's part of what I love about her. Probably because until right about now she's had nothing to lie about, but that night she saw something else there. I know it because when I asked about Ben's grandmother's last words she said they were "goodbye." Nobody's last words are "goodbye." Least of all a Navajo elder. I almost laughed. Fair enough. If she doesn't want to tell, she doesn't have to. I have enough trouble keeping the rational parts of my brain from mutiny with the information I already have. I'm swimming out beyond my depth here, so that first week after everything went down, I did what any sane medical practitioner does when they don't understand something: I researched the hell out of it.

I started with medical explanations for visual and auditory hallucinations of the sort that might explain why Joey Flatwood seemed to phase in and out of view. I looked for literature related to degenerative eye conditions, something akin to a temporary glaucoma-like symptom that would affect frontal vision but not peripheral. I mostly did this just to make myself feel better. To do some sort of due diligence. If it was a visual phenomenon, it would have had to affect Ben and me at the same time, and in the same way. And there's also the fact that Joey isn't an instance of ocular flashing or a visual blind spot. He is a person. A person who appeared and then disappeared. He was no hallucination. I saw Ben grab him by the coat. So what, then? Some illusion? A sleight of hand or a smoke and mirror trick? Everyone knows your brain sees what it wants to see. And yes, maybe he could have fooled me. Or Ben. But both of us? And afterwards to elude the FBI and a platoon of policemen?

There was no explaining it from a medical perspective, so I flipped the table around and tried it from Joey's end, and from what I overheard when he and Ben spoke face-to-face.

The next night I start researching crow totems and invisible men.

I go down the internet rabbit hole into some pretty crazy conspiracy websites. Eventually I know I'm just clicking through this garbage to keep myself from calling Caroline, which I want to do more than anything. The problem is there's really no reason for me to talk to her. I'm not sure what I'd even say aside from rehashing that we all broke down last night and then tacking on a *wasn't that crazy?*

I have this absurd idea early in the morning of calling Caroline to ask her on a date. After another hour of pacing the apartment and delving deeper into the underbelly of the web, I decide to table that, thank God. Essentially I'd be hitting on a girl just after a funeral, like some hornball. It's not like me at all, but then again I'm not really myself these days. I'm increasingly coming to see that whatever happened that afternoon with Ben and Jocy has fundamentally changed me. It is the sum measure of a path I took up when I volunteered to attend at CHC. I gained speed on that path when Caroline stepped on the scene, and then Ben. I'm usually not one for preordination, but this kind of trend is hard to ignore. The Harvard medical student Owen, the staunch atheist, would scoff at the Doctor Bennet sitting up until the dead of night thinking more and more that it's possible that out there somewhere is a man who can disappear into space.

I stumble across a chat room on the topic of ancient cabals. The usual tropes: old orders of men and women whose job it is to shepherd the interests of humanity, typical One World Order crap that doesn't hold a candle to reason. Even the new Owen Bennet refuses to believe that the big banks are financed by aliens intent on keeping the masses from acquiring super-technology that a handful of privileged humans currently employ. That's a common theme in these whack job forums. But in my glassy-eyed state I recall a point of the conversation between Joey and Ben: Joey took his crow off a dead man. He said there are other crows. He said that the agents want to get them all.

I sleep fitfully, and I awake in cold sweats from nightmares I half remember. I start seeing things out of the corner of my eye that I know are not there. I keep a hammer underneath my pillow because it's the only thing I have in my apartment that resembles a weapon. I don't even own a good set of kitchen knives. By the end of the week, I've convinced myself I have to get off the conspiracy kick and back to the common denominator here: the Navajo connection. Ben's grandmother had a crow. Joey has a crow. The crow is turquoise, a powerful stone in Navajo lore. The crow functions as a totem, which is a Navajo token. I get out of the chatrooms and back to the academic articles where I've lived most of my professional life. This time I look up the Navajo.

I find an interesting bit about Chantways that invoke symbolism. The Blessingway and the Evilway and the Enemyway are the most famous, but there are others. Hundreds. Historians have no idea what most of them were like or what sort of function they served. The names of some of these extinct Chantways are all that survives. Names like the Hailway, the Mothway, the Dogway, the Waterway, the Big Godway, and then one that strikes me: the Ravenway. But that's where the line ends. There's no way to know what the Ravenway might have done, or been. It's lost to time along with the rest of the extinct Chantways. It's infuriating, because I have a feeling that I was getting close. Closer than aliens running JP Morgan, at least.

I stare at crows all the next day: out of windows, from my car. Daring them to make a move. But other than the fact that there seem to be an awful lot of them, they don't take any notice of me whatsoever. And as for the numbers, well, they flock in the winter, and it's just about winter.

A week goes by like this. Agonizing. Plodding. No word from Ben, and no word from Caroline. We aren't scheduled to work together for some time. I just need an excuse to call her. You'd think *I'm in love with you* is a pretty good one, but that has the unfortunate effect of making things awfully uncomfortable if the sentiment's not returned. Call me what you will. You don't have to stare at the phone like I do. You aren't the one with his heart on the line.

Then, late Saturday evening, an excuse drops right onto my plate: Ben's most recent chart, filed by Caroline on the second regimen of chemotherapy she'd delivered just the night before.

Increased visual impairment.

Reported diplopia.

Noted word aphasia.

Noted slurred speech.

Bruising on right hip and right elbow from a fall.

He can't see right, he can't speak right, and he can't stand right. Ben is getting worse.

I dial the phone. Caroline picks up on the first ring.

"Owen," she says, and as soon as she gets my name out, she starts crying. I can tell by the lack of sound, by the clipped silence that comes when you cover a receiver.

"I saw the report."

"It's worse than that. He's...he's giving up."

"We need to bring him in to the hospital, Caroline. Full time. If he's to have any chance of surviving, he needs radical radiation therapy to shrink these tumors. I don't think he's responding to the chemotherapy."

"I know that. He won't go."

"He will when he collapses."

"That's what it's going to take, I think," she says.

"What is he doing that is so important? More important than his own life?"

"He wants them."

I almost ask who *they* are, but then I already know who he wants: the people he thinks killed his family.

"He's stubborn," she says. "He has to right the wrong if it kills him. He has to restore the balance. You didn't see his house, Owen. You didn't see what I saw."

In the depths of all this insanity, it occurs to me that she is using my first name. It sounds wonderful coming from her. It sounds like she's been saying it for a thousand years.

"What did you see?" I ask.

"I...I can't say, really. I'm not sure."

So she's in shock too. The both of us adrift at sea, the mainsail snapped.

"Caroline, you have to listen to me. You need to convince him to come here, to ABQ General. You too. Both of you have to come."

"I think we will," she says flatly. "I just think it's gonna be when it's too late for him."

I swallow, and it hitches in my throat. There's no way I can make Ben come to the hospital myself. My entire career I've been fighting to get the Navajo people *out* of the IHS revolving door. It seems perversely fitting that this upending of my life should culminate in my trying to drag a Navajo back *in*.

"I wasn't crying until you called," Caroline says, with quiet pride.

"That's always nice to hear, when a guy calls a girl."

"No, I mean that I haven't just been sitting around crying the whole time."

"I know, Caroline."

"I just want to help him."

"Me too. I think it's...it's very important that we help him. However we can. Do you know what I'm saying?" I walk to the window and I stare out at where the crows massed in the tree before. It's barren, now.

"I do," says Caroline.

"You have to get him to come to ABQ. You have to try."

"I will."

"And be careful, for Christ's sake."

"You too, Owen."

She hangs up. God, I love the way she says my name.

17

CAROLINE ADAMS

Usually I'm good with patients in shock. You know it immediately. It's the vacant stare, the ridges on the sides of the eye. Anxious patients have ridges around the forehead. Shell-shocked patients have ridges around the eyes. I have this theory that it's because they're running through slides in their mind and can't turn away, can't even blink. They may be quiet, but they're having a full-blown conversation with themselves in their heads. You can see it in the twitches in the bags under their eyes.

That's how Ben looks during chemo today. His house is still a crime scene, so I administer the regimen in a disgusting hotel outside of the reservation, past the casino. The kind of place a gambler would stay with his last forty bucks. This is where I meet his mom, Sitsi Dejooli. I arrive as he is in the middle of explaining who I am.

As soon as I walk in, I hear her go, "You have cancer?" in a shrill, panicky voice. Ben moves back to sit on the brown comforter draped over the lumpy twin bed. He looks pleadingly at me for a moment, then drops his head in his hands and gives a weak nod. His mother is a small woman, thin, like Ben, and with his frame. She has the dark hair of the Navajo, but it's cut short and pixie-like around her head. She wears trim, straight-legged jeans and two-toned leather boots with thick heels. She's standing in the middle of the room clutching her purse to herself with one hand and clutching the collar of her sweater with the other. She's quite pretty, but she has that look of an older woman trying too hard to stay in her thirties. She also looks like she doesn't want to touch anything. Which I can understand.

"Cancer?" she screeches again. I get the sense she's been repeating herself. She looks at me toting my radioactive cooler like I'm here to rob them.

"This is Caroline. She's my nurse," Ben says. His face twitches. He's here, but he's not here. His color is roiling in black. It looks like clay mixed with blood. He must have seen something at the house that sapped him completely. He's barely there.

"Hi, Mrs. Dejooli," I say. She ignores me.

"No, this isn't right. You can't have...did you check with other people? How many opinions did you get?"

Ben never told his mother. Most likely never would have if his life hadn't fallen around his feet. I can see that he's not comfortable with her. He doesn't trust her. He feels like she's turned her back on him, on all of them. He thinks she doesn't love him. It all centers on Ana. I can feel this. I'm getting better at reading the colors by the day.

For what it's worth, he's wrong. Looking at this woman it's impossible not to see it. She's terrified of losing him. It's coming off of her in bursts of yellow, like popping gasoline bubbles. She wants to see him grow older. She wants to die before him. She's afraid of being alone. Which is pretty rich coming from a woman who left her entire family to carve out a new life for herself off the rez.

Ben looks over at me with unfocused eyes. He holds out a hand weakly to me, and I come over to him.

"Tell her, Caroline. I can't right now."

I sit down and hold his arm, much thinner now even than last week. I cradle it in my lap as I swab it with an alcohol pad.

"It's no mistake, Mrs. Dejooli. He has a late stage brain cancer. It's very real, and very serious."

She breaks down completely. She sits in a smoke-stained chair by the faded table in the corner and cries for basically the entire session.

A couple of times she stops and looks up at me like I've betrayed her or something, then she goes back to holding her head in her hands and wiping her face with a Kleenex. I'd had such plans. I wanted to tell him myself what I'd whitewashed for the police report. I wanted to tell him about his grandmother's last minutes. About what he couldn't hear over the phone. About her calm confidence and her strange words, and, of course, about the hollow bell that hung from my neck like a ball of iced lead.

But there is no place for that. Not with his mother here. Not with the way he's lying on the bed and taking the drip and staring at the flaking ceiling like he wants to float up and through it and away. I might as well set it and forget it. I think he's forgotten about me completely until I get up to use the bathroom and he grips me by the arm for a moment. I can see he's afraid I'm leaving him. He looks lost. Like he's floundering in the deep end of his life and is about to give up and sink under. I refuse to cry in front of his mother, who is, quite frankly, putting on a disgusting little show, heartfelt or not. Tears are not what Ben needs right now.

That's about all I get from Ben this time: that one look. I wrap up my stuff to leave, and he thanks me and hugs me with a creepy finality. He made some sort of decision on that bed. Some decision that is final.

On the drive home I'm looking for any excuse to turn around, and it's Owen who gives me one. My notes. I'd submitted them to the system in my car before hitting the road while they were still fresh in my mind, and they are blatantly indicative of a worsening condition. Ben looked so bad on the inside that the diplopia and aphasia and the bruising I noticed seemed secondary to me, but of course they were huge red flags. He is getting worse. He has to go to a hospital. He needs full-time care. I just needed someone with guts to tell me to go do it, and as usual, Owen Bennet is that man.

You have to get him to come to ABQ. You have to try.

I flip my car around and bounce over the median, kicking up dust and wincing when I hear the scrape of metal on rock, but I don't care. I'm going back to him, and this time I'm not leaving without him. I turn up the radio to drown out my mind, but I still second-guess myself sick. Nothing is harder than treating a patient who doesn't want to be treated. I've seen that look before, that black look that settled over him. It's a look of pure despair that lives on the cancer floor, and you have to constantly chase it away or else it'll find a home in you. But I've also felt that tug before. That small tug that he gave me when he thought I was leaving. If you're completely gone, you don't tug like that. He has it in him to fight. If he's given up, I just gotta make him un-give up. That's all.

But when I get back to the hotel, he's gone anyway. And so is his mother. Or she's not answering the door. Either way, nothing stirs behind the shabby curtains when I slam the knocker down again and again until someone down the row screams at me to shut up.

I go back down and sit in my car in the dark and try to think. I check the clock. It's been a little under two hours since his chemo. He'll be feeling like warmed over crap right about now. There is no reason he shouldn't be on the couch or in a bed trying to sleep off nausea. It takes a lot to get a chemo patient to move. Last time it took the FBI and Joey Flatwood. This time it's gotta be something as serious as that. He looked terrified today, but there was also a cold fury deep within him, like a frozen black soup boiling at the edges of the pot. It had to have been because of what he saw at the house. That sort of scene would shock anyone, but it was more. He saw something else there. Something that he needs to deal with.

I take a deep breath and let it out, and it fogs the inside of my windshield. I grip the steering wheel. I know where he is, but I want to go back to that house about as much as I want this damn bell hanging around my neck.

It doesn't help that it's as dark as a pit around Chaco at night. On the side streets like the one where Ben lives (or used to live, anyway) the lighting is spaced way out. A lot of the streetlights are in disrepair, if they're there at all. There are bright orange cones of light every couple of blocks, but that only serves to make the homes in between darker than ever. His is the darkest of all.

It looks like everything that was once good about the Dejooli home has fled this place, and the bad that is left is seeping out from underneath. The other side of the duplex is black, too. As is the neighbor's house across the street, and the one kitty-corner as well. It makes sense, since the Navajo really hate death and the places where things die, but it gives me the impression that Ben's place is slowly infecting everything around it. I check every angle before getting out of my car and make a lame attempt at protecting myself by gripping my keys so they extend between my fingers like cat's claws. Lot of good that would do me. Probably just make me lose my keys before getting mugged.

My footsteps on the concrete are the loudest thing around. I take to creeping, and if someone were to glance outside they might think I was the one out for trouble, but nobody looks. There's nobody here at all, that I can see. But I feel Ben. I can feel his coloring like a whiff of smoke on the wind, and he's terribly weak.

The house is boarded up and locked and taped over. I won't be getting inside through the front door, so I walk around, slowly. I keep my eyes on the sky for birds, and I strain my ears for any sound as I cut through an alley that leads through to the back yard. The gate there is open, and I pause. That's when I hear the retching. It's quiet, like he's trying to muffle it, but in this silence it's still clear enough.

I peek around the corner and see Ben on his hands and knees in the backyard near where his father died. His whole body tenses with the retches and the effort to keep them quiet. Then, a moment later, he collapses on his side and spits and makes this soft mewl that rips me to pieces. I have to pull back behind the house and sit with my head against the side and scrunch up my face not to lose it. I'm supposed to be helping him. There's no excuse for this right now, not even a breaking heart. I stand and smooth my shirt and then walk out back. Ben is still on his side and doesn't seem to hear my approach.

"Ben?" I ask quietly. He tenses and turns his head to me, but he's like a lamed animal. He can't quite turn the rest of his body.

"Ben, it's me. It's Caroline."

A faint trickle of the beautiful, rich red comes back to him. I rush over, get down on my knees next to him, and brush his stringy hair from his watery, bloodshot eyes. The floodlight kicks on, and I can see just how bad he's become. His neck and head jut out like a turtle's from his hollowing body. He has vomit on his uniform.

"Caroline. What are you doing here? You can't be here," he says, but he holds on to my arm for dear life.

"Me? What are *you* doing here?"

"This is my home."

"Don't give me that bullshit. You need to be inside, warm, comfortable. With liquids and anti-nausea meds and ice cream and a terrible midnight movie playing in the background." Is that a hint of a smile? Maybe. I hope so.

"This one's pretty bad. Worse than the first one. I think I'm gonna stop this chemo stuff."

"No you're not. If you do, you'll die," I say, and I barely manage to keep my voice from clipping high at the end.

"Eh," he says. "I'm going to die anyway." He says this like he might say it's dark out tonight. "I think we both know that. It's just killing what time I have left. Which isn't much."

"We could try other regimens," I say. "Maybe...maybe you—" but he quiets me with a soft squeeze.

"Maybe nothing. I can feel it. And so can you. But I have to do something first. Here. And you need to go."

"No, Ben—"

"Yes. It's not safe for you. The people that I love get hurt, Caroline. Do you understand me? This thing begins and ends with me. Once I'm out of the way, it'll leave you alone."

Oh, I understand all right. I understand that I think that he might have said, in some roundabout, guy-like, obscure Navajo way, that he loves me. If I could see myself, I'd be leaking gold, darkness and death be damned. Talk about food for thought at three a.m. I'll be chewing on this one for years.

"Caroline? Do you understand? You have to go. He'll be here soon."

I shake my head again, and he tries to interject, but I stop him by putting my face right in front of his. "No, Ben. This didn't begin with you. And it won't end with you either. Whatever is happening here, it's an old thing. Very old. And it's bigger than you and me."

Ben tries to shake his head. "He's got Gam's crow, but I got something of his. Something that is important to him. Something he wants back," Ben says, and he holds out an old beaded lanyard of some sort. I don't quite understand him, but there's no time to hash it out.

"Yeah well, I got something else important," I say, and my hand touches the cold metal resting on my chest. "And I need to talk to you about it—"

But that's when we hear the sound.

It's a strange whistling. Low, and in pockets, like the sound of a staff being waved through the air, followed by a small pop, like a ball hitting a glove. It's out on the street first, and then closer: *whistle, pop. Whistle, pop.* Then, impossibly, it's inside the house, without a door opening or closing. Both of us can hear it, low and muffled, but there.

Whistle, pop. Whistle, pop.

Moving from room to room. There's a haphazard crash then, and some rough shoving of furniture from Ben's grandmother's room. We can hear it loud and clear from the backyard because her broken window looks out on us.

We can see it, too. Or him, rather. A massive dark shape straightens and turns towards the window, and two black glints of eyes blink once then stare solidly at us. There is a flash of teeth, either a smile or a snarl.

"Too late," Ben says and shuffles back to sitting. His hand goes to his gun and there is one more *whistle, pop.* Then he's there in front of us. Like he stepped out of the air itself.

"Hello, Danny," Ben says.

Danny's a massive Indian in full war paint, his face dyed red from his forehead down to below his eyes, and his long hair is straight and as smooth as black water. He is shirtless despite the cold, but he steams like a bull, and all along his arms are spots and whorls of paint. He wears buckskin chaps and has bare feet, and in his hand is a knife the size of my forearm. It flashes in the moonlight as he adjusts his grip on it.

"Ben," he grunts. As if he ran across us at the supermarket. His face is as telling as stone.

"Forget something?" Ben asks.

Danny nods slowly. Ben holds out a leather string of beads. Danny looks at it and laughs. It's a great, booming laugh. One that I can tell is seldom used, since it sets Ben on edge as much as it does me.

"No. Not that. I no longer concern myself with trinkets of this realm. They mean nothing to me."

"What?"

"Where did they put out your grandmother, Ben?" Danny asks, his voice quiet.

Whistle, pop, and then he's there in front of Ben. He shoves me aside with as much care as he would a curtain of beads. He grabs Ben, heedless of the gun, and pulls him up to his face, his feet dangling in the air. Ben's eyes are wide with shock. Danny's so close now that I can see that what I took for spotted markings are actually scabbed tears and claw marks. I remember the dead crow. The crow that didn't go quietly.

"I have no time for this, Ben. It calls to me. It is near. I must have it. I believe your grandmother was the Keeper. I must know where they put her out for the cliff burial. Perhaps the crows took it from her body." His eyes are full of madness, brimming in the darkness. He never raises his voice, but he speaks each word carefully and each one drips with malice.

And then Ben spits in his face. "Fuck you. You're insane. You killed her, and my dad, and now you want to desecrate her burial? You stole her totem, Danny," Ben says. He pulls his gun up and places it between them, right at Danny's gut. "But now you're gonna give it back."

Danny looks down at the gun with mild interest.

"Always fighting. A rookie, but a fighter nonetheless. You would have made the circle stronger. But you are dying, so you are worthless to me. Your grandmother was strong, too. She fought, too, but she was old. No longer fit to be the Keeper. Your father was a loose end. Always at the wrong place at the wrong time."

He ticks each of them off like he's reading a grocery list.

"The gambler was unfit. Flatwood is too," he says.

Ben peers into his eyes with growing horror, looking for any light, but he can see as well as I can that there is none there. "You killed all of them," he says.

"Not Flatwood. Not yet. But I did convince you to banish him while I continued my search for the bell. He's an industrious rat, though, and he found a totem despite his banishment. But I will find him and take it. Then I will have three. Triple the power. Better to find the bell. It took me years to find my first totem with the gambler, and then your grandmother's dropped in my lap at the Evilway. Things are moving faster. More becomes clear to me every day."

"But why? Why?" Ben asks, and his color fades, guttering.

"We are the first people, Ben. And we will be the last. A Navajo must be the Keeper of the Bell. A *worthy* Navajo. Strong in the old ways. Not an old crone, or a hopeless addict, or worthless trailer trash like your friend Flatwood. Me. It must be *me*." His voice is a fervent whisper now. Like a muttered chant.

"Go to hell, Ninepoint," Ben says. And then he fires his gun.

Whoosh, pop. Danny flicks in and out of existence at the same time. Ben drops heavily to the ground, and a moment later Danny is standing just as he was, unscathed. He looks down upon Ben and narrows his eyes.

"You would have killed me?" he says, and his tone is tinged with surprise. "*You?* You would have killed *me*?"

Ben looks blankly at his gun, then up at Danny. He swallows and tries to kick away, but Danny is there, grabbing him by the lapel and jerking him up to standing.

"Fool. I have two crows. I am untouchable. And now I must kill *you*," he says. "It is only fitting. In the end, I'm just bringing about the inevitable."

It all happened so quickly—in the span of half a minute. The gunshot is still ringing in my ears, and everything around me, the very black of the night itself, seems to sway and hitch. I wonder if I'm having a panic attack or passing out, but when Danny Ninepoint grabs Ben, everything snaps back into focus. I throw myself at Danny. I don't care how big he is. I don't care how strong. I don't give a shit who this man is, or about the crow totems or even about the bell. All I know is that nobody should speak to Ben like that. That condescending *"you,"* as if he were less than human. Nobody should speak to anybody like that, but especially not to Ben, a guy who is ripping precious days from the jaws of death itself just to set things right, a man who cares nothing for himself and everything for those around him. That is the type of man who deserves the most respect. Buckets full of respect. Not a fucking *"you?"*

I catch his knife hand on the windup. He wants to slash across Ben's throat, but I grip him by his arm like I'm climbing a tree, and he hitches mid-swipe. I pull down his arm and try for the knife. I manage to turn it in his hand a bit and yank it free. I feel a quick, cold pain across my palm, then a terrible running warmth. The knife falls to the ground. He goes for it, but I grab at his face, flinging blood, dark and glittering in the moonlight, all over him, and press my bloody palm into his eyes.

"You bitch!" he says, and he backhands me. I stagger back. I feel like I took a frying pan to the head.

"Unclean," he says, wiping at his face. He mutters more, but I can't hear him. My head feels like someone poured boiling water over it. My hearing is wavering, and my face stings like fire. He picks up his knife again and wipes my blood off on his chaps. "I'll deal with you afterwards," he says, then turns back to Ben and points a finger at him as if Ben were a child. "You should have come alone." He steps towards him. Ben is watching me with blank shock, his hand loose around his gun. He sits like a worn teddy bear: slouched, tipping. Danny grabs Ben's hair and grimaces when a tuft of it comes off in his hand. Ben looks up at him. Then beyond him. Danny pauses.

That's when I hear it too. It's a tittering sound. And the wavering in my vision is back, but this time it's not from any slap to the face. The entire night is moving.

"What's that?" Danny asks.

Ben's blank stare falls slowly back into focus. Then it's Ben's turn to smile.

"You're wrong, Danny."

Danny's face shows a crack of fear. Faint, but there. He looks around himself as if he's lost. He can hear it, too.

"What...what are you doing? What are you saying?"

"I said you're wrong."

"Why?" Danny asks, looking all around to pinpoint the source of the sound we're hearing, but it's no use. It's the night itself, oozing black.

"Because I was never alone."

There's a brief stillness then, an expectant hush when I can hear everyone breathing. Then, from out of the darkness, three sharp calls of a crow, and then the night explodes around us.

I didn't see any birds because there was nothing to see *but* birds. Crows everywhere. They painted the roofs and weighed down the trees. They bowed the wires and covered the fence lines. They'd sat still as stone upon the grass and the dirt, watching the three of us until that very moment, and then every single one of them flew right at Danny Ninepoint.

He's there one moment, and then he's not. But this time he doesn't disappear. The crows won't let him. They cover him like tar, raking at him and slashing and tearing, and only his screams can be heard. Then even his screams succumb to the rush of feathers, a sound like the shaking of a forest in the wind. I hide my head, I scream, I scramble to Ben. He holds me, and I bury my head in his arms as the black vortex rages around us.

And then it's gone.

When I look up, there is nothing but blood on the grass and feathers floating in the air. And there, on the ground where Danny had stood, are two small stone crows. One that had belonged to the gambler, and one that had belonged to Ben's grandmother. We watch in stunned silence as one black feather floats to the ground in front of our faces.

I turned to Ben. I want to kiss him. To tell him he's saved us, somehow, by calling down the night. He's figured it all out. I am in his arms. This is the perfect time for a kiss. This is textbook. This is it. If it's ever going to happen, it's going to happen now.

But Ben is crying. He is in a ball sobbing quietly to himself on my shoulder and saying their names over and over again. All of them: Gam, Dad, Ana, Joey, and yes, even Danny. All of them. So instead I just turn towards him and hold him.

And that's when the agents come.

They walk slowly into the floodlight, one after the other, stirring tufts of feathers with each step. They have eyes only for the crow totems. Each snatches one with greedy abandon, their eyes glimmering. As they touch the totems with their bare hands, they flicker a bit in and out of focus, and terrible grins spread across their faces. I'm beginning to think they don't know that we're here, but then Parsons speaks.

"Thank you, Mr. Dejooli," he says. "We'll take it from here."

Then both of them blink out of existence.

BEN DEJOOLI

She saved me from the knife. From Danny's huge knife. The knife that's hung at Danny's side as long as I've known him. The same knife that Danny would casually click in and out of its sheath when things got tense on calls. He used to use the bone handle to crush beer cans at station BBQs. He once plucked a two-inch splinter from my palm with the tip of it. Caroline stopped that same knife from ripping my throat open. That's my first thought when I wake up in the hospital bed.

The second thought is that it was a lot of work on her part to buy me another couple of days. Don't get me wrong: the last thing I wanted was to get killed by my two-faced partner. When I go, I can count him being swallowed by a million crows among the top five most beautiful things I've ever seen in my life. Ana being another one. Caroline being another. I would have missed that sight if it weren't for her, but part of me wonders if she shouldn't have bothered.

The other two in my top five, in case you're wondering, are kind of like memory snapshots. One is of a sunrise. Danny and I were coming off a nightshift one warm summer night two years ago. I had the next two days off. We were driving the fringes, the northern border of the rez, just flying across the desert in the cruiser, and the sun was rising over the sand and it painted the whole thing purple. It doesn't sound like much, but it was. If you were there, you'd have thought so too. The way things ended up with Danny doesn't change that sunrise. That picture. That's forever.

The second is a snapshot of a bonfire out at the Arroyo. It was a Saturday night, and I was with Joey Flatwood. Both of us were fourteen, tearing circles around the fire pit while our folks drank beers and talked and sang. I have this picture in my mind of us running around and around like a long exposure of light in the dark, and we're leaving these phosphorescent firefly trails behind us. Even when I banished Joey, even when I thought he knew what happened to Ana and was keeping it from me, nothing could ruin that picture either. That's forever, too.

It's funny how you take stock of these things when your life is coming to a close. You don't really do it because you're getting all sentimental, either. A lot of it is boredom. There's not a lot to do in a hospital bed when you're waiting to die.

I'm pretty far gone, now, I think. There isn't a lot of pain. The morphine drip killed all that, along with most of my hospital phobia. Funny how high-powered drugs will do that for you. So I'm not nauseous anymore and I'm not aching, but I am sort of being packed away. I feel like I'm being swaddled, slowly, from the feet up. I lose chunks of time. First it was hours, but the chunks are getting bigger. Half a day? A whole day? All I know is that the times between when I open my eyes are getting longer, and I suspect that when I actually die it'll be just that: the time between when I open my eyes will be forever.

I can't really talk anymore, but I can think, and I can listen. I know that people are here with me. And that people are coming and going. Caroline has been the most constant. She holds my hand and speaks to me about everything, and I suspect that she knows I can listen. I think she can see more than most people. Can understand more. It's like she can sense when I surface, even if I don't open my eyes. She whispers to me about the bell. She doesn't know what to do with it. I don't either. She says it's mine, by rights, but I don't think it is. I don't think it's anybody's. I don't think it even belongs here at all. I can feel it, resting on her chest. It has this dull hum that seems to get stronger as I get weaker. She tells me that I'm flipping through the pages of my life. Setting the numbers in order. She whispers to me that she wishes she could be in there with me, flipping the pages. She wishes she could see it all. I can feel her tears, hot, falling on my cheeks, before she wipes them away. It feels good, to have someone cry for you. That may sound like an asshole thing to say, but it's true.

Mom is here too, although less frequently. I don't blame her. I think her mind is breaking. I think it cracked when Ana died, but now it's breaking. She'll have lost everyone, when this is all over. I think she's learning that it's one thing to push everyone away when they're still here and it's another thing to have them disappear altogether. She talks to me, too, although she sounds off. She talks about the day Ana disappeared. She says it was just like this. Over and over again she says that: *Just like this. Just like this.*

"It's happening again," she says, when I float back. She's panicky, and her hand is trembling as it holds mine. I want to help her. She was dealt a heavy hand of grief in life and she folded with it, gave up early on, but I'm not sure I can begrudge her that. She couldn't deal. Is that her fault? I'm not sure I could deal, either, if I was her. Maybe that's why I joined the force. Not because I was dealing with Ana's loss, but because I wasn't dealing with Ana's loss. I spent my days patching up other people's problems instead of dealing with mine.

I manage a squeeze, and she latches on to it. I open my eyes and mumble, "S'okay, Mom." Kind of a stupid thing to say, especially given that pretty much nothing is okay. But there's nothing she can do about it. I expect her to break down or something, but she doesn't. She gets real close to me and says, "Stay, Benny. Stay here."

That's pretty rich. I don't exactly feel like running these days, Mom. But she's serious.

"Ana didn't stay," she says. "You must stay. No matter what Gam or anyone says."

Gam's gone, Mom. Dead. Ana's dead, too. And I'm going. I hope she gets the help she needs, my mom. This is going to pretty much destroy her. Is it bad that I take just a tiny measure of comfort in the fact that I won't be around to see it?

I get the sense that Caroline's right. I've been flipping through my book, setting the pages in order, but here at the end there are a bunch of blanks. The pages are there, the numbers are right. They're the end, but there's nothing on them.

Not yet, anyway.

Something is coming. Something has to happen for me to close my book. It's why I'm not dead just yet. It's why I can still hear them. I'd heard that right before people die, some of them get really lucid. Sort of come back for one last big push. I think that's what's happening to me. I think I have one last big push stored up, and I'm terrified to think of what it's for.

The people around my bed are like pieces shifting on a combination lock. Doctor Bennet, Caroline, Mom, they need to be here, I feel it, but one is missing, and when that fourth shows up, I know it is time.

Joey Flatwood.

It's late at night when he comes to me. I hear the *whoosh, pop,* and for one horrible minute I think Danny is back. I actually open my eyes. It startles me back to the surface, almost above the surface. *This is it,* I think. *This is the push. This is the end.*

Joey is stunned, looking at me. He's like a bull charging into the china shop only to find it's a butcher's. He reaches one trembling hand out towards me, and it hangs in the air.

"Jesus, Ben. I mean...Jesus."

"Hello," I say. It comes out a croak.

Caroline stirs in the chair next to me. Mom stirs in the makeshift bed next to Caroline. Doctor Bennet walks by the door. I know he's done that many times, many more times than he needs to, always with the pretense of checking my vitals or reading my charts, but I know it's more than that. I wish I had more time to get to know the good doctor. I think we'd have liked each other.

When Bennet sees Joey, he stops still, looks back and forth along the hallway, then steps inside the room and closes the door.

The gang's all here.

"This is bad," Joey says, staring at me as he walks over to my bedside.

"Well, it's not good, Joey," I say. I try to smile. My lips are goopy from Vaseline.

Joey looks from me to the other three, who watch him carefully, but everyone seems to know to stay quiet.

"No. I mean they're coming," he says. "They know about the bell. They think you have it."

"Who?"

"The agents," he says, then he freezes and pricks his ears. He looks over his shoulder at the door. He turns back to me, and I can see that he's genuinely afraid.

"It's here, isn't it? I can feel it, too. It pulls at the crow."

We are all silent. Bennet looks at me. I have to make a conscious effort not to look at Caroline.

"It's here," I say, at last. Then I ask him a question, very carefully, because I know a lot hinges on it. "Do you want it, Joey?"

He looks at me without blinking, and he works his jaw around.

"No," he says. "No, I don't think I do. I don't think anyone can have it. Especially not them. It's too...too much. Too dangerous. Too...everything."

"What is the bell?" Caroline asks quietly. Joey flicks his gaze over to her. He zeroes in on the leather strap around her neck, and I know he knows. I know he knows it's right there, with her. But all he does is nod. And right then I know something else, too: Joey had nothing to do with Ana's vanishing. Far from it. In fact, it wouldn't surprise me to learn that from the second I banished him, Joey spent every waking day trying to make sense of what happened to her, just like me.

"It's what took Ana," Joey says.

"What?" Mom asks. "What?" She's getting louder. Bennet tries to quiet her, but she ignores him. She runs to Joey, grabs him with both hands, and shakes him. "What are you saying? You can't just say

things like that. You can't just come in here and say things like that."
She slaps him, and he takes it. "What do you *mean*?" she wails. She is
unraveling. Bennet grabs her with both arms and pulls her away. I
hear movement outside.

"I don't know," Joey says, and I see that he's crying. "I don't
fucking know. It's all I've ever wanted to know. You have to believe me.
Ben, please. I don't know how. I don't know why. But that bell took
her away from me right before my eyes."

"I believe you," I say, and I sound stronger than I have in what
feels like weeks. The push is upon me. The crest is here. "Joey, I really
fucked up, man. I really fucked up, and if you never forgive me, I
understand."

"It was Danny, Ben. Danny planted the seed. Danny brought the
hearing. Danny pulled all the right strings, with the council, with
your family, with your heart. He wanted the bell for himself. He knew
I wanted it too. But I don't want it like he did."

"Nah," I say, and it's a sort of wail. The beginning of a cry. "Nah. I
fucked up. I did."

There's a subtle shift in the air, and we all feel it. A *whistle, pop*
from down the hall. There's shouting outside the room. They're here.
Joey turns to me. His eyes are swimming, but his teeth are gritted.

"I want you to know, man. I want you to know that you never
stopped being my best friend. Never. Not when you screamed at me
at the hospital that day she disappeared. Not when you spoke against
me in front of the court. Not when you stood and watched me cross
that line out of Chaco. Never. And you never will."

Bennet locks the door. Joey looks at him. "Locks don't matter," he
says, and just then there's a *whistle, pop* and one of the agents is there.
It's Douglas, the bulldog one with the stained teeth. His face lights
up, and his eyes are like tar-dipped coins.

"Here you are," he says, staring at me with wild, hungry eyes. He
sniffs the air. "And it's here, too."

Joey steps between us, and I see Bennet position himself in front
of Mom and Caroline.

Douglas snaps away, and then in a blink he's back with Parsons, who looks fresh from a conference call, as always. Both of them stare at me, unblinking. They suck in the air as if mad for the scent of the bell.

"Where is it, Mr. Dejooli?" Parsons asks. He's like a schoolteacher giving an unruly pupil one last chance. But Joey steps in between us.

"It's not for you to have," Joey says. "You don't know what you're doing. The crows are meant to protect the bell. To keep it secret. And safe."

Parsons and Douglas turn to Joey as if seeing him for the first time.

"It will be safe," Parsons says. "With us. And only with us."

Douglas steps towards me, but Joey holds out his hand and stops him. Douglas bumps into it and stares at it like it's a tumbleweed bumped against a fence.

"Back off," Joey says.

Douglas looks back at Parsons, who cocks an eyebrow. Then both of them laugh. It's not a good laugh. It's the strange, low laugh of the far gone, and I know there is nothing we can say that will stop these two men. Douglas unbuttons his jacket with one hand.

"Don't do this," Joey says. "None of us knows what that thing can do."

"It's more powerful than any crow. More powerful than all of the crows," Douglas says, with strained patience, reaching in his pocket. "And if the crows can do this—" He grasps the totem in his bare hand. In a hissing blink he's behind Joey, right next to my bed. He reeks of sulfur, like a pack-a-day habit of the devil's own cigarettes. He grabs the sheets of my bed and throws them off, his eyes wild and probing. "—Then we must have it," he says.

There's another pop, and suddenly Douglas goes sprawling back into the door, splintering the jamb and throwing it open with his bulk. In his place is Joey once more. It's like Joey left us and then came back at a charge and checked Douglas straight in the chest. Parsons looks impassively at him. Douglas looks ridiculous, sitting like a child in the doorway with both legs out. He nods to himself and cracks his neck.

"I said back the fuck off, suit. Both of you," Joey says.

"Impressive, Mr. Flatwood," says Parsons. "I'll admit, you know your way around the crow. But then again, you've had more time with yours."

He doesn't sound impressed. He sounds pleased, actually. One look at Douglas confirms it. He's smiling, too, from the floor. They both look like prize fighters at the title bout.

"Last chance, Mr. Flatwood. All of you. Give us the bell, and we'll let you live," Parsons says, as Douglas stands and dusts off his jacket. "For a little while, at least," he adds, looking at me with a wan smile.

Joey starts to speak, but I beat him to it. "You aren't worthy," I say, surprising myself. Thinking of Gam. Thinking of Caroline. Gam carried it all her life and never said a word. Caroline carries it now, as it's supposed to be carried. As a burden. A quiet burden. I don't know exactly what this bell is, but I know that's how it's supposed to be worn: heavy and soft. As if he can hear my thoughts, Joey looks back at me and nods. It's a thankful nod. It's like he's come back. Like we've seen each other in the airport and hit the bar, and it's all the same. In my mind another page is written and numbered, and it has everyone here on it. I'm that much closer. I have minutes. Minutes until I'm gone. But there's one more page yet to write.

My words hit Douglas. He seems to me like the idiot of the pair. Proud. Quick to anger. His bureaucratic smile turns to a snarl. There's a puff of air as he slips out of space, and I know he's coming for me. For my neck. For my face. And I can do nothing. I am passing from this world, and if it's Douglas that does it or the poison cells in my brain—six of one, half dozen of the other.

Whistle, pop, and he's there, in front of me. But so is Joey.

Douglas brings his hand down, ripping through the air, trying to grab at my throat, but Joey stops him with a sledgehammer blow to the side that sends him sprawling again. Whatever plane the crows flip them to, it seems like Joey gets a running start before they flip back. Joey is not a big man and the drugs have drained him, but somehow he's hitting like a fire hydrant. Joey doesn't even blink before he throws himself at Douglas again. Douglas tries to phase out, but Joey catches him. What happens from there is like a movie seen in snapshots, like frames have been removed from the reel of a fistfight. They dance around each other, pummeling each other. They flip in and out of sync, coming back bloodied and torn. Douglas reaches for his gun at one point, but Joey grabs him and phases both of them out before he can fire. This time the blood comes back before they do, spraying out like whipped washing, and then they are with us again, Douglas's head snapped back and his mouth split and Joey grazed at the shoulder. They blink out again, and a piece of a tooth is all that remains, clattering to the floor in their absence. I smile grimly. Joey always knew his way around a fistfight. I suppose an existential fistfight is still a fistfight.

But then there's Parsons. He watches the popping, whooshing, sucking explosions with a cold smile, like he's hanging over the pit of a dog fight, and then he begins to walk toward me, adjusting his tie, sniffing at the air. Bennet swipes at him, but he phases in and out and takes no notice. Bennet lunges forward again, and again comes up with air. Parsons stops at the head of my bed as calm as a Sunday morning while Douglas and Joey rip at each other like desert coyotes.

He is disturbingly gentle as he brushes my scrub top apart and pulls my palsied hands flat. No bell. He sniffs the air again, then he turns to Caroline. I try to scream at him, to lunge at him, to do anything. But my time is up. I'm being packed in. I can feel the weight upon me. The first words on the final page are being written, and I can see them in my mind. They say, *A crow flew down the hall.*

Which is insane, because we're in a hospital. And yet there is the crow. It passes across the open doorway at normal speed, but everything else seems to have hit a time pocket. No one else notices it, and I know that this is because no one else can see it. Then, in a blink, everything catches back up.

I look back at Caroline, who is gripping the bell under her shirt like it's pulling her down to the ground. Parsons walks towards her like a golem. He reaches for her, but Bennet throws himself towards him, and this time Parsons doesn't phase out. He's done with dancing between our two planes. He's been snake charmed by the call of the bell, and he doesn't count on Bennet's reach. His haymaker staggers Parsons, who looks at Bennet as if he's just arrived. Bennet takes advantage and slams his shoulder into Parsons, pushing him away, battering him back, putting distance between the agent and Caroline. He's pummeling Parsons' face bloody, and I think for one glorious minute that we've done it, that we've beaten them. Then Parsons takes out his gun.

"Unworthy," he says, echoing the madness of Danny Ninepoint as he levels it at Caroline.

Bennet throws himself in front of the line of fire just as the gun blast echoes and we hit another time pocket. And on cue, there's another crow. This one makes a sloppy landing out in the hallway in front of the door, flapping and hopping to a standstill in the time it takes for the bullet to leave the chamber. The crow stares at me. The sulfur hits me like a smoke ring to the face. People are caught in mid-scream outside, but they are like shadows of themselves—bugs rolled in sap, caught in time. Then there is another crow. It flutters down from the top of the splintered door, much more gracefully than the first, and then another that seems to swagger into the room. This one ponders the bullet leaving Parsons' gun with a cosmic cloud of gunpowder—a misshapen lump of lead that inches forward even as it spins over itself, like a curve ball in slow motion.

If I could reach out I could grab it, I could pluck it from the air like a lazy bumblebee. But I can't reach out. There is a weight on me that I know has stopped my lungs, and I will never breathe again. That was the last one, the final breath. I've taken in all of the oxygen that will ever reach my blood. I can only watch as Bennet dives in front of Caroline with his eyes closed, and I can't help but admire him. What a strong, crazy bastard he is. I know he loves her. Loves her madly. I also know he is worthy of her. It's a slow motion game of angles and trajectories between him and the bullet, one that was written out long ago, and the crows hop up on my bed to watch with me. They rest on my headboard and perch on my feet. There are many of them—first ten, then twenty, then thirty. They gather around and watch with me as the bullet, in a game of millimeters, misses

Bennet's heart and rips into his shoulder. And then they all titter, like an applause. I want to jump up and hoot.

I turn towards Joey and Douglas, locked around each other's necks like lions on the savannah. Joey has him. I turn back to Parsons, who is frozen in an implacable look of dismay. We've been slowed by the thousandth now. His look is such that he knows that was the only shot he had, because I can feel the last page of this story being inked, and I know it ends with this: *Ana.*

Ana walks through the door after the crows. She walks with the same girlish bounce she always had, and the crows move aside for her. One sits on her shoulder and bows its head to her. She is pale, so pale, paler than she ever was before. And she wears a child's dress of black and lace that is resplendent one moment and tattered the next.

And she is smiling. And illusion, vision, demon, or nothing at all, when my sister smiles like that, I've never been able to resist it. I smile too.

"Hello, brother," she says.

"What are you doing here?" I ask.

"I've come for you," she says. "At last."

"Am I dead?" I ask.

Ana cocks her head in such a perfect imitation of how she used to listen to us when we tried to get her to come in from the back, or eat her dinner, or close her eyes to go to sleep, that it's as if the years of her absence never happened at all.

"No," she says, after a moment. "Not yet. But I can wait."

She steps over to Bennet, the bullet still ripping the sinew of his shoulder. She grabs at the rippling air that marked its passage as if she could stop it, but her hand passes right through. And that's when I see that Caroline is with us in the pocket of time. She looks up at me with huge eyes. Blinking wildly, she takes a staggering breath and touches her own face, as if to confirm it's still there.

"Am I dead?" Caroline asks.

Ana listens to the air again, and it chills me to the bone. Such a childish expression, like she's listening to a tin-can phone, but I'm terrified of whatever is on the other end.

"No," she says, nodding to herself. "Not yet."

Caroline stands heavily. She lifts her head as if it is yoked. Then she freezes. Very carefully, very slowly, she reaches down her collar and grasps the bell. She pulls it out and over her like it is a link of iron chains. She holds it out in front of her and opens her palm.

"The clapper. It's back," she says.

Ana nods cheerfully.

"It only appears when someone is dying," Caroline says.

"Yes," Ana says. "My brother is dying."

She hops up, scattering the crows, and she comes to the foot of my bed. Her little head barely reaches over the footboard.

"Is this really you, Ana?" I ask, my voice hoarse.

Ana listens to the invisible wind again.

"Yes, and no," she says.

"How?"

"Because I am Ana. But I am Death," she says, and she smiles. It's pure and young and good. But there is something in her eyes. Something just as natural as the smile, but far blacker. She walks around my bed, trailing one small finger, and now she looks embarrassed. She scrunches up one side of her face as if she's about to cry.

"I missed you, Ben," she says, nodding at the truth of it.

I start to weep, and I grab her to me. She lets me take her in. I feel as though I'm leaving my body. I know I have seconds left, but seconds stretch. I smell her hair. I kiss her forehead. I wrap my arms around her tiny frame, and she hugs me back, giggling. "Ana, why didn't you come to me before?"

"Silly," she says, smiling up at me. "Because you weren't dying before. I can only take the dead people away."

The air chills again. And when I look at her I see that the deep black is leaking from her eyes again, just like it did when I saw her in the Evilway, when the chant breached our two planes.

"It's almost time," she says, and the black leaks like tears from her, dripping down in triangles from her eyes.

"But how, Ana? How did you come to take all the dead people away?" It's all I can think to ask as I watch the child in her morph, turn darker, blacker, longer. But she still has that same puckish voice as always.

"I rang the bell that Gam gave me," she says. "That's how. She told me to keep it very secret, and if I felt like I was going away, to ring it. So I did."

Caroline looks at the bell in her hands, bowing down her arms with its unseen weight. Ana ponders it, then nods.

"That's it," Ana says. Then she laughs with a strange, unsettling darkness. "I saw her pick it up from my bed after I left it. Careful. If you ring it, you have to take dead people away too."

The page is almost done, the ink almost dry.

"Ana," I say. "Are you tired?"

She thinks for a second, then shakes her head.

"Are you lonely?"

She nods.

"Are you ready to go?" I ask, because I know now. I know what the bell is and what the bell does.

She looks at me for a second, then throws a fierce hug over me. I can feel her changing, feel her moving, but inside all of it is my little sister. The girl I've dreamed of seeing gives me the hug I've dreamed of getting. The one that I used to weep over when I woke up before it happened. It's happening now. She holds me. And she is warm, and small, and she is Ana. She is finally here. And she and I come to an understanding then.

"I'm ready to go now," she whispers.

And that's when I look at Caroline.

"Can I have the bell?" I ask.

She shakes her head vigorously, throwing tears left and right. "No." She knows, too. She knows what happens if I ring the bell. She knows what I become. "No. You're going to live. You're going to get better. You're going to beat this, and we're going to live together and have kids and dance around the fire together and grow old and die holding each other's hands." She shakes her head again. "No. Absolutely not."

"Caroline," I whisper. "Look."

I turn towards my vital monitor. It's flat. No beats. Nothing. I am sitting up talking to her, and I am lying down dead at the same time. We've caught a window, but that window is closing. I listen carefully, and I can hear the flat buzz of the machines in the time outside of our time. I hear the alarm of the code. I see the soft pulsing of the blue light outside of my room. It's slow and subtle, but it is there.

"Caroline, I'm already gone," I say. "In a heartbeat I'll be beyond you forever anyway."

Caroline hears the sounds, she sees the lights. Ana looks curiously at us, her face melting further and further.

"Hurry," Ana whispers. "Please hurry. Or I have to take you."

"Please, Caroline," I say. "Ana isn't meant for this. She was thrown into this. She needs to go home with Gam and Dad."

"What happens to you?" Caroline asks, weeping. Snotting. She sniffs and coughs and cries, still holding the bell like it's a ten-pound stick of dynamite.

"What happens to me?" I ask Ana.

"You become me," she says, as if that explains everything. "It's a lot of work," she adds, knowingly. And in a blink her face has become that of a monster. Her eyes have dripped down to nothing. Her face is two strips of terrible black ripped through an orb of pure white.

"It's time," she says, and her voice is changed too. It is layered beyond itself into endless echoes. She reaches for my hand. For the first time in my life, I refuse my little sister.

"The bell, Caroline. Last chance. If I go with her, it's all over."

Caroline sobs, but she stumbles forward, her thumb in the bell. She falls onto me, and my hand grasps the bell. Our lips find each other, and we are given a kiss outside of time that lasts longer than the lives of many people. It lifts me. It unwraps me. And then it is over.

"Goodbye, Ben," she says.

"Goodbye, Caroline," I say. "Go. Live."

The thing Ana has become grasps my hand with cold finality, but I ring the bell first, and the time that had been slowed truly stops.

In a blink Ana is herself again. She laughs and jumps and

stretches—and she begins to fade. I am not afraid of this. I know this is what is supposed to happen. It's a one in, one out policy.

"Goodbye, Ana," I say. "Say hi to everyone for me."

She giggles and spins in circles and runs up to me and grabs me around the waist, but her grip is like the brushing of a feather.

"It's hard," she says. "What you go to do."

"I am sure."

"You'll do good," she says, nodding. Then she pushes back. "Remember," she says, pointing at the machines that blare and the flat lines. "You're gone too, Benny. When the bell rings again, you come to be with us."

She fades and fades. Soon she's just a smile. "Love you, Benny. See you later."

"Love you, Ana."

Then she has truly passed. In the silence, one of the many crows that nobody but I can see hops onto my shoulder and turns to look at me. He ruffles his feathers and stretches himself, and somehow he seems to grow, and grow, and shocks of red tinge his feathers until I recognize him once more.

"Hiya," he says.

"Hello."

"Time to clean all this up, I'd say," he says, nodding at the slow motion spectacle that is happening around me. Bennet is about to hit the floor. Joey and Douglas still spar for each other's necks. Parsons watches with cold fury.

"Ben? Where are you?" It's Caroline. "Ben?" But her voice slows, matches the pace of the world around us as she passes out of the pocket of time and we are gone to each other.

I stand.

All of my pain is gone. Everything that marked my understanding of the world is gone. In its place I have what I can only describe as a black map that is marked with pins of light. Millions upon millions of pins of light, more popping into existence all the time, but as soon as they do, they start to fade, each in their turn, by infinitesimal degrees. And I am there, with each of them. But I am here, too, completely. I am where I need to be, exactly as I need to be. Because I walk the map, and I tend to the lights when they are dim enough. I have been called Death before, but I already know that's not accurate. Better to call me the Walker.

Where I once lay, the covers softly cave. My body is not there. My body is gone. Nothing remains of me on the plane where these humans stand, screaming and fighting and bleeding. I am separate from them. Separate and alone. And yet I remember. I remember them. All of them. I see the agents, but I do not feel anger towards them. I mark their time. I can measure the strings of their lives.

I see my mom. She is screaming in madness, and her string is weak, fraying. I am troubled by this only in the sense that I know it is not yet her time.

I see Owen Bennet. He is bleeding, but he will survive. His string is stronger than he shows. Stronger than he knows.

And I see Caroline Adams and am shocked by the force of feeling that swells within me. The crow cocks his head at me, and the light brushes his beak such that it seems to smile.

"You don't lose everything of yourself," he says. "Kind of a curse, though, because you can't do anything with what remains."

"She's special."

"I'd say so," the crow says. His voice has a bit of a drawl to it. If you were to close your eyes and listen to him, you'd think a twenty-something beach bum was talking to you.

"Look at her string," I say. "It's beautiful. Colorful."

"I'll take your word for it. She does have that glow though."

"I have to save her. These men will hurt her."

"Can't do that."

"Why not?"

"Direct interference. Strictly off limits. Them's the rules."

"Rules? Horseshit." I take a swipe at Douglas, who's still moving at a snail's pace. My arms pass right through him.

"Told ya," says the crow.

"So she's going to die..."

"Not necessarily."

"What?"

"It's the bell they want. Not the girl."

"But I can't give them the bell."

"Oh, you can't let them have the bell. That would be a terrible idea. You're right. They suck. What you can do, though, is take it out of the equation."

I look at the bell in my hand. I see the clapper is fading, and my grip on it is slipping as well.

"Quickly now. Once the clapper's done for, it's back in their plane again. Those bastards will snatch it up, and that's all she wrote."

"What do I do?"

"If I were you, I'd take it out back and chuck it as far as you can."

"Out back?"

"Way out back, if you catch my meaning."

I think I do. I focus beyond the hospital room and grab on to the map of lights, but this time I also step into it. It's like opening up a heavy trap door at the bottom of my mind, and jumping in. The lights zip around me and spin wildly, and I start to scream. It's like falling in a dream, but endlessly. There's no waking up from this one.

"Stop flailing around, dumbass. Your little sister got it on the first try," says the crow. He's flapping his wings next to me, keeping steady with my head.

So I stop. And the lights settle around me. I see them for what they are. I'm floating inside a map of souls. The bell is still in my hand, but it feels lighter and lighter.

"Get rid of it, man! Throw it!"

"But where will it go?"

"Who cares? Not here!"

So I wind up and throw it. I throw it forever. It's like a golf ball in space. It sails and sails and sails, and then it's gone, like a coin disappearing into the ocean.

"Where did it go?"

"Somewhere else on their plane. Don't you worry about that bell. Worrying about the bell is my job. Frickin' thing has a propensity to show up at inopportune times. To say the least. The point is, I'll find it, and if I know these two scumbags, you bought your friends some time. Look."

The crow flips in the air with all the grace of a flying rag, but he manages to turn around and look back where we came. I follow him, shakily, like I'm turning around in close quarters on a bike.

I see nothing but the soul map. Billions of lights pulsing in an orb around my head.

"Where'd they go?"

"You tell me, bro. You saw their threads. You can find them again."

"How?"

"Hell if I know. I'm just the bird. You're the Walker. That's why you get paid the big bucks." The crow titters.

He's a wiseass, but he's been helpful so far, and even though he sounds flip, I get the feeling he really believes in me. I'll chalk that up to being related to Ana, who I can already tell he was fond of. I focus on the threads I saw back in the hospital. It's hard to picture all four of them, though, so instead I think of only one: Caroline's. It shimmered like a rip of sunset through campfire smoke, if the fire burned in every color of the rainbow: flare red, sparkler white, gas-rich blue, the green of flaming sap, and more— purples and pinks and so many shades of white I don't have the words to describe them, from soft to hard, all burning at a million degrees. This was her line of life.

And then I see it. I reach for it, and in a smashing blur I'm back in the room. Standing by the bed. My clothes ripple and still. I notice that the hospital gown is gone. In its place is a uniform, not unlike my NNPD getup: crisp slacks and a trim buttoned shirt, but it's pure black. I don't wear shoes. I can see the veins in my feet, and in my hands. They are very thick and very clear, and they pulse black.

There are many crows still in the room, including the one that talks to me, and all of them turn to watch me. I hold my hands out to the one that speaks and show him the pale underside of my wrists and the black veins there. He shrugs.

"Comes with the territory. The soul map is a powerful place. It leaves its mark. Only you can walk it for that long and live. And me, of course." He preens his glossy feathers, and I see the red marks there more clearly than ever. "What do you think of your new threads?"

"Not bad."

"Ana figured you'd like 'em. All right, get ready now," the crow says.

"For what?"

"As soon as the map closes, we're back on their time."

The window into the fiber-optic cityscape of the soul map is closing like water going down a drain. As it spins away, time catches up with itself. And then, with an audible pop, the commercial break is over.

And the agents scream.

They scream louder than Bennet does, because they know the bell is gone, and they see that my bed is empty, which can only mean one thing. They missed their chance.

"Where is he?" Douglas screams, frothing. He forgets about Joey entirely and runs to my bed, ripping up the sheets. He passes right through me as he throws the monitoring equipment aside. Joey looks at him with his hands still out, stunned and panting.

"You know where he is," Parsons says, his gun still trained on Caroline. I snarl, helpless to intervene. "He's right here. But he's beyond us, now."

Douglas takes a mad swipe around the room. I can't even feel the wind of his passing. The code alarm is blaring and people are running into the room and then out of the room at the same time, once they see the gun. Douglas tilts his head, sniffing, as if chasing the noise. Parsons turns the gun on Joey, then on Bennet, keeping all of them at bay.

"I can still smell it," Douglas says. "The bell. But it's fading."

"Better than nothing," Parsons says.

Without another word, Douglas snaps out of mortal view, and a shade of him flits by me, only this time I think I can feel a touch of wind. Then he's out of the room, and then out of the hallway, and soon out of the building entirely. On the trail of the bell.

Parsons looks around at the mess and then turns briefly towards where Caroline has run to Bennet, who's bleeding on the floor. My mother is screaming in her madness. Joey watches him carefully, his hands still out, waiting for Parsons to shoot, but instead Parsons spits in disgust. He holsters his weapon, and I breathe a sigh of relief. Then he speaks to me.

"I know you're here, Mr. Dejooli. I know about the bell, not everything, but enough to find it again, no matter where it is. I know about the map, too. Is it beautiful? I can almost picture it. And one day it will be mine, with all of the power that comes with it. So don't get used to it. You may have rung the bell, but you're still a two-bit cop to me."

His flat, vanilla gaze melts slowly into a wicked smile. "The bell is out there. I can feel it. When I find it, I'm coming for you."

In a flash, he's gone. But I can watch him still. When he flits out of his realm, he's a shadow in mine, but he cannot see me. He is passing between our realms when he grabs the crow totem. He is neither here nor there. Soon enough, he's gone too.

The big crow is tapping his beak against the metal of the bed in mocking applause. "Hear that? He's gonna getcha! What a dick, am I right?"

He's joking, and I smile, but I'm still unnerved. Parsons and Douglas know more about where I am and who I am than I do, and it bothers me. Those two aren't just going to go away.

All around me the room has exploded into action again. Police and doctors and nurses swarm about, treating Bennet and shuffling my mother and Caroline out and under blankets and into locked rooms.

Joey becomes a shadow, and I know he's holding his crow and is invisible to those around him, but I can see him.

"Ben! Are you there?" he yells, but his voice is muffled and whipped, like he's screaming into a gale force wind. I can also tell that it's hurting him, flitting between realities like this, and suddenly I know why he was taking the drugs. They help with the pain of phasing out. Allow him to walk in shadows for longer than he should.

"Go, Joey! You'll kill yourself!" I scream, but he can't hear me, or see me. His crow shines like the sun in his hand.

"I'll watch over the doc and the girl! Don't worry! Those fuckers won't touch them!"

I can't help but smile at his bravado. Old school Joey, right there. The first flicker of it I've seen since this whole mess started years and years ago. As if he can sense me, he smiles too.

"I'm glad it's you, buddy. I hope you said goodbye to Ana."

I nod to him. He was right. He found her after all, even if he couldn't see her.

Then he's out of the room in a flash, and it's just me and the crows. I'm surrounded by people, but I can't touch them. I can't speak to them. I feel terribly alone. It's like the first soft pressure of a crushing weight that threatens to drown me, but then the big crow is there. He flies to my shoulder and settles there as if born to it, and I feel instantly better.

"It's not so bad," he says. "Ana was a good Walker, very good. But I don't think she was the one we need now. It's good that you let her go."

I turn to him, puzzled. "What makes a good Walker?"

"All in good time. We'll start simple."

"I can already feel that I need to be in places."

"People die," says the crow, shrugging his shoulders. "It's the one constant on this plane."

"Then I will go to them," I say.

The crow nods. It's a sort of excited bob that makes me smile again.

"What's your name?" I ask.

"Don't know. I've had countless names."

"What did Ana call you?"

"Well, she called me a lot of things. Flappy, Blackie, Birdie, Dummy, mostly Birdie. When she got lonely and reached for me sometimes she'd call me Ben," he says quietly. "Or Chaco."

"Chaco," I say. "I like that one."

"Chaco it is then, chief."

The lights are calling me, they are fading, and they need me to tend to their end. I know I can do this. It's what I am meant to do.

"Well, Chaco. I think my time is done here."

"For now..." Chaco says.

"Then let's get going. We have work to do."

I reach out my black-veined hand and press through the air. A pinprick of darkness appears, and I swirl the matter that makes up this plane like I'm spinning batter in a bowl. The soul map whorls into view, bigger, bigger, until it is all that is in front of me, staggering and infinite.

"I like the swirl move," Chaco says. "Nice touch."

I gaze flatly at him. "Try to keep up," I say, grinning.

Then I'm off.

19

THE WALKER

When I was dying, I spoke of life as a book, of our experiences as a series of pages fluttering to an eventual close. Now that I'm on the other side of it I can tell you that's not true. Not exactly, anyway. The idea that each of us has a book to write, and then once it's done we shelve it in the great library of existence, that's ludicrous. No story is separate. If you could see this map, this beautiful, glowing map, you'd understand that.

I've walked the map a bit by now, and I often catch myself thinking about how I could explain this to you, or to Caroline, or to anyone. The best I can come up with right now is this: you know those huge fiber optic cables that span the oceans like enormous ropes? Imagine one as wide as the sun, and cut it in half so you see the countless individual fibers pulsing with light. That's about as close as I can get to describing it. Your life isn't a book: your life is a string of light, wrapped up with every other string into infinity.

I walk these strings. I walk the rope. Sometimes Chaco joins me, but mostly I do what I do alone. When a thread is breaking, I'm called to it. The life it belongs to can see me then, although I don't know what they see when their eyes are opened in death. Sometimes they call me the names of people they knew, or loved. Sometimes they weep. Sometimes they cheer. The old are happier than the young. The old often cheer. The young are often heartbroken. I can understand. It's hard to let go of life. Even if it sucks, it's hard to let go.

I do not frighten them, for the most part. Perhaps they expect the cowl and scythe. They get me, instead. Or whatever their impression of me is. On a handful of occasions so far I have had people run. The first guy I actually chased, too. The old cop instincts kicked in, and I ended up running down a beach after the guy for half a mile before I remembered I could slow time. Good thing, too, because he was a young guy and I hadn't used my lungs for quite a while by then and was out of shape. In a footrace he would have kicked my ass. As it was, I pulled the fabric of time down a notch and walked right up to him. He screamed the whole time, screamed bloody murder with nobody to hear but me. These runners are the only people that I've seen so far that are truly afraid when I come for them. Everyone's afraid of death until they die, then the hard part is over. The ones who are *still* afraid when I come are the ones that know that whatever lies beyond me won't be good to them.

What lies beyond me? Wish I could tell you. I walk the rope, and I can't drop off the sides. But something does lie beyond me. I get whispers of it when I work. Rustlings from beyond the veil, and not all of them are good.

It came naturally, what I do. In a nutshell I clip the fading string of light and pack it away into the rope. Sort of like cosmic sewing. Left alone, the string will fade and weaken, but it will hold on. Like I said, life is pretty tenacious that way. Thing is, it's not supposed to linger once it's faded past a certain point. It's bad if strings linger. It upsets the order of things. It's unnatural, and its unnaturalness calls to me, tugs at me until I walk the rope and find it and clip it.

No scythe, either. Not even a pair of store-bought scissors. I use my fingers. Pointer and middle, I tease it out of them, and I snip it. There is no pain. It actually feels quite tremendous for the both of us, like finally sneezing after waiting what seems like a lifetime. After I clip a string, a seam opens in space, not unlike when I open the soul map, but it's red and it billows like a curtain. I can't walk through. I tried. Something stops me. All I can do is usher them through. Sometimes I hold their hand and send them off. Sometimes I just point. Sometimes I have to shove. But they all go through the veil eventually.

I'm getting better at it. The first couple of snips were disasters. There was the runner, and then there was this young kid who wept and wept and wouldn't go through the curtain. The longer you wait, the bigger the curtain gets, until it takes up everything. This only scared the kid more, and I'm not ashamed to admit I panicked a little myself. I started getting pressed back, and the kid screamed until I basically tossed him in. Just kind of picked him up under the armpits and chucked him through. Not my proudest moment, but it worked. And like I said, the veil gets you in the end. It's just a matter of how you go through it.

At first I got backed up. Way backed up. Think about it. People die every second on earth, but there's just one Walker. It took me a while to figure out how to split myself. To be in many places at once. The key is to not think about it. Just let it happen, smooth your mind. The stoners we used to bust out by the Arroyo were closer to transcendence than I gave them credit for, because that's what it is I do. When I stop thinking of myself as being in one place, I allow myself to be in every place. I sucked at it for a while, still sort of do, but I'm getting better, thanks to Chaco.

Chaco's a strange thing. I'm learning about him just like I'm learning about everything else. Slowly, but surely. First, he's not a bird. Not exactly. There is only one creature like him, just like there's only one creature like me. I think the best way to describe him would be as a 'thinning.' There are animals on the earth that are 'thinner' than others. Animals that are just more aware of what is beyond the earth plane. I'm sure you know what I'm talking about. Cats are probably the best example. When they sit and stare at walls, do you really think they're staring at walls? Nope. Crows are another. Sloths also, believe it or not. Elephants have some capacity for it, and wolves. There are others, too. Many of them. Chaco can take on any of their forms. He just likes the crow the best.

He's been helping me when he can, but mostly he's been looking for the bell. Or rather, waiting for someone to find the bell and become the new Keeper. Chaco watches over the Keeper, just like Gam's iteration of Chaco watched over her and gave its life for her in the end, to protect her from Danny Ninepoint and allow her to pass the bell to Caroline. I was a little disappointed to hear that Chaco served the bell, not me, because I thought he was like my sidekick, sort of like every wizard has an owl. He put a short end to that line of thought though, by laughing his ass off when I tried to give him an order.

I asked him how all the crows killed Danny Ninepoint, if they weren't ordered to do something like that. He said they killed him because they loved Ana, and Ana loved me, and they knew Danny meant me harm. He said this like he was explaining that the sky was blue. Good enough for me. They came in in the clutch, and Chaco does the same. He almost always comes when I call for him, but I try not to call him unless I need him. But right now I need him. I need his help to get the crow totems back from the agents.

See, it turns out that just like there are thin creatures, there are also thin *things*. The crow totems are one of these thin things: they exist on more than one plane. In the case of the crows, they're on the earth plane most of the time, and on my plane when they're activated, but only briefly. We're talking seconds. And seconds I can't slow down. Chaco had always known it could be done, he just hadn't seen it, and it's no wonder, because it's hard as hell to get the timing right.

I couldn't tell you how long I followed those two agents. I stepped out of time for quite a while, practicing my grab while they criss-crossed the globe looking for the bell. Chaco tells me it's almost impossible to find the bell on its own, but once it presents itself to a Keeper, the race is on. For now, though, it's sort of dormant. He tells me they'd literally have to stumble across it.

Still, I can't even chance a stumble. Even a blind squirrel has a shot at a nut, and the more I follow them, the more it becomes clear to me that I have to keep the bell from them at all costs. They have strange ideas. Unnatural ideas. They have a sense of the map, and the veil, although I'm not sure how. They speak of forcing the veil. Of bending the map to their will. Cutting strings that aren't fading and sewing fading strings back to strength. I haven't been on the job long, but even I know that stuff would spell disaster.

Chaco assures me these things can't be done. But I'm not so sure. He's the thinning. He doesn't deal with the strings or the veil or the map. I'm the Walker; I do. I learn new things every day. Just because I can't do something now, like cut a healthy string, doesn't mean it can't be done. It's just that I have the good sense not to try it.

I know if I can take their totems, it will at least slow them down. There are others on earth, as many as twenty that I know of, but most likely more, so the agents could theoretically get another pair. But it won't be easy. I know a little bit about who carries these crows. They call themselves the Circle of the Crow, and they're sworn to protect the bell. Joey is one of them, but there are others, and some of them make Joey look like a punk. Safe to say, the crows won't be easy to replace, even by a couple of lunatics like the agents. So I practice the timing, and I learn to find the subtle signs that the two of them are jumping. I learn to read the fabric of their plane so I'll know when the crow begins to part it. And I wait. I know I'll get one shot at this. I'm guessing there are ways to protect the crow even during the phasing. I don't want to tip them off.

When the agents meet up together to sniff out New York City, a big task that requires both of them at once, I know my time has come. They are walking down the street—prowling down the street, is more like it—and even the hard-eyed New Yorkers know to move out of their way. Humans have a sense of when not to mess with people that could get them in trouble. More than I give them credit for. They range from dull to Caroline-status, but everyone has at least something of what you might call a sixth sense. Everyone knows to leave the agents alone to their dark work.

Everyone except me.

I keep pace with them. Walking backward, keeping a measured distance. They know nothing of me. Not until they phase out, that is. Then they see me there for half a heartbeat. I know they see me there because they pause, but that is all it takes. It's like a baton passing gone wrong. They try to jump forward in space, but I snatch the crows from their hands. One in my left, one in my right. Their bodies pass through me, untouchable, but the crow totems are thin, and for that one moment, they're as real on my plane as they are on theirs. I pluck them from their hands like flowers, and the agents tumble back to the New York City sidewalk in a heap. Parsons knows immediately what has happened, and I see the hate burn silent within him as he scans the empty air in front of him. Douglas screams and swipes madly at the air, and an entire sidewalk full of people crosses to the other side of the street immediately. But all the spitting and swearing and raving in the world can't help him now. Once I bring the crows to my side, they're lost to him. I couldn't bring them across again even if I wanted to. I and everything with me walk the rope. I can observe their world. Nothing more. Unless the bell rings.

Parsons quiets Douglas and says, "Patience, patience." He looks around at the empty air, passing blindly over as I pump my fists in the air.

"There are other crows," he says quietly. "Other ways."

"I'll be ready!" I scream, right into his face, but he can't hear me, and eventually they turn away. I know that's not the last I'll see of the agents. I have the feeling that Parsons in particular is the kind of guy who only gets more pissed off when you needle him. I remember his golem stare, and I shudder as I watch them walk away, side by side.

Now. What do I do with these two crows?

I call Chaco. I use the two-fingered whistle he taught me, but I think he's just messing with me. I think he knows when I need him, he just wants to make me spit through my fingers. I'm not a good whistler. I can hear him careening through time even before I take a breath. He blows through the soul map and pops out in New York City. He flares his wings and settles on my shoulder.

"What can I do ya for, chief?" he asks.

"Any luck with the bell?"

"Not yet. But I've narrowed it down. When it finds a Keeper, I'll know. I'll be the first there. Although let me tell you, they're gonna have to work pretty damn hard to beat your grandmother. That old lady could kick some ass."

I nodded. Chaco often talks about Gam. He's been through thousands of Keepers, but he keeps coming back to Gam. Sometimes I wonder if Gam didn't have all this in mind when she gave Ana the bell. She was patient even for a Navajo, which basically put her at guru status. Me ending up here, with this gig, at this time, this is exactly the sort of long play she would drum up. The thought makes me smile, but it also worries me. Gam never did anything without good reason.

"I wonder if you could help me," I ask Chaco.

"Maybe. That's eighteen favors to zero now. I'm keeping track."

"Yeah, yeah. Listen. I can't pass through to the human plane, right?"

"That's why you dragged me all the way here? I was in a pretty awesome beach town, my man."

I ignore him. "But you can, right?"

He quiets.

"I know you can, Chaco. You did it with Gam. And I saw you too, back when I was Ben. A couple of times. One time you shit on my car."

He titters in what I can only assume is a bird laugh. "Yes. Yes, okay? I can. When a Keeper is declared—"

"But what about now? When there's no Keeper."

Chaco pauses.

"I dunno, bro. It's not good to mess around with the rules of this place. You don't want to piss off what's behind that curtain."

"Please. I have to get these crows to the other side."

"You mean to the girl you love and the doctor."

I pause. Am I that obvious? I suppose so.

"You know you can never be with her," Chaco says. "You know that, right? I mean, there ain't no *way*—"

"Yeah, yeah. I get it," I say. And I do. I think. "But I know they would be great allies of ours. Both her and Owen Bennet. I think you know this too."

Chaco puffs up in a birdish sigh. Then he bobs his beak. "Yes. I think so too."

"So you'll do it? You'll cross over?"

Chaco eyes me with cold calculation, then squawks in frustration. "I can tell this is going to be a hell of a run, with you."

"Chaco—"

"Yes, Walker. Yes, I'll carry the crows," he says.

I hold them out, one in each hand. He snatches them in his claws and then takes off in a whirl. I watch him rise, rise, and then blink out of view.

20

CAROLINE ADAMS

I magine going to work again like it was just your typical Monday after meeting Death herself in a patient's room.

Imagine falling in love and then watching the one you love taken from you. Not even into death, but into something else. Something just as distant, but even less understood. And then the hospital gives you two working days off to pull yourself together, and then it's Monday and you're back at work again, answering your phone, helping your patients to the bathroom, administering meds, all while trying to ignore the fact that your world has fundamentally changed.

Owen is a hero. I expected nothing less. He was borderline adored on the floor to begin with, and then he got himself shot in my place and that just threw the entire hospital into a frenzy. The CEO met him personally. They gave him a ceremonial key to the complex at a big dinner a week later that was attended by every C-level executive. I think I was the only nurse. It was surreal. I thought they only did that stuff in movies. In typical Owen Bennet fashion he demurred and shrugged adorably through everything, one arm in a sling, the other resting softly over it.

The aftermath of the shooting went by in a blur of police questioning, mandatory counseling, and cleanup. There was no way

Owen or I could tell the truth about what happened in that room. We'd be committed along with Sitsi Dejooli, Ben's mother, so we kept our lie simple. Two men claiming they were FBI agents barged into Ben Dejooli's room. Owen Bennet and I confronted them, and Owen took a bullet for me. Then the two men took Ben from his bed and disappeared. The agents never showed up on camera. All the police had was our testimony, as well as that of two nurses who were the first on the code. They said they saw at least one man in a suit, which would have been Parsons, but couldn't say what happened to him. When they turned back around, he was gone, along with Ben.

The police put out an APB for the agents, but there was no trace of them. We were told the FBI had no record of employing an Agent Douglas or an Agent Parsons, and they declined further comment on what they deemed a state matter. The bullet markings didn't match anything on file, nor did any of the blood samples found. Not surprising.

It's also not surprising that this series of events was finally what broke Sitsi Dejooli's mind. She wouldn't respond to anybody: not the police, not me or Owen, not anyone. But in her quiet, staring pondering I sensed a certain measure of peace. I could see it in her coloring, too. Her yellow is tinged with a soft pink now, barely there, but consistent. It looks like the color of a woman who has seen more than her mind will allow. Rather than fight it and make sense of it, her mind has simply decided to close itself for a time. I'd be lying if I said part of me doesn't envy her. She recovered at ABQ General for two days. The only words I ever heard her say after the whole ordeal was her verbal consent to a transfer upstate to Los Alamos, where the Navajo Nation had arranged for her to live in a step-up care mental facility indefinitely. She turned her back on the Navajo, but it would appear that the Navajo hadn't turned their backs on her. The Council said it was the least they could do, given her loss. She was blood, after all.

And all the while I had a decision looming. I had entirely forgotten about it until I received the papers in the mail. My five years were up. My debt was forgiven. If I wished to stay at ABQ General I was to notify my nurse manager in writing by the end of the week. If not, they wished me well, thanked me for my service at the CHC, and would be happy to write a reference on my behalf wherever I decided to go.

Check the box yes or no. Sign your name. Drop it off with your supervisor. Three simple steps that will define the trajectory of my life. It's enough to make you laugh out loud. They clearly don't know me. I am not good with decisions. I sweat over dinner plans. So I made lists: a pros list and a cons list. The old high-school approach.

Pros:

- The job is pretty good. Not wildly good. Not something I wake up every morning super jazzed for, but pretty good. Good enough, I decide.
- I'm already here. I'm settled. I have an apartment and a car, and I know the city.
- I can work at the rez. Which makes me feel like I'm doing something worthwhile. And I like the Navajo. For the most part.
- Owen Bennet.

I've avoided thinking about my feelings for Owen, because they're all wrapped up in crazy right now. But the bottom line is he would give his life for me. He proved that much back when Parsons tried to shoot me. I know what that means. Ben told me that he loved me. Owen showed it. To think that the world was within two inches of swapping him out for me is insane. It makes me go beet red and feel slightly ill at the same time. Let's be honest, of the two of us, he is the one you want on your team. He's Owen Bennet. I'm just...me. I put *x2* next to his bullet point. Then I crossed it out and put *x3*. He deserves to be weighted more heavily.

Cons:

- If I keep it up here for much longer, there's a good chance this is where I'll play out the rest of my days.

I'm nearly thirty. All the girls say it gets harder to make stupid choices after thirty, even if they might make your life better in the long run. Things like traveling or nursing abroad. ABQ is okay, but let's face it, it's not exactly Paris.

- Ben is dead. And it's hitting me way harder than I thought it would.

I knew he was going to die. I knew the second the chemo regimen didn't stick. I had weeks with him to prepare myself, but it still hit me like a dump truck because I loved him. I hope I let him know that, but the more I think about our time together, the more I'm afraid I fretted so much about whether or not he loved me that I missed a chance to tell him I loved him. Typical.

- Ben isn't gone.

I put this on as a con because it's an argument against me staying here. I wake up in the middle of the night sometimes and for a split second I think I can still feel the soft pressure of his hand. I have to tell myself that whatever happened to him, he is beyond me now. I am slowly coming to peace with that—but I still want to know what happened to him. What it means. What the bell is. And I don't think I can do that if I stay here.

So there you have it. I stare at the list, two columns. It's hard not to call it what it is: Ben vs. Owen. Ben's dead. Owen is alive. So why is this so hard? At three in the morning it's easier to convince myself that I need to go. Nothing seems right around me anymore. The shadows of that day haunt me. The Ben factor has a heavy weighting, too. So heavy I'm not sure it can be measured. In the end, it's enough to make me check the 'No' box. I decide to pack it up. But then, the next day, I run into Owen as I'm about to hand in my resignation. I think he knows what I'm doing. I think he was on the lookout for me.

"Caroline," he says. "Wait. Please." He reaches out for me, and his fingers flutter briefly towards my hand before he drops his arm and looks at the ground. "You're leaving, aren't you," he says.

The *Bennet x3* flashes in my mind. He looks so sad. Like the resignation letter in my hand is a personal rejection, when it's not. This place is all screwed up for me, now, that's all.

"I wish..." He grits his teeth and shakes his head. "I wish I was better at this. I wish I could stop you. Ben could have. I know that."

"Owen, please..." My mind is already full up on regrets. If Owen throws his hat in the ring, I'll never sleep again.

"No, I understand," he says, smiling sadly. "He...he was special. I just hope that I let you know..." He stutters and smooths at his white coat. "I hope I was able to make myself clear, that you are special too. I know he thought so. But so do I. I hope you know that."

I can't take this. These men have ruined me. I want to do the cowardly thing. I want to run away.

"I can't stop you. I know that," he says. "But I also can't help but think that if I had more time. If we had more time...maybe I could."

I'm crying as I push the letter through the slot. He watches it like it's the tail end of a train carrying his life away from him. It clinks inside the box with a hollow ping. I want him to shake his head and shuffle away. I want him to get mad at me, give me a disparaging look, even. But instead when I look back up at him he's still there, smiling sadly.

"Can I at least walk you to your car?" he asks.

Dammit, Owen. Of course you can walk me to my car, you beautiful man.

We're quiet on the walk out, our hands shoved into the pockets of our coats against the first real winter wind of the season. I turn to him, and the wind cuts at my face and streaks my tears sideways. "I wouldn't have left without saying goodbye to you. You know that, right? I owe you my life, Owen."

He shrugs. "I believe you," he says. At my car we pause. "I was thinking," he says, struggling. He puffs his coat out from the pockets.

"What?"

"I was thinking of doing something crazy and stupid. But I'm not sure I can."

I want to draw more out of him, but there's a subtle ringing in the distance, just barely sounding above the wind and a ripple in the sky draws our attention to the horizon at the same time. He steps closer to me, so we're shoulder to shoulder. I know he feels it too: something broke through.

"Not again," he says.

"No. Look."

There, on the horizon, is a black speck. And it's growing.

Still, Owen pulls his hands from his pockets and angles himself in front of me, even after we watch as the speck grows into a bird, a huge bird, with a dull glint of red upon its head. A bird I recognize. A bird I saw die.

"How the hell?" I begin, but then I know. Somehow Ben is behind it.

The bird flies in near silence. Slowly, languorously flapping its wings like an ancient beast, which I suddenly know it is, in one form or another.

"My God, it's huge," Owen says. "Is it coming after us?"

"No. Not in that way. I don't think it'll hurt us."

Now it's careening out of the sky, slowing, and dropping down straight for us, and I'm rethinking what I just said. But in an instant it flares its wings and pulls up before flopping rather unceremoniously on the hood of my car. It sort of tumbles down the windshield and then manages to stop itself on the bonnet by gripping a windshield wiper in its beak. It shakes its head, and I swear if I could hear it talk it would be telling us to keep that landing between the three of us. I can't blame it, though, because I see it's got something in both claws. Something it deposits on the hood after a preliminary, twitchy look about itself.

With one final glance at both of us, it lets out a deafening trio of *caws* and swoops up into the sky. I can feel the wind from its wings on my face as it's up, up, and out. I feel that distortion again, like a popping bubble: the world's cabin re-pressurizing. And it's gone. In its place are two crow totems, side by side, touching wing tips.

We stare at them, dumbfounded. Owen is the first to speak. "Well, that's about all the providence I need."

He picks up one in his gloved hand, and tucks it in his pocket. "I believe the other is for you," he says.

I pick mine up as well. It seems to hum, in a way only I can hear. It feels right. I grasp it tightly, protectively, then I tuck it away. When I look up again, Owen is watching me carefully.

"That stupid thing I was thinking," he says. "I think I can do it, now. Maybe."

"Maybe?"

"I can't stop you from leaving," he says. "But I was wondering if you'd let me leave with you." He cringes a bit, looking slightly ill with anticipation. "It doesn't have to be like that, or anything, of course. I'd just...it's just that I have this strange feeling. And it's been growing stronger. And it's that Ben, or whoever he is now after all that happened to him...I don't think he's gone. He's just changed. And I think he'll be needing our help. Am I weird in thinking that? Am I going insane?"

I shush him by basically running into him. Before I know what I'm doing I've thrown myself into his arms and am hugging him. No passionate kiss. No longing look into anyone's eyes. The last time I expected that to happen things didn't work out. I'm done with perfect moments. From here on out, I'm just going to work on taking advantage of whatever moments I'm given. Perfect or not.

Owen puts his arms around me in delayed shock, and even that thought makes me want to giggle like a teenager. But I compose myself and step away from him, holding both of his hands in mine like I'm physically keeping him here with me. If things are about to go down, there's nobody on earth I'd rather have on my side than Doctor Owen Bennet.

"No," I say.

His face falls.

"No no no. I mean *no* as in 'no, you're not crazy.' Yes to everything else."

He looks back up at me with a wry grin, still hesitant.

"Sorry. I always screw these kind of things up."

He lets out a big laugh. I've never heard him laugh before, I realize. And as he does, a flock of crows flies by overhead, an enormous flock—hundreds of them, blotting the sky like dribbled ink. They seem to catch his laugh as one, and all of them call out against the winter wind together.

Maybe it's just a coincidence. But I doubt it.

ACKNOWLEDGMENTS

Several people helped me out at various stages of this novel, and I'd like to take a moment to give thanks. First and foremost, to my wife, Emily, whose experience as an oncology nurse proved invaluable in crafting the perspective of Caroline Adams. I'd also like to thank Emily in general for her patience and fortitude in being married to a writer. That can't be easy.

I'd like to thank my editor Laura and the editing crew at Red Adept Publishing, along with Kit, my beta reader, for their work in polishing the story. They all have eagle eyes.

In writing the Navajo lore, I drew in part upon the research and essays of Leland C. Wyman ("Navajo Ceremonial System") and R. W. Shufeldt ("Mortuary Customs of the Navajo Indians"). I also learned from Tony Hillerman's work; his *Joe Leaphorn* novels are an education in the Navajo culture in and of themselves.

Finally, I'd like to thank you, the reader, for taking a chance on my book. Whether or not you liked *Follow the Crow*, please leave a review to help others decide on the novel. There's more to come, and if you'd like to be notified when I have another book out, you can join my mailing list here: http://eepurl.com/SObZj. It is an entirely spam-free experience. I promise.

I can also be reached over at my digital home: bbgriffith.com.

Feel free to drop me a line. I'd love to hear from you.

Happy reading,

-BBG

BEYOND THE VEIL

B. B. GRIFFITH

To Dad.
For believing in my stories.

Shall any gazer see with mortal eyes,
Or any searcher know by mortal mind;
Veil after veil will lift—but there must be
Veil upon veil behind.

-Edwin Arnold
The Light of Asia

1

GRANT ROMER

My name is Grant Romer, and I'll ride my bike almost anywhere, but I especially like this graveyard. I ain't scared. Pap says I shouldn't play here, even though the whole time I've been biking around and through it, it's been nothing but quiet. Which is for at least a year. Which is a lot for me, since my whole life is only eight years so far.

Pap thinks I'm settin' at Mom and Dad's plot when I come here, but I'm not. Not always. Mostly I just like to ride my bike around and listen to things fly by me, like the trees and the gravestones and the little flags they put in front of the gravestones, because it's pretty quiet here and you can hear the *whoosh* each thing makes when you ride by it fast. Plus it cools me down. In the summer I do lots of things just to stay cool. Pap says there ain't no place on earth hotter in the summer than Midland, Texas. I ain't been nowhere else, but I believe it.

Every time on my ride over I think how Pap says I should stop coming here, and every time I just pass under the Fairview Cemetery arch anyway, and up until now for an entire year of my life it's been nothing but quiet. And this time it's quiet too. But it's different quiet. It's bad quiet.

For starters, there's no mowing sounds, not even coming over the air from a distance where it sounds like not much more than a buzzing bee. And the tons of birds that chirp all day long, they ain't just ain't chirping; they're gone. All I can see is three big crows sitting like drops of mud on the top of the arch as I go under. They watch me ride under them with little ticking movements of their heads, but they don't make a sound neither.

I skid my bike to a stop when I'm a little ways inside. There's nobody here. I mean, there usually ain't a lot of people here to begin with, but there's bound to be *some* people. Not today. I look back at the fat crows, they look at me, then they look down the hill to the center of the grounds where there's a big old house. It's where the graveyard people work. Usually there's a car or two. Now there's nobody. No cars. It's getting on in the afternoon, but it's still a weekday, and during the weekday grownups work even in the summertime, so I know people should be there, but they ain't.

I hear Pap in my head, and he says, "*Son, you stay away from that graveyard. It ain't for the young.*" I think for a second about turning around. But when's the last time you ever had a whole graveyard to yourself? I decide to make my circle. With nobody to see me or get in my way, I get going real fast. The gravestones and the trees don't just flutter in my ears, they start to whine. The air makes tears in my eyes, and they trickle back and behind my head, and I'm smiling, and Pap's voice is gone, and there's nothing in my brain but air that feels double cold 'cause Pap just gave me a buzz cut, and my mind goes blank, and that's why I almost eat it on the rock in the middle of the road.

I swerve at the last second, and my foot slips off the pedal and skids on the ground, and my front tire goes all wobbly, so I jump off the bike onto the grass and roll about a bit until I come to a stop sitting right on my butt. Good thing ain't nobody around to see it. That's not how I ride bikes. I hardly ever fall.

I pick grass from my elbow and walk back to my bike, which looks good enough. I pick it up then look back at the rock. It's glinting in the late sunlight. I set my bike down again and walk over to it and stop. It ain't just any rock. It's a gravestone. Right there in the middle of the road. It reads Andrew Gordon Masterson, and it has the date 1968 on it, which is the born date, but there's no dead date. It has a price tag on it, too. $799. Which is a *lot* of money for a rock. I don't care how glinty it is; that's almost eight hundred dollars. It's chipped on one side pretty bad, and I can see the bit that came off just a little ways away. Like it was dropped there. I wonder if Andrew Gordon Masterson dropped it there, or if somebody tried to steal it, but ain't nobody stupid enough to steal another man's gravestone. Maybe Andrew Gordon Masterson was trying to steal it. Come to think of it, this whole place has that empty, stolen feeling about it, like the grocery store on Wadley Avenue at the end of the week after the roughnecks pick it clean and all that's left is some cans of spinach and pickled things and the ugly fruits and veggies.

I decide to go talk to Mom and Dad about it.

Their place is on top of a low hill overlooking the old house, not far from where I almost bit it on my bike. It's still as hot as it was at noon, but the shadows of the gravestones are getting long now, so I know it must be gettin' on. I decide to sit with my back against Mom's this time. No offense to Dad or nothin'. I sat under his shadow last time. I like to switch it up.

"What the heck's goin' on here, Mom?" I ask. Don't worry, I know she's not gonna answer. I'm not stupid. I still talk though. Not quite sure why. A big beetle walks slow as an elephant across the top of Mom's rock. I pick it up and set it on the ground. I like beetles, but I can't have them on Mom's rock. It ain't right. I wonder if Pap paid $799 for Mom's and Dad's rocks. They're almost two years old now, and they still look brand new, so I bet they were expensive. No wonder Pap had to go back to work on the rigs.

I can hear when the crows take off from the arch back at the entrance—that's how quiet it is. They come my way, circle over my head up high, and then shoot over to the old house, where they land with the sound of bouncing marbles on the metal gutter at the edge of the roof.

"I think those crows want me to follow 'em," I say. "So that's what I'm gonna do."

I pull myself up using Mom's rock and then slap the top of both of them like I'm giving Mom and Dad high fives. Then I pick up my bike, hop on, and coast my way toward the old house. When I get there I stop hard, and my brakes squeak so loud I think the folks underground might catch a note or two. There's junk all over outside the house. Papers caught in the bushes and receipts smashed into the pebbles that line the walkway, like they were pounded there by boots. A strip of caution tape flutters off one side of the door in what little bit of breeze there is. The front door is closed, but the wood is splintered near the lock. I try it. It opens. I stare inside for a second. The crows nearly set me runnin' when they clack their way toward me on the ledge, walking like stick figures.

"Git outta here," I whisper at them, fluttering my hands, but it's halfhearted and kinda chickenshit, and I think they know it. Right now I don't mind the company, even if they're birds. One cocks his head at me, but none of them move.

The place has been run through. That much is easy to see, even from the porch. Looks like it was shut down in a hurry, then maybe some kids got a mind to pick it over—maybe somebody like Otis and his crew from up the street from me. They'd do something like that. Or maybe Andrew Gordon Masterson. But Otis and Andrew ain't here now. Nobody's here. This place is hollow. I can feel it.

I reach inside and flick the light switch. Nothing. Which concerns me, seeing as a light's clearly coming from somewhere in there. It's reflecting off the walls leading around the corner to the garden in the middle of the place. It's not a normal light, neither. It's a shimmery, electric blue light, like one of those underwater lights at the swimming pool. It looks like the kind of light that might have run a kid like Otis straight out of this house.

Not me, though. For some reason, some reason that I can't rightly explain, that shimmering blue light tugs at me. It's something I want to see. Pap told me a story once about how sometimes when the weather is just right, lightning doesn't shoot straight up and down. Sometimes it can become a floaty ball. He saw it once, working late on the rig. A floating, crackling ball of lightning creeping around out in the flat desert. He said two men tore off after it in their truck, like moths to a flame, but it popped before they got near it, and it was a good thing, too, 'cause it popped like a grenade going off. Pap said that wasn't even the scary part, though. The scary part was how much he wanted to go after it right along with them. Like he was hypnotized.

That's what I'm feeling right now. I'm one of those dumbasses in the truck that went after the lightning. I know it, and still I walk inside.

The last sunshine of the day is cutting through the big stained glass window set in the side of the wall to my left, and it colors the floating dust kicked up from all the scattered books and the over-turned chairs purple and red and yellow. I walk past a desk to my right that's all pulled apart like whoever worked there lost their keys and freaked out and then just ran.

Ran from whatever's in that courtyard, probably—so I walk toward the courtyard. I'm no wussy. It's been two years since I was really scared, and I said to myself that I'd never be that scared again.

I'm expecting some sort of fresh hell when I turn the corner, but that ain't what I see. It's actually kind of pretty. I walk through the open screen door into the garden, and there it is, floating in the air above the flowers under the sunset sky. It looks like a patch of water in the air. It's shimmering and blue, kind of like a little pond that got lost. I walk slowly around it. It's wide, but it's thinner than paper. If I look at it side-on, it nearly disappears, like the edge of a knife. And that's when I see that something is testing the surface of it. Just little pokes, like a finger trying to push through a balloon.

That stops me cold. Because that ain't right. Nothing about this is exactly *normal*, but the floating pond thing feels like a *right* thing. It's hard to explain how I know this, but I do. It feels like it's got every right to be there, same as the flowers and the bushes. I bet most times it's quiet and flat. But the poking? Nothing about that is right at all.

It's especially not right when I see what I think is the outline of a face pressing through. I can't make out what kind of face because it's still covered, but it's trying to look around, and it's pushing forward here and there like it's testing for a weak spot.

Then it looks at me.

Every hair on my body stands straight up. Even my buzzed hair feels like it stands up a little straighter. But that's not the worst part of it. When I move to the side, it follows me. It sees me. Then it opens its mouth into a silent scream.

What does it sound like? Hell if I know. I'm no wussy, but I told you I ain't stupid, neither—I get the hell out of there. I run as fast as I can. I don't look back. I don't do anything except jump on my bike and pedal and pedal until the wind is ripping at me again and I'm free of that old house. Then I'm under the arch and out of the grave-yard. I can hear the crows squawking at me, but they can stuff it. They can keep the graveyard for themselves.

PAP IS WORKING ALL the way over near Lubbock these days so I thought I'd beat him home from the rig, but I lost track of time in the graveyard, and when I get home it's dark and he's reading the *Midland Reporter* on his old chair. The nightly news is on low on the TV in front of him so I know I blew it, missed dinner. News is after dinner for Pap. That's the way it goes.

"Sorry, Pap," I say before he can say anything. He rustles the paper a bit then sets it down on his lap. He doesn't look mad. I've never seen Pap mad. I never want to. I work hard not to. So he's not mad, but he does look tired. And I know it's because of me. But not just for being tardy tonight—for everything. Because Mom and Dad died and I was still around so he had to stop working on his wood things and go back to the rig jobs for money. He's never said this, of course, but I know it. He's pretty old. He should be working on wood things right now, not driving to and from Lubbock and working on rigs.

Pap picks up a small glass of whisky carefully with his four-fingered hand and takes a sip. "Food's in the fridge, son," he says. He calls me *son* even though I'm not his *son* son. He's always called me *son.* He called Dad *son* too, which was sometimes confusing. Back then.

"Yessir," I say, and I trudge to the kitchen to open the fridge. It's fried chicken—my favorite. I'll eat it cold. I don't care. I carry the bucket out to the living room and sit across from Pap on the old bench he made by the window. Our house ain't too big. The living room is kind of the dining room too. And the sitting room. And TV room. I chomp on the chicken while Pap rustles the paper and sips his drink.

"The reason you're coming in so late have anything to do with this?" he asks, tossing a folded section of the paper my way. I catch it with greasy fingers and open it up like a napkin. The front page reads, *Fairview Cemetery Abandoned* and beneath that in smaller letters, *Former customers encouraged to claim their headstones.*

"What's a headstone?" I ask, partly to buy time.

"It's a grave marker," Pap says, looking at me carefully. "The article says ol' Andy Arnaud, who owns Fairview, up and vanished a little over a week ago. Abandoned the whole place. His employees have no idea where he is, but not a one of them'll go back to work. Won't set foot there."

I cough a little as a bit of chicken goes down the wrong pipe.

"Somethin' tells me you are of a different mind," Pap says, which is his grandpa way of saying he knows I was running around the graveyard. I look at the ground. I can hear him sip the last of his drink and wipe the wet ring the glass made from the side table before he gets up.

"Son, I ain't mad about you exploring that place," he says, which gets me to look up again. "I understand the draw. I really do. I just want you to be safe is all. Hear?"

"Yessir."

He rustles my hair and pats my shoulder. The skin of his hand feels rough and strong, and he smells like fresh oil and sawdust. He walks past me and sets his glass in the sink.

"I'm headed to sleep. Don't stay up. Just 'cause it's summer don't mean you can stay up all night."

"Yessir."

He pauses before the door to his room. He glances at me over his shoulder. "You'd tell me if you saw anything there that wasn't supposed to be there, right?"

This catches me so out of the blue it's like I'm hit upside the head for a second. Does he know? If he doesn't, would he think I'm crazy? The last thing Pap needs is a crazy grandson running around sucking up all the money he works hard for. The way he says it makes me think he knows more than he's letting on. But what did I see? I'm not even sure myself. A floating pond? A weird face? You don't just go around saying crap like that. Not in Midland.

"Y-yessir," is all I can stammer out. He nods before going in and closing the door softly behind him.

Pap's got a lot on his plate. Whatever this is, he don't need it too. I make a promise to myself then and there that I won't ever go near that house again.

Out of sight, out of mind.

Right?

2

THE WALKER

It's a strange time to be dead.

Depending on how you look at it, I've been dead either for a year, or for forever and ever, so forth and so on, ad infinitum. The brain tumor got me about a year ago, but what I became has been around since the dawn of time. So you tell me how old I am. You know what? Save it. Let's just go with thirty. A year isn't a long time on the job, so in a sense I'm still a rookie, but even I know something isn't right beyond the veil, in the land of the dead.

I go by a lot of names, Death being the most accurate and the most boring. The Ferryman is another, but I've never been on a boat in my life. I used to get carsick on the rides from Chaco Indian Reservation to Albuquerque General Hospital back when I was getting chemo, so I doubt I'd last long on a boat. Then there's Azrael, if you're into the whole fallen-angel thing, but I'm no angel. Not even a fallen one. There's the Grim Reaper, of course. Pale guy in a cosmic bathrobe who carries around an enormous farming tool. About the only thing similar between me and that guy is that we're both pale, although I didn't used to be. Oh, and we're both barefoot. No robe for me. I was a cop with the Navajo Nation Police Department when I was alive, and I feel most comfortable in uniform, although the one that I wear now is black. No badge. And no gun. I don't carry any weapons, actually. Well, except my fingers. Which I'll get to in a sec.

My bird, Chaco, he calls me Walker. He's been around for a long while and goes by a million names himself, but I call him Chaco because it reminds me of my roots on the rez. He's a bit of a smart-ass, but he generally knows what he's talking about, being as old as time. Since he's the only thing I regularly talk to, I guess I get called Walker a lot. It makes the most sense, too, since my job is to walk the soul map. I find souls ready to go (whether or not they want it is another matter), and I cut the fraying cord of their essence that keeps them tied to the living world. I use my fingers. Pointer and middle. Snip, snip. Go ahead. Try it yourself. Just like that. I tuck the remainder of their soul string back up into the soul map, button up their life story with the stories of everyone else, and then I escort them to the veil.

How do you get this job, you ask?

Well, there's this bell. A special bell. A one-of-a-kind bell that was forged with the essence of the living world and the world of the dead and everything in between. And if I was to ring this bell at the right time, say when my poor brain has decided to crap out on me and I'm seconds from death, well, then I'm spared from death... but I become the Walker. I become Death himself. That's some serious irony, right there.

Don't get me wrong. What I do must be done. But I'm not gonna sit here staring at a soul map full of billions of life forces that I cannot touch until their final moments and then tell you that I don't occasionally get lonely.

One-of-a-kind bell, one-of-a-kind veil, one-of-a-kind job.

The veil is a big, billowing, red curtain that comes in as you're going out. It's freestanding. Like the big puppeteer in the sky plunked down a busker stage right where you kicked the bucket. I can't cross the veil. That's not my territory. I'm the Walker. I inhabit no land—not the land of the living, not the land of the dead, not even the thin place in-between. Only fully severed souls can cross the veil. Most people go willingly enough—some skip, some dance, some sob their way through. Some try to run away. Trust me when I say running never works. The veil follows you, and so do I.

But lately the veil has been... acting strangely. If such a thing can be said of a spooky sheet of fabric. When I started this gig, this was how it went: When someone died I was drawn to their fraying soul string, I cut them free, and in came the veil. The dead went through the veil (or I tossed them through the veil, if they were being dicks about it) and then the veil disappeared. Ta-da! Job well done. On to the next.

But lately things with the veil have changed. I'm losing ground to it. I don't know how else to explain it, but trust me. Like I said, I was Navajo. Still am. Once a Navajo, always a Navajo. I know a thing or two about having my ground taken from me.

Maybe it's best if I just show you what I mean.

I get a tug that takes me to a forest at the base of Mount Fuji in Japan. A place called *Aokigahara*. It's also called the Suicide Forest. The place is known for its silence. The trees here are so dense, they cut all the wind. Your normal forest creatures don't come here. The trees are too thick to run from predators. Chaco told me once that there are certain places that the birds avoid, and at the top of that list is any place without wind. No chattering squirrels, no birds, no wind, dense forest—it all makes for a great place to go hang yourself if you never want to be found.

If you guessed this isn't the first time I've been to the Suicide Forest, you guessed right. About a hundred people kill themselves here every year. Only a fraction are ever found by the living. I find every one. It's what I do.

I step off the soul map and into a bubble of forested silence, like I've dropped down to a garden at the bottom of the sea. The undergrowth is thick. The trees themselves aren't huge, but there are tons of little ones, maybe as thick as my wrist. I reach out and touch one. It bends and snaps back, and it rustles the trees around it, but the sound seems caught up in the canopy, like it was snatched away and stowed in the treetops. I don't immediately see the soul, but I do see a long, satin ribbon stretching out of view.

In the year or so that I've been doing this, I've found suicides come in two camps: those who go through with it wanting to die, and those who go through with it not wanting to die. In the Suicide Forest, if you *kind of* want to die but aren't real sure of it yet, you bring a long ribbon or piece of string along with the rope you're thinking about using on your neck. When you trek off the beaten path, a little ways in you tie the ribbon to a tree, then a little ways later you tie another ribbon, or loop the string around a bush, and so on. There's a ranger here; his name is Honji. It is his sole job to follow these strings when he finds them. Sometimes he finds a troubled case on the other end that he can talk to. Sometimes just a body swinging from the end of a rope. Honji is one of those people who has a deeper sense for the world beyond the veil. A sixth sense, you might say. He is eighty-eight years old. He volunteered for ribbon-duty a lifetime ago, and still does it every day without complaint, and still sheds quiet tears every time he is too late. He is a beautiful soul. In a lot of ways, the color of his soul string reminds me of Caroline's.

This time around, I beat Honji to the punch. I'm drawn by the sound of laughter toward a dense area of brush where I see a fluttering red ribbon. I push through the wall of green, and there I find a young Japanese man at the base of an old oak tree. He's sitting on the ground, hunched like a rag doll in a rumpled suit, and he's laughing so hard that tears roll down his face. He hears me, and his head snaps up. He's smiling. When I come to clip a soul string, I appear differently to each person who sees me. I never know who they are seeing, but this time I must not have looked too out of place, because he still laughs, and it's a relieved laugh.

"After all that," he says, speaking in Japanese. "Everything I did and said, all of the veiled goodbyes and donating everything I own, I jump from the branch and the rope breaks." He wipes tears from his eyes and smiles wider. "And you know what? I'm happy about it! That's all it took! I see now. I see! I can live. I will live!"

He laughs again and leans back on his hands and sighs contentedly, like this was all a big ruse. There's only one problem. I don't get called to big ruses. Something in the quiet way I watch him stills his laughter and drops his smile a notch.

"What is it?" he asks.

I point above his head. There, his body spins slowly from a rope wrapped around the branch he jumped from moments ago. A rope that is very much intact. His tongue bulges out at twice the normal length, red and purple like a cut of pork tenderloin. His neck looks bunched and crumpled on one side. His head rests nearly on his shoulder. He died instantly.

"Oh..." he says, as if he's just scared away a bird he was watching. He eventually turns back to me, and there's no hint of laughter about him now. "So that would make you..."

"Yep."

This startles him. People are always shocked when I talk to them. It goes back to the movie thing. The ol' point and leer of the man in black. I may point, but I hardly ever leer. Talking to recently dead people is my new equivalent of a Saturday night. I don't waste the chance. It's about all I've got these days.

"But... but... no. How could... how could this happen?" he asks. He's rubbing his face. I think the newly dead still get an echo of the old sensation of touch. He still feels the world around him. But it's not his world anymore.

"Well, jumping from a tree with a rope around your neck might have something to do with it," I say.

"A joke? Really?"

"Sorry." I forget that the freshly dead don't have a real sense of humor. Neither do I, not really, although I'm trying. The Navajo have a... unique sense of humor. When we crack jokes, you can't tell. Maybe it's a joke, maybe it's a grocery list. That's where the humor comes from. If you're laughing right now, there's a good chance you're an Indian.

Anyway, the last thing I want is to become some sort of dour visage of death during the only time I actually get to talk to people, so I'm working on my material with each visit. It's not going so great.

"Look," I say. "What's done is done. Whatever was hurting you back there"—I point up to his swaying body—"that can't get you here anymore. I'm just gonna clip your soul string—it's frayed beyond repair now—and show you through the veil. It'll be all right."

"That thing?" he asks, pointing a shaking finger over my shoulder.

I turn around, and there it is. It startles me, too. "Yeah. That's it."

"Well it doesn't *look* all right," he says, and I can see that he's gone paler still. Paler even than the ankles hanging above his head. And I can see why.

The veil isn't the veil anymore.

It's supposed to be a red curtain. Softly billowing in the breeze, like a rich man's laundry on the line. But this thing is just... wrong. There's a brownish-black color creeping up it now, like the bottom has been sitting in a pool of oil. And it's twitchy, as if a bunch of tiny fists are punching it from behind. This thing looks more like boiling lake water than the veil I've come to know. When did this happen? Come to think of it, the color *had* been changing recently, but I thought maybe it was a trick of the light, or the darkness, or whatever. I go a lot of places at a lot of times. To be honest, after about a month on the job, I kind of tuned the veil out. It's always there eventually. It's the people that I have to be concerned with. The souls I need to cut free.

"Oh shit," I say. Which is exactly the wrong thing to say in front of a skittish soul.

"'Oh shit?' What's 'oh shit?'" he asks, really panicking now. He jumps up into a crouch. He's gone past pale into a shade of milky green, like he's gonna puke. Which would be a first. A dead guy puking. What would even come up?

"It's n-nothing. Listen to me, you have to go beyond the veil. It's what you do. It's gonna get you in the end." But I know my words are falling on deaf ears.

We got a runner.

He springs up and tears off through the trees behind him, leaving his swinging body behind. My old cop instincts kick in, and I take off after him. You'd be surprised how fast a guy can negotiate a thick forest when he's scared to death and he can't quite feel it when he bounces off trees and gets thrashed by branches. Me? I still get winded. I think it's a product of being as close to the living world as I am, even without being a part of it. I get shades of experience and feeling as well. It takes me almost a whole minute of weaving and slipping and shoving through brambles and over a rotten layer cake of dead leaves before I remember, again, that while I might not have him in a footrace, I sure as shit have him beat when it comes to time.

When I want to walk the soul map, I swirl a hole in the living world. It creates a time bubble that I step through, and off I go. If I swirl it just a little bit, it creates the time bubble without the hole. Think of it like a DJ on the turntables, but instead of music, I'm screwing with time. Just call me DJ Time. You'd laugh if I told you how many footraces I had to gut out before I figured out this little trick. So I reach out in front of me and I swirl the space, just like I'm waxing a car. If anyone could see me, I'm sure I'd look like a shitty mime lost in the forest. Everything around me slows, and suddenly the world is my movie on slo-mo, only here I am walking through it all like normal. I'm not gonna lie: this is definitely a perk of the job.

I walk through the slowed world around me, and in about a hundred steps I catch up to the guy. He's turning his head in tiny increments, and I can see that he catches me out of the corner of his eye because his pupils start to pinprick by degrees. To him, I bet I look like I'm moving at hundreds of miles an hour. Like I'm a streak of black light. I stop in front of him, crack my neck, and get a good hold on his arm with one hand. I let out a breath, then I swirl the other way with my free hand.

Time snaps back, and the guy snaps around with it, spinning around my body like a tetherball as I fling him to the ground. I dive on him and pin him. He swings at me, and his fists glance off me. I feel an echo of pressure. Nothing really.

"Hey!" I yell, slapping his face. "Hey! Stop it!" He pushes at my face and muffles my mouth, but I shake him off. "Stop! You're making an ass of yourself, man."

"No!" he yells. "I'm not going in that floating rag! Let me go!"

I fight to pin his arms to his chest like I'm packing him away. "I told you. The veil always wins. Look!"

I point over his head, and he cranes his neck around. There it is. Just like before. Only closer. A lot closer. Closer than it usually is at this point in a chase. I crinkle my nose. It smells now, too. Like dirty, drying mud. I try to keep the disgusted look off my face.

"So you can either run your ass off in the world you left behind until this thing crushes you and keeps crushing you forever, or you can let me cut your string and you go where you're supposed to go."

He stills.

"Will it hurt?" he asks.

"The cut? No. Actually people say it feels like finally popping your ears after a lifetime of being stuffed up."

"No, the veil." I can tell the fight is out of him. I ease up on him, and he sits up, eyes wide with terror. The veil creeps toward him even still.

"I told you, man. I don't know. But it's where you go. End of story."

He drops his hands to the dead leaves on either side of him and lowers his head. "Shit. Just... shit. It wasn't even that bad, you know? What I had here. It just... it wasn't that bad."

Moments like this—when all the shine of sweet release and whatnot is stripped off and these poor souls are faced with their choices and hindsight is crystal clear—they're tough to take. Not much can tug at me anymore, but this does.

"It is what it is." I know it comes out sounding cold, but it's not meant to.

"Easy for you to say. You don't have to go through that thing."

"I know more than you think about the consequences of a single choice," I say, my voice flat.

I think of the bell. I think of Caroline. I think of the last seconds I had with her. The kiss that should have been the first of hundreds, thousands. And I think of my sister Ana, trapped in this job before me. She didn't have a choice. She was only eight years old. She had no idea what the bell meant, what happens when it chimes. How it saves the ringer from death by making him Death itself. "Sometimes one choice can ring out louder than hell," I say. "But it is what it is."

He looks at me as I bring my hand over his head. I make like scissors with my fingers. He nods. I gently grasp his frayed soul string, sick and struggling, like a lightbulb on its last leg. It was strong once and shined like woven silver, but it's done for now. His eyelids flutter in anticipation as I snip it cleanly. Then he actually smiles.

"You're right," he says. "That feels... awesome."

I fold the frayed string up and into the swirled air above him, sewing it into the fabric of the soul map along with all those that came before it. Their experiences form the base of the map. The foundation itself.

"Time to go," I say, and I pull him up. When I turn around again, the veil is three feet from my face. I barely keep myself from screaming in surprise. The guy is tensed under my grip. He's tugging away, and I don't blame him. I've been wondering what's beyond the veil ever since I got this job, but looking at it right now, I think I can wait a little longer to figure it out. Just when I think the guy is fixing to bolt again, the veil doesn't give him a choice.

It reaches out and eats him. Eats him right out of my hand like a dog would a piece of meat when you aren't watching close enough. One second he's there, the next the veil has swept up and around him, and he's gone in a blink. I pull back my hands like it's electric.

"What has gotten into you?" I ask. I realize I'm talking to a cosmic piece of cloth, but right now it doesn't really feel like a doorway. It feels like an entity. It feels like it's trying to tell me something. The little punches from the other side are intensifying right around where I'm standing. One big one comes out, like a bowling ball thrown against the back of a sheet of canvas, and it's too fast for me to get away from. The veil sweeps out and around me, and I flinch and squint... until it falls back away. It passes through me. I feel nothing. It makes me a little relieved and a little bummed out at the same time.

"You can't touch me," I say, but all the same I back up. It doesn't follow. "I'm the Walker. You have no power over me." I'm feeling cockier now, ten or so steps back. "Nothing has power over me but the bell, you old rag. You got your soul. Now leave."

The veil should leave. There are rules about these things. Guy goes through veil, veil disappears. But the veil isn't leaving. Which is not good, because if this rule is breaking down, other rules are breaking down, and I work in a business where if the rules break down, shit hits the fan. The rules keep things in balance. I don't want to know what happens if the balance between the worlds falls apart. In fact, right now, with the veil staring me down, I'm about the most terrified I've been since I died. Which is saying a lot.

That is, until something pushes from the other side, stretching the veil tight around the five points of what look like five fingertips. It's quick, but it's undeniable. Then they're gone.

Now I'm the most terrified I've ever been.

If you ever visit Chaco Rez, which I wouldn't suggest you ever do without a Navajo guide, you'll see a fair number of Navajo who have just rolled over with what the US government and the Tribal Council give them every month. That's one type of Navajo. But there are others. Some of us, and it's more than you might think, if we're backed into a corner, we can turn the tables by talking. Then there are guys like me, who snap back. The more we're scared, the harder we snap. I think it's part of the reason I was kind of a shitty cop. A good investigator but a shitty cop.

"Listen to me, you piece of toilet paper. You did your part. Now you get the fuck out of here. Take your fingers and shove them up your ass."

The veil billows in waves, almost like it's laughing, or something is laughing behind it. Then it begins to dissipate slowly, blowing away like sand in an invisible wind until I'm alone in the forest. I blow out a big breath.

This has something to do with the bell and the two agents that are on the hunt for it. I just know it. Chaco, my bird, is on the hunt too, and he's a better hunter, what with him being an immortal creature tied to the bell and all, but still, it would make me and all the good people who make up the Circle of the Crow back in the land of the living feel a whole lot better if he just hurried up and found the damn thing already. He says he's close, but the bell doesn't fully present itself until it's found a new Keeper. I told him maybe he should have been a bloodhound or a homing pigeon or something instead of a crow, and he told me that the Walkers never understand. He likes to remind me that, while there have been thousands of me over the years, there has only ever been one of him.

I feel another tug on the soul map. I look around myself at the forest and shake my head in the silence. Duty calls. And this time, if the poor soul doesn't walk freely into that damn veil, I'm tossing them in from a few feet out.

CAROLINE ADAMS

I have a hunch that the bell has already passed us by, but I'm still new to this Circle of the Crow thing, so I keep my feelings to myself. Then there's a knocking on the front door of our RV. Owen opens it up, and Big Hill is standing there. I take one look at him and know my hunch is right. It's time to move on.

Big Hill was a swamp bear in another life. If there is such a thing. I'd say swamp alligator, but he's too hairy and fat for an alligator, and he doesn't have near the amount of teeth. He also has quite a soft side. He's squishing up his nose as he says, "I don't feel the bell no more," because it means we have to go, and I think Big Hill has grown attached to us over these past three months. I can't say I'm sad to say goodbye to the outskirts of Shreveport—I was expecting charming and mysterious Louisiana, and this area is more like muddy, backwater, weird Louisiana—but I will miss Big Hill.

Owen looks from him to me then back to him. "What do you mean you don't feel it anymore?"

"I 'spect it was thinking about touchin' down here. But it ain't thinkin' no such thing no more. It's moved on," Big Hill says in his thick, mumbling, bayou accent, pulling his stained and faded baseball cap off his head and dusting it off with one hand. His chin quivers.

"You mean this thing has a mind of its own?" Owen asks.

"'Course it does. It's the bell. But it ain't here no more, and the Circle, we know the job you've been given, and if it ain't here, you gotta be movin' on." Big Hill clears his throat heavily. It sounds like a downshifting truck.

"Big Hill, are you crying?" I ask, trying to peer up at his wooly face.

"Aw, hell," he says. "I suppose I am. It's just that I like the two o' you." He pulls out a handkerchief the size of a placemat and honks into it.

"We like you too, Big Hill! No tears. You can grab on to your crow totem and walk to us anytime, anyway."

Every member of the Circle has a crow totem. That's the ticket to ride. The crow totems are carved from turquoise and fit nicely in your hand. They depict a crow midflight. They're an extremely old, extremely powerful type of magic... although magic isn't quite the right word for it. More like they're keys that can open up the doors behind our world. If you hold one in your bare hand, against your skin, you can step through the doors for a bit into what we call the thin place. The totem is sort of like a backstage pass to the guts of the living world. The fabric of our world gets very thin, and everything feels much more intense, like you're in the engine room of the world, getting blasted with heat from the furnace. You disappear from the living world as long as you hold on tight to your crow, but it starts to hurt after a while. It's not a natural place for normal, living people to be, but it has its advantages. One step in the thin world is a giant leap in the living world. Owen calls this type of travel "phasing." Big Hill calls it "blinking."

"Hell, you know it ain't the same as havin' ya here," Big Hill says, folding his kerchief and stuffing it back down the front of his overalls. Owen awkwardly pats at Big Hill's hairy arm. He's trying to be nice and consoling, but he's a doctor. He still doesn't have that one down yet. I'm a nurse. I've got the comfort gene in spades. I step right down to where Big Hill is standing and put my arm around him even though I can't reach much higher than his butt. He hangs his big shaggy head. "Plus," he says, "you'n Owen shouldn't be blinkin' if you don't got cause to. There's strange things in the thin place these days."

"Strange things?" Owen asks, stepping down from the RV to join us. "Like what?"

Big Hill looks at both of us for a moment. I can see he's trying to describe what he means, but he's having some trouble. Instead he says, "I brought you some catfish for the road," and nods over at his rusted-out truck. "Help me load you up."

"Oh... really, Big Hill, you shouldn't have," I say. If I never eat another catfish it'll be too soon. Living at the edge of Big Hill's property, catfish is a once- or twice-a-week thing. Big Hill says he's known all around this area for his catfish. I don't doubt it. If a man his size gives you catfish, you take catfish, even if it tastes like glue.

"No, no," Big Hill says modestly. "Think nothing of it. It's a partin' gift from Big Hill."

We've only met two Circle members so far. I'm told it's because they're very private on the whole. The first we met was Joey Flatwood. Before Ben Dejooli died, Joey was his best friend. Ben's dead but not really *gone* gone—he's the Walker now—so maybe they're still best friends. You never know with Ben. Things with him are... complicated. The first time Joey showed up was on a vintage motorcycle, druggie-thin, wearing a leather jacket that swallowed him up and an Indian hair braid that went down to where his butt would have been if he had enough meat on him to *have* a butt. The first time I saw him, in Ben's hospital room, I wasn't sure whether he was there to rob us or kill us. Turns out he was there to fight for us.

Joey is very, very good at phasing and at using the crow in general. Owen and I are still new at it. When we walk in the thin place, it hurts us. It's a slow, steady pain that increases, like something's scraping at your teeth, until you let go of the crow and blink back. Not Joey. Joey could run across the country in no time flat if he wanted to. Of course, he paid a price for it. He pumped himself full of painkillers in order to stand the pain and get as good at phasing as he is. We've seen him a handful of times since that showdown back in Ben's hospital room, and at first he was completely addicted. I could see it in his smoke. His addiction rolled off his skin in putrid green and weeping yellow. He knew I could see it, too. He knows about my little gift. He just didn't care. He said he had a higher calling and that using the crow to its full potential was more important than his own health.

I told him if he was really devoted to that higher calling, he'd be able to do it without drugs. If you really want to rile up a young Navajo man, all you gotta do is suggest that he's too scared to do something. Works like a charm. I know because I worked with the Navajo for years at the Chaco Health Clinic. Here's another pro tip: this strategy is not limited to young Navajo men.

Recently Joey's been looking a lot better. Stronger. Healthier. His smoke shows up pearl white now when he talks about what the Circle must do, how we are to protect the bell at all costs. *Watch after it, and keep it secret.*

Of course, we need to find the dang thing first.

So, about the colors. If you're the carnival sideshow type, you might call what I have *aura sight.* If you aren't into that mumbo jumbo, you could say I just have a really, really good bead on people. I'm a heck of a nurse. I was back at ABQ Medical and Chaco Health Clinic, and I am now as a travel nurse. Not to toot my own horn, but everywhere I go people want me to stay and work full time. It's not because I have endless patience or because I'm super medically inclined like Owen is; it's because I see what is wrong with people. Literally, I can see it, in colors that come off of them like misty breath on a cold day. It makes for a lot of awkward conversations with Owen when I can see how he's feeling about the road warrior life he took on with me. And how he feels about me in general. Which is, in a word, strongly.

"Here," Big Hill says, shifting a Styrofoam cooler to the edge of the rusted bed of his truck. "Take one end of this and hold tight, hear? This'n is a live one. And a big sucker. You save this'n for a special time with your lady."

Owen blushes wildly, his face turning almost as red as his hair. I can't help but smile. He looks like a deer in headlights, still. As if I didn't know what he was feeling. It was pretty clear that he was falling for me when he asked if he could join me on the hunt for the Keeper. He didn't do it because he loves RVing.

But Owen and I aren't together. Or sleeping together. Or even hooking up. No heavy petting. No light petting. We almost kissed once after I'd had a bit too much of Big Hill's moonshine, which I think is just radiator fluid mixed with grain alcohol. I pulled out of the Kiss That Never Happened. Owen said he understood. He knows how I felt about Ben, which is funny, because *I* don't even know for sure how I felt about Ben. How I feel about him still. All I know is I didn't get enough time with Ben. But Owen understands. He always "understands." He's always willing to "give me as much time as I need." He's always concerned that he doesn't "make it weird." He just wants me to know that he's "here for me." And the bell, of course. But mostly me, I think.

It's not that I don't think he's attractive. He is. He's smart and trim and always well dressed and professional, and when he's in doctor mode he straight-up kicks butt. He's good enough to be a full-blown partner at a top clinic somewhere in the Boston circuit or up in Rochester at the Mayo Clinic, to say nothing of these tiny temp offices we ended up working in Shreveport so that we could keep up pretenses and not completely bleed money. He's the best doctor any of these joints have ever seen. That's his world, and he is the king of it. But outside of his world he's completely lost. His fire puffs away, and he becomes the ultimate nice guy, which isn't all bad, but sometimes it drives me nuts.

The fish bucks in the cooler, and both men pause to steady it. After a moment's stillness, Big Hill nods. They load it into the underbelly of the RV.

"It's packed in ice, but sometimes they still kick. The good ones, anyway. Got a couple more things for your journey," he says, and motions Owen back to the truck bed.

"Where did it go?" Owen asks. "The bell. If it's not here, any idea where it went? Should we just start driving?"

Big Hill walks around to the passenger-side door and opens it with a squeal. I think I can see the rust flake down from the joints. "Follow your crow totem, 'course."

I absently reach for my jeans pocket, where I keep my crow. "I still don't know what these things are, Big Hill. Neither you nor Joey can give me a straight answer."

Big Hill steps back from the back seat, and he holds his hands behind his back as if he's stepped up in front of the class.

"They the stuff o' the vein o' the earth," Big Hill says.

"You keep saying that, but what is the vein of the earth?" Owen asks.

"Ain't seen it m'self. But it's where they came from. Now. Guess what's in my right hand."

Owen sighs. Big Hill is tough to understand when he's talking about swamp fishing, much less opining on the powers that hold the balance between worlds. He takes it for granted that there's a bell out there with the power over death. But Owen is in the business of facts. Diagnosis. Science. That a rock carved into the shape of a crow could defy the laws of physics bothers him a great deal. Not Big Hill. Big Hill wants us to guess what's behind his back.

"More catfish?" I guess, trying to hide a cringe.

"Nah, you got plenty in the icebox. It's a jug of 'shine!" He pulls his right hand in front of him, and in it is a bell jar of grainy moonshine. It looks like pond water distilled through a sock. It gives me a hang-over just to see it.

"Guess what's in my left hand," Big Hill says, still grinning. I already know. I can see it coming off of him in waves. He's an open book, Big Hill.

"More moonshine?" I guess.

"How the hell did you know!" he says, laughing loudly. "You're a special one. Both of you are. A jug for each of you. Least I could do for the ones the Walker chose."

I take my moonshine. I can smell it through the glass. Big Hill says the two of us are the only members of the Circle in living memory to have received their crows from the Walker himself. They think this makes us special. I tried to tell him how Ben was just a patient of mine, and of Owen's. He won't have it. Ben's the Walker. As far as he's concerned, Ben was never anything else. He's right, and he's wrong. Ben is the Walker, but he was much more. To me.

"Now go," Big Hill says. "'Fore I start bawlin' again. Head west. That's as good as I got."

Owen nods. He feels the tug, too, just like I do. The bell is somewhere west. Big Hill hugs us each for a suffocating few seconds, then he practically pushes us up the steps of the RV. "G'on now. Get gone. And remember, don't blink. Hear me? There's things in the thin place. Things watching. Things that shouldn't be there. It's not safe."

Owen settles behind the wheel, wider around than he is. I stand at the top of the stairs.

"Thanks, Big Hill, for everything. Be seeing ya."

Big Hill has his handkerchief out again. He blows loudly into and nods. "I hope so," he says.

4

GRANT ROMER

The city of Midland is different from the outskirts where Pap and I live. The city has a lot going on, what with people walking around in suits and driving all sorts of nice cars and carrying briefcases during the day. I asked Pap one day how many people were in Midland, and he said feels like twice as many after each boom and half as many after each bust, by which he means oil, of course. We're in a boom right now. There are people everywhere.

I feel best in quiet places like the graveyard, but I ain't never going back there, so I gotta find a new place to ride. I suppose I could cruise the neighborhood, but I've done that a million times already and I might run into Otis and his crew, which wouldn't be good since I know they'd rather ride without me on account of they think I'm weird.

I'm not crazy about it, but I got this feeling that I should go toward the city. Sometimes I get these feelings about places, like I forgot something there even if I know I've never been there before. The graveyard gave me that feeling too. It's why I kept going back again and again. I know I'd have gone ridin' there even if Mom and Dad weren't there.

Pap is working hard on the rig near Lubbock until real late, so I have enough time to wait out the worst of the heat and get started in the late afternoon. Where we live is up north of the city just a bit, and if you look out on it as the sun is setting, Midland stands like a big lightbulb in the center of two patches of dark desert. But if you stare at the dark for a while you'll see it ain't really that dark—it's shot through with tiny dots of light. Those dots are the rigs out in the desert, drilling for oil and gas, day and night. Pap is out there on one right now, and even though I know he's too far away, I like to think I could still maybe see him. Like maybe he's one of the very farthest dots to the north. I wave at him even though I know it's a stupid thing to do.

I can already see the line of trucks off in the distance to my left like one long, glowing caterpillar. They're going to the man camp, which is sort of like a city of oil workers that popped up on the edge of town during the boom 'cause all the people had no place to stay. I don't want to go that way. That's no place for kids. I want to go where the people are walking in their suits and with their briefcases. There's a pretty nice street that runs around the big buildings and has trees and grass in the middle and shops all down both sides. That might be a good place to ride. I cut to my right, down a small, winding road that heads off that way. But I must have gotten my directions wrong because after a couple of minutes the road winds back, and by the time I stop and set down the kickstand, I'm looking toward the man camp again in the distance.

I start off again, but this time I go hard right, down a straight street that I know will take me to the city. Instead I hit construction. A big man smoking a cigarette and holding a stop sign shakes his head at me and points left. I have to pedal up another hill and cross over a park just to get back to where I started. And I'm staring at the man camp again. I hit the brakes and skid as best I can. I check out my skid mark in the streetlights and nod. It's a good one. But that doesn't change the fact that twice I've tried to cut right and twice I got nowhere. The long line of trucks is still there, creeping forward. The lights in the rows of the man camp houses turn on all at once. I spit.

Pap would hate me spitting, but I figure it's okay right now 'cause I got a problem: I gotta go left. I gotta follow the trucks. And I gotta ride toward the man camp.

Sometimes things work like that with me, when I get that feeling about a place. Maybe it's true and Otis is right and I am weird, but I ain't supposed to go to the right today. I slide my back tire around until I'm facing the trucks.

Fine. If I'm goin' left, I'm goin' left.

The truck caterpillar came along with the oil boom. It's been there pretty much nonstop for a while now. Pap says the problem is that there's only one main road to the camp and the rigs beyond and it's an old road with two lanes, one going each way. He says it worked just fine for fifty years and even through the first oil boom, thank you very much, but the rigs are bigger now and all smart and whatnot and so they need a lot of trucks. So the rigs changed, but the road didn't. It's still the same ol' two-lane road with stop signs and no stop-lights, and now there's a hundred big trucks stopping and going at every stop sign. It backs up for a mile sometimes. Stop and go. Stop and go. I bet it takes a whole day for a truck to get from the back all the way to the man camp.

Better to have a bike at top speed.

I whizz past the trucks in a blur like they are gravestones back at the cemetery. Some of them honk at me, but I think it's just 'cause they're bored. I'd be bored too, sitting in a truck and not on a bike.

The man camp ain't much to look at. It's mostly a bunch of big sheds spread out in rows, like the kind you keep tools and old cars in. Except these ones hold people, and some of them sell things like food and drinks. I've also seen people selling beer and cigarettes out of them, and one has this man who sits in front of it and brings men inside, and I think there's girls in that one that they pay to kiss. But mostly it's just people living. New people come in when they take jobs on the rigs, and old people leave when their job is up or their rig goes away to find oil somewhere else.

I shouldn't be going near the man camp at all, much less at night, but I can't go against that feeling. Even so, I try to keep to the outskirts where big light stands shine down the dirt roads between the sheds like there's a football game goin' on or something. I wish I could go faster, but there's lots of ruts to deal with from the big haulers and there's people about too. Some of them call after me or whoop. Some of them are falling around like zombies, and I know they're drunk. I have to make a hard right to skirt a big rut, and my bike skids out on tiny rocks. By the time I get hold of it again, I almost run into two men falling into each other, trying to fight. They stumble around and stop cussin' at each other long enough to turn and look at me.

"Hey!" one yells, his eyes puffy and his mouth open. "Git over here, kid!" But I'm already gone. I kick up dirt and rocks behind me and pedal as hard as I can. I hear a whistle by my ear, and a beer bottle explodes on a stack of crates to my right. I pedal harder. I hear a flat-footed thumping behind me, and I know someone is chasing me, probably for my bike, probably 'cause it's a ten-speed. I ain't givin' it up.

I pedal harder than I ever have before, out of the lights, out of the camp, and soon I'm shooting through the tumbleweeds and out on the hard desert floor in the dark, and I'm basically riding blind. My legs won't stop pumping, even though the thumping sound is long gone now and all I can hear is the clicking of my teeth. Without those lights and with no moon to speak of, it's as dark as a basement out here, and I'm praying I don't hit a pothole or a rattler den or fly into a ditch.

By the time I get my legs to stop, I'm way out, like I'm floating in the middle of a lake at night. The camp is behind me, but it looks like a blob of light in the distance. There's a working rig ahead, about the length of my finger. I can see the gas flare like a dancing yellow hat on top of the derrick. There's some clanking, and the revving sound of a big engine floats softly over to me, but other than that, it's quiet. Which is good. Out here, in the dark, what you don't want to hear is rattling. I was snake bit once two years ago, but it wasn't a rattler. Got me right in the crook of my elbow. If it had been a rattler, even a baby rattler, I'd have been dead. Especially a baby rattler. They're the worst 'cause they don't know when to let go.

I shouldn't have started on about snakes because there's a rustling in the bushes that I bet is just a mouse of some sort, but it gets me up on my bike and out like a flash. Before I know it I'm even deeper in the desert and closer to the rig. I feel better closer to the circle of light it's putting out, so I glide my bike as quietly as I can to the edge of the equipment, and in order to calm myself down, I start naming all the things Pap taught me about the rigs.

The first time I saw a drilling rig, I thought it was a giraffe. I don't remember this, 'cause I was just a baby, but I know it's true 'cause that's how Pap taught me about rigs from then on out, as parts of the giraffe. I see the head of the giraffe, the crown block with its little fenced-in fort way up high that I always thought was like the top of a pirate ship. The neck of the giraffe is the derrick, and there's a cord with a hook moving around in there that makes it look like the giraffe is swallowing. The body and back of the giraffe is the platform, where most of the men are now, hooking pipe up to feed the giraffe. Its butt is the engine, which is farting smoke into the air. Below is the blowout preventer, the guts of the giraffe. When I used to cry about Pap leaving to Odessa or Permian or somewhere to run a giraffe for a while, he'd say not to worry, he'd be back because the guts keep him and his crew safe.

I breathe. My heart is back to normal again. The desert behind me is just as big and just as black, but I'm all right with it. The blood stops screaming through my ears. I can actually make out what the roughnecks are saying on the rig. Two men are talking next to the control shack.

"Had to move the whole goddamn pad, is what I'm sayin'," says one. He's in a monkey suit, but he's carrying around a big black notebook, which means he's probably the tool pusher. The crew chief. Like Pap.

"The whole thing?" says the guy he's talking to. He's in a full-blown suit and tie. Not a rig guy. A money guy.

"I been drilling in the Permian for fifty years, Don. Fifty fucking years. And in that time I've moved pads for a lot of reasons, usually because of a geologist or geophysicist or engineer or some other rock licker telling me they think horizontal pay dirt is a hundred feet to the left or right of where we're standing. That's nothing new to me. But that? That shit was too much. We broke five straight bits."

"Jesus," Don says, pulling his hair back with one hand.

"You know how much five drill bits cost? Not to mention the downtime on a rig in this basin? We had to push our whole schedule back."

"You think I don't know what the cost is?" Don asks. "We're already near a million over AFE because of this little shuffle job you did." He shakes his head. "A quarter section to the left. For a million bucks. This shit better be worth it."

I can tell the tool pusher ain't used to being talked to by a guy in a suit like that. He steps right up into the guy's face. "I'll tell you what you would have got a quarter section back, compadre. You woulda got another five broken bits, at least. I got the drill plan from your engineers. We can hit the zone here. We will hit the zone here."

They keep talking, but I'm not listening anymore. Now I'm looking a quarter section to the right, where the rig broke five bits trying to drill a well. It looks like nothing but a flat spot of black earth under a moonless sky. Like a huge tent was there that just broke camp.

I get that feeling again. Like I lost something there even though it's the first time I've ever set eyes on it.

I leave the rig behind and bike out toward that spot. My bike jumps and bumps over yucca and big clods of dirt. The shocks kick back and forth with a quiet hiss. A quarter section is about a hundred and sixty acres of land, and it's dark as mud by the time I hit the taped-off zone that the rig left behind. The desert is churned up around the old spot and pounded down inside of it. I set my bike down outside of the line and duck under the tape. I don't have a flashlight or a cell phone or anything, so I'm not exactly sure what the heck I think I'm gonna find, but I do have that feeling, and it's telling me to check the place out.

I feel in front of myself with my hands and my feet, like a wall might jump out at me at any time. I trip over a big wheel rut and scramble to standing again. No rattling. That's good. In fact, there's really no sound at all. It's as still as the graveyard was. It feels a lot like the graveyard, too. I look all around me for anything that might look like a blue pool or a creepy hand, but there's nothing. I'm in a pool of black, but it's a quiet pool.

Once I'm where the old rig stood, the footing gets better. The dirt is all hammered down. I can see where the rig was centered. The earth is plated over by a huge manhole. I walk on top of it, and my steps clang out. I jump up and down because at least it's *some* sort of sound.

Then I hear the bird.

I stop jumping like a trampoline's broke under me. The bird's doing nothing but flying, and still it's so loud in the quiet that it sounds like an airplane. It's a darker spot on the black, and I wouldn't be able to track it at all except that I see a streak of red in it that must catch a stray part of rig light that would have died otherwise.

It scares the crap out of me. My feet move so fast I slip on the metal pad cover and scrape up my knee before I can get traction. I pound the dirt back to my bike and slam it upright, but this time I stop before I hit the road.

I've been hitting the road a lot lately when things get scary, which is a chicken thing to do, and I'm tired of it. I told you I'm no wuss. Plus, I don't want to get any deeper into this desert than I already am. It takes all I got to keep my hands on the handlebars and my feet on the ground, but I do it. I scan the flat ground behind the tape until I find it. The bird. It's a crow. And no wonder it sounded so loud coming in—it's the size of a dog. A red stripe starts at its head and runs down its right wing like a racing stripe. The clouds break for a second, and the red glints in the starlight, along with two black eyes. And they're staring right at me.

"What do you want?" I say, and my voice breaks at the end, which is just great.

The crow says nothing, doesn't move a muscle.

"What are you," I say, because I don't need anyone to tell me that this crow is not normal. I can figure that out on my own just fine. For all I know, it might not even be a crow. It might be a monster that just looks like a crow. It stares at me with its beady eyes long enough that I get to thinking about taking up my bike again and leaving this whole mess behind me, but then the crow looks behind its left wing with a slow, steady motion.

"Aw, crap," I say. 'Cause I know what the thing wants. It wants me to go over into that dark where it's pointing. "Seriously?"

The crow looks back at me and nods. I swear to God.

What am I supposed to do when a crow nods at me? I can't *not* at least check it out. Even though where it's pointing is dark as all hell. Darker than it should be. It's dark like a rain cloud dropped right down on the ground. But the crow nodded at me. I'm not gonna bike home and go to bed and wait for Pap to come back and think the entire time about how a bird told me to check something out but I was too chicken to walk through some soupy dark.

"All right then," I say. I set my bike down again. I walk under the tape and over the slammed-down earth and under the tape again across the old pad, going wide around the bird. He watches me, blinks once. I hit the edge of the dark. I puff myself up and walk forward. It's like walking through a mist. I step again and again, hands out, feet out. Then I hear a rattle. I freeze. I step back as slow as molasses. I hear another rattle.

Most rattlers sound like bean shakers. This one doesn't. It sounds more like bird bones banging against a can. I freeze again, but I don't want to, because I know why the bird told me to go here. Why I rode here through the man camp and past the rig. It's because the thing I don't know I forgot is here. Right here. And I know this place isn't what it looks like. It's not just desert. It's where our world flickers in and out. Where things like birds might not be birds. And things like snakes might not be snakes.

There's another break in the coat of clouds, and I see a glint in the desert dirt about ten feet from me. It looks like a piece of tinfoil. I want to step toward it; I feel like I *need* to step toward it. Like every bike ride I've ever had led me to this moment, where I'm just a step away. Two steps at most. I move toward it. There's another rattle, louder this time, and another glint, but this one is like a slick of grease in a parking lot. And it's moving toward me, which I know ain't right. The one good thing about rattlers is that they stay where they're at. Not this one. It's going toward the shiny thing, same as me. I take another step, and it quickly coils up with its head like a floating fist. It looks at me, and its tail rattles hollow, like rocks clacking down a well forever. I don't know why, but I know sure as the night is black that I can't let that snake get to whatever shines in the sand in front of us. I know it the same way that I know I didn't end up here by chance. The same way I know that Pap knows about my feelings. I saw it in his face when he said goodnight after I came back from the graveyard, but I missed my chance to come clean.

I'm not missing this chance.

I dive for the shine. The snake coils back like a spring for a half second then lunges at me. I can see its fangs in the dark. They drip with venom, and I think in that split second how they look like rusty wire. Brown and sick. And they're going to get to me. The rattler shoots forward right at the crook of my elbow as I reach out. I'm not quick enough. Nothing in the desert is quicker than a rattler.

Except the crow.

The snake is inches from the meat of my arm when the crow crushes it from the air. I feel the brush of black wings on my face, then the snake is on the ground, thrashing like an out-of-control garden hose. And it can thrash all it likes, 'cause the crow has it right at the back of its head, and the crow don't look scared. I think it makes a point of looking at me before it snaps its beak shut and clips the snake's head clean off. It even fluffs its own feathers a bit afterward, puffing up and settling down with one claw over the head of the snake. Then it points its arrowhead beak at the glint again.

I dig it up from the desert with my fingers and hold it to the weak light of the stars. It's a silver bell, but it's not. It's the lightest and the heaviest thing I've ever held in my hands.

"What's up?" the crow says. And I almost drop the bell.

His feet are still on the dead snake, but he's looking up at me, expecting an answer.

"You talk?" I ask, then I shake my head. "This is a dream."

Truth be told, I sometimes think I've been dreaming since Mom and Dad died. Like I was in the car with them that night and maybe I'm in a coma. Or dead. It would be easier in a lot of ways. At least I wouldn't worry anymore about Pap. No need to worry if you're just a dream. Somehow the bird seems to know what I'm thinking. And I can feel that the bird gets sad. You ever seen a sad bird? It sort of dips its head.

"This is no dream," the bird says. "And that bell is no ordinary bell."

I look at the silver bell in my hands. As if I needed any proof it ain't a normal bell, it's cold. Nothing normal is cold in Midland in August. I clutch it to my chest. I'm afraid of losing it already.

"My name is Chaco," says the crow. "That bell is yours. It's my job to make sure it stays that way."

5

THE WALKER

We got a Keeper!

Now that the bell has found its partner, I find myself studying the boy. He has in his possession the bell that put me here. If he wanted to, he could off himself and take my job. I know it's unlikely and improbable, but if he wanted to, he could do it. Ring the bell in that space between life and death, and he slips into my role and I fade away across the veil, just like Ana did before me. The thought turns my stomach. It's something I both want and want to run from. Sure, sometimes the job sucks, but other times I feel like I'm a king and the soul map is my domain. A lone king, sure. But a king. Plus, I need to figure out what is happening to the walls between worlds. I can't go fading away just yet.

I trace his soul string, which is sort of the equivalent of rewinding his life. A bit nosy, but who's gonna judge me? I realize I hardly need to worry about the kid taking my job. He has no intention of leaving his world behind and his Pap all alone, even though he thinks, in the shortsighted way that eight-year-olds do, that it might be easier on the man if he wasn't around. He's seen mysteries, too. Places where the world thins. He has a gift for finding them. I suspect it's part of the reason the bell came to him. He has a drive to set things right, even if he can't yet describe precisely why he feels that they're wrong in the first place.

Grant accepts the absurdity of his new job, the realities of the bell and what it means to be the Keeper, in the way only a child can: totally and without reservation. Chaco is amazing with him. For a timeless bird, he's pretty good with kids. I can see why Ana loved him. I felt him calling for me as soon as he felt the bell, and I zipped through the soul map to Midland, Texas, of all places, and watched the finding unfold. If I could have, I'd have ripped that rattlesnake apart myself, but his world is beyond my reach. I was powerless to help. Thankfully, Chaco wasn't.

Afterward, Chaco makes sure Grant gets safely back home. He perches right on the handlebars of his bike, making himself smaller so the kid can see. The whole ride back he talks to him.

"So there's this place you go after you die," Chaco says.

"Of course there is. Mom and Dad are there," Grant says, leaning in close to get a look at Chaco's red stripe. Chaco blinks. That was easy enough.

"And the bell. Let's see. The bell. How to describe the bell? Your bell summons the Walker, who guards the gate between here and there and walks our world keeping things straight."

"Like Death?" Grant asks, stepping off one pedal and coasting back to his driveway. Chaco flutters up and settles on Grant's head. Grant looks up and laughs but doesn't seem to mind.

"Yeah, sort of, but he's not such a bad guy. He's here right now," Chaco says, before *tsking* at himself. Way to go, bird. Just tell the kid that Death Walking is right next to him, why don'tcha.

"He's here right now? Awesome!"

Chaco looks at me. I shake my head, but I can't help smiling.

"Yeah, he's right there." Chaco points with one wing. "But you can't see him. Only I can see him. He's not always around you, though, okay? And he won't hurt you. He just wanted to see you. Pretty soon he'll get pulled away on work."

"You mean killin' people." Grant stashes his bike behind a bush. He holds the bell tight in one hand, his knuckles white.

"Well, he doesn't kill 'em. He just cleans up their souls after they die. He guards the gate between here and there, and he watches over a map that has everyone's soul written into it."

Grant stares at the empty space I take up. "Makes sense. Somebody's got to, I guess."

I like this kid.

"So... what are you?" Grant asks Chaco.

"A smart-ass," I chime in. Chaco ignores me.

"Well, I go where the bell goes. I'm its buddy. And the bell chose you, so now I'm your buddy too. Like it or not."

There's a little uptick of a smile at the corner of Grant's mouth. I get the feeling he hasn't smiled much recently. I think it's safe to say he probably doesn't have many buddies either.

"You really a bird?" Grant asks.

"Not really. Close enough, though." I guess Chaco doesn't want to get into what it means to be a thin creature just yet. Although I'm pretty sure Grant would get it.

"And you go by Chaco?"

"That's right," Chaco says, fluffing up his feathers a little defensively. I grin. He and I give each other a lot of shit, but I gave him that name, and he likes it. That little flutter says a lot, coming from a thing that has had a million names.

"It's a good name," Grant says.

"So's Grant."

And just like that, Chaco and Grant are buddies.

Grant's soul thread, like every thread caught up in the pull of the bell, is hard to read. Ever changing. Its color morphs from a healthy, shimmering silver to a dusty, faded white and back again. One moment it is as strong as an anchor tie, the next it's frayed and weak. What's for certain is that his life has become a good bit more dangerous than it was when he woke up this morning. And also a hell of a lot more interesting.

I wince a little when I feel that little pricking that tells me it's time to go back to work, and not just because I want to stick around and hang out with Chaco and Grant, even if it's essentially watching them through the window. I wince because it's getting so that every time I hit the scene to clip a soul, it's a dice roll as to whether or not what I see is in my job description. More and more I'm coming up craps. In short, the weird shit is getting weirder.

But work waits for no man. I turn away from our new Keeper, swirl open the soul map, and step through. When I walk the map it's like I'm walking along a massive rope made up of countless smaller strings weaving in and around and through each other. These are the souls of every living person. Think of it like a cross section of a massive fiber-optic cable—millions of points of light that shine and pulse with life, which makes it easy to find the departed soul. It looks like a flickering, broken pixel on a big-screen TV. I zip over to it, stop there, and stand still on the rope.

Something doesn't look right.

Soul strings on their way out look weathered, like creeping vines in winter. This one looks young, but it flickers nonetheless. It's unnatural. It puts me on edge. But it still needs tending to, so I take a deep breath, sweep open the living world, and step off the map and back to earth.

I don't know what I'm expecting. A murder scene, maybe. An atrocity. Or perhaps something just as staggering but on a small scale, like an infant, cold in its crib. What I get is a woman sitting on a park bench on the Strip outside of the Palazzio Casino in Las Vegas, Nevada.

Now, I've paid more than my fair share of visits to Las Vegas. Trust me. This place is like Grand Central Station for me. But this time is different, and I immediately know it's wrong. She's holding a map of the Strip, and she's asking people walking by for directions. People who no longer see her. People who can never answer her. She's older, perhaps sixty, but she looks healthy. In fact, she's wearing beads and a frilly sash and a dress that sparkles, along with running shoes. A yard glass of beer sits next to a cheap, tattered sombrero at her feet. She looks like she's been trying to get the attention of the world she left behind for some time; she's sat down with the effort of it. That's strange in and of itself. I'm usually on the scene moments after death.

"Excuse me?" she says, lifting her arm at a passing couple before letting it flop back to her lap. She looks drunk and in shock. And her soul thread isn't right at all. It's done for, all right, but not like I've ever seen. It looks hacked at, like a broken guitar string.

"Please," she says, holding out her hand again as a young woman clacks by on heels, uncaring, unknowing.

"I'm right here," I say, as if I could do something. As if I could bring her back. I've never said it like that before. I don't know why I say it now. But this woman is in pain she can't understand, and I want to acknowledge that.

"Oh, thank God," she says, and she tries to rise but can't. She looks at her legs like they aren't hers anymore. I hold out my hand for her to stay put, and then I move in and sit beside her. Both of us, on a bench, the Strip seething around us and through us. She looks desperately at me and holds up a phone that is an echo of the one she had in the world she's left, which is another thing that's wrong with this scene. Souls usually stick close to their bodies. There is no body anywhere near us. "I can't get reception," she says. "I've lost my friends. We were just at the tables, and then we went to that bar, and then..." She trails off for a second before starting again. "It's a girls' weekend," she says quietly. "We were supposed to stick together. Why would they leave me? Have you seen them? My name is Karen Mulaney. Have they been asking for me?" She looks up at me for answers, and the terrible sadness in her face fogs my eyes with tears. Not because a poor woman died in Vegas alone. Plenty of people die alone. It's because she shouldn't be dead. And what's left of her soul knows it and is crying out in pain.

I have seen terrible things in my line of work. The most unjust, unfair, unbelievable endings to existence you can imagine. They happen every day. But even those unbearable deaths have a *place*. They have a *place* on the rope I walk, which tells me that they have a purpose, too. They may not know what that purpose was, but it was there nonetheless. I know it because when I cut their souls free, their life story fits back in the map same as every other, and the balance of the map holds.

But this is new. This poor woman, lost and alone in Sin City, shouldn't be dead. I know that as soon as I see her chewed-up soul thread. I also know this: no matter how she got here, it's my job to see her across. I look around for the veil. I can see it down the street, coming my way. It moves like a broom, sweeping over the living with no effect, but the dead have nowhere to run. The veil is entirely black now, which worries me, but not as much as the newfound calm it has. It no longer ripples or bulges or flickers. It's as slack as a curtain in the far corner of an empty house.

"Karen, I'm sure that your friends are looking for you," I say, resting my elbows on my knees. "But they're not gonna find you. You're beyond them now."

"No, I'm not." She shakes her head. "I'm right here. They're close."

So is the veil.

"Karen, can you tell me what happened when you lost them? How you lost them and ended up here?" But Karen has lost interest in me. She's looking at the veil. It has swept its way down the strip and is maybe a hundred feet from us.

"Oh, no," Karen says. She blinks rapidly and scratches at her head then all over her body, like the tweakers we used to deal with back at Chaco. She stretches her neck out like she's wearing a rough wool sweater. Her soul string twitches and frays. I can see that it's causing her pain, not physical pain—she can't feel that anymore—but spiritual pain, which, in a way, is much worse. Her soul is rebelling against being here. It's rebelling against the veil. And with good reason. It's been cheated out of its full lifetime of experiences. Karen's mouth is slack, her eyes wide and rolling. I think about asking her again how she got this way. About who, or what, cut her soul line like this, and how, but I can't bear it any longer.

I place one hand on her shoulder, and with the other, I scissor the soul and set it free. The pop is big this time, like the first crack of a frozen lake in thaw. Karen slumps on the bench, and I hold her upright. I'm surprised to find tears rolling down my face, and I wipe them away quickly.

"It's okay," I say, although I'm not sure if I'm reassuring her or myself. "I had to do it. There's no going back once it's as tattered as that. It was the only way..."

The veil has crept up on us. And before I can finish my blubbering, it sweeps over Karen like limp fingers and pulls her from my hands. It doesn't stick around to gloat this time, either. Once it has her, it pops out of this plane. Then it's just me on the bench, my arm resting on nothing but air.

Now that Karen's gone, my eyes are clear and hard. This is really starting to piss me off. Not just because the veil is sick, or dead, or evil, or whatever the hell it's become, and not just because the things that are supposed to be happening in death aren't happening right anymore. I'm pissed off because I have a job to do here and something out of my power is messing with that. In fact, if I didn't know any better, I'd say some fly-by-night poser trying to play Death did a hack job on poor Karen's soul before it was her time to go.

But that can't be right, because the only one that gets to cut strings around here is me, goddammit. Or so I thought. I mean, the evidence was right there. Her string was mangled. She looked like a shell-shocked soldier wandering around holding a limb she'd just lost. I only wish I could have talked to her longer; maybe we could have retraced her steps...

Or I could just do it myself. I whap my own forehead. Of course. When I get runners, I slow time to catch them. Wax left, that's the slowdown move. I do it now, slowly circle left in the air, and I watch the Strip cut to half-time, then quarter-time, then to a trickle. I pull the Strip to a full stop. Then I keep swiping left.

Karen is back on the bench with me, but she's just an echo of the past. I roll back some more and watch as she pleads in reverse for attention from a crowd that can't see her. I watch as she stands up and walks backward, retracing her steps. I pause. I want to walk through the end of her life as she did. I grab the frayed end of her soul string with my free hand, then I zip in reverse. Las Vegas becomes a blur of colors and lights streaming over me. When I slow the roll, I'm at the bar next to her, frozen in time. She's drinking in the middle of the crowd of friends that she would later think had forgotten her. I start from there.

I walk beside her as I live her final hours. I watch as they pay and leave and she spills her yard of beer, her sombrero flopping over her face. She and her friends walk to the blackjack table at the Palazzio, and she sets a single chip down. She hits a blackjack right off the bat. She cheers, and the table cheers, and her friends slowly pare off to tables of their own as she keeps playing. She doesn't notice. She splits at the right time, doubles down at the right time. She's an aggressive bettor. They bring her martini after martini. She keeps winning. In one stupid bet she drunkenly splits tens over the protests of the entire table. She puts in everything. She hits twenty-one on both hands. The cheers sound muted on the replay, like the soundtrack to her life is playing underwater.

Karen chips out; she's a thousand up. She tips the dealer a hundred. She gets pats on the back. Her eyes are glossy, and her face is red with the win and the booze. She backs away from the table and looks for her friends, but she can't see them, even though I can. They're at the nearby roulette table and hovering around the craps table. One of them stands almost directly to her right, but she misses her. I want to scream at her and point. *They didn't go anywhere, Karen! They're right here!* But this is a replay. There's nothing I can do but watch as she tries to shake off the booze and walk to the elevators. Either she thinks her friends are in their room or she wants to stash her chips. Either way, she leaves the casino floor alone.

In the elevator, she talks with another couple off to see a show. She weaves in place. The couple gets off on the floor below hers, and she exits alone. The twenty-second floor of the Palazzio Hotel and Casino is completely empty when she walks out. It's a long, straight hallway. The elevator bay is in the dead center. The carpet is dark and patterned. The lights are low. Every twenty feet or so stands an alcove with a vase of flowers or a cheap sculpture. I know on cop instinct that this is where it goes south for Karen, but when I look up and down the hallways, I see nothing. There's an ice machine. That's it. But the dread lingers.

I walk beside Karen as she makes her way down the long hallway. I look behind us. Nothing. She stumbles against the wall, and I almost move to help her before I check myself. I look behind us again. Nothing. She stops in front of her door and opens her purse. She fumbles through it then drops it, and her chips spill out all over the hallway. She laughs and curses. And suddenly there's someone there to help her pick them up.

He's on the scene so quickly it even scares the shit out of me. I jump a foot back. Karen was there alone, and in a blink Karen is with a man. I stop the replay with several quick swipes to the left like a teenaged kid pausing a horror flick to mute the scare. Once the world is frozen again, I take a bunch of deep breaths and get myself together. I'm breathing fine until I see who it is.

It's a man in a boring suit, black or dark blue depending on the light, and a white shirt and black tie. He has light brown hair parted neatly with gel. He looks like the kind of man you acknowledge as doing some sort of important job and then immediately forget when you look away. But if you don't look away—if you get a look at his face — then things change. He's bending down, so Karen hasn't seen it yet, but his eyes are completely black and his skin is as pale as snow.

I know this man. Agent Parsons. I know him because he was the one who came to me at the end of my life, thinking I had the bell. He would have killed me for it, had the cancer not killed me first. I didn't have the bell then, but Caroline did. And he tried to kill her instead. Owen took a bullet for her as she passed the bell to me. I rang it, and here I am today. But that doesn't change the fact that this fucker tried to kill Caroline. I spit at him, but it passes through him. I look down the hall again, and this time I see another figure. I'm not surprised. Agent Douglas always travels with Agent Parsons. The two of them are like dogs that lick each other clean of blood.

I should have known. I press play, my stomach in my throat.

Parsons takes his hand from his jacket pocket where he's been holding something. I know that move. That's a move the Circle uses because they often hold their crow totems in their pockets when they skip through space, but I took the agents' crows. I gave them to Caroline and Owen. And yet here they are appearing out of nowhere again. I rewind it several times. I see the telltale ripple. I can hear the *whoosh, pop*. There's no denying it.

Here's the problem: whatever he has in his pocket, it's no crow totem I've ever seen. I know every crow totem, and every member of the Circle that carries them, from Joey Flatwood all the way across the world and back again to Owen and Caroline. None of the crow totems are unaccounted for. They're using something else.

The Circle has been on the lookout for these two assholes for almost a year, ever since they jumped me at ABQ General while I was on my deathbed. Even though I call them agents, they're not really FBI agents. We figured out that much back at Chaco when the Navajo Police Department ran them down with the FBI but the feds had no record of them. Precisely who they are is still a mystery, even to me.

I've been watching them, too. Their souls are warped and hollow, but they still have them, and if you have a soul, I can find you. I made it a point to check in on them from time to time after I stripped them of their totems, just to make sure they weren't plotting again. They spend a bunch of time in libraries, searching old survey maps and flitting through old microform on creaky machines. They have no social life to speak of. They live in extended-stay hotels wherever they happen to be. They pack a single suitcase each with a second suit identical to the ones they always wear, a pair of spare white dress shirts, and several pairs of black socks and underwear. They meditate at night. At least, that's what it looks like they're doing. They don't drink. They don't chase women. They don't thug around. They're like strange monks. In short, they bored me. And I had a shitload of work to do and a new lifestyle to get accustomed to, so I admit it: I checked on them less and less.

Then one day they were just gone. Both of them.

I found their soul threads on the map, but when I walked to where they should have been in the living world, they weren't there. I waited. I walked a big perimeter, but I found nothing. I searched as long as I could, until I got another tug to get back to work. Four days later I found them again, and it was like nothing had happened—

same routine, same libraries, same old maps of new-world America and ancient Europe, same hotels. The next day they were gone again. This time for quite a while. But they always came back, until recently, when they disappeared for nearly a month. I knew it was too much to hope that they'd died, because I would know, but that's what it was like. Their souls were clouded and obscured on the map. Barely present at all. It was like they were dead.

But now here they are again, at least in replay. And they are both dramatically changed. I walk around Parsons, bent over and picking up Karen's chips, and I'm shocked at how white he is. His brown hair is turning ashen. His face is as white as milk, and thin, so thin you can see his veins through his skin. And they're black, too. Just like mine. The white skin, the black veins, it's what happens when you spend too much time phasing. I'm this way because it's part of my DNA now. With me, it's the new normal. Parsons looks alien. Like the kind of thing that would walk out of a deep cave. And that's when I figure it out. I can't find them because they're living in the thin world. Joey Flatwood had to medicate himself to near death to take the pain of all the phasing he was doing. These guys have taken it even further. And it's taken its toll on them. They look like mannequins come to life.

I watch as she stumbles and rights herself, still smiling, thanking Parsons for his help and cursing her clumsiness. Until she sees his face. Then she screams. Or tries to. In a blink, Douglas is there, phasing down the hall right up into her face, his dead-white hand jammed over her mouth as he pulls her into him, clipping her struggles. Parsons reaches into her purse and finds the room key she was about to use and opens the door. The two of them walk inside her room. Parsons looks both ways down the hall, and satisfied nobody sees them, he closes the door behind them.

I follow the agents into the room, Douglas with his hand over Karen's face, Parsons calmly walking in after him. Douglas looks like an albino pit bull. His jaw is locked. The veins of his forehead are black as ink, and they bulge from the skin. I have a sick feeling in my stomach as Parsons opens his jacket and reaches into his breast pocket. Douglas lets go of Karen's mouth to reach into his own jacket. Karen pulls in a breath to scream. I don't want to watch whatever is going to happen, but I know I have to. I steel myself and cringe.

Then they all vanish.

I scream in the empty room. I stop the tape, rewind, play again. But it's no use. If they phased, I should still be able to see an echo of them, but they've gone entirely. I swirl open the soul map thinking maybe I can follow a trace of them there, but the soul map is in real time. No rewinding allowed.

They're gone. And they took Karen with them. But I know Karen came back. She had to, to meet me on the bench. So I fast forward. The lights of the Strip blink in triple time outside the big bay window of the hotel room. The world continues to turn. And then Karen snaps back, along with both agents.

Karen falls to the floor. Douglas picks her up and tosses her onto the bed. Both agents step back and watch her, like scientists might a monkey in a cage. Cold, clinical, detached. Karen looks lobotomized. Her eyes are open but unseeing. And that's where she dies. Unmarked and unbloodied but severed at the soul. Parsons looks at Douglas and nods. Douglas smiles. I realize that the two of them haven't spoken a word since they arrived. Somehow it makes what happened here even more unnatural.

Karen's soul leaves her body and wanders through the hotel room in a lost zigzag. She looks around the room as if she's never seen it before. The agents can't see her, but she can see them. Still, she doesn't recognize the men who killed her. She seems embarrassed and tries to start up halting conversations with them before losing her train of thought. Dazed, she walks through the door and out of the room, on her way to the bench outside where I'll find her. I let her go. It's the agents I'm interested in now. They have something that is allowing them to phase more powerfully than anything I've encountered with the Circle. Worse, they have some sort of weapon. A weapon that strikes at the soul. I get up close to them, trying to find any clue, but whatever it is, it's hidden from me. It's infuriating. I swipe at the imprint of the agents in frustration, but my hands pass right through them.

I let the rest of the encounter play out, fuming at the two men who don't seem like men anymore. They look at each other and seem ready to bounce out, but then they both freeze. Their black eyes darken a shade more, like a dollop of ink has been dropped onto their irises. They are frozen for a moment as if hypnotized, and when they snap out of it they blink rapidly and look to each other.

Parsons speaks his first words of the night, and they chill me to the bone.

"The bell has been found," he says. And he smiles. He's so white it makes his teeth look yellow. Douglas nods. They both reach in their jacket pockets and vanish.

6

OWEN BENNET

Since you're already thinking it, I might as well just say it. I'm kind of pathetic when it comes to women. Or, at least, I'm kind of pathetic when it comes to Caroline, who is the only woman I can remember ever feeling this way about. Like I have this raging, five-alarm fire in my chest. Like my heart has at least second-degree burns, inching every day toward third-degree classification, and perhaps it ought to be admitted to the Burn Intensive Care Unit.

What I can't quite manage to do is fan the fire in her direction, see if maybe she can catch a similar spark.

I apologize for that dose of saccharine. Earlier I said *kind of* pathetic. I think maybe we can throw out the modifier here altogether and just go with *pathetic*. But you probably already figured that out when you realized that I'd been traveling across the country right next to her, side by side, for basically a year, and I still sleep on the modified sofa/table/couch in the main room of the RV. That's a pretty big tip-off that I've crossed from a "romantic candidate" into the friend zone. *Really, really* good friends, to be sure, but you can take your *reallys* and shove them up your ass.

How was that? That was pretty good. That was some genuine anger. I've been trying to back out of the "nice guy" corner that I seem to have painted myself into. I know Caroline doesn't like nice guys. I mean, she likes them, because who doesn't, but she likes them in the way you like your favorite grocery bagger at the supermarket. He's just so nice. What a *pleasant* guy he is. Then you're in the parking lot and you've already forgotten him.

What Caroline *really* likes—I would go so far as to say *loves*—is darker guys, with devil-may-care attitudes, who are willing to risk it all, even to die, to make things right. I know this because that's what Ben Dejooli was. Or is. I don't know for sure where he stands cosmically. Which is another thing. How am I supposed to compete with an ageless demigod who can walk the space between life and death and who singlehandedly has the power to set your soul free? How the hell am I supposed to compete with that? I'm an oncologist. Which I thought was pretty cool until I tried to stack myself up against a demigod. Honestly. Ben and I are basically opposites. We even look opposite. He's this swarthy Navajo badass, and I'm a lanky, freckled redhead.

This is the stuff I think about when Caroline thinks I'm concentrating on the road. We've been cruising west at a consistent seventy miles per hour on I-20 on our way to the Texas border. I like to establish myself in the right-hand lane and really own it. We're following crows, which sounds insane, but if you had the crow totems that we have, you'd know it just feels right to be going this way. Caroline sits in the big captain's seat on the passenger side in her comfy clothes, which she likes to call her "loungeabouts" like the RV was some east coast estate. I love it. It's things like this that stoke the five-alarm fire.

Her feet are up on the dash, and she's flipping through a magazine we picked up at our last six-hundred-dollar fill-up. She'll read it until she starts to feel carsick then put it in the pile with the rest.

When she jumps a little in her seat and drops the magazine, at first I think it's because she's about to vomit, but then I feel it myself. My pocket is hot. My front pocket. Where I keep my crow totem.

"What the hell?" I slap at my pants like an ember dropped there. I swerve the boat a little bit and get a honk from somewhere to my left before I right us again. The crow is still hot. Not burning, but definitely hot. Caroline has hopped up and is dancing in place. She must really be feeling it. Her loungeabouts are pretty thin, which I also love, but that's beside the point. She starts to reach in her pocket.

"No! Don't touch it! You'll phase right out of the RV! Hold up, I'm pulling over."

I flick on the hazards and shift into a long, slow stop on the shoulder of an exit for a town I've never heard of just east of the Texas border. I'm tapping my leg the whole time. Caroline bunches the cloth of her pants around the crow like she's carrying a hot skillet with nothing but a napkin. I see the outline of the totem. It's pulsing with rich, yellow light.

"What should we do?" she asks. "What does this mean?"

"I don't know," I say, holding my own crow off my leg over my jeans. "Your guess is as good as mine. But *something* just happened."

"I mean, should we phase? What if it's like a page or something?"

"We could try." I'm not crazy about it though. Big Hill's warning to stay clear of the thin world comes back to me. I know Caroline remembers, too, because she's furrowing her brow in that way she does when she's weighing options.

"It's really hot, Owen."

"Well, you could take off your pants," I say before I realize what I'm saying. She cocks an eyebrow at me, but I think there's a hint of a smile there nonetheless.

"It's definitely trying to tell us something," she says.

I see my window. Mr. Nice Guy would most likely advise against phasing. It's the sober, rational thing to do given Big Hill's warning, a man who is infinitely more versed in the crow totem than the two of us are.

But Mr. Nice Guy bags Caroline's groceries.

"On the count of three. Ready?" I say. She looks at me with wide eyes then nods. "One, two... three!"

We both grab our burning crows at once and blink out of the living world and into the thin world. The colors bleed into harsh basics, like an over-touched photograph. The sounds of the world are dulled and distant. Things move at strange speeds. Time seems more arbitrary here, less consistent. I have a theory about time in the thin place. The closer you get to the world of the dead, or wherever departed souls go, the less time matters. There, theoretically, it doesn't matter at all.

The pain is slight, at first. The shock of the color switch and the time dilation is more staggering than the initial pain, but the pain is there. When we get our feet under ourselves, it's more apparent. It's like a slow pinch, but you can't quite source it. That's because it's not on your body. It's deeper, past muscle and bone. I reach out to touch Caroline's shoulder.

"You all right?" I ask. My voice sounds like I'm talking through a tin can phone, but she nods.

"This place sucks," she says, looking around in distaste. "We're not supposed to be here. The living should stay in the land of the living."

My sentiments exactly, but only nice guys call uncle. "The other Circle members use this place as a tool. So should we. We're just not used to it yet, that's all. C'mon, let's walk." I hold out my hand, and she grabs it. Then we take a step. We walk a city block in a blink. We stop again and get our bearings. We've left the RV well behind us. The first time we tried this we ended up hundreds of feet from each other as well and couldn't right the distance in the thin world. We had to phase back and walk it out in real time. Now we hold hands. I don't mind it. I don't think Caroline does either, honestly, if for no other reason than she doesn't want to skip off alone in this place.

The pinch is getting stronger. Was it always like this? I'm no Circle pro or anything, but I've phased a few times. It feels like it's getting worse.

"Does the color here seem off to you?" Caroline asks, echoing my thoughts. "I mean, it's always kind of sepia, but doesn't it seem darker..." And just then a black hand rips through the shimmering wall of the thin world and latches on to her hand, the one that grasps her crow. It grips her so that Caroline can't let go and phase back. For a second she stares at it like you might stare at a bad cut in the seconds before the pain hits, then she starts screaming. She can't scream long, though, because a second hand rips through space and clutches at her neck. She sputters. It all happens in an instant.

I try to pull her my way with the hand that still holds hers, but it's no use. The dark arms jut from thin air, but they're anchored somewhere else, somewhere beyond the thin place, and they won't budge. In fact, they're pulling Caroline backward, and the air is bulging around her, straining with surface tension.

"Let her go!" I scream, but I'm trapped myself. I need a free hand, but I don't dare let go of my crow. I'd phase out, and I could lose her forever.

I swing under the arm that holds her neck and brace it with my shoulder, trying to break the grip. I gasp at the touch of the thing. It sets my heart racing with a rising panic, like it's an amphetamine of some sort. I'm overcome with feelings of disorder and mayhem, but I refuse to let it take her. I strain against the hand, against the panic, and against the boiling of my blood just from being in this godforsaken place. Tears come to my eyes because I know I'm going to lose her. I look over at her, and she's turning blue. She tries to shake her head at me to go.

"I won't leave you!" I scream through gritted teeth, and I feel the walls of the reality of this place start to give.

But then there's a pop, loud and clear, and I know someone is there with the two of us. At first he's a blur—he seems to move as fast in this place as we would phasing through the living world. He coasts on a wave of momentum and slams his fists into the smoky black arm around Caroline's neck. I hear a crack, and the arm caves in. The long, thin fingers fog away, and Caroline jerks her neck forward, sucking in a monster breath.

The third man slides behind Caroline and flips to the other side of the hand that holds her crow. He grabs it as he would the hilt of a sword and wrenches it around and over his head. It disjoints, and he moves to snap it over his knee, but it flits back through the wall and disappears, leaving only a trace of black smoke behind it. Caroline drops to her knees, the crow tumbles from her fist, and she blinks back to the land of the living. I follow her a second later.

Caroline is on her knees on the hot concrete of the shoulder of the highway, and she's vomiting. I drop to my knees myself and suck in gulp after gulp of warm Louisiana air. I reach for Caroline. She's shivering uncontrollably. She leans back and sits on the concrete and reaches back for me. I realize I'm shivering, too. And my hands have that soft-blue coloring that I always associate with cyanosis from hypothermia.

"Told you... that place... sucks," Caroline says, and before she can say another word, there's a *whoosh, pop,* and knowing my luck it's nothing but trouble. All I want to do is lie down on the shoulder of I-20 like a dead armadillo, but I force myself to stand.

I nearly faint with relief when I see Joey Flatwood standing there.

"It doesn't suck," he says, in his quiet Navajo accent where he emphasizes every word carefully. "It's getting taken over."

Flatwood repositions his own crow, which he wears around his neck, to rest over a leather collar piece he's fashioned to keep it from his skin. Then he reaches a hand out to Caroline. She takes it and allows herself to be pulled up. "It's good to walk afterward," he says. "Takes the chill away."

Flatwood looks like he's done a lot more than walk since we last saw him. He's bulked up at the shoulders, and now he fills out his leather jacket. He wears jeans and heavy black boots that buckle at the side. His face filled out, too, but in that angular, Indian way that looks cut from flint. His hair is long but no longer greasy. It's braided with beads and two big black crow feathers that flash in the sun.

He looks like a complete badass, naturally, and while I could weep with joy from seeing him, I can't help but realize that the Indian version of James Dean kicked the hell out of whatever was holding Caroline hostage in the thin place and saved the day for both of us while I was stuck to her hand like some sort of awful figure skating partner. And he's Ben's best friend, no less.

Flatwood is bleeding at the knuckles, but he ignores it. "I thought Big Hill told you not to walk the thin world. It's not safe. The walls are breaking down." He says this without judgment, only as a statement of fact, in that uniquely Navajo way that reminds me of being back at

Chaco. And for a fleeting moment, as the cold still seeps from me, it makes me wish I was still there. In my nine-to-five job. A couple days a week at the Navajo clinic. Living safely behind a curtain of my own.

"The crow totems were burning," I say. "We thought it might be a call of some sort. That's why we phased."

Flatwood turns to me, his eyes alight. "So you felt it too! I swore it was burning, but back in my using days, everything burned. I thought it was ghost pain. I didn't get my hopes up."

Caroline still holds his hand, unsteady. She looks like she's been locked in a walk-in freezer. Her teeth are chattering.

"Hopes up?" I ask. "What's going on?"

"The totem flares when the bell's been found. There's a new Keeper. A young boy. Somewhere in the plains of Texas. I don't know where. Those are the visions the crows have given me." Once he's sure Caroline is steady, he gently withdraws his hand. He looks between the two of us, his brown eyes flashing. "You must go to him. You must protect him. That is your part."

"Us?" Caroline says, wheezy. "Joey, we can't even take two steps in the thin place without nearly getting killed. You should be the one going."

"She's right," I say, even though it burns me. "I mean, look at us. We're rookies. And... look at you."

But Joey Flatwood shakes his head adamantly. "No. You are the Walker's chosen ones. And I am meant to be elsewhere. I have another calling."

"It can't be more important than protecting the Keeper," Caroline says.

"Everything that is done has one importance," Flatwood says simply. I try not to roll my eyes. "You must go to the Keeper, and I must rally the Circle."

"Why?" I ask.

"Because the time is coming when we must fight to keep this world as it is. To hold the balance," Flatwood says, nodding to himself. He tucks one feather-braided strand of hair behind his ear. "Now go. The crows above will lead you. But beware. The crows above are seen by all. Those that would help the Keeper and those that would hurt him."

He looks at both of us one last time then grasps the lanyard that holds his totem. He flips it so it rests against the bare skin of his chest and phases out of existence. Caroline and I are left alone.

We walk back toward the RV, nearly a half mile behind us, not daring to touch our totems again. We're quiet the whole time, walking side by side, but I sneak glances at Caroline the entire way. She looks forward, her eyes unfocused. I keep expecting to have to catch her, she looks so weak.

Once we strap in the front seats of the RV, she lets out a deep breath. The engine roars to life, and I feel the first real measure of comfort since we phased. I wait for an open lane and gun it, and just like that we're back on the highway. As if in answer, a flock of crows soars above us, flying in our direction hundreds of feet in the air like a black wisp of smoke.

After nearly half an hour on the road, I turn to Caroline. "What is it?" I ask. "What did you see?" Because I know she is attuned in ways others are not. I know she sees things in people, sees what sort of mood they project. I also think she can see what state their soul is in. That is both her blessing and her curse.

"The hands," she says. "They... gave me pictures, in my mind." She turns to me, and her eyes are frightened, her nose runny from the cold she's just been through. "I don't know how to explain them." She looks out the window, gathering her thoughts. "They were pictures of chaos. There was nothing else to them. Just chaos."

GRANT ROMER

I like having a crow for a best friend. I know it may seem weird that I could get a best friend so quick, but if you knew Chaco you wouldn't think so. He's an easy bird to like. With the guys up the street like Otis and his crew, you never know if what they are saying is true when they say they are my friends. I asked Otis once, and he sort of nodded and said *yeah* but in the way you say *yeah, why not?* Like he ain't got nothing better to do at the time.

With Chaco it's not like that. Chaco never lies. That was one of the first things he told me. I asked him why, and he said it's 'cause he has no reason to. Lying is a human thing. I believe him because when he says he's my friend, it sounds *heavy*. Like it has the weight of a million years behind it. More than that, even, because Chaco says he came around when the world came around. He wouldn't say to meet up to ride bikes and then ditch me. Things like that don't matter to a super old bird. He's got other things to care about. And the most important one of them is me.

My most important thing is supposed to be the bell. I know the bell is important, but I don't quite know if it's my *most* important thing, because I think my real most important thing is still Pap. I told

Chaco this, and Chaco nodded and said he understood but that in time I'd come to see just how much the bell means.

I haven't told Pap about Chaco yet. I haven't told him about the bell, either, which I keep around my neck on a metal chain. At first I was afraid that the chain might break while I'm on my bike or rolling around in my sleep or something and it'd fall off and roll away and I'd never find it again, but Chaco says once the bell is found, it's never lost. It can only be taken or given. That makes me feel a little better and a little worse. I don't want anyone to take the bell from me, and I don't think the bell does either. It sits in this little pit in the middle of my chest that seems meant for it. It hardly moves. It's not hot or cold anymore, and it hardly weighs anything, but I know it's there all the time. It feels *right*, like a brand-new fifty-cent piece or a smooth river stone.

When I get home that night, the night I find the bell, Pap knows something is up. But I just can't lay it all out for him. I don't think I have the words. He asks me point-blank, "You didn't go back to that cemetery, did you, son?"

"No," I say. Which is true. But it's also not true because what happened at the cemetery and what happened when I found the bell are connected. I know it. But I don't know how, so I just sit quietly and stare at the ground. I want to look at Chaco, who is outside in the trees, but I make myself look up at Pap. He looks so tired. His shoulders seem to disappear more and more every day, like he's slumping into himself. He watches me for a second and then nods.

"Pap, are you okay?"

He smiles at me and comes over to me and pats the back of my head, and I breathe in the scent of wood and oil and hard soap.

"Of course, son," he says. "Just got a long week ahead in Lubbock. That's all. Gotta turn in a bit early. Food is in the ice box."

He pads off to his room and softly closes the door, and I know he's not telling me the truth. He's not lying, exactly, but I know he's not *okay*. I know he misses Mom and Dad, and he misses his shop in the garage and the big pile of raw wood he has in there that's doing nothin' but sitting under a dusty tarp. All these things make him sad.

When I open up the refrigerator, I see a small meal of fried chicken. Not the big bucket, just a few chicken strips, enough for me. Not enough for him. I wonder if he didn't eat dinner so that I could eat dinner, and it makes me want to run into his room and throw the chicken strips at his head and curl up next to him in bed at the same time. He's the one that has a job. He needs the food. And if he works just so I can eat, then there's only one thing I can do: I gotta work so he can eat.

I got a plan.

Back when Mom and Dad were alive and I wanted to buy my bike, I didn't have enough money. I thought Pap might give it to me because he was always giving me a secret five bucks here and there, so I went to him and I showed him the ad in the paper and I asked him for it.

"You know how much this is?" he asked me.

I hadn't looked. I just saw the picture and wanted it so bad that when I ripped it out it tore the price off, so I shook my head. Then he asked how much I had, and I told him almost fifteen dollars. Which was all I had in the world, and I'd saved from Christmas and the last few times he'd handed me a five. Pap said that wasn't enough, which I remember almost had me in tears since I was smaller then and I cried more. But Pap said, "Hold on a minute, now. If you're willing to work for it, I'll make sure you get it." So that's what I did. I set up a stand and sold water and pop from a cooler on Cotton Flat Road, which is a pretty crowded street. That was during May and it was starting to get real hot again, but it was still early enough that people were surprised by the heat and didn't bring water or Cokes along on their errands. I sold a lot of Cokes that day. Made nearly forty bucks. I took it to Pap. He nodded and patted my head with his four fingers, and the next day I had the bike at my house. I'm pretty sure the bike was more than forty bucks, or even fifty bucks, but that was when Mom and Dad were alive and Pap still had some cash, and so I think he spotted me. He ain't never called me on it neither. Now I think it's time I spotted him.

I take my last ten bucks and go down to the gas station and buy two twenty-four packs of different types of Cokes and haul them back in a cooler I strap to the back of my bike. Chaco watches my back the whole way. He seems nervous. He says I shouldn't be out running around because things on his end—the world of talking animals and dead people—are pretty noisy. But I keep thinking of Pap going to bed hungry, and it stings me in the heart. If I sell all the Cokes, I'll make my ten bucks back plus maybe another forty bucks. And it's hot out today. I think I'll sell them all. Especially because I have a great idea, which is to post up near the four-way stop into the man camp and sell to the truck caterpillar. That's a guaranteed crowd.

I dump the two packs of Coke into the roller cooler then take the whole ice tray out of the refrigerator and dump it all over the Coke. I rope the cooler extra tight to the back of my bike seat. I test ride for a few feet. If I go slow, I'll have no problem.

Chaco lands on my handlebars and nearly tips me over as I'm riding.

"What's going on here, my man?" Chaco asks, walking back and forth until he settles right in the middle.

"I can't see when you sit right there," I say. He hops up and onto my shoulder and then my head.

"That's not helping either."

"Remember how I told you to lay low? This isn't laying low." I can see by Chaco's shadow that he's looking everywhere at once.

"Pap didn't eat anything last night. He gets paid at the end of the month. That's two more nights he might not eat, or might have scraps 'cause he feeds me first. Well, I ain't havin' that."

Chaco looks down at me, and I grit my teeth because all of a sudden my throat is clenching up because I'm mad-sad again. "He looks so old and sad, and I don't want him to be that way anymore, but I think it's too late because what's done is done and Mom and Dad ain't coming back, and I'm not old enough to get a real job yet so this is what I got." It sort of pours out of me the way the tears usually do, but because the words came out first the tears stay in and I feel a bit better. Chaco is still looking at me. Then he sort of fluffs himself down on my head.

"Are you hugging me?" I ask, smiling.

"Yeah," Chaco says.

"Bird hugs are funny."

"Just go with it."

"Thanks, Chaco," I say, after a few seconds of riding.

"Well, a man's gotta do what a man's gotta do. Or so I hear. But you promise me a couple of things. First: don't sell to the weird guys. You know 'em. I know 'em. If they look weird or it doesn't feel right, you back away. Second: they put the cash in the can, you toss them the Coke. Cool? You're not getting up near anybody." He leans over and looks down at me with that cocked-head stare that I think means he's being really serious.

"Jeez, Chaco. Nobody's gonna kidnap me in the middle of the day with all those people all around." But actually I'm getting kind of nervous. I was just trying to make some extra cash, but the way Chaco is talking makes me think I'm going into enemy territory or something.

"You haven't seen what I've seen, man," Chaco says. "We got a deal?"

"Deal."

The four-way stop outside is just like I expected. Jammed up and noisy with creeping trucks going back almost as far as I can see. It's hot and humid, and all the heat from the trucks makes it worse, plus the whole place smells like exhaust. Perfect for sellin' Cokes. I chain my bike to a tree nearby and put up my sign, and I'm not set up for five minutes before I get my first beep—a big silver eighteen-wheeler with the round back that looks like a medicine pill and means it's carrying water or oil. I glance at Chaco, who sits in the shade of the tree, high up where he can see everything. He doesn't tell me anything or try to fly out or stop me, so I go up to the passenger door. The driver reaches over to push it open. He's a big fat guy wearing an old T-shirt with the state of Texas on it and some faded words I can't make out. He looks all right.

"You got Diet Coke?" he asks.

"Yessir."

"How much?"

"Dollar for one."

"No shit?" He starts laughing then checks the line through his windshield. He won't be moving far anytime soon.

"Pretty steep, boy. But you got the best of me. Maybe I should go into the roadside pop business. I'll take two."

I toss him the cash can. He seems to know what to do with it, plopping two bucks in. He tosses it back, and I dig around for two Diet Cokes, which I toss up to him. He catches them both then cracks one open. "Cheers," he says. Then he idles on another ten feet, and I go back to my stand.

I try not to grin because I need to look all business, but already that's two bucks I made off of cans that cost me maybe a quarter each. Things are looking good. As soon as I pocket the cash, I get another beep. Then another. I get to each of them in turn. One's a skinny younger guy, and the other is a big army guy, but they both look all right, too. The Army guy gives me two bucks for one Coke and says to keep the change. Then there's a bit of a break, but soon enough another beep. I keep tossing Cokes, and in about an hour I'm over halfway done. I got seven Cokes left and thirty-five bucks in my pocket. That's a lot of fried chicken.

I take a break and pull my stand into the shade under Chaco's tree and lean back against the trunk. I wipe my face with my shirt, and it comes away like a mask of sweat.

"You all right down there?" Chaco asks.

"Yeah," I whisper back. "Almost empty."

"That's pretty good. What say we pack it in?"

I look up and try to find him in the shadows, and when I do, I see he's out as far as he can be while staying in the shade, away from eyes. He's not looking at me. He's watching the skies. I follow his gaze, and I can see why. A whole mess of crows are on the horizon. And more still even farther out, like thin black lines of pencil. They're coming in waves.

"Wow," I say. "What's with all the crows? Is that... are they bad?"

"No," Chaco says. "They just sense a disturbance, that's all. But whatever got them riled up could be bad news. Plus, they're basically pointing a huge finger down at us right now."

Before I can ask more, I hear another beep. I step out from under the tree almost on instinct, looking for the truck it came from. One last sale and then we're off.

"Hey, hombre. How about we let this one be?" Chaco says, his sharp black head flitting from the sky to the row of trucks. I get the beep again, and this time I see where from: a shiny white truck a little larger than an ice cream truck about five spaces back. It looks brand new. I take another step forward, and just then it's like the bell takes a step backward, like it's trying to burrow into me. It doesn't hurt, but it feels heavy, and it makes it hard to walk. I clutch at it, and as I do the truck swims around in my vision. It goes from brand-new to hazy and milky, like an old faded picture of a new truck. I blink, and the picture is gone. But I know something is wrong.

"Yeah, we oughta get outta here," I start to say, but my words are slow. I can't look away as the door rattles open and two men jump out. They wear black suits and black sunglasses, but their skin is whiter than the truck. One stands tall, and the other is sort of hunched over with his hands out. Even their brown hair is faded, like their heads were dusted in powder.

They both take off their sunglasses, and their eyes are like black marbles. I know because they're looking right at me. When they see me, the eyes widen, but they're still black all through. I try to run, but my feet don't seem to be working like they should. Everything feels muddled. I look up for Chaco, but I don't see him. That's when I really get scared.

The two men look at each other, and the tall one nods at the thicker one, who pops his neck back and forth and disappears. There's a *whoosh, pop*, and then he's inches from me, his hand out like a claw going for my neck. This close, I notice his skin has black veins and that a turquoise glow comes from underneath his jacket, but all I can really see are his eyes. They say one thing: *I am going to kill you.*

His long fingernails brush my throat, but that's as far as they get. A river of black pours out of the sky, and wings rush all around me.

All I hear is the sound of a million feathers along with a fast clapping sound as the birds slam into the man. He staggers back, punching at them with his fists, but it's no use. For every one he hits, ten more are behind. The man roars like a bear, raging forward, and he almost gets to me until one crow, my crow, the biggest crow of all, passes right over my head and rakes him with talons as big as your finger. The man's head snaps back, and Chaco takes a strip of his face with him as he circles up and around for another go, but the man has already disappeared. In a blink he's back with the other guy by the truck, one arm over his eyes.

"Let's go!" Chaco says to me, flapping in front of my face, and it's like the birds are part of him. They flow through and around him like water, like they're his wings. "They will buy us time!"

I flick off the cooler hitch, hop on my bike, and tear away, not even looking behind me, not even caring about the seven Cokes. Chaco is above, just in my sight. More and more birds are whipping by us, all going back at the two men. I try not to think how each beak is as sharp as a razor and missing my face by inches, but none of the crows touch me. Not even a feather. I only feel the wind from their passing, and I try to focus on following Chaco. He's like a living GPS, ticking right and left just before I get to turns so I know where to go. I pump the brakes to skid into turns. I pedal so hard I kick up gravel behind me. The wind brings tears to my eyes, and I remember how it did the same thing back at the graveyard when I listened to the rows of gravestones fly by. That seems like a lifetime ago now.

It took me almost thirty minutes to get down to the four-way stop sign, but it feels like I get back home in about a minute. I stash my bike in the bushes where nobody will see it and open up the front door and turn around and actually lock it, which I almost never do, and then I run into my room and squeeze in the small space between my bed and the dresser. I haven't squeezed in between there since the days and weeks just after Mom and Dad died. It's a lot tighter than it was then, but I still fit. A few seconds later there's a light tapping on the window above my head. I look up and see Chaco there, taking up most of the window.

"You all right in there?" he asks.

I shake my head.

"You hurt?"

I shake my head again.

"You scared?" he asks after a minute.

I nod.

"You wanna talk about it?"

I shake my head. I just want to sit here for a second and hug my knees.

"D'you, uh... You want me to leave you alone?"

I tilt my head up to look at him, and I see him looking down at me. His eyes are sad. I didn't think it was possible for bird eyes to be sad, but his are. I shake my head again, hard this time. He sort of fluffs up, and when he settles again his eyes are less sad.

"All right then. I'll just stay right here, okay? Sometimes you need to sit and chill in the corner for a bit. I get that."

And that's where Pap finds me when he comes home that night. Still sitting in the corner, my knees to my chest. He calls my name a few times, and I call back but it sounds weak and like a baby, so Pap opens my door really slow.

"Grant?" he asks, switching on the light. He looks around until he finds me, then he's quiet for a second, hard hat in hand. "Are you all right, son?"

Everything wells up inside me then, and it's like my head is a full bucket of water that tips over, and for some reason all I can think to say is, "I left the cooler and my Cokes," and then I start crying. I cry so hard it's completely silent. Pap gets down on one knee, then both knees, and then he sits down, and then he takes one of my hands from where it clutches my legs and he presses it between both of his hands, and they're cool and rough and clean. After a minute, it calms me down enough that I can talk again.

"I have a friend who's a bird," I say. I don't know why I say it. I'm tired of holding things from Pap. I never want to hold anything from him again.

"I had a lot of friends like that too when I was your age," Pap says.

"I wish some of them had stuck around, sometimes. They were so... I dunno. It's like they were real."

"He's still here," I say.

"Yeah?" Pap says, his voice gentle. "Where?"

"He's right out of the window."

Pap looks up. "Holy Jesus!" he says, and his hand shoots to his mouth because he never says that. I know I should be shocked, but it's so out of place and the look on his face is so open mouthed and wide eyed that I start to laugh.

"His name is Chaco. He can talk, but only to me I think." I watch Pap watch Chaco, and I smile more as Chaco does this funny little bow thing that smashes his head against the glass. "You think I'm crazy, don't you? And a liar," I say, looking down again. "Maybe I am. Maybe this is a big dream, and I was in that car too. I think that sometimes."

"No," Pap says quickly. "No. Never. You're not crazy, and you weren't in that car, thank God Almighty. And you sure as hell ain't a liar. Pardon my mouth tonight." His eyes are still on Chaco. "That is one big bird, son."

"He's probably my best friend. I met him when I found this bell." I take the bell out from under my shirt and hold it out to him. There's no ringer, which is good. It has a heavy shine to it. Not bright or polished. Heavy. I know Pap knows it ain't normal. He doesn't try to touch it or hold it, which I like. After a second, I tuck it back away. "But you can't tell no one about the bell, Pap."

Pap looks me square in the face for a second, and I can tell he's thinking hard, digging deep in his brain. He looks up at Chaco, who watches both of us with a flat gaze.

"Where'd you find the bell?" he asks me.

"In the desert past the man camp. Maybe a half mile in."

"There's the Wilmington rig out near there," Pap says, thinking. "They just moved the pad."

"Yeah, that's the one. Near there. How did you know?"

"Because that's a thin place," Pap says. "A place where things are different."

Above me, Chaco nods. "I knew it!" Chaco says. "I knew it! He's like you, my man!"

I look at Pap cockeyed for a second. "The graveyard is the same way."

"I guessed as much. That's why I told you to keep out. Those types of places, they ain't bad, exactly, but they ain't good either. They're just..."

"Thin," I say.

Pap nods.

"And sometimes thin places don't sit right with people who don't know about them. Now, I don't know nothin' 'bout no bell, but I do know this. You are a special boy. I think your father had some of it too, rest his soul. He didn't get the time to use it. But you're special too. You're like me. You can see the thin places. You feel them."

"They give me this feeling like I lost something there even though I've never been there," I say, and all of a sudden I feel this warm sense of relief. If you ever thought you were going crazy and then found out you weren't, you'd know what I feel like. If not, I just can't explain it to you. It's like something big breaks inside you for the better.

"But you saw something there today," Pap says, his face darkening. "Something scary."

I shake my head. "Not there. No. I saw it near the four-way stop on the road that leads to the camp. In the middle of the truck caterpillar. Two guys. But they weren't guys. They weren't even people like I've ever seen." I look up at Chaco, who is watching me carefully. "And I think they knew. I think they knew about the bell. And they wanted it *so bad*."

Chaco nods. "They did. I'm not gonna sugarcoat this because that's not what I do, so here's the truth. They've wanted that bell for a long time, and they're about the worst kind of thing you can imagine. Now that they know you've got it, they're looking for you."

"What do we do?" I ask, and my voice is quiet and mousey, and I think how strange it must be for Pap to hear a one-sided conversation like this. "If a million birds can't stop 'em, what can the three of us do?"

Chaco spreads his wings, and they shoot out past the edges of the window. "You're never as alone as you think, hombre. Remember how I told you that everyone could see all those crows in the sky? Well, there are people that are as good as those two are bad, and they saw the crows too. They're coming our way. We just gotta make sure it's them that find us first."

8

THE WALKER

All I want to do is go after the agents. I know they're headed for Grant and Chaco. Two pictures float in my mind. The first is Grant, still just a kid, clutching the bell like he just snatched a hundred bucks off the sidewalk, trying to figure out what it all means and what his part in it is. The other is Karen. Her soul butchered—hanging by a thread before its time. Grant could end up like that. And that doesn't sit well with me. The lifespan of a soul is written well before its thread is first spun. From day one, I took comfort in knowing that no matter what kind of fresh hell the agents want to rain down on the world of the living, no matter how thin the walls between the worlds have become, all of it was already written into the souls that play a part. It has been since they were created.

What happened to Karen is shaking that faith. It sure as hell looked to me like what happened to her wasn't part of any plan.

I step out of Vegas and into the soul map and start sifting through strands, looking for Parsons and Douglas again. Even if they were in the thin world and hidden from me, their last steps in the living world would at least give me a clue as to where they were. But when I walk the map in their footsteps, it's like a huge game of Twister. One foot in Vegas, the next in California, then to Arizona, then New

Mexico, and on and on. These guys are phasing on a level I didn't think possible, striding across entire states at a time. But this time I'm not going to lose them. I'm tracking them step-by-step when I get called away again. That's me, always on the clock.

I walk the map until I find the flickering soul, and again I stop. This one is all sorts of weird. If a soul is like a shining lightbulb, and a soul on its way out is a dim, flickering lightbulb, then this thing, if it can be called a soul, is a lightbulb that rattles hollow with a blown filament, just a shell now.

At times like this, where I get one weird call after the next, I really wish Chaco was around. But he has a new job now. And it's time I did mine. I swirl open the map and step into the living world.

I land outside of the Albuquerque foothills. Not all that far from Chaco Reservation, as the crow flies. I recognize Palomas Peak to the south and what looks to be a single bright streetlight illuminating I-85 to the distant west.

I'm looking at a man named Stanley Vickers. He's a sixty-seven-year-old accountant who lives and works in Plymouth, Virginia. He has two kids in their late thirties and is divorced going on ten years now. He died of a heart attack while sitting behind his desk.

I know all of this because I walked Stanley through the veil a week ago, back in Plymouth. And yet here Stanley is again, wandering around in the middle of nowhere, New Mexico.

"Stanley? What the hell are you doing here?"

Stanley seems to register my voice, but when he turns around and looks at me, his face has this slack blankness to it that reminds me of the paint huffers back on the rez. He weaves in place. His eyes slowly close then slowly open again. He doesn't answer me. I walk up to him. He doesn't move. I wave my hand in front of his face and snap my fingers a few times. His skin seems to mist away a little bit, as if he's not quite whole.

"Stanley. Hello? You in there, Stan?" I wave my hand above his head. No soul string there. I shouldn't be surprised since I snipped it myself barely a blink ago, but I snip all around him anyway just in case. His hair and skin swirl around as if they're losing consistency, but nothing else happens. No pop, no release. Whatever this thing is, it's not Stanley. I put my hands on my hips and look around the desert in the failing light.

"Where is that damn veil," I mutter, and sure enough, there it is, gliding toward us across the darkening plains in complete silence. It doesn't catch the light so much as poke a hole through what remains. It is entirely black, and it's as flat and dead as a lake surface. To be honest, it's scary as hell, so I do what I do to all things that I'm confronted with that scare me. I start cussing at it.

"Why don't you do your fucking job, huh? I cut the strings, you take the souls. Where is the major breakdown here..." But as it approaches, I trail off. This thing is nonresponsive. It's as much of the veil I once knew as this shell wandering the desert is Stanley Vickers.

"Are you gonna take him?" I ask, stammering a little. "Look at him. He's just standing there."

The veil doesn't move. I feel like I'm talking to a corpse. But of course it wouldn't recognize him. It already took him once. As far as the veil knows, Stanley is on the other side. It must have sensed the disturbance same as I did, but it's blind to Stanley. I see that I'm gonna have to walk him right up and push him through myself, which doesn't exactly excite me, because I don't want to get anywhere near the veil.

I go wide around Stanley and put my hand to his back. "All right, Stan. Time to go. Again." He shambles forward with my hand at his back like he's had ten too many shots at Sancho's Bar. My touch sinks partway into him, which is more than a little gross. I get unsettling flashes of his past life, pictures of his wife and his desk and his yard and a little yapping dog. It depresses me. I aim him at the veil and narrow my eyes.

"No funny business," I say.

Nothing.

I brace myself and shove Stan toward the veil. He falls through it like a rock through a black cloud. The veil doesn't rustle. Doesn't move at all. Which by now I'm finding more unsettling than when it was getting handsy. Then it pops out of sight.

Now, to figure out just what happened to my man Stan.

I open the soul map and find where I tucked Stan's soul string away. I mark it then step back into the living world and start to swipe back along the line of his life, just like I did with Karen. I backtrack a week. Before Karen met her end, before Grant found the bell. The world whips and blurs until I land in Plymouth, Virginia, once more. On the third story of a big brick corporate building, where he worked in a corner office. I recognize all of it. There's Stan, typing away at a spreadsheet but pulling every now and then at the collar of his shirt. His coloring isn't good. He keeps flicking the fingers of his left hand in and out, rubbing them. He feels constricted. His arm is going numb. Warning signs, Stan. C'mon, man... and there he goes. Mid-report. So it was a massive coronary that got him. He was alive one moment then dead the next, eyes still open, his face on his keyboard.

Enter: me. I watch myself step from the soul map and survey the scene. I take a point of pride at my response time. Less than thirty seconds.

I watch myself help Stan's soul up from his seat. He's a little disoriented, but he gets it faster than most. More than anything he's pissed off. He says he was voted most likely to work himself to death in high school, and here it actually fucking happened. "Can you believe that?" he asks me.

Sure can, Stan. Time to go.

He's still shaking his head, as if he's pissed off at his dead body, as the veil snaps him up. I watch myself look around the room for a minute then swirl open the map and step through. Job well done.

So here I am, watching the credit reel of a job I just did, which just so happens to be in a corner office with a dead, soulless body slumped over a keyboard. Nothing too out of the ordinary, but something has to happen to bring Stan back. So I wait.

I wait, and I wait, and I wait. I see the entire aftermath. The screaming secretary who stumbles across the body. The ambulance call. The medics that come in, take a pulse, and start prepping the gurney in no particular hurry. The office is in shock; they shut down early. I'm still there in a darkened room. Nothing strange yet. Nada. But somehow Stanley ended up wandering the New Mexico desert.

If it ain't happening here, maybe it's happening there.

I whip back to where I ran into Stanley in the foothills. It's still several hours before I find him, but all is quiet here, too. It occurs to me that he could have been wandering around for hours out here even before I came across him. Who knows where he started. I spin in a circle, but see no sign of him. Nothing but cracked earth, dry, brittle bushes, and barren desert trees. Nothing on the horizon but the mountains one way and the highway with its lone light in the other. I squint at it. Kind of strange for I-85 to have a streetlight this far out in the desert. Usually it's just you and your headlights.

In fact, the light looks way too green to be a streetlight. It's almost turquoise, actually. Like the crow totems...

I start walking toward it. Then I start running, which I don't need to do, since I'm still in replay mode, but I'm running nonetheless. Because I know this ain't gonna be good.

Sure enough, the "streetlight" isn't a streetlight at all. I'm deeper in the desert than I thought. The light is coming from the desert itself, pulsing with the time of a heartbeat. It's leaking from the mouth of a spillover that looks to have serviced a river system long gone dry.

I walk into the riverbed following the light, taking the subtle bends and turns slowly, until I stop at the mouth of a cave, where the light is strong. Ancient marks surround the opening. Marks I recognize as crows, some drawn with fingers and some chipped into the rock itself. Two large boulders look like they once guarded the entrance, but they've been pushed aside, the earth ripped beneath them. The mouth has been exposed for what I feel must be the first time in generations. The turquoise light pulses in low, measured time like the heartbeat of the earth. I run my hands over the rough cave paintings as I walk inside, and their paint takes on a turquoise sheen. I have a sudden flashback to crawling through the open mouth of the hogan when Gam performed my Evilway ceremony. This is like that. I feel like I am entering a sacred, delicate place. I pull my hand from the walls, afraid, even in this echo of events, that I'll kill something special just by intruding here. I feel strongly that nobody should be here. Ever.

But somebody is. I can hear a distant squealing sound, like nails on a chalkboard. I walk toward the sound, and every inch of me is on edge, even though I know that nothing can hurt me. But old habits die hard. It's the sound that's doing it. It's a scream. I can hear it more clearly with every step. Someone is being tortured.

I'm deep in the cave now. The only color is turquoise. It's like I'm walking through the middle of a crow totem that is being destroyed. The sound is too much, so I run toward it, if only to get it over with. To see what I came here to see and be done with it.

I follow the guts of the cave around a final bend, and it opens up into a low cavern. I skid to a halt on grainy rock. In front of me, Parsons and Douglas are naked, facing away from me. The white skin of their broad backs is thickly veined in black, and their hair is slicked with sweat. They are hacking at a vein of beautiful turquoise that feathers through the earth and widens just at their feet. It is the source of the light, so powerful now that it's nearly blinding. Perhaps it *is* blinding, to them. Perhaps it is what has turned their eyes black. This one vein pulses enough light to travel through the cave and sift over the riverbed, where it's still strong enough that I mistook it for a streetlight.

It's also screaming. With every blow the agents rain down upon it, it screams. Not like any animal or human might—not out of fear or anger—but out of pure pain. It hits me like a staggering punch to the gut, worse than any sucker punch I ever felt while I was alive. It's the ground itself screaming. This is a vein of the stuff that knits together the heart of the living world, and it's being ripped apart by the agents.

I lose it. I scream at them and run toward them, as if I could hammer away at an echo of the past. As if I could change what was written. The rational part of me knows I can't, but like I said, I'm a cusser.

"You fuckers! What are you doing? You're killing her!" I don't even know who *she* is, but I know they're killing her. I swing at their imprints. My fists pass through them. I fall to the ground against the vein and am washed in light like blood, and I feel like I'm gonna cry. But I'll be damned if I cry in front of the agents. Even in front of a picture of them. So I watch.

They're hammering at something inside the vein. Smashing away like children at a piñata. Their naked bodies are bright, and slick lines of sweat seem to trace their black veins and pool in the crooks of their skin. Their eyes are manic. They both step away at the same time, in total silence, heaving with the effort, and I see that they are each holding pure turquoise.

So this is the source of the totems. This, or something very like this. Although here the agents are taking what the earth freely gave to the Circle. I've held the totems. There is nothing of this scene about them. They are like nuggets of gold that unearth themselves and tumble down the rivers to be found. This is pure theft.

My point is proven when I get a better look at what exactly they are holding, because it sure as shit ain't a crow. Douglas holds a rough chunk of turquoise in an oiled rag. It's flat on one side, like a crude whetstone. Which makes sense because Parsons holds a knife. It's jagged and unfinished, but it's clearly a knife. The blade is maybe six inches long and roughly chipped, but it still glints sharply, just like an old arrowhead or traditional skinning knife. The hilt is turquoise too but wrapped in silver wire. Parsons holds it up above him and checks its edge. His eyes flash black when he sees it. He breaks into this horrid grin, and suddenly I know what the agents have been doing all this time when I should have been watching them like a dog. They were here, hacking away at the lifeblood of the living world. Fashioning some sort of weapon from the same material the crow totems came from.

And it all comes together for me. This was how poor Karen's soul was clipped before its time. What I do with my fingers, the agents have found a way to do with a knife. It's sloppy, it's ugly, and it's a perversion, but it works. I remember seeing the glow of the thing from beneath Parsons's jacket in the Vegas hotel room.

If I ate anything anymore, I think I'd have puked it up by now.

That's how wrong it feels to see a weapon crafted from the vein in front of me. As it is, I just get this phantom nausea, which is almost worse.

I have answers, but they just lead to more questions. Why would the agents care about cutting souls? If they wanted to kill someone, they could have saved themselves a lot of time and exposure to the turquoise vein if they'd just shot them. Something tells me getting rid of a dead body wouldn't be a problem for these two. And for that matter, how did they find this place? It was walled over, left in peace for generations. They must have been told by someone. A Circle member? Did we have a traitor in our ranks? If not, then that meant someone else out there knew about this place, this pulse point to the heart of our world, and told the agents. Neither option was good.

Which brings us back to our friend Stan. This shit-show ended up with a departed soul wandering the New Mexico desert. I want to know how.

I don't have to wait long.

Douglas is pacing around, psyching himself up for something. He flaps his arms back and forth like he's about to swim a few laps then slaps at his pecs, muttering to himself. He rolls his head around on his neck and pushes against the glittering rocks of the cavern, like he could move the cave. Naked and powder-white and crazed, he looks even more like a bulldog than before. Caged and prodded, ready to rip. Then Parsons hands him the knife. He takes it by the handle with both hands, and he raises it above his head, like he's about to drive a stake into the ground. But instead, he runs at the wall of the cavern, bellowing like a midnight train.

I scream with him as I watch him slam the knife into the rock wall, but it's not precisely in the rock; it's in the space before the rock. It's in the wall of the living world itself. Once it catches, Douglas rips down on it, practically hanging off the floor from the hilt. I can see the wall between the worlds slice open in a thin white line, like a paper cut before the blood seeps out. The knife moves about a foot downward, then it catches and sticks. Douglas screams in rage, and I smile grimly. He wanted more. They wanted to get through. I can see it in the disappointment in Parsons's face as he looks away in disgust.

Nice try, assholes. Maybe you could throw a ferret through that thing, but you ain't getting through. You're staying right here.

Douglas jerks the knife back out and hands it to Parsons, who takes it and covers it with an oiled cloth of his own. Parsons walks over to where he has laid his suit over a boulder. He carefully dresses himself, but I can tell his mind is racing. Douglas slams his fist into the rock wall of the cave a few times then puts his own suit back on, leaving blood marks on the cuffs. At the mouth of the cave, the agents pause. Parsons turns to Douglas, who still seethes.

"It was lazy and foolish to think we could get through using the knife alone," he says, his voice flat and slow. "There is only one way across to the land of the dead, and we have known it all along."

Douglas nods once.

"If the knife can cut a soul, it will serve its purpose on the other side. Let us test it, someplace where we will not be noticed. Someplace with enough chaos. Then we will redouble our efforts to find the bell."

Douglas nods again. Parsons reaches in his jacket and touches the knife then disappears in a flash. Douglas reaches in his jacket, touches the whetstone, and follows him a moment later. I know where they're going, of course. Off to Vegas, where Karen will be in the wrong place at the wrong time. Spoiler alert: the knife works.

Once again I'm left alone. I walk over to the vein they've ripped apart and try to see what damage they've done, but it's so bright it almost seems to buzz. I can't see anything but retina burn. When I blink my eyes clear again, I notice smoke drifting in from the cut Douglas made. More and more seeps through, and as it hits the air of this world it starts to change into something else. That something else is Stanley Vickers. He fumbles himself together and ends up sitting on the floor of the cave like he woke up there halfway through a ten-day bender. He gets up, completely lost. He staggers into the walls and falls on the floor and scrabbles his way toward the mouth of the cave and out.

I know how this one ends, too. Soon enough his presence will start to weigh on the soul map, and in a couple of days I'll feel it, too. I'll find Stan about a quarter mile from here, for the second time. He doesn't get very far. Poor guy.

But it's not Stan that worries me anymore. What worries me is that the agents somehow found a way to this place, and they have crafted a weapon that they intend to use in the land of the dead. I remember the way their black eyes glimmered in the hotel room, when they realized, somehow, that the bell had been found.

Parsons said there's only one way across, and he's right. It's the veil. The veil that has been rotting away as the knife was being ripped out of the earth. As the knife was being constructed, the veil was breaking down. The walls of the living world might hold up to the knife, but the veil sure as shit won't. Not now.

But Parsons knows as well as I do that he can't see the veil. Even if he's prepared to slice it open, he won't find it. As far as I know, the only way you can see the veil is if you're dead, or if you're me.

So that's it then. The puzzle is snapping together. The agents are gonna take the bell, then take my job, then take the knife across the veil, and by the time they do whatever evil shit they plan on doing over there, I'll be too dead to care.

9

CAROLINE ADAMS

The crows have led us to Midland, Texas. I guess Paris will have to wait.

It's probably for the best. I'm not really the Paris type. I've seen too much weirdness to sit and smoke at sidewalk cafes and get in touch with my artistic side. Someone who sees colored smoke coming off people might be a little too in touch with her artistic side as it is. Plus there's only so much espresso I can drink before my hands start to shake. And smoking kills you. Don't even get me started on that.

I chase the bell now. I deal with the thin space between the land of the living and the land of the dead. And I'm not bummed about it, either. When the chaos things tried to latch on to me and drag me into oblivion off the highway, sure, I had a moment where I thought maybe Paris might have been a better choice. How about you take a walk down the street and then have a surprise chaos hand rip through the fabric of the air and go after your jugular? You'd be doubting your direction in life as well. But once we got on the road and the highway was sliding under us and the summer sun was shining through the window of the RV onto the front seat, I started feeling better. I love road trips. When I was a kid and couldn't sleep,

Mom used to put me in the back seat of our old station wagon and drive around the neighborhood until I conked out. It still works.

Cruising aside, it's really Owen who calms me down. Warms me up. Helps bring me back. And he does it just by driving and giving me time. Although it helps that I can see the worry coming off of him in waves. He wants badly to comfort me. To reach out and touch me and reassure himself that I'm thawing out. There's another color on him, too. I've seen it in others, and it's different for each person. For Owen it's a rich cream, like foamed milk or melted white chocolate. It started to tinge his smoke when he took that bullet for me back at ABQ General Hospital, when he decided he'd rather I be around than him.

There's another word for that smoke. A four-letter word. But I don't even want to go down that road because that's just crazy, and it kind of breaks my heart to know Owen feels that way without him saying anything. It seems like a thing I shouldn't know before he wants me to know. It's a thing that's partly made real by speaking it. So until that happens, I try not to think about what his feelings mean for us. I also try not to think about how I'd answer him if he said it— and how my answer might disappoint him. Or worse, how my answer might snuff out that beautiful color of smoke. Because the truth is, right now I'm not in a position to love anyone back. I can't keep my own head on straight, much less bring someone else on board in the front seat of my life.

And now I'm starting to freak out again just sitting here. I'd say I'm seventy-five percent convinced that I'm not a complete freak of nature because of the things I see in people. That last twenty-five percent is still on the fence, though. And sometimes when I start to think too hard about it, my life gets thrown all out of whack and I wonder what the hell I'm doing with myself in an RV with a guy I like —and maybe *more* than like but maybe not—but definitely *need*. And a magic crow in my pocket. And a special bell in my sights.

Just lock me up and throw away the key. I wouldn't blame you.

I force myself to look out of the window at the desert floating by out on the horizon, and I feel a little better. I look over at Owen, and I feel even better still. I give a little fist pump. See? Old Caroline would have been paralyzed by these thoughts, her eyes open like some shocked baby who'd just tasted her first lemon, except that it would last all day and night and sometimes roll into the next day and affect every aspect of her life. Now at least I'm keeping my neurosis contained. That deserves a fist pump.

Sometimes I think if I could just make Owen realize how weird I am it might make him think twice about me. Pull over the boat and usher me out. But what I call weird, Owen thinks is special and unique. Which is true. But it's also weird. He's nice-guy under-standing about it when sometimes what I need most is for someone to call a spade a spade.

We hit the outskirts of Midland, and now all of a sudden it's stop and go. Then we find ourselves in a long line of semi-trucks, and we hit full-blown stop for thirty seconds at a time. I'm not sure who lives here, but I'm willing to bet it's not the type of people I see getting in and out of these trucks and walking around with huge packs on their backs. We idle next to a supermarket, and I see a big line of conver-sion vans in the back of the parking lot that look set up for the long haul. A couple of two-seater cars are even set up with chairs around them that don't look like they're going anywhere anytime soon.

"What's with all the people?" I ask.

"We're in the middle of oil country," Owen says. "I suspect these are people looking for temp work on the rigs, trying to cash in on the boom."

I try to think of the kind of life someone has to have to give it all up, head to Midland, and camp out in their car in a parking lot in the hopes of finding a temp job. It makes me feel like a complete bitch for freaking out about crossing the country in this boat of an RV with my own bed and a flat-screen TV and an endless supply of gossip rags. And Owen by my side.

"It's kind of hard to follow the crows when the crows are every-where. And they're acting very un-crow-like," I say, leaning over to look up and out of the windshield. The crows seem as confused about what they're doing here as we are. They're floating this way and that like ribbons in the breeze or hopping from tree to tree in mass movements of black. We're not the only ones taking notice, either. Stuck in standstill traffic, people are getting out of their cars and filming with their phones.

"This is as far as I think we're going to get for a bit. No sense in sitting in traffic for the sake of it," Owen says and turns off the road into the supermarket parking lot. He parks the RV in the far corner in the last free spot tailored for it. He kills the engine and sits back in his seat then looks over at me. I'm expecting a *what now*? What I get is "I think we have to move on instinct. If Joey Flatwood and Big Hill are right, the crow totems will lead us to the Keeper and the bell. Are you ready?"

I smile. There's the Doctor Bennet I remember from ABQ General and Chaco Medical Clinic. Maybe something about the attack in the thin place steeled him. Like he saw what he was up against, saw it hurt me, and it pissed him off.

"It's like a crow convention out there," I say. "The agents aren't stupid. If we followed the crows here, they can't be far away."

Owen nods stoically. "We better move our asses then," he says. I think about asking him exactly what he thinks the two of us can do to protect the Keeper—which the rest of the Circle apparently thinks Ben hand-picked us to do—when we can barely take two steps in the thin world without getting jumped. But I think that last line of his was sort of his action-movie exit, which is cute. So I let it go. Regardless, we're on a path, and that path has led us here. No point stopping now.

We start to walk east, leaving the long line of trucks behind. It's getting into the late afternoon; the sun is at our backs, but it's still sticky hot. The streetlights are flickering on one by one. Several crows sit atop each and watch us as we walk.

SOON WE'RE WALKING through the middle of the city. I take off my long-sleeved shirt and tie it around my waist. It's still hot even in a tank top. Owen looks like he's regretting his "forever in a button-down" policy. He looks sunburned, which you'd think would be impossible given that we stepped out of the RV at six p.m., but it's true.

"You feeling anything?" he asks.

"I dunno. Would I know it if I did?"

He shrugs and dabs at his forehead with the underside of his sleeve. "Maybe it's working already. Maybe it's been working this whole time. I should have brought water." He pauses, and we lean against the still-warm brick of an office building. I can see that he doesn't have a lot of faith in wandering around waiting for feelings, and I also see annoyance, probably because he knows that I know that he doesn't have a lot of faith. He looks at me sideways.

"You know that thing you're doing? Where you know everything about me? Can you turn it off?"

I look down, and my face reddens. "I'm sorry, Owen. Sometimes I wish I could." That's a lie. I love knowing things about people. So sue me. And when I look back up at him, I know he sees through me. He's sporting the *yeah, right*, cocked-eye look.

"It's okay," he says. "If I could know how you really feel about things, I'd be all over it." His smile ticks up one corner of his mouth.

"I know it sort of... puts you at a serious disadvantage in this whole"—I pass my hand between us—"this *thing* we've got going on here."

Owen lets out a breath. "Yeah. It's quite a *thing* we've got. Just awesome. You read me like a book, and I get to take it."

"I'm a mess," I say. "You, you're ordered. It's clear as day with you. If you could see what my smoke looks like... It's a cat's cradle with a million different colors of string. I'm all over the place."

It looks like this isn't what Owen wants to hear. In fact, he kind of looks like I'm pissing him off. Which is why it's good when a stream of crows thumps its way around the corner—the heavy flapping of their wings feels like it stirs the air around me. They're flying low, by the windows, and they look like they know what they're doing. So we run after them.

We run with the crows above us as long as we can, cutting across streets and whipping around corners. We run until my lungs burn, and then we run some more. I'm sweating like a pig. I taste salt. My eyes sting. And still we run. If I ever had my bearings to begin with, I'm totally lost now. Eventually we just can't keep up with the flock. The last one passes overhead, and Owen staggers to a halt. I've got serious sweavage, and my thighs are sticking together. I double over and put my hands on my knees to catch my breath. Owen does the same. After a minute, when I feel like I can talk again, I stand. The air doesn't move here. It's like we're in a bubble. If I could, I'd strip down. I look over at Owen and see that he's allowed himself to unbutton the top button on his shirt. I laugh. It's ridiculous. He's ridiculous. I kind of love it. He looks at me and laughs, too, which means I must look much more like a farm animal than I think. Then we both look for more crows.

They're circling high over a subdivision of small houses, most of them not much bigger than a double-wide trailer. They're flat and low but well kept and brightly lit. Most have dirt front yards, but some have that crazy, thick super grass out front that can live in this type of climate. My crow totem stirs, like when you have your phone in your pocket and it phantom buzzes on you.

"The bell is close," I say. "I think it may be in that group of houses somewhere."

Owen nods. I know he can feel it too. We take a step toward the neighborhood and then freeze at the same time. Something else is here. Something close that shouldn't be. It feels like a vague muscle cramp you can't quite rub away. The crow totems are rebelling against it like opposite ends of a magnet. Whatever is coming, it's like an anti-totem.

"We gotta move," I say, but Owen is already one step ahead of me.

10

GRANT ROMER

Pap moves his sitting chair into my room so I can sleep. The last thing I remember is hearing the rustling of the newspaper and the tinkling of the ice in his drink as he takes a sip, then I'm so tired that I just nod off.

I have this dream that I'm back at the graveyard by the floating pond. The 'thin place' is what Pap called it. Everything is still strewn about, and the light is all weird and off, like an old movie. There's nobody else there, just like at the real Fairview Cemetery. Pap said other people can't see the thin places like I can, but they can feel them. And if things ain't right with a thin place, it sort of bleeds over into the people around it, and sometimes they get up and go. In my dream, things ain't right. In fact, *things* are coming out of the thin place, smoky black things that are inching toward me and molding together into arms and hands. I turn around to run, and standing right there are the bone-white men with black eyes. They smile with their yellow teeth and grab at my chest where the bell is. It burns so bad that I bolt upright in bed and cry out.

Pap is by my side in a second. "It's all right, son. It's all right. I'm right here. Just a dream."

I clutch at my chest and nearly collapse back into bed. I feel the bell still there, and I'm relieved the dream things didn't get it. You're probably thinking that would be impossible, but you wouldn't be so sure if you'd felt how hot the bell is in my hand. That's when Chaco taps on the glass. And it's not a *how you doing?* tap. It's a quick, rapid-fire tap that I already know means we got trouble. I throw open the window.

I say, "The bone men—"

"They're almost here," Chaco says. "They're both phasing again. I don't know how. They must have found another way." He's puffing in and out really fast now, talking to himself and to me. I turn to Pap to translate, but one look from me and he seems to get it.

"Can we fight them?" Pap asks, balling his huge hands into rough fists. Chaco shakes his head in a blur. "They're much faster now than they ever were, and stronger. They let the thin place possess them. They're hardly even a part of the living world now. Our only chance is to run."

I turn to Pap. "We can't fight them," I whisper.

"Then we run." Pap says to Chaco, "Meet you round back." He grabs my hand, and together we cut through the house and through the back door. We don't even close it. We run over the lawn and through the back gate, and then we're running down the alleyway between all the houses before I even really wake up completely. I'm still in my PJs, even. I look above us and see Chaco like a dark drop of oil on the black sky.

"Where we goin'?" I ask.

"Camp," Pap says. "I figure if these guys are as bad as I think they are, only thing we can do is distract them and maybe lose them. Ain't nothin' more full of distractions than that damn camp."

Pap never liked the man camp. He told me once it was full of the new kind of field worker. He called them "cocky drunks who think they're oilmen." I remember it because Pap hardly says a bad word about anyone.

"They can't take my bell, Pap," I say. "Not the bone men, not the cocky drunks who think they're oilmen, not nobody. It's a really important bell." I clutch it in one hand as I run. I speak in whispers and pull up my pajama pants. I feel like a burglar in the night.

"I know. I don't know how, or why, but I get the same feeling from it that you do. That thing is more important than me, might even be as important as you. And you're about the most important thing in the world." Pap is wheezing a bit, and I try to slow up so that he can catch his breath, but he just pulls me along faster. My heart is jackhammering in my ears. I'm trying to listen for that *whoosh, pop* that the bone men made when they first came after me, but now I imagine that I hear it everywhere. One thing's for sure: we're being followed. I feel it even before Chaco's shrieking *caw* tips us off.

I clear my throat. "There's somebody back there."

Pap nods. "It's two of them, I think. Too dark to make out for sure. C'mon now, this way."

Pap knows this area even better than me. We run in silence this way and that, cutting through neighborhoods and over flat plots of dirt, and we only slow just as we get to the edge of town. We cross the last paved road before the man camp breathing hard and trying to look like we didn't just run a mile. I try to find Chaco ahead, but my heart is pounding too hard, and my eyeballs feel like they're shaking. I can't see him above me, but I know he's there, somewhere. A lot of men are stoop-sittin' outside of their sheds. They eye us as they smoke or drink, and almost all of them stop whatever they were doing to look our way. A couple of big guys who look drunk stumble to their feet. I don't know if they think they recognize us or what, but one calls after us. Pap pulls me along faster again. He looks left and right and then decides left, trotting now and muttering to himself, "Stupid, stupid, stupid idea."

"It's not stupid, Pap," I say. "Maybe if there are a ton of scary things around us at once, they'll all just holler 'n' go after each other and leave us alone."

Pap smiles even though I know he's scared, too. He stops to look down at me. "Now that right there, some might say is life in a nutshell." He ruffles my hair. And that's when someone grabs me from behind, and I go from feeling a little better to screaming in one second.

Chaco swoops down and flaps his wings, and the air around us seems to swim in black. "Whoa, whoa! Grant, it's all right! It's all right, my man! These are the people I told you about! They're cool!"

Chaco perches on my head, and I sag a little with his weight and stare at the two people who came out of the shadows. One is a tall, thin guy with red hair who looks like a schoolteacher, and the other is a lady with soft eyes and a nice-looking face who is holding her hair up off her neck and fanning herself with her hand. They both stare at Chaco, but they don't look surprised that a huge bird is on my head. I think they've seen him before. Pap is balling his fists, but I put a hand on his and hold it like he held mine back at home in my small space.

"My bird Chaco knows you," I say. They nod. "He says you're good people."

The lady nods. The man shrugs. "Comparatively, for sure," he says. The lady elbows him.

"My name is Caroline. This is Owen. Are you... do you have the bell?" she asks, dropping her voice, although from the way she's looking at me, I think she already knows I do. I think she knows that and a lot more about me. Still, I clutch at the bell. Chaco titters on my head.

"It's all good, man. All good. They're with us," he says.

I look back to them and nod. The lady smiles at me, and her smile makes me feel warm. The man crouches down and cocks his head at me, then he laughs. "Incredible," he says. "It's... it's ludicrous, but also it's inspired. A child. It's perfect. You're perfect."

I don't know whether to snap at the guy or blush, but Pap saves me the trouble. "We better keep moving."

He starts to press at my back to move again when we hear another scream. At first the new guys look at me like I did it, but I was just surprised that first time. I hardly ever scream. Chaco knows it wasn't me. He snaps his arrowed head to the right, back the way we came. That was a grown-man scream, which is a thing you hardly ever hear, and that sounds terrible.

"Remember how you talked about running trouble into trouble

and hoping it doesn't notice you?" Chaco asks. I nod, and he bobs along. "There's a rough crowd hanging out at this makeshift booze hut. They're fixing for something. Follow me." Chaco lifts up off my head in big swoops. I turn to Pap.

"Let's follow him." I think he hears that my voice is kind of soft, because he thumps my back and pulls together a small smile for me. I straighten up.

"All right then," Pap says. The new guys nod. We all take off after Chaco.

We stand out in this place like four sore thumbs, and everyone outside of this shop Chaco takes us to knows it. I'm expecting a restaurant or something like the Roadhouse where Pap sometimes used to go with Dad. It's not like the Roadhouse. The Roadhouse has a bright sign with some letters missing on it so it reads *Radhus*. This place has no sign. It's not really a place, either. It's the same type of cheap-looking shack as every other building here; this one just has the door wide open and cigarette smoke pouring out of it and a big crowd milling around on the dirt outside getting into each other's faces. Not fighting, exactly, but fixin' to. Until they see us, that is. Then they pour it on us.

"Look at this fuckin' guy," someone yells, and I don't know who they're talking about exactly, but I think it's probably Owen. I think I like Owen, but even I know he stands out the most. He'd stand out in downtown Midland. Then I hear another person say, "Hey sweetheart, what's he pay to fuck you? I'll double it." Which I don't really follow, but I know ain't what you're supposed to say to people.

Owen surprises me by stepping forward and saying, "Keep drinking, you fat-ass. It's either going to be diabetes or cirrhosis that gets you. Then you'll be praying to God that people like her can save your pathetic life."

I don't really get what Owen's talking about, but that's okay 'cause I can tell these men don't either and they've got about twenty years on me. The fat guy shoves a few people out of the way and steps forward.

"The fuck you just say to me, boy?" he says, stomping forward. This time I expect Owen to turn tail for sure, but still he doesn't back down. Chaco lands heavily on the flat roof of the place. He squawks loudly, and I can see he's looking from the crowd here down the mud pathway back toward the entrance, where I hear another scream.

Then a *whoosh, pop.*

Pap hears it too, and even though he ain't never had the *whoosh, pop* happen to him before, he squeezes my shoulder even tighter and tries to move me behind him.

Caroline hears it and steps up between Owen and the big man before he can get to him.

"You men are gonna die here tonight if you don't start running," she says. "Fair warning."

Whoosh, pop. Closer this time. The men laugh. One spits a stream of tobacco juice at her feet, and it dangles in his beard and on his shirt, which is crossed with dark lines of the stuff. "Only ones in trouble tonight are you and your boyfriend. The old man and the kid can fuck off if they know what's good for them."

Caroline doesn't look mad, but she is looking. She's looking at this guy the way she looked at me, as if she can see more of him than anyone else on earth. Only this time she doesn't like what she sees, and it makes her sad.

"That's what I thought," she says, almost whispering.

"You first, ginger," the big guy says, and he swings a big ol' punch at Owen, wide as a house. Only when it's supposed to hit Owen, it doesn't. It hits nothing. Owen's gone. The big guy just about chucks himself over. Then there's Owen, in a blink, standing behind the guy, and he looks as surprised as anyone that he's there. Then he breaks out into this huge grin.

"Caroline, I did it! Did you see that? It's less of a step, you know? More of a pivot sort of thing and you aren't so far away when you..." He trails off when he seems to remember what he's doing there, and he lays a big heel into the fat guy's butt right as he's trying to stand. The guy goes down hard right on his chin.

"Owen, behind you!" Caroline yells and runs toward him, but it's too late. A bottle zips through the air and clocks him right in the back of the head, and now it's Owen that's staggering. Then he's on the ground, and there's a pile-on. Caroline tries to pull them off him, but she gets wrapped up herself by another man. I want to go to them and help, even though I know I stand no chance of doing anything worthwhile, but Pap holds me back. I was really starting to like these guys, and here they are going down in a cloud of screaming and sweat and dirt and the smell of dirty metal and dog crap. We get shoved away, pushed to the outside, and I look up at Pap to tell him to let me go, but he's looking past the pile. Down the mud road. At the bone men.

Both of them are there, like powder wearing a suit and tie. There's a *whoosh, pop* and they're gone, but now it's me who's pushing Pap to get away. I can't even get out the word *run* before both bone men are in the mess of people in front of us. The tall one cocks his head, and I'm reminded of this one time when I watched a lizard for a whole hour. Just watched it look at things. That's how he looks at each man he picks up. Then he tosses them a good twenty feet with a flick.

"Where is the child?" he asks.

Another roughneck grabs at the bone man but screams as soon as he touches him and lets go like he's been burned. Pap pushes me behind him.

"Where is the bell?" he screams again, and his voice sounds so jagged and harsh that it even pauses the brawl. The tall one stares at the pile. He thinks I'm underneath, like maybe the bell is what everyone here is fightin' for. He nods at the short one, the one built like a brick wall, and this one steps forward. I almost give up the ghost by screaming when I see him. He's the one who went after me, and he's the one Chaco ripped up. His face has two huge gashes running down it, from his forehead all the way down to his chin, and they go through his eyes, which are like bleeding black marbles. He squats down and shoves his arms underneath the pile like a tractor, then in one lift he flips four or five people up and spinning in the air. They scream until they land in clumps with a sound like smashed tomatoes. He does it again. More people fly. Then there's Caroline. Her clothes are ripped up, and she's crying. The guy holding her drops everything and runs, and she falls to the ground and crawls over to Owen, who ain't moving. He's sort of crumpled, his arms and legs at weird angles and his face mushed and puffy. When the tall one sees him, his eyes flash.

"You two. I know you two. We must be close," I hear him say, even over all the running and all the fighting that's still going on at the fringes and pouring out of the smoky door to the makeshift restaurant. The tall one moves toward Caroline, who starts to back away but then stops herself. She stands tall, slowly, but she does it. Then she walks over to Owen and stands over him, inches from the tall one. She doesn't say anything. She's looking the bone man up and down.

"I can see what you were," she says. "But you aren't that man anymore."

"Less and less. Soon I will leave humanity behind altogether," he says. "The child is here. The bell is with him. We know it. Perhaps all he needs is to be drawn out." He grabs her by the arm with one hand, and with the other he reaches inside his jacket pocket. He pulls out a knife that seems to burn the air and that stains them both a weird green color. I don't need to know what type of knife it is to know that it's just *wrong*. I know in my heart that I can't let that thing touch anyone.

I scream again. "No!"

I can't even take another breath before the bulldog bone man is in front of me. This close, the *whoosh, pop* shakes my ears. His cut-up face is inches from me. His slashed eyes don't move, but I know they see me. He takes a deep sniff and looks down at my chest. Then, faster than a blink, he grabs the bell and rips it through my shirt and off my neck. The force yanks me down, and I'm on my knees. I see the other one walk up to me. His shoes stop at my hands.

"I knew you'd betray yourself, child," he says. "Compassion is a uniquely human failing. You cling to the belief that there is a way that things should be, but that is wrong. That implies order." He lifts me standing by the nape of my shirt. "You can't be blamed for thinking thus. Even we did, once. The thin place burns what is human away from you bit by bit and shows you the true nature of things."

"Go," I say. I think it comes out as a groan. I think I'm trying to say *go away*, but his grip is so cold that it burns. Everything burns. The green knife burns. The place where the bell rested near my heart burns. The bell wants to come back to me, but the short bone man grips it with his whole fist. It has no chance of escape.

"Oh, we will go. But first we need a death. That is the way of the bell." Everything becomes green as he raises the knife above me. But Pap is there. He screams and throws himself at the arm holding the knife, but it's not enough. I barely feel the bone man move. He keeps raising the knife over my head until Chaco hits him like a cannonball. He staggers backward, one hand protecting his face as Chaco rips at the knife, but as soon as he touches it, he screeches and shrinks away like he's been stung bad, which gives the bone man an opening. He snatches Chaco around the neck and slams him to the ground. Chaco twitches and flops then goes still.

"Chaco!" I scream. "That's my best friend! What did you do to my best friend?"

The bone man doesn't care. Why would he? I bet he never had a best friend in his life. He grabs me by the neck and brings the knife up again. Pap is scrabbling, and I'm pulling against him, but we're not moving a muscle on the bone man, until Pap spits in his face. He spits right in his eyes. That catches him up.

"Leave him be!" Pap yells. "You're perversions. Both of you. You ain't fit to touch my grandson."

The tall one turns to him, and that lizard-like interest comes back. He blinks the spit away, which is the first time I think I've seen him blink. He drops me.

"One death is as good as another," he says. Then he plunges the knife into Pap's stomach, and Pap drops to the ground before I can even scream. His eyes are open, but there's nothing behind them.

Even though I can't hold it, I feel the bell start to pull itself together. Chaco lets loose a heartbreaking cry, and I feel him rushing toward me. I watch the black eyes of the bone men widen as the glow of the silver grows, and grows, and grows.

"Ring it," the tall one says.

The bell is rung. It sounds like a shotgun, and it sounds like a whisper, but mostly it just sounds sad.

11

THE WALKER

I am there.

I am there when the agents come to Midland. I walk behind them as they reach the camp. I reach for Caroline as she is swallowed up in the brawl, but my hands swipe nothing. I scream for Chaco to help, but he says that his charge is Grant. He says it again and again like he has to constantly remind himself or he'd be diving in.

And when the bell is ripped from Grant and Chaco does dive in, I see him dashed to the floor. I scream when Parsons plunges the turquoise knife into Grant's grandfather. I watch as it cuts a soul that is still strong, that still had time. I watch as the knife destroys the natural order of things and rewrites a small portion of the soul map in one jagged, muddy swipe. My world lurches. I get a sense of drunken vertigo, and everything leers to one side for a second before righting itself again. I can do nothing. I am worthless.

Now all Parsons or Douglas needs to do is stab himself and ring the bell. Then I hand over the keys to the car and cross over forever, and one of them takes my place. I close my eyes. In a way, I want it to happen. In a way, it's bittersweet. I wish I could tell Caroline goodbye, but my life has never been on point in the timing department anyway. It makes sense that it would end like this. Like I got hung up on.

Parsons says, "Ring the bell." I squeeze my eyes shut. I hear the bell chime like a hammer striking a brass pipe that's as big as a car...

...And nothing happens to me.

I open my eyes and find both agents very much alive and the bell very much rung. The sound's shockwave has formed a bubble around the agents that is distorting time. I remember it well from when I died and rang the bell. The shockwave pushes outward slowly, like a kid blowing a bubble. But that was when I was in the thick of it. It never occurred to me that someone might ring the bell in the presence of death and not actually be dying themselves. But now that it's happening, I remember Caroline and her last moments with Gam. The bell formed then, but Gam told her not to ring it. She could have, but she didn't. The agents just did. And now the agents are waiting inside their bubble of time. They can only be waiting for one thing.

I feel the tug of the soul map calling me to a man named Abernathy Romer, but I don't need the hint, because I'm already there. I watch as the soul of Abernathy sits up from his dead body and turns to his grandson, who is huddled over him. He reaches for Grant, and his hand passes right through the kid. He knows in that second that he's been cut from his grandson, and he weeps. It's a soft, hitching sound that is all the more heartbreaking for the fact that I know from his soul string that he's only cried twice in his adult life: once when his grandson was born and once at the death of his son and daughter-in-law. He calls their names first.

"James? Becca?"

He gets no answer. He stands and watches Grant slump over him, shaking with silent tears. "So I am alone, then," he says.

"No, sir," I say.

He flips around and puts his hands up, eyes wide.

"No more fighting, Ab. All we can do now is watch and wait." I point at the agents in the bubble of the bell and add acidly, "Like them." I don't know if they can see us, too, but they aren't on the lookout for us anyway. They're on the lookout for the veil. They watch with fierce intensity, scanning the horizon like stranded sailors looking for rescue.

Ab's hands lower slowly. His eyes stay wide. "Are you..." He trails off. I nod. I want to sit down with him over a beer. I want to shoot the shit. I want to tell him how he was robbed of years he should have had with Grant. But the veil is here. Funny how even outside of time, there's never enough time.

"What in God's name is that thing?" Ab asks.

"That's what everyone's waiting for." The veil sweeps down the dry, cracked mud street of the camp with all the presence of a strip of iron, and when it enters the bubble of the bell, the agents see it, along with everyone else.

It's sort of like if a big stage prop falls down in the play that is our living world, and all the people working behind the scenes in black are suddenly bang on in the spotlight. Everyone's focus meets at once, and everything within the bubble is revealed. The agents see me. Grant sees his grandfather's soul standing over him. Owen sees us both. I see Caroline.

Caroline sees me.

My name is on her lips. I can see it. And I see something else, too. Something I haven't seen for a long time. I see someone who misses me. I can't tell you what that feels like after what seems like an eternity of people terrified to see me. Here's a woman who misses Ben Dejooli. Not the Walker. Just Ben. She doesn't cry out or yell or run to me. She just smiles through her tears. Until the agents step between us.

"Benjamin Dejooli," Parsons says slowly, splitting into a yellow smile. "Remember us?"

"You screwed up, Parsons. If you wanted my job, you had to off yourself and ring the bell at the same time. You two are such fanboys that I'd have thought you'd have picked up on that by now."

Douglas laughs. It's a disturbing, hyena laugh. Quick and clipped. "We don't care about your job anymore, Ben," Douglas says.

Parsons nods slowly in agreement. "You see, you're the ferryman. Nothing more than a glorified day laborer. You hold every soul by the hand and escort them to the threshold like you were their arm candy. You are doomed to this for eternity. Giving everything, getting nothing. Why in this world or the next would I want that?"

I consider myself pretty quick on the draw when it comes to swapping barbs, but shit, this one floors me. I was just starting to feel good about my job.

"You have no idea what I do," I say. "You can't. If you walked the soul map, it would destroy you."

"We don't come to walk the soul map, Mr. Dejooli. We come to own the map on which you walk," Parsons says. "Your peasant's day job doesn't concern me. I know what you do. I also know what you can't do. You can't cross the threshold. You take the souls to the veil, never beyond."

"The veil is closed to the living. Those are the rules."

"Those *were* the rules." Parsons's black eyes are like pits of coal in his face.

He trades Douglas the knife for the bell. Douglas positions the knife in his hand with the care of a boxer wrapping tape. Then he eyes the veil just as he did the wall back at the cave. He has an audience this time: Caroline, Owen, and Grant, along with the soul of Abernathy. Anyone from the camp in the land of the living who is paying attention is seeing what they can't possibly understand, and many are struck dumb in the middle of the brawl.

Of all of them, Grant is the worst to see. With one hand he clutches at his heart, where his bell was ripped from him. With the other hand he reaches for a living picture of his grandfather only feet from him but beyond his grasp. It's not fair that he should have to see this. None of it is fair. But it's the way it is.

Douglas runs at the veil the way a bear sprints, his body seemingly falling over itself. He screams like a demon and then jumps with the knife high above his head. He brings it down on the veil, and it sticks. He uses his body to drag it down, and down, and down. He falls to the ground with the knife in his hand, laughing like a maniac, because he's ripped it right open.

There's a loss of pressure so great that it brings every living thing near the bubble to their knees. Only Ab and I are standing. Even the agents are buckled over, but they recover. They grit through it and stand tall and suck in the pain that must be pummeling them. I realize that this is what they've been training for. This is their moment. Parsons screams in triumph and holds his hands out wide.

"Do you see, Benjamin? Do you see? Nothing can keep us from him now!" Parsons screams.

Him? I don't like the sound of that, but I don't have a lot of time to think about it. I'm scared shitless. I admit that freely. I'm looking around this place like I stepped into a bad party and all I want to do is turn around before the guys with guns realize I'm there. And I may have done just that—swirled open the map, walked through, taken a stroll over to Cancun for a couple of personal days to piece all of this together—if it weren't for Caroline. Caroline is on the ground with her hands pressed against her ears. I want to run to her and envelop her, but I know I can't. I want to tackle the agents, but I know I can't. Still, I feel I owe it to everybody to watch. So I watch. That's me. Fuck the Walker; they should just call me the Watcher.

But you know who doesn't just stand around feeling sorry for himself? Abernathy Romer. He's been seething at Parsons the whole time. When Parsons holds his hands out, palms open, swimming in victory, Ab swats the bell out of his hand.

While the bell rings, it exists on every plane, but Ab doesn't know that. Ab doesn't care. He sees something that is precious to his grandson, stolen from him, and he wants to give it back. His hand passes right through Parsons, but it connects with the ringing bell. It's out and spinning in space before anyone knows what happens.

Scratch that. I should say "before anyone but Grant knows what happens."

Grant sees it all. He's on top of it. He's so quick on the draw that he scampers out and snatches it mid-air like one last handshake from his grandfather. He clutches it to his chest, and the kid smiles. Finally, he smiles. When Ab nods at him in approval, he smiles wider.

Parsons looks at his empty hand, confused. Douglas pushes him toward the split veil. "Let's go!" Douglas says. "Forget the bell! We don't need it anymore!"

As broken as it is, the veil is already slowly oozing together again. The hole the agents cut is closing, just like it did back in the cave. They don't have enough time to go for both the bell and the veil. Parsons turns to Grant, and the look he gives would probably kill a normal kid, but Grant isn't a normal kid. Grant squares his shoulders.

"Go!" Douglas screams again. It seems like it takes an effort of will from him, but he rips his gaze from the bell and turns to the veil. He doesn't hesitate. He runs and leaps through the crack. Douglas follows without so much as a word back toward us.

And now I've got a problem on my hands.

Whatever those powder-haired freaks want to do on the other side, I guarantee you it's not gonna be good for any of us. Not good for the living world, the dead world, or any world in between. Parsons is the brains of the duo, and he's pissed about losing the bell back to Grant, which is good, but these two are like crocodiles. They're not going away; they just keep swimming until they get what they want.

And now they're swimming around unchecked on the other side.

Ab looks at me. Grant looks at me. Owen looks at me. Caroline looks at me. All of them watch me even as the ringing—and their vision of me—begins to fade.

"Ah, shit," I say. Because I know what it might mean. When Death takes a holiday, the dead go on vacation. But I can see it in Caroline's eyes. I've got no choice. "After you," I tell Ab. He nods. He turns to Grant and clutches at his heart, then he holds his hands out. "I love you, son," he says. Even if he can't hear it, Grant gets it. He's crying silently, but he nods.

Ab walks through the veil.

I have seconds left. I take one last look at Caroline and Owen, then I go for the rip. It's just about shoulder width. I dive for it. It catches on my waist. I push through and fall out and over like a newborn animal. And just like that, the living world and the world in between are lost to me.

I'm beyond the veil now, in the land of the dead.

12

OWEN BENNET

When Parsons stabs Grant's grandfather, I'm thinking subcutaneous perforation for sure, and probable bowel piercing. Almost certainly there will be internal bleeding. But it's in the stomach proper, not the liver, and Parsons pulls the knife out cleanly and doesn't go for more. I'm thinking that if there's a medical building in this camp, there's a good chance we can save his life. Instead the man drops dead instantly.

It's the knife. Something about that knife is an aberration. I recognize the rock it's made from, of course. I put that together as soon as Parsons took it from his jacket. It's the same as my totem. But in shaping it into a weapon, the agents created something terrible.

When the bell rings, I can see it all—the world of the Walker. Of Ben. And, of course, like a knight in shining armor, there's the man himself. If he is a man anymore. Whatever he is, it's done him good. He's standing there like he's just pushed open the doors as a late entrant into a black-tie party and he's the guy everyone's been waiting for. Especially Caroline. I don't even need to look at her to know. But I look at her anyway. I can't tell if she's in awe or if she's scared out of her mind. All I know is that there's a connection there. A strong one. One I've never quite been able to spark between us. And I can't even be mad. I can't even blame her. This man died for his sister, took up the mantle of Death, and has been keeping the balance between life and death like some sort of dark king for the past year. Meanwhile a man has just died, and I—the doctor, mind you—am standing around blinking like a cow.

I'm seeing Grant's grandfather in two places now, so I know there's a good chance my mind has finally broken. There's his body, and then, through the hole the bell ripped into the air, I see him again. It takes me a second to realize that it's his soul. The agents and Ben are talking, but the ringing of the bell is still shaking my head. Plus my left ear feels puffy and useless from when one of the camp meatheads socked me, so I can't hear what they're saying.

Douglas, the thick one, gets a running start and lashes out with the knife at what looks like a barrier of burned paper. It splits open, and then it's like the barometer drops fifty points. I'm thinking we've lost everything. We lost a good man to the knife, we lost the bell to the agents, and now we're going to lose the agents to whatever lies beyond. Then Grant's grandfather swipes out at Parsons. There's a glinting in the air, and Grant dashes from his crouch and makes a spectacular, cross-dimensional catch. His grandfather reaches for him in farewell, but with the bell safely on our side, the rift is sealing fast. Soon they're parted. What's on that side will stay there, and the agents are on that side.

The aftermath of the opening and closing and of the ringing of the bell sits on everyone within eyeshot like an elephant. I'm the first to speak.

"Caroline," I say, and I admit it, it's partly to break her train of thought, which I'm sure is careening around Ben Dejooli Mountain. But mostly because I know that we have to pick ourselves up and dust ourselves off. The agents succeeded in something. And anything they succeed in is bound to be a mess for us. Caroline is staring at the spot where Ben disappeared. She doesn't even know I'm calling for her until I touch her shoulder.

"Caroline," I say gently. She starts. She's bleeding from the lip. I roll my cuff to a clean spot and gently dab at it. I find myself pushing a damp strand of hair back off her face. She either allows it or is too stunned by events to stop me. I'd like to assume the former, but after seeing Ben across time and space, it's most likely the latter. "The agents," I say. "We have to find them."

Caroline shakes her head. "They're gone."

I stand back and check her over. The dirt and the tears and the scrapes only serve to make her more beautiful. I'm reminded of those times when we were on shift together at ABQ General and running around from patient to patient, both of us rumpled and disheveled and tired, but fighting the same fight. Those times she'd smile at me at four in the morning as we passed in the hall. That was when I started to fall in love with her, I think.

And suddenly she's looking at me and her face is softened and she's back here, in the land of the living, with me. And I remember how she can basically read me like a book, so I shake my head as if that will clear my thoughts. I'm sure I'm as red as a fire hydrant. I touch my face. It comes away red, all right. With blood. "God, I must be a mess," I say. I try to dab at my face, but she holds my hand away and keeps it in hers.

"Let it coagulate. Just a few cuts. You'll get your shirt all bloody," she says.

As much as I want to stand here, my hand in hers, I can't shake the image of Douglas running full tilt with that horrid knife held high. "We've got to go after them."

"They're beyond us now," she says. "Beyond even the thin world. They're in the world of the dead. The world beyond." She turns to Grant, who is sitting again, slumped over, near his grandfather. He's holding the bell, but it's Chaco he's looking at. Poor Chaco, a broken mound of feathers on the cracked mud. The camp men have mostly scattered now, but I know they'll be back. I know we have to get out of here, but I'm not about to rush Grant. Without speaking, Caroline moves over to him and lowers herself down to both knees.

"I'm so sorry, Grant," Caroline says, and she's looking at him, but I know she's also looking into him. At the color of him. At his essence. She lays one hand gently on his shaking back. The other she passes lightly over him, grabbing smoke. Whatever she sees makes her eyes well with tears, but I can see her mind working. Then, out of nowhere, she says, "You weren't a burden to your grandfather. You gave him such joy. If he was ever sad, it was only because of how he wished you could have made your mom and dad as happy as you made him."

Grant's shaking subsides a little. He looks up at Caroline. "How do you know?"

"Because I saw it. How much he loved you... it came off him in waves. He blazed with it." Caroline holds out a hand to him. He takes it, and she helps him up. The three of us stand around Chaco, and the dusty wind tousles his feathers.

"He was an awesome bird..." I begin, but Grant stops me by stepping forward and kneeling down next to him.

"Chaco," he says. "I have the bell. I'm the Keeper still." He presses his little finger gently to Chaco's head, brushing the small feathers of his face. "That means we're still best friends. You told me. That means you have to get up."

I want to take the kid and hug him. I don't think I can watch him talk to his broken best friend. I think it'll rip my heart out.

The good news is I don't have to for long, because Chaco stirs.

Chaco's broken wing stretches out and snaps together again. His bulging neck straightens. His claws flex. His black eyes open, and they find Grant. Chaco twitters. Grant smiles and holds out his little arm, and Chaco flips himself up. He shakes his head like he's taken a bad fall then takes a wobbly walk up to perch on Grant's head.

The wind drops on a dime and the dust settles, but I don't get the feeling that the storm has ended, only that we're standing in the eye of it. Grant looks up at Chaco, and I think they're having some sort of silent conversation. When he looks down at us again, I can see in his eyes that my hunch is correct.

"The bone men, you call them the agents. They did a really bad thing. They ripped open the veil. It was sick to begin with because of them, but then they pretty much broke it." Grant says. "And Chaco says that if it's broken, things can come through."

"What things?" I ask. Grant and Chaco look over at me at the same time. The double weight of their gaze gives me goose bumps but not as much as what Grant says.

"Things from the other side. Things that shouldn't be here. Bad things."

Grant and Chaco look at each other again.

"What else does Chaco say?" I ask.

Grant smiles at me through all his pain and all his loss.

"He says he'd be my best friend even if I didn't have the bell."

13

THE WALKER

So now that I'm over here on the other side, beyond the veil, I bet I know what you wanna know.

You want to know if I'm seeing God. Maybe you think I'm staring at a blazing figure sitting on a throne behind a set of gleaming pearly gates. Maybe you think that by crossing the veil I'm somehow free of my job and am getting reborn. Maybe you think what I see over here is so crazy, so awe inspiring and beyond description, that I'm struck dumb. Maybe you think I'm seeing beyond the racing edges of the universe, like I'm surfing the Big Bang.

Well, you're all wrong.

Don't feel bad about it. Hell, the Navajo don't even have what you might call a totally formed idea of what happens after we die. We're fine with the multiple worlds thing—I remember Gam used to tell Joey and me about how we humans had to go through five worlds just to get to the one we lived on, so I shouldn't fuck it up by tossing my cigarette butts on the ground. But as to what happens after we die? The Navajo don't really go in for that. In fact, my people believe that chances are after we die we sort of hang around because we're pissed off at those of us that are still living. We give the dead some things in the forms of offerings, mostly to get them to stop lingering. Best-case scenario is they disappear back into the great balance of things.

In fact, now that I think about it, and after having dealt with poor Karen and Stan 2.0, maybe the Navajo aren't so far off. No more so than anyone else. But don't worry, we didn't get it exactly right either.

What I'm staring at is a river. It's a massive, glowing river that looks like it's floating a billion flashlights. I know instantly that these are the souls I deliver. When I push them through the veil, I'm delivering them to this river. Ab and I stand on the shore just watching them. Neither of us can speak. The souls provide all the light there is in this place, but it is plenty. Everything has this mesmerizing glow about it, and for a second I forget everything, even the agents who ducked in here minutes before me. It's just Ab and me, standing side by side, following the souls, like fireflies, with our eyes.

Then Ab says, "I gotta go." It startles me.

"Yeah? Where? Into the river?" It looks kind of nice. Like swimming with a bunch of glowing fish.

"Yeah, but not just anywhere in there. I gotta go thatta way." Ab points down the right side of the riverbank.

"You act like you've been here before or something," I say, my mouth still not quite working right. "Why not that way?" I point down the left bank.

Ab shakes his head. "Nope. No way. That's not my way. My way is that way."

"You mean you can't go left?"

"I could, I suppose," Ab says. "But I don't want to." He steps forward into the river, and his feet leave no mark upon the sand. He goes into the water up to his knees then pauses. He turns back to me.

"Grant," he says. "What will happen to him?"

"I don't know. But if he's with Caroline and Owen, he's in good hands."

Ab lowers his head a bit, his brow furrowed. He takes another step in the water, and it starts to glow around him.

"I'm sorry, Ab," I blurt out. "I fucked up, man. I should have seen the knife coming. I should have followed the agents, and when I lost them, I should have known it was trouble. I let my guard down, man. I let it down and you died. That knife never should have happened." I look at my own feet. I make two heavy prints in the sand. When I look up again, Ab is smiling sadly at me.

"It's all part of the plan, young man."

"No, it's not. You don't understand. That knife, its purpose is to destroy the plan. It was created to ruin the plan. I saw your soul string, Ab. You had time left. You shouldn't be here. You should be back at home, with Grant, drinking a glass of whisky on the rocks and reading the Midland Reporter." I feel tears come to my eyes, and in a stupid act of defiance, I refuse to wipe them, as if that will make them go away. "You know, you think you know your job, and then you start feeling good about it, and that's when you fuck up. That's prime fuck-up time."

"Hey," Ab says, not harsh but enough to stop my blubbering. "I don't know much. Even after all these years living, I feel I'm going out knowing less than the day I came in. But I do know this. If I wasn't supposed to be here, I wouldn't be here."

I put my hands on my hips. I don't know how I can make him understand about the knife. I think he sees the frustration in my face because he says, "I get it, son. That knife is bad news. But I want you to consider for a second that even it has its place. Maybe breaking the plan is part of the plan."

I try to consider it. A thing that can alter the soul map, which is essentially the plan of the living world, also being a part of the plan? It's too much for me. I shake my head.

"Don't worry about it," Ab says. "You just keep going. Do me a favor. Watch out for my grandson. If you can." Ab sinks into the water up to his chest. His lower half disappears. The glow around him grows.

"I will."

"Now you go get those rat bastards that stuck me." He's up to his neck now. "They ain't supposed to be here." I nod. He smiles at me. Then he dips under, and he's gone. He's a glow now. I watch his glow spin around and then float peacefully down the river to the right. I can't help but smile myself. If I were to hazard a guess, even though I think he was a content man, I'd say Abernathy Romer hadn't smiled like that in years.

Now it's just me on the shore. Wherever Ab is going, that's not where the agents went. I turn to the left. I walk about fifty feet, scanning the ground. I see what remains of two sets of footprints, which tells me that the vein rock won't work here—there's no phasing or skipping space. The agents are hoofing it on foot. I look in their direction, but the river bends and twists and the shoreline changes terrain, following it. I can't see the men themselves, so I start running.

I get about five hundred feet down the shore before I realize that the veil isn't following me. It sits like a sad, lost dog right where I came in. Its tattered, broken silence serves as a reminder: as long as I'm over here, I'm not doing my job. This hits home harder when I look back the way I came and see that the bobbing soul lights have floated away from where I came in, and nothing else has replaced them. The water is blank. Empty. The inflow has stopped.

I pick up the pace, running full tilt now, following the footprints of the agents, which seem to fill with oily water like parking lot puddles.

The scenery begins to shift on me. No more flat beach. Soon I'm running over pebbles, then rocks, then I'm dodging around boulders. Another couple hundred feet, and the earth starts to jut up around me. Soon I'm running through a canyon that zigzags all over the place. The soul light flickers and wavers like a flashlight under water. I look to my right and see the souls down this way are acting up, zipping all over the place, sometimes surging out and taking almost human form before crashing down into the water again. I feel it too: the farther I go down this side of the river, the more chaotic everything becomes. I don't think it's the agents doing it, either. I think it's the river itself. It flows two ways. There's the way Ab went, and then there's this way. The other way.

Soon even the terrain itself can't seem to decide on a form. The inlets and breaks in the rock walls that border the river shift before my eyes. It's like I'm running through a scatterbrained formation of a river. New earth pushes up through splits in the ground then breaks down seconds later. The river cuts one way through the canyon, then in a blink it changes course and cuts another way. The walls of rock recede and expand, almost as if they're breathing. The flow is in the same direction, but at one glance it seems to go uphill, then down, then around, then through overhangs that break apart the second I pass them. I focus on putting one foot in front of the other and scan the horizon when I can.

A pillar of stone shoots into the air, missing me by an inch, and when I stop to right myself, I see the agents up ahead. Parsons is in the lead, and Douglas lopes just behind him. Douglas carries the knife in his closed fist, tip down, hilt up, pumping it in time with his stride. Parsons carries something, too. It looks like a small book. He holds it up and runs blindly forward behind it.

I feel that this side of the river is normally a place of chaos but that the presence of the knife has really revved things into overdrive. The earth around Douglas blurs and stutters. The soul light ebbs and flows around him. The two agents look like glitches in the program out here.

Parsons comes to a skidding stop, with Douglas a few paces after. Parsons flips the book around, looking to his right at the river. This is my chance to catch them. I pick up speed.

Douglas hears me first, and he lets out this low growl that gets Parsons's attention. I don't get any patronizing smile this time—this time Parsons is pissed off. It's a minor victory, but I'll take it.

"I don't have time for you right now, Dejooli. Go back to your boat, ferryman."

"I don't give two shits what you've got time for. Clearly you've got enough time to stick the laws of the universe in a blender with that damn knife of yours. I feel like you can take a second here to explain to me what exactly it is that you're planning on doing. You know, before you really, cosmically fuck everything up. I'd ask you where the hell you're going, but judging by the way you're reading that book, I'm about ninety percent sure you don't know yourself."

Parsons, who was never a real talker to begin with, even before he went and bleached himself, doesn't even give me the time of day. He just nods at Douglas, who grins and takes a step forward. The jagged cuts that span his face seem not to bother him in the slightest. "Wait," Parsons says, and Douglas pauses. "Give me the knife. We can't risk losing it." Douglas shrugs and hands Parsons the knife, then he balls both hands into fists and walks toward me.

I smirk. I'm not worried. It's easy to feel cocky about yourself when you're already dead. I spit on the sand. "Really, Douglas? Are you that much of a dumbass? You know you can't hurt me." I hold my hands out as if I'm welcoming him. Douglas cocks one arm and throws a haymaker mid-stride that shuts me right up. It knocks me off my feet and sprawls me out along the shuddering, shifting riverbank.

"Forgot what it feels like to get hit, Dejooli?" Douglas asks. He saunters over to me and grabs me by the shirt. "The thing about this place is that there are no laws. No rules. Only form and destruction. Here, you're just another form." He pulls me up by the collar. "And I am destruction." He slams his fist across my face, and I see stars. He drops me, and I scrabble for footing. He seems to enjoy it. He revs up for a kick, but when he lashes out, I catch his foot and wrench it like a bottle cap. He howls and goes down hard on his side.

"Cuts both ways, Douglas," I say. "If you can hit, I can hit. And you don't have the strength of ten men out here. Just one. And barely that."

Douglas curls his lip and stands, limping. "I've never killed a dead man before. But I guess there's a first time for everything." He throws himself forward and uses his momentum to snatch me into a bear hug. I see it coming, but I'm not that big of a guy. Every time I got into a fight back at Chaco, all the bigger guys—which was almost all of them—would use this same approach, like they could just crush me out of existence. The first few times I ended up on the wrong side of it, it sort of did feel that way until my old partner Danny Ninepoint had to save my ass. But then I learned to use their momentum against them. I sidestep Douglas and fling him behind me like a duped bull. He falls flat on his stomach. This is my opening. I jump up in the air with my knee out, ready to crack down on his back, but just then the lay of the land switches on us. The ground rolls and cracks, and I'm caught in an upthrust of rock that slams into my knee and flattens me even as it carries me up into the air. It tumbles Douglas onto the floor like a hamster in a wheel, end over end until everything comes to rest. Except that I'm fifty feet in the air now, marooned on a square patch of rock.

Douglas slowly stands, dusting himself off. He shields his eyes and looks up at me. Then he laughs. "I hope you like the view, Dejooli!" he screams. "You may be there a while!"

I look over the edge and immediately feel sick. This is a true mesa. The sides are sheer and smooth. I always hated heights. It's in my blood. The Navajo are a plains people for a reason. It's hard to tumble to your death in miles of open grassland. I always appreciated that. Never more than right now. I do the only thing I can: I spit down at him. Like some kid leaning over a bridge. Real mature, I know. He sidesteps it easily. Then he's forced to dodge another jut of earth himself. It almost takes his legs right out from under him. All around us, the land is going haywire. Dust coats the air like mist. It's as bright as midday one second, then pitch black for a blink, then everything is in this gloaming color, then marine blue, then bright again. There's no rhyme or reason to it, but it does seem to be getting worse. When I look around, I think I can see why.

We're at the edge of things. Just beyond where Douglas limps over to Parsons, the river disappears. The horizon is a thin line of black, and beyond that is just a void, like a spot between stars. It turns my stomach a bit, so I flip around, back the way I came. I can see the river wind off beyond sight, and the world seems to settle along with it. Form, function, order. Just seeing it helps calm my racing heart. I think I'm getting a hint of what Ab meant when he said he felt that this way was best for him. I almost reach out to it. Only Parsons's triumphant laugh gives me pause. I snap around and find him holding the book out at arm's length.

"Now!" he says. "This is it! But quickly! Already it changes!"

And without a second's hesitation, he runs right into the river.

Douglas takes one last look up at me. He gives me a dismissive shake of the head, the kind that says I ended up being even less of a factor than he thought I would be. Ninepoint used to give me those from time to time. They burned me every single time. Then Douglas is splashing off after Parsons. The bobbing soul lights seem to vibrate as he passes. They zip out of the way of the two men then spin around them like embers caught in an updraft. The agents sink and sink, and then they're gone, just like that. I scramble to the edge of the ledge, scanning the river. Crazy or not, they're still human, both of them. I figure they gotta come up some time. But they don't. And then a minute goes by. And another. And I realize it's just me here now. Alone again. Stuck on a shifty ledge above a churning world.

14

CAROLINE ADAMS

I think I pined. I didn't mean to pine, but I think I pined when I saw Ben through that rip in the air. Which sucks, because not only am I not a piner—I pride myself on not being a piner—but that was about the worst time in the world to get starry eyed. A man had just been murdered, for crying out loud. We were in the middle of man-camp hell. Dust flying, people yelling and fighting—and a little boy screaming. It's times like that when I'm supposed to be managing the situation, but instead I got zapped by the sight of Ben. You know who managed the situation? Owen. You know who I stand to hurt the most by all this nonsense with Ben? Owen.

It's a joke, really. A cruel joke. Just when I think the guy is beyond me, he pops up. He did that for months and months in my brain. I'd be at the gas station waiting for the boat to fill up and—*bam!*—surprise Ben thoughts! We played blackjack while he took his chemo regimen with those same blue-faced cards they were selling by the cash register. Or when we got waved through a cone zone back in Louisiana and there was a cop who looked just like him, even wore his pants a little high on his hips like Ben did. I'm doing nothing but flipping through a gossip rag when I see that cop and—*bam!*—surprise Ben thoughts!

But this time it was surprise Ben. Surprise *the guy himself.* In a way it was a blessing that I only had seconds to see him, to process him. Like one last voice message from someone who is gone forever, just a few seconds long, a quick hi and goodbye. You can delete that without going too crazy over it. Any longer and I would have made even more of an ass out of myself than I did.

When I turn to Grant, my skills finally kick in, and I become the nurse I'm supposed to be. Grant's grandfather is gone. Grant's smoke is weak. He's going into a state of shock, which makes sense since he saw the soul of his grandfather pass into the great beyond. I had to go talk to my school counselor for a while because I accidentally locked myself in the basement storeroom at school when I was about his age. I thought that was bad. This kind of thing would have sent little girl Caroline right off the deep end. So I do the first thing that all nurses do when they deal with a patient in shock. I let him know I'm here in a completely nonthreatening way. I reach out and gently touch his shoulder, heaving with sobs. He looks up at me, and I can see why he is in pain. I can read it dancing on his skin, leaking from his eyes, and swirling like unformed words around his chapped lips. It has less to do with his grandfather dying than it does with how he feels like crap for dragging his grandfather down during what would be the man's final days. He accepts death in the way a child can—because he has to. What he can't accept is how his grandfather had to live after Grant's parents died. I see all of this as clear as a book, and the clarity almost staggers me.

I hold myself together because one thought cuts through: he's wrong. Grant is wrong to think his grandfather found him a burden. I know he's wrong, because I saw his grandfather's smoke too. And I saw how it only really shone true when he was with Grant, the two of them, running along with Owen and me.

And just like that, I know how to help him. I know how to fix his color. I see his pain as gaps in his smoke, and I know how to smooth them over. I know the words. So I say them. It's like I'm smoothing over a cracked vase with fresh clay. In fact, I see it happening. My own smoke comes off of me and flows over his. Changes it. It doesn't quite bring it back to the brilliant color it was when I first saw him—he's far too sad for that shine right now—but it turns it into something close. Something that could one day get back to that color.

Grant stands. He takes my hand. It takes a lot to floor the little guy. It takes even more to floor Chaco, who literally rises from the dust in front of us and hops up onto Grant's head. I remember Ben's grandmother's bird, just like this. Probably the same one, in the way that these creatures span across time and space. It stuck with her to the end, as I held her hand. I have no doubt Chaco will be around for the end of Grant, too, and will do his best to make sure it doesn't happen anytime soon.

Chaco snaps his gaze down the dirt road, past the crowd that is slowly pooling at the edges of our group. The crow caws, and Grant scrambles around me to where he can see around the buildings at the edge of the camp and out into the desert. I follow his eyes. There's an oil rig not far out there, painted red in the sunset, but that's about it. I turn back to Grant. His eyes are unfocused, almost like he's in a trance. I think he can see more than I do, just like I see more than others do, but his talent is different.

"What's out there?" I ask.

"A thin place," Grant says. "It's where I found the bell."

Owen steps up to us, still stemming the blood on his face with his cuff, despite my fussing. "Guys, I hate to break up the party. It's been such a lovely time. Charming little camp you've got here. But the natives are getting restless again. If we don't get out of here soon, we're going to end up in another fight or in jail. And one brawl a day is plenty for me."

"Grant, we have to get you someplace safe," I say.

Chaco caws again and leaps from Grant's head with a swoop. "There's nowhere safe," Grant says, translating for us. "We're the only ones who can stop it."

He's in full-blown Keeper mode now. I recognize the look from Ben's grandmother, when she gave me the bell back at Chaco. It's an ageless look. Focused but distant.

"Stop what, buddy?" Owen asks, his voice plugged up by his swollen nose.

"That thin place is breaking," Grant says, and then he takes two running steps down the dirt road before pausing and turning around again. In a second, he switches back to the little boy he is at heart. His face softens and his brow furrows as he looks down at where his grandfather's body lies. His smoke stirs and slows and darkens, but his color stays true, even deepens a little.

"You all right, Grant?" I ask, which is a ridiculous thing to ask. Of course he's not. None of us are, in the grand scheme, but he looks up at me and nods.

"I know Pap's not there," he says, looking at the body. "That's not him. But still, it..." He pauses, swallows.

"Sucks." Owen says, taking his hand away from his face. Grant looks at him and then nods. "We're with you, Grant," Owen says. "Take us to where we need to be." Owen's eyes harden, and he balls his hands into fists. Tattered and torn and bloody, he's not bowed. I feel heat rising to my chest, which I know I can't one hundred percent attribute to adrenaline, and I feel like I'm staring again, this time at Owen. Funny how your hormones don't care if you're on the threshold of hell.

And while I'm thinking about hormones, Owen and Grant are already running toward the desert. Owen looks back at me. He ticks his head for me to join them, and I see a hint of a smile. His smoke is dark, too. Thick. Settled. I have this bizarre urge to snort it, like some sort of junkie. I think it might give me guts. I rub at my face as if that could straighten out my thoughts. This last half hour has given me enough fodder for a decade of sleepless rendezvous with 3:00 a.m.

I take off after them, and soon we break through the edge of the camp, the three of us running through the desert at a dead sprint, streaking smoke behind us like the tail of a comet, with Chaco crowing high above us.

We follow Grant's lead, and the kid can run. He seems to know the best route, jumping over pits and pointing out rocks to watch. He's not tiring, and neither is Owen. Or if he is, he's hiding it well. So

I don't slow either. I try not to think of the kinds of things that scamper and slither around the desert soaking up the last of the sun. I tell myself it's probably mostly fluffy little prairie dogs, but then I see a flash of banded scales. Not a fluffy prairie dog. There's no stopping now. In fact, I pick up the pace and fall in step with Owen. He's sweating profusely. There is no wind in this desert, and we're baked twice: once from what's left of the sun and once from the heat seeping out of the dirt below.

Grant skids to a stop. Above him, Chaco wheels hard right and flares his feathers out behind us in a low loop. He coasts right over my shoulder and settles on Grant's head. Grant ticks forward with the force of his landing but keeps his eyes focused on a bare patch of land in front of us ringed by caution tape. It's almost a perfect square—I'd say two hundred feet or so per side. The dirt looks hammered down here. Like a big square elephant sat on it. Grant won't go past the tape, and when Owen tries to step past him, Grant tugs him back.

"Is this the place?" I ask. "The thin place?"

Grant nods, his eyes sweeping the flat land. "See that rig over there?" He points at the rig I saw from the distance without looking at it. Now that it's near dark and the rig is lit up, I see at least ten people moving about underneath the spotlights.

"This was where that rig was first set up. 'Cept they couldn't set up right cause the bell was here. They broke a bunch of drill bits. Those cost a ton of cash. So they moved the rig over there."

Chaco chirrups, and Grant nods. "Well, yeah. Other things went wrong too. The rig sort of broke down. It all kind of went to chaos."

Chaco caws.

Grant's eyes are unfocused again. "This is a thin place close to chaos, but it's broken. It's leaking."

"Leaking what?" I ask, still catching my breath.

Grant seems to struggle with this. I can see him talking to Chaco in silence.

"Souls," Grant says. "But not like Pap's soul. Pap is good where he's at. This is the other kind of soul. From the other side of the river. The kind that don't care where they're at."

Rivers and souls aside, I can't see anything. I squint and still can't see anything. Just the desert at sunset, and all I can hear are the distant clanks and calls of men at work. Beside me, I see Owen squinting too, with his hands on his hips.

"I can't see anything," Owen says, echoing my thoughts. "Are you sure, Grant?"

Chaco chirrups again from Grant's shoulder, and this time he flares out his wings. They reach twice again the width of Grant's shoulders. Grant steps back and holds the fist that clutches the bell out in front of him.

"Chaco says to grab your crows," Grant says.

Owen reaches in his pocket, and I grab my totem at the same time. In an instant, we blink into the thin world. The first thing I notice is Grant, standing like a toy soldier in front of us, his body a faint outline of smoke, but the bell that he holds in his hand blazes like the sun. So does Chaco sitting atop his head. In fact, I don't think I could rightly call Chaco a bird any longer. He's a changing thing. A bird one moment, then a lithe, leonine thing prowling across Grant's shoulders the next before returning to bird form again. The two of them stand like pillars of white against what I see beyond them.

I see the thinning that Grant is talking about. It floats in the air like a swimming pool, reflecting light in crazy, distorting ways. And in the middle, it's leaking. Strange lights float on the far side of the pool. They zip and shake and spin spastically, but they're all slowly moving toward the crack, like hundreds of strange fish pulled toward a leak in a billion-gallon aquarium.

"Get ready," Grant says. "If you have to let go of your crow, get away. Don't let them touch you. And don't worry about me. Chaco says they hate the bell because the bell has rules to it and they hate rules."

Chaco's wings flare out larger than a beach umbrella over Grant. I can feel the subtle pinch of the thin place already starting to squeeze me, but I ignore it. I grab Owen's hand. Owen squeezes back. There is a moment of pure desert silence. Then I hear a powerful splintering sound, like a windshield cracking, and I see the thin place break.

The bobbing lights drop out of the fissure one by one, and as they do, they change. They become a misty black smoke that sifts and clumps together into ever-changing shapes of two- and four-legged creatures. Each of them is different but for one thing. Every one of them has a hollow, swirling black pit where their face should be.

These things look and lurch like monsters from the darkest closet of my imagination, but I don't sense malice from them. The color of their smoke, the way it drips from them, I recognize it. Some of the worst cases I dealt with at Chaco Health Clinic had a touch of it—usually the poor men and women who were beyond themselves with addiction, people who didn't know who they were anymore, only that nothing around them made sense and everything was spiraling out of control. Their new normal was chaos. They had a touch of this black. These things *are* that black.

"If you can push them back through the break, chances are they'll go their own way on the other side," Grant says.

"Chances are?" Owen asks. "That's the best we got?"

"Just kick them back where they came from. We gotta hold them here, in this stretch of desert. No further," Grant says, with boyish simplicity.

Owen looks at me with a wide-eyed, terrified smile. "Hold them here. Why the hell not? Like the little Dutch boy."

He lets out a nervous chuckle, and that's when they seem to notice us. A four-legged thing half trips, half leaps toward Owen as he's talking to me. I step forward and grab it where I guess its neck would be. It shifts and turns in my hands, wriggling like a snake. I scream and drop it. The slimy-but-dry feeling of its scales sets me wiping my free hand on my jeans. I let out a string of *ews* that I'm not proud of, but what can I say? I hate snakes.

My hopping around draws more of them our way, all of them still shifting but settling on a human form. Owen doesn't let them. He's got his hands up and in fists, one with the crow in it, and he goes boxing. He gets one good, clean uppercut to the first thing then kicks the rest over. He looks a bit like a disgruntled postman taking it out on some boxes, but it works. I watch as he drags one soul back under the break and then drop-kicks it upward. He staggers and winces, limping a bit, but the thing is sucked up, back through the crack. It's like a vacuum. The middle of the break drops the souls out, but the edges suck them back up. It's a balance, albeit a broken one.

Owen turns to me and gives me a look that says *if I can do it, so can you*. Which makes me pull my shoulders back, put my own hands up, and get to work. A smaller form floats over to me, and I catch it with my free hand. It shifts under my grip, first into a four-legged thing of some sort, then a flapping bird, then a hissing rodent. I almost drop it then, but I manage to rear back and chuck it into the updraft, where it's sucked away again. Owen's drop-kicking like it's his job, but still more come. For every one we kick out, two slip in. This is a losing fight.

I notice that when the souls hit the ground they change the ground as well. They create divots and mounds where none were before, like their very touch rewrites the world. Even the air they pass through smears and clouds. I try to get Owen's attention to show him what I mean, but my initial butt-kicking adrenaline is wearing off and the painful pinch of the crow is seeping in. It makes my teeth rattle. I have to let go of my totem.

In a blink I'm back in the living world, standing in the middle of an empty patch of desert. I can't see the souls, but I can see how they muddy the world as they slip through the break in the sky above me. Ten feet away I know Owen struggles with something out of my sight because I can see how it blurs everything around him. Behind me, Grant stands stock still like a tiny shaman, his eyes blank and distant, his bell hand out. Above me, Chaco dives with a screaming call and blinks out of sight and into a battle of his own. I shake my hand off like I touched a hot stove and take in several gulps of hot desert air. I grab my totem again.

Chaco slams into some roiling black shape that looks near enough to a person. It whips and boils around him as he drags it back to the break and flings it in the updraft. Owen is tiring, not only from struggling with the souls but also from the bite of his crow totem. His teeth grind; his face is pale and splotchy. He shoves another creature high into the air. It's sucked away from him, but he staggers and sits hard on the ground before blinking away to the real world. When he flits back to the other side, he's a murky outline to me, but I can clearly see two of the souls focus on him, as if suddenly picking up a different scent. His living, breathing scent. They start to make their way toward him, bulky blocks of smoke that fall into form and shape as they lumber forward, and that he cannot see. Above, Chaco screeches, and Grant translates, his voice shrill and cracking.

"Don't let them touch you in the living world! They'll change you forever if they touch you! You gotta hold the totems!"

Owen seems not to have heard; he's still panting and flexing the hand that held his totem, now on the desert floor next to him. The souls march nearer to him, ten feet away now, but he can't see them. They've turned the air and the earth around them into rifts and rivets and bubbles and streaks, charring some bits and smoothing others but forever changing everything, and I know that they'll do the same to Owen if they touch him. So I grip my crow tightly, lower my head, and come at them sideways.

The lead figure reaches out to Owen, trailing a sooty mess where its arm passes, and it grabs his lapel before I can slam my shoulder into it. I sink into it like squeezing a sponge, only instead of water coming out, I'm inundated with a muddy blast of chaotic pictures and images until it staggers away from me. My shoulder tingles, but I'm otherwise unchanged.

Owen looks at his shirt collar in horror. It's smeared. Not burned, not tattered or torn or broken, but smeared. Like an impressionist painting. Its essence has been changed.

"Good lord!" Owen says then scrambles to grab his totem. He blinks into the thin world next to me just in time to see the second figure a few feet from him, reaching out to him. It pauses as Owen leaves the living world, almost like it's disappointed. Then Owen grabs it by the neck, spins around so he's behind it, and drags it one-handed back to the updraft. He squats and encircles the thing's trunk with both hands then grunts and heaves it up into the break, where it's sucked away. He reaches for me and grabs my hand, and together we carefully step away, back to Grant. As we do, another soul slips out and another. We blink back to the living world, and I steady myself with both hands on the ground.

"What the hell are these things?" Owen asks.

"Chaco says they're souls that went down the chaos side of the river," Grant says, his voice distant.

"I can feel it, when I touch them in the thin world. I get these—"

"Bad thoughts," Grant finishes.

Owen nods, working his fingers like he's trying to get the blood flow back.

I know even without being able to see them that the souls have turned their attention back toward us. Owen shakes his head.

"The pinch of the thin place is getting worse. It's like one long bee sting," Owen says, gasping in the warm air. "I'm gonna be pretty worthless here after too much longer, but maybe I can lead them away from you guys for a bit. Give you a chance to fix that break."

"Owen." I shake my head, but he interrupts me, even as his eyes flick across the deceivingly empty desert around us. They're coming for us, right now. It makes me wince.

"You're more important than I am, Caroline. Always have been. You can do things nobody else can... maybe you can fix that break."

"No," Grant says, interrupting us both. "If you're tired, stay behind me." Chaco swoops down and lands on his head then turns to us and nods.

"Seriously?" I ask.

Chaco nods hard. "Quick!" Grant says, pleading.

Owen and I look at each other, then at Grant, and then scamper to stand right behind him, each of us with one hand on his shoulder. I take a breath and grip my totem, and when I snap into the thin world I have to stifle a scream.

The souls are surrounding us. I count fifteen of them, maybe ten feet from us and pressing in. I grip Grant's shoulder harder than I mean to and try to focus on breathing as Chaco caws loudly.

"Hold still," Grant says. As if I could move a muscle anyway. The four of us stand as still as statues, like we're posing for some ridiculous family portrait. They shamble forward, and I begin to think that maybe Grant just wanted us all to be together when we're smeared out of existence by these things, but when the first soul gets within a couple of feet of us, the bell starts to glow. It's soft at first but enough to give the souls pause. The closest souls press forward again. But the bell glows brighter with each inch they take, and it's as if the light itself is a hardening barrier. The closer the souls get, the more they struggle, until they're stopped cold inches from us, and the bell is blazing like a spotlight from Grant's fist. It's so bright I have to close my eyes. Chaco caws again, and Grant speaks for him.

"The bell is a symbol of order. It's been passed down forever. It creates each Walker, which is a job that keeps order between the worlds. These things are its opposite. Souls that have chosen chaos. They're like opposite ends of a magnet." He looks up at me and smiles. "Stick with me and they can't touch you."

Owen laughs, his eyes dazzling in the light of the bell. I almost sag with relief, but I don't want even another inch of separation between us.

"Take that, you stupid things!" Grant yells. Chaco fluffs his breast up and titters.

"Yeah, you... frickin' stupid things!" Owen says, steering away from a swear word I know he wants to grab. "You ruined my shirt!"

I find myself laughing, too, especially when I see the chaos souls start to fade back, inching away from us, leaving a greasy stain in their wake. Then something grabs their attention. They all turn as one to the right. I follow their line of sight and see that they've turned to the oil rig in the near distance. An engine has revved to life, and another battery of floodlights have kicked on, illuminating a handful of people working on the platform there. I stop laughing. When the souls begin to move toward the oil rig, Owen does too. Grant falls silent. "Oh, no," I whisper.

"We're not easy prey anymore," Owen says. "So they're moving on to what is."

"We gotta stop 'em," Grant whispers, his voice breaking. "Pap worked on a rig like that once. There's someone else's Pap out there. Maybe a bunch of them."

Chaco caws again and lifts off into the air, wheeling above us. "Chaco says to stay behind the bell, do what we can near the break," Grant says quietly.

"It's like spitting into the wind," Owen says. "There's more by the minute. And they're all heading off toward the rig."

"Unless we can plug that hole, we'll just be running in place," I say.

"Chaco says he's working on that," Grant says. I follow Chaco's flight and watch as he dives straight for the break, changing his own form until he's a pencil-thin streak of black feathers. I squeeze Grant's shoulder even harder as he shoots for the break, and in a blink he's gone. For a second I think maybe he's plugged the hole himself, but half a minute later another black soul slips through and hits the battered and scarred ground below the break. Another follows. They form themselves, take one look at us, and then head off in the direction of the rig with the others.

"I think it may be up to us," Owen says.

15

THE WALKER

I thought about jumping. I don't want you thinking that I just counted that out, because that makes me sound like a chicken. But you tell me what you would do in my situation. First of all, the agents are long gone. They were long gone the minute they ducked under the river. The second thing is that I'm in pain for the first time in a while. My jaw feels like a balloon where Douglas hit me, and my knee is all swollen where the earth slammed into it on its way to taking me up into the sky and plunking me here on this magic-carpet-sized mesa about a hundred feet up.

I know I can't die. I'm already dead. When I lose this job, I'll become just another soul in the river—and I pray to who or whatever runs this place that I float the other way when that time comes—but even knowing this, I'm still not so sure that jumping off a hundred-foot cliff would be good for me. And don't get me started on how I'd be jumping in water. You ever jump off a big cliff? The Chaco flats flooded one time when Joey and I were thirteen, and this deep desert pool formed in the middle of the valley for a while. All the kids liked to jump into it from the cliff edges. On a dare, I jumped from what I swore at the time was fifty feet, but now I'm thinking it was more like twenty. I didn't pencil my legs right, and when I hit, I tweaked my knee and got a slap right to the balls that I felt for the next three months. At this height, water turns to cement. Maybe not soul-river water, but still...

The third thing is, the whole landscape is bucking and shifting at random, and I have this terrible feeling that as soon as I chuck myself off this cliff it'll shift and melt, and I'll become a smashed bug for no reason.

So that's why I'm still up here. If you're wondering. Now that I hear myself, it does sort of sound chickenshit. I wonder what Caroline would think of me, flat as a door on this mesa, batting back and forth the idea of jumping. She'd see right through me. That's her gift. She'd see that I'm really thinking about whether it matters in the long run anyway. I'm either solo up here forever or solo down there forever. Say I catch the agents, stop them from ruining things, then what? It's back to the solo workday. Forever. Neither choice gets me closer to her.

Plus, what Parsons said back when the bell rang still stings a bit. Here I was thinking that the agents wanted my job so bad that they'd go to the ends of the earth and beyond for it, but it turns out they just wanted to get beyond the veil. Then he called me a day-laboring peasant.

What an asshole.

All I'm saying is things have me in kind of a funk right now. I know that time is precious, but I'm getting jaded. Time is slowly losing its importance to me. I'm like the annoying guru at the top of the mountain who pisses off the pilgrims. Everyone dies at one time or another. Sure, they may bottleneck at the veil without me there to snip their lines, but why not just sit on a fucking rock until the dam bursts?

Anyway, I'm not proud of it, but that's what I'm thinking on my rock, when out of the corner of my eye I spy a long slice of black shoot from the river, like the edge of an obsidian knife. As I watch, the back half of the slice catches up with the front half to form a beak and tail feathers, and two wings shoot out with an audible bang. I hop up. It's Chaco! I suspected Chaco might be able to travel through the break, but I didn't dare hope he'd come for me. I leap up and wave my hands.

"Hey! Over here! Chaco!" I laugh and then cut it short as a wave of vertigo hits me, or maybe the plateau shifts a little. I have to catch my balance. Then I get to waving again. "Over here!"

Chaco wheels around. "Yeah, yeah. I see you. I see you," he says. And he doesn't sound happy. I step back, and he lands in a fit of dust at my feet, flaps his wings a few times before tucking them in, then just stares up at me.

"What?" I ask.

"Where are the agents? I only ask because I swear when I last saw you, you were going after them. And yet here you are without them."

"They jumped in the river." Chaco follows where I point and furrows the fine feathers on his head. He turns back to me.

"And what the fuck are you doing? Working on your tan?"

"No," I say, fully aware I sound like a child. "It's just... I dunno... did you know I can get hurt here? What's up with that?"

"Of course you can get hurt here. This is the doorway to chaos. The rules don't apply. Or if they do, it's on and off. Nothing is for sure. I'd have thought the freaky landscape might have tipped you off on that one."

"Well, that's another thing, I thought maybe this plateau would... sort of... go back down." I'm reaching now.

"Or stay up here for eternity," Chaco says. "Which it has an equal chance of doing. Given that there are no rules here."

I know I don't have much of a leg to stand on, so I do what I always do when pressed against the wall. I get pissed. It helps, a little. "Hey, fuck you, man. Excuse me if I have to think about it for a bit before I throw myself off a cliff. You're not on this side of the coin."

I should know by now that this type of shit doesn't work on Chaco.

"Do you have any idea what is going on in the mortal world right now?" he asks, clawing his way up my front until he's right in my face. I open my mouth then close it. I assume things are going downhill fast, but I don't really know. I don't really know anything about what is going on, to be honest.

"Owen and Caroline are standing with Grant against a frickin' platoon of chaos souls. A platoon, Walker. They're coming from a break in the thin place where the bell landed. It's sourced directly from this end of the river. Right down there. And if we don't close it, I got reason to believe all the thin places will start to break down. Everywhere."

"What are chaos souls?" I ask quietly, my mind racing.

Chaco turns to the river and points with his wing. "Those are chaos souls. This side of the river is chock full of them. The river only exists on this plane, but it's very deep. Sometimes it gets close to other planes. There are thin places where the bottom of that river gets too close to the living world, and the thin places are cracking because those two assholes have been screwing with things. The river is leaking, and your friends are caught up in it." He's puffing rapidly now.

"Chaos souls..." I repeat. That doesn't sound good. "Are those like... like demons or something?" The Navajo believe that demons are trapped souls that wander the earth. It fits. But Chaco shakes his head.

"Demons," he says, as if I'm stuck in the Stone Age. "What did you see when you first came through with Abernathy?"

"Nothing. I mean, a shore. The river. It was calm."

"No judge, no jury weighing Ab's life?"

"No."

"No winged St. Peter behind his ledger, looking your name up, running your life down, telling you which way to go?"

"No. Ab seemed to know which way to go. He felt called to the other side."

Chaco nods. "Toward the side of order. The side of light. That's because that's the kind of man he was in life. But if you happened to cross over with any of those guys down there, they'd tell you that it just felt right for them to go toward the other side. This side. Where you are right now. Sitting on your ass."

I look down on the churning souls below. "So they're here of their own accord."

"That's right. These souls brought themselves here. They aren't demons, they aren't ghosts, they're souls that feel that the end of this side of the river is where they belong. Now if that's damned, so be it. Damned can mean a lot of things in my book."

"What's at the end of this side of the river?"

Chaco settles his feathers for the first time. Sort of slumps a bit. "That's something you gotta find out for yourself. Because that's where the agents went."

I know Chaco knows what's at the end of the river. "Is it... is it a lonely place?" I ask. I know full well how lame it sounds coming out. I also know I'm showing my hand to Chaco. Showing him what's really bothering me. So it's good of him when he softens his bird brow. He understands.

"It's a place of chaos, Walker. Sometimes lonely, sometimes not. What I do know is that it's never one thing for long. It's not a place of peace."

"And I gotta go there, huh?"

"If you don't, the living world you knew will be overrun. The girl you love will be wiped away forever. These souls don't just want chaos. When they're this far down the river, they *are* chaos. They rewrite everything they touch in the living world. You and I both know Caroline. We know she's a soul that would follow Ab's path down the river. But if one of those things touches her, they could change her, and she'd be powerless to stop it. Maybe she'd end up down there. Maybe she'd be of two minds, ripped apart."

I find myself locking my jaw. I find myself balling my fists. I step to the edge. And damn if it isn't still just as far down.

"I know what you're thinking, Walker. You've been running through a *woe is me* scenario up here. You're getting the itch. I've seen it before, with past Walkers. It's really hitting you now that you are all you've got out here. You're getting thoughts that aren't like you. Thoughts like 'What is it to me if the world goes to hell?' But you gotta remember, man. Remember them. Remember her. And she's not alone. But if things go wrong here—and they're going very wrong right now, my man—if they keep it up, she could be lost forever. Do you want that? Remember her."

And I do. I remember her. It's the color of her soul string that I remember first. The *colors*, actually, because she has way more than one. I got to see them for a bit, before I left. The best way I can describe them is like the swirling colors on the skin of a floating bubble when the sunlight catches it just right. And then I think of that bubble popping. Or worse, being *smeared* somehow. Smudged out by the chaos souls dripping from the crack at the bottom of the river. The river I gotta jump into.

"Fine. Fuck it. For her," I say. "See you, Chaco."

And I jump.

I fall a long time. It's like the land drops out below me, farther and farther. I tell myself not to flail, but I flail. I flail like a ragdoll. I scream too. Guess I haven't learned anything since the Chaco flats jump. I get ready for another ball whacking.

But then, just when I can see the souls roiling the water, I feel Chaco's claws on my back, ripping my shirt to get a grip under my arms, and the earth stops rushing at me. Instead it only zooms. Then it floats toward me.

"Chaco! You could do this the whole time?"

"Yep," Chaco says, his big beak above my head. "But I had to see if you would jump."

Before I can piece together the weight behind that statement, Chaco says, "Good luck, Walker. Give 'em hell." And he drops me into the river.

16

GRANT ROMER

Back before Mom and Dad died, the three of us and Pap would sometimes go to church. Mostly for Easter and Christmas, but sometimes Mom would get the idea to go on a random Sunday, so I've been to church a bunch of times. After Mom and Dad died, I think Pap kinda turned on the whole thing, so the two of us never went. But I still remember Sunday school, and I know about souls and how they're the real *you* inside you. Chaco says these black smoke monsters are souls, but if they are, they sure ain't any kind of soul I've ever heard of.

I always thought that you got your soul, and if you believe in God and do all right with your life, you'll end up in Heaven and get to see your mom and dad and pap again. If you don't do those things, well, you'll be sorry and sent to Hell. These chaos souls sure look like they come from Hell. But they don't look sorry. They don't look like they're burning or hollerin' in pain, neither. I'll tell you what they look like: they look like sick animals. Crazy, smoking animals that are wandering around doing what they do because that's all they know now. Like the mangy, rabid coyotes that sometimes come in from the desert and have to be put down.

When that bunch of them got real close to Caroline, Owen,

Chaco, and me, I didn't feel like they wanted to get at *me,* Grant Romer. They wanted to get at everything that made it so I was standing there in that spot. It was like the bell formed a little snow globe around us, and the chaos souls wanted to turn all of us to water and mix up the snow globe so there wasn't nothin' recognizable in it but a bunch of bits. They weren't angry about it, or scary like the agents are scary. I think it's just what they are.

And what they're doing right now is heading straight for a drilling rig, like ants to a kitchen. I think it's the noise—or maybe the smell— but mostly the way it's all working together: people and machine. There's no chaos there. But it's coming. The souls are messin' up the desert where they step and screwing up the sky where they pass. One steps through a tumbleweed, and the tumbleweed stretches out like putty until it's a dripping line.

"We can't just sit here and watch all those men get smeared," I say. "I don't care what Chaco said."

I look up at Caroline and Owen, and they both nod.

"Really?" I ask. "You ain't gonna try to stop me or nothin'?"

"He said stay behind the bell. He didn't say where the bell could go," Caroline says. "I know we can't stop these things; there's too many of them. But what we can do is warn those men at least."

"Convince a bunch of good ol' boy roughnecks that an army of cell-destroying chaos souls is at their doorstep," Owen says. "Sounds easy enough." He's rolling up his sleeves. I can't tell if he's joking or if he's dead serious. I'm beginning to think with him it's always a little bit of both, because Caroline smiles.

"Leave the convincing to me," Caroline says. "I'll know what to say."

Owen looks at her then looks down at me. I shrug. I've seen weirder things today.

"Let's roll," Owen says. "You're in the lead, big guy. We follow you."

I start running toward the rig and thinking about giraffes again, and then all of a sudden I'm crying. Thankfully we're running pretty fast, and I'm in the lead so Caroline and Owen don't see.

The last of the sun still shines off the tip of the rig. The giraffe stands tall, but if the chaos souls get to it, it won't for much longer. For everything to be okay, so many different parts have to keep working together. Especially the blowout preventer, the guts of the giraffe that kept Pap safe. It has to keep working to keep these men safe too.

We cut wide around the march of the souls. Caroline holds on to my hand, and every now and then Owen stops, grabs his crow, and checks to make sure we won't run into any of the souls and wipe ourselves out by mistake. We keep running, and he catches up a little bit sweatier each time with some added directions. *Cut left. Shoot straight through. This is the front of them. Now they're behind us.*

The sun is nearly set now, and the shadows are long. I look behind us and see a flat stretch of desert that's shifting and moving in little ways with the touch of the souls, like it's made of new paint that's getting rained on. You might miss it if you didn't know what to look for, but once you see it, it's impossible to unsee. It's like the desert is playing tricks on us.

"How far back are they?" Caroline asks. The hands we hold are sweaty, but she hasn't let go, and neither have I.

"Closest one is about fifty yards or so. They're wandering but with a purpose. I think we've got five or so minutes max to get all these people out of here," Owen says. Then he looks at Caroline. "What do you need from me?"

Caroline scans the rig. It's loud and smells like gas. She squints, looking for something beyond what we can see, but she shakes her head. "We gotta get someone who's in charge."

"Oh, I can do that!" I say. "He'll be in the toolbox. C'mon." I grab their hands and pull them after me toward the side where there's a shed. A few men in hard hats look at us with questions in their eyes, but we ignore them and they don't say anything. I stop in front of a makeshift staircase made out of big bricks that leads to an open door. I hop up and in the shed with Caroline and Owen close behind. Inside, three men stare at a bunch of computers with all sorts of numbers and shapes running up the screen. All three wear hard hats, but two of them are in nice clothes, and one is in a greasy brown monkey suit. He has a big brown beard with bits of grey in it, and his hands are tanned and thick and strong like Pap's. I run up to him.

"Excuse me, sir. Are you the tool pusher?" I ask. He looks to his right above my head, then he looks down.

"What the fu... heck is this? Sam, is this your kid?" he asks.

One of the two men sitting down swivels around. He blinks at me. "No. This yours, Don?" The other man turns around for a second then turns back.

"I don't have kids," he says.

"He's with us," Caroline says.

"And who are you?" the tool pusher asks. "This is a tight hole, ma'am. That means no visitors allowed. And it certainly ain't no place for a kid."

"You're in danger," Caroline says, stepping forward, stopping him. "You and your whole crew. All of you need to leave this place now. It's life or death."

This gets everyone's attention. Both men swivel back around. The tool pusher squints at us. He has the same lines shooting from the sides of his eyes that Pap had, and I almost step closer to him. But then I feel Owen squeeze my shoulder a bit, and I fight the feeling down. Pap would be the first to say that this ain't the time for stuff like that.

"Who the hell put you up to this?" one of the clean men asks. "Did corporate do this? This shit isn't funny."

"No, it's not," Owen says. "You have less than five minutes to get everyone off this rig." His voice is rising, but Caroline stops him with a touch. She hasn't stopped looking at the tool pusher. I mean *looking* at him. The way she looked at me that helped me get up off Pap when Pap was gone.

"You know what I'm talking about, don't you?" Caroline says.

The tool pusher shakes his head, but I can tell she's getting to him. If anything, he looks scared. Caroline steps forward, and he steps back.

"Now just a minute," the other clean man says, getting up from his seat, but Owen steps in front of him.

"Sit down, kid," he says. Which is funny, because he doesn't look like a kid to me. He looks about the same age as Owen. But the guy listens. He sits down.

"Nothing about this operation has been going right," Caroline says, looking carefully at the tool pusher. "You had to move the rig, even. Things are breaking. Your veteran men are screwing up." The tool pusher licks his lips and straightens his hat, his eyes on her. "You think you've lost it. You're wondering if you're too old. You think maybe the men don't respect you anymore. That you can't do your job."

The tool pusher lets out this tiny little huff of breath, like he was hugged real hard.

"It's not your equipment, it's not your men, and it sure as heck isn't you. It's this place. And this place just broke open. Now, please. For the love of God. Get your men and yourselves out of here." Caroline stands up straight again. It's quiet for a couple of seconds.

"Sound the alarm, Don," the tool pusher says quietly.

"What? Just because some crazy lady came in here and—"

"Sound the goddamn alarm! Clear the floor! Get everyone out! Now!"

"Just calm down, Jerry—"

"Oh, for fuck's sake," Jerry says, pushing the man aside as he flips open a box and presses a big red button. An alarm goes off that sounds like a truck horn on repeat. He looks back at us, eyes wide. "You better be right, ma'am, or you just cost us a boatload of money. And our jobs."

But Caroline isn't looking at him, and I'm not sure she even hears him. Her head is cocked like she's straining to hear something out the door. I run to the doorway, but I can't see anything but bright lights and, beyond that, complete blackness. Desert night and worse. But I don't need to see anything to hear the screaming.

All six of us rush out of the toolbox and look around to see where it's coming from, which is probably why none of the workers notice when Caroline and Owen disappear into the thin place to get a better look. They're back in a blink.

"Over there," Owen says. He's pointing at the butt of the giraffe, and it's blowing a lot of smoke. Way too much smoke. The screaming is coming from the men on the drilling floor. I know it's the smoke that's scaring them, but if they looked carefully they'd have a lot more to scream about. The engine is smoking because it's being warped. And it's being warped because a chaos soul is walking right through it, trying to get to the men on the platform. With each step, the metal and gears and belts change, some to sand, some to drippy goop, some to black smoke. It looks like a big thumb is slowly wiping right through it.

The tool pusher and his friends take off toward it before any of us can scream at them to stop, but they get about ten feet before the engine catches fire. It's just a little fire, just a lick of a thing, but a fire on a rig is very, very bad.

"Clear the rig!" the tool pusher screams, waving his hands. He cuts right and grabs a red spray-bottle fire extinguisher while the other two just sort of stand there staring at it. He blows right past them with the big bottle in his hand, fiddling with a lever on top.

"He's gonna run right into them," Owen says. He turns to Caroline. "Stay here with Grant. I'll be back." Before Caroline or I can say anything, he puts his hand in his pocket and disappears. I try to step forward, but Caroline holds me tight. I look up at her, and I can see in her eyes that she's holding herself as still as she is me. She wants to be out there with him.

"I'm just gonna look," she says. "I'll still be right here." She disappears too. I watch the tool pusher running around hell-bent on getting to that fire. He has the spray bottle out in front of him. Caroline comes back. Her face is white. "They're all over," she says.

"Owen?" I ask.

"He's fighting them, but he can only push them away. He's gonna get overwhelmed."

Owen just about scares the snot out of the tool pusher when he blinks back right in front of him and takes him out at the waist. Both of them go down to the ground in a mess of limbs. Owen presses him flat, like a big invisible axe is passing over them both, and I bet in a lot of ways it probably is.

"Forget the fire!" I hear Owen scream. "It's too late for that! Go!"

The tool pusher is sitting as if he just fell smack off his bike and onto the concrete, and he's checking to see if he's still in one piece. So Owen just gets behind him and pulls him up and out of the way, his boots dragging through the dirt. And good thing too, 'cause that's when the engine starts making this heavy hammering sound, then a whine, and then it blows to pieces.

There are still men on the giraffe's back when the engine blows. It smacks all of them flat as pancakes. At first I think they're all dead because the bell gets heavy and I can feel it come together. I hold it real still until it passes. Then two of the men start to move on the ground, and I see the smearing of chaos souls moving toward them. The souls didn't stop at the engine. They don't want the engine. They want the people. At least three souls are cutting their way toward the crew like nails slowly scraping through butter. The giraffe makes a big groan, and its neck bobs a little to the right. I look back at the men crawling around on the platform. Sure, they could be like the guys at the man camp that said mean things to Owen and Caroline. But maybe they're guys like Pap. Little Paps. Working at becoming tool pushers. Guys with grandsons.

"I can't let them die," I say. And I run. I slip through Caroline's grip like we're playing Red Rover. She screams after me, but I'm pretty fast, and I'm already halfway across the grounds in a flash. I feel a whump of air to my right, and then she's right there keeping pace.

"I'm the only one that can keep the souls away from them," I say, before she can get mad at me. I glance up at her. She's not mad at me. She wants this as much as I do. We go wide around the body of the giraffe and up the metal steps on the far side from the engine fire. I'm up top first. There are three men, two of them rolling around and crying and one not moving at all. The souls are slicing butter our way.

They're just a couple of feet from the one that's not moving. I start to go to him when Caroline grabs me.

"No," she says, and her voice is heavy. "He's gone. These other two. Stand in front of them."

So I do. I stand in front of them with my feet apart and set and my hands on my hips, and I feel the bell start to shine in my fist. Behind me, Caroline corrals the two men until they're in a row at my back, then she comes back to me and puts her arm around me. She squeezes. It makes me puff out my chest more.

The two men are shaking it off, touching their bodies and poking at their ears because I bet they can't hear nothin' but ringing. One gets up and weaves away behind us and off the platform, but the other has a cut-up leg. He left a trail of blood when Caroline dragged him behind me. He tries to scoot away, but Caroline grabs him by the scruff and leans down and whispers something. His eyes get all big, but he stays put. The three of us watch as the souls reach the dead man. One cuts right through him. It's exactly like you'd expect and worse. Just this past Fourth of July I brought out my firework collection and my bucket of army men and played war with 'em. I dug a pit in the sand out back of Pap's house and started a fireworks fire with a bunch of sparklers and threw in a few of the army men to watch them melt. I picked one up with a sparkler and it stuck to it, so I wiped it off on the wood edge of the sandbox. This is just like that, only more red. The man behind us screams, but he stays put. Thank God the guy was dead. If he wasn't, I'd probably be screaming right with him.

The bell shines real bright, enough to make me squint, and I know that the chaos souls are here. Right next to me. Maybe inches from me.

"Stay still!" Caroline yells. All three of us do. It's just like back in the desert. They can't get to me or any of us. But back there it was solid earth we were standing on. Here, it's a sheet of metal above the ground. It starts to bubble where I know the soul is standing. Then it melts and flakes away, turning to ash and dripping to sand at the same time. One hole forms then another, and the souls drop below the platform like a hot iron through ice, leaving a muddy, dead-bug streak behind them. Which would be good, 'cept that they're dropping on the guts of the giraffe.

I look down through the holes and see the drill pipe slice in two, and all of a sudden the giraffe is barfing oil. It blows out high in the air in one big black spew, and then it shuts off just as quick. The blowout preventer clamped it down, and I have enough time to wipe my face and eyes off and look back down to see the blowout preventer start to bubble and shift like a soul is sitting right on top of it.

I look up at Caroline. She sees it too. The man behind us is throwing a fit. It sounds like he's making enough racket for two men. I turn my head to tell him to shush, but I see he's looking up the neck of the giraffe. I follow his eyes, and sure enough, there's another man. Way up high in the crow's nest. Sitting right on the head of the giraffe. He was probably repairing a line or something up there, which is just terrible luck. I don't know why he hasn't used the escape route. They usually have a zip line that leads all the way to the ground, but then I see the line dangling off the side like a leash, useless. At first I think he's hollerin' to get us to save him, but then I see he's hollerin' and pointing at the engine, because it's leaking gas in a long, burning line that's running right toward the bubbling guts of the giraffe.

17

THE WALKER

The first thing I realize when I hit the water, other than that I want to hug my bird friend and punch him in the beak at the same time, is the feel of the souls.

The "water" isn't even water, so to speak. It's not wet. Which makes sense. I assumed this setup was a bit more complex than a bunch of souls floating down a river like rubber ducks. The feeling isn't so different from the soul map, actually, the sense of being totally enveloped by a place. But with the soul map I'm sewing up the strings of those that leave—tucking away their connection to the living world. It's cosmic housekeeping. The soul itself I don't deal with anymore, because I send it here.

Well, here they all are. And, man oh man, do I have to deal with them. I try for a pencil- straight landing but screw it up and hit the river at a jackknife. And I'm surrounded by souls. Not all of them can get out of my way. Not all of them want to get out of my way. And the ones I end up touching sizzle with images and echoes of the lives and experiences that made them what they are.

I don't think it'll surprise you when I say they are in complete chaos.

Each brush against a soul brings me a rapid-fire slideshow of pictures that makes no sense to me. A car wreck as seen by a pedestrian, a slab of snow breaking from the side of a mountain, a roiling anthill, a broken tile set among a thousand whole tiles, a stream of water blown by the wind. Things like that, but millions of them, all in a blink. And there's a feeling, too, coming from each of them. It's just an imprint, an echo, but it's there. Each is a shade different, but they all rub me the same way. The closest I can come to explaining it is this: You know that feeling you get when you're driving your car and you come up on a wreck and you know it's a bad one? That feeling that you don't want to see what happened, but you do at the same time? Everybody has a little bit of that tendency in them. Back on patrol in Chaco, we'd get bad wrecks on the straightaways north through the flats, and sometimes we'd have to have one officer whose sole job it was to keep the rubberneckers moving through. It's human nature to have some interest in the mess and the destruction. Well, these souls have a lot more than just *some* interest. The feeling I get is that these are the guys that would stop traffic whole. Or maybe even cause another wreck from looking too hard. They feed off of it.

And after a while, it gets to me. I feel my own brain turning a bit. I'm getting panicky. I take a bunch of deep breaths, but I keep running into souls. They're everywhere, all around me, lighting the river a fogged-over, electric white. It takes me a bit to position myself to best avoid them. I shift and arch, ducking low and swimming high. The souls only illuminate more souls as I drop further. The pressure doesn't change, but the souls do thin out a bit as I go lower. I touch for the bottom with my toes. It feels spongy and soft, but it holds me. I start walking.

I get to the break Chaco was talking about after just a few minutes. The souls are slowly spinning around it, sort of like when you swirl water around a bottle and create a tornado. This is much more subtle, but it's here. The break is pulling the souls down into it. I watch one spin slowly, like a floating leaf, down, down, and then disappear. I walk up to the spot with caution. After all it took to get me here in the first place, the last thing I want to do is get sucked out.

I stand just outside of the pull and crouch down. The break is really more like a jagged tear. I wish there was something I could do to plug it somehow, but there's nothing here. The closer I get, the more pieces break away. I can see through it to the darkness beyond, and it's different from the darkness of the bottom of the river. It's a dark I know. A desert dark. I get the feeling that in order to close this thing, I'm gonna have to get rid of the agents and the knife first.

I stand. Above me, another soul is caught in a slow, looping spiral downward. I skirt the edge of the break and pick up the pace down the riverbed. The souls zip and shiver and buzz and weave all around me. I keep my hands up in front of my face, partly out of self-defense and partly because I don't want to run into anything. From my perch on high, I saw that the river flattened to nothing not too far from where I jumped in—for whatever that's worth in a world that changes from moment to moment.

And just like that, I'm at the end. I don't hit a wall or a dam but a cavern. A huge, domed cavern. The river feeds into it at the bottom of one side. I thought the river was big, but now it looks like a little stream trickling into the ocean. I can see through the ether of the place, up, up, and all around myself. I feel like I'm a grain of sand inside a giant eggcup, the kind Gam used to have a pair of—porcelain things she always kept clean but that I never saw her use. Countless souls light the cavern a pulsing, electric blue. And hanging from the center of this massive eggcup is a big, black pearl that would fit nicely inside of a crater. It hangs like an earring and shines with a wicked black patina, and it's where all the souls are going. It's also where I see Parsons and Douglas.

The agents stand out like two floating specks of black in a snow globe on crack. Also, the souls seem to want no part of them, and especially no part of what I see in Parsons's hand, glowing green like a toxic splinter.

"Hey!" I yell. My voice is scratchy, and I clear my throat. "Hey, assholes! What do you think you're doing with that thing?" I kick off the ground and push myself forward, swimming up in the cavern, but they're even farther away than I thought. It takes a second for my voice to reach them, but it does, and Parsons turns around briefly. He has the book in one hand and the knife in the other, and at that moment, he slams the book closed and passes it to Douglas, says a few words, then takes off himself, pushing upward, skirting the shimmering black surface of the massive pearl on his way to the top.

"Parsons! Whatever you're doing, cut that shit out right now! Don't be a dumbass! This place is way too powerful for you, or me, or any of us. None of us should be here!"

Parsons isn't stopping. He's floating up, his suit billowing around him. I can see the bone white of his legs above his black socks. I kick harder. I'm coming up on Douglas now. Fucking Douglas. Always my roadblock. How many times am I gonna have to run into this guy? He pops his shoulders back and squares up at me, but all I can look at is this big pearl. It's hypnotizing, so big that the curvature seems flat, and it shines like a black mirror. I feel like I get a taste of what drives moths to a flame. It takes an effort to pull up, to go after Parsons. Which is what Douglas was waiting for, of course, because he plows into me right as I stretch upward.

I fold over him like a piece of paper, and the two of us go spinning back out into the soup of souls. I lose my breath for a second, but without anything hard to land on, we just spin out into nothing until we slow down. He swings at me, but the momentum of pulling the punch back pushes him backward too. When he throws it, I block, and he does a somersault over my right shoulder.

Forget him. It's Parsons who has the knife. Parsons who's fixing to do something stupid. I kick off back toward the pearl, leaving Douglas behind.

"Parsons! Do you *want* to destroy the world? Is that what gets you off?" I kick harder, and I'm getting close until Douglas grabs my ankle. He yanks me backward and sails over my shoulder to try and get between me and Parsons, but I'm not about to let that happen. I grab his balls as his crotch floats over me and yank him backward again. I crush 'em up a bit for good measure. He curls around himself and groans, spinning in a crouch out to my right. Parsons is two-thirds of the way up the pearl. I go into sprint mode.

I'm sweating like a pig, swimming my ass off through nothing, surrounded by souls. While I gasp for whatever passes as air in this place, I notice what the souls are doing. They're thinking. At least, that's what it looks like they're doing. They're spinning around the pearl thinking, and when they've thought hard enough, they either back off, flowing back toward the river, or they shoot forward and hit the pearl, cracking like eggs. I see it happen right in front of me. A soul zooms by and smacks into the pearl, spreading out like a yoke until it's absorbed and becomes part of the thing.

"Parsons! Hey! You pansy ass! Come fight me!" I scream, gasping and swimming. Hurling insults: the last refuge of the truly desperate. It's not the first time I've been here, but it's definitely the worst. Parsons doesn't buy it. I know he can hear me, but he doesn't care about me. I chance a look over my shoulder. Sure enough, there's Douglas. It's like he's on PCP. Nothing stops the guy. At least he has stubby little legs. He's not gaining on me.

But I'm gonna be too late. I know it. I think I knew it before I even entered this place. I think about what Abernathy said. How he asked if I'd ever considered whether maybe a knife that destroys the plan might also be part of the plan. True or not, right now it doesn't make me feel any better.

I scramble up the pearl, my hands and feet slipping. To either side of me, souls slam into its glossy surface. I get a little soul splash-back. It's like climbing a mirror. I churn my hands and feet, anything to get speed. Then I get too much speed. I fly past Parsons at the top and let out a string of curse words. I flare out like a skydiver above the pearl, trying to slow myself. And that's how I see Parsons win—me floating above him like some sort of sweaty flying squirrel while he stands at the top of the pearl, holding on with one hand to the thin strand that connects the pearl to the top of the cavern. He watches me sail past without interest. Without joy. Without hate. He watches me like I'm a fly buzzing the picnic, on my way to do fly things.

There's a sleeve in the strand anchoring the pearl. Sort of like a pachinko machine, where you'd drop a token and watch it bounce off the pegs, only this thing has one path and one path only, and it runs down the outer side of the pearl. It's the only seam that I can see on the pearl, which is otherwise an alien sort of perfect. Parsons takes the knife and slaps it broadside against the sleeve. He looks up at me again with his dead eyes.

"Parsons. Please. Whatever this thing is, let it lie." My voice is weak. I wouldn't convince myself. And I realize it's because I'm scared shitless again. "There's nothing but destruction in there," I say. And I know it's true.

For the first time, I think Parsons really sees me. He doesn't gloat or smile or laugh triumphantly. None of that. He actually shakes his head.

"No destruction," he says. "Only chaos." As if the two were different. As if I should understand that.

Then he drops the knife.

It slides with purpose, like it was built for that slot. An absurdly out-of-place memory hits me of when I used to play with a marble track as a kid. You dropped marbles onto it, and they'd slide up and down and around a roller coaster track depending on where you dropped them. They stuck like glue to that track. This is like that. The knife slides as smoothly as water down a spout until it hits a chunk of something, then it starts to hiss and bubble. I kick my way down after it until I get close and can see the stoppage is a chunk of rock on top of rock on top of rock like rolled steel, a lock as thick as my thigh. The kind of thing that would stand the test of eternity, unless you had the pick. And the knife is the pick. It burns into it, sizzling brightly like an acetylene torch under water. And it's working.

Before I can reach the knife, it cuts through the rock, breaking it in two. The pearl splits open a tiny bit. I see the fissure, and then I feel the fissure like the kickback of Dad's old twelve-gauge shotgun we used to shoot at yucca in the desert. I reach for the knife, but it slides out of reach, on its way down to the next lock. This one is bigger, nearly the size of my entire body. I think I can catch it there.

Unless Douglas grabs me around the neck, of course. I spin my leg around in a big, looping roundhouse kick that's meant for his face, but he catches that, too. "Dammit, Douglas! If this is how the world ends, if it's because of guys like you, I'm gonna be really pissed off."

Douglas is smiling at me. It's a vacant, black smile shot through with brittle, white teeth. Whatever these two men once were, they aren't that anymore. They've hit ground zero. DEFCON 1. I pull the leg Douglas holds into my body and then snap out with my free foot. It's a pull-push combo, and it hits home hard. Douglas explodes off of me, spread-eagled and floating, falling, spinning until he's far out in the souls and beyond my sight.

I turn back to the knife. It's already halfway through the second lock. My own kick pushed me back a ways, so it takes me a second to get back to where I was and then far too long to get close to the knife. It's almost as if the knife is getting sharper as it cuts, like it's hitting its stride. It even looks different. It's no longer the homemade hack job I saw back in the desert. It's gone military. It reminds me unsettlingly of the scalp knife Danny Ninepoint always carried around with him. The knife that killed my grandmother and my father. And then it cuts through the second lock.

This time it's no shotgun blast that we get. It's a straight-up underwater explosion. It throws me end over end away from the pearl and out into the ether. I don't know which way is up. All I can do is spread out and hope the spinning stops, and when my body finally does stop, it takes another good while for my head to stop spinning. When I right myself, I'm at least a football field away from the pearl.

Like I said. I failed. Whatever it was I was hoping to do here, I didn't do it. Now the only thing left is to see how badly I failed.

The only comfort I have is that it looks like Parsons and Douglas were no more prepared for that explosion than I was. Douglas is about a hundred feet below me, shaking his head and treading ether like he's about to go under. I think Parsons had some sort of grand idea of standing on top of the pearl while his master plan came to be, but that ain't happenin' anymore. He got thrown damn near a hundred feet past me, and he's still spinning. He has that floppy-rag-doll look of someone who's been knocked out.

I want to scream at them, but I don't think there's any *them* anymore. I think they've become tools, and there's no use screaming at your screwdriver. You just look like a fool. Instead I look back at the pearl. There is one more lock. This one is as big as a car. I can see the tiny white light of the knife burning through it, and it's already halfway done.

I don't know what kind of opinion you've formed of me by now. I'm sure it's not *great*, but I hope it's not garbage either. So I hope you'll understand me when I say I'm not the type of guy to go running into oblivion and believe me when I tell you that going after that knife would be oblivion right now. A stupid, foolish, admirable gesture of suicide.

That's not me.

I'm more the type of guy who says if the world is gonna end when that pearl opens, we need to find a way to tackle that problem on level footing. Not floating and spinning. In other words, I have this stupid notion that there's gonna be another day. Maybe that's what comes with a job that gives you a zillion and one days. And that's why I start booking it back toward the river entrance where I came in. My back is to the pearl when the final lock blows. I'd say it goes with about the strength of a car wreck, but I've never been in a car wreck. That's just the biggest, wrenching trauma I can think of in the silent, blue moment before the concussion wave hits me. It's like I'm a puppet getting yanked off stage, but instead of going up, I go down and out. Ass first and half-conscious, I'm flushed out of the eggcup and back into the river, along with a million souls, both agents, and— I catch a glimpse of it—the knife as well, glowing brighter than anything around me. I land on hard ground and flop around like a prize catch in some hick dynamite-fishing contest.

I black out. I'm not sure for how long but not long enough for the aching and buzzing to subside. Caroline's voice echoes in my ears, and it sounds close, but my mind has played tricks on me before where Caroline is concerned. The ground under me shudders and keeps shuddering, which is what I think finally brings me back. I roll over on my stomach. Everything hurts in that way your body hurts before a really disgusting set of bruises shows up. The kind of bruises you have a really hard time explaining away. I'm gonna get those bruises, and I'm dead. That's how bad it is.

I expect to see the river, but what I do see is a trickle of a stream. The rest of the river is gone, and I'm lying on the dry riverbed. Splayed out not even twenty feet from me are the agents. They aren't moving. Around them a few souls linger like beached jellyfish.

In the middle of them all is the knife.

My first thought is to get to the knife, and I do try, but my body won't quite respond. I honestly think if I was alive, I'd be dead for sure after that, but since I'm already dead, my body has to adjust to being dead twice, which it isn't too happy about. I manage a few flops in the knife's direction before I have to steady my head again.

My second thought is to wonder where the hell all the souls went. There were millions of them. That kind of volume doesn't just disappear. I'm looking at one of them now like a stoned teenager, trying to piece my head together, when I hear the sound. It's a rushing sound, like a jet seconds from breaking the sound barrier. I raise my head enough to look down the river, and that's when I see the wave.

The explosion kicked everything out, but now everything is coming back, and it's coming back with force. The wave is higher than I was when I was having my pity party on top of the mesa. It's the biggest wave I've ever seen. It's a tsunami from hell.

I scramble up, forcing my limbs to get it together. I rake my hands and knees over the riverbed. I have to get to that knife. The sound is deafening, and I can feel the air sucking out like the tide would in the ocean. I throw myself toward the knife and grab it with my outstretched hand, but then I feel another hand clamp on mine. I look up; it's Douglas, his black eyes bleeding again. Then Parsons grabs it too, his eyes closed, as if feeling on instinct.

Together they raise the knife up, and I have no choice but to let them. The three of us hold the knife over the river bed as the soul wave bears down on us, and when I think I'm about to black out from the sound and the fury, I see Caroline. She's below me, through the break, like she's floating behind glass. I have to get the knife out of here. I have to get it to her. She'll know what to do, just like she did back at Chaco Rez. Just like she did with me.

I use every last ounce of strength I have to plunge the knife into the riverbed. I reach for Caroline. In my addled state, I think I actually feel her. Then the wave hits, and I lose my grip on everything.

18

CAROLINE ADAMS

I 'm going to be honest with you. I took up the crow totem and joined the Circle to find Ben. That's it. There it is. That's the splat of gravy on the kitchen table. Sure, I wanted to follow the rabbit hole. Sure, I was staggered by what I'd just seen with the bell and Ben dying and the crows and my sight coming into its own. All of that made me curious, but the reason I took the crow in that parking lot was to find Ben. Just like I know Owen did it to be near me.

Joey and Big Hill said looking for the Keeper would be dangerous. They said we might even die. In my line of work, I've been in plenty of situations where the doctor or head surgeon has to deliver that type of news to a patient, and when they do, usually one of two things happens: either the patient gets it, or they flat-out don't believe it.

You'd be surprised how many people flat-out don't believe that they are in the valley of the shadow of death. It's something about humans. We never believe it can happen to us. I saw it all the time back on the oncology floor. So you'd think I'd take it seriously when the warning happened to me. But *oh, no.* I thought of the Circle's warning like you think of those travel warnings the government issues at airports. *Are you feeling ill?* Yes, always. *Please notify the TSA if you are experiencing any flu-like symptoms.* I just got off an airplane. I'm a walking flu-like symptom. *You may be at risk for the H1N1 virus.* I think I'll take my chances at home, thank you. I'm a nurse. I'd know.

In other words, it could never happen to me.

But then it does. Then you realize you're gonna die on an oil rig in Midland, Texas. And Joey Flatwood's warning rings loud in your ears, and you wonder if it was all worth it. You start to stack up your life. List it—pros and cons. But you don't have time for that, because a thin stream of fiery diesel fuel is snaking toward the blowout preventer ten feet below where you stand, and it's about to blow you and your stupid list right off the face of the earth. And you're scared shitless. So you look to your friends. And you find them looking right back at you. And then the thin scream of a rig worker stranded way up high at the top of the structure snaps you out of your inner monologue.

"Go!" he's screaming. "Run!" And you look back at Owen and you can see what he's thinking because at that moment he's the kindest, bravest, most beautiful idiot you've ever seen, and it's practically bleeding off his skin that he's going to try to save that man. He's going to tell you to run and to take Grant, and he's gonna try to maneuver his way up to the crow's nest using his totem, and he's gonna die trying to save a man he doesn't know because that's who he is. He thinks that his Hippocratic Oath somehow signed him up as a super-hero and not a physician. If there's a one percent chance of saving a life, he's willing to take it. With me. With Grant. With the crows. And now with this guy, who is literally screaming at us to get away and save ourselves. The guy behind us gets it—he has a busted-up leg and he still starts shuffle-running away. But not Owen.

Owen reaches for his pocket, so I grab him. I grab him, and I kiss him. This is no little peck on the cheek, no adrenaline-fueled *let's see what it feels like* type thing, either. This one is the real deal. Now, what it means, precisely, whether I'm doing it to keep him from throwing his life away or because I'm falling for him, I don't know. That's 3:00 a.m. talk. That's not fiery-diesel-fuel-coming-at-me talk.

All I know is I want to kiss him. So I do. He freezes. His hand stops going for his pocket.

"You're staying with me," I whisper. And I pull him and Grant off the platform. With one of their hands in each of mine, I literally pull them after me, and I try to block out the screams of the poor man trapped on high. And in a lifetime of tough decisions and of dealing with those decisions, I know that this one will be the worst yet. I know those screams will tear at me forever, but I know losing Owen would tear at me more. Sometimes you have to make a goddamn choice.

We stumble down the warping metal stairs, and Grant instinctively pushes in front of us, holding the bell out straight, allowing us a chance to run into the black desert and at least giving us a fighting chance to avoid the chaos souls. I don't need to blink out to know that they are everywhere. I don't need to see the flare of the bell to know that they have saturated this place. When it blazes, Grant pulls us in another direction. We run through a minefield we can't see until Grant trips, or I trip, or maybe I'm just too exhausted to keep running, and we go down in a tumble right onto a yucca about fifty yards from the rig.

The plant slices at my arms and spears through my pants. I hit the ground hard on my wrists. I'm turned back around and facing the rig. I can see the man waving at the top, and the pain is dulled then replaced by another pain that stings me even deeper. *I'm sorry*, I think, looking at him. But I don't say it. Because that wouldn't do us any good right now. Still, I don't turn away. I feel like I owe it to the man to watch.

Owen screams something, but I'm not sure what. I'm watching the rig. And soon I have to shade my eyes, squint out to see through the blinding light of the bell. I know the souls are everywhere around us. Owen pulls me closer to Grant and tries to back away, but Grant grabs him.

"No!" Grant screams. "I have to protect you!"

"There are too many! You can't protect us. You must protect yourself. We'll be fine as long as we hold the crows!"

In a daze, I reach into my pocket and grab my crow. Owen does too. And in an instant I see that he's right. It's as if the blackest cloud of pollution you ever saw is being blended up inches from my face. The souls are barely recognizable as individual figures anymore. Only a mass of jutting hands and heads and pressing limbs. I turn to Owen, and he grabs my hand, gritting his teeth. "Hold on as long as you can," he says, his voice warped and tinny. At our backs, Grant blazes white with the protection of the bell, but it's pressed so close to him that it's basically a sheath. We'll get no more protection there.

So it's me and the crow and the pain of the thin place. The second I let go, I know I'll be smeared into paste. But already the sting of the thin place is starting, like a dull pinch. I have this bizarre flashback to elementary school when every kid had to hold a chin-up as long as they could in PE, in front of the whole class. I held my head up until my whole body shook, then I fell to the mat below. I didn't last too long.

Already my body is starting to shake with the pain. But there's no mat below me this time. Still, I can't take my eyes off the man on the rig. It's almost worse seeing him through the lens of the thin place. His soul shines brighter. It's terrified, billowing with fear but also with relief that the three of us got away. It's like a cloud around him, as if it burns twice as bright knowing it has so little time left.

Then it blinks out. Just like that, it's gone. The rig explodes. I see it as a shattering picture of greys and greens and blacks, like a great crystal sculpture blown to pieces. It doesn't so much break apart as it fragments before my eyes into a billion different shards. The flame isn't red; it's black, but I feel it like a blistering shower. I cover my face and scream, and I hear Owen and Grant do the same. But Owen never lets go of me, and Grant never scrambles or runs. He presses closer to us, as if he could still save us, and he yells for his pap.

The initial blast of heat subsides and leaves me feeling raw and sunburned, but it doesn't stop there. My teeth are ringing with the pain of the thin place, and my eyes are watery, but I can see the souls still all around us, unaffected. A thin, splattering line of black shoots high into the sky—the oil itself, pressured to blow, and it, too, is on fire. Like a live wire straight from the guts of the earth, it bellows black flames and rolling bursts of smoke into the air. Everything around us smells like burned hair and cloying oil. I'm gasping from the pain and the smells, and my knuckles are white against Owen's. He's tearing up beside me with the effort of holding his crow.

It's really hard to fight through pain when you know it's just prolonging the inevitable. I mean, if all that stands between you and death is pain, why the hell suffer pain? Everything I've ever said to the chemo patients who passed under my care about perseverance, grit, and positive attitudes—all of it sounds so hollow to me now. My words wash back over me, and I'm humiliated by them because I don't think I have the soul to back them up. My grip loosens.

Then Owen clamps his free hand over mine. His face is shaking, his brow ridged and sweating, his eyes nearly closed, but for the first time I think it's him that's reading me, not the other way around.

"You... never... know..." he stammers.

You never know? I want to ask him what he means, but the pain has clamped my mouth shut as sure as if I'm being fried in the electric chair. Why hang on?

Because Owen is hanging on. That's why.

"You... never... know... what..." Owen says again, until the pain courses through his face and the tendons in his neck jut out, and he throws his head back and screams, but he still hangs on.

And then I get it. I get what he's saying. And I get it because there's a *whoosh, pop* followed by a ripping war cry that I swear could have come from an entire canyon full of Navajo warriors but really comes from just one: Joey Flatwood. He's wearing nothing but leather breeches and eagle feathers, and his face is streaked in white and dotted with red. In his left hand he holds his crow totem. Under his right arm, he holds the rig worker from the crow's nest. He's carried him through the thin place, which I didn't think possible. He drops him, unconscious, to the desert floor, and still screaming, he lowers his head, his black hair streaming out behind him. He hits the cloud of chaos souls like some ancient, powerful comet that's finally swung around the galaxy and come back for retribution. He clears through them like a wheat thresher. His cry alone is enough to make those nearest kick and squirm away.

It's like Owen was trying to say: you never know what one more second might bring.

I let go of my crow. Owen does the same, and we collapse onto the sand and let the warm desert night wash over us. Even the diesel-fuel-tinged air smells sweeter than an ocean breeze. We gulp it like water while around us Flatwood blinks in and out of the living world, each time with more speed and momentum than the last. Only minutes later he stands before us, dripping sweat, his muscles corded and shining bright with the distant firelight.

"*Ya'at'eeh,* Keeper!" he says, his face a jubilation. "Greetings!" Then he turns his face to the sky and screams, "They're here! Hill! Over here!"

I hear a thumping, lumbering sound, and for a second I think the rig is collapsing a second time. But then there's a *whoosh, pop,* and there in front of us, handkerchief in hand and on the verge of blubbering, is Big Hill the Bayou Bear.

"Friends!" he roars, reaching down and scooping all three of us up in his arms. He manages two seconds of a crushing hug before he starts sobbing. "I thought I'd lost you! But here you are. I knew the Walker chose true 'nuff when he said you was to guard the Keeper. And Keeper!" His blubbering reaches a new pitch. "Bah gawd, bah gawd, if it ain't you true and true," he says, as if he's known Grant for a lifetime. Grant, to his credit, is taking all of this in with wide-eyed appreciation. He nods numbly where I might have run screaming into the desert.

"The black souls regroup even now, Hill," Joey says, blinking in and out of view, as fast as lightning, and reappearing each time in a different place, his hands up and ready for a fight. Big Hill doesn't even seem to hear him. He's smiling and crying and snotting at the same time.

"Injun Joe come outta the air like thunder one day, and he says to me, he says,

'Hill, we's gatherin' the Circle,' and I says, 'Why?' And he says we gotta fight for the new kids and the Keeper, and that's all he needed to say to me 'cause I always will rememba' when the two of you stayed overn' Hill's Hill as the best time I had, and some o' the best catfishin' I ever had the privilege of fishin' was with the two of you—"

"Hill! Heads up, big man!" Joey says.

Hill looks up. "'Scuse me," he says, and he reaches into his hand-kerchief for his crow and blinks out. I grab my crow to watch, and Hill squares his shoulders and steps right up to a creeping line of black souls. With three swift haymaker swings, two from his right, one from his left, he belts the whole front line about twenty feet back. He turns back to us and folds his crow back away.

"Now, as I was sayin', at first when Injun Joe tells me this, I asked if you was hurt, and he said not yet but that you was fixin' to get into something soon. So this whole time I've been mixed up inside for worry. I mean, my gut wasn't right for *days* while we checked up on these thinnings. I had scuttlebutt and everything. But now we found you and—"

I think Big Hill would have gone on for a day, but he's interrupted by a spectacular cracking sound that seems to shut the whole desert up. Streaks of lightning feather the air just above our heads. Hill has to duck as tendrils of it flit right over us, and every hair on my body feels like it's doing the wave. The lightning moves toward the break, turning the desert purple.

"Hill, where are the others?" Joey asks, his voice quiet but his eyes wide and burning.

"They on their way," Hill says.

"That's good," Joey says. "We're gonna need 'em."

I hear a sound then, like the distant roar of a jet. I grab my crow and watch the lightning coalesce over the thin place, getting brighter and brighter. No more souls are dropping from the break, which should be a good thing, but in my gut I know something has gone badly wrong on the other side. A black line zips out from the break and transforms into a bird mid-flight.

"Chaco!" Grant yells, waving his hands. "We got help, Chaco! Look!"

Chaco caws three times and banks his way over to Grant. He pulls up in a whirl of feathers and settles on Grant's head. The two look at each other.

"Uh oh," Grant says, after a minute.

"What's 'uh oh'?" Owen asks. "I don't like 'uh oh.'"

"There's a wave comin'," Grant says. "Chaco says the Walker is on the other side of the thin place right now. Fighting for us. Against the agents. It's not going great."

I make a conscious effort not to look at Owen. Not to look at anything really, but I find myself peering hard into the dark, as if I could make Ben out across the veil. He's right there... but he's not. He's as far away as he ever was.

"We gotta make our way to the break," Grant says. "Be there for the Walker."

Chaco squawks loudly and caws three times.

"There are hundreds and hundreds of the souls now," I say. "And they're as thick as thieves under the break. We can't make it there ourselves. Even with Joey and Big Hill." But it's Owen I'm thinking of. Owen is the one who would throw himself into that mess headfirst. I didn't drag him out of a burning oil rig to see him off himself in a sea of black souls.

"Don't worry, Ms. Caroline," Big Hill says, rolling his ham hock sized shoulders. "Ain't no member of the Circle fights alone."

"Pardon?"

Joey Flatwood walks slowly up to the front of our line. "What my redneck friend is trying to say is that we won't be doing it ourselves." He wraps the beaded lanyard of his crow tightly around his ropey forearm. The stone hangs just off his hand, ready to grab. The wave sounds like a stampede now, a thundering herd, but below it I hear another sound: *whoosh, pop!* Then another. And another as the Circle comes to our aid. A tall African woman appears at my side, and the air broken in her arrival pushes softly at my hair. She looks tribal, with a series of thin brass rings around her neck and thick bone gauges in her earlobes. She is completely bald, and when she nods, the purple light glints off her head. She faces the break and pulls a crow totem from her robes. It is wrapped loosely in a big green leaf.

There is another *whoosh, pop*, and an old man dressed in a three-piece suit walks out of thin air into the desert. He surveys the scene like we're standing on a chessboard. He turns to the break and twirls a cane in his right hand. At its top is a stone crow.

Whoosh, pop! A young man in fatigues drops a massive pack from his back and digs into the dirt with combat boots. He wears his crow around his neck, sandwiched between dog tags.

Whoosh, pop! A monk walks out of the sky like he's on a Sunday stroll and stops to set his feet on top of a small rock in a position that would have me falling right on my butt. He turns and smiles at me like a kid in a candy store, tucking his crow into the orange folds of his robes.

Whoosh, pop! A woman in a pantsuit and wearing high heels steps into the desert sand and sinks three inches. She steps out of them and with a gloved hand drops her crow into a designer clutch she carries at her side. She winks at me.

Again and again it's like this. Ten, eleven, twelve times. An Australian aboriginal lands twenty feet to my left and swipes a wide and perfect circle around himself with his right toe. His crow is in his hair; it seems to glow in the moonlight, wrapped in messy dreads. A small man wearing an animal pelt and with a beard so long and thick it obscures everything but his eyes steps out nearby. His crow peeks out near his chin, through his beard. He unclasps a coat that looks to be made of the wool of at least ten sheep and lets it fall to the ground before he screams bloody murder at the blackness underneath the break. I lose count of all those that arrive, each of them unique. Some elegant, some wild, but all dangerous. And all of them with one goal in mind: protecting the bell. And to do that, we gotta close that break.

The *we* strikes me as absurd. I have no place among these people, right? I mean, we've got warriors here. I'm a neurotic nurse. Not even a nurse anymore, technically. More of a neurotic RVer. I look over at Owen. He's too open mouthed to even look back, so I know he's feeling the same thing. But something about the way each Circle member nods at us settles me. It's like we're already part of the team. Like we're at a big, crazy family reunion at the end of the world.

"*Ya'at'eeh*, Circle!" Joey cries. "Welcome! We fix the break today." It's not a question. Not an entreaty. It's a fact. We're *going* to fix the break. "We fight for the bell. We fight for the Walker. We fight for *this* place. This is *our* place." Joey scoops up some desert dust with his hand and sprinkles it over his head. He spits in his hand and wipes the paste under his eyes.

"Our place," he says again. He turns to the break. "We go."

Just like that. Not a pep talk for the ages, perhaps, but one that rings true. I know because anything that makes me want to reach up and rub dirt on my own face must be persuasive. I hate dirt.

Joey starts to run, and before he hits his second stride, he lets loose another ripping war cry of the sort I'm going to go ahead and say hasn't been heard for centuries. It's a thing taken from the top shelf of his people, dusted off, and pumped full of nitro gas. It would have sent a whole army of men running, but these things aren't men any longer. I find myself sprinting at them. Owen is right beside me, the Circle to both sides, and Grant at our heels clutching the bell in his hand. We run at them like our own rushing wave.

The chaos souls are actually drawn to us. I think they feel the energy, the coordination of the attack, and the unity of purpose, and they want to ruin it. So they come at us, and even with this crew, I can't see a way to get through the masses of black. But that's before I see how hard the Circle hits. It's the spinning cane of the older man that I see first. He's doesn't seem so old now, though, and his crow blurs in a turquoise circle like it's a flaming blue staff. When it hits the chaos souls, it shreds them like an airplane propeller. They are blown to black dust that is sucked back up and away.

Joey Flatwood is a force of nature. He walks through the thin place like it's his own personal garden and he's pruning dead leaves. He looks more at home here than he does in the real world. The souls he hits are turned into Rorschach inkblots with the force of his fists. Even so, he's leading this charge, and there's a terrible moment where he's separated from the rest of us. The oily black pools around the back of him, and suddenly he's on an island. The bald woman yells and points, but it's too late. They're all around him, and even Joey can't guard the blind side of his back. Owen throws himself forward and lowers his shoulder into the souls, but he's thrown back. I can only watch as they reach for Joey's grip on his crow and manage to pry it away finger by finger. He fights like a bull but can't hold on and blinks back. A soul swipes at his chest, and its fingers rake into him, pulling flesh like sand. He screams and rips his crow back, blinking back in time to save himself, but he drops to the ground.

Big Hill is there. He is a human cannonball. A rolling boulder. He plows his way through the souls and reaches Joey. He picks him up like he's made of straw and sets him on his feet. He's frantic, crying and seething at the same time.

Joey shakes his head and pats Big Hill's chest. I see him nod. I am more relieved by this than perhaps anything that has happened to me on this insane day. The rest of the Circle sees Joey rise again, and a wild cheer goes up. We redouble our efforts. A host of different war cries washes over the desert, and all around me the turquoise crows glow bright in the hollow darkness of the desert in the thin place. The burn of holding the crow seems to lessen.

Grant walks past me as cool as a cucumber with Chaco bobbing along on his head. The souls shy away from him. He takes up my hand at the last second and tugs me along through a sea of chaos. I try to pull him back, but he's not having it. He shakes his head again and again.

Chaco screeches louder than I've ever heard him. The sound itself makes the press of souls back off. Grant nods in agreement. Grant says, "We only got one shot at this."

"One shot at what?" I ask. "And if you've only got one shot at a thing, maybe you should get Joey or somebody else. Anybody else."

Grant shakes his head. "Not Joey."

"Then get Owen." My mouth is dry, really dry. Not just because of the war going on around me but because I know where he's taking me. He's taking me right under the break. "Owen!" I scream.

Owen looks up from where he's attending to Joey's wound while Big Hill gives them cover. He makes toward us, but Grant shakes his head.

"Not Owen," Grant says. He tugs me along harder. Chaco turns and looks at me. He's right at my eye level, and he's doing that bird thing where his body moves with every step Grant takes, but his head stays dead still.

"We don't have much time," Grant says, pulling me faster. Now we're really in the thick of it. Grant blazes like a lighthouse, but I'm not so immune. They pull at me and go for my crow, so I tuck it under my armpit and throw my elbows like I'm breaking down a door just to take each step. Now that we're this near the break, I can hear the wave again, and it's like how I'd imagine sticking my head under the hood of a semi-truck barreling down a mountain might sound. I can see up and through it now, and there on the other side I see the faint outline of three bodies. Two of them are bone white and dressed in suits. The other is Ben. They aren't moving. This evidently pisses Chaco off, because he caws about as loud as I've ever heard him caw. They shift a little bit. In the middle of the three of them sits the knife. The air smokes and bubbles around it.

We're right underneath the break now. No more souls drop through, but I know they're coming. They're coming on the crest of that tsunami I'm hearing. It's all I can hear now. The sound is so loud it's become a physical thing that vibrates my teeth and tries to push me back.

"He has to wake up. He has to get to the knife," Grant says, his voice dazed, his head cricked back all the way like he's stargazing. Chaco is staring at me. Then Grant turns to look at me too. "Chaco says you need to call him."

"Ben!" I shout. "Ben! It's me! It's Caroline! Please, Ben. You gotta get the knife."

He moves.

"Ben! Can you... can you hear me?"

The break is getting bigger. Pieces of the ground Ben lies on flake off and shift to smoke above us. I think of the last time I spoke to Ben. Of the kiss before he walked away from his body, away from me forever. They call him the Walker, but I remember the man who was dying from cancer and from the chemo that we used to try and kill it, vomiting in his back yard, giving everything he had left to try and find some closure for his family, for himself.

"Ben, we need you," I say. "I need you."

He shakes his head a bit and rolls onto his back. He's coming back, slowly. Unfortunately, so are the agents. Douglas is the fastest to orient himself. And to remember the knife. He reaches for it, and I see in his scarred face that he is intent on using it on Ben. But Ben grabs it at the same time. Ben has a better grip on the knife, and I think he's going to yank it free until Parsons makes a grab too. Then Ben is overmatched. My heart slumps. And that's when Ben sees me.

The sound is a high-pitched keening roar now. The three of them look like they're in a vacuum. Their clothes and hair are pulled back toward the force bearing down on them, and the agents' ties flip and turn. The wave is pulling everything out before it slams back in. Ben's black hair flutters out over his eyes, but he's looking at me, and I really see him for the first time in almost a year.

I wave.

I know. It's a stupid thing to do, but it's the only thing I can think of. So I wave at him like a ten-year-old girl saying hello to her grand-parents. His mouth opens a little so that I think he may start to smile, but the agents yank at the knife. Whatever smile there was turns into a grimace as he strains to keep control.

"Catch," he says. Or I think he says it. I read it on his lips. All three hands slam down on the break. The knife slips through and tumbles from the sky, glinting green as it falls as if in slow motion, spinning end over end. The agents follow it, reaching and falling through themselves, grasping after it like it's a golden coin dropped in the ocean. I step back from it, terrified to touch the blade.

Joey Flatwood catches it out of midair. His hand strikes out like a cobra, and he snatches it right by the hilt, one handed, despite his bleeding chest. The wave of souls is almost on top of Ben. I can see it like a skyscraper above him.

He reaches out for me. Reaches through the break. His hand comes through, floats in midair. I reach up and touch his finger. I swear I touch his finger. I'm not making this up. I know because it's not like I just feel the smoke of a ghost. I feel the rough fold of his knuckle and the smooth slip of his nail. Real things. He smiles at me. It's a sad smile. It's not the smile of a man who is coming back. It's the smile of a man who knows he has to go away.

Then the wave hits him, and his arm is snapped back, and he's gone in a blink. The sky shudders with a long, low rumble of thunder, and it feels like the very air is weighted down on our heads like a balloon seconds from bursting. Joey Flatwood takes the knife, jams it between two rocks at our feet, takes a big jump in the air, and lands square on the handle with both heels.

The blade snaps with a crack like lightning. The chaos souls are blown to dust and sucked instantly away. Every member of the Circle takes cover, expecting the thin place to blow apart, but the shattering doesn't come. Nothing comes. The sky eases back into itself, straightening, flattening. The break starts to knit, layers and layers of shining thread moving over and through the patch in the sky until there's nothing but the faint, vague thinning that made this stretch of desert what it is in the first place.

I don't know how long I stand staring at the empty sky. There is movement all around me, the men and women of the Circle calling roll and tending to their own injuries. I must look like a lost kid in a supermarket, but I don't care. I want to try to remember that touch. I want to think about it for a while.

Eventually Owen brings me back. He taps me lightly on the shoulder. I turn to him. He doesn't speak. No hint of anger or jealousy mars his smoke. They might have been there once, but not anymore. Now there is understanding. And worry. And love. And a question that I don't give him time to ask, because he shouldn't have to. Not anymore. I lay my head against his chest, and he holds me.

"I love you, Owen," I say. But Owen surprises me.

"I'm not so sure you do, Caroline."

I look up at him, my brow furrowed. My mouth works, but nothing comes out. He just laughs and presses his lips to my forehead. Not a kiss, exactly, but something kinder. Something better.

"I don't know what we've got, you and I," he says. "But I'm willing to take a lifetime to figure it out."

I nod, pressing my cheek to his chest. "Me too."

"And what about these two crazies?" Grant asks, standing over by the agents, who lie still on the desert floor. Chaco squawks loudly.

"Get away from them, Grant," Owen says and reaches for his hand. He pulls him over to us. "They'll kill you as soon as look at you just to get that bell."

Grant squints at them. "I dunno. I think they might be... broken."

I creep forward with my hands raised like I expect the agents to pull a jack-in-the-box at any second, but when I get close enough to see their faces clearly, I think Grant may be right. They aren't dead, but they aren't with us, either. Their eyes are closed, but their faces look like they're being forced to watch something horrible. Douglas twitches minutely, almost as if he's trying to shake his head. Parsons's eyes flit wildly underneath their pale, black-veined lids. His mouth looks like it wants to turn down but can't.

"They both look like they want to cry or something," Grant says.

Joey Flatwood circles around and watches them with his arms crossed over his chest. His wound seems not to bother him at all. In fact, it sort of goes with his look, like a wolf or maybe a bear swiped a claw across his pec right before Joey kicked its ass. And that's not too far from the truth.

"It's the knife," Joey says. "They put too much of themselves into it. When it broke, so did they."

I know I should throw out a "serves them right" and walk away. These two have put us through unrelenting hell for a year now. Parsons tried to kill me, and nearly did kill Owen. They're lunatics. Obsessive. They walked over us in their quest for the bell and would do it all again if they had the chance. I try to turn away and leave them for the coyotes and the rattlesnakes, I really do, and I'm sure if I were the first to turn away, the others would follow. Even now Joey looks at me, and his smoke says, *Your kill.*

But it's not in me. I surprise myself by kneeling down over Parsons, and before I know it, I'm sweeping over him with my other sight. I've never been this close to the agents without being afraid for my life, and now that they're here, I can see that they still smoke. Meaning they're not dead. Meaning they still have souls somewhere in there. Parsons's smoke is black, true, but it's a broken black now. I scoop some of it up, and it pools in my hand. I look carefully at it. There is definitely another color in there, underneath the black. I see flashes of it, like a gemstone buried in mud. It's a soft yellow. Not unlike Owen's was when I first met him. Professional. Straightforward. Meticulous.

I picture the yellow in my mind and all the things that yellow could represent. A man with a job he was proud of. A man who worked hard. Perhaps too hard. A man who was swallowed up in something but before that might have been like us. And with all this in my mind, I blow on the smoke in my hand... and the black dissipates a little. And with it, the pulsing twitch at Parsons's temple calms.

I know what I have to do.

I move around Parsons to his head, where I see his smoke at its root. I'm not sure how the soul works or where it leads, but I see a clear connection here to the other plane in everyone, and Parsons's is still roiling in broken black smoke. I put my hand on his forehead, and I hear Owen stir. He wants to come take me away from this man. He took a bullet from this man for me once. I look up at him and smile.

"I can do this," I say. "It's what I do."

He calms himself with a big breath and crosses his arms. Chaco watches me carefully but nods.

I picture the yellow again. Parsons's yellow. Driven, practical, meticulous, perhaps overbearing. But pure, uncorrupted. Then I place my hand over his face and brush upward toward his forehead. It's a strange, plucking sensation, like I'm pulling a rotten sheaf from a head of corn, but underneath is the pure yellow. And with each inch, his tremors still, and before my eyes, his color returns. The white fills in, the black veins fade away. With one last push, I dissipate the black smoke fully, and it falls away entirely.

He calms. His body stills, relaxes into the warm desert floor. He takes a big, shuddering breath. Then he opens his eyes. They are clear and green. Owen steps forward along with Joey Flatwood, but I hold up my hand. They pause.

"Parsons?" I ask, my voice barely above a whisper. His eyes find me and focus then blink. He takes me in then turns his head and marks each of us surrounding him. He pushes up onto his elbows, and I step back a little bit. He rubs at his face and his eyes, then he looks back at me.

"Who the hell are you people? And what have you done to me?"

"It's a long story," I say. I try not to smile, since I know that would probably seem creepy to a man who just woke up from a nightmare to find himself in the desert surrounded by a strange host that includes an Indian, a man as big as a hill, and a boy with a crow on his head.

He looks over at his partner, still on the ground, still twitching.

"Allen?" he asks, trying to get up and nearly collapsing. "Hey! Allen!" He turns to me, frantic. "Is he okay? What have you done to him?"

"He'll be fine, soon enough. We didn't do anything to him. We're here to help you. What is the last thing you remember, Parsons? Think back to the last thing you did. What case you were on."

Parsons looks strangely at me. "Case?"

"Yes, you were tracking a man named Joey Flatwood. You thought he was running drugs."

"Flatwood? Drugs? What the hell are you talking about? Allen and I are archivists."

"Get the fuck outta here," Owen blurts out in the dead silence that follows. I glare at him. He coughs. "Sorry, it's just... you guys? Librarians?"

"Not librarians, *archivists*." Parsons stands slowly and dusts his hands off. He walks carefully over to Douglas, and I see the worry in his eyes. He gasps at the scarred claw marks that rake Douglas's face. I move over to Douglas and start focusing to find his hidden color. I hear Owen talking in the background of my mind.

"It's just that we thought you guys were FBI agents. You had badges and suits. And you were pretty handy with a gun," he says. "For a librarian."

I see Douglas's color. It's a pale blue. I almost think I have it wrong, because what I see is a kind-hearted man, gentle, not at all in line with the brutish thug I know. If anything, he is too meek. Too soft-spoken. The type of man who would take easily to being told what to do. I focus on that color and push away his darkness. He comes back to us by degrees just like Parsons did. Even the scars on his face fade, although they don't disappear altogether.

Parsons drops to his side and grabs his hand. "Allen? Can you hear me, Allen?"

Douglas opens his eyes. They are clear and blue, not unlike his smoke color, with no hint of the trauma that left him bloody. The hard lines of his face are gone. The scars are soft pink. His entire person has softened.

"James? What happened?" He slowly sits up, with our help. He looks all around him at the desert night. "Where are all the books? Oh, dear. Did I have too much wine again?"

Parsons pauses. He looks over at me, still holding Douglas's hand. "That's it. Books. We were at work. We do work for the government but not like you think. We're senior archivists at the Library of Congress. Which I take it is not anywhere near where we are right now."

"You're in the west Texas desert," Grant says.

"That's a long way from the stacks in DC," Owen adds.

"Yes!" Parsons says. "The stacks! We were retrieving a book in the restricted stacks! It was a little thing, almost like a lady's black book or something. A strange thing. It was unmarked..."

"Yes," Douglas says, nodding. "It was an old, leather-bound book. I remember pulling it from the stacks, and taking it from its sheath, and handing it to you, and... that's it."

"I tried to read it, to check it was the correct volume, but every page was blank. I felt very odd, though, like the words were just out of sight. Looking at it made me feel a little ill, so I put it away. And then I heard something. Something calling my name. I *felt* something. Right there with us. And…"

"And?" Owen prompts.

"And that's it. Just like Allen. Here I am. In the desert. With a splitting headache."

Each of us mutters a curse in our own way. We were that close. Whatever it was Parsons and Douglas retrieved, it is the key to understanding this whole thing. The attack on the veil. The knife. Their obsessive mission. All of it. Without it, we're just shell-shocked survivors of a battle we don't quite understand. I see the colors around me, the smoke of the Circle, dampened by disappointment. Only Grant seems undaunted.

"Well, where did you put it away?" he asks.

Parsons looks over at him, at the crow on his head, and blinks. "Put it away?"

"The book. You said you put it away. Before the other thing came up on ya."

"Yes…" Parsons pats at his pants pockets, then his jacket pockets, then reaches into his breast pocket. He freezes.

"Oh, shit," he says, his eyes wide. He slowly pulls his hand out, and in his grasp is a small, leather-bound book, black as night, about the size of an address book. "I took it from the stacks," he whispers.

All of us stare at it. Chaco shivers his feathers. I sense no power in the book itself, no malice, but it is a heavy thing, despite its size. It has weight to it that spans across the planes, just like the bell, although if the bell is like solid silver, this is like solid lead.

The book might look blank to others but not to me. Its title is written in smoke that I can see quite clearly. It says *The Book of the Dark Walker*.

"Oooh, James," Douglas says quietly. "You are *so* fired."

19

THE WALKER

I'm gonna let you in on a little secret.

I wanted the knife for myself.

Yes, I know it was ripped unwilling from the vein of the earth. Yes, I know that the turquoise was perverted when the agents hammered and chipped it into a weapon. Yes, I am aware that it nearly destroyed the balance between the living world, the thin world, and the world of the dead. All of this I know.

But it was a key. It was my way out, back into the land of the living, if I so chose. Not sayin' I would choose that, but it'd be nice to have in my back pocket. The whole time I was getting my ass kicked by Douglas then stranded on top of the mesa then chasing after the agents down the river, in the back of my mind I was thinking, *How can I get these assholes out of here but keep that knife?*

Then Caroline looked at me, and all that went out the window. That's all it took to give it up for the greater good. She looked at me, and I *think* she even touched me. I knew then the only way I could stop the balance from breaking and the world from spinning out of control was to give her the knife. So I did. Like a prisoner who finally snatches the cell keys from the wall then decides to chuck them out the window.

At least I didn't have long to think about it. A tsunami of souls smashing into your body will do that to you. Back at Chaco Rez, we'd usually get one or two big snowstorms every winter, and afterward Gam, Mom, and Dad would take Ana and me to this place south of the Arroyo where the basin leveled out but there was still a good-sized hill for sledding. We'd drive through the Arroyo proper to pick up Joey, and Gam would stop by to check on a few people. At the time I thought this was just her seeing friends, but looking back on it, I think Gam wanted to make sure the Arroyo old-timers survived the storm, which wasn't a given back then and ain't a given now either. Then they'd set up camp at the top of the hill with the other families and watch the three of us kids sled and sled and sled. I mean hundreds of times. All day long. And every time we'd make sure they were watching, and they'd wave and then go back to their knitting or their beers or their magazines.

Ana was just little, so she couldn't do much more than roll around and slide a little down the hill, but Joey and I built big jumps and competed with each other for who could take the one good tube down the hill fastest and get the biggest air. One time we built a kicker too well. This thing was perfect. Joey wanted to be the first down, but I grabbed the tube from him and got a running start and everything just came together. I was flying. Then I hit the kicker and basically rag-dolled. I lost my gloves before I even hit the ground, and when I did hit, I lost my boots and my hat and my jacket ripped open. I was spinning and spinning and spinning, and then all of a sudden I couldn't breathe, there was a huge thump, and everything went white.

That's what it was like when the wave of souls hit me. If I had gloves, they'd be halfway across the world right now. If I had a hat, it would be in another dimension. On the hill, turns out I couldn't breathe because I had snow in my throat, and everything went white because I was stuck ass up in a big drift at the bottom. My throat opened after a panicked half minute, and Joey was there to pull me out of the drift. Gam patched me up. We kept sledding.

This time what chokes me is the weight of billions of individual images. The imprints of thousands upon thousands of souls. I'm crushed by them without them ever weighing me down, and this time there's nobody to pull me out. The pure emotional attack is too much even for me to take—and I walk a map of souls for a job. Thankfully I still have that fail-safe off switch: eventually I just black out.

When I come around again, I'm back in the cavern. The wash has driven me all of the way down and under again. I'm floating around like a dead fish near the top, where the pearl is connected to the eggcup by that long strand. I actually bump my head against the pearl. It's what wakes me up, and it's not forgiving.

When I look around, it seems to me like everything is back to normal. The souls have settled in their own way and are back to their slow spinning circle around the pearl, and after blinking and rubbing my face to get some sense back, I kick off toward the inlet where the river lets off. Two visits to this weird-ass chaos globe are plenty for me. I'd be perfectly fine never seeing this place again.

It's only when I chance a look back over my shoulder to see the whole of the cavern one last time that I notice that things are definitely *not* back to normal. As a matter of fact, things may never be normal again.

The pearl has split wide open. I couldn't see it from the back, but it's opened like a massive clam from the front, right down the seam where the knife blew through those locks. I sort of float there, staring at it for a minute. Once I'm reasonably sure it's not gonna blow up on me again, I swim toward it.

I stop at the edge of the pearl. The shiny veneer is pretty thin, actually, only an arm's length or so deep on a thing the size of a domed football stadium. The rest of it looks like it's made up of thick, black coral pitted and grooved with tiny rivulets and pathways, almost like veins, leading from the outside inward.

I look back toward the inlet, where the shore lies just beyond. Nothing but floating silence out there. I look back inward, to the center of the pearl. Nothing but floating silence in there, either. And when you're stuck between two empty places, you'd be surprised how willing you are to check out the one you haven't seen. Even if it is spooky. Either way, whatever the agents wanted is in here. I'm not leaving until I figure out what it is.

I kick along with one hand lightly touching the inner wall. I get sensations from the touch that are sort of like when a soul hits me but less powerful, more diluted. As if these thousands of capillaries etched along the inside of the pearl are sifting the emotions and echoes, refining them. The grooves get bigger the deeper I go. Soon they are the thickness of my arm, then my leg, then my whole body. When I see a vein the size of a car, I start to sweat. This thing is looking more and more like the shell of a living creature. I kick harder, shooting toward the center. The veins get bigger and bigger, and soon they're the size of a school bus... and then they stop.

By now the light from the souls floating around outside is very weak, so it takes me a second to see what happened. The main veins collapse very quickly into a hundred different cones. The cones start wide, but they narrow fast, and as I swim forward, I see them for what they are. Needles. They're essentially needles that channel the chaos souls from the outside, refine them, and then shoot them right to the center.

I want out of here.

I'm tearing forward to see what's there, then I'm getting out. This whole place is messing with me, scattering my thoughts. I can hardly keep moving in a straight line. Even the echo of what was here is enough to muddle my brain. I focus on swimming. I focus on things I know. Ana, Joey, Owen, Caroline.

And then I'm there. I'm at the center of the pearl. And what finally makes me turn around, what makes me hightail my ass out of there at double the clip I went in, isn't that I find what the agents wanted. It's that I find nothing at all.

Literally, I find a hollow. But it's a hollow in the shape of a person. All the chaos energy from all the souls that have ever existed gets shot into here. Right into this hollow. And the hollow is empty.

The locks weren't set on the pearl to keep something from getting in. They were set to keep something from getting out.

And now it's out.

. . .

I'M FOLLOWING footprints in the sand, and they aren't mine. I noticed them as soon as I kicked my way out of the river of souls and got back to the beach. At first they were hard to follow because the ever-changing landscape at the chaos end of the river messed around with their placement. The earth shifted under me, and I lost them for a time. But I reasoned that whatever came out of the pearl was on its way down the beach, so I ran, figuring I'd pick them up again after I got out of the crazy fun-house nightmare of the chaos end of things.

I was right. Now that the riverbank is more level and the world isn't bucking under me, I can see that the footprints are human. Look to be male. The gait is such that it's a tall guy, or a man running, but the pressure points don't suggest running. Just a big fella with a big stride.

Just when I'm about to congratulate myself for the old cop instincts kicking in, the footprints change. I don't mean change pace. I mean they change entirely. Now they're children's footprints, barely bigger than the palm of my hand, and they indicate a quick step. Then, impossibly, the tiny footprints space farther and farther apart until this child is walking with the gait of a giant. Then something bigger than a giant. Then they change again. I stop and stare at the print where the change happens. The front half is the print of a child's toes. The back half is a hoof. I stare at that one for a while. The next print is a full-on hoof. Then the hoofprints are spaced wildly apart.

Then come the claw prints. I break out in a cold sweat at these. No way around it. They give me the shivers, which is why I nearly bury my head in the sand when I hear a snapping sound and see a dark line shoot out of the river like an obsidian spear chucked from below. I'm seriously halfway dug in with my feet before I realize it's just Chaco. He spies me and soars my way.

"Hate to cut your vacation short, Walker," he says, "but there are, like, a hundred thousand souls backed up in the pipes here, man, and you gotta get back to work."

"How'd you get here? I thought I sealed the break. Not that I'm not overjoyed to see you."

"I'm a thinning. I can travel through all thin places. I don't need no stinkin' break. But seriously, what the hell are you waiting for? The veil is almost back to one hundred percent..."

He trails off as he gets closer to me and sees the dark imprints of the tracks. This claw print would be hard to miss, even from the air. He flutters down to my shoulder, and we stare at them for a second.

"Who let the dinosaur in?" Chaco says, finally.

I point my finger down the way I came. "Dinosaur-thing, goat-thing, demon-spawn child-thing, big-ass man-thing. Lots of things."

"And one thing," Chaco says. We follow the trail in silence. The claws dig huge rivets in the sand... until they don't. About a hundred yards down, they change into a man's footprint again in a single step. They continue for another ten paces, then they disappear. I look at Chaco, and he takes off, shooting down the beach toward dead center, where I left the veil. He flies for a time, sweeping low, his head snapping this way and that, as if he's looking for a mouse to eat. He goes on down until I can't see him anymore. Then, after a time, he comes back. He pumps his wings to gain speed then flares out right before me to plop on my shoulder again.

"Nothing," he says.

"What? What do you mean nothing?"

"I mean nothing. Nada. Zilch. No more tracks. Not at the veil, not past the veil, not anywhere."

"You're telling me this thing just disappeared?"

Chaco is eyeing the tracks with unblinking bird focus. "He didn't use the veil. And he didn't cross over through a thin place, because I would know. So... yeah. He pretty much disappeared. I don't get it."

"Great. I thought you got everything. That's been our MO. I fuck around and nearly destroy the world, and you patch it all up after me with your timeless wisdom."

"You fuck around with the best of intentions, of course," Chaco says, absently.

"Of course."

"Where the hell did this thing come from, Walker?"

"A big pearl in the chaos eggshell."

"Say what?"

"It came from inside a big black pearl at the chaos end of the river."

Chaco snaps his head back to me. "What did you say?" He sounds deadly serious. "Did you say a big black pearl?"

"Yes, bird. That's what I'm saying."

He walks slowly along my shoulder until he is inches from me, then he tilts his beak down and walks closer until his feathered head and beady eyes are centimeters from mine.

"I want to be very clear here. Super-duper clear. This thing came from inside the black pearl? You're sure of it?"

I've tilted my head back as far as it goes, but Chaco doesn't move. He stares me down.

"Yes! The agents broke the locks to the pearl with the knife. It blew us out of the chamber when they broke. We fought for the knife on the riverbed, and I tossed it through. The tsunami hit me, and I blacked out. When I came to, I was back in the chamber. The pearl was open. I swam inside to have a look around and found a sort of sarcophagus thing that looked like it once held a man. I swam out here and found these tracks."

Chaco stares at me for a good ten seconds.

"So what is it?" I ask.

"I don't know." That's twice now Chaco has been stumped, and it feels as unnatural as these claw prints look. "The pearls anchor the river. Chaos on one side and order on the other. It's been that way since the dawn of time. Since before the dawn of time, actually, because I came around at the dawn of time, when the river started wearing away at its banks and bed, which rivers will do, and created the first thinning. Yours truly."

"So this thing is... older than you?"

"I didn't even know there was a *thing* there. I've only ever seen the pearls. I thought they were just inanimate lightning rods for their respective types of souls. Maybe inside was millions of years of soul goo. That's it. It never occurred to me that an entity could be in there. Much less an entity that makes tracks like this."

"So we know where it came from," I say, trying to talk through things, to order them in my mind and keep me from running around doing something stupid—which is usually what happens when I panic. "The next question would be—"

"Where the hell did it go?" Chaco says, taking the words from my mouth.

And this is one question that shuts us both up.

I GET BACK through the veil. Actually, the veil seems all too eager to get me back on the other side of it where I belong. It basically pulls me in and through itself once I get within arm's length of where it billows at the middle of the river, robustly red once more. I fall out on my ass in the middle of the desert, right where the thick of the mess happened. I see the whole gang still here, patching themselves up, gathering themselves, but once again, I'm in my own world. They can't see me, they can't hear me, and they can't touch me.

Yep. The good ol' days are back again.

The first thing I notice is that the agents don't look like the agents anymore. They look more like overworked accountants, and they're talking to the Circle members like they've never seen anything like them before. I know immediately that this is Caroline's doing. That she fixed them or helped them in some way, because that's what she does, what she was made for.

Then I find Caroline. She stands next to Owen. He has his arm around her shoulder. Between them is Grant, and I don't need to case the place to realize that the Keeper has a new family now.

I try to get jealous. I try to get pissed. I can't do either. But I do ache. My body aches, and my heart aches. I don't begrudge Owen anything. That man has been a class act since day one. But I do begrudge his arm. The arm that he has resting around Caroline when mine would pass right through her. It's the little things that get to you.

Chaco is already resting on Grant's head. "He's right over there,"

Chaco says, nudging his beak my way. Grant stares into the open space that is me on the side of the living, and he gives a small wave. He smiles, too. It's an awesome smile. I wave back, even though I know damn well he can't see me.

Caroline asks him who he's waving to. "Nobody," he says. Which tells me he's more perceptive than I thought. That maybe he figured out about this whole mess of hearts without anyone saying anything and doesn't want to get involved. But Caroline knows. She looks my way too, and she smiles. It's exhausted and a little sad, but it's genuine. It hits me that she's sad for me. Caroline feels sorry for me.

If you ever want to light a fire under a Navajo's ass, or under any red-blooded man's ass, really, all you gotta do is tell them you feel sorry for them.

I straighten up. I roll my shoulders back until I hear a crack. I ball my fists. Chaco looks at me and puffs up as well.

I got work to do. I got souls to settle. Then I got a monster to find.

And since you've been along for this whole ride so far, I might as well stick with the honesty thing. I want to find this creepy Other Walker for two reasons: First, because I want to right the balance of the river. It won't do to have millions of souls swirling around an empty pearl for too much longer. Even I know that.

Second, because I want to see what it is. Specifically, how it can just flit in and out of worlds. And I've got a completely selfish motive for this one. I've got a strong hunch, a near certain hunch, that this thing, whatever it is, is walking the world of the living.

And if it can walk with the living, maybe one day I can too.

THE
COYOTE
WAY

B. B. GRIFFITH

"Coyote is always out there waiting, and Coyote is always hungry."

-Navajo Proverb

1

THE WALKER

There is a room at Green Mesa Psychiatric Hospital in Los Alamos, New Mexico, called the Serenity Room. Attendants deliver medicine in soft whispers, waking dozing patients only when they must. Some patients read, some mutter, some simply sit by the huge bay window that faces the chunky orange cliffs of the Pajarito Plateau. The Serenity Room is a place set outside of the day-to-day, where the driving white noise the world makes as it turns can't be heard. Where the sick can live out the remainder of their troubled lives undisturbed.

Then I walk in.

I do my job alone—nobody can see me or hear me or touch me—but over the past six years that I've walked the soul map, snipping frayed threads and sending the dead through the veil and on their way, I've noticed that some people do seem to sense me. For instance, babies don't much like it when I'm near. They start fussing pretty bad. Everyone in the living world can pass right through me, but once a blind guy in Rome walked around me. I stood there blinking like a sheep while he went on his way. A deaf woman at a call I answered in Reno, Nevada, pricked her ear my way when I was talking to myself. I swear that sometimes the very old can track me with their milky eyes, although I'm not sure they know what they're looking at. Stuff like that. But by far the most perceptive are the insane.

The two men who were muttering to each other in the corner a second ago? Now they're crying. The woman who was putting together a puzzle, one that she's been working on diligently for nearly a year? Now she's dismantling it piece by piece. The young man who's been reading the same book over and over again for months? Now he's ripping the pages out and letting them flutter to the floor. It's because of me. Because of what I am. I make them uncomfortable when I'm nearby. They're already half in and half out of the world they live in. They fight every day to cling to whatever frayed strings of sanity they have left, and I'm the type of guy whose job it is to cut threads.

The staff can't figure out why this happens every so often, and they never will. They can only curse under their breaths and scamper around trying to keep these delicate people from falling apart like dried flowers in a sudden wind. One of these dried flowers, perhaps the most delicate of all, is my mother.

You heard that right. Death has a mom.

Mom sits in a decorative wheelchair with a plump pillow at her back, staring blankly out of the bay window at the soft pink New Mexico sunset. When she left us, not long after Ana died, she cut her long black hair short and spiky. It's grown out again now, down past her shoulders, and it's as white as snow. She neglects it, but her attendants don't. It's pulled back and banded behind her head with a beaded leather thong. One of the handful of things she kept from her life before. Something Ana made in school. She wears a clean and neat dressing gown of blue and gold, one of several that the staff rotate throughout the week.

She's not sickly looking, or gaunt. Her skin still has that Navajo cinnamon coloring, even if it's a bit ruddy at the cheeks. In a lot of ways, she looks just like the woman she was back when we all lived in one half of a little duplex on Chaco rez, about an hour north of Albuquerque. The same woman who bundled Ana and me up for the walk to school, who packed our lunches and washed our clothes.

Who helped Gam cook dinner and kept Dad's drinking at bay. Who tanned my hide when I chipped a tooth racing around the campers out at the Arroyo at dusk, Joey and I weaving in and out, slapping the corrugated metal of each with the flat of our hands and tearing off before we got something chucked at us, laughing like hell. Our twenty-first-century, dirt-poor version of counting coup.

On the outside she looks just like she did back then, just older. Inside, she's a mess. Many of the patients around her fuss and fidget and mewl as I walk toward her. She takes no notice. Just stares forward until her eyes water and she's forced to blink.

I come here a lot in between calls, but not because I feel I owe it to Mom. I know that she's well taken care of at Green Mesa, which is just about the cushiest extended-stay psychiatric hospital in the Southwest. They have cucumber water *and* lemon water *and* lime water in the front lobby. Water trickles into little ponds, and fountains burble everywhere. The only people who work harder than the doctors around here are the groundskeepers. The place costs a fortune, but the Navajo Nation is footing Mom's entire bill. Medical costs, room and board, extra expenses, the whole thing. The Council took pity on her after she lost everyone. With the Navajo, you take your mother's clan. The Dejooli branch of our clan is going to end with her. It sucks, but in a twisted way it's kind of fitting. Dejooli is Navajo for *up in the air*. I always took it to mean *gone*.

So Mom hasn't paid a dime since the day she got here, almost six years ago now. Good thing too. Mom's broke. But worse than that, she no longer has the wherewithal to pay anything anyway. I don't even think she knows where she is anymore. The day Ana disappeared, Mom started to fade. She backed away from Chaco, and eventually from the Navajo Way altogether. I found Ana, eventually, right as I died. Turns out she was the one who came for me, to take me away, just like I'm the one who will one day come for you. Except I rang a special bell, took her job, and set her free. Mom was already cracked, but when she saw that happen, it broke her.

I take a seat next to her, away from the rest of the patients, who start to settle now that I've settled myself and it turns out I'm not coming for them. I'm barely taller than her, and only slightly thicker. Danny Ninepoint, my old partner back at the Navajo Nation Police Department, used to say that I have tricky muscles, which was his way of saying I look like a wuss but somehow could still hold up my end of a fight. I still wear an NNPD uniform, but it's all black now. It looks out of place, here. I think there's some sort of rule against the color black at Green Mesa.

"Hi, Mom," I say, knowing full well she won't answer. She continues to stare out of the window. Her right finger twitches a little. I cross my arms and watch as a murder of crows spans the horizon, flying away. It's midsummer. Not crow season in this part of the country. But lately the crows have been gathering anyway. Which is never a good sign.

When Mom first came to Green Mesa she didn't need a wheelchair. She was in a state of shock from losing her family, but she was functional. She even showed signs of getting better. She made a few friends, spoke to each of the attendants and doctors by name, had a few lunch dates at the fancy buffet, but then, just about a year after her arrival, she started going downhill. Stopped smiling, then stopped talking. She eventually stopped eating on her own, and then stopped walking. The doctors are at a loss, but I'm not.

Right around the time she started to withdraw, a turquoise knife nearly ripped a hole in the fabric between our worlds. Caroline, Owen, Grant, and I managed to shore it up, but not before something came through. I think she felt it. As whatever *it* is grows in strength, she is weakening.

It is some form of chaos. That's all I know. Since it broke through into the land of the living, it's disappeared, but I think it has some sort of connection with sick people like her. Broken minds are attuned to it. My mother more than most. She's had more exposure to my line of work than your average mental patient. Hell, both of her children ended up as Walkers. She was there when the bell rang and I started my watch. She shares my blood. So you see, I have an ulterior motive here. These visits aren't just one-sided social calls. Mom is a canary in a coal mine.

I look over at her again. Her pointer finger is twitching still, more like scratching now. I try to put my hand over it, to calm it. I pass right through her. Her eyes water, and she blinks free a rivulet of tears. It rolls down her cheek. I try to brush it, but my finger cannot touch her.

"I know, Mom. I can feel it too. Whatever's been simmering for the past five years is about to come to a boil. The chaos thing, the Dark Walker, it's making its move, but I can't find it. Chaco can't find it. Nobody can find it."

I watch the crows wheel and float in the distance like a flock of starlings, which is entirely unlike them. The sun is setting with this feeling of pressure, like it's trying to jam itself into a horizon that's already full up and ready to spill. I think about the river of souls. Five years' worth of souls following a path down the chaos side of the river, swarming around an empty pearl. We stitched up the walls between worlds, but the balance of the river is off. The thing that anchors the chaos end of things is walking free as you please in the world of the living, has been for years now, and it's eluded all of us.

When I turn back to Mom, she's looking right at me. I nearly jump up from my seat. Her finger is still. Her eyes are focused. The canary senses something coming from the deeps of the mine.

"Go home, Ben," she whispers in Navajo.

I reach for her again, my hands shaking. These are the first words she's spoken in years, and the first Navajo words I can ever remember her voluntarily speaking. I reach out as if I could grab them, maybe keep them in my pocket. She still looks at me.

"Go home," she says again. She uses the old Navajo word *Bikeyah*, which means *homeland*. The place of my people. Then she turns slowly to the window again, where the crows have disappeared into the gloaming.

"Mom?" I ask. "Mom, can you hear me?" I repeat myself again in Navajo. Nothing. Her face is blank once more. But my canary has spoken, and moments later I get a tug from the soul map. I stand and swirl it open then turn back to her. My mind races. These things are connected. I raise my hand in a farewell she's blind to, then I step through.

I walk the rope of intertwined souls, looking for the break that calls me, looking for the dimming of a life that needs to be set free. I see it, like a flickering bulb in a sea of warm light. I step up to it, swirl the map open once more, and by this time I have a pretty good hunch about where I'm going to step out. It's the *why* that I can't figure.

The day is coming to a close, but the desert is still hot under foot. It creaks a little, like a massive settling house, with the roof open to a sky that goes on forever. It smells like baked clay and untouched wind. It smells like home.

I'm back on the rez.

2

CAROLINE ADAMS

I'm about the last girl on earth you'd pick as having a little black book. Seriously. You could count on one hand the number of guys I've hooked up with, and you wouldn't need your thumb. To be fair, I'm not exactly hitting the scene these days. I hang out in an RV with two people most of the time, and one of them is a four-teen-year-old kid with a bird for a best friend. The other is Owen Bennet. If what I carried actually *was* a little black book, his name would be the only entry on any of the pages for the past five years, which would make it less of a "little black book" and more of a "pen-manship exercise," but like I said, what I carry isn't a little black book.

Sure, it *looks* like one. It's small, thin, and bound in black leather (or at least what I really hope is black leather), but it's also a key. A clue. A map. Some sort of Rosetta stone that can help explain what came through to our world when the barriers broke down all those years ago. The cover says *The Book of the Dark Walker*. Ben is called the Walker too. What I'm really hoping is that somewhere inside I'll find a little bit about Ben Dejooli, about how his world works, maybe even how I can reach him. I don't tell Owen about this last part, of course, but I don't have to. He knows. And it makes me feel like a bad person.

"Does that make me a bad person?" I ask James Parsons, hereto-fore Agent Parsons and now of AJ's Villa, a four-star bed-and-break-fast on the West Sound of Orcas Island in upstate Washington. It's a bit of a bear to get here, if you're not traveling by crow. That's exactly why James and Allen chose it.

"Well, it doesn't make you a *great* person," James says. He's setting the breakfast table. It looks like they have two couples staying with them.

"It's not my fault I'm the type of girl who needs closure. Ben and I shared something that changed me, but he died before I could figure it out," I say, flopping down on one of their puffy living-room chairs that face the bay.

"Did you just blame a guy for dying of cancer?" James asks. He adjusts the alignment of a fork.

I put my head in my hands. "God. Maybe I really am a bad person."

"Don't listen to him, Caroline," Allen chirps from the kitchen. I hear the sizzling of eggs and bacon and the clunk of the oven door opening and closing. "He's just grumpy. It's completely normal to take five years to figure out where your heart lies."

I hear the *glugluglug* of coffee being poured. Allen Douglas comes around the corner with two mugs. He uses neutral cover-up to mask the light-pink scarring that Chaco left on his face back when Allen was trying to kill all of us. He's gained weight since then too. Happy weight. He holds one cup out to me.

"I can't tell if you're being serious or not." I take a sip. The mug is a ceramic pineapple. The decor here is a little too tropical for my tastes. The San Juan Islands always struck me as more *hot toddy* while AJ's is clearly channeling *mai tai*. But their coffee is outstanding, and Allen is a heck of a cook, and the view ain't bad, either. I watch the sunrise over the choppy waters of the sound, always hoping to see an actual orca. I haven't seen one yet, but I do see lots of crows. Even way out here. I phase over here sometimes when living in an RV day after day with Owen and Grant starts to grate on me. Don't get me wrong, I love the guys, but Owen is too bright to be as bored as he is, and Grant is... well, Grant is fourteen.

"I *am* being serious," Allen says, sitting down for a moment then getting right back up when something dings in the kitchen. "Just look at the two of us. This took five years," he says over his shoulder.

"That doesn't count. You were in a fugue state," I say.

"I'm just saying," he calls back.

"Have you at least gotten rid of that disgusting book?" James asks, turning to look at me. I reach involuntarily to my jacket pocket. He notices.

"Caroline Adams," James says, in a remarkable imitation of my mother. "What did I tell you about bringing that thing into our house?"

"It's not gonna hurt you. It doesn't *do* anything. That's the problem."

"You mean besides push you and Owen apart? When it's not brainwashing people?" He lowers his voice and glances toward the kitchen. These two hate the book, with good reason. They were following it when they broke through beyond the veil, but whatever they saw in it has been wiped away, along with their memories. Allen in particular is terrified of it. He has the scars as souvenirs.

"I can't just throw it away," I whisper. "It's says it's the *Book of the Dark Walker*. What if it helps us catch that thing that came through?"

"It's blank inside, Caroline. Has been for five years," James whispers. "Whatever we were reading, it's gone."

"What if it comes back?"

"If you ask me, I think you're less interested in finding whatever came though and more interested in seeing if it'll tell you how to find a certain Walker in particular. One named Ben Dejooli."

I can't claim otherwise, so I hide behind a big sip of coffee. I dream sometimes that it's a two-way journal. That I write things in it and they go to the other side and Ben can read them, and that Ben can write things in it that I can read. Things about that last kiss we shared before he died. Or the time our fingertips touched through the thin place. Chaco says the agents followed it like a map when they were beyond the veil. A map can lead to a lot of things. Maybe even to Ben.

"Are you two whispering?" Allen asks, bringing out steaming bread in a covered basket in one hand and a plate of food in the other. James turns back to the place settings. I prolong my sip of coffee.

"This is about that awful book, isn't it?" Allen asks primly, setting the bread basket down with a bit more force than necessary. "We already told you we can't read it. I don't even remember carrying it. It's blank to us too, and God willing it will stay that way forever."

"I'm sorry Allen. I just. . ."

"Can't let it go. I know. But be careful. That's how it starts." Allen pats my shoulder kindly. "Now eat. Before the guests come down and we have to explain you away. You look thin."

"I'm definitely not thin. You should see Owen. *That* is thin." But I take a hefty bite anyway as Allen refills my coffee.

"Maybe it's those crow totems," James says, sitting down next to me. "Watch out with them. You need to get outside. Less thin place. More sunshine."

"We know what we're doing with the totems now," I say, but now that he mentions it, I do look paler. I was never a tan girl to begin with, but these days I have that milquetoast, sat-in-front-of-the-TV-all-day look. I think it's less from the phasing, though, and more from the fact that we've been spinning our wheels for a while now, going from place to place, always stuck in transition. I wear a lot of loose, functional travel clothes, and my hair is in an endless string of pony-tails. I look rootless. I *am* rootless, and it shows.

"Don't listen to him," Allen says again. "You look beautiful. He's just grumpy."

3

OWEN BENNET

You would be absolutely flabbergasted if you saw how many wires and circuits are in a large RV. Ours is technically called a motor coach, but let's not glamorize things: it's a single-wide on wheels. Still, looking at this fuse box, you'd think I was driving the space shuttle *Endeavor* around the country. I've never really had a good look at the guts of it before. Aside from the handful of times Caroline's tried to dry her hair while Grant's played his videogames and a breaker got tripped, I've really had no cause to go rooting around down here. But then I decided to do my little project.

Caroline thinks I'm losing it. Like this is my Bridge to Nowhere and I'll be chipping away at it until I die because I've got nothing better to do. Fine. Let her think that. While she's off obsessing over that book I'm here trying to plan a future. Grant is indifferent, but he's indifferent to most things lately, except the color black. I do catch him occasionally watching me tinker, wearing this look like he's watching a squirrel bobbing around on one of those trick bird feeders.

After ten years in medical school, another ten years working the hospital floor, and another five traveling the country carrying the crow totems and the bell—tools that are essentially the nails that keep the tapestry of the living world hanging straight—it's amazing how much you *don't* know. Like how to wire a trailer hitch for a 240-volt electrical system, for instance.

I'm lying on my back on the floor at the rear of the RV, which we affectionately call the boat, the top half of my gangly frame stuffed awkwardly under the aft paneling, one hand holding a green wire. I've got a penlight in my mouth. I'm about to make a risky soldering decision when I hear Grant from up front.

"He's back," he says.

I freeze. I mumble around the penlight, "Seriously?"

"Seriously."

I sigh, scoot out front underneath the paneling like a dog scooting along the carpet, then sit up. Grant is looking at me with one earbud still in, the other dangling down his front. He gestures out the big side window with his head.

"What is with this guy?" I ask. It's rhetorical, of course, but these days Grant isn't one to skip an opportunity to fire off a droll answer.

"I think you know. I think we all know. If it's not this guy, it's the weird lady back in Pagosa, or that hick in the Pawnee Buttes, or those drunk college kids in Mendocino. They've all got the same thing."

I button my shirt up and straighten my rolled cuffs. "The itch. Yeah, I get it. Thank you, Grant."

Grant nods. That was sarcasm, but that seems to roll right off Grant these days as well. He's only capable of giving it, hasn't quite figured out how to take it.

"Stay behind me, out of sight," I say, moving toward the door. Grant gets up anyway and follows me, but he does stay back. *The itch* is a term I came up with, one of very few new diagnoses I do these days.

If Caroline were here, she could use her second sight to see what is bothering him, figure out exactly what to say, exactly what buttons to push to make the guy go away. She could see the script written in his "smoke," wafting off him in waves. If Chaco were here, he might be able to scare him off by virtue of being an enormous crow perched on top of the RV, but he's off too, looking for the thing that came through. So as it stands, it's just me. The only thing I can sense wafting off this guy is booze.

"Can I help you?" I ask, stepping down from the RV and closing the door behind me. He wears a tattered red T-shirt under oil-stained coveralls. His work boots are frayed at the steel toe. The guy looks like a mechanic, but then again, that's sort of the de facto dress code at this RV park. For all I know he could be the mayor.

"Whatcha buildin'?" he asks. His eyes flit to the trailer addition but always settle back to me and then behind me, to the right, where Grant watches behind the curtains. He's got the itch all right.

Most people are completely normal around the bell. Most wouldn't even know Grant carries the thing. But every now and then somebody gets the itch. These people, they come in all shapes and sizes, some mean, some just curious. Mostly mean, these days. It's been getting worse and worse ever since that thing broke through. They're troubled people, drawn to the world beyond ours. Drawn to the bell that could get them there. They end up in front of the RV without knowing why. They're the reason Grant, Caroline, and I have to pack up and head out every couple of months. They're the reason we can't ever establish ourselves anywhere.

"Just a trailer hitch. Now, I think you should move on, sir," I say.

"Uh-huh." The man nods without seeming to hear me. He takes a step forward.

"Stay back," I say. "I'm warning you." I'm not really sure what I'll do. I was not a fighter before I met Caroline. I've been in a fair amount of scrapes since, but every time I'm confronted with another one I feel like a mathlete trying to talk down the captain of the football team. I wish I'd kept the soldering iron. I could at least threaten to solder the man.

"I just want to check it out," he says. I don't think he means the trailer hitch. He steps forward again, and this time I take no chances. I step into him and try to push him back, but he hangs on to me. I'm taller than him, but he's bigger than me. He could bowl me over if he wanted to, but instead he just flails behind me, like I'm a stuck turnstile. He's got a one-track mind, this one. This is as focused as I've ever seen an Itch, and I'm dreading what I'll have to do to subdue the guy, when the door to the RV opens and Grant steps out. He has a gun.

"Get the fuck away from us," Grant growls. He levels the gun at the man. I don't know a thing about handguns, only that I hate them. This one looks as heavy and gray and dully evil as the rest of them. Grant is decked from head to toe in black, and with his shaved head he looks like that crazy type of fourteen. Child-soldier fourteen. I'm so shocked that I put my hands up right along with the Itch. Grant furrows his brow at me.

"I didn't mean nothin'," the Itch says. He blinks. His eyes seem to have cleared a bit. I can see that he's not quite sure how he got here, only that he needs to get out. He backs away for several paces then turns tail and scampers. I'm still holding my hands up.

"You have a gun?"

"Put your hands down, Owen."

"You have a *gun*?"

"Come on. That dude'll be back. They always are."

I step up and into the RV, close the door, and lock it behind us. Grant looks sheepish now, much more like the young boy from Midland that I know.

"Grant, this is not acceptable. Does Caroline know about this? What does Chaco think?"

"It's fake. See?" He points to a plastic ring around the muzzle. "Stop freaking out." He tosses it on the couch. I lean against the wall, less relieved than I thought I'd be. Grant sounds disappointed that it's fake. "I traded some kid at the edge of the park a bunch of games for it. And good thing, huh?" He looks up at me pointedly.

"I could have de-escalated the situation," I say.

"Uh-huh."

"And now we have to get out of here, of course. So there goes that."

"Good. This place sucks anyway. It smells like dog food." He flops down on the couch himself, which is something he does when he's frustrated. He learned it from Caroline.

"And stop cussing. You never cussed before. Don't start now. It's classless."

"I had to get my point across to the Itch," he says, rubbing at his head. I see a flash there, at his wrist. A bead bracelet. I have one of my own, a gift from a Navajo girl I treated back at the Chaco Health Clinic. I'm not naive enough to think he wants to be like me, though. The only thing Grant likes more than the color black is Joey Flatwood. He worships the man. Grant collects crow feathers wherever we go, swapping out for the best ones. I want to tell him that if he plans on weaving them into his hair like Joey, he'd better start growing it out, but no doubt that would blow up in my face too. I decide to leave well enough alone.

I step into the cockpit and fire up the boat to warm up the engine. "Batten down the hatches," I say. Grant gets up and starts to pack the RV away while I do a perimeter sweep, picking up a few loose odds and ends. I text Caroline *on the run*, which is our code for a quick getaway. I'll text her again when we fill up the tank outside of town so she can phase back to us. I survey the camp one more time. We've been here for three months, but I'm not sad to go. It does smell like dog food.

4

THE WALKER

There's no room for coincidences in the Navajo Way. No such thing. So all I can do is nod when I step out of the soul map and find that the tug takes me to Chaco Canyon. In a lot of ways, the whole reason I'm here is because of this canyon and what came from it.

Chaco Navajo Reservation is named for Chaco Canyon, which is this big jagged scoop in the earth in northwest New Mexico. The wash from the canyon created the Arroyo to the north, which edges up to the main camp of Chaco rez, and which is where all this began for me all those years ago when I started digging for more info on an Arroyo man everyone called the gambler. The old-timers and hard-line Navajo that ring the Arroyo in their tents and car camps like to say that they are the Chaco Wash themselves: they are the stones that rumbled down from the canyon over the years in the great rains. They are the pure deposits that were unearthed and the strongest that remain.

The old Chaco River chopped the canyon up into a bunch of jagged mesas to either side of the banks. They look sort of like teeth from far away, and they harbor a lot of old Pueblo and Navajo ruins in their ridges and flats. I'm standing in the shadow of the west mesa, I'd say about forty miles from the rez as the crow flies, and I'm looking at a dead Navajo man.

The soul map tells me this man is Bidzill Halkini. I knew Bidzill Halkini. He was a sheep farmer. An eccentric guy that we occasionally drove out to check on when I was with the NNPD. He wore a New York Yankees baseball cap all the time and wanted everyone to call him Bill instead of Bidzill. Every rookie at one point or another had to make the drive to check on Bilagaana Bill, as we called him. *Bilagaana* is a sorta loaded word we Navajo use for white people. It's not bad, exactly. But it's not good either. With Bidzill Halkini it was a joke because he was about as Navajo as they come—I mean, he was a sheep farmer, after all, and he lived more or less alone for most of the year in what was basically a lean-to out here near the west mesa. Just him, his animals, and the Navajo Way. But he had the Yankees cap and wanted to be called Bill, so there you go.

And now, here he is. But something about him doesn't sit right with me.

The Bilagaana Bill I knew was a desert-hardened, savvy Navajo. Not the type of guy to end up in the middle of Chaco Canyon, miles from anything, without so much as a stitch of supplies. Where are his sheep? Where is his sheep switch? Where is his Yankees hat? And most of all, where the hell is his soul?

I perch my hands on my hips and furrow my brow. I feel this strange, creeping dread that's timed perfectly with the slow wash of the setting sun as it coats the canyon in front of us, cutting a dividing line between the open canyon and our dark corner. I don't know as much as I'd like about how death works, even after all my time walking the map, but I do know that when things in my profession don't line up, it's very bad news. For everyone. And it usually starts like this. With little glitches in the system.

I drop in as the soul pops out, so it should be here somewhere close by. I scan the canyon. Nothing. I turn around and trace the edges of the west mesa where the fading sunlight is strongest. Nothing. I look up in the sky. Nothing. Which is another strange thing. The New Mexico desert is hard country. When something dies in it, something that could provide food for the creatures that live out here, it doesn't take long for the animal kingdom to realize it. Starting with the birds. But there are no birds in sight. No flies, either. No bugs of any kind. It's as if everything is avoiding this man.

"Hey!" I yell. "Bill! Come out! I wanna talk with you!"

Nothing. Not even an echo. This is a strange place even for a wanderer like Bilagaana Bill to end up, and without even a water bottle to his name. His car camp is at least five miles north. Time to do a little rewind, see exactly how he got here.

One of the best perks of walking the soul map is that if I want to see the story behind a death, I can track back the soul thread. Basically just rewind the life of the recently departed. I do this more than you'd think. More than I need to, that's for sure. The last moments of people's lives give me a lot to ponder. A bit ghoulish, I know, especially coming from a Navajo, where we're taught to stay the hell away from death, but I don't exactly have a lot of entertainment options here. You binge-watch TV shows. I do this. So sue me.

I swipe backward on the map, watch the dead man carefully. Swipe backward some more. Keep watching. The guy is still face down on the desert floor. The wind rustles his hair and kicks some dust up against his cheek, but that's about it. For hours he's like this. Which makes the lack of carrion feeders all the more suspicious. Then it's sunrise past, and all of a sudden I see a coyote. A mangy, feral-looking thing. Maybe even rabid. I take the thread back a bit and watch it approach. It senses the dead man and raises its hackles, but it keeps moving forward, almost like it can't help it. Once it's even with the body, it lunges at the dead man's mouth like it was shocked in the haunch, rips around a bit, then takes off down the canyon. I follow it for a few steps, but it's hauling ass and I'm not getting any closer to settling this soul, so I turn around.

I trace the rest of Bilagaana Bill's soul back, and as far as I can tell, here's how he died: He got up from his lean-to, neglected everything he owned, from his water to his gear all the way to his hat, then he walked out into the desert in complete silence for five miles, where he laid down right here and died. And then nothing came out.

Now I'm starting to freak out. We've got a body with nothing to tie it to the world beyond. I let out a big breath. Take another one in. And then yell as loud as I can for my bird friend.

"Chaco! Chaco, I need some help here!"

I wait. Wait some more. I start to get a little sweaty thinking about how I'm gonna deal with this on my own, and just when I suck in a breath to yell again, I hear the telltale *snap* of Chaco breaking through the plane. There he is, just a thin black line in the sky, until the line whips back on itself and sprouts wings and tail feathers and a sharp-beaked head. He spots me and dives right for my face, hoping I'll flinch. I don't flinch anymore. He pulls up and catches himself on my shoulder.

"Walker," he begins, already annoyed, "I got a lot on my plate these days. If this is another one of your sob stories, I'm gonna peck your face off."

Chaco doesn't understand how I can get wrapped up in my work sometimes. I admit I tend to get sentimental. Especially when I use rewind. But this ain't no sob story. Not yet.

Instead I just point at the body. "What the hell is that?"

"You're the expert and everything, but it looks to me like a dead guy."

"I know that, thank you. He's Bilagaana Bill. But where's his soul?"

"Billa-what?"

"His soul never left him," I say, holding out my hands, staring at the space between them as if it holds the answers.

Chaco twitches his head like he's shaking off water. "That's ridiculous. Of course it did. You just missed it."

"I didn't miss anything. Could the map be wrong somehow?"

"The map has never been wrong. *Never*. And it's been around *forever*. Walkers, on the other hand, have been known to fuck up a fair amount. No offense."

I crouch down again, and Chaco walks up my shoulder to perch on my head. Both of us peer down at the body. "I ran his thread back all the way. He walked out here and died, but nothing came out of him."

Chaco hops off my head and flutters down toward Bill but then flares his wings out at the last second. "Whoa, whoa," he says, skittering to rest on the dirt beside him. "He doesn't smell right."

"Well, he is dead."

"There's a right dead smell and a wrong dead smell. This is a wrong dead smell. And probably why none of my kind are anywhere near this thing." Chaco scans the sky above him with little ticks of his head.

"I thought that was strange too. Although there was one coyote. . ." My eyes trace the path the coyote took when it bolted. I feel like I'm missing something vital here.

Chaco looks up at me and tucks his wings in to make his back streamline straight, almost like he's pointing at me. "You're sure that you ran this thing back?"

I nod.

"And you're *sure* that you looked all around this place for his soul?"

I nod again.

"You'd better be really sure, Walker. This isn't *where the hell did I put my car keys?* stuff. This is *you're telling me up is down and down is up* stuff."

"I'm sure. And you know as well as I that for the past five years, up has seemed a little down and the other way around."

"Maybe the veil took it without you. Maybe your department is getting downsized, as they say. Maybe this is your cosmic pink slip and they got a robot to do your job."

"Ha ha. I gotta cut 'em loose first, asshole. There are rules. You know that."

"Yeah, yeah. So what are we gonna do?"

"Maybe we should call Caroline in," I say, trying to seem nonchalant. "See what her sight shows her. Maybe she picks something up that we can't see."

Chaco is quiet, and I pretend to be looking the body over again in the silence until it drags out too long. When I glance at him, he's staring right at me. "What? It's just a thought," I say.

"Uh-huh."

"Am I wrong? She's very perceptive."

"She's also deep in the trenches of some *matters of the heart* that seem to continuously feature you, despite the fact that you both know you're dead."

"I can't help that." I'm glad that I don't have the blood to blush.

"You could by leaving her alone," Chaco says, taking slow bird-steps around the body until he's on my side again. He looks askew at Bilagaana Bill and puffs up his breast in a sigh. "But you're right. We gotta get this straightened out. And the crew is on the move again anyway. Maybe they can swing by here."

"I'll be here," I say. "And Bill ain't going nowhere."

Chaco gives me one last look that says *watch yourself*, and I know he's meaning around the body, but also with Caroline. But Chaco isn't my bird, and I don't work for him either. We're just two poor saps trying to keep the balance between worlds, and I'll take any excuse I can to see Caroline. He's up, up, and gone, and then it's just me and Bill and the rez. All of us waiting.

5

GRANT ROMER

We pick up Caroline at a 7-11 outside of Pueblo, Colorado. She phases into the parking lot behind the boat, where I'm sitting watching the gauge at the gas pump tick over again and again. She blinks into reality mid-stride. She's getting really good at it. Both of them are. I remember when I first met them, they couldn't hold on to the thin place for more than a few minutes at a time, and if they walked in the thin place, there was no tellin' where they'd end up. It ain't that way no more. Sorry. It *isn't* that way *anymore*. I'm working on that. How I talk. I'm tired of people thinking I'm some dumb hick from Nowhere, Texas, especially when that place isn't my home anymore.

"Itch?" she asks, glancing toward the store where Owen is stocking up.

"Yep," I say, fingering my bracelet. Joey Flatwood gave it to me when we crossed paths a few years ago. He's always off somewhere with something to do, someplace to be. We're always off somewhere too, but the difference is we never seem to know where we're going.

"That was quick," Caroline says. "What, two weeks?"

"Three." But Caroline was only there for two of them. The rest of the time she was chasing after what might or might not be inside that book. She's quiet until I look up at her and find her watching me.

"Shit," I mutter. She's reading me again. "I thought you said you weren't going to do that."

"Watch your language, buddy. And I said I'd *try* not to read you. I didn't say how hard I'd try. And I'm already well aware of how you and Owen feel about the book."

The gas pump finally snaps off. Caroline and I look at the total, and we both clear our throats. Owen isn't gonna like that. He's been more and more concerned about cash lately, which I think means we have less and less of it.

"It's Owen who doesn't like that book. I don't care about it." Which is true. If it could help us find what came through, or figure out what the Dark Walker of the title is, we'd know by now. Personally, I think it ain't much more than a creepy doorstop. Although I do think it's a convenient way for Caroline to get away from us and call it "research." Or maybe just get away from me. Because I have a tendency to be a bit of a drag on people who end up taking care of me. Even before I got the bell and became the Keeper and started attracting all sorts of weirdness that makes us pick up shop every few weeks, I was a problem. Pap had to come out of retirement to provide for me after Mom and Dad died. I always muddy the waters wherever I am.

Joey doesn't need anybody. He can fend for himself. I can't, yet. But I will be able to one day. Sooner rather than later. Caroline is looking at me still. I don't know how much of this she can read in my smoke. Not all of it, but enough. My look is a challenge to her, to tell me otherwise if she understands me. She looks away.

Owen comes around the corner with two baggies full of drinks and gas-station food. He passes each of us a scratch ticket. This is his gas-stop ritual. He calls it our only chance at retirement, and I think he's only half joking.

"Welcome back," he says to Caroline, letting his words linger for just a second. He gives her a delayed hug. I can't take the awkwardness, so I push around them and walk up into the boat. "How are the agents?" Owen asks her, both of them stepping up after me.

"Oh, fine. Not a lot of help, as usual. They hate the book more than you do, but it's good to see them anyway." Caroline settles in the co-captain's chair up front. She kicks her shoes off and tucks her feet underneath her, rummaging around for her sunglasses. The August sunshine cuts right through the enormous front window. You get a full-body blast when you sit up front, which is why I never do.

"I don't hate it. I just don't trust it," Owen says.

"It's a book, Owen. Not a car salesman."

"I don't like how much of your time it takes up," Owen begins, before stopping himself. "But you already know that, and you know that I've said everything I'm gonna say about that thing. Did you know Grant has a gun?" he asks, completely throwing me under the bus just because he can't talk straight with her.

"Fake gun," I say quickly as Caroline turns to me. Owen does this stuff sometimes when he gets annoyed. Throws out hand grenades to see if Caroline has already picked up on their smoke. "It's an air gun, Caroline. No big deal. Jesus. And it's how we got away from the Itch too."

"So that's what you two were fighting about," Caroline says.

"We weren't *fighting*," Owen says, starting the boat up with a rolling roar of the engine. "Guys don't *fight* like that. I was just letting Grant know that I don't like guns. Of any kind." His pale skin blushes bright red. He was always pale, but he's gotten paler. It's a side effect of being good with the crow totem. Well worth it, I'd say. I'd love to have that freedom. To go across the country in a few steps, see some friends, be back whenever I wanted. The bell is sort of the opposite of that. It hangs around my neck and keeps me here. It's heavy. It pulls other people toward me, in fact.

Caroline sets her hand over Owen's for a moment, tries to get him to look at her, but he's flustered. He doesn't shake it off, exactly, but he gently moves his hand to the steering wheel, and hers falls away. I take notice of these things. I've been tryin' to figure the two of them out for years, and I'm still guessing. I think I have it figured out, then one of them stops talking to the other, or Caroline blinks out for a couple days, and it's just me and Owen and an awkward elephant in the boat.

One time, about a year ago, I walked in on them having sex. In the boat there's not a lot of privacy. They have the back bedroom, and I have a couch bed that pops out of the side and can fold up for some extra space. For whatever reason, the door to the back bedroom was open, and I came home early from walking to get dinner at the burger place that was across from the Alamo Placita RV park where we were camped at the time, and there they were. Owen was on top of Caroline, his skinny white back to me. Thankfully his butt was covered by the sheets, but it was definitely moving. Caroline practically threw him off of her when she heard the outside door open, and then they scrambled to cover up, but I saw basically everything. All that evening Caroline was too embarrassed even to talk to me, and Owen talked too much: explaining everything at once in birds-and-bees style like I was still ten years old.

I know what sex is. I know how it works. And it's not like I was scarred or anything. It's not like I walked in on my parents. Owen and Caroline aren't my parents, despite what they sometimes think. They're more like my older friends. So it wasn't gross, just awkward. The next day during homeschool Owen still hadn't come off it. He was babbling and stammering and trying to explain penises and vaginas using terms like *genitalia* and *ejaculate* and *menses*. I sat there and nodded, but all I was thinking about is how it'd be nice to have someone to do that stuff with. Or even to hang out with, without the sex.

There's been no repeat of anything resembling that little run-in since, though. At least not that I've seen, and I've been a bit more on the lookout for it. If anything, it seems like they were the ones that got the most awkward about everything. Now there's that extra little half-beat pause before they hug, or when they decide to hold hands. Like they're thinking too hard about it.

Day in and day out I have to see this stuff, and then they wonder why I want to just put on my headphones or zone out with video

games or go off by myself to see what other kids are doing. Then I
end up trading games for an air gun and suddenly they get pissed?
Thank God for Chaco. Having him around reminds me that the
world is a lot bigger than the boat, which makes me happy but also
makes me a little sad since so far I haven't been able to experience
any of it. Oh, I *see* a lot of it all right. It's rolling by underneath the
wheels right now. But I can't *touch* any of it.

"Bird incoming," I say, and Owen looks back at me from the
rearview mirror and nods. I get up, pop open and slide back the large
side window, and Owen slows the boat a bit. I hold out my arm and
watch the wind flutter the loose tie straps of the bracelet Joey gave
me. Don't worry, I double knotted it and made Joey promise that if I
somehow lost it he'd make me another one. But I don't lose things.
Ever. I'm the Keeper, after all.

Chaco isn't there and then suddenly he is, pumping his huge
black wings and flattening his arrowed head until he's level with the
window and on pace, then he reaches out and snatches my arm. It
doesn't hurt. He's pretty good at it by now. I carefully pull him inside
the boat, and he walks up my arm to perch on my shoulder. He used
to be able to perch on my head in the boat, but I got taller, and he's
not exactly a small bird.

"On the move again, eh?" he says, moving down to rest on my
knee as I sit back on the couch. Only the Walker and I can hear
Chaco. His voice is like a thought in my head. I answer him the same
way, without ever opening my mouth. He's what he calls a thinning.
Some creatures are closer to the thin world and the land of the dead
than others. Cats, bats, some dogs, supposedly elephants and sloths
too, according to Chaco. And crows, of course. Chaco represents all of
them. He's their presence across the planes. It's his job to protect the
Keeper. Me. He's been around in one form or another since the dawn
of time, but if you heard his voice, you'd think he sounds like a
twenty-something beach bum.

"It was the fat mechanic guy," I say. "He came back." I talk aloud
this time to let Caroline and Owen know. And to gloat, a little. I'd
warned them about that guy a week ago when he was hanging

around the cigarette shop across from our parking spot for hours every day. Owen was too busy working on his trailer, and Caroline was too busy with her book.

Owen looks back at me through the mirror and rolls his eyes. "Hey, Chaco. Where to now? Any thoughts?"

"It doesn't matter where we go," I say. "We'll last two or three weeks, if we're lucky, and then we'll run away from there too." I eye Chaco's feathers. They're huge. They'd be great for my collection, but Chaco knows what I'm thinking and squares up to me with a *don't even think about it* look.

"We're not *running away*, Grant," Owen says. "We're making a tactical move. For the good of the bell. Tell him, Caroline."

Caroline looks up from her magazine and blinks. "Hm? Oh. Tactical, yes. Although. . ."

Owen stares at her for a little longer than is safe when you're piloting a ten-ton vehicle. "Although what?"

"I was just thinking about Ben's grandmother, you know. The last Keeper. She stayed in one place for decades."

"Yeah, the rez. In the middle of nowhere. And that was before that thing came through," Owen says.

"Well, maybe we should go to the rez," I say softly. I finger my bead bracelet. I think of my crow feathers. Two of the strongest men I know came from the rez. Maybe if I go there, I can figure out how to hack it like they did. Like they do. Chaco titters and fluffs and watches me carefully.

"I don't think you know what you're saying, Grant," Owen says. "Chaco rez is not like some teepee camp where the Navajo ride war horses and hunt buffalo." He shakes his head, almost laughing. "And it's not exactly an easy place for a white kid to grow up. Tell him, Caroline."

Caroline is looking out of the side window at the crows on the horizon, the slow passing of the plains, and the even slower passing of the sheet-flat clouds in the distance.

"Go ahead, Caroline," Owen says again.

"I dunno," she says, shrugging.

"What? Are you serious? You were the one who wanted to leave that place five years ago. Remember?"

"I can leave whenever I want, now. I can go anywhere. And I can come back. This is about finding a place for Grant to stick," Caroline says, with an edge to her voice. "Might as well give it a shot. Worst case scenario, we're out of there in a couple weeks."

"Chaco," Owen says, turning briefly to look at him properly before facing forward again. "Can you talk some sense into these two? Neither the rez nor the surrounding areas are what I would call a great place for an outsider to grow up. Right? Heck, even Albuquerque is questionable depending on who you ask."

Chaco hops up to the couch and settles there in a plop of black. "Funny you all should say this," he says. "Because I was just with the Walker. And we were just in the Chaco canyon, where we found something."

Now he doesn't want to look at me. I narrow my eyes.

"What kind of something?" I ask.

"Something I was hoping you could check out. Some*one*, actually. And maybe *identify* is a better word."

"What are you two talking about?" Owen asks. "What's he saying?"

I contemplate repeating Chaco word for word, but Owen is already jittery about the move and Caroline can and often does change her mind from second to second. I gotta jump on it.

"Chaco wants our help checking something out in Chaco canyon."

"Well," Owen says acidly, "isn't that convenient. Right on the rez. How about that."

"Yeah," I say. "How 'bout that."

6

CAROLINE ADAMS

The dead guy in the desert doesn't bother me so much. I've seen a lot of death, unfortunately. When you work on an oncology floor for as long as I did at ABQ General, it's hard to avoid. It comes to you. Walks your halls. Sometimes seems to perch at the corner of every bed, waiting patiently. You never get used to death, not exactly, but you do eventually get so saturated with it that you become a little blind to it. And that was before I knew it was essentially Ben waiting there. Ben perched on the bed. I wonder, if I had known then what I know now, would it have been any easier working that floor?

Probably not. Cancer sucks. Always has. Always will.

This body looks like it's a set piece. It seems to have drifted down to earth from the sky in the middle of a wide canyon, like a piece of paper carried by the wind, and I'm having a hard time focusing on it because all I want to do is stare at the place where I know Ben is standing. Right now. I know Ben is standing there because Chaco is looking there, speaking with him, then relaying all this to Grant, who interprets for us.

Back at ABQ General we used to have this service called the IP: the Interpreter Phone. We'd get a lot of Navajo and Mexicans coming in and had only a handful of people on staff who could effectively speak Spanish and basically nobody who spoke conversational Navajo. Big problem, right? But fear not! IP was there for us. We'd dial a special number on our shift phones that would patch us through to Spanish and Navajo interpreters, hand the phone to the patients, then get the scoop ourselves.

Chaco is sorta like an interpreter phone with wings. And Grant is like the nurse doing the relay, like I was, standing there getting the scoop, telling it to the room. Ben is the lifesaver on the other end that you can't see. The one tapped in to another world. I have to stop myself from staring into his space. I can feel Owen watching me. Owen's smoke is a strange color these days. When we started on this trip, all those years ago, it was this beautiful aquiline blue, like his eyes. It's changed since then. Not in a bad way, not exactly, but different. It's tinged with a weary color of earthen brown. There's a lot wrapped up in that color. A bit of jealousy, a bit of regret, a bit of sadness, but mostly that unique weariness that comes with Owen's kind of determination to do what's right by us. It's the color of a man growing older. I know that sounds bad, but it's not. Not entirely. In a way, it's just as natural as the blue was, but it's still a little sad.

"The Walker says he just found the guy here," Grant says. He's trying to play it cool, but I can see he's enamored. Ben, like Joey, is a rock star to him. I don't think he's blinked since we got here. "Just like this," he says, pointing at the dead man. "No trace of a soul."

Chaco chirrups then caws. "The Walker wants to know if you can see anything," Grant says, looking to me.

I kneel closer to the body. Look all around it. I cup my hands over his heart, touch his forehead. I stand and turn back to Grant and Chaco, both watching me intently. My eyes flick over to the empty space that is Ben. "I can't see anything," I say, and the sad weight that comes out with the words makes Owen shift uncomfortably behind me. He knows I'm not just talking about the body, I'm talking about Ben too. "But that's not surprising," I add, standing from my crouch then slapping my hands together and rubbing them on my jeans.

"When a person dies, their smoke goes with them. This man's soul has gone somewhere."

"You're sure?" Grant asks.

I nod, thinking of Oren Dejooli, Ben's father. When I came across his body in Ben's backyard, after Danny Ninepoint went on his killing spree, his body was just as empty as this man's in front of me. "I can't say where it went, but it went somewhere."

Grant slumps a little. Chaco mimics him on top of his head. "Well that's just great," Grant says. "What good are we if we can't help out when the Walker needs us?"

"Hey," I say sharply. "Take it easy. I can't make smoke where there's no smoke. I don't know what to tell you."

Grant moves over to the body and kicks a rock near its hip so that it clatters against the canyon wall. I can tell Chaco is trying to talk to him. Grant has been getting more and more pissy lately. I always thought boys were supposed to be the easy ones to navigate through puberty. Although I know I'm not exactly the best navigator. Sometimes I feel like I'm still going through puberty myself.

"Did Ben trace back the string?" Owen asks, startling me. I'd forgotten he was there for a moment.

"He did," Grant says. "The guy acted weird. Basically just came out here and gave up."

"That's it?" Owen asks. "Nothing else?"

Grant listens. "Well, there was this coyote." Chaco flutters to the ground near an incoming stream of paw prints. He follows them over to the body, but then he looks lost. There's some back-and-forth, and Grant looks confused.

"The tracks are gone," Grant says. "They go up to the body, but then they disappear. The Walker says he saw the coyote take off down the canyon. There should be tracks."

All of us move in closer to the body, which by now should at least be putrefying a little bit. It's sundown on the second day. We should be seeing some swelling of the gut or staining of the face, but instead it looks eerily fresh.

"No tracks? Then what the heck is that thing?" Owen asks,

pointing at the canyon floor just beyond Grant. We all turn to look, and there, sure enough, is a paw print. A single paw print leading away from the body, down the canyon.

"Chaco says that wasn't here before," Grant says quietly. I can almost feel Ben rushing over to it along with us. Almost.

I can't quite believe what I'm seeing. The paw print looks like it's sitting a hair above the sand, and it seems to glow slightly in the shadow of the mesa. Grant slowly drags the toe of his sneaker across the outer edge. The movement cuts a rivulet through the desert floor, but the track remains whole. Chaco hops over and peers closely at it, then he looks around, no doubt thinking what all of us are thinking. Where are the rest of the tracks?

Grant takes a tentative step past the paw print, farther into the Canyon shadow. The first track fades as he passes it, but a second is illuminated. Chaco hops behind as Grant walks. Each print is illuminated, then fades as he passes. The blurred edges of each print remind me of the tracks the chaos souls made as they smeared their way across the desert back in Texas. My stomach does a little roll.

"It's the bell," Grant says, pulling it out and grasping its chain in his hand. "They light up when it's near." He waves it over the sand, and the prints illuminate, then fade. Chaco squawks, and Grant listens, then turns to us.

"This guy had a run-in with something bad," Grant says.

"Our monster?" Owen asks. There is wary hope in his smoke, that maybe we've found a trail worth following after all, but he knows as well as I do that this stuff never comes easily. Our new jobs make our old jobs look positively orderly. Night shift at ABQ General was a game of croquet compared to watching over the bell and the Keeper. But I still get my hopes up. Why can't something break our way for once? You know, just fall our way without a fight? Without the world teetering on its edge first? It happens to other people all the time. Open, closed. Why not us?

"The coyote took off into the canyon," Grant says, twenty feet away now, following the prints. The tracks cut to the canyon wall, much harder to see in the light. If you weren't looking for them, you would miss them. They trace the edge, until they jump up on a rock, then to another a bit higher. Grant follows the tracks as far as he can, peering closely at the rock face, until he hits an old gravel slide. The tracks race up it, but Grant can't get far. Nobody could. I'd guess it's at a forty-five-degree angle. "Looks like he went up and out."

"What's up there?" I ask, my voice wavering.

"There's the canyon visitor's center a few miles that way," Owen says, pointing.

Chaco caws once. "That's not where it's going," Grant says.

"No, I don't think so either. Another few miles past that you start to hit the rez proper."

Chaco caws again.

"That's where it's going," Grant says, nodding.

We all crane our necks to look up the canyon, as if we could see out and beyond the lip. After a minute, Grant speaks again.

"The Walker says it just looked like a damn coyote. Nothing more."

Owen shakes his head. He looks over to where I think Ben is standing, but only briefly. As if even the empty space is too much for him. When he speaks, his voice sounds defeated already, although I don't think it has anything to do with our monster. "If there's ever a place where a coyote isn't just a coyote," he says, "it's right here."

7

THE WALKER

I know I'm not supposed to play favorites in my job, but you'd better believe I'm nicer to some souls than I am to others. A lot of assholes die every day. With the assholes, I play into the Death stereotype a little more. Ham it up a bit. I try to make it easy on the good people. Help explain things when I can. Sit with them or pray with them or chat with them for a bit, whatever they want to do, until the veil comes.

I'm especially partial to Navajos. Surprise, surprise.

When Caroline, Owen, and Grant leave Chaco Canyon to go call in the body, I stick around. It's just the two of us. Both of us dead, and in a way, neither of us able to move on. It's kind of depressing to realize how much I have in common with this stiff out here in the desert. I'm still not sure what was going through Bilagaana Bill's mind when he walked out here. I don't know what the coyote was, or why it came to him, but I do know that this man was someone, once. He lived on the fringes, but he had a place on the map. There's one less Navajo walking the Way right now, and that hits me hard. So I sing for him.

I sing an old song Gam used to sing to me. It's not a mourning song, or a song about good-byes or anything like that. I don't know any of those. It's actually just a song Gam always sang to Ana and me when we were young to get us up for school. It's about the sunrise, and it's the only song I know by heart. Whenever I'm called to Navajo deaths, I sing this song with the soul as we wait for the veil. It seems to help. Even with the younger generation, who sometimes don't give a shit about the chants or songs or even the Navajo Way, really. Until they're dead. Funny how once they're dead they start to care real quick.

As I sing I get to thinking. I've been singing this song a lot recently. A whole lot of people die every day, and I'm there for every one of them. When you walk the soul map, you have to be a lot of places at once. That's what happens when you clip well over a hundred thousand souls a day: they start to blend together. But this song takes me back to all the Navajo I've been seeing out, and it seems to me like I've been working overtime in this neck of the woods lately. A lot of singing. And I don't like it.

My song done, I swirl open the map and step through. It's time to do some digging and find out where Bill's soul went. I take a few steps and walk out onto my old street at Chaco rez. Here seems as good a place as any to orient myself to the rez once again.

My family used to live in one half of a split duplex on a quiet road about a quarter mile north of the police station. We were pretty broke, all things considered, but the place was always clean and neat. Comfy in its simplicity. Because of Gam. Her mind was as ordered as the rugs she wove, and she was the Keeper of more than just the bell in her time. She kept the house too. Especially after Mom left. Danny Ninepoint ruined all that. He turned our home from something beautiful into something stained.

My people wrap death and dying up in all sorts of superstitions. One of them is ghost sickness. We think death is literally contagious. Even the young generation, the kids who say they're scared of nothing and think more about their cell phones than the Navajo Way, even they won't stick around a place like this. It's been over five years since Gam and Dad died here, and nobody on the rez will touch the place, not even to tear it down.

Joey and I used to laugh at the old-timers who seemed scared of death. These were supposed to be the champions of the Navajo Way. Men and women who walked in balance, who were so even keeled that if the entire rez was on fire they'd nod and smoke and sweat and say to themselves, "Well, the world can't hold everything." But then when someone dies they won't mention their names because they're too afraid that person's *chindi*, its restless spirit, might come back to haunt them. Might touch them and give them ghost sickness and then they'd die too. The Arroyo crew'll tell you don't even look too long at the dead. Don't even stand too long where they died.

Crazy, right? Stupid superstitious nonsense, right?

I thought so too. Up until I saw a restless spirit wandering the desert five years ago, his soul cut by the turquoise knife we destroyed. I thought so too, right up until I jumped into a river of restless spirits, and I touched them, and I felt like their chaos was catching. Up until restless spirits tried to kill my friends. If Gam saw those things and how they acted, she'd be calling them *chindi*.

I don't laugh at the old-timers anymore. They claim the world can't hold everything. I know it can't. It's my job to keep it balanced. Which is why I'm not especially surprised to find a coyote waiting for me, standing in the shadow of my front porch, looking right at home in the gloom.

The coyote's paws rest on piled leaves, its tail swishing through little fragments of broken glass. It's the same brown and burned-orange color as the faded graffiti that streaks across the door.

If you ask a Navajo about Coyote, the Coyote of our legends, you'll get all sorts of answers. Some will tell you he's funny, some'll say he's tricky. Everyone will agree he's trouble. Coyotes are bad omens. Old-timers say if a coyote crosses your path, turn back. Forget your journey. So I'd take notice even if the damn thing wasn't staring right at me.

I can't see its tracks without the bell around, but I'd bet my best hat that if I had the bell in my hand, this old house would be lit up with glowing paw prints. This is our dark visitor. And it's waiting for me. It's expecting me.

"What did you do to Bilagaana Bill," I ask. I don't know why I expect it to answer. I talk to things all the time in my job. People, rocks, clouds. I've never expected an answer until now.

I don't get one. The coyote looks like it's chewing on something that's giving it trouble. In the low light it looks blurry about the face. Like it's shaking its head really fast. Then it freezes and stares at me again. Then it shoots off into the street at a dead sprint. It moves so fast I can't even react. I watch it stop on a dime in the intersection, oblivious to traffic, like a rabid dog. A car swerves and honks, missing it by an inch. It shakes its head in a blur again. Waits. It turns to stare at me with unblinking eyes the color of gold coated in oil. Then it yips at me a bunch of times in succession, and the sound gives me shivers. It sounds like a thing laughing as it's dying.

I follow it. I get to the end of my block, and it's already moved a hundred feet farther down the street, almost to the service route that leads to the main drag and the NNPD station. It's really twitching now, and not just like it needs to be put down either. It seems like it's double exposed. It keeps gnawing at itself, then something seems to grip its attention and its head snaps up. Down the street there's a couple walking toward the main drag. A boy and a girl, maybe in their twenties. They're facing away from us and don't notice the coyote. It prowls toward them.

"Hey! What the fuck do you think you're doing?"

It prowls a second step, looking back at me like a mischievous two-year-old holding a glass of red juice over white carpet.

"Don't you take another step. Leave them alone. I don't know what you want, but I'm the one you gotta deal with out here."

It doesn't take another step—

It flat out takes off. It sprints after the couple in dead silence, flying over the hard packed dirt in bounds that seem way too long for its legs. Its big ears are flattened to its head. Its tail jets out like in a streamer behind it. All I can do is yell after it as it leaps to collide with the girl and nails her square in the small of the back with the crown of its head, sending her sprawling to the ground. In a blink it's at her face, snapping and chewing. Its growl is high pitched and whiny, like a power drill.

The man she's with kicks at it. He's calling her name over and over again. It sounds like Polly or Molly. I can't quite tell through his panic. He lands one, then two solid kicks right to the torso of the coyote. The third connects just as I get there and finally pops the coyote away. It scrabbles in the dirt, flailing like a dog running in its dreams, then it flips itself up.

"You little bastard," I growl. I have my hands out like a grappler and reach for it, but my fingers pass right through, which surprises me. This thing and I had a clear connection. But now that I'm close to it, I think maybe I was seeing things. The coyote looks as surprised as the couple, and it's in a good deal of pain too, from the kicking, that it doesn't seem to understand. "What did you do that for?" I ask, pointing at the girl. She's on her back, her hands up in front of her, while her partner strokes her face and calls for help on his phone. Blood from her wounds trickles into her mouth, and she coughs it up right into the man's face.

The coyote is wide eyed, startled. It's trying to slink away. Run from all this. If it ever saw me, it doesn't anymore. It looks like it woke up in the wrong county with a malt-liquor hangover. It takes a few tentative steps before it limps its way off without looking back.

My gut tells me to leave it. I turn to the girl. I hold my hands out, as if I could touch them. Help them. As if I could even offer words of support. I still sometimes forget that I can do none of these things, even after all these years. They wouldn't want the kind of help I can give. It's a bit more permanent than a coyote bite.

The girl is bit up on the left cheek where it looks like the coyote tried to get at her mouth, but other than that she's not terribly hurt. Nothing a few stitches and a bunch of rabies shots can't fix. Already I see a group of people jogging her way down from the service route. I hear a siren. I turn to the guy, wishing I could pat him on the back. Buy him a beer. But he's gone. His bright-red shoes are beating down the opposite side of the street toward the oncoming group. He's high-tailing it. Then he cuts across the street at the last second and nearly plows into them, two women and another man wearing the black polo shirts of Manuelitas—the tamale shop a few blocks away.

I look down at his girlfriend. She moans, unaware. Red Shoes hugs one of the women like he knows her, which is lucky. Then he gets real close to her, which starts a shoving match with one of the men. Maybe not so lucky, after all. Of all the times to pick a fight, right?

Red Shoes gets knocked to the ground and has his hands up in protest. I can't hear what he says, but it's enough to mollify the man, who points toward us. Red Shoes gets up, shakes himself off, and starts running back our way. The man follows, along with one of the two women. The third woman, the one Red Shoes hugged, stands stock-still. The other three don't seem to notice that she's not following them my way. That instead she's staring right at me.

I take a few steps toward her. Her eyes definitely follow me. The group rushes right through me on their way to the girl on the ground. I notice that Red Shoes seems a bit disoriented. He looks behind him like he's trying to figure out how he ever left her side. He looks an awful lot like the coyote did after it got up. I start walking toward the Manuelitas girl, and soon I'm close enough to notice that her face is a little twitchy, her cheeks a bit stretched as if her skin is colored just a touch outside the lines of her face.

"Don't move," I say, but it doesn't come out too strong. I've got goose bumps running up my neck that make me want to jump around in the hot desert sun for about an hour. I take another step forward, she takes one back. I take another step, she does the same. Her eyes light up with manic glee. She smiles so hard I think it's gonna break her face. Then she winks at me. Before I can react she takes off at a dead sprint down the street away from me, her strides longer than they should be. She covers more ground than she should, just like Red Shoes did. Just like the coyote did. Before I can get even fifty feet after her, she's turned the corner in front of the police station onto the main drag.

I turn the corner barely a minute later. I find her, but already I know that whatever possessed her is gone. She's leaning against the chipped stucco of the Navajo Gas building barely twenty feet away. Her hands are on her hips. She's taking big gulps of air and trying to figure out how she got there. I'm right in front of her, but she doesn't see me. I spin around, scanning the crowd. An awful lot of people are out here today. A lot of trucks. Flatbeds loading and unloading things. A van of tourists crawls by, not knowing where to park or where to turn off to get to Old Town. A lot of movement. I don't see anybody else looking at me, but I can feel the thing. I can feel it here, and I can see evidence of it everywhere. Two men start arguing in front of Manuelitas. Just a disagreement, or something more? What about the young guy perched at the mouth of the alley half a block down, weaving and drinking from a bag? Is he looking at me, or just drunk? A souped-up sport truck peels around the corner, north toward Wapati Casino. Just some kid trying to swagger a bit? Or maybe the Manuelitas girl got up in his face seconds before? The street seems chaotic—it's everywhere you look, once you start looking. And I think I know why.

Gam used to walk everywhere back when I was young. She'd sometimes take me with her on easy little hikes around the piñon hills not far from the house. They're more like lumps than hills, actually. I'd race around the lumps and cut between the yuccas, thinking I was following animals when I was only tracing the path the water made when the rains washed everything out every year in late summer. I'd never stray too far from Gam, who walked in her slow way, her bony hands clasped behind her back, but I can remember one time when I was running around and she yelled at me to stop. Gam never yelled. She got plenty angry sometimes, but she wasn't a yeller. So you better believe when I heard her yell my name I stopped in my tracks.

I waited as she walked up to me in her own time and then looked down at the path I'd been following. She pointed down at a little furrow there where it looked like someone had run a stick along the dirt. My little shoe print cut a waffle in the dust right next to it.

"You know what this is?" Gam asked, speaking in Navajo.

I shook my head.

"Snake. That's a snake track," she said, tracing it all the way back into a hole on the nearest hill with one sharp finger. "And you just stepped over it."

I stared up at Gam, trying to divine if she was joking with me or scolding me. With her it was sometimes hard to tell. With most old-timers it still is.

"Scuff it out," she said, scraping her leather boots on the dirt to show me. When I asked why, she said, "Because if you don't, the snake will follow you home."

I started scuffing that dirt like my life depended on it. And every time I crossed a snake's path after that I scuffed the track out. All my life. Maybe after I died I got lazy. Maybe I got cocky. Because I crossed something's path beyond the veil, on the shores of the river, and I forgot to scuff out my tracks.

And maybe it's being back here, surrounded by everything I used to be, thinking about Gam and all the other old-timers and their little sayings and wards and superstitions, but if you ask me, I think I got a pretty good idea whose path I crossed.

A coyote can be a lot of things.

If Joey and I got caught raising hell around the rez or goofing off at school and Gam really wanted to scare some sense into us, she didn't talk about snakes. She talked about shape-shifters. Things that could take the form of coyotes, if they wanted. Things that could move faster than people. Things that snuck up on you and took you down, then moved on to sow more evil before you even knew what hit you.

There's one thing that the Navajo hate talking about even more than the names of the dead, and that's witchcraft.

Gam spoke of these witches in low, cautious quiet, telling me how they'd get me if I didn't stop screwing around. I was terrified of them as a kid. As a teenager, I stopped being afraid because I convinced myself that Gam was just telling me stories to keep me in line, to get me to finish my chores or do my homework. That she didn't actually believe them herself.

I was wrong.

Gam called these creatures by their Navajo word: *at'latai*. Kids these days use the English slang: skinwalkers.

I think I crossed paths with a creature of chaos beyond the veil, and I think it followed me home. It's wearing the lore of my people like a disguise. Preying on the Navajo like a skinwalker would. Taking on the most dangerous form of Coyote. The trickster. The witch.

8

GRANT ROMER

We'd intended to go all the way up to Chaco City proper, but Owen got lost on the Navajo roads, and we ended up swinging too far southwest. We have no phone service, and since Owen shorted the dash GPS doing all his trailer-hitch tinkering, we drive for over an hour through the flats with our asses in the air, Caroline trying to politely tell Owen he's completely lost and Owen trying to politely take her advice without turning the boat into oncoming traffic.

Then we start seeing crows. A lot of crows.

We end up pulling in to a rez town called Crownrock, on account of all the crows we see flying overhead, and also so Owen can get out of the boat before he busts a button on his collared shirt.

The dinged-up Navajo Nation sign off Highway 371 says the population of Crownrock is three thousand. At first glance I think that may be generous. I notice the population number is written on an interchangeable metal plate. I'd say it's due to be knocked down a peg. Still, I'm excited. I can't tell if it's the bell stirring itself on my chest or my heartbeat shaking it, but I haven't felt this excited about a new place since we left Texas.

The crows are flocking here for some reason, and wherever crows flock, something is out of whack. They line the side of the street and watch us pass like a crowd at a parade. They hop out of the way of people and cars a little slower than they ought to. They perch twenty and thirty deep on the overhead wires, and bunches of them swarm here and there, worrying at scraps of trash in the gutters and road kill on the shoulders.

The thing about crows is, they're not bad, but they're not good either. They're just crows. They've got their own agenda. Chaco will be the first to tell you. Most of the time it's in line with ours. Sometimes they just want to sit back and watch the carnage and wait to clean up. But wherever there are a bunch of them, something's up.

The whole town isn't much more than a mile across. We spot a KOA-style campground a little ways in where we can plug in and dump out the boat, and all of us get out to stretch our legs and wait for Chaco, who's gone ahead to get the lay of things. I can see him soaring above. The crows here are like ribbons of smoke in a wildfire, but he's impossible to miss. I want to start checking things out immediately, but I can see both Owen and Caroline are exhausted.

Wandering around a new town like zombies won't do any of us any good. They pack it in, and I busy myself in the main room, listening to music, playing video games, messing with my feathers, until eventually I nod off too.

Owen wakes me up on his way outside. I'm shocked at how late it is, already mid-morning. I must have been more exhausted than I thought.

"I remember this place," Owen says, stretching his back. He starts doing old-man calisthenics right there in the middle of the parking lot, and for the first time in a while I thank God I don't know anybody here. "Crownrock. Yeah. We did some off-site work here for the CHC back in the day. House calls and all that. Mostly smiling and shaking hands. Checking insulin pumps and blood pressure levels. Making the Tribal Council look good. Pretty quiet town."

"Well, something's going on," Caroline says. "This place feels. . . troubled." She walks out to the street and carefully watches the people walking by. She shakes her head. They look fine to me, a little twitchy maybe, but that's about it. Then again, I can't see feelings like she can.

What I can see is tracks. Faint paw prints everywhere I step, fading in and out of view.

"Uh, guys," I say, pointing. Owen and Caroline say nothing. They just stare. A definite path of those weird paw prints runs down the main street.

"Looks like our coyote beat us here," Owen said. "Damn back-country roads. Would it kill them to put up a few more road signs?"

"I'm sure the Tribal Council is all over that. Top of the list," Caroline mutters, kneeling down to get a better look at the crisscrossing tracks in front of me. "But I don't think it matters how fast we got here. These things are layered all over one another. The coyote has been all around here for some time."

"Looks like a bunch of coyotes to me," I say as Chaco floats down our way in big, looping pinwheels. He lands with a series of hops and surveys the tracks, ticking his head along them like a typewriter.

"This thing has been all over the rez," he says to me. "The Walker is up north, in Chaco City. He ran into the bastard itself yesterday."

"What?" I yelp, causing heads to turn. "Did he catch it?"

Chaco shakes his head.

Owen clears his throat. "I'm guessing this has to do with Ben," he says, and there's this tiny sigh in his voice.

Caroline watches Chaco and me intently as Chaco relates the story. I can't quite believe it myself, and I'm sure I sound as confused as I feel when I tell it to Owen and Caroline.

"It's a shape-shifter. Jumps from body to body, leaving hell in its wake. He says it's a lot like something the Navajo call a skinwalker. Fast, strong. Can be anywhere, or anyone."

Owen grimaces. "Skinwalker, huh? I think I liked it better when we called it just your garden-variety Dark Walker. Or the *thing*."

"It looks to me like it prefers the coyote," Caroline says, following close behind me, eyeing the prints. If the bell could light up the whole street, it would look like a coyote run.

"So what's it want?" Owen asks.

"This thing came from the black pearl," Chaco says to me. "Its job is chaos. That's what it's doing. Problem is, chaos takes many forms. This bad boy tricked the agents into breaking it out of the pearl. It fought its way through the veil. I have a hard time believing it's just here to start street fights and make everyone nervous, or even to kill someone like Bilagaana Bill. It wants more."

"Something big," I say, translating. "It wants a big meltdown."

"And there's another thing," Chaco says, perching on my shoulder. "It could be anywhere in the world. It's clearly fast as hell, and it can disguise itself as anyone. But it's here. Right here. On the rez."

"It's personal," I say, turning back to Owen and Caroline. "It wants chaos, and it wants us to be in the middle of it. All of us. The Walker too. It brought us all here because it knows you have history here. The Walker is from here." I didn't add that it was essentially my idea to get us out here. There's no way this coyote could have known that, right? About how I'd always wanted to see where Joey and Ben came from myself? About my feathers? I fiddle with my bead bracelet. Does it know about that too? It's been here for five years. What if it was watching us the whole time?

"So it's leading us into a trap?" Caroline asks.

Chaco nods. "Smells like it to me, but what can ya do?" he says to me. "When you don't know the game, you gotta get played a bit until you can figure it out." Chaco spreads his wings and lifts off in three slow blasts. "I can see better from up high. Coming in here, it looked like a lot of people headed thataway for some reason, down the street."

"A lot of the coyote tracks go that way too," I say, stepping forward, studying the ground. Owen and Caroline get that I mean to follow, but I look back at them anyway and wait for them to decide. Sometimes I think they like to think they're still in charge of what happens here. Owen particularly.

Owen puffs out his cheeks and lets out a breath, shrugging. "By all means the smart thing to do here is follow the coyote's exact steps into whatever trap it's setting. Sounds completely rational to me. A lot healthier than a candy trail into the oven, that's for sure. In terms of sugar intake."

Caroline lets out a snort, and I turn around before he can see me smile. I know he's kidding. His sense of humor is drier than the desert sometimes. But I bet Ben and Joey ain't laughing at a time like this. Chaco ain't either. Sorry. *Isn't.* Chaco *isn't* laughing.

"All right, then. It's settled," I say.

We start following the tracks.

9

OWEN BENNET

When CHC would have us do courtesy calls across the rez, we'd sometimes come here to Crownrock. You can count on both hands the number of towns across Chaco rez that have more than a thousand people in them, and we made it a point to visit each at least once a year. Memories come back to me as we walk the street. There's a great hole-in-the-wall Mexican food joint somewhere here. It doesn't have a name, just "Mexican Food," but it does the best Christmas-style enchiladas you'll ever have. Half green chili, half red. One hundred percent glorious indigestion. The volunteer crew would stop there whenever we passed through, usually me, another resident, and a nurse looking to help out a community we had no idea how to approach. We were full of righteous medical science then. There to make a difference. We were looking for *Heart of Darkness* experiences. To get deep in it. We were convinced we were the real deal, and everyone else was just a tourist.

You wouldn't know that looking at me now, walking down the center of Crownrock like I'm lost in Manhattan. All I'm missing is the oversized map and the sandals with black socks. The man I was would watch me now with narrowed eyes. At least until I was able to explain to younger me about Caroline. About how she still looks to me every now and then like I know what I'm doing, like we're back on the hospital floor and not out here navigating the rest of life together. About the way we sometimes find ourselves holding hands without meaning to. I think the man I was might start to understand. I didn't know Caroline back then. That was years before she came to ABQ General. But I had a place in my heart waiting for her.

Young Me might ask about Grant too. *Your kid?*

Not exactly, I'd say. Definitely not if you go by what he says. And as for Caroline, she's not in that place with me. Might never be. When we have sex it's more like the kind of sex you have because you're stranded on an island with someone. You have your pride and your principles in one hand, and in the other you hold some small part of a beautiful woman's heart. All that she's willing to give right now. At first you're stalwart. You insist you'll wait for true, fully reciprocal love to seal the deal. Then the days turn to months and the months turn to years and you're still on the island, and all of your principles start to seem foolish. Eventually you take whatever piece of her she's willing to give you.

I hope it's worth it, Young Me would say. *What would Dad say? What would Grandfather say?*

I think about it every day, I'd reply. They'd tell me to weigh what was lost when I forwent my cause here to be with her. And I do think about it every day. And it's still worth it in moments like this one, when she nudges me softly with her shoulder as we walk side by side, following Grant as he scampers after the tracks. It doesn't seem like a lot, man. I know. But it is. You'll understand one day.

"Everyone is going over there," Grant says, pointing at a big square building one block off the main street. It's built of whitewashed concrete inset with thin windows at regular intervals. It looks like a prison, but it's actually a school. Crownrock High School. We used to hold community health meetings there and give our little talks about heart health and weight management. We had to give out free pizza to get people to come. Which is sort of counterintuitive, if you think about it.

We pass row upon row of trucks in the parking lot, most of them battered F-150s, which we used to call the Chaco state car. We fall in with a steady line of Navajo walking toward the open double doors of what looks like a big gymnasium. It has a large stenciled eagle on one wall and Home of the Eagles written in thick black lettering underneath. We always did our presentations in the classrooms. We never got this much attention. This looks like some sort of town forum. Grant stares up at the eagle until I have to pull him along. I'm more interested in the three NNPD squad cars parked front and center near the entrance.

Inside, the hallways are scuffed and narrow, the lockers are dented, and the paint on the walls is chipped and cracked. The school has that stale basement smell that seems to permeate all high schools. Above a leaking water fountain the wall is peppered with signs for the upcoming Enchanted Desert Homecoming Dance along with several flyers that read, "If you live in a shelter, a car-park, abandoned building, or train station *you may qualify for certain benefits under the federal McKinney-Vento act.*"

The doors to the gymnasium are propped open, and on each hangs a big, colorful poster advertising the upcoming Native Market of Santa Fe. It occurs to me that this might be a community gathering in preparation for the market. It's a pretty big deal. I went a couple of times back when I lived in Albuquerque. Hundreds of Indian artists with works of all kinds, from beaded dolls and woven coasters all the way up to sand-cast silver and turquoise jewelry that can run you in the thousands. It's also a bit of a zoo. Santa Fe tourism cranked up to eleven.

At a glance I'd say the gym has about two hundred people in it already, and more are filing in with us. Someone is already talking at the front of the room, and it takes me a second to recognize that it's Sani Yokana, the NNPD chief of police. Back at ABQ General we'd see a fair number of Navajo with criminal records. The guys that were repeat offenders in our neck of the woods were often repeat offenders in Sani Yokana's as well, so I had some dealings with him. I remembered him as a stout, powerful-looking man with a wide head, like a stone mountain with long gray hair. I'm shocked to see how much older he looks. His bulk seems deflated. His long hair is grayer and receding a bit at the temples, but he still has that flinty gleam in his eye that hints of the kind of mettle that's kept him in his position for all these years. He's addressing the crowd, and the tension is palpable. His tone is flat, professional, and deliberate.

"You know me, many of you personally. I'm telling it to you straight, and I'm telling you what I know. That's why I'm here today, because there are a lot of rumors out there already, and people are getting concerned. First, the facts. We have three separate incidents here where we've found unmarked bodies, two men and one woman, all three Navajo. One in the Escavada Wash, another south of Nageezi, and now this third in Chaco Canyon. Without going further into it, suffice it to say we think all three are connected."

The crowd murmurs, hushed and low. I notice teenagers here too, standing with their parents. Most likely Crownrock students. This is definitely a neighborhood affair.

"Now it's important to note that all three were discovered in remote locations. Not within the cities or even the settlements. We've doubled the officers on each shift, and they're out patrolling Crownrock and the other towns right now, nonstop. This is a time to remain vigilant, not a time to panic. Normally we'd keep all this in the department, but recently everyone seems to be on edge and talking anyway, so we're going around to head off rumors and calm some fears."

"Is it a serial killer? One of our people?" someone shouts from the crowd.

Yokana flinches as if the thought physically twinges him. I'm sure he, and any number of the other old-timers here, think the idea of a Navajo killing another Navajo is basically tantamount to treason.

"What did I just say about not panicking? About rumors?" Yokana says. "*Serial killer* is about as loaded a word as my job's got. I wouldn't use that, no."

If the NNPD found three bodies in quick succession, and they are in fact connected with Biligaana Bill, then they don't need to worry about the killer being Navajo. The killer isn't from this world at all.

The way that Caroline squeezes my hand, like she's on a rollercoaster ride about to drop, I know she wants to tell Yokana as much, just like me. Grant is pointedly not looking at us, as if he might give us away if he did. All of us want to say it. None of us can. At best they'd think we're insane. At worst they'd think we're involved. I called in an anonymous tip from just outside the canyon, and Chaco says he brushed our prints from the scene, but that wouldn't matter if we start talking like we know what happened to Biligaana Bill.

"Three dead," Caroline whispers to me, her lips brushing my ear, confusing my body. "Busy couple of nights for Ben."

"Is the market still on?" comes another shout from the crowd.

"Yes. I want to be absolutely clear here," Yokana says, holding up his hands. "The Native Market is on as planned. Our department is teaming up with the Santa Fe PD to boost security there and help keep an eye on our people. If you've participated in the Native Market, we urge you to do so again. It's important that the Diné are represented."

The faces I see are flat and unreadable in that uniquely Navajo way, but I see determination in the way heads nod. I think it would take a lot to shut down the Native Market, or even to postpone it. The market is a serious source of revenue and publicity for the rez, and not just for the Navajo either. Hundreds of tribes gather in Santa Fe. One of my first years at ABQ General I helped coordinate a medical tent for the market thinking I'd be helping out the rez. I spent seven straight hours giving water to fat white people who had too many margaritas and forgot they were at eight thousand feet. 150,000 people came that year. That's a lot of water for a lot of sunburned tourists. I was sort of put off the whole experience for a while. I'd planned to go back and drink and shop on my own, maybe buy some art I definitely didn't need, but then I met Caroline.

More people are shouting out questions now, but Yokana preempts them by saying he's said his piece but will stick around for a while to speak with whomever wants to chat with him. I wish I had his dogged calm. A lot of it comes from his heritage, but a lot of it is learned. I need to work on that. I used to have it, but I think it's left me. On the drive over here yesterday I was about ready to chuck myself out of the driver's-side window listening to everyone's thoughts on how to find our way back to the 387. We've got a coyote prowling the countryside that can change shapes, for crying out loud —the fact that I made a wrong turn or two means nothing in the long run, but we're still at each other's throats. This whole rez is on edge. It's infectious.

Most of the crowd disperses. A few of the latecomers stick around to speak with Yokana in person. He addresses each of them in turn, quickly but warmly, shaking hands and patting backs. I turn to corral Grant so we can get back to the boat and talk this over, but he's disappeared again. He does this more often, now. You'd think we have bars on the boat the way he scampers away whenever we park it somewhere and open the door.

"Did you see where Grant went?" I ask Caroline. She's looking carefully at every single person in the room. Testing for smoke like a drug dog at the airport. It's important, I know, but so is Grant. He's our first charge, after all. I think Caroline senses my annoyance, because she focuses on me again.

"He's around here somewhere," she says, scanning the room for his smoke. She senses something, peers around a crowd of Navajo speaking to each other quietly in their rhythmic way, as if every word was already written and they were just reading it out loud to one another. I walk around them and stop. Grant is in the far corner of the gym, with the other kids, talking to a Navajo girl. A girl his age. And he's *smiling*. I mean, he looks like he doesn't know what to do with his hands, but he's smiling.

"Dr. Bennet, I thought that was you." Yokana steps over my way after disengaging himself. "I wasn't sure we'd ever see you again our way," he says. He grasps my hand warmly, and although I know he doesn't intend it, Yokana's words hit me with a wave of guilt, as surely as if Young Me were standing in the corner, watching, shaking his head in disappointment.

"Are you in town for the market?" Yokana asks.

You were a tourist after all.

"No," I say. "We're. . . we're back for a while."

Yokana looks pleasantly surprised, and I feel a bit better. Young Me shuts up at least.

"We?" he asks.

"I'm with Caroline Adams. I'm not sure if you remember her. She worked the CHC too. And that one—" I point to where Grant has now thankfully put his hands in his pockets while he's talking to the girl, instead of holding them out like claws. "He's with us too. Checking out the school and all."

Yokana nods. Thankfully doesn't delve. I've always loved that about the Navajo. I disappear for five years and show up with a four-teen-year-old kid, and all I get is a placid nod.

"Crownrock High is a good place. Open enrollment. They'll take him if he's interested. It's not very diverse, but that's the rez for you. And you've never had a problem with that."

It takes me several seconds to realize he thinks Grant wants to attend Crownrock High School. I look over at him again, surrounded by kids his age for once. Yokana is right. There's only one other white kid that I can see. He's watching Grant carefully.

"Dr. Bennet," Yokana says, quietly drawing my attention again. "If you're here for a time, I was wondering if you might do me a favor." Suddenly he looks tired. As if he's spent all his energy keeping his face together for the crowd, and now that they've mostly dispersed he's drooping.

"Sure," I say. "Name it."

"We have three bodies at the CHC morgue that nobody can make heads or tails of, in terms of cause of death," he says softly. "Maybe you could take a look at them."

"Me? I'm not sure what I could do."

"As strange as it might sound, I'm not all that surprised to see you here, Dr. Bennet. These cases, they give me the same type of feeling that I got with Dejooli and Ninepoint. Before they disappeared. Back when you were nearly killed. And if we don't get it settled soon, it's gonna attract the attention of Gallup, just like last time. Or something worse than Gallup. Maybe you'll see something the morgue missed. You and Ms. Adams are quite... perceptive."

I can't tell how much he knows or believes about what happened the last time we were all at Chaco rez and the agents hit the hospital. Certainly not the whole of it, but maybe little parts. By Gallup he means the FBI. They've got a station there. Parsons and Douglas couldn't be traced back to the FBI, but Yokana didn't see what we saw. He was convinced they were federal operatives of some sort, and he doesn't want their kind of trouble again. The way he says *or something worse* makes me wonder if he doesn't sense a bit of what's at work here now. He's an old-school Navajo, after all. And a cop. That's a double whammy.

"Sure. I'll check it out." I give him my phone number and tell him to call me to arrange a time. He nods again, takes a deep breath, and puts his face back on.

"Now if you'll excuse me, I have two other towns to visit on this little tour, and then I've got to go try and make sure a hundred thousand tourists get what they pay for at the Native Market, and nothing more. Good seeing you, Dr. Bennet."

He turns and makes his slow way to the exit, stopping here and there to say good-bye to everyone who greeted him.

A hundred thousand people. That's a lot of bodies that could harbor our coyote shape-shifter. That's a lot of potential for chaos that I don't think it would pass up. My stomach sours, and I turn to Caroline. She's watching people, but she catches my gaze, shakes her head. No skinwalker here. But still, I feel like it wanted us here. We followed its tracks here, after all. Maybe it wanted us to hear about the trouble it's already causing. Maybe it wants us to think about what it could do if it had a real crowd to whip into a frenzy. Say, a crowd of over a hundred thousand people at the Native Market.

When we finally get Grant's attention and take our leave, the afternoon has settled over Crownrock like a heavy blanket, and pinning it down along the edges are rows and rows of silent black crows.

10

CAROLINE ADAMS

I t's three in the morning, and I'm making a list for us in case one of us gets snagged by the coyote and turns into a skinwalker, so we'll know. I have two columns next to each of our names. The first is for the tell, the hint that we need to pick up on in order to realize that we're no longer ourselves. The second column is tips for how to take us down, if it comes to that.

First, Grant. I was going to say watch out if he drops his accent, but he's been doing that already. When we finally had to pull him away from the gaggle of kids he'd found at Crownrock High he was speaking slowly, carefully, making sure all the drawl was gone. He sounded like a politician. Devoid of accent. I suppose if he comes out dressed in any sort of color, or maybe if he were to ask either Owen or me how our day was, that would be major red- flag material. Very out of the ordinary.

How to take him down? Give him a hug. It paralyzes him. He hangs there like a sheet drying on the line.

Next, Owen. I'd know things were amiss if he wore his shirt two buttons down or untucked. Other than that, I suppose if I caught him dismantling his Trailer to Nowhere after nearly killing himself running an electrical line to it, I'd know he was a skinwalker. Or if his smoke ever stopped reaching for mine. If that ever happened, I'm not sure what I'd do. I'd be too shocked to even try to take him down.

As for me, it's easy. If I ever get a good night's sleep, you need to take me out back and shoot me because I am not in my right mind and am most likely a skinwalker. Worry and insomnia are the normal for me. I worry about Owen, about Grant, about how my new family can fit with Ben. All of it. Sometimes when Grant is quiet or moody I ask him what he's thinking about and he says *nothing*. What the heck is that? How can you think of *nothing*? What's that even like? Is that like what a cow thinks of? What I wouldn't give to just go into cow mode when I'm up yet again in the middle of the night. It gets so bad sometimes that I even miss Big Hill's moonshine. The stuff tasted like socks, but even a thimble of it would put me out for the count. I'd wake up feeling like poo, but sometimes it was worth it. Come to think of it, that's how you can take me out if I'm a skinwalker. A shot of moonshine. Either that or take away my magazines. Or you could make me cold. I hate being cold. I'd just complain a lot and then be really easy to shoot.

I'm actually listing all this, by the way. Writing it all down in my journal under the thin blue light of my bedside lamp. Owen is sleeping softly next to me, one long arm wrapped under his pillow, the other tucked in to his chest. He doesn't fit this bed. His feet hang over by a few inches, which would drive me nuts, but he's never complained. He doesn't complain about anything. Ever. Even when I can see it on him, in his smoke, that the Ben situation makes him feel like a fool. He's outrageously in love with me. Every fiber of him. All he wants is the same in kind from me. And I do love him. Just not with every fiber. Some fibers are wrapped up elsewhere, and he knows it, and it makes him feel like a chump.

Owen thinks I'm obsessing over this book because it offers me a link to Ben's world, and I want that connection because I want Ben. But it's not like that. At least not completely. I'm not some love-struck tween. I know how long five years is. I know the life I chose. More and more I just want those fibers back. I want to close that chapter. And to do that I need to see Ben again. I need to speak with him. But Owen wouldn't understand that, even if I found the guts to tell him, and the words came out the way I wanted them to.

What Owen does understand is that we need to figure out a way to stop these murders and corral this coyote. And for that, we need the book.

I think.

The truth is, I have no idea what's in the book, and I'm no closer to figuring it out than I was when the agents gave it to me five years ago. It might be a detailed history of the coyote we seek, or step-by-step instructions to cross between the lands of the living and the dead like the coyote did, or maybe it's a book of its favorite Crock-Pot recipes. Nobody knows. Not Chaco, not Ben, not Joey Flatwood or Big Hill. I've used microscopes and magnifying glasses. I've used black-light and firelight and UV light. I put out an APB to the Circle for ideas and got a bunch of shrugs. The general consensus was don't worry about it unless it starts causing trouble.

Now people are dying. We don't have the luxury of blank pages anymore. If there's any way the book can help us, I need to figure it out right now. So that's what I'm gonna do.

I slowly sit up, my legs hanging off the bed. I ease open the flip lock on my built-in nightstand, I pull the book out from under the makeup and lotion and even a few condoms that I set on top of it to discourage Grant, or anyone else, from browsing. Not that it matters. Grant couldn't care less about the book. He's got a big bird that serves as his connection to the other side, if he wants it, but he'd rather listen to his music and play video games. He's got other things on his mind. Most likely that Navajo girl he was gawking at over at the school. Basically all the condoms do is serve to remind me that I'm not having enough sex with Owen, or that I'm having too much sex with Owen for the wrong reasons. Did you know it's possible to have too much sex and not enough at the same time? Neither did I! Then Ben and Owen happened.

I shove those thoughts out of my mind and flip through the book. Blank as always, but the pages have felt a little different ever since we crossed over to the rez. They feel heavier, like before we came they were your standard-issue paperback, and now they're that fancy pressed paper chock-full of weird fibers that costs a fortune at the stationery store. I think it's reacting to the coyote, being close to the thing, surrounded by its tracks that seem to stain the very air and refuse to go away.

Which got me thinking about the agents. They've got a few marks of their own that don't seem to wash off, and I'm not just talking about the special mark Allen's brunches have left on my heart. Or even the scars on his face, although they aren't going anywhere. I'm talking about the searing marks they have on their palms, where they held the knife that ripped a hole through the veil. They hide them well. I mean, how many times do you look at someone's palms, after all, but they're there, and when you see it, you see it. The knife had some serious firepower behind it. And when they held it, they could also read the book. Maybe it's a coincidence, maybe not, but it's all I've got to go on.

Now, since the knife is gone forever and we're immensely better off for it, I need to use the next best thing: my totem. The knife was made of the same vein of turquoise as the totems. In the past, I've only held the book while phasing in and out of the thin space. Once or twice I gave it a glance while traveling but saw nothing. This time, I'm betting things might be different if I stick out the cold burn of the place and really hunker down with my crow totem and refuse to quit.

I look over at Owen as I slide my totem pouch from its spot underneath my pillow. He doesn't stir. He breathes softly, his lips barely parted. I loosen the pull on the worn leather bag, the first gift Owen ever gave me, and one that matches his own. I take a deep breath and tighten my grip on the book with one hand then reach inside the bag with the other.

The world snaps into a windblown sepia color around me where all that I see are faint outlines and shapes of the living world, like a rough-draft artist's sketch. Owen's own totem glows warmly beneath his pillow. In the next room I can see Grant sleeping splayed out like a ragdoll, the covers on the daybed askew, but the bell around his neck glints and shimmers with a drowsy power. It's asleep now too, but it's always waiting.

The pain is already starting, but I've gotten used to it by now. Living people like you and me aren't supposed to hang out in this in-between space, neither fully dead nor fully alive. It's unnatural, and our bodies rebel from it after a while. The stinging cold used to take my breath away instantly, but I'm not such a lightweight anymore. I've got the body to prove it too. The agents were right, my skin has this super-attractive midwinter coloring that seems to stick around no matter how many hours I lay out on the roof of the boat under the summer sun. Owen calls it Arctic chic.

I flip open the book one handed and leaf through a couple of the pages. They're still heavy, but in the thin place they glisten too. As if they're running with invisible ink. I put the book right up to my face, as if I'm an old lady with a dinner menu. I think I see something, but it looks more like those little floaties you have at the corner of your eye, the little strings of pearls that flit away from you when you look right at them. I flip through another few pages with my thumb, staring, and then another few. I'm starting to get a headache. I pull myself away from the book, muttering all sorts of swear words. I massage my temple with the hand that holds the crow, but the headache isn't going away. The stinging burn of the thin place is strong. Stronger than it should be. It comes at me in a wave, like the stinging pinch of getting a shot at the doctor—at first you don't feel it at all, then the pain comes, then it comes hard and you try not to embarrass yourself by crying as a grown woman. I drop my crow.

I snap back to the bedroom. The crow lands on the book with a thump that makes Owen shift around for a second before settling again. The boat feels wonderfully warm. I realize that I'm trembling. I look at the clock on my nightstand. It tells me nearly thirty minutes have passed. That can't be right. I was in the thin place for two, three minutes tops. Maybe Owen shorted out the clocks or something doing his "improvements." I light up my phone, and the time checks out.

I was in the thin place for half an hour. I've never been in it for that long. What happened? It's as though I was in some sort of trance. The book bewitched me. But I was so *close*. I could see something! I could see the place where letters would be, if they weren't. . . not there. Sort of like in the old days when you used to use correction fluid to cover mistakes but unless you really coated your paper with the stuff, a hint of the word shone through. I was getting hints!

I lay my hand flat and hold it out in front of me. I watch it shake, then tremble, then shimmy, then twitch. Then nothing. When it's as calm as a lake, I grab my totem again.

11

OWEN BENNET

I'm back at ABQ General on the ninth floor, and I'm late for my shift. I slept in, forgot to set my alarm, doesn't matter how. All that matters is that I've left all my patients on the line. I had a full schedule, twenty-minute visits through to lunch, half an hour for lunch and charting, then a full afternoon of twenty-minute visits. I've let them all down—they'll have to be rescheduled too, so I've let down my staff as well. The other oncologists, my nurses, Caroline in particular. I'm running around the floor, going door to door to try and catch up, papers flying everywhere, my lab coat fluttering behind me, but I can't find anyone I'm supposed to see. All the patients look the same: faceless lumps in hospital gowns staring silently at me as I run. All I can hear is this strange tapping noise, like a man with a cane following me. Or maybe the clicking claws of a coyote.

I sprint around the *U* shape of the floor, trying to match my appointments with the charts on beds and on exam-room doors, but everyone is staring at me in faceless silence. There's only this tapping, and it's getting louder. I spin all around trying to find the source of the sound. My heart feels like it's in my throat. I have no idea how I can save these people if I can't see them, if I don't know who they are. The tapping burrows into my skull—

I shoot up from bed. My head is pounding, and my chest heaves with great big breaths of air. The tapping continues, rattling everything, and it takes me a moment to understand that it's Chaco at the window. He looks like he's trying to break in. Just then Grant bursts into the bedroom, his hair sleep-crazy and his boxer shorts crooked. The bell on its chain bounces off his bony sternum.

"Where's Caroline?" he asks.

Before I can answer that she's obviously right here next to me, he's already at her side of the bed, flipping the covers back. And her side's empty.

"Where did she go, Owen?" he asks again, his voice cracking in panic.

I haven't worked moisture into my mouth quite yet, but my eyes are focusing, and the first thing I see is her bedside drawer open and the book gone.

"She took that damn book somewhere," I say. "Maybe back to the agents?" Chaco is still slamming his head against the window again and again. He lets out a raucous trio of caws. "What's his problem?"

"He says she's not gone. She's here. She's stuck phasing or something."

"Stuck?" I ask as Grant swipes at the place where Caroline should be, and finally everything clicks into place. I reach under my pillow, tear at the tie to my pouch, and grab my totem. The cold sting of the thin place slams over me, and suddenly I see her. She's right there, sitting on the bed. Grant is swiping right through her. I call her name, but she doesn't answer. My words sound as though I'm screaming through a windstorm. I carefully pivot myself around the bed, taking care not to walk in this place, or else I might find myself a mile away in the blink of an eye. She's upright, and her eyes are open—staring, actually—and they glisten with an icy film. She's shivering uncontrollably, the black book tremoring in her hand. She has her crow pressed to the page like it's a penlight.

"Caroline! Let go!"

She hears me, but none of my panic registers. She looks up at me slowly, like a sloth, and the white in her eyes slips a little as she recognizes me.

"I can almost read it, Owen," she says. "I get whispers. It's beautiful and it's awful and I. . ." Tears well in her eyes and freeze to pearled drops on her cheeks. "I can't look away." She slowly reverts her gaze to the book.

"Help me," she whispers.

I fall upon her hand, tearing at her crow while holding my own in place, but her grip is locked. Frozen. It's as cold as a butcher's block. She lets out a frightened sigh that's oddly sexual, as if it's both pain and pleasure in one, and I see that with both our crows on the book, the page is darkening in waves of a script, like a scrolling computer code full of characters new and ancient. The effect is like when your brain shifts to finally comprehend those 3-D pictures, only this picture is the equivalent of the Sistine Chapel if it were painted above the devil's own throne. It paralyzes me, but the characters only click for a minute, then they scramble. The sight of them drills into my eyes like windblown sand. The pain is immense, but I don't care. I'm only thinking about how to get Caroline out of here.

If she won't let go of her crow, maybe she'll let go of the book. I wind up and slap the black book with a flat-palmed forehand and it goes spinning from her, vanishing from the thin place back into the living world, where it falls to the floor like lead. Caroline crumples, and I seize the opportunity, punching her crow from her grip. She blinks back, and I follow in the next instant.

Caroline falls forward and off the bed like a badly positioned mannequin. Grant catches her head before it bounces off the floor. Chaco is frozen, staring through the window at her, not even blinking. I whip our blanket off the bed and wrap it around her, trying to warm her hands in mine, pressing my cheek against her forehead. She feels like she's just been dredged from the bottom of a lake. At first she's still, her eyes on the book, her blue lips trying to form words that won't come, and this is when I'm so scared I think I'm going to vomit. I'm going to vomit from fear. It's a new sensation for me, the thought of such horrible outcomes, such terrifying potentialities, striking me in the stomach with the force of rotten meat. I think I'm going to have to grab the trash can, but then she starts to shiver. Trembling at first, but then she starts shaking so badly the blanket slips off her. I battle my nausea down. Shivering is good. Shivering means her body is still with it enough to fight, to contract to keep her warm. If she can fight she can live.

I take off my shirt and bear hug her. Grant unhooks the window so Chaco can hop in and float down inside, then Grant steps between Caroline and the book and sits down. Something about Grant—and the bell—being between her and the black book finally snaps her out of her trance. She blinks and looks up at him, and this time the tears are able to roll down her cheek instead of freezing there.

"What did you do?" Grant asks, his eyes wide, confused. Almost like he's angry at her. "Why did you do that? You could have been killed." I see in his eyes that he's grappling with the same fear as I am. Likely he feels about ready to vomit too.

"It. . . it was like staring into. . . the darkest part. . . of the sky. . ." she stammers. "The sky between stars. It. . . sucked me in. . ."

Chaco walks over to the book and nudges it open with his beak, tittering to himself. The cover thuds to the ground, and moments later Chaco squawks loudly and hop-flies backward, settling in a crouch on Grant's head. Grant turns around and goes to the book. He picks it up, unafraid. He holds it out to us, open to the first page. The one Caroline was looking at. The one both of our crows illuminated in the thin place. I flinch, expecting to see the flowing of those horrible words, but the page is white again, except for three words scrawled as if by a dripping pen quill across the top.

It reads: The Coyote Way.

12

THE WALKER

In between work calls I walk the streets of Chaco looking for our coyote. I jump around to the different rez towns and off-map settlements at random: Matagorda, Ponca City, Wheeling, Las Cruces. I drop in on Crownrock a fair amount too. I don't feel like so much of a stalker now that I actually have an excuse to check in on Caroline. But I spend most of my time in Chaco City, my old stomping grounds. I used to walk all over these streets as a kid, both the pretty paved main streets and the beaten dirt outskirts. I know the people and the feel, so it's easy for me to see how much the coyote has changed things. I got called to two other deaths not long after Bilagaana Bill, same scenario. Unmarked bodies without souls. The coyote ramped up its game real quick. The way things have escalated feels chaotic, which would be in keeping with the thing, but part of me also feels like it cased this place for years. Maybe waiting for us.

When I was a rookie at the NNPD, back before I got partnered with Ninepoint, I had to use my own truck for calls. We only had so many cruisers, and they went out based on seniority, so I puttered around the rez in a beater Toyota that Mom left me because I think she was embarrassed to be seen in it in Santa Fe. It had a couple hundred thousand miles on it and desert dust caked into the paint job. The AC had all the power of a panting dog, and the whole time I drove it I kept thinking how I wanted a new one. Soon enough the universe started rubbing it in, because I was seeing new trucks every-where. That's what it's like now with the coyote's trail. I haven't seen anyone outright staring at me, but now that I'm looking for it, I can see evidence of the thing everywhere. I can feel it in that plucking sensation you get when you know someone's staring at your back, but when you turn around nobody's there.

This used to be a tight neighborhood, but now people don't talk to each other on the streets. No *ya-at-eeh*s. No tipping of the hat. When people do run into each other it's prickly. People seem rubbed raw. Hungover without being drunk first.

If you didn't know better, you'd think that the upcoming Santa Fe Native Market was the reason. People are working on their booths in the streets and alleys. Loading trailers and packing up artwork. Some are painting signs and assembling costumes. Especially on the main drag, where the more established pottery and rug places are located to catch tourists. The market runs all weekend, but the first day is the big day and the big party night. Most of these people can't afford a hotel in Santa Fe during the winter dead season, much less during the market, so they'll be driving in and out all weekend. Two hours each way. Usually everyone does it happily. The market's where they make a good chunk of cash for the year. But nothing about them looks happy now.

I see people muttering to themselves, shielding their work from others, closing the blinds of shops and galleries, rushing boxes to and from trucks, locking the doors each time. You'd think the market is a big competition with one winner instead of a huge celebration.

Now, I'm not crazy about the Native Market, but I know how important it is to a lot of people on the rez. There's a lot of shuckin' and jivin' going on there, true. You see a lot of stunning pottery and silver and whatnot, but sometimes it's right next to mass-produced corn-husk dolls and beaded jewelry that you'll swear came from China. And I won't deny that pretty much everyone selling there is hoping the white people with the twelve-dollar frozen margaritas take out their wallets, but the market is more than that. It shines a spotlight on a group of people that the rest of the country seems to constantly want to forget. It's supposed to be an opportunity to bring together a bunch of tribes and peoples, always has been, so I know all this shade everyone is throwing is coming from something else. From the coyote.

I feel the pressure pop of Chaco coming into my plane. I don't break stride as he flares his wings out over me and settles on my shoulder, just like the old times, back before he had a Keeper to look after. His weight feels good. Substantial. I live in a world where sometimes I wonder if I have any weight at all, or if I'll float away one day like the souls I bring to the veil. Chaco seems to understand this in that silent way he has of reading me. He fluffs up and plunks down harder.

"How is she?" I ask.

"She's fine. Still drinking a lot of hot coffee."

I knew she'd recover fast. Caroline has techniques of pulling others out of tailspins, knitting together broken hearts and frayed souls. I have no doubt she used them on herself. Any other person who spent that long in the thin space with that book would be dead or insane. Except maybe Joey. But he's a little crazy already. Always has been. After I heard what happened to her I stepped over to see her for myself, but it's too hard to watch her in pain when there's nothing I can do. After the fourth time I tried to touch her hair and my hand slid right through her, I got up and left. I told Chaco not to tell anyone I was ever there.

"Nothing more from the book?" I ask.

Chaco shakes his head and sighs, puffing out his chest feathers. "It still just says *The Coyote Way*, and we're still drawing a blank. Caroline wants to take it to the Circle, maybe someone has some idea. I don't know, maybe it's some dark self-help mantra. You know? Like a twelve-step program to achieving your inner chaotic potential?"

"I don't think so, bird."

"Oh yeah? And I suppose you got a better idea?"

"I might," I say, which surprises him. "What, you think I just walk around all day in between calls, taking in the beautiful views of back-water Chaco?"

"No, you spend a lot of time staring at Caroline too."

"Shut up. Here, follow me for a second."

Before he can reply I swirl open the soul map and step through. He shoots in behind me. It's a quick trip, just a skip away on the map, the souls shooting by us like stars in warp. I hold up my hand to stop us and swipe my way out again. Chaco blinks onto the scene a heart-beat later. He flops onto my shoulder again and looks around us, the sunset reflecting off his eyes like red marbles in a bucket of black.

"The desert? So what? I've been seeing a lot of desert lately. Been hoping for less desert, actually. More beach."

"The Arroyo is behind us, about a quarter mile back, where a lot of old-timers and hard liners live, alongside your run-of-the-mill bootleggers and meth cooks." I start to walk up a low rise, and when I crest it we see a broken string of rounded huts in the distance. The sunlight cuts just over their tops, where you can see a black opening in the ruddy brown mud ceiling of each. Three of them are close to us, but none of the three are standing the way they should. They're slumped, half exposed, their wooden bones bleached by the sunlight.

"The hogans?" Chaco asks.

I shield my eyes from the last of the sun.

"I've been thinking a lot about Gam. About the old-timers back down the way. About how Joey and I used to laugh at all the things they used to tell us. The old ways and the old warnings and all that. None of that seems so funny now."

I know Chaco thinks a lot about Gam too. She was his last Keeper, and no matter how much he loves Grant, he was with her for decades. He watches the hogans quietly. He looks tired. He has to keep tabs on Grant on top of all this coyote business. Gam was an eighty-year-old woman at the end. Grant offers entirely new chal-lenges, of the exhausting teenaged variety.

"What happened to them?" Chaco asks, his head bobbing along with my steps as I walk toward them.

"There used to be six here that I knew of. They were pristine.

Status symbols for their clans. They used to meet here from time to time. Perform ceremonies and cleanses. Or just sweat it out. But then the elders kept dying and the younger kids stopped caring so much."

"That sucks," Chaco says.

"It happens. Every generation thinks the old ways are forgotten, lost on the young shits running around in their lifted trucks blaring their rap music. But it ain't the end of the world. The Navajo seem to go through cycles. Tipping too far off the path, then eventually coming back to what's in our blood. We can never stray far from the Way for long. It's a balance. Or at least it was until the coyote came to town."

We pass all three run-down hogans. Hollow, brittle shells of themselves. Even the smoke stains are barely visible.

"I gotta tell you, Walker, I don't see what you're seeing here. This place looks forgotten to me."

"Not totally," I say. "Not yet."

We pass around the third hogan, and we're faced with about a thousand feet of desert, clumped and pitted by shadows that looked bigger than they are, the sunset playing tricks on us. At the edge of the sunlight, just now plunged into darkness, stands a complete hogan, smaller than even the broken ones we'd passed, but tended and whole. As we approach it, I point out the smoke hole up top, patched and trimmed. I point out the eastward-facing door, the mud fresh. I pass my hand through the mantel above it and can almost feel the pollen there. We walk in, and I can almost smell the traces of pinon smoke. I know Chaco can, because his beak noses this way and that. The fire pit is brushed clean, and its rocks are placed neatly in a circle. The dirt floor looks swept.

"This one is still used," Chaco says.

"This is my clan's hogan. Gam brought me here once, when I first found out I had cancer all those years ago. She sang over me. Performed a Way chant that I thought was for healing. But now I'm not so sure. I think she knew I was going to die."

I point at the swept floor beyond the fire. "Two old men sand-painted the Holy People right there, but there was a fifth figure in addition to the four. A dark figure with turquoise eyes. I saw Ana during the chant. Up until about a week ago I still thought she was a vision. Now I think maybe I really saw her. I think the chant called her and opened my eyes for a short time. Maybe Gam wanted me to see what was in store for me so it'd be easier for me to take it when the time came."

"A Way chant," Chaco said softly.

"That's right. We have a bunch of them. The Blessingway and the Evilway are the most famous, but there are a ton more. Enemyway, Nightway, Shootingway. There was even a Ravenway and a Dogway a long time ago, and more that are lost to time. Each calls the Holy Family's attention in a different way, for a different reason. Brings them to the song."

"The Coyote Way," Chaco says, amazed. "It's a song. A Navajo chant."

"Why not? And think about this: the coyote is untouchable right now. It's a skinwalker. It can be anyone and anywhere. But what if we could bring it right here? Right to this hogan. What if we could call it?"

"We could trap it," Chaco says excitedly.

"Why not?" I say again.

Chaco and I stare at the cold fire pit in silence. It's the logistics of the thing that are tricky. If there ever was a Coyoteway chant, it's an ancient memory now. The instructions might be in the black book, but is it worth risking Caroline's life for them? And even if we did know what to do, what to say, it takes talent and preparation to sing. Gam brought Ana to me, but she was an accomplished Singer with decades of experience under her belt and a full Singer's pouch. And what if we actually catch the damn thing? What then? We got a lot on our plate, and time is running out.

Still, I can't help but smile a little. Maybe we caught a break. And what's more, maybe we can catch another. Somebody is keeping this hogan clean. If we can find them, maybe they can help us before this becomes coyote country once and for all.

13

GRANT ROMER

I'm talking to Chaco on the way to school. That's right. I'm going to school. And not school where Owen is the math teacher and the science teacher and the history teacher and whatever other teacher, either, with Caroline showing up every now and then to tell me I should read more literature and do some art. Like she reads much more than her magazines anyway. No, this is a real school, with real kids, and real lockers, and real desks, and a real football team.

Chaco ain't so keen on the idea. Sorry. He *isn't* so *happy* with the idea. Texans get *keen*. Other people get *happy*. He sort of slow-floats above me, riding thermals, but we still talk. Every now and then he passes behind a slew of other crows floating the thermals too as they careen to get out of his way.

"Something is wrong with this place," he says. "I can feel it."

"Something is wrong with every place," I say, muttering some of the words, thinking the rest. I've been doing a lot of talking out loud to Chaco when I don't need to. Now that I'm around other kids, I need to keep him on the downlow.

"You know what I mean, bro." And he's right. I do. I can see paw prints all around Crownpoint High if I look close enough. The town itself is pretty bad, but this place is bad in particular. It's a good thing nobody else notices what I see. They might not leave their houses. Which would suck because I want to meet them. That girl in particular. I didn't catch her last name, but I sure remember her first name. Kai. It sounds good. It sounds like how she looks. I don't speak any Navajo yet, but if I was to guess, I'd say a *Kai* is that little tiny smile she has on the corner of her mouth. Or maybe a *Kai* is when you wink your eye without winking your eye, like she can.

"Well, you watch my back, right? I mean, if something is going on here, one of us needs to figure out what."

"I can't always be there for you. I do my best, but you're growing up, man. You're in all sorts of different situations now, and it's all I can do just to keep up."

"Maybe I don't always need you lookin' after me," I say, and the way Chaco suddenly gets distant, in the sky and in my mind, makes me immediately regret it. After an awkward silence Chaco chimes in again.

"The things that are coming after you aren't always as easy to spot as the agents. Snakes don't always look like snakes, Grant."

"I'll be careful, man. Why can't you be happy for me? I'm finally off the boat."

And with those words hanging in the air, I walk under the eagle painted above the doors of Crownrock High for my first day of school.

THEY PAIR me with a white kid to show me around the place, which I'm sure they think will make me more comfortable or something, but it isn't exactly what I was looking for. His name is Mick, and he's as pale and scrawny as I am. He wears these baggy gangster clothes, big printed T-shirts that go down past his butt, and baggy b-ball shorts with huge work boots, and they sort of swallow him up. We talked for a minute or two at the town meeting in the gym. I meet him in the hall outside of the front office after I hand in my enrollment papers.

"It's you," he says. "I wondered if I'd see you again. Thought maybe you'd be scared off the place."

"Scared off?" I ask, trying not to sound nervous. "Why?"

"Well, you saw. At the meeting. There aren't a lot of white kids here. Matter of fact, I think you're number ten or so in the whole school now."

"I don't mind."

"Not yet you don't. But you just walked through the doors."

I don't know what to say to that, so I just shrug.

"C'mon," he says. "Your locker is over here."

We walk down the halls and everything is quiet. Mick is quiet. I can feel Chaco nearby, but if I can't see him I have trouble talking to him, so even he's quiet. I can see everyone already in class as I pass the doors.

"It's first period right now. Which I hate, so thanks for getting me out of it."

I can't tell if Mick is being friendly or not. I think maybe he is. He looks at the ground a lot, almost like he's following some invisible tracks of his own. I think he's just one of those people who doesn't like looking straight at you. "You'll start at second period." He snatches my schedule from my hand. "Which looks like Geometry for you. Good luck with that shit. Room 108, right over there, after the bell rings."

We walk past a row of small lockers, some of them hanging open. A few have little hearts and hand-drawn signs on them with things like Go 18! Beat Sargaso!

"What's Sargaso?" I ask.

"High school in Santa Fe. We always play them in football the Thursday before the market. It's a big stupid deal. Why do you wear all black?"

He asks this like it's right in line with football and big stupid deals.

"Just like it is all. Doesn't stain."

Mick doesn't laugh. He does nod, though, like it was good advice or something. I think my sense of humor is getting a little dusty. More Navajo, hopefully.

"Here's yours," he says, popping his fist on the farthest locker in the line. "Upperclassmen get all the good ones," he says, reading my mind. "Your code is in your folder. Put your shit in there, we still got a few minutes to walk."

Mick shows me the cafeteria. "There's where you get the food, there's where you eat it. Can you eat lunch?"

"You mean like do I have lunch?"

"Can you pay for it. You got money?"

"A little," I say. Owen gave me twenty for lunch, even after I told him I wanted to walk solo.

"A'ight, well, if you got money trouble, they help you out. There's programs and stuff." He shoves his hands in his pockets. "But if you do got money, keep that shit to yourself."

We walk again without talking much. Just the sounds of Mick's boots squeaking against the tracked floor. He points out the art-and-music hall, where I see the wooden framing of a booth.

"It's the Crownpoint booth for the market." He sneers. "I gotta help paint it 'cause I got busted skipping first period last week. If you wanna check it out after class, I could use the company."

He vaguely gestures out a big window in the rear toward the sports fields. I see one half of a dusty baseball diamond and take his word on a football field just out of sight. All in all the place is old, pretty small, and well worn. Discolored paths snake along the concrete floor where kids have walked for years. But I don't mind. I'm used to old places. Pap's house was old before he bought it. I'm used to small places too. I live in a car—a big car, but still a car. As for well worn, well, I got no problem with that. The bell I wear around my neck might be the most well-worn thing on this planet.

Mick looks at his watch. A big, plastic, cheap-looking thing. "Shit," he says. "Time's up."

The bell rings. The period switches over, and a couple hundred kids go from in the classrooms to in the halls in a blink. I try to keep my eye out for anything weird, or for anyone eyeing me funny, sensing the bell, but all I see is kids. Tons of them. More than I've seen in my life. And all of them look at me as they pass: I'm the new kid. One of a handful of white kids in the whole place. Of course they're gonna look at me. But still I feel as hot as I've ever felt in my life. And that's before I spot Kai.

She's walking out of a classroom, talking with two other girls at her side, and putting a notebook away into a woven bag at her hip. She's wearing a Lobos Football T-shirt and very short pink shorts. The way the shirt falls, it almost looks like she's not wearing shorts at all. She laughs at something one of her friends says, then she looks up, and then she sees me staring like a cow. I know I should look away, pretend I was just scanning the hall, but I can't. She recognizes me. She looks surprised, but not in a bad way. She opens her mouth a little, then she's surrounded by a group of older guys who come laughing down the hallway, and soon all of them go off in the same direction.

When I turn back to Mick, he's already looking at me with a smirk on his face. His mouth twitches a little, like he wants to say something, but he just shakes his head. The hallway is already clearing out. The passing period is winding down.

"Remember, you're in Room 108. Good luck, lover boy."

14

CAROLINE ADAMS

I'm freezing. I mean, I know I get cold. I always have. I'm the type of girl to blow dry my feet for ten minutes after I do my hair, just because I can. In the winter, if it were socially acceptable for me to walk around in one of those huge Carhartt monkey suits the rig workers have, I would do it. I'd sleep in it too. But it's August, in the desert, and I'm way too cold for August in the desert.

The book almost killed me. The thought of how close I came to having my life sucked out of me in the thin place makes me a bit dizzy. So now I'm cold and dizzy. It's been a few days since that night, and I'm still not right. I came close to slipping away forever. Really, really close. I try not to tip Owen and Grant off about just how close, but I think they know. It might have something to do with the fact that I reheat my steaming-hot tea in the microwave every thirty seconds. Or that I'm drinking cup after cup of steaming-hot tea in the first place, in the co-captain's chair, under the blazing windshield.

Anybody else wouldn't have made it back. I don't want to toot my own horn here, but it's the truth. I had to coax my own smoke back to life, which is tough, because I can't exactly see it on myself. All I know is I felt it guttering, like a little spark at the bottom of a pile of straw, only the pile is on the desert plains and a big wind is trying to scatter it far and wide. I had to put my hands around it, breathe on it, whisper to it, just like I did with the agents when they first tumbled out of the break in the river, when they were half dead too.

I focused on thoughts that would warm me. Not things like tropical islands and Carhartt monkey suits, which would warm my body, but things that would warm my soul. Things like remembering Grant when he stood like a little superhero, holding the bell out in front of us to protect us in the Texas desert. Things like Ben. Everything I can remember about Ben, actually. But the problem is, I'm remembering less and less about Ben. I have a bunch of core memories that I go back to all the time. Playing cards with him when he was getting chemo, holding him in the dry grass of his backyard when he got sick, kissing him for the first and last time before he left me. These are all important to me, but I've been bringing them out of their special memory box and shining them up too much, and I think I've forgotten other stuff. I had a lot more Ben material once. I know I did. Every moment I spent with him was special in some way, but all I have now are the superstars, and the more I bring them out, the less shiny and the more bronzed they get. The rest seem to have faded altogether. That, more than anything, reminds me of all the years that have gone by.

The Ben memories helped, but they didn't bring me back. They're more the type of thing I talk to James and Allen about over a cup of French press up at Friday Harbor. They're great "last thoughts," the kind of things you run up the flagpole right as you're checking out, and I thought I was checking out, until a stupid memory popped into my head. It was of Owen, frazzled and red faced and damp about the ironed neck of his button-down, trying to make a twenty-point U-turn in the boat when we were lost on some Navajo road west of Chaco Canyon, and even though I couldn't laugh with my frozen mouth I ended up laughing with my soul. And just like that, the icy-iron grip of the thin place and the creeping insanity of the book were snapped. I'd live. What can I say? I guess I have a soft spot for frazzled men.

Speaking of frazzled, Owen has been in a constant state of mild frazzlement for days now, ever since he slapped that book away and pulled me back. He grasps my fingers like straws whenever he sees me, as if they were thermometers that could measure my core temperature. He does this without talking sometimes, just reaches over and grasps my fingers, and, yes, they're cold. I tell him that they're always cold, which is true, but I can tell he doesn't buy it. His smoke is so gentle. It's this softly resting blue, like a cloud plunked over a mountain, afraid to leave. Which is why he's really not happy about what we're about to do.

"Are you sure they're all gonna show up? I mean, if it's just you and me, we're really underprepared for this. Criminally underprepared," Owen says. He's pacing the main room of the boat, his head cocked at forty-five degrees so it doesn't bump the ceiling.

"Chaco got word out. Everyone will be there," I say, trying to grab him as he passes, but he's lost in his analytical world again. The one that measures outcomes and risk and determines best practice. The oncologist's world.

"You *just* stopped shivering in your sleep, Caroline."

"We don't have any more time. You've seen this place. It's falling apart. And Grant is in the middle of it. Ben thinks this could be the key to trapping this thing. If there's a chance we can get any more info out of the book, we have to take it." I check the dash clock on the boat. It's almost time.

Owen mutters to himself, still pacing. I hear the words *Grant wouldn't even let me walk him halfway* and *goddamn book*, but I know he's in with me. He's pulling his totem pouch from inside his shirt. He chose to wear it there because his neckties used to cover up the bulge. He doesn't wear ties anymore, but he still keeps it there. He has racks and racks of ties in the closet that he hasn't touched in years, but he still keeps them too.

"Are you ready?" I ask gently.

"No."

"Owen."

"Fine."

I count down from ten. I have the book in one hand, flipped open to the Coyote Way page. At one, I grab my totem. Owen phases right along with me, his hand grasped around my fingers.

The bite is immediate and twice as painful as I've ever felt it, so soon.

"Don't look at it!" Owen screams. He brushes my cheek with the hand that holds his totem and nudges my line of sight toward him. "Not yet!"

We're alone. Each second that ticks by makes us more alone. I think maybe I was wrong and Owen was right. Maybe this was another stupid decision in a long line of stupid decisions with this stupid book. And if you peg this book as stupid, and me as stupid for getting it, then the whole house of my life starts to look like a stupid deck of cards.

I shake my head. That's just the melancholy of this place talking. I can't let it win. But there's no denying that we're here alone and I'm holding on to a mental time bomb with the hand that doesn't hold my totem. I stare into Owen's eyes, as muted and sepia-blown as they are, and he stares into mine, both of us willing each other not even to glance at the book. Another interminable number of seconds ticks by. I want to leave. I want to blink back. I dip my gaze, but Owen squeezes my fingers. I look up at him again.

Then there's a weird sucking sensation, like when you're bobbing in the ocean and caught in the retreat of a wave that pulls your legs out from under you. Another hand falls on my shoulder, bracing me. I turn to find Joey Flatwood watching me with calm eyes, his long black hair spread out behind him like a ribbon, splintering into fragmented strands of gray that blend into the thin place. He says nothing, only clamps his hand onto my shoulder and nods.

I feel another pull, a big one this time. All three of us bob like bottles in the waves as the refrigerator form of Big Hill pops into sight, mid-lumber. He settles next to Owen and clamps one hand on his shoulder. He's washed in gray, a charcoal painting of a man, but I can see one of his constant kerchiefs around his neck. He looks like the world's hugest train robber.

"Hold on now, hear?" he bellows. "They comin'!"

More distortions around us. I feel like my body is floating on the crest of where two seas meet. The first, the thin place, is freezing. The second, the Circle, is warmer, and with each wave that hits me the gripping cold lessens. I close my eyes and let the current take me, confident that Owen's grip, and Joey's, will keep me from floating away. When I open my eyes again I see our chain has become a circle at least twenty strong. Most I recognize from when we fought with them in the desert. I see the old Aborigine and the staid gentleman with his cane. I see the soldier next to the businesswoman. I see the tribeswoman and the monk, and several I've never seen before—a young girl and a man hunched and bent at the back, and three tall women who look like triplets—all of them swathed in gray, smudged and blurred, but standing determined. Outside of Joey Flatwood, I don't know any of their names. I don't even know Big Hill's real name. But I don't have to know who they are to know that we're a sisterhood and a brotherhood. It's like a family reunion. We all have our separate battles, but when the time comes to do our part, we pick up right where we left off, mid-conversation even.

With all of us here, the chain unbroken, the bite of the thin place is bearable, but I know we can't sit on our duffs. The book is already responding, just as I'd hoped it would. My theory is simple. If Owen's totem combined with mine made a few words appear, maybe a whole mess of totems would make a whole mess of words appear. Two totems brought a little stick to the fight. I want to bring a big stick. Looking around me now in the wind-tunnel scream of the thin place, it's pretty clear I brought a big damn stick. I brought a log.

I step into the middle of the Circle members, and their chain wraps around me. They eye the book warily, flinching away from it already. Glancing at it in snatches like you would a solar eclipse. It's time to play cheer captain.

"Bring it in!" I yell. The Circle closes in, totems out. Their collective turquoise burn is blinding. Even if I wanted to look at the book, I couldn't. Instead I close my eyes and feel as each member plunks an edge of their totem onto the page. I feel like those scientists who watch bomb blasts from behind lead walls with mega goggles over their eyes. Even the backs of my eyes are bright. After the last plunk the book gets noticeably heavier. I can feel the words forming, their ink soaking in, the pages saturating.

Owen squeezes my hand, and if I could see him I know he'd be grimacing. Despite all of our power, the thin place is fighting back. The bite is getting stronger. There's no beating it back for long. But that's fine, because I think we have what we need.

"I think we did it!" I yell. I have this absurd urge to break it up like a cheer captain again. *Circle on three! One, two, three, CIRCLE!* But instead I just drop the book. It blinks out of the thin place and falls to the floor of the boat. The Circle members blink out, each stepping back to where they came from. Joey gives me a thumping pat on the back first and then blinks away himself. Owen and I are the last to go.

This time I don't collapse. Neither does Owen. He looks for my eyes. I nod to reassure him, then both of us stare at the book, open, on the floor. The page still says The Coyote Way, but now there's more. Much more.

15

GRANT ROMER

C haco ain't happy with me right now. He's hanging over me all the time, chiming in when I'm trying to talk to people, chirping off opinions here and there about classes and teachers and kids I'm trying to be friends with.

"They needed you there, Grant," he says. He's sitting on top of this huge window well outside of the art department. I hear his voice in my mind. The other ten kids painting the front face of this booth are oblivious to our conversation.

"They're fine," I say, hoping he gets the tone of my thoughts. "They had Joey, they had twenty Circle members. They got what they needed."

Chaco shakes his head. I can tell by his shadow. He nearly blots out all the light coming in from the window. After class that first day, when my head was still sort of spinning, Mick came up to me and reminded me about his work duty on the booth. I told him I wasn't much of a painter, but then he said that Kai was on the market crew too. So here I am.

I'm trying not to get red and blue paint on my black jeans and sort of succeeding. I'm dabbing at a glob that landed on my T-shirt with my thumb, trying to ignore Chaco, when someone says, "You should just take it off." I look up with my thumb still pressed to my gut, and I see Kai.

"Seriously, the way you paint, you oughta just take your shirt off. It's not staying clean."

My mouth suddenly seems too dry to form words, but I do manage to put my thumb down. She smells like paint and sawdust in a way that makes me think strangely of my grandpa, of the way he used to smell coming out of the shop. But his was on top of a glass of whisky, and hers is on top of this flower smell that's either on her skin or in her hair and that I have a crazy urge just to huff. She cocks her head, waiting for me to talk. I work spit into my mouth.

"How do you paint, then?" I ask. I absolutely am not about to take my shirt off. I'm a hundred and twenty pounds soaking wet, and she'd be blinded by how white I am. She grabs my hand and steps in to direct me, and I have to tell myself to close my mouth.

"You slide, see? Up and down. Slide it. Don't slap it." She slides my hand a few more times, letting the brush flip over itself, up and down the corner post of the booth. I'm stumbling around saying *thank you* when my words die in my mouth. Three older guys have come into the room and are standing a few paces back. They're all Navajo, and they're watching me like I'm taking a leak on their car door. Kai sees my look and seems to know instantly what's up, even without turning around. Her face falls. No more wink. No more hint of a grin. She plucks her hand from mine. Goes over to her side of the booth. Acts like they aren't there. But the whole room is silent. The older guys let her go, but they're still looking at me. I recognize them from the first day. They were the swaggering crew that swallowed Kai up in the hallway.

I almost apologize to them, but at the last second I wonder what Joey would do. He damn sure wouldn't apologize for no reason. So I return their gaze, paintbrush in hand, blue droplets trailing up my sleeve.

The lead kid, the one in front, isn't a big guy. He's my height, maybe ten pounds heavier, but he's cut. He wears a sleeveless T-shirt from some local diner that I don't know, cut open at the sides near to his ribs. He wears b-ball shorts and tan work boots too, just like Mick, but somehow I doubt this kid is following Mick's cue. More like the other way around. The two guys behind him are big, thick boys with creased necks and pudgy foreheads and open mouths. I notice Mick in the back with the stencils and spray-paint. He meets my eyes for one second then shakes his head and gets back to spraying. I look out the window and see Chaco's shadow standing stock-still.

The front kid says something, and for a second I think maybe I'm messed up in the head because it's coming out in gibberish. My second thought is that I've found our skinwalker. This guy is why the crows are perched two- and three-deep on the roof and cars, this is why the place has all those coyote tracks. This guy. Right here.

Then my head clears, and I recognize that he's speaking Navajo and he ain't even talking to me. He's talking to Kai while he's looking at me. I can't understand a word of it, obviously, but I catch a few other kids grinning, looking away. I know it ain't good. I catch one phrase in English: Indian lover. That one gets Kai's attention too, and she snaps something back at him. I've talked with Owen enough about these things to know that if you call a white man an Indian lover he's at best a tourist and a fanboy. At worst he's a pervert. Someone here to taint the blood.

"Whoa, whoa man," I say, holding up my hands in a way I hope doesn't look too wussy. "I'm just here to paint. No big deal."

"Just here to paint." He has no accent at all. He shakes his head like I can't read the writing on the wall, but forget the writing, I don't even see any wall. "You make sure it stays that way," he says.

Before I can dig myself into anything deeper, he nods at a few of the boys in the back by Mick, and a bunch of them head off into the corner where they speak in low Navajo. They look shady, but they've apparently forgotten all about me, so I'm OK with that. I spend another minute or so halfheartedly trying to paint the cross post before the lead kid calls Kai away from her friends. She chances an unreadable glance my way out of the corner of her eye as she goes over to him. I see Chaco's shadow tip its head; he's trying to listen as hard as I am, but it's no use. They argue a bit, not much on her part, before he leads all of them out.

After another minute the air cools enough that people start to get back to work, and the low hum of conversation returns. I'm not sure what the heck just happened. I feel sweaty and red and like I'm breathing too loudly. Mick scares me half to death when he taps on my back. I didn't hear him take a step my way.

"See what I'm telling you, man?" he says under his breath, dipping a brush into my bucket to paint along with me. "If you're trying to find a place here, I'm just gonna tell you, it's not with them."

"Is that her boyfriend or something?" I try to keep my stroke even, keep it from shaking with the adrenaline I feel coursing through me. I've never run into anything like that before. Heck, before I stepped foot into Crownrock High I hadn't really had more than a passing confrontation with anybody my age, ever. Not since the boys in Midland would chase me on their bikes. And even then it was mostly them hollering at me and me pedaling for my life, hoping they got bored before I got tired.

"Her boyfriend? No. Worse. That's Hosteen Bodrey. Everyone calls him Hos. He's her big brother." Mick scratches at his neck and looks away. "Don't take it personal man, it's called the Native Market, after all."

"Meaning what?"

"Meaning I'm only doing this 'cause I got caught ditching and they made me. It's the Native Market. It's for Native Americans. They don't want us doing it no more than we want to be here doing it. Sorry you had to learn that the hard way."

I'm not so sure. Kai didn't look like she didn't want me here. Looking around the room now I see a lot of eyes watching me with distant expressions, but they're not angry, not mean, just distant. Quiet. Even as they work in their own groups on other parts of the booth, they seem quiet. Mick sees what I see and murmurs while he whaps his paintbrush clean.

"Like I said. Don't take it personal. It makes me want to burn the place down sometimes too. And I've been here for a year now."

He stands up and tosses his brush down. His post looks more cat scratched than painted. "That's good enough. You guys got the rest, right?" he asks the group. "For your big show?" A couple of the nearest kids look up at him and roll their eyes. They aren't unfriendly, though. Mick may be as much of an outsider as me, but he's an accepted outsider. His section leader ticks her head toward the door and tells him to get gone if he wants to leave.

"Adios, then," he says. "C'mon, Grant, I got something I want to show you."

But I'm not feeling like leaving yet. Taking off right now feels a bit too much like running scared, which isn't something Joey or Ben would do. I may be the new white kid, and I may have no family save the two who took me on and one bird, and them more on account of what hangs around my neck than on account of me. But I'm still Pap's grandson. I'm still here walking through more hell than these kids have seen in all their lifetimes, Navajo or not. I don't feel like leaving just yet. I feel like painting my goddamn post, the right way, sliding, not slapping.

"You go on ahead," I say.

Mick cocks his eye at me. He looks around. He holds out his hands and spins a little, shrugging. "Fine by me," he says, his voice quiet and flat. He shakes his head as he leaves.

"That guy is trouble," I mutter to Chaco, dipping my brush again.

"Which one?" Chaco asks. He fluffs and settles in the shadows, and I realize he's been about ready to break through the glass this whole time. "They all seem like trouble. Everything here seems like trouble." I can sense him staring at me through the wall. As if I'm the one to blame.

"So it's my fault I decided to take the front lines of this mess?" I ask, starting to slap and stopping myself. I take a deep breath.

"That's the problem. Do you know what they might do to you if they knew what you have around your neck? What anyone might do to you? What if they smoosh your head into the floor and notice the tracks running up and down the halls here? Ever thought of that?"

"I'm not some stupid kid riding his bike in the dark anymore. I know what I'm about. Did you at least catch anything Hos and his crew said?"

Chaco is silent, and I think I've gone too far. In the quiet seconds, while I'm standing alone doing someone else's work, nobody taking notice, I wonder what it might be like without Chaco. Without Owen or Caroline, without any of them. I was basically alone before them. Pap and I were together, but we were both alone. I hacked it then, and I was just a kid. What could I do now, just me and the bell? But then Chaco chimes into my thoughts.

"After he got done telling her not to touch you, he and his boys said something about the market. Something about being ready for it." Chaco's voice is quiet. I wonder, not for the first time, how much of my thoughts he can read. If he hears more than I let on. But this only pisses me off more.

"Yeah, that's what this stupid booth is for," I say.

"I don't think he was talking about the school art booth, bro," Chaco says, his voice full of snark. "He wanted Kai to come with his crew, to get ready for something. She didn't want to. I think he's got some other plan, but I couldn't make anything else out. Sorry, your highness. Is that enough for you? Can I have my shiny bauble now like a good crow?"

"Shut up, Chaco." That's the first time I've ever said it to him and meant it. And I expect him to snap something back at me, but he doesn't. He shuts up. He hops up and takes flight, and I expect him to leave me. Go somewhere to blow off steam or maybe just check out altogether for a bit like Caroline does with the agents sometimes. But not Chaco. I still feel him near, just higher up, trying to get a better view of what I've thrown myself into.

16

OWEN BENNET

I'm lying on my back on the floor inside the trailer hitch. It's the only part of the thing I've managed to finish completely, but no need for applause. It's just a ten-by-six-foot slab of carpet. And it's the thin stuff too. The stuff you find on the floor of elevators. You can glue it down without much work. I managed to wire a 240 line, but now I've got nothing to hook to it. The walls are bare, the ceiling is bare. It's dark, but that's because I closed the back. It's also outrageously hot, but I feel like I need the heat. Like it might give me some sort of clarity. The Navajo sweat it out. I figure I ought to give it a try. Of course, I'm drinking a glass of bourbon as well, which isn't part of the Navajo ritual. I'm dribbling it into my mouth a half sip at a time and swirling it around my teeth.

I don't really know what purpose I thought this trailer would serve. When I started it, all I wanted was to be doing *something*. I guess serving as a place to swish bourbon around my teeth in the dark is as good as anything. Sort of like a hick sensory-deprivation chamber. I supply the darkness. The bourbon supplies the weightlessness. It's good bourbon too. Not the plastic bottle trash I used to drink back at my apartment. That, at least, is an improvement in my life. Something to hang your hat on. Not in here, though. There's nothing in here on which to hang a hat.

The good thing about bourbon, one of several, actually, is that it sets aside noise. Chaco rez is buzzing with noise, and it's about ready to break the people here, even if they don't know it yet. It's about ready to break me, and Caroline, and Grant, and even Chaco too. Grant used to tell me about this place he had in his bedroom back in Midland, between the dresser and his bed, where he would go to shut out the noise. Maybe this is my place like that. Grant doesn't tell me much of anything anymore, but after a few dribbled sips of bourbon, that doesn't sting quite as much.

Caroline is with the agents. She thinks they may be able to make sense of what we found in the book. They won't. I know it. They want nothing to do with the book. Caroline knows this too, which tells me she's more comfortable in upstate Washington with two guys that tried to kill us, however entranced they may have been, than she is with me right now. But after a few more dribbles and a big swish, that shuts up too.

With the noise turned down, the reality of our situation steps up. We've got a killer coyote on the loose, one that can take on the personage of any living person it comes across. It taints the ground it walks on, like lead seeping into the water, until the whole place is putrid and ready to blow. It wants to bring our world crashing down around us, and house odds are that it wants to do all the crashing at the Native Market. So we've got three days.

The Coyote Way might be able to trap it. Ben tells us it's a chant-way. One of the spiritual ceremonies of the Navajo where Singers try to get the attention of the Navajo gods to bestow favors. Cure illness. Lend strength. It's the exact type of nonsense I spent a decade as a CHC doc trying to tiptoe around, being politically correct enough to acknowledge that yes, your spiritual beliefs have merit, but no, a heavy sweat will not cure your son or daughter of tuberculosis. Your grandfather will not be cured of his chronic emphysema by inhaling piñon smoke. Your husband's jaundice will not go away if he's chanted over for three days, no matter how expensive the Singer is.

You need medicine for these things, or your people will die. I still believe that. Even after all I've seen. There's magic out there, but there's also medicine. And maybe they aren't so different.

And yet here I am. I pat my breast pocket, where the words of the book are transcribed. Each of us has a copy, in case the book gets fickle again and sucks up all the ink we only recently got it to bleed out. I've already memorized it, and I'll spare you the anticipation: the directions make no sense. The three of us and Chaco brainstormed all night over them without getting far. Maybe if I recite them out loud in the hollow of the trailer, the acoustics will make sense of them. Sort of like singing in the shower. Which is what Caroline does. I used to go over some of my trickier biopsy procedures in the shower. Same difference. Here goes. Number one:

"A birth bag," I say. Not sure what that is. Medically, it could be a lot of things, none of them appealing outside of a hospital setting. Don't blame me, I'm just telling you what the book says.

"A burned stick." Which shouldn't be too hard. In a sane world, you just go out, find a stick, and burn it. There you go. Or how about a match? That's a burned stick. Can it possibly be that easy?

"A broken pot." Same deal. Do I just break a pot? Caroline said that we have a Crock- Pot we sometimes use. She likes to cook enough for several days at a time when she can. It has her most recent concoction in it right now, a peccadillo that didn't go over very well. I can toss it. It'll be a shame to lose the ceramic piece, but if it means saving the world, I can part with it.

"A cane." There are plenty of those around here. We used to give them out for free at the CHC. We took up a donation in Albuquerque for them. Most of them were used walkers, though. Would that work?

"A whisk broom." We use a Hoover to keep the RV clean. Caroline said that's like a modern whisk broom. Maybe we toss the Hoover in?

"A broken stirring stick." We're at a loss here. I'm not quite sure what a stirring stick is. Grant suggested using our soup ladle.

I laugh out loud. If you think we can catch our coyote with a match, a crock pot, a walker, our vacuum, and a soup ladle, all wrapped up in whatever the hell a birth bag is, I've got a bridge in

Brooklyn I'd like to sell you. Once again that damn book provides us more questions than answers. I dribble more bourbon into my mouth. Maybe I'll just sit in here until all the chaos blows over. Or until the world blows over into chaos. The latter is looking more likely these days...

A sharp series of knocks makes me literally jump up from my back in complete darkness. I forget where I am. All I know is that I'm sweating profusely. It must be a hundred degrees. I feel out wildly for anything, and my hands slap against the sides of what I slowly come to realize is the trailer. I stumble around in the darkness, slam my head against the back hatch, and knock over my bottle of bourbon. I scramble to pick it up then feel around the trailer handle for the lever that pops it open. The door snaps up into the ceiling in a jarring rattle, and I'm left peering out into the afternoon sun. My shirt is drenched in bourbon and sweat, and my hair sticks straight up like the tuft of some sort of tropical bird. What's left of the booze swirls around the bottle hanging from my left hand. I shade my eyes from the blinding sun. I can't even tell who's standing on the dirt in front of me.

"Can I help you?" I ask, trying to make it sound polite but challenging at the same time. The first thing that comes to mind is that another Itch found us.

"Everything all right, Dr. Bennet? It's three o'clock. We're supposed to be at the CHC in half an hour."

My eyes adjust, and I see the bulky outline of a big Navajo. A few single strands of his long hair hover about over his shoulders in the rising heat. He's dressed in a worn linen button-up and well-washed jeans. He wears creased leather cowboy boots and sports a shiny silver police badge on his hip, offset of a shinier silver belt buckle.

"Oh God. Chief Yokana. I'm sorry. I lost track of time." Truth be told, I lost track of the fact that we were supposed to meet to go to the CHC morgue in the first place. He knows it too. I can tell by the way he looks at me sidelong then peers behind me into the empty trailer where there's a wet outline of my head on the floor. He glances at the bottle of bourbon I have absolutely nowhere to hide. He sees me deflate. There are a million things he could say right now. Any number of accusations.

What he says is: "All right, then. Let's get goin'."

God bless the Navajo.

"Great," I say, a little too eagerly. "Let me just change my shirt."

WE DRIVE over in Yokana's SUV, a well-traveled Ford Explorer with NNPD plates but no other markings. It has a dusty clean to it—no trash, not even a stray coffee cup—but everywhere bits of the desert, even down to the cracked-earth smell of the AC. I get the feeling he could have a nicer car. He's the chief of police, after all, but I think he doesn't have one for the same reason he's traveling the rez to try and calm people down, and for the same reason he knocked on my trailer and picked me up today. Because he's more interested in actually doing the job than just looking like he's doing the job.

As we roll down the double-lane road out of Crownrock and onto the Navajo Service Route he just starts to talk. Not a lot, not consistently, but a few words here and there. Observations about what he's seen in the towns and outposts, none of them good. The one thing I can say I definitely learned working with the Navajo over the years is to shut up and listen if they're talking, so that's what I do.

"There's a backwater trading post ten or so miles north of Crownrock. It's where I was before I came to you. A man named Burner Forbath runs it with his wife. Has for decades. It works on the barter system still. If you want to set up a house account, you leave what you got as collateral, take what you need. All sorts of things get left and taken. He's had no trouble. Ever. Until his own son robbed him then ended up dead several miles west near White Rock. No visible cause of death. Nothing but coyote tracks around him. That was two days ago. Yesterday I got another call. I'll tell you about that when we get there. Just know that now we're up to five."

Yokana is quiet then. He shakes his head once then shifts his hardened gaze to the road. He doesn't need to embellish. That is implication enough. A two-fold betrayal: Navajo stealing from Navajo, and son stealing from father.

"Burner's boy was a good kid. I didn't believe him until I saw the boy's body myself, surrounded by the house bank he stole. You'll see for yourself, but our team found no cause of death, no markings. It's like the gods struck him down for what he did."

Sani turns north on 191 toward Chaco City. He seems to be working words around in his mouth, behind his closed lips. I know what he wants to say, that this makes no sense. That Burner's boy was struck mad. That the whole rez has been struck mad. That maybe this goes beyond the police work he's accustomed to, into another realm. If he said that, maybe I could shift this load I've been carrying, tell him he's right. That the bodies I'm about to see all were most likely struck by madness. That we've got a coyote skinwalker in our midst. That Burner Forbath's son didn't betray his own family and clan. The coyote did, using him.

But Sani Yokana didn't get to be where he is by swiping at shadows and ghosts. He charged real people with real crimes and put them behind real bars. Just like I used to practice real medicine on real people with real ailments.

"Maybe he didn't steal the house bank," I say. It's as close as I can come to saying what I feel without chancing Yokana pulling a U-turn and taking me right back to Crownrock with a *good day to you, sir*. He looks over at me.

"Burner has one key to the store safe. He gave it to the boy before he left for business in Crownrock that day. It was him."

"What I mean is, maybe Burner's son was ill. Mentally unwell." I look pointedly out the window at all the crows weaving above me, casting shadows like running clouds on the flats and across the heat-beaten road. Yokana follows my eyes, and together we watch a line of four crows flank the car then cut high and right. One tracks us with eerie calm before all are lost to view.

"If I remember correctly, the crows started to show up last time too," he says. "You know I sometimes wonder if they follow me? You believe that?" He smiles sadly and shakes his head.

The rest of the drive, Yokana outlines what he knows about the rest of the bodies. One of them is Bilagaana Bill. I already know his story, but I listen to Yokana tell me about him again. The one they found in the Escavada Wash is a woman from a little town called Los Cristos. An older loner, like Bill. It took three days for someone in her family to get to the CHC to identify her. The third they found the same day: a farm hand who worked seasonally in Nageezi for years. The ranch foreman identified him but couldn't say much other than that he always did his work well then left after harvest.

We pull into the CHC parking lot as the sun turns from the light brightness of high noon to the heavy, cutting rays of a New Mexico afternoon. I reflexively straighten the tie I put on when I changed my shirt, the first I've worn in months, and I'm struck by a nearly over-whelming nostalgia. I remember the heady, antiseptic smell of the place with such force that I can nearly taste it in my mouth. The sunlight reflects off the uniform windows of the squat, four-story building like each has a raging bonfire behind it, and most likely, many do. Not physical fires, but mental ones. Most of my time here was spent putting out fires with Caroline and nurses not nearly as good as Caroline.

We walk through the doors, and I see the front-desk receptionist, a Navajo woman named Lelah who was fairly old before I came around a decade ago. She looks up, mid-phone call, and smiles. Then she ends the call and stands up. She laughs when she sees my surprise. For the first five years I knew Lelah, she couldn't walk right. She was on the receiving end of the walker donations we started in Albuquerque. She walks evenly over to me and gives me a big hug and says, "All it took was every day." I don't know what she's talking about at first, until I see that she's holding out a tattered single sheet of paper with a series of physical therapy exercises on it. "Just like you said, Dr. Bennet," she adds as she hands me the sheet. I sense it's important to her that I take it. Like it signals the end of a long struggle.

I return her smile, and I laugh along with her, but inside I find I'm disappointed in myself. I've let her down by not walking in these doors a few times a week over the past five years. I cheated by handing her the instructions and leaving for half a decade and then walking in when her battle is done. I should have been here. I don't deserve her smile, but she pats me on the back and mutters over me in broken English and Navajo anyway until I have to excuse myself to follow Yokana.

He leads me past the elevator bay, where I'd usually wait to ride to the top floor then make my way down methodically from there, getting as far as I could, one patient at a time. Instead we walk to the stairs at the back of the main floor. They lead down to the morgue.

The formaldehyde tang washes over us slowly along with the increasing cold, all of it gradual, until we find ourselves standing under buzzing blue lights between cold lockers and stainless-steel tables. A medical examiner and his assistant work quietly on a naked body on a cold slab in the far back of the room. I recognize Tim Bentley, a mortician who comes up from Gallup twice a week on behalf of IHS. He's a good guy, if a little weird. But what mortician isn't?

Bentley looks up at us as we approach. "Dr. Bennet," he says, "thanks for coming down." I wonder if he knows I've been gone for five years. Bentley never got out much. He ushers the assistant aside and makes way for us to approach the table. "We've been trying to make heads or tails of this one for almost a week now. He was the first. Take a look."

On the table is Bilagaana Bill. He's looked better, but I've definitely seen corpses look worse. I think whatever kept the grubs away is still lingering on him. The chaos. If it's anything like what we felt with the book, I'd want to stay away too. Yokana clears his throat.

"Got a tip from a group of hikers that said they saw something in the middle of the canyon near the west mesa. This is Bidzill Halkini, the one I told you about. Who went by Bill."

I hope it doesn't show that I've seen him before. That we were the ones that found him. That I was the one who called in the tip from a pay phone at the Chaco Canyon Visitor's Center, muffling the receiver a bit with my hand when I spoke.

"What's your cause of death?" I ask Bentley.

"On paper, organ failure. Same as the other four."

"On paper?"

The assistant glances at Bentley. He looks uncomfortable. So does Bentley, in his own way. He takes off his magnifying glasses and picks at some sleep in the corner of his eye. "There's some indication here of a. . . I'd almost call it a type of encephalopathy, although it doesn't follow modern examples of the disease. The blood flow in the brain was not normal."

"Do you have any postmortem scans?" I ask, slipping on latex gloves. It comes back remarkably easily. Like I've fallen back into the routine of flicking on the coffee pot and stepping outside to get the morning paper. Yokana steps back and rests against the wall, watching.

"Mr. Yokana petitioned for two—one on Halkini, because he came in first, and then on Burner, because he was significantly younger than the first three victims." He moves over to Bill's file and rifles through it until he finds a photo printout of the man's brain. He hands it to me.

"Burner's looks much the same as Halkini's, in terms of blood flow."

As soon as I touch the glossy printout, I'm taken back to that moment in my apartment when Radiology patched through a brain scan of Ben Dejooli, effectively hammering the last nail in his coffin. I remember the way the crows exploded from the big tree outside of my apartment window after I read the scan. I'd been drinking bourbon then too. I half expect more crows now, their claws clacking against the flooring as they come hopping down the stairs. I get no such thing, only the low-grade buzz of fluorescent lights and Tim Bentley looking at me strangely.

Brains are not my specialty, outside of when they're anomalous with cancerous growth. This man's brain is not. I recognize no outstanding masses of any sort, nothing that would indicate a tumor or clot. But I've seen enough postmortem CT scans of brains to recognize what a normal one looks like.

Bilagaana Bill's scan does not look normal. Some areas of his brain look devoid of blood flow entirely. As if they've been cut off. Others are suffused with blood, bright white on the scan, like they've been overexposed. I bend over him and pull up his right eyelid. The tiny capillaries that web the eye are burst in places. Their red is softened to a muted purple by the milky film of death.

"When was this taken?"

"As soon as we got him in, five days ago."

I take a big breath. "On its face it looks like some sort of massive stroke."

"Except that—"

"Except that there are no clots or blockages of any sort," I say.

Bentley nods. "I thought the error might have been mechanical until I took his front plate off. The tissue samples corroborate."

I stare at the scans for another minute in silence, until Bentley says, "Thoughts, Dr. Bennet?"

"I'm not sure you want to know what I think, Dr. Bentley."

"Try me."

I weigh my thoughts. Test my words in my mind first. "I think his brain looks like it was changing, and his body couldn't take it. Let me guess, no indications of why his major organs gave out?"

Bentley shakes his head.

"He shut down," I say.

"Why?" Bentley's tone is academic. Distant.

"Maybe he didn't want the alternative." By which I mean whatever chaos was poisoning his brain. I wish I could just tell them, without Yokana taking me out in handcuffs.

"He does look like something got at his mouth," I offer, since it's all I can do.

"All of them do," Yokana says. "Paw prints around them too. Probably just a coyote worrying at the mouths. They do that sometimes."

"The rest of the decomposition process is occurring remarkably slowly," Bentley says.

More overhead buzzing. I look at Bentley only to find he's already looking at me. I tuck the scan back in the folder. "Can I see the other bodies?"

Bentley moves down the cold locker, snapping open clasps and sliding out corpses like a tailor pulling an assortment of fabrics. Soon the other four are stretched out before me. I'm looking for anything that might link them, besides the coyote bite. Something that might give me a clue as to the type of person the coyote wants. I feel like more of a cop than a doctor. But then again, maybe that's why Yokana brought me along. Because the best cop he knew for this type of stuff is dead.

After Bilagaana Bill is the woman they found in Escavada Wash. She's squat, fatter than Bill. There are no marks on her that might indicate how she died, but her face has the same creases from age and sun. The farmer they found near Nageezi looks similarly worn. Deep crow's feet around the eyes. Chapped lips and chapped hands. There's a slight crease around his forehead, and when Yokana sees me looking at it, he chimes in.

"That's from an ancient Stetson he always wore."

"These people are all old," I say.

"That was our first connection too. Until Burner's son came in."

I move down the line to Burner. He's darkened by the sun, but otherwise he looks like a normal young man. He's filled out at the shoulders, but his face still has a hint of that pudgy, teenaged veneer.

"How old was Burner's son?"

"Nineteen," Bentley says.

I walk as calmly as I'm able to the last slab down the line. A thin girl with waist-length black hair lies here. She has muddy feet. She's quite pretty.

"And this girl. How old was she?"

"She's our most recent," Yokana says. "Sixteen. She comes from a family who owns a used-tire shop in a one-horse town off 57 called Animas. One of three daughters and two sons. She set fire to the building before she apparently walked five miles barefoot to the north bank of the Chaco River and laid down to die. No priors, no record of any kind. All anybody the NNPD questioned could say about her was that she was the quiet one of the family."

"Isn't it a bit strange that all of them seem to have been bitten?" I ask carefully, still looking at the girl. She has the gnaw marks on her face too, around the lower lip. Just like the rest of them. I look up at Bentley. "Maybe that ought to be looked into more carefully. There's a chance we need to tell people to look out for coyotes—"

Bentley winks at me.

Half of his mouth turns up into a grin, the other half down into a snarl. It's an awful, two-faced grimace that lasts maybe half of a second. I shake my head, take a deep breath, and when I look up again he's watching me calmly.

"Yes?" he asks.

I turn to Yokana. He seems to have seen nothing.

"Dr. Bentley has told me that they see this quite a bit," Yokana says, flipping through the chart in his hand as he speaks. "The coyotes get at the mouths of exposure victims pretty regularly."

I look at Bentley again. He's grinding his teeth softly.

"It's just what they do," Bentley says, staring at me, unblinking. "It's the softest meat." I take a step back.

"I can't help you," I say quickly. "I'm sorry. I wish I could. Chief Yokana, I need to go. I've forgotten I need to pick Grant up from school."

I've forgotten no such thing. Grant won't let me walk him to school or pick him up. But I have to get out of here. The air is suddenly thick. I'm having trouble getting a breath. I look at the assistant, and he seems strangely doped. Oddly quiet. Has he spoken since I got here?

"Chief," I say. "We need to leave."

Bentley smiles and waves good-bye like a kid at a bus stop. I turn and just start walking up the stairs. It takes every fiber of my being not to run as fast as I can. I hear Yokana behind me with his slow, deliberate steps. I don't say a word until we're both out and in the baking sun, and only then can I finally breathe. I let the sun wash over me like a shower, craning my neck toward it.

"You OK, Dr. Bennet?" Yokana asks.

I watch the door. Nobody comes after us. Not Bentley, not anybody.

"I am now. Sorry. I haven't been around all that for a while." I wonder what I can possibly say to convince Yokana that every policeman on the rez needs to descend on the CHC morgue right now and shoot Bentley on sight. I almost start to say it, and Yokana is watching me, concerned, but after a few more moments in the Navajo sun I've calmed myself. No, that wouldn't do. The skinwalker will have thought of that, after all. It wanted to show me what it was doing, toy with me, and it said its piece. If I were to go back down those steps right now I'd probably find Tim Bentley dazed and confused, the skinwalker already gone.

"Did you see something down there?" Yokana asks, and not for the first time do I wonder if he knows more than he lets on.

"You brought me to hear what I think. Well, I think these people were attacked by something. Something that broke their minds. They wandered out into the desert because they couldn't take it anymore."

Yokana cocks his head. "What kind of thing would do that?"

A coyote. I almost say it. But it won't come out. I shake my head in frustration. "And they're getting younger. The victims. From Bill on down to the girl."

If this was already obvious to him, Yokana doesn't let on. He only nods, his face falling another centimeter, lower and lower. Grayer and grayer. I wonder how much longer a man like him can stay standing if every day he gets lower and grayer. But I can't dwell on that now. Right now I'm wondering about who will come next. Who comes after the sixteen-year-old? A fifteen-year-old? Fourteen?

All I can think of is Grant.

17
_____

THE WALKER

I'm sitting inside my clan hogan watching the daylight fade. The sun seems to be pulled through the smoke hole at the top as if someone is sucking it up with a straw. Gam used to call this type of light *dust light*, the last, sideways beams that catch the dust and the pollen floating in the air. There's no dust at my passing, though. I disturb nothing. I'm the only one here, and I'm not even really here, not like the fire pit is, or the swept earth, or the pollen-dusted beams. I've been the only one here for days. I come back in between calls, hoping to catch whoever keeps this place, but so far I've only seen crows. I think they can see me, or almost see me. They hop in through the eastward-facing door and cock their heads at me before turning around and hopping right out again. Maybe they don't like what they see.

I'm probably looking a little grim. I'm definitely feeling grim. We've got three days until the Native Market, where our coyote may be primed to pop off. The rez is slowly falling apart under the weight of the chaos it brings, and our only weapon against it reads like a shitty garage sale.

Something about all this is going over my head, and I can almost hear the *whoosh*. Something fundamental about the coyote, as a skinwalker. I'm missing something, and it's driving me nuts. If you think about it, this coyote and I have a lot in common. It's a mean bastard, but it has a job too, just like I do. It anchors the chaos side of the river. It absorbs the souls that are drawn there. It may look like the coyote has free rein here—it can change hosts with a touch, turn them into skinwalkers too, and moves with unnatural speed and strength—but the world it inhabits now still has rules. I take a swipe at the rocks ringing the fire pit, and my hand passes through. That's one rule. I can't interact with this world unless it's to take a soul to the veil. And as far as unnatural speed and strength, well, I bet if you were to ask some of the poor saps I have to chase down and drag to the veil, they'd say much the same about me. But I still have limits, so this thing must too. It's just a matter of finding them.

I wish Gam was here. I wish I could knock on some camper doors and rattle some tents at the Arroyo and figure this out NNPD style like in the old days. I wish I was a better Navajo and knew what a Coyoteway was in the first place. I wish Joey Flatwood had any idea. I wish I was with Caroline right now, playing cards on a TV table in my house while we talked all this over. I'd even be willing to take the chemo again. See what I mean about being a bad Navajo? My people aren't supposed to dwell. We don't look forward much, either. We take what is and work with it. But what *is* sucks, and all I find myself doing these days is looking back. Sorry, Gam, I know you'd be sucking your teeth at me, shaking your head, but can you really blame me? What's *back* is all I have.

I'm roused from my one-person pity party by a shuffling sound coming from outside. I walk out and take a lap around the hogan, tracing the sound back toward the Arroyo until I see two figures crest the rise, taking a well-worn path in my direction. The sunset falls right on them, and I see it's two men. Two old men. They're walking along the path in silence, backs bent with age, their eyes on the ground in front of them. They don't pick up their feet so much as slide them, right foot, left foot, with a sound like the slow sweeping of a broom, one in front, the other behind.

They pass the first three derelict hogans without a glance. As they make their slow way down the path it dawns on me that I know these men. They were at my chant. They're the sand painters. Two brothers, as old as the hills, who used to perform with Gam on the rare occasions she still sang. They're dressed in light jackets despite the summer heat, in that universal way of all old people, but theirs are over what looks like traditional garb: woven tunics and buckskin breeches worn as thin and white as paper at the knees. They wear beaded moccasins that look patched and patched again. I know they could walk right through me, but I step aside for them anyway. They pause briefly at the open entrance to the hogan, and the first reaches into his tunic. He takes a pinch of pollen in his hands and slaps the mantel. They gently help each other with the slight bending and crouching required to get inside, and once there they silently go about sweeping the place and shoring up the four corners of the framing by dusting pollen in each direction.

One builds a fire in the pit while the other smooths the dirt beside it like he's priming a canvas, and when the hogan is nice and hot, they take off their jackets. Then they take off their tunics. And then they take off their slippers and breeches. They're stripped down to saggy old-man underwear. I'm starting to wonder if maybe I ought to give these fellas their privacy, but that's where they stop. One nods at the other and then creaks his way downward until he's lying flat on the dirt between the fire and the canvas. His brother takes up several handfuls of piñon leaves and stuffs them in a paper grocery bag. I'm thinking maybe he's going to burn the whole thing, but instead he sets it carefully on the floor and kneels on it to save his bony knees from the hard-packed dirt of the floor. Now we've got one lying flat, the other kneeling over him, and the fire crackling and smoking. The kneeling man extends his right hand out over his brother, and he touches his dirt canvas with the knobby pointer finger of his left hand. Then he closes his eyes and begins to sing.

I don't recognize his song, but that's hardly surprising. Gam sang all the time, walking the foothills with me, cooking around the house, when she weaved and when she knitted. She sang Ana and me to sleep when I was younger, and it seemed like no two songs were exactly the same. The sand painter sings over his brother in a softy rhythmic chant that's surprisingly high and on key, considering I bet the guy is well into his eighties. His right hand still hovers above his brother. He draws in the dirt with his finger.

I peer over his shoulder and watch as he traces symbols. I recognize the hard lines and basic shapes that make up the symbols of power and the outlines of the Holy People, but I get the sense that he's improvising, moving his finger in time with his voice—deeper gouges when his song counts out beats, softer strokes as his words soften and his voice keens. He draws circles one way then traces them back in the opposite direction. I'm so lost in the finger painting that I don't realize he's opened his eyes and is staring now at his right hand. It's a complicated one-man dance that he's doing. Singing, painting, and now moving his right hand slowly, evenly over his brother's body. His eyes never waver, and neither does his right hand. It cuts the air in a slow and steady slice. There aren't even any old-man shakes. That's when I figure out what's going on. This is a hand-trembling ceremony. This man is a hand-trembler, a Navajo medicine-man, although not quite like what Gam was. Tremblers can tell you if you're sick with something, then they send you to people like Gam, Singers who can perform chantways to get your spirit patched up and back in line with the Navajo Way.

After a time, the first brother abruptly stops, evidently satisfied with how still his right hand was the whole time. He gently wipes his tapestry clear, and then the two switch places. Both brothers are Tremblers, then. I can't help but smile. These two and Gam must have made quite the team back in the day. Gam didn't sing nearly as much near the end of her life, but I can only imagine what they must have been like in their prime. Gam was good. One of the best. I bet the brothers are too, if you believe that sort of thing. And if you were here, in the smoke and heat, and you saw the painting, the singing, and now the surgical stillness of the second brother's hand, I don't care how skeptical you are, some part of you might start to wonder.

The brothers now stand facing each other, which is odd. I don't remember this sizing-up as part of any hand-trembling ceremony I ever saw or heard about from Gam. As a matter of fact, they look like they're checking each other for blemishes, like they're pieces of meat at the butcher. They slowly circle each other. One turns his back on the other, and he scans it from top to bottom, even stretching out the underwear band for a glance down below. They check each other's sparse hair, like they're looking for ticks. They lift up one leg and then the other like old donkeys and check the soles of each other's feet. Last, they check each other's mouths, up and down. Then they both speak the first words I've heard them say all evening. It's in Navajo, but it's clear and I understand it: "No bead, no bone."

They nod to each other. They seem as pleased as they were to find their right hands steady over one another, and it occurs to me that this trembling ceremony wasn't to diagnose an illness of some sort but to pronounce a clean bill of health.

At the sound of the words, memories flood into my head, one after the other. I remember walking with Gam, both Ana and me, taking care to brush our feet over any track we saw, in case it was a snake's, and Gam laughed at us and said we just wiped out a lizard's slow *swish*-and-*clomp* track, not a snake's. Ana said something like, "Aren't they bad too?" But Gam shook her head. "The Gila gave us the trembling power," she said. "Its scales harden the Navajo warriors. It keeps us safe." And that afternoon, outside the front door, she stopped us and ran her still-nimble fingers through our hair playfully. "See?" she said. "No bead, no bone. The Gila has kept you safe from the witches."

No bead, no bone. The sign of a Navajo witch, of the skinwalker, is supposed to be a bead made from bone, embedded just under the skin. The sand painters wanted to make sure they were clean. They've been coming here time and again, judging from the pollen, to check each other for a bead.

And now other images hit me like bolts out of the blue. The first time I saw the coyote it was gnawing on its own cheek. It tackled the woman in green and lashed out at her mouth, and then she spat at her boyfriend in the red shoes. I remember the blood, the way it hit his mouth too. Then, while I was looking at her, he disappeared. I try to picture what happened next, and I go blank. I panic and take some deep breaths. The sand painters are packing up, and I watch them go in a daze, the very last of the light showing them the path that they seem to know by heart. Their slow, methodical gait calms me.

I remember now. There was a fight. A fight between Red Shoes and another man over an embrace with the waitress. Perhaps a kiss? Then the skinwalker jumped again, to the waitress, who then ran around the corner, where I lost her.

The coyote, gnawing at its mouth. The woman in green, bitten at the lip. Red Shoes, who took a full gob of blood to the face himself. The waitress he then kissed. A bone bead transferred to each. The hallmark of the skinwalker. Its source of power.

I call for Chaco. I call again and again like an annoying neighbor ringing the doorbell fifteen times. Eventually I hear the pop and feel the pressure drop, and he floats out of the sky like a piece of darker night.

"Walker, you better have a damn good reason to call me like this. Grant is in the trenches at that damn high school, and he's chosen right now to fall into puppy love. We got darkness closing in on all sides, man. I don't have the time to—"

"It's a bead, Chaco. A bead made from bone. That's what we're looking for. Everybody that became a skinwalker had it in their mouths. The five dead people that hit me one after the next, all soul-less, they had it in their mouths, but it broke their minds. Maybe they carried it for too long, or maybe they fought against it. Either way they tried to take it away, lay down and die in a place where it might be forgotten, buried by the desert in the Chaco Canyon or Escavada Wash or wherever. But this thing has forged a connection to the coyote, and the coyote found it every time."

Chaco stills and half floats, half flops his way to the ground in front of me. "A bead. Another object of power." He's talking to himself more than to me, but I nod. "Of course," he says. "Your object of power is the bell. You're a Walker, this thing is a Walker. Why wouldn't this thing have one too?"

"The coyote carries it in its mouth. We find the coyote, we rip it out like a bad tooth, we destroy it."

Chaco flutters. "Then it's all over."

18

CAROLINE ADAMS

Owen is actually making Grant open up his mouth. He's got a penlight and everything, and he's telling him to move his tongue around. I'm torn between laughing and crying. This is what it's come to around here. The boat is getting weird.

"OK, no beads. You're looking good. Now you check me," he says. He holds the penlight out to Grant, but Grant just crosses his arms and shakes his head pityingly.

"You're not a skinwalker, Owen. I don't need to look in your mouth to know that," he says.

Owen shrugs. "Fine. Caroline, you can check me."

"How about we all just stop looking in each other's mouths, OK? None of us is the coyote. I would know," I say.

"Oh yeah, how?"

It's best not to get into how I have a detailed skinwalker checklist for both of them, wherein I would determine that Owen doing this type of fretting is actually *normal* for him. And Grant looking bored out of his mind is *normal* for him too. Instead I say, "I'd see it in your smoke."

"You don't know that. You've never seen it."

"I'd know." Although he's right, I haven't seen it. Still, I think there'd be some indication from the smoke that a body is possessed, being molded, being shifted by this thing into a vessel it can ride until it dies. Owen just got finished telling us his uplifting theory that the coyote needs a kid. A young person, at least. The bodies he saw were trending younger, and Owen thinks it's because it's harder for the coyote to take control of an old person, with set routines and embedded prejudices and experiences. Young people are malleable. Easier to warp because there's less to change.

"The point is that we all need to see that we're who we say we are, right now, right here, before we go to the Arroyo. It's a baseline panel. Do you know what a baseline panel is, Grant?"

Good old Owen, always finding a teachable moment. He's such a dad, which is remarkable considering Grant doesn't consider himself Owen's son. Predictably, Grant says nothing, just resigns himself to listening as Owen plods on.

"It's an establishment of control levels. For instance, a baseline lipid panel is something I recommend you get at twenty years old to establish cholesterol levels and enzyme activity for that moment in your life. Then we'll know in subsequent panels if there's cause for alarm."

"All right, can we go?" Grant asks. He looks at me with pleading eyes.

"What he's trying to say is that we need to know that at this moment we're bone-bead free," I say, snatching the penlight and doing a cursory check in Owen's mouth, more to get this show on the road than anything. "Because we're going into a dangerous area, and if something does happen and one of us starts acting weird from here out, we'll know at least we were all good here. And it's a good idea."

Owen gives me a proud smile that is surprisingly catching, considering we're on the edge of what you might call the rez war zone. It was my idea. Most of the really insane ones are. Chaco said Ben divined his bead theory from watching these two old hand-tremblers that sandpainted during his chantway years ago. I said it would have been great to ask them about the Coyote Way, seeing as they're old as the hills and might have some idea as to what the six odd ingredients are. If this creature attacks like a skinwalker and has some sort of affinity to the Coyote of Navajo lore, maybe we could use the lore it's wrapped itself in to catch it. I was just spitballing, you know? Just saying the first thing that came to mind. Like, it would also be great if I had a chai tea latte right now. Except instead of getting a delicious, warm drink the four of us now have to walk into Navajo skid row looking for two old guys.

"You're clear," I say, then I slap the penlight into his hand and pop open my mouth and say *ahhhh*. I hear Chaco squawk on the steps of the RV, where's he's waiting. After all these years I can tell when crow squawk sounds impatient.

"Chaco says it's not the coyote we need to worry about here. This crew is old-school. Way too much work to turn into a skinwalker. It's getting our asses kicked that we need to worry about."

"That's lovely. Thank you, Chaco. Quite helpful," Owen says.

Chaco squawks again. Grant translates, his voice droll. "He says if you know anyone else who's willing to translate old geezer Navajo, be his guest."

I do, actually. Joey Flatwood. But he's still not willing to break his banishment. Certainly not to show himself at the Arroyo again. He's stubborn like that. Just like Ben was, and still is. Chaco says Ben is going with us, but we obviously can't expect any help from his corner, not that it's his fault. Chaco says that for the record Ben isn't all that hot on this idea. He suggested we bring Yokana in, but that's easy for him to say. He's not the one that would have to explain the existence of worlds beyond worlds to the Navajo chief of police. And the bottom line is, we have two days before the Native Market. We're running out of time. It's now or never.

We parked the boat in a well-tracked dirt shoulder just before the turnoff to the Arroyo proper. It's still a five-minute walk from here, and we could have gone closer, but the last thing we need to do is show up to this place in our suburban war-vehicle. The boat is nice. Not Liberace-On-Tour nice, but we've got about a hundred grand wrapped up in it (OK, Owen's got about a hundred grand wrapped up in it), and it would look obnoxious rolling up on old tents and tarp-covered lean-tos and cars on blocks. The idea is to look exactly as desperate as we are.

Owen clicks on a flashlight, and we set off in the silence down the rutted road to the Arroyo. The night is black in the rez in general, but it's blacker out on the fringes. Eventually we see lights in the distance, soft glows from inside cars and here and there tents lit up like wish lanterns. The clunky turning sound of a few small generators provides a hum of background noise over which snippets of conversation can be heard, blown our way by the soft night breeze. It's not late yet, just dark, and the Arroyo is still alive. You could even call it sort of pretty. This is the time to see the place if you have to, when the drop-off beyond looks like the velvety black entrance to some sort of mysterious cave and not the pit full of trash and rusted metal that it is. When the camp looks like a half moon of bobbing lanterns, you can almost believe it isn't full of people too poor to own a house or rent an apartment, right next to bootleggers and meth cooks and addicts. The rough parts are muted, covered in a blanket of velvet night and soft moonlight. I might actually like to take it all in, if it weren't for the fact that we were being followed.

I tug on Owen's cuff, and he turns to me.

"We've attracted some attention," I say. I can see the smoke of two or three people in the darkness to our right and left, like faint wisps of ground fog in strange colors. The people themselves blend in seamlessly with the dark horizon.

Owen and Grant slow, and Chaco stills. We wait. But neither the smoke nor the bodies it comes from move toward us, which you'd think would be heartening. Until you realize that all they want us to do is keep walking, farther from the main road. Farther from the boat. I can read it in the way their colors bubble and waft. But they're not roiling, either. They're not angry, or cruel. They're curious, and maybe a little bit opportunistic, but I think that's the game out here at the Arroyo.

"Let's keep walking if we're gonna keep walking," I say. "Act like you know what you're doing, Owen."

And he does. He straightens up and fixes the tuck of his shirt. He clears his throat and nods at the rest of us. I see the people around us pausing, reassessing. Maybe it's Owen, maybe it's the huge bird that sits on Grant's head. Either way, they follow at a distance, but more join. By the time we reach the inlet at the camp's edge, basically a big, rusted swinging gate bolted into the ground in the middle of nowhere, we've got six different smokes at the fringes that I can see, but so far they all hold back.

At the gate is a young man. He leans heavily against it, and his body makes the slight sways and constant adjustments of the veteran drunks we'd see at ABQ General. He smokes a cigarette that burns a soft red in the dark. He wears a stained Cleveland Indians jersey and sagging gym shorts with sandals covered in duct tape, and he watches us plainly as we approach. I hold Owen and Grant back a few paces from the guy. An element of everyone's smoke here is harsh, rough, but it's more of an undercurrent than what surfaces up top. Up top is still curiosity.

"You're definitely lost," he says. Then he takes a quick drag of his cigarette.

"No, we came here for help," Owen says, and although I can see that he's near to trembling on the inside, his voice is level and calm. Doctoral. I wonder, if I'd had the sight I have now back when I worked on the floor with him, how many times his outside would have belied his inside. When you work an oncology floor, you're almost always terrified. It's all about how you control it. I'm not at all surprised that Owen does it well.

"We're looking for two old men, sand painters. We were told they live here," he says.

The man is quiet, but inside he's surprised. First, three white people show up, then they ask about two old-timers who probably haven't been off the Arroyo in years. I think we've chosen the right approach, but then he shatters my confidence.

"Get the fuck out of here, *bilagaana*," he says. "Before you get hurt."

"We need help," Owen says again.

"Navajo medicine works best on Navajo. Go back to your pretty city."

"It's not for us, it's for the rez," Owen says.

"The *rez*? What do you care about the *rez*?" he asks. The six who lurk in the darkness start to move in as soon as he raises his voice. Owen senses that he's been too familiar. He takes a step back, another smart move. Now the smoker sees Grant fully for the first time, with Chaco on his head, doubling his height.

"What the fuck is that?" he asks, and I see his color rise for a moment.

"It's my bird," Grant says, calm as a lake. Chaco rises to his full height.

The smoker is afraid, but not of Chaco, not exactly. He's afraid because in his past he had a friend who lived by the crow totem, but he died. A Circle member, although the smoker didn't know it. I see the words play over his head and his heart. They read, "Oka Chalk."

"That's a big fucking bird," the smoker says, speaking around his cigarette, taking in a long drag now.

"He's. . . not your normal type of crow," Grant says.

"Listen," says the smoker. "You take this circus and walk your asses back the way you came. Hear me? This ain't no place for you."

The six others are coming toward us, and now they're not so curious anymore. Now they've got one thing on their mind: getting us out. Maybe taking a bit of a road tax along the way. Chaco sees them too, and he snaps his head to the side, eyeing the closest. He shifts himself to fly. I speak first, loudly.

"Oka Chalk is the reason we're here. He was the start of all this. You remember him?"

Everyone freezes. The smoker comes a few steps closer. I sense Owen tense but keep a hand on him. "What do you know about Oka Chalk?" he asks, peering at me over the cherry of his cigarette, through half-hooded eyes. He smells like bad beer.

"He had a crow too, once. Different from the one there." I nod at Chaco. "But—"

"A bad omen," he finishes. "That stone crow of Chalk's, it was bad luck. He started his own totem pile with it. I bet it told him he was gonna die. Now the fuckin' things are everywhere—the sky, the roads. They're in the middle of the pit by the hundreds." He gestures vaguely with his cigarette behind him

I don't know what the man is talking about with totem piles and premonitions of death, but I know I have his attention. The problem is he's just getting more scared now, no more willing to take us beyond the gate. We need to play our cards quickly, or we're going to get the hook. As if Chaco can understand me, he lets out three shrill *caws* that are immediately echoed from the desert behind us and built upon by the crows in the trash pit. From the sound of the birds, their collective voices slamming against the dirt and the desert like they're all right next to our ears, there are more than a hundred in that pit. It sounds like an army, and it's worse for being nighttime. If you think about it, you never hear crows at night. You never really hear birds of any kind at night. There's a reason. It's not natural. And it's terrifying. Still, I sense a new respect for us in the smoker. If it's born from fear, so be it.

"Do you want us to get rid of the crows?" I ask.

The smoker eyes me. He's sizing us all up in a new light, especially Chaco and Grant.

"You know we can do it," I say. "We know why they're here. But we need to talk to the sand painters first. And we need to do it soon."

The six that surround us are still moving in, inching closer while the smoker thinks. At the last second, just as I see Chaco's beak flashing to strike, the smoker holds up a hand.

"Follow me," he says. "And stay on the path."

WE WALK single file behind the smoker, and his sandals make loud clicks in the heavy silence that falls after the cacophony of the crows. Two of the six people that surrounded us follow in the rear. The rest fade away again, back to watch the road, I suppose. The first thing we pass is a big-wheeled Jeep. The tires look more expensive than the car, which is missing its back doors, and when the smoker passes the driver's-side door he taps the window three times. Someone is inside, and they honk three times. The honk is echoed across the camp. A warning that outsiders are coming in. Hide anything you don't want strangers seeing.

I'm not exactly sure what I expected to see at the Arroyo. Albuquerque has a pretty big drug problem and the vagrant problem that goes along with it, so I guess I was expecting something like Commons Park in ABQ, which isn't too far from my old apartment: a bunch of homeless kids mixed in with grizzled drifters, all of them milling around giving each other shady handshakes, rifling through piles of their belongings looking for some odd or end.

The Arroyo isn't like that. I don't know if it's the culture of the place, where they sort of police their own, or if it's the more private nature of the Navajo in general, but I don't see any trouble. I sense trouble behind shuttered camper windows or in zipped tents where lights are snuffed as we pass, but that's where it stays. What I do see is men drinking around a campfire, laughing. Quieting when we pass and watching us carefully, then laughing again (probably at our expense). I smell people cooking meat and beans and grease. I hear kids shouting and running, and I think of Ben and Joey dashing all over this place. Climbing and jumping and racing between campsites.

We round the corner and move from the more ramshackle tenements to places that look almost homey. These are clean and swept. Some campers have welcome mats and potted desert flowers. Most of the cars look functional. The far side is where the reserved spots are. In the lights of the campers, I see people who look older, some very old. The smoker catches me peering, and I look straight ahead, embarrassed.

We walk the entire perimeter, to the opposite side of the entrance from the road, where the semicircle camp butts up against a low rock rise that isn't level enough to set a tent or a camper upon. The smoker stops us ten or so feet back from a pop-up camper that looks as though it popped up decades ago and stayed that way. In the low light that leaks from the windows I see pruned flowers and old-growth brush hemming it in on all sides. It looks like something that sprouted up from the desert itself, with the same sand coloring and the same stark lines.

"Wait," says the smoker. "Don't wander." He dusts ash off the front of his jersey and hitches up his shorts a little then walks up to the front door of the camper and knocks softly, stepping back to wait. After several minutes, a woman opens the door. She's dressed in a light- blue nightgown covered by a faded pink robe. He speaks with her quietly, but Chaco can hear.

Grant whispers to us the gist of what they're saying: "This is where both of the brothers live. She's related somehow. He's asking if they can talk to us. He's calling us outsiders but says we know the crows."

The woman takes a step down and peers out into the darkness at us. She shakes her head several times then speaks with the smoker. "She says no way. They're getting ready for bed." Grant's voice is low with disappointment. The smoker seems to understand. He's already turning away. The woman takes one last look at us, squinting into the dark. Her body turns to go inside, but her head lingers for another moment, as if she's confused. She stops and turns back fully to face us. Then she takes a step down.

"Doctor?" she says. All of us turn to Owen, who looks as surprised as anyone.

"Yes?" he replies.

"O," she says. "Doctor O."

"That's right. I'm Owen. Owen Bennet. Do I know you?"

The woman ignores his question and bustles down the last step and over to us. She holds out her hands to Owen, and he takes them. She's smiling, and her smoke is suddenly warm and reaching. She takes one hand and points at a small scar on her neck, where her thyroid is. Or was. I can see what happened there. Faint purple stretch marks circle the lower edge of her neck, where Owen most likely treated a goiter. It was probably large, but it's all but invisible now, save for the scar and what remains of the stretch marks. Owen laughs once.

"I remember you," he says faintly, his eyes wide. "Right when I first came here, the CHC volunteer crew arranged to pick you up for treatment near the turnoff. That was well over a decade ago, though. You still remember me?"

She doesn't understand, but she beams at his words anyway. "Maya," she says.

"That's right. You're Maya. My God, you look like a different person."

She smiles until her eyes nearly disappear. Then she looks at me and Grant. She takes Chaco strangely in stride, which I think is a good sign. She takes Owen's hand and brings him forward then motions for all of us. "Come," she says.

Owen follows her up and inside the main room of the camper, which is bisected into two equal sides, with two beds made neatly with similar woven blankets. The kitchen smells vaguely of a rich spice I can't place, but it's orderly as well, all the dishes freshly washed, still dripping on the rack. I'm wondering how the heck she thinks all of us are going to fit in here, especially since the smoker still isn't willing to leave us, for better or worse, but my fears are put to rest when she takes another few steps and exits down and out of the opposite door on the side of the camper facing the Arroyo.

Here there's a small fire in a raised fire pit about the size of a hubcap. Enough light to see close up, but not enough to mute the stars that seem scattered above the desert like an arc of thrown glitter. Two men look up at us, both seated in old loungers, the type you'd find in a frat house common room. They wear light jackets, and their legs are covered with woven throws. They're small men, diminished by age, but they sit still with a solid presence and seem absolutely unsurprised to see us here. Even Chaco. Maybe especially Chaco.

"Chaco remembers these two," Grant says quietly. "From his time before me. When he was a different bird, with Ben's grandmother."

Both men nod at Chaco first, and Chaco nods back. Each of us steps forward and introduces ourselves, and when it's done, all of us wait in silence. The men turn to each other and mutter something I don't think anyone could possibly hear, much less understand, but afterward the one on the left says, "Tsosi," and the one on the right says, "Tsasa."

That done, Maya starts fussing around looking for four seats in a square patch of land no more than twenty feet wide. I try to tell her not to worry, that we'll stand, but she's not having it. Eventually I end up in a slightly busted lawn chair, Owen and Grant on two glazed stumps of wood. The smoker seems content to stand out by the periphery of the light, toward the stars, where he lights up another cigarette and waits.

Everyone waits. I wait too, until I realize everyone is waiting for me. They want me to say something, to kick all this off, but to be honest with you I never really thought we'd get much past the turnoff. Also, I'm not sure what these people can understand, or what they can tell me, in English. So I'm sort of in a bit of a pickle, here. With no better ideas jumping to mind, I start by taking out the black book. As soon as they see it, the brothers frown, and Tsosi makes a sucking sound with his teeth that reminds me so much of Ben's grandmother that I have to take a breath to steady my head.

"Do you know what this is?" I ask. The brothers still frown. Maya looks back and forth between us and then shrugs, but I think it's because she can't understand what I'm asking. I look at Chaco, who squawks, and for one insane moment I think maybe they can understand bird squawk. I let it hang in the air for a second, but it does us no good. The sand painters don't understand bird—nobody does but Grant and Ben. I take a deep breath and rub at my face. This is going to be harder than I thought. Then the smoker chimes in from the dark. In Navajo. The brothers respond, and he interprets for us.

"They don't. Not exactly. But they don't like it," he says.

I glance at Chaco, who nods. We're all on the straight here.

"Neither do I. Not exactly," I say. "But it's important, because I think it can help us catch the skinwalker."

The word slips out before I can stop it, and it has an immediate effect. The smoke of both men, heavy and still and a rich chestnut in color, freezes. Maya's face is drawn, and the smoker hisses at us, then spits. "We don't talk witchcraft here. Not with the old generation. And definitely not now." The smoker looks carefully behind him at the trash pit, where the crows sleep again. He shivers, like we just sneezed in the cave of a sleeping bear and everyone's waiting to see if it'll wake up.

"But how will we ask them anything? It's what we came here for," Grant says.

"You talk about the crows. They'll get your meaning."

"But the crows aren't the problem. They're just here because they go where things are out of balance," Owen says, before the smoker cuts him off.

"Listen, *Dr. O*," he says, making it clear he doesn't have quite the shine for Owen's position that Maya does. "You and your friends gotta learn how to talk around what you mean, or you'll never get anywhere with the old-timers. It's not their way to be direct."

Owen sits back a little, and I can tell he's stung. That's something he should have known. Something I should have remembered too. But we've been gone too long. I hold up my hands in apology.

The brothers' smoke stirs again, tentatively.

"There's a list of things in this book that I was hoping you two could explain to us. Tell us what they mean. Tell us what to do."

That came off as desperate, all right. Which was my initial plan. But now that I realize how desperate it sounds I'm wondering if I should rethink my approach. The brothers' smoke is stilling again. Maya looks awkwardly at us from out of the corner of her eye. I can hear the smoker shaking his head, spitting again. I was too direct. That's not the way. But what is the way? I'm starting to panic. I scratch at my neck, and I can feel it puff up with irritation. Suddenly I'm thinking about my puffy scratches and not about the book or what's inside of it, and now my train of thought is totally derailed and I'm thinking again about that stupid chai tea latte, which is *so* irresponsible at a time like this—downright *rude*—but I have nothing else to say. I feel like I'm breathing way too fast.

"Tell us about the Coyote Way," Grant says quietly. The tension snaps. The brothers seem to understand him, or at least those few words. Their smoke stirs then breaks and starts to flow over them again. They start talking to one another, nodding, not speaking to us, but letting us in on the conversation. The smoker interprets.

"The Coyoteway is a Way Chant. A healing ceremony. With a Singer and all that. Tsosi is saying how he went to one as a child, by Shiprock. His dad was the Singer. Tsasa was off chasing some girl, and he missed it. Their dad was pissed. They're laughing about it, because the Coyoteway is a super-long chant. Nine days long, if it's done right. That's a long time to chase after tail."

A healing ceremony doesn't sound like what we need. What we need is a plan to catch a coyote, not heal it. I don't think it can *be* healed. What it is, what it's made of, isn't something that can be cured. But even if a Coyoteway is the key, nine days is way too long. We have two until the market. The way Owen looks at me, I know he's thinking the same thing. If we started right now, we'd still be too late. It's a dead end.

I look at the book, and I'm feeling numb. The brothers' words wash over me, talking about their own stories, talking circles around our problem, and I stop paying attention. I see the strange objects written down in the book, glittering in ink that's impossibly black. I want to spit them all out at the feet of the brothers and see what sticks, but I know that would do us no good and only serve to still their smoke again. What would Ben do? I look desperately at Chaco, who titters at me, low and sad.

"Just talk," Ben would say. I can almost hear him say it too, and I wonder if he's here right now. I bet he is. He wouldn't miss this. I try to feel his presence, walking around us. I reach out desperately in my mind for the rich earthen red of his smoke. I knew it, once. I think of one of the first times I saw it, when I was in his house and he was strapped to the chemo, and I asked him what he wanted to do, to take his mind off the poison that was coursing through him.

"Just talk," he said. When I asked him what he wanted to talk about, he said, "Anything. You first."

We need to take another step back, here. What if we're not talking about a specific chant, but something bigger? Something like the *way* of the coyote?

"Tell us about the coyote," I say, interrupting, then cover my mouth. "Sorry, I uh. Was that too direct?"

The smoker actually smiles. "Sometimes the only way to get these two to shut up is to interrupt them. Otherwise you'll be here 'til you're as old as them."

He poses my question. The brothers take it in stride. Their conversation never misses a beat. In fact, they seem more animated, and Maya is even smiling now. I catch Owen's eye, and he grins at me. Grant seems transfixed by the old men and the loping sound of their voices. The smoker interprets.

"Coyote is a lot of things. A shifter. A trickster. He's good and bad. He can even be a god."

"How do you catch Coyote?" Owen asks. "If he's a trickster and a shifter and a god?"

The smoker speaks and then listens with us, his cigarette forgotten.

"Coyote may be a shifter and a god, but he's also a gambler, and sometimes a fool. He falls for tricks as often as he dishes them out, and he'll put it all on the line to get his prize."

Tsosi points to the sky as he speaks, and all of us follow his voice as it lifts up into the night above us.

"Coyote did that," the smoker says. "The Milky Way. Black God was putting the stars into the sky real careful like, one at a time, in all the right shapes, but Coyote was bored, impatient, so he threw the rest up to make the Milky Way. He's powerful, but reckless. To catch Coyote you just need to take away his warning signs. Without them he will run headlong into your trap."

"Warning signs?" I ask. I feel like we're getting closer, still circling around what we need to know, but the circles are tightening. The wood in the pit collapses to red ash, and Maya puts another log on. A desert wind kicks up, and it scatters tiny embers into the sky, where they glow for a heartbeat before they snuff out. Tsosi confers with Tsasa then clears his throat and begins to speak, and the smoker follows a few moments later.

"One day Coyote woke up at camp and decided to walk. He set

out toward the east but started growling, you know? Like how dogs growl for no reason. So he turned back. Then he started south, but his nose began to twitch, like he smelled something bad, so he turned back again. He's wondering what all this means, right?"

The smoker's cigarette dangles in his mouth as he talks.

"He sets off west this time, but his ears start ringing, so he turns around again. All that's left is north, but as he starts off that way he gets all itchy. His skin twitches, and he can't take it, so he turns around again and goes back to camp."

The smoker pauses and lets the brothers roll on for a bit. Then he starts in, talking low so they'll keep going.

"So Coyote does this four times, right? And the whole time he's freaking out about all these weird feelings he's getting. He's trying to figure it all out when this guy emerges, right from the desert." The smoker cocks his head and listens then reassesses. "Well, not just a guy, but a thing too. Sort of both. And he says, 'I'm your birth bag, Coyote. I'm what you came from. And I say your home is that way.'"

Thankfully, it's dark enough and Maya and the smoker are so wrapped up in the story that the fact that the three of us are suddenly sitting like we've got steel rods for spines goes unnoticed. This is what we're looking for. I doubt there are a ton of stories about birth bags and coyotes in Navajo lore, and this night feels like it doesn't have any room for coincidences.

"So Coyote walks the way he was told, until he makes camp again. In the morning he sets out, runs into the same problems. The buzzing, the growling, the itching, the smells. He's stuck, until another thing comes up from the desert. This time it's a burned stick, but *not* a burned stick, you know? Something more, to Coyote. And the burned stick tells him where to go from there."

I imagine even Ben is still, now. If he ever was pacing around the fire, I bet he's not anymore. The smoker seems to struggle with his translation when he gets to the birth bag that isn't quite a birth bag, and the burned stick that isn't quite a burned stick, but I get it. I know all about things that aren't what they seem. All three of us carry objects that are more than they appear.

"Coyote does this four more times. Each morning he wakes up, he's lost again. He can't figure out what to do, where to go, but each morning he gets help from these things. On the third day it's a broken pot. On the fourth day it's a ratty old cane. On the fifth it's a little broom. The sixth day it's a broken stirring stick, like for a cook pot. They tell him where to go, and he eventually finds himself at his home, where he sacrifices again and again and again until he becomes a god himself."

Sacrifices again, and again, and again. I think of Owen telling me about the bodies pulled from the lockers one at a time so he could examine each. Of the way the mortician twitched. Bit at his own tongue. Could that really have been something like the Navajo Coyote, showing himself for a brief time? Gambling by laying out his cards face up on the table, showing us that his hand is almost full? The brothers suddenly laugh to each other, nodding in agreement. It's a warm *kyuk kyuk kyuk* that both men share. I look over at the smoker expectantly.

"They think it's funny that Coyote was warned again and again not to go the wrong way, but he didn't recognize it. Like most men. Without direction, we would be lost. Coyote came to see that the things he was feeling, the itching and the growling and all that, those were his warning signs. The things from the desert showed him that. Without those things, he'd be doomed."

"These things that warn Coyote," Owen begins then stops, obviously choosing his words carefully. I can tell this part frustrates him the most. His entire life, until he met me, he lived in a world where things were exactly what they looked like. Things worked exactly as they were supposed to. Treatments had outcomes. Things were documented, ordered, peer-reviewed. But not anymore. "Can we find these things here? Now? They seem so simple."

The smoker speaks with the brothers for a moment. They lob these beautiful words back and forth like a slow tennis match, where everyone playing doesn't have to move much because nobody cares too much about winning. Then he turns to us.

"They're simple, but they're not," he says. "They're things that Coyote took and made his own."

Tsasa leans forward and with his bare hands plucks a small strip of half-burned wood from the fire pit in front of us. The brothers watch it for a moment as it fades from angry red to dull then puffs a wisp of smoke into the air, the fire gone out. Tsasa starts speaking again, and the smoker interprets.

"Yesterday this would have been just a burned stick, right? Nothing more, nothing less. Eventually it would turn to ash and be forgotten. It's Coyote's stick just like every stick could be Coyote's."

Tsasa passes it to Maya then indicates for her to give it to us. It goes around the circle until Grant hands it to me.

"But today it's much more. Now it takes on your journey. Your strength in coming here. It has the Arroyo in it. It has all of us, this night, this sky where these stars look just like they do. Now it's much more. Now it's powerful. Now you have taken it back from Coyote."

Maybe it's just the night, or the fire, or the fact that I've got two ancient Navajo guys telling me an ancient story under the stars when half an hour ago I thought I was gonna lose my purse and maybe have my Chuck Taylors tossed over whatever passes for the equivalent of a telephone wire here at the Arroyo, but I feel it. The burned stick is heavier than it has any right to be. Its colors are richer. Its wood-smoke smell is stronger.

"Keep it," the smoker says. "They think you're gonna need it."

Both brothers watch us carefully now, their eyes reflective pools in the firelight. It occurs to me that when we asked how to catch a coyote, they immediately started in on the Navajo figure. They didn't go into, oh, say, how to hunt and kill an actual coyote, which might be the sane thing to discuss. Tsosi says something quietly, and the smoker speaks.

"If you find the rest of Coyote's warning signs, they invite you to the hogan over the hill. They say it's as good a place as any to set a trap."

The brothers seem half asleep when we say our good-byes, but they pat our hands and nod farewell. Maya clasps Owen's hands once more and says good-bye in a way that sounds more like *good luck*. On the walk back around the crescent, the Arroyo is much quieter, the lanterns fewer and farther between. There are no more laughing men or playing children. I get the sense that things should be different, maybe even had been different as recently as a few months ago, but people are circling the wagons even at the Arroyo. Afraid of what is happening outside.

"You gonna catch a coyote and get rid of my crows?" the smoker asks at the gate.

"We'll do what we can," I say.

He nods. "That one and his friends can stay, though," he says, pointing at Chaco. "I like that one." He takes a drag. "Old-timers talk in circles, but now that they're back there and we're up here, I'll go ahead and say it. Coyote may be a god—sometimes he is, sometimes he ain't. But for my money, he's definitely a witch. And a mean one at that."

Before any of us can answer, the smoker nods again, then he simply turns around and walks away.

19

GRANT ROMER

I'm walking to school with Mick. For the past couple of days he's been waiting for me at the edge of the Crownrock RV Park in the morning. He doesn't say much, just leans against the rusted park sign with his hands in the baggy pockets of his shorts then walks with me when I come down the path. I'm not sure how I feel about it, since the only reason he's doing it is 'cause I'm white. I mean, he can't know me yet as a person. I've been at Crownrock High for a week. But I suppose it's better than walking alone.

I know my mind should be on broken pots and stirring sticks and birth bags and all that crap, but instead it keeps coming back to the market and the Crownrock booth there that I gotta take apart and reattach after the dumbass morning crew drilled an unpainted cross-beam right through the middle of it on accident. And then there's Kai. And Hosteen, her brother, who now comes to every prep session I'm at and manages to get into an argument every time with Kai over something I still can't quite figure. Chaco thinks I'm nuts. He's flying high above us now, making a point not to talk to me, which is fine by me because I know what he'd say: "You're screwing around in this high-school-drama crap when the devil is at the gates." And I'd say what I've been saying: If Crownrock High is good enough for the coyote to case—and it definitely is, its tracks are everywhere, worse by the day—then it's good enough for me.

Mick isn't happy that I stuck with market prep. He doesn't understand why I'd want to do something for the Navajo, who never did a damn thing for him or his family and he thinks won't do a damn thing for me. Mick's family works in construction and got some contract on the rez that he says the Navajo are constantly messing with and rewriting and "dragging ass on."

"You sure you don't want to chill with me after school?" he asks. "I got some cool places to show you around here. Some cool shit." Mick hitches up his shorts and walks with a bit of a fake limp.

"Market's in two days, Mick. I wanna finish this thing, then you can show me whatever you want."

"You know Hos is gonna kick your ass if you make a move on Kai. You know that, right? He's been walking around for weeks now just looking for someone's ass to kick."

Of all the people in school, Hosteen is probably the one I should be trying to avoid. I've heard people talking at lunch about how he and his family go way back at the Arroyo and rumors of some bootlegging gambit his family runs. But of all the people in school, he's the one that shows the most signs of being wrapped up in whatever our coyote has planned.

"I dunno, man. I don't think it's me he's pissed at. It's something else. Like you said, he's been thugged up for weeks now. He's got something else in mind."

"I heard he's got something planned for the market, something big," Mick says, and I wait quietly, in case he knows more than he's letting on, but his mouth is shut.

"You got any idea what it might be?" I ask.

"What the fuck do I care what these Injuns do? If you're worried about it, stay away from the market."

We walk the rest of the way in silence, but Mick gives me a fist bump when he turns off at the stairs for his first class on the second floor. Mick is weird like that. He talks like he's pissed off, then he's friendly like nothing happened. I've been trying to get a feel for what the rest of the school thinks of the guy, but all I've found out is that nobody talks about him. Same as me. I sort of came one day, everyone checked me out, then everyone moved on the way they've been moving all year. Everyone except for Kai, that is. Kai looks for me in the halls. I've seen it. She sort of cranes her neck around to look for me every day when she comes out of first period near my locker. She's the only one outside of Mick who really acknowledges that I exist here, but two is better than none.

The classes are fine. The classes are classes. Pretty easy, actually. I think Owen went a little crazy with his Professor Bennet's Education Emporium routine. From what I gather, I'm at least a grade, maybe two, ahead of the rest of the kids my age. I don't let it show. I try not to let anything about where I come from show. Not any cash, not any smarts, and definitely not the bell. I've got one shot here to make myself what I want to be, which is a kid who maybe could call this place home. Mick would say no chance, but I think Mick is kind of a loser.

The Crownrock booth has been moved outside into the back parking lot and roughly disassembled. It lies in five different pieces that will eventually join together to make a decent- sized, three-walled enclosure with a stage in the middle. The stage is for the dance crew. Crownrock has a dance crew that does your standard popular music routines but also traditional Navajo stuff. Sometimes a mix of the two. The three walls also exhibit student art, which is for sale. The art is OK. A few things are pretty good. But they tell me they sell out every year.

I fall in with the crew holding up the top part of one wall while another two guys take apart the bottom with power drills so we can get to the bare crossbar. A few people nod at me, sort of. At least they shuffle to make room for me. That's a victory, I guess. I find myself looking at people's mouths, trying to see what Ben saw on the street with the coyote and the bead, or what Owen saw with the guy in the morgue. It's tough, though. Everybody in high school chews gum all the time. And as for acting weird, well, hell. Take your pick. There's this guy in my history class who talks to himself all the time. Another kid in English lit blurts out cuss words at strange times, and nobody acts like it's weird at all.

I get pretty into the woodworking part. Pap would be proud. I picked up a good base from him, so I actually know a bit about this stuff. I break open the existing joint without cracking things then pull out the crossbar with the help of two or three other kids. We set it on a bunch of flat cardboard that we spread out so we don't get paint all over the parking lot, then get to painting. The other kids still don't talk to me, but I get the feeling that they're more comfortable every day talking *around* me. It sounds pathetic, but it's true. I think it helps just being here. I get to dippin' and slidin'.

I think I lose track of time a bit, because the next thing I know I'm done with the base coat and it's time to put in the designs, which are the type of traditional Navajo connected triangles that you see all over New Mexico, painted in the colors of Crownrock High, which I only just learned are the blue and red I've been getting all over my clothes for a week. Could be worse, I suppose. The Sargaso kids have to deal with adobe pink. That's rough.

I'm about to go search for the right buckets when two of them plunk down right next to me, and then Kai plunks down too. She's wearing paint-streaked jean shorts and an old art smock, which is really just a ratty men's dress shirt about ten sizes too big that she wears backward. She's got flecks of paint in her jet-black hair and a few little drops on her thighs. She sits cross-legged, leans back on her palms, and watches me for a second.

I think I must be staring, because eventually she looks down at her smock and then says, "What? I think it's a pretty good look for me."

"It works."

"What's your deal, Grant?" she asks. She's not smiling at me, not exactly, but her words sound like she's smiling. I think it's something the Navajo can do.

"My deal?"

"You've been here, what, a week? And instead of checking out the football team or the lacrosse club or just bugging out with the other white kids, you've been here every day, painting a market booth for stuff you have nothing to do with."

I shrug. "I dunno. Maybe because I want to have something to do with it. Plus, I'm not really the football or lacrosse type."

She nods. She's chewing gum too. I hope. Yeah, I know. It's just gum.

"Kind of hard to play in black jeans," she says.

"They ain't so black anymore." Two days ago I dumped a blot of white primer on my jeans. It won't scrub out. They're sort of motley now.

"*Aren't.*" I correct myself, awkwardly late.

"Yeah, well then maybe you *ain't* gonna mind getting a little blue and red here and there," she says, and she pops open both cans, stirring each up with one side of the same stick. She hands me a washed brush. "Stick between the lines."

We paint in silence for a while. Or maybe I should say she paints in silence. I test about a million lines of dialogue in my head, and I'm about ready to sweat with how much I'm trying to stay between the lines when she says, "Since you basically painted the whole thing, are you gonna go to market to see it in action?"

To be honest, I'd been so focused on the setup and hopefully seeing Kai, exactly the way that's happening right now, that I haven't given much thought to actually going to the market or not.

"'Cause if you were," she says, turning back to the design, "there's this big party some of the alumni kids throw at Marcy Park—"

"Of course he's gonna go," says a voice from behind me. It's deadly even, and I know exactly who it is without looking. My shoulders want to sag, but I don't let them. "That's who the market's for," he says. "*Bilagáana* like him, right? Look at me when I'm talking to you."

I set down my brush carefully on a corner of cardboard and stand up. I turn around, and Hos is about a foot from me, his entourage of ogres with him. He's shorter than me, but not by much, and the way he's looking at me is like I'm about an inch tall anyway. He's wearing another cutoff T-shirt and loose jeans with boots. His shoulders sport a bunch of tattoos that look Navajo that I never noticed before. He's probably no more than two years older than me, but it looks like he and I are on opposite sides of the spectrum of life.

"Right, kid?"

I'm stunned. I think adrenaline has wiped my brain. I have no idea what he's talking about. "What?" I ask.

"The market, fucknuts. That's where your kind peruses our kind. Right? Like a zoo, sort of, except we dance for you and hold out pots and beads for you?"

"I dunno, man," I stammer. "I ain't never been to the market before." The other kids have stopped working, once again, and are gathering around the fringes. Hos is on a roll.

"Let me tell you, then. It basically goes like this." He takes the stick Kai stirred the paint with and wipes it on his hands. "A bunch of Indians from all around the country paint themselves up like this and hope white people notice them and give them money." He slams my chest with his open palm and leaves a blue-and-red palm print. I back up a pace but keep my feet. "And white people like you look for great deals on authentic Indian shit for their condos and then hope that the actual Indians will just go back to wherever they came from once the big show is over."

"Leave him alone, Hosteen," Kai says. She's still sitting down, facing forward, but all that hidden shine that she had is gone once again. "It's not his fault."

Hos looks at her and shakes his head. "I know that, Sister." He crouches down until his face is right behind her head, but she still won't look at him. "It's *our* fault. For not doing something about it. For letting them walk all over us. But all that's about to end. And it's not too late for you to join us. There's still time to make your clan proud."

He stands again and turns to me. He looks at his print on my shirt and smirks. "Looks better than it did before." He moves the paint stick closer to me. "Maybe we oughta mark you up a little more, huh?" His two ogre bodyguards move to the other side of me, and now Kai is looking up at me. She looks scared. And that's the first time in this whole fracas that *I* start to get scared. Hos takes another step and raises the stick to swipe it across my face, but then I hear a beating of wings. Big wings. It sounds like somebody is shaking out a sheet. And I know what's coming, so I duck. Chaco lets out a single explosive call, and all I see is a shadow with inch-long talons swipe at Hos from behind. I can actually hear one talon strike home on his forearm. It makes a *zip* sound as it cuts him from his elbow all the way up to his hand, then Chaco is away again.

I stand up and find Hos staring at his bleeding forearm. I can already see that it'll scab but won't scar. Chaco held back, but the paint stick is basically gone. Just a nub of it remains in his hand. Some of the kids start yelling, not sure what they just saw. They're pointing at the roof of the gym, where Chaco perches with the stick in his grasp. Even at this distance he looks big. Kai stands and shields her eyes to get a better view of him, then she starts to laugh. She points at Hos's big buddies. There's a clear line of bird shit running over both of them, shoulders and heads and all. It's as if I dipped my brush in a bucket of the stuff and flung it at 'em in a big arc. All three of them start fuming. They want to be mad at me, but they can't. I didn't do anything.

"Stupid fucking bird," Hos mutters. "Must have thought the stick was food or some shit."

"Maybe," I say.

He looks at me with fire in his eyes. "Maybe? The fuck does that mean, *maybe*?"

I shrug. "It means maybe."

He looks at me sidelong for a cold ten seconds or so then turns to Kai. "Get up. Time to go. This booth is as done as it's gonna get."

I can see that Kai doesn't want to leave, but she gets up anyway and shoulders her bag. She looks at me briefly, and her eyes say *sorry*. She shoulders past Hos and his crew, and they close ranks behind her. I can't see her, but I can hear her walking away.

Hos takes one last look at Chaco, who takes this moment to let out three opportune *caws*. Hos looks to be weighing something care-fully in his mind, then he shakes his head.

"See you at the big dance, *bilagaana*. Make sure you're there." Then he winks at me.

He walks off, his bleeding arm seemingly forgotten. The rest of his crew don't even spare me a glance as they follow him. Once they're gone, all of my adrenaline dumps, and I'm instantly exhausted. I feel like I'm gonna fall asleep onto the fresh paint, but I finish the design. When the crew leader, a big senior gal, says that's a wrap and that we'll reassemble everything in Santa Fe, I clap along with everyone else then grab my backpack and go. Nobody seems to notice except for Chaco. He flies right above me.

"You all right there, boss?" he asks me, the first words he's spoken to me all day.

"Yeah," I say. "Thanks for helping me out back there."

"No prob. You know, I think you're right, man. That one is trouble. He may be wrapped up in all this. Maybe our coyote."

"And all I did was piss him off."

Suddenly I feel like an idiot. Maybe Mick was right when he said I was crazy to help out with the market crew. Nobody seemed to give a damn if I was there or not. Even Kai thought it was weird. What was the point of all that? What was I trying to do? Be an Indian? Did I think some paint and a few nails would turn me Navajo?

"It was all a waste of time, man," I say.

"You never know," Chaco replies. I can hear him coming in low. "Heads up," he says.

He backpedals above me and drops something from his claws. I snatch it out of the air and slow to a stop. It's the paint stick, half red, half blue. I can see little imprints where Kai's fingers smudged the paint. I can't stop staring at it. The paint is so bright it almost sparkles in the sun, and her fingerprints are cleanly pressed, like whorled ice crystals. Even the jagged end where it broke looks beautiful, like the splinters could tell a story. It feels heavy.

"What's that look like to you?" Chaco asks.

"A paint stick." But already I know it's not. It's more.

"See, to me that looks like a certain broken stirring stick we've been on the hunt for."

He's right. The story of my arrival at Crownrock is wrapped up in this stick. It might have been the coyote's once, before I came, but I took it back. Kai helped, and Chaco helped. Even Hos helped in his own way. I grin to think that our coyote himself might have handed me one of his warning signs.

Either way, that's two down, four to go.

20

THE WALKER

It's almost three in the morning, the night before the market, and I'm walking the soft streets of Santa Fe. They literally look soft. They're so old in places that the stones and bricks dip and crest like frozen ripples in a pond. A lot of Navajo kind of roll their eyes at Santa Fe. Part of it is because white people love it so much. Part of it is because for a while in the 1900s it was a place where the Navajo could actually live and work. Now it's a place where rich people eat and shop. I don't know a single Navajo who could afford a place in this city, so I get where they're coming from. But don't blame the city. It's old as hell. Since I died, I've gotten a lot of perspective. Forget what happened in the 1900s, try the 1500s. Or the 900s. People were here then too. You don't have that much history without also getting a little magic. You can feel it here, in the old streets, the old churches, the old hills dotted with old graves. This city is an old rock in the desert. It's been hot and cold and hot again, and it doesn't seem to care what anybody thinks. I like it. So sue me.

Usually Santa Fe is a pretty quiet city too, despite all the tourists, but not tonight. Not even at 3:00 a.m., and it certainly won't be tomorrow. Whatever creeping unease taints the rez has spread here. I know the coyote has been here too. His breath seems to hang dead in the night air. Distrust is everywhere, even between the volunteers and cops that sit at the intersections. These guys should be shootin' the shit, sneaking off to get arepas and maybe even a beer if they aren't in uniform. Every year the NNPD sends a couple lucky bastards to represent here. I was chosen one year when Chief Yokana felt particularly sorry for me about everything around Ana. It's a cakewalk. A paid vacation. But not today. Today everybody is yelling at everybody. Micromanaging things like cordons and cones that nobody really needs. Waving cars off and getting pissy whenever the booth people ask for something.

I'm trying to mark these things more than just in passing. I'm trying to look for patterns, maybe find a way to track the coyote, to be where he wants to be before he brings down the house, because I think he's gonna bring down the house. We've got a way to catch him now, if we can beat the clock, thanks to the sand painters, and thanks to Caroline, but we've got to act fast.

You should have seen her by the campfire. She was unreal in the night light of the Arroyo. I couldn't quite believe what I was seeing. Caroline, right there where Joey and I used to raise hell. Caroline, walking into the very place the NNPD tells even the Navajo to steer clear of if they can help it. I never thought I'd live to see the day an Arroyo campfire would play off the warmth of her eyes. Turns out I didn't live to see it. But what I got was the next best thing. At one point, I swear she looked for me. I was there, listening, next to the smoker (which, at the rate that guy rips cigs, I bet I'll be seeing again pretty soon), but her eyes passed right through me just as sure as my hands pass right through booth after booth after booth under the heavy moonlight.

I feel the telltale pressure drop of a Chaco arrival, like an itch in my ear. There's the pop, and then I feel the wind of his wings and the heavy weight of him as he settles on my shoulders. I relax without knowing I was ever tense. Sometimes when your fingers pass through too many things, it starts to key you up, I guess. The solid weight of Chaco feels good. Like a fat file folder of finished work. Not that I'd ever tell the ungrateful bastard.

"We got two," he says.

"No kidding?"

"Yeah, the stirring stick. It came from the school. It came around because of Grant."

I smile. That kid surprises at every turn. Here I was thinking maybe he'd give up and join a metal band. Instead he insists on enrolling at a Navajo high school and, for better or for worse, seems like he's hacking it. That can't be easy. They picked on me in high school because I was small, but even a small Navajo is still a Navajo. In the circles I ran with in high school the social scene went from the popular-jock-badass Navajo kids at the top to the skinny white boys like Grant at the bottom. What he's doing takes guts.

"I also think maybe he's right about the market," Chaco says. "Something big is gonna happen here, tomorrow night during the dances, most likely. Keep an eye on a kid everybody calls Hos." Chaco settles into the crook of my neck and gets small. He hasn't done that in years.

"That's a lead, Chaco. Why do you sound like you ate some bad Chinese?"

"I didn't believe him. I should have, but I didn't."

"Don't start moping now, right when we gotta get to work." I kind of gloat. I can't help it. Usually it's me whining and crying imaginary tears at one of my pity parties. I never get to sit at the other end of the table. He says nothing, only gets smaller.

"Look, man. The kid is fourteen. I'm sure he wasn't exactly being a good friend to you, either. His brain just got soaked in puberty. He'll even out eventually."

Chaco titters on my shoulder, which is his way of laughing. Then he gets bigger. "You'd think I'd know that after a couple thousand years. But I forget every time. Every Keeper is new for me, and I. . ."

"You care," I say. "It's a good thing. But if you're right about the dances, then we gotta bust our asses. They start in like twelve hours."

"Can we make a move on this Hosteen kid? If he's really a skin-walker, could the Circle jump him right now and take the bead?"

I shake my head. "The coyote is too tricky for that. If we make a move and it senses us coming, it could jump from Hosteen, maybe change up its plan totally, and then we've got what cops call an unknown. Unknowns are dangerous. Especially with this thing."

We walk down Canyon Road toward St. Francis Cathedral, which is this big church made out of stone that takes on a copper color at night. The cathedral marks the west boundary of Santa Fe Plaza, which is normally a big open square where people hang out and eat or drink around the obelisk statue at the center. A circle stage has been constructed around the center statue. It's where the dances will be performed. Beyond the viewing area, the entire square is cross-hatched with rows of booths like mini city blocks on a grid. The booths spill out into adjacent streets in every direction. I see twenty or thirty people still setting up. The real procrastinators.

Then again, you could say the same about me right now. I should be hunting down artifacts of my own, I should be running around like a chicken with its head cut off, but instead I have this strange calm. Like I used to get in the car with Ninepoint when we'd quickly sketch out our approach to bringing in whomever we were after. I got some ideas that I want to run by Chaco first. I want to sketch out my approach like I used to.

"Man oh man," Chaco says, surveying the scene. "This is gonna be a beehive."

"The booths seem to go on forever this year. There's a great park at the edge of all this mess. You got a second to check it out?"

Chaco nods, and we set out, walking through the honeycombed streets without turning a single head.

The walk from the plaza to Marcy Park is a pleasant one. I take the uphill approach, through the old neighborhoods, every one of them the same type of covenant-controlled adobe and wood pillared construction. You get the sense that you've walked back in time, especially when you come across the houses that were built well before the covenant came around. The original adobe, patched and repatched, and still strong.

"I've been thinking about this bone bead," I say. "I don't think we're gonna be able to beat the coyote unless we destroy it. It moves too fast. It jumps from person to person. It's made of chaos, so there's no way we can reason with it. And if we do manage to trap it, it's gonna be mad as hell."

Chaco cocks his head. "I think you're right. But we gotta tread carefully. No doubt this bone bead is a super powerful object. Think of it as a chaos bell."

"Then you're saying we shouldn't destroy it?"

Chaco does this *tiktiktik* thing with his throat that I've learned is the same as when humans say, "Well, hold on just a second, now. . ."

"From what you said you saw in that cavern with the black pearl, I got a hunch that the pearl uses chaos souls to form the bead. The coyote has a place at the center of that pearl, and at the center of the coyote is the bead. So if I'm right, and we can fix all this by destroying the bead, the souls will just go back to making another bead for the coyote, only the coyote will be back where it's supposed to be. No harm, no foul."

"And if you're wrong?"

"Hellfire and brimstone. Take your biggest pile of shit and throw it right at the biggest fan you've got. Then throw in a bunch of crow feathers for giggles."

"I'm serious, bird."

"So am I. But it's no worse than what will happen if the coyote roams free. Either way, the river is out of whack, man. For all I know, beyond the veil is already a huge cluster. This bastard has been on a joyride from hell, not doing his *job* for *five years*."

Chaco hates when people don't do their jobs. That's what happens when you diligently do yours for a couple millennia.

We crest the hill and come up on Marcy Park from on high. It looks like a concert is being set up here. Tents and merchandise booths flank a big stage at the far end of a wide grass field. A handful of technicians are turtling around, checking stage equipment and lighting.

The two of us are quiet for a moment, taking in that strange stillness that can fall over a place in the twilight hours before it gets jammed with people.

"What happens when the bead is destroyed?" I ask quietly. "I mean, I imagine that it's more than just a little crack of breaking bone."

"I'd imagine so, yeah."

"You don't know, do you?"

"I'm in new territory here, brother. Right along with you. I do know that no anchor object like that has ever been broken in living memory."

I suspect Chaco knows more than he's telling me. I can sense it in the way he's looking away from me, focusing on the park below. But that's OK, because I have some thoughts of my own about what happens when one of these things breaks, and I want to keep them to myself for a bit too.

"We're still a ways away from breaking the thing, Walker," Chaco says evenly. "We need to catch it first. We've got two of the coyote's artifacts. We're four short."

"Three," I say.

Chaco looks at me, his bird brow raised.

"We're three short. I think I know where one of them is. The broken pot. But it's not in any place any of the five of us can reach it."

"So what do we do?"

"I got an idea. The four of you keep at it. It's about time I visited my old buddy Joey."

21

CAROLINE ADAMS

It's just before dawn on Saturday, the kickoff for the market. We've got twelve hours before the dances begin. Usually my 3:00 a.m. insomnia centers on obsessing over what passes for my love life. This time I've been up all night thinking about a whisk broom.

I'm not going to lie to you, I had to look online even to see what a whisk broom is. Turns out it's a little hand-held straw broom. Something old farm women dressed in babushkas would use to dust out their cook fires. I had an absurd urge just to buy one, right then. Enter my credit card information, pay for same-day shipping. Voilà. An individually packaged whisk broom, brought to my door. But I get the feeling that's not what the sand painters meant when they said the object is about the journey. A journey from a warehouse in Albuquerque to an RV park mail room doesn't have an ounce of spiritual weight to it, no matter how expedited.

None of us has slept. There's no time for sleep anymore. Not right now. Grant is already at Crownrock High with the setup crew, packing up for their trip to Santa Fe on a school bus. He was as chipper as he usually is, which is to say not at all, but at least his eyes were open. I have that gritty feeling that I used to get doing night shift at ABQ General. The one where it feels like the sandman comes by to knock you into sweet oblivion, except you have to tell him that no, in fact, you won't be sleeping tonight because you have to do rounds on a thirty-six-bed floor, but the sandman doesn't take that too well—he's the jealous type—so instead of sprinkling his dust on your forehead he chucks the whole bag right at your face. It fuzzes up your teeth and gets behind your eyes, and I know it won't be going away any time soon, so I put a pot of coffee on our little stove and get down to more thinking.

I'm halfway through my second cup when it occurs to me that Owen and I haven't had sex in a month. Don't ask me why this hits me out of the blue. It certainly has nothing to do with whisk brooms, but just like that I'm very disappointed in myself. I look out of the back window of the boat, where Owen is standing and watching the sunrise. He's been walking back and forth, checking odds and ends on the hitch and around the outside of the RV without actually doing anything. That's how he thinks. I can see it on him: he's completely invested in this, every ounce of his smoke is wrapped up in it, and I can't believe I haven't noticed the change in him before now.

In a way, he looks the same as he always did on the floor. He's driven, totally focused on the problem at hand, and you'd think that would be a good thing, but I also know that when he was that way on the floor—blind to everything else but the patients he was tasked with getting healthy again—it was a willful blindness. He told me so. He told me that work was the only thing that could take his mind off me.

I search the smoke sifting off him in the early-morning light in slow, thick waves, and I can see it. I can see that longing, but it's tamped down. Packed under. He's doing it again. He's swapped one distraction for another. He's doing everything he can not to think about me, about us, about loving me the way that he does, and it's working. But it's also blocking him, plugging up his soul. The colors I see on him now aren't the true colors I know. His blue isn't as blue. Sure, there's a lot of it—he's throwing himself into this search with everything he's got—but it isn't as strong. And it makes me feel like garbage.

I set my coffee down and walk outside. He sees me coming and musters a heartbreaking smile. His hair, normally meticulously combed and evenly parted, is tufted here and there where it looks like he's been running his hands through it again and again. He's frustrated and stumped.

"I know I'm missing something with that damn broken cane." He lets his hands drop to his sides. "It's right there, on the tip of my brain, but I can't..."

I don't even say anything. I just take one hand and pull him gently toward the boat. He looks confused at first, then I see him understand, and a few things cross his smoke. At first he's incredibly hungry for me, in every way. I don't do this type of stuff. I'm not one of those girls that does this, grabs a guy by the hand and whispers something into his ear and takes him away to the bedroom on a whim. I'm a planner. Even when it comes to sex. I think of it in terms of time frames and schedules and recommended amounts. I know it's not romantic in the movie-star sense, but then again, I find weird things romantic. Opposite things. Things like the fact that there's no physical way Ben and I could ever be together, but sometimes I can still feel him reach for me. Things like I'm very probably ruined emotionally by what I've seen and done, but Owen still stays with me, by my side, and he loves me so fiercely he's afraid to let it show because he thinks it'll scare me. And it does. And I sort of like it.

The second thing I see in Owen's smoke is hesitation, and he pulls back gently.

"Caroline," he says, "I don't want this. I can't keep doing this."

He's not lying, not exactly, but his color tells me more of what he's thinking than his brain can right now. He does want this, and he can keep doing this, but it's taken him a long time to get right with living with half of my heart, and when we do things like this and I lose myself and he does too, there are a few seconds of eternity where I'm his completely. It's a beautiful lie that our bodies speak to each other.

And it's a lie we both need right now. I just need to let him know this without hurting more of him than I already do every day.

"I don't know why I can't move on from him, Owen. I'm split in half, and I don't know how to fix it. I wish I could tell you how awful I feel. I wish you could see it on me like I see it on you. You've been walking around with half of a companion. Half of a friend too. And I have no right to ask you to see it my way, but if you could, just think about what it's like to *be* half there. To live life with part of yourself missing. You help me. You shoulder some of that loss for me. Your heart is so huge, it makes up for what I'm missing. Not all of it, but enough to make it OK for a while. So I know it may not be right, or healthy, or whatever, but I'm just gonna say it: I need this. From you."

It works. I can see it immediately. Owen likes to know he's needed. Just like me. Just like everybody. He lets me take his hand again and follows me inside. We lock the little door and pull down the little blinds and clear off our little bed. We undress, and he hangs his shirt in the closet to keep it off the ground and lays his socks over his shoes, right to right, left to left. He folds his slacks at the crease and lays them over the pull-out dressing table. His little routine always makes me smile. I have one too: shorts folded under shirt, folded under bra, all set on my tiny nightstand, and panties off and in the hamper. No socks or shoes for me. I haven't worn shoes since May. Just flip flops. We do this in comfortable silence, like we have ever since that first time years ago, when it was a hilariously awkward dance around this box of a bedroom— but one that I had planned down to the minute while Grant was off getting groceries. All went according to plan, of course. I think you could actually hear the bubble of sexual tension pop that time. It was long overdue.

Owen gets in bed and makes a place for me under his arm, and I get in bed and fit there, and that's how it starts. We know each other now. I could sketch the dimple in his shoulder from the bullet he took for me, entry and exit. I know it by heart. I've felt it with my hand and with my arm and with my mouth. I also know he can fit the entire back of my head in the long palm of his hand. We know where we fit with each other, and that is exactly what we both need right now, when we don't know where we fit with everything else. We forget all that. All the to-dos, the artifacts, the ticking time bomb at the market, it's all blown from our minds for about twenty minutes on a scorching summer morning in the Navajo desert.

Afterward, Owen's smoke sifts peacefully down and around him, pooling in that teacup spot at the base of his neck, and it matches the blue of his eyes again. He's staring at the ceiling but seeing through it. It's like he's been abraded of something, scrubbed clean, which is why he says: "It's not the cane."

"What is it, then?"

"It's the exercises. Lelah, the secretary at CHC, she gave me the PT sheet I gave her with the donated walker, years ago. She didn't need the exercises anymore. Her pain was gone."

I sit up on one elbow. Now I'm really confused.

"It's been staring me in the face for days now. That was my journey, right there. That program was the first walk I took with the Navajo, with the CHC. The coyote tried to take it from me. I took it back."

Owen gets up and goes over to his nightstand, opens it up, and starts pulling things out. He shakes his head, moves over to the built-in table, lifts a stack of wiring instructions for the trailer, then lifts my magazines and rifles through all the pages. He shakes his head again. I can see him thinking for a minute before he goes over to his little closet and flips through it to find the slacks he wore that day. He frisks his pockets. Nothing. He turns around with his hands on his naked hips.

"It's in Chief Yokana's car," Owen says heavily. "I left it in his damn car."

He picks up his watch and clicks it over his wrist. He checks the time and frowns. I know what he's thinking. We're in the final hours now. I slide out of bed, walk over to my little pile of clothes, and get dressed. He does the same, careful to put the correct socks on the correct feet. I smile again, even with the seconds on the clock hammering home.

"Let's go find him, then," I say. He looks up at me and nods, and I feel like something that was coming loose between us is tied tightly again. We reach underneath our pillows for our totem pouches, and as soon as I grab mine it's like I'm stunned. It feels heavier, richer, like it's made of velvet and it's carrying thousands of diamonds instead of an ancient lump of turquoise fashioned into a crow. Owen has already pocketed his and is moving to the door, but he pauses when he sees me.

"Something wrong?"

I open up the pouch and pour it out on the bed, expecting something more than the crow, expecting that stream of diamonds to come pouring out, but it's just my totem, tumbling onto the bed. Solid as ever. I see the irregular notches in its wings, the sharp point of its searching beak. Its head, slightly turned, mid-flight, as always. And I realize it isn't the crow totem that shocked me this time. It's the pouch I'm still holding in my hand.

"What's up?" Owen asks, moving over to me now. He relaxes when he sees my totem, safe and whole.

I hold the pouch out to him. "Take it and tell me I'm not crazy. Touch it."

He takes it, and his eyes widen. He pulls his own pouch out of his pocket and squints at both, weighing them up and down in his hand.

"Is this the same one I gave you?" he asks. "It definitely feels different from mine. It's like it's in high def or something."

"It's the same old pouch."

"But I picked up both of them in that truck stop in Alamosa. They were a pair." He tosses mine back over to me. I catch it, and I'm struck again by how soft and full it feels. Like it's woven silk, when I know it's just old leather. Then I get it. It's not just old leather. It never was. It's more.

"You gave it to me," I say. "It's because you gave it to me. Only I never realized it until now."

"That I gave it to you?"

"No, what it meant. It's about the journey, right? That's what the sand painters said. When we got those crows and you said you wanted to come with me, it was because you wanted me then. Just me. But when you gave me the bag, and you got the same, it was because you wanted to do all of this *with* me. You weren't just there for me, you were there alongside me. Both of us were born into this new life together."

I see it dawn on him. "The birth bag," he says.

I blow out a breath, and a little bit of the weight that is pressing on me is lifted. "Thank God. I thought that one was gonna be really gross."

22

THE WALKER

Joey lives in an old conversion van just like his grandfather did at the Arroyo. Matter of fact, it's his gramp's van. After Joey drove off the rez that day when the tribal council turned their backs on him, and I did too, he kept going north, almost like he wanted to drive himself off the map altogether. I often picture him as he must have been then. Blinded by sadness and pain but refusing to give up until he made things right for my family. He was on a cannonball run, fleeing some demons, chasing others down. He must have been a hell of a sight.

For some reason he hit the brakes in Montana, just south of the Canadian border. He was running from the agents then, and the cops, so a border run was risky. He needed a place to lay low and figure things out, so he rolled his van into Hamm, a speck of a town fifty miles west of I-25 in the middle of the plains. He pulled up under an abandoned carport that was once attached to a tiny house, but the house collapsed who the hell knows how long ago, certainly well before he and I were racing around the rez together.

He parked the van, and it promptly died. And that's where it still sits to this day, over a decade later. Joey doesn't like to let anyone in the Circle know about it, but that's where he still lives most of the time. He might call it home, if he called any place home. But he doesn't call any place home anymore, and that's the problem.

Hamm, Montana, is one of those little towns you don't even catch a whiff of when you're cruising by. There are small towns—the kind where you might stop to gas up or grab a coffee to keep you going— and then there are *really* small towns. The kind that have four or five businesses on half a block, and that's Main Street. The kind that have one crossroad and no real trees and every single building is a flat, single-story square. And if you step back a few paces, you can take in the whole of the town in one look, underneath an enormous open sky that seems twice as big for how small everything else is. There are only ever a handful of people there, and they come and go all the time. A guy living out of his van, even a guy who looks a little rough and haunted like Joey, can do whatever the hell he pleases so long as he doesn't bother anybody, and Joey never does, because all Joey does is work on phasing.

Joey was the type of guy who did anything to get out of work back in the day. He and I were always looking for corners to cut, ways to slip away and do our own thing, which usually involved drinking beers or smoking cigarettes or throwing things at other things to see what happened. If you'd told me all those years ago that Joey would devote all of his time to studying and practice, I'd have laughed you out of the rez. It just wasn't him. Then again, he probably thought the same thing when he heard I became a cop. Sometimes shit doesn't go the way you think. People change.

His work with the crow totem damn near killed him. It would have killed him at first, the way he just dived into the thin space and held the phase as long as he could, but he took so many drugs that his body stopped rebelling like it should. He overrode his instincts with chemicals. Soon he was able to spend hours in the thin space, then days. He started meditating in the thin space. I watched him as he sat in one place, cross-legged, crow in hand, until I thought he'd blow away into the cold, sepia dust that the thin place seems made of. But he never blew away.

Joey learned to do what the agents did, which was essentially to live in the thin place. Of course, the agents were driven by our coyote at the time. They had a connection with him through the book that I think was the only reason they were kept alive. Joey had drugs. Still, he was able to inhabit the place for long stretches of time, test what it had to offer. He came out of his meditations and trances with a connection to the world beyond that I haven't seen in anybody else, except maybe Caroline. That, and a raging pill habit.

I've watched Joey a long time. For a while I thought the pills would get him. That I'd get the tug and show up at his van and find him conked out against the door in a puddle of his own vomit. One time, about two years after I died, I checked in on him and saw him down one pill after another for about three hours, then he snorted one for good measure, and I just lost it. I screamed my lungs out at him. Forget that he and I are on separate planes and that nobody on earth could hear me. I yelled and I yelled at him about everything. Got it all off my chest, saying stuff like how Caroline and Owen needed him, and even pulling out the big trump cards like how Ana would be disappointed in him and how his own grandfather would turn his back on him if he saw him right now. About fifteen minutes into my tirade, he said, "I'm done."

That's when I figured out that he could sense me.

He dumped all his pills, locked himself inside his van with a jug of water and a tin of jerky, and got clean over a hellacious forty-eight hours in which I spent every free second I had next to him. I can't touch him, of course, or hold a conversation with him. Nothing like that. But all the time Joey spent in the thin place changed him just like it changes everybody, and it made him more aware of me. He knew I was with him in the van over those two days. At the end of it he emerged sweaty and stinking into this lucidity that still allowed him to walk the thin place but kept him from killing himself with pills, and he thanked me.

So Joey knows when I'm there. Which is good, because I owe him something, and it's time I gave it to him.

When Gam was murdered, she essentially had three things to her name: her Singer's bag, the bell, and her crow totem, which she kept in a little bone box. The bell was never mine to have, and it found its next owner all on its own. As for the Singer's bag, well, singing was Gam's talent. I never had the will or the brains to get the chants and the ceremonies right, plus, each Singer's bag is personalized, filled with things that have a powerful connection to the individual Singer. With her gone, it became just a bag of things. Ninepoint stole her crow totem, and then the agents stole it from him, but I got it back and gave it to Caroline at the same time I gave Owen the gambler's totem. That leaves the bone box.

The bone box is a holder of things. Important things. Much like a pot. And it just so happened to break when Ninepoint ransacked it. It has the story of that night wrapped up into it, and that night means so much. I keep thinking about how the coyote was there, at my front door, when I came back. In a way, when I left the rez, the coyote moved in and took that box. I know in my heart that the bone box is our broken pot, and it's time I took it back. The problem is, I can't get to it.

When I walk into the lean-to I see the van door is closed and locked and the windows are rolled up, but it's basically hotboxed: the windows are white with smoke, and there's a big hole cut in the top where Joey rigged up an exit pipe. Good thing there's nobody around here for acres in either direction, because I bet it reeks of piñon smoke, and probably a few other things too, of the more hallucinogenic sort. He's essentially created a makeshift hogan out of his grandpa's old conversion van. The sliding door is even facing east, now that I notice it. I gotta admit, I'm impressed. I walk inside.

Joey's head, which had been resting peacefully on the back of the inside wall, straightens as soon as I take a second step inside the van, which is roomier than you'd think.

"Hi, Joey," I say. "Nice setup you have here."

He doesn't answer, of course. Like I said, our connection isn't like that, but he does look everywhere with his eyes for a bit before taking a deep breath of whatever mixture he's thrown in this little coffee can he has smoldering on a piece of corrugated metal siding in the middle of the floor.

"Walker," he whispers. "*Ya at eeh.*"

I shake my head. "Will you cut it with the Walker crap? I'm Ben. Just Ben."

No answer, of course. Which is going to present a problem, because while I know that the bone box is our broken pot, I also know Joey has to deliver it to Owen and Caroline, which is hard for two reasons. First, the bone box is still at the rez. Second, Joey won't go back to the rez. He's still abiding by his banishment. Part of him still thinks he was thrown from the Navajo Way, even after all that came to light. Even though we know he had nothing to do with Ana's disappearance.

The artifacts are about the journey, and Joey needs to make the journey back to his home. His real home. That's how the bone box becomes the broken pot. But it's not like I can tell him that. He can't hear me. I've tried so many times to get anyone to hear me. It's never gonna happen. There are rules.

Joey looks troubled. His eyeballs dart around under his lids like he's having a bad dream, but I can't shake him out of it. Joey was always sensitive, even before he hazed himself in the thin place, so it would make sense that he's feeling the crush of the coyote here too. If the balance of the river is off, the balance of the living world is off as well. Soon enough, even Hamm, Montana, will feel it.

When Ana was having bad dreams, I'd tell her stories. You can't go to bed again right after a nightmare. You'll fall right back into it if you do, so you have to switch things up. Get a glass of water, go pee, or in the case of Ana and me, tell each other stories. But I can't just tell stories here, can I? Joey can't hear me. Unless, of course, he doesn't need to hear me. Not my words, anyway. He's pretty far under right now. You never know what kinds of things can cross over during a sweat. I have firsthand experience. I saw Ana during one.

So I sit back in the smoke and tell him stories. Just like I used to with Ana. Just like Joey and I used to as well, back around the campfires we'd make in my backyard.

"Remember that one time we made a big fire out back of my place, in the pit there by the rocks, and we tried to jump it?

Remember how dumb we were?" I say, and I laugh out loud. That was a huge fire. The neighbors who had the other half of our duplex were not too happy with us, but then again, they never were.

"And then Ana came out and saw us and said she was gonna jump it too, and she ran for it, but you caught her up just in time and swung her up on your shoulders instead? Remember that?"

I remember. That's a big memory. A special one that I almost don't want to think about too much because I'm afraid I'll change it by how badly I want to be back there again. Like I'll make up things that weren't there because I want more from it. But it's now or never.

"We were all whooping around that fire, you, me, and Ana on your shoulders. Then we convinced Ana to go sneak us some of Dad's beer. Of course she would have done anything for you, bro. So she ran off, but she didn't know what she was doing, remember? She came back with Gam's knitting. How the hell do you get *knitting* out of *beer*? That crazy girl."

She came back so proudly with Gam's knitting that we didn't have the heart to tell her it wasn't remotely what we asked for. We cracked up, and she cracked up along with us, which always used to worry me because she had a weak heart, even then. We all just laughed until we were lying on the grass and the fire was soaring above us.

"So you say, 'Listen, man. I'm not getting your Gam pissed off at me. She's a big deal. We gotta sneak this shit back.' And you were right, but turns out Gam was watching TV right outside her room, so we try to send in Ana again, but now she's having none of it when we tell her to put it back."

Joey's eyes are still closed, but they aren't flitting as much anymore. And is that a smile on his lips? Maybe a ghost of a smile?

"It was up to us, remember? So we had Ana go in and do a little song and dance in front of Gam to distract her and then you and I snuck into her room. You almost lost it when you saw how Gam was watching Ana, like *what the hell is this child doing now.*"

Is that a nod? No, no nod. Just his chin falling gently to rest on his chest. The makeshift sweat brazier he rigged up here is slowly dying out. Which is good. I look out of the foggy window of his van, and I see that the sun is past high noon already. Montana time is New Mexico time. And we're running out of both.

"We did it, though. We snuck in, on our bellies, thinking we were Hoskininni sneaking around in the valley or some shit like that. Trying to ambush the white man. But you thought her knitting went up on her shelf, remember? Up high. So you put it up there at first, and I kept whispering to you that it's supposed to go in the basket by her bed, but you were up there and you weren't listening because you were staring at that box. Remember that box, Joey?"

Somehow I think that Joey remembers that box. Maybe he's even having some sort of vision of that box. Maybe in his vision it's half box, half pot.

"I didn't know what that was, man. Not then. I forgot about it five minutes later. But I bet you didn't. You always had a head for this type of shit. All of it. The world I live in now. The thing I am. I can't tell you how many times I thought you'd be better at this than I am. I think a lot of people would be better than I am. But at the end of the day, I'm on this side of things, and you're on that side of things, and hell if I know if any of this is even getting through to you. It shouldn't be. Because there are rules, and the rules say it shouldn't be."

I can see the sun moving down the line. I can feel the gathering pressure of the coyote. Suddenly all this seems like grasping at straws. We're chasing after legends when there's a killer at the doorstep. But then Joey laughs. I snap up and watch him carefully. He's laughing and nodding. The way he did when he had Ana on his back and we were dancing.

"I need you to get that box, Joey," I say. He quiets, and his face slackens again. I don't know if he's listening or if his mind is on some other faraway fantasy, but it's getting late.

"It's on the rez, man. The NNPD took it to bag and tag it as evidence in a case they never closed, just shuffled off once I disappeared, and Ninepoint disappeared, and the agents disappeared. It's in the evidence room."

I get up and move over to Joey so I'm right by his ear.

"Joey, you gotta get that box, and you gotta take it to the hogan today. Before five. I know you're afraid of the rez. You don't want to go back there, but you gotta think about Ana. About me. About your home there. What you did for my family. . . nobody I know is a better Navajo than you. Please, man. Do this for all of us."

He's very still now. I want to say more, want to plead more, maybe scream in his ear just in case louder is better, but I get a tug. The job never waits. I open up the map and step through and do what I need to do, which is escort a very polite Swedish guy through the veil. He puts up no fuss. Doesn't even seem scared. Of the two of us, I bet I'm the one that looks scared. I'm checking the position of the sun, making mental calculations in my head as our time ticks away from us.

When I get back to Joey's van and step inside again, the air is clear, the coffee can is clean, and Joey is gone.

23

GRANT ROMER

This whole Native Market thing is nuts. I've never seen so many people in one place before. We left for Santa Fe early, took the school bus all the way up with a rickety trailer attached that held the parts of our booth, but when we get here the place is already crowded. People are milling about on the back streets, and all the cafes are jammed. They put us in a section of booths a little ways off the main plaza, where the local schools are all set up, and we get to work.

Chaco hops from terrace to terrace, watching me, watching the crowds. He finally agreed that it's OK that I'm even here. With Owen and Caroline tracking down the rest of the artifacts then heading to the hogan, it makes sense that somebody actually shows up where we all think the coyote is going to do work.

Once the booth is up and ready, I retreat into the crowd. None of the art is mine, of course, and I don't really feel up to explaining the indigenous programs of the high school I've been at for a little over a week to potential donors, so it makes sense, but more than that I sort of get the feeling that people want to see Navajo kids at the Navajo high school booth. The bottom line is this is a fundraiser. They're showing art, yeah, but also trying to drum up money and community buy-in, and I'm not the type of kid that tourists think of when they think of a high school on the rez.

You'd think this might piss me off. It doesn't. I knew what I was getting into when I suggested we head out this way in the first place way back when we got chased out of Pueblo by the guy with the itch. It's guys like Mick who can't seem to get over it, which is why I let out a bit of a groan when I see him milling through the crowd around ten in the morning, heading toward our booth. He sees me, and his eyes light up. He worms his way to where I stand under the shade of a wooden awning, my back against stucco that's already getting hot. It's a bluebird New Mexico day, and the sun shines so bright already you'd think it was plunked right there on the hills just to the west.

"What's up?" he says, not quite looking at me. He turns his back to the wall too and wipes his hands nervously up and down his shorts.

"I thought you said this place sucks," I say.

He's bobbing his head, watching the crowd intently. "Somethin' to do. You see any weird shit yet?"

"Naw, man. Looks to me like everybody is having a decent time."

That isn't exactly true. I've seen some fights over prices, I've seen a lot of shoving, and I've heard a lot of grumbling, but that's the coyote effect. I can see his greasy steps here already. Mostly walking around the big statue at the center of the plaza, almost like he was doing some sort of pilgrimage or something. There's even some tracks by our booth. But all I've seen so far are the tracks, never the thing making them. This is a prime place to pass that bead around, but I'm not about to get into all this with Mick. The guy gets on my nerves. I don't like how he assumes I'm his friend.

"C'mon, man," Mick says, pushing off the wall. "They're already pre-gaming at the house party off Marcy Park. I got some stuff in my trunk. Come check it out."

I look at my watch. "It's eleven in the morning, man."

"It's the kickoff party. Tradition and all that."

"You go ahead. I gotta make sure they got what they need here until the afternoon crew comes."

Mick shakes his head, jams his hands in his pockets. "Whatever," he says, then he slinks off. He doesn't go far, though. Already a crowd has started to gather around the obelisk statue where the plaza stage is. I can just see the edge of it from where our booth stands. Kai finishes talking to some old couple who claim to be alumni and comes my way to catch a look. I've been carefully trying to bump into her all morning, but she was always busy, either with her friends or chatting to someone who stopped by the booth. Now she swoops in where Mick left. A pretty damn good trade, I'd say, although she does look uneasy.

"You all right?" I ask. I give her my best Clint Eastwood squint and hope she doesn't see how much the sun is making my forehead sweat. Someone is talking into the microphone. The sound is mashed with the crowd noise, so I can't quite make it out. I hear scattered applause.

"You seen my brother?" she asks.

"To be honest, I've kind of been on the lookout to avoid him. But no."

She swallows hard. "Don't take it personally. It's not you he has a problem with. It's *all* of you." She gestures around me, at the scene just behind me of rows and rows of white people wearing sunhats and running shoes, scurrying toward the stage.

"Should that make me feel better?" I ask.

"I guess not." She's still looking for Hos. She's distracted, biting down gently on the dark pink of her lower lip.

"C'mon," she says. "Let's go check it out. We'll stay back from all the mess of people."

She could have asked if I wanted to go straight into the black pearl of chaos itself just then, and I probably woulda said the same thing: "All right."

She actually takes my hand and weaves her way through the crowd, around the booths. Our grip sweats, but she doesn't let go. I *was* looking for Hos because I think he may have a bead in his mouth, but now I'm looking for him because if he sees his little sister holding my hand, I think he'll kick my ass, coyote or not. We skirt the plaza, moving along the outer square until we reach the big cathedral, and she hops up on a low brick wall. She drops my hand and uses both of hers to shade her eyes. She pans the crowd slowly, breathing fast.

On stage, four Navajo women dressed in long blue gowns and leather moccasins are holding up what look like thatched shields in the shadow of the statue. One drummer at the edge of the stage starts banging out a quick-time rhythm. The women bob on the balls of their feet then start to gently hop forward and back in four distinct lines as the drummer chants in a rolling rhythm.

"It's the Basket Dance," Kai says. She's still nervous about something, but I hear a note of pride in her voice. "That's Navajo. We're kicking off the dance competition."

The women are mesmerizing. They do everything twice. Move up, move back. Circle right, circle left. Lift up the baskets, lower them down. It's like they're writing a poem in dance then erasing it again. They walk off stage just as they came on, but the air around them is somehow cleaner.

Kai feels it too, the brief calm that follows the dance as the Navajo walk off and another tribe sets up in the wings. People are feeling the way this place should be, if it weren't for the trail of the coyote. I look over at Kai and find her smiling at me.

"Looks like Hosteen and his buddies decided not to come," she says. "And right about now the afternoon crew is taking over the booth. How about you and I head over to the Marcy Park party? I bet it's ramping up."

Chaco sits above us on a worn stone eave of the church, his head just visible if you were to look up from the square. He ticks his ears downward, the way other crows might listen for worms in the ground. I know what he's trying to figure out. There's relief in Kai's voice—whatever she thought Hos was going to do, maybe he isn't going to do it after all. Maybe that was his window, when his people were on stage, and he missed it. But Chaco doesn't buy it, and I don't either.

"We ain't out of the woods yet, chief," Chaco says to me. "No matter how pretty Kai smiles."

Already whatever brief calm the Basket Dance settled upon the crowd is unraveling. The coyote still prowls these parts. Waiting. I can feel it.

Kai takes my nod as agreement, so she grabs my hand and hops down from the wall. She looks back at me and smiles. The spark is back, but I feel like the air is heavier than ever. Still, it is one hell of a smile she's got. I can't do anything but let her lead me wherever she wants to go.

24

OWEN BENNET

We've got an hour until we're supposed to be at the hogan. Grant is in the thick of coyote country in Santa Fe, and Caroline and I are about to break into the NNPD chief of police's car.

The first place we tried was the NNPD main office in Chaco City. We asked for Yokana at the desk and were told he wasn't there. Caroline pressed, in her unique way. Soon enough she had the secretaries up front laughing and chatting away like they were all best friends. We learned Yokana was actually dealing with something at CHC, so off we went. And here we are, staring at his old Ford Explorer, parked in the same spot in the CHC parking lot as it was when we both first visited.

I don't think I need to tell you that I have no experience breaking and entering. It's not really my cup of tea. Once, back when I was a resident working myself blind and prone to all sorts of brain farts, I was trying to warm up my old box of a Subaru for the drive to work in the dead of February, and I locked the keys in the car while it was running. I fiddled around with a clothes hanger for an hour as if I knew what I was doing, praying the neighbors weren't watching, before I gave up and called a locksmith. Still, I know the basic idea, and I did manage to swipe a wire hanger from the coat rack at the CHC without anyone noticing, so here we go.

I take two deep breaths, step out from behind a docked service truck, and walk slowly and evenly to the SUV. Caroline follows behind. She keeps a lookout while I try to worm the hook end in and through the upper window like a blind man trying to thread a sewing needle. I've got my tongue out and everything, wincing at every scrape, until Caroline says, "It's open."

I slowly pull my hanger out then simply open the passenger-side door. Of course it's open. Why would the chief of police lock his car? What lunatic would try to break in to the chief of police's car?

I pop my head in. I left the tattered paper in the cup holder sometime during the car ride, but it's gone now. The car is as clean as it ever was. Same brushed cloth seats, same mud-mats devoid of mud, same baking smell of trapped desert heat. Nothing else. I pop open the glove compartment. It has the owner's manual, a first aid kit, a wind-up flashlight, and his registration in a plastic sleeve. That's it. I'm thinking that perhaps he threw it in the back, or it was blown back there if he was cruising the service roads with the windows down, but as I'm moving to open the back right door, Caroline whispers again.

"He's coming."

"Really? Shit. How long?"

"Whoops, he sees us."

I turn around in time to find Sani Yokana and another policeman I don't recognize watching us from across the lot. Thank God I closed the passenger door. There's a chance he thinks we're just hanging around his car for some reason I can't imagine, but as he starts walking again I see in his face that chance is pretty slim. He knows what we were doing. It's obvious in the way he takes off his sunglasses. Thankfully, for us, I also see he has bigger problems. Between him and the other officer stands Tim Bentley, the mortician, looking very out of sorts. His hair and clothes are disheveled. He seems to be missing a shoe. His face is scruffy. They're not escorting him, not exactly, but they're very clearly keeping him between them as they approach us.

"Something I can help you with, Dr. Bennet?" Yokana asks, glancing at me then at Caroline. The lines in his face seem a hair more dug out even than when I saw him last. A notepad sags in his breast pocket, his shirt is tucked in, and his jeans are still clean, but they look two- or three-day clean, not one-day clean. He's wearing his gun this time too. It's hooked to his belt next to the badge and the buckle.

"Dr. Bennet?" Bentley is squinting at me, slack jawed. "When did you get to town?"

Yokana and I exchange a knowing glance. Yokana's face darkens further.

"Can you take me away from here, Owen?" Bentley asks. He scratches violently at the side of his face and then rubs his head like he's clearing it of sand. "I don't feel right, you know?"

"We're gonna get you out of here, Dr. Bentley," the other officer says, gently holding on to his shoulder.

"Where do you want to go, Tim?" I ask.

He shrugs hugely, lets out a big *harrumpf*. He tries to scratch at his face again, but the officer prevents him. He doesn't seem to notice or care.

"Anywhere. I just need to walk. I've got these thoughts. These terrible pictures in my head. They itch. My brain itches."

Caroline steps in. "Does he have anything in his mouth?" she asks point blank.

Yokana shakes his head. "He was causing a scene in the morgue. His assistant said he tried to drink formaldehyde and swallow some tools, saying he had to clean his brain. We checked his mouth to make sure he wasn't hiding anything else."

"I'm gonna sit him in the car, chief," the officer says. "Before he gets really out of hand."

Yokana nods, and the officer leads Bentley away to his squad car two spots down. Bentley drags his feet, and he seems unsteady. He keeps looking at the desert to our right and reaching for it.

"We've seen a lot of cases like this recently," Yokana says, watching him along with us. "People seem disoriented. My first thought was severe dehydration, but the few we've checked out are fine. Physically, at least."

Yokana turns back to us. "He didn't remember our first visit at all."

"I think he had. . . some type of fever then." I'm trying to think of the best way to phrase this so that I sound like a doctor and not a lunatic. Bentley doesn't have the bead in his mouth any longer, but the hangover seems to linger, and it looks awful.

"The fever broke, but he's going to be very disoriented for a time. Depending on how long he was ill."

"A fever, huh."

"Something like that, yes."

I'm an awful liar, but Yokana doesn't call me on it. Instead he reaches in his pocket and hands me a tattered sheet of white paper. My gift from Lelah. Her journey from hobbled to healthy is wrapped up within it, and my journey is too.

"I was gonna throw this away, but when I grabbed it I sort of just held on to it. Not sure I can say why. Seemed like something I should get back to you. I suspect that's what you were looking for in my car?"

Caroline clears her throat. "Sorry about that. We needed the paper. You're right. It's more important than it looks. Also, is there any chance you might have stumbled across a broom that feels equally important? A little broom?"

"A broom?"

"Yeah, a little broom." She holds her hands out a foot apart. "About yea big?"

"No, can't say I have," he says, his tone uninterpretable. Maybe droll, maybe sarcastic, but definitely honest. His phone rings in his pocket, and he picks it up, looks at it, then shakes his head.

"If you'll both excuse me, I was due in Santa Fe hours ago. We doubled our force there, but my men still feel like things are more unruly than usual. Looks like a lot of people are feeling off today."

We step aside as he gets in his car and starts it up after several rolls of the engine. He slowly shifts into reverse. He's exhausted, but he's got his job to do, and Sani Yokana is the type of guy to work himself into the ground if that's what's required of him. He rolls down his window and plops his elbow out.

"Can I ask what you expected to find in his mouth, Ms. Adams?"

Caroline looks to me. I shrug. *What the hell.* I think Yokana has always been more aware than what he lets on, and what he lets on is that he's aware of quite a lot.

"A bead," Caroline says.

He taps his teeth. I wait for him to press us, but he doesn't. Instead he says, "The funniest thing happened to me earlier today. I was going through some files in the basement back at NNPD, and I swore I saw Joseph Flatwood in the evidence room."

Caroline shuffles her feet. I can't think of anything to say either that won't dig us any deeper than we already are. Thankfully, Yokana doesn't seem to mind.

"I did a bit of a double take. I looked up again, and nobody was there. Walked around the whole evidence room thinking I'd lost my mind. Nobody. Funny thing is, I was happy to see him. And sad when I realized he wasn't there. Maybe I got a touch of that fever myself."

"You don't," I say. "I'd know."

He takes a deep breath. "No, I 'spect not. Not yet, at least. I'll see you folks around."

With that he backs up and makes his way out of the parking lot, the sand and grit crackling beneath his tires. He gives us a slow, single wave then pulls out onto the street.

I take the tattered sheet of paper and tuck it carefully in my bag along with the burned stick and the stirring stick. Caroline has the birth bag, her crow still inside. It sounds like Ben and Joey may have come through with the broken pot. The sun is hitting us sideways now. Our time is almost up.

"We need to get to the hogan," I say.

"We're missing the broom, though."

"We've got no leads on that one, nothing at all. Maybe it isn't ours to get. At the very least, if we're all together, maybe we can come up with something."

Caroline looks unconvinced. I'm right there along with her. But we're out of time. Five is better than none, but five isn't six, and I get the feeling when it comes to these things, there are no half measures.

"Come on," I say. "If Yokana can keep going, and Joey, and Ben, and Grant over there in the middle of it all, we can too."

Caroline holds out her hand, and I grasp it, then together we grab our crows and snap into the thin place, on our way to a line of hogans in the desert.

25

GRANT ROMER

Marcy Park is about a fifteen-minute walk from the Plaza, but it feels a world away. By the time we get there the afternoon shadows are long, and the park—which seems lower than the rest of the city, as if it's dug out of the rock—is dark while the hills are still bright. There's a crowd here too, but it's younger, spread out in pockets around a big stage set against the far side. A band is playing country rock. Where Kai and I stand at the lip of the park, we catch snatches of music. The wind has picked up, and it's blowing most of the sound away from us, along with clouds of smoke that puff up from the pockets of people.

As Kai leads me down and through the park, past the crowds and the music into a low-lying neighborhood, Chaco is talking nonstop. His shadow flits across the green, right to left, left to right.

"They're all gathering at the hogan, man. Maybe you oughta think about laying low while they call for the coyote. Nobody knows what's gonna happen."

His voice is louder than usual in my head. I think he knows I'm only half listening. And almost completely helpless, hand in hand with this girl.

"The coyote is here somewhere," I say. "I know it, and you know it. We need to get a bead on it before the dances are over."

"Is that a pun? At a time like this?"

"When the others call it, don't you think it would be good to know exactly what, or who, it is they're calling?" I'm spitballing, because I know and Chaco knows that there isn't anything on this plane or the next that would keep me from this party with Kai, but I still think it's a valid point. Nobody likes to just open the door to their home without checking through the peephole first.

She takes me through an older, simpler neighborhood than the one immediately surrounding the park. Here the cars are more like the stuff I see in the RV park, and the houses are smaller and closer. Blaring dance music comes from one of them, a long, flat ranch house at the end of the block. I smell a loaded grill and can see its smoke coming up from the backyard. A cul-de-sac circles up to the front, and it's already a parking lot full of cars. Souped-up trucks and beater sedans, mostly. I recognize a lot of them from the Crownrock parking lot. A few kids hang out front sipping from plastic cups and talking loudly. Kai leads me inside, but she drops my hand.

This is my first party. Unless you count my birthday parties, which basically consisted of a bird and two people twenty years older than me sitting around a grocery-store birthday cake on a table bolted to the floor of an RV. We made the best of it, and all of them ended up being more fun than they sound, but still. That's not a party. This is a party.

People are everywhere, almost all of them Navajo, but a few white kids and some Mexicans too. The air smells like BBQ and beer and cigarettes and weed. The music is stupidly loud for five in the afternoon. I lose track of Kai in the crush of people, and suddenly I'm alone. A few kids look my way, but most ignore me, until I'm pulled aside by Mick. He's smiling and weaving, his eyes already glassy. He's grinding his teeth a bit too. Owen sat me down years ago and told me all about the stuff he saw at the CHC, and a lot of the bad cases were people without teeth on account of drugs. Mick's got a sloshing cup of beer in his hand, but I wonder what else he has in his system.

"'Bout time you showed up," he says. My guess is he's spent more time here than he has at the market. He leans toward me and sort of bounces off the bell under my shirt. I have to catch him, but then he seems to come to. He nods. "Sorry, man. I think I got started a little early. Hey, listen." He leans in again. "Hos and his crew, they're here. I wanted to catch you before you did anything stupid like show up with Kai. Whoops."

I hear sound coming from the back of the house. It sounds more urgent, angrier than the rest of the party noise. I hear Chaco from somewhere outside, his voice faint. "It's the Hos kid," he says. "Grant, be carefu—"

And then he's there in front of me, with his whole crew. And they're dressed to kill. Literally. They've painted their faces like Navajo warriors. Black smeared around the eyes, and red down the face. Some have dots of white peppering the base colors. The loud room tapers to quiet. Kai is pushing back on Hos but getting nowhere. She whispers urgent Navajo at him that he doesn't seem to hear, pointing down at a lumpy duffel bag, one of several that his crew is carrying.

He's trying to head out the door. He's not expecting to see me. This isn't like one of those moments when the new kid confronts his bully and turns him around or makes him see the light. For that to happen Hos would actually have to care about me, have me on his radar, and he doesn't. He never has. When he grabs my shirt in a bunch in his fist, he's looking at me, but he's not seeing Grant. He's seeing a white kid at a Navajo party for a Navajo school in a part of the country that was once full of Indians and is now full of white people.

"What are you doing here?" he says simply. I turn to look to Mick for help, but Mick is slinking away again. It's just me. "Your place is up at the market, walking booth to booth."

"I ain't got a place," I say then wish I could bite back the *ain't*. But it's already out there. "I figured maybe this was everyone's place right now."

I'm not sure what I think that's gonna do. Change his mind? He's painted up for war and smells like whisky, and he's carrying what I really hope isn't a duffel bag full of guns. He jerks me right into his face. His eye is twitching, rapid fire.

"Wrong, *bilagaana*. It *ain't* everybody's place. It's *our* place. We're taking it back."

He pushes me against the wall and watches me for another span of seconds. I realize that this is my moment. This is when I try to stop him. You think about this stuff sometimes, when you're bored and staring out the window of the boat as the miles roll by. You think about all the crazy shooting and ultra-violence that happens every-where you go, especially nowadays, when this stuff seems to happen more than usual, and you wonder if, say, you were there that night when some asshole decided to shoot up something or raise some hell somewhere, and he came at you first. Say he's stalking the cubicles or walking the pews or something with destruction in his eyes, and everybody just wants to live, so they shove themselves deeper down into whatever foxhole they've dug, but you've got a chance. You could smash the guy in the face, or better yet call him out before he gets violent. At least ask him to open up the duffel bags and explain himself. Face what he's doing before he gets crazy.

Sitting safe and sound on the boat, watching the miles roll by, you think, "Of course I'd call him out. No brainer." But then it actually happens, and you know what I do?

Nothing. And neither does anybody else.

I watch as he shoulders his duffel and gives one last look my way. I can see he's already forgotten me. His mind is on whatever lies ahead. Then he shuffles off. His crew follows him. There are five of them, all guys painted like him, all grim looking. And then they're gone. Kai yells something in Navajo after him, stopping at the front door. It does no good. Kai watches after them for a second, and the room watches after Kai, and then the music comes back. Maybe it was always playing, but the ringing in my ears that started when Hos grabbed me cancelled it out until I got my brains together again. I can hear Chaco, faint but freaked out.

"You all right, my man? Hos and his gang are moving in the back alleys and neighborhoods toward the plaza. The dances are almost over, but he still has time to pull something."

"It's up to Owen and Caroline to pull him back now." I'm a little numb at how much of a wuss I was. How much of a wuss I am. Mick is looking at me with this gleam in his eye, and it says to me, "Your only hope for the next four years is to stick with me," and what gets me down most is that he's probably right. He's a bit of a goof and a little weird, but Hos didn't grab him on his way out. Nobody told Mick to get back to shopping the booths where he belongs. It occurs to me that I've given Mick a bum rap. The guy is quiet and down low, but he keeps his head above water. Nobody messes with him, even though nobody really brings him in either, but maybe that's the best I can hope for.

Kai turns around from the doorway with a strange gleam in her eye. I wouldn't call it the Kai shine, not the one I saw in her when she sat next to me and told me to stop slapping and start sliding. This is twice as dangerous, and when she turns it on me, I go twice as numb.

"Well that's that," she says. "He never listened to me anyway. Never once." She forces a smile, and I see that her eyes glisten with damp. She walks past me and grabs my hand again. I was facing the door all ready to go out, all ready to leave with Chaco, maybe call Sani Yokana or one of the officers for help, but then Kai spins me around and I'm back in the party. I'm following her past the living room, into the kitchen, where a bunch of kids are sitting around a table with full cups, and they're spinning a bottle.

"People actually do this?" I ask Kai, and my voice seems distant. "I thought this was just something on TV or whatever."

Kai says nothing, just plops me down in a seat and takes the one next to me. I recognize some of the kids from class. They're all my age, and they're laughing and smiling. I don't think they saw Hos leave. They've been out back drinking the whole time. Mick finds his way to the table soon after and shoulders in as well. He looks pretty far gone now. Chaco is trying to say something to me about getting out of here. He says he has eyes on Hos and his crew, but he'll lose them soon.

"What are we gonna do?" I ask out loud. I mean it for Chaco. And it's not really a question. But Kai answers.

"You spin the bottle. If it lands on a guy, he's gotta drink. If it lands on a girl. . ." Her smile is dangerous. Her words trail off. "Just a little kiss. You go first."

I spin the empty rum bottle. It has smooth edges and seems to spin forever, around and around and around, until it lands on Mick. I'm sure I look disappointed, because Mick snuffs out a breath and says, "Sorry, friend." But his eyes are narrow and angry. I think he's gonna chug his drink, but all he does is take one dainty sip. Then he says, "My turn," and spins. The bottle turns and turns, and Mick stares at it without blinking until it lands on Kai. He says nothing, but I get the weirdest feeling he was expecting this.

Kai's a good sport. Either that or she wants it over with. Either way she pops up, goes over to him, and leans down for a peck, but he grabs her and kisses her deeply. At first she tries to pull back, but then she leans in to him, almost falling on top of him, until she climbs off and away and stares at him for a second. I think maybe she's gonna slap him. The circle is hooting, and some of the girls are calling Mick an asshole, but Kai doesn't do anything to him. She walks quietly back to my side of the table with this strange grin on her face.

"My turn," she whispers. She's standing behind me, but she reaches over me, pressing her chest to my back, and spins the bottle right in front of me. I look at Mick, and he seems lost. He's staring at his hands, at the table, at the spinning bottle. He looks at the circle of people as if seeing them for the first time. Then he looks at me.

"Grant?" he says, as if surprised to see me sitting across the table from him. "My head. . ." He sags in his chair and presses his palms to his forehead. His gaze runs a thousand yards.

Chaco slams against the back window. The whole party jumps in fright, and Chaco slams again. The glass splinters, and kids scream and run from the kitchen, everyone but Mick and me and Kai. The bell starts to push at me, to push me away from here, from this place, but it seems to realize things at the same time I do. Which is too late.

The bottle stops dead to rights on me. Kai grabs my head and wrenches it around and pries my mouth open with her tongue. Her lips seal against mine.

Everything hits me. A million flashes of a million jagged edges of a million shattered memories where everything is falling apart. People, things, emotions, all of it splintered and scattered at random. The bell is burning like a white coal pressed to my chest. My heart feels stuck in an endless loop of the terrible space between beats, flopping out of rhythm inside of me like it's lost and will never get right again, and still I'm hammered with these memories that aren't mine, over and over and over and ov—

26

CAROLINE ADAMS

The line of hogans is mostly falling apart, and their cracked mud tops go: bleached white, bleached white, bleached white, then black as night. We take a well-worn path that snakes down and around the bumps and rolls of the desert, and as we approach I see that the black we mistook for the roof of the last one is actually about a hundred silent crows. A hundred black beaks pointing, and two hundred black eyes following our movements. When they shuffle a bit to keep us in view, it makes a sound like flipping through a huge phone book. It gives me goose bumps.

"Here for the show, huh?" Owen asks them, stopping before the low entrance. No answer. Just blinking. As creepy as they are, I'm not entirely against them being here. We've been in more than a few scrapes where a curtain of black crows has come in handy. Although if it comes to that, somebody is usually dead or dying, so I hope they stay right where they are in the peanut gallery.

Inside, the sand painters are waiting. They sit together in one corner, shirtless, their scrawny brown chests hairless. They wear leather breeches and sit cross-legged on a bed of pinion leaves. They watch us in silence until we both eventually sit too. We have no Chaco/Grant combo to translate this time, and no smoker to be our voice. I expected the smoker, but when we walked through the Arroyo to get here, it was quiet and closed, like a town battened down for an incoming storm. We didn't see anybody, and nobody approached us.

One of the brothers—I don't know if it's Tsosi or Tsasa now that they're out of their recliners—points at the fire pit in the center, where berries, wood, leaves, and pine needles are clumped in two neat piles, one large and one small. He takes a pack of wooden matches from a pouch at his waist and tosses them to Owen, who bobbles the catch but snatches them up from the ground.

"Me?"

The sand painter nods.

"Small," he says, pointing at the little pile. Owen crawls over on his hands and knees and strikes a few matches until he gets the needles to burn. The rest takes care of itself. The pile is already burning fast and putting out a great deal of smoke. The brothers watch the smoke waft until it envelops all four corners of the hogan, then they close their eyes and breathe deeply. Owen and I do the same and immediately start coughing. The smell isn't bad, necessarily, it's just strong. Like a gin martini. But as the fire fades, the smoke eases. We sit still until the hogan is almost completely clear again. I get the feeling that was a prep round, maybe a burst of purification to ready the place for the big pile.

"Broken pot," says the other brother. Owen and I look at each other. That was Joey's task, and Joey isn't here.

"Looks like we didn't get very far," Owen whispers to me, his face grave.

I rub my smoke-irritated eyes and think about how I'm gonna explain that it looks like we're missing step one in this business, when I hear the telltale *whoosh, pop* of a Circle member arriving. When I blink my eyes I see a shadow outside of the entrance. A leather vest falls to the desert floor outside, followed by a shower of pollen, and then in comes Joey. His eyes are wide as he looks at Owen and me, but it's really the sand painters that he seeks. When he finds them he bows his head, as if awaiting sentencing from them.

The two men watch him coldly for a moment, and in the silence Joey chances a sad little glance at them. When he does, they can't hold their scowls any longer and both burst out laughing, their smiles genuine. Joey looks up again and after a moment starts to grin. The brothers gesture him over to them, and they scooch apart then slap the space between them with their hands. Joey sidles in between and smiles at us sheepishly, which is something I've never seen him do before. It gives me a quick glance at the type of guy he might have been when he was young and it was just him and Ben here, running around the Arroyo like it was their personal playground.

Joey Flatwood has been welcomed home.

"Broken pot," the sand painter says again, and this time Joey reaches in his own pouch and pulls from it a small box that looks like it's been carved from bone and hardened with glaze. I recognize it immediately from the night I said good-bye to Ben's grandmother. It was on the ground next to her. It's cracked at the back, where its two leather hinges have been snapped, and Joey takes the top entirely off.

The sand painters nod. Crisis one is averted. I think about confessing that we don't have the broom, but it looks like things are on a roll here, and basically I don't want to have to see the looks on everyone's faces when I tell them our recipe is missing something and our cake isn't gonna rise. So I don't. Besides, the guy sitting right next to me once told me to hold on if you can, because you never know what one more second might bring.

"Burned stick," says one brother. Owen reaches in his satchel and pulls out the first artifact we found, given to us, actually, by the sand painters themselves. One brother mimics putting things in the bone box. Joey holds it out to us, and Owen drops the stick in. The burned part juts out over the side.

"Broken stirring stick," says the other brother, struggling with the words. Owen places the second stick in the box, and the brother read-justs it so that they cross each other and stick out evenly.

"Old cane" is next. Owen plucks the tattered page from his bag and looks at it for a moment, smiling. The brothers mime sliding it under the sticks in the box, and he does.

"Birth bag." I pull out my totem pouch and frown. And here I pause. I know it's crazy, but I don't want to part from the old thing. I know it's to save the rez, and maybe the world, but it still sort of sucks. This thing has been under my pillow for years. It's rubbed silky smooth on one side where it sits against my skin when I wear it. I look over at Owen, and I'm surprised to realize that I have tears in my eyes again, and not from the smoke.

Owen gives me a soft smile and leans over to me. "I'll find you a new pouch."

"You too. We do this together. Same pouches."

"Same pouches."

I sniff and nod. Then I open it and let my crow totem tumble to the floor of the hogan. The brothers pass me a strip of cloth, and I wrap my crow then tuck it in my pocket. I place the pouch on top of the sticks in the box.

I know what's coming next.

"Whisk broom."

And here we've hit our wall. I take a deep breath, look the brothers in the eye, and shake my head. They don't frown or *tsk tsk*. They don't do anything, really. Their faces are impassive as they speak to Joey between them. After a minute Joey gets up and lights the big pile, and I think we may have dodged a bullet. Maybe the artifacts were more like guidelines after all.

"Are we good?" I ask. But Joey shakes his head.

"We wait," he says.

"For what?" Owen asks.

"For the whisk broom."

What's that supposed to mean? Wait for the whisk broom? What's it gonna do—come waltzing into the hogan like one of those talking candy bars in the movie theater ads?

"What's the fire for, then?" Owen asks. I can tell he's as disappointed as I am. In the fact that we can't move forward without the broom, but mostly in himself. We've let everybody down.

"That's how much time we have to wait," Joey says. "When the fire dies, the window closes."

Owen looks like he wants to say more, but suddenly he twitches and paws at his own totem pouch. I feel it too, at the same time. The crows are deadly cold. So cold that I can feel it through the cloth wrapping of mine. We pull them out of our pockets at the same time and set them down on the dirt. The cloth around mine is already frosting, despite the heat.

"Something is wrong," Joey says. I look up to find him holding his bead-wrapped crow before he, too, sets it down, working the chill from his fingers. "The bell is calling for help."

The three of us—Joey, Owen, and I—stare mutely at each other until the sand painters break the silence.

"They say I am needed here, and Caroline is needed here," Joey says. He looks at Owen and shrugs. "I don't know why, Owen. But that leaves you to go to the bell."

Owen looks down, nodding to himself. Grant is foremost in his mind. He's more than willing, but his smoke still takes a hit at the fact that he's not "needed." When I touch the small of his back, he perks up a little. Not much, but a little.

"All right," he says. "I'll go."

"The market," Joey says as Owen flutters his fingers over his crow on the dirt floor.

"Be careful," I say.

He turns to me. Kisses me on the forehead. "You too," he says. Then he grabs his totem and pops out of sight.

The sand painters take all this in as evenly as if they were watching the sun setting behind their camper. Joey takes a deep breath of smoke from the new fire, and I watch as it streams out of the top of the hogan. The pile is bigger, but it's burning fast.

We wait.

27

OWEN BENNET

I step from the tense quiet of the hogan into a madhouse of people at the Santa Fe Plaza. I hold my phase for now, reasoning that it'll be easier to spot the bell in the crush of people if I'm in the thin place. And it truly is a crush. The blurred effect of the thin place seems to double the mayhem. All around me people are shoving and yelling. Walking over each other to get away from the main stage for some reason. There, someone holds the microphone. A young man with a painted face. A security guard appears to be unconscious on the ground next to him, and two others are being held back by a group of other young men painted similarly. So this is Hos. This is our coyote. I'm not sure what he's saying—sounds are muted by the whipping wind of the thin place—but judging by how badly everyone wants to get away from him, I know it's not good.

He lifts up a duffel bag and drops the mic. A sea of panicked people passes right through me, but none of them is Grant. I chance a quick scan of the plaza, looking for the glow of the bell, but I don't see it anywhere. Back on stage, the coyote and his pack are fishing through the duffel and each pulling out what look like duct-taped aerosol cans. They fan out around the stage. Policemen on the perimeter are struggling to get to them, but they look like fish fighting a waterfall. Every step forward is two steps back.

Hos holds up his bomb and screams, "My people are not entertainment!" so loudly that even I can hear it. Then he chucks his bomb at the obelisk statue in the center of the stage. His gang follows his lead. There's a split second when I see six floating packages sailing toward the center, and I realize we blew it. We missed our chance. We couldn't bait the trap in time. I wonder what fire feels like in the thin place. Will I live through this? Does it matter?

I can't hear the bombs explode, but I can see them. They send out great gouts of color, all of it tinged a glittering black to my eyes. Then I tense for the blast, but it never comes. The crowd has pushed their way through me, and my way is clear now, save a few people injured in the stampede. I blink into reality.

"This symbolizes the blood of our people, shed for the benefit of yours, year after year after year!" yells Hos, just before he's tackled by police along with the rest of his gang. Behind him, the plaza statue is glistening, absolutely soaked in red paint.

Paint? That's it? That's what the coyote had planned? It almost makes me want to laugh. They've got Hos rolled over, they're cuffing him, and all the while he's still screaming about Native American rights. I let out a deep breath. Maybe we misjudged this whole affair after all. Then a piercing scream rings through the crowd. Everyone hears it, even the cops. Even Hos stops his tirade. All of us look west. There, high in the sky, I see Chaco. Immediately I know something isn't right. He's diving down fifty or so feet then pulling up. Diving down again then pulling up. He looks harried, like when a bunch of smaller birds chase away one large bird, but this is worse. Panicked. He calls again, and it sounds like he's in pain.

I look at the square. Hos is back to his tirade. The crowd is calming down at the edges. This isn't the right place. The coyote tricked us.

I position Chaco in my mind, do some quick thin-place calculations, then snatch my totem and blink out.

28

THE WALKER

I sit at Caroline's side, and both of us watch as the fire burns down. I want to hold her, reassure her that everything will be all right, but the fact is, I don't think it will. The simple cloth that covers her totem is frosted completely over. Soon the fire will be down to embers. But neither of us needs those things to know how south all this has gone. She can feel it as well as I can. Grant is in serious trouble, and now Owen is too.

One brother says, "Sweep," but Caroline shakes her head. "Sweep," he says again, pointing to the little ash pile from the first fire and then to the box. He wants the whisk broom to sweep the ash into the box, but Caroline can't, and she starts to cry.

"We don't have the broom, old man!" I yell, and maybe I see a flicker from Joey's eyes, but otherwise it falls on deaf ears, as always.

"Sweep," the brother says again, gently this time. Caroline reaches for the ash with her hands, but the second brother is up on his knees quickly and stills her arm. He's firm but not unkind. He has sad eyes. His grip tells us that each artifact is integral.

"Please," he says, his voice breaking. "Sweep."

That's when Caroline gets it. But it doesn't lift her spirits any.

She takes the black book from her breast pocket and looks at it.

She bends it this way and that, fluttering the pages. They flop heavily. For Caroline the book was always weighty. To her, it represents a link. A chance. A possibility to reach me. Her heart is tangled up with memories of me in the blank pages of that thing.

She holds it by the spine and carefully sweeps the small pile of ashes into the box that Joey still holds. Then Joey caps it. The brothers mime that the book goes on top, to hold the box top in place and press down on the package. And then the whole thing goes into the fire.

Joey holds out the box, but Caroline still holds the book.

"I'm sorry, Ben," she whispers. I know she can't see me, but I also think she knows I'm here. She's really speaking to me.

"You have nothing to be sorry about," I say, even though my words will not reach her.

"I was hoping I might be able to finish our story some day," she says. "All these blank pages. Why couldn't one be for us?"

Tears are rolling down her face now, dripping off her cheeks and onto the book. I reach out to try and wipe them again, but this time I stop myself before I pass through her. If I passed through her right now, it might break me apart.

"You've had half of my heart ever since I first met you," she says. "If we'd had time, I think I'd have given you the whole thing, but we didn't, and over the years what I had left has gone to Owen, piece by piece. Even I didn't realize it until it happened. But it happened, and I can't live like this anymore. Half measures don't work when it comes to hearts."

Her head droops low, she speaks into her lap, but her words are for me.

"Ever since you died, all I've wanted is closure. I didn't even have to have you back, if I could just figure out how to say good-bye to you properly. But I know now, I don't need closure. If it means that I have to forget you, forget who I was when I was with you and forget the person you helped me to become, I don't want it. And that piece of my heart you have, it's always going to have a bit of you in it, but I want to give it to Owen. I need to give it to Owen."

"I know," I say. "I know you do."

I didn't think I had any tears left. I thought they all dried up when I rang the bell. Boy was I wrong.

Caroline takes a shuddering breath. "I can't ask you to give back to me what I gave to you. It's up to me to reach out and take hold of it again myself, so that's what I'm doing."

She gently sets the book on the box and nods to Joey, who moves over to the fire and places the whole package in the searing coals. It's alight in moments. Now both Caroline and I are slumped over ourselves, as if the strings that bonded us, that moved us together and mixed us up and were hopelessly tangled when I died, have finally been cut.

As the coyote's warning signs catch fire, I feel a sea change. The hole at the top of the hogan seems to be pulling more than just smoke up and out. It's subtle but definite: the wind from outside is pulled in, then a bit of desert sand. The hogan darkens as if a stream of the rising night itself is being pulled in from the eastern door.

One of the brothers says, "Now we wait."

I feel like a wrung-out towel, but I know that this is my time to get to work. I'm the one that has to catch this thing in between planes. Keep it from jumping from person to person and away from us again. I don't know how I can do anything but collapse with Caroline's words still bouncing around my head, but I have to do my part too.

I stand, but as I do, I feel the tug. I'm getting a call.

"You've got to be kidding me," I say. "Now? Really?"

It's insistent, much more insistent than it usually is, and it makes my stomach flip. I swirl open the map looking for the fray, for the guttering soul string that calls to me, and I find it almost immediately. It's very close. Someone is dying, and they're dying in Marcy Park.

29

OWEN BENNET

My half step in the thin place takes me to a park, where I'm thrown into mayhem of a different sort. A band plays on a stand in the distance with a large crowd all pressed together, but the wind makes their music sound whiny and off key. The stage lights are rattling in the gusts, and one falls from the overhead rigging, spinning wildly and throwing a chaotic beam across the darkening green before it shatters behind the band in an electric flare that shorts out all the music. Now all I can hear is the wind and a screaming crow.

Chaco is behind the stage, off to the right, above a bunch of houses. I sprint toward where he dips and hovers, still struggling. The wind seems to be pushing back at me, and the sound is as loud as if I was back in the thin place, but this wind is real. It throws dirt and grass and grit in my eyes and mouth, but I carve through.

I break free of the park and into a small neighborhood, and now I can hear Chaco's wings beating just under the cut of the wind. He's in the sky over a house at the end of the block, but he's moving my way, because Grant is moving my way. I almost collapse with relief.

"Grant! Are you OK? Where's the bell?"

Grant stops dead in his tracks and looks at me. Chaco lets loose another painful cry, twice as loud.

"Grant?"

He runs toward me with this insane smile on his face, but there's nothing happy about it. It's the type of smile I used to see back on my psych rotations in medical school. It's the smile of the mentally broken. The unhinged.

He's in front of me in the blink of an eye, and then he's grabbing my throat with one hand. My air shuts off full stop. His grip feels like a knot in my windpipe.

Chaco dives again and pulls up, and now I see why. This is not Grant. This is the coyote. He's turned Grant into a skinwalker, and Chaco doesn't know whether to attack him or help him. I try to speak but can't. My words feel like they back up from my mouth all the way to my brain. My head is about to burst, but then he drops me.

I suck in a crackling breath on my hands and knees. But the air isn't coming fast enough. My vision dims, tunneling to a pinpoint, but then I feel the soft head of Chaco brushing against my arm. I've never actually touched Chaco before, not in five years, but here he is, standing beside me, and I focus on that touch until my vision clears. When I look up again, I see that the whole party is outside on the front porch watching. But then Grant's insane smile is right in my face again.

"Let him go," I say. It comes out in a growl. The coyote wears Grant's grin, stretches it wider than it should be, and he shakes his head like an ornery child. I push myself standing, and the coyote follows me, inches away. The crowd of kids behind him is half cheering, half terrified, and totally unaware of what is happening. He backs up their way, and I stagger after him. He sticks out his tongue, and I see it. The bone bead. It's the size of a pea. How could such a small thing cause so much destruction?

"Spit it out!" I say. I lurch after him, but he dodges me at the last second, lurching this way and that like we're playing tag. He zips his tongue back in and clamps the bead behind a mad grin that bares his full set of teeth. I lunge for him and grab him by the shoulders.

"Give me my *son* back, you bastard!"

The coyote backhands me across the face so hard that I end up spitting out a molar. Now the crowd silences. One girl starts to scream. I see Kai, the girl Grant is so fond of, sitting down outside on the grass, her head between her knees. She's moaning, "No, no, no, no, get out of my head!"

The coyote pulls me straight again. "Your son is mine," he says. "Until he dies."

"I'm not going anywhere," I say, my words bubbling with blood. "Take me! Take me, but leave him!"

The coyote shakes his head very slowly, his eyes wide. It's hard to imagine that Grant ever had those eyes.

"No," the coyote whispers. "I want the Keeper."

"Then you're gonna have to kill me first."

The coyote looks behind me, and his eyes light up. He takes in a big, overjoyed breath.

"I don't have to kill you," he says, pointing behind me with all five trembling fingers. "Because he will."

I spin around to find a small figure standing alone in the middle of the block. He's talking to himself. Hitting his head, muttering loudly then quietly. It's Grant's friend Mick. And Mick has a gun in his hand.

"I told you," Mick says. "I told you they'd never like you. I told you I told you I told you to come see what I had. To come check it out." He raises his gun. He's pointing it at Grant, but he's aiming through me. With his other hand he's hitting and scratching at his head, just like Tim Bentley was. He's trying to shake free the cobwebs that chaos left there. "Nobody wants to see what I got. Nobody. Well, fine. If you don't want to come see, I'll just *show it to you anyway!*"

Mick shoots three times, and all of the bullets punch into me. The first thing I think is how different it feels from when I was hit in the shoulder years ago, back at the hospital. That time the shot passed clean through. This is so much worse. These hit the meat of me. They scramble all the beautiful things that are packed inside of me, the things I studied all my life to learn. I picture them now. My stomach, miles and miles of delicate instrumentation for converting food to energy, pulverized to mush. My liver, that miracle machine, which I've mistreated from time to time. I'm sorry you had to go like this, punctured and riddled with filthy lead, your delicate connections to my bloodstream destroyed. My lungs, with their millions of tiny balloons keeping me afloat, popped forever. It hurts terribly. It hurts worse than I'd ever imagined anything could hurt. It hurts for the blink of an eye.

And then I die.

30

THE WALKER

When I step out of the soul map, I don't understand what I'm seeing.

First, I see Grant. He's standing tall with his arms out like he's taking in the adulation of a crowd, but all I hear is screaming. He's smiling, so at first I think he's happy, that maybe we got the coyote, maybe it's finally all over, but then the true nature of his smile creeps over me. When he turns to look right at me, I know it's true. I'm face to face with the creature of chaos that has fashioned himself after Coyote, and he's taken over Grant.

"Welcome, Walker," he hisses. It's Grant's boyish voice, but it's *off* somehow. Like it's slightly out of tune for a human range. It makes me sick to hear it.

Then I see Owen on the ground, and a lot of blood. I feel like my mind is lagging way behind my eyes, because I can't put together that the holes in Owen's body made all that blood. I feel like I'm looking at a tricky math problem, letters as numbers, numbers as letters, none of it making any sense.

"What did you do?" I ask.

"He killed me," Owen says. Then his soul sits up from his body and looks down around him. "What a waste."

Owen's soul stands and walks over to me. "Hello, Ben. Long time no see."

I back up. "No, no. What the fuck are you doing? Get back in there, Owen."

"I can't."

"Get back in your body. Now."

"Ben," he says, reaching out to me. And he touches me. He touches my shoulder. That can only happen when people die. That's my window to interact. But I never wanted this from Owen. Ever. I throw it off.

"Don't you fucking *touch me*, Owen. You get back in your body *right now!*"

"Ben, it's over."

But I'm not having that. I don't care if the coyote is in Grant's body or not. I'm taking that thing down. Grant's bones can heal. I launch myself at the coyote. But once again, I fly right through. And the coyote laughs like a maniac.

"You'll never cross over, Walker. Ever. But I will. Again and again. Now that I have the bell, this world is mine to remake."

He rips the bell from Grant's neck and holds it high. "Do it, Mick!" he yells.

That's when I see the boy. He's been warped by the coyote, and he has a gun. Owen tries to stand in front of Grant's body again, the poor bastard. As if he had any physical body left to take the bullets. And finally it dawns on me what the coyote wanted all along: the bell, just like everybody else. With the bead and the bell he'd be unstoppable. His chaos would smother the rez and then the world. And we brought it right to him.

Mick raises the gun again, but then my world lurches, just a touch. It feels like an invisible train just blew by, and my clothes and hair are sucked back a bit. The coyote doesn't seem to notice anything.

"Owen, get over here," I whisper.

The coyote closes his eyes, waiting to die. Waiting to ring the bell.

Double his power. And Owen still won't move, so I run over and grab him.

"Hold on."

"What?"

I felt a warning sign. And the coyote missed it. The crew at the hogan did their job. When you wear the robes of Coyote, you play by the history of Coyote. I see the veil in the distance. Closing fast. It's here to take Owen away from me. From Caroline. Forever. But not yet. It's gotta catch us first.

"Just hold on tight."

If what I felt before was a breath of the train's passing, what I feel now is the full damn train. The coyote opens his eyes at the last second, but he still doesn't understand. He's confused. Mick fires his gun, but the coyote is yanked backward by another lurch, this time across both of our worlds. The bullet misses, careening off the pavement. The coyote growls, slaps his hands over his mouth, but he can't keep the bone bead from the pull of the hogan now. It leaps from Grant's mouth, a little white dot, like a floating snowflake, and Grant collapses next to Owen's body. That's all I see before I'm pulled away along with the bead like a fish yanked out of water.

We blow though the soul map, and I see a coyote form itself around the bead, muzzle first. Both of us are dragged by the nape toward the hogan, helpless to fight the pull. The coyote growls, but I grit my teeth in silence, my arms straining, because I'm carrying Owen's soul right along with me.

THE WALKER

All three of us hit the dirt of the hogan with enough force to kill us, if any of us were alive in the first place. We bounce and stagger, and my vision spins. All three of us seem confined here by the ceremony, but the only thing that makes an actual impression on the living world is the bead that the coyote still holds in its mouth. It's real on every plane, just like the bell. It rips into the dirt when the coyote's chin hits, digging a little trench on the ground, but the coyote holds on. The brothers notice it, Joey notices it, and so does Caroline. They watch it with strange calm.

When I find my focus again, one of the sand painters is saying something quickly, and I hear Joey's voice quietly translating.

"Nobody move."

Apparently I'm the last to wake up at the party, because when I sit up I see Owen's soul quietly getting to his feet. The coyote is already prowling the edge of the hogan, testing the walls, bead in mouth, his oil-dipped eyes furious. The fire is still burning bright. The bone box is in the middle of it, glowing red, the warning signs vaporized. The sand painters start singing in tandem, their voices rising and falling easily. I recognize the song too. It has nothing to do with Coyote. It's not even a Chant. It's what Gam sang to Ana and me at night. The song about the coming sunrise.

"You've been duped," Owen says.

The coyote growls.

"You should have stayed on your side of the veil," I say. "And done your job."

Owen moves around behind him, and the coyote lunges at him, but it's just a feint. I take the opposite tack, coming at him from the front. I stop when I'm standing right behind Caroline.

"I told you to spit it out," Owen says. "I told you."

The coyote laughs. It's a grating, high-pitched yipping, and it makes me cringe, then he jumps at Owen. Owen falls back, but the coyote changes direction at the last second, bounces over Owen's head, and heads straight for Caroline.

Time seems to slow without me having a thing to do with it. The coyote leaps, his mouth open, the bead bared, aiming to jam it into Caroline and take her as well, and he looks like he's grinning. He sees his way out. But I know something the coyote doesn't know. I know Caroline. And I know that no matter how crazy this may be, somewhere, somehow, through all those sleepless nights, Caroline thought of this. Thought of how it might come down to this, and how the coyote might come for her, and she's been watching the bead carefully.

At the last second, Caroline shifts her head to the right. The coyote's bead misses her mouth by a centimeter. His spirit body passes right through her, but not through me. I catch him by the neck and hold on for dear life. The coyote bucks and twists in my arms, yipping and growling. Owen jumps on the coyote's hind legs to keep them from raking at me, and together we wrestle him still, but it's a tense, primal type of stillness that won't last if we give it an inch.

"Now you have a choice, Walker," the coyote says. I shove its face against my chest to keep it from talking. I shove it hard, because I know what it's talking about. I think I knew the choice I'd be faced with back when I danced around the subject with Chaco while we walked the streets of Santa Fe.

I can feel the veil coming. I look at Owen and know that he feels it too. The curtain call is here. Throughout everything, agents of chaos, runaway souls, skinwalkers, and coyotes, one thing has always remained constant: the veil comes for everyone eventually.

Even Owen.

A moment of strained silence, then the veil's shadow falls over the hogan.

"It's here," Owen says, looking out of the eastern door, still holding tight to the coyote with me.

You'd think I'd be the one with the stone jaw here. I've seen the veil millions of times. I've had long-winded, one-sided conversations with the damn thing over the years. But suddenly I'm the one blubbering.

"Wait. Owen. We can think of something here." I ease my grip, and the coyote bucks and twists, and I almost lose him. Owen and I slam together to still it. "Just hold on a second, man."

Owen shakes his head. "I've got to go out there, Ben. I've got to meet it like a man."

He looks me in the eye until I nod.

"Together, then. This thing crosses back over too. Carefully."

Owen takes a deep breath, and then he looks at Caroline. She's watching the bead. The only thing she can see, but I sense that she understands. Her face is falling. Her whole being is falling. She's like a sandcastle being slowly picked apart by waves. But it's Owen's look that hits me hardest. He's saying good-bye to her in the only way that he knows how. With his entire heart wrapped up in one last, longing gaze.

We walk out of the hogan together, with the coyote between us, and there's the veil. It's as tall and as still and as red as I've ever seen it. And it's creeping toward Owen.

"Jesus," Owen says numbly. "It's a lot bigger than I thought it would be."

Owen might be intimidated, but I sure as hell ain't.

"Listen, you old rag. I know you don't like me crossing over, but we got something here that shouldn't be here, and you know it. See?"

The coyote bucks again, and we have to wrestle him still. It's like hauling in a hundred- pound catfish. The veil pauses its relentless approach.

"Yeah, you see it. Now, the only way we can get this thing back where it belongs is if Owen and I take it together. So are you gonna let me cross over or not?"

The veil hesitates. It's always been a stickler for the rules. But it knows better than any of us that since the coyote has been gone, things have gone to seed on the other side. It flutters slightly. That's a yes in my book.

"C'mon, Owen," I say.

"You're coming with me?"

"Let's get a move on. Before Big Red here changes its mind."

So it is that Owen Bennet and I cross over into the land of the dead, wrestling the coyote the whole way, together.

32

OWEN BENNET

It's not bad, if that's what you're wondering. Death doesn't feel bad. Except for the solid weight of the coyote between Ben and I, like a python trapped in a bag, I don't feel anything, really. I just feel dead. But then I see the river.

The river of souls is beautiful. It reminds me of flying over LA at night, but instead of a million different roads and a million different people going a million different directions, it's one road. Billions of people. Two directions. Left, or right.

"Man oh man, has this place gone to shit," Ben says.

I lose my focus. I feel this crazy pull toward the water. To float to the right. That's all I want to do. I want to do it as badly as I've wanted anything, as badly as I wanted Caroline, even. And I drop the coyote.

Immediately the coyote starts bucking, throwing itself left and right, and Ben can't hang on. He throws him down on the sand and sets up in front of the veil like a goalkeeper. The coyote rights himself and shakes his fur free of sand. He slowly raises his head and snaps his teeth a few times, showing us a few flashes of the bead, then he starts to prowl the perimeter of the veil, looking for a chance to jump back through.

"Owen, a little help," Ben says.

"It's just that this river. . ."

"I know, man. I know. But not yet. We gotta deal with this thing first."

I shake my head. The pull of the river lessens if I look away, turn back toward the veil, toward whatever was beyond it. I try to focus on Caroline. Not on how she looks but on how she feels. The color of her. It's the color of the skin of a bubble, and I want to be with it again. I finally understand what she sees on people all the time. What she calls "smoke."

I step up next to Ben, both of us eyeing the coyote as it walks back and forth in front of us, its eye on the veil.

"The bead and the bell," Ben says. "That would have been a pretty sweet deal for you. Eh?"

The coyote snuffs and kicks up a divot of sand.

"You'd have the soul map, so you could go anywhere. You'd have your pick of the dead, the ordered and the chaotic both, it wouldn't matter. All of them would have been yours. And you could take any of them at any time." Ben whistles. "That would have been one powerful setup."

The coyote growls. I'm not sure what Ben's going for here, but he taps my leg gently in a way that says *get ready*.

"Turns out you blew it, though. We took your warning signs from you. Took back the world you were trying to steal from us. And then you never saw us coming."

The coyote snaps at us, and I see a flash of white bone in his mouth.

"As a matter of fact, I doubt you can even make a run at the veil anymore. You got nothing left in the tank, old man," Ben says.

The coyote stops prowling. Ben taps on my leg again, down low, by my knee. Then the coyote jumps.

We take him down together. I hit low, Ben hits high. Together we stun him, throw him to the sand, his tongue lolling. I see the bead.

"Grab it!" Ben screams. "Grab the bead!"

I jam my hand in the coyote's mouth. He bites down, but I feel nothing. No pain, no pressure, nothing. That, more than anything, drives home that I'm gone. I've left the living world behind me. But I snag the bone bead.

"You should have spit it out when I told you to," I say, then I rip it from the coyote's mouth. The coyote howls, leaps at me as he sees the bead leave him. Then he starts changing. He goes from coyote to person in a blink. It's Bilagaana Bill, then its Burner's boy, then it's the young girl. All the while it's screaming, its voice changing as its body changes. It flickers faster, through hundreds, then thousands of people. For a split second I see myself there, and Ben, and Caroline. I try to remember that Coyote is a trickster, so this creature of chaos might be showing me things to try and throw off my nerve, but it doesn't help much. Not when you see yourself screaming.

Ben isn't fooled. Ben holds on when I scramble back. Ben picks up this chaotic blur of a thing and wrestles it to the river.

"Time to go home," he says. "Your souls are calling for you."

He tosses the coyote up and kicks it out, like he was busting down a door. The coyote flies out and over the river, and the river reaches for it. The river is overflowing with souls that strain toward it, souls stacked upon souls stacked upon souls, and no matter how much the coyote kicks, there is no escaping them. They grasp and coil and stick to the coyote like tar, then they start to pull it down.

The coyote stops fighting. Its flickering muzzle forms a translucent grin. "Now for your choice, Walker," it says. Then it's swept under the river. I see its form like a shark under water, jetting down the left side of the river, toward its home in the pearl.

That isn't my way. My way is to the right, and as I face my way, the pull of the river is twice as strong. It's like a glass of cold water in the desert. You never realize how much you want water until water is gone from you forever.

I stagger forward, but Ben comes around and presses a gentle hand against my chest. "Owen, we need to talk."

It hurts quite a lot now, turning from the river. It's like fighting sleep after staying awake for days, but I figure after all we've been through, I at least owe Ben a chat. He turns me around so I'm facing the veil again. The pull is less, but not by much.

"You have the bead?" he asks.

The bead. I'd forgotten about the bead. I suppose I do still have it. I hold out my hand and open my palm. "Take it," I say, but Ben recoils. He steps back and then shudders, and in the way that this place strips emotions bare, I realize that he wants to take it more than anything he's ever wanted in his life. It takes every ounce of him to do what he's doing right now, to keep from touching it.

"What?" I ask. "What is it? Take the bead, Ben. We've won."

"It's not worth it," Ben says.

"Of course it is. Just take it."

"No! It's not worth it if we lose you. If they lose you. If *she* loses you."

"What are you talking about?" My head turns toward the river. The pull is insistent now. Ben slaps me in the face, and when I look back at him I see he's trembling with the effort it takes to stay away from the bead.

"We need to break that thing," Ben says.

"So break it." My voice sounds clouded. Dreamy.

"Here's the thing. When we do, a big hole is going to be ripped between worlds. Look at me, Owen. A big one. One that someone could walk through without anything stopping them."

I feel as though I come around again for a minute. "Anyone could walk through?"

"Anyone," Ben says. "No matter what. Free pass. But it's one for one. That's the way things work here. Balance rules."

I get it now. I'm happy for him, really. I thought I'd be angry, but it makes so much sense now.

"You did it, Ben," I say. "This is your chance. Cross over, man. For God's sake, do it. You have no idea how much she loves you."

"Don't say that," Ben says.

Enough of this. I didn't get killed to sit here and bandy the obvious with Ben. I set the bone bead on a rock at the edge of the river and a grab a bigger rock. I'll make his choice for him. Before he can say anything I slam one rock into the other, and the veil is blown open with a staggering *crack*, like all the thunder in the world saved up for one massive explosion. It sloshes the river like a child would a bucket of water and kicks the sand into a dust-devil frenzy until we're thrown to the ground.

When both of us can stand again, and the sand of the riverbank is settled enough to see, we find the veil is parted. Not in the way that it parted to take me across, either. It's as if a hole has been blown completely through it. No rules need apply for this one time, in order to right the balance of years and years of the coyote prowling and taking what wasn't his to take. As if in emphasis, the five souls he stole seem to crawl from the rock where we shattered the bead. Bill, Burner, and all the rest. They pay us no mind but go directly to the river, which is where I should be.

"Go, Ben," I say.

"Don't say that!" Ben screams.

"Then just cross!"

"I can't," Ben says, sobbing. He drops to the sand. "I can't."

"Why?"

"Because I belong here, and you belong there."

"Are you kidding me? *Belong there?* They don't need me. I spent a year of my life wiring a goddamn trailer hitch. I've got a fourteen-year-old boy who doesn't care if I'm alive or dead. And as for Caroline, she's spent five straight years just trying to *talk* to you. She'd *kill* to have just *one moment* of what I'm doing right now. So cross over. Take the bell from Grant. Take the burden from both of them. You could be everything to them, the Walker and a father and a husband."

"That's not how it works. I know that now." Ben's hands are limply brushing the sand, his knees digging divots. "I don't know what else to say except that when you thought you were spinning your wheels, you were winning her heart. Both of them. You were building a family, and you didn't even realize it."

Ben comes to some sort of decision, and he stands up. He looks at me in a way not entirely different from the way he looked before, when he grappled with the coyote.

"What are you doing, Ben? Think for a second."

"Oh, I've thought," he says. "I get a lot of time to think. Sometimes I feel like it's all I ever do. And I've made my decision."

I back up, look toward the river. I can feel its warmth calling to me, but Ben's voice pulls me back.

"I think a lot about my grandmother these days, about the stories she told me." He swings slowly to the right, pacing in the still-fresh tracks of the coyote. I realize he's herding me. "My favorite, always, is about the Slayer Twins. Have you heard of them?"

"Ben, this thing isn't going to stay open forever."

He ignores me. "All the young Navajo kids love the Slayer Twins. Monster Slayer and Born For Water are their names. We used to pretend we were fighting with them, running around with sticks, slapping at yucca and dirt like they were the monsters the twins were sent to fight."

I start to walk toward the river without realizing it. I'm almost at the bank when Ben steps in front of me and shoves me back. He's not gentle either.

"They're the twin sons of Changing Woman. She's the Big Deal for us. Basically the Earth itself. And the twins, they had this huge job to do. They had to rid the earth of monsters like the thing we just dragged to the river. So that people could live their lives."

He's backing me up now, so I just rush at him. He grabs me, and we grapple for a minute while the souls behind us swirl and hop. Ben gets me in a headlock pretty quickly. I never claimed to be a good fighter. I'm facing the river again, and its pull is enough to start me writhing and kicking, but Ben flips me around so that I face the veil again. He presses my face to his chest.

"The Slayer Twins cleared the earth so we people could live there, but I always wondered *what then*? I asked Gam, when I was a kid, what happens if the monsters come back."

Ben's dragging me toward the break in the veil. I hit him in the arm, in the shoulder, in the face. He doesn't flinch.

"You wanna know what she said?"

I spin Ben around again so his back is at the veil. He's right there. He could go through. I get this wild idea to just push with my legs and fling him backward, but as soon as I tense he reads me and flips me facing forward. Facing the veil myself. The scene just beyond the veil is the hospital for half a heartbeat. The room where Ben died. That's where he would step back to. He'd walk out of ABQ General whole again. But now that I face it fully the scene shifts. Now I see my body lying in the street, and Grant's body stirring slightly next to me, both of us resting in my blood. Ben sees what I see.

"Gam said, well, if monsters come back, then somebody will have to stand up in their own way. Fight them back again. I used to think that was me. The problem is, I can't fight in the land of the living anymore. My time there is over. But you can. You and Grant and Caroline and the rest of the Circle."

"Ben, don't do this," I croak. "She won't be able to take it if I tell her you had a chance to go to her and you didn't take it."

"She's already made her choice. I was there. And she's right."

Ben lowers his head to me, loosens his grip, and presses his forehead to mine.

"It's not your time to die, Owen. Watch your son grow tall and strong. Be there to wipe away her tears. And whatever you do, don't ever let go of her."

Ben tosses me forward just like he tossed the coyote. The veil is all around me, like an ocean of red, and then it's behind me, and all worlds go black.

33

GRANT ROMER

I come to face down on the hot concrete street, and my cheek is lying in a pool of cooling blood. I have no idea what happened to me, only that it was very, very bad. I do the first thing that I do every morning when I get up. I feel for the bell around my neck. But it's not there.

I sit up, and a string of blood comes up with me, drips down my face. My hands are painted in it, my clothes are saturated. And my head is killing me. It feels foggy and scratched up. I have shadows of strange memories, and I don't think all of them are mine. I feel like I needed to do something terrible, but I forgot what it was.

I see the bell and let out what I feel must be my first breath in hours. It's lying by my shoes, like it was dropped there. The necklace is broken, and both bell and necklace are smeared in blood. Then I see Owen. He's facing away from me, his nice shirt soaked.

"Hey, Owen? Get up, man. Something bad happened here."

Owen doesn't move, but that's OK, because I know he will. He's just pulling it together, like me. I shake him a little bit.

"Get up, Owen. We gotta find the coyote. C'mon."

Owen still isn't moving, and at the very back of my brain I know why, but I'm keeping it there, in the back. I refuse to let it come to the front. I shake my head hard, and it's jarring. The shadows of the terrible thoughts threaten to make noise until I sit very still again.

"Owen?"

The truth of what I see is creeping to the front of my brain an inch at a time. I'm remembering Pap. He was lying on the ground like this, and there wasn't even any of the blood then that there is now. And I know how that ended.

"Owen. Please." I pull him over, and he flops on his back. His front is a mess. His nice shirt. It's a mess. It's way too big of a mess for anything to ever be right in my life ever again. That's when it hits me that all this blood is *his* blood. I don't know whose blood I thought it was before, but it's *his* now.

"No, no, no." I scoop a little bit of it up and hold it in my hand. I don't know what I'm doing with it, so I set it on Owen, like I could maybe put it back in him or something, even though I know that's not how these things work, but this just *can't be*. Owen being dead is also *not how things work*. There is not a scenario in which the world can exist without Owen in it.

I sort of choke then, with the weight of it all. I don't cry, I just start coughing, and I close my eyes because I don't want to see any of this anymore, and I lay my head down on Owen's ruined stomach, and I just want to go to sleep.

With my eyes closed, the sounds of everything wash over me. Kids are screaming. I hear sirens in the distance, and over everything is the roar of the wind. The only completely silent thing is Owen. Then I hear footsteps. I look up and see Mick standing above me. He's looking down at me, and he has a gun hanging limply in his hand, but he looks completely lost. There's a big gust of wind and the light brush of black feathers over my face as Chaco lands between us. He snaps at Mick, but Mick doesn't even seem to notice him.

"My dad is dead," I say. I don't know what else to say. I don't even know who I'm talking to. Chaco lowers his head and folds his wings in and turns around to tuck himself between Owen and me. Mick shakes his head, and I hear a big clunk as he drops the gun before he shuffles over to the curb and collapses there.

I don't know how long Chaco and I lay like this, resting on Owen. Certainly until I fall asleep, because I know I must be dreaming when I start to hear a small beat in Owen's chest. It's like his heart is telling me a secret, it's so quiet, and then I think it goes away again, and it was nothing after all. But the bell heard the secret too, because it gets a little bit warmer in my hand. I try to listen, and even Chaco presses himself closer. He hears it too.

Another beat. Another whisper. Louder now. I can hear it. And I know what it's saying. It's saying *not yet*.

Not yet. Not yet. Thump-thump. Thump-thump. Stronger and stronger and stronger. *Not yet. Not yet. Not yet.*

Chaco rises, then I sit up, and when we look at Owen, we find he's looking back at us. He rolls on his side to grab my hand, and there are three soft *tink, tink, tink* sounds as the bullets that were inside of him fall to the ground.

"Not yet," he says, smiling at me. "Not just yet."

34

THE WALKER

The Serenity Room at Green Mesa is back to normal. Well, normal for a psychiatric hospital, anyway. I guess I was giving myself too much credit when I said it was me that was spooking all these people. It was the combo of the coyote running loose everywhere and then me walking in on top of that. This time, with the coyote back where he belongs, I only get a few mutters when I pass. That's it.

Mom is in her usual spot, by the big bay window, and she's watching the Jemez Mountains again. Only this time, when I sit down next to her, I see that she's actually seeing them. The sunset is an explosion of soft pink, and the clouds look like strings of cotton candy. She's watching the crows fly under them, away from here. They're scattering again. That, as much as anything, tells me our job is done for now.

"You look good, Mom," I say. She says nothing, but she does smile. I know it has nothing to do with me talking to her. That's the rub with a job like mine. When you do it right, nobody notices you. If things are going the way they should, you're invisible.

"She's moving on," I say. "Caroline is. Which is good, because until she told me, I didn't realize how tightly I was holding on to her.

To the past. To my life. I've been dead for six years. You'd think I would have realized it by now. But it took her showing me. It took her letting go to get me to ease my grip too."

Mom reaches back and brushes her fingers through her silky hair, still watching the sky. Her eyes are moving from cloud to cloud.

"She's good at helping people realize things that are staring them in the face. Like the rez. How it needed help. It still needs help, but at least its problems are normal problems now. They're gonna stick around, all three of them. She told Owen that if he was gonna keep screwing around with that trailer hitch, he ought to at least put it to work. He's turning it into a mobile doc's office. He and Caroline are gonna work the rez."

It makes me absurdly happy to know that they're staying on Chaco rez. That when I need to find them, I won't have to search the map. No more uprooting. Grant's staying at Crownrock High. Even after all that happened. He said he was done running. Caroline is helping with that too. The coyote messed with a lot of people's minds, and she's got a knack for fixing them. Grant's and Kai's. Even Mick's. Although that kid was troubled for a long time, maybe even before the coyote came through. The cops found an arsenal in the back of his car and journals with all sorts of terrible plans. He was ripe for the coyote to begin with. Still, Caroline got permission to visit him at UNM's acute care psych ward, where he's under lock and key. She says she at least wants to undo whatever the coyote did, and I know she can. The rest is up to the docs.

Things at Chaco are settling down again. Life is moving forward.

"I think I was afraid that for me, there was no such thing as forward. All I had was what lay behind me. Like when Ben died and I became the Walker, that was it for Ben. I thought the two were totally separate things. So I held on to Caroline for dear life, thinking that if I let go, not only would I lose her, but I'd lose Ben too, forever. I looked high and low for a way to get back to her, for a chance to be Ben again. But that's the thing. Ben's still here. Ben never left. And the Walker is still here too. It's all one thing. It's all me."

Mom's gaze is broken when another patient sits down in the chair next to her. A woman her age. One that used to sit with her all the time, until Mom started to go downhill.

"Evening, Sitsi," she says. "It's almost dinnertime. Any interest?"

"I think so," Mom says, and hearing her voice brings tears to my eyes. "I think that would be nice."

The two women help each other up, and together they walk right through me, on their way out.

I don't mind. Not anymore. It makes me smile, actually. It makes me feel good. This is my job. This is my journey, and it's moving forward now. Caroline, Owen, Grant, they all walk it with me. We're all still in it together. For now. And even though they can't see me, I know they can feel that I'm there, walking next to them.

It's what I do. I am the Walker, after all.

AUTHOR'S NOTE

Coyote is one of the most fascinating and contradictory beings in Navajo lore. Karl W. Luckert, a mythology scholar on the subject, calls him, among other things, a "fool-gambler-imitator-trickster-witch-hero-savior-god."

Signs of Warning, the tale told in Chapter 18 of this novel, was taken from the Curly To Aheedlinii version of *Navajo Coyote Tales*, translated from the original Navajo by Father Berard Haile, OFM (and interpreted by the smoker in the narrative). The six objects that present themselves to Coyote (birth bag, burned stick, broken pot, cane, whisk broom, and broken stirring stick) are all accurate at their origin.

Signs of Warning is but one of many tales about Coyote, and anyone looking to learn more will benefit from both Haile's compilation and Karl W. Luckert's essay on the theoretical and historical framework of Coyote that is presented as the introduction.

Ready for more from the Rez? The Wind Thief (Vanished, #4) is out now!

ABOUT THE AUTHOR

B. B. Griffith writes best-selling fantasy and thriller books. He lives in Denver, CO, where he is often seen sitting on his porch staring off into the distance or wandering to and from local watering holes with his family.

See more at his digital HQ: bbgriffith.com

If you like his books, you can sign up for his mailing list here: http://eepurl.com/SObZj. It is an entirely spam free experience

Ready for more? The Wind Thief (Vanished, #4) is out now!

ALSO BY B. B. GRIFFITH

The Vanished Series

Follow the Crow (Vanished, #1)

Beyond the Veil (Vanished, #2)

The Coyote Way (Vanished, #3)

The Wind Thief (Vanished, #4)

Child of the Sky (Vanished, #5)

Gordon Pope Thrillers

The Sleepwalkers (Gordon Pope, #1)

Mind Games (Gordon Pope, #2)

Shadow Land (Gordon Pope, #3)

The Tournament Series

Blue Fall (The Tournament, #1)

Grey Winter (The Tournament, #2)

Black Spring (The Tournament, #3)

Summer Crush (The Tournament, #4)

Luck Magic Series

Las Vegas Luck Magic (Luck Magic, #1)

Standalone

Witch of the Water: A Novella

Made in the USA
Las Vegas, NV
22 October 2023

79546791R00371

Microsoft® Office XP INSIDE OUT

The CD that helps you put your software to work!

Dig in—for the work-ready tools and resources that help you go way beyond just using Office XP. You'll conquer it! Just like the INSIDE OUT book, we've designed your INSIDE OUT CD to be both comprehensive and supremely easy to use. All the tools, utilities, and add-ins have been tested against final Office XP code—not beta. The sample chapters from other INSIDE OUT books help take your Office XP learning experience even deeper. You get essential links to online software updates, product support, and more—direct from the Microsoft Office team. And with the CD's intuitive HTML interface, you'll always know exactly where you are and what else you can do!

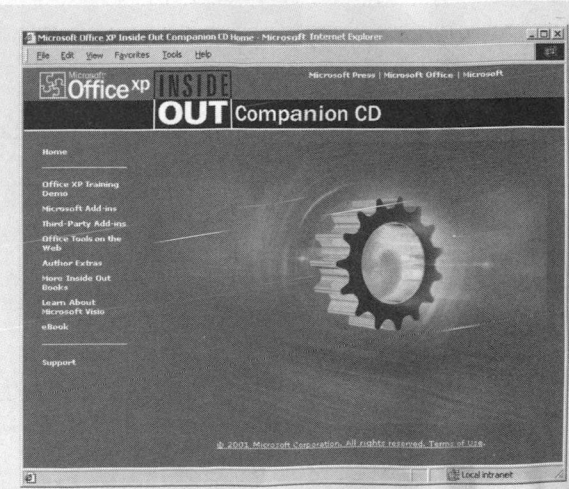

Your Inside Out CD features:

- Microsoft and Third-Party Add-ins—dozens of must-have tools, utilities, demos, and trial software

- Office Tools on the Web—complete descriptions and links to official Microsoft Office resources on line

- Author Extras—sample files and macros

- More INSIDE OUT Books—sample chapters from INSIDE OUT books for indiv[...] Office XP applications

- Complete Microsoft Press® eBook—the entire MICROSOFT OFFICE [...] book in easy-search electronic format

- Step by Step Interactive Tutorials—trial version of offic[...] training for Office XP

Want to learn more? Read on for full details, including Sy[...] Requirements (last page of this section).

Microsoft Office ᵡᵖ
INSIDE OUT

Microsoft Add-Ins

Get Microsoft add-ins and tools for Office—straight from the source.

Includes:

- **MSN® MoneyCentral™ Stock Quotes Add-In**—get refreshable stock quotes right in Microsoft Excel. This gives you the flexibility to calculate formulas based on the function's return values so you can easily create your own financial analysis.

- **Microsoft Office Internet Free/Busy Service Wizard**—publish the blocks of time when you are free and when you are busy to a shared Internet location, so people who don't normally have access to your Microsoft Outlook® Calendar can check your schedule on the Web.

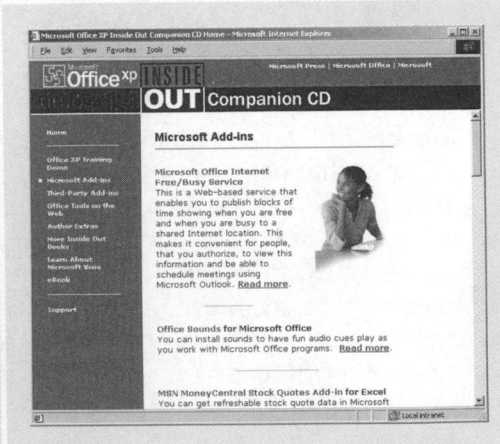

- **Microsoft Excel templates**—kick-start your projects and learn more about Excel with templates for world currency rates, currency conversion, major U.S. stock indices, stock quotes, and loan calculations.

- **Web Template Maker**—copy any open Web site as a reusable template

- **Microsoft Office Visual Keyboard**—type in multiple languages on the same computer by using an on-screen keyboard for other languages.

- **Microsoft Visio® Auto-Demos**—use these customizable auto-demos to see how to ᵖᵘᵗ Visio diagramming software to work on your next project.

- **ᵇʸ Step Interactive Tutorials**—try official Microsoft interactive training for ᵒ ˣP, and teach yourself common tasks and key features and functions.

- **ᵒffice Sounds**—hear fun audio cues when you use toolbars, ᵃⁿᵈ dialog boxes, when you zoom in or out, or when you

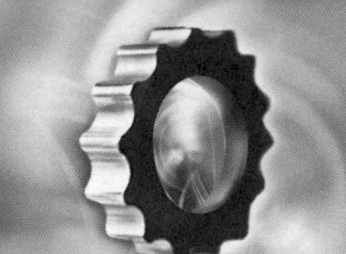

Microsoft Office xp INSIDE OUT

Third-Party Utilities, Demos, and Trials

All the third-party add-ins on this CD have been tested for use with Office XP. In this section, you'll find all the details you need about each tool—including a full description, application size, system requirements, and installation instructions.

Includes:

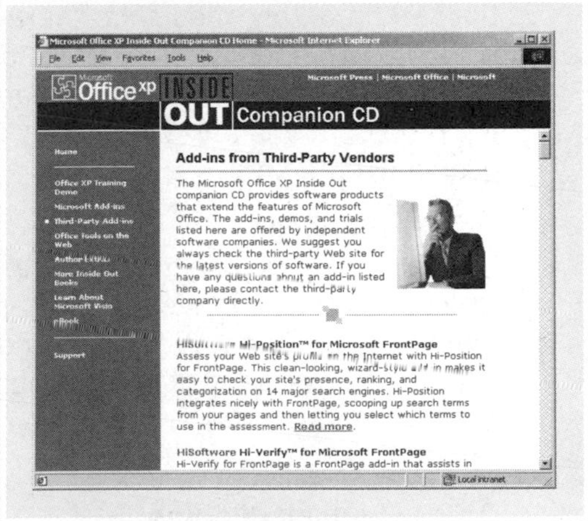

- **HiSoftware's metaPackager™**—encapsulate your files in pure XML so they're easy to index and manage.
- **Nereosoft's ProWrite™**—use existing information from the contact manager to create new e-mail and letter merges in a flash.
- **MacroSystems' Spreadsheet Assistant**—use this tool to knock off time-consuming tasks, such as selecting cells without scrolling or performing arithmetic functions on an entire range.
- **GlobeSoft's MultiNetworkManger**—connect to multiple networks the easy way.
- **AnvilLogic's AcroWizard**—collect acronyms and their definitions from your docs, build a list, and update a database of acronyms for reuse.
- **ConvertAll Ltd. ConvertAll**—as unobtrusive as "Find & Replace" and works with the same ease and efficiency! Every conversion from $ to €, km to miles, lbs to kilos is executed quickly and effortlessly.

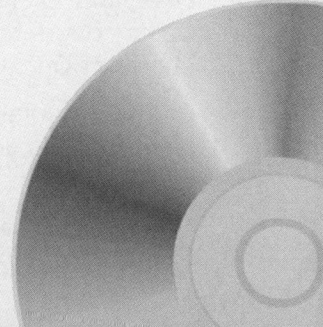

Microsoft
Office xp
INSIDE
OUT

Office Tools on the Web

Here you'll find ready links to the most helpful and informative online resources for Office XP, direct from Microsoft. Find out exactly how each site can help you get your work done—then click and go!

Office Assistance Center

Get help using Office products with articles, tips, and monthly spotlights. Learn more about working with documents, data, and graphics; using e-mail and collaboration features; creating presentations and Web pages; and using everyday time savers.

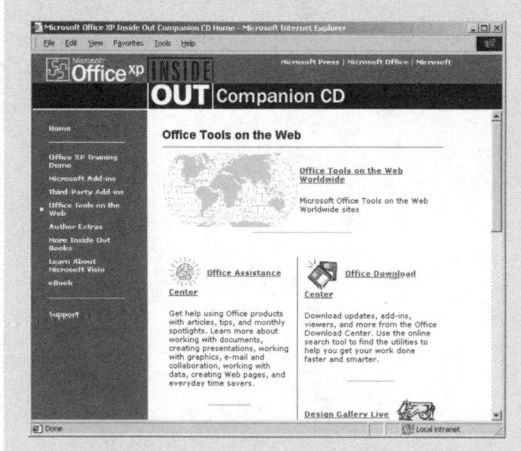

Office eServices

Use these Web services to get the most from Office. Learn how to store and share files on the Web; build and host Web sites; find communication services, language translation, learning and reference, and online postage resources; tune up your computer; and much more!

Office Product Updates

Obtain recommended and critical updates to enhance your Office XP experience.

Office Download Center

Download updates, add-ins, viewers, and more from the Office Download Center. Use the online search tool to find the utilities to help you work faster and smarter.

Design Gallery Live

Pick out clip art or photos for your Office project from this huge royalty-free selection. New items are constantly added to meet your needs. The advanced search facility makes finding the right artwork quick and easy.

Microsoft Office Template Gallery

Instead of starting from scratch, download a template from the Template Gallery. From calendars to business cards, marketing material, and legal documents, Template Gallery offers hundreds of professionally authored and formatted documents for Microsoft Office.

Online Troubleshooters

Microsoft has developed Office XP online troubleshooters to help you solve problems on the fly. Access them using the links on the CD—and get the diagnostic and problem-solving information you need.

Microsoft Office XP INSIDE OUT

Author Extras

Here's where your INSIDE OUT author went the extra mile: great sample files on CD for you to take apart and study! It's an excellent way to make the examples used inside the book come to life on your PC.

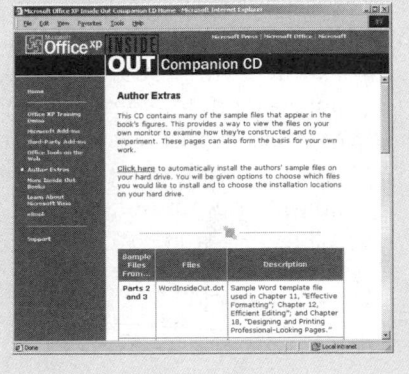

Includes:

- **Sample files used in book examples**—study these demonstrations of common Office techniques, which include example Microsoft Word documents and ready-to-run Word macros
- **Sample macros**—all you have to do to run them is open the practice files in Microsoft Word and press Alt+F8 to see the macro list
- **Sample code**—examine the code used to write the sample macros, and use what you learn to develop your own
- **Sample Access databases**—see Access working from the inside, and build on these to create your own inventories
- **Sample Excel spreadsheets and workbooks**—copy these tricks for advanced formatting, organizing, number crunching, and analysis

More Inside Out Books

The INSIDE OUT series from Microsoft Press delivers comprehensive reference on the Office XP suite of applications. On this CD, you'll find sample chapters from the companion titles listed below, along with details about the entire line of books:

- Microsoft FrontPage® Version 2002 Inside Out
- Microsoft Excel Version 2002 Inside Out
- Microsoft Outlook Version 2002 Inside Out
- Microsoft Word Version 2002 Inside Out

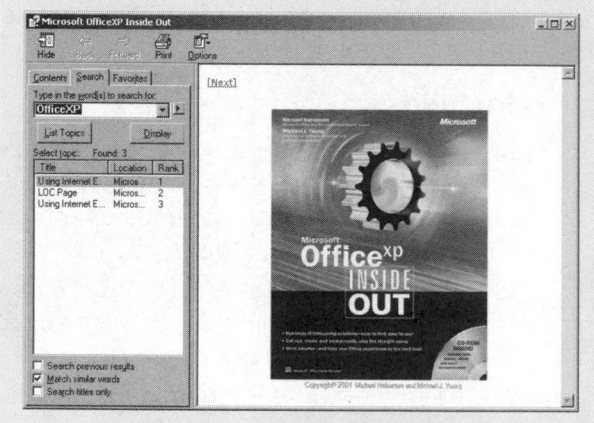

Complete Microsoft Press eBook

You get the entire MICROSOFT OFFICE XP INSIDE OUT book on CD—along with sample chapters from other INSIDE OUT books— as searchable electronic books. These Microsoft Press eBooks install quickly and easily on your computer (see System Requirements for details) and enable rapid full-text search.

Features:

- Super-fast HTML full-text search
- Full-size graphics and screen shots
- Copy, paste, and *print* functions
- Bookmarking capabilities
- A saved history of every file viewed during a session

CD Minimum System Requirements

- Microsoft Windows® 95 or later operating system (including Windows 98, Windows Millennium Edition, Windows NT® 4.0 with Service Pack 3, Windows 2000, or Windows XP)
- 266-MHz or higher Pentium-compatible CPU
- 64 MB RAM
- 8X CD-ROM drive or faster
- 46 MB of free hard disk space (to install the eBook and interactive tutorials)
- 800 x 600 with high color (16-bit) display settings
- Microsoft Windows compatible sound card and speakers
- Microsoft Internet Explorer 4.01 or higher
- Microsoft Mouse or compatible pointing device

NOTE

System Requirements may be higher for the add-ins available on the CD. Individual add-in system requirements are specified on the CD. An Internet connection is necessary to access the hyperlinks in the Office Tools on the Web section. Connect time charges may apply.

Michael Halvorson
Microsoft Office and Microsoft Visual Basic® expert

Michael J. Young
*Professional software developer and
computer book author*

Microsoft®
Office xp
INSIDE
OUT

- **Hundreds of timesaving solutions—easy to find, easy to use!**
- **Get tips, tricks, and workarounds, plus the straight scoop**
- **Work smarter—and take your Office experience to the next level**

PUBLISHED BY
Microsoft Press
A Division of Microsoft Corporation
One Microsoft Way
Redmond, Washington 98052-6399

Library of Congress Cataloging-in-Publication Data
Halvorson, Michael.
     Microsoft Office XP Inside Out / Michael Halvorson, Michael Young.
          p. cm.
     Includes index.
     ISBN 0-7356-1277-3
     1. Microsoft Office.   2. Business--Computer programs.   I. Young, Michael J.   II. Title.

   HF5548.4.M525 H353   2001
   005.369--dc21   2001030208

Printed and bound in the United States of America.

1 2 3 4 5 6 7 8 9   QWT   6 5 4 3 2 1

Distributed in Canada by Penguin Books Canada Limited.

A CIP catalogue record for this book is available from the British Library.

Microsoft Press books are available through booksellers and distributors worldwide. For further information about international editions, contact your local Microsoft Corporation office or contact Microsoft Press International directly at fax (425) 936-7329. Visit our Web site at mspress.microsoft.com. Send comments to *mspinput@microsoft.com*.

FoxPro, FrontPage, Microsoft, Microsoft Press, MSN, NetMeeting, Outlook, PhotoDraw, PowerPoint, SharePoint, Visual Basic, Windows, and Windows Media are either registered trademarks or trademarks of Microsoft Corporation in the United States and/or other countries. Other product and company names mentioned herein may be the trademarks of their respective owners.

The example companies, organizations, products, domain names, e-mail addresses, logos, people, places, and events depicted herein are fictitious. No association with any real company, organization, product, domain name, e-mail address, logo, person, place, or event is intended or should be inferred.

Acquisitions Editor: Kong Cheung
Series Editor: Sandra Haynes
Project Editor: Judith Bloch
Technical Editor: Don Lesser, Pioneer Training

Body Part No. X08-03785

Contents At A Glance

Contents At A Glance

Table of Contents

Chapter 17
Proofing Word Documents   475

new feature!

Chapter 18
Designing and Printing
Professional-Looking Pages   509

new feature!

newfeature!

Chapter 27

Advanced Worksheet Charts   753

Chapter 28

Power Database Techniques: Lists, Filters, and Pivot Tables   777

Chapter 32

Advanced Presentation Formatting 875

Chapter 33

Mastering Tables, Graphics, and Drawings 897

Chapter 38
Managing Messages and Appointments   1021

Chapter 39
Managing Contacts, Tasks, and Other Types of Information   1057

Chapter 40
Customizing Outlook   1089

Part 9
Publisher   1377

Chapter 51
Essential Publisher Techniques   1379

Chapter 52
Creating Professional Brochures
and Newsletters   1411

We'd Like to Hear from You!

Our goal at Microsoft Press is to create books that help you find the information you need to get the most out of your software.

The INSIDE OUT series was created with you in mind. As part of an effort to ensure that we're creating the best, most useful books we can, we talked to our customers and asked them to tell us what they need from a Microsoft Press series. Help us continue to help you. Let us know what you like about this book and what we can do to make it better. When you write, please include the title and author of this book in your e-mail, as well as your name and contact information. We look forward to hearing from you.

How to Reach Us

E-mail: nsideout@microsoft.com
Mail: Inside Out Series Editor
            Microsoft Press
            One Microsoft Way
            Redmond, WA 98052

Note: Unfortunately, we can't provide support for any software problems you might experience. Please go to http://support.microsoft.com *for help with any software issues.*

Introduction

Microsoft Office XP has more power, more application integration, and greater sharing of features than any previous version of Office. Microsoft has worked hard to make the Office applications easy to use, but the Office suite's sheer size and complexity can make it challenging to find your way around the software, to learn the applications and the ways they work together, and to solve the problems that result from the software's intricacy. *Microsoft Office XP Inside Out* is designed to help you meet this challenge.

Who This Book Is For

This book is written for the power user, the software enthusiast, the consultant, the solutions developer, or the company guru—the one others come to for help. It's designed for the person who wants to learn the essentials quickly and then go on to more interesting topics—advanced timesaving techniques, bug workarounds, trouble-shooting advice, and insights into Office's inner workings. It's written for the computer user who needs to solve the problems that will inevitably occur with software as complex as Office. And it's targeted to the reader who wants an honest, objective evaluation of the different Office components, clarifying which features to use and which to avoid.

Rest assured that the book also covers the essentials. Contrary to the typical media depiction of a computer genius, even the savviest computer expert needs to learn the basics of a new program. In this book, however, the essentials are taught as they would be in a graduate seminar rather than in a freshman 101 course—quickly and concisely, relying on your general computer understanding and your ability to translate your current insights and skills to the topic at hand.

Consequently, to get the most out of this book, you should know the basics of computer hardware and software. You should know Microsoft Windows. You should know how to use the file system, how to access the Internet, and how to manage your e-mail. You should have used a word processor and spreadsheet program before, so that the essential concepts are familiar to you. But most important, you should be excited about exploring the fascinating territory that lies just beyond the surface of Office XP.

How This Book Is Organized

Part 1, "Getting Going with Office XP," is designed to get you started with Office in as few pages as possible. Chapter 1, "An Office XP Overview," includes a concise Office road map to help you quickly choose the Office application or applications you need to accomplish your intended tasks, plus a comprehensive summary of the new Office features, which will be especially valuable if you've used previous Office versions. Chapter 2, "Installing and Configuring Office XP," provides succinct instructions to help you install Office and maintain your Office installation, either on a freestanding computer or in a networked environment. And Chapter 3, "Getting Expert Help on Office XP," shows you how to make the most of the online help provided with Office and lists valuable Office resources located on the Internet and elsewhere.

Part 2, "Common Office XP Techniques," focuses on the shared features of the Office applications and on the ways to take advantage of Office application integration. For instance, this part explains how to use the new Office task panes, the revamped search feature, the new speech recognition and handwriting interfaces, the enhanced Office Clipboard, and the many commands for adding graphics to documents, including the new Clip Organizer and diagram features. It also shows how to create compound documents that combine data from several applications; how to use Office applications to share documents and information on Web servers running the new SharePoint Team Services from Microsoft; and how to customize the menus, toolbars, and other features of the common Office application interface.

Parts 3 through 9 provide in-depth coverage of each of the major Office applications: Microsoft Word, Excel, PowerPoint, Outlook, FrontPage, Access, and Publisher. For a brief rundown on each of these applications, see "An Office XP Map," on page 6, as well as the first chapter of each application part.

Finally, Part 10, "Supercharging Office XP with Macros and VBA," covers the common macro and development language of the Office applications: Visual Basic for Applications (VBA). These chapters explain how to use VBA to automate tasks within individual Office applications, as well as ways to create sophisticated multiple-application solutions.

Keep in mind that *Microsoft Office XP Inside Out* isn't the type of book you need to read through from the beginning. Nor must you read an individual chapter in its entirety. Rather, the book has been designed so that you need to consult only the specific section or sections that are relevant to completing your pending Office task or to solving your current Office problem. The sections in this book are concise, down-to-business, and are largely self-sufficient. If a section does depend on material found elsewhere, you'll find a cross-reference to the chapter, section, or page containing that information.

In addition to cross-references, you'll find many notes and sidebars that provide supplemental and in-depth insights and techniques, as well as tips presenting advanced tricks and workarounds. You'll also discover candid Inside Out elements in each chapter, which typically point out flaws and shortcomings in the Office software and suggest ways to deal with them. And finally, the chapters include special troubleshooting sidebars to help you solve specific problems that you're likely to encounter.

To quickly find the section or sections you need to read, be sure to take advantage of the book's comprehensive table of contents and indexes, including a separate index of troubleshooting sidebars, which should be the first resource you consult when Office trouble strikes.

Contacting the Authors

The authors welcome your feedback and comments and will try to help you with problems you encounter in using the techniques covered in this book.

● For comments or questions about the parts of the book on common Office techniques, Word, Outlook, FrontPage, or Access, you can contact Michael J. Young through his Web site at *www.mjyOnline.com*.

● For comments or questions about the parts of the book on Excel, PowerPoint, Publisher, or Visual Basic for Applications (VBA), you can e-mail Michael Halvorson at *Mike_Halvorson@msn.com*.

● For comments or suggestions about this book specifically or about the Inside Out series in general, please see page xxxiv.

Acknowledgments

The authors would like to express their heartfelt gratitude to the team of dedicated and talented professionals who planned, produced, and supported this book. In particular, we would like to offer a warm *thank you*:

To Kong Cheung, Acquisitions Editor, for initiating the project, for doing a great job of organizing the author summit where all the *Inside Out* authors got together to plan their books, and for your ongoing support and enthusiasm.

To Judith Bloch, Project Editor, for smoothly coordinating and facilitating the entire project. We truly appreciate your thoughtful accommodation of our many requests, as well as all those words of encouragement and humor cheering us on at just the right moments. Thanks for making this challenging project a much easier one!

To Sandra Haynes, *Inside Out* Series Editor, for your insightful work during the initial stages of the project in planning the book's content and implementation.

To Kathie Werner, who revised the PowerPoint and Publisher sections, and to Eric Stroo, who revised the Excel section. Thanks for all your helpful and wise additions, and especially for your good humor throughout the project. We couldn't have done it without you.

To the team at nSight, for your huge role in producing this book: Sue McClung, Project Manager; Don Lesser, Lead Technical Editor; Kathleen Cinelli, Kitty Dougherty, Margaret Lampron, Kate McLean, Doug Slaughter, and Mannie White, Technical Editors; Joseph Gustaitis and Teresa F. Horton, Copy Editors; Patty Fagan, Mary Beth McDaniel, and Joanna Zito, Desktop Production Specialists; Janet Cocker, Proofreader; and Rebecca Merz and Katie Pickett, Editorial Assistants.

To Karin Meier, Program Manager for the companion CD, for putting together a truly useful CD for this book. And to Angela Cummings, Tess McMillan, Fredd Stephens, Bill Teel, and Leslie Phillips, for your work on the eBook.

It was a great pleasure working with all of you!

Conventions and Features Used in This Book

This book uses special text and design conventions to make it easier for you to find the information you need.

Text Conventions

Convention	Meaning
Abbreviated menu commands	For your convenience, this book uses abbreviated menu commands. For example, "Choose Tools, Track Changes, Highlight Changes" means that you should click the Tools menu, point to Track Changes, and select the Highlight Changes command.
Boldface type	**Boldface** type is used to indicate text that you enter or type.
Initial Capital Letters	The first letters of the names of menus, dialog boxes, dialog box elements, and commands are capitalized. Example: the Save As dialog box.
Italicized type	*Italicized* type is used to indicate new terms.
Plus sign (+) in text	Keyboard shortcuts are indicated by a plus sign (+) separating two key names. For example, Ctrl+Alt+Delete means that you press the Ctrl, Alt, and Delete keys at the same time.

Design Conventions

newfeature!

This text identifies a new or significantly updated feature in this version of the software.

InsideOut

These are the book's signature tips. In these tips, you'll find get the straight scoop on what's going on with the software—inside information on why a feature works the way it does. You'll also find handy workarounds to deal with some of these software problems.

tip Tips provide helpful hints, timesaving tricks, or alternative procedures related to the task being discussed.

Troubleshooting

Look for these sidebars to find solutions to common problems you might encounter. Troubleshooting sidebars appear next to related information in the chapters. You can also use the Troubleshooting Topics index at the back of the book to look up problems by topic.

Cross-references point you to other locations in the book that offer additional information on the topic being discussed.

 This icon indicates sample files or text found on the companion CD.

caution Cautions identify potential problems that you should look out for when you're completing a task or problems that you must address before you can complete a task.

note Notes offer additional information related to the task being discussed.

Sidebar

The sidebars sprinkled throughout these chapters provide ancillary information on the topic being discussed. Go to sidebars to learn more about the technology or a feature.

Part 1

Getting Going with Office XP

1

Chapter 1

An Office XP Overview

A Rundown on Office XP

The Microsoft Office XP suite provides more applications and utility programs than ever before. Which ones you have depends upon which edition of Office XP you own or which individual Office applications you've obtained. This book covers all the major Office XP applications:

- Microsoft Word (Part 3)
- Microsoft Excel (Part 4)
- Microsoft PowerPoint (Part 5)
- Microsoft Outlook (Part 6)
- Microsoft FrontPage (Part 7)
- Microsoft Access (Part 8)
- Microsoft Publisher (Part 9)

The book also covers many of the valuable utility programs and add-ons that are included with Office XP (or are available on the Web) and that help you work with the main applications:

- Office Shortcut Bar (Chapter 4)
- Clip Organizer (Chapter 6). See Figure 1-1 on page 4.
- Microsoft Graph (Chapter 6)
- Microsoft Equation (Chapter 6)
- Save My Settings Wizard (Chapter 9)
- Office Resource Kit, including the Custom Installation Wizard (Chapter 2)

Part 1: Getting Going with Office XP

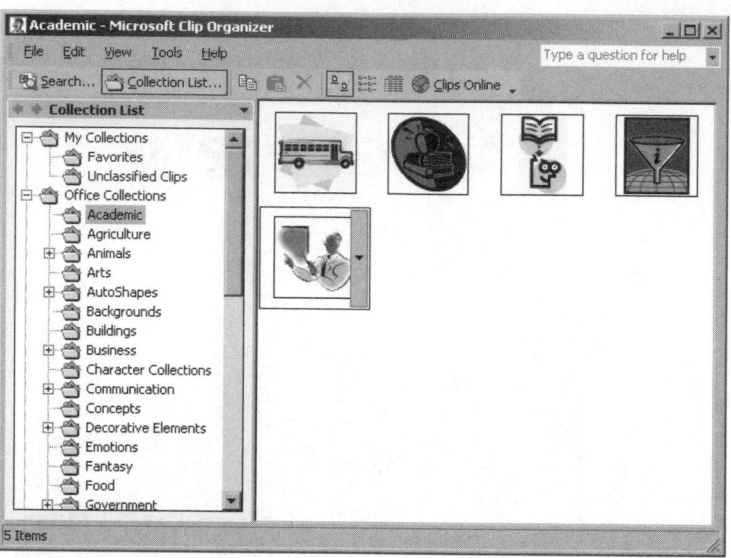

Figure 1-1. You can run the new Clip Organizer program in its own window, shown here, or through the new Insert Clip Art task pane.

Even if you don't have one or more of the applications covered in this book, you might want to read some of the information about these applications to help you decide whether to add an Office program to your software collection or whether you're better off using the applications you already have.

Advantages of the Office XP Suite

Obtaining and installing the Office XP application suite, rather than acquiring individual applications here and there, isn't just a way to economize by buying programs "cheaper by the dozen." The real advantages of a software suite such as Office XP lie in the common user interface and the application integration features.

In Office XP, the individual applications share more common features than in any previous Office version. An obvious advantage of a common user interface is that once you learn one application, it's much easier to learn another. Also, as you switch between applications, you won't have to switch working modes quite so radically. And, perhaps most important, a common user interface frees your focus from the individual applications and their idiosyncrasies and lets you concentrate on the documents you're creating. The following are examples of important common features in the Office XP suite:

- The menus, toolbars, shortcut keys, and the methods for customizing these features.

- The common dialog boxes (notably, the Open and Save As dialog boxes), with shared features such as the Search command that now lets you find either files or Outlook items.

Chapter 1: An Office XP Overview

● The task panes (described later in this chapter). See Figure 1-2.

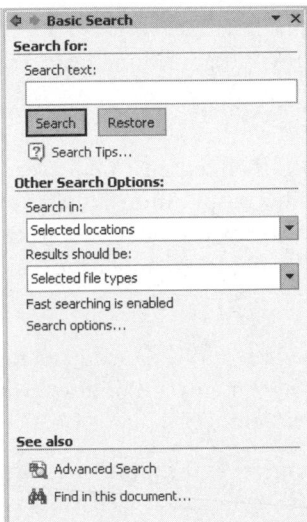

Figure 1-2. The new Search task pane, which is available in most Office applications, lets you locate either disk files or Outlook items.

● The methods for displaying and setting document properties.

● The speech and handwriting interfaces.

● The drawing features (Drawing toolbar, AutoShapes, Diagrams, WordArt, and others). See Figure 1-3.

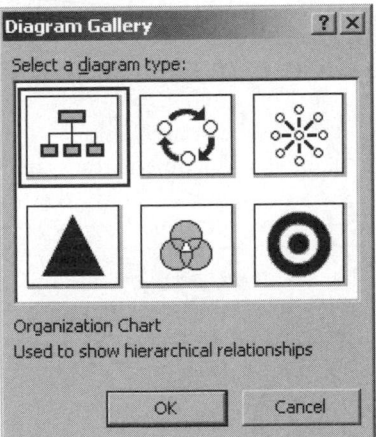

Figure 1-3. The new Diagram Gallery dialog box lets you quickly insert a variety of ready-made conceptual drawings.

● The proofing tools (Spelling, Thesaurus, AutoCorrect, and others).

● The help interface and the Detect And Repair command.

● The Visual Basic for Applications (VBA) programming features.

● The ability to store and share documents on SharePoint team Web sites.

The Office XP applications are also more tightly integrated than ever. Application integration extends the usefulness of the individual applications. It lets you combine applications in a synergistic way to solve more complex problems and to easily accomplish otherwise difficult tasks. The following are examples of application integration features available in Office XP:

● The Office Shortcut Bar, as well as the New Office Document and Open Office Document commands on the Start menu in Windows, which let you create or open any type of Office document

● The ability of Office applications to import and export each other's documents (using the Open and Save As dialog boxes, as well as special purpose commands for importing and exporting documents or data)

● The capability of using data stored in Outlook or Access when creating mail-merge documents in Word

● Commands for linking and embedding data from several Office applications in a single compound document

● VBA, the common programming language of the Office applications and the most powerful way to create solutions using multiple Office applications

An Office XP Map

If you're not sure where to start with Office, you can use Table 1-1 to select the best Office application to use for creating the type of document you want or for performing the task you need to complete.

> **note** For a more detailed rundown on an Office XP application, see the first chapter in the part of the book that covers that application.

Chapter 1: An Office XP Overview

Table 1-1. **The Best Office XP Application to Use for Performing Specific Tasks**

Office XP Application to Use	Task
Word	• Create general printed or online documents of all kinds—for example, memos, letters, faxes, reports, contracts, résumés, manuals, theses, and books.
	• Enter and organize research notes, outlines, and other types of free-form text information.
	• Generate form letters, envelopes, labels, and other mail-merge documents (see Figure 1-4, on page 9).
	• Print individual labels and envelopes.
	• Create general-purpose, relatively simple Web pages, which can include almost any Word document element, plus movies, sounds, forms, frames, visual themes, navigation bars, and components for accessing information on a SharePoint team Web site. Use templates to create personal Web pages and other types of pages or use the Web Page Wizard to create simple Web sites.
Excel	• Save, organize, calculate, analyze, and chart numeric business or personal data in a spreadsheet (row and column) format. For example, balance checking accounts, prepare invoices, plan budgets, track orders, or maintain general accounting ledgers.
	• Store relatively simple text or numeric data in lists that organize the information into records (rows) and fields (columns)—for example, a product inventory or descriptions of members of your ski racing team. Sort, find, filter, automatically fill, summarize, group, outline, or subtotal data. Display data in varying combinations using pivot tables or pivot charts.
	• Publish static or interactive spreadsheets, charts, or pivot tables, for displaying numeric, text, or graphic information on the Web. Publish forms on the Web for collecting data in lists or other databases.
PowerPoint	• Create multimedia presentations consisting of sets of slides to teach, sell, communicate, or persuade. Include text, graphics, animations, sound, and video in your presentations. Present multimedia information using 35 mm slides, transparencies for overhead projectors, speaker notes, printed handouts, or live slide shows on a computer or computer projector.
	• Publish presentations on the Web that consist of a series of multimedia slides displaying text, graphics, animations, sounds, or videos.

(continued)

Table 1-1. *(continued)*

Office XP Application to Use	Task
Outlook	● Send, receive, and organize e-mail messages. Exchange instant Internet messages. ● Store and manage personal information (appointments, names and addresses, to-do lists, journal entries, or free-form notes). ● Communicate and coordinate with members of your workgroup (schedule meetings, manage group projects, and share information and files). ● Access files on local or network disks and explore Web sites. ● Publish snapshots of your calendar on the Web.
FrontPage	● Create entire Web sites using templates or wizards—such as a site for establishing a corporate presence, displaying personal information, conducting an online discussion, managing a project, or accessing shared information stored on a SharePoint team Web site (see Figure 1-5). Use visual themes to apply consistent formatting to all pages in your site. ● Manage your Web site (maintain files and folders, display reports, create and update hyperlinks, track tasks, publish your site, or control the source in workgroups). ● Create a Web page quickly using a template or wizard (for example, a page containing a bibliography, a feedback form, or a table of contents). ● Create or edit a Web page using a full-featured HTML (Hypertext Markup Language) editor, which supports all standard Web page elements and provides ready-to-use Web-page components (date and time stamps, comments, hover buttons and other dynamic effects, forms for searching the site, spreadsheets and charts, hit counters, galleries of photos, included files, link bars, tables of contents, site usage statistics, views of information stored on a SharePoint team Web site, and controls that display information from Web sites such as MSN).
Access	● Store, organize, select, and present data in a relational database, which allows you to easily manage large amounts of complex or interrelated data and to divide data into separate, related tables to maximize storage efficiency. ● Publish an interactive form on an intranet that allows users to view or update information from a database.
Publisher	● Use wizards to create brochures, flyers, signs, greeting cards, business cards, menus, catalogs, newsletters, and other relatively short documents that have precise page layouts integrating text and graphics. ● Create coordinated sets of publications (business cards, letterheads, envelopes, fax cover sheets, and so on). ● Use wizards to create graphical Web pages.

Chapter 1: An Office XP Overview

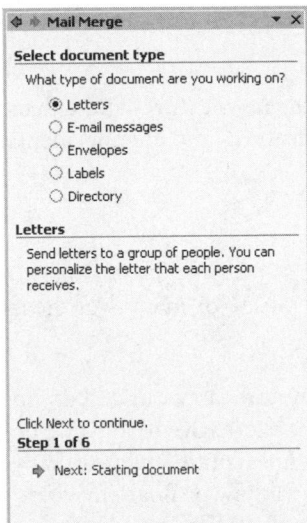

Figure 1-4. Word's new Mail Merge task pane makes it easy to create and print form letters, envelopes, labels, and other mail-merge documents.

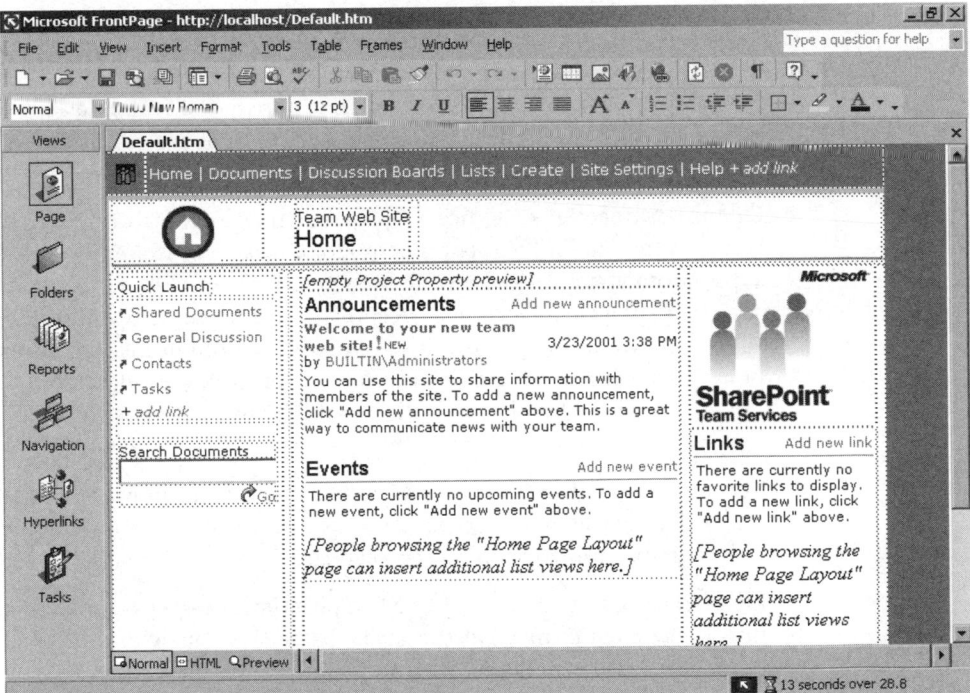

Figure 1-5. In FrontPage you can create a new team Web site on a Web server running SharePoint Team Services from Microsoft. This figure shows the home page of a newly created team site.

newfeature!

What's New in Office XP

The following sections briefly describe many of the new features and enhancements found in Office XP. (Office XP has so many new features and enhancements that it would be difficult to list them all!)

New Common Office XP Features

Each of the following new features is available in most—or many—of the main Office XP applications.

● **Task panes** In Office applications you can now carry out certain operations or choose selected options using a new alternative to a dialog box known as a *task pane*. A task pane is a Web-style command area that you can dock along the right or left edge of the window or float anywhere on the screen. Most Office applications provide the following common task panes: New Document (the name varies with the specific application), Clipboard, and Search. (For examples of task panes, see Figures 1-2, on page 5, and 1-4, on page 9.)

● **Search feature** Office XP includes a new search feature that you can use to locate files on local disks, network drives, or Web sites or to find items in Outlook folders. You can run the search feature in the Search task pane (see Figure 1-2, on page 5), or in a dialog box that you display from the Open or Open Office Document dialog box.

● **Document recovery** Office XP provides many new features to help you recover your data in the event of a program crash. For example, Office applications attempt to save your document when a crash occurs, and, on restarting, provide a Document Recovery task pane to help you restore your document. Also, you can use the new Office Application Recovery utility to break into a hung application so it can save your data. And you can use the Open And Repair option in the Open dialog box to attempt to repair a corrupted document.

● **Speech recognition** In Office XP applications you can now dictate text rather than type it, and you can issue basic commands by speaking them rather than by using the mouse or keyboard.

● **Handwriting interface** Office XP applications now let you enter text into a document using an electronic tablet and pen or (with difficulty) an ordinary mouse. You can either insert handwritten characters (such as your signature), or you can have Office *recognize* your handwritten characters and convert them to regular text.

Chapter 1: An Office XP Overview

- **Smart tags**   Office XP applications can now recognize a wide range of different data types entered into a document (such as names, dates, addresses, and stock ticker symbols). The application converts each recognized piece of data into a smart tag, and you can then use a menu attached to the smart tag to perform useful actions on that data, automatically invoking the required Windows program.

- **AutoCorrect Options button**   After the Office AutoCorrect feature makes a change, you can modify the correction using the new AutoCorrect Options button.

- **Paste Options button**   When you paste data into an Office XP document, a Paste Options button appears, allowing you to select the desired format of the pasted data and to switch among different formats to determine the one you want.

- **XML (Extensible Markup Language) support**   Excel and Access 2002 can now import and export data from and to XML documents. Also, you can have FrontPage 2002 apply XML formatting rules when generating the HTML source for the Web pages you create.

- **Diagrams**   In Office XP applications you can now get a head start in building a conceptual drawing—such as an organization chart or a Venn diagram—by inserting a ready-made Office diagram. (See Figure 1-3, on page 5.)

- **Windows in Taskbar option**   You can now display documents in top-level windows with buttons in the Windows Taskbar (as in Office 2000), *or* you can display them in child windows within a single top-level application window without displaying a toolbar button for each document window (as in Office 97 and earlier).

- **New From Existing command**   You can now create a new document based on an existing document as an alternative to using a template.

- **SharePoint access**   In Office XP applications you can now open or save documents stored on a SharePoint team Web site, you can participate in online discussions hosted by the site, and in some types of Office documents you can insert Web components that allow you to view and modify shared information stored on a team site. (A team Web site is hosted by a Web server that runs SharePoint Team Services, and it provides collaboration features that allow workgroups to share documents and exchange information. See Figure 1-5, on page 9.)

New Word Features

● **New formatting features**   Word 2002 now saves and lets you reapply directly assigned formatting features as an alternative to using styles. In addition to character and paragraph styles, Word provides table and list styles for applying predefined formatting features to tables and to multi-level lists. To find out what formatting and style (or styles) have been applied to characters in your document, you can use the new Reveal Formatting task pane. To remove all formatting from text, you can use the new Clear Formatting command. To find text that's inconsistently formatted with the rest of the document, you can use Word's new formatting consistency checker. To select all text that has the same style or saved format as the current selection, you can use the new Select All command. And you can simultaneously select multiple blocks of text or graphics in a document so that you can format or edit all of them at once.

● **Change tracking**   The change tracking feature has been completely revamped—for example, you can have Word mark changes using margin balloons without disturbing the line and page breaks in the document.

● **Comments**   In Word 2002, comments have also been extensively redesigned—for instance, you can have Word display comment text in margin balloons, making it easy to insert, view, or edit the comment text.

● **Document security**   Document security has been enhanced—for example, the Options dialog box provides a new Security tab, and you can attach a digital signature to a document.

● **Document statistics**   You can display the number of words, characters, lines, pages, or paragraphs in the current document using the new Word Count toolbar.

● **Text translation**   You can use Word's new Translate task pane to translate into a different language either a word, or—by means of a translation service on the Web—a phrase, a block of text, or an entire document.

● **Watermarks**   Word's new Printed Watermark command makes it easy to add a document watermark, which consists of faint text or graphics displayed across every page in the document or in a document section.

● **Booklet printing**   Word provides new page setup and printing options that make it easy to directly print a booklet or even a book.

● **Mail Merge Wizard**   Word's new Mail Merge Wizard, which runs in the Mail Merge task pane, makes it easy to create form letters, envelopes, labels and other mail-merge documents. (See Figure 1-4, on page 9.)

Chapter 1: An Office XP Overview

● **New Web page formats**   Word now lets you save a Web page in the Web Archive (*.mht, *.mhtml) format, which saves everything in a single Web archive file. You can also filter a Web page when you save it, which generates a smaller and "cleaner" HTML file by preserving only the essential document information (but with the possible loss of document features).

New Excel Features

● **Unlocking data**   A number of new tools make it easier to find, analyze, and publish data associated with worksheets in Excel 2002. Web queries make it easier to link to data on the Web. Web Page AutoRepublish automatically keeps Web pages in sync every time you save your document. Copy Paste Web Query automatically links to data on the Web when you paste it from a Web page. Import Data allows you to easily find and share data sources.

● **Improved pivot tables**   Pivot tables have been improved with drop-down menus and other user interface enhancements. The automatic GetPivotData formula streamlines the analysis of pivot table data.

● **Access to more data**   Excel 2002 works with more data types, including common data sources on the Web. XML is supported as a data interchange format, and worksheets can be linked directly to XML data on the Web. The new real-time data (RTD) function brings real-time data into Excel for analysis.

● **Command and feature enhancements**   Numerous menu command and product feature enhancements make Excel even easier to use in fundamental areas, including link management, Find and Replace searches, hyperlink navigation, sorting, drawing borders, inserting international number formats, editing cells vertically, error checking, and customizing headers and footers with graphics and additional information. The IntelliPrint feature eliminates the printing of blank pages, an enhancement designed to conserve your printing and paper resources.

New PowerPoint Features

● **Collaboration**   Several tools make it easier to edit and review PowerPoint 2002 presentations in workgroup environments. You can now save presentations with password protection, so that reviewers can view presentations in PowerPoint but not edit or save them. Web broadcasting is now easier to use. Authors can now attach digital signatures to their presentations to increase security and reviewer confidence. Presentation review cycles in workgroups have been made easier through routing and reconciliation features, which manage change requests from multiple reviewers. Comments have been revised so that in addition to allowing reviewers the chance to insert "hidden" notes in presentations, they can be compared to one another, merged together, and printed in a new way.

- **Animation** You can now apply a combination of animation and transition schemes to your whole presentation at once—a significant time saver. New slide transition effects include Comb, Fade Smoothly, Newsflash, Push, Shape, Wedge, and Wheel. Custom animation effects are easier and more impressive now that PowerPoint lets you control exit animations, path animations, and timed/simultaneous animations.

- **Everyday tasks made easy** The Copy and Paste commands are better able to handle inserting different content types and a larger volume of information. Print Preview allows you to determine how a presentation prints and lets you make fine-tuning adjustments. Slide formatting is easier with "one-click" formatting. You can apply more than one design template to the same presentation. Thumbnail views of your slides are now available in Normal View.

New Outlook Features

- **Single configuration** Outlook 2002 no longer has the separate Corporate Or Workgroup and Internet Only configurations. The features of both these configurations are combined in a unified configuration.

- **Enhanced Preview pane** If you select an item in the Calendar, Contacts, or Journal folder, the Preview pane now displays the item within its form (that is, within the form used to display the item when you open it).

- **Outlook item search** You can search for Outlook items, as well as disk files, by using the new Search task pane in Office applications. (See Figure 1-2, on page 5.)

- **Account groups** If you have more than one e-mail account, you can now set up account groups to control exactly which accounts Outlook uses to send and receive e-mail when you initiate a send and receive operation and also to have Outlook automatically send and receive e-mail at fixed intervals using specific accounts.

- **Easier management of e-mail headers** Outlook provides an easier interface for downloading and screening e-mail message headers before you download the full content of your messages.

- **Mailbox Cleanup** You can use the new Mailbox Cleanup dialog box to weed out messages when your Inbox starts growing out of control.

- **Appointment color coding**   You can now tag your appointments using colors—for example, red for an important appointment, blue for a business appointment, green for a personal appointment, and so on.

- **Alternative meeting times**   When you use Outlook to plan a meeting, an attendee can now reply by proposing a new meeting time, rather than simply accepting or declining the invitation.

- **Enhanced meeting planner**   You can now consult the meeting planner whenever the Calendar folder is open, without actually scheduling a meeting.

- **Unified Reminders dialog box**   All pending appointment reminders are now displayed in a single Reminders dialog box, so you don't have to view and close a separate dialog box for each one.

- **Instant Messaging**   You can now use Instant Messaging to communicate from Outlook in real time.

- **Address Bar**   You can use the new Address Bar to explore Web pages within the Outlook window.

New FrontPage Features

- **Customization of SharePoint Web sites**   You can now create or customize a SharePoint team Web site. You can add new custom document libraries, surveys, and other types of lists to a team site. You can view team site usage statistics. You can add a Document Library View or List View Web component to a page, which allows you to view the contents of a document library or a list on a team site. And you can create a custom form for adding, editing, or displaying items in a document library or other type of team site list. (See Figure 1-5, on page 9.)

- **Navigation pane**   You can view a web's navigation structure in Page view by opening the new Navigation pane.

- **Report publishing**   You can now copy a web report to a Web page, so that you can publish the report on the Web.

- **Enhanced Web publishing**   The Web publishing feature has been completely revamped. For instance, you can publish individual files that belong to a web. And when you publish, the Web Publish dialog box lets you select exactly which files to publish and enables you to manage files in the local web as well as files on the destination server (you can cut, copy, paste, rename, or delete files, or copy files between the source and the destination).

- **Tabs in Page view**   You can now quickly switch between pages opened in Page view by clicking the tabs at the top of the window.

- **Language formatting**   You can now mark foreign text contained in a Web page so that Outlook uses the correct dictionary for checking its spelling and looking up synonyms.

- **Added graphics features**   You can now quickly add and arrange a collection of images by inserting a Photo Gallery Web component. You can create drawings within FrontPage using AutoShapes and the Drawing toolbar. And you can add decorative text by inserting a WordArt object.

- **Automatic table fill**   If you've added text to one table cell, you can now have FrontPage automatically copy that text to other cells.

- **Enhanced shared borders**   You can now assign a separate background color or picture to an individual shared border as well as to the main part of a page.

- **Collapsible outlines**   You can now convert a simple list to a multilevel outline that the page visitor can collapse or expand.

- **Inline frames**   As an alternative to creating a frames page to view multiple pages, you can now insert an *inline frame*, which is a rectangular element that displays another page and lets you scroll through it.

- **New Web components**   FrontPage provides new Web components, including new types of custom link bars, components that let you display information from the MSN or MSNBC Web sites, and components for SharePoint team Web sites (mentioned previously in this list). You can also download additional Web components from the Web.

New Access Features

- **New database format**   Access 2002 provides a new database file format that offers better performance for larger databases. You can open and save databases in either the old format or the new one, and you can easily convert databases between formats.

- **Enhanced spelling checker**   You can modify the way the spelling checker works by using the new Spelling tab in the Options dialog box.

- **Convert objects to data access pages**   You can now convert a table, query, form, or report to a data access page.

- **XML support**   You can now import or export data from or to XML documents.

Chapter 1: An Office XP Overview

New Publisher Features

- **Prepress preparation**   Publisher 2002 offers enhanced commercial printing functionality, including support for up to 12 "spot colors" in a single publication and the ability to combine process and spot colors in the same publication. Publisher also includes a new version of the EPS (Encapsulated PostScript) filter, which provides improved handling and previews of text, as well as improved handling of named colors to properly separate EPS graphics in spot-color publications.

- **Common features and improvements**   Font schemes make it easy to give your publication a new look. Choose one of 25 coordinated font sets, and it will be consistently applied to your publication. Publisher now makes it easy to prepare Word documents with great-looking professional designs by using the Word Import Wizard. Fifteen new Design Sets aimed at producing streamlined, professional-quality business publications have been added to Publisher. Many Publisher features—wizards, designs, and color schemes—have been redesigned for easy access in the task pane. Publisher includes a style inspector that describes the properties of the current style, allowing you to make better use of styles. Now you can save and open documents in HTML file format. The new mail-merge feature in Publisher is more like mail merge in Word, making it easier to use.

- **Drawing tool**   Publisher 2002 uses the same drawing tools, including AutoShapes, used by other Office applications. You can now move objects inline with text in text frames. Once moved inline, graphics flow with text in frames. Publisher now supports cyan-magenta-yellow-black (CMYK) TIFFs internally. You're no longer required to link to externally stored TIFFs. Publisher can separate vector and bitmap red-green-blue (RGB) images. Publisher supports print previews of the current publication, using the characteristics of the current printer to render the preview. If you're using either process or spot color, print preview can display both a composite preview and previews of individual ink plates. Printing is easier now that the Print Setup and Page Setup dialog boxes have been merged into a single dialog box.

- **International support**   Publisher 2002 now includes support for complex scripts and bidirectional languages, such as Arabic and Hebrew. Publisher uses Office "word-breaking" technology to detect word breaks in Japanese and Chinese text for easy selection and editing of your text. Publisher now supports the Office Language Settings tool to let users enable language-specific editing features and the language used in online Help.

Chapter 2

Installing and Configuring Office XP

Installing Office XP from the CD

To install Microsoft Office XP on your computer from the product CD, perform the following steps:

1 Insert the first Office CD into your CD-ROM drive. If AutoPlay is enabled on your computer, the Office Setup program will run automatically. If for some reason Setup doesn't start, you'll need to manually run the Setup.exe program in the root folder of the Office CD.

Using the Windows Installer program, Setup will now guide you through the process of installing Office XP.

2 Complete the first two Setup dialog boxes. In the User Information dialog box, you need to enter your name, initials, organization, and the product key displayed on the label on the Office CD container. In the End-User License Agreement dialog box, you need to accept the Office XP license agreement.

note To see an explanation of the options in the currently displayed Setup dialog box, click the Help button in the lower-left corner.

3 In the third Setup dialog box, shown in Figure 2-1, on page 20, choose the type of installation you want.

19

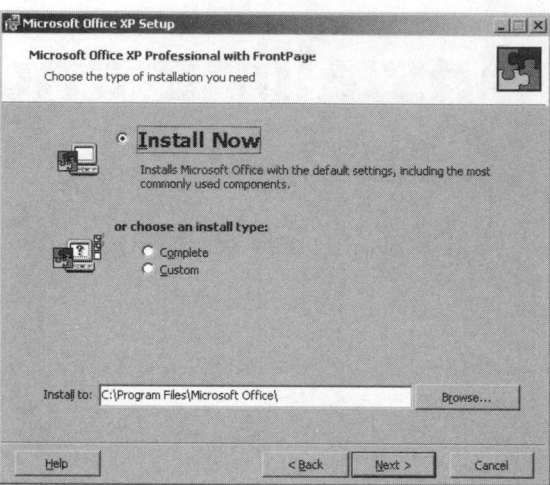

Figure 2-1. The installation type you select in the third Setup dialog box determines the basic set of components that are installed.

If a previous version of Office *isn't* currently installed on your computer, select an option as follows:

■ To quickly install the most commonly used Office XP applications, tools, and features, select the Install Now option.

■ To install everything, including all optional tools and features, select the Complete option.

■ To control exactly which applications, tools, and features are installed, select the Custom option.

With any of these three choices, you can change the default installation location by typing a new folder path into the Install To text box or by clicking the Browse button to select an installation folder.

note Keep in mind that the set of Office XP components you choose to install isn't final. You can later rerun Office Setup to add or remove components, as explained in "Revisiting Office Setup," on page 27. Setup will remember and display the exact set of applications, tools, and features you previously installed. You can then adjust that set, adding or removing specific features.

If a previous version of Office *was* installed on your computer when you ran Setup, you'll see a slightly different set of options in the third dialog box. Select an option as follows:

■ To remove your previous Office version, replacing each application and feature of your previous installation with the new version, select the Upgrade Now option.

Chapter 2: Installing and Configuring Office XP

■ To quickly install the most commonly used Office XP applications, tools, and features, select the Typical option.

■ To install everything, including all optional tools and features, select the Complete option.

■ To control exactly which applications, tools, and features are installed, select the Custom option.

> **note** The remaining steps in this procedure apply only if you selected the Custom option (whether or not you had a previous Office version installed).

4 In the fourth Setup dialog box, shown in Figure 2-2, check the major Office XP applications you want to install. Then, select one of the following installation options:

■ To quickly install the common features for the applications you selected, as well as the typical Office tools, select Install Applications With The Typical Options.

■ To choose the specific application features and Office tools that will be installed, select Choose Detailed Installation Options For Each Application.

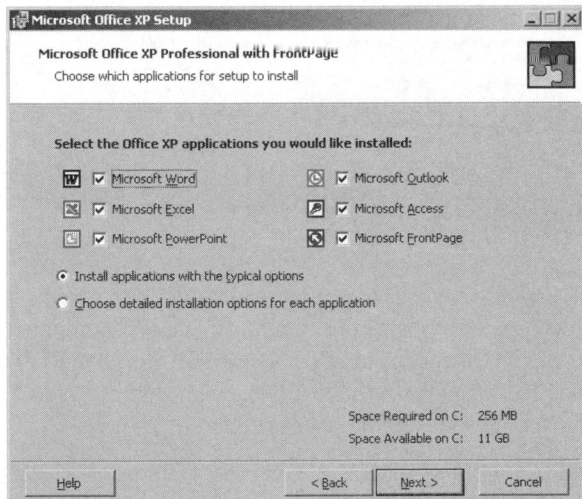

Figure 2-2. In the fourth Office Setup dialog box, you can select the main Office applications that will be installed.

5 If, in the fourth Setup dialog box, you selected Choose Detailed Installation Options For Each Application, Setup now displays the Choose Installation Options dialog box, shown in Figure 2-3, on page 22, where you can select the specific application features and Office tools that you want to install.

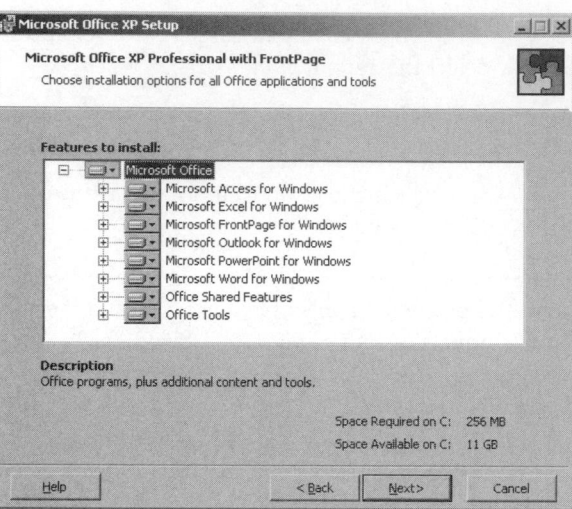

Figure 2-3. In this Setup dialog box, you can select the specific application features and Office XP tools you want to install.

To control the installation of a particular application, tool, or feature, expand the hierarchy if necessary to reveal the component and click the down arrow to open the menu of choices, as shown below:

Then, choose Run From My Computer to install the component, choose Run All From My Computer to install the component plus all components underlying it in the hierarchy, choose Installed On First Use to have Office automatically install the component the first time you attempt to use it, or choose Not Available to omit installing the component.

6 If you had a previous version of Office installed on your computer when you ran Setup, you'll now see the Remove Previous Versions dialog box. In this dialog box, choose whether to have Setup remove your previous Office version, preserve your complete previous Office installation, or remove one or more specific applications from your previous installation.

7 Setup now displays the Begin Installation dialog box, which shows a list of the applications that will be installed. Click the Install button to complete the installation.

Installing Office XP from a Network

In a networked environment, provided that you've obtained the required licenses from Microsoft, you can copy all of the Office XP files to a single shared network folder and then allow all users to install Office XP directly from that folder over the network, rather than from the product CD. Not only does this method eliminate the need to distribute Office CDs to all users, but also it allows you to fully customize and automate the Office XP installation. (That is, users won't need to enter options into the Setup dialog boxes. Rather, Setup will automatically create a standard Office XP installation— or one of several standard installations—that you've defined.)

The following is a procedure you can use for setting up and installing Office XP on a network. This procedure allows you to fully automate and customize Office XP installations on users' computers. Keep in mind, however, that Microsoft provides many additional techniques, options, and tools for setting up custom network installations of Office XP. You'll find all the required documentation and tools in the Office Resource Kit. If you don't have the Office Resource Kit, you can download it from Microsoft's Web site at *http://www.microsoft.com/office/ork/*.

1 Create an *administrative installation point*, which is a shared network folder that contains all of the Office files required to install Office on users' computers. To convert a shared network folder to an administrative installation point, run Office Setup using the /a flag. For instance, if the Office CD is on drive D, you could choose Run from the Start menu in Windows and type the following into the Run dialog box:

```
d:\Setup.exe /a
```

Next, in the Administrative Installation Setup dialog box, enter your organization name, the path of the shared folder you want to use as the administrative installation point, and the product key. (If you omit the product key, each user will have to enter a valid product key when installing Office XP.) Then in the End-User License Agreement dialog box, accept the license agreement and click the Install button.

2 Use the Custom Installation Wizard to create a *transform* (.mst) file for automating and customizing the installation of Office XP on users' computers. The Custom Installation Wizard is included in the Office Resource Kit. When you run it, it begins by displaying the informational dialog box shown in Figure 2-4, on page 24.

Part 1: Getting Going with Office XP

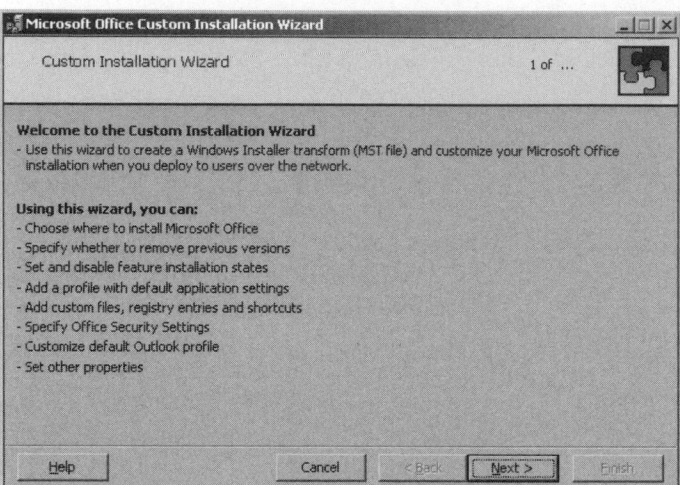

Figure 2-4. The Custom Installation Wizard begins by displaying this informational dialog box.

In the second wizard dialog box, you'll need to enter the path of the *Windows Installer package file* that will be used to install Office XP. You'll find this file in the administrative installation point folder that you set up in step 1. (The file will have a name such as Proplus.msi. This file contains default settings that Setup uses to install Office XP on a computer. These settings will be modified by the transform file that you create in the current step.)

In the third dialog box, you'll need to enter a name and location for the transform file that will be created. The best place to save it is in the administrative installation point folder you set up in step 1.

In the next series of wizard dialog boxes (about 20 of them!), select all the options that you want to apply when users install Office XP on their individual computers. You can click the Finish button in any of these dialog boxes to use the defaults for all installation options you haven't yet set. The final wizard dialog box, shown in Figure 2-5, provides further instructions.

Chapter 2: Installing and Configuring Office XP

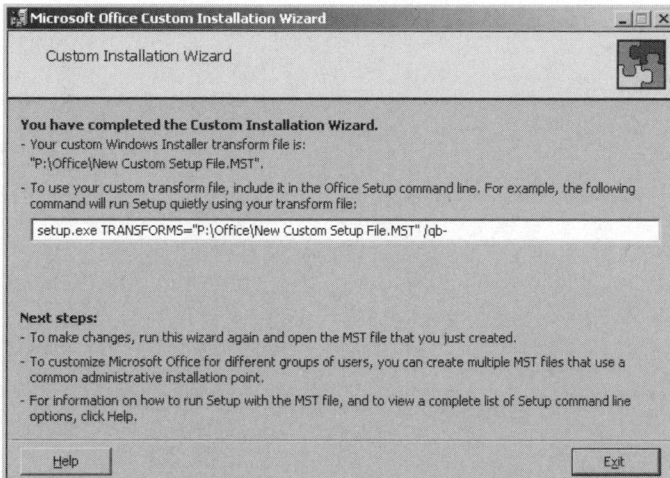

Figure 2-5. The final Custom Installation Wizard dialog box provides instructions for using the transform file that it creates.

3 Have each user install Office XP by running the Setup.exe program in the administrative installation point folder you created in step 1. When running Setup.exe, the user must pass the TRANSFORMS command-line parameter specifying the location of the transform file you created in step 2. For instance, if you created the administrative installation point in the \\admin\c\AdminInstallPoint\ network folder, and you named the transform file New Custom Setup File.mst, a user could install Office XP by choosing Run from the Start menu in Windows and entering the following into the Run dialog box:

```
\\admin\c\AdminInstallPoint\setup
TRANSFORMS="\\admin\c\AdminInstallPoint
\New Custom Setup File.mst" /qb-
```

(You should enter the entire command given above on a single line in the Run dialog box, with a space setween setup and TRANSFORMS.)

The Setup program will then run, without requiring the user to enter choices, and will automatically install Office XP using the options you specified in step 2. (The */qb-* command-line option suppresses the display of dialog boxes that allow the user to enter choices or require the user to respond. If you *omit* this option, the user will be able to override the default installation options specified in the transform file. For an explanation of other Setup command-line options, see the Office Resource Kit documentation.)

Chapter 2

> **tip** To make it easier for users to install Office XP, create a shortcut file containing the required command line for running Setup and then distribute the shortcut to all users.

newfeature!
Activating Office XP

After you install Office XP on your computer, you're required to *activate* it. If you don't activate Office, you'll be able to start an Office application only 50 times, and then you'll be required to activate it. Activation involves connecting with Microsoft on the Internet or by telephone.

> **note** If you haven't activated Office XP after running Office applications 50 times, you'll still be able to start an application, but it will run in Reduced Functionality Mode, which will prevent you from saving or creating new documents and possibly from using certain other features. You can activate Office XP at any time before or after reaching the Reduced Functionality Mode, and you'll then have unlimited use of Office.

The first time you run an Office application, it displays the Office Activation Wizard, shown in Figure 2-6, which allows you to activate Office XP. You can now do one of the following:

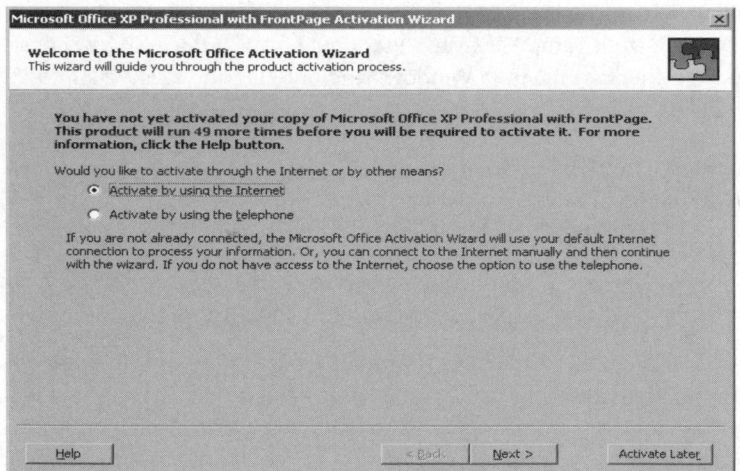

Figure 2-6. The Office Activation Wizard allows you to activate Office XP through the Internet or by telephone.

● To activate Office XP via the Internet, select the Activate By Using The Internet option and then click the Next button and follow the instructions in the remaining wizard dialog boxes to connect to Microsoft's Office XP activation site and complete the activation. You can manually connect to the Internet before clicking Next to use a specific connection if you have more than one or just click Next to have the wizard use your default Internet connection. You'll need to provide only your country of residence; supplying additional personal information is optional. The wizard will automatically activate your Office XP installation.

● To activate the product by telephoning a Microsoft customer service agent, select the Activate By Using The Telephone option and then click the Next button to see complete instructions for calling the agent and completing the activation process.

The next dialog box will provide the telephone number for calling the agent from your country and will display your unique Installation ID. You'll need to provide that ID to the agent, who will then give you a Confirmation ID. When you enter the Confirmation ID into the wizard dialog box and continue, the wizard will activate your Office XP installation.

● To skip the activation and immediately run the application, click the Activate Later button. Keep in mind, however, that you'll be able to run the product a total of only 50 times before activating, and in the meantime the Office Activation Wizard will keep coming up every time you start an Office XP application.

You can run the Office Activation Wizard at any time by doing one of the following:

● Choose Activate Product from the Help menu of an Office XP application

● From the Start menu in Windows, choose Programs, Microsoft Office Tools, Activate Product.

Revisiting Office Setup

You can rerun Office Setup in *maintenance mode* at any time to add or remove specific features, to reinstall Office XP if you've been having serious problems with one or more programs or features and you suspect that program files or Registry settings may have become corrupted, or to remove Office XP from your computer. To use Setup in maintenance mode, complete the following steps:

1 Open the Add/Remove Programs item in the Windows Control Panel, select the Microsoft Office XP item in the list, and click the Add/Remove button. The first Setup maintenance-mode dialog box will appear, which is shown in Figure 2-7, on page 28.

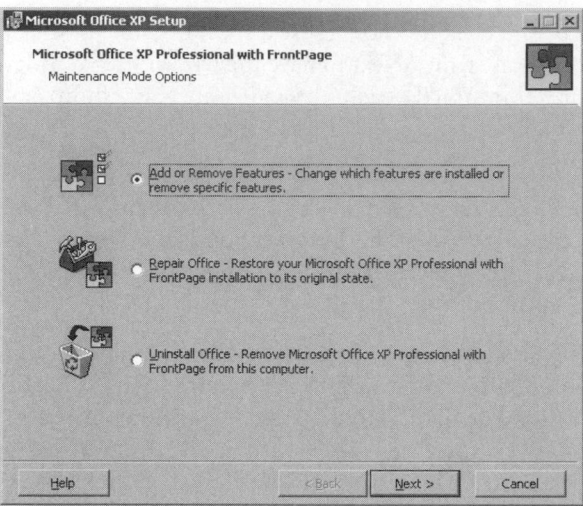

Figure 2-7. When you run the Office Setup program after installing Office XP, it begins by displaying the Maintenance Mode Options dialog box.

2 In the opening Setup dialog box, select an option (as explained in the following list), click the Next button, and fill in any additional dialog boxes or message boxes that are displayed.

■ To add or remove one or more Office applications or features, select Add Or Remove Features. Setup will display the same installation options you selected when you most recently ran Setup. You need to change only the installation options for features you want to add or remove; the rest of your installation won't be disturbed.

■ To reinstall all Office applications and features that have already been installed, select the Repair Office option. In the next dialog box you can then select one of the following options:

● To force Setup to reinstall all Office XP files and redo all Registry settings, whether or not they appear to be defective, select Reinstall Office.

● To have Setup detect defective files or settings and make just the repairs that are necessary, select Detect And Repair Errors In My Office Installation. If in doubt about which option to select, you might choose this simpler option first and select the more radical Reinstall Office option only if your problem persists.

note Another way to have Office XP detect and repair errors in your Office XP installation is to choose the Detect And Repair command from the Help menu of any Office application. This command provides an additional option that discards your customized settings and restores all defaults.

■ To remove Office XP from your computer, select Uninstall Office.

Chapter 3

Getting Expert
Help on Office XP

Getting the Most Out of the Office Online Help

Microsoft Office XP provides three main ways to access the online help information:

- The Assistant
- The Ask A Question list
- The Help Window

> **note**   To see a brief explanation of a program feature, choose Help,
> What's This? or press Shift+F1, and then click a toolbar button,
> choose a menu command, or click some other interface object
> (such as the ruler or status bar). If you click on text in a
> Microsoft Word document, Word displays the new Reveal For-
> matting task pane, which fully describes the text's formatting.

Getting Help with the Assistant

In Office XP you can use the Assistant, shown below, to get help quickly by typing plain English questions or phrases.

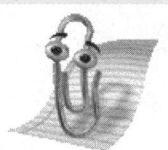

To use the Assistant, complete the following steps:

1 If the Assistant isn't visible, choose Help, Show The Office Assistant.

> **note** When you choose the Show The Office Assistant command, the Assistant is *turned on*—if it hasn't already been turned on—and it will remain turned on until you explicitly turn it off, as described later in this section. When the Assistant is turned on, you can quickly display the Assistant and its balloon by choosing Help, Microsoft Word Help, by clicking the Help toolbar button, or by pressing F1.
>
> **Help**
>
> Note that you can modify this behavior, as well as other Assistant behaviors discussed in these steps, by using the procedure for customizing the Assistant given later in this section.

2 If the Assistant balloon isn't visible, click the Assistant to display it:

(To hide the balloon, click the Assistant again.)

> **note** When the Assistant is displayed on the screen, Office shows messages using the Assistant balloon rather than the usual message box. For example, if you close a document containing unsaved changes, it will display the "Do you want to save the changes to the document?" message in the Assistant balloon rather than in a standard message box.
>
> Messages appear in the Assistant, however, only if the Display Alerts option is checked in the Options tab of the Office Assistant dialog box, described later in this section.

3 Type a question or phrase, in ordinary English, into the Assistant balloon—for example, "How do I use help?"—and click the Search button. The Assistant will then display a list of help topics matching your question, as shown at the top of the next page.

Chapter 3: Getting Expert Help on Office XP

4 Scroll through the topics, if necessary, by clicking See More or See Previous. Then click the topic you want to view. The help text will be displayed in the Help Window, described later in this chapter.

If you don't find a relevant topic in the list, you can click None Of The Above Look For More Help On The Web, which is the last option in the Assistant balloon, to connect to the Office Update Web site and perform a search for relevant help information on the Microsoft Web site. But before you do this, see the Inside Out on page 34.

You can work with the Assistant in the following ways:

● To hide the Assistant, choose Help, Hide The Office Assistant, or right-click the Assistant and choose Hide from the shortcut menu.

note Don't confuse merely *hiding* the Assistant with *turning off* the Assistant. When you hide the Assistant, it's removed from the screen but it will still appear if you choose Help, Microsoft Word Help, click the Help toolbar button, or press F1. When you turn off the Assistant, as described next, these three help commands display the Office Help window rather than the Assistant.

● To turn off or to customize the Assistant, click the Options button in the Assistant balloon, or right-click the Assistant itself and choose Options from the shortcut menu. This will display the Office Assistant dialog box.

In the Options tab of the Office Assistant dialog box, shown in Figure 3-1, you can turn off the Assistant by clearing the Use The Office Assistant check box and you can modify the way the Assistant works by checking or clearing other options. If the Guess Help Topics option is checked, when the Assistant is turned on it occasionally appears and automatically displays suggested help topics—for example, when you start writing a letter. Also, if one or more of the options in the Show Tips About area are checked, the Assistant periodically displays a light bulb to indicate that it has a tip relevant to your current actions. To read the tip, click the bulb. (If the Assistant is turned on but hidden, the light bulb is displayed on the Help toolbar button, which you can click to read the tip.)

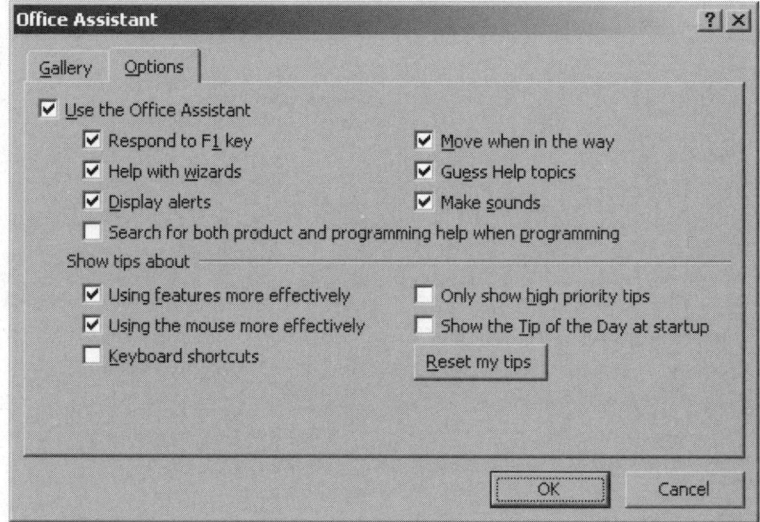

Figure 3-1. The Options tab of the Office Assistant dialog box lets you turn off the Assistant or modify the Assistant's behavior.

> **tip** In the Options tab of the Office Assistant dialog box, if you check Use The Office Assistant but clear Respond To F1 Key, you can easily display either the Help Window (by pressing F1) or the Assistant (by choosing Help, Microsoft Word Help or clicking the Help toolbar button).

In the Gallery tab, shown in Figure 3-2, you can select a different Assistant, such as The Dot, F1, or Office Logo (Clippit is the default Assistant, which is shown in the figures in this chapter). The Assistant options you select in these two tabs affect all Office applications.

Chapter 3

Chapter 3: Getting Expert Help on Office XP

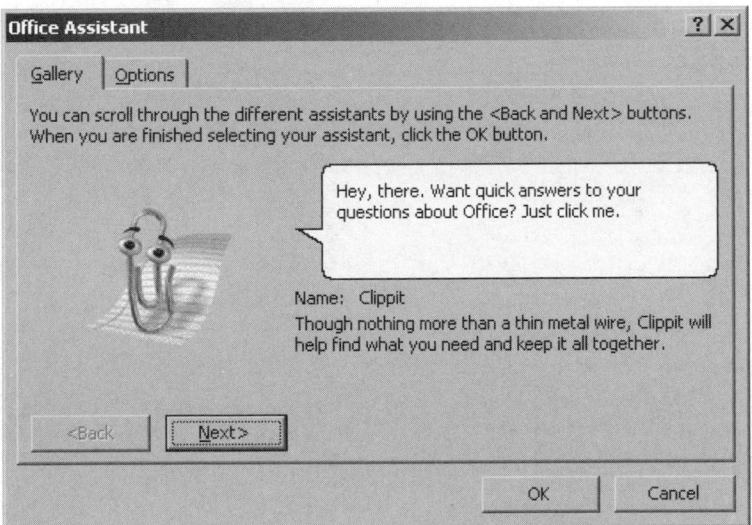

Figure 3-2. The Gallery tab of the Office Assistant dialog box lets you view different Assistants and select the one you want.

tip   You can download additional Assistants by choosing Help, Office On The Web to connect to the Microsoft Office Update Web site.

newfeature!
Getting Help with the Ask A Question List

Office XP provides a convenient new alternative to using the Assistant: the Ask A Question list. You can now get help by typing a question or phrase, in plain English, into the Ask A Question drop-down list that you'll find in the upper-right corner of every major Office application and then pressing Enter.

note   If you want to repeat a question you've already typed into the Ask A Question list during the current application session, you can simply select the question from the drop-down list.

The Ask A Question list works just like the Assistant, and it will find and display the identical list of topics:

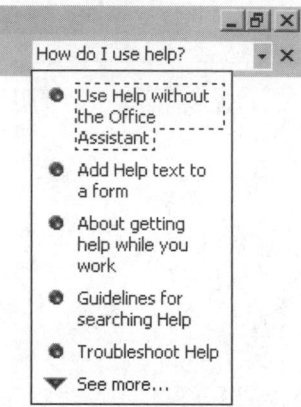

Before you click the None Of The Above Look For More Help On The Web option at the end of the list, however, see the Inside Out below.

InsideOut

If the Office help feature finds more than nine relevant topics, the Assistant or the Ask A Question list shows only the first nine. Although theoretically the first nine topics are the most relevant ones (the help engine attempts to list "hits" in the order of their relevance), the most useful topic might not be among the first nine. If you don't see the topic you want in the Assistant or Ask A Question list, use the Answer Wizard tab in the Help window, which displays *all* topics that are found. For example, in response to the question "How do I use help?" the Answer Wizard listed 20 topics, while the Assistant and Ask A Question list showed only the first nine of these topics. The next section explains how to use the Help window.

Getting Help Using the Help Window

Although it's not as convenient to use, the Help window provides more options than either the Assistant or the Ask A Question list. To use the Help window to obtain help information for the Office application you're currently running, follow these steps:

1 Make sure the Assistant is turned off, as described in "Getting Help with the Assistant" earlier in the chapter.

2 Choose Help, Microsoft Word Help, or click the Help toolbar button, or press F1.

3 In the Help window do one of the following actions:

Chapter 3: Getting Expert Help on Office XP

note If the tabs aren't visible in the Help window, click the Show/Hide button (see Figure 3-3).

■ To browse through the list of help topics and select the topic you want, use the Contents tab, shown in Figure 3-3.

Auto Tile
Show/Hide
Back
Forward
Print
Options

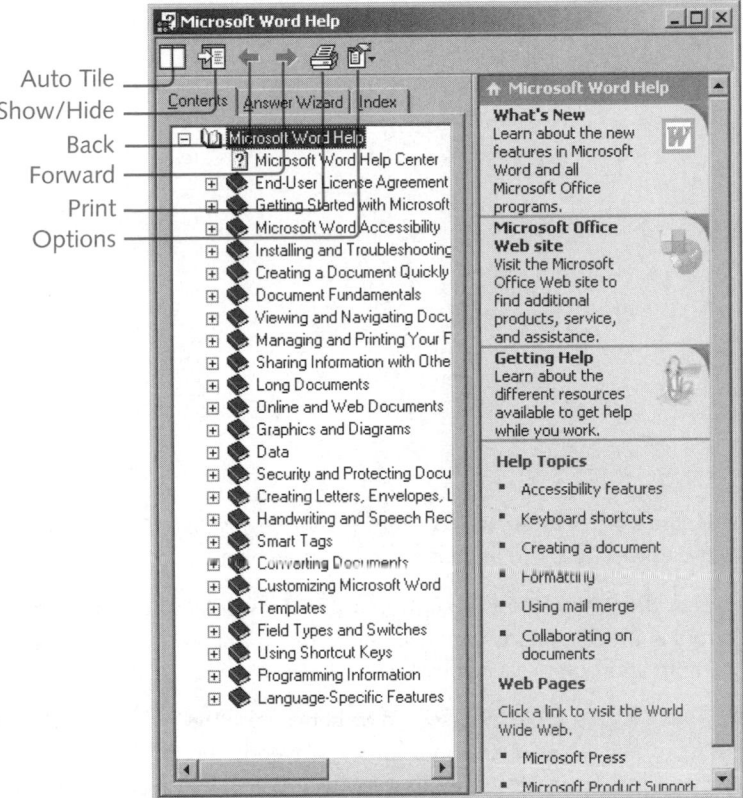

Figure 3-3. The Contents tab of the Help window displays the contents of the help file(s) for the current application (here, Word).

note You can fully expand or fully collapse the list of help topics in the Contents pane by right-clicking anywhere within the pane and choosing Open All or Close All from the shortcut menu.

■ To get help by typing in a plain English question or phrase (as you do with the Assistant or the Ask A Question list), use the Answer Wizard tab, shown in Figure 3-4.

Part 1: Getting Going with Office XP

Figure 3-4. The Answer Wizard tab works just like the Assistant or the Ask A Question list but shows *all* matching topics.

Click the Search On Web button in the Answer Wizard tab to connect to the Office Update Web site and perform a search for relevant help information on the Microsoft Web site.

To find a help topic by keyword or phrase, use the Index tab, shown in Figure 3-5. All valid keywords are displayed in the Or Choose Keywords list. The fastest way to select one is to begin typing a keyword into the Type Keywords text box, and the Help feature will automatically select the first matching keyword in the list and complete your entry. Keep typing until the desired keyword is selected in the list and entered into the text box (if you can find the keyword you want). To narrow the number of matching topics, you can enter several keywords into the list, separating them with semicolons. Click the Search button to see all matching topics.

Chapter 3: Getting Expert Help on Office XP

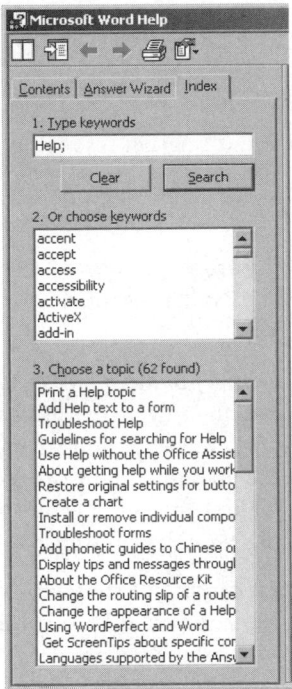

Figure 3-5. The Index tab lets you search using one or more pre-defined keywords or phrases.

---

tip **Open Help Files Directly**

Using the application help commands discussed in this chapter, you can access the help text for the current Office application only. To view the help text for *any* application without running that application, you can directly open the corresponding help file. The English language help files are located in the Program Files\Microsoft Office\Office10\1033 folder, and have the .chm (compiled HTML help) extension. For instance, you could double-click the Wdmain10.chm file in this folder to view the help text for Word. To quickly access a help file you use frequently, you can create a shortcut to that file in a file folder, on the Windows desktop, or on the Quick Launch toolbar. Note, however, that the Help window you display by directly opening a help file won't include the Answer Wizard and Index tabs.

For more information on creating shortcuts on the Quick Launch toolbar, see "Running the Office Applications," on page 43.

Chapter 3

Accessing Office Help Resources on the Web

The following are some useful Web sites and Internet resources where you can obtain information on Office applications, find answers to questions or solutions to problems, or download templates, updates, tools, and other useful files.

- **Microsoft Office site at *www.microsoft.com/office/*** This Microsoft site provides general information on evaluating, buying, installing, using, updating, and supporting Office XP.

- **Microsoft Office Update site at *officeupdate.microsoft.com*** This Microsoft site provides resources for all Office applications, including answers to frequently asked questions and other information, news and announcements, important product updates, online services, as well as templates, clip art, and other useful files you can download. You can open this site by choosing Help, Office On The Web in any major Office application.

- **Microsoft Product Support Services site at *support.microsoft.com/directory/*** This site is Microsoft's main portal for obtaining help information on all Microsoft products, for asking technical support questions online, for downloading files, and for finding out about all of Microsoft's support offerings, including phone numbers you can call for help.

- **Microsoft Knowledge Base at *search.support.microsoft.com/kb/*** This site is possibly the single most important Web resource for Office XP users and developers. It lets you search through an extensive set of articles containing detailed instructions, problem solutions, and links to files you can download, covering all aspects of Office XP.

- **Microsoft Download Center at *www.microsoft.com/downloads/*** For users of Office XP and other Microsoft products, this site is Microsoft's main portal for downloading free files. You can search for files by product, category, or keyword. The site will either let you download immediately or it will send you to the appropriate Microsoft page where you can find more information on the file and then download it.

- **Author's Web site at *www.mjyOnline.com*** Michael J. Young's Web site provides a companion Web page for *Microsoft Office XP Inside Out* (including book information, error reports, and links to related sites), an Office Tips page (including Office XP help resources and reader questions and answers), Office XP book recommendations, and information on contacting the author.

- **Microsoft Press site at *mspress.microsoft.com*** This site provides information on all Microsoft Press books.

- **Microsoft Office XP newsgroups**   You can post questions or comments in the general Office newsgroup on Microsoft's public news server at *news://msnews.microsoft.com/microsoft.public.office.misc* or in one of the other newsgroups on this same server that contain the word *Office* or the name of a specific Office application (for example, *news://msnews.microsoft.com/microsoft.public.word.tables*).

Using Other Help Resources

This section lists some additional Office XP help resources that you might find useful.

- **Microsoft TechNet**   Provides monthly CD-ROMs containing advanced information on Microsoft business products such as Office XP. Each CD-ROM includes many articles, technical notes, and tips, as well as service packs and patches. To subscribe in the United States or Canada, call (800) 344-2121.

- **Microsoft Developer Network (MSDN)**   Provides Windows and Office XP developers with programming information and toolkits. Subscribers receive regular deliveries of information, a newsletter, and access to other information sources. To subscribe in the United States or Canada, call (800) 759-5474 or visit MSDN Online at *msdn.microsoft.com*.

- **Microsoft Office XP Resource Kit**   Provides extensive information and a complete set of tools to help you install, configure, and support Office XP in a corporate setting. It's aimed at system administrators, consultants, and power users. You can obtain a printed copy (including a CD-ROM) from a computer book seller or directly from Microsoft press at *mspress.microsoft.com/*. Or you can download an up-to-date version of the text and utilities, without charge, from *www.microsoft.com/office/ork/*.

Chapter 3

Part 2

Common Office XP Techniques

Working with Office XP Applications, Documents, and Program Windows

Running the Office Applications

When the Setup program finishes installing Microsoft Office XP on your computer, you won't be at a loss for ways to run the Office programs. Office provides many ways for you to run its applications and utilities. Here's a summary of these techniques to help you find the easiest method to use in various situations.

● **Programs submenu.**   You can run any of the major Office applications you've installed by choosing the application from the Start menu in Microsoft Windows; click Start, Programs, and then choose the application. In Word, Excel, and PowerPoint, the application opens with a new, blank document.

note   In this chapter, the expression "all major Office applications" refers to Microsoft Word, Excel, PowerPoint, Outlook, FrontPage, Access, and Publisher.

● **New Office Document command.**   You can create a new Office document based on a template and run the corresponding Office application by clicking the Start button and choosing New Office Document. This will display the New Office Document dialog box.

> The New Office Document dialog box is explained in "Creating New Office Documents," on page 53.

- **Open Office Document command.** You can open an existing Office document and run the appropriate Office application by clicking the Start button and choosing Open Office Document. This will display the Open Office Document dialog box.

> The Open Office Document dialog box is explained in "Opening Existing Office Documents," on page 61.

- **Office Shortcut Bar.** This tool lets you open or create an Office document, or simply start an Office application, by merely clicking a button.

> The Office Shortcut Bar is discussed in "Using the Office Shortcut Bar," on page 46.

- **Quick Launch toolbar.** You can run Outlook by clicking the Launch Microsoft Outlook button on the Quick Launch toolbar displayed on the Windows taskbar. Note that the icon for Outlook doesn't appear on the Quick Launch toolbar until you configure Outlook.

  You can easily install additional buttons on the Quick Launch toolbar for running Office applications, opening documents, or displaying folders (see Figure 4-1).

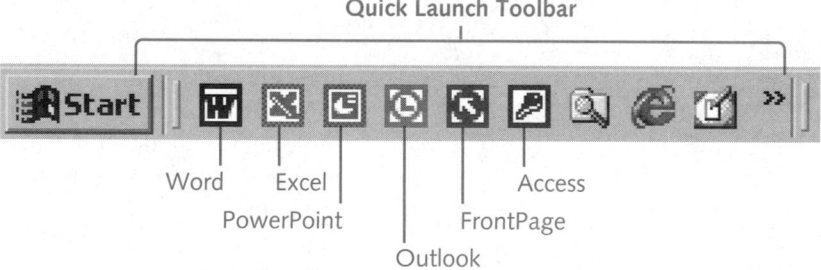

Figure 4-1. You can set up the Quick Launch toolbar so that it allows you to quickly open any of the major Office applications.

The fastest way to add a button to Quick Launch toolbar is to *right-drag*—drag using the right mouse button—the appropriate object (file, shortcut, or folder) from a folder (displayed in Windows Explorer, a folder window, or the desktop), drop it on the Quick Launch toolbar, and then choose Create Shortcut(s) Here from the shortcut menu, as shown here:

You can also drag a command from the Start menu using this same method. This is a good way to quickly add buttons to the Quick Launch toolbar for running programs.

- **Folder.** You can run an Office application and open an existing Office document by double-clicking the document—or a shortcut to the document—in a folder displayed in Windows Explorer, a folder window, or the Windows desktop. You can run an Office application by double-clicking a shortcut to that program.

note If you have enabled Web-style single-clicking in Windows, substitute "single-click" for "double-click" in these instructions.

Initially, you'll find a shortcut for running Microsoft Outlook on the Windows desktop. You can easily include additional shortcuts on the desktop (or in any other folder) for running Office applications, opening documents, or displaying folders. To do this, right-drag as discussed under the previous item in this list, but drop the object on the desktop (or in the folder) rather than on the Quick Launch toolbar.

tip Double-clicking an Office template or a wizard file creates a new document based on that template.

For information on templates and wizards, see "Creating New Office Documents," on page 53.

Chapter 4

45

● **Microsoft Office Tools submenu.** You can run the tools or utilities provided with Office from the Microsoft Office Tools submenu, which you open by choosing Programs, Microsoft Office Tools from the Start menu in Windows, as shown here:

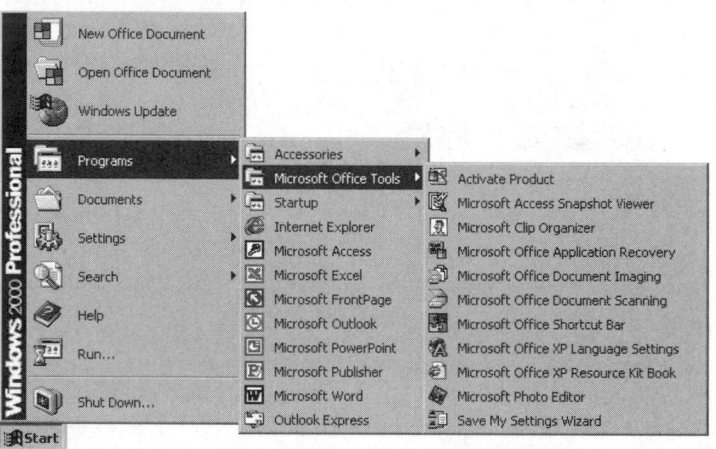

> **note** Some of the Office tools run only when you embed an object in an Office document and can't be run as freestanding programs. These applications, which include Microsoft Graph and Microsoft Equation, are known as OLE (object linking and embedding) servers. They are discussed in Chapter 6, "Adding Professional Graphics and Special Effects to Office XP Documents."

Using the Office Shortcut Bar

The Office Shortcut Bar (shown in Figure 4-2) doesn't let you do anything you can't do by other means. Its chief advantage, however, is that you can set it up so that its buttons are always visible on the screen, allowing you to open or create an Office document or run an Office application with a single click, rather than having to open a menu, switch to a particular program, or perform some other lengthier task. You can dock the Office Shortcut Bar along an edge of the screen or float it anywhere on the desktop, and you can configure it so it won't get covered by program windows. In other words, the Office Shortcut Bar behaves just like the Windows taskbar.

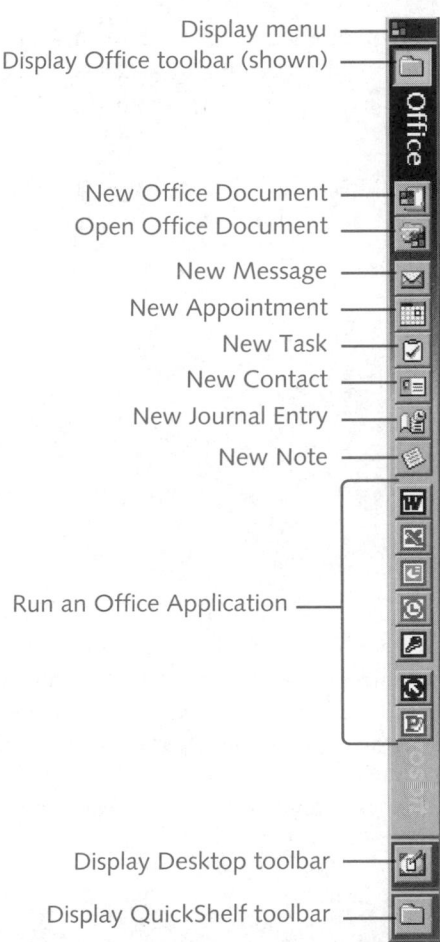

Display menu
Display Office toolbar (shown)

New Office Document
Open Office Document
New Message
New Appointment
New Task
New Contact
New Journal Entry
New Note

Run an Office Application

Display Desktop toolbar
Display QuickShelf toolbar

Figure 4-2. This figure shows the Office Shortcut Bar displaying the Office toolbar.

To display the Office Shortcut Bar, click the Start button, and then choose Programs, Microsoft Office Tools, Microsoft Office Shortcut Bar. You will then see a message box that gives you the option to have the Office Shortcut Bar appear automatically whenever you start Windows. This is a good choice if you regularly use the Office Shortcut Bar.

tip To stop displaying the Office Shortcut Bar automatically at Windows startup, quit the Office Shortcut Bar by choosing Exit from its menu, and then click No in the message box that appears.

The Office Shortcut Bar can include one or more separate toolbars. Initially, it includes only a single toolbar titled "Office," which is shown in Figure 4-2. (Before preparing this figure, we added two toolbars.) You display a particular toolbar by clicking its button on the Office Shortcut Bar.

To add or remove toolbars or toolbar buttons, or to customize the Office Shortcut Bar in other ways, click the icon in its title bar, and from the shortcut menu choose Customize, as shown here:

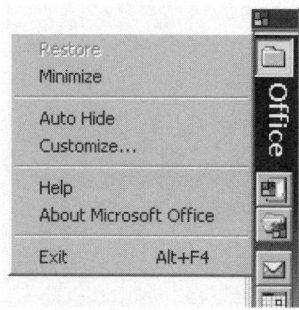

This action opens the Customize dialog box. To add toolbars to the Office Shortcut Bar, click the Toolbars tab of this dialog box (shown in Figure 4-3). To add a predefined toolbar simply check the toolbar name in the list. The predefined QuickShelf toolbar is initially empty and allows you to add any buttons you want; the other predefined toolbars give you immediate access through the Office Shortcut Bar to important Windows folders, such as Favorites, Programs, and Desktop. To create a new, blank toolbar, click the Add Toolbar button.

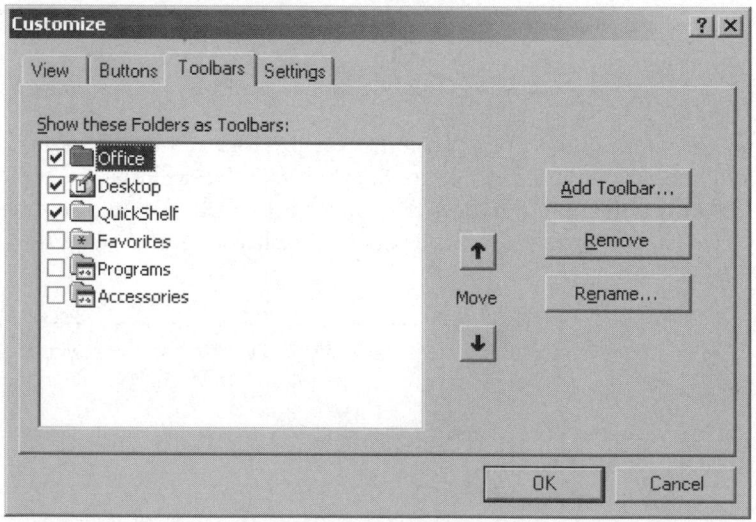

Figure 4-3. The Toolbars tab of the Customize dialog box lets you add or remove toolbars displayed on the Office Shortcut Bar.

To add, remove, hide, or show buttons on any of the currently displayed toolbars, click the Buttons tab of the Customize dialog box (shown in Figure 4-4). You can create buttons in the Office Shortcut Bar for performing the following Office tasks:

- Running an Office application or other program

- Opening an Office document or other file in the appropriate program

- Opening a folder

- Displaying the New Office Document dialog box to create a new document

- Displaying the Open Office Document dialog box to open an existing document

- Quickly creating an Outlook item (such as a message or appointment) without running Outlook

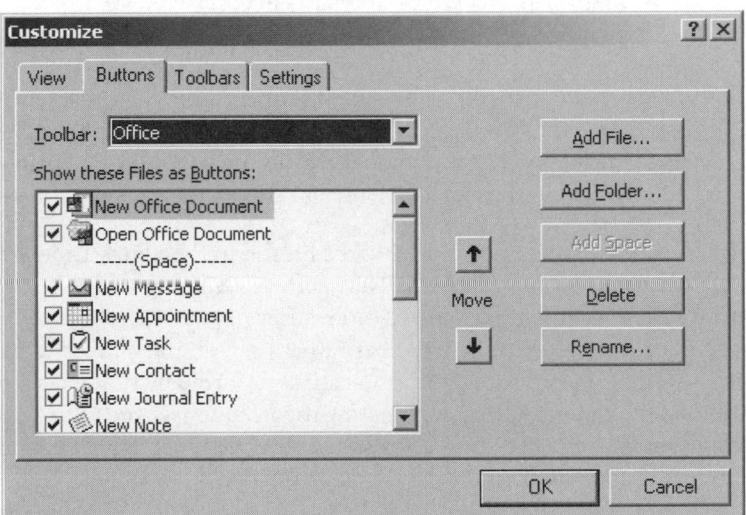

Figure 4-4. The Buttons tab of the Customize dialog box lets you work with toolbar buttons on the Office Shortcut Bar.

caution Don't delete any of the buttons in the Office toolbar of the Office Shortcut Bar. If you need a deleted button later, you might not be able to re-create it. Hide the button instead.

You can easily create one of the first two types of buttons in the list by clicking the Add File button on the Buttons tab and selecting the desired program or document. You can create a button of the third type by clicking the Add Folder button and selecting the folder you want the button to open. Alternatively, you can create any of these types of buttons by dragging the appropriate object from a Windows folder and dropping it directly on the toolbar displayed on the Office Shortcut Bar.

Adding one of the last three types of buttons, however, is a bit tricky. These buttons represent a special type of shortcut that you can't create using the normal methods. You can, however, create one of these types of buttons by following these steps:

1 In Windows Explorer, open the Office folder, which contains the actual shortcut for each of the buttons on the Office toolbar of the Office Shortcut Bar. You'll find the Office folder in one of the following locations (the particular folder depends on your Windows version and setup):

  ▪ Documents and Settings*UserName*\\Application Data\\Microsoft\\Office\\Shortcut Bar\\Office

  ▪ WinNT\\Profiles*UserName*\\Application Data\\Microsoft\\Office\\Shortcut Bar\\Office

  ▪ Windows\\Profiles*UserName*\\Application Data\\Microsoft\\Office\\Shortcut Bar\\Office

  ▪ Windows\\Application Data\\Microsoft\\Office\\Shortcut Bar\\Office

2 While pressing Ctrl, drag the desired shortcut from the Office folder and drop it on the Office Shortcut Bar toolbar where you want to add the button. For example, to add a button that creates a new Outlook appointment, press Ctrl as you drag the New Appointment shortcut and drop it on the toolbar.

You can use this same technique to add a button to the Quick Launch toolbar (on the Windows taskbar) for opening the New Office Document dialog box, displaying the Open Office Document dialog box, or creating a new Outlook item. Just drop the shortcut on the Quick Launch toolbar rather than on the Office Shortcut Bar. You can thus customize the Quick Launch toolbar to perform any of the tasks you can perform with the Office Shortcut Bar, eliminating the need to run the Office Shortcut Bar and saving some screen space. You can also use this basic technique to add one of these shortcuts to the Windows desktop or to any folder.

You can modify a particular button on the Office Shortcut Bar by right clicking it and choosing a command from the shortcut menu that appears:

newfeature!
Using the Task Panes in Office Applications

The new Office application *task panes* can—or must—be used to execute many of the commands discussed in this book. You will find them in all the major Office applications. A task pane is a Web-style area that you can either dock along the right or left edge of the window or float anywhere on the screen. It displays information, commands, and controls for choosing options (check boxes, buttons, lists, and so on). Like links on a Web page, the commands on a task pane are highlighted in blue text, they are underlined when you move the mouse pointer over them, and you run them with a single click (see Figure 4-5).

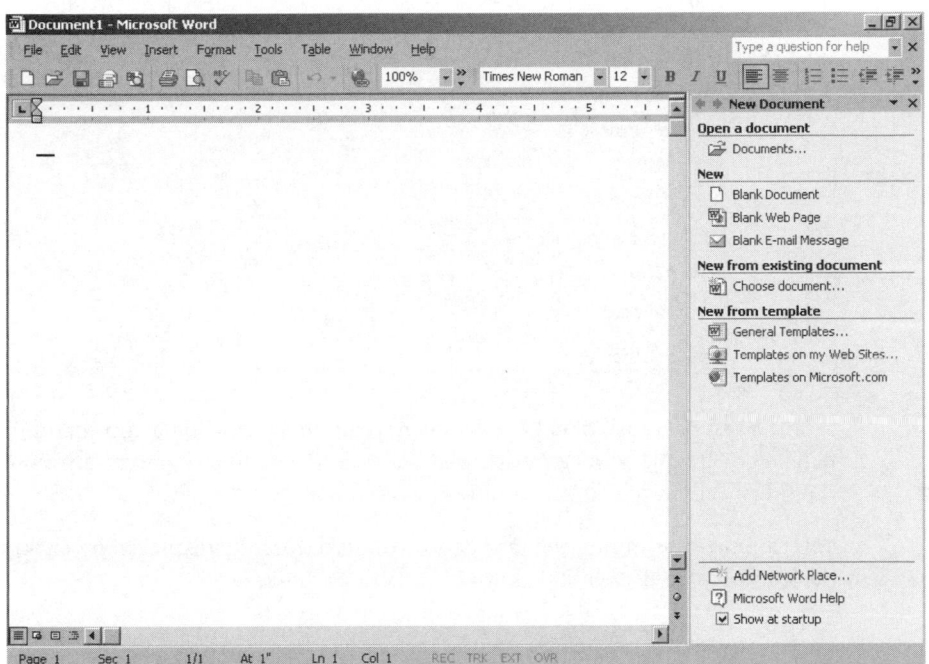

Figure 4-5. The New Document task pane is shown here displayed on the right side of a Word window.

Although a task pane takes up a lot of space on the screen and adds to the many different ways to perform tasks, it has some unique advantages over a dialog box—primarily that you can easily work with a task pane and with your document at the same time. A task pane doesn't cover your work, nor does it require that you close it before resuming other tasks. It's especially valuable for performing fairly complex jobs, such as creating form letters in Word or searching for files using multiple criteria.

A task pane pops up automatically when you perform certain tasks—for example, when you choose File, New to create a new document. To display a task pane at any time, choose View, Task Pane (if available). Or, use any of the standard methods for displaying a toolbar, namely:

- Choose View, Toolbars, Task Pane.

- Right-click the menu bar or any toolbar and choose Task Pane from the shortcut menu.

You then need to navigate to the particular task pane you want to work with. You can display any of the main task panes that are available by clicking the down arrow near the upper right corner of the pane that's displayed initially, and then choosing the name of the pane you want to open from the drop-down menu, as shown here:

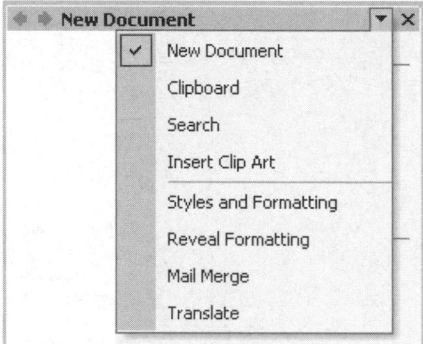

(Some subsidiary task panes can be displayed only by clicking a command in another pane. For example, you can display the Advanced Search task pane only by selecting the Advanced Search command in the Search pane.)

You can navigate among the task panes you have recently displayed by clicking the Back and Forward Web-style buttons, as shown here:

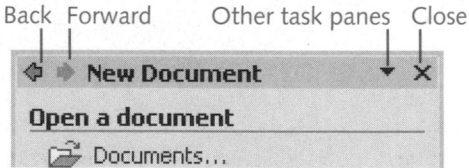

Each task pane contains a set of related commands. The particular panes that are available depend on the Office application you are running. However, most applications provide the following standard panes:

- **New**   for creating and opening documents. The actual title of the task pane varies by application; for example in Word it's the New Document pane and in Excel it's the New Workbook pane.

- **Clipboard**   for working with the enhanced Office Clipboard.
- **Search**   for finding files or Outlook items.

> This task pane is discussed in "Creating a Document Using the New Document Task Pane," on page 58. The enhanced Office Clipboard is covered in "Using the Enhanced Office Clipboard Task Pane," on page 109. The Search task pane is explained in "Finding Office Files or Outlook Items Using the Search Feature," on page 69.

> **note**   Outlook has only the Clipboard task pane.

Creating New Office Documents

The methods for creating new Office documents are quite uniform among most of the major Office applications—namely, Word, Excel, PowerPoint, FrontPage, Access, and Publisher. The three basic methods for creating new Office documents are the following:

- Using the New Office Document dialog box
- Creating an empty Office document in a folder
- Using the New Document task pane

You can use the first two methods from Windows without first starting an Office program. With the third method you have to first decide which application you want to use to create the document and then run that application.

Creating a Document Using the New Office Document Dialog Box

The New Office Document dialog box (shown in Figure 4-6) lets you create almost any type of Office document. To use this dialog box, complete the following steps:

1 From the Start menu in Windows, open the dialog box by choosing New Office Document, or, on the Office Shortcut Bar, by clicking the New Office Document button.

2 Click the tab corresponding to the general category of document you want to create (General, Letters & Faxes, Presentations, Web Pages, and so on).

3 Double-click the icon for the specific type of document you want to create. This runs the appropriate application and creates the document. When you select a particular icon, the Preview area shows a preview image of the document, if one is available.

53

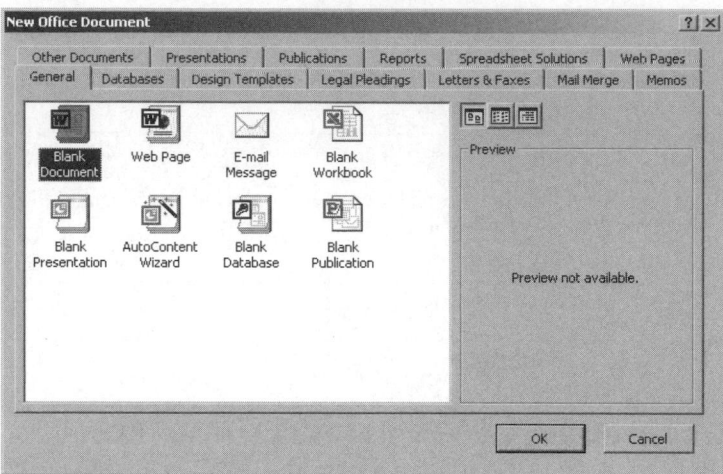

Figure 4-6. The New Office Document dialog box lets you open an Office document from Windows.

Almost all the icons in the New Office Document dialog box create a document by using a template or by running a wizard, giving you a head start in putting together a particular type of document. A *template* contains a blueprint for a specific document type and immediately creates the document, usually adding initial content to get you started. A *wizard* first displays a series of dialog boxes that let you customize the new document's content. An icon that runs a wizard is marked with a magic wand and usually has "wizard" in its name.

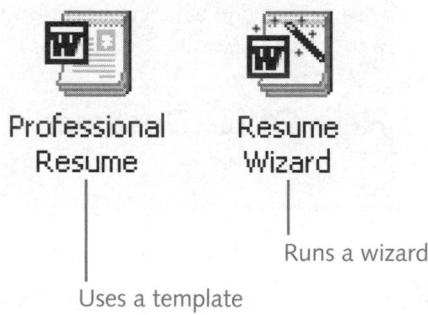

Professional
Resume

Resume
Wizard

Runs a wizard

Uses a template

InsideOut

FrontPage provides a large internal set of templates and wizards that you can use to create webs (FrontPage-managed Web sites) or Web pages. Likewise, Publisher offers many internal wizards for creating publications. These templates and wizards, however, *are not* available through the New Office Document dialog box. To use them, you need to run the application and create a new web, Web page, or publication using the program's commands, as explained in the part of this book pertaining to FrontPage or Publisher.

Chapter 4

In the New Office Document dialog box, it might not be obvious which application will be used to create the document type you've selected. This dialog box conforms to the document-centric philosophy that the type of document you are creating is more important than the particular application that you use to create it. In the real world, however, you'll probably want to know which application is used (maybe you're a whiz at Word, but a klutz with PowerPoint). The image in the icon indicates the application, not always obviously (yes, the big W stands for Word and the big X for Excel, but the others aren't so apparent). To be certain, click the Details button to switch into the Details view. This view also clearly indicates whether the icon uses a template or runs a wizard (see Figure 4-7). You'll learn about the templates provided by specific applications—and how to work with them—in the parts of the book that cover individual applications.

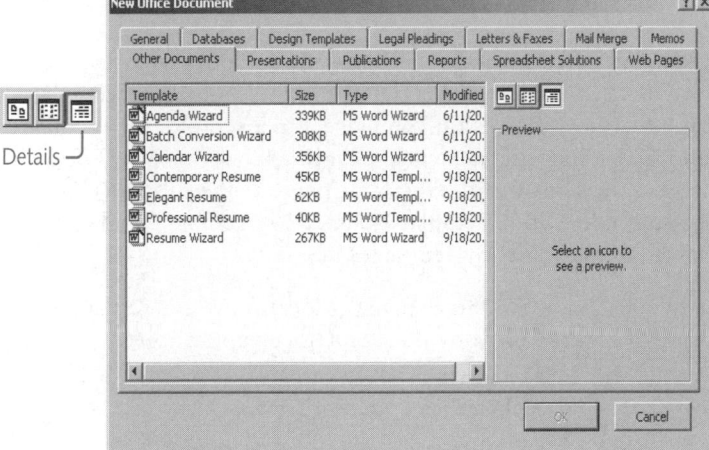

Figure 4-7. Viewing document types in Details view indicates which application is used to create a document.

Table 4-1 shows the extensions used for files that store Office templates and wizards.

Table 4-1. Extensions Used for Template and Wizard Files

Type of Template or Wizard	Extension of Template or Wizard File
Access database wizard	.mdz
Excel template	.xlt
Outlook item template	.oft
PowerPoint template	.pot
Publisher	.pub (a Publisher "template" is stored in the normal document format)
Word template	.dot
Word wizard	.wiz

Word, Excel, and PowerPoint let you modify the standard templates that come with Office and create new custom templates. You'll learn the details in the chapters on these individual applications.

The standard Office templates are stored in subfolders of your Program Files\Microsoft Office\Templates folder. However, you should normally store any custom templates you create in one of the following folders (the particular folder depends on your Windows version and setup):

- Documents and Settings*UserName*\Application Data\Microsoft\Templates
- WinNT\Profiles*UserName*\Application Data\Microsoft\Templates
- Windows\Profiles*UserName*\Application Data\Microsoft\Templates
- Windows\Application Data\Microsoft\Templates

If you store a custom template directly within the Templates folder, it will appear in the General tab of the New Office Document dialog box (or in the Templates dialog box displayed by individual Office applications). If you place it in a subfolder that you create within the Templates folder, the template will appear in a tab of the New Office Document (or Templates) dialog box that has the same name as the subfolder. For instance, if you create a subfolder within Templates named My Templates, all templates you put in that folder will appear in the My Templates tab.

Be aware, however, that you can use Word to change the location where you store templates, and the settings you make in Word affect all Office applications.

For more information, see "Customizing and Creating Document Templates," on page 405.

InsideOut

The New Office Document (or Templates) dialog box displays the standard templates supplied with Office that are stored within subfolders of Program Files\Microsoft Office\Templates. However, for some reason it won't display any new custom templates that you create and store in this area. Therefore, be sure to follow the guidelines given in this section for storing your templates, and don't attempt to save them in the same location as the standard templates.

To make sure that you save a custom template in the right place, follow these steps:

1 After you have completed the Word document, Excel workbook, or PowerPoint presentation that you want to use as a template, choose File, Save As.

2 In the Save As dialog box, from the Save As Type drop-down list, select the Template item. This item will be labeled Document Template in Word, Template in Excel, and Design Template in PowerPoint. The Save As dialog box will automatically switch to the proper folder for storing custom templates.

3 Enter a name for your template and save it in the current folder—in this case the template will appear in the General tab of the New Office Document (or Templates) dialog box. Or, save it in a subfolder of the current folder—in this case, the template will appear in a tab that is labeled with the name of the subfolder. You can quickly create a subfolder by clicking the Create New Folder button near the top of the Save As dialog box or by pressing Alt+5.

InsideOut

As explained in "Creating a Document Using the New Document Task Pane," on page 58, in Office XP you can use a standard document as if it were a template. This new feature makes modifying templates and creating custom templates less important.

Creating an Empty Office Document in a Folder

You can use the New command in Windows to quickly create and save a new Word, Excel, PowerPoint, Access, or Publisher document—ready for later editing—without even running an Office application. To do so, perform the following steps:

1 In Windows Explorer or in a folder window, open the folder in which you want to store the document.

2 Choose File, New, or right click on a blank area within the folder and choose New from the shortcut menu.

3 Choose the appropriate command from the New submenu, as shown here:

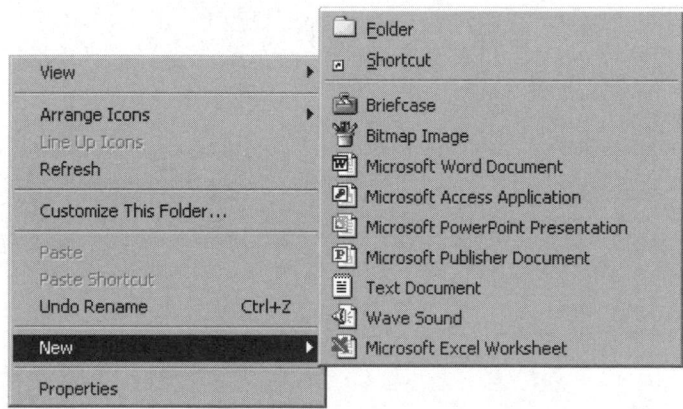

Windows and Office then create and save a new document, giving it a default name and highlighting the name so that you can change it if you wish. You can open the document later for editing.

Normally, the New command creates a blank document. However, you can customize the content of the documents that New creates for a particular application by editing the appropriate file in the WINNT\ShellNew or Windows\ShellNew folder, as shown in Table 4-2.

Table 4-2. The Applications and Files Used by the New Command

Office Application Used by New Command	File Used for New Documents
Word	Winword8.doc
Excel	Excel9.xls
PowerPoint	Pwrpnt10.pot
Access	Access9.mdb
Publisher	Mspub.pub

For example, if you frequently write memos in Word, you could edit the WINNT \ShellNew\Winword8.doc file so that it contains the basic content—text, formatting, graphics, and so on—for a memo. Whenever you subsequently use the New command, the new document created will already contain the basic memo content. All you would then need to do is to open the document and type in the message.

newfeature!
Creating a Document Using the New Document Task Pane

The third main way to create a new Office document is to open the application you want to use and then click the New toolbar button (labeled New Blank Document in Word), or, choose File, New. Details vary among applications, but typically, clicking the New button immediately creates a new blank document, and choosing the New menu command opens the New Document task pane, as shown in Figure 4-8. You'll find this pane in all the major Office applications except Outlook. The actual label of this pane varies by application—for example, in Word it's labeled New Document, and in Excel it's labeled New Workbook.

For general information on using task panes, see "Using the Task Panes in Office Applications," on page 51.

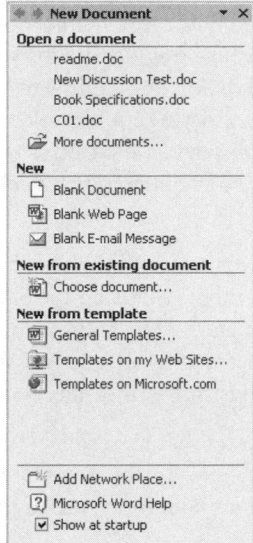

Figure 4-8. This is the New Document task pane that's displayed in Word.

---

tip **Use Other Methods to Open the New Document Task Pane**

Rather than choosing File, New, you can use any of the general methods for opening a task pane that were explained in "Using the Task Panes in Office Applications," on page 51. In fact, if the Show At Startup option at the bottom of the pane is checked, the pane will appear automatically when you first start the application. (This option affects only the current Office application. You can also set this option by checking or clearing the Startup Task Pane check box in the View or General tab of the Options dialog box, which you can open by choosing Tools, Options.)

To create a new document in the task pane, use one of the following methods:

- To create a new blank document, click one of the commands in the New group. Most Office applications provide several commands in this group to let you create various types of documents. For example, in Word you can click Blank Document to create an empty Word document based on the Normal template, Blank Web Page to create an empty document in HTML (Hypertext Markup Language) format, or Blank E-Mail Message to create a new e-mail message that you can send using Outlook.

newfeature!
- To create a new document based on an existing one, click the Choose Document command in the New From Existing Document group. This opens the New From Existing Document dialog box, which lets you select

an existing document. The new document created will contain all of the content from the existing document, just as if the existing document were a template. (The label of the command group and dialog box again varies by application; for example, in Excel it is New From Existing Workbook.) The New From Existing Document dialog box lets you select a file from a local, network, or Internet location. It's similar to the Open dialog box, which is explained in the next section.

The "new from existing" feature provides a safe alternative to the somewhat precarious practice of opening a boilerplate document, choosing the Save As command to create a new copy of that document, and then customizing the document (precarious because it's too easy to forget to use the Save As command *before* you edit and save the document, thus overwriting your boilerplate).

● To create a document based on one of the templates that are available for the current application, choose a command in the New From Template group. Most Office applications let you select a template from one of three different sources:

■ To use one of the templates stored on your computer, click the General Templates command to open the Templates dialog box. This dialog box is similar to the New Office Document dialog box discussed in "Creating a Document Using the New Office Document Dialog Box," on page 53, except that it shows only those templates used by the current application.

■ To open a template that is stored on a Web site, click Templates On My Web Sites. This action displays the New From Templates On My Web Sites dialog box, which lets you view or open a Web site that has been set up in your My Network Places folder (or Web Folders in versions of Windows prior to Windows Me and Windows 2000).

Using My Network Places (Web Folders) is discussed in "Accessing SharePoint Document Libraries from Office Applications," on page 189.

● To use one of the additional Office templates stored on Microsoft's Web site, click Templates On Microsoft.com.

Templates and wizards are discussed in "Creating a Document Using the New Office Document Dialog Box," on page 53.

Chapter 4

> **tip** **Use Drag-and-Drop to Open a Document**
>
> Another way to open an existing document in an Office application is to drag the document file from Windows Explorer, or from a folder window, and drop it on the window of the application in which you want to open it. The surest way to simply open the document is to drop it on the application window's title bar. The effect of dropping it within a document window varies with the application and the type of file you've dragged.

Opening Existing Office Documents

The basic methods for opening existing Office documents are the same across most of the major Office applications—namely, Word, Excel, PowerPoint, FrontPage, Access, and Publisher. (In FrontPage, the procedures differ somewhat because you can open either a file or a *web*, which as mentioned earlier in the chapter, is a FrontPage-managed Web site.)

> The FrontPage-specific techniques are described in Part 7 of this book.

The following are the two basic methods for opening Office documents:

- Using the Open Office Document dialog box to open any Office document
- Running an Office application and opening a document specific to that application

Keep in mind that you can also open an Office document by double-clicking (or single-clicking) a document file or a shortcut to that file in a folder, as discussed in "Running the Office Applications," on page 43.

Opening an Existing Document Using the Open Office Document Dialog Box

You can use the Open Office Document dialog box (shown in Figure 4-9) to open any kind of Office document without having to first start an application. The document will be opened in the particular Office application that is registered to open that document type, as determined by the document's file extension. For example, Word is registered by default to open files with the .doc extension, Excel files with the .xls extension, and Notepad files with the .txt extension.

> **newfeature!**
>
> **note** In Office XP you can adjust the size of the Open dialog box. You can't, however, make the box smaller than its original size.

Chapter 4

To display the Open Office Document dialog box, from the Start menu in Windows, choose Open Office Document, or click the Open Office Document button on the Office Shortcut Bar. To use this dialog box, complete the following steps:

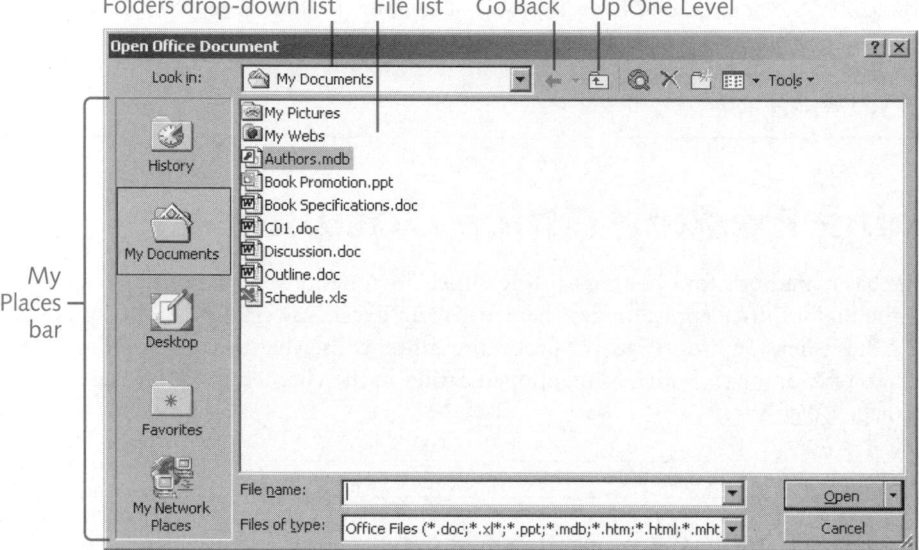

Folders drop-down list   File list   Go Back   Up One Level

My Places bar

Figure 4-9. The Open Office Document dialog box lets you open any type of Office document.

1 In the Files Of Type drop-down list, select the type of the document you want to open. This will narrow the number of files you will have to look at. The default selection, Office Files, shows all the standard Office document types, which is quite a large collection of file types.

2 In the My Places bar, select a folder to look in. Alternately, use the File list, together with the Folders drop-down list, Go Back button, and Up One Level button at the top of the dialog box to navigate to the folder that contains the document.

3 Type the filename into the File Name text box or click the filename in the File list.

4 Click Open. As an alternative to steps 3 and 4, you can just double-click the filename in the File list.

---

tip   **Convert a Document**

If you want to open a document that is in a non-native format (for example, you want to open a WordPerfect 5.x document in Word), you have to first run the application in which you want to open the document, and then use the Open dialog box, as discussed in the next section. The Files Of Type list in the Open Office Document dialog box does *not* list the non-native formats.

To open an Office document stored in a location other than on a local disk, use one of the following techniques in the Open Office Document dialog box:

● To open a document on a shared drive on your network, click My Network Places in the My Places bar to view or open your network drives. With versions of Windows prior to Windows 2000 and Windows Me, you will have to navigate to the network drive using the Network Neighborhood folder in the Folders drop-down list. In any version of Windows, you can also get to a network location via a mapped network drive if you have created one.

● To open a document on a Web site that has SharePoint Team Services or other Microsoft server extensions, click My Network Places (or Web Folders with versions of Windows prior to Windows 2000 and Windows Me) in the My Places bar. You can then use a shortcut to a particular Web site to display the documents stored on that site. You can also save the document back to the site when you have finished editing it.

For information on using My Network Places (Web Folders), and for setting up shortcuts to Web sites, see "Accessing SharePoint Document Libraries from Office Applications," on page 189.

● To open a document from a Web site that does *not* have Microsoft server extensions that allow you to save documents, type the file's URL directly into the File Name box. Alternately, select a shortcut to that file—these are usually stored in your Favorites folder and in its subfolders, which you can access by clicking Favorites on the My Places bar. The file will be opened in read-only mode. You can edit it and save a local copy by using the File menu's Save As command.

● To open a document on a File Transfer Protocol (FTP) Internet site, type the *full* URL into the File Name text box (for example, *ftp://ftp.microsoft.com*). Or, navigate to the site using the FTP Locations folder in the Folders drop-down list of the Open Office Document dialog box. FTP Locations lists the FTP sites you've previously accessed. To add a new site to FTP Locations, double-click Add/Modify FTP Locations in the FTP Locations folder, as shown here:

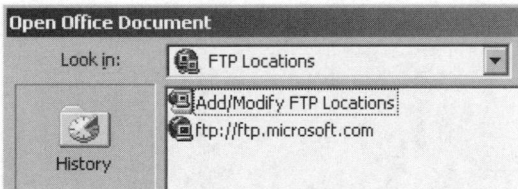

You can save the document back to the FTP site (or save any document to the site through the Save As dialog box), provided that you have the required permissions.

You can select multiple files in the File List of the Open Office Document dialog box to open them all at once. To select an adjoining set of files, click the first one and then click the last one while pressing the Shift key. To select nonadjoining files, click the first one and then click each additional one while pressing the Ctrl key.

> For tips on managing several open documents, see "Working with Multiple Documents," on page 79.

To open a file in alternative ways, click the down arrow on the Open button and choose a command from the drop-down list shown here:

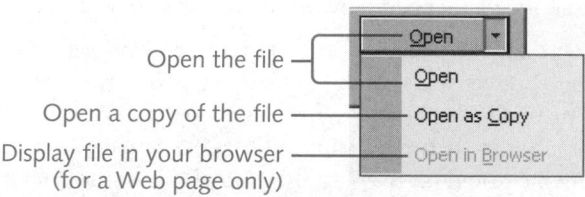

Open the file ————

Open a copy of the file ————

Display file in your browser ———— (for a Web page only)

InsideOut

The Open As Copy command creates a copy of the selected document and saves it in the same folder as the original. The name of the copy is based on the original filename (for instance, if you select Memo.doc, the copy will be called Copy(1) of Memo.doc). Usually, however, a better way to create a new document based on an existing one is to use the New From Existing... feature of the New Document task pane, described in "Creating a Document Using the New Document Task Pane," on page 58. The New From Existing... feature is preferable because it lets you name the new document yourself, and it doesn't automatically save a document to disk (which would leave clutter on your disk if you decide to abandon the new document).

You can perform many file and folder management tasks right within the Open Office Document dialog box by using the controls at the top right of the dialog box, as shown here:

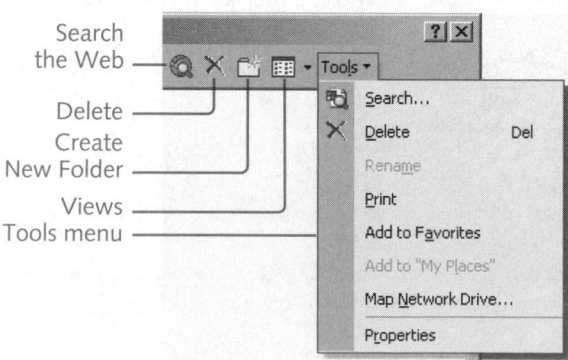

Search the Web ————

Delete ————
Create New Folder ————
Views ————
Tools menu ————

Chapter 4

You can also perform many management tasks by right-clicking on a blank area in the current folder:

or on a file or folder:

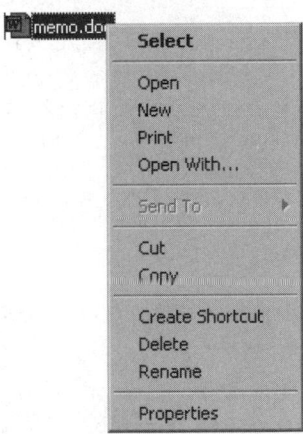

and choosing a command from the shortcut menu. (The commands on the shortcut menu that appears when you right-click a file vary according to the type of file.)

new feature!

In Office XP you can easily customize the My Places bar in the Open Office Document dialog box (without editing the Windows Registry, which was required in Office 2000). Here's how:

- To add a folder to the bar, select it in the File list, click the Tools button, and choose Add To "My Places" from the drop-down menu.

- To remove, rename, or change the position of a folder in the bar, right click it and choose the appropriate command from the shortcut menu, as shown on the next page.

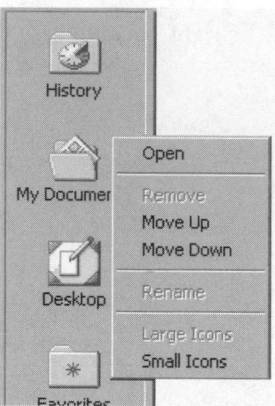

You can remove or rename only folders you have added, not the standard ones that are originally displayed in the bar.

Once you have added one or more folders, you might need to scroll through the My Places bar to get to a particular folder. To scroll, just click the small arrow at the top or bottom of the bar. To avoid having to scroll, you can reduce the size of the icons by choosing Small Icons from the shortcut menu that appears when you right click anywhere in the bar. You can later restore the icons to their original size by choosing Large Icons.

The following are some general methods that will make it easier to locate the documents you want to open:

- To make it easier to identify documents, click the Views button and choose the Details, Properties, or Preview view, as shown here:

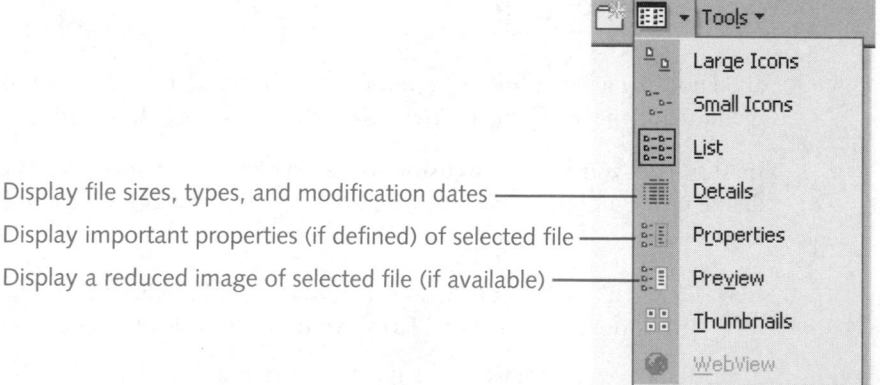

Display file sizes, types, and modification dates ——— Details
Display important properties (if defined) of selected file ——— Properties
Display a reduced image of selected file (if available) ——— Preview

- To view *all* properties of the selected file—and to be able to set many of them—choose Properties from the Tools drop-down menu.

- To find documents based on a wide variety of criteria, use Office XP's new Search feature.

You can learn more about the new Search feature in "Finding Office Files or Outlook Items Using the Search Feature," on page 69.

● To make it easier to identify documents, assign distinguishing properties to documents before you save them.

Assigning properties is explained in "Using Office Document Properties," on page 82.

Opening Documents Within Office Applications

Rather than displaying the Open Office Document dialog box, you can run the particular Office application in which you want to open the document and then display the Open dialog box (shown in Figure 4-10), using one of the following methods:

● Click the Open toolbar button.

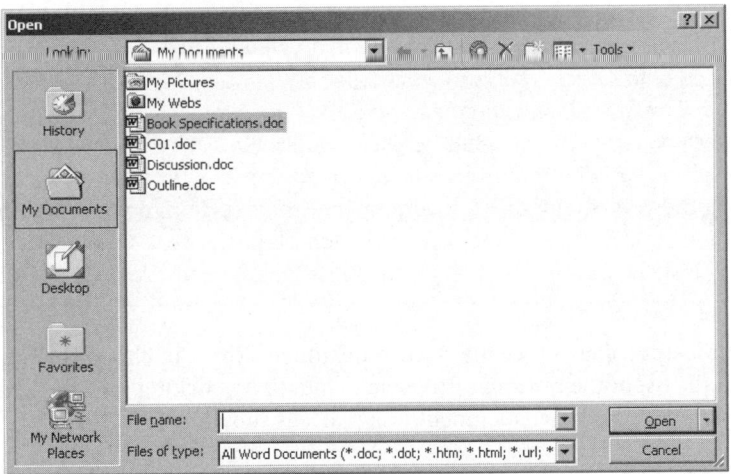

Open

● Choose File, Open.

● Press Ctrl+O.

● Click the appropriate command in the New Document task pane. For example, in Word's New Document task pane, click the More Documents command; in Excel's New Workbook task pane, click the More Workbooks command.

Figure 4-10.   This figure shows the Open dialog box displayed in Word.

Chapter 4

The Open dialog box works just like the Open Office Document dialog box described in the previous section, except for these unique features:

● The Files Of Type drop-down list displays *all* of the different file types that the current application can open. (The Open Office Document dialog box displays only the native Office document types.)

To open a file with a non-native format in a particular Office application (for example, to open a Lotus 1-2-3 file in Excel), run the application, display the Open dialog box, and select the file's format in the Files Of Type drop-down list, which will display all formats that the application can open and convert to its native format.

● The file you select will usually be opened in the current application, rather than in the application that is registered to open that file type. This feature can be good or bad. For example, if you open an Excel workbook in Word, the workbook is opened as an embedded object in a new Word document (a helpful action). On the other hand, if you open a PowerPoint presentation in Word, Word simply displays the content of the presentation as unreadable binary data (which is not helpful).

---

tip **Convert More File Formats**

If, in the Files Of Type drop-down list, you don't find a description of the format of the file you want to import, make sure that you've installed all the text converters supplied with Office. (You should also do this if you are saving a document to a non-native format and don't see the desired format in the Files Of Type list.) To install all converters, rerun Office Setup, as explained in "Revisiting Office Setup" on page 27, and select the Run From My Computer option for the Text Converters feature. You will find this feature in the Converters And Filters section, under the Office Shared Features group. Because the converters don't take up a lot of disk space, we recommend installing all of them, rather than just the one you currently need.

To quickly reopen a recently opened document, you can choose it from the recently used file list at the bottom of the File menu, or by clicking it in the identical list displayed in the New Document task pane, as shown here:

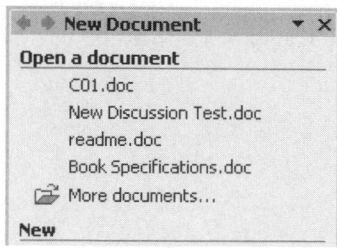

Windows also lets you reopen a document that was recently opened in any program by choosing it from the Start menu's Documents submenu. (This list is distinct from the ones maintained by Office applications.)

> **tip** **Adjust the Length of the Recently Used File List**
>
> In Word, Excel, PowerPoint, and Access you can modify the number of documents displayed in the recently used file list—on the File menu and in the New Document task pane—by choosing Tools, Options, clicking the General tab, and changing the number in the Recently Used File List text box. Clearing the Recently Used File List check box completely removes the recently used file list from the File menu and from the New Document task pane.

newfeature! Finding Office Files or Outlook Items Using the Search Feature

You can quickly locate Office document files, as well as Outlook items, using the new Search feature in Office XP. The Search feature is a completely revamped version of the Find command that you could run through the Open Office Document and Open dialog boxes in Office 2000. An important improvement of the new Search feature is that it makes it easy to search for Office files containing specified text, a common task that was quite cumbersome with the former Find command.

> The more common way of finding Outlook items is using Outlook's Find command or Advanced Find command, discussed in "Finding Outlook Items or Disk Files," on page 1010.

In Office XP, you can find the Search feature in the Search task pane in all the major applications except Outlook. You can also access it via the Search dialog box, which you open by choosing Search from the Tools drop-down menu in the Open Office Document dialog box, as shown here, or in the Open dialog box in all major Office applications.

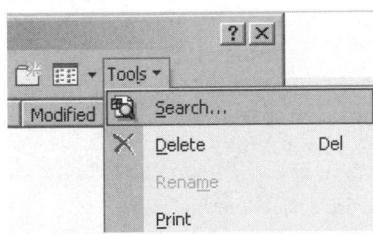

The options in the Search task pane and in the Search dialog box are arranged differently, and the Search task pane provides two additional options (a command to modify the Indexing Service, and in Word and Excel, a command to open the Find And Replace dialog box to search the current document). Otherwise, they work the same, so this section covers just the Search task pane.

Search

To display the Search task pane, click the Search button on the Standard toolbar (the Database toolbar in Access) or choose File, Search. Alternatively, if a task pane is currently displayed, you can navigate to the Search task pane by clicking the down arrow in the upper right corner of the pane and choosing Search from the drop-down menu.

The Search task pane consists of a basic pane, an advanced pane, and a results pane that shows the files found through the search. To quickly search for files or Outlook items containing specified text, use the basic Search task pane (shown in Figure 4-11) as follows:

1 If the advanced pane is currently displayed, switch to the basic pane by clicking the Basic Search command near the bottom of the pane.

2 In the Search Text box, enter the text you want to find.

3 In the Search In drop-down list, select the specific file folders or Outlook folders you want to search, or select Everywhere to search all of them.

4 In the Results Should Be drop-down list, select the specific types of files or Outlook items you want to search for.

5 Click Search to start.

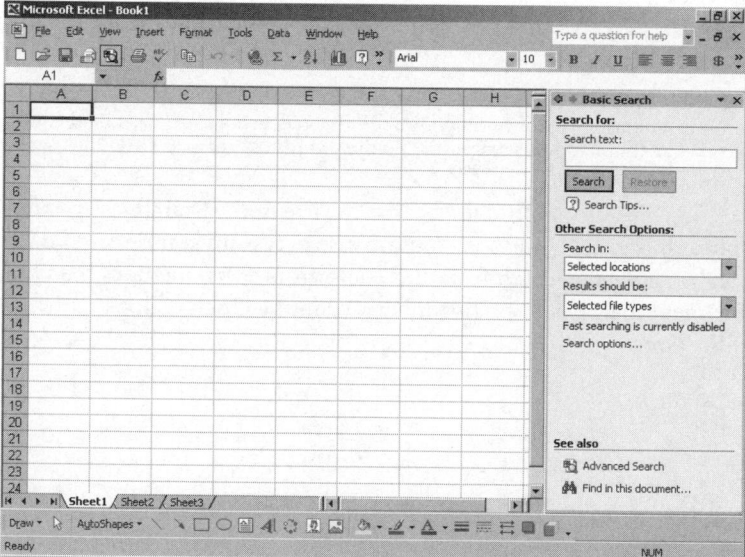

Figure 4-11. The basic Search task pane is displayed in Excel.

In the basic Search task pane, you can also perform the following tasks:

● To recall your previous search (after you have entered options for a new search), click the Restore button.

● To open the Advanced Search task pane, described later in this section, click the Advanced Search command.

● In Word or Excel, to open the application's Find And Replace dialog box for searching the currently opened document, click the Find In This Document command.

To learn more about the Find In This Document command, see "Finding and Replacing Text and Formatting," on page 281.

● To modify the Office Indexing Service, click the Search Options button to open the Indexing Service Settings dialog box, shown here:

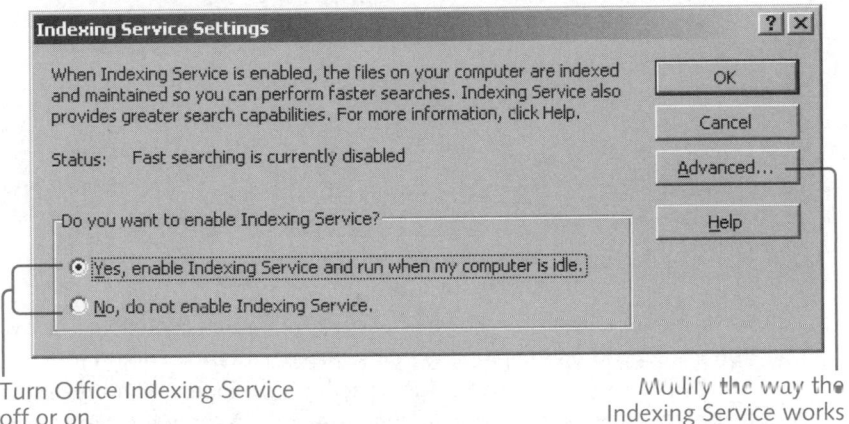

Turn Office Indexing Service off or on

Modify the way the Indexing Service works

When enabled, the Office Indexing Service runs in the background and maintains an index of the contents of your Office files. This index allows the Search feature to work more quickly. However, if you discover that the Indexing Service slows down applications you are running, or if you find the disk activity that it generates annoying, consider modifying the service's behavior by clicking the Advanced button, or turning it off completely by selecting No, Do Not Enable Indexing Service.

The Advanced Search task pane (shown in Figure 4-12) lets you search for files or Outlook items based on the values of one or more properties of the file or item. In this task pane, you can perform a simple property search by using the following steps:

1 In the Property drop-down list, select the property you want to use as a search criteria—for example, Author or Last Modified. Choosing the Contents item lets you search for specific text in the content of the document file, as you do in the basic Search task pane. Choosing Text Or Property lets you search for all Office files that contain specific text in either the document content or in the value of a document property.

Chapter 4

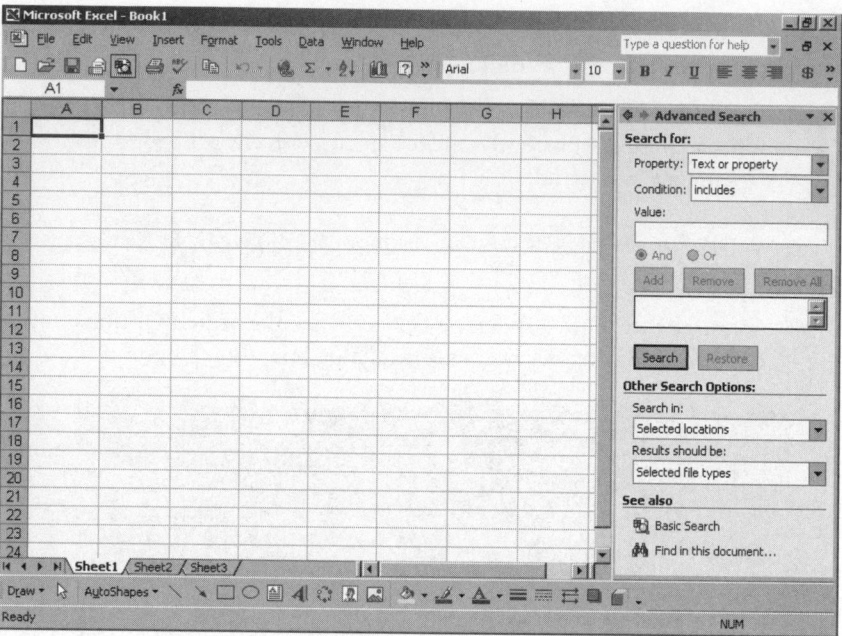

Figure 4-12. This figure shows the Advanced Search task pane displayed in Excel.

2 From the Condition drop-down list, select the search condition. The available options depend on the property you selected in step 1. For instance, with the Author property, you can select Is (Exactly) or Includes. With the Last Modified property, you can select On, On Or After, On Or Before, Today, and so on. With the Contents or Text Or Property properties, you can select only Includes.

3 In the Value text box, type the property value you want to search for.

4 In the Search In drop-down list, indicate *where* you want to search; that is, select the file folders or Outlook folders you want to search, or select Everywhere to search them all.

5 In the Results Should Be drop-down list, indicate *what* you want to search for. That is, select the types of files you want to search for: Office files (Word files, Excel files, and so on), Outlook items (e-mail messages, appointments, and so on), or Web pages.

6 Click the Search button to start the search.

You can perform a more precise search by combining criteria, as follows:

1 Define the first criterion by specifying the property, search condition, and value as explained in steps 1 through 3 in the preceding instruction list.

2 Click the Add button to add the criterion to the list near the center of the task pane.

3 Define another criteria and select either the And or the Or option to specify the way you want to combine this criterion with the previously defined one.

4 Click Add to add the new criterion to the list.

5 Repeat steps 3 and 4 for any additional criteria you would like to use in your search.

6 Complete the search by following steps 4 through 6 in the preceding instruction list.

You can perform the following additional tasks in the Advanced Search task pane:

● To remove the selected criterion from the list, click the Remove button.

● To remove all criteria from the list, click the Remove All button.

● To return to the basic Search task pane, click the Basic Search command.

When you click the Search button in either the basic or the Advanced Search task pane, Office displays the Search results task pane, which lists any files or Outlook items it found (see Figure 4-13).

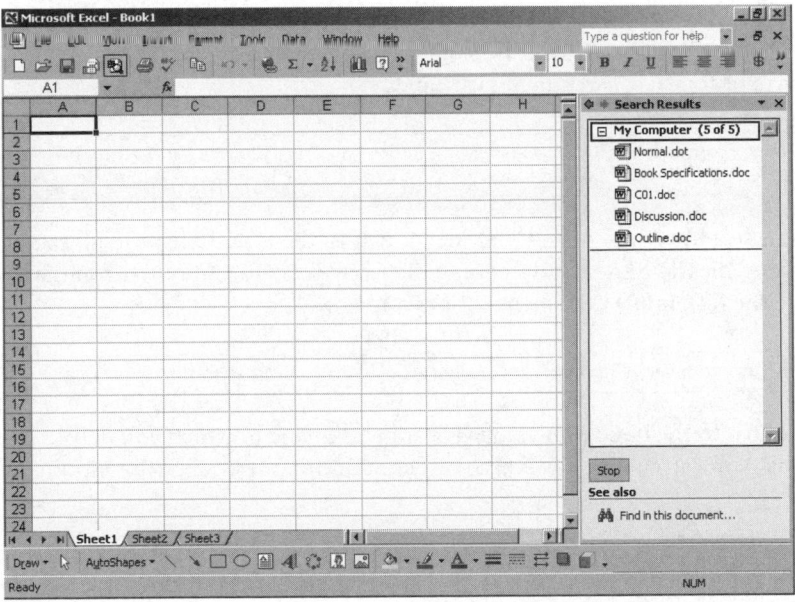

Figure 4-13. This figure shows the Search results task pane displayed in Excel.

When you hold the pointer over a particular file or item listed in the Search results task pane, detailed information on the file or item will appear in a ScreenTip. To open a file or item, click it. To perform other actions on the file or item, click the down arrow that appears when you move the pointer over the name and choose a command from the drop-down menu, as shown here:

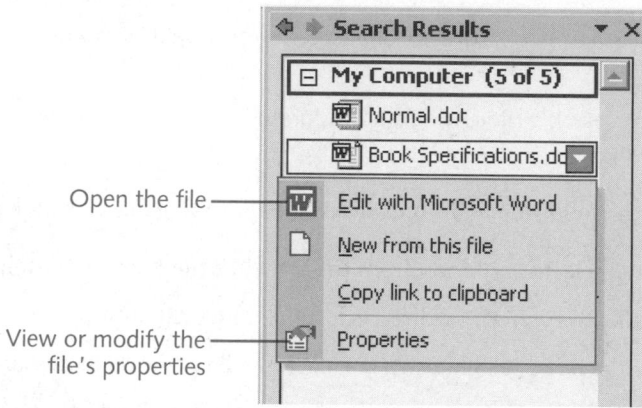

Open the file ─── Edit with Microsoft Word

View or modify the ─── Properties
file's properties

> For information on document properties, see "Using Office Document Properties," on page 82.

To create a new document, using the found document as if it were a template, choose New From This File. (This command works just like the New From Existing Document feature of the New Document task pane.)

> The New From Existing Document feature is described in "Creating a Document Using the New Document Task Pane," on page 58.

To create a hyperlink in an Office document to the found file or item, rather than opening the file or item now, choose the Copy Link To Clipboard command, and then paste the link into a document.

> For information on using hyperlinks, see "Adding and Using Hyperlinks," on page 583.

To return to the basic or Advanced Search task pane in which you defined the search, so that you can modify the search or define another one, click the Modify button.

Saving Office Documents

Like the methods for creating and opening Office documents, the methods for saving documents are fairly similar across most of the major Office applications—namely, Word, Excel, PowerPoint, FrontPage, and Publisher.

Save

To save a document that you have created or edited in an Office application, click the Save button on the application's Standard toolbar button, choose File, Save, or press Ctrl+S.

> **tip** **Have Office Automatically Save Your Work**
>
> You can use the AutoRecover feature to have an Office application automatically save changes to your document at regular intervals so that you can recover your work in the event of a power outage or program crash. To enable AutoRecover, choose Tools, Options, click the Save tab, check the Save AutoRecover Info Every option, and enter the desired frequency of automatic saves into the adjoining text box.

The first time you save a new document, the application displays the Save As dialog box where you can specify a name and location for the file (see Figure 4-14). If you want to create a copy of a document under a new filename or in a new location, you can open the Save As dialog box at any time by choosing File, Save As.

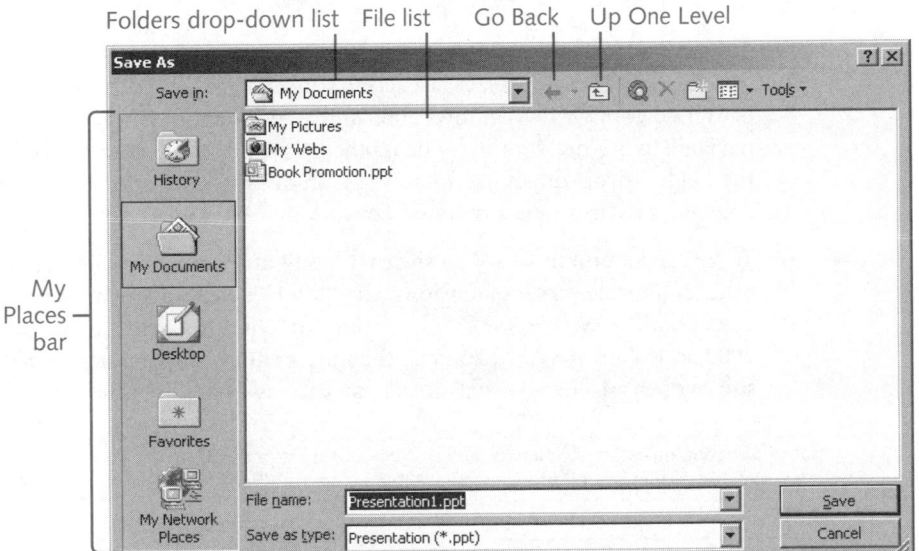

Figure 4-14. The Save As dialog box is displayed in PowerPoint.

To save a document using the Save As dialog box, complete the following steps:

1 In the My Places bar, select the folder in which you want to save the document, or use the File list, together with the Folders drop-down list, Go Back button, and Up One Level button at the top of the dialog box to navigate to the desired folder.

2 Type a name for your document into the File Name text box, or accept the default name.

3 Click the Save button.

75

newfeature!

note In Office XP you can adjust the size of the Save As dialog box. You can't, however, make the box smaller than its original size.

If you want to convert the saved copy of the file to a different format (for example, you want to convert a Word 2002 document to a WordPerfect 5.0 document), choose the desired format in the Save As Type drop-down list before you type in the document name and click the Save button. Note that if the filename entered into the File Name text box doesn't include the file extension, Office saves it with the standard extension for the selected format. In Word, for example, if you type the filename **Bonzo** into the File Name text box and select the Document Template format in the Save As Type drop-down list, the document will be saved as Bonzo.dot.

If you don't find the format you want in the Save As Type list, see the tip "Convert More File Formats," on page 68.

To save an Office document to a location that's not on a local disk, use one of the following techniques in the Save As dialog box:

- To save a document to a shared drive on your network, in the My Places bar, click My Network Places to access your network drives. With versions of Windows prior to Windows 2000 and Windows Me, you will have to navigate to the network drive using the Network Neighborhood folder in the Folders drop-down list. In any version of Windows, you can also access a network location via a mapped network drive if you have created one.

- To save a document to a Web site that has SharePoint Team Services or other Microsoft server extensions, click My Network Places in the My Places bar (or Web Folders with versions of Windows prior to Windows 2000 and Windows Me). You can then use a shortcut to a particular Web site to open a folder on that site so you can save your document there.

For information on using My Network Places (Web Folders), and on setting up shortcuts to Web sites, see "Accessing SharePoint Document Libraries from Office Applications," on page 189.

tip   Use the Templates On My Web Site Command

If you store a custom document template that you have created on a Web site that has Microsoft server extensions, you or any member of your workgroup can subsequently use that template to create new documents by means of the Templates On My Web Site command in the New Document task pane. See "Sharing Documents on SharePoint," on page 187.

- To save a document to an FTP Internet site on which you have the required permissions, type the *full* URL into the File Name text box (for example, *ftp://ftp.marketing^.com*). Or, navigate to the site using the FTP Locations folder in the Folders drop-down list of the Open Office Document dialog box. The FTP Locations folder lists the FTP sites you've previously accessed. To add a new site to FTP Locations, double-click Add/Modify FTP Locations in the FTP Locations folder, as shown here:

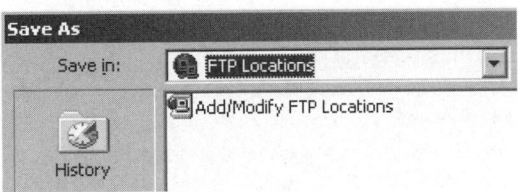

As with the Open Office Document and Open dialog boxes, you can perform many file and folder management tasks in the Save As dialog box. You can also customize the My Places bar. In fact, the Open Office Document, Open, and Save As dialog boxes all share the same My Places bar: Changes you make to the bar in one dialog box will affect the bar in the other dialog boxes in all Office applications.

For information on these topics, see "Opening an Existing Document Using the Open Office Document Dialog Box," on page 61.

Keep in mind, however, that in the Save As dialog box, the Tools drop-down menu has a slightly different set of commands. Here's the Tools menu in PowerPoint's Save As dialog box:

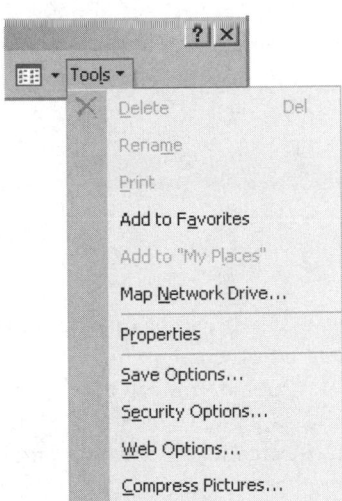

The commands on the Tools menu below Properties vary among the different Office applications.

newfeature!

| tip | Guard Your Privacy |

You can have Word, Excel, PowerPoint, or Access remove personal information from a document when you save it. The information removed includes any text assigned to the Author, Manager, and Company document properties. Also, the author's actual name is removed from all comments, tracked changes (in Word), and macros, and is replaced with the word *Author*. To enable this feature, choose Tools, Options, click the Security tab, and check the Remove Personal Information From This File On Save option. (In Access, click the General tab and check Remove Personal Information From This File.)

Saving a Document as a Web Page

One of the most important features of Word, Excel, PowerPoint, FrontPage, Access, and Publisher is the ability to save a document as a Web page—that is, in HTML format—so that you can publish it on the World Wide Web or on a company intranet.

For information on choosing the best Office application for creating the particular type of Web page you want to publish, see "An Office XP Map," on page 6.

In each application's part of the book, you'll learn how to use that application to publish effectively on the Web. When you create a Web page in a particular Office application, the page will contain the identity of the creating application. You can determine which application was used to create a particular Web page by looking at the page's icon in the folder where it is stored, as shown here:

Data Access Page Created in Access.htm
Page Created in Excel.htm
Page Created in FrontPage.htm
Page Created in PowerPoint.htm
Page Created in Word.htm

If you double-click the icon for a Web page in a folder, it will be displayed in your browser, rather than being opened for editing. To edit the page, you can right click the icon and choose Edit from the shortcut menu. Of course, you can also open the page for editing through the Open Office Document dialog box (which will open the page in the creating Office application) or you can run the creating application and use its Open dialog box.

Office normally opens a page for editing in the application that created it. For example, if you use the Open dialog box in Word to open a Web page created in PowerPoint, the page will be opened in PowerPoint, not in Word. This design helps to prevent loss of features; for example, Word might not be able to view or edit a feature in a Web page that was created by PowerPoint. To circumvent this limitation and edit a page in an application other than the one that created it, follow these steps:

1 Open the page in Microsoft Internet Explorer, for example, by double-clicking the page's icon in the folder where it is stored.

2 In Internet Explorer, on the Standard Buttons toolbar, click the down arrow on the Edit button and choose the name of the application you want to use to edit the page, as shown here:

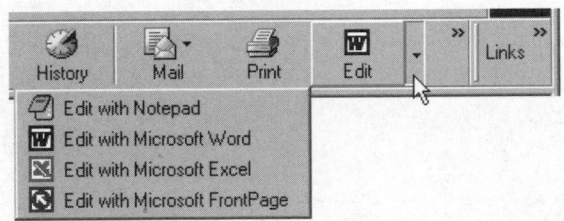

Working with Multiple Documents

In Word, Excel, and PowerPoint, you can have several documents open at the same time. In these Office XP applications, you can now work with multiple documents using one of two different interfaces: single document interface (SDI) or multiple document interface (MDI).

Using SDI

With SDI, each document is opened in a separate top-level window with its own title bar, menu, toolbars, status bar, and other interface objects. Documents were opened in Office 2000 in this way. The main advantage of SDI is that because each document window is a top-level window, it has its own button in the Windows taskbar and you can use these buttons to quickly switch among documents.

To enable SDI, choose Tools, Options, click the View tab, and check the Windows In Taskbar option. With SDI, the upper right corner of the window displays two Close buttons, as seen here:

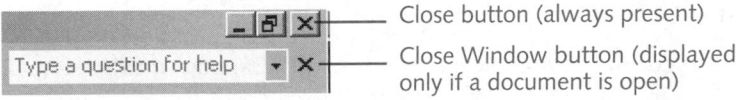

Close button (always present)

Close Window button (displayed only if a document is open)

The way some window management commands work depends on whether SDI or MDI is active. Table 4-3 shows window management procedures specific to the SDI mode.

Table 4-3. Window Management Procedures in SDI

Window Management Task	Procedure in SDI
Closing a document window	• If only one document window is open, click Close Window button or press Ctrl+W (leaves empty application window). • If more than one document window is open, click Close Window button, press Ctrl+W, click Close button, or press Alt+F4.
Closing the application	• If only one document window is open, click Close button, press Alt+F4, or choose File, Exit. • If more than one document window is open, choose File, Exit.
Switching to another document window	Click the Taskbar button for that document window, press Ctrl+F6, or choose the document window name from Window menu.

Using MDI

With MDI, each document is opened in a separate *child window* of the application window. A child window has the following properties:

- It can't be moved beyond the boundaries of the application window.
- It doesn't have its own menu bar, toolbars, or status bar (although it might have a ruler or other interface object).
- It doesn't have a separate button on the Windows taskbar.

The main advantage of MDI is that if you like to work with document windows side by side, you can fit more of them on the screen without wasting screen space with duplicate copies of the menu bars, toolbars, and the status bar.

To enable MDI, choose Tools, Options, click the View tab, and clear the Windows In Taskbar check box.

In MDI, each document window has it own set of minimize, maximize, and close buttons. Here are the buttons on a non-maximized document window:

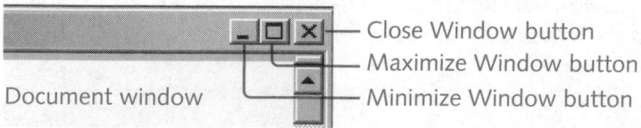

Close Window button
Maximize Window button
Document window
Minimize Window button

Chapter 4

If the document windows are maximized, the buttons for the active document window appear to the right of the menu bar of the application window, as seen here.

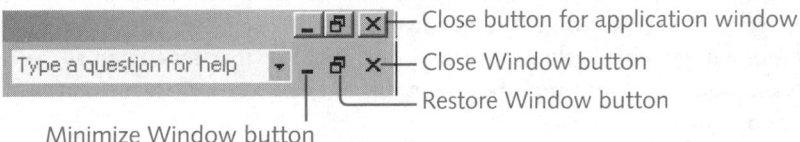

Close button for application window
Close Window button
Restore Window button
Minimize Window button

Table 4-4 shows window management procedures specific to the MDI mode.

Table 4-4. Window Management Procedures in MDI

Window Management Task	Procedure in MDI
Closing a document window	Click Close Window button for the document window or press Ctrl+W.
Closing the application	Click Close button for the application window, press Alt+F4, or choose File, Exit.
Switching to another document window	Press Ctrl+F6 or choose document window name from Window menu.

Common MDI and SDI Procedures

Table 4-5 shows useful window management procedures that will work with either SDI or MDI.

Table 4-5. Window Management Procedures in SDI or MDI

Window Management Task	Procedure for Either SDI or MDI
Tiling all document windows	Choose Arrange All (Arrange in Excel) from Window menu.
Splitting the active document window into two views	Choose Split from Window menu or drag split box toward bottom of window.
Opening the active document in an additional window	Choose Window, New Window.
Closing all windows displaying the active document	Choose File, Close.
Closing all windows for all open documents	Press Shift key while opening File menu and then choose Close All.
Saving all open documents (saves only documents with unsaved changes)	Press Shift key while opening File menu and then choose Save All.

Using Office Document Properties

A Word, Excel, or PowerPoint document—as well as an Access database—has a set of properties that are saved in the document file together with the document content. Assigning meaningful values to various document properties—such as the Subject, Category, or Keywords properties—can make it easier to organize, identify, and find your documents.

To give you an idea how useful and ubiquitous document properties are, the following is a list of ways properties are used or displayed in Office and Windows.

- The Office Search feature can find documents on local or network drives using property values or combinations of property values as search criteria.

For more information about the Office Search feature, see "Finding Office Files or Outlook Items Using the Search Feature," on page 69.

- In the Open Office Document and Open dialog boxes, you can display a brief summary of the properties of the selected document by switching to the Properties view. You can see all properties of the selected document—and set many of them—by choosing Properties from the Tools drop-down menu.

- For Word, Excel, and PowerPoint documents, Windows Explorer—as well as a folder window or the Windows desktop—will display the Author, Title, Subject, and Comments properties in a ScreenTip when you hold the mouse pointer over the document. It will display and let you set many of a document's properties if you right click the document and choose Properties from the shortcut menu. Also, if you have enabled Web content in your folders (the name of this option and the way you set it varies among versions of Windows), Windows Explorer or a file folder will display some of the properties of the selected document at the left of the window (the specific properties shown depend on the version of Windows you're using).

- Outlook's Integrated File Management feature displays document properties if you activate a column view. You can customize the specific properties that are shown, and you can group, filter, and sort files according to property values (for example, you could group all documents in a particular folder by author).

For more information on the Integrated File Management feature, see "Accessing File Folders," on page 975.

- A Visual Basic for Applications (VBA) program can read or set a document's properties. You can thus use properties as a part of a custom Office application.

VBA is covered in Part 10 of this book.

If you want to make use of properties, you should set them before you first save a document. To set properties, choose File, Properties (Database Properties in Access), and then enter the desired property values into the tabs of the Properties dialog box (see Figure 4-15).

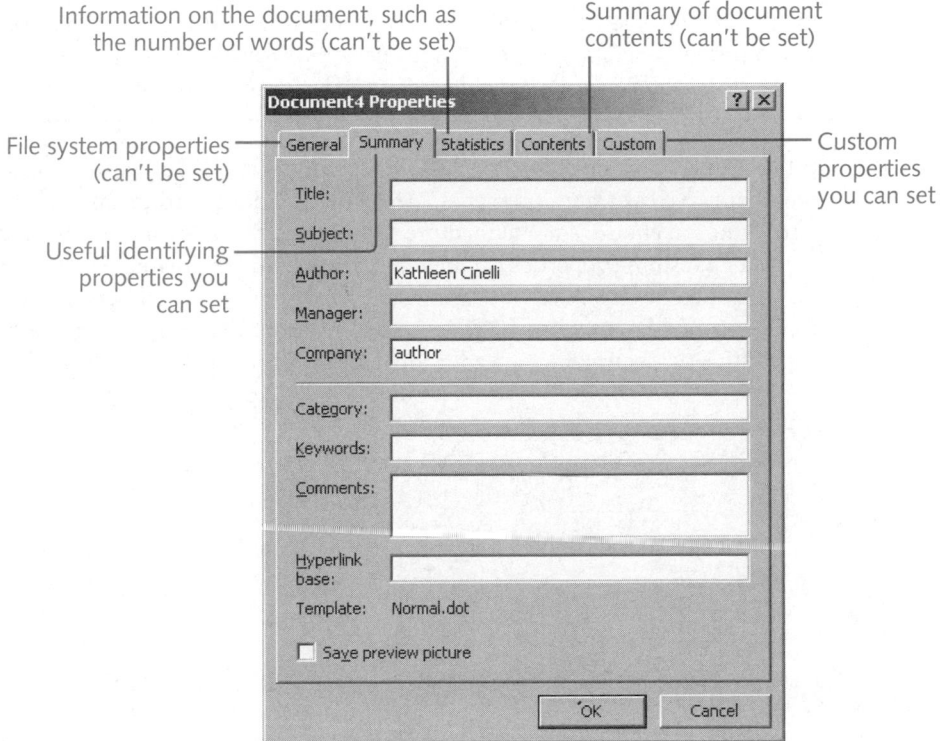

Information on the document, such as the number of words (can't be set)

Summary of document contents (can't be set)

File system properties (can't be set)

Useful identifying properties you can set

Custom properties you can set

Figure 4-15. The Properties dialog box is displayed for a new Word document.

When you create a new document, the Office application you use will automatically assign values to the Author and Company properties using the information you supplied when you installed Office. Word, PowerPoint, and Access also assign a tentative value to the Title property. When you first save a document, Windows automatically stores the file system properties displayed on the General tab (this tab doesn't display information before the first save).

> **tip** **Have Office Remind You to Set Properties**
>
> You can have Word, Excel, or PowerPoint automatically display the Properties dialog box the first time you save a document. To do this, choose Tools, Options, click the Save tab (the General tab in Excel), and check the Prompt For Document Properties option (the option is worded slightly differently in Excel and PowerPoint).

In the Properties dialog box, the Custom tab allows you to add custom properties to a document, such as Date Completed, Department, Editor, Group, and Status (see Figure 4-16). You can choose a predefined property or create a new property with any name you want. Custom properties can be especially useful for organizing, tracking, and locating documents shared by a workgroup, provided that members of the workgroup use the properties consistently. To set a custom property, complete the following steps (repeat this procedure for each additional custom property you want to define):

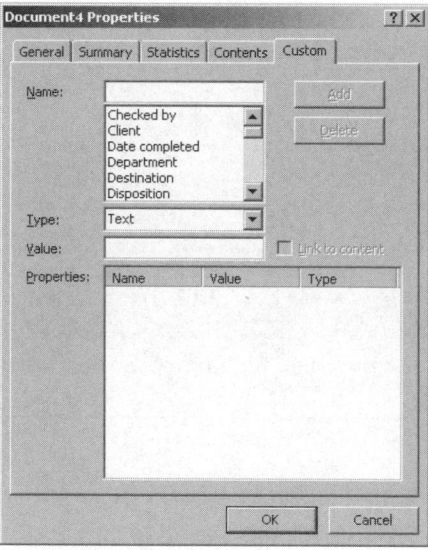

Figure 4-16. The Custom tab of the Properties dialog box allows you to add custom properties.

1 Select a predefined property in the Name list, or type a new property into the Name text box at the top of the list.

2 In the Type drop-down list, choose the type of data you want the property to contain.

3 Enter a property value into the Value text box. (The value you enter must conform to the type you chose in step 2.)

note Rather than assigning a fixed value to a property, you can derive its value from a named block of text in the document (a Word bookmark, an Excel named range, or PowerPoint selected text). To do this, check the Link To Content option and then select the specific named block of text in the Source drop-down list, which will replace the Value text box. The property's value will then be derived from the named text, and therefore its value will change whenever that text changes.

4 Click the Add button to save the property in the document. The new property will be displayed in the Properties list at the bottom of the Custom tab.

5 To remove a custom property, select it in the Properties list and click the Delete button.

Chapter 4

Chapter 5

New Editing and Formatting Techniques in Office XP

newfeature!

Talking to Office: Using Speech Recognition

Microsoft Office XP has added a major new capability to its interface: speech recognition, a long-anticipated feature that is finally becoming a practical reality. With speech recognition you can dictate text rather than type it, and you can issue basic commands by speaking them rather than by using a mouse or keyboard. You can use speech recognition in Microsoft Word, Excel, PowerPoint, Outlook, FrontPage, Access, and Publisher.

Speech recognition technology is still in its relative infancy. It's not perfect, and it certainly won't free you completely from the keyboard. It's good enough, however, to make working with Office more efficient and enjoyable and to provide a welcome break from incessant typing and the strained posture that usually accompanies it.

To use speech recognition, first make sure that your microphone is attached to the correct output jack on your computer and—if the microphone has a switch—that it's turned on. If you're using a headset with both a microphone and earphones, you'll also need to plug the earphone jack into the correct output jack on your computer.

Then, turn on speech recognition by choosing Tools, Speech in any Office application. You'll then be able to use speech recognition in any of the Office applications that support it.

(Speech recognition is an operating system resource. It works basically the same way in all Office applications, and settings that you make in one application affect the way it works in all applications.)

---

tip   **Install Speech Recognition**

If the Speech command isn't on the Tools menu of your Office applications, then speech recognition hasn't been installed. To install it, rerun Office Setup, and select the Run From My Computer option for the Speech feature. You can find this feature in the Office Shared Features section, under the Alternative User Input group (see Figure 5-1).

Rerunning Office Setup is explained in "Revisiting Office Setup," on page 27.

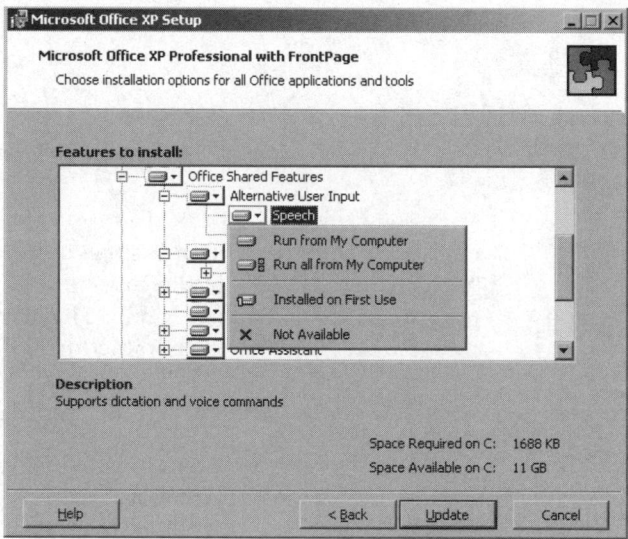

Figure 5-1.   Choose the Run From My Computer option to install Office speech recognition.

Training Speech Recognition

To enhance the reliability and accuracy of speech recognition, you need to adjust your microphone and speakers and train Office to recognize your personal speech patterns. When you first activate speech recognition, Office runs two wizards to accomplish these tasks.

First, Office runs the Microphone Wizard (shown in Figure 5-2).

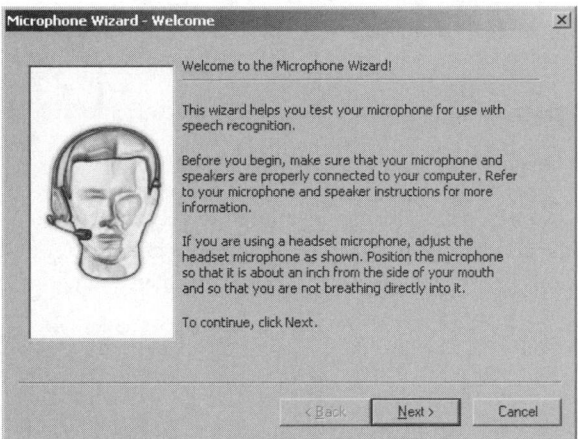

Figure 5-2. The Microphone Wizard displays an introductory dialog box upon opening.

Click the Next button and follow the instructions in the remaining Microphone Wizard dialog boxes. These dialog boxes do the following actions:

● They test and adjust the volume of your microphone.

● They help you to position the microphone properly.

Next, Office runs the Speech Recognition Training Wizard. Make sure that the room is quiet, and keep the microphone in the position you used when you worked with the Microphone Wizard. The training process should take about 10 minutes. In the first Training Wizard dialog box (shown in Figure 5-3), click the Next button and follow the instructions in the remaining dialog boxes. The Speech Recognition Training Wizard does the actions listed on page 90.

Figure 5-3. The first Speech Recognition Training Wizard dialog box displays a welcome message.

- It gathers some information about you to help the Training Wizard ascertain your voice type.

- It lets you speak a series of sentences so it can analyze your speech patterns.

- It saves the data it has collected on your personal speech patterns.

The introductory training session will probably be enough to get you started using speech recognition. To enhance the accuracy of speech recognition, however, you should complete two or more training sessions. You can run additional sessions later, at any time.

For information on running additional training sessions, see "Customizing Speech Recognition," on page 97.

When you have finished running the Speech Recognition Training Wizard, Office will attempt to run the Microsoft Voice Training video. You may need to download the Flash 5.0 player in order to use this video. The video will explain the basics of using voice recognition in Office XP.

tip **Speak Naturally**

When you use the speech recognition Training Wizard, be sure to speak in your natural tone of voice, pronouncing words the way you normally do, so that you can speak that way when you use speech recognition to dictate text and issue commands. You might, however, need to speak a little more slowly and distinctly than you normally do.

Troubleshooting

Speech Recognition Is Slow or Unreliable

Speech recognition seems to be working, but recognition of your words lags behind your speech, even when you speak slowly. Or speech recognition fails to understand many of your words.

The *minimum* requirements for speech recognition are a 200-MHz computer, with 64 MB of RAM for Windows 95, Windows 98, or Windows Me; and 96 MB for Windows NT or Windows 2000. However, if you use speech recognition regularly, you probably won't be happy with the response time using less than a 400-MHz computer with 128 MB of RAM.

You also need a high-quality sound card or integrated sound on your computer.

In addition, you need a good microphone. The best kind is a close-talk headset microphone with noise cancellation. With this type of microphone, you should adjust the microphone so that it's about a thumb's width to one side of your mouth to avoid

Chapter 5

> **Troubleshooting** *(continued)*   breathing directly into it. The primary advantage of a headset microphone is that the relative position of the microphone with respect to your mouth can easily be kept constant. If you use a microphone on your desktop or computer, you'll tend to get inconsistent results as you move closer to or further away from the microphone.
>
> Finally, if you meet the hardware requirements but speech recognition fails to understand quite a few of your words, try running additional training sessions.

Using Speech Recognition

The Language Bar, shown here, is your primary tool for using speech recognition. It automatically appears on the screen when you turn on speech recognition.

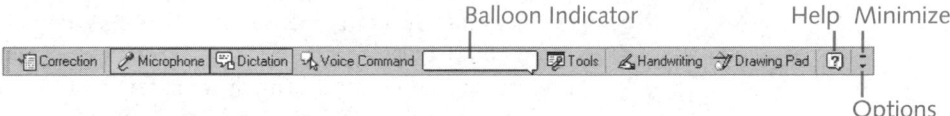

You can hide the Language Bar by clicking the small Minimize button. The Language Bar then appears as an icon in the system tray at the right (or bottom) of the Windows Taskbar. You can redisplay the Language Bar by clicking this icon and choosing Show Language Bar from the menu, shown here:

You can move the Language Bar anywhere on the screen by dragging its left border, shown here:

Unlike the standard Office application toolbars, the Language Bar and its settings are shared by all Office applications. For example, if you display and position the Language Bar when Word is active, it remains displayed in that position if you then switch to Excel, PowerPoint, or another application.

Table 5-1 contains brief descriptions of the Language Bar buttons.

> **note** The commands that are available on the Language Bar vary according to the Office application you're using.

Chapter 5

Table 5-1. **The Buttons On the Language Bar**

Language Bar Button	Purpose/Effect
Correction	Displays a list of alternative words for the dictated word under the insertion point.
Microphone	Turns the microphone on or off, enabling or disabling speech recognition.
Dictation	Turns on *dictation mode*, in which your spoken words are inserted into text as if you had typed them.
Voice Command	Turns on *voice command mode*, in which a spoken command is executed as if you had used the mouse or keyboard to issue the command.
Balloon Indicator	Displays messages. For example, in voice command mode, it displays the names of the commands you speak or execute using the mouse or keyboard. And in dictation mode, it displays the message "Dictating..." when speech recognition is processing dictated text and "Too soft" when you're speaking too quietly.
Tools	Displays a menu that lets you modify different speech recognition settings.
Handwriting	Displays a menu of commands for accessing the Office XP handwriting interface, described in "Using Handwriting in Office," on page 101.
Writing Pad, Drawing Pad, and so on	Displays or hides the handwriting tool that's currently selected on the Handwriting menu. The button name indicates the currently selected tool.
Help	Displays the Language Bar Help command, which you can use to display online help explaining how to use the Language Bar.
Minimize	Hides the Language Bar and displays the Language Bar icon in the system tray in the Windows Taskbar.
Options	Displays a menu that lets you modify the Language Bar or change the text input language settings.

To use speech recognition successfully, place the microphone in the same position you used with the Microphone Wizard and speak in the same natural tone of voice you employed when using the Training Wizard.

To begin using speech recognition, make sure that the Microphone button is in the enabled (highlighted) state (this button toggles between on and off). When the Microphone button is off, the Balloon Indicator, Dictation, and Voice Command buttons are hidden. You can also use the Speech option on the application's Tools menu to turn the microphone on or off. (The button and the menu option are tied together—turning one on or off turns the other on or off.)

Using Speech Recognition Dictation Mode

You can use speech recognition's *dictation mode* to enter text into an Office application by speaking. For example, you can enter text into the body of a Word document, into an Excel worksheet, into a PowerPoint slide, or into a text box in a dialog box. To dictate text, click the Dictation button—if it's not already enabled—to switch on dictation mode, and then begin speaking the words you want to enter (see Figure 5-4).

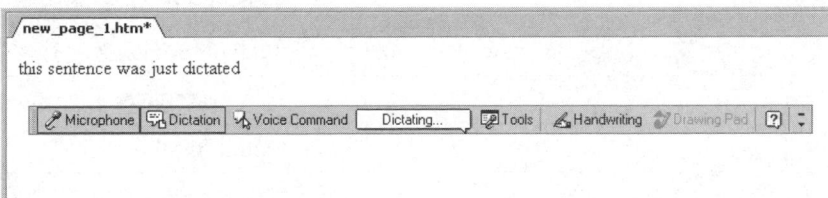

Figure 5-4. In this figure, text has been dictated into a Web page in FrontPage.

To insert a punctuation character, say the name of the character as given in Table 5-2.

Table 5-2. Phrases for Dictating Punctuation Characters

To Insert This Punctuation Character	Say This
&	"Ampersand"
*	"Asterisk"
@	"At sign" or "At"
\	"Backslash"
[	"Open bracket"
)	"Close paren"
:	"Colon"
,	"Comma"
—	"Double dash"
…	"Ellipsis"
=	"Equals"
!	"Exclamation" or "Exclamation point"
>	"Greater than"

(continued)

2: Common Office XP
Techniques

Chapter 5

Table 5-2. *(continued)*

To Insert This Punctuation Character	Say This
-	"Hyphen" or "Dash"
{	"Open brace"
<	"Less than"
Enter	"New line"
Enter twice	"New paragraph"
(	"Open paren" or "Paren"
%	"Percent" or "Percent sign"
.	"Period" or "Dot"
+	"Plus" or "Plus sign"
#	"Pound sign"
?	"Question mark"
'	"Single quote"
"	"Quote" or "Open quote"
}	"Close brace"
]	"Right bracket"
;	"Semicolon"
/	"Slash"
Tab	"Tab"
~	"Tilde"
		"Vertical bar"

Troubleshooting

Speech Recognition Inserts Extra Spaces

Speech recognition dictation mode inserts a space character between a word and the following punctuation character.

To make a punctuation character come immediately after a word without an intervening space, say the name of the punctuation character immediately after saying the word. For example, say "QUOTEhelloQUOTE" rather than "QUOTE hello QUOTE."

If either you or speech recognition makes a mistake while you're dictating text, you can make a correction by right-clicking a recently dictated word to display the shortcut menu (see Figure 5-5).

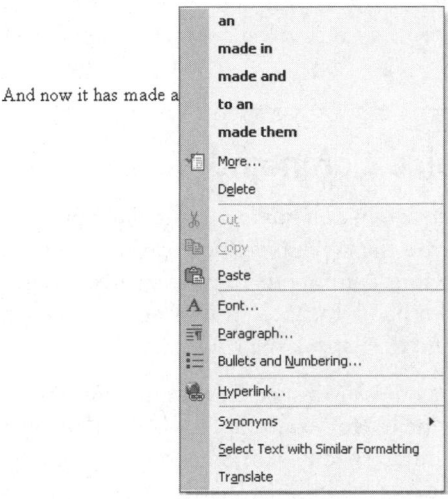

Figure 5-5. This shortcut menu is displayed in Word when you right-click an erroneous word that speech recognition has inserted.

Then choose an item from the shortcut menu, as follows:

- If the correct word is among the alternatives displayed in bold type at the top of the shortcut menu, click the word to insert it and replace the original word you right-clicked.

- If you don't see the correct word, choose the More command to display a longer list of alternatives, as shown in this example:

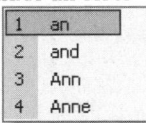

If you find the correct word on the expanded list, click it to make the replacement. Another way to display the expanded list of alternatives is to place the insertion point on the erroneous word and click the Correction button on the Language Bar.

- If you don't find the right word among the alternatives, you can choose Delete—or erase the word using any editing method—and then either dictate it again (if you're stubborn) or just type it in.

> **tip** **Replace a Misspelled Word**
>
> If the application's while-you-type spelling checker has underlined a mistakenly inserted word, the shortcut menu won't display the alternative words or commands described here. However, you can choose the Speech Alternatives command at the bottom of the shortcut menu to display speech recognition's expanded list of alternatives.

Using Speech Recognition Voice Command Mode

You can use speech recognition's *voice command mode* to issue basic program commands by voice—for example, to save a file, to change the document view, to apply bold formatting, or to undo the previous command. To issue a verbal command, on the Language Bar click the Voice Command button—if it's not already enabled—to switch into voice command mode and then speak the command.

How do you know which words to say to issue a specific command? To issue a menu command, first say the name of the menu (for example, "file," "edit," or "view") to open the menu. Then say the name of the specific command on the menu you want to execute (for example, "close," "find," or "ruler"). In Word, for example, saying "file close" would choose the Close command on the File menu, closing the current document. If the command is on a submenu, first say the name of the main menu, then the name of the submenu, and then the name of the specific command. In Word, for example, saying "view toolbars formatting" would display the Formatting toolbar.

To issue a toolbar button command, make sure that toolbar is displayed and then say the button name (the one that appears in the ScreenTip when you hold the mouse pointer over the button). For example, saying "bold" when the Word Formatting toolbar is displayed applies bold formatting to the currently selected text, just as it would if you clicked the Bold button.

In voice command mode you can also issue a keyboard command by saying the name of the command key, as shown in Table 5-3.

Table 5-3. **Spoken Commands for Issuing Keyboard Commands**

To Issue This Keyboard Command	Say This
Left arrow key	"Left"
Right arrow key	"Right"
Up arrow key	"Up"
Down arrow key	"Down"
Home key	"Home"
End key	"End"
Enter key	"Enter"
Esc key	"Escape"

Notice that whenever you issue a menu or toolbar command—verbally or by using the mouse or keyboard—the Balloon Indicator on the Language Bar displays a description of the command. For example, if you open the Edit menu, the Balloon Indicator displays the word *Edit,* as shown here:

Customizing Speech Recognition

To modify the way speech recognition works, click the Tools button on the Language Bar to open the drop-down menu shown here:

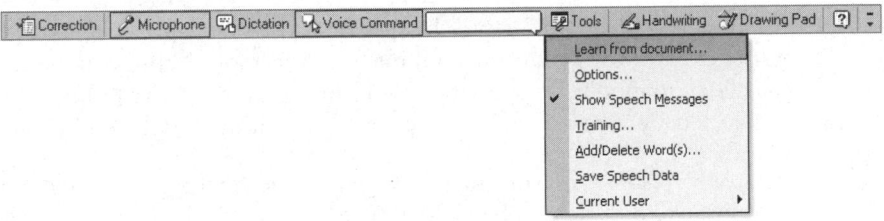

Then, choose the appropriate command, as shown in Table 5-4.

Table 5-4. Using the Tools Menu Commands on the Language Bar

To Do This	Choose This Command
Scan the document for words to add to the speech dictionary	Learn From Document
Open the Speech Properties dialog box	Options
Display or hide the balloon indicator on the Language Bar	Show Speech Messages
Run one or more speech recognition training sessions using the Voice Training wizard	Training
Add or remove words from the speech dictionary	Add/Delete Word(s)
In Word, turn on or turn off permanent saving of the recordings that speech recognition makes of each word you dictate. (See the note following this table.)	Save Speech Data
Change to a different speech recognition *user* (also known as a *profile*, as explained later in this section)	Current User

97

> **note** In Word, speech recognition records your actual speech sounds for each word you dictate. You can play back the sounds for a dictated word by right-clicking that word in the document and choosing More from the shortcut menu, or by placing the insertion point within the word and clicking the Correction button on the Language Bar. If the Embed Linguistic Data option is checked in Word and if the Save Speech Data option is enabled on the Tools menu on the Language Bar (described in Table 5-4), Word will permanently save these recordings within the document, along with the lists of corrections it displays on the shortcut menus. If both of these options are not enabled, Word will discard the recordings and corrections whenever you close the document. You access the Embed Linguistic Data option in Word by choosing Tools, Options and clicking the Save tab.

To view or change the properties of the speech recognition system, open the Speech Properties dialog box by choosing Options from the Tools drop-down menu on the Language Bar. To modify the speech recognition engine, the active profile, or your hardware, change options as follows in the Speech Recognition tab (shown in Figure 5-6):

- If you've installed one or more third-party speech recognition engines in addition to the one supplied with Office XP, you can use a specific speech recognition engine by selecting it in the Language drop-down list. To be able to use a third-party speech recognition engine with Office XP, the engine must use Speech Application Program Interface version 5 (SAPI 5). Activating an engine you haven't recently used will run the Microphone Wizard (explained below) and a training session so that the engine will be properly set up and trained.

- To modify a third-party speech recognition engine, select it in the Language drop-down list and click the Settings button. (You can't click the Settings button if you've selected the speech recognition supplied with Office.) The settings you can make are specific to each engine type.

- To activate a particular speech recognition profile, check it in the Recognition Profiles list. Speech recognition will then use the training data and settings stored in that profile.

> **tip** You can also open the Speech Properties dialog box by running the Speech program in the Windows Control Panel folder, using this icon:
>
>
> Speech

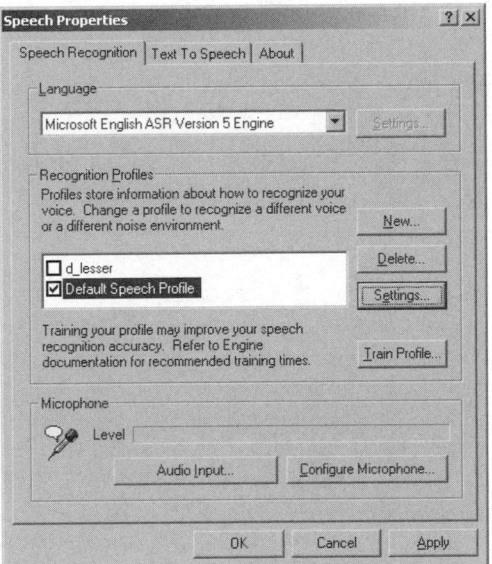

Figure 5-6. To modify the speech recognition engine, profile, or hardware, use the Speech Recognition tab of the Speech Properties dialog box.

> **note**   A speech recognition *profile* (also known as a *user*) contains a set of speech recognition settings as well as speech recognition training data. Each person who uses speech recognition should have a unique profile that matches the person's voice and preferences. If you use your computer in different rooms or attach different microphones, you might also want to create a separate profile for each environment.

- To change the properties of the activated profile, click the Settings button.

- To run one or more speech recognition training sessions for the activated profile, click the Train Profile button to run the Voice Training Wizard.

> The Voice Training Wizard was explained in "Training Speech Recognition," on page 88.

- To remove the activated profile, click the Delete button.

- To create a new speech recognition profile, click the New button. This will run the Profile Wizard, which sets up the new profile and runs the Microphone Wizard and then the Voice Training Wizard.

- To select the microphone that's used for speech recognition, click the Audio Input button.

- To run the Microphone Wizard, click the Configure Microphone button.

tip You can quickly change the active profile by clicking the Tools button on the Language Bar and choosing the desired profile from the Current User submenu, shown here:

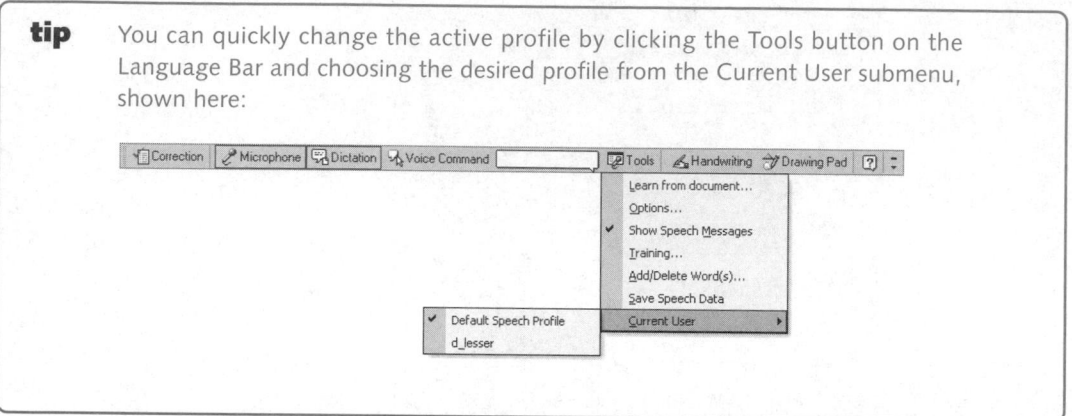

For information on the Microphone Wizard, see "Training Speech Recognition," on page 88.

To modify the Office text-to-speech feature, click the Text To Speech tab of the Speech Properties dialog box (shown in Figure 5-7). Change options as follows:

● To activate a particular voice personality from those that are installed, select the voice description you want to use in the Voice Selection drop-down list. When you activate a new voice, a preview of the voice begins playing. To change the text spoken by the voice, edit the text in the Use The Following Text To Preview The Voice text box.

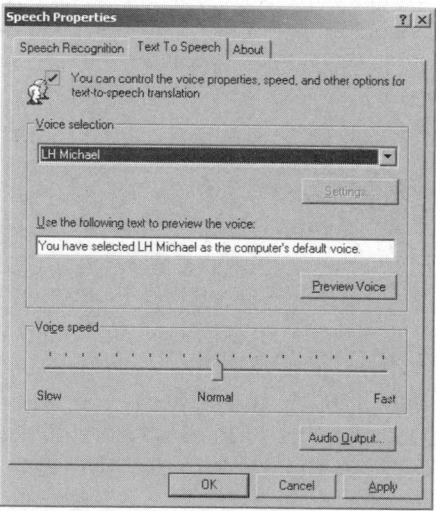

Figure 5-7. To modify the text-to-speech feature, use the Text To Speech tab of the Speech Properties dialog box.

● To select the audio output device (speaker or headphone) used for text-to-speech, click the Audio Output button.

Chapter 5

● To adjust the speed of the active voice, use the Voice Speed slider.

Customizing the Language Bar

To modify the Language Bar itself or to change the input language settings, click the Options button on the bar (the small down arrow at the right end) to open the menu shown here:

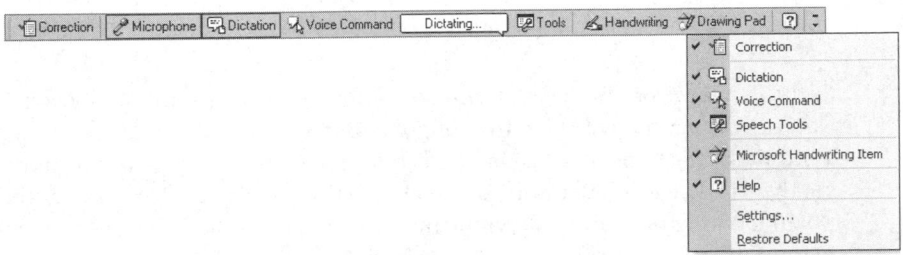

To hide or display one of the Language Bar buttons, choose the corresponding command from this menu. (To return to the set of buttons shown by default, choose Restore Defaults.) Choosing the Settings command opens the Text Services dialog box, which lets you modify input languages and to change Language Bar settings (by clicking the Language Bar button). You can also open the Text Services dialog box by running the Text Services program in the Windows Control Panel, using the following icon:

Text Services

Using Handwriting in Office

The new handwriting interface in Office XP lets you enter text into a document using an electronic tablet and pen or (with difficulty) an ordinary mouse. Specifically, the handwriting feature lets you do any of the following:

● Insert handwritten characters into a document. For example, you could insert your signature at the end of a letter or an e-mail message.

● Convert handwritten characters to regular document text.

● Quickly insert a freehand sketch.

● Issue a keyboard command (Enter, Backspace, Up arrow, Down arrow, Left arrow, Right arrow, or Tab) using an electronic pen or a mouse.

● Type a keyboard character, insert a symbol, or issue a keyboard command using an onscreen keyboard and an electronic pen or mouse, without using an actual keyboard. (Not every keyboard shortcut works, but most do.)

Accessing the Handwriting Interface

To access the handwriting interface, you begin by clicking the Handwriting button on the Language Bar and choosing a writing option from the drop-down menu, displayed here. These options are explained in the following sections.

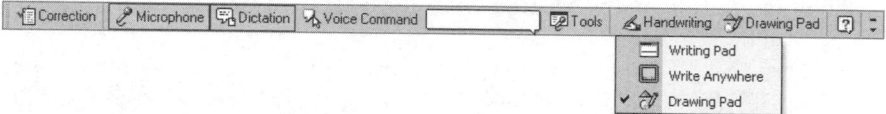

If the Language Bar has been minimized so that it isn't currently visible on the screen, you can display it by clicking the Language Bar icon in the system tray at the right (or bottom) of the Windows Taskbar and choosing Show Language Bar from the menu. If neither the Language Bar nor its system-tray icon are present, or if either the Handwriting button or its drop-down menu is missing from the Language Bar, you need to rerun Office Setup and install the Handwriting component. (That is, you must select Run From My Computer for this component.) You can find the Handwriting component in the Office Shared Features section, under the Alternative User Input group.

For information on rerunning Setup, see the tip "Install Speech Recognition," on page 88.

Entering Handwriting

To enter handwriting into an Office document, click the Handwriting button on the Language Bar and choose the Writing Pad option from the drop-down menu. This will open the Writing Pad window, shown in Figure 5-8. When the Writing Pad option is selected on the Handwriting drop-down menu, the button to the right is labeled Writing Pad, and you can click it to hide or redisplay the Writing Pad window.

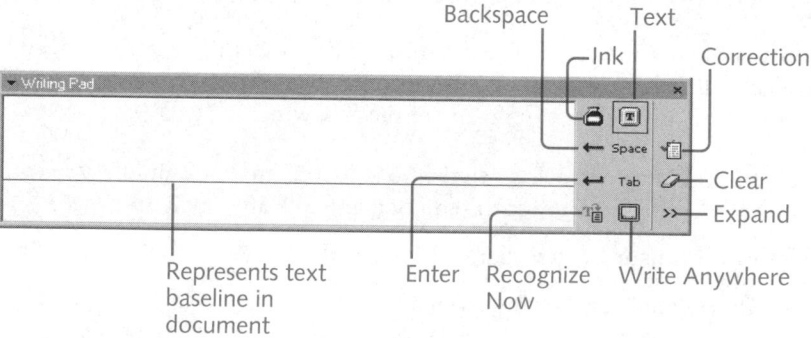

Figure 5-8. The Writing Pad window lets you enter handwriting using a separate program window.

---

tip **Move the Writing Pad Window to a Convenient Place**

You can drag the Writing Pad window to any convenient position on the screen. For example, you might want to drag it almost completely off the screen to temporarily make room for other work.

To enter handwritten characters directly into the document, so that the characters appear just as you sketch them, click the Ink button in the Writing Pad window to turn on the *ink mode*. You could use this mode, for example, to enter a signature. After switching on ink mode, use the pen with your electronic tablet (or use your mouse) to write in the Writing Pad window. To write, just press the main pen or mouse button and drag. Here's an example of a handwritten signature produced using this method:

Ink button

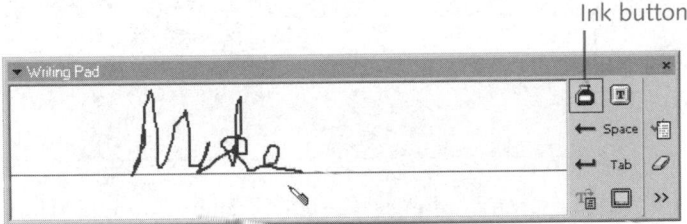

If you pause writing for a second or longer, the text you've written will be inserted into the document as an embedded Ink object, which displays the characters (or anything else you've scrawled) exactly as you sketched them, as shown in this example:

Until then, I remain
Yours very truly,
Mike

(Later in this section, you'll learn how to change the length of the pause before the Ink object is inserted.)

For more information on embedded objects, see "Embedding Data," on page 175.

An Ink object is a graphic object, not text, so you can't edit it in the document using text editing techniques. You can, however, format the text of an Ink object using standard character formatting methods. For example, you can change the characters' point size, make them bold or italic, change their color, and so on. To apply character formatting to an Ink object, complete the following steps:

1 Click the Ink object to select it. (All characters in an Ink object will be formatted the same way—you can't select or format individual characters.)

2 Apply the desired character formatting features using the controls on the Formatting toolbar (such as the Bold button), keyboard commands (such as Ctrl+I for italic), or the Font dialog box (to open it, choose Format, Font).

Chapter 5

103

Character formatting techniques for Word are described in "Formatting Characters Directly," on page 298.

Some character formats have no effect—or a very minimal effect—on an Ink object, for example, All Caps or changing the font.

To have the Handwriting interface *recognize* your handwritten letters and insert them into the document as regular text, click the Text button in the Writing Pad window to turn on text mode. Then use the pen with your electronic table (or use your mouse) to write the characters into the Writing Pad window. To write, just press the main pen or mouse button and drag. Here is an example:

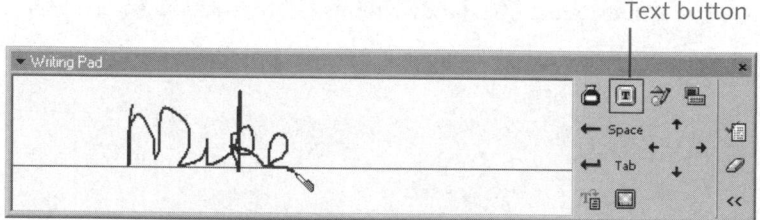

Text button

If you pause writing for a second or longer, the letters entered into the window are recognized and inserted as regular text into the document. (Later in this section, you'll learn how to change the length of this pause.)

Like speech recognition, handwriting recognition can make mistakes. If it inserts the wrong word, you can right-click the word and use the shortcut menu, shown here, to make a correction:

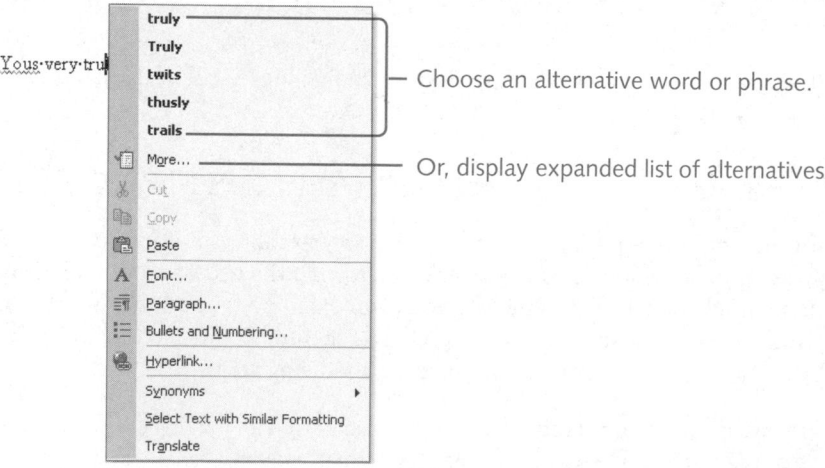

Choose an alternative word or phrase.

Or, display expanded list of alternatives.

The expanded list of alternatives looks like the one at the top of the next page.

Chapter 5

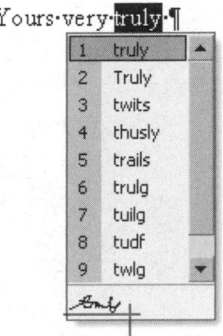

Ink Object command

Another way to display the expanded list is to place the insertion point on the erroneous word and click the Correction button on the Language Bar. To insert the characters you've written as an Ink object rather than as text, so that they appear exactly as you wrote them, choose the Ink Object command below the expanded list.

If you don't find the right word among the alternatives, you can delete the erroneous letters and rewrite them in the Handwriting window or just type them in. Unlike an Ink object, recognized text is regular text so you can fully edit or format it in the document.

In either ink mode or text mode, you can click the buttons displayed along the side of the Handwriting window to issue common keyboard commands: Enter, Space, Up arrow, Right arrow, Backspace, Tab, Down arrow, or Left arrow. Using these buttons frees you from the need to use a keyboard to navigate, edit text, or add space between words.

In either ink mode or text mode, you can use your electronic pen or mouse to write text within the document window itself, rather than within the Handwriting window, by clicking the Write Anywhere button in the Writing Pad window to enable write anywhere mode, as shown here:

Notice that in write anywhere mode, the Writing Pad window is converted to a toolbar containing the same buttons that were displayed around the edges of the Writing Pad window.

> **note** Another way to activate the write anywhere mode is to click the Handwriting button on the Language Bar, choose Write Anywhere from the drop-down menu.

Finally, to change the way the handwriting interface works, click the Options button in the upper-left corner of the Writing Pad window and choose Options from the menu, as shown here:

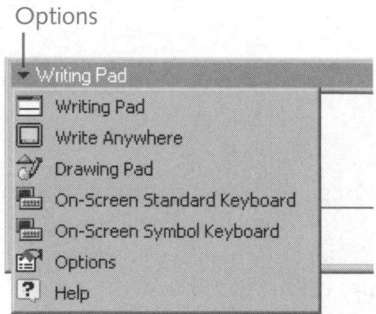

Then, select the options you want in the tabs of the Handwriting Options dialog box, shown in Figure 5-9.

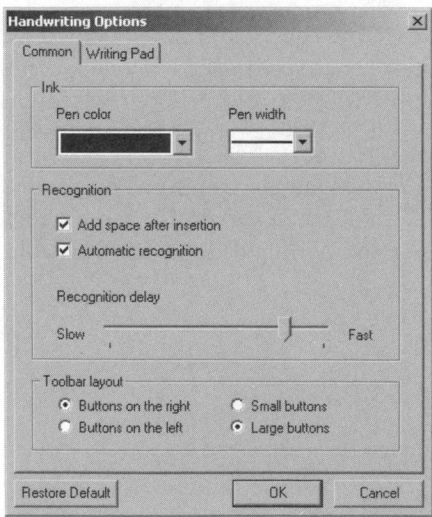

Figure 5-9. You use the Handwriting Options dialog box to modify the features of handwriting recognition.

> **tip** **Replace a Misspelled Word**
>
> If the application's while-you-type spelling checker has underlined a mistakenly inserted word, the shortcut menu won't display the alternative words or the More command. However, you can choose the Handwriting Alternatives command at the bottom of the shortcut menu to display handwriting recognition's expanded list of alternatives.

Chapter 5

Inserting Sketches

To insert freehand sketches into your documents, click the Handwriting button on the Language Bar and choose the Drawing Pad option from the drop-down menu, if it's not already selected, as shown here:

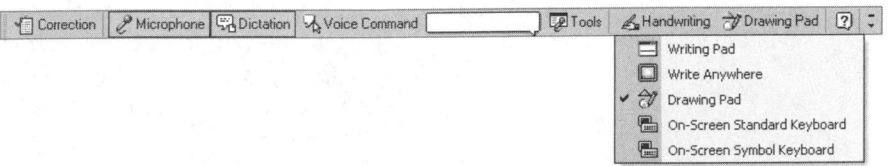

The Drawing Pad window, shown in Figure 5-10, will then appear. If the Drawing Pad option is already selected on the Handwriting drop-down menu, display the Drawing Pad window by clicking the Drawing Pad button on the Language Bar.

Then, create your sketch in the Drawing Pad window as follows:

● To draw, press the main pen or mouse button and drag in the window.

● To insert your sketch into the document, click the Insert Drawing button.

Figure 5-10. You can create a freehand sketch in the Sketch window.

The sketch will be inserted into your document at the current position of the insertion point as an embedded graphic object known as a *Drawing object*. Unlike an Ink object, a sketch isn't inserted automatically after you pause in drawing. Rather, you need to click the Insert Drawing button.

For more information on embedded objects, see "Embedding Data," on page 175.

Chapter 5

Table 5-5 provides a summary of the tasks you can perform in the Drawing Pad window.

Table 5-5. Using the Drawing Pad Window

To Perform This Task in the Drawing Pad Window	Do This
Close the Drawing Pad window and open the Writing Pad instead	Click the Writing Pad button, or click the Options button (the down arrow in the upper left corner of the Drawing Pad window) and choose Writing Pad from the menu.
Erase the entire contents of the Drawing Pad window	Click the Clear button.
Erase the most recent sketch element drawn	Click the Remove Last Stroke button.
Copy the current contents of the Drawing Pad window to the Clipboard, so that you can paste the sketch anywhere in a document	Click the Copy To Clipboard button.
Insert the current contents of the Drawing Pad window into the document	Click the Insert Drawing button.
Modify the color or thickness of the lines in the sketch or the size or the position of the buttons (on left or right)	Click the Options button (the down-arrow in the upper-left corner of the Drawing Pad window) and choose Options from the menu.
Close the Drawing Pad window	Click the Close button (the x in the upper right corner of the Drawing Pad window).

Using the On-Screen Keyboards

To use the pen with an electronic tablet or a mouse, to enter any keyboard character, or to issue any keyboard command, click the Handwriting button on the Language Bar and choose On-Screen Standard Keyboard from the drop-down menu. Then, use your pen or mouse to click buttons on the standard keyboard image displayed on your screen.

Clicking a button has the same effect as pressing the corresponding key on a keyboard. To "press" a key combination, such as Shift+A for a capital A or Ctrl+F6 to issue a command, first click the Shift, Ctrl, or Alt key (or several of these keys) and then click the letter or command key.

To use a pen or mouse to insert symbols, as well as to issue keyboard commands, click the Handwriting button on the Language Bar and choose On-Screen Symbol Keyboard from the drop-down menu. Then, use your pen or mouse to click buttons on the symbol keyboard image displayed on your screen.

> **note** When either On-Screen Standard Keyboard or On-Screen Symbol Keyboard is selected on the Handwriting drop-down menu, you can hide or redisplay the on-screen keyboard by clicking the On-Screen Keyboard button on the Language Bar.

newfeature!
Using the Enhanced Office Clipboard Task Pane

The Clipboard is a Windows system feature that allows you to copy or move text or graphics within a document, between two documents in the same application, or between separate Windows applications. Traditionally, when you issue the Copy or Cut command to copy content to the Clipboard, any previous content in the Clipboard is lost. Consequently, the Paste command inserts only the content that was most recently copied to the Clipboard.

The enhanced Office Clipboard, however, allows you to copy or cut several blocks of text or graphics and store them all in the Clipboard so that you can later paste any or all of these blocks into a document. The enhanced Office Clipboard even collects multiple blocks copied from non-Office applications; however, in a non-Office application, you can paste only the most recently copied block, as usual.

To work with the Office Clipboard, you use the Clipboard task pane and the Clipboard icon in the system tray at the right (or bottom) of the Windows Taskbar. These elements replace the Clipboard toolbar found in Office 2000.

The Office Clipboard stores multiple blocks of text or graphics only when it's *active*. If the Office Clipboard isn't active, only the most recently copied or cut block is retained, as with the traditional Windows Clipboard. To activate the Office Clipboard, use any of the following methods:

- Display the Clipboard task pane in the Office application by choosing Edit, Office Clipboard or by using any of the other available methods for displaying a particular task pane. (See Figure 5-11 for an example of the Clipboard task pane in Excel.) *The Office Clipboard is always active when the Clipboard pane is displayed in at least one Office application.*

> The general methods for displaying task panes are described in "Using the Task Panes in Office Applications," on page 51.

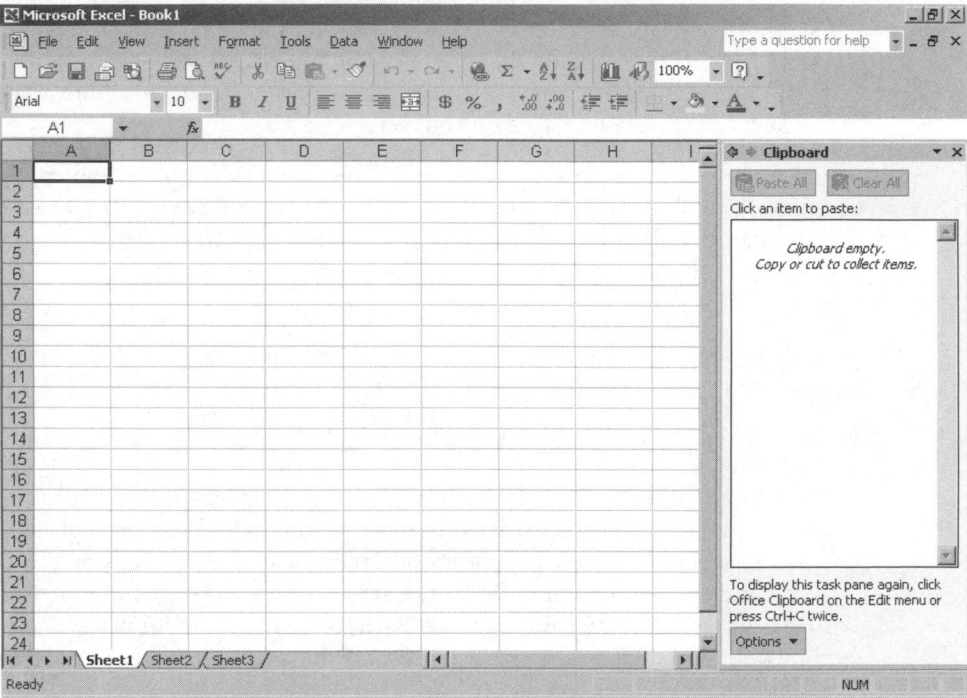

Figure 5-11. This figure shows the Clipboard task pane displayed in Excel.

● If the Show Office Clipboard Automatically option is selected, the Clipboard task pane opens automatically if you copy a block of text or graphics to the Clipboard using the Cut or Copy command and then copy another block *without* issuing an intervening command (such as editing, formatting, or saving the document). When the Clipboard task pane appears, it displays items for both of the blocks you copied (plus any previously copied blocks).

To turn the Show Office Clipboard Automatically option—or another Clipboard option—on or off, click the Options button near the bottom of the Clipboard task pane and choose the option from the menu, shown here:

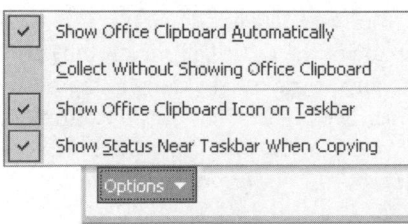

● If you turn on the Collect Without Showing Office Clipboard option, the Office Clipboard is always active, even when the Clipboard task pane isn't displayed in any application.

Chapter 5

While the Office Clipboard is active, each block of text or graphics that you copy or cut to the Clipboard is stored, up to a maximum of 24 blocks. If you copy a 25th block, the Office Clipboard discards the first one.

To paste one or more blocks into a document, open the Clipboard task pane if it isn't already visible. The pane will display a preview of each stored block, together with an icon indicating the block's source program. The blocks are listed in order from the most recently copied one to the least recently copied one (see Figure 5-12).

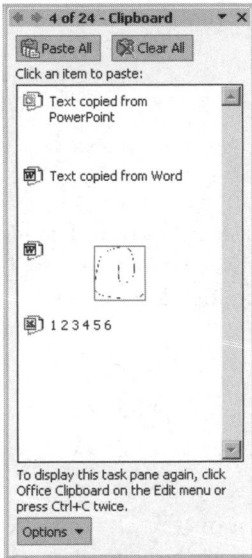

Figure 5-12. Here, the Clipboard task pane lists four blocks of text or graphics that have been copied to the Clipboard.

To paste a particular block into your document at the position of the insertion point, simply click the description of the block in the list, as shown in this example:

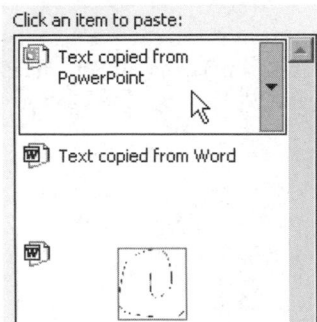

You can also paste a block—or delete it from the Clipboard—by clicking the down arrow that appears to the right of the description when you move the pointer over it and choosing a command from the drop-down menu, shown here:

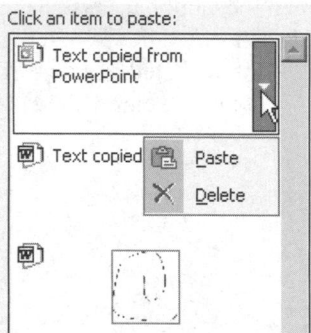

To paste all blocks stored in the Clipboard, click the Paste All button. The blocks will be inserted into the document in the order in which they were copied to the Clipboard (that is, the bottom item will be pasted first and the top item last). To remove all blocks from the Clipboard, click the Clear All button seen here:

If the Show Office Clipboard Icon On Taskbar option is on, the Clipboard icon appears in the system tray at the right (or bottom) of the Windows Taskbar whenever the Office Clipboard is active, as shown here:

Clipboard icon

If the Show Status Near Taskbar When Copying option is on, each time you copy a block to the Clipboard (even from a non-Office program), a small ScreenTip will appear above the Clipboard icon indicating that the block was added to the Clipboard, as in this example:

To display the Clipboard task pane if it's hidden, you can double-click the Clipboard icon. To customize the Office Clipboard, right-click the Clipboard icon to display the shortcut menu shown at the top of the next page.

Chapter 5

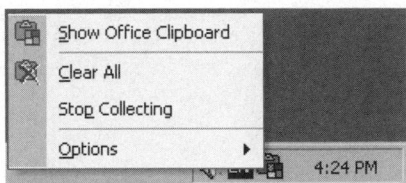

Then choose a command from the shortcut menu. Table 5-6 provides a summary of these commands.

Table 5-6. **Using the Clipboard Icon Shortcut Menu**

To Do This	Choose This Command from the Clipboard Icon Shortcut Menu
Display the Clipboard task pane	Show Office Clipboard
Remove all blocks currently stored in the Office Clipboard	Clear All
Close the Clipboard task pane and turn off the Always Copy To Office Clipboard option	Stop Collecting
Set Office Clipboard options	Options, which opens a submenu containing the same four options you can set through the Options button at the bottom of the Clipboard task pane (as explained earlier in this section)

Troubleshooting

Missing Clipboard Blocks

You copied several blocks of text to the Clipboard but don't find them in the Clipboard task pane when you open it.

The Office Clipboard doesn't store multiple blocks of text or graphics unless the Office Clipboard is active. The Office Clipboard isn't active unless the Clipboard task pane is displayed in at least one Office application or the Collect Without Showing Office Clipboard option is on.

Adding Professional Graphics and Special Effects to Office XP Documents

Inserting Pictures into Office Documents

This section explains how to insert pictures into a Microsoft Office document. In Office, the term *picture* refers to a graphic object that is derived from outside of the Office application. Specifically, you will learn how to:

- Insert a picture from the Clip Organizer program

- Import a picture from a graphics file or from another Microsoft Windows program

newfeature!

Inserting Pictures with the Clip Organizer

You can use the new Office Clip Organizer program to organize, find, preview, and insert into your documents the contents of media files (picture, movie, or sound) that are stored on your computer. The Clip Organizer replaces the Microsoft Clip Gallery program that was included with Microsoft Office 2000.

The Clip Organizer provides access only to those media files that have been imported into the program. In the Clip Organizer, these imported files are known as *media clips*. The Office Setup program automatically imports a set of media files that

115

are provided with Office. If you wish, you can import additional media files stored on your local or network drives.

For each imported media file, the Clip Organizer stores the file's location and description, as well as a list of keywords (to help you find an appropriate clip) and a thumbnail image of the file's contents (to let you preview the clip). The file itself remains in its original location.

Some of the Clip Organizer clips provided with Office insert AutoShapes, not pictures. For information on AutoShapes, see "Using AutoShapes to Create Drawings," on page 132.

Insert
Clip Art

In Microsoft Word, Excel, PowerPoint, or FrontPage, the fastest way to use the Clip Organizer to insert a graphic clip into a document is to place the insertion point at the position in your document where you want to display the picture, and then either choose Picture, Clip Art from the Insert menu or click the Insert Clip Art button on the Drawing toolbar (if it's displayed). This displays the Insert Clip Art task pane within the Office application you're using (see Figure 6-1).

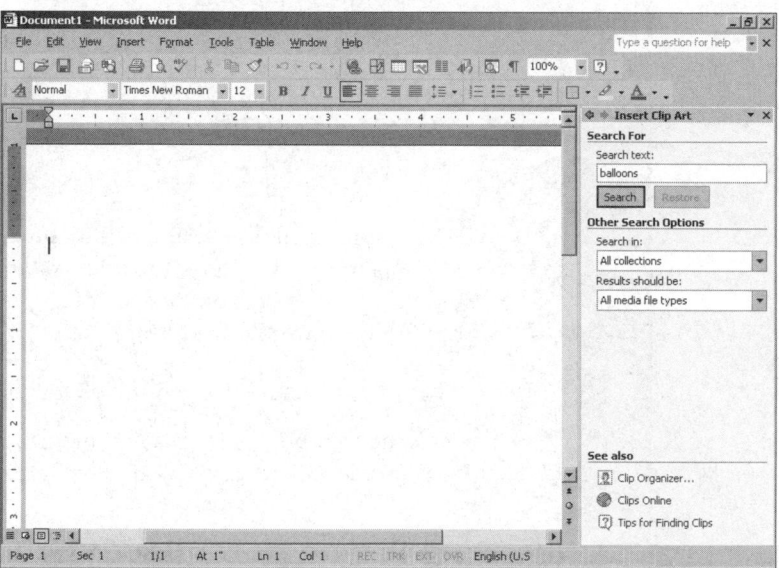

Figure 6-1. This figure shows the Insert Clip Art task pane displayed in Word.

When you first display the Insert Clip Art task pane (or run the freestanding Clip Organizer program, as explained later), you'll see the following dialog box:

Chapter 6

Click to specify which folders
are searched for clips.

If you click the Now button, the Clip Organizer finds and imports media files that are currently located on your computer. (These are imported in addition to the previously imported clips provided with Office.) The Clip Organizer categorizes the imported clips (that is, adds each one to a particular collection that is named according to the folder where the clip is stored) and assigns keywords to each clip. If you let the Clip Organizer perform this search, you might discover clips you didn't know you had stored on your computer. If you want to start using the Clip Organizer without importing additional clips, click the Later button.

For information on other ways to import clips into the Clip Organizer, see "Importing Clips into the Clip Organizer," on page 124.

To search for clips using keywords in the Insert Clip Art task pane, perform the following steps:

1 Enter one or more keywords in the Search Text box. For example:

- To find all pictures of leaves, enter **leaves**.

- To find all pictures that depict seasons, enter **seasons**.

- To find pictures of leaves that also depict seasons, enter either **leaves seasons** or **leaves and seasons**.

2 In the Search In drop-down list, select the collections you want to search, or select Everywhere to search all your collections. As explained later, the Clip Organizer stores clips within separate *collections*, which are analogous to folders in the file system.

tip **Browse a Collection**

If you want to view all clips in a particular collection, select that collection in the Search In drop-down list and leave the Search Text box empty.

3 In the Results Should Be drop-down list, select the specific types of clips you want to find—Clip Art, Photographs, Movies, or Sounds—or select All Media Types to find all types. To insert a picture into your document, select Clip Art, Photographs, or both types. (Graphics of the Photographs type typically have a large number of colors and are in JPEG format.)

> **tip** After you have started entering new search criteria, you can quickly restore your previous set of search criteria (if any) by clicking the Restore button in the Insert Clip Art task pane.

4 Click the Search button to begin the search.

> If you're creating a document meant to be viewed online (rather than printed) or if you're designing a Web page, you might want to insert movie or sound clips, as well as pictures. For information on inserting movie and sound clips in Word documents, see "Adding Movies and Sounds," on page 589.

When you click the Search button, the Insert Clip Art task pane displays all matching clips (see Figure 6-2).

Display results in a wider list.

Return to search pane to do another search.

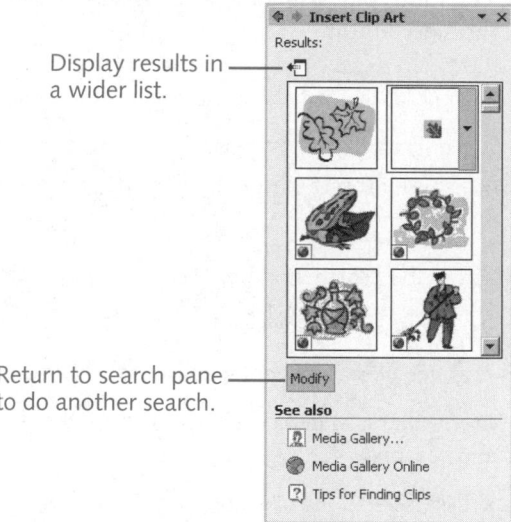

Figure 6-2. This screen shows the results of searching for "leaves" in the Insert Clip Art task pane.

The fastest way to insert a particular clip is to just click on it, as shown here:

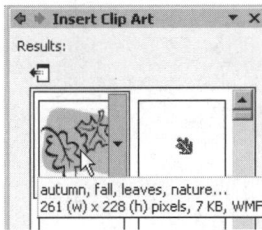

You can also insert a clip, or manage it in other ways, by clicking the down arrow that appears when you move the pointer over the clip and choosing a command from the drop-down menu shown here:

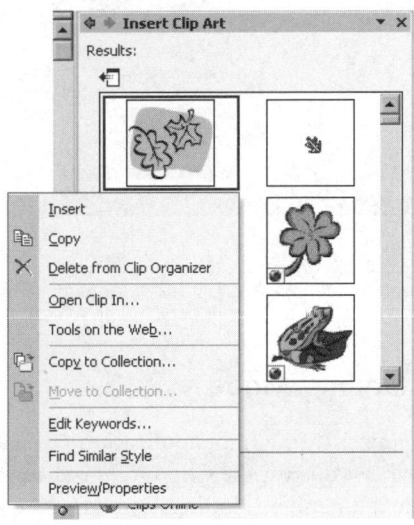

When you insert a clip, it appears as a picture in your document, as shown in this example:

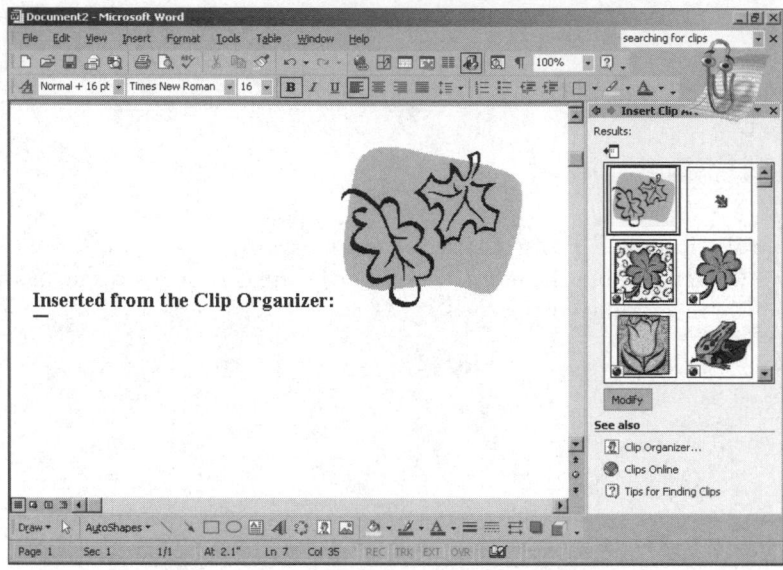

> For instructions on modifying the picture once you've inserted it into the document, see "Modifying Pictures," on page 127, and "Modifying Graphic Objects," on page 150.

Running the Clip Organizer in Freestanding Mode

Rather than working with the Clip Organizer through an application task pane, you can run it as a freestanding program. When you run the Clip Organizer in freestanding mode, you can't paste a clip directly into a document. Rather, you have to copy the clip into the Clipboard and then insert it into your document using the Paste command. However, the freestanding program lets you view and work with your clips in ways that aren't possible in the task pane. It also lets you add clips to a Microsoft Outlook item or a Microsoft Access database object (these applications don't display the Insert Clip Art task pane).

If you are currently displaying the Insert Clip Art task pane in an Office application, the fastest way to run the Clip Organizer in freestanding mode is to click the Clip Organizer command in the task pane, shown here:

You can also run the freestanding program by choosing the Start, Programs, Microsoft Office Tools, Microsoft Clip Organizer command in Windows.

To use the freestanding Clip Organizer, first select one of its two main views: Search or Collection List. To perform a keyword search for a clip, click the Search button to open the Search view, shown in Figure 6-3. Then, perform your search using the Search task pane in the Clip Organizer window, which works just like the Insert Clip Art task pane that appears in other Office applications, as explained in the previous section. The search results will appear in the main part of the program window.

Activate Search or Collection list view.

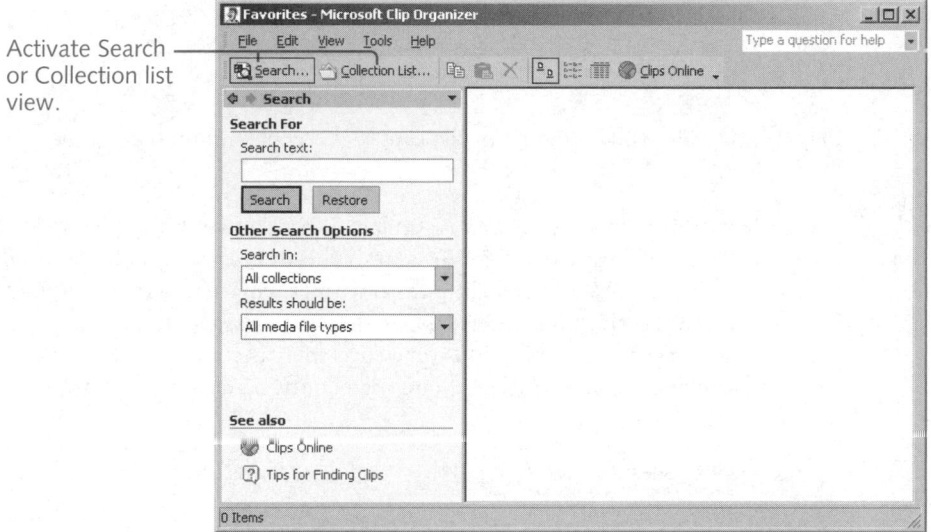

Figure 6-3. The freestanding Clip Organizer program is shown in Search view.

tip You can modify the way the Clip Organizer displays clips by choosing the Thumbnails, List, or Details option on the View menu (the figures in this chapter show the Thumbnails view).

To work with a particular clip, click the down arrow that appears when you move the pointer over the clip and choose a command from the drop-down menu (see Figure 6-4).

121

Figure 6-4. To work with one of the clips that has been found, open the drop-down menu.

Notice that this drop-down menu is similar to that shown in the Insert Clip Art task pane of other Office applications. To insert a clip into a document, you need to choose the Copy command. Then, switch to the document, place the insertion point where you want to insert the clip, and use the application's Paste command to insert it. You can also perform several operations on a clip (such as copying it to a different collection) by clicking the clip to select it and then choosing a command from the Edit menu, as shown here:

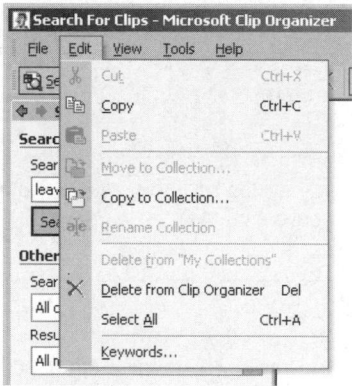

---

tip **Insert a Clip Using Drag-and-Drop**

An alternative way to insert a Clip Organizer clip into any type of Office document is to drag the clip and drop it at the position in your document where you want to display it. You can use this technique with either the freestanding Clip Organizer program or with the Insert Clip Art task pane displayed in another Office application.

To browse the available clips or to organize your clips, click the Collection List button to display the Collection List view, shown in Figure 6-5. The Clip Organizer stores your clips within different named collections, such as Academic, Fantasy, or Nature. Like file folders, collections are arranged in a hierarchical treelike structure, with collections stored within other collections. To open a particular collection, expand the hierarchy (if necessary) in the Collection List task pane and then click on the collection. Its contents will then appear in the main part of the window.

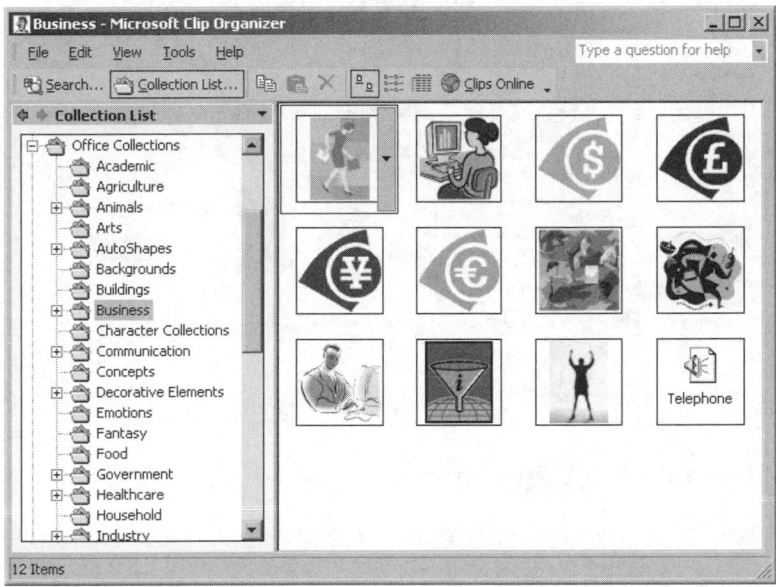

Figure 6-5. This figure shows the freestanding Clip Organizer program in Collection List view, displaying the clips in the Business collection.

In the Collection List view you can also manage your collections by right-clicking a particular collection in the Collection List task pane, and then choosing a command from the shortcut menu, shown here:

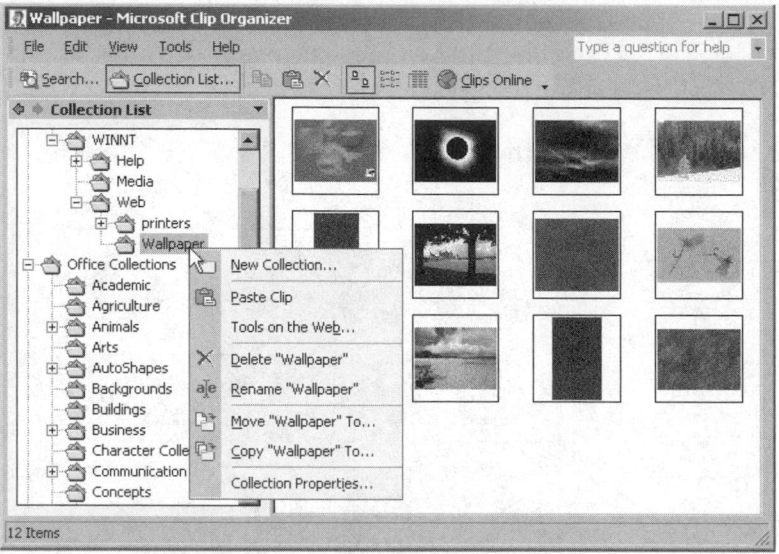

Importing Clips into the Clip Organizer

The fastest way to have the Clip Organizer import all the media files stored on your computer is to run the automatic import feature through the Add Clips to Organizer dialog box that is displayed when you start Clip Organizer. After you use the automatic import feature, the dialog box no longer appears automatically. However, you can display it and use the automatic import feature at any time by choosing, from the File menu of the freestanding Clip Organizer program, Add Clips To Organizer, Automatically.

> The Microsoft Clip Organizer dialog box is explained in "Inserting Pictures with the Clip Organizer," on page 115.

You can also import an individual clip into the Clip Organizer using any of the following methods. (You can import the clip to any collection *except* one of the collections in the predefined Office Collections or Web Collections group.)

- To import a clip from a media file, from the File menu in the freestanding Clip Organizer program, choose Add Clips To Organizer, On My Own.

- To import a graphic object that is displayed in a document (such as a Word document), drag the object and, in the freestanding Clip Organizer program, drop it on the collection in which you want to store it, as shown at the top of the next page.

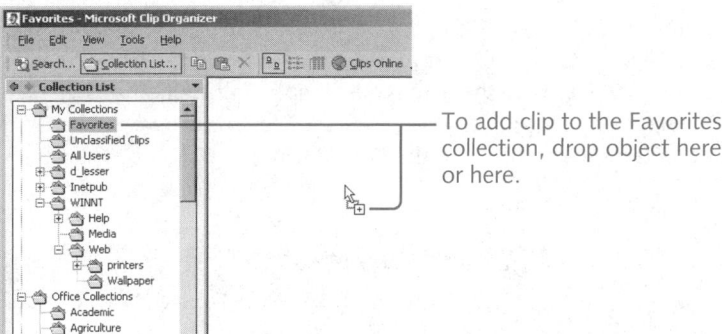

To add clip to the Favorites collection, drop object here or here.

● Another way to import a graphic object displayed in a document is to copy the graphic to the Clipboard, switch to the freestanding Clip Organizer program, open the collection where you want to store the clip, and choose Edit, Paste or press Ctrl+V.

InsideOut

The Clip Organizer automatically assigns keywords to a clip that you import. However, it derives these keywords not from the actual content of the clip but rather from fairly irrelevant information, such as the folder where the media file is stored, the format of the clip, and even the name of the current Windows user. To make it easier to find the clip when you need it, you should add meaningful keywords based on the actual content of the clip. To do this, select the clip in the main window of the freestanding Clip Organizer program. Then choose Edit, Keywords. To assign the same keywords to an entire set of clips, select them all prior to choosing the Keywords command. You can select several clips by pressing Ctrl while clicking each one (to select adjoining clips, click the first one in the range and then press Shift and click the last one).

Importing Pictures

You can import a picture into a Word, Excel, PowerPoint, or FrontPage document either by inserting the contents of an entire graphics file or by copying a block of graphics from another program and pasting it into the document.

To import a picture from a graphics file, do the following:

1 Place the insertion point at the position in your document where you want to insert the picture.

2 Choose Insert, Picture, From File. This opens the Insert Picture dialog box, which is similar to the Open dialog box for opening documents (see Figure 6-6).

3 In the Insert Picture dialog box, locate and select the graphics file you want to import. You can import graphics files in a wide variety of formats—for example, files with the extensions .bmp, .wmf, .gif, and .jpg. To see preview images of your graphics files, click the Views button and choose the Preview or Thumbnails view from the drop-down menu.

4 Click the Insert button.

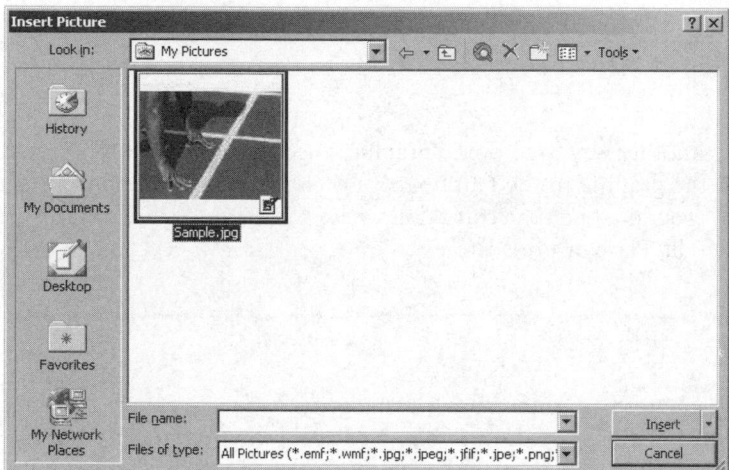

Figure 6-6. The Insert Picture dialog box is shown in the Thumbnails view.

---

tip **Import More Graphics Formats**

To maximize the number of graphics formats that you can import into an Office document, make sure that all of the Office graphics filters are installed. To do this, rerun Office Setup and select the Run From My Computer option for the Graphics Filters feature. You'll find this feature in the Converters And Filters section, under the Office Shared Features group (see Figure 6-7). Because the filters don't take up a lot of disk space, we recommend installing all of them, rather than just the one you currently need.

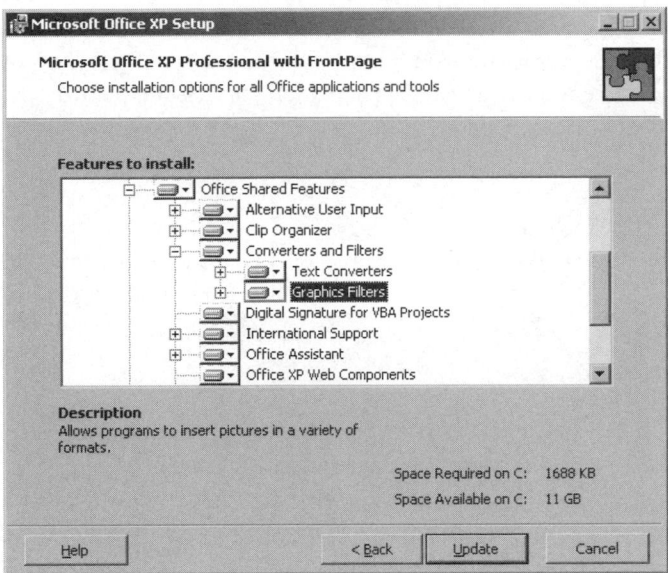

Figure 6-7. Installing all Office graphics filters is recommended.

Rerunning Office Setup is explained in "Revisiting Office Setup," on page 27.

To insert a picture into an Office document by copying graphics from another program (such as the Paint program that comes with Windows), perform the following steps:

1 Select the graphics in the other program, and from that program's Edit menu, choose Copy.

2 Place the insertion point at the approximate position in the Office document where you want to insert the picture.

3 From the Office application's Edit menu, choose Paste or press Ctrl+V.

For instructions on modifying the picture once you've inserted it into the document, see the next section.

Modifying Pictures

This section explains how to modify pictures using the commands and options provided by the Picture toolbar and the Picture tab of the Format Picture dialog box that apply specifically to pictures.

To learn about the common techniques, commands, and options for modifying pictures and other types of graphic objects, see "Modifying Graphic Objects," on page 150.

Chapter 6

The fastest way to modify a picture is to use the Picture toolbar, shown below. Unless you previously hid the Picture toolbar, it appears whenever you click on a picture to select it. (If the Picture toolbar doesn't appear when you select a picture, choose View, Toolbars, Picture.)

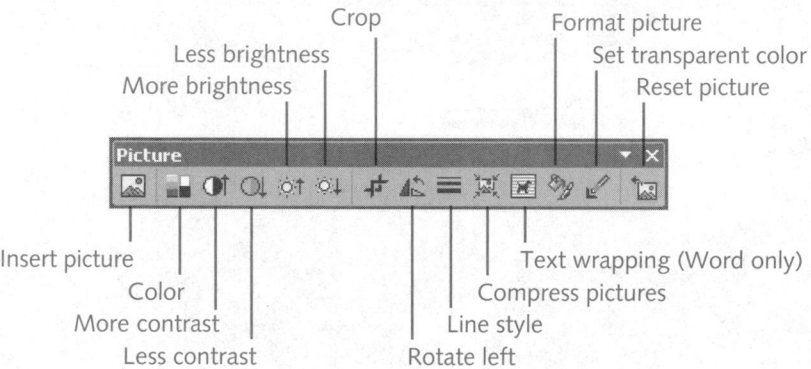

To modify the selected picture use the Picture toolbar, as shown in Table 6-1.

Table 6-1. **Methods for Modifying the Selected Picture Using the Picture Toolbar**

To Modify the Selected Picture Like This	Do This with the Picture Toolbar
Add a new picture from a graphics file	Click the Insert Picture button. (Clicking this button is equivalent to choosing Insert, Picture, From File.)
Set the picture colors to Grayscale (shades of gray), Black & White, Washout (faded tones), or Automatic (the original color values)	Click the Color button and choose an option from the drop-down menu.
Make light colors lighter and dark colors darker	Click the More Contrast button, repeatedly if necessary, to achieve the result you want.
Make light colors darker and dark colors lighter	Click the Less Contrast button, repeatedly if necessary, to achieve the result you want.
Make all colors lighter	Click the More Brightness button, repeatedly if necessary, to achieve the result you want.
Make all colors darker	Click the Less Brightness button, repeatedly if necessary, to achieve the result you want.

Table 6-1. *(continued)*

To Modify the Selected Picture Like This	Do This with the Picture Toolbar
Crop the picture. (For more information on cropping, see "Cropping a Picture," on page 130.)	Click the Crop button, and then drag one of the sizing handles displayed around the picture.
Rotate the picture image 90 degrees counterclockwise	Click the Rotate Left button.
Select a style of line to be used for drawing an AutoShape, or to be drawn around an AutoShape, Drawing Canvas, Diagram, or Organization Chart (this button doesn't apply to pictures)	Click the Line Style button and choose a style from the drop-down menu.
Modify either the selected picture or all pictures in the document in one or more of the following ways: ● Optimize the picture resolution for either the Web or for printing ● Compress the graphic data for the pictures ● Delete cropped areas of pictures (if you do this, you won't be able to restore cropped areas)	Click the Compress Pictures button and select the desired options in the Compress Pictures dialog box.
Change a picture's text wrapping style (available in Word only). (For information on wrapping styles, see "Combining Text with Graphic Objects and Text Boxes," on page 515.)	Click the Text Wrapping button (displayed in Word only) and choose a wrapping style from the drop-down menu.
Open the Format Picture dialog box. (For more information, see "Using the Format *Object* Dialog Box to Format Graphic Objects," on page 156.)	Click the Format Picture button.
Make a particular color in a picture transparent	Click the Set Transparent Color button and then click an area in the picture with the color you want to make transparent. (This command isn't available for pictures in certain for mats, such as a picture in .wmf format inserted from the Clip Organizer)
Restore the size, cropping, and colors of the picture to their original values	Click the Reset Picture button.

Chapter 6

> **note** FrontPage displays an extended version of the Picture toolbar known as the Pictures toolbar. You can display it by choosing View, Toolbars, Pictures.

The Picture tab of the Format Picture dialog box provides an alternative way to crop a picture, to change the color (to Grayscale, Black & White, Washout, or Automatic), to adjust the contrast or brightness, or to reset a picture. Although less convenient than the Picture toolbar, it lets you crop by entering precise measurements. You can also adjust the brightness and contrast by entering exact percentages. Here's the procedure:

1 Click on the picture to select it.

Format
Picture

2 Choose Format, Picture. Or, click the Format Picture button on the Picture toolbar.

3 Set options in the Picture tab of the Format Picture dialog box (see Figure 6-8).

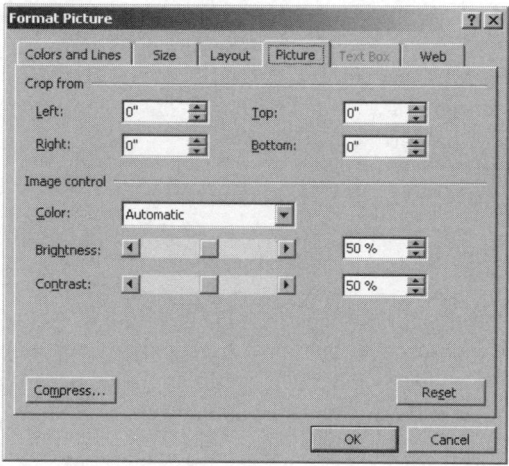

Figure 6-8. The Picture tab of the Format Picture dialog box is shown.

> **tip** **Compress Pictures When Saving a Document**
>
> You can also display the Compress Pictures dialog box when you save a Word, Excel, or PowerPoint document. In the Save As dialog box, choose Compress Pictures from the Tools drop-down menu.

Cropping a Picture

Changing the size of a picture by dragging a sizing handle or by using the Size tab of the Format Picture dialog box *scales* the picture—that is, it compresses or expands the graphics contained in the picture.

The techniques for scaling pictures are covered in "Modifying Graphic Objects," on page 150.

Alternatively, with a picture you can use the Picture toolbar's Crop button, or the Picture tab in the Format Picture dialog box (shown in Figure 6-8) to *crop* a picture. Cropping a picture changes the size or proportions of the picture itself without changing the size or proportions of the graphics it contains. Cropping results in either cutting off some of the graphics or adding additional white space around them. Figure 6-9 shows the difference.

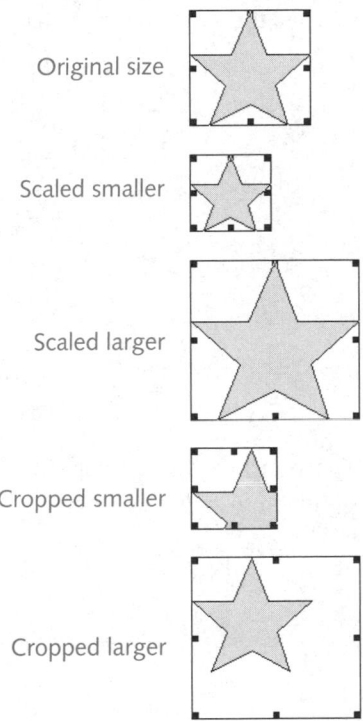

Original size

Scaled smaller

Scaled larger

Cropped smaller

Cropped larger

Figure 6-9. Scaling versus cropping a picture provides different results.

To crop using the Picture toolbar's Crop button, select the picture, click the button, and then drag any sizing handle on the picture. To use the Picture tab of the Format Picture dialog box, enter the amount that you want to crop each side of the picture— as a positive or negative number—into the Left, Right, Top, or Bottom box.

Using AutoShapes to Create Drawings

As an alternative to importing graphics, you can create drawings within Word, Excel, PowerPoint, or FrontPage by using AutoShapes. An AutoShape is a predefined or free-form figure—such as a line, oval, cube, flowchart symbol, banner, or free-form scribble—that you can quickly insert into a document and then customize.

To insert an AutoShape, perform the following steps:

1 Choose Insert, Picture, AutoShapes to display the AutoShapes toolbar shown here:

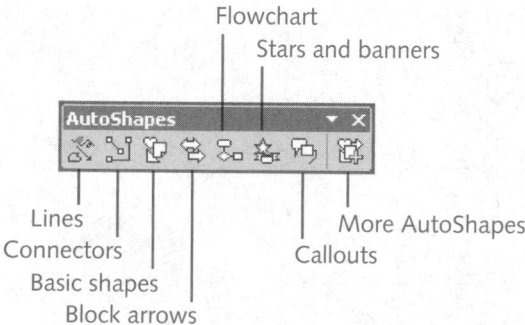

2 On the AutoShapes toolbar, click the button for the type of shape you want to insert. This action opens a drop-down menu of AutoShapes belonging to that category, as shown in this example:

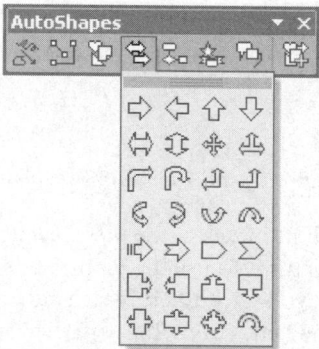

InsideOut

Don't be misled by the label of the More AutoShapes button. It doesn't insert just AutoShapes. Rather, it displays the Insert Clip Art task pane so you can insert pictures or other media clips, in addition to the AutoShapes contained in the Clip Organizer.

3 Click the button for the particular shape you want to insert. Notice that when you hold the mouse pointer over a button, a ToolTip displays a description of the shape, as shown here:

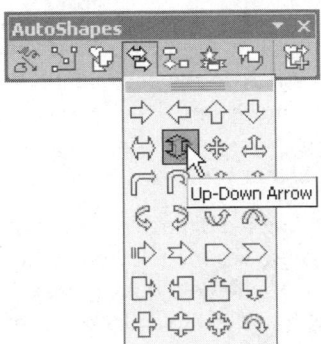

4 To insert a standard-sized AutoShape, click the position in your document where you want to display the figure, as shown here. (You can later change its size, shape, or position.)

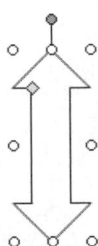

To give the AutoShape a specific initial size and shape, press the mouse button and drag to create the figure, as in this example:

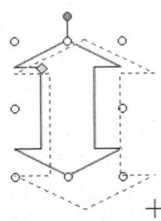

Drawing Canvases

In a Word document, when you click a button to insert an AutoShape, Word automatically inserts a graphic object known as a *drawing canvas*. A drawing canvas is a rectangular area that can contain one or more AutoShapes. The automatically inserted drawing canvas initially contains the message "Create Your Drawing Here." However, you can insert the AutoShape anywhere in the document—you don't need to put it within the drawing canvas. (Word removes the drawing canvas if you place the AutoShape outside of it.) You can also remove the drawing canvas by pressing the Esc key after you select a drawing tool but before you begin drawing.

A drawing canvas is primarily useful for creating a drawing consisting of two or more separate AutoShapes. The drawing canvas preserves the relative positions of these AutoShapes and prevents them from getting separated by page breaks or intervening text. The drawing canvas also makes it easy to move the entire set of AutoShapes in the drawing as a unit.

You can insert a blank drawing canvas in a Word document by choosing Insert, Picture, New Drawing.

Drawing

If the Drawing toolbar is currently displayed, you might find it more convenient to use the Drawing toolbar to insert an AutoShape rather than the AutoShape toolbar. (To display the Drawing toolbar, choose View, Toolbars, Drawing, or click the Drawing toolbar button if it's displayed in the application you're using.) The Drawing toolbar lets you insert any type of AutoShape, with a single button click for some of the more common ones, shown here:

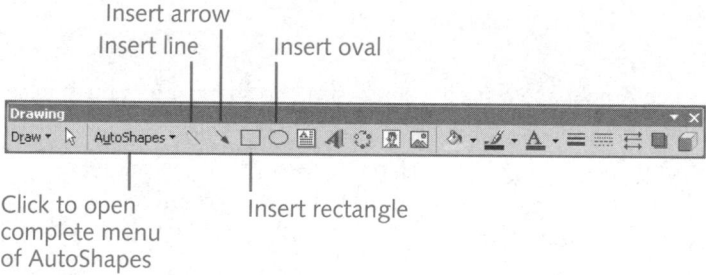

For information on changing the size, shape, position, and other features of an AutoShape, see "Modifying Graphic Objects," on page 150.

Troubleshooting

AutoShapes Disappear in Word

You inserted one or more AutoShapes, diagrams, or organization charts into a Word document. However, you no longer see them in the document.

The following are two situations in which AutoShapes, diagrams, or organization charts are hidden from view:

- You are viewing the document in Normal or Outline view. To insert or view AutoShapes, diagrams, or organization charts, however, you must be in Web Layout, Print Layout, or Print Preview view. If you aren't in one of these views when you insert one of these objects, Word automatically switches to Print Layout view. However, if you later change to Normal or Outline view, the objects disappear.

- The Drawings view option is turned off. Word won't display these graphic objects—even in Web Layout or Print Layout view—if this option is off. (Print Preview always displays graphics objects.) To turn on the option, choose Tools, Options, click the View tab, and check the Drawings option in the Print And Web Layout Options area.

newfeature!
Generating Conceptual Drawings Using Office Diagrams

You can create almost any type of conceptual drawing by using one or more individual AutoShapes, as described in the previous section. However, in Word, Excel, or PowerPoint you can get a head start in building a conceptual drawing—such as an organization chart or a Venn diagram—by inserting a ready-made Office *diagram*. When you insert a diagram, Office instantly adds all the necessary AutoShapes and places them within a rectangular drawing area (which is similar to a Word drawing canvas, described in the previous section). Office also provides tools that make it easy to customize the drawing and add text to it.

Creating an Organization Chart

You can insert an organization chart into a document to illustrate the structure of an organization or to depict other hierarchical relationships—for example, the families, genera, and species of a particular order of biological organisms. To add an organization chart, perform the following steps:

1 Choose Insert, Picture, Organization Chart.

135

Office will then insert an organization chart with a single top-level box and three subordinate boxes, and it will display the Organization Chart toolbar, shown in Figure 6-10. (This toolbar appears automatically whenever you select an organization chart.)

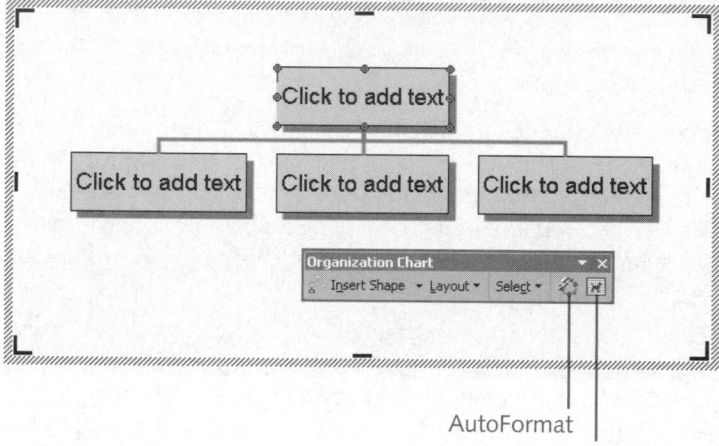

AutoFormat

Text wrapping (Word only)

Figure 6-10.   This figure shows an organization chart inserted into a Word document.

> For information on text wrapping in Word, see "Combining Text with Graphic Objects and Text Boxes," on page 515.

2 To add text to a box, click in it and type the desired text.

3 To add a new box, click an existing box to select it, click the Insert Shape button on the Organization Chart toolbar, and from the drop-down menu choose the desired relationship of the new box to the selected box, as shown here:

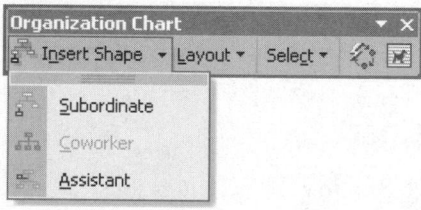

To delete a box, click on it to select it and then press Delete.

4 To modify the overall structure of the organization chart, on the Organization Chart toolbar, click the Layout button, and choose the structure you want from the drop-down menu, as shown here:

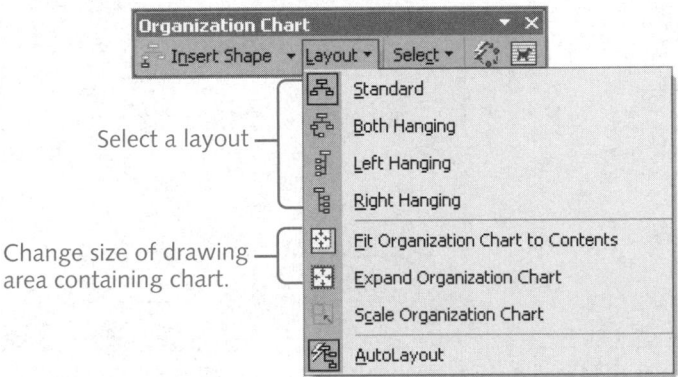

Select a layout

Change size of drawing
area containing chart.

You can move a particular box within the chart by dragging it and dropping it on another box.

---

tip **Control Automatic Layout**

The AutoLayout option on the Layout drop-down menu (which is on by default) causes Office to automatically maintain the positions and sizes of the individual AutoShape objects that make up an organization chart (or one of the other types of diagrams you will see later). This option restricts the ways you can modify the AutoShapes—for example, you might not be able to drag an AutoShape to a particular position if this option is on. If you are customizing a diagram and can't modify an AutoShape the way you want, try turning this option off. Otherwise, you should leave it on.

---

5 To modify the overall style of the organization chart, click the AutoFormat button and choose a style in the Organization Chart Style Gallery dialog box (shown in Figure 6-11).

To learn how to modify the individual AutoShapes in an organization chart, see "Modifying Graphic Objects," on page 150.

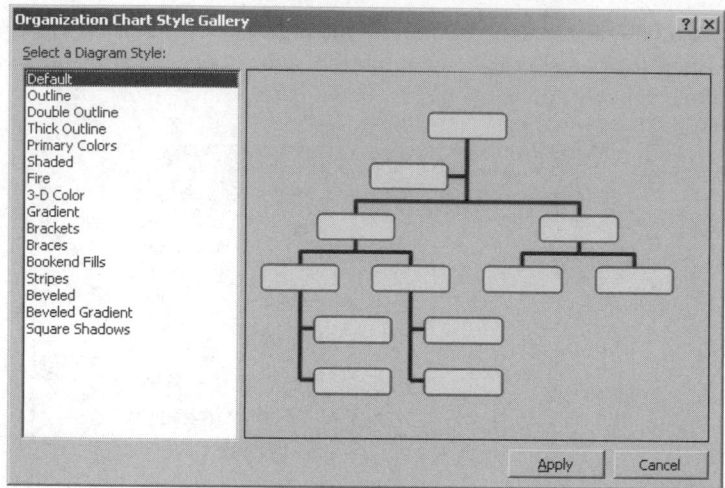

Figure 6-11. The Organization Chart Style Gallery dialog box allows you to customize the overall style of an organization chart.

Creating Other Types of Diagrams

To insert a cycle, radial, pyramid, Venn, or target diagram, perform the following steps:

1 Choose Insert, Diagram.

2 In the Diagram Gallery dialog box, click the particular type of diagram you want to create and then click the OK button. Or, just double-click the diagram type, as shown here:

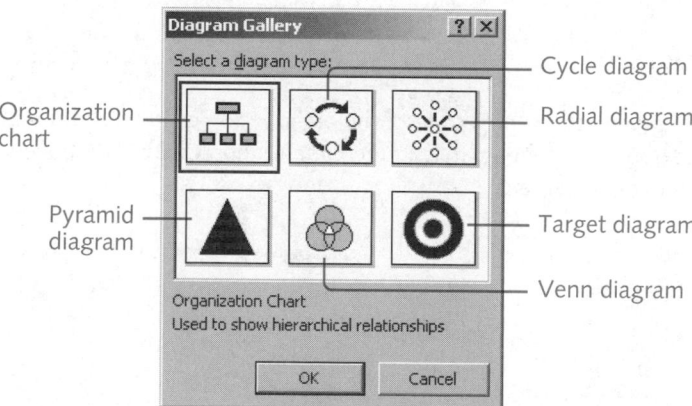

Selecting the Organization Chart diagram type has the same effect as choosing Insert, Picture, Organization Chart. The procedure for creating an organization chart is different from that for creating the other diagram types. If you want an organization chart, follow the instructions given in the previous section.

Office will insert the basic diagram and will display the Diagram toolbar. (This toolbar appears automatically whenever you select a diagram other than an organization chart.) The diagram will consist of a collection of AutoShapes and text boxes for adding labels, all inside of a rectangular drawing area (see Figure 6-12).

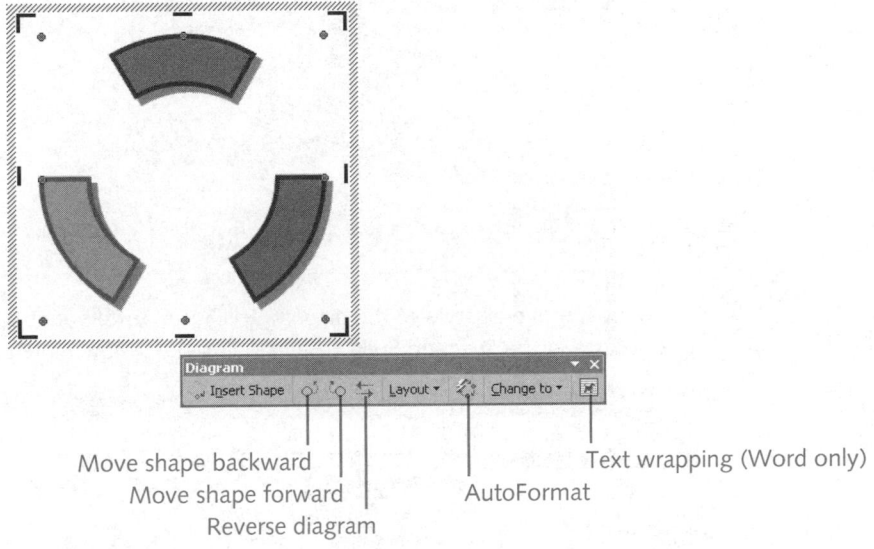

Move shape backward

Move shape forward

Reverse diagram

AutoFormat

Text wrapping (Word only)

Figure 6-12. This is a cycle diagram inserted into a Word document, showing the Diagram toolbar as it appears when you select an AutoShape within the diagram.

Text boxes are discussed in "Using Text Boxes to Create Precise Page Layouts," on page 510. For information on text wrapping in Word, see "Combining Text with Graphic Objects and Text Boxes," on page 515.

3 To add text to the diagram, click in a text box and type. Some diagrams also contain AutoShapes that you can add text to.

4 To add a new shape to the diagram (for example, a new sector to a cycle diagram or a new level to a pyramid diagram), on the Diagram toolbar, click the Insert Shape button. To delete a shape, click it and press Delete.

5 To rearrange your text labels within the diagram, select the text box or AutoShape containing the particular label you want to move, and then on the Diagram toolbar, click the Move Shape Backward button to rotate the label within the diagram in one direction or the Move Shape Forward button to rotate it in the other direction.

6 To reverse the order of the shapes in the diagram, on the Diagram toolbar, click the Reverse Diagram button.

7 To adjust the size of the drawing area containing the diagram, on the Diagram toolbar, click the Layout button and choose an option from the drop-down menu, shown here:

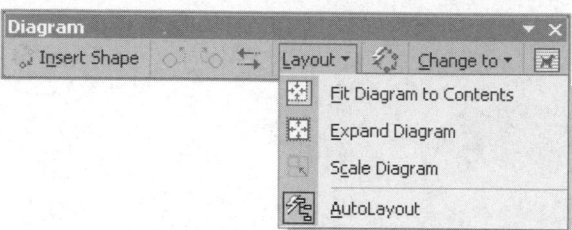

For an explanation of the AutoLayout option on the Layout drop-down menu, see the tip "Control Automatic Layout," on page 137.

8 To modify the overall style of the diagram, click the AutoFormat button and select a style in the Diagram Style Gallery dialog box, shown in Figure 6-13.

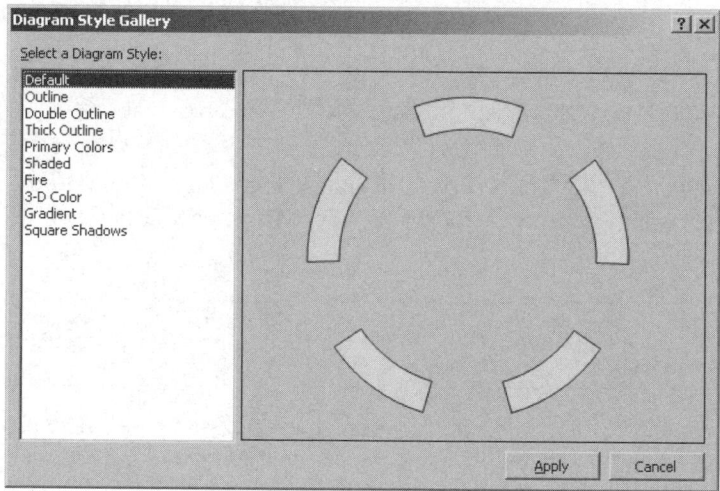

Figure 6-13. The Diagram Style Gallery dialog box is used to customize the overall style of an Office diagram.

9 To convert the diagram to another type (for example, to change a cycle diagram to a Venn diagram), click the Change To button on the Diagram toolbar, and choose the drawing type you want from the drop-down menu, shown at the top of the next page.

To learn how to modify the AutoShapes in a diagram, see "Modifying Graphic Objects," on page 150.

Using WordArt to Produce Special Text Effects

In a Word, Excel, PowerPoint, or FrontPage document you can add unusually formatted text—for example, curved, slanted, or three-dimensional text—by inserting a WordArt object. To do this, perform the following steps:

1 Choose Insert, Picture, WordArt. Or, if the Drawing toolbar is displayed, you can click the WordArt button.

2 In the WordArt Gallery dialog box (shown in Figure 6-14), double-click the style you want.

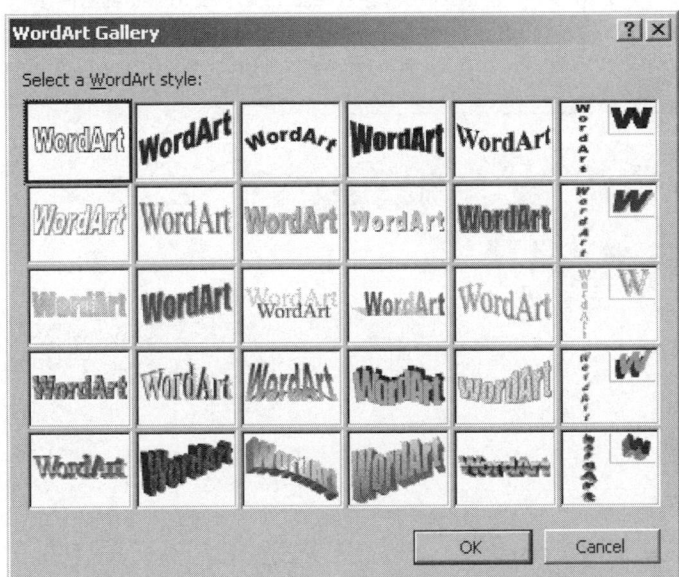

Figure 6-14. The WordArt Gallery dialog box is used to insert special text effects.

Chapter 6

3 In the Edit WordArt Text dialog box (shown in Figure 6-15), type your text and select the desired font and size.

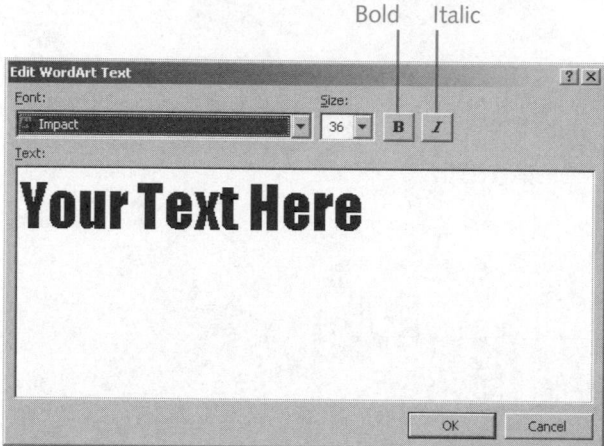

Figure 6-15. In the Edit WordArt Text dialog box, you enter the text and select the desired font, size, and style.

Click the Bold or Italic button to make *all* text bold or italic. (You can't apply bold or italic to a selected portion of the text.)

4 In the Edit WordArt Text dialog box, click the OK button. Office will insert your text into the document.

Whenever the WordArt object is selected, Office displays the WordArt toolbar (shown in Figure 6-16). If this toolbar isn't visible when you've selected a WordArt object, choose View, Toolbars, WordArt to display it.

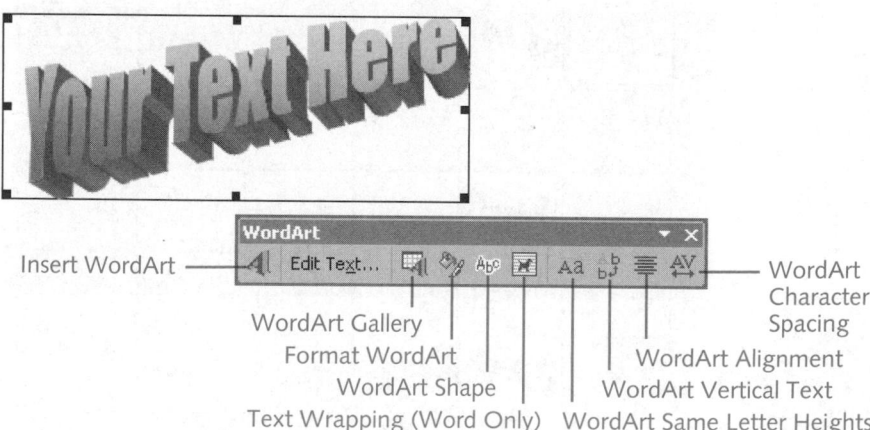

Figure 6-16. The WordArt toolbar lets you insert and work with WordArt objects.

For information on text wrapping in Word, see "Combining Text with Graphic Objects and Text Boxes," on page 515.

5 If you want to modify the WordArt object, use the WordArt toolbar, as shown in Table 6-2.

Table 6-2. Using the WordArt Toolbar

To Modify a WordArt Object Like This	Click This WordArt Toolbar Button
Add a new WordArt object	Insert WordArt
Open the Edit WordArt Text dialog box, where you can edit the text, change the text font or size, or apply bold or italic	Edit Text
Open the WordArt Gallery dialog box, where you can select a different text style	WordArt Gallery
Open the Format WordArt dialog box, where you can change many features of the WordArt object. (For general instructions on using this dialog box, see "Using the Format *Object* Dialog Box to Format Graphic Objects," on page 156.)	Format WordArt
Display a drop-down menu from which you can choose a different text pattern (for example, various types of curved or slanted text)	WordArt Shape
Toggle between text with same-height letters and text in which the first letter of each word is higher	WordArt Same Letter Heights
Toggle between vertical and horizontal text	WordArt Vertical Text
Display a drop-down menu from which you can choose a text alignment style	WordArt Alignment
Display a drop-down menu from which you can choose a character spacing style	WordArt Character Spacing

For information on common formatting techniques that you can use to modify a WordArt object, see "Modifying Graphic Objects," on page 150.

Constructing Charts Using Microsoft Graph

Using the Microsoft Graph program, you can insert charts into your Office documents. Graph supports a wide variety of chart types and provides a handy alternative to using Excel charts.

The fastest way to create a chart with the Graph program is to use a Word table (you can later move the chart to a different Office application). Here's how you do this:

1 Insert a table into a Word document, enter into this table the data that you want to graph, and then select the entire table. An example is shown in Figure 6-17.

Contract	Gross Profit
Corn	6,392.00
Oats	3,920.00
Soybean Meal	-1,560.00
Soybean Oil	1,598.00
Soybeans	-2,598.00
Wheat	9,403.00

Figure 6-17. Select the Word table containing the data that you want to graph.

For information on Word tables, see "Arranging Text with Tables," on page 339. For details on creating charts in Excel, see Chapter 27, "Advanced Worksheet Charts."

2 Choose Insert, Picture, Chart.

Graph will immediately embed a chart into the document that depicts the data contained in the Word table. Graph will also display a datasheet containing the chart data (see Figure 6-18).

For more information on embedded objects, see "Embedding Data," on page 175.

Table entered into the
Word document in step 1

Menu commands and toolbar
buttons provided by Microsoft Graph

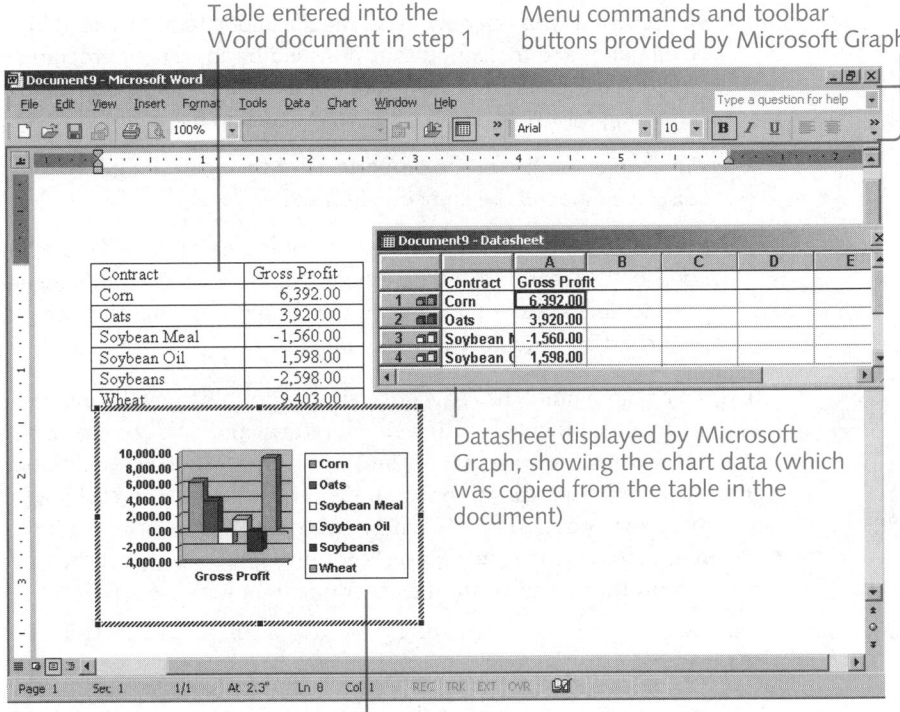

Datasheet displayed by Microsoft
Graph, showing the chart data (which
was copied from the table in the
document)

Chart that Microsoft Graph inserted into
the document as an embedded object

Figure 6-18. This figure shows a Chart object, based on the Word table shown in Figure 6-17, embedded in a Word document.

3 The datasheet contains a copy of the data from the original Word table that you selected. If you want to change the values plotted on the chart, you must edit the numbers within the datasheet, not within the original table.

InsideOut

Once the chart is inserted, a copy of the data from the table in the Word document is stored independently within the embedded chart object. Changing the table data won't affect the chart; in fact, you can delete the Word table if you want to.

4 If you want, you can now make modifications to the chart using the menu commands and toolbar buttons provided by the Graph program. You can access detailed online information on using the Graph commands by choosing Microsoft Graph Help from the Help menu or by pressing F1.

5 To change the size or the proportions of the chart, drag the sizing handles displayed around the embedded object.

6 When you've finished modifying the chart, click in the Word document outside the chart and the datasheet. The datasheet and the menu commands and toolbar buttons provided by the Graph program will disappear, leaving the chart embedded in your document.

View
Datasheet

If you want to modify the chart later, simply double-click the embedded chart object. The commands provided by Graph will return, and you can change the features of the chart. If the datasheet isn't visible and you need to change the numbers shown on the chart, you can display it by choosing View, Datasheet or by clicking the View Datasheet button on the Graph toolbar. If you want to display the chart within another Office document (for example, in a PowerPoint presentation), select the Chart object, cut or copy it, and then paste it into the other document.

> You can modify the appearance of a chart using the Picture toolbar or the Picture tab of the Format Object dialog box, which were explained in "Modifying Pictures," on page 127.

InsideOut

If you embed a new Graph object within a program other than Word (by choosing the Object command from the program's Insert menu and selecting the Microsoft Graph Chart object type), or if you embed a new Graph object in a Word document without first selecting a table containing valid chart data, Graph will create an example chart displaying example data. You then need to manually enter the actual data, as well as the row and column headings, cell by cell, into the Graph datasheet.

> For information on common formatting techniques that you can use to modify a chart, see "Modifying Graphic Objects," on page 150.

Chapter 6

Building Equations with Microsoft Equation

If you create Office documents that involve mathematics, you will find the little-publicized Microsoft Equation program useful for accurately formatting equations in your documents. You can insert an equation into Word, Excel, PowerPoint, Outlook (in the large text box of an item opened in a form), Access (in an OLE Object type field), or Publisher. To enter an equation, perform the following steps:

1 Choose Insert, Object.

2 In the Object dialog box, click the Create New tab, choose the Microsoft Equation 3.0 object type, and click OK. Equation will insert a blank working area into your document, and the Equation toolbar and menus will appear within the Office application's window (see Figure 6-19).

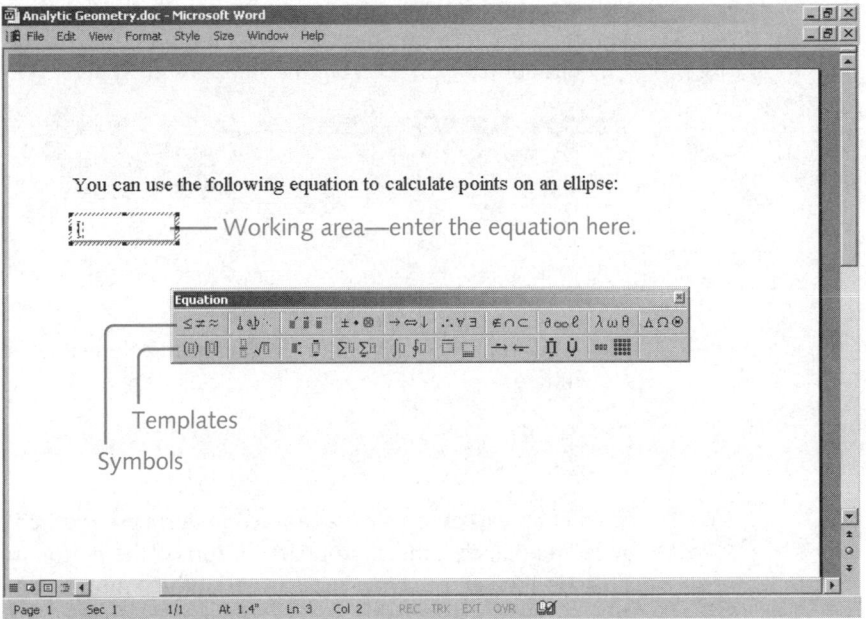

Figure 6-19. This figure shows an Equation object embedded in a Word document.

> The equation you insert is an embedded object created by the Equation program. For more information on embedded objects, see "Embedding Data," on page 175.

3 Use the following instructions to create a mathematical expression:

Chapter 6

- To enter numbers or variables, simply type them using the keyboard, such as the *y* typed to begin the following example equation:

- To enter a mathematical operator that appears on the keyboard, such as the plus sign (+), the minus sign (–), or the equals sign (=), you can simply type it. For instance, you could add an equals sign to the example equation, as shown here:

- To enter an operator or symbol that doesn't appear on the keyboard, click the appropriate button on the top row of the Equation toolbar, and then click the desired symbol on the drop-down palette of symbols. For example, clicking the symbol shown here:

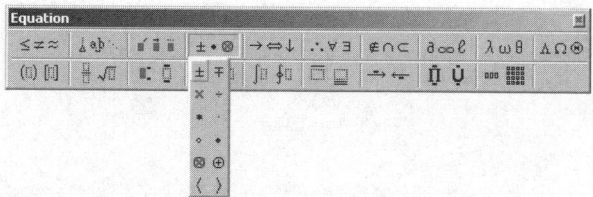

   adds a plus-or-minus symbol (±) to the example equation, as shown here:

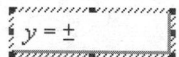

- To enter an expression such as a fraction, a square root, an exponent, or an integral, click the appropriate button on the bottom row of the Equation toolbar, and then choose one of the templates on the drop-down palette. For example, you would click the following template:

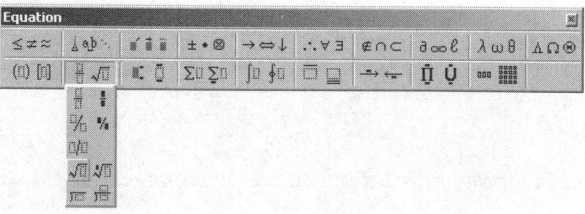

   to add a square-root expression to the example equation, as shown here:

Chapter 6

$$y = \pm\sqrt{}$$

Then enter the desired numbers and variables into the area marked by dotted lines within the template. For example, you could type the following into the radical expression in the example equation:

$$y = \pm\sqrt{1+a}$$

You can insert templates within other templates to create nested operator expressions, such as a fraction within a square-root operator.

You can modify the font, font size, or format (that is, normal, bold, or italic) of characters or symbols by choosing commands from the Style and Size menus.

Troubleshooting

Can't Enter Spaces into an Equation

The Equation Editor won't let you enter space characters when you're typing an expression.

To create consistent spacing, Equation Editor automatically sets the spacing between the numbers and symbols that you enter and won't let you type in space characters manually. You can adjust the spacing or alignment of symbols, however, by selecting symbols from the Spaces And Ellipses palette, as shown in the following screen, or by choosing commands from the Format menu.

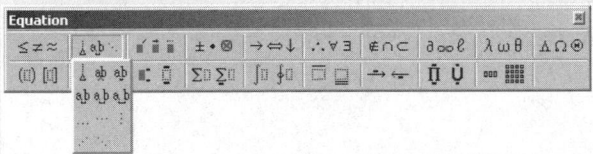

149

Chapter 6

> **tip** **Format an Equation**
>
> You can display an equation in faded letters via the Picture toolbar by clicking the Color button and choosing Washout from the drop-down menu. You can also crop (rather than scale) an equation via the Picture toolbar by clicking the Crop button or by using the Picture tab of the Format Object dialog box.

> These techniques are explained in "Modifying Pictures," on page 127. For a description of common formatting methods you can use with an equation, see "Modifying Graphic Objects," below.

Modifying Graphic Objects

This section summarizes the general methods that you can use to modify any of the types of graphic objects described previously in this chapter: pictures, AutoShapes, organization charts and other types of diagrams, WordArt objects, Graph objects, and equations (as well as text boxes, described in Chapter 18, "Designing and Printing Professional-Looking Pages"). Keep in mind that the particular commands and features that are available for working with a given graphic object depend on the Office application you're using, the type of object, and the formatting features currently assigned to the object. The best way to work with a particular type of graphic object is to explore the three general approaches introduced in the following sections—using the mouse, using the Drawing toolbar, and using the Format *Object* dialog box—and discover exactly which commands are available for the object you're working with.

Using the Mouse to Resize, Reshape, Rotate, or Move Graphic Objects

To change the dimensions of a graphic object, click it to select it and then drag one of the uncolored, round sizing handles that appear around the object, as shown here:

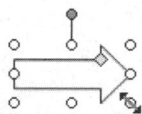

To maintain the original proportions of the object as you change its size, press Shift while dragging one of the corner sizing handles. To resize the object symmetrically about its center (that is, to change the size of the object without moving the position of its center), hold down the Ctrl key while dragging a sizing handle.

> Changing the size of a picture using the technique given here scales the picture. To learn about cropping a picture instead of scaling, see "Cropping a Picture," on page 130.

With WordArt objects, as well as some AutoShapes, Office displays a yellow, diamond-shaped reshaping handle. Dragging this handle lets you change some aspect of the object's shape, such as the angle of the sides of a trapezoid, or the thickness of the shaft of an arrow, as shown here:

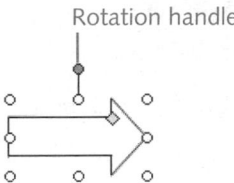 — Reshaping handle

The effect of dragging a reshaping handle varies widely among different types of AutoShape and WordArt objects.

To rotate a graphic object, drag the green, round rotation handle, shown in this example:

Rotation handle

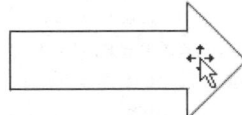

To move a graphic object to a different position in your document, place the mouse pointer over the object (but not over a handle if the object is selected), and when the pointer displays cross-arrows, drag the object to the desired location, as shown here:

Drawing

To copy rather than move the object, hold down the Ctrl key while you drag. Alternatively, when an object is selected, you can use the keyboard to move it by pressing the appropriate arrow key: Up, Down, Left, or Right. (You can't copy the object using the keyboard method.)

Chapter 6

InsideOut

When you select a graphic object in Word that is assigned the In Line With Text wrapping style, Word sometimes displays rectangular sizing handles only, and you can't reshape or rotate the object using the methods described here. See "Combining Text with Graphic Objects and Text Boxes," on page 515. Also, because such an object is an integral part of the text and is treated like a single text character, you must move or copy it to a different position in the text using the standard methods for moving and copying text, which are discussed in "Editing the Selection," on page 275.

Using the Drawing Toolbar to Modify Graphic Objects

The Drawing toolbar in Word, Excel, PowerPoint, and FrontPage provides a large, heterogeneous set of commands for creating and modifying graphic objects. To display this toolbar, choose View, Toolbars, Drawing, or click the Drawing toolbar button (if available). The Drawing toolbar is shown here:

The Drawing toolbar contains three groups of buttons. To select and modify graphic objects, use the first group, as seen here:

Select Objects

As when you work with document text, the general procedure for working with a graphic object is to first select the object and then perform an action on it. You can often select a graphic object by simply clicking on it when you are in the normal text editing mode. Alternatively, you can click the Select Objects button to switch into selection mode, which lets you easily select several objects at once.

Selection mode also lets you select a Word object that is contained in the layer underneath text. Layers are explained in "Combining Text with Graphic Objects and Text Boxes," on page 515.

When you click the Select Objects button to switch into selection mode, the pointer turns into an arrow slanting up and to the left. While in this mode, click the object you want to select. To select several objects so that you can perform some action on them simultaneously, drag a selection rectangle around all of them, as shown in the example on the next page.

Chapter 6

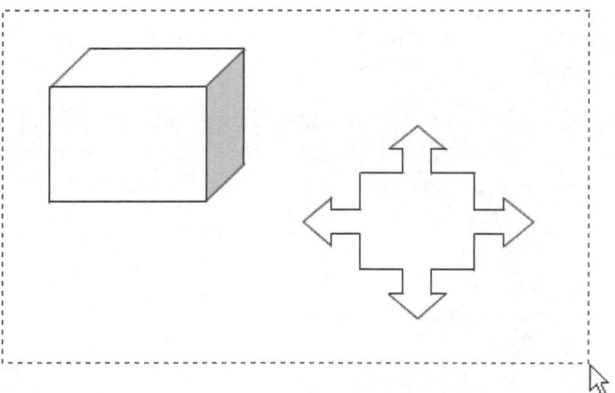

Alternatively, you can select several objects at once by pressing Shift while you click each one. This method allows you to select several objects in an area without selecting all the objects in this area. (To remove the selection from one of the objects, press Shift and click it again.) To switch off selection mode so that you can work with text, click the Select Objects button again (this button toggles selection mode on and off).

To delete the selected graphic object or objects, press the Delete key.

To modify the selected graphic object or objects, you can click the Draw button and choose a command from the menu seen here:

> The Draw menu in Word also has a Text Wrapping submenu, which allows you to change the wrapping style of the selected object, as explained in "Combining Text with Graphic Objects and Text Boxes," on page 515.

If you have selected several graphic objects, you can combine them into a single object so that you can work with them as a unit. To do this, from the Draw menu, choose the Group command. You can later break apart the group into its constituent objects by selecting the group and choosing Ungroup from this same menu. (You can later choose

Regroup to reestablish this same group without first selecting the individual objects that belonged to the group.)

To control the overlapping order of different drawing objects that intersect on the page, select an object. On the Drawing toolbar, click the Draw button, point to Order on the menu, and choose the appropriate command from the submenu, as shown here:

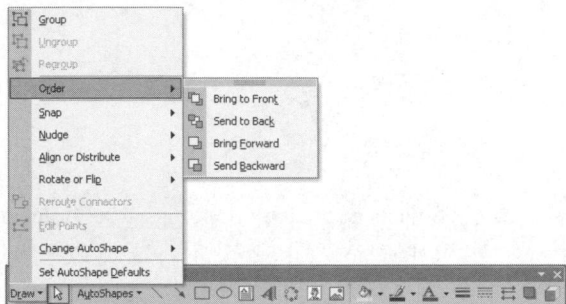

You can also use commands on the Draw menu to align, move, rotate, or flip the selected object or objects, as seen here:

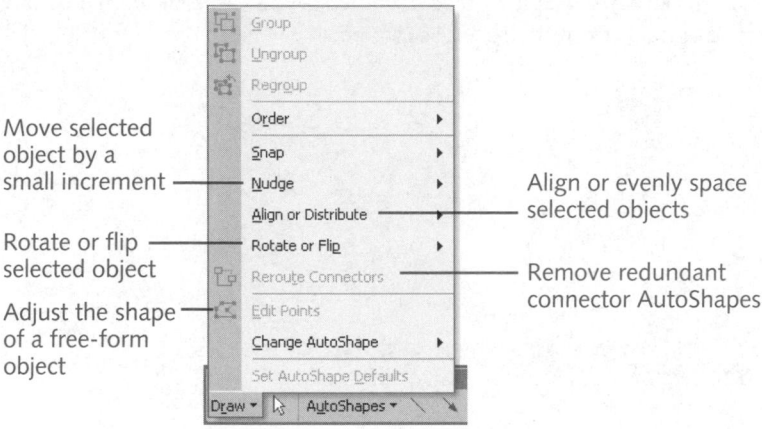

Move selected object by a small increment

Rotate or flip selected object

Adjust the shape of a free-form object

Align or evenly space selected objects

Remove redundant connector AutoShapes

> **tip** **Transform an AutoShape**
>
> If you've spent some time inserting, sizing, and formatting a particular AutoShape and then realize that you'd rather be working with a different type of AutoShape, you don't need to delete the object and start over. Rather, you can simply convert it to the AutoShape object you want. To do this, select the object and choose the new type of AutoShape object you want from the Change AutoShape submenu of the Draw menu on the Drawing toolbar.

You can experiment freely with all of the features discussed in this section. If you don't like the result of applying a particular feature or effect, just issue the Undo command to remove it. If you do like the result of a particular combination of effects that you've applied to an AutoShape, you can make them the default effects to be applied to all AutoShapes that you subsequently draw. To do this, select the object that has the combination of effects you want, and then, choose Set AutoShape Defaults from the Draw menu.

To quickly insert new graphic objects, use the second group of buttons on the Drawing toolbar, shown here:

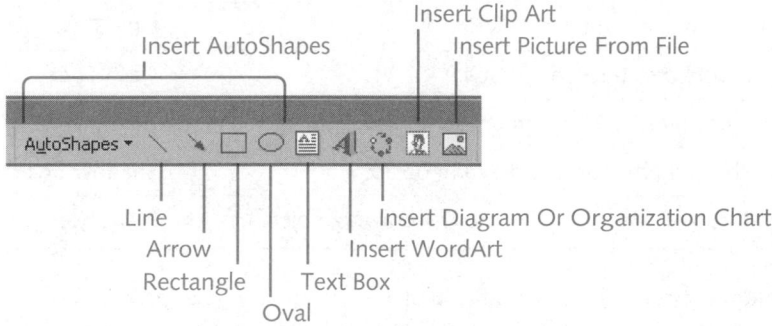

To change the selected object's fill color or pattern, line color or style, or font color, or to add shadow or three-dimensional effects to the object, use the buttons in the third group on the Drawing toolbar, as seen here:

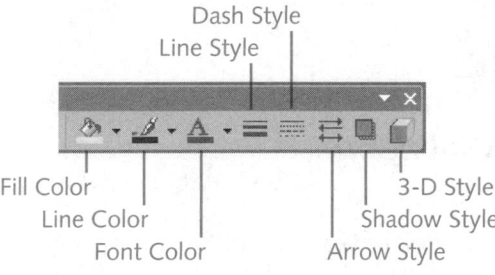

Table 6-3 shows how to modify the selected graphic object(s) with these buttons.

Table 6-3. Modifying Graphic Objects Using the Drawing Toolbar

To Modify the Selected Graphic Object(s) Like This	Click This Drawing Toolbar Button
Select a fill color or effect	Fill Color
Select a line color or line pattern	Line Color
Select a color for text in a text box or in an AutoShape	Font Color
Select a solid line style	Line Style
Select a dotted or dashed line style	Dash Style
Add (or change) an arrow on an AutoShape line	Arrow Style
Add a shadow effect to the drawing object	Shadow Style
Add a three-dimensional effect to the drawing object	3-D Style

The following example shows an AutoShape rectangle as it appeared when it was first inserted, and then as it appears after a fill color and a three-dimensional effect are applied.

 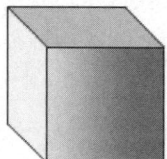

Using the Format *Object* Dialog Box to Format Graphic Objects

The Format *Object* dialog box provides the largest set of formatting options. The actual title of the dialog box depends on the type of the selected graphic object—for example, Format Picture, Format AutoShape, or Format Diagram. To format an object using this dialog box, perform the following steps:

1 Click the object to select it. (To select an object that's behind text in Word, you must first click the Select Objects button on the Drawing toolbar.)

2 From the Format menu, choose the Picture, AutoShape, Organization Chart, Diagram, WordArt, or Object command. The command name depends on the type of object you've selected. (The command will be Format Object if you've selected a Graph or Equation object.) This action opens the Format *Object* dialog box.

3 Select formatting options in the tabs of the Format *Object* dialog box. The specific tabs and options that are available depend on the type of graphic object you've selected and the application you're using. Figure 6-20 shows the Format Picture dialog box that would be displayed if you selected a picture in Word.

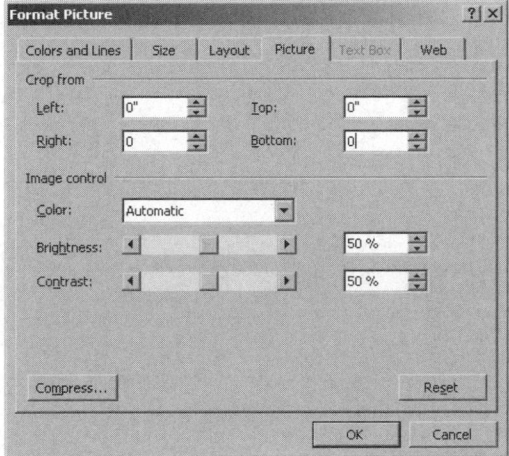

Figure 6-20. This is the Format Picture dialog box shown in Word.

Table 6-4 shows what you can do in the six tabs of the Format *Object* dialog box.

Table 6-4. Modifying Graphic Objects Using the Format *Object* Dialog Box

To Modify the Selected Graphic Object(s) Like This	Use This Tab in the Format *Object* Dialog Box
● Select a background fill color *or* ● Set the color, style, and thickness of the lines used for drawing an AutoShape, or to draw a border around other kinds of objects *or* ● Add arrows at the ends of an AutoShape line (or to modify existing arrows)	Colors And Lines
Resize or rotate the object, or restore its original size	Size
Select the wrapping style and horizontal alignment of the object (Word only)	Layout
For a picture, to crop the picture, to convert the picture colors (to grayscale, black and white, or washout), or to set the brightness and contrast of the picture colors	Picture

(continued)

Table 6-4. *(continued)*

To Modify the Selected Graphic Object(s) Like This	Use This Tab in the Format *Object* Dialog Box
For a text box, to modify the margins between the text and the edges of the text box	Text Box
Assign alternative text that a Web browser will display while the object is downloading, if the object's file is missing, or if graphics are disabled in the browser	Web

> Wrapping styles are explained in "Combining Text with Graphic Objects and Text Boxes," on page 515. Text boxes are discussed in "Using Text Boxes to Create Precise Page Layouts," on page 510. Creating Web pages in Word is covered in Chapter 20, "Creating Web Pages and Other Online Documents."

Modifying a Graphic Object Using the Shortcut Menu

You can perform several of the operations discussed in this section by right-clicking a drawing object and choosing the command that accomplishes what you want from the shortcut menu that appears. The commands provided on this menu depend on the application you're using, the type of the drawing object, and the features you have applied to it. Here's the shortcut menu shown for an AutoShape in Word:

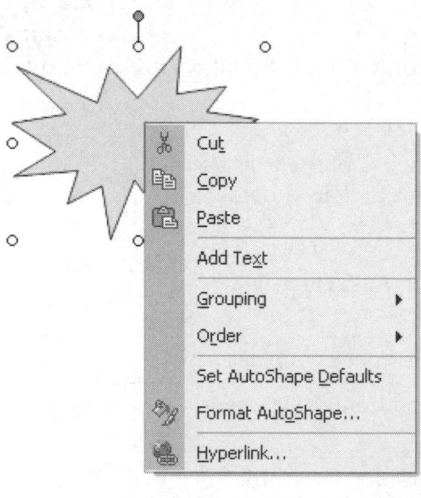

Modifying a Graphic Object Using the Shortcut Menu *(continued)* If you right-click a closed AutoShape figure, such as an oval or star, the shortcut menu provides an interesting command that isn't available elsewhere: Add Text. This command lets you add text to the AutoShape object, so that it functions just like a text box, but with an interesting shape, as in the following example:

Chapter 7

Sharing Data Among Office XP Applications

Different Ways to Share Data

In the parts of this book covering the individual Office XP applications, you'll learn how to copy and move data within a single document or among separate documents within a single program. In this chapter, you'll learn the different ways of exchanging data among separate Office applications.

This section provides a general overview of the three basic ways to exchange data among separate Office applications:

- Static copying or moving of data
- Linking of data
- Embedding of data

This discussion will help you choose the most appropriate method. The following sections discuss the specific techniques for performing each method.

With *static copying* or *static moving*, the data that you insert becomes an integral part of the receiving document and retains no link or connection with the document or program from which it was obtained. This is the type of copying or moving that you normally use when you work within a single document or application, using the techniques discussed in the later parts of the book. When you statically copy or move data from one application to another, you might or might not be able to edit the data within the receiving document. If the data can be converted to a format that the receiving program understands, you'll be able to edit it—for example, when you copy text from a Microsoft Excel worksheet and paste it into a Microsoft Word document. If, however, the data can't be converted into a format native to the receiving program, the data can be displayed and printed but not edited in the receiving program—for example, when you copy a bitmapped graphic from a drawing program such as Microsoft Paint and paste it as static data into a Word document.

With *linking*, the data that you insert retains its connection with the document and the program from which it was obtained. In fact, a complete copy of the data is stored only within the source document; the receiving document stores only the linking information and the information required to display the data. When the data in the source document is edited (by you or by someone else), the linked data in the receiving document can be updated automatically or manually to reflect the changes.

With *embedding*, the inserted data retains its connection with the source program but not with the source document. In fact, there might not even be a source document, because you can create new embedded data contained only in the receiving document. The receiving document stores a complete copy of the information, just as it does with statically copied data. However, because of the connection between this data and the source program, you can use the source program's tools to edit the data.

A document that contains linked or embedded data from other programs is known as a *compound document*.

You should use linking rather than embedding when you want to store and maintain data within a single document and merely display an up-to-date copy of the data in one or more other documents. Linking would be especially useful in the following situations:

- You want to display only part of the source document within the receiving document. For example, in a Word document you want to display only a totals line from a large Excel worksheet. (If you embedded the data, the entire workbook would be copied into the receiving document.)

- You maintain a single master document that you want to display in several other documents. For example, you have a Word document containing instructions that you want to display within several other Word documents and Microsoft PowerPoint presentations. By using linking, you need to update the data in only one place—the source Word document—to ensure that all copies of the information displayed in other documents are identical.

- You want to minimize the size of the receiving document. (In linking, the receiving document stores only the linking information plus the data required to display the object.)

You should use embedding rather than linking when you want to store an independent block of data as an integral part of the document in which it is displayed. Maintaining documents that contain embedded data is simpler than maintaining documents that contain linked data, because you don't have to keep track of source documents. (To update linked data, the source document must be present in its original location under its original filename.) And you can easily share with other users a document containing only embedded data, without having to provide linked source documents along with it.

In later parts of the book, you'll learn how to copy or move data within an Office application using the drag-and-drop technique, as well as by using the Copy or Cut command followed by the Paste command. You'll also learn how to use the new Office XP Paste Options button that usually appears after you paste data. You can use any of these techniques to copy or move data among separate Office applications, as well as within a single application. When you use these general-purpose methods, however, you have less control over how the data is transferred (even with the Paste Options button). The data might be copied or moved statically, or it might be embedded in the receiving document, depending on the nature of the data and the specific applications involved. Because of the importance of the way the data is copied or moved, in the following sections, you'll learn how to use the Copy or Cut command followed by the Paste Special command to precisely control the format and the manner in which the data is transferred.

> You can use many of the techniques given in Chapter 6, "Adding Professional Graphics and Special Effects to Office XP Documents," to modify the appearance of embedded data, as well as linked data in certain formats. In particular, see "Modifying Pictures," on page 127, and "Modifying Graphic Objects," on page 150.

Copying and Moving Data Statically

To copy or move data statically from one Office application to another, as explained in the previous section, perform the following steps:

1 Select the data in the source program, and from the program's Edit menu, choose Cut or Copy.

2 Switch to the receiving program and place the insertion point at the position in the receiving document where you want to insert the data.

3 From the receiving program's Edit menu, choose Paste Special to open the Paste Special dialog box.

> **note** When you choose the Paste Special command in Microsoft FrontPage, rather than displaying the standard Paste Special dialog box, the program displays the Convert Text dialog box, shown here, which has fewer options.

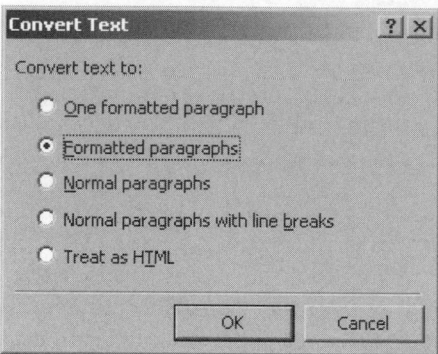

4 In the Paste Special dialog box, select the Paste option, and in the As list select the desired format. Select any format except one containing the word *object*. (Selecting an object format would embed the data rather than copy it statically.)

The formats listed depend on the source program and the nature of the data. Notice that when you select a format in the As list, a description of that format appears in the Result area near the bottom of the dialog box (shown in Figure 7-1).

Select Paste to paste
data statically.

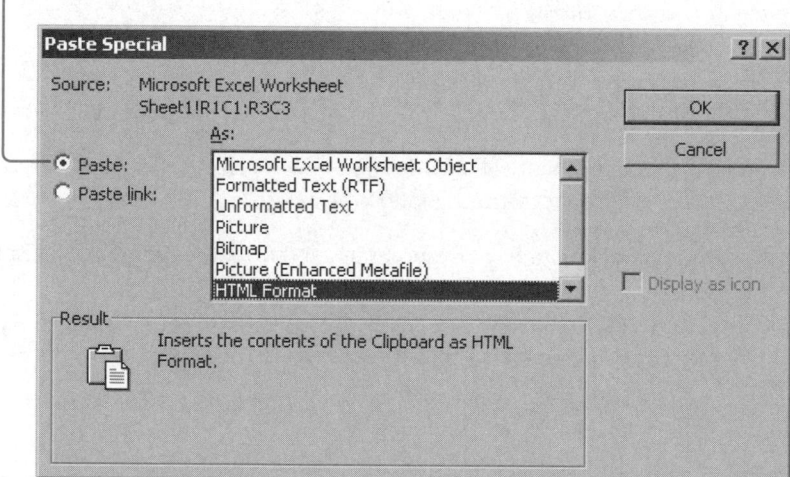

Figure 7-1. You can paste data statically between applications using the Paste Special dialog box.

5 Click the OK button to paste the data.

---

tip   **Drop the Formatting of Pasted Data**

One very useful format is Unformatted Text, which lets you paste only the text you copied without including the formatting that was assigned to the text in the source program. The text is inserted just as if you typed it on the keyboard in the receiving program.

A faster, although less reliable, alternative to steps 3, 4, and 5, is to press Ctrl+V or choose Edit, Paste. The data are then pasted in a default format and, in most cases, the receiving application displays a temporary Paste Options button, shown here, following the data.

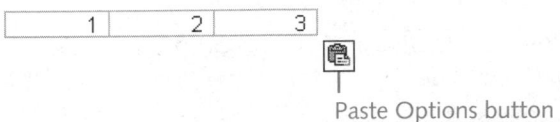

Paste Options button

Click this button and choose the desired format from the drop-down menu, as seen here.

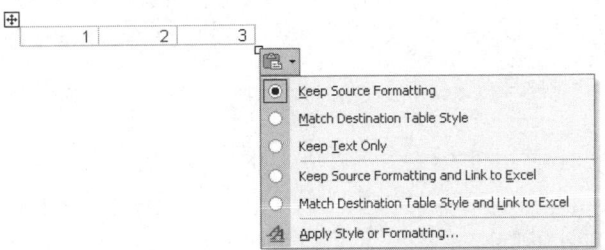

Choose any format except one containing the word *link* (which would link the data) or the name of the source application, such as "Excel Table (entire workbook)," which appears when you pass Excel data into PowerPoint and would embed the data. (That format doesn't appear in the above example.)

InsideOut

Although pasting and using the Paste Options button is faster than employing the Paste Special dialog box, the Paste Options button offers fewer alternative formats, and the somewhat vague wording of the options makes it difficult to determine whether you're pasting statically, linking, or embedding. Also, the options it provides differ wildly from one situation to another. In general, it's safer to use the Paste Special dialog box when copying data across applications and to limit your use of the Paste Options button to data transfers within a single application.

> **tip** You can also use the Paste Special dialog box when copying or moving data within a single Office application to gain more control over the format of the pasted data.

Linking Data

You can transfer and link many kinds of data among Office applications. The following are a few examples:

- You can insert and link part or all of an Excel worksheet or an Excel chart into a Word document or a PowerPoint slide.

- You can insert and link part or all of a Word document into an Excel worksheet or a PowerPoint slide.

- You can insert and link a PowerPoint slide into a Word document or an Excel worksheet.

> **note** You can't link data from the Microsoft Graph or Microsoft Equation programs provided with Office, which were discussed in Chapter 6, "Adding Professional Graphics and Special Effects to Office XP Documents." These programs can be used only to embed data.

You can transfer and link either a selected part of a document or an entire document. To transfer and link part of a document, do the following:

1 Select the data in the source document, and from the source program's Edit menu, choose Copy (don't choose Cut!) to copy the data to the Clipboard.

2 Place the insertion point at the position in the receiving document where you want to insert the data, and from the receiving program's Edit menu, choose Paste Special.

3 In the Paste Special dialog box, select the Paste Link option, select the desired data format in the As list, and click the OK button (shown in Figure 7-2).

Select Paste Link
to link data.

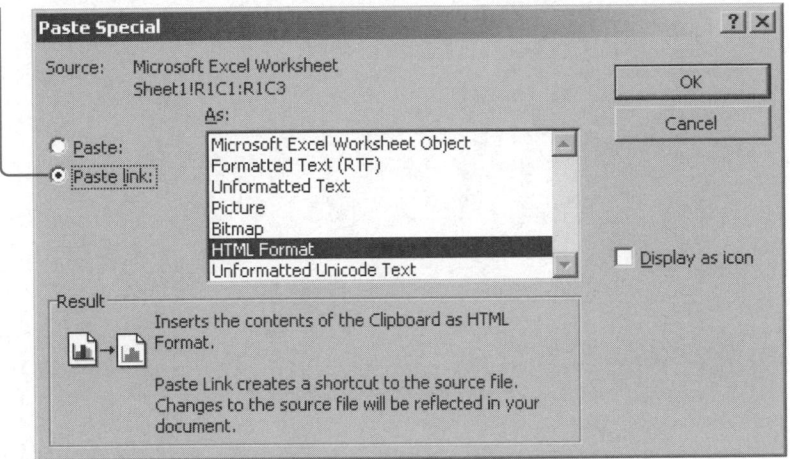

Figure 7-2. You can use the Paste Special dialog box to link data.

> **note** If the Paste Link option isn't available, this means that the data in the Clipboard can't be linked or that the source program doesn't support linking.

To link an entire document, use the following method:

1 Place the insertion point at the position in the receiving document where you want to insert the data.

2 From the receiving program's Insert menu, choose Object. In the Object dialog box, shown in Figure 7-3, click the Create From File tab. (In PowerPoint and Access, the dialog box is titled Insert Object, and Create From File is an option button that you select, rather than a tab.)

3 Select the Link To File option, and in the File Name box, enter the filename of the document you want to insert. (In PowerPoint and Access, the option is called Link and the text box is called File.) Click the Browse button if you need help locating the file.

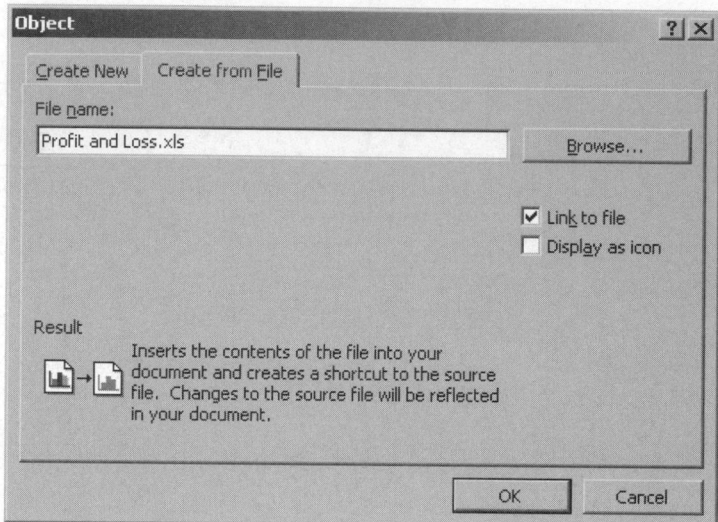

Figure 7-3. You can use the Object dialog box to insert and link an entire document.

4 Click the OK button to link the document.

Troubleshooting

You Can't Link Data from PowerPoint

You copied data from a PowerPoint slide or you copied several slides, but in other Office applications, in the Paste Special dialog box, the Paste Link option is disabled.

To link data from a PowerPoint presentation, you must either link a single slide in its entirety or link the whole presentation. You can't link part of a slide, nor can you link two or more slides out of a presentation without linking the entire presentation.

To link a single slide, switch to Slide Sorter view in PowerPoint (by choosing View, Slide Sorter), select a single slide by clicking on it, and then choose Edit, Copy or press Ctrl+C. You can then switch to the receiving document and link the slide using the Paste Special dialog box as described in the three-step procedure for linking part of a document, given earlier in this section.

To link an entire PowerPoint presentation, you must use the Object dialog box as described in the four-step procedure for linking an entire document, given previously in this section.

tip **Display Your Data as an Icon**

If you select the Display As Icon option in either the Paste Special or the Object dialog box (the Insert Object dialog box in PowerPoint and Access), the receiving program displays an icon representing the linked data rather than displaying the data itself. Also, when you print the document, only the icon is printed. After you select Display As Icon, you can click the Change Icon button—which will appear in the Paste Special, Object, or Insert Object dialog box—to change the icon and the caption that are displayed in the document. To view the linked data within the source program, use one of the methods for editing linked data described next. Using icons to display linked data is a convenient way to present various types of information in a compact format within a document intended to be viewed on the screen.

To edit linked data you must make the changes within the source document. To do this, you can use one of the following methods:

- Run the source program and open the source document.

- Select the block of linked data in the receiving document (or the icon that represents it), or simply place the insertion point anywhere within the data. Then, on the Edit menu, point to Linked *Item* (where *Item* is a description of the selected data, such as Worksheet Object), and choose either Edit Link or Open Link from the submenu that appears, as shown here:

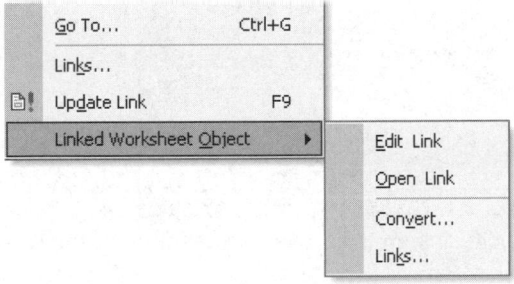

(The specific commands that appear on this submenu depend on the source program and the nature of the data.) The source document will then be opened in the source program, and you can edit the data.

- For some types of linked data formats (for example, Picture or Bitmap in a Word document), you can open the source document in the source program by simply double-clicking the linked data in the receiving document.

> **caution** Although you might be able to edit certain types of linked data directly within the receiving document (for example, Unformatted Text in a Word document), your changes will be overwritten the next time the data is updated! However, formatting changes (such as applying bold or italic to text) will be preserved when the data is updated, provided that, in the Links dialog box, the Preserve Formatting After Update option is selected, as described later in this section.

You can modify one or more links within a document by choosing Edit, Links to open the Links dialog box, which lists all the links contained in the active document. The options available in the dialog box vary among Office applications; Figure 7-4 shows the Links dialog box displayed in Word. To modify a link, select it in the list. To simultaneously modify several links, select them by clicking the first one and then pressing the Ctrl key while clicking each additional link. You can now modify the link or links you have selected. Note that although all of these actions are available in Word, some of them aren't available in other Office applications.

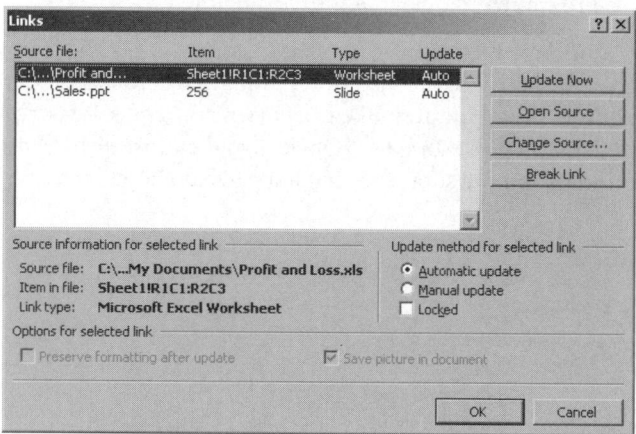

Figure 7-4. You can modify links in the active document using the Links dialog box.

- To make a link either automatic or manual, in the Update Method For Selected Link area of the Links dialog box, select the Automatic Update or Manual Update option. By default, a link is automatic, which means that the data is automatically updated whenever the receiving document is opened and whenever the data is modified in the source document while the receiving document is open. If you make a link manual, it won't be updated until you explicitly issue a command (described next). You might want to make links manual to avoid slowdowns while working with a document that contains many links or linked data whose source is modified frequently.

- To update a manual link, click the Update Now button. (You can also manually update a link without opening the Links dialog box, by selecting

it—or just placing the insertion point within it—and choosing Edit,
Update Link or pressing F9.)

● To modify the link so that updating the link will update the data but will
leave unchanged any formatting you have applied to the linked data in the
receiving document, check the Preserve Formatting After Update option.

● To change the name or location of the source document for the linked data,
click the Change Source button to open the Change Source dialog box,
which is similar to the Open dialog box (shown in Figure 7-5). (You might
also be able to change the description of the data location within the
source document—for example, the range of cells in a spreadsheet.) You
would need to do this to repair a link after the source document has been
moved or renamed.

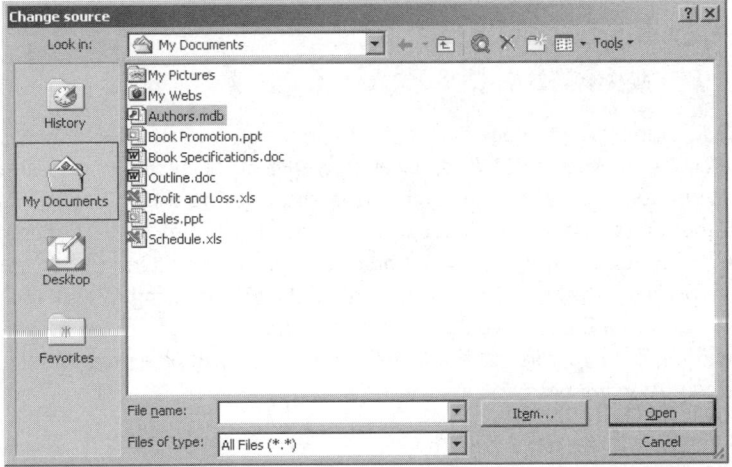

Figure 7-5. Use the Change Source dialog box to change the document
that is the source of linked data.

To specify a new source document, in the Change Source dialog box, open the
folder that contains that document and enter its filename into the File Name
box. To select a new data location within the source document, click the Item
button and enter a description of the location into the Set Item dialog box. For
a Word document, you would enter a bookmark name. For an Excel workbook, you would enter the name of the worksheet and the row and column
range within this worksheet, as in the following example:

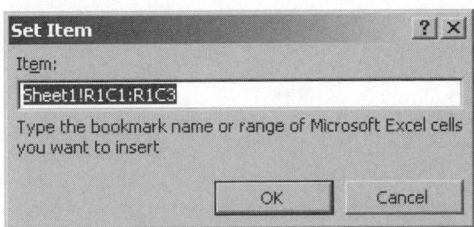

- To open the source document within the source program, click the Open Source button. This action has the same effect as using one of the techniques for editing linked data, which were described previously.

- To remove the link, click the Break Link button. The data will become an integral part of the receiving document, just as if you had copied it statically. After doing this, you won't be able to restore the link.

- In Word, to prevent the link from being updated, select the Locked option.

tip   A good way to help ensure that the source document is always available to maintain the link is to store both the source document and the receiving document together in the same folder.

Using Hyperlinks to Link Data

Instead of inserting a block of data that's linked to a source document, as described in this section, in Microsoft Word, Excel, PowerPoint, or Access you can insert a simple *hyperlink* to the data in the source document. Clicking the link opens the source document and scrolls to the specific data that's the target of the hyperlink.
Using this method, the data won't be displayed or printed in the document containing the hyperlink, which can be a disadvantage. However, using a hyperlink is simpler and less error prone than conventional linking, it consumes less space in the document containing the hyperlink, and it is more in keeping with the increasingly popular Web model of working with documents.

To create the hyperlink in Word, Excel, or PowerPoint, select the data in the source document and drag it to the destination document using the right mouse button. When you release the mouse button to drop the data, choose Create Hyperlink Here from the shortcut menu that appears, as shown here:

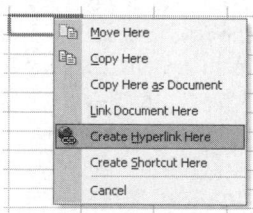

Chapter 7

Using Hyperlinks to Link Data *(continued)*   You can also create a hyperlink in Word, Excel, PowerPoint, or Access by first copying the text from the source document into the Clipboard, and then pasting it into the destination document choosing Edit, Paste As Hyperlink (this command, however, isn't available in Microsoft Outlook or FrontPage).

With either method, the text you copy must be from a file that has been saved on disk. Otherwise the command for creating the hyperlink won't be available.

A Linking Example

Imagine that you have created an Excel worksheet containing the daily prices of a commodity—wheat—for a historical period, together with a chart illustrating those prices for 25 days within that period. Figure 7-6 presents such a spreadsheet. You now want to write an article in Word that describes the price action over that period. To link a copy of the Excel chart to your report, you would perform the following steps:

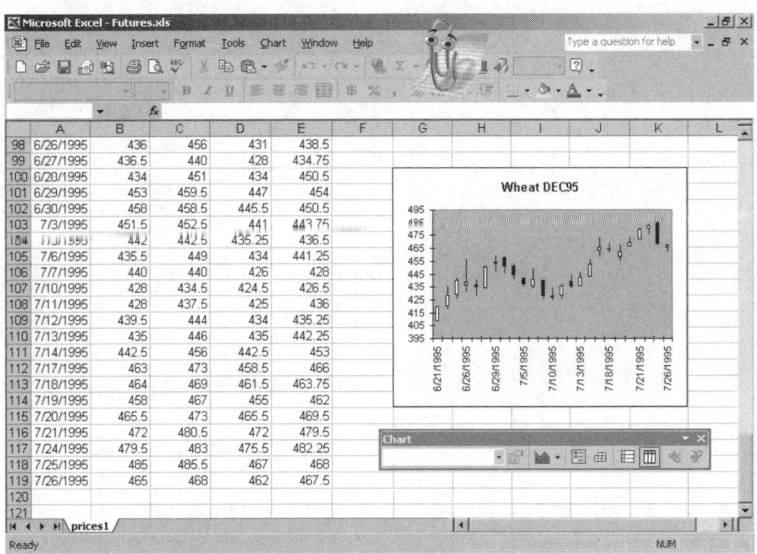

Figure 7-6.   An Excel worksheet is shown together with a chart.

1 In the Excel worksheet, click the chart to select it. From Excel's Edit menu, choose Copy.

2 In the Word document containing your report, place the insertion point at the position where you want the chart. From Word's Edit menu, choose Paste Special. Complete the dialog box as shown in Figure 7-7, and click the OK button. The resulting report is shown in Figure 7-8.

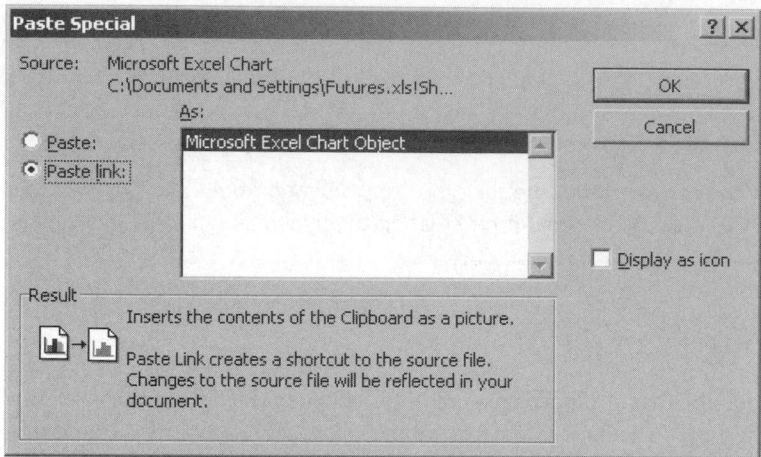

Figure 7-7. Here, the Paste Special dialog box is used to link the Excel chart to a Word document.

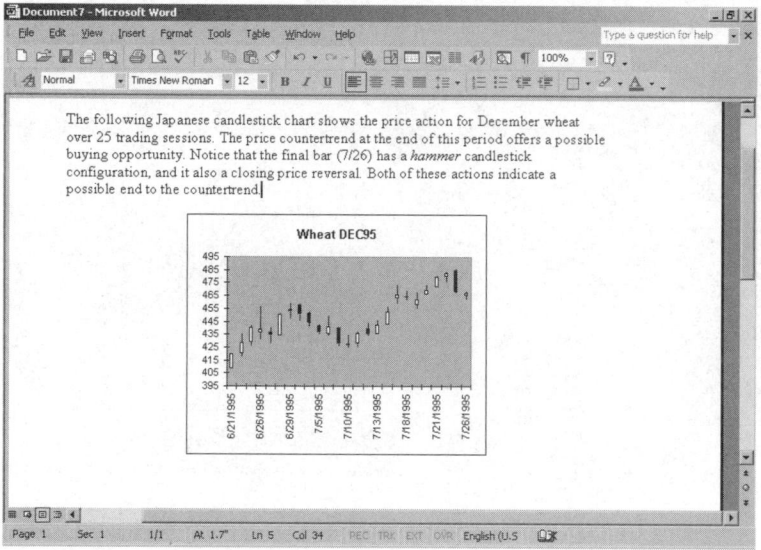

Figure 7-8. This figure shows the Excel chart seen in Figure 7-6, linked to a Word document.

The following are some advantages of linking this chart rather than embedding it:

● Only the linking information and the data required to draw the chart are copied into the receiving document. If you embedded the chart, the entire workbook, including all the price data, would be copied into the receiving document, significantly increasing its size. (Although you would normally see only the chart, the workbook data is also stored in the document so that you can edit both the data and the chart.)

- The same chart could be linked to additional Word documents, PowerPoint presentations, or other documents. The chart would then be updated within all receiving documents whenever you changed the price data in the Excel worksheet.

Embedding Data

A block of embedded data is known as an *embedded object.* In an Office XP document, you can embed data that you have created in another Office application, including the Microsoft Graph and Microsoft Equation programs discussed in Chapter 6, "Adding Professional Graphics and Special Effects to Office XP Documents," or in any other Microsoft Windows–based program that is designed to be a source of embedded data, such as Microsoft Visio. You can create an embedded object in three ways, which differ in how you obtain the data for the object.

First, you can obtain the data for an embedded object from a portion of an existing document, as follows:

1 Select the data in the source document, and from the source program's Edit menu, choose Copy or Cut.

2 Place the insertion point at the position in the receiving document where you want to add the embedded object. From the receiving application's Edit menu, choose Paste Special.

3 In the Paste Special dialog box, select the Paste option, and in the As list, choose the first format description that contains the word *object* (see Figure 7-9). Click OK.

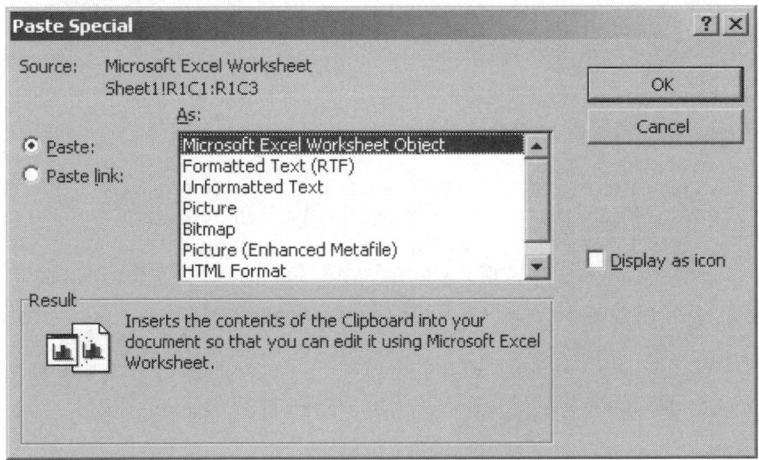

Figure 7-9. In this figure, the Paste Special dialog box is used to embed an Excel worksheet object.

The second way to create an embedded object is to use an entire existing document as the source of the data, as follows:

1 Place the insertion point at the position in the receiving document where you want to embed the object. From the receiving program's Insert menu, choose Object, and click the Create From File tab (or option button) in the Object (or Insert Object) dialog box.

2 Make sure that the Link To File (or Link) option is not selected, and either type the filename of the source document into the File Name (or File) text box, or click the Browse button to locate the file (see Figure 7-10). Click OK.

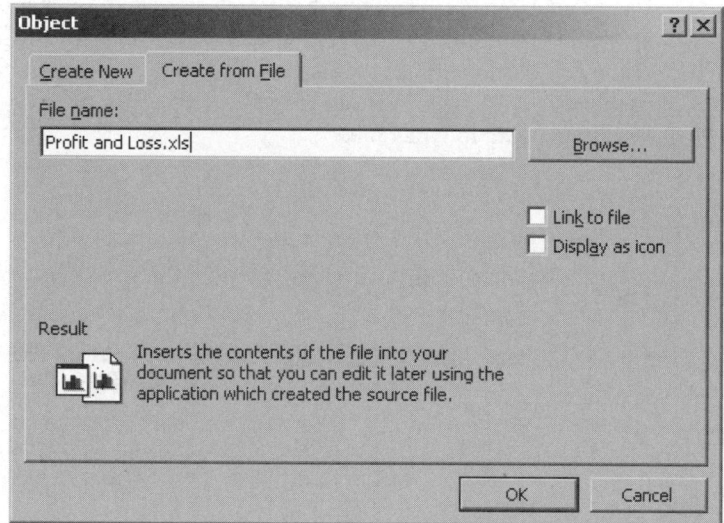

Figure 7-10. Here, the Create From File tab of the Create Object dialog box is used to embed an entire document.

The third way to embed an object is to create new data for the object using the source program's tools, as follows:

1 Place the insertion point at the position in the receiving document where you want to embed the object. From the receiving program's Insert menu, choose Object, and click the Create New tab (or option button) in the Object (or Insert Object) dialog box.

2 In the Object Type list, select the type of object that you want to embed. This list contains one or more items for every installed Windows program that can be the source of an embedded object. Click OK, and one of two things then happens, depending on the source application.

▪ A blank working area appears within the receiving document, and the source program's menus and buttons are displayed within the receiving program's window. The source program's keyboard commands are also available.

or

▪ The source program's window opens and displays a blank working area (for example, blank worksheet cells) or other tools (for example, a set of commands for working with a media clip).

3 In either case, use the source program's commands to enter the data for the embedded object into the working area.

4 When you have finished entering the data, exit the editing mode. If you're working in the receiving program's window, simply click in the receiving document outside the object.

If you're working in the source program's window, exit the editing mode by choosing File, Exit. (The command might have a label such as Exit And Return To MyDocument.) You can also use any other method to quit the source program. Click Yes if the source program displays a message box asking whether you want to update the object in the receiving document (some programs update the object automatically).

With the Microsoft Graph and Microsoft Equation programs discussed in Chapter 6, "Adding Professional Graphics and Special Effects to Office XP Documents," you must use this third method for creating an embedded object, because these programs can't create independent documents.

When you use any of these three methods for embedding an object, you might be able to select the Display As Icon option in the Object dialog box. For an explanation of this option, be sure to see the tip "Display Your Data as an Icon," on page 169.

To edit an embedded object, simply double-click it. The object is then opened for editing either within the source program or, more commonly, within the receiving program. (The action that occurs depends on how the source application is designed.)

---

note For some types of embedded objects, double-clicking the object doesn't open it for editing. For example, if you double-click an object containing a sound or video clip, the clip is played. To edit the object, you must use the alternative method, given below.

An alternative way to edit an embedded object is to select the object by clicking it, and then, on the receiving program's Edit menu, point to *Item* Object (where *Item* is a description of the selected object, such as Worksheet) to display the submenu shown here.

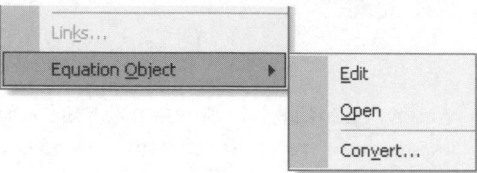

Choose one of the following commands from this submenu:

- To edit the object within the receiving program's window using the source program's menus, toolbars, and keyboard commands, choose the Edit command, if present.

- To edit the object within a separate window provided by the source program, choose the Open command, if present.

These are the typical commands and their actions. The actual commands that appear on the submenu—and their actions—depend on the source program and the nature of the embedded data.

When you have finished editing the object, exit the editing mode. If you're editing in the source program, do this by exiting from the source program and clicking the Yes button in the message box if the source program asks whether you want to update the object in the receiving document. If you're editing in the receiving program, click in the receiving document outside the object.

---

tip **Convert Objects to the Format You Prefer**

If the Object submenu includes a Convert command, you can choose it to change the embedded object to a different object type. The available object types depend on the object you have selected. For example, if you select a PowerPoint Slide object, you can convert it to a PowerPoint Presentation object. This would allow you to add additional slides to the object (a presentation is composed of a group of slides), or to display the presentation in a slide show by double-clicking the object.

An Embedding Example

Imagine that you're preparing a PowerPoint presentation and you want to include a table of numeric values in a slide. By embedding an Excel Worksheet object, you can use all the features provided by Excel for creating the table. You could do this as follows:

1 Run Excel, open a new document, and enter the data into a worksheet.

2 Select the worksheet cells that you want to display in the PowerPoint slide, as shown in Figure 7-11, and from Excel's Edit menu, choose Copy.

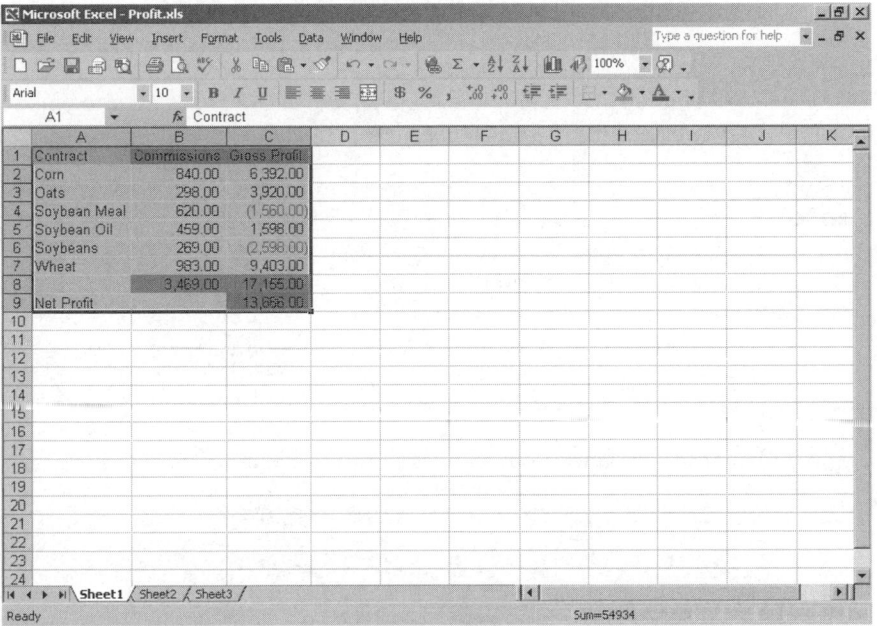

Figure 7-11. Here, cells are selected in an Excel worksheet prior to copying the data to a PowerPoint slide.

3 Open the slide in the PowerPoint presentation in which you want to display the worksheet cells. (You must be in PowerPoint's Normal view; to switch to this view, from PowerPoint's View menu, choose Normal.)

4 From PowerPoint's Edit menu, choose Paste Special. In the Paste Special dialog box, select the Paste option and select the Microsoft Excel Worksheet Object item in the list, as shown in Figure 7-12. Click OK.

5 To adjust the size of the embedded object, drag one of the uncolored, round sizing handles that appear around the object when it's selected.

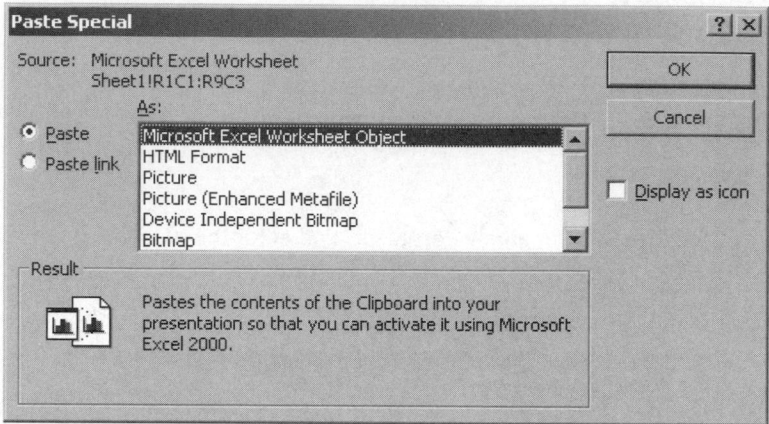

Figure 7-12. Here, the Paste Special dialog box is used to embed the Excel worksheet cells shown in Figure 7-11 into a PowerPoint slide.

note After you have pasted the worksheet cells into the slide, you can either save or discard the original Excel document. In the example, we created the embedded object by copying cells from an Excel document—rather than choosing Object from PowerPoint's Insert menu to create new data—because the copying method lets you specify the exact number of cells to display in the slide and makes it easier to scale the worksheet within the PowerPoint slide.

The resulting PowerPoint slide is shown in Figure 7-13.

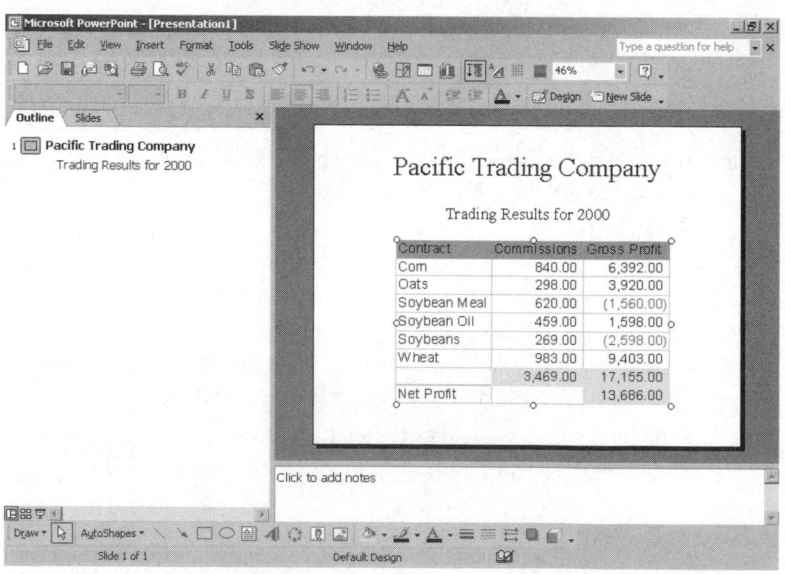

Figure 7-13. This figure shows the Excel worksheet cells embedded in a PowerPoint slide.

After embedding the worksheet into the slide, you can edit it within PowerPoint by double-clicking the worksheet. The Excel menu and toolbar are then displayed within the PowerPoint window to let you edit the object (see Figure 7-14).

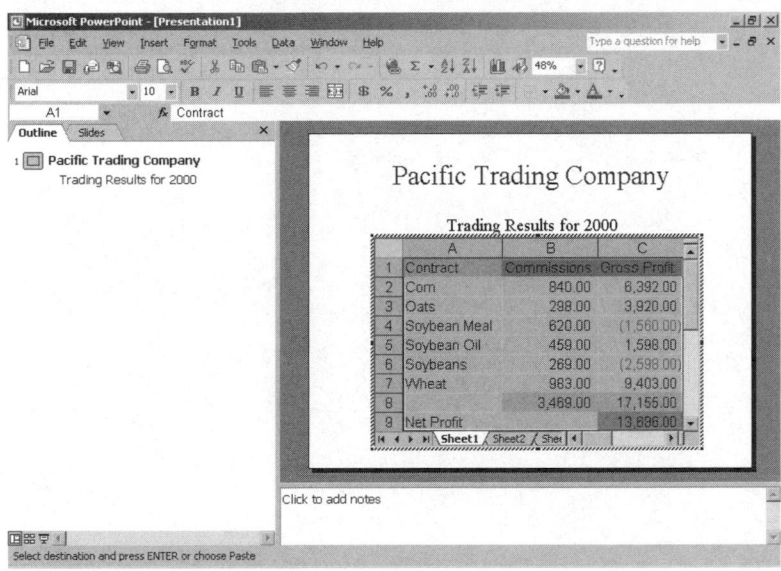

Figure 7-14. You can edit Excel worksheet cells embedded in a PowerPoint slide.

Using SharePoint Team Services in Professional Workgroups

SharePoint Team Services Essentials

SharePoint Team Services from Microsoft is a set of program extensions that can be installed on a Web server—the software that manages a site on the World Wide Web or on a company intranet—to add features that a Web server normally doesn't provide.

SharePoint is new with Office XP. The concept of Web server extensions, however, isn't new. For example, the Microsoft FrontPage Server Extensions have been used for years to make it easy to publish Web sites from FrontPage and to add dynamic features, such as hit counters and search forms, to FrontPage Web sites. Also, the Microsoft Office 2000 Server Extensions allowed users of Office 2000 to save and share files on a Web site, to conduct newsgroup-like discussions about any online document, and to subscribe to online documents or folders in order to be notified by e-mail whenever the document or folder changed.

SharePoint Team Services includes all the features offered by its Office 2000 Server Extensions predecessor. However, rather than simply providing an empty folder for storing documents, plus support for discussions and subscriptions, it provides an entire customizable Web site. This site is known as a *team Web site*, and it offers extensive collaboration features

183

that allow workgroups to share documents, exchange information, and work together on projects. Here are some of the main features of a SharePoint team Web site:

- Customizable *document libraries* (that is, folders) for storing and sharing Office XP documents. Each document library can be assigned a default template for quickly creating a particular type of Office document.

- *Discussion boards* that allow members to conduct online discussions.

- Standard *lists* that allow team members to post announcements, contact descriptions, event notices, favorite Internet links, surveys for collecting member responses, and summaries of tasks that need to be performed.

- Custom lists for sharing any type of information.

- Web pages that allow members to customize document libraries, discussion boards, lists, or the entire Web site.

As with the Office 2000 Server Extensions, you can access a team Web site through the My Network Places folder in Microsoft Windows (known as Web Folders in versions of Windows prior to Me and 2000). This folder appears in Windows Explorer, as well as in the Office Open and Save As dialog boxes. Also like its predecessor, SharePoint lets you conduct document discussions and subscribe to documents using the Web Discussions toolbar in Office applications. However, because SharePoint provides a complete Web site, the main new way for Office users to access it is through their browsers.

In this chapter, you'll learn how to use a team Web site on the World Wide Web or on a company intranet.

Connecting to a SharePoint Team Web Site

To access a team Web site, enter the site's URL (Uniform Resource Locator) into your browser. This will open the home page of the site. Figure 8-1 shows the home page of a newly created team Web site, before documents have been stored, information has been entered, or customizations have been performed.

Navigation bar

Links

Search tools

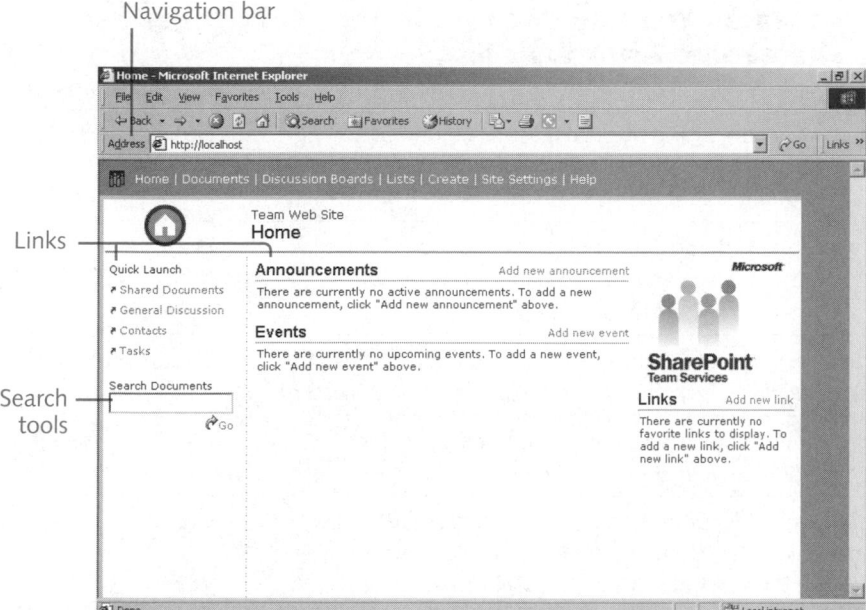

Figure 8-1. Here, the home page of a newly setup SharePoint team Web site is opened in Microsoft Internet Explorer.

From the home page, you can perform three main tasks:

- To navigate to one of the main site pages, click a link on the navigation bar at the top of the home page. See Table 8-1 for instructions on which page you should visit to perform various tasks.

- To quickly go to a particular page, you can click one of the links displayed on the home page below the navigation bar. For example, to go to the page where you can view the announcements that have been posted, click the Announcements link in the main part of the home page. To post a new event notice, click the Add New Event link. To work with the contents of the Shared Documents document library, click the Shared Documents link in the Quick Launch area.

- To find specific Office documents that are stored on the site, use the search tools on the left of the home page. To search for documents containing specific text, enter that text into the Search Documents text box and click Go.

Table 8-1. **Tasks You Can Perform in the Main Pages of a SharePoint Team Web Site**

To Perform This Task	Go to This Page
Get an overview of the site, navigate to commonly used pages, or search for Office documents stored in document libraries on the site	Home
Browse any of the document libraries that store Office documents on the site; open, upload, or create Office documents; or create new document libraries	Documents
Participate in any of the discussion boards set up on the site, create a new discussion board, or discuss a specific document	Discussion Boards
Access any of the site lists (announcements, contacts, events, links, surveys, tasks, or custom)	Lists
Create a new document library, discussion board, or list (announcements, contacts, events, links, surveys, tasks, or custom); import a list from an Excel spreadsheet	Create
Change the site name or description, add new users to the site, create a new team Web site, perform other administrative tasks, or customize a specific document library, discussion board, or list (announcements, contacts, events, links, surveys, tasks, or custom)	Site Settings
Read online help explaining how to use the SharePoint team Web site	Help

On a team Web site, the term *list* is used in two senses. In the broad sense, a list is a collection of documents (a document library), discussion remarks (a discussion board), announcements, contacts, events, links, survey responses, tasks, or custom information items (these are all the types of information that can be managed by SharePoint). In other words, it's a place where documents or information items of a particular type can be stored, and is closely analogous to a *folder* in Microsoft Outlook. On the team Web site, each list is stored in a separate file folder.

The term *list* is also used in a narrow sense to refer specifically to a collection of announcements, contacts, events, links, survey responses, tasks, or custom information items. Hence, the Lists page accesses just these types of items.

Table 8-2 describes the kind of information stored in each type of list—in the broad sense of the word—as well as the names of the initial lists that SharePoint sets up. (As you'll learn later in the chapter, you can create additional lists.)

Table 8-2. **The Uses for SharePoint Lists**

To Store This Type of Information	Use This List Type	Default List Set Up by SharePoint
Office documents that are to be shared by site members	Document library	Shared Documents
A newsgroup-style online discussion	Discussion board	General Discussion
Bulletins and news items relevant to your SharePoint team	Announcements	Announcements
Names, addresses, and other information on people that team members work with	Contacts	Contacts
Descriptions of upcoming events, such as meetings, due dates, and social occasions	Events	Events
A collection of useful Web links	Links	Links
A survey (a question and list of possible answers) for polling site members, and the results of that survey	Survey	None
Summaries of jobs that need to be completed by you or other members of your team	Tasks	Tasks
Any type of information that doesn't fit into one of the standard list types, such as an inventory, a membership roster, or a bibliography	Custom list	None

Sharing Documents on SharePoint

Office documents stored in a document library on a team Web site can be shared by the members of the site. You can access the document libraries on a team Web site either using your browser or through the My Network Places (or Web Folders) folder in Office applications or in Windows Explorer.

Accessing SharePoint Document Libraries Using Your Browser

To access SharePoint document libraries using your browser, perform the following steps:

1 Connect to the team Web site and open the Documents page on the team Web site, which will list all the document libraries contained on the site (see Figure 8-2).

Chapter 8

187

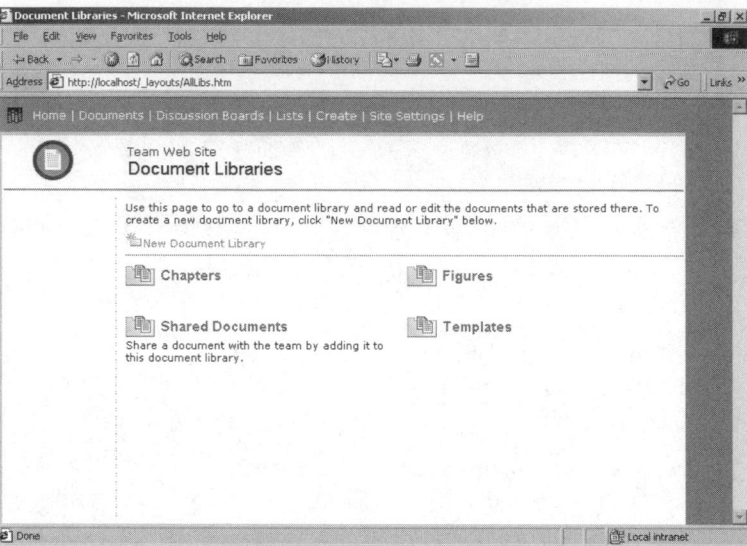

Figure 8-2. The SharePoint Documents page displays the document libraries contained on the site.

2 Click the name of the particular document library you want to access. (For example, on the page shown in Figure 8-2, you would click Chapters, Figures, Shared Documents, or Templates.) This will open the page for that document library (see Figure 8-3).

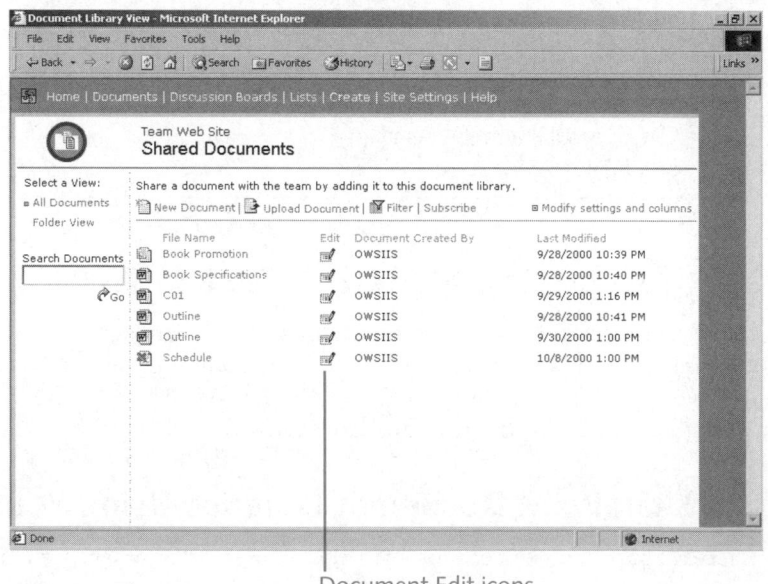

Document Edit icons

Figure 8-3. The SharePoint page for the Shared Documents document library is displayed.

3 In the document library page, you can do any of the following:

　▓ To open a document for viewing and editing in your browser (or to save a copy of the document on your computer), click the document's name.

　▓ To open the SharePoint Web page for a document, click the document's Edit icon (shown in Figure 8-3). In the document's page, you can open the document for editing in the appropriate application, send the document to someone else for review, change the document's title property, or delete the document.

　▓ To create a new document, click New Document. The new document will be based on the template assigned to the library (if the library hasn't been assigned a template, a Microsoft Word document based on the Normal template will be created).

> For information on assigning templates to a document library, see "Use Templates for Document Libraries," on page 203.

　▓ To transfer an Office document from your computer to the library on the Web site, click Upload Document.

　▓ To control which documents are shown, click Filter.

　▓ To change the way the documents are displayed, click a view in the Select A View column at the left of the page.

Accessing SharePoint Document Libraries from Office Applications

To open a document stored in a SharePoint document library, perform the following steps:

1 In the Office application, choose File, Open.

2 Click the My Network Places (or Web Folders) folder in the My Places bar at the left of the Open dialog box.

3 If a shortcut to your team Web site doesn't already exist, double-click the Add Network Place (or Add Web Folder) item. In the first dialog box of the wizard that runs, choose the Create A Shortcut To An Existing Network Place (or Create A Shortcut To An Existing Web Folder) option. Then, complete the wizard, specifying the URL of the root folder of the team site you want to access.

> **note** Choosing the Create A New Network Place (or Create A New Web Folder) option in the first wizard dialog box allows you to create a FrontPage Web site or some other type of content on the site that you specify. The type of content you can create depends on the server program managing the site and the type of extensions that are installed on that server.

4 Double-click the shortcut to your team Web site (see Figure 8-4). If you are prompted to establish a dial-up connection, click the Connect button. The Open dialog box will then display a list of the document libraries on your site (see Figure 8-5).

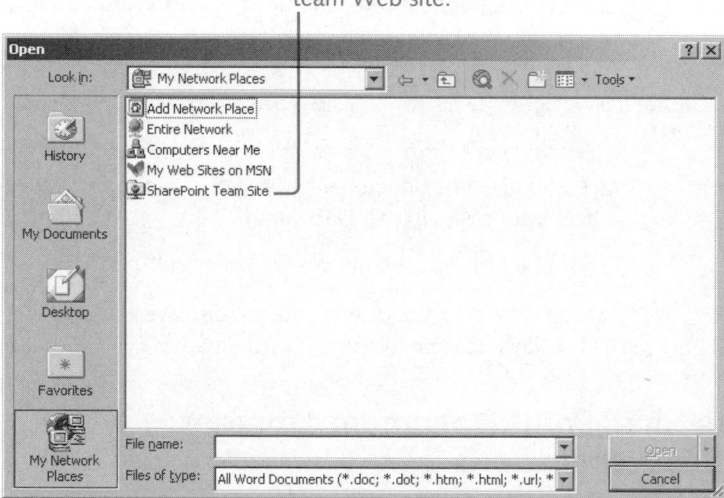

Double-click to open this team Web site.

Figure 8-4. Here, a team Web site is opened using the Open dialog box.

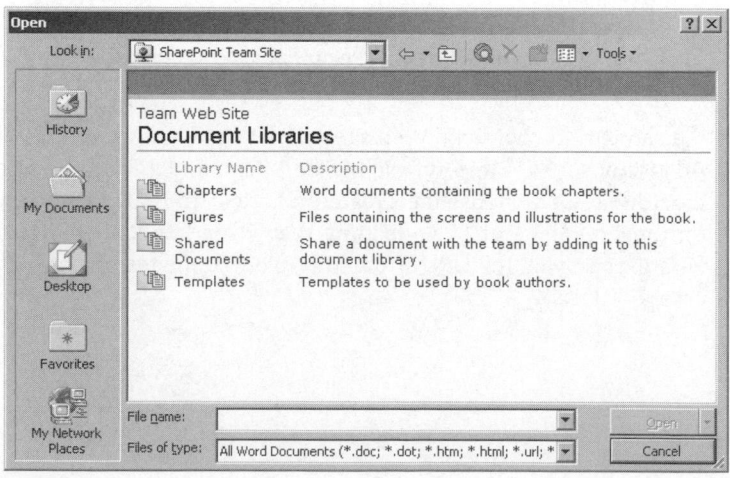

Figure 8-5. A list of the document libraries on a team Web site is shown.

5 Navigate to the library containing the document you want, and then open that document. Use the same methods you would use for a document in a folder on a local or network disk.

See "Opening an Existing Document Using the Open Office Document Dialog Box," on page 61.

note You can also use this technique to open a document on a Web site that has one of the earlier types of Microsoft server extensions, such as the FrontPage Server Extensions or the Office 2000 Server Extensions.

To save a document in a SharePoint document library, follow these steps:

1 In the Office application, choose File, Save As.

2 Access your team Web site using the My Network Places (or Web Folders) folder, navigate to the document library where you want to store your document, and save your document using the techniques outlined in steps 2 through 5 in the previous instruction list.

Create a New Document Using a Shared Template

Team members can use Office templates stored in document libraries on a team Web site to create new documents. Using shared templates on a team Web site is a good way to help ensure that the new documents team members create will have a consistent layout, as well as uniform formatting and possibly boilerplate content. To store a document template in a document library, use any of the techniques for storing Office documents given previously in the chapter.

To use a shared template to create a new Office document, perform the following steps:

1 In the Office application, choose File, New.

2 In the New *Document* task pane, click the Templates On My Web Sites command. (The name of the task pane depends on the particular application you're using. For instance, it's New Document in Word and New Workbook in Excel.)

3 In the New From Templates On My Web Sites dialog box, open your team Web site using the instructions given in the previous section, and select the template you want to use.

4 Click the Create New button in the dialog box to create your new Office document, which will be based on the selected template.

Using SharePoint Discussions and Subscriptions

Using a team Web site, you can communicate with your fellow team members by participating in a discussion board or by joining an online discussion about a shared document. You can also subscribe to a SharePoint document library, discussion board, or list in order to be notified by e-mail about changes in one of these areas.

Participating in a Discussion Board

Your team Web site may have one or more active discussion boards set up for conferring about various topics. To participate in a discussion board, do the following:

1 In your browser, navigate to the Discussion Boards page of your team Web site (shown in Figure 8-6). This page will display all of the discussion boards that have been set up on the site.

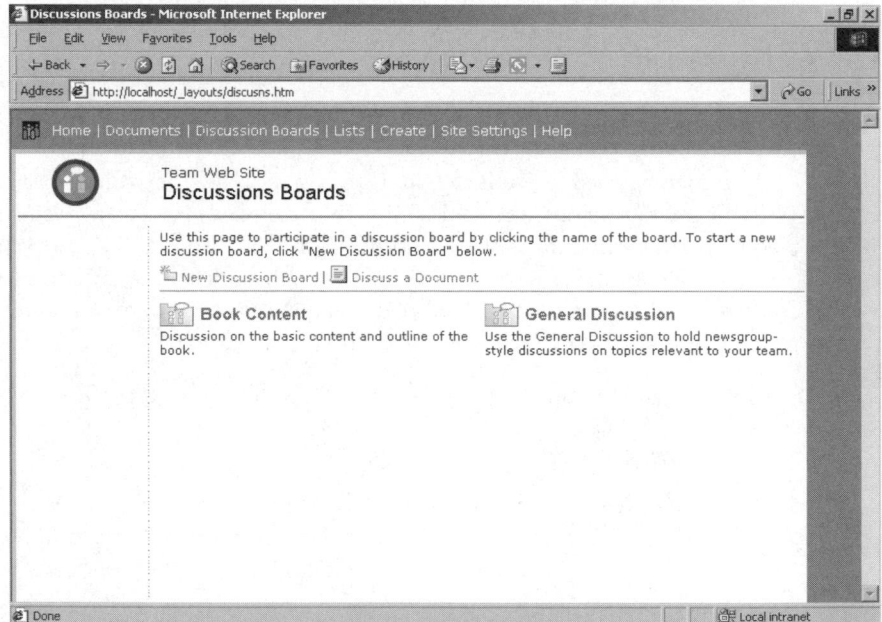

Figure 8-6. The Discussion Boards page displays the discussion boards set up on the team Web site.

2 Click the name of the particular discussion board you want to access. (For example, on the page shown in Figure 8-6, you would click Book Content or General Discussion.) This will open the page for that discussion, which will display all the discussion items that members have posted, organized by subject (see Figure 8-7).

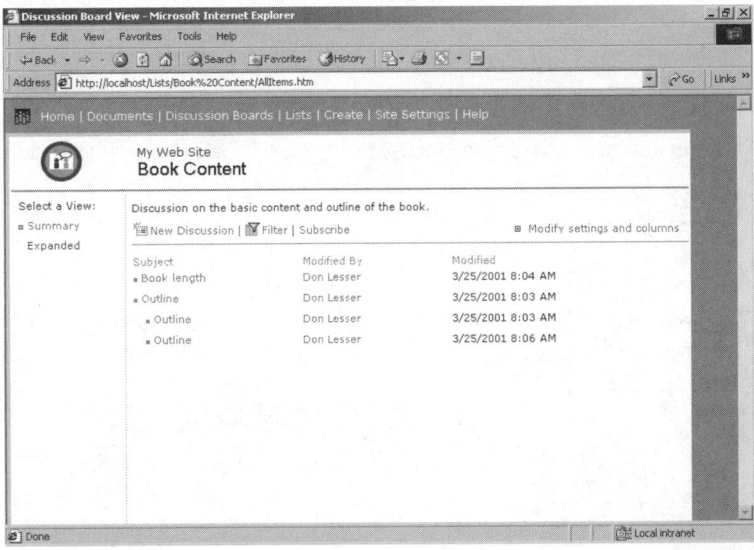

Figure 8-7. This figure shows the SharePoint page for the Book Content example discussion.

3 In the discussion board's page, you can do any of the following:

■ To read, reply to, edit, or delete a discussion item—as well as other discussion items on the same topic—click the name of the discussion item.

■ To create a discussion item on a new topic, click New Discussion.

■ To control which discussion items are shown, click Filter.

■ To change the way the discussion items are displayed, click a view in the Select a View column at the left of the page.

Discussing an Online Document

You and your fellow team Web site members can conduct a discussion about an Office document or page located on the Web. A member of the team Web site can add discussion remarks about the document and can view remarks added by other members.

A database on the team Web site stores all the discussion remarks on each document, together with the address of the document. Because the remarks aren't stored in the document itself, using a SharePoint discussion is a good way for a workgroup to comment on a document without altering the document's content. Also, because a discussion doesn't require write access to the document, the document doesn't need to be stored on the team Web site itself—it can be located anywhere on the Web where members can view it.

You can participate in a document discussion using Word, Microsoft Excel, or Microsoft PowerPoint. This works just like it did in Office 2000:

1 Open the document in the application by choosing File, Open, selecting the document you want to discuss in the Open dialog box, and clicking OK.

For instructions on opening a document on the Web using the My Network Places (or Web Folders) folder, see "Accessing SharePoint Document Libraries from Office Applications," on page 189.

2 From the application's Tools menu, choose Online Collaboration, Web Discussions. This will display the Web Discussions toolbar, shown here:

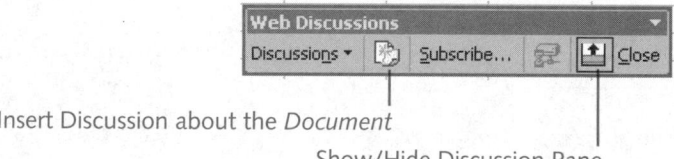

Insert Discussion about the *Document*

Show/Hide Discussion Pane

3 If the document you've opened for discussion isn't located on your team Web site, you may need to set up your SharePoint discussion server before the commands on the Web Discussions toolbar become available. To do this, click the Discussions button on the Web Discussions toolbar and choose Discussion Options from the shortcut menu, as shown here:

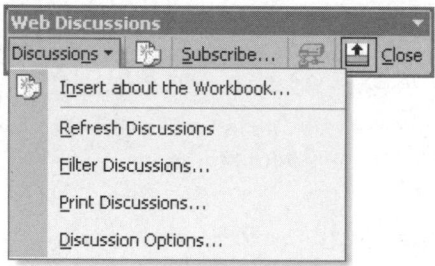

Then, in the Discussion Options dialog box, click the Add button and enter the requested information about your team Web site (you will need to know its URL).

4 In the Discussion Pane at the bottom of the Office application window, you can view any discussion remarks that team Web site members have previously added (see Figure 8-8). If this pane isn't visible, click the Show/Hide Discussion Pane button on the Web Discussions toolbar.

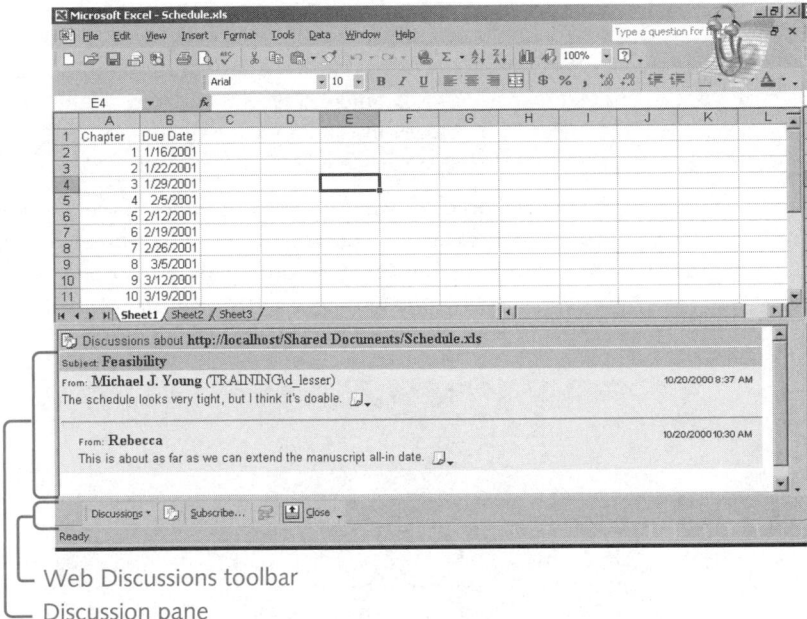

Web Discussions toolbar

Discussion pane

Figure 8-8. Conducting a discussion on an Excel workbook is shown in this example.

5 To reply to an existing discussion remark, click the button at the end of the remark in the Discussion pane, and choose Reply from the shortcut menu that appears, shown here:

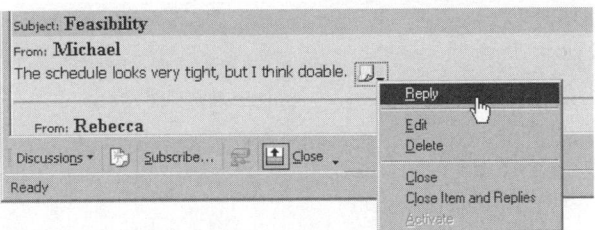

Then, in the Enter Discussion Text dialog box, enter your reply in the Discussion Text box. (Don't modify the subject, otherwise your reply won't be listed under the remark you're replying to.)

6 To add a new discussion remark, click the Insert Discussion About The *Document* button on the Web Discussions toolbar and enter the subject and your remark text into the Enter Discussion Text dialog box. (The button's actual ScreenTip text depends on the application you're using. In Excel, for example, it's Insert Discussion About The Workbook.)

> **note** The Web Discussions toolbar in Word also has an Insert Discussion In The Document button that inserts an *inline* discussion, which is a discussion remark attached to specific document text, like a Word comment. (Keep in mind, though, that unlike a comment, the remark text isn't actually inserted into the document content.)

7 To track future modifications, you can *subscribe* either to the document or to the folder or library that contains the document. Doing so prompts the team Web site to send you e-mail when changes are made to the document or to the folder. To subscribe, click the Subscribe button on the Web Discussions toolbar and fill in the Document Subscription dialog box (see Figure 8-9).

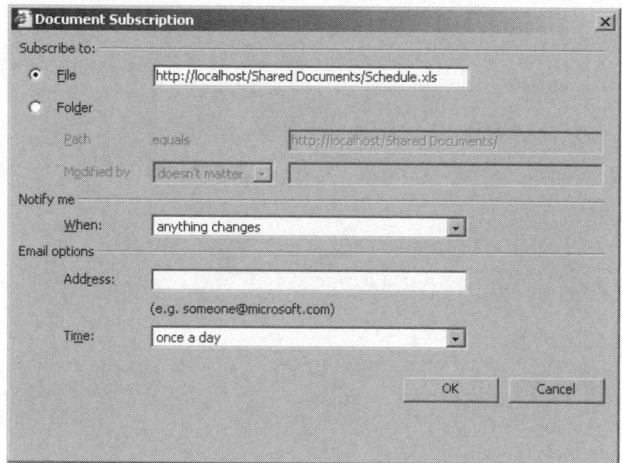

Figure 8-9. The Document Subscription dialog box is used to subscribe to a document or folder.

> **note** To subscribe to a document folder, it must be stored on the SharePoint team Web site that is used as the discussion server, and the Active Document's Server item must be selected in the Discussion Options dialog box.

8 To terminate the discussion, click the Close button on the Web Discussions toolbar. Both the Web Discussions toolbar and the Discussion pane will be removed.

---

tip **Join a Document Discussion Through the SharePoint Team Web Site**

Another way to participate in a discussion about a document that's stored on your team Web site is to connect to the site in Microsoft Internet Explorer, open the page for the document (as explained in "Accessing SharePoint Document Libraries Using Your Browser," on page 187), and click Discuss. Internet Explorer might then display the File Download dialog box; if it does, be sure to choose the Open This File From Its Current Location option. Internet Explorer will then open the document in the Internet Explorer window and display its Discussion pane and Discuss bar, which you can use to view and add discussion remarks or to subscribe to a document or folder. Use the same techniques employed in an Office application, described earlier in this section.

Subscribing to a SharePoint Document Library, Discussion Board, or List to Track Changes

In the previous section, you learned how to track changes to a specific document or folder (that is, library) by subscribing to that document or folder using the discussion feature of an Office application or Internet Explorer. On a team Web site, you can subscribe not only to any document library, but also to any discussion board or list (announcements, contacts, events, links, surveys, tasks, or custom). SharePoint will then notify you by e-mail whenever an item contained in the document library, discussion board, or list is added, changed, or removed. To subscribe, perform the following steps:

1 Connect to the team Web site in your browser.

2 Open the Web page for the document library, discussion board, or list, using the techniques described earlier in this chapter.

3 Click Subscribe, as shown in Figure 8-10. SharePoint will then open its general New Subscription page.

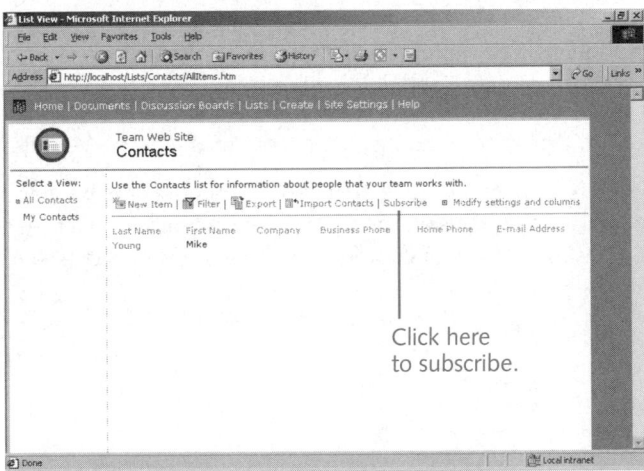

Figure 8-10. The Web page for the Contacts list is shown here.

197

4 On the New Subscription page, shown in Figure 8-11, specify the details of your subscription, and click the OK button. Note that you can use this page to subscribe to any document library, discussion board, or list, by selecting it in the Subscribe To drop-down list.

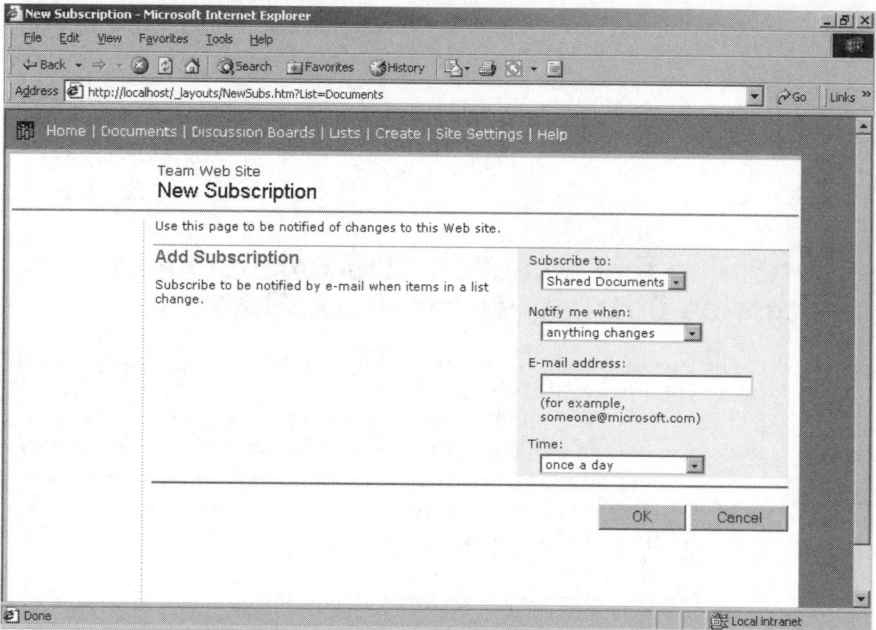

Figure 8-11. The New Subscription Web page allows you to subscribe to a document library, discussion board, or list.

Exchanging Information on SharePoint

To view or add items to a SharePoint list (announcements, contacts, events, links, surveys, tasks, or custom) perform the following steps:

1 In your browser, connect to the home page of the team Web site.

2 Click the Lists link in the navigation bar at the top of the page to open the Lists page, which will display all the announcements, contacts, events, links, surveys, tasks, or custom lists stored on the team Web site (see Figure 8-12).

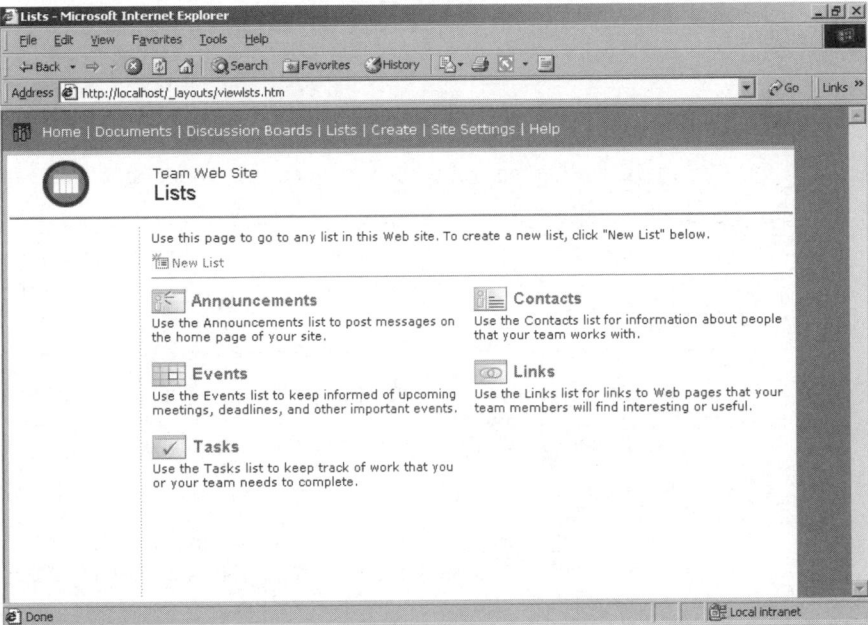

Figure 8-12. This figure shows the SharePoint Lists page.

3 Click the name of the particular list you want to access. This will open the page for that list, which will display all the list items that members have posted. For example, Figure 8-13 shows the page for the Events list.

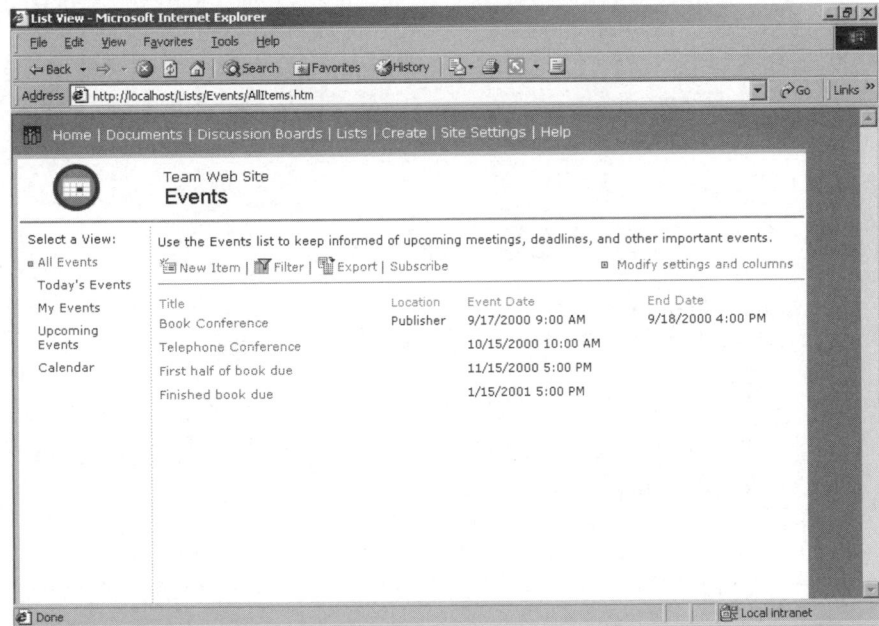

Figure 8-13. This page displays the Events list.

4 In the list's page, you can do any of the following:

- To open an item's page, where you can view, edit, or delete the item, click the name of the list item. (For a link item, click Edit at the left of the item to open the page where you can view, edit, or delete the link. Click the name of the link to open the link's target Web page.)

> **tip** You can copy an events or contacts list item to your Outlook Calendar or Contacts folder. This provides you with a personal copy of the event description or contact information. To do this, click Export Event or Export Contact in the item's page.

- To add a new item to the list, click New Item.

- To control which items are displayed, click Filter.

- To copy the list into an Excel workbook, click Export.

- To change the way the items are displayed, click a view in the Select A View column at the left of the page. (For some types of lists, such as an announcements list, only one view is initially available. You can define additional views for any type of list.)

> **tip** **Go Directly to a List or List Item**
>
> You can go directly from the SharePoint home page to a list or list item, provided that a link has been set up for that list or item. The initial home page contains links for going to the Announcements, Events, and Links lists, as well as individual items belonging to these lists. And the Quick Launch area (at the left of the home page) has links for opening the Shared Documents document library, the General Discussion discussion board, and the Contacts and Tasks lists.

Customizing SharePoint

You can use your browser to customize a team Web site. The site provides pages that allow you to do any of the following:

- Add a new document library, discussion board, or list.

- Customize a document library, discussion board, or list.

- Modify the overall look and behavior of the site.

To add a new document library, discussion board, or list (announcements, contacts, events, links, surveys, tasks, or custom), perform the following steps:

1 Connect to the team Web site in your browser.

2 Open the Documents, Discussion Boards, or Lists page on the team Web site.

3 Click New Document Library, New Discussion Board, or New List.

Alternatively, you can click the Create link in the navigation bar at the top of the SharePoint page to open the Create page. Then, click Document Library, Discussion Board, or the command for the particular type of list item you want to create (Announcements, Team Contacts, Events, and so on; see Figure 8-14). On the Create page, you can also click Import Spreadsheet (at the bottom of the page) to create a new list by importing information from an Excel workbook.

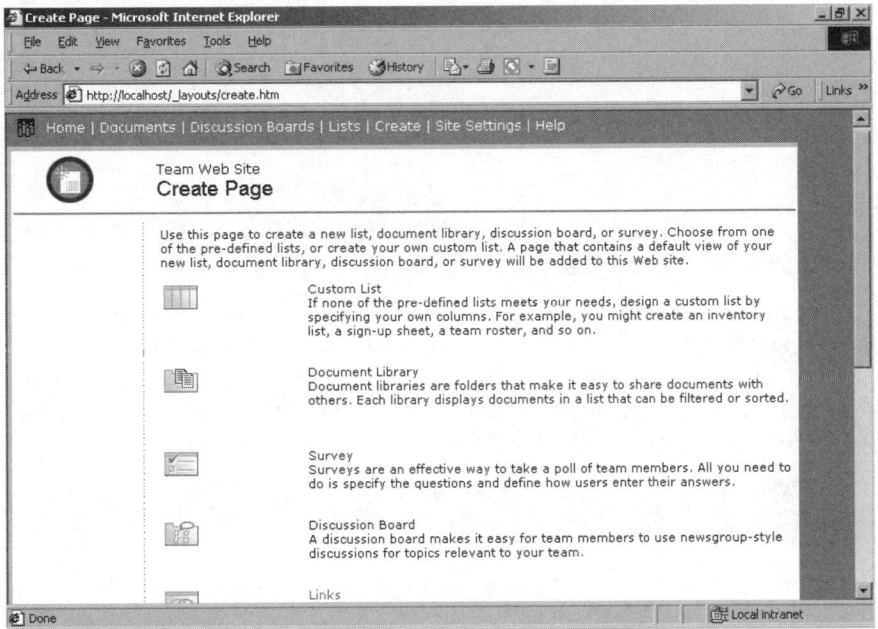

Figure 8-14. On the Create page, you can add a new document library, discussion board, or list.

To customize a document library, discussion board, or list (announcements, contacts, events, links, surveys, tasks, or custom) do the following:

1 On the team Web site, open the page for the document library, discussion board, or list you want to customize.

2 Click Modify Settings And Columns, which will open the Customize page for the specific document library, discussion board, or list (see Figure 8-15).

3 Make the changes you want in the Customize page.

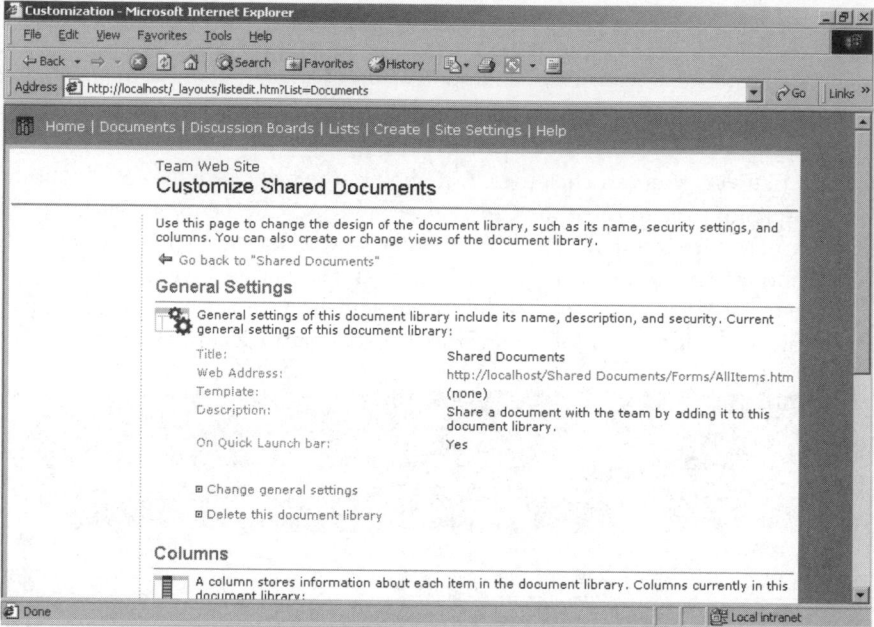

Figure 8-15. Use the Customize page to modify the Shared Documents document library.

An alternative way to customize a document library, discussion board, or list is to click the Site Settings link in the navigation bar at the top of a SharePoint page to open the Site Settings page. Then, in the Modify Site Content area at the bottom of this page, click the Customize command for the particular document library, discussion board, or list you want to modify (see Figure 8-16).

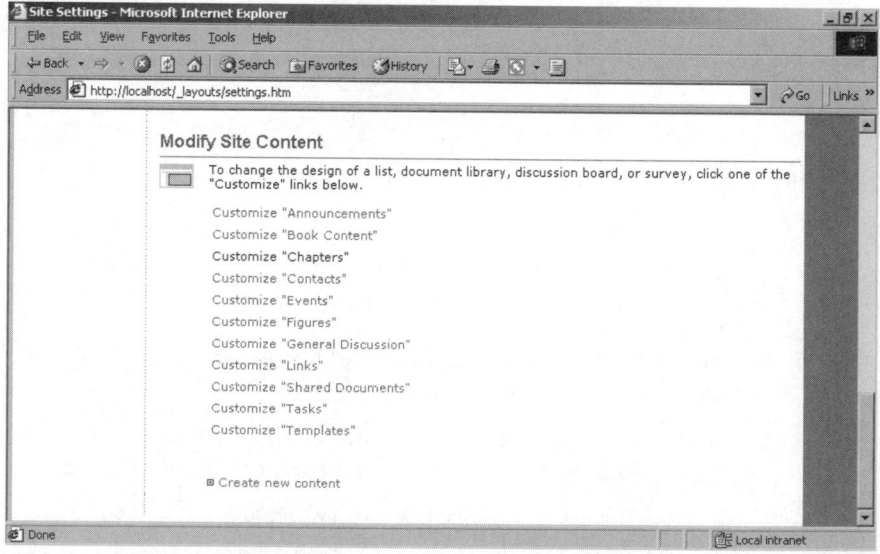

Figure 8-16. These commands are provided at the bottom of the Site Settings page for customizing document libraries, discussion boards, or lists.

---

tip   **Use Templates for Document Libraries**

You can assign a Word, Excel, PowerPoint, or Microsoft Access template to a SharePoint document library so that whenever a member creates a new document in that library by clicking New Document on the library's page, the new document will be based on the assigned template. (If no template is assigned, clicking New Document creates a Word document based on the Normal template.) This feature allows you to use each document library for creating and sharing a specific type of Office document. To assign a template to a document library, upload the template file to that document library. Then, in the Customize page for the document library, click Change The General Settings (see Figure 8-15) and enter the path for the uploaded template into the Template URL text box. For example, if you uploaded the template Outline.dot to the Shared Documents document library, you would enter **Shared Documents/Outline.dot** into the Template URL text box.

To modify features of the overall team Web site, perform the following steps:

1 Click the Site Settings link in the navigation bar at the top of a SharePoint page to open the Site Settings page (see Figure 8-17).

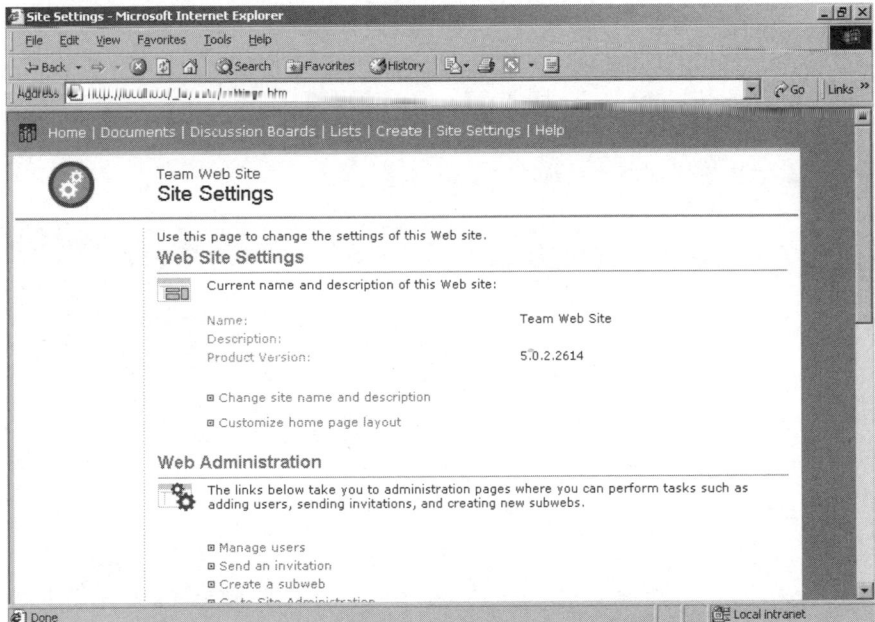

Figure 8-17. The Site Settings page allows you to modify features of the overall team Web site.

2 To change the name or description of the site, click Change The Site Name And Description.

3 To change the contents or arrangement of the site's home page, click Customize Home Page Layout.

4 To manage members of the site, click one of the following commands: Manage Users, Send An Invitation, Edit My Information, or View User Information.

5 To create a new Web site within the current team Web site, which is known as a *subweb,* click Create A Subweb.

6 To manage users and their roles, to control Web discussions and subscriptions, to configure usage analysis, to check for server problems, to enable or disable version control, or to manage subwebs, click Go To Site Administration.

> You can use FrontPage to customize a team Web site much more extensively than you can by administering the site in your browser. For information, see "Customizing and Creating SharePoint Team Web Sites," on page 1121.

Customizing the Office XP Application Interface

Customizing Toolbars, Menus, and Shortcut Keys

You can extensively modify the interface of any of the major Microsoft Office XP applications—Word, Excel, PowerPoint, Outlook, FrontPage, Access, and Publisher—to suit your working style. You can create new custom toolbars and you can modify existing toolbars and menus. In Word, you can define new shortcut keys for quickly executing commands or running macros. You can also set a variety of other options that affect the application interface. In Office XP, you can run a utility to save your Office settings so that you can restore them on another computer where you use Office. This section discusses several general principles that apply to all ways of customizing the Office application interface. The following sections then present the specific techniques for making each type of modification.

In Word, when you create a toolbar, modify a toolbar or menu, or define a shortcut key, you can choose where to save your modification by selecting an item in the Make Toolbar Available To, Save In, or Save Changes In drop-down list, which is displayed at the bottom of the dialog box in which you make the modification. In most cases, you must choose an item in this list before you make the modification in the dialog box (choosing a new item in the list might not affect modifications that you've already made). If you choose the Normal.dot (or

205

Normal) item, the modification will be stored in the Normal template and will be in effect while you work on any document. This choice is best for designing a general-purpose toolbar or menu or for defining a shortcut key that you'll use frequently.

Alternatively, you can choose the name of the current document's template (assuming that the document is based on a template other than Normal). In this case, the modification will be in effect only while you work on a document based on the same template. This choice is best when you make changes that are useful for a specific type of document. For example, if you want to create a menu with commands for writing faxes, you could save your modifications in the Word template you use for creating faxes.

For information on Word templates, see "Creating New Office Documents," on page 53, and "Customizing and Creating Document Templates," on page 405.

Finally, you can choose the name of the document itself. In this case, the modification will be in effect only when you work on that particular document. This choice is best for highly specific modifications.

Display or
Hide Assistant

Note that while you use the Customize dialog box to make modifications, you can get help from the Office Assistant. If the Office Assistant isn't visible, click the Display or Hide Assistant button in the lower-left corner of the Customize dialog box.

The Office Assistant is described in "Getting the Most Out of the Office Online Help," on page 29.

caution Making extensive modifications to the toolbars, menus, or shortcut keys in one or more Office applications may make it difficult to learn tasks from this book or from the Office online Help, because these sources refer to the standard configurations. You might therefore want to wait until you're familiar with the Office skills involved before making extensive customizations.

Creating and Managing Custom Toolbars

You can create new custom toolbars that you can display in addition to the toolbars that are supplied with the Office application. To create a custom toolbar, perform the following steps:

1 Choose Tools, Customize. In the Customize dialog box, click the Toolbars tab. The particular toolbars you'll see listed depend on the Office application you're using (see Figure 9-1 for an example of the Toolbars tab in Word).

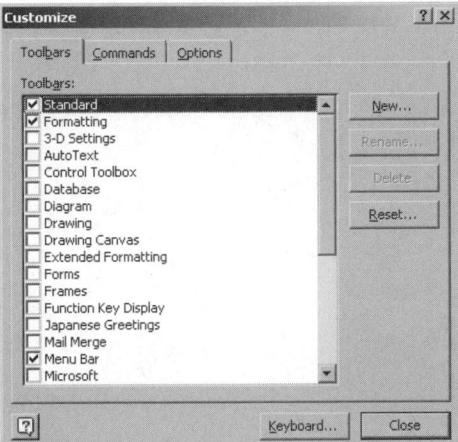

Figure 9-1. This is the Toolbars tab of the Customize dialog box that is displayed in Word.

Another way to open the Customize dialog box is to click the down arrow on the right end of a toolbar, and then choose Add Or Remove Buttons, Customize from the shortcut menu, shown here:

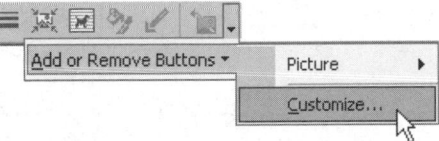

2 Click the New button to open the New Toolbar dialog box (shown in Figure 9-2).

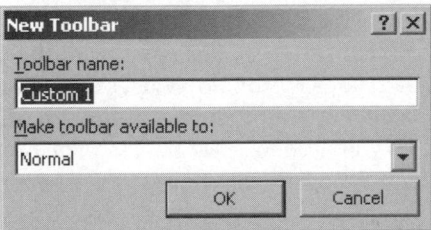

Figure 9-2. This is the New Toolbar dialog box that is displayed in Word.

3 Type a name for your toolbar in the Toolbar Name text box.

4 If you're customizing Word, select an item in the Make Toolbar Available To drop-down list. If you choose Normal.dot (or Normal), the toolbar can be displayed when you work on any document; if you choose the name of the document template, it can be displayed only when you work on a document based on this same template; and if you choose the name of the current document, it can be displayed only when you work on that document. These choices were explained in greater detail in the previous section.

207

Chapter 9

5 Click OK. The Office application will display your new toolbar (which initially won't contain any buttons), and will return you to the Toolbars tab.

6 Add buttons to your toolbar using the Customize dialog box Commands tab, as explained in the next section.

> Although Task Pane is listed in the Toolbars tab, as well as on the Toolbars submenu of the View menu, a task pane isn't an actual toolbar and you can't modify it using the techniques given in this chapter. For more information, see "Using the Task Panes in Office Applications," on page 51.

In the Toolbars tab of the Customize dialog box, you can also show, hide, rename, delete, or reset a toolbar, as follows:

● To show a toolbar that isn't currently visible (a custom or built-in toolbar), check the box to the left of the toolbar name in the Toolbars list. To hide the toolbar, clear the check box.

> **tip**   **Display Toolbars More Quickly**
>
> To quickly show or hide a commonly used toolbar, on the View menu, click Toolbars, or click any toolbar or the menu bar with the right mouse button, and then choose the name of the toolbar from the menu. If the toolbar you want to show or hide doesn't appear on the menu, open the Toolbars tab of the Customize dialog box, which shows all toolbars available in the application.

● To rename or delete a custom toolbar you've created (not a built-in one), select the toolbar in the Toolbars list and click the Rename or Delete button.

● To remove any modifications that you have made to one of the built-in toolbars supplied with Office (not a custom toolbar), select the toolbar in the Toolbars list and click the Reset button. In Word, you'll see the Reset Toolbar dialog box, in which you need to select the template or document for which you want to reset the toolbar (the choices were explained in the previous section). In other applications, you'll see a message box asking you to confirm that you want to reset the toolbar. The methods for making modifications to toolbars are discussed in the next section.

> For instructions on using the Word Organizer to copy, delete, or rename a custom toolbar you've created in Word, see "Using the Organizer," on page 409.

Modifying Toolbars and Menus

Office applications let you extensively modify menus and both custom and built-in toolbars. The different objects you can work with are so interchangeable that the terminology becomes a bit confusing. The following terms are used in this chapter to describe three of the basic objects you work with when you customize toolbars and menus:

- A *menu* is one of the drop-down lists of items that appear on the application's menu bar, such as the File menu or the Edit menu. A menu can also be displayed as an item on another menu, where it is known as a *submenu*. In addition, a menu can be displayed as a button on a toolbar, where you can open it by clicking a down arrow. A menu label consists of text only—it can't include an icon.

- A *menu item* is one of the objects listed on a menu. A menu item can be a *command*, which immediately performs an action, sets an option, or opens a dialog box. It can also be another menu, which in this context is known as a submenu. The label for a command on a menu can consist of both text and an icon, or text only.

- A *toolbar button* is one of the objects that appear on a toolbar, such as the Standard or Formatting toolbar. It can be a command or it can be a menu. The label for a command on a toolbar can consist of an icon only, text only, or both an icon and text.

> **note** A command can be either a simple object that you click to execute the command or a drop-down list control from which you select an item or type in a value (such as the Style, Font, and Font Size drop-down lists on the Formatting toolbar in Word).

You can add, remove, or rearrange toolbar buttons, menu items, or menus. You can also change the text or the icon that is associated with a command on a toolbar or menu, and you can change the name of a menu. And, you can specify whether a toolbar or menu command displays text only, an icon only (on a toolbar), or both text and an icon.

To make any of these modifications, the first step is to choose Tools, Customize, which displays the Customize dialog box. If you want to modify a toolbar that isn't currently visible, you must first display it by clicking the Toolbars tab of the Customize dialog box and checking the box next to the toolbar name. Then, click the Commands tab (shown in Figure 9-3, on page 210).

Chapter 9

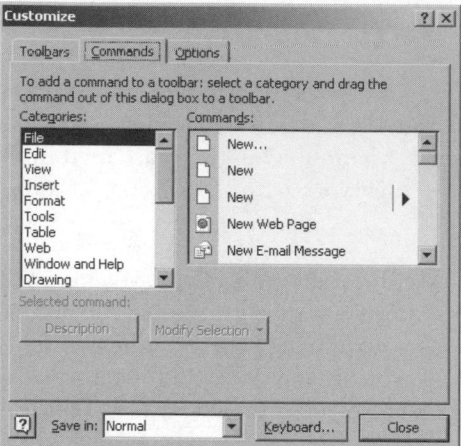

Figure 9-3. This is the Commands tab of the Customize dialog box that is displayed in Word.

---

tip **Modify a Shortcut Menu**

In Word, PowerPoint, and Access, you can modify the shortcut menus the program displays when you right-click various items. To modify a shortcut menu, click the Toolbars tab in the Customize dialog box, then check the Shortcut Menus item. This action will temporarily display a special floating toolbar—labeled Shortcut Menus—on which you'll find copies of the application's shortcut menus, arranged by category. (This toolbar will be hidden when you close the Customize dialog box.) Then, to modify a particular shortcut menu, use the techniques given in this section to modify the copy of the shortcut menu found on the Shortcut Menus toolbar.

If you're working in Word, before you make any of the modifications described in this section, choose the appropriate item in the Save In drop-down list at the bottom of the Customize dialog box. If you choose Normal.dot (or Normal), the modifications will be in effect when you work on any document; if you choose the name of the document template, they will be in effect only when you work on a document based on this same template; and if you choose the name of the current document, they will be in effect only when you work on this document.

These choices were explained in greater detail at the beginning of "Customizing Toolbars, Menus, and Shortcut Keys," on page 205.

To add a new toolbar button, menu item, or menu perform the following steps:

1 Select an item in the Categories list, as follows:

  ■ If you want to add a command that executes a built-in application command, select a command category (File, Edit, View, and so on).

■ If you want to add a command that runs a macro, assigns a font, inserts an AutoText entry, or applies a style, select the Macros, Fonts, AutoText, or Styles item (Fonts, AutoText, and Styles are available in Word only).

■ If you want to add a menu to the menu bar, to a toolbar, or to another menu, select Built-In Menus to add a copy of one of the application's standard menus (File, Edit, View, and so on). Or, select New Menu to add an empty menu (you can then add items to it using this numbered procedure). You can also add one of the application's standard submenus by selecting the name of the application menu that contains the desired submenu (for example, File, View, or Insert).

For information on Office macros, see Part 10 of the book. Fonts are discussed in "Formatting Characters Directly," on page 298; AutoText in "Reusing Text with the AutoText Feature," on page 252; and styles in "Applying Styles and Reusing Formats," on page 320.

2 In the Commands list, select the specific application command, other command (macro, font, AutoText entry, or style), or menu that you want to add. To see an explanation of the selected application command, click the Description button. (Word automatically shows a description or preview of a selected macro, font, AutoText entry, or style.) Then, use the mouse to drag the command or menu directly to the position on the toolbar, menu bar, or menu where you want to insert it. Note that when you drag an object to a menu, Office automatically opens the menu when the mouse pointer moves over the menu label.

While the Customize dialog box is displayed, you can *move* a toolbar button, menu item, or menu to any position on a toolbar, menu, or the menu bar by simply dragging the object to the new location. To make a *copy*, press the Ctrl key while you drag. When you've dragged an object to a position where you can insert it, the mouse pointer displays a + sign and also an I-beam symbol at the point of insertion, as shown here:

To *remove* a toolbar button, menu item, or menu, drag it away from its current position and drop it anywhere except on a toolbar, a menu, or the menu bar. When you've dragged the object to a position where dropping it will remove the object, the mouse pointer displays an X, as seen here:

Chapter 9

While the Customize dialog box is open, you can also modify a specific toolbar button, menu item, or menu by clicking the button, the menu item, or the menu name (Office draws a selection border around the object you click). In the Commands tab, click the Modify Selection button and choose the appropriate command from the menu that pops up, which is shown here:

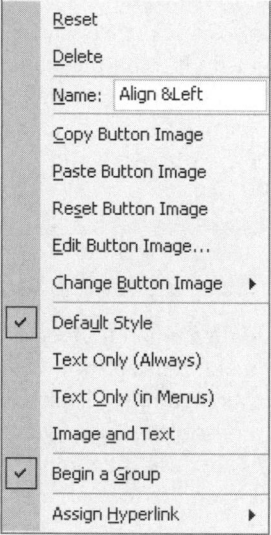

Table 9-1 lists what you can do using the commands on this menu.

Table 9-1. **Modifying a Toolbar Button, Menu Item, or Menu Using the Modify Selection Menu**

To Do This	Perform This Action on the Modify Selection Menu
Undo any changes you have made to the selected toolbar button, menu item, or menu	Choose Reset.
Remove the selected toolbar button, menu item, or menu	Choose Delete.
Change the label text for the selected toolbar button, menu item, or menu (this command also changes the text of the ScreenTip for a toolbar button)	Type the new text into the Name text box. You can specify a shortcut key by inserting an & in front of one of the characters in the label (that character will be underlined in the label, indicating that it's a shortcut key).

212

Table 9-1. *(continued)*

To Do This	Perform This Action on the Modify Selection Menu
Copy the selected toolbar or menu command's icon (if any) into the Clipboard	Choose Copy Button Image.
Assign the previously copied icon to the currently selected command on a toolbar or menu	Choose Paste Button Image.
Restore the selected toolbar or menu command's default icon (if the command doesn't have a default icon—like the Save As command on the File menu— the icon will simply be removed)	Choose Reset Button Image.
Open the Button Editor, in which you can modify the toolbar or menu command's icon or design a new, custom icon	Choose Edit Button Image.
Assign a stock icon to a toolbar command or menu command	Choose the icon from the Change Button Image submenu.
• Display the icon only on a toolbar command or • Display the text label plus the icon on a menu command	Choose Default Style.
Display the text label only on either a toolbar command or menu command	Choose Text Only (Always).
• Display the icon only on a toolbar command or • Display the text label only on menu command	Choose Text Only (In Menus).
Display both the text label and the icon (if there is one) on either a toolbar command or menu command	Choose Image And Text.
Display a dividing line before the selected toolbar button, menu item, or menu	Choose Begin a Group.

(continued)

Chapter 9

Table 9-1. *(continued)*

To Do This	Perform This Action on the Modify Selection Menu
Assign or remove a hyperlink from a toolbar command or menu command	Choose one of the following commands from the Assign Hyperlink submenu (not available in FrontPage or Publisher): ● Open: To assign the command a hyperlink that opens a document ● Insert Picture: To assign the command a hyperlink that inserts a picture into the active document ● Remove Link: To remove a previously assigned hyperlink from the command

This shortcut menu is referred to as the Modify Selection menu throughout the remainder of this discussion. Note that while the Customize dialog box is open, you can select an object and open this same menu (as a shortcut menu) by simply clicking a toolbar button, a menu item, or a menu label using the right mouse button.

If you selected a menu prior to opening the Modify Selection menu, the command you choose will affect the entire menu. However, only the Reset, Delete, Name, and Begin A Group commands will be available; that is, you can only reset the menu, delete the menu, change the menu label, or insert a dividing line before the menu.

Most of the commands that you can add to a toolbar or menu have a default icon. For example, the Open command in the File category has a default icon that depicts an opened file folder, as shown here:

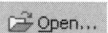

If you don't like the default icon for the selected toolbar or menu command (or if there is no icon), you can replace the icon (or add an icon) in one of three ways. First, from the Modify Selection menu, you can choose Change Button Image and choose an icon from the palette of images that Office displays, shown on the following page:

Second, you can modify the icon or draw a new one by choosing the Edit Button Image command and designing the image you want in the Button Editor dialog box.

Finally, if you have spotted an attractive icon on another toolbar or menu command, you can copy that icon to your command, as follows:

1 Right-click on the command that has the icon you want to copy.

2 Choose Copy Button Image from the shortcut menu.

3 Right-click the button or menu item you want to modify.

4 Choose Paste Button Image from the shortcut menu.

You can restore the default icon for the selected toolbar or menu command by choosing the Reset Button Image command from the Modify Selection menu.

If you choose the Reset command with a toolbar or menu command selected, any change that you've made to the command will be removed. If you choose Reset with a menu selected, the menu will be restored to its default configuration—that is, any item you have added to the menu will be removed, any item you have removed will be restored, and any item you have modified will be returned to its default state.

You can also reset the entire menu bar by opening the Toolbars tab of the Customize dialog box, selecting the Menu Bar item in the list, and clicking the Reset button. This action removes any menus you have added and restores any menus you have removed. It doesn't, however, reset individual menus to their default configurations; you must reset each menu separately using the method given in the previous paragraph.

Finally, to restore a built-in toolbar to its default configuration, select the name of the toolbar in the Toolbars tab and click Reset. Note, however, that you can't use this method for a custom toolbar.

A Quick Way to Add or Remove Toolbar Buttons

You can quickly add or remove a button from a built-in toolbar by clicking the down arrow at the right end of the toolbar (or the arrow at the bottom of a vertically positioned toolbar), clicking the Add Or Remove Buttons command, clicking the command that has the same name as the toolbar, and then choosing the button you want to add or remove, as shown here:

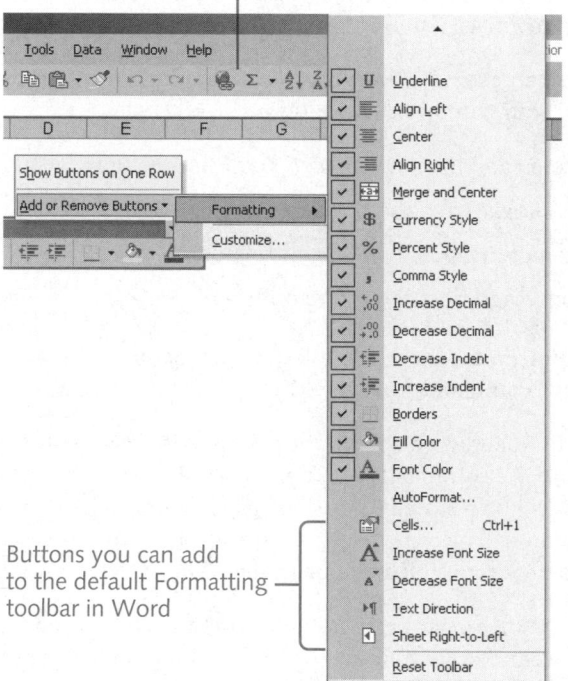

Buttons you can add to the default Formatting toolbar in Word

Although this is a fast way to add a button, typically the menu includes only a few buttons—if any—that aren't already displayed on the default toolbar. The technique is useful mainly for reducing the size of a toolbar by hiding buttons that you seldom use. Note that you can't use this technique with a custom toolbar you've created.

Choosing the Reset Toolbar command on the bottom of the menu has the same effect as clicking the Reset button in the Toolbars tab of the Customize dialog box, as explained in "Creating and Managing Custom Toolbars," on page 206.

Defining Shortcut Keys (Word Only)

In Word, you can assign a built-in application command, a macro, a font, an AutoText entry, a style, or a symbol to a shortcut key. Pressing the shortcut key immediately executes the command, runs the macro, applies the font, inserts the AutoText entry, assigns the style, or inserts the symbol.

To assign one of these items to a shortcut key, perform the following steps:

1 Choose Tools, Customize. At the bottom of the Customize dialog box, click the Keyboard button. (You can be in any tab of the Customize dialog box when you do this.) Word will open the Customize Keyboard dialog box, shown here.

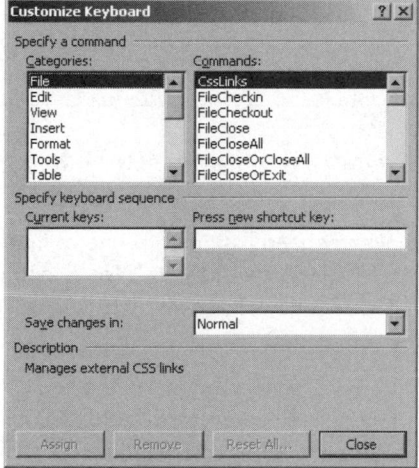

2 Select an item displayed in the Save Changes In drop-down list. If you choose Normal.dot (or Normal), the shortcut key will be available when you work on any document; if you choose the name of the document template, it will be available only when you work on a document based on this same template; and if you choose the name of the current document, it will be available only when you work on this document.

> These choices were explained in greater detail at the beginning of "Customizing Toolbars, Menus, and Shortcut Keys," on page 205.

3 Select a category in the Categories list. Notice that in addition to the categories available for adding commands to toolbars or menus (described previously in the chapter), you can select the Common Symbols category to assign a symbol to a key combination so that you can quickly insert a symbol that doesn't appear on the keyboard.

4 In the list to the right of the Categories list, select the specific command that you want to assign to the shortcut key. (This list is named Commands,

Macros, Fonts, AutoText, Styles, or Common Symbols, according to the current selection in the Categories list. To simplify the remainder of the discussion, the term *command* is used to refer to a built-in Word command, macro, font, AutoText entry, style, or symbol that you select in the list.) You'll see a description of the selected command in the Description area at the bottom of the dialog box.

If you've chosen the Common Symbols category but don't see the character you want in the Common Symbols list, select the Insert category and the Symbol command, click the Symbol button that Word displays, and choose the character you want in the Symbol dialog box.

note If the name of a command in the Commands list ends with a colon (such as the Symbol command in the Insert category), you'll need to supply additional information using the control or controls that appear in the Customize Keyboard dialog box when you select the command.

For information on using the Symbol dialog box, see "Inserting Symbols and Foreign Characters," on page 246.

If the selected command has already been assigned to one or more shortcut keys, these keys will be shown in the Current Keys list. Note that you can assign a command to several shortcut keys; each shortcut key will provide an alternate way to carry out the command.

5 Click in the Press New Shortcut Key text box and press the key combination to which you want to assign the selected command. Word then displays a message below the box indicating whether a command has already been assigned to that shortcut key. If a command has already been assigned, the new command you assign will replace the former one. In general, you should try to find a key combination that hasn't already been assigned a command, so that you don't lose keyboard functionality in Word.

6 Click the Assign button. The key combination is then added to the Current Keys list.

tip **Assign Any Style to a Shortcut Key**

If you've selected the Styles category in the Customize Keyboard dialog box but don't see the style you want in the Styles list, you can assign *any* paragraph, character, or list style to a shortcut key by opening that style in the Modify Style dialog box, clicking the Format button at the bottom of the dialog box, and choosing Shortcut Key from the shortcut menu. See "Customizing Styles Using the Modify Style Dialog Box," on page 390.

7 To make additional shortcut key assignments, repeat steps 3 through 6 for each one. Click the Close button when you're done.

You can remove a specific shortcut key assignment by selecting the key combination in the Current Keys list and clicking the Remove button. You can remove all shortcut key assignments you have made for all commands by clicking the Reset All button. (Note that this action removes the assignments only from the template or document currently selected in the Save Changes In list.)

Setting Interface Options

To set options that affect toolbars, menus, and other interface elements, in the Customize dialog box, click the Options tab, as seen here:

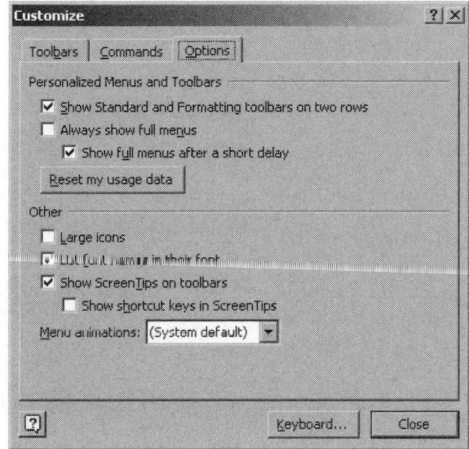

Then, proceed as explained in Table 9-2.

Table 9-2. Modifying the Application Interface Using the Options Tab of the Customize Dialog Box

To Do This	Perform This Action in the Options Tab
Dock the Standard and Formatting toolbars on separate rows	Check the Show Standard And Formatting Toolbars On Two Rows option. When the option isn't selected, these two toolbars share a single row, which conserves screen space but usually hides some of the buttons. You can also turn this option on (or off) by clicking the down arrow on the right end of either toolbar and choosing Show Buttons On One Row (Two Rows) from the shortcut menu.

(continued)

Chapter 9

Table 9-2. *(continued)*

To Do This	Perform This Action in the Options Tab
Enable personalized menus, which display only the most basic commands plus the commands you use most frequently	Clear the Always Show Full Menus option. When this option is cleared, you can still display all commands by double-clicking the menu label, or by clicking the double down arrow displayed at the bottom of a partially displayed menu, shown here:
Make all menu commands belonging to a personalized menu appear if you hold the pointer over the menu label for about six seconds	Check the Show Full Menus After A Short Delay option. This option is available only if you've cleared the Always Show Full Menus option.
Remove the information that Office stores on the menu and toolbar commands you use most frequently	Click the Reset My Usage Data button.
Display big toolbar buttons, making it easier to see the buttons, but also consuming a large amount of screen space (this option doesn't affect menu items)	Check the Large Icons option.
Display each font name in a drop-down toolbar list (such as the Style or Font list) using the named font, providing a sample of how the font looks	Check the List Font Names In Their Font option. Turning this option off results in a faster display of font lists. This option doesn't affect the way font names are displayed in the Font dialog box or the way styles and formats are displayed in Word's Styles And Formatting task pane.

(continued)

220

Table 9-2. *(continued)*

To Do This	Perform This Action in the Options Tab
Display a description of a toolbar button—that is, a ScreenTip—when you hold the mouse pointer over the button (a ScreenTip displays the text that is set through the Name item on the Modify Selection menu, described in "Modifying Toolbars and Menus," on page 209)	Check the Show ScreenTips On Toolbars option.
Include a description of the shortcut key for the command (if it has one) in the text of a toolbar button's ScreenTip	Check the Show Shortcut Keys In ScreenTips option. This option is available only if you've checked the Show ScreenTips On Toolbars option.
Add an animation effect to the opening of menus	Select an animation from the Menu Animations drop-down list, or select (System Default) to eliminate special Office menu animation effects.

You can change settings in the Options tab of any of the main Office applications—Word, Excel, PowerPoint, Outlook, FrontPage, Access, or Publisher—and your settings will affect all of these applications.

If you position two or more toolbars on the same row (or even if you place only one toolbar on a row but have a small window size or a low screen resolution), there might not be enough room to display all of the toolbar buttons. In this case, with a built-in toolbar, Office shows the buttons you use most frequently based on data it collects as you work. To click a button that has been hidden, click the chevron on the right end of the toolbar. This action displays a palette of all the buttons that have been hidden from toolbars on the current row, as shown here, and you can click the button you want.

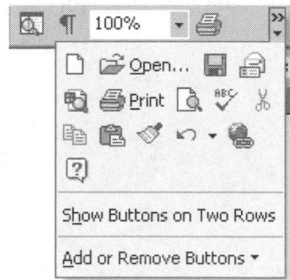

Office also selects the items it shows on personalized menus based on the data it collects about your usage. (Office displays personalized menus if the Always Show Full Menus option is not selected.) If you click the Reset My Usage Data button, Office discards the usage data it has collected and begins showing the toolbar commands and menu items that it considers most important, without regard to your personal usage habits. (This method is also how Office selects the buttons to display on a custom toolbar.) Office then starts collecting usage data again and gradually adjusts the set of buttons it displays on built-in toolbars and the set of items it displays on personalized menus based on which buttons you use most frequently.

newfeature!
Saving and Restoring Your Office Settings

You can use the Save My Settings Wizard to save the customizations and other settings you've made in Office applications, and then later restore these settings on the same computer or on a different one. For example, if you've been using Office on one computer and now want to start using it on a second computer, you could use the Save My Settings Wizard to transfer your Office settings to the second computer, eliminating the need to re-create them one at a time. The settings that the wizard saves and restores include the following:

- Customizations you've made through the Customize toolbar, as discussed in this chapter

- Options you've selected through the Options command on the Tools menu

- Settings you've made through common menu options, such as the Ruler option on the View menu

- Your arrangements of the application toolbars

To save or restore your Office settings, perform the following steps:

1 Quit all Office applications.

2 From the Start menu in Windows, choose Programs, Microsoft Office Tools, Save My Settings Wizard. This action displays the first dialog box of the Save My Settings Wizard, shown here:

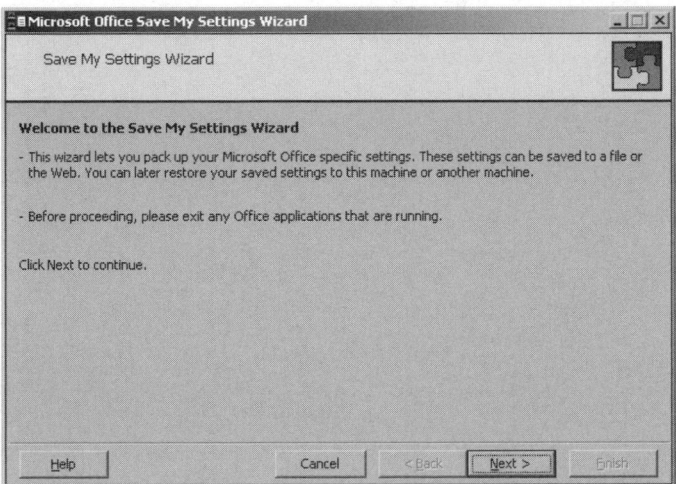

3 Click the Next button, and in the second wizard dialog box select the Save The Settings From This Machine option, as shown here, to save your settings, or select Restore Previously Saved Settings To This Machine to restore them.

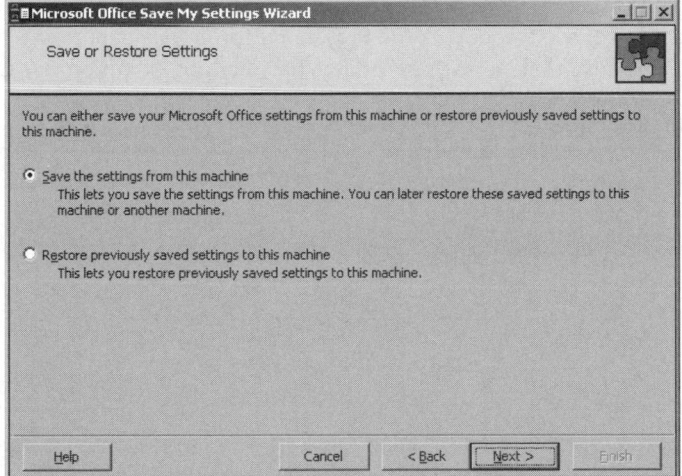

4 Click Next, and in the final wizard dialog box, indicate whether you want to save or restore your settings from the Web, or from a file on a local or network disk, as shown here, and then click Finish.

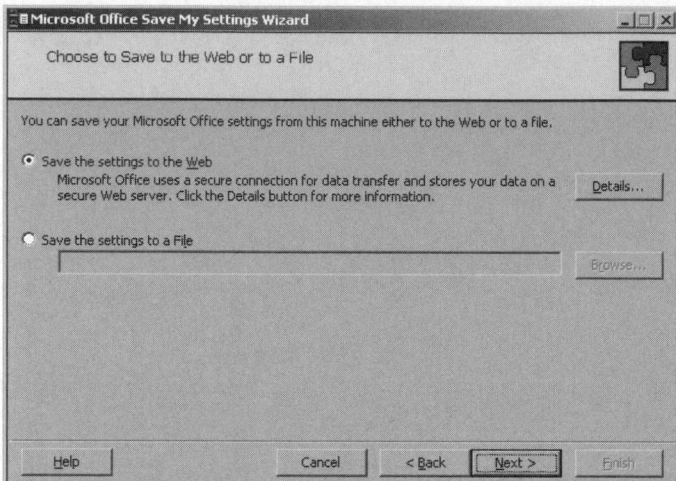

If you store your settings on the Web, they are kept on a secure site that Microsoft has provided for this purpose. Storing your settings on the Web frees you from the need to create a file and transfer it to another computer. For more information on this option, click the Details button in the dialog box.

If you choose to store or restore your settings from a file, you'll need to enter the path of the file, or click the Browse button to navigate to the file's location. The file that stores your settings has the .ops extension (for Office Profile Settings).

> **tip** To learn about ways to customize the Save My Settings Wizard, about exactly what's stored in an Office Profile Settings file, and about how to migrate settings from an Office 2000 installation to Office XP, click the Help button in any of the wizard dialog boxes.

Part 3

Word

Chapter 10

Word Fundamentals

A Rundown on Word

Microsoft Word 2002 is an incredibly powerful, general-purpose, word processing program that you can use to create basic documents of all kinds—memos, letters, faxes, reports, contracts, resumes, manuals, theses, and books—to mention only some of the possibilities. Word is also surprisingly good at creating complex or specialized documents that are normally the province of more specialized software applications—for example:

● **Web pages.** Although it's not as good at creating Web pages and managing Web sites as Microsoft FrontPage (see Part 7 of this book), Word now has more Web publishing features than ever, and it lets you easily create attractive and dynamic Web pages.

> For more information on creating Web pages with Word, see Chapter 20, "Creating Web Pages and Other Online Documents."

● **Brochures, newsletters, and other documents with complex page layouts.** You might be able to do a better job at creating short, layout-intensive documents using Microsoft Publisher (see Part 9 of this book). However, Word's improved drawing and layout features make it a highly viable tool for creating these kinds of documents.

> For more information on creating complex layouts using Word, see Chapter 18, "Designing and Printing Professional-Looking Pages."

● **Printer-ready publications.** Dedicated desktop publishing packages (such as Adobe PageMaker,

Corel Ventura, or Quark XPress) do a superb job of creating printer-ready publications with precise page layouts, cross-references, indexes, tables of contents, and so on. Word is ideal for the initial organizing, writing, editing, and proofing of a publication. However, you can also do quite a good job in Word of preparing the final printer-ready publication. (Many books and other manuscripts have gone directly from Word to the printer.) If your page layout needs are a bit demanding for Word's tools, you can always transfer your Word document to a dedicated desktop publishing program to create the final layout.

For more information on desktop publishing techniques in Word, see Chapter 15, "Managing Large or Complex Documents," and Chapter 18, "Designing and Printing Professional-Looking Pages."

● **Tables of numbers or other data.** Clearly, Microsoft Excel is the tool of choice for working with numbers, and Microsoft Access for working with databases (for more information on those applications, see Parts 4 and 8 of this book). However, Word tables can be used to store and display reasonable amounts of numeric or textual data. Word even provides mathematical functions for working with numbers in tables, as well as database tools for working with data fields and records in tables.

Why use Word for a task that can be performed with a more specialized software program, perhaps one already installed on your computer? The main reason is that you probably already know how to use Word, and the extra features of a more specialized program might not be worth the time required to learn a new software package, especially if you create only an occasional Web page, brochure, or other specialized document. You might also have existing Word documents that you can quickly convert to Web pages or other specialized formats. You can thus use Word to leverage not only your current skills, but also your existing collection of documents.

For a description of the new features included in Word 2002, see "New Word Features," on page 12.

The first eight chapters in this part of the book are basically about laying down the content of a Word document—organizing, editing, formatting, arranging, footnoting, indexing, annotating, and proofing the document text. These chapters present techniques for creating simple documents yourself, as well as methods for generating complex publications in a workgroup.

The last three chapters in this part deal with producing the final end product. Chapter 18 covers the methods for laying out and printing a traditional hard copy document. Chapter 19 explains the techniques for producing multiple, customized copies of a document—form letters, labels, envelopes, faxes, or e-mail messages. And Chapter 20 presents the methods for creating an increasingly important end product: the online document, which is intended to be read on a computer. Online documents not only save trees, but also—unlike printed documents—they can include background colors and patterns, interactive forms, hyperlinks, and other dynamic elements. An online document can be a Word file stored on a network disk or on a SharePoint team Web site; or, it can be an HTML (Hypertext Markup Language) page on the Web or on a company intranet.

This chapter summarizes the unique features and tools you'll find in the Word workplace, and shows you how to set up the Word interface—the windows, task panes, document view, zoom factor, ruler, and other elements—to suit your working style, before you begin creating and editing documents.

Using the Word Workplace

If you run Word without opening an existing document—for example, you choose the Programs, Microsoft Word command on the Start menu in Windows—Word will automatically create a new, blank document. Figure 10-1 shows the Word window as it might appear when you first start Word. Because Word is so highly customizable, your window might look quite different. In "Setting Up the Word Interface," on page 234, you'll learn the basic techniques for adding and removing interface elements and for modifying the interface in other ways.

> For information on the ways to start Word and other Microsoft Office XP applications, see "Running the Office Applications," on page 43.

> **note** Figure 10-1 shows the Word window as it appears when the Windows In Taskbar option is off. When this option is off, Word displays all document windows within a single, top-level program window. For information on this option, as well as the techniques for working with windows in Office applications, see "Working with Multiple Documents," on page 79.

> For general information on working with application task panes, such as the New Document task pane shown in Figure 10-1, see "Using the Task Panes in Office Applications," on page 51.

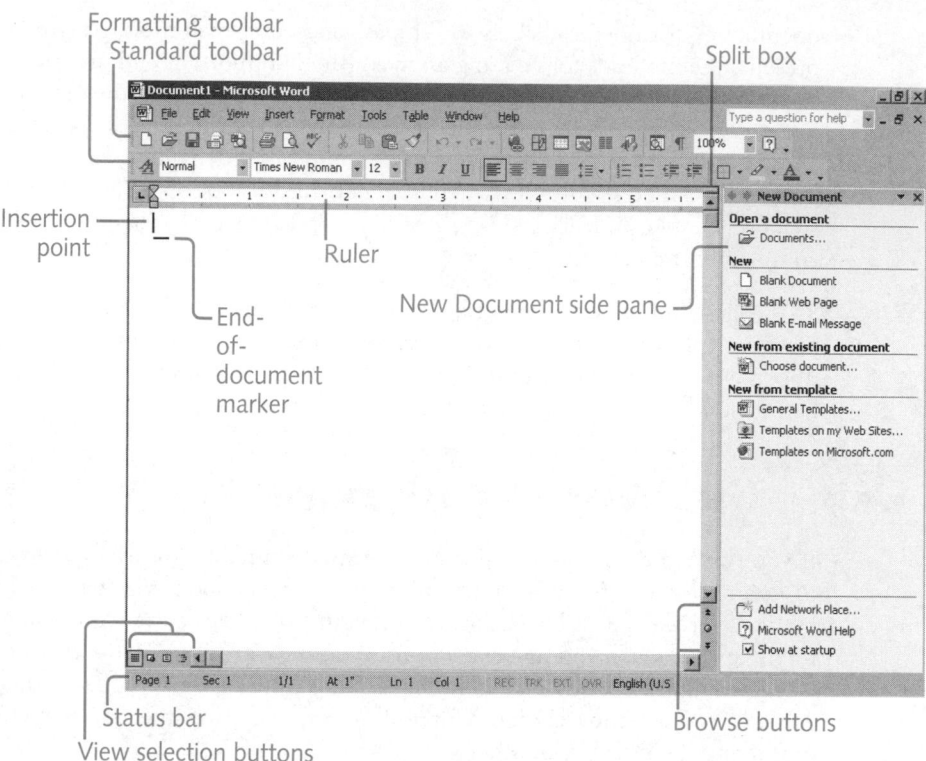

Formatting toolbar
Standard toolbar
Split box
Insertion point
Ruler
End-of-document marker
New Document side pane
Status bar
View selection buttons
Browse buttons

Figure 10-1. When you start Word, this window appears.

Table 10-1 explains what you can do using Word's main task panes. These are the task panes you can display by clicking the down arrow near the upper right corner of the pane and choosing the name of a pane from the drop-down menu, shown here:

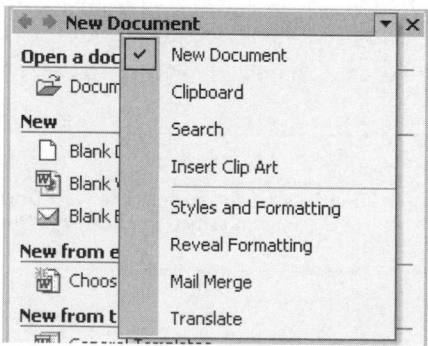

Table 10-1. **Tasks You Can Perform in Word's Main Task Panes**

To Do This	Use This Word Task Pane
Open an existing document or create a new Word document, Web page, or e-mail message (the new document can be blank or based on a special-purpose template)	New Document (see "Creating a Document Using the New Document Task Pane," on page 58)
Work with the Office Clipboard	Clipboard (see "Using the Enhanced Office Clipboard Task Pane," on page 109)
Search for Word documents, other types of files, or Microsoft Outlook items	Search (see "Finding Office Files or Outlook Items Using the Search Feature," on page 69)
Insert clip art, photographs, movies, or sounds into a document	Insert Clip Art (see "Inserting Pictures with the Clip Organizer," on page 115)
Apply or customize Word styles or reuse document formats	Styles And Formatting (see "Applying Styles and Reusing Formats," on page 320)
View, modify, or clear any formatting feature	Reveal Formatting (see "Using the Reveal Formatting Task Pane to View or Modify Formatting Features," on page 332)
Create form letters or multiple labels, envelopes, or e-mail messages	Mail Merge (see Chapter 19, "Using Word to Automate Mailings")
Translate text to a different language	Translate (see "Translating Text," on page 497)

The Word status bar (shown in Figure 10-2) provides information about the operation of the program. To display or hide the status bar, choose Tools, Options. In the Options dialog box, click the View tab and check or clear the Status Bar option in the Show group. Each piece of information in the status bar is displayed in a separate indicator, as shown in Figure 10-2.

note The status bar will also include a Default Language Indicator if you've enabled one or more languages in addition to the default Office language, using the Microsoft Office Language Settings program. You run this program in Windows by choosing Start, Programs, Microsoft Office Tools, Microsoft Office XP Language Settings.

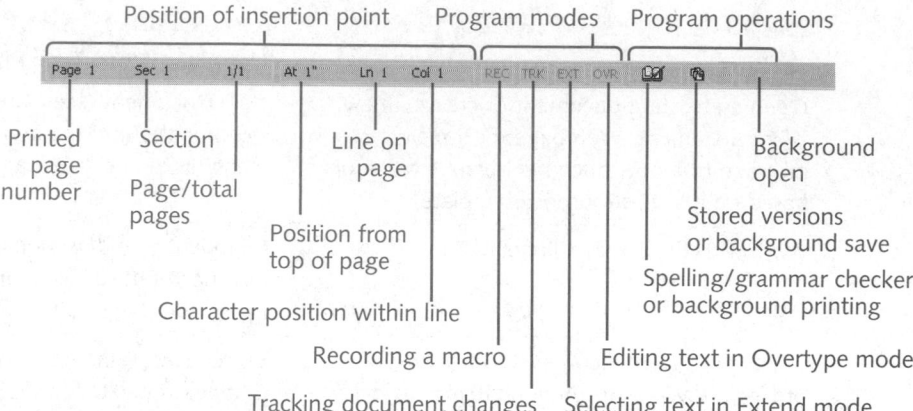

Position of insertion point   Program modes   Program operations

Printed page number

Section

Page/total pages

Line on page

Position from top of page

Character position within line

Recording a macro

Tracking document changes

Selecting text in Extend mode

Editing text in Overtype mode

Spelling/grammar checker or background printing

Stored versions or background save

Background open

Figure 10-2. The Word status bar provides information about the program's operation.

You can double-click indicators in the status bar to quickly issue certain Word commands, as shown in Table 10-2.

Table 10-2. **Performing Actions by Double-Clicking Status Bar Indicators**

To Do This	Double-Click This Status Bar Indicator
Issue the Go To command (see "Moving the Insertion Point with the Go To Command," on page 292)	Any of the first six indicators (which give the position of the insertion point)
Start (or stop) recording a macro (see Part 10 of the book)	REC
Start tracking document changes and display the Reviewing toolbar, or stop tracking document changes (see "Tracking and Reviewing Document Changes," on page 445)	TRK
Switch the Extend selecting mode on or off (see "Selecting by Using the Keyboard," on page 270)	EXT
Turn Overtype mode on or off (see "Adding Text," on page 245)	OVR
Mark the language of the selected text (see "Marking the Language," on page 504)	Default language (if present)

Table 10-2. *(continued)*

To Do This	Double-Click This Status Bar Indicator
Display suggested spellings for the next spelling error in the document that has been marked by the as-you-type spelling checker (see "Checking Your Spelling as You Type," on page 476)	Spelling/grammar checker (You can perform this action only when you see the Spelling And Grammar icon, which is displayed after the as-you-type spelling or grammar checker has examined text in the document.)
Open the Versions dialog box (see "Storing Different Document Versions," on page 243)	Stored versions (You can perform this action only when you see the Versions icon, which is displayed only if you've stored one or more document versions in the current file.)

If you have enabled ScreenTips, placing the mouse pointer over an indicator on the status bar displays a ScreenTip describing the effect of double-clicking that indicator, as shown in this example:

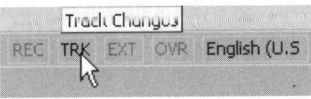

ScreenTips are also displayed when you place the pointer over a toolbar button or other type of button on the Word interface (such as a browse button or view selection button). To enable ScreenTips, choose Tools, Customize, click the Options tab in the Customize dialog box, and check the Show ScreenTips On Toolbars option. Changing this option affects other Office applications as well. If you want the ScreenTips to display the key combination for executing each command, also check Show Shortcut Keys In ScreenTips.

Table 10-3 shows what you can do with some of the other visible interface elements that are unique to Word (see Figure 10-1 for the locations of these elements).

Table 10-3. **Using Word Interface Elements**

To Do This	Use This Interface Element
Change the document margins and set the indents and tab stops for individual paragraphs, using the mouse	Ruler. To display or hide the ruler, choose View, Ruler. You can display it temporarily by moving the pointer over the horizontal gray bar at the top of the document area of the window. (See "Formatting Paragraphs with the Ruler," on page 317.)
Divide the document window into two panes	Split box. (See "Setting Up the Word Interface.")
Navigate quickly through the document by going to the next or previous browse object (page, section, target of Find command, and so on)	Browse buttons. (See "Navigating with the Browse Buttons," on page 294.)
Select a document view	View selection buttons. (See "Setting Up the Word Interface.")
Identify the end of the document in Normal or Outline view	End-of-document marker.
Open, save, or print a document; copy text or formats; obtain help; or perform other basic tasks	Standard toolbar. To display a particular toolbar, choose View, Toolbars, or right-click any toolbar or the menu bar, and then choose the name of the toolbar from the submenu or shortcut menu.
Modify the format of characters or paragraphs	Formatting toolbar. The Formatting toolbar is typical of a special-purpose Word toolbar. (See Chapter 12, "Effective Formatting in Word.")

For general information on displaying and customizing toolbars, see Chapter 9, "Customizing the Office XP Application Interface."

Setting Up the Word Interface

Chapter 9, "Customizing the Office XP Application Interface," explained how to make serious modifications to the toolbar, menu, and keyboard interface of Word or other Office applications. This section focuses on quick ways to set up the Word interface and arrange the Word tools to suit your working style, using menu commands and dialog box options. This discussion focuses on Word-specific techniques (although some of them are available in Excel or other applications).

Changing the View

You can modify the basic way that Word displays a document—as well as the way you work with it—by changing the document *view*. Table 10-4 lists the different document views, briefly describes each, and identifies the chapters in which you can find fuller discussions on each one.

Table 10-4. **Word Document Views**

View	Description	For More Information
Normal	Shows the document in a general-purpose format for efficient editing and formatting. Does not display margins, headers, or footers.	See Chapter 11, "Efficient Editing in Word"
Web Layout	Displays the document in a format that is easy to read on the screen. Ideal for previewing Web pages or for reading regular Word documents online. The text is shown without page breaks and with only minimal margins. Lines of text are wrapped to fit within the window, and any background color or image assigned to the document is visible.	See Chapter 20, "Creating Web Pages and Other Online Documents"
Print Layout	Displays text and graphics exactly as they will appear on the printed page, showing all margins, headers, and footers. All editing and formatting commands are available, but Word runs somewhat more slowly than in Normal view and scrolling is not as smooth.	See Chapter 18, "Designing and Printing Professional-Looking Pages"
Outline	Shows the organization of the document. Lets you view various levels of detail and rapidly rearrange document text.	See Chapter 15, "Managing Large or Complex Documents"
Print Preview	Displays an image of one (or more) entire printed page and lets you adjust the page setup.	See Chapter 18, "Designing and Printing Professional-Looking Pages"

To switch the view of a document to any view except Print Preview, choose the appropriate option from the View menu, as shown at the top of the next page.

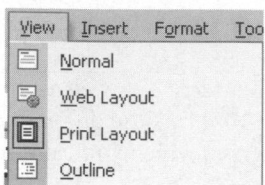

You can also switch to Normal, Web Layout, Print Layout, or Outline view by clicking a button at the left end of the horizontal scroll bar, as seen here:

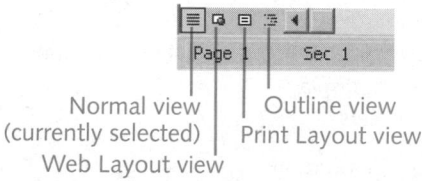

Print
Preview

If the horizontal scroll bar isn't visible, choose Tools, Options and in the Options dialog box, click the View tab (shown in Figure 10-3) and check the Horizontal Scroll Bar option. To switch to Print Preview view, choose File, Print Preview, or click the Print Preview button on the Standard toolbar. Changing the view affects only the document in the active document window; you can set the view of each open document independently.

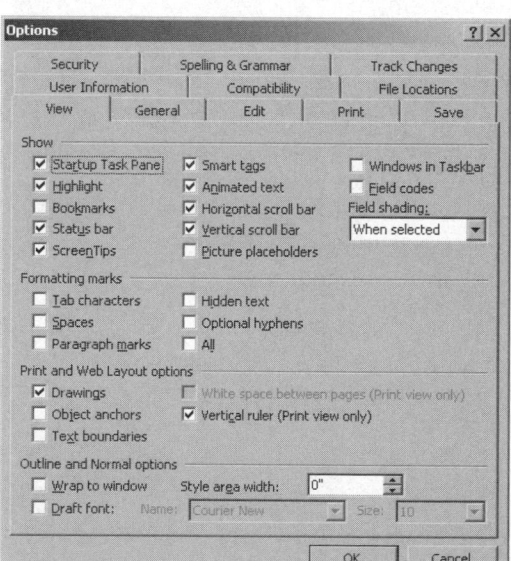

Figure 10-3. The View tab of the Options dialog box allows you to set many options that affect the Word interface. Some options affect only certain views.

> If you have several documents open at once in Word, each is displayed in a separate document window. For information on setting up and working with multiple document windows, see "Working with Multiple Documents," on page 79.

Modifying the Way Documents Are Displayed

In addition to changing the basic view, you can also set a variety of options that affect the way a document is displayed in the current view.

To divide the document window into two panes, click the split box and drag the pane divider to the desired position, as shown here:

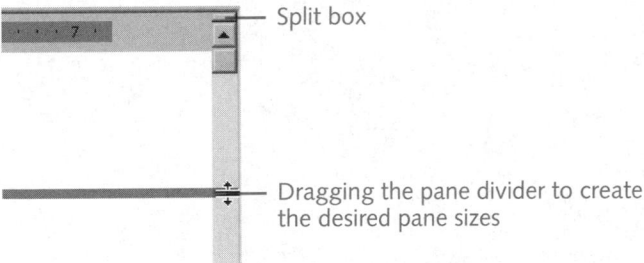

— Split box

— Dragging the pane divider to create the desired pane sizes

You can then scroll each pane independently, so that you can view and work with two portions of the document at the same time.

Troubleshooting

The Split Box Isn't Visible

You want to divide the document window into two panes but the split box isn't present.

The following are two possible reasons for the absence of the split box:

- The Document Map is displayed. You can hide (or show) the document map by choosing View, Document Map.

> For an explanation of the Document Map, see "Navigating Through an Outline," on page 426.

- The vertical scroll bar isn't visible. The split box is an integral part of this scroll bar. Display the vertical scroll by choosing Tools, Options and in the Options dialog box clicking the View tab and checking the Vertical Scroll Bar option.

To scale the characters and graphics on the screen choose View, Zoom and enter a scaling factor into the Zoom dialog box (shown in Figure 10-4). You can specify the scaling factor by typing or selecting a percentage of the normal size of the text and graphics or by selecting the Page Width, Text Width, or Whole Page zooming option. In Print Layout view, you can select the Many Pages option to display several full pages on the screen at once (as you can in Print Preview view). Click the button immediately below the Many Pages option to select the number of pages you want to display (from 1 to 24) and their arrangement. Displaying multiple pages might make it impossible to read the text, but it can be useful for examining the overall layout of a group of adjoining pages.

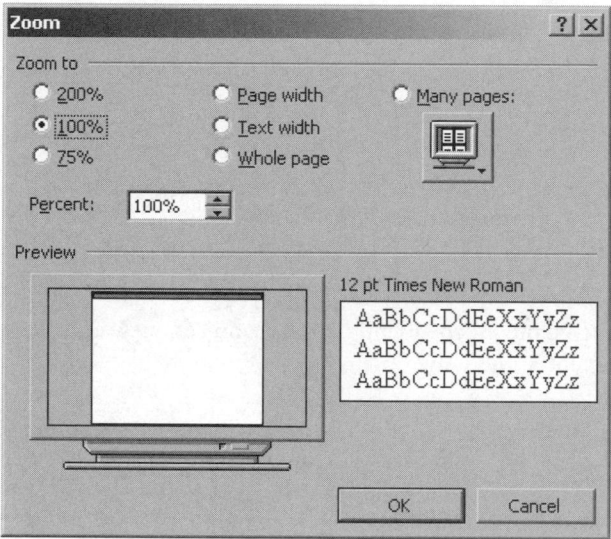

Figure 10-4.   This figure shows the Zoom dialog box as it's displayed in Print Layout view.

An alternative way to change the zooming factor is by using the Zoom drop-down list on the Standard toolbar (or on the Print Preview toolbar if you're in Print Preview view), as seen here:

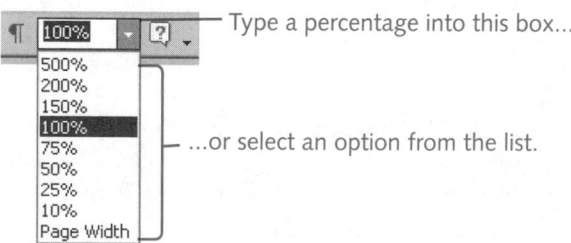

Zooming is available in all views. However, the particular zooming options that are available vary by view (the Print Layout and Print Preview views support them all). Zooming affects only the view in which you set it, so you need to set it separately for each view you work with. Rest assured that zooming does *not* change the actual size of the text or graphics that are printed and stored in the document; rather, it affects only the level of magnification at which you view the document in the window.

To expand the Word workspace to fill the entire screen—hiding all menus, toolbars, and other tools—choose View, Full Screen. You can use this command in any view. To restore the normal Word window, press the Escape key or click the Close Full Screen button that Word displays on the Full Screen toolbar, as shown here:

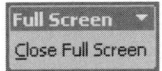

---

tip　**Access Menus and Toolbars in Full-Screen Mode**

In full-screen mode, you can temporarily display the menu bar by simply moving the mouse pointer to the top of the window. After you choose a menu command, the menu bar will disappear again.

You can also display any Word toolbar while you're in full-screen mode by right-clicking the Full Screen toolbar (or the menu bar while it's displayed) and choosing the name of the toolbar from the shortcut menu. The toolbar will remain displayed whenever you use full-screen mode.

Alternatively, to avoid cluttering up the full-screen window with additional toolbars, you can add buttons for your favorite commands directly to the Full Screen toolbar, using the methods explained in "Modifying Toolbars and Menus," on page 209.

To display all characters in the document using the same font and size, regardless of the applied formatting, you can turn on the *draft font* option. This option affects only the way the document is displayed on the screen in Normal or Outline view. It doesn't change the formatting information stored in the document, nor does it affect the way the document is printed. As soon as you turn the option off, the document goes back to its original appearance. In the days of slow computer displays, the draft font option was useful for speeding up scrolling. But even with fast displays, it has two possible uses:

● You might find it easier to type in document text if you select an easy-to-read, monospace draft font (such as Courier New) that clearly shows the number of spaces between words. You can turn off the draft font before formatting the document.

● If you have trouble reading characters on the screen, you can select a large, easy-to-read draft font to facilitate typing in text. (Although you can use zooming to increase the character size, you can't use it to switch to an easier-to-read font.)

To switch on the draft font option, choose Tools, Options and in the Options dialog box, click the View tab, check the Draft Font option, and select a character font and size for the draft font in the Name and Size drop-down lists, as shown here:

---

tip **Prevent Eye Strain by Using the Blue Background, White Text Option**

You can have Word display document text in white characters on a blue background by clicking the General tab in the Options dialog box and checking the Blue Background, White Text option. This option affects all views except Print Preview and can help prevent eye strain. (Some Microsoft Windows users find looking at a white screen similar to trying to read the wattage on a burning light bulb.)

Troubleshooting

Document Is Too Wide to View

The lines in your Word document are too wide to view within the Word window, so you have to scroll horizontally to read each line.

This problem might crop up if you've formatted your document with wide lines, or if you're using a low graphics resolution (typical with a notebook computer or a computer with a small monitor). The following are several ways to alleviate or remove the problem:

- First, be sure to maximize the Word program window and hide any task pane that's currently displayed.

- You can gain a little more window width by choosing Full Screen from the View menu to work in full-screen mode.

- If you're using Normal or Outline view, you can have Word wrap all lines so that they fit within the current window width. To do this, choose Tools, Options, click the View tab, and check the Wrap To Window option in the Outline And Normal Options area near the bottom of the dialog box.

- You can switch to the Web Layout view, which always wraps lines so they fit within the window.

- In any view, you can scale the size of the text on the screen so that the lines just fit within the width of the window by selecting the appropriate option in the Zoom drop-down list on the Standard toolbar, or in the Zoom dialog box (opened by choosing View, Zoom). In Normal or Outline view, the appropriate option is Page Width. In Print Layout view, the appropriate option is Text Width. Web Layout view doesn't have an option for fitting the lines to the screen, but zooming isn't necessary because this view always wraps lines to fit.

Creating, Opening, and Saving Word Documents

Chapter 4, "Working with Office XP Applications, Documents, and Program Windows," discussed the different ways to create, open, and save documents in Word and other Office applications. The remainder of this chapter explains some of the techniques and options that are specific to Word.

When you first display the Open or Save As dialog box to open or save a Word document, it normally displays the contents of your My Documents folder. However, you can change the folder that's initially displayed in these dialog boxes by choosing Tools, Options, clicking the File Locations tab in the Options dialog box, selecting the Documents item in the list, and clicking the Modify button (see Figure 10-5).

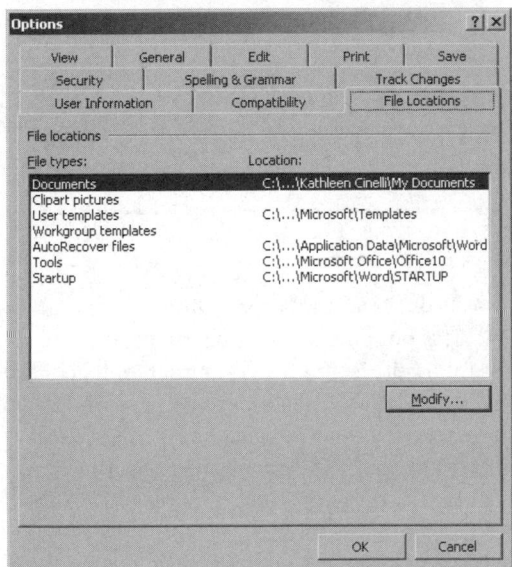

Figure 10-5.   The File Locations tab of the Options dialog box allows you to change the default folder displayed in the Open and Save As dialog boxes.

You can change the way Word saves documents by selecting options in the Save tab of the Options dialog box (shown in Figure 10-6). To change the default format that Word displays in the Save As Type list in the Save As dialog box, select a format in the Save Word Files As drop-down list in the Save tab.

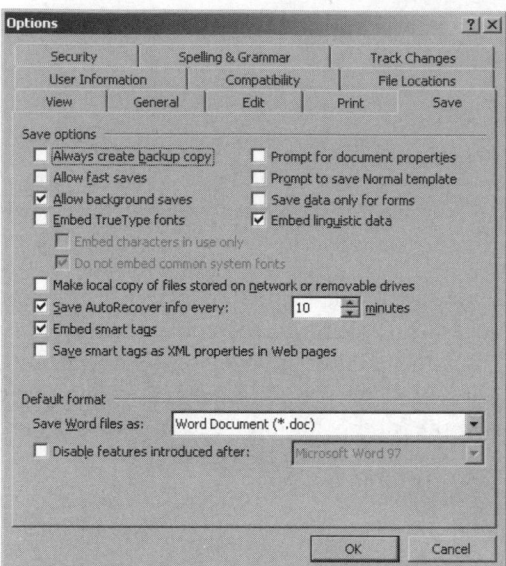

Figure 10-6. The Save tab of the Options dialog box allows you to change the way Word saves documents.

InsideOut

The Allow Fast Saves option causes Word to use a faster—although less safe—method for saving your documents to disk. This option may have been useful in the days of slow computers, but now it's best to disable it. If a fast save operation is interrupted (by a power outage, for example), your document can become severely corrupted. With a reasonably fast computer—especially if you enable background saves (by checking the Allow Background Saves option)—fast saves aren't needed. You can access the Allow Fast Saves and Allow Background Saves options in the Save tab of the Options dialog box.

Converting Groups of Files

Chapter 4, "Working with Office XP Applications, Documents, and Program Windows," explained how to convert files in various formats to Office XP documents and how to convert Office XP documents to other formats.

In Word, you can use the Conversion Wizard to efficiently convert an entire group of files to Word 2002 format, or to convert a group of Word 2002 files to another format. The Conversion Wizard eliminates the need to separately open and convert each file. The files that you convert must all be contained in the same folder.

Chapter 10: Word Fundamentals

To convert files, choose File, New, click the General Templates command in the New Document task pane, click the Other Documents tab in the Templates dialog box, and double-click the Batch Conversion Wizard item. Then, complete the dialog boxes displayed by the Conversion Wizard (shown in Figure 10-7). You'll need to specify the format you want to covert to or from, the source and destination folders, and the specific files to be converted.

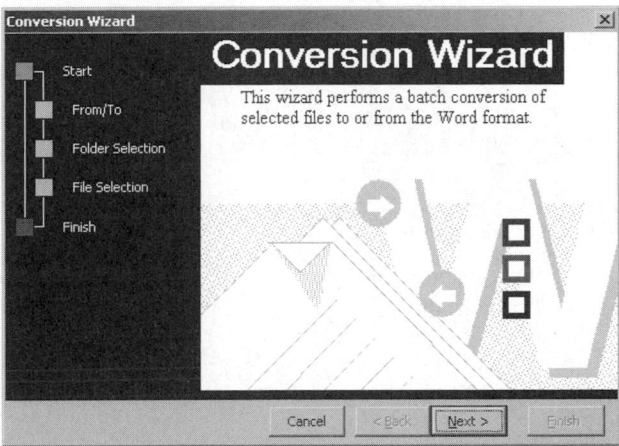

Figure 10-7. This is the opening dialog box displayed by Word's Conversion Wizard.

Storing Different Document Versions

You can use Word's Versions command to store several separate versions of a document, all within a single document file. Say, for example, that you have written Chapter 1 for your latest novel, and you saved the current version in a file named Chapter1. You now want to revise the chapter, but you also want to keep the original version intact so that you can refer back to it if necessary. Without the Versions command, you would have to save the current version in a separate file. Using the Versions command, however, you can save a copy of the current document version right within the Chapter1.doc file, so that you can easily refer back to it later and avoid having to keep track of separate files.

To do this, choose File, Versions (or double-click the Versions indicator in the status bar if it's present) and in the Versions dialog box, click the Save Now button. Word will prompt you to add a descriptive comment for the version. You can then proceed to revise your chapter and save your work in the usual way. Now, both versions of the document will be stored within the Chapter1.doc file. However, when you open the document you won't see the original version unless you again choose Versions from the File menu and use the Versions dialog box to open the original version in a separate window, as shown in Figure 10-8. You can use this technique to store additional document versions within the same document file.

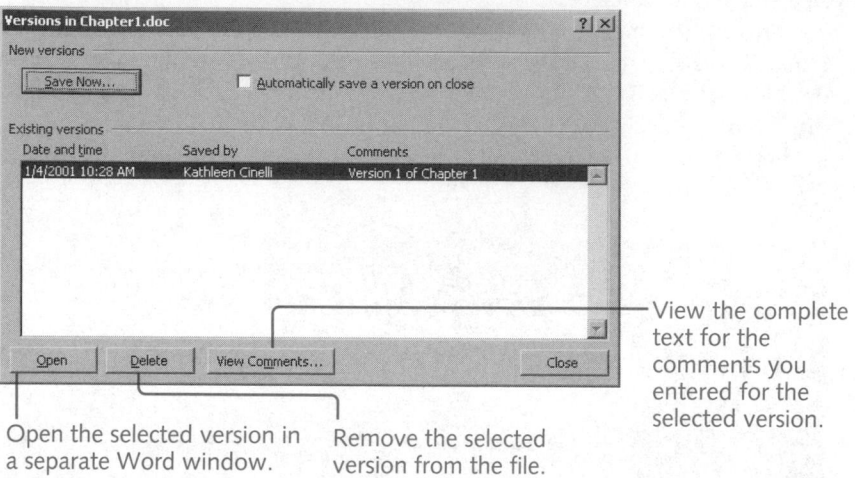

View the complete text for the comments you entered for the selected version.

Open the selected version in a separate Word window.

Remove the selected version from the file.

Figure 10-8. You can use the Versions dialog box to work with separate document versions stored in a single document file.

Chapter 11

Efficient Editing in Word

Adding Text

This chapter focuses on the *content* of a Microsoft Word 2002 document—that is, the characters, words, sentences, and paragraphs that compose a document. You'll learn about the many ways to add, edit, find, and navigate through document text. The next chapter focuses on the *format* of a Word document—that is, the appearance of the characters and paragraphs. These two topics are treated separately to make your learning task easier, not to imply that you must finish editing the entire document before you begin formatting it. Typically, you will use formatting techniques as you are entering and editing the text.

To enter text, simply move the insertion point to the desired location in the document and type the text. Word provides two editing modes: *Insert* and *Overtype*. In Insert mode (the most common mode), any existing characters beyond the insertion point are moved ahead in the document as you type. In Overtype mode, the new characters you type replace any existing characters. When Overtype mode is active, the OVR indicator on the status bar is darkened. To switch between the two modes, double-click the OVR indicator. You can also use the Insert key to do this, provided that the Use The INS Key For Paste option isn't checked (to access this option, choose Tools, Options, and then click the Edit tab).

For a description of the techniques for moving the insertion point, see "Positioning the Insertion Point," on page 267.

> **tip** **Create a New Line Within a Paragraph**
>
> To create a new line within a paragraph, press Shift+Enter. Why not just press Enter and create a new paragraph? Some paragraph formatting affects only the first or last line of the paragraph, such as an initial indent or additional space above or below the paragraph. By pressing Shift+Enter, you can create a new line without introducing this formatting. The section "Combining Text with Graphic Objects and Text Boxes," on page 515 explains how to add a *text wrapping* line break, which causes the following line to be moved below an adjoining text box or graphic object.

Pressing Enter creates a new paragraph. Word marks the end of each paragraph by inserting a *paragraph mark*. A paragraph mark (¶) is one of the nonprinting characters that can be contained in a Word document. Nonprinting characters never appear on the final printed copy of the document. Normally, they are also invisible on the screen. You can, however, make them visible on the screen by clicking the Show/Hide ¶ button on the Standard toolbar. The following is an example of some document text on the screen after nonprinting characters have been made visible:

¶

Show
/Hide ¶

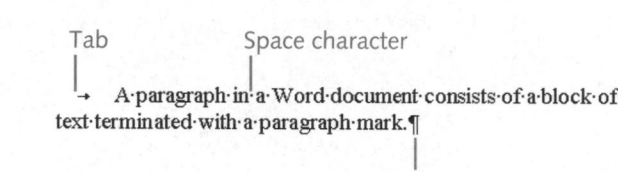

Tab   Space character

→ A·paragraph·in·a·Word·document·consists·of·a·block·of·
text·terminated·with·a·paragraph·mark.¶

Paragraph mark

> **caution**   Avoid deleting a paragraph mark unintentionally. (It can be deleted whether or not it's visible.) Deleting this mark will merge the paragraphs on either side of the mark, and any paragraph formatting assigned to the second paragraph will be lost. (Paragraph formatting is discussed in Chapter 12, "Effective Formatting in Word.")

You can also display or hide specific nonprinting characters by choosing Tools, Options, clicking the View tab, and selecting the appropriate options in the Formatting Marks area.

Inserting Symbols and Foreign Characters

You can use the Symbol dialog box to insert into your text a variety of symbols and foreign characters that you won't find on your keyboard. To insert a symbol or foreign character at the current position of the insertion point, perform the following steps:

1 Choose Insert, Symbol to open the Symbol dialog box.

2 Click the Symbols tab (shown in Figure 11-1) if it is not already displayed.

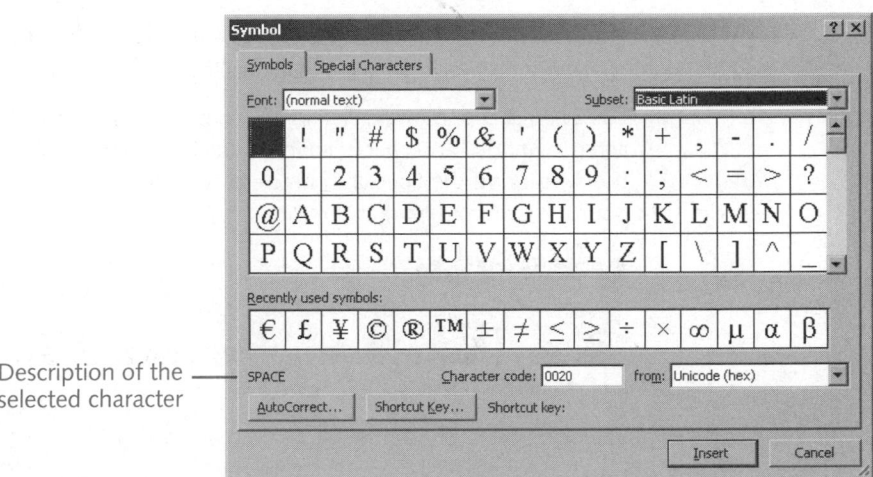

Description of the ———— selected character

Figure 11-1. The Symbols tab of the Symbol dialog box lets you find and insert any of the characters belonging to your installed fonts.

3 In the character list, double-click the character you want to insert. Or, select the character by clicking it and then click the Insert button. The symbol will appear in your document at the position of the insertion point, just as if you had typed it. The following tips will help you find the character you want:

- If you don't find the character you want in the list, or if you'd prefer to enter a character using a different font, select a different font name in the Font drop-down list. This will display all the characters belonging to that font. The (normal text) item at the beginning of the list of fonts displays the set of characters belonging to the font at the current position of the insertion point in your document. The following are special *symbol fonts* that contain only symbols, and not the ordinary keyboard characters (such as a, A, 1, !, and so on): Marlett, MS Outlook, MT Extra, Symbol, Webdings, Wingdings, Wingdings 2, and Wingdings 3.

- You can scroll through the character list to view additional characters, or—for a font that isn't a symbol font—you can go immediately to a particular character group by choosing an item (such as Basic Greek, General Punctuation, or Mathematical Operators) in the Subset drop-down list box.

- If you've selected a font that isn't a symbol font and want to see the full set of characters belonging to that font, make sure that the Unicode (Hex) item is selected in the From drop-down list in the lower right corner of the Symbols tab. Selecting the ASCII (Decimal) or the ASCII (Hex) item will display only the first part of the character set (namely, the font's ASCII character set, which consists of less than 255 visible characters).

Chapter 11

247

■ You can reuse a character that you recently inserted by double-clicking an item in the Recently Used Symbols area.

■ You can insert one of a collection of commonly used punctuation characters, symbols, and special space characters from the Symbol dialog box by clicking the Special Characters tab (shown in Figure 11-2) and double-clicking an item in the list.

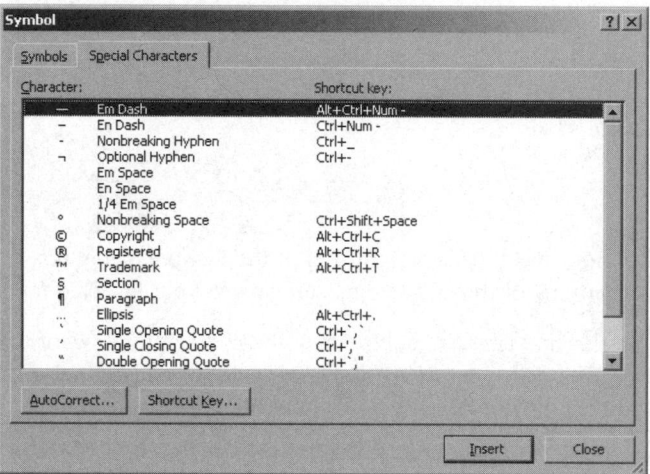

Figure 11-2. The Special Characters tab of the Symbol dialog box allows you to insert commonly used special characters in a document.

4 After you have inserted the symbols you need, click the Close button to close the dialog box.

note In Word 2002 you can resize the Symbol dialog box by dragging an edge or corner.

You can also use the keyboard to insert any of the characters displayed in the Symbol dialog box's Symbols tab.

For a character belonging to a symbol font, you'll have to define your own shortcut key as explained in the tip "Set Up Shortcut Keys for Symbols You Frequently Use," on page 250.

Word provides built-in shortcut keys for all characters belonging to the regular character fonts. When you select a character from one of these fonts that can't be typed on the keyboard, the shortcut key for inserting the character is displayed following the Shortcut Key label near the bottom of the dialog box, as shown at the top of the next page.

Chapter 11: Efficient Editing in Word

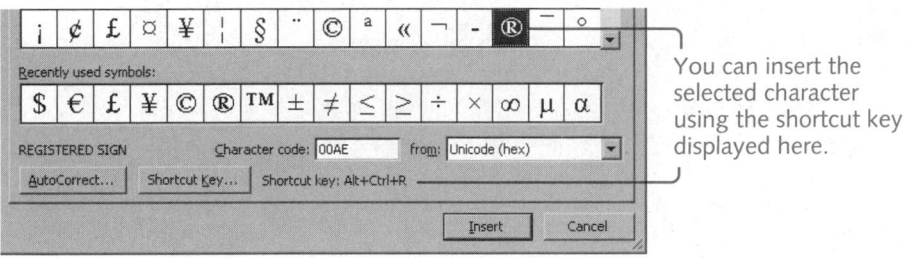

You can insert the selected character using the shortcut key displayed here.

Table 11-1 gives examples of the different kinds of shortcut keys displayed following the Shortcut Key label, and how you would type each one. Make sure that Num Lock is on before you try to use the Keypad numbers.

Table 11-1. Examples of Shortcut Key Descriptions and How You Type Them

Shortcut Key Description Displayed After the Shortcut Key Label	Character Inserted	How to Type the Shortcut Key
Alt+Ctrl+C	©	Press Alt, Ctrl, and C simultaneously.
Alt+Ctrl+!	¡	Press Alt, Ctrl, Shift, and 1 simultaneously (you need to press Shift to type ! rather than 1).
Alt+0163	£	Hold down Alt and type **0163** on the numeric keypad with NumLock on. The character will be inserted when you release the Alt key.
Ctrl+/, C	¢	Press Ctrl and / simultaneously. Release both keys. Then, press C.
03A3, Alt+X	Σ	Type **03A3**. Then, press Alt and X simultaneously. (The number you type is the Unicode value for the character in hexadecimal. This type of shortcut key lets you insert a character that isn't included in the standard ASCII set, a new feature of Word 2002.)

Of course, once the Symbol dialog box is open you could just insert the character by double-clicking it. However, for a symbol or foreign character that you use frequently, you can learn the keystroke and use it in the future to quickly insert the character without having to open the Symbol dialog box.

note The Symbol dialog box's Symbols tab displays the character code for the selected character in the Character Code text box. The code is displayed in decimal if a *decimal* item is selected in the adjoining From drop-down list, such as ASCII (Decimal). It's displayed in hexadecimal if a *hex* item is selected in the From list, such as Unicode (Hex). To select a particular character, you can type its code into the Character Code box (use decimal or hexadecimal according to the current selection in the From list).

tip   **Set Up Shortcut Keys for Symbols You Frequently Use**

You can define your own shortcut key for a character in a symbol font (such as Symbol or Wingdings) or an alternative shortcut key for a character in a regular character font. To do this, in the Symbol dialog box, click the Symbols tab, select the character in the list, and click the Shortcut Key button. This will display the Customize Keyboard dialog box, which is explained in "Defining Shortcut Keys (Word Only)," on page 217.

You can also define a character or group of characters—such as "(ae)"—that Word will automatically replace with a specified symbol—such as æ. To do this, in the Symbols tab, select the symbol you want to use as the replacement and click the AutoCorrect button. The AutoCorrect feature is explained in "Automatically Fixing Your Text with AutoCorrect," on page 258.

For information on entering symbols using an on-screen symbol keyboard, together with a pen and electronic tablet, or a mouse, see "Using the On-Screen Keyboards," on page 108.

Inserting the Date and Time

To insert the current date, the current time, or both into your document, perform the following steps:

1 Choose Insert, Date And Time, to open the Date And Time dialog box (shown in Figure 11-3).

2 Select the desired date or time format in the Available Formats list.

3 To have the date or time automatically updated whenever you print the document, check Update Automatically. If this option isn't checked, the date or time remains the same as it was when you inserted it.

Chapter 11: Efficient Editing in Word

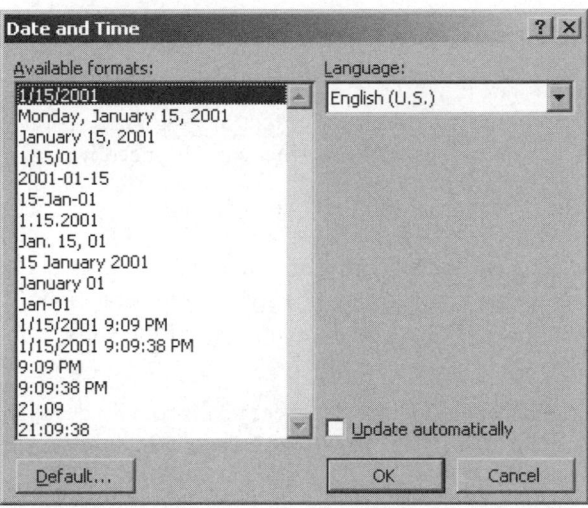

Figure 11-3. You can insert the current date or time using the Date And Time dialog box.

4 To have your current settings in the Date And Time dialog box displayed by default the next time you open the dialog box, click the Default button.

5 Click the OK button.

Replaying Your Editing Actions with the Repeat Command

If you've just typed a block of text, you can have Word insert that same text at any location in a document. Perform the following steps:

1 Type the original text.

2 Move the insertion point to the location where you want to repeat the text (in the same Word document or in a different Word document).

3 Choose Edit, Repeat Typing, or press Ctrl+Y or F4. Word will automatically insert the text you originally typed. You can do this repeatedly to insert multiple copies of this text.

Undo

If you don't like the result, you can reverse it by immediately choosing Edit, Undo Typing, pressing Ctrl+Z, or clicking the Undo button on the Standard toolbar. (The Undo command is described later in the chapter.)

note Repeat Typing is only one example of how the Repeat command can be used. The Repeat command repeats any editing or formatting action, not simply text that you have typed. As explained later in the chapter, this command will also redo an action that you have just reversed by using the Undo command.

251

Reusing Text with the AutoText Feature

A second way to automate the insertion of text is to use the AutoText feature, which allows you to save commonly used blocks of text or graphics as *AutoText entries* and lets you quickly insert one of these blocks wherever you need it.

To create an AutoText entry, perform the following steps:

1 Type into a document the block of text that you want to save. (Typing the text into a paragraph that has the same style as the paragraphs in which you'll later use the text can make it easier to insert the entry from the AutoText submenu, as you'll see later.)

2 Select the block of text. One way to select text is to hold down the Shift key while pressing the appropriate arrow key. Selection methods are discussed later in the chapter.

3 Choose Insert, AutoText, New. Alternatively, you can press Alt+F3. Word will display the Create AutoText dialog box.

4 Type a name for your AutoText entry into the text box and click OK. Word proposes a name based on the selected text, but you'll probably want to invent a name of your own. If you type the name of an existing entry, Word will ask whether you want to redefine that entry; click Yes to replace the original text for the entry or No to choose a new name.

To make it faster to insert your entry, you might want to use one of these two approaches:

■ Enter a short name so you can type it in quickly when you want to insert the text (for example, **w** for an entry containing the text "World Wide Web").

or

■ Enter a fully descriptive name, but make sure that the first four letters are different from the first four letters of any of your other AutoText entries (later in the chapter, you will see how to view the list of your AutoText entries). Then, the AutoComplete feature (explained later) will let you quickly insert the entry after typing just the first four letters of the name. For example, if you assigned the name "hypertext" to an entry containing the text "Hypertext Markup Language," you could insert the entry by typing **hype**, provided that no other AutoText entry begins with those letters.

Figure 11-4 shows an example.

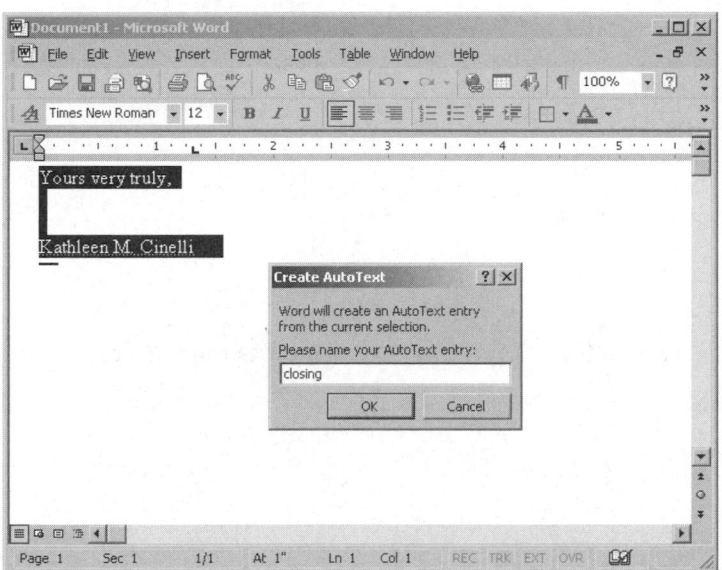

Figure 11-4. In this example, a standard letter closing is stored as an AutoText entry named "closing."

After you create an AutoText entry, it is stored permanently. You can insert an AutoText entry into a document by performing the following steps:

1 Place the insertion point at the position in your document where you want to insert the text.

2 Type the name of the AutoText entry as a separate word. This means that you must type the name at the beginning of a line or following a space, tab, or punctuation symbol. The case of the letters you type doesn't matter. You need type only a sufficient number of characters to distinguish the name from the names of all other AutoText entries.

3 Press F3 or Ctrl+Alt+V. Word will immediately replace the entry name with the entry text. For example, if you had defined the AutoText entry shown in Figure 11-4, at the end of a letter you could simply press Enter, type **closing** (or perhaps just **cl** if none of the names of your other entries begins with those letters), and then press F3 or Ctrl+Alt+V, as seen here:

I am looking forward to hearing from you soon.

closing

Press F3 or Ctrl+Alt+V here.

Word would replace the word "closing" with your standard letter closing, as shown here:

I am looking forward to hearing from you soon.

Yours very truly,

Kathleen M. Cinelli

---

tip   **Use AutoComplete to Insert AutoText Entries and Dates More Quickly**

If the Show AutoComplete Suggestions option is checked, as you begin typing an AutoText entry name into a document, Word displays the entry text (or at least part of the text) in a box near the insertion point. The box appears as soon as you have typed at least four characters and enough of the name to identify the entry. You can then insert the entry text by simply pressing Enter (or the usual F3 or Ctrl+Alt+V shortcut key) without typing the complete entry name. If Show AutoComplete Suggestions is on, you can also have Word complete partially typed dates using the same method. To turn this option on or off, choose Insert, AutoText, AutoText. In the AutoText tab, check or clear the Show AutoComplete Suggestions check box. (The AutoText tab is located within the AutoCorrect dialog box, discussed in the following section.)

As an alternative to steps 2 and 3, you can insert an AutoText entry by choosing it from the Insert menu's AutoText submenu, seen here:

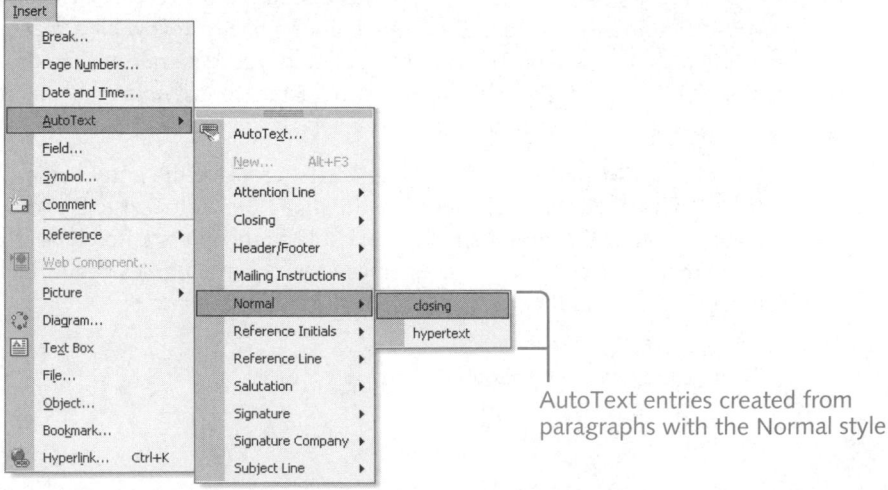

AutoText entries created from paragraphs with the Normal style

The AutoText submenu lists all AutoText entries you have defined. Each entry is placed on a submenu labeled according to the style of the paragraph from which the entry was originally obtained; for example, if you created an entry by selecting text in a paragraph with the Normal style, the entry is placed on a submenu labeled Normal. (This arrangement helps you locate entries that are relevant to the type of paragraph you're currently working on.)

The AutoText submenu also displays a large collection of entries defined by Word, grouped on submenus named according to their functions (for example, Attention Line, Salutation, and Signature). To get the most use out of the predefined AutoText entries, be sure to check the Show AutoComplete Suggestions option, described in the tip "Use AutoComplete to Insert AutoText Entries and Dates More Quickly," on page 254. Then, as you type documents, an AutoComplete suggestion occasionally pops up for one of these entries, as shown here, allowing you to save a little typing.

```
Yours truly, (Press ENTER to Insert)
        Your
```

Note, however, that if the insertion point is currently in a paragraph with a style other than Normal, and if you created one or more AutoText entries from paragraphs having that style, the AutoText submenu lists only entries created from paragraphs with the same style. In this case, if you want to see all AutoText entries, hold down the Shift key when you open the AutoText submenu.

> **tip** **Change the Text for an AutoText Entry**
>
> To modify the contents of an AutoText entry without having to delete it and reenter it, insert the entry text into the document (using one of the methods just described), make the changes you want, and then use the procedure given at the beginning of this section to save the text again as an AutoText entry, using its original name. You must answer Yes when Word asks whether you want to redefine the entry.

Using the AutoText Tab of the AutoCorrect Dialog Box

You can use the AutoText tab of the AutoCorrect dialog box to create AutoText entries, to view their contents, or to delete them. You can open this tab using either of the following methods:

- Choose Insert, AutoText, AutoText.

   or

- Choose Tools, AutoCorrect Options. In the AutoCorrect dialog box click the AutoText tab. (The other tabs in the AutoCorrect dialog box are discussed later in the book.)

To create an AutoText entry using the AutoText tab, perform the following steps:

1   Select the document text you want to save.

2   Display the AutoText tab using one of the methods just given.

3   Type a name for the AutoText entry into the Enter AutoText Entries Here text box. Note that if you type the same name as an existing entry, the existing entry will be overwritten.

4   In the Look In drop-down list, select the template in which you want to store the AutoText entry. If you select All Active Templates or Normal.dot (Global Template), the Normal template will store the entry and all Word documents will have access to it. If the current document is attached to a template other than Normal, and if you select the name of that template in the Look In drop-down list, then the attached template will store the entry and it will be available only to documents attached to this same template.

Chapter 14, "Advanced Word Formatting Techniques," explains how templates are attached to documents and shows how to copy AutoText entries from one template to another, as well as how to rename entries.

Note that your selection in this list also affects the location where AutoText entries are subsequently stored when you create entries using the Insert, AutoText, New command, as described in the previous section.

5   Click the Add button.

Figure 11-5 shows a completed AutoText tab just before the Add button is clicked.

To view the contents of an AutoText entry or to delete or insert an entry, perform the following steps:

1   Display the AutoText tab using one of the methods given previously.

2   Select a template in the Look In drop-down list. Word will list only the AutoText entries stored in the template you select. Note that if you choose All Active Templates, Word will list all entries stored in the Normal template, in the template attached to the document (if other than Normal), and in any other loaded templates.

Your selection in the Look In drop-down list also affects the AutoText entries that are subsequently displayed on the Insert menu's AutoText submenu, as well as those that are displayed by the AutoText toolbar, which is described in the next section.

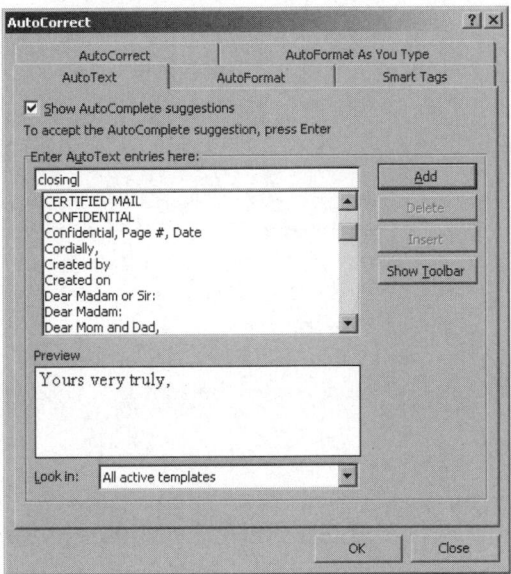

Figure 11-5. You can create an AutoText entry using the AutoText tab of the AutoCorrect dialog box.

3 Select the name of an AutoText entry in the Enter AutoText Entries Here list. You can now do one of the following:

- You can view the current contents of the entry in the Preview area.

- You can delete the entry by clicking the Delete button.

- You can insert the entry into your document by clicking the Insert button. (The advantage of inserting an entry from the AutoCorrect dialog box is that it allows you to preview the contents of any entry immediately before you insert it.)

Displaying the AutoText Toolbar

If you use AutoText frequently, you can save time by displaying the AutoText toolbar, shown in Figure 11-6. To display it, choose View, Toolbars, AutoText. You can also display the toolbar by clicking the Show Toolbar button in the AutoText tab, described in the previous section.

AutoText

Figure 11-6. The AutoText toolbar can save you time in working with AutoText.

Chapter 11

257

You can work with the AutoText toolbar as follows:

- To display the AutoText tab of the AutoCorrect dialog box, click the AutoText button.

- To insert an AutoText entry, click the All Entries button and choose an entry from the menu.

> **note** If the insertion point is currently in a paragraph with a style other than Normal, and if you created one or more AutoText entries from paragraphs having that style, the middle button on the AutoText toolbar is labeled with the name of the paragraph style rather than All Entries, and it lists only entries created from paragraphs with the same style. If you want to see all AutoText entries, hold down the Shift key while clicking the middle button.

- To create a new AutoText entry, select the text or graphics in your document and click the New button. This displays the Create AutoText dialog box, shown in Figure 11-4.

Automatically Fixing Your Text with AutoCorrect

A final way to automate text insertion is to use the AutoCorrect feature, which is similar to the AutoText feature. The primary difference between the two is that after you've typed the name of an AutoCorrect entry followed by a space or a punctuation symbol, Word automatically replaces the name with the entry text; you don't need to press a special key or issue a command. Thus, you might want to use AutoCorrect rather than AutoText for text that you insert frequently. You can also have AutoCorrect perform certain general text replacements; for example, you can have it automatically capitalize the first letter of a sentence if you fail to do so.

To enable AutoCorrect text replacements and define one or more AutoCorrect entries, perform the following steps:

1 If the text or graphics you want to save in the AutoCorrect entry has already been entered in a document, select it. (If the content you want to save consists of text only, this step is optional because you can type in text later.)

2 Choose Tools, AutoCorrect Options to open the AutoCorrect dialog box. Click the AutoCorrect tab if it isn't already displayed.

3 Make sure the Replace Text As You Type option is checked to activate the AutoCorrect entries.

4 In the Replace text box, type a name for the AutoCorrect entry you want to define. Keep in mind that whenever you subsequently type this name into a document, followed by a space or a punctuation symbol, Word will automatically insert the AutoCorrect entry content.

> **caution** Make sure that the name you choose for an AutoCorrect entry is not a word that you might need to type into a document. For example, if you assigned the name *a*, each time you tried to enter the word *a* into a document, Word would insert the associated AutoCorrect entry. Also, if you type the name in capital letters, you will always have to type it in capital letters for Word to insert the AutoCorrect entry.

5 If you selected text or graphics prior to opening the AutoCorrect dialog box, that content will already be contained in the With text box. To save your selected content without including its formatting, select the Plain Text option above the With box. To save the selected content together with its formatting, select the Formatted Text option.

6 If you didn't select content, type the text for the entry into the With box.

7 Click the Add button (or the Replace button if the entry name has already been used) to define the new entry and to add it to the list. Figure 11-7 shows the AutoCorrect dialog box after a new entry has been defined.

The list in the AutoCorrect tab displays the AutoCorrect entries that have already been defined. Notice that the list initially contains a collection of useful predefined entries for inserting frequently used symbols (for example, *(c)* will be replaced with ©) and correcting common spelling errors and typos (for example, *acheive* will be replaced with *achieve*, and *hte* with *the*).

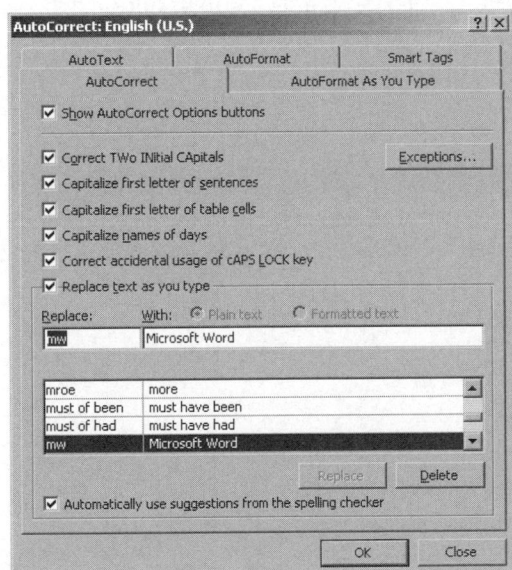

Figure 11-7. This figure shows the AutoCorrect tab after a new entry named *mw* has been added.

8 To remove an AutoText entry, click on it in the list and then click the Delete button.

9 To define an additional entry, repeat steps 4 through 7. When you're finished adding AutoCorrect entries, click the OK button to save your entries and close the dialog box.

---

tip   **Create an AutoCorrect Entry for a Symbol**

As mentioned in the tip "Set Up Shortcut Keys for Symbols You Frequently Use," on page 250, in the Symbol dialog box (which you can open by choosing Insert, Symbol), you can select a symbol and then click the AutoCorrect button to quickly create an AutoCorrect entry for that symbol.

After you have performed these steps, Word will immediately replace the name of the AutoCorrect entry you defined with the entry text whenever you type the name followed by a space, tab, punctuation character, or line break (inserted by pressing Enter or Shift+Enter). Note that you must type the entry name as a separate word; that is, the word must immediately follow a space, tab, or punctuation character, or be typed at the beginning of a line. For example, if you had defined the entry shown in Figure 11-7, typing **mw** followed by a space would cause Word to erase the "mw" and insert "Microsoft Word" in its place.

You can also have Word perform several kinds of general text replacements by checking one or more of the options in the upper part of the AutoCorrect dialog box. For example, if you check the Correct TWo INitial CApitals option, whenever you type a word beginning with two capital letters (with the rest of the characters lowercase), Word will automatically correct the error by converting the second letter to lowercase. If you select the second option (Capitalize First Letter Of Sentences), Word will automatically capitalize the first letter of a sentence if you fail to do so.

To add or delete exceptions to corrections made by the Capitalize First Letter Of Sentences or Correct TWo INitial CApitals options, click the Exceptions button in the AutoCorrect dialog box. Word will display the AutoCorrect Exceptions dialog box, shown here:

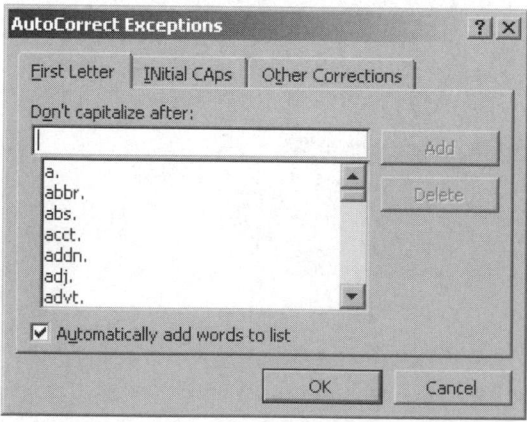

In the AutoCorrect Exceptions dialog box, you can do the following:

● The Capitalize First Letter Of Sentences option normally capitalizes a word that comes after an abbreviation ending in a period, because a period usually ends a sentence. To prevent Word from capitalizing a word that comes after a specific abbreviation ending in a period, click the First Letter tab, type the abbreviation—including the period—into the Don't Capitalize After text box, and click the Add button. (Notice that the list initially includes quite a few predefined exceptions.) To remove an exception, click on it and then click the Delete button.

● To specify a word containing two initial capital letters (such as *POs* for *purchase orders*) that you don't want the Correct TWo INitial CApitals option to correct, click the INitial CAps tab, type the word into the Don't Correct text box, and click the Add button. To remove an exception, click on it and then click the Delete button.

● To add a word to your default custom spelling dictionary, so that the spelling checker will no longer flag the word, click the Other Corrections tab, type the word into the Don't Correct text box, and click the Add button. To remove a word from the custom dictionary, click on it in the list and then click the Delete button.

For information on custom spelling dictionaries, see "Using Custom Dictionaries," on page 483.

InsideOut

The Other Corrections tab, which affects the spelling checker and not AutoCorrect, is rather misplaced and confusing. In fact, if your Replace Text As You Type list in the AutoCorrect tab contains an entry for correcting a misspelling (for example, replacing *colour* with *color*), entering *colour* into the Other Corrections tab will stop the spelling checker from flagging that word, but it *won't* prevent AutoText from making the replacement. To stop the AutoText replacements, you'll have to delete the AutoCorrect entry.

● To have Word automatically add words to the First Letter or the INitial CAps exceptions list, check the Automatically Add Words To List option in any of the tabs. Then, if the Capitalize First Letter Of Sentences or the Correct TWo INitial CApitals option makes a correction, and you reverse that correction by issuing the Undo command or by backspacing and retyping, Word will automatically add the word to the corresponding exceptions list.

In the AutoCorrect tab, if the Show AutoCorrect Options Buttons option is checked, Word 2002 lets you modify an AutoCorrect correction using the new AutoCorrect Options button. After AutoCorrect has made a correction, use this button as follows:

1 Move the mouse pointer (or the insertion point) to the text that AutoCorrect has inserted. A bar will appear below the left end of the text indicating that an options button is available, as shown here:

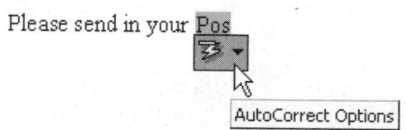

2 Move the pointer over the bar. The AutoCorrect Options button then appears, as seen here:

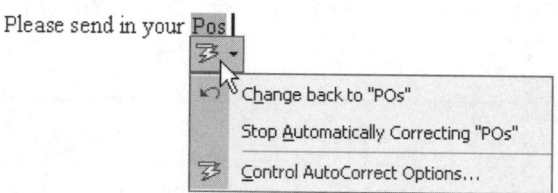

3 Click the button and choose a command from the drop-down menu shown here:

Please send in your Pos |

Change back to "POs"

Stop Automatically Correcting "POs"

Control AutoCorrect Options...

■ To reverse the correction, choose the Change Back... command. (The full wording of the command depends on the correction AutoCorrect made.)

■ To prevent AutoCorrect from making similar corrections in the future, choose the Stop... command. The wording of the command depends on the particular type of correction AutoCorrect made. Choosing the command either turns off the corresponding AutoCorrect option or adds an exception to the appropriate exception list.

■ To open the AutoCorrect tab of the AutoCorrect dialog box, choose Control AutoCorrect Options.

4 If you later change your mind about reversing an AutoCorrect correction, you can reopen the drop-down menu and choose Redo AutoCorrect.

> **tip** **Use AutoCorrect to Correct Your Spelling**
>
> The collection of AutoCorrect entries predefined by Word includes many that correct common misspellings (such as *accomodate*, *acheive*, and *embarass*). Additionally, when you use the Spelling And Grammar command to check your spelling, whenever Word finds a spelling error, you can quickly create an AutoCorrect entry that will automatically correct that error in the future.
>
> In the AutoCorrect tab, if you check the Automatically Use Suggestions From The Spelling Checker option (shown in Figure 11-7), whenever you misspell a word, Word will immediately replace it with a word from the spelling checker's suggestion list rather than simply marking the misspelling with a wavy red underline. This feature works, however, only if there is a *single* word on the suggestion list. Also, the as-you-type spelling checker must be turned on (choose Tools, Options; click the Spelling & Grammar tab; and check the Check Spelling As You Type option).

For information on the spelling checker and on using its suggestions for AutoCorrect, see "Checking Spelling," on page 475.

newfeature!
Using Smart Tags

The most recent previous versions of Word have been able to recognize hyperlinks and e-mail addresses contained in a Microsoft Office document and have performed an appropriate action when you click on the data (namely, opening the target document of a hyperlink or sending an e-mail message). Word 2002 has greatly extended this type of capability with the introduction of *smart tags*. Word can now recognize a wide range of different data types entered into a document (such as names, dates, addresses, and stock ticker symbols). It converts each recognized piece of data into a smart tag, and you can then use a menu attached to the smart tag to perform useful actions on that data, automatically invoking the required Microsoft Windows program. For instance, for a smart tag containing a person's name, you could open the Microsoft Outlook Contacts item for that person or send the person an e-mail message. For a stock ticker symbol marked as a smart tag, you could connect to the Internet and view the current stock price. The particular types of data that Word can convert to smart tags depend on the specific smart tag *recognizers* installed on your computer and activated in Word. Smart tag recognizers are included with Office, and additional recognizers can be obtained from various third-party companies or developers.

To enable smart tags in Word and to activate one or more specific smart tag recognizers, perform the following steps:

1   Choose Tools, AutoCorrect Options.

2   In the AutoCorrect dialog box, click the Smart Tags tab (shown in Figure 11-8).

Chapter 11

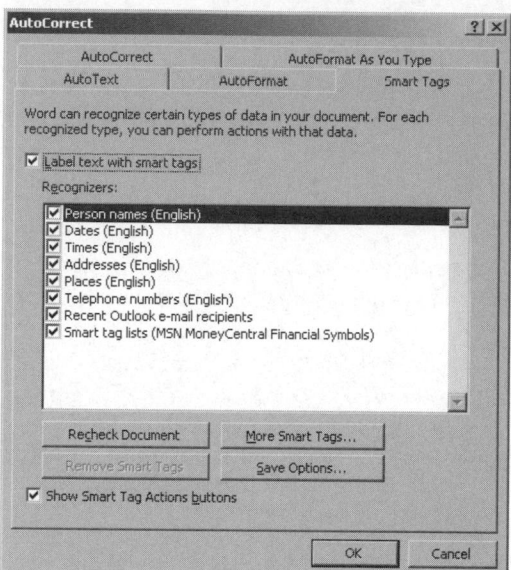

Figure 11-8. The Smart Tags tab of the AutoCorrect dialog box is shown. The settings displayed enable smart tag recognition, activate all available smart tag recognizers, and display smart tag menu buttons.

3 Check the Label Text With Smart Tags option to have Word recognize smart tags contained in a document.

4 Check the Show Smart Tag Actions Buttons to have Word display smart tag buttons so that you can perform actions on smart tag data in your documents.

5 Activate the specific smart tag recognizers you want to use by checking them in the list. (The Smart Tags shown in Figure 11-8 feature eight recognizers you could activate—Person Names, Dates, Times, Addresses, Places, Telephone Numbers, Recent Outlook E-Mail Recipients, and Smart Tag Lists (MSN MoneyCentral Financial Symbols).)

6 To download additional smart tag recognizers from Microsoft, click the More Smart Tags button.

7 To change the way smart tags are saved, click the Save Options button.

8 Click the OK button.

Assuming that you have activated the Person Names recognizer shown in Figure 11-8, whenever you type a proper name into a document, Word will convert the name to a smart tag as soon as you press Enter at the end of the paragraph containing the name. If the Smart Tags option is checked in the View tab of the Options dialog box (opened by choosing Tools, Options), Word will mark the smart tag with a dotted underline like this:

Mike Halvorson

Chapter 11: Efficient Editing in Word

If the Smart Tags option isn't checked, the smart tag will look like ordinary text.

To work with the smart tag, do the following:

1 Move the mouse pointer (or insertion point) over the smart tag. Word will display an "information" icon above and to the left of the text, shown here, to indicate that it is a smart tag.

2 Move the pointer over the icon. The smart tag button will now appear, as seen here:

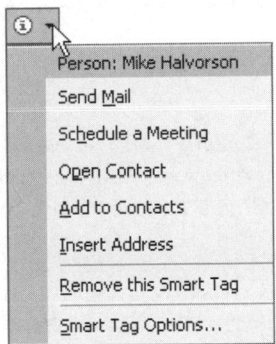

3 Click the button and choose a command from the drop-down menu shown here:

The particular items you see on the menu depend entirely on the type of data contained in the smart tag and the recognizer that is used to convert the text to a smart tag. In the preceding example shown, you could perform the following actions:

- ■ To send an e-mail message to the person, choose Send Mail.

- ■ To send that person a meeting invitation using Outlook, choose Schedule A Meeting.

- ■ To search for an Outlook Contacts item for the person and open the item if found, choose Open Contact.

- ■ To create a new item in your Outlook Contacts folder for that person, choose Add To Contacts.

■ To search for an Outlook Contacts item for that person and insert the person's address if the item is found, choose Insert Address.

■ To remove the smart tag, converting the data to ordinary document text, choose Remove This Smart Tag.

■ To open the Smart Tags tab, shown in Figure 11-8, choose Smart Tag Options.

---

tip **Remove or Add Smart Tags**

To remove all smart tags in the document, converting the smart tag data to ordinary text, open the Smart Tags tab and click the Remove Smart Tags button. To have Word scan the whole document, converting all recognized blocks of text to smart tags, click the Recheck Document button.

For information on scheduling Outlook meetings, see Chapter 38, "Managing Messages and Appointments." For information on the Outlook Contacts folder, see Chapter 39, "Managing Contacts, Tasks, and Other Types of Information."

Troubleshooting

You Would Rather Do It Yourself

Word keeps making automatic changes to your documents as you work on them, even after you turn off all AutoCorrect options. You would really like to turn off all automatic editing and formatting changes so that you have complete control over editing and formatting your document.

Word's automatic editing and formatting features become more pervasive with every edition, so it's difficult to know where to turn them all off. To turn off every automatic editing or formatting feature that we could think of, go through the following list. (To open the AutoCorrect dialog box, choose Tools, AutoCorrect Options.)

● To turn off AutoCorrect, in the AutoCorrect dialog box, click the AutoCorrect tab and clear every check box. (Unfortunately, there isn't a master option that turns off AutoCorrect. Instead, you have to turn off each option and then try to remember which options you had used if you decide to enable AutoCorrect again.)

● To turn off automatic formatting as you type, in the AutoCorrect dialog box, click the AutoFormat As You Type tab and clear every check box. (Don't worry about the options in the AutoFormat tab of the AutoCorrect dialog box, because they aren't applied unless you explicitly choose AutoFormat from the Format menu.)

Troubleshooting: You Would Rather Do It Yourself *(continued)*

- To turn off automatic completion of AutoText entries, in the AutoCorrect dialog box, click the AutoText tab and clear the Show AutoComplete Suggestions check box. If this option is enabled, Word sometimes automatically inserts an AutoText entry if you type the first part of the entry name and press Enter. For example, if you type your first name and press Enter, Word may insert your full name, even though your intention may have been to simply insert your first name and then start a new paragraph.

- To turn off automatic conversion of text to smart tags, in the AutoCorrect dialog box, click the Smart Tags tab and clear the Label Text With Smart Tags option.

- To turn off automatic updating of a particular style, open the Modify Style dialog box for that style and clear the Automatically Update check box. If the Automatically Update option is turned on for a style, when you manually reformat one paragraph with that style, Word automatically reformats all other paragraphs in the document that have the same style.

For information on using the Modify Style dialog box, see "Customizing Styles Using the Modify Style Dialog Box," on page 390.

- To stop Word from modifying styles in your document whenever you or someone else modifies the corresponding style in the document's template, choose Tools, Templates And Add-Ins. In the Templates And Add-Ins dialog box, clear the Automatically Update Document Styles option.

For information on the Automatically Update Document Styles option, see "Copying Styles from a Template to a Document," on page 403.

Positioning the Insertion Point

After you have created a document, the first step in editing it is to move the insertion point to the position where you want to make the change. Word provides many ways to move quickly through your documents. This section describes some of the essential ones.

To learn advanced methods for navigating through a document, see "Moving Quickly Through a Document," on page 289.

The easiest way to move the insertion point to a document position that is currently visible in the window is to simply click the position using the left (primary) mouse button. You can use the shortcut keys listed in Table 11-2 to move the insertion point to any position in a document.

Table 11-2. Shortcut Keys for Moving the Insertion Point

To Move	Use This Shortcut Key
To previous character	←
To next character	→
One line up	↑
One line down	↓
Backward through the document one word at a time	Ctrl+←
Forward through the document one word at a time	Ctrl+→
Backward through the document one paragraph at a time	Ctrl+↑
Forward through the document one paragraph at a time	Ctrl+↓
To the beginning of the line	Home
To the end of the line	End
To the beginning of the document	Ctrl+Home
To the end of the document	Ctrl+End
One window up (that is, up a distance equal to the height of the window)	Page Up
One window down	Page Down

For information on searching for text, see "Finding and Replacing Text and Formatting," on page 281.

You can also use the horizontal and vertical scroll bars to bring text into view in a document window. If either scroll bar is currently hidden, you can display it by choosing Tools, Options, clicking the View tab, and checking the Horizontal Scroll Bar or the Vertical Scroll Bar option. Note that when you navigate using a scroll bar, the insertion point isn't moved; in fact, after you scroll, the insertion point is often not even visible in the window. To move the insertion point, scroll and then click the position in the document where you want the insertion point to appear.

> **tip** **Scroll Without Losing Your Place**
>
> To temporarily view another part of your document, use the vertical scroll bar to move to that location. Provided that you don't click the text at the new location, you can instantly return to your original position by simply pressing an arrow key. Word will automatically scroll back to the position of the insertion point (which isn't moved when you use a scroll bar).

Editing Document Text

Once you have moved the insertion point to the position in your document where you want to make a change, the next step is to apply a Word editing command. Word provides an assortment of editing commands for deleting, replacing, copying, moving, or capitalizing text.

You can delete a limited number of characters by simply positioning the insertion point and pressing one of the shortcut keys shown in Table 11-3.

Table 11-3. **Shortcut Keys for Deleting Text**

To Delete	Press This Shortcut Key
The character after the insertion point	Delete
Through the end of the word containing (or following) the insertion point	Ctrl+Delete
The character before the insertion point	Backspace
Through the beginning of the word containing (or preceding) the insertion point	Ctrl+Backspace

Undo

You can hold down any of these shortcut keys to delete several characters or words. Remember that you can choose Undo from the Edit menu, click the Undo button on the Standard toolbar, or press Ctrl+Z to restore text that you've deleted by mistake. If you held down the Backspace key to delete a group of characters, the Undo command restores all of them. If you used any of the other deletion shortcut keys, Undo restores only the most recently deleted character or word. (You can then repeat the Undo command to restore additional characters or words.)

For more information on using the Undo button, see the sidebar "Undoing and Redoing Editing and Formatting Actions," on page 272.

Chapter 11

Selecting the Text

Most of the Word editing techniques—as well as the formatting techniques discussed in the next chapter—require that you first *select* (that is, highlight) one or more blocks of text, and then issue a command that affects that text. The highlighted block or blocks of text constitute the current *selection*. Selecting lets you precisely control the part or parts of your document that are affected by a Word command, from one or more single characters or graphic objects to the entire document. This example shows two blocks of selected text.

This text is selected. In Word, you first select text and
then act on the selection. This text is also selected.

For example, you could first select one or more blocks of text, and then press the Delete key. Having a selection changes the usual effect of the Delete command—it erases one or more entire blocks of characters rather than erasing a single space or character. Selecting text removes the normal insertion point; that is, at a given time a document has either a selection or an insertion point, but never both. You can select text or graphics using either the keyboard or the mouse.

Selecting by Using the Keyboard

The basic method for using the keyboard to select a single block of text or graphics is to hold down the Shift key, and then press any of the shortcut keys for moving the insertion point that were described in Table 11-2 on page 268. With the Shift key pressed, the keyboard command selects text rather than merely moving the insertion point. For example, you can hold down Shift and an arrow key to extend the selection character by character or line by line in the direction you want.

Using the keyboard method alone, you can select only a single block of text. To select an additional block, you have to use the mouse as described in the next section.

Table 11-4 summarizes the shortcut keys for selecting text. Keep in mind that these shortcut keys simply combine the Shift key with the shortcut keys used to move the insertion point which were described in Table 11-2.

Table 11-4. **Shortcut Keys for Extending a Selection**

To Extend the Selection	Press This Shortcut Key
Through the previous character	Shift+←
Through the next character	Shift+→
One line up	Shift+↑
One line down	Shift+↓
Through the beginning of the current word (or previous word if already at the beginning of a word)	Shift+Ctrl+←

Table 11-4. *(continued)*

To Extend the Selection	Press This Shortcut Key
Through the beginning of the next word	Shift+Ctrl+→
Through the beginning of the current paragraph (or previous paragraph if already at the beginning of a paragraph)	Shift+Ctrl+↑
Through the end of the current paragraph	Shift+Ctrl+↓
Through the beginning of the line	Shift+Home
Through the end of the line	Shift+End
Through the beginning of the document	Shift+Ctrl+Home
Through the end of the document	Shift+Ctrl+End
One window up (that is, extend up a distance equal to the height of the window)	Shift+Page Up
One window down	Shift+Page Down

An alternative way to use the keyboard to select a single block of text is to press the F8 key or double-click the EXT indicator on the status bar to activate the *Extend mode*. (When the Extend mode is active, the EXT indicator is displayed in darker characters.) While working in Extend mode, you can make selections by pressing any of the shortcut keys given in Table 11-4 *without* pressing the Shift key. For example, you can select all characters through the end of the line by pressing F8 and then pressing End. To turn off Extend mode, either press the Esc key or double-click the EXT status bar indicator. (This action won't remove the selection, but will merely end Extend mode.) Also, Extend mode will be canceled automatically if you perform any editing or formatting action on the selected text.

---

tip   **Use F8 to Select Parts of a Document**

You can press F8 repeatedly to select increasingly larger portions of your document. The first press activates the Extend mode, the second press selects the current word, the third press selects the current sentence, the fourth press selects the current paragraph, and the fifth press selects the entire document.

You can also extend the selection through the next occurrence of a character by pressing F8 and then typing the character.

Finally you can select the entire document by choosing Edit, Select All or by pressing Ctrl+A.

To cancel a selection—and display the insertion point instead—simply press an arrow key or click at any position in the document. (If you're in Extend mode, you must first press Esc or double-click the EXT indicator on the status bar.)

Chapter 11

Selecting by Using the Mouse

The basic technique for using the mouse to select a block of text or graphics is to move the pointer to the beginning of the desired selection, press the left mouse button, and then drag over the text or graphics you want to select. If you reach a window border while dragging, Word will scroll the document so that you can keep extending the selection. If one or more blocks of text are already selected, you can select an additional block of text by pressing the Ctrl key while you drag. If you don't press Ctrl while dragging, the selection will be removed from any previously selected blocks.

note If the When Selecting, Automatically Select Entire Word option is checked, dragging selects text word by word rather than character by character. That is, as the selection is extended, entire words are added to the selection rather than individual characters. If you prefer to select text character by character, clear this option. To access the option, choose Tools, Options and click the Edit tab.

You can also select a single block of text or graphics by performing the following steps (using this method removes the selection from any previously selected block or blocks):

1 Click the position where you want to start the selection.

2 Hold down the Shift key while you click the position where you want to end the selection.

Undoing and Redoing Editing and Formatting Actions

Undo

You can reverse the effect of your most recent editing or formatting action by choosing Edit, Undo or by pressing Ctrl+Z. Clicking the Undo button on the Standard toolbar has the same effect.

If you repeat the Undo command, Word will undo your next most recent action. Suppose, for example, that you type a word, format a paragraph, and then delete a character. If you subsequently issue the Undo command three times, Word will replace the character, restore the paragraph to its original format, and then erase the word.

Also, as a shortcut for undoing multiple actions, you can click the down arrow next to the Undo button, drag the pointer down to highlight all the actions you want to undo, and then release the button, as shown in this example:

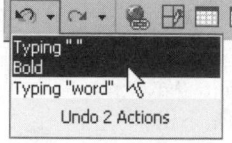

Undoing and Redoing Editing and Formatting Actions *(continued)* (The actions are listed in order from the most recent to the least recent, and you can select them for undoing only in this order.)

As explained in "Replaying Your Editing Actions with the Repeat Command," on page 251, you can issue the Repeat command (by choosing Edit, Repeat, or by pressing Ctrl+Y or F4) to perform again your most recent editing or formatting operation. If, however, your most recent operation was to undo an action using any of the methods just described, the Repeat command will redo the action. (In this case, the command on the Edit menu will be labeled Redo rather than Repeat.) For example, if you delete a word and then press Ctrl+Z, the word will be restored; if you then press Ctrl+Y, the word will again be removed. (It makes sense for the Repeat command to perform this action, because repeating an undo action "undoes the undo"; that is, it reverses the effect of the Undo command.)

You can also redo an action by clicking the Redo button on the Standard toolbar.

Redo

Like the Undo button, the Redo button has an adjoining down arrow you can click to select the exact actions you want to redo. (Unlike the Ctrl+Y and F4 shortcut keys and the Repeat [Redo] Edit menu command, the Redo button can be used only to redo an action; it can't be used to repeat an action.)

Table 11-5, on page 274, lists some mouse shortcuts you can use to select various amounts of text. Perform the action in the third column to preserve any current selection; if you don't, the current selection will be canceled. The *selection bar* referenced in this table is the area within the document window to the immediate left of the text. It's easy to tell when the mouse pointer is within the selection bar because the pointer changes to an arrow pointing up and to the right, as seen here:

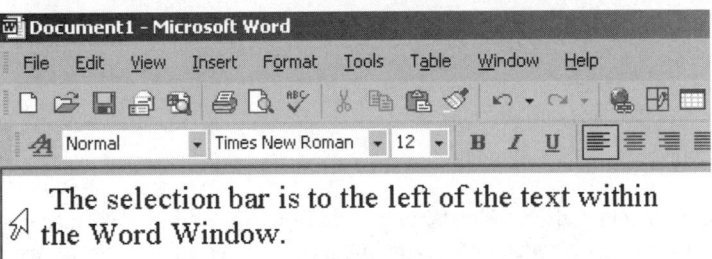

Table 11-5. Mouse Shortcuts for Selecting Text

To Select	Do This	To Add to a Current Selection, Also Do This
A word	Double-click the word.	Press Ctrl while clicking.
A sentence	Hold down the Ctrl key while clicking within the sentence.	This technique works only if there is no current selection.
A line	Click in the selection bar next to the line.	Press Ctrl while clicking.
Several lines	Drag down or up in the selection bar.	Press Ctrl while dragging.
A paragraph	Double-click in the selection bar next to the paragraph.	This technique won't work if you press Ctrl while clicking, so it always removes any current selection.
Several paragraphs	Double-click in the selection bar, and then drag down or up.	This technique won't work if you press Ctrl while clicking, so it always removes any current selection.
The entire document	Hold down the Ctrl key while clicking in the selection bar.	This technique works only if there is no current selection.

You can select a column of text by holding down the Alt key and dragging over the area you want to select (this technique always removes any current selection), as shown in the example:

To select a column of text, hold
down the Alt key while
dragging over the desired block
of text.

Pressing the Delete key after selecting as shown above would erase the first character of each line. Note that an editing or formatting action won't affect a character unless it's *entirely* selected. (In the preceding example, even though parts of the *r* and *f* in the last two lines are selected, these characters aren't deleted.)

To cancel the selection, either click at any position in the document or press an arrow key. If more than one block of text is selected, you can cancel the selection from a single block by clicking it while holding down Ctrl.

Editing the Selection

Once you have selected one or more blocks of text, you're ready to apply an editing or formatting command to the selection. This section describes the essential editing commands you can apply to selections.

> As you use these techniques, keep in mind that you can reverse your editing action by issuing the Undo command, as described in the sidebar "Undoing and Redoing Editing and Formatting Actions," on page 272, even if the amount of text deleted or altered is large.

If the Typing Replaces Selection option is checked, you can replace the selection by simply typing the new text. When you type the first letter, the entire selection is automatically deleted, and the new text you type is inserted in its place. If Typing Replaces Selection isn't checked, the selected text is left in place, the selection is canceled, and the new text is inserted in front of the formerly selected text. To access the Typing Replaces Selection option, choose Tools, Options and in the Options dialog box, click the Edit tab.

To erase the selected text, press the Delete key or the Backspace key, or choose Edit, Clear, Contents.

To change the case of the letters in the selection (to Sentence case, lowercase, UPPER-CASE, or Title Case), or to toggle all letters between uppercase and lowercase, choose Format, Change Case and select the desired capitalization option in the Change Case dialog box (Figure 11-9). Alternatively, you can press Shift+F3—repeatedly if necessary—to switch among various capitalization styles.

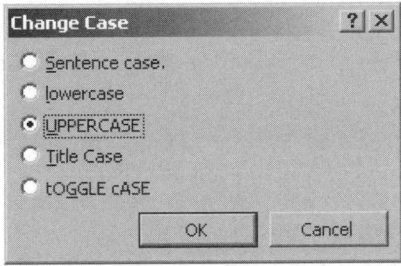

Figure 11-9. The Change Case dialog box allows you to change the capitalization style of the selected text.

Moving and Copying Text Using the Mouse

To use the mouse to quickly move or copy text, perform the following steps:

1 Select the text.

InsideOut

If several blocks of text are selected, using drag-and-drop to move or copy one of them moves or copies them all. However, when you drop the text, Word inserts extraneous paragraph breaks following each moved or copied block, so the results might not be what you expect. A better way to copy or move multiple blocks of text is to use the enhanced Office Clipboard, which gives you much more control over the way the copied or moved blocks are inserted into your document. See "Using the Enhanced Office Clipboard Task Pane," on page 109.

2 Place the mouse pointer over the selection (the pointer will change from an I-beam to an arrow), and hold down the left mouse button, as seen here.

3 To move the text, simply drag it to its new location. To copy the text, hold down the Ctrl key while you drag. If the target location isn't visible, just drag the text to the edge of the window, and the document will automatically be scrolled in the corresponding direction. The target location can be within the same Word document, within a different Word document, or even within a document in another Office application (such as a Microsoft Excel worksheet). If a target location in a different document isn't currently visible, drag the text to the target document's button on the Windows taskbar and hold the pointer there for a few seconds. The target document's window is then activated, and you can complete the drag operation (keep the left mouse button pressed the whole time).

When the text is inserted in its new location, Word will display the Paste Options button, as seen here, at the end of the moved or copied text.

This text was just moved to a new location using drag-and-drop.

Paste Options button

note To use the Paste Options button, the Show Paste Options Buttons option must be enabled. To access this option, choose Tools, Options and click the Edit tab.

4   Normally, when you copy or move text, the text's formatting is copied or moved along with it. If you want to copy or move the text without transferring its formatting, click the Paste Options button and choose Match Destination Formatting or Keep Text Only from the drop-down menu, shown here:

This text was just moved to a new location using drag-and-drop.

⊙ Keep Source Formatting
○ Match Destination Formatting
○ Keep Text Only
🅰 Apply Style or Formatting...

---

tip   **Use Shortcut Keys to Move a Paragraph Up or Down**

You can select and move an entire paragraph by pressing a single key combination. First place the insertion point anywhere within the paragraph. Then, to move the paragraph up (that is, before the previous paragraph), press Shift+Alt+Up arrow. To move it down (that is, after the next paragraph), press Shift+Alt+Down arrow.

Troubleshooting

Drag-and-Drop Editing Doesn't Work

When you try to drag a block of selected text, the selection changes rather than the text moving.

To drag selected text, make sure that when you press the mouse button to start dragging, the tip of the arrow pointer is within the selected area. Otherwise, you'll merely change the selection.

Also, to move or copy text using the drag-and-drop method, the Drag-And-Drop Text Editing option must be checked. To access this option, choose Tools, Options and then click the Edit tab.

For information on moving blocks of text in Outline view, see "Working with Documents in Outline View," on page 415.

Moving and Copying Text Using the Clipboard

You can also move or copy text using the Clipboard, by performing the following steps:

1   Select the text.

Chapter 11

InsideOut

If several blocks of text are selected when you issue the Cut or Copy command, the Clipboard stores them all. However, when you paste the text, Word inserts extraneous paragraph breaks following each moved or copied block, so the results might not be what you expect. A better way to copy or move multiple blocks of text is to use the Office Clipboard, which gives you much more control over the way the copied or moved blocks are inserted into your document. See "Using the Enhanced Office Clipboard Task Pane," on page 109.

2 To move the text, choose Edit, Cut or press Ctrl+X. This *cuts* the text; that is, it removes it from the document and places it in the Clipboard.

To copy the text, choose Edit, Copy or press Ctrl+C. This *copies* the text; that is, it leaves the text in the document and places a copy of it in the Clipboard.

3 Place the insertion point at the position where you want to insert the text that has been cut or copied to the Clipboard. The target location can be within the original document or within a different document.

4 Choose Edit, Paste or press Ctrl+V. This action *pastes* the text; that is, it inserts it into the document.

Word will display the Paste Options button at the end of the moved or copied text, as seen here:

This text was just pasted into the document.

Paste Options button

5 Normally, when you copy or move text, the text's formatting is copied or moved along with it. If you want to copy or move the text without transferring its formatting, click the Paste Options button and choose Keep Text Only from the drop-down menu, shown here:

This text was just pasted into the document.

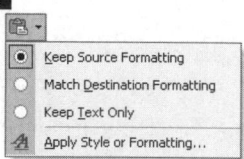

note To use the Paste Options button, the Show Paste Options Buttons option must be checked. You'll find this option by choosing Tools, Options and then clicking the Edit tab.

Chapter 11: Efficient Editing in Word

Word provides two additional ways to cut, copy, or paste text with the Clipboard. One method is to click the appropriate buttons on the Standard toolbar, shown here:

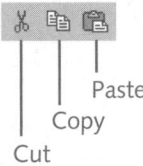

Another way to cut or copy a block of selected text is to right-click it and then choose Cut or Copy from the shortcut menu that is displayed, as seen here:

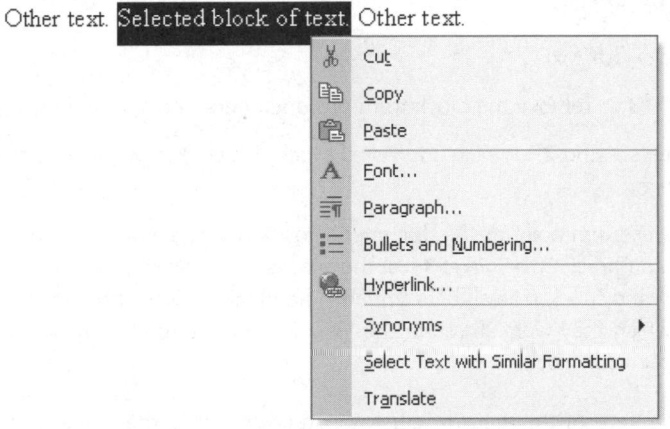

Likewise, to paste the text, you can right-click the target location and then choose Paste from the shortcut menu. To remove the shortcut menu without choosing a command, press the Esc key or click anywhere within the document.

An advantage of using the Clipboard is that you can move or copy text or graphics between separate Windows-based programs. (The Clipboard is a shared Windows facility.) Another advantage is that the text is retained in the Clipboard after you paste, allowing you to insert several copies of the text by pasting repeatedly.

For information on different ways to use the Clipboard to transfer data between Office applications, see Chapter 7, "Sharing Data Among Office XP Applications."

This section has explained the techniques for cutting or copying a single block of data into the Clipboard and then pasting that block. Alternatively, you can use the enhanced Office Clipboard to store multiple blocks of text or graphics and then paste any of them into a document.

Chapter 11

For information on activating and using the Office Clipboard, see "Using the Enhanced Office Clipboard Task Pane," on page 109.

To transfer multiple blocks of text or data, you can also use the Spike, described in the next section.

Using the Spike

You can use the *Spike* to remove several blocks of text from a document and then insert all these blocks together at a single document location. The Spike is based on a special-purpose AutoText entry that is assigned the name "Spike." (This name derives from the old days when newspaper editors would cut out blocks of lines from typed copy and impale them on a metal spike for possible later use.) The following is the usual procedure for using the Spike:

1 Select a block of text.

2 Press Ctrl+F3 to remove the block from the document and store it in the Spike.

3 Repeat steps 1 and 2 for each additional block of text you would like to add to the Spike.

4 Place the insertion point at the document position where you want to insert the text, and press Ctrl+Shift+F3. All the blocks of text will appear in the document and the Spike will be emptied. The blocks will be inserted in the order in which they were stored in the Spike, and a paragraph break will be added after each block.

In the first three steps of the preceding list, Word adds text to the Spike AutoText entry. In step 4, Word inserts all the entry text into the document and deletes the entry. You can insert the text without deleting the entry by typing **Spike** and then pressing F3. You can also use any of the other AutoText insertion techniques discussed in "Reusing Text with the AutoText Feature," on page 252.

Setting Clipboard Options

Word provides several options that affect moving and copying text with the Clipboard. To set these options, choose Tools, Options and click the Edit tab.

If you want to be able to paste by pressing the Insert key (in addition to the other methods), check the Use The INS Key For Paste option. (If the Use The INS Key For Paste option is checked, you can double-click the OVR indicator in the Word status bar to toggle between Insert and Overtype editing modes, which is the function of the Insert key when this option is off.)

Setting Clipboard Options *(continued)*   To have Word display the Paste Options button whenever you move or copy text using drag-and-drop or the Clipboard, check the Show Paste Options Buttons option.

To have Word remove extraneous spaces that remain after you cut text (or after you delete it by choosing Edit, Clear, Contents or by pressing the Delete or Backspace key), check the Smart Cut And Paste option. For example, if this option is enabled and you cut only the word "expression," without removing any spaces, from the text "(a parenthetical expression)," Word would automatically remove the space following "parenthetical."

To set a variety of additional options that affect pasting and other editing functions in Word, click the Settings button to open the Settings dialog box, shown here:

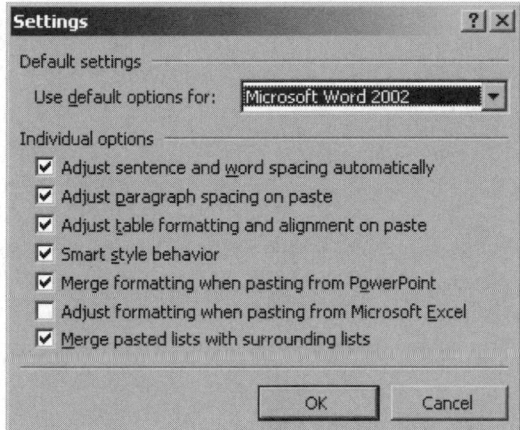

In the Settings dialog box, you can select a version of Word (Word 2002 or Word 97 through 2000) to use the default editing settings for that version, or you can check or uncheck individual options to create custom settings.

Finding and Replacing Text and Formatting

You can easily search for text, formats, or special items such as paragraph marks and graphics using the Find command. The following is the essential procedure for using this command to conduct a search in Word:

1 If you want to limit the search to one or more specific blocks of text, select that text.

2 Choose Edit, Find or press Ctrl+F to display the Find tab of the Find And Replace dialog box (shown in Figure 11-10).

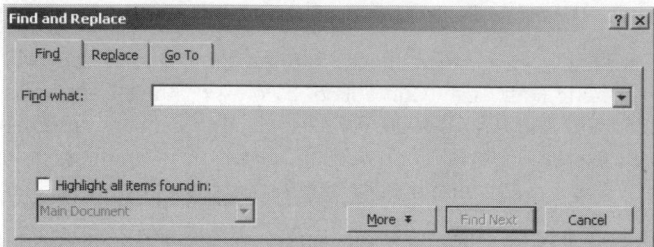

Figure 11-10. The Find tab of the Find And Replace dialog box is shown without the search options displayed.

3 To perform a search using the options you set the previous time you used the Find command, skip to step 6 now. Otherwise, complete steps 4 and 5 to select the search options you want.

4 To have the Search command immediately select all matching blocks of text it finds, check Highlight All Items Found In. In the drop-down list, select the part of the document that you want Word to search; you can select Main Document, Current Selection (if you've selected text), or—for documents that contain these items—Headers And Footers, Footnotes, or Comments. For instance, if you've added comments to a document, you could have Word search and highlight in either the main document or in your comment text, as shown here:

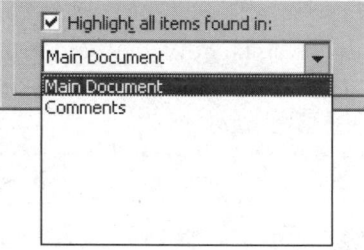

To have the Search command select matching blocks one at a time so that you can view or work with each one separately, clear the Highlight All Items Found In check box.

5 To set one or more additional search options, click the More button to display the options, if they aren't already shown, and select the ones you want (see Figure 11-11). The search options are summarized in Table 11-6. (If you selected text in step 1 and want Word to search only within the selection, you must choose Down or Up in the Search drop-down list. If the All option is selected, Word will search the entire document.)

Chapter 11

Chapter 11: Efficient Editing in Word

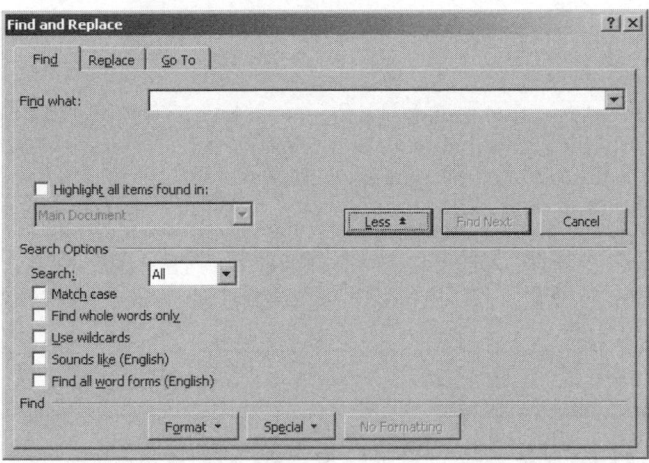

Figure 11-11.   The Find tab of the Find And Replace dialog box is shown displaying all options.

Table 11-6. **Search Options on the Find Tab of the Find And Replace Dialog Box**

To Search Like This	Select This Option
To search the entire document from the insertion point (or start of the selection) to the end of the document, and then from the beginning of the document down to the insertion point (or start of the selection), including headers, footers, comments, and footnotes	Select All in the Search drop-down list.
To search from the insertion point (or start of the selection) to the end of the document (or selection), excluding headers, footers, comments, and footnotes	Select Down in the Search drop-down list.
To search from the insertion point (or end of the selection) to the beginning of the document (or selection), excluding headers, footers, comments, and footnotes	Select Up in the Search drop-down list.
To search only for text that matches the case of each letter in the search text you enter	Check the Match Case option.
To exclude matching text that is part of another word (for example, if searching for *cat*, don't match *catatonic*)	Check the Find Whole Words Only option.
To include wildcards in your search text (for an explanation of this option, see the sidebar "Using Wildcards in Your Search Text," on page 284)	Check the Use Wildcards option.

(continued)

Table 11-6. *(continued)*

To Search Like This	Select This Option
To search for all text that sounds like the search text you enter into the Find What text box (for example, if the search text is *there*, this option would find *their* as well as *there*).	Check the Sounds Like (English) option.
To find all forms of the search text (for example, if the search text is *go*, this option finds *go*, *goes*, *gone*, and *went*)	Check the Find All Word Forms (English) option.

Using Wildcards in Your Search Text

If you check the Use Wildcards option in the Find tab or in the Replace tab of the Find And Replace dialog box, you can include wildcards in the search text you enter into the Find What text box. A *wildcard* is a special character that matches a particular class of characters or text strings. For example, the ? wildcard matches any character (hence, c?t matches cat, cot, cut, and so on). The * wildcard matches any string of characters (hence, b*d matches bad, bard, board, and so on). To search for an actual wildcard character, precede it with a backslash (\)—for example, \? to find "?" and * to find "*."

The fastest way to insert wildcards into your search text is to click the Special button and from the menu choose the type of character or string you want to find. Be sure that you check the Use Wildcards option *before* choosing an item from the Special menu. (Otherwise, the Special menu lists standard Word search codes rather than wildcards, and also allows you to insert several codes that aren't compatible with the wildcard option.)

Wildcards are often combined in fairly complex expressions, known as *regular expressions*. After inserting an item from the Special menu, you might therefore need to manually complete the wildcard expression in the Find What text box, as well as type in the rest of your search text. You can also manually type wildcards into the Find What box rather than using the Special menu. For details on the specific wildcards and wildcard expressions you can use, look up *wildcards* in the Word online Help.

The primary advantage of using wildcards is that they give you greater control in searching for text. When you use wildcards, however, you might need to look up the syntax and manually type in (or complete) fairly complex expressions. We recommend using them only if you're comfortable with regular expressions, or if you're unable to find the text you want without using wildcards.

6 If you want to search for text (that is, specific words or phrases), enter that text into the Find What box. (You can click the down arrow to select previous search text from the drop-down list.)

To include a nonprinting character or other document element in your search text (for example, a tab character or a graphic object), click the Special button and choose the appropriate item from the menu. (If the Special button or other button mentioned in these instructions isn't visible, click the More button to reveal it.) This will insert into your search text a code for finding the item (for example, ^t to find a tab character or ^g to find a graphic object). If you've checked the Use Wildcards option, the Special menu also lets you insert wildcard expressions.

7 If you want to search for a particular format or combination of formats, click the Format button, choose a formatting type, and specify the format in the dialog box that's displayed. Alternatively, if Word provides a shortcut key for applying a specific format (such as Ctrl+B for bold text or Ctrl+E for centered paragraph alignment), you can specify that format by pressing the shortcut key when the insertion point is within the Find What text box.

> Formatting and the shortcut keys you can use for formatting are described in Chapter 12, "Effective Formatting in Word."

When searching for certain formats (such as bold or superscript text), you can search either for text that has the format or for text that does not have the format. For example, you can select Bold (to search for text that is bold and meets other criteria) or Not Bold (to search for text that is not bold and meets other criteria), or you can select neither option (to search for text that meets other criteria whether it is bold or not). The formatting that you choose is displayed below the Find What box.

> **note** If you specify a search format in a dialog box, a check box that has just a check mark means to find text that has the format, an empty check box means to find text that does not have the format, and a check box with a gray background and a check mark means the format isn't part of your search criteria. If you specify a search format using a shortcut key (for example, Ctrl+B for bold text), repeatedly pressing the key toggles between these three states (for example, Bold, Not Bold, and either Bold or Not Bold).

You can enter search text into the Find What text box *and* choose formatting. In this case, Word will search for text that matches your search text and has the specified formatting. To remove all your formatting specifications, click the No Formatting button.

8 If you checked the Highlight All Items Found In option, click the Find All button to have Word select all instances of the search text or formatting all at once.

If you *didn't* check Highlight All Items Found In, click the Find Next button to have Word find and select each occurrence of the search text or formatting one at a time. You can edit your document while the Find And Replace dialog box is open; simply click the document when you want to edit it, and then click in the Find And Replace dialog box to continue searching. (If the Find And Replace dialog box covers the text you want to edit, point to the title bar of the dialog box and drag the box out of the way.)

9 To close the Find And Replace dialog box, click the Cancel button.

After the dialog box is closed, you can continue to search for the same text or formatting using the keyboard. Each time you press Shift+F4, Word searches for the next occurrence of the text or formatting, moving in the direction you specified in the Find And Replace dialog box. Each time you press Ctrl+Page Down, Word searches for the next occurrence moving down in the document, and each time you press Ctrl+Page Up, Word searches for the next occurrence moving up in the document. You can also have Word search for the next occurrence by clicking the Next browse button, or search for the previous occurrence by clicking the Previous browse button. These buttons are described in "Navigating with the Browse Buttons," on page 294.

tip If you're searching for multiple occurrences of text or formatting, you'll probably find it most convenient to use the Find And Replace dialog box to locate the first occurrence, and then close the dialog box to get it out of your way and use the keystrokes described here to find additional occurrences.

InsideOut

Keep in mind that the Ctrl+Page Up, Ctrl+Page Down, and Shift+F4 keystrokes, as well as the Previous and Next browse buttons, are multipurpose commands that browse through instances of whatever *browse object* you last specified. The browse object can be the search text of the Find command, a target set up in the Go To tab, or a target selected through the Select Browse Object browse button. (The Go To tab is covered in "Moving the Insertion Point with the Go To Command," on page 292.)

Consider, for example, that you just closed the Find tab and are now navigating through instances of your search text using the Ctrl+Page Up and Ctrl+Page Down keystrokes or the Previous and Next browse buttons. However, you now use the Go To command to locate a comment. You'll then discover that these keystrokes and buttons no longer locate instances of your search text, but rather move through comments. To resume browsing through instances of your search text using the keystrokes or browse buttons, you'll need to reopen the Find tab and use it to find at least one instance of the search text.

For information on using Word's new Styles And Formatting task pane to find or reformat all text throughout the document that has a particular style or formatting, see "Selecting All Text with the Same Style or Formatting," on page 328.

Replacing Text and Formatting

You can find and replace text or formatting using the Replace command. Like the Find command, Replace allows you to search for text, formatting, or a combination of text and formatting. You can replace the text that is found, change its formatting, or both replace the text and change its formatting. The following are the essential steps. (See the instructions in the previous section for more information on the steps that are common to both finding and replacing text.)

1 If you want to replace only within one or more specific blocks of text, select the text.

2 Choose Edit, Replace or press Ctrl+H to display the Replace tab of the Find And Replace dialog box.

3 If you want to perform a replace operation using the options you set the previous time you used the Replace command, proceed now to step 4. If, however, you want to set one or more search options, click the More button to display the options—if they aren't already shown—and select the ones you want (see Figure 11-12). These options are the same as those available in the Find tab, as summarized in Table 11-6. (If you selected text in step 1 and want Word to search only within the selection, you must choose Down or Up in the Search drop-down list. If the All option is selected, Word will search the entire document.)

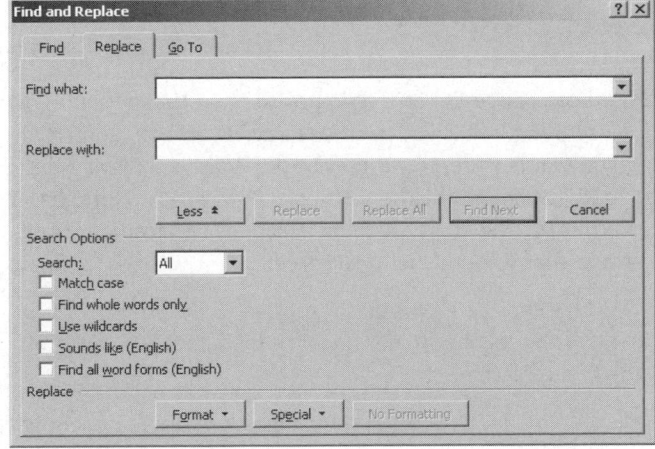

Figure 11-12. The Replace tab of the Find And Replace dialog box is shown displaying all options.

4 If you want to search for text, type it into the Find What box. (You can click the down arrow to select previous search text from the drop-down list.) To include a nonprinting character or other document element in your search text (for example, a tab character or a graphic object), click the Special button and choose the appropriate item from the menu.

5 If you want to search for a particular format or combination of formats, make sure that the insertion point is within the Find What box. Then, click the Format button, choose a formatting type, and specify the format you want in the dialog box that is displayed. Alternatively, if Word provides a shortcut key for applying a specific format (such as Ctrl+B for bold text), you can specify that format by pressing the shortcut key when the insertion point is within the Find What text box.

> For information on choosing formatting, see Chapter 12, "Effective Formatting in Word."

6 If you want to replace the text that is found, type the replacement text into the Replace With box. To include a special character in the replacement text (such as a paragraph mark), click the Special button. Word will display only those special characters that are appropriate for replacement text.

tip **Replace Text with Graphics**

You might want to replace text with graphics throughout your document. (Perhaps, for example, you have inserted placeholder text in your document for a particular icon and now want to replace each placeholder with the actual graphic object.) Although you can't insert a graphic object directly into the Replace With text box, you can copy the graphic object into the Clipboard prior to opening the Find And Replace dialog box, and then type ^c into the Replace With text box, causing Word to use the current contents of the Clipboard (that is, your graphic object) as the replacement text.

7 If you want to change the formatting of the text that is found, make sure that the insertion point is within the Replace With box, and choose the formatting you want, as described previously. Word will display the replacement format you have chosen below the Replace With box. Note that if you leave the Replace With box empty and don't choose replacement formatting, each block of text that is found will be deleted.

8 Either click the Replace All button to replace all occurrences of the text or formatting, without confirmation, or click the Find Next button to view and verify the first replacement.

9 If you clicked Find Next, Word will highlight the first matching text. You can then click Replace to replace the text or formatting and find the next occurrence, or you can click Find Next to leave the text unaltered and continue to the next occurrence. You can repeat this step until all text has been replaced.

Or, at any time, you can click Close to close the dialog box and stop the process, or Replace All to replace all remaining occurrences without confirmation. (The Cancel button is labeled Close after the first replacement, reminding you that you can't cancel replacements you've already made.) Recall that you can leave the Find And Replace dialog box displayed while you manually edit the document. (You might have to move the dialog box out of the way by dragging its title bar.)

---

tip   **Reverse Your Replacements**

If you replaced all occurrences of text in your document by clicking the Replace All button in the Replace tab, issuing the Undo command immediately afterward reverses all these replacements at once. If you replaced occurrences one at a time by clicking the Replace button, the Undo command reverses only your most recent replacement. (You can then repeat the Undo command to reverse previous replacements.)

For information on searching for specified text or properties in multiple Office documents or in Outlook items, see "Finding Office Files or Outlook Items Using the Search Feature," on page 69.

Moving Quickly Through a Document

"Positioning the Insertion Point," on page 267, summarized the keystrokes you can use to move the insertion point through a document. The following sections explain how to move through a document quickly, especially useful for larger documents.

Using Bookmarks to Label and Locate Text

You can use Word's bookmarks to mark and then quickly return to specific positions in a document.

To mark a position in a document, you need to define a bookmark using the following steps:

1 Place the insertion point at the position you want to mark, or select a single block of text to mark. (You can't assign a bookmark if you've selected more than one block of text.)

2 Choose Insert, Bookmark, or press Ctrl+Shift+F5. Word will open the Bookmark dialog box.

3 Type an identifying name into the Bookmark Name box, and click the Add button (shown in Figure 11-13).

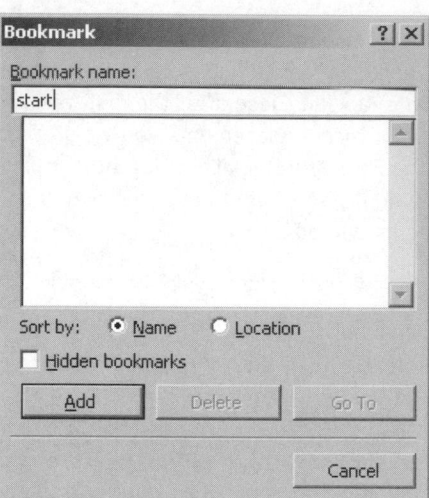

Figure 11-13. This example shows how to define a bookmark named *start* in the Bookmark dialog box.

You can use this technique to mark any number of positions in a document. Note that you can make bookmarks visible by choosing Tools, Options. In the Options dialog box, click the View tab and check the Bookmarks option (in the Show area). Word will then display an I-beam symbol at the location of each bookmark, or, if you marked a block of text, Word will place bracket markers around the bookmark text.

> **note** Bookmarks can be used for a variety of other purposes, some of which are discussed later in the book—for example, for specifying the target of a hyperlink (discussed in "Adding and Using Hyperlinks," on page 583), for defining cross-references, and for creating index entries that refer to a range of pages. Indexes are discussed in "Generating Indexes and Tables of Contents," on page 435.

To move the insertion point to a position marked with a bookmark, open the Bookmark dialog box (choose Insert, Bookmark, or press Ctrl+Shift+F5), select the name that you assigned when you defined the bookmark (in step 3 above), and click the Go To button. Word will immediately move the insertion point to the marked position. You can also use the Go To command, discussed in the next section, to move to a particular bookmark.

> **note** If you select a block of text prior to defining a bookmark, the bookmark will be assigned to the entire selection. In this case, when you go to the bookmark, Word will select the text.

Writing Macros for Saving and Restoring Your Place in a Document

This sidebar presents an invaluable pair of macros that use bookmarks for saving your place in a document and rapidly returning to that place. (It's surprising that Word doesn't provide build-in commands for doing this!) You can enter these macros yourself using the Visual Basic for Applications (VBA) Editor, following the brief instructions given here. (For complete information on macros and using the VBA Editor, see Part 10 of this book.) Alternatively, you can use the Organizer to copy the macros from the WordInsideOut module in the WordInsideOut.dot file provided on the book's companion CD into your own Normal template. For instructions on using the Organizer, see "Using the Organizer," on page 409.

To enter these macros, perform the following steps:

1 From the Tools menu in Word, choose Macro, Visual Basic Editor. This runs the Microsoft Visual Basic editor.

2 In the Project Explorer pane at the upper left of the Visual Basic editor window, double-click the Normal/Microsoft Word Objects/This Document item. (Expand the tree, if necessary, to access this item. If the Project Explorer pane isn't displayed, choose View, Project Explorer.) This will open a code window where you can enter code that is stored in your Normal template.

3 Type the following macro code into the code window:

```
Sub SavePlace()
'SavePlace Macro
   With ActiveDocument.Bookmarks
      .Add Range:=Selection.Range, Name:="MarkedLocation"
   End With
End Sub


Sub ReturnToPlace()
'ReturnToPlace Macro
   Selection.GoTo What:=wdGoToBookmark, Name:="MarkedLocation"
End Sub
```

4 In the Visual Basic editor, choose File, Close And Return To Microsoft Word.

5 Use the procedures described in "Defining Shortcut Keys (Word Only)," on page 217 to define a shortcut key for the SavePlace macro and a shortcut key for the ReturnToPlace macro.

You can now test these macros as follows: Place the insertion point anywhere in a document (or select a single block of text), and then press the shortcut key you defined for the SavePlace macro. This will save your position (or selection).

(continued)

Chapter 11

> **Writing Macros for Saving and Restoring Your Place in a Document**
>
> *(continued)* Then move the insertion point anywhere else within the same document and perform any editing or formatting actions you want. When you're ready to go back to your original location in the document, press the shortcut key you defined for the ReturnToPlace macro. Word will immediately move the insertion point back to its original position (or restore the original selection).

Moving the Insertion Point with the Go To Command

You can use the Go To command to move the insertion point (or the selection highlight) to a position marked by a bookmark (described in the previous section) or to one of a variety of other locations in a document, as follows:

1 Choose Edit, Go To, press Ctrl+G or F5, or double-click anywhere on the left half of the status bar (to the left of the REC indicator). Word will display the Go To tab of the Find And Replace dialog box (shown in Figure 11-14).

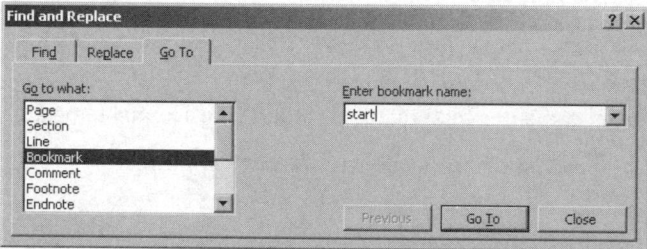

Figure 11-14. The Go To tab of the Find And Replace dialog box is shown as you would fill it out to go to a bookmark named *start*.

2 In the Go To What list, select the type of target you want to navigate to. For example, to go to a particular bookmark, select Bookmark in the list; or, to go to a particular page, select Page.

3 Enter the name or number for the specific target into the text box on the right side of the dialog box and click the Go To button. The text box is labeled according to the type of target you selected in step 1. For instance, if you selected Bookmark it is labeled Enter Bookmark Name, or if you selected Page it is labeled Enter Page Number. For certain types of targets, such as bookmarks or comments, you can select the name of the target from a drop-down list.

> **note** To go to a particular document line, select Line in the Go To What list and type the line number into the Enter Line Number box. For the Go To command, line numbering begins at 1 with the first line in the document and is incremented throughout the rest of the document. In contrast, the line number displayed on the status bar refers to the number of the line within the current page.

For any type of target except a bookmark, if you don't enter a specific target into the text box, the dialog box displays buttons labeled Next and Previous. You can use these buttons to browse through the different instances of the target item. For example, if you select Section in the Go To What list and leave the Enter Section Number text box blank, clicking Next will take you to the beginning of the next document section and clicking Previous will take you to the beginning of the previous one. (Document sections are discussed in Chapter 13, "Arranging Text Using Tables, Columns, and Lists," and Chapter 18, "Designing and Printing Professional-Looking Pages.")

You can also enter into the text box a plus (+) or minus (−) sign followed by a number to move forward or back by a certain number of objects. For example, if you've selected Page in the Go To What list, you can enter +4 in the Enter Page Number box to move forward by four pages.

You can leave the Go To tab of the Find And Replace dialog box displayed while you work in your document. Whether or not the dialog box is displayed, you can navigate to the next instance of the type of target you specified in the Go To tab (for example, the next page, section, or bookmark) by pressing Ctrl+Page Down or by clicking the Next browse button. You can navigate to the previous instance of your Go To target by pressing Ctrl+Page Up or by clicking the Previous browse button. (The browse buttons are discussed in the next section.) If you entered a specific target in the Go To tab (such as a specific page number or a particular named bookmark), you can press Shift+F4 to go back to that target (if you didn't enter a specific target, Shift+F4 works just like Ctrl+Page Down).

InsideOut

Keep in mind that the Ctrl+Page Up, Ctrl+Page Down, and Shift+F4 keystrokes, as well as the Previous and Next browse buttons, are multipurpose commands that browse through instances of whatever *browse object* you last specified. The browse object can be the search text of the Find command, a target set up in the Go To tab, or a target selected through the Select Browse Object browse button.

Consider, for example, that you selected the Comment target in the Go To tab and are now happily navigating through your document's comments using the Ctrl+Page Up and Ctrl+Page Down keystrokes or the Previous and Next browse buttons. However, you now use the Find command to locate a text item. You'll then discover that these keystrokes and buttons no longer navigate through comments, but rather move though instances of your search text. To resume browsing through comments using the keystrokes or browse buttons, you'll need to reopen the Go To tab and use it to go to at least one comment (or, you could use the Select Browse Object button described in the next section to reselect the comment browse object).

Another way to move through a document is to press Shift+F5, the Go Back key. Pressing Shift+F5 moves you back through the locations where you most recently performed editing or formatting actions or moved to using a navigation command (Find, Go To, or browse button). You can move to three prior positions, at most. If you press the key a fourth time, the insertion point will cycle back to its original position.

Navigating with the Browse Buttons

To use the browse buttons to quickly locate various types of objects within your documents perform the following steps:

1 If the vertical scroll bar isn't displayed, choose Tools, Options. In the Options dialog box, click the View tab, and check the Vertical Scroll Bar option. You'll find the three browse buttons at the bottom of the vertical scroll bar, as shown here:

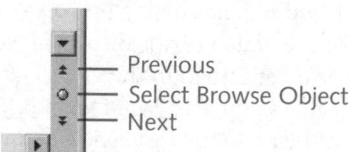

Previous
Select Browse Object
Next

2 If you've previously selected a browse object—search text in the Find tab, a target in the Go To tab, or an object in the Select Browse Object menu—you can click the Next button to go to the next instance of this object in your document or click the Previous button to go to the Previous instance of the object. The ScreenTips displayed on the Next and Previous buttons indicate your most recently selected browse object. For example, if your most recent browsing action was to use the Find command to search for text, the buttons are labeled Next Find/Go To and Previous Find/Go To, and they cause Word to locate the next or previous instance of your search text.

Note that pressing Ctrl+Page Down is equivalent to clicking the Next button, and pressing Ctrl+Page Up is equivalent to clicking the Ctrl+Page Up button.

3 If you haven't selected a browse object, or if you want to select a new one, click the Select Browse Object button and choose a target from the menu, shown here:

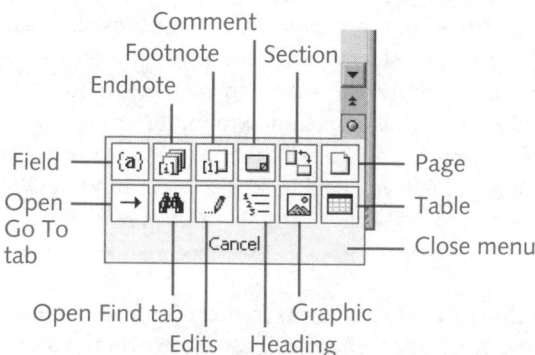

Comment
Footnote   Section
Endnote

Field ——
Open
Go To
tab

—— Page
—— Table
—— Close menu

Open Find tab
Edits   Heading
Graphic

When you choose an object type from the menu (field, endnote, footnote, comment, section, page, edits, heading, graphic, or table) Word moves the insertion point to the next object of that type (the next field, endnote, comment, and so on). You can subsequently use the Next and Previous buttons to navigate to additional objects of the same type.

note Choosing the Edits browse object moves you through the locations where you've performed your most recent editing or formatting actions, just like the Go Back key (Shift+F5) described in the previous section.

Should you use the browse buttons rather than the Go To command? On the negative side, the browse buttons don't provide some of the targets that the Go To command offers (such as Line and Bookmark). Also, you can't specify a particular item number (for example, you can't go directly to page 25); you can only browse forward or back through the objects. However, the browse buttons are quicker to use. Also, if you've previously used the Find command or the Go To command, you can just click the Next or Previous browse button to instantly go to the next or previous Find or Go To target, without the need to first select a browse object on the menu.

You can also use hyperlinks as a navigation tool in a document. For information, see "Adding and Using Hyperlinks," on page 583.

Chapter 12

Effective Formatting in Word

Directly Formatting a Word Document

You can directly format a Microsoft Word 2002 document at four main levels:

- You can format individual characters—for example, changing the font or making the characters bold or italic. This level of formatting is covered primarily in this chapter.

- You can format individual paragraphs—for example, changing the alignment, indentation, or line spacing. This level of formatting is also covered primarily in this chapter.

- You can format document sections. A *section* is a division of a document that you create specifically for applying unique formatting to that part of the document. The types of formatting that you can apply to document sections include newspaper-style columns, page borders, page numbering, headers and footers, margins, and the page layout. This level of formatting is covered in Chapter 13, "Arranging Text Using Tables, Columns, and Lists," and Chapter 18, "Designing and Printing Professional-Looking Pages."

- You can format the entire document. The types of formatting you can apply to an entire document are the same as those you can apply to individual document sections.

For information on finding and replacing formatting or formatting styles within a document, using the Find command or the Find And Replace command, see "Finding and Replacing Text and Formatting," on page 281.

tip   Remember the Undo Command

As you learn the techniques presented in this chapter, keep in mind that you can reverse the effect of any formatting command by issuing the Undo command, using any of the methods discussed in the sidebar "Undoing and Redoing Editing and Formatting Actions," on page 272.

Formatting Characters Directly

Directly applying individual formatting features to characters within your document gives you the finest level of control over character formatting. The paragraph style specifies the predominant character formatting of the paragraph text. You typically apply direct character formatting to one or more characters *within* a paragraph to emphasize or modify them in some way. For example, you might italicize a word or convert a character to superscript. The character formatting that you directly apply overrides the character formatting that is specified by the paragraph style or by any character style assigned to the text.

Styles are discussed in "Applying Styles and Reusing Formats," on page 320.

tip   Don't Overuse Direct Character Formatting

Avoid directly applying character formatting to entire paragraphs or groups of paragraphs. It's better to assign each paragraph a paragraph style that includes the basic character formatting that you want and to use direct character formatting only to modify smaller blocks of text within paragraphs. This approach makes it easier to change the basic character formatting of your text and tends to make your character formatting more consistent throughout the document.

To directly apply character formatting, perform the following steps:

1   Select one or more blocks of text, or to apply the formatting to the text you're about to type, place the insertion point at the position where you want your new text to appear.

For a description of text selection methods, see "Selecting the Text," on page 270.

Chapter 12: Effective Formatting in Word

> **tip** **Format a Word Without Selecting It**
>
> To apply character formatting to a word, you can simply place the insertion point any-where within the word rather than selecting the word. This technique works, however, only if the When Selecting Automatically Select Entire Word option is checked. To access this option, choose Tools, Options and click the Edit tab.

2 Apply the character formatting. Table 12-1 summarizes the different types of character formatting you can apply. For each type, it indicates which of the three basic methods you can use to apply the formatting:

- The Font dialog box, which you open by choosing Format, Font.

> For details, see "Formatting Characters with the Font Dialog Box," on page 303.

- The Formatting toolbar, which you can display by choosing View, Toolbars, Formatting.

> For details, see "Formatting Characters with the Formatting Toolbar," on page 308.

- Shortcut keys.

> For details, see "Formatting Characters with Shortcut Keys," on page 308.

Table 12-1. Types of Character Formatting You Can Apply to Text

Character Formatting Type	Description	Methods You Can Use to Apply the Formatting
Font		
Font	The general type of the characters: Times New Roman, Arial, Courier New, and so on.	● Font dialog box (Font tab) ● Formatting toolbar (Font drop-down list)
Font style	The basic look of the characters: regular, italic, bold, or bold italic.	● Font dialog box (Font tab) ● Formatting toolbar ● Shortcut keys
Size	The height of the characters, measured in points (1 point = $1/72$ inch).	● Font dialog box (Font tab) ● Formatting toolbar (Font Size drop-down list) ● Shortcut keys (to increase or decrease size)

(continued)

Table 12-1. *(continued)*

Character Formatting Type	Description	Methods You Can Use to Apply the Formatting
Underline	Character underlining, which can be single, double, thick, dashed, dotted, or in one of many other styles. You can also select Words Only underlining to apply single underlining that skips spaces.	● Font dialog box (Font tab) ● Formatting toolbar (single underline only) ● Shortcut keys (single, double, or Words Only underlining)
Underline color	The color of the underlining. You can select a standard color, create a custom color, or choose Automatic (which uses the Window Font color selected in the Display program of the Windows Control Panel).	● Font dialog box (Font tab)
Color	The color of the characters. You can select a standard color, create a custom color, or choose Automatic (which uses the Window Font color selected in the Display program of the Windows Control Panel).	● Font dialog box (Font tab) ● Formatting toolbar (Font Color drop-down palette)
Effects	Character enhancements: strikethrough, double strikethrough, superscript, subscript, shadow, outline, emboss, engrave, small caps, all caps, and hidden.	● Font dialog box (Font tab) ● Shortcut keys (superscript, subscript, hidden, small caps, or all caps)
Character Spacing		
Scale	The amount by which the characters are increased or decreased in width, expressed as a percentage of the normal character width.	● Font dialog box (Character Spacing tab)
Spacing	The amount added to or subtracted from the intercharacter spacing to produce expanded or condensed text.	● Font dialog box (Character Spacing tab)

Table 12-1. *(continued)*

Character Formatting Type	Description	Methods You Can Use to Apply the Formatting
Position	Amount by which the characters are raised or lowered from the baseline. (Unlike the subscript or superscript effects, the character size is not reduced.)	● Font dialog box (Character Spacing tab)
Kerning for fonts	Moving certain character pairs (for example, *A* and *W*) closer together.	● Font dialog box (Character Spacing tab)

Other Character Formatting Types

Animations	Visual special effects displayed by text, such as blinking, shimmering, sparkling, and so on. Intended primarily for regular Word documents that will be read online. Text animation, of course, won't print. If it's applied to a Web page document, it won't be displayed by popular browsers (such as Microsoft Internet Explorer 5).	● Font dialog box (Text Effects tab) To view animated text, the Animated Text option must be checked in View tab of the Options dialog box (opened by choosing Tools, Options, View).
Language	Controls which dictionary (English, French, or German, for example) the Word proofing tools (such as the spelling and grammar checkers) use to correct the text. Can also be used to exclude text from proofing. The proofing tools are discussed in Chapter 17, "Proofing Word Documents."	● Language dialog box, described in "Marking the Language," on page 504
Borders and shading	Borders around the text and background shading. (Borders and shading can be applied either as a character format to one or more characters or as a paragraph format to one or more entire paragraphs.)	● Borders And Shading dialog box and Tables And Borders toolbar, both discussed in "Adding Borders and Shading," on page 356

Chapter 12

3 If you didn't select characters in step 1, begin typing. The character formatting will be applied to all characters you type until you move the insertion point or press Ctrl+Spacebar or Ctrl+Shift+Z.

> **note** A newly inserted character normally acquires the character formatting of the previous character. Or, if you type the character at the beginning of a new paragraph, it acquires the formatting of the *following* character. However, in either case, this formatting is overridden by any character formatting you select immediately before typing the character.

For information on applying character formatting to handwriting you've inserted into a Word document, see "Entering Handwriting," on page 102.

To remove directly applied character formatting and restore the character formatting specified by the paragraph's style, select the text and press Ctrl+Spacebar or Ctrl+ Shift+Z. Also, if you're inserting new text, you can press one of these key combinations to discard any directly applied character formatting acquired from the adjoining text. For example, if you're inserting text following an italicized phrase, you can press Ctrl+ Spacebar to begin inserting nonitalicized text—assuming the italics were directly applied and aren't part of the paragraph style.

For information on using Word's new Clear Formatting command to remove formatting, see "Removing All Formatting," on page 326.

newfeature!

To find out what formatting and style (or styles) have been applied to characters in your document, you can use the new Reveal Formatting task pane.

The Reveal Formatting task pane is described in "Using the Reveal Formatting Task Pane to View or Modify Formatting Features," on page 332.

---

tip   **Control Font Substitution**

If you open a document that contains text in a font that isn't installed on your machine, Word chooses one of your installed fonts and uses it to display the text. If you'd rather substitute a different font, choose Tools, Options, click the Compatibility tab in the Options dialog box, and click the Font Substitution button. Then, in the Font Substitution dialog box (shown in Figure 12-1), select the missing font in the Font Substitutions list and select the substitute font that you want to use to display the text in the Substituted Font drop-down list.

If you want to permanently convert the missing font to the specified substitute font, click the Convert Permanently button. If you don't click this button, selecting a new substitute font won't change the font designation in the document itself (the original font will still be used if the document is opened on a computer where the font is installed), but will merely change the font that Word uses to display and print the text.

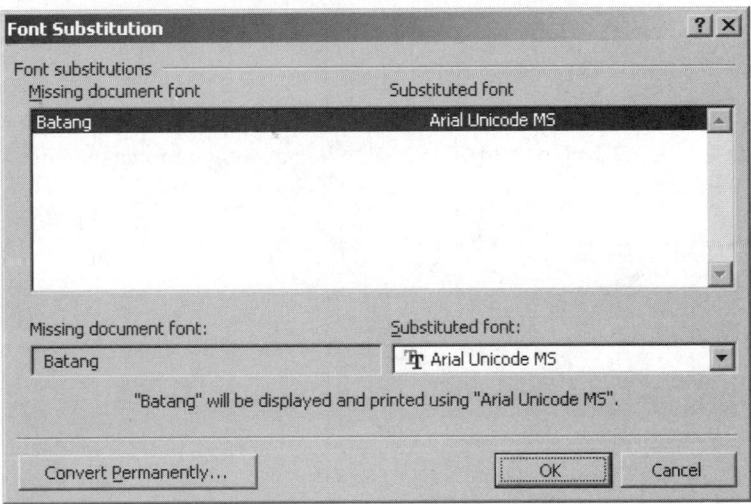

Figure 12-1. The Font Substitution dialog box allows you to temporarily or permanently assign substitute fonts.

Formatting Characters with the Font Dialog Box

To open the Font dialog box, choose Format, Font, or right-click the selected text and choose Font from the shortcut menu. To apply character formatting, click the appropriate tab—Font, Character Spacing, or Text Effects—and select the features you want. The three tabs are shown in Figures 12-2, 12-3, and 12-4, on pages 304 and 305. Selecting the formatting you want is easy because the Preview area in all tabs of the Font dialog box shows a text example formatted with the formatting selected in all the tabs.

For tips on entering measurement values into the text boxes of the Font dialog box, see the sidebar "Entering Measurements into Dialog Boxes," on page 306.

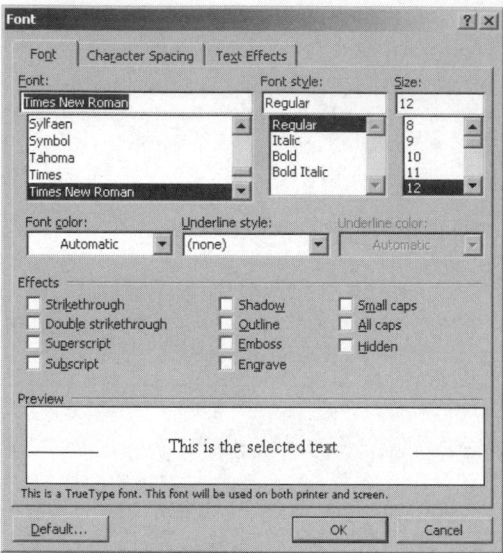

Figure 12-2. The Font tab of the Font dialog box allows you to change many text formatting features.

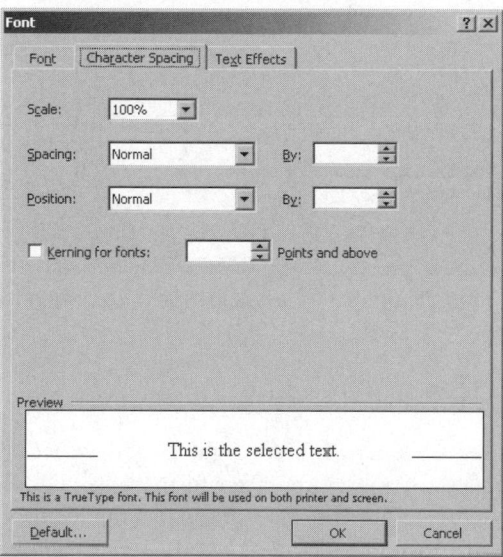

Figure 12-3. The Character Spacing tab of the Font dialog box lets you adjust the spacing and positioning of text.

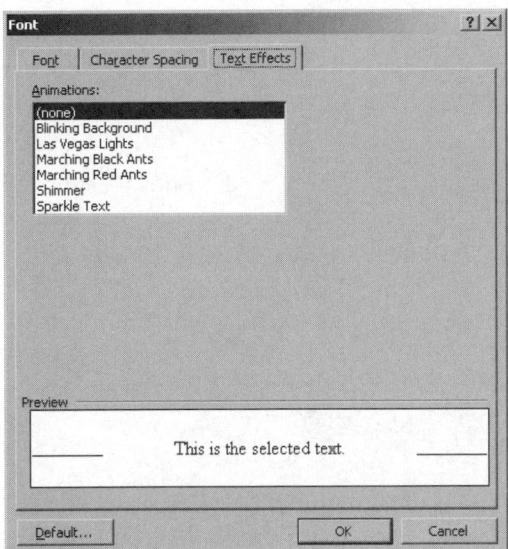

Figure 12-4. The Text Effects tab of the Font dialog box allows you to apply text animations.

When the Font dialog box is first displayed, it shows the current formatting of the selected text. If a particular formatting feature varies within the selected text (for example, part of the text is bold and part is not bold), the box indicating the formatting is left blank. Or, if the formatting is selected by checking an option, the check box contains a check mark with a shaded background. If you select a formatting option, it will be applied to all text in the selection.

Notice that Word displays information on the font that's currently selected in the Font list box on the Font tab. This information is shown at the bottom of the tab and indicates, for example, whether the font is a *TrueType* font. A TrueType font is a scalable font (one that you can make any size) that is installed in Windows. A TrueType font produces high-quality characters on almost any screen or printer and is a good choice if you want to be able to display the characters in a range of sizes or if you want to be able to print your document on a variety of printers.

Clicking the Superscript or Subscript box (also on the Font tab) raises or lowers the text by a standard amount and reduces the character size. To raise or lower the text by any amount without changing its size, open the Character Spacing tab and select either Raised or Lowered in the Position drop-down list (see Figure 12-3). Then enter into the By box the exact amount that the text should be moved, in points (1 point = 1/72 inch).

If you check the Hidden option on the Font tab, you can make the text invisible on the screen or on a printed copy of the document. To control the visibility of hidden text, choose Tools, Options. Hidden text will be visible on the screen only if the Hidden Text effect is checked on the View tab, and it will be visible on a printed copy of the document only if the Hidden Text option is checked on the Print tab.

Note that the Small Caps and All Caps effects on the Font tab change only the way the text is displayed and printed; they don't change the actual characters stored in the document. Therefore, if you remove the effect, the original capitalization of the text reappears.

When you specify a value other than 100% in the Scale drop-down list on the Character Spacing tab, you change the width of each character. In contrast, when you select Expanded or Condensed in the Spacing drop-down list, you affect the spaces between the characters, but you leave the widths of the characters themselves unchanged, as shown here.

200% Scale

Expanded Spacing

If you check the Kerning For Fonts option on the Character Spacing tab, Word reduces the spacing between certain character pairs— such as *A* and *W*—to give the text a more compact appearance. (In contrast, selecting the Condensed option in the Spacing drop-down list reduces the spacing between *all* characters in the selected text.) Word performs kerning only on characters that have a size equal to or greater than the size you enter into the Points And Above text box. Also, the selected font must be a TrueType (or Adobe Type 1) font.

You can click the Default button, displayed on all tabs of the Font dialog box, to change the default character formatting so that it conforms to the styles that you have selected in the Font, Character Spacing, and Text Effects tabs. Clicking Default (and responding Yes when prompted) assigns the selected formatting to the Normal style of the document and to the Normal style of the template that was used to create the document. (As explained in Chapter 14, "Advanced Word Formatting Techniques," modifying Normal affects all the other styles that are based on Normal.) As a result, whenever you create a new document using this template, the document text will display the new formatting. (Clicking Default will not, however, affect other documents that have already been created using the template.)

Entering Measurements into Dialog Boxes

Some of the text boxes in Word dialog boxes require you to enter measurements (for example, the By boxes following the Spacing and Position drop-down lists on the Character Spacing tab of the Font dialog box). Word displays the current value as a number followed by an abbreviation for the units. If you enter a new value, you should generally use the same units.

For example, consider a box in which Word displays the value 3 pt, meaning 3 points. If you type either **5** or **5 pt** into this box, the value is changed to 5 points. You can use another unit of measurement, provided that you specify the units. For example, you

Entering Measurements into Dialog Boxes *(continued)* could type **.05 in** into this box, and the value would be changed to .05 inches. The next time you opened the dialog box, Word would display this value in points—that is, 3.6 pt. (In some cases, Word will adjust the measurement to match its internal rules. For example, text can be raised or lowered only in half-point increments; therefore, in the By box following the Position drop-down list, Word would change .05 in to 3.5 pt.)

Note that you can change the standard units that Word uses for many of the values entered into dialog boxes. To do this, choose Tools, Options. Then click the General tab and select the units you want in the Measurement Units list.

The following table will help you work with the different units of measurement that Word recognizes.

Units	Abbreviation	Points	Picas	Lines	Centimeters	Millimeters	Inches
Points	pt	1	1/12	1/12	.035	.35	1/72
Picas	pi	12	1	1	.42	4.2	1/6
Lines	li	12	1	1	.42	4.2	1/6
Centimeters	cm	28.35	2.36	2.36	1	10	.39
Millimeters	mm	2.83	.24	.24	.10	1	.04
Inches	in *or* "	72	6	6	2.54	25.4	1

Troubleshooting

Cannot Underline Trailing Spaces

You want to use one of Word's fancy underlining styles (double, thick, dotted, dashed, wavy, or one of the others) to underline spaces at the end of a line, but Word won't display the underlining.

Word underlines spaces between two characters on a line, but it doesn't underline spaces that occur between the last nonspace character on a line and the end of the line. In the following example, Word underlines the spaces between the *e* and the *x*:

Sign here_____x

However, if you delete the *x*, the underlining disappears. To get around this limitation, you can replace the *x* with a nonbreaking space, which you insert by pressing Ctrl+Shift+Spacebar. Although a nonbreaking space is invisible, it's treated as a text character and preserves the underlining, as shown here:

Sign here_____

Formatting Characters with the Formatting Toolbar

You can use the buttons on the Formatting toolbar, shown here, to apply character formatting features to the current selection (or to the position of the insertion point).

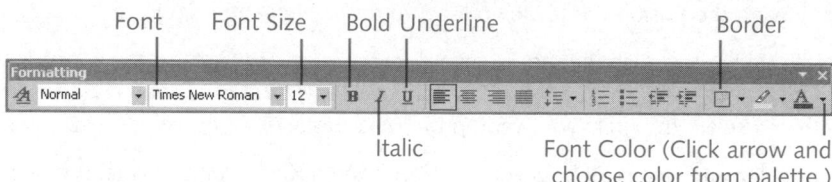

If the formatting applied by a button is currently assigned to *all* characters in the selection, the button is highlighted (that is, displayed with a box around it and a darker background color). The Bold, Italic, and Underline buttons *toggle* the formatting, as follows: If the first character of the selection doesn't have the formatting, clicking the button applies the format to all characters. If the first character of the selection already has the formatting, clicking the button removes the formatting from all characters. For example, if you select text in which the first character is not bold and click the Bold button, all the text will become bold; if you click Bold again, all the text will become nonbold.

To make it easier to find fonts, Word lists the recently applied fonts at the top of the Font drop-down list. Below these fonts (and separated by a double line), Word lists all available fonts in alphabetical order.

Formatting Characters with Shortcut Keys

You can also use the shortcut keys listed in Table 12-2 to apply character formatting to the selected text (or to the position of the insertion point).

Table 12-2. **Character Formatting Shortcut Keys**

Character Formatting Option	Shortcut Key	Toggles?
Bold	Ctrl+B	Yes
Italic	Ctrl+I	Yes
<u>Underline</u>	Ctrl+U	Yes

Table 12-2. *(continued)*

Character Formatting Option	Shortcut Key	Toggles?
<u>Double Underline</u>	Ctrl+Shift+D	Yes
<u>Words</u> <u>Only</u> <u>Underline</u>	Ctrl+Shift+W	Yes
Subscript (P_1)	Ctrl+=	Yes
Superscript (1st)	Ctrl+Shift+=	Yes
Hidden	Ctrl+Shift+H	Yes
SMALL CAPS	Ctrl+Shift+K	Yes
ALL CAPS	Ctrl+Shift+A	Yes
Increase font size to next size in Font Size list	Ctrl+> (that is, Ctrl+Shift+period)	No
Decrease font size to previous size in Font Size list	Ctrl+< (that is, Ctrl+Shift+comma)	No
Increase font size by exactly 1 point	Ctrl+]	No
Decrease font size by exactly 1 point	Ctrl+[	No
Assign Symbol font	Ctrl+Shift+Q	No

The shortcut keys that toggle work as follows: If the first character of the selection doesn't have the formatting, pressing the key applies the format to all characters. If the first character of the selection already has the formatting, pressing the key removes the formatting from all characters. For example, if you select text in which the first character is not bold and press Ctrl+B, all the text will become bold. If you press Ctrl+B again, all the text will become nonbold.

Formatting Paragraphs Directly

Paragraph formatting affects the appearance of entire paragraphs. In general, the best way to format your paragraphs is by applying appropriate styles. Doing so makes your formatting easier to modify and helps enhance its uniformity. (If you don't have a suitable style for a particular type of paragraph, you can modify an existing style or define a new one, as explained in Chapter 14, "Advanced Word Formatting Techniques.") However, you might want to directly apply paragraph formatting to make an occasional adjustment to the appearance of a paragraph.

For example, you might want to center a specific paragraph or increase its left indent. (Directly applied paragraph formatting overrides the formatting specified by the paragraph's style.) Also, even if you use only styles for formatting your paragraphs, you'll need to know the techniques presented here to be able to customize or create styles.

Styles are discussed in "Applying Styles and Reusing Formats," on page 320.

To directly apply paragraph formatting, perform the following steps:

1 To format a single paragraph, place the insertion point anywhere within the paragraph, or select all or part of the paragraph. To format several paragraphs, select at least a portion of each one.

2 Apply the paragraph formatting. Table 12-3 summarizes the different types of paragraph formatting you can apply, and for each type, it indicates which of the four basic methods you can use to apply the formatting:

- The Paragraph dialog box, which you open by choosing Format, Paragraph.

- The Formatting toolbar, which you can display by choosing View, Toolbars, Formatting.

- The ruler, which you can display by choosing View, Ruler.

- Shortcut keys.

For a description of text selection methods, see "Selecting the Text," on page 270. For details on paragraph formatting, see "Formatting Paragraphs with the Paragraph Dialog Box," on page 314. For details about the Formatting toolbar, see "Formatting Paragraphs with the Formatting Toolbar," on page 316. For details about using the ruler, see "Formatting Paragraphs with the Ruler," on page 317. For details on using shortcut keys, see "Formatting Paragraphs with Shortcut Keys," on page 317.

note When you press Enter within an existing paragraph to create a new paragraph, the new paragraph automatically acquires the paragraph formatting you assigned to the existing paragraph.

Table 12-3. **Types of Paragraph Formatting**

Paragraph Formatting Type	Description	Methods You Can Use to Apply the Formatting
Indents and Spacing		
Alignment	Justification of the paragraph text: left (text aligned with left indent), right (aligned with right indent), centered (centered between left and right indents), or justified (aligned with both indents).	• Paragraph dialog box (Indents And Spacing tab) • Formatting toolbar • Shortcut keys
Indentation	Horizontal position of the paragraph text relative to document margins: left indent, right indent, first line indent, or hanging indent. If you're creating a Web page, keep in mind that a negative left or right indent may cause text to be cut off in the browser (because a browser doesn't show the full margin areas).	• Paragraph dialog box (Indents And Spacing tab) • Formatting toolbar (left indent only) • Ruler • Shortcut keys (left or hanging indent only)
Spacing before	Additional space inserted above the paragraph.	• Paragraph dialog box (Indents And Spacing tab) • Shortcut keys (only to add or remove 12 points of spacing before the paragraph)
Spacing after	Additional space inserted below the paragraph.	• Paragraph dialog box (Indents And Spacing tab)
Line spacing	Height of each line of text in the paragraph—for example, single or double spacing, or an exact line height.	• Paragraph dialog box (Indents And Spacing tab) • Formatting toolbar • Shortcut keys (single, 1.5, and double spacing only)
Line and Page Breaks		
Widow/ orphan control	Prevents printing the last line of the paragraph by itself at the top of a new page (a *widow*) or printing the first line by itself at the bottom of a page (an *orphan*).	• Paragraph dialog box (Line And Page Breaks tab)

(continued)

Table 12-3. *(continued)*

Paragraph Formatting Type	Description	Methods You Can Use to Apply the Formatting
Keep lines together	All lines in the paragraph are printed on the same page—that is, Word does not insert a page break within the paragraph.	● Paragraph dialog box (Line And Page Breaks)
Keep with next	Prevents Word from inserting a page break between the paragraph and the next paragraph.	● Paragraph dialog box (Line And Page Breaks)
Page break before	The paragraph is printed at the top of a new page.	● Paragraph dialog box (Line And Page Breaks)
Suppress line numbers	If you apply line numbering to the document, the paragraph is excluded from numbering. (See "Adjusting the Page Layout," on page 545.)	● Paragraph dialog box (Line And Page Breaks)
Don't hyphenate	If you hyphenate the document, the paragraph is excluded from hyphenation. (See "Hyphenating Your Documents," on page 498.)	● Paragraph dialog box (Line And Page Breaks)
Other Character Formatting Types		
Outline level	Converts the paragraph to a heading that you can work with in Outline view.	● Paragraph dialog box (Indents And Spacing tab) Outline level paragraph formatting is discussed in "Changing Outline Levels," on page 418.
Tabs	Position and type of tab stops in effect within a paragraph.	● Ruler ● Tabs dialog box You can set tab stops in the selected paragraph by using the ruler, or by choosing Format, Tabs to open the Tabs dialog box.

Table 12-3. *(continued)*

Paragraph Formatting Type	Description	Methods You Can Use to Apply the Formatting
Borders and shading	Borders around the text and background shading. Borders and shading can be applied either as a character format to one or more characters or as a paragraph format to one or more entire paragraphs.	● Borders And Shading dialog box ● Tables And Borders toolbar Using the Borders And Shading dialog box or the Tables And Borders toolbar to apply borders or background shading to paragraphs is covered in "Adding Borders and Shading," on page 356.
Bullets and numbering	Automatic display of a bullet character or number for a paragraph in a list.	● Formatting toolbar ● Bullets And Numbering dialog box Using the Formatting toolbar or the Bullets And Numbering dialog box to apply bullets or numbering to paragraphs is covered in "Ordering Text in Bulleted and Numbered Lists," on page 372.

To remove directly applied paragraph formatting and restore the paragraph formatting that is specified by the paragraph's style, select the paragraph or paragraphs as described in step 1, and then press Ctrl+Q. Also, if you press Enter within an existing paragraph to create a new paragraph, you can press Ctrl+Q before typing in the new paragraph to discard any directly applied paragraph formatting acquired from the existing paragraph. For example, if you typed in a heading and assigned it centered alignment, when you press Enter to begin typing in the body text following the heading, you can press Ctrl+Q to discard the centered alignment format (and, as explained earlier in the chapter, you can press Ctrl+Spacebar or Ctrl+Shift+Z to discard any character formatting you directly applied to the heading).

> For information on using Word's new Clear Formatting command to remove formatting, see "Removing All Formatting," on page 326.

newfeature!

To find out what formatting and style (or styles) have been applied to characters in your document, you can use the new Reveal Formatting task pane.

> The Reveal Formatting task pane is described in "Using the Reveal Formatting Task Pane to View or Modify Formatting Features," on page 332.

Formatting Paragraphs with the Paragraph Dialog Box

To open the Paragraph dialog box, choose Format, Paragraph, or right-click within the selected text, and then choose Paragraph from the shortcut menu. To apply paragraph formatting, click either the Indents And Spacing tab (shown in Figure 12-5) or the Line And Page Breaks tab (shown in Figure 12-6), and then select the features you want. As with the Font dialog box, choosing formatting features in the Paragraph dialog box is easy because Word displays a text example formatted with the selected features in the Preview area of both tabs.

> For tips on entering measurement values into the text boxes of the Paragraph dialog box, see the sidebar "Entering Measurements into Dialog Boxes," on page 306.

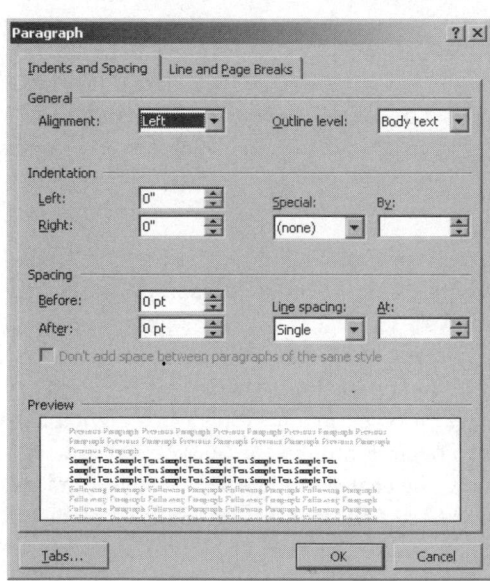

Figure 12-5. The Indents And Spacing tab of the Paragraph dialog box lets you adjust the alignment, indentation, and spacing of paragraphs.

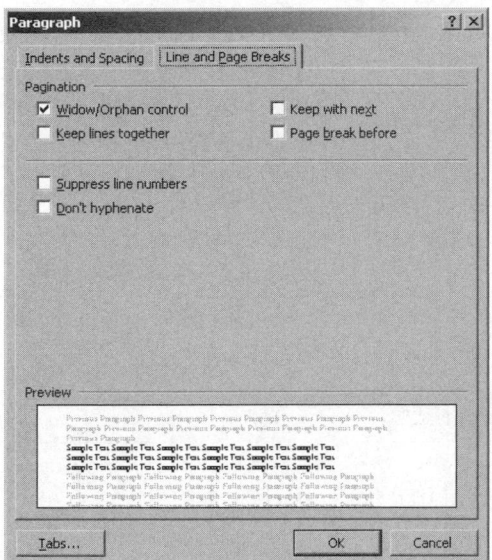

Figure 12-6. The Line And Page Breaks tab of the Paragraph dialog box allows you to control pagination, line numbering, and hyphenation of paragraphs.

The *left paragraph indent* is the distance that the left edge of the paragraph text is moved in from the left margin area (a positive indent) or out into the left margin area (a negative indent). Likewise, the *right paragraph indent* is the distance the right edge of the text is moved in from the right margin area (a positive indent) or out into the right margin area (a negative indent). The *margins* are the distances between the text and the edges of the page when the indents are set to 0. You set the margins when you adjust the page setup. The easiest way to learn how to use the various indentation settings is to change the values and observe the effects on the preview text.

Adjusting the page setup is described in Chapter 18, "Designing and Printing Professional-Looking Pages." For instructions on setting the document margins and a description of the difference between margins and indents, see "Setting the Margins and Page Orientation," on page 536.

If you select First Line in the Special drop-down list on the Indents and Spacing tab, the first line of the paragraph will be moved to the right of the other paragraph lines (by the amount you enter into the following By text box). If you select the Hanging option in the Special list, all lines except the first will be moved to the right (by the amount you enter into the following By text box).

Line spacing is the total height of each line of text in a paragraph. Table 12-4 shows how to use the options in the Line Spacing drop-down list to achieve various line spacing effects.

Chapter 12

Table 12-4. Creating Different Types of Paragraph Line Spacing

To Produce this Line Spacing Effect	Do This Using the Line Spacing Drop-Down List and the At Text Box
Make each line just high enough to accommodate the characters in the line. (If a particular line contains an unusually tall character, that line will be made higher than the others.)	In the Line Spacing drop-down list, select Single.
Make the height of each line 1.5 times its height with Single spacing. (If a particular line contains an unusually tall character, that line will be made higher than the others.)	In the Line Spacing drop-down list, select 1.5 Lines.
Make the height of each line 2 times its height with Single spacing. (If a particular line contains an unusually tall character, that line will be made higher than the others.)	In the Line Spacing drop-down list, select Double.
Set the *minimum* height of a line. (If a character in a line is taller than this value, the height of that line will be increased.)	In the Line Spacing drop-down list, select At Least and enter the desired line height into the At text box.
Set the *exact* height of each line. (This option makes all lines evenly spaced. However, if a character in a line is taller than the line height specified, it will be cut off.)	In the Line Spacing drop-down list, select Exactly and enter the desired line height into the At text box.
Make the height of each line any multiple of its height with Single spacing. (If a particular line contains an unusually tall character, that line will be made higher than the others.)	In the Line Spacing drop-down list, select Multiple and enter the desired multiple into the At text box.

Formatting Paragraphs with the Formatting Toolbar

You can use the buttons on the Formatting toolbar, shown here, to apply paragraph formatting features to the currently selected paragraph or paragraphs.

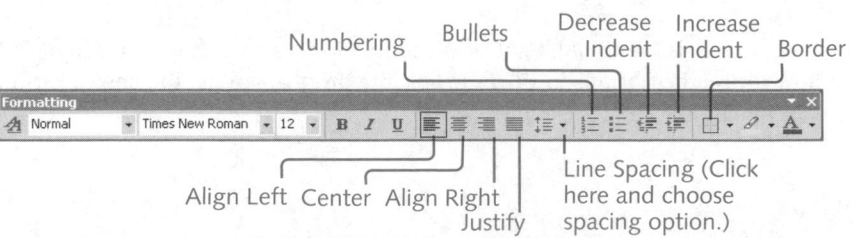

Chapter 12: Effective Formatting in Word

> **note** The Decrease Indent and Increase Indent buttons affect the *left* paragraph indent.

Formatting Paragraphs with the Ruler

You can also use the ruler to apply paragraph formatting. If the ruler isn't displayed, choose View, Ruler. You can also display it temporarily by placing the mouse pointer over the gray band at the top of the document area of the window, as shown here:

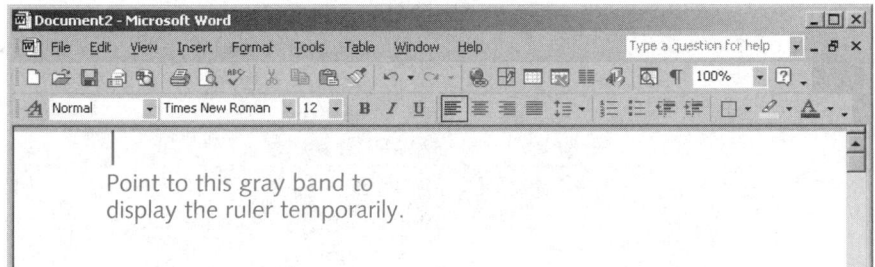

Point to this gray band to display the ruler temporarily.

You can use the ruler to set paragraph indents, as shown here:

Drag to set left indent of first line only.

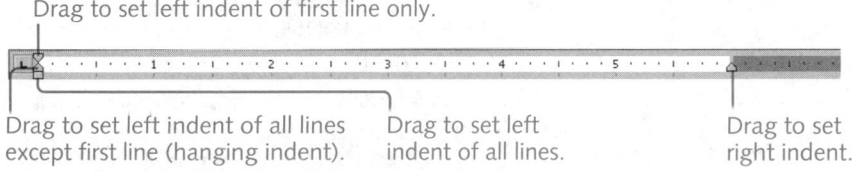

Drag to set left indent of all lines except first line (hanging indent).

Drag to set left indent of all lines.

Drag to set right indent.

Formatting Paragraphs with Shortcut Keys

You can use the shortcut keys listed in Table 12-5 to quickly apply paragraph formatting to the selected paragraph or paragraphs.

Table 12-5. **Paragraph Formatting Shortcut Keys**

Paragraph Formatting Action	Shortcut Key	Comment
Increase left paragraph indent	Ctrl+M	Indent is moved to the next tab stop.
Decrease left paragraph indent	Ctrl+Shift+M	Indent is moved to the previous tab stop. This key cannot be used to create a negative left indent.
Increase hanging indent	Ctrl+T	All paragraph lines are indented except the first line. Each time you press the shortcut key, the hanging indent is moved right to the next tab stop.

(continued)

Table 12-5. *(continued)*

Paragraph Formatting Action	Shortcut Key	Comment
Decrease hanging indent	Ctrl+Shift+T	Hanging indent is moved left to the previous tab stop.
Add or remove 12 points of extra space above the paragraph	Ctrl+0 (zero at top of keyboard, *not* on numeric keypad)	Toggles feature on or off.
Create single spacing	Ctrl+1 (1 at top of keyboard, *not* on numeric keypad)	Same as Single option in the Paragraph dialog box.
Create 1.5 spacing	Ctrl+5 (5 at top of keyboard, *not* on numeric keypad)	Same as 1.5 Lines option in the Paragraph dialog box.
Create double spacing	Ctrl+2 (2 at top of keyboard, *not* on numeric keypad)	Same as Double option in the Paragraph dialog box.
Left-align paragraph	Ctrl+L	Text is aligned with left indent.
Right-align paragraph	Ctrl+R	Text is aligned with right indent.
Center paragraph	Ctrl+E	Text is centered between left and right indents.
Justify paragraph	Ctrl+J	Text is aligned with both left and right indents. (Word adjusts the character spacing as necessary.)

Writing Macros That Apply Formats Quickly

If you frequently use a particular character or paragraph formatting feature that doesn't have a built-in toolbar button or shortcut key (for example, the Strikethrough character format or the Keep Lines Together paragraph format), you might want to add a toolbar button or define a shortcut key to apply the feature quickly. Doing so can save you from having to open a dialog box every time you want to use the format. Although you can't directly assign a formatting feature to a button or shortcut key, you can assign a macro or a style to a button or shortcut key. However, a macro that you record or a style that you define applies an entire *set* of formatting features, not just the one you want to apply.

Writing Macros That Apply Formats Quickly *(continued)*   One possible solution is to record a macro to apply the format, and then manually edit the macro to remove the unwanted formats. (If, while recording a macro, you make a setting in a dialog box, such as the Font or Paragraph dialog box, *all* the settings in the dialog box are stored in the macro, not just the one that you changed to apply a specific formatting feature.)

Another solution is to use the Visual Basic for Applications (VBA) Editor to write a simple macro, such as the StrikeThru macro presented here, which applies the Strikethrough character format, leaving all other character and paragraph formats unchanged. You can enter this macro yourself using the VBA Editor, following the brief instructions given here. Or, you can use the Organizer to copy the macros from the WordInsideOut module in the WordInsideOut.dot file provided on the book's companion CD into your own Normal template.

1   From the Tools menu in Word, choose Macro, Visual Basic Editor. This will run the Microsoft Visual Basic editor.

2   In the Project Explorer pane at the upper left of the Visual Basic editor window, double-click the Normal/Microsoft Word Objects/This Document item. (Expand the tree, if necessary, to access this item. If the Project Explorer pane isn't displayed, choose View, Project Explorer.) This will open a code window where you can enter code that will be stored in your Normal template.

3   Type the following macro code into the code window:

```
Sub StrikeThru()
'StrikeThru macro
   With Selection.Font
      .StrikeThrough = True
   End With
End Sub
```

4   In the Visual Basic editor, choose File, Close And Return To Microsoft Word.

5   Use the procedures described in "Defining Shortcut Keys (Word Only)," on page 217, to define a shortcut key for the StrikeThru macro. You can also use the techniques given in "Modifying Toolbars and Menus," on page 209, to add a toolbar button for running the macro.

You can now test this macro as follows: Select a block of text, and then press the shortcut key you defined—or the button you added—for running the StrikeThru macro. The StrikeThrough format will be applied to the text, and all current formatting features will be left unaltered.

(continued)

Chapter 12

> **Writing Macros That Apply Formats Quickly** *(continued)*   To ascertain the Visual Basic properties required to apply formatting features other than StrikeThrough, you can press F2 in the Visual Basic editor and use the Object Browser to look up the properties, or you can record macros that set various formatting features and then inspect the resulting code to determine the property values for each feature.
>
> Chapter 9, "Customizing the Office XP Application Interface," explains how to add toolbar buttons and define shortcut keys. For information on recording and editing macros, see Part 10 of this book." For instructions on using the Organizer, see "Using the Organizer," on page 409.

Applying Styles and Reusing Formats

A style is a named collection of formatting features that you can apply to text in your document. For example, the built-in Normal style supplied with Word consists of the Times New Roman font, a 12-point font size, left paragraph alignment, single line spacing, and widow and orphan control. If you assign the Normal style to a paragraph of text, the text instantly acquires this entire set of formatting features. The advantages of applying a style, rather than assigning individual character and formatting features as described earlier in the chapter, include the following:

● If you want to assign an entire set of formatting features, applying a style can be faster than assigning the individual formatting features one at a time. And you can easily assign the style to a toolbar button or shortcut key to make it even faster to apply the features.

● Using styles helps you maintain consistent formatting within a document. For example, to maintain uniform-looking top-level headings in a document, it would be much easier to simply assign all those headings the Heading 1 built-in style, rather than to try to remember the individual formatting features you use for headings and assign them directly. And because a style can be stored in a document template, copied between templates and documents, and shared by members of your workgroup, you can easily maintain consistent formatting within *all* your documents.

● If you use styles, it's much easier to globally modify the format of a particular element. For example, if all the top-level headings in a document have the Heading 1 style, you can quickly reformat all of them by modifying the Heading 1 style, rather than having to find and change each heading separately. You can even apply your modifications to existing or new documents by using the modified Heading 1 style in those documents.

Chapter 12: Effective Formatting in Word

For information on creating and modifying styles and on copying styles between documents and templates, see Chapter 14, "Advanced Word Formatting Techniques."

Word uses four different types of styles:

- **Paragraph styles.** A paragraph style includes both paragraph and character formatting features and applies to one or more entire paragraphs. It fully specifies the format of the paragraph—the font, font size, alignment, and line spacing, plus optional features such as italic characters, an indentation, or widow and orphan control. Every paragraph in a Word document has a paragraph style. The paragraphs in a new document usually have the Normal paragraph style unless you explicitly assign a different one. (Certain templates, however, might create paragraphs assigned other styles, such as Body Text.) The methods for applying paragraph styles are covered in the next section.

- **Character styles.** A character style includes one or more character formatting features and can be assigned to any block of characters. Unlike a paragraph style, a character style doesn't need to fully specify the character format. For example, a particular character style might specify only bold and italic formatting. If you assigned this style to a block of text, Word would remove any directly applied character formatting, apply the bold and italic formats to the text, and preserve all the other character formatting specified by the paragraph style, such as the character font, size, and effects. The methods for applying character styles are covered in the next section.

Because Word provides relatively few built-in character styles, the techniques you learn in this chapter won't be truly useful until you learn how to create custom character styles in Chapter 14, "Advanced Word Formatting Techniques."

note If a character style includes formatting that's also part of the paragraph's style, applying the character style can result in turning off the formatting. This happens with optional formatting features that can be turned on or off, such as bold, italic, all caps, and strikethrough. For example, if a character style includes italic, applying the character style to text within a paragraph whose style also includes italic removes the italics. This is in accord with common writing practices; for example, a typical way to emphasize a word within an all-italic heading is to remove the italics from that word.

newfeature!
- **Table styles.** A table style includes a set of formatting features and table properties. You can apply a table style to a Word table to quickly change the overall look of the table.

Chapter 12

newfeature!
● **List styles.**   A list style includes a set of formatting features that create a particular type of outline numbered list (that is, a multilevel numbered or bulleted list).

> Table styles are discussed in "Formatting Tables by Applying Table Styles," on page 352, and list styles are discussed in "Ordering Text in Bulleted and Numbered Lists," on page 372.

newfeature!
Word 2002 provides a new alternative to defining and using styles: *automatically saved formats*. Whenever you apply a unique set of formatting features to a block of text in a document, Word automatically saves a description of that format combination and lists it along with your available styles (in the Styles And Formatting task pane and in the Style drop-down list on the Formatting toolbar, which is described in the following sections). You can later apply one of these saved formats to additional text in the document in the same way you would apply a style.

> **note**   Word saves and displays saved formats only if the Keep Track Of Formatting option is checked. To access this option, choose Tools, Options and click the Edit tab.

Saved formats offer some of the advantages of styles. Primarily, you can use them to maintain consistent document formatting. Consider, for example, that you type the first top-level heading into a new document, and then directly apply a bold, 16-point font to the whole paragraph, together with centered alignment. Word will automatically save the format and list its description ("16 pt, Bold, Centered") together with your styles. When you type another top-level heading later in the document, you can simply apply this saved format rather than trying to remember the different formatting features you used previously and apply them individually. The methods for applying your saved formats are discussed in the next section.

InsideOut

Although saved formats eliminate the need to define styles, and are thus somewhat more convenient, they aren't as easy to use as styles (once they're defined), nor are they as effective as styles at maintaining formatting consistency. First, because saved formats don't have names that indicate their purposes as styles do (such as Heading 1, Body Text, and List Bullet), it can be difficult to pick the appropriate one; and the more saved formats you accumulate, the harder it becomes. Also, because you can't store saved formats in templates or copy them between documents and templates (as you can with styles), they don't help you maintain formatting consistency among the separate documents that you or your workgroup create.

newfeature!
Checking the Consistency of Your Formatting

If the Keep Track Of Formatting option is checked (enabling saved formats, as discussed in the previous section), you can also check Mark Formatting Inconsistencies option, which turns on Word's new *formatting consistency checker*. (You access both options by choosing Tools, Options and clicking the Edit tab.) If the formatting consistency checker is on, as you type in and format your document, Word will display a wavy, blue underline under any text it considers inconsistently formatted with the rest of the document. To change the formatting—or to have Word ignore the inconsistency—right-click the underlined text and choose a command from the top of the shortcut menu shown here:

Inconsistently Formatted Heading

> Make this text consistent with formatting Arial, 14 pt, Bold
>
> Ignore Once
>
> Ignore Rule
>
> Cut

newfeature!
Assigning Paragraph Styles, Character Styles, and Saved Formats

To apply paragraph or character style, or a saved format, to text in your document, perform the following steps:

1 Select the text as follows:

- To apply a paragraph style (or a saved format containing paragraph formatting) to a single paragraph, place the insertion point anywhere within the paragraph. To apply the style or saved format to several paragraphs, select at least a portion of all of the paragraphs. To apply the style or saved format to a new paragraph that doesn't yet contain text, place the insertion point before the paragraph mark for that paragraph (you can do this whether or not the paragraph mark is visible).

- To apply a character style (or a saved format containing only character formatting), select the text. Or, to apply the style or saved format to the text you're about to type, place the insertion point at the position where you want to insert the text.

> **tip** **Apply a Style to a Word Without Selecting It**
>
> To apply a character style (or a saved format containing only character formatting) to a single word, you can place the insertion point anywhere within the word rather than selecting the word. This technique works, however, only if the When Selecting Automatically Select Entire Word option is checked. To access this option, choose Tools, Options and click the Edit tab.

2 Choose Format, Styles And Formatting, or click the Styles And Formatting button on the Formatting toolbar. This will open the Styles And Formatting task pane (shown in Figure 12-7).

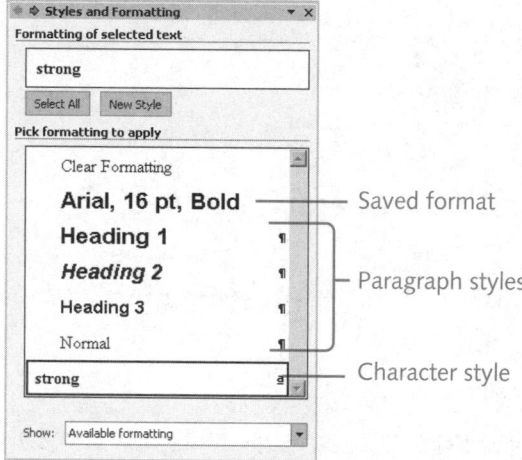

Figure 12-7. This figure shows the Styles And Formatting task pane with Available Formatting selected in the Show drop-down list.

3 In the Show drop-down list near the bottom of the task pane, select a category to control the styles that are displayed, as shown here:

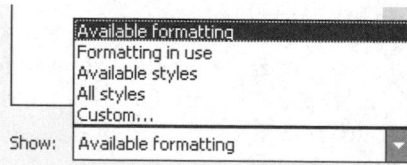

- To show all styles and saved formats currently used in the document, styles stored in the document, and frequently used heading styles (Heading 1, Heading 2, and Heading 3), select Available Formatting.

- To show all styles and saved formats currently used in the document, select Formatting In Use.

Chapter 12: Effective Formatting in Word

- To show all styles currently used in the document, and frequently used heading styles (Heading 1, Heading 2, and Heading 3), select Available Styles.

- To show all user-defined styles and most built-in styles that are available to the document, but not saved formats, select All Styles.

note Word displays saved formats only if the Keep Track Of Formatting option is checked. To access this option, choose Tools, Options and click the Edit tab. If the Keep Track Of Formatting option is cleared, the Show drop-down list omits the Available Formatting option and it replaces the Formatting In Use option with the Styles In Use option.

tip **Control Which Styles Are Displayed**

To specify exactly which styles and saved formats Word displays in the Styles And Formatting task pane, at the bottom of the Show drop-down list, click the Custom item, which opens the Format Settings dialog box (shown in Figure 12-8). Using this dialog box, you will be able to display some built-in styles that aren't normally shown even if you select the All Styles option in the Show list (such as Caption and Comment Text).

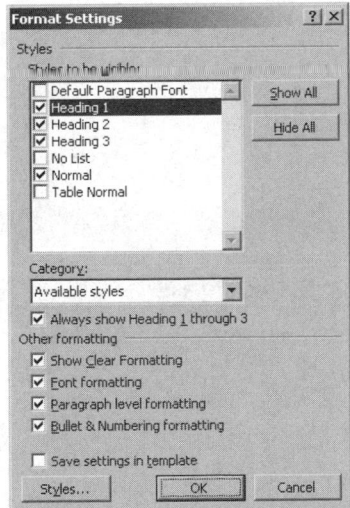

Figure 12-8. The Format Settings dialog box allows you to specify exactly which styles and saved formats Word displays in the Styles And Formatting task pane.

4 To apply a particular style or saved format to the selected text, click the item name in the Styles And Formatting task pane. Paragraph and character styles each have a name (such as Heading 2 or Strong). A paragraph style is marked with ¶ and a character style is marked with a̲. A saved format has a format description (such as "16 pt, Bold, Centered") rather than an name and isn't marked with a symbol. To help you select the appropriate style or saved format, Word displays each item using the item's formatting.

> **note** Some of the built-in styles are used for standard Word elements. For example, Word automatically assigns the Comment Text style to comment text and the Header style to page headers. You can, however, assign these styles to any paragraphs in your document.

Notice that at the top of the Styles And Formatting task pane, the Formatting Of Selected Text box displays the style or saved format currently assigned to the selected text. You can click the down arrow to work with the selection or with other styles, as seen here:

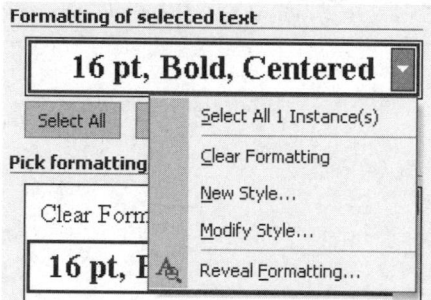

> The first two commands on this menu are discussed in the following sections. The New Style and the Modify Style commands, which create a new style or modify an existing one, are discussed in Chapter 14, "Advanced Word Formatting Techniques." The Reveal Formatting command displays the Reveal Formatting task pane, explained in "Using the Reveal Formatting Task Pane to View or Modify Formatting Features," on page 332.

newfeature!
Removing All Formatting

To use the new Clear Formatting command to remove all formatting from text, perform the following steps:

1 Select the text like this:

Chapter 12: Effective Formatting in Word

■ To remove directly applied character formatting or a character style, select the characters with the formatting or style you want to remove, but be sure *not* to select all the text in a paragraph. The Clear Formatting command will then remove all character formatting or a character style and restore the character formatting specified by the paragraph style of the paragraph containing the text. That is, Clear Formatting will have the same effect as the Ctrl+Spacebar or Ctrl+Shift+Z shortcut keys.

The Ctrl+Spacebar and Ctrl+Shift+Z shortcut keys are described in "Formatting Characters Directly," on page 298.

■ To remove directly applied paragraph formatting plus the paragraph style, place the insertion point within the paragraph or select all text in the paragraph (you don't need to include the paragraph mark). Clear Formatting will then remove all directly applied paragraph formatting, and—if the paragraph has a style other than Normal—it will convert the paragraph's style to Normal. Note that this is *not* the same as the effect of the Ctrl+Q shortcut key, which removes directly applied paragraph formatting but doesn't remove the style.

The Ctrl+Q shortcut key was explained in "Formatting Paragraphs Directly," on page 309.

2 Issue the Clear Formatting command in one of the following ways:

■ In the Styles And Formatting task pane, click the Clear Formatting item at the top of the list, as shown here:

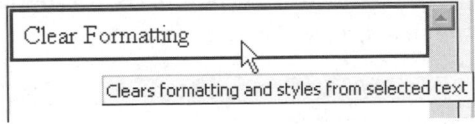

(This item doesn't appear if you select All Styles in the Show drop-down list.)

■ From the Formatting Of Selected Text menu at the top of the Styles And Formatting task pane (shown in Figure 12-7), choose Clear Formatting.

■ In the Style drop-down list on the Formatting toolbar, select the Clear Formatting item.

■ Choose Edit, Clear, Formats.

> **note** The Clear Formatting command preserves all hyperlinks in the text, as well as the formatting of the hyperlinks (usually a blue font color with underlining).

newfeature!
Selecting All Text with the Same Style or Formatting

You can instantly select all text throughout the document that has a particular style or saved format. Once you do this, you can apply a new style or saved format to the text, directly apply new formatting, use the Clear Formatting command to remove all formatting from the text, or work with the text in other ways.

To select all text that has the same style or saved format as the current selection, at the top of the Styles And Formatting task pane, click the Select All button, or choose Select All from the Formatting Of Selected Text menu shown here:

Click this button...   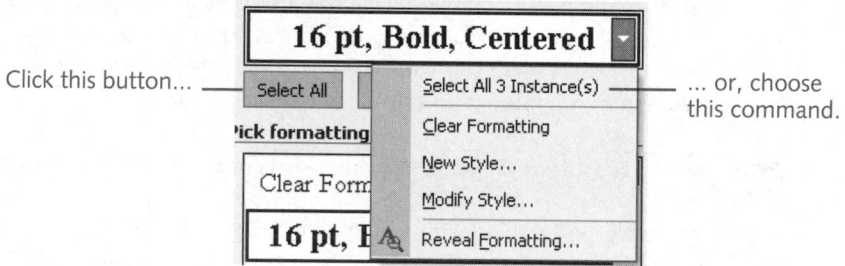   ... or, choose this command.

To select all text that has one of the styles or saved formats listed in the Styles And Formatting task pane, click the down arrow next to the style or saved format and choose the Select All command, as seen here:

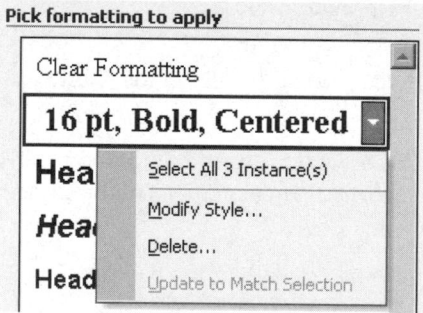

For example, if you have been using a particular saved format (for example, "16 pt, Bold, Centered") to consistently format your top-level headings throughout a document, but then decide you'd like to globally change the font size to 18 points, you could select all text that has this saved format and then directly apply an 18-point font size (using the Font dialog box or the Font Size drop-down list on the Formatting toolbar). This would reformat all your headings and also update the saved format description in the Styles And Formatting task pane.

> For information on using Word 2002's enhanced Find or Replace command to globally select or reformat all text with a particular format or style, see "Finding and Replacing Text and Formatting" on page 281. For a description of the commands in the Styles And Formatting task pane that are used to create, modify, or delete styles, see Chapter 14, "Advanced Word Formatting Techniques."

Working with Paragraph Styles

When you press Enter at the end of a paragraph, the new paragraph that is inserted generally has the same style as the previous paragraph. Some styles, however, are defined so that the new paragraph has a different style. For example, if you press Enter while in a paragraph with the Heading 1 style, the new paragraph will typically be assigned the Normal style.

tip **Use the Body Text Style for More Formatting Control**

If you use the Body Text style—rather than Normal—for the body text in your document, you'll be able to easily modify the formatting of the body text without altering other text in your document. (Changing Normal alters most other paragraph styles as well, because these styles are *based on* Normal. In contrast, other styles aren't commonly based on Body Text. This topic is discussed fully in Chapter 14, "Advanced Word Formatting Techniques.")

tip **Take Advantage of the Predefined Heading Styles**

Use the predefined styles Heading 1 through Heading 9 for the headings in your document whenever possible. Not only do these styles provide appropriate and consistent formatting for various levels of headings, but using them allows you to view the organization of your document in Outline view, to navigate quickly through your document with the Document Map, and to generate tables of contents easily.

Additionally, when you drag the scroll box on the vertical scroll bar, Word displays the text of each heading to make it simpler to find the desired location in your document. (Headings, outlines, the Document Map, and tables of contents are covered in Chapter 15, "Managing Large or Complex Documents.")

Assigning Styles and Saved Formats Using the Formatting Toolbar

An alternative way to apply a style or saved format is to select it from the Style drop-down list on the Formatting toolbar (or by typing the style name or the saved format description into the box at the top of the list), as shown here:

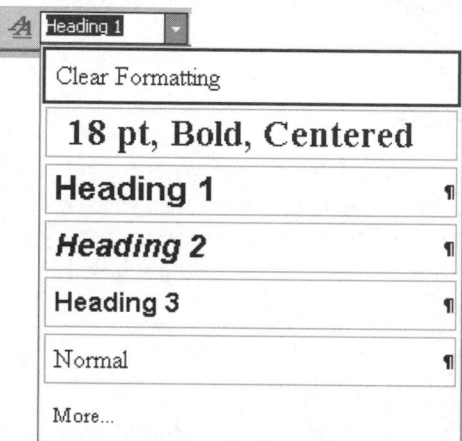

The drop-down list displays the same set of styles and saved formats that you previously displayed in the Styles And Formatting task pane. If this task pane isn't currently displayed, you can select the More item at the bottom of the Styles list to display the task pane, thereby accessing additional styles and saved formats. Also, if you click Shift when you open the Styles drop-down list, the list will show all or most of your available styles. (It will show the same set of items that are displayed in the Styles And Formatting task pane if you select All Styles in the Show drop-down list. Remember that with this option saved formats won't be included.)

Assigning Styles Using Shortcut Keys

Word provides the shortcut keys shown in Table 12-6 for applying several of the built-in paragraph styles.

Table 12-6. **Shortcut Keys for Applying Common Paragraph Styles**

To Apply This Style	Press This Shortcut Key
Normal	Ctrl+Shift+N
List Bullet	Ctrl+Shift+L
Heading 1	Alt+Ctrl+1
Heading 2	Alt+Ctrl+2
Heading 3	Alt+Ctrl+3

For details on defining your own shortcut keys for quickly applying any styles, see "Defining Shortcut Keys (Word Only)," on page 217, and "Inserting Symbols and Foreign Characters," on page 246.

Troubleshooting

Formatting Changes Mysteriously

You have your document formatted the way you want it. However, as you work on the document, you notice certain formatting features changing by themselves.

The following Word options can cause automatic formatting changes in a document.

- If the Automatically Update feature is enabled for a particular paragraph style, when you make changes to text that is assigned that style, Word will automatically update the style and all text throughout the document that is assigned that style.

- If the Automatically Update Document Styles option is enabled for the document, whenever you or a co-worker updates a style within your document's template, the next time you open the document Word will update the style in the document to match.

For information on the Automatically Update feature, see "Customizing Styles Using the Modify Style Dialog Box," on page 390. For information on the Automatically Update Document Styles option, see "Copying Styles from a Template to a Document," on page 403.

newfeature!
Using the Reveal Formatting Task Pane to View or Modify Formatting Features

Word's new Reveal Formatting task pane lets you view a detailed description of the formatting of any text in your document. It describes directly applied character and paragraph formatting features, as well as formatting features derived from the paragraph style or any character style assigned to the text. You can also use this task pane to modify or clear formatting, to compare the formatting of different selections, or to find blocks of text with similar formatting.

To use the Reveal Formatting task pane, perform the following steps:

1 Select the text you want to examine or reformat.

> **note** When you use Word's old method for finding formatting information—that is, choosing What's This? from the Help menu or pressing Shift+F1 and then clicking text—Word now displays the Reveal Formatting task pane (if it isn't already displayed) instead of showing the formatting information in a balloon-style dialog box.

2 Choose Format, Reveal Formatting to display the Reveal Formatting task pane (shown in Figure 12-9).

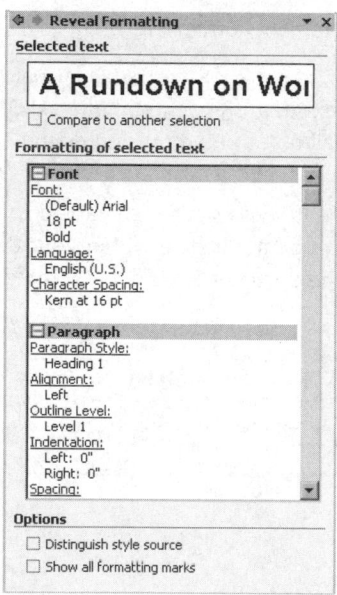

Figure 12-9. Here, the Reveal Formatting task pane shows the formatting features of a paragraph that's been assigned the built-in Heading 1 style.

3 To work with the formatting of the selection, do one or more of the following:

■ To modify the formatting of the selection, click one of the underlined commands in the format description, as shown here:

Click one of these commands to modify the selection's formatting.

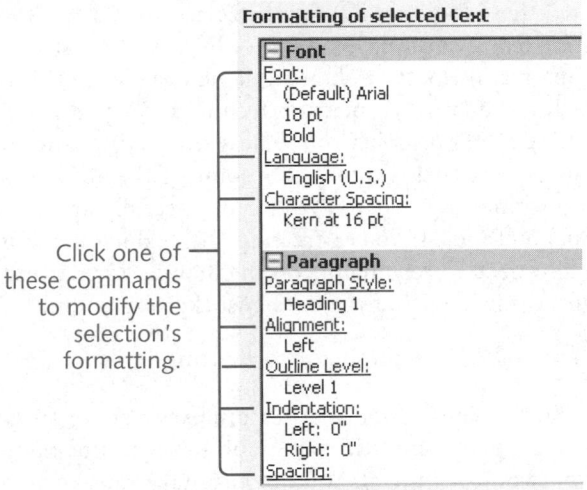

For example, clicking Font opens the Font dialog box for changing the character formatting; clicking Language opens the Language dialog box for setting the text's language; clicking Alignment, Outline Level, Indentation, or Spacing opens the Paragraph dialog box for setting the paragraph formatting; and clicking Character Style or Paragraph Style opens the Style dialog box, where you can apply a character style or change the paragraph style.

■ To view a feature-by-feature comparison of the selection's formatting with the formatting of another block of text, check the Compare To Another Selection option and then select the other block of text.

■ To work with the selected text in other ways, click the down arrow in the Selected Text box and choose a command from the drop-down menu shown here:

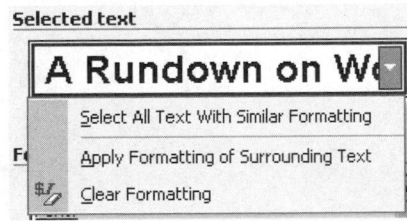

333

Formatting Your Documents Automatically

Word provides a number of tools that automatically format documents in various ways. Although you will probably discover a few useful automatic formatting features, in general, these tools are not for the Microsoft Office XP expert. The automatic formatting features can help an Office beginner get started. However, once you learn the manual formatting skills explained earlier in this chapter (and in Chapter 14, "Advanced Word Formatting Techniques"), you will probably find the manual formatting methods easier to use, less frustrating, and much more precise than the automatic formatting tools. Also, some of the automatic tools can literally wreak havoc on formatting that you've already carefully applied using the more exacting manual methods. If you're creating Office documents in a workgroup, you will probably also need to rely mainly on the manual formatting methods to make your document formatting conform to the workgroup's standards.

Here's a summary of Word's automatic formatting tools:

- **AutoFormat.** The AutoFormat feature uses a set of simple rules to apply appropriate, built-in paragraph styles to the paragraphs throughout your document. You can also have AutoFormat make certain replacements in your document text—for example, it can replace straight quotes (" ") with smart (that is, curly) quotes (" "). To control the way AutoFormat works, choose Tools, AutoCorrect Options and in the AutoCorrect dialog box, click the AutoFormat tab (shown in Figure 12-10). To have AutoFormat format your document, choose Format, AutoFormat, select the desired options in the AutoFormat dialog box (shown in Figure 12-11), and click OK.

Chapter 12: Effective Formatting in Word

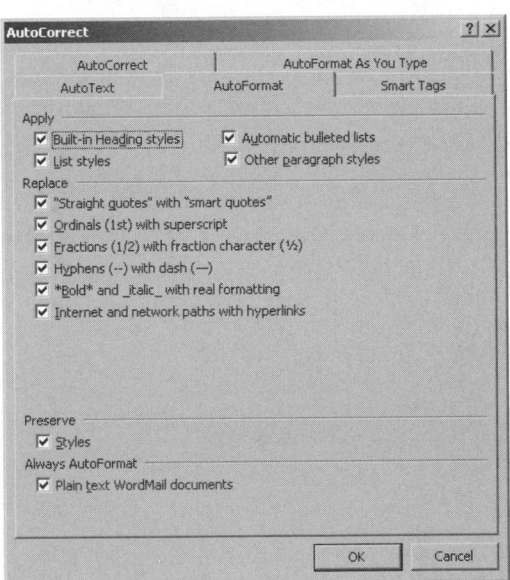

Figure 12-10. The AutoFormat tab of the AutoCorrect dialog box allows you to select options that affect the way AutoFormat works.

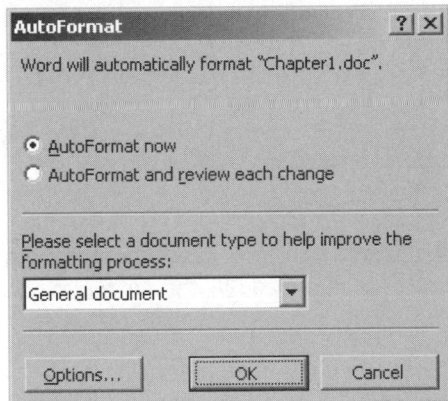

Figure 12-11. You use the AutoFormat dialog box to run the AutoFormat feature.

● **AutoFormat As You Type.**   The AutoFormat As You Type feature automatically makes formatting changes as you type in your document text.
You can have it make text replacements (for example, change fractions
like 1/2 to single-character fractions like ½), apply paragraph styles (for
instance, apply built-in heading styles to document headings), and perform other automatic changes. To control the specific changes this feature
makes, choose Tools, AutoCorrect Options and click the AutoFormat As
You Type tab (shown in Figure 12-12). To turn AutoFormat As You Type
completely off, you need to clear all check boxes on this tab.

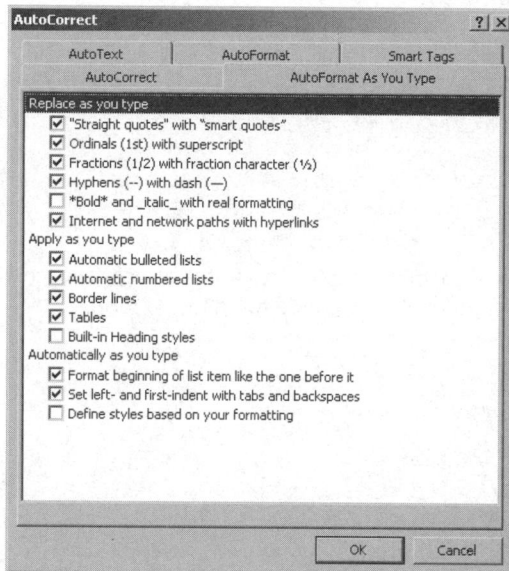

Figure 12-12.   The AutoFormat As You Type tab of the AutoCorrect dialog
box allows you to control the changes made by the AutoFormat As You
Type feature.

● **Themes.**   A theme is a predesigned visual scheme that applies consistent
formatting to elements throughout a document. You use a theme by choosing
Formatting, Theme. Themes are primarily useful for formatting Web pages.

Themes are covered in "Applying a Web Page Theme," on page 598.

● **Style Gallery.**   The Style Gallery lets you copy the styles from any document template into your current document, instantly changing the overall
document formatting. You should use the Style Gallery only after you have
already applied appropriate styles to various document elements, such as
headings, lists, and body text. The Style Gallery will then replace each of
these styles with the same-named style from a different template, quickly
(but somewhat dangerously) altering the overall appearance of your document. To use the Style Gallery, choose Format, Theme and click the Style
Gallery button at the bottom of the Theme dialog box. Then, in the Style
Gallery dialog box (shown in Figure 12-13), select a template and click OK.

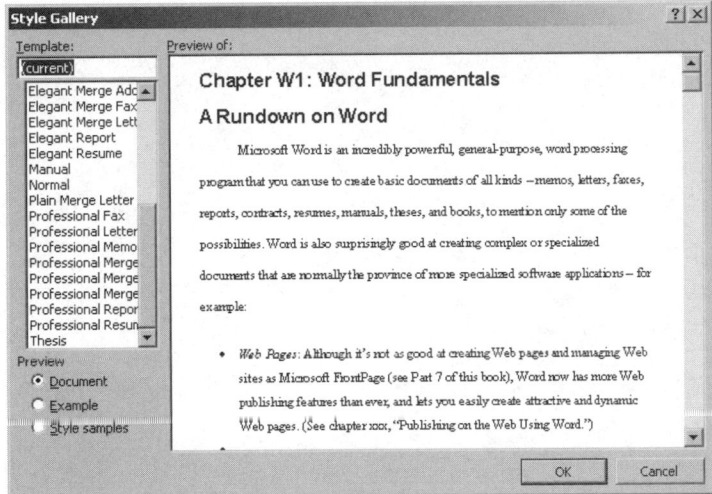

Figure 12-13.   The Style Gallery dialog box lets you change the overall
formatting of a document by copying styles from a template.

Chapter 13

Arranging Text Using Tables, Columns, and Lists

Arranging Text with Tables

A Microsoft Word 2002 *table* is a highly versatile tool for arranging text in rows and columns. Figure 13-1 shows a Word table as it appears on the screen. Using a table offers many advantages over arranging text using tab characters or other methods. For example, if a particular text item doesn't fit on a single line, Word automatically creates a new line and increases the height of the row. (The table shown in Figure 13-1, for instance, would be difficult to create using tabs.) Also, when you use tables, you can easily rearrange and adjust the size of the rows and columns, and you can emphasize table items by using borders and background shading.

Paragraph formatting action	Shortcut key	Comment
To increase left paragraph indent	Ctrl+M	Indent is moved to the next tab stop.
To decrease left paragraph indent	Ctrl+Shift+M	Indent is moved to the previous tab stop. This key cannot be used to create a negative left indent.
To increase hanging indent	Ctrl+T	All paragraph lines are indented except the first line. Each time you press the shortcut key, the hanging indent is moved right to the next tab stop.
To decrease hanging indent	Ctrl+Shift+T	Hanging indent is moved left to the previous tab stop.
To add or remove 12 points of extra space above the paragraph	Ctrl+0 (zero at top of keyboard, *not* on numeric key pad)	Toggles feature on or off.

Figure 13-1. This figure shows a Word table as it appears on the screen.

Creating a Table

To construct a table at the position of the insertion point, perform the following steps:

1 Point to the Insert Table button on the Standard toolbar, shown here:

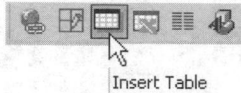

2 Press the left mouse button and drag down and to the right to select the number and arrangement of table cells that you want, as seen here:

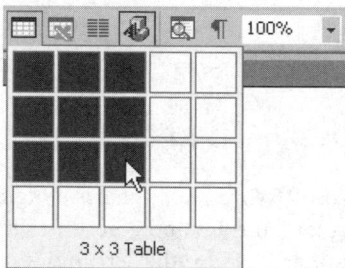

The new table will consist of rows and columns of empty *cells*. The lines defining these cells are known as *gridlines* and they can be shown in a variety of ways. The gridlines in a newly created table are usually marked with thin, solid *borders*. A border is a line that is visible on the screen in Word, on a printed copy of the document, and on a Web page document viewed in a browser. (Borders can also be added to paragraphs and other objects.) As explained later in the chapter, you can modify or remove one or more borders from a table. If you remove a border, the gridline will be marked with a light gray line that appears on the screen in Word, but won't be printed or show in a browser. This line will appear on the screen, however, only if the Show Gridlines option is selected on the Table menu.

> For information on adding or modifying borders in tables and applying background shading to tables, see "Adding Borders and Shading," on page 356.

> **tip** **Don't Worry About the Number of Rows**
>
> If you don't know how many rows you'll need when you insert a table, just choose a single row. It's easy to add new rows to the end of a table as you enter the table text by pressing Tab in the last cell. You should, however, try to choose the actual number of columns, because inserting additional columns is not as easy.

> **tip** **Insert Text Above a Table**
>
> If you add a table at the very beginning of a document, and then want to insert text above the table, you won't be able to move the insertion point to the necessary position above the table to type the text. To get around this, place the insertion point anywhere in the first row of the table and press Ctrl+Shift+Enter. This will insert a new paragraph above the table. You can then move the insertion point to that paragraph and type text.

Adding Content to a Table

To add text or graphics to a cell in a table, click in the cell and type the text or insert the graphics in the same way that you would in an ordinary paragraph. Notice that if you reach the right border of the cell, Word wraps the text down to the next line and increases the height of the entire row, if necessary, to accommodate the new text. If you press Enter while typing in a cell, Word will insert a new paragraph *within* the cell. (Each cell contains one or more entire paragraphs.) You can edit and format text within a cell using the standard Word editing and formatting techniques given in the previous chapters.

> **tip** **Nest Tables for Complex Layouts**
>
> You can insert a table within a cell of another table, creating a nested table. To do this, place the insertion point at the position in the cell where you want the nested table and use any of the methods given in this chapter for inserting a table.

To move the insertion point to another cell, click in the cell or use the arrow keys to move the insertion point. To move to the next cell (in row-by-row order) and select any text it contains, press Tab. To move to the previous cell and select any text it contains, press Shift+Tab. When you're in the last cell of the table, pressing Tab adds a new row to the end of the table.

> **tip** **Insert Tabs in Tables**
>
> To insert a tab character into a table cell, press Ctrl+Tab. You can set the position of tab stops as in a paragraph outside of a table. Watch for one oddity, though—if you set a decimal tab, the text in the cell is moved to that tab stop without you manually inserting a tab character in front of it.

Adding and Removing Table Cells, Rows, and Columns

To insert or delete rows, columns, or groups of cells, you must first select the appropriate portion of the table. You can easily select a cell, row, or column as shown here:

Click here to select a single cell.

Units	Abbreviation	Points	Picas	Centimeters	Inches
Points	pt	1	1/12	.035	1/72
Picas	pi	12	1	.42	1/6
Centimeters	cm	28.35	2.38	1	.39
Inches	in or "	72	6	2.54	1

Click here to select a row.

Units	Abbreviation	Points	Picas	Centimeters	Inches
Points	pt	1	1/12	.035	1/72
Picas	pi	12	1	.42	1/6
Centimeters	cm	28.35	2.38	1	.39
Inches	in or "	72	6	2.54	1

Click the mouse pointer to select a column.

Units	Abbreviation	Points	Picas	Centimeters	Inches
Points	pt	1	1/12	.035	1/72
Picas	pi	12	1	.42	1/6
Centimeters	cm	28.35	2.38	1	.39
Inches	in or "	72	6	2.54	1

After you have selected a single cell, row, or column, you can drag to select additional cells, rows, or columns. Alternatively, you can select any block of cells by placing the insertion point within a cell and then pressing an arrow key while holding down Shift. You can select the entire table by placing the insertion point anywhere within it and pressing Alt+5 (the 5 on the numeric keypad with Num Lock off).

To add entire rows or columns to an existing table, perform the following steps:

1 To insert rows at a particular position in a table, select existing rows just below that position; select the same number of rows as the number you want to add, as in this example:

Row 1		
Row 2		
Row 3		
Row 4		

To insert two rows above row 2, select two rows as shown here.

Likewise, to insert columns, select an equal number of columns to the right of the position where you want to add the new ones.

Chapter 13: Arranging Text Using Tables, Columns, and Lists

To insert one or more new rows at the bottom of a table, you can place the insertion point immediately below the table without selecting text. (You can also insert a single row at the end of a table by pressing Tab when the insertion point is in the last cell, rather than using this two-step procedure.)

  2 If you're inserting rows, click the Insert Rows button on the Standard toolbar. If you're inserting columns, click the Insert Columns button.

Insert Insert
Rows Columns

> **note** The Standard toolbar actually has only one button for table insertion. When table rows, columns, or cells are selected, the button's ScreenTip reads Insert Rows, Insert Columns, or Insert Cells. If no text is selected (or if text is selected outside of a table), the ScreenTip reads Insert Table, and the button inserts a new table (outside of or within an existing table). As the selection changes, the image on the button changes to indicate its function.

Alternatively, you can right-click the selection and choose Insert Rows or Insert Columns from the shortcut menu. (The command on the shortcut menu changes depending on whether you have selected rows or columns.) If you placed the insertion point immediately below the table to add rows at the bottom, Word will now prompt you for the number of rows to insert.

After you click the Insert Rows button or choose Insert Rows from the shortcut menu, the example table shown earlier (under step 1) would look like this:

Row 1		
Row 2		
Row 3		
Row 4		

Two new rows have been inserted above row 2.

Word marks the end of each table cell with an end-of-cell mark and it marks the end of each table row with an end-of-row mark to the right of the row, outside of the table. You can make these marks visible by clicking the Show/Hide ¶ button on the Standard toolbar. In step 1, if you want to insert rows, you must include the end-of-row marks in your selection whether or not they are visible. (Selecting a row by clicking to the left of the row, outside the table, automatically includes the end-of-row mark.) To insert a column at the right end of a table, select the entire column of end-of-row marks, as shown here, before clicking the Insert Columns button. (You can select these marks whether or not they're visible.)

Show/
Hide ¶

343

Click the mouse pointer to insert a new — column to the right of the table.

Row·1□	□	□	
Row·2□	□	□	
Row·3□	□	□	
Row·4□	□	□	

End-of-cell mark   End-of-row mark

To insert a block of one or more cells without inserting entire rows or columns, perform the following steps:

1 Select a block of existing cells that has the number and arrangement of the cells you want to insert.

2 Click the Insert Cells button on the Standard toolbar. Word will display the Insert Cells dialog box, shown in Figure 13-2.

Insert Cells

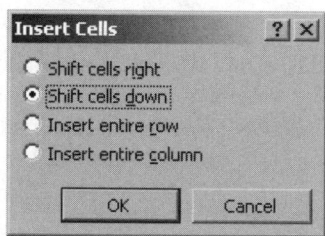

Figure 13-2. The Insert Cells dialog box gives you options for including new cells in a table.

3 Select Shift Cells Right to have Word move the existing cells to the right when it inserts the new cells, or select Shift Cells Down to have it move the cells down. You can also select Insert Entire Row or Insert Entire Column to insert complete rows or columns even though you didn't select complete rows or columns.

note When you have Word move cells down, Word adds extra cells, if necessary, at the bottom of the table to complete the rows.

To delete table rows, columns, or cells, simply select them, right-click the selection, and choose Delete Rows, Delete Columns, or Delete Cells from the shortcut menu. (The command will be labeled according to the current selection.) Alternatively, you can choose Table, Delete, and then choose Rows, Columns, or Cells from the submenu. (You can also choose Table from this submenu to remove the entire table.) If you selected a block that doesn't include complete rows or columns and you choose to delete cells, Word will display the Delete Cells dialog box (shown in Figure 13-3), which lets you choose how the remaining cells are rearranged after the deletion.

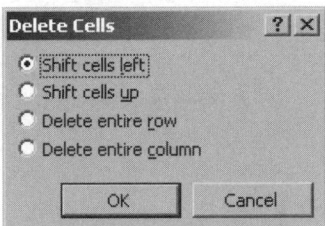

Figure 13-3. The Delete Cells dialog box gives you options when removing cells from a table.

To delete the *contents* of rows, columns, or cells—that is, the text or graphics contained within them—without removing the cells themselves, select the rows, columns, or cells and press Delete.

Resizing Table Cells

You can adjust the width of a table column by dragging its right vertical gridline, as shown here:

To change the
width of this column...   ...drag this vertical gridline.

Units	Abbreviation	Points	Picas	Centimeters	Inches
Points	pt	1	1/12	.035	1/72
Picas	pi	12	1	.42	1/6
Centimeters	cm	28.35	2.38	1	.39
Inches	in *or* "	72	6	2.54	1

To adjust the width of one or more specific cells in a column (rather than the entire column), select the cells before dragging. The cells in a single column can vary in width.

When adjusting the width of a column, you can modify the way Word changes the widths of the cells to the right of the column, if any exist, by pressing additional keys while dragging (see Table 13-1 on page 346). Of course, if you drag the rightmost vertical gridline in a table, you'll always change the overall table width. (Pressing Ctrl or Shift will have no effect.) Note that if you drag the leftmost vertical gridline in the table, you'll change the indent of the selected rows (or of the entire table if no rows are selected) from the left document margin.

Table 13-1. **Different Ways to Modify Table Column Widths**

To Modify Column Widths Like This	Press This Key While Dragging the Vertical Gridline
Change the width of only the column to the immediate right of the gridline, without changing the overall table width	No key
Display the width of each column in the ruler while you drag the gridline (has the same effect on column widths as pressing no key)	Alt
Change the width of all cells to the right proportionately, without changing the overall table width (for example, if the cells to the right have equal widths, they remain equal in width after you drag)	Ctrl
Change the overall table width, rather than changing the widths of the columns to the right	Shift

You can also rapidly adjust the width of one or more cells to accommodate the current contents of the cells. To do this, select the cell or cells and double-click the rightmost vertical gridline of the selection. To adjust one entire column of cells, you can simply double-click the right gridline without selecting cells. Here's an example:

Units	Abbreviation	Points	Picas	Centimeters	Inches
Points	pt	1	1/12	.035	1/72
Picas	pi	12	1	.42	1/6
Centimeters	cm	28.35	2.38	1	.39
Inches	in *or* "	72	6	2.54	1

To have Word adjust the width of this column to accommodate the widest cell entry...   ...double-click anywhere on this vertical gridline.

Here's how the example looks after double-clicking:

Units	Abbreviation	Points	Picas	Centimeters	Inches
Points	pt	1	1/12	.035	1/72
Picas	pi	12	1	.42	1/6
Centimeters	cm	28.35	2.38	1	.39
Inches	in *or* "	72	6	2.54	1

(If Word adjusts more than one cell in a particular column, it resizes them equally to accommodate the widest block of text in a cell.) If you later change the contents of a cell, you'll have to read just the cell or column width.

Alternatively, you can apply the AutoFit command to a table to have Word adjust the widths of all columns to fit the cell contents or the window width and to dynamically maintain the adjustment as you change the contents or window width. To do this,

Chapter 13: Arranging Text Using Tables, Columns, and Lists

right-click anywhere in the table and choose AutoFit from the shortcut menu to open the submenu shown here:

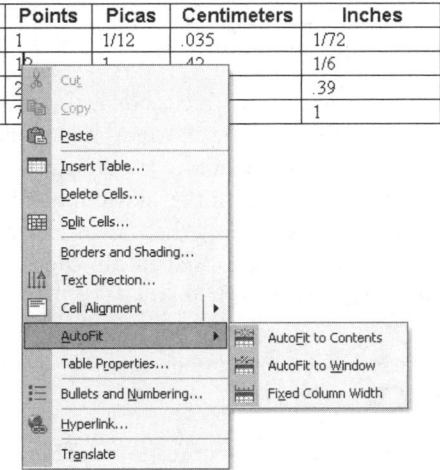

Then choose one of the three commands, as in Table 13-2.

Table 13-2. **Using the Commands on the AutoFit Submenu**

To Apply AutoFit Like This	Choose This AutoFit Submenu Command
Have Word immediately adjust the width of each column in the table to accommodate the widest block of text in that column, and then dynamically adjust the column widths to maintain the fit as you add or delete text	AutoFit To Contents
Have Word expand the overall table width, if necessary, so the table fills the entire width of the window, and then dynamically adjust the width to maintain this fit if the window is resized (this command works only when you view the document in the Web Layout view of Word, or when you view a Web page document in a browser)	AutoFit To Window
Keep the column widths constant unless you manually adjust them using one of the techniques described previously in this section	Fixed Column Width

Alternatively, you can place the insertion point within the table and choose one of these three commands from the AutoFit submenu on the Table menu.

Chapter 13

Word automatically adjusts the height of a table row to accommodate the text contained in the row. You can also manually adjust the height of a row by dragging the horizontal gridline at the bottom of the row. To do this, you must be in Web Layout or Print Layout view. Note that you can't adjust the height of selected cells within a row—you always have to change the height of all the cells in the row.

You can give two or more rows the same height by selecting them, right-clicking the selection, and choosing Distribute Rows Evenly from the shortcut menu. Likewise, you can give two or more columns the same width by selecting them, right-clicking the selection, and choosing Distribute Columns Evenly from the shortcut menu. Note that to use this method, you must select entire rows (including the end-of-row markers) or entire columns. (Alternatively, after you make the selection, you can choose either of these commands from the AutoFit submenu on the Table menu.)

Move or Resize a Table Quickly

In Web Layout or Print Layout view, you can easily move or resize an entire table by performing the following steps:

1 Hold the mouse pointer over the table until the Move and Resize handles appear, as seen here:

Move handle

Units	Abbreviation	Points	Picas	Centimeters	Inches
Points	pt	1	1/12	.035	1/72
Picas	pi	12	1	.42	1/6
Centimeters	cm	28.35	2.38	1	.39
Inches	in or "	72	6	2.54	1

Handles appear when you point to the table.

Resize handle

2 To move the table to a new position in your document, drag the Move handle.

3 To change the overall size and proportions of the table, drag the Resize handle. Word will change the sizes of all the cells in the table proportionately.

Moving and Copying Table Cells, Rows, and Columns

To move rows or columns within a table, select entire rows or entire columns, and then use the mouse to drag them to a new location. The rows or columns will be removed from their current location and inserted into the table at the new location. To copy rows or columns, press the Ctrl key while you drag. When you select rows, you must include the end-of-row marks; otherwise, you'll merely move or copy the contents of the cells.

Changing the Text Orientation and Alignment in a Table Cell

You can modify the orientation of the text in a table cell so that rather than the text reading from left to right, it reads from bottom to top or top to bottom. You might want to do this to make information fit into a particular table or to improve the appearance or readability of a table. If you're creating a Web page, however, keep in mind that a browser will ignore vertical text and will display the text in the conventional left-to-right orientation.

To change the text orientation within a table, select one or more cells, right-click within the selection, and choose Text Direction from the shortcut menu. (To change a single cell, you can right-click within the cell without selecting it.) Then select the desired orientation by clicking one of the three options in the Orientation area of the Text Direction dialog box, shown here:

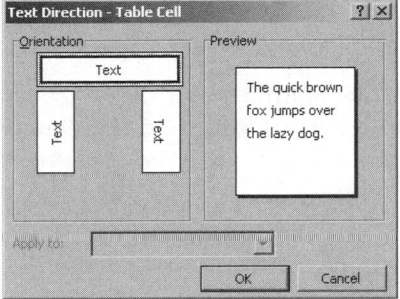

To change the alignment of the text within one or more cells, select them and right-click the selection. (To change a single cell, you can just right-click it.) Then choose Cell Alignment from the shortcut menu and choose an alignment style from the submenu shown here:

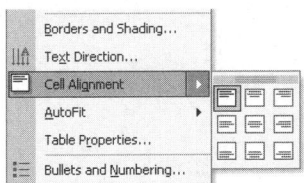

Note that Word creates the horizontal component of the alignment by assigning the Left, Center, or Right paragraph formatting features to the paragraphs in the cell.

---

note To use the techniques discussed in this section, the Drag-And-Drop Text Editing option must be checked. To locate this option, choose Tools, Options, and click the Edit tab.

To move the contents of table cells, select the cells and drag them to a new location in the table. Word will delete the contents of the cells you selected (leaving empty cells behind) and it will insert these contents into the cells at the target location, overwriting the current contents of the target cells. To copy the contents of table cells, press the Ctrl key while you drag. (To move or copy cell contents, you must not select entire columns. You can select entire rows as long as you don't include the end-of-row marks.)

You can also move or copy text from one cell to another without overwriting the contents of the second cell. To move text this way, select only the text within the first cell (rather than selecting the entire cell), and then drag the selection to the new location. Press Ctrl while you drag to copy. The moved or copied text will be added to the contents of the second cell.

Creating Tables with the Table Drawing Tools

Tables And Borders

Another way to insert a table is to interactively draw it, in much the same way that you would draw lines or rectangles in a drawing program. To draw a table, choose Table, Draw Table, or click the Tables And Borders button on the Standard toolbar. When you choose Draw Table or click the Tables And Borders button, Word does the following:

● If you're in Normal view, Word switches to Print Layout view. (You must be in either Print Layout or Web Layout view to draw a table. If you're currently in Outline view, you must manually switch to one of these views.)

● Word displays the Tables And Borders toolbar, which provides buttons for working with tables, borders, and shading. This toolbar is shown in Figure 13-4.

● Word selects the Draw Table button on the Tables And Borders toolbar, which converts the mouse pointer into a pencil and switches to table-drawing mode. (Clicking the Draw Table button toggles this mode on or off.)

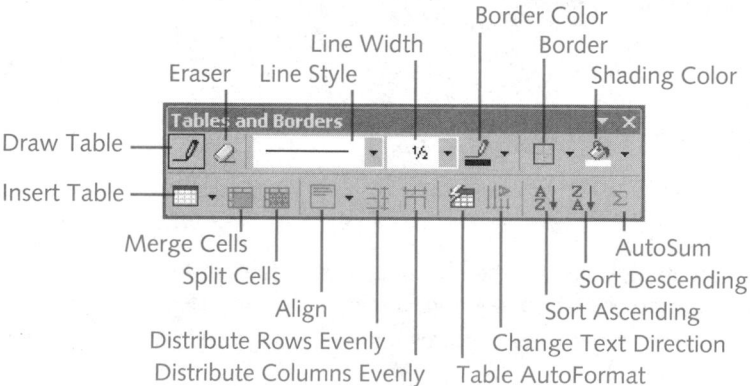

Figure 13-4. The Tables And Borders toolbar provides buttons for working with tables, borders, and shading.

Chapter 13: Arranging Text Using Tables, Columns, and Lists

To create a table, perform the following steps:

1 Place the pencil-shaped pointer at one corner of the position in your document where you want to insert the table, press the mouse button, and drag
the pointer to the opposite corner. (If you don't have the pencil pointer, click
the Draw Table button on the Tables And Borders toolbar.) The rectangle you
draw defines the outside gridlines of the table, which initially consists of a
single cell, as seen here:

Click here to start
drawing the table.

Then, drag to
draw the outside
gridlines of the
table.

If you draw the gridlines around an existing paragraph of text, that paragraph will be included within the table cell.

2 You can divide the table into any number of cells by using the mouse to
draw internal cell gridlines. Drag the pencil-shaped pointer to draw each
gridline, as shown here:

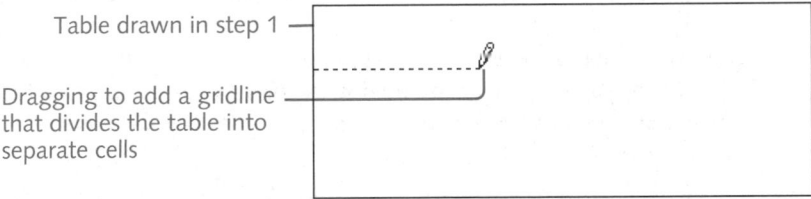

Table drawn in step 1

Dragging to add a gridline
that divides the table into
separate cells

3 To remove a table gridline, click the Eraser button on the Tables And Borders
toolbar, which changes the mouse pointer to an eraser. Then, drag over the
gridline. As you drag, the gridline will be highlighted, and when you release
the mouse button, the gridline will be removed. To erase several gridlines at
once, you can use the eraser-shaped pointer to drag a selection rectangle
around the gridlines; the gridlines will be removed when you release the mouse
button. When you're finished, click the Eraser button again to deselect it.

---

tip **Remove a Gridline While Drawing**

When the Draw Table button is selected and you have the pencil-shaped pointer, you
can press Shift to temporarily convert the pointer to an eraser for conveniently removing one or more gridlines. When you release Shift, the pointer will change back to a
pencil and you can continue drawing gridlines.

When you draw a table, the way the gridlines are marked depends on the current selections in the Line Style, Line Weight, and Border Color buttons on the Tables And Borders toolbar. If you choose No Border in the Line Style drop-down list, the gridlines will be marked with light gray lines, provided that the Show Gridlines option on the Table menu is selected. These lines will appear on the screen in Word but won't be printed and won't be visible in a browser. If you choose a border style in the Line Style list (such as a single, double, or dotted line), the gridlines will be marked with borders that appear on the screen in Word, on a printed copy, and in a Web browser. The appearance of these borders will be affected by the current settings in the Line Weight and Border Color buttons.

In "Adding Borders and Shading," on page 356, you'll learn how to add, modify, or remove borders in a table you have already drawn, and also how to apply shading to table cells. Borders and shading are discussed in a separate section because you can apply them to text outside of tables, as well as to tables.

InsideOut

Changing a setting in the Line Style, Line Weight, or Border Color button affects only the table gridlines that you subsequently draw or redraw with the mouse (or borders that you subsequently apply using the Border button). It *doesn't* affect table gridlines that you have already drawn even if the cells are selected.

As you can see in Figure 13-4, the Tables And Borders toolbar provides a number of buttons that you can use for modifying existing tables. You might therefore want to display this toolbar whenever you work with tables, even if you don't use the mouse to draw the table.

newfeature!
Formatting Tables by Applying Table Styles

You can instantly change the overall appearance of a table by applying one of the built-in table styles provided with Word. Applying an appropriate style can make your table stand out on the page, rendering it both more attractive and easier to read. A table style can apply borders and background shading to the table itself and character formatting features to the text within the table. Figures 13-5 and 13-6 show a table (one used in previous examples in this chapter) formatted with two of the built-in styles, giving you an idea of the range of effects you can achieve.

Units	Abbreviation	Points	Picas	Centimeters	Inches
Points	pt	1	1/12	.035	1/72
Picas	pi	12	1	.42	1/6
Centimeters	cm	28.35	2.38	1	.39
Inches	in *or* "	72	6	2.54	1

Figure 13-5. This table was formatted with the Table 3D Effects 2 built-in table style.

Chapter 13: Arranging Text Using Tables, Columns, and Lists

Units	Abbreviation	Points	Picas	Centimeters	Inches
Points	pt	1	1/12	.035	1/72
Picas	pi	12	1	.42	1/6
Centimeters	cm	28.35	2.38	1	.39
Inches	in *or* "	72	6	2.54	1

Figure 13-6. This table was formatted with the Table Columns 3 built-in table style.

The following procedure is the fastest way to apply a table style to a table:

1 Place the insertion point within the table.

2 Choose Table, Table AutoFormat.

3 Select a style in the Table Styles list in the Table AutoFormat dialog box (shown in Figure 13-7).

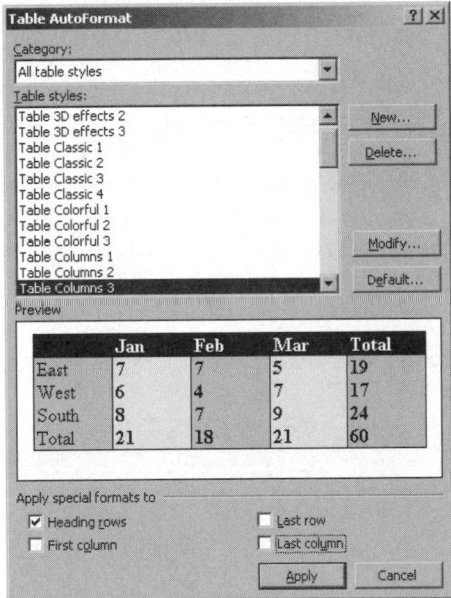

Figure 13-7. The Table AutoFormat dialog box allows you to apply a style to a table.

4 Select any other options you want in the Table AutoFormat dialog box and click the Apply button. To help you make your choices, the dialog box displays a table in the Preview area that shows the effect of the currently selected style and options.

> You can create, remove, or customize a table style by clicking the New, Delete, or Modify button in the Table AutoFormat dialog box, or by using the Styles And Formatting task pane. These techniques are discussed in Chapter 14, "Advanced Word Formatting Techniques."

If you want to reuse a particular style, click the Default button in the Table AutoFormat dialog box to make that style the default (either for the current document or for all documents you create based on the document's template). Word will then automatically apply that style whenever you create a new table using the Insert Table button on the Standard toolbar or the Insert Table dialog box (opened by choosing Table, Insert, Table). The style won't be applied to tables that you draw using the Tables And Borders toolbar.

note Because table styles are standard Word styles, you can also apply them using the Styles And Formatting task pane or the Style drop-down list on the Formatting toolbar. In these places, a table style is marked with this icon: ⊞

For information on applying and modifying individual table borders, as well as background shading, see "Adding Borders and Shading," on page 356.

Using Other Methods for Creating and Modifying Tables

The previous sections have focused on working with tables using the Standard toolbar, mouse, and shortcut menus. In general, these interactive methods are the fastest and most convenient. The Table menu provides alternative methods for inserting and modifying tables; it also allows you to perform some additional table operations not possible using the interactive techniques. Table 13-3 summarizes the ways you can work with tables using these commands. Keep in mind that for many of these commands, merely placing the insertion point within a table, row, column, or cell is equivalent to selecting that element.

note You can perform some of the commands listed in Table 13-3 by right-clicking a table—or a selection within a table—and choosing the command from the shortcut menu.

Table 13-3. **Tasks You Can Perform Using the Table Menu**

To Perform This Task	Do This on the Table Menu
Draw a table using the mouse, as explained in "Creating Tables with the Table Drawing Tools," on page 350.	Choose the Draw Table command.
Insert a new table into a document or into a table cell, to insert columns (to the left or right of the selection), to insert rows (above or below the selection), or to insert cells (specifying the direction in which the existing cells are shifted). The effects of these commands depend on the current selection or position of the insertion point.	Choose the appropriate command from the Insert submenu.
Delete the selected cells, columns, rows, or the entire table.	Choose the appropriate command from the Delete submenu.
Select the column(s), row(s), cell(s), or the entire table containing the insertion point or selection.	Choose the appropriate command from the Select submenu.

Table 13-3. *(continued)*

To Perform This Task	Do This on the Table Menu
Combine selected adjacent cells into a single cell.	Choose the Merge Cells command.
Divide the selected cell (or each cell in a group of selected cells) into two or more cells. You can specify the resulting number of rows and columns of cells.	Choose the Split Cells command.
Divide a table into two separate tables and insert a regular (Normal style) paragraph between the two tables. The division occurs above the selected row.	Choose the Split Table command (or press Ctrl+Shift+Enter).
Instantly modify the overall look of the selected table by applying a table style, as explained in the previous section.	Choose the Table AutoFormat command.
Apply the AutoFit command to the selected table or distribute rows or columns evenly. (These features were described in "Resizing Table Cells," on page 345.)	Choose the appropriate command from the AutoFit submenu.
Mark the selected row or rows at the top of a table as a heading. If a page break occurs within a table, Word repeats the heading row(s) at the top of the next page.	Choose the Heading Rows Repeat command.
Convert the selected table to text (removes the table and converts the text it contains to ordinary paragraphs), or convert selected text outside a table to a table (creates a new table and inserts the selected text into the table)	Choose Text To Table or Table To Text from the Convert submenu.
Sort the contents of the selected rows and columns within a table. If the selection is outside a table, the command sorts paragraphs of text. For information on this command, see "Sorting Lists and Tables," on page 380.	Choose the Sort command.
Insert a formula into a table cell. A formula displays the result of a mathematical computation on numbers within table cells. This command lets you create a Word table that functions as a simple spreadsheet.	Choose the Formula command and type or select the formula you want in the Formula dialog box (shown in Figure 13-8, on page 356).
Mark the gridlines around cells in all tables using light gray lines. These lines are visible only on the screen in Word (they don't print or show in a Web browser) where borders haven't been applied. Note that when the option is selected, it's labeled Hide Gridlines; when it isn't selected, it's labeled Show Gridlines.	Choose the Show Gridlines option.
Display the Table Properties dialog box, which allows you to modify the size, alignment, indent, and text-wrapping style of the selected table; the height and page-breaking style of rows; the height of columns; and the width and vertical text alignment style (top, center, or bottom) of the selected cell or cells. By modifying the text-wrapping style, you can have adjoining text wrap around the table rather than staying above and below it.	Choose the Table Properties command.

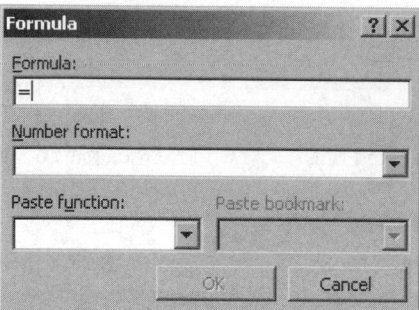

Figure 13-8. The Formula dialog box is used to insert a formula that performs a calculation on numbers in a table.

Troubleshooting

Table Text Is Cut Off

The text in a table cell is cut off horizontally (that is, you can't see the beginnings or you can't see the endings of the lines). Or, it's cut off vertically (that is, you can't see the bottom part of the text).

You won't be able to see the left ends of the lines if the paragraph in a table cell has a negative left indent. You won't be able to see the right ends of the lines if it has a negative right indent. The hidden text will be inaccessible—you won't even be able to scroll to it.

> You can remove the negative indents using the techniques discussed in "Formatting Paragraphs Directly," on page 309.

The bottom part of the text in a table row might be cut off (even in the middle of a line of text) if it's assigned an exact height. To remove the exact height setting, right-click in the row, choose Table Properties from the shortcut menu, click the Row tab in the Table Properties dialog box, and select the At Least item in the Row Height Is drop-down list.

Adding Borders and Shading

You can emphasize, organize, or set apart portions of your document by adding borders or background shading to entire tables, to cells within tables, or to blocks of characters or paragraphs outside of tables (see Figure 13-9). You can also have Word print borders around entire pages in your document (see Figure 13-10).

Chapter 13: Arranging Text Using Tables, Columns, and Lists

You can apply borders and shading to blocks of characters *within* a paragraph.

You can apply borders and shading to entire paragraphs.

You can apply borders and shading to tables:

Units	Points	Picas	Centimeters	Inches
Points	1	1/12	.035	1/72
Picas	12	1	.42	1/6
Centimeters	28.35	2.38	1	.39
Inches	72	6	2.54	1

Figure 13-9. You can apply borders and shading to a block of characters, a paragraph, or a table.

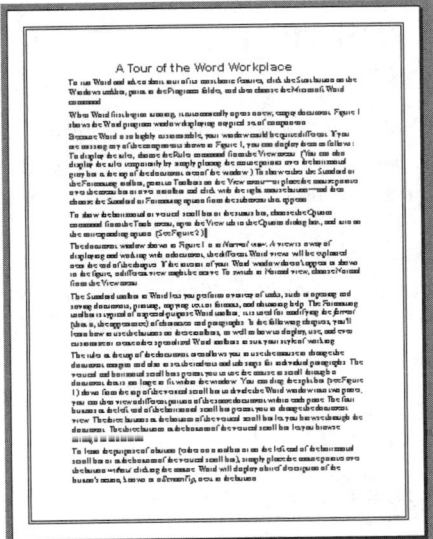

Figure 13-10. You can have Word include borders around a document page.

note If you create a table using the Insert Table toolbar button or the Table, Insert, Table menu command, it will initially be assigned the borders (and other formatting features) specified by the default table style. If you create a table using the Draw Table button on the Tables And Borders toolbar, you can use any style of borders (or no borders). In this section, you'll learn how to modify, remove, or add borders to a table that has already been created. Recall also that if you remove a border, Word will mark the cell gridline with a light gray line (which appears on the screen in Word but doesn't print or show in a browser), provided that the Show Gridlines option on the Table menu is selected.

For information on adding borders, background shading, and character formatting to a table by applying a table style, see "Formatting Tables by Applying Table Styles," on page 352.

To apply borders and shading to characters, paragraphs, or tables, you can use either the Tables And Borders toolbar or the Borders And Shading dialog box. To apply borders to pages, you must use the Borders And Shading dialog box.

> **note** If you're creating a Web page, remember that a browser won't display a border applied to a block of characters (you'll need to apply the border to the entire paragraph). Also, regardless of the line style you assign to a border, a browser will display either single or double solid lines.

Applying Borders and Shading with the Tables And Borders Toolbar

This section explains how to use the Tables And Borders toolbar to apply (or modify) borders or shading around characters, paragraphs, cells within tables, or entire tables. Figure 13-11 shows the Tables And Borders toolbar, labeling each of the buttons that you use for applying borders and shading. Table 13-3 briefly explains the tasks you can perform with these buttons (the following discussion provides more details on using these buttons). If the toolbar isn't visible, you can display it by choosing View, Toolbars, or by right-clicking the menu bar or another toolbar, and then choosing Tables And Borders.

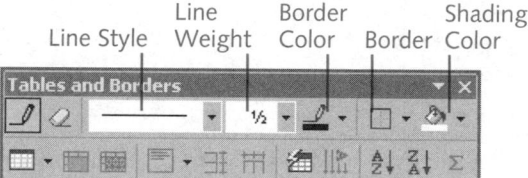

Figure 13-11. You can use these buttons on the Tables And Borders toolbar to apply borders and shading.

Table 13-3. **Using the Tables And Borders Toolbar to Apply Borders and Shading**

To Do This	Perform This Action on the Tables And Borders Toolbar
Select the style of the borders that you subsequently apply.	Select a style from the Line Style drop-down list, or select No Border to remove borders.
Select the thickness of the borders that you subsequently apply.	Select a thickness in points from the Line Weight drop-down list.
Set the color of the borders that you subsequently apply.	Choose a color from the Border Color drop-down palette. Or, to make the border color the same as your current Windows font color, choose Automatic.

(continued)

Table 13-3. *(continued)*

To Do This	Perform This Action on the Tables And Borders Toolbar
Apply or remove border(s). The border(s) will have the features that are currently selected in the Line Style, Line Weight, and Border Color controls.	Click the down arrow on the Border button and choose a border arrangement from the drop-down palette.
Apply or remove background shading.	Click the down arrow on the Shading Color button and choose a color from the drop-down palette, or choose No Fill to remove background shading.

The first step in adding borders or shading is to make an appropriate selection in one of the following ways.

● To add borders or shading to a block of characters, select the characters *without* including the paragraph mark at the end of the paragraph.

● To add borders or shading to one or more entire paragraphs, select the paragraphs. To add borders or shading to a single paragraph, include the paragraph mark in your selection, or place the insertion point anywhere within the paragraph without selecting text.

● To add borders or shading to table cells, select one or more entire cells. To add borders or shading to the whole table, you must select all cells in the table. To format a single cell, you can just place the insertion point within the cell without selecting any text.

● To add borders or shading to text within a table cell, without assigning borders or shading to the cell itself, select just that text. Note, however, that selecting *all* of the text in the cell causes the borders or shading to be applied to the cell, not to the text. To apply a border or shading to all of the text, you can temporarily add a character that you leave out of your selection.

Applying Borders

To apply borders to your selection, perform the following steps:

1 From the Line Style, Line Weight, and Border Color drop-down lists or palettes on the Tables And Borders toolbar, select the desired style, thickness, and color of the border or borders you want to apply.

note Choosing Automatic from the Border Color drop-down palette applies the current Window Font color, which is usually black. You set the Window Font color by running the Display program in the Windows Control Panel, opening the Appearance tab in the Display Properties dialog box, selecting Window in the Item drop-down list, and then choosing the color you want from the Font Color drop-down palette.

2 Click the down arrow on the Border button, and on the drop-down palette click the button for the specific border or combination of borders that you want to apply to the selection. As you position the pointer over each button on the palette, Word displays a ScreenTip describing the border—or combination of borders—that will be applied (Outside Border, Top Border, Left Border, Bottom Border, and so on), as shown in this example:

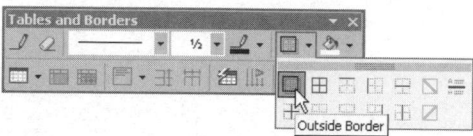

Borders labeled Inside are applicable only if you have selected more than one paragraph or table cell. (They will be added between the paragraphs or cells.) Diagonal borders can be applied only to table cells. (If you're creating a Web page, note that browser won't display diagonal borders.) Clicking the Horizontal Line button inserts a horizontal dividing line, not a border. When you click a button on the palette, Word will immediately apply the border or borders to the selection in your document.

> Horizontal dividing lines are described in "Inserting Horizontal Dividing Lines," on page 586.

> **note** If ScreenTips don't appear, you can enable them by choosing Tools, Customize, clicking the Options tab in the Customize dialog box, and checking the Show ScreenTips On Toolbars option.

If the Border drop-down palette doesn't have a button for the particular combination of borders you want to add, you can apply the borders one at a time. For example, to apply borders to the left and right of a paragraph, you could first click the Left Border button and then click the Right Border button.

If you want the borders you apply to have varying properties (for example, you want each border to have a different color), return to step 1 before applying each border.

> **note** The Border button also appears on the Formatting toolbar. On either the Formatting toolbar or the Tables And Borders toolbar, you can simply click the Border button (rather than opening and using the palette) to apply the border style you most recently applied. The button's icon and ScreenTip indicate the type of border that will be applied (Outside Border, All Borders, Top Border, and so on).

To remove a border from the selection, you can click the same button on the Border drop-down palette that is used to apply that border. Repeatedly clicking the button will toggle the border off and on. If you've changed the style, weight, or color settings on the Tables And Borders toolbar since you originally applied a border, clicking the button will apply the new border type; to remove the border, just click again.

You can remove all borders from the selection by clicking the No Border button on the Border palette. Note, however, that clicking this button again won't restore the borders.

---

tip **Change an Existing Border**

To modify the properties of a border that has already been applied, select the new properties using the Line Style, Line Weight, and Border Color buttons on the Tables And Borders toolbar (as described in step 1, given earlier). Then, use the Border button to reapply the border (as described in step 2).

Applying Shading

To apply shading to the selected paragraph or table cells, click the down arrow on the Shading Color button on the Tables And Borders toolbar to display the palette of color choices, shown here:

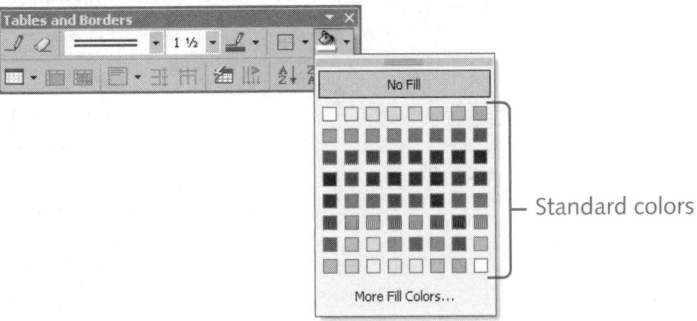

Then, choose one of the following options:

- To apply a standard shading color, click one of the standard colors on the palette.

- To select from a larger collection of standard colors or to create a custom color, click More Fill Colors.

- To remove background shading from the selection, click No Fill.

Applying Borders and Shading with the Borders And Shading Dialog Box

The Borders And Shading dialog box is not quite as easy to use as the Tables And Borders toolbar, but it provides the following additional options:

- You can create borders that have a shadow or 3-D effect.

- You can specify the distance between the borders and the text.

Chapter 13

- You can apply a background shading pattern as well as a solid shading color. (The Tables And Borders toolbar lets you apply only a solid background shading color.) If you're creating a Web page, keep in mind that a browser will display a patterned background as a solid color.

- You can place a border around entire document pages.

The first step is to select the document elements to which you want to apply borders or shading, using one of the following methods:

- To add borders or shading to a block of characters, select the characters *without* including the paragraph mark at the end of the paragraph.

- To add borders or shading to one or more entire paragraphs, select the paragraphs. To add borders or shading to a single paragraph, include the paragraph mark in your selection, or place the insertion point anywhere within the paragraph without selecting text.

- To add borders or shading to table cells, select them. To add borders or shading to the entire table, place the insertion point anywhere within the table.

- To add borders or shading to text within a table cell without assigning borders or shading to the cell itself, select just that text. Note, however, that selecting all of the text in the cell causes the borders or shading to be applied to the cell, not to the text. To apply a border or shading to all of the text, you can temporarily add a character that you leave out of your selection.

To apply one or more borders to your selection, perform the following steps:

1 Choose Format, Borders And Shading. In the Borders And Shading dialog box, click the Borders tab, as shown here:

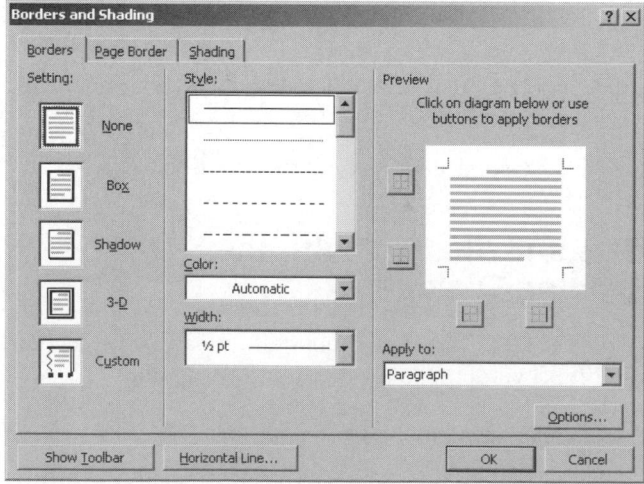

2 From the Style, Color, and Width lists, choose the properties of the border or borders you want to apply.

3 Click one of the items in the Setting area to specify the basic look and arrangement of the border or borders. Pick the one that's closest to what you want—you can customize it later.

The specific choices in the Setting area depend on what you selected prior to opening the Borders And Shading dialog box. (If you begin customizing borders, as explained in the next step, the Custom item will be automatically selected so you don't need to click it yourself.) If you want to remove all borders, click None, and then click OK to close the dialog box. In this case, you can skip the remaining steps.

4 To add or remove specific borders, click the appropriate buttons in the Preview area (each button toggles between applying and removing the corresponding border). If you want to modify the properties of a specific border, make the desired selections in the Style, Color, and Width lists just before clicking the button to add the border. (You can thus assign different properties to each border.)

5 If you selected paragraphs prior to opening the Borders And Shading dialog box, you can modify the clearance between the borders and the text by clicking the Options button. Then, in the Border And Shading Options dialog box, adjust the measurements in the From Text area. If you selected characters, a table, or table cells, you can't adjust the clearance.

> **tip** After you have applied borders to one or more paragraphs, you can adjust the clearance between a border and the text by dragging the border with the mouse.

6 To modify the portion of your document that receives borders, choose an item in the Apply To drop-down list. For example, if you selected one or more paragraphs prior to opening the Borders And Shading dialog box, the Paragraph item will initially be selected in the list, causing Word to apply borders to the entire paragraph or paragraphs. If you choose the Text item, however, Word will place the borders around each line of characters rather than around the entire paragraph(s).

7 When the example borders shown in the Preview area have the look you want, click the OK button.

> **note** When applying borders or shading, keep in mind that the Automatic color choice applies the current Window Font color, which is usually black. You set the Window Font color by running the Display program in the Windows Control Panel, clicking the Appearances tab in the Display Properties dialog box, selecting Window in the Item drop-down list, and then choosing the color you want from the Font Color drop-down palette.

To apply shading to your selection, perform the following steps.

1 Choose Format, Borders And Shading and click the Shading tab of the Borders And Shading dialog box, as shown here:

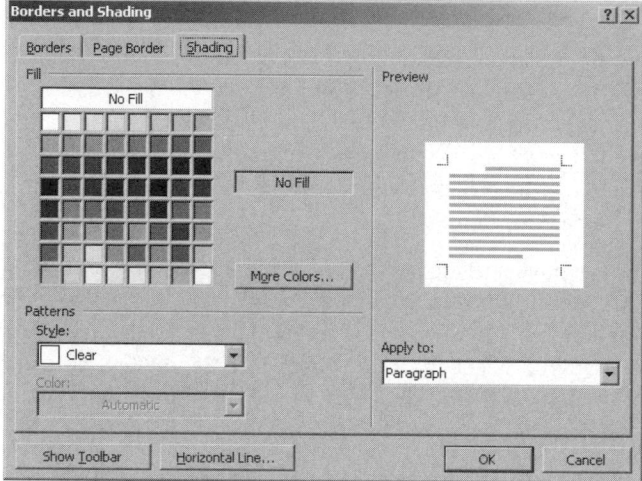

2 To apply a solid shading color, select a color in the Fill area. To pick a standard color, click one of the colors in the palette. To choose from a larger set of standard colors or to create a custom color, click the More Colors button and make your choice in the Colors dialog box. If you don't want a solid shading color, select No Fill at the top of the palette.

3 To apply a shading pattern, select a pattern from the Style drop-down list in the Patterns area. Then, select a color for the pattern in the Color drop-down palette. If you don't want a pattern, choose Clear in the Style list.

> **note** You can apply both a solid shading color and a shading pattern to your selection.

4 If you want to change the portion of your document that is to be shaded, select an item in the Apply To list box as explained in step 6 of the previous procedure for applying borders.

5 When the example shading shown in the Preview area has the look you want, click the OK button.

> You can also apply background shading to an entire Word document. You can view this shading in Web Layout view, or if you've saved the document as a Web page, in a browser. For information, see "Applying a Background Color or Pattern," on page 597.

Applying Borders to Pages

To give your document a polished or decorative look, you can have Word draw borders around entire pages. You can add page borders to the entire document or to just part of it. Borders will be visible in Print Layout view, in Print Preview, and of course, on the printed page. If you're creating a Web page, however, page borders aren't for you—they won't be displayed in a browser.

To add page borders, perform the following steps:

1 Choose Format, Borders And Shading to open the Borders And Shading dialog box, and click the Page Border tab, as shown here:

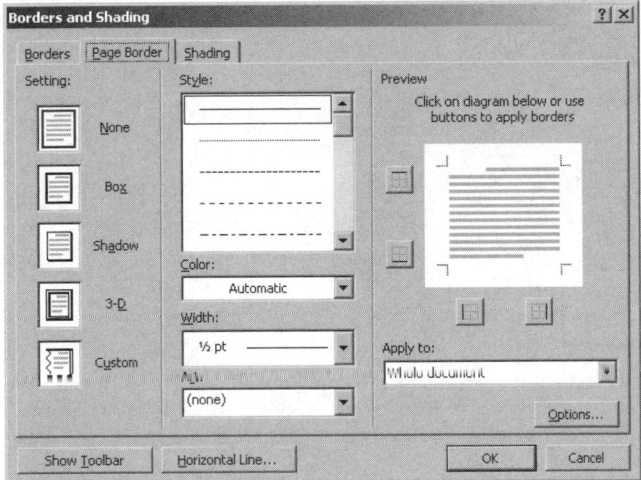

2 Using the techniques described in the previous section for applying borders to characters, paragraphs, or tables, choose options until the example borders shown in the Preview area have the look you want.

When you apply a page border, however, as an alternative to selecting a particular style of line from the Style list, you can select an "artwork" border from the Art drop-down list to create a highly decorative border, consisting of apples, ice cream cones, stars, or one of many other patterns. Choose (None) to remove an artwork border and restore whatever border type is currently selected in the Style list. (Figure 13-10, on page 357, shows one of the artwork borders.)

3 In the Apply To list box, select one of the following options to specify which part of the document is to be given page borders.

- To apply borders to the entire document, select Whole Document.

- If you have divided your document into sections, to apply borders to the current section only, select This Section.

■ To apply borders to the first page of the document, or to the first page of the current section if you've created sections, select This Section - First Page Only.

■ To apply borders to all the pages except the first page of the document, or to all pages except the first page of the current section if you've created sections, select This Section - All Except First Page.

4 To modify the clearance between the page border and either the edge of the page or the text, or to set other page border options, click the Options button, select the settings you want in the Border And Shading Options dialog box, shown here, and click OK.

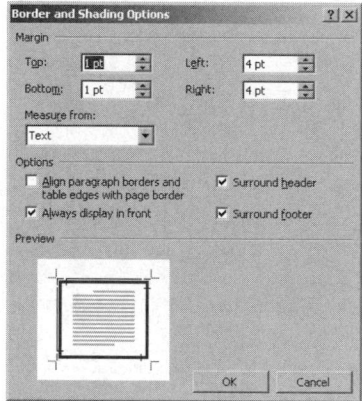

5 When the example border in the Preview area of the Page Border tab has the look you want, click OK.

Arranging Text in Newspaper-Style Columns

Unlike the columns created with tables, newspaper-style columns aren't divided into rows of side-by-side items. Rather, the text flows from the bottom of one column to the top of the next column, just like it does in the familiar columns of newspapers and magazines (see Figure 13-12). Newspaper-style columns are intended for regular Word documents that you're going to print or view online in Word. If you're creating a Web page document, forget about newspaper-style columns—they won't display in a browser; rather, the text will be displayed in a single column.

If you want to view newspaper-style columns on the screen, you must switch to Print Layout view or to Print Preview. In the other Word views, text is always displayed in a single column. You can create newspaper-style columns using either the Columns button on the Standard toolbar or the Columns dialog box.

Chapter 13: Arranging Text Using Tables, Columns, and Lists

Figure 13-12. In this Word document page, the text following the heading is divided into two newspaper-style columns.

Applying Columns with the Columns Button

To set up equal-width newspaper-style columns throughout your entire document or in a part of the document, perform the following steps:

1 To create columns in a part of your document, select that part. To create columns throughout your entire document, place the insertion point anywhere in the document.

2 Click the Columns button and drag to indicate the number of columns you want (from 1 to 6), as in this example:

Word will divide the selected text, or the entire document, into the specified number of columns. The columns will be equal in width and will be separated by 0.5 inches.

If you selected part of the document in step 1, Word will insert *section breaks* before and after your selection; that is, the selected text will be placed in a separate document section, and newspaper-style columns will be applied to that section. In general, a Word document can be divided into separate sections, and each section can be assigned different page setup features, such as margins, headers, footers, and newspaper-style columns. Sections allow you to vary page setup features within a document. You can manually divide a document into sections using the Insert, Break menu command. The steps given in this part of the chapter work somewhat differently if you have previously divided your document into sections.

> For more information on sections, as well as on the formatting features that can be applied to sections, see Chapter 18, "Designing and Printing Professional-Looking Pages."

Applying Columns with the Columns Dialog Box

Although using the Columns dialog box isn't as quick as creating columns with the Columns button, it provides the following additional options:

- You can create columns of unequal widths.

- For each column, you can specify the exact column width and the amount of space between that column and the next.

- You can force the columns and column spacings to remain equal in width, even if you later adjust the width of a particular column.

- You can add vertical lines between the columns.

To set up newspaper-style columns with the Columns dialog box, perform the following steps:

1 To create columns in a part of your document, select that part. To create columns from a specific position in the document through the end of the document, place the insertion point at that position. To create columns throughout the entire document, place the insertion point anywhere within the document.

2 Choose Format, Columns to open the Columns dialog box, shown in Figure 13-13.

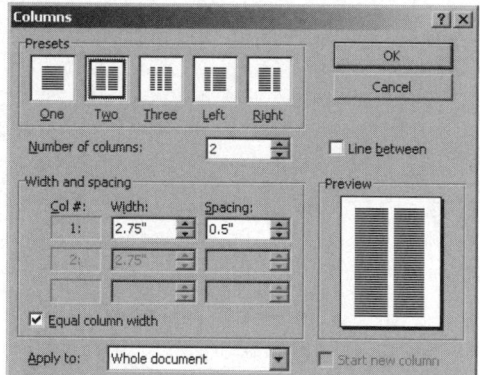

Figure 13-13. You can use the Columns dialog box to apply newspaper-style columns.

3 Choose an option in the Apply To list box to tell Word which portion of your document to modify. If you selected text prior to opening the Columns dialog box, choose Selected Text to add columns to the selection only or Whole Document to add columns to the entire document. If you didn't select text, choose Whole Document to add columns to the entire document or This

Point Forward to add columns from the position of the insertion point through the end of the document.

InsideOut

The name of the Start New Column option in the Columns dialog box is misleading. This option is available only if you've selected This Point Forward in the Apply To list, and in most situations it actually inserts a *page break* before the beginning of the section containing the columns that you are applying.

4 Choose a column arrangement as follows:

- To use a standard column arrangement, choose one of the items in the Presets area.

- To create a custom column arrangement, enter the number of columns you want into the Number Of Columns text box. Then, for each column, specify the column width in the Width box and enter the space you want between that column and the next column in the Spacing box. (To enter separate widths and spacings, the Equal Column Width option, discussed next, must not be checked.)

5 To force Word to keep the column widths and spacings equal, check the Equal Column Width option. If this option is checked, adjusting the column width—using the procedures described in the next section—will affect all columns simultaneously. If this option isn't checked, you can adjust the width of each column individually. Note that if you choose the One, Two, or Three option in the Presets area, Equal Column Width is checked automatically.

6 To add a vertical line between each column, check the Line Between option.

7 Click the OK button to apply the columns. Word might insert one or more section breaks, as discussed under the previous heading.

Fine Tuning Columns

Once you have applied newspaper-style columns, you can change the column widths, insert breaks within columns, and adjust other features.

The easiest way to change column widths is as follows:

1 If you're not in Print Layout view, activate it by choosing View, Print Layout.

2 If the horizontal ruler isn't visible, display it by choosing View, Ruler.

3 If the columns you want to adjust are contained within a particular document section, click in that section.

4 Drag the appropriate "Move Column" marker on the horizontal ruler, as shown here:

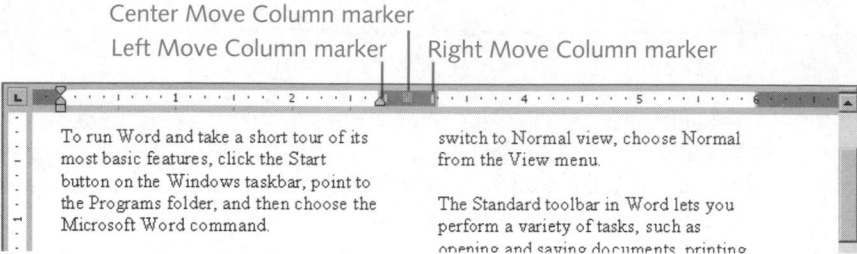

To change the width of the column on the left, drag the left Move Column marker. (This will alter the column spacing.)

To change the width of the column on the right, drag the right Move Column marker. (This will also alter the column spacing.)

To change the width of both columns simultaneously, drag the center Move Column marker. (This will increase the width of one column and decrease the width of the other without altering the column spacing.)

note The instructions here assume that you haven't checked the Equal Column Width option in the Columns dialog box. If this option is checked, dragging the left or right Move Column marker adjusts the widths of all columns simultaneously, keeping their widths equal, and the ruler won't display a center Move Column marker.

When the pointer is over one of the Move Column markers, it changes to a two-headed arrow and you'll see "Move Column" in a ScreenTip, as seen here:

You can force Word to move text into the next column by inserting a *column break* anywhere within a column (as shown in Figure 13-14). To do this, place the insertion point where you want to break the column. Then choose Insert, Break and select the Column Break option; or, just press Ctrl+Shift+Enter.

You can prevent Word from inserting a column break within a particular paragraph by selecting that paragraph, choosing Format, Paragraph, clicking the Line And Page Breaks tab, and checking the Keep Lines Together option. Then, if the paragraph won't fit at the end of a column, Word will move the entire paragraph to the beginning of the next column rather than breaking the paragraph across columns.

If you want to change any of the other column features, such as the number of columns, just repeat the procedure for setting up columns given in the previous section.

Chapter 13: Arranging Text Using Tables, Columns, and Lists

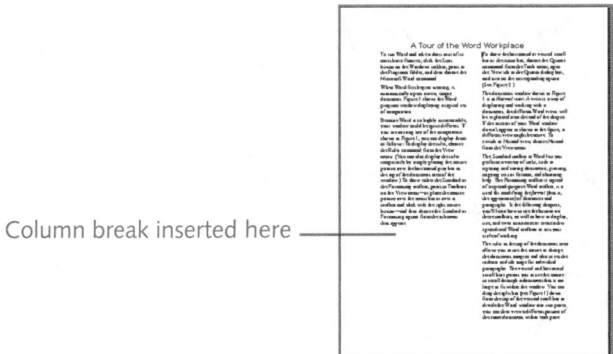

Column break inserted here —————

Figure 13-14. This figure shows a column break inserted within a newspaper-style column.

---

tip   **Do You Know Where Your Columns Are?**

To see the exact boundaries of your columns in Page Layout view, you can have Word draw dotted lines around them. Choose Tools, Options, click the View tab, and check the Text Boundaries option (see Figure 13-15).

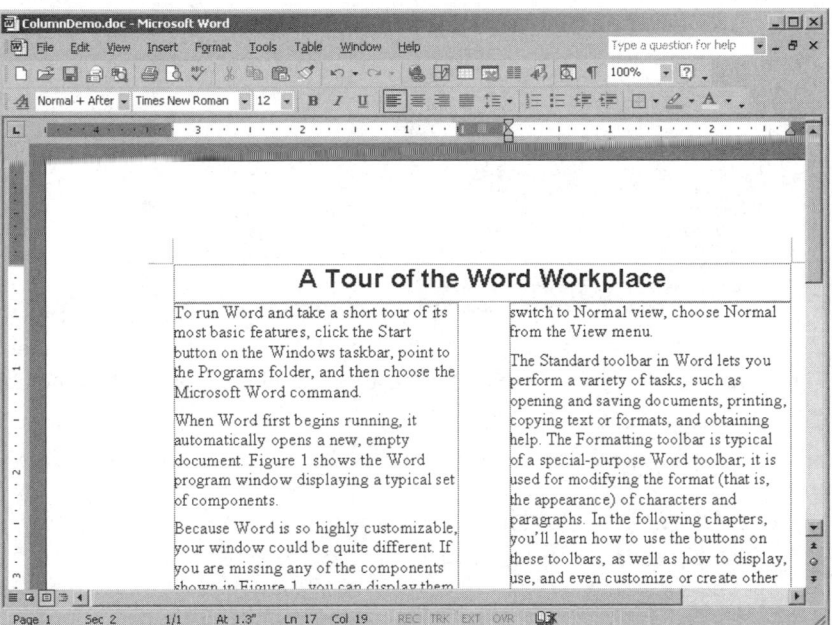

Figure 13-15. This figure shows a document in Print Layout view with boundary lines drawn around paragraphs and columns.

Ordering Text in Bulleted and Numbered Lists

You can create lists in your document by having Word add bullet characters or automatic numbering, together with hanging indents. These bullets and numbering are part of the paragraph formatting. Unlike any bullet characters or numbers you might type in manually, you can't select or perform normal editing on automatic bullets or numbers. Also, if you rearrange the paragraphs in a numbered list, Word renumbers the list for you. Figure 13-16 shows examples of the three kinds of lists you can create by adding automatic bullets or numbers.

You can apply bullets and numbers using the Formatting toolbar or using the Bullets And Numbering dialog box.

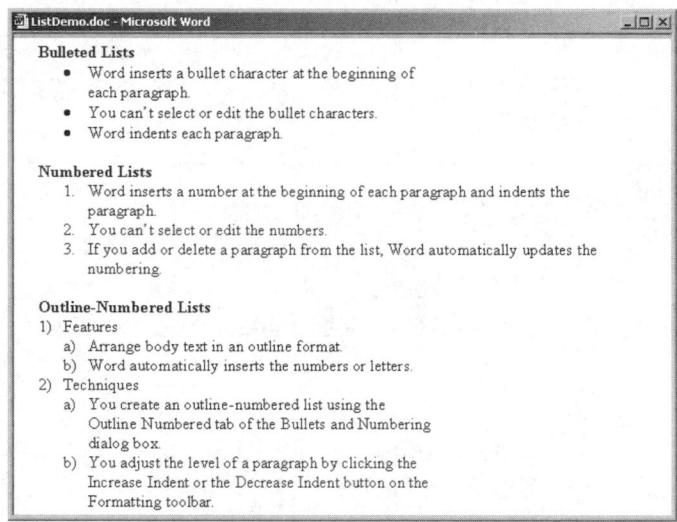

Figure 13-16. These are examples of bulleted, numbered, and outline-numbered lists.

note Because bullets and numbering are considered to be paragraph formatting, you can use most of the techniques for paragraph formatting that are covered in Chapter 12, "Effective Formatting in Word," and Chapter 14, "Advanced Word Formatting Techniques." For example, you can apply bullets or numbering by using a saved format in the Styles And Formatting task pane, or you can assign bullet or numbering formatting to a paragraph style.

Creating Lists with the Formatting Toolbar

The fastest way to have Word apply bullets or numbering to a list is to use the Bullets button or the Numbering button on the Formatting toolbar, using the following steps:

1 Type the list. Press Enter at the end of each list item so that each is contained in a separate paragraph.

2 Select all the paragraphs in the list.

3 Click the Bullets button to apply bullets, or click the Numbering button to apply numbering, as shown here:

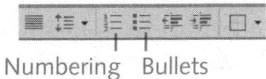

    Numbering Bullets

If you apply numbering to a series of paragraphs and then delete or rearrange one or more of them, Word will update the numbering. If you place the insertion point at the end of a bulleted or numbered paragraph and press Enter, the new paragraph will also be bulleted or numbered. If, however, you press Enter twice without typing text, the new paragraphs will not be bulleted or numbered; this is a convenient way to stop adding bullets or numbering when you reach the end of your list.

For instructions on numbering the lines in a document, see "Adjusting the Page Layout," on page 545.

You can remove bullets or numbering by selecting one or more paragraphs and clicking the Bullets button or Numbering button again. You can also remove the bullet or number from a single paragraph by placing the insertion point immediately following the bullet or number and pressing Backspace.

To control the starting number for a list of automatically numbered paragraphs, use the Bullets And Numbering dialog box, described in the next section.

tip   **Number Cells in Tables**

You can number the cells in a Word table by selecting the cells and clicking the Numbering button. Word will number the cells beginning with the upper left cell and progressing through each row from left to right. The cells you number don't have to be adjoining, as shown in this example.

To select nonadjacent cells, click at the left of the first one, and then click at the left of each additional cell while pressing Ctrl.

newfeature!
Creating Lists with the Bullets And Numbering Dialog Box and List Styles

If you apply bullets or numbering using the Bullets And Numbering dialog box rather than using the Formatting toolbar, you have the following additional options:

● You can choose any character or graphic image for the bullets in a bulleted list.

● You can specify the starting number for a numbered list.

● You can modify the appearance and position of the bullet characters or images or the numbers.

● You can create and customize an outline numbered list. An outline numbered list displays text in an attractive outline format, without using the Heading styles or Outline view. The list items can be automatically numbered in various ways or marked with bullet characters. You can create an outline numbered list by directly applying the features you want, or by assigning a list style (a new feature in Microsoft Office XP) to the selected paragraphs.

● You can automatically number your document's headings.

To apply or modify any kind of list formatting, perform the following steps:

1 Select all the paragraphs in the list.

2 Open the Bullets And Numbering dialog box by choosing Format, Bullets And Numbering, or by right-clicking the selection and choosing Bullets And Numbering from the shortcut menu.

3 Follow the instructions given in the following sections to apply a specific type of list formatting.

Creating a Bulleted List Using the Bulleted Tab

To create a bulleted list, click the Bulleted tab of the Bullets And Numbering dialog box (shown in Figure 13-17) and do one or more of the following actions:

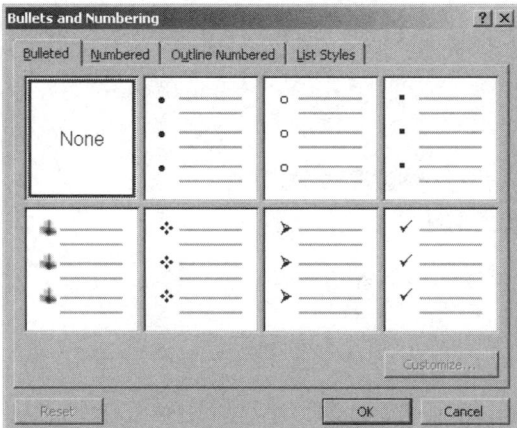

Figure 13-17. You can apply one of a variety of bullet types by using the Bulleted tab of the Bullets And Numbering dialog box.

● To apply one of the standard bullet types, double-click one of the seven types displayed in the "gallery" of bullet types in the dialog box.

- To customize one of the standard bullet types, click it to select it and then click Customize. This will display the Customize Bulleted List dialog box, in which you can select a different bullet character or graphic, modify the indent of the bullet or the text, and adjust the size of the tab space between the bullet and the first line of text. Use the preview image to guide your selections.

- To restore a bullet type that you've customized, select it and click the Reset button.

- To remove bullets that were previously applied, double-click the None option at the upper left of the tab.

> **note** Applying a theme to your document modifies the bullets in bulleted lists throughout the document. Themes are discussed in "Applying a Web Page Theme," on page 598.

Creating a Numbered List Using the Numbered Tab

To create a numbered list, open the Numbered tab of the Bullets And Numbering dialog box (shown in Figure 13-18) and do one or more of the following actions:

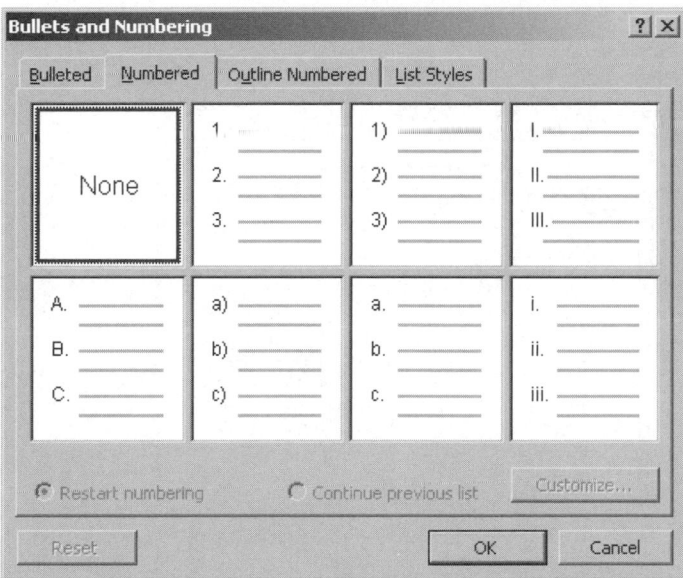

Figure 13-18. You can apply any one of several numbering types using the Numbered tab of the Bullets And Numbering dialog box.

- To apply one of the standard numbering types, double-click one of the seven types displayed in the "gallery" of numbering types in the dialog box.

- To customize one of the standard numbering types, click it to select it and then click the Customize button. This will display the Customize Numbered List dialog box, in which you can modify the number format, style, starting number, and position, as well as the position of the text. Use the preview image to guide your selections.

● To restore a numbering type that you've customized, select it and click the Reset button.

● To continue the numbering sequence from the previous numbered list in the document, select the Continue Previous List option. To start numbering with 1 (or with a custom starting number you select through the Customize Numbered List dialog box), select Restart Numbering. These options are available only if the document contains a numbered list prior to the paragraphs you selected.

● To remove numbering that was previously applied, double-click the None option at the upper left of the tab.

Creating an Outline Numbered List Using the Outline Numbered Tab

To create an outline numbered list by directly applying the formatting features you want, click the Outline Numbered tab of the Bullets And Numbering dialog box (shown in Figure 13-19) and do one or more of the following actions:

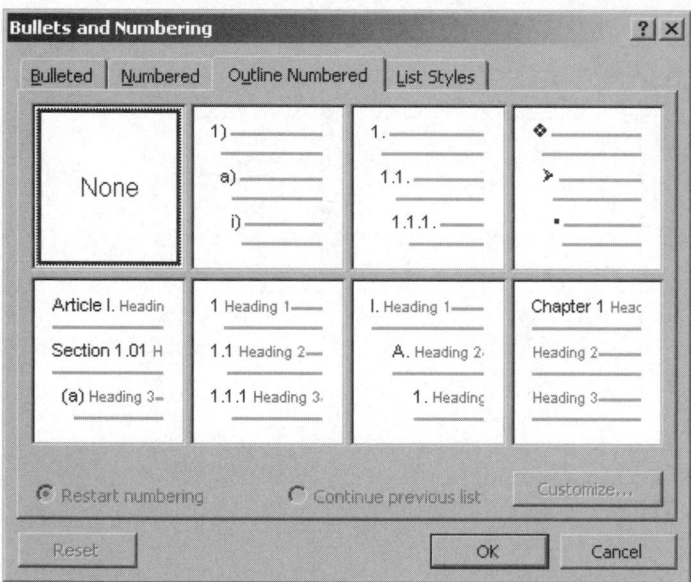

Figure 13-19.   You can create an outline numbered list using the Outline Numbered tab of the Bullets And Numbering dialog box.

● To apply one of the standard types of outline numbering, double-click one of the three outline numbering types displayed on the *first row* of types in the Outline Numbered tab. (The types in the second row are explained later in this section.)

- To customize one of the standard outline numbering types, click it to select it and then click Customize. This will display the Customize Outline Numbered List dialog box, in which you can modify the number format, style, starting number, and position—as well as the text position and other features—for any of the levels of the outline numbered list. Use the preview image to guide your selections.

- To restore an outline numbering type that you've customized, select it and click the Reset button.

- To continue the numbering sequence from the previous numbered list in the document, select the Continue Previous List option. To start numbering with 1 (or with a custom starting number you select through the Customize Outline Numbered List dialog box), select Restart Numbering. These options are available only if the document contains a numbered list prior to the paragraphs you select.

- To remove outline numbering that was previously applied, double-click the None option at the upper left of the tab.

InsideOut

Decrease
Indent

Double-clicking the None option might leave the paragraphs with various levels of indentation. You can remove an indentation by clicking the Decrease Indent button on the Formatting toolbar, repeatedly if necessary.

note The Outline Numbered List feature is convenient for permanently formatting any amount of document text as an attractive outline. In contrast, the Outline view allows you to temporarily view an entire document in outline form so that you can quickly organize the text. (Outline view is covered in "Working with Documents in Outline View," on page 415.)

Once you have applied an outline numbered list format to a series of paragraphs using this procedure, you can adjust the level of each paragraph as follows:

Increase
Indent

- To demote a paragraph (that is, convert it to a lower level list item), place the insertion point in the paragraph and press Alt+Shift+Right Arrow or click the Increase Indent button on the Formatting toolbar.

Decrease
Indent

- To promote a paragraph (that is, convert it to a higher level list item), place the insertion point in the paragraph and press Alt+Shift+Left Arrow or click the Decrease Indent button on the Formatting toolbar.

---

tip   **Convert a Simple Bulleted or Numbered List to an Outline**

You can convert a simple bulleted or numbered list (created using the Bulleted or Numbered tab or the Bullets or Numbering toolbar button) to an outline numbered list by demoting some of the paragraphs in the list. When you do this, Word will apply default bullet characters or numbering to the lower outline levels. If you want to choose the style of all levels, you must create or modify the outline numbered list using the Outline Numbered tab of the Bullets And Numbering dialog box, as explained previously in this section, or by applying a list style, as covered in the next section.

You can also use the Outline Numbered tab of the Bullets And Numbering dialog box to apply automatic outline numbering to all the headings throughout your document, even though they aren't contained in a list of adjoining paragraphs, provided that you have assigned all your heading paragraphs the standard Heading styles, Heading 1 through Heading 9. To do this, place the insertion point within any heading in the document, click the Outline Numbered tab of the Bullets And Numbering dialog box, and select one of the four outline numbering types in the bottom row, shown in Figure 13-19. Notice that the sample in the Outline Numbered tab for each of these types contains the names of Heading styles.

---

newfeature!

tip   **Control Numbering When You Copy a List Item**

If you cut or copy and then paste a paragraph formatted as a numbered list or outline numbered list, you can use the Paste Options button to control whether the list item at the new position will continue numbering from the previous document list or restart numbering, as shown here:

3.   Third list item.

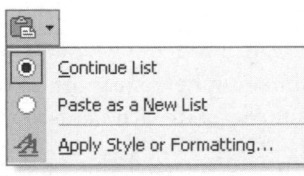

---

newfeature!

Creating an Outline Numbered List by Applying a List Style

An alternative way to create an outline numbered list is to apply a *list style* to the selected paragraphs. A list style is one of the four types of Word styles (the other three are paragraph, character, and table). Using a style to create your outline numbered lists gives you the following advantages:

- Because a style can be stored in a template, copied between templates and documents, and shared by members of your workgroup, you can easily maintain consistent formatting of your outline numbered lists within all your documents.

- You can quickly update all your outline numbered lists by modifying the style, rather than changing each list.

- You can easily assign a list style to a toolbar button or shortcut key for quick application.

The fastest way to assign a list style to the selected paragraphs is to click the List Styles tab of the Bullets And Numbering dialog box (shown in Figure 13-20) and do one or more of the following actions:

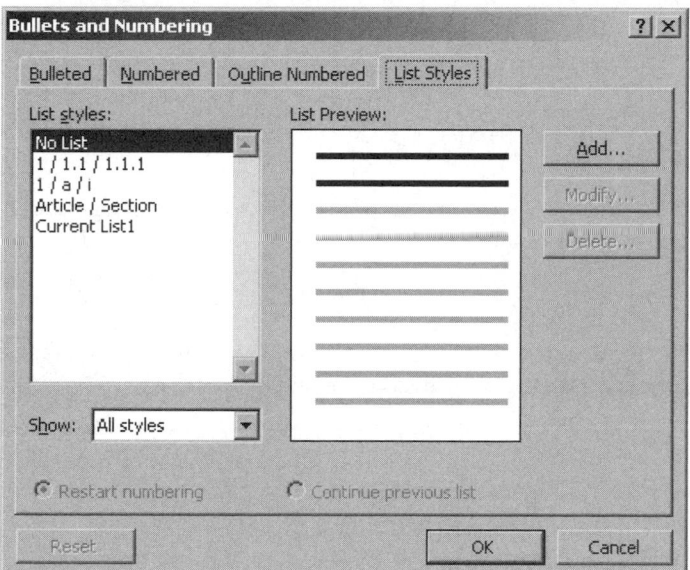

Figure 13-20.   You can assign list styles using the List Styles tab of the Bullets And Numbering dialog box.

- To apply one of the built-in styles, double-click one of the styles (other than No List) in the List Styles list. To control which styles are shown, select an item in the Show drop-down list.

- To customize a list style, select it in the List Styles list and click the Modify button. This will display the Modify Style dialog box, in which you can change any formatting feature of the style.

379

● To create a new list style, click the Add button and define the formatting features in the New Style dialog box.

● To remove a style in the List Styles list, select it and click the Delete button.

● To continue the numbering sequence from the previous numbered list in the document, select the Continue Previous List option. To start number-ing with 1 (or with a custom starting number you select through the Modify Style dialog box), select Restart Numbering. These options are available only if the document contains a numbered list prior to the para-graphs you selected.

● To remove a list style that was applied previously, double-click the No List item in the list.

> For information on creating, modifying, removing, or copying list styles (as well as other types of Word styles), see Chapter 14, "Advanced Word Formatting Techniques." For information on adjusting the level of a paragraph in an outline numbered list, see the previous section. You can also apply, modify, or delete a list style using the Styles And Formatting task pane, as dis-cussed in Chapter 12, "Effective Formatting in Word," and Chapter 14, "Advanced Word For-matting Techniques."

Sorting Lists and Tables

You can have Word sort the items in a list consisting of a series of paragraphs. You can also have it sort rows within a table.

To sort a list of paragraphs, perform the following steps:

1 Select all the paragraphs that make up the list. (Recall that a paragraph con-sists of any amount of text followed by a paragraph mark.)

2 Choose Table, Sort to open the Sort Text dialog box, shown here:

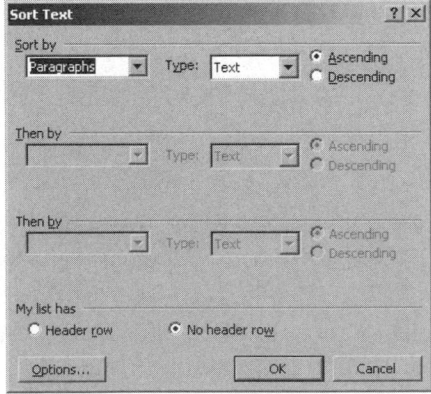

3 In the Sort By drop-down list, choose the part of the text that is to be used as the sort criterion. To sort a list of paragraphs, you normally choose Paragraphs to base the sort on all text in each paragraph. If, however, each paragraph is divided into *fields* (entries within the paragraphs separated with tabs, commas, or another character), you can base the sort on a specific field by choosing Field 1, Field 2, and so on. For instance, if you wanted to sort the following list by birth date, you would select Field 2:

John, December 18
Sue, April 25
Pete, April 25
Joan, June 10

You can also choose a second and a third sort field in the Then By controls, which Word will use if the previous sort fields are identical. In this example, if you chose Field 1 in the second Then By box, Word would use the names to sort the paragraphs for Sue and Pete, who have identical birthdays—that is, it would place Pete before Sue.

4 Select an item in the Type drop-down list to indicate the way the text should be sorted. You can choose Text to sort alphabetically. If the information you're sorting by consists of numbers, you can choose Number to sort it numerically. If it consists of dates, you can choose Date to sort it chronologically. (In the previous example, you would choose Date for the first sort field and Text for the second.)

5 Select Ascending to sort text from the beginning to the end of the alphabet, numbers from smaller to larger, and dates from earlier to later. Select Descending to sort in the opposite order.

6 Select Header Row to eliminate the first paragraph from the sort, or No Header Row to sort all selected paragraphs. When Header Row is selected, the items in the first row are used to name the fields; in this case, you can select a name from the Sort By or Then By list (rather than selecting Field 1, Field 2, and so on).

7 If you want to modify the way Word sorts text, click the Options button to open the Sort Options dialog box (see Figure 13-21, on page 382). This dialog box lets you specify the character used to separate fields. (The example in step 3 uses commas.) Also, if you check the Case Sensitive option, Word considers a lowercase letter to come before the same letter in uppercase (if you sort text in ascending order). If Case Sensitive isn't checked, Word ignores the case of letters. You can select a specific language in the Sorting Language drop-down list to cause Word to use the sorting rules defined by that language.

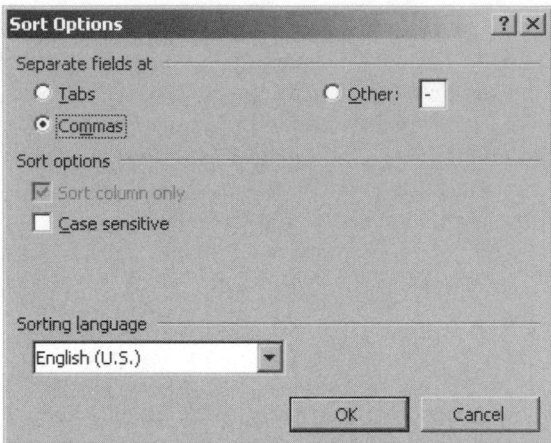

Figure 13-21. You can define sorting criteria in the Sort Options dialog box.

> **note** If you sort a list of paragraphs to which you have applied automatic numbering, Word renumbers it properly.

You can also use the steps listed previously to sort rows within a Word table, with the following provisos:

newfeature!

● The dialog box is titled Sort and has several additional controls (Using drop-down lists), as shown in Figure 13-22.

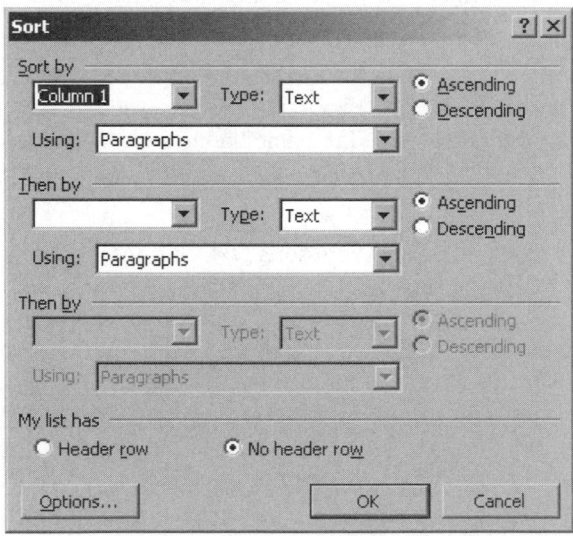

Figure 13-22. This figure shows the Sort dialog box, as it's displayed when you have selected text in a table.

382

Chapter 13: Arranging Text Using Tables, Columns, and Lists

- In step 1, select the rows and columns you want to sort. To sort the entire table, place the insertion point anywhere within the table. Note that Word sorts only vertically; you cannot, for example, select a single row and have Word sort the cells in that row.

- In the Sort By and Then By lists, choose the table columns that you want to use as sort criteria (assuming that you have selected more than one column in the table).

newfeature!

- If the text in one of the columns you're sorting by is divided into fields (using tabs, commas, or another character), in the Using drop-down list you can select a particular field to sort by (just as you do in the Sort By drop-down list when you sort paragraphs outside of a table, as explained in step 3).

- In the Sort Options dialog box, you can select the Sort Column Only option to have Word sort only the selected column or columns. Otherwise, Word will sort entire rows even if you haven't selected all the columns.

After you have sorted a list of paragraphs or the contents of a table, you can unsort it by immediately issuing the Undo command.

For information on using the Undo command, see the sidebar "Undoing and Redoing Editing and Formatting Actions," on page 272.

tip   **Arrange Text Using Dividing Lines**

Another way to arrange or organize the text in your document is to insert horizontal dividing lines, which commonly appear in Web pages but can be added to any type of document. For information, see "Inserting Horizontal Dividing Lines," on page 586.

Chapter 14

Advanced Word Formatting Techniques

Customizing Styles

All documents have access to the general-purpose, built-in styles that are provided by Microsoft Word 2002—for example, Normal, Body Text, Heading 1 through Heading 9, and List. Also, when you first create a document, the document obtains a copy of any user-defined styles or customized versions of built-in styles that are stored within the template on which the document is based. Many of the special-purpose templates supplied with Word store user-defined or customized versions of built-in styles that are useful for formatting the types of documents these templates are designed to create. An example is the Professional Report template, which stores many user-defined styles (for example, the Company Name, Title Cover, and Subtitle Cover styles that are used for formatting elements on the report's title page), as well as versions of built-in styles that have been customized for creating professional reports. When you create a document based on the Professional Report template, all of the user-defined and customized styles it contains are copied into your document and are stored in the document file.

If you later create a user-defined style or customize a built-in style within your document, the new or modified style definition is also stored in the document file. When you format text in the document, you can use any of the styles stored in the document file in addition to any of the original built-in Word styles.

Built-In vs. User-Defined Styles

A *built-in* style is one that is hard-coded into Word and is available to every docu-ment. Examples are Normal, Block Text, Body Text (and the Body Text variations such as Body Text 2 and Body Text Indent), Emphasis, Footer, Header, Heading 1 through Heading 9, List and the many List variations such as List 2 and List Bullet, Plain Text, and Strong. (There are many others.) If a built-in style is modified, the modified ver-sion of the style is stored in the document or template where the modification was made. The modified style can later be copied to another document or template. (When you create a new document, any modified built-in styles in the template are automatically copied into the document.) If a modified version of a built-in style is stored in a document, it takes precedence over the unmodified version of the style.

A *user-defined* style is a new style that has been created in a document or template. You or a co-worker can create user-defined styles. User-defined styles are also included in some of the templates shipped with Word (in this case, the *user* would be the Microsoft devel-oper who defined the style). User-defined styles are stored in a document or template and may be copied to another document or template. (When you create a new document, any user-defined styles in the template are automatically copied into the document.) In a document, you can use only those user-defined styles stored within the document's file.

> Creating user-defined styles is explained in "Creating New Styles," on page 399.

You can determine which of the styles available to your document are user-defined— as opposed to original or modified built-in styles—as follows:

1 If the Styles And Formatting task pane isn't visible, choose Format, Styles And Formatting.

2 Near the bottom of the Styles And Formatting task pane, select Custom in the Show drop-down list.

3 At the bottom of the Format Settings dialog box, click the Styles button.

4 In the Style dialog box, select User-Defined Styles in the Category drop-down list. The Styles list will then display all user-defined styles stored in the document. Figure 14-1 shows the list of user-defined styles that you would find in a new document created by using the Professional Report template.

You can modify any of the styles to which your document has access—those stored in the document, plus the built-in Word styles. When you modify a style, all text in your docu-ment that is assigned that style automatically acquires the style's new format—an impor-tant advantage of using styles rather than directly formatting text. Modifying a style initially affects only the document itself; it doesn't affect the document's template or other docu-ments based on that template. (When you modify a built-in style in a document, the modi-fied version of that style is stored only within the document.) As explained later in the chapter, however, you can easily copy styles between documents and templates to make any of the style definitions stored in a document available to other documents.

Chapter 14: Advanced Word Formatting Techniques

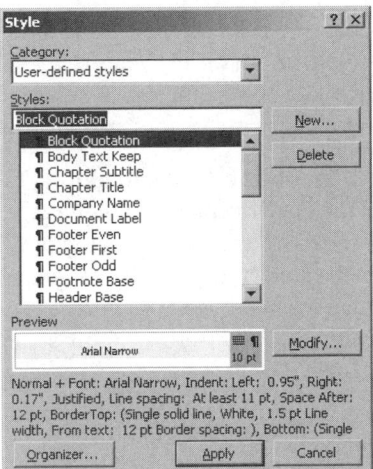

Figure 14-1. You can view all of the document's user-defined styles in the Style dialog box.

> Applying a theme to a document, as described in "Applying a Web Page Theme," on page 598, modifies the document's Normal style as well as its Heading styles (Heading 1 through Heading 9). These styles are given a look that's consistent with the theme.

When you modify or create a paragraph or character style, keep in mind that one style can be based on another style. The Normal paragraph style is the base style for most of the other built-in paragraph styles. For example, Body Text is defined as "Normal plus 6 points of space following the paragraph." This definition means that Body Text has all the formatting stored in Normal except the amount of space after the paragraph— Normal has 0 points of space after the paragraph, whereas Body Text has 6 points of space. (Normal itself isn't based on any other style.) Any formatting specifically assigned to a style supersedes the formatting of the base style.

If you change a style such as Normal, all styles based on it instantly change. For example, if you assigned the Courier New font and "10 points of space following the paragraph" to the Normal style, Body Text would acquire the Courier New font. Body Text would not, however, acquire "10 points of space following the paragraph" because it contains an explicit "space following" value (that is, it does not derive this formatting from Normal).

---

tip **Use Built-In Styles to Change the Appearance of Standard Document Elements**

Word assigns certain built-in styles to standard elements in your document. For example, it assigns the Comment Text style to comment text, the Footer style to page footers, and the Page Number style to page numbers. You can therefore change the appearance of one of these standard elements by changing the corresponding style. For example, if you change the Header style, you'll modify the appearance of the headers on all pages of your document. (Assigning headers, footers, and page numbers is discussed in Chapter 18, "Designing and Printing Professional-Looking Pages." Comments are discussed in "Inserting Comments in Documents," on page 457.)

Chapter 14

Basing one style on another fosters formatting consistency. For example, if you assign a new font to the Normal style, derived styles will automatically acquire the new font, and you'll avoid having dissimilar fonts throughout your document. (The only derived styles that won't acquire the new font are any that include a font specification.)

Chapter 12, "Effective Formatting in Word," described one way to modify the Normal style: When you click the Default button in the Font dialog box, you change the character formatting stored in Normal to the features selected in the dialog box. You can also modify the Normal style by clicking the Default button in the Language dialog box, which is discussed in "Marking the Language," on page 504. The next two sections of this chapter explain the two basic ways to modify any feature of any style:

- Modifying styles using example text
- Modifying styles using the Modify Style dialog box

tip **Display Style Names**

You can have Word display the name of each paragraph's style in a separate *style area* at the left of the document window—in Normal or Outline view only—by choosing Tools, Options, clicking the View tab, and entering a nonzero measurement into the Style Area Width box. If the width value is 0, Word doesn't display the style area. Don't worry about the exact value you enter; once the style area is displayed, you can easily change its width by dragging the right border, as seen here:

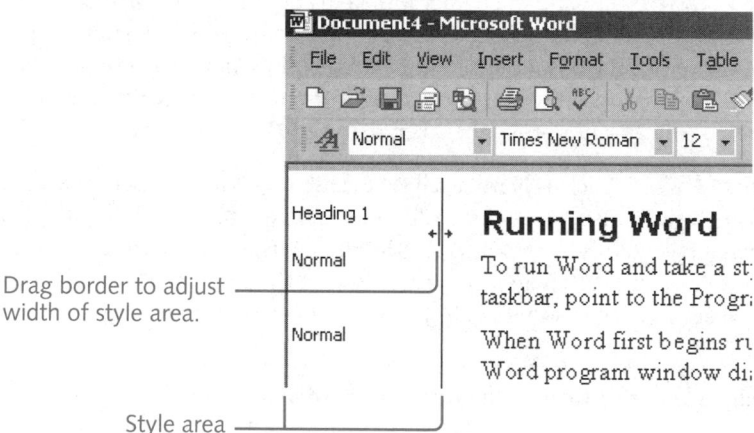

Drag border to adjust width of style area.

Style area

You can quickly remove the style area by dragging the border all the way to the left of the window.

Also, you can print a description of the document styles by choosing File, Print and selecting Styles in the Print What drop-down list.

Customizing Paragraph and Character Styles by Example

newfeature!

The fastest way to modify a paragraph or character style is to use example text. This method instantly updates the style definition to match the formatting of example text you have selected in your document. You can use this technique to modify any style except Normal by performing the following steps:

1 Select the example text you want to use to update the style. To save time, select text with formatting that's as close as possible to the formatting you want to assign to the style. You can select text that has been assigned the same style that you want to modify, or text with a different style.

2 If necessary, modify the formatting of the selected text so that it has the exact formatting you want to assign to the style you're customizing. Apply the new formatting directly to the text. You can use any of the methods for directly formatting text that were described in Chapter 12, "Effective Formatting in Word." Be sure to leave the text you modified selected.

3 If the Styles And Formatting task pane isn't currently shown, display it by choosing Format, Styles And Formatting.

4 Locate the name of the style you're modifying in the list in the Styles And Formatting task pane, click the down arrow that appears when you move the pointer over the style name, and choose Update To Match Selection from the drop-down menu. The following example shows how you would modify the Heading 1 style with the formatting features of the selected paragraph:

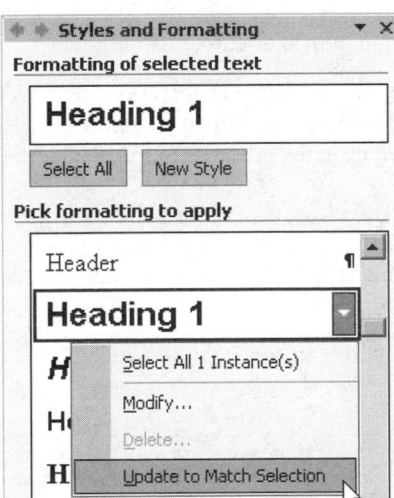

Word will now assign the formatting of the selected text to the style.

caution When you display the style's drop-down menu in the Styles And Formatting task pane, be sure to click the down arrow. Don't accidentally click the style name itself, which would immediately remove any formatting you applied in step 2 and would apply the unmodified style to the text.

For information on directly formatting text, see "Formatting Characters Directly," on page 298, and "Formatting Paragraphs Directly," on page 309.

Customizing Styles Using the Modify Style Dialog Box

Modifying a style by using the Style dialog box is not as fast as modifying the style by example, but it provides the following additional options:

- You can modify any type of style: paragraph, character, table, or list.

- You can rename the style or assign it one or more aliases (explained later).

- You can change the style on which a paragraph, character, or table style is based.

- For a paragraph style, you can change the style that Word automatically assigns to a paragraph that follows a paragraph that's assigned the modified style.

- You can define a shortcut key for quickly applying a paragraph, character, or list style.

- You can copy the modified style to the document's template.

- You can have Word automatically update a paragraph style. With automatic updating, whenever you apply direct formatting to a paragraph that's assigned the style, Word updates the style to match the new format.

To modify a style using the Style dialog box, perform the following steps:

1 If the Styles And Formatting task pane isn't currently shown, display it by choosing Format, Styles And Formatting.

2 Locate the style you want to modify in the list in the Styles And Formatting task pane.

If you don't see the style you want, see "Assigning Paragraph Styles, Character Styles, and Saved Formats," on page 323, for information on controlling the styles that are displayed.

3 Click the down arrow that appears when you move the pointer over the style name, and choose Modify from the drop-down menu, as shown here (for modifying the Heading 1 style):

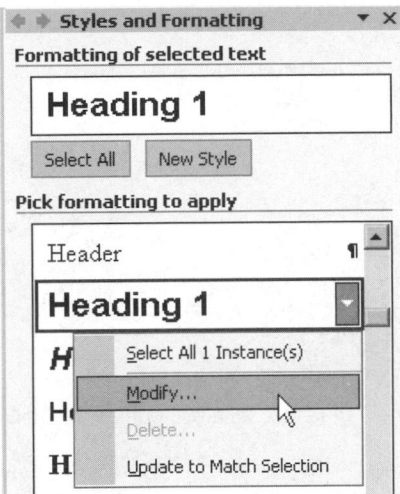

Word will display the Modify Style dialog box. Figures 14-2 through 14-5 show the Modify Style dialog box as it appears for each of the four types of Word styles.

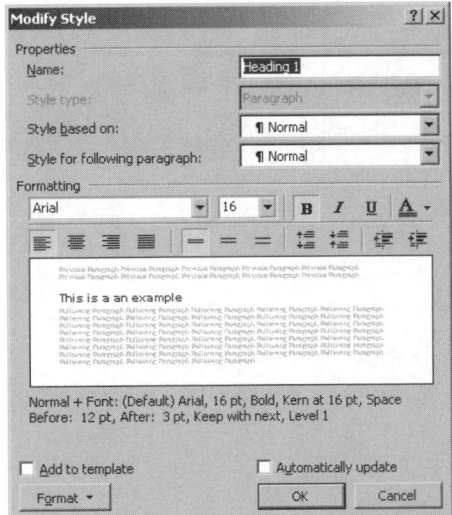

Figure 14-2. In this figure, the Heading 1 paragraph style is modified in the Modify Style dialog box.

391

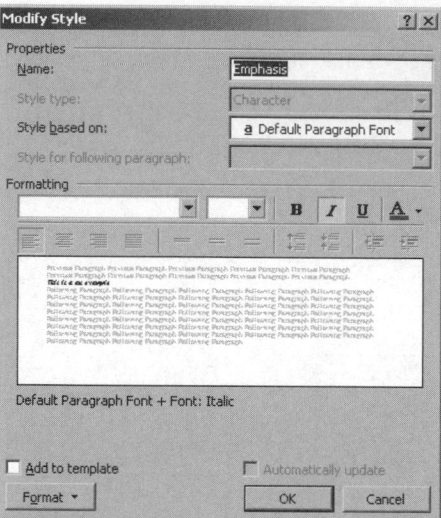

Figure 14-3. Here, the Emphasis character style is modified in the Modify Style dialog box.

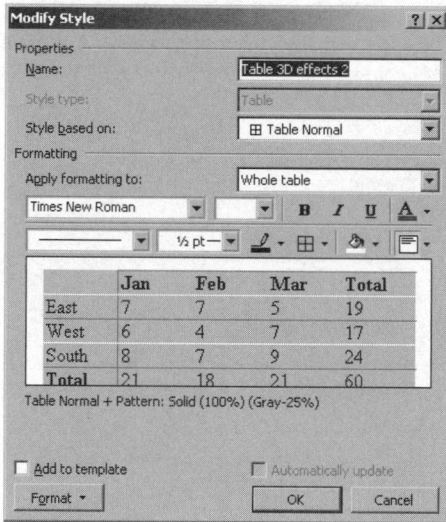

Figure 14-4. In this figure, the Table 3D Effects 2 table style is modified in the Modify Style dialog box.

Chapter 14

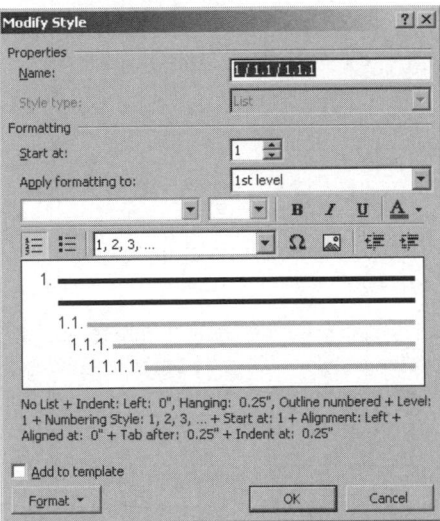

Figure 14-5. Here, the "1/1.1/1.1.1" list style is modified in the Modify Style dialog box.

4 In the Modify Style dialog box, perform one or more of the following actions:

- To change the name of a user-defined style, type a new name into the Name text box.

    Each style must have a unique name, and style names are case-sensitive—for example, *List* and *list* are considered different styles. You can include spaces in the name. Also, for a user-defined or built-in style, you can define one or more *aliases,* or alternative names for a style, by typing them after the style name in the Name box, separating the names with commas. (If you attempt to rename a built-in style, Word will add the new name you type as an alias for the style.)

InsideOut

Before you spend a lot of time creating aliases, keep in mind that in Word 2002 they aren't nearly as useful for applying styles as they used to be. With previous versions of Word, you could quickly apply a style by typing a short alias into the box at the top of the Style drop-down list on the Formatting toolbar, and immediately pressing Enter. Word 2002, however, attempts to autocomplete an alias, often coming up with a different style.

Consider, for example, that b is an alias for the Body Text style. As soon as you type **b** into the Style box, however, Word might fill in the style name Block Text. Pressing Enter would then apply the Block Text style rather than the Body Text style.

To get rid of any autocompleted text in the style drop-down list, press the Delete key right after you type the name of the alias but before you press Enter. You don't have to select the autocompleted text because Word selects it automatically.

■ To change the base style (for a paragraph, character, or table style), select a style name from the Style Based On drop-down list.

The result of basing one style on another was discussed in "Customizing Styles," on page 385.

For a paragraph style, if you choose the (No Style) option, the style will not be based on another style, and it will contain its own complete set of paragraph and character formatting features. (The Normal style can't be based on another style.)

For a character style, if you choose the Default Paragraph Font or (Underlying Properties) option, the style will not be based on another character style. Rather, it will store only the character formatting features that are explicitly assigned to the style.

A table style must always be based on another table style (usually, Table Normal, which has minimal formatting features).

■ For a paragraph style, to change the style for the following paragraph, choose a style name in the Style For Following Paragraph drop-down list.

For example, if you were modifying the Heading 1 style, you might choose Body Text in the Style For Following Paragraph list. As a result, if you pressed Enter after typing a paragraph with the Heading 1 style, Word would assign the Body Text style to the newly inserted paragraph. (For most styles, you typically choose the same style in the Style For Following Paragraph list so that the style doesn't change when you press Enter.)

InsideOut

Keep in mind that the Style For Following Paragraph option doesn't work in the following two situations:

1 If there are one or more characters, even a single space character, between the insertion point and the paragraph mark at the end of the paragraph.

2 If you're working in Outline view.

In both these cases, the following paragraph is assigned the *same* style as the current paragraph, regardless of the style assigned to the Style For Following Paragraph option.

■ To copy the modified style to the document's template, check the Add To Template option. In this case, the modified style will be available to any documents you subsequently create using that template (but not documents that have already been created from the template). If you don't check this option, modifying the style will affect only the current document.

- To have Word automatically modify a paragraph style (and instantly apply the new formatting to all other paragraphs in the document that have this style) whenever you directly apply formatting to a paragraph that has been assigned the style, check the Automatically Update option.

  The Automatically Update option helps ensure that all text throughout the document that has a particular style will remain consistent in formatting. However, if you aren't fond of Word making automatic changes to your documents, you'll probably want to turn it off.

- To change the formatting stored in the style, use the Style, Font, Font Size, Bold, Italic, Underline, or Font Color controls displayed in the Modify Style dialog box, shown here:

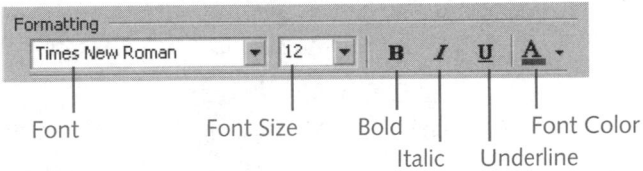

  You can also use any of the other controls that appear in the Modify Style dialog box. The particular controls you'll see depend on which type of style you're modifying (see Figures 14-2 through 14-5).

  Alternatively, you can select the formatting features for the style by using one of the standard dialog boxes used for directly applying formatting. This approach provides you with more formatting options and gives you a finer level of control over the formatting. To open a formatting dialog box, click the Format button at the bottom of the Modify Style dialog box and choose the appropriate command from the menu, as shown here:

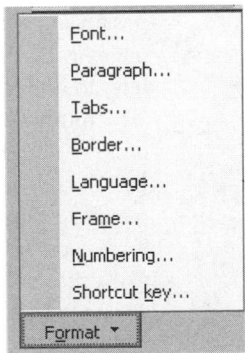

395

Table 14-1 shows which command to use to open a particular dialog box and provides additional information on the commands. When you have made the changes you want in each of the dialog boxes, click OK in the dialog box to return to the Modify Style dialog box.

Table 14-1. **Using the Format Menu in the Modify Style Dialog Box**

To Open This Formatting Dialog Box	Choose This Command	For These Style Types	Comments
Font	Font	● Paragraph ● Character ● Table ● List	See "Formatting Characters with the Font Dialog Box," on page 303.
Paragraph	Paragraph	● Paragraph ● Table	See "Formatting Paragraphs with the Paragraph Dialog Box," on page 314.
Tabs	Tabs	● Paragraph ● Table	This dialog box lets you assign the positions and the types of tab stops that are used in the paragraph.
Borders And Shading	Border	● Paragraph ● Table	See "Applying Borders and Shading with the Borders And Shading Dialog Box," on page 361.
Language	Language	● Paragraph ● Character	See "Marking the Language," on page 504.
Frame	Frame	● Paragraph	A *frame* is an obsolete element for positioning a block of text on the page. (In this context, *frame* doesn't refer to one of the panes used to view multiple documents in a Web browser.) Rather than using frames, you should use *text boxes* (which are handled as graphic objects rather than as paragraph formatting), as explained in "Using Text Boxes to Create Precise Page Layouts," on page 510.

Table 14-1. *(continued)*

To Open This Formatting Dialog Box	Choose This Command	For These Style Types	Comments
Bullets And Numbering	Numbering	● Paragraph ● List	See "Creating Lists with the Bullets And Numbering Dialog Box and List Styles," on page 373.
Table Properties	Table Properties	● Table	See "Using Other Methods for Creating and Modifying Tables," on page 354.
Borders And Shading	Borders And Shading	● Table	See "Applying Borders and Shading with the Borders And Shading Dialog Box," on page 361.
Format Stripes	Stripes	● Table	Applies shading to alternate rows or columns to make the table easier to read. Techniques for manually applying table shading are covered in "Adding Borders and Shading," on page 356.

▥ To assign a paragraph, character, or list style to a shortcut key so that you can quickly apply the style to selected text, choose Shortcut Key from the Format menu, as shown here:

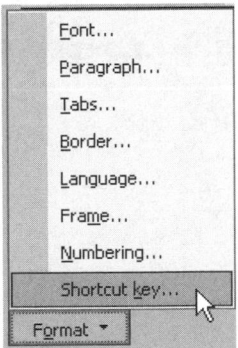

Then, define the shortcut key in the Customize Keyboard dialog box.

Defining shortcut keys is explained in "Defining Shortcut Keys (Word Only)," on page 217.

5 When you have finished making changes to the style, click OK in the Modify Style dialog box to save your modifications.

If you modified a style that was stored in your document, the modified version of the style will replace it. If you modified the original version of a built-in style, Word will save the modified style definition in your document.

Word will also copy the modified style definition to the template attached to the document if you checked the Add To Template option in the Modify Style dialog box.

For information on ways to copy the modified style to other templates or documents, see "Reusing Your Styles by Making Copies," on page 403.

Deleting a Style

To delete any user-defined style stored in the current document, perform the following steps:

1 If the Styles And Formatting task pane isn't visible, choose Format, Styles And Formatting.

2 Locate the style you want to delete in the list, click the down arrow next to the style name, and choose Delete, as shown here:

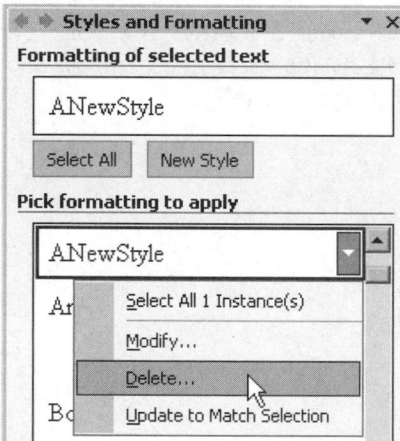

3 Click the Yes button when Word asks whether you want to delete the style. Word will then remove the style definition from the document. Word will also remove the style from any text that it was assigned to. A paragraph that was assigned a deleted paragraph style will be converted to Normal. Text that was assigned a deleted character, table, or list style will simply be left without a character, table, or list style.

You can use this same procedure to delete any built-in style that is stored in the document, *except* the Normal paragraph style or the Heading paragraph styles (Heading 1 through Heading 9). This method works as follows:

- Deleting a *modified* built-in style erases the modified style definition from the document and removes the style from all text to which it was assigned. A paragraph assigned a deleted paragraph style will be converted to Normal. Text assigned a deleted character, table, or list style will be left without a character, table, or list style. Although the modified style definition will no longer be available, you can still apply the original built-in style to text. Deleting a modified built-in style is a convenient way to reset the style to its "factory settings."

   For example, if you've modified the built-in paragraph style Body Text, you can delete it. This will remove the modified Body Text definition from the document and will convert all Body Text paragraphs to Normal. Although the modified Body Text style definition will no longer be available, you can still assign Body Text to paragraphs; doing so will format them with the original, built-in Body Text features.

- Deleting an *unmodified* built-in style removes the copy of the style from the document and removes the style from all text to which it was assigned. (The only unmodified built-in styles that are stored in the document and that you can therefore delete are ones that have been assigned to text within the document.) A paragraph assigned a deleted paragraph style will be converted to Normal. Text assigned a deleted character, table, or list style will be left without a character, table, or list style. The built-in style will still be available for applying to text. This is a convenient way to globally remove a style from text in a document.

> For a description of the different types of styles that can be stored in a document file, see the sidebar "Types of Styles Stored in a Document or Template," on page 407.

> **tip**   **Delete a Group of Styles Quickly**
>
> To delete multiple styles quickly and efficiently, you can use the Organizer, as explained in "Using the Organizer," on page 409.

Creating New Styles

If you find yourself frequently applying the same set of formatting features to characters or paragraphs, it's probably time to define a new user-defined style. Doing so will save you time and help improve the consistency of your formatting. For example, if you routinely format figure captions by applying an italic, 12-point Arial font, double line spacing, and 6 points of space following the paragraph, you could define a paragraph style—perhaps named Label—that has all these features. Likewise, if you frequently emphasize words by assigning a 14-point font and a red font color, you could define a character style—named, say, Big Red—that has these two features. And if you normally display numbers in a table with a particular design, you could define a table style—maybe called Number Table—that stores the table design.

You can quickly create a user-defined paragraph style by example and you can create any kind of style using the New Style dialog box.

Creating Paragraph Styles by Example

The fastest way to create a user-defined paragraph style is by example. (You can't use this method to create a character, table, or list style, though.) To do so, perform the following steps:

1 Select or place the insertion point within a paragraph in a document. You can save time if you choose a paragraph that already has formatting close to the formatting you want to assign to the user-defined style.

2 Directly apply any additional character or paragraph formatting that you want to assign to the style, using the methods given in Chapter 12, "Effective Formatting in Word." When you're done applying formatting, be sure to leave the text selected.

3 Type a unique name for the new style into the box at the top of the Style drop-down list on the Formatting toolbar, and press Enter.

As you type in a style name, Word's Autocomplete feature may attempt to fill in the name of an existing style. If this happens, be sure to edit the entry so that the Style box contains the name you want to assign to your new style before you press Enter. (Otherwise, the existing style will be applied to the text and your directly applied formatting will be lost!)

Word will add the new user-defined paragraph style to the styles stored in the document and it will apply the style to the example paragraph. The new style will be based on the style that was originally assigned to the example paragraph, and it will store all the paragraph and character formatting you directly applied to the example paragraph.

For information on formatting text directly, see "Formatting Characters Directly," on page 298, and "Formatting Paragraphs Directly," on page 309.

Creating Styles with the New Style Dialog Box

Although using the New Style dialog box to create a user-defined style is a little less convenient than using the Style control on the Formatting toolbar, it provides the following additional options:

- You can create any type of user-defined style: paragraph, character, table, or list.

- You can choose the style on which a new paragraph, character, or table style is based.

- For a user-defined paragraph style, you can change the style that Word automatically assigns to a paragraph that follows a paragraph that's assigned the modified style.

- You can define a shortcut key for quickly applying a paragraph, character, or list style.

- You can copy the new style to the document's template.

- You can have Word automatically update a new paragraph style. With automatic updating, whenever you apply direct formatting to a paragraph that's assigned the style, Word will update the style to match the new format.

To define a new style using the New Style dialog box, follow this basic procedure:

1 To save time, select—or just place the insertion point within—text that has formatting similar to the formatting you want to assign to the new style. (This step is optional because you can select all the formatting features you want later in the procedure.)

2 If the Styles And Formatting task pane isn't currently shown, display it by choosing Format, Styles And Formatting.

3 Click the down arrow that appears when you move the pointer over the Formatting Of Selected Text box and choose New Style from the menu, as shown here:

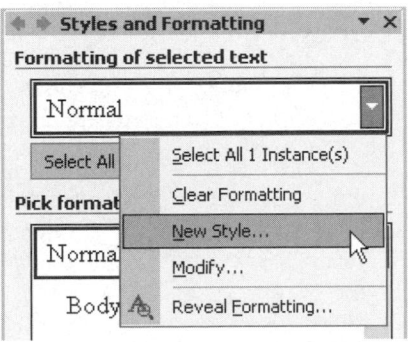

401

Or just click the New Style button near the top of the Styles And Formatting task pane. Word will display the New Style dialog box. Word will initially assign the new style a tentative name, such as Style1, which you can easily change. The formatting features of the text that is selected in the document already will be entered into the New Style dialog box, saving you time in defining a style with similar formatting. Except for the dialog title (and the availability of the Style Type drop-down list) this dialog box is the same as the Modify Style dialog box. Figures 14-2 through 14-5 earlier in this chapter show the Modify Style dialog box as it appears for each of the four types of Word styles.

4 In the Style Type drop-down list, select Paragraph, Character, Table, or List to specify the type of style you want to create.

5 Select the formatting and other features you want for your new user-defined style, following the instructions that were given under step 4 of the procedure for modifying an existing style (see page 393). As you apply those instructions, note the following:

- Word initially sets the base style to the style that's assigned to the selected text in the document. To base the new style on a different style—or on no style—choose the appropriate option in the Style Based On drop-down list.

- For a paragraph style, Word initially makes the style for the following paragraph the same as the new style. To have Word assign a different style to a paragraph that follows a paragraph with the new style, choose a style in the Style For Following Paragraph drop-down list.

6 When you have finished making changes to the style, click OK in the New Style dialog box to save your new user-defined style.

Word will save the new style definition within the current document. It will also copy the new style to the template attached to the document if you checked the Add To Template option in the New Style dialog box. For information on ways to copy the new style to other templates or documents, see the next section.

---

tip   Work with Table and List Styles in Other Ways

An alternative way to modify, create, or delete Table styles is to choose Table, Table AutoFormat, and use the Modify, New, or Delete button in the Table AutoFormat dialog box, discussed in "Formatting Tables by Applying Table Styles," on page 352.

Another way to modify, create, or delete List Styles is to choose Format, Bullets And Numbering, and use the Modify, Add, or Delete button in the List Styles tab of the Bullets And Numbering dialog box, described in "Creating an Outline Numbered List By Applying a List Style," on page 378.

Reusing Your Styles by Making Copies

Each document and each template stores its own private set of user-defined styles and modified built-in styles. Therefore, adding or modifying a style in a document doesn't normally affect the template, and adding or modifying a style in a template doesn't normally affect documents that were already created using the template. You can, however, use several Word options and commands to copy these types of styles from a document or template to another document or template. Copying styles allows you to take advantage of any style that is contained in any document or template and to share styles with other members of your workgroup. The next three sections describe various ways to copy styles between documents and templates.

Copying Styles from a Template to a Document

To take advantage of a style that is stored in a template, you must copy it into a document. Styles can be copied from a template to a document in the following ways.

- When you create a new document, it automatically acquires a copy of all the user-defined styles and modified built-in styles that are stored in the template that the document is based on.

- To have Word automatically copy all styles from a document's template into the document each time you open the document, choose Tools, Templates And Add-Ins and check the Automatically Update Document Styles option in the Templates And Add-Ins dialog box (shown in Figure 14-6). This option is useful if you periodically update the styles stored in the template and want a particular document to always have the latest style versions.

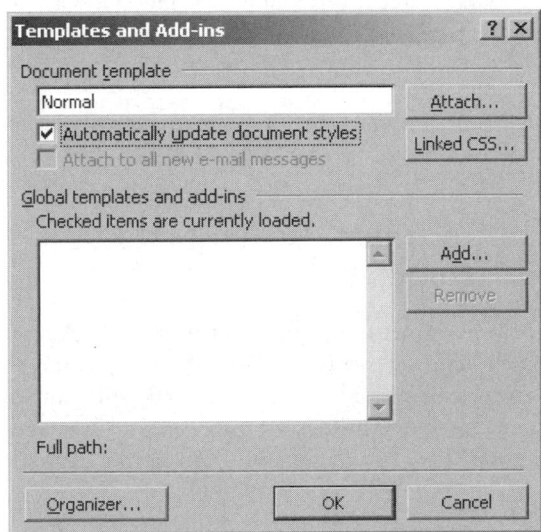

Figure 14-6. Use the Templates And Add-Ins dialog box to have Word copy styles from a document's template.

403

● You can use the Style Gallery to copy entire sets of styles from any template into your current document, thereby rapidly changing the overall look of the document.

● You can use the Organizer to copy as many or as few styles as you want from a template to a document.

> Using the Style Gallery is explained in "Formatting Your Documents Automatically," on page 334. For information on the Organizer, see "Using the Organizer," on page 409.

Copying Styles from a Document to a Template

When you create or modify a style in a document, you might want to copy the style into a template so that it will be stored there and will be available in any document you subsequently create using that template. You can do this several different ways.

● When you modify or create a style in the Modify Style or the New Style dialog box, you can check the Add To Template option. Word will then copy the modified or new style to the document template, as explained earlier in the chapter. (If you want to copy a style without changing it, you can open the Modify Style dialog box for that style, click the Add To Template option, and click OK without altering any of the formatting settings.)

● When you select character formatting in the Font or Language dialog boxes, you can click the Default button and respond Yes when prompted. Word will assign the selected formatting to the document's Normal style and it will copy the updated Normal style to the document template.

● You can use the Organizer to copy as many or as few styles as you want from a document to a template.

> For a description of the Font dialog box, see "Formatting Characters with the Font Dialog Box," on page 303. For a description of the Language dialog box, see "Marking the Language," on page 504. For information on the Organizer, see "Using the Organizer," on page 409.

Copying Styles from a Document or Template to Another Document or Template

The Organizer has already been mentioned several times in the previous sections. The Organizer is the ultimate tool for copying styles. It lets you copy individual styles or groups of styles from any document or template to any other document or template. It also lets you delete or rename one or more styles. To run the Organizer, choose Tools, Templates And Add-Ins and click the Organizer button in the Templates And Add-Ins dialog box.

> The Organizer is discussed in "Using the Organizer," on page 409.

Customizing and Creating Document Templates

A template stores a variety of items that form the basis of a Word document. When you create a new document, some of the items, such as text and styles, are copied into the document from the template that you select. Other items, such as AutoText entries and macros, are kept in the template. The template, however, remains attached to the document so that the document can access these items.

> **note** Every Word document is based on a template. If you create a document using the File, New command (together with the New Document task pane), the Start, New Office Document command in Microsoft Windows, or the New Office Document button on the Office Shortcut Bar, you can choose the template. If you create a new document by clicking the New button on the Standard toolbar, the document will be based on the Normal template. Note that the template that the document is based on is also called the *document template* or the *template attached to the document*. As explained later in this chapter, you can change the document template after you have created the document.

Table 14-2 lists the template items that are copied into a new document. Once you have created a new document, the document and the template have separate copies of these items. Normally, changing one of these items in the document won't affect the template, and changing an item in the template won't affect the document.

> **note** Word *will* copy style changes from documents to templates or vice versa if you check Add To Template in the Modify Style dialog box or if you select Automatically Update Document Styles in the Templates And Add-Ins dialog box. For more information, see "Reusing Your Styles by Making Copies," on page 403.

Table 14-2. Template Items That Are Copied to a New Document

Template Item	Comments
Text and graphics, together with the formatting assigned to them	Includes headers, footers, footnotes, and comments.

(continued)

Table 14-2. *(continued)*

Template Item	Comments
Page setup	Includes the margins, paper size and source, page layout, and other features (explained in Chapter 18, "Designing and Printing Professional-Looking Pages"). Also includes the default tab stop setting (which you define by choosing Format, Tabs and entering a value into the Default Tab Stops text box).
Styles	All the styles stored in the template are copied to the document. See the sidebar "Types of Styles Stored in a Document or Template," on page 407.

For information on choosing a template when you create a new document, see "Creating a Document Using the New Office Document Dialog Box," on page 53.

Table 14-3 lists the items that are kept in the template when a new document is created. A document can access any item stored in the document template. It can also access any item stored in the Normal template. (Of course, if the document is based on Normal, the document template and Normal are the same.) In addition, a document can access any item that is stored in a template that has been explicitly loaded as a *global template.*

Loading global templates is discussed in "Loading Global Templates and Word Add-Ins," on page 413.

For example, if an AutoText entry named Close is defined in either the document template or the Normal template, you can insert it into your document using any of the methods discussed in "Reusing Text with the AutoText Feature," on page 252. If an AutoText entry named Close is defined in both the document template and the Normal template, Word inserts the text defined in the document template. (That is, an item defined in the document template overrides a similarly named item in the Normal template or other global template.)

Table 14-3. Template Items Kept Within the Document Template

Template Item	Comments
AutoText entries	An AutoText entry is a stored block of text or graphics that you can insert anywhere into a document, as explained in "Reusing Text with the AutoText Feature," on page 252.
Macros	A macro is a script for automating a Word task, as discussed in Part 10 of this book.

Table 14-3. *(continued)*

Template Item	Comments
Custom toolbars, as well as modifications to toolbars, menus, or shortcut keys	Creating custom toolbars and modifying toolbars and menus is discussed in Chapter 9, "Customizing the Office XP Application Interface."
Shortcut key definitions	Defining shortcut keys to run commands, apply styles, or perform other tasks is covered in "Defining Shortcut Keys (Word Only)," on page 217.

note When you create a macro, a custom toolbar or menu, or a shortcut key definition, you have the option of storing it within the document rather than within a template so that the item will be private to that document. AutoText entries, however, can be stored only in a template.

Types of Styles Stored in a Document or Template

The following types of styles can be stored directly within a document or template file:

● All documents and templates store four basic "default" built-in styles (whether or not these styles have been used in the document or have been modified): Normal, Default Paragraph Font, No List, and Table Normal.

Default Paragraph Font, No List, and Table Normal are atypical styles that are applied to text to remove character, list, or table styles or formatting. They can't be modified.

● Any built-in style that was used in the document, even if it is no longer applied to document text and even if it hasn't been modified.

● Modified versions of built-in styles.

● User-defined styles.

You can view a complete list of the styles currently stored in a document or template by using the Styles tab of the Organizer, discussed later in this chapter.

Keep in mind that when you apply styles to text in a document or template, you can use any of the styles that are actually stored in the document or template, *plus* any of the built-in styles stored in Word.

Customizing Templates

You can modify Word templates in a variety of ways. First, performing any of the following common Word actions can automatically modify a template.

● Creating any of the items listed in Table 14-3, on pages 406 and 407: an AutoText entry, a macro, a custom toolbar or menu, or a shortcut key. When you create any of these items, you can save it in the Normal template or in the document template if it is other than Normal. (You also have the option of saving any of these items, except an AutoText entry, right within the document.)

● Clicking the Default button in the Font, Language, or Page Setup dialog box and responding Yes when prompted. Clicking Default saves the character formatting, language, or page setup in the document template. The character formatting and language are stored within the Normal style of the document template.

● Selecting the Add To Template option when modifying or creating a style (in the Modify Style or New Style dialog box) will copy the modified or new style to the document template.

Another way to modify a template is to open the template file and edit it in the same way you edit a document. To do so, perform the following general steps:

1 Choose File, Open.

2 In the Open dialog box, select Document Templates (*.dot) in the Files Of Type drop-down list, and then select the template file you want to modify.

The templates supplied with Word (except Normal) are stored in subfolders of C:\Program Files\Microsoft Office\Templates. The Normal template, plus any templates you create, are usually stored within one of the following folders, or subfolders of these folders: C:\Documents And Settings\User Name\Application Data\Microsoft\Templates, C:\Windows\Application Data\Microsoft\Templates, or C:\Windows\Profiles\UserName\Application Data\Microsoft\Templates (here, substitute the actual name of your Windows folder if necessary; for example, WINNTYO). The specific folder depends on your Windows version and setup.

You can change the locations where Normal and user-created templates are stored, as explained in the tip "Choose Locations for Your Templates," on page 412.

3 Edit and format the template using the same techniques used for documents. You can add or modify any of the template items listed in Table 14-2 (on page 405) or Table 14-3 (on page 406). For the items listed in Table 14-3, be sure to save your changes in the template itself rather than in the Normal template.

4 Choose File, Save, or click the Save button to save your changes.

Chapter 14: Advanced Word Formatting Techniques

---

tip   **Open a Template File for Editing**

In Microsoft Windows Explorer or in a folder window, double-clicking a Word template file (such as Elegant Fax.dot) will create a Word document based on that template. To open the template file itself, right-click the file and choose Open from the shortcut menu, as shown here:

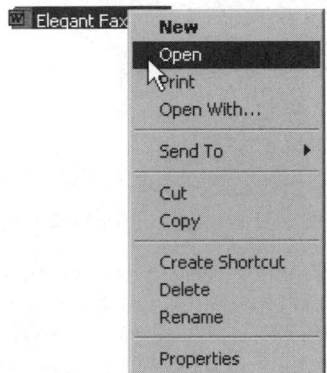

(Choosing New would have the same effect as double-clicking the file.)

Using the Organizer

You can also directly change the contents of one or more templates by using the Organizer. With the Organizer you can delete, rename, or copy styles, AutoText entries, custom toolbars, or macro project items (macro modules or forms). You can copy styles, custom toolbars, or macro project items from a template or document to another template or document. You can copy AutoText entries only from one template to another.

To use the Organizer, perform the following steps:

1 Choose Tools, Templates And Add-Ins, and then click the Organizer button in the Templates And Add-Ins dialog box. This will open the Organizer dialog box (shown in Figure 14-7).

2 In the Organizer dialog box, click the tab corresponding to the type of template item you want to manage: styles, AutoText entries, custom toolbars, or macro project item.

A tab in the Organizer displays two lists, each of which displays the items belonging to a particular template or document. (In this discussion, *item* is used to refer to a style, AutoText entry, custom toolbar, or macro project item.)

The lists in the Styles tab itemize all of the styles currently stored within the template or document file. For details, see the sidebar "Types of Styles Stored in a Document or Template," on page 407.

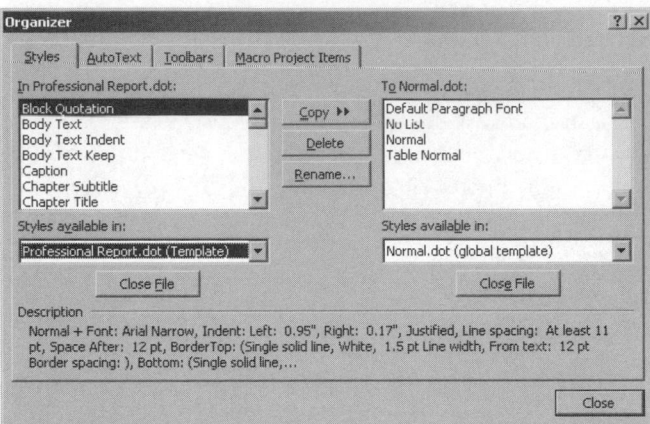

Figure 14-7. This figure shows the Styles tab of the Organizer dialog box.

3 If you want to work with the items in a different document or template (that is, one whose items aren't currently displayed in the tab), select the file from either of the Styles Available In drop-down lists. (In this discussion, *file* refers to either a document or a template.) If you don't find the file in either list, click one of the Close File buttons to close the currently displayed file, and then click the button again (it will then be labeled Open File) and select the file in the Open dialog box.

4 In the appropriate list, select the item or items you want to work with. To select a single item, click it. To select a range of items in a list, click the first one and then press Shift and click the last one. To select several items that are not adjoining, click the first one and then press Ctrl and click each additional item.

5 Perform one of the following actions:

- To copy the selected item or items into the file whose items are shown in the other list, click the Copy button.

- To rename the selected item, click the Rename button. (Only a single item can be selected.)

- To delete the selected item or items, click the Delete button.

note You can delete, copy, or rename styles, custom toolbars, or macros stored in either a document or a template. AutoText entries, however, are stored only in templates.

tip **Don't Forget to Copy Macros**

If you copy a custom toolbar that contains buttons to which you've assigned macros, be sure to also copy the module or modules containing those macros!

Creating New Templates

The procedure for creating a new template is similar to that for creating a new document. Perform the following basic steps.

1 Choose File, New.

2 In the New Document task pane, click the General Templates command in the New From Template area.

3 In the Templates dialog box, select the Template option in the Create New area in the lower right corner, as shown here.

4 In the Templates dialog box, select an existing template to use as the starting point for your new template, and click OK. Your new template will be opened and will acquire the contents of the template you chose.

The Templates dialog box works just like the New Office Document dialog box, discussed in "Creating a Document Using the New Office Document Dialog Box," on page 53.

5 Enter text and graphics, edit, and format the new template using the same techniques used for documents. You can add any of the items listed in Table 14-2 (on page 405) and Table 14-3 (on page 406). For the items listed in Table 14-3, be sure to save your changes in the template itself rather than in the Normal template.

6 Choose File, Save, or click the Save button to save the new template.

The first time you save the template, Word will open the Save As dialog box and will automatically switch to your current User Templates folder. If you want the Templates dialog box to display the template you have created, you must save it in the file folder designated as your User Templates folder, or in one of its subfolders. The default User Templates folder is C:\Documents and Settings*User Name*\Application Data\Microsoft\Templates, C:\Windows\Application Data\Microsoft\Templates, or C:\Windows\Profiles*UserName*\Application Data\Microsoft\Templates (here, substitute the actual name of your Windows folder if necessary; for example, WINNTYO). The specific folder depends on your Windows version and setup.

You can save the template directly within your User Templates folder; in this case, the template will be displayed in the General tab of the Templates (or New Office Document) dialog box. Alternatively, you can place it within a subfolder of your User Templates folder (an existing subfolder or a new one that you create); in this case, the template will be displayed in the Templates (or New Office Document) dialog box in a tab that's labeled with the name of the subfolder. Also, you must name the template file with the .dot extension or omit the extension. (If you omit it, Word will add the .dot.)

Note that file extensions might not be displayed when you list files, depending on the options you have chosen in Windows.

tip **Choose Locations for Your Templates**

You can designate a different folder as your User Templates folder, causing the Templates (or New Office Document) dialog box to display the templates stored in the new folder you specify, rather than in the original User Templates folder. To do this, choose Tools, Options, click the File Locations tab, click User Templates in the list, click the Modify button, and enter the new folder path. This change will affect all Office applications that use templates, not just Word.

Notice that in the File Locations tab, you can also designate a Workgroup Templates folder. (Initially, no folder is designated for this item.) If you do so, the Templates (or New Office Document) dialog box will display the templates in the Workgroup Templates folder in addition to those in your User Templates folder. Typically, the Workgroup Templates folder is located on a network and contains a set of templates that you share with co-workers.

You can also set your User Templates and Workgroup Templates locations in the Settings tab of the Customize dialog box of the Office Shortcut Bar, which is explained in "Using the Office Shortcut Bar," on page 46.

In addition to the new and customized templates stored in the User Templates and Workgroup Templates folders, the Templates (or New Office Document) dialog box displays the templates that are supplied with Word, such as Contemporary Letter and Professional Memo.

Note also that when Word creates a Normal.dot template file (when you first start using Word or if Normal.dot has been deleted) it stores it in the current User Templates folder.

tip newfeature! **Base a New Template on an Existing Document**

If an existing document already contains many of the features you want to add to a new template, you can save time by basing the new template on that document. To do this, choose File, New, and then click the Choose Document command in the New From Existing Document area of the New Document task pane. In the New From Existing Document dialog box, select the document you want to use as a basis for your template and then click the Create New button. When you first save the new document after editing it, be sure to select the Document Template (*.dot) item in the Save As Type drop-down list of the Save As dialog box.

Attaching a Template to a Document

You can change the template that is attached to a document. When you do this, all the AutoText entries, custom toolbars, interface modifications (toolbar, menu, and short-cut key), and macros that are stored in the new template become available to the document in place of the items stored in the previous template. To change the document template for the current document, perform the following steps:

1 Choose Tools, Templates And Add-Ins. Word will display the Templates And Add-Ins dialog box (shown in Figure 14-6 on page 403).

2 Click the Attach button.

3 Select the desired template in the Attach Template dialog box, which works just like the standard Open dialog box for opening a Word document. Make sure that Document Templates (*.dot) is selected in the Files Of Type drop-down list. Then click the Open button.

Loading Global Templates and Word Add-Ins

Word allows you to load one or more templates *in addition* to the document template. An additional template that you have loaded is known as a *global template*. All the AutoText entries, custom toolbars, interface modifications (toolbar, menu, and short-cut key), and macros that are stored in a global template become available to *any* document currently open in Word. (An item defined in a document template, however, overrides a similarly named item in any of the global templates you load.) To load a global template, choose Tools, Templates And Add-Ins, and perform one of the following actions in the Templates And Add-Ins dialog box:

● If the template is listed within the Global Templates And Add-Ins list, simply check the adjoining check box.

● If the template isn't in the list, click the Add button to open the Add Template dialog box. In this dialog box, make sure that the Document Templates (*.dot) item is selected in the Files Of Type drop-down list, select the template you want, and click OK. The template will be added to the Global Templates And Add-Ins list and will be checked.

> **note** You can also load a Word add-in, which is a utility program that supplies enhancement features to Word. (You can obtain Word add-ins from various software vendors.) To do this, follow the procedure for opening an additional template, except that in the Add Template dialog box you must choose the Word Add-Ins (*.wll) item in the Files Of Type drop-down list.

A global template or add-in will remain loaded only for the remainder of your current Word session. When you exit and restart Word, you'll need to reload it by checking it in the Global Templates And Add-Ins list. (The template or add-in will still be in the list, although it won't be checked.)

Troubleshooting

Missing AutoText, Macros, or Customizations

You moved or copied a document to a different computer or network location (perhaps you sent the file to a co-worker), and now you or your co-worker can no longer access the AutoText entries, the macros, or the menu, toolbar, and keyboard customizations that you previously used with that document.

The most likely reason that the items are missing is that they are stored in the document's template (or in the Normal template) and Word can't access that template from the document's new location. Here are two possible solutions to this problem:

- Before you move or copy the document, use the Organizer to copy all macros and custom toolbars from the document template directly into the document. This method won't work, however, for AutoText entries (which can be stored only in a template) or for other customizations (that is, modifications to toolbars, menus, or shortcut keys, which you can't copy using the Organizer).

- Create a new template located in the same folder as the document on your computer, attach the template to your document, and use the Organizer to copy all needed items into the new template. (Be sure *not* to name the new template Normal.dot.) Then, copy or move both the document and its new template to the new location.

The techniques mentioned have all been discussed in this chapter.

Chapter 15

Managing Large or Complex Documents

Working with Documents in Outline View

Outline view can be a great help while you're planning or organizing a document, and even while you're entering the bulk of the document text. The following are among the important features and advantages of Outline view:

- The outline headings in the document—and the text that follows them—are indented by various amounts, so that you can immediately see the hierarchical structure of your document.

- You can control the level of detail that is visible in the outline. For example, you can hide all body text and view only the headings to see the overall organization of your document. Or, you can hide the content under all top-level headings except the one you're working on to help you focus on that part of the document.

- You can quickly move an individual paragraph or an entire heading together with all text and subheadings that follow it.

- You can usually see more text on the screen in Outline view than in other views because all text is single spaced, regardless of the paragraph formatting.

InsideOut

In Outline view, paragraph formatting isn't displayed and you can't open the Paragraph dialog box to apply paragraph formatting. (You can control whether or not character formatting is displayed, as explained later.) Therefore, to modify the formatting of your paragraphs, you should switch out of Outline view.

note This chapter explains how to organize, footnote, index, and add tables of contents to your Microsoft Word 2002 documents. Although these techniques are especially useful for developing long or complex documents, such as books, manuals, and academic papers, you can use them when writing any type of document.

Switching to Outline View

To activate Outline view, choose View, Outline, or click the Outline View button on the left end of the horizontal scroll bar shown here:

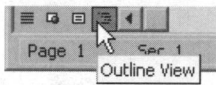

Word will display the document as an outline, and it will show the Outlining toolbar, shown in Figure 15-1. In Outline view, *heading* refers to any paragraph that has been assigned one of the built-in Heading styles, Heading 1 through Heading 9. A heading assigned the Heading 1 style is at the highest level and is not indented. A heading assigned Heading 2 is at a lower level and is indented a small amount when displayed in Outline view. A heading assigned Heading 3 is at an even lower level and is indented more in Outline view, and so on. *Body text* refers to all paragraphs displayed in Outline view that have not been assigned a Heading style.

note Switching to Outline view doesn't change the content or format of your document. It merely displays the document in a different way and allows you to work with it differently.

In Outline view, Word displays one of the symbols shown in Table 15-1 in front of each paragraph. *Subtext* refers to either subheadings or body text that immediately follows a heading.

Chapter 15: Managing Large or Complex Documents

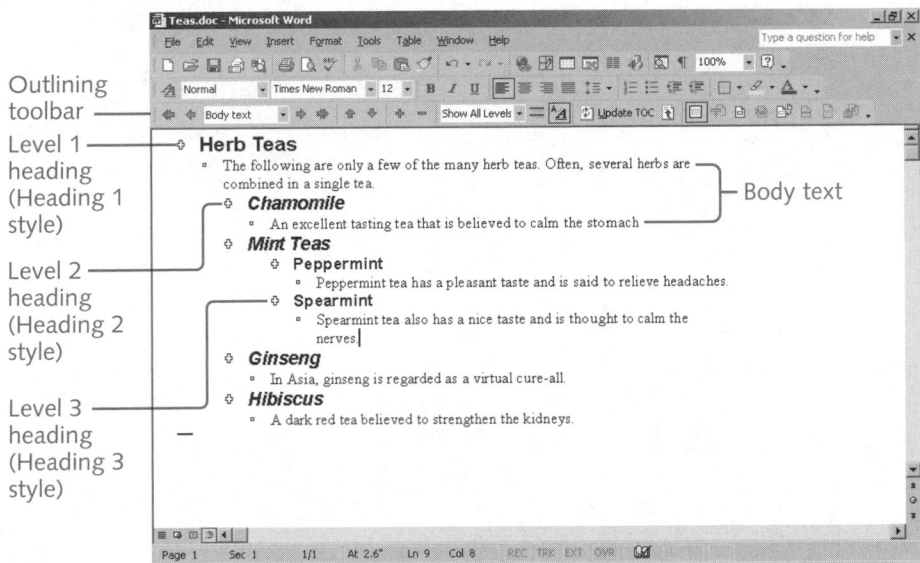

Outlining toolbar

Level 1 heading (Heading 1 style)

Level 2 heading (Heading 2 style)

Level 3 heading (Heading 3 style)

Body text

Figure 15-1.   This figure shows a Word document in Outline view.

Table 15-1. Symbols Used in Outline View

Symbol	Type of Paragraph
◇	Heading with subtext
⌴	Heading without subtext
▫	Body text

If you have already assigned the Heading 1 through Heading 9 styles to your document headings (as recommended in Chapter 12, "Effective Formatting in Word"), Word will indent the headings appropriately in Outline view and the document will look like an outline, as shown in Figure 15-1. If, however, you haven't already assigned the built-in Heading styles to your heading paragraphs, the document will consist of a simple list of body text paragraphs, as shown in Figure 15-2 on page 418, and it won't look much like an outline. Don't worry—by using the buttons on the Outlining toolbar, you can easily apply Heading styles and convert the document into outline form.

> **note**   Because each level of heading is assigned a different Heading style, each generally has different formatting. Higher-level headings are typically formatted with larger, bold fonts to convey their relative importance; lower-level headings are typically formatted with smaller, nonbold fonts.

Chapter 15

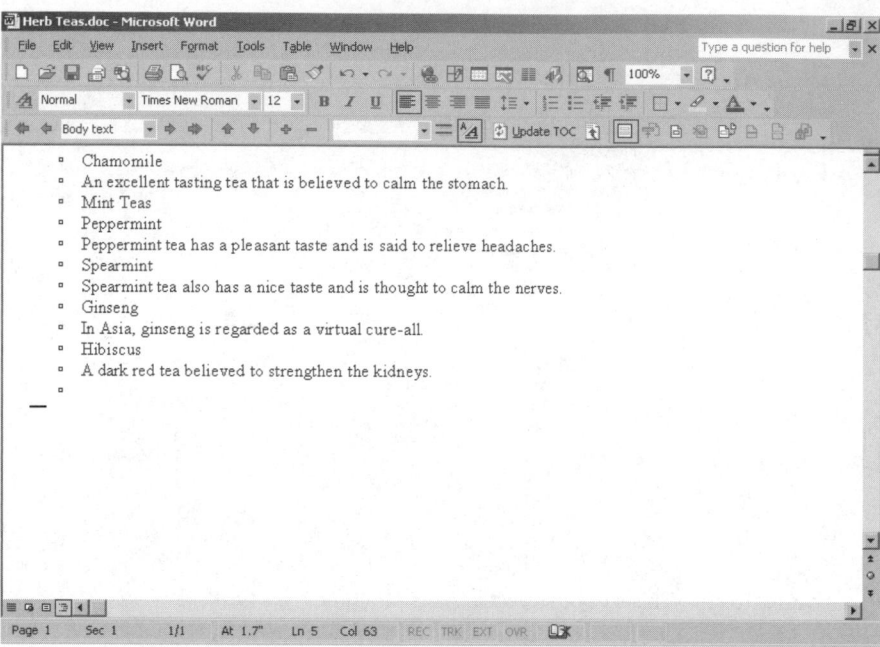

Figure 15-2. A document containing headings that haven't been assigned the built-in Heading styles looks like a simple list of paragraphs in Outline view.

> To quickly change the appearance of a particular level of heading throughout your document, you can modify the corresponding built-in Heading style, as explained in "Customizing Styles," on page 385.

Changing Outline Levels

You can use the first five controls on the Outlining toolbar, shown below, to change the level of a heading, to convert a paragraph of body text to a heading, or to convert a heading to a paragraph of body text:

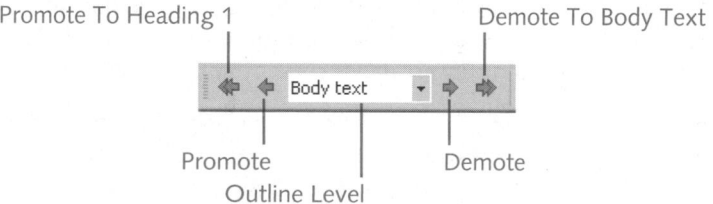

In general, you can perform outlining operations on more than one paragraph (headings or body text) by selecting several paragraphs prior to issuing the command. For simplicity, however, the discussions on outlining use the singular terms *heading* or *paragraph*.

---

tip   **Select a Heading and Its Contents Quickly**

To select a heading together with all its subtext, just click the symbol in front of the heading, as shown here:

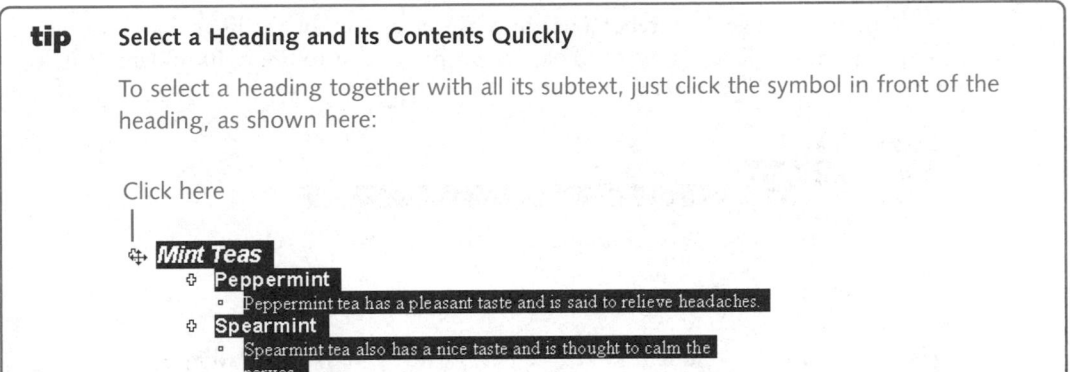

To change the level of a heading, perform the following steps:

1 Place the insertion point in the heading you want to change (or select several headings).

2 Do one of the following:

■ To promote the heading to the next higher level, click the Promote button, or press Alt+Shift+Left Arrow or Shift+Tab.

■ To demote the heading to the next lower level, click the Demote button, or press Alt+Shift+Right Arrow or Tab.

■ To promote the heading to a level 1 heading in a single step, assigning it the Heading 1 style, click the Promote To Heading 1 button.

■ To promote or demote the heading directly to any level—or to convert it to body text—select an outline level from the Outline Level drop-down list on the Outlining toolbar, shown here:

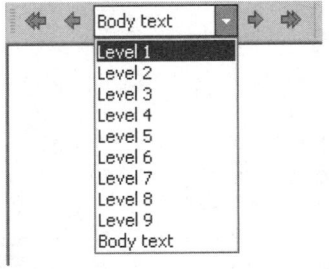

---

tip   To enter a tab character while you're in Outline view, press Ctrl+Tab.

Chapter 15

You can also change the level of a heading, as well as any subheadings that follow it, by dragging the heading symbol to the left to promote it, or to the right to demote it, as seen here:

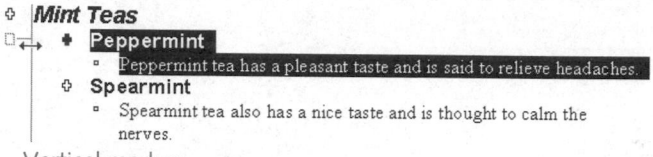

Vertical marker

The vertical marker that temporarily appears when you drag a heading horizontally indicates the new level that would be assigned to the highest-level heading in the selection if you released the mouse button at the current position.

When Word changes the level of a heading, it assigns it a new Heading style. For example, if you demote a top-level heading, Word changes the style from Heading 1 to Heading 2.

You can convert a paragraph of body text (that is, a paragraph that isn't assigned one of the built-in Heading styles) to an outline heading by either promoting it or demoting it, using any of the methods just described. You can select more than one paragraph of body text, but don't include a heading in the selection. If you promote a paragraph of body text by one level, it's converted into a heading at the same level as the preceding heading. If you demote it by one level, it's converted into a heading one level lower than the preceding heading. If you click the Promote To Heading 1 button on the Outlining toolbar, it becomes a top-level (Heading 1) heading. And if you promote or demote it by selecting a level in the Outline Level drop-down list on the Outlining toolbar, it's converted directly to the heading level you select.

> **tip** **Use Styles to Change Outline Levels**
>
> You can also change the level of a heading, convert body text to a heading, or convert a heading to body text by directly assigning the paragraph the appropriate style (Heading 1 through Heading 9 for a heading, or a style such as Normal or Body Text for body text). You can quickly apply the Heading 1, Heading 2, or Heading 3 style by pressing Alt+Ctrl+1, Alt+Ctrl+2, or Alt+Ctrl+3, respectively, and you can apply the Normal paragraph style by pressing Ctrl+Shift+N.

To convert a heading to body text, place the insertion point within the heading (or select a number of headings), and click the Demote To Body Text button or press Alt+Shift+5 (5 on the numeric keypad with Num Lock off). Word will assign the paragraph the Normal style.

---

tip   **Number Your Outline Headings Automatically**

You can apply automatic outline numbering to all the outline headings throughout your document (that is, to all paragraphs assigned the built-in Heading styles, Heading 1 through Heading 9). To do this, place the insertion point within any heading, choose Format, Bullets And Numbering, click the Outline Numbered tab in the Bullets And Numbering dialog box, select one of the four outline numbering styles on the bottom row, and click OK. (Notice that the sample in the Outline Numbered tab for each of these styles contains the names of Heading styles.) For more information, see "Creating an Outline Numbered List Using the Outline Numbered Tab," on page 376.

Creating Headings Using Outline-Level Formatting

The discussions in this chapter assume that your outline headings are assigned the built-in Heading styles (Heading 1 through Heading 9). However, you can also create an outline heading by assigning outline-level formatting to a paragraph that hasn't been assigned a Heading style. To do this, switch out of Outline view, select the paragraph, choose Format, Paragraph, click the Indents And Spacing tab, and choose the desired heading level (Level 1 through Level 9) in the Outline Level drop-down list. (You can choose the Body Text item in this list to convert an outline heading to outline body text.)

In general, however, it's easier to create outline headings by assigning the Heading 1 through Heading 9 built-in styles for several reasons:

- In Outline view, you can rapidly and easily assign a Heading style using the Outlining toolbar or the shortcut keys that were described. (In contrast, to assign outline-level formatting, you have to switch out of Outline view and perform the time-consuming procedure just described.)

- If you're not using the Heading styles, when you work in Outline view it's likely that you'll lose the style (and the style's formatting) that you've applied to a paragraph. Some of the controls on the Outlining toolbar (such as the Promote To Heading 1 button) will apply a Heading style, overwriting the paragraph's original style.

- Assigning a Heading style will apply appropriate formatting for a heading (such as a larger font, bold type, and so on). Using the Heading styles will also make it easier to maintain consistent formatting of your headings and to quickly modify this formatting throughout the document.

- You can have Word number Heading styles, as explained in the tip "Number Your Outline Headings Automatically," on page above. (You can also do this with non-Heading styles, but only by defining a custom outline numbering type.)

Moving Blocks of Text

You can quickly move one or more paragraphs by using the two buttons shown here on the Outlining toolbar:

Move up ——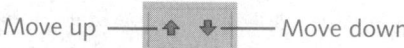—— Move down

The paragraphs can be either headings or body text. To move these paragraphs, perform the following steps:

1 Place the insertion point within the paragraph you want to move (or select several paragraphs).

2 Do one of the following:

- To move the paragraph above the previous paragraph, click the Move Up button or press Alt+Shift+Up Arrow.

- To move the paragraph below the following paragraph, click the Move Down button or press Alt+Shift+Down Arrow.

3 Repeat step 2 as necessary to move the paragraph to the desired final position.

You can also quickly move a paragraph by dragging the paragraph symbol up or down in the document, as shown here:

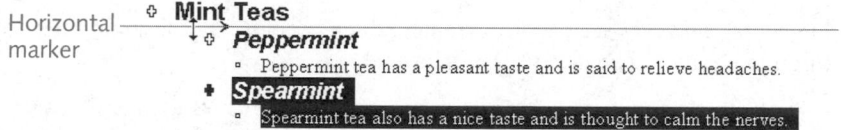

Horizontal marker

The horizontal marker that temporarily appears when you drag a heading vertically indicates the new position the paragraph would occupy if you released the mouse button at the current position. If you use this method to move a heading, it moves all the heading's subtext as well, because both the heading and its subtext are selected when you begin dragging the symbol.

Collapsing and Expanding Outline Text

You can use the buttons on the Outlining toolbar shown here to change the level of detail that is visible in the outline:

Expand   Collapse

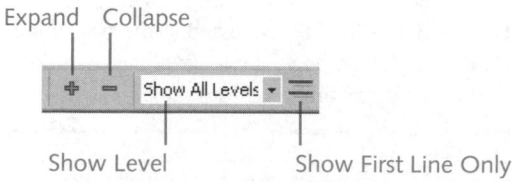

Show Level   Show First Line Only

To hide the subtext—subheadings or body text—that follows a particular heading, perform these steps:

1 Place the insertion point within the heading (or select several headings).

2 Click the Collapse button, press Alt+Shift+- (the hyphen key on the top row of the keyboard), or press – (the minus key on the numeric keypad). Word will hide the lowest level of subtext that is currently visible.

For example, if your cursor is in a level 1 heading and the level 1 heading is followed by level 2 headings, level 3 headings, and body text, the first time you click the Collapse button, the body text will be hidden. (Body text is considered to be at the lowest level.) The next time you click Collapse, the level 3 headings will be hidden, and the third time you click Collapse, the level 2 headings will be hidden.

3 Repeat step 2 as necessary to hide the desired amount of subtext.

To redisplay collapsed subtext, use this same procedure, but in step 2, click the Expand button, press Alt+Shift+=, or press + (plus key) on the numeric keypad.

You can also fully collapse a heading (that is, hide all its subtext) by double-clicking the paragraph symbol, as shown here:

Double-click to hide all subtext.

▫ **Mint Teas**
　　◊ **Peppermint**
　　　　▫ Peppermint tea has a pleasant taste and is said to relieve headaches.
　　◊ **Spearmint**
　　　　▫ Spearmint tea also has a nice taste and is thought to calm the nerves.

To fully expand the heading, double-click again. Notice that when a heading contains collapsed subtext, Word marks it with thick underlining, as seen here:

Double-click here to show all subtext.

◊ **Mint Teas**

Underline indicates hidden subtext.

To change the levels of headings displayed throughout the entire document, open the Show Level drop-down list on the Outlining toolbar, shown here:

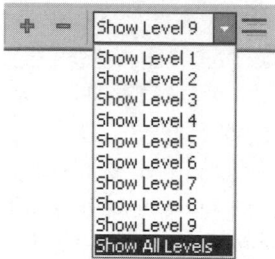

Then, select an item in the list, as follows:

- To display all headings through a particular heading level, hiding body text, select an item in the range from Show Level 1 through Show Level 9. For example, selecting Show Level 3 would show all level 1, level 2, and level 3 headings. Selecting Show Level 9 would show all headings in the document. Rather than selecting a specific level in the Show Level list, you can press the equivalent shortcut key, Alt+Shift+1, Alt+Shift+2, Alt+Shift+3, and so on (press the number on the top row of the keyboard, *not* on the numeric keypad).

- To show all headings in the document, plus all body text, select Show All Levels. Rather than using the Show Level list, you can press the equivalent shortcut key, Alt+Shift+A, or * (asterisk) on the numeric keypad. Pressing the shortcut key repeatedly toggles between Show All Levels and Show Level 9.

If body text is shown, you can have Word display only the first line of each paragraph of body text by turning on the Show First Line Only mode. You can turn this mode on or off by clicking the Show First Line Only button on the Outlining toolbar or by pressing the Alt+Shift+L shortcut key. Word will indicate the presence of hidden body text by displaying an ellipsis (…) at the end of the first line of each body text paragraph.

To display all text in the outline (including headings) using the character formatting currently assigned to the Normal style, rather than the actual formatting assigned to each paragraph, turn off the Show Formatting mode. You can turn this mode off or on by clicking the Show Formatting button on the Outlining toolbar, shown here, or by pressing the / (slash) key on the numeric keypad. The Show Formatting mode doesn't remove character formatting, but merely suppresses its display.

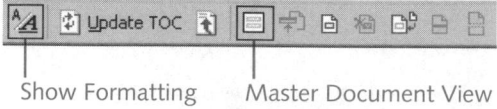

Show Formatting   Master Document View

Master Document View is a special mode of Outline view that allows you to divide a long Word document into separate subdocuments, all of which belong to a single *master document*. If you're creating a very large manuscript (such as a book) and want to be able to format, print, and work with the entire manuscript as a unit, creating a master document—together with subdocuments—might be a more manageable solution than attempting to store the entire manuscript in a single document file.

You can turn the Master Document View mode on or off by clicking the Master Document View button on the Outlining toolbar. The buttons on the Outlining toolbar to the right of the Master Document View button are displayed only when the Master Document View mode is active, and are provided for working with master documents. For information on creating and using master documents, look up the topic "master documents" in the Word online Help.

---

tip   **Include Documents Using an Alternative Method**

You can also tie together separate documents so that you can print them in series and work with them as a unit by creating a single overview document (analogous to a master document created in Master Document View). Then, include each of the separate Word documents that make up your manuscript by inserting an IncludeText field. To insert this field, choose Insert, Field, select IncludeText in the Field Names list, fill in the other options in the Field dialog box, and click the OK button (see Figure 15-3).

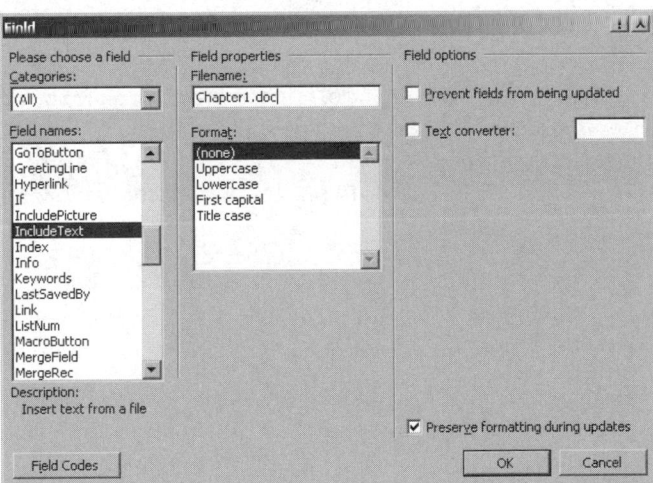

Figure 15-3. You can include a document in another Word document using the IncludeText field.

Chapter 15

Troubleshooting

Your Document Is Too Big to Save

You issue the Save command but you get a message indicating that your document is too large to save.

Don't panic. Nothing has been lost yet. Word is just unable to put all the pieces of your document together in a single disk file. What you should do first is cut part of the document's text into the Clipboard, paste it into a new document, and then save both documents on disk. Once you've safely saved all your text on disk, you can think about how to organize the text contained in the separate document files.

One way to organize a collection of separate document files that make up a single, large manuscript is to create a Master Document and include each of the separate document files within it as subdocuments, as discussed in "Collapsing and Expanding Outline Text," on page 422. Alternatively, you can tie together separate documents in a single overview document by using IncludeText fields, as explained in the tip "Include Documents Using an Alternative Method," on page 425.

Navigating Through an Outline

Word provides two features that let you quickly scroll to a particular document heading that is formatted with one of the built-in Heading styles. These features offer additional reasons to use the built-in Heading styles.

When you drag the scroll box on the vertical scroll bar, Word displays the page number of the current position as well as the text of the preceding outline heading (or at least the first part of the text), as shown in Figure 15-4. This feature works only if the Show ScreenTips On Toolbars option is selected. To set this option, choose Tools, Customize, and click the Options tab.

To locate a particular outline heading, simply drag the scroll box until you see the heading displayed, and then release the mouse button. Note that you don't need to be in Outline view to use this feature.

Document Map

A second feature that makes it easy to scroll to a particular heading is the Document Map, which is displayed in a separate pane at the left of the Word window (see Figure 15-5). To display the Document Map, choose View, Document Map, or click the Document Map button on the Standard toolbar.

Chapter 15: Managing Large or Complex Documents

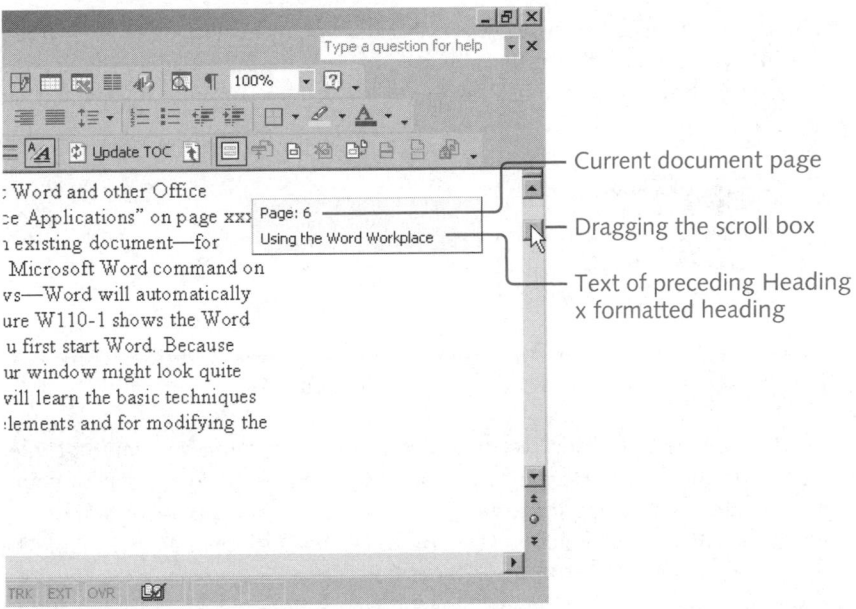

— Current document page

— Dragging the scroll box

— Text of preceding Heading x formatted heading

Figure 15-4. The ScreenTip shown here displays your current document position as you scroll.

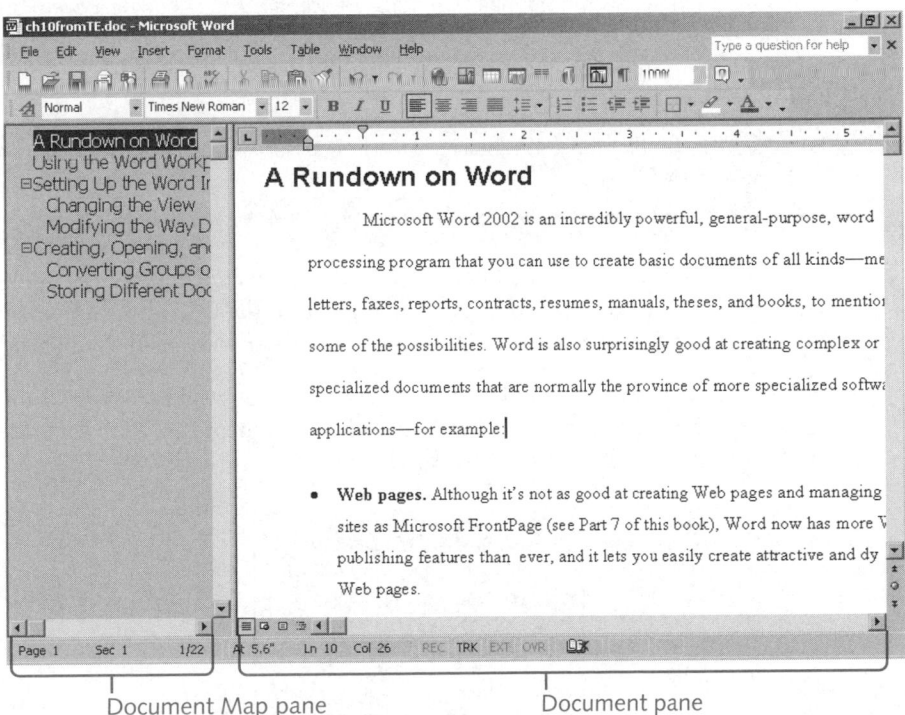

Document Map pane   Document pane

Figure 15-5. The Document Map makes it easy to display and scroll to headings in a document.

The Document Map lets you see all your document headings even if you're not in Outline view. Notice that if the full text of a heading isn't visible, you can display a ScreenTip showing the full heading text by placing the pointer over the heading, as shown in this example:

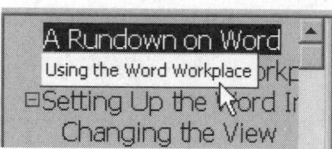

InsideOut

The Document Map works well if you've consistently formatted your document headings using the built-in Heading styles. If you've formatted some or all of your headings by directly applying formatting features (such as a large font size, bold, and so on) rather than using a built-in Heading style, the Document Map attempts to identify document headings by their formatting, but it often mistakenly identifies document elements such as figure captions, notes, sidebar titles, and so on, as headings, and displays them in the Document Map. It displays suspected headings in the Document Map by permanently changing their paragraph formatting to include outline-level formatting (discussed in the sidebar "Creating Headings Using Outline-Level Formatting," on page 421). The next time you view the document in Outline view, you might be quite surprised to see many of your document elements (such as figure captions) appearing as outline headings.

To avoid this problem, use the built-in Heading styles to format *all* your document headings!

To have Word scroll your document to a particular heading, just click that heading within the Document Map. If not all headings fit in the Document Map, you can use the vertical scroll bar within the Document Map pane to see additional headings.

Notice that if a heading is followed by one or more subheadings, Word displays a square symbol to the left of the heading in the Document Map. You can hide the subheadings in the Document Map by clicking that box, as shown here:

Click here to hide subheadings.

This symbol means subheadings are currently visible.

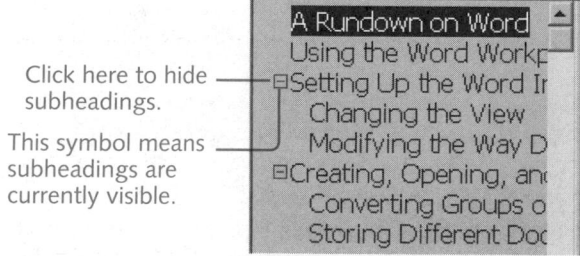

Chapter 15

You can show the subheadings by clicking the box again, as seen here:

This symbol means subheadings are currently hidden. ⎯⎯

Click here to show subheadings. ⎯⎯

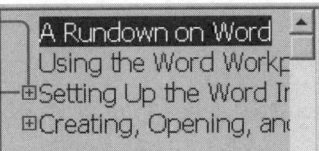

You can also collapse or expand the selected heading in the Document Map or change the level of headings shown throughout the Document Map by right-clicking in the Document Map pane and choosing the appropriate command from the shortcut menu.

If you're in Outline view, hiding or showing headings in the Document Map also hides or shows them in the document pane. In Normal, Web Layout, and Print Layout views, hiding or showing headings in the Document Map doesn't affect the document pane.

InsideOut

You can't display the Document Map when an additional pane is opened in the document window (such as the Reviewing pane, the Footnotes pane, or a second document pane opened by choosing Window, Split). If you open the Document Pane when an additional pane is open, Word will close the additional pane before displaying the Document Map.

Also, if you change the Word view, the Document Map may disappear. You need to control whether or not it's displayed separately in each view.

Printing an Outline

When you print a document while in Outline view, Word prints only the headings and body text that are currently visible. To print the whole document, click the All button on the Outlining toolbar or switch out of Outline view before printing.

InsideOut

Create a Better Looking Printed Outline

The appearance of a document printed in Outline view is often disappointing. Paragraph formatting features don't show, lines are always single spaced, and you can't add extra space between paragraphs. Also, the small box symbols that visually separate paragraphs of body text on the screen don't print, so the paragraphs of body text all run together. To print an attractively formatted outline, consider switching out of Outline view and formatting the text in the document as an outline numbered list, as explained in "Creating Lists with the Bullets And Numbering Dialog Box and List Styles," on page 373.

For information on printing documents, see "Previewing and Printing Documents," on page 547.

Troubleshooting

You Have Trouble Copying Outline Headings

Your editor has asked you to submit a Word document containing an outline of the chapter you're writing. You open the chapter, switch into Outline view, and display the levels of headings you want to include. However, when you try to copy those headings to a different document, all body text and subheadings are included with it. The only solution seems to be to manually copy all the headings one at a time.

To solve this problem, try the following method:

1 Insert a table of contents anywhere in the document. In the Table Of Contents tab, clear the Show Page Numbers and the Use Hyperlinks Instead Of Page Numbers options to eliminate page numbers and hyperlinks from the table of contents.

For details on inserting a table of contents, see "Generating a Table of Contents," on page 440.

2 Select the entire table of contents, press Ctrl+Shift+F9 to convert the table of contents from a Word field to regular document text, and press Ctrl+X to move the text into the Clipboard.

3 Open the document that you want to contain the outline and press Ctrl+V to paste the outline headings.

4 Format the outline as desired.

Inserting Footnotes and Endnotes

Word makes it easy to add footnotes or endnotes to your document. The text for a *footnote* is placed at the bottom of the page that contains the reference mark (or you can choose to place a footnote just beneath the text on the page that contains the reference mark). The text for an *endnote* is placed at the end of the document (or you can choose to place an endnote at the end of the section that contains the reference mark). Figure 15-6 shows a footnote.

To add a footnote or endnote to your document, perform the following steps:

1 Place the insertion point where you want to insert the footnote or endnote reference mark.

Footnote reference mark

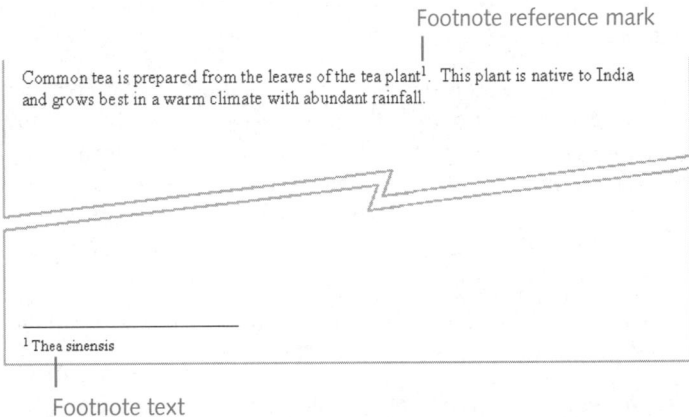

Common tea is prepared from the leaves of the tea plant[1]. This plant is native to India and grows best in a warm climate with abundant rainfall.

¹ Thea sinensis

Footnote text

Figure 15-6. This figure shows a footnote in a Word document.

2 Choose Insert, Reference, Footnote. This will open the Footnote And Endnote dialog box, shown here:

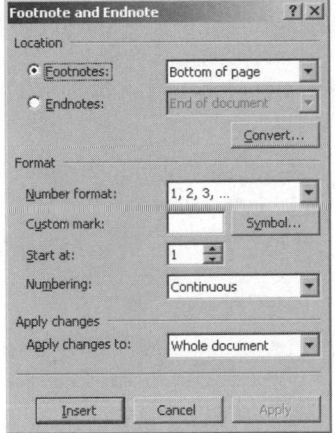

3 In the Footnote And Endnote dialog box, do one of the following:

- To insert a footnote, select the Footnotes option, and specify where you want the footnote positioned by selecting Bottom Of Page or Below Text from the adjoining drop-down list.

- To insert an endnote, select the Endnotes option, and specify where you want the endnote positioned by selecting End Of Document or End Of Section from the adjoining drop-down list.

> **tip** **Move Endnotes**
>
> If you have displayed endnotes at the end of a particular document section, you can move those endnotes to the end of the *next* document section (if any), where they will be displayed before the endnotes belonging to the next section. To do this, place the insertion point in the section containing the endnotes you want to move, choose File, Page Setup, click the Layout tab in the Page Setup dialog box, select This Section in the Apply To drop-down list, and check the Suppress Endnotes option.

4 Specify the numbering format of the footnote or endnote reference marks in one of the following two ways:

   ▪ To use automatically incremented numbers or symbols (*, †, ‡, §, …), select the type of number you want (or the symbol set) from the Number Format drop-down list, specify the starting number (or symbol) in the Start At text box, and select the way you want the numbering to restart from the Numbering drop-down list. Also, if you've divided your document into sections, select This Section or Whole Document to specify the part of the document where you want to use the numbering format you specified. (If you select the "i, ii, iii, …" format, keep in mind that lowercase roman numerals can be difficult for many readers to comprehend after about xv, or 15.)

   ▪ To use a custom reference mark (such as *), type the symbol into the Custom Mark text box, or click the Symbol button to select the symbol from the Symbol dialog box.

> For information on using the Symbol dialog box, see "Inserting Symbols and Foreign Characters," on page 246.

> **note** If you select an automatically incremented number or symbol for your reference marks, the format you specify will be applied to all automatic reference marks in the document (or in the current document section if the document is divided into sections and you selected This Section in the Apply Changes To list).
>
> If you want to change the format of the automatic reference marks without inserting a mark, you can open the Footnote And Endnote dialog box, specify the format, and click the Apply button rather than the Insert button.
>
> If you specify a custom reference mark, your selection will apply only to the mark you insert, not to other reference marks in the document.

5 Click the Insert button.

   Word will insert the reference mark into the body text. Also, in Normal, Web Layout, or Outline view, it will open a separate footnote pane and position the insertion point in this pane, as shown in Figure 15-7.

Chapter 15: Managing Large or Complex Documents

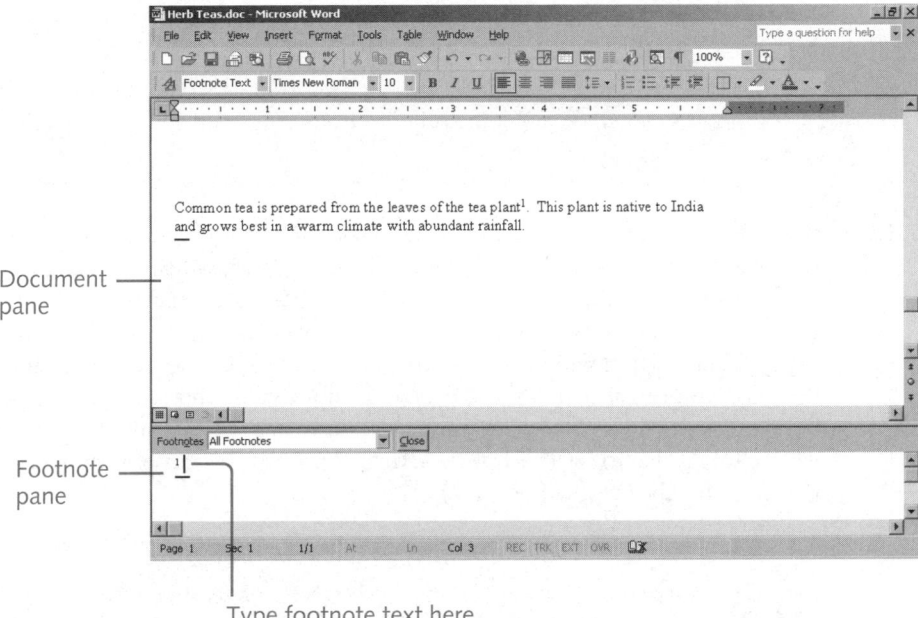

Document pane

Footnote pane

Type footnote text here.

Figure 15-7. In Normal view, you enter footnote text in the footnote pane.

In Print Layout view or Print Preview, Word will place the insertion point at the actual position of the footnote or endnote on the page.

6 Type the footnote or endnote text.

7 In Normal, Web Layout, or Outline view, if you want to close the footnote pane when you have finished typing the footnote or endnote text, click the Close button at the top of the pane. The insertion point will be moved back to the position where you inserted the footnote or endnote reference in the document text. If you want to leave the footnote pane open, you can switch back and forth between that pane and your current position in the document pane by pressing F6.

In Print Layout view or Print Preview, after you finish typing the footnote text, you can move the insertion point back to the position in the document text where you inserted the footnote or endnote reference by pressing Shift+F5 or by using any other navigation method.

---

tip   Insert a Note with a Shortcut Key

To quickly add a footnote or endnote using the options you previously chose in the Footnote And Endnote dialog box (or using default options if you didn't choose any), place the insertion point where you want the reference mark, and press Alt+Ctrl+F for a footnote or Alt+Ctrl+D for an endnote.

> **tip** **Convert Note Types**
>
> You can click the Convert button in the Footnote And Endnote dialog box to convert all footnotes in your document to endnotes, to convert all endnotes to footnotes, or to swap footnotes and endnotes.

If you later want to view or edit your footnote or endnote text, choose View, Footnotes. If you have both footnotes and endnotes, Word will ask which you want to view. You can also simply double-click a footnote or endnote reference mark. In Normal, Web Layout, or Outline view, Word will open the footnote pane. In Print Layout view or Print Preview, Word will move the insertion point to the footnote or endnote area of the page. You can also view the text of your footnote or endnote by holding the mouse pointer over the reference mark, as shown in the following example. (This feature works only if the ScreenTips option is turned on. You set this option by choosing Tools, Options and clicking the View tab.)

Thea sinensis

Common tea is prepared from the leaves of the tea plant[1] This plant is native to India and grows best in a warm climate with abundant rainfall.

To move or copy a footnote or endnote, move or copy the reference mark to the desired document location using any of the editing methods explained in Chapter 11, "Efficient Editing in Word." If you used automatically incremented reference marks, Word will automatically renumber your reference marks if necessary. If you copy the reference mark, Word will make a copy of the footnote or endnote text.

For techniques on moving or copying text, see "Editing the Selection," on page 275.

> **tip** **Reformat Footnotes or Endnotes Globally**
>
> To change the formatting of footnote or endnote reference marks or text throughout your document, you can modify the built-in character style Footnote Reference or Endnote Reference, or the built-in paragraph style Footnote Text or Endnote Text. (These styles aren't normally displayed in the Styles And Formatting task pane. To list them, select Custom in the Show drop-down list near the bottom of the task pane, and in the Format Settings dialog box, select All Styles in the Category drop-down list and then check the style or styles you want to modify.)

To delete a footnote or endnote, select the reference mark and press Delete. Word deletes both the reference mark and all the footnote or endnote text.

Generating Indexes and Tables of Contents

You can have Word generate an index or a table of contents for your document. A comprehensive index and an accurate table of contents are important assets for a document, especially a lengthy or technical one.

---

tip   **Use a Table of Contents for a Web Page**

If you're creating a Web page document, you should use a table of contents rather than an index. The page numbers given in an index are meaningless in a Web page displayed in a browser, because the browser doesn't divide the document into separate pages. However, a table of contents displayed in a browser normally consists of a list of hyperlinks that a visitor can click to navigate to different parts of the document, making it quite useful.

---

note   If you have inserted captions using the Insert, Reference, Caption command, you can have Word generate a table of figures. You can also have it generate a table of authorities for a legal brief. These sorts of tables aren't as common as indexes and tables of contents and aren't discussed in this book. For information, look up the following topics in the Word online Help: "captions," "tables of figures," and "tables of authorities."

Generating an Index

Preparing an index in Word is a two-step process: First, you mark a series of index entries, and then you compile and insert the index itself, based on these entries.

A typical index entry consists of the name of a topic followed by the number of the page on which the topic is discussed, as seen here:

oolong tea, 1

When you mark an index entry, you specify the topic name and you tag the location of the topic in the document so that Word can determine its page number when you compile the index. To mark an index entry, perform the following steps:

1   If all or part of the word or phrase that you want to appear in the index entry (such as *oolong tea* in the preceding example) is contained in the document text to be indexed, select this word or phrase, as shown here:

Select the text you want to
appear in the index entry.

There are three types of tea: green, black, and oolong. The leaves for black and oolong teas are first fermented and are then dried and heated. The leaves for green tea are dried and heated without fermentation.

Otherwise, simply place the insertion point at the beginning of the document text you want to index.

2 Choose Insert, Reference, Index And Tables. Then click the Mark Entry button on the Index tab of the Index And Tables dialog box to open the Mark Index Entry dialog box, shown here. An alternative way to open this dialog box is to press the Alt+Shift+X key combination.

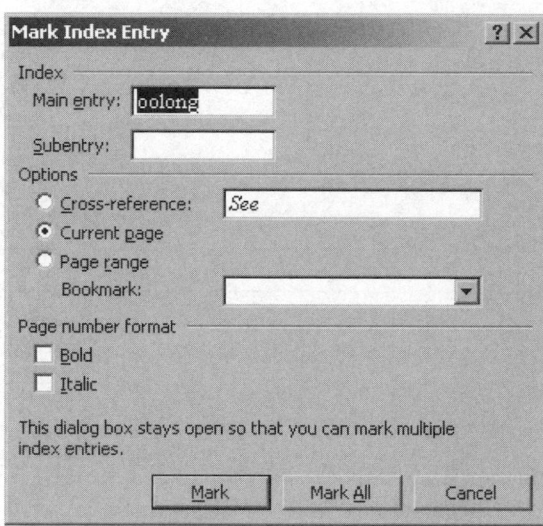

3 If you selected text in step 1, it will appear in the Main Entry text box; otherwise, the box will be empty. If necessary, edit the contents of this box so that it contains the exact text you want to appear in the index, as shown here:

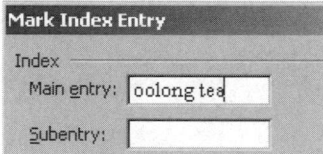

4 If you want to create an index subentry, enter the subentry text in the Subentry text box.

For example, typing the following into the Main Entry and Subentry text boxes

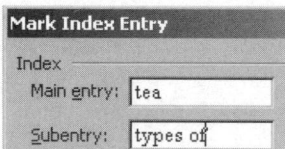

would create the following index entry and subentry:

tea
    types of, 1

5 Make sure the Current Page option is selected so that the index entry will display the number of the page that contains the indexed topic.

> **note** Rather than selecting the Current Page option, you can select the Cross-Reference option or the Page Range option. If you select Cross-Reference, the index entry will display the cross-reference that you type into the adjoining text box, for example, "*See* herb teas," rather than a page number. If you select Page Range, the index entry will display the range of pages that are marked with the bookmark that you select in the Bookmark list. Bookmarks are discussed in "Using Bookmarks to Label and Locate Text," on page 289.

6 To modify the format of the page number in the index entry, check Bold, Italic, or both.

7 Click the Mark button.

> **tip** **Mark the Selected Text Globally**
>
> If you selected text in step 1, you can have Word globally mark as index entries all occurrences of that text within your document. To do this, click the Mark All button rather than the Mark button. Word will apply the entry, subentry, and other settings that you've entered in the Mark Index Entry dialog box to all marked occurrences.

8 If you want to mark additional index entries, you can leave the Mark Index Entry dialog box open while you move the insertion point to additional locations in your document. When you have finished marking entries, click Close to remove the dialog box.

> **note**
> Show/
> Hide ¶
> Word marks an index entry by inserting a block of instructions known as a *field* into the document. The field contains the XE field name (for *index entry*), and it is formatted as hidden text. If you can't see these fields in your document, you can make them appear by clicking the Show/Hide ¶ button on the Standard toolbar. (You can also choose Tools, Options, click the View tab, and check the Hidden Text option.)

When you have marked all the index entries, the next step is to compile and insert the index itself. To do this perform the following steps:

1 Place the insertion point at the position in your document where you want to display the index.

2 Choose Insert, Reference, Index And Tables to display the Index And Tables dialog box, and click the Index tab, shown here:

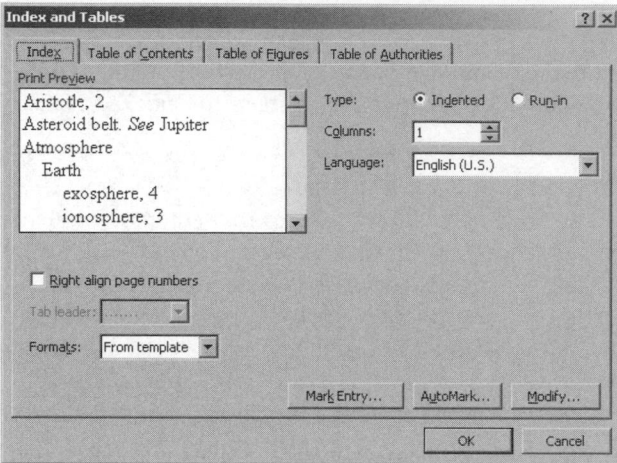

3 If you want to modify the appearance of the index, choose options in the Index tab until the model index in the Print Preview area has the look you want for your index. You can set the index type, the number of columns, the language, the alignment of page numbers, the tab leader character, and the overall format of the index.

4 Click the OK button. Word will compile the index and insert it into the document. Word will also add section breaks before and after the index so that it's contained in its own document section.

---

tip **Customize Your Index Entries**

When you generate an index using the Index tab of the Index And Tables dialog box, you can create custom formatting for your index entries. To do this, select the From Template item in the Formats drop-down list. Then, click the Modify button to open the Style dialog box, which lets you modify the built-in styles that Word assigns to index entries: Index 1 for main entries and Index 2 through Index 9 for subentries. To customize a style, select it in the Styles list and click the Modify button.

You can also change the formatting of index headings (that is, the A, B, and C headings, and so on, that precede each index section) by using the Styles And Formatting side pane to modify the Index Heading built-in style. (This style isn't normally displayed in the Styles And Formatting side pane. To list it, select Custom in the Show drop-down list near the bottom of the side pane. In the Format Settings dialog box, select All Styles in the Category drop-down list and check the Index Heading item in the Styles To Be Visible list.)

For instructions on modifying styles, see "Customizing Styles," on page 385.

Word creates the index by inserting an INDEX field into the document. Under certain circumstances, rather than seeing the index itself, you might see the field code for the index, which would look something like this:

{ INDEX \c "2" \z "1033" }

The switches following the field name, INDEX, indicate the options that you selected in the Index And Tables dialog box. The switches in this example have the meanings given in Table 15-2.

Table 15-2. INDEX Field Code Switches

INDEX Field Code Switch	Meaning
\c "2"	Arrange the index in two columns.
\z "1033"	Use the English (U.S.) language.

If you see the field code rather than the actual index, you can make the index appear by placing the insertion point within the field code and pressing Shift+F9.

If your document changes after you insert an index, you can update the index by placing the insertion point anywhere within the index and pressing F9. To have Word automatically update the index when you print the document, choose Tools, Options, click the Print tab, and make sure that the Update Fields option is checked.

Troubleshooting

Spelling Errors in Index

You notice outrageous spelling errors in your index and you're wondering why Word didn't catch them.

Word formats the XE fields that mark your index entries as hidden text. If hidden text isn't visible, neither the as-you-type spelling checker nor the spelling checker you run by choosing Tools, Spelling And Grammar, checks the spelling of the words contained in the text. Also, because the index itself is generated from a field, neither spelling checker checks its contents.

To check the spelling of your index entries, make hidden text visible by clicking the Show/Hide ¶ button on the Standard toolbar, or by choosing Tools, Options, clicking the View tab, and checking the Hidden Text option. You can then use either spelling checker to check the spelling of the text directly within the XE fields, which will be used to build the index entries the next time you insert or update the index.

Chapter 15

Generating a Table of Contents

You can also use Word to compile and insert a table of contents, which lists the document headings, in your document. When you view a table of contents in any Word view except Web Layout, each entry typically includes the page number of the heading and functions as a hyperlink that you can click to navigate to that heading. When you view a table of contents in Web Layout view or when you view a Web page document in a browser, each entry usually consists of only a hyperlink without a page number. (Page numbers would be meaningless in a browser, which doesn't divide a document into separate pages.) When you generate the table of contents, however, you can choose whether or not to include page numbers or hyperlinks.

The following is the fastest way to create a table of contents:

1 Make sure that every heading you want to include in the table of contents has been assigned one of the built-in Heading styles, Heading 1 through Heading 9. You can assign these styles using Outline view, as explained earlier in this chapter.

> You can also assign styles using the methods given in "Assigning Paragraph Styles, Character Styles, and Saved Formats," on page 323.

2 Place the insertion point at the position in your document where you want to display the table of contents.

3 Choose Insert, Reference, Index And Tables. Then click the Table Of Contents tab, shown here:

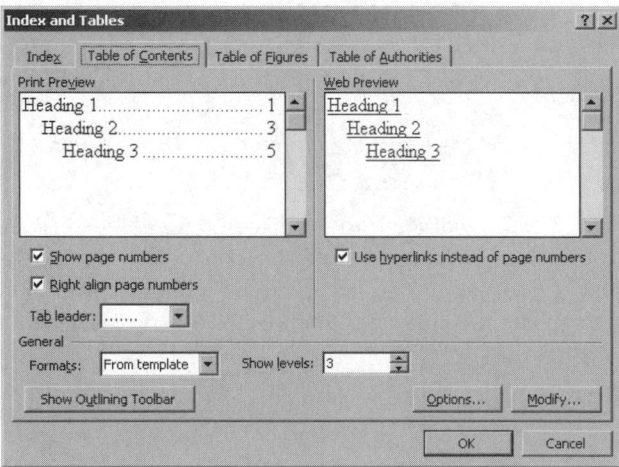

4 If you want to modify the appearance of the table of contents, choose options in the Table Of Contents tab until the model table of contents in the Print Preview or Web Preview area has the look you want.

Chapter 15: Managing Large or Complex Documents

The Print Preview area shows how the table of contents will appear in any Word view except Web Layout, and the Web Preview area shows how it will look in Web Layout view or when a Web page document is viewed in a browser. You can specify the alignment of page numbers, the tab leader character, the overall format of the table of contents, and the number of heading levels that should be included in the table of contents.

Clearing the Use Hyperlinks Instead Of Page Numbers option has two results:

- Hyperlinks won't be included in the table of contents, whether the document is viewed in Normal, Print Layout, or Outline view in Word, or it's viewed in Web Layout view or in a browser.

- When the document is viewed in Web Layout view or in a browser, page numbers are displayed *unless* you've cleared the Show Page Numbers option, which eliminates the display of page numbers from all views.

5 Click the OK button.

---

tip　**Customize Your Table of Contents**

When you generate a table of contents using the Table Of Contents tab of the Index And Tables dialog box, you can create custom formatting for the table of contents. To do this, select From Template in the Formats drop-down list. Then, click the Modify button to open the Style dialog box, which lets you modify the built-in styles that Word assigns to table of contents entries: TOC 1 through TOC 9 for each of the different heading levels shown in the table of contents. To customize a style, select it in the Styles list and click the Modify button. Also, you can click the Options button in the Table Of Contents tab to have Word build the table of contents using paragraphs with styles other than the built-in Heading styles, instead of—or in addition to—using paragraphs with the built-in Heading styles.

For instructions on modifying styles, see "Customizing Styles," on page 385.

Word creates a table of contents by inserting a TOC field. Under certain circumstances, rather than seeing the table of contents itself, you might see the field code for the table of contents, which would look something like this:

{ TOC \o "1-3" \h \z \u }

The switches following the field name, TOC, indicate the options you selected in the Index And Tables dialog box. The switches in this example have the meanings shown in Table 15-3, on page 442.

Table 15-3. TOC Field Code Switches

TOC Field Code Switch	Meaning
\o "1-3"	Build the table of contents from document paragraphs that are assigned the built-in Heading styles Heading 1 through Heading 3.
\h	Assign a hyperlink to each table of contents entry.
\z	In Web Layout view, hide the page numbers, as well as the tab leader (the dots, dashes, or underlining between the end of the entry text and the page number).
\u	In addition to using the headings with the built-in heading styles to build the table of contents, use paragraphs that have been assigned outline-level formatting. (Outline-level formatting is assigned to a paragraph by choosing Format, Paragraph, clicking the Indents And Spacing tab, and selecting a level in the Outline Level drop-down list.)

If you see the field code for the table of contents rather than the table of contents itself, you can make the table of contents appear by selecting the *entire* field code and pressing Shift+F9. Note that a table of contents usually includes nested HYPERLINK and PAGEREF fields; if you see any of these field codes rather than the field contents, you can likewise select the entire field code and press Shift+F9 to show the contents.

If you chose to include hyperlinks in your table of contents, when you view the document in Word or in a browser, you can click a table of contents entry to navigate to the referenced heading. In Word, if the Use Ctrl + Click To Follow Hyperlink option is checked, you'll have to press Ctrl when you click a hyperlink. You access this option by choosing Tools, Options and clicking the Edit tab.

If the content or page locations of your outline headings change—or if you added or removed headings—after you insert a table of contents, you can update the table of contents by clicking the Update TOC button on the Outlining toolbar, shown here:

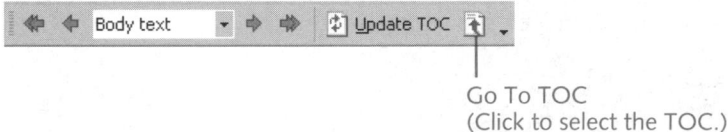

Go To TOC
(Click to select the TOC.)

You can also select or place the insertion point within the table of contents and press F9. Word will ask whether you want to update the page numbers only or update the entire table of contents. To have Word automatically update the table of contents when you print the document, choose Tools, Options, click the Print tab, and make sure that the Update Fields option is checked.

---

tip   **Change a Table of Contents to Regular Text**

As explained in this section, a table of contents consists of a dynamic Word field, so that it can be automatically updated to reflect changes in the document headings. If you want to convert it to regular, static text, select the entire table of contents and press Ctrl+Shift+F9. You can then edit, format, or copy the table of contents like any other regular document text.

Troubleshooting

Edits to Index or Table of Contents Are Lost

You edited text within an index or a table of contents. However, when you updated the index or table of contents, or when you printed the document, your edits disappeared.

Remember that an index or a table of contents is a dynamic *field*, not regular text. Any edits you make directly to an index or table of contents will be overwritten when Word updates the field. Therefore, to edit index entries, you should edit the contents of the XE fields in the document that are used to build the index (if you don't see them, click the Show/Hide ¶ button on the Standard toolbar). Likewise, to edit the entries in a table of contents, you should edit the document headings that are used to build the table of contents.

Using Word in Workgroups

newfeature!

Tracking and Reviewing Document Changes

You can have Microsoft Word 2002 track and mark all changes you make to a document so that you or a co-worker can later review these changes and either accept them to make them permanent or reject them to restore the original text. When Word tracks changes, it always stores the details on every change made to the document—the exact modification that was made, the name of the person making the change, and the date and the time of the change. (The name used to indicate the author of a change is the name that was contained in the Name box on the User Information tab of the Options dialog box at the time the revision was made.) You can display this information when you review the revisions. You can also have Word mark the revisions on the screen in various ways so you can see at a glance the proposed corrections and changes to the document. Or, you can temporarily hide the markings, letting Word store the change information internally only.

This version of Word has significantly revamped the change-tracking feature of previous Word versions and offers new ways to display and work with tracked changes. Working with tracked changes can be divided into two phases:

● Tracking and marking your changes as you edit a document

● Reviewing tracked document changes made by you or a co-worker

note The Word document merging and comparing feature also generates tracked changes—automatically—to mark merged text or to indicate differences between two document versions. See "Merging and Comparing Documents," on page 455.

Tracking Your Document Changes

You can turn on change tracking whenever you want to start saving a record of all modifications you make to a document so that the modifications can be viewed and later either accepted or rejected. For example, you could turn on change tracking before making tentative document alterations that you might want to reverse later. You could also turn on change tracking in order to communicate to a co-worker the exact ways that you edit a document.

To track your document changes, perform the following steps:

1 To take advantage of Word's new ways of showing changes, switch to either Web Layout or Print Layout view. In these views—as well as in Print Preview and on the printed document—Word 2002 displays all deletions and indicates all formatting changes within margin "balloons." Displaying deleted text in the margins makes it easier to read your modified paragraphs and avoids throwing off the positions of line and page breaks (see Figure 16-1). Although you *can* track and view changes in Normal or Outline view, Word will use its old method for marking tracked changes, in which deleted text is left in place, making it more difficult to read the document and visualize the way the final text will actually appear on the page (see Figure 16-2). The discussions in this section assume that you're in Web Layout or Print Layout view.

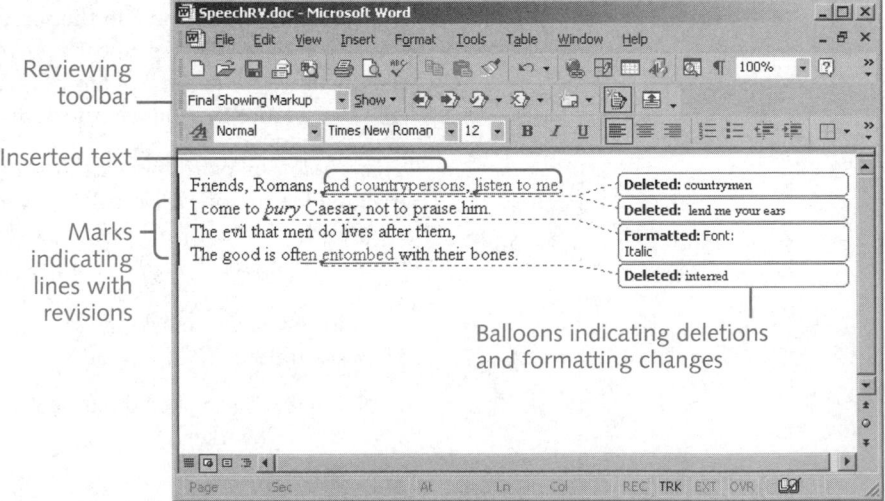

Figure 16-1. When displayed in Web Layout view, a Word document containing tracked changes shows the changes in balloons in the margin.

Chapter 16: Using Word in Workgroups

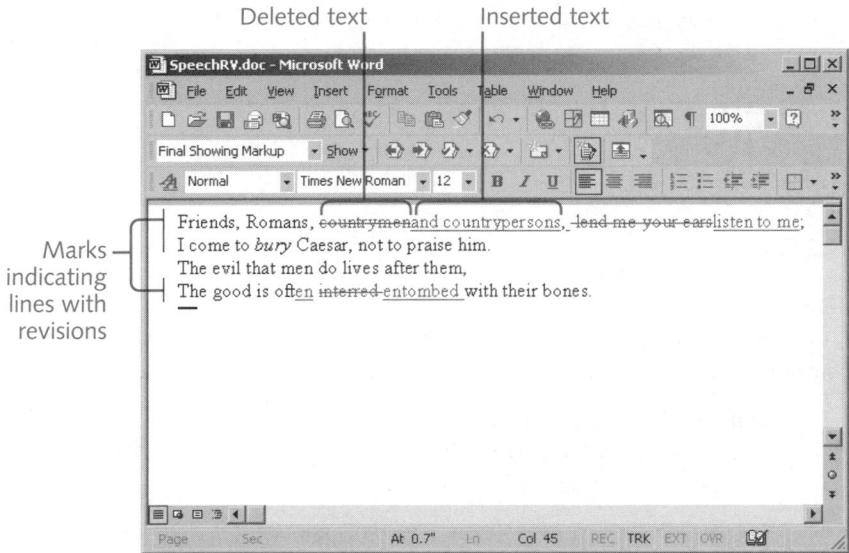

Figure 16-2. A Word document containing tracked changes displayed in Normal view shows the changes within the text itself.

2 Turn on change tracking by double-clicking the TRK indicator in the status bar, by choosing Tools, Track Changes, or by pressing the Ctrl+Shift+E shortcut key. Word will now start tracking all insertions, deletions, and formatting changes you make to the document. When change tracking is turned on, the TRK indicator in the status bar is displayed in darker type.

To turn change tracking off, repeat any of these three commands. When you turn off change tracking, Word retains its record of all changes that have already been tracked, but it doesn't track changes that you subsequently make.

note If the Reviewing toolbar is currently displayed, you can turn change tracking on or off by clicking the Track Changes button.

When you turn on change tracking, Word will automatically display the Reviewing toolbar (shown in Figure 16-3).

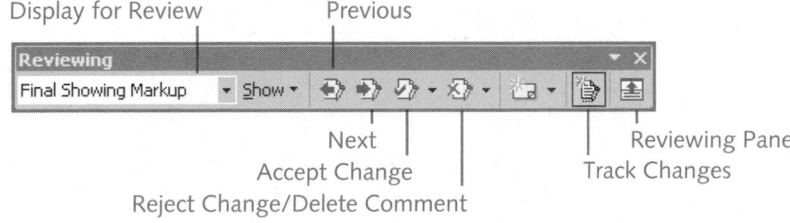

Figure 16-3. The controls on the Reviewing toolbar are used for working with change tracking.

3 To adjust the change marking mode, open the Display For Review drop-down list on the Reviewing toolbar, shown here:

Then, select one of the following two change marking options from the list (the other two options are more suitable for reviewing changes and are discussed in the next section):

■ To have Word mark all your changes as you edit the document, choose Final Showing Markup. Use this option if you want to monitor your changes as you make them.

■ To turn off marking of changes, choose Final. Word will continue to track changes and store the change information internally, and you can have Word show the changes later if you want. (The only way to permanently remove a tracked change is to accept or reject it, as described in the next section.) Use this option if you want to record your changes but don't want the window to be cluttered with markings while you edit. In this mode, Word works *almost* as it does when change tracking is off. However, you'll occasionally notice minor quirks; for example, once in a while you might have to press the Backspace key several times before it erases the preceding character.

4 To filter the particular changes that Word shows, click the Show button on the Reviewing toolbar, shown here:

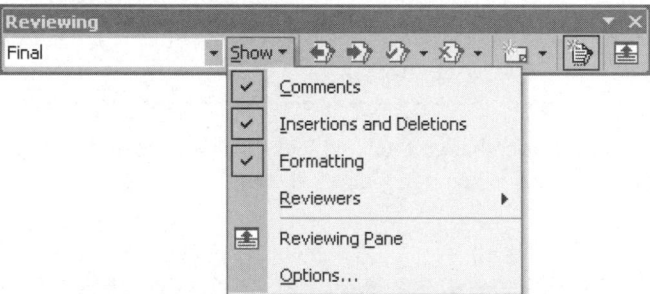

Then, choose an option from the drop-down menu, as follows:

■ To show or hide markings for all insertions and deletions, choose Insertions And Deletions. The markings are shown when the menu item is checked.

■ To show or hide markings for all formatting changes, choose Formatting.

■ To show or hide markings for changes made by a particular Word user, click Reviewers and choose a user name from the submenu seen here (or choose All Reviewers to show or hide markings for all users):

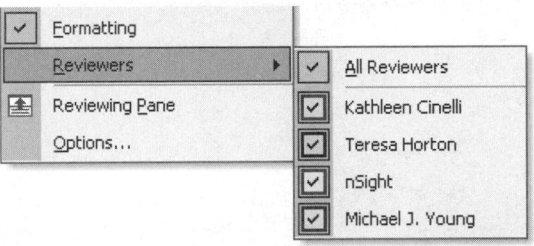

Note that your choice affects only the items that are *shown*. As long as change tracking is on, Word will continue to record all changes to the document, and you can later show any changes that aren't currently marked.

5 To modify the way Word marks changes, choose Options from the Show drop-down menu, and select the desired options in the Track Changes tab (see Figure 16-4 on page 450). Another way to display this tab is to choose Tools, Options in Word and click the Track Changes tab in the Options dialog box. In the Track Changes tab you can modify the types of markings and colors that Word uses to mark insertions, formatting changes, and revised lines. You can adjust features of the balloons that show changes in the margins, or you can turn off the balloons by clearing the Use Balloons In Print And Web Layout option. (Word 2002 will then mark all changes in the body of the text, as did previous versions of Word.) And, you can choose the Preserve, Force Landscape, or Auto page orientation option for printing the document. The Preserve option prints the document with the orientation— either portrait or landscape—that is currently set in the Margins tab of the Page Setup dialog (displayed by choosing File, Page Setup). The Force Landscape option always prints in landscape orientation, providing the most room for displaying margin balloons. With Auto, Word selects the page orientation that provides the best layout for the document.

note When selecting a color for change markings in the Track Changes tab, keep in mind that the Auto item refers to your normal Window Font color, which is usually black. (The Window Font color is selected in the Display program of the Windows Control Panel.)

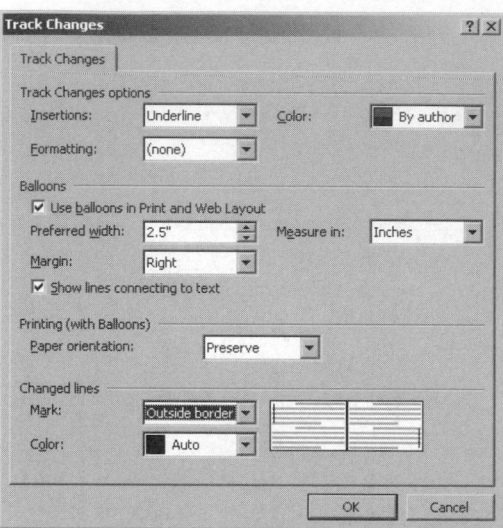

Figure 16-4. The Track Changes tab lets you modify the way Word marks tracked changes.

Reviewing Tracked Document Changes

If you want to convert a document containing tracked changes to its final form, you'll need to review the tracked changes, accepting or rejecting each one. The document might be one that you or a co-worker has edited with change tracking turned on, or a document generated by the Word document merging or comparing feature.

The merging and comparing features are discussed in "Merging and Comparing Documents," on page 455.

Adjusting the Way Changes Are Shown

While reviewing tracked changes, you might want to modify the way Word displays the changes, as follows:

● To view the modified version of the document with changes marked, select the Final Showing Markup option in the Display For Review drop-down list on the Reviewing toolbar, as shown here:

Figure 16-1, on page 446, shows the result of selecting this change marking option.

- To view the modified version of the document without changes marked, select Final. This option shows the document as it would appear if you accepted all changes (see Figure 16-5).

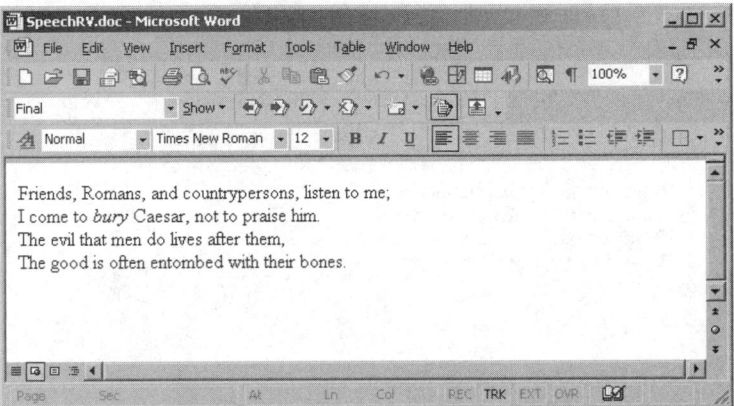

Figure 16-5. The example document is displayed with the Final change marking option.

- To view the unmodified version of the document (that is, the version before you made any tracked changes) with changes marked, choose Original Showing Markup. With this option, you'll notice that deletions are left in the body of the text, and insertions are displayed in margin balloons (the opposite of the way changes are shown with the Final Showing Markup option; see Figure 16-6).

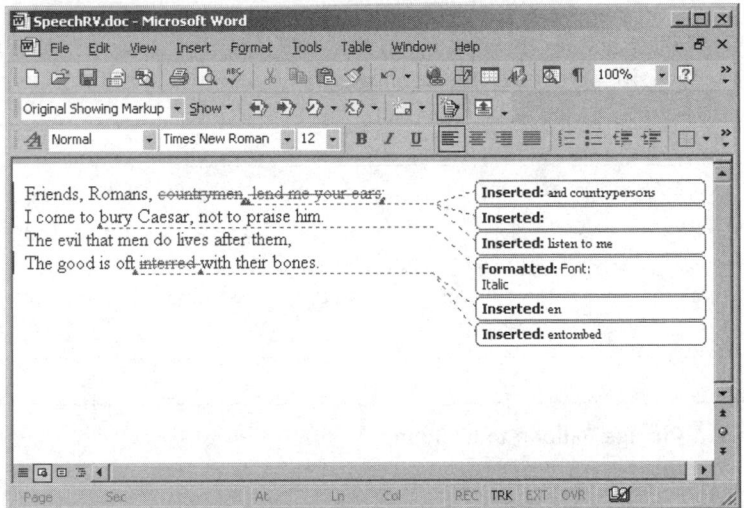

Figure 16-6. The example document is displayed with the Original Showing Markup change marking option.

- To view the unmodified version of the document without changes marked, choose Original. This option shows the document as it would appear if you rejected all changes (see Figure 16-7).

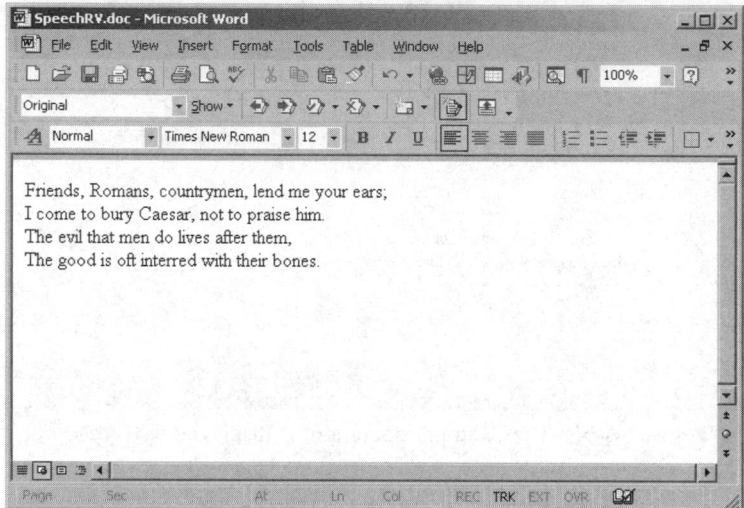

Figure 16-7.   The example document is displayed with the Original change marking option.

> **note**   In Outline or Normal view, the Final Showing Markup option and the Original Showing Markup option have the same effect.

- If changes are shown, you can filter the specific changes that are marked by choosing options from the Show drop-down menu on the Reviewing toolbar, as explained in the previous section.

> **note**   If you've selected either the Final Showing Markup or the Final change marking mode, you can toggle back and forth between these modes by choosing View, Markup. Likewise, if you've selected either the Original Showing Markup or the Original change marking mode, you can toggle back and forth between these modes by choosing View, Markup.

> **tip**   **Track a Change Balloon to Its Source**
>
> If more than one tracked change occurs on the same line (as in the first line of the example document shown in Figure 16-6), it can be hard to determine which part of a sentence a change balloon refers to. However, if you click a particular balloon, it will display a thick line that points more clearly to the location of the change.

Viewing Change Details

You can view the details of each change, using one of the following methods:

- Hold the mouse pointer over either the marked change itself or over its balloon in the margin to see details about the change in a ScreenTip, as seen here:

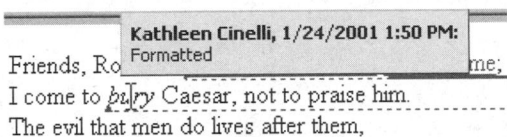

Kathleen Cinelli, 1/24/2001 1:50 PM:
Formatted

Friends, Ro_____me;
I come to *bury* Caesar, not to praise him.
The evil that men do lives after them,

> **note** If you don't see the ScreenTips, choose Tools, Options, click the View tab, and check the ScreenTips option.

- Click the Reviewing Pane button on the Reviewing toolbar (shown in Figure 16-3, on page 447) to display the Reviewing pane at the bottom of the document window. This pane always lists details about all tracked changes (as well as comments, discussed later in the chapter), regardless of the current change marking mode in effect in the document window. The tracked changes are grouped according to the part of the document that contains them (main document, header and footer, text box, header and footer text box, footnote, and endnote; see Figure 16-8). To close the Reviewing pane, click the Reviewing Pane button again. To switch the insertion point back and forth between the Reviewing pane and the document pane, press F6.

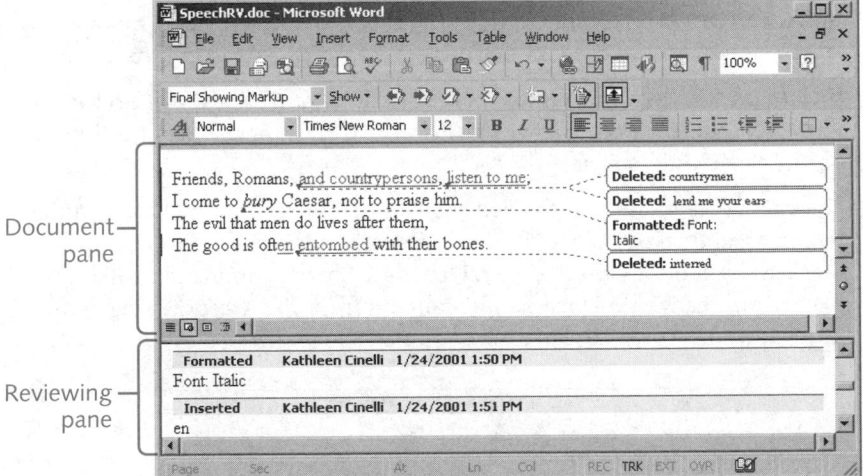

Figure 16-8. The Reviewing pane shows details on all tracked changes and comments in a document.

453

> **note** If several Word users have created tracked changes in a single document, each user's changes are usually marked in a distinct color, helping you to identify the author of each change. However, in the Track Changes tab, shown in Figure 16-4 on page 450, you can choose to use a single color for marking all users' changes.

> **tip** **Find Change Details in the Reviewing Pane**
>
> To find information about a particular change in the Reviewing pane, click on the margin balloon for that change. The Reviewing pane will scroll immediately to the change's description.

Accepting or Rejecting Changes

When you accept a revision change, Word discards the information it has stored on that change, it removes the change marking, and it permanently incorporates the change into the document. When you reject a change, Word discards the change information, removes the change marking, and permanently reverses the change in the document.

To accept or reject changes, use the following techniques:

- Whether or not changes are marked on the screen, you can accept or reverse all changes in a particular portion of the document by selecting the affected text and clicking the Accept Change or the Reject Change/Delete Comment button on the Reviewing toolbar (shown in Figure 16-3).

- If changes are currently marked on the screen, you can accept or reject a particular marked change by right-clicking the changed text and choosing the Accept or Reject command from the shortcut menu. (The command label will indicate the type of the change—for example, Accept Insertion.)

- If changes are currently marked on the screen, you can have Word select the next or the previous change by clicking the Next or the Previous button on the Reviewing toolbar.

- You can globally accept all tracked changes that are currently shown on the screen or all tracked changes in the document (whether or not they're marked) by choosing the Accept All Changes Shown command or the Accept All Changes In Document command from the Accept Change drop-down menu on the Reviewing toolbar, shown here:

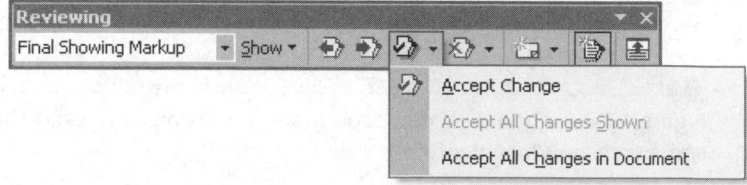

● You can globally reject all tracked changes that are currently shown on the screen or all tracked changes in the document (whether or not they're marked) by choosing the Reject All Changes Shown command or the Reject All Changes In Document command from the Reject Change/Delete Comment drop-down menu on the Reviewing toolbar, as seen here:

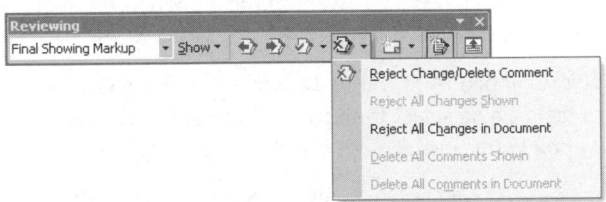

> **note** The Accept All Changes Shown and Reject All Changes Shown commands are enabled only if you've filtered out some of the change markings (using the Show drop-down menu on the Reviewing toolbar).

> **tip** **Process Tracked Changes in Batches**
>
> To accept or reject an entire batch of tracked changes, first use the commands on the Show drop-down menu to display the set of tracked changes you want to modify. Then choose the Accept All Changes Shown or the Reject All Changes Shown command on the Accept Change or the Reject Change/Delete Comment drop-down menu.

Merging and Comparing Documents

If you have two different versions of a document, you can have Word merge or compare the two versions. Word uses change marking to indicate the merged text resulting from merging documents or the differences between two documents that you are comparing. This is the same type of change marking that Word employs when you turn on change tracking, as described in the previous sections.

Merging would be useful, for example, if you and a co-worker have been editing separate copies of the same document, and you now want to create a single document that includes both your edits. The merged document will contain all of the text from both documents, and any text that is contained in one document but not in the other will be marked as inserted text using standard change marking. You can then accept or reject each instance to control exactly what text is kept in the final merged document.

If formatting differs between two merged documents (for example, the headings have been italicized in only one of the two documents), and if you choose to have Word find formatting, Word will prompt you to decide which document's formatting to display.

Although the formatting from only one document will be displayed, all formatting differences will be indicated with change marking. By accepting or rejecting these tracked changes, you can decide which version of the formatting to use for each instance.

To merge two documents, perform the following steps:

1 Open either of the documents you want to merge; it doesn't matter which one you open first. (The remaining instructions refer to this as the *first* document.)

2 Choose Tools, Compare And Merge Documents. In the Compare And Merge Documents dialog box, select the second document you want to merge. (This dialog box works just like the standard Open dialog box.)

3 In the Compare And Merge Documents dialog box, clear the Legal Blackline check box.

4 If you want Word to mark formatting differences so you can later choose which formatting to use wherever there's a difference, check the Find Formatting option.

5 In the Compare And Merge Documents dialog box, do one of the following:

- To overwrite the second document with the resulting merged document, click the Merge button. This will preserve the current contents of the first document.

- To overwrite the first document with the resulting merged document, click the down arrow on the Merge button and choose Merge Into Current Document. This will preserve the current contents of the second document.

- To store the merged document in a new file, choose Merge Into New Document from the Merge drop-down menu. This will preserve the current contents of both the first and the second document.

> **note** If you choose the name of an existing document when you save a document using the Save As dialog box, Word will display a message box giving you the opportunity to merge the two documents into the existing document, rather than simply overwriting it. Also, if you attempt to open a shared network document that is currently locked by another user, Word will display a message box; one of the options in this message box lets you create a local copy of the document and then later merge that copy with the original document.

Whenever you simply want to determine the differences between two documents, you can compare rather than merge them, by performing the following steps:

1 Open one of the documents you want to compare. (In the remaining instructions, this is referred to as the *first* document.)

2   Choose Tools, Compare And Merge Documents. In the Compare And Merge Documents dialog box, select the second document for the comparison. (This dialog box works just like the standard Open dialog box.)

3   Check the Legal Blackline option.

4   If you want Word to mark formatting differences, check the Find Formatting option.

5   Click the Compare button.

Word will then create a new document that contains the text from the second document, *plus* all the marked changes that would be required to produce the first document—just as if you had opened the second document, turned on change tracking, and then edited the text so that it matched the first document. If you rejected all marked changes in the new document, you would end up with the second document, but if you accepted all marked changes, you would end up with the first document. (That sentence might take a moment's thought to understand!)

Inserting Comments in Documents

You can add comments that refer to specific blocks of text within a Word document without altering the main document text. You can use comments to store alternative text, criticisms, ideas for other topics, research notes, and other information useful in developing a document. Or, you can use them for communicating ideas, corrections, requests, or other information to others who are working on the document.

You can exchange comments about a shared online document using the Web Discussions feature in Word, or through a SharePoint team Web site. For more information, see "Discussing an Online Document," on page 193.

Inserting Comments

You can insert comments while you are in Web Layout or Print Layout view, or in Normal or Outline view. (You can't insert a comment while in Print Preview view.) In the former two views, a comment's text is displayed in a balloon in the margin (just like a tracked change), which makes it easy to insert, view, or edit the text (see Figure 16-9, on page 458). In the latter two views, you must enter or edit the comment text in a separate Reviewing pane at the bottom of the document window (as in previous versions of Word), making it less convenient to insert, view, or edit comment text (see Figure 16-10, on page 458). In all views, revisions are marked in the main part of the document with thin bracket symbols, which don't take up space in the text and don't throw off line and page breaks.

Reviewing toolbar

Comment marker for a comment that's not attached to text

Comment markers for a comment that's attached to a block of text

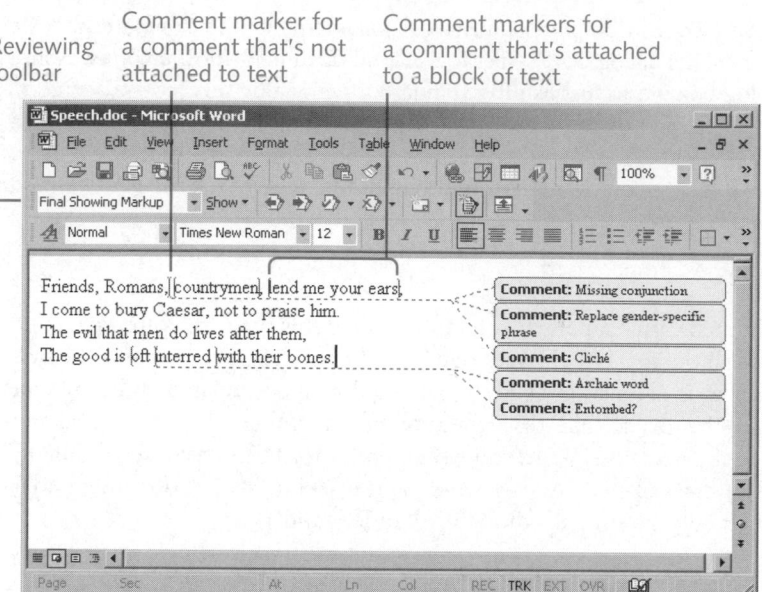

Figure 16-9. A document with comments is displayed in Web Layout view.

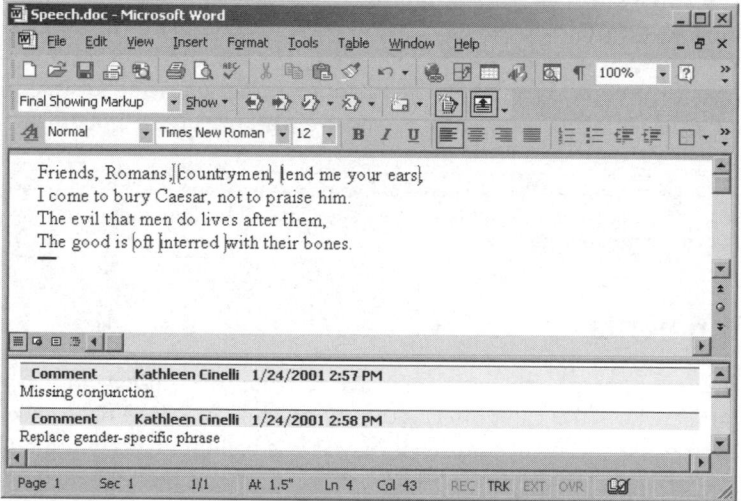

Figure 16-10. A document with comments is displayed in Normal view, showing the text of the first two comments in the Reviewing pane.

note You can turn off the balloons in Web Layout or Print Layout view by choosing Tools, Options, clicking the Track Changes tab, and clearing the Use Balloons In Print And Web Layout option. You'll then need to enter or edit comment text in the Reviewing pane, as in the Normal or Outline view.

To insert a comment, perform the following steps:

1 If the comment pertains to a specific block of text, select that text. In this case, the comment will be attached to that text, the comment-marking brackets will surround the text, and you'll be able to work with the comment by placing the insertion point anywhere within the text. If the comment isn't associated with a specific block of text (or the related text is more than you want to mark), just place the insertion point at the appropriate position in the document. In this case, the comment won't be attached to text and the comment will be marked with two brackets placed one on top of the other. (The two types of markings are labeled in Figure 16-9.)

2 Choose Insert, Comment. In Web Layout or Print Layout view, this will open a new comment balloon and place the insertion point within it, as shown here:

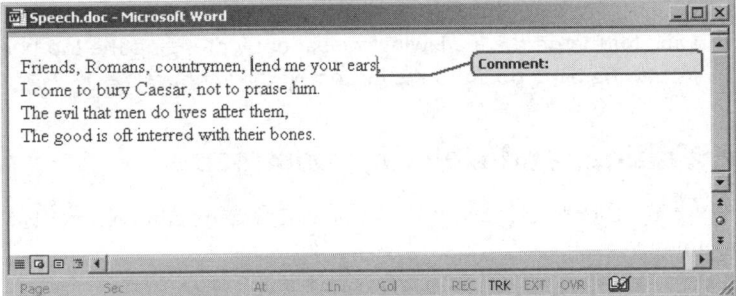

In Normal or Outline view, this will open the Reviewing pane and place the insertion point within a new, blank comment, as shown here:

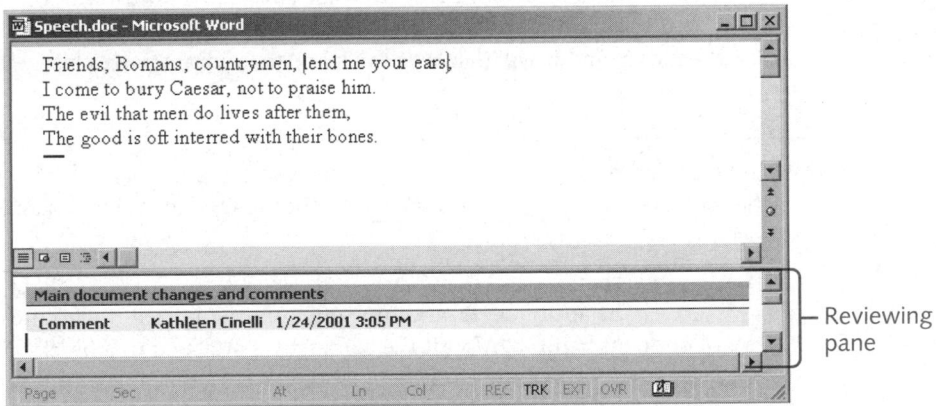

Reviewing pane

When you insert a comment, Word automatically displays the Reviewing toolbar (see Figure 16-11, on page 460). Once it's displayed, you can insert a comment by clicking the New Comment button.

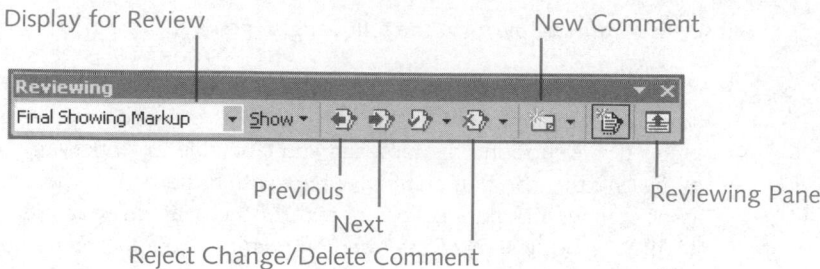

Figure 16-11. The controls on the Reviewing toolbar labeled in this figure are used for working with comments.

3 Type the comment text into the balloon or into the Reviewing pane. When you're done, click back in the document. You can move the insertion point back and forth between the Reviewing pane and the document pane by pressing F6. You can close the Reviewing pane by clicking the Reviewing Pane button on the Reviewing toolbar or by dragging the top border of the Reviewing pane down to the bottom of the window.

Viewing, Editing, and Deleting Comments

In Web Layout or Print Layout view, you can view or edit comments by following these guidelines:

- You can easily read the comment text in the margin balloons. However, if more than one comment (or tracked change) occurs on the same line (as in the first and last lines of the example document shown in Figure 16-9), it can be hard to determine which block of text or position in the line a particular comment balloon is associated with. In this case, you can click the balloon, and it will display a thick line that points more clearly to the associated text.

note The name used to indicate the author of a comment is the name that was contained in the Name box on the User Information tab of the Options dialog box at the time the comment was inserted.

- To see the author, date, and time of a comment, hold the pointer over the comment balloon. Also, if the comment is attached to a block of text, you can hold the pointer over that text (you can't use this method if the comment isn't attached to text). With either method, the comment information will be displayed in a ScreenTip, as seen here:

> **Kathleen Cinelli, 1/24/2001 2:58 PM:**
> Commented

Friends, Romans, countrymen, lend me your ears

Chapter 16: Using Word in Workgroups

- If the text for a comment is long, it might not all be displayed in the balloon. In this case, or if you simply prefer to read the comment in a separate pane, open the Reviewing pane (if it's not already shown) by clicking the Reviewing Pane button on the Reviewing toolbar (see Figure 16-11). Once the Reviewing pane is open, you can navigate to any comment's information and full text by clicking the corresponding balloon.

- You can edit the comment text either in the balloon or in the Reviewing pane.

In Normal or Outline view, you can view or edit comments by following these guidelines:

- If a comment is attached to a block of text, you can view the author, date, time, and content of the comment in a ScreenTip by holding the pointer over the block of text, as shown here:

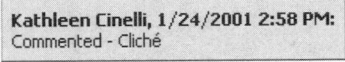

Friends, Romans, countrymen, lend me your ears

- If a comment isn't attached to text, if a comment's text is too long to fit in a ScreenTip, or if you want to edit a comment, place the insertion point anywhere within the commented text (or on the double brackets if the comment isn't associated with a block of text), and choose Edit Comment from the New Comment drop-down menu on the Reviewing toolbar shown here:

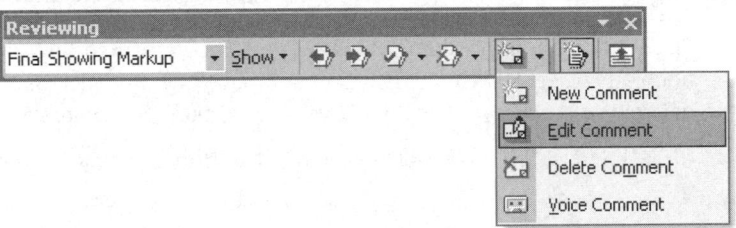

Word will open the Reviewing pane and scroll to the entry for that comment, where you can view the comment information and full text or edit the text. Note that you can also open the Reviewing pane by clicking the Reviewing Pane button on the Reviewing toolbar.

If you have a microphone attached to your sound card, you can add a voice comment, which is an embedded sound object that contains a sound clip that you record (this would usually be a verbal comment about the document). You can add a voice comment to the text of a regular comment or you can add it directly to the main text in your document. You can insert a voice comment in any view except Print Preview by performing the following steps:

1 Place the insertion point at the position in the text where you want to insert it (if text is selected, the voice comment object will be inserted before the selected text). You can insert a voice comment within comment text (in a comment balloon, or in the Reviewing pane) or anywhere within the main document text. However, keep in mind that adding a voice comment to the main text will insert an obtrusive embedded object that will take up space in the document, will throw off line breaks, and will be included on a printed copy of the document.

2 From the New Comment drop-down menu on the Reviewing toolbar, choose Voice Comment.

3 Record your comment using the Sound Object dialog box, seen here:

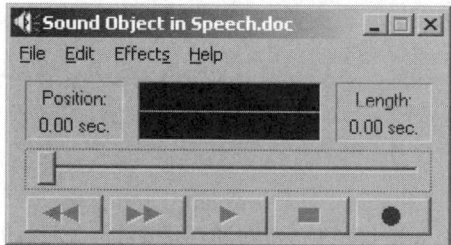

When you're done, choose File, Exit & Return in the Sound Object dialog box. This will insert an embedded sound object into your document. You can double-click this object to play back the sound clip.

You can delete a single comment in any view by performing the following steps:

1 Place the insertion point anywhere within the commented text (or on the double brackets if the comment isn't associated with a block of text). Alternatively, in Web Layout or Print Layout view, click the comment balloon.

2 Click the Reject Change/Delete Comment button on the Reviewing toolbar.

> **note** In Web Layout or Print Layout view, you can also delete a single comment by right-clicking the comment balloon and choosing Delete Comment from the shortcut menu.

To delete a group of comments or all comments, in any view, perform the following steps:

1 If you want to delete only the comments created by one or more particular authors who have added comments to the document, check just those authors on the Reviewers submenu of the Show drop-down menu on the Reviewing toolbar. Word will then display only the comments created by the selected authors.

2 Click the down arrow on the Reject Change/Delete Comment button on the
Review toolbar to open the drop-down menu shown here:

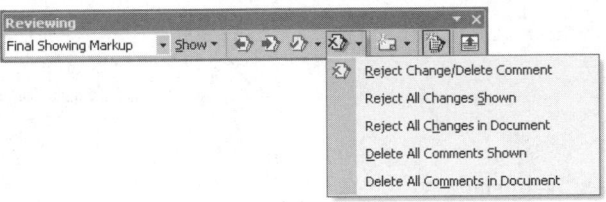

Then, choose a command as follows:

- If you displayed only the comments created by selected authors in step
  1, you can remove just those comments by choosing Delete All Comments Shown.

- To remove *all* comments, whether or not they are currently displayed,
  choose Delete All Comments In Document.

---

tip **Edit or Delete a Comment Using the Shortcut Menu**

If a comment is associated with a block of text, you can edit or delete it in any
view by right-clicking anywhere within the commented text and then choosing Edit
Comment or Delete Comment from the shortcut menu.

Troubleshooting

You Need to Scroll to See Change or Comment Balloons

*You're working in Print Layout view, but you can't see both the document text and all of
the change or comment balloons in the margin, which forces you to scroll back and forth.*

If you don't need the features of Print Layout view (such as the display of page
breaks, margins, and headers and footers), switch to Web Layout view, which automatically wraps the text so that you can see both the text and the change and comment balloons at once. If you do require Print Layout, reduce the zooming factor as
explained in "Modifying the Way Documents Are Displayed," on page 237.

To navigate through the comments in the document in any view, perform the
following steps:

- To select the next comment following the insertion point, the text selection, or
  the selected comment, click the Next button on the Reviewing toolbar. Word
  will select the next comment balloon (in Web Layout or Print Layout view) or
  the next comment entry in the Reviewing pane (in Normal or Outline view).

- To select the previous comment, click the Previous button.

> **note** If there isn't a next or a previous comment in the document, Word—after prompting you—will wrap around and start searching from the beginning or from the end of the document.

Troubleshooting

Comments Have Disappeared!

When you entered comments into the document, you could see the comment marking brackets in the main text, and in Web Layout and Print Layout views you could see the comment balloons in the margin. Later, however, both disappeared and you're wondering what happened to your comments.

To see comment markings, the Final Showing Markup or the Original Showing Markup mode must be selected in the Display For Review drop-down list on the Reviewing toolbar, *and* the Comments item must be checked on the Show drop-down menu.

> **tip** To switch both these options on at once, you can choose View, Markup.

If comments still don't show up, make sure that the comment author or authors are checked on the Reviewers submenu of the Show drop-down menu on the Reviewing toolbar, or that the All Reviewers option is checked on this submenu.

If the comment markers are shown in Web Layout, Print Layout, or Print Preview view, but not the comment balloons, choose Tools, Options, click the Track Changes tab, and check the Use Balloons In Print And Web Layout option.

Highlighting Text

You can use the Highlight button in Word to permanently mark blocks of text in a document, much the same way you use a colored marker to highlight text on a printed page. The text you mark is highlighted both on the screen and on the printed copy of the document. Highlighting is useful for drawing attention to specific blocks of text, either for your own benefit or to communicate with other members of your workgroup. Word provides a variety of highlighting colors, so you can color-code your highlighted text (for example, you could highlight important text in yellow, potential deletions in green, and so on).

To highlight a block of text, perform the following steps:

1 Select the text you want to highlight.

Highlight

2 To highlight using the color currently shown on the Highlight button on the Formatting toolbar (which is the most recently selected color), just click the Highlight button. To highlight using a different color, click the down arrow on the right side of this button, and then click the color you want on the drop-down palette shown here:

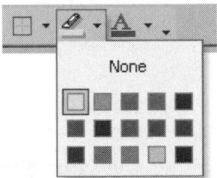

You can rapidly highlight several blocks of text as follows:

1 Without selecting text beforehand, click the Highlight button or click a color on its drop-down palette, as described previously.

2 Using the mouse, drag over each block of text that you want to highlight.

3 When you have finished highlighting text, click the Highlight button again or press Esc to return to normal editing mode.

---

tip **Find Highlighting**

You can easily locate blocks of highlighted text in your document by using the Find command. Choose Edit, Find, and in the Find tab, click the More button (if the Search Options are not displayed), click the Format button, and choose Highlight from the menu shown here:

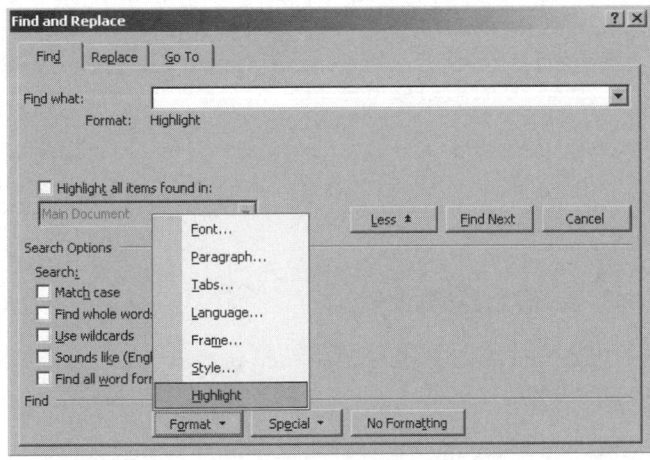

You can remove highlighting by doing the following:

1 Select the text from which you want to remove the highlighting.

2 Click the down arrow on the right side of the Highlight button, and click None on the drop-down palette, as shown here:

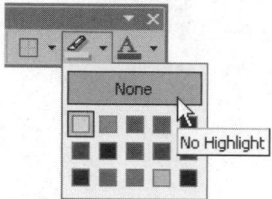

Alternatively, if the Highlight button currently shows the same color as the highlighting applied to the text, you can simply click the button. (You could also remove highlighting by choosing the same color from the drop-down palette, but it's probably easier to choose None.)

---

tip **Hide Highlighting**

You can temporarily hide all highlighting on the screen by choosing Tools, Options, clicking the View tab, and clearing the Highlight option in the Show area. You can make highlighting reappear by checking this same option. Also, highlighting will automatically become visible if you add new highlighting to a document. If highlighting is hidden on the screen, it will also be hidden on printed copies of the document.

You can quickly remove highlighting from several blocks of text using the same technique described for highlighting several blocks. In step 1, simply click the None item on the palette.

---

tip **Print Highlighting Effectively**

If you print a document containing highlighting on a monochrome printer, the highlight color will be converted to a shade of gray. For best results on a monochrome printer, choose a light highlighting color, such as yellow, bright green, or turquoise.

Sharing Word Documents

You can easily share Word documents with other members of your workgroup, using any of the following methods:

- Store documents on a shared network drive to which members of your workgroup have access.

- Store documents on a Web site running SharePoint Team Services or other Microsoft server extensions.

- Store documents on an FTP site on the Internet or on a company intranet.

- Store documents in shared Exchange Server folders.

- Exchange documents using e-mail.

- Exchange documents using floppy disks or other portable media.

> For information on saving or opening documents on a network drive, an FTP site, or a Web site, see Chapter 4, "Working with Office XP Applications, Documents, and Program Windows."

The remaining sections in this chapter discuss the following topics related to sharing Word documents:

- Sharing documents on a network

- Sharing documents using e-mail

- Protecting your shared documents

- Sharing fonts

Sharing Word Documents on a Network

Chapter 4, "Working with Office XP Applications, Documents, and Program Windows," discussed the general methods for saving and opening Office documents on shared network drives to which you have access. When a network user has a document open in Word, the document is locked to prevent other network users from opening and editing the document in a way that would cause conflicts or loss of edits. If you attempt to open a locked document, Word will display this message box:

Choose an option as follows:

- To open the document in read-only mode, select Open A Read Only Copy. You'll actually be able to freely edit the document. However, when you issue the Save command, Word will display the Save As dialog box and you'll have to select a new filename or location, saving a separate copy of the document rather than overwriting the original copy. If you wish, you can later merge the two document versions.

467

> To merge document versions, use the techniques discussed in "Merging and Comparing Documents," on page 455.

● To open the document in read-only mode and later merge your copy of the document with the original, select Create A Local Copy And Merge Your Changes Later. This option is almost the same as Open A Read Only Copy, except that if you still have the document open when the first user closes the original copy of the document, Word will display a message box that lets you merge your copy of the document with the original, as shown here:

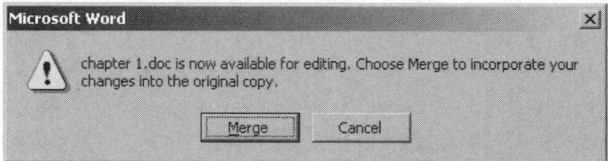

If you choose to merge, Word will add the resulting merged document to the original document copy, and you can accept or reject any of the merged text or formatting.

> Merging documents is discussed in "Merging and Comparing Documents," on page 455

● To open the document in read-only mode but have Word notify you when the original copy is closed, select Receive Notification When The Original Copy Is Available. This option is the same as Open A Read Only Copy, except that when the first user closes the original copy, Word will display the message box shown here, which lets you open the original copy in normal read-write mode:

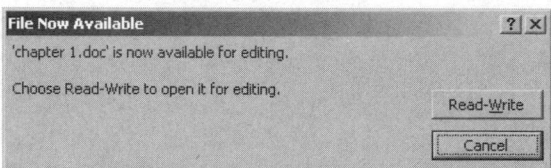

If you wish, you can later merge any edits you made in the read-only copy with the original copy.

> To merge edits, use the techniques discussed in "Merging and Comparing Documents," on page 455.

Sharing Word Documents Using E-Mail

You can easily send a Word document to a co-worker by attaching it to an e-mail message. You can also send a Word document to a co-worker via e-mail by opening the document in Word and choosing a command from the File, Send To submenu, shown at the top of the next page.

Chapter 16: Using Word in Workgroups

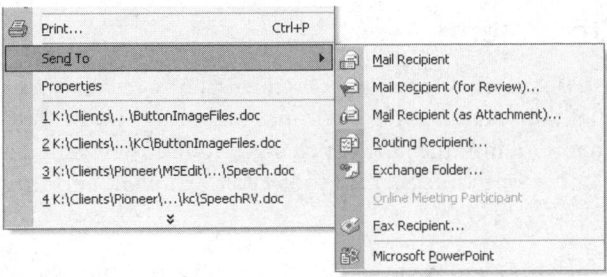

Choose a command as follows:

E-Mail

- To send a copy of the document in the body of an e-mail message, choose Mail Recipient. You can also do this by clicking the E-Mail button on the Standard toolbar.

- To e-mail the document to one or more reviewers, choose Mail Recipient (For Review). This will create an e-mail message that includes the document either as a link (if the document is contained in a shared network or Web location) or as an attachment (if the document isn't contained in a shared location). The document will be specially marked for review. As a result, Word will automatically display the reviewing tools when a recipient opens the document and, when the reviewed copy of the document is returned to you, Word will prompt you to merge the changes back into the original document.

- To create an e-mail message and send a copy of the document as an attachment to that message, choose Mail Recipient (As Attachment).

- To e-mail the document to a group of co-workers, either sequentially or all at once, choose Routing Recipient. Word will open the Routing Slip dialog box, in which you can enter a list of recipients from your Outlook address book, type a subject and a message, protect the document if you wish (as described in the next section), and set other options. Word will create an e-mail message and include a copy of the document as an attachment to this message. The attached document will internally store a *routing slip* containing the list of recipients and their e-mail addresses. When a recipient has finished reading or editing the document, he or she can choose File, Send To, Other Routing Recipient in Word to send the document to the next recipient on the list. Eventually, the document will come back to you.

- To use Word's Fax Wizard to fax a copy of the document to a co-worker using your fax modem, choose Fax Recipient.

> For information on how to send e-mail message attachments with Microsoft Outlook 2002, or how to work with attachments you've received, see "Receiving and Sending E-mail Messages Using the E-mail Folders," on page 1021.

Protecting Shared Documents

Before you distribute a document—or copies of a document—to other members of your workgroup so that they can review, edit, or make additions to the document, you can protect the document to limit the kinds of changes your co-workers can make, thereby ensuring the document's integrity. To protect a document, perform the following steps:

1 Make sure the document you want to protect is displayed in the active document window.

2 Choose Tools, Protect Document to open the Protect Document dialog box, shown here:

3 Choose one of these three types of protection in the Protect Document For area of the dialog box:

■ To permanently turn on change tracking for the document, select the Tracked Changes option. With this option, change tracking can't be disabled, nor can tracked changes be accepted or rejected. (After you remove the document protection, you'll be able to review, accept, or reject any of the changes that reviewers made.) Note that selecting this option also permits comments to be added to the document.

■ To allow reviewers to add comments to the document, but to prevent them from changing the actual document text, select the Comments option.

■ If you added a *form* to the document, to prevent changes except within form fields (such as check boxes or text boxes), select the Forms option. (A form is a collection of check boxes, text boxes, and other fields that you add to a Word document for collecting information.) Also, if you have divided your document into sections, you can select the Forms option to disallow all changes within one or more specific document sections. Click the Sections button to select the particular section or sections you want to protect.

4 To prevent reviewers from removing the protection, type a password into the Password box. (Word will display only asterisk characters as you type.) You'll be asked to retype the password after you click OK.

Note that the protection you choose will apply to you as well as to other users. However, because you have the password, you'll be able to remove the protection when necessary.

If you have routed a single copy of the document among the members of your workgroup, when you receive the document back, you'll probably want to remove the protection. You can do so by choosing Tools, Unprotect Document. (When the document is protected, Unprotect Document replaces the Protect Document command.) If you entered a password when you protected the document, Word will prompt you for it.

If you have distributed a separate copy of the document to each member of the workgroup, when these documents are returned to you, you can merge the changes they contain into the original document.

Merging changes is explained in "Merging and Comparing Documents," on page 455.

File-Sharing Protection

You can also protect a document against unauthorized changes by selecting file-sharing options, using the following steps:

1 Open the document you want to protect.

2 Choose Tools, Options, and click the new Security tab (Figure 16-12). If the Save As dialog box is currently displayed, you can open the Security tab by choosing Security Options from the Tools drop-down menu.

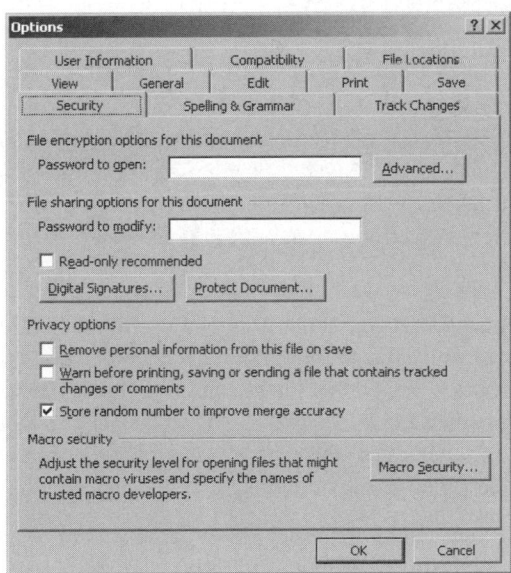

Figure 16-12. This figure shows the Security tab of the Options dialog box.

3 Set one or more of the options in the top portion of the Security tab, as follows:

- To encrypt the document and prevent unauthorized users from open-ing (and decrypting) the document, type a password into the Password To Open text box. Word will ask you to retype the password when you click OK. No user will be able to open the document in Word without typing this password, and because the document is encrypted, no one will be able to read its contents by using other software. To select the type of encryption that Word uses, click the Advanced button.

> **note** An open password or a modify password is case-sensitive—that is, you'll always have to type it with the same combination of uppercase and lowercase letters.

- To prevent unauthorized users from changing the document, type a password into the Password To Modify text box. Word will ask you to retype the password when you click OK. Any user will be able to open the document in read-only mode, which doesn't allow the user to save changes to the original copy of the document. Only users who know the password, however, will be able to open the document in the nor-mal read-write mode, which allows them to save changes to the origi-nal document copy.

> **caution** If you forget a document-protecting password, you won't be able to open the document (for an open password) or modify the document (for a modify password), nor will you be able to recover the password.

- To have Word suggest that users open the document in read-only mode, check the Read-Only Recommended option. When any user opens the document, Word will display a message suggesting that the document be opened in read-only mode. The user, however, can choose whether to open the document in read-only or in normal read-write mode.

newfeature!

- If you have obtained a digital certificate from a certification authority (such as VeriSign, Inc.) you can digitally sign the document by clicking the Digi-tal Signatures button and adding the certificate to the Signatures tab in the Digital Signature dialog box. A digital signature attached to a document verifies to all document recipients that you created the document and that it hasn't been modified since you signed it.

- To open the Protect Document dialog box, discussed in the previous section, click the Protect Document button.

You can turn off file-sharing protection (assuming that the document is open in the normal read-write mode) by opening the Security tab again and then deleting the pass-word or deselecting the Read-Only Recommended option.

Note that you can open any document in read-only mode—even one that's not protected—by choosing File, Open, clicking the down arrow to the right of the Open button, and choosing the Open Read-Only option from the drop-down menu shown here:

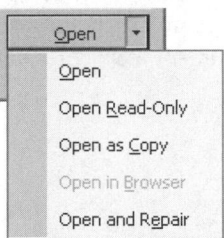

When you open a document in read-only mode, you can freely make changes to its contents. You can't, however, save the modified document under the same name (that is, you can't overwrite the original document version with the changed version), although you can save a copy of the modified document under a different name by choosing File, Save As.

> When you share Word documents with others, you should take precautions against receiving viruses contained in Word macros. For information on macro security, see "Setting Macro Security," on page 1479.

Sharing Fonts

One problem that you might encounter when you work in a workgroup is that a co-worker might not be able to view or print a particular font that you have assigned to text in a document. To avoid this problem, you should make sure that your document uses only TrueType fonts, which are widely available and don't depend on using a particular printer. Common TrueType fonts (such as Times New Roman, Arial, and Courier New) are installed on virtually every computer that runs Windows. If, however, you use one or more TrueType fonts that might not be installed on a co-worker's computer, you can embed TrueType fonts in your document so that your co-worker can view and print them even on a machine that doesn't have them installed. (Doing so, however, will increase the size of the document.)

> For a brief description of TrueType fonts, see "Formatting Characters with the Font Dialog Box," on page 303.

To embed TrueType fonts, perform the following steps:

1 Open the document in which you want to embed fonts.

2 Choose Tools, Options, and click the Save tab.

3 Check the Embed TrueType Fonts option. To reduce the size of the document, you can also check the Embed Characters In Use Only option, which causes Word to save font information only for those characters that actually appear in the document. You can also check Do Not Embed Common System Fonts to avoid wasting space by including common fonts—such as Times New Roman, Arial, and Courier New—that the document recipient is sure to have on his or her computer.

Chapter 17

Proofing Word Documents

Using the Word Proofing Tools

Microsoft Word 2002's proofing tools help you polish your writing and improve the appearance of your documents. Word provides some proofing tools that you can use while you enter the text into a document: namely, the as-you-type spelling and grammar checkers and the thesaurus. It provides other proofing tools—the full-featured spelling and grammar checkers and the hyphenation command—that you generally use after you have finished entering, editing, and formatting the text in your document, but before you preview the printed appearance of the document and make the final adjustments to the page setup, as discussed in the next chapter.

For information on using Word's new formatting consistency checker, see "Checking the Consistency of Your Formatting," on page 323.

Checking Spelling

You can use the Word spelling checker to verify and to help you correct the spelling of the text in your document. You can have Word automatically check your spelling as you type, or you can manually run the full-featured version of the spelling checker to check text that you have already entered.

If your document contains text in a foreign language or text that you want to exclude from proofing, you should perform the steps discussed in "Marking the Language," on page 504, before using the Word spelling, grammar, thesaurus, or hyphenation tools.

Part 3: Word

Checking Your Spelling as You Type

To have Word check your spelling as you type, choose Tools, Options, click the Spelling & Grammar tab, and check the Check Spelling As You Type option in the Spelling section at the top of the tab (see Figure 17-1).

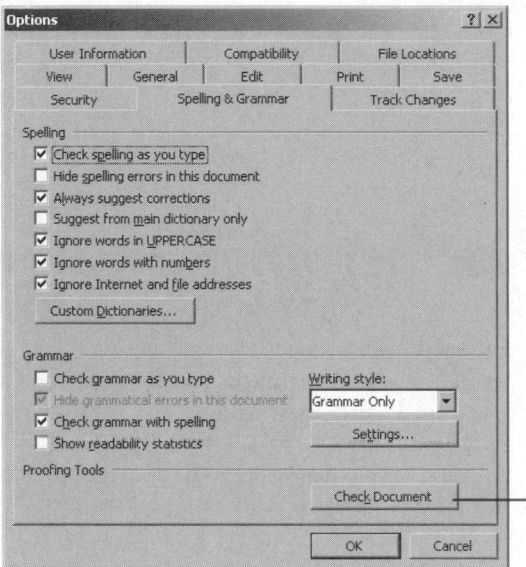

This button is labeled Recheck Document if you have previously checked spelling or grammar in the current document.

Figure 17-1. The Spelling & Grammar tab of the Options dialog box allows you to select options for the spelling checker.

Word will then check the spelling of any text that has already been entered into your document, and it will check the spelling of each new word immediately after you type it. If the spelling checker encounters a word that it judges to be misspelled (that is, a word that it doesn't find in its dictionary), it marks the word with a wavy red underline. You can ignore the word, correct it manually, or right-click it to display the following shortcut menu:

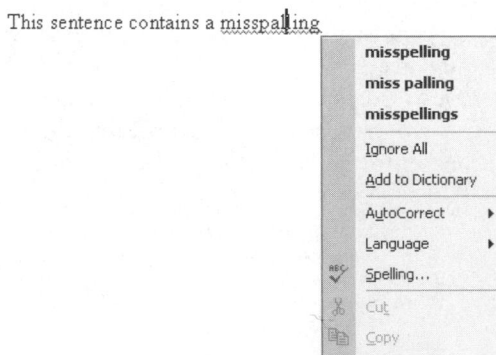

Chapter 17: Proofing Word Documents

From the shortcut menu, choose one of the following options:

- To correct the word, choose one of the suggested spellings in bold type at the top of the menu (if any are shown).

- To have the spelling checker stop marking the word, choose Ignore All. Word will stop marking the word in all documents until you click the Recheck Document button in the Spelling & Grammar tab.

- To add the word to the default custom dictionary so that Word will permanently stop marking it as misspelled, choose Add To Dictionary.

> Custom dictionaries are discussed in "Using Custom Dictionaries," on page 483.

- To correct the word and add the word to AutoCorrect, choose one of the suggested spellings from the AutoCorrect submenu shown here:

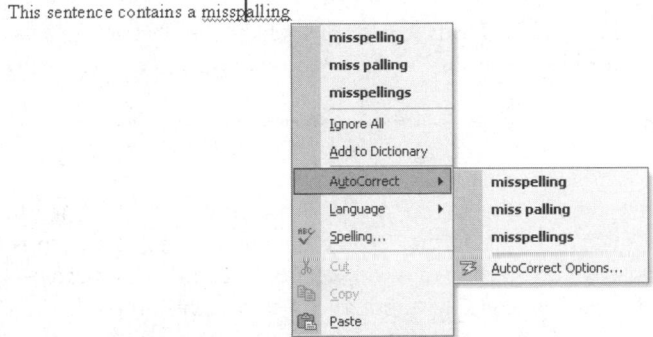

Word will then correct the word in your document and it will add the correction to the Replace Text As You Type list of the AutoCorrect feature. From then on, Word will automatically correct—not just mark—the misspelling whenever you type it, provided that you have checked the Replace Text As You Type option. To locate this option, choose Tools, AutoCorrect Options, and click the AutoCorrect tab in the AutoCorrect dialog box.

- To change the language formatting of the wavy underlined text, use the Language submenu.

> Language formatting is discussed in "Marking the Language," on page 504.

- To open the Spelling dialog box, choose Spelling. This dialog box provides several additional options for correcting spelling and is described in the next section.

> **note** If the Replace Text As You Type option of the AutoCorrect feature is turned on, Word immediately corrects many common misspellings before the as-you-type spelling checker has a chance to underline the word. For information on this option and on using AutoCorrect, see "Automatically Fixing Your Text with AutoCorrect," on page 258, and see the tip "Use AutoCorrect to Correct Your Spelling," on page 263.

If the as-you-type spelling checker (or the as-you-type grammar checker) has marked one or more words in your document, you can locate (and correct) these words by double-clicking the Spelling And Grammar Status icon on the Word status bar, shown here:

Spelling And Grammar Status

Each time you double-click this icon, Word selects the next marked word or phrase and displays the shortcut menu shown earlier so that you can correct the spelling.

InsideOut

Once you've turned on the as-you-type spelling checker (by checking the Check Spelling As You Type option in the Spelling & Grammar tab, shown in Figure 17-1), the option will stay on as you work with various documents and as you quit and restart Word, until you explicitly turn it off. Once you've turned the option on, can you therefore trust that any word you subsequently type will be correctly spelled unless it has a red underline? Unfortunately, no, because of the Hide Spelling Errors In This Document option, also in the Spelling & Grammar tab. Unlike the Check Spelling As You Type option, Hide Spelling Errors In This Document applies only to the current document. If you or someone else has checked this option for a particular document or for the template used to create that document, even though you've turned on the as-you-type spelling checker and are relying on it to flag your misspellings, misspelled words *won't* be underlined in the document.

So, if you've been using the as-you-type spelling checker, but suspect that Word isn't catching misspellings in the document you're currently typing, make sure that the Hide Spelling Errors In This Document option *isn't* checked. And if this option is always checked for the new documents you create based on a particular template, open that template, clear the option, and resave the template file. You might also routinely verify that this option is off before sending out important documents to avoid embarrassing spelling errors.

Checking the Spelling of Existing Text

Another way to check your spelling is to manually run the full-featured, dialog-box version of the spelling checker *after* you've entered a block of text or an entire document. If you're planning to run the full-featured spelling checker, you might want to turn off the as-you-type spelling checker so you won't be bothered with the wavy underlines while you write.

To check the spelling of text you have already entered, perform the following steps:

1 If you want to check the spelling of your entire document, place the insertion point anywhere in the document. (Word will check spelling from the position of the insertion point to the end of the document, and then from the beginning of the document down to the insertion point.) If you want to check the spelling of a portion of your document, select that portion. (Recall that you can quickly select a single word by double-clicking it.)

Spelling
And
Grammar

2 Begin the spelling check by choosing Tools, Spelling And Grammar, by clicking the Spelling And Grammar button on the Standard toolbar, or by pressing F7.

3 Whenever the spelling checker encounters a word that it can't find in its dictionary, it selects the word in the document and displays the Spelling And Grammar dialog box (see Figure 17-2). Within this dialog box, the Not In Dictionary box displays a copy of the sentence containing the questionable word (which is shown in red). The Suggestions list contains one or more possible correct spellings for the word (provided that the spelling checker can derive any, and that the Always Suggest Corrections option is selected, as discussed later).

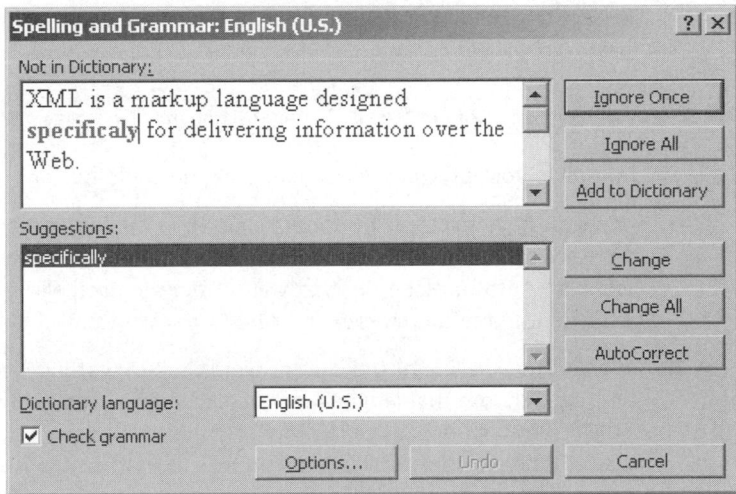

Figure 17-2. The Spelling And Grammar dialog box flags each spelling error.

To deal with this word, you should do one or more of the following:

- To change the word and then search for the next misspelling, either correct the spelling of the word within the Not In Dictionary box (for your convenience, Word places the insertion point just after the word), or simply select the correct spelling—if present—in the Suggestions list. Then click the Change button or the Change All button. Clicking Change will replace only the current occurrence of the word. Clicking Change All will replace the current occurrence of the word plus all occurrences that the spelling checker subsequently finds in the document. (It won't correct any occurrences that the spelling checker previously encountered and you chose to ignore; nor will it correct occurrences in text that you don't check—for example, if you're checking only a selected block of text or if you stop the spelling checker before it has finished checking the whole document, the word won't be corrected in the unchecked portions of the document.)

  If you edit the word within the Not In Dictionary box, you can click the Undo Edit button (which replaces the Ignore button) before you click another button, to restore the word. Also, if you retype the word in the Not In Dictionary box and Word still doesn't recognize the spelling, it will flag the word again.

- To leave the word unchanged and search for the next misspelling, click the Ignore Once or Ignore All button. If you click Ignore Once, the spelling checker will continue to flag other occurrences of the word that it subsequently finds. If you click Ignore All, Word will not flag the word again during the remainder of the spelling check or during any future spelling check in any document (even if you quit and restart Word) until you click the Recheck Document button in the Spelling & Grammar tab (as described in Table 17-1 in the next section).

- To leave the word unchanged and add it to your default custom dictionary so that Word will permanently stop flagging it, click the Add To Dictionary button.

Custom dictionaries are discussed in "Using Custom Dictionaries," on page 483.

- To reverse your previous correction, click the Undo button.

- After you have selected the correct spelling in the Suggestions list or have manually corrected the word in the Not In Dictionary box, to have Word define an AutoCorrect entry that will correct the misspelling whenever you type it in the future, click the AutoCorrect button.

- To check the spelling of the current word using a word list for a different language, choose that language in the Dictionary Language drop-down list. (The Dictionary Language drop-down list is displayed only if you've enabled one or more additional languages using the Microsoft Office Language Settings dialog box. This list contains the languages for which dictionaries have been installed—initially, dialects of English, French, and

Spanish.) For example, if the current word is *colour* and you choose English (U.K.) in the Dictionary Language list, the spelling checker would accept the spelling and search for the next misspelling. (However, if the word is *coluor*, it would remain displayed as a misspelling.)

See "Taking Advantage of Automatic Language Detection, on page 506, for information on enabling languages using the Microsoft Office Language Settings dialog box.

■ To have Word start or stop checking your grammar throughout the remainder of the document or selection, check or clear the Check Grammar option (near the bottom of the Spelling And Grammar dialog box).

note If the Check Grammar With Spelling option in the Spelling & Grammar tab of the Options dialog box (opened by choosing Tools, Options) was checked before you ran the spelling check, after Word checks the spelling of the words in each sentence, it checks the grammar of the sentence. You can start or stop grammar checking during a spelling check by checking or clearing the Check Grammar option in the Spelling And Grammar dialog box. Checking grammar is discussed in "Checking Your Grammar," on page 486.

■ To change the way Word checks your spelling, click the Options button. (Spelling options are discussed in the next section.)

4 The spelling checker will also stop at any word that repeats the previous word (except for words that are commonly repeated, such as *that* and *had*). When the spelling checker encounters a repeated word, it replaces the Change button with the Delete button. You can click Ignore Once to leave the repeated word in the document or click Delete to delete the second word.

tip **Edit While You Display the Spelling And Grammar Dialog Box**

You can edit your document while the Spelling And Grammar dialog box remains displayed. To edit, click in the document. To start checking spelling again, click the Resume button in the Spelling And Grammar dialog box. Word will start checking from the current position of the insertion point, or within the current selection, not necessarily from the point where it left off.

If the Check Grammar With Spelling and the Show Readability Statistics options were checked before you ran the spelling check, after Word completes the spelling and grammar check, it will display readability statistics. (You access these options by choosing Tools, Options and clicking the Spelling & Grammar tab. You can't check Show Readability Statistics unless Check Grammar With Spelling is also checked.)

These readability statistics are described in "Checking the Grammar of Existing Text," on page 489.

Customizing the Spelling Checker

You can tailor the way Word checks your spelling by clicking the Options button in the Spelling And Grammar dialog box to open the Spelling & Grammar tab, which was shown in Figure 17-1, on page 476. You can also display the Spelling & Grammar tab by choosing Tools, Options and then clicking this tab in the Options dialog box. Table 17-1 describes the ways you can use the Spelling & Grammar tab to modify the spelling checker. Note that changes you make affect both the as-you-type spelling checker and the full-featured spelling checker unless otherwise noted in the table.

> The Check Spelling As You Type and Hide Spelling Errors In This Document options were discussed in the previous section, and the options that affect the grammar checker are covered in "Customizing the Grammar Checker," on page 492.

Table 17-1. **Modifying the Word Spelling Checker in the Spelling & Grammar Tab**

To Do This	Perform This Action in the Spelling & Grammar Tab
Have Word display, if possible, one or more replacement words in the Suggestions list in the Spelling And Grammar dialog box, whenever the spelling checker finds a misspelled word. You can choose an appropriate replacement word from this list to instantly correct your misspelling. This option doesn't affect the as-you-type spelling checker.	Check the Always Suggest Corrections option.
Have the spelling checker suggest words only from its main dictionary and not from any custom dictionaries. Word, however, will continue to use both its main dictionaries and all custom dictionaries to check spelling. (Custom dictionaries are discussed in the next section.)	Check the Suggest From Main Dictionary Only option.
Have the spelling checker omit checking the spelling of words that are in all capital letters. This option prevents the spelling checker from flagging acronyms.	Check the Ignore Words In UPPERCASE option.
Have the spelling checker omit checking the spelling of words that contain one or more numbers, such as 3-D.	Check the Ignore Words With Numbers option.
Have the spelling checker omit checking the spelling of Internet addresses (such as *http://www.microsoft.com*) or file paths (such as C:\Book\Chapter1.doc).	Check the Ignore Internet And File Addresses option.

Table 17-1. *(continued)*

To Do This	Perform This Action in the Spelling & Grammar Tab
Display the Custom Dictionaries dialog box, which allows you to create, open, remove, or edit custom dictionaries, as discussed in the next section.	Click the Custom Dictionaries button.
Have the spelling checker delete its list of ignored words (that is, words for which you chose the Ignore All option), and to begin flagging them again. Also, have the grammar checker delete its list of grammatical errors for which you chose the "ignore rule" option and start flagging them again, as explained later in the chapter.	Click the Recheck Document button (labeled Check Document if you haven't checked spelling or grammar in the current document).

Using Custom Dictionaries

Both the as-you-type spelling checker and the full-featured spelling checker look up words in the main spelling dictionary and in one or more custom dictionaries. When Word is installed, a single custom dictionary file named Custom.dic is created. Initially, this dictionary file is empty. However, every time you click the Add To Dictionary button in the Spelling And Grammar dialog box, and whenever you choose Add To Dictionary from the shortcut menu while you're correcting a word underlined by the as-you-type spelling checker, the current word is added to Custom.dic so that the word will no longer be flagged as misspelled.

If using a single custom dictionary meets your needs, you don't need to do anything except occasionally add a word to it by using the Add To Dictionary command. You might, however, want to create and use one or more special-purpose custom dictionaries. For example, if you write both computer books and science fiction, you might create one dictionary that contains the technical terms you use when writing computer books (perhaps named Computer.dic) and another dictionary that contains the invented words you use when writing science fiction (perhaps named Fiction.dic).

To create a new custom dictionary, perform the following steps:

1 Choose Tools, Options and click the Spelling & Grammar tab, or click the Options button in the Spelling And Grammar dialog box that appears during a spelling check, to open the Spelling & Grammar tab (see Figure 17-1, on page 476).

2 Click the Custom Dictionaries button in the Spelling & Grammar tab to open the Custom Dictionaries dialog box, shown here:

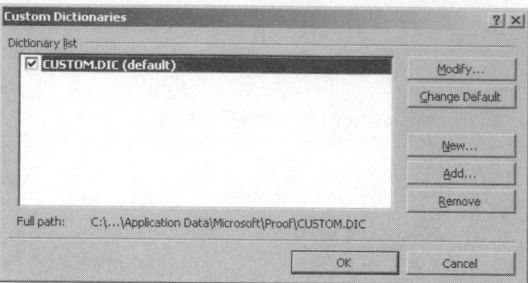

3 Click the New button, and in the Create Custom Dictionary dialog box, type a filename for the dictionary into the File Name text box, seen here:

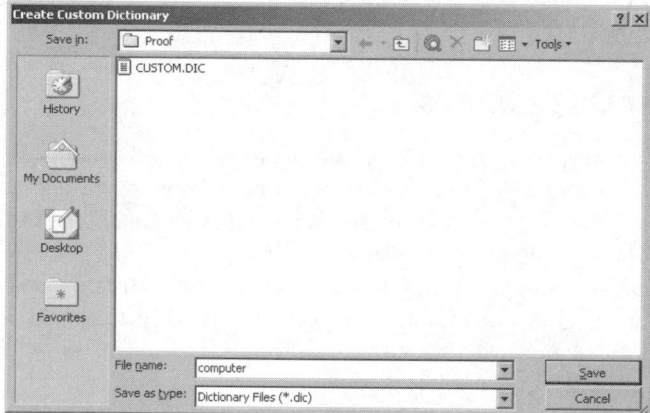

You can either include the .dic extension in the name you type, or omit adding an extension. (In the latter case, Word will add the .dic extension for you.) You can accept the default file location that Word initially selected or you can select a new one. When you click the Save button, Word will create a new, empty custom dictionary. Also, it will add this dictionary to the Dictionary List in the Custom Dictionaries dialog box, and it will check the box next to the dictionary name to indicate that the dictionary has been activated. (Activating custom dictionaries is explained later.)

4 Click the OK button.

To begin using a custom dictionary that you have created or one that you have purchased or obtained from someone else, perform the following steps:

1 *Activate* the dictionary. (If you created a new dictionary using the preceding steps, it should already be activated and you can skip this step.) To activate a dictionary, click the Custom Dictionaries button on the Spelling & Grammar tab (shown in Figure 17-1, on page 476), and check the box next to the name of the dictionary in the Dictionary List, as shown at the top of the next page.

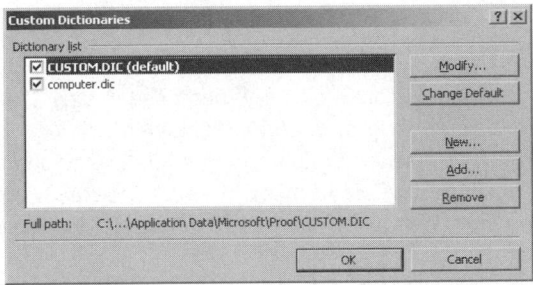

If the dictionary isn't in the list, click the Add button and select the dictionary file. Leave the Custom Dictionaries dialog box open for the next steps.

The spelling checker will look up words in all custom dictionaries that have been activated. To deactivate a dictionary and have Word not use the words it contains, repeat this step but clear the check box next to the dictionary name in the Custom Dictionaries dialog box.

tip **Remove a Dictionary**

While the Custom Dictionaries dialog box is open, you can remove a custom dictionary from the Dictionary List by clicking on it to select it and then clicking the Remove button. This doesn't delete the dictionary file itself, but merely takes it out of the list.

2 To manually add words to your new dictionary, select it in the Dictionary List of the Custom Dictionaries dialog box and click the Modify button. Then, add new words to the dictionary using the dialog box that appears (the name of the dictionary is displayed as the dialog box title), as shown in this example:

You can use this procedure to add or remove words from any custom dictionary.

InsideOut

The dialog box for modifying a custom dictionary (described in step 2) misleadingly allows you to enter phrases consisting of more than one word. However, these entries won't work. For example, if you added the phrase *Thea sinensis* to a custom dictionary, Word would continue to flag occurrences of *Thea sinensis* in your documents. To stop the flagging, you would have to add *Thea* as one word and *sinensis* as another word.

note   If you want a custom dictionary to check text in a specific language, choose that language in the Language drop-down list at the bottom of the dialog box in which you modify the dictionary (described in step 2). The spelling checker will use the dictionary only for text that has been marked for that language, or text that Word's automatic language detection has determined to be in that language. (Marking the language of text is described in "Marking the Language," on page 504.) If you select All Languages in the Language list, the dictionary will be used for all text; regardless of its language.

3 To have Word automatically add words to your custom dictionary, make it the *default* custom dictionary by selecting it in the Dictionary List in the Custom Dictionaries dialog box and clicking the Change Default button. Whenever you click the Add To Dictionary button in the Spelling And Grammar dialog box or choose Add To Dictionary from the shortcut menu of the as-you-type spelling checker, Word adds the current word to the default custom dictionary.

4 Click the OK button in the Custom Dictionaries dialog box and in the Spelling & Grammar tab.

Checking Your Grammar

You can use the Word grammar checker to help polish your writing. The grammar checker indicates possible grammatical errors, such as a disagreement between subject and verb, a double negative, or incorrect punctuation (such as extra spaces inserted between words). It also flags expressions that exhibit possible poor writing style, such as clichés, misused words, or long sentences (more than 60 words). You can have Word automatically check your grammar as you type, or you can manually run the full-featured grammar checker (along with the spelling checker) to check text that you've already entered. When you run the grammar checker manually, you can have it display statistics on the general readability of your document after it has completed its check.

If your document contains text in a foreign language or text that you want to exclude from proofing, you should perform the steps discussed in "Marking the Language," on page 504, before using the Word spelling, grammar, thesaurus, or hyphenation tools.

Checking Your Grammar as You Type

To have Word check your grammar as you type, choose Tools, Options, click the Spelling & Grammar tab, and check the Check Grammar As You Type option (see Figure 17-3).

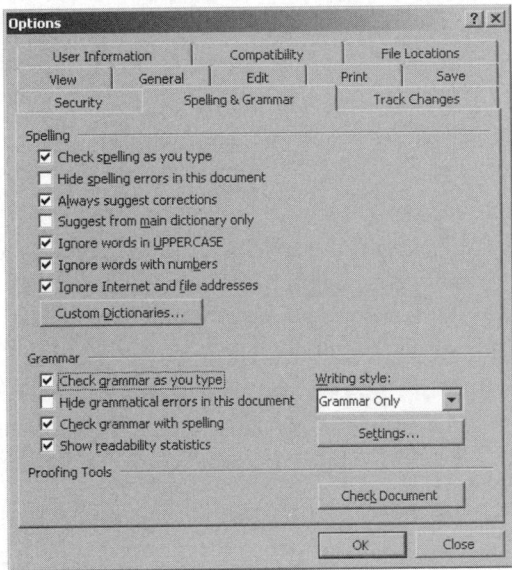

Figure 17-3. The Spelling & Grammar tab of the Options dialog box allows you to activate the as-you-type grammar checker.

Word will then check the grammar of any text that has already been entered into your document, and it will begin checking the grammar of each new sentence you enter, immediately after you finish typing it. If the grammar checker encounters a sentence that violates one of its current grammar or style rules (later you'll see how to modify these rules), it marks the offending portions of the sentence with a wavy green underline. (Recall that Word marks a misspelled word with a wavy *red* underline.) You can then ignore the mark, correct the sentence manually, or right-click the underlined portion to display the following shortcut menu:

This grammar isn't no good.

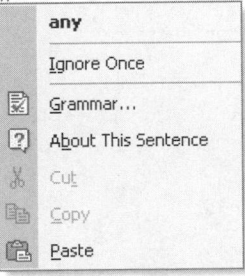

On the shortcut menu, choose one of the following options:

● To have Word correct the sentence, choose one of the suggested grammar corrections displayed in bold type at the top of the menu (if any are given). Note that rather than displaying actual substitute text that you can choose, the menu might display a tip for manually correcting the sentence. For example, if the checker encounters a sentence fragment, the menu displays Fragment (Consider Revising).

● To have the grammar checker ignore the error and remove the wavy underline from the word or words, choose Ignore Once. (Word will, however, continue to search for violations of the same grammar or style rule.)

● To open the Grammar dialog box, which provides additional options for correcting grammatical errors, choose Grammar. This dialog box is the same (except for its title) as the Spelling And Grammar dialog box displayed when you manually run the grammar checker, described in the next section.

● Choose About This Sentence to display an explanation of the grammatical error that was flagged, as shown in the following example. (This command is available only if the Office Assistant is currently enabled.)

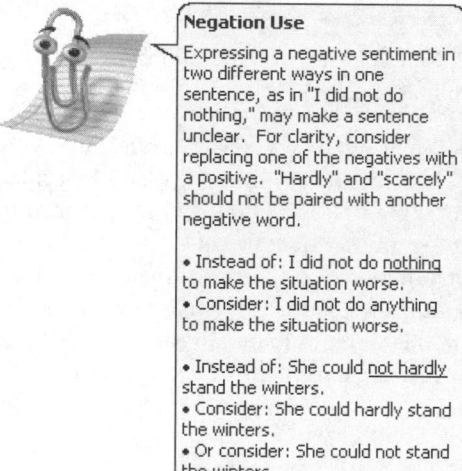

Negation Use

Expressing a negative sentiment in two different ways in one sentence, as in "I did not do nothing," may make a sentence unclear. For clarity, consider replacing one of the negatives with a positive. "Hardly" and "scarcely" should not be paired with another negative word.

• Instead of: I did not do <u>nothing</u> to make the situation worse.
• Consider: I did not do anything to make the situation worse.

• Instead of: She could <u>not hardly</u> stand the winters.
• Consider: She could hardly stand the winters.
• Or consider: She could not stand the winters.

If the as-you-type grammar checker (or the as-you-type spelling checker) has marked one or more errors in your document, you can locate and correct them by double-clicking the Spelling And Grammar Status icon on the Word status bar, shown here:

English (U.S

Spelling And Grammar Status

Each time you double-click this icon, Word moves the insertion point to the next flagged error and displays a shortcut menu for correcting the error.

> **note** If you check the Hide Grammatical Errors In This Document option in the Spelling & Grammar tab of the Options dialog box, Word will remove the wavy lines from all grammar errors in the active document and stop marking them in new text you type into that document. If you rely on Word to flag your grammar errors, see the Inside Out on page 478 regarding the Hide Spelling Errors In This Document option for the as-you-type spelling checker (which works just like Hide Grammatical Errors In This Document).

Checking the Grammar of Existing Text

You might prefer to manually run the full-featured, dialog-box version of the grammar checker to examine the grammar of a block of text—or an entire document—after you have typed it, rather than having to deal with possible grammatical errors while you write. In this case, you can turn off the as-you-type grammar checker or just ignore the wavy underlines. Then, when you're ready to check your grammar, you can run the grammar checker.

To use the full-featured grammar checker, choose Tools, Options, click the Spelling & Grammar tab, and make sure that the Check Grammar With Spelling option is checked. If you want to see readability statistics, make sure that the Show Readability Statistics option is also checked (you can't check this option unless you've also checked the Check Grammar With Spelling option).

When the Check Grammar With Spelling option is checked, Word will run the grammar checker whenever you run the full-featured spelling checker, as described in "Checking the Spelling of Existing Text," on page 479. The specific steps for checking your grammar are as follows:

1 If you want to check your entire document, place the insertion point anywhere in the document. (Word will check grammar from the sentence containing the insertion point to the end of the document, then from the beginning of the document down to the sentence before the one with the insertion point.) If you want to check only a portion of your document, select that portion.

Spelling And Grammar

2 Choose Tools, Spelling And Grammar, click the Spelling And Grammar button on the Standard toolbar, or press F7.

3 For each sentence in the document (or selection), Word first checks the spelling of the words it contains. To handle any word that is flagged as a possible misspelling, follow the instructions that were given in step 3 of the process for checking your spelling on page 479.

4 After checking the spelling of a sentence, Word will check the grammar. If the grammar checker finds a violation of one of its grammar or style rules, it opens the Spelling And Grammar dialog box (see Figure 17-4). At the top of this dialog box is a description of the possible grammar or style violation, together with a copy of the sentence showing the offending words in green. Below this, the Suggestions list displays one or more blocks of replacement text (if the grammar checker can generate a replacement), or a general suggestion to help you manually edit the sentence; for example, Negation Use (Consider Revising).

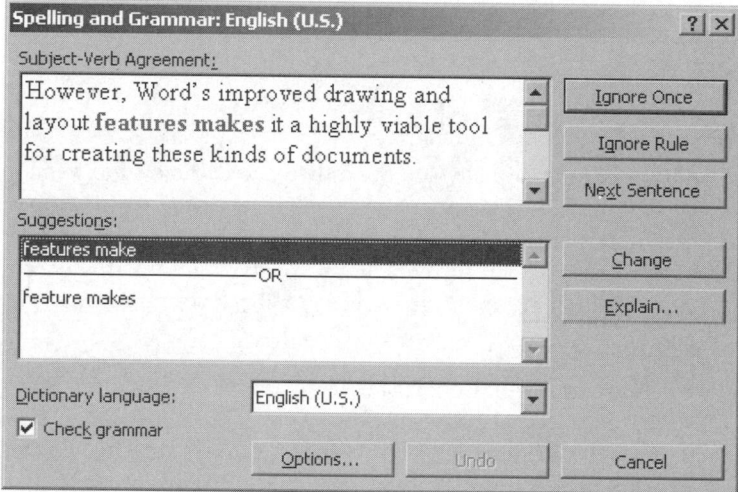

Figure 17-4. The Spelling And Grammar dialog box flags each grammatical error.

To deal with the possible error, do one or more of the following:

- To correct or improve your sentence, either directly edit the copy of the sentence displayed at the top of the Spelling And Grammar dialog box or select a block of replacement text in the Suggestions list (if one is present). Then click the Change button.

- To ignore the suggestions and move on to the next error, click the Ignore Once button. The next error might be in the same sentence.

- To ignore the suggestions for the current sentence and to move on to the next sentence, click the Next Sentence button. If the current sentence has additional errors, the grammar checker will skip them.

- To ignore the suggestions and stop Word from flagging violations of the same grammar or style rule, click Ignore Rule. Violations of the rule won't be flagged again during the remainder of the grammar check, or during any future grammar check in any document (even if you quit and restart Word), until you click the Recheck Document button in the Spelling & Grammar tab, as described in Table 17-1, on page 482. The checker will then move on to the next error.

490

- To reverse your previous correction, click the Undo button.

- To check the current error using the rules for a different language, choose that language in the Dictionary Language drop-down list. (This list contains the languages for which dictionaries have been installed—initially, dialects of English, French, and Spanish.)

- To stop Word from checking your grammar, clear the Check Grammar option. Word will then check only your spelling until you check the option again.

- To modify the way the grammar checker works, click the Options button. (Setting options is explained in the next section.)

---

tip   **Edit While You Display the Spelling And Grammar Dialog Box**

You can edit your document while the Spelling And Grammar dialog box remains displayed. To edit, click in the document. To start checking grammar again, click the Resume button in the Spelling And Grammar dialog box. Word will start checking from the current position of the insertion point, or within the current selection, not necessarily from the point where it left off.

If the Show Readability Statistics option was checked in the Spelling & Grammar tab before you started the spelling and grammar check, Word will display the Readability Statistics dialog box after it has finished the check. This dialog box shows statistics about the text that was checked, including several standard indicators of the general readability of the text. For an explanation of any of the information in the dialog box, click the question-mark icon at the upper-right corner of the dialog box and then click the part of the dialog box displaying the information. Figure 17-5 shows the statistics that Word displayed for the original draft of the chapter you're reading.

Readability Statistics

Counts	
Words	10057
Characters	50795
Paragraphs	379
Sentences	395

Averages	
Sentences per Paragraph	2.1
Words per Sentence	20.3
Characters per Word	4.8

Readability	
Passive Sentences	12%
Flesch Reading Ease	50.8
Flesch-Kincaid Grade Level	11.1

OK

Figure 17-5. This figure shows the Readability Statistics dialog box that was displayed after running a spelling and grammar check on a preliminary draft of this chapter.

newfeature!

tip **Other Ways to Display Document Statistics**

You can display statistics about the number of pages, words, characters, and so on in your document by choosing File, Properties and clicking the Statistics tab, or by choosing Tools, Word Count. You can also display the number of words, characters, lines, pages, or paragraphs by choosing View, Toolbars, Word Count to display the new Word Count toolbar, shown here:

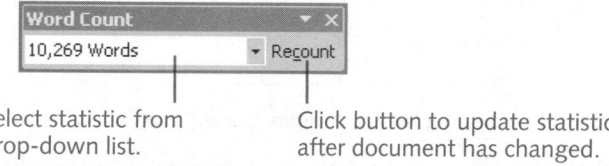

Select statistic from drop-down list.

Click button to update statistic after document has changed.

Customizing the Grammar Checker

You can modify the way the grammar checker works by choosing Tools, Options and clicking the Spelling & Grammar tab in the Options dialog box, shown in Figure 17-3, on page 487. You can also display this tab by clicking the Options button in the Spelling And Grammar dialog box. The options discussed in this section affect both the as-you-type grammar checker and the full-featured grammar checker that you run manually through the Spelling And Grammar command.

To have the grammar checker flag grammatical errors only, select Grammar Only in the Writing Style drop-down list. The checker will then apply only its grammar rules. To have it flag both grammatical errors and stylistic weaknesses, applying both its grammar and its style rules, select Grammar & Style. You can also customize either of these options, specifying exactly which rules the grammar checker applies when you select that option. For example, you could change the Grammar Only option so that it would cause Word to apply some of its grammar rules and some of its style rules. (Doing this, however, would make the name of the option, Grammar Only, a misnomer. Unfortunately, Word doesn't let you create new options with appropriate names.) To customize a Writing Style option, perform the following steps:

1 In the Spelling & Grammar tab, click the Settings button to display the Grammar Settings dialog box (shown in Figure 17-6).

2 Select the option that you want to modify in the Writing Style drop-down list at the top of the Grammar Settings dialog box.

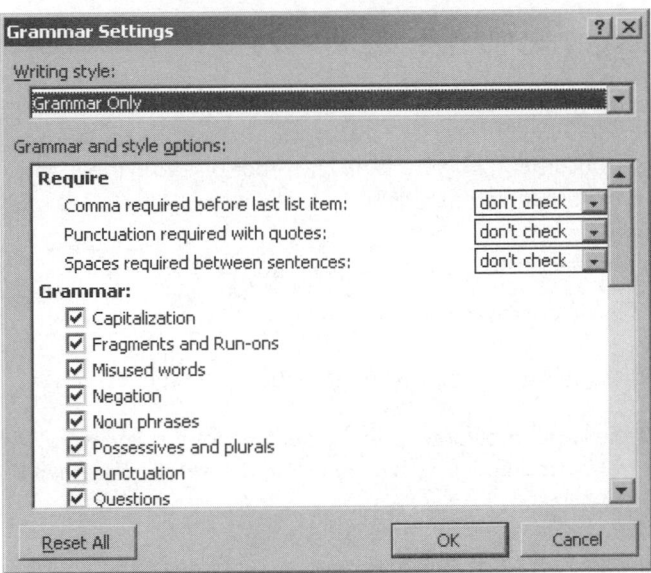

Figure 17-6. The Grammar Settings dialog box allows you to customize the grammar checker Writing Style options.

3 Check or clear the individual grammar or style rules that you want the modified option to apply. (By default, the Grammar Only option applies all the Grammar rules, while the Grammar & Style option applies all the grammar rules plus all the Style rules except Use Of First Person.) Additionally, you can have the option apply one of the three Require rules given at the top of the list, by choosing an option in the drop-down list other than Don't Check. For example, to have Word check your use of a comma after the last item in a list, you would select Always (comma required) or Never (comma not allowed) in the Comma Required Before Last List Item drop-down list, shown here:

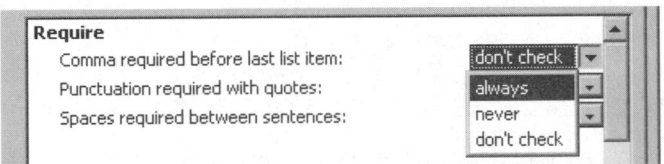

4 To restore the option that's currently selected in the Writing Style drop-down list (Grammar Only or Grammar & Style) to its default set of rules, click the Reset All button.

5 Click the OK button.

Finding Synonyms with the Thesaurus

You can use the Word thesaurus to look up synonyms or antonyms for a word or phrase in your document. You'll probably want to use the thesaurus as you are entering text into your document, in contrast to the other proofing tools, which you often use after you have finished entering text.

> If your document contains text in a foreign language or text that you want to exclude from proofing, you should perform the steps discussed in "Marking the Language," on page 504, before using the Word spelling, grammar, thesaurus, or hyphenation tools.

To use the thesaurus, perform the following basic steps:

1 Select the word or phrase. To find synonyms for a single word, you can just place the insertion point anywhere within the word rather than selecting it, as shown here:

Although perhaps mentally negligible, Bertie Wooster was certainly an agreeable person.

2 Choose Tools, Language, Thesaurus, or press Shift+F7. Word will open the Thesaurus dialog box. Here's the Thesaurus dialog box as it would appear if the word *agreeable* were selected in the document:

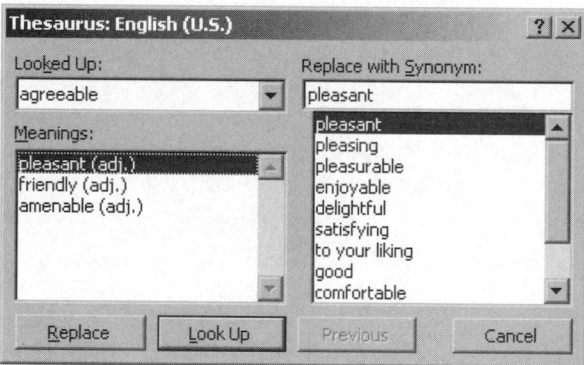

3 In the Meanings list, select the intended meaning of the word. (Note the part of speech following most words: *adj.* for adjective, *adv.* for adverb, *n.* for noun, and so on.) The thesaurus will then list synonyms for this meaning in the Replace With Synonym list.

The Replace With Synonym list might also display one or more antonyms for the selected meaning of the word. Each antonym will be marked with (Antonym), such as the word *unwilling* in the Thesaurus dialog box shown in step 4.

The Meanings list will sometimes contain the item Related Words. Selecting this item displays one or more other forms of the word in the Replace With Synonym list. For example, if the word in the Looked Up box is *going*, the Replace With Synonym list would display *go*.

If the thesaurus doesn't have information on the selected word, it displays an alphabetical list of words with similar spellings. You can select one of these words and click the Look Up button to find synonyms.

---

tip   **Use the Shortcut Menu to Access the Thesaurus**

An alternative way to use the thesaurus is to right-click a word or a selected phrase to display the shortcut menu. Then, from the Synonyms submenu, shown here, either choose a synonym or antonym (if any are displayed), or choose the Thesaurus command to open the Thesaurus dialog box discussed in this procedure.

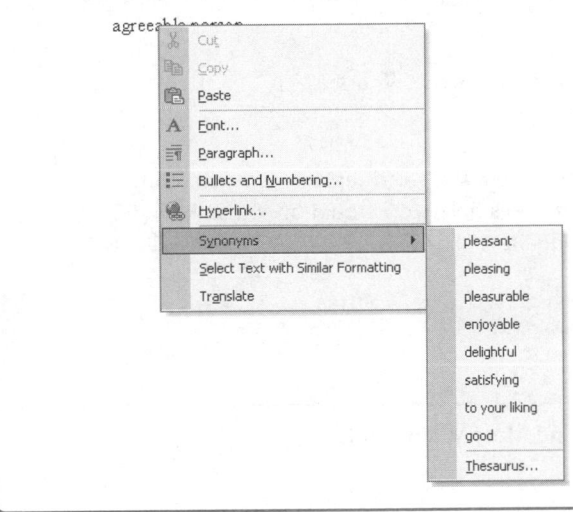

---

4 Click the best synonym (or the best antonym or related word) in the Replace With Synonym list, and click the Replace button. Here's how the Thesaurus dialog box would appear if you looked up *agreeable* and then chose the meaning *amenable* and the synonym *compliant*:

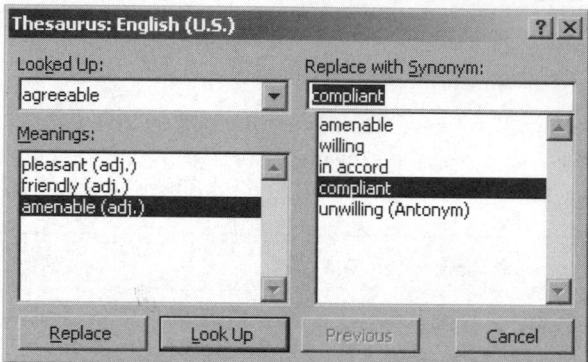

When you click Replace, Word will replace the selected word in the document with the chosen synonym, matching the capitalization of the original word, as in this example:

Although perhaps mentally negligible, Bertie Wooster was certainly an compliant person.

Don't forget to correct the sentence if the word replacement altered the grammar of the sentence. In this example, you would of course have to change the *an* preceding *compliant* to *a*:

Although perhaps mentally negligible, Bertie Wooster was certainly a compliant person.

---

tip **Use the Synonyms Dialog Box to Find More Word Choices**

After selecting a synonym in step 4, you can click the Look Up button to find synonyms for the synonym. (You can also do this by simply double-clicking a synonym in the Replace With Synonym list.) Doing this one or more times might help you find precisely the word you want. Consider this scenario: You look up the word *pretty* and select the synonym *beautiful*, which is better than *pretty* but not perfect. You therefore click the Look Up button again and find the perfect synonym, *gorgeous*.

Also, while the Thesaurus dialog box is displayed, you can look up a synonym for any word by typing the word into the Replace With Synonym text box at the top of the list and then clicking Look Up or pressing Enter.

To return to the previous looked-up word, click the Previous button. To return to any word you looked up while the Thesaurus dialog box was displayed, choose the word from the Looked Up drop-down list.

Chapter 17: Proofing Word Documents

Translating Text

You can use Word's new Translate task pane to translate into a different language either a word, or—by means of a translation service on the Web—a phrase, a block of text, or an entire document. To do so, perform the following steps:

1 Choose Tools, Language, Translate to display the Translate task pane, which is shown in Figure 17-7.

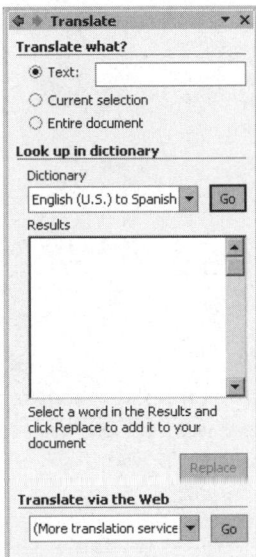

Figure 17-7. The Translate task pane provides you with options for translating text.

2 If you want to translate a word, phrase, or block of text contained in your document, select it.

3 In the Translate What area of the task pane, specify the text that you want to translate, as follows:

- To translate a word or phrase that you enter, select the Text option and type the text into the box.

- To translate text you selected in the document in step 2, select Current Selection.

- To translate the whole document, select Entire Document.

4 Generate the translation, as follows:

- To translate a single word or a phrase of two words, in the Dictionary drop-down list select an item to indicate the languages you want to translate from and to. For example, to translate an English word to Spanish, you could select

Chapter 17

English (U.S.) To Spanish (Spain-Modern Sort). Then, click the Go button. The translation will appear in the Results area, as shown here:

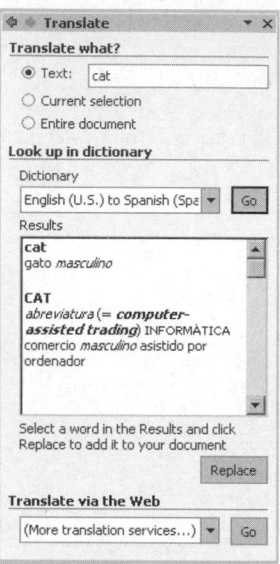

If you selected or entered two words, Word will translate them separately and display both translations in the Results area. If you selected or entered more than two words, rather than displaying a translation, Word will suggest using the Translate Via The Web option, described next.

■ To translate a phrase of more than two words or an entire document using a translation service on the Web, select a specific service in the Translate Via The Web drop-down list, or select (More Translation Services…) to connect to a Web site that will help you choose a service, and then click the Go button to the right of the list.

5 If you selected a word in step 2, you can replace that word with its translation by selecting the translated word in the Results area and clicking the Replace button. If you didn't select text in your document, clicking the Replace button will insert the selected translated word at the position of the insertion point.

Hyphenating Your Documents

You can improve the appearance of a document by hyphenating words at the ends of the lines. Once hyphenated, text that is not justified will be less ragged at the right indent, and justified text will have more uniform spacing between the characters. You can hyphenate your document in one of three ways.

● You can have Word automatically hyphenate your document. The advantage of automatic hyphenation is that it's applied instantly (Word won't ask you to confirm each hyphenation, as it does with manual hyphenation). Also, if you later edit or reformat the document, Word will automatically rehyphenate it as needed. (When you apply automatic hyphenation, Word stores syllable information for all words in the document, so it can immediately hyphenate any word.) If you're creating a Web page, keep in mind that automatic hyphenation will work when you view the page in Word; however, it won't work when you display the page in a browser.

● You can manually hyphenate your document. With manual hyphenation, Word lets you confirm or adjust the placement of each hyphen. If you later edit or reformat the document, however, you'll probably have to rehyphenate the modified text to maintain consistent hyphenation throughout the document. The advantage of manual hyphenation is that it gives you more control over the way words are hyphenated; you can specify the exact location of each hyphen. If you're creating a Web page, keep in mind that manual hyphenation will probably not be very effective when the page is viewed in a browser. (A manually hyphenated word will break properly if it falls at the end of a line. However, because the line lengths are unpredictable in a browser, you would have to hyphenate almost every word to maintain consistent hyphenation.)

● You can insert various types of hyphen characters one at a time.

> If your document contains text in a foreign language or text that you want to exclude from proofing, you should perform the steps discussed in "Marking the Language," on page 504, before using the Word spelling, grammar, thesaurus, or hyphenation tools.

Automatically Hyphenating a Document

To have Word automatically hyphenate the current document, perform the following steps:

1 If you want to exclude one or more paragraphs in your document from hyphenation, select them. Choose Format, Paragraph, click the Line And Page Breaks tab, and check the Don't Hyphenate option.

Automatic hyphenation will affect all paragraphs in the document, except those with Don't Hyphenate paragraph formatting, even if you select only a portion of the document before proceeding. Note that if you later remove the Don't Hyphenate formatting from a paragraph, automatic hyphenation will begin working in that paragraph—you won't have to reapply automatic hyphenation.

> **note** The Don't Hyphenate paragraph formatting excludes a paragraph only from automatic or manual hyphenation. In contrast, the Do Not Check Spelling Or Grammar character formatting (discussed in "Marking the Language," on page 504) excludes text from *all* proofing (spelling, grammar, and hyphenation).

2 Choose Tools, Language, Hyphenation. This will open the Hyphenation dialog box, shown here:

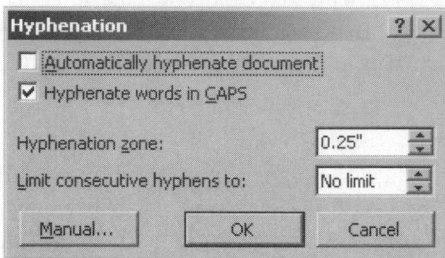

3 In the Hyphenation dialog box, check the Automatically Hyphenate Document option.

4 Choose any other hyphenation options you want in the Hyphenation dialog box, as follows:

- To have Word hyphenate words in all capital letters, such as acronyms, check the Hyphenate Words In CAPS option.

- To adjust the hyphenation zone, explained later, enter a new value into the Hyphenation Zone text box.

- To limit the number of consecutive lines Word will hyphenate, enter a number into the Limit Consecutive Hyphens To text box. Limiting consecutive hyphenations prevents unsightly "stacking" of hyphen characters along the right margin.

5 Click the OK button.

The *hyphenation zone* affects the particular hyphenations that Word performs. It works as follows: When Word encounters a word that extends beyond the right indent, it must decide whether to simply wrap the word (that is, move the entire word down to the next line) or whether to attempt to hyphenate the word. If wrapping the word would leave space at the end of the line that is narrower than the hyphenation zone (.25 inch wide by default), Word wraps it, as shown here:

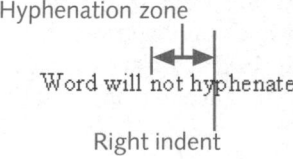

If, however, wrapping the word would leave a space wider than the hyphenation zone, Word attempts to hyphenate it, as seen at the top of the next page.

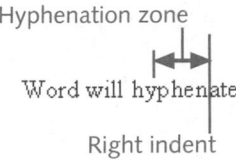

Hyphenation zone

Word will hyphenate

Right indent

(However, if Word can't hyphenate the word so that it fits within the right indent, it will wrap it.)

Choosing a wide hyphenation zone reduces the number of hyphenations that Word will perform, but it increases the raggedness of the margin (or makes the intercharacter spacing less uniform in justified text).

To remove automatic hyphenation from a document, reopen the Hyphenation dialog box, clear the Automatically Hyphenate Document option, and click the OK button.

Manually Hyphenating a Document

To manually hyphenate the current document, perform the following steps:

1 If you want to hyphenate your entire document, place the insertion point anywhere in the document. If you want to hyphenate only part of your document, select the block or blocks of text you want to hyphenate.

2 Choose Tools, Language, Hyphenation. This will open the Hyphenation dialog box, as seen here:

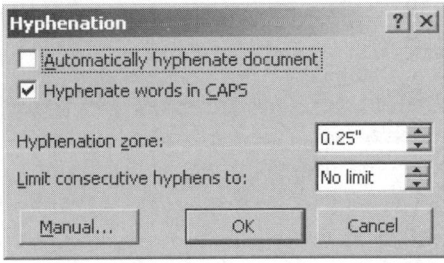

3 In the Hyphenation dialog box, set the hyphenation options you want, but make sure that the Automatically Hyphenate Document option is not checked. These options were explained in the previous section.

4 Click the Manual button. Word will activate Print Layout view and begin looking for possible hyphenations. (When Word is finished hyphenating, it will restore your original document view.)

5 Whenever Word encounters a word that requires hyphenation, it displays the Manual Hyphenation dialog box, which shows the word and the proposed position of the hyphen, together with all other possible hyphen positions in the word, as shown here:

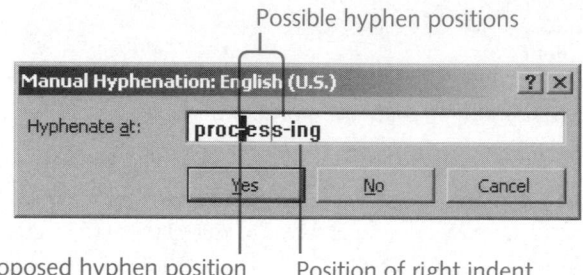

Possible hyphen positions

Proposed hyphen position   Position of right indent

Each possible hyphenation position is marked with a hyphen. The proposed hyphenation position is marked with a blinking highlight in addition to the hyphen. The position of the right indent is marked with a vertical line. Word also carries out the proposed hyphenation in the document and highlights the hyphen character.

You should now do one of the following:

- To hyphenate the word at the proposed position, just click the Yes button.

- To hyphenate the word at a different position (say, to avoid a hyphen after only the first two letters of a long word), use the Left or Right arrow key to move the blinking highlight to that position, and then click Yes.

- To skip hyphenating the word, click No. The word will be wrapped rather than hyphenated.

note You can assign a paragraph the Don't Hyphenate paragraph formatting to exclude it from manual or automatic hyphenation. You can also assign a block of text the Do Not Check Spelling Or Grammar character formatting to exclude the text from *all* proofing (spelling, grammar, and hyphenation).

For information on applying the Don't Hyphenate and other paragraph formatting features, see "Formatting Paragraphs Directly," on page 309. For information on applying the Do Not Check Spelling Or Grammar feature to a block of text, see "Marking the Language," on page 504.

When Word manually hyphenates a word, it inserts a special character known as an *optional hyphen*. If a word containing an optional hyphen is shifted so that it no longer falls at the end of a line, the hyphen is hidden and the letters on either side of the hyphen come together. However, the optional hyphen remains within the word, and it will reappear and allow the word to be broken if the word shifts back to the end of a line.

To remove a manually applied hyphenation, you need to delete the optional hyphen character. You can delete one or more of these characters using either of the following methods:

Show/
Hide ¶

- Make optional hyphens visible by clicking the Show/Hide ¶ button on the Standard toolbar (which displays all nonprinting characters). Or, you can choose Tools, Options, click the View tab, and check the Optional Hyphens option in the Formatting Marks area to make just optional hyphens visible. Then, use standard editing methods to delete the optional hyphen characters.

- To quickly delete optional hyphens throughout your document, choose Edit, Replace, enter the code for an optional hyphen into the Find What box by choosing Optional Hyphen from the Special menu, leave the Replace With box empty, and click Replace or Replace All.

For details on using the Replace command, see "Replacing Text and Formatting," on page 287.

Inserting Hyphen Characters

You can manually insert optional hyphens (discussed in the previous section), as well as several other related special characters, as shown in Table 17-2. If you click the Show/Hide ¶ button on the Standard toolbar, Word will display on the screen all the characters listed here, using the symbols shown in the second column.

Table 17-2. **Manually Inserted Hyphens and Nonbreaking Spaces**

Special Character	Symbol Shown on Screen	Shortcut Key for Inserting Character	Character Properties
Optional hyphen	¬	Ctrl+hyphen (the hyphen key on the top row of the keyboard, *not* on the numeric keypad)	When an optional hyphen falls at the end of a line, it is displayed and the word that contains it is broken. When it falls within a line, it's hidden and the characters on either side come together (unless you make it visible on the screen).

(continued)

Chapter 17

Table 17-2. *(continued)*

Special Character	Symbol Shown on Screen	Shortcut Key for Inserting Character	Character Properties
Nonbreaking hyphen	–	Ctrl+Shift+hyphen (the hyphen key on the top row of the keyboard, *not* on the numeric keypad)	A nonbreaking hyphen is always displayed. A word is never broken at the position of a nonbreaking hyphen. It can be used to keep a hyphenated word or expression (such as *Stratford-Upon-Avon*) together on a single line.
Normal hyphen	-	Hyphen (the hyphen key on the top row of the keyboard *or* on the numeric keypad)	A normal hyphen is always displayed. Word breaks a word at the position of a normal hyphen if it falls at the end of a line.
Nonbreaking space	°	Ctrl+Shift+Spacebar	A line break can't occur at the position of a nonbreaking space. This character can be used to keep several words together on a single line.

Marking the Language

If your document contains text in a foreign language, or text that you want to exclude from proofing, you should perform the steps discussed in this section and in "Taking Advantage of Automatic Language Detection," on page 506, before using the proofing tools; otherwise, you can safely skip these sections.

In the version of Word sold in the United States, all text is initially marked as English (U.S.), meaning English as written in the United States. If all or some of the text in your document is written in a different language or in non-U.S. English and you want to be able to proof this text, you should mark each block of such text by performing the following steps:

1 Select the non-U.S. English text in your document.

2 Choose Tools, Language, Set Language to open the Language dialog box (see Figure 17-8).

Chapter 17: Proofing Word Documents

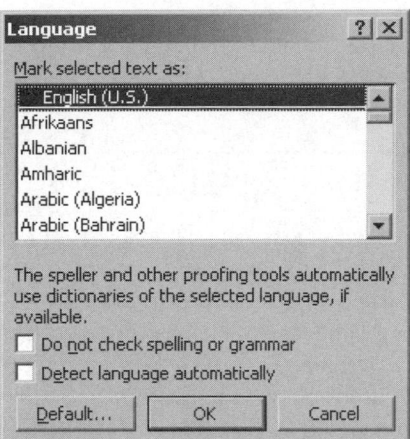

Figure 17-8. The Language dialog box lets you mark the language of the selected text.

3 In the Mark Selected Text As list, click the language you want to use to mark the selected text.

The languages that are available for the proofing tools are marked with an *ABC* spelling check icon, as seen here:

᠊ᵛEnglish (U.S.)

The available languages supplied with the English language version of Word are the various dialects of English, French, and Spanish. If you choose a different language, you'll need to obtain the Microsoft Office XP Proofing Tools. For information about this product, look up *proofing tools* in the Word online help.

4 Click the OK button.

Your document might also contain blocks of text that you want to exclude from proofing. For example, if you're writing a paper on *Beowulf*, you might want to exclude direct quotations that come from the poem so that the spelling checker won't flag all the archaic words and the grammar checker won't attempt to "improve" the writing style. To do this, perform the following steps:

1 Select the text you want to exclude from proofing.

2 Choose Tools, Language, Set Language to open the Language dialog box (see Figure 17-8).

3 In the Language dialog box, check the Do Not Check Spelling Or Grammar option.

Chapter 17

> **note** Applying the Do Not Check Spelling Or Grammar formatting to a block of text won't affect the functioning of the Thesaurus within that text.

> **tip** **Use Styles to Assign Language to Text**
>
> If you frequently mark blocks of text with a particular language (or to exclude proofing), you can save time by assigning that language (or the Do Not Check Spelling Or Grammar option) to a style that you can apply to all blocks of text written in that language (or that you want to exclude). Language marking is a form of character formatting, which you can apply directly as described in this section, or you can assign it to a paragraph or character style. For information on assigning character formatting to a style, see "Customizing Styles," on page 385.

If you click the Default button in the Language dialog box, Word will add the selected language format to the Normal style of the document and to the document's template. As a result, the language (or the Do Not Check Spelling Or Grammar option) will be assigned to all text based on the Normal style in the current document as well as in all new documents you subsequently create using the same template.

Taking Advantage of Automatic Language Detection

Rather than marking each block of foreign language text individually, you can have Word automatically detect the language of text in your document and use the appropriate dictionary (if available) for proofing that text. Word will detect only those languages that you explicitly enable for Office applications. To have Word automatically detect one or more languages, perform the following steps:

1 In Windows, choose Start, Programs, Microsoft Office Tools, Microsoft Office XP Language Settings. This will open the Microsoft Office Language Settings dialog box.

2 For each language you want Word to detect, click the language in the list in the Enabled Languages tab of the Microsoft Office Language Settings dialog box (shown in Figure 17-9), and then click the Add button. Click the OK button when you're done.

3 If Word is currently running, you'll have to stop it and then restart it for the changes you made in the Microsoft Office Language Settings dialog box to take effect.

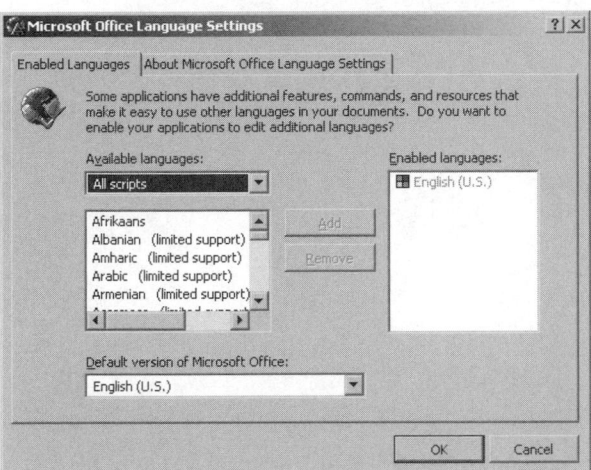

Figure 17-9. Choose languages for automatic detection in the Enabled Languages tab of the Microsoft Office Language Settings dialog box.

4 In Word, choose Tools, Language, Set Language.

5 In the Language dialog box, make sure that the Detect Language Automatically option is checked and click OK (see Figure 17-8). Word will then begin detecting the language in all open documents and in all documents you subsequently open.

This procedure causes Word to detect each enabled language and to look for the appropriate proofing dictionary. (If Word doesn't find the dictionary for a detected language, it doesn't proof that text.) The languages that are available for the proofing tools are marked with an *ABC* spelling check icon in the Language dialog box, as seen here:

ABC English (U.S.)

The available languages supplied with the English-language version of Word are the various dialects of English, French, and Spanish. If you've enabled one or more languages other than these, you'll need to obtain the Microsoft Office XP Proofing Tools. For information about this product, look up *proofing tools* in the Word online help.

---

tip **Use Manual Formatting If Automatic Detection Fails**

Automatic language detection isn't foolproof. It's especially prone to failure with small blocks of text in a particular language (which don't give Word enough of a sample to work with).

If you've set up automatic language detection properly and Word still fails to detect the language of a particular block of text, apply the appropriate language formatting manually to that text, as described in the previous section.

Chapter 17

507

Chapter 18

Designing and Printing Professional-Looking Pages

Designing Pages

The previous chapters in this part of the book have dealt with entering the content of a Microsoft Word 2002 document and adjusting the appearance of individual document elements, such as characters, paragraphs, headings, lists, tables, and graphic objects. This chapter is about the appearance of the document pages, which appear in Print Layout view, Print Preview, and on the printed copy of a document. It focuses on the way document elements—those just listed, as well as headers, footers, and watermarks—are arranged on the individual pages of the document.

This chapter will be of interest primarily if you're creating a traditional hard copy document consisting of a series of pages, such as a memo, letter, résumé, form, report, pamphlet, brochure, newsletter, manual, thesis, or book. However, if you're using Word to create Web pages, online documents, labels, envelopes, e-mail messages, or other end products, you'll still find some of the information in this chapter important. For example, the text-wrapping styles discussed in "Combining Text with Graphic Objects and Text Boxes," on page 515, affect the display of a graphic object in a Web browser or on a mailing label, as well as on a full printed page. And some of the page setup features discussed in "Modifying the Page Setup," on page 535, as well as the printing techniques covered in "Previewing and Printing Documents," on page 547, affect the printing of labels and envelopes. The sections in this chapter indicate the techniques that aren't suitable for creating Web pages.

509

> Creating Web pages and online document is covered in Chapter 20, "Creating Web Pages and Other Online Documents." Creating labels, envelopes, or multiple e-mail messages is covered in Chapter 19, "Using Word to Automate Mailings." Creating individual e-mail messages is discussed in "Sharing Word Documents Using E-Mail," on page 468.

Some of the techniques presented in this chapter affect the look of a specific page; namely, adding text boxes and formatting graphic objects. Other techniques affect the general look of pages throughout a document or document section—for example, adding watermarks, headers, or footers, or adjusting the margins or page orientation.

> Using newspaper-style columns is another way to arrange text and graphics on the pages throughout a document or document section. For information, see "Arranging Text in Newspaper-Style Columns," on page 366.

tip   **Consider Publisher for Some of Your Projects**

If you're creating a small, layout-intensive printed publication—such as a postcard, business card, sign, flyer, menu, brochure, or newsletter—you might prefer using Microsoft Publisher, which is designed specifically for these tasks and provides a large set of wizards and templates to get you started. For more information, see Part 9 of this book.

Using Text Boxes to Create Precise Page Layouts

The text in the body of a document is contained in a stream of characters that flows from line to line and from page to page. This section describes how use a *text box* to place a block of text or graphics outside of the normal stream of characters in the body text, at a precise position on the page or at a specific position relative to the adjoining text. You can use text boxes to position margin notes, figures, tables, sidebars, and other elements that you want to set apart from the main text. By adjusting the *wrapping style* of a text box, you can have it overlap the body text (either in front of or behind the text) or you can have the body text wrap around the text box. (You can also place a text box inline with the body text, although you can then no longer freely position it outside of the main flow of text.)

> Wrapping styles are discussed in "Combining Text with Graphic Objects and Text Boxes," on page 515.

Chapter 18: Designing and Printing Professional-Looking Pages

Figure 18-1 shows a Word document containing a margin note created by inserting text into a text box, and an inset table created by inserting a Word table into a text box. (The margin note text box was assigned the In Front Of Text wrapping style. The table text box was assigned the Square wrapping style, which causes the adjoining body text to wrap around the text box.)

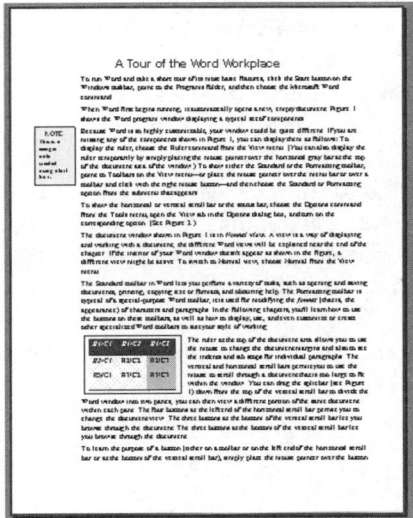

Figure 18-1.   This figure shows a margin note and an inset Word table, both created using text boxes.

To place a text box around existing text in your document, perform the following steps:

1   Select the text you want to include in the text box. You can include one or more characters or paragraphs or a Word table.

2   Choose Insert, Text Box, or click the Text Box button on the Drawing toolbar.

Text Box

Word will then create a new text box, and it will move the selected text into the text box. You'll now probably need to adjust the size, position, and format of the text box, as described later in this section.

You can also create an empty text box and then insert text into it, using the following steps:

1   Without selecting text, choose Insert, Text Box or click the Text Box button on the Drawing toolbar. The insertion point can be anywhere within the document.

2 Word will insert a drawing canvas graphic object, which will contain the label "Create your drawing here." For best results, press Esc to remove the drawing canvas.

InsideOut

Although a drawing canvas is useful for containing a drawing that consists of several AutoShape objects, placing a text box within a drawing canvas only complicates working with the text box. (A text box can be positioned, sized, and formatted by itself—it doesn't need to be inserted within another graphic object.) When you add a text box without selecting text, Word automatically inserts a drawing canvas and invites you to put your text box within it. Fortunately, however, you can easily remove the drawing canvas by pressing Esc before you click or drag to insert the text box. For information on drawing canvases, see the sidebar "Drawing Canvases," on page 134.

3 Drag the mouse pointer to indicate the size and position you want for the text box, as shown here:

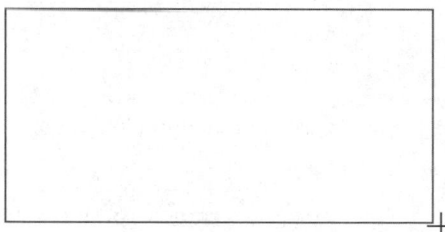

Or, simply click in the document to insert a default-sized text box.

4 You can now insert text into the text box. If the insertion point isn't already in the text box, click *within* the box (not on one of its borders), so that the insertion point appears in the box. You can then enter, edit, and format text just as you would in the main body of a document. A text box can contain one or more paragraphs.

caution   If you're creating a Web page document, don't place a text box in a margin area, because it will probably be partially or completely cut off when the page is viewed in a browser. Neither Web browsers nor Word's Web Layout view display the full document margins.

Chapter 18: Designing and Printing Professional-Looking Pages

As you type text in a text box, Word will wrap the text when you reach the right text box edge. Word *won't*, however, automatically increase the height of the box when you reach the bottom; you'll have to manually increase the height of the box to make the text at the bottom visible. (Or, as you'll see later, you can link the text box to another text box so that excess text automatically flows into the second box.)

To change the height or width of a text box, perform the following steps:

1 Click anywhere on the text box to select it. When a text box is selected, Word displays a thick band around it, which contains eight round sizing handles, as shown here:

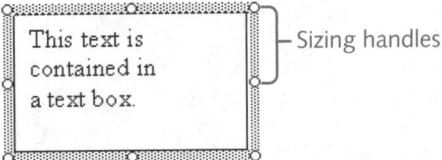

2 Drag any of the sizing handles to resize the box. To maintain the original proportions of the text box as you change its size, press Shift while dragging one of the *corner* sizing handles. To resize the text box symmetrically about its center (that is, to change the box size without moving the center of the box), hold down Ctrl while dragging any sizing handle.

To move or copy a text box, perform the following steps:

1 Place the pointer over one of the edges of the text box (but *not* over a sizing handle if the text box is selected). Cross-arrows will appear at the tip of the mouse pointer, as seen here:

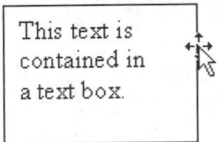

2 Drag the text box to the position you want on the page. If you want to copy the text box rather than move it, hold down Ctrl while you drag.

If you move or copy a text box onto an area of the page occupied by text, you'll notice one of the following two types of behavior:

- If you selected existing text in the document before inserting the text box (that is, if you used the first method given for creating a text box), the document text will wrap around (that is, move away from) the text box. (The text box has the Square wrapping style.)

- If you didn't select text before inserting the text box (that is, if you used the second method for creating a text box), the text box will overlap the document text. (The text box has the In Front Of Text wrapping style.)

The next section explains how to change the wrapping style of a text box.

When a text box is selected, Word will usually display the Text Box toolbar, shown here. (If it isn't displayed when a text box is selected, choose View, Toolbars, Text Box.)

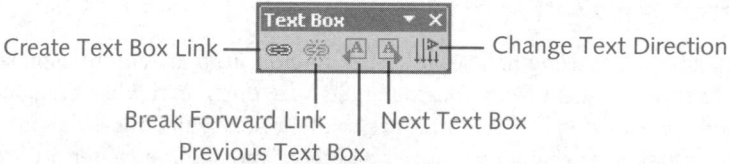

Create Text Box Link ——— Change Text Direction

Break Forward Link | Next Text Box
Previous Text Box

You can use the Text Box toolbar to create a series of two or more linked text boxes. Text will flow from one text box to the next one in the linked series. That is, any text that doesn't fit in a text box will be moved to the next one, in the same way that document text flows from one page to the next. To create a set of linked text boxes, perform these steps:

1 Add the text boxes to your document. All text boxes except the first one in the series must be empty.

2 Click the first text box in the series to select it, click the Create Text Box Link button on the Text Box toolbar, and then click the second text box. This will create the first link.

3 If you want to add additional text boxes to the linked series, repeat step 2 for each additional text box you want to link.

You can remove the link between a text box and the next one in the series by clicking the text box and then clicking the Break Forward Link button on the Text Box toolbar.

If one of the text boxes in a linked series is selected, you can move the selection to other boxes in the series by clicking the Next Text Box button to select the next box in the series or by clicking the Previous Text Box button to select the previous one.

To modify the direction of the text in the selected text box and in any text boxes that are linked to it, click the Change Text Direction button. The button will toggle the text direction from left to right, to top to bottom, to bottom to top.

To remove a text box, plus the text it contains, select it by clicking one of its *edges*, and then press Delete. (If you select the text box by clicking inside the edges, Word will place the insertion point within the text, and pressing Delete will delete only a single character.) If you want to move text from a text box into the main part of the document, be sure to copy the text from the text box and paste it into the document *before* you delete the box. Note, however, that if a text box is linked to one or more others, deleting the text box won't erase the text, but will merely shift it to the remaining linked text boxes.

> For information on changing the formatting features of text boxes, other than the wrapping style, see the general instructions for modifying graphic objects in "Modifying Graphic Objects," on page 150. Changing the wrapping style is covered in the next section.

Troubleshooting

Text Boxes Disappeared

You inserted one or more text boxes into your document, but you can no longer see them.

To view text boxes, you must be in Word's Web Layout, Print Layout, or Print Preview view. If you're not in one of these three views when you choose Insert, Text Box or click the Text Box button on the Drawing toolbar, Word will switch automatically into Print Layout view. However, if you later switch to Normal or Outline view, your text boxes will be hidden.

Text boxes will also be hidden, even in Web Layout and Print Layout views, if the Drawings view option isn't checked. You'll find this option by choosing Tools, Options, clicking the View tab, and looking in the Print And Web Layout Options area of the tab.

Combining Text with Graphic Objects and Text Boxes

"Modifying Graphic Objects," on page 150, explained the general methods for formatting graphic objects in Office applications. Because a text box is a type of graphic object, you can use these methods to modify text boxes that you've added to a Word document. One type of formatting that is unique to Word is the *wrapping style*, which affects the way a graphic object—such as a picture, AutoShape, diagram, or text box— is positioned on the page and its relation to the text in the body of the document.

To modify the wrapping style of the selected object, choose the name of the object from the Format menu (such as Picture, AutoShape, Diagram, or Text Box), and click the Layout tab of the Format dialog box (as shown in Figure 18-2).

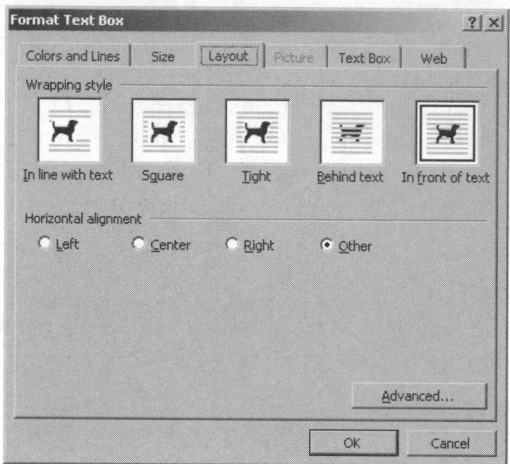

Figure 18-2. This figure shows the Layout tab of the Format dialog box as displayed when a Text Box is selected.

> **note** You can also change the wrapping style of the selected graphic object by clicking the Text Wrapping button on the Picture toolbar and choosing a wrapping style from the drop-down menu. Or, you can click the Draw button on the Drawing toolbar and choose a wrapping style from the Text Wrapping submenu on the menu. The Picture and Drawing toolbars are discussed in Chapter 6, "Adding Professional Graphics and Special Effects to Office XP Documents."

In the Layout tab, you can choose from five different wrapping styles. To choose from a larger selection of wrapping styles, and to fine-tune the positioning of the object, click the Advanced button in the Layout tab to open the Advanced Layout dialog box and then use the Text Wrapping Tab in the dialog box. When selecting a wrapping style, keep in mind that the styles can be broken down into three basic groups:

- **Square, Tight, Through, and Top And Bottom**   With these styles, you can place the object anywhere on the page. Document text will wrap around the object in various ways.

- **In Front Of Text and Behind Text**   With these styles, you can also position the object anywhere on the page. However, if the object intersects document text, it will overlap the text and will appear either in front of the text or behind it.

● **In Line With Text** With this style, the object is an integral part of the body text in the document. It's positioned as if it were a single text character, and you can move or copy it using the standard text editing methods.

Standard text editing methods are discussed in Chapter 11, "Efficient Editing in Word."

newfeature!

You can also change the initial wrapping style that Word will assign to the following types of graphic objects when you first insert them:

● Pictures

● WordArt objects

● Microsoft Graph chart objects

● Equation objects

● Other types of embedded objects

To change the initial wrapping style for these graphic object types, choose Tools, Options, click the Edit tab, and select the wrapping style you want from the Insert/Paste Pictures As drop-down list, shown here:

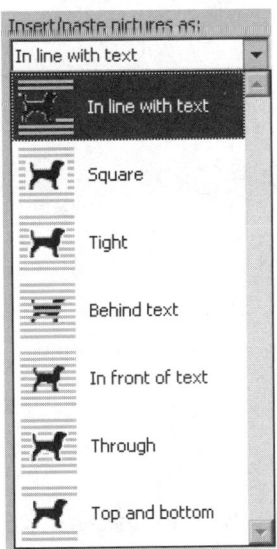

For information on adding pictures, AutoShapes, diagrams, WordArt objects, Microsoft Graph charts, and Equation objects to Word documents (as well as other types of Office documents), see Chapter 6, "Adding Professional Graphics and Special Effects to Office XP Documents." For information on adding other types of embedded objects, see Chapter 7, "Sharing Data Among Office XP Applications."

---

tip   **Use a Text Wrapping Break**

If an object is assigned the Square, Tight, or Through wrapping style, you can insert a special line break known as a *text wrapping break* into a line of text that's to the right or to the left of the object. The text following this break will be moved down below the object. To insert the break, place the insertion point at the position where you want to break the text, choose Insert, Break, and select the Text Wrapping Break option in the Break dialog box.

---

newfeature!
Displaying Watermarks

Word now makes it easy to add a watermark to a document. A watermark consists of faint text or graphics displayed across every page in the document or in a document section. A text watermark, for example, might consist of the words *Confidential*, *Draft*, *Urgent*, or *Top Secret*, as shown in Figure 18-3.

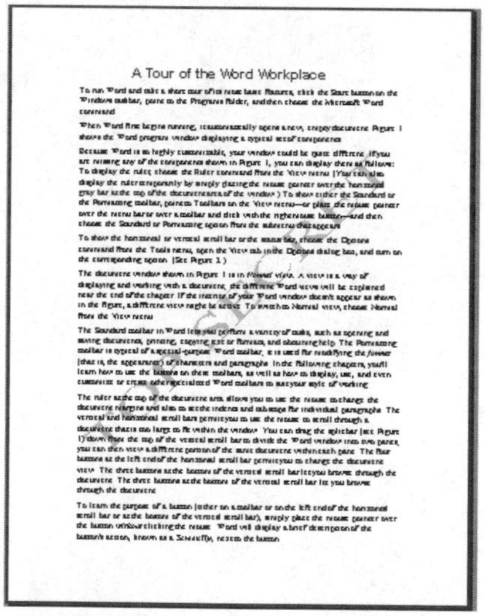

Figure 18-3.   This document has a text watermark that displays the message *TOP SECRET*.

Chapter 18: Designing and Printing Professional-Looking Pages

To add a watermark, follow these steps:

1 If you're in Web Layout view, switch to any other view.

2 Choose Format, Background, Printed Watermark to open the Printed Watermark dialog box.

3 In the Printed Watermark dialog box, do one of the following:

 ■ To display the contents of a graphic file as the watermark, select the Picture Watermark option, click the Select Picture button, and select the file in the Insert Picture dialog box, which works just like the standard Open dialog box. To adjust the scale of the graphic, select a scaling percentage in the Scale drop-down list, or select Auto to have Word scale the graphic so that it just fits on the page. The Washout option, which is checked by default, displays the graphic in light tones.

 ■ To display text as the watermark, select Text Watermark. Then, type or select the text in the Text drop-down list, and choose the font, font size, and text color in the other drop-down lists. Specify the text direction by selecting Diagonal (selected for the watermark shown in Figure 18-4) or Horizontal. The Semitransparent option, which is checked by default, lightens the color of the text.

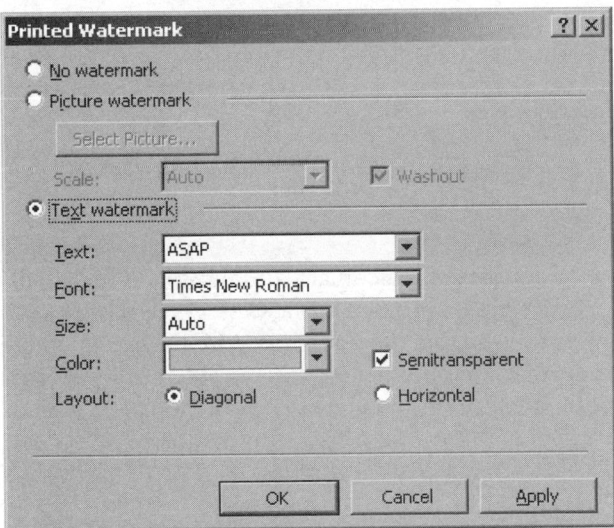

Figure 18-4. In this figure a text watermark is defined in the Printed Watermark dialog box.

 ■ To remove a watermark you added previously, select No Watermark.

4 Click the OK button.

> **note** To create the watermark, Word adds a picture (for a graphic watermark) or a WordArt object (for a text watermark) to the document's headers, which causes the watermark to appear on every document page. Headers are described in the next section.

> **tip** **Remove or Modify Watermarks in Document Sections**
>
> When you create a watermark using the method explained in this section, Word adds the watermark to *all* pages in the document, even if you divided your document into separate sections and selected one or more specific sections before creating the watermark.
>
> However, if you have divided your document into sections, you can remove the watermark from a particular section by deleting the picture or WordArt object from that section's header, using the techniques discussed in the next section for working with headers. (For information on document sections, see the sidebar "Working with Document Sections," on page 524.) You can also directly modify the watermark object in the header, rather than using the Printed Watermark dialog box to change it.

> **note** Watermarks aren't visible in Web pages displayed in a browser because they are part of the document's headers, which aren't shown in Web pages.

Adding Page Numbering, Headers, and Footers

A *header* is a block of text or graphics that Word displays at the top of every page in your document, or every page in a document section. Likewise, a *footer* is text or graphics displayed at the bottom of every page. With the exception of page numbers, the text or graphics that appear in the headers or footers of a document—or of a document section—are the same on every page. You don't see headers and footers in Normal, Web Layout, or Outline view. They appear, however, in Print Layout view, Print Preview, and on printed document pages.

The following section explains how to create simple headers or footers consisting of just automatic page numbers. The section after that shows how to create headers and footers containing any text, graphics, or formatting you want.

> **note** If you're creating a Web page in Word, forget about headers and footers because they won't be displayed in a browser.

Adding Automatic Page Numbering

You can use the Page Numbers dialog box to quickly add automatic page numbering to the pages in your document. You can display numbers within headers at the top of each page or within footers at the bottom of each page, and you can choose from a variety of numbering formats. If your document doesn't already have headers or footers when you add page numbers using the Page Numbers dialog box, Word creates simple headers or footers consisting of only the page number.

To add automatic page numbering to the currently opened document, perform the following steps:

1 Switch into Normal or Print Layout view, if necessary, and choose Insert, Page Numbers to open the Page Numbers dialog box, shown here:

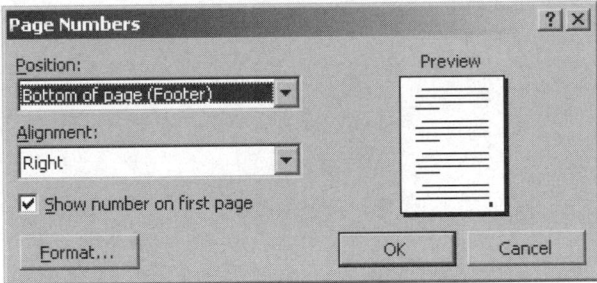

2 In the Position list, select Top Of Page (Header) to place the page numbers at the top of each page (that is, within headers), or Bottom Of Page (Footer) to place the page numbers at the bottom of each page (that is, within footers).

3 In the Alignment list, choose the position of the page numbers within the headers or footers, as follows:

- To place the page numbers at the left margin, centered between the margins, or at the right margin on each page, choose Left, Center, or Right.

- To place the page numbers at the right on even-numbered pages and at the left on odd-numbered pages, choose Inside.

- To place the page numbers at the left on even-numbered pages and at the right on odd-numbered pages (as in this book), choose Outside.

4 If you want to eliminate the page number from the first page of the document, clear the Show Number On First Page check box.

If you clear Show Number On First Page, Word will omit the page number from the first page, although it will count the first page in numbering the pages. For example, if you start numbering at 1, Word won't display a number on the first page, but it will number the second page with 2.

5 If you want to modify the style of the numbering or change the starting number, click the Format button to open the Page Number Format dialog box, shown here:

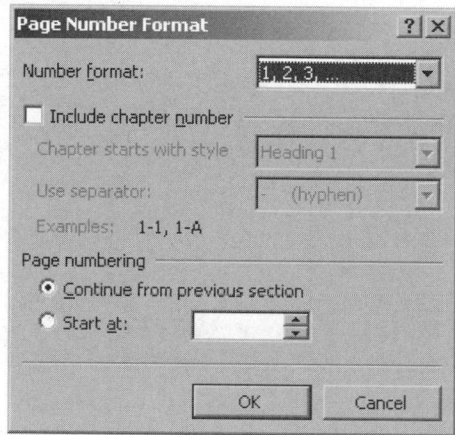

In the Page Number Format dialog box, do one or more of the following:

■ To select the type of numbering, choose an item in the Number Format drop-down list. You can select various styles of Arabic numbers, letters of the alphabet, or Roman numerals.

■ To add chapter numbers to the page numbering (for example, 1-1 and 1-2 on the first two pages of Chapter 1), check Include Chapter Number, select the style used to format your chapter headings in the Chapter Starts With Style drop-down list, and select the character you want to use between the chapter and page number (such as a hyphen, period, or colon) in the Use Separator drop-down list.

> **note** To add chapter numbers to your page numbering, you must have formatted all your chapter headings using the same built-in Heading style (Heading 1 through Heading 9), and you must have applied automatic outline numbering to these headings, as explained in "Creating an Outline Numbered List Using the Outline Numbered Tab," on page 376.

■ To start numbering the pages with 1, select Continue From Previous Section.

> If you've divided your document into sections, the Continue From Previous Section option will cause the numbering in the current section to continue the numbering from any previous section. For more information, see the Inside Out below.

■ To start numbering the pages with a specific number, select the Start At option and enter the desired starting number in the adjoining text box.

To modify page numbering that you previously added, you can reopen the Page Numbers or Page Number Format dialog box and change any of the options. You can also edit or delete page numbering by using the View, Header And Footer command, as described in "Adding Headers and Footers," on page 526. (Even though you can see page numbers in Print Layout view, you can't edit them unless you choose the Header And Footer command or double-click the header or footer area.)

InsideOut

If you've divided your document into separate sections, adding page numbering using the Insert, Page Numbers command is a bit confusing. The command will add page numbering to *all* document sections, even if you haven't selected all sections. (An exception: If you've turned off the Same As Previous option in a section following the current one, numbering won't be added to that section or any sections following it. This option is discussed later in the chapter.) However (and here's where it gets confusing), changing the status of the Show Number On First Page option or changing any of the settings in the Page Number Format dialog box affects the numbering *only within the currently selected section or sections* (even if the Same As Previous option is turned on for all sections, supposedly making all headings identical). For instance, clearing Show Number On First Page removes the page number from the first page of only the selected section or sections.

If you want to apply your selected options to the entire document, press Ctrl+A to select all document sections before you choose Insert, Page Numbers. After you've added numbering, you can later modify the numbering options (such as the Start At option to vary the starting number) in a specific section by placing the insertion point in that section, reissuing the Page Numbers command, and selecting the new options you want. (Keep in mind that you can "select" a single section by simply placing the insertion point within it.)

For information on document sections, see the sidebar "Working with Document Sections," on page 524.

tip **Reformat Your Document's Page Numbering Quickly**

To change the character formatting of page numbering throughout your document, modify the Page Number character style. Word assigns this style to automatic page numbers. For information on modifying styles, see "Customizing Styles," on page 385.

Working with Document Sections

You can divide a document into separate sections and then assign different formatting features to each section. The following are the features that you can vary from section to section:

- Page borders (discussed in "Applying Borders to Pages," on page 365).
- The number of columns (discussed in "Arranging Text in Newspaper-Style Columns," on page 366).
- Headers and footers, including page numbering (discussed in "Adding Page Numbering, Headers, and Footers," on page 520), as well as watermarks (which are part of headers and are discussed in "Displaying Watermarks," on page 518).
- The features that you set using the Page Setup dialog box, such as the margins and the paper size (discussed in "Modifying the Page Setup," on page 535).

To divide your document into separate sections, perform the following steps:

1 Place the insertion point at the position where you want to insert a section break.

2 Choose Insert, Break to open the Break dialog box, seen here:

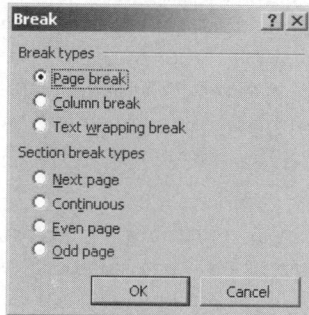

3 Select one of the options in the Section Break Types area, as follows:

- To start the following section's text at the beginning of a new page, select Next Page.

- To start the following section's text immediately following the text in the previous section, with no line or page break, select Continuous.

- To start the following section's text at the beginning of the next even-numbered page, select Even Page. (If the next page is odd-numbered, this option will create a blank page. Note that a blank page will be shown in Print Preview, but not in Print Layout view.)

- To start the following section's text at the beginning of the next odd-numbered page, select Odd Page. (If the next page is even-numbered, this option will create a blank page.)

Chapter 18: Designing and Printing Professional-Looking Pages

Working with Document Sections *(continued)*   In Normal view, Word marks a
section break as shown here:

This is the last line of the previous section.

———————————————————————————————Section Break (Next Page)———————————————————————

This is the first line of the next section.

Show/
Hide ¶

The text in parentheses varies according to the type of break you insert. In Web Layout, Print Layout, or Outline view, section breaks are marked only if the All viewing
mode is on. (You can turn this mode on or off by checking or clearing the All option in
the View tab of the Options dialog box, or by clicking the Show/Hide ¶ button on the
Standard toolbar.) Here's how a section break is marked in Print Layout view:

This·is·the·last·line·of·the·previous·section.¶————————————Section Break (Next Page)————————————

Section breaks aren't marked in Print Preview.

To remove a section break, follow these steps:

1 Switch into Normal view.

2 Select the section-break mark and press Delete.

Word will merge the sections before and after the break into a single section, which
will acquire the section formatting features (those listed at the beginning of this
sidebar) of the section that *followed* the mark. Any section formatting features that
you assigned to the section preceding the mark will be lost. Conceptually, a section-
break mark stores the formatting features of the preceding section, so if you delete
the section mark, you delete these features.

To copy section formatting to a different part of the same document or to a different
document, go into Normal view, select the section-break mark at the end of the section
with the formatting you want to copy, and then copy the mark to the new location using
any of the standard techniques for copying text. The text preceding the copied section
mark will then acquire the section formatting stored in the section mark.

You can conveniently store an entire collection of section formatting features by
selecting the section-break mark at the end of a section that has these features and
creating an AutoText entry that contains just that mark. You can then quickly apply
all of the section formatting features by simply inserting this AutoText entry at the
end of the text you want to format.

Chapter 18

525

Adding Headers and Footers

This section explains how to create full-featured headers and footers containing any text, graphics, or formatting you want. If you used the Page Numbers dialog box to create simple headers or footers consisting of only page numbers, you can use the techniques given here to edit or delete these headers or footers, or to add additional header or footer content. If you're creating a Web page document, keep in mind that headers and footers won't be displayed in a browser.

To create or edit headers or footers throughout the currently opened document, perform the following steps:

1 Choose View, Header And Footer. (If you're in Print Layout view or Print Preview, you can edit existing headers or footers by double-clicking the header area at the top of the page or the footer area at the bottom of the page.) Word will then do the following:

- Switch to Print Layout view, if it's not already active.

- Mark the header and footer areas on the page with dotted lines and activate these areas so that you can work within them.

- Dim all text outside the header or footer area. (You won't be able to work on this text.)

- Display the Header And Footer toolbar, which provides commands for working on the headers and footers.

Figure 18-5 shows the header area in the Word window after the Header And Footer command has been chosen. The footer area at the bottom of the page is similar.

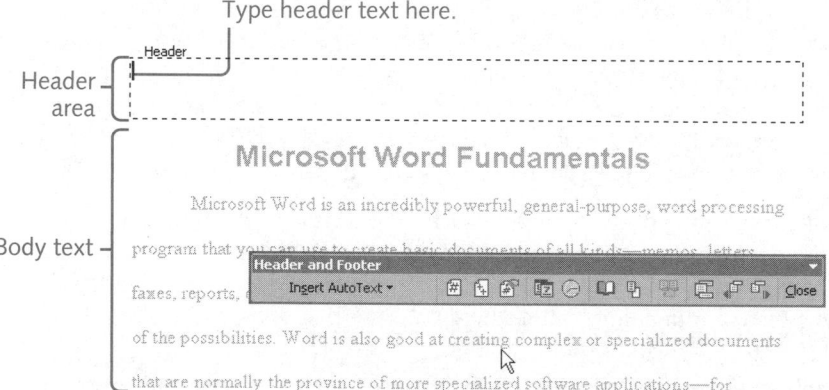

Figure 18-5. This figure shows the header area and the Header And Footer toolbar.

2 If you need to move the insertion point from the header to the footer area, or from the footer to the header area, press the Down or Up arrow key, or click the Switch Between Header And Footer button on the Header And Footer toolbar (shown in Figure 18-6).

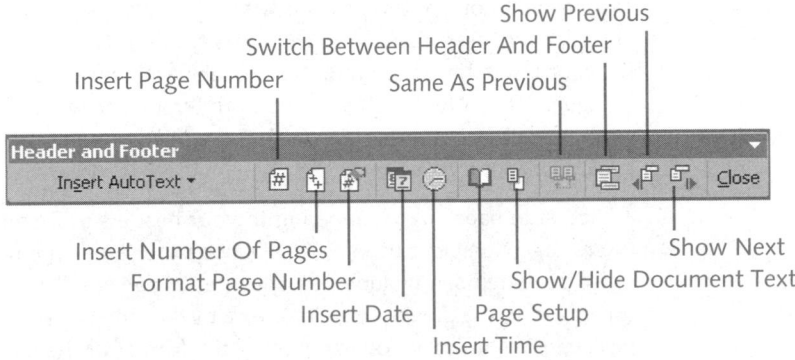

Figure 18-6. The Header And Footer toolbar provides tools for working with headers and footers.

> **note** Using the arrow keys or other navigation key combinations, you can move to the header or footer area on any page in the document. Usually, it doesn't matter which page you work on because the headers and footers are the same throughout the document. However, as explained in "Varying Headers or Footers Within a Document," on page 532, you can vary the headers or footers within the document (to reflect, for example, different section or chapter names in the document). In this case, you must move to the appropriate page before working on the header or footer.

3 Type the text for the header or footer into the header area or the footer area. You can enter one or more paragraphs of text into a header or footer, and you can edit and format the text in the same way that you edit and format text in the body of a document.

> You can also insert graphic objects or text boxes into a header or footer, using the techniques covered in Chapter 6, "Adding Professional Graphics and Special Effects to Office XP Documents," and "Using Text Boxes to Create Precise Page Layouts," on page 510.

The following are some techniques that will help you build your header or footer content:

■ To align your text on one of the two predefined tab stops in the header or footer area, press Tab. The first tab stop aligns text in the center of the header or footer, and the second tab stop right-aligns text at the right edge of the header or footer. (Note that the tabs might be set differently in documents based on certain templates.)

■ To remove headers or footers, just delete all the text or graphic objects in the header or footer area.

■ To quickly insert the page number, the total number of pages in the document, the date, or the time into your header or footer text, place the insertion point at the position where you want the information, and click the Insert Page Number, Insert Number Of Pages, Insert Date, or Insert Time button on the Header And Footer toolbar (shown in Figure 18-6). Note that when you print your document, the number of pages, the date, or the time that you insert will be updated to reflect the current value.

■ To add automatic page numbering to your headers or footers, click the Insert Page Number button. This will insert the same type of automatic page numbering added by the Insert, Page Numbers command (described in the previous section), except that the page number isn't placed inside a frame. You can modify the format of the numbers or the starting number by clicking the Format Page Number button on the Header And Footer toolbar to open the Page Number Format dialog box, also described in the previous section.

For an explanation of frames, see "Adjusting the Size and Position of Headers or Footers," on page 529.

■ To quickly insert various types of information into your header or footer, click the Insert AutoText button and choose an item from the submenu shown here:

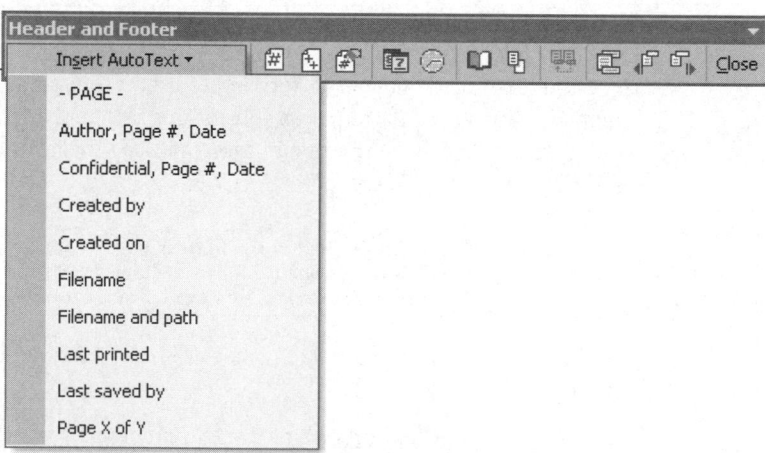

For example, you can choose Filename to insert the name of the current document. Or, you can choose "Author, Page #, Date" to insert your name, the page number, and the date. (The items on this menu are predefined AutoText entries provided with Word.)

---

tip **Hide Body Text**

To reduce distraction while you work on headers or footers, you can completely hide the body text on the page by clicking the Show/Hide Document Text button on the Header And Footer toolbar. (Normally, when you work on headers and footers, document text is shown in a dimmed font.)

---

4 When you have finished creating or modifying the headers or footers, click the Close button on the Header And Footer toolbar, or choose View, Header And Footer to return to the view you were using previously.

---

tip **Use Styles to Format Headers, Footers, and Page Numbers**

Word assigns the Header paragraph style to header text, the Footer paragraph style to footer text, and the Page Number character style to automatic page numbers within headers or footers. You can therefore uniformly change the formatting of headers, footers, or page numbers throughout your entire document by modifying the corresponding style. Doing this will affect headers or footers in all document sections, even if the headers or footers vary from section to section.

You might, for example, assign to a style borders or shading, distinctive character formatting (such as a font, style, size, color, or enhancement), or other formatting to emphasize your headers or footers and make them stand apart from the text in the body of the document.

For information on modifying styles, see "Customizing Styles," on page 385.

Adjusting the Size and Position of Headers or Footers

The header or footer text you enter is normally confined within the header area or the footer area at the top or bottom of each page. You can change the size or position of these areas, however, or extend the header or footer text outside the header or footer area using one or more of the following techniques listed on the next page.

- To adjust the top or bottom boundary of the header area, click in the header area and then drag the Top Margin marker or the Bottom Margin marker up or down on the vertical ruler, as shown here:

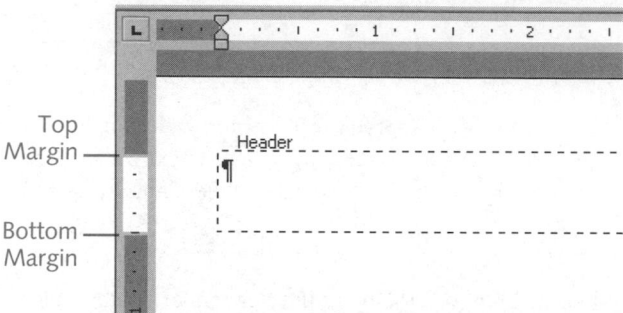

If the vertical ruler doesn't appear when the View, Ruler option is selected, choose Tools, Options, click the View tab, and check the Vertical Ruler (Print View Only) option.

- To adjust the top boundary of the footer area, click in the footer area and drag the Top Margin marker up or down on the vertical ruler, as shown here:

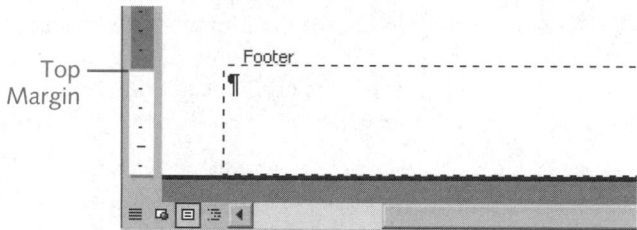

> **note** If the text or graphics you insert into a header is higher than the current header area, Word will move the bottom boundary of the header area down so that the header won't overlap the main document text. Likewise, if the text or graphics you insert into a footer is higher than the footer area, Word will move the top boundary of the footer area up.

- To adjust the height of the header or footer area by entering exact measurements, click the Page Setup button on the Header And Footer toolbar (shown in Figure 18-6), and enter the measurements you want into the Header box or Footer box in the From Edge area of the Layout tab.

Chapter 18

- To move text to the left or to the right of the header or footer area, assign a negative left indent or a negative right indent to one or more paragraphs of header or footer text. To do this, you can use the horizontal ruler or the Paragraph dialog box.

> The horizontal ruler and Paragraph dialog box are explained in "Formatting Paragraphs Directly," on page 309.

> **note** A page number inserted by the Page Numbers dialog box is placed within a *frame*, which is an obsolete Word element similar to a text box. Like a text box, it can be dragged to any position on the page. To change a frame's properties, click it to select it and then choose Format, Frame.

- To position header or footer text anywhere on the page, place the insertion point within the header or footer, add a text box as described in "Using Text Boxes to Create Precise Page Layouts," on page 510, and assign the text box a wrapping style *other than* In Line With Text, as explained in "Combining Text with Graphic Objects and Text Boxes," on page 515. You can then drag the text box to any position on the page. Because the header or footer area was active when you inserted the text box, it remains an integral part of the header or footer, and it is therefore displayed on all pages in the document or section, and you can modify it only after you activate the header or footer area (by choosing View, Header And Footer or by double clicking in the area).

> **note** If a text box or a graphic object you've added to a header or footer overlaps the document's body text, the text in the text box or the graphic object is displayed behind the text (even if you've assigned the text box the In Front Of Text wrapping style) and it is displayed in fainter tones.

- To display a graphic object—such as a picture, AutoShape, or WordArt object—on every page of the document or section, insert it into the header or footer. If the object is assigned a text wrapping style other than In Line With Text, you can drag it to any position on the page. (Note that when you create a watermark by choosing Format, Background, Printed Watermark, Word adds a picture or a WordArt object to the document's header, but positions it in the middle of the page.)

> **tip**   **Overlap Headings and Body Text to Create Special Effects**
>
> Normally, if you extend the header or footer area beyond the current top or bottom margin area, Word will automatically adjust the top or bottom margin so that the header or footer text doesn't overlap the text in the body of the document. However, if you enter a minus sign before the Top or Bottom margin setting in the Margins tab of the Page Setup dialog box (discussed in "Setting the Margins and Page Orientation," on page 536), Word will not adjust the margins. Doing this will allow you to extend the header or footer area into the area occupied by the body text and to enter text or graphics into the header or footer that overlaps the body text. When header or footer text overlaps body text, the header or footer text is displayed behind the body text and in fainter tones. You can use this technique as an alternative way to create watermarks or to create other special effects.

Varying Headers or Footers Within a Document

Normally, the same header or footer is printed on every page in the document. There are, however, three ways that you can vary headers and footers within your document.

You can create a different header or footer on the first page of the document, or on the first page of a section if you have divided your document into sections that begin on a new page. (This procedure doesn't work for continuous section breaks.) You might want to do this, for example, to eliminate the header from the title page of a report or to avoid placing a page number on the first page of a letter. To do so, perform the following steps:

1   If you have divided your document into sections, and if you want to create a different first-page header for a specific section or for a specific section plus all following sections, place the insertion point in that section.

2   Choose View, Header And Footer.

3   Click the Page Setup button on the Header And Footer toolbar (shown in Figure 18-6, on page 527) to open the Layout tab of the Page Setup dialog box.

4   Check the Different First Page option.

5   Select an option in the Apply To drop-down list, as follows:

- ■   To create a different header for the first page of your document, or for the first page in all document sections if you've divided the document into sections, select Whole Document.

Chapter 18: Designing and Printing Professional-Looking Pages

- To create a different header on the first page of the section containing the insertion point, select This Section.

- To create a different header on the first page of the section containing the insertion point and on the first page of every section following it, select This Point Forward.

6 Click the OK button.

In addition, you can create different headers and footers on odd and even pages. You might do this, for example, if you're writing a book and want the book title at the top of the left page of facing pages (called the *verso* page by book designers), and the chapter title at the top of the right page (called the *recto* page). To do this, follow these steps:

1 Choose View, Header And Footer. (The insertion point can be anywhere in the document.)

2 Click the Page Setup button on the Header And Footer toolbar to open the Layout tab of the Page Setup dialog box.

3 Check the Different Odd And Even option, and click OK.

Word will always create odd and even headers throughout your entire document, even if it's divided into sections and regardless of your choice in the Apply To drop-down list in the Layout tab.

Finally, if you have divided your document into sections, the headers or footers in separate sections can have different contents. Initially, the headers and footers in every section (except the first) are connected to the headers and footers in the previous section, meaning that they'll be exactly the same as those in the previous section. When headers and footers are all connected this way, making a change (except for reformatting numbering) in a header or footer in any section will change the headers and footers in all sections. To create different headers and footers in different sections, perform the following steps:

1 Place the insertion point within the section where you want the headers and footers to be different from the previous section.

2 Choose View, Header And Footer.

3 Click the Same As Previous button on the Header And Footer toolbar to toggle this setting off. This will remove the connection between the current section and the previous one. You can now modify the headers or footers for the current section without changing those of the previous section. (Your changes will, however, modify any following sections that are still connected to the current section.)

Modify Automatic Page Numbering in a Specific Section

If you have inserted automatic page numbering into your headers or footers—either by choosing Insert, Page Numbers or by clicking Insert Page Number on the Header And Footer toolbar—you can modify the format and starting number of the numbering or add chapter numbers to the numbering within a particular document section.

To do this, place the insertion point in the section you want to modify, choose View, Header And Footer, click the Format Page Number button on the Header And Footer toolbar, and change options as desired in the Page Number Format dialog box, which was explained in "Adding Automatic Page Numbering," on page 521. The options you set in this dialog box will apply only to the current document section (even if the Same As Previous option is turned on for all sections, supposedly making all headings identical).

The most important numbering change you might want to make for a particular section is to select the Continue From Previous Section option to continue the numbering sequence from the previous section, or to select the Start At option to restart the numbering of the current section with a specific page number.

Troubleshooting

Headers or Footers Cut Off

When you print a document, part or all of the header or footer text is cut off.

The header or footer text might be too close to the edge of the page. Find out from your printer's documentation how close it can print to the edge of the paper. Then choose File, Page Setup, click the Layout tab of the Page Setup dialog box, and adjust the distances of the headers or footers from the edge of the page in the Header or Footer text boxes (in the From Edge area near the center of the dialog box).

If you have varied the headers and footers using any of the three methods just described, then you must, when you choose the Header And Footer command, move to an appropriate document page to enter or modify each of the different headers or footers. For example, if you have created a different first-page header, you must move to the first page to enter or modify the first-page header or footer. You must then move to any other page to enter or modify the headers or footers for the other pages. The area for each header or footer is labeled to help you find the right one, for example, *Header -Section 2-* or *First Page Footer*, as shown here:

Chapter 18: Designing and Printing Professional-Looking Pages

To quickly move to the header or footer on the appropriate page, you can click the Show Previous or Show Next button on the Header And Footer toolbar, seen here:

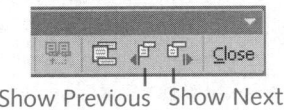

Show Previous   Show Next

Modifying the Page Setup

The Page Setup dialog box allows you to adjust a wide variety of options that affect the general appearance of the pages throughout your entire document or in one or more document sections. These options include the document margins, the paper size, the vertical alignment of text on the page, and line numbering.

> **note** If you're creating a Web page document, keep in mind that none of the settings you make in the Page Setup dialog box will affect the way the page appears in a browser.

To set any of these options, follow these steps:

1 Select the portion of your document that you want to modify by doing one of the following:

- If you want to modify the entire document, place the insertion point anywhere within the document.

- If you want to modify the document from a given position through the end of the document, place the insertion point at that position.

- If you want to modify a portion of the document, select that portion.

- If you have divided the document into sections, place the insertion point in the section you want to modify, or select several sections.

2 Choose File, Page Setup to open the Page Setup dialog box, which has three tabs: Margins, Paper, and Layout.

3 In the Apply To drop-down list (which appears in all tabs), choose the part of the document you want to modify, as shown here:

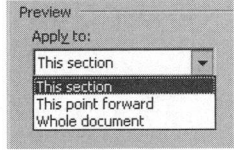

The selection you make in the Apply To drop-down list in one tab will change the selection in this list in all tabs and will control the part of the document that settings in *all* tabs will be applied to. In general, you can modify either the entire document or one or more document sections. The specific choices that

535

appear in the Apply To drop-down list depend on the part of the document that you have selected and whether you have divided your document into sections. Note that if you choose the This Point Forward option (which appears if you didn't select text), Word will insert a section break at the position of the insertion point, and if you choose the Selected Text option (which appears if you selected text), Word will insert a section break at the beginning and at the end of the selected text. Choosing one of these options is a convenient way to divide your document into sections without having to manually insert section breaks.

4 If you want to use the options you select as the default settings, click the Default button (which appears in all tabs) and respond Yes. Word will assign the current settings in each of the four tabs to the document and to the document template so that the settings will apply to any new documents you create based on this template.

5 Select the page setup options you want. The options displayed on each of the three tabs are discussed in the following three sections. Use the document model in the Preview area as an aid in selecting the options you want.

Setting the Margins and Page Orientation

To set the page margins and the orientation of the text on the page, perform the following steps:

1 Click the Margins tab of the Page Setup dialog box (shown in Figure 18-7).

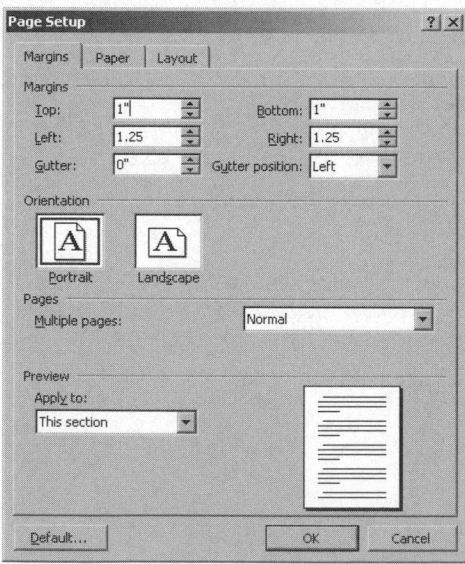

Figure 18-7. You can set the margins for a documents in the Margins tab of the Page Setup dialog box.

Chapter 18: Designing and Printing Professional-Looking Pages

2 In the Orientation area of the dialog box, choose Portrait (the usual setting) to print the lines of text at right angles to the direction of the paper feed, or choose Landscape to print the lines of text in the direction of the paper feed, as shown here:

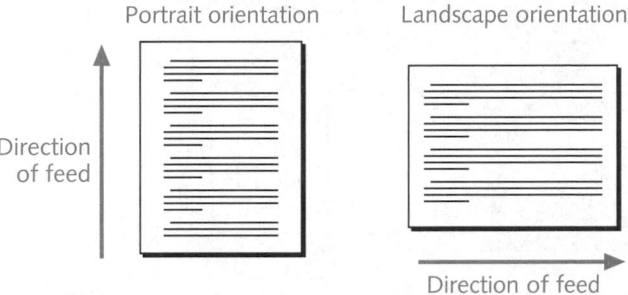

If, for example, your document contains a wide table, you might place the table in its own section and assign the Landscape orientation to that section, leaving the other document sections in Portrait orientation. Word would then print the table sideways so that it would fit on the paper.

> **note** When you switch paper orientations, Word automatically swaps the current settings of the top and bottom margins for the settings of the left and right margins so that the text occupies the same area on the page.

3 Select an item in the Multiple Pages drop-down list to specify the way you want the text laid out on the sheets of paper, as follows:

■ To print a single document page on each sheet of paper (or on each side of a sheet if you're printing on both sides) using the same margins for all pages, select Normal, as shown here. This is the usual printing option.

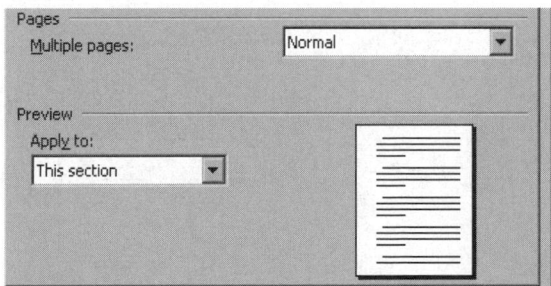

■ To print a single document page on each sheet of paper (or on each side of a sheet if you're printing on both sides) with symmetric margins on even and odd pages, select Mirror Margins, as seen in the following example. With this option the left margin on an even-numbered page will match the right margin on an odd-numbered page (this margin is known as the *outside* margin), and the right margin on an even-numbered page will match the left margin on an odd-numbered page (this margin is known as the *inside* margin).

- To print two half-sized document pages on each sheet of paper (or on each side of a sheet if you're printing on both sides) with symmetric margins, select 2 Pages Per Sheet. If you choose the Portrait orientation, the pages will be printed one above the other, as seen here:

If you choose the Landscape orientation, the pages will be printed side by side, as shown here:

With the 2 Pages Per Sheet option, the pages are printed in the order they occur in the document. If you think about that, you'll realize that you won't be able to create a booklet by simply printing on both sides of the paper and then folding the stack of sheets in half—to do that, you'll want to select the option discussed next.

newfeature!

■ To print two pages on each side of a sheet of paper with symmetric margins, so that you can create a booklet or book directly from the printed sheets, select Book Fold, as shown in the following example. This option uses the Landscape orientation only (you won't be able to switch to Portrait). To be able to make a booklet directly from the printed sheets, you'll need to print on both sides of each sheet (that is, you must print in duplex mode).

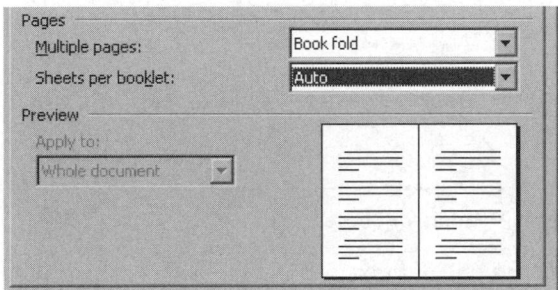

As you can see, the placement of the pages on a sheet with the Book Fold option is the same as that with the 2 Pages Per Sheet option in Landscape orientation. However, rather than printing the pages in the order they occur in the document, the Book Fold option prints the pages in the proper order so that you can quickly create a booklet by folding the stack of sheets in half and stapling in the center. If you've selected this option, you can divide the document into a series of separate booklets by selecting a specific number of sheets in the Sheets Per Booklet drop-down list.

For step-by-step instructions, see the sidebar "Creating a Booklet or Book," on page 543.

4 Set the page margins in the four text boxes in the Margins area at the top of the Margins tab. The labels on the boxes will correspond to the option that is currently selected in the Multiple Pages drop-down list. For example, if the Normal option is selected, the boxes will be labeled Top, Bottom, Left, and Right, and they will set the margins as shown here:

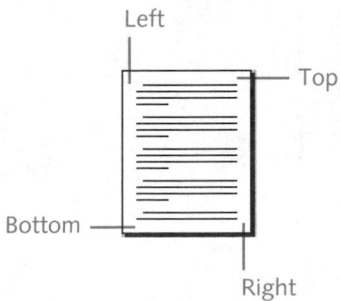

And, if you selected Mirror Margins, the boxes will be labeled Top, Bottom, Inside, and Outside, and they will set the margins as shown here:

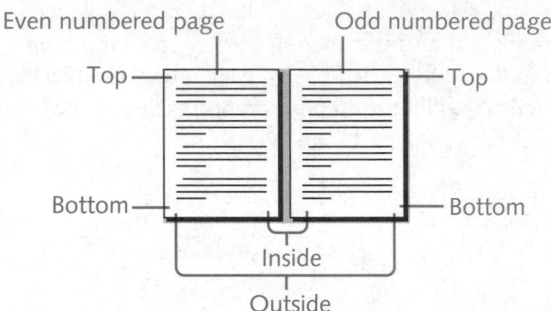

tip   **Create Symmetric Headers or Footers**

If you have selected one of the options in the Multiple Pages drop-down list that creates symmetric margins (Mirror Margins, 2 Pages Per Sheet, or Book Fold), you might also want to create symmetric headers or footers. You can do this by checking the Different Odd And Even option in the Layout tab of the Page Setup dialog box and formatting your headers and footers appropriately, as explained in "Adding Headers and Footers," on page 526.

5 You can add extra space to the left, top, or inside margin on each page to make room for the binding. To do this, enter the desired amount of space into the Gutter text box. If you've selected the Normal option in the Multiple Pages drop-down list, you can select either Left or Top in the Gutter Position drop-down list to specify the page margin where you want to add the gutter.

If you've selected Mirror Margins, 2 Pages Per Sheet, or Book Fold in the Multiple Pages list, Word places the gutter on the inside margin and you can't change its position. The position of the gutter with the Mirror Margins option and the Portrait orientation would be as shown here:

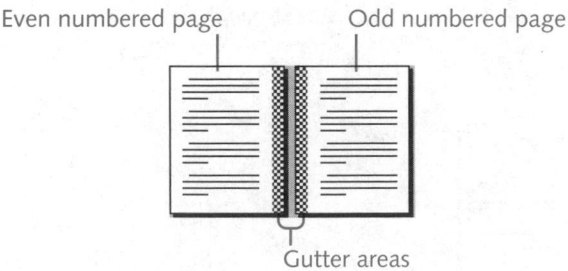

Chapter 18: Designing and Printing Professional-Looking Pages

---

tip   Mark Your Margins

In Print Layout or Web Layout view, you can have Word mark with dotted lines the inside boundaries of the page margins (as well as the boundaries of multiple columns, if you've applied them to the text). To show these marker lines, choose Tools, Options, click the View tab, and check the Text Boundaries option in the Print And Web Layout Options area.

Setting Margins Using the Rulers

Another way to adjust the page margins is by using the horizontal and vertical rulers, following these steps:

1 If you have divided your document into sections, place the insertion point in the section you want to modify, or select several sections to modify all of them.

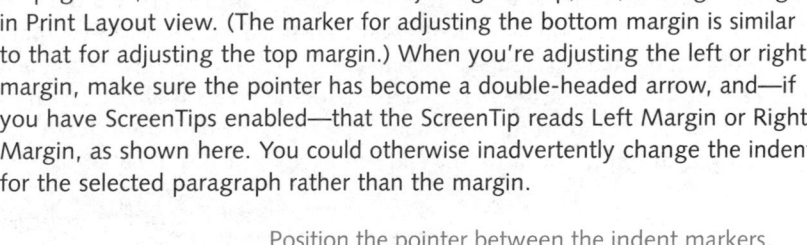

View Ruler

2 Switch to Print Layout view or to Print Preview and display the horizontal and vertical ruler. To display the rulers in Print Layout view, choose View, Ruler. If the vertical ruler still isn't visible, choose Tools, Options, click the View tab, and check the Vertical Ruler (Print View Only) option. To display both rulers in Print Preview, click the View Ruler button on the Print Preview toolbar.

3 Drag the appropriate marker on the horizontal or vertical ruler. Figure 18-8, on page 542, shows the markers for adjusting the top, left, and right margins in Print Layout view. (The marker for adjusting the bottom margin is similar to that for adjusting the top margin.) When you're adjusting the left or right margin, make sure the pointer has become a double-headed arrow, and—if you have ScreenTips enabled—that the ScreenTip reads Left Margin or Right Margin, as shown here. You could otherwise inadvertently change the indent for the selected paragraph rather than the margin.

Position the pointer between the indent markers.

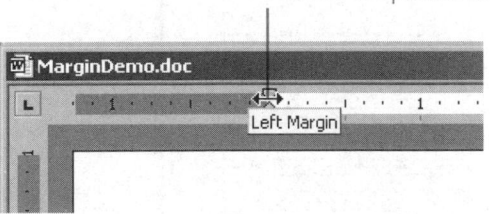

Chapter 18

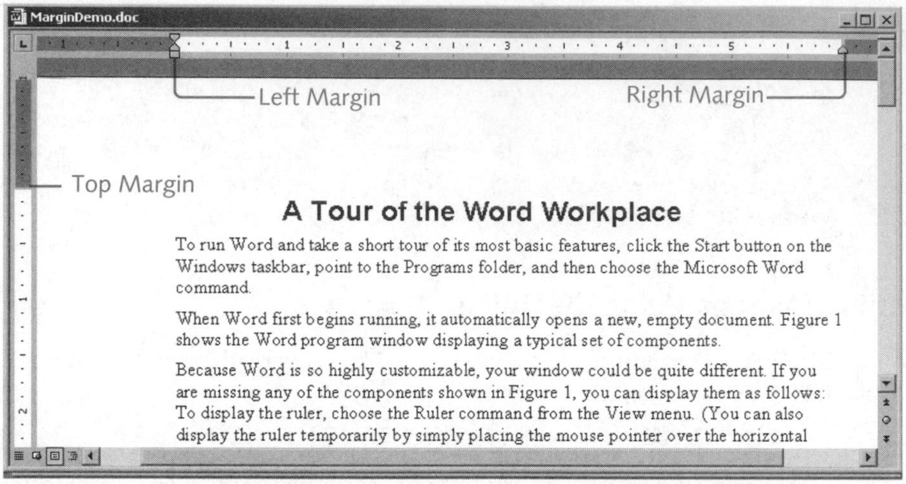

> **MarginDemo.doc**

Left Margin   *Right Margin*

Top Margin

A Tour of the Word Workplace

To run Word and take a short tour of its most basic features, click the Start button on the Windows taskbar, point to the Programs folder, and then choose the Microsoft Word command.

When Word first begins running, it automatically opens a new, empty document. Figure 1 shows the Word program window displaying a typical set of components.

Because Word is so highly customizable, your window could be quite different. If you are missing any of the components shown in Figure 1, you can display them as follows: To display the ruler, choose the Ruler command from the View menu. (You can also display the ruler temporarily by simply placing the mouse pointer over the horizontal

Figure 18-8. This figure shows the markers on the horizontal and vertical rulers for adjusting the top, left, and right margins in Print Layout view.

> **tip** To see the exact margin measurements, hold down the Alt key while you drag a margin marker on a ruler.

Don't confuse the left and right *margins* with the left and right *indents*. A margin is the normal distance between the text and the edge of the paper, and it applies to an entire document or section. An indent is an adjustment to this distance that applies to one or more individual paragraphs. (An indent is a paragraph formatting feature.) If the left or right indent measurement is 0, the paragraph text is aligned with the left or right margin. If the indent measurement is positive, the paragraph text is moved in from the margin, and if it's negative the text is moved out from the margin (see Figure 18-9).

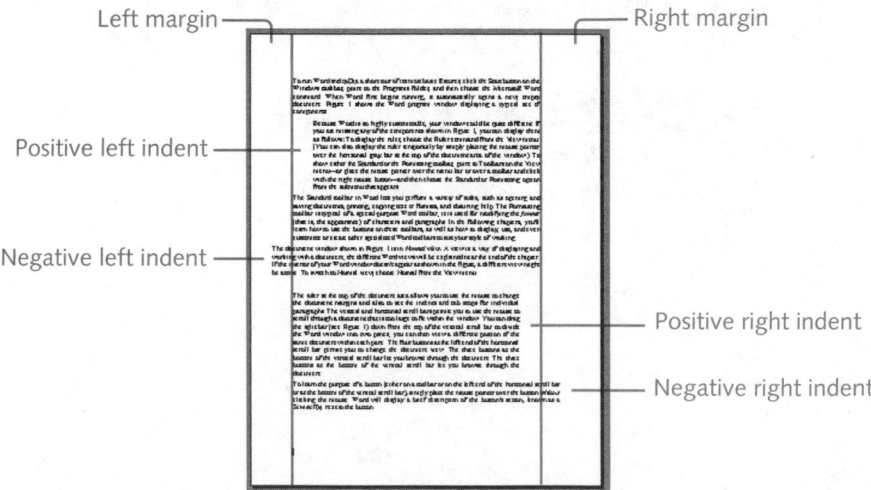

Left margin — — Right margin

Positive left indent —

Negative left indent —

— Positive right indent

— Negative right indent

Figure 18-9. This figure shows different types of margins and indents.

Chapter 18

Setting indents is discussed in "Formatting Paragraphs Directly," on page 309.

newfeature!
Creating a Booklet or Book

In Word 2002 you can now directly print the pages for a booklet, or even a book. Each page will be printed on one half of a side of a sheet of paper. So if you're using 8½-inch by 11-inch paper, each booklet page will measure 5½-inches wide by 8½-inches high. It might take some trial and error to perfect the process for your printer, so *be sure to start by printing a small test booklet.*

To create a booklet from the currently opened document, perform the following steps:

1 Choose File, Page Setup and click the Margins tab in the Page Setup dialog box (see Figure 18-7, on page 536).

2 In the Multiple Pages drop-down list, select Book Fold.

3 Make sure that All is selected in the Sheets For Booklet drop-down list.

4 Set the margins, make any other adjustments to the page setup that you want in the Page Setup dialog box, and click OK.

5 When you print the document, be sure to print on both sides of the paper (that is, print in *duplex* mode). If you have a duplex printer, you should be able to select duplex printing by clicking the Properties button in the Print dialog box.

Details on printing are given in "Previewing and Printing Documents," on page 547.

If you don't have a duplex printer, you can print on both sides of the paper manually by checking the new Manual Duplex option in the Print dialog box. Word will print the first side of each sheet of paper, prompt you to flip the stack of sheets over and reinsert them into your paper tray, and then print the second sides. (Discovering the correct way to flip the sheets over for your printer will probably take a little trial and error. Again, start with a small test booklet!)

6 After the pages are printed, fold the stack of sheets down the center and staple them together in the center using a long-reach stapler.

Rather than printing all of the pages of a large document as a single booklet, you can print them as a series of separate booklets. To do this, follow the same procedure, but in step 3 select the number of pages you want to include in each booklet from the Sheets Per Booklet drop-down list, rather than selecting All (because four pages are printed on each sheet of paper, the numbers you can select are multiples of four). To create a book, you could bind the separate booklets together using appropriate book-binding methods. (Book designers call each one of these booklets a *signature*.)

Adjusting the Paper Size and Source

Word normally assumes that you're printing on 8½-inch by 11-inch paper. If you're using a different paper size, you must change the paper size setting, by following these steps:

1 Click the Paper tab of the Page Setup dialog box (shown in Figure 18-10).

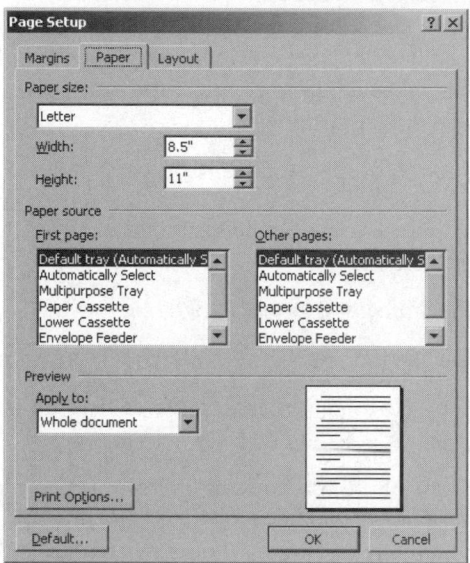

Figure 18-10. The Paper tab of the Page Setup dialog box lets you specify the paper size and source.

2 If you're using a standard paper size, choose that size in the Paper Size drop-down list. (The contents of this list depend on your current default printer.)

3 If you can't find the size of your paper in the Paper Size list, enter the correct size into the Width and Height boxes.

If your printer has more than one paper tray, a manual feed slot, or another paper source, you can print the first page of the document (or of the section) on paper from one source and print all remaining pages on paper from a different source. You could use this technique, for example, to print the first page of a letter on letterhead stock and the remaining pages on blank stock. To set the paper source, perform the following steps:

1 Click the Paper tab of the Page Setup dialog box (see Figure 18-10).

2 Select a paper source for the first page in the document (or document section) from the First Page list.

Chapter 18: Designing and Printing Professional-Looking Pages

3 Select a paper source for the remaining document (or section) pages from the Other Pages list.

note To set printer options, click the Print Options button in the Paper tab to open the Print tab. Another way to access this tab is to choose Tools, Options.

Adjusting the Page Layout

You can adjust a variety of page setup options in the Layout tab of the Page Setup dialog box, shown in Figure 18-11, as follows:

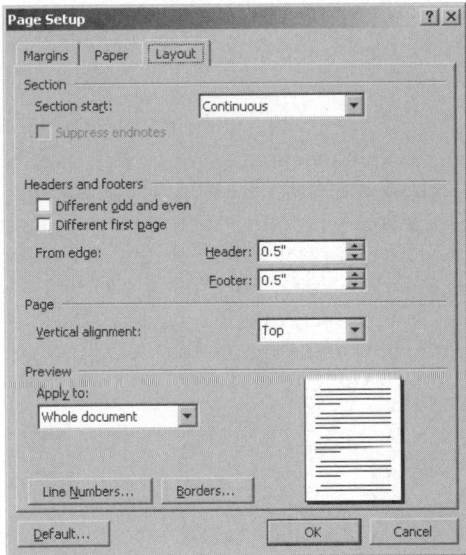

Figure 18-11. You can set several layout options in the Layout tab of the Page Setup dialog box.

- To control the location of the text at the beginning of the selected document section or sections, choose an item in the Section Start drop-down list.

- To affect the way Word arranges paragraphs—in the vertical direction—on pages that are not completely filled with text, choose an option in the Vertical Alignment list. Figure 18-12, on page 546, shows the effects of the different options. You might, for example, choose the Center option for the title page of a report.

Top   Center   Justified

Figure 18-12. This figure shows the effect of each of the Vertical Alignment options.

> **note** The effect of the Vertical Alignment option you have chosen will be visible only in Print Layout view, in Print Preview, and on the printed pages.

● To have Word print line numbers in the left margin within one or more document sections, click the Line Numbers button. In the Line Numbers dialog box (see Figure 18-13), check the Add Line Numbering option, and select the line numbering options you want. Line numbers are displayed only in Print Layout view, Print Preview, and on the printed copy of the document. Lawyers and publishers often use line numbering to facilitate discussion of specific lines among several people. Note that you can block line numbering for a specific paragraph by applying the Suppress Line Numbers paragraph formatting option, which you'll find in the Line And Page Breaks tab of the Paragraph dialog box.

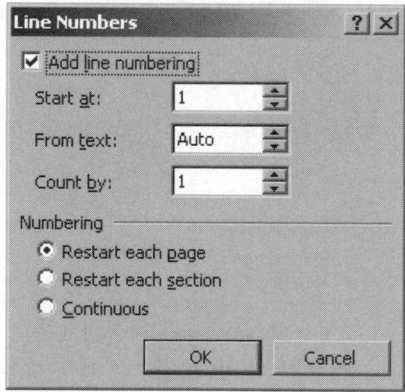

Figure 18-13. The Line Numbers dialog box allows you to add line numbering to a document.

For a description of the Paragraph dialog box, see "Formatting Paragraphs with the Paragraph Dialog Box," on page 314.

> **tip** **Reformat Line Numbers**
>
> You can change the character formatting of line numbers throughout your document by modifying the Line Number character style, using the techniques given in Chapter 14, "Advanced Word Formatting Techniques."

● To apply a page border to the pages in your document or in one or more document sections, click the Borders button to open the Page Border tab of the Borders And Shading dialog box.

> The procedure for applying page borders is described in "Applying Borders to Pages," on page 365. For information on the Different Odd And Even and the Different First Page options in the Layout tab, see "Varying Headers or Footers Within a Document," on page 532. For an explanation of the Header and Footer text boxes in the From Edge area of the Layout tab, see "Adjusting the Size and Position of Headers or Footers," on page 529, and the Troubleshooting sidebar "Headers or Footers Cut Off," on page 534. And for instructions on using the Suppress Endnotes option, see "Inserting Footnotes and Endnotes," on page 430.

Previewing and Printing Documents

When you have finally finished entering text and graphics into your document, as well as editing, formatting, proofing, and adjusting the page design, you're ready to print the document. Before doing so, however, you might want to preview the printed appearance of the document on the screen and possibly make a few last-minute adjustments.

Word provides two document views that display the document exactly as it will be printed: Print Layout and Print Preview. These two views have many features in common; in general, however, Print Layout view is best for editing the document and working with text boxes and graphics, and Print Preview is best for viewing the overall appearance of the document pages immediately before printing.

> **newfeature!**
>
> **tip** **Compress Top and Bottom Margins in Print Layout View**
>
> Normally, Print Layout view shows the complete document page, including the top and bottom margin areas, as well as some background between the pages. These areas take up a lot of screen space and also cause the insertion point to jump when you use an arrow key to move it from one page to the next. In Word 2002, you can see more of your document in Print Layout view and make scrolling smoother by hiding the top and bottom margin areas. To do this, choose View, Options, click the View tab, and clear the White Space Between Pages (Print View Only) option.

Print
Preview

To switch to Print Preview, choose File, Print Preview or click the Print Preview button on the Standard toolbar. The Print Preview screen is shown in Figure 18-14. To edit your document while in Print Preview, click the Magnifier button on the toolbar to disable the Magnifier. Click the Close button to close Print Preview and return to the view you were working in earlier.

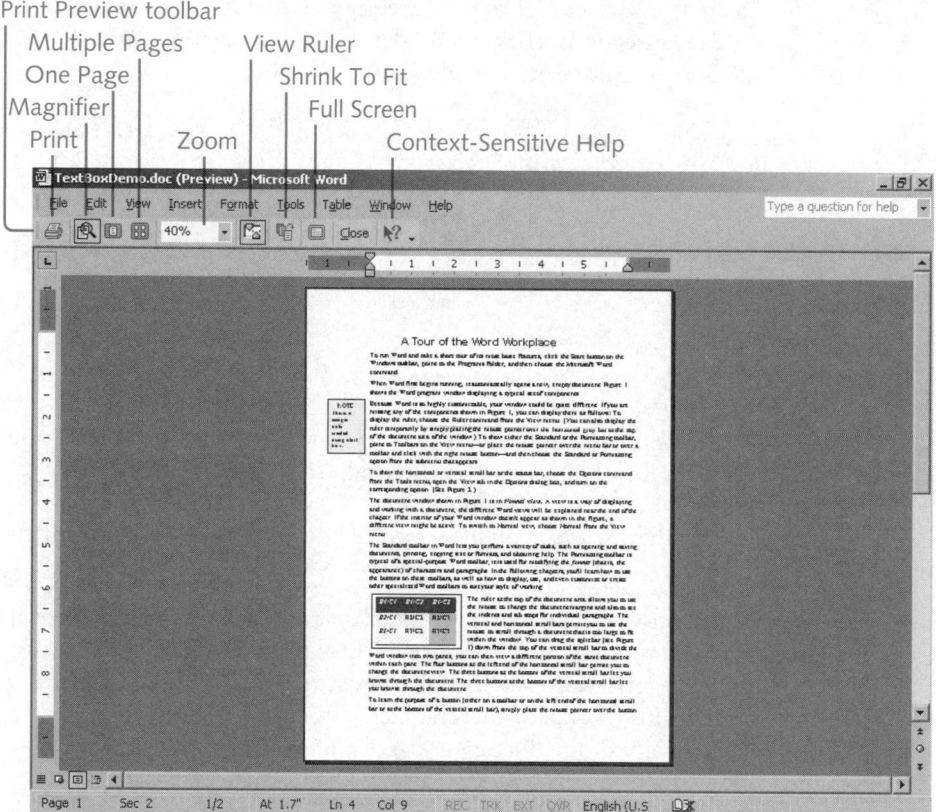

Figure 18-14. This figure shows a document displayed in Print Preview.

When you're ready to print your document, choose File, Print or press Ctrl+P. Word will display the Print dialog box, which is shown in Figure 18-15. Before clicking the OK button to start printing, you can choose the printer, change printer settings, and select printing options.

Chapter 18: Designing and Printing Professional-Looking Pages

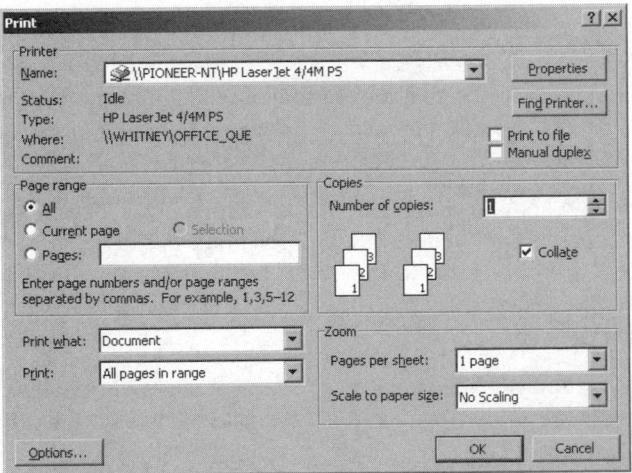

Figure 18-15. The Print dialog box lets you set options before printing a document.

Rather than printing the document itself, you can print various document elements by choosing an item other than Document in the Print What drop-down list of the Print dialog box, as follows:

- To print the information displayed and set by the File, Properties command, select Document Properties.

- To print the document plus all tracked change markings and comments that have been added to it, select Document Showing Markup.

- To print a list of all tracked changes and all comments, including the page, author, date, and time of each, select List Of Markup. Word will print the same information that it displays in the Reviewing pane.

- To print a description of the document styles, select Styles.

- To print the contents of the document's AutoText entries, select AutoText Entries.

- To print a list of the document's current shortcut key assignments, select Key Assignments.

Print

Alternatively, you can quickly print your document using the current default printer and the default print settings by simply clicking the Print button on the Standard toolbar or on the Print Preview toolbar (which is displayed when you switch to Print Preview).

Adjusting the Pagination

Before printing your document, you might want to view and adjust the positions of the page breaks. You should do this after editing, formatting, and proofing your document because these actions can change the positions of page breaks.

In Print Layout view or in Print Preview, you can easily see the positions of page breaks because each page is displayed exactly as it will print. In Normal view, Word marks the position of each page break with a dotted horizontal line if you have checked the Background Repagination option. (To access this option, choose Tools, Options and click the General tab.)

The following paragraph formatting features can affect the positions of page breaks: Widow/Orphan Control, Keep Lines Together, Keep With Next, and Page Break Before.

> These paragraph formatting features are explained in detail in Chapter 12, "Effective Formatting in Word." See Table 12-3, on page 311, for an explanation of each of them.

Also, the positions of page breaks can be affected by the current settings of the print options that tell Word what to include in the printed copy of the document. These options are contained in the Include With Document area of the Print tab of the Options dialog box, shown in Figure 18-16. To access this tab, choose Tools, Options, or click the Options button in the Print dialog box, shown in Figure 18-15.

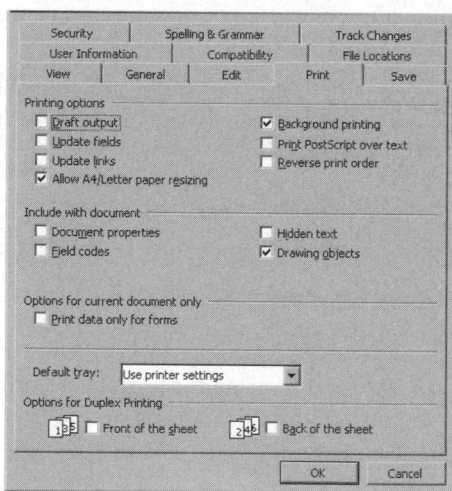

Figure 18-16. You can select several printing options in the Print tab of the Options dialog box.

Adjusting the Pagination *(continued)*   A page break that Word automatically generates when the text reaches the bottom of a page is known as a *soft page break*. You can also force a page break at any position in a document by inserting a *hard page break*. The position of a hard page break is fixed, and it always causes a page break regardless of its location on the page. To insert a hard page break at the insertion point, press Ctrl+Enter, or choose Insert, Break and select the Page Break option. In Normal view, Word marks the position of a hard page break with a horizontal dotted line labeled Page Break, as shown here (in contrast, the horizontal line marking the position of a soft page break is not labeled):

Soft page break mark   ···

Hard page break mark   ···Page Break·································

Show/
Hide ¶

In Print Layout view, the text following a hard page break is forced to a new page, but the mark itself appears only if all nonprinting characters are displayed. (To display all nonprinting characters, select All under Formatting Marks in the View tab of the Options dialog box, or click the Show/Hide ¶ button on the Standard toolbar.

To remove a hard page break, just select the mark and press Delete.

Writing a Macro for Printing the Current Selection Quickly

This sidebar presents a useful macro for printing the current selection in the document using the default printer settings. You can quickly print bits and pieces of a document by selecting the text or graphics and running this macro, rather than having to open the Print dialog box, select the Selection option, and click OK.

You can enter the macro yourself using the VBA Editor, following the brief instructions given here. Or you can use the Organizer to copy the macro from the WordInsideOut module in the WordInsideOut.dot file provided on the book's companion CD into your own Normal template.

For complete information on macros and using the VBA Editor, see Part 10 of this book. For instructions on working with the Organizer, see "Using the Organizer," on page 409.

1   In Word, choose Tools, Macro, Visual Basic Editor. This will run the Microsoft Visual Basic editor.

(continued)

> **Writing a Macro for Printing the Current Selection Quickly** *(continued)*
>
> **2** In the Project Explorer pane at the upper-left of the Visual Basic editor window, double-click the Normal/Microsoft Word Objects/This Document item. (Expand the tree, if necessary, to access this item. If the Project Explorer pane isn't displayed, choose View, Project Explorer.) This will open a code window where you can enter code that will be stored in your Normal template.
>
> **3** Type the following macro code into the code window:
>
> ```
> Sub PrintSelection()
> 'PrintSelection macro
> Application.PrintOut Range:=wdPrintSelection
> End Sub
> ```
>
> **4** In the Visual Basic editor, choose File, Close And Return To Microsoft Word.
>
> **5** Use the procedures described in "Defining Shortcut Keys (Word Only)," on page 217, to define a shortcut key for the PrintSelection macro. You can also use the techniques given in "Modifying Toolbars and Menus," on page 209, to add a toolbar button for running this macro.
>
> You can now test the macro as follows: Select a block of text or graphics in a document and press the shortcut key or click the toolbar button that you defined for the macro. Word should now print just the selected text or graphics using the default printer settings.

Chapter 19

Using Word to Automate Mailings

new feature!
Using the Mail Merge Wizard to Automate Large Mailings

The Microsoft Word 2002 *mail merge* feature merges a main document with a recipient list to generate a set of output documents:

- The *main document* is a specially marked Word document that serves as a blueprint for creating the output documents. It contains the basic text that is the same in every output document—for example, a letterhead, the main body of a letter, and a letter closing—plus instructions (known as *merge fields*) for inserting the text that varies from one output document to another—for example, the recipient names and addresses.

- The *recipient list* is a database—for example, a Microsoft Access 2002 database file or a Microsoft Excel 2002 workbook—that contains the data that is to be merged into the output documents. Typically, it stores a list of names, mailing addresses, e-mail addresses, fax numbers, and so on.

- The end product of the mail merge feature is a set of *output documents*. Some of the text is the same in all output documents, while some varies from document to document. You can use mail merge to create any of the following types of output documents:

    - Form letters
    - E-mail messages
    - Faxes

Part 3: Word

- Envelopes
- Labels
- A directory (a list of names and addresses or other information that is printed or is stored in a single Word document)

Figure 19-1 shows how mail merge works when you create a set of form letters.

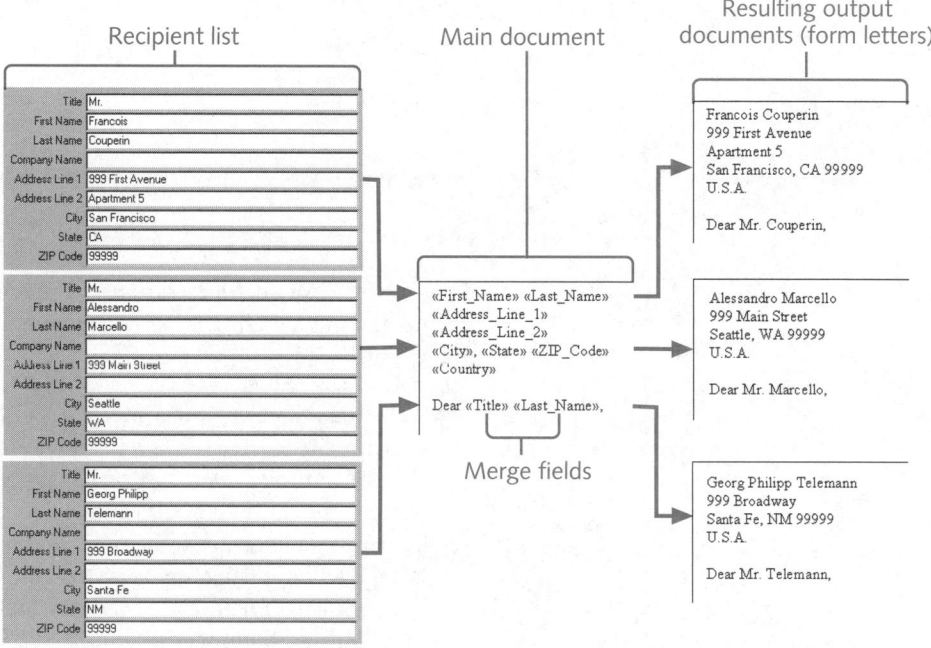

Figure 19-1. This figure shows the process of merging a recipient list with a main mail merge document to generate a set of form letters.

The fastest way to use the mail merge feature is to run the Mail Merge wizard. The following basic method lets you create any of the types of output documents just listed, except faxes (a method for creating faxes is given later in this section):

1 If you want to use an existing document for your mail merge main document, open it now. Otherwise, just open a blank document.

2 Choose Tools, Letters And Mailings, Mail Merge wizard. This will display the Step 1 Mail Merge task pane, the first of six Mail Merge panes.

3 In the Step 1 Mail Merge task pane, titled Select Document Type, choose one of the five options displayed at the top of the pane to specify the type of output documents you want to create (see Figure 19-2). Then, click the Next command to display the next Mail Merge task pane. (In the wizard panes, the Next command is labeled according to the title of the following pane—for example, Next: Starting Document or Next: Select Recipients.)

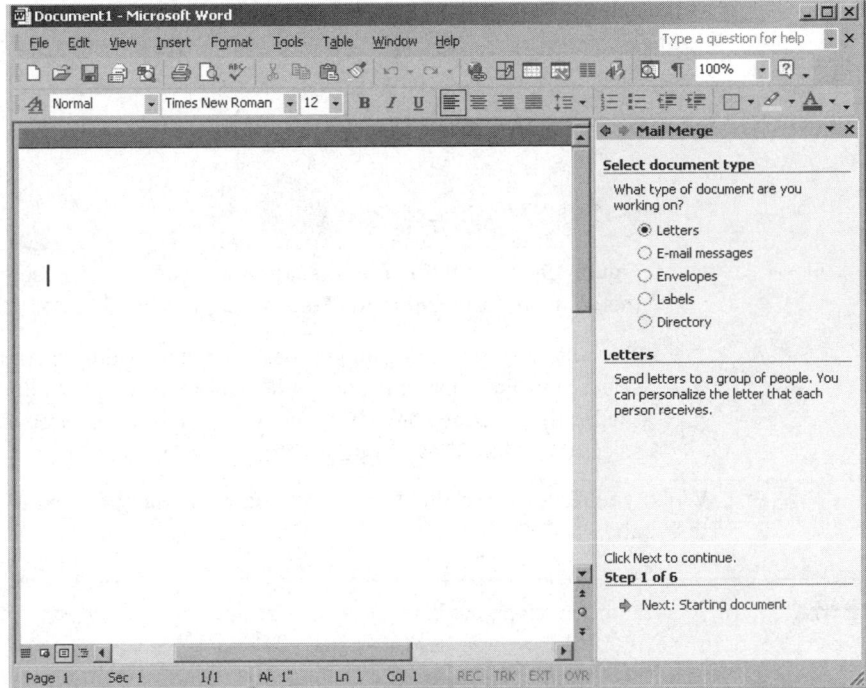

Figure 19-2. Here, the Letters output document type is selected in the Step 1 pane of the Mail Merge wizard to generate form letters.

4 In the Step 2 Mail Merge task pane, titled Select Starting Document, select an option to tell the wizard how to create your mail merge main document.

- To convert the document in the active document window to a mail merge main document, select Use The Current Document (see Figure 19-3, on page 556).

- To create a new main document based on a template, select Start From A Template, and then click the Select Templates command that appears to choose the template you want to use.

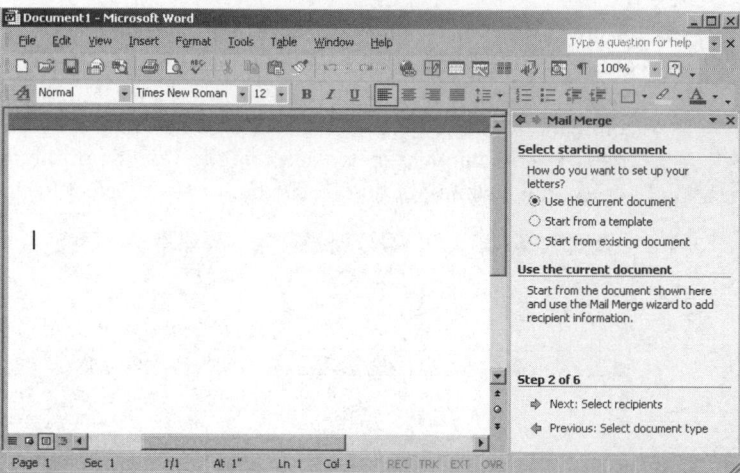

Figure 19-3. In this figure, the current document is chosen as the mail merge main document in the Step 2 task pane of the Mail Merge wizard.

- To create a new main document based on an existing document file, select Start From Existing Document, and then select the document in the list that appears, or to use a document that doesn't appear in the list, select the (More Files...) option. Then click the Open button.

When you're done, click the Next command to display the next Mail Merge task pane.

---

note If you're creating envelopes or labels, the Step 2 task pane provides the following two options, rather than the three just listed:

- To set up a custom layout for your envelopes or labels, select Change Document Layout. Then click the Envelope Options (or Label Options) button that appears and select the layout and printing options you want in the dialog box that's displayed.

- To use an existing mail merge main document containing an envelope or label layout, select Start From Existing Document, and then select the document in the list that appears—or select the (More Files) option to choose a document that doesn't appear in the list—and then click the Open button.

---

tip In the Mail Merge Step 2 through Step 6 task panes, you can click the Previous command to go back to a previous pane and modify your selections.

5 In the Step 3 Mail Merge task pane, titled Select Recipients, specify what you want to use as your recipient list—that is, as the source of your mail merge data:

▪ To use an existing database file that contains the names and addresses or other data you want to merge, select Use An Existing List, and then click the Browse command that appears to select the file.

▪ To use a Microsoft Outlook Contacts folder as the source of the mail merge data, select the Select From Outlook Contacts option, and then click the Choose Contacts Folder command that appears to pick the contacts folder you want to use.

▪ To create a new recipient list by typing in the data, select Type A New list, and then click the Create command that appears and type each entry into the New Address List dialog box (see Figure 19-4 and Figure 19-5, on page 558). When you close the dialog box, Word will display the Save Address List dialog box (similar to the Save As dialog box), so that you can select a filename and location for your new recipient list. The wizard will save the recipient list as an Access database file (with the .mdb extension). Finally, the wizard will display the Mail Merge Recipients dialog box, in which you can sort or filter the entries in the recipient list, if you like, or work with them in other ways.

When you're done, click the Next command to display the next Mail Merge task pane.

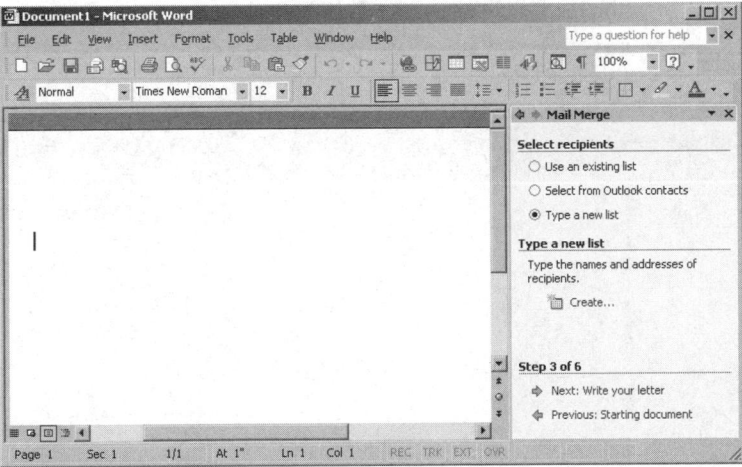

Figure 19-4. Here, a new recipient list is created in the Step 3 task pane of the Mail Merge wizard.

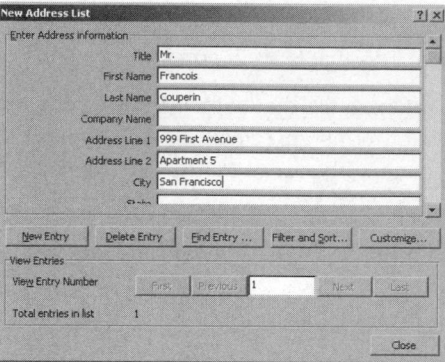

Figure 19-5. In this figure, a new recipient list entry is typed in the New Address List dialog box.

6 When the wizard displays the Step 4 Mail Merge task pane, you can enter or edit the mail merge main document that's displayed in the active document window (which you selected in step 4), as follows:

- To enter the text that remains the same in all of the output documents (such as a letterhead, the main body of a letter, or a letter closing) use standard Word editing and formatting methods.

- To enter the text that varies from one output document to another, insert the appropriate merge fields using the commands displayed in the Step 4 task pane (shown in Figure 19-6). Table 19-1 describes these commands and what they do.

Mail Merge toolbar

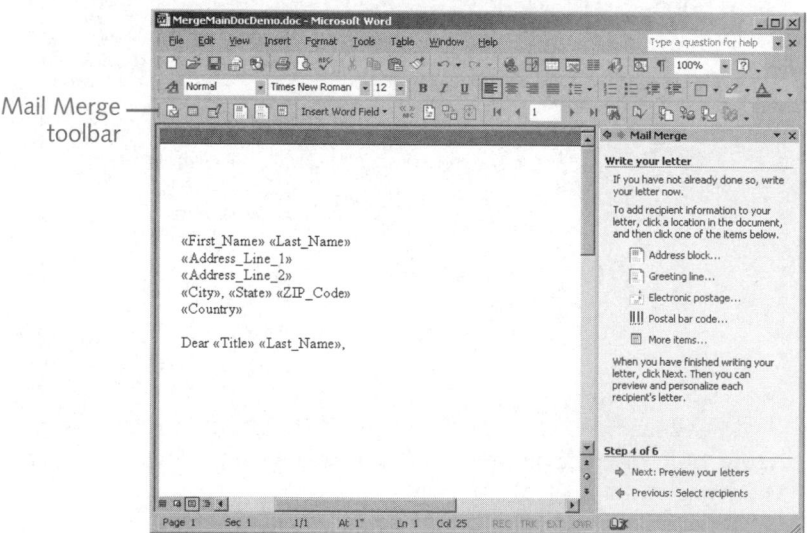

Figure 19-6. This figure shows a completed mail merge main document, written using the commands displayed in the Step 4 pane of the Mail Merge wizard.

Chapter 19: Using Word to Automate Mailings

Table 19-1. **The Commands in the Step 4 Mail Merge Task Pane**

To Insert These Merge Fields	Click This Command in the Step 4 Task Pane
Name and address fields, in various formats—for example: *Francois Couperin* *999 First Avenue* *Apartment 5* *San Francisco, CA 99999* *U.S.A.*	Address Block
Salutation field, in various formats—for example: *Dear Mr. Couperin,*	Greeting Line
E-postage field (several software programs let you print your own postage on envelopes or mailing labels). For information, see the Office Update Web site at *http://officeupdate.microsoft.com/*.	Electronic Postage
Postal bar code field (a postal bar code is a machine-readable representation of the ZIP code, and including it on an envelope or label might expedite mail delivery).	Postal Bar Code
Merge fields for specific fields in your recipient list, such as the Title, First Name, Last Name, Company Name, or Address Line 1 field	More Items

note An alternative way to insert merge fields, to work with your mail merge main document, or to run a mail merge, is to use the Mail Merge toolbar that Word displays when you open the Step 4 Mail Merge task pane (see Figure 19-6, on page 558). You can also display this toolbar at any time by choosing Tools, Letters And Mailings, Show Mail Merge Toolbar.

Although the Mail Merge toolbar isn't as easy to use as the Mail Merge wizard (especially if you employ mail merge only occasionally) if you become a mail merge expert, you might find it faster to display and use the toolbar rather than running the wizard. The Mail Merge toolbar provides all the commands you need to run a mail merge. In fact, the toolbar provides several commands not included in the Mail Merge wizard task panes. For example, you can use the Insert Word Field drop-down menu on the Mail Merge toolbar to insert Word fields for controlling the merge process (for instance an IF field that inserts text only if a particular merge field has a specified value). Or, you can click the Check For Errors button to have Word run the mail merge and report any errors contained in the main document.

> **note** The Step 4 Mail Merge task pane is labeled according to the type of output document you're creating—Write Your E-Mail Message, Arrange Your Envelope, and so on.
>
> If you're creating labels, you can click the Update All Labels button in the task pane to copy the layout of your first label to all other labels on the sheet.

When you've finished writing the main document, save your work and then click the Next command in the Mail Merge task pane to display the next pane.

7 When the wizard displays the Step 5 Mail Merge task pane, it replaces each of the merge fields in the main document with the actual text from the first entry of the recipient list, so you can see what your first output document will look like (see Figure 19-7). You can now work with your output documents as follows:

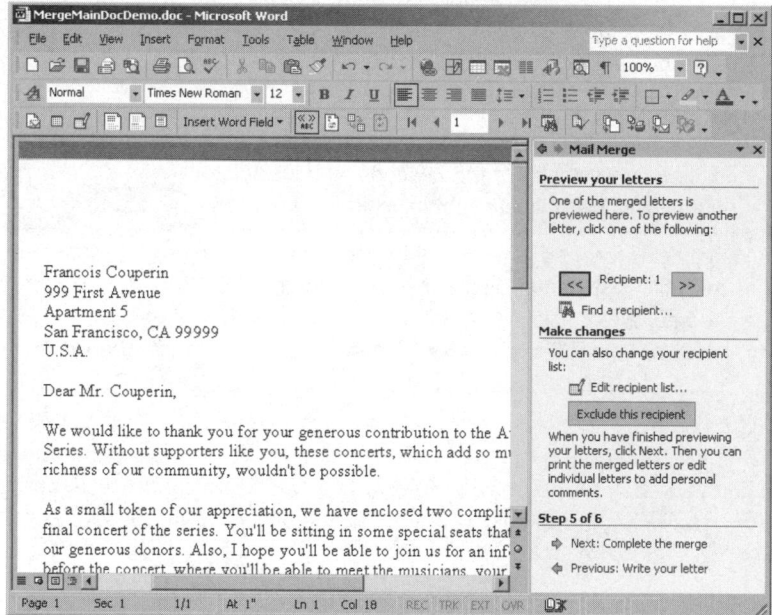

Figure 19-7. You can view and work with output form letters using the commands displayed in the Step 5 pane of the Mail Merge wizard.

- To view other output documents, click the << and >> buttons.

- To find an entry in your recipient list that contains specific text and to view the output document showing that entry's information, click the Find A Recipient command and type the text into the Find Entry dialog box.

- To modify the recipient list (which you selected or created in step 5), click the Edit Recipient List command.

- To remove the currently displayed output document from the final output (that is, from the printed copies, Word document, e-mail messages, and so on), click the Exclude This Recipient button.

> **note** The Step 5 Mail Merge task pane is labeled according to the type of output document you're creating—Preview Your Letters, Preview Your E-Mail Messages, and so on.

When you're done previewing and working with the output documents, click the Next command to display the final Mail Merge task pane.

8 In the Step 6 (and final) Mail Merge task pane, labeled Complete The Merge, generate your final output documents by clicking the appropriate command (see Figure 19-8).

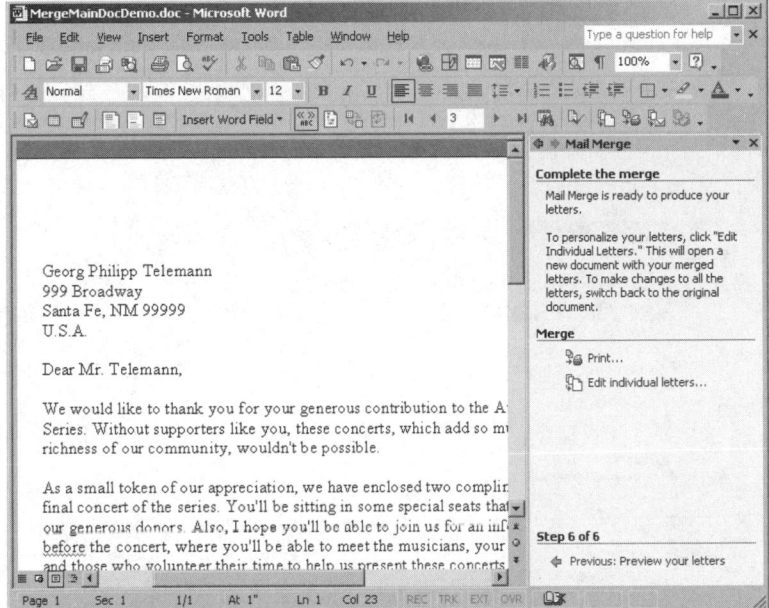

Figure 19-8. The Step 6 Mail Merge task pane lets you print the form letters or output them all to a single Word document.

If you're creating form letters, envelopes, or labels, you can do one of the following actions:

- To print the letters, envelopes, or labels immediately, click the Print command.

- To store all the letters, envelopes, or labels within a single, new Word document, click the Edit Individual Letters (or Edit Individual Envelopes or Edit Individual Labels) command. The advantage of using this command is that it gives you the chance to double check the output, touch up its content or formatting, and then print or reprint the items whenever you want. However, if you find that you're making the same change to all letters, envelopes, or labels, you'll probably save time by going back to the Mail Merge wizard, editing the main document or recipient list, and regenerating the output.

Part 3: Word

> **note** If you're creating e-mail messages, click the Electronic Mail command to create the messages. If you're creating a directory, click the To New Document command to store the resulting directory in a Word document. And if you're creating faxes (as explained below), click Print to print the faxes or click Fax to send the faxes out using your fax modem.

The following alternative way to use the Mail Merge wizard lets you create faxes, as well as form letters or a directory:

1 Choose File, New to open the New task pane.

2 Click the General Templates command to open the Templates dialog box.

3 In the Templates dialog box, click the Mail Merge tab (as shown in Figure 19-9) and double-click the template you want to use. Word provides mail merge templates for creating faxes, letters, or an "address list" (another term for a directory).

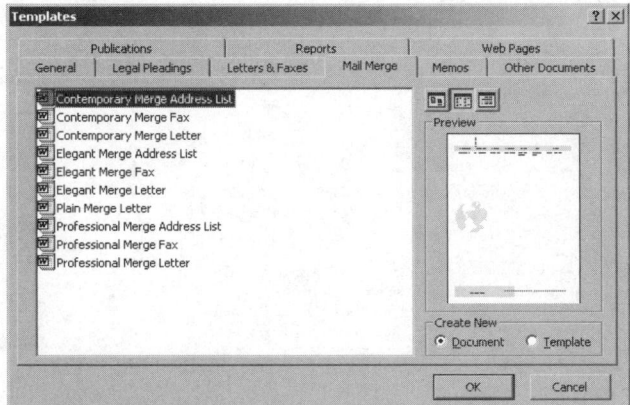

Figure 19-9. The Mail Merge tab of the Templates dialog box allows you to create a mail merge document by using a template.

Word will then create the new document based on the selected template and it will open the Mail Merge task pane. By selecting a specific mail merge template, you have already completed the first two steps of the Mail Merge wizard. Therefore, the wizard displays the task panes for only the final four steps.

> **note** If you want to use a mail merge template stored on a Web site, click the Templates On My Web Sites command. To look for a mail merge template on Microsoft's Web site, click Templates On Microsoft.com. For information on creating documents using templates, see "Creating a Document Using the New Document Task Pane," on page 58.

4 Complete the four Mail Merge wizard task panes as explained in the previous procedure in this section. However, keep in mind that the Step 1 through Step 4 panes are equivalent to the Step 3 through Step 6 panes referenced in the previous procedure.

Generating Individual Envelopes and Labels

You can print an individual envelope or label using the Envelopes And Labels command. This command is especially useful for addressing an envelope or label for a letter that you have just finished typing.

> For information on using Word's mail merge feature to print envelopes or labels for an entire group of delivery addresses, see "Using the Mail Merge Wizard to Automate Large Mailings," on page 553.

Generating Individual Envelopes

To print a single envelope, perform the following steps:

1 If you have already typed the delivery address into a document (for example, in the heading of a letter), open that document. (This step is optional because you can type the address later.)

2 Choose Tools, Letters And Mailings, Envelopes And Labels. Then, in the Envelopes And Labels dialog box, click the Envelopes tab, shown here:

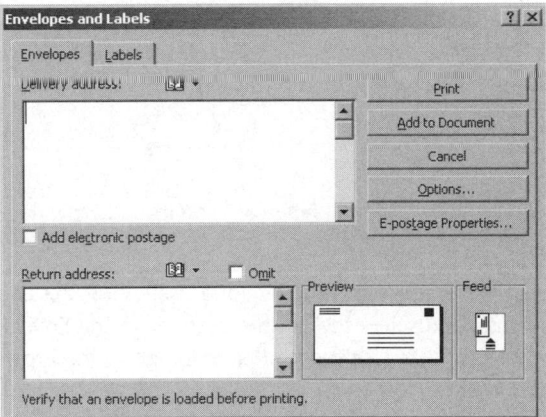

3 Type the delivery address into the Delivery Address text box.

If Word finds an address in the document, this address will already be contained in the Delivery Address box. In this case, you can simply edit the text, if necessary.

4 If you want to print a return address, type it into the Return Address text box.

If you have specified a personal mailing address in Word, this address will automatically appear in the Return Address box. In this case, you can edit the text, if necessary. (To specify a personal mailing address, choose Tools, Options, click the

User Information tab, and type the address into the Mailing Address text box. Be sure to include your name at the beginning of the return address if you want your name to be included automatically in the Return Address box in the Envelopes tab.) Note that if you enter or edit text in the Return Address box of the Envelopes tab, when you click the Print or Add To Document button (in step 7), Word will ask whether you want to save the new address as your default return address. If you click Yes, Word saves the text as your personal mailing address.

If you don't want to print a return address (perhaps you're using preprinted envelopes), you can either delete any text in the Return Address box or just check the Omit option above the box.

---

tip   **Save Time by Getting an Address from Outlook**

If you have entered names and addresses into your Outlook Contacts folder, you can use the Insert Address button above the Delivery Address box or above the Return Address box to select an address from Outlook rather than typing one.

Insert
Address

- To select any of the contact items stored in your Outlook Contacts folder, click the main part of the Insert Address button and choose a name in the Select Name dialog box.
- To quickly select a contact item you've used previously, click the down arrow on the button and choose a name from the drop-down menu.

Either action will insert both the name and the address of the selected contact. If you've defined more than one address for the contact, the one designated as the mailing address will be inserted.

For information on working with the Contacts folder in Outlook, see "Maintaining Your Address List with the Contacts Folder," on page 1057.

5   If you want to change features of the envelope itself, click the Options button on the Envelopes tab, and select the desired settings in the Envelope Options tab (shown in Figure 19-10). Use the model envelope in the Preview area to guide your selections.

---

newfeature!

tip   **Print Your Postage**

If you have installed e-postage add-in software, you can have Word print postage directly on your envelopes (or mailing labels) rather than affixing a postage stamp or using a postage meter. To do this, check the Add Electronic Postage option. If you want to modify e-postage features, click the E-Postage Properties button. For information on e-postage, see the Office Update Web site at *http://officeupdate.microsoft.com/*.

Chapter 19: Using Word to Automate Mailings

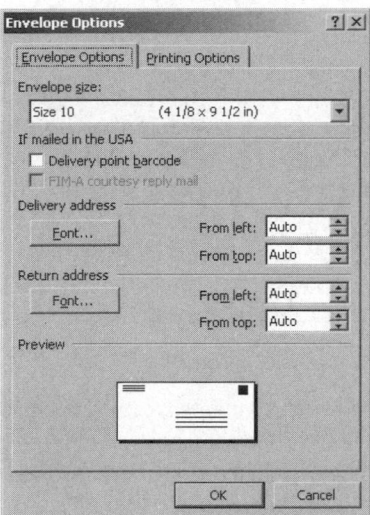

Figure 19-10. You can change features of an envelope in the Envelope Options tab of the Envelope Options dialog box.

6 If you want to modify the way the envelope is printed, click the Options button in the Envelopes tab, and select the desired settings in the Printing Options tab (shown in Figure 19-11). If you've changed any settings in the Printing Options tab, you can click the Reset button to restore Word's default settings.

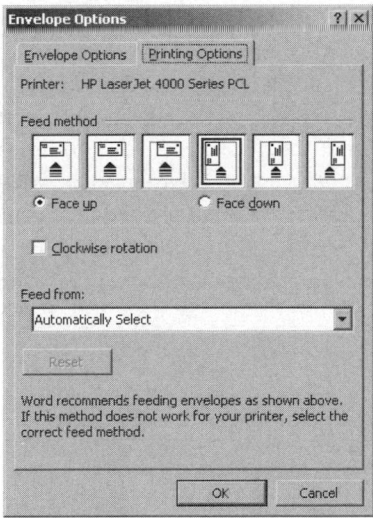

Figure 19-11. You can modify the way an envelope is printed using the Printing Options tab of the Envelope Options dialog box.

> **tip** **Vary the Formatting of Your Envelope Text**
>
> The Envelope Options tab lets you select the basic formatting of all the delivery address and return address text. You can also change the formatting of one or more individual characters within the Delivery Address or Return Address box in the Envelopes tab (overriding the basic formatting). To do this, select the text, and press the shortcut key for applying (or removing) character formatting—for example Ctrl+B, Ctrl+I, or Ctrl+U to apply (or remove) bold, italics, or underlining, respectively. You can use any of the first 10 shortcut keys that are listed in Table 12-2, on page 308.

7 To complete the envelope, do either of the following:

- To print the envelope immediately, place an envelope in your printer and click the Print button. You should insert the envelope into the printer so that it has the orientation shown in the Feed area in the lower right corner of the Envelopes tab. (You select the orientation in the Printing Options tab of the Envelope Options dialog box, shown in Figure 19-11. You can quickly display this tab by clicking in the Feed area.)

- To add the text for the envelope to the document in the active window, click the Add To Document button. (If you have already added envelope information to the document, this button will be labeled Change Document, and it will replace the former envelope text with the new text.) Word will insert the envelope text into a separate section at the beginning of the document, and it will assign to this section the correct margins, paper size, printing orientation, and paper source for printing the envelope. If necessary, you can edit the envelope text or add text or graphics to it. Thereafter, the envelope will automatically be printed whenever you print the document. You can use this technique to include the text for both a letter and its envelope within a single document, so that you can print both using only one print command.

> For information on setting the margins, paper size, printing orientation, paper source, and other page setup options for a document section, see "Modifying the Page Setup," on page 535.

Generating Individual Labels

You can print a single label, or you can print the same text on every label on a full sheet of labels, by performing the following steps:

1 If you have already typed the label text into a document (for example, an address in a letter heading), open that document. (This step is optional because you can type the text later.)

2 Choose Tools, Letters And Mailings, Envelopes And Labels. Then click the Labels tab In the Envelopes And Labels dialog box, shown at the top of the next page.

Chapter 19: Using Word to Automate Mailings

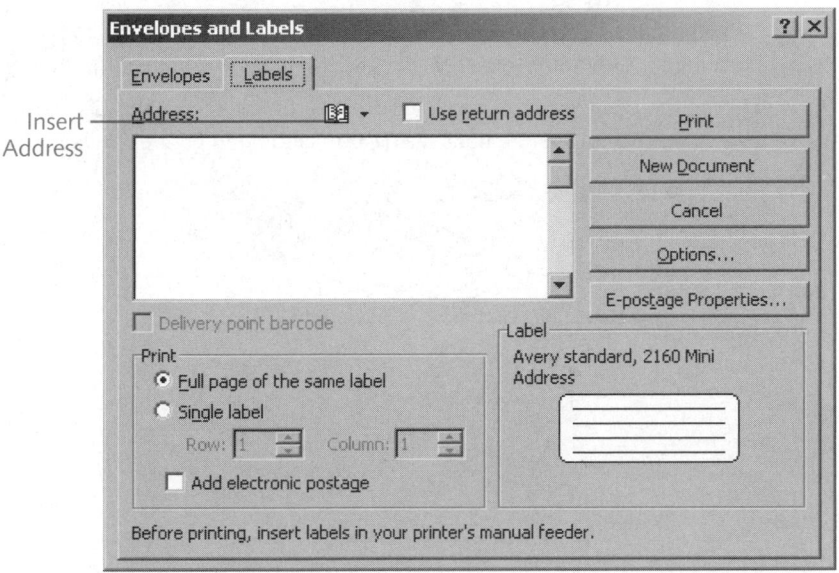

Insert Address

3 Type the label text into the Address box. If Word finds an address in the document, this text will already be contained in the Address box. In this case, you can simply edit the text, if necessary.

Alternatively, you can check the Use Return Address option to have Word copy into the Address box your personal mailing address (the address you set by using the User Information tab of the Options dialog box, as described in the previous section). You could do this to print return address labels for yourself.

Also, if you have entered names and addresses into your Outlook Contacts folder, you can use the Insert Address button above the Address box to select an address.

For more information, see the tip "Save Time by Getting an Address from Outlook," on page 564.

tip **Format Your Label Text**

You can change the formatting of any block of text in the Address box in the Labels tab. To do this, select the text, and press the shortcut key for applying (or removing) character formatting—for example Ctrl+B, Ctrl+I, or Ctrl+U to apply (or remove) bold, italics, or underlining, respectively. You can use any of the first 10 shortcut keys that are listed in Table 12-2 on page 308.

4 To tell Word how many labels to print, do either of the following:

- To print a full page of labels that has the same text on each label, select the Full Page Of The Same Label option. You might select this option, for example, to prepare a full sheet of return address labels.

■ To print a single label, select Single Label and enter the row and column position on the label sheet of the label you want to print.

5 If you need to change any of the label printing options, click the Options button to open the Label Options dialog box (shown in Figure 19-12).

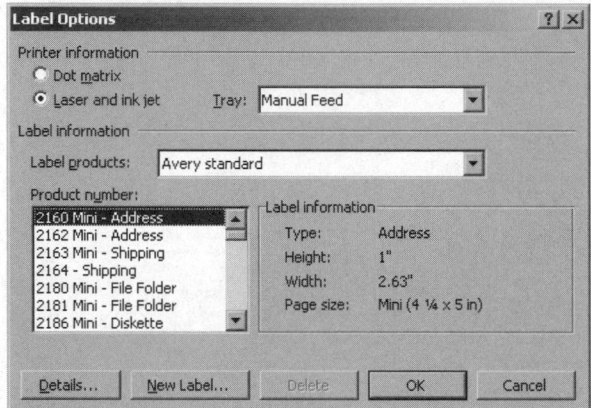

Figure 19-12. You can select options for printing labels in the Label Options dialog box.

If your label sheet doesn't match any of the standard labels listed in the Product Number list of the Label Options dialog box, you can specify custom label measurements by selecting the closest standard label, clicking the New Label button, and modifying the measurements in the New Custom dialog box (shown in Figure 19-13). You must give your custom label a name. You can later delete the custom label by selecting its name in the Product Number list of the Label Options dialog box and clicking the Delete button.

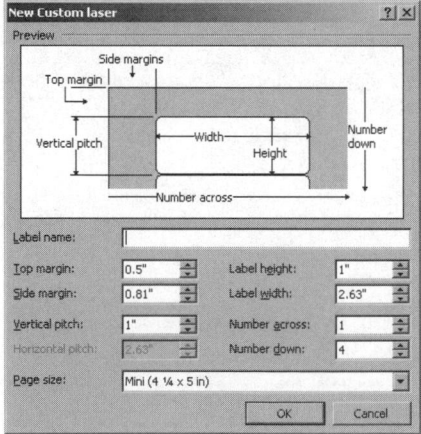

Figure 19-13. The New Custom dialog box allows you to create custom label measurements.

note You can click the Details button in the Label Options dialog box to see the exact measurements of the selected label in an information dialog box. An alternative way to create a custom label is to modify one or more measurements in this dialog box, enter a new name for your custom label into the Label Name text box, and click OK. (You can't change the measurements of one of the standard labels.)

When you click OK in the Label Options dialog box, you'll return to the Labels tab of the Envelopes And Labels dialog box.

tip **Insert Postal Bar Codes for Faster Delivery**

If you have selected a sufficiently large label and if the label text contains a valid ZIP code, you can check the Delivery Point Barcode option in the Labels tab of the Envelopes And Labels dialog box to have Word print a postal bar code at the top of the label. The bar code is a machine-readable representation of the ZIP code, and including it might expedite mail delivery.

6 To finish the label, do either of the following:

- To print the label immediately, insert a label sheet into your printer, and click the Print button.

- If you're printing a full page of labels (that is, if you chose the Full Page Of The Same Label option), you can click the New Document button to have Word store the label text in a new document. You can then modify the labels if you want (perhaps adding a graphic logo to each label or applying formatting), and you can print the labels by printing this document. You can save the document so that you can print the same labels again in the future. (In this document, you'll notice that Word has created a table and has inserted each label into a separate table cell.)

For information on printing e-postage on your labels, see the tip "Print Your Postage," on page 564.

tip **Have Word Write Your Letters**

You can have Word automatically insert into a document all the basic elements of a letter (the date line, return and recipient's addresses, salutation, closing, and so on), and format them according to your specifications. To do this, choose Tools, Letters And Mailings, Letter Wizard to open the Letter Wizard dialog box. Then, in the tabs of this dialog box, choose the options you want and supply the required information about the letter sender and recipient. Of course, you'll still have to type in the text for the body of the letter!

Chapter 20

Creating Web Pages and Other Online Documents

Online Documents

Not too many years ago, Microsoft Word was used almost exclusively for creating traditional printed documents. With the move toward the paperless office, however, each version of Word has provided more features for creating an alternative end product: the online document. An online document is one that's designed to be read and worked with on a computer, rather than being sent to a printer. It can be a Word document in native format that's made accessible to—or distributed among—a group of readers. Or, more commonly now, it can be a Web page document in HTML (Hypertext Markup Language) format that's posted on a server on the World Wide Web or on a company intranet.

For a description of different ways to share native Microsoft Word 2002 documents, as well as a discussion on related techniques, see "Sharing Word Documents," on page 466.

In addition to saving trees, the main advantage offered by an online document is that it can be made dynamic and interactive. For example, an online document can contain hyperlinks for navigating to other locations; interactive forms for collecting information; frames for viewing several documents at once; a background color, pattern, or sound; animated text or graphics; or movie or sound clips. An online document can also contain ActiveX controls, Microsoft Visual Basic for Applications (VBA) macros, or scripts for performing a wide variety of tasks.

571

> For information on VBA macros, see Part 10 of this book.

When you create a Web page or online Word document, you primarily use the general Word editing and formatting techniques presented in the previous chapters in this part of the book, as well as in Part 2, "Common Office XP Techniques." You can also use the techniques and Word elements described in this chapter, which are unique to Web pages or online Word documents, or are especially useful for creating these types of documents.

Keep in mind that although the next section, "Creating and Publishing a Web Page," focuses exclusively on Web pages, almost all of the techniques covered in the remaining two sections ("Adding Web Page Elements" and "Formatting Web Pages") can be used for online documents in native Word format as well as for Web page documents, although you'll have to view the document in Web Layout view to see Web-style features such as background images. (These sections note any techniques or elements that aren't suited for native Word documents. In addition, they point out a few features that work *only* in native-format documents.)

tip **Use Linking or Embedding in Online Documents**

Using object linking or embedding with the Display As Icon option lets you include a great variety of information in a small amount of space within an online document that's in native Word format. Each block of information is represented by an icon that the reader can click to view the full text or graphics. For instructions, see Chapter 7, "Sharing Data Among Office XP Applications."

Using Fields in Online Word Documents

Fields are dynamic document elements that you can use to add interactivity to online documents, primarily documents in native Word format. To cite only a few examples, you can add fields for displaying the date and time, going to another document location, running a macro, downloading commands to a printer, displaying the document author or the number of characters, performing calculations, numbering document items, or prompting the user for text. The previous chapters in this part of the book have described several common fields—for example merge fields used in mail merge main documents, IncludeText fields for including other documents within the current one, and the fields used to create index entries, indexes, and tables of contents.

To insert a field, perform the following steps:

1 Choose Insert, Field to display the Field dialog box (shown in Figure 20-1).

Using Fields in Online Word Documents *(continued)*

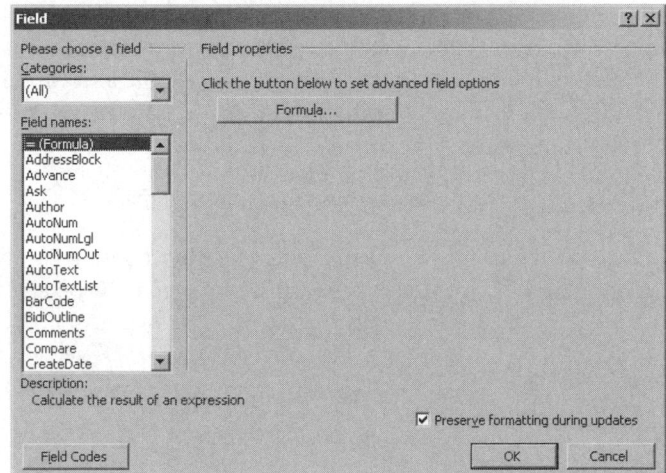

Figure 20-1. You can insert many types of fields using the Field dialog box.

2 Select the general category of the field you want in the Categories drop-down list.

3 Select the specific field in the Field Names list. Below the list you'll see a description of the currently selected field.

4 Select the desired field properties and options, which vary according to the field you've selected.

For further details, see the Word online help topic "Field Types and Switches."

Creating and Publishing a Web Page

With some of the earlier versions of Word (in particular, Microsoft Word 97), explaining how to create Web pages would have required several chapters, if not an entire book. When you created a Web page, the entire interface changed—familiar commands disappeared and new ones became available. And you had to be careful about saving a document as a Web page, because many document features would be irretrievably lost. Since the introduction of Word 2000, however, creating a Web page is hardly different than creating a regular Word document. The Word commands, interface, and features are basically the same whether you're creating a regular document in native Word format or a Web page in HTML format (a few exceptions are noted in this chapter).

Because HTML is now one of the standard Word formats—like the native .doc format or Rich Text Format (.rtf)—when you save a Word document in HTML, the vast majority of document features are preserved (again, a few exceptions are noted in this chapter). Even if a feature isn't used by a browser (such as the page margins set through the Page Setup dialog box in Word), all of the feature's settings (for example, the margin sizes) are carefully saved in the HTML file or in a supporting file. These features will be used whenever you open the document in Word (for instance, the margins will be shown unless you're in Web Layout view). Because you can save a native Word document in an HTML file, and then later reopen the HTML file and convert it back to a native Word document if you wish, with almost no loss of features, Word is said to provide "round-trip" support for HTML.

To create a Web page in Word, follow these three basic steps:

1 Open the document. You can open a document by choosing File, New to display the New Document task pane (shown in Figure 20-2), and then doing one of the following actions:

Figure 20-2. The New Document task pane allows you to open a new document.

- To create a new, blank Web page document, click the Blank Web Page command.

- To create a new Web page based on a Web page template, click the General Templates command, click the Web Pages tab (shown in Figure 20-3), and select a template for the type of page you want to create. If you use one of these templates, your new Web page will contain an initial layout of text and graphics that's suitable for a particular kind of Web page, such as a personal Web page or a table of contents. (Note that the Web page templates appear with an icon that represents your default browser instead of the W icon that appears with templates that create regular Word documents.) You can then modify the page and add your own content.

Chapter 20: Creating Web Pages and Other Online Documents

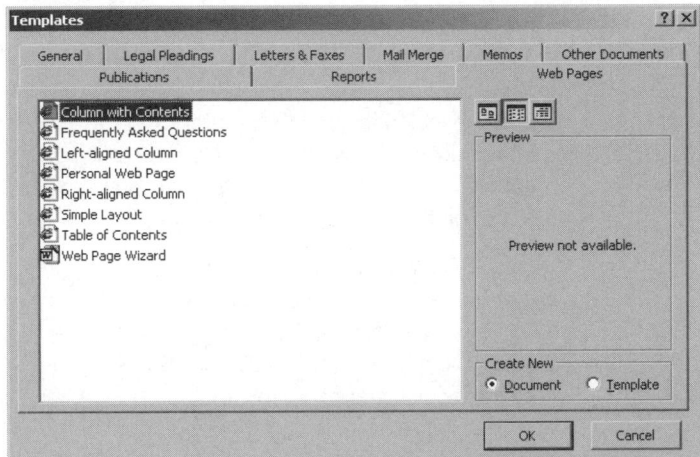

Figure 20-3. The Web Pages tab of the Templates dialog box displays Word templates designed for creating Web pages, as well as the Web Page Wizard.

- To create an entire set of linked Web pages (that is, a Web site), you can select the Web Page Wizard item in the Web Pages tab described in the previous instruction. The Web Page Wizard will let you add pages to the site (you can choose a template for each one) and will allow you to specify the folder where the pages are stored, the organization of the hyperlinks that connect the pages, and the visual theme of the pages. (Hyperlinks and themes are covered later in this chapter.) After the wizard generates the Web site, you can open, modify, and add content to any of the individual pages.

- To open an existing Web page or native Word document, click the Documents command (which will be labeled More Documents if the task pane lists recently opened documents), and select the file in the Open dialog box.

> For general instructions on using the Templates and Open dialog boxes, see Chapter 4, "Working with Office XP Applications, Documents, and Program Windows."

2 Enter or edit the text and graphic content of your page and format the document using the standard Word techniques discussed in the previous chapters in this part of the book, as well as in Part 2, "Common Office XP Techniques." But keep in mind the following points:

- Some Word features aren't displayed or supported by common browsers. Examples of these features are negative paragraph indents; diagonal table borders; vertical text in table cells; character, nonsolid, or page borders; newspaper-style columns; automatic hyphenation; watermarks; headers and footers; margins and other settings made in the Page Setup dialog box; and certain character formatting features such as an underline color or style, some of the effects like Shadow, and text animations (for example, Blinking Background). Most of the features that aren't supported in browsers have been noted as such in the previous chapters. Also, some features will look different in a browser from the way they appear in Word; for instance, tabs might not align correctly, patterned shading will become solid, and a text-wrapped graphic object or table will be moved to the left or right of the adjoining paragraph.

When you edit a Web page, Word generally lets you go ahead and apply most of the features that aren't supported by common browsers. (As mentioned, it will save these features in the HTML file and use them whenever you open the page in Word.) You can, however, have Word block most of the character, paragraph, or table formatting features that are incompatible with specific browsers. To do this, choose Tools, Options, click the General tab, click the Web Options button, and click the Browsers tab. Then, in the drop-down list, select the browser versions that readers of your Web page will be using, and in the list below, check the Disable Features Not Supported By These Browsers option (as shown in Figure 20-4). Word will then disable the nonsupported features in the dialog boxes you use to apply them (the Font dialog box, the Borders And Shading dialog box, and so on). And, if your document already contained one of these features before you blocked them, when you save the document, Word will first warn you and will then convert the feature, if possible, to a similar supported feature. Note that Word will disable these features only for a Web page. So, if you're working on a native Word document that you're going to convert to HTML and want to take advantage of the blocking feature, save your document in HTML before formatting it.

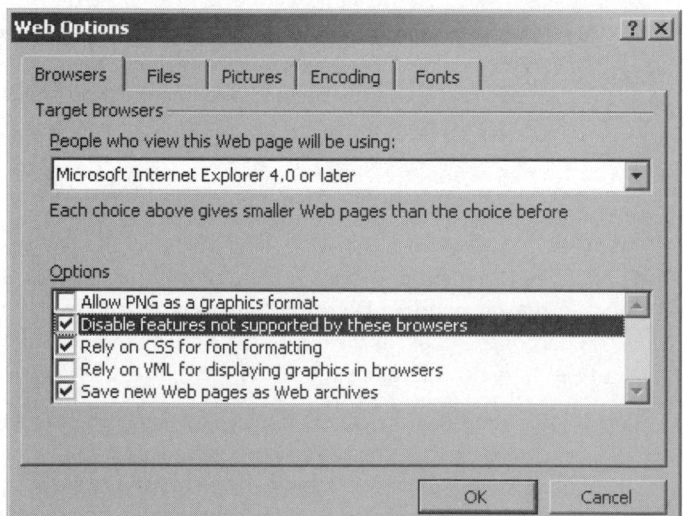

Figure 20-4. The settings shown here cause Word to disable formatting features not supported in Microsoft Internet Explorer 4.0 or later.

■ When you work on a Web page, you'll notice a few changes in the Word interface from the way it appears when you work on a regular Word document. For example, the New Blank Document button becomes the New Web Page button and clicking it creates a blank Web page. The Versions command is disabled on the File menu. And the HTML Source command appears on the View menu to let you work directly with the HTML source for the Web page.

■ In addition to the basic Word features discussed in the previous chapters, Word provides elements and formatting features that are especially useful for creating Web pages (as well as online Word documents). The elements include hyperlinks, horizontal dividing lines, movie and sound clips, background sounds, scrolling text, Web forms for collecting information, frames for viewing several pages or Word documents simultaneously, and Web components for navigating to other pages or viewing information on a SharePoint team Web site. The formatting features include background colors or patterns and themes.

The elements used to create Web pages are described in "Adding Web Page Elements," on page 582. Formatting features useful for Web pages are explained in "Formatting Web Pages," on page 596.

■ It's best to create a Web page document using the Web Layout view, which displays the document in much the same way that popular browsers would display it. For a more accurate preview, you can open the document in your browser by choosing File, Web Page Preview.

3 Save the document. If you created a new Web page or opened an existing Web page in step 1, you can use the usual Save or Save As command to save your work, and your document will be stored by default in the HTML format. If, however, you created or opened a native Word document in step 1, you should choose File, Save As Web Page. This will open the Save As dialog box and will select an HTML format in the Save As Type drop-down list.

Word uses several different HTML formats. You can choose the specific format in which to save the document by selecting one of the following items in the Save As Type drop-down list in the Save As dialog box:

■ **Web Page (*.htm; *.html)** This format saves the Web page in an HTML file, but saves graphics and other supporting data in separate files. The format provides round-trip support for HTML; that is, it saves all Word features contained in the document, as explained previously in this section.

newfeature!

■ **Web Archive (*.mht; *.mhtml)** This format saves everything in a single Web archive file. It also provides round-trip support for HTML.

newfeature!

■ **Web Page, Filtered (*.htm; *.html)** This format is like the first one [Web Page (*.htm; *.html)], except that it saves only the essential

document information, and therefore does *not* provide round-trip support for HTML.

---

caution Although the filtered format generates a smaller and "cleaner" HTML file (one
that's perhaps easier to edit in other programs), if you reopen the file in Word, some
of the document's original features—such as headers or footers—might no longer be
present. Therefore, if you create a filtered HTML file from a document, you might also
want to save a copy of the document in regular HTML format [Web Page (*.htm;
*.html)] to preserve all the document's features.

InsideOut

If you've checked the Always Create Backup Copy option (in the Save tab of the
Options dialog box) and have been relying on Word always making a backup copy of
a document when you save it, keep in mind that Word *won't* make a backup copy
of a Web page when you save it, even if this option is checked. (This is probably due
to the complexities of making backups of the page's supporting files.)

---

note When an HTML format is selected in the Save As Type list, the Change Title button
appears in the Save As dialog box. You can click this button to change the page's title.
(The title appears in the browser's title bar when it displays the page.) You can also
change the title by choosing File, Properties, opening the Summary tab, and editing
the contents of the Title text box.

For general information on saving documents in Office, see "Saving Office Documents," on
page 74. For information on choosing the application that a Web page is opened in, see "Saving a Document as a Web Page," on page 78.

Publishing Your Page

When you've finished creating your Web page, you need to *publish* it—that is, copy it
to the appropriate folder on the computer on which your Web server is installed, so
that the page will be available on the World Wide Web or on your company intranet.

You might be able to save the page in the appropriate Web server folder directly
from Word. This may be possible, for instance, if the Web server folder is on your
computer, if it's on your network, if it's on an FTP site where you have the required
permissions, or if it's on a Web site on which Microsoft server extensions (such as
SharePoint Team Services from Microsoft) have been installed.

> For information on saving files to each of these locations, see "Saving Office Documents," on page 74.

If you can't publish your Web page directly from Word, you'll have to post it to the Web server using an FTP utility or feature (such as the one supplied with Microsoft Internet Explorer), Microsoft Web Publishing Wizard (supplied with Microsoft Windows), or by other means. Use the method that your Web hosting service, company webmaster, or network administrator recommends.

Setting Web Page Options

You can set a variety of options that affect the way Word manages the Web pages you create by choosing Tools, Options, clicking the General tab, and clicking the Web Options button to open the Web Options dialog box. You can also open this dialog box by choosing Web Options from the Tools drop-down menu in the Save As dialog box. Then select the settings you want in the tabs of the Web Options dialog box, as follows:

- To have Word disable formatting features that aren't supported by specified browsers (as explained under step 2, on page 575), and to set general Web options, use the Browsers tab (see Figure 20-4, on page 576). Note that when you select a particular browser in the drop-down list at the top, Word automatically checks the general options in the list below that are compatible with that browser.

- To modify the way Word saves your Web pages, use the Files tab (shown in Figure 20-5).

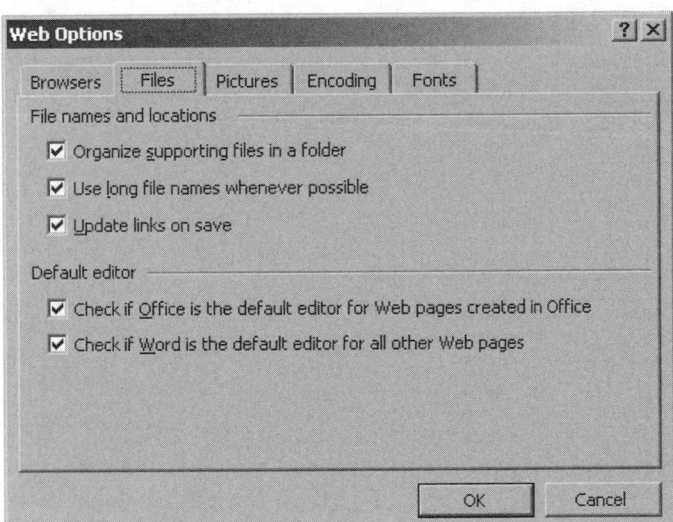

Figure 20-5. You can change the way Word saves your Web pages in the Files tab of the Web Options dialog box.

(continued)

Setting Web Page Options *(continued)*

- To specify the size and resolution of the typical monitor on which your Web pages will be viewed (if you know this information), so that Word can optimize the display of graphics in a page, use the Pictures tab (shown in Figure 20-6).

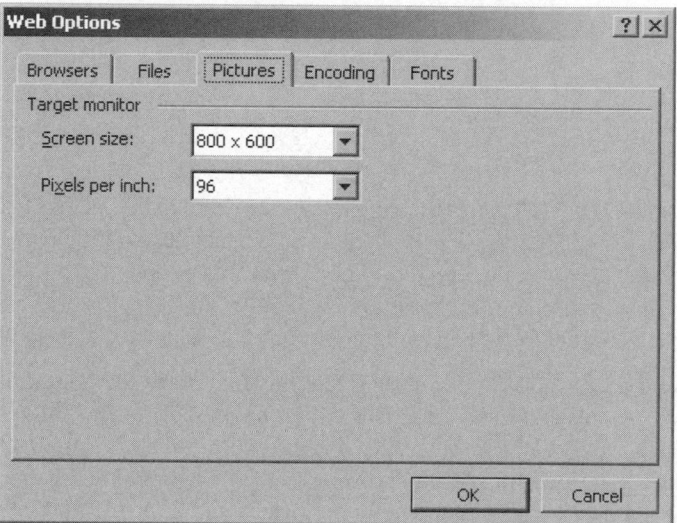

Figure 20-6. You can change the monitor settings in the Pictures tab of the Web Options dialog box.

- To specify the language used for your Web pages, use the Encoding tab (shown in Figure 20-7).

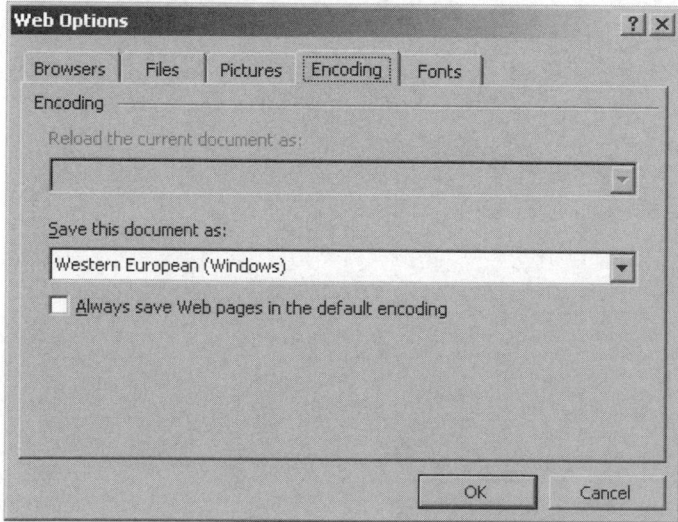

Figure 20-7. The Encoding tab of the Web Options dialog box allows you to specify the language used for your Web pages.

Setting Web Page Options *(continued)*

● To select the appropriate character set for the language used in your Web pages, or to choose the default Web page fonts and font sizes, use the Fonts tab (as shown in Figure 20-8).

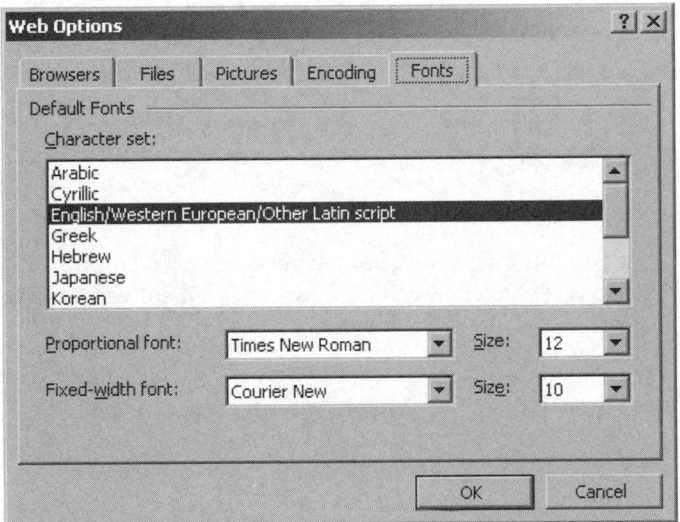

Figure 20-8. You can choose the character set and default font settings for your Web pages in the Fonts tab of the Web Options dialog box.

Also, you can have Word use pixels as the default unit of measurement in some of the dialog boxes that affect the display of Web pages (such as the Paragraph and Tabs dialog boxes). To do this, check the Show Pixels For HTML Features option in the General tab of the Options dialog box.

Troubleshooting

HTML Markup Appears Rather Than the Document Content

You opened an HTML file that doesn't have one of the standard extensions (such as .htm, .html, .mht, .mhtml, or .asp) and you see the HTML tags like <HEAD>, <BODY>, and <P> rather than seeing the page's content as it would appear in a browser.

Because of the nonstandard file extension, Word doesn't know that the file contains HTML, so it displays the HTML source as literal text rather than rendering the content as a browser would. To view the document's content rather than its HTML markup, perform the following steps:

1 Choose Tools, Options and click the General tab.

(continued)

HTML Markup Appears Rather Than the Document Content *(continued)*

2 Check the Confirm Conversion At Open option.

3 Close and reopen the document.

4 In the Convert File dialog box that Word displays on opening the document, select HTML Document and click OK.

Troubleshooting

Lost Document Versions

You created a document containing several versions and then saved the document as a Web page. However, you now can't access the document versions other than the one that's displayed.

If a document file stores several document versions, when you save the document in HTML format (by choosing File, Save As Web Page, for example), Word stores in the HTML file only the document version that is currently displayed, and any saved document versions are lost. (You'll notice that the Versions command on the File menu is dimmed for a Web page document.) This occurrence is an exception to the general rule that Word saves all your document information—even features not supported by Web browsers—when you convert it to HTML format. Word will warn you about losing saved versions only if you've checked the Disable Features Not Supported By These Browsers option, shown in Figure 20-4 on page 576.

To access your other versions, you'll have to open the original native Word (.doc) document in which you stored these versions. *Be sure to save this file if you want to be able to access the document versions it contains.*

For information on storing multiple versions in a document, see "Storing Different Document Versions," on page 243.

Adding Web Page Elements

The following Word elements, which are described in the sections that follow, are especially valuable for Web pages, or—with the exception of Web components—for native Word documents that are intended to be read online:

- Hyperlinks
- Horizontal dividing lines
- Movie clips, sound clips, and background sounds

- Scrolling text
- Web forms
- Frames
- Web components

Adding and Using Hyperlinks

You can assign a hyperlink to a block of text or to a picture in a Word document. The hyperlink connects the text or picture to a target location. The target location can be a Web page, an Office document or other file, or a folder, which can be located on a disk, network drive, or Internet site. The target location can also be a specific place within the current document or within another file. Or, it can be an e-mail address. Clicking the hyperlink displays the target location or sends a message to the target e-mail address. You can click a hyperlink when a document is open in Word, or—for a Web page document—when it's displayed in a browser. Hyperlinks can be useful in any type of Word document, but they are especially important in Web pages, where you can use them to tie together the pages in your Web site or to connect to other sites.

---

note If the Use CTRL + Click To Follow Hyperlink option is checked, clicking a hyperlink in Word while pressing Ctrl displays the target location, and clicking the hyperlink without pressing Ctrl places the insertion point within a text hyperlink (so you can edit the text) or selects a picture hyperlink (so you can modify the picture). If the Use CTRL + Click To Follow Hyperlink option isn't checked, the opposite occurs. That is, clicking a hyperlink while pressing Ctrl places the insertion point within it or selects it, and clicking the hyperlink without pressing Ctrl displays the target location. When you place the pointer over a hyperlink, Word shows a ScreenTip that indicates whether you need to press Ctrl and click or just click the hyperlink to follow the link.

You'll find the Use CTRL + Click To Follow Hyperlink option by choosing Tools, Options, clicking the Edit tab, and looking in the Editing Options area.

To create a hyperlink, perform the following steps:

1 Select the text or picture to which you want to assign the hyperlink, or simply place the insertion point at the position in your document where you want Word to insert the hyperlink text that you later specify.

Insert
Hyperlink

2 Open the Insert Hyperlink dialog box (shown in Figure 20-9, on page 584) by choosing Insert, Hyperlink, by clicking the Insert Hyperlink button on the Standard toolbar, or by pressing Ctrl+K.

Browse The Web

Up One Folder   Browse For File

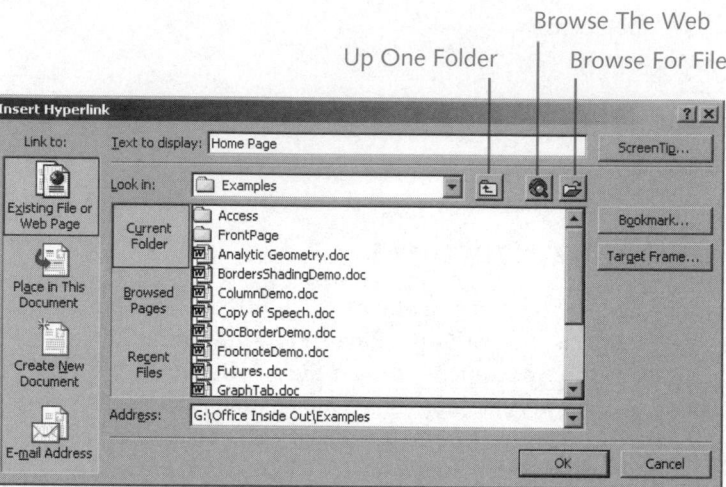

Figure 20-9. You create hyperlinks using the Insert Hyperlink dialog box.

3 Enter or edit the hypertext text in the Text To Display box. Skip this step if you selected the desired text in step 1 or if you are assigning the hyperlink to a picture.

4 In the Link To bar at the left of the Insert Hyperlink dialog box, select the general category of hyperlink you want to create:

- To link to a different existing document or Web page, select Existing File Or Web Page.

- To link to a different location within the current document, select Place In This Document.

- To create a new document or Web page and link to it, select Create New Document.

- To link to an e-mail address, so that clicking the hyperlink sends a message to that address, select E-Mail Address.

The controls that Word displays in the rest of the dialog box depend on which of these options is selected.

5 If you selected Existing File Or Web Page in step 4, select the target document or Web page using one of the following methods (the controls you use are shown in Figure 20-9):

- To specify any target, type the target's file path or URL into the Address text box.

- To select a target file or folder on a local or network disk, click the Current Folder bar item, and then select the file in the main list. To navigate to a different folder, use the Look In drop-down list and the Up One Folder button, which work just like they do in the standard Open dialog box. Alternatively, you can click the Browse For File button to select the target file or folder in the Link To File dialog box, which is modeled after the standard Open dialog box.

- To link to an Internet location or disk file that you've recently browsed, click the Browsed Pages bar item and then select the specific browsed target in the main list.

- To link to a disk file that you've recently opened, click the Recent Files bar item and select the file in the main list.

- To run your browser to search for a target on the Internet, click the Browse The Web button.

To link to a specific location within the target file, click the Bookmark button and indicate the target location by selecting a document heading or bookmark in the Select Place In Document dialog box.

> **note** If in step 4 you selected any of the Link To bar items except E-Mail Address, you can select the specific frame where the target file will be displayed—if you've added frames to your document—or you can have the target file opened in a separate browser window if the link is clicked in a browser. To do this, click the Target Frame button and select the option you want in the Set Target Frame dialog box.

> Frames are briefly discussed in "Use Frames to View Several Documents at Once," on page 594.

6 If you selected Place In This Document in step 4, specify the target location by selecting a document heading or bookmark in the main list.

7 If you selected Create New Document in step 4, specify the name and location of the new document or Web page as follows:

- To create a file in the current directory, just type its name into the Name Of New Document text box.

- To create a file in a different directory, click the Change button to select the directory.

8 If you selected E-Mail Address in step 4, type the target e-mail address into the E-Mail Address text box and, if you want, type a message subject in the Subject text box.

9 To have Word or the browser (Internet Explorer 4.0 or later) display a specific message when you hold the pointer over the hyperlink, click the ScreenTip button and type the message into the Set Hyperlink ScreenTip dialog box.

10 Click the OK button.

> **tip** **Change Hyperlink Formatting**
>
> By default, hyperlink text is initially blue and underlined. After you have *followed* the hyperlink (that is, clicked it in Word or in a browser, to open the target), the color will change to violet. You can change the format of an unfollowed or a followed hyperlink by modifying the Hyperlink or FollowedHyperlink built-in Word style. (For instructions, see "Customizing Styles," on page 385.) The hyperlink colors are also modified when you apply a theme to the document, as discussed later in this chapter.

To modify a hyperlink you have already defined, select the text or picture again, and then use any of the techniques that were given for opening the Insert Hyperlink dialog box. The dialog box will now be labeled Edit Hyperlink. You can use it to modify the hyperlink, or you can click the Remove Link button in the lower right corner of the dialog box to remove the hyperlink from the text or picture in your document.

If you click a hyperlink in Word, and if the target of that hyperlink is a regular Office document (that is, one saved in native format, not HTML), you can use the Web toolbar to navigate back and forth through the document locations you have visited or to open other documents (as shown in Figure 20-10). When you first click the hyperlink, the Web toolbar is displayed automatically. (You can display it at any time by choosing View, Toolbars, Web, or by right-clicking a toolbar and then choosing Web from the shortcut menu.)

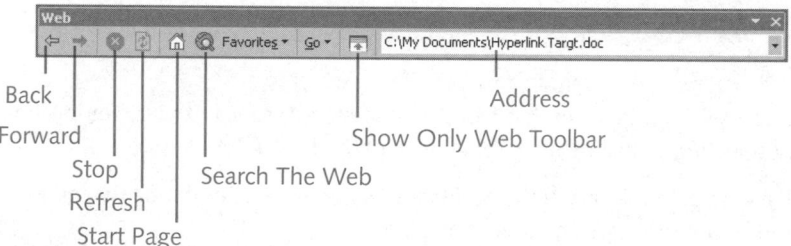

Figure 20-10. You can navigate among document locations you have visited using the Web toolbar.

Inserting Horizontal Dividing Lines

You can use horizontal dividing lines to separate different parts of your document. Although horizontal dividing lines are typically used in Web pages, you can insert them into any type of Word document to help organize the document's contents. Adding a horizontal dividing line provides an alternative to applying a horizontal border above or below a paragraph. Unlike a border, a horizontal dividing line is a separate document element that you can independently select, move, delete, or format. You can insert a plain, standard dividing line; or you can use a graphic image for a dividing

Chapter 20: Creating Web Pages and Other Online Documents

line, so it can serve as a decorative element consistent with the overall look of your document.

To insert a horizontal dividing line, perform the following steps:

1 Place the insertion point at the position where you want to divide your document. The horizontal dividing line will be inserted immediately before the insertion point and will be placed on a separate document line (in its own paragraph).

2 Choose Format, Borders And Shading, and click the Horizontal Line button at the bottom of the Borders And Shading dialog box. This will open the Horizontal Line dialog box (shown in Figure 20-11), which displays a gallery of your available dividing lines.

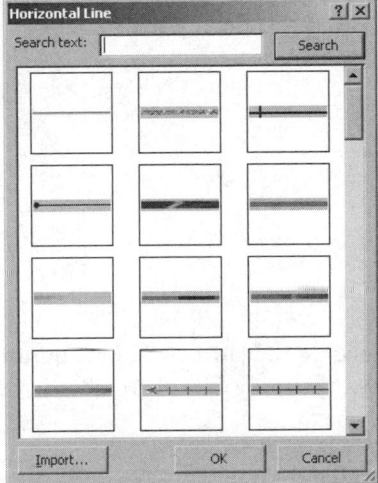

Figure 20-11. The Horizontal Line dialog box displays the available dividing lines you can insert.

3 Select the line style you want.

The first item in the list (at the upper left corner) inserts a plain, standard dividing line. (Word creates the line by adding an <HR>, horizontal rule, HTML element, which causes a browser to display its standard dividing line.) Each of the other items inserts a dividing line created from a graphics file. (Word generates the line by adding an <IMG>, image, HTML element, which causes a browser to display the specified graphics file.)

To add a new line to the list from a graphics file, click the Import button and select the file in the Add Clips To Gallery dialog box (which works just like the standard Open dialog box).

4 Click OK.

In the Horizontal Line dialog box, you can search for lines by keyword, by entering a word into the Search Text box and clicking the Search button. (Like clips in the Microsoft Clip Organizer, each line is assigned one or more keywords.) However, it's not easy to guess what type of keywords would be assigned to dividing lines. After trying many keywords (*plain*, *modern*, *decorative*, *classic*, *corporate*, and so on), we finally got two matches from the word *nature*. To show all line styles, delete the contents of the Search Text box and click the Search button.

Once you've used this procedure to select and insert a horizontal dividing line, you can quickly insert additional dividing lines that have the same style. You do this by clicking the down arrow next to the Borders button on the Formatting toolbar or on the Tables And Borders toolbar and then clicking the Horizontal Line item on the palette, shown here:

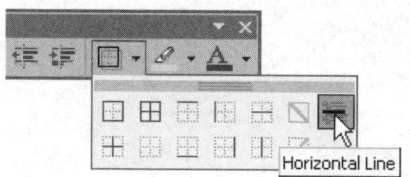

As a further shortcut, once you have clicked the Horizontal Line button on the palette, you can insert additional dividing lines by simply clicking the Borders button on the Formatting or Tables And Borders toolbar.

To modify a horizontal dividing line you have inserted into a document, click it to select it. You can then drag it up or down to move it to a new location in the document, or you can press Delete to remove it.

To format the selected horizontal dividing line, choose Format, Horizontal Line (or just double-click the line) to open the Format Horizontal Line dialog box. In this dialog box, you can adjust the width, height, or alignment of any type of line. You can change the color of a standard line. And you can change the cropping, color control, brightness, or contrast of a graphic line. Note that applying a theme to the document will modify the horizontal dividing lines throughout the document.

Themes are discussed in "Applying a Web Page Theme," on page 598.

Adding Movies and Sounds

You can add a movie clip or a background sound to liven up your Web page or online Word document. These elements function when a document is viewed in Word, as well as when a Web page is displayed in a browser.

You can add movie clip or background sound using the Web Tools toolbar (shown in Figure 20-12). To display it, choose View, Toolbars, Web Tools, or choose Web Tools from the shortcut menu that appears when you right-click a toolbar.

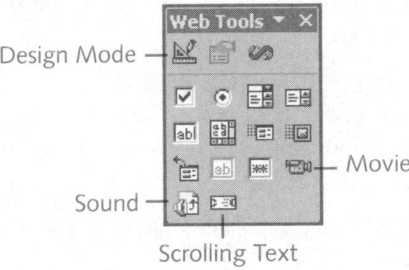

Design Mode

Sound

Scrolling Text

Movie

Figure 20-12. You can use the Web Tools toolbar to add various items to a document or Web page.

A movie clip displays a video sequence, with sound, in a rectangular area in your page or document. To insert a movie clip, perform the following steps:

1 Click the Movie button on the Web Tools toolbar to open the Movie Clip dialog box (shown in Figure 20-13).

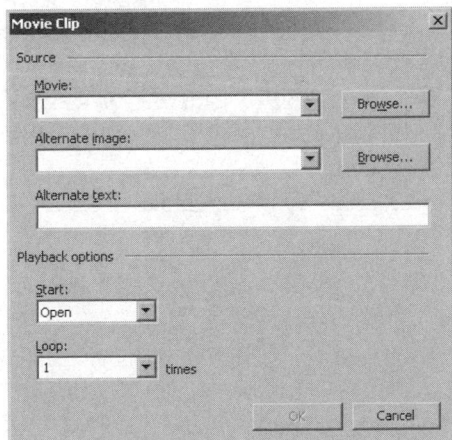

Figure 20-13. Use the Movie Clip dialog box to insert a movie clip into your Web page.

2 Type the path of the file containing the movie clip into the Movie text box, or click the adjoining Browse button to locate the file in the Open dialog box (this is a compact version of the standard Open dialog box for opening documents).

589

note Movie clips are contained in files using a variety of different formats. The following are the standard file extensions for movie files in the formats that Word supports: .avi, .mov, .movie, .mp2, .mpeg, .mpg, and .qt.

3 If you wish, you can set or modify any of the following options in the Movie Clip dialog box:

■ To have a browser display a static picture if movie clips aren't enabled, type the path of a graphics file into the Alternate Image text box or click the adjoining Browse button to locate the file. You should select a .gif or .jpeg graphic file.

■ To have a browser display text if neither movie clips nor pictures are enabled, type the text into the Alternate Text box. Some browsers also display the alternate text while downloading the movie clip or if the clip is missing.

■ To control *when* the movie clip is played, select an item in the Start drop-down list.

■ To control *how many times* the movie clip is played each time it's started, select an item in the Loop drop-down list. Select Infinite to keep playing the movie clip continuously.

4 Click OK.

If you later want to modify a movie clip, right-click the clip in Word and choose Properties from the shortcut menu, or just double-click the clip to reopen the Movie Clip dialog box.

To play the movie clip in Word or in Internet Explorer at any time—in addition to the playing times you specified when you added the clip—right-click the clip and choose Play from the shortcut menu. To stop a movie clip from playing, right-click it and choose Stop.

tip **Make Big Movies Optional**

A movie clip in a Web page can take a long time to download over a slow Internet connection. To avoid forcing the reader to wait for a large movie clip to download, you can make viewing the movie optional by inserting a hyperlink to a movie clip file, rather than inserting the movie clip directly into the page as described in this section. Hyperlinks are discussed in "Adding and Using Hyperlinks," on page 583.

If you assign a background sound to a Web page or document, Word or a browser will play that sound when you first open the file. To add a background sound, perform the following steps:

Chapter 20: Creating Web Pages and Other Online Documents

1 Click the Sound button on the Web Tools toolbar to open the Background Sound dialog box (shown in Figure 20-14).

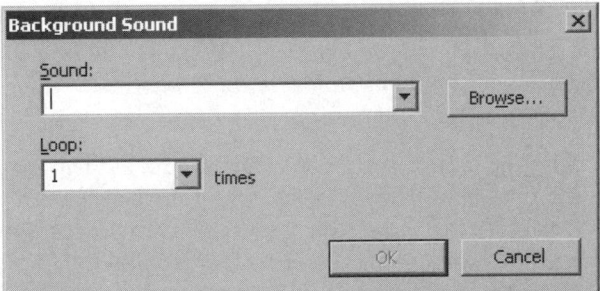

Figure 20-14. Use the Background Sound dialog box to add a background sound to a Web page.

2 Type the path of the file containing the sound you want to use as a background sound into the Sound text box, or click the Browse button to locate the file using the Open dialog box.

note Sounds are stored in files using a variety of different formats. The following are the standard file extensions for sound files in the formats that Word supports: .wav, .mid, .midi, .rmi, .au, .aif, .aiff, and .snd.

3 To control how many times the sound is played, select an item in the Loop drop-down list. Select Infinite to keep playing the sound continuously.

4 Click OK.

You can turn off the background sound while you work on a document in Word by switching on design mode. You can turn design mode on or off by clicking the Design Mode button on the Web Tools toolbar.

tip **Use the Clip Organizer to Add Clips**

You can use the Microsoft Clip Organizer—through the Insert Clip Art task pane or by running the freestanding Clip Organizer program—to insert a movie or sound clip. A sound clip is analogous to a movie clip. Adding a sound clip to your document displays a sound object, which you can double-click to play the sound. For instructions on using the Clip Organizer, see "Inserting Pictures with the Clip Organizer," on page 115.

When you add a movie or sound clip, Word inserts an embedded object or a control, which you can format using some of the methods discussed in "Modifying Graphic Objects," on page 150.

Troubleshooting

Can't Remove a Background Sound

You want to remove a background sound from a Web page or document but the Background Sound dialog box doesn't provide a control for removing the sound, and when you delete the contents of the Sound text box, the OK button is disabled.

When you add a background sound, Word inserts a control at the position of the insertion point, but formats it as hidden text so it's not normally visible. To remove the background sound, click the Show/Hide ¶ button on the Standard toolbar to temporarily display hidden text, click the background sound object (which displays a small image of a speaker), and press Delete to remove the object.

Adding Scrolling Text

You can use a *marquee,* a block of scrolling text that travels repeatedly across the width of your Web page or document, to draw attention to a message. To insert scrolling text, click the Scrolling Text button on the Web Tools toolbar (shown in Figure 20-12, on page 589) and enter the text and display options that you want into the Scrolling Text dialog box (shown in Figure 20-15).

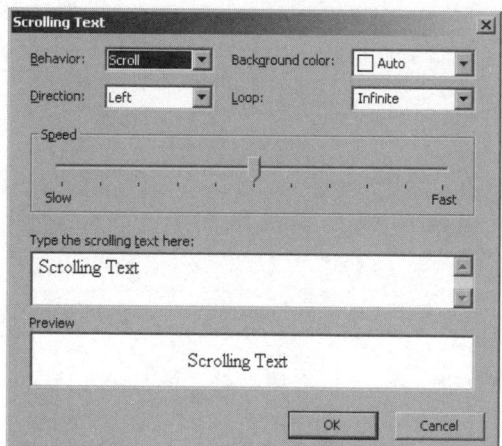

Figure 20-15. Add a marquee to a document using the Scrolling Text dialog box.

Creating Web Forms to Gather Information

A Web form is a collection of controls—such as check boxes, option buttons, lists, text boxes, and buttons—that allow you to collect information from readers of your online Word document or Web page. For example, you could add a form to a Web page that

Chapter 20: Creating Web Pages and Other Online Documents

allows visitors to your site to sign up for a newsletter that you send out, to request information, or to enter their names and comments in a guest log.

To add a form to a document or Web page, perform the following steps:

1 Place the insertion point at the position in your document or page where you want to add the first form control.

2 Display the Web Tools toolbar (shown in Figure 20-16) by choosing View, Toolbars, Web Tools.

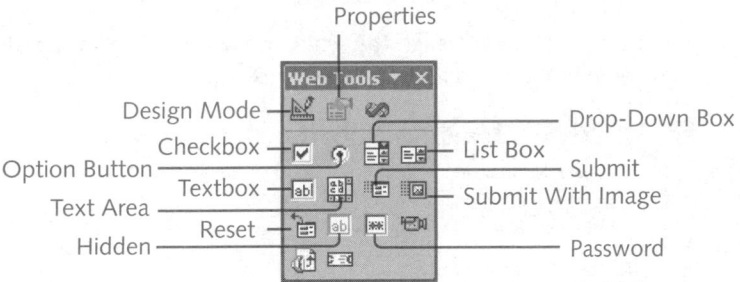

Figure 20-16. This figure labels the buttons on the Web Tools toolbar that are used for creating Web forms.

3 Add the controls. To add each control, click the appropriate button on the Web Tools toolbar. When you add the first control, Word will do the following:

■ It will insert a top-of-form and a bottom-of-form boundary. Be sure to add all additional controls that belong to the form you're creating within these boundaries, as seen here:

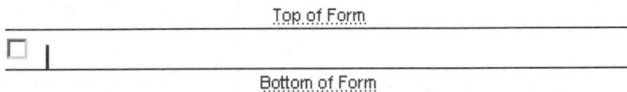

■ It will switch into *design mode*, which lets you add or modify form controls. (When you're out of design mode, the controls will function as intended; for example, you'll be able to check a check box or enter text into a text box.) You can switch design mode off or on by clicking the Design Mode button on the Web Tools toolbar.

Be sure to add either a *submit button* (click the Submit button on the Web Tools toolbar) or a *submit image* (click the Submit With Image button). A submit button or image allows the user to send you the information that they've entered into the form.

In addition to adding controls to the form area, you can type any text you want for labeling the controls, providing instructions, or displaying other information.

4 Customize the controls as necessary. To customize a control, double-click it and set the desired properties in the Properties dialog box.

For a submit button or a submit image, you must assign the Action property the URL of the custom program or script on the server that receives and processes the form information (consult your Web hosting service or webmaster about creating this program or script).

Alternatively, you can assign the Action property your e-mail address, using the *mailto* protocol, as in the following example:

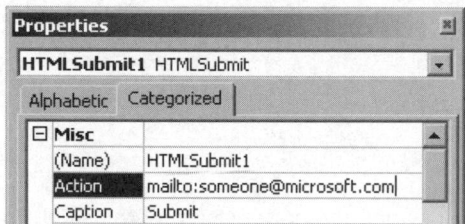

As a result, clicking the submit button or image will send the current contents of the form in an e-mail message addressed to you.

> **note** For a description of each type of control and its properties, see the Word online help topic "Form controls you can use on a Web page."

5 When you're done creating the form, click the Design Mode button (now labeled Exit Design Mode) to return to normal editing mode.

Use Frames to View Several Documents at Once

You can show several documents simultaneously in the Word or Web browser window by displaying each document within a separate *frame*, which is an adjustable pane within the window.

> **note** In Word, the term *frame* also refers to a seldom-used element for positioning text on a page, which is similar to a text box.

The fastest way to create a set of Web pages that are displayed in frames is to use the Web Page Wizard. You can also use the Frames submenu on the Format menu to create a document that displays frames (known as a *frames document* or *frames page*), or to add individual frames to such a document. And you can use the Frames toolbar to add or remove frames, or to modify the properties of the frames document or of one or more frames. Note that you can use either the submenu or the toolbar to add a frame containing a table of contents, which lets the viewer select the document or document section that's displayed in another frame.

For instructions on Using the Web Page Wizard, see step 1 of the procedure in "Creating and Publishing a Web Page," on page 573. For detailed information on using frames in Word, see the Word online help topic "Frames and Frames Pages." For general information on frames and for instructions on creating them in Microsoft FrontPage, see "Using Frames to Display Multiple Pages," on page 1240.

newfeature!
Adding Web Components

Word 2002 provides several prebuilt components that you can quickly add to a Web page you create in Word. These components let the reader of the page navigate to other pages or view the information stored on a SharePoint team Web site. Note that you can add these components only to a Web page, *not* to a native Word document, and the Web page must be posted to a Web site with the appropriate Microsoft server extensions (the specific required extensions are given in the list below). The following are the Web components you can add in Word:

- **Link Bar** A link bar is a ready-made set of hyperlink buttons that let the page reader navigate to other pages or documents on the current Web site or on other Internet sites. To use a Link Bar component, you must post the page to a Web server that is running the Microsoft Office 2000 Web Server Extensions SharePoint Team Services.

- **List View** This component lets the page reader view and track the items stored in a list on a SharePoint team Web site. Each list contains a different type of information: discussion postings, announcements, contact descriptions, event notices, links to Internet sites, a survey, summaries of tasks that need to be performed, or custom information items. To use a List View component, you must post the page to a Web server that is running SharePoint Team Services.

- **Document Library View** This component lets the page reader view documents stored in document libraries on a SharePoint Web site. To use a Document Library View component, you must post the page to a Web server that is running SharePoint.

SharePoint Team Services is discussed in Chapter 8, "Using Microsoft SharePoint Team Services in Professional Workgroups."

To add one of these components to your Web page, perform the following steps:

1 Place the insertion point at the position in the page where you want to display the component.

2 Choose Insert, Web Component to open the Insert Web Component dialog box (shown in Figure 20-17).

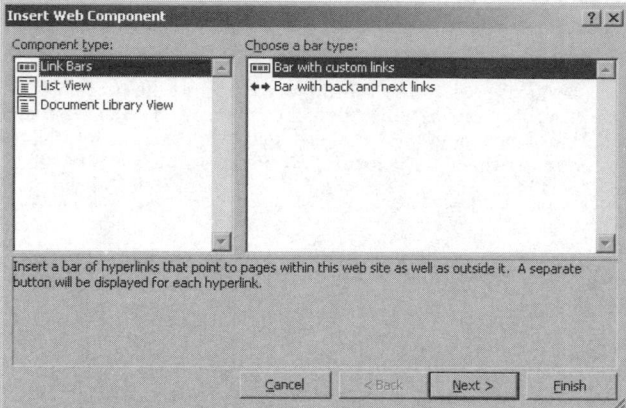

Figure 20-17. You can add Web components to a Web page in the Insert Web Component dialog box.

3 In the Component Type list at the left of the Insert Web Component dialog box, select the Web component you want to add.

4 In the list at the right of the dialog box, select a type or style for the selected component. (The name of the list and the items it contains vary according to the selected component.)

5 If you're adding a List View or Document Library View component, click the Finish button.

6 If you're adding a Link Bar component, click the Next button, select a bar style, and then click Finish.

Formatting Web Pages

Word provides the following formatting features that are especially useful for a Web page or an online Word document:

- A background color or pattern
- A theme

For information on general Word formatting techniques, see Chapter 12, "Effective Formatting in Word."

Applying a Background Color or Pattern

You can assign your Web page or document a solid background color, a standard background pattern, or a background picture derived from a graphics file that you select, by choosing an option from the Format, Background submenu, shown here:

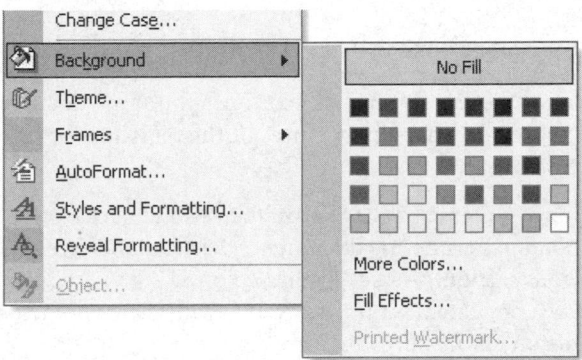

- To apply a standard, solid background color, choose one of the colors directly from the palette on the submenu.

- To select from a larger set of solid colors, or to create a custom solid color, choose More Colors.

- To apply a background pattern or picture, choose Fill Effects, which opens the Fill Effects dialog box. The first three tabs of this dialog box (Gradient, Texture, and Pattern) let you select from a large collection of standard background patterns. The fourth tab (Picture) lets you display a picture in the document background by selecting any graphics file.

- To remove a previously applied background, choose No Fill.

Troubleshooting

Page Background Isn't Visible

You applied a background color or pattern to a document. It was visible at first, but it has now disappeared.

A background color or pattern is visible only in Web Layout view. Word automatically switches to that view when you first apply a background, but if you later change to a different view, the background will disappear. To see the background, switch back to Web Layout view (by choosing View, Web Layout, or by clicking the Web Layout View button at the left end of the horizontal scroll bar).

Applying a Web Page Theme

You can modify the overall appearance of your Web page or native Word document by applying a *theme*, which is a predesigned visual scheme that applies a consistent look to elements throughout the document. You can choose from a list of almost 70 themes provided with Office XP.

Applying a theme affects the following document elements:

- The font, size, color, and other features of text throughout the document. (The theme modifies text by changing features of the built-in Normal and Heading styles.)

- The page background. A theme might apply either a solid background color or a background pattern to the document. (Backgrounds are discussed in the previous section.) A background color or pattern is visible only when you view a document in Word's Web Layout view or when you view a Web page document in a browser.

- The images used for horizontal dividing lines and for bullets in bulleted lists.

- Hyperlink text colors (for both unfollowed and followed hyperlinks).

- The color of table borders.

To apply a theme to the current Web page or document, perform the following steps:

1 Choose Format, Theme to open the Theme dialog box (shown in Figure 20-18).

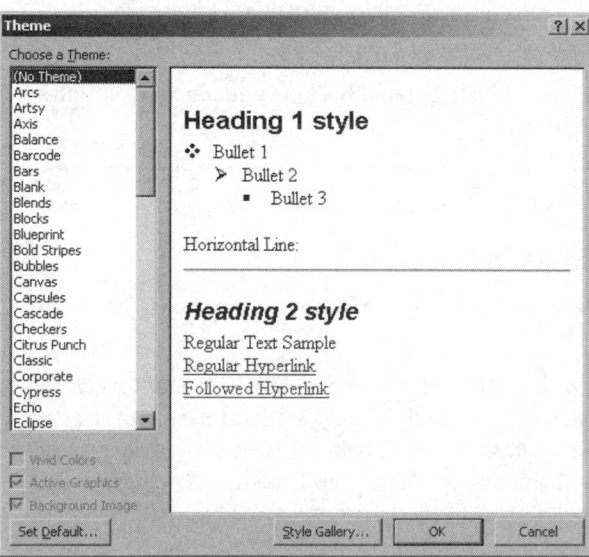

Figure 20-18. The Theme dialog box provides a collection of themes that you can apply to Web pages.

2 Select the theme you want in the Choose A Theme list, or select (No Theme) to remove a previously applied theme.

The Sample area of the dialog box shows the visual effect of the selected theme and theme options.

3 Choose options, as follows:

- To apply bright colors to the document text, table borders, and background, check Vivid Colors.

- To display any animated pictures included with the theme, check Active Graphics.

- To display the background pattern included with the theme, check Background Image. (Clearing this option displays a solid background color rather than a pattern.)

- To use the selected theme as the default for all new Web pages you create in Word, click the Set Default button (this won't affect the new native-format Word documents you create).

Part 4

Excel

Chapter 21

Worksheet Construction Essentials

Microsoft Excel 2002 is a general-purpose electronic spreadsheet used to organize, calculate, and analyze data. The tasks you can perform with Excel range from preparing a simple invoice for your house-painting service or planning a budget for a family vacation to creating elaborate 3-D charts or managing a complex accounting ledger for a medium-sized business. This section of the book introduces Excel and teaches you how to accomplish a variety of tasks with the newest version of Microsoft's flagship spreadsheet application. You'll receive training and support for virtually all your Excel needs, from creating a simple worksheet to forecasting expenses and publishing spreadsheets on the Web. Along the way, you'll learn how to use Excel's newest features and how to customize Excel to work the way you do. We'll also share our favorite Excel productivity tips, including several that come directly from the Excel development team.

This introductory chapter gives you a quick tour of the Excel workplace and shows you how to build a simple worksheet from start to finish. A *worksheet* is an Excel document containing rows and columns of information that can be formatted, sorted, analyzed, and charted. Building a worksheet involves starting Excel, entering information, adding formulas, and saving your data. If you want to get fancy, you can even add hyperlinks to your worksheet to access supporting files on your hard disk or on the Internet.

Starting Excel and Getting Comfortable

You start Excel like you start most programs in the Microsoft Office XP application suite; click the Start button on the taskbar, and then choose Programs, Microsoft Excel (the icon is shown here).

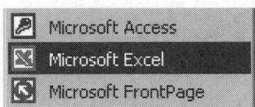

When Excel first starts, it displays a new, empty workbook (which will be defined shortly) in the application workplace. Figure 21-1 shows the default opening Excel screen, featuring many of the common window elements for Office applications: a standard menu bar, toolbars, a formula bar, and a status bar. The application window has been maximized to display all the elements of the Excel user interface. If your application window doesn't appear maximized when you start it, you can click the Maximize button on the Excel title bar to give you more space to work with.

> **tip** **Display Other Toolbars**
>
> To display other toolbars—or to hide toolbars that appear by default—point to the toolbar region with your mouse and click the right mouse button. The checked items are toolbars that are currently displayed. Select an unchecked item from the list to display the associated toolbar; select a checked item to hide the associated toolbar.

Like most Office applications, the Excel application window also contains *sizing buttons* you can use to minimize, maximize, restore, and close windows, plus a *status bar* that shows the state of various keyboard keys, including Num Lock. A special feature of the Excel status bar is the *AutoCalculate box*, which displays the result of the selected function (SUM by default) using the highlighted cells in the active worksheet. To get additional help with the Excel interface or with any Excel command, click the Microsoft Excel Help button on the right side of the Standard toolbar. If the animated Office Assistant isn't already running, clicking this button will start it.

Troubleshooting

Installation Revisited

Errors surface when you start Excel that point to missing program components.

In this chapter, we assume that Excel is installed and ready to go on your computer. If Excel displays an error message or notes a problem when you start it, try evaluating and repairing your software with the new Detect And Repair command. For more information, see "Revisiting Office Setup," on page 27.

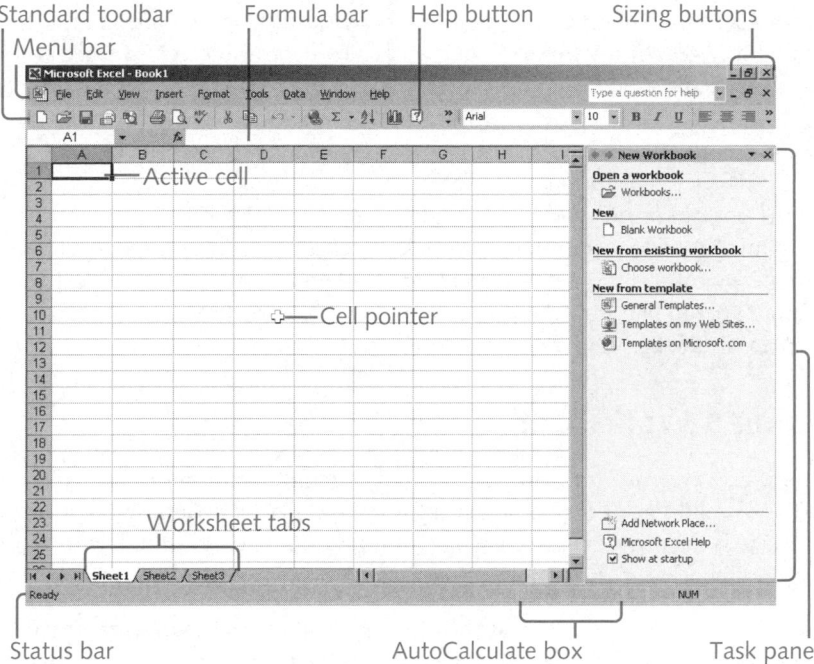

Figure 21-1. The Microsoft Excel user interface features many important elements (labeled).

> For more information about using menus, dialog boxes, toolbars, and application windows, see Chapter 4, "Working with Office XP Applications, Documents, and Program Windows." For more details about starting and configuring the Office Assistant, see Chapter 3, "Getting Expert Help on Office XP."

When you first open Excel, the default workbook (Book1) appears on the screen and displays the first worksheet (Sheet1). A worksheet is divided into a grid of rows and columns, as shown in Figure 21-1. (An Excel worksheet can contain up to 65,536 rows and 256 columns.) A letter is assigned to each column of the worksheet, and a number is assigned to each row. The intersection of each row and column is a worksheet *cell*, which is referenced individually by its *cell name*. For example, the cell at the intersection of column A and row 1 is known as cell A1. Cell names are also called *cell addresses* or *cell references*.

> For information about managing the worksheets in a workbook and opening additional workbooks, see Chapter 24, "Power Organizing with Workbooks."

A *workbook* is a collection of one or more worksheets, plus (optionally) chart sheets containing graphic pictures of your worksheet data. You can also store special macros in Visual Basic modules in the workbook, but they aren't listed among the worksheets.

You'll learn how to create Visual Basic macros to boost your productivity in Part 10.

At the bottom of the workbook window are tabs that give you instant access to the remaining worksheets in the workbook. Excel allows you to name your worksheets, add new worksheets, or delete blank or obsolete worksheets. Each workbook window contains scroll bars you can use to move from one worksheet to the next or from place to place in the active worksheet.

Navigating a Worksheet

To create a typical Excel worksheet, you'll store information in dozens or even hundreds of cells. Each time you enter information in a cell, you must first move to the cell to make it the *active cell*. Accordingly, you need to be comfortable with several methods for moving around in, or *navigating*, a worksheet.

To activate a cell, you can press the arrow keys (the Up, Down, Left, and Right arrow keys), or you can click the cell you want to activate with the mouse. This is called *selecting* or *highlighting* a cell. The name of the selected cell appears in the Name box, as shown in Figure 21-2. Also notice that when you first move the mouse pointer onto the worksheet, it changes its shape to the *cell pointer*. You can use the cell pointer to select individual cells or ranges of cells, as you'll learn later in this chapter.

To view part of a worksheet that isn't currently visible in the workbook window, you can click the vertical or horizontal scroll bars. Each time you click a scroll arrow at the top or bottom of the vertical scroll bar, the active worksheet scrolls vertically one row. Each time you click a scroll arrow at the left or right end of the horizontal scroll bar, the active worksheet scrolls horizontally one column. Note that when you scroll with the scroll bars, you change only your view of the worksheet—scrolling moves the screen but doesn't change the active cell. Your relative position in the worksheet is identified by the scroll boxes in each scroll bar. These boxes change size as your worksheet changes size, representing the relative portion of the entire worksheet that's currently visible.

tip   If you scroll far from the active cell so that it's no longer visible, you can redisplay the active cell by pressing Ctrl + Backspace, as noted in Table 21-1 on page 608.

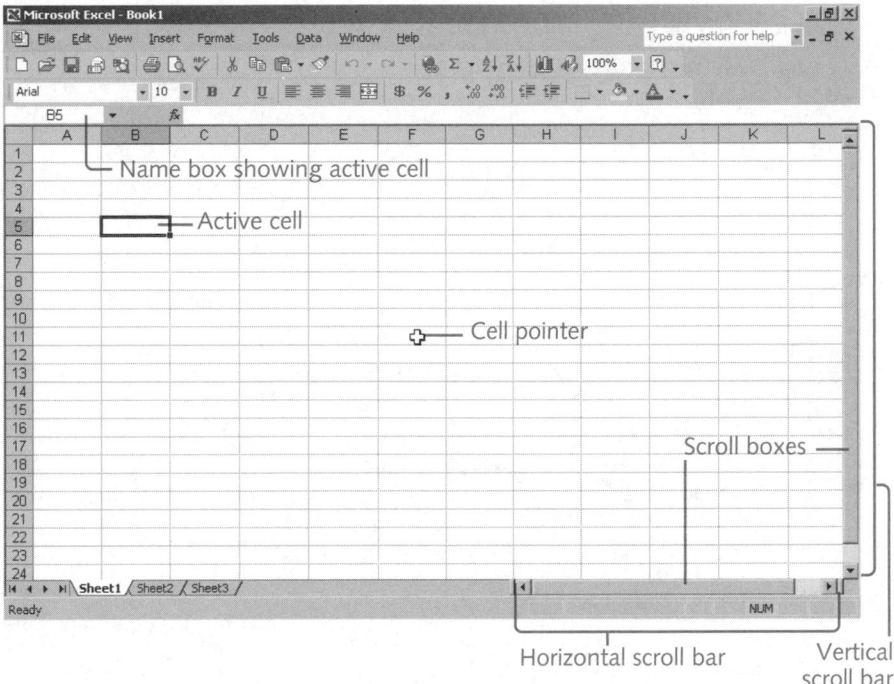

Figure 21-2. Use the cell pointer to select a cell in the worksheet or use the scroll bars to move to cells not currently visible.

To move among the worksheets in your workbook, you can click the worksheet tabs. If necessary, first use the tab scroll buttons to display worksheet tabs that are not visible because of limited space. Be careful not to confuse the tab scroll buttons with the buttons for the horizontal scroll bar.

Using the Keyboard

Several key combinations let you move quickly throughout your worksheet. Unlike scroll bar movements, these key combinations also select a new active cell. Table 21-1 lists the most useful keyboard navigation keys in a worksheet.

Table 21-1. **Useful Worksheet Navigation Keys**

Use This Key or Key Combination	To Move
↑, ↓, →, ←	To the next cell in the direction pressed
Ctrl+↑, Ctrl+↓, Ctrl+←, Ctrl+→	To the next cell containing data (the next nonblank cell) in the direction pressed
Home	To column A of current row
Page Up	Up one screen
Page Down	Down one screen
Alt+Page Up	One screen to the left
Alt+Page Down	One screen to the right
Ctrl+Home	To cell A1
Ctrl+End	To the cell in the last row and last column that contains data
Ctrl+Backspace	To reposition the visible portion of the worksheet to display the active cell or selected ranges that have scrolled out of view

Jumping to a Specific Cell with the GO TO Command

To highlight a specific cell in the active worksheet by name, you can choose Edit, Go To or press F5. When you choose the GO TO command, Excel displays the Go To dialog box, as shown in Figure 21-3. You can jump to a specific cell by typing the name of the cell in the Reference text box and clicking OK. (You can also double-click the name of the cell if it appears in the list box. As you'll see in Chapter 26, "Crunching Numbers with Formulas and Functions," Excel lets you assign a meaningful name, such as Salary or SalesTax, to a cell or range of cells.)

If you'd like to highlight a range of cells based on a special attribute, such as all the cells containing formulas or comments, click the Special button and specify the cell contents you're interested in.

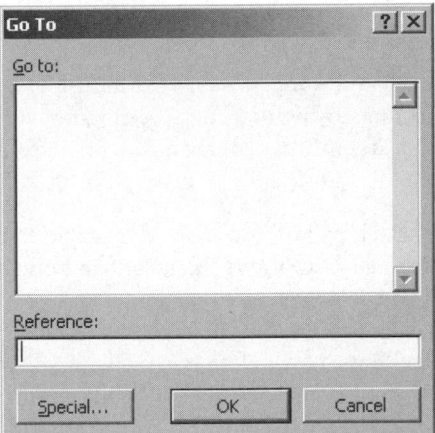

Figure 21-3. The Go To dialog box lets you jump instantly to a certain cell.

tip   Notice that the cell name (location) of the active cell appears in the Name box, which is located to the left of the formula bar. You can also move to a specific cell by clicking the Name box, typing the cell name, and pressing Enter (see Figure 21-2 on page 607).

Entering Information

Excel lets you enter the following types of information into a worksheet cell:

- Numeric values, such as the numbers 22,000, $29.95, and 33%

- Text values, such as the words *Total*, *1st Quarter*, and *1820 Warren Avenue*

- Dates and times, such as Feb-97, 11/19/63, or 1:00 P.M.

- Comments to yourself or others, such as *This region leads in sales*, or an appropriate recorded sound or voice message

- Formulas, such as =B5*1.081 or =SUM(B3:B7)

- Hyperlinks to Internet sites or other documents

- Electronic artwork, such as clip art, scanned photographs, maps, and illustrations

Each kind of information has its own formatting characteristics, meaning that Excel stores and displays each entry type differently. The following sections show you how to enter these values into a worksheet.

Chapter 21

Entering Numeric Values

To enter a number in a cell, select the cell you want by using the mouse or keyboard, type the number, and press Enter. Selecting, or highlighting, a cell makes it the active cell. Then, as you type, the number appears simultaneously in the active cell and on the *formula bar* above the worksheet.

The formula bar serves as an editing scratch pad. If you make a mistake entering a long cell entry, you can click within the formula bar to move the insertion point and then correct the entry without having to retype it. Conveniently, you can also double-click the active cell, and then move the insertion point within the cell to edit your entry. To the left of the formula bar is a Cancel button, which you can click to discard an unwanted entry on the formula bar (if you haven't already accepted the entry by pressing Enter). Alongside the Cancel button is an Enter button, which you can click to accept or *lock in* a revised entry. See Figure 21-4.

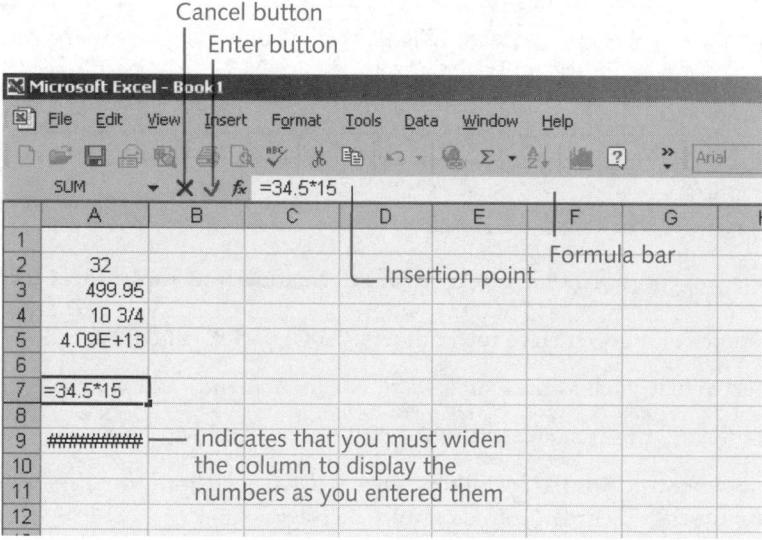

Figure 21-4.   New values appear both on the formula bar and in the cell when you enter them.

A numeric value can be an integer (such as 32), a decimal number (such as 499.95), an integer fraction (such as 10 3/4), or a number in scientific notation (such as 4.09E+13). You can use several mathematical symbols in numbers, including plus (+), minus (−), percent (%), fraction (/), and exponent (E), as well as the dollar sign ($). If you enter a number that's too large to fit into a cell, Excel will automatically widen the cell to accommodate the number or adjust its display of the number by using scientific notation or by showing fewer decimal places. If Excel displays the number in scientific notation or places a row of number signs (#######) in the cell, you'll need to increase the column width manually to see the number in its entirety.

Troubleshooting

When you use a slash to create a fraction in a numeric entry, be sure to include a leading zero (0) and a space if the fractional value is less than 1. If you don't, Excel interprets your fraction as a date. For example, Excel interprets the fraction 3/4 as the date March 4 unless you enter the fraction as 0 3/4. You'll learn more about date and time formatting in Chapter 23, "Expert Formatting Techniques."

Excel always stores the actual number you typed internally, no matter how it's displayed in the cell, and you can view this *underlying value* on the formula bar whenever the cell is active. By default, numeric values are aligned to the right edge of a cell.

tip   **Use Arrow Keys to Move from Cell to Cell**

If you plan to enter additional numbers, you can use the arrow keys to enter a number and move to a new cell in one step. For instance, if you type a number and press the Down arrow key, the cell pointer moves down one line. The Left, Up, and Right arrow keys move the pointer one cell left, up, or right.

Entering Text Values

To enter a text value into a cell, select the cell, type your text, and press Enter. A text value, or *label*, can be any combination of alphanumeric characters, including uppercase and lowercase letters, numbers, and symbols. Excel recognizes text values and aligns them to the left margin of each cell. If no information appears in adjacent cells, Excel allows longer text entries to overlap the cells on the right. If the adjacent cells do contain information, the display of the text is cut off, or truncated; however, just as with a truncated value, Excel correctly stores the full text internally, and you can see it on the formula bar when the cell is active.

For details about changing column widths to make room for more information in cells, see "Changing Column Widths and Row Heights," on page 665.

If you want Excel to store as text a value such as a numeric address, date, or part number, precede the value with a single quotation mark. For example, if you enter '55 in a cell, the number 55 will appear left-aligned in the cell without a quotation mark. A quotation mark will appear on the formula bar to identify the number as a text value.

newfeature!

Numeric values that are inadvertently stored as text can be troublesome, especially if they are expected to behave as numbers in formulas. To flag cells that contain these values, Excel 2002 includes a comment in such a cell that alerts you to the discrepancy. To display the pop-up comment, activate the cell and move the mouse pointer over the caution indicator alongside the cell. To eliminate the comment, right-click the indicator and choose Ignore Error. This background checking—to anticipate potential difficulties—is a new (optional) feature called Error Checking.

For more information about Error Checking, see "Checking for Common Errors," on page 646.

Figure 21-5 shows several examples of text entries: a cell that has overlapping text, a few cells that have truncated text, and several numeric text entries (that is, numbers stored internally as text).

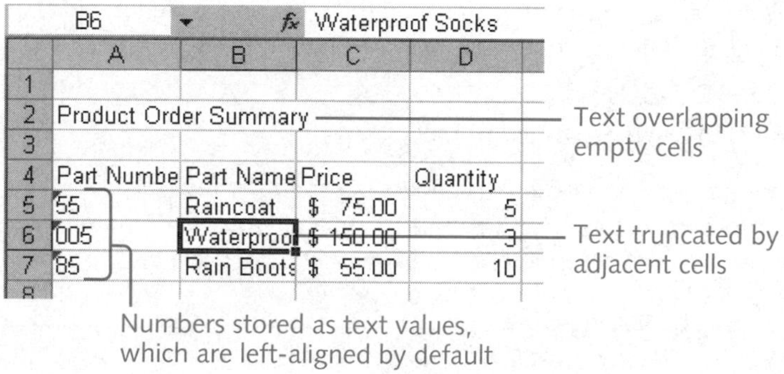

Figure 21-5. Text values are left-aligned and can overlap adjacent cells if they don't contain information.

tip **Speed Up Your Work with AutoComplete**

If Excel recognizes the pattern you're typing when you enter a sequence of characters, it will attempt to complete the pattern using a feature called *AutoComplete*. AutoComplete can be a major time-saver for you if you manage lists in Excel or find that you're entering the same values or functions over and over again. If you use the AutoComplete feature while entering data, review the characters Excel inserts and if they make sense to you, press Enter and move on.

For information about turning off AutoComplete, see "Customizing Editing Options," on page 729.

Entering Dates and Times

If you want to store a date or a time in a worksheet cell, you should use one of Excel's predefined date and time formats to enter the value so that Excel will recognize the number as a chronological entity and apply appropriate formatting. (Internally, Excel stores identifiable dates and times as *serial numbers*, counters that commence with January 1, 1900. In this form the dates and times are easier to use in functions and formulas.) As you'll learn in Chapter 23, "Expert Formatting Techniques," Excel lets you specify the format of times and dates with a few simple commands.

> **tip** To enter the current date in the active cell, press Ctrl+; (the semicolon key). Excel will use the format *m/d/yyyy* for the date.

Table 21-2 shows you some of the time and date formats Excel supports. Date formats with a four-digit placeholder for the current year (the patterns *m/d/yyyy* and *d-mmm-yyyy*) are included to help manage the year 2000 problem. This confusion arises in spreadsheets and accounting ledgers when the century portion of a numeric entry is recorded ambiguously. (For example, the date 3/14/02 could be read as March 14, 1902 or March 14, 2002.) As a rule Excel treats a date with a two-digit year as belonging to the twenty-first century if it precedes 1/1/30; subsequent dates entered in this form fall in the twentieth century. To clarify which century you mean, use one of the new four-digit-year date formats.

Table 21-2. Popular Date and Time Formats Supported by Excel

Format	Pattern	Example
Date	m/d/yy	10/1/99
Date	d mmm yy	1-Oct-99
Date	d-mmm	1-Oct
Date	mmm-yy	Oct-99
Date (four-digit year)	m/d/yyyy	10/1/1999
Date (four-digit year)	d-mmm-yyyy	1-Oct-2002
Time	h:mm AM/PM	10:22 PM
Time	h:mm:ss AM/PM	10:22:30 PM
Time	h:mm	22:22
Time	h:mm:ss	22:22:30
Time	mm:ss.0	22:30.3
Combined	m/d/yy h:mm	10/1/99 22:22

Figure 21-6 shows working examples of the most popular date and time formats and the procedure to enter them. You can change the format of a date or time in the active cell by choosing Format, Cells, clicking the Number tab, and then choosing a different pattern in the Date or Time category.

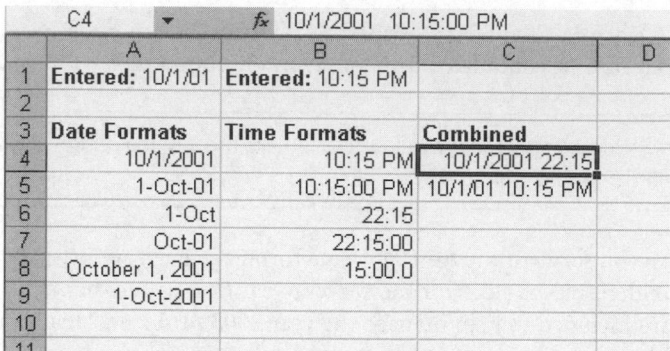

Figure 21-6. Enter time and date values in one of these popular formats.

> For information about changing the format of date and time values, see "Changing Number Formats," on page 655.

Entering Comments

If you plan to share your Excel worksheets with other users, you might want to anno-tate a few important cells by using *comments* to provide instructions or to highlight critical information. You can add a pop-up comment to a cell by selecting the cell and choosing Insert, Comment. Choosing the Comment command displays a pop-up win-dow that contains a blinking pointer and your name; type a short note in the cell, as illustrated in Figure 21-7. When you're finished typing the comment, click another cell to lock in the note.

> **tip** To change the name that appears when you enter a comment, choose Tools, Options, click the General tab, and change the name in the User Name text box.

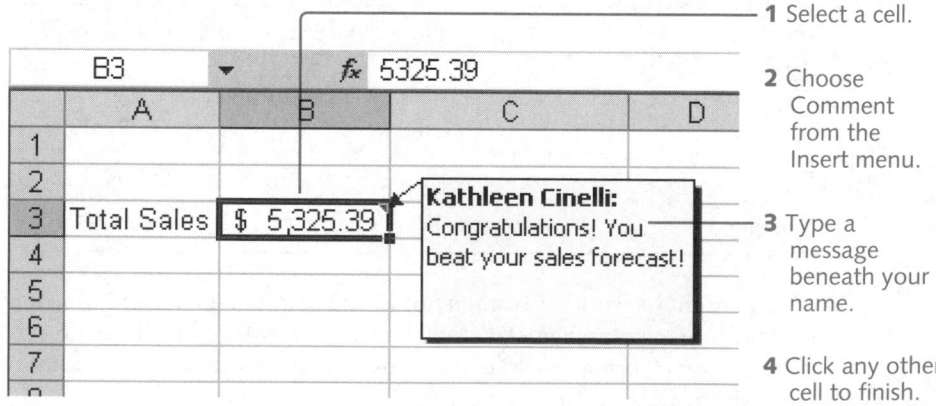

1 Select a cell.

2 Choose Comment from the Insert menu.

3 Type a message beneath your name.

4 Click any other cell to finish.

Figure 21-7. The Comment command allows you to add a descriptive note to a cell.

614

Active comments are identified by tiny red dots in the upper right corner of a cell. To display a comment in a worksheet, hold the mouse pointer over the annotated cell until a pop-up comment box appears. Remember that because comments are cell annotations, they exist in *addition* to the other entries in cells—they don't *replace* them. To delete an existing comment, select the cell containing the comment in the worksheet, choose Edit, Clear, and click Comments on the Clear submenu.

Managing Comments

You can view all the comments in your workbook by enabling the Comments command on the View menu. The Comments command is a toggle that is either off or on; when it's enabled, all the comments in your workbook appear in pop-up windows; when it's disabled, a comment appears only when you move the mouse pointer over the cell in which it resides. The Comments command also activates the Reviewing toolbar, which contains a number of useful command buttons. To edit an existing comment, click the Edit Comment button on the toolbar or right-click the cell containing the comment that needs editing and choose Edit Comment from the shortcut menu.

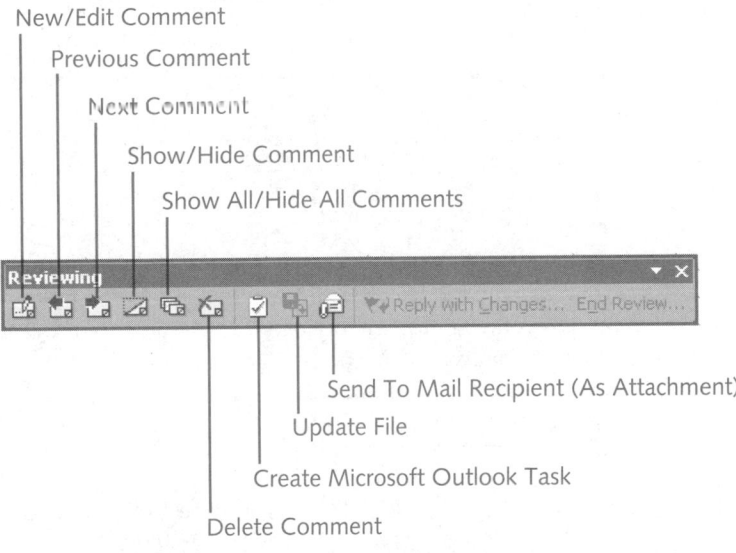

New/Edit Comment

Previous Comment

Next Comment

Show/Hide Comment

Show All/Hide All Comments

Send To Mail Recipient (As Attachment)

Update File

Create Microsoft Outlook Task

Delete Comment

Entering Formulas

A *formula* is an equation that calculates a new value from existing values. Excel lets you enter a formula in a cell and display the calculated result in your worksheet. For example, a simple formula could calculate the total cost of an item by adding its price, sales tax, and shipping costs.

Formulas can contain numbers, mathematical operators, cell references, and built-in equations called *functions*. One of Excel's great strengths is its vast collection of powerful and easy-to-use functions. These functions can help you perform a wide range of tasks, from rounding a number to the nearest integer to determining the one-tailed probability of the chi-squared distribution (yes, statistics).

All formulas in Excel begin with an equal sign (=). The equal sign signals the beginning of a mathematical operation and tells Excel to store the expression that follows as a formula. For example, the following formula calculates the sum of three numbers:

```
=10+20+30
```

Excel stores your formulas internally (you can see them on the formula bar), but it displays the result of each calculation in the cell in which you placed the formula. You can use the standard mathematical operators in a formula—addition (+), subtraction (–), multiplication (*), division (/), and exponentiation (^), as well as a few specialty operators described in Chapter 26, "Crunching Numbers with Formulas and Functions." Figure 21-8 lists the steps to follow to enter a simple formula in a worksheet cell.

For detailed information about formula syntax, see "Building a Formula," on page 733. For detailed information about Excel's collection of built-in functions, see "Using Built-In Functions," on page 739.

Troubleshooting

Does Not Compute

Excel doesn't calculate the result of your formula.

If you don't begin formulas with an equal sign (=), Excel will interpret the equation as a text value and the formula won't be calculated. If you make this common mistake, press F2 to edit the cell, press the Home key to move the insertion point to the beginning of the formula, type an equal sign (=), and then press Enter.

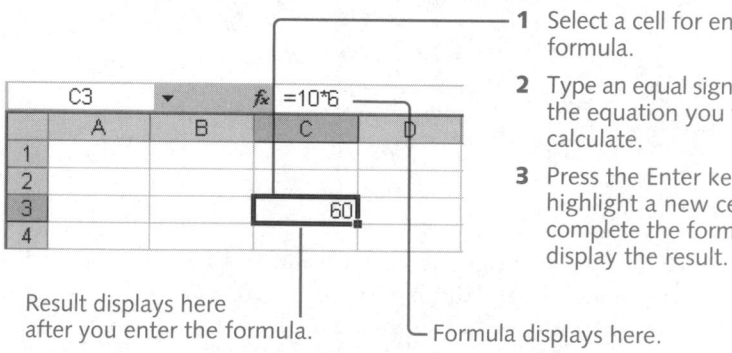

1 Select a cell for entering a formula.

2 Type an equal sign (=) and the equation you want to calculate.

3 Press the Enter key or highlight a new cell to complete the formula and display the result.

Result displays here after you enter the formula.

Formula displays here.

Figure 21-8. A simple formula might involve only a few numbers and operators.

Chapter 21

Using Cell References in Formulas

Formulas can also contain worksheet *cell references*—cell names such as A1 or B5—so that you can include the contents of cells in formulas and combine them in any way you choose. You can use cell references along with numbers, mathematical operators, and built-in functions. To specify a cell reference while you're entering a formula, you can

● Type in the cell name, such as **B5**

● Highlight the cell individually using the mouse

● Highlight the cell using the keyboard

For example, to add the contents of cell B5 to the contents of cell C5, you'd create the following formula:

```
=B5+C5
```

> You can also include groups of cells, such as A3:A9, in formulas. See "Selecting Cells and Ranges," on page 628.

Figure 21-9 shows the results of such a calculation.

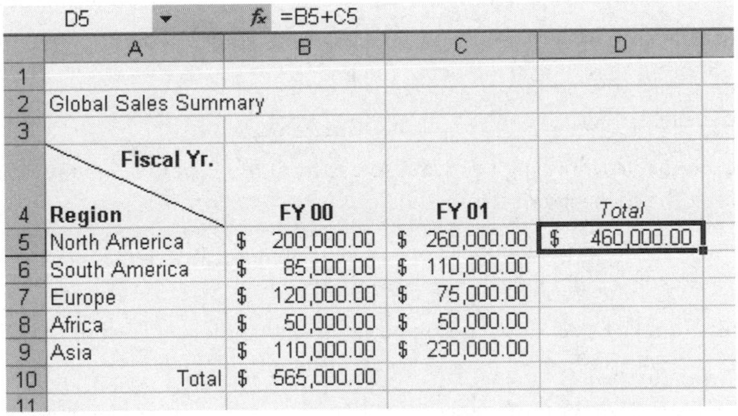

D5	▼	f_x =B5+C5		
	A	B	C	D
1				
2	Global Sales Summary			
3				
4	Fiscal Yr. Region	FY 00	FY 01	Total
5	North America	$ 200,000.00	$ 260,000.00	$ 460,000.00
6	South America	$ 85,000.00	$ 110,000.00	
7	Europe	$ 120,000.00	$ 75,000.00	
8	Africa	$ 50,000.00	$ 50,000.00	
9	Asia	$ 110,000.00	$ 230,000.00	
10	Total	$ 565,000.00		
11				

Figure 21-9. To use the contents of cells in a formula, include cell references in the equation.

To create a formula such as the one in Figure 21-9, complete the following steps. This procedure includes cell references you highlight with the mouse, but you could easily substitute other methods for including the cell references.

1 Select the cell—D5, for example—in which you want to place the formula.

2 Type an equal sign (=) to start the formula. Click the first cell you want to place in the formula, and then type a mathematical operator. For example, click cell B5, and then press the plus (+) key to add B5+ to the formula bar.

When you click the cell, a flashing border surrounds the cell, and its name appears on the formula bar. The flashing border disappears when you type the operator. The border and cell address are colored blue.

3 Click the second cell you want to place in the formula. If the cell you want isn't currently visible, use the scroll bars to locate it. If you want to include additional mathematical operators and cell names, you can add them now. Each additional cell address and border appears in a different color.

4 Press the Enter key to store the formula. Excel calculates the result and displays it in the cell. (The result is 0 if the cells you're adding are empty.) All colors and borders disappear when you press Enter.

Adding Artwork

After you enter your worksheet's basic facts and figures into Excel, you might want to spruce things up a bit by adding some electronic artwork such as clip art, scanned photographs, background images, organization charts, or hand-drawn illustrations. The basic technique for adding these items to worksheet cells is the same in all Office applications: click a command on the Picture submenu of the Insert menu.

Follow these steps to add a piece of electronic artwork to a worksheet:

1 Select the cell in which you want to place the artwork. (Allow some room in neighboring cells to accommodate the image.)

2 Choose Insert, Picture.

3 Choose the artwork type you want to use from the Picture submenu. You will see the following options:

- **Clip Art**   A picture gallery containing thousands of pieces of electronic art for presentations, reports, and brochures

- **From File**   An Open dialog box that lets you locate existing artwork on your system

- **From Scanner Or Camera**   A utility that helps you insert scanned images and photographs into worksheet cells

- **Organization Chart**   A utility that helps you build corporate organization charts

- **AutoShapes**   A toolbar that lets you add arrows, lines, and other shapes

- **WordArt**   A wizard and toolbar that helps you build creative banners, headlines, and text elements

4 Move or resize the artwork as desired in the worksheet.

5 If you want to delete the image later, select the artwork object you inserted and press Delete.

Inserting a Background Graphic

If the worksheet you're creating will take center stage in a report or presentation, you might want to embellish it further by adding a subtle piece of artwork to the background. When you add background artwork, Excel places the image you specify behind (below) the current worksheet or chart. (The data in your worksheet cells will appear on top of the image.) If you specify a small pattern rather than a complete image, Excel automatically repeats, or *tiles*, the pattern to fill the entire worksheet or chart.

To add a bitmap, metafile, or other electronic image to the background of your worksheet, follow these steps:

1 Display the worksheet you want to customize by adding background artwork.

2 Choose Format, Sheet, and then click Background on the Sheet submenu. The Sheet Background dialog box appears.

3 Browse the folders on your hard disk or network to locate the electronic artwork you want to display as a background graphic. When you find and select it, click the Insert button to insert the graphic. (You'll find several useful images in the Program Files\Microsoft Office\Office10\Bitmaps\Styles folder, in the Windows folder, and in your clip art folders.)

> **tip** Try to use simple, light-colored background images in your worksheets and charts so that the artwork doesn't overpower the text you're using for labels and numbers. Subtle, light gray images often work best.

If at some point you decide you don't want the background image, choose Format, Sheet, Delete Background to remove it.

Inserting Hyperlinks

Excel includes an enhanced feature that allows you to add *hyperlinks* to cells in your workbook, connecting them to other electronic documents on your hard disk, the Internet, or an attached computer network. Hyperlinks in Excel give you a handy way to combine a series of related workbooks or let you provide your users with on-demand access to supporting documents, Web pages, or other reference materials on the Internet. You create a hyperlink using the Hyperlink command on the Insert menu, and the command prompts you for the name of the supporting file or Web page and underlines the text in the worksheet cell that was selected when you ran the command. (The underlined word appears in a special color and looks similar to linked topics that appear in the Office online Help.) After a hyperlink to another document has been established, you can activate it by clicking the underlined word in your worksheet.

> **note** You can specify any supporting document for your hyperlink—provided that you have the application necessary to open the document on your computer. Similarly, if you have Microsoft Internet Explorer or another Internet browser, you can create a hyperlink to any resource on the Internet for which you have a proper address.

Creating a Hyperlink in Your Worksheet

To add to your worksheet a hyperlink that opens a document on your hard disk, the Internet, or a network to which you're attached, complete the following steps:

1 In your worksheet, select the cell with which you want to associate the hyperlink. You can create a hyperlink in an empty cell or in a cell containing information, artwork, or a formula.

Insert
Hyperlink

2 Choose Insert, Hyperlink or click the Insert Hyperlink button on the Standard toolbar. The Insert Hyperlink dialog box appears, as shown in Figure 21-10. Excel now asks you two fundamental questions about your selection: what type of hyperlink are you creating, and what content should the hyperlink contain?

Troubleshooting

Can't Insert a Hyperlink

The Insert Hyperlink command is unavailable.

Does the Insert Hyperlink command appear dimmed? If so, the command is unavailable, probably because the workbook is being shared. For more information, see "Managing Shared Workbooks," on page 698.

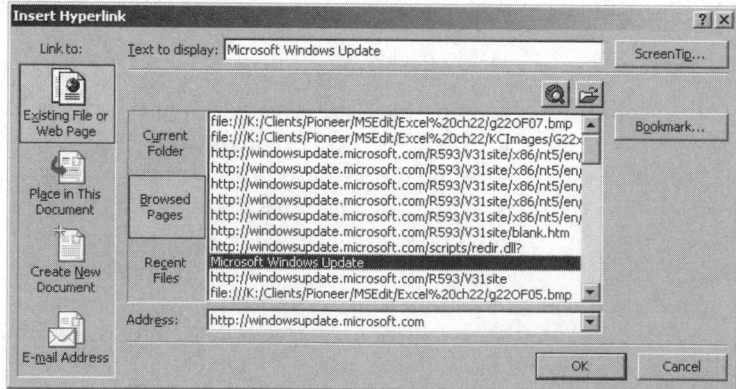

Figure 21-10. The Insert Hyperlink dialog box gives you several options when creating hyperlinks.

3 Answer the first question by clicking one of the four buttons on the left side of the dialog box. The Existing File Or Web Page button creates a link in your worksheet to a file on your hard disk or a home page on the Web. On a day-to-day basis, this option will probably cover most of your hyperlink needs because it's the fastest way to create links to useful files and Internet resources within your worksheet.

You have three additional options.

- The second button, Place In This Document, creates a link to a different location in the current workbook. Use this option if you want to jump quickly from one location in a spreadsheet to another. (It works like the Go To command but is more convenient.)

- The third button, Create New Document, allows you to open a new Office document from within your worksheet, which can be another Excel spreadsheet, a Word document, a PowerPoint presentation, and so on. This option gives users a quick way to write notes or jot down estimates while using a worksheet.

- Finally, E-Mail Address (the fourth button on the left side) allows you to create a link in your worksheet that automatically sends an e-mail message to another user, complete with a custom subject header and a handy screen tip.

4 Fill out the dialog box options corresponding to the type of hyperlink you're creating.

If you're identifying a particular document name or Web page that should be loaded when the user clicks the hyperlink, locate it on your system by using one of the browse buttons (Browse The Web or Browse For File), and specify a descriptive label in the cell by typing it in the Text To Display text box. (This text box is available only if the cell is blank or contains a text label.) You can also use three buttons within the dialog box corresponding to frequently used documents: Current Folder, Browsed Pages, and Recent Files.

---

tip   **Use a Web Page as a Hyperlink**

When you browse for a Web page link, Office opens your Internet browser and allows you to locate the Web page you want to use. After you locate the page you want to use, return to the Insert Hyperlink dialog box (with your Internet browser still running), select any additional options you want, and click OK. The trick here is to jump back to the Insert Hyperlink dialog box while your browser is still running, or you won't get the right Web page.

---

5 When you're finished identifying the content of your hyperlink, click OK to add the hyperlink to your worksheet. When the Insert Hyperlink dialog box closes, the text in the highlighted cell appears in underlined type and the

Web toolbar opens. If you specified a descriptive label, it also appears when
you hold the mouse pointer over the hyperlink.

E17	▼		*fx*			
	A	B	C	D	E	F	G
1							
2							
3							
4							
5			MSN Home Page				
6							
7			http://www.msn.com/ - Click once to follow. Click and hold to select this cell.				
8							
9							

Activating a Hyperlink

To activate a hyperlink in a worksheet, click the underlined cell containing the hyperlink, and Excel will start any necessary applications and load the linked document.
If the hyperlink requires an Internet or other network connection, you might be
prompted for a member ID (also called a *user name*) and password when your
browser activates the link.

The Web Toolbar

After you activate a hyperlink in Excel, a special Web toolbar appears on the screen
that lets you switch back and forth between open hyperlinks, establish additional
Internet connections, or run special network-related commands. If the toolbar doesn't
appear, click View, Toolbars and choose Web on the submenu. You don't have to use
the Web toolbar when using hyperlinks to switch to other Excel workbooks (you can
also use the Excel Window menu), but in many cases you will benefit from doing so.
To close the Web toolbar, click the Close button on the toolbar's title bar.

The Web toolbar is shown here as a freestanding toolbar, which you can duplicate by
dragging the toolbar from its default locked position beneath the Formatting toolbar.

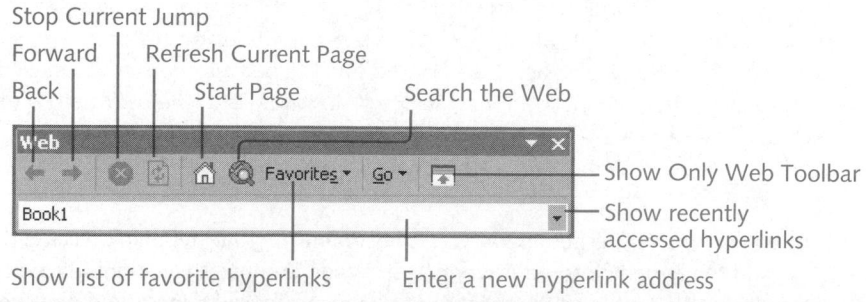

Chapter 21

tip If you're not sure whether an underlined word represents a hyperlink, place the mouse pointer directly over the cell and see if the mouse pointer changes shape. The mouse pointer over a cell containing a hyperlink resembles a hand with a pointing finger and often displays a descriptive label.

After a hyperlink has been activated, you can jump back and forth between the home document and any hyperlinks in the same workbook by clicking the Back and Forward buttons, respectively, on the Web toolbar. If the hyperlink launched a separate Microsoft Windows application to load the document—say, the hyperlink started Microsoft Word or Internet Explorer—you can also use the Windows taskbar to move back and forth quickly between the applications. When you're finished viewing a hyperlinked Excel workbook, close it by choosing Close from the Excel File menu. When you're finished using documents associated with other applications, simply close those applications. (If you're using the Internet, this will end your connection.)

Editing and Removing Hyperlinks

To edit or remove a hyperlink from a worksheet cell, follow these steps:

note Don't left-click the cell containing the hyperlink or you'll activate it.

1 Right-click the cell containing the hyperlink to display a shortcut menu of commands used to manipulate spreadsheet cells.

2 On the shortcut menu, choose Edit Hyperlink if you want to customize or alter the hyperlink in the cell you clicked. To remove the hyperlink, click Remove Hyperlink.

Saving the Workbook

After you enter information into a new workbook, it's a good idea to save the data to disk—before you make some phone calls and get distracted or go to lunch! This way you can protect the information and use it again later. Each workbook is stored in its own file on disk and is assigned a filename that's unique to the folder in which it's stored. To assign a new filename to a workbook, use the Save As command on the File menu. To save edits you've made to an existing workbook file, use the Save command on the File menu.

For more information about saving workbooks, see "Saving Office Documents," on page 74. For information about including worksheets in document libraries using SharePoint Team Services, see "Sharing Documents on SharePoint," on page 187.

Using the SAVE AS Command

Figure 21-11 shows you the steps to follow to save your workbook to disk. Choose Save As from the File menu. The Save As dialog box appears, prompting you for a filename, as shown in Figure 21-11.

InsideOut

Save Your Favorite Files in a Special Folder

We recommend that you place the files you use most often in the My Documents folder. This folder is located on your hard drive and is set aside for particularly useful files. (If you like, you can also create subfolders in this folder.) You'll see a button for this folder on the left side of the Save As and Open dialog boxes when you use Office applications.

---

1 Click a folder icon to choose one of the standard folder options...

Or, select a folder location in the Save In list...

Or, use any of these availability tools to specify a location.

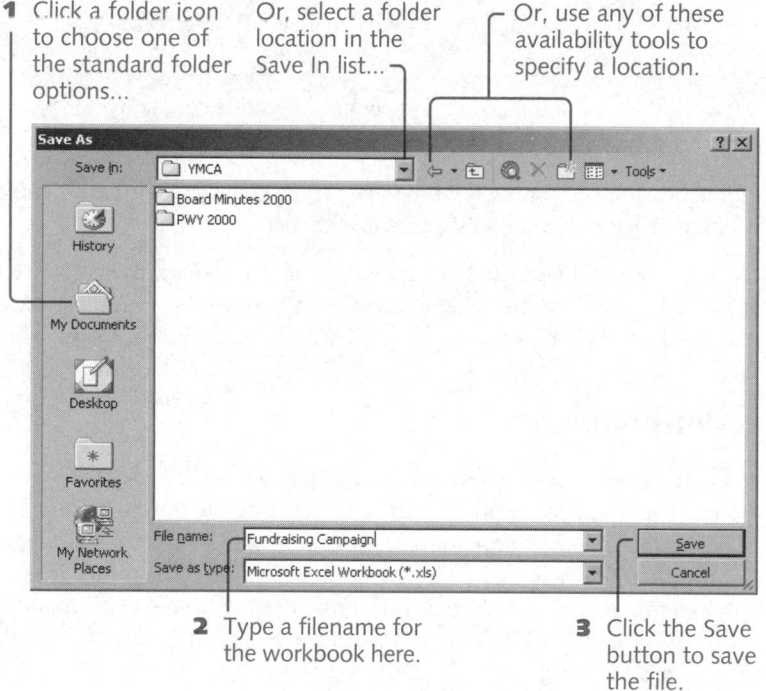

2 Type a filename for the workbook here.

3 Click the Save button to save the file.

Figure 21-11. The Save As command lets you save your workbook to disk using a new filename.

Using the Save Command

To save revisions you've made to a workbook that already has a filename, choose File, Save. That's all there is to it—choosing Save updates your file on disk automatically. If you decide you want to create a new version of the file while preserving the original, choose Save As and specify a new filename.

---

tip **Do Quick Saves**

Save

You can also save your file by clicking the Save button on the Standard toolbar or by pressing Ctrl+S on your keyboard.

Quitting Excel (A Few Points to Remember)

All right, you've finished building an awesome worksheet and you're ready to get on to other tasks. Before you do, however, you should perform the following steps:

1 Save your workbook to disk with a clear, easy-to-remember filename. You can do this at any time by choosing File, Save As (for new files) or by choosing File, Save (for existing files).

---

tip Please don't wait until you've finished creating your document to save it to disk. We recommend saving your work to disk every 10 minutes or so to avoid losing data in a power outage or system crash.

---

2 Give the spelling of labels and text in your worksheet a once-over by choosing the Spelling command from the Tools menu. Since the spelling checker is smart and only checks the words in your worksheet, this step shouldn't slow you down.

3 (Optional) Print your worksheet by choosing File, Print. If you want to adjust the margins, headers, or footers in your worksheet before you print it, choose File, Page Setup and File, Print Preview.

For more information on issues related to managing files and printing, see Chapter 3, "Getting Expert Help on Office XP."

---

4 When you're finished working, choose File, Exit to quit Excel rather than simply turning off your computer. If you want to retain the changes in your worksheet, click Yes when Excel prompts you.

5 (Optional) Make a backup copy of your valuable workbook files on a floppy disk once in a while by using Windows Explorer. This is the best way to keep your data safe in the sometimes uncertain world of electromagnetic media.

Advanced Worksheet Editing

If you make a mistake while building a worksheet, you're not expected to live with it. Microsoft Excel 2002 features a variety of traditional and innovative electronic editing techniques. They enable you to fix your typos, of course, and also to reorganize your data, find and replace data, check for common input errors, fill cells with data, and create room for more information. In this chapter you'll learn the essential editing techniques you'll need when managing worksheet data in Excel. You'll also learn how to use innovative features such as AutoFill and the new Office Clipboard to replicate and rearrange vital information.

Essential Editing Techniques

When you need to remember how data is moved from cell to cell in Excel, refer to this part of the book. In this section you'll learn the following editing techniques:

- How to select cells and ranges
- How to clear cells and delete cells
- How to copy data from one cell to another
- How to use the new Office Clipboard
- How to move cells by dragging
- How to add new rows and columns to the worksheet
- How to undo and repeat commands

For information about tracking and approving edits in a multiuser environment, see "Accepting or Rejecting Revisions," page 701.

Selecting Cells and Ranges

Several Excel commands work with individual cells or groups of cells called *ranges*. Selecting a cell means making it the active cell; as a result, its name appears in the Name box to the left of the formula bar. To select an individual cell or a range of cells, you can use either the mouse or the keyboard.

> **tip** To make cell ranges easier to work with, you can assign a name to a cell range and then use the name in place of the cell reference. See "Using Names in Functions," on page 749.

When you select a range of cells, Excel indicates the range with a bold border (the same border that identifies a single active cell), and the background color within the range changes from the default white to a shade of blue. (If you've used versions of Excel prior to Excel 2000, you'll notice that this cool blue has replaced black as the default highlight color for a selected range.)

A range of cells in Excel is always a contiguous rectangular block. In expressions—such as formulas—Excel uses a simple notation for a range of cells: the first cell (at the upper left corner of the block), followed by a colon, and then the last cell (at the lower right corner of the block). For example, A1:E1 represents a single row of five cells along the top edge of the worksheet, and E5:F8 represents two adjacent columns of four cells in the worksheet. You'll use cell ranges in many of the formulas and functions you create in Excel worksheets. In this illustration the user has selected a rectangular block of 45 cells (nine rows by five columns) named A1:E9.

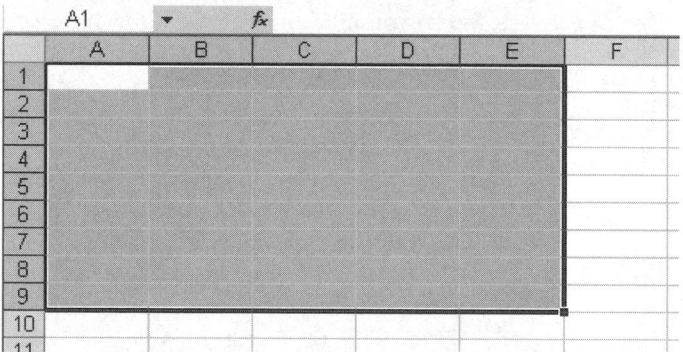

Selecting a Range Using the Mouse

To select a range of cells using the mouse, complete the following steps:

1 Position the cell pointer over the first cell you want to select, which is normally the top left cell in the range.

2 Hold down the mouse button, and then drag the mouse over the remaining cells in the selection. Release the mouse button.

3 If you want to select multiple cell ranges simultaneously, drag the mouse over the first range and release the mouse button to highlight the first range; then hold down the Ctrl key, use your mouse to make another selection, and release the Ctrl key. You can continue to add ranges to a selection using the Ctrl key each time. Figure 22-1 shows a multiple-range selection.

note In Figure 22-1 two ranges of cells are selected (A5:A9 and C5:C9). Only one of the cells, however, is the active cell—C5—denoted by the Name box and the bar around the cell. Most commands will affect all the selected cells, including the active cell, but there are exceptions. Entering new information, for example, affects only the active cell and won't change anything in the other selected, or highlighted, cells.

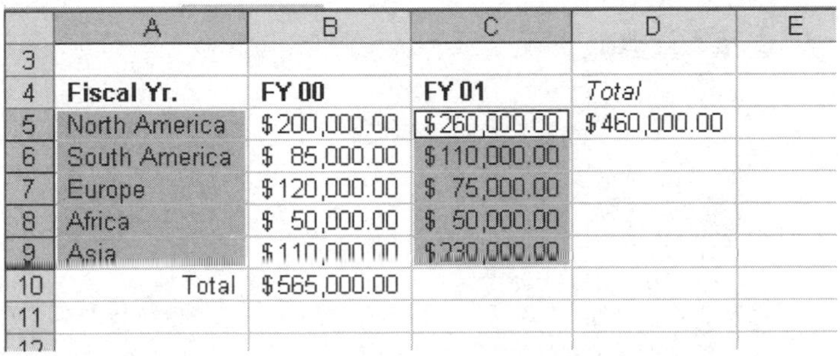

	A	B	C	D	E
3					
4	**Fiscal Yr.**	**FY 00**	**FY 01**	*Total*	
5	North America	$ 200,000.00	$ 260,000.00	$ 460,000.00	
6	South America	$ 85,000.00	$ 110,000.00		
7	Europe	$ 120,000.00	$ 75,000.00		
8	Africa	$ 50,000.00	$ 50,000.00		
9	Asia	$ 110,000.00	$ 230,000.00		
10	Total	$ 565,000.00			
11					
12					

Figure 22-1. To select noncontiguous ranges using the mouse, hold down the Ctrl key.

Selecting a Range Using the Keyboard

To select a range of cells using the keyboard, complete the following steps:

1 Use the arrow keys to move to the first cell you want to select.

2 Hold down the Shift key, and then press the appropriate arrow key to select the remaining cells in the range. Release the Shift key.

3 To select additional, noncontiguous cell ranges, press Shift+F8. The Add indicator appears on the status bar, indicating that you can add a range to the selection. Repeat steps 1 and 2 to add another range. You can continue to add ranges to a selection using Shift+F8 each time.

Selecting Rows and Columns Using the Mouse

If you want to select quickly part or all of your worksheet, you can click one of several hot spots on your screen.

To select an entire column with a single mouse click, click the column letter at the top of the column. To select an entire row, click the row number on the left edge of the row. You can also select multiple columns or rows by selecting a row or column head and dragging across the heads of the rows or columns you want to select. Be careful when you select multiple rows or columns: If the row numbers or column letters aren't consecutive, the sheet probably has some hidden rows or columns. If you clear or delete the visible range, you'll do likewise to the hidden data.

If you need to select the entire worksheet, you can click the Select All box in the upper left corner of the worksheet. Here is a worksheet that has two columns selected.

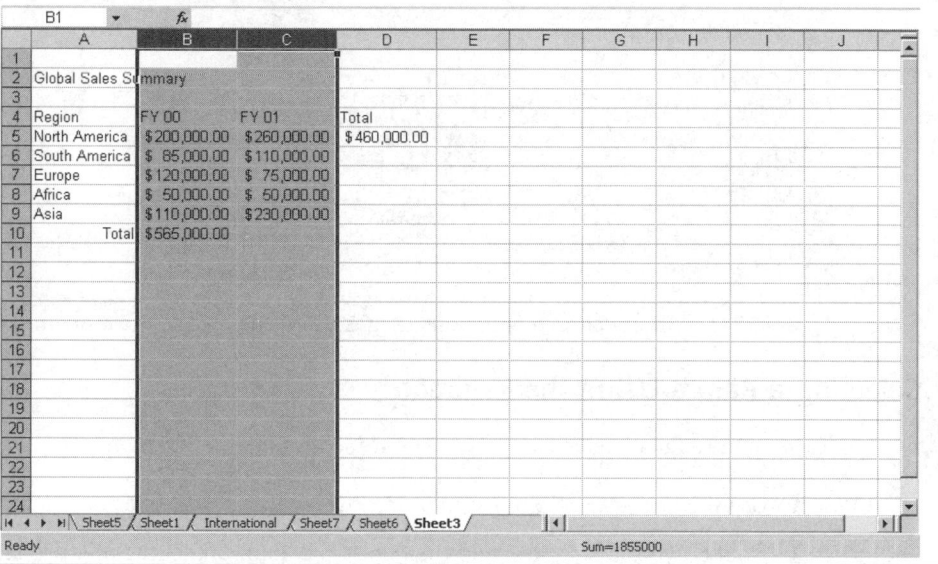

Clearing Cells and Deleting Cells

Now that you know how to select ranges of cells, you can put your new skill to work clearing and deleting cells. If you want to clear the contents from a group of cells, select the cells, right-click within the selection, and choose Clear Contents from the shortcut menu. Excel removes the content but keeps the cell formatting so that you can enter new values in the same format. (For example, if you clear cells formatted for dollar values, the next time you place a number in one of these cells it will be formatted for dollars.) To see the complete range of clear options, choose Clear from the Edit menu, and Excel will display a submenu that contains commands for clearing the formatting, the contents, the comments, or all three items together.

Chapter 22

InsideOut

You can also clear the contents of the active cell (or a selection) by pressing the Delete key. It's not the most intuitive way to distinguish between clearing and deleting—to use the Delete key to clear contents—but it's quick if you can keep it straight.

If you'd rather delete a single cell from the worksheet, moving the rows below it up or shifting columns over to the left, display the Edit menu and choose the Delete command rather than the Clear command. In many applications the terms *delete* and *clear* have the same meaning, but in Excel there's a distinct difference between the two commands. Clearing a cell is like using an eraser to remove the contents or the format from a cell, but deleting a cell is like cutting it out with a tiny pocketknife and then moving the remaining cells up or over to fill the gap.

To use the Delete command to delete cell ranges, entire rows, or entire columns from a worksheet, complete the following steps:

1 Place the cell pointer in the cell, row, or column you want to delete from the worksheet. If you want to delete a range of cells, select the range.

2 Choose Edit, Delete. The dialog box shown in Figure 22-2 appears.

3 Click the option button that corresponds to the way you want remaining cells moved after the deletion.

In Figure 22-2, for example, where B3 is the selected cell, to delete cell B3 and move cells over to fill the gap, click Shift Cells Left. To delete cell B3 and move cells up to fill the gap, click Shift Cells Up. You can also click Entire Row or Entire Column to remove all the selected rows or columns. In Figure 22-2 you could, for example, remove row 3 or column B.

4 Click OK to delete the selected cells and move other cells to fill the gap.

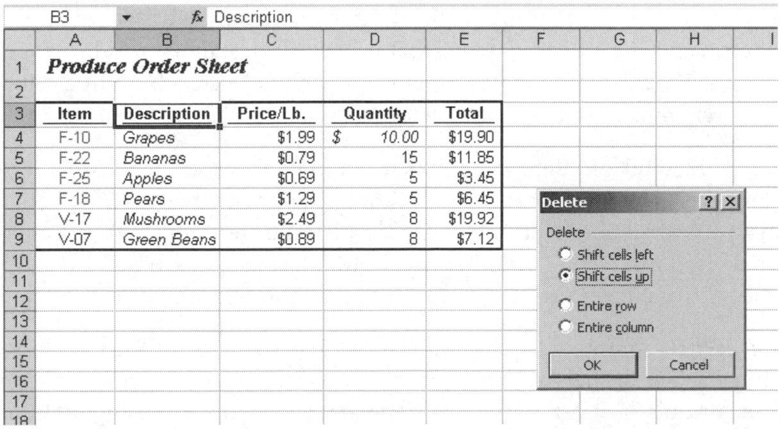

	B3	▼	*fx* Description					
	A	B	C	D	E	F	G	H	I
1	*Produce Order Sheet*							
2								
3	Item	Description	Price/Lb.	Quantity	Total			
4	F-10	Grapes	$1.99	$ 10.00	$19.90			
5	F-22	Bananas	$0.79	15	$11.85			
6	F-25	Apples	$0.69	5	$3.45			
7	F-18	Pears	$1.29	5	$6.45			
8	V-17	Mushrooms	$2.49	8	$19.92			
9	V-07	Green Beans	$0.89	8	$7.12			

Delete ? X

Delete
○ Shift cells left
● Shift cells up
○ Entire row
○ Entire column

OK   Cancel

Figure 22-2. The Delete command lets you remove a cell, row, or column from the worksheet and fill the gap with adjacent cells.

Chapter 22

Finding and Replacing Data

The Find command on the Edit menu is handy both for navigating and editing worksheets that are extensive or densely packed with data. Find lets you specify a string of characters and move directly to each instance of that string. The string can be any series of characters: a word or part of a word, a numeric value, a cell name or range, or the functions and operators in a formula.

After you find a string, Excel can automate the process of revising the string. Allied to the Find command is a Replace command, the second tab shown in Figure 22-3. With Replace you can substitute a replacement string for any or all instances of the target string.

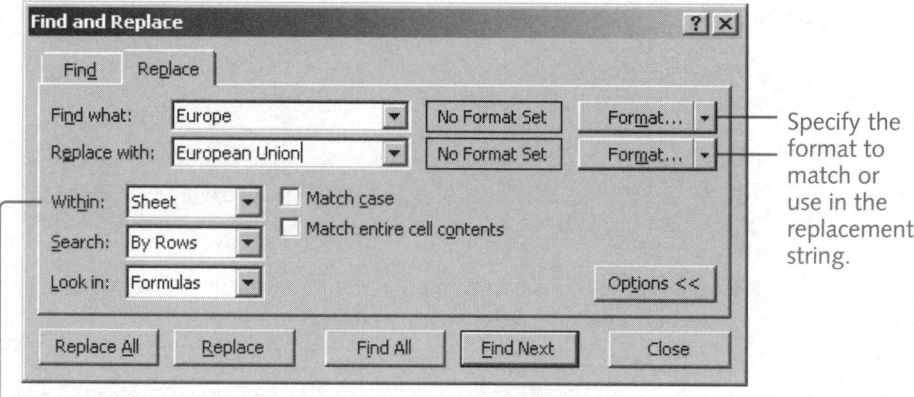

Specify the format to match or use in the replacement string.

Search the current worksheet or the entire workbook.

Figure 22-3. The Replace command offers flexible options for targeting the replacement.

The options in the Replace tab help you streamline your search. You can specify that you want to match only strings with the same (upper and lower) case characters as those in the search string. And you can narrow the search with the Match Entire Cell Contents check box so that the search string matches only cells for which the search string represents the entire contents; that is, the cell contains no additional characters. In that case, *Yankees* would match a cell that contains *Yankees* but not a cell that contains *New York Yankees*.

In Excel 2002, Find and Replace are enhanced to let you specify a format to match for the search string and a format to use for the replacement string. When you click these options, you can define the formats either by hand or by choosing a cell that already has the desired formatting. Another new option lets you search beyond the current worksheet across the entire workbook. Both new features are labeled in Figure 22-3.

A powerful new command is Find All, which generates a list of the matching instances, including their worksheet and cell location and the type of matching cell contents, value, or formula. You can select any of the matches in the list to highlight the matching cell and to make replacements as appropriate.

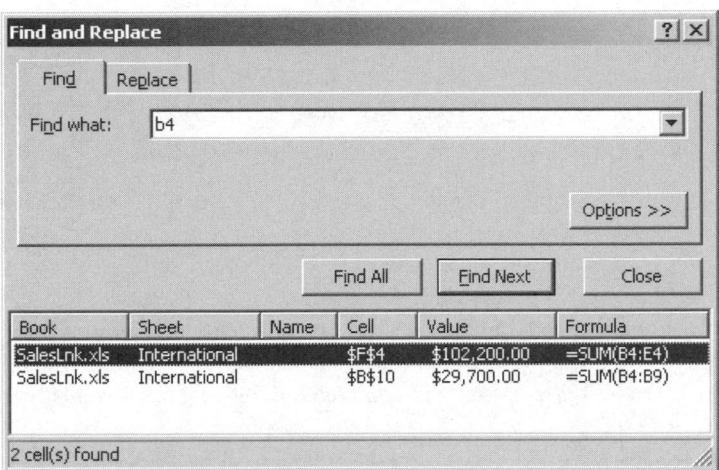

Undoing Commands

If you make a mistake when executing an Excel command, you can undo your mistake by immediately choosing Edit, Undo. For example, if you deleted a range of cells in error, choosing Undo will return the cells to the worksheet as if you had never deleted them.

Undo

You can also click the Undo button on the Standard toolbar, or press Ctrl+Z, to undo a command.

The Undo button on the Standard toolbar also has multiple levels of undo (like Microsoft Word). This extremely useful feature lets you "go back in time" to fix editing mistakes you made 3, 4, or 10 commands back. Now and then you'll probably think better of a modification you made that took several steps to accomplish. By clicking the small arrow attached to the Undo button, you can scroll through a list of the edits you've made and determine how many actions you want to undo, as shown in Figure 22-4. Excel will then undo each command, from your most recent action back to and including the one you just picked.

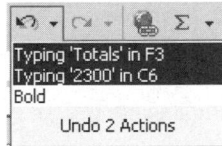

Figure 22-4. Using the Undo button, you can undo one or more of your previous editing mistakes.

Undo has a few limitations. For example, you can't undo the actions of adding a new worksheet to your workbook or deleting an existing worksheet. You also can't undo the actions of saving revisions to a file or customizing the Excel interface. If Undo isn't available for a particular command or action, the Undo command on the Edit menu is dimmed and reads "Can't Undo."

Chapter 22

Troubleshooting

Undo Unavailable

The Undo command isn't available for the action you want to undo.

Excel is smart about tracking your actions during a given work session. It doesn't create an Undo command when you use the scroll bars, press keyboard navigation keys, run online Help, or look for cell data using the Go To or Find commands. Remember, however, that your ability to undo ends when you save or close your workbook. Saving frequently is encouraged, of course, but if you're editing a workbook in which you have invested a great deal of time and effort, consider saving changes to a new location or keep a backup for recovery until you are confident that you want to retain the new version.

Redoing Commands

What happens if you decide to, well, undo an Undo command? For example, what do you do if you delete a range of cells, restore them with Undo, and then, on reflection, decide to remove them after all? One option is to select the cells again and choose Delete. But Excel makes it even easier to be fickle. Excel adds the commands you've reversed to the Redo button on the Standard toolbar, letting you redo commands one by one or several commands at once. (This makes the Redo button the functional opposite of the Undo button, allowing you to restore and remove edits you've made.)

Redo

note The Redo and Repeat commands are different, although easy to confuse. Redo reverses one or more actions that you un-did, whereas Repeat enables you to re-execute (with a different selection) the command that you last used.

Repeating Commands

Below the Undo command on the Edit menu is the Repeat command, which allows you to repeat the command you just executed—but at a different place in the worksheet. Here's how it works: Let's say you just used the Cells command on the Format menu to place a border around cell B3. Excel then displays a Repeat Format Cells command on the Edit menu, enabling you to add the same border to a new cell by simply highlighting the new cell and clicking Repeat on the Edit menu. An even faster way is to press F4 or the shortcut key combination Ctrl+Y.

tip **Think About Repetitive Actions**

The Repeat command is a speed feature designed to help you work faster in Excel. But most people forget to use it because they don't anticipate repetitive actions. Think about how you work, and you might discover several clever uses for the Repeat command. (We use Repeat most often for formatting labels and changing number formats.)

Using Cut and Paste to Move Data

At times you'll want to move cell entries from one place to another on your worksheet. To do this, you can use the Cut and the Paste commands on the Edit menu. When you cut a cell or range of cells using the Cut command, Excel places a dotted-line marquee around the selection to indicate which cells will be moved, and then it moves the cell contents (including comments and formatting) to a temporary storage location known as the Clipboard. Excel lets you move a rectangular range of cells only—no noncontiguous blocks.

When you select a new location for the data and choose Paste, the cells and their formatting are pasted from the Clipboard into their new location and the original cells are replaced. (If you're pasting a range of cells, they're inserted in a block.) To cancel the move after the marquee appears, press the Esc key.

> **note** In contrast to other Microsoft Windows applications, Excel lets you paste only once after you cut. Use the Copy command to paste multiple times. Using Copy you can also paste the contents of a single cell to all the cells in a selection.

Figure 22-5 shows a group of cells after the Cut command was chosen (notice the marquee), while Figure 22-6 shows the same worksheet after the Paste command was chosen. Note that when you use the Paste command, you can also copy over cells containing data that you don't want to delete, so be cautious when moving information. As alternatives to using the Edit menu's Cut and Paste commands, you can use the Cut and Paste buttons on the Standard toolbar or the standard Windows key combinations Ctrl+X and Ctrl+V.

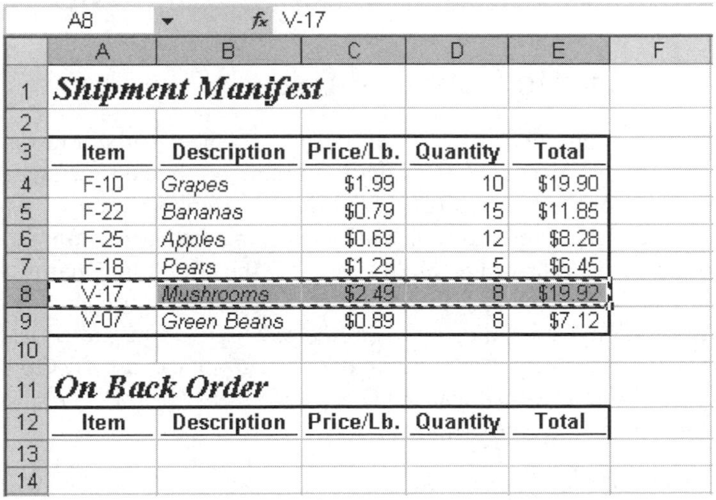

	A	B	C	D	E	F
	Shipment Manifest					
3	Item	Description	Price/Lb.	Quantity	Total	
4	F-10	Grapes	$1.99	10	$19.90	
5	F-22	Bananas	$0.79	15	$11.85	
6	F-25	Apples	$0.69	12	$8.28	
7	F-18	Pears	$1.29	5	$6.45	
8	V-17	Mushrooms	$2.49	8	$19.92	
9	V-07	Green Beans	$0.89	8	$7.12	
10						
11	*On Back Order*					
12	Item	Description	Price/Lb.	Quantity	Total	
13						
14						

A8 ▼ *fx* V-17

Figure 22-5. The Cut command marks the selected cells with a marquee.

Chapter 22

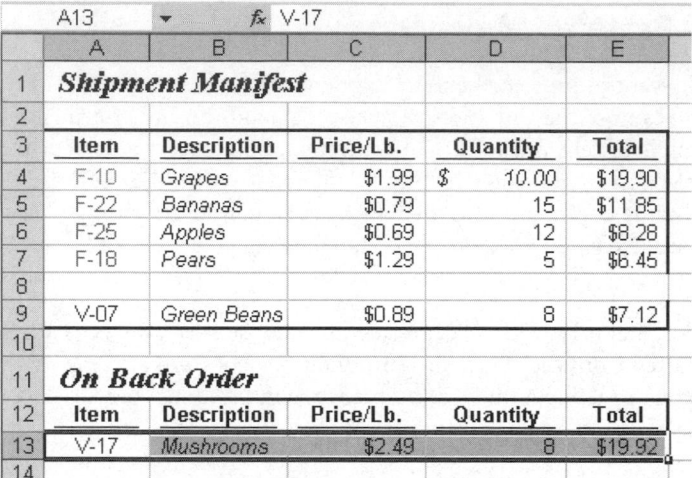

	A	B	C	D	E
1	*Shipment Manifest*				
2					
3	**Item**	**Description**	**Price/Lb.**	**Quantity**	**Total**
4	F-10	Grapes	$1.99	$ 10.00	$19.90
5	F-22	Bananas	$0.79	15	$11.85
6	F-25	Apples	$0.69	12	$8.28
7	F-18	Pears	$1.29	5	$6.45
8					
9	V-07	Green Beans	$0.89	8	$7.12
10					
11	*On Back Order*				
12	**Item**	**Description**	**Price/Lb.**	**Quantity**	**Total**
13	V-17	Mushrooms	$2.49	8	$19.92
14					

(Cell reference A13, formula bar: V-17)

Figure 22-6.   The Paste command moves data from the Clipboard to the active cell.

To move a range of cells using the Cut and Paste commands, complete the following steps:

1 Select the group of cells you want to move.

Cut

2 Choose Edit, Cut. (You can also click the Cut button on the toolbar or press the Ctrl+X key combination.)

3 Click the cell to which you want to move the data. (If you're moving a group of cells, highlight the cell in the upper left corner of the area you're copying to.)

Paste

4 Choose Edit, Paste. (Or click the Paste button on the toolbar or press the Ctrl+V key combination.)

Using Copy and Paste to Duplicate Data

If you just want to duplicate a range of cells in the worksheet, and not move them from their current location, you can use the Copy command on the Edit menu. This command places a copy of the cells you've selected into the Clipboard, and you can transfer these cells any number of times to your worksheet using the Paste command. The Copy command indicates the cells you're duplicating with the dotted-line marquee so that you can see what you're copying as you do it. As when you use the Cut command, when you use the Copy command you're limited to copying contiguous (touching) blocks of cells. If you cut or copy a series of data items, you can use the Office Clipboard (discussed in "Using the Enhanced Office Clipboard," below) to paste an item other than the one most recently copied.

To speed up your copy operations, you can use the Copy button on the Standard toolbar or press the Ctrl+C key combination.

To copy a range of cells using the Copy and Paste commands, complete the following steps:

1 Select the group of cells you want to copy.

Copy

2 Choose Edit, Copy. (You can also click the Copy button on the toolbar or press Ctrl+C.)

3 Click the cell into which you want to copy the data. (If you're duplicating a group of cells, highlight the cell in the upper left corner of the area you're copying to.)

4 Choose Edit, Paste. (Or click the Paste button on the toolbar or press Ctrl+V.)

Using the Enhanced Office Clipboard

newfeature!

Once you've cut or copied two pieces of data to the Clipboard, Excel displays the Office Clipboard in the task pane, a new interface feature in Microsoft Office XP. If the Clipboard doesn't appear automatically, choose Office Clipboard from the Edit menu.

The Office Clipboard is a special editing tool that retains the last 24 items moved to the Clipboard by *any* Windows application. Figure 22-7 shows the Clipboard in action. At the moment depicted in the figure, the Clipboard contains four data items from the current work session (two Excel worksheet ranges, one Word document selection, and a bitmap image).

Office XP applications use the task pane not only to display the Office Clipboard but also to execute a search and to launch a new document. See "Using the Task Pane, in Office Applications," on page 51, for an overview of the task pane and its various uses.

InsideOut

If you've used earlier versions of Excel, you might recognize this aggravating situation: You copy a range of cells, causing the marquee to appear; then, before you paste the date, you become briefly sidetracked (to edit a cell or the like) only to find that the marquee has disappeared and the Paste command has become unavailable. In Excel 2002 nothing has changed, *but* with the Office Clipboard you're no longer reduced to repeating the select-and-copy procedure. The copied data is there on the Clipboard, so you can highlight the destination and paste the data from the Clipboard even though the Paste command on the Edit menu is dimmed.

Chapter 22

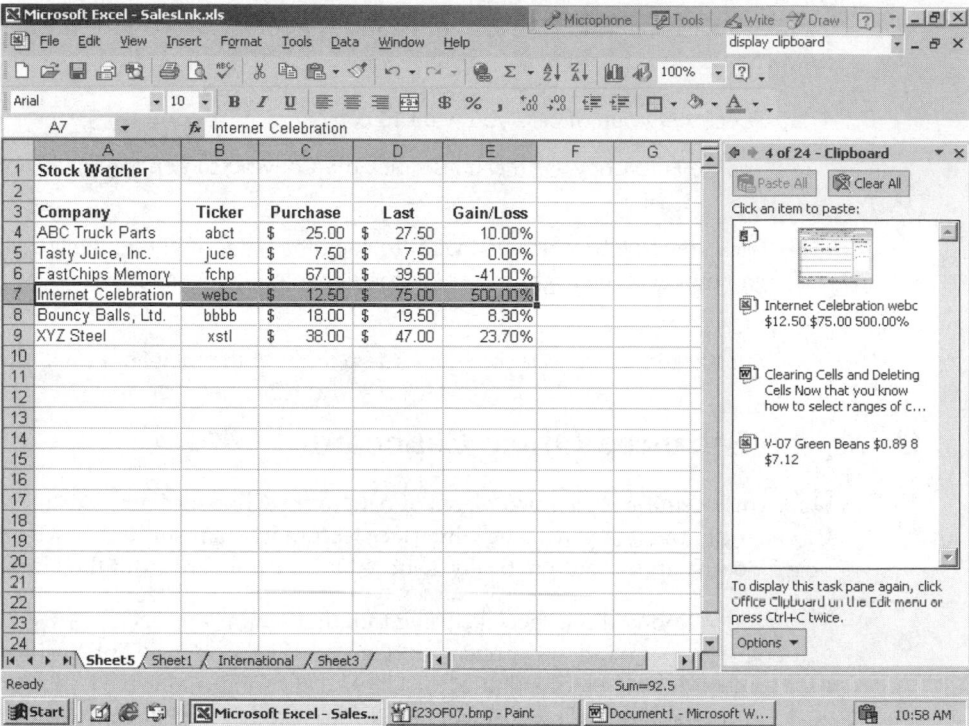

Figure 22-7. The Clipboard stores up to 24 data items from cut or copy operations for future use.

The Office Clipboard is a last-in, first-out *stack* that places the data from the most recent cut or copy operation at the top of the list in the Office Clipboard. After the Clipboard list reaches 24 items, the toolbar discards the oldest items in the Clipboard as you cut or copy new items. To discard an item yourself, move the mouse pointer to the item. When you point to the item, a solid border appears with a down arrow. Click the arrow to display a menu of commands and choose Delete. To empty the Office Clipboard and start fresh, click the Clear All button.

You can paste any one of the Office Clipboard items into your worksheet. Just select the cell in which you want to place the data and click the item in the Clipboard corresponding to the data you want to paste. To paste all the items in the Office Clipboard, click the Paste All button. Excel pastes the list of Clipboard contents into a series of cells. Note that undoing the Paste All action entails undoing each paste operation separately.

When you're finished using the Office Clipboard, click the Close button (the x) in the upper right corner of the task pane.

Moving Cells by Dragging

The fastest way to move a group of worksheet cells is by dragging. By using the drag-and-drop technique, you can edit a worksheet in an efficient and visibly uncomplicated way—by dragging a group of cells from one location to another. To enable drag-and-drop editing, you need to select cells (usually with the mouse), release the mouse button, and then move the cell pointer toward an outside edge of the selected cells until the cell pointer changes to a white arrow pointer (pointing to a four-way arrow). When the pointer changes shape, you can hold down the left mouse button and drag the selection to a new location. As you move the cells, Excel displays both an outline of the range and the current range address, so that you can align the cells properly in your worksheet. See Figure 22-8 for an illustration of the drag-and-drop procedure.

1 Select the range you want to move.

2 Point to a border of the box around the selected cells. The cell pointer changes to an arrow.

3 Drag the selected range to its new location. An outline of the selected range follows the cell pointer. Release the mouse button to complete the move.

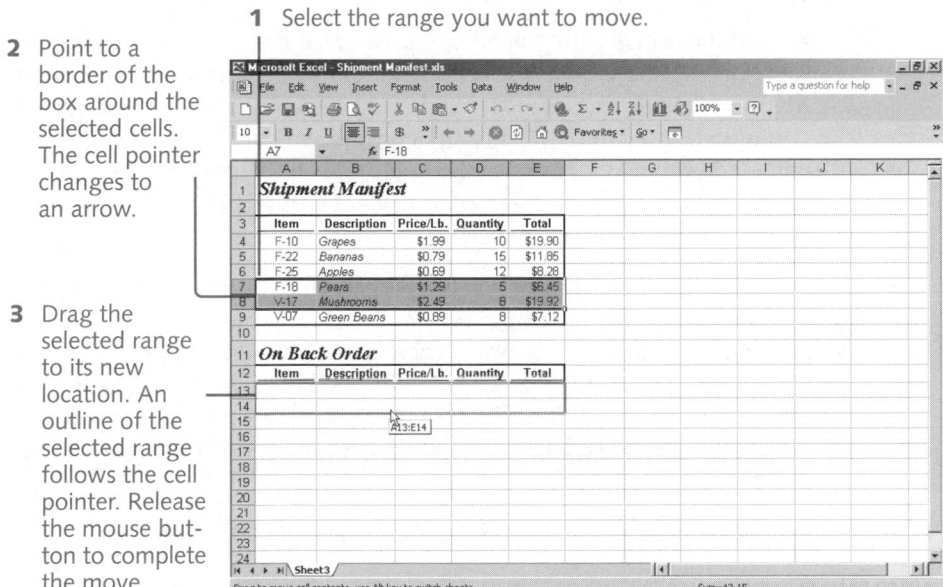

Figure 22-8. The quickest way to move cells in the worksheet is by using the drag-and-drop mouse technique.

To copy (rather than move) cells by dragging, hold down the Ctrl key while you drag the selected cells. When you drag with the Crtl key down, a plus (+) sign appears beside the arrow pointer to let you know that you're copying data.

note If you drop cells onto existing data when you are moving them, Excel will warn you that you're about to replace the contents of your copy destination. Click OK if you want to replace the old cells, or click Cancel if you want to choose a new place for the data.

Chapter 22

InsideOut

A consistently satisfactory way to copy or move cells is to click and hold the right mouse button on the border of the selected cell or range and then drag the data to the destination. When you release the right button, Excel presents a list of actions, including Move Here and Copy Here and Cancel. Other options let you elect how to deal with any overlapping data in the destination cells. This technique often produces an extra step, but it helps you check yourself to be sure that you are performing the action you intend.

Adding Rows and Columns to the Worksheet

Now and then you'll want to add new rows or columns to your worksheet to create space. You might decide to add cells because your existing data is too crowded, or perhaps you're creating a report that has changed in scope and requires a new layout to communicate effectively. You add new rows and columns to your worksheet by using the Rows and Columns commands on the Insert menu. When you add rows or columns to your worksheet, the existing data shifts down to accommodate new rows or shifts to the right to allow for new columns.

If you're rearranging rows or columns of cells in a worksheet, you can avoid the extra steps involved in creating empty rows or columns to paste data into. Select the row(s) or column(s) you want to relocate, choose the Cut command from the Edit menu or press Ctrl+X. The dotted marquee appears and highlights the range to be deleted. Then select the row below or the column to the right of the intended destination and choose Insert, Cut Cells. Excel deletes the cells marked for removal and inserts the row(s) or column(s) into the intended location.

To add a blank row to your worksheet, complete the following steps:

1 Select the row *below* the place you want to enter a new row. (Select the row by clicking the row number.)

2 Choose Insert, Rows.

To add a column to your worksheet, complete the following steps:

1 Select the column to the *right* of the place where you want to enter a new column. (Select the column by clicking the column letter.)

2 Choose Insert, Columns.

Inserting Individual Cells

Excel lets you add individual cells to your worksheet's rows or columns by choosing Cells from the Insert menu. Before you use the Cells command, you should select the worksheet cell below or to the right of the new cell you want. For example, if you want to add a new cell to column B between cells B3 and B4, highlight cell B4 before choosing the Cells command. When you choose Cells, the Insert dialog box appears.

Use the Insert dialog box to tell Excel to shift the cells to the right or down. If you're adding a cell to a column, click Shift Cells Down. If you're adding a cell to a row, click Shift Cells Right.

You can also insert entire rows and columns by using the Insert Rows and Insert Columns commands, shown below. Excel inserts as many rows or columns as you select. If you select three cells in a column (C7:C9, for example) and choose the Insert Rows command, Excel inserts three rows above your selection.

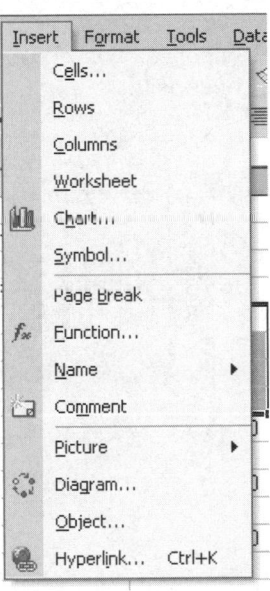

Entering a Series of Labels, Numbers, and Dates

Excel streamlines the task of entering worksheet data by allowing you to fill a range of cells with one repeating value or a sequence of values, called a *series*. This capability saves you time when you're entering groups of labels, numbers, or dates in a report. For example, you can replicate the same price for many products in a report or create

Chapter 22

part numbers that increment predictably. To enter a series of values into a range of cells, you use the Fill command on the Insert menu or a mouse technique called *AutoFill*. The following sections show you how you can enter data automatically using these commands.

> For information about replicating formulas in a worksheet, see "Replicating a Formula," on page 736.

Using AutoFill to Create a Series

The easiest method for entering repeating or incrementing data is to use Excel's AutoFill feature. Begin by locating the *fill handle*, a tiny black square located in the lower right corner of the active cell or a selected range of cells, as shown in Figure 22-9. When you position the cell pointer over the fill handle, the cell pointer changes to a plus sign (+), indicating that the AutoFill feature is enabled. To create a series of labels, numbers, or dates, select two or more cells (to establish a pattern for the series) and then click the fill handle and drag it over the cells you want to fill with information. (Notice that Excel shows the next value in the series in a pop-up box.) When you release the mouse button, you have, like magic, a list of new values!

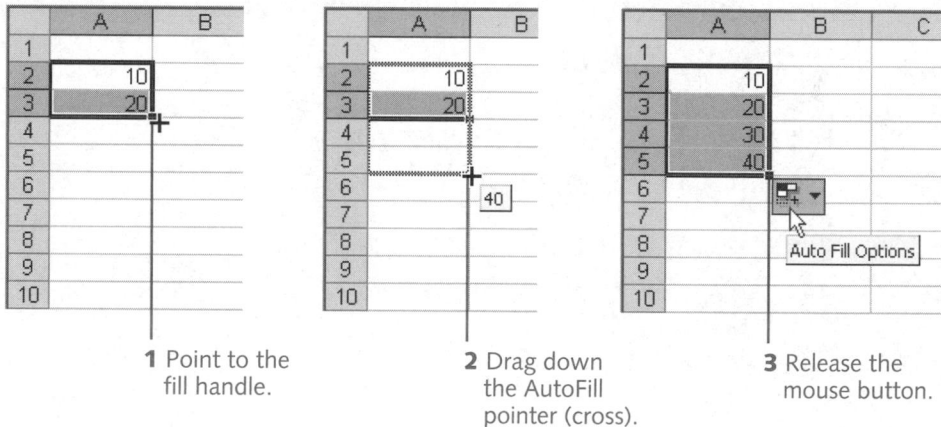

1 Point to the fill handle.

2 Drag down the AutoFill pointer (cross).

3 Release the mouse button.

Figure 22-9. Follow these steps to AutoFill a series of cells.

The AutoFill feature obeys a clear set of rules when it replicates data in cells, as shown in Table 22-1. When you drag the fill handle down or to the right, AutoFill creates values that increase based on the pattern in the range of cells you first select. When you drag the fill handle up or to the left, AutoFill creates values that decrease based on the pattern. If AutoFill doesn't recognize the pattern, it simply duplicates the selected cells.

> **tip** To suppress the AutoFill feature (and just duplicate the selected cells), hold down the Ctrl key while you drag the fill handle. Another technique is to click and hold the right mouse button when you drag, release the button, and then choose Copy Cells from the pop-up menu.

Table 22-1. **AutoFill Insertion Patterns**

Pattern Type	Series	Example
Label (Text)	No pattern, text is duplicated	Units, Units, Units
Number	Values increase based on pattern	10, 20, 30
Text with number	Series created by changing number based on pattern	Unit 1, Unit 2, Unit 3
Day	Series created to match day format	Mon, Tues, Wed
Month	Series created to match month format	Jan, Feb, Mar
Year	Series created to match year format based on pattern	1998, 1999, 2000
Time	Series created to match time interval	1:30 PM, 2:00 PM, 2:30 PM

Using the Fill Commands

The mouse-driven AutoFill feature is designed to handle most of the data copying and replication in a worksheet, but you can also use a collection of Fill commands on the Edit menu to accomplish simple copying tasks. You'll find these commands useful if you want to copy one cell into many adjacent cells, or if you want to fine-tune the way patterns in an AutoFill series are created.

Filling Up, Down, Right, and Left

When you choose Fill from the Edit menu, a submenu appears that contains several replication commands, including Up, Down, Right, and Left. These commands let you copy information from a cell (or series of cells) to a group of selected, adjacent cells. Figure 22-10 shows how to use the Fill Down command to copy the contents of cell A2 to cells A3 through A5. Note that cell comments aren't copied when you use the Fill commands (because comments aren't considered essential to the calculation process).

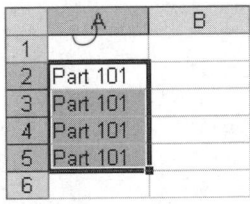

Figure 22-10. Select the range you want to fill and choose Up, Down, Right, or Left from the Fill submenu.

> **note** The Excel key combination for the Copy Down command is Ctrl+D. The key combination for the Copy Right command is Ctrl+R.

Using the Fill Series Dialog Box

If you want to specify a custom series, such as a number that increments in fractional portions or a maximum value for the series, enter the starting number, select your fill range and choose the Series command from the Edit menu's Fill submenu. The dialog box shown in Figure 22-11 appears. This dialog box allows you to specify the value type and date type—characteristics that are usually set automatically when you use the AutoFill feature. A Linear series is incremented by adding the Step Value; a Growth series is incremented by multiplying by the Step Value.

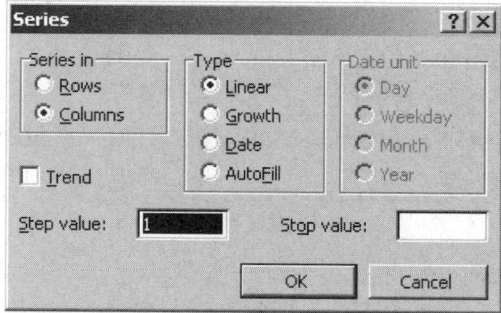

Figure 22-11. The Series dialog box lets you create custom fill sequences.

What makes the Series dialog box handy is the Step Value and Stop Value text boxes, which let you control how the specified series increments and specify its final value. For example, if you want to increment a numeric series by 1.5, type *1.5* in the Step Value text box. Similarly, if you want to set 10 as the highest number in the series, type *10* in the Stop Value text box. Figure 22-12 shows the results you get when you start with the number 1 and create a linear series that uses both the step and stop values mentioned above. Notice that although cells A8, A9, and A10 were selected in the fill range (just as a guess), they were left empty because the stop value in the Series dialog box (10) had been reached.

	A	B
1	1	
2	2.5	
3	4	
4	5.5	
5	7	
6	8.5	
7	10	
8		
9		
10		
11		

Figure 22-12. The Series command lets you increment by an amount you specify and stop when a limit you set has been reached.

Checking for Errors

Checking your data entries for errors is a great way to maintain your professional profile! You'll locate mistakes that would trip up your users and avoid confusion (and embarrassment) down the road. Excel provides two tools that work in a smooth and well-integrated fashion with your worksheet-building efforts: Spell Checking and Error Checking.

Correcting Your Spelling

How often have you noticed a glaring spelling error just as you've begun to pass out copies of your document at a meeting? And you've sworn from that moment on to proofread and spell check without fail every document and e-mail you create. The resolve may crumble under time pressure, but spell checking in Excel is easy enough to do. You simply click the Spelling button to check the current worksheet, or choose Tools, Spelling. Excel checks entries from the active cell to the end of the sheet, row by row. It then prompts you before continuing to check from the top of the sheet.

To focus your efforts further, you can select a range of cells, and the Spelling command will check for errors only in the selection. Better yet, you can stop in the middle of entering data in a cell, click the Spelling button, and Excel will check only the current entry—the contents of the formula bar.

The Spelling window is shown in Figure 22-13. Most of the buttons can be readily understood. Note that AutoCorrect catches and fixes many common typos. Clicking the AutoCorrect button for a particular misspelled word has the following effects: First, it replaces the misspelled word with the word you chose from the list of suggestions or with the word you typed in its place in the Not In Dictionary field. Second, it adds the replacement to its list of AutoCorrect items. And third, it corrects any other instances of this misspelling as it moves through the remainder of the worksheet (as if you had chosen Replace All).

The spelling checker is essentially the same throughout Office applications, although you will find minor differences in behavior and options. Unlike Word, Excel doesn't offer grammar checking, nor does it present the option of flagging misspelled words as you type. Numeric entries are never flagged, of course, and you can exempt any words that combine alphabetic characters and numerals (such as V8), any words or acronyms typed in all caps (such as ASCII), or Internet addresses (which are recognized by their syntax). The Options button on the main Spelling window lets you indicate these preferences.

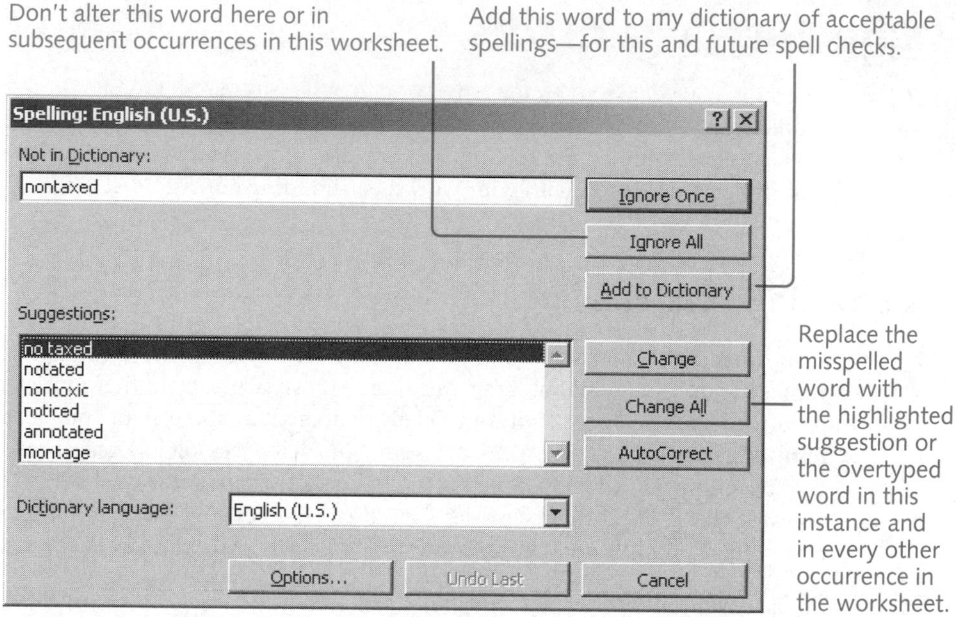

Don't alter this word here or in subsequent occurrences in this worksheet.

Add this word to my dictionary of acceptable spellings—for this and future spell checks.

Replace the misspelled word with the highlighted suggestion or the overtyped word in this instance and in every other occurrence in the worksheet.

Figure 22-13. The spelling checker identifies words that are not listed in the specified language/dictionary and suggests replacements from the dictionary that are similar in spelling.

InsideOut

Error Checking has been implemented with people's variable work styles in mind. Some people will turn off the background function and use it only in a troubleshooting situation. Others will find it comfortable to have the tool functioning in the background, providing security in much the same way that automatic spell checking flags words as you type, enabling you to catch typos while you work in much the same way that automatic spell checking in Word flags misspellings as you type.

newfeature!
Checking for Common Errors

After years of supporting customers using versions of Excel, Microsoft has identified seven of the most common situations that typically frustrate users. To search for these situations, choose Error Checking from the Tools menu. The seven error situations that Excel detects are listed on the Error Checking tab of the Options dialog box displayed with the Tools menu, shown on page 647.

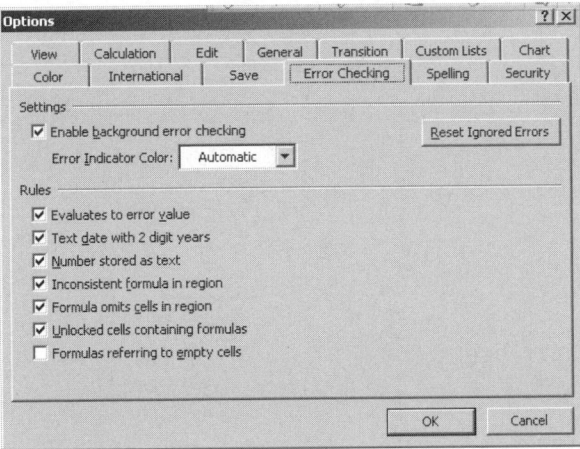

If Excel detects a potential error, it displays a dialog box like the one in Figure 22-14. This box locates and identifies the potential error and suggests responses, including ignoring the situation. After you choose a response, you can navigate to other errors with the Prev and Next buttons.

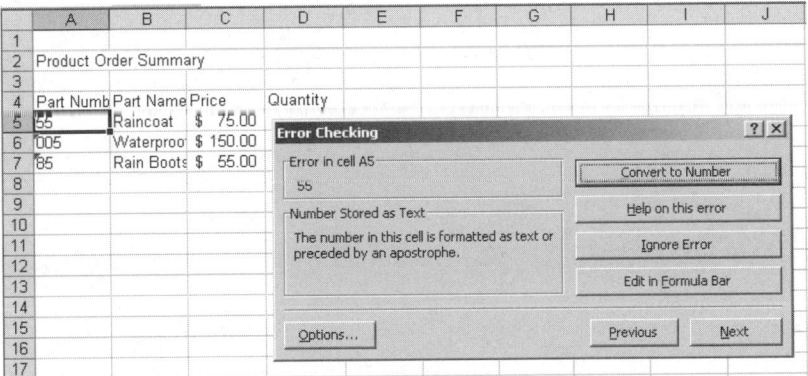

Figure 22-14. Error Checking alerts you to possible oversights that commonly plague Excel users.

Any of these potential error situations could occur intentionally, especially during the creation of a worksheet. But in general the errors deserve attention because they arise so commonly by accident. You can turn off each one by using the check box. And error checking can occur as a background activity, generating comments and colored indicators in the affected cells. If you prefer, you can also turn off error checking as a background activity on the Error Checking tab.

Expert Formatting Techniques

After you enter and edit the information in worksheet cells, you can format the data to highlight important facts and make the worksheet easier to read. In this chapter you'll learn how to format worksheet cells, change column widths and row heights, add and remove page breaks, use formatting styles, and work with predesigned worksheet templates. You'll be surprised how easily you can improve the appearance of your Microsoft Excel 2002 worksheets by using the powerful techniques discussed in this chapter.

InsideOut

It's worthwhile to note that there's formatting, and then there's *formatting*. That is, some types of formatting are quite different from others, and it would be helpful if Excel could distinguish them more clearly. In particular, the formatting that tells Excel what data type a cell contains can be critical for calculations. If Excel recognizes 3/4 as a fraction rather than a date, you will be able to use the cell in some calculations, but you won't be able to apply date-oriented functions to the cell contents. This chapter is, however, primarily concerned with cosmetic formatting—which is often vital to the usability of a worksheet but not necessary for the accuracy of the results.

Formatting the elements of a chart involves some different commands, which are discussed in "Formatting a Chart," on page 764.

Formatting Cells

Effective worksheet formatting is crucial when you present important information. Formatting the contents of a cell doesn't change how Excel stores the data internally; rather, it changes how the information looks on your screen and how it appears in print. In this section you'll learn the following techniques for formatting the data in cells:

- How to change the vertical and horizontal alignment of data in a cell

- How to change number formats

- How to change the font, text color, and background color

- How to add decorative borders and patterns to cells

- How to apply combinations of formatting effects using the AutoFormat command

Once you're familiar with these formatting options, you'll see (later in this chapter) how Excel can apply many formatting features automatically. This capability, called conditional formatting, means that Excel can format the contents of a cell depending on the value stored in the cell.

Changing Alignment

The gateway to Excel's formatting commands is the Cells command on the Format menu. To apply the command, you begin by highlighting the cell you want to format or by selecting a range of cells. Then choose the Cells command to display the Format Cells dialog box, as shown in Figure 23-1. The Format Cells dialog box contains six tabs of formatting options that you can use to adjust the appearance of information in worksheet cells. You use the Alignment tab shown in Figure 23-1 to change the alignment and orientation of information in worksheet cells. You can also use the Formatting toolbar to set the most popular alignment options.

> **tip** You can display the Format Cells dialog box by selecting the range of cells you want to format, right-clicking the range, and then choosing Format Cells from the shortcut menu.

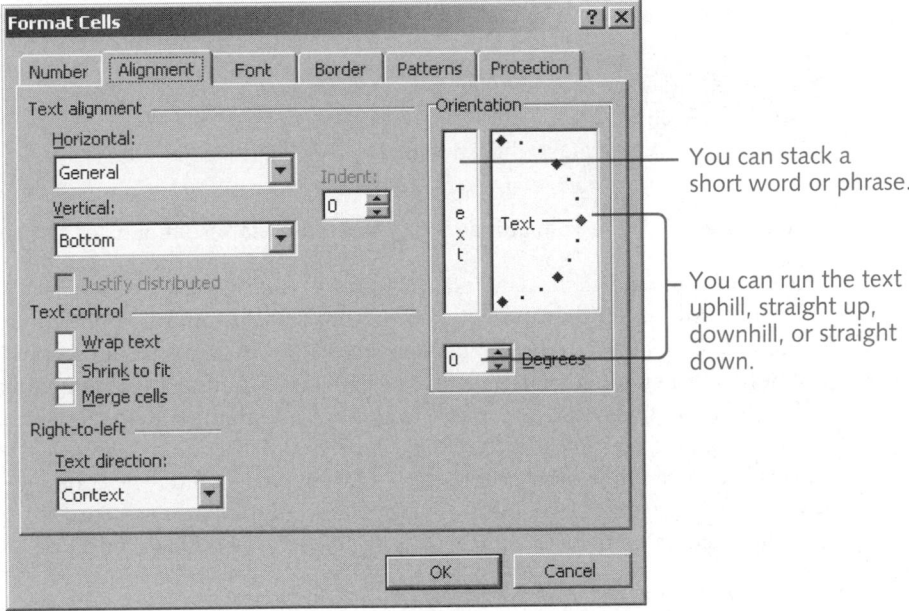

Figure 23-1. Alignment tab of the Format Cells dialog box.

Adjusting Horizontal Alignment

To adjust the *horizontal* (side-to-side) alignment of data in a range of cells, select the range you want to align, choose Format, Cells, click the Alignment tab, and choose one of the eight alignment options in the Horizontal drop-down list box. General alignment (the default) aligns information one of two ways, depending on the type of information you enter: it aligns text to the left edge of the cell, and it aligns numbers to the right edge. This basic alignment will be suitable for most entries. Left, Center, and Right enforce the indicated alignment in the cell, regardless of the type of information (text or numeric) you enter. You can also use toolbar buttons to set these common formatting options, as shown in Figure 23-2.

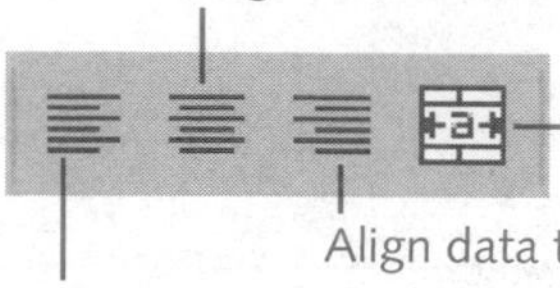

Align data to the center of selected cells.

———Center text across the selected range of columns.

Align data to the right edge of selected cells.
Align data to the left edge of selected cells.

Figure 23-2. Use the Formatting toolbar to set the more common cell formats.

The Fill option repeats the data in a cell to fill all the cells selected in the row, although the data is still stored only in the first cell. Note that this option applies only to a horizontal range, not to a vertical range. The Justify option aligns text evenly between the cell borders when longer entries wrap within a cell. (Turn text wrapping on and off using the Wrap text check box, which is also on the Alignment tab.) The next option in the Horizontal drop-down list box is Center Across Selection, which centers the data in one cell across a range of adjacent cells. For example, to center the contents of cell A1 across columns A, B, C, and D, select cells A1 through D1, choose Format, Cells, click the Alignment tab, and select the Center Across Selection option in the Horizontal list box.

To achieve a similar result (to Center Across Selection alignment), you can select cells A1 through D1, and then click the Merge and Center button on the Formatting toolbar. The further effect of this command (which you can toggle on and off in Excel 2002), is that Excel treats the merged cells as a single cell. If you attempt to select cell C1, for example, after you have used the Merge and Center command in the example above, Excel displays your location (in the Name Box) as cell A1.

By the way, Center Across Selection won't display text over occupied cells, so for the command to function properly, cells B1 through D1 must be empty. When you choose the command, Excel aligns the data to the center of the selection and merges the selected cells into a single cell with the cell name of the leftmost cell.

> **tip** For Horizontal alignment options that are followed by the word Indent (in parentheses), you can specify a measurement in the Indent box. For example, text that is formatted for Left alignment with an Indent value of 2 is aligned two picas from the left cell wall rather than immediately against the cell wall (the default).

newfeature!

The Horizontal list box contains one final item, Distributed, which is new in Excel 2002. This option, similar to Justify, evenly distributes text across the cell width and multiplies the height of the cell if necessary so that all the text is visible when wrapped. The appearance is similar to that of justified text except that incomplete lines are centered rather than left aligned. Figure 23-3 shows examples of several types of horizontal alignment formatting.

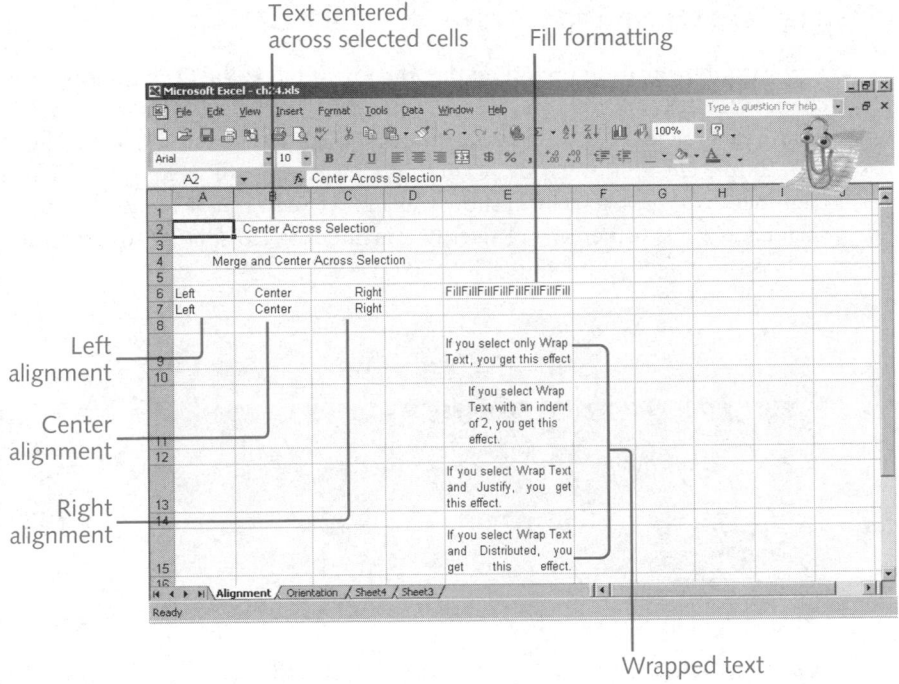

Figure 23-3. The Horizontal alignment options can create a variety of useful formatting effects.

Adjusting Vertical Alignment

The Alignment tab also allows you to adjust the *vertical* (top to bottom) alignment in cells. The default vertical alignment is Bottom, meaning the cell contents are aligned to the bottom of the cell. However, if you change the row height to add additional white space to cells (you'll learn how to do this later in the chapter), you might enhance the appearance of your worksheet by selecting the Top or Center option in the Vertical drop-down list box (see Figure 23-1).

> **tip** An easy way to create multiline text in a cell—and control where the text wraps—is to press Alt+Enter where you want a line break within the cell. The cell must, of course, be wide enough to accommodate the line lengths you specify.

If you have multiple lines of text in a cell, you can also use the Justify or Distributed alignment option to spread complete lines of text evenly between the top and bottom edges of the cell, multiplying cell height as necessary. If text is oriented vertically (as explained in the next section), the Justify and Distributed options differ just as they do for horizontal alignment: defaulting to left (top) and centered alignment respectively for incomplete lines of text.

653

Adjusting Text Orientation

A powerful formatting option on the Alignment tab is the Orientation setting, which changes the text orientation in the selected cells from the default horizontal orientation to an exact angle (measured in degrees) on a 180-degree semicircle. In the Orientation box, simply click the angle you want to use for the text or drag the word *Text* on the alignment compass. Excel will show you a preview of the orientation you select. This slick feature lets you create a ledger that includes space-saving, attractive column labels such as those shown in Figure 23-4.

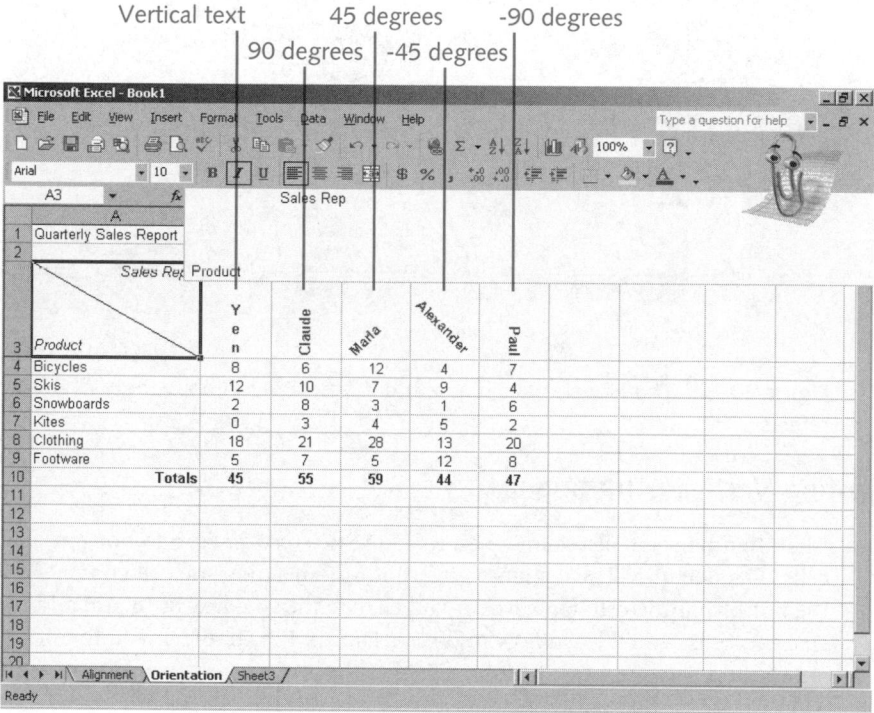

Figure 23-4. The Orientation option in the Alignment tab lets you specify an exact angle for your text—just like using a protractor in art class.

> **note** Using the Degrees scroll box, you can specify an exact text angle from -90 degrees to +90 degrees.

One further option in this Orientation setting is the button you use to "stack" letters vertically in worksheet cells. To create this neat effect, select the Vertical orientation of Center, and click the vertical bar on the Alignment tab labeled *Text* (see Figure 23-1). When this bar is highlighted, Excel creates the stacked-letter effect shown in cell B3 in Figure 23-4. (The text orientation will be set to zero degrees.) This is a useful and visually interesting effect for labeling a column, especially if the text is brief.

 The Format.xls example is on the companion CD to this book.

Changing Number Formats

Excel allows you to change the appearance of your numeric entries by using several formatting options on the Number tab of the Format Cells dialog box, shown in Figure 23-5. To change the number format for a range of cells, begin by selecting the cells. If the first cell in the range contains a number, Excel uses that number in the Sample box to illustrate the changes in format. Next, choose Format, Cells, click the Number tab, and choose a category in the Category list box.

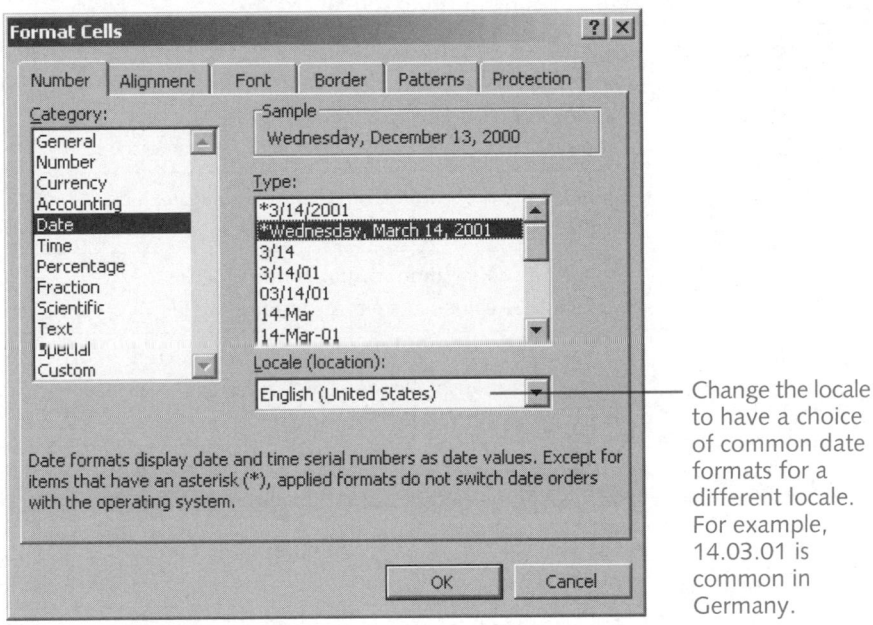

Change the locale to have a choice of common date formats for a different locale. For example, 14.03.01 is common in Germany.

Figure 23-5. The Number tab lets you change the format of your numeric entries.

When you choose a category, the tab changes, in most cases presenting additional format options that are appropriate to the category. If you choose Currency, for example, you can specify a number of decimal places to display, a currency symbol, and a format for presenting negative amounts. On the other hand, if you're formatting a range of dates, the Date category presents a variety of date formats. Among them are two that use four-digit year formats. Excel includes these, of course, to eliminate the confusion that surrounded the Y2K rollover. After you make your format choices, you can click OK or move to another tab.

Table 23-1, on page 656, describes the purpose of each numeric format category on the Number tab and shows examples of each.

Table 23-1. **The Numeric Formats on the Number Tab**

Category	Purpose	Examples
General	The default number format, right-aligned, with no special formatting codes.	15.75 5425
Number	A flexible numeric format that can be enhanced with commas, variable decimal places, and (for negative numbers) colors and parentheses.	3.14159 (1,575.32)
Currency	A general monetary format that can be enhanced with dollar signs, variable decimal places, and (for negative numbers) colors and parentheses. Excel 2002 supports the Euro format.	$75.35 ($1,234.10)
Accounting	A special currency format designed to align columns of monetary values along the decimal point. (The dollar sign appears along the left side of the cell.)	$ 75.00 $500.75
Date	A general-purpose date format that displays calendar dates in several standard styles.	1/15/2000 Jan-15-00
Time	A general-purpose time format that displays chronological values in several standard styles.	3:30 PM 15:30:58
Percentage	A format that multiplies the value in the selected cell by 100 and displays the result using a percentage symbol (%).	175% 15.125%
Fraction	A format that expresses numbers as fractional values. (You specify the number of digits and denominator.)	1/8 2/16
Scientific	An exponential notation for numbers that contain a lot of digits.	1.25E-08 4.58E+12
Text	A format that treats numbers and formulas like text. (It aligns them on the left edge of the cell and displays them exactly as they are entered.)	500.35 12345.0
Special	A collection of useful formats that follow an alphanumeric pattern, including Zip Code, Phone Number, and Social Security Number.	98109-1234 535-65-2342
Custom	A list of all standard formats (such as formats for foreign currency) and any custom numeric formats you create. (For more information, see "Creating a Custom Number Format," on page 657.)	INV-0075 £150.50

In addition to the options on the Number tab, you can use the Formatting toolbar buttons shown in Figure 23-6 to format the numeric entries in selected cells.

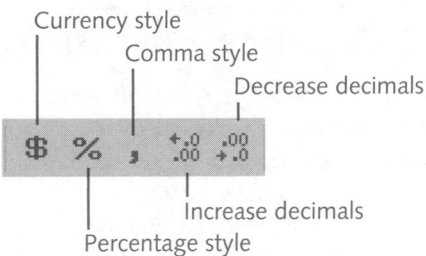

Figure 23-6. The Formatting toolbar provides buttons for commonly used numeric formats.

Creating a Custom Number Format

If you routinely enter numeric values in a format that Excel doesn't recognize, you should consider creating a custom number format. For example, you might want to create a custom number format for part numbers or invoice numbers that include both letters and numbers or a monetary format that features international currency symbols. To create this type of custom format, choose Format, Cells, click the Number tab, select Custom from the Category list box, and then either

● modify an existing format by selecting it in the list box and then editing it in the Type box, or

● enter a new format in the Type box using characters and one or more of Excel's special formatting symbols.

Figure 23-7 shows the Custom option on the Number tab after a currency format using the British pound (£) symbol has been created. (You enter the £ symbol by holding down the Alt key and typing 0163 on the numeric keypad. Make sure Num Lock is on.)

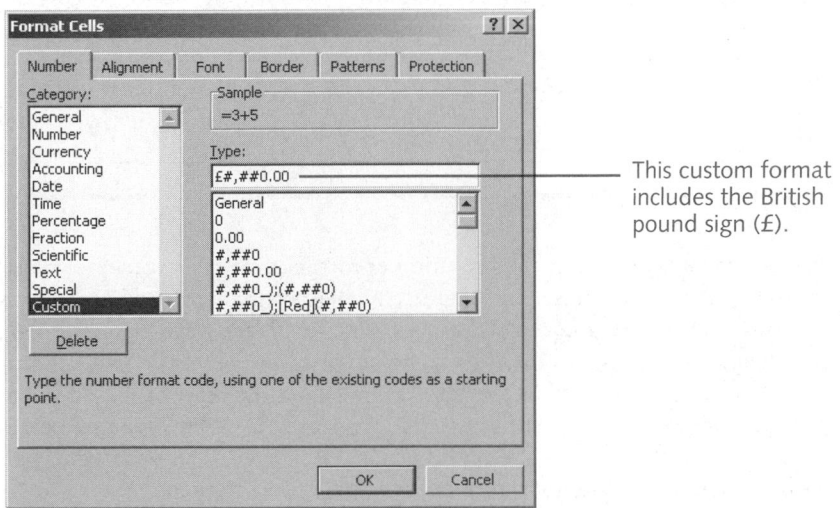

This custom format includes the British pound sign (£).

Figure 23-7. To create a custom number format, select the Custom option and either modify an existing format or create a completely new one.

Chapter 23

Changing Excel's Default Currency Symbol

You can change the currency symbol used in Excel and other Microsoft Windows–based applications. In Windows Me, open the Control Panel, double-click the Regional Settings icon, and then select the appropriate language and country or region in the Regional Settings tab. Then click the Currency tab and select the symbol you want to use in the Currency Symbol drop-down list box. For example, if you want Excel to display the British pound sign (£) as its default currency symbol, choose English in the Language drop-down list box and United Kingdom for the Region/Country on the Regional Settings tab, and then click OK. Windows will reconfigure your Windows–based applications so that the pound sign (£) is used as the default rather than the dollar sign ($) in all your documents. For Windows 95, Windows 98, and Windows 2000, select the country that uses the preferred currency symbol in the drop-down list box on the Regional Settings (Regional Options in Windows 2000) tab.

If you want to change only particular currency symbols on a worksheet, enter them individually in cells or customize a number format to display them as needed. If standard alphabetical letters or other symbols normally represented on your keyboard are used for the symbol, type them in the appropriate format. For example, the currency symbol for German marks is DM and the symbol follows the monetary value, such as 550.57 DM. If a special ANSI (American National Standards Institute) code is required for the symbol, make sure Num Lock is turned on, hold down the Alt key, and type the appropriate four-digit code. Table 23-2 lists some of the most popular currency symbols and their ANSI codes.

Table 23-2. Currency Symbols and ANSI Codes for Entering Them

Country	Denomination	Symbol	ANSI Code
United Kingdom	Pound	£	Alt+0163
Japan	Yen	¥	Alt+0165
United States	Cent	¢	Alt+0162

To help you organize your custom number format, Excel lets you enter placeholders for digits, special symbols, and other useful characters using the formatting symbols shown in Table 23-3. You can also enter characters (such as currency symbols or useful abbreviations such as *Part* or *INV*) to be included in the format. For example, to create a custom part number format that translates the cell value 25 to the formatted part number *Part AA-025*, enter the code *Part AA-000* in the Type text box. To use the custom format later, click the Number tab, click the Custom Category, and then double-click the custom format in the list box. You can also delete custom formats by highlighting the format and clicking the Delete button. (Excel won't let you delete the default formats.)

InsideOut

Custom and Special formats are especially useful if you need to enter a lot of data that combines numbers and punctuation, such as phone numbers or Social Security numbers. Creating a format can insert routine punctuation or prevent Excel from dropping a leading zero in a series of digits. The Special format for Social Security numbers, for instance, lets you enter the digits without the punctuation. Excel inserts the hyphens in their standard locations after you press Enter or move to a different cell.

Table 23-3. Useful Formatting Characters for Building Custom Number Formats

Character	Purpose	Example	Number Entered	Result
#	Creates a placeholder for significant digits, rounding to fit if necessary.	##.###	50.0048 2.30	50.005 2.3
0	Rounds numbers to fit like the # character, but fills any empty positions with zeros to align numbers and to fill all specified positions.	00.00	50.1 5	50.10 05.00
?	Also rounds numbers to fit, but fills any empty positions with spaces rather than extra zeros (if necessary) to align numbers and fill positions.	??.??	5.6 .70 73.27	5.6 .7 73.27
"text"	Adds the characters specified to the value in the cell.	"ID " ##	75 2	ID 75 ID 2
comma (,)	Separates thousands in numbers.	#,###	5600	5,600
$, -, +, :, /, (,), space	Standard formatting characters. Each appears as specified in the custom numeric format.	$#.000	500.5	$500.500
%	Multiplies value by 100 and adds percentage symbol.	##%	.25	25%

Changing Text Font and Text Color

To emphasize headings and distinguish different kinds of information in your worksheet, you can use the Font tab in the Format Cells dialog box, shown in Figure 23-8. The Font tab lets you change the font, style, size, and color of the data in selected cells. It also controls whether data is underlined and allows you to create special formatting effects such as strikethrough, superscript, and subscript. The fonts displayed on the Font tab depend on the type of printer you're connected to and the fonts installed on your system. Fonts preceded by a TrueType symbol are TrueType fonts designed to appear in print exactly as they do on the screen. You might also see fonts on the Font tab that have tiny printer icons in front of them; these are scalable fonts, which will look sharp when printed but might not display accurately on the screen. (The size will probably be right but the character shapes might not exactly match.)

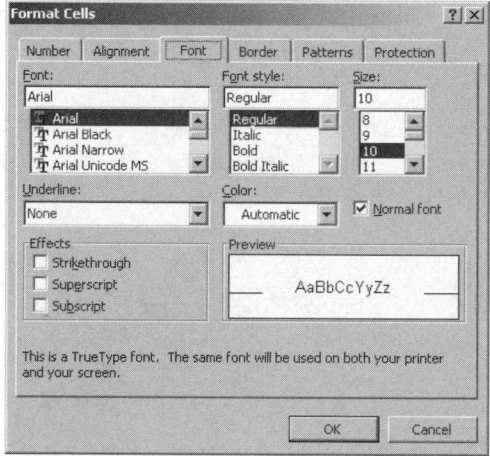

Figure 23-8. You can change the font and text color for selected cells in the Font tab in the Format Cells dialog box.

In addition to selecting formatting options in the Font tab, you can also use Excel's Formatting toolbar to change several font and text color options. Figure 23-9 shows the buttons you can use to increase your formatting speed.

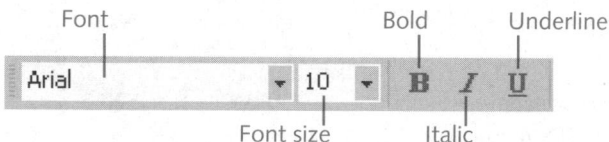

Figure 23-9. You can format selected text cells by using these Formatting toolbar buttons.

When you display the drop-down list of fonts on the Formatting toolbar, Excel shows each font in characters that match the font itself. If you don't need these visual cues, you can eliminate this somewhat cumbersome feature by choosing Tools, Customize and clicking the Options tab. Clear the option List Font Names In Their Font.

To change the font and text color formatting in one or more cells, select the cells you want to format. (To format individual characters in a cell, see the sidebar called "Formatting Individual Characters in a Cell," on page 662.) Choose Format, Cells, click the Font tab, and then use the list boxes and check boxes on the Font tab to adjust the font characteristics you want to change. The Preview window helps you verify that the appearance is what you want, especially if the font is unfamiliar. When you're finished, click OK.

> **tip**   If you want to return to the default font setting, select the Normal Font check box on the Font tab.

Adding Borders to Cells

Another useful technique for highlighting specific information in a worksheet is adding borders to important cells using the Border tab of the Format Cells dialog box, shown in Figure 23-10. The Border tab lets you place a solid or dashed line along one or more cell edges, and you can use the diagonal lines to divide cells from corner to corner. Borders help make the information in a worksheet easier to comprehend. You can emphasize particular cells, rows, and columns such as those containing headings or totals.

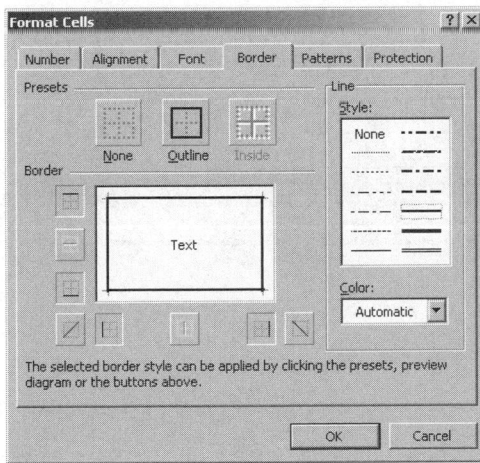

Figure 23-10.   The Border tab lets you add borders and grids to selected cells.

To specify borders for the cells you've selected, first click one of the 14 line styles in the Style box (the None style removes existing borders). Then click the lines you want on the preview diagram in the Border box or click the buttons along the left and bottom of the Border box for the same result. As a shortcut, you can also use one of the three border styles in the Presets box: None (to remove an existing border), Outline (to place a border around the outside edge of the selected cells), or Inside (to draw lines along the inside edges of selected cells). You can also change the color of the border by opening the Color list box. Remember to select the color prior to selecting your borders.

Formatting Individual Characters in a Cell

You can also format individual characters in a cell if the entry contains text. This useful feature lets you emphasize important words in a long entry or create dramatic effects in headings. For example, you can italicize one word in a cell containing many words or change the first letter of a heading to a larger point size. To format individual characters in a cell, double-click the cell and select the characters you want to change. Then choose the Cells command on the Format menu and change the attributes you want or click the appropriate buttons on the Formatting toolbar. When you press Enter, the formatting will take effect.

Figure 23-11 shows an example of combined border styles. In the example we selected various ranges of cells and then applied outlines, partial outlines, and internal grids of different line weights as described in the labels.

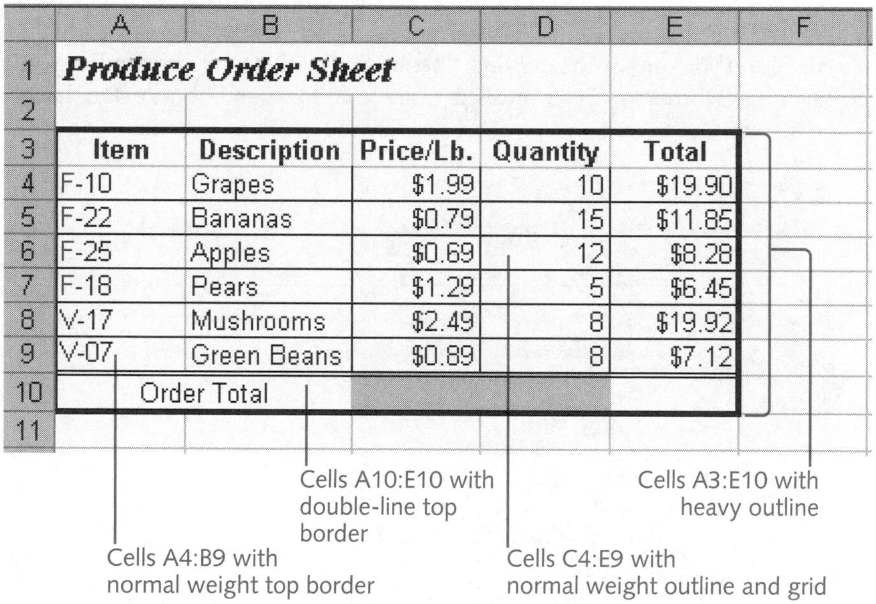

	A	B	C	D	E	F
1	*Produce Order Sheet*					
2						
3	**Item**	**Description**	**Price/Lb.**	**Quantity**	**Total**	
4	F-10	Grapes	$1.99	10	$19.90	
5	F-22	Bananas	$0.79	15	$11.85	
6	F-25	Apples	$0.69	12	$8.28	
7	F-18	Pears	$1.29	5	$6.45	
8	V-17	Mushrooms	$2.49	8	$19.92	
9	V-07	Green Beans	$0.89	8	$7.12	
10		Order Total				
11						

Cells A10:E10 with double-line top border

Cells A3:E10 with heavy outline

Cells A4:B9 with normal weight top border

Cells C4:E9 with normal weight outline and grid

Figure 23-11. Clicking the Outline button adds a box around the selected text.

 The Orderfrm.xls example is on the companion CD to this book.

Adding Instant Borders

A handy alternative to using the Border tab is clicking the Borders button on Excel's Formatting toolbar. In this case using the Formatting toolbar is much faster than using the Format Cells dialog box, and the toolbar also gives you single-step access to some formatting designs that require multiple steps using the Format Cells dialog box.

To use the Borders button, select the range of cells you want to highlight, click the drop-down arrow to the right of the Borders button, and then pick from the 12 border options that appear on the Borders toolbar, as shown in Figure 23-12 below. The bottom left style is useful for creating worksheet tables; it places a light border on the top of the cell and a heavier border on the bottom of the cell. Learning to use these border styles will save you considerable time as you format your worksheets.

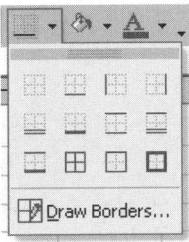

Figure 23-12.   The Borders button quickly applies commonly used border options to the selected range of cells.

newfeature!
Drawing Borders with the Borders Toolbar

If you're already comfortable with electronic drawing tools, you will immediately like the new border drawing capability, which you can launch from the Borders button shown in Figure 23-12 above. Click the Draw Borders option on the Borders button to display the toolbar shown here.

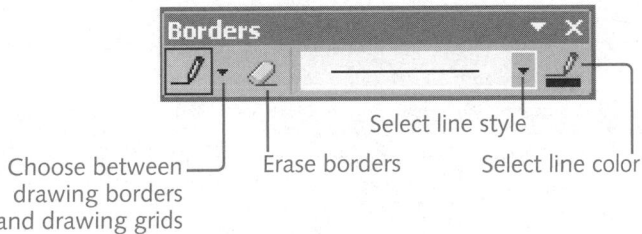

The Borders toolbar gives you access to all the features Excel offers for creating borders, and it lets you work directly on your worksheet cells. To draw lines, select the line style and color you want to use, and then use the cursor (which appears as a pencil) to add borders. Either click a cell border to add a line or click and drag to form a border. If you want clicking and dragging to form a complete grid rather than an outside border, use the drop-down box for the leftmost button on the Borders toolbar to select the Draw Border Grid option. Click the button itself to activate and deactivate the drawing cursor (pencil) itself.

663

Adding Shading to Cells

If you would like to create effects that complement the borders produced by the Border tab, the Patterns tab in the Format Cells dialog box shown in Figure 23-13 lets you add a background color and optional colored pattern to one or more cells in your worksheet. By default, the color you select has no pattern added to it, so you see a solid color in your cells. However, you can also add a background pattern and change its color from the default black to any of the colors displayed in the Pattern drop-down list box. To do the procedure, perform the following steps:

1 Select the cells you want to format.

2 Choose Format, Cells.

3 Click the Patterns tab, select a cell shading color, and then select a shading pattern (in a second color) from the Pattern drop-down list box.

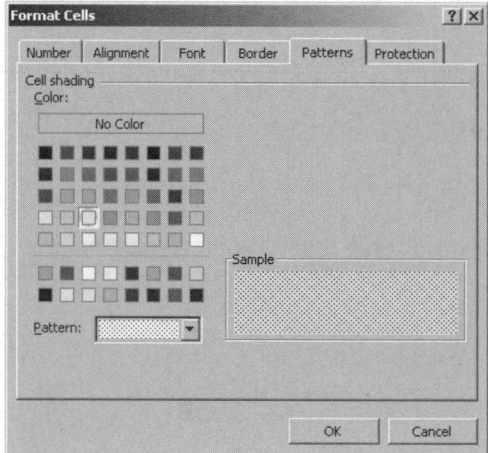

Figure 23-13. The Patterns tab lets you add color background shading and patterns to your cells.

> **tip** An excellent practical use for background color is to shade every other row of a wide worksheet so that a reader can more easily glance across a row without confusion.

Color can make a striking addition to your worksheet and is ideal—if used in moderation—for documents created to be viewed electronically, such as status reports, departmental ledgers, sales projections, and the like. If you don't have a color printer, your color shading effects will be converted to gray tones when you print. (Not to worry, Excel usually does a good job at this.) To see what this conversion is like, you can view your worksheet using the File, Print Preview command.

664

Fill Color

You can also use the Fill Color button on the Formatting toolbar to change the background color (but not the pattern) used in worksheet cells. To remove the existing color in worksheet cells, click the No Fill option.

Copying Formatting Using the Format Painter Button

Format
Painter

Occasionally you'll need to copy the formats from one cell to another cell without copying the data in the cell. For example, you might want to copy the cell formats you used to create a 14-point, bold, Times New Roman heading that has a thick border to a second heading you're creating later in the worksheet. Excel allows you to accomplish this task by using the Format Painter button on the Standard toolbar. To copy formatting using the Format Painter button, follow these steps:

1 Select the cell from which you want to copy formats.

2 Click the Format Painter button on the toolbar. A marquee will appear around the selected cell and a paintbrush will be added to the mouse pointer.

3 Select the range of cells you want to change to the new format. You can change worksheets using the lower tabs and navigate using the scroll bars without canceling the format copy.

If you decide you don't like the format you copied, remember that you can choose Undo from the Edit menu to remove it. To remove the selection marquee, press Esc.

> **tip** If you want to copy formats to cells or ranges that aren't contiguous, double-click the Format Painter button, and then select one by one the cells you want to format. When you've finished, click the Format Painter button again.

Changing Column Widths and Row Heights

Excel gives you room for about eight digits in a worksheet cell if you use the default 10-point Arial font. Worksheet cells are automatically resized whenever a number doesn't fit, unless you intentionally reduce a cell width so that a number won't fit—in that case Excel displays the number using the overflow characters, #######. Fortunately, it's easy to fiddle with your column widths and row heights if you want to format them in a special way. You can resize rows and columns by dragging with the mouse (the fastest method) or by using commands on the Format menu. We'll cover both techniques in this section.

> **note** Different columns can be different widths in a worksheet, but all the cells in a particular column must be the same width. Likewise, different rows in the worksheet can have different heights, but all the cells in a particular row must be the same height.

Chapter 23

Adjusting the Height or Width Manually

You can widen or narrow a column by dragging the right column edge with the mouse or by specifying a new width by using the Width command on the Column submenu of the Format menu. Also, you can change a row's height by dragging the row's lower edge or by specifying a new height by means of the Height command on the Row submenu of the Format menu. Each method is described in the following sections.

For an automatic means of fitting spaces to dates, see "Using the AutoFit Command," on page 668.

Changing Column Width or Row Height Using the Mouse

Figure 23-14 shows how to change column width using the mouse. The process requires that you drag the right edge of the column at the top of the column, the heading row. When the pointer is the right location for resizing, its shape changes to a sizing pointer with arrows pointing in opposite directions. To change row height using the mouse, follow a similar procedure: drag the lower edge of the row heading to increase or decrease the height.

The Formula.xls example is on the companion CD to this book.

1 Position the mouse pointer at the right edge of the column heading and drag the column border, which appears as a dotted line.

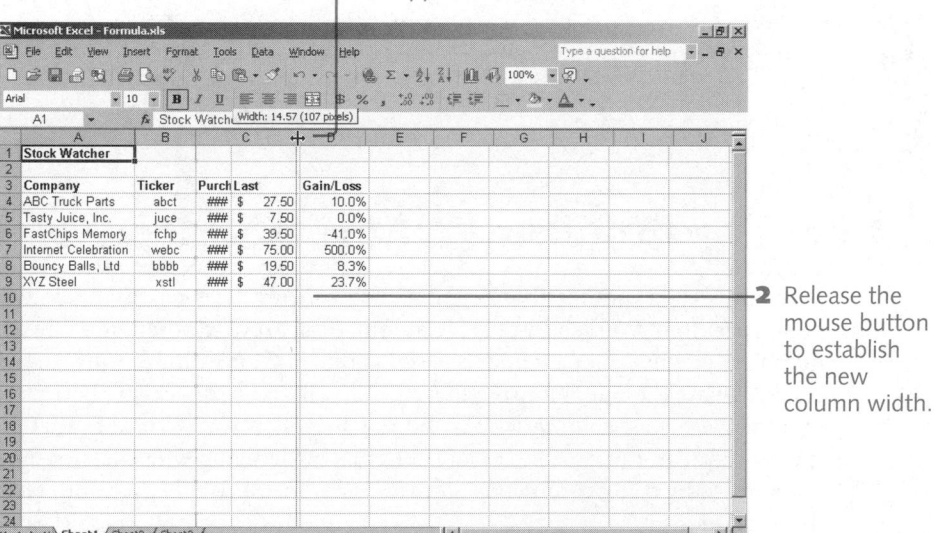

2 Release the mouse button to establish the new column width.

Figure 23-14. Follow these steps to change the column width using the mouse. A pop-up box displays the column width.

To change the width of multiple columns with the mouse, select the columns you want to resize, and then drag and adjust one of the columns. When you release the mouse button, each of the columns will be the width of the one you changed. The same process applies to changing row heights. Select the rows and resize one of the rows in the selection.

Using the Column Width and Row Height Commands

The Width command on the Column submenu is useful if you want to type an exact width for the column you're resizing. Select a cell in the column you want to resize. (To resize multiple columns, select a cell in each of the columns you want to adjust.) Choose Format, Column, and then choose Width from the submenu. The number you specify in the Cell Width dialog box is the average number of characters that will fit in the cell using the default font (defined as part of the Normal style). Click OK to resize the column.

In a like manner, the Height command on the Row submenu is useful if you want to type an exact height for the row you're resizing. Highlight a cell in the row you want to resize. If you want to resize multiple rows, select a cell in each of the rows you want to adjust. Display the Format menu, and from the Row submenu, choose Height. Specify the row height in the Row Height dialog box in points, and click OK. The standard height is based on the size of the default font.

InsideOut

Set Your Preferred Column Widths Instantly

To set the default (or standard) width of columns in your worksheet, choose Standard Width from the Column submenu and type in the width you want. This command adjusts the width of every worksheet column that hasn't already been resized or every column you select. To select all the columns of the worksheet, even those you've previously changed, first click the Select All button above row 1 and to the left of column A. This is a good way to customize the cells in your worksheet if you always want them to be a certain shape.

Hiding Rows and Columns

Note that you can use any of these resizing techniques to hide one or more rows or columns completely. Hiding a column, for example, is equivalent to setting its width to zero. Sometimes hiding data is desirable, either to shield the data from unauthorized glances or to keep it out of your way while you work.

Excel provides yet another way to hide one or more rows or columns: select the row or column you want to hide and choose Hide from the Row or Column submenu. To restore the hidden row or column, select the rows or columns on both sides of the

Chapter 23

hidden entry, and then choose Unhide from the Row or Column submenu. The hidden row or column will appear as you last saw it.

When you choose this command, the entire row or column, including the row number or column letter, will seem to disappear from the worksheet (though it hasn't actually been deleted).

> **caution** Hiding a column or row can be a great convenience but it can also be a risk. Be careful, for example, when deleting a range of rows and columns so that you don't inadvertently delete hidden rows and columns in the process.

Although Excel doesn't permit you to specify different widths for cells in the same column (or different heights for cells in the same row), it does allow you to merge consecutive cells so that they're identified and treated as a single cell. (Also see "Adjusting Horizontal Alignment," on page 651.)

Using the AutoFit Command

If you want Excel to size your rows or columns automatically for you, use the AutoFit command on the Column and Row submenus. When you select a column and choose AutoFit Selection from the Column submenu, Excel resizes the column to fit the widest entry in the column. This saves you the trouble of manually calculating point sizes or scanning every entry in a column as you drag the mouse. If you select a group of cells in a column, Excel adjusts the width based on the widest cell value in the selection, not the entire column.

Excel automatically resizes rows when you modify the font, so the row AutoFit command is less dramatic. When you select a row and choose AutoFit from the Row submenu, Excel returns the row to the default height for the largest font being used in the row.

Applying a Combination of Effects Using AutoFormat

If you're formatting a block or table of cells, you can apply several formatting effects in one fell swoop by using the AutoFormat command on the Format menu. The AutoFormat command displays a dialog box that features several predesigned table styles in the Table Format list box. Figure 23-15 shows one of the two table formats that create a three-dimensional effect. When you find the style you want, click OK to format the block of cells you selected as a table. You might try several styles on your own data to get the true visual effect and determine which one offers the most impact.

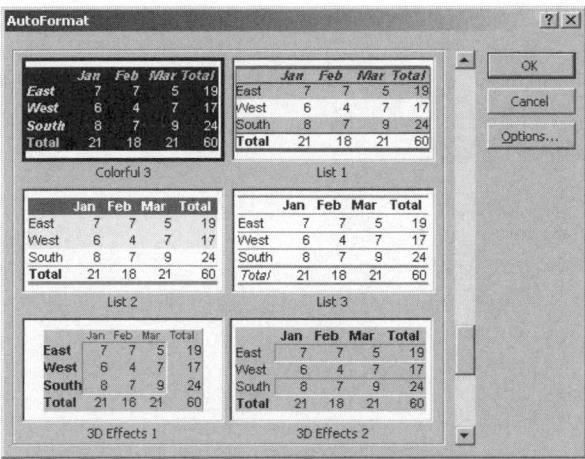

Figure 23-15.   The 3D Effects 2 style is only one of many AutoFormats requiring just a single click to format your worksheet. Excel shows each table style in its own preview window.

By default, the AutoFormat command sets the Number, Border, Font, Patterns, Alignment, and Width/Height options to match the table style you select. You can limit the options used in AutoFormat by clicking the Options button in the dialog box and clearing the formats you don't want. For example, if you like a particular table but don't want the border that's included, clear the Border check box (by clicking it), and click OK to apply the format's other characteristics.

Creating Conditional Formatting

Another slick feature of Excel is the ability it gives you to add *conditional formatting*—formatting that automatically adjusts depending on the contents of cells—to your worksheet. In plain English, this means that you can highlight important trends in your data—such as the rise in a stock price, a missed milestone, or a sudden spurt in your college expenses—based on conditions you set in advance using the Conditional Formatting dialog box. With this feature, an out-of-the-ordinary number "jumps out" at anyone who routinely uses the worksheet.

The following example shows how to add conditional formatting to a sample worksheet that tracks stock prices. If a stock in the Gain/Loss column rises by more than 20 percent, the conditional formatting will display numbers in bold type on a light blue background. If a stock in the Gain/Loss column falls by more than 20 percent, the number will be displayed in bold type on a solid red background. (The worksheet is shown in Figure 23-16, on page 670.)

 The Condform.xls example is on the companion CD to this book.

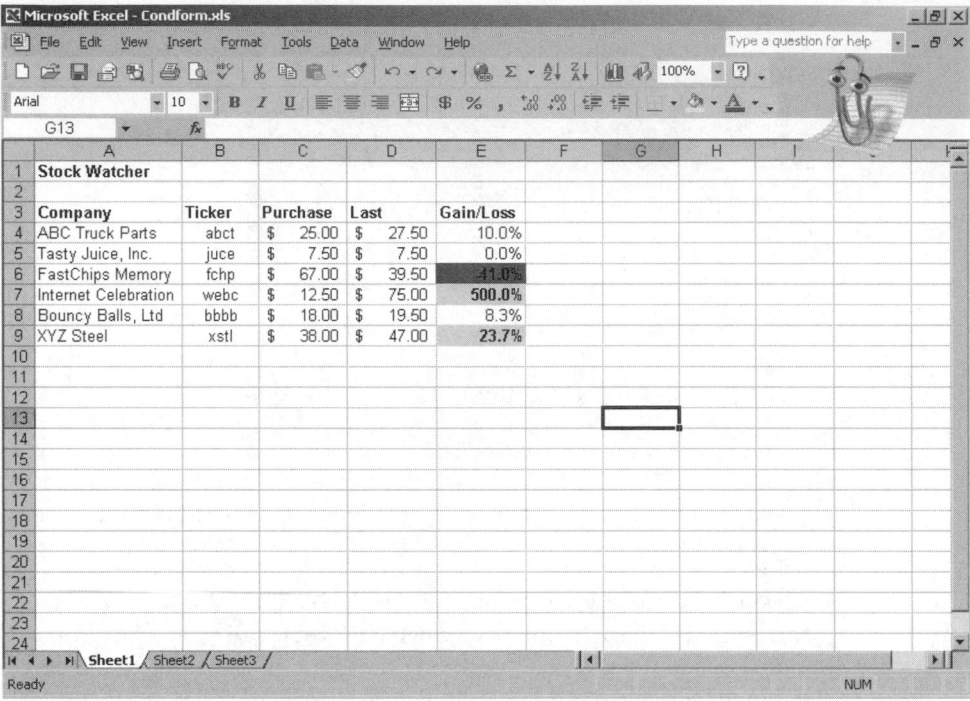

Figure 23-16. Conditional formatting highlights noteworthy numbers automatically, according to your specifications.

To create such a conditional format, complete the following steps:

1 Create a worksheet containing one or more cells of numeric information. (The worksheet can be an invoice, a financial document, a sales report, or any other document with useful numeric data.)

2 Select the cell range to which you want to apply the conditional formatting. (Note that each cell can maintain its own, unique conditional formatting, so that you can set up several different conditions.)

3 Choose Format, Conditional Formatting. The Conditional Formatting dialog box appears, containing several drop-down list boxes.

4 In the first list box, indicate whether you want Excel to use the current formula or the current value from the cells that you've selected. (In most cases you will want to use the cell value.)

5 In the second list box, indicate the comparison operator you would like to use in the conditional formatting. For our example, we selected greater than, because we're looking for stock returns greater than 20 percent.

6 In the third list box, type the number you want to use in the comparison. We typed 20%, or 0.2, because we want to isolate gains over 20 percent.

InsideOut

You can use dates for comparisons, but Excel requires that you enter the date as a serial value, an integer incremented for each day beginning with January 1, 1900. To determine the appropriate value, enter the date in a cell and then reformat the cell to use General format. You can undo the formatting to restore the date.

7 Click the Format button and specify the formatting you will use for the cells if the conditional statement you specified in steps 4 through 6 becomes true.

A modified Format Cells dialog box appears that has three formatting tabs. We selected Bold style on the Fonts tab and Light Blue on the Patterns tab and then clicked OK.

8 If necessary, click the Add button in the Conditional Formatting dialog box to add another condition to the scenario. (We took this opportunity to add a condition that highlighted losses of more than 20 percent in the worksheet.) The dialog box expands to accept an additional condition.

note The Add button lets you add up to three conditions. The Delete button removes conditions you no longer want.

9 Specify the operator you want to use in the second drop-down list box, and then type a value in the third list box. We specified less than as the operator, and then typed -20%. (We could have typed -0.2 as well.)

10 If you specified a second condition, click the Format button for Condition 2 and select a unique formatting color or type style. We chose Bold for the font style on the Font tab, and then, using the Patterns tab, we specified red shading. Our screen looks like this:

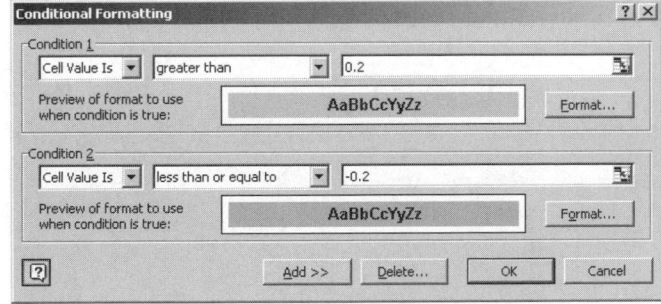

11 Click OK to close the dialog box and the conditional formatting will be applied to the selected text. If any numbers fall into the ranges you specified, the formatting you specified will be applied. Figure 23-16 shows two gains and one loss highlighted by the conditional formatting we entered for this

671

Chapter 23

example. Our efforts certainly paid off, especially if we now act on the knowledge of our profits and losses!

---

tip   **Find Conditional Formats**

If you try to apply or remove formatting to a cell and find Excel strangely non-compliant, it might be that you've forgotten the conditional formats that you've applied. Excel can help. To locate all cells that have conditional formatting, display the Edit menu and choose Go To. Click Special, select Conditional Formats, and (below Data Validation) be sure All is selected. (Select Same rather than All to find all cells with conditional formatting identical to the currently selected cell.) When you click OK, Excel indicates (with shading) all the cells with conditional formats.

Using Styles

If you routinely use the same formatting options for cells in your worksheets, you might want to consider creating a formatting *style* (a collection of formatting choices) that you can save with your workbook and use whenever you format information with the same attributes. After you create a new formatting style, or modify an existing one, you can use that style in any worksheet in your workbook, or you can copy the style to other open workbooks. In this section you will learn the following techniques:

- How to create your own styles

- How to apply existing styles

- How to copy or *merge* styles from other workbooks

Creating Your Own Styles

You create styles by using the Style command on the Format menu. When you choose Style, the Style dialog box appears, as shown in Figure 23-17.

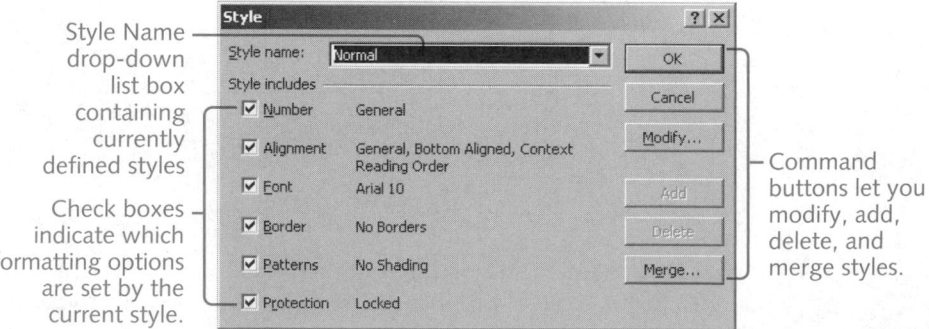

Style Name drop-down list box containing currently defined styles

Check boxes indicate which formatting options are set by the current style.

Command buttons let you modify, add, delete, and merge styles.

Figure 23-17. You can use the Style dialog box to manage the formatting styles in your worksheet.

The easiest way to create a new style is by selecting a cell that has the formatting characteristics you want to apply, choosing the Style command, and giving the style a new name. This is called creating a style *by example*, because you use your own worksheet formatting to define the style.

If the cell you selected before choosing the Style command hasn't yet been formatted with a style, the Normal style will be displayed in the Style Name box. Excel predefines several styles in addition to the Normal style, including Comma, Currency, and Percent styles. If you want to modify one of these styles (or any other style that you previously defined) throughout the workbook, select the style in the Style Name drop-down list box, click the Modify button, update the style using the tabs in the Format Cells dialog box, and click OK to return to the Style dialog box. When you click OK in the Style dialog box, the updated style will be changed throughout your workbook.

tip You can also create styles from scratch by using the Add button in the Style dialog box.

The following steps show how to create a new style by example. The style we created is the vertically oriented column heading for Claude, shown in cell C3 in Figure 23-18. The heading is bold, dark blue, center-aligned, and rotated up 90 degrees in the cell. We call it Vertical Head.

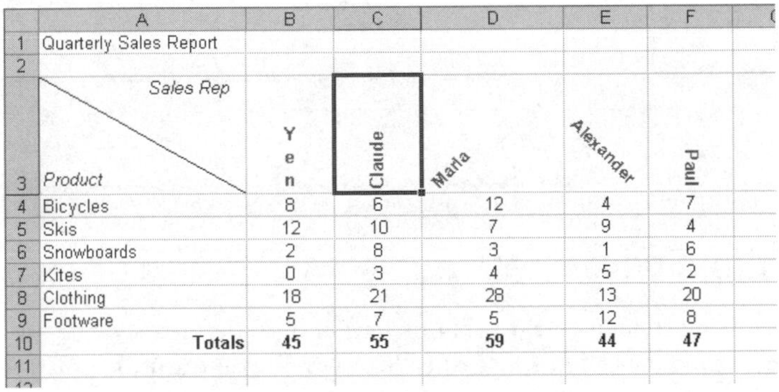

	A	B	C	D	E	F
1	Quarterly Sales Report					
2						
3	Sales Rep / Product	Yen	Claude	Maria	Alexander	Paul
4	Bicycles	8	6	12	4	7
5	Skis	12	10	7	9	4
6	Snowboards	2	8	3	1	6
7	Kites	0	3	4	5	2
8	Clothing	18	21	28	13	20
9	Footware	5	7	5	12	8
10	**Totals**	**45**	**55**	**59**	**44**	**47**
11						

Figure 23-18. To create a new style by example, you select a cell in your worksheet that has the formatting you want to save for the new style.

To create the Vertical Head style by example, follow these steps:

1. Format the cell you want to create your style from. For example, you could use the Alignment tab in the Format Cells dialog box to center the text horizontally and change the orientation, and then use the Font tab to change the font style to bold and dark blue.
2. Select the cell you just formatted.
3. Choose Format, Style.

4 Type *Vertical Head* (or another name
of your choice) in the Style Name textbox.

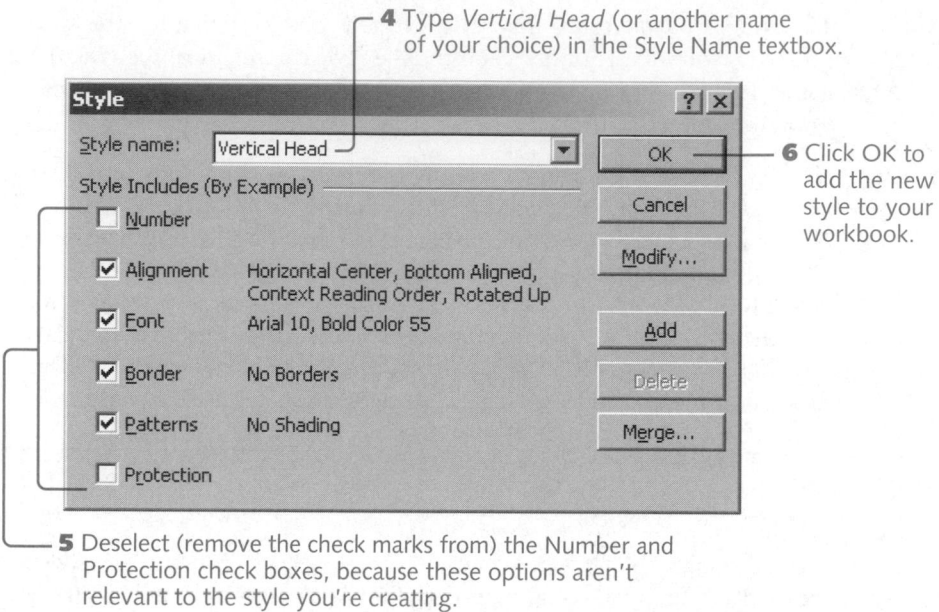

6 Click OK to
add the new
style to your
workbook.

5 Deselect (remove the check marks from) the Number and
Protection check boxes, because these options aren't
relevant to the style you're creating.

When a style option is cleared (there's no check mark in its check box), it means that
any time you apply the associated style, the selected cells will keep their existing formatting for these categories.

> **tip** To delete a custom style you no longer want, select the style in the Style Name drop-
> down list box and click Delete.

Applying Existing Styles

To apply an existing style in your workbook, either a predefined style or one that
you've created, select the cell or range of cells to which you want to apply the style and
choose Style from the Format menu to open the Style dialog box. Then click the Style
Name drop-down list box to display the styles available in your workbook, select the
style you want, and click OK.

Merging Styles from Other Workbooks

When you create a new style, you can use it only in the workbook where you create
it—the new style is saved in the current workbook and won't appear in other workbooks. (This way, you won't mix up styles for your stock portfolio with those for your
college expense budget.) However, you can copy or merge styles from other workbooks
into the current workbook by using the Merge button in the Style dialog box.

Chapter 23

note   Merging is a powerful tool, but use it with some caution. If the workbook into which you merge styles has matching style names, the new styles can override those existing styles and be applied throughout your workbook.

tip   Merging styles is a useful way to give your workbooks a consistent look. You can also use Excel templates (discussed in the next section) to format documents in a standard manner.

To merge styles from other Excel workbooks, follow these steps:

1   Open the *source* workbook (the workbook you want to copy styles from) and the *destination* workbook (the workbook you want to copy the styles to).

2   In the Window menu, click the destination workbook (its name should appear near the bottom of the Window menu) to make it the active window.

3   From the Format menu, choose Style.

4   Click the Merge button to display the Merge Styles dialog box shown below:

Other workbooks currently open in Excel

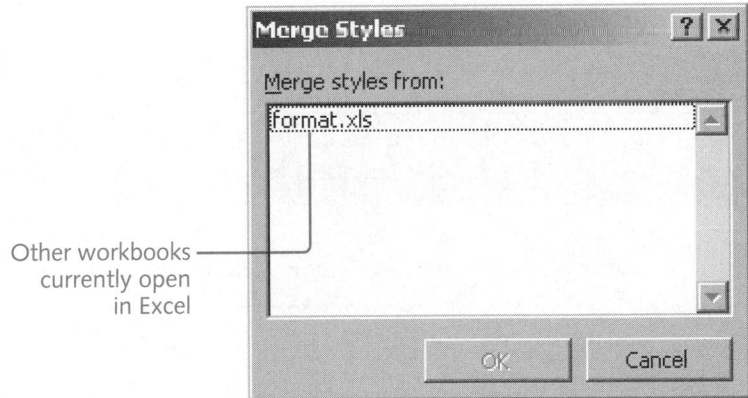

5   Select the name of the workbook you want to copy styles from (the source workbook), and then click OK.

Excel copies all the styles from the source workbook to the destination workbook. If the source workbook contains formatting styles that have the same names as styles in the destination workbook, a warning message will appear asking whether you want to merge the styles with matching names anyway. If you click Yes, the styles will be merged, and the source styles will be applied throughout the workbook.

> **note** The Undo command does *not* reverse the effects of the Merge Styles dialog box. Be sure you want to copy over *all* the styles from the source workbook to the destination workbook before you click the Merge button. (Remember that you can delete unwanted styles before the merge by using the Delete button in the Style dialog box.)

Creating and Modifying Templates

Using formatting styles is a good way to organize existing data in a standard format. If you routinely create similar documents from scratch, however—such as monthly reports, purchase orders, or product invoices—consider creating an Excel template. A *template* is a file that serves as a model for worksheets you create in your workbooks. The template can include file content as well as styles and macros. You can use the many preformatted templates that are included with the Microsoft Office XP software or available at *www.microsoft.com*, or you can tell Excel to treat any of your own workbooks as a template. In this section, you'll learn

● How to create a new template file

● How to open and modify an existing template file

> **tip** **Use an Existing Template**
>
> If you want to use an existing Excel template to create a new worksheet (rather than modifying a template to create a new type of worksheet), choose New from the File menu. Select one of the three sources of templates in the task pane under the heading New From Template: General Templates, Templates On My Web Sites, and Templates On Microsoft.com. Finally, highlight the template (navigating the Web or file structure, as necessary), and click OK. For more information on using Office XP templates and wizards to create documents, see "Creating New Office Documents," on page 53.

InsideOut

Excel users have long recognized that using a template—or even an existing data file—to get a head start on file creation is simply smart and efficient. The only problem with using an existing data file rather than a template as a starting point was the danger that arose when you saved the new file—unintentionally overwriting the data file that you used as a head start.

Happily, Excel 2002 has finally adapted to the work habits of users by allowing you to create a new file based on an existing data file and then protecting you from inadvertently overwriting your original file. The provisional filename for the new file is a unique name, such as MyFile2, derived from, but not identical to, your original data file.

Creating a New Template File

To make a new template file using one of your own workbooks as a model, complete the following steps. When you're finished, you will have a template you can use each time you want to create a worksheet that has the formatting you've included.

1 Open the workbook you want to save as a template file.

2 Choose File, Save As. The Save As dialog box appears.

3 Select Template in the Save As Type drop-down list box.

4 Enter a name for the template in the File Name text box, specify a folder location for the template by using the Save In list box, and then click Save. The location is, by default, an automatically created Templates folder.

> **tip** For your own convenience, be sure to specify one of the Office template folders (or a subfolder) for the location of your template. If you do, then the template will show up as an option under General Templates when you choose File, New.

5 Close the workbook you saved as a template. The next time you want to use the template as a worksheet model, choose File, New, locate the template, and double-click it.

Opening and Modifying an Existing Template File

To open an existing template file—either a template included with Office XP or one you created on your own—choose Open from the Excel File menu, specify Templates (*.xlt) in the Files Of Type list box, and double-click the template file icon in the files list box. Unless you intend to make changes to the original template, your first step after opening a template should be to save the workbook under a new filename to protect the original template.

To open an existing template, follow these steps:

Open

1 Choose File, Open, or click the Open button on the Standard toolbar. The Open dialog box appears.

2 In the Files Of Type drop-down list box, select Templates, as shown on the next page.

> **note** Excel templates have the .xlt file extension on disk. When you use the Save As command to save a file as a template, Excel stores the file (by default) in a Templates folder, and those templates appear (as General Templates in the task pane) when you create a new workbook using the File, New command.

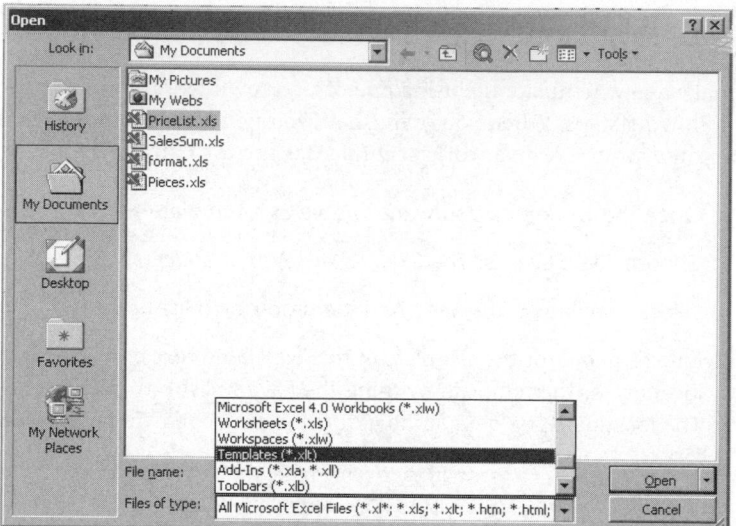

3 Browse to the folder or Web site containing the template you want to open. Office creates a Templates folder in the folder in which you installed Office. (Usually this is C:\Program Files\Microsoft Office\Templates.) The Templates folder contains several folders of its own for each of the Office applications. You'll find several useful Excel templates in the folder shown above.

tip For a description of each of the templates included in Excel, search for "Templates" in the Excel online Help.

4 Double-click the template file you want to open. The template appears in a window. If the template was included with the Office XP software, it typically contains several worksheet tabs and operating instructions. It may also contain a useful template toolbar that has custom template commands and online Help for the template.

5 Choose File, Save As. When the Save As dialog box appears, give the template a new filename. You must place it in the Templates folder or a subfolder of Templates for the file to appear in the File New dialog box. Click Save to save the template file to disk.

6 Your new template is now ready to be customized. When you're finished adding the touches you want, save your changes and close the template. Each time you open this template in the future, it will be ready to use as a boilerplate worksheet.

Changing Page Breaks

After you format your worksheet, you might want to adjust where the page breaks fall, particularly for longer worksheets. A *page break* is a formatting code that tells your printer to stop printing information on one page and start printing on the next page. Excel adds a page break to your worksheet when a page is full and identifies the division with a light dashed line. (Excel adds both vertical and horizontal page breaks.) If you don't want to see these breaks as you work, choose Options from the Tools menu, click the View tab, and then clear the Page Breaks option in the Window Options area.

You can set your own page breaks manually in the worksheet. For example, you might choose to place a page break between a table and a remittance form to keep all the table entries separate from the mail-back form. To set a manual page break in the worksheet, follow the steps shown in Figure 23-19.

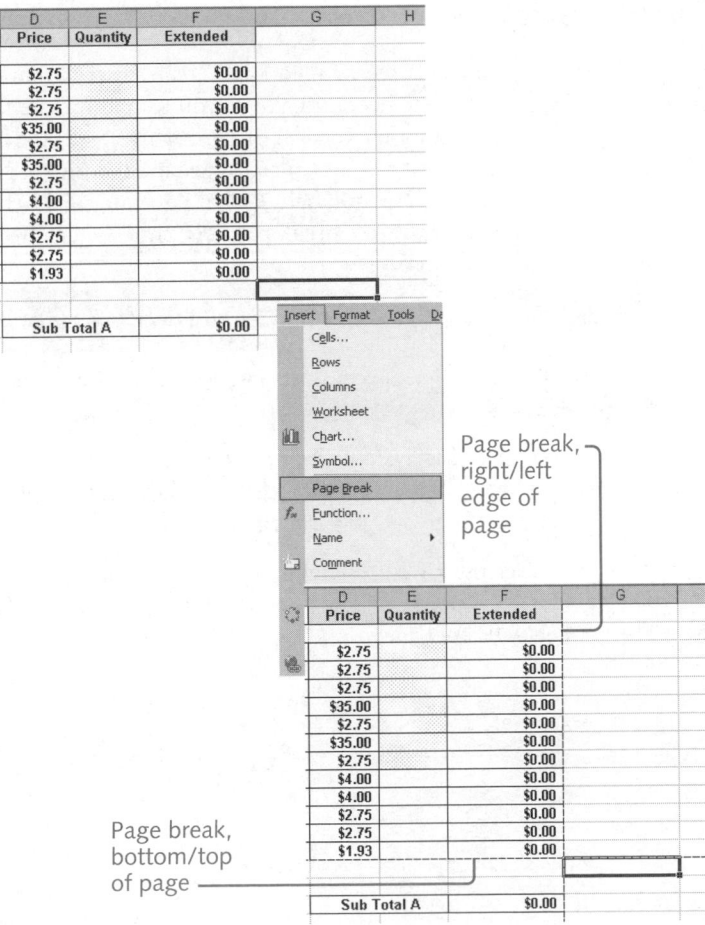

Figure 23-19.   In Normal view, Excel indicates page breaks with bold dashed lines.

The highlighted cell will become the upper left corner of a new page, and the manual page break will appear as a bold dashed line.

 The Invoice.xls example is on the companion CD to this book.

> **tip** **Remove a Manual Page Break**
>
> To remove both the bottom and right edges of a manual page break, click the cell below and to the right of the page break, and choose Insert, Remove Page Break. You can also remove just the bottom of the page break or just the right side by clicking any cell directly below or directly to the right of the page break.

Using Page Break Preview

Excel also provides a special worksheet view called Page Break Preview that quickly identifies the page breaks in your worksheet and allows you to manipulate them easily. Page Break Preview shows you a miniature version of your worksheet (a little like the Print Preview command on the File menu), but marks page breaks with a thick bold line and highlights page numbers with giant labels so that you can quickly find your place (see Figure 23-20). To display the page break preview, choose Page Break Preview from the View menu; to clear it, choose View, Normal.

To view and modify page breaks in Page Break Preview, follow these steps:

1 Choose View, Page Break Preview. Excel starts Page Break Preview mode, as shown in Figure 23-20.

2 If you see a dialog box that displays a welcome message, read the instructions about modifying page breaks, and then click OK. (You can suppress this dialog box by clicking Do Not Show This Dialog Again.)

3 Examine the page breaks in your worksheet by using the vertical and horizontal scroll bars. Individual pages will be marked with large labels, and page breaks will be marked with bold lines.

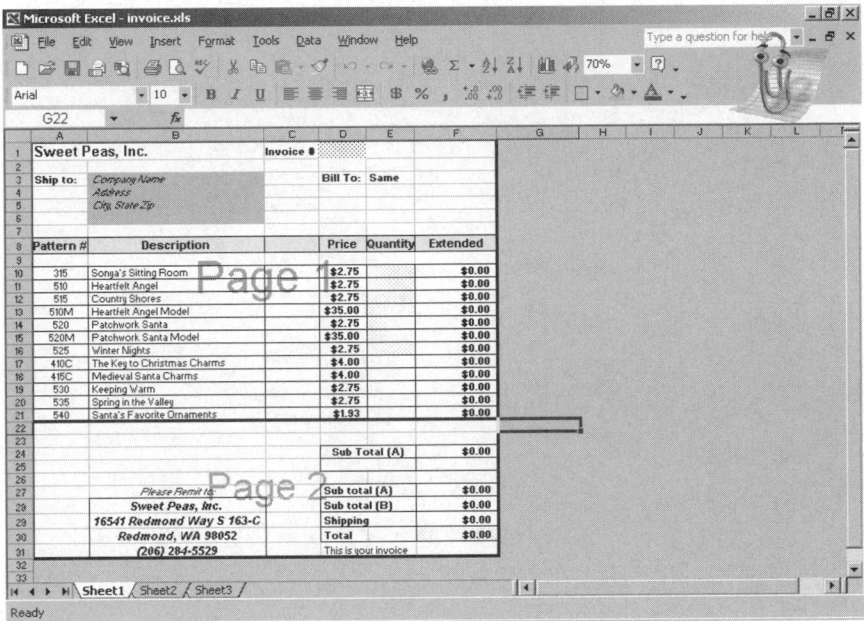

Figure 23-20. To change a page break, simply drag a break line to a new location.

> **note** Page Break Preview is an active editing mode, so you can add information to worksheet cells, select ranges, issue commands, or edit individual entries while you preview your page breaks. However, you'll probably find it easier to read the contents of worksheet cells in Normal view.

4 To change a page break marked with a bold line, drag the break line with the mouse to a new location in the worksheet. When you release the mouse button, Excel will repaginate the worksheet and display the new page break. (If you want to reverse the change, you can reinstate the old page break by simply clicking the Undo button on the Standard toolbar.)

5 When you're finished working in Page Break Preview, choose Normal from the View menu.

Power Organizing with Workbooks

Worksheets are the basic building blocks used to store information in Microsoft Excel 2002, and workbooks are the organizational tools you can use to manage your worksheets effectively. By default, each Excel workbook contains three worksheets. In this chapter you'll learn how to switch between worksheets, name worksheets, add worksheets to a workbook, delete unwanted worksheets from a workbook, and rearrange worksheets. You will also learn how to work with more than one workbook at a time, link information between worksheets and workbooks, create and manage shared workbooks on a network, and hide and protect worksheets and workbooks. When you're finished, you'll have all the tools you need to manage workbooks effectively.

Managing Worksheets

Workbooks help you organize the reports, ledgers, tables, and forms you use every day. In the early days of electronic spreadsheets, users typically created a new file for each worksheet they built. This approach worked fine for casual spreadsheet users, but experienced business users, who often worked with literally hundreds of worksheets, were soon swamped with files and folders. (If this sounds like you now, you'll like this section!)

Excel now provides the ability to create workbooks containing up to 255 worksheets. Although you're not actually required to save more than one worksheet in a workbook, this organizational feature gives you the option of collecting similar worksheets in one place. People use this capability in a variety of effective ways. For example, you can store all the annual worksheets related to product development costs (research, manufacturing, marketing, packaging, and so on) in one workbook entitled Development Costs 2001. Or you can break out the manufacturing cost estimates in one workbook, where each worksheet is a detailed cost estimate for a different product or a different estimate for the same product from a different vendor.

The value of worksheets is often apparent by the ease with which you can switch among them to print or edit information of different types. Changing worksheets is usually far easier than jumping or scrolling to locate subsections within the expanse of a single worksheet. Some workbooks, for example, have two or three sheets: the first for entering variable data, the second to present a chart or other analysis of the data, and perhaps a third that formalizes the results in a report.

In the first part of this chapter you'll learn the basic skills needed to manage worksheets in workbooks. You'll learn how to

- Switch between worksheets in a workbook
- Name your worksheets
- Delete worksheets from a workbook
- Add worksheets to a workbook
- Change the order of worksheets in a workbook
- Group worksheets for easier manipulation

Switching Between Worksheets

By default, each new Excel workbook contains three identical worksheets named Sheet1, Sheet2, and Sheet3. Each worksheet is identified by a *worksheet tab* at the bottom of the worksheet window, as shown in Figure 24-1. To switch between worksheets, you click the worksheet tab you want to display; and that worksheet then appears as the active worksheet in the workplace. To the left of the worksheet tabs are the *tab scroll buttons*, which you can use to display worksheet tabs not currently visible. Clicking the outside navigation arrows displays the first and last tabs in the workbook, and clicking the inside arrows displays tabs that aren't visible immediately to the left and right. To switch between worksheets in a workbook, follow the steps in Figure 24-1.

Naming Worksheets

The default names for worksheets—Sheet1, Sheet2, and so on—are just placeholders for more useful and intuitive names that you devise. You can name or rename a worksheet at any time by double-clicking the worksheet tab to select the title and then typing a new name. Figure 24-2 shows the two-step process. (To cancel your edit, press the Esc key.)

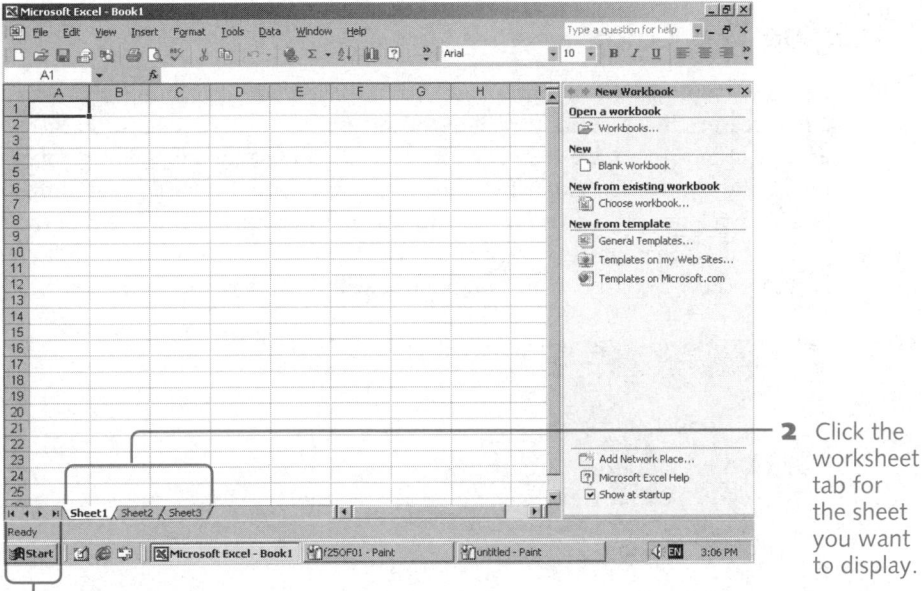

2 Click the worksheet tab for the sheet you want to display.

1 Use the tab scroll buttons (if necessary) to bring into view any worksheet tabs that may be hidden.

Figure 24-1. Use the worksheet tabs at the bottom of the window to switch between worksheets.

You can use up to 31 characters in your worksheet names (including spaces), but remember that the more characters you use, the less room you leave for other worksheet tabs. It's a good idea to strike a balance between meaningful and brief names.

You can also use a menu command to rename the worksheet that's currently visible. To do that, choose Format, Sheet, choose Rename from the submenu, and then type the new worksheet name and press Enter.

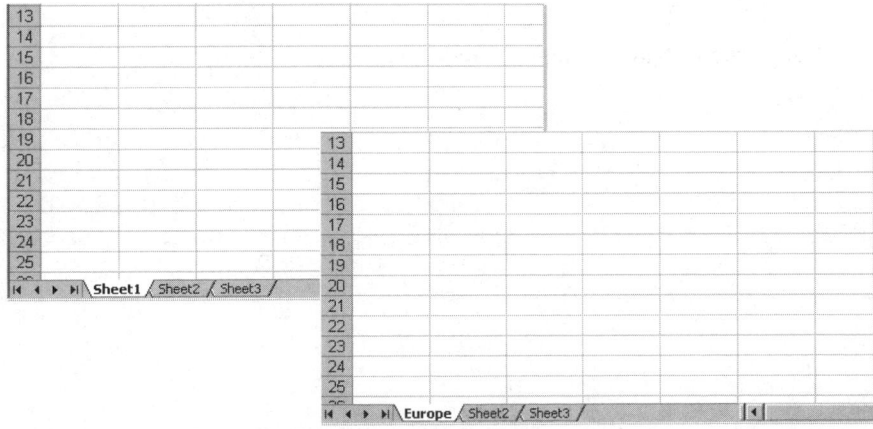

Figure 24-2. To rename a worksheet tab, double-click it and type a new name.

Changing Tab Color

Besides assigning a meaningful name to a tab, you can also change the tab color. This is a new feature that's useful for color-coding tabs for easier recognition or for indicating groups of tabs that have a similar function. To change the tab color, display the Format menu and choose Tab Color from the Sheet submenu. In the Format Tab Color dialog box shown below select a color for the tab and then click OK. Note that the tab color will be fully apparent only when you click to a different worksheet; while the worksheet is active, the tab will be white and the text will be underlined in the selected color.

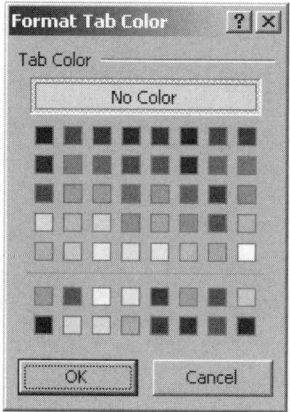

Deleting Worksheets

While each empty worksheet in a workbook takes up only about 500 bytes of disk space, if you don't plan to use all the worksheets in a workbook, you can delete the unused worksheets to save space. (You can always add new worksheets later.) To delete a worksheet, display it in the workplace window, and then choose Edit, Delete Sheet.

---

tip   **Change the Default Number of Worksheets**

By default, Excel displays three worksheets in a workbook. However, you can adjust this number by choosing Tools, Options and specifying a new number on the General tab. In the Sheets In New Workbook text box, specify the number of worksheets you want, either by typing a new number in the text box or by using the text box scroll arrows to increase or decrease the current value. You can specify any number from 1 through 255.

> **caution** Once you delete a worksheet—even if it contains several rows and columns of data—the worksheet will be permanently erased and you won't be able to undo the command.

Inserting Worksheets

Excel lets you add a new, empty worksheet to your workbook at any time by choosing the Insert, Worksheet command. When you insert a new worksheet, Excel places it before the active worksheet and numbers it consecutively; that is, the eleventh worksheet will be given the name Sheet11. Figure 24-3 shows how a new sheet will be inserted if your workbook contains three worksheets and if Europe is the active worksheet. After you insert a new worksheet, you can change its name, as described in "Naming Worksheets," page 684.

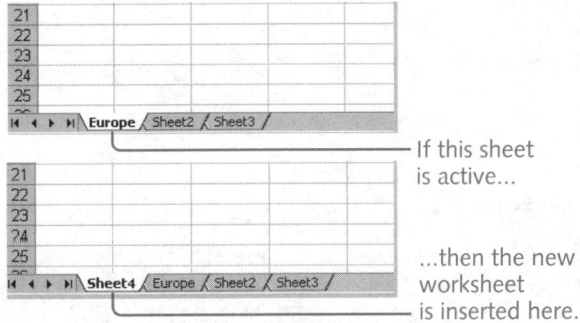

If this sheet is active...

...then the new worksheet is inserted here.

Figure 24-3. Excel inserts a new worksheet before the active worksheet in the workbook.

> **tip** If you right-click a worksheet tab, a shortcut menu appears with commands that let you accomplish common tasks with the active worksheet: deleting, renaming, copying, and the like. You can use this technique to speed up many of your workbook management tasks.

Moving or Copying Worksheets

If you don't like the placement of the worksheets you've created, you can easily move them within the workbook by using a simple drag-and-drop technique. To relocate a worksheet, click the worksheet tab you want to move, and then drag it between two other worksheet tabs. (A tiny arrow appears to help you place the worksheet.) Figure 24-4 shows how the three-step process works.

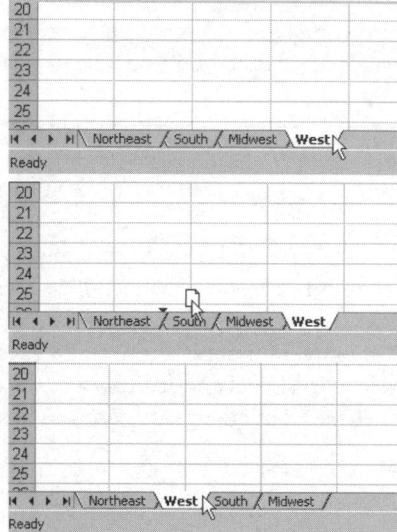

Figure 24-4. To move a worksheet, drag the worksheet tab to a new location.

InsideOut

Working with Grouped Worksheets

To specify a group of worksheets, Excel uses a technique that's relatively consistent across Microsoft Office XP applications. First, activate one sheet in the group and then hold the Ctrl key as you click the tab for each additional sheet. To select a series of consecutive worksheets, activate the first sheet, hold the Shift key, and click the tab for the last sheet. A quick way to select all the worksheets in the workbook is to point to a tab, display the shortcut menu, and then choose Select All Sheets. The word [*Group*] in the title bar indicates that you're working in group mode.

You can perform many actions on a selected group of worksheets rather than repeating the same action on each one individually. For example you can print, delete, move, or copy sheets, add headers and footers, or use many of the formatting commands on a group of sheets. To cancel the selection, click a tab that isn't in the group or select Ungroup Sheets from the shortcut menu; if all the sheets are selected, you can click any tab other than the one that's currently active.

You can copy a worksheet in a workbook by holding down the Ctrl key while you drag a tab from one location to another. This procedure creates a duplicate of the worksheet in the workbook. The name and any tab color is copied also, and a "(2)" is added to show that it's the second worksheet with that name. To remind you that you're duplicating a worksheet, the mouse pointer includes a plus (+) sign during the drag-and-drop operation.

Excel also makes it easy to move or copy a worksheet from one workbook to another. To begin, open both the source and destination workbooks. (If you want to move or copy the sheet to a new workbook, however, you don't need to open a blank work-book.) Then choose the Edit, Move Or Copy Sheet command. This command displays the dialog box shown in Figure 24-5.

Figure 24-5. To copy rather than move a worksheet, be sure the Create A Copy check box is selected after you specify the destination workbook and position.

From the first drop-down list, select the destination workbook. If you select (*new book*) for the destination, Excel inserts the sheet in an otherwise empty workbook—but it doesn't create the default number of blank sheets in addition to the moved or copied work-sheet. If you want those default blank sheets to be included, click the New Blank Work-book button from the standard toolbar before you begin the move or copy process.

After you specify the destination in the To Book list box, choose the location for the sheet in the Before Sheet list box. Excel generates the list of sheets from the worksheet names in the destination workbook. Finally, if you want to copy rather than move the worksheet to the destination workbook, select the Create A Copy check box.

Referencing Cells in Other Worksheets

When you create a workbook containing several worksheets, you will often want to ref-erence the data in one worksheet when you build a formula in another worksheet. Set-ting up a connection between worksheets is sometimes called creating a *link* in Excel terminology, although nowadays the term tends to be associated with references in one file to objects located in another.

To learn how to link worksheets together in different workbooks, see "Linking Information Between Workbooks," on page 693.

Let's consider an example. If your workbook contains a separate worksheet for each sales region in the country, you could create a summary worksheet that includes sales data from each of the supporting worksheets. This use of references to other worksheets provides an additional advantage: when you change the source worksheet, Excel updates the related information in the dependent worksheet.

The following procedure shows you how to create formulas that reference other worksheets. The sample workbook contains five worksheet tabs—Summary, Northwest, South, Midwest, and West. Four of these tabs contain regional worksheets that present quarterly sales data for each of a company's sales representatives active in the region. (The sales reps are listed individually by name.) The Summary worksheet presents an overview of the sales activity throughout the year and uses several SUM functions to calculate the quarterly totals from each of the linked worksheets. You might want to use this worksheet structure in your own workbooks.

To create formulas that calculate totals from other worksheets and place them on a single summary worksheet, follow these steps:

1 Create your regional worksheets in a workbook, or use your own data containing a similar pattern of detail-level worksheets that you want to sum up in a summary worksheet.

The following screen shows the sample worksheet named Northeast, which contains quarterly sales figures for the six sales reps active in the Northeast sales region.

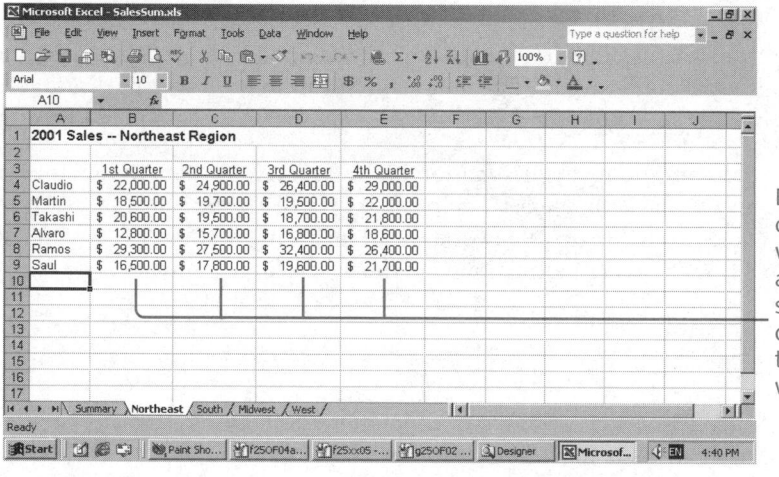

Each column of sales figures will be summed, and those sums will be displayed in the Summary worksheet.

The SalesSum.xls example is on the companion CD to this book.

2 Add a new worksheet to your workbook to display the totals from the other worksheets. (Add the worksheet by choosing Insert, Worksheet, and then change the name to *Summary* or another appropriate name.)

3 Using the SUM function, add formulas to the Summary worksheet that compute totals. Begin each formula by typing *=SUM(*.

4 To specify a range for the SUM function, click the worksheet tab you want to include in the formula, and then select the range of cells you want to use within the link. For example, to add the six sales figures from the 1st Quarter

Chapter 24

column in the Northeast worksheet, click the Northeast worksheet tab, and then select cells B4 through B9. The customized formula appears in the formula bar; the worksheet name and cell range are separated by an exclamation mark (Northeast!B4:B9).

5 Press the Enter key to complete the formula. Excel adds a closing parenthesis to complete the function.

Excel calculates the result and displays it in cell B4 of the Summary worksheet, as shown in the following illustration. The completed formula also appears in the formula bar.

Formula for cell B4 —

Sum of 1st Quarter Sales from the Northeast worksheet —

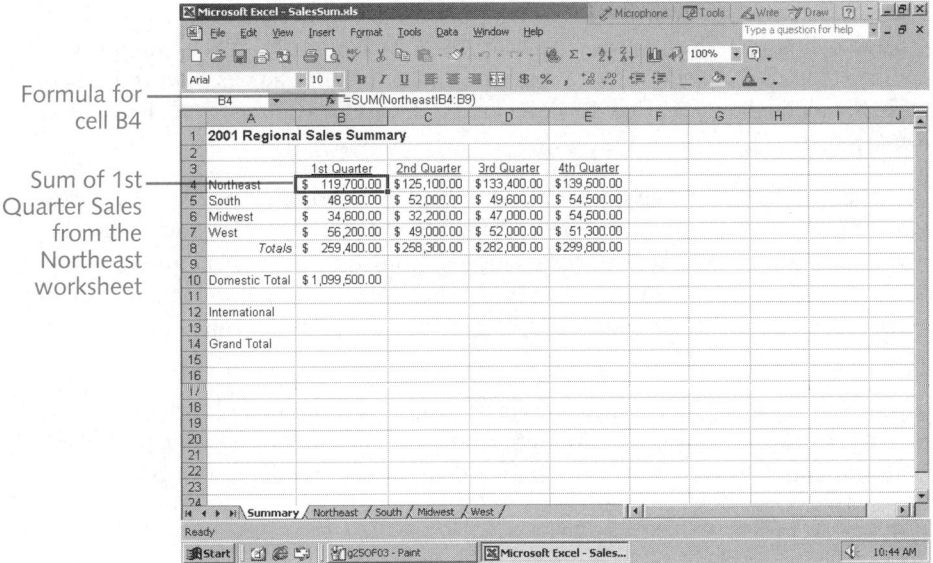

6 Repeat steps 2 through 5 to add linking formulas for the remaining summation cells.

Using More Than One Workbook

As you complete daily tasks with Excel, you'll often find it necessary to open additional workbooks to review sales figures, prepare an invoice, copy data, or complete other work. Excel allows you to load as many workbooks into memory as your system can handle. Each workbook appears in its own window and is given a separate icon on the Windows taskbar. (If you don't see separate icons for multiple open workbooks on your taskbar, choose Tools, Options, click the View tab, and choose the Windows In Taskbar option.) You can switch between workbooks by clicking the workbook icons on the taskbar or by choosing the workbook's filename from the Window menu. (Excel lists files on the Window menu in the order that you open them.) The following section shows you how to

● Switch between workbook windows

- Link information between open workbooks

- Consolidate information from a series of similar sheets

- Use multiuser workbooks in a network setting

Switching Between Workbooks

You can open additional workbooks in Excel by choosing File, Open, locating the workbook you want to open in the Open dialog box, and then double-clicking it. In this version of Excel you can also choose File, New, and then create a new workbook or open an existing workbook using the task pane. The most recently used documents are listed as links that open immediately when you click on them. When multiple workbooks are loaded, you can view them one at a time in maximized windows (the default), or side by side in the workplace. To view workbook windows side by side, choose Window, Arrange.

The Arrange dialog box includes four useful window orientation options that display different parts of the workbook: Tiled, Horizontal, Vertical, and Cascade. Figure 24-6 shows how two open workbooks are arranged if you click the Vertical option button and click OK. To switch between these open workbooks, click the workbook you want to work with. (The active workbook's title bar will be displayed using your system's Active Title Bar color settings.)

You can also switch between open workbook windows by pressing the key combination Ctrl+F6 or by choosing filenames from the Window menu. When you display the Window menu, the active workbook is identified by a check mark next to its filename.

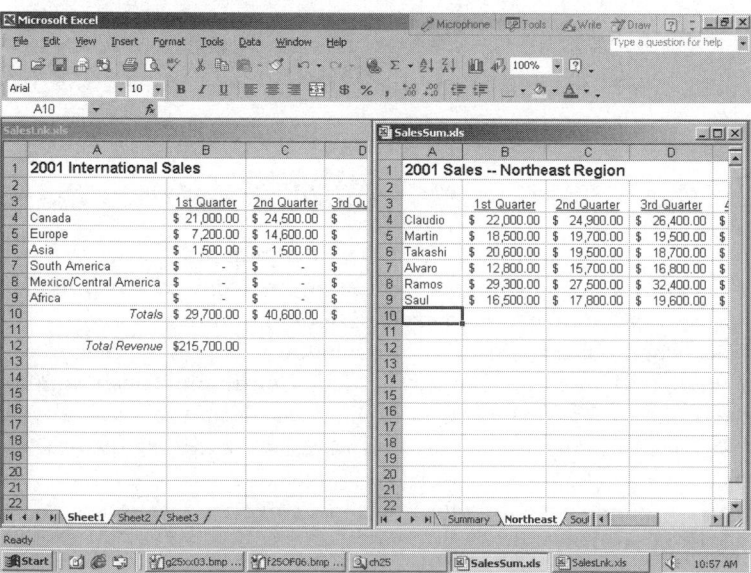

Figure 24-6. The Arrange command lets you view more than one workbook at a time.

Linking Information Between Workbooks

Earlier in this chapter you learned how to build formulas that reference other worksheets in the workbook. You can also build formulas that reference worksheets in other workbooks. Before you create the linked formula, however, you must open each of the workbooks you plan to use. The following example adds the total revenue from a workbook named SalesLnk (containing international sales data) to the domestic sales total calculated in the SalesSum workbook.

If you want to create formulas that reference other workbooks, follow these steps:

1 Open the workbooks you plan to reference in your formulas.

You can practice by opening SalesSum and SalesLnk on your companion CD. The following screen shows the sample workbook named SalesLnk, which computes the total revenue received by a company from areas outside the United States:

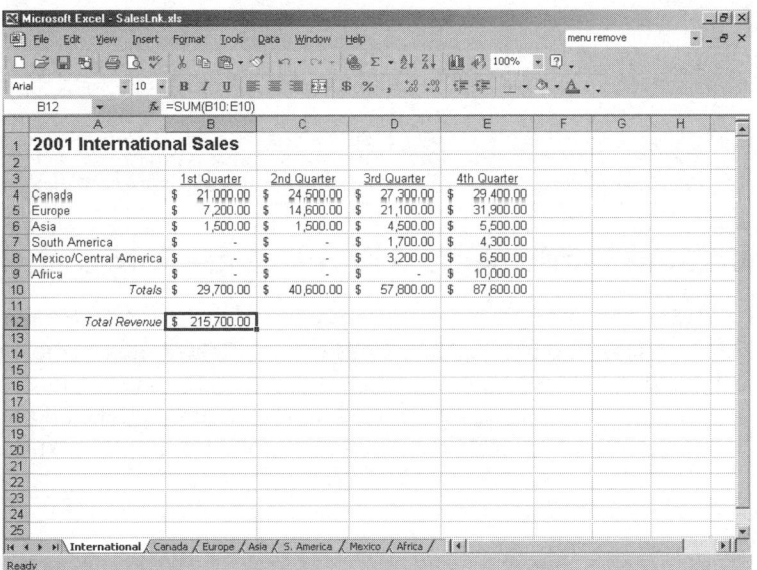

on the CD SalesLnk.xls, SalesSum.xls, and the South SalesSum workbook are on the companion CD to this book.

2 Add a formula to your worksheet that references cells in other workbooks.

For example, to copy a grand total from the International worksheet in the SalesLnk workbook to SalesSum, start in the cell in the Summary worksheet where you want to display the data, type an equal sign (=), click the SalesLnk workbook on the Windows taskbar, click the International worksheet tab, click the cell with the total you want to incorporate (B12 in this example), and press Enter. The linking formula appears in the formula bar; if you examine the formula notation, you'll find the workbook filename enclosed in square brackets, the worksheet name followed by an exclamation mark, and dollar signs ($) preceding the linked cell's column letter and row number. Your screen will look similar to this one:

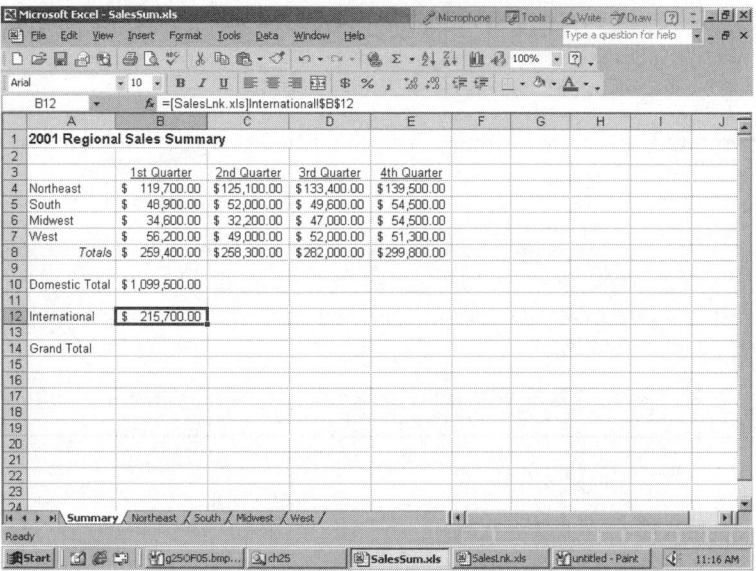

Consolidating Worksheets with Identical Formats

If you want to link together several worksheets that share a common organizational format, you can also use the Data, Consolidate command to assemble workbook information. When you consolidate worksheets, you can use one or more *statistical functions* on the cell ranges you select to obtain useful information about your data. The statistical functions available include Sum, Count, Average, Max, Min, and StdDev.

> You'll learn more about using statistical functions in Chapter 26, "Crunching Numbers with Formulas and Functions."

Consider, for example, a series of quarterly sales reports presented as a set of worksheets such as the ones shown on the next page. You can load this workbook, South SalesSum, from the companion CD. If each quarterly report has the same layout, as is the case in this sample workbook, you can create a consolidated view, to present (for example) the total annual sales for each of the sales reps.

Chapter 24

694

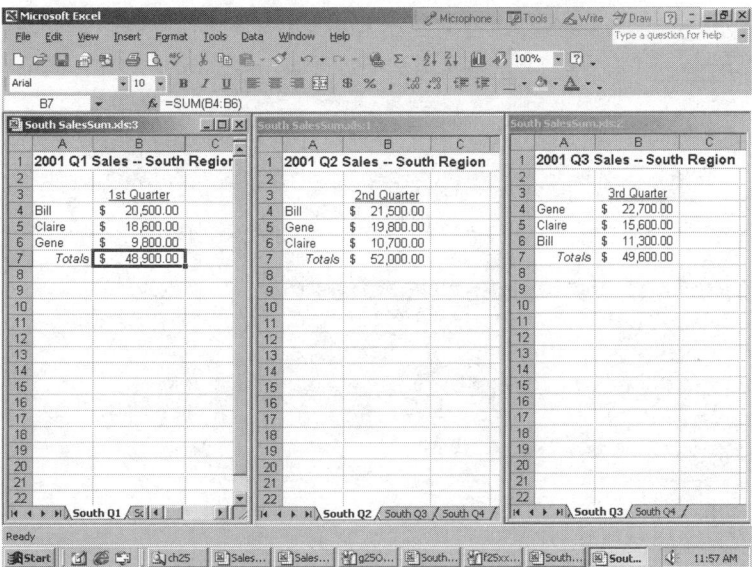

To use the Consolidation command to create a summary view, activate a blank worksheet or insert one at the front of the workbook. Rename the sheet Sales Summary. Now follow these steps:

1 Add the headings shown below to the blank worksheet.

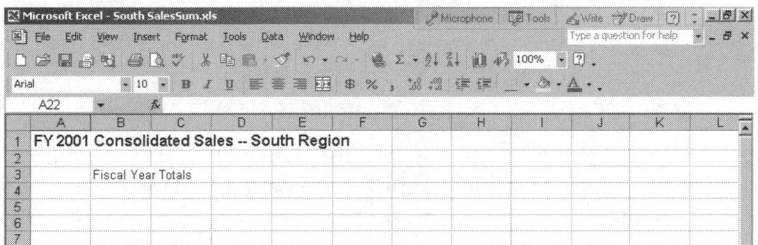

2 Make cell A4 the active cell and then choose the Consolidate command from the Data menu.

3 In the Consolidate dialog box (shown in Figure 24-7), we'll use the Sum function, which is selected by default. This function sums data from corresponding cells in each of the ranges that you specify in the next step. You could open the list box and choose another function if you wanted a different result, such as average quarterly sales.

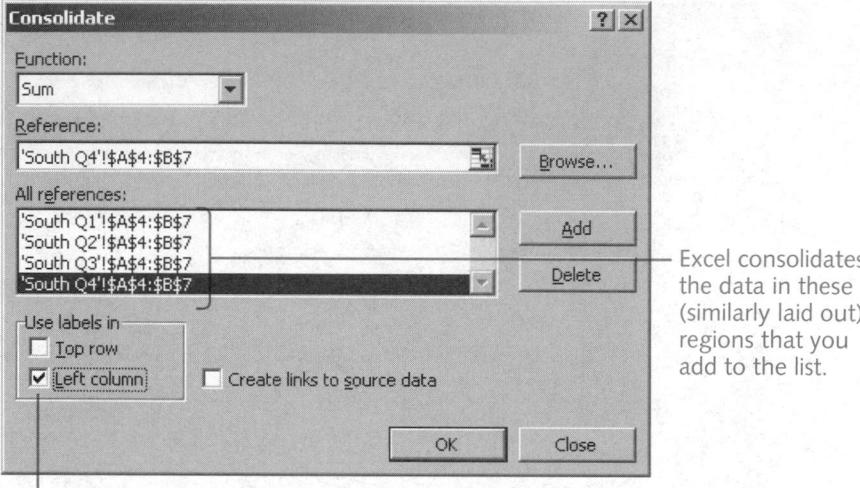

Excel consolidates the data in these (similarly laid out) regions that you add to the list.

Using column labels means that Excel associates rows with the same labels rather than those with exactly the same position.

Figure 24-7. The Consolidate command lets you identify the corresponding ranges of cells and the function to apply in the consolidation.

4 Click the Reference box and then indicate the first reference by choosing the South Q1 tab and selecting the sales reps and results (including totals) in the first two columns, cells A4:B7. Click Add to add the range to the All References list.

5 Repeat the procedure in step 4 to add the same cell range from each of the other quarterly sales worksheets. When all four ranges are specified, the dialog box appears as shown in Figure 24-7.

6 Select the Left Column button to use the labels in that column for correlating the data. Why is this important? In every quarter the sales reps are listed in order of performance, with the best sales results on top. This means that their order may change from quarter to quarter. To ensure that the sums, when consolidated, correctly follow the figures for each sales rep rather than simply totaling cell contents in corresponding locations, you specify that Excel should use the labels in the left column.

7 Press the OK button to generate the consolidation. The result is shown in the illustration at the top of the next page.

Saving a Workspace File

If you often use the same collection of workbooks in Excel, consider creating a *workspace file* to save information about which workbooks are open and how they appear on the screen. The next time you want to use the workbooks, simply open the workspace file, and each workbook will appear as it did when you last saved the workspace, including toolbars, cell selections, and other tools in the user interface. The workspace file doesn't include unsaved changes you make to your worksheets— you need to save these separately by using the Save or Save As command—but it does keep track of your open windows and worksheets, so that you can pick up right where you left off.

To save the arrangement of open workbooks in a workspace file, follow these steps:

1 Open and organize your workbooks as you would like them saved in the workspace file. (Creating a workspace file is a little like taking a picture, so get everything positioned just where you want it.)

2 Choose File, Save Workspace. The Save Workspace dialog box appears. (It works basically like a Save As dialog box.)

3 Type a name for the workspace file in the File Name text box and specify a folder location if necessary.

4 Click the Save button to save the workspace file. (You might also be prompted to save one or more of the open workbooks.)

When you're ready to open the workspace file later, locate the document and open it as you would any Excel document. Your workbooks and worksheets will appear just as you last saved them, including any cell selections you made.

Managing Shared Workbooks

If you have access to a shared folder on an attached network, you can create shared workbooks that can be opened and used by several people simultaneously. This powerful feature allows you to distribute the responsibility for group tasks, such as revolving product inventories, incoming customer orders, or corporate mailing lists. The following steps show you how to create and maintain a shared workbook.

> If your workbook contains information arranged under uniform headings, you can set it up as an Excel database. See Chapter 28, "Power Database Techniques: Lists, Filters, and Pivot Tables."

Troubleshooting

Features Unavailable in Shared Workbooks

Excel does not support a feature that you want to use in a shared workbook.

If you work on a shared workbook, you'll eventually try to make a change that Excel does not allow or support for shared data. These limitations are detailed in Excel online Help under "Features That Are Not Available in Shared Workbooks." As you'll see, this excellent Help item suggests alternatives for many situations. For example, although you can't insert or delete a block of cells, you can insert and delete entire rows and columns.

tip   **How to Use a Shared Workbook**

To use a shared workbook, you need access to a shared folder on a computer network (not on an Internet server). If you or your colleagues don't have access to such a shared folder, ask your network system administrator how to get one or how to create one on your own computer.

Creating a Shared Workbook

To create a *shared* workbook, which can be used by several users simultaneously, follow these steps:

1 Build the workbook you want to share as you normally would. Because a number of users will be working with the worksheets in your workbook, take extra care to format the contents clearly and concisely. You might also want to add cell comments that contain operation instructions and tips.

2 Choose Tools, Share Workbook. When the Share Workbook dialog box appears, click the Editing tab, as shown in the following illustration.

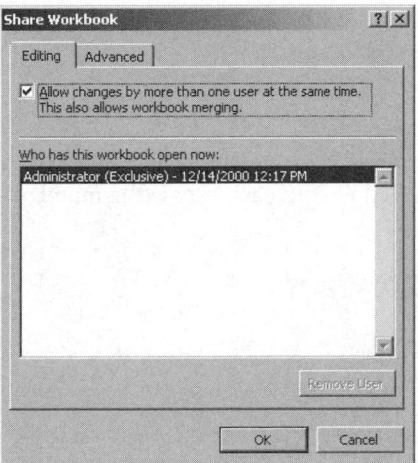

3 Select the Allow Changes check box to define the workbook as a shared workbook, and then click OK. A dialog box appears asking you if it's all right to save your workbook (a requirement if the workbook is to be shared).

4 Click OK to save the workbook.

To learn how to add comments to worksheet cells, see "Entering Comments," on page 614.

After you save the workbook, the word *Shared* appears in the title bar between brackets, indicating that you're now editing a multiuser or shared workbook. As long as the Allow Changes check box is selected on the Editing tab, you will be able to save formulas in the workbook and modify any cell formatting.

tip For the shared workbook to operate properly, your co-workers need to open the same copy of the shared workbook from a shared network folder, *not* separate ones from their own individual hard disks. Users will know the workbook is shared if the word *Shared* appears in the title bar when it's loaded in Excel.

5 Use Windows Explorer to copy the shared workbook to a shared folder on your network, and then notify your associates that the file is available for use. From now on, each time User A saves changes to the shared workbook, the changes will be copied to the shared list and any changes made by other users will be uploaded into User A's system as well. Excel handles and distributes the revisions automatically!

Monitoring a Shared Workbook

Once a shared workbook is active, you (as the owner of the file) can monitor it by choosing the Share Workbook command to find out who's using it. To see a list of the users working on the file, follow these steps:

1 Choose Tools, Share Workbook. The Share Workbook dialog box appears.

2 A list of the users working on the file appears on the Editing tab, as shown in Figure 24-8. The time displayed next to each user is the moment that user started editing the workbook.

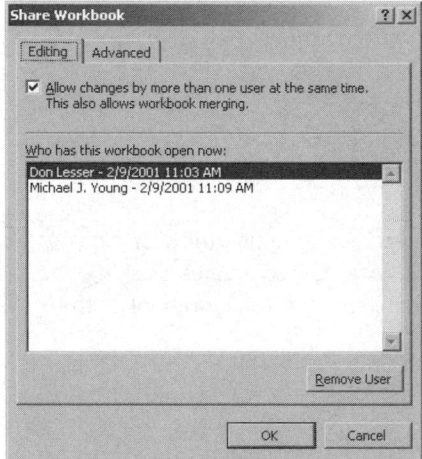

Figure 24-8. To see who is working on a shared workbook with you, use the Editing tab of the Share Workbook dialog box.

3 If you want to prohibit a user from working on the shared workbook, select the user's name and click Remove User. The user will be excluded from the editing session and won't be able to modify the shared copy of the file.

To turn off the shared workbook feature and disable multiuser editing in a workbook, choose Tools, Share Workbook, click the Editing tab, and clear the Allow Changes check box.

> **caution** As owner of a shared worksheet, you should not disable the Share Worksheet feature until each of your users has finished editing the workbook and has saved the changes, or you'll lock them out of the file. Closing a shared workbook discards any revision information in the file and prohibits users from saving their changes to the multiuser copy of the workbook, even if you reopen sharing.

Accepting or Rejecting Revisions

If users enter or change data in different cells, each change is accepted automatically and updated in everyone's workbook as each user saves his or her workbook. The changes to the workbook coming from other users are highlighted after each save. Moving the cell pointer over each highlight opens a window showing who made the change, as shown in the following illustration:

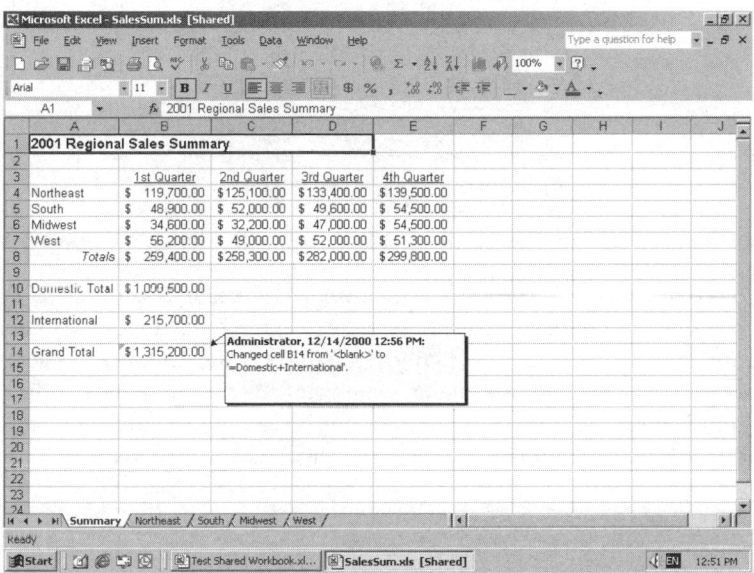

An interesting problem arises, however, when two or more users change the same cells in different ways. Whose entry for the shared workbook should Excel accept? You have two methods for resolving the conflict.

In the first method, the values in the most recently saved workbook replace the values that were entered into the cells on an earlier save. Choose this approach when you feel confident that later changes are always more accurate than earlier changes, such as when entering order numbers or tracking inventory quantities.

The second method enables the user saving the shared workbook to review the conflicting cells and decide whose changes take precedence. The user saving the workbook can accept all of his own changes, accept all of another's changes, or decide cell by cell. Choose this method if you want to review the accuracy of changes before accepting them, or if you want to give one person's changes precedence over another's. These choices and other multiuser options are provided in the Advanced tab of the Share Workbook dialog box, shown in Figure 24-9. To customize how your shared workbook handles conflicts in a multiuser environment, use these settings.

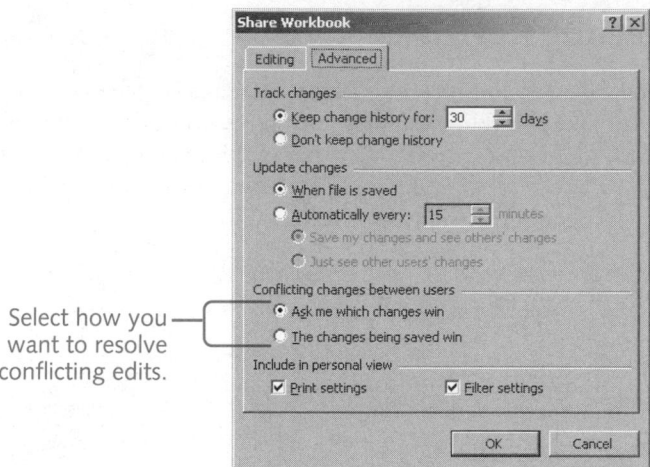

Select how you
want to resolve
conflicting edits.

Figure 24-9. You can use the Advanced tab to customize how workbooks are shared.

When you're ready to examine the list of editing activities in a shared workbook, choose Tools, Track Changes, and choose either Highlight Changes or Accept Or Reject Changes from the submenu. The Highlight Changes command displays a dialog box asking you to specify the editing changes you want Excel to highlight in the workbook, as shown in Figure 24-10. (If your workbook isn't currently shared, you can also use the Highlight Changes command to start sharing it as a workbook.)

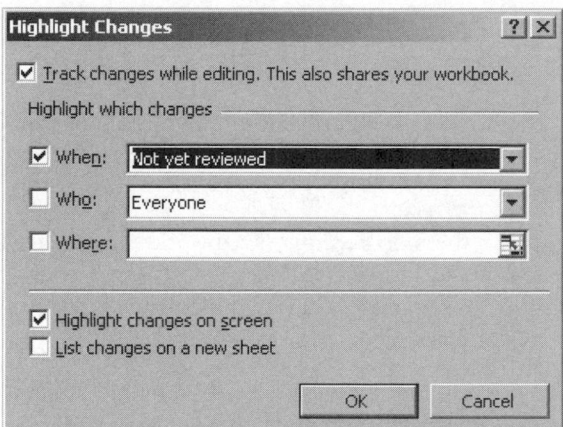

Figure 24-10. Excel automatically highlights new edits in a shared workbook. To set options, use the Highlight Changes command on the Track Changes submenu.

You can highlight changes that were made at a particular time, by a particular user, or in a particular worksheet range. When you click OK, Excel outlines in blue each modified cell in the workbook that matches your search criteria and places a small triangle in the upper left corner of each affected cell. To see how a highlighted cell was changed, place the mouse pointer over the cell, and Excel displays a comment box containing the user name, date, time, and substance of the edit.

If you want to step through the list of revisions in the workbook and either accept or reject them, use the Accept Or Reject Changes command on the Track Changes submenu. When you choose this command, Excel saves the workbook and then displays a dialog box asking for your search criteria.

As you do when you choose Highlight Changes, you specify the time, person, and location of the edits you're looking for using the drop-down list boxes in the dialog box. When you click OK, Excel displays the changes one at a time in the Accept Or Reject Changes dialog box, as shown in Figure 24-11. (If more than one user wants to modify a cell, Excel identifies each user and the edits they're requesting.)

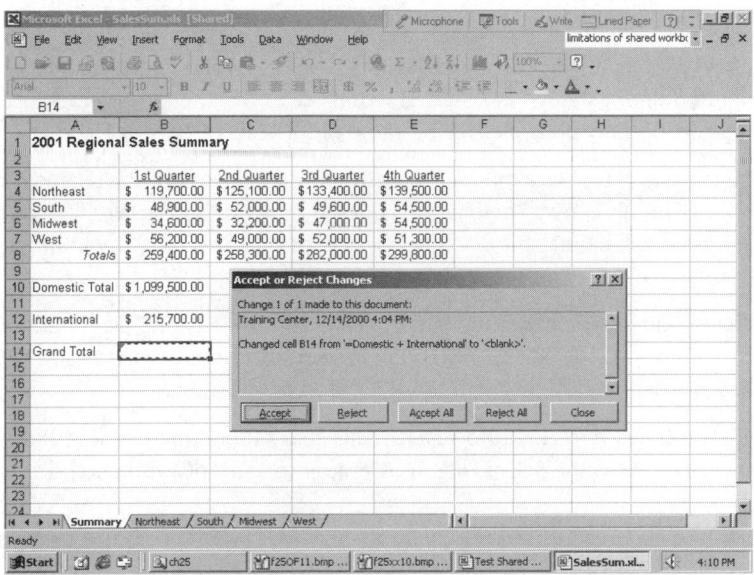

Figure 24-11. Excel tracks each edit in a shared workbook and lets you accept or reject it. If a change made by another user is inappropriate, you can discard it.

To accept an edit and store it in the shared workbook, click the Accept button. To reject the change, click the Reject button. Some cells might have more than one edit, in which case you must click the edit you want to accept. After you accept or reject an edit, Excel removes the revision highlighting from that cell.

Chapter 24

703

Merging Workbooks

Another method (less sophisticated than tracking changes) for consolidating edits to a shared workbook is to merge two copies of the workbook together using the Tools, Merge Workbooks command. Merging workbooks is a useful technique when two users are working with slightly different copies of the same file and one user wants to incorporate all the changes the other user has made.

Merging workbooks is a one-step process—you simply choose the Merge Workbooks command and the file you want to merge with the active workbook, and Excel compares the two workbooks and copies any revisions from the merge file to the active file. Changes that you've made to your copy remain, unless the second user (working on the copy) has revised those same cells.

Unlike the Accept Or Reject Changes command, however, the Merge Workbooks command doesn't give you a chance to compare or sort out the differences between the different copies. Its sole purpose is to update one copy of a workbook with another.

To merge two copies of a shared workbook, follow these steps:

1 Before you make any edits, use the Tools, Share Workbook command to identify the original file as a shared workbook. (The Merge Workbooks command works only on copies of the same file that have been marked as shared.)

2 Use the File, Save As command to create a second copy of the shared workbook. Give this copy of the file a unique name, and then deliver it to another user (who will be making the edits) by means of a network, the Internet, or a removable disk.

3 When you're ready to consolidate the changes made to the file, open your original copy of the shared workbook in Excel, and then choose Tools, Compare and Merge Workbooks to access the updated copy.

4 When prompted, click OK to save the file to disk, and then choose the copy of the workbook in the Select Files To Merge Into Current Workbook dialog box.

Troubleshooting

Merge with Caution

Your attempt to merge two workbooks produces an error.

It's easy to generate an error when you're trying to merge workbooks. The file you specify for merging must be a copy of the original file that has a unique filename. Be sure that you have the original open and the copy closed when you initiate the Merge process. The copy, like the original, must be saved as shared.

5 Click OK to merge the files. After a moment, Excel updates the original file by adding the changes from the merge file. (If there are no changes, Excel notifies you in a dialog box.) That's all there is to it!

> **tip** Remember, the Merge Workbooks command doesn't give you a chance to accept or reject changes, so use it only if you want all revisions merged into your original file.

Protecting Worksheets and Workbooks

In Chapter 23 you learned how to hide rows and columns in your worksheet from unauthorized glances. (Turn to "Hiding Rows and Columns," on page 667, if you'd like a refresher.) Excel also lets you hide complete worksheets, as described in the tip below. But for a more powerful combination of openness and control, you can apply *password protection* to a worksheet or to an entire workbook. When you guard worksheets or workbooks by requiring a password, users can open the file but they can't change the parts you've protected. If you want to share your workbooks with others while protecting them from modification, this is the feature for you.

> You can even require a password from users when they open a workbook. See "Requiring a Password for File Access," on page 709.

> **tip** **Hide Individual Worksheets**
>
> Being visible, as it turns out, is just another formatting option. To hide the active worksheet, open the Format menu and choose Hide from the Sheet submenu. Reverse the process by choosing Unhide from the Sheet submenu. Note that Excel doesn't let you hide a sheet in a workbook whose structure is protected (this detail is discussed later in this chapter).

Protecting Worksheets

To protect a worksheet in the workbook from modification, follow these steps:

1 Click the worksheet tab corresponding to the worksheet you want to protect.

2 Choose Tools, Protection, and then choose Protect Sheet from the submenu. The Protect Sheet dialog box appears, as shown in Figure 24-12.

Chapter 24

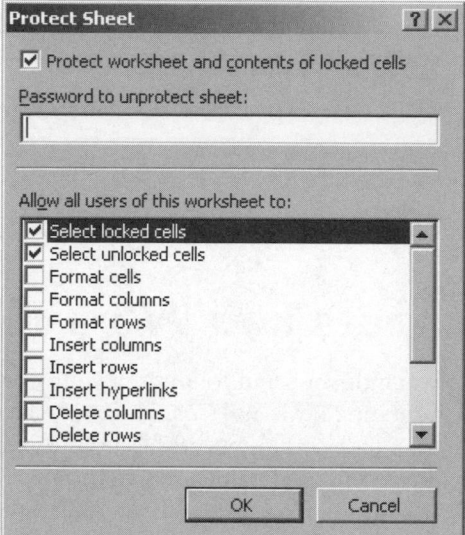

Figure 24-12. The Protect Sheet dialog box lists capabilities you might want the user to retain.

The Protect Sheet dialog box contains a password text box and a set of protection check boxes that list the ways in which you allow users to manipulate the worksheet. These range from selecting and reformatting cells to deleting entire columns and rows. By default, two boxes are checked, enabling users to select cells, both locked and unlocked. Review the options and select any types of protection you *don't* require.

Troubleshooting

Protection Unavailable

You want to protect your worksheet or workbook, but the commands for doing so are dimmed.

Note that you won't be able to use Protect Sheet or Protect Workbook on a workbook that's shared. A separate command, Protect Shared Workbook, is available to let you add change tracking, but you won't be able to assign a password until the file is unshared.

3 Type a short (optional) password in the Password To Unprotect Sheet text box and click OK. Note that Excel distinguishes uppercase letters from lowercase letters, so remember any variations you make in your password's capitalization. If you forget this password, you won't be able to unprotect the worksheet.

Use a Password (If Any) with Care

A password isn't required to protect worksheets. And most users have had the experience of concocting a clever "easy-to-remember" password only to forget it an hour later. If you're afraid you'll forget the password, set worksheet protection without entering a password: You'll preserve the worksheet from accidental entries and mistakes, and you won't risk losing the ability to modify the file. (However, a renegade user could easily disable worksheet protection and then modify your document.)

4 When Excel asks you to verify your password, type it in again (and be sure to remember it). If anyone attempts to modify this protected worksheet in the future, Excel will display the following dialog box:

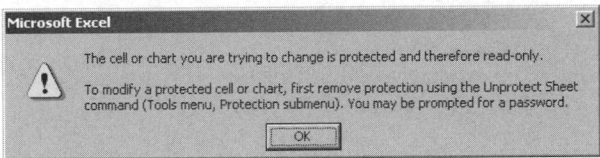

5 To remove worksheet protection later, choose Tools, Protection, and choose the Unprotect Sheet command from the submenu. If you didn't originally use a password, that's all there is to it! If you did, enter the worksheet password when the prompt appears.

Locking by Not Unlocking

If you want to let users modify some cells in your worksheet, Excel provides a rather circuitous route that requires you to think of protection as a tool and also as a format option. First, select the cells that you want to leave unprotected and clear the Locked option on the Protection tab of the Format Cells dialog box. As the note on the Protection tab explains, what you've just done has no immediate effect: locking or unlocking has no consequence until you protect the sheet. After you apply protection, all cells are locked except those that you explicitly formatted as unlocked.

This technique is useful (if confusing to apply) if you have a field for comments or an area in the worksheet that is typically used for data entry. And if you've ever wondered, protection isn't defeated if you selected the Format Cells option on the Protect Sheet dialog box. Remember, this would allow a user to format the cells on the protected sheet, which (you might have figured) enables the user to change the locked/unlocked setting and (voilà) get around protection. Nope. Excel eliminates the Protection tab from the Format Cells dialog box until the sheet is unprotected.

707

Chapter 24

Protecting Workbook Structure

To protect the structure of an entire workbook from modification (that is, to guard the names and the order of the worksheets), follow these steps:

1 Choose Tools, Protection, and then choose Protect Workbook from the submenu. The Protect Workbook dialog box appears, as shown in Figure 24-13.

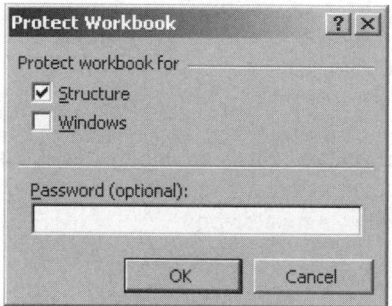

Figure 24-13. The Protect Workbook dialog box lets you protect the structure of an entire workbook from modification.

The Protect Workbook dialog box contains a password text box and two protection check boxes. When the Structure check box is selected, users can't insert, delete, hide, rename, copy, or move worksheets in the workbook, although they *can* modify data in the worksheets if worksheet protection isn't set. When the Windows check box is selected, users can't resize the windows displaying the workbook.

2 Type a password in the password text box and click OK. Note any variations you make in your password's capitalization and take steps to remember the name. You can also click OK without typing a name to set workbook protection without a password.

3 Retype the password when Excel asks for it. From this point on, no user will be able to modify the worksheet's structure without first unprotecting the workbook by choosing the Unprotect Workbook command from the Protection submenu (and supplying the password if you assigned one).

> **tip** If you work regularly in a multiuser environment, you might also enjoy the protection provided by the Protect Shared Workbook command on the Protection submenu of the Tools menu. When you enable this toggle, it prevents users from modifying a shared workbook's revision history.

Requiring a Password for File Access

If you're using Excel to track confidential information, you might want to limit access to your file by requiring a password to open it. This control goes further than protecting the content and structure of the workbook: it prevents anyone lacking an entry key (the password) from viewing your workbook at all.

> **caution**   Take care when using password protection. If you forget your password, you'll have no way to open the protected file.

To save a file that has password protection, follow these steps:

1   Create your workbook as you normally would. You don't need to hide or protect confidential parts of the file—your password protection limits access to every component.

2   Choose File, Save As to display the Save As dialog box. If you haven't already specified a filename, type one now in the File Name text box.

3   Click the Tools drop-down arrow in the upper right corner of the Save As dialog box, and then click the General Options command.

4   The Save Options dialog box appears, as shown in Figure 24-14. It contains two password protection text boxes: Password To Open, which prohibits users from opening the file unless they know the specified password, and Password To Modify, which prohibits users from saving changes to the file without knowing the password.

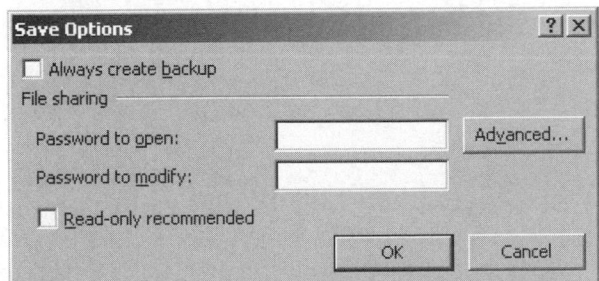

Figure 24-14.   To protect your file from unauthorized access, type a password in the Save Options dialog box.

> **tip**   If you want to recommend—but not require—that users open the file as a read-only document, select the Read-Only Recommended check box. Users who modify a read-only file can save their changes to a different filename but are blocked from overwriting the original file.

709

5 To limit access to your workbook, type a password in the Password To Open text box, and then click OK. When Excel asks for it, reenter the password to verify that you typed it as intended.

6 The next time you (or another user) tries to open the file, Excel will prompt for the password in a dialog box. To remove password protection, choose Save As, click the Options button, and remove the password from the Password To Open text box.

Chapter 25

Customizing Excel to Work the Way You Do

A short time ago one of the editors of this book moved into a new office. Our first visit to her new digs was a shock; in place of the familiar, delightfully idiosyncratic workspace stood an empty desk, a computer wrapped in packing tape, several boxes of books and supplies, and four white walls bathed in pale, phosphorescent light. However, after several hours of patient adjustment and tinkering, her simple 10' × 10' room again reflected her personality and interests. Books and treasures lined the walls, a soft lamp replaced the cold overhead lighting, and the computer displayed a familiar electronic photograph. In a way, this routine relocation reminded us of one of the many aspects we really like about Microsoft Office XP applications—they're eminently adaptable to your preferences and work style.

You can also change how toolbars and menus are presented in the Excel interface. For more information about these customization options, see "Customizing Toolbars, Menus, and Shortcut Keys," on page 205.

This chapter gives you several techniques for customizing Microsoft Excel 2002 and making it work the way you want it to. As you read about each technique, notice that some affect a particular worksheet or workbook and others apply across Excel to each workbook you open or create. You'll learn how to magnify the worksheet and save your favorite views, set your typical printing options, and configure a timesaving feature called AutoComplete. You'll also learn how to control recalculation and adjust other hidden settings by using the Options dialog box, and how to install add-in commands and wizards. When you're finished, you'll have all the techniques you need to create your own personalized Excel interface.

711

Adjusting Views

In Chapter 23, "Expert Formatting Techniques," you learned how to increase the point size in worksheet cells to make numbers and headings more readable. You can also change the magnification of the worksheet to zoom in on information or back up to view it from a distance. In this section you'll learn how to use the Zoom command to vary the magnification in your workbook, and you'll discover how to save different views using the Custom Views command.

Using the Zoom Command

The Zoom command on the View menu changes the magnification of the selected worksheets. You can enlarge the worksheet temporarily to examine a group of cells, or you can shrink the worksheet so that you can judge its overall appearance. (This change doesn't affect any of your data or formatting, and it doesn't alter the way your worksheets appear when printed.) When you choose the Zoom command, the Zoom dialog box appears, as shown in Figure 25-1.

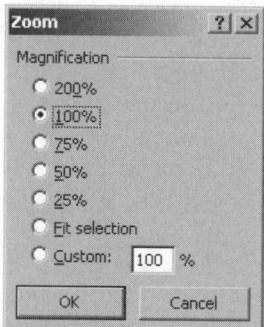

Figure 25-1. The Zoom dialog box lets you enlarge or shrink the selected worksheets without changing cell formatting.

The default worksheet magnification is 100%, or Normal view. To enlarge the worksheet to twice its normal size, select the 200% option button. To shrink the worksheet, select the 75%, 50%, or 25% option button. After you select a magnification percentage and click OK, your worksheet is resized and displayed in the workplace window. If you save it to disk, the zoomed view appears when you reopen the workbook.

Perhaps the most useful option button is Fit Selection, which adjusts the magnification to display only the cells you select before choosing the Zoom command. Its effect is illustrated in Figure 25-2. Finally, the Custom option button lets you specify an exact magnification percentage, from 10% reduction to 400% enlargement.

> **note** The size of displayed text in Normal view is variable, of course. It depends on the resolution of the image on your monitor. You can adjust the screen size by pointing to Settings on the Start menu and choosing the Control Panel. Then double-click the Display icon, click the Settings tab and adjust the slider control for Screen Area to the left or right.

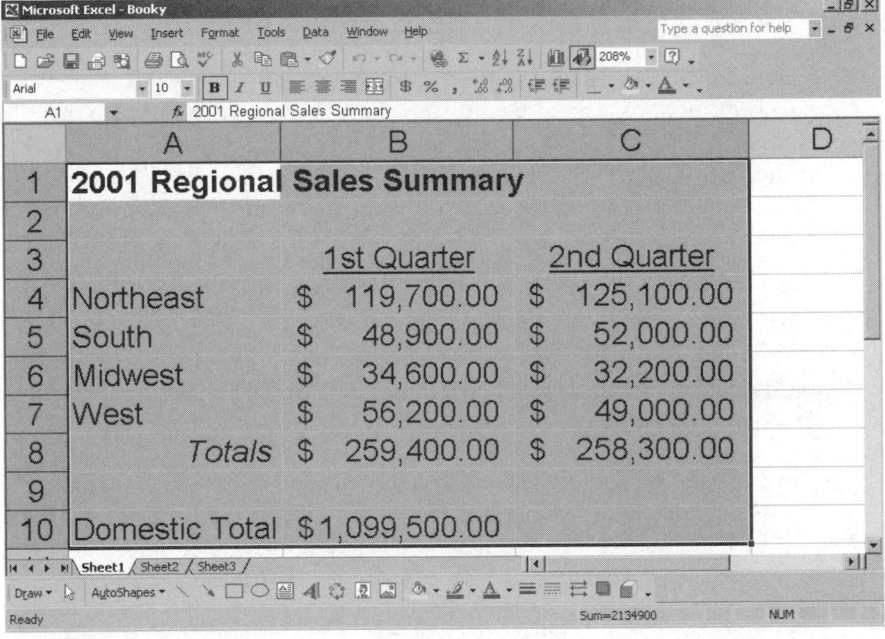

Figure 25-2. The Fit Selection option button zooms the worksheet to show only the selected cells. Before we chose the Zoom command, we selected cells A1 through C10.

The Zoom control on Excel's Standard toolbar also gives you access to many of the magnification options in the Zoom dialog box. To use the Zoom control, follow these steps:

1 If you plan to magnify your worksheet based on a selection, highlight a range of cells in the worksheet. If you want to magnify several worksheets in the workbook, hold down Ctrl and click the worksheet tabs you want resized.

2 Click the Zoom control. Your toolbar will look similar to the one shown here:

3 Select the magnification option you want. Excel resizes the selected worksheets.

> **tip** Not all the worksheets in a workbook need to be viewed at the same magnification. Occasionally, you might want to vary how your worksheets appear within the workbook.

Saving Views Using the Custom Views Command

If you find you like rotating between two or three different views when you work in your workbook, you can save your views to disk and switch between them freely by using the Custom Views command on the View menu. Custom Views is a replacement for the View Manager add-in available in previous versions of Excel. Note, however, that Custom Views are not saved when you convert a file to XML (Extensible Markup Language) using the Save As command and that the Custom Views will be deleted from your workbook.

When you save a view, you give it a name, and Excel records the display options, window settings, printing options, and current selection in your worksheet. You can quickly switch back and forth between saved views. To save a view using the Custom Views command, follow these steps:

1 Set the view and display settings you want to save as a custom view. For example, set the magnification of the worksheet, click a cell to make it the current selection each time you use the view, hide columns that are unnecessary for a given update task, or resize the workplace window.

2 Choose View, Custom Views. The Custom Views dialog box opens, and any custom views you've previously defined appear in the list box.

3 Click the Add button. You'll see the Add View dialog box shown here:

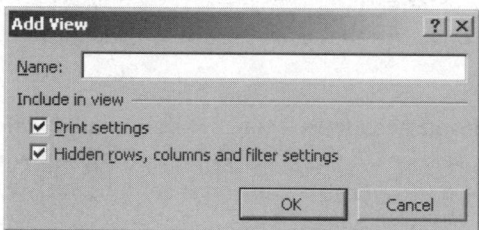

4 Type a descriptive name for your worksheet view, such as *Sales Update*, and then click OK. Excel saves your custom view and stores it in the current worksheet. To display a custom view later, open the workbook, click the worksheet tab containing the named view, and choose Views, Custom Views. The Custom Views dialog box appears, as shown here:

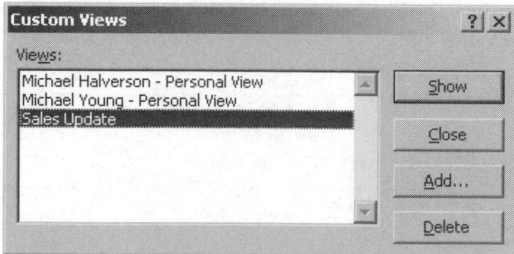

5 Double-click the view you want to show. The dialog box closes and the worksheet adjusts to your custom settings.

InsideOut

Selecting the Correct Worksheet

Each worksheet in a workbook contains different named views, including the default or personal view associated with each registered user of the product. (Be sure to click only one worksheet before you select Custom Views—if more than one worksheet is selected, the Custom Views command won't be available.) To delete a custom view, select the view in the Custom Views dialog box, and then click Delete.

Setting Printing Options

Few changes to a workbook turn out to be as noticeable as the options you select before printing. Using the Page Setup command on the File menu, you can control the orientation of your page, the width of your margins, the text or pictures placed in headers and footers, and the presence of extra elements such as gridlines and cell notes. The Page Setup dialog box contains four tabs (Page, Margins, Header/Footer, and Sheet) that control how worksheets are printed. We'll cover each tab in this section.

Controlling Page Orientation

To customize your printing options, choose File, Page Setup. The Page tab, shown in Figure 25-3 on page 716, lets you control orientation and other options related to the physical page you will be printing on. Orientation governs the direction in which your worksheet appears on the printed page. Portrait, the default, is a vertical orientation designed for worksheets that are longer than they are wide. If your worksheet is too wide to fit on one page in this orientation, which is often the case, choose the Landscape option to orient your document horizontally.

The Scaling options let you reduce or enlarge your worksheet so that it fits in the specified number of pages. The percentage you enter in the Adjust To text box is similar to the percentage you specify when you create custom views using the Custom Views command. For a description, see "Saving Views Using the Custom Views Command," on page 714. In this case, however, the scaling affects the printed page, not the view on your screen.

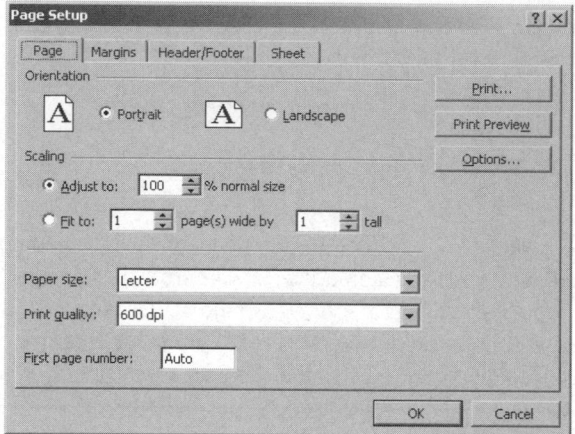

Figure 25-3. The Page tab lets you adjust page orientation and other paper options.

The Paper Size and Print Quality options let you specify a custom paper size and printing resolution. These options are drawn from the settings of your selected Microsoft Windows–based printer. To set the unique attributes of your printer, click the Options button in the Page Setup dialog box and make your changes in the dialog box tabs.

Adjusting the Margins

The Margins tab of the Page Setup dialog box allows you to adjust the margins in your workbook (see Figure 25-4). Typical margin settings are 1 inch for the top and bottom, and 0.75 inch for the left and right. As you change the margins, Excel shows you in the preview window which margin in your document is affected. Customizing the margin settings is especially useful if you're printing on letterhead paper or other sheets that contain graphics or text you don't want to overprint.

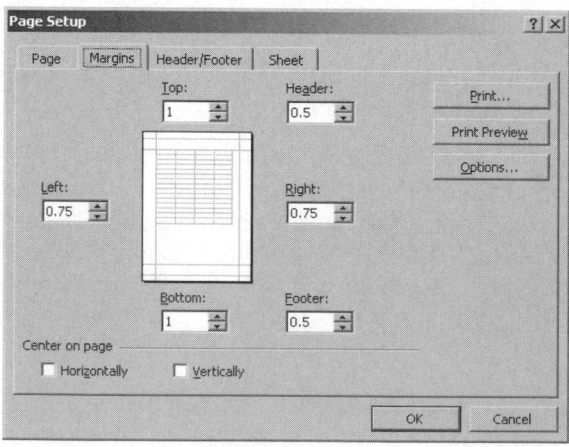

Figure 25-4. The Margins tab gives you control over the placement of your worksheet relative to the edges of the paper you print it on.

If you want to center your worksheet between the margin settings, select the Horizontally check box at the bottom of the Margins tab to center the printout from left to right; select the Vertically check box to center the printout from top to bottom.

Adding Headers and Footers

The Header/Footer tab of the Page Setup dialog box (shown in Figure 25-5) lets you add a header or a footer to your worksheet when it prints. Headers and footers typically contain reference information about a document, such as the worksheet name, the time or date, or the current page number. Excel permits you to pick headers and footers from a predefined list in the Header/Footer tab, or you can create your own custom entries by clicking the Custom Header or Custom Footer buttons. As an enhancement, this version of Excel offers the option of inserting and formatting a picture as part of a custom header or footer.

> **tip**   You can display the Page Setup dialog box by choosing Page Setup on the File menu—or you can choose View, Header And Footer.

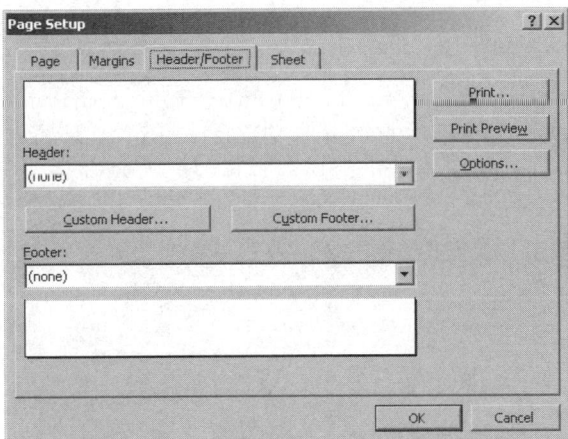

Figure 25-5.   The Header/Footer tab lets you choose a header or footer from a predefined list or create your own version.

To choose predefined headers and footers from the Page Setup dialog box, complete the following steps:

1   Choose File, Page Setup. When the Page Setup dialog box opens, click the Header/Footer tab.

2   To pick a new header, click the Header list box, and choose one of the formats listed. The first format—(None)—removes the header. Note that commas between items separate the header or footer components, which are aligned to the left, center, and right margins.

717

When you select a format (and release the mouse button), the header is shown in the preview window above the list box.

3 To pick a new footer, click the Footer drop-down list box, and choose one of the formats listed. Again, the (None) option removes the footer from the document.

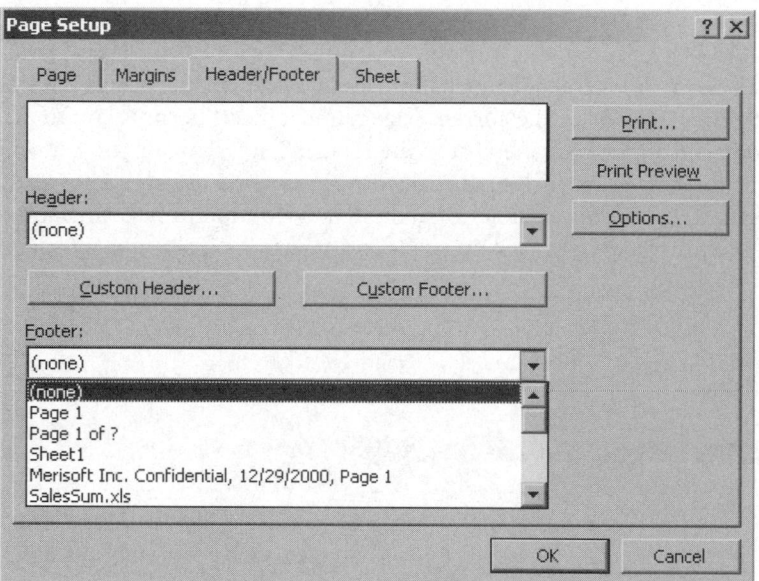

After you set headers and footers, your screen should resemble the following:

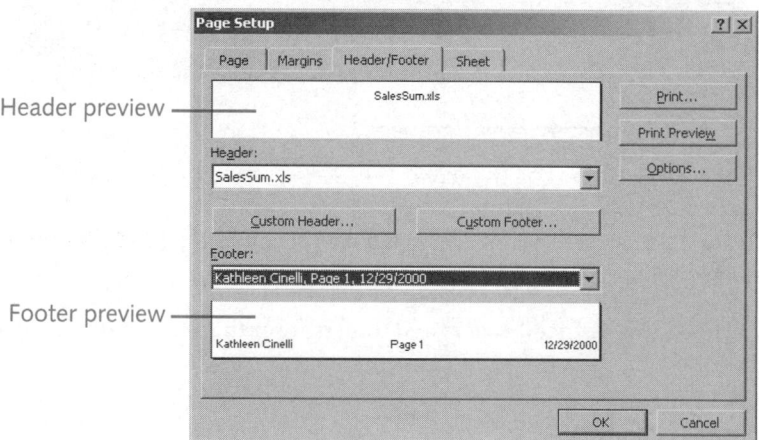

4 When you're finished, click OK. The specified headers and footers appear on each page of your document when you print it.

> **tip** To remove all headers and footers from a document, select the (None) option in both the Header and Footer drop-down list boxes.

If you don't like the predefined headers and footers, you can create your own by clicking the Custom Header and Custom Footer buttons in the Header/Footer tab. To do that, complete the following steps:

1 Choose File, Page Setup. When the Page Setup dialog box opens, click the Header/Footer tab.

2 To create a custom header, click the Custom Header button. The following dialog box appears:

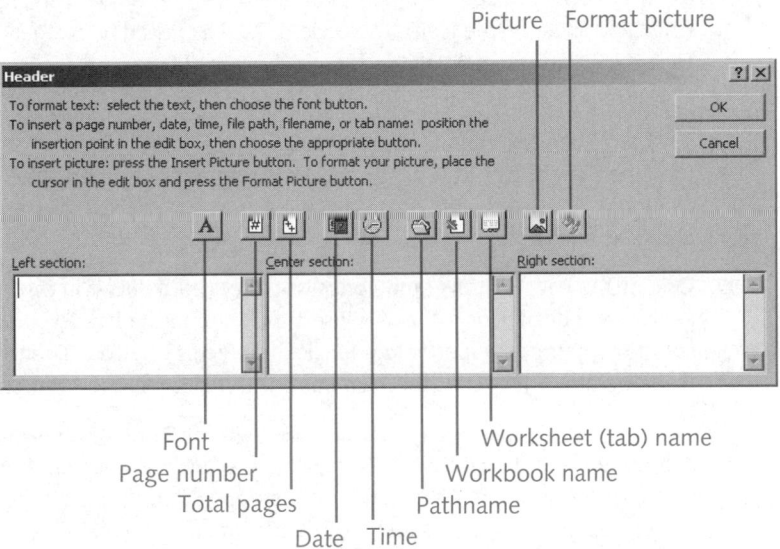

The Header dialog box lets you specify your header in three sections: left, center, and right.

3 Click in one of the sections, and then type the text you want.

InsideOut

Customizing Default Printer Options

The options in the Page Setup dialog box affect the current worksheet. When you save your workbook, the printer options are saved with it, but the default values are used whenever you create a new workbook with the standard Workbook template. Excel doesn't exactly invite you to open this Workbook template to modify it—say, with your own preferred header or footer—but you can do the next best thing. Open a new document with the Workbook template; make changes that reflect your preferences for view, toolbars, headers and footers, margins, orientation, and the like; and then save the document as a template, calling it perhaps My Blank Workbook.xlt. Select this template when you create a new document using the File, New command.

You can supplement the text you type by clicking any of the special buttons to enter codes in your document. For example, if you click the eighth button (the Worksheet Name icon), the code &[Tab] is placed in the header. This is Excel's special formatting code for inserting the name of the current worksheet of your workbook at this location in the header.

4 To change the text formatting, select the portion you want to format and click the Font button (the first one). Selecting and formatting the code for an element (such as &[Tab]) causes Excel to format the text that the code generates at print time.

5 One of the new buttons (and codes) for Excel 2002 lets you insert a picture as part of a header or footer. To insert a picture in the header, place the cursor in the desired header field and click the Picture button. Then browse the file structure to highlight the filename for the picture, and then choose Insert.

6 After you insert a picture, the Format Picture button is active, enabling you to adjust the picture's size, orientation, cropping, and print effects. Place (or leave) the cursor in the header field that contains the picture code and click the Format Picture button.

The Format Picture dialog box has two tabs. The first, the Size tab, lets you resize the picture: the entire image is sized to fit the dimensions you specify. Don't cancel the Lock Aspect Ratio unless you want the picture to be distorted as it's resized. After you decide on the proper size for the image, go to the second tab, the Picture tab. Here you have settings for cropping and other effects. Cropping (as opposed to sizing) eliminates part of the picture. Figure 25-6 shows the Picture tab.

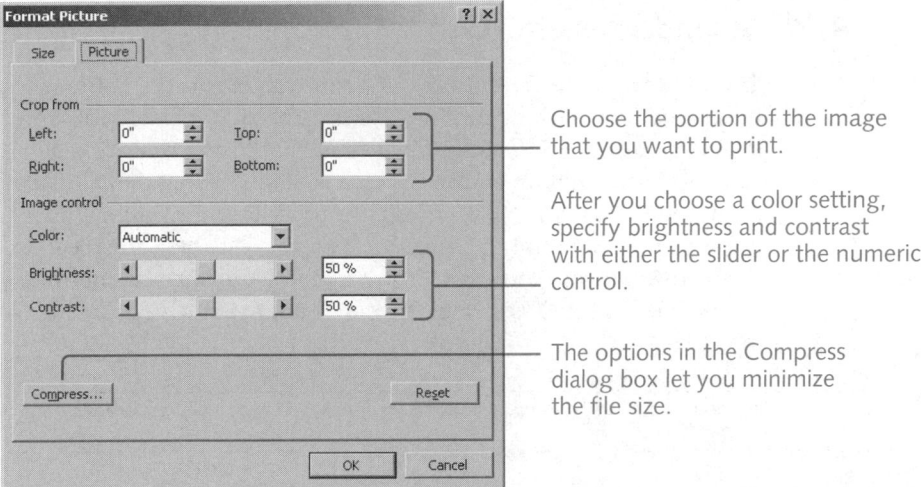

Choose the portion of the image that you want to print.

After you choose a color setting, specify brightness and contrast with either the slider or the numeric control.

The options in the Compress dialog box let you minimize the file size.

Figure 25-6. The Picture tab provides a number of ways to fine-tune a graphic for presentation in the header or footer.

7 Click the Compress button if you want Excel to save the embedded picture in ways that optimize the file size. This might mean matching the saved resolution to the printer, discarding the cropped regions from the file, and so forth.

When you're finished with the header, click OK to view the customized header in the preview window. If you don't like the results, repeat the above steps and make further changes. Click OK to return to the Format Picture dialog box, then click OK again to return to the Custom Header/Footer dialog box.

> **tip** If you want to include an ampersand in header or footer text, be aware that you'll need to type two of them, like this: &&. Excel treats the first ampersand as a control character to initiate special formatting codes. Also, you cannot format text in headers and footers for color. A possible workaround is to use print titles.

That's the procedure. If you want to create a custom footer, click the Custom Footer button and follow steps 3 through 7 as you would for creating a custom header. Use the Print Preview button to see the entire page; this is especially helpful if you insert a picture that's larger than the preview window in the dialog box. (If you do this, use the Setup button to return to the Page Setup dialog box.) When your header and footer are the way you want them, click OK.

> **tip** To create multiline headers or footers, press Enter at the end of the line in the section portion of the Header or the Footer dialog box.

Adding Gridlines and Other Options

The Sheet tab of the Page Setup dialog box (see Figure 25-7) lets you include visual or interpretive aids such as gridlines, comments, and repeating row and column headings in your printout. *Gridlines* are the dividing lines you normally see on your screen that run down each column and across each row, identifying the cells in the worksheet. To print gridlines with your worksheet, simply select the Gridlines check box in the Print category. *Cell comments* are special notes you create by using the Comments command on the Insert menu. You can specify how they're printed by choosing a selection in the Comments list box. The default (None) is not to print any comments the worksheet might contain.

> To learn more about using comments in your worksheet, see "Entering Comments," on page 614.

> **tip** To remove gridlines from your screen, choose Tools, Options, click the View tab, and clear the Gridlines check box. To print only certain gridlines, outline cells using the Borders tab in the Format Cells dialog box, as discussed in Chapter 23, "Expert Formatting Techniques," on page 649.

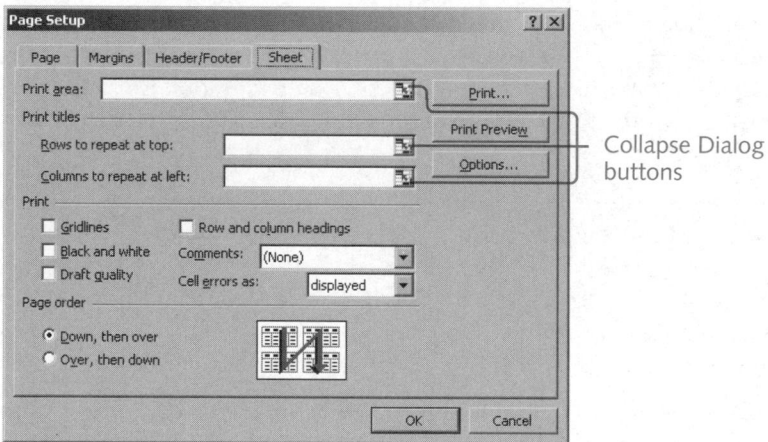

Figure 25-7. The Sheet tab lets you include extras such as gridlines and cell comments in your printout.

Two other useful features in the Sheet tab are the Print Area and Print Titles text boxes. Both these features let you select ranges for printing. In the Print Area text box, you specify the worksheet range that will be printed. In the two Print Titles text boxes, you can choose to repeat either row or column headings (or both) on multipage printouts.

Specifying a Print Area

To use the Print Area feature, follow these steps:

1 Choose File, Page Setup.

2 When the Page Setup dialog box opens, click the Sheet tab.

3 Click the Collapse Dialog Box button at the right edge of the Print Area text box. The dialog box temporarily shrinks to enable you to see your worksheet. If it still obscures your view, drag its title bar to move it out of the way.

4 Select the cells you want to print in the worksheet.

As you select the cells, a marquee appears around the range, a pop-up box shows the number of rows and columns you're selecting, and a description of the cells appears in the Print Area text box, as shown here:

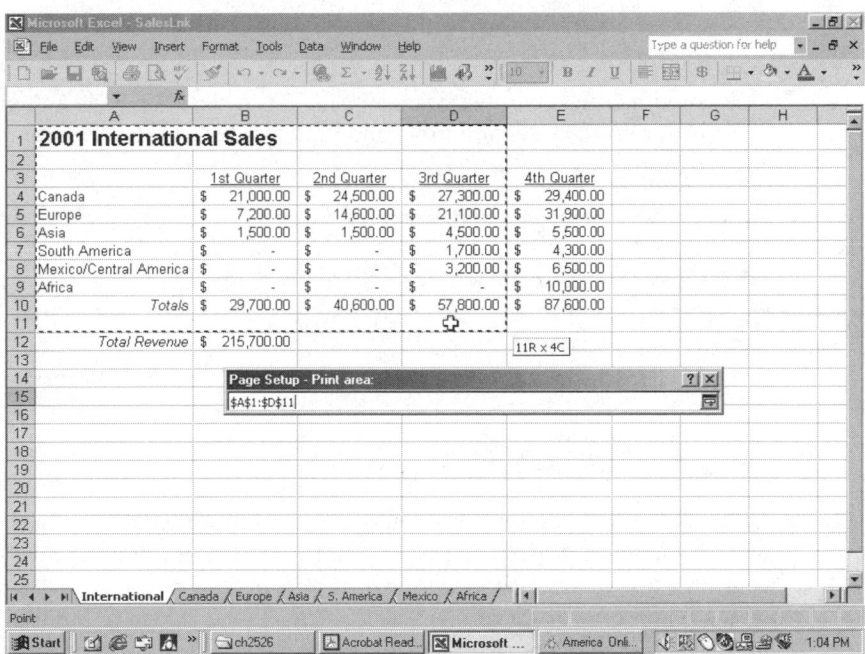

5 When you've selected the cells you want, click the Collapse Dialog Box button again.

6 After making any other changes, click the Print button, and then click OK in the Print dialog box to print the cells you selected.

> **tip** To delete a print area or to choose a different one (without changing your data), click the Sheet tab and delete the cell range in the Print Area text box. Leave it blank or draw a new range on your worksheet.

Repeating Row or Column Headings

To repeat row or column headings (or both) on each printed page of a long (or wide) worksheet, follow these steps:

1 Choose File, Page Setup.

2 When the Page Setup dialog box opens, click the Sheet tab.

3 Click one of the Collapse Dialog Box buttons under the Print Titles heading to select repeating rows or repeating columns.

4 Select the rows or columns you want to have repeated on each page. Excel highlights the entire rows or columns you select by surrounding them with a marquee.

5 Click the Collapse Dialog Box again to complete your selection.

6 You can repeat steps 3–5 if you want to repeat both rows and columns on your printed worksheet.

7 After making any other changes, click OK to close the Page Setup dialog box, or click the Print button, and then click OK in the Print dialog box to print the worksheet.

> **tip** You can verify how your print options look by clicking the Print Preview button in the Page Setup dialog box or by choosing File, Print Preview. This allows you to decide whether to make cosmetic adjustments and ensures that you've chosen the portion of the worksheet you want.

Using Multiple Panes

In the last section you saw how you can repeat rows and columns when you print a worksheet, which is useful when you want to see the headings or refer to a summary column while you review a multipage document. You can achieve the same convenience when you edit or review a worksheet on your screen by splitting the worksheet into multiple panes. The panes let you see different parts of a worksheet at the same time.

Excel saves the pane divisions that you create as part of the worksheet. If you don't want to save them with the workbook, you might save them as an attribute of a custom view.

Splitting a Worksheet into Panes

To split a sheet, first highlight a cell in the row or column to the right of or below the pane division that you want to establish. Next, point with your mouse to one of the *split boxes,* inconspicuous rectangles in the scroll bars that are located above the up scroll arrow and to the right of the right scroll arrow. When your mouse pointer is located on a split box, it changes to a double line with opposing arrows, as shown in Figure 25-8.

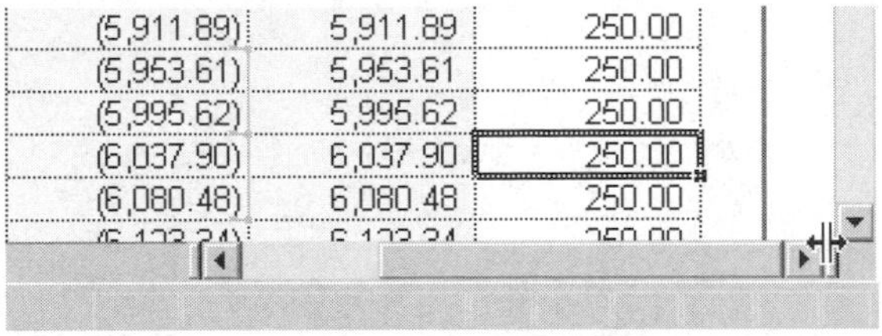

Figure 25-8. The mouse pointer appears as a double-headed arrow when you place it over the split box. Drag the box or double-click to create a new pane.

> **note** When you split a sheet, Excel doesn't prevent you from scrolling in one pane to the same rows or columns that are displayed in another pane. This can be confusing when you find repetition on the screen, such as a duplicate column A or row 1. Freezing panes prevents this duplication, as you'll learn in the next section.

Double-click a split box to establish two panes at the selected cell. The split box on the horizontal scroll bar creates a vertical split; the split box on the vertical scroll bar creates a horizontal split. You can also drag the split box to specify a dividing line between two panes. Using both split boxes (or using the Window, Split command), you can create four separate panes in a worksheet. When you're ready to remove a split, double-click the pane divider or choose Window, Remove Split.

Freezing Panes in a Worksheet

Freezing a pane is a variation on splitting panes: columns or rows to the left of or above a certain line remain visible while the rest of the worksheet scrolls indefinitely. It's a useful feature when you're working on a large database and want to keep the row headings (field names) visible as you scroll through the rows (records). Alternatively (or additionally), you can freeze the first column or two to keep a key field visible as you scroll to the right.

To freeze a pane, select the entire row or column immediately below or to the right of the region to be frozen and choose Window, Freeze Panes. Select a single cell, as shown in Figure 25-9, to freeze both the rows above and the columns to the left of the cell.

Scrolling a frozen pane is limited until you unfreeze the pane. To do so, choose Window, Unfreeze Pane.

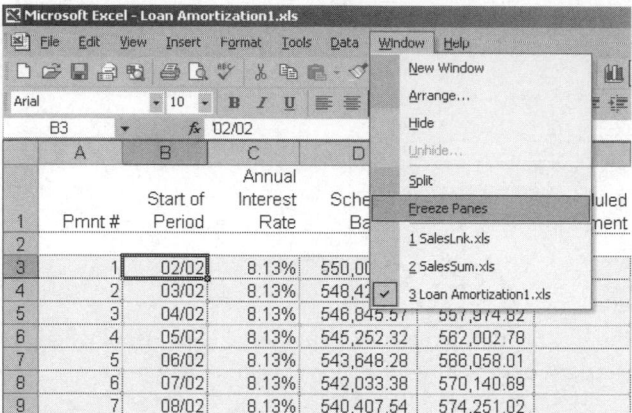

Figure 25-9. Select cell B3 and then choose Freeze Panes from the Window menu to freeze column A and rows 1 and 2.

Customizing Excel Using the Options Dialog Box

To change the way Excel looks and works, experiment with the customization choices in the Options dialog box shown in Figure 25-10. As you do in Word, you display the Options dialog box by choosing Tools, Options. The Options dialog box contains tabs that control virtually every aspect of the Excel interface. Although some tabs customize features that you might be unfamiliar with, such as the settings that help you transfer data from other spreadsheet programs, you can often learn a lot about how Excel works just by browsing through the tabs in this dialog box. In this section you'll experiment with the following options:

- Formula calculation settings, such as manual recalculation and updating remote references

- Worksheet appearance options, such as scroll bars and colors

- Editing options, such as drag-and-drop settings and default decimal places

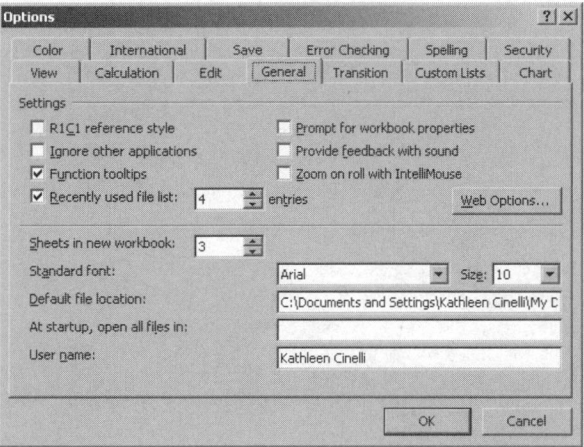

Figure 25-10. The Options dialog box lets you customize many of Excel's commands and options. The General tab controls basic options such as the standard font.

Controlling Calculation

When you enter a formula, Excel automatically computes the result or recalculates. Most of the time you'll want Excel to recalculate automatically when you modify cells that are included in formulas—it makes sense to keep your numbers up to date. But occasionally you'll want to configure Excel so that it recalculates only at your command. For example, you might want to refer to the previous result of a calculation while you enter new values in a worksheet. Or you might want to disable recalculation temporarily if you're entering several complex formulas in a worksheet, because lengthy calculations can take some time to finish.

To customize formula calculation in your worksheet, choose Tools, Options, and then click the Calculation tab of the Options dialog box. You will see the dialog box shown in Figure 25-11, on page 728.

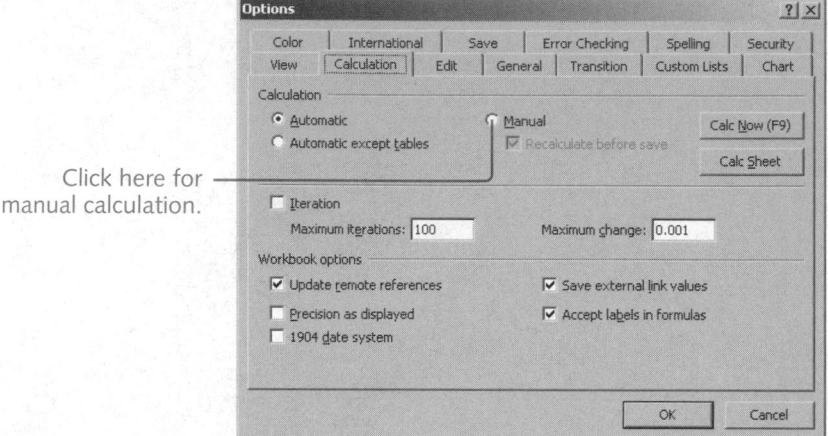

Click here for manual calculation.

Figure 25-11. To control recalculation in a worksheet, click the Calculation tab.

For manual calculation, select the Manual option button in the Calculation area, and then click OK. From this point on, Excel recalculates formulas only when you enter or edit them, when you press F9 to calculate manually, or when you return to the Calculation tab and click the Calc Now (F9) button. If you're disabling automatic recalculation, you might also want to disable automatic updating from other applications linked to your worksheet. To remove this option, clear the Update Remote References check box in the Workbook Options portion of the Calculation tab, and Excel won't update links that rely on other programs for data.

tip Remember to select the Automatic option in the Calculation area and to select the Update Remote References check box when you're finished entering data. Otherwise your workbook might display out-of-date information and present incorrect results.

Customizing Worksheet Appearance

You've already learned how to add toolbars to your workspace and change the layout of workbook windows. Using the View tab in the Options dialog box, you can further adjust your worksheet's appearance. The View tab includes option buttons and check boxes that enable and disable several visual characteristics, as shown in Figure 25-12. If you prefer not to have the task pane visible when you launch Excel, for example, clear the Startup Task Pane check box. Or you can remove the formula bar and status bar from the screen, giving you more real estate for your worksheet, by clearing the Formula Bar and Status Bar check boxes. If you don't like the red triangle that signifies that a comment has been placed in a cell, you can choose None in the Comments category. The red indicators disappear, but the comments remain.

For a refresher course on using toolbars and working with document windows, see Chapter 4, "Working with Office XP Applications, Documents, and Program Windows."

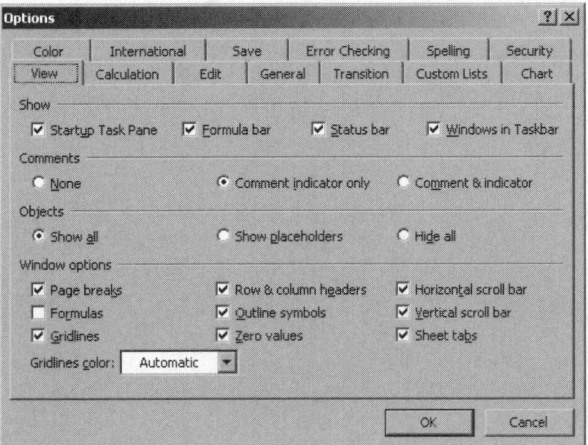

Figure 25-12. The View tab controls how your worksheet appears on the screen.

You might also find it useful to examine the selections in the Window Options category of the View tab. You can use these options to choose whether to view automatic page breaks, gridlines (you can also alter their color), scroll bars, and other visual qualities of your worksheet. When you're finished customizing your worksheet's appearance, click OK to close the Options dialog box.

Customizing Editing Options

If you want to change how Excel responds to your editing instructions, you can modify several special settings, including the way the drag-and-drop technique works, the way Excel responds to the Enter key, and the action the AutoComplete feature takes. Figure 25-13, on page 730, shows the Edit tab in the Options dialog box, which controls these customizations and more.

To disable direct cell editing—the option that lets you move the insertion point into cells when you double-click a cell—cancel the Edit Directly In Cell check box. You might want to cancel this option if you often accidentally double-click cells when selecting ranges. When this option is disabled, you must edit the cell's contents in the formula bar.

A related option is Allow Cell Drag And Drop, which enables the drag-and-drop method for copying and moving cells. If you tend to drag cells unintentionally, you can disable the option by clearing the check box.

> **caution** We recommend that you *never* disable the Alert Before Overwriting Cells safety feature, which protects you from inadvertently copying one piece of data over another.

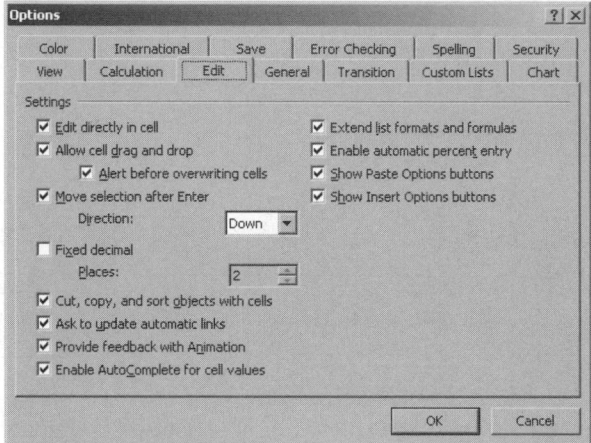

Figure 25-13. You can personalize Excel's editing behavior by enabling or disabling options on the Edit tab.

If you spend a lot of time keying in data a row at a time, you might prefer that Excel move the selection box to the right when you press Enter (rather than down, which is the default). To make this change, the Move Selection After Enter check box must remain selected, and you'll need to select Right from the drop-down list box associated with that option. Clearing the Move Selection After Enter check box indicates that you want to "lock in" the entry but not change the active cell when you press Enter.

You might consider disabling the AutoComplete feature if you grow weary of Excel automatically entering data for you based on your last entry. While this capability is extremely useful, it can also be tiresome if Excel doesn't guess your intentions correctly. To stop AutoComplete, clear the Enable AutoComplete For Cell Values check box. When you're finished selecting your editing choices, click OK to close the Options dialog box.

Installing Add-In Commands and Wizards

As you learned in Part 1, the applications in the Office XP software suite can customize menus and toolbars on their own to hide seldom-used commands and install specific options *on demand* (or as they are needed). You can also use the Add-Ins command on the Excel Tools menu to install useful tools known as add-in commands and wizards, which further extend the Excel application's functionality. Typical add-in commands included with Excel 2002 are Solver and Analysis Toolpak, which appear on the Tools menu after you install them. A popular wizard included with Excel is the Template

Wizard, which creates form templates that have the data tracking option enabled. You can also acquire add-in commands and wizards from third-party software developers.

To install add-in commands and wizards, complete the following steps:

1 Choose Tools, Add-Ins. The Add-Ins dialog box appears, as shown in Figure 25-14.

2 Select the add-in command or wizard that you want to have appear as a menu command. To locate a command that doesn't appear in this dialog box, click the Browse button and find it on your hard disk.

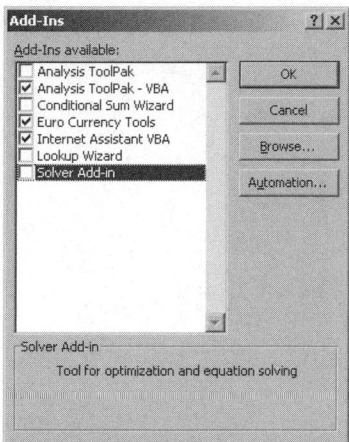

Figure 25-14. The Add-Ins command on the Tools menu allows you to add and remove add-in commands and wizards. The checked items in the figure are all new for Excel 2002.

> **tip** To remove an add-in command or wizard from a menu, clear the add-in or wizard in the Add-Ins dialog box. The add-in command will be removed when you next start Excel.

3 Click OK to save your changes and reconfigure the menu. Excel searches for the tool on your system and prompts you for your Office XP installation disks, if necessary.

> To see the Solver Add-In at work, see Chapter 29, "Advanced Business Analysis."

Most add-in commands appear on the Tools menu after you've installed them, but this location is arbitrary. And occasionally the utility's designer will opt to locate it some-place else in the menu structure after installation.

Crunching Numbers with Formulas and Functions

A *formula* is an equation that calculates a new value from existing values. In Chapter 21 you learned how to build simple formulas using numbers and cell references, and in Chapter 24 you expanded your skills by creating formulas that referenced cells from other worksheets and workbooks. In this chapter you'll discover how to build more sophisticated formulas. You'll learn how to use arithmetic operators and parentheses to control how your formulas are evaluated, you'll explore techniques for replicating formulas, and you'll practice using names to make your formulas easier to read and modify.

In addition, you'll learn how to use Microsoft Excel 2002's impressive collection of built-in functions for specialized tasks such as totaling rows and columns, computing averages, and calculating monthly loan payments. Using well-organized formulas and functions, you can evaluate business data in new ways, spot important trends, and plan your financial future.

Building a Formula

Figure 26-1, on page 734, shows two basic Excel formulas. The first calculates a value by adding the contents of a series of cells, and the second uses an Excel function to find the sum of a range of cells and then multiplies that sum by a number. These formulas have several characteristics in common.

● Each begins with an equal sign (=). The equal sign tells Excel that the following characters are part of a formula that should be calculated and that the result should be displayed in a cell. (If you omit the equal sign, Excel treats the formula as plain text and doesn't compute the result.)

733

- Each formula uses one or more arithmetic operators. An arithmetic operator is not required, however; you might easily create a formula that uses one or more functions to do all the necessary calculating. Each formula includes values that are being combined by using arithmetic operators. When you use Excel formulas, you can combine numbers, cell references, results of functions, and other values.

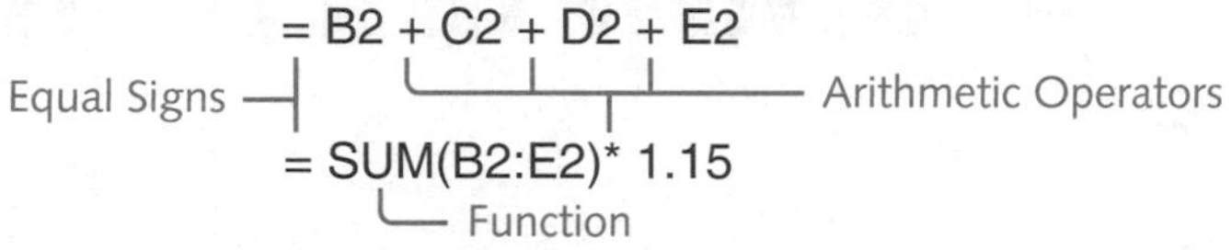

Figure 26-1. Simple formulas can combine numeric values, operators, cell references, and Excel functions.

The examples in this chapter feature an order-form worksheet that catalogs the merchandise sold in a small pet shop. It's the type of worksheet that pet shop employees might use to take orders over the phone or that customers might use to purchase mail-order items. As you work through this chapter, you will see how to use Excel formulas and functions to add information to the order-form worksheet. You can load the worksheet from the companion CD or Web site (or create it yourself) and follow the examples exactly if you want to, or you can customize the worksheet for your own purposes.

Multiplying Numbers

Formulas that multiply the numbers in two cells are among the most basic and easy to enter. To multiply a price cell and a quantity cell to create a subtotal, complete the following steps:

1 Create a product order form, price list, or another worksheet containing well-organized Price, Quantity, and Subtotal columns. The order-form worksheet we'll use looks like this:

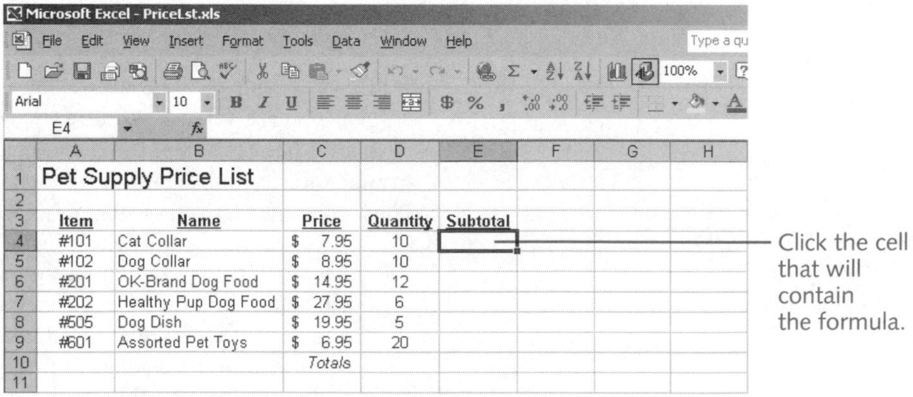

Click the cell that will contain the formula.

For your convenience as you follow the example, the PriceLst sample worksheet (PriceLst.exe) is on the companion CD.

2 In the Subtotal column, click the cell that will contain the multiplication formula (E4, in our example).

3 Type the equal sign (=) to begin the formula.

An equal sign appears on the formula bar and in the highlighted cell. From this point on, any numbers, cell references, arithmetic operators, or functions that you type will be included in the formula.

To learn more about entering simple formulas, referencing cells, and using the formula bar, see "Entering Formulas," on page 615.

4 In the Price column, click the cell containing the first number to be multiplied (C4, in this example). A dotted-line marquee appears around the highlighted cell, and the cell reference appears in the formula bar.

5 Type an asterisk (*) to add the multiplication operator to the formula.

6 In the Quantity column, click the cell containing the second number to be multiplied (D4, in this example). The complete formula now appears in the highlighted cell and on the formula bar. Your worksheet should look similar to this one:

The formula bar records your formula as you build it.

	A	B	C	D	E	F	G	H
1	Pet Supply Price List							
2								
3	**Item**	**Name**	**Price**	**Quantity**	**Subtotal**			
4	#101	Cat Collar	$ 7.95	10	=C4*D4			
5	#102	Dog Collar	$ 8.95	10				
6	#201	OK-Brand Dog Food	$ 14.95	12				
7	#202	Healthy Pup Dog Food	$ 27.95	6				
8	#505	Dog Dish	$ 19.95	5				
9	#601	Assorted Pet Toys	$ 6.95	20				
10			Totals					
11								

Microsoft Excel - PriceLst.xls — SUM =C4*D4

7 Press Enter to end the formula. Excel calculates the result (79.5, in this example), and displays it in the cell containing the formula. The number automatically appears in currency format.

Chapter 26

Replicating a Formula

Excel makes it easy to copy, or *replicate*, a formula into neighboring cells, using the Fill submenu of the Edit menu. The slick thing about the Fill submenu is that its commands automatically adjust the cell references in your formula to match the rows and columns you're copying to. For example, if you replicate a formula (that averages the values in the row) down a column with the Down command, Excel adjusts the row numbers so that the formula includes appropriate references in each cell. (Excel automatically adjusts cell references when you delete cells, too.)

For more information about the commands on the Fill submenu, see "Using the Fill Commands," on page 643.

The following example uses the same order-form worksheet to demonstrate formula replication. To replicate a formula, complete the following steps:

1 Highlight the cell that has the formula and expand the selection to include the empty cells you want to fill.

To control how Excel calculates formulas, see "Controlling Calculation," on page 727.

2 Choose Edit, Fill. Then choose Down if your formula is at the top of the selected range (or choose Right, Left, or Up as appropriate). Your formula is replicated within the selected cells, as shown here:

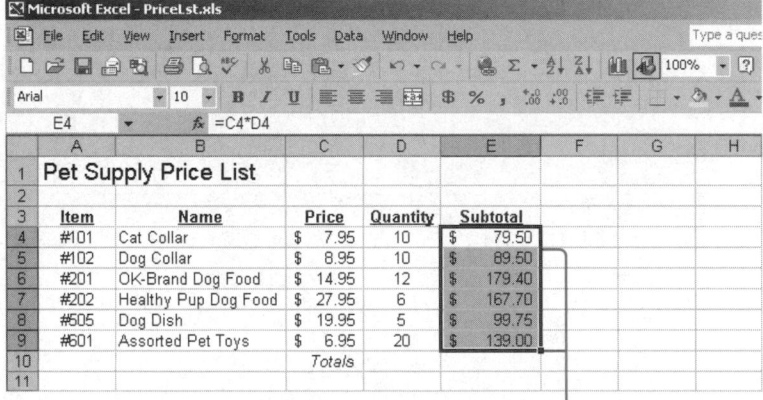

Excel replicates the formula.

tip You can also replicate a formula by using the AutoFill mouse technique. Simply select the cell you want to replicate, click the tiny box in the lower right corner of the cell, and drag it over the cells you want to fill.

Using Relative and Absolute Cell References

When you replicate a formula, Excel adjusts cell references relative to each new location of the formula. So a formula in cell D8 that references cell C8 is, as a matter of *relative* location, referencing the cell immediately to the left of the cell containing the formula. Copy the formula to D9, and the cell that's referenced becomes C9; paste the formula to G12, and the referenced cell in the formula becomes F12—the cell located to the left of the one containing the formula.

To override this behavior, you need to indicate that a cell location in a formula is *absolute* rather than relative, and you do this by inserting a dollar sign ($) before the column and row indicators. So as an absolute reference, H8 becomes *$H$8*. The formula *=$H$8 * 2* when copied to any other cell in the worksheet remains *=$H$8 * 2*.

The example below calculates a mileage reimbursement for trips taken in a personal vehicle. The formula in cell C6 references the reimbursement rate as an absolute cell reference, *$B$3*, and the miles driven as a relative reference to cell B6. When you replicate the formula to other cells in column C, the reimbursement rate correctly references the same location while the location referenced in column B changes to match the current row.

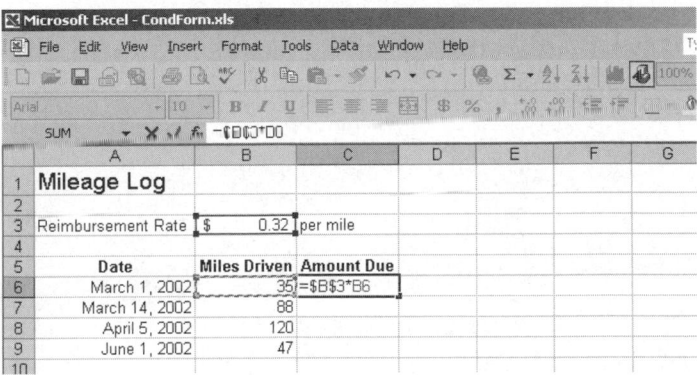

A third type of cell reference is called a *mixed* reference because it mixes relative and absolute notation. The cell referenced as $C8, for instance, has an absolute column location. Wherever you replicate a formula that contains a reference to $C8, it continues to reference column C, although the relative row indicator might change. Similarly, C$8 is a mixed reference, although here the row number is fixed, whereas the column reference is subject to change.

---

tip   **Cycling Through Reference Types**

When you're entering or editing a formula in the formula bar, pressing F4 changes the reference type for the cell reference nearest the insertion point. Thus, if the cell reference is relative (A5, for example), press F4 to change it to absolute ($A$5); press F4 again to change it to a mixed reference (A$5), again to change it to the other mixed reference ($A5), and yet again to change it back to a relative reference again.

737

Editing Formulas

Excel allows you to edit formulas in the same way that you edit any other cell entry. Simply double-click the cell, locate the mistake using the mouse or the arrow keys, make your correction, and press Enter.

You can insert new cell references while editing a formula by positioning the mouse pointer (or highlighting a cell reference or range to replace) on the formula bar and highlighting new cells with the mouse. Notice that Excel uses colors to identify cell references on the formula bar and like-colored boxes to indicate the corresponding cells in the worksheet. To cancel an edit, press Esc.

Combining Arithmetic Operators

Table 26-1 shows a complete list of the arithmetic operators you can use in a formula. When you enter more than one arithmetic operator, Excel follows standard algebraic rules to determine which calculations to accomplish first in the formula. These rules—called Excel's *order of evaluation*—dictate that exponential calculations are performed first, multiplication and division calculations second, and addition and subtraction last. If more than one calculation exists in the same category, Excel evaluates them from left to right. For example, when evaluating the formula =6-5+3*4, Excel computes the answer using these steps:

=6-5+3*4

=6-5+12

=1+12

=13

Table 26-1. Excel's Arithmetic Operators, in Order of Evaluation

Operator	Description	Example	Result
( )	Parentheses	(3+6)*3	27
^	Exponential	10^2	100
*	Multiplication	7*5	35
/	Division	15/3	5
+	Addition	5+5	10
-	Subtraction	12-8	4

Parentheses and Order of Evaluation

As you can see in Table 26-1, parentheses come first, letting you override Excel's normal order of evaluation. For example, consider how parentheses create a difference in evaluation between these two formulas:

=10+2*0.25

=(10+2)*0.25

The first formula produces a result of 10.5, while the second formula produces a result of 3. By modifying Excel's order of evaluation in the second formula, you wind up with a different answer.

Troubleshooting

Enforcing Operator Precedence

A complicated mathematical formula calculates unexpected results.

Parentheses can make a formula easier to read and therefore easier to troubleshoot or revise. If you get unexpected results from a formula, the problem might be that your assumptions about the order of evaluation are incorrect. You can add parentheses to enforce the order of evaluation you expect, even if you believe the expected order is the one Excel would normally use.

In fact, you can add any number of parentheses to a formula as long as you use them in matching pairs. For example, although the following formulas both produce the answer 15, the first formula is a bit easier to decipher.

=((5*4)/2)+(10/2)

=5*4/2+10/2

If you specify an uneven number of parentheses in a formula or a pair of parentheses that don't match, Excel displays a message saying that it found an error in the formula and proposes a correction. Click Yes to accept Excel's proposed correction, or click No so you can correct the mistake on the formula bar or in the cell directly.

Using Built-In Functions

To accomplish more sophisticated numerical and text processing operations in your worksheets, Excel allows you to add functions to your formulas. A *function* is a predefined equation that operates on one or more values and returns a single value. Excel includes a collection of more than 200 functions in several useful categories, as shown in Table 26-2, on page 560. For example, you can use the PMT (payment) function from the Financial category to calculate the periodic payment for a loan based on the interest rate charged, the number of payments desired, and the principal amount.

For more information on the PMT function, see "Using PMT to Determine Loan Payments," on page 744.

Table 26-2. Categories of Excel Functions

Category	Used For
Financial	Loan payments, appreciation, and depreciation
Date & Time	Calculations involving dates and times
Math & Trig	Mathematical and trigonometric calculations like those found on a scientific calculator
Statistical	Average, sum, variance, and standard-deviation calculations
Lookup & Reference	Calculations involving tables of data
Database	Working with lists and external databases
Text	Comparing, converting, and reformatting text in cells
Logical	Calculations that produce the result TRUE or FALSE
Information	Determining whether an error has occurred in a calculation

You must enter each function with a particular *syntax*, or structure, so that Excel can process the results correctly. For example, the PMT function has a function syntax that looks like this:

PMT(**rate,nper,pv**,fv,type)

The abbreviated words shown between the parentheses are called *arguments*; these are the values that you supply so that the function can return its result, enabling your formula to complete its calculations. In this function, *rate* is the interest rate, *nper* is the number of payments you will make, and *pv* is the principal amount. To use a function correctly, you must specify a value for each of these required (**boldfaced**) arguments, and you must separate the arguments with commas. The arguments *not* shown in bold are optional. For the PMT function, the arguments fv and type are optional. (Each is explained in online Help.)

To use the PMT function to calculate the monthly loan payment on a $1,000 loan at 19 percent annual interest over 36 months, for example, you could type the following formula:

=PMT(19%/12,36,1000)

When Excel evaluates this function, it places the answer ($36.66) in the cell containing the formula. (The answer is negative, as indicated by the parentheses, because it's money you must pay out.) Note that the first argument (the interest rate) is divided by 12 in this example to create a monthly rate for the formula. This demonstrates an important point—you can use other calculations, including other functions, as the arguments for a function. Although it takes a little time to master the way these arguments are structured, you will find that functions produce results that can otherwise take hours to calculate by hand.

The Versatile SUM Function

Perhaps the most commonly used function in Excel's collection is SUM, which totals the range of cells you select. Because SUM is used so often, the Standard toolbar includes an AutoSum button to make adding numbers faster. In the following example, we will use the AutoSum button to sum the values in the Subtotal column in our order-form worksheet.

To total a column of numbers using the SUM function, follow these steps:

1 Click the cell in which you want to place the SUM function. (If you're totaling a column of numbers, select the cell directly below the last number in the column.)

2 Click the AutoSum button.

Excel places the SUM function on the formula bar, and (if possible) automatically selects a range of neighboring cells as an argument for the function. If you selected a cell directly below a column of numbers, your screen will look similar to the one in Figure 26-2.

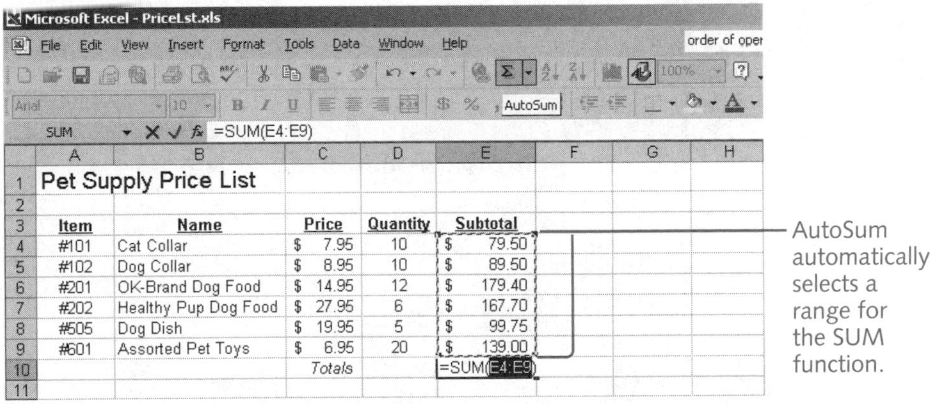

AutoSum automatically selects a range for the SUM function.

Figure 26-2. The AutoSum button inserts the SUM function and automatically suggests the cells to use for the argument.

3 If Excel selected the range you want to total, press Enter to complete the function and compute the sum. If Excel didn't select the range you want to add up, select a new range by dragging the mouse over the range and pressing Enter. (You can specify any block of cells in any open workbook to be an argument to the SUM function.) To cancel the AutoSum command, press the Esc key.

> **tip** **Use SUM to Add Nonadjacent Ranges**
>
> You can use the SUM function to add multiple noncontiguous ranges by separating the cell ranges with commas. For example, =SUM(A3:A8,C3:C8) adds six cells in column A to six cells in column C and displays the total. You might find it easier to use the mouse and select cells by clicking each cell or range of cells while pressing the Ctrl key.

The Insert Function Command

With so many functions to choose from, it might seem daunting to experiment with unfamiliar features on your own. Excel makes it easier by providing a special command on the Insert menu named Function to help you learn about functions and enter them into formulas.

The Insert Function dialog box, shown in Figure 26-3, lets you type a question to get help (a list of suggested functions) or browse through the function categories and then pick just the function you want. When you highlight a function, the dialog box displays a brief description of the function that explains its syntax and purpose.

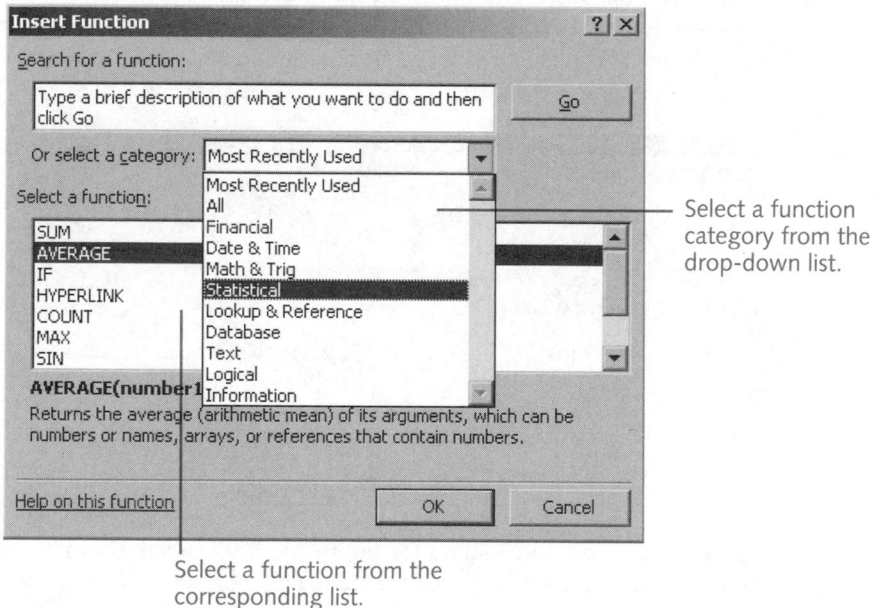

Select a function category from the drop-down list.

Select a function from the corresponding list.

Figure 26-3. The Insert Function dialog box lists function names by category.

> **note** In the Insert Function dialog box, all arguments in the function syntax appear in bold, but not all are required. Use the Office Assistant and online Help for more detailed documentation of each function and its arguments.

Chapter 26

When you double-click a function in the Select A Function list box, Excel displays a second dialog box prompting you for the arguments. If the note for an argument says that it can be omitted, the argument is optional. Give it a try now with a useful statistical function called AVERAGE.

To use AVERAGE to calculate the average of a list of numbers, follow these steps:

1 Click the cell in which you want to place the results of the AVERAGE function. (In the pet shop example, this is B12. The label Avg. Price has been added in A12.)

2 Choose Insert, Function to display the Insert Function dialog box.

3 Open the drop-down list of categories and select Statistical. The mathematical functions in the Statistical category appear in the list of functions.

4 Click the AVERAGE function, and then click OK. A second dialog box appears, asking you for the arguments in the function. In the AVERAGE function, you can specify either individual values to compute the average or a cell range. This time you will specify a cell range.

5 Click the Collapse Dialog Box button (at the right edge of the Number1 text box shown below), and the dialog box shrinks to show only the text box you're about to fill.

6 Select the cells you want to average. In our example, we selected the numbers in the Price column (cells C4 through C9) to determine the average price of pet supplies in the store.

7 After you release the mouse button, press Enter or return to the collapsed dialog box and click the button at the right of the argument field. The dialog box returns to its normal size, and the cell range you selected appears in the dialog box and in the AVERAGE function on the formula bar. Our dialog box looks like this:

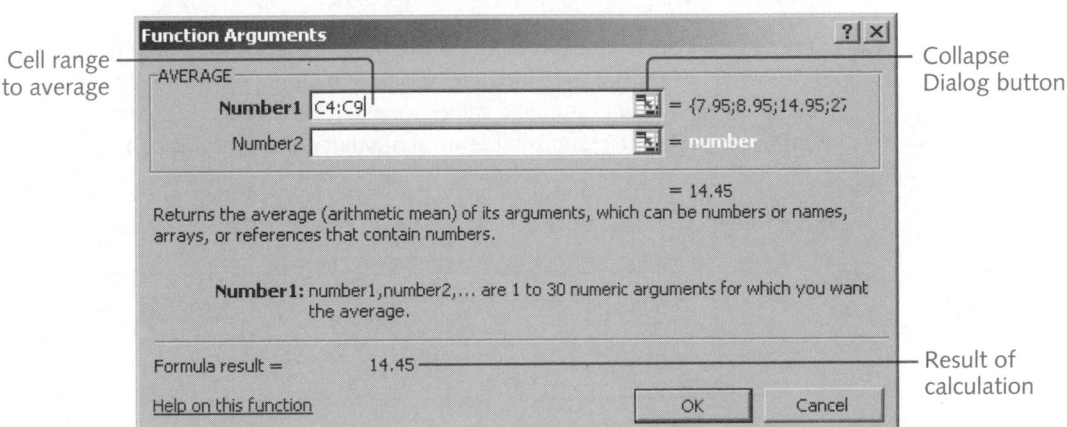

Chapter 26

743

8 Click OK to complete the formula and calculate the result. The average, $14.45, appears in the cell containing the AVERAGE formula.

> **tip** You can include one function as an argument in another function if the result is compatible. For example, the formula =SUM(5,SQRT(9)) adds together the number 5 and the square root of 9, and then displays the result (8).

Using Functions to Analyze Finances

Although Excel includes too many functions to discuss exhaustively in this book, we thought you might enjoy seeing a few more examples of functions and formulas to prompt your own exploration. We've decided to highlight three of Excel's most useful financial functions: PMT, FV, and RATE. Using these functions, you can precisely calculate loan payments, the future value of an investment, or the rate of return produced by an investment.

Using PMT to Determine Loan Payments

The PMT function returns the periodic payment required to amortize a loan over a set number of periods. In plain English, this means that you can estimate what your car payments will be if you take out an auto loan or what your mortgage payments will be if you buy a house. Try using the PMT function now to determine what the monthly payments will be for a $10,000 auto loan at 9 percent interest over a 3-year period.

To use the PMT function, follow these steps:

1 Click the worksheet cell in which you want to display the monthly payment.

2 Choose Insert, Function, or click the Insert Function button on the Standard toolbar. The Insert Function dialog box appears.

3 Choose the Financial category from the drop-down list box, and then double-click PMT in the list of function names. The Function Arguments dialog box appears. You will enter numeric values for rate (the interest rate), nper (the number of payments), and pv (the present value, or loan principal).

4 Type **9%/12** for the monthly rate and press Tab, type **36** and press Tab, and type **10000**. The dialog box should look like the one on the next page.

> **newfeature!**
> **tip** As you grow accustomed to using functions, you might simply type them in your formula without using the Insert Function command. As you begin to type the arguments for the function, Excel 2002 provides pop-up Help that walks you through the syntax.

744

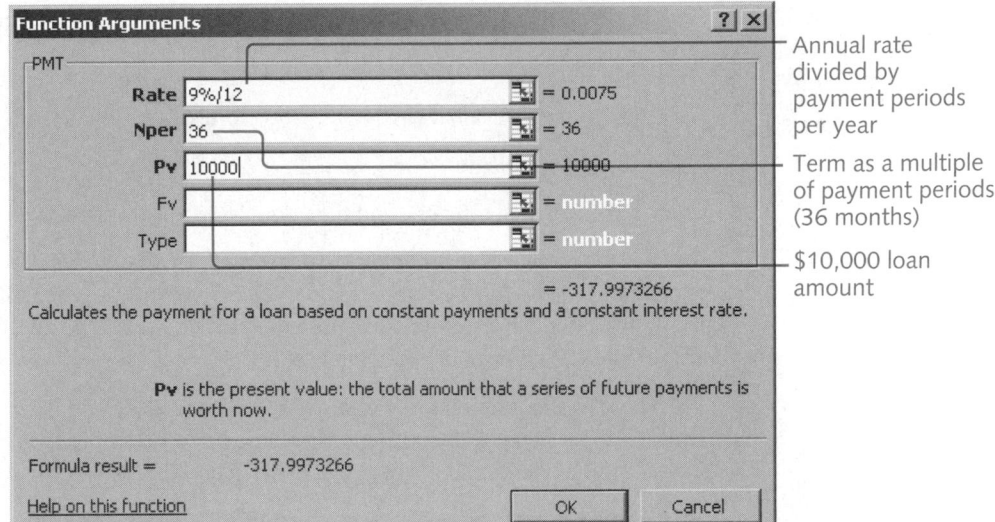

The result of the calculation (-317.9973266) appears near the bottom of the dialog box.

> **tip** To calculate monthly payments, be sure to type the annual interest using a percent sign and divide it by 12 to create a monthly interest rate. Likewise, be sure to specify the number of payments in months (36), not years (3).

5 Click OK to complete the function and display the result. Your monthly loan payment, less any applicable loan fees, appears in the cell you highlighted. The result, formatted as currency, appears as ($318.00) in the worksheet (Excel has rounded off the original number). The amount appears in red and between parentheses because it represents money that you must pay out.

Using FV to Compute Future Value

Although monthly loan payments are often a fact of life, Excel can help you with more than just debt planning. If you enjoy squirreling away money for the future, you can use the FV (future value) function to determine the future value of an investment. Financial planners use this tool when they help you determine the future value of an annuity, Individual Retirement Account (IRA), or Simplified Employee Pension (SEP) account. The following example shows you how to compute the future value of an IRA in which you deposit $2,000 per year for 30 years at a 10 percent annual interest rate—a possible scenario if you invest $2,000 per year between the ages of 35 and 65.

To use the FV function to calculate the value of your investment at retirement, follow these steps:

1 Click the worksheet cell in which you want to display the investment total.

2 Open the Insert Function dialog box.

3 Choose the Financial category, and then double-click FV for the function name.

A dialog box appears that contains a description of the FV function and five text boxes for the function arguments. (The arguments are related to those of the PMT function, but now a Pmt field is added so that you can enter the amount you're contributing each period.)

4 Type **10%** in the Rate text box and press Tab, type **30** in the Nper text box and press Tab, type **-2000** in the Pmt text box and press Tab twice, and then type **1** in the Type text box. Your dialog box should look like the following:

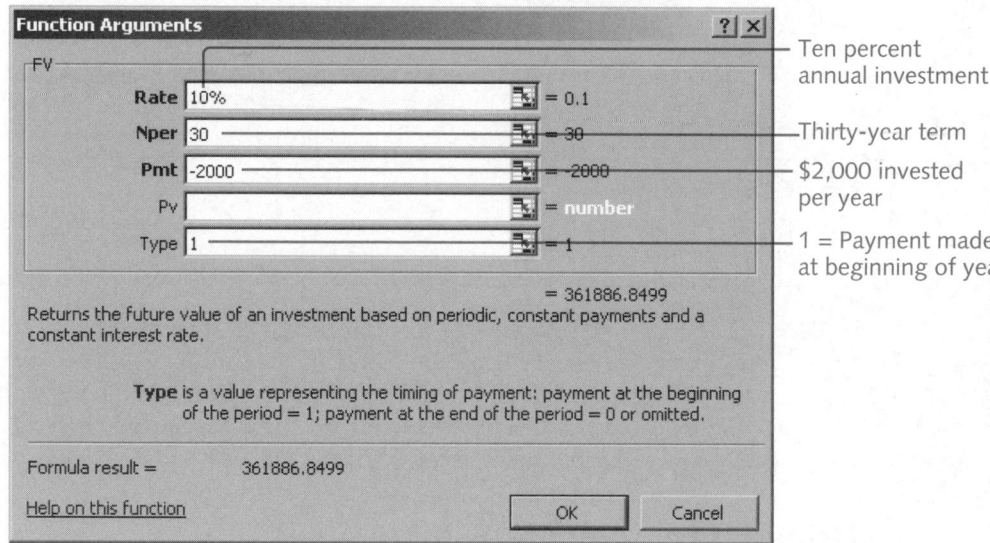

- Ten percent annual investment
- Thirty-year term
- $2,000 invested per year
- 1 = Payment made at beginning of year

5 Click OK to display the result. In our example the 30-year IRA has a future value of $361,886.85. Not bad for a total investment of $60,000.

> **note** By placing a 1 in the Type text box, you direct Excel to start calculating each year's interest at the beginning of the year—a sensible move if you place one lump sum in your IRA at the same time each year. If you omit this argument, Excel calculates each year's interest at the end of the year, and because of the lost compounding the total future value will be smaller—about $33,000 less in this example.

Troubleshooting

Money Troubles

The results of a financial formula are way off.

If you use a financial function and get results that are far different than you expected, consider the following common sources of error:

- Rate and Nper arguments must be based on the same units of time. In the previous examples, months were the basis in one case, years in another.

- Payments and loans are treated as negative or positive in the sense of a ledger: incoming amounts are positive, and outgoing amounts are negative.

- Formatting can be misleading: an argument might represent thousands (an entry of 17.3 might actually be $17,300), but if the cell that holds the formula result is formatted as a currency amount with two places after the decimal point, the displayed result won't appear to be accurate.

Using the RATE Function to Evaluate Rate of Return

You will often want to evaluate how a current investment is doing or how a new business proposition looks. For example, suppose that a contractor friend suggests you lend him $10,000 for a laundromat/brew pub project and agrees to pay you $3,200 per year for four years as a minimum return on your investment. So what's the projected rate of return for this investment opportunity? You can figure it out quickly using the RATE function, which allows you to determine the rate of return for any investment that generates a series of periodic payments or a single lump-sum payment.

To use the RATE function to determine the rate of return for an investment, follow these steps:

1 Click the worksheet cell in which you want to display the rate of return.

2 Open the Insert Function dialog box.

3 Choose the Financial category, scroll down the list of function names, and double-click RATE.

A dialog box appears that contains a description of the RATE function and six text boxes for the function arguments. (Scroll down to see the sixth text box, Guess.) The arguments are similar to the ones you've used in previous financial functions, but they appear in a slightly different order.

4 Type **4** in the Nper text box and press Tab, type **3200** in the Pmt text box and press Tab, and type **-10000** in the Pv text box. Be sure to enter the third argument—the loan value—as a negative number. Your dialog box should look like this:

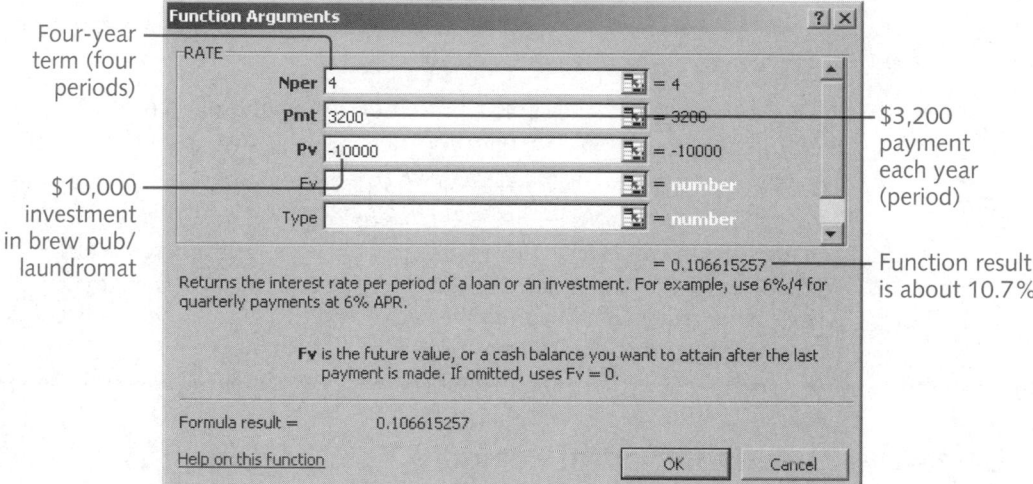

Four-year term (four periods)

$10,000 investment in brew pub/ laundromat

$3,200 payment each year (period)

Function result is about 10.7%

5 Click OK to display the result. In this example, your investment of $10,000 today will return 11 percent. With this information in hand, you can decide whether the projected rate of return is enough for you or whether you would rather try something less risky—or renegotiate the deal.

In short, Excel functions can't guarantee your financial success, but when used correctly they can help you analyze your choices.

Using Function Error Values

The Insert Function dialog box makes entering functions relatively straightforward. If you do make a mistake when typing a function, you might receive a code called an *error value* in one or more cells. Error values begin with a pound (#) symbol and usually end with an exclamation point. For example, the error value #NUM! means that the function arguments you supplied aren't appropriate to calculate the function—one of the arguments might be too big or too small.

If you see an error value in a cell, simply click the cell and fix your mistake on the formula bar, or delete the formula and enter it again. You can also click the Error button for a list of responses, such as using online Help, ignoring or tracing the error, and displaying the Formula Auditing toolbar. Table 26-3 shows the most common Excel error values and their meanings.

tip If you want to suppress the error values when you print a worksheet, choose File, Page Setup; in the Sheet tab, open the Cell Errors As list box and select an option other than *displayed* (such as *<blank>*) and click OK.

Table 26-3. **Common Error Values in Excel Formulas**

Error Value	Description
#DIV/0!	You're dividing by zero in this formula. Verify that no cell references refer to blank cells.
#NA	You might have omitted a function argument. No value is available.
#NAME?	You're using a name in this formula that hasn't been defined in the workbook. (See the next section, "Using Names in Functions.")
#NULL!	In a formula, you referred to the intersection of two ranges that don't intersect.
#NUM!	Your function arguments might be out of range or otherwise invalid, or an iterative function you're using might not have computed long enough to reach a solution. (Entering a rough answer in the *Guess* argument might reduce the number of iterations Excel needs.)
#REF!	Your formula includes range references that have been deleted.
#VALUE!	Your formula is using a text entry as an argument.
######	Your calculation results were too wide to fit in the cell. Increase the column width.

Using Names in Functions

To make your functions more readable and easier to type, you can name a cell or range of cells in your worksheet and then use the name in place of cell references throughout your workbook. For example, you could give the cells E4 through E9 the name Subtotal and then use the SUM function to add the six cells by entering the following formula:

=SUM(Subtotal)

After you assign a name to a cell or range, you can use the name in any formula in your workbook.

Creating Cell and Range Names

Excel gives you two techniques for creating names in a workbook: you can click the Name box and type a name or you can use the Create command on the Name submenu. If you have a column heading already in place, using the Create command is slightly faster.

Names must begin with a letter and can't include spaces. We recommend that you limit your names to 15 characters or fewer so they fit easily into the Name box and you can type them quickly in formulas.

Assigning Names with the Name Command

To create a name using the Create command, follow these steps:

1 Select a range of cells, and include a label or heading in the selection to define the name. For example, the following selection includes the text label Subtotal for the range name:

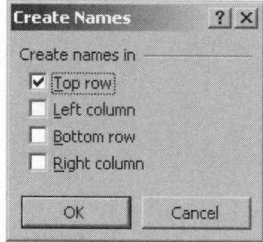

Quantity	Subtotal
10	$ 79.50
10	$ 89.50
12	$ 179.40
6	$ 167.70
5	$ 99.75
20	$ 139.00
	$ 754.85

2 Choose Insert, Name, and then Create.

The Create Names dialog box appears, prompting you for the location of the name within your selection:

3 Click OK to accept Excel's default selection if you included a row or column heading in your range; otherwise, click the option to tell Excel where to find the labels.

In this example Excel has detected the text label Subtotal at the top of your selection. You can use this name in computations in any worksheet in the workbook.

Assigning Names with the Name Box

To create a name by selecting, clicking, and typing, follow the steps shown in Figure 26-4. This direct approach is handy if you want to name cells in a different, perhaps more economical, way than the headings used in the worksheet. If you name an individual cell, the name appears in the Name Box whenever you select the cell. If you assign a name to a range of cells, the name won't appear unless you select the complete range.

750

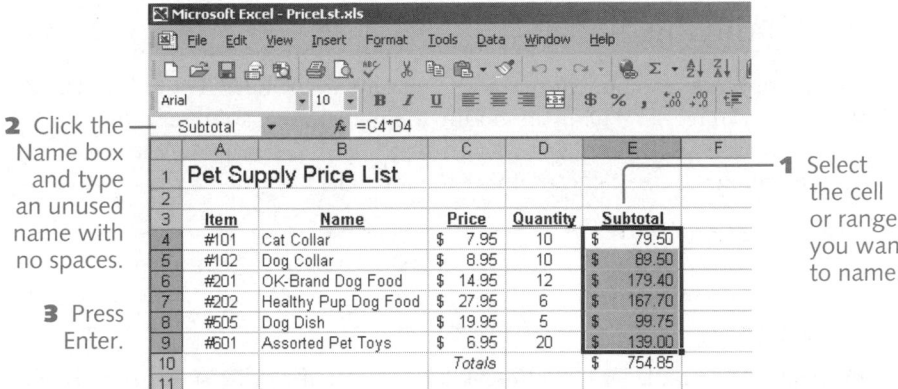

2 Click the
Name box
and type
an unused
name with
no spaces.

3 Press
Enter.

1 Select
the cell
or range
you want
to name.

Figure 26-4. You can create a named range by hand.

Putting Names to Work

You can use names as arguments in functions wherever they're appropriate. For example, you could use the Subtotal range name in the SUM and AVERAGE functions because they accept ranges as arguments, but you couldn't use Subtotal in the PMT function because each of the PMT arguments must be a single number.

To insert a name into a formula or function, follow these steps:

1 Create the formula or function as you normally would. For example, to determine the average of the cells in the Subtotal range, begin your formula as follows:

=AVERAGE(

2 When it's time to specify a range of cells as an argument, type the named range in the formula:

=AVERAGE(Subtotal)

When you've finished entering the formula, press Enter.

Troubleshooting

Trouble with Names

A formula returns the error code #NAME?.

If your formula returns the error code #NAME?, you might have incorrectly remembered a name you assigned in the workbook. To be safe, you can choose names from a list by using the Paste Name dialog box. To insert names in this manner, type your formula, and when it's time to insert a name, choose Insert, Name, Paste, and then double-click the name that you want to include. The error might also arise if you delete or modify a name that you used in the formula (as described in the next section). Redefine the name or update the reference in your formula to correct the error.

751

Deleting and Modifying Names

Names are an important component of well-documented formulas. They also make your formulas easy to revise. When you modify the name, Excel automatically updates all your formulas. If you delete a name that's used in a formula, the error value #NAME? appears in the cell containing the formula.

> **tip** You can't undo a name deletion. To fix the problem, you will need to replace the name in the formula with an actual cell reference or with a valid name.

The Define command on the Name submenu lets you modify or delete a name. Delete a name by highlighting the entry in the Names In Workbook list and clicking Delete. Modify a reference using the Refers To text box. You can add cells to, or remove cells from, a reference either by typing in the Refers To text box or by highlighting a new cell reference or range in the worksheet.

To modify the cells included in a name, follow these steps:

1 Choose Insert, Name, and then Define.

 The Define Name dialog box includes a list of the names in your workbook and a Refers To text box listing the cells they reference.

2 Click the name that you want to modify.

3 Change the cell references in the Refers To text box, or select a new cell or range of cells directly in the worksheet. Just click the Collapse Dialog button in the Refers To box to shrink the dialog box. Then select the cells and press Enter. Click OK to save your changes.

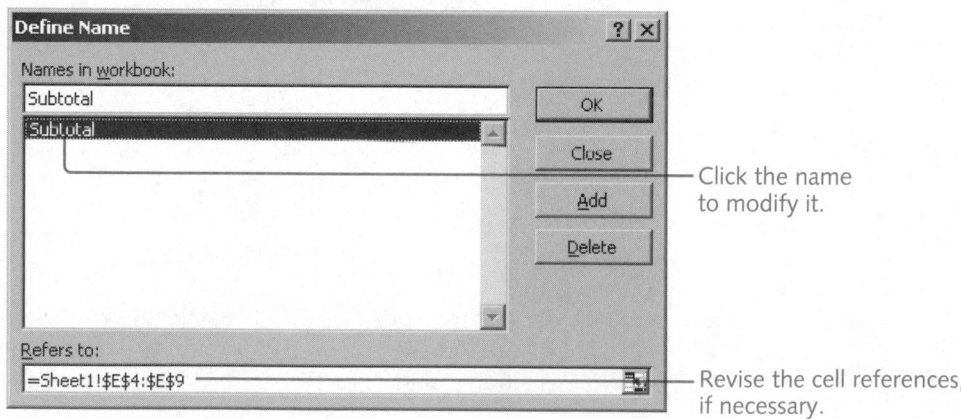

Click the name to modify it.

Revise the cell references, if necessary.

Advanced Worksheet Charts

When you have worksheet data that you need to present to others, it often makes sense to display some of the facts and figures as a *chart*. Charts are graphical representations of data that transform rows and columns of information into meaningful images. Charts can help you to identify numerical trends that can be difficult to spot in worksheets, and they can add color and flair to an important presentation. In this chapter you'll learn how to create a Microsoft Excel 2002 chart from worksheet data, format your chart's appearance, add special effects, and print your chart. If it's your job to plan for the future or to analyze the past, you'll find Excel's charting tools both useful and addictive.

Planning a Chart

Before you can create a chart, you need to do some planning. You create an Excel chart from the data in an existing Excel worksheet, so before you build a chart, you need to create a worksheet that contains the necessary facts and figures. Excel can create a chart from data that's distributed throughout a worksheet, but you'll make the process easier if you organize your numbers so that they can be combined and selected easily. For example, Figure 27-1 shows a sales worksheet that contains rows and columns of data you can easily convert into several types of charts.

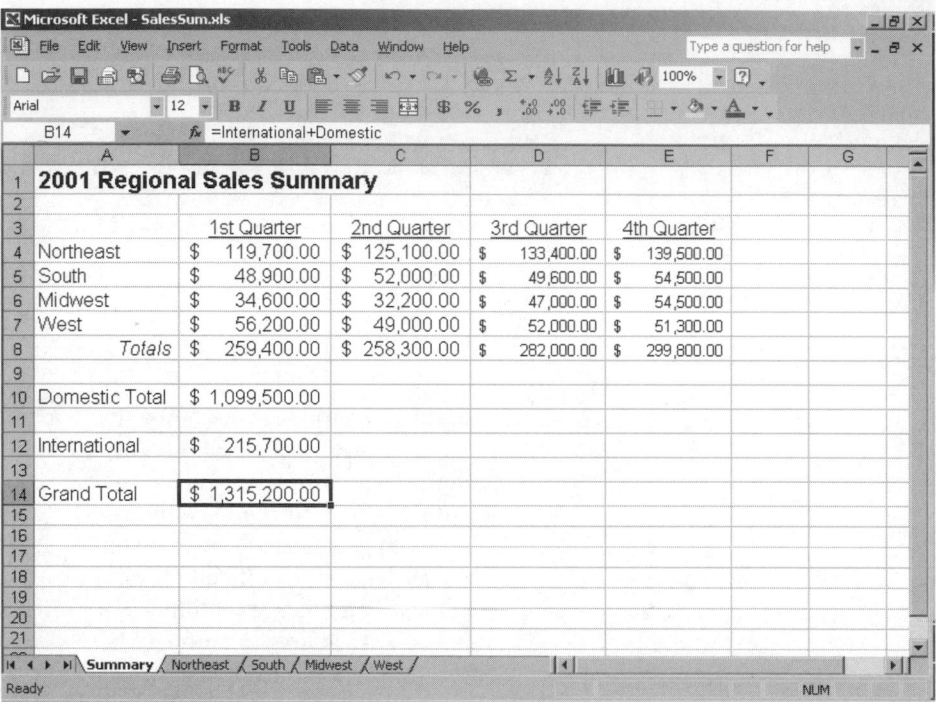

Figure 27-1. Creating charts is easier when you make neatly organized rows and columns of data.

Choosing a Chart Type

As you plan, give some thought to the type of chart you'll be creating. Excel provides 14 chart types that you can use to present worksheet data, and there are several variations for each chart type. The basic chart types are shown in Table 27-1 along with each one's typical uses. For example, you can use a pie chart to describe the relationship of parts to a whole or a bar chart to compare different categories of data with each other. If you're gathering information for an annual sales report, you might want to try out both of these chart types.

If you have your worksheet set up with fields and records like a database, you can also create an interactive chart called a pivot chart. For more information about this powerful charting feature, see "Creating Pivot Tables and Pivot Charts," on page 795.

Table 27-1. **Excel Chart Types and Typical Uses for Each One**

Chart Symbol	Chart Type	Typical Use
	Column	Compares categories of data with each other vertically
	Bar	Compares categories of data with each other horizontally
	Line	Shows trends by category over a period of time
	Pie	Describes the relationship of the parts to the whole in a single group
	XY (Scatter)	Depicts the relationship between two kinds of related data
	Area	Emphasizes the relative importance of values over a period of time
	Doughnut	Compares the parts to the whole in one or more data categories; a more flexible pie chart that has a hole in the middle
	Radar	Shows changes in data or data frequency relative to a center point
	Surface	Tracks changes in two variables as a third variable (such as time) changes; a three-dimensional (3-D) chart
	Bubble	Highlights clusters of values; similar to a scatter chart
	Stock	Combines column chart and line chart; especially designed to track stock prices
	Cylinder	Uses a unique cylinder shape to present bar or column chart data
	Cone	Emphasizes the peaks in data; a bar or column chart
	Pyramid	Emphasizes the peaks in bars or columns; similar to the cone chart

Chapter 27

Measure Twice, Chart Once

Charting requires some up-front planning to get the best results. Just as a carpenter measures a length of wood twice before cutting it, you would be well advised to take your time and think about your goals for a chart before creating it. As you plan your charting strategy, ask yourself the following questions:

● Which worksheet data would I like to highlight in a chart? Can I build my worksheet so that I can copy data directly to the chart?

● How will I present my chart? Do I want to store it as a separate sheet in my workbook, in an existing worksheet, or as part of a Microsoft Word document or a Microsoft PowerPoint presentation?

● Which chart type do I plan to use? Do I want to show one category of data (such as first-quarter sales by geographic region), or several (such as the four most recent quarters of sales by geographic region)?

Understanding Chart Elements, Excel-Style

Finally, to help you map your data to the representation in the various chart types, you need to master the terms that Excel uses—terms that apply to the worksheet data that it charts and terms that apply to the various chart elements that you can format or otherwise modify.

As an example, you might create a standard column chart from the data selected in Figure 27-2. For a column chart, Excel assumes initially that the columns of values that you select are the *data series*, and the column headings become the series *names* in the Legend box, as shown in Figure 27-3. (You can correct these assumptions as necessary.) The *legend* explains the way Excel uses colors or patterns to correspond to particular names of data values or data series.

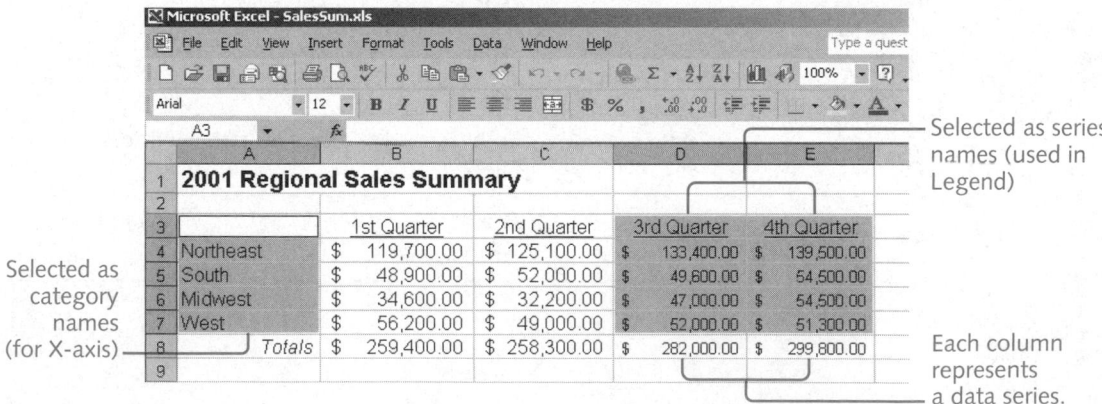

Figure 27-2. Select the data that you want to be represented graphically.

In a two-dimensional chart, Excel refers to the horizontal axis, or *x*-axis, as the *Category axis* and it refers to the vertical axis, or *y*-axis, as the *Value axis*. The chart in Figure 27-3 uses the row headings in column A to identify the values on the Category axis. Lines that mark distance along the axes are called *tick marks*, and the horizontal and vertical extensions of these marks within the plot area are *gridlines*. The chart also illustrates the use of *labels*, which refer here to the text attached to the plotted values themselves.

> **note** In a 3-D chart, the vertical axis is the z-axis—and is still called the Value axis—whereas the "depth" axis is the y-axis, which Excel refers to as the Series axis.

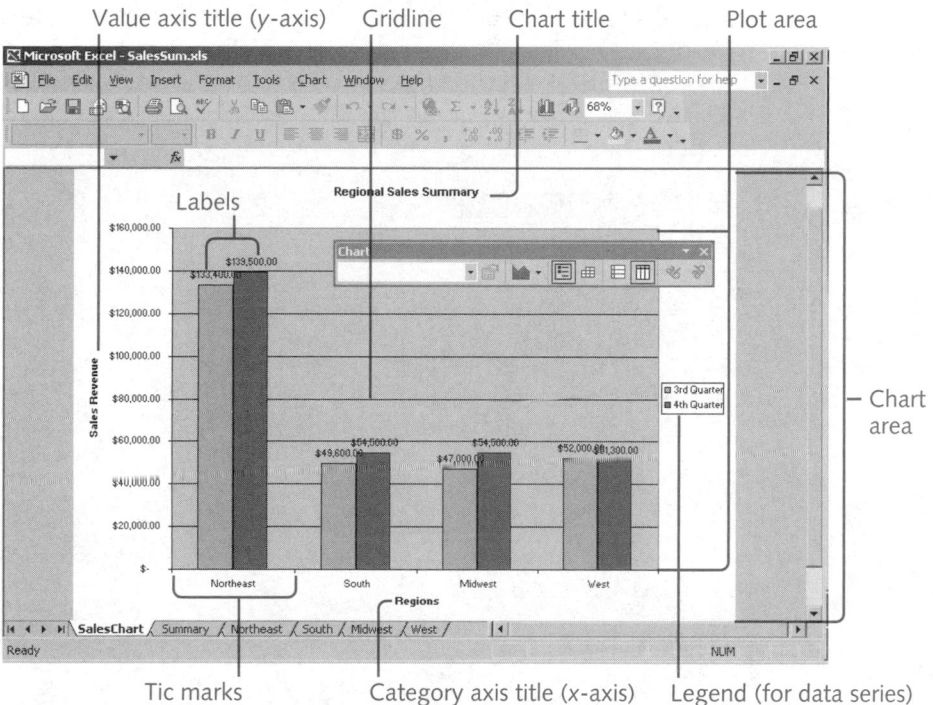

Figure 27-3. Understand the terms Excel applies to chart elements so that you can use the various tools to modify and format them.

Creating a Chart

When you have a well-organized worksheet in place, you're ready to create a chart. In the following examples we'll use the 2001 Regional Sales Summary workbook (SalesSum.xls) shown earlier in Figure 27-1 to create a pie chart and a column chart. Because charting often involves experimenting with different chart types, feel free to follow your own impulses as you complete the instructions.

 The SalesSum.xls example is on the companion CD to this book.

To create a pie chart in a new sheet in the workbook, follow these steps:

1 Prepare a worksheet that has rows and columns of information that you can use in the chart. Add row and column labels if you want them included in the chart.

> **tip** If you select headings along with the data for your chart before you create the chart, Excel will add the names to the chart automatically.

2 Select the cell range containing the data to be plotted. In this example we'll be creating a pie chart, so we want to select one series of values (one row or column). The following screen shows how you would select numbers in the 1st Quarter column for a pie chart, including text that you want to use as chart labels:

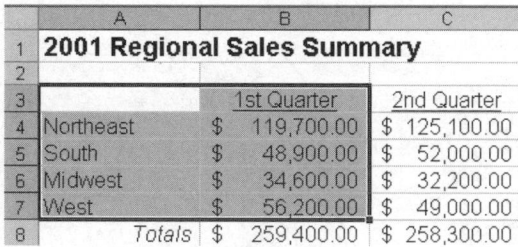

	A	B	C
1	**2001 Regional Sales Summary**		
2			
3		1st Quarter	2nd Quarter
4	Northeast	$ 119,700.00	$ 125,100.00
5	South	$ 48,900.00	$ 52,000.00
6	Midwest	$ 34,600.00	$ 32,200.00
7	West	$ 56,200.00	$ 49,000.00
8	Totals	$ 259,400.00	$ 258,300.00

Chart Wizard

3 Create the chart. Choose Insert, Chart, or click the Chart Wizard button on the Standard toolbar.

The Chart Wizard starts, and you will see the following dialog box asking you to select a chart type:

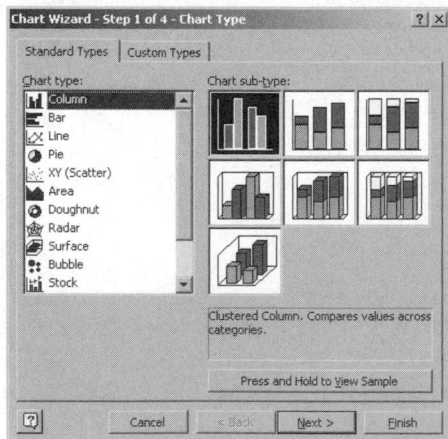

Chapter 27

4 If Office Assistant appears, click the Help button to close it so that you will have a better view of the worksheet.

5 Click the Pie chart type in the Chart Type list box, and then click the Exploded 3-D Pie in the Chart Sub-Type box. (The names of the sub-types appear as you click each one.)

6 Click Next to display the dialog box prompting you for the worksheet cells to include in the chart. The cells you selected in step 2 appear in the Data Range text box (cells A3 through B7).

note If you organized your worksheet well, and if you selected the proper data, your chart should now contain the correct information (although the names might be too small to see). If your chart doesn't look right, use the option buttons and list boxes in this dialog box to change the cells used for the data series, names, and chart title.

7 Click Next to display the Chart Wizard dialog box that controls the chart's titles, legend, and data labels. Your pie chart appears in a sample window with the default settings, as shown here:

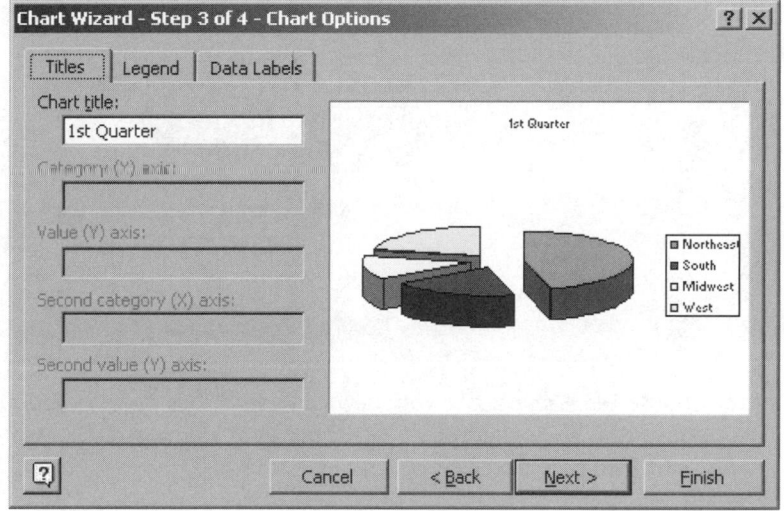

8 Starting from the Titles tab, change the chart title by typing **2001 Regional Sales Summary**; click the Legend tab, and clear the Show Legend check box. Then click the Data Labels tab and select both Category Name and Value for labels. Clear the Show Leader Lines option because the pie sections are few and the labels should be clear without leader lines.

tip It's often wise to use labels rather than relying on the legend if you will be printing and photocopying a chart and you fear that the distinctions in grayscales will be lost.

Finally, click Next to proceed to the final step. The Chart Wizard displays a dialog box asking you for the location of your new chart. You can either create a new workbook tab for the chart or place it as an object in one of your existing worksheets.

9 Click the As New Sheet button, type **Summary Chart** in the highlighted text box, and then click Finish.

Excel completes the pie chart and displays it in a new sheet with the name you assigned, Summary Chart. Excel adjusts the Zoom control on the Standard toolbar so that the entire chart is visible. The Charting toolbar also appears; we will cover that feature in "Formatting a Chart," on page 764.

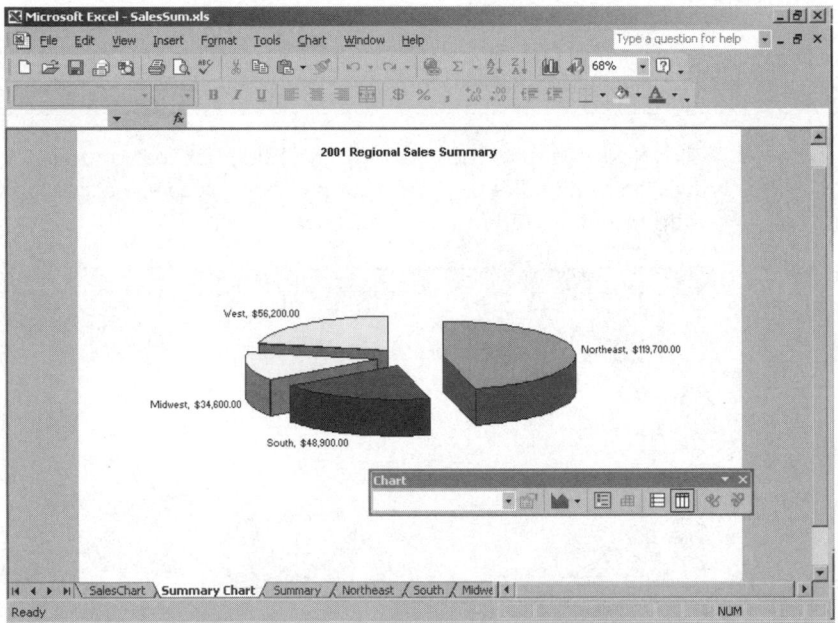

10 Choose File, Save to save your new chart to disk as part of your open workbook. You can now display the pie chart at any time by clicking the Summary Chart tab.

tip To get a better look at the title, labels, and data in your new chart, click the Zoom control on the Standard toolbar, and select a higher viewing percentage. You will find that 75% or 100% usually works well for reading the text in your chart and for formatting names.

Creating an Embedded Chart

Excel also allows you to create an in-place, or *embedded*, chart in an existing worksheet. This technique allows you to closely associate graphical images with the data in your worksheet. For example, within a bakery worksheet that contains inventory and sales data, you could create an area chart depicting bagel production. In the following example, we will show you how to add a column sales chart to a sales-summary worksheet.

> **tip** Another way to present the chart in close association with its underlying data (without embedding it) is to choose the chart option that displays the data within the chart area.

To create an embedded chart in a worksheet, follow these steps:

1 Prepare a worksheet that has rows and columns of data that you can chart. As you create the worksheet, set aside some room for a rectangular column chart.

2 Select the cell range containing the data that you want to plot. In our example we'll be creating the chart in Figure 27-3 that has groups of columns representing sales regions, so if you want to follow our example, you will need to select several columns of data. For this example, let's select two columns, as shown below:

	A	B	C	D	E	F
1	2001 Regional Sales Summary					
2						
3		1st Quarter	2nd Quarter	3rd Quarter	4th Quarter	
4	Northeast	$ 119,700.00	$ 125,100.00	$ 133,400.00	$ 139,500.00	
5	South	$ 48,900.00	$ 52,000.00	$ 49,600.00	$ 54,500.00	
6	Midwest	$ 34,600.00	$ 32,200.00	$ 47,000.00	$ 54,500.00	
7	West	$ 56,200.00	$ 49,000.00	$ 52,000.00	$ 51,300.00	
8	Totals	$ 259,400.00	$ 258,300.00	$ 282,000.00	$ 299,800.00	
9						

3 Click the Chart Wizard button on the Standard toolbar. (Creating an embedded chart is exactly like creating a stand-alone chart, except for specifying the chart location in the last step of the Chart Wizard.)

4 In the Chart Type dialog box, specify the chart type you want to use and click Next. (In this example, we'll use the default column chart type.)

5 The Chart Source Data dialog box reflects the data range selected in step 2. To add region names for the Category axis, choose the Series tab and click the Collapse Dialog Box button in the text box opposite Category (X) Axis Labels. Select cells A4:A7 and press Enter so that the dialog box appears as shown below. Click Next to proceed to the next step.

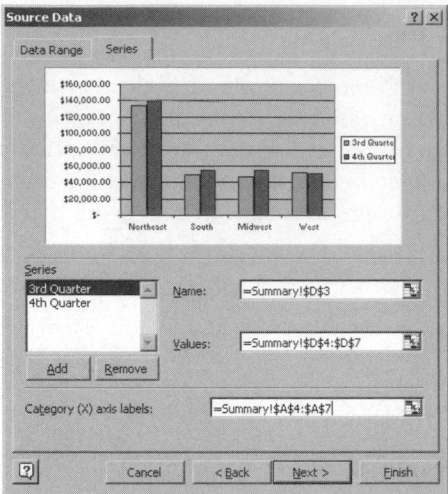

6 Customize your chart by choosing from the options presented in the Chart Options dialog box or accept Excel's settings. Notice that you have a different set of options for the column chart than you did for the pie chart.

In our chart, let's add a title for the chart and for each axis. On the Titles tab, type **Regional Sales Summary** for the Chart Title text box, **Regions** for the Category (X) Axis, and **Sales Revenue** for the Value (Y) Axis. Next, choose the Data Labels tab and select the Value check box to add labels that contain the exact value that each column represents.

> To modify fonts and numeric formats as shown in Figure 27-3, use the techniques described in "Formatting a Chart," on page 764.

7 When you're finished, click the Next button to display the Chart Location dialog box:

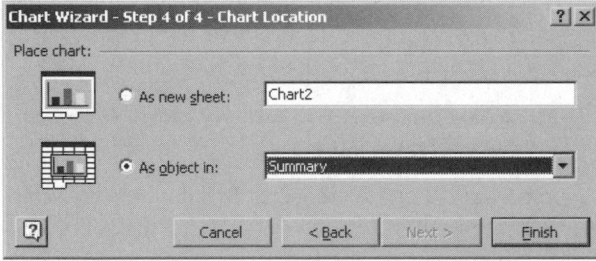

8 Click the As Object In option button, and then specify the worksheet in which you want to place the new chart by using the adjacent drop-down list. (We placed our chart in the Summary worksheet.)

9 Click Finish to complete the chart.

10 The Chart Wizard builds the chart to your specifications and places it in the middle of the worksheet, as shown in the following illustration. (Note that the chart is currently selected and has eight selection handles.)

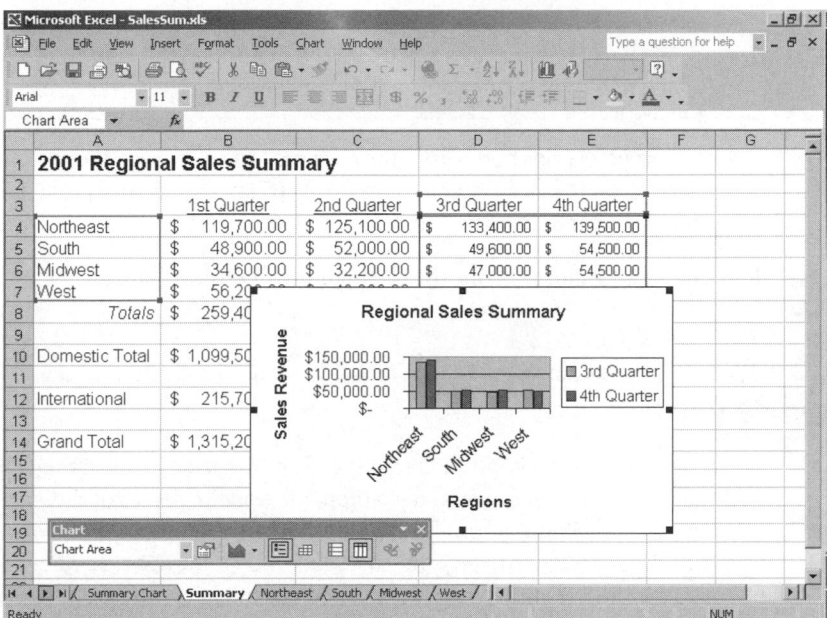

Working with Embedded Charts

When you embed an Excel chart in a worksheet, you create an object that can be resized, formatted, moved, and deleted like clip art or any other object. You can use the following editing techniques on embedded charts:

- To resize an embedded chart, move the mouse pointer to the edge of the chart and drag one of the selection handles.

- To format an embedded chart, double-click the chart (in its background area), and the Format Chart Area dialog box appears. Add borders to the chart from the Patterns tab or choose other commands from the Font or Properties tabs.

For more information, see "Formatting a Chart," on page 764.

- To move an embedded chart from one location to another in the worksheet, click within the object and drag it to a new location. To move the chart to a new worksheet, click the chart, and then choose Chart, Location. To move the chart to another workbook or Microsoft Office XP application, click the chart, choose Edit, Cut; open or switch to the destination document; and then choose Edit Paste.

- To delete an embedded chart, select the chart and press the Delete key.

11 Drag the chart to the desired location in the worksheet and resize it to display the amount of detail you want. (Drag the chart by one of its edges so that you don't inadvertently rearrange the chart components.)

> **tip** Excel creates embedded charts small to make them easy to move and format. However, your chart usually looks better if you enlarge it.

12 When you're finished, click outside the chart to remove the selection handles and lock it in place on your worksheet. (Click the chart to reactivate the selection handles in the future.)

 The Charts.xls example is on the companion CD to this book.

InsideOut

Whether you embed a chart or create it on a new sheet, Excel changes the chart as you change its data. In general, this automatic updating is a good thing: your chart remains current without your making a deliberate effort. But what if you *want* to freeze the chart? You can copy the chart to another workbook, but even then, Excel updates the chart (as long as you choose to update links when prompted) because the program establishes a link between the chart and its external data set.

Should you want to freeze the chart, your best bet is to break the link. Copy the chart to an external workbook. Then open that workbook, choose Edit, Links, select the link between the chart and its data (if more than one link is present), and click the Break Link button. When Excel warns you about the consequences of breaking the link, click Break Links.

Formatting a Chart

If you're content to use Excel's default formatting for your chart, you're all finished—just tidy up your chart and print it. If you're like most people, however, you probably can't resist adding a label here or changing the point size there. In this section you will learn how to format charts by changing the chart type, editing titles and gridlines, adjusting the legend, adding text, and controlling character formatting. What you learn will apply both to embedded charts and to stand-alone chart sheets in the workbook.

> **tip** To reverse the order of the items on an axis, you can make the change in the Format dialog box. Select the axis, choose Format, Selected Axis, and display the Scale tab. Select the check box for reversing the order, which is labeled to reflect the axis itself, whether it contain values, categories, or series (for 3-D charts only).

Exploring the Chart Menu

When you created the pie chart in the first example in this chapter, you might not have noticed that a Chart menu replaced the Data menu on the menu bar and that several commands on the remaining menus changed. Excel's Chart menu includes commands that are specifically designed for charting, as shown below. (Note that your Chart menu might be customized differently.)

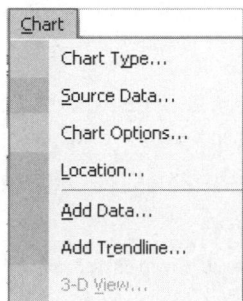

> **note** The Chart menu replaces the Data menu whenever a chart is the active object—either because you select a sheet that contains only a chart or because you click on some element of an embedded chart.

Using the Chart Toolbar

The Chart toolbar shown in Figure 27-4 contains several buttons designed to help you format your chart. This toolbar also contains the Chart Objects list box, which you can use to select different components of your chart for editing (such as the chart title, legend, and plot areas). Many of the buttons on the Chart toolbar correspond to commands on the Chart menu, as you will see in the following sections. Display the Chart toolbar at any time by choosing it from the Toolbars submenu of the View menu.

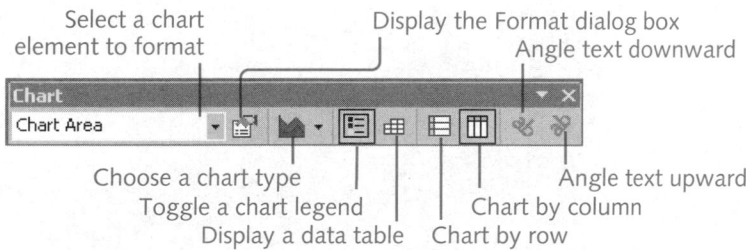

Figure 27-4. The Chart toolbar appears when a chart is active in the workbook. To remove it, click the Close button.

Changing the Chart Type

Even after you create a chart, you're not locked in to one particular chart type. If your data supports it, you can reformat your chart to use any of Excel's 14 chart types. (For example, you can change your pie chart into a column chart.) To switch between chart types, click the Chart Type button on the Chart toolbar or choose the Chart menu and then Chart Type.

To change the pie chart you created earlier into a column chart by using the Chart toolbar, follow these steps:

1 If the chart is embedded, click it to select it, and then click the Chart toolbar. If the chart appears in its own worksheet, simply display the worksheet.

2 Click the arrow on the Chart Type button on the Chart toolbar to display pictures of the various chart types.

3 Click the 3-D Column Chart button. (When you move the pointer over each chart type, its name appears.)

Your chart changes shape to match the selected chart type. The following screen shows how your pie chart looks when it's changed into a 3-D column chart. (The value labels for the data points were "tweaked" for better visibility.)

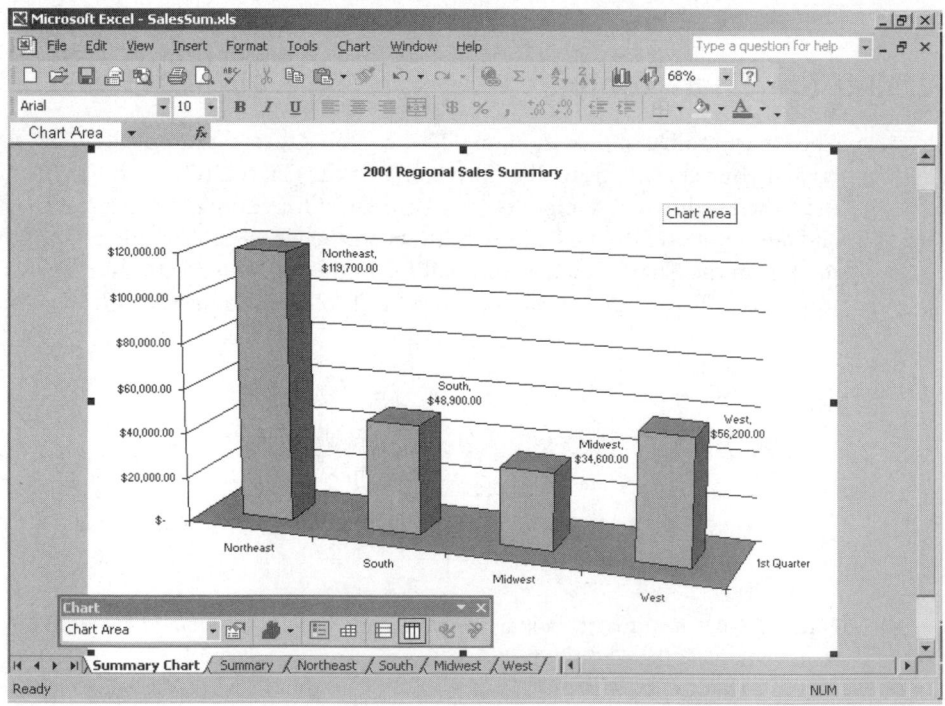

---

note **Choosing Additional Chart Sub-Types**

For a wider selection of chart types (for example, to change from 3-D view to 2-D view), select the chart, and choose Chart and then Chart Type. Here you can pick from over 70 choices in the Chart Sub-Type list boxes for each chart type.

Changing Titles and Labels

You can edit the text in your chart's titles and labels as well as modify the font, alignment, and background pattern. If you select a data label, you can change its numeric formatting.

To edit title or label text, follow these steps:

1 Display the chart that you want to modify. If the chart is embedded in a worksheet, click the chart to activate it. Excel displays its charting commands and tools.

Troubleshooting

Selecting Accurately in a Chart

It's difficult or impossible to select the item desired in the chart.

Check that you've selected the part of the chart you want to edit by making sure the selection handles indicate the specific object and not the entire chart. If you can't select the specific item (a label along the Category axis, for example), you might have to edit that item in the underlying data to have the change reflected in the chart.

---

2 Use the Zoom control to zoom in on the title or label so that you can read it, if necessary. The best view for editing text is usually 100%.

3 Click the title or label in the chart. (If you're selecting a label, click a second time to select a particular label in the series.) Selection handles surround the text.

4 Click again to insert the text pointer at the spot you want to edit. You can insert new text and use the Backspace and Delete keys to delete unwanted text.

---

tip You can check the spelling of the text in a chart by selecting the text object and choosing Spelling from the Tools menu.

---

5 When you've completed your edits, press the Esc key once to remove the text insertion marker and then press Esc a second time to remove the selection handles. (You can also click outside the chart to remove the selection handles.)

Changing Character Formatting

To change a title or label font, alignment, or pattern, follow these steps:

1 Click the chart title or an axis title or a label. Selection handles appear around the text.

2 Choose Format, and then Selected Chart Title or Selected Axis Title (for a title) or Selected Data Labels (for a label). Only one of the commands will be available. You will see a dialog box similar to the one shown in Figure 27-5.

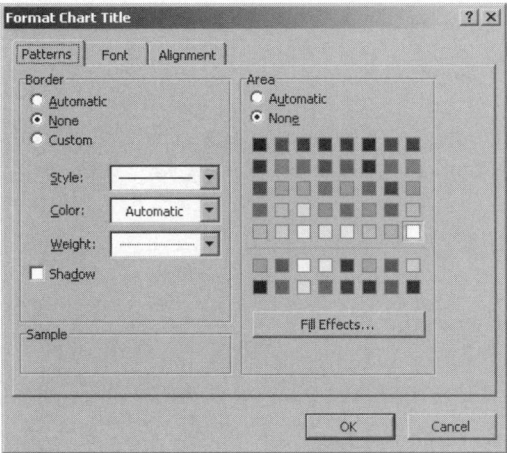

Figure 27-5. You can format chart titles and labels in the same way as regular worksheet text.

> **note** If you're formatting a label, the dialog box will also have a Number tab. We'll discuss this tab in the next example.

3 Use the Patterns, Font, and Alignment tabs to modify the borders or colors, adjust the character formatting in the text, or adjust the text orientation. For example, if you plan to print your chart, you might want to increase the text's point size using the Font tab.

4 When you've finished formatting the text, click OK.

> To learn more about formatting text, see Chapter 23, "Expert Formatting Techniques."

Adjusting Numeric Formatting in Labels

If you selected a label in your chart, your dialog box includes a Number tab, as shown in Figure 27-6. To use the Number tab to adjust the numeric formatting in labels, complete the following steps:

1 Click a label or an axis that contains numeric data such as percentages or dollar amounts. By selecting an axis, you also select the numeric values associated with the intersection of the gridlines and the axis.

---

tip   To add or change data labels, use the Chart Options command on the Chart menu.

---

2 Choose Format, Selected Axis. (If you selected a label, choose the Selected Data Labels command.)

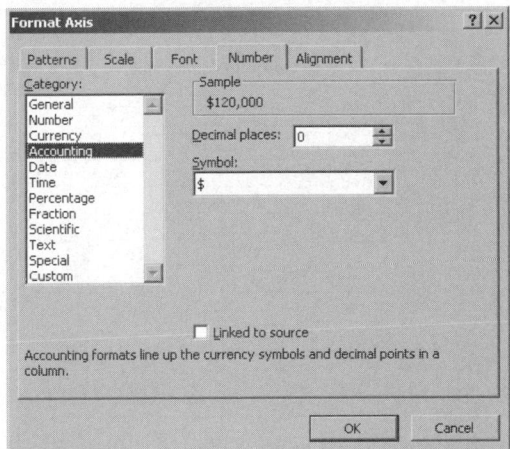

Figure 27-6.   The Number tab lets you change the number formatting in chart labels.

3 Click the Number tab of the Format dialog box. Your screen will look like the one shown in Figure 27-6. (If you're formatting an axis, the dialog box also has a Scale tab, which you can use to adjust the numbers and tick marks along the axis.)

4 Click the numeric category that you want to use and specify a new number of decimal places if necessary. Because our labels are in the Currency format, we'll set the decimal places to zero to remove cents and make more room on our chart.

5 When you finish formatting, click OK.

Chapter 27

Adjusting Gridlines

With most chart types (the exceptions being pie and doughnut charts), you can include gridlines that extend horizontally from the x-axis or vertically from the y-axis. Gridlines help you to associate numbers accurately with the pictures in your chart, and they're especially useful if you need to make exact comparisons between categories of data.

To add gridlines to your chart, follow these steps:

1 Display the chart. If your chart is embedded in a worksheet, click the chart to activate Excel's charting commands and tools.

2 Choose Chart, and then Chart Options to display the Chart Options dialog box. Then click the Gridlines tab (see Figure 27-7).

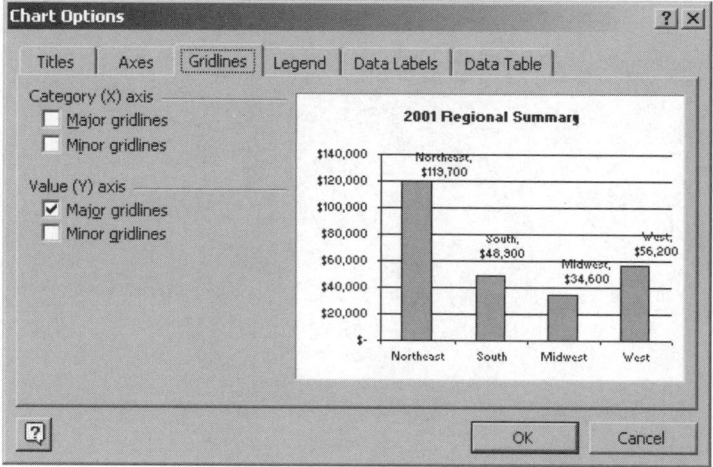

Figure 27-7. The check boxes in the Gridlines tab determine which gridlines appear.

3 To add gridlines to one or more axes, select the corresponding Major Gridlines check boxes. If you want to create a denser pattern of gridlines, select one or more Minor Gridlines check boxes also.

4 Click OK to add the gridlines. To remove the gridlines, simply remove all the check marks from the Gridlines check boxes and click OK.

tip You can also remove gridlines by clicking the gridlines in your chart and pressing Delete.

Modifying the Chart Legend

A chart *legend* describes what each color or pattern represents in a chart so that you can compare the values in a category. Excel lets you change the font, colors, and location of an existing chart legend by using a special dialog box. You can add a legend to a chart when you first build the chart using the Chart Wizard, or later by clicking the

Legend button on the Chart toolbar. Because the Legend button is an on or off toggle, you can add or remove a chart legend quickly, to see whether you like it. If you remove the chart legend, you will have more room on your chart for graphing the data.

To modify the font, colors, or location of a chart legend, follow these steps:

1 Display the chart and click the legend, which is then surrounded by selection handles. (You can resize the legend by dragging any of these handles.)

2 Choose Format, Selected Legend to display the Format Legend dialog box. The dialog box contains three tabs that let you control the border, colors, and patterns used for the legend box; the font used for the legend text; and the location of the legend in relation to the chart.

3 Use the Patterns, Font, and Placement tabs to customize the legend. When you finish, click OK.

tip To quickly format the text in a chart legend, you can also use the Font, Font Size, Bold, Italic, and Underline buttons on the toolbar.

Changing the Viewing Angle in 3-D Charts

Excel offers you 3-D chart types in the Area, Bar, Column, Line, Pie, Radar, Surface, Cylinder, Cone, and Pyramid categories. Three-dimensional charts have much in common with two-dimensional charts, but they add a feeling of depth that brings realism and visual interest to your data. You can change the orientation, or *viewing angle*, of a 3-D chart by selecting the chart and choosing 3-D View from the Chart menu, as shown here:

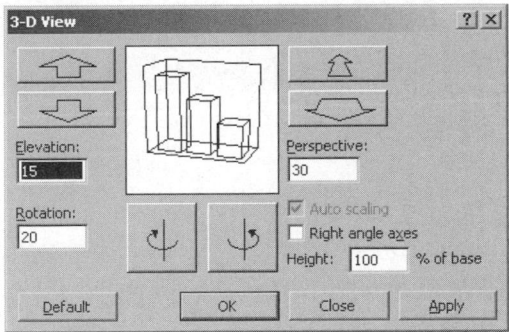

To tilt the chart up or back, click the large up or down buttons in the 3-D View dialog box above the Elevation text box. To rotate the chart left or right, click the clockwise or counterclockwise buttons beneath the chart preview window. You can also change the perspective or line-of-sight angle by clicking the up or down buttons above the Perspective text box after you type a value. (However, these settings are only available for 3-D charts.)

Copying Chart Formats

If you're creating a number of charts that you intend to present as a set, you can ensure that they are formatted consistently by copying the formats of one to each of the others. This technique is similar to format painting as you might use it in worksheets or in other Office XP applications. To copy chart formats, complete the following steps:

1 Select the chart area (rather than a specific element) of the chart that you want to model the other charts after.

2 Choose Edit, Copy.

3 Activate the chart to which you want the new formatting to apply.

4 Choose Edit, Paste Special. In the Paste Special dialog box, select the Formats option and click OK.

Excel reformats the second chart to match the first, possibly including some aspects that you didn't intend to change, such as the chart type or the scaling of the axis. You can undo the Paste Special operation or reverse the unwanted changes individually.

Adding Labels and Arrows

Have you ever been lost in a shopping mall, unable to determine your location or find the store you're looking for? When this happens, it's comforting to find the mall map, with its familiar *You Are Here* arrow and message that identify your location and help you get your bearings. As you design your charts, you can use Excel's charting commands to add similar pointers to your own pictures. If you have important aspects that you want to highlight, this could be the perfect tool.

To highlight a chart attribute by adding an arrow, follow these steps:

1 Display the chart that you want to embellish with an arrow. If the chart is embedded in a worksheet, click the chart to activate Excel's charting commands and tools.

2 Click the Drawing button on Excel's Standard toolbar.

Drawing

Excel then displays its multipurpose Drawing toolbar (typically in the lower part of the screen, just above the status bar), as shown in the illustration at the top of the next page.

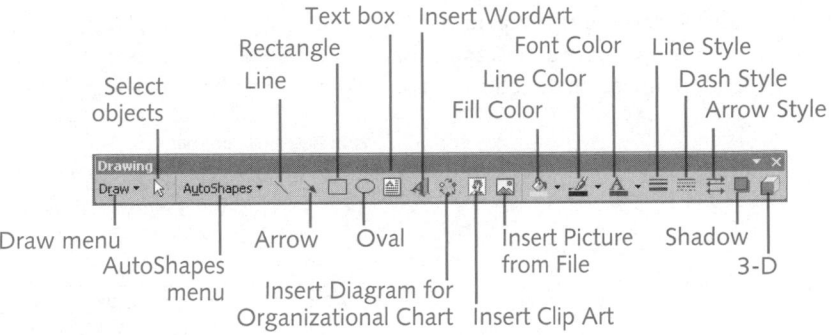

3 Click the Arrow button on the Drawing toolbar. The mouse pointer changes to drawing crosshairs.

4 Draw the line that will be your arrow—clicking and holding at the arrow's tail, dragging and then releasing at the arrow's head. When you release the mouse button, a default-style arrow appears.

5 Customize the arrow by adjusting the line's weight with the Line Style button, selecting a dashed line style with the Dash Style button, or adjusting the arrow's head and tail with the Arrow Style button.

> The Drawing toolbar contains several tools to further embellish your charts and worksheets. For more information, see Chapter 6, "Adding Professional Graphics and Special Effects to Office XP Documents."

To add text to the arrow, follow these steps:

1 Click the Text Box button on the Drawing toolbar.

2 Use the drag technique to draw a rectangle to hold your label text. When it's approximately the right size, release the mouse button.

3 Type the label text and click near the border of the text box to select it.

4 Use the Formatting toolbar to set the text's font, size, and style. Use the Drawing toolbar to change the text's color (click the Font Color button), to add an outline to the text box (click the Line Style button), and to set the outline's color (click the Line Color button).

> **tip** You can reposition free-floating text boxes and arrows in your chart by selecting them and dragging them with the mouse. To delete a text box or arrow, select the object and press Delete.

Chapter 27

773

5 Resize the text box using the selection handles and place the text box where you want it by dragging the border. Then click outside the chart area to remove the selection handles. Our chart now looks like this one:

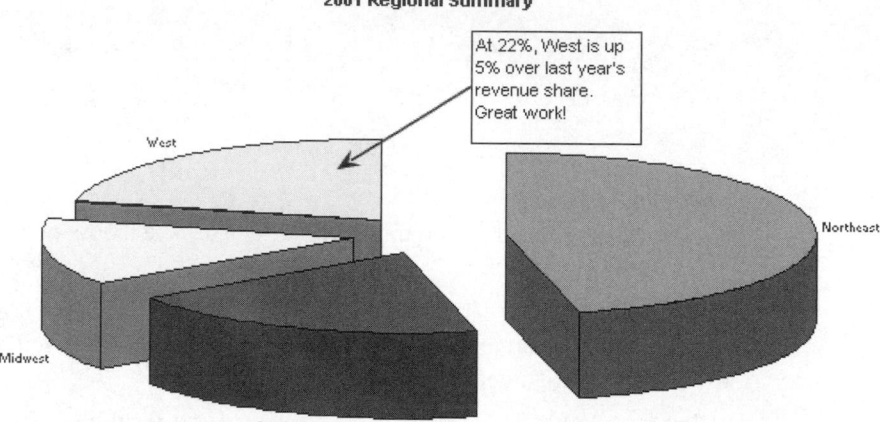

2001 Regional Summary

At 22%, West is up 5% over last year's revenue share. Great work!

West

Northeast

Midwest

South

6 Click the Close button on the Drawing toolbar to remove it from the screen. (If you don't see a Close button, right-click the Drawing toolbar and clear Drawing to remove it from the screen.)

Printing a Chart

When you've finished creating attractive charts, you will most certainly want to print them. Printing charts isn't much different from printing worksheets, but you have a few extra options. If you're using a black-and-white printer, you will want to examine your chart in Print Preview to verify that its colors have been properly converted to grayscale shading. If you're printing an embedded chart, you have the option of printing the chart with or without the worksheet data around it.

To double-check chart colors in Print Preview, follow these steps:

Print Preview

1 Display the chart that you want to print, and then click the Print Preview button on the Standard toolbar.

2 Verify the chart shading—you should be able to distinguish one shade of gray from another. (If you're using a color printer, you will, of course, see everything in color.)

3 Click Close to exit Print Preview.

Troubleshooting

Move Beyond Shades of Difference

Differences in shading are not sufficient to distinguish data series in printed charts.

If you're not happy with the shading—especially with any lack of contrast between supposedly distinct data series or data points—double-click the chart piece you want to change and specify a new color or pattern. Depending on the chart type, you will be working with either the Format Data Series or the Format Data Point dialog box.

In the Patterns tab, click the Fill Effects button and look at the options on the Pattern tab. These are effective for creating readily distinguishable regions for black-and-white printing. In fact, if you choose File, Page Setup and click the Chart tab, you will find a check box for black-and-white printing under the Print Quality options. This option goes beyond grayscaling; it substitutes patterns for colors to provide clear distinctions in the printed output.

To print a chart, follow these steps:

1 Display the chart that you want to print, either as a stand-alone chart sheet or as an embedded chart in the worksheet.

2 If you want to print an embedded chart only, and not the surrounding worksheet data as well, click the chart first.

3 Choose File, Print to open the Print dialog box.

4 Specify the print options that you want and then click OK to send your chart to the printer.

Troubleshooting

Chart "Scalability"

Excel is printing the chart larger than expected.

By default, Excel prints a chart on an entire page. If you want your printed chart to be the same size as the chart in your worksheet, choose File, Page Setup, click the Chart tab, and then select the Custom option before printing. This option tells Excel to render the chart on paper exactly as it appears in your worksheet. Use Print Preview to get an idea of the size differences.

Power Database Techniques: Lists, Filters, and Pivot Tables

If you routinely track large amounts of information in your business—customer mailing lists, phone lists, product inventories, sales transactions, and so on—you can use the extensive list-management capabilities of Microsoft Excel 2002 to make your job easier. A *list* is a table of data stored in a worksheet, organized into columns of fields and rows of records. A list is essentially a *database*, but because lists are stored in Excel workbooks and not in formatted files created by database programs such as Microsoft Access or Microsoft FoxPro, Microsoft has chosen to use the word *list* as the preferred term.

In this chapter you'll learn how to create a list in a workbook, sort the list based on one or more fields, locate important records by using filters, organize and analyze entries by using subtotals, and create summary information by using pivot tables and pivot charts. The lists that you create will be compatible with Access, and, if you're not already familiar with Access, the techniques that you learn here will give you a head start on learning several database commands and terms.

Using a List as a Database

A list is a collection of rows and columns of consistently formatted data adhering to somewhat stricter rules than an ordinary worksheet. To build a list that works with all of Excel's list-management commands, you need to follow a few guide-

777

 lines. Figure 28-1 shows a simple sales-history list that has five columns, or *fields*, and a dozen sales transaction *records*. This list is saved in Pivot.xls, which you can load from the companion CD to this book.

Each row represents a record in the list.

Each column represents a field containing one type of information.

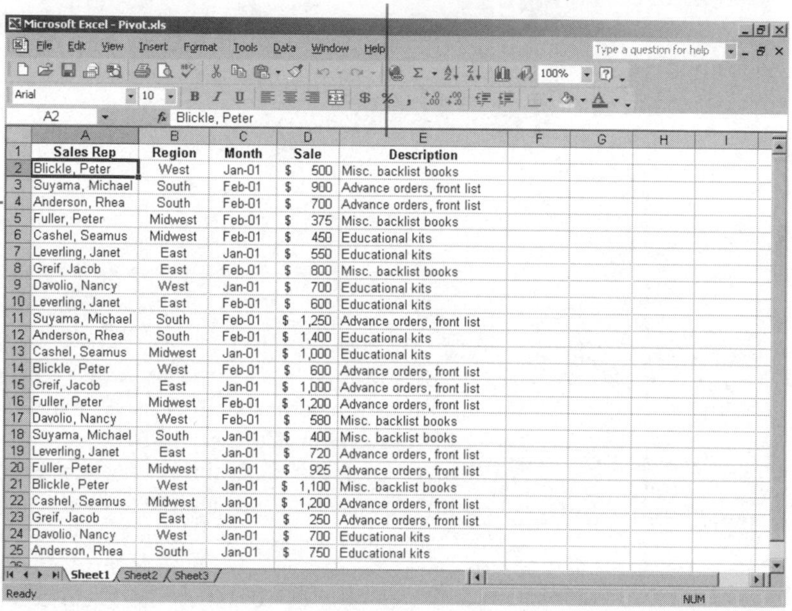

	A	B	C	D	E	F	G	H	I
1	**Sales Rep**	**Region**	**Month**	**Sale**	**Description**				
2	Blickle, Peter	West	Jan-01	$ 500	Misc. backlist books				
3	Suyama, Michael	South	Feb-01	$ 900	Advance orders, front list				
4	Anderson, Rhea	South	Feb-01	$ 700	Advance orders, front list				
5	Fuller, Peter	Midwest	Feb-01	$ 375	Misc. backlist books				
6	Cashel, Seamus	Midwest	Feb-01	$ 450	Educational kits				
7	Leverling, Janet	East	Jan-01	$ 550	Educational kits				
8	Greif, Jacob	East	Feb-01	$ 800	Misc. backlist books				
9	Davolio, Nancy	West	Jan-01	$ 700	Educational kits				
10	Leverling, Janet	East	Feb-01	$ 600	Educational kits				
11	Suyama, Michael	South	Feb-01	$ 1,250	Advance orders, front list				
12	Anderson, Rhea	South	Feb-01	$ 1,400	Educational kits				
13	Cashel, Seamus	Midwest	Jan-01	$ 1,000	Educational kits				
14	Blickle, Peter	West	Feb-01	$ 600	Advance orders, front list				
15	Greif, Jacob	East	Jan-01	$ 1,000	Advance orders, front list				
16	Fuller, Peter	Midwest	Feb-01	$ 1,200	Advance orders, front list				
17	Davolio, Nancy	West	Feb-01	$ 580	Misc. backlist books				
18	Suyama, Michael	South	Jan-01	$ 400	Misc. backlist books				
19	Leverling, Janet	East	Jan-01	$ 720	Advance orders, front list				
20	Fuller, Peter	Midwest	Jan-01	$ 925	Advance orders, front list				
21	Blickle, Peter	West	Jan-01	$ 1,100	Misc. backlist books				
22	Cashel, Seamus	Midwest	Jan-01	$ 1,200	Advance orders, front list				
23	Greif, Jacob	East	Jan-01	$ 250	Advance orders, front list				
24	Davolio, Nancy	West	Jan-01	$ 700	Educational kits				
25	Anderson, Rhea	South	Jan-01	$ 750	Educational kits				

Figure 28-1. In an Excel worksheet, a list typically includes column headings, for easier manipulation.

When you create a list, keep the following in mind:

- Maintain a fixed number of columns (or categories) of information; you can alter the number of rows as you add, delete, or rearrange records to keep your list up to date.

- Use each column to hold the same type of information.

- Don't leave blank rows or columns in the list area; you can leave blank cells, if necessary.

- Make your list the only information in the worksheet so that Excel can more easily recognize the data as a list.

- Maintain your data's integrity by entering identical information consistently. For example, don't enter an expense category as *Ad* in one row, *Adv* in another, and *Advertising* in a third if all belong to the same classification.

To create a list in Excel, follow these steps:

1 Open a new workbook or a new sheet in an existing workbook.

2 Create a column heading for each field in the list, format the headings in bold type, and adjust their alignment.

3 Format the cells below the column headings for the data that you plan to use. This can include number formats (such as currency or date), alignment, or any other formats.

 The Pivot.xls example is on the companion CD to this book.

For information about sharing a list with other users over a network, see "Managing Shared Workbooks," on page 698.

4 Add new records (your data) below the column headings, taking care to be consistent in your use of words and titles so that you can organize related records into groups later. Enter as many rows as you need, making sure that there are no empty rows in your list, not even between the column headings and the first record. See Figure 28-1 for a sample list of information. When you've finished, save your workbook. If your list grows to include many records, consider keeping a separate backup copy in a safe place as an extra precaution.

InsideOut

Let AutoComplete Finish Typing Your Words

Excel's AutoComplete feature helps you insert repetitive list entries consistently by recognizing the words you type and finishing them for you. A nice alternative is to right-click the cell and choose the Pick From List command to reuse a previously typed entry.

To activate the AutoComplete feature, choose Tools, Options, click the Edit tab, and select the Enable AutoComplete For Cell Values check box. It's important that repeated names and other data (such as *January*, *Midwest Region*, and so on) be entered identically from record to record, to enable Excel to recognize the data for grouping, sorting, and calculating.

Using a Form for Data Entry

To make it easy to manage the data in your list, Excel lets you add, delete, and search for records by using the Data, Form command. When you choose Form, a customized dialog box appears, showing the fields in your list and several list-management command buttons (see Figure 28-2, on page 780). The name of the current worksheet also appears on the dialog box title bar.

Chapter 28

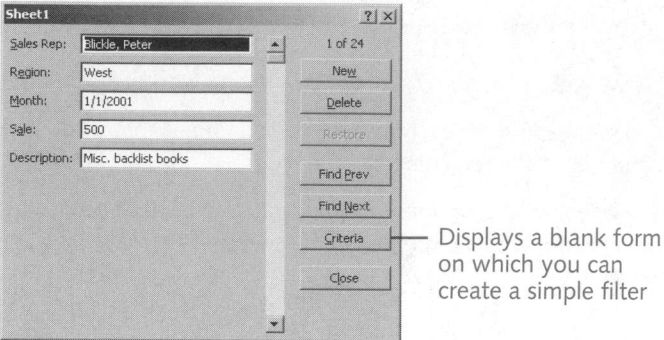

Displays a blank form
on which you can
create a simple filter

Figure 28-2. The Form command gives you another way to enter data into the rows and columns of a list.

When you choose the Form command, the first record in the list appears. You can scroll to other records by clicking the vertical scroll bar. To display a blank record, you can scroll to the bottom of the list or click New. Excel adds new records to the end of the list. Although you'll often add records by typing them directly into the worksheet, using the Form command is a useful alternative (for, say, a less-experienced colleague you've asked to help enter data), and in some cases you'll find that it works faster.

The Criteria button lets you limit the records that you see in the Form window by applying a simple filter. When you click it, Excel lets you enter search criteria on a blank form to match entries in the corresponding field; your search criteria can include relational operators, such as < and >. When you specify criteria for fields that contain text, Excel finds matches when you supply only initial letters (*St* matches *Stevens* or *Stewart*), much as it would if you were using the Find command. It also accepts the familiar wildcard characters ? (to match any single character) and * (to match any string).

In Figure 28-3, three sample criteria are entered. Click Find Prev to move to the first matching record that precedes the current record (row); click Find Next to move to the first record after the current record. Click Criteria to refine the search information; click Close to return to the list (and clear the criteria).

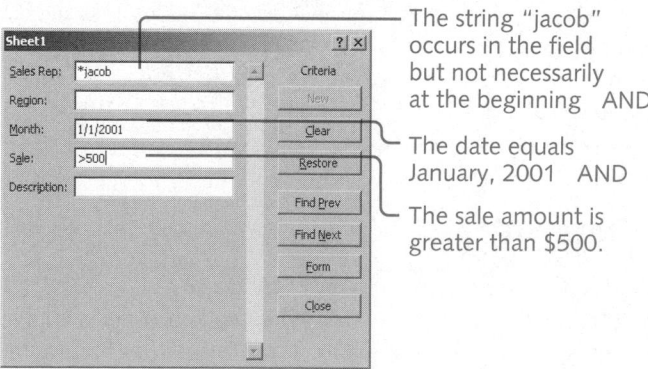

The string "jacob"
occurs in the field
but not necessarily
at the beginning   AND

The date equals
January, 2001   AND

The sale amount is
greater than $500.

Figure 28-3. The Criteria button displays a blank form with fields into which you can enter search information.

Chapter 28

Validating Data As You Enter It

If several people are using your Excel list, you might want to control the type of information they're allowed to enter into worksheet cells in order to minimize typing mistakes. For example, you might want to require that only January or February dates can be entered into the Month column or that only dollar values in a particular range (say, $0–$5,000) can be entered into the Sale column. With Excel you can enforce input requirements such as these by using a formatting option called *data validation*. When you use data validation, you protect part or all of your worksheet from invalid input that might cause formulas or list-management tools to produce incorrect results.

> **tip** Remember too that Excel also lets you protect parts of your sheet from changes by a user. See "Protecting Worksheets and Workbooks," on page 705.

To enforce data validation of a particular range of worksheet cells, follow these steps:

1 Select the cells in the column that you want to protect with data validation. This should include cells already containing data as well as the blank cells below, where you'll be adding new records. (If you're not sure how long your list will be, you may want to select the entire column.)

2 Choose Data, Validation. The Data Validation dialog box opens. Click the Settings tab.

3 In the Allow drop-down list, specify the input format you want to require for the selected cells. Your options are Any Value (used to remove existing data validation), Whole Number, Decimal, List, Date, Time, Text Length, and Custom (a format you specify by writing your own formula).

When you select a value in the Allow drop-down list, additional text boxes appear, as shown below, that let you specify extra input conditions or *restrictions*, such as the smallest number and the largest number Excel will accept.

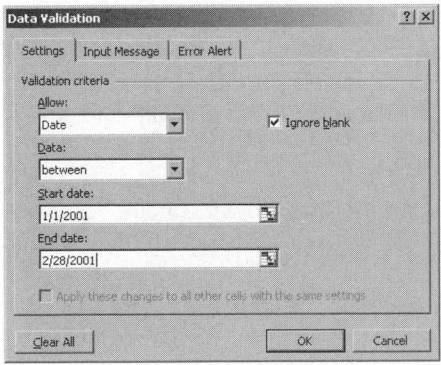

4 Click the Input Message tab, as shown below, and select Show Input Message When Cell Is Selected to specify a message that will appear when the cell is selected.

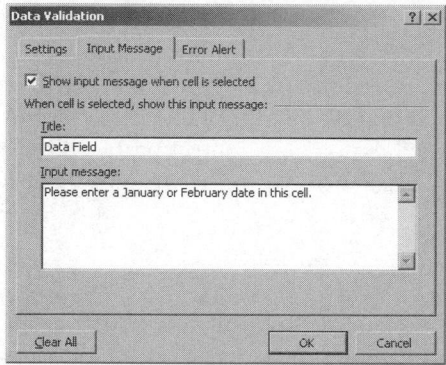

In the Input Message text box, type the words you want displayed in the pop-up box that appears when a user selects a cell containing the data validation formatting. (This box is optional, but using it helps your users discover the requirements you've established *before* they make a mistake.)

5 Click the Error Alert tab, as shown below, and select Show Error Alert After Invalid Data Is Entered to specify the type of error message you want Excel to display if a user enters inappropriate information into a cell.

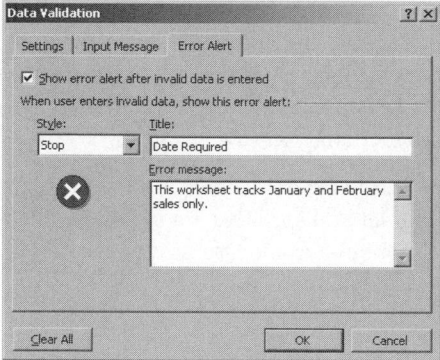

6 In the Style drop-down list, select one of the following options:

- Stop (to block the input)

- Warning (to caution the user but allow the input)

- Information (to display a note but allow the input)

7 In the Error Message text box, type the words you want displayed in the error message dialog box that appears if the user enters invalid data. For example, a useful phrase might be *This worksheet tracks January and*

February sales only. (The Title text box lets you enter text that will appear as the title of the Error Message dialog box.)

8 Click OK to complete the Data Validation dialog box. If you specified the options shown in step 6, you'll see a gentle error message similar to the following if you enter the wrong type of data in a cell that has active data validation:

Sorting Rows and Columns

Once your records are organized into a list, you can use several commands on the Data menu to rearrange and analyze the data. The Sort command allows you to arrange the records in a different order based on the values in one or more columns. You can sort records in ascending or descending order or in a custom order, such as by days of the week, months of the year, or job title.

The Pivot.xls example is on the companion CD to this book.

To sort a list based on one column, follow these steps:

1 Click a cell in the column that you want to use as the basis for sorting the list.

2 Choose Data, Sort. Excel selects all the records in your list and displays the following dialog box:

3 The Sort By drop-down list contains the heading for the column you selected. If you like, you can now select a different column in the list box for the sort.

4 Click one of the sort order option buttons to specify ascending order (A to Z, lowest to highest, earliest date to latest) or descending order (Z to A, highest to lowest, latest date to earliest).

5 Click OK to run the sort. If you sorted the first column in ascending order, your screen will look similar to this:

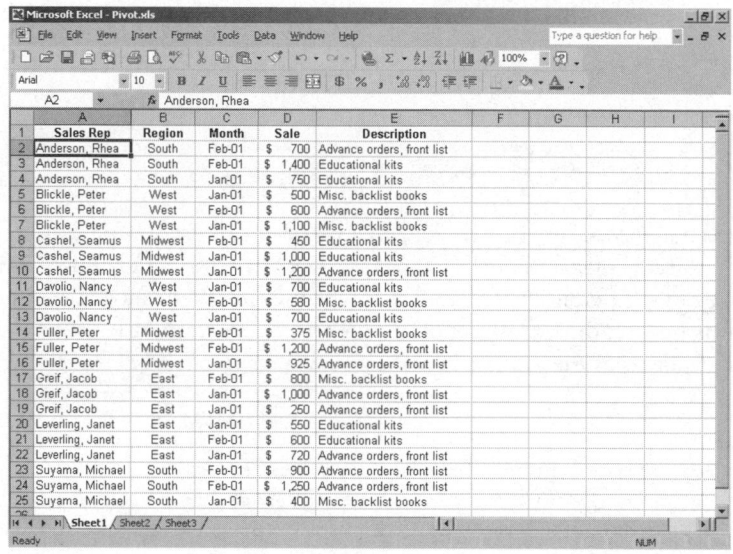

---

tip **Click a Cell, Sort a List**

Sort Ascending

Sort Descending

To quickly sort a list based on a single column, click a cell in the column, and then click either the Sort Ascending or Sort Descending button on the Standard toolbar. Excel rearranges the list in the order that you selected. If you select an entire column and attempt to sort it, Excel displays a dialog box that lets you either sort the entire list (by expanding the selected region) or sort only the entries in the column. If you sort only the column entries, they won't remain in the same rows with the records to which they belong.

Sorting on More Than One Column

If you have records in your list that have identical entries in the column you're sorting with, you can specify additional sorting criteria to further organize your list. To sort a list based on two or three columns, follow these steps:

1 Click a cell in the list that you want to sort.

2 Choose Data, Sort. Excel selects the records in your list and displays the Sort dialog box.

3 Select the primary field for the sort in the Sort By drop-down list. Specify ascending or descending order for that column.

4 Click the first Then By drop-down list and pick a second column for the sort to further sort any records that have identical entries in the primary field. Specify ascending or descending order for the second sort as well.

5 If it's required, click the next Then By drop-down list and pick a third column for the sort. Once more, specify ascending or descending order. (Your sorts needn't all be in the same direction.) A Sort dialog box that has three levels of sorting is shown here:

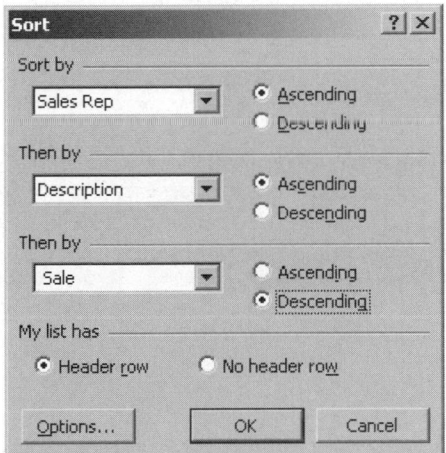

6 Click OK to run the sort.

The example on page 786 shows how a sort would look based on the options shown above.

These three records demonstrate how the three sort fields
are applied. The primary field is Sales Rep (ascending),
followed by Description (ascending), and then Sale (descending).

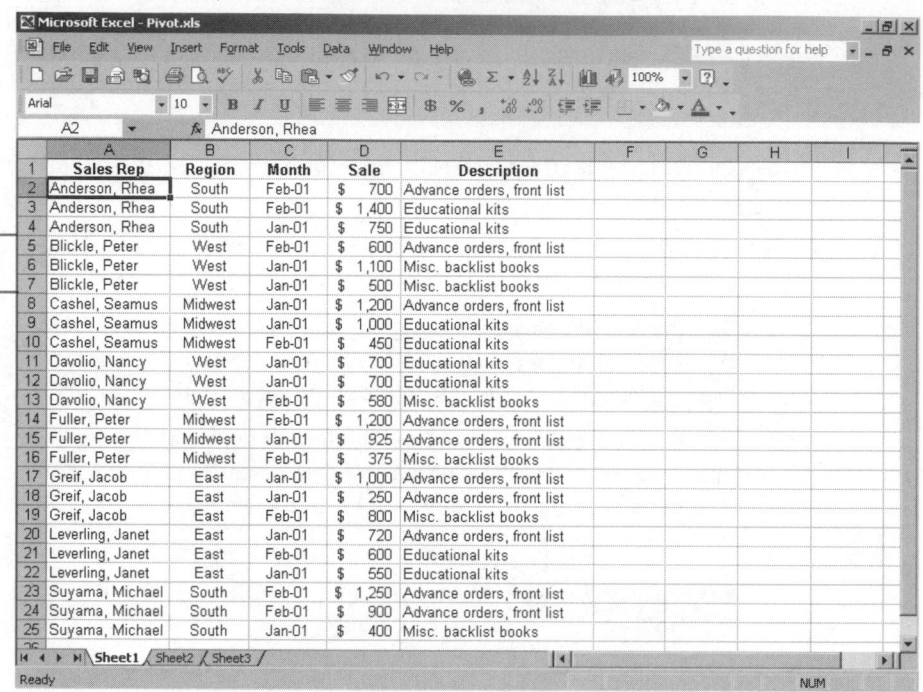

Note that the columns you specify in the Then By sections are used only to arrange
records that are otherwise identical for sorting purposes—not to control the entire
sort. (For this reason, numbers in the Sale column are only in descending order when
both the Sales Rep and the Description fields are identical.)

Troubleshooting

Cell Reference Roulette

Sorting a list created invalid results or error values for cells containing formulas.

Sorting a list that contains formulas can make a fine mess of the cell references within
the formulas. If you sort by row, you'll be all right only if the formulas in each row
refer only to other cells in the same row. Otherwise, undo the sort and change cell
references in formulas to absolute references to cells outside the list, preferably on a
different worksheet. To restore a list to its original order after a sort, choose Edit,
Undo Sort immediately after running the sort or display the Undo button's drop-down
list and click an earlier sort action to reverse it. (Keep in mind that selecting an earlier
sort action using the Undo list will reverse all actions up to and including the sort.)

Creating Your Own Custom Sort Order

Excel allows you to create custom sort orders so that you can rearrange lists that don't follow predictable alphanumeric or chronologic patterns. For example, you can create a custom sort order for the regions of the country (West, Midwest, East, South) to tell Excel to sort the regions in the way *you* want rather than by strict alphabetic rules. When you define a custom sort order, it appears in the Options dialog box and is available to all the workbooks in your system.

To create a custom sort order, follow these steps:

1 Choose Tools, Options, and then click the Custom Lists tab.

2 Click the line NEW LIST under Custom Lists, and the text pointer appears in the List Entries list box. This is where you'll type the items in your custom list. (In this example you'll create the custom order West, Midwest, South, East.)

3 Type **West, Midwest, South, East**, and then click Add. You can either separate each value with a comma or type each one on a separate line.

The new custom order appears in the Custom Lists list box, as shown in Figure 28-4. You can now use this sorting order to sort your columns, as described in the next section of this chapter, "Using a Custom Sort Order."

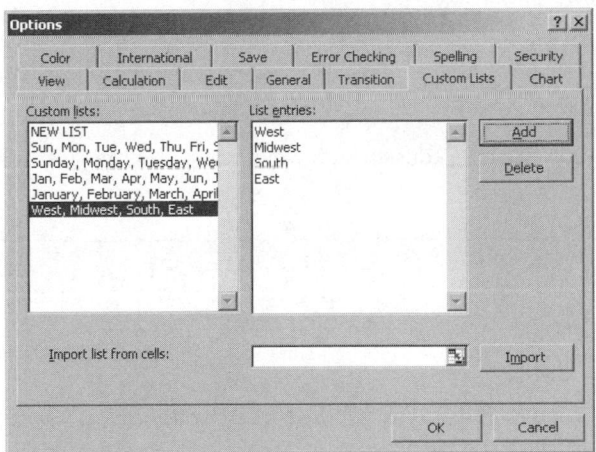

Figure 28-4. The Custom Lists tab lets you add, delete, and edit Excel's collection of custom sorting orders.

4 Click OK to close the Options dialog box.

> **tip** You can also use the Custom Lists tab to edit and delete other list formats in your system. For example, you could rearrange the days-of-the-week sorting order so that Monday appears as the first day of the week and Sunday appears as the last.

Using a Custom Sort Order

When you want to sort based on an order that isn't alphabetical or numerical—the days of the week, for example, or the months of the year that have been entered as text rather than dates—you can click the Options button in the Sort dialog box and specify a custom sort order to use for the comparison. To use a custom sort order, follow these steps:

1 Click any cell in your list.

2 Choose Data, Sort. Excel selects the records in your list and displays the Sort dialog box.

3 Select the primary field for the sort in the Sort By list box. Specify ascending or descending order. (The direction you specify also applies to the custom sort, where Ascending is the custom order as shown, and Descending is the reverse order.) In our example, we selected the Region field, ascending order.

4 Click Options to display the Sort Options dialog box, as shown here:

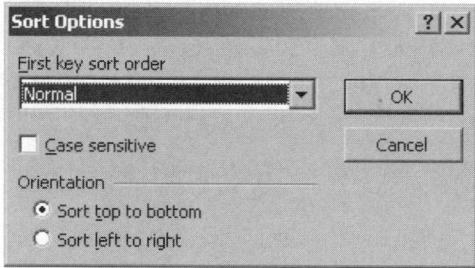

5 Click the First Key Sort Order drop-down list, and click the custom order that you want to use.

> **tip** You can also specify custom sort orders for the second and third sort options if you want to, in which case the title of the sort order drop-down list changes to match the key that you're defining.

6 Click OK in each dialog box to run the sort. Your list appears sorted with the custom criteria you specified.

Using AutoFilter to Find Records

When you want to hide all the records (rows) in your list except those that meet certain criteria, you can use the AutoFilter command on the Filter submenu of the Data menu. The AutoFilter command places a drop-down list at the top of each column in your list (in the heading row). To display a particular group of records, select the criteria that you want in one or more of the drop-down lists. For example, to display the sales

Chapter 28

history for all employees that had $1,000 orders in January, you could select January in the Month column drop-down list and $1,000 in the Sale drop-down list.

To use the AutoFilter command to find records, follow these steps:

1 Click any cell in the list.

2 Choose Data, Filter, and then choose AutoFilter from the submenu. Each column head now displays a down arrow.

3 Click the down arrow next to the heading that you want to use for the filter. A list box that contains filter options appears, similar to the one shown in Figure 28-5.

	A	B	C	D	E	F
1	Sales Rep ▾	Region ▾	Month ▾	Sale ▾	Description ▾	
2	Anderson, Rhea	(All)	Feb-01	$ 700	Advance orders, front list	
3	Anderson, Rhea	(Top 10...)	Feb-01	$ 1,400	Educational kits	
4	Anderson, Rhea	(Custom...)	Jan-01	$ 750	Educational kits	
5	Blickle, Peter	East	Feb-01	$ 600	Advance orders, front list	
6	Blickle, Peter	Midwest	Jan-01	$ 1,100	Misc. backlist books	
7	Blickle, Peter	South	Jan-01	$ 500	Misc. backlist books	
8	Cashel, Seamus	West	Jan-01	$ 1,200	Advance orders, front list	
9	Cashel, Seamus	Midwest	Jan-01	$ 1,000	Educational kits	

Figure 28-5. The AutoFilter command places filter arrows at the top of each column in your list.

4 If a column in your list contains one or more blank cells, you'll also see (Blanks) and (NonBlanks) options at the bottom of the list. The (Blanks) option displays only the records containing an empty cell (blank field) in the filter column, so that you can locate any missing items quickly. The (NonBlanks) option displays the opposite—all records that have an entry in the filter column. Click the value that you want to use for the filter.

Excel hides the entries that don't match the criterion you specified and highlights the active filter arrow. Figure 28-6 shows the results of using East as the criterion in the Region column.

	A	B	C	D	E	F
1	Sales Rep ▾	Region ▾	Month ▾	Sale ▾	Description ▾	
17	Greif, Jacob	East	Jan-01	$ 1,000	Advance orders, front list	
18	Greif, Jacob	East	Jan-01	$ 250	Advance orders, front list	
19	Greif, Jacob	East	Feb-01	$ 800	Misc. backlist books	
20	Leverling, Janet	East	Jan-01	$ 720	Advance orders, front list	
21	Leverling, Janet	East	Feb-01	$ 600	Educational kits	
22	Leverling, Janet	East	Jan-01	$ 550	Educational kits	
26						

Figure 28-6. A list that's filtered for East region entries hides all records that don't match.

You can use more than one filter arrow to further narrow your list—a useful strategy if your list is many records long. To continue working with AutoFilter but to also redisplay all your records, choose Data, Filter, Show All. Excel displays all your records again. To remove the AutoFilter drop-down lists, disable the AutoFilter command on the Filter submenu.

Creating a Custom AutoFilter

When you want to display a numeric range of data or customize a column filter in other ways, choose Custom from the AutoFilter drop-down list to display the Custom AutoFilter dialog box. The dialog box contains two relational list boxes and two value list boxes that you can use to build a custom range for the filter. For example, you could display all sales greater than $1,000 or, as shown in Figure 28-7, all sales between $500 and $800. The list boxes are easy to deal with because the most useful values and relationships are already listed in them—all you have to do is point and click. You can further fine-tune your criteria by using the And and Or option buttons as well as the ? and * wildcard characters.

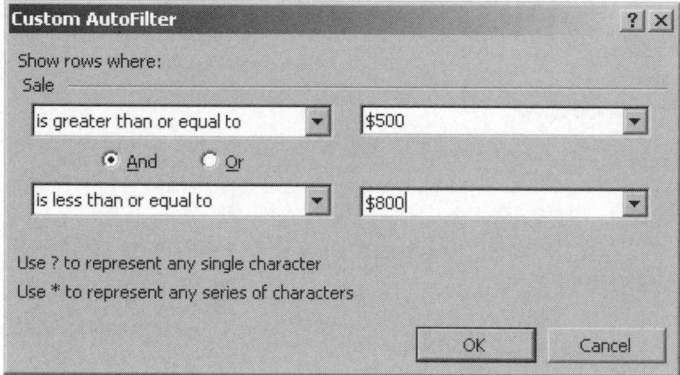

Figure 28-7. The custom AutoFilter dialog box lets you build your own filter.

To create a custom AutoFilter, follow these steps:

1 Click any cell in the list.

2 If AutoFilter isn't already enabled, choose Data, Filter, and then choose AutoFilter from the submenu. A drop-down list appears at the top of each column in the list.

3 Click the arrow next to the heading that you want to use for the customized filter and select (Custom) from the list of choices. The Custom AutoFilter dialog box opens.

4 Click the first relational operator list box and specify the relationship (equals, is greater than, is less than, and so on) that you want to use for the filter, and then click the first value list box and specify the boundary that you want to set. (For example, you could specify *is greater than or equal to $500*.)

5 If you want to specify a second range, click And to indicate that the records must meet both criteria or click Or to indicate that the records can match either criterion. Then specify a relationship in the second relational operator list box and a range boundary in the second value list box. Figure 28-7 shows a Custom AutoFilter dialog box with two range criteria specified.

6 Click OK to apply the custom AutoFilter. The records selected by the filter are displayed in your worksheet.

InsideOut

Refining the Filter

If Custom AutoFilter doesn't provide enough options to create the filter you need, the Advanced Filter command (on the Filter submenu) might offer adequate flexibility. Using advanced criteria, you can specify more than two criteria for a single column, joined with AND or OR, and you can include calculations in your criteria. You might, for example, filter a portfolio list to find only those investments that have increased in value by 20 percent over the last year. For details, see the online Help topic "Filter by Using Advanced Criteria."

Analyzing a List with the Subtotals Command

The Subtotals command on the Data menu helps you organize and analyze a list by displaying records in groups and inserting summary information, such as subtotals, averages, maximum values, or minimum values. The Subtotals command can also display a grand total at the top or bottom of your list, letting you quickly add up columns of numbers. As a bonus, Subtotals displays your list in Outline view so that you can expand or shrink each section in the list simply by clicking.

InsideOut

Subtotals vs. Pivot Tables

Be sure to sort and filter your list as much as you require before you add subtotals, because Excel sorts and filters the subtotal rows as if they were individual records (and yes, this can get messy). Pivot tables (discussed in "Creating Pivot Tables and Pivot Charts," on page 795) are generally more useful than the Subtotals command if you want to continue experimenting with sorts and filters. With a pivot table, unlike subtotals, you can continue to make changes that affect the sorting, such as swapping the primary and secondary sort fields.

To add subtotals to a list, follow these steps:

1 Arrange the list so that the records for each group are located together. An easy way to do this is to sort on the field on which you're basing your groups. For example, you could sort based on employee, region, or store.

2 Choose Data, Subtotals. Excel opens the Subtotal dialog box and selects the list.

3 In the At Each Change In list box, choose a group whose subtotal you want to define. This should be the same column that you sorted the list with. Each time this value changes, Excel inserts a row and computes a subtotal for the numeric fields in this group of records.

4 In the Use Function list box, choose a function to use in the subtotal. SUM is the most popular, but other options are available, as described in Table 28-1.

5 In the Add Subtotal To list box, choose the column or columns to use in the subtotal calculation. You can subtotal more than one column by selecting multiple boxes, but you'll apply the same function in all columns. The following screen shows the settings for a typical use of the Subtotals command:

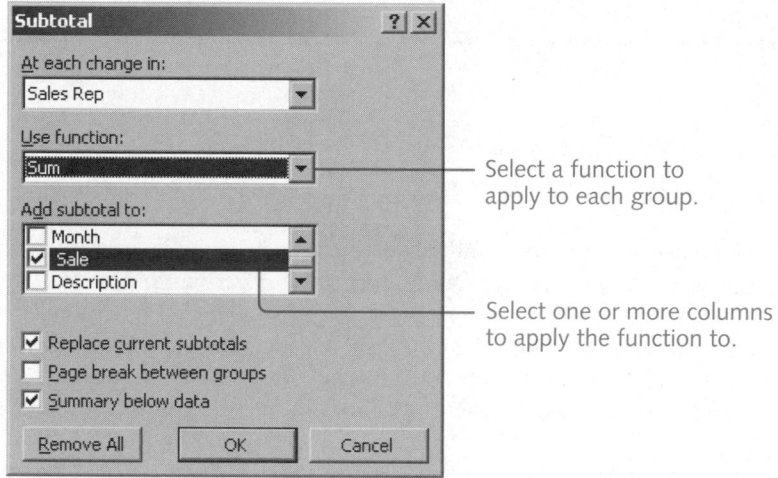

Select a function to apply to each group.

Select one or more columns to apply the function to.

6 Click OK to add the subtotals to the list. You'll see a screen similar to the one in Figure 28-8, complete with subtotals, outlining, and a grand total.

> **note** You can choose the Subtotals command as often as necessary to modify your groupings or calculations. When you've finished using the Subtotals command, click Remove All in the Subtotal dialog box.

Table 28-1. Summary Functions in the Subtotal Dialog Box

Function	Description
SUM	Add up the numbers in the subtotal group
COUNT	Count the number of nonblank cells in the group
AVERAGE	Calculate the average of the numbers in the group
MAX	Display the largest number in the group
MIN	Display the smallest number in the group
PRODUCT	Multiply together all the numbers in the group
COUNT NUMS	Count the number of cells containing numeric values in the group
STDDEV	Estimate the standard deviation based on a sample
STDDEVP	Calculate the standard deviation for an entire population
VAR	Estimate the variance in the group based on a sample
VARP	Calculate the variance for an entire population

Click the minus button to collapse the subtotal details.

These three buttons give the display options: 1=Grand Total Only, 2=Grand Total and Subtotals, 3=All Records.

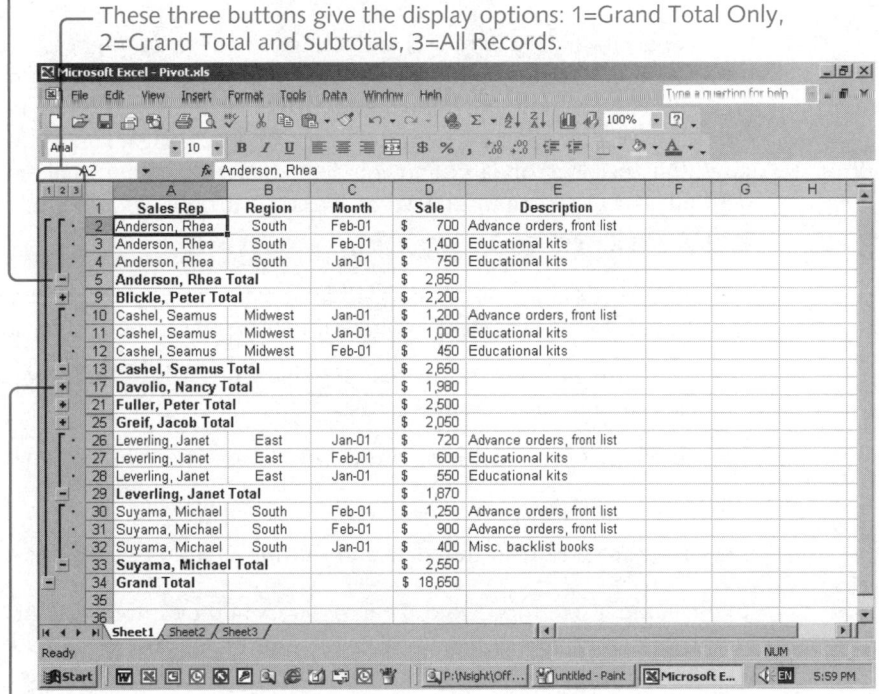

Click the plus button to expand the subtotal to show details.

Figure 28-8. The Subtotals command creates an outline view of your list.

Working in Outline View

When you use the Subtotals command in Excel to create outlines, you can examine different parts of a list by clicking buttons in the left margin, as shown in Figure 28-8. Click the numbers at the top of the left margin to choose how many levels of data you want to see. Click the plus or minus button to expand or collapse specific subgroups of data. (Note that this is similar to the way you expand and collapse parts of a Microsoft Word document in its Outline view.)

Converting an Excel List into an Access Database

If you have the Professional or Premium Edition of Microsoft Office XP, you also have Access, Microsoft's relational database management system.

> **tip** If you have data stored in Word in a table format, you can paste it directly to Excel, which converts the table to rows and columns. For a plain text file, use the Text to Columns command to add column breaks, or import the text file using the Data, Get External Data command.

If you've been working with lists in Excel for a while, you might be wondering whether your lists are compatible with Access, and when, if ever, you should move up to a more sophisticated database. What are the real differences between these two products? The short answer is that Excel is perfectly suited to list management as long as your databases don't become too large and you don't need to track unusual data or run especially advanced commands. However, Excel has the following limitations when it's dealing with databases:

- Worksheets are limited to 65,536 rows, meaning that you can't have more than 65,535 records (names in your mailing list, sales transactions, and the like).

- Fields can't contain more than 256 characters, which limits you to shorter descriptions or notes in your lists.

- Excel can't store pictures, sounds, and other types of special data in fields.

- Excel lacks advanced data protection or sophisticated backup features.

- You can't create custom data entry forms without using Access.

If you would like to move your list into Access in the future, be assured that the transition will be relatively painless. To convert your Excel list into an Access database, you start Access, click More Files in the New Files task pane, and use the Open dialog box to locate and open your Excel workbook. If you are opening Access for the first time, the task pane will say Files instead of More Files. (If Access is already running, you can use the File, Get External Data, Import command.)

When you open an Excel workbook in Access, Access launches a wizard that saves your list as an Access table. (To complete the conversion, you need to specify the worksheet that the list is in.) Figure 28-9 shows the Pivot.xls worksheet used in this chapter organized as an Access database.

After you import and save the table, you'll find many familiar data management and formatting commands on the Access menus. You can learn more about specific Access commands in Part 8 of this book.

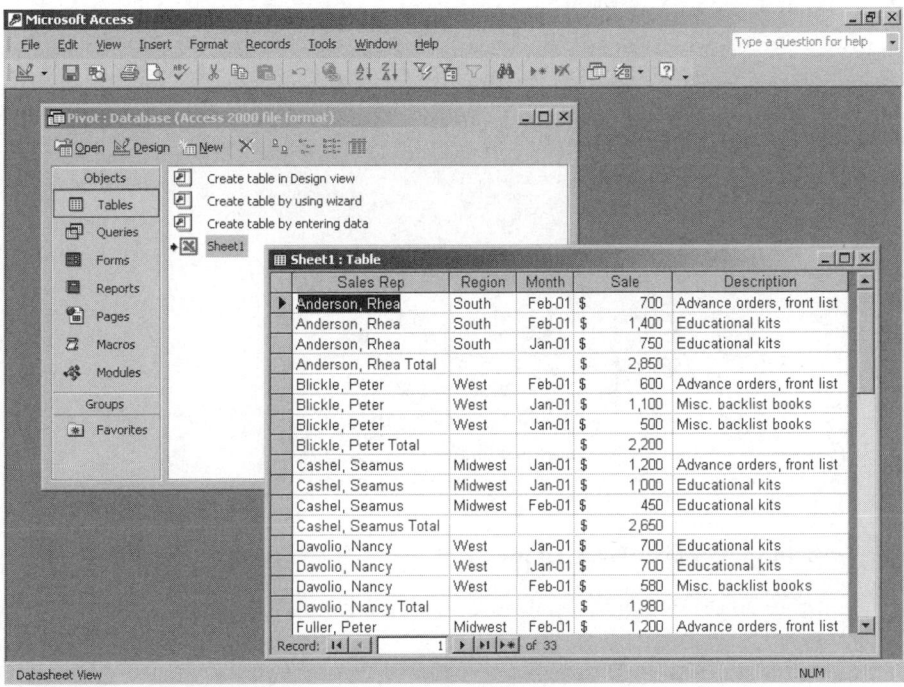

Figure 28-9. Excel lists appear as database tables in Access.

Creating Pivot Tables and Pivot Charts

The most sophisticated data-analysis feature in Excel is the *pivot table*, an organization and analysis tool that displays the fields and records in your list in new and potentially useful combinations. Pivot tables are made easy in Excel by a powerful wizard on the Data menu. The wizard goes further to create not only tables but also colorful *pivot charts*: compelling graphical reports that display pivot table information visually.

In this section you'll learn how to create both pivot tables and pivot charts by using the PivotTable And PivotChart Wizard, and you'll learn how to connect to external data sources to apply this command in powerful new ways.

Using the PivotTable And PivotChart Wizard

The best way to learn about a pivot table is to create one. Fortunately, the PivotTable And PivotChart Wizard gives you complete control over the position of row and column headings in your table, so that you can rearrange all the important variables down the road. To create a pivot table, follow these steps:

1 Click a cell in the list that you want to view as a pivot table.

2 Choose Data, PivotTable And PivotChart Report. The PivotTable And PivotChart Wizard starts and prompts you for the source of data for the table, as shown here:

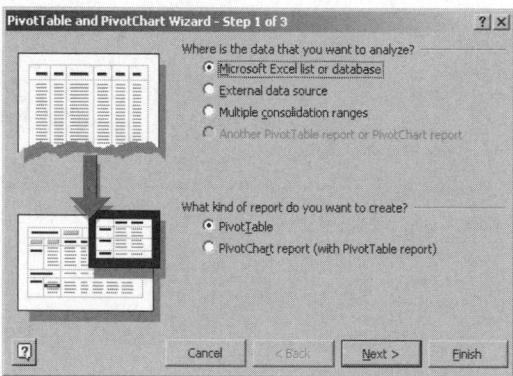

tip   **Learn More About Pivot Tables**

If the Office Assistant is enabled, you'll have an opportunity now to learn more about pivot tables and the various options you have when creating a database report. Feel free to seek guidance from the Office Assistant as you use the PivotTable And PivotChart Wizard. When you no longer need it, click the Excel Help button in the lower left-hand corner of the wizard dialog box to dismiss the Office Assistant.

3 Verify that the first option, Microsoft Excel List Or Database, is selected, and click Next.

In this example, you'll create a pivot table from a list in your worksheet. However, you can also create pivot tables from external data (such as records received by Microsoft Query), multiple consolidation ranges, or another pivot table or pivot chart. After you select a data source, Excel prompts you for a data range.

4 If you had a list active when you started the wizard, Excel might have already selected it for you. If not, select data from an Excel list now using the mouse. (Be sure to include the column headings.)

Don't worry about the dialog box getting in the way—Excel will minimize it when you start selecting cells, giving you a full-window look at your data. Our sample screen looks like this:

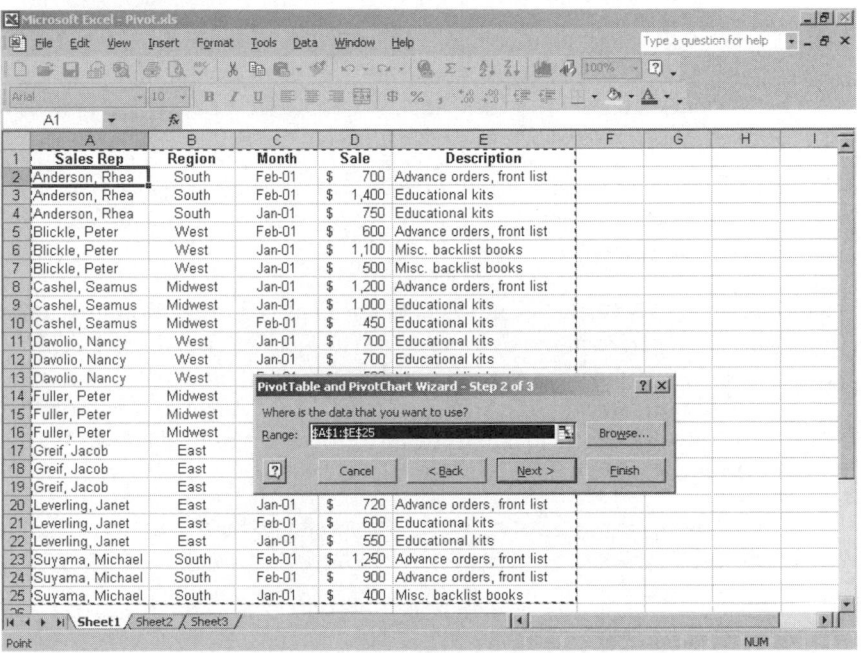

5   Click Next to display the final screen of the PivotTable And PivotChart Wizard, shown below. By default, Excel creates pivot tables in new worksheets, though you can also specify an existing worksheet and even an exact location within a worksheet.

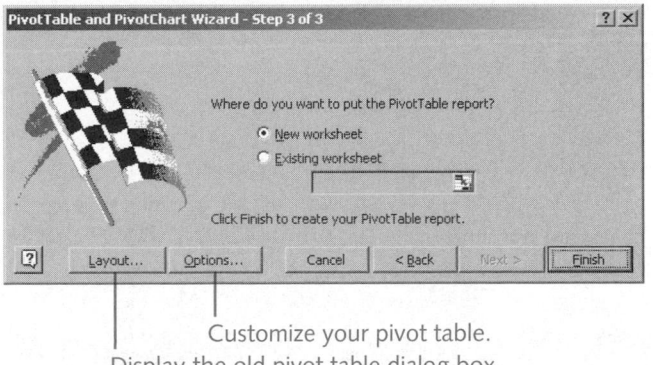

Customize your pivot table.
Display the old pivot table dialog box.

In Excel 97, the PivotTable Wizard displayed a layout grid at this point to help you build your pivot table, but this feature is now provided directly in the worksheet by means of an enhanced PivotTable toolbar. However, you can use the old pivot table "construction" dialog box if you like by clicking the Layout button in the final wizard screen. In addition, you can use the Options button now or in the future to fine-tune how your pivot table or pivot chart appears.

6 Click Finish to accept the default settings and continue building your pivot table. The PivotTable And PivotChart Wizard opens a new worksheet, creates a blank pivot table and a list of available data fields, and displays the PivotTable toolbar, as shown in Figure 28-10.

7 Define the initial layout of your pivot table by dragging fields from the PivotTable Field List into the Row, Column, Data, and Page Fields areas in the worksheet.

In Figure 28-10, the Month field has been placed in the Row area and the Region field has been placed in the Column area. The Sale field is being selected on the PivotTable Field List and will be dragged to the Data area. Fields placed in the Data area are added together with the SUM function. You can arrange, or pivot, these values later, so don't worry too much about the final placement of fields now. (We'll look at the Page area in "Using the Page Area," on page 800.)

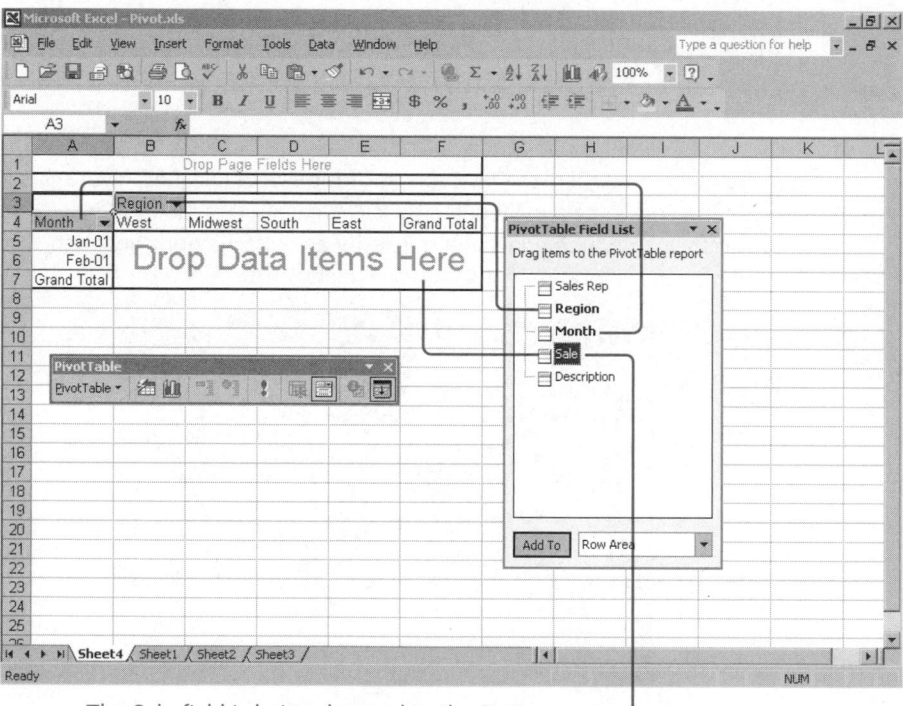

The Sale field is being dragged to the Data area.

Figure 28-10. A pivot table lets you try new arrangements of the data in your worksheet.

After you place a field in the Data area, Excel finalizes the pivot table, as shown below:

	A	B	C	D	E	F
1			Drop Page Fields Here			
2						
3	Sum of Sale	Region ▼				
4	Month ▼	West	Midwest	South	East	Grand Total
5	Jan-01	3000	3125	1150	2520	9795
6	Feb-01	1180	2025	4250	1400	8855
7	Grand Total	4180	5150	5400	3920	18650

Evaluating a Pivot Table

It might take you a moment to recognize the data in your pivot table, because it presents an entirely new view of your list. It's almost as if you had created new row and column headings, typed all the data again, and used the Subtotals command to summarize the results! However, you didn't have to rearrange your worksheet manually—the PivotTable And PivotChart Wizard did it for you. Best of all, you can easily transpose one or more fields and use new functions to highlight other trends in your list.

To help you work with the pivot table and create pivot charts, Excel displays the PivotTable toolbar, shown in Figure 28-11. You'll find this toolbar useful when evaluating and customizing your pivot tables and pivot charts. Take a moment to examine the buttons and commands on the PivotTable toolbar, and then read the summary data in your new pivot table, especially the Grand Total row and column.

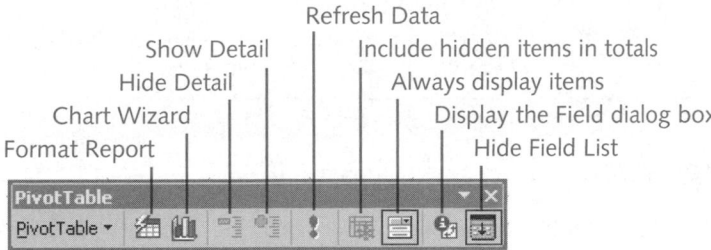

Figure 28-11. The PivotTable toolbar contains commands and buttons specifically designed for manipulating pivot tables.

Rearranging Fields in a Pivot Table

To rearrange, or pivot, the data in your pivot table, just click the fields in the table and move them to new locations. You can also remove unwanted fields by dragging them out of the pivot table and add new fields by dragging field names from the list onto the pivot table.

To demonstrate this capability, let's swap the Row and Column fields in the pivot table we created above. Drag the Month button from the Row area to the Column area, and the Region button from the Column area to the Row area. Then drag the Sales Rep field from the PivotTable Field List to the Row area, being sure to drop it to the right side of the Region button. (If the table gets confusing, you can always drag a field button—or all the field buttons—out of the pivot table.) The resulting table is shown in Figure 28-12.

	A	B	C	D	E
1	Sale	(All) ▼			
2					
3	Sum of Sale		Month ▼		
4	Region ▼	Sales Rep ▼	Jan-01	Feb-01	Grand Total
5	West	Blickle, Peter	1600	600	2200
6		Davolio, Nancy	1400	580	1980
7	West Total		3000	1180	4180
8	Midwest	Cashel, Seamus	2200	450	2650
9		Fuller, Peter	925	1575	2500
10	Midwest Total		3125	2025	5150
11	South	Anderson, Rhea	750	2100	2850
12		Suyama, Michael	400	2150	2550
13	South Total		1150	4250	5400
14	East	Greif, Jacob	1250	800	2050
15		Leverling, Janet	1270	600	1870
16	East Total		2520	1400	3920
17	Grand Total		9795	8855	18650

Figure 28-12. You can rearrange pivot tables to provide new views and new insights on the same data.

---

tip **A Degree of Independence**

As you edit or rearrange the data in the pivot table, note that your changes don't affect the data in your list (which is in its own worksheet)—your original rows and columns remain the same. However, if you change the cells in your list, you'll need to click the Refresh Data button on the PivotTable toolbar to see the changes.

Using the Page Area

Even a well-designed table can present an overwhelming amount of information—or at least more information than a person can focus on at a given moment. The Page area lets you interact with the pivot table to choose the data series you want to display. It lets you view multiple data series as if each were on a separate page. Alternatively, you can use the Show Pages command to send each of the page views to its own worksheet. Let's see how the Page area works in an example.

If you've followed the steps in the foregoing sections, you've created a pivot table and then rearranged the fields to develop the version shown in Figure 28-12. To use the Page area, you can simply drag the Region button from the Row area to the Page area (at the top of the worksheet). When you release the field, Excel changes the pivot table to the simplified version shown in Figure 28-13.

InsideOut

Dividing, but Not Always Conquering

Moving a field to the Page area gives you the powerful option of viewing the pages individually. But it also limits your options. When the same field was in the Row area, you could drop down a list of field entries and select any combination of items. The drop-down list for the Page area lets you choose one at a time or all at once, but not the combination of your choice.

Click the arrow and then select a region from the list.

	A	B	C	D
1	Region	(All) ▼		
2				
3	Sum of Sale	Month ▼		
4	Sales Rep ▼	Jan-01	Feb-01	Grand Total
5	Anderson, Rhea	750	2100	2850
6	Blickle, Peter	1600	600	2200
7	Cashel, Seamus	2200	450	2650
8	Davolio, Nancy	1400	580	1980
9	Fuller, Peter	925	1575	2500
10	Greif, Jacob	1250	800	2050
11	Leverling, Janet	1270	600	1870
12	Suyama, Michael	400	2150	2550
13	Grand Total	9795	8855	18650

Figure 28-13. Moving a field to the Page area lets you see your data all at once or as a series of separate pages.

In this latest version of the pivot table, the data for all the regions is presented, but you can easily focus the table on any one region. Click the down arrow beside the Region button. Although the initial value is (All), the drop-down list lets you select any region and view its data separately.

After you've experimented with this feature, open the PivotTable command list on the PivotTable toolbar and select Show Pages. (Be sure that the active cell is within the pivot table.) Excel then displays the Show Pages dialog box; confirm that you want to show pages for the Region field. The command then creates four new worksheets, one for each page, labeled West, Midwest, South, and East. On each sheet is a pivot table, linked to the original, that contains the page for the corresponding region. The following table, for example, is on the tab labeled East.

	A	B	C	D
1	Region	East ▼		
2				
3	Sum of Sale	Month ▼		
4	Sales Rep ▼	Jan-01	Feb-01	Grand Total
5	Greif, Jacob	1250	800	2050
6	Leverling, Janet	1270	600	1870
7	Grand Total	2520	1400	3920

Chapter 23

4: Excel

Changing the Function in a Pivot Table

By default, the PivotTable And PivotChart Wizard uses the SUM function to add up values in the Data area of your pivot table, but you can easily change the function to calculate another value. For example, you could use the AVERAGE function to calculate the average sales in a month, or the COUNT function to total up the number of sales orders written by a particular employee. The list of functions available is identical to the set employed by the Subtotals command, described in Table 28-1, on page 793.

To change the function used in a pivot table, follow these steps:

1 Open the sheet containing your (primary) Excel pivot table, if it isn't already open.

2 In the upper left corner of your pivot table (the cell above the Row field and to the left of the Column field), double-click the Data field name. In our example, the cell's location is A3 and contains the title Sum of Sale.

You'll see the PivotTable Field dialog box, as shown in Figure 28-14.

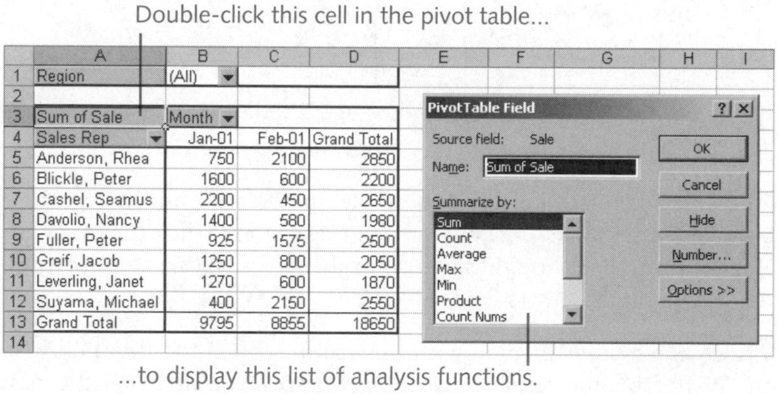

Double-click this cell in the pivot table...

	A	B	C	D	E	F	G	H	I
1	Region	(All) ▼							
2									
3	Sum of Sale	Month ▼			PivotTable Field		?×		
4	Sales Rep ▼	Jan-01	Feb-01	Grand Total	Source field: Sale			OK	
5	Anderson, Rhea	750	2100	2850	Name: Sum of Sale				
6	Blickle, Peter	1600	600	2200				Cancel	
7	Cashel, Seamus	2200	450	2650	Summarize by:				
8	Davolio, Nancy	1400	580	1980	Sum			Hide	
9	Fuller, Peter	925	1575	2500	Count / Average				
10	Greif, Jacob	1250	800	2050	Max			Number...	
11	Leverling, Janet	1270	600	1870	Min			Options >>	
12	Suyama, Michael	400	2150	2550	Product				
13	Grand Total	9795	8855	18650	Count Nums				
14									

...to display this list of analysis functions.

Figure 28-14. Double-click the cell containing the current function and field to display the PivotTable Field dialog box.

3 In the Summarize By list box, select the new function that you want to use. (For example, select the MAX function to display the largest sales total in the field.)

tip You can also use the Field Settings button on the PivotTable toolbar to display the PivotTable Field dialog box and change the function used to summarize a field in your pivot table. The PivotTable Field dialog box displays different options, depending on the type of entry selected.

Adjusting the Formatting in a Pivot Table

When you use the PivotTable And PivotChart Wizard to modify a pivot table, Excel automatically reformats the table to match the data in your list and to calculate the result of the function that you're using. Avoid making manual changes to the table formatting, because the AutoFormat table feature overwrites them each time you rearrange the pivot table.

However, you can make lasting changes to the numeric formatting in the Data area by following these steps:

1 Click any numeric data cell in the pivot table (not a row or column heading).

2 Click the Field Settings button on the PivotTable toolbar. The PivotTable Field dialog box opens.

3 Click the Number button. The familiar Format Cells dialog box appears, which allows you to adjust the formatting of the numbers in the Data area.

4 Select a type of numeric format in the Category list box, and then select a formatting style. For example, to add currency formatting to numbers, click the Currency category, specify the number of decimal places you want, and specify a style for negative numbers.

5 Click OK to close the Format Cells dialog box, and then click OK to close the PivotTable Field dialog box. Excel changes the numeric formatting in the table, and these changes persist each time you modify the pivot table.

---

tip **Use AutoFormat for Fast Style Makeovers**

To change the heading and line style, highlight a cell in the pivot table, and choose Format, AutoFormat. Excel displays a list of table styles for you to choose from. Select the style you want, and then click OK to reformat and recalculate the pivot table.

Displaying Pivot Charts

If you find pivot tables addictive, you'll want to take advantage of a closely related data analysis tool, the pivot chart. A pivot chart is a graphical version of an Excel pivot table. Pivot charts are created from existing pivot tables and are placed in new charting worksheets in the workbook. Like pivot tables, pivot charts have dynamic, customizable fields that you can drag back and forth to the PivotTable Field List and move around the charting area. You can also modify the functions used to analyze data in a pivot chart.

To analyze an Excel list using a pivot table chart, follow these steps: (If you already have an existing pivot table in your workbook, click a cell in the pivot table, and start with step 4.)

Chapter 28

803

1 Click a cell in the list that you want to view as a pivot chart.

2 Choose Data, PivotTable And PivotChart Report.

> **note** Although the PivotTable And PivotChart Wizard gives you the option of creating a pivot chart in the first wizard step, you'll still be required to create a pivot table in the third wizard step to base the pivot chart on. For this reason, we recommend that you simply follow the default pivot table options when you create a pivot chart. (You won't lose any time doing so.)

3 Answer the questions posed by the PivotTable And PivotChart Wizard, and then create a new pivot table by dragging the appropriate row, column, and data values from the PivotTable toolbar to your new pivot table.

Chart
Wizard

4 On the PivotTable toolbar, click the Chart Wizard button to open a charting worksheet and build a new pivot chart based on the selected pivot table. You'll see a chart that looks similar to the one in Figure 28-15.

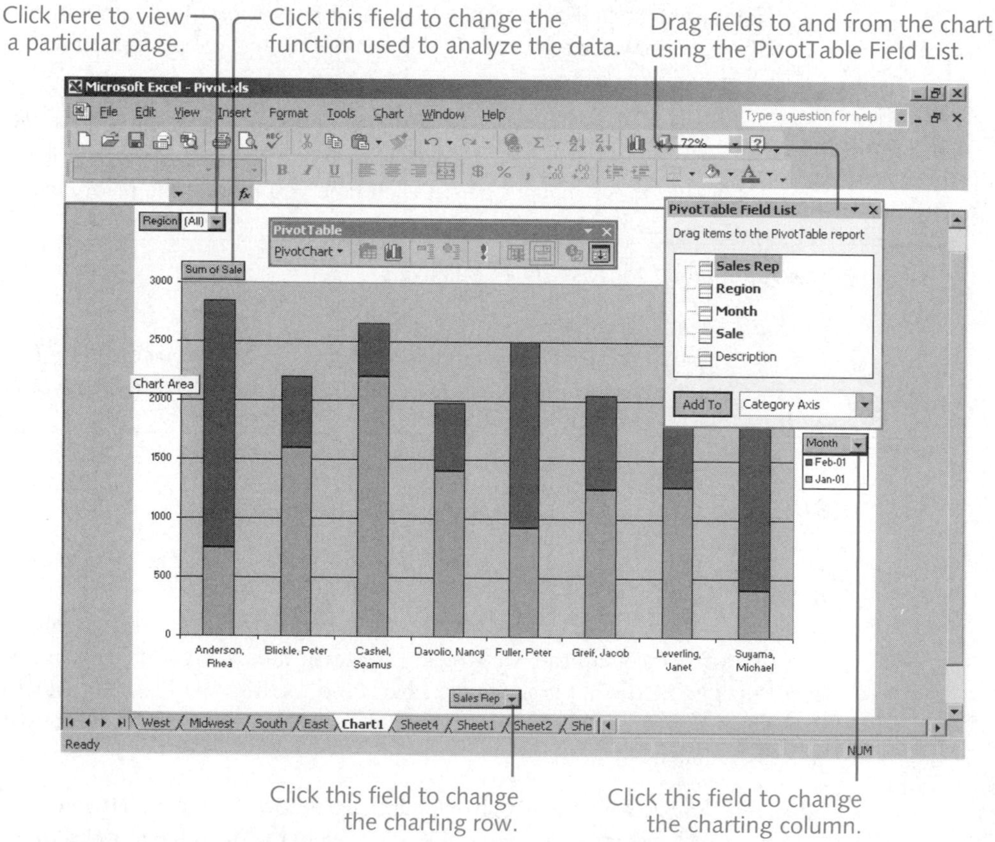

Click here to view a particular page.　Click this field to change the function used to analyze the data.　Drag fields to and from the chart using the PivotTable Field List.

Click this field to change the charting row.　Click this field to change the charting column.

Figure 28-15. Excel 2002 allows you to analyze your database lists with customizable pivot charts.

Chapter 28

5 You're now free to customize and format the pivot chart as you see fit. The labels in Figure 28-15 suggest some ways to customize the chart.

> **tip** In a pivot chart, the legend represents the column field and the charting category represents the row field. To customize either of these values, right-click the associated field button in the chart and choose a command from the shortcut menu that appears.

Using External Data Sources in Pivot Tables

When you created your pivot table by using the PivotTable And PivotChart Wizard, you had the option of using external data as the source of your information. One method of extracting external data for your pivot table is by using Query, a program shipped with Office that you can use to connect to external data sources using a software driver called open database connectivity (ODBC). Query acts as a link between Excel and database files that have diverse data formats, such as Access, FoxPro, SQL Server, dBASE, Paradox, and Btrieve. With Excel 2000, you gained the ability (using Query) to access yet another type of external data source, known as an *OLAP cube*. OLAP stands for online analytical processing, a format designed to consolidate massive amounts of corporate information using units that are sometimes referred to as *data warehouses*.

Query uses ODBC to translate complex data-filtering questions, or *queries*, into a language called SQL (structured query language), which is usually pronounced "sequel." As a result, you can use Query to extract information about compatible database files in sophisticated ways. For example, your query might be, "How many sales reps do we have who sell more than $20,000 in products per year and who work in the South or the Midwest?"

When you want to work with external database files, consider using Query as a standalone tool or as a utility to import your data into Excel. Start Query in Excel by clicking the Data menu and picking a command from the Import External Data submenu. To use Query for accessing data in constructing a PivotTable, select External Data Source in Step 1 of the PivotTable And PivotChart Wizard, and then click Get Data in Step 2. (Query is an add-in program, so you'll have to install it using the Office Setup program before it can be accessed.)

> **tip** For more information about using Query to manage external data sources, search for "Query (Microsoft)" in the Excel Help Index. You can also access a series of helpful cue cards from within the Query Help menu.

Advanced Business Analysis

Running a successful business requires many important skills. One of your best management tools is the capacity to build what-if models to help you plan for the future. How many $1.75 coffees do you need to sell to gross $30,000? What will happen to your bottom line if you lower the price of caffe latte but increase advertising expenses? Fortunately, Microsoft Excel 2002 provides several planning tools to help you map out a robust future. In this chapter you'll learn how to use the Goal Seek command to find an unknown value that produces a desired result, the Solver add-in to calculate an optimum solution based on several variables and constraints, and the Scenario Manager to create and evaluate a collection of what-if scenarios containing multiple input values.

Using the Goal Seek Command to Forecast

Excel's basic forecasting command is Goal Seek, which is located on the Tools menu. The Goal Seek command determines the unknown value that produces a desired result, such as the number of $14 compact discs a company must sell to reach its goal of $1,000,000 in CD sales. Goal Seek is simple because it's streamlined—it can adjust only one variable to complete its iterative calculation. If you need to consider additional variables in your forecasting, such as the effects of advertising or quantity discounts on pricing, use the Solver command (described in "Using the Solver to Set Quantity and Pricing," on page 810).

To use Goal Seek, set up your worksheet to contain the following:

● A formula that calculates your goal

● An empty cell for the missing number that will get you there

● Any other values required in the formula

The empty cell should be referenced in your formula; it serves as the variable that Excel changes.

> **note** When you run the Tools, Goal Seek command, the cell containing the formula is called the Set Cell, because it *sets* the terms that produce a result.

When the Goal Seek command starts to run, it repeatedly tries new values in the variable cell to find a solution to the problem you've set. This process is called *iteration*, and it continues until Excel has run the problem 100 times or has found an answer within .001 of the target value you specified. (You can adjust these iteration settings by choosing Tools, Options and adjusting the Iteration options in the Calculations tab.) Because it calculates so fast, the Goal Seek command can save you significant time and effort over the brute force method of trying one number after another in the formula.

To forecast using the Goal Seek command, follow these steps:

1 Create a worksheet that contains a formula, an empty *variable* cell that will hold your solution, and any data you need to use in your calculation. For example, Figure 29-1 shows how you might set up a worksheet to determine the number of cups of coffee priced at $1.75 that you would have to sell to gross $30,000.

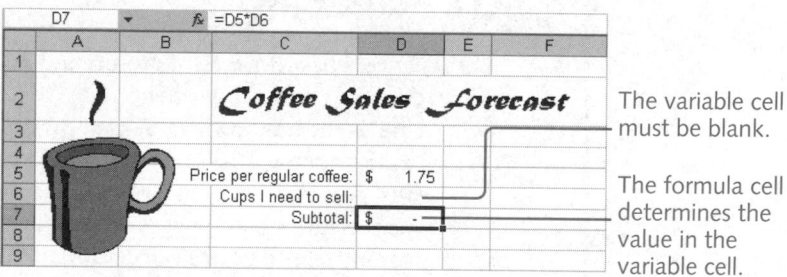

The variable cell must be blank.

The formula cell determines the value in the variable cell.

Figure 29-1. The Goal Seek command requires a formula and a blank variable cell.

The Goalseek.xls example is on the companion CD to this book.

2 In your worksheet, select the cell containing the formula.

3 Choose Tools, Goal Seek. The Goal Seek dialog box opens, as shown here. The dialog box asks you to complete a sentence, "Set cell <blank_1> to value <blank_2> by changing cell <blank_3>." The cell name you selected appears in the first text box, and a marquee appears around the cell in your worksheet.

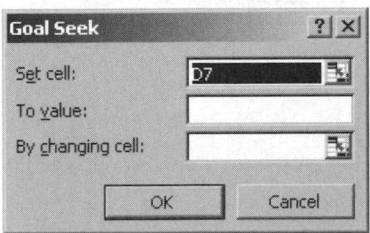

4 Press Tab, and then type the goal that you want to reach in the To Value text box. For example, to reach $30,000 in sales, type **30000** in the To Value text box.

Press Tab to select the By Changing Cell text box, collapse the Goal Seek dialog box, if necessary, and then click the blank cell that's to contain your answer (the variable cell). The Goal Seek command calculates the value for this blank cell using your goal and the formula in the Set Cell. The variable cell is indicated by a selection marquee (cell D6 in this example):

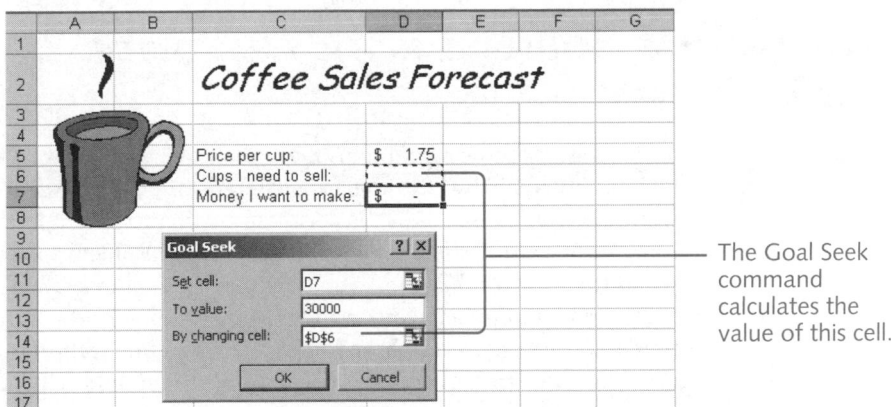

The Goal Seek command calculates the value of this cell.

5 Click OK to find a solution for your sales goal.

The Goal Seek Status dialog box displays a message when the iteration is complete, and the result of your forecast appears in the worksheet, as shown in Figure 29-2. This forecast shows that you need to sell 17,143 coffees at $1.75 per cup to reach your sales goal of $30,000.

Chapter 29

6 Click OK to close the Goal Seek Status dialog box.

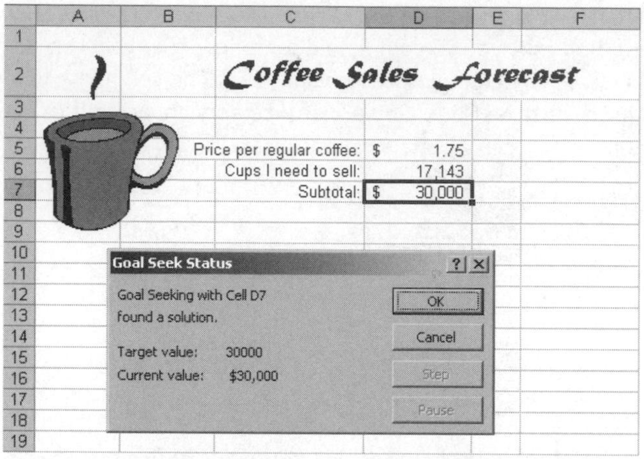

Figure 29-2. The Goal Seek command displays its result in the empty variable cell that you specified in your worksheet.

> **tip** In a time-consuming calculation, such as a computation that involves several financial functions, you can click the Pause button in the Goal Seek Status dialog box to stop the iteration or the Step button to view one iteration at a time.

Using the Solver to Set Quantity and Pricing

When your forecasting problem contains more than one variable, you need to use the Solver add-in utility to analyze the scenario. Veterans of business school will happily remember multivariable case studies as part of their finance and operations management training. While a full explanation of multivariable problem solving and optimization is beyond the scope of this book, you don't need a business school background to use the Solver command to help you decide how much of a product to produce, or how to price goods and services. We'll show you the basics in this section by illustrating how a small coffee shop determines which coffee beverages it should sell and what its potential revenue is.

In our example we're running a coffee shop that currently sells three beverages: regular fresh-brewed coffee, premium caffe latte, and premium caffe mocha. We currently price regular coffee at $1.25, caffe latte at $2.00, and caffe mocha at $2.25, but we're not sure what our revenue potential is and what emphasis we should give to each of the beverages. (Although the premium coffees bring in more money, their ingredients are more expensive and they take more time to make than regular coffee.) We can make some basic calculations by hand, but we want to structure our sales data in a worksheet so that we can periodically add to it and analyze it using the Solver.

> **note** The Solver is an add-in utility, so you should verify that it's installed on your system before you get started. If the Solver command isn't on your Tools menu, choose Tools, Add-Ins, and select the Solver Add-In option in the Add-Ins dialog box. If Solver isn't in the list, you'll need to install it by running the Office Setup program again and selecting it from the list of Excel add-ins. For more information, see "Installing Add-In Commands and Wizards," on page 730.

Setting Up the Problem

The first step in using the Solver command is to build a Solver-friendly worksheet. This involves creating a *target cell* to be the goal of your problem—for example, a formula that calculates total revenue—and assigning one or more *variable cells* that the Solver can change to reach your goal. Your worksheet can also contain other values and formulas that use the target cell and the variable cells. In fact, for the Solver to do its job, each of your variable cells must be *precedents* of the target cell. (In other words, the formula in the target cell must depend on the variable cells for part of its calculation.) If you don't set it up this way, when you run the Solver you'll get the error message, "The Set Target Cell values do not converge."

Figure 29-3 shows a simple worksheet that we can use to estimate the weekly revenue for our example coffee shop and to determine how many cups of coffee we will need to sell. The worksheet in the figure appears in Formula Auditing mode, which you choose from the Formula Auditing submenu on the Tools menu. Cell G4 is the target cell that calculates the total revenue that the three coffee drinks generate. The three lines that converge in cell G4 were drawn by the Trace Precedents command on the Formula Auditing toolbar. The arrows show how the formula in cell G4 depends on three other calculations for its result. (The Formula Auditing toolbar contains commands that expose the links between formulas in a worksheet.)

The three variable cells in the worksheet are cells D5, D9, and D13—these are the blank cells whose values we want the Solver to determine when it finds a way to maximize our weekly revenue.

 The Solver.xls example is on the companion CD to this book.

In the bottom-right corner of our screen is a list of constraints we plan to use in our forecasting. A *constraint* is a limiting rule or guiding principle that dictates how the business is run. For example, because of storage facilities and merchandising constraints, we're currently able to produce only 500 cups of coffee (both regular and premium) per week. In addition, our supply of chocolate restricts the production of caffe mochas to 125 per week, and a milk refrigeration limitation restricts the production of premium coffee drinks to 350 per week.

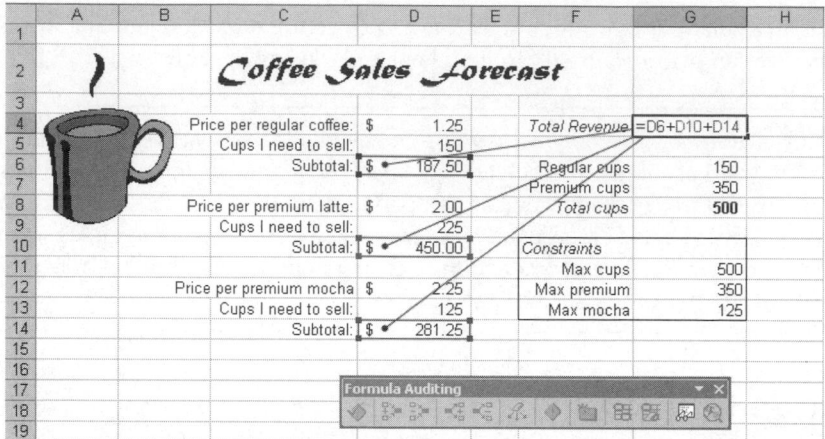

Figure 29-3. The Auditing submenu helps you visualize the relationship between cells. Here the target cell depends on three other cells, each of which contains a formula.

These constraints structure the problem, and we'll enter them in a special dialog box when we run the Solver command. Your worksheet must contain cells that calculate the values used as constraints (in this example, G6 through G8). The limiting values for the constraints are listed in cells G11 through G13. Although listing the constraints isn't necessary, it makes the worksheet easier to follow.

---

tip **Name Key Cells**

If your Solver problem contains several variables and constraints, you'll find it easiest to enter data if you name key cells and ranges in your worksheet by using the Define command on the Name submenu of the Insert menu. Using cell names also makes it easy to read your Solver constraints later. For more information about naming, see "Using Names in Functions," on page 749.

Running the Solver

After you've defined your forecasting problem in the worksheet, you're ready to run the Solver add-in. The following steps show you how to use the Solver to determine the maximum weekly revenue for your coffee shop given the following constraints:

- No more than 500 total cups of coffee (both regular and premium)

- No more than 350 cups of premium coffee (both caffe latte and caffe mocha)

- No more than 125 caffe mochas

In addition to telling you the maximum revenue, the Solver tells the optimum distribution of coffees in the three coffee groups. To use the Solver, complete the following steps:

1 Click the target cell—the one containing the formula that's based on the variable cells you want the Solver to determine. In Figure 29-3, the target cell is G4.

2 Choose Tools, Solver.

The Solver Parameters dialog box opens, as shown here. Select the Set Target Cell text box (unless it already contains the correct reference), and then click cell G4 to insert $G$4 as the target cell. The Equal To option button (Max) that's already selected is the correct one, because you want to find the maximum value for the target cell.

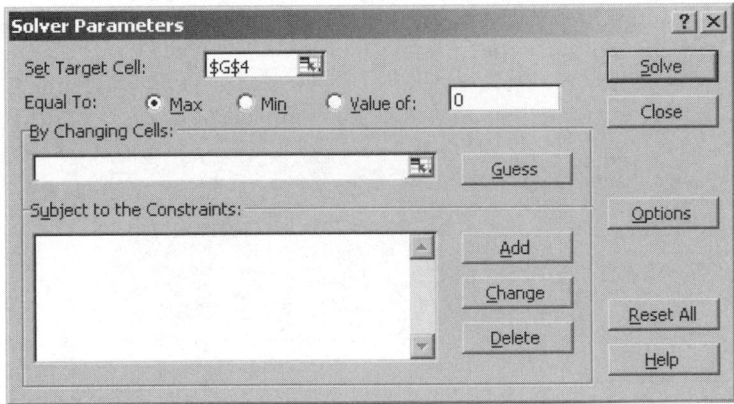

3 Select the By Changing Cells text box. Click the button in the text box to collapse the dialog box. Select each of the variable cells. If the cells adjoin one another, simply select the group by dragging across the cells. If the cells are noncontiguous, as in our example, hold down the Ctrl key and click each cell. This places commas between the three cell entries in the text box: $D$5,$D$9,$D$13.

In the following illustration the three blank cells reserved for the number of coffee drinks in each category are selected:

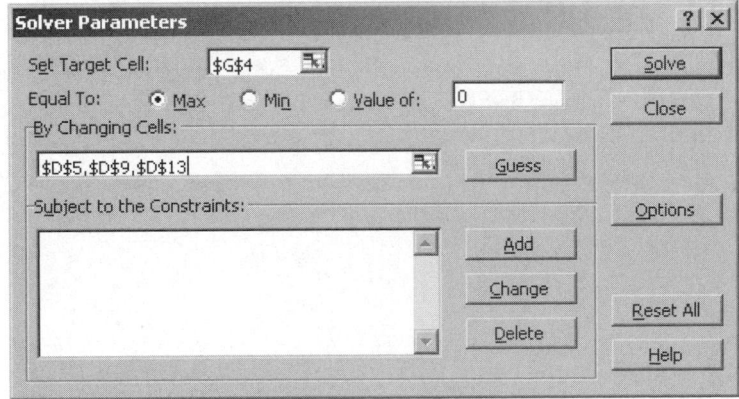

813

> **tip** Use the Guess Button to Preview the Result
>
> If you click the Guess button, the Solver tries to guess at the variable cells in your forecasting problem. The Solver creates the guess by looking at the cells referenced in the target cell formula. Don't rely on this guess, though—it's often incorrect!

4 Constraints aren't required in all Solver problems, but this problem has three. Click Add to add the first constraint in the Add Constraint dialog box.

5 The first constraint is that you can sell only 500 cups of coffee in one week. To enter this constraint, click cell G8 (the cell containing the total cups formula), click <= in the operator drop-down list, and with the insertion point in the Constraint text box, click G11 or type **Max_cups**, using the underline character to link the words. (Max_cups is the name of cell G11 in our example.)

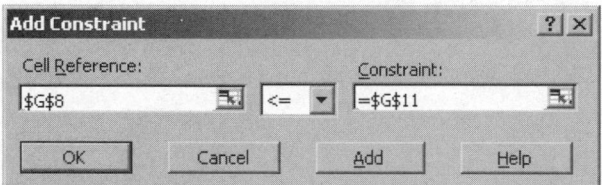

> **note** You have the option of typing a value, clicking a cell, or entering a cell name in the Constraint text box. If you click a cell that has a defined name, Excel uses that name when you add the constraint.

6 Click Add to enter the first constraint and begin the second constraint—you can sell only 350 premium coffees in one week. With the insertion point in the Cell Reference text box, click cell G7 (the cell containing the premium cups formula), click <= in the operator drop-down list, and in the Constraint text box, type **Max_ premium** (the name of cell G12) or click cell G12.

7 Click Add to enter the second constraint and begin the third—you can sell only 125 caffe mochas in one week. Click cell D13 (the variable cell containing the number of mocha cups), click <= in the operator drop-down list, and in the Constraint text box, type **Max_mocha** (the name of cell G13) or click cell G13.

8 Click OK to add all three constraints to the Solver Parameters dialog box. It should look like the one on the next page.

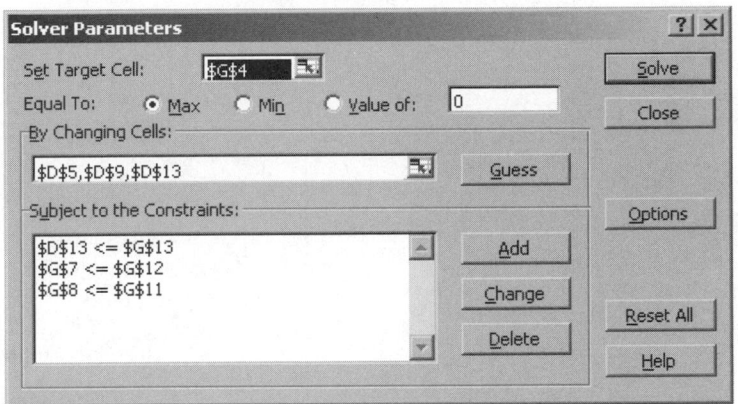

> **tip** To modify one of the constraints displayed in the Solver Parameters dialog box, select the constraint and click Change. To customize the iteration and calculation parameters in the Solver utility, click Options and make your adjustments.

9 Your forecasting problem is ready to go, so click Solve to calculate the result.

After a few moments the Solver displays a dialog box describing how the optimization analysis went. If the Solver runs into a problem, you see an error message, and you can click the Help button to learn more about the difficulty. If the Solver finds a solution, you see the following dialog box:

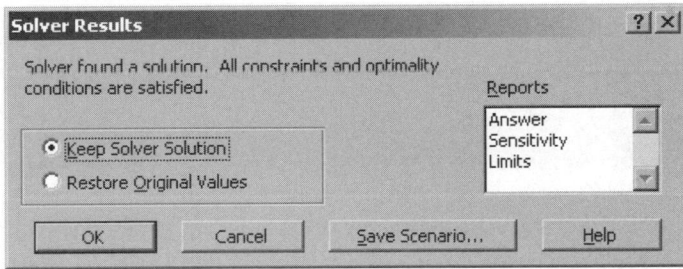

10 To display the new solution in your worksheet, click the Keep Solver Solution option button, and then click OK. The Solver places an optimum value in the target cell and fills the variable cells with the solutions that best match the constraints you specified, as shown in Figure 29-4.

In this example, you've learned that if you're limited to selling 500 cups of coffee per week, you can expect a maximum of $918.75 in revenue and your optimum drink distribution is 150 cups of regular coffee, 225 cups of caffe latte, and 125 cups of caffe mocha. Although this financial model doesn't consider several realistic business variables, such as the costs associated with running a shop and the benefits of making volume purchases, it does help you to forecast much more easily and quickly than you could using pencil and paper.

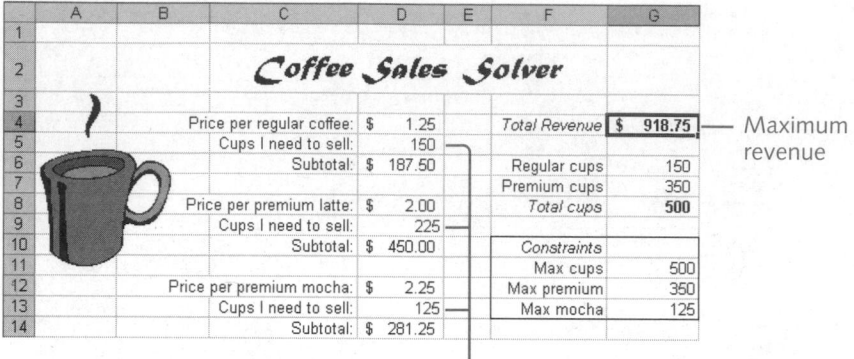

Figure 29-4.   When the Solver finishes, it displays the values that produce the optimum result in the target cell.

Editing Your Solver Forecast

Perhaps the best feature of a Solver forecast is that you can easily edit it to evaluate new goals and contingencies. For example, if you decide that you want to earn exactly $700 per week from coffee drinks, you can use the Solver to tell you what the optimum combination of drinks would be. Setting a target value in the Solver is a little like using the Goal Seek command to determine a value for an unknown variable, although with Solver you can use more than one variable.

InsideOut

Excel saves your Solver parameters when you save the workbook. But you can save only one complete set of parameters per workbook, including the constraints and all the values they rely upon. The Scenario Manager, which is described in the section "Using the Scenario Manager to Evaluate What-If Questions," on page 818, can help somewhat by saving the values in the variable cells (the ones in the By Changing Cells text box) in a named scenario. In the Solver Results dialog box, choose the Save Scenario button, assign a name, and choose OK. Notice, however, one potential glitch. Restoring the scenario restores only the values in the variable cells (and the target). If you've changed constraints or other critical cells since Excel calculated the saved results (such as the values of cells referenced in the constraints), you might need to run the Solver again to see whether the results change.

To edit your Solver forecast to find the variables to reach a specific goal, follow these steps:

1 Choose Tools, Solver. The Solver Parameters dialog box appears, still displaying the variables and constraints of your last Solver problem. You'll adjust these to compute a new forecasting goal.

2 Click the Value Of option button and type **700** in the text box to the right. The Value Of option button sets the target cell to a particular goal so that you can determine the variable mix you need to reach your milestone. (In this example, the variable cells represent cups of coffee.) Your dialog box should look like this:

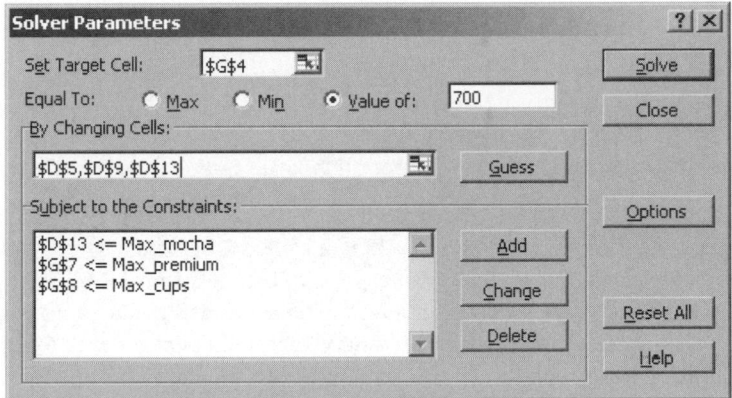

3 Click Solve to find a solution to your forecasting problem. When the Solver has finished, click OK to display the new solution in your worksheet.

Figure 29-5 shows the solution the Solver generates if the variable cells contain the values you entered in the previous example. (You can make $700 by selling approximately 100 mochas, 175 lattes, and 100 regular coffees. The Solver calculates an exact answer, but because you can't sell partial cups of coffee, the variable cells are formatted to show integer—whole-number—values.)

	A	B	C	D	E	F	G
1							
2			*Coffee Sales Solver*				
3							
4			Price per regular coffee:	$ 1.25		Total Revenue	$ 700.00
5			Cups I need to sell:	100			
6			Subtotal:	$ 125.00		Regular cups	100
7						Premium cups	275
8			Price per premium latte:	$ 2.00		Total cups	375
9			Cups I need to sell:	175			
10			Subtotal:	$ 350.00		Constraints	
11						Max cups	500
12			Price per premium mocha:	$ 2.25		Max premium	350
13			Cups I need to sell:	100		Max mocha	125
14			Subtotal:	$ 225.00			

Figure 29-5. When you specify a target goal, the Solver computes an optimum product mix that meets your constraints.

What If There Is More Than One Solution to the Problem?

In the previous example, the Solver determined that you could sell 100 mochas, 175 lattes, and 100 regular coffees to reach your sales goal of $700. But you can also reach the $700 mark using a different product mix; for example, you could sell approximately 125 mochas and 210 lattes to reach $700. (Using this mix, your revenue would actually be $701.25.) So how *did* the Solver decide what the optimum product mix would be? The Solver simply started with the numbers in the variable cells and incremented them until it found an acceptable solution (subject to the constraints described in the previous example). This is why, if you use different starting values, you can get different results from a nonlinear problem with multiple solutions.

> ## Troubleshooting
>
> ### Solver Doesn't Find a Solution
>
> *Solver reaches its iteration limit without finding a solution.*
>
> Starting values in variable cells can affect the solution: Solver might fail to find a solution or it might time out before reaching a solution, especially when you're working with nonlinear formulas. Enter values in variable cells that fall close to what you believe the final values will be. If Solver still reaches its iteration limit without arriving at a solution, you can adjust the starting values and restart or click Continue to use the maximum solution time. You can adjust both the iterations and Max Time using the Options button in the Solver Parameters dialog box.

If you would like to use a particular product mix, you can take advantage of the way the Solver reaches its results. Enter the values that you think might be acceptable in the variable cells before you run the Solver, and Excel uses those as starting values when it computes the solution. If you prefer to find a true optimal solution, you need to add extra constraints to the Solver Parameters dialog box before you run the forecast. For example, you might specify that a certain minimum must be met in each category or that you'd like to minimize the number of products sold to reach your goal. You can have two constraints for each variable cell (an upper bounds and a lower bounds) to structure the computation and reach an optimal solution to your problem.

Using the Scenario Manager to Evaluate What-If Questions

Although the Goal Seek and Solver commands are extremely useful, if you run several forecasts you can quickly forget what your original values were. More important, you have no real way to compare the results of the Goal Seek and Solver commands. Each time you change the data, the previous solution is lost. To address this limitation, the Scenario Manager helps you keep track of multiple what-if models. Using the Scenarios command on the Tools menu, you can create new forecasting scenarios, view existing scenarios, run scenario management commands, and display consolidated scenario reports. We'll show you each technique in this section.

Creating a Scenario

A *scenario* is a named what-if model that includes variable cells linked together by one or more formulas. Before you create a scenario, you must design your worksheet so that it contains at least one formula that's dependent on cells that can be fed different values. For example, you might want to compare best-case and worst-case scenarios for sales in a coffee shop based on the number of cups of coffee sold in a week. Figure 29-6 shows a worksheet that contains three variable cells and several formulas that can serve as the basis for several scenarios. (This coffee sales worksheet is the same one we used in the Solver example, without the constraints table.) In the following example, we will use this worksheet to show how to create a best-case and a worst-case sales scenario.

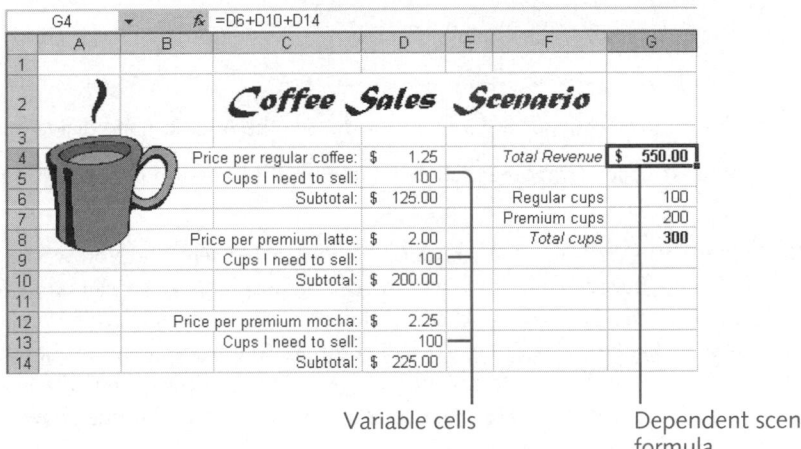

Variable cells   Dependent scenario formula

Figure 29-6. Before you create a scenario, you need to build a worksheet with one or more formulas that depend on variable cells.

 The Scenario.xls example is on the companion CD to this book.

To create a scenario, follow these steps:

1 Choose Tools, Scenarios. The Scenario Manager dialog box appears, as shown here:

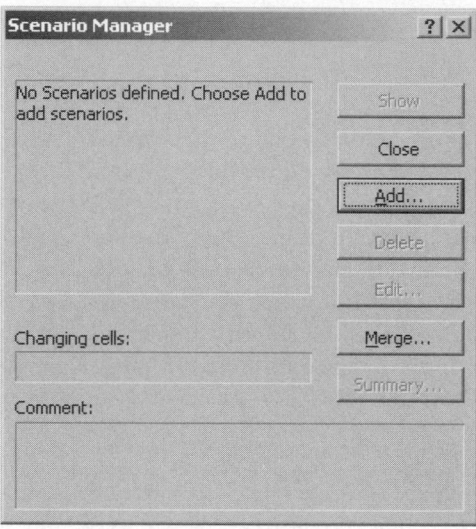

2 Click Add to create your first scenario. You'll see the Add Scenario dialog box.

3 Type **Best Case** (or another suitable name) in the Scenario Name text box, and press the Tab key.

4 In the Changing Cells text box, specify the variable cells that you want to modify in your scenario. You can type cell names, highlight a cell range, or hold down the Ctrl key and click individual cells to add them to the text box. (If you hold down the Ctrl key, Excel automatically places commas between the cells that you click.) To follow our example, hold down the Ctrl key and click cells D5, D9, and D13. Your screen should look like the one shown at the top of the next page.

> **tip** You might want to define cell names for your variable cells. That way, you'll have an easier time identifying your variables when you create your scenarios and when you type in arguments later.

5 Click OK to add your scenario to the Scenario Manager. You'll see the Scenario Values dialog box, which asks you for your model's variables. The default values are the numbers that were already in the cells.

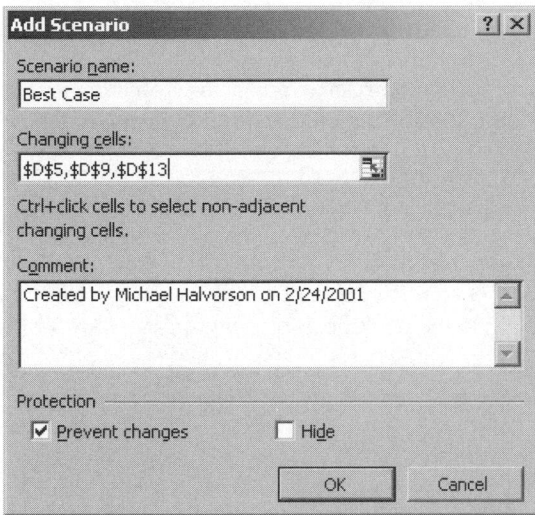

6 Type **150**, press Tab, type **225**, press Tab, and type **125**. These are the values (derived by the Solver in the previous section) that will produce the revenue in your best-case scenario based on the constraints described in "Setting Up the Problem," on page 811. Your screen looks like the one here:

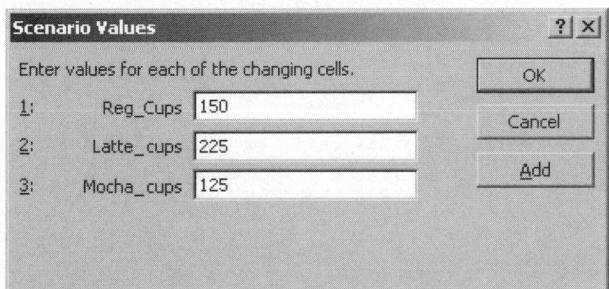

7 Click Add to create a second scenario. Type **Worst Case**, and click OK to display the Scenario Values dialog box.

8 Type **50**, **40**, and **30** in the variable cells, and then click OK. (These values represent our guess at the worst case.) The Scenario Manager dialog box appears and lists the Best Case and Worst Case scenarios. Now you're ready to view the results of your forecasting models.

9 Click Close to close the Scenario Manager dialog box.

tip You can save Solver problems as scenarios for future trials by clicking the Save Scenario button in the Solver Results dialog box when the Solver computes a new forecast. The Solver prompts you for a name, which you can use later to view the scenario in the Scenario Manager.

Viewing a Scenario

Excel keeps track of each of your worksheet scenarios. You can view them by choosing the Scenarios command on the Tools menu whenever your worksheet is open.

InsideOut

When you view a scenario, Excel replaces the current values in your worksheet with the values stored in the scenario. If you want to load a scenario but still be able to restore the previous values in the worksheet, be sure to save your file before loading the scenario.

To view a scenario, follow these steps:

1 Choose Tools, Scenarios. You'll see a dialog box similar to the one in Figure 29-7.

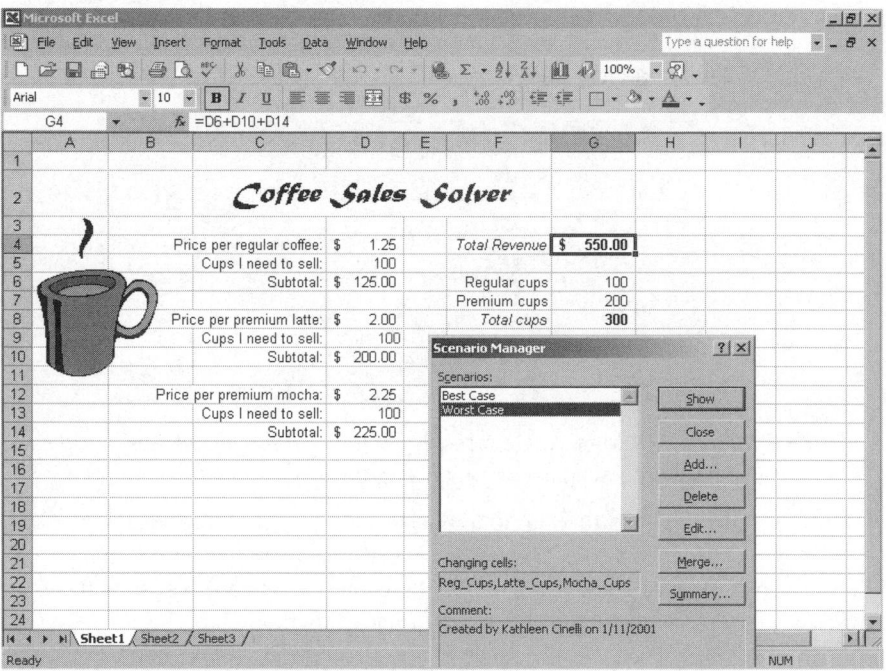

Figure 29-7. The Show button lets you compare the results of different what-if scenarios in your worksheet.

2 In the Scenarios list box, select the scenario that you want to view.

3 Click Show. Excel substitutes the values in the scenario for the variables in your worksheet and displays the results in your worksheet, as shown in

Chapter 29

Figure 29-7. (You might need to move the Scenario Manager dialog box to view the results.)

4 Select additional scenarios, and click Show to compare and contrast the what-if models in your worksheet. When you've finished, click Close. The last active scenario remains in your worksheet.

Creating Scenario Reports

Although you can easily compare different scenarios by switching between them using the Show button in the Scenario Manager dialog box, you might occasionally want to view a report that contains consolidated information about the scenarios in your worksheet. You can accomplish this quickly by clicking the Summary button in the Scenario Manager dialog box. Excel automatically formats the summary report and copies it to a new worksheet in your workbook.

To create a scenario report, follow these steps:

1 Choose Tools, Scenarios. The Scenario Manager dialog box opens.

For more information about viewing pivot table reports, see "Rearranging Fields in a Pivot Table," on page 799.

2 Click the Summary button.

The Scenario Summary dialog box opens, prompting you for a result cell to total in the report and also for a report type. A *scenario summary report* is a formatted table displayed in its own worksheet. A pivot table is a special summary table whose rows and columns can be rearranged, or *pivoted*:

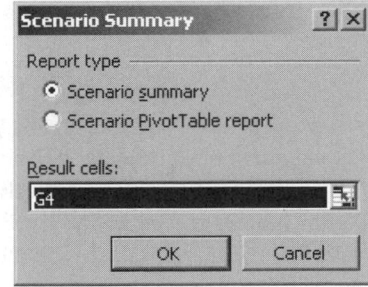

3 Select the result cell that you want to total (cell G4 in this example), click the report option button that you want to use (accept the Scenario Summary default if you're not sure), and then click OK.

After a few moments, a new Scenario Summary tab appears in your workbook, as shown in Figure 29-8. The outlining buttons in your report's left and top margins will help you shrink or expand the rows and columns in your scenario summary.

823

note Each time you click the Summary button in the Scenario Manager dialog box, Excel creates a new summary worksheet in your workbook. To delete unwanted summary reports, click the unwanted scenario's summary tab in the workbook, and then choose Edit, Delete Sheet.

Excel uses the defined names for variable cells D5, D9, and D13, which results in a more comprehensible summary.

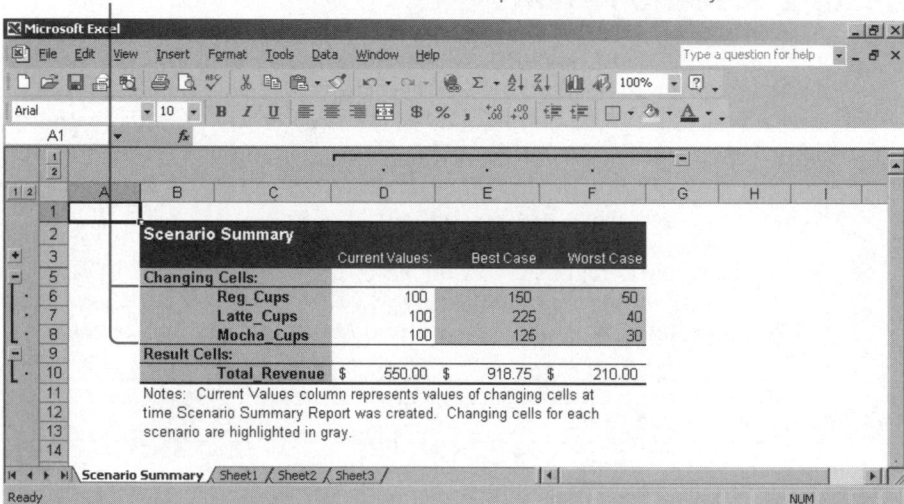

Figure 29-8. The Summary button creates a scenario summary report in a new worksheet in your workbook.

Managing Your Scenarios

Once you've defined a scenario using the Add button, luckily you're not stuck with that scenario forever. You can edit and delete scenarios by clicking the Edit and Delete buttons in the Scenario Manager dialog box. The Edit button lets you change the name of the scenario, remove existing variable cells, add new variable cells, or even choose a completely new group of variables. To assign different values to the variable cells in a scenario, clear the Prevent Changes check box on the Edit Scenario dialog box. After you click OK, Excel displays the Scenario Values dialog box. Make any changes you want to make, and then click OK.

To remove a particular scenario permanently, simply highlight it in the Scenario Manager dialog box and click Delete. Finally, you can copy scenarios from other open workbooks or worksheets into your current worksheet by clicking the Merge button in the Scenario Manager dialog box and specifying a source workbook and worksheet in the Merge Scenarios dialog box.

Expert Web Publishing and Querying Techniques

So far in this book, you've used Microsoft Excel 2002 to create reports, invoices, charts, lists, and pivot tables that are ready for use on your own computer or for traditional printing and paper distribution. However, with Excel, you can also save your worksheets in HTML (Hypertext Markup Language) or XML (Extensible Markup Language) format for electronic circulation on the World Wide Web. Several new features make this process straightforward and useful.

And it's a two-way street: another feature of Excel lets you import data from the Internet into a worksheet. This capability is not only easy to use, but it's also powerful in that it allows for regular updates to reflect the volatile nature of Web content.

In this chapter, you'll learn how to prepare your worksheet so that it can be saved in a Web page format, and you'll learn how to set special publication options that make your workbook more accessible and useful on the Internet. You'll also learn the simple commands that both save and preview completed Web pages, and you'll learn how to use Microsoft Office Web toolbars to issue Excel commands in Microsoft Internet Explorer. Finally, you'll step through the process of creating and revising Web queries. When you're finished, you'll have the skills necessary to create and distribute your own Excel Web pages and to import data from the Internet.

Designing a Web Page

Web pages are documents that contain special formatting codes known as HTML. These formatting codes have been optimized for speedy transmission over the Internet and for displaying information attractively in Web browsers, such as Internet Explorer and Netscape Navigator. In the past, only special-purpose application programs such as Microsoft FrontPage allowed you to create HTML documents for the Web, but now you can create Web pages using each of the applications in the Office XP software suite. The program you choose depends on the features you want to provide and the type of Web site you're constructing.

Naturally, the most effective Excel Web pages use Excel's rich worksheet formatting, calculation, and data analysis capabilities. We recommend that you build Excel Web pages when you need to distribute the following types of information:

- Electronic invoices and order forms, such as an invoice for a new car or a price sheet for a furniture store

- Database analysis tools, such as summary reporting and pivot tables for a corporate database

- Tables of image collections, such as employee photographs, company clip art, and links to other Web sites

- Statistics and demographic information presented in tables, such as government population statistics, traffic patterns, or water usage

- Testing and survey information presented in worksheets, such as online practice tests, government surveys, or customer satisfaction questionnaires

- Excel charts that present important facts and figures graphically, such as revenue reports and cost comparisons

Creating an Excel Web page is no different than building a regular worksheet from scratch. You enter information in rows and columns, edit the data, and use formulas and formatting commands as you normally would. However, take care to use fonts and colors in a way that's aesthetically compatible with the other documents on your home page and use hyperlinks when necessary to connect your Excel Web page to other Internet sites. And be sure to preview your documents carefully to verify that the HTML file conversion created a Web page that matches your expectations.

In addition, be aware that some of the more advanced features in your Excel worksheet might not be available to your users when the document is published on the Web. Because the Excel application itself won't be available on the Web site (only the HTML file you create), your users won't have the ability to employ add-in programs such as the Solver, and some of the more advanced features such as tracking changes, comments, macros, and forms will be disabled. However, if you're planning to view the Excel Web page using Internet Explorer 4.0 or later, you can use Office Web Components to work inter-actively with formulas, filters, pivot tables, charts, and worksheet formatting com-mands. (You'll learn more about these options later in this chapter.)

Why Save in XML Format?

Excel offers the option of saving your workbook as the file type XML Spreadsheet (.xml). You might wonder when that option would be desirable. By some measures, XML is the most promising language for storing and delivering information on the Web. Its flexible, structured syntax lets you describe virtually any kind of informa-tion—from a simple recipe to a complex business database—and to sort, filter, search, and manipulate that information in powerful ways. XML, as opposed to HTML, tags the data in your file to indicate the structure and meaning of the information, not just its appearance.

XML tags are not especially important if the worksheet data is intended simply to be published and viewed in some fixed format. But if the content of your file is meant to be acted on by programs and scripts, then storing data with XML tagging can be cru-cial. For example, if you want a program, such as a script in a Web page, to be able to examine your file and determine not only that it contains cells with characters that appear to be dates, but also that some of the dates are birthdates and others are expi-ration dates, then your needs are extending into the realm of XML.

For a hands-on guide to the basics of XML, see *XML Step by Step*, by Michael J. Young (Microsoft Press, 2000). The book clearly explains the basics of XML and shows both non-programmers and Web developers how to create XML documents and display them on the Web.

Static Pages vs. Interactive Pages

Fundamentally, you have two options when presenting Excel Web pages: you can dis-play a static, noninteractive Excel worksheet (in other words, a snapshot of your work-sheet that can't be modified), or you can display a working, interactive worksheet that users can modify directly in Internet Explorer. The option you select depends on the purpose of your Web site and your particular design goals. Static Web pages are best for showing purchase orders, sales data, and other tabular information that should be viewed but not modified. Interactive Web pages are best for budgeting, calculation, and analysis tools that invite remote colleagues and other Internet users to experiment with their own facts and figures. (For example, a mortgage calculator that prompts users for their own loan information.)

You can also share and discuss Excel workbooks with other users on the Web using an Internet connectivity feature known as Online Collaboration. For more information about this feature, see "Discussing an Online Document," on page 193.

Setting Web Publication Options

The Save As Web Page command on the Excel File menu saves an existing Excel worksheet or workbook as a Web page and allows you to set a number of useful publication options. Before you use this command, verify that your worksheet contains the proper document style and content for your Web page and that it presents information in a clear format that includes the necessary operating instructions. And remember: users with no knowledge of you or your worksheet open and run this document on the Internet or an intranet (provided that they have the necessary permissions), so take care to make the worksheet's user interface simple and intuitive.

To save or publish an Excel worksheet or workbook as a Web page, follow these steps:

1 Open the worksheet you plan to save as an HTML document. In this example, we'll save the Invoice.xls worksheet (an order form for sewing patterns) as an interactive Web page.

The Invoice.xls example is on the Microsoft Office XP Inside Out companion CD.

2 Choose File, Save As Web Page. You'll see a dialog box similar to the one shown in Figure 30-1.

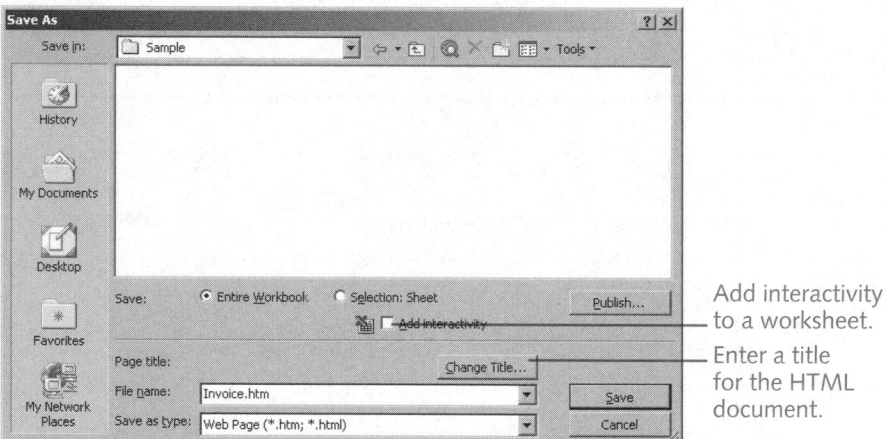

Figure 30-1. The Save As Web Page command displays this dialog box, which offers options that control how your Excel worksheet is converted into an HTML document.

The Save As Web Page dialog box looks similar to the standard Save As dialog box displayed by all Office applications. However, you see the following four new options related to Web publishing:

■ You can specify which part of your workbook you want to publish (the entire workbook or the active worksheet).

- You can specify whether you want the document to be interactive or not (an option that's valid for worksheets only, not entire workbooks).

- You can add an HTML document title to the Web page.

- You can select advanced options by clicking Publish.

3 Click the Selection: Sheet option button to save the active worksheet as a Web page.

4 If you want to make your worksheet interactive, verify that the Add Interactivity check box is selected.

5 Click Change Title, and modify the HTML page title that appears above the Web page in your browser. In this example, we typed "Use This Invoice to Calculate Your Order."

6 Click OK to lock in the page title. The Save As dialog box shows any changes you made.

7 (Optional) Type a new filename in the File Name text box. This isn't a requirement, because Excel can use your existing filename, but you might want to give your Web page a new title now. By default, Excel Web pages have the .htm filename extension.

> **note** After you type a filename, you can select a different file type. You might, for example, choose XML Spreadsheet in the Save As File Type drop-down list; however, note that you will be able to save a file of this type, *but you won't be able to publish it.*

8 Click Publish to display the advanced options in the Publish As Web Page dialog box. You see a list of choices that looks similar to Figure 30-2.

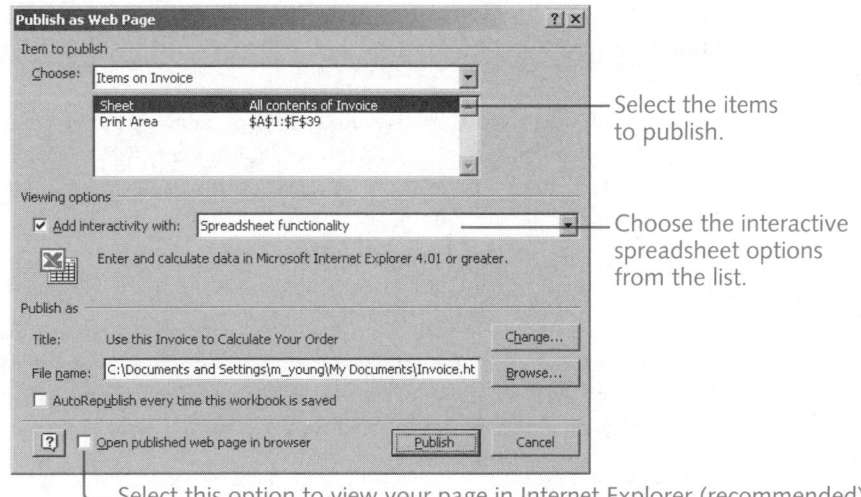

Figure 30-2. The Publish As Web Page dialog box lists the entire collection of options available to you.

The top list box gives you the option of selecting only a portion of your worksheet for the Web page. Although we typically include the whole sheet in our interactive Excel pages to allow the user some maneuvering room, this option is nice if you want to limit what users can see and do on the screen.

The Interactivity options control what the user can do with the worksheet when it appears in the browser. To make the Web page static and non-interactive, clear the Add Interactivity With check box. To specify the type of interactivity you want to use, select the Spreadsheet Functionality option in the list box in Figure 30-2. Excel Web pages support general spreadsheet functionality, pivot table functionality, and charting functionality. (To get the chart functionality option, you need to open a chart in Excel.)

Interestingly, the interactivity features listed here aren't provided by the Excel application itself, but by small ActiveX controls called *Office Web Components* that Excel places in the HTML document when it builds the Web page. When your completed page is viewed in Internet Explorer version 4.0 or later, these components spring to life as toolbars and simulate the capabilities of a real Excel worksheet.

---

tip   **Planning for Change**

Just in case you need to make changes, be sure to save the Excel document that you published. If you publish an interactive Web page, you won't be able to modify it in Excel. Instead, open the original Excel workbook, make your changes there, and republish the sheet.

The Publish As Web Page dialog box also lets you change the HTML document title and filename—the same options you saw in the Save As dialog box earlier.

newfeature!

A new feature in Excel 2002 is AutoRepublish, which you can select or clear in the corresponding check box, AutoRepublish Every Time This Workbook Is Saved. This feature assures that any changes you save to the workbook also get propagated to the Web page.

Finally, the Open Published Web Page In Browser check box gives you a chance to display the completed Web page in Internet Explorer now. (If you choose this option, Excel starts Internet Explorer when you click Publish.) We recommend that you habitually use this preview option whenever you publish Web pages so that you can see early in the development process how the page will appear to users on the Web.

9 Select the Open Published Web Page In Browser check box, and then click Publish. Excel launches Internet Explorer and displays the Web page. Figure 30-3 shows the result for the Invoice worksheet we've been working with. Note that if you have a different browser installed, you get different results.

> **tip** **Another Way to Preview**
>
> If you don't select the Open Published Web Page In Browser check box while you're saving your Web page, you can preview the document later by choosing Web Page Preview from the Excel File menu. Both actions launch the current Excel Web page in Internet Explorer or the default browser for your system.

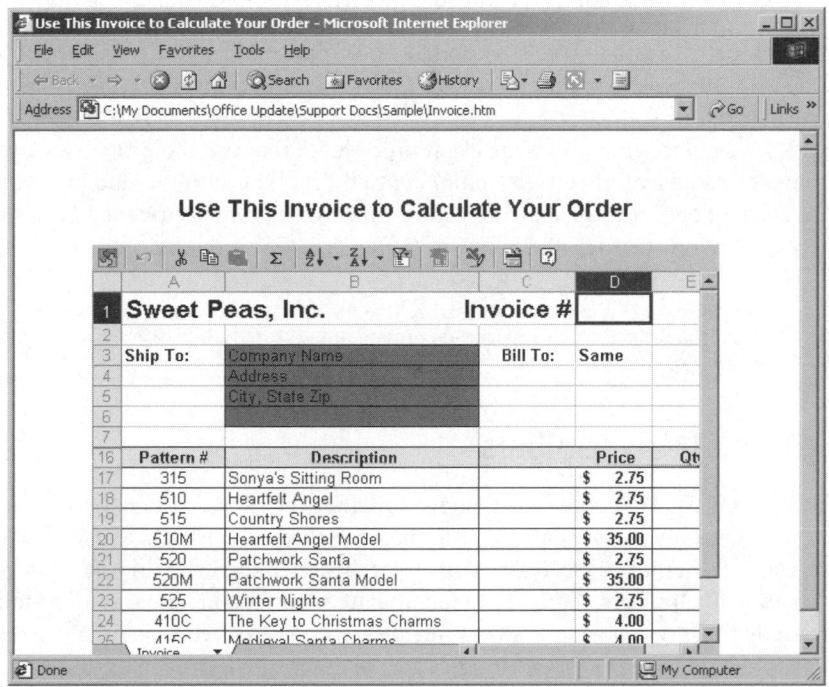

Figure 30-3. The Open Published Web Page In Browser option lets you preview your worksheet as it appears in your browser—Internet Explorer in this case.

Running Excel Web Pages on the Internet

If you created a static Excel Web page, your options for manipulating the Web page in your Internet browser are rather limited. You can use the scroll bars to view all aspects of the page, and you can copy cell data from the page to the Clipboard by selecting the desired cells, right-clicking the selection, and choosing Copy. However, if you requested an interactive Web page when you saved the Excel worksheet using the Save As Web Page command, you can perform a number of useful editing and calculation activities on your Web page, including filling the worksheet with data, editing and formatting cells, adding new formulas, running filters, modifying charts (if you started with one), and manipulating pivot tables.

831

As mentioned earlier, the spreadsheet functionality that Excel Web pages provide comes not from Excel itself, but from a collection of ActiveX controls used in the worksheet called Office Web Components. Internet Explorer versions 4.0 and later recognize these components, which offer a subset of Excel's data analysis features to those using Excel worksheets on the Web. You can identify the presence of Office Web Components in Internet Explorer by the special toolbars that appear directly above Excel HTML documents and by the Office Web icon that appears on the left side of Office Web toolbars. If you click one of these icons in Internet Explorer, you see an Office Web Components dialog box.

You can control Office Web Components programmatically by using development tools that support Component Object Model (COM) technology. For example, you could load an Excel-interactive Web page into the Microsoft Visual Basic 6.0 Dynamic HTML Page Designer and write event procedures that use the properties, methods, and events exposed by Office Web Component objects. The result would be an interactive Excel Web page customized with features that you designed in Visual Basic and slick new commands that use the power of Office Web Components.

> For more information about using Microsoft Visual Basic 6.0 to customize HTML documents, check out Michael Halvorson's self-paced programming tutorial *Microsoft Visual Basic 6.0 Professional Step by Step* (Redmond, Wash.: Microsoft Press, 1998).

Using Office Web Toolbars

Interactive Excel Web pages allow you to move the cell pointer around the worksheet to enter and edit data. If you enter data into cells that are linked to a formula, a new result is calculated immediately in the worksheet when you press the Enter key. In addition, the Office Web Components toolbars allow you to manipulate your data in new ways. The following example shows you how to work with an interactive worksheet in Internet Explorer.

> **note** To follow these steps exactly in a sample document, you can open the Invoice.xls example on the Microsoft Office XP Inside Out companion CD, save the worksheet as an interactive spreadsheet by choosing the Save As Web Page command, and open the page in Internet Explorer.

To manipulate an Excel Web page using the Office Web spreadsheet toolbar, follow these steps:

1 Open the Excel Web page you want to use in Internet Explorer using either the Publish button in the Publish As Web Page dialog box or the Web Page Preview command on the File menu.

If your Web page is interactive, it will feature an Office Web toolbar, as shown in the following illustration:

Spreadsheet functionality toolbar provided by Office Web components

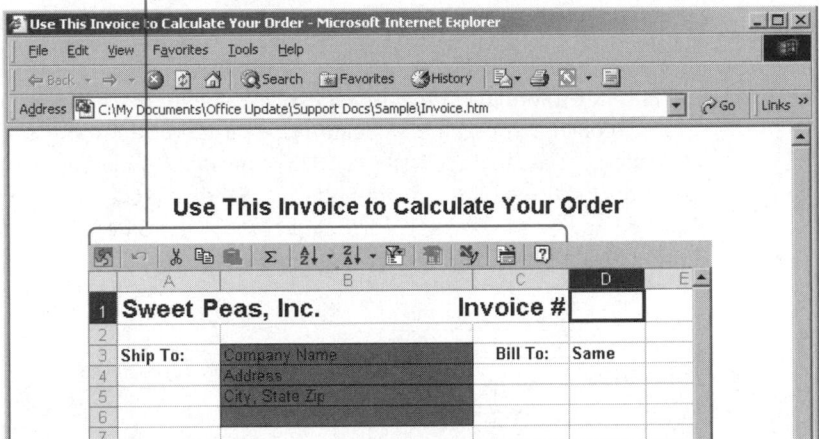

2 If the Web page is a worksheet that welcomes data entry, enter some information now by clicking cells on the Web page, typing numbers and labels, and pressing the Enter key.

The following illustration shows what the Invoice Web page looks like when three quantity numbers are entered into the order portion of the interactive worksheet.

You can enter data in an interactive worksheet.

	Description	C	Price	Qty	Extended
16	Description		Price	Qty	Extended
17	Sonya's Sitting Room		$2.75	2	$5.50
18	Heartfelt Angel		$2.75	1	$2.75
19	Country Shores		$2.75	3	$8.25
20	Heartfelt Angel Model		$35.00		$0.00
21	Patchwork Santa		$2.75		$0.00
22	Patchwork Santa Model		$35.00		$0.00
23	Winter Nights		$2.75		$0.00
24	The Key To Christmas Charms		$4.00		$0.00
25	Medieval Santa Charms		$4.00		$0.00
26	Keeping Warm		$2.75		$0.00
27	Spring In The Valley		$2.75		$0.00
28	Santa's Favorite Ornaments		$1.93		$0.00
29					
30					
31			Subtotal (A)		$16.50
32					
33					
34	Please Remit to:		Subtotal (A)		$16.50

Formulas are calculated automatically.

3 Scroll to the bottom of the Web page, if necessary, to see the results of any calculations you've entered. (In our example the page automatically calculated a total of $16.50.)

4 Try entering a formula in the interactive Web page. If you have the Invoice example open, scroll to the Shipping cell near the bottom of the worksheet, click the cell next to it (containing $0.00), press the equal sign (=), press the Up Arrow key twice to highlight Subtotal (A), type ***0.2**, and press Enter. Excel computes a hypothetical shipping cost for the order (20 percent of the total, or $3.30) and displays it in the highlighted cell:

Subtotal (A)	$16.50
Subtotal (B)	
Shipping	=F34*0.2
Total	$16.50
This is your invoice	

— Entering a new formula here...

Subtotal (A)	$16.50
Subtotal (B)	
Shipping	$3.30
Total	$19.80

— ...produces a new result immediately.

Sort
Ascending

5 Now try sorting a group of rows in the worksheet. If you have the Invoice example open, scroll to the product list part of the worksheet, select the region that lists the products (A17:F28), click the down arrow alongside the Sort Ascending button on the Office Web toolbar, and then click the Description field.

	A			C	D	E	
6		Pattern #					
7		Description					
16	Pattern #	Price			Price	Qty	
17	315	Sonya's S	Qty		$2.75	2	
18	510	Heartfelt A	Ext		$2.75	1	
19	515	Country Shores			$2.75	3	
20	510M	Heartfelt Angel Model			$35.00		
21	520	Patchwork Santa			$2.75		
22	520M	Patchwork Santa Model			$35.00		
23	525	Winter Nights			$2.75		
24	410C	The Key to Christmas Charms			$4.00		
25	415C	Medieval Santa Charms			$4.00		
26	530	Keeping Warm			$2.75		
27	535	Spring in the Valley			$2.75		
28	540	Santa's Favorite Ornaments			$1.93		

— After you select the rows and columns you want to sort, open the list for the Sort Ascending button and choose Description, the field on which you want to sort.

The worksheet sorts the selected rows alphabetically in ascending order, based on the product descriptions in column B:

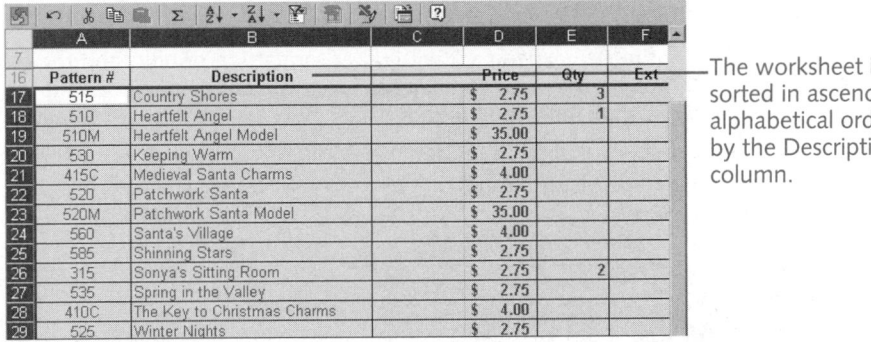

The worksheet is sorted in ascending alphabetical order by the Description column.

6 With the sorted rows and columns still selected, click the Commands And Options button on the Office Web toolbar to modify the formatting in the selected worksheet cells.

You see a menu bar that has several command categories that are applicable to the active worksheet.

7 Click the Format tab to display the valid formatting commands for the current selection of cells. You'll see the following dialog box:

Commands and Options

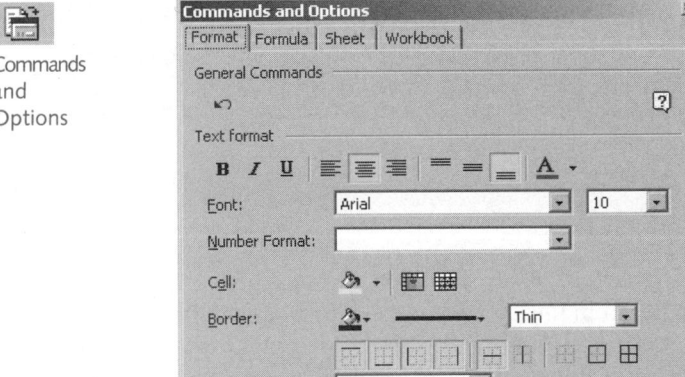

8 Click the Font Color button's drop-down arrow, click the red color, and then click the Font drop-down arrow and choose Times New Roman from the list of available fonts. The formatting options you pick are immediately updated on the Web page as you select them.

9 Continue to experiment with other formatting options and the remaining Office Web toolbar commands if you want to. When you're finished, close the Commands And Options dialog box, and then exit Internet Explorer.

You're done working with Office Web toolbars for now. If you like, copy the .htm file you created (and any supporting files) to a server on the Internet and see how it runs live on the Web!

InsideOut

Are Web Pages Read-Only?

After your Web page has closed, you might start wondering what it will look like the next time you open it. After all, you made several changes to the interactive Excel Web page. Will those be part of the HTML document the next time you display it in *your* browser? The answer is no: Your Web page will appear exactly as it did when you finished creating it in Excel: the data entry, sorting, and formatting changes are lost as soon as you close the Web page. In this sense, you should think of Excel Web pages as read-only documents. Users on the Internet can modify them, but each time you reopen the file it appears as it did the first time. If transmitting a modified document on the Web is what you're looking for, experiment with the commands on Excel's Online Collaboration submenu, which are discussed along with other Office applications in Chapter 3, "Getting Expert Help on Office XP."

Using Web Queries

Excel not only publishes to the Web, it also gives you convenient ways—via Web queries—to pull data seamlessly from the Web into Excel worksheets. With the explosion of data available on the Web, this is a crucial capability to exploit. And because data on the Web is often valuable for its timeliness, Excel builds automatic background refresh capabilities into Web queries, so that you can be sure that the external data you import from the Web is up-to-the-minute.

Importing Data from the Web

You can use Web queries to import data from the Web into Excel. The process is interactive and easy to follow, much like a wizard, enabling you to select just the information you want. Of course, you need Internet access to display the data source you intend to use and make your selection. As an example, let's import some stock data from MSN to see how the process works.

To begin, establish an Internet connection and open a new Excel worksheet. (You also can use this process to import data to an already-existing worksheet.) Then complete the following steps:

1 Select cell A1 on the worksheet. Open the Data menu, and from the Import External Data submenu, choose New Web Query. Excel displays the New Web Query dialog box.

2 Enter the web address for the site you want to display. For this example, enter www.moneycentral.msn.com. The site will appear in the browser window within the dialog box, as shown below:

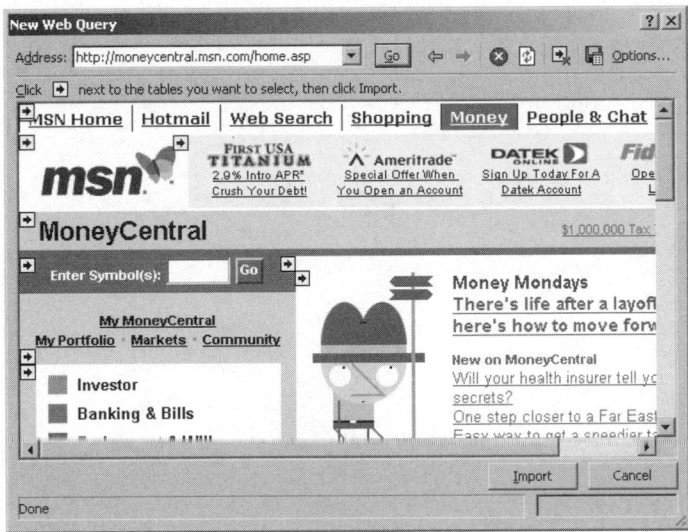

3 In the MoneyCentral homepage, enter the following series of ticker symbols (or symbols of your own choosing) in the Enter Symbol(s) text box: **BA**, **COST**, **IMNX**, **MSFT**, **WM**, **WY**.

Then click the Go button to display the current trading price for each stock. If the market is open at the time of the query, the price reflects a 15-minute delay. If the market is closed, the price is the last trading price at the closing bell.

caution Web sites seem to be constantly in flux. So although this example was devised with stability in mind, there is no guarantee that the MSN screens will match or that eventual redesign of the Web site will not invalidate the specific instructions. Stock prices reflect the trading date on March 12, 2001.

4 In the browser window of the New Web Query dialog box, each pane of information on the MoneyCentral screen is displayed with a small selection box in its upper left corner: a square yellow icon that contains a black arrow. In this example, click the arrow for the table of stock data. The icon becomes green (with a check mark instead of an arrow), and the data table is highlighted.

5 Select the Options toolbar button to display the Web Query Options dialog box. From among the Formatting options, select Full HTML Formatting, and then click OK.

6 You are now ready to import the selected information into your worksheet. Click the Import button. Excel displays a dialog box to verify the destination of the imported information—the upper left cell in the target area. In this example, use cell A1 to indicate the destination. For now, ignore the Properties button, which displays the Data Range Properties dialog box.

7 Click OK to finish the import process. Excel fetches the data and then presents it in a block of cells in your worksheet, as shown in Figure 30-4.

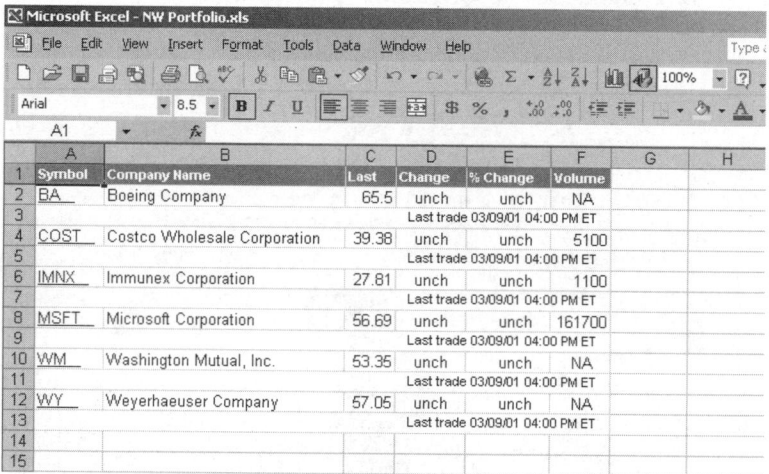

Figure 30-4 The Web query results in a block of imported data, which can be unformatted or can retain formatting, as shown here.

Because we chose, in this example, to retain HTML formatting, the imported data retains a full set of formatting attributes: colored backgrounds, font attributes—even hyperlinks that jump to activity data for individual stocks. Also notice that Excel displays the External Data toolbar near the imported table. We'll look at some of these tools in the next section.

Revising Web Queries

To revise a Web query, select any cell in the external data table, and then click the appropriate button in the External Data toolbar. You can edit the query itself or change the properties assigned to the data range. You can also use your mouse to right-click a cell in the data table and choose a command from the shortcut menu.

Editing Web Queries

When you choose the Edit Query button on the External Data toolbar, Excel displays the Edit Web Query dialog box. You can navigate to a different Web address or select different tables at the current site. Click a green, checkmarked icon to clear a selection; click additional yellow icons to add them to the current selection. If no table is selected before you click the Import button, Excel imports all the selectable items on the current Web page.

Click the Options button to change the Web Query options. You can change the formatting that is preserved in the external data, or alter other import settings. Among the Web Query formatting options, Rich Text Formatting is generally a good middle-of-the-road choice. It preserves most character formatting but does not retain hyperlinks and other attributes that might be overkill in a simple presentation.

> **tip** If you choose Full HTML Formatting when you create or edit a Web query, Excel includes any hyperlinks in the imported data, but you won't be able to retain (through the refresh process) any formatting you subsequently apply to the external data in Excel.

Changing Data Range Properties

On the External Data toolbar, choose Data Range Properties to display the corresponding dialog box, shown below:

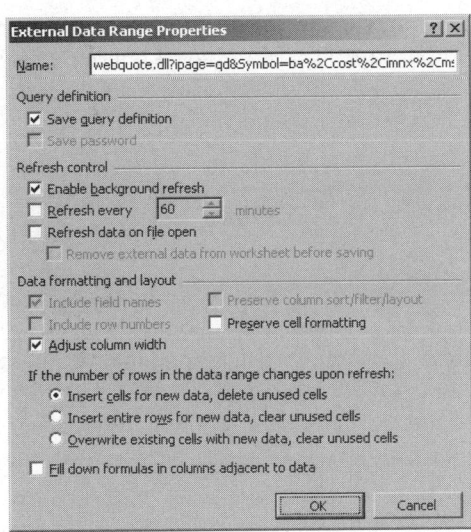

This dialog box is particularly valuable for setting the refresh options you want for the Web data. You might want to experiment using the Web query defined in the previous example (for tracking stock prices). When you finish adjusting the options, click OK to save your changes.

By default, the Save Web Query check box is selected. If you clear this box, the rest of the options are dimmed: without a saved query, Excel has no query definition to consult for automatic refresh. The Save Password option retains the password (if you need one to access the data source) as part of the query. This option is dimmed for Web queries.

Troubleshooting

External Data Tools Unavailable

The commands available through the External Data toolbar are dimmed.

The External Data toolbar has seven toolbar buttons. Various buttons are dimmed at different times. Here are some clues to what's going on. All the buttons except Refresh All are dimmed if the sheet is password-protected or if the selected cell is not part of an external data table. Query Parameters is always dimmed for Web Queries.

Cancel Refresh and Refresh Status are available only if a refresh is in progress. During a refresh, Edit Query and Data Range Properties are dimmed so that you can't redefine a query that is currently being applied.

The Refresh Control options are important if you intend to work on a file that contains Web data. If you clear the Enable Background Refresh check box, you will not be able to use Excel until the refresh process is finished. Other options let you determine the frequency at which your data is automatically refreshed. Only integer values (minutes) are accepted for the refresh interval.

Among the formatting options, don't worry about the dimmed items. They generally apply to external database queries rather than typical Web data queries. Preserve Cell Formatting can be a useful option. If you select it, refreshed data acquires the formatting you applied (while working in Excel) to the previously imported data.

InsideOut

Keeping a Snapshot of Web Data

If you want to save a snapshot of Web data such as stock price information, you'll need to frustrate the Automatic Refresh features that will change the data right out from under you. It might occur to you to save a copy of the external data to a new worksheet, so you could then format the table and present the snapshot of Web data later. But you'd be in for a surprise: the copy would be refreshed whenever the original data is refreshed.

To freeze the data, you need to choose Edit, Paste Special when you paste the Web data to a new worksheet. Among the Paste options, select Values And Number Formats, and then click OK. You can use Paste Special a second time with the same selected range to paste the Column Widths, as well. Then, you might want to do some additional cell formatting by hand, but the values will remain static.

Part 5

PowerPoint

Chapter 31

Essential PowerPoint Techniques

Microsoft PowerPoint 2002 is presentation graphics software. Using PowerPoint, you can create and display sets of slides that combine text with diagrams, photos, clip art, media files, and animated special effects. You can then turn your work into 35-mm slides, transparencies, or printed handouts that you can present electronically or interactively on the World Wide Web.

Furthermore, because PowerPoint is part of the Microsoft Office XP suite of applications, you can easily blend Microsoft Word outlines, Microsoft Excel worksheets, and Microsoft Clip Organizer illustrations into your own original PowerPoint text and graphics.

When you need to teach, persuade, or explain, PowerPoint can help you create clear, attention-getting presentations.

In this introductory chapter, you'll learn:

- The main features of the PowerPoint window
- How to build a simple presentation quickly
- How to add and edit text in placeholders and in an outline
- How to add comments to slides
- How to check spelling and style guidelines
- How to select a file format to save a presentation

Exploring the PowerPoint Window

The PowerPoint window, shown in Figure 31-1, opens by default displaying a slide and three work areas—an Outline tab, a Slides tab, and an area for notes. Normal view also opens with the task pane displayed, which contains information, commands, and controls for creating or opening a presentation, displayed like links on a Web page.

> For details on using the task pane, see Chapter 4, "Working with Office XP Applications, Documents, and Program Windows."

Outline tab
Slides tab

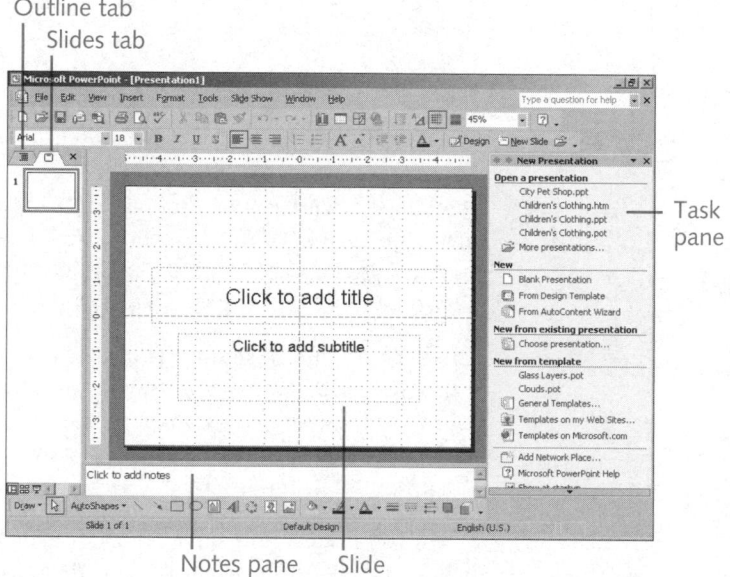

Task pane

Notes pane   Slide

Figure 31-1. Important parts of the PowerPoint window are shown in Normal view.

The PowerPoint interface elements, many of which are shared with other Office programs, are the following:

- A menu bar provides access to the most important commands in PowerPoint. To choose a command from a PowerPoint menu, click the menu you want, point to the desired submenu (if applicable), and then click the command you want to run.

- The toolbars provide one-click access to frequently used commands. Placing the mouse pointer on a tool displays a ScreenTip that briefly describes the tool's function. The Common Tasks toolbar has been replaced in this version of PowerPoint by two new buttons on the Formatting toolbar: Design (for slide design options) and New Slide (with slide layout options), with both of them opening in the task pane.

- The task pane is where you find options for creating a new presentation or working with existing presentations. Although you can also access many of these commands from the menu bar, you'll find the convenience of working with the Web-like interface useful, particularly when creating presentations in a hurry.

- Like most Office application windows, the PowerPoint application window also contains sizing buttons that you can use to minimize, maximize, restore, and close windows, plus a status bar at the bottom of the screen that displays the number of the slide you're working on as well as the type of presentation you're creating.

- The scroll box moves you from slide to slide, not up or down through the slide's text (as happens in a Word document, for example). In addition, PowerPoint displays the number and title of each slide as you drag the scroll box.

- The two buttons displaying double arrows at the bottom of the vertical scroll bar give you another way to move through slides. Click the button with the upward-pointing arrows to go to the previous slide; click the button with the downward-pointing arrows to move to the next slide.

- The View buttons below the Slide and Outline tabs let you quickly switch to different PowerPoint views. Each view is designed to make some aspect of creating and viewing a slide show as effective as possible. Views are described in more detail in the next section.

- The Office Assistant button on the right side of the Standard toolbar provides access to all the PowerPoint Help documentation and the animated Office Assistant. If the Office Assistant isn't already running, clicking this button starts it.

> For more information about using menus, dialog boxes, toolbars, and application windows, see Chapter 4, "Working with Office XP Applications, Documents, and Program Windows." For more information about starting and configuring the Office Assistant, see Chapter 2, "Installing and Configuring Office XP."

Elements of a Slide

After you're comfortable with the PowerPoint window, take a look at what is typically included on a slide, shown in Figure 31-2, on page 846.

A basic slide contains the following elements:

- **A background**   A slide with a design template applied comes with predesigned background graphics, fills, and color schemes, all of which can be modified or scrapped if you choose to create your own.

- **A title**   Each slide is generally titled, as shown in Figure 31-2. Each presentation usually also has a title slide that contains the title of the presentation, the

Part 5: PowerPoint

Title   Body text   Design elements from template

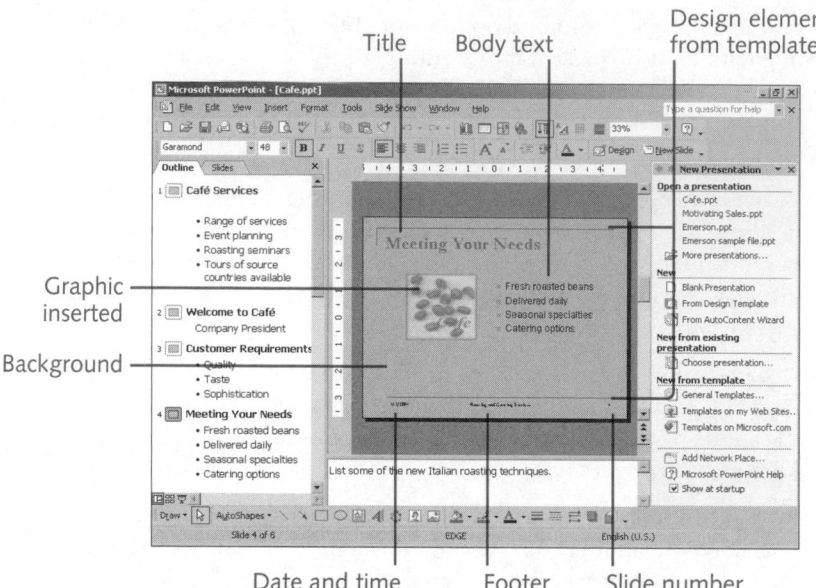

Graphic inserted

Background

Date and time   Footer   Slide number

Figure 31-2.   Content of a typical slide is shown here.

subtitle, and information about the presentation, such as what audience it was created for.

● **Body text**   This consists of content that you enter, often formatted as a bulleted or numbered list.

● **Placeholders**   These are boxes outlined with dotted lines that serve as containers for text and objects (such as diagrams, tables, photos, or media files) that you can add to the slide. In PowerPoint 2002, some placeholders also contain a rotate handle so you can manipulate the placeholder position.

● **Footer**   This is an area at the bottom of a slide that you can use to specify your organization name or slide show theme. You can also delete this section.

● **Date and time**   Also displayed at the bottom of a slide, this setting can be set to update automatically or can be deleted.

● **Slide number**   By default, this is displayed at the bottom of a slide, although you can move it anywhere you like or delete it.

Understanding PowerPoint Views

To use PowerPoint effectively to create and modify presentations, you need to become comfortable with PowerPoint's views. By default, PowerPoint opens in Normal view, but you can display the other views by clicking their buttons in the lower left corner of the PowerPoint window. PowerPoint displays your slides in any of four basic views:

Chapter 31: Essential PowerPoint Techniques

● Normal view is the default view in this version of PowerPoint. It contains a current slide, an Outline tab, and a Slides tab containing thumbnails of all the slides in the presentation, as well as a pane for adding notes. The task pane opens in Normal view (as shown in Figure 31-1), which gives you options to work on text, graphics, sound, animation, and other effects as well. You can also enlarge the tabbed areas to work more comfortably in the work area you prefer.

InsideOut

You can specify in which view you want PowerPoint to always open. Choose Tools, Options, and then click the View tab. In the View tab, in the Default View drop-down list, select the view you are most comfortable using to create presentations.

● Slide Sorter view, shown in Figure 31-3, arranges all your slides across and down the screen so that you can see the entire presentation. Use Slide Sorter view when you want to see your presentation as a whole and when you want to view or add transitions between slides, although the newly enhanced Normal view lets you apply transitions and animations without leaving that view.

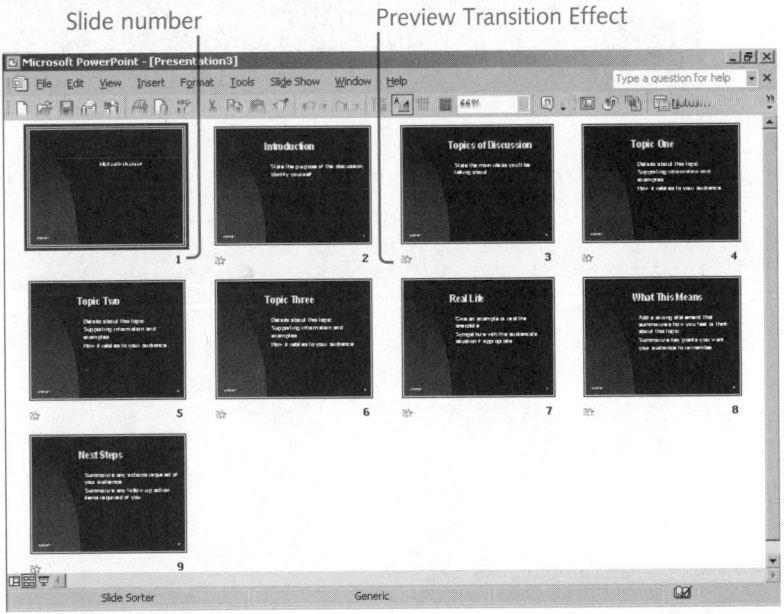

Figure 31-3. Slide Sorter view is useful for working on presentations as a whole.

● Slide Show view, shown in Figure 31-4, lets you preview the show itself by displaying each slide as a full screen. In Slide Show view, you can see the results of transitions (how the screen changes when moving between slides) as well as any animation or sound effects you have added to the presentation. You can navigate in this view by simply right-clicking and using the shortcut menu options to move through your slides.

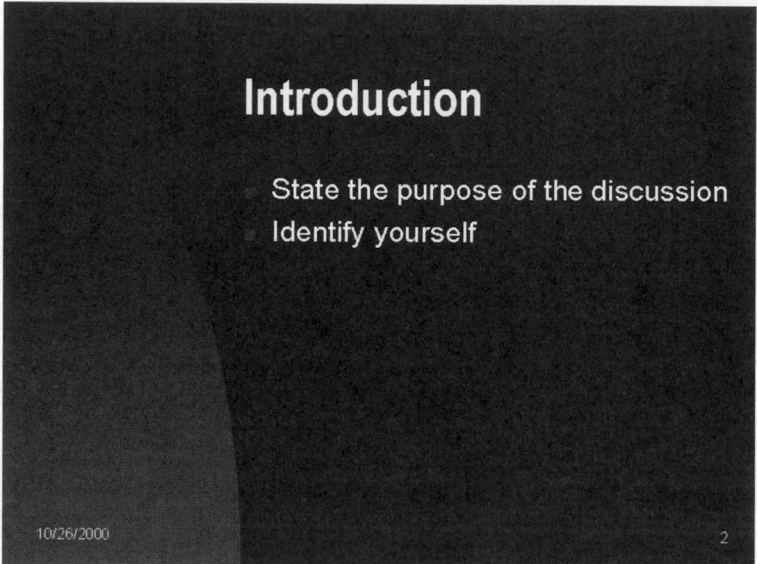

Figure 31-4. Slide Show view lets you preview slides in a full screen.

● Notes Page view, a subsection of Normal view, allows you to add notes to your slides. To add notes, click inside the Notes area in Normal view or choose View, Notes Page. When you choose this option, the Notes page looks like the one shown in Figure 31-5. There is only one Notes page per slide, so you should use the new Print Preview button on the Standard toolbar to see if all your notes fit on a page. You can also make the slide smaller in this view to fit in more notes per page.

Chapter 31: Essential PowerPoint Techniques

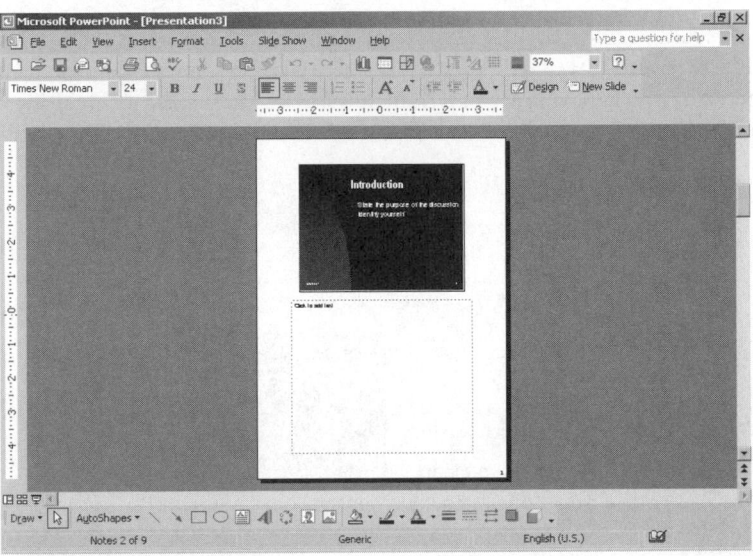

Figure 31-5. In Notes Page view, you can also format the text or background of your notes.

Using a Web Browser to View a Presentation

You can make your PowerPoint presentations available for viewing on the Web by saving or publishing them as Web pages. If you are working on a presentation that you know will be viewed on the Web, choose File, Web Page Preview to check how the slides look in a browser.

> Chapter 35, "Setting Up and Presenting the Slide Show," discusses formatting a presentation for the Web in greater detail.

note By default, PowerPoint presentations saved as Web pages are optimized for viewing in Microsoft Internet Explorer 4.0 or later. Be aware that aspects of your presentation, such as animations, slide scaling to fit the browser window, or media files, can be adversely affected when viewed in other browsers.

newfeature! Using Print Preview to View a Presentation

You can view your slides as they will look in printed form using Print Preview, a new command in PowerPoint 2002. This command is found on the File menu. Print Preview opens in its own window. It is a streamlined view in which to set options for printing not just slides, but also handouts, notes pages, and outlines. Because you typically print presentations in black and white or grayscale, but view them on your computer screen in color, it is useful to preview how they will actually look in black and white or grayscale before you print them.

The Print Preview toolbar also provides quick access to options for setting the orientation for handouts, notes, or an outline; adding a frame around each slide when printed; determining how many slides to print per page in handouts; printing hidden slides; and editing the slide headers and footers. A slide in Print Preview is shown here:

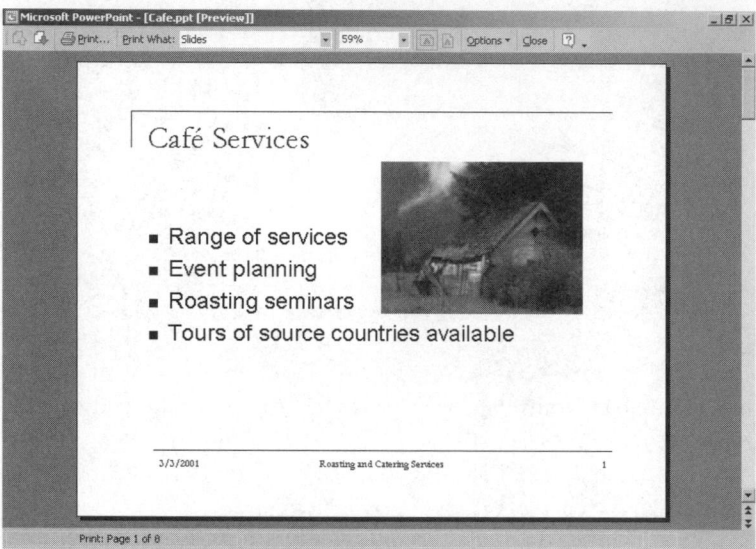

Creating a Presentation

After you're comfortable with the PowerPoint window and its views, the next step is creating a presentation. PowerPoint, like most Office XP applications, offers you a variety of choices. You see them listed in the task pane, shown in Figure 31-1, when you first open PowerPoint.

- Clicking More Presentations under Open A Presentation causes the Open dialog box to appear, which gives you access to all PowerPoint files on your computer, whether they're saved as presentations, Web pages, slide shows, design templates, or PowerPoint add-ons, such as PhotoAlbum. (The More Presentations option is called Presentations until you create and save a presentation.)

- Clicking Blank Presentation under New gives you a plain canvas on which to create a single slide. This option offers the most flexibility but, as you'd expect, it also assumes that you know what you want to do and how to do it. You start with a single, blank slide and create additional slides chosen from the Slide Layout suggestions in the task pane. Then you can add color, background, and objects of your choosing. You can make your own templates and save them as custom Blank Presentation templates.

● Clicking From Design Template under New lets you apply a PowerPoint design concept to your presentation, including predesigned fonts, color schemes, and backgrounds that create a cohesive design for a set of slides. You can also create custom templates to add to the Design Templates folder.

● Clicking From AutoContent Wizard under New is by far the easiest approach to creating a new presentation. The AutoContent Wizard asks for information and then creates a set of slides built around the theme you specify. The wizard applies an initial color scheme most suitable for the type of output you specify, although you can change the content suggestions, formatting, and color scheme. You can also add your own presentations to the AutoContent Wizard.

● Clicking Choose Presentation under New From Existing Presentation lets you choose a PowerPoint presentation that you have already created and saved and build a new presentation on it. In PowerPoint 2002, clicking this option opens the New From Existing Presentation dialog box, where you can search for presentations on your computer, network, or a Web folder. A copy of the selected presentation is created so you can enhance it and save it as a new, different presentation.

● Clicking General Templates under New From Template lets you browse in the Templates dialog box that provides access to general templates (the AutoContent Wizard, Blank Presentations, and custom templates that you've created and stored there), templates that are stored on a team Web site, and additional templates in the Microsoft Office Template Gallery.

Using the AutoContent Wizard

The AutoContent Wizard is often the simplest way to start a new presentation when you're either new to the software or working under deadline pressure. The AutoContent wizard provides a sample slide show of 8 to 12 slides organized in content categories such as Corporate, Projects, or Sales/Marketing, already formatted with a design. To start the AutoContent Wizard, open PowerPoint in Normal view with the task pane open, then perform the following steps:

1 In the task pane, click From AutoContent Wizard. After reading the introductory wizard page, click Next.

If you have been working in PowerPoint and the New Presentation task pane isn't displayed, then choose File, New. Click From AutoContent Wizard in the task pane.

Part 5: PowerPoint

2 In the second dialog box, select the type of presentation you're going to give by clicking one of the six topics displayed. For example, to see a list of the business presentations, click Corporate. You then see the dialog box illustrated here:

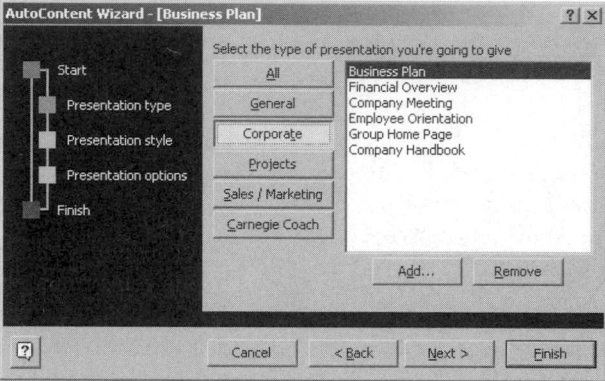

3 Click an appropriate presentation from the list for the category you selected, and then click Next.

> **note** You might select a presentation template that has not been installed. When prompted by PowerPoint, you can install the template, but you must have the Office XP CD or network connection to install from. To avoid doing this each time you select an uninstalled template, you can go back to Office Setup and install all the templates at once.

4 In the next dialog box, select the output style for the presentation you'll be making. PowerPoint comes with a number of built-in templates designed for the different output options. You can choose to play your presentation either on-screen or on the Web, and you can specify whether you need black-and-white or color overheads, or 35-mm slides. Click Next.

5 Enter information to be displayed on the opening, or title, slide. By default, the wizard includes your name. You provide the name of your presentation and the information you want included in the footer on each slide, and then click Finish.

The AutoContent Wizard creates a basic set of slides built around the choices you made, and ends up by displaying the presentation in Normal view, as shown in Figure 31-6.

With the preliminary work done, you can add or remove slides, modify the suggested text and graphics, and change the formatting to make the presentation your own.

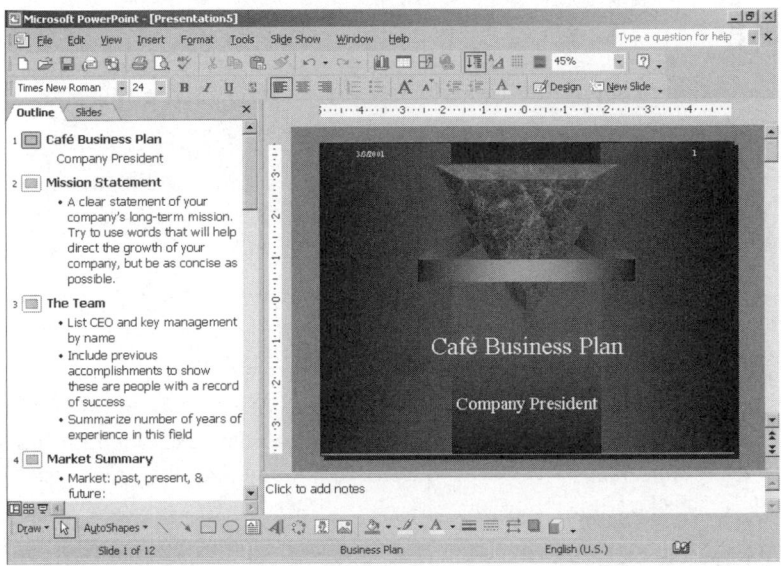

Figure 31-6. The AutoContent Wizard displays a new presentation with options for modifying the design or color scheme or adding animation schemes.

Adding Templates to the AutoContent Wizard

You can add templates that you've created for other presentations to the list of available templates in the AutoContent Wizard.

To add a template of your own to the AutoContent Wizard, open the AutoContent Wizard from the task pane, and follow these steps:

1 Click Next in the introductory wizard page.

2 Select the category of presentation you want to place your template in, and click Add.

3 In the Select Presentation Template dialog box, select the Design template or Presentation you want to use as a template, and then click OK. Your template appears in the list of presentation templates.

4 Click Finish, and PowerPoint opens that template for you to use for a new presentation.

You can always delete the template by going back to the AutoContent Wizard and clicking the Remove button after selecting your template.

Starting a Blank Presentation

When you want to opt for full creativity instead of relying on the AutoContent Wizard, follow these steps:

1 If the New Presentation task pane is open, click Blank Presentation under New. Otherwise, click File, New to open the new Presentation task pane. A title slide with a white background appears.

2 If you want to keep the title slide that is displayed by default, add your text directly to the placeholder on the slide or in outline view. You can also select a different layout from the Slide Layout pane to the right.

3 To add slides, use the Slide Layout pane that opens in the task pane. Place your mouse pointer over the layout you want to use, and when the arrow button appears, click it to view the shortcut menu, and then click Insert New Slide, which results in the following:

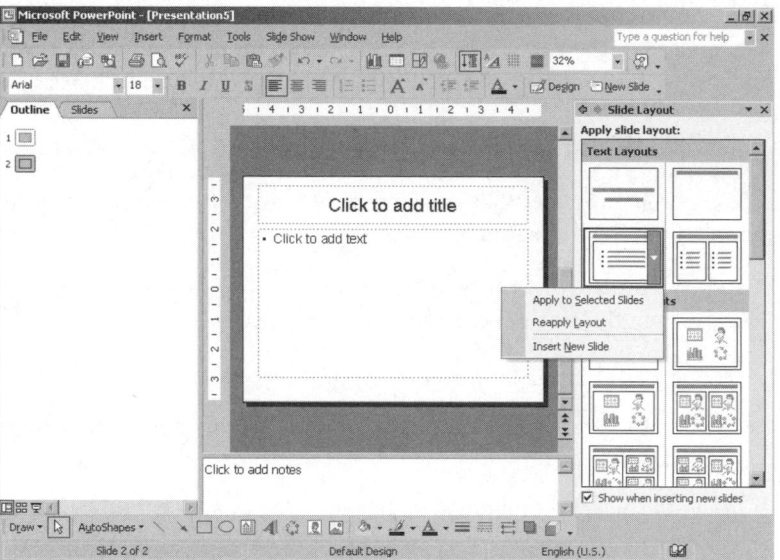

Once you have chosen the basic layout for your blank slide, you can enter, edit, and format its contents, as well as add design elements and animations from the task pane. PowerPoint uses certain fonts and font sizes by default even in a blank presentation, but you can easily change them. Following basic design guidelines can make your slides eye-catching and easy to read:

● Apply no more than two fonts per slide.

● Obey the 6 by 6 rule: No more than six words per line and no more than six lines per slide.

- Select fonts that suit your audience: Tempus Sans ITC is casual, Times New Roman is conservative, and Verdana is good for the Web.

- Select dark backgrounds for on-screen slide shows and light backgrounds for overhead transparencies.

> You'll learn more about text formatting in Chapter 32, "Advanced Presentation Formatting."

Creating a Custom Blank Presentation Template

You can add templates of your own to the Blank Presentations templates folder, which are stored as blank .pot template files. You can use this method to store particular elements, such as a logo, slogan, or background graphic that your company or organization inserts on every slide or on selected slides in a presentation. To create your own blank presentation template, perform the following steps:

1 Add the repeating elements to a blank presentation and then choose File, Save As.

2 In the Save As dialog box, in the Save as type box, click Design Template. This stores the new template in the default folder for templates, usually C:\Windows\Application Data\Microsoft\Templates.

3 In the File Name box, type **My Blank Presentation**.

4 Click Save to save your new template.

Your new blank presentation template is then available under General Templates in the task pane. The New Blank Presentation option in the task pane still opens a standard, blank presentation.

Using a Design Template

Design templates help you apply a consistent design and color scheme to an entire set of slides. They have names such as Compass, Glass Layers, Digital Dots, and Blends. These templates combine a background color and design with a set of eight complementary colors that PowerPoint uses for elements such as titles, backgrounds, slide text, shadow effects, and so on.

InsideOut

PowerPoint and Microsoft Publisher share some design templates (called design sets in Publisher): If you choose Blends or another shared design, you could create a brochure handout in Publisher, for example, that matched your on-screen PowerPoint presentation. Using shared design templates provides a cohesive look across your various documents.

The following illustration shows a title slide based on the Crayons design template—suitably whimsical for a children's clothing business, but unsuitable for a stockholders' meeting:

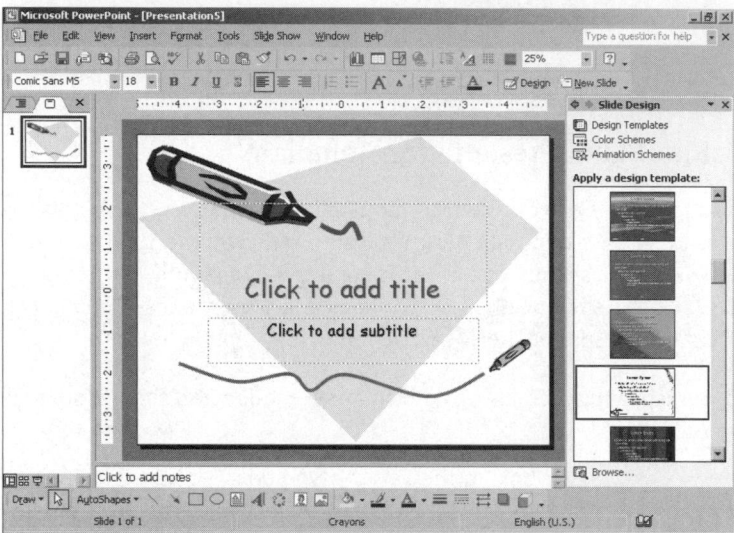

To start a presentation from a design template, follow this procedure:

1 If the New Presentation task pane is open, choose From Design Template under New. If you have been working on a different presentation, save it (if necessary), and then choose File, New. Either way, the Slide Design pane appears, as shown here:

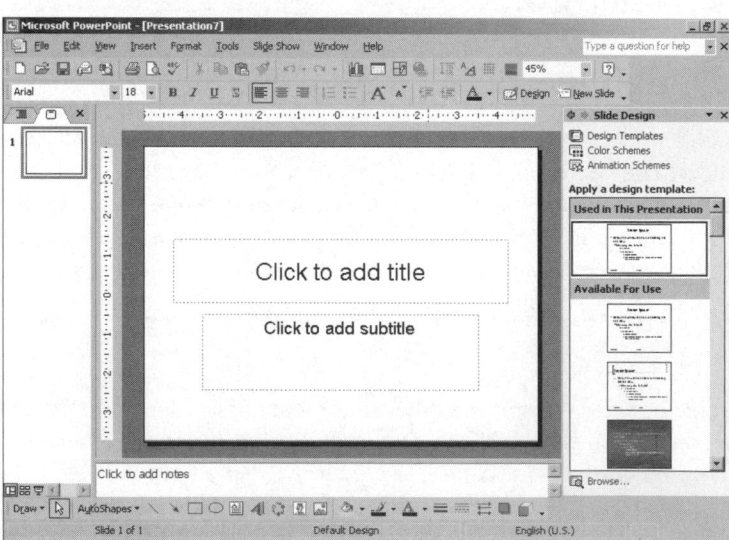

2 Under Apply a design template, scroll the list of Used In This Presentation design templates and Available For Use design templates, and click to insert the template you want to use. You can also click Browse to install more templates.

3 Click the arrow button next to the design template thumbnail to view options for inserting the template onto all slides or selected slides, or to change the size of the thumbnail previews.

In PowerPoint 2002, you can apply more than one design template to the same presentation. For example, you can insert slides created by a team member and retain their formatting without having that affect the design template your own presentation is based on. This new feature is referred to as support for *multiple masters*.

> Using the Title and Slide Master is covered in Chapter 32, "Advanced Presentation Formatting."

4 To continue building a presentation, choose Formats, Slide Layout on the Formatting toolbar and apply the layout you want to use for each slide in the rest of your presentation.

5 Click the Back arrow in the Slide Layout task pane to return to the Design Templates pane. Here you find additional options for editing the color scheme or adding animation schemes.

Animation schemes are also new in PowerPoint 2002. They are a combination of animations and transitions that can be applied without leaving the Normal view.

> For more information on animation schemes and transitions, see Chapter 34, "Adding Special Effects and Hyperlinks."

Creating a Custom Design Template

If you modify a PowerPoint design template and want to save your version as a template, in the Save As dialog box simply specify Design Template as the file type you are saving. You must save it to the folder that PowerPoint defaults to when saving a Design Template, or PowerPoint won't be able to find it. The default folder for templates, where selecting Design Template in the Save As box should place your template, is usually C:\Windows\Application Data\Microsoft\Templates (for Microsoft Windows 95 and Windows 98) or C:\Documents and settings\user_name\Application Data \Microsoft\Templates (for Microsoft Windows 2000). You can find your custom templates in the General tab of the Templates dialog box, accessed by clicking General Templates in the task pane.

Using an Existing Presentation as a Model

In PowerPoint 2002, you can use the Choose Presentation command in the task pane to open a copy of any PowerPoint presentation you'd like to use as the basis for a new presentation. This command allows you to use any presentation as a template and can make creating new templates less critical.

> For more information on how this command works in other Office XP programs, see "Creating a Document Using the New Document Task Pane," on page 58.

To create a new presentation based on an existing one, perform the following steps:

1 Click Choose Presentation under New From Existing Presentation in the New Presentation task pane. The New From Existing Presentation dialog box opens, as shown here:

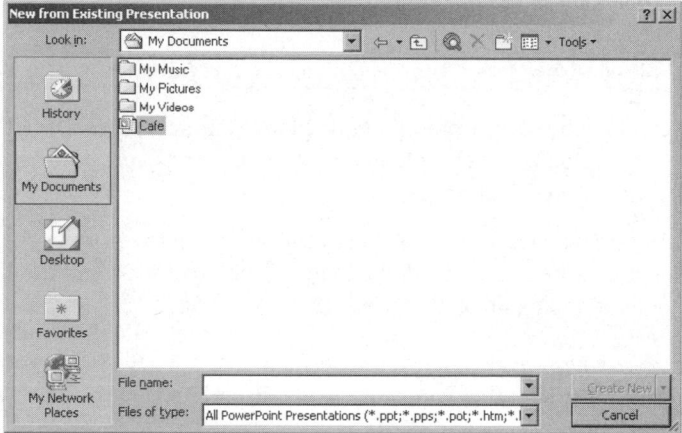

2 Click the presentation you want from the file list or the File Name list, and then click Create New.

3 Modify the existing presentation, and then choose File, Save As.

4 Type a new name for the presentation in the File Name box, and then click Save.

Starting a Presentation from a Template

There are several ways to access templates in PowerPoint 2002:

● Click From Design Template in the task pane to open a presentation with a preformatted design and color scheme.

● Click From AutoContent Wizard in the task pane for help in creating a presentation based on suggested content with a design applied to it.

● Click any of the options under New From Template.

Under New From Template in the task pane, you'll see a list of recently opened templates if you have previously worked with any. General Templates takes you to the Templates dialog box, which contains three tabs, General, Design Templates, and Presentations. Note that your custom templates are displayed in the General tab, shown in Figure 31-7.

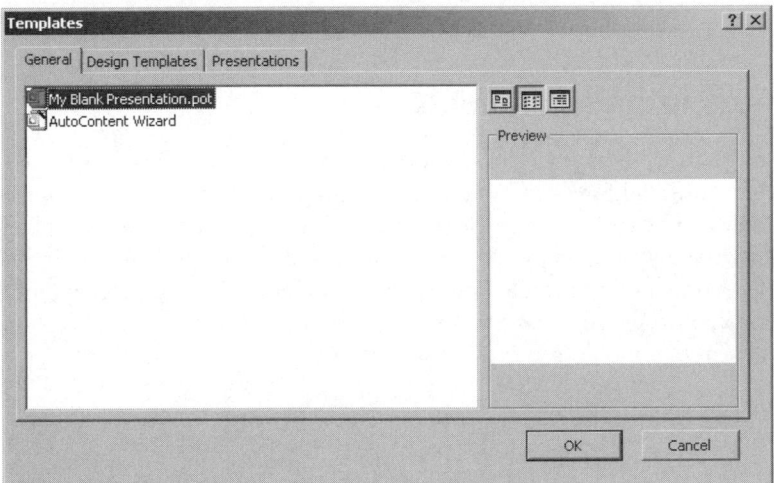

Figure 31-7. Both PowerPoint and custom templates are stored in the Templates dialog box.

Any templates that you have created are available in the General tab. For example, if you create a blank presentation to use as a template, it can be found here. The Design Templates tab stores both installed and uninstalled design templates. The Presentations tab contains the kinds of presentation templates that the AutoContent Wizard provides, covering suggested topics such as Company Meeting, Motivating a Team, or Business Plan.

To start a new presentation from a template, simply click the template and then click OK to open a presentation based on that template.

Entering and Editing Text

Whether you start a new presentation by choosing a template, a blank presentation, or one the AutoContent Wizard creates for you, entering text is a matter of replacing the text that PowerPoint provides on each slide placeholder with your own text. This section describes ways to build the body of a presentation using text. The text you enter into placeholders, such as titles, subtitles, and bulleted lists, can be entered and edited in the Slide tab or in the Outline tab.

> **note** This section deals with adding text to placeholders on a slide. PowerPoint also lets you add text to an AutoShape, add text to a text box for use as a caption or label for graphics, and insert WordArt. However, these three options treat text as an object and are created using the Drawing toolbar, which is covered in Chapter 33, "Mastering Tables, Graphics, and Drawings."

Entering Text into Placeholders

Dotted or shaded borders surround placeholders, which come preformatted with a particular font and font size. Placeholders contain text that you replace with your own text. They can be resized using the sizing handles that appear when the placeholder is selected, rotated using the rotate handle, or moved when the mouse pointer becomes a four-headed arrow. By default, PowerPoint automatically wraps text within the placeholder as you type, so press Enter only when you want to start a new paragraph. To enter text in placeholders, perform the following steps:

1 Select the placeholder.

2 Type your own text.

3 When you have finished typing text, click anywhere outside the placeholder to make the border disappear.

Tips for Positioning Placeholders

When you're working with placeholders, here are some tips to keep in mind:

● If you're having trouble fitting text onto a slide, try resizing or repositioning another placeholder before enlarging the one in which you want more text. To reposition a placeholder, point to a part of the border other than a sizing handle and drag the placeholder up or down on the slide. Moving a title higher, for example, results in extra space for a bulleted list below it.

● Because PowerPoint automatically wraps text, you can use placeholder resizing as a quick-and-dirty way to realign text. To turn a two-line paragraph into a one-line paragraph, for instance, widen the placeholder box. To force text to fill more vertical space, make the box narrower and longer.

● You can resize or realign placeholders to make room for an object, such as a graphic, that isn't provided for on your slide layout.

You can also choose a new anchor point for your text. Normally, PowerPoint adds text from the top down. By choosing a different anchor point, you can have PowerPoint add text from the bottom or from the middle of an object instead. This feature is useful when text doesn't completely fill the placeholder. To select a new anchor point in a placeholder, follow these steps:

1 Select the placeholder you want to modify, and then choose Format, Placeholder.

2 In the Text Box tab, select a new text anchor point in the Format Placeholder dialog box, as shown here:

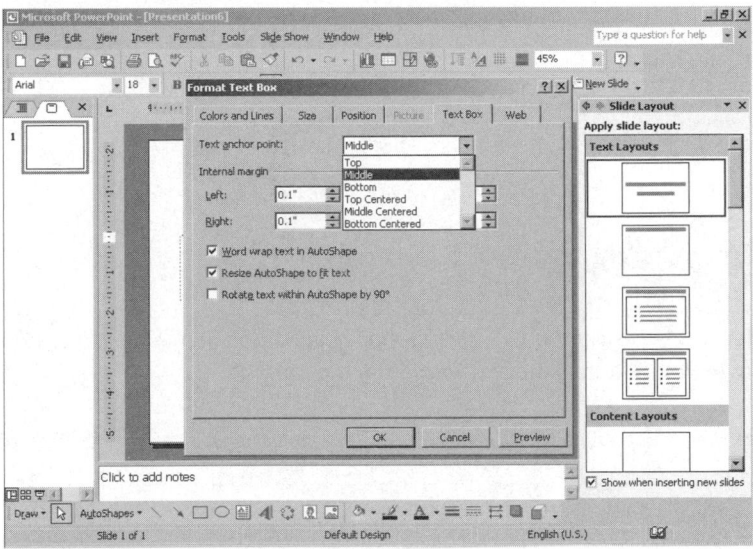

Working with Automatic Text Formatting

When you type more text than the placeholder can hold, PowerPoint, by default, doesn't expand the placeholder to contain the overflow. Instead, it automatically resizes the text in placeholders if the font size you've chosen doesn't fit. After this kind of automatic formatting action, what PowerPoint 2002 refers to as a smart tag appears. *Smart tags* are buttons that contain a menu of options that you can choose from to control the automatic formatting or layout decisions that PowerPoint makes. The smart tag buttons that you'll run into when entering and editing text are likely to include the following:

● AutoCorrect Options button

● Paste Options button

● AutoFit Options button

● Automatic Layout Options button

You can use these buttons to undo the automatic formatting in this instance, turn it off completely, or go to the AutoCorrect Options dialog box (also available from the Tools menu) to set your own AutoCorrect and AutoFormat options. The AutoFormat tab of the AutoCorrect Options dialog box is shown in Figure 31-8.

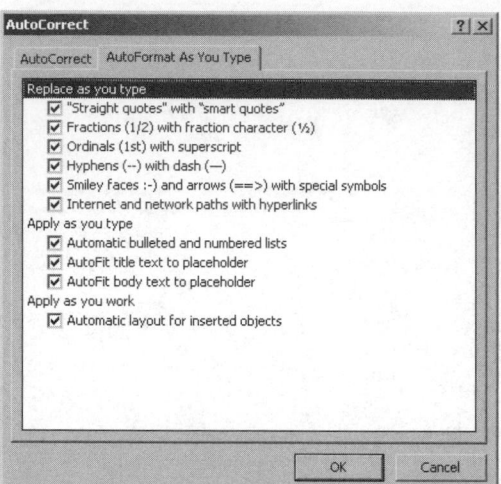

Figure 31-8. The AutoCorrect Options dialog box allows you to customize many of PowerPoint's automatic text formatting options.

For more information on the AutoCorrect dialog box options, see "Checking Spelling and Style," on page 871.

Editing Text

To edit text, you must first select it. In PowerPoint, in addition to dragging the mouse over the text you want to select, you can use the following mouse shortcuts:

● In Normal view, click a slide icon in the Outline or Slide tab to select the entire slide.

● In Normal view, select any bulleted item by clicking anywhere in the placeholder, and then moving the mouse pointer to the left of the item and clicking when the pointer becomes a four-headed arrow.

Using the keyboard, you can choose one of these methods:

● To move to the beginning of a line, press Home; to move to the end, press End.

● To select to the beginning or to the end of a line from the insertion point, press Shift+End or Shift+Home.

● To select consecutive lines, press the Shift key as you press End or Home.

You can replace any amount of text just by selecting it and typing something else. You can also duplicate text quickly, using the standard Office cut-and-paste technique. In PowerPoint 2002, when you click Paste, the Paste Options button appears. The options available on its menu let you choose if you want the item or items you're pasting to match the design of your presentation, retain their own design, or use a Design Template format. You can also choose Edit, Paste Special to more precisely control how and in what format data is transferred, which can be particularly useful when pasting Excel files or graphics files.

> For more information on copying and moving data in Office programs, see Chapter 7, "Sharing Data Among Office XP Applications."

To move text, select it, and then use one of the following methods:

- If you're working in Normal view, select the text and drag it to its new location.

- If you're working in the Slides tab, use the Cut and Paste buttons on the Standard toolbar. Using these buttons causes the Office Clipboard to open in the task pane (as well as the Paste Options button under the text you're pasting). The Office Clipboard lists each item you've cut in the task pane. Clicking the item inserts it into the slide.

- Right-click the selected text and use the Cut and Paste commands on the shortcut menu.

- To delete text, select it and press Delete or choose Edit, Clear.

- To delete an entire slide, display it (in Slide view) or select it (in Normal view), and choose Edit, Delete Slide.

Using Outlines

Instead of—or in addition to—entering text into placeholders provided by templates and built-in layouts, you can organize your thoughts in outline form and then turn your outline into slides. An outline provides a summary of a presentation arranged in headings and subheadings. If you're creating a complex presentation or if you're a person who values structure and likes to see how the parts contribute to the whole, working with an outline is probably a good choice for you.

Outlines in PowerPoint are created or edited using the Outline tab in Normal view, as shown in Figure 31-9 on page 864, with the splitter bar moved to the right to reveal more of the outline pane.

If you have opened an existing presentation or if you're using a presentation template, you see the text displayed in outline form, as shown in Figure 31-9. If you're working on a blank presentation, you see a slide number and a slide icon, but no text appears until you type some.

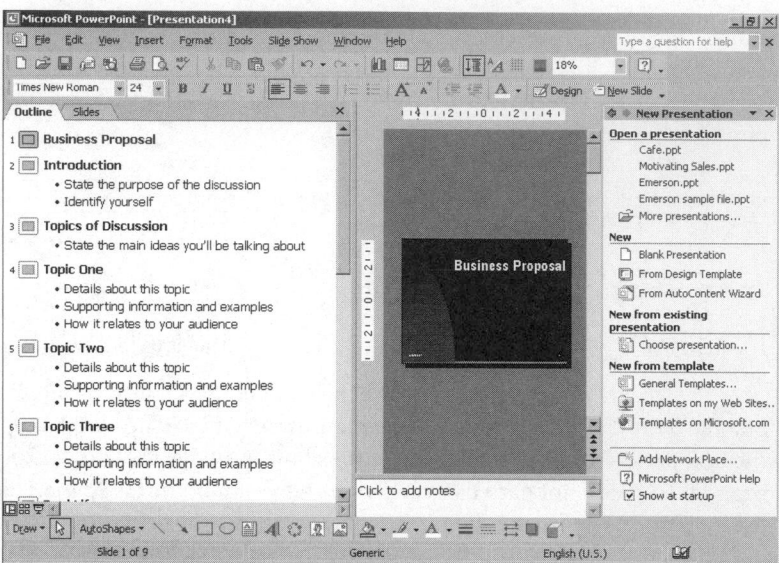

Figure 31-9. You can shape presentation content using the Outline tab.

When you begin entering text into the Outline tab, you can use the tools on the Standard and Formatting toolbar to help you order your content. Using these tools lets you increase or decrease an indent, which moves the selected text to a higher or lower outline level, collapse or expand content so that you can see only headings or all subheads too, and also show or hide formatting. It's useful at this point to open the Outlining toolbar in its default position, docked on the left side of the PowerPoint window next to the Outline tab area. To open the Outlining toolbar, perform the following steps:

1 Choose View, Toolbars.

2 Click Outlining. The Outlining toolbar opens, as shown here:

> **tip**   If you tend to use the Outline tab a lot to organize presentations, you might want to customize PowerPoint options so that the Outlining toolbar opens every time you open the program. To do so, choose Tools, Customize. In the Toolbars tab, check the Outlining check box.

Entering an Outline from Scratch

When you have displayed a blank presentation in the Outline tab, generating an outline feels as if you're working on a cross between a Microsoft Word document and a PowerPoint slide. The outline tab shows a numbered slide icon. You can enter text next to the icon for a heading to be used as a title, and enter your body text under the title, which can be formatted in up to five outline levels.

- Pressing Enter creates a new paragraph exactly like the preceding one. That is, if the last character you typed was a bullet, press Enter to create another bullet; if the last character you typed was a slide title, press Enter to create a new slide.

- Depending on the preceding outline level you typed, the key combination Ctrl+Enter toggles between creating a new slide and creating a bulleted item. That is, if the last text you typed was a slide title, Ctrl+Enter creates a bulleted item; if the last text you typed was a bulleted item, Ctrl+Enter creates a new slide.

- If you want to create an outline that has several sublevels, use the Promote and Demote buttons on the vertical Outlining toolbar.

- Click the Promote button to raise the importance of a paragraph one heading level.

- Click the Demote button to lower the importance of a paragraph one heading level. You can also use the Demote button to move the top heading on one slide to the previous slide.

Modifying an Outline

When you're comfortable creating an outline in Normal view, use the following procedures to control and refine either an outline that you have created from scratch or one that you're revising by using the suggestions in a template or the headings in another document that you're inserting into PowerPoint:

- To select a slide title in an outline, drag the mouse pointer over the title.

- To select a bulleted item and all its subitems, click the bullet (when the pointer becomes a four-headed arrow).

- To select several consecutive bulleted items, press the Shift key as you click. (Although pressing Ctrl while you click lets you select nonconsecutive items in other Office XP applications, it doesn't work that way in PowerPoint.)

- To select an entire slide, click the slide icon.

- To move a paragraph, select it and either drag it to its new location or use the Move Up and Move Down buttons on the Outlining toolbar.

> **note** When you drag text, a small empty box appears when you click the pointer to drag the text. If it doesn't, make sure that drag-and-drop editing is turned on. Choose Tools, Options. In the Edit tab, check the Drag-and-Drop Text Editing check box.

- Use the buttons on the Outlining toolbar to change outline levels and to control how much of the outline you see on screen.

Rearranging Slides on the Outline Tab

As you're working with your slides, you might find that you need to rearrange some of them. You can easily do so by dragging them to new locations in Slide Sorter view, but when you're working on an outline in Normal view, the drag-and-drop technique works just as well. To reorder your slides, follow these steps:

1 Select the slide you want to move. Be sure to select all of it by clicking the slide icon.

2 Place the mouse pointer on the slide icon and drag the slide to a new location. As you drag, watch the horizontal line that shows where you're dragging the slide. To avoid inserting the slide into the body of another slide, don't release the mouse button until the line is completely above or below your target.

3 To undo a move, either choose Edit, Undo Move, or click the Undo button.

When you move slides, PowerPoint automatically renumbers them for you.

Expanding and Duplicating Slides

Other useful slide management capabilities that PowerPoint 2002 offers you are the ability to expand one slide into several slides and the ability to quickly duplicate a slide.

Using the Outlining toolbar, you can easily turn each text element on a slide—text place-holder, bullet, or paragraph—into a new, separate slide. To expand one slide into several slides, follow these steps:

1 Display the slide you want to expand in the Outline tab of Normal view.

2 To select a text element (such as a bulleted item in a list), click the element when the pointer becomes a four-headed arrow. To select several consecutive text elements, press the Shift key as you click.

3 Click the Promote button on the Outlining toolbar.

   If you selected one text element, it is expanded into a new slide. If you selected several text elements, each one is expanded into a new slide.

4 Repeat these steps to expand as many items as you choose into separate slides. To remove the new slides, choose Edit, Undo.

tip You can also use the AutoFit Options button that appears when you type too much text for a placeholder on a slide. If you click this button when it appears, you can split the text into two slides or continue the text onto a new slide using options on the list of options offered.

To create an identical copy of a slide in your presentation, perform the following steps:

1 Select the slide in the Outline tab.

2 Choose Insert, Duplicate Slide. PowerPoint creates a copy of the slide and places it immediately after the selected slide in the presentation. If you want to move the duplicated slide to a new location, you can use the drag-and-drop technique.

Using Word to Create an Outline

To Microsoft Office, an outline is an outline, whether it's created in PowerPoint or in Word, so you can easily turn a Word outline into a set of slides. Some familiarity with Word's heading-level styles is helpful, because heading levels in a Word document become bulleted items on PowerPoint slides. To use a Word document that contains heading styles as the basis for a presentation, follow this procedure:

1 Click File, New to open a new PowerPoint presentation. By default, PowerPoint opens with a blank title slide.

Part 5: PowerPoint

2   Choose Insert, Slides From Files. The Slide Finder dialog box appears, as
    shown here:

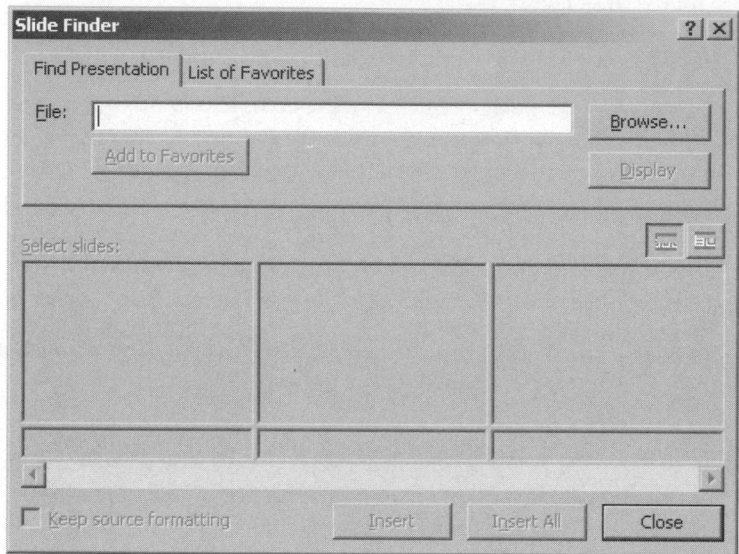

3   Click Browse, and in the Files Of Type box, select All Files.

4   Double-click the appropriate document name to insert it into the open presen-
    tation. The imported Word outline opens in PowerPoint, beginning with the
    second slide. PowerPoint leaves the title slide empty so you can enter suitable
    text there.

note   The first time you choose Insert, Slides From Outline or Files (other than PowerPoint
files), you might receive a PowerPoint message box telling you that PowerPoint needs
to install a converter to display this type of file correctly. Click Yes to install the converter, and have your Office CD or network connection available.

You can also use the procedures listed in the preceding steps to insert a Word outline into a
PowerPoint presentation. In this instance, choose Insert, Slides From Outlines, and make
your selection from the Insert Outline dialog box that appears, as shown on the next page.

Chapter 31: Essential PowerPoint Techniques

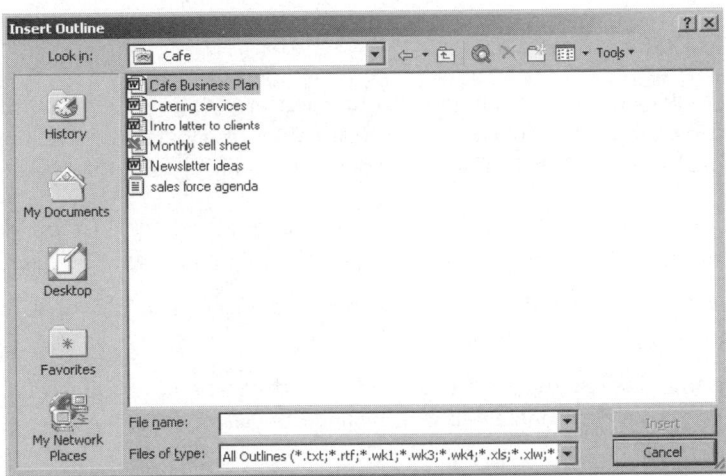

You can also import outlines into PowerPoint that have been saved as text files (.txt), Rich Text Format files (.rtf), Hypertext Markup Language (HTML) documents (.html), and Excel worksheets (.xls).

To turn a Word document that doesn't use heading styles into a PowerPoint outline, use these same procedures, selecting All Files in the Files Of Type box. Each paragraph in the document you insert becomes the title of a new slide. If your Word document contains five paragraphs, for example, PowerPoint turns those paragraphs into the titles of five slides—a useful technique if you have nothing else to start with.

> For more information on applying styles in Word, see Chapter 12, "Effective Formatting in Word." For details on using outlines in Word, see Chapter 15, "Managing Large or Complex Documents."

Creating a Summary Slide

You can use a summary slide, a bulleted list of all or selected slide titles, to introduce your presentation; this is often called an *agenda slide*. You can also insert a summary slide at the end of your presentation to recap the points you covered. To create a summary slide, perform the following steps:

1 In the Outline tab, select the slides you want to include on the summary slide.

2 Click Summary Slide on the Outlining toolbar. The summary slide appears before the first slide you selected. If you selected several slides, the summary slide may be more than one slide.

3 Change the title of the summary slide and select and delete any bulleted items that you want to edit or delete.

4 Move the summary slide to the location where you want to use it.

Adding Comments

If you plan to share your presentations with other users, you might want to annotate a few important slides with comments to provide instructions or highlight critical information. In PowerPoint, you can add a comment and post it to a slide by following these steps:

1 Display the slide in Normal view and choose Insert, Comment. This displays a comment box that contains a blinking pointer, your name, and the date.

2 To move a comment, drag it with the mouse, or delete it by clicking its place-holder border and pressing Delete.

3 To change the reviewer name at the top of the comment, Choose Tools, Options. Click the General tab and then edit the Name field.

4 If you type or receive a lengthy comment, use the scroll bars that appear on the right side of the comment box to view the entire comment.

5 When you finish typing the comment, click another object on your slide to lock in the comment. The comment box closes and appears with just your initials and the number of the comment showing.

The comment appears on your slide in each view as long as View, Markup is selected. The Markup command is a toggle that is activated when you enter your first comment. You can also use the Reviewing toolbar to manage your comments; it appears when you create your first comment.

Here's what a comment looks like on a slide after you enter your text into it:

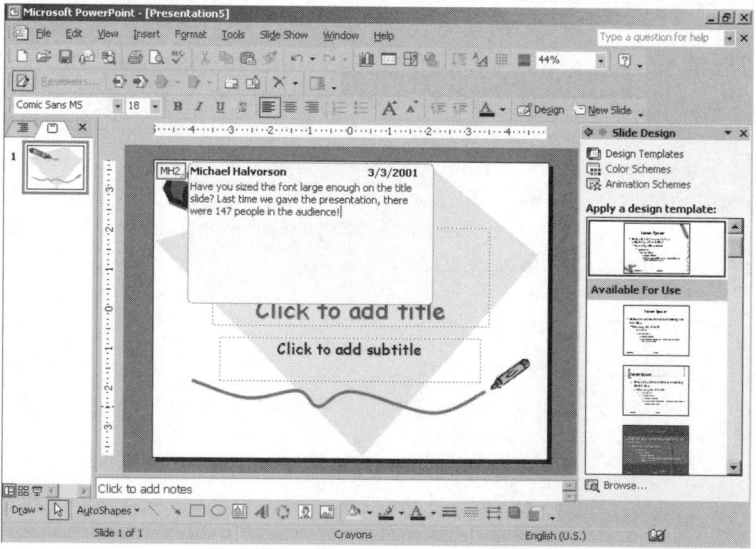

Checking Spelling and Style

Misspellings loom large when your slide show is projected onto a big screen. PowerPoint's Spelling feature finds and highlights misspellings in your outlines, notes (less important, because they're not being projected), and text on slides, such as titles and bulleted lists.

> For more information on using the Spelling feature and custom dictionaries, see Chapter 17, "Proofing Word Documents." To learn more about AutoCorrect, see "Automatically Fixing Your Text with AutoCorrect" on page 258.

By default, PowerPoint checks your spelling as you type and marks any misspelled words with a wavy red underline. Right-click the word and choose an option from the shortcut menu to correct the spelling at that moment.

Using AutoCorrect Options

PowerPoint's AutoCorrect feature catches and corrects common spelling, capitalization, and punctuation mistakes as you type. When you break one of PowerPoint's rules, a light bulb appears over the incorrect entry if you have the Office Assistant turned on. Clicking the light bulb opens the Office Assistant and gives you the opportunity to change or ignore the instance or go to the Style Options dialog box to change the rule for all presentations, as shown here.

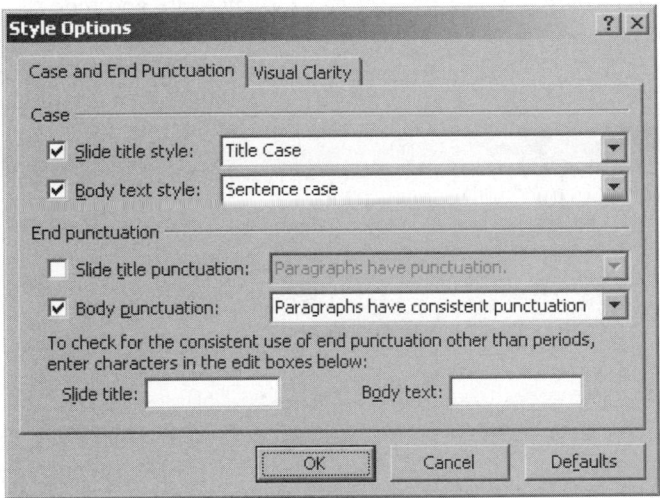

In addition, PowerPoint also notes presentation errors, such as too much text in a bulleted item. One of the smart tags, the AutoFit button in this case, appears and gives you a list of options or takes you to the AutoCorrect dialog box, shown below with the AutoCorrect tab selected, where you can specify options and exceptions for punctuation in all presentations.

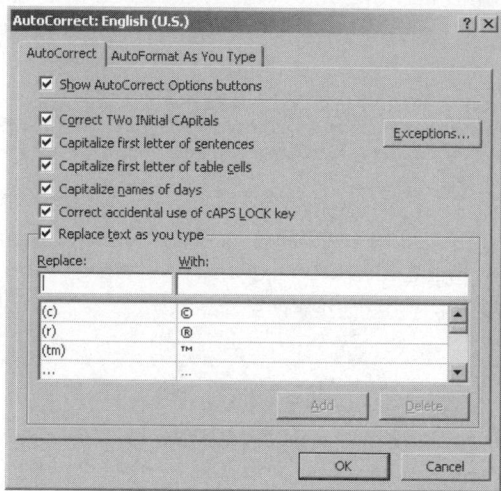

To see what PowerPoint means by *visual clarity*, follow these steps:

1 Choose Tools, and then click Options.

2 In the Options dialog box, click the Spelling and Style tab, and then click Style Options.

3 In the Style Options dialog box, click the Visual Clarity tab, as shown here:

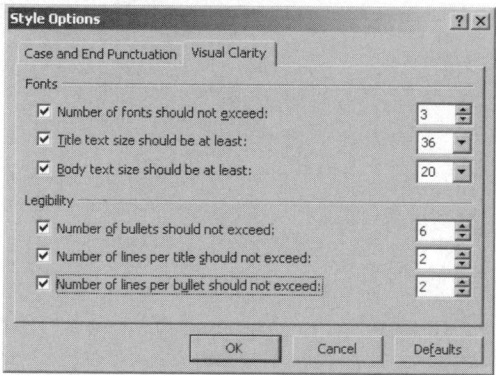

Notice that Visual Clarity encompasses not only fonts and font sizes, but also legibility. When PowerPoint checks your slides, it uses the default settings as guidelines, notifies you of any slides that don't match the settings, and offers suggestions for addressing the style issue.

Saving a Presentation

By default, PowerPoint saves your presentations as .ppt files, which saves and opens them as typical presentations, but you can use the Save As dialog box to specify in what format you want to save a particular presentation. You can also choose Tools, Options, and in the Save tab, set options that change the default type of file that PowerPoint uses to store your presentations.

The Save As dialog box also lists other file formats for saving presentations, such as HTML for Web presentations, or for saving a PowerPoint 2002 presentation to a format suitable for opening in an earlier version of PowerPoint.

InsideOut

You can have PowerPoint remove personal information from your presentations when you save them. The information removed includes any text assigned to the Author, Manager, and Company presentation properties. Also, your actual name is removed from all comments and macros and replaced with the word Author. You might find this a useful option if you are creating presentations for the Web or a public kiosk, and would prefer not to have your name visible. To set these options, choose Tools, Options. In the Security tab, check the Remove Personal Information From This File On Save check box.

Chapter 32

Advanced Presentation Formatting

An effective PowerPoint presentation communicates information and affects your audience in some way. The effect varies with the purpose of your presentation, but what doesn't vary is the importance of arranging content on your slides so that your message has the greatest impact.

You want the text to be clearly readable, titles quickly grasped, lists well placed, and related information logically aligned. To support the words in your presentation, you want to select color, backgrounds, and repeating design elements that enhance the feeling and theme of your presentation.

PowerPoint comes with templates that make all the design choices for you. However, the more familiar you (and your audience) are with PowerPoint, the more interested you'll become in crafting original presentations.

In this chapter, you'll learn about:

- Formatting text

- Formatting bulleted and numbered lists

- Working with paragraph indentation, alignment, and line spacing

- Modifying color and color schemes

- Working with backgrounds and creating custom backgrounds

- Editing master slides and working with multiple masters

875

Formatting Text

Font, font size, style, and color are defined by settings in the design template assigned to each text placeholder in your presentation. You can reformat text properties by making changes on an individual slide or by making global changes to a master slide. In this section, you'll learn to make formatting changes to individual slides. Figure 32-1 shows how a few, simple formatting changes can make a slide fit better with its subject.

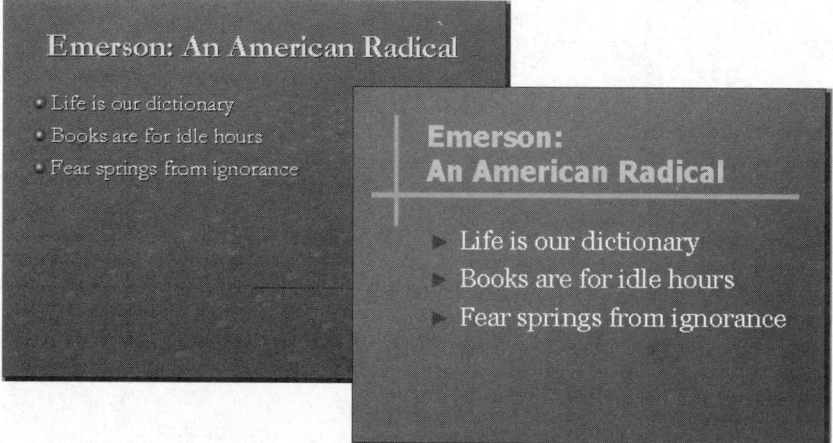

Figure 32-1. Changing the design template, color scheme, and font choices makes this slide better for a classroom presentation.

> Working with master slides and multiple masters is covered in "Editing Master Slides," on page 892.

To apply a different formatting to text, you must first select it. To change all the text in a text object, perform the following steps:

1 Click the text object's border to select both it and all the text it contains.

2 To change the formatting of just some of the text in a text object, select the text you want to change, and then issue your formatting command.

You can make changes to text by working in the Font dialog box or by using the buttons on the Formatting toolbar, which control many of the most common changes that you might want to make.

Formatting Text Using the Formatting Toolbar

The Formatting toolbar contains the Font list box, which contains samples of the fonts, the Font Size box, Increase Font and Decrease Font buttons, and the Font Color button. You can also apply different font styles or attributes to your font selection by selecting the text and then clicking the appropriate font style button. The term *font style* refers to variations from the basic look of the font. Although it's best to use no more than two fonts for all the text in your presentation, you can often add variety and emphasis by changing the font style.

The most common font styles, bold and italic, can be used for drawing attention to text in a presentation. However, avoid using italics for emphasis or to define a word, because they can look blurry when projected on a screen. Instead consider underlining by using a decorative rule to highlight a text item, as shown in Figure 32-2.

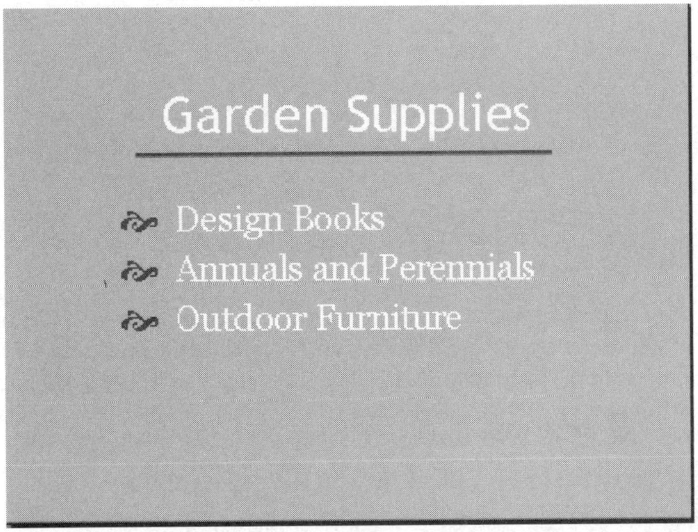

Figure 32-2. If the title had been underlined using the underline attribute, it would have cut off the descenders of the characters.

InsideOut

Using a line or *rule* to underline text is generally a better choice than applying the underline attribute to text. Assigning the underline attribute in the Font dialog box (or by using the Underline button on the Formatting toolbar) doesn't permit you to specify where to put the line in relation to the text above it. Most often, the result is a line that is too close to the text, which can cut off the descenders of characters (the tail of a lowercase *g* or *p*, for example). To remedy this, create a rule using the Line tool on the Drawing toolbar. Click Format, AutoShape, and then in the Format AutoShape dialog box, click the Colors and Lines tab to format its style, color, and size using the available options. You can position the line using the mouse or the options on the Position tab of the Format AutoShape dialog box.

Text Formatting Using the Font Dialog Box

When you want to create several formatting effects at once, you can also use the Font dialog box, shown here, by choosing Format, Font.

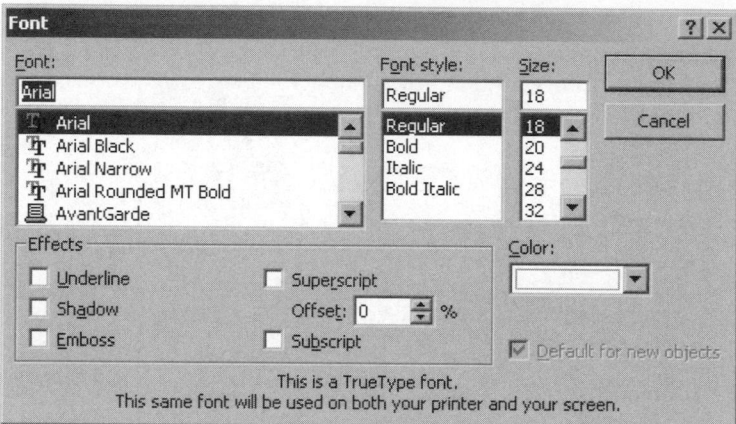

Use this standard dialog box to make all the formatting changes covered in the previous section. In addition, you can apply a few other special effects, such as embossing and superscript, using the Font command.

To format text using the Font dialog box, select the text, and then do one or more of the following:

- To change the text color, pick a new color in the Color drop-down list. By adding color to your text, you can emphasize important words or phrases on your slide.

- To add a shadow effect, check the Shadow check box. The shadow effect adds a shadow at the bottom and to the right of each character, making the text appear three-dimensional. However, it is more effective when applied to graphics and objects than to text used in presentations.

- To add the embossing attribute to text, check the Emboss check box. PowerPoint surrounds each character with a combination of light and dark outlines so the letters appear to be raised. The color depends on the slide's background color. Embossing generally works best with fonts that produce thick characters or with headline-sized text that is formatted as bold.

Replacing Fonts

To replace one font with another throughout an entire presentation, you will typically want to use the slide master. However, if you've added individual formatting to some slides, the slide master may not be linked to every instance of the font in your presentation. To make sure that you're replacing all the instances of the font, select the text and then perform the following steps:

1 Choose Format, Replace Fonts.

2 In the Replace Font dialog box, specify the font you want to replace in the Replace drop-down list, which contains only fonts used in your presentation.

3 Specify the new font in the With drop-down list, shown here, which contains all available PowerPoint fonts:

4 Click Replace and then click Close to return to your presentation.

All the fonts are automatically replaced in the presentation with the one you selected, except for fonts in WordArt objects.

Copying Formatting

When you want to copy the look and style of text or other formatting, use the Format Painter button on the Standard toolbar. This technique also works with other PowerPoint objects, such as AutoShapes, pictures, clip art, and WordArt. To copy text formatting from one word, phrase, or placeholder to another, follow these steps:

1 Select the first item, and then click the Format Painter button on the Standard toolbar.

2 Click the item you want to copy to.

Working with Bullets and Numbering

Bulleted lists are frequently used to organize information on slides in PowerPoint. When you use a bulleted-list placeholder, PowerPoint enters the bullets automatically. You can also insert a bullet in front of any paragraph that you type, including those in text boxes or drawing objects that you create. Simply type a paragraph (usually consisting of a single line of text, which must be followed by pressing Enter) on the slide, and then click the Bullets button on the Formatting toolbar. PowerPoint adds a bullet at the beginning of your text. If you no longer want the bullet, click anywhere in the paragraph that contains the bullet, and then click the Bullets button again to remove it.

To insert a numbered list on a slide, follow the same procedure, but instead of clicking the Bullets button, click the Numbering button on the Formatting toolbar.

Both of these methods result in standard bullets selected by PowerPoint. To choose a different bullet, perform the following steps:

1 Select the text to reformat, and choose Format, Bullets and Numbering. The Bullets and Numbering dialog box appears, as shown here:

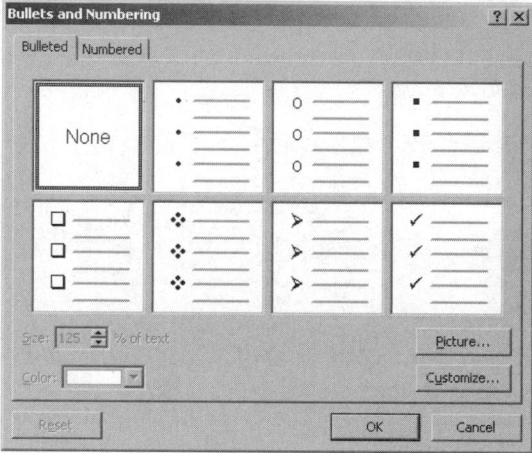

> **note** You cannot select the actual bullet character. Instead, select the text that immediately follows the bullet character you want to format.

2 In the Bullets and Numbering dialog box, click one of the suggested bullets, select its size as a percentage of the text, specify the color of the bullet shape, and then click OK.

To insert a picture bullet supplied by PowerPoint, do the following:

1 Select the text you want to format, and then choose Format, Bullets and Numbering.

2 In the Bullets and Numbering dialog box, click Picture to choose a picture bullet from the Clip Organizer. The Picture Bullet dialog box opens.

3 Double-click the picture bullet from the list to insert it. Figure 32-3 shows picture bullets inserted on a slide.

Chapter 32: Advanced Presentation Formatting

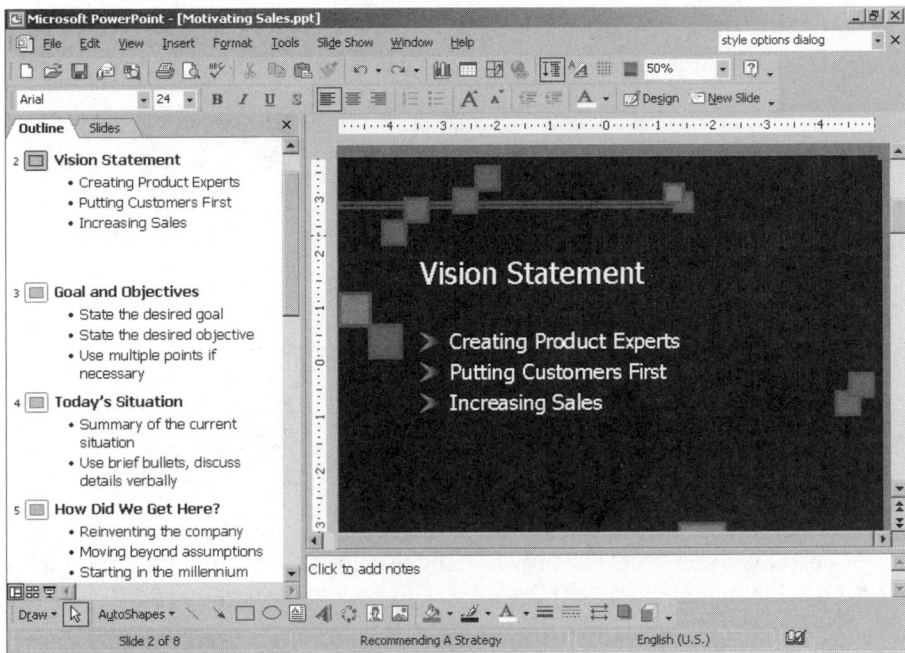

Figure 32-3. On a PowerPoint slide, you can use decorative symbols instead of standard bullets.

To insert a picture from your files, follow these steps:

1 Select the text you want to format with a custom bullet, and then choose Format, Bullets and Numbering.

2 In the Bullets and Numbering dialog box, click Picture. The Picture Bullet dialog box opens.

3 Click Import within the Picture Bullet dialog box, and when the Add Clips to Organizer dialog box opens, select the file you want to insert, and then click Add.

4 Make sure that the correct image is now selected in the Picture Bullet dialog box, and then click OK.

Now the image appears in your presentation and is included in the Clip Organizer's Picture Bullet list.

To create a bullet from the font symbols and wingdings in the Symbol dialog box, follow these steps:

1 Select the text for which you want to create a symbol bullet, and choose Format, Bullets and Numbering.

Chapter 32

2 In the Bullets and Numbering dialog box, click Customize and select a character from those listed in the Symbol dialog box, shown here:

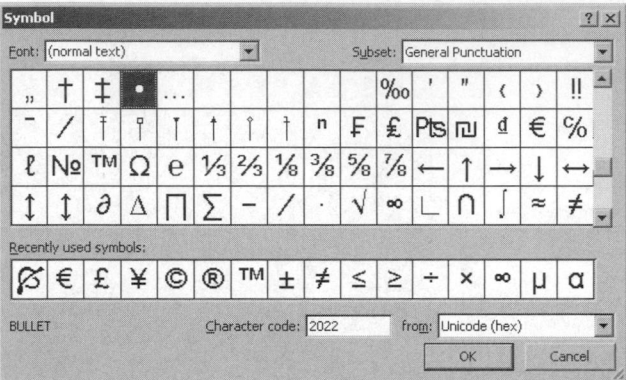

When you increase the size of the bullet relative to the font, you might need to add space before your text to provide enough room for the bullet. (This kerning problem is evident in Figure 32-3.) To correct this problem, you need to adjust the paragraph indentation, as described in the next section.

Formatting Indents and Tab Settings

An indent is a paragraph formatting attribute. The tab settings or tab stops are the small, gray markers on the horizontal ruler that you move to set new paragraph indentations. When you work with bulleted and numbered lists in PowerPoint, you often need to adjust the paragraph indentation in the template so that enough space exists between the text and bullets and the text aligns correctly. To do this, follow these steps:

1 Choose View, Ruler to turn on the horizontal and vertical rulers.

2 Click within the text object you want to modify. The ruler shows the markers for the template's default indentation. PowerPoint provides preset indents for five levels of bullets or numbers and body text.

3 Drag the upper triangle-shaped marker to move the first line of the paragraph or the bullet character or number in your list.

4 Drag the top of the lower triangle-shaped indent marker to move the text following the bullet or number and to align any additional lines in the paragraph at the same point, as shown in Figure 32-4.

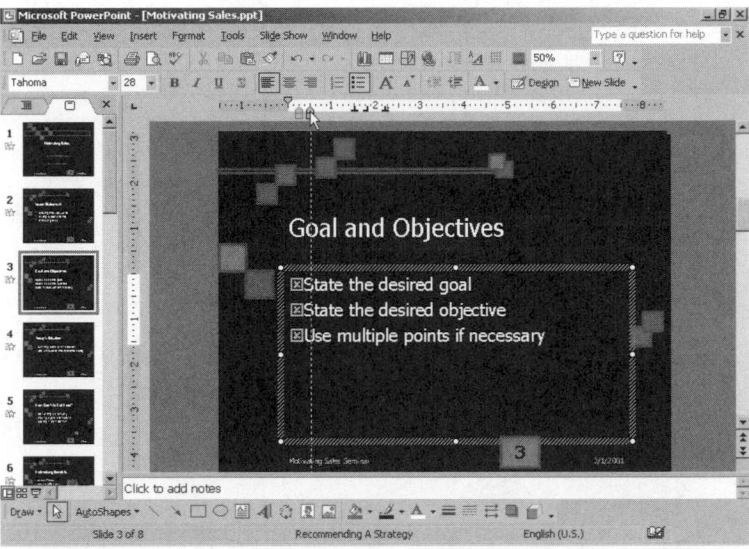

Figure 32-4. Creating custom bullets often requires formatting the paragraph indentation in the list.

As you drag, you'll see a vertical dotted line, which helps you position the marker. You'll typically be dragging these first two markers in opposite directions when adding space between a bullet or number and the text following it.

5 Drag the rectangular portion of the lower indent marker to maintain the distance between the text and the number or bullet while moving the list.

As in Word, you can set tab stops to left-align text at the tab stop, to center text at the tab stop, or to right-align it at the tab stop. You can use the decimal tab stop to align decimal points at the tab stop. To do so, click the button at the left end of the horizontal ruler until you get to the type you want to use. Clear the tab stops by dragging them off the ruler, which restores the default tab stops.

Changing Text Alignment and Line Spacing

PowerPoint templates include default text alignment settings for placeholders. Titles are often centered and text is usually aligned flush left. When you want to modify alignment, choose from among the Align Left, Center, Align Right, and Justify (both margins even) alignment options.

To change text alignment, follow these steps:

1 Select the text you want to align. (Either select individual lines of text using the mouse or select entire text placeholders.)

2 Click one of the alignment buttons on the Formatting toolbar (Align Left, Center, or Align Right).

3 To apply justified alignment—a formatting option that aligns text to both left and right margins—choose Format, Alignment, and then click Justify.

You can also adjust line spacing before or after selected paragraphs and change the amount of line spacing between the lines. For example, to increase the line spacing between each item in a bulleted or numbered list, perform the following steps:

1 Select the text for which you want to change the line or paragraph spacing. If you're changing the spacing in a bulleted list, select the entire text object so that your choices apply to the entire list.

2 Choose Format, Line Spacing to display the Line Spacing dialog box, shown here, and then make your formatting selections.

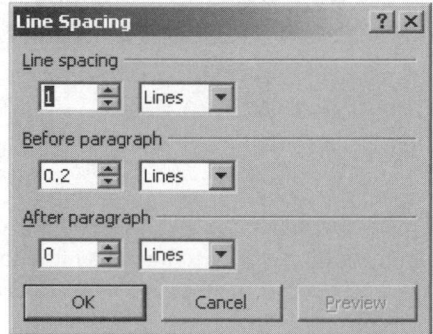

Working with Color and Color Schemes

The design template you apply to a presentation controls the color scheme of the slides. The color scheme, which consists of eight colors selected by PowerPoint, affects the background, text, lines, shadows, fills, accents such as bullets, and hyperlinks on your slides. You can use color to add contrast, to attract attention to a particular slide or element such as a table or chart, or to create a mood or feeling in your audience.

Whatever the goal involved in your color choices, the first factor you should consider is the medium you will use to display the slide show. When giving an electronic presentation, using a display device to project the image in a well-darkened room, you are safe in relying on this basic rule: Use a darker background and a lighter foreground to hold your audience's attention. Too much light color on the screen ultimately annoys your viewers: Their eyes can't quickly adjust to a white background in a dark room and they get tired of looking at it for too long. When using overheads, slides, or printed presentations, use the opposite tenet: Keep the foreground dark and the background light.

To change the color scheme, select the slide, and display the Slide Design task pane by clicking the down arrow in the upper right corner of the task pane, and then clicking Slide Design - Color Schemes. The Slide Design task pane opens with thumbnails of suggested color schemes, as seen at the top of the next page.

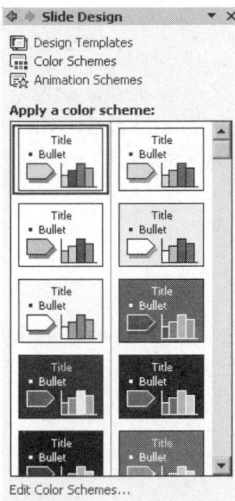

You can apply color changes to a single slide, to several slides, to notes pages, and to handouts. When you modify a color scheme, the new color you've added is displayed on the color palette below the eight preselected colors of the scheme, which is displayed when you click the Fill Color, Line Color, or Font Color buttons on the Drawing and Formatting toolbars. In this way, you can keep track of which colors you're using on slides: When modifying color schemes, consistency is a good thing.

Creating a Custom Scheme

When you want to create your own color scheme, select the colors from PowerPoint's version of the color wheel, like the one illustrated here in the Standard tab of the Colors dialog box:

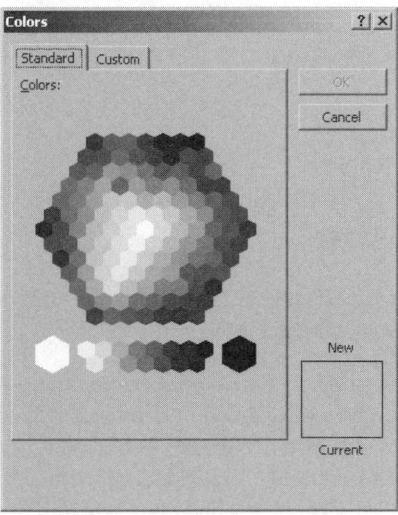

A color wheel shows relationships among colors. Choosing colors that are adjacent on the color wheel creates more harmonious schemes, but with little contrast. (When you hear designers say that a color combination really "pops," they are usually referring to the effect of contrast.) Choosing colors that are located opposite each other on the color wheel creates contrast. Professional designers often achieve successful contrast by choosing three colors about equidistant from each other on the color wheel; for example, red, yellow, and blue work well together.

To create your own color scheme, perform the following steps:

1 Click the Edit Color Schemes command at the bottom of the Slide Design task pane. The Edit Color Scheme dialog box appears, as shown here:

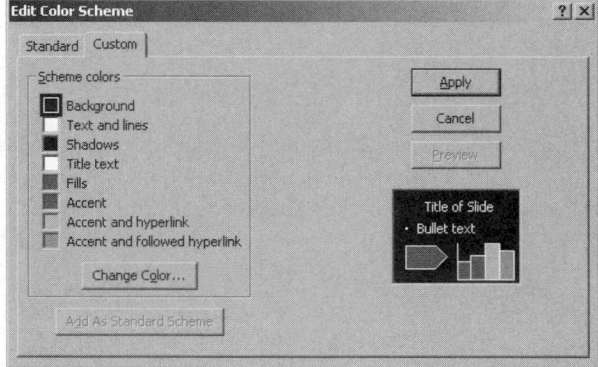

2 In the Edit Color Scheme dialog box, click the presentation element you want to adjust (the current color is displayed in a box beside the element name). Then click Change Color and pick a new color.

Use this technique to change the color for elements in your presentation.

3 When you're finished, click Add As Standard Scheme. PowerPoint saves your custom scheme and displays it in the list of available color schemes in the Slide Design task pane.

4 Click Apply to close the dialog box.

Changing the Background

PowerPoint templates come with ready-made background designs that include some or all of these elements: color, shading, pattern, texture, and pictures.

You'll want to change the background of a slide or slides in many instances—when you're inserting a chart, diagram, picture, or table that won't show up well against the prescribed background; when you want your audience to really focus on a slide or section of a presentation; or when you want to include a logo, rule, border, or graphics on the background. Figure 32-5 shows a logo inserted on a slide background.

Chapter 32: Advanced Presentation Formatting

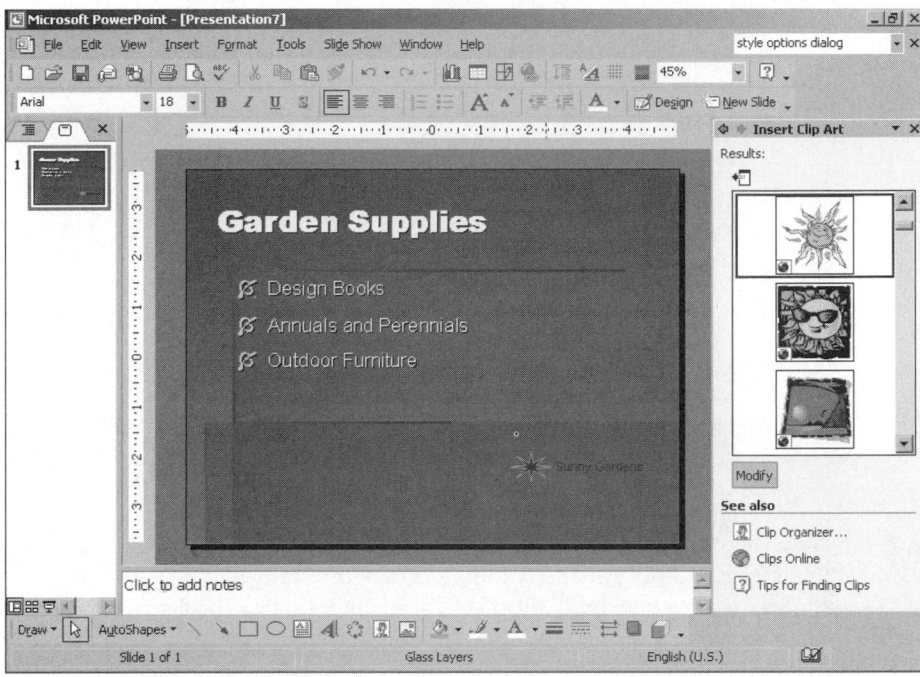

Figure 32-5. This example shows a logo placed on the background of a slide.

When you make changes to the background, you can apply them to individual slides, to notes pages, to handouts, and to the master slides.

> For more details on making changes to master slides, see "Editing Master Slides," on page 892.

> **note** Changes to the background of notes pages can be applied to the selected notes page or to all notes pages. Background changes to handouts, however, apply to all hand-outs for that presentation, as well as to the printed outline.

To modify the background of a slide, perform the following steps:

1 In Normal or Slide Sorter view, select the slide or slides that you want the change to apply to. Otherwise, the change applies to all the slides that share the design template of the current slide.

2 Choose Format, Background. The Background dialog box appears.

3 In the Background dialog box, under Background fill, click the arrow to the right of the empty field, as shown in Figure 32-6, on page 884.

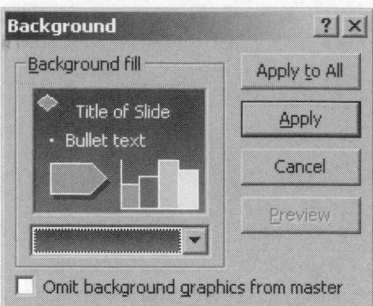

Figure 32-6. The down arrow in the Background dialog box opens the color scheme and fill effects toolbar.

4 Select a color from the Color Scheme palette, or click More Colors and either select a color from the Standard tab or click the Custom tab to create your own.

Now you can apply PowerPoint fill effects (or import your own) to apply to the color. Fill effects add pattern and texture to a background, which in turn adds depth to your slide design. As you apply fill effects, remember that the background is the *backdrop* for the message of your presentation. It's not the whole story and shouldn't overshadow the foreground, where you'll do the job of spelling out your message.

Fill effects let you apply gradient fills (a color transition effect) or a texture, including one you've designed from scratch, or import a graphics file that is automatically sized to fit the background of a PowerPoint slide. To apply a background fill effect, follow these steps:

1 Choose Format, Background, or right-click anywhere (except in a place-holder) on the slide that you want to change and choose Background from the shortcut menu. The Background dialog box appears.

2 If you have not already selected the color scheme for the background, do so by making your selections from the Color palette, as described in the previous set of steps.

3 In the Background dialog box, click the down arrow in the empty field box, and then click Fill Effects. The Fill Effects dialog box appears, as shown at the top of the next page.

4 Pick the settings for your new background, including the option to insert a picture that will be stretched to encompass the whole background, and then click OK to close the Fill Effects dialog box.

5 In the Background dialog box, click Apply to apply the effects to the selected slides. Click Apply To All to also update the master slide.

Chapter 32: Advanced Presentation Formatting

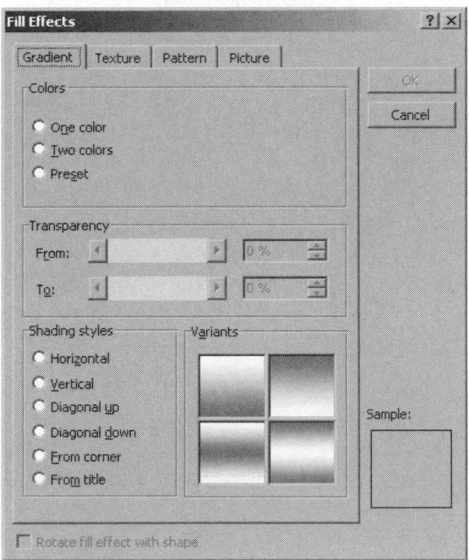

When you create a background that you want to reuse in other presentations, you can preserve its formatting in the following ways:

- Save the slide that contains the background as a picture file.

- Make this slide the default design for new, blank presentations by saving as a Blank.pot file. It's a good idea to delete all slides, text, graphics, and effects that you don't want on your default slide before you save it.

- Save it as a design template, which makes it available in the Slide Design task pane. It's a good idea to delete all slides, text, graphics, and effects that you don't want in your template before you save it.

The options to save a presentation as a template are covered in Chapter 31, "Essential PowerPoint Techniques."

- Save the presentation and build new ones based on it, using the New From Existing Presentation command in the New Presentation task pane.

To save a slide background containing a texture or a picture as a picture, perform the following steps:

1 Select the slide that contains the background you want to save.

2 Click the background of the slide in a section outside any text or object placeholders.

3 Right-click the slide, and then select Save Background from the shortcut menu.

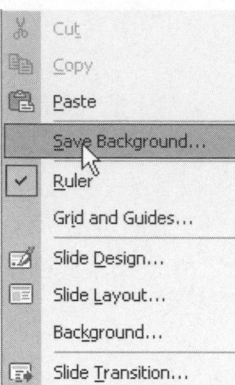

4 Type a name for the background in the File Name box.

5 Select the graphics file format that you want to save it in, and then click Save.

> **tip** When selecting a graphics file format for saving, note that some picture file formats let you ungroup and edit the elements in the picture, such as Windows metafiles (.wmf). Some file formats don't, however; the most common type in this category is bitmap files.

The simple technique of modifying a PowerPoint background and saving it as a graphics file helps you build a design library of useful backgrounds. To really put an individual stamp on your PowerPoint presentations, however, you can easily put together your own backgrounds from scratch with impressive results.

Creating Custom Backgrounds

To create custom backgrounds that set your presentations apart from the standard familiar ones, you need three things:

- A scanner
- Image-editing software, such as Microsoft PhotoDraw or Adobe Photoshop
- Found objects

Scanned objects make great backgrounds. Keep in mind, however, that the background is the background: The foreground is where you want your audience to focus. Found objects are the raw materials of backgrounds. Examples of items you might scan include marble or granite pieces, sheets of metal, wood with a grain, fabric, tiles, flowers, leaves, feathers, stones, shells, coins, buttons, and food items.

> **note** Many designs are covered under the pictorial and graphic category of U.S. copyright laws. If you scan a product that contains a design that is the intellectual property of someone else, you are violating those laws. That's why it's a good idea to choose objects found in nature or items like antique pieces of fabric or tiles. The use of such found items is not limited by copyright regulations.

The procedures for creating a background from a scanned image vary according to the hardware you are using. To scan an item for use as a background in a slide, follow these general steps:

1 Scan the item.

> **tip** You'll want the file size of the scan to be as small as possible so that you can store, transfer, and print it conveniently. Make use of any options your scanning software gives you to reduce file size. You can usually crop out portions of the item, set the scanner resolution to a lower value, or change the color model you're using to scan. Also store the scan in an image file format, such as .png, .wmf, or .jpeg, which both compresses the file and is recognized by PowerPoint as an acceptable graphics file format.

2 Open the scan in the image-editing software of your choice.

3 Apply effects to the scan to make it suitable for a background, such as:

- Applying a color gradient
- Adding shapes
- Blurring the background
- Applying a transparency effect so text is legible against it

4 Save the file in a format that can be imported into PowerPoint.

For more information on the graphics filters included in Office XP, see Chapter 6, "Adding Professional Graphics and Special Effects to Office XP Documents."

InsideOut

Before you insert the image file into PowerPoint, it's good practice to make a backup copy of the file in the file format native to the image-editing program you're using. This lets you return to that file and edit it again. Whenever you want to make a few changes to the image (for example, to make it more transparent to work better with new title formatting on a slide), you can use the saved file without having to start from scratch.

To insert the picture as a custom background in PowerPoint, do the following steps:

1 Open the presentation and display the slide into which you want to insert the custom background, and then choose Format, Background.

2 Click the drop-down arrow that displays the current fill effects of the background and select Fill Effects from the list.

3 Select the Picture tab and click Select Picture.

4 Display the picture you want to use, changing folders and/or drives as necessary, and double-click the picture. Click OK.

5 If you want this picture to be a custom background in this slide only, choose Apply. If you want the custom background on every slide, choose Apply to All.

Figure 32-7 displays an example of a slide with a custom background.

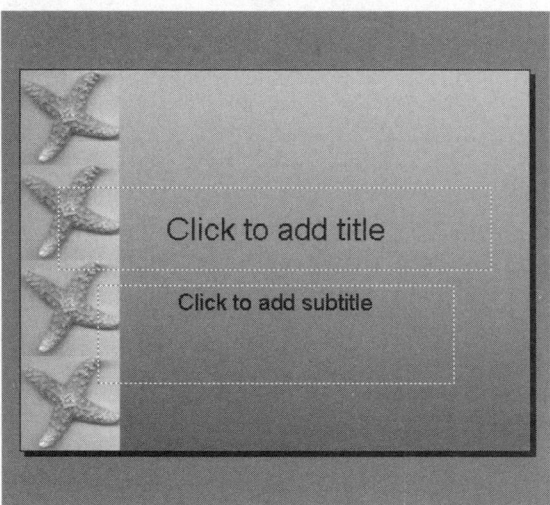

Figure 32-7. A scanned image is used as a custom background.

Editing Master Slides

Master slides control the default formatting of the design template (or templates) applied to your presentations. There are four masters: the Title Master, the Slide Master, the Notes Master, and the Handout Master. To display the toolbar for each of these masters, take the following steps:

1 Choose View, Master, and then select the appropriate one.

2 To display the Title Master, click Slide Master to display the Slide-Title master pairs.

Chapter 32: Advanced Presentation Formatting

3 The Slide Master View toolbar appears, containing options to Insert New Slide Master, Insert New Title Master, Delete Master, Preserve Master, Rename Master, and Master Layout, which contains options to restore placeholders to master slides.

Use master slides to make global changes that affect all the slides that are based on that master. In PowerPoint 2002, you can insert more than one design template into a presentation. Because each design template automatically inserts a Title and Slide master into your presentation, using more than one design template per presentation means that you can end up with more than one set of Slide-Title master pairs. This feature is known as *multiple masters*. To help you sort out what slides will be affected by formatting changes you apply to master slides, the Slide and Title masters are paired and displayed as thumbnails in the Slides tab in Normal view, as shown in Figure 32-8.

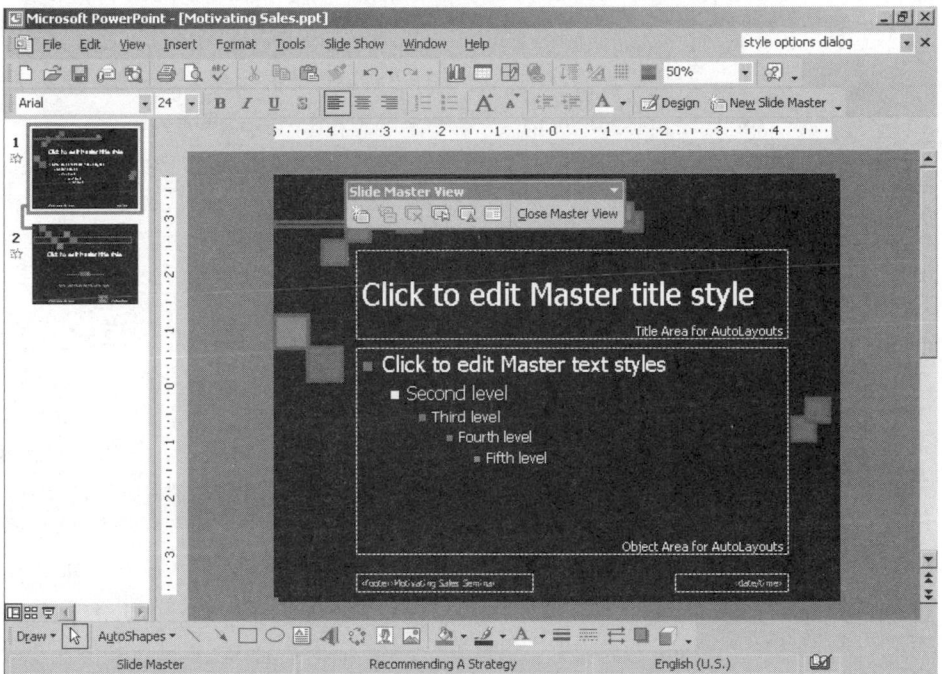

Figure 32-8. Slide-Title pairs appear for each design template in use.

When you move the mouse pointer over one of these master thumbnails, a ScreenTip appears, telling you which master you are viewing and what slides in the list of slide thumbnails it controls.

Formatting the Slide Master

All slides in your presentation are initially formatted based on the Slide Master, which sets the font formatting, bullet styles, placeholder size and position, background design, and color schemes for all the slides (except the title slides) that follow a specified design template in your presentation. You can use the placeholders on the Slide Master to control the formatting and position of the title and body text on any slide in your presentation.

To customize the Slide Master, perform the following steps:

1 Choose View, Master, and then select Slide Master from the submenu. The Slide Master appears, as shown in Figure 32-8.

2 Choose "Click To Edit Master Title Style" to format the title for your slides.

The Slide Master also shows several text entries in the main body of the slide. Each of these entries corresponds to one bullet level of text on the slide.

3 Select the placeholder for the area that you want to change.

4 Make any changes that you want using the Formatting toolbar's controls and the Format menu's commands, such as changing a bullet style or adjusting the indentation settings on the ruler.

> **note** The font formatting changes you make here are inherited by the Title master, although you can make changes to the font directly on the Title master, which are reflected on all title slides using that design template.

5 Type any information in the Date, Footer, and Number areas that you want to appear on all slides. To edit the contents of the header or footer, you must choose View, Header And Footer.

6 When you're finished, click the Close button on the Master toolbar that floats above the Slide Master to return to Normal view.

Formatting the Title Master

You lead off your presentations with a slide that contains the title of the presentation and the subtitle, if any. This slide is called the *title slide* and might also contain information about the presentation such as when it was created or for what audience, which is contained in a header or footer. In addition, you might use more than one title slide within a presentation to separate major sections or summarize what you've covered.

You can position and format five areas on the Title Master: Title, Subtitle, Date, Footer, and Number. To create and customize the Title Master, complete the following steps, similar to those used with the Slide Master:

1 Choose View, Master, and then select Slide Master from the submenu. Click the Title Master thumbnail in the Slide tab or click Insert New Title Master button on the Slide Master View toolbar.

2 Select the text placeholder that you want to change.

3 Use the tools on the Formatting toolbar or the commands on the Format menu to apply formatting effects. When you're finished, click the Close Master View button on the Slide Master toolbar to return to Normal view.

Any formatting changes that you make to the text objects on the Title Master are then applied to any title slides within your presentation. Only information that is still in the standard format is changed. If you have made manual changes to the formatting of a title slide (using the techniques discussed in "Formatting Text," on page 876), that formatting is maintained. You can also change the position of objects on your title slides by moving the objects on the Title Master.

If you find working with multiple masters confusing and determine that it is a feature you're not likely to implement, the solution is simple: To disable multiple masters, perform the following steps:

1 Choose Tools, Options.

2 In the Edit tab, under Disable New Features, check the Multiple Masters check box to disable them.

Chapter 33

Mastering Tables, Graphics, and Drawings

The basic formatting effects in Microsoft PowerPoint 2002 create solid, compelling presentations. To further enliven your presentations, you can add graphics. Tables, diagrams, organization charts, Microsoft Excel worksheets, clip art, or your own drawings all work to illustrate conceptual information. By using visual effects throughout your slide show, you can make your point quickly and effectively.

If the computer or projector you're using to present the slide show supports sound and video, you should consider adding one or more multimedia elements to your presentation. PowerPoint makes it easy to insert video, sound, and music clips in your show.

When you use well-chosen graphics to support the information you're presenting, you can make complicated information clear and intelligible to your audience.

In this chapter, you'll learn to:

- Create tables, diagrams, and charts
- Work with drawn objects
- Insert clip art and pictures
- Create WordArt
- Position objects using grids and guides
- Insert media files

Adding Graphics

The techniques for adding graphics to slides in PowerPoint are the same as those used in other Microsoft Office XP programs. In this chapter, the term *graphics* is meant to include diagrams, charts, linked documents created in other Office programs, pictures, clip art, and media files.

> For more details on adding graphics, see Chapter 6, "Adding Professional Graphics and Special Effects to Office XP Documents."

Creating Tables

newfeature!

Adding tables to your slide presentation is an excellent way to show important trends and relationships among groups of data. Typically, PowerPoint tables look best when they're kept small and concise, with no more than two or three columns and three or four rows, as shown in Figure 33-1.

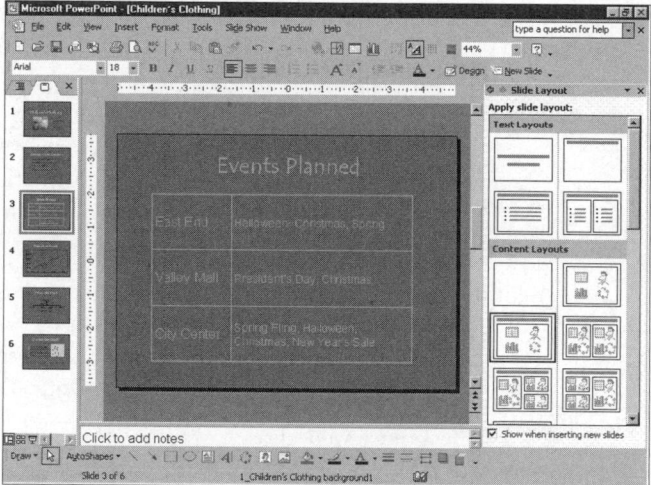

Figure 33-1. It's good design practice to keep tables simple when including them on a slide.

You can create a table that has numbers, words, or both in a PowerPoint slide. To insert a basic table, perform the following steps:

1 Display the slide in which you're going to create the table.

2 On the Standard toolbar, click Insert Table.

3 In the table grid, point to select the number of columns and rows that you need. When you click, the blank table is inserted into the current slide.

4 Add your data to the cells. When you're finished adding data to the table, click the slide background to close the table.

Another way to add a table to your presentation is to simply add a slide with one of the content layouts that includes a table icon. Double-click the table icon in the place-holder, and specify the number of columns and rows that you need in the Insert Table dialog box.

You can quickly perform simple editing tasks by double-clicking within the table area and making your changes, as follows:

● Use the Tab key to move from one cell to another within the table.

● To correct typos and make simple changes to the data, use the standard editing conventions such as overtype, insert, delete, copy, and move.

● If a column or row is too narrow or too wide, move the mouse pointer to the border until the pointer changes to a double vertical bar, and then drag the border to change the width of the column.

● Resize the entire table by dragging the resizing handles that appear on the outer edges of the table when it is selected.

To create a more complex table, follow these steps:

1 On the Tables and Borders toolbar, click the Draw Table button.

2 Use the pointer, which is a pencil now, to draw the boundaries of your table, and then drag the pointer to create the columns and rows.

3 To remove a column or row, click the Eraser button, and then click the line you want to remove.

The Tables and Borders toolbar includes two useful commands (borrowed from the Table toolbar in Microsoft Word 2002) to help you resize table elements on slides: Distribute Rows Evenly and Distribute Columns Evenly. If necessary, you can use these buttons to revise the row and column widths in your table.

Formatting a Table

Use table formatting to add clarity to your presentations; for example, you can emphasize relationships among groups of data by adding shading to a column heading, or distinguish groups of cells by giving them their own color scheme.

You can make changes to your table (inserting and deleting rows and columns, adding fill colors to cells, applying borders, or changing the text alignment within cells, and so on) by using the formatting options available from the Tables And Borders toolbar. When the table is active on your slide, click Table on the Tables And Borders toolbar, and then click Borders and Fill. The Borders tab of the Format Table dialog box appears, as shown in Figure 33-2, on page 900.

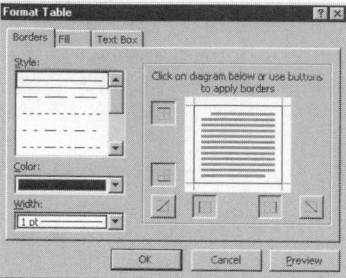

Figure 33-2. Apply borders to a table using the Borders tab of the Format Table dialog box.

Use the appropriate tab to make changes:

- To modify the style, color, and width of the border around each cell, column, row, or the entire table, click the Border tab if it is not already selected.

- To select a fill or background color for the table or elements in the table, click the Fill tab.

- To adjust the center point, change the internal margins of the cells, or rotate the text within the cells of your table, click the Text Box tab. (Rotating text in a column or row is often a convenient way to make information fit into a cell and keep it readable.)

To add a picture to a table, click the cell you want to place it in, and then choose Insert, Picture, as shown in this example:

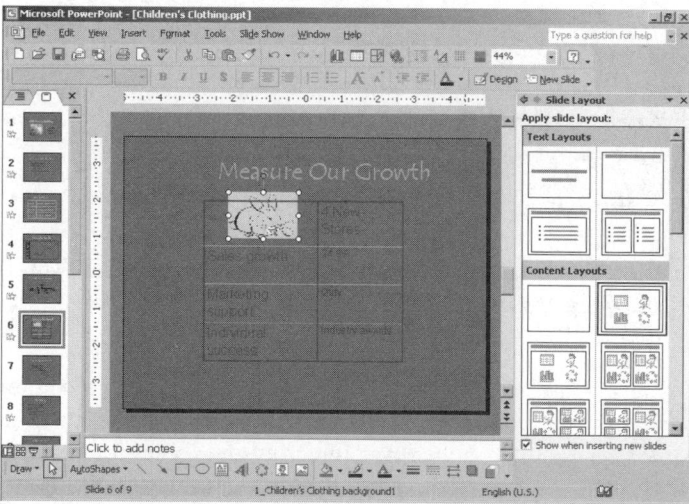

Troubleshooting

The Picture Doesn't Fit Into the Cell or Table

After you insert a picture into the table, it doesn't fit into the cell you selected. After you insert a picture into a table, the picture doesn't move with the table. After you insert a picture into a table as a fill effect, the picture appears distorted.

The following are possible reasons for these problems:

- The first two problems occur because the picture is simply layered on top of the table when you insert it. You must group the picture and the table after either resizing the picture to fit the cell or table, or resizing the cell or table to fit the picture. Note that to group a picture with a table, you must first ungroup the table, then group all table cells and the picture. (For instructions on how to group objects, see "Grouping Objects," on page 908.)

- When you insert a picture into a cell or table as a fill effect, the picture is automatically resized to fit the cell, which can cause it to look distorted. Resize the cell or table until the distortion is eliminated.

Adding Diagrams and Charts

newfeature!

In PowerPoint 2002, you can insert predesigned diagrams using the tools on the Drawing toolbar. Diagrams are used to demonstrate how something works or to illustrate relationships among parts of a whole, as shown in Figure 33-3.

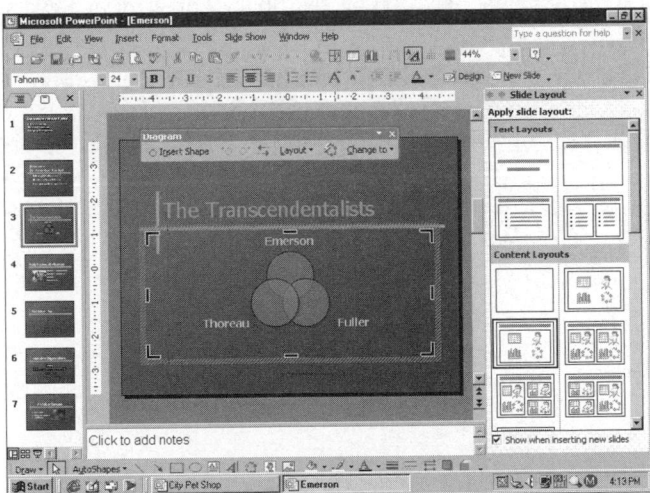

Figure 33-3. A Venn diagram demonstrates how topics overlap.

Organization charts, which demonstrate the hierarchy or structure of an organization, now open directly in PowerPoint. They are also formatted using PowerPoint's drawing tools. To add a diagram or an organization chart, follow the steps listed on the following page.

901

1   Click in the slide to which you want to add a diagram or chart.

2   On the Drawing toolbar, click the Insert Diagram or Organization Chart button. The Diagram Gallery appears, as seen here:

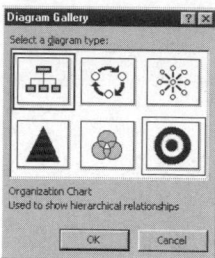

3   Click one of the diagram types to show a description of it in the dialog box. Once you have made your choice, click OK to insert it.

If you click Organization Chart, the Organization Chart toolbar opens, which contains options for inserting a shape, adjusting the layout of a chart, or selecting an element of the chart.

If you click one of the other diagrams, the Diagram toolbar opens.

You can make changes to a diagram in the following ways:

● To add a shape, select the shape next to where you want to add the new one. On the Diagram toolbar, click the Insert Shape button.

● To move a shape in the drawing layer, on the Diagram toolbar, click one of these buttons: Move Shape Backward, Move Shape Forward, or Reverse Diagram.

● To add text to a shape in a diagram, click in the shape and enter your text. To edit the text, click on the text or right-click the shape, click Edit Text, and enter your text.

> **note**   In certain diagrams, text can only be entered in the placeholders provided in the pre-designed pattern. In Target and Cycle diagrams, you can only add text to the text boxes provided for you.

● To change design schemes, on the Diagram toolbar, click the Change to button and choose a new style of diagram or chart.

- To apply color to a diagram or chart, click the shape you want to affect. On the Drawing toolbar, click the Fill Color button. You can change the fill color back to its preformatted color by clicking Automatic, or you can pick a new color from the ones listed.

- To modify fill effects, on the Drawing toolbar, click the Fill Effects button. Choose from options in the Gradient, Texture, Picture, or Pattern tabs.

- To modify the line color or style of a shape in a diagram or chart, click the line or connector you want to change. On the Drawing toolbar, click either the Line Color or Line Style button to make your changes.

Adding Charts

Many slide presentations include a set of numbers of some kind—projected sales figures for next year, for example, or comparisons of market trends. Long rows of numbers are difficult to understand, especially in the short time your audience has to grasp their meaning. A chart can provide quick visual cues to trends and comparisons.

To add a chart to a slide, select the slide and then either select a slide layout that has a chart placeholder from the Slide Layout task pane or choose Insert, Chart; or on the Standard toolbar, click the Insert Chart button. There are two ways to work with charts in PowerPoint.

- You can use Excel to create the chart, copy it to the Office Clipboard, and then paste it onto your slide. The advantage of this technique is that you can use all of Excel's tools for managing your data and creating your graph. In addition, you can use existing charts that have already been created and saved in Excel workbooks. To add an Excel chart to a slide, you can simply paste it onto any slide; you do not have to insert it or use a slide layout containing a chart.

- You can use Microsoft Graph, a utility that's included in Office XP. To open Graph, simply double-click the chart placeholder on your slide or click the Insert Chart button on PowerPoint's Standard toolbar.

When Graph opens in PowerPoint, you'll see a new menu bar, a new toolbar, and a datasheet, which is a table that contains sample information that shows you where to type your own data for your chart. Beneath the datasheet is a column chart, as shown in Figure 33-4, on page 904.

Part 5: PowerPoint

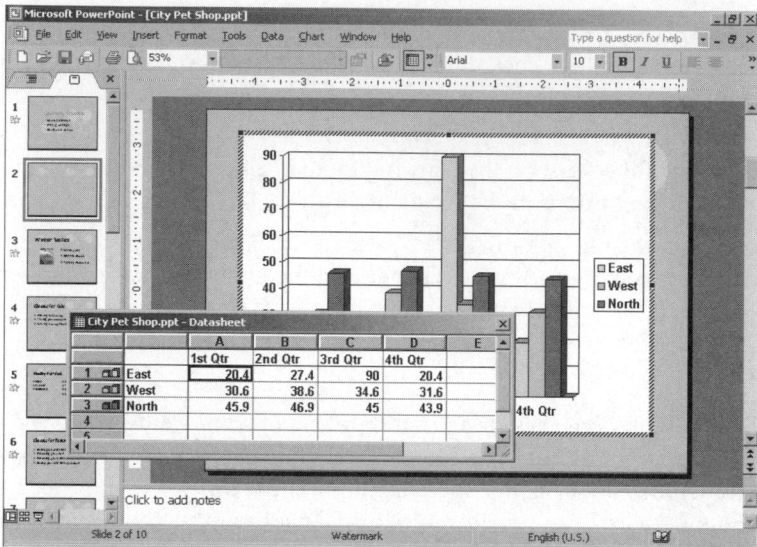

Figure 33-4. Microsoft Graph opens a placeholder datasheet when you open a chart in PowerPoint.

> Using Graph and its various tools is also discussed in Chapter 7, "Sharing Data Among Office XP Applications."

To customize this chart with your own information, perform the following steps:

1 Modify the placeholder information one cell at a time.

or

Right-click the button in the upper-left corner of the datasheet, and then click Delete to clear all the sample information and rebuild the whole chart.

2 Use the buttons on the Graph Standard toolbar to import data from Excel worksheets to replace the data in the current datasheet, change the chart type from the default vertical-column chart to one of a variety of 2-D or 3-D charts, turn the display of the datasheet window on or off, and modify the chart colors.

To create a chart that updates information automatically when you open it, you must insert a linked Excel chart. To do so, follow these steps:

1 In the Excel worksheet, select the range of cells you want to use, and choose Edit, Copy.

2 In PowerPoint, click the slide or notes page where you want to insert the Excel data, and choose Edit, Paste Special. The Paste Special dialog box appears, as shown here:

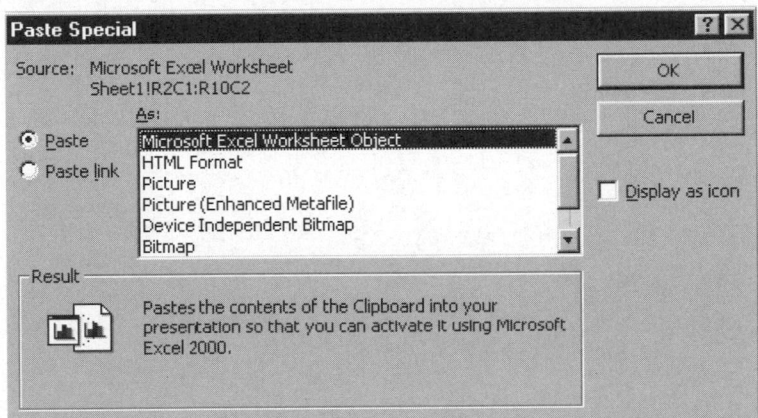

3 In the Paste Special dialog box, select Microsoft Excel Worksheet Object, check Paste Link, and then click OK.

Now you can use all the functionality of Excel to edit this chart and update the chart data automatically from the source file whenever you open it. If you don't want the chart to update automatically, change the default settings in PowerPoint using the following procedure:

1 Choose Edit, Links.

2 In the Links dialog box, specify breaking the link, updating it manually, or changing the location of the source file.

Working with Drawn Objects

By default, the Drawing toolbar appears at the bottom of the PowerPoint window. If you have only a few minutes to experiment with creating drawing objects, you should begin with the AutoShapes menu on the Drawing toolbar, because it contains a variety of predefined shapes, including flowchart symbols, arrows, banners, and action buttons, that you can use to illustrate points on a slide. In PowerPoint, the flowchart AutoShape and Connector lines are often used to present information, as shown in Figure 33-5, on page 906.

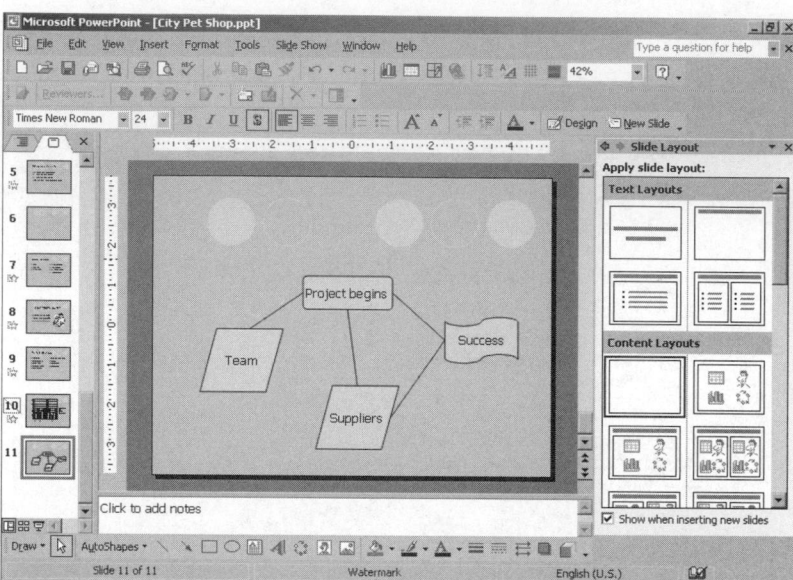

Figure 33-5. Flowchart shapes often use locked connector lines.

You can also create your own free-form drawings by selecting one of the pen shapes in the Lines category. For example, the table chart line shown in Figure 33-6 was created using the Freeform tool, which lets you draw a line that has both straight and curved elements.

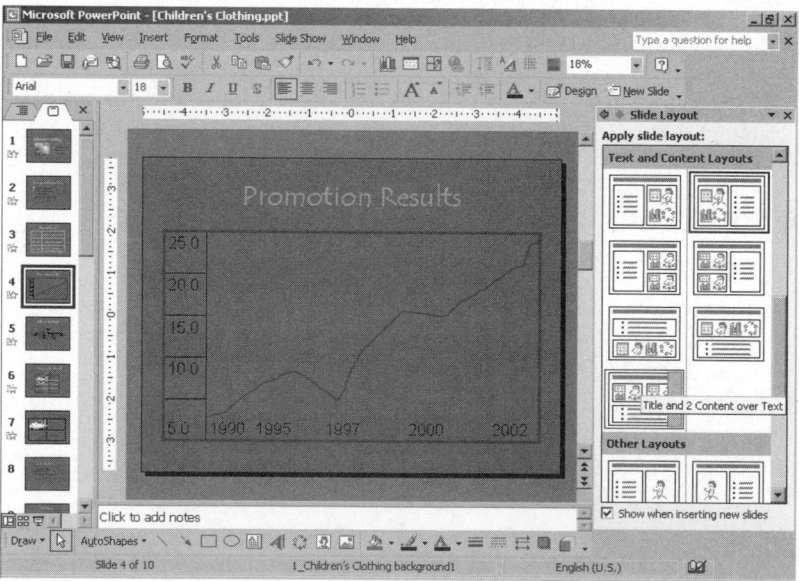

Figure 33-6. Use Drawing tools allows you to create custom charts and tables.

Chapter 33

> **tip** To make it easier to control the movement of the drawing tools, you can increase the zoom so that you can see what you're doing, and also slow down the mouse tracking speed, using settings in the Microsoft Windows Control Panel.

When you use the Drawing toolbar to create an image on your slide, it becomes an object that you can resize, copy, move, format, and delete. Before you can change an attribute of a drawing object, you must select it.

> **note** Drawn objects or pictures can be added to notes only by switching from the Notes pane in Normal view to Notes Page view. (Choose View, Notes Page.) Add your illustrations in this view. When you switch back to Normal view, the objects you just added are not displayed, but they print and display in Notes Page view.

After you create your illustration, you can use commands on the Drawing toolbar's Draw menu to format or edit your object.

> The formatting options detailed in "Adding Diagrams and Charts," on page 901, are available for drawn shapes as well.

Troubleshooting

An Object Can't Be Selected

You can't select an object, or you can't see the object you want to select.

These problems occur for the following possible reasons:

- If you can't select an object, it might be placed on the slide background. To select it, first you must choose Format, Background. Then you can select the object and make formatting changes to it.

- If you can't select an object, it might be placed on a master slide. To select this object, choose View, point to Master, and then click the appropriate master. Make your changes to the selected object, and then click Close Master View to return to Normal view.

- If you can't see the object that you added to the Slide or Title Master on other slides, you might have checked the Omit Background Graphics From Master check box. To reverse that setting, choose Format, Background, and in the Background dialog box, clear the Omit Background Graphics From Master check box.

- Another reason why you can't see an object might be because it is hidden behind another object. You can solve this problem by changing the order in which the objects are stacked. For information on doing this, see "Working with the Drawing Layer," on page 908.

Grouping Objects

A useful set of commands on the Draw menu lets you create groups of objects. By creating a group, you can use a single command to change all the objects at once. To group objects, perform the following steps:

1 Select the first object and then press the Shift key while you select additional objects.

2 Choose Group from the Draw menu seen here:

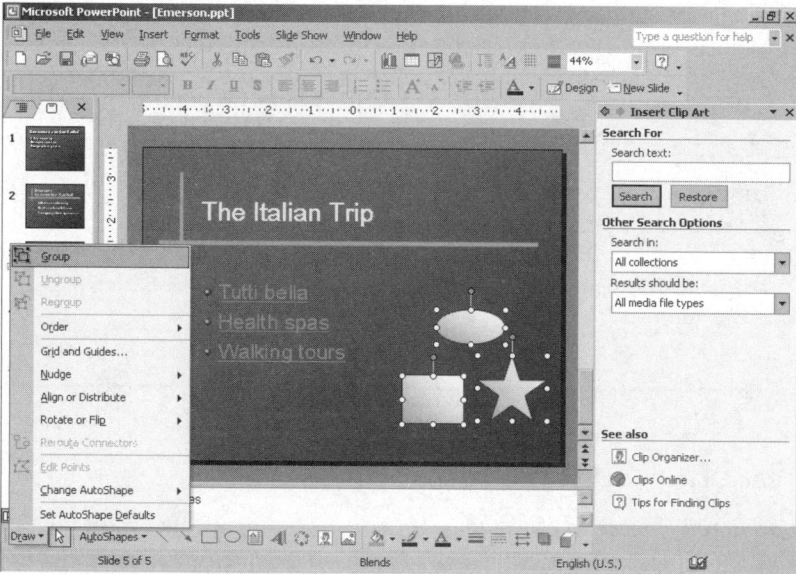

The objects are now grouped together into one object and all the objects in the group share a single set of sizing handles.

3 If you no longer want to group a collection of objects, select the object group and choose Draw, Ungroup.

Working with the Drawing Layer

Each drawing object that is placed on a slide exists on its own layer. This means that some drawing objects can appear to cover up parts of other objects, so it's often necessary to change the order of the objects. To change the stacking order of objects, use these procedures:

● If you want an object to appear behind all the other objects, select the object, choose Draw, Order. Select Send To Back from the submenu.

● If you want an object to appear at the very front of the slide (so that all of it is visible and it covers up parts of the objects behind it), select the object and then choose Bring To Front from the Order submenu.

● If you're setting the order for a large number of objects, you can fine-tune the sequence using the Send Backward and Bring Forward commands, which move objects through the stacking order one step at a time. You can also select an object and press Tab to move through each object in the stack (except for tables).

Inserting Pictures, Clip Art, and WordArt

The Clip Organizer contains clip art, picture, and media files. You can use the Clip Organizer to store and organize additional graphic objects as you import or create them. When you want to insert one of these objects onto a slide, you click either the Insert Clip Art button or the Insert Picture button on the Drawing toolbar. You can also select an appropriate slide from the Content Layouts in the Slide Layouts task pane.

> For more information about the Clip Organizer, see Chapter 6, "Adding Professional Graphics and Special Effects to Office XP Documents."

To insert a picture, perform the following steps:

1 On the Drawing toolbar, click the Insert Picture button. The Insert Picture dialog box appears, as shown here:

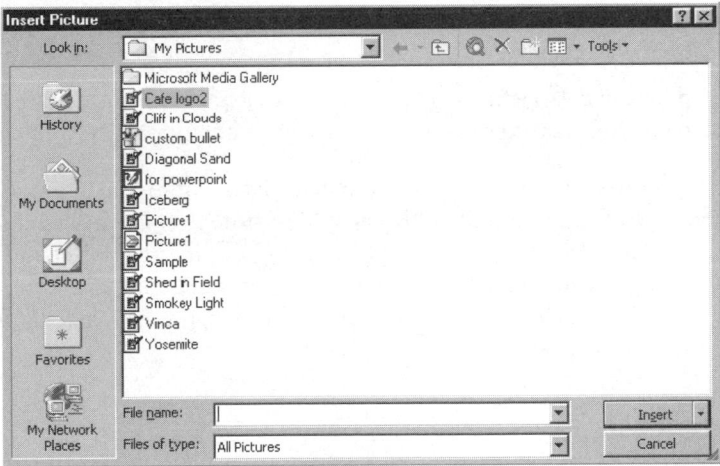

2 In the Insert Picture dialog box, select the file that contains the picture you want to insert.

or

Choose Insert, Picture, and then click From Scanner Or Camera to insert a picture directly from another electronic device.

3 Click Insert.

909

You can apply formatting to pictures as you can to other objects in PowerPoint by going to the Format menu. Select Picture, and in the Format Picture dialog box's Picture tab, shown here, you find tools that let you compress, recolor, crop, and make adjustments to the image color, brightness, and contrast of a picture.

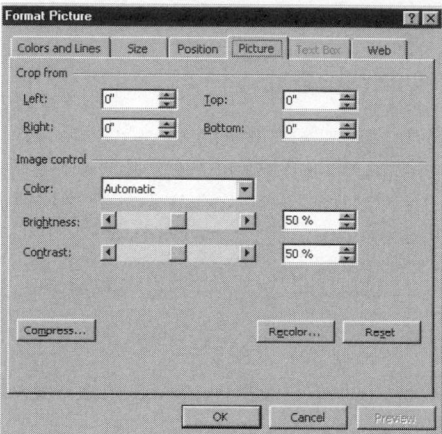

When you create or modify an object, such as a customized AutoShape or recolored clip, and then want to preserve the new object, you can save it as a picture, using the following procedure:

1 Right-click the object, and then click Save As Picture on the shortcut menu.

2 In the Save As Picture dialog box, type a filename for the picture, specify the folder you want to store it in, and select an appropriate type of file format.

If you want to edit the parts of an AutoShape later, you need to save it as a Window metafile (.wmf) graphics file, which is used to store vector graphics. You can edit a drawn object, which is a vector graphic, by ungrouping the object and then manipulating the various components of it, such as recoloring it. (You cannot ungroup a raster image, of which the most common type is a bitmap, but you can edit it by using a paint or photo-editing program.)

InsideOut

When saving graphics, you will often want to reduce the file size. Reducing the graphic's file size saves room on your hard disk and, if you're using the graphic on the Web, makes it easier to download quickly. Use the new Compress button in the Format Picture dialog box to make needed adjustments: change the resolution to print, Web, or screen; delete cropped areas; and compress selected pictures.

You can search for interesting clip art images in the Clip Organizer, purchase collections of clip art, create your own art in a vector drawing program, or visit the Office

Chapter 33

Update Web site to download clips from the Microsoft Clip Gallery Live site. Clips can add life to your text, as shown in Figure 33-7.

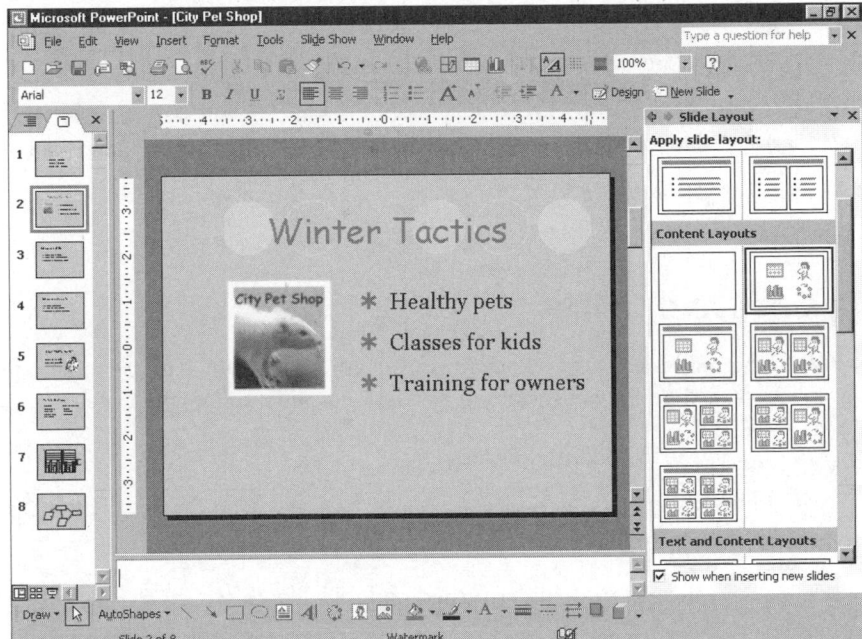

Figure 33-7. Placing a clip art object next to bulleted text adds visual interest to your presentation.

To insert clip art, perform the following steps:

1 On the Drawing toolbar, click the Insert Clip Art button or select a slide layout with an appropriate placeholder.

2 In the Insert Clip Art task pane, search for a clip by keyword or category. Moving your pointer over the clip lets you see the ScreenTip containing the file category, dimensions, size, and format.

3 Click the arrow that appears to the right of the clip for options to insert, copy, or manipulate the clip.

To open the Clip Organizer as a freestanding program, select the Insert Clip Art task pane, and then click the Clip Organizer link.

Applying WordArt Effects

WordArt is useful for creating special text effects to add to your slides. When you create graphics in other programs, by scanning or using an image-editing program, often the text effects that you add there end up looking blurry or fuzzy when inserted on a

911

PowerPoint slide. To create crisper text effects directly on a slide, you can use the WordArt toolbar. To insert WordArt, follow this procedure:

1 Click the Insert WordArt button on the Drawing toolbar.

2 In the WordArt Gallery, click the effect you want to use.

3 In the Edit WordArt Text dialog box, type the text you want to use, and make the formatting changes you want to the font, font size, and font style.

4 Click OK to return to your slide. The WordArt toolbar appears so you can continue formatting the object.

Using Grids and Guides

Grids and guides are viewable, nonprinting guides that you can use to help position objects on a slide. To view grids and guides on a slide, follow these steps:

1 Choose View, Grid And Guides.

2 In the Grids and Guides dialog box, click Display Grid On Screen and Display Drawing Guides On Screen.

A slide with the grid and guides turned on looks like this:

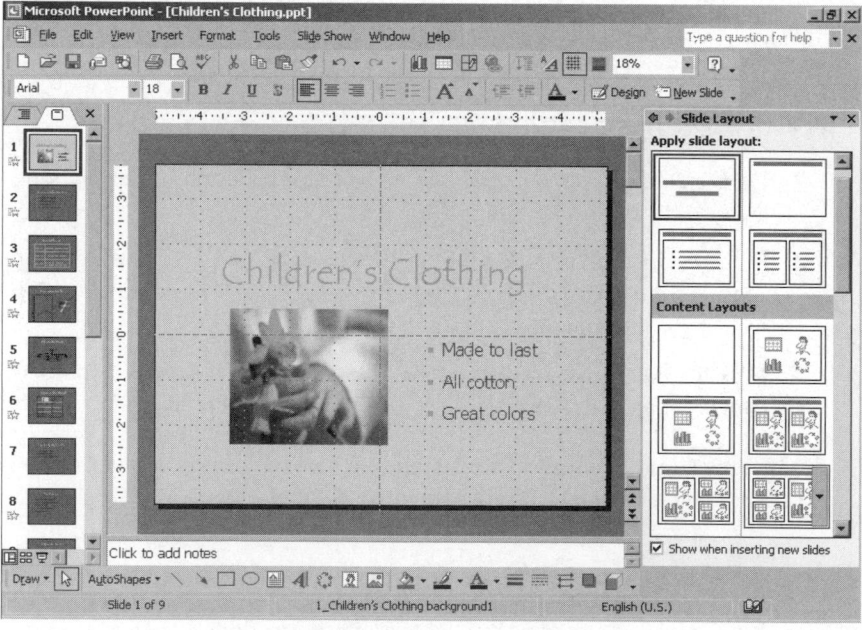

Chapter 33: Mastering Tables, Graphics, and Drawings

The guide, by default two intersecting straight lines, is helpful in arranging objects evenly on a slide. To manipulate guides, perform the following steps:

- Move the guides by selecting them and then dragging them to another location on the slide. When you drag a guide, a ScreenTip appears, telling you where on the vertical or horizontal ruler you are moving the guide.

- To delete a guide, drag it off the slide.

- To add a new guide, press Ctrl while dragging the guide.

The gridlines, which are a set of many intersecting lines, help you position objects precisely on a slide. To manipulate grids, perform the following steps:

1 Choose View, Grid And Guides. The Grid And Guides dialog box appears, as shown here:

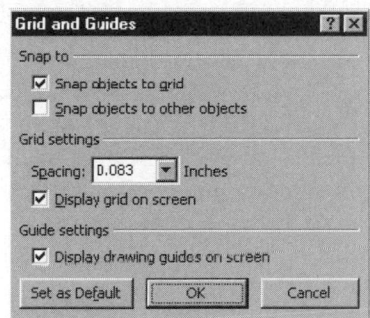

2 In the Grid And Guides dialog box, under Grid Settings, click the arrow in the Spacing list, and select the spacing you want to use between gridlines.

3 By default, Snap Objects To Grid is checked. You can clear that check box or override it on an ad hoc basis by pressing Alt as you move an object.

4 Check the Snap Objects To Other Objects check box to align objects with each other.

In addition to positioning objects by using grids and guides, you can also click Draw on the Drawing toolbar, and then choose Align or Distribute to set alignment options, or click Nudge to move an object in small increments.

Adding Media Files

Media files store sound, music, and movie clips that you can add to your slides. Inserting a media file on a slide can add interest to your presentation, but relying on multimedia effects to carry your presentation often backfires. Too much sound and motion during a presentation is ultimately confusing to your audience. Used judiciously, however, multimedia effects can quickly catch your viewers' attention.

913

Inserting Video Clips

You can insert one or more video objects (movies) into any slide. You might want to play a video quote from your product manager, for example, or run a short documentary movie for a fund-raising event. You could even create a video for product tutorials and educational materials.

> **note** Most of the movie clips stored in the Clip Organizer are simply animated .gif files, small files that contain an animated sequence of images. If you imported your own movie files into the Clip Organizer, you will find them there too, generally stored in .avi format. You can find additional movie clips on your network, intranet, or the Internet.

When presenting your slide show, you can play the video clip or movie—or you can have PowerPoint play it for you. If PowerPoint doesn't support the media file you want to play, you can often use the Microsoft Windows Media Player to run the file.

Before you insert any video objects, think about the environment you'll be presenting in. Does the computer or projector you'll use have the necessary hardware (such as a sound card, speakers, and an enhanced video card) for playing the multimedia items during your presentation? You might consider adding a few multimedia elements just in case. If the machine you give your presentation on doesn't support them, plan an alternate way to make your presentation compelling. With this basic detail considered, you'll find that adding media objects is the same as adding any other object to your slides, and the special effects are truly exciting.

To insert a movie into a slide, follow these steps:

1 If the slide has the Insert Media Clip icon, just double-click the icon.

2 If the slide doesn't have the Insert Media Clip icon, you will need to locate the clip you want to insert. If you want to browse the Clip Organizer for a movie clip, choose Insert, Movies And Sounds, and then choose Movie From Clip Organizer from the submenu. PowerPoint opens the Insert Clip Art task pane, with options that let you search your computer system for video clips. Double-click the movie you want to add to your slide.

3 If you want to insert a movie from an existing movie file on your hard disk, choose Insert, Movies And Sounds, and then choose Movie From File from the submenu. Select the movie file in the dialog box that appears, and then click OK. To play the movie automatically when the slide is displayed, click Yes. If you want to start the movie only after you click the icon, click No.

   Don't worry about the slide layout or the placeholders on the slide. Video clips are always inserted directly onto the slide, not into a placeholder.

4 To customize how your video is presented, select the video object on the slide, choose Slide Show, Custom Animation, and click Add Effect and select the dropdown arrow beside the video clip on the Custom Animated task pane to modify how the video runs.

5 Resize the video window, if necessary, using the sizing tools attached to the video window. By default, PowerPoint retains the original proportions of the clip as you drag to resize it by locking in its aspect ratio.

The video plays during your slide show until either the clip ends or you move to the next slide. You can also set it to loop continuously on the slide. In addition, you can configure a custom animation so that the movie plays as part of an animation sequence.

You can preview movies by displaying the slide and clicking Slide Show (From Current Slide) in the lower left corner of the PowerPoint window, or by selecting the slide, and then clicking Play in the Custom Animation task pane. When you insert a video clip, it is automatically linked to your presentation. Keep this in mind if you are going to present your slide show on another computer, as you'll need to take these linked files also.

> For more information on slide shows, see Chapter 35, "Setting Up and Presenting the Slide Show."

> **note** If you have any problems playing your videos, make sure that the video and Media Player settings are correct. Open the Windows Control Panel and choose Sounds And Multimedia. Check the sound device, the hardware setup, and the sound setup—and check all cable connections. Also check the volume control by double-clicking the Volume icon on the taskbar.

Inserting Sounds

Sound effects, such as music and voice recordings, can add another level of professionalism to your slide presentations. Music is an effective way to introduce or end a presentation and it gives your audience something to listen to as they enter and leave the presentation room. You could play a movie theme song as background music for several slides, or play a voice recording that contains advertising slogans to insert on a single slide, for example.

> **tip** Before you add sound to your show, make sure that your sound card is Windows-compatible and that sound files are available on your system. Otherwise, PowerPoint can't play or record sounds. To record sound, you'll also need a microphone or another type of input device.

You can find sound files in several places—in the Clip Organizer, in the folder where you've chosen to store your audio files, on the Internet, or from a network folder. There are two primary types of sound file formats—.wav (often called "wave" files) and .mid or MIDI files. After you add a sound to a slide, you'll see a Sound icon, as shown in Figure 33-8, on page 916.

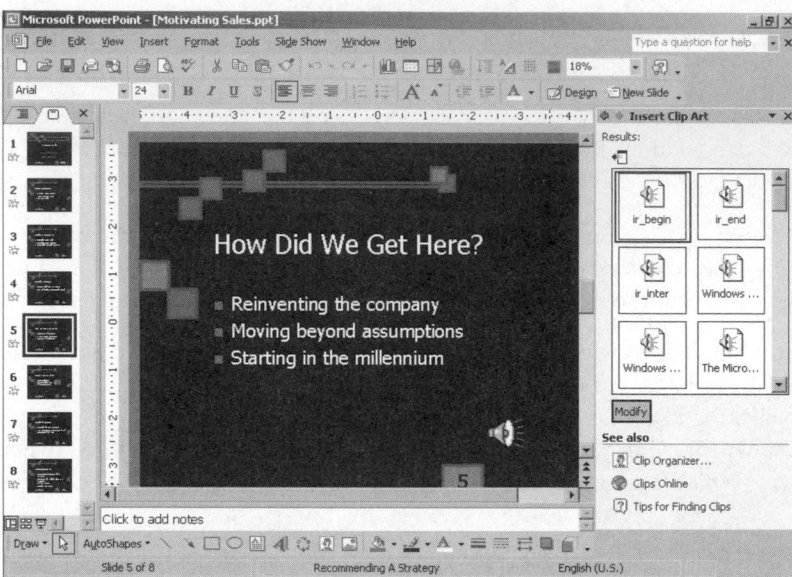

Figure 33-8. PowerPoint inserts a Sound icon on your slides when you select a sound file.

To add sound to your slide show, perform the following steps:

1 Display the slide to which you want to add sound.

2 If you want to browse for a sound file, choose Insert, Movies And Sounds, and then choose Sound From the Clip Organizer. In the Insert Clip Art task pane, double-click the sound file to add it to your slide. To play the sound automatically when the slide is displayed, click Yes. If you want to play the sound only after you click the icon, click No.

3 Alternatively, to insert a sound from an existing .wav or .mid file on your hard disk, if you haven't imported the file into the Clip Organizer, choose Insert, Movies And Sounds, and then choose Sound From File. The Insert Sound dialog box appears. Select the sound file that you want, and then click OK. To play the sound automatically when the slide is displayed, click Yes. If you want to play the sound only after you click the icon, click No.

PowerPoint automatically links sound files to your presentation file, rather than embedding them, if they are larger than 100 KB, although you can change the default specification. As when using any linked files, remember to copy the linked files with your presentation if you'll be presenting at a different computer than the one you used to create your presentation.

> **note** If you have problems using sound, make sure that the audio and Musical Instrument Digital Interface (MIDI) settings are correct. Open the Windows Control Panel and double-click Sounds And Multimedia. Check the sound device, the hardware setup, and the sound setup. Click the Volume icon on the taskbar to check the volume control.

To edit the sound or movie clips, perform the following steps:

1 Right-click the Sound icon on the slide, and then click Edit Sound Object or Edit Movie Object. The Sound Options dialog box, shown on the next page, or the Movie Options dialog box appears.

2 In the Sound Options or Movie Options dialog box, specify if you want the sound to loop continuously, or the movie to loop until stopped or rewind movie when done playing.

InsideOut

When you insert movies and sounds on your slides, PowerPoint inserts a small icon on the slide that contains the object. If you don't want the icon there, you can set the file to play automatically, and then drag the icon off the slide. You can also set effect options in the Custom Animation task pane to hide the icon when the media file is not playing.

Playing CD Audio Tracks

PowerPoint can locate and play a particular track from a CD during your presentation. You can choose to have an entire track play or specify a segment of it.

To insert a CD audio selection, perform the following steps:

1 Choose Insert, Movies And Sounds, and then click Play CD Audio Track. The Movie and Sound Options dialog box appears, as shown in Figure 33-9 on page 918.

2 In the Movie And Sound Options dialog box, enter a Start and End track number in the Track boxes. If you want, enter a particular point during each track at which it should start and end.

3 Click OK to insert the audio specifications. PowerPoint asks if you want the sound tracks to play automatically during the presentation.

4 Click Yes if you want the sound to begin when the slide appears; click No if you want to click the CD icon to start the music. A Sound icon appears, which you can move anywhere on your slide.

Figure 33-9. Set play options in the Movie And Sounds dialog box.

You can also set options in the Custom Animation task pane for these tracks. To edit the CD audio selection, follow these steps:

1 Right-click the CD icon on the slide.

2 Then click Custom Animation to open the Custom Animation task pane.

3 In the Custom Animation task pane, click the down arrow to the right of the Media item you want to edit, and choose Effect Options. Use the Effect tab to specify hiding the CD icon, or timings, or triggers to start or stop the play, as shown in Figure 33-10.

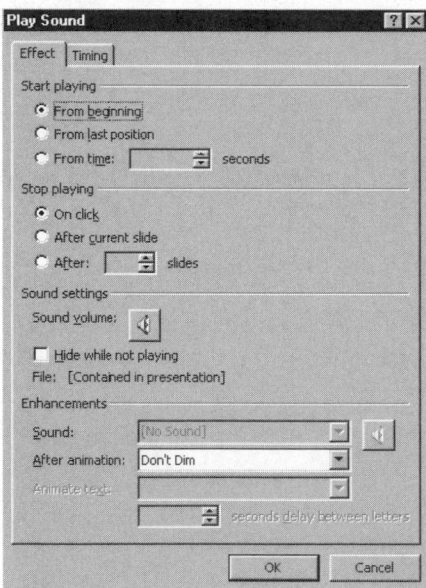

Figure 33-10. Use the options in the Play Sound dialog box to refine your music presentation.

Chapter 34

Adding Special Effects and Hyperlinks

The animation effects in Microsoft PowerPoint 2002 can help you focus your audience's attention on a particular slide or element on a slide. Animating a text item or an object means adding a special visual or sound effect to it. For example, you can have each slide title zoom in to the sound of a drum roll, or each bullet point fly in to the sound of wind. Using PowerPoint's new animation schemes, you can apply pre-designed animation and transitions to selected slides or an entire slide show with one click. When you use transitions, you can have one slide appear to dissolve or wipe into another, or choose from other filmlike transition effects.

In addition, you can create hyperlinks and action buttons that let you move to a specific slide, a custom show, a particular file, or a Web page during your presentation. By carefully balancing this combination of special effects—animation, sounds, transitions, and links to network and Web resources— you can fill your slide show with life and energy.

In this chapter, you'll learn about

- Applying animation schemes
- Animating chart elements
- Creating a motion path
- Setting timings
- Adding transitions to individual slides
- Creating hyperlinks
- Adding action buttons

Applying Animation

When you animate the text and objects in your presentations, you can help focus your audience's attention on your major points and give them something interesting to look at in the process.

newfeature!

PowerPoint 2002 introduces more sophisticated tools for controlling how information appears on a slide, which are contained in the new animation schemes. Animation schemes apply a set of animation effects and transitions to an entire presentation. You no longer have to animate each bullet point or apply a transition between each slide in your presentation. You can select a preset scheme and simply click to apply it to selected slides or your whole presentation. To get an idea of what is included in a preset animation scheme, move your mouse pointer over the scheme name in the Animation Schemes task pane. A ScreenTip appears, as shown in Figure 34-1, containing information about which elements on the slide are animated and if a transition is included in the scheme.

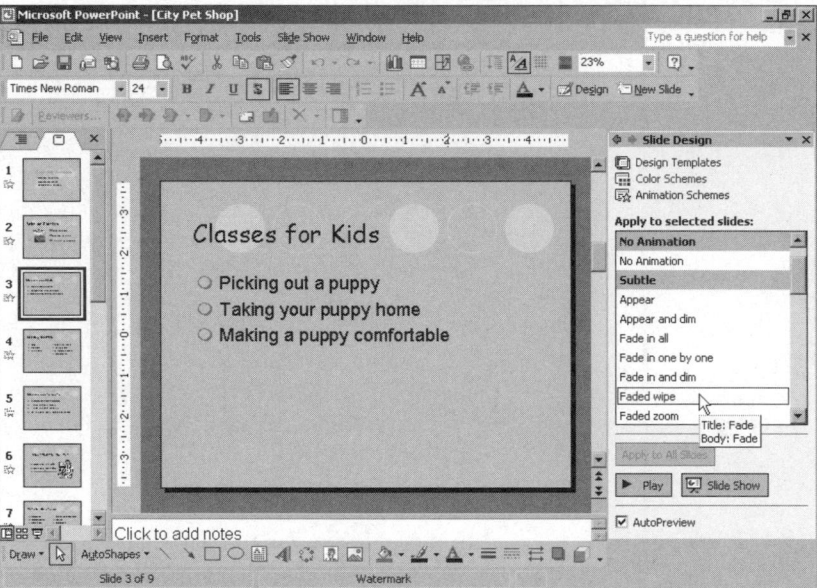

Figure 34-1. A ScreenTip provides a description of the components of an animation scheme.

To apply an animation scheme to a slide show, perform the following steps:

1 Open the slide show you want to animate in Normal view.

2 To open the Animation Schemes task pane, choose Slide Design—Animation Schemes.

3 In the Animation Schemes task pane, from the animation effects list, select an animation scheme from those organized in Subtle, Moderate, and Exciting categories.

4 Select the thumbnails in the Slides tab that you want to animate, if you don't want to animate the entire show.

tip You don't have to leave Normal view in PowerPoint to select slides to animate. Click the slide thumbnails in the Slides tab. To select noncontiguous slides, press Ctrl while clicking the thumbnails.

5 Click the name of the animation scheme to apply it to the selected slides or click Apply To All Slides.

Customizing Animation

To customize an animation sequence, choose Slide Show, Custom Animation when the slide is visible in Normal view. You'll see the Custom Animation category in the task pane, presenting animation options, as shown in Figure 34-2.

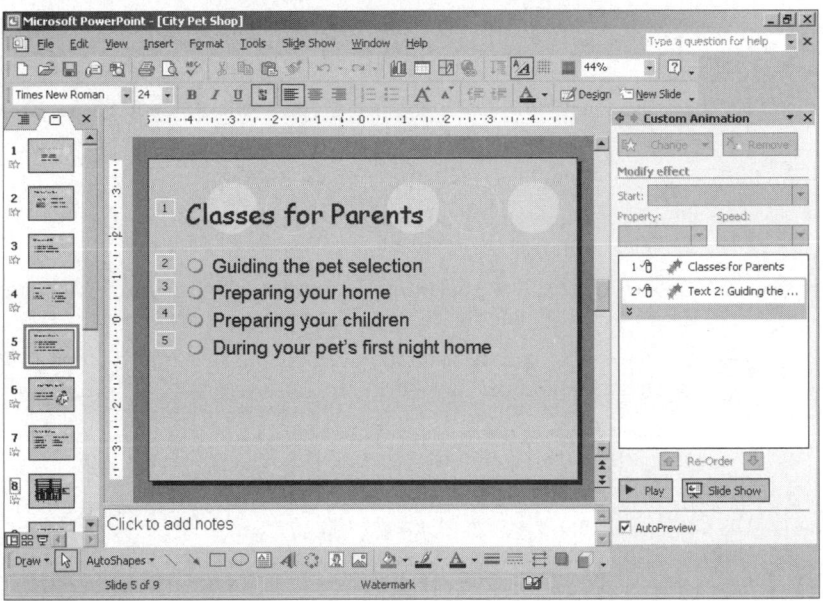

Figure 34-2. Specify animation for each element in the Custom Animation list.

The large text box in the task pane contains the Custom Animation list, which you can use to set the order in which the objects on your slide are animated. For example, you might want to display the title first to let the viewers know what the subject is, a piece of clip art second to plant a visual image in viewers' minds, and a bulleted list third to flesh out the image with text. Items are listed in the Custom Animation list in the order in which they are applied, from top to bottom in the list box. You can set additional options for effects using the Effects Options list, which appears when you click the down arrow next to an added effect.

921

The task pane also contains buttons and options that control advanced aspects of the animation sequence you're customizing, as follows:

- The Add Effect button lets you add entrance, emphasis, exit, and motion paths.
- The Start list box lets you pick which event starts the animation.
- The Property list box lets you change the propertie0s of the selected animation effect. This box changes to Direction, Path, or Font Size, depending on the animation effect you select.
- The Speed list box lets you set the speed at which the animation runs.
- The Reorder buttons (at the bottom of the task pane) let you rearrange the order of the animation elements you have selected.

For example, when you want to apply a particular animation effect to a title on a slide and different effects to each of the bulleted items in the list that follows it, you must apply custom animation effects. To do so, perform the following steps:

1 In Normal view, display the slide to which you want to add animation effects, and then select the part of the slide you wish to animate, such as the title.

2 If the Custom Animation task pane is not open, choose Slide Show, Custom Animation.

3 In the Custom Animation task pane, click Add Effect.

- Choose Entrance to specify animation effects that occur as the item appears on the slide.
- Choose Emphasis to specify animation effects that occur after the item appears on the slide.
- Choose Exit to specify animation effects that occur at the end of the animation sequence.
- Choose Motion Paths to specify the exact route the item will take as it moves through its animation sequence.

4 Click the particular animation effect you want to apply to each item.

Troubleshooting

You Can't Get an Element to Leave the Slide

The element for which you created an exit path doesn't leave the slide.

When you apply an Exit effect, the item doesn't actually leave the slide. Unless you set additional options, it simply reappears in the same place it started in after the animation sequence is over. See "Creating Motion Paths," on page 9250, for information on creating an effect that moves the item off the slide after the sequence ends.

After you apply the animation effects, the title for each animation appears in the Custom Animation task pane. In addition, an icon appears that represents the type of animation selected, its speed, when the animation starts, if clicking another object will trigger the animation, and a drop-down list with more options for refining the sequence. Also, as shown in Figure 34-3, the slide now contains a nonprinting numbered list that indicates the order in which the animation effects occur.

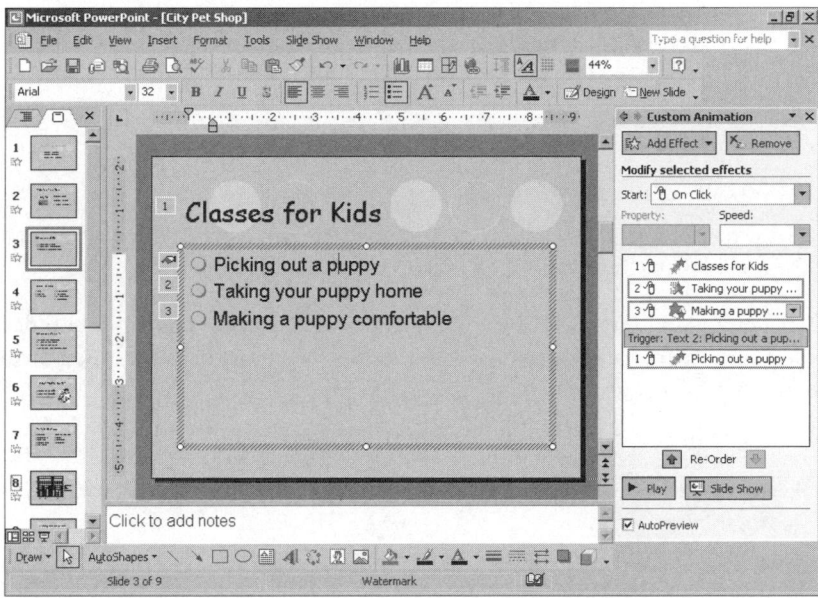

Figure 34-3. The labels on the slide items are not visible and do not print when you present your slide show.

Animating Diagrams and Chart Elements

You can add animation to individual elements in a chart, diagram, or organization chart to add impact to your presentation of their values. For example, you can bring each category in a bar chart onto the slide one at a time for emphasis or to prolong the suspense. However, to add animation to the individual elements of a Microsoft Excel chart or worksheet, you must first convert the Excel file to a PowerPoint chart. To do so, follow these steps:

1 In PowerPoint, add a new slide by clicking the New Slide button on the Standard toolbar.

2 In the Slide Layout task pane, click one of the Content Layouts that contains a placeholder for a chart.

3 Double-click the Insert Chart icon to open the Microsoft Graph utility.

4 On the Edit menu, click Import File.

5 In the Import File dialog box, select the workbook that contains the chart, and click Open. The Import Data Options dialog box appears, as shown here:

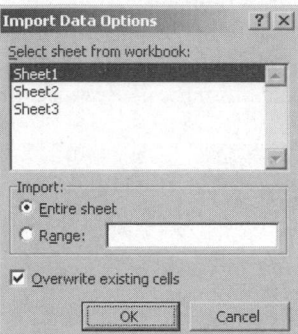

6 In the Import Data Options dialog box, click the worksheet or range that contains the chart, and then click OK.

After PowerPoint imports the Excel file and places it in the chart placeholder on the slide, you can animate the individual elements, but Excel does not open or update the chart when you double-click it.

To animate individual elements of a chart or diagram, follow these steps:

1 In Normal view, select the slide that contains the chart or diagram you want to animate.

2 Choose Slide Show, Custom Animation, if the Custom Animation task pane is not already open.

3 Select the chart, and in the Custom Animation task pane, click Add Effect to apply an animation to the chart or diagram as a whole.

4 Click the down arrow next to the effect you just applied to see the collapsed list of options, and then click Effect Options. The Effect Options dialog box appears.

5 In the Chart (or Diagram) Animation tab, in the Group Chart (or Group Diagram) list, select how you want to animate the elements of your chart or diagram, as seen here:

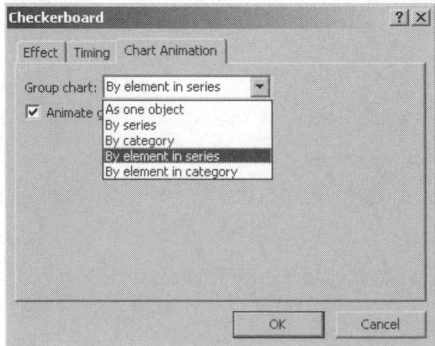

The animations you apply are listed in order in nonprinting numbered labels next to the element in Normal view when the Custom Animation task pane is open, as shown in Figure 34-4.

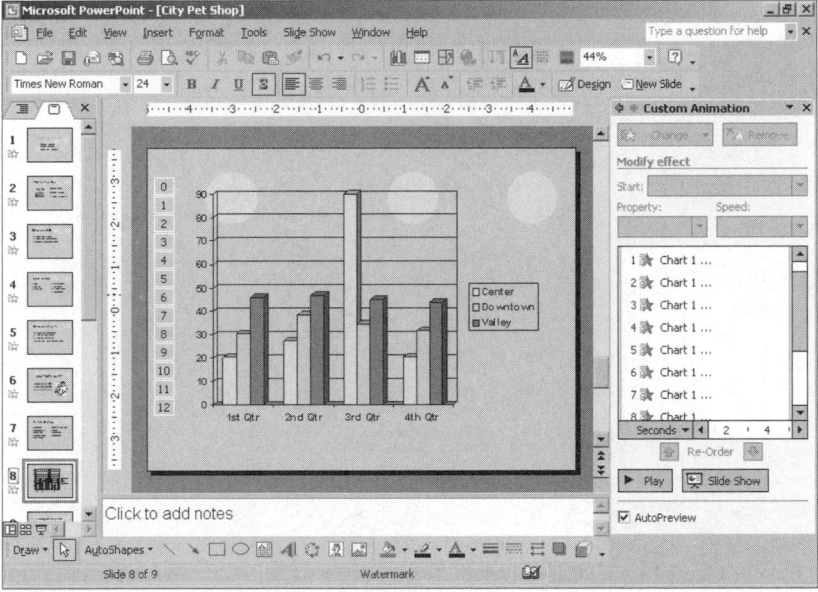

Figure 34-4. Animation sequences are numbered in order of application.

Creating Motion Paths

One of the new features in PowerPoint 2002 gives you the ability to draw the motion path that you want an object to follow during an animation. Creating a custom motion path is useful when you're creating several custom animation effects, and you need to bring in another element that must navigate among the pieces you've already placed on the slide. You can use the preset motion paths, but most of them follow a closed path: They begin and end at the same point. If you're creating a fairly complex animation sequence and want to use an open motion path, you can create a custom motion path using the familiar tools from the Drawing toolbar. An open motion path lets you draw your animated object's path so it begins at one part of the slide and ends at another.

To add a preset motion path, perform the following steps:

1 In Normal view, select the slide you want to add a motion path to.

2 Choose Slide Show, Custom Animation to open the Custom Animation task pane, if necessary.

3 Select the text or object to animate.

4 Click Add Effect in the Custom Animation task pane, point to Motion Paths, and click one of the predesigned paths, or click More Motion Paths to apply one of PowerPoint's additional motion paths. Figure 34-5 shows a bulleted item that follows a preset motion path as it moves right across a slide.

Figure 34-5. The preset motion path added here is indicated by the green and red arrows on the slide.

After you click the selected path, the motion path is previewed for you and an outline of the path appears in Normal view when you have the Custom Animation task pane open.

InsideOut

When you create a motion path for text or an object, typically you want it to move off the slide and disappear after it follows its path. To do so, you must either draw a custom path and drag the line off the slide or apply an enhancement to the effect that makes the text or object appear to exit. To apply an effect option, in the Custom Animation task pane, click the arrow next to the item in the list, and then click Effect Options to open the Effect Options dialog box. In the Effects tab, in the After Animation list, select Hide After Animation, and then click OK.

PowerPoint also makes it easy for you to draw your own motion path for an object. To create a custom motion path, follow the preceding procedure, but in the Custom Animation task pane, click Add Effect, point to Motion Paths, point to Draw Custom Path, and then click one of the following tools:

● Click Freeform to draw paths that contain both curves and straight segments.

> **tip** To gain more control over mouse movements when drawing shapes, you can adjust the tracking speed of your mouse in Microsoft Windows Control Panel to make it move slower.

- Click Scribble to draw paths that have smooth curves, and drag the pointer to create penlike lines.

- Click Line to draw a linear path, and press the Shift key while dragging the pointer to create perfectly straight lines.

- Click Curve to draw a curved path. Click where you want the path to start, move the pointer, and then click where you want another curve.

When you are finished creating the custom motion path, press Esc to stop drawing. You will see an outline of the path on your slide in Normal view when the Custom Animation task pane is open, as shown in Figure 34-6.

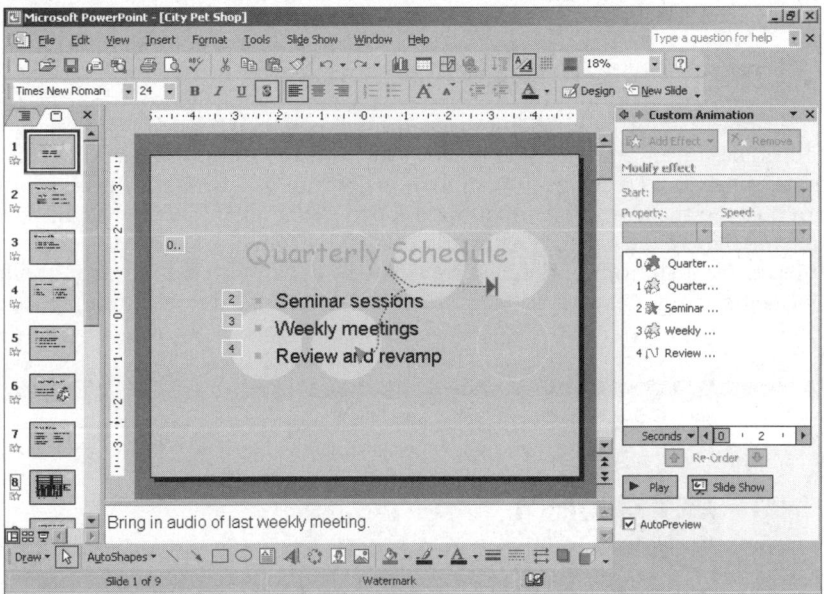

Figure 34-6. The custom motion path shown here moves between graphic elements on the background.

To edit this path, you can right-click it and then choose from the options on the shortcut menu. If you select Edit Points on the shortcut menu, you can move the start or end point of a motion path by dragging the small black squares, which are called *edit points*, to a new location, as shown in Figure 34-7, on page 924.

927

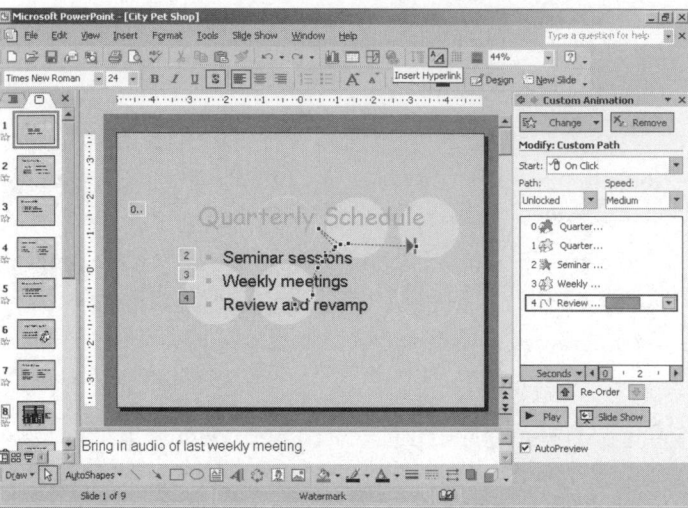

Figure 34-7.   Moving the edit points changes a motion path.

Setting Timings for Animations

PowerPoint's animation schemes have timings attached to them. PowerPoint contains additional timing controls that let you synchronize multiple text and object animations. When you create custom animations or want to change the preset timings, you can do so in the Custom Animation task pane. When you preview an animation (by clicking Play in the Custom Animation task pane when the slide is selected), a timeline appears at the bottom of the task pane. Here you can watch a moving timeline that clocks the seconds each item takes to move through its animation sequence, as shown in Figure 34-8.

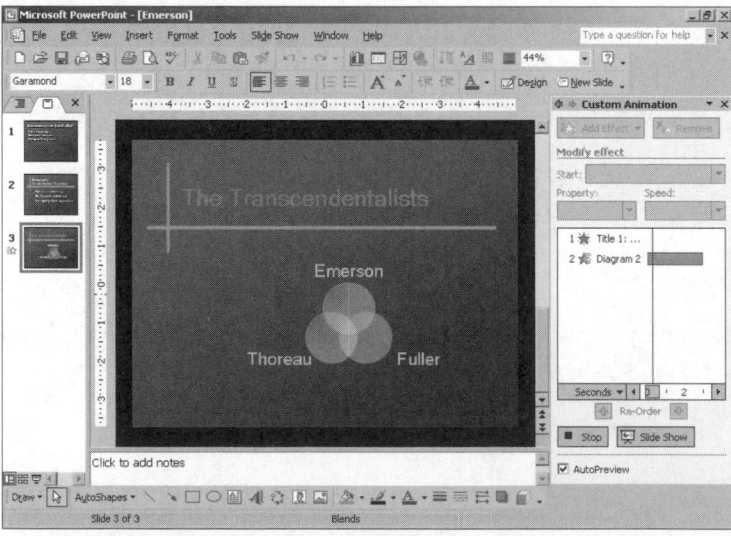

Figure 34-8.   Timings can be refined in the Custom Animation task pane.

Chapter 34

To set timing, perform the following steps:

1 In the Custom Animation task pane, select the slide for which you want to set timings.

2 Click the down arrow next to the item whose timings you want to modify, and then click Timing. The Timing dialog box appears, as shown here:

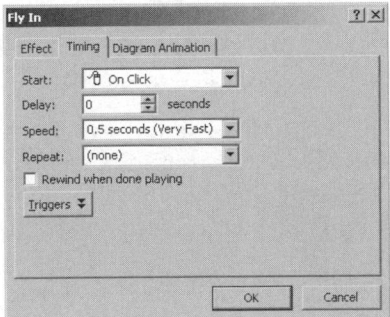

3 In the Start drop-down list, select On Click to specify starting the animation on a mouse click, select With Previous to specify starting at the same time as the previous animation, or select After Previous to start this animation right after the previous one.

4 To delay between animations, click the arrows in the Delay box to specify the amount of delay.

5 In the Speed drop-down list, specify the speed or duration of the animation.

6 To select looping options, in the Repeat drop-down list, click None, or the number of times you want the animation to repeat, or click Until Next Click, or click Until End of Slide.

7 Check the Rewind When Done Playing check box to automatically have PowerPoint rewind the animation, thus bringing it back to its starting point on the slide.

8 Click the Triggers button to add further control to when an animation occurs, as shown here:

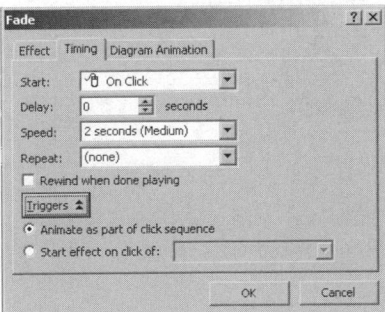

To change the sequence of animations, simply select the slide or slide element containing the effect, and drag it to a new location in the Custom Animation list in the Custom Animation task pane.

Applying Transitions

The purpose of a transition is to add visual interest as you move from one slide to the next. If you choose an animation scheme for your presentation, your slide show has built-in transitions. However, you may wish to fine-tune the look of your show by changing the default transition between one or more slides, or you may need to add transitions to a presentation that doesn't have a default scheme. The best way to do this is in Normal view, where you can select one or more slides using the Slides tab and then select transition effects using the Custom Animation task pane.

If you want to apply a new transition effect to all the slides in your presentation, you don't need to select the slides first. Instead, click the transition you want in the task pane and then click the Apply To All Slides button at the bottom of the task pane. PowerPoint immediately applies the transition you've selected to all the slides.

To apply transitions to selected slides, follow these steps:

1 Choose View, Normal, if it is not already selected.

2 In the Slides tab, click one or more slides that you want to change the animation transitions for. To select multiple slides, press Shift while you click. Press Ctrl to select noncontiguous slides.

3 Choose Slide Show, Slide Transition to open the Slide Transition task pane. The Slide Transition task pane opens, as shown in Figure 34-9.

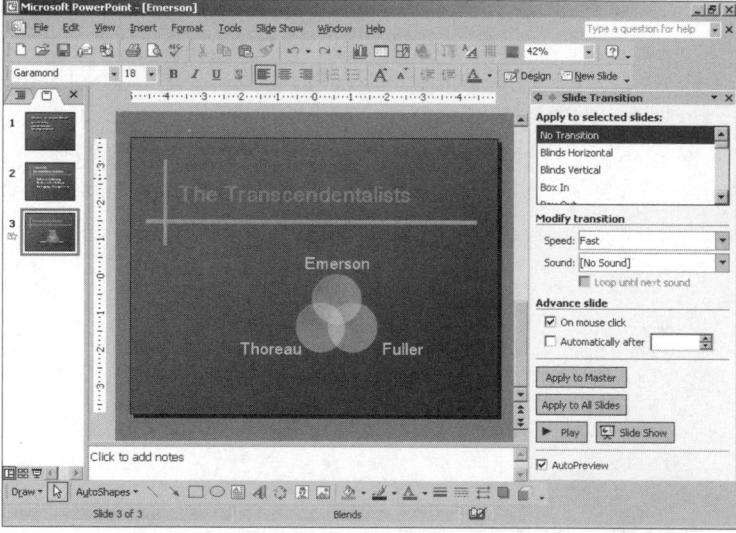

Figure 34-9. The Slide Transition task pane includes options for customizing slide transitions.

4 Select a transition from the task pane and use the other available options to control the speed and movement characteristics of the transition.

After you specify a transition for a slide, PowerPoint runs a preview of the transition. When you switch to the Custom Animation task pane, an icon of a star that appears to be in motion appears next to the slide in the Custom Animation list, identifying the presence of a slide transition.

5 To preview the transition again, select the slide you want to view, and then click Play in the Custom Animation task pane, or click Slide Show to view all the animations and transitions for your slides.

You can apply different transitions to different slides or groups of slides, so you may want to select groups of similar slides and assign each group a transition type. The transition effect appears when the slide is first opened, although if you add a similar exit animation, it can mimic the transition that introduces the slide.

Creating Hyperlinks and Action Buttons

Hyperlinks can provide connections between nonsequential slides, other PowerPoint presentations, documents created in other Microsoft Office programs, and, if the computer you're using to present your show has an Internet connection, Web pages.

Hyperlinks can be either text, which is underlined in a color you specify, or an object, such as a picture or a chart. You can add action settings for hyperlinks so that a sound plays or highlighting occurs when you click or move your pointer over the hyperlink. By default, PowerPoint creates a hyperlink every time you type an e-mail address or URL on a slide.

To create a hyperlink, perform the following steps:

1 Select the text or object you want to create a hyperlink for.

2 Choose Insert, Hyperlink, or click the Insert Hyperlink button on the Standard toolbar to open the Insert Hyperlink dialog box.

3 Enter the location of the link to the item and edit the text in the Text To Display text box, if you want. (If you're linking an object, the Text To Display box is not available.)

4 If you're linking to a Web page, click the ScreenTip button to supply text to be displayed when you move the pointer over the hyperlink in the Set Hyperlink ScreenTip dialog box, shown here:

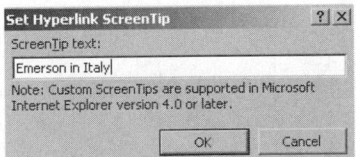

When you select the destination of the hyperlink, other than one connecting to another slide, its location is formulated as a URL or address on the Internet or an intranet. When you create a hyperlink to a file on your own computer, the hyperlink destination is called a *path*. An example of a path is shown in Figure 34-10.

Chapter 34

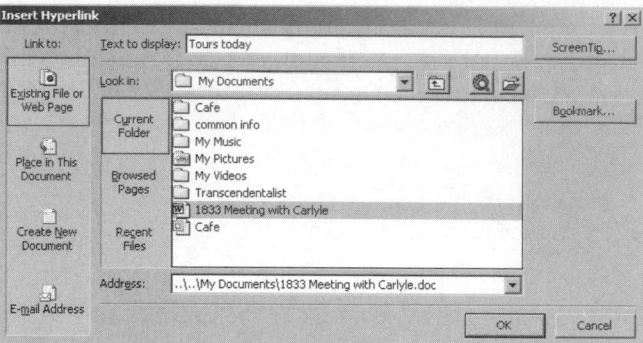

Figure 34-10. You can enter a path to a Microsoft Word document stored on the presenter's hard drive.

The link between the destination file and the hyperlink can be broken in several ways: if you move the file that is linked, if the URL changes, if the location of a shared folder changes, or if you misspell the URL. Always click each link in Slide Show view to test it before you present your show. Make sure that the Internet links open correctly in your browser. (Hyperlinks are not active in Normal view, but when you run your presentation in Slide Show view, you can activate them with a click.)

Adding Action Buttons

Action buttons are predesigned buttons that you can insert into a presentation and specify a hyperlink for. Within the presentation, the action buttons appear as icons on a slide, as shown in this example, and you just click the button to jump to a new location.

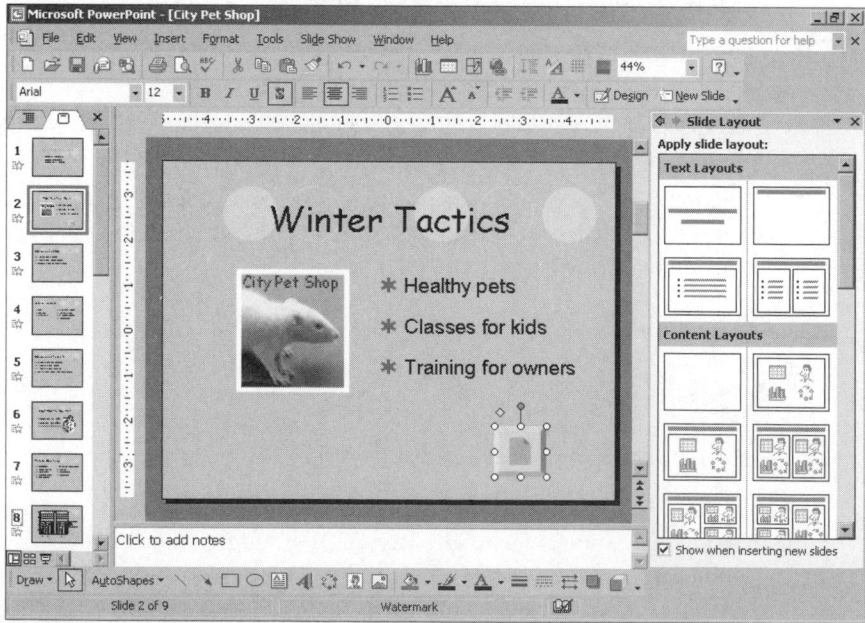

Chapter 34: Adding Special Effects and Hyperlinks

Typically, action buttons are used because the icons are easy-to-understand navigational elements (such as Home, Help, Back, or Forward), and are most often applied to self-running presentations. Action buttons let users interact easily with a presentation, such as one running in a trade-show booth or kiosk.

When you create an action button on a slide, you specify the button you want to use, identify the mouse movement you want to trigger the action, and then specify where you want to move to. When you run the presentation in Slide Show view, the buttons are enabled, and when you click one, PowerPoint immediately moves to that specific assigned location.

To create an action button to a specific slide or file, perform the following steps:

1 In Normal view, display the slide on which you want to create the hyperlink.

2 Choose Slide Show, Action Buttons and choose one of the action buttons on the submenu.

PowerPoint supplies several intuitive shapes for different types of hyperlinks you might want to create. The Return button is shown in Figure 34-11. Different shapes are especially useful when you're adding more than one button to a slide.

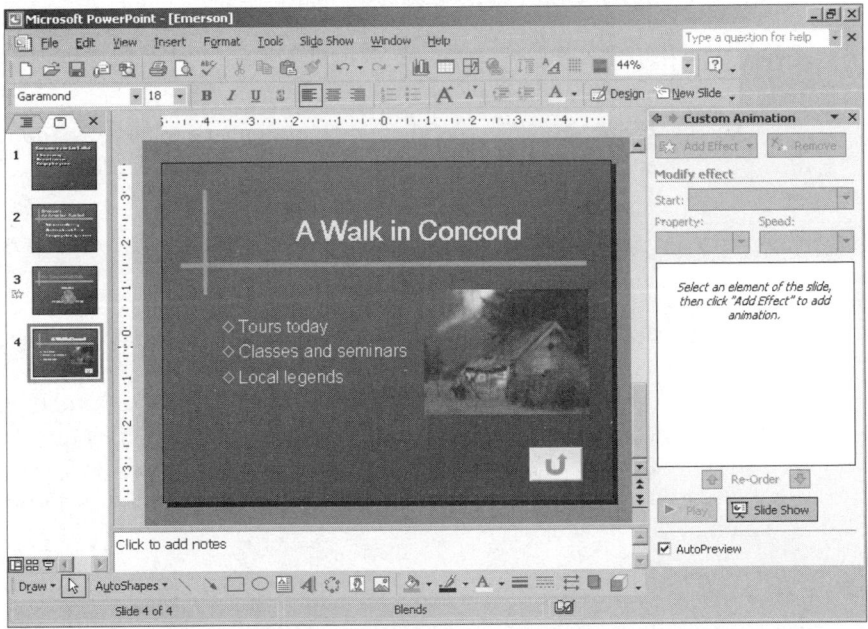

Figure 34-11. This slide's action button lets you return to another source of information during your presentation.

3 Drag the mouse on the slide to create the action button. When you release the mouse button, the Action Settings dialog box appears, as seen here:

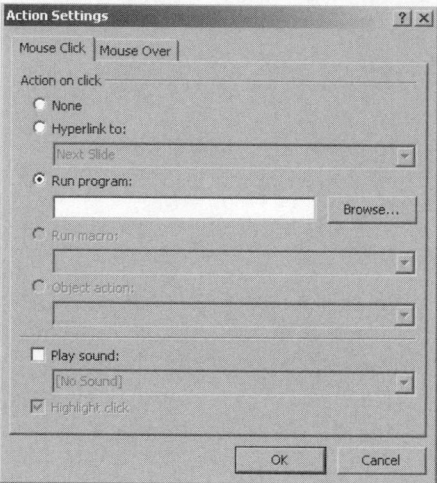

4 If you want to activate the hyperlink by clicking, use the Mouse Click tab. If you'd rather activate the link by simply placing the mouse pointer over the button, click the Mouse Over tab. Both tabs have identical controls.

5 In the Hyperlink To drop-down list, choose the location you want to move to using your action button.

6 If you want to play a sound during the jump, check the Play Sound check box and select a sound in the drop-down list, and then click OK.

Running Another Program

If you want to open a Windows-based application without loading a specific file, you can click the Run Program option in the Action Settings dialog box and use the Browse button to select the name of an application program (.exe file) on your system. You might find this technique useful if you want the ability to respond to audience requests during a presentation, such as demonstrating an application feature during a training session. When you activate the action button during your show, you'll launch another application. To return to your presentation at the current slide, exit the application as you normally would.

Chapter 35

Setting Up and Presenting the Slide Show

After you've created a slide show that makes your points as clearly as possible, rehearse your presentation so that you are comfortable with the content, flow, and timing of your material. Then decide on the medium that you'll use to present your slides. You can deliver your presentation on-screen, using a computer and a projector, or over the Web, either by saving the presentation as a Web page or by broadcasting a live presentation. You can also transform your slides into overhead transparencies, 35mm slides, or printed handouts.

If you travel and you want to run your slide show from another computer, just use the Pack And Go Wizard to compress your presentation and copy it to disk. Then you or any other presenter can run the slide show from another computer, even if it doesn't have PowerPoint installed on it.

When you're working on presentations with a team, you can incorporate comments from multiple reviewers, using the options in the new Revisions task pane. This chapter discusses how you can fine-tune your presentation before you run your slide show, how to actually run a presentation, how to create notes and handouts to accompany it, and how to collaborate with others by sending presentations for review.

In this chapter, you'll learn about

- Rehearsing slide timings
- Recording narration
- Creating a custom show
- Creating notes and handouts
- Delivering an electronic presentation

935

- Delivering presentations on the Web
- Broadcasting presentations
- Reviewing presentations

Picking a Presentation Medium

PowerPoint 2002 includes a number of presentation options to let you display your slide show. You can deliver an electronic slide show, typically presented from a notebook computer connected to a projector; a presentation of overhead transparencies or 35mm slides projected on a large screen; a Web-based presentation of slides saved in HTML; or a live presentation broadcast over the Web.

If you choose an electronic presentation, you can set up your slide show in three ways:

- To be presented full screen by an individual—the most common method. With this method, you'll have complete control of the slide show from beginning to end. You can skip slides, stop the presentation, add meeting minutes, and so on.

- To be presented in a window along with navigation controls—designed for presentations that you want to distribute to colleagues or send out over a network.

- To be presented at an automated kiosk—a method that creates a self-running presentation suitable for a demonstration at a kiosk or trade show.

In addition, you can control which slides are included in the final presentation, how narration and animation are used, and how the slides advance.

To pick the show type, complete the following steps:

1 Choose Slide Show, Set Up Show. You'll see the following dialog box:

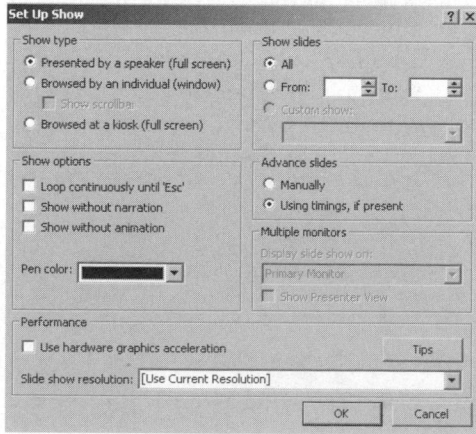

2 Specify the show type—speaker (full screen), individual (window), or kiosk (full screen).

3 Specify which slides you want included in the show. You can include all the slides (the default), a slide range, or a custom slide show. (For more information about custom shows, see "Creating a Custom Show," on page 942.)

4 Under Advance slides, specify whether you want to advance the slides manually or by using timings if they're present. (You create slide timings by using the Rehearsal toolbar, as you'll learn in "Rehearsing the Show," on page 938.)

5 When you're finished setting up the show, click OK. To see how your choices have affected the presentation, choose Slide Show, View Show, or click the Slide Show button in the Slide Design – Animation, Custom Animation, or Slide Transition task pane.

Using Overheads

If you have an inkjet or laser printer, you can load the printer's paper tray with overhead transparencies made especially for such printers. Before you print your slides on overheads, you must check the page setup. Choose File, Page Setup to open the Page Setup dialog box, shown here:

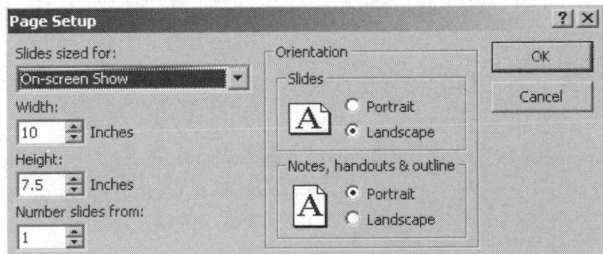

Use the options here to change to Overheads as the medium for which the slides are sized, and adjust the dimensions of the printed page to fit your overheads, as well as specify the orientation of the slides and other handout pages.

You can print your slides in grayscale, black and white, or color on transparencies, just as if they were paper. When you're ready to print, choose File, Print. To print your presentation in color on transparencies, you must choose a color printer from the Name list in the Printer section of the Print dialog box. You'll produce a set of high-quality transparencies that you can project on an overhead projector. However, if you need higher resolution and richer color reproduction than your printer provides, you can send your overheads to a service bureau to have digital color overheads made.

Ordering 35mm Slides

When your slide show includes technical images that require high-quality image resolution and contrast, your solution is to project 35mm slides onto a large screen. Make sure that the room in which you're going to use the slide projector is darkened as much as possible. For high-quality image resolution, have a service bureau turn the presentation files into professional 35mm slides for you. Before you do this, contact the service bureau, and ask if they have any special instructions for preparing your files. You can often send your files electronically and get your presentation materials back via overnight delivery.

Preparing an Electronic Presentation

A professional-looking electronic presentation fills a computer screen with your slides and keeps the audience interested with various special effects such as animation, transitions, and timings. For a small audience, you can use a desktop or notebook computer. For a large audience, you'll need a larger monitor or projection technology such as an LCD (liquid crystal display) projector that connects directly to your computer, as well as a non-glare projection screen.

Rehearsing the Show

Rehearsals are the backbone of any professional production, whether it's a Broadway play or a company slide show. Rehearsing your presentation is important so that you know what to say and when to say it, as well as to make sure that you don't run over or under your allotted time. You don't want to have to improvise if you run short or race through your material if you run long. Even worse, if you run over your time limit at a busy conference, you could be asked to leave the podium whether you're finished or not.

PowerPoint can time your presentation so that it fits precisely into the allotted time. There are two ways to rehearse timings: automatically and manually.

You can have PowerPoint automatically determine the length of time to display each slide by recording the timings while you rehearse your presentation. To use the Rehearse Timings feature, follow these steps:

1 Open the presentation that you want to rehearse and choose Slide Show, Set Up Show to specify the slides that you want to include. The Set Up Show dialog box appears, as seen here:

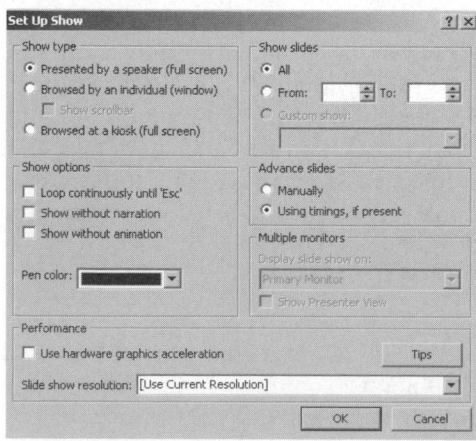

Make your changes and close the dialog box.

2 Choose Slide Show, Rehearse Timings. When the full-screen version of your first slide appears on screen, rehearse exactly what you'll tell your audience about this slide, using your notes and moving through the animation and transitions you've applied. The Rehearsal toolbar counts the seconds that the slide remains on screen, as shown in Figure 35-1.

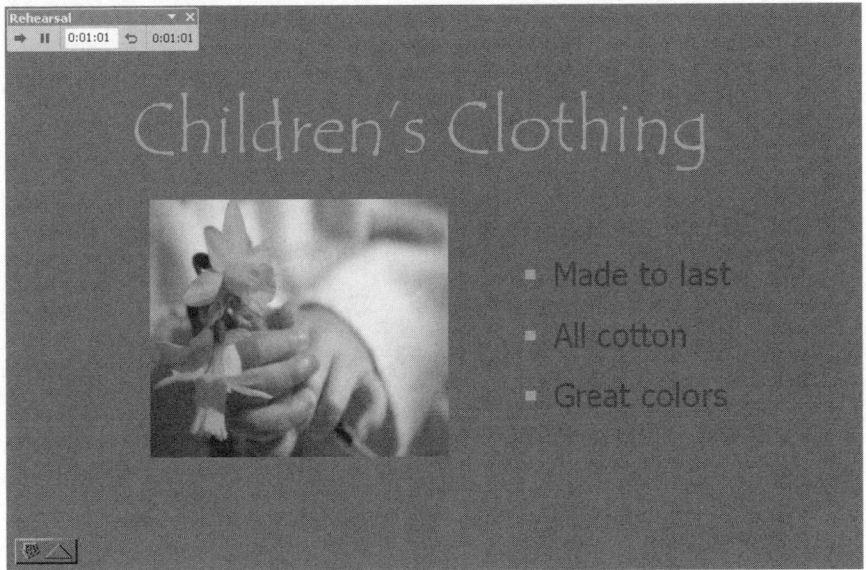

Figure 35-1. You can time slides by using the Rehearsal toolbar.

> **tip** Your audience's attention can wander if you spend too much time on a slide. If you intend to spend more than two or three minutes on the topic covered on one slide, make two or three slides for this subject. On the other hand, if a slide takes only a few seconds to discuss, it's probably too elementary and could be combined with another slide.

To move to the next element on your slide (bulleted item or graphical element) or to the next slide, click the Next button to advance the slides manually. This resets the counter in the center, which measures the time spent on the current slide.

To pause a slide and temporarily stop both time counters, click the Pause button. When you want to continue, click the Pause button again.

To start over with a slide, click the Repeat button.

3 To stop rehearsing and return to Normal view, click the Close button on the Rehearsal toolbar.

4 If you know the exact timing you want to assign to a slide, you can enter it in the Slide Time box on the Rehearsal toolbar.

After you have finished with the last slide, the timing information box appears, giving you the total elapsed time for your presentation.

5 If you want to accept the timings, click Yes. If you want to rehearse again, click No. If you click Yes, the slides open in Slide Sorter view with the timing displayed beneath each slide, as shown in Figure 35-2.

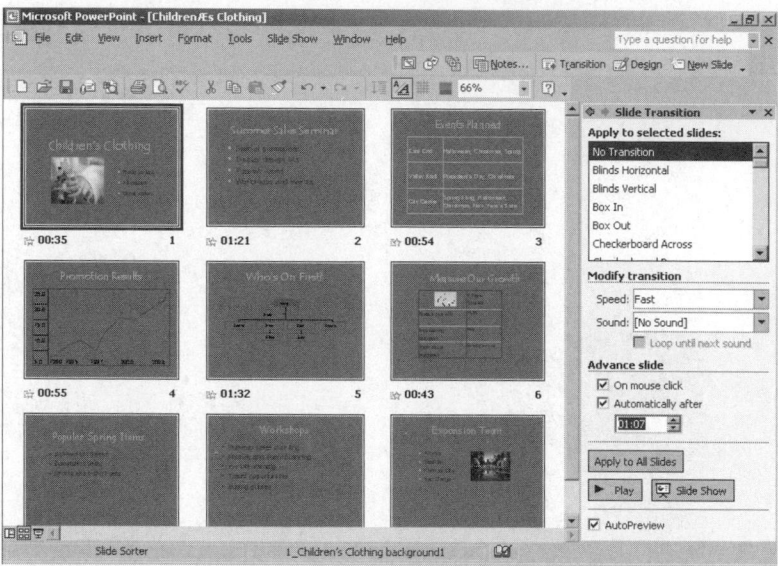

Figure 35-2. The rehearsal timings in Slide Sorter view.

Setting Timings Manually

When you want tight control over the pace of your presentation, you can set timings manually for the exact amount of time that you want each slide to remain on the screen. To set slide timings manually:

1 In Normal view, select the slide or slides you want to set timings for on the Slides tab.

2 Choose Slide Show, Slide Transition. The Slide Transition task pane appears. If you had already set a timing for the slide, you'll see a timing in the task pane, as shown in Figure 35-2.

3 Under Advance Slide, select the Automatically After check box, and use the arrows in the list box to enter the time in seconds that you want the slide to remain on the screen.

4 Repeat the above steps for each slide in your show.

After you rehearse the timings for your slide show, you can either run the show using the timings or remove the slide timings and advance the slides manually.

To advance slides manually:

1 On the Slides tab in Normal view, select those slides you want to control manually.

2 In the Slide Transition task pane under Advance Slide, select On Mouse Click and clear Automatically After in the Advance section of the Slide Transition dialog box.

If both Advance options are selected, the slides will advance automatically after the specified number of seconds has elapsed; to advance the slide sooner, you can do so manually by clicking the mouse.

Recording Narration

If you want to include narration during your slide show, a feature typically used in presentations that are self-running or Web-based, you can easily do this. With PowerPoint, you can add voice narration to a slide show so that you can prepare a final presentation in advance, complete with recorded material in your own voice. If you want to record narration or comments for single slides, you can do so, but PowerPoint treats these as individual .wav files, displayed with a sound icon on each slide that you must click to play the sound.

To record a voice narration, you'll need a sound card, a microphone, and a set of speakers.

Complete these steps:

1 Choose Slide Show, Record Narration. The Record Narration dialog box appears, showing the amount of free disk space and the number of minutes you can record, as shown here:

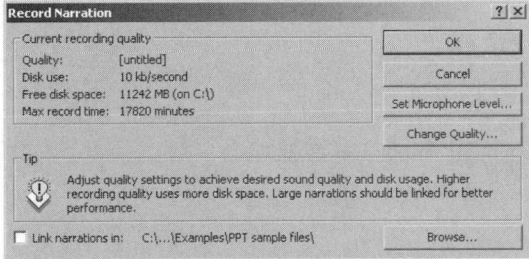

2 Click the Set Microphone Level button to calibrate your microphone.

3 Click the Change Quality button and use the options in the Sound Selection dialog box to customize the recording or playback.

4 To begin recording, click OK in the Record Narration dialog box.

5 Record voice content for each slide in your presentation, clicking to move from one slide to the next. PowerPoint records the narration with timings for each slide.

6 If you want to stop the narration for any reason, right-click anywhere in the slide, and then click Pause Narration on the shortcut menu. When you're ready to resume, right-click and then click Resume Narration.

7 When you're finished with the recording, PowerPoint displays a dialog box asking whether to save your narration with your slide timings. To do this, click Save. To

Chapter 35

Part 5: PowerPoint

save the narration only, click Don't Save. Your presentation will then open in Slide Sorter view with a sound icon displayed in the lower right corner of each slide.

If you want to synchronize your narration with each slide it accompanies, you must click Save.

When you run the slide show, the narration will play automatically. The narration overrides any other sounds you've added to the slide show, so you'll hear only your narration. If you want to hear additional sounds, consider adding them to the narration as background. If the sound clips are important for a particular audience, you can run the slide show without narration by choosing Slide Show, Set Up Show and then selecting the Show Without Narration check box.

Creating a Custom Show

The Custom Shows command on the Slide Show menu lets you create a short list of alternate slide shows based on the slides in your presentation. For example, you might want to drop out a few slides for sales reps in your organization who don't need to know your production staff's editorial policies. After you create a custom show, you can then specify it when you're configuring your show's presentation options in the Set Up Show dialog box.

To create a custom show:

1 Open the slide show you want to select slides from, and choose Slide Show, Custom Shows. The Custom Shows dialog box appears, as seen here, listing your current collection of custom shows (if any).

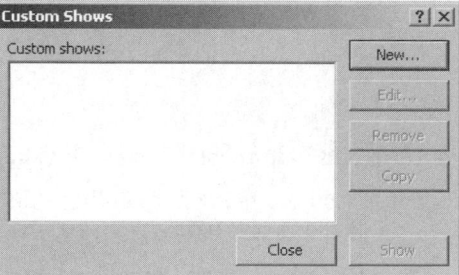

2 To edit, remove, copy, or show one of these presentations, click the appropriate buttons in the dialog box.

3 To define a new custom show, click the New button, type a name for your custom show, and then specify the slides you want to include by selecting the slide titles and clicking Add.

The following illustration shows how to create a custom slide show using the Define Custom Show dialog box:

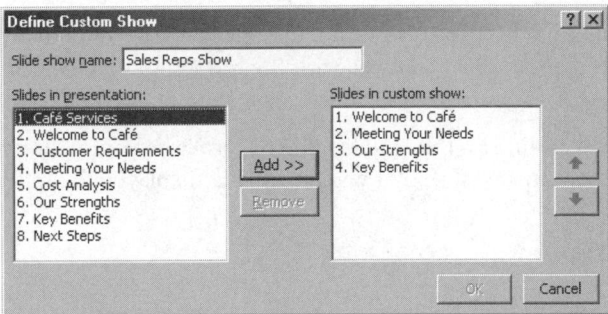

Hiding Slides

You can place information you want to reveal only to a certain audience or only at a certain time on a hidden slide. To hide a slide, select the slide on the Slide tab in Normal view, and choose Slide Show, Hide Slide. The slide will appear on the Slides tab with a strikethrough on its slide number, as shown in Figure 35-3.

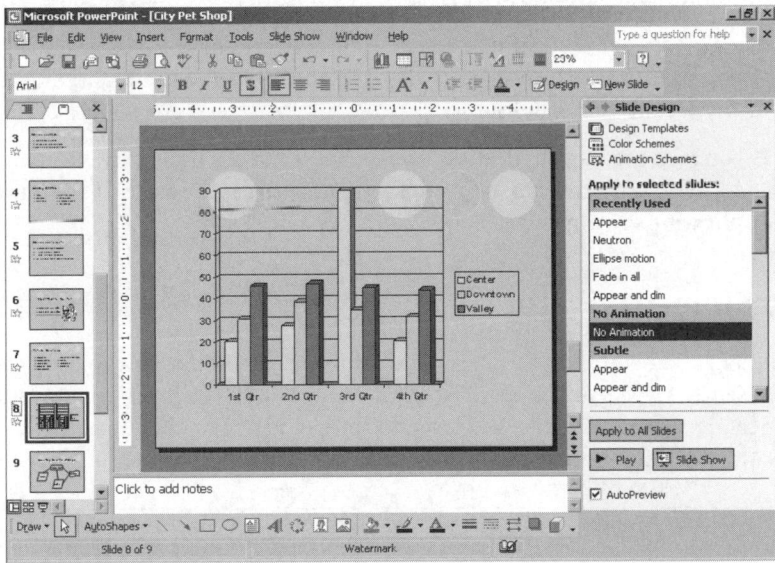

Figure 35-3. A hidden slide is marked with a slash through the slide number on the Slides tab, as well as in Slide Sorter view and in the Slide Navigator. (In this figure, slide 8 is hidden.)

To reveal a hidden slide when you show a presentation, do one of the following actions:

- From the slide that precedes the hidden slide, press H to unveil the hidden slide.

- From the slide that logically precedes the hidden slide (for example, from the slide that asks the question you answer with the hidden one), create a hyperlink to the hidden slide.

- Create another hyperlink on the hidden slide to return to your slide show. This way your audience won't realize that you're actually displaying a hidden slide.

Using Action Buttons

When you arrive at a slide that contains an action button, click the button to branch to another slide, to begin another presentation, to start another Microsoft Office XP program, or to connect to the Web.

For more information about action buttons, see "Creating Hyperlinks and Action Buttons," on page 931.

- If you created an action button on the slide to which you branched, click that button to return to the original slide or to move to a different slide.

- If you branched to another presentation, PowerPoint automatically returns you to the slide from which you branched in your original presentation at the end of the second presentation.

- If you launched an application, you can edit the document live for your audience. When you're ready to move to the next slide, choose Exit from the application's File menu.

Using the Slide Navigator

When navigating your way through a slide show, if you're not able to use PowerPoint's new Presenter view, you can click a slide or use the shortcut menu to move to slides in sequence or to a specific slide. However, to find a particular slide that you want to discuss with your audience, use Slide Navigator.

Presenter view is described in detail in "Working in Presenter View," on page 948.

To use the Slide Navigator, follow these steps:

1 In Slide Show view, right click a slide.

2 On the shortcut menu, point to Go, and then choose Slide Navigator from the submenu. You'll see the following dialog box:

Slide Navigator contains a list of all the slides in your show and displays the name of the last slide shown. Notice that the slide number for a hidden slide is enclosed in parentheses.

3 To jump to a slide that's out of sequence, find the slide in the Slide Titles list, and double-click it.

Using the Pen to Mark Slides

When you want to annotate your PowerPoint slides, you can use the Pen feature during an electronic slide show, just as you would use a marking pen on overhead transparencies.

To use the Pen feature during a slide show:

1 Right-click a slide, point to Pointer Options, Pen on the shortcut menu, and then click Pen.

2 Using the pen-shaped pointer, hold down the mouse button to draw on a slide, as shown here:

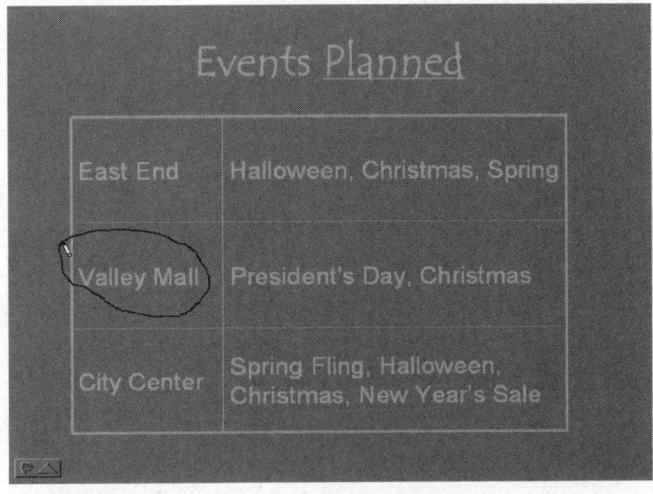

945

3 Press Enter or the spacebar to move to the next animation or slide.

> **note** The writing or drawing that you add to a slide during a show is a temporary overlay; it doesn't stay on the slide once you've moved on to another slide in your show.

4 To change the pen color, right-click a slide, point to Pointer Options, point to the Pen Color submenu, and pick a new color.

5 To return to the regular mouse pointer, press Ctrl+A.

6 To erase the pen markings, press E.

Using Meeting Minder

PowerPoint's Meeting Minder is a helpful reminder tool that lets you create action items and record minutes of the meeting—as well as schedule appointments in Outlook—while you're delivering your presentation. Use Meeting Minder to record the minutes as the meeting progresses, typing up the important points or items to be acted on. After the meeting, transfer your minutes to your note pages or to a new Microsoft Word document. From there, you can print them and distribute copies to all the attendees and to those people who couldn't attend.

Finally, you can start Outlook from the Meeting Minder to update your schedule or handle other administrative tasks. To select this option, you need a working copy of Outlook on your system that has a copy of your schedule.

Follow these steps to work with Meeting Minder:

1 During your show, right-click a slide and choose Meeting Minder from the shortcut menu.

2 Click the appropriate tab that indicates what you'd like to do, or click Schedule to start Outlook.

3 If you're adding an action item or meeting minute, type it in the space provided, as shown in the following dialog box:

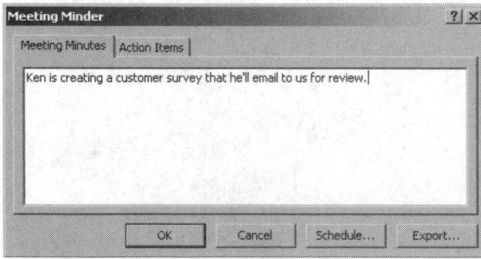

4 To export action items and meeting minutes to a Word document, click Export. Edit the text in Word, if necessary, then save the document and exit Word. When you are finished with the Meeting Minder, click OK.

Chapter 35: Setting Up and Presenting the Slide Show

Action items are added to a new slide at the end of the current presentation. You can refine this information into a finished slide or print it the same way that you print other note pages and slides.

Giving an Electronic Presentation

To launch your presentation on the big screen:

- From Windows Explorer, right-click the PowerPoint presentation file, and choose Show from the shortcut menu. During the presentation, your slides appear in Slide Show view. When you finish the show, you're returned to Windows Explorer.

- Within PowerPoint, open your show in Normal view and move to the slide that you want to show first. To start, click the Slide Show button at the bottom of the Slide Design – Animation, Custom Animation, or Slide Transition task pane, or click the Slide Show icon at the bottom left of the PowerPoint window.

- To start your show by using a command, choose Slide Show, View Show, or choose View, Slide Show.

Whichever method you use to start your slide show, the first slide appears on screen. You'll talk about your first slide, and then, if your show is automatically timed, the slide disappears from the screen, using the transition effect you've specified, and the ncxt slide immediately appears. If your show doesn't have timings, simply click the slide when you're finished with it and advance to the next slide.

During your show, an icon with an up arrow button appears in the lower left corner of your screen as soon as you move the mouse. When you click this button, you see a shortcut menu. (You can also display this menu by right-clicking a slide.) This menu appears only in Slide Show view, and it's specifically designed to give you fast access to all the commands you need while a show is running.

947

The simplest way to move manually to the next slide in sequence is to click the slide. If you prefer to use the shortcut menu, choose Next or Previous from it. To move to a specific slide, type the slide number, and press Enter.

The mouse pointer arrow appears on the screen when you move the mouse, but you can change its color or remove it by using commands on the Pointer Options submenu. The arrow is often useful for pointing to various text and objects on your slides. If you don't want the mouse arrow pointer or the shortcut menu button to appear on screen, you can hide both of them. Press Ctrl+H to hide the pointer and button for the entire show. Even when you've hidden the pointer, you can still click your mouse to move to the next slide.

> **tip**   **Call for Help with F1**
>
> If, in the middle of delivering your presentation, you suddenly forget which slide show controls to use—for example, the actions and keys for moving between slides, or for hiding and displaying the arrow pointer, button, or hidden slides—all you have to do is press the F1 key. This key displays a list of controls anytime during your presentation.

Working in Presenter View

If you have Windows 98, Windows Millennium Edition (Me), or Windows 2000 installed on your desktop computer and two video cards (one for each monitor), you can run your slide show from one computer and let your audience view it on another monitor. PowerPoint 2002 supports dual-monitor capability.

One monitor can present the slide show to your audience, and your own computer monitor can display PowerPoint's Presenter view, which makes it easy for you to navigate through your presentation, as shown in Figure 35-4.

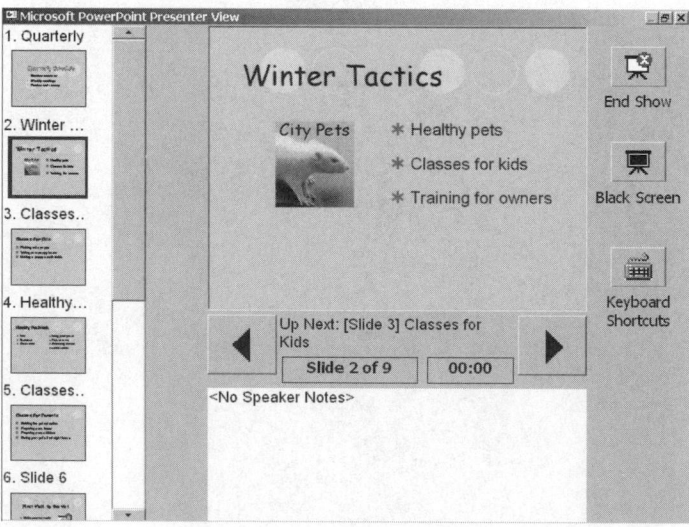

Figure 35-4.   Presenter view provides a preview of what's up next in your slide show.

> **note** Dual-monitor support for laptop or portable computers is not currently supported by the Windows 2000 or Windows Me operating systems. When you want to run a slide show from a laptop that will be displayed on two monitors, you must have Windows 98 installed on the laptop. In this case, you do not need to install two video cards, the video card feature is built into most portable computers shipping today. However, you can run your slide show on two desktop monitors when you have Windows 98 or later versions of the operating system installed on your computer.

To work in Presenter view, you must turn on dual-monitor support. To set up dual-monitor support, you need to consult the display settings in the Control Panel in Windows and the hardware specifications for your monitor. After you've set up dual-monitor support, you can access Presenter view by following these steps:

1   Choose Slide Show, Set Up Show.

2   In the Set Up Show dialog box, under Multiple Monitors, click the Show Presenter View check box to select it.

3   Under Display Slide Show On, specify the monitor you will use to present your slide show and click OK.

In this view, you can perform the following actions:

● Select slides out of sequence on the Slides tab to spontaneously create custom shows.

● View preview text displayed under the slide area that tells you what your next click brings to the screen, whether it is an animation sequence, a media clip, or a new slide.

● Read speaker notes in a special, enlarged point size.

● Black out your screen during a slide show and then return to the slide you left on the screen.

Printing Slides, Notes Pages, and Handouts

In many cases, you'll want to print your entire presentation, including your outline, slides, notes, and audience handouts. Even when you're presenting your material electronically, you can print your notes and handouts to rehearse with, to pass around to colleagues for a critique, or to fill information gaps.

The process for producing the actual material for your presentation is the same, no matter what type of output you choose:

1   Determine which printer you want to use, and open the presentation that you want to print.

Part 5: PowerPoint

2 Set up your slides by choosing the output medium (paper or transparencies, for example) and orientation, such as portrait or landscape.

3 Start producing the material.

To print your presentation, follow these steps:

1 Open the presentation that you want to print, choose File, Page Setup, and select the appropriate size for your medium in the Slides sized for list. Click OK.

2 Choose File, Print. The Print dialog box for the default printer opens. The default printer in the following dialog box is an HP Laserjet 4/4M.

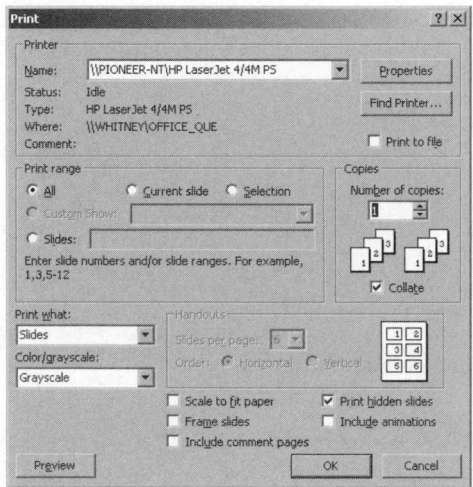

3 Specify the slides that you want to print in the Print range area, and in the Print What drop-down list, select the material to be printed. Your options are slides, handouts, notes, or an outline of your presentation.

You can print your entire presentation, the current slide, selected slides, a custom show, or a particular slide range.

4 To print hidden slides, select the appropriate boxes, and click OK to begin printing the selected portion of your presentation.

Creating Notes Pages

When you print your slides in Notes Page view, by default, PowerPoint prints the notes below a placeholder containing the slide. (For more information on creating notes, see "Understanding PowerPoint Views," on page 846) You can add richer content to the Notes Page view by adding a picture, diagram, or chart to the page to further illustrate your points. In fact, it's a good idea to include additional information in the notes and handouts that you supply your audience, and not just distribute in print the exact presentation that you deliver to them electronically.

Chapter 35: Setting Up and Presenting the Slide Show

To add content to the Notes Page:

1 Choose View, Notes Page.

2 Choose Format, Notes Layout to add or remove the slide image or body text placeholder from the page, or reapply the Notes Master.

3 Choose Format, Notes Background to edit the background or color scheme of the page.

4 In Notes Page view, click the slide or body text placeholder to reposition, resize, delete, or reshape them.

5 Click the Body text placeholder, and then on the Insert menu, choose the appropriate command (Picture, Diagram, Chart, Table, etc.) to add an object that further illustrates your point. Figure 36-5 shows an organizational chart inserted on a notes page.

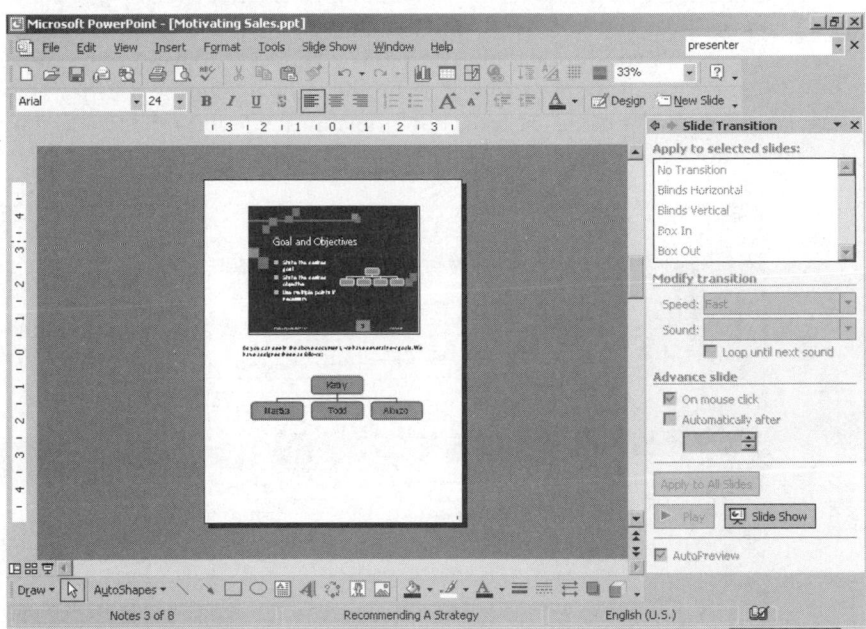

Figure 35-5. Adding more detailed information to a notes page increases its value as a handout.

6 Choose File, Print Preview, and select Notes Pages from the Print What list to view how your notes pages will print with the graphics or background you've added. The Notes pane in Normal view does not reflect how your notes pages will look when printed.

For more information on the Print Preview window, see "Using Print Preview to View a Presentation," on page 849.

7 To make global changes to your notes pages, choose View, Master, and then click Notes Master. On the Notes Master, you can format the header and footer, as well as apply any repeating graphic element that you want to appear on every notes page.

Updating Your Speaker Notes

You can also amend your speaker notes during a presentation by choosing Speaker Notes from the Slide Show view's shortcut menu. You might find this command useful if you find a mistake in your notes while you're giving a presentation, or if you think of a new analogy for explaining a tricky point. Your edits will appear in the Notes pane of Normal view the next time you need them.

Creating Handouts

You can create handouts in PowerPoint, which are printed pages containing one or more slides (up to nine) that you can distribute to your audience to help them follow along with your presentation. When you choose the layout that features three slides to a page, you also can provide lines on the right side of the page for your audience to take notes. The lined space is not visible until you view the handout in Print Preview, as shown in Figure 35-6.

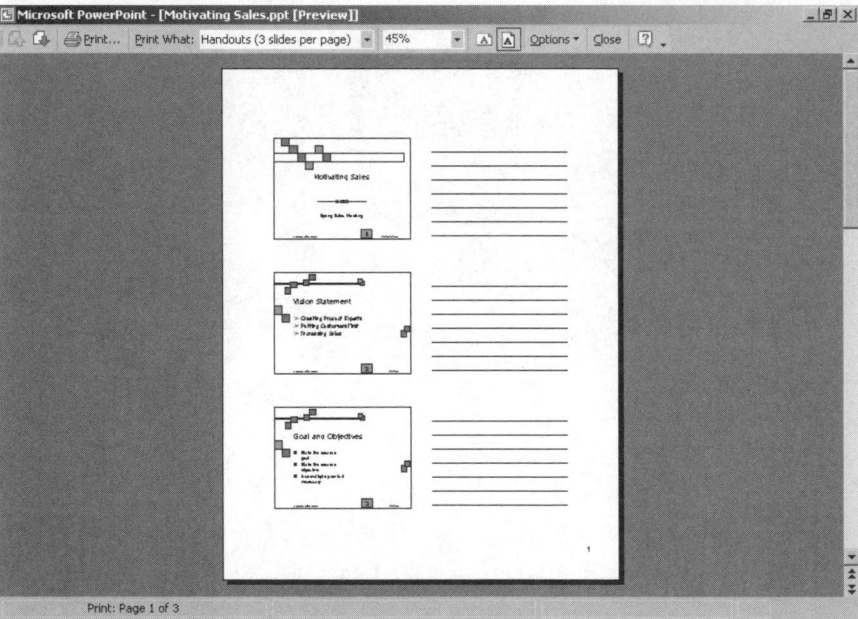

Figure 36-6. Switch to Print Preview to see the lined notes area.

As when working with Notes pages, you can format global changes to your handouts by using the master slide for this view—the Handouts master in this case.

Using Pack and Go

Many presenters run their presentations on a computer that is waiting for them at their destination. If that computer doesn't have PowerPoint installed on it, you can still run the slide show from that computer using PowerPoint's Pack and Go feature. Pack and Go creates a package, which contains a compressed copy of your presentation, along with all its multimedia files that you copy to disks, as well as the PowerPoint Viewer. The PowerPoint Viewer is a mini-application that lets you run your slide show from a computer that doesn't have PowerPoint installed on it.

To pack up your presentation to go, follow these instructions:

1 Open the presentation that you want to compress and save to disks.

2 Choose File, Pack And Go. The Pack And Go Wizard opens, as shown here:

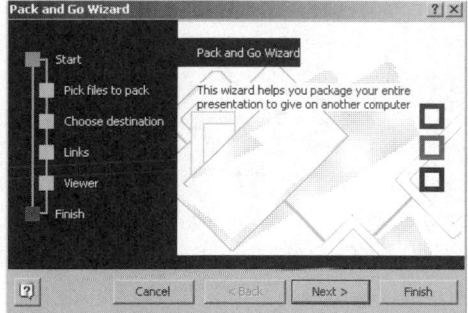

3 Follow the instructions in the Pack And Go Wizard dialog boxes.

tip To ensure maximum portability, select the Include Linked Files and Embed TrueType fonts options when the Pack And Go Wizard prompts you. If you don't select these options, you might need to copy additional files to make your presentation run smoothly. Also, be aware that some TrueType fonts have copyright restrictions built into them, and can't be packaged by Pack and Go.

Publishing to the Web

To widen the distribution of your presentation, you can take your slides, complete with special effects and hyperlinks, and publish them to the Web so your colleagues can view them. PowerPoint 2002 makes giving a presentation on the Web as easy as giving one on your laptop in a conference room down the hall.

By using the Save As Web Page command, you can save your slides in HTML format so that your slide show can be made available on the Web, including a navigation bar created from the contents of the Outline tab and text narration in the form of your speaker notes.

Chapter 35

Saving as a Web Page

To save your slide show in a format suitable for the Web, follow these steps:

1 Open the presentation you want to make ready for the Web.

2 Choose File, Save As Web Page. The Save As dialog box appears, as shown here:

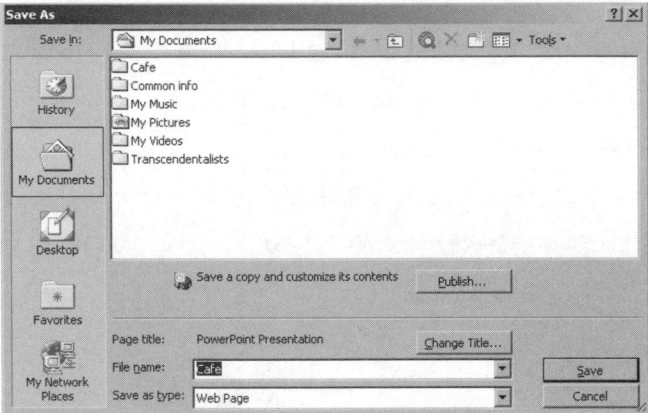

3 In the Save As dialog box, enter the filename you want to use for your Web presentation in the File Name text box.

4 Click Change Title to change the page title that will appear when someone views it on the Web, and then click Save when you're finished.

PowerPoint codes your presentation in HTML and stores it along with all your graphics, animations, and special effects in a folder that you can upload to the server that hosts your Web site.

InsideOut

When you save your presentation as a Web page, it is no longer password protected, and you cannot create a password for the presentation. To retain the password for this file, save the presentation in its original file format before you apply the Save As Web page command.

To see how this slide show will look as a Web presentation, choose File, Web Page Preview. (You can choose this option first, even before you save your PowerPoint presentation as a Web page.)

The slide show opens in your browser, as shown in Figure 35-7.

Chapter 35: Setting Up and Presenting the Slide Show

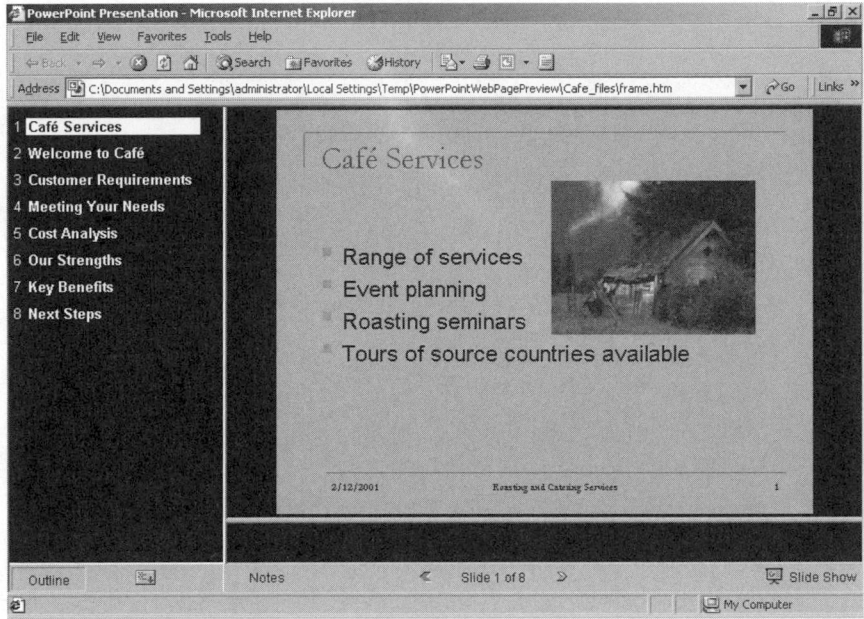

Figure 35-7. A slide previewed as a Web page.

Web Page Preview might give you some ideas on how to improve your presentation for a Web audience. For example, timing animations to advance automatically instead of after a mouse click is probably a better choice for a Web-based presentation. To edit your slide show, close the browser window, and you'll be back in PowerPoint. Make any changes you want to your slides before you publish them to the Web.

When you're ready to set options for viewing your Web-based presentation, follow this procedure:

1 Choose File, Save As Web Page, and check that the filename and page title are correct, and then click Publish. The Publish As Web Page dialog box appears, as shown below:

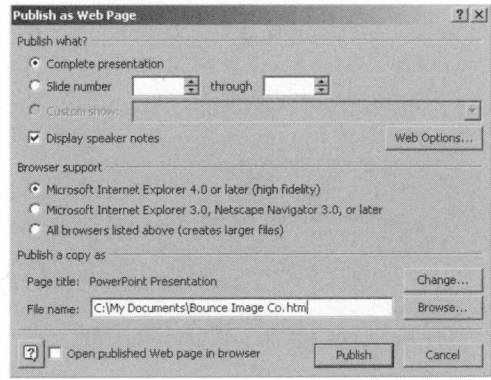

2 Select the options you want for your presentation. You can choose to present a few slides as Web pages, or use your entire presentation.

3 Click Web Options to find more formatting and display options. The Web Options dialog box appears, as shown here:

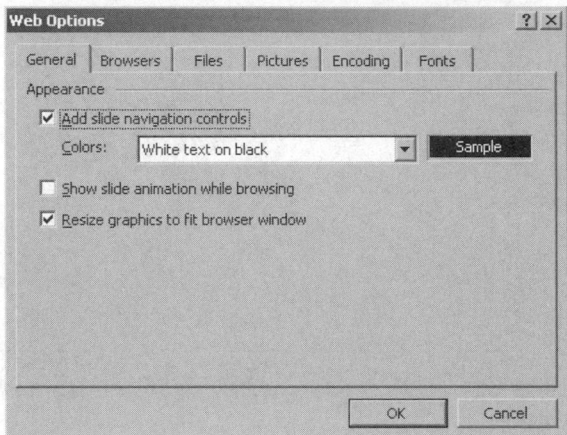

If you want to include slide transitions and animation effects in your Web presentation, select Show Slide Animation While Browsing. You can also choose to hide or display your speaker notes on the Publish As Web Page dialog box.

4 Click the Files tab in the Web Options dialog box. If you accept the default settings for managing the files and folder for your Web presentation, PowerPoint keeps all the necessary related files together to post to the Web. None of your graphic elements or links will be broken.

5 Click the Browsers tab to customize the presentation for viewing in a particular version and type of browser, as well as to set options for displaying graphics and archiving new Web pages.

6 When you're finished selecting Web options for your show, click OK in the Web Options dialog box.

7 To view your presentation as it will look to your Web audience, select Open Published Web Page In Browser in the Publish As Web Page dialog box.

Here's the place to thoroughly test your site before you finally publish it: make sure that your links go where you say they will and that your animations and special effects are displayed properly.

8 Click Publish to complete the procedure.

Your slide show is now in a format ready to be viewed on the Web. PowerPoint organizes all the images, bullets, animations, and hyperlinks to other Web sites in a supporting folder so that your links will display properly when your presentation is published as a Web page. When you upload your presentation to a Web server, FTP site, or company intranet, you must include this supporting folder.

Broadcasting Your Presentation

If you want to do the slide show live and include all the sophisticated effects you have employed, you can use PowerPoint 2002's broadcast capabilities to bring your show dynamically to the Web.

The basic difference between broadcasting a presentation and saving one as a Web page is that broadcasting is a live performance and publishing as a Web page is static. Broadcasting is a more complex procedure and includes options to use audio and video streaming. The purpose of presentation broadcasting is to actually give the presentation and capture it, including the presentation, the presenter, and the voice of the presenter.

If you need to broadcast to more than 10 computers, you must use Windows Media Services and select a shared location on a network server for viewers to access during your presentation. If you are broadcasting video, which requires a fast computer and a video card that uses hardware compression, you should also use Windows Media Services for your broadcast, even if you are sending it to fewer than 10 people.

If you're in charge of the broadcast, it could be your responsibility to schedule it, decide whether you will record and save the broadcast, and select which attributes you want to offer your audience. If you're the presenter, you need Microsoft Internet 5.0 or higher, a connected video camera, and a microphone for broadcasting with live narration.

Scheduling a Broadcast

If your audience is fewer than 10 people and you want to broadcast your slide show on the Web, you don't need a server. You can broadcast a presentation from your own computer by following these steps:

1 Choose Slide Show, Online Broadcast, and then click Schedule A Live Broadcast.

2 In the Schedule Presentation Broadcast dialog box, in the Description field, type the information that will identify your presentation.

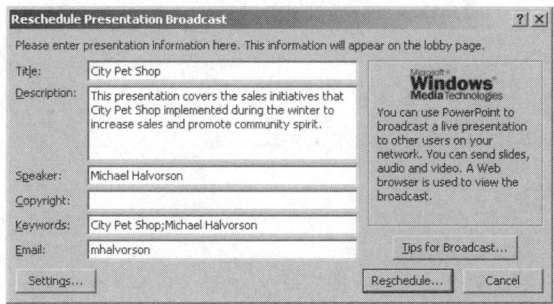

Part 5: PowerPoint

3 Click Settings, and on the Presenter tab, under File Location, type the location of your presentation file in the Save Broadcast Files field as shown below.

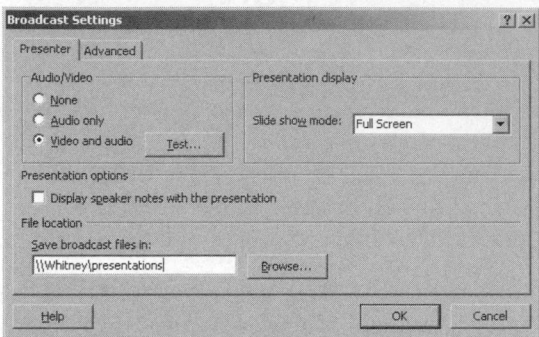

4 Make your changes to Audio/Video settings, if necessary. If you aren't using these functions, click None. Click OK when you are done.

5 In the Schedule Broadcast dialog box, click Schedule. Microsoft Outlook, or whichever e-mail program you use, opens and you can finish scheduling your meeting.

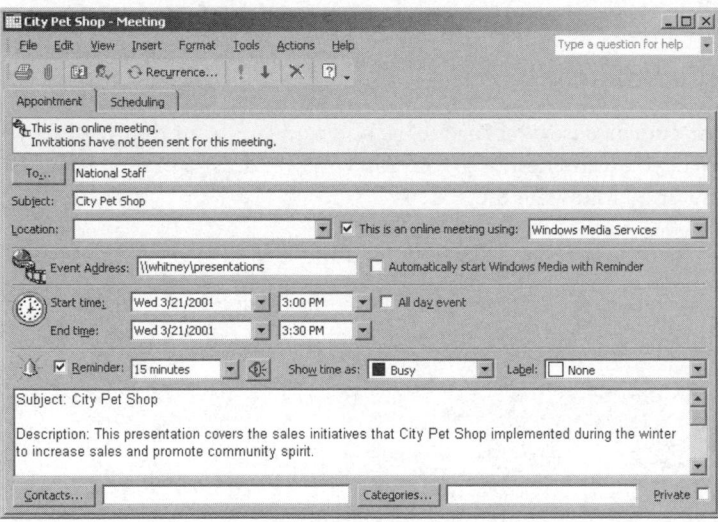

tip Rehearse before you broadcast your presentation. You won't be able to see yourself as you're broadcasting, so in addition to not moving from the position you started in after you tested the video capabilities, you can also follow this tip: Use the Record And Save A Broadcast command on the Slide Show menu to create a broadcast that you can view later when you want to critique your work.

Troubleshooting

A Scheduled Broadcast Needs To Be Updated

You want to update the content in a PowerPoint presentation that is scheduled for broadcast.

You have to reschedule a broadcast in order to update it. The following is the procedure for making changes to a presentation that you've already scheduled:

● To update the content, open the presentation and make changes. Then save the presentation and reschedule it.

● To reschedule the presentation, choose Slide Show, Online Broadcast, and then click Reschedule. When Outlook or the e-mail program you're using to notify viewers opens, save and close the message. The changes you made are saved for this presentation.

Conducting a Broadcast

You should prepare to deliver your broadcast at least 30 minutes before it's scheduled to begin so that the file can be uploaded to the Windows Media Server (if you're using one), and you can send out reminder e-mail messages to your audience. About half an hour before your broadcast is scheduled, follow these steps:

1 Open the presentation you're broadcasting, and choose Slide Show, Start Live Broadcast Now. In the Live Presentation Broadcast dialog box, click the broadcast you want to deliver, and then click Broadcast.

2 If you specified audio, the Microphone Check window opens, as shown here:

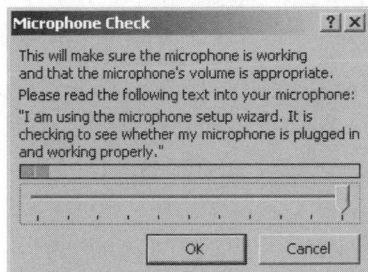

After checking your microphone, click OK.

3 In the Broadcast Presentation dialog box, shown on the next page, you can view the countdown until your presentation begins. Click Audience Message to send a reminder e-mail message or update, or click Preview Lobby Page to see the what your viewers will see when they click the link you've sent them in the invitation to the broadcast.

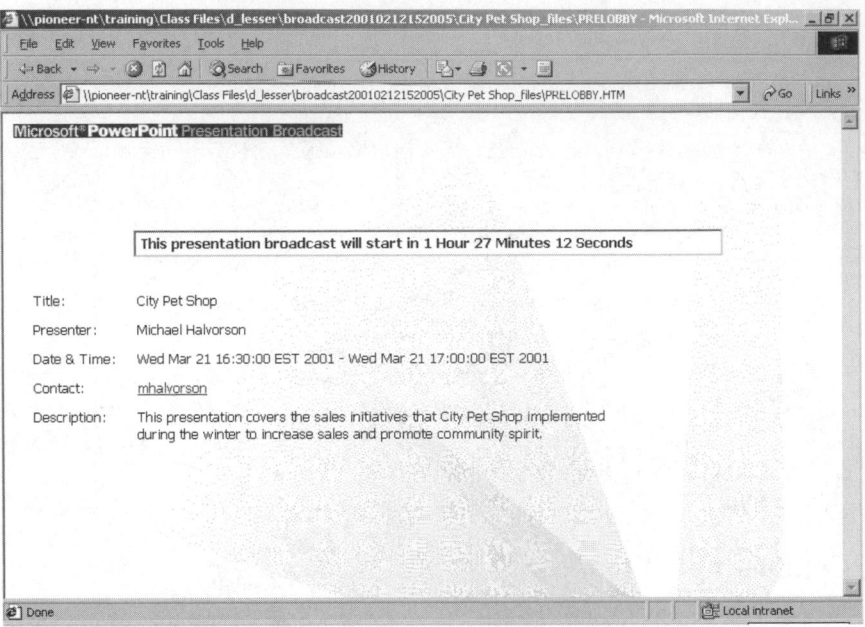

4 When the countdown is over, click Yes in the dialog box asking if you want to start the broadcast.

5 Give your presentation just as you would in a room with the audience physically present.

6 When you reach the end of the presentation, exit the show in the final black screen, and then click Yes in the dialog box asking if you want to end the broadcast.

Viewing a Presentation Broadcast

When you receive an invitation to a broadcast in Outlook or another e-mail program, it contains a URL for the shared folder that contains the broadcast. To view a broadcast, follow these steps:

1 About 15 minutes before the broadcast is scheduled to begin, click the URL for the broadcast. (Check in early in case the presenter has made any changes you need to know about.)

2 Check the Lobby page for a countdown to the broadcast, as well as a description of the presentation and information about the presenter.

newfeature!
Reviewing Presentations

Another way of sharing a presentation with a team is to collaborate on it. PowerPoint works with Microsoft Outlook to make it easy to send a presentation to team members for review. Then, using PowerPoint 2002's new Revisions task pane and Reviewing toolbar, you can look at multiple reviewers' suggestions, accept or reject each one, and merge them into a new, collaborative work.

To send a presentation for review using Microsoft Outlook, Microsoft Exchange, or another 32-bit email program that is compatible with the Messaging Application Programming Interface, follow these steps:

1 Save the original copy of a presentation that you want to send for review, and on the File menu in PowerPoint, point to Send To, and then click Mail Recipient (for Review).

2 In the Outlook window, which opens if that is your email program, enter the name and address of the recipient, type any instructions in the message area, as shown in Figure 35-8, and then click Send.

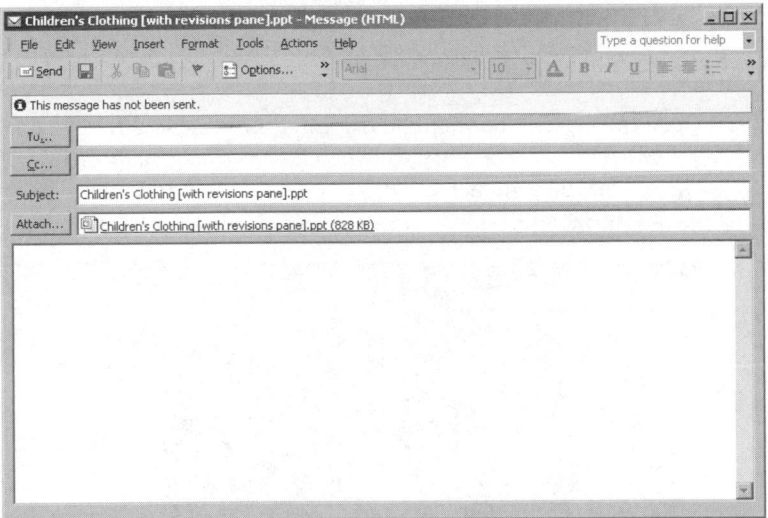

Figure 35-8. Using Outlook to send a presentation to reviewers.

Your entire presentation is sent as an attachment for review: you cannot select only a few slides to send.

InsideOut

If you want your entire presentation, including linked files and images, to be available to your reviewer, you must also include them in the attachment or embed them in the presentation.

When your reviewers respond, you can automatically combine their revisions with your original presentation if you're using Outlook by doing the following procedure:

1 In Outlook, double-click the attached PowerPoint presentation.

2 In the message box, click Yes, and the reviewer's changes will be merged with your file.

> **note** When you use this approach, the changes that reviewers have made to the master slides in your original presentation are not reflected in the merged result.

3 If you're not using Outlook, open the PowerPoint presentation you sent for review.

4 Choose Tools, Compare And Merge Presentations.

5 In the Choose Files To Merge With Current Presentation dialog box, select the reviewed presentations to combine with your original one, and then click Merge.

To apply selected changes from reviewers to a presentation, use the Revisions task pane by doing the following steps:

1 Open the presentation returned to you from review. When PowerPoint asks if you want to merge these changes with your original presentation, click Yes. The original presentation opens with the Revisions task pane displayed, as shown in Figure 35-9.

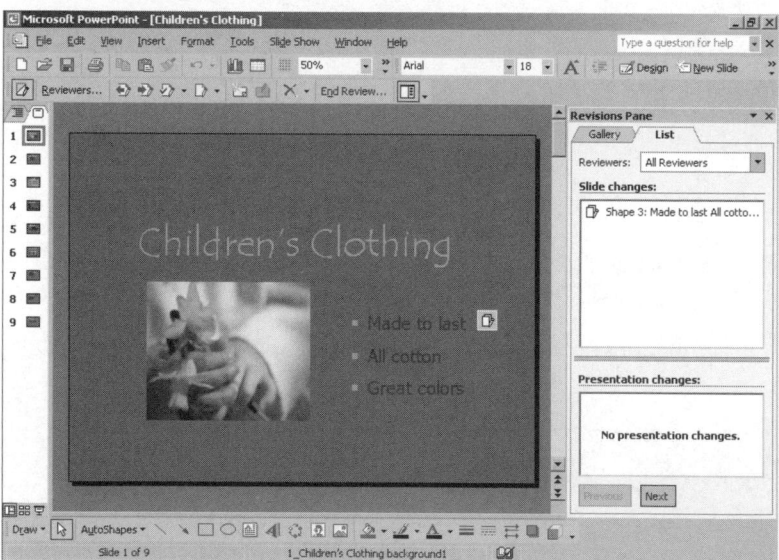

Figure 35-9. The Revisions task pane marks changes with the change marker icon.

2 On the List tab in the Revisions task pane, click a change marker and then select the changes you want to apply.

3 On the Reviewing toolbar, click Apply, and then click Apply, Apply All Changes To The Current Slide, or Apply All Changes To The Presentation.

4 If you want to select which changes you'll incorporate from multiple reviewers, click Multiple Reviewers on the Reviewing toolbar, and then select the individual changes to apply.

If you are the reviewer, you simply open the attachment that contains the PowerPoint presentation and make changes to it. Your changes apply to a copy of the presentation and do not alter the original presentation when you send the file back to the sender. If you're using Outlook as your e-mail program, in PowerPoint, choose File, Send To, and then click Original Sender when you're ready to return the presentation with your changes.

Part 6

Outlook

Outlook Fundamentals

A Rundown on Outlook

You can use Microsoft Outlook 2002 to organize and track your personal information, to communicate with other people in your organization or anywhere on the Internet, and to share information with members of your workgroup. The following are some of the important tasks you can perform with Outlook:

- Send, receive, store, and systematize e-mail messages.

- Maintain a personal calendar of appointments, events, and meetings.

- Schedule meetings with your co-workers.

- Store names, addresses, and other information about your business and personal contacts. And quickly communicate with any of your contacts.

- Use Instant Messaging to communicate in real time with friends and associates on the Internet.

- Create to-do lists and manage personal or group projects.

- Keep a journal of messages you send or receive, Microsoft Office XP documents you access, or other business or personal events.

- Jot down miscellaneous information on electronic "sticky notes."

- Access and maintain the files on your local or network disks.

- Explore sites on the Internet and your company's intranet.

For a description of the new features included in Outlook 2002, see "New Outlook Features," on page 14.

Setting Up Outlook

In addition to the general ways to start Office applications (which are discussed in "Running the Office Applications," on page 43), the Office Setup program provides two convenient shortcuts for running Outlook, one on the Microsoft Windows Desktop and the other on the Quick Launch toolbar displayed on the Windows Taskbar, shown here:

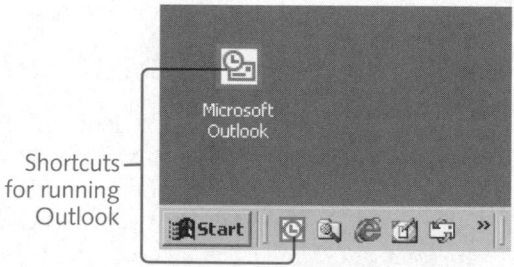

Shortcuts for running Outlook

The first time you run Outlook, you might see a series of dialog boxes asking for information required to set up Outlook and create an Outlook account for sending and receiving e-mail messages. The specific dialog boxes and options that Outlook displays depend on whether you previously had Outlook or another e-mail program installed on your computer and on that program's configuration. The dialog boxes also vary according to the choices you make during the setup process. The following typical scenario will give you an idea of the information you need to supply. The following setup steps occur if you install Outlook on a computer without a previous installation of Outlook or another e-mail program—except for Microsoft Outlook Express, which is supplied with Microsoft Internet Explorer—and if you choose to set up a standard Internet POP3 e-mail account:

1 Outlook displays the opening startup dialog box shown in Figure 36-1. Click the Next button to continue.

Outlook vs. Outlook Express

Don't confuse Outlook 2002 with Outlook Express. Outlook is a full-featured personal information manager and messaging client, and it's one of the major members of the Microsoft Office XP family of applications. Outlook Express, by contrast, is a specialized e-mail and newsreader program that's included with Internet Explorer. Note that choosing View, Go To, News in Outlook runs the newsreader feature of Outlook Express.

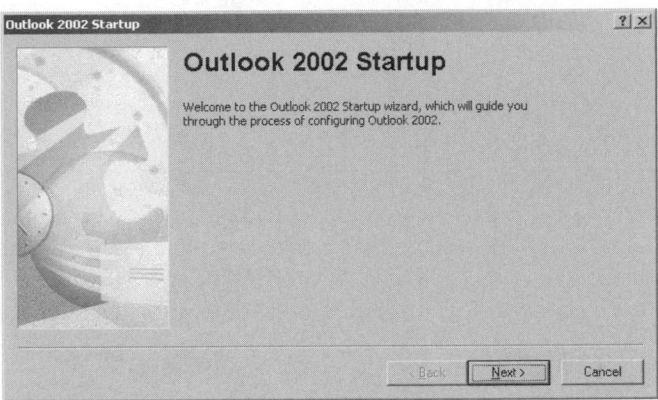

Figure 36-1. The setup of Outlook begins with the opening Outlook startup dialog box.

2 Outlook displays the E-mail Upgrade Options dialog box, which allows you to import the e-mail messages, stored addresses, and settings from an e-mail program that's currently installed on your computer. Doing this allows you to keep using your same e-mail service and setup without interruption. (E-mail programs that Outlook can import from include Netscape Mail, Qualcomm Eudora, and Outlook Express.) In this dialog box, do one of the following:

- To import settings, select the Upgrade From option and then select the program in the list.

- To set up Outlook without importing settings, select Do Not Upgrade (see Figure 36-2).

Then, click the Next button. The remaining steps are those that occur if you *don't* import settings from another e-mail program.

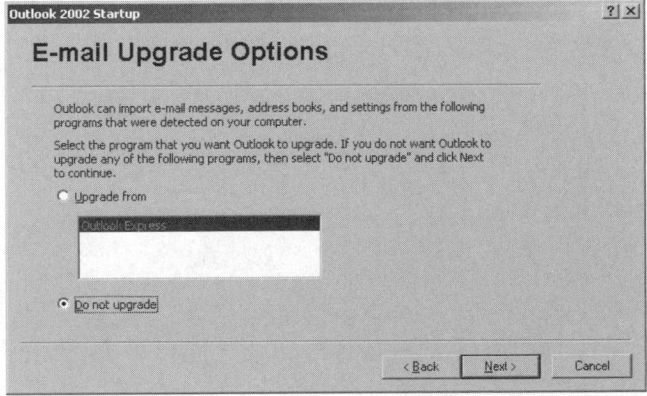

Figure 36-2. The E-Mail Upgrade Options dialog box lets you import messages and settings from an e-mail program that's currently installed on your computer.

> **note** You can import e-mail messages, stored addresses, and settings from another e-mail program later by choosing the Import And Export command from the File menu in Outlook. For information, see "Adding, Modifying, and Removing Outlook Accounts," on page 1093.

3 Outlook displays the E-mail Accounts dialog box, which lets you decide whether to set up an account that lets you send and receive e-mail messages in Outlook. Select Yes or No and click the Next button. The remaining steps occur if you select Yes to set up an e-mail account (see Figure 36-3).

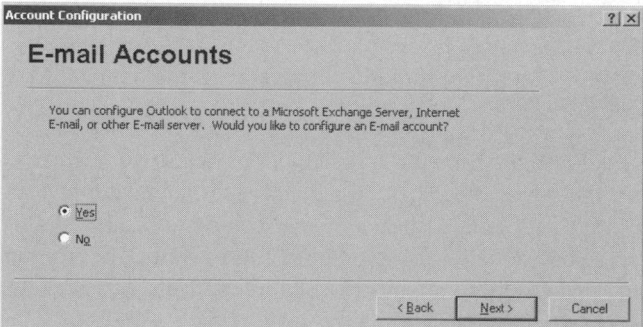

Figure 36-3. The E-mail Accounts dialog box asks you if you want to set up an e-mail account.

4 Outlook displays the Server Type dialog box (shown in Figure 36-4), in which you select the *type* of e-mail account you want to set up. Select an account type and click Next. If you're in doubt about which of these types is appropriate for the e-mail service you're using, consult the Internet service provider (ISP) or network administrator who manages your e-mail server. The remaining steps take place if you select the POP3 e-mail account type.

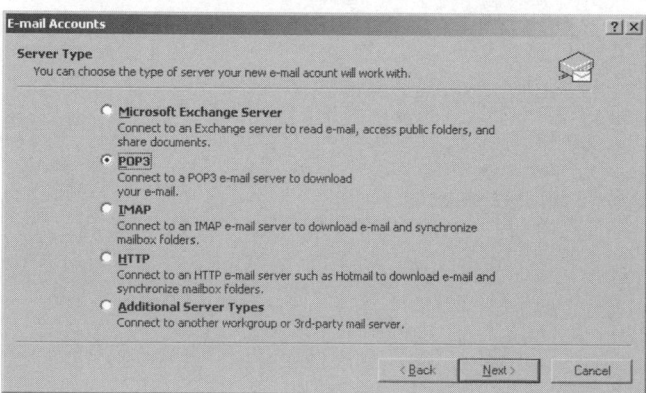

Figure 36-4. The Server Type dialog box allows you to select the type of e-mail account you want.

Chapter 36

> **note** POP3 (Post Office Protocol version 3) is the most common nonproprietary server protocol used for receiving e-mail from the Internet. An Outlook account that uses a POP3 e-mail server for *receiving* messages uses an SMTP (Simple Mail Transfer Protocol) e-mail server for *sending* messages on the Internet.

5 Outlook displays one or more dialog boxes that let you set up the type of e-mail account that you selected. Figure 36-5 shows the dialog box for setting up a POP3 account. You should be able to obtain all the required information from the ISP or network administrator who manages your e-mail server. Click the Next button when you're done.

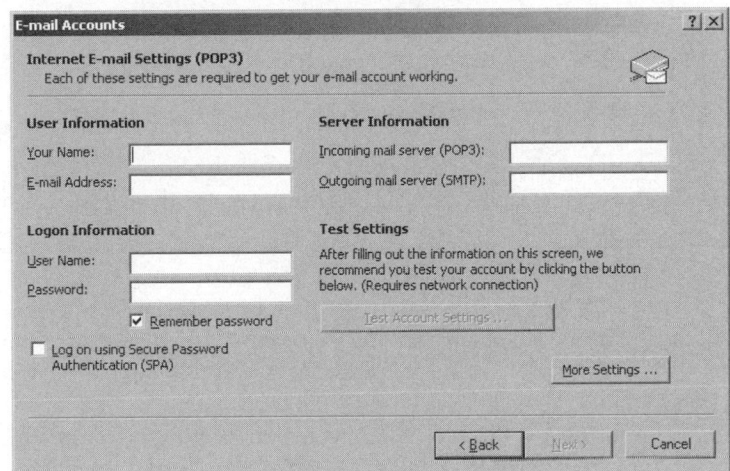

Figure 36-5. This Outlook setup dialog box lets you create a POP3 e-mail account.

6 When Outlook has all the information it needs to set up your e-mail account, it displays a concluding dialog box (shown in Figure 36-6). Click the Finish button.

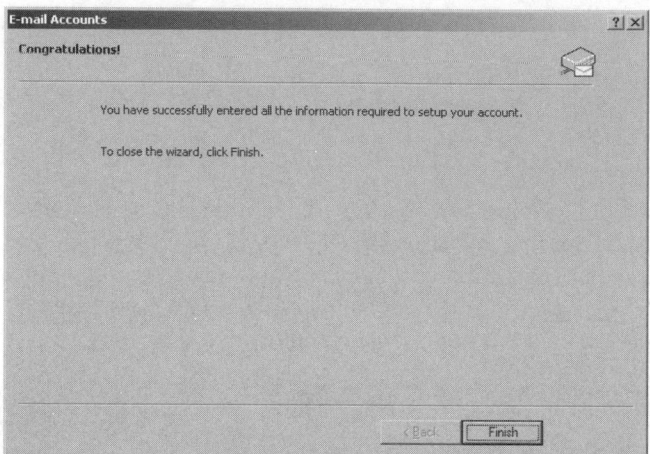

Figure 36-6. This is the concluding Outlook setup dialog box.

When you complete the setup process, Outlook adds shortcuts to the Outlook Bar, inserts a Welcome message into your Inbox folder, and then starts running.

InsideOut

During the initial setup Outlook prompts you for only the minimum amount of information that's required to run the program and it makes a number of configuration choices for you—such as the type, name, and location of the file that stores your Outlook data. Presumably, it does this to get you started using the program as quickly as possible, although some of the choices Outlook makes might not be the ones you prefer. Later, however, you can add, remove, or modify Outlook accounts or data files. For information, see "Adding, Modifying, and Removing Outlook Accounts," on page 1093, and "Managing Outlook Data Files," on page 1101.

Viewing Information in Outlook

Each type of information that Outlook manages is stored in a separate *Outlook folder*. Table 36-1 lists the type or types of information stored in each of the default Outlook folders that Outlook initially sets up. (As explained in Chapter 37, "Working with Outlook Items and Folders," you can create one or more additional folders for storing each information type.) A particular piece of information stored in an Outlook folder is known as an *item*—for example, an e-mail message stored in the Inbox folder, an appointment stored in the Calendar folder, or a task description stored in the Tasks folder.

note In the Outlook chapters the term *folder* is used to refer to an Outlook folder—rather than a file folder—unless otherwise qualified.

Table 36-1. Information Stored in Default Outlook Folders

Default Outlook Folder	Type(s) of Outlook Items Stored in the Folder
Calendar	Appointments, all-day events, and meetings.
Contacts	Contact descriptions (names, addresses, phone numbers, and other information on your personal or business contacts) and distribution lists (each of which stores an entire set of contact descriptions).
Deleted Items	Outlook items and folders that you've removed, before they're permanently deleted.
Drafts	E-mail messages. The Drafts folder stores a message that you're writing before you send it.
Inbox	E-mail messages. The Inbox receives your incoming e-mail messages.
Journal	Records of events that have occurred, such as accessing an Office file, sending an e-mail message, or making a phone call.
Notes	Electronic "sticky notes," each of which stores text information.
Outbox	E-mail messages. The Outbox folder temporarily stores a message that you've sent before it's uploaded to the outgoing e-mail server and transmitted to the recipient.
Sent Items	E-mail messages. The Sent Items folder stores a copy of each message after it has been sent and uploaded to the outgoing e-mail server.
Tasks	Descriptions of tasks you need to perform or personal or group projects you're managing.
Outlook Today	Displays an overview of the current information in other Outlook folders.

Chapter 36

Figure 36-7 shows the Outlook window as it appears when you first run the program.

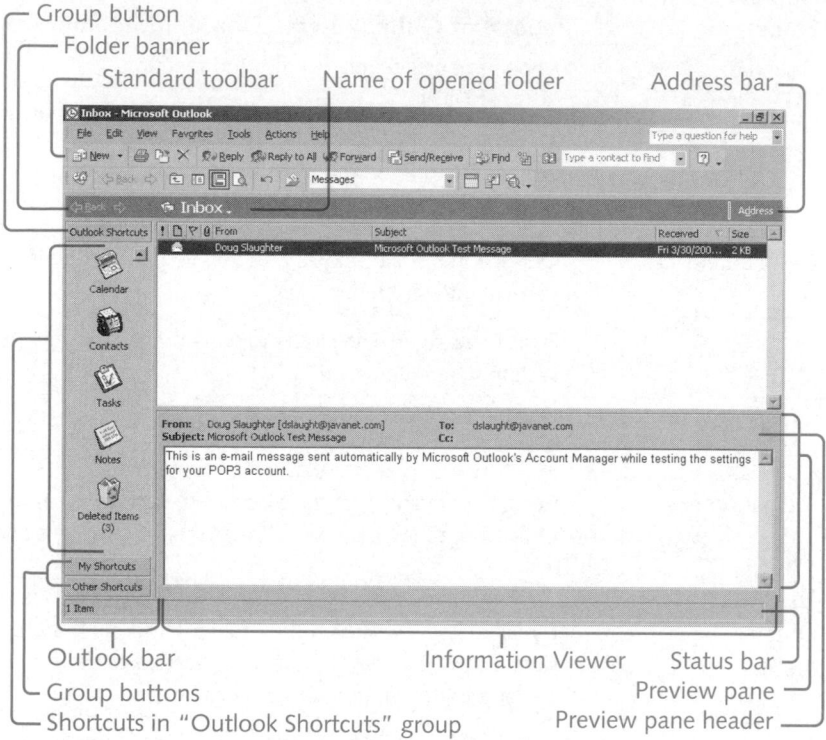

Group button
Folder banner
Standard toolbar   Name of opened folder   Address bar

Outlook bar
Group buttons
Shortcuts in "Outlook Shortcuts" group

Information Viewer   Status bar
Preview pane
Preview pane header

Figure 36-7. This figure shows the Outlook program window as it appears when you start Outlook. (Depending on your Outlook configuration, you might also see a welcome message from Outlook in your Inbox.)

To view and work with the items of information stored in a particular folder, you need to *open* that folder. Outlook will then display the folder's items in the Information Viewer of the Outlook window, and the Outlook menu commands and toolbar buttons will change to provide the commands you need to manage the type of information kept in that folder. (In the Outlook window shown in Figure 36-7, the Inbox folder is opened.)

The fastest way to open an Outlook folder is to use the Outlook Bar. You do that by completing the following steps:

1 If the shortcut for the folder you want to open isn't currently displayed in the Outlook Bar (keep in mind that you might be able to scroll the Outlook Bar to see additional shortcuts), open the group that contains the shortcut by clicking the appropriate button. Outlook initially provides the following two groups of shortcuts for opening Outlook folders:

■ The Outlook Shortcuts group contains shortcuts for opening the following Outlook folders: Outlook Today, Inbox, Calendar, Contacts, Tasks, Notes, and Deleted Items.

■ The My Shortcuts group contains shortcuts for opening the following Outlook folders: Drafts, Outbox, Sent Items, and Journal. (It also contains a shortcut to the Outlook Update page on Microsoft's Web site.)

> **note** You can hide or display the Outlook Bar by choosing View, Outlook Bar.

2 Click the shortcut for the folder you want to open.

> **note** The Outlook Bar can contain shortcuts for opening Outlook folders, file folders, disk files, or Web sites. For information on adding, removing, or renaming shortcuts or shortcut groups in the Outlook Bar, see "Customizing the Outlook Bar," on page 1089.

> Chapter 37, "Working with Outlook Items and Folders," explains the general techniques for viewing and working with the Outlook items contained in the opened Outlook folder. Chapter 38, "Managing Messages and Appointments," and Chapter 39, "Managing Contacts, Tasks, and Other Types of Information," then describe the methods for working with the items in specific Outlook folders, namely Inbox (and other e-mail folders), Calendar, Contacts, Tasks, Journal, and Notes.

Accessing File Folders

With Outlook's integrated file management feature, you can view and work with the contents of file folders on local or network disks. To open a file folder in Outlook, complete the following steps:

1 Click the Other Shortcuts group button on the Outlook Bar to open the Other Shortcuts group.

2 Click one of the shortcuts contained in that group to open the corresponding file folder:

■ My Computer

■ My Documents

■ Favorites

> **note** In the initial Outlook setup, shortcuts to file folders are all put in the Other Shortcuts group. However, you can add them to any Outlook Bar group, using the techniques covered in "Customizing the Outlook Bar," on page 1089.

3 To navigate from the opened file folder to other file folders, you can use the navigation techniques discussed in "Using Other Methods to Open Folders," on page 978.

> **tip** **View a Folder in a Separate Window**
>
> You can open an Outlook folder or a file folder in a separate Outlook window, rather than having it replace the view of the currently opened folder. To do this, right-click the folder's shortcut in the Outlook Bar and choose Open In New Window from the shortcut menu. The second window will be the same as the originally opened Outlook window, except that initially the Outlook Bar won't be displayed. This technique allows you to have several folders opened at once and is especially useful if you want to view another folder without disturbing your view of the current folder. For instance, if you've found a particular e-mail message and are reading it in the Preview pane, you could view another folder without losing your place by opening it in a separate window (switching folders in the current window would scroll you back to the beginning of the list of e-mail messages).

When you open a file folder, Outlook displays the files and subfolders contained in that folder within the Information Viewer of the main Outlook window (see Figure 36-8). Outlook displays files and file folders in much the same way as Microsoft Windows Explorer. However, it shows more information on each file and file folder than does Windows Explorer, and it provides many more ways to view a folder's contents.

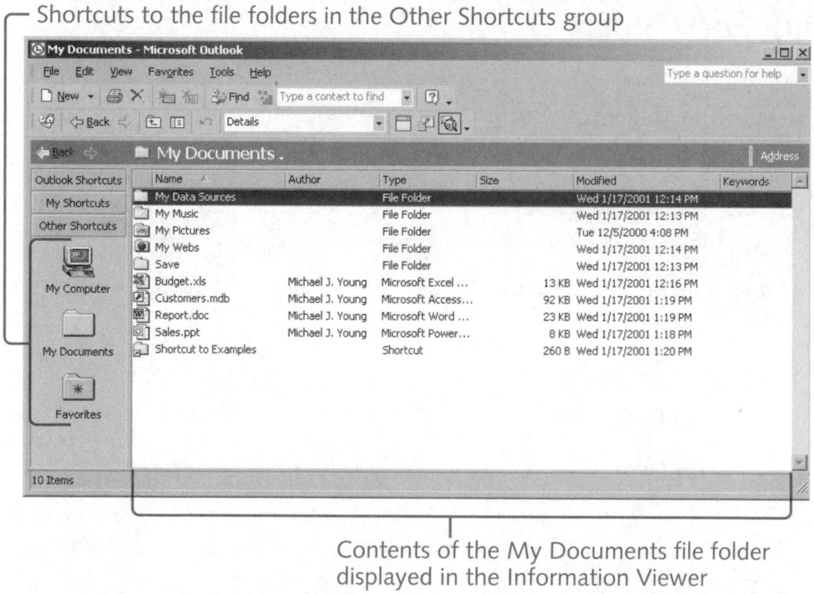

Shortcuts to the file folders in the Other Shortcuts group

Contents of the My Documents file folder
displayed in the Information Viewer

Figure 36-8. This figure shows the My Documents file folder opened in Outlook, using the Details view. The Advanced toolbar is displayed.

To change the way you view a file folder in Outlook, complete the following steps:

1 Open the file folder for which you want to change the view. (Outlook stores different view settings for each file folder.)

2 If the Advanced toolbar isn't shown, display it by choosing View, Toolbars, Advanced. To switch to a different file folder view, open the Current View drop-down list on the Advanced toolbar

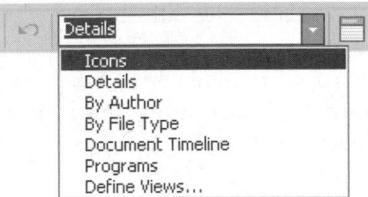

and select a view as follows:

■ To display all file folders and files as icons, select Icons.

■ To display all file folders and files in a table format, showing the name, author, type, size, modification date, and keyword properties of each file, select Details (as shown in Figure 36-8).

■ To display the file folders and files in a table format, with a grouping or filter applied, select By Author, By File Type, or Programs.

■ To arrange the file folders and files in a timeline according to their creation dates, select Document Timeline.

> **note** Selecting Define Views in the Current View drop-down list opens the Define Views dialog box, which is explained in "Switching and Customizing Views," on page 1000.

3 To change features that are specific to the current view, choose View, Current View, Customize Current View, and then click the Other Settings button in the View Summary dialog box. This will open one of three dialog boxes: the Format Icon View dialog box for the Icon view (see Figure 36-9), the Format Timeline View dialog box for the Document Timeline view, or the Other Settings dialog box for a table view (Details, By Author, By File Type, or Programs).

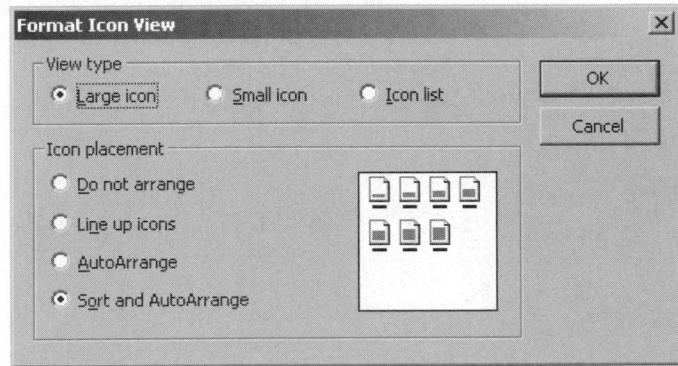

Figure 36-9. When you're in Icon view, clicking the Other Settings button in the View Summary dialog box reveals the Format Icon View dialog box.

977

Chapter 36

> For a general discussion on using and customizing Outlook views, including the methods for sorting, grouping, and filtering the items or files shown in the view, see "Changing the Way You View Items," on page 999.

Once you've opened a particular file folder and have adjusted the view to your liking, you can open, run, copy, move, rename, print, or delete files in the folder. You can also copy, move, rename, print, or delete file folders. And you can view or modify the properties of a file or folder. You can perform these tasks using the same basic methods you use in Windows Explorer or in an opened file folder in Windows.

> For information on using the Advance Find command in Outlook to search for files, see "Finding Outlook Items or Disk Files," on page 1010.

Using Other Methods to Open Folders

Folder
List

You can also open Outlook folders or file folders by using the hierarchical Folder List. The advantage of using the Folder List rather than the Outlook Bar is that you can readily locate and open *any* Outlook folder or file folder, not just those for which Outlook Bar shortcuts have been defined. You can open (or close) a permanent Folder List by choosing View, Folder List or by clicking the Folder List button on the Advanced toolbar. (If this toolbar isn't visible, choose View, Toolbars, Advanced.) Alternatively, you can open (or close) a temporary Folder List by clicking the name of the opened folder in the Folder Banner.

A permanent Folder List is displayed in a separate pane and remains displayed until you choose the Folder List menu command or click the Folder List button again, or until you click the Close button in the upper right corner of the list. A temporary Folder List overlaps the information in the Information Viewer and disappears as soon as you either use it to open a folder or click anywhere in Outlook outside the list. You can convert a temporary Folder List to a permanent one by clicking the push-pin button displayed in the list's upper right corner.

You use the Folder List just like the list in the left pane of Windows Explorer. To expand or contract a branch, click the square button displaying the plus (+) or minus (–) symbol; to open a folder, click the folder name. If you have an Outlook folder opened, the Folder List shows all your Outlook folders (see Figure 36-10); if you have a file folder opened, it shows all your file folders (see Figure 36-11).

Folder List

Click here
to collapse
(or expand)
list.

Folder
contains
1 message.

Permanent
Folder List

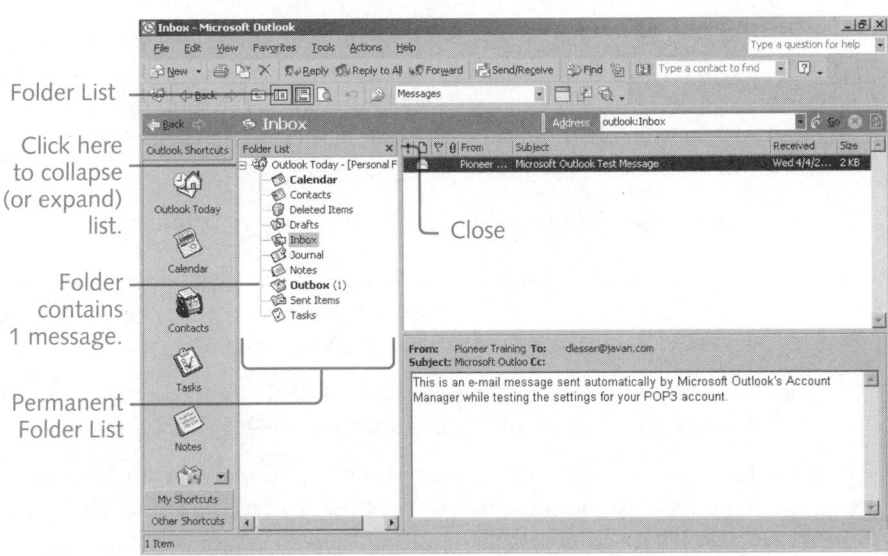

Close

Figure 36-10. Here, a permanent Folder List shows the Outlook folders.

Click here to open or close
temporary Folder List.

Click here to convert Folder List
from temporary to permanent.

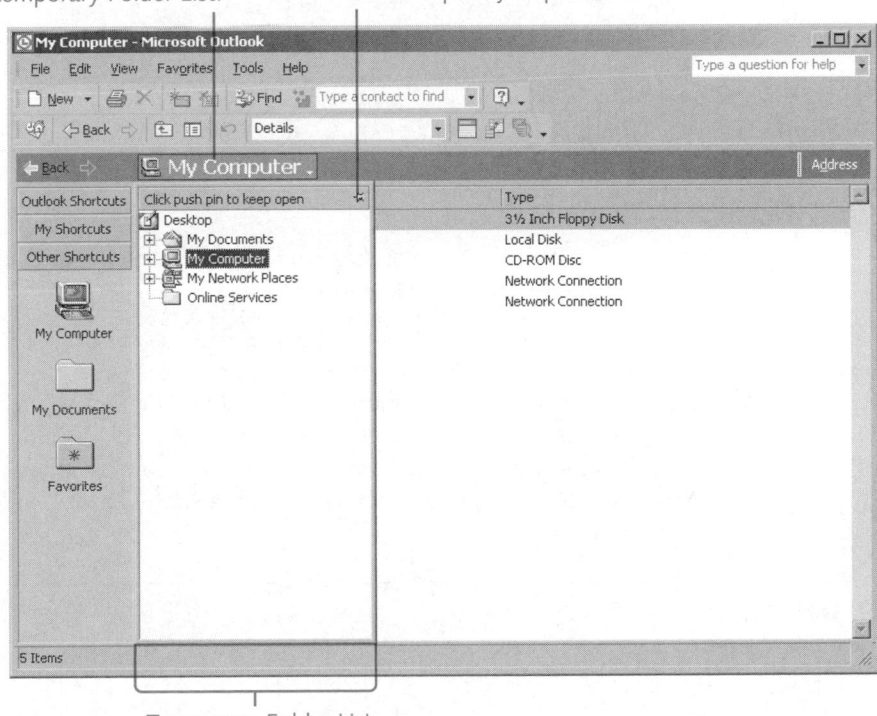

Temporary Folder List

Figure 36-11. Here, a temporary Folder List shows the local and network disk folders.

If an e-mail folder or the Deleted Items folder contains one or more unread messages, the folder name in the File List is formatted in bold and the number of unread messages is displayed in parentheses. (Note, however, that the number displayed next to the Drafts or Outbox folder indicates the *total* number of messages contained in the folder, read or unread.)

The following are additional ways to open either Outlook folders or file folders:

Outlook
Today

● To open one of the commonly used default Outlook folders (namely, Outlook Today, Inbox, Drafts, Calendar, Contacts, or Tasks) choose the folder name from the Go To subfolder on the View menu.

● To quickly open the Inbox, press Ctrl+Shift+I. To quickly open Outlook Today, click the Outlook Today button on the Advanced toolbar.

● To reopen the folder you previously had open, click the Back button on either the Advanced toolbar or on the left end of the Folder Banner, shown at the top of the next page.

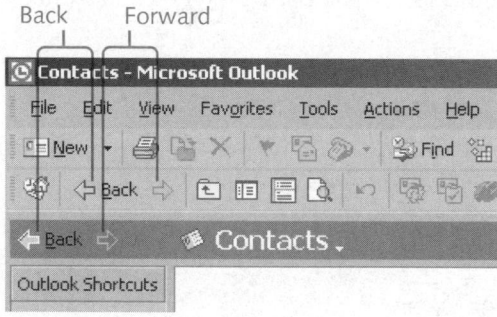

● After you've gone back one or more times, you can go forward again by clicking either of the Forward buttons.

Up One
Level

● You can open the next folder up in the hierarchy by clicking the Up One Level button on the Advanced toolbar. For example, if the Inbox Outlook folder is open, clicking Up One Level opens Outlook Today—because Outlook Today is the next folder up in the hierarchy of Outlook folders. Or if the Favorites file folder is open, clicking Up One Level opens the Windows folder—assuming that Favorites is a subfolder of Windows on your computer.

> **note** As you can see in Figure 36-10, Outlook folders—like file folders—are arranged in a hierarchy of folders and subfolders. Outlook Today (also labeled as "Personal Folders") is at the top and all other Outlook folders fall within it. As explained in Chapter 37, "Working with Outlook Items and Folders," when you create a new Outlook folder, you can make it a subfolder of any other Outlook folder.

● You can open a subfolder of a file folder by double-clicking the subfolder name in the Information Viewer.

● You can locate and open any Outlook folder or file folder by choosing View, Go To, Folder, or by pressing Ctrl+Y to open the Go To Folder dialog box (shown in Figure 36-12). In the Look In drop-down list, select Outlook if you want to open an Outlook folder or choose File System if you want to open a file folder. Next, type the name of the folder into the Folder Name box, or select a folder in the Folder Name drop-down list of previously opened folders, or select a folder in the hierarchical list at the bottom of the dialog box. Then, click the OK button. This technique is useful primarily for locating and opening file folders or for locating and opening Outlook folders if you've added quite a few new ones, some of which might be buried in the hierarchy.

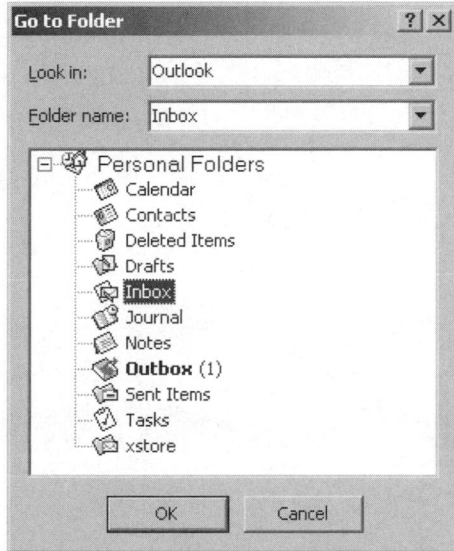

Figure 36-12. You can use the Go To Folder dialog box to locate and open any Outlook folder or file folder.

In addition to using Outlook to view items in Outlook folders and files in file folders, you can use it to view Web pages. For information, see "Opening Web Sites," on page 1085.

Working with Outlook Items and Folders

Working with Outlook Items

An individual piece of information stored in a Microsoft Outlook 2002 folder is known as an *item*—for example, an e-mail message stored in the Inbox, a contact description stored in the Contacts folder, or a record of an event stored in the Journal folder. For a summary of the different type or types of items that are stored in each of the default Outlook folders, see Table 36-1, on page 973.

The first step in working with a particular type of Outlook item is to open the folder that contains the items. To open a folder, you can use any of the techniques discussed in "Viewing Information in Outlook," on page 972. The following sections explain how to work with the items in the currently opened folder in the following ways:

- Creating new items
- Editing items
- Moving and copying items
- Removing and archiving items
- Changing the folder view and sorting, filtering, and grouping items
- Finding items
- Organizing items

Creating New Items

The way you enter information into an Outlook folder is to create a new item. Although Outlook sometimes lets you create a new item right within the Information Viewer of the main Outlook window, you usually create an item by opening an Outlook *form*. A form is a separate window that displays a set of controls—text boxes, buttons, drop-down lists, check boxes, and so on—in which you enter each piece of information that's to be stored in the item, such as the recipient of an e-mail message, the name of a contact, or the subject of a task. Each of these pieces of information is known as a *field*.

To create a new Outlook item, complete the following steps:

1 Open the Outlook folder where you want to store the item.

> **note** To create an e-mail message, open any e-mail folder. The default e-mail folders are Inbox, Drafts, Outbox, and Sent Items.

2 Open a form for defining the new item using either of the following methods:

New Form

■ To create the most common type of item stored in the opened folder, click the New button on the Standard toolbar or press Ctrl+N. The following are the types of items that this command creates in each of the default Outlook folders:

Table 37-1. Types of Items Created by the New Command

Default Outlook Folder	Type of Item Created by the New Command
Inbox, Drafts, Outbox, Saved Items	E-mail message
Calendar	Appointment
Contacts	Contact
Tasks	Task
Journal	Journal entry
Notes	Note

■ To create a specific type of item in a folder that manages several item types, choose the appropriate command from the Actions menu. For example, in the Calendar folder, you can create a new appointment, all-day event, meeting request, recurring appointment, or recurring meeting by choosing the corresponding command from the Actions menu:

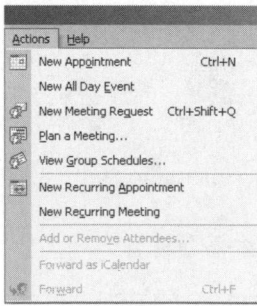

Outlook will then open a blank form for you to fill in. The form that Outlook displays is one designed specifically for defining the type of item you're creating. Figures 37-1 to 37-3 show three examples of these forms.

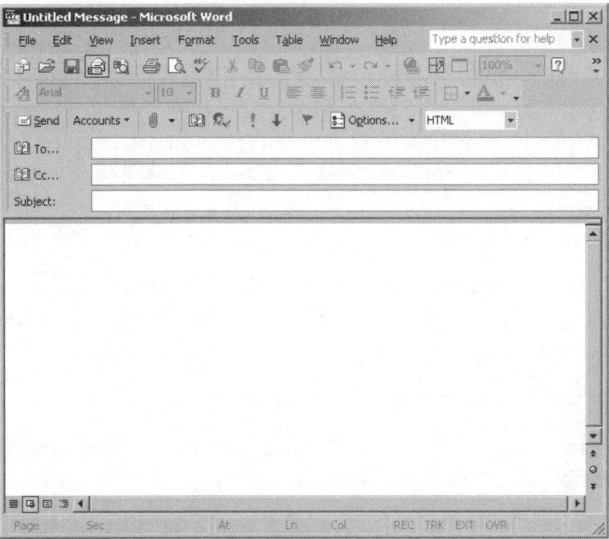

Figure 37-1. This is the form that Outlook displays for creating a new e-mail message (here, Microsoft Word is used as the Outlook e-mail editor).

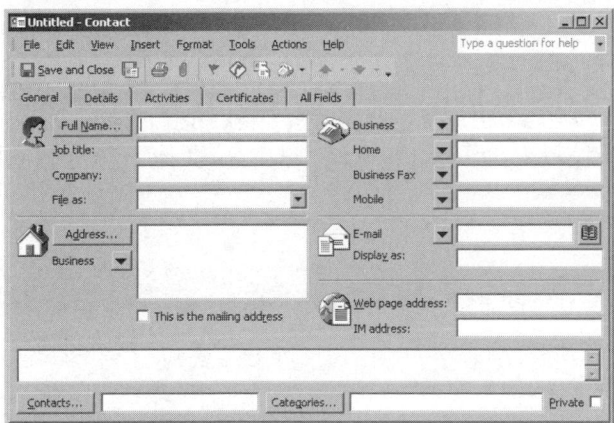

Figure 37-2. This is the form that Outlook displays for defining a new contact in the Contacts folder.

Figure 37-3. This is the form that Outlook displays for entering a new note into the Notes folder.

3 Enter the information for the item into the controls in the form.

A form provides toolbar buttons and menu commands to assist you in completing the form and formatting your text. For convenience, a form also provides general-purpose menu commands that are the same as menu commands found in the main Outlook window—for example, the commands on the New submenu on the File menu for creating new Outlook items. (The Notes form provides only a few menu commands and no toolbars.)

The next section provides some general information on entering or editing information in a form, and the following chapters describe the specific information that you enter into each type of Outlook item.

4 Close the form and save the item as follows:

■ For an e-mail message, meeting request, or assigned task, click the Send button to save the item and send it to the recipient.

■ For a note, click the Close button in the form's upper-right corner.

■ For all other types of items, click the Save And Close button on the form's Standard toolbar.

■ For any item except a note, you can save the current contents of the form without closing the form by choosing Save from the File menu or by pressing Ctrl+S. To close the form and discard the information you've entered, choose File, Close, click the Close button in the upper-right corner of the form, or press Esc or Alt+F4. (Outlook will warn you and let you save your changes if you want.) Outlook automatically saves the text you type into a note.

tip **Use an Item to Create an Item of a Different Type**

You can use an existing item to quickly create a new item of a different type by dragging the existing item from the Information Viewer and dropping it on the Outlook Bar shortcut for an Outlook folder of a different type. (You can also drag it to the destination folder's name in a permanently displayed Folder List.) The new item will contain information from the existing item. For example, dragging an appointment from the Calendar folder and dropping it on the shortcut for the Tasks folder will create a new task that contains the description and date (which becomes the task's due date) from the appointment. Dragging an e-mail message from the Inbox and dropping it on the Contacts shortcut creates a new contact containing the name and e-mail address of the person who sent the message as well as the body of the message (which is stored in the contact item's large text box). And dragging an item from the Contacts folder to the Inbox shortcut creates a new e-mail message addressed to the contact. (You can then fill in the subject and message text.) If the shortcut for the target folder isn't visible, while you drag you can hold the pointer over a group button to open that group, or you can hold it over the top or bottom of a group to scroll through the shortcuts.

Outlook will now save your item in the opened folder and will display it in the Information Viewer, together with the folder's other items. The next section explains how to reopen an item in a form so you can view all of the item's information or edit that information.

An alternative way to create a new Outlook item, which you can use regardless of which folder is currently open, is to choose a command from the New submenu on the File menu, or from the equivalent menu that appears when you click the down-arrow on the New button on the Standard toolbar:

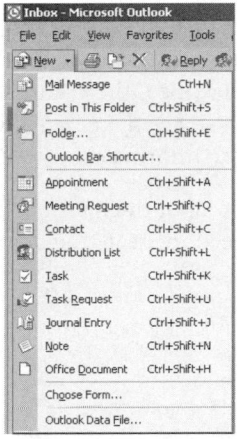

Or, you can press the equivalent shortcut key. The shortcut keys are displayed on the menu shown above, but note that to create a new e-mail message when an e-mail folder is *not* open, you need to press Ctrl+Shift+M. (The above figure shows the menu as it's displayed when the Inbox, or another e-mail folder, is opened. The menu indicates that you can create an e-mail message by pressing Ctrl+N because that's the shortcut key for creating the default item type for the currently opened folder.)

If the opened folder is displayed in a table view (a view consisting of rows and columns) you can create a new item right in the Information Viewer of the main Outlook window by clicking in the top row, typing information into each column, and pressing Enter:

Create a new item by entering it into the top row.

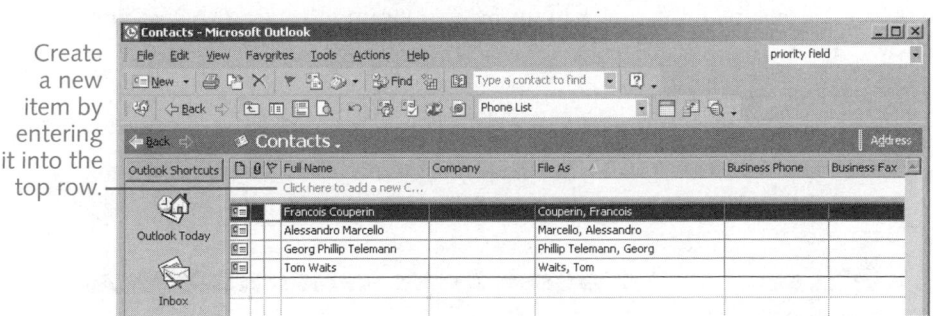

Chapter 37

> **note** The icon and ScreenTip text on the New button on the Standard toolbar change to match the open folder, such as "New Mail Message" or "New Contact."

> Views are discussed in "Changing the Way You View Items," on page 999.

> **note** You can also open an empty form by double-clicking in the top row.

To add items to a particular folder in this way, the Allow In-Cell Editing and Show "New Item" Row options must be selected for the current view. To find these options, choose View, Current View, Customize Current View, click the Other Settings button, and look in the Rows area of the Other Settings dialog box. See the next section for a discussion on entering or editing item information in the Information Viewer.

Typically, however, the Information Viewer doesn't show all of the item's fields. If one or more fields you want to define aren't shown, you'll need to create the item using a form, as described previously in this section.

> **tip** **Use an Item to Create an Item of the Same Type**
>
> If you want to create a new item that's similar to an existing item of the same type (for example, you want to create a new contact for a person in the same household), make a copy of the existing item (as explained later in the chapter) and then edit the copy.

Editing Items

With most views, you can directly edit an item in the Information Viewer in the main Outlook window without opening the item in a form, provided that the Allow In-Cell Editing option is checked for that view. (To access this option for a view, switch to that view, choose View, Current View, Customize Current View, click the Other Settings button, and look in the dialog box that's displayed, the title of which varies according to the view.) To edit an item, click in the field you want to enter or change, and type the new text:

Click in Full Name field to edit it.

	Full Name	Company	File As	Business Phone	Business Fax
	Click here to add a new C...				
	Tommaso Albinoni		Albinoni, Tommaso		
	John Bull		Bull, John	(999) 999-9999	
	Francois Couperin		Couperin, Francois		
	Alessandro Marcello		Marcello, Alessandro		
	Georg Phillip Telemann		Phillip Telemann, Georg		
	Tom Waits		Waits, Tom		

Contacts. / Outlook Shortcuts / Outlook Today / Inbox / Back / Address

You can set the value of some fields by clicking in the field and selecting a value from a drop-down list:

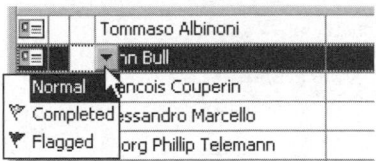

And you can set the value of other fields (such as the completion status) by checking a check box.

Views are discussed in "Changing the Way You View Items," on page 999.

The Information Viewer, however, typically shows only a portion of an item's fields, and you can't edit some of those fields in the Information Viewer (such as the File As field of a contact). Also, some views don't allow you to edit any of the fields (such as a timeline or icons view).

To view or edit *any* field, you can open the item. When you open an item, Outlook displays it in the same form that's used to create that type of item (see Figure 37-4). You can open an item using one of the following methods:

● Double-click the item in the Information Viewer.

● Click the item to select it and press Ctrl+O or Enter.

● Right-click the item and choose Open from the shortcut menu.

> **note** You can open several items simultaneously by selecting all of them and then using either of the last two methods in the list above. To select several adjoining items, click the first and then click the last while pressing Shift. To select nonadjoining items, click the first and then click each additional one while pressing Ctrl. To select *all* items in the opened folder, choose Edit, Select All or press Ctrl+A.
>
> To close all open items, choose File, Close All Items from the main Outlook window.

Large text box

Figure 37-4. This figure shows a contact opened for editing in the Contact form.

---

tip **Use a Form to Browse Items**

Once you've opened an item in a form, you can open other items in the same Outlook folder without leaving the form. To open the previous or next item, click the Previous Item or Next Item button on the form's Standard toolbar, shown here, or press Ctrl+< or Ctrl+>.

Previous Item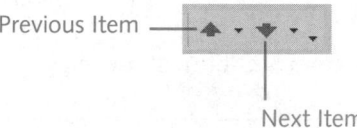

Next Item

To open a specific item, click the down-arrow on the Previous Item or Next Item button and choose a command from the drop-down menu, as shown here:

The commands that the form provides for entering, editing, selecting, formatting, moving, copying, or finding text, as well as those for checking your spelling or undoing your actions, are similar to commands available in Word and other Microsoft Office applications. For detailed instructions, see the Outlook online help topic "Format and Text" and "Check Spelling."

> **tip** **Enter a Date Using English**
>
> You can enter a date or time into a form's date or time field (such as a task's due date or an appointment's start time) by typing a normal English expression into the text box, such as "one week from now" or "midnight." Entering "noon" or "midnight" is useful if you've never quite figured out whether these times are 12 A.M. or P.M.!

Most Outlook forms provide a large, unlabeled text box where you can enter free-form information—such as the body of an e-mail message, a description of an appointment, or comments about a contact (see Figure 37-4). When entering information into this text box, you can insert a disk file, another Outlook item, or a linked or embedded item as follows:

- To insert a disk file, choose File from the form's Insert menu or click the Insert File button on the form's Standard toolbar, and select the file in the Insert File dialog box. Click the Insert button to insert the file as an attachment to the item, or click the down-arrow on this button to select an alternative way to insert the file:

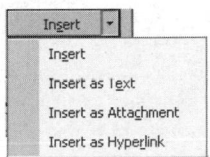

Clicking the button, choosing Insert, or choosing Insert As Attachment causes Outlook to store a copy of the file within the item but to display it as an icon that you must double-click to view the copy. Choosing Insert As Text causes Outlook to insert and display the full text from the file in the text box. Choosing Insert As Hyperlink causes Outlook to insert just a hyper-link to the file without storing the contents of the file in the item.

> **note** The Insert button in the Insert File dialog box for an e-mail message doesn't provide the Insert As Hyperlink command. And if you're using Word as your e-mail editor, the Insert button also lacks the Insert As Attachment command (although simply clicking the Insert button will insert the file as an attachment).

Inserting a file is a common way to send information with an e-mail message.

> **note** An alternative way to insert a file as an attachment is to drag the file from a file folder (displayed in Outlook, in Microsoft Windows Explorer, or in Microsoft Windows) and drop it in the large text box.

● To Insert an Outlook item, choose Insert, Item and select the item in the Insert Item dialog box. In the Insert As area of the dialog box, you can choose to insert the file as text, as an attachment, or as a shortcut. Inserting as text adds the full content of the item. Inserting as an attachment stores a copy of the inserted item within the receiving item but displays the inserted item as an icon. Inserting as a shortcut causes Outlook to insert just a link to the inserted item. Alternatively, to insert the item as an attachment, you can drag the item from the Information Viewer in the main Outlook window and drop it in the large text box.

note If you're using Word as your e-mail editor, to insert an Outlook item into the body of an e-mail message, you need to click the down-arrow on the Insert File button in the message header and choose Item from the drop-down menu. You can insert the item only as an attachment.

For example, you might attach an appointment to an e-mail message so that the recipient can add that appointment to his or her Calendar folder (by dragging it from the e-mail message to the Calendar folder).

note In a note, you can insert an Outlook item as text by dragging the item and dropping it in the note form. You can also insert a document's properties as text by opening the folder containing the document in Outlook and then dragging the document from the Information Viewer and dropping it on the note.

tip **Insert an Item into an E-Mail Message Quickly**

If you've selected an Outlook item in the Information Viewer or opened it in a form, you can create an e-mail message and insert that item as an attachment using a single command. Just choose Forward from the Actions menu in Outlook or in the form, or press Ctrl+F.

Also, in the Calendar and Contacts folders, Outlook provides commands for attaching an item to an e-mail message using a generic format that can be read by some personal information managers in addition to Outlook. Namely, if you've selected an appointment or other item in the Calendar folder, you can choose Actions, Forward As iCalendar; and, if you've selected a contact in the Contacts folder, you can choose Actions, Forward As vCard.

● To insert a linked or embedded item, choose Object from the Insert menu and select the object and insertion options in the Insert Object dialog box. For details on linked and embedded items, see Chapter 7, "Sharing Data Among Office XP Applications."

992

---

tip   **Include Hyperlinks in Your Outlook Items**

In the large text box of an Outlook form (including the body of a note), you can insert a hyperlink that opens an Internet site or sends an e-mail address by simply typing in the URL. For a hyperlink target other than a Web site, be sure to type the full URL, including the protocol (such as *mailto:* or *ftp:*), as in this example:

mailto:someone@microsoft.com/

Outlook will automatically convert your text to a blue, underlined hyperlink.

Alternatively, if you use Word as your e-mail editor, you can create a hyperlink by choosing Insert, Hyperlink, clicking the Insert Hyperlink button on the Standard toolbar, or pressing Ctrl+K. Adding hyperlinks in Word is discussed in "Adding and Using Hyperlinks," on page 583.

For instructions on closing the form and saving (or discarding) your changes, see step 4 of the procedure for creating a new item, on page 986.

---

tip   **Save Outlook Information on Disk**

You can save a copy of an Outlook item in a disk file. To do this, select the item in the Information Viewer or open it in a form, and choose Save As from the File menu in Outlook or in the form. Before saving the item, select the desired format from the Save As Type drop-down list in the Save As dialog box.

You can also save an item in a disk file with the Message Format (that is, as an .msg file) by dragging it from the information viewer and dropping it on a file folder or on the Windows Desktop. Opening such a file (for example, by double-clicking it) opens the saved copy of the Outlook item in a form, even if Outlook isn't currently running.

Keep in mind that a copy of an Outlook item stored in a disk file *isn't* linked to the original item and won't be updated if the original item is changed.

Also, you can export an entire Outlook folder to a disk file in a variety of different formats, and you can import data from a range of file types (such as a Microsoft Access database or another Outlook data file) to an Outlook folder. To import or export items, run the Import And Export Wizard by choosing File, Import And Export in Outlook.

Moving and Copying Items

You can move an Outlook item to a different folder, and you can copy an item to the same folder or to a different folder. In either case the destination folder can be of the same type as the folder storing the original item or it can be of a different type. Copying or moving an item to a folder of a different type creates a new item in the destination folder, which contains information from the original item.

Moving or copying items can be useful in a variety of situations. For example, you could organize the e-mail messages you've received by creating several new e-mail folders (perhaps named Client Messages, Personal Messages, and News Server Messages) and then moving messages to these folders from your Inbox. Also, you could make a copy of an item in the same folder as the original item (or in a different folder of the same type) to get a head start in creating a new item that will contain much of the same information (perhaps a contact who works for the same company as an existing contact). And, you could copy an item to a different type of folder to create a new item based upon an existing one, as explained in the tip "Use an Item to Create an Item of a Different Type," on page 986.

To move or copy an item, complete the following steps:

1 In the Outlook window, select the item or items you want to move or copy.

> **note** To select several adjoining items, click the first and then click the last while pressing Shift. To select nonadjoining items, click the first and then click each additional one while pressing Ctrl. To select *all* items in the opened folder, choose Select All from the Edit menu or press Ctrl+A.

1 Choose Edit, Move To Folder or Edit, Copy To Folder to move or copy the item. (To move the item, you can also press Ctrl+Shift+V.) This will open the Move Items or the Copy Items dialog box (see Figure 37-5).

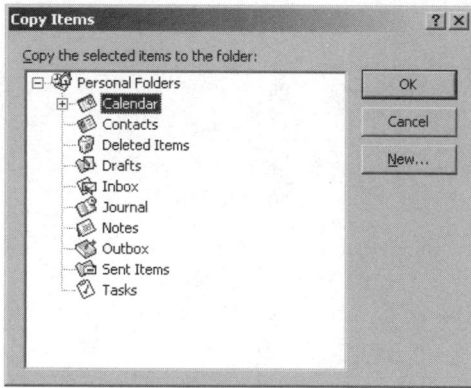

Figure 37-5.   You can use the Copy Items dialog box to copy an item.

note An alternative way to open the Move Items dialog box is to click the Move To Folder button on the Standard toolbar and choose Move To Folder from the drop-down menu. (The Move To Folder button isn't available when you're viewing the Calendar.) Also, you can immediately move the selected item or items to one of the folders that you've recently moved or copied an item to by choosing the folder name from this menu:

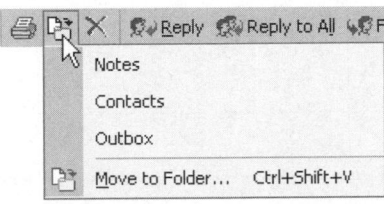

3 In the Move Items or Copy Items dialog box select the destination folder, or click the New button to create a new destination folder.

4 Click OK.

When you move or copy an item to a destination folder of a different type, the method just given uses a default method to move or copy. For example, if you copy an e-mail message from the Inbox to your Contacts folder, Outlook creates a new contact containing text from the e-mail message. (It copies the message sender's name to the contact's Full Name field, the sender's e-mail address to the contact's E-Mail field, and the body of the message to the contact's large text box).

To choose the exact way the item is transferred from the source folder to the destination folder, drag the item using the right mouse button from the Information Viewer in the Outlook window, drop it on the Outlook Bar shortcut for the destination folder, and choose the transfer method you want from the shortcut menu that appears. The following is the shortcut menu that Outlook displays when you right-drag an e-mail message from an e-mail folder to the shortcut for the Contacts folder:

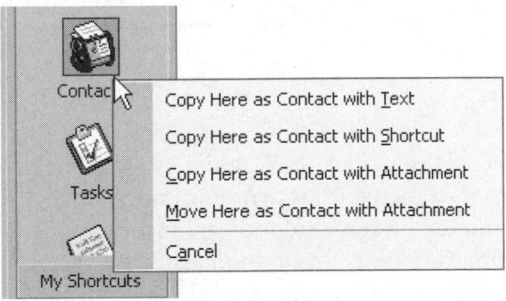

note If you've opened an item in a form, you can move or copy it by choosing File, Move To Folder or File, Copy To Folder. These commands work just like the identically named commands on the Edit menu in Outlook, which are explained in this procedure.

If the shortcut for the target folder isn't visible in the Outlook Bar, while you drag you can hold the pointer over a group button to open that group, or you can hold it over the top or bottom of a group to scroll through the shortcuts.

---

tip **Unmove or Uncopy an Item**

Undo

Issuing the Undo command *immediately* after moving or copying an item reverses the move or copy operation. Either choose Undo Move (or Undo Copy) from the Edit menu, or click the Undo button on the Advanced toolbar.

Troubleshooting

Attached Item Not Updated

You created an appointment in your Calendar folder, and you inserted an item from your Contacts folder into the appointment's large text box as an attachment using one of the methods discussed in "Editing Items," on page 988, or in "Moving And Copying Items," on page 993. Your purpose was to provide ready access to information on the person with whom you have the appointment. However, when you updated the contact in your Contacts folder, the copy of that contact attached to your appointment wasn't updated.

Attaching an item creates a separate copy of that item, which isn't updated when the original item is changed. If you want to insert an item and have it updated when the original item changes, you should insert it as a *shortcut* rather than as an attachment. If you're using the Insert Item dialog box to insert the contact (as described in "Editing Items") select the Shortcut option in the Insert As area. If you're creating a new appointment by copying a contact into your Calendar folder, right-drag the contact, drop it on the Calendar shortcut, and choose Copy Here As Appointment With Shortcut, as explained in "Moving and Copying Items."

Removing and Archiving Items

Delete

You can remove one or more items from an Outlook folder by selecting the item or items in the Information Viewer of the Outlook window and then choosing Edit, Delete, clicking the Delete button on the Standard toolbar, or pressing Ctrl+D. If you've opened an item in a form, you can remove it by clicking the Delete button on the form's toolbar, choosing File, Delete, or pressing Ctrl+D (a particular form might not have all of these commands).

When you remove an item, it's not permanently deleted right away. Rather, it's initially moved to the Deleted Items folder. As long as an item is still contained in the Deleted

Items folder, you can restore it to the folder that originally contained it by simply moving it back into that folder using any of the methods described in the previous section.

> **note** To select several adjoining items, click the first and then click the last while pressing Shift. To select nonadjoining items, click the first and then click each additional one while pressing Ctrl. To select *all* items in the opened folder, choose Select All from the Edit menu or press Ctrl+A.

If you want to permanently delete the item, remove it from the Deleted Items folder using any of the methods just described. You can also permanently delete *all* items in the Deleted Items folder by choosing Tools, Empty "Deleted Items" Folder. Or, you can have Outlook permanently delete all items in the Deleted Items folder each time you exit the program by choosing Tools, Options, clicking the Other tab in the Options dialog box, and checking Empty The Deleted Items Folder Upon Exiting. To see a message before an item is permanently deleted, click the Advanced Options button in the Other tab and make sure the Warn Before Permanently Deleting Items option is checked.

Also, if you archive your Outlook folders, as discussed next, you can have Outlook permanently delete all items in the Deleted Items folder that are older than a specified age. This method is usually safer for permanently deleting items because it generally gives you a longer period of time in which you can recover removed items from the Deleted Items folder.

Archiving Items

You can clean up your Outlook folders by *archiving*. Archiving removes Outlook items either by moving them to a separate Outlook data file, from which you can later recover them, or by permanently deleting them. You can have Outlook archive automatically at specified intervals, or you can archive manually.

To have Outlook archive automatically, complete the following steps:

1 For each folder you want to archive, right-click the folder's shortcut in the Outlook Bar, choose Properties from the shortcut menu, click the AutoArchive tab (shown in Figure 37-6), and do one of the following:

- ■ To use Outlook's default AutoArchive settings, select the Archive Items In This Folder Using The Default Settings option. (You can change these default settings by clicking the Default Archive Settings button.)

- ■ To override the default AutoArchive settings for the current folder, select Archive This Folder Using These Settings, and then select the specific AutoArchive options you want.

This enables archiving for the particular folder and tells Outlook how to do it. Click OK when you're done.

997

> **note** Because items in a Contacts folder don't normally become obsolete with time—as messages, appointments, and other items do—you can't have Outlook automatically archive your Contacts folder (its Properties dialog box doesn't have an AutoArchive tab). You can, however, manually archive this folder, as described later.

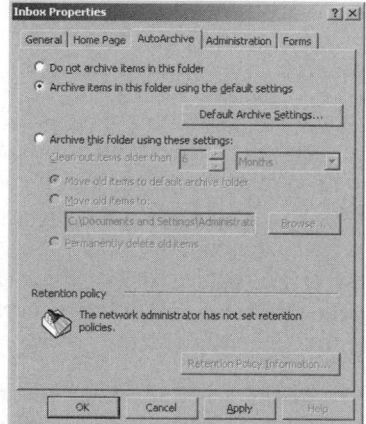

Figure 37-6. You can set up automatic archiving for a folder using the AutoArchive tab of the Properties dialog box.

2 Choose Tools, Options, click the Other tab in the Options dialog box, click the AutoArchive button, check the Run AutoArchive Every option, and in the adjoining text box enter the desired frequency of automatic archiving in days. This will cause Outlook to begin automatically archiving at the specified frequency all folders for which you turned on archiving in step 1.

3 In the AutoArchive dialog box, choose any other automatic archiving options you want and click the OK button. Note that you can override the settings in the Default Folder Settings For Archiving area for a particular folder by selecting Archive This Folder Using These Settings in the AutoArchive tab of that folder's Properties dialog box, as explained in step 1.

To archive manually, complete the following steps:

1 Choose File, Archive to open the Archive dialog box (shown in Figure 37-7).

2 Do one of the following:

■ To archive all folders for which archiving is enabled in the AutoArchive tab of the folder's Properties dialog box, using the settings made in that tab (as explained in step 1 of the previous procedure), select the Archive All Folders According To Their AutoArchive Settings option.

■ To archive a single folder, select Archive This Folder And All Subfolders and select the archiving options that you want.

3 Click OK to start archiving.

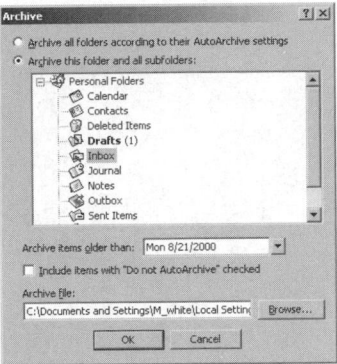

Figure 37-7. The Archive dialog box lets you archive your Outlook folders manually.

---

tip   **Preserve Individual Items**

You can exempt an important item from being automatically archived by opening the item in a form, choosing Properties from the form's File menu, and checking Do Not AutoArchive This Item. Note, however, that if you perform a manual archiving, you can override this setting by checking Include Items With "Do Not AutoArchive" Checked in the Archive dialog box.

To recover an archived item, you can choose File, Open, Outlook Data File and select the Outlook data file where you stored the archived item (you specify this folder when you set up automatic archiving or perform a manual archive). Outlook will open the archive file and display its contents (together with the contents of your main data file) in the Folder List. You can then use the Folder List to open the folder containing the archived item and copy it back into its original folder.

For information on opening and working with Outlook data files, see "Managing Outlook Data Files," on page 1101.

Changing the Way You View Items

You can change the way you view Outlook items displayed in the Information Viewer of the main Outlook window in the following ways:

- Switching and customizing views
- Sorting, filtering, and grouping items
- Using the Preview pane

These techniques are discussed in the following three sections.

> **note** Keep in mind that although this chapter focuses on Outlook items and folders, you can use the first two methods to modify the way you view the contents of file folders when you use Outlook's integrated file management feature. For information on viewing files in Outlook, as well as details on the views that are available when you open a file folder, see "Accessing File Folders," on page 975. (Outlook doesn't provide a Preview pane for viewing the contents of disk files.)

Switching and Customizing Views

You can work with an Outlook or file folder using a variety of different *views*, which vary—often radically—in the way the information is organized and in the amount of detail that's shown in the Information Viewer of the main Outlook window. For example, Figure 37-8 shows the Contacts folder in the Phone List view, which displays all contacts in a table, with each contact in a separate row and each contact field (such as Full Name, Company, File As, and so on) in a separate column. Figure 37-9 shows Contacts in the By Category view, which also displays the contacts in a table but groups them according to the contents of their Category fields. And Figure 37-10 shows the Contacts folder in the Address Cards view, which displays each contact in a business card format.

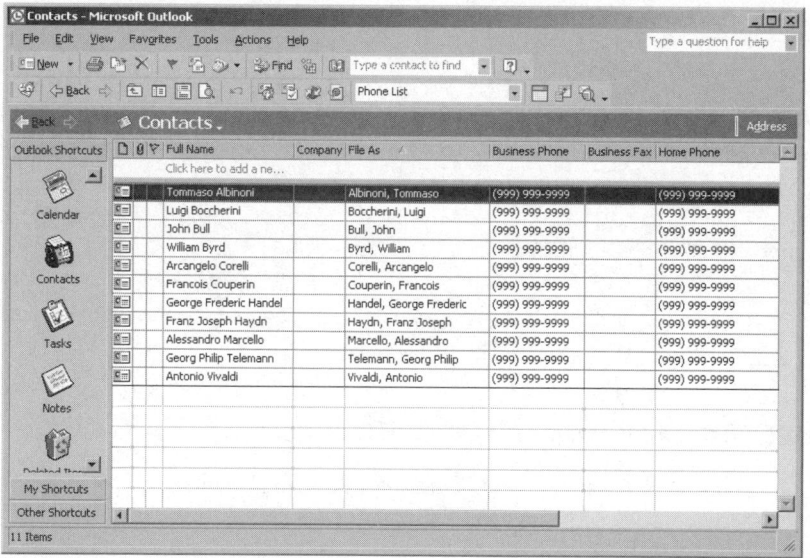

Figure 37-8. This figure shows the Contacts folder in the Phone List view.

> **note** You can assign each of your Outlook items one or more different categories, which you can use to group, filter, sort, or find items. The following chapters explain the details of assigning categories to different types of items. Grouping items is covered in the next section.

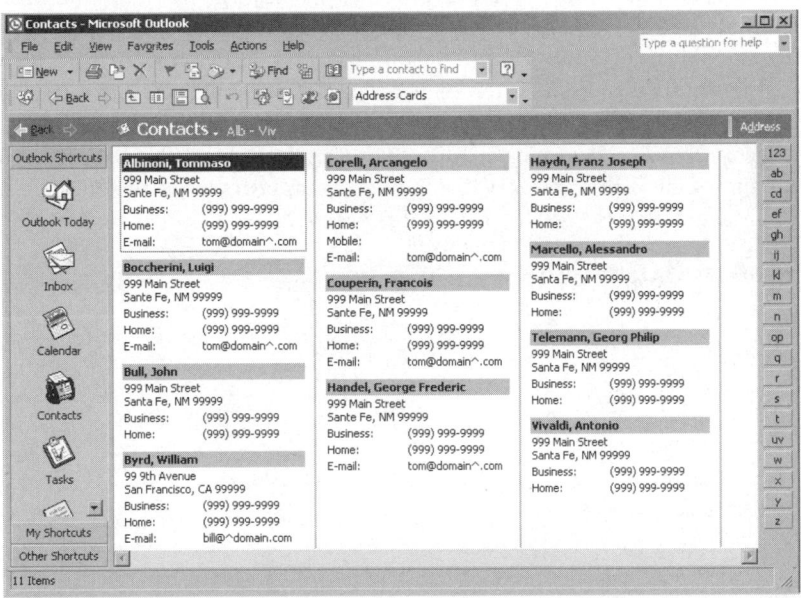

Figure 37-9. This figure shows the Contacts folder in the By Category view.

Figure 37-10. This figure shows the Contacts folder in the Address Cards view.

Each folder has available a set of default views that are appropriate for the type of information stored in that folder. To change the view of the opened folder, simply select another item in the Current View drop-down list on the Advanced toolbar. For example, the available views for the Contacts folder are shown at the top of the next page.

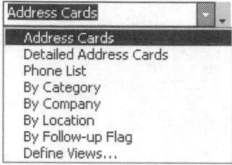

Alternatively, you can choose the view from the Current View submenu of the View menu.

For certain views, such as the Day/Week/Month view of the Calendar folder and the Message Timeline view of the Inbox folder, you can control the number of days shown on the screen by choosing the Day, Week, or Month option from the View menu, or by clicking the Day, Week, or Month button on the Standard toolbar. Some views (such as the Day/Week/Month view of the Calendar folder) also have a Work Week option.

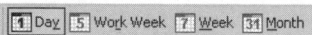

You can modify any view by choosing View, Current View, Customize Current View. Choosing this command displays the View Summary dialog box, which contains a set of buttons you can click to change various features of the current view. Note that in certain views, some of these buttons are disabled because the corresponding features don't apply to that view. For example, if Day/Week/Month is the current view of the Calendar folder, the Group By and Sort buttons are disabled. Also, the information displayed to the right of each button depends on the particular view that's active and the options that have been selected for that view. This information either gives the current settings or describes the type of settings you can make by clicking the button. Figure 37-11 shows the View Summary dialog box as it appears when the Phone List view of the Contacts folder (with default settings) is active.

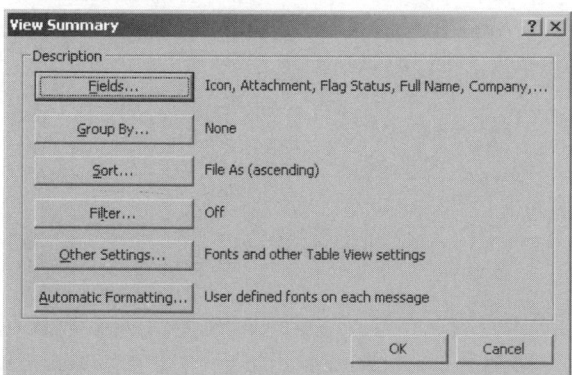

Figure 37-11. Opening the View Summary dialog box is the first step in modifying the current view.

You can click the Other Settings button in the View Summary dialog box to change the fonts used in the view and to modify other features, which vary according to the current view. In some views—such as the Messages view of the Inbox folder or the Day/Week/Month view of the Calendar folder—you can click the Automatic Formatting button to apply distinguishing formatting to certain items. For example, in the Messages view of the Inbox folder, you could have the headings for all unread messages displayed in an italic green font. Or, in the Day/Week/Month view of the Calendar folder, you could have all meetings organized by your boss displayed in red text to indicate their importance.

The features set by the Fields button are discussed in the sidebar "Modifying Columns in a Table View," on page 1004, while those set by the Group By, Sort, and Filter buttons are discussed in the next section.

Finally, you can choose View, Current View, Define Views to open the Define Views dialog box (shown in Figure 37-12), in which you can modify any of the views available for the current folder, restore any of these views to its default settings, rename a view, or create a new custom view.

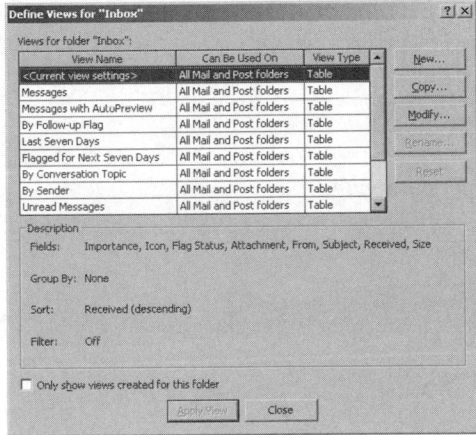

Figure 37-12. The Define Views dialog box allows you to work with any of the views available for the current folder.

Modifying Columns in a Table View

In many of the views of Outlook or file folders, the information is arranged in a table consisting of rows and columns (for instance, the Messages view of the Inbox folder shown in Figure 36-7 on page 974, the Details view of the My Document file folder shown in Figure 36-8 on page 976, and the Phone List view of the Contacts folder shown in Figure 37-8). Each column displays the values of a given field of information. A *field* is an individual unit of information within an Outlook item—for example, the subject or date received of a message in the Inbox folder.

In a table view, you can modify the columns in a variety of ways. For example, you can change the width of a column by dragging the right border of the *column heading* (the button-like bar, containing a label, at the top of the column). You can adjust the width of a column to accommodate its contents by double-clicking the column heading's right border. You can move a column by dragging its heading to a new position in the column heading row. And you can remove a column by dragging the heading to any position on the screen outside the column heading row. (When the mouse pointer turns into an *X*, releasing the mouse button will remove the column.)

You can add, remove, or rearrange columns in a table view by choosing options in the Show Fields dialog box. To open this dialog box, choose View, Current View, Customize Current View, and then click the Fields button in the View Summary dialog box (shown in Figure 37-11).

To modify a column from within the Information Viewer, right-click the column's heading to display the following shortcut menu:

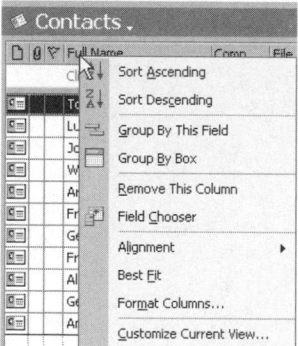

Then choose a command as described in Table 37-2.

Modifying Columns in a Table View *(continued)*

Table 37-2. **Modifying Columns Using the Shortcut Menu**

To Modify the Column Like This	Do This on the Shortcut Menu
Delete the column	Choose Remove This Column.
Display a dialog box that lets you add a new column by simply dragging a field name from the dialog box to the desired position in the heading row	Choose Field Chooser.
Apply left (the default), right, or centered alignment to the contents of the column	Choose a command from the Alignment submenu.
Make the column just wide enough to display the column contents	Choose Best Fit. This command has the same effect as double-clicking the right border of the column heading.
Change the format, label, width, or alignment of one or more columns in the table	Choose Format Columns and select options in the Format Columns dialog box. You can also display this dialog box by choosing View, Current View, Format Columns.
Display the View Summary dialog box	Choose Customize Current View.

Sorting, Filtering, and Grouping Items in Folders

You can further refine the way information is displayed in a particular view of an Outlook or file folder by sorting, filtering, or grouping the items in the folder. You can assign different sorting, filtering, or grouping settings to each view, and the settings will stay with the view until you explicitly change them.

note You can sort, filter, or group items in any table view (that is, any view consisting of rows and columns with a row of column headings at the top). You can also perform one or more of these operations in certain other views. For example, in the Address Cards view of the Contacts folder, you can sort or filter items, and in the By Type view of the Journal folder, you can filter or group items. You can tell which operations are possible when a particular view is selected by the buttons that are enabled in the View Summary dialog box (These buttons are discussed next.)

To sort, filter, or group items in the current view, choose View, Current View, Customize Current View to open the View Summary dialog box (shown in Figure 37-11, on page 1002). Alternatively, you can open this dialog box by right-clicking anywhere in the heading row of a table view, or in a blank area of any type of view, and then choosing the Customize Current View command from the shortcut menu.

To sort the items in a folder, click the Sort button in the View Summary dialog box. This will open the Sort dialog box (shown in Figure 37-13), which lets you sort the items by the values of one or more fields, in either ascending or descending order. Alternatively, you can sort the items in a table view by the values in one of the columns by simply clicking the heading above that column. Each click of the heading toggles between an ascending and a descending sort. An arrow is displayed in the heading of a column currently used for sorting—an up-arrow for an ascending sort or a down-arrow for a descending sort. (If the column is too narrow, however, the arrow won't appear in the header.) You can use multiple fields for sorting by clicking each header while pressing Shift; Outlook will sort using the fields in the order you click them.

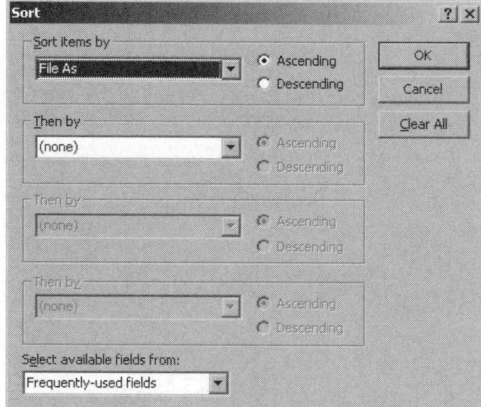

Figure 37-13. The Sort dialog box lets you sort the items in a folder.

When you open a folder, Outlook normally displays all items stored in that folder. However, you can click the Filter button in the View Summary dialog box to open the Filter dialog box (Figure 37-14), where you can set conditions to determine which items will be displayed. For example, you could display only those messages in the Inbox that contain the word *manuscript* in the message text, or only those messages that are marked as high importance. The criteria you can select are the same as those displayed in the Advanced Find dialog box, which is discussed in "Finding Outlook Items or Disk Files," on page 1010.

Chapter 37

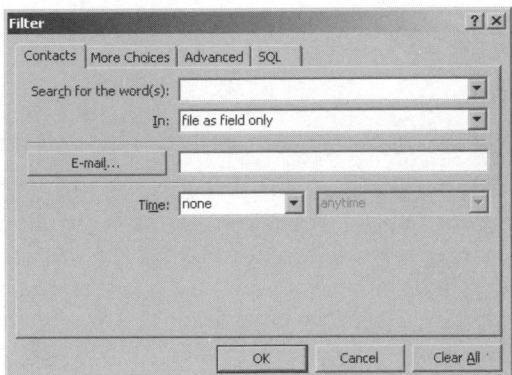

Figure 37-14. The Filter dialog box lets you control the items that are displayed in a folder.

You can click the Group By button in the View Summary dialog box to open the Group By dialog box (Figure 37-15), which lets you group items by the values of one or more fields, rather than displaying the items in a simple list. For example, if you grouped the messages in your Inbox by the Importance field, Outlook would list all high-importance messages in one group, followed by all normal-importance messages in a second group, followed by all low-importance messages in a third group. You can define groups within other groups, creating up to four levels of nested groups. For instance, in the previous example, within each importance group you could group the messages by their sensitivities. Figure 37-9 shows the Contacts folder grouped by the Category field (in this case the grouping is part of the definition of the By Category view).

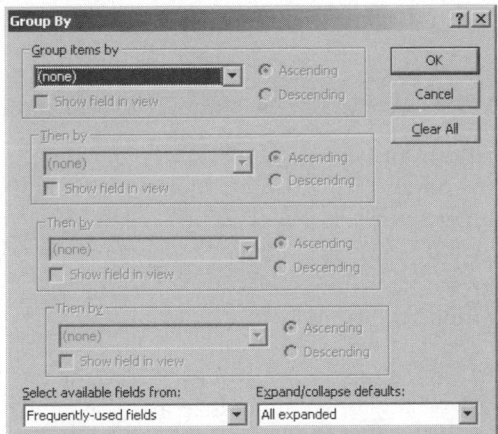

Figure 37-15. The Group By dialog box lets you group items by one or more fields.

Troubleshooting

Outlook Items Mysteriously Disappear

You switched to a different view and some of the items in the Outlook folder disappeared.

When you apply a filter (or a sort or grouping), you're actually modifying the definition of the current view. The filter (or the sort or grouping) will stay with the view and will be reapplied whenever you switch back to that view. If you suspect that Outlook isn't displaying all of the items in the opened folder, look for the words "Filter Applied" in the Folder Banner (to the right of the folder name), as shown below:

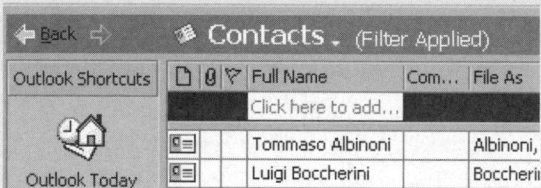

("Filter Applied" is also displayed at the left end of the Outlook status bar.)

To remove the filter, choose View, Current View, Customize Current View, click the Filter button, and click the Clear All button in the Filter dialog box (as shown in Figure 37-14, on page 1007). (You can likewise remove sorting and grouping by clicking the Clear All button in the Sort or Group By dialog box.)

Outlook provides the following two alternative ways to group items in a table view:

- You can group the items by the values in a column by right-clicking the column's heading and choosing Group By This Field from the shortcut menu.

Group
By Box

- You can choose Group By Box from this same shortcut menu (or click the Group By Box button on the Advanced toolbar) to display the Group By box at the top of the Information Viewer. Once this box is displayed, you can drag one or more column headings into the box to group the items by the associated field or fields. You can change the order of the groupings by dragging the field names within the Group By box.

When items are grouped, you can expand or collapse groups by clicking the + or − button at the top of the group, or by using the commands on the Expand/Collapse submenu on the View menu.

You can use the Categories command on the Edit menu to assign categories to the selected item or items in your Outlook folders. For example, you might assign some messages the Business category and others the Personal category. (As explained in Chapter 38, "Managing Message and Appointments," and Chapter 39, "Managing Contacts, Tasks, and Other Types of Information," you can also assign a category to an item when you create or edit it in a form.) You can then sort, filter, or group the items based on their categories. You can also locate and display items that belong to a given category using the Advanced Find command, which is covered in "Using the Advanced Find Dialog Box," on page 1011.

newfeature!
Using the Preview Pane

Preview
Pane

You can use the Preview pane to view the contents of an Outlook item without having to open it in a form. You can display or hide the Preview pane by choosing Preview Pane from the View menu, or by clicking the Preview Pane button on the Advanced toolbar. Once you display the Preview pane within a particular view, the pane will be displayed whenever you use that view—until you hide it.

If you've opened the Tasks folder, the Notes folder, or an e-mail folder such as Inbox, the Preview pane works just like it did with Outlook 2000. That is, it shows selected item fields in a header and it displays the contents of the item's large text box (such as the body of an e-mail message) below that. (See Figure 36-7, on page 974, which shows the Inbox folder with the Preview pane displayed.)

If, however, you've opened one of the other default Outlook folders, the Preview pane in Outlook 2002 displays the selected item within the item's form—that is, within the form used to display the item when you open it (see Figure 37-16). The Preview pane shows only the main tab of the form and doesn't let you edit its contents. You might have to expand the size of the Preview pane to see the complete form. You can adjust the size of the Preview pane by dragging its upper border.

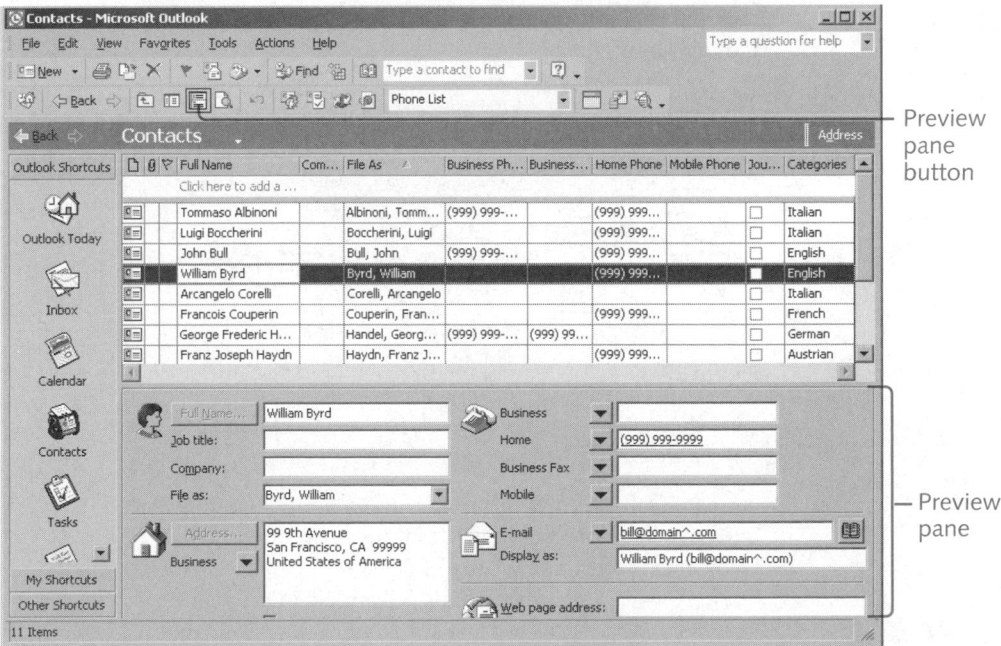

Figure 37-16. In this figure a Contacts item is viewed in the Preview pane.

When the Preview pane is displayed, you can normally display different items by pressing the Spacebar to display the next item or by pressing Shift+Spacebar to display the previous item. To modify this or other features of the Preview pane, choose Tools, Options, click the Other tab, and click the Preview Pane button.

tip **Preview an Item's Text**

AutoPreview In a table view, you can display the text contained in each item's large text box—or at least the first part of that text—below each item in the Information Viewer by turning on the AutoPreview feature. You can turn AutoPreview on or off by choosing View, AutoPreview or by clicking the AutoPreview button on the Advanced toolbar.

Finding Outlook Items or Disk Files

The fastest way to find Outlook items that contain specified text in any field is to use the Find pane, which is displayed at the top of the Information Viewer. (To search for disk files, you'll have to use Advanced Find, discussed in the next section.) To use the Find pane, follow these steps:

1 Open the Outlook folder that you want to search and switch to the view you want to use to display the found items.

Find

2 Click the Find button on the Standard toolbar, choose Tools, Find, or press Ctrl+E to display the Find pane (see Figure 37-17). (To hide the Find pane, click the Find button, choose Tools, Find again, or click the Close button at the right of the pane.)

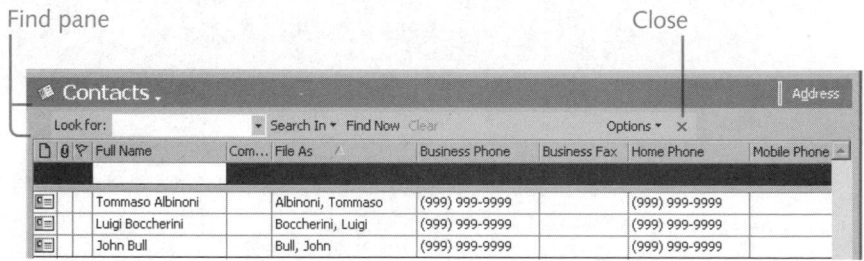

Figure 37-17. The Find pane displayed in the Contacts folder.

3 Type the text you want to search for into the Look For box, or select previously entered search text from the drop-down list.

4 To search a folder other than the currently opened one, click the Search In button and choose the folder from the drop-down menu, or choose Choose Folders and select one or more folders in the Select Folder(s) dialog box. Outlook will list the search folder or folders in the text box to the right of the Search In button (this box initially contains just the name of the currently opened folder).

InsideOut

Although the Find pane lets you search in one or more folders besides the current one, it uses the current view of the opened folder to display the search results, which might not show much of the information of the found items. Consider, for example, that the Contacts folder is opened and the Phone List view is active. If you search for items in the Inbox folder, the Phone List view won't show the information for a found item because this view displays the wrong fields (Full Name, Company, and so on, rather than From, Subject, and so on). So if you're searching a single folder, you should open that folder before you use the Find pane.

Options

5   To look for your search text in all item fields, click the Options button and check Search All Text In Each Message. To speed up the search, you can clear this option to search only the most common fields.

6   Click the Find Now button.

Outlook will then display any found items within the Information Viewer. (Outlook may switch to a different view to better present the results.) To clear the found items from the Information Viewer and redisplay the items that were listed there before you performed the search, click the Clear button in the Find pane.

Using the Advanced Find Dialog Box

The main advantages of using the Advanced Find dialog box rather than the Find pane are that you can fine-tune your search criteria, you can search for files in addition to Outlook items, you can stop the search at any time, and you can run a search from Windows even if Outlook isn't running. Also, because an Advanced Find search runs in the background, you can continue working in Outlook during a long search.

You can search for items in one or more Outlook folders, and you can search either for items of a particular type (such as messages, contacts, or journal entries) or for items of any type. For example, you could search the Inbox folder for all messages that were sent by a given person. Or, you could search all your Outlook folders for items of any type that are assigned a particular category, such as Business or Personal.

Likewise, you can search for files in one or more file folders. You can search for files of a certain type (such as Word or Microsoft Excel documents), or for files of any type. For example, you could search for all Word document files on your hard disk that contain a specific word or phrase.

Whether you search for Outlook items or disk files, the Find command lets you specify a wide variety of search criteria. To use the Advanced Find dialog box, complete the following steps:

1   Display the Advanced Find dialog box (shown in Figure 37-18) by choosing Tools, Advanced Find, by pressing Ctrl+Shift+F, or by right-clicking a shortcut

in the Outlook Bar and choosing Advanced Find from the shortcut menu. Also, you can open the Advanced Find dialog box at any time—even when you aren't running Outlook—by choosing Start, Search, Using Microsoft Outlook in Windows.

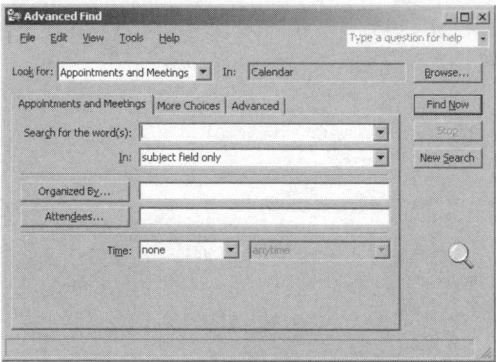

Figure 37-18. The Advanced Find dialog box provides the most powerful way to search for Outlook items.

2 In the Look For drop-down list, select the type of Outlook item, or other kind of file, that you want to search for.

3 Click the Browse button and select the specific Outlook folders or file folders that you want to search. The folder(s) you select will be displayed in the In box. Or you can just accept the default folder displayed in the In box.

4 Specify basic search criteria in the first tab, which is labeled according to the item you've selected in the Look For list, such as "Contacts" or "Files." You can specify more advanced search criteria in the other tabs. The particular search options that appear on the tabs of the Advanced Find dialog box depend on the type of item or file you're searching for (which is selected in the Look For drop-down list). Keep in mind that you can get help on using a particular control by choosing What's This? from the Help menu and then clicking the control.

5 Click the Find Now button to start the search.

You can resume working in Outlook while a search takes place. If you want to stop a search before it has finished, click the Stop button.

After the search is completed, Outlook displays all matching items or files in a list that's added to the bottom of the Advanced Find dialog box. You can open an Outlook item or a disk file by double-clicking it within this list. Keep in mind that the Advanced Find dialog box provides many of the same commands that the main Outlook window provides for customizing the view, sorting and grouping the items, and so on.

If you want to perform another search, click the New Search button to remove the found items and to clear the search criteria you've typed in.

You can also save all of the criteria you've entered into the Advanced Find dialog box by choosing Save Search from the File menu and then specifying the name of the file in which you want to store the search criteria. (The file will be given the .oss extension.) You can quickly rerun the same search later by choosing File, Open Search and selecting this file. Or, if the Advanced Find dialog box isn't currently displayed, you can display it and rerun the search by double-clicking the .oss file in Windows Explorer or in a file-folder window.

> **newfeature!**
> **note** In Office XP you can also search for Outlook items, as well as disk files, by using the new Search task pane in Word, Excel, Microsoft PowerPoint, or Access. Or you can use the similar features found in the Search dialog box, which you open by choosing Search from the Tools drop-down menu in the Open dialog box and related dialog boxes. For more information, see "Finding Office Files or Outlook Items Using the Search Feature," on page 69.

Organizing Items Using the Organize Pane

The Organize pane is a Web-style page that you can display at the top of the Information Viewer and use for working with Outlook items. Although it doesn't let you do anything you can't do by using the program's conventional commands, it provides fast, easy alternative methods for performing some of the more common tasks.

You can perform the following tasks in the Organize pane. These tasks aren't available in all folders. In the Organize pane displayed for each folder, Outlook provides only the capabilities that are most useful for working with the types of items stored in that folder.

- Move selected items in the folder to another folder. Or have Outlook automatically move items in the future, according to rules that you specify. For example, you could have all future e-mail messages that your boss sends automatically moved to a specific folder.

- Assign categories to items—such as Business or Personal—or create new categories.

- Change the current view.

- Organize messages by color-coding certain ones. Or automatically color-code, move, or delete junk e-mail or adult-content e-mail.

> These features are discussed in "Organizing Your E-Mail Messages and Handling Junk E-Mail," on page 1036.

To use the Organize pane, follow these steps:

Organize

1 Open the folder you want to work with.

2 Choose Tools, Organize or click the Organize button on the Standard toolbar. The Organize pane will then be displayed at the top of the Information Viewer. The features that the Organize pane includes vary depending on the current folder. Figure 37-19 shows the Organize pane for the Calendar folder.

You can remove the Organize pane by choosing the Organize command, by clicking the Organize button again, or by clicking the Close button in the pane's upper right corner.

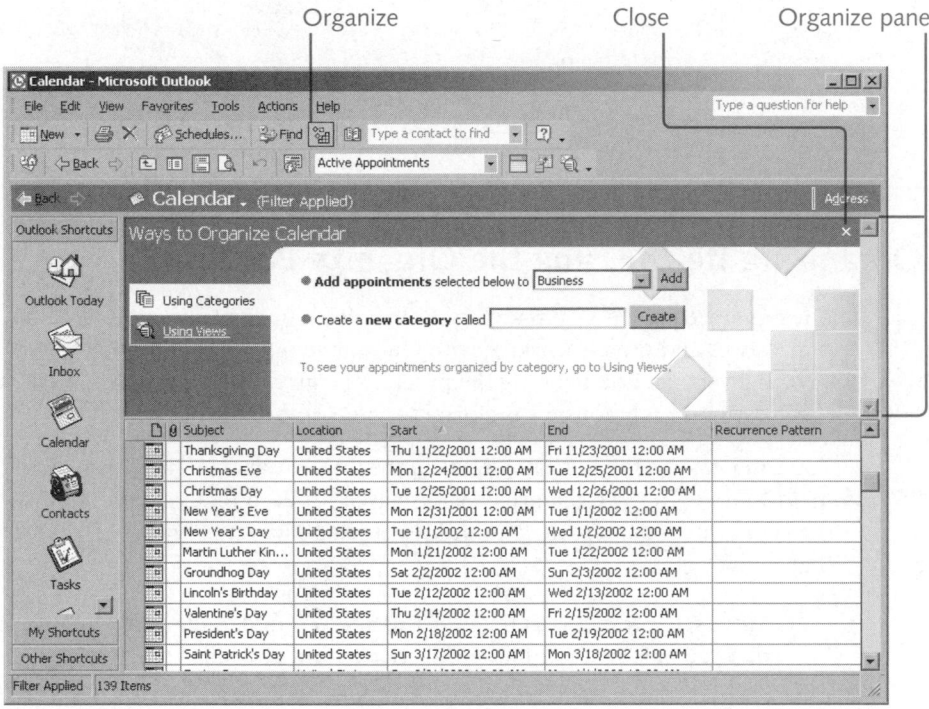

Figure 37-19. This figure shows the Organize pane displayed in the Calendar folder.

3 Click a command at the left of the Organize pane—such as Using Categories or Using Views—to indicate the way you want to organize the folder. This will open a tab on the right that contains the necessary controls.

4 Use the controls on the right side of the pane to carry out the organizing tasks.

Working with Outlook Folders

The Outlook folders described in this book are the default folders created by the Outlook program. You can create additional folders to store specific types of Outlook items. For example, you might create one or more folders for storing saved e-mail messages, rather than keeping them all in your Inbox. Also, you might create a new folder for storing appointments so that you can have one calendar for your personal appointments and another for your business appointments.

To create a new Outlook folder, complete the following steps:

1 Choose File, New, Folder; choose File, Folder, New Folder; or press Ctrl+Shift+E. This will open the Create New Folder dialog box (shown in Figure 37-20).

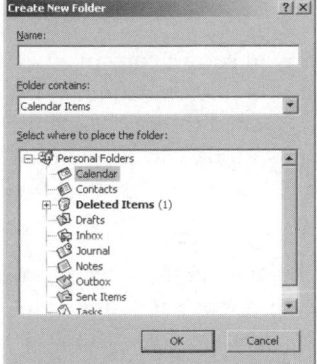

Figure 37-20. Use the Create New Folder dialog box to create a new Outlook folder.

2 Type a name for your new folder into the Name text box.

3 In the Folder Contains drop-down list, select the type of Outlook item the new folder will contain, as follows:

- To create a folder for storing e-mail messages, select Mail And Post Items.

- To create a folder for storing appointments, events, or meetings, select Calendar Items.

- To create a folder for storing contact descriptions and distribution lists, select Contact Items.

- To create a folder for storing tasks, notes, or journal entries, select Task Items, Note Items, or Journal Items.

4 In the Select Where To Place The Folder list, click the folder in which you want to store the new folder. Your new folder will be made a subfolder of the folder you select and will be displayed under that folder in the Folder List.

1015

> **note** Outlook folders—like file folders—are arranged in a hierarchy of folders and subfolders. This hierarchy is shown in the Folder List. Outlook Today (which also has a data file name, usually "Personal Folders") is at the top of the hierarchy. The default Outlook folders are all direct subfolders of Outlook Today. You can store your new folder at the same level as the default Outlook folders by selecting the top item (usually labeled "Personal Folders") in the Select Where To Place The Folder list in the Create New Folder dialog box.

5 Click the OK button.

6 If you want to add a shortcut for your new folder to the Outlook Bar, click Yes in the message box that Outlook now displays. If you choose not to do this, you can access the folder using the Folder List. Also, you can add a shortcut later using the method described in "Customizing the Outlook Bar," on page 1089.

You can also create a new Outlook folder by making a copy of an existing folder and its contents. To do this, open the folder you want to copy, choose File, Folder, Copy "*Folder*" (where *Folder* is the name of the opened folder). You'll then have to select the folder where you want to store the copy. Outlook will copy the folder plus any subfolders it contains, together with the contents of these folders, and it will assign the copy a default name. You can rename it later.

You can't move, rename, or remove any of the default Outlook folders (Inbox, Calendar, and so on), but you can move, rename, or remove an Outlook folder that you've created. To perform one of these operations, open the folder, and then on the Folder submenu of the File menu, choose Move "*Folder*," Rename "*Folder*," or Delete "*Folder*" (where *Folder* is the name of the open folder).

As when you remove an Outlook item, when you remove an Outlook folder, it isn't permanently deleted at that moment. Rather, it's moved to the Deleted Items folder, where it becomes a subfolder of Deleted Items. You can permanently delete it using the same techniques described for items in "Removing and Archiving Items," on page 996. And you can restore a folder by moving it back to its original location in the folder hierarchy. Be aware that if you've selected the Empty The Deleted Items Folder Upon Exiting option on the Other tab of the Options dialog box (opened by choosing Tools, Options), the items in your Deleted Items folder are permanently deleted when you exit Outlook.

> **note** Rather than choosing the menu commands discussed in this section from the Folder submenu of the File menu, you can choose them from the shortcut menu that appears when you right-click the Folder Banner above the Information Viewer.

> **tip** **Use the Folder List to Work with Folders**
>
> An alternative way to perform the operations explained in this section is to display a permanent Folder List, right-click an Outlook folder name, and then choose a command from the shortcut menu that appears. Using the Folder List, you can also move an Outlook folder by simply dragging it or copy a folder by pressing Ctrl while you drag. And you can remove an Outlook folder by selecting it and pressing the Delete key. For information on displaying the Folder List, see "Using Other Methods to Open Folders," on page 978.

Printing Outlook Information

Outlook lets you print the information stored in any of your Outlook folders. For example, you could print a message stored in the Inbox folder, a day (or a range of days) in the Calendar folder, or, to create an address book that you can carry with you, the entire contents of your Contacts folder. Also, if you've opened a file folder in Outlook, you can print the list of files and file folders currently displayed in the Information Viewer or you can print the actual contents of the selected file or files (provided that you have a program installed on your computer that's registered to print the type of file that's selected).

Outlook provides a variety of methods for printing. The following is a flexible, general procedure that you can use for printing any kind of Outlook information:

1 Open the folder containing the information you want to print and switch to the view that displays the items the way you want to print them. (The current view affects the printing options that the Print dialog box provides when you open it.)

2 If you want to print one or more specific items—for example, messages in the Inbox folder or contacts in the Contacts folder—select the item or items. To select an item, click it; to select additional items, press Ctrl while you click each one.

3 Choose File, Print, or press Ctrl+P to open the Print dialog box, which is shown in Figure 37-21, on page 1018.

Chapter 37

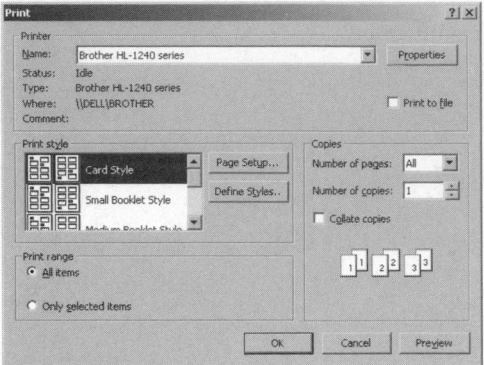

Figure 37-21. This figure shows the Print dialog box as it would appear if you opened the Contacts folder in the Address Cards view and selected a single contact prior to opening the dialog box.

4 In the Print Style list near the center of the dialog box, select a printing style to specify the general way the information will be organized on the printed copy and the level of detail that will be shown.

5 If you want to modify the selected printing style for the current print job, click the Page Setup button to open the Page Setup dialog box, which lets you modify the fonts, paper size, headers or footers, and other features of the printed pages. If you want to permanently modify one of the default printing styles or create a custom style, click the Define Styles button.

6 Change other print options in the Print dialog box, as necessary. The specific options available depend on the folder you opened and the items you selected prior to opening the dialog box. For example, if you opened the Contacts folder, you can choose whether to print all contacts or only the contact or contacts that you selected.

7 To preview the appearance of the printed output and to see the effect of all the options you've selected, click the Preview button. When you're done previewing, click the Print button in the Print Preview window to return to the Print dialog box.

8 To begin printing, click the OK button in the Print dialog box.

InsideOut

Print

Printing by simply clicking the Print button on the Standard toolbar creates somewhat random results. In some situations Outlook prints immediately, while in other situations it first opens the Print dialog box so you can select the print settings you want. To get predictable results, it's generally better to use the Print dialog box as discussed in this section.

Using Outlook Today to Get an Overview

The Outlook Today folder displays a Web page that provides you with an overview of some of your current Outlook information and allows you to access other Outlook folders. It's shown in Figure 37-22.

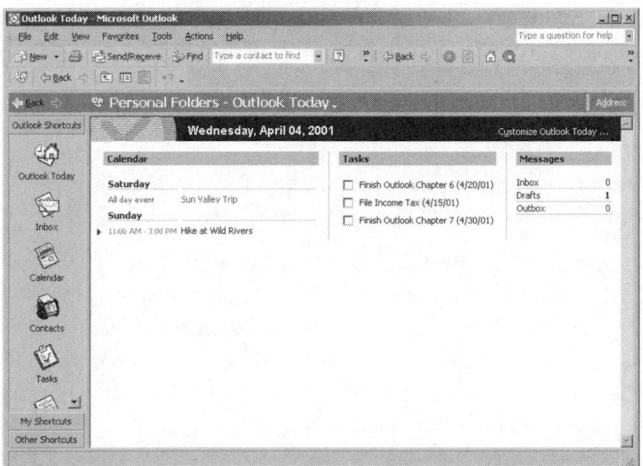

Figure 37-22. The Outlook Today folder displays a Web page that gives you an overview of your Outlook information.

You can use Outlook Today as your starting point for working in Outlook. You can use the default Outlook Today folder shown in Figure 37-22 in the following ways:

- To open the Calendar, Tasks, or Inbox folder, click Calendar, Tasks, or Messages.

- The Calendar area displays your appointments, all-day events, and meetings for the next five days. To open one of these items, click it.

- The Tasks area lists all your pending tasks, showing their subjects and due dates. To mark a task as completed, check the check box (Outlook will then draw a line through the task). To open a task, click the task subject or due date.

- The Messages area shows the number of unread messages in your Inbox, as well as the total numbers of messages in your Drafts and Outbox folders. To open one of these folders, click the folder name.

- To customize the Outlook Today folder, click the Customize Outlook Today command near the upper-right corner of the page to open the Customize Outlook Today page. Here you can check the When Starting Go Directly To Outlook Today option to have Outlook display the Outlook Today folder (rather than the Inbox) when you first run the program. You can also modify the information that Outlook Today displays from your Calendar, Tasks, and E-mail folders. And, you can select an alternative page style.

InsideOut

The Web page displayed in the Outlook Today folder is known as the folder's *home page*. You can assign a home page to *any* Outlook folder. A home page might be useful for displaying instructions or other information about the folder. Unfortunately, however, Microsoft removed the Show Folder Home Page command from the View menu, which made it relatively easy to switch between viewing the folder's home page and viewing its contents in Outlook 2000. In Outlook 2002, a better way to display a Web page in the Outlook window is to add a shortcut to the Outlook Bar for opening that page. You can then easily display the page by clicking the Web-page shortcut, and then quickly switch to viewing a folder's contents by clicking the folder's shortcut. For information on adding a shortcut to the Outlook Bar for opening a Web page, see "Working with Outlook Bar Shortcuts," on page 1090.

(If you still want to assign a home page to a folder, right-click the folder's shortcut in the Outlook Bar, choose Properties from the shortcut menu, open the Home Page tab, and either type in the file path of the Web page you want to use as the home page or click the Browse button to locate and select the page. To display the folder's home page rather than its contents, check the Show Home Page By Default For This Folder option. To display the page's contents, you have to go back into this tab and clear this option.)

Managing Messages and Appointments

Receiving and Sending E-Mail Messages Using the E-Mail Folders

If you've set up one or more e-mail accounts in Microsoft Outlook 2002, you can use Outlook to receive and send e-mail and to organize your e-mail messages. Outlook uses the default e-mail folders it has created as follows:

- Incoming e-mail messages are delivered to your Inbox folder.

- While you compose a message using the e-mail editor, Outlook normally stores the message in your Drafts folder.

- When you send a message, Outlook temporarily stores it in your Outbox folder until the message is transmitted to your outgoing e-mail server and delivered to the recipient. (In some cases, when you send a message it's transmitted immediately to the outgoing server rather than being stored in the Outbox.)

- When a message is transmitted to the outgoing e-mail server, Outlook normally stores a copy of the message in your Sent Items folder.

> **note** You can control whether Outlook automatically saves unsent messages that you are composing and whether it saves copies of your outgoing messages in the Sent Items folder, and you can set other e-mail handling options, by choosing Tools, Options, and clicking the E-Mail Options button in the Preferences tab of the Options dialog box to open the E-Mail Options dialog box (shown in Figure 38-1).
>
> You can specify the folder where Outlook saves unsent messages and how often it saves them, as well as set other advanced e-mail processing options, by clicking the Advanced E-Mail Options button in the E-Mail Options dialog box to open the Advanced E-Mail Options dialog box (shown in Figure 38-2).

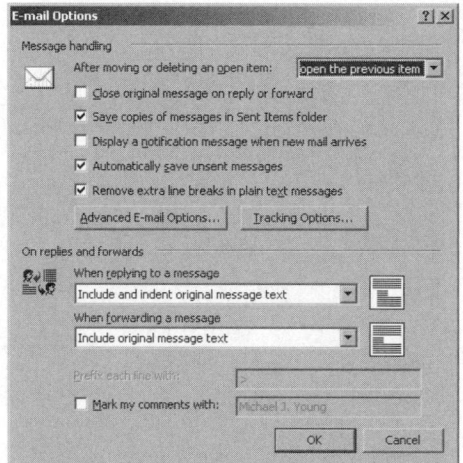

Figure 38-1. The E-Mail Options dialog box provides a basic set of e-mail options.

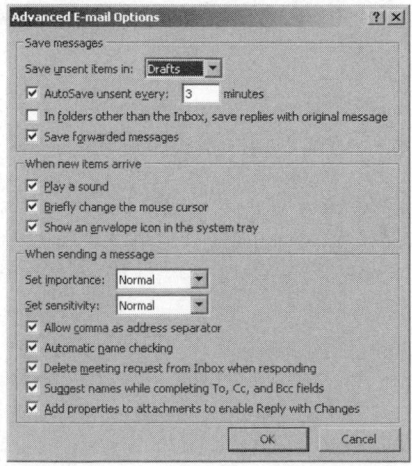

Figure 38-2. Further e-mail options are available in the Advanced E-Mail Options dialog box.

For information on sending messages in real time using Instant Messaging, see "Using Your Contacts Folder," on page 1065. For information on setting up an e-mail account when you first run Outlook, see "Setting Up Outlook," on page 968. For information on working with e-mail accounts at any time, see "Adding, Modifying, and Removing Outlook Accounts," on page 1093.

Receiving and Viewing E-Mail Messages

To receive and view your e-mail messages, complete the following steps:

1 In Outlook, open the Inbox folder.

2 Click the Send/Receive button on the Standard toolbar or press F9.

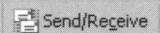 Outlook will then download all messages from your incoming e-mail server and add them to your Inbox. (It will also transmit any outgoing messages in your Outbox folder, as discussed in "Composing and Sending E-Mail Messages" later in the chapter.) Figure 38-3 shows how messages are displayed in your Inbox if you've selected the Messages view.

note In an e-mail folder such as the Inbox, the descriptions of incoming messages you haven't read or replied to are displayed in bold type. You can mark any message as read (nonbold) by selecting it and choosing Edit, Mark As Read or by pressing Ctrl+Q. You can mark the selected message as Unread (bold) by choosing Edit, Mark As Unread. And you can mark all messages in your Inbox as read (nonbold) by choosing Edit, Mark All As Read.

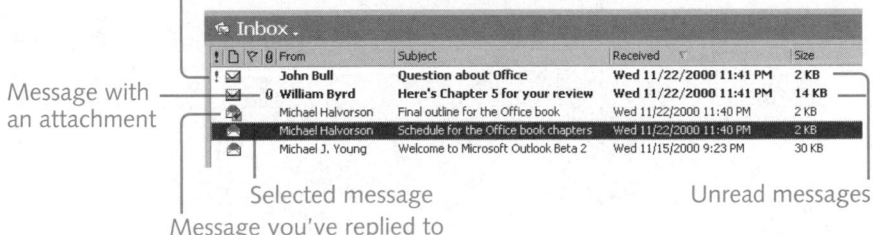

Figure 38-3. This figure shows a set of incoming e-mail messages in the Inbox folder, displayed with the Messages view

3 You can read your messages by viewing them in the Preview pane (see Figure 38-4 and "Using the Preview Pane," on page 1009) or by opening them in the Message form (see Figure 38-5, on page 1024; and "Editing Items," on page 988). The Message form provides commands for replying to or forwarding the message, printing it, moving it to a different Outlook folder, deleting it, or adding a message flag (a comment such as *Call* or *Follow up* attached to the message). In the Message form, you can also open other messages, create new messages, and perform additional operations.

1023

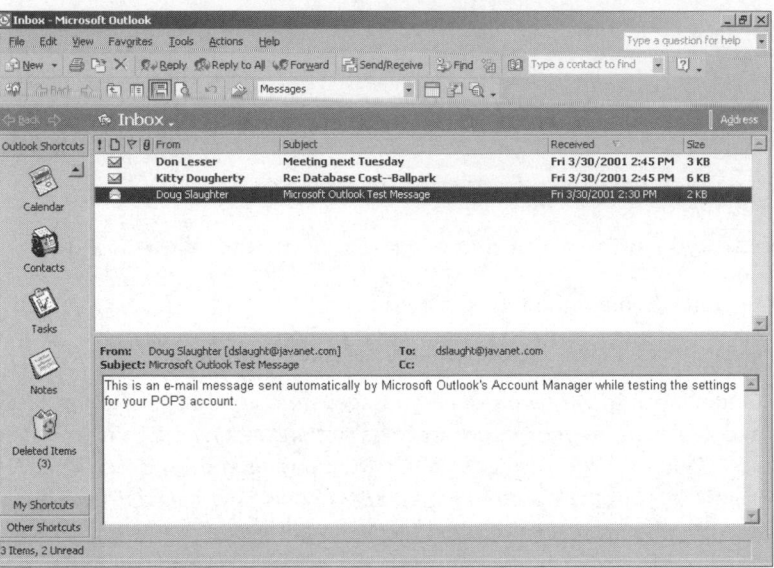

Figure 38-4. You can view an e-mail message in the Preview pane.

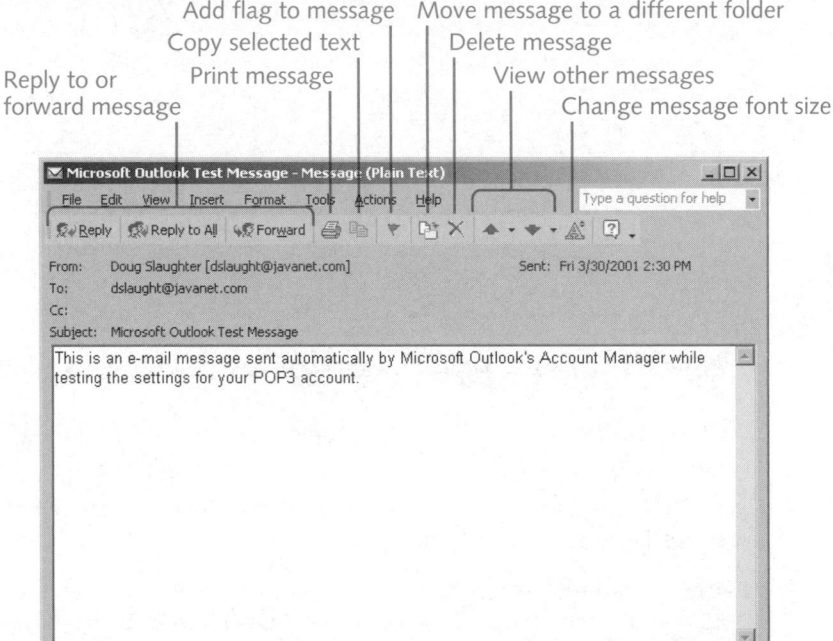

Figure 38-5. You can also view an e-mail message by opening it in the Message form.

Chapter 38

Chapter 38 *(right margin vertical)*

> **note** If you have more than one e-mail account, be sure to read the next section, "Using Groups to Manage Several E-Mail Accounts." And, if you want to download and work with your e-mail message headers before downloading the full content of the messages, see "Working with E-Mail Headers," on page 1028.

If a message includes an attachment, it's marked with a paper-clip icon (shown in Figure 38-3) in the Outlook window. When you've opened a message in the Message form, you can open the attachment by double-clicking the icon representing the attachment in the body of the message as shown here:

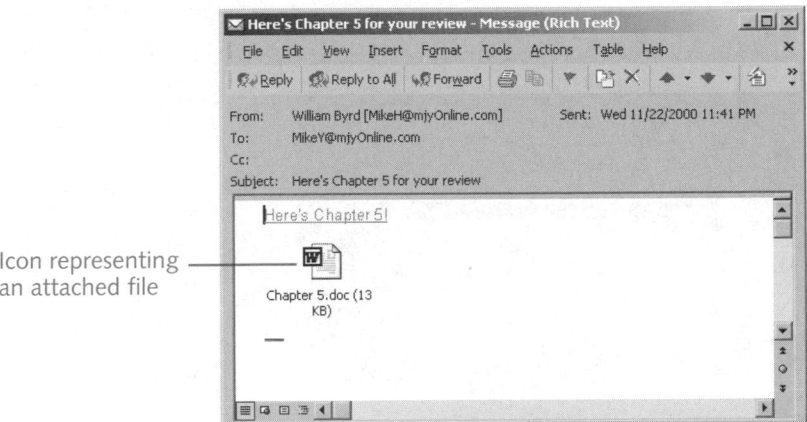

Icon representing an attached file

If the format of the message is HTML or plain text, the icon will appear below the Subject line in the message header. You can save an attachment to a disk file by selecting the message in the Outlook window and choosing the appropriate command from the Save Attachments submenu of the File menu. Or, you can open the message in a form and choose Save Attachments from the form's File menu.

> **caution** Because certain types of message attachments can contain viruses, never open or save an attachment in a message from an unknown source. And even if the message is from someone you know, you should verify with that person that they have intentionally sent you a file with an attachment. (Certain viruses cause messages to be sent out using addresses from an address book without the user's knowledge.) For more information, see "Setting Macro Security," on page 1479.

> **tip** **View a Message's Internet Headers**
>
> With most types of e-mail accounts, you can view the Internet header for a message by right-clicking the message in the Outlook window, choosing Options from the shortcut menu, and looking in the Internet Headers area near the bottom of the Message Options dialog box. Internet headers reveal interesting information (if you know how to interpret it!) regarding the sending and routing of the message on the Internet.

newfeature!
Using Groups to Manage Several E-Mail Accounts

If you have more than one e-mail account (perhaps one provided by your company for business e-mail and another you use for personal messages), you can set up account *groups*. These groups let you control exactly which accounts Outlook uses to send and receive e-mail when you initiate a send and receive operation and also let you have Outlook automatically send and receive e-mail at fixed intervals using specific accounts.

Initially, Outlook creates a single group called All Accounts that includes all your e-mail accounts. To create a new group, complete the following steps:

1 Choose Tools, Send/Receive Settings, Define Send/Receive Groups, or press Ctrl+Alt+S to open the Send/Receive Groups dialog box (shown in Figure 38-6).

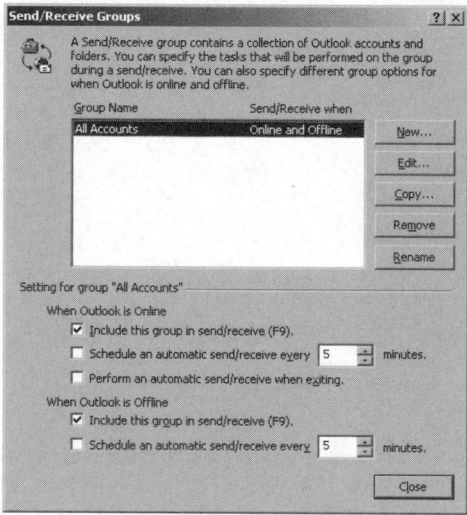

Figure 38-6. The Send/Receive Groups dialog box lets you set up and modify e-mail account groups.

2 Click the New button, and in the dialog boxes that Outlook displays, enter a name for the group, add the accounts you want to belong to the group, and select the options you want for each account in the group.

3 When you get back to the Send/Receive Groups dialog box, you can select your new group in the list and select options for the entire group. These options let you include or exclude the group from the accounts that Outlook uses when you click the Send/Receive button or press F9, as described in the previous section (or when you choose Tools, Send/Receive, Send And Receive All). You can also have Outlook automatically send and receive messages using the group's accounts at specified intervals. Notice that you can set separate options for working online or offline in Outlook. You switch between working offline and online by choosing File, Work Offline.

> **note** Outlook initially defines the All Accounts group so that Outlook will always use all your e-mail accounts (whether you're working online or offline) when you click the Send/Receive button, press F9, or choose Tools, Send/Receive, Send And Receive All. If you want to control the specific accounts that Outlook uses when you issue one of these commands, you can redefine this group (or delete it).

Once you've set up groups, you can send and receive your e-mail messages selectively by choosing the appropriate command from the Send/Receive submenu of the Tools menu, as shown here:

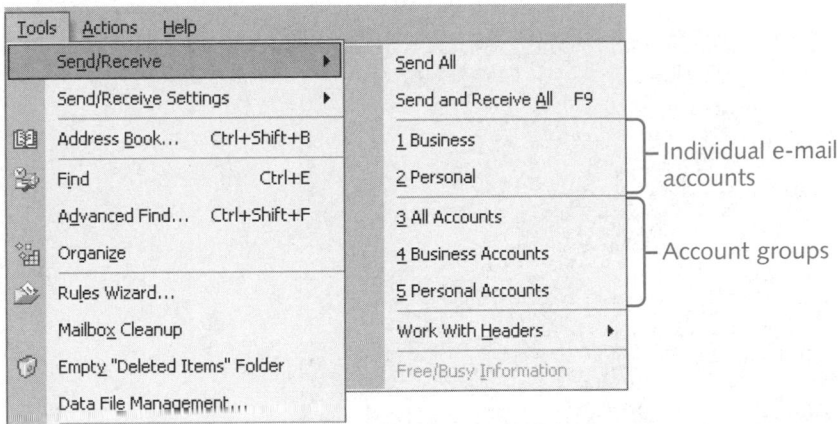

> **note** If you've set up one or more groups for automatic sending and receiving of e-mail, you can turn off (or turn back on) automatic transfers by choosing Tools, Send/Receive Settings, Disable Scheduled Send/Receive.

- Choose Send And Receive All to send and receive e-mail using all account groups for which the Include This Group In Send/Receive (F9) option is checked in the Send/Receive Groups dialog box (shown in Figure 38-6 and explained in step 3 above).

InsideOut

Keep in mind that the Send And Receive All command, in spite of its name, does *not* necessarily send and receive e-mail using all your e-mail accounts.

- Choose the name of an individual e-mail account to send and receive e-mail using just that account, regardless of the groups that are set up and their settings.

- Choose the name of an account group to send and receive e-mail using all accounts defined and enabled in that group. (Sending or receiving can be disabled for a particular account in a group by settings you make when you add the account to the group.)

> **note** If you receive and send e-mail using a dial-up service (that is, a service you access with a modem and telephone line), you can control the way Outlook connects to your account by choosing Tools, Options, clicking the Mail Setup tab, and selecting or checking options in the Dial-Up area at the bottom of the tab (see Figure 38-7).

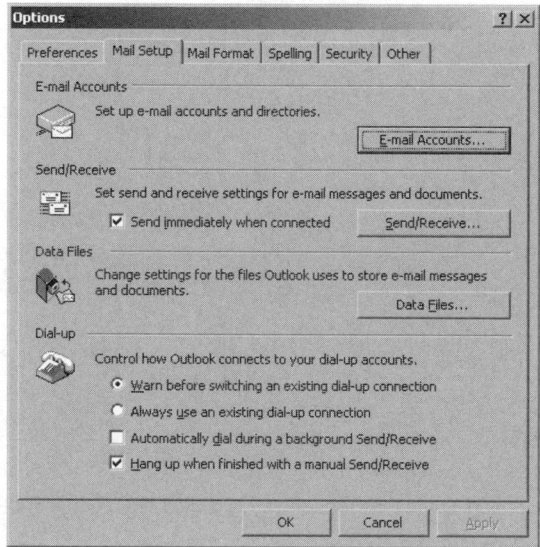

Figure 38-7. You can use the Mail Setup tab of the Options dialog box to manage your e-mail accounts, accounts groups, and data files, and to modify the way Outlook connects to dial-up accounts.

Working with E-Mail Headers

For most types of e-mail accounts, Outlook lets you work with the headers of the messages that are waiting on your incoming e-mail server, before you download the full message content. This feature is especially useful if you receive e-mail over a relatively slow Internet connection. It lets you first download just the message headers, which contain the Importance, Attachment, From, Subject, Received (date), and Size fields only. You can then mark the messages you want to download and those you want to delete. You then download a second time, and Outlook retrieves the messages marked for download and removes from the server the messages marked for deletion without downloading them.

To work with e-mail message headers, perform these steps:

1 Open the Inbox folder.

2 Perform the first download by choosing Tools, Send/Receive, Work With Headers, Download Headers.

> **note** If you've set up more than one e-mail account, download headers by choosing Tools, Send/Receive, Work With Headers, Download Headers From. Then, from the submenu that opens, choose the particular account you want to use to download headers or choose All Accounts to use all your accounts.

Outlook will now download the headers of all messages on your incoming e-mail server and store them in your Inbox. When you first download headers, Outlook adds a Header Status column to the Messages view, which displays an icon next to each message item that consists of only a header. (This icon changes to indicate the way you've marked the message, as explained in the next step.) Figure 38-8 shows an example.

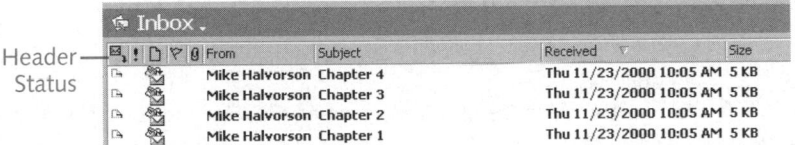

Figure 38-8. Downloaded headers are displayed in the Inbox, using the Messages view.

3 Mark each message to indicate how you want it handled when you download again. Do this by selecting each message, choosing Tools, Send/Receive, Work With Headers, Mark/Unmark Messages, and then choosing the appropriate command from the submenu that's displayed, as shown here:

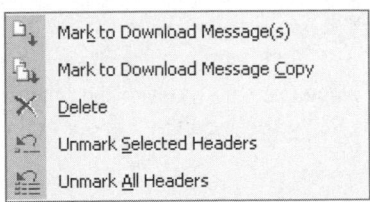

The Mark To Download Message(s) command causes Outlook to download the message and remove the message from the server, as usual. With some e-mail servers, Mark To Download Message Copy causes Outlook to leave the original message on the server after it downloads it.

4 Perform the second download by choosing Tools, Send/Receive, Work With Headers, Process Marked Headers.

InsideOut

Don't rely on the Mark To Download Message Copy command to preserve the message on your incoming e-mail server. On some servers the original message is removed when you choose this command.

note If you've set up more than one e-mail account, perform the second download by choosing Tools, Send/Receive, Work With Headers, Process Marked Headers From. Then, from the submenu that opens, choose the particular account you want to use to download your messages or choose All Accounts to use all your accounts.

Outlook will now download each message whose header you've marked for downloading. You can now read or reply to these messages as usual. Outlook will remove from the server each message whose header you've marked to delete, without downloading it.

Composing and Sending E-Mail Messages

To create and send an e-mail message, complete the following steps:

1 Create the message using one of the following methods:

■ To reply to a message you've received, select the message in the Outlook window and click the Reply button on the Standard toolbar; choose Actions, Reply; or press Ctrl+R. Outlook will create a new message and open it in the Message form. The message will be addressed to the sender of the original message, will have the same Subject field as the original, prefaced with *RE:*, and will contain the original message's header, body, and attachments . (You'll add your message above the original one.)

   Reply   Reply to All   Forward

■ To send a message reply to all people who received the selected message (including yourself), click the Reply To All button; choose Actions, Reply To All; or press Ctrl+Shift+R.

■ To forward the selected message, click the Forward button; choose Actions, Forward; or press Ctrl+F. Outlook will create a new message and open it in the Message form. The message will have the same Subject field as the original, prefaced with *FW:*, and will contain the original message's header, body and attachments. (You'll add your message, if any, above the original one and enter the message recipient in the To text box.)

■ To create a new message, make sure that an e-mail folder is open and choose Actions, New Mail Message; click the New button on the Standard

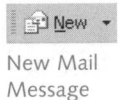

New Mail
Message

toolbar; or press Ctrl+N. (If don't have an e-mail folder open, you can create a new message by clicking the down arrow on the New button and choosing Mail Message from the drop-down menu or by pressing Ctrl+Shift+M.) Outlook will open a blank Message form for you to fill in.

note You can also issue any of the commands described here for creating a message by opening a message in a form and choosing the command from within the form.

Setting the E-Mail Format and Editor

When you create a new e-mail message by choosing Actions, New Mail Message, by pressing Ctrl+N, or by using an equivalent command, Outlook creates the new message using your default e-mail format—plain text, rich text, or HTML (Hypertext Markup Language)—and it opens the message in your default e-mail editor—Outlook or Microsoft Word. (When you reply to or forward a message, Outlook uses the format of the original message you received and opens it in your default e-mail editor.) You can change both of these defaults—and set other e-mail formatting options—by choosing Tools, Options and clicking the Mail Format tab (shown in Figure 38-9, on page 1032).

If you select HTML as your default e-mail format, you can also select default HTML *stationery* that will be used as the basis for the new e-mail messages you create. HTML stationery adds initial content to new messages, which might include a background color, background graphics, or boilerplate text. After you create a message using stationery, you can customize these elements if you wish and you can add your own text. To specify default stationery, select the name of the stationery from the Use This Stationery By Default drop-down list in the Mail Format tab or click the Stationery Picker button to select stationery in the Stationery Picker dialog box, which lets you preview each stationery style.

You can create a new message and override either your default format or your default editor by choosing a command from the New Mail Message Using submenu on the Actions menu. If your default format is HTML and your default editor is Word, this submenu appears as follows:

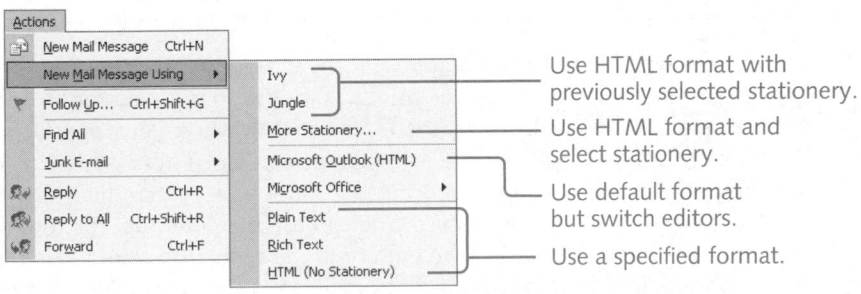

(continued)

Setting the E-Mail Format and Editor *(continued)*   You can also override your default format after you've opened a new message in Word by selecting a format from the Message Format drop-down list in the message header (see Figure 38-10). If you've opened the new message in the built-in Outlook editor, you can change the format by choosing a command from the form's Format menu.

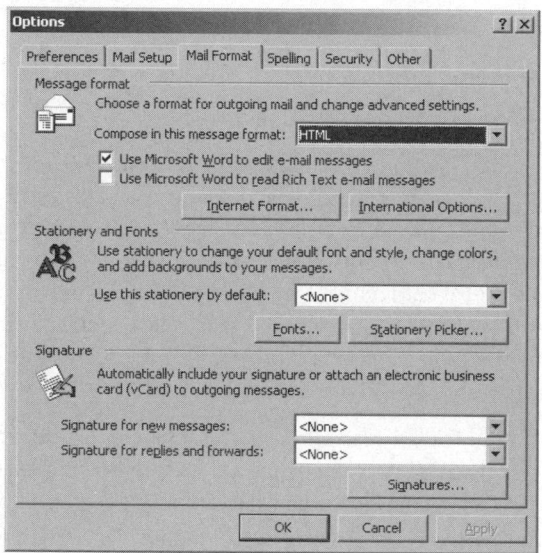

Figure 38-9.   The Mail Format tab of the Options dialog box lets you select the format, editor, stationery, fonts, signature, and other features of your e-mail messages.

2 Complete the message header in the Message form and type your message into the large text box. Figure 38-10 shows the Message form displayed by Word.

note To hide or show the message header in the Message form, click the E-Mail button on the Standard toolbar (in Word) or choose View, Message Header (in the Outlook e-mail editor).

You can type the recipient's address directly into the To or Cc text box (such as *someone@microsoft.com*), or you can click the To or Cc button to open the Select Names dialog box (see Figure 38-11), where you can select a recipient or a distribution list (a collection of recipients) from your Contacts folder or—if you've set up a directory account—look up an e-mail address using an Internet directory service. You can use the buttons at the top of the message header in Word (or the buttons in the form's Standard toolbar in the Outlook editor) to work with your message as explained in Table 38-1 on page 1034.

For information on setting up and using directory accounts for looking up e-mail addresses on the Internet, see "Adding, Modifying, and Removing Outlook Accounts," on page 1093.

Check Names Importance: High
Address Book Importance: Low
Insert File Message Flag Message Format

Message header

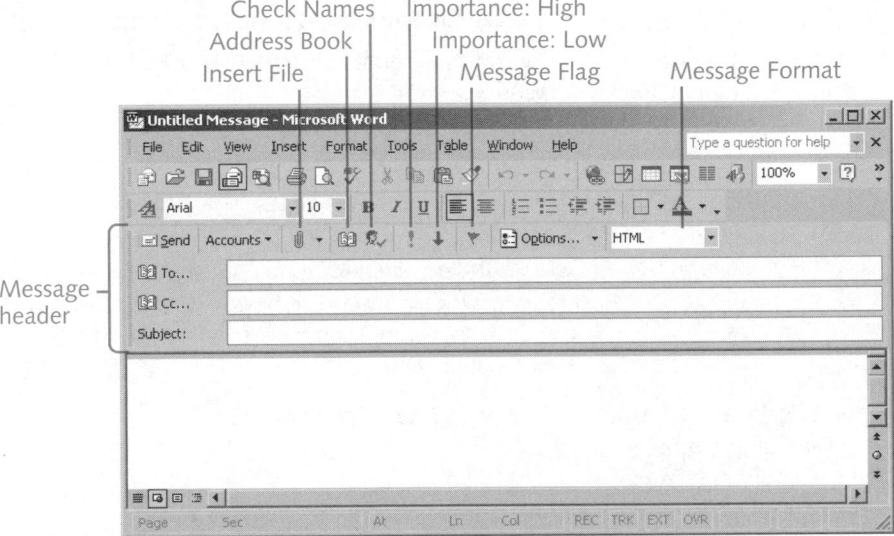

Figure 38-10. When you use Word as the e-mail editor, you see a blank message form like this one.

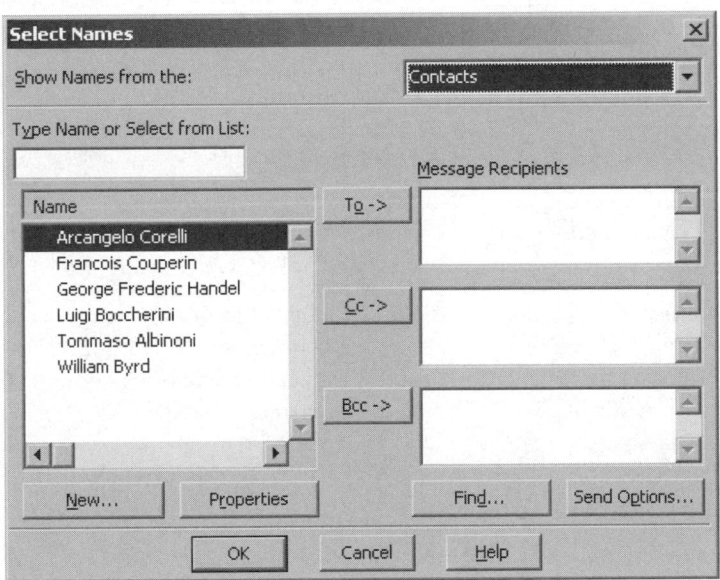

Figure 38-11. You can select a recipient or look up an e-mail address in the Select Names dialog box.

Chapter 38

Table 38-1. **Using the Buttons on the Message Header (in Word) or the Standard Toolbar (in Outlook)**

To Do This	Perform This Action Using the Message Header (or Standard Toolbar) Buttons
Specify the account you want Outlook to use to send your message, if you have more than one account.	Choose an account from the Accounts drop-down menu.
Insert a file or an Outlook item into the message.	Choose File or Item from the Insert File drop-down menu and then select the file or item in the Insert File or Insert Item dialog box. (In the Outlook editor, click the Insert File button to insert a file or choose Item from the form's Insert menu to insert an Outlook item.)
Open the Select Names dialog box (the same dialog box opened by clicking the To or Cc button).	Click the Address Book button.
Have Outlook replace names you've typed into the To or Cc boxes with the e-mail addresses from your Contacts folder.	Click the Check Names button.
Mark the message as *high importance*.	Click the Importance: High button.
Mark the message as *low importance*.	Click the Importance: Low button.
Add a flag (such as *Follow Up* or *No Response Necessary*).	Click the Message Flag button and select the flag in the Flag For Follow Up dialog box.
Display the Message Options dialog box (shown in Figure 38-12). This dialog box lets you modify many message features, including assigning associated contacts and categories to the message.	Click the Options button. In Word only, you can also click the down arrow on this button and choose several additional e-mail options from the drop-down menu.
Change the message's format.	Select a format in the Message Format drop-down list. (In the Outlook editor, choose an option from the form's Format menu.)

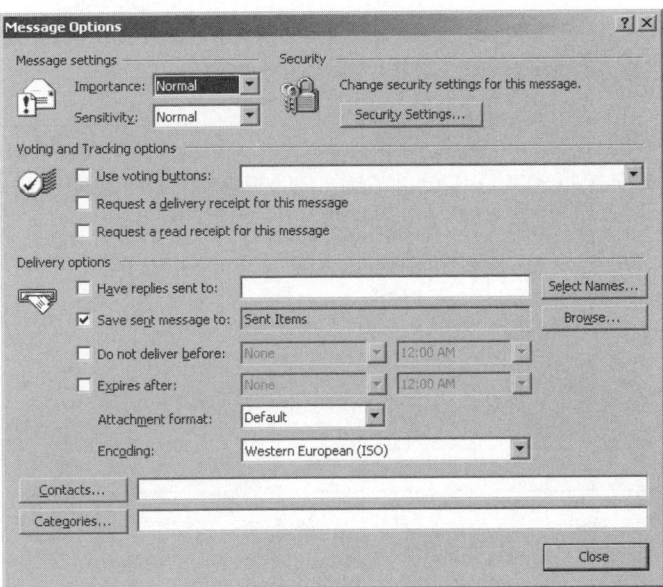

Figure 38-12. The Message Options dialog box lets you change message settings.

---

tip **Preserve Your Recipient's Anonymity**

If you're sending an e-mail message to several recipients and you don't want to reveal the list of e-mail addresses to each message recipient, insert each of the recipient's addresses into the Bcc text box rather than into the To or Cc box. (If you wish, you can insert your own e-mail address into the To box or just leave that box blank.) To display the Bcc text box in the message header, choose Bcc from the Options drop-down menu on the message header (in Word), or choose View, Bcc Field (in the Outlook e-mail editor).

---

3 When you've completed entering the message content and setting message options, click the Send button on the message header (in Word) or on the Standard toolbar (in the Outlook editor) to move your message to the Outbox and mark it for delivery.

---

note The description of the message in your Outbox that's marked for delivery is formatted in italics. If you reopen the message, be sure to click the Send button again. Otherwise, it will no longer be marked for delivery and will just sit in your Outbox when you perform a send and receive operation.

Chapter 38

4 Transmit your message (plus any other messages in your Outbox) to your outgoing e-mail server for delivery as follows:

- To send messages only, choose Tools, Send/Receive, Send All. If you have more than one e-mail account, Outlook will transmit each message in your Outbox using the account designated for that message (see the first item in Table 38-1, on page 1034).

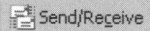

- To send and receive messages, click the Send/Receive button on the Standard toolbar or press F9.

> If you have more than one e-mail account, see "Using Groups to Manage Several E-Mail Accounts," on page 1026, for important information on using account groups, along with the commands on the Send/Receive submenu of the Tools menu, to control exactly which accounts are used to send and receive e-mail.

> **note** If the Send Immediately When Connected option is checked and you're working online, Outlook will immediately transmit a message when you click the Send button in the Message form, rather than storing it in the Outbox. (If you access your e-mail server using a dial-up connection, Outlook will dial that connection if you're not already connected.) You'll find this option by choosing Tools, Options and clicking the Mail Setup tab (shown in Figure 38-7). You switch between working offline and online by choosing File, Work Offline.

> **tip** **Resend a Message**
>
> If you want to resend a message (perhaps to remind the recipient to reply), open the copy of the message stored in your Sent Items folder and choose Resend This Message from the Message form's Actions menu.

Organizing Your E-Mail Messages and Handling Junk E-Mail

You'll probably want to move all messages that you've read or replied to out of your Inbox and into one or more other folders to store and categorize them. If you don't do this on a regular basis, the number of messages in your Inbox can rapidly get out of hand. The techniques for creating new folders and moving items between folders are explained in "Working with Outlook Folders," on page1015, and "Moving and Copying Items," on page 993.

Outlook's Organize pane can help you manage your e-mail messages. The general techniques for using the Organize pane are discussed in "Organizing Items Using the Organize Pane," on page 1013. The following are some additional tasks you can perform with the Organize pane that are unique to e-mail folders:

---

tip   **Find Related Messages**

You can find all messages in the Inbox, Drafts, and Sent Items folders that have the same sender—or are about the same subject—as the message that's currently selected in the Outlook window. To do this, choose either Messages From Sender or Related Messages from the Find All submenu of the Actions menu. (If a message is opened in a form, you can choose these commands from the form's Actions menu.)

● You can create a rule that automatically moves messages that are sent from or to a particular person as soon as each message is delivered to the Inbox. To do this, select a message from or to the person whose e-mail you want to have moved (if possible), open the Using Folders tab of the Organize pane, and select and enter appropriate values in the Create A Rule item (shown in Figure 38-13).

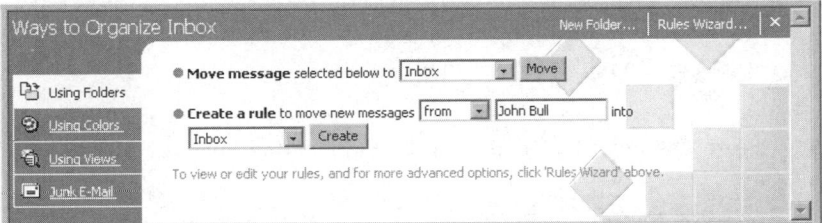

Figure 38-13.   When the Inbox folder is open, the Using Folders tab of the Organize pane looks like the figure above.

● You can have Outlook automatically color-code messages from or to a particular person or messages that are sent only to you. To do this, select an e-mail message from or to the person whose e-mail you want to color-code (if possible), open the Using Colors tab of the Organize pane (shown in Figure 38-14), and select and enter the appropriate values into the controls.

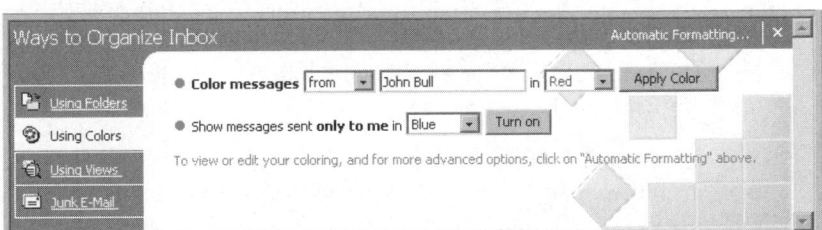

Figure 38-14.   When the Inbox folder is open, the Organize pane includes a Using Colors tab.

● You can have Outlook color-code or move all messages that it judges to be junk or adult-content e-mail. To do this, open the Junk E-Mail tab of the Organize pane (shown in Figure 38-15) and select the options you want. To read more information about Outlook's junk and adult-content e-mail

1037

handling, or to set additional options, click the Click Here command near the bottom of the pane.

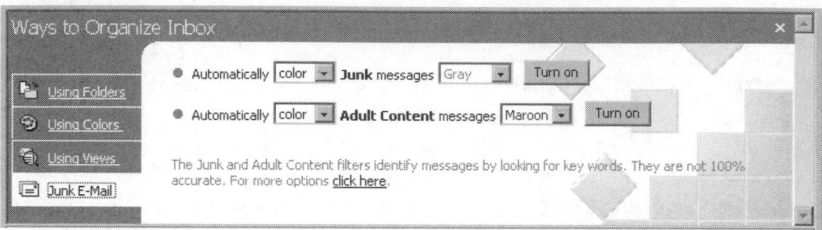

Figure 38-15. When the Inbox folder is open, the Organize pane includes a Junk E-Mail tab.

Outlook's junk and adult e-mail handling feature uses filtering rules that identify junk or adult-content messages by looking for specific key phrases in the subject or body fields of the message. For example, if the subject contains "$$" Outlook would identify the message as junk e-mail, and if the body contains "over 21" it would identify the message as adult-content e-mail.

> **tip** **Learn Outlook's Junk and Adult E-Mail Filtering Rules**
>
> To see an exact description of all the rules Outlook uses to filter junk and adult e-mail, open the following file: C:\Program Files\Microsoft Office\Office10\1033\Filters.txt.

Whenever you receive a junk or adult-content message that Outlook doesn't filter, you can add the message sender to Outlook's junk e-mail or adult-content sender list. From then on, messages from that sender will be processed as junk or adult e-mail, regardless of their content. To do this, select the message and choose Actions, Junk E-Mail, Add To Junk Senders List or choose Actions, Junk E-Mail, Add To Adult Content Senders List. You can edit the senders you've added to either list by clicking the Click Here command in the Junk E-Mail tab of the Organizer pane and then clicking the Edit Junk Senders or Edit Adult Content Senders command on the new page that Outlook displays. To download improved junk and adult message filters, click the Outlook Web Site command on this same page.

You can also add a particular sender to an exception list so that Outlook won't classify messages from this sender as junk or adult e-mail (even if Outlook's filtering rules indicate otherwise). To do this, follow these steps:

1 Choose Tools, Rules Wizard to open the Rules Wizard dialog box.

2 In the Apply Rules In The Following Order list, select the Exception List item.

3 In the Rule Description list, click Exception List.

4 Click the Add button in the Edit Exception List dialog box and type in the e-mail address you want to exempt from filtering.

InsideOut

A Better Way to Handle Junk or Adult E-Mail Messages

Outlook's handling of junk and adult messages isn't really practical. It would be much more usable if you could turn off the filtering rules and have Outlook move only messages from those senders that you've explicitly added to the junk or adult e-mail senders lists, so that you would no longer have to look at messages from those senders. The problem with the filtering rules is that Outlook can easily move or color-code a message you want to read (for example, a message from your friend with the subject "I've got the $$ I owe you"), so you always have to manually review the moved or color-coded messages, eliminating most of the feature's potential benefit.

Here's a more practical way to have Outlook move junk or adult e-mail messages: When you actually receive an undesirable message, select the message, open the Using Folders tab of the Organize pane, and create a rule to have Outlook move all messages from the message's sender to a specific folder (perhaps a folder you've created called Junk E-Mail). Then, you no longer have to look at messages from that sender (except for maybe an occasional review of the messages stored in your Junk E-Mail folder, just to be safe), and you need have very little concern about missing an important message.

newfeature!

Finally, if your Inbox starts growing out of control, you can choose Tools, Mailbox Cleanup to display the new Mailbox Cleanup dialog box (shown in Figure 38-16). This dialog box can help you find large or old e-mail messages so that you can move or delete them. You can also use it to display the current size of any of your Outlook folders, to run the AutoArchive feature, or to empty your Deleted Items folder.

For information on archiving and on the Deleted Items folder, see "Removing and Archiving Items," on page 996.

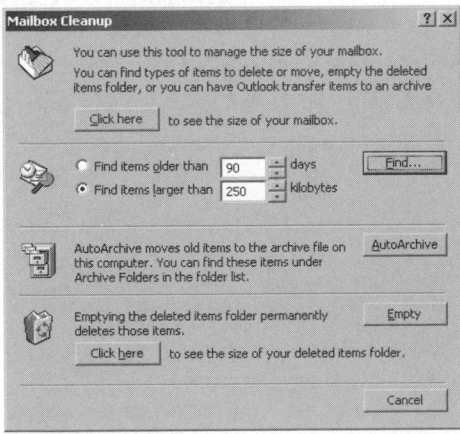

Figure 38-16. The new Mailbox Cleanup dialog box helps you find large or old e-mail messages and perform other maintenance tasks.

Maintaining Your Schedule with the Calendar Folder

You can use the default Outlook Calendar folder, or another Calendar-type folder you've created, to schedule appointments, events, or meetings—terms that have specific meanings in Outlook. An *appointment* is an activity that can be scheduled for any time period and consumes a block of your own time. For example, an interview that you're planning to conduct next Wednesday morning from 9 to 9:30 would be an appointment. An *event* (sometimes called an *all-day event*) is an occurrence that lasts for one or more entire days but doesn't necessarily fully consume your time. For example, your birthday next May 21 would be an event. A *meeting* is similar to an appointment but involves other people and resources *that you schedule using Outlook*. For example, a conference with your team of programmers that takes place in a conference room and uses a computer projector *and* that you've scheduled using Outlook would be a meeting. The following sections explain how to work with each of these three types of Calendar items.

Scheduling Appointments

You can schedule a one-time appointment, which is added to a single time slot in your Calendar folder, or you can schedule a recurring appointment, which is added to a series of time slots in your Calendar according to a daily, weekly, monthly, or yearly recurrence pattern that you specify. In either case, begin by opening your default Calendar folder or another Calendar-type folder in which you want to schedule the appointment.

Then, to schedule a one-time appointment, complete the following steps:

1 Select the time period for the appointment in the Information Viewer of the Outlook window (shown in Figure 38-17). (If you do this, Outlook will save you time by filling in the appointment times when it displays the Appointment form. However, this step is optional because you can specify any time period you want in the form.)

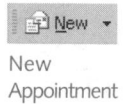

New
Appointment

2 Choose Actions, New Appointment, click the New button on the Standard toolbar, or press Ctrl+N. Outlook will then open an empty Appointment form, as shown in Figure 38-18.

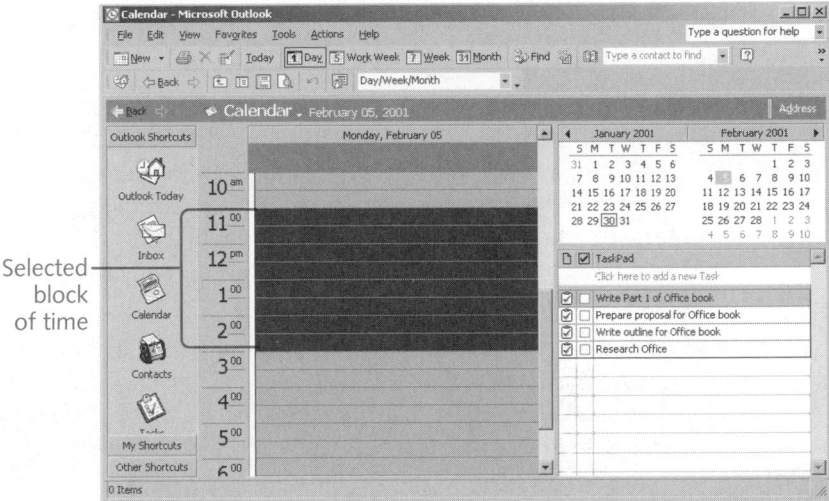

Selected block of time

Figure 38-17. You can save time by selecting a time period prior to defining an appointment for that time.

Insert File
Print
Importance: Low
Importance: High
Delete

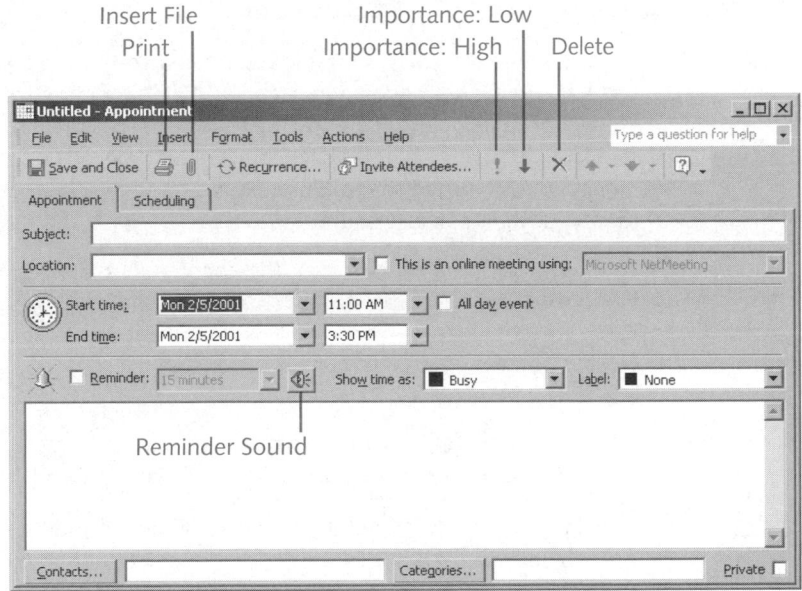

Reminder Sound

Figure 38-18. This figure shows an empty Appointment form for scheduling a new appointment.

3 Fill in the Appointment form as follows:

- Describe the appointment by entering a short description into the Subject text box. You can also enter a longer appointment description, comments, or other information into the large text box.

Chapter 38

■ To indicate where the appointment will take place, type a location into the Location text box or select a previously entered location from the drop-down list.

■ To schedule an online appointment, check the This Is An Online Meeting Using option, and then select the online meeting software you're using in the following drop-down list (for example, Microsoft NetMeeting) and enter information on the meeting into the other controls that appear as soon as you check This Is An Online Meeting Using.

■ If you didn't select the meeting time in step 1, enter the starting and ending dates and times for the meeting into the Start Time and End Time controls. (You can click the down arrow in one of these controls to select a date from a Calendar or a time from a list of times.)

> **note** Don't check the All Day Event option unless you want to convert the appointment to an event. An event is a different type of Calendar item and is described in the next section.

■ To have Outlook display a message to remind you of the appointment, check the Reminder option and in the adjoining text box enter the amount of time in advance of the appointment that the message should be displayed, or select a time from the drop-down list. To modify or turn off the sound Outlook plays when it displays the message, click the Reminder Sound button.

■ To specify your availability during the appointment time, select an item in the Show Time As drop-down list, as shown here:

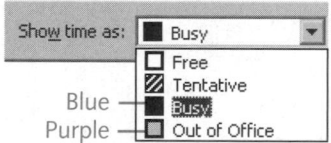

In certain views of the Calendar folder, Outlook will indicate your availability by displaying a border around the appointment time using the pattern shown on the drop-down menu (a white border for free time, a cross-hatched border for tentative time, a blue border for busy time, or a purple border for out-of-office time).

■ To color-code your appointment, select an item other than None in the Label drop-down list, as shown at the top of the next page:

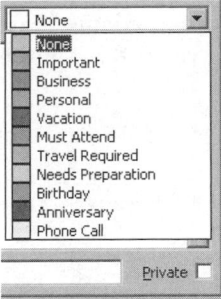

In the Outlook window, the appointment text will be displayed with a background using the color you select: red for an important appointment, blue for a business appointment, green for a personal appointment, and so on.

- To enter one or more contacts who are associated with the appointment (perhaps the person you're going to interview), click the Contacts button and select one or more items from your Contacts folder (or from another Contact-type folder you've created). Outlook will then display the contact(s) in the adjoining text box. Entering a contact here links the appointment to the contact; as a result, the Activities tab of the form for that contact will list the appointment as well as other linked Outlook items. You can double-click a contact name in the box to open the contact.

- To assign one or more categories to the appointment, click the Categories button and in the Categories dialog box (shown in Figure 38-19) check any of the predefined categories you want to assign in the Available Categories list. To add a custom category to the list (and check it), type it into the Item(s) Belong To These Categories text box and click the Add To List button. You can use categories for finding, sorting, filtering, or grouping Outlook items (see "Finding Outlook Items or Disk Files," on page 1010, and "Sorting, Filtering, and Grouping Items in Folders," on page 1005).

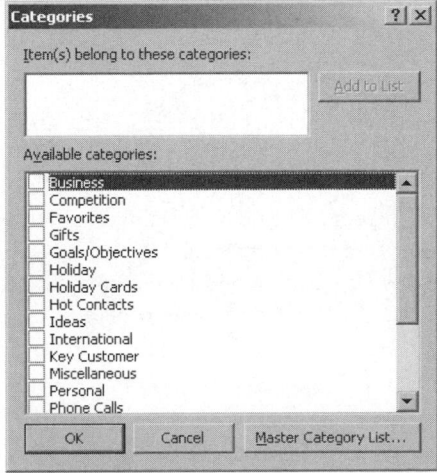

Figure 38-19. Use the Categories dialog box to assign one or more categories to an appointment.

■ To mark your appointment as private, check the Private option. (The appointment will then be hidden if you share your Calendar folder with others.)

4 Click the Save And Close button on the form's Standard toolbar.

Troubleshooting

Trouble with Custom Categories

You've been assigning custom categories (for example, Foreign and Domestic) to your Outlook items by typing them directly into the Categories text box in the item forms. However, when you sort, filter, group, or search by category, some of the items are missing from categories and extraneous categories appear.

Outlook lets you assign new custom categories by typing them directly into the Categories text box. However, if you make a minor typo, you inadvertently create a new category, so that items you want in the same category end up in different categories. A better way to create a custom category is to click the Categories button and enter it into the Categories dialog box (shown in Figure 38-19), as explained on page 1043. With this method, the category is added to the *master category list,* and subsequently it will always appear in the Categories dialog box. To assign the same category to additional items, open this dialog box and check the category in the list, rather than typing it directly into the form.

Note that you can also assign categories to the selected item or items in the Outlook window—without opening the item(s) in a form—by choosing Edit, Categories, which also opens the Categories dialog box.

Note also that in the Categories dialog box, you can click the Master Category button to open the Master Category List dialog box, where you can add or remove categories from the master list or reset the master list back to the original set of categories defined by Outlook.

To create a recurring appointment, perform the steps given above, *except* rather than entering the starting and ending times in the Appointment form, click the Recurrence button on the Standard toolbar (shown in Figure 38-18) and enter the desired recurrence pattern into the Appointment Recurrence dialog box (shown in Figure 38-20). Or, you can create the appointment by choosing Actions, New Recurring Appointment (rather than New Appointment); Outlook will then display the Appointment Recurrence dialog box before it displays the Appointment form.

> **note** To change the recurrence pattern, click the Recurrence button in the form. Then, in the Appointment Recurrence dialog box, enter new information or click the Remove Recurrence button to convert the recurring appointment to a one-time appointment.

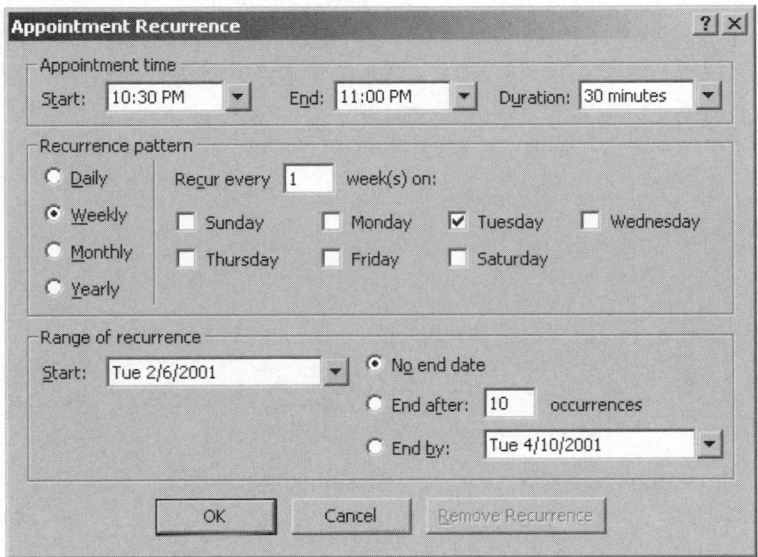

Figure 38-20. Use the Appointment Recurrence dialog box to create a recurring appointment.

Setting Up Events

To schedule a one-time or recurring event, complete the following steps:

1 In the Calendar folder, select the day or days on which the event will occur. (If you do this, Outlook saves you time by filling in the event days when it displays the Event form. However, this step is optional because you can specify any day or range of days in the form.)

2 Choose Actions, New All Day Event. Outlook will then open an empty Event form, as shown in Figure 38-21.

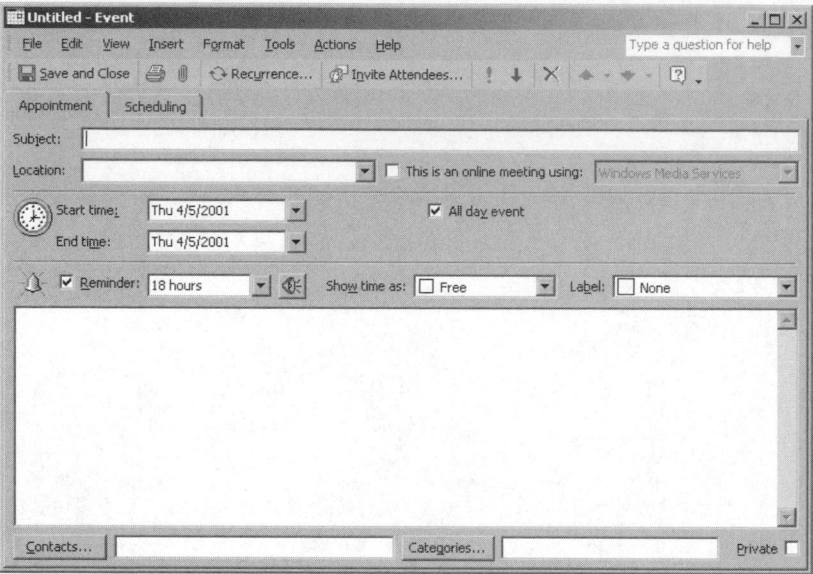

Figure 38-21. You use an empty Event form for scheduling a new event.

3 Fill in the form as described (for an appointment) in step 3 of the previous section, but be sure to leave the All Day Event option checked. Also, because an event is always scheduled for one or more complete days, the form doesn't include controls for specifying starting and ending times.

> **note** To create a recurring event, which is analogous to a recurring appointment, click the Recurrence button and fill in the (mislabeled) Appointment Recurrence dialog box rather than entering starting and ending dates in the form. To remove the recurrence, which converts the item to a one-time event, click the Recurrence button again and click the Remove Recurrence button in the Appointment Recurrence dialog box.

4 Click the Save And Close button on the form's Standard toolbar.

> **note** You can convert an appointment to an event by simply checking the All Day Event option in the Appointment form.

Planning Meetings

To schedule a meeting with one or more people, do the following:

1 Select the time period for the meeting in the Information Viewer of the Outlook window. (If you do this, Outlook will save you time by filling in the meeting times when it displays the Meeting form. However, this step is optional because you can specify any time period you want in the form.)

2 Choose Actions, New Meeting Request, or press Ctrl+Shift+Q. Outlook will then open an empty Meeting form, as shown in Figure 38-22.

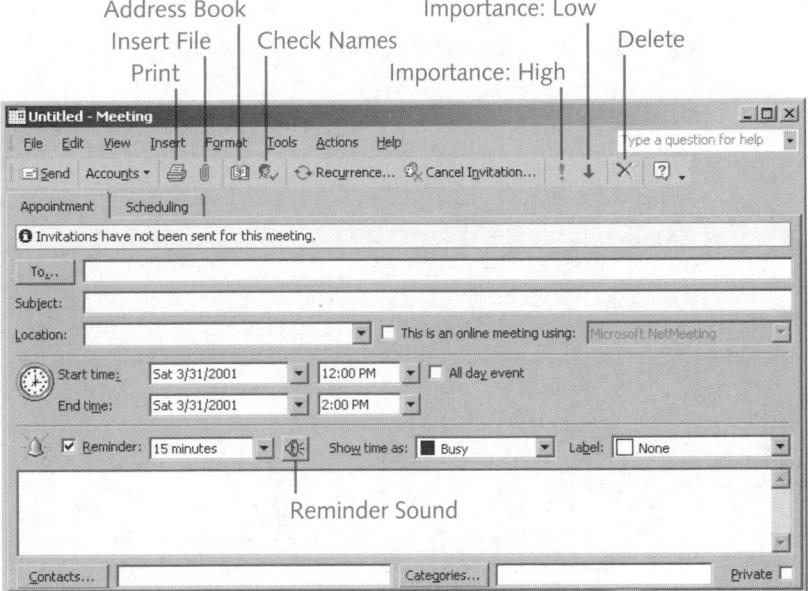

Figure 38-22. You use an empty Meeting form for scheduling a new meeting.

note To schedule a recurring meeting (analogous to a recurring appointment), create the meeting by choosing Actions, New Recurring Meeting rather than choosing Actions, New Meeting Request. Then, before Outlook displays the Meeting form, it will then display the (mislabeled) Appointment Recurrence dialog box in which you can specify the recurrence pattern (shown in Figure 38-20, on page 1045).

Also, you can convert a one-time meeting to a recurring one by clicking the Recurrence button on the form's Standard toolbar and entering the recurrence pattern into the Appointment Recurrence dialog box. (And you can convert a recurring meeting to a one-time meeting by clicking the Remove Recurrence button in this same dialog box.)

3 Type the e-mail addresses of the people you want to invite to the meeting (the meeting *attendees*) into the To text box, separating each address with a semicolon. Or click the To button to select the addresses from your Outlook Contacts folder.

For information on entering or selecting addresses, see "Composing and Sending E-Mail Messages," on page 1030.

4 Fill in the other controls in the Meeting form following the instructions given under step 3 in "Scheduling Appointments," on page 1041 (see Figure 38-23).

> **note** To invite other people to an all-day event, rather than a meeting, check the All Day Event option in the Event form. This coverts the meeting to an *invited event*.

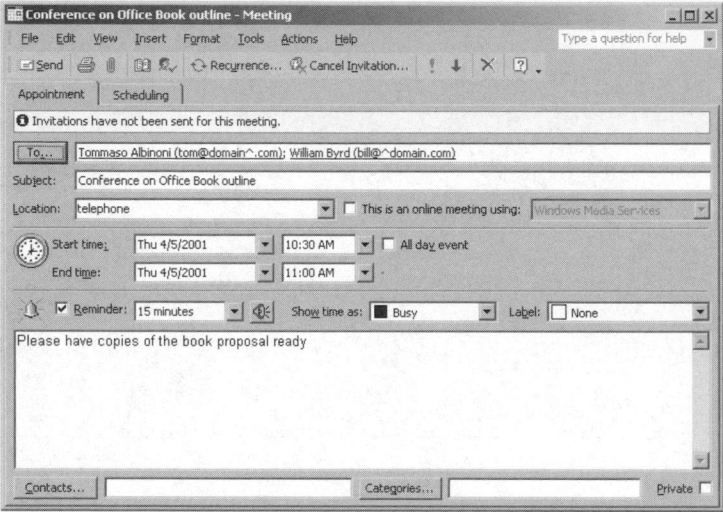

Figure 38-23. This completed Meeting form is ready to send.

5 Select an e-mail account (if you have more than one) from the Accounts drop-down menu on the Standard toolbar. Then click the Send button on this same toolbar to place a meeting-request e-mail message in your Outbox, and then transmit this message to your outgoing e-mail server so that the requests will be delivered to the attendees, as explained in "Composing and Sending E-Mail Messages," on page 1030.

Outlook will place a copy of the meeting in the scheduled time slot in your Calendar folder, and a meeting request will appear in the Inbox of each attendee you invited. An attendee can open the meeting request or just view the request in the Preview pane of the Inbox (shown in Figure 38-24), and the attendee can reply by clicking the Accept, Tentative, or Decline button in the form or on the Preview pane header.

newfeature!

The attendee can also click the Propose New Time button to send a reply with a proposal for a new time. (To help the attendee pick a suitable new time, when the attendee clicks this button, Outlook displays the Propose New Time dialog box, which lets the attendee use the meeting planner as discussed in the sidebar "Planning a Meeting," on page 1051.) If the attendee clicks any of the four reply buttons except Decline, a copy of the meeting will be added to the scheduled time slot in the attendee's Calendar folder. Whichever button the attendee clicks, the meeting request will be removed from the attendee's Inbox.

The attendee's reply will be e-mailed back to you, and when you receive it, Outlook will record the response in the copy of the meeting in your Calendar folder.

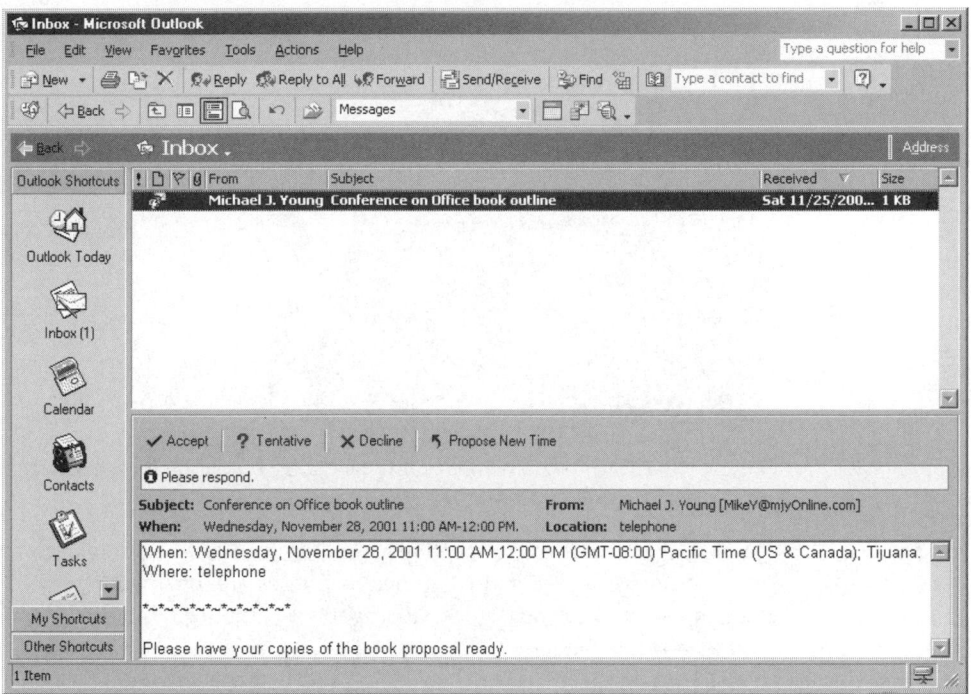

Figure 38-24. This figure shows the meeting request in the Inbox of one of the invited attendees, viewed in the Preview pane.

note Your attendees can propose new meeting times only if the Allow Attendees To Propose New Time For Meetings You Organize option is checked. To find this option, choose Tools, Options, click the Calendar Options button in the Preferences tab of the Options dialog box, and look in the Calendar Options area of the Calendar Options dialog box (shown in Figure 38-25).

In the Calendar Options dialog box, you can also customize the way the Calendar folder displays weeks, add standard holidays to your Calendar folder, and make other settings that affect the look or operation of your Calendar folder.

tip **Reach a Wider Audience by Using iCalendar**

If you send out your meeting requests using the standard iCalendar Internet format—rather than the proprietary Outlook meeting format—you can invite anyone who uses a calendaring program that supports iCalendar, not just Outlook users. To use iCalendar, choose Tools, Options, click the Calendar Options button in the Preferences tab of the Options dialog box, and make sure that the When Sending Meeting Requests Over The Internet Use iCalendar Format option is checked in the Calendar Options dialog box (as shown in Figure 38-25, on page 1050).

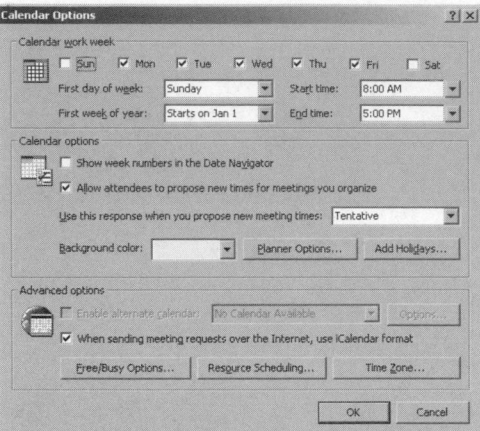

Figure 38-25. In the Calendar Options dialog box you can make settings that affect the operation of your Calendar folder.

6 To view the records of the meeting replies, so you can see at a glance which attendees have replied and what their responses are, open your copy of the meeting in your Calendar folder and open the Tracking tab of the Meeting form (shown in Figure 38-26).

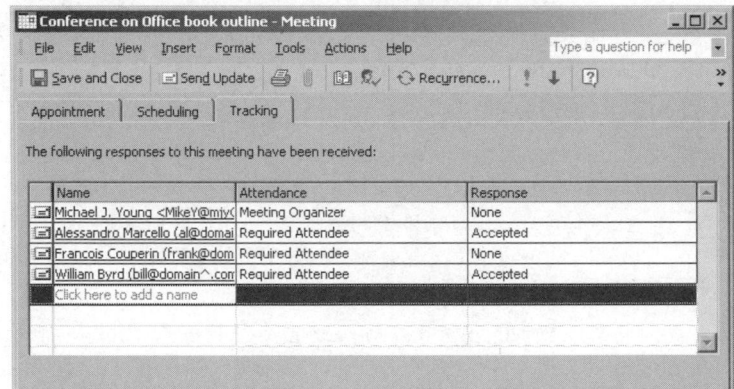

Figure 38-26. You can view the replies to your meeting requests in the Tracking tab of the Meeting form.

note You can convert an appointment to a meeting by clicking the Invite Attendees button on the Appointment form's Standard toolbar. And you can convert a meeting to an appointment by clicking the Cancel Invitation button on this same toolbar.

Planning a Meeting

If you and all your attendees connect to the same Microsoft Exchange Server network, or if you and all attendees have published their free/busy on the Internet, you can use Outlook's meeting planner to quickly select a time for the meeting when all attendees (and all required resources) are free. You can use the meeting planner in the following ways:

- When you've opened a Meeting form to define a meeting (as described previously), you can click the Scheduling tab of the meeting form to access the meeting planner (as shown in Figure 38-27).

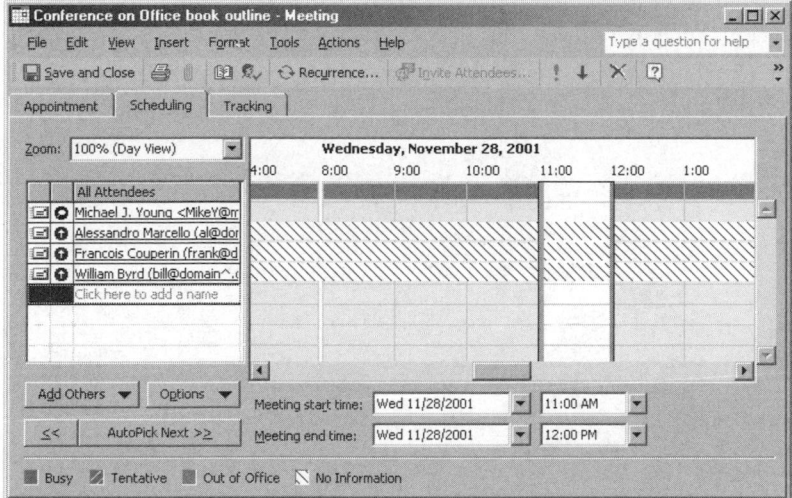

Figure 38-27. You can use the meeting planner through the Scheduling tab of the Meeting form.

- When you schedule a new meeting, you can choose Actions, Plan A Meeting (rather than choosing New Meeting Request). Outlook will then display the Plan A Meeting dialog box, which lets you use the meeting planner, before it displays the Meeting form.

newfeature!

- If an attendee opens a meeting request in his or her Inbox—or views it in the Preview pane—and clicks the Propose New Time button, Outlook opens the Propose New Time dialog box, which displays the meeting planner.

newfeature!

- You can consult the meeting planner whenever the Calendar folder is open, without actually scheduling a meeting, by choosing Actions, View Group Schedules.

(continued)

Planning a Meeting *(continued)* If you want to schedule meetings over the Internet (rather than using Exchange Server) you and your attendees must publish their free/busy times, and you must tell Outlook where to locate each attendee's free/busy information by completing the following basic steps:

1 To publish free/busy times, you (as well as each attendee) should choose Tools, Options, click the Calendar Options button in the Preferences tab of the Options dialog box to open the Calendar Options dialog box (shown in Figure 38-25), click the Free/Busy Options button, and fill in the publishing options in the Free/Busy Options dialog box (shown in Figure 38-28).

Note that you can have Outlook update your free/busy information at any time by opening the Calendar folder and choosing Tools, Send/Receive, Free/Busy Information.

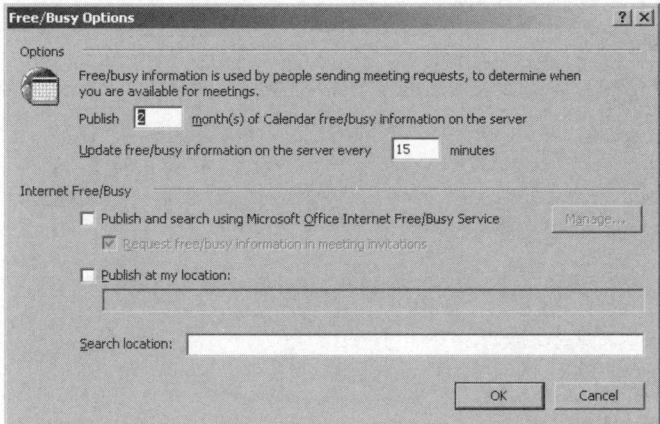

Figure 38-28. The Free/Busy Options dialog box lets you control the way Outlook publishes your free/busy information.

2 To tell Outlook where to look for each attendee's free/busy information, you can enter a default free/busy location into the Search Location text box in the Free/Busy Options dialog box. You can also enter a free/busy location for a specific contact by opening that contact, opening the Details tab in the Contact form, and entering the URL of the contact's free/busy location into the Address text box in the Internet Free-Busy area. If you provide a free/busy location for a contact, Outlook will look for that contact's free/busy schedule at that location rather than at the default free/busy location.

Working with Your Calendar Folder

Chapter 37, "Working with Outlook Items and Folders," describes the general methods for working with Outlook views, items, and folders. In the Calendar folder, the most common view is Day/Week/Month, which displays your Calendar items (appointments, events, and meetings) in the Information Viewer in a layout that resembles a printed calendar or appointment book. In this view (shown in Figure 38-29), you can click the Day, Work Week, Week, or Month toolbar button to adjust the view's range.

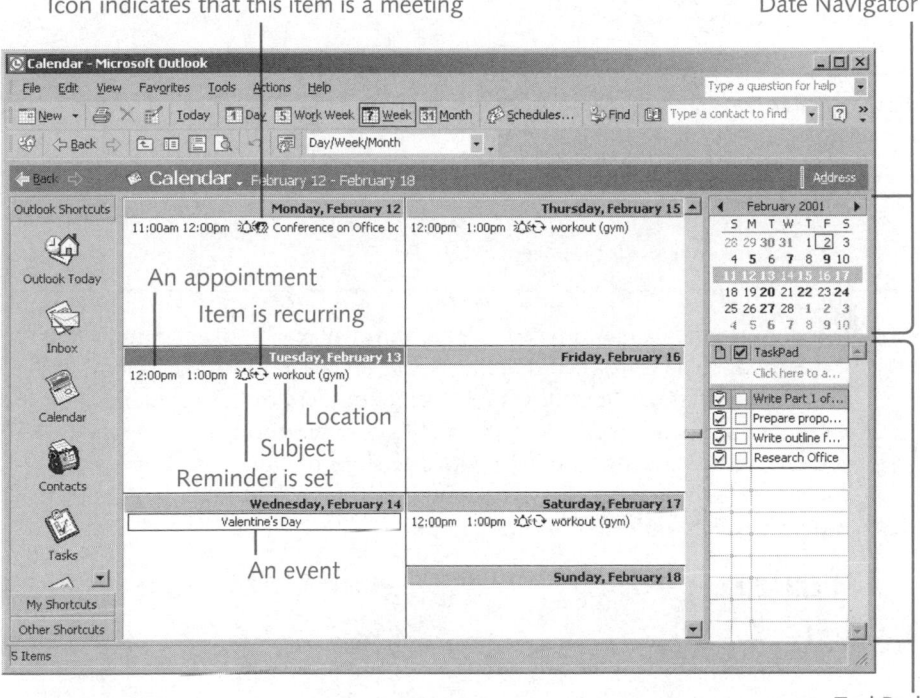

Figure 38-29. This figure shows the Day/Week/Month view of the Calendar folder, with the Week range displayed.

The following are some unique techniques you can use in the Day/Week/Month view of the Calendar folder (some of these techniques aren't available in all ranges):

● You can resize the different panes (such as that holding the Date Navigator) by dragging the appropriate border between panes.

● You can quickly view particular time slots by clicking objects within the Date Navigator. You can view any date by choosing View, Go To, Go To Date or pressing Ctrl+G, and entering the date into the Go To Date dialog box. And you can select the current day by clicking the Today button on the Standard toolbar.

● You can view, open, or add items in your Tasks folder (described in Chapter 39, "Managing Contacts, Tasks, and Other Types of Information") by using the Task Pad.

1053

- You can add a new appointment or event (the item type depends on the current range and where you click) by clicking a time slot and typing the subject. And you can edit an item's subject by clicking it and typing.

- You can change an item's time by dragging it to a new time slot (press Ctrl while you drag to make a copy). And you can change an item's duration by dragging its border.

---

tip **Publish Your Calendar on the Web**

You can publish a snapshot of your Calendar on the Web by choosing File, Save As Web Page to save your Calendar in an HTML file, and then posting that file to your Web server. Keep in mind that if any items change, you'll have to repeat this process to update your published Calendar.

---

newfeature!

If you specified a reminder for an appointment, event, or meeting, when the item is nearly due (or if it's past due but you just started Outlook), Outlook will display a reminder message. In Outlook 2002, all reminders are displayed in a single dialog box (shown in Figure 38-30), so you don't have to view and close a separate dialog box for each due item (as you did in previous versions of Outlook). To view all due Calendar items that you haven't dismissed, you can display this dialog box at any time by choosing View, Reminders Window.

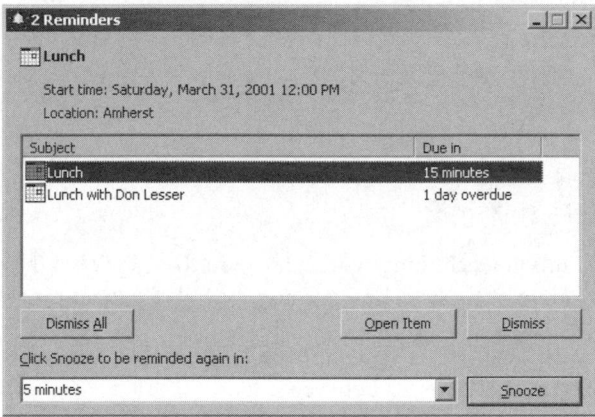

Figure 38-30.   This figure shows Outlook's new unified reminder dialog box.

In addition to the Calendar folder options you can set in the Calendar Options dialog box (shown in Figure 38-25), you can make the following settings to customize your Calendar folder:

- To have the reminder feature turned on by default when you open a new Appointment, Event, or Meeting form and to specify the default reminder time, choose Tools, Options, check the Default Reminder option in the Preferences tab of the Options dialog box, and select the time in the adjoining drop-down list.

- To modify the font used in the Date Navigator or to customize the reminder feature, click the Other tab of the Options dialog box, click the Advanced Options button, and click the Font button to set the Date Navigator font or click the Reminder Options button to change the reminder feature.

---

tip   **Import Events from Your Team Web Site**

If you have access to a team Web site on a Web server running SharePoint Team Services from Microsoft, you can copy an event from the site to your Calendar folder so that you'll have a personal copy of the event description. To do this, open the event in the particular events list that contains it on the SharePoint team Web site, and click the Export Event command in the event's page, and — if prompted — choose to open the file from its current location. The event will then be opened in an Appointment form, which you can use to read, modify, and save the item in your Calendar folder. You will then have to import the event file by using either the Import And Export option on the File menu or by dragging the file and dropping it into your Calendar folder.

Chapter 38

Managing Contacts, Tasks, and Other Types of Information

Maintaining Your Address List with the Contacts Folder

You can use the default Contacts folder—or any folder you've created that contains Contact items—to store names, mailing addresses, phone numbers, e-mail and Web addresses, and many other types of information for your business or personal contacts. Once you've added a collection of contacts to your Contacts folder, you can use Microsoft Outlook 2002 commands to find a contact quickly, and then send an e-mail message or an instant message to the contact, write the contact a letter, telephone the contact, visit the contact's Web site, or communicate with the contact in other ways.

Defining Contacts and Distribution Lists

You can add individual contacts as well as distribution lists to your Contacts folder. A *distribution list* is a single item that contains an entire set of contact descriptions (known as *members* of the distribution list)—for example, everyone in your department or all the members of your volleyball team. A member of a distribution list can be a reference to one of the contacts already stored in your Contacts folder, or it can be an independent description consisting of just a person's or company's name and e-mail address. When you address an e-mail message (or a meeting request or task assignment), you can easily send it to all of the members of a distribution

1057

list you've created. You can do that by clicking the To (or Cc or Bcc) button in the message header and selecting the distribution list in the Select Names dialog box.

> For information on addressing e-mail messages, see "Composing and Sending E-Mail Messages," on page 1030.

To define a new contact, complete the following steps:

1 Open a blank Contact form (shown in Figure 39-1) using one of the following methods:

New Contact

- Open the Contacts folder and choose Actions, New Contact, click the New button on the Standard toolbar, or press Ctrl+N.

- With any folder open, choose Contact from the New drop-down list on the Standard toolbar or press Ctrl+Shift+C.

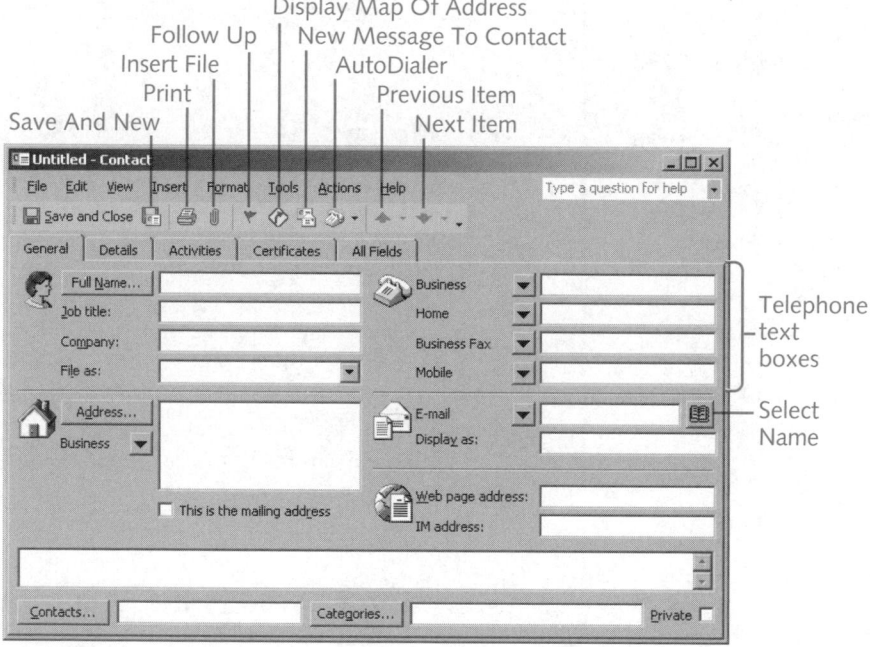

Figure 39-1. This is a blank Contact form, which you use for defining a new contact.

---

tip **Use an Existing Contact**

If you want to create a new contact that has some of the same information as an existing contact (perhaps a contact who works for the same company), select the existing contact in the Contacts folder, and then choose Actions, New Contact From Same Company (rather than New Contact). When the Contact form is opened, it will initially contain the company name, business address, business telephone number(s), and Web page address from the existing contact.

2 Fill in the Contacts form as follows:

- If the contact is an individual (rather than a company), type the contact's full name into the Full Name text box.

> **note** Outlook stores the name you type into the Full Name text box as a set of separate fields—Title, First, Middle, and Last. This feature allows you to search, sort, filter, or group items by one of these individual fields. To see how Outlook has divided the name you typed into separate fields, and to make corrections if necessary, click the Full Name button to display the Check Full Name dialog box. (If Outlook can't decipher the name you've typed, it will display this dialog box automatically.)

- If the contact has a job title, type it into the Job Title text box.

- If the contact is associated with a company, or if you're defining the item for a company rather than an individual, enter the name into the Company text box.

- You can enter up to three different street or post office box addresses for the contact. To enter each one, click the down arrow to the left of the Address text box and select a description for the address—Business, Home, or Other. Then type the full address into the Address text box.

To designate one of the addresses you enter as the contact's mailing address, check the This Is The Mailing Address option when that address is displayed. If you use Microsoft Word to print an individual envelope or label for the contact, or if you use Word's mail merge feature to create form letters or other output documents using your Contacts folder as the recipient list, Word will use the designated mailing address.

> **note** Outlook stores an address you type into the Address text box as a set of separate fields—Street, City, State/Province, ZIP/Postal Code, and Country/Region. This feature allows you to search, sort, filter, or group items by one of these individual fields. To see how Outlook has divided the address you typed into separate fields and to make corrections if necessary, click the Address button to display the Check Address dialog box. (If Outlook can't decipher an address you've typed, it will display this dialog box automatically.)

- You can enter up to four telephone numbers for the contact, one in each of the telephone text boxes. To enter each, click the down arrow next to a box, select the type of phone number (Business, Business Fax, Home, Home Fax, Pager, and so on), and then type the number into the box. If you skip the area code, Outlook will insert your current area code (which you can set using the Modems program in the Control Panel and in other places in Windows).

1059

■ You can enter up to three e-mail addresses for the contact. To enter each one, click the down arrow to the left of the E-Mail text box and select E-Mail, E-Mail 2, or E-Mail 3. Then, either type the address into the E-Mail text box or click the adjoining Select Name button to select the address in the Select Name dialog box.

note The Select Name dialog box is similar to the Select Names dialog box that's displayed when you click the To, Cc, Bcc, or Address Book button in a Message form. If you've set up a directory account, you can search an Internet directory service for the contact's e-mail address. Directory accounts are discussed in "Adding, Modifying, and Removing Outlook Accounts," on page 1093.

newfeature!

■ When you address an e-mail message to the contact, Outlook will display the contents of the Display As text box in the To, Cc, or Bcc field of the Message form. When you enter an e-mail address into the Contact form, Outlook will add default text (the contact's name followed by the e-mail address) to the Display As text box, but you can change this text if you wish.

■ If the contact has a Web page, type the URL into the Web Page Address text box.

■ If the contact has an address for receiving Instant Messaging messages, type it into the IM Address text box.

Using Instant Messaging is described in "Using Your Contacts Folder," on page 1065.

■ Type any free-form information you wish into the Contact form's large text box.

■ To enter one or more other contacts who are associated with the current contact (perhaps members of the same family), click the Contacts button and select one or more other contacts from your Contacts folder (or from another folder you've created to contain Contacts items). Outlook will then display the contact(s) you selected in the adjoining text box.

tip   **Link a Contact to Related Information**

Entering one or more other contacts into the Contacts text box of the Contacts form *links* those contacts to the current contact (and also links the current contact to the other contacts). You can link any other Outlook item to the current contact by entering the current contact into the Contact text box of the other Outlook item.

You can also link any Outlook item or disk file to the current contact by choosing Actions, Link, Items or choosing Actions, Link, File in the Contact form (or in the main Outlook window if the contact is selected in the Information Viewer). The following are a few examples of items or files you might want to link to the current contact:

● An appointment you have with the contact.

● An item in the Notes folder containing free-form information relating to the contact.

● A Word document the contact sent you.

If you send or receive a message to or from a contact, Outlook *automatically* links the message to the contact in your Contacts folder (this includes a regular e-mail message, as well as a meeting or task request or reply and the corresponding item in the Calendar or Tasks folder).

If one or more items or files are linked to the current contact, you can view them by opening the Activities tab of the Contact form (shown in Figure 39-2). To open an item or file, double-click it in the Activities tab.

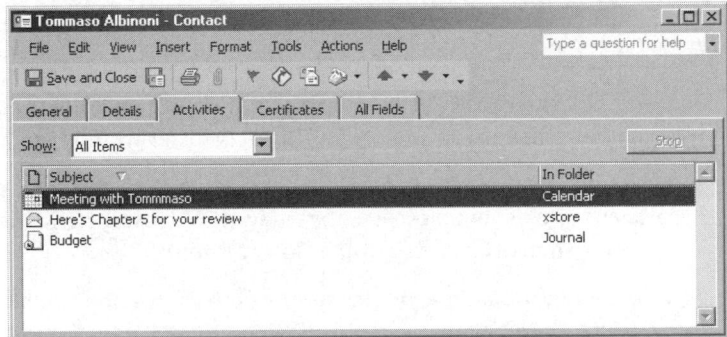

Figure 39-2. You can view linked Outlook items and files in the Activities tab of the Contact form.

To assign one or more categories to the contact, click the Categories button, and in the Categories dialog box (see Figure 39-3, on page 1062), check any of the predefined categories you want to assign in the Available Categories list. To add a custom category to the list (and check it), type it into the Item(s) Belong To These Categories text box and click the Add To List button. You can use categories for finding, sorting, filtering, or grouping Outlook items.

> To learn more about using categories for finding, sorting, filtering, or grouping Outlook items, see "Finding Outlook Items or Disk Files," on page 1010, and "Sorting, Filtering, and Grouping Items in Folders," on page 1005.

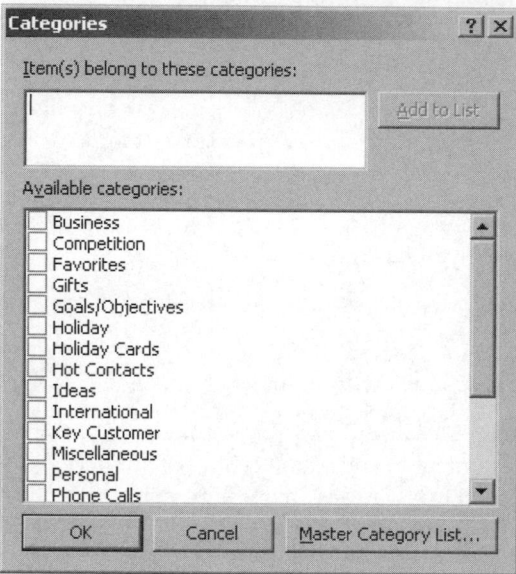

Figure 39-3. Use the Categories dialog box to assign one or more categories to the contact.

> For important information on creating custom categories, see the sidebar "Trouble with Custom Categories," on page 1044.

- To mark the contact as private, check the Private option. (The contact will then be hidden if you share your Contacts folder with others.)

- To enter additional information on the contact—such as the contact's department, profession, nickname, birthday, or Microsoft NetMeeting settings—open the Details tab of the Contacts form.

- To view, modify, or add certificates for the contact, use the Certificates tab. A contact's certificate is a digital ID that Outlook uses to send encrypted e-mail to that contact.

- To access all fields of information for the contact, or to create custom fields, use the All Fields tab.

3 Click the Save And Close button on the form's Standard toolbar.

To define a distribution list, follow these steps:

1 Open a blank Distribution List form (shown in Figure 39-4) using one of the following methods:

- Open the Contacts folder and choose Actions, New Distribution List.

- With any folder open, choose Distribution List from the New drop-down list on the Standard toolbar or press Ctrl+Shift+L.

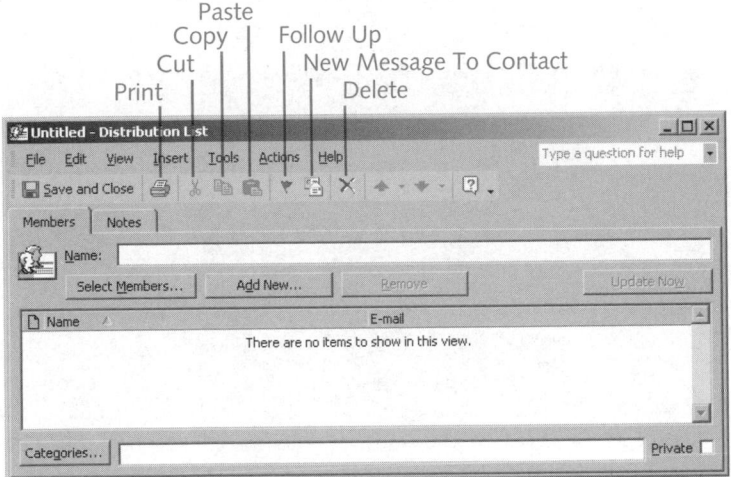

Figure 39-4. This is a blank Distribution List form, which you use for defining a new distribution list.

2 Type a name for the distribution list into the Name text box.

3 Add members to the distribution list. To add each member, do one of the following actions:

- To add a member from a contact stored in your Contacts folder, click Select Members and choose the contact from the list in the Select Members dialog box. The member will be linked to the contact, so that if you change any of the information on the contact in the Contacts folder, the member in the distribution list will reflect that change.

- To add a new member, click the Add New button and enter the person's or company's name, e-mail address, and e-mail address type into the Add New Member dialog box (see Figure 39-5). If you leave the Add To Contacts option clear, the new member will consist of an independent description and will not be linked to a contact in the Contacts folder. If you check Add To Contacts, Outlook will create a new contact in your Contacts folder containing the information you supplied and it will link the new member to that contact, as described above.

The new members you add will be displayed in the list in the Distribution List form. If you double-click a member based on a contact, Outlook will open the linked contact in the Contact form. If you double-click a new, independent member, Outlook will open the member in the E-Mail Properties dialog box, which displays the same controls as the Add New Member dialog box in which you originally created the member (except that it doesn't have an Add To Contacts option). In either case, you can modify the member's information. You can remove a member by selecting it and clicking the Remove button (this removes only the distribution list member, *not* a contact to which it's linked).

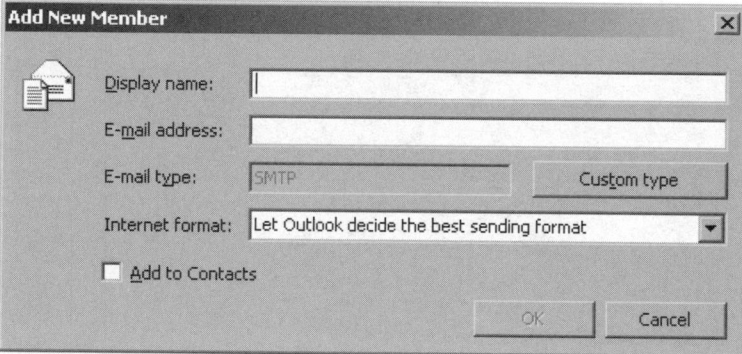

Figure 39-5. You use the Add New Member dialog box to create a new distribution list member.

4 If you wish, add categories to the Categories box or check the Private control, as explained in step 2 of the procedure for defining a contact, given previously in this section.

5 If you wish, you can enter free-form information about the distribution list by opening the Notes tab and typing the information into the large text box.

6 Click the Save And Close button on the form's Standard toolbar.

In the Information Viewer, Outlook marks a distribution list using a double-head icon. Here's how one would appear in the Address Cards view:

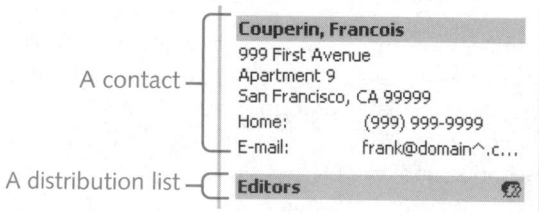

> **tip** **Keep Your Distribution List Private**
>
> Unless you want to reveal to all message recipients the entire list of e-mail addresses in your distribution list, add the distribution list to the Bcc field when you address an e-mail message, rather than adding it to the To or Cc field. To display the Bcc field in the Message form's header, choose Bcc from the Options drop-down menu on the message header (in Word), or choose Bcc Field from the View menu (in the Outlook e-mail editor).

Troubleshooting

Distribution List Displays Out-Of-Date Information

You've added members to a distribution list from your Contacts folder. However, when you change or delete a contact and then open the distribution list, the information displayed in the Distribution List form doesn't show your changes.

Although a distribution list member you create from a contact is linked to that contact, and Outlook will use the current e-mail address contained in the contact if you address a message with the distribution list, the information displayed in the Distribution List form will become out of date if you change the contact's Display As or E-Mail field (these are the two fields displayed in the Distribution List form). Also, if you delete the contact a member is linked to, the member will remain displayed in the Distribution List form. To update all the information displayed in the Distribution List form, click the Update Now button within the form.

> **tip** **Import Contacts from Your Team Web Site**
>
> If you have access to a team Web site on a Web server running SharePoint Team Services from Microsoft, you can copy a contact description from the site to your Contacts folder so that you'll have a personal copy of the contact description. To do this, open the contact in the contacts list that contains it on the SharePoint team Web site and click the Export Contact command in the contact's page, and—if prompted—choose to open the file from its current location. The contact will then be opened in a Contact form, which you can use to read, modify, and save the item in your Contacts folder.

Using Your Contacts Folder

Figure 39-6, on page 1066, shows a set of contacts that have been added to the Contacts folder displayed in the commonly used Address Cards view. This section explains how to quickly find or communicate with a contact you've added to your Contacts folder and how to set several Contacts folder options.

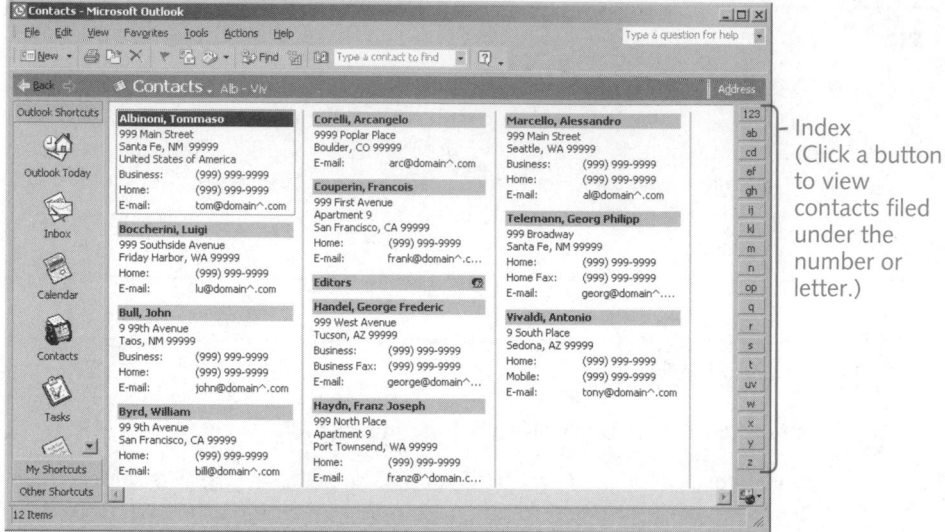

Figure 39-6. This figure shows the Contacts folder in the Address Cards view.

In addition to the general methods for finding Outlook items discussed in "Finding Outlook Items or Disk Files," on page 1010, you can quickly locate a contact when working in any folder by typing the contact's name (or part of the name) into the Find A Contact box on the Standard toolbar and pressing Enter:

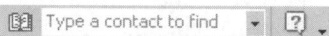

You can also select a previously entered name from the drop-down list.

You can communicate with a contact in a variety of ways by selecting the contact in the Information Viewer and then using Outlook commands, as follows:

- To send an e-mail message to the contact, choose Actions, New Message To Contact. (For more information, see "Receiving and Sending E-Mail Messages with the E-Mail Folders," on page 1021.)

- To use Word and the Word Letter Wizard to write a letter to the contact, choose Actions, New Letter To Contact. (See the tip, "Have Word Write Your Letters," on page 569.)

- To run Word's mail-merge feature from within Outlook, select the contacts you want to receive the form letter (or other mail-merge output document), choose Tools, Mail Merge, fill in the Mail Merge Contacts dialog box, and then complete the mail merge operation in Word. Once Outlook transfers you to Word, the easiest way to complete the merge is to choose Tools, Letters And Mailings, Mail Merge Wizard in Word to display the Mail Merge task pane. For details on using mail merge in Word, see "Using the Mail Merge Wizard to Automate Large Mailings," on page 553.

New Meeting
RequestTo
Contact

- To send a meeting request to the contact, choose Actions, New Meeting Request To Contact or click the New Meeting Request To Contact button on the Advanced toolbar. (For more information, see "Planning Meetings," on page 1046.)

- To schedule an appointment with the contact, choose Actions, New Appointment With Contact. Outlook will open a new appointment in a form and will link the appointment with the contact by entering the contact's name into the Appointment form's Contacts box. (For more information, see "Scheduling Appointments," on page 1040.)

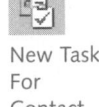

New Task
For
Contact

- To assign a task to the contact, choose Actions, New Task For Contact or click the New Task For Contact button on the Advanced toolbar. (See "Managing Tasks and Projects with the Tasks Folder," on page 1069.)

- To create a new journal entry that's linked to the contact (and has the contact's name as the subject), choose Actions, New Journal Entry For Contact. (See "Recording Events with the Journal Folder," on page 1076.)

- If you have a modem attached to the same line as your telephone, you can place a call to the contact by using the commands on the Call Contact submenu of the Actions menu:

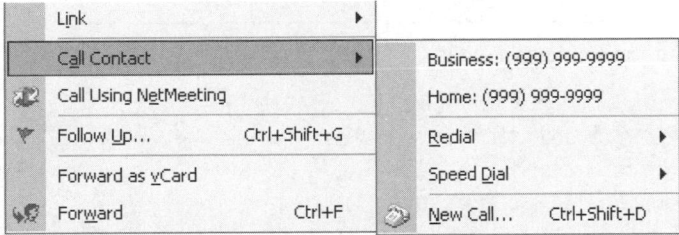

Dial

or on the menu that appears when you click the down arrow on the Dial button on the Standard toolbar.

Call Using
NetMeeting

- If you've defined NetMeeting settings for the contact (in the Contact form's Details tab) you can establish a NetMeeting connection with that contact by choosing Actions, Call Using NetMeeting or by clicking the Call Using NetMeeting button on the Advanced toolbar.

newfeature!

- If the contact has an Instant Messaging account and if you've entered the contact's Instant Messaging address into the IM Address text box in the General tab of the Contact form, you can use Instant Messaging to communicate with the contact in real time—provided that the person is currently logged onto Instant Messaging—by opening the contact in the Contact form and choosing Actions, New Instant Message in the form. To enable Instant Messaging in Outlook, choose Tools, Options, click the Other tab in the Options dialog box, check Enable Instant Messaging In

Chapter 39

1067

Microsoft Outlook, and click the adjoining Options button to set up Instant Messaging. (You might be prompted to download the MSN Messenger software from the Web.) To log onto or off Instant Messaging, to check your Instant Messaging status, or to set Instant Messaging options, you can use the commands on the Instant Messaging submenu of the Tools menu. (This submenu is present in any folder you've opened.)

Explore Web Page

● If you've entered a URL into the Web Page Address text box in the contact's form, you can open that page in your browser by clicking the Explore Web Page button on the Advanced toolbar or by pressing Ctrl+Shift+X.

Display Map Of Address

● You can display a map showing the location of the contact's address by opening the contact and choosing Actions, Display Map Of Address in the Contact form or by clicking the Display Map Of Address button on the form's Standard toolbar. Outlook will then connect to the Microsoft Expedia site on the Web and attempt to locate and display the map.

> **note** If you've opened a contact in the Contact form, keep in mind that most of the commands mentioned in this list are also available in the form. (The Display Map Of Address and New Instant Message commands are available *only* in the Contacts form.)

> **tip** **Customize the Contacts Folder**
>
> To specify the order in which you enter contact names into the Full Name text box (such as "First (Middle) Last" or "Last First") so that Outlook knows how to divide the names into separate fields, or to change the default way Outlook files contacts ("Last, First," "First Last," "Company," and so on), choose Tools, Options, click the Contact Options button in the Preferences tab of the Options dialog box, and make your changes in the Contact Options dialog box (shown in Figure 39-7).

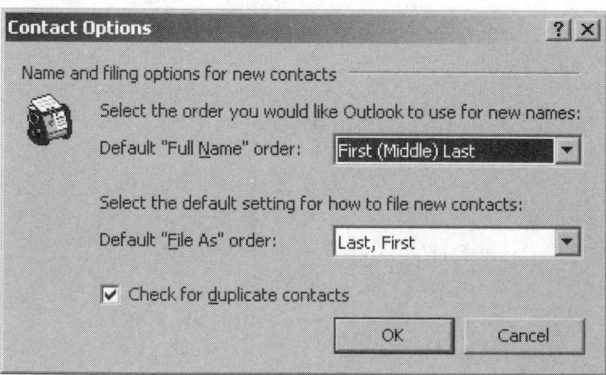

Figure 39-7. The Contact Options dialog box lets you change the order in which you enter names and other features of the Contacts folder.

Chapter 39

Managing Tasks and Projects with the Tasks Folder

Each item in the Tasks folder—or in any folder you've created that holds Task items—stores information on a task or project that needs to be completed, including a description of the task, as well as the task's due date, priority, completion status, and other details. You can create a *personal task* to keep tabs on a task you're undertaking by yourself. A personal task is stored in your Tasks folder only and you're the *owner* of the task.

You can also create an *assigned task* by sending a task request to someone else, who becomes the task owner and is responsible for completing the task. The task itself is stored in the owner's Tasks folder, although Outlook places a copy of the task in your Tasks folder and updates your copy whenever the owner changes the task information (for example, if the owner changes the value in the % Complete field). All task requests, replies, and updates are transmitted using e-mail messages.

You can manage a group project by assigning the individual project tasks to different members of your workgroup (as well as to yourself). For a complex project, you might want to create a separate folder to store all of the project's tasks.

Defining Tasks

To create a personal task, complete the following steps:

1 Open a blank Task form (shown in Figure 39-8) using one of the following methods:

New Task

■ Open the Tasks folder and choose Actions, New Task, click the New button on the Standard toolbar, or press Ctrl+N.

■ With any folder open, choose Task from the New drop-down list on the Standard toolbar or press Ctrl+Shift+K.

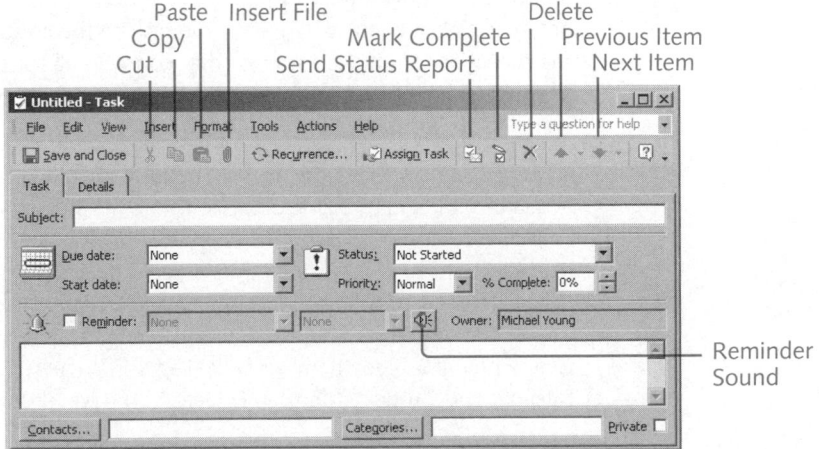

Figure 39-8. This figure shows a blank Task form as it appears when you define a new personal task.

1069

2 Fill in the Task form as follows:

■ Enter a brief description of the task into the Subject text box. If you want, you can type a more complete task description, as well as instructions, comments, or any free-form information into the large text box.

■ If the task has specific starting and due dates, enter those into the Due Date and Start Date text boxes. (You can click the down-arrow button on either box to select the date from a drop-down calendar.)

■ Select a priority for the task—Low, Normal, or High—in the Priority drop-down list.

■ If you've already started working on the task, indicate its current completion status by selecting a value in the Status drop-down list and entering the completion percentage into the % Complete box. If you haven't started the task, just leave the default values—Not Started and 0%—in these controls and update their values as you begin working on the task.

■ To have Outlook display a message to remind you when the task is due, check the Reminder option and in the following controls, type or select the date and time you want Outlook to display the reminder (by default, Outlook displays it at 8 A.M. on the day the task is due). To modify or turn off the sound Outlook plays when it displays the reminder message, click the Reminder Sound button.

■ To enter one or more contacts who are associated with the task (perhaps people you need to ask for information or assistance), click the Contacts button and select one or more items from your Contacts folder (or from another folder you've created for storing Contact items). Outlook will then display the contact(s) in the adjoining text box. Entering a contact here links the task to the contact; as a result, the Activities tab of the form for that contact will list the appointment as well as other linked Outlook items. You can double-click a contact name in the Contacts box to open the contact.

■ To assign one or more categories to the task, click the Categories button and in the Categories dialog box (see Figure 39-3), check any of the predefined categories you want to assign in the Available Categories list. To add a custom category to the list (and check it), type it into the Item(s) Belong To These Categories text box and click the Add To List button. You can use categories for finding, sorting, filtering, or grouping Outlook items (see "Finding Outlook Items or Disk Files," on page 1010, and "Sorting, Filtering, and Grouping Items in Folders," on page 1005).

For important information on creating custom categories, see the sidebar "Trouble with Custom Categories," on page 1044.

■ To mark the task as private, check the Private option. (The task will then be hidden if you share your Contacts folder with others.)

■ To enter additional task information, open the Details tab. Here you can add the names of companies associated with the task, billing information, and mileage for the task. When you complete the task, you can also enter in this tab the date completed, the total estimated work hours, and the actual work hours.

---

note If the task you're defining is one that repeats—that is, it needs to be completed at regular intervals—click the Recurrence button on the Standard toolbar of the Task form and specify the daily, weekly, monthly, or yearly recurrence pattern in the Task Recurrence dialog box (see Figure 39-9). Outlook will add only the first task in the series to your Tasks folder. When you mark that task as completed (by selecting Completed in the Status drop-down list in the Task form or by simply checking the Completed column displayed in the task's description in the Information Viewer of the Outlook window), Outlook will add the next task in the repeated series. And it will keep on adding tasks like this one at a time.

You can have Outlook change a recurring task's due date to the due date for the *next* task in the series by opening the task and choosing Skip Occurrence from the form's Actions menu. (This command won't be available if you selected the Regenerate New Task option in the Task Recurrence dialog box.) This is a convenient way to extend the deadline for a particular task in the series.

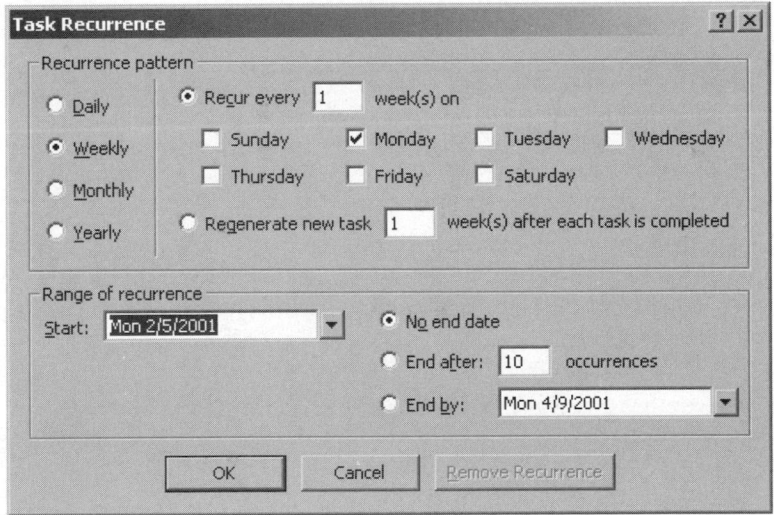

Figure 39-9.   Use the Task Recurrence dialog box when the task you're defining is one that's repeated.

3 Click the Save And Close button on the form's Standard toolbar.

To create an assigned task, complete the following steps:

1 Open a blank Task form for an assigned task (shown in Figure 39-10) by opening the Tasks folder and choosing Actions, New Task Request or by pressing Ctrl+Shift+U.

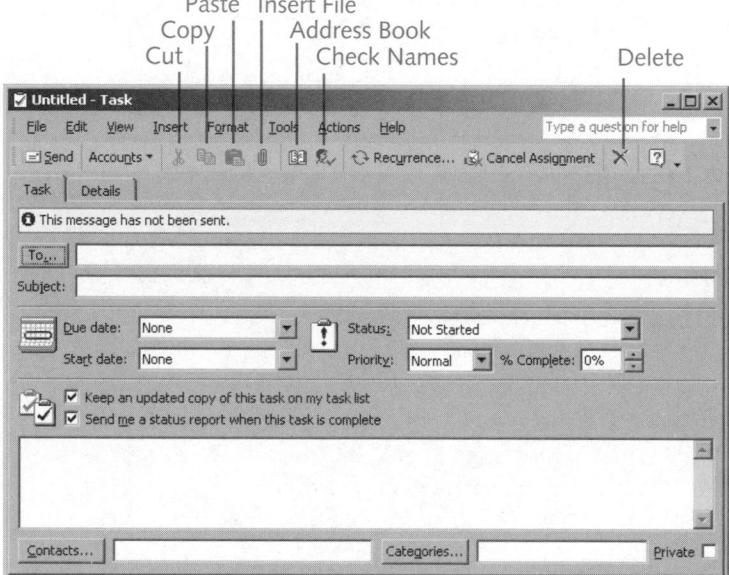

Figure 39-10. This figure shows a blank Task form as it appears when you define a new assigned task.

> **note** You can convert a personal task to an assigned task by clicking the Assign Task button on the form's Standard toolbar, and you can convert an assigned task to a personal task by clicking the Cancel Assignment button.

2 Enter the e-mail address of the person to whom you want to assign the task. This person will become the task owner. Either type the address into the To text box or click the To button to select the address from your Outlook Contacts folder.

> For information on entering or selecting addresses, see "Composing and Sending E-Mail Messages," on page 1030.

note To store a copy of the assigned task in your own Tasks folder, check the Keep An Updated Copy Of This Task On My Task List option. Although you won't be able to directly modify this copy of the task, Outlook will automatically update it when the task owner changes the task in his or her Tasks folder. (You can, however, convert your task copy to a task that you own by opening the Details tab of the Task form and clicking the Create Unassigned Copy button. If you do this, you'll no longer receive updates, but you'll be able to use the task yourself or to click the Assign Task button on the form's Standard toolbar to assign the task to someone else.)

To receive an e-mail message when the task owner marks the task as completed, check the Send Me A Status Report When This Task Is Complete option.

3 Fill in the remaining controls in the tabs of the Task form, following the instructions in step 2 of the procedure for creating a personal task, given on page 1070. However, note the following:

- The Task form doesn't contain the Owner text box because you aren't the owner of a task you assign. This box appears only in the actual task, which is stored in the owner's Tasks folder.

- The Task form doesn't include the Reminder controls. Only the task owner is allowed to set a reminder.

4 Select an e-mail account (if you have more than one) from the Accounts drop-down menu on the Standard toolbar. Then click the Send button on this same toolbar to place a task assignment e-mail message in your Outbox, and then transmit the message to your outgoing e-mail server as explained in "Composing and Sending E-Mail Messages," on page 1030. The following is typical of the series of events that now occur:

- Outlook stores a copy of the task in your Tasks folder, provided that you checked the Keep An Updated Copy Of This Task On My Task List option.

- The task owner receives a task request as an e-mail message.

- newfeature! The task owner views the task request in the Preview pane and clicks the Accept or Decline button displayed in the Preview pane header to accept or relinquish ownership of the task (see Figure 39-11, on page 1074). You'll receive an e-mail message indicating the owner's reply.

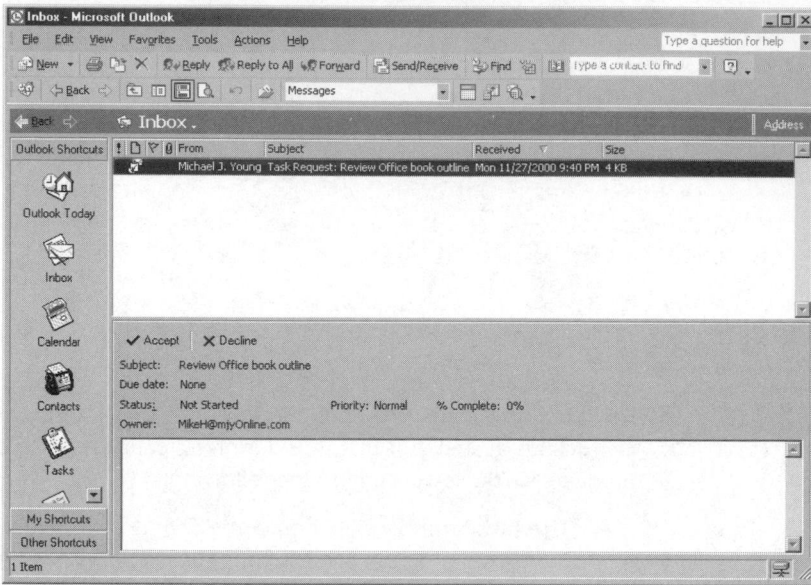

Figure 39-11. This figure shows a task request received in the owner's Inbox.

- If the owner accepted the task request, the task is added to the owner's Tasks folder (and the task request is removed from the Inbox). Whenever the owner modifies the task, your copy of the task will be updated (by means of a special e-mail message).

- When the owner marks the task as completed, you'll receive an e-mail message notifying you, provided that you checked the Send Me A Status Report When This Task Is Complete option in the original task request form.

note The task owner can click the Assign Task button on the Standard toolbar to assign the task to someone else. All people who have assigned the task to another person and who have checked the Keep An Updated Copy Of This Task On My Task List option in the Task form will be included in the Update List of the task stored in the current owner's Tasks folder (the Update List is shown in the Details tab of the Task form).

Working with Your Tasks Folder

The Task Timeline view of the Tasks folder arranges your tasks in a timeline according to their due dates. All of the other views display the tasks in a table, some of them applying a filter or grouping the tasks (see Figure 39-12).

Chapter 39

---

tip **Navigate Quickly Through the Task Timeline**

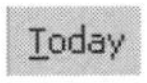

In the Tasks Timeline view, you can go directly to a particular time period by clicking the gray banner at the top of the Information Viewer and choosing a date from the calendar that drops down. Or, you can choose Go To, Go To Date from the View menu or press Ctrl+G to display the Go To Date dialog box. To go to the time period

Today   displaying the current date, you can click the Today button on the Standard toolbar. You can change the range of days shown in the window by clicking the Day, Week, or Month button on the Standard toolbar.

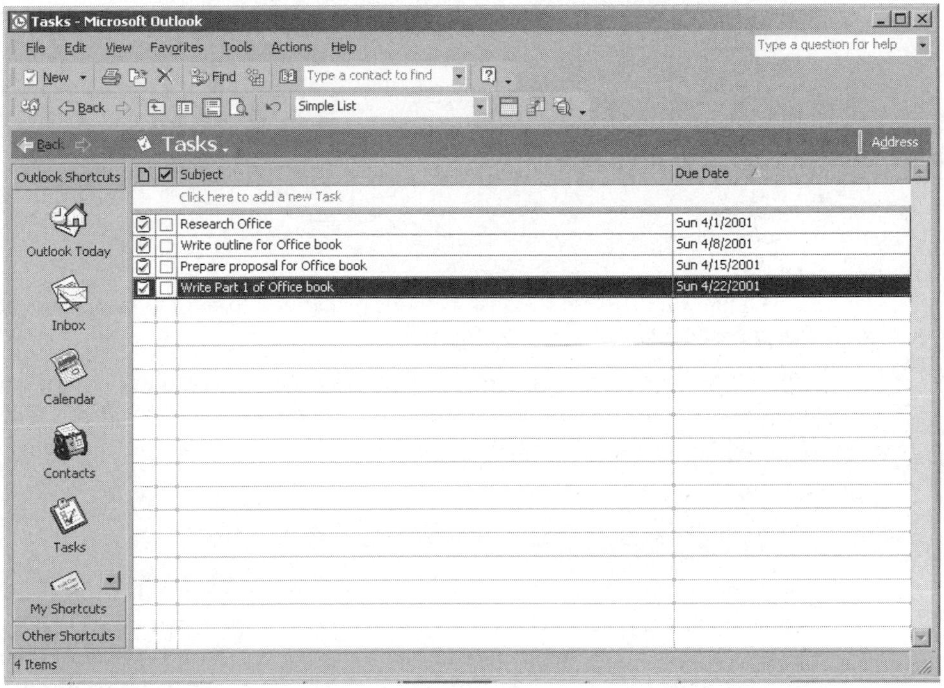

Figure 39-12. The Tasks folder in the Simple List view displays the Subject and Due Date of all tasks and has check boxes that you can click to mark tasks as completed.

---

tip **Arrange Tasks in Any Order**

If you remove all sorting from a table view of the Tasks folder, you can drag the tasks to arrange them in any order you want. To remove sorting, choose View, Current View, Customize Current View, click the Sort button in the View Summary dialog box, and click the Clear All button in the Sort dialog box.

You can modify the appearance or behavior of the Tasks folder in the following ways:

● To change the default time of day when a reminder is displayed for a task due on that date, choose Tools, Options and select a time in the Reminder Time drop-down list in the Preferences tab. You can modify task colors and other features by clicking the Task Options button in this same tab to open the Task Options dialog box (see Figure 39-13).

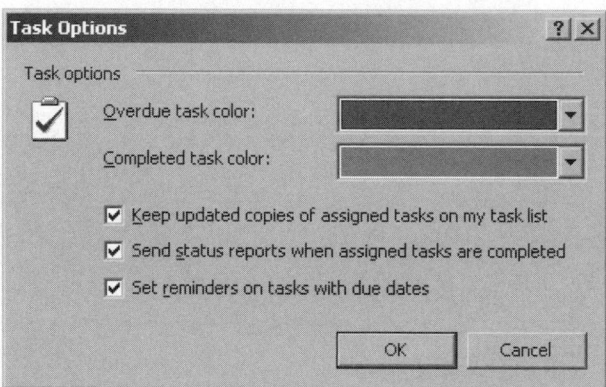

Figure 39-13. Use the Task Options dialog box to modify task colors and other features of the Tasks folder.

● You can set additional options that affect the Tasks folder by clicking the Other tab in the Options dialog box and clicking the Advanced Options button.

Recording Events with the Journal Folder

Each item in the default Journal folder—or in a Journal-type folder that you create—stores a journal entry that contains information on a particular event that occurred, such as receiving an e-mail message or a task request, creating a Microsoft Excel 2002 workbook or editing a Word document, sending a letter, or making a phone call. You can have Outlook *automatically* create a journal entry whenever you send or receive a message (e-mail message, meeting request, task request, and so on) to or from a particular contact or whenever you open a document in a particular Microsoft Office XP application. You can also *manually* create a journal entry to record any type of event.

InsideOut

If you simply want to keep track of messages for one or more contacts, you do *not* need to turn on automatic journaling, because when you send or receive a message to or from a contact, Outlook *automatically* links the message to that contact (this includes a regular e-mail message as well as a meeting or task request or reply and the corresponding item in the Calendar or Tasks folder). You can view all of the contact's messages by opening the contact and looking in the Activities tab of the Contact form.

1076

Recording Entries in Your Journal Folder

To have Outlook begin automatically recording journal entries, do the following:

1 Open your Journal folder. If you haven't already turned on automatic recording of journal entries, Outlook may display a message box giving you the option to turn on automatic journaling. Click the Yes button in this message box to display the Journal Options dialog box (shown in Figure 39-14). You can open this dialog box at any time by choosing Tools, Options and clicking the Journal Options button in the Preferences tab.

> **note** Outlook initially puts the shortcut for your Journal folder in the My Shortcuts group within the Outlook Bar.

InsideOut

Turning on automatic journal recording can slow Outlook's response time and also rapidly expand the size of your Outlook data file. Therefore, if you use automatic recording, you should enable it for only the messages and document accesses you truly need to record. Keep in mind that you can use the Activities tab in the Contacts form to view all of a contact's messages without incurring the overhead of automatic journaling, as explained in the "Inside Out" on page 1076. To control the growth of your Outlook data file that's caused by automatic journaling, archive your Journal folder regularly, using the instructions given in "Archiving Items," on page 997.

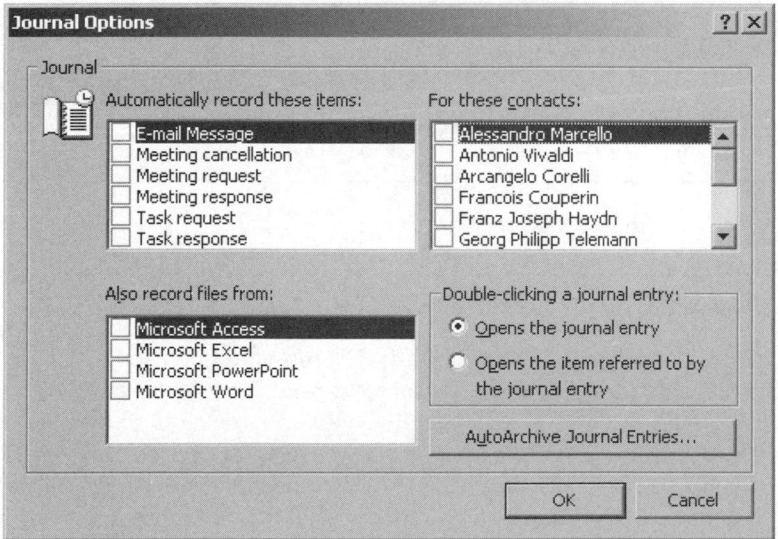

Figure 39-14. The Journal Options dialog box lets you set up automatic recording of journal entries.

1077

Chapter 39

2 To have Outlook automatically create a journal entry whenever you receive or send a message from or to a contact, check the specific types of messages you want to record in the Automatically Record These Items list and then check the contacts you want to record messages for in the For These Contacts list. (This list shows all the contacts contained in your default Contacts folder. You won't be able to select contacts in another Contacts-type folder you've created.)

3 To have Outlook automatically record a journal entry whenever you open a document in an Office application, check the specific Office applications whose documents you want to record in the Also Record Files From list, which will display the applications currently installed on your computer.

---

tip **Control the Way You Open Journal Entries**

When Outlook automatically creates a journal entry, it inserts into the entry's large text box a shortcut to the message (which is an Outlook item) or to the disk file that's associated with the entry. (When you create a manual journal entry using the method given in the next section, you can also insert an Outlook item shortcut or a file shortcut, as explained in "Editing Items," on page 988.)

If you select the Opens The Journal Entry option in the Journal Options dialog box (shown in Figure 39-14), whenever you double-click a journal entry that contains a shortcut (or use any other method to open the item), Outlook will open the journal entry itself in the Journal Entry form. To open the item or file targeted by the shortcut, you can right-click the entry and choose Open The Item Referred To from the shortcut menu. An Outlook item will be opened in the appropriate form and a file will be opened in the application that was used to create it.

If, however, you select Opens The Item Referred To By The Journal Entry, double-clicking an entry with a shortcut will open the item or file targeted by the shortcut. To open the entry itself, right-click it and choose Open Journal Entry from the shortcut menu.

---

4 Click the OK button.

---

tip **View Automatically Recorded Entries for a Contact**

When Outlook automatically records a journal entry for a contact, it links the entry to that contact (by inserting the contact's name into the Contacts text box, discussed later in this section). You can therefore view at a glance all of the automatically recorded journal entries for a contact by opening that contact and looking in the Activities tab of the Contact form. You can choose Journal in the Show drop-down list at the top of the tab to display just the linked journal entries and not other linked Outlook items.

1078

Troubleshooting

Journal Entries for Document Accesses Don't Appear

You turned on automatic journal entries for accessing Office documents, but the entries don't appear in your Journal folder.

If the Journal folder is currently opened in Outlook, automatically recorded journal entries for document accesses won't appear until you close the Journal folder by opening another folder in Outlook and then reopen the Journal folder.

To manually record any type of event, complete the following steps:

1 Open a blank Journal Entry form (shown in Figure 39-15) using one of the following methods:

New
Journal

■ Open the Journal folder and choose Actions, New Journal Entry, click the New button on the Standard toolbar, or press Ctrl+N.

■ With any folder open, choose Journal Entry from the New drop-down list on the Standard toolbar or press Ctrl+Shift+J.

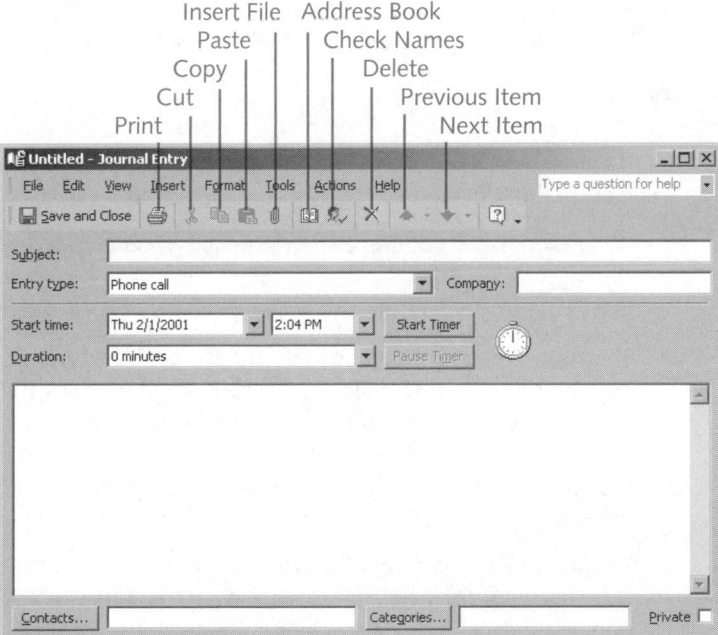

Figure 39-15. This figure shows a blank Journal Entry form, which you use for manually recording a new journal entry.

2 Fill in the Journal Entry form as follows:

■ Enter a short description for the entry into the Subject text box. If you wish, you can enter a full description, comments, or any free-form information into the large text box.

■ Select the item from the Entry Type drop-down list that most closely describes the event you're recording—Conversation, Document, E-Mail Message, Fax, Phone Call, and so on.

> **note** The By Type view of the Journal folder groups your journal entries by the value of the Entry Type field.

InsideOut

Surprisingly, the Journal Entry form doesn't let you create custom types, which would make the Journal folder more useful as a general-purpose journaling tool. And the collection of built-in types is quite limited. If an event you want to record (such as selling shares of a mutual fund at a particular time and price) doesn't fit one of the built-in types, the best you can do is to choose one of the less-specific types, such as note, and then possibly assign a custom category (such as Sale Of Shares) to indicate a more precise classification. You could then find, sort, filter, or group your Journal entries using the categories. Categories are described later in this list.

■ If a company is associated with the entry, enter its name into the Company text box.

■ If the event occurs during a specific period of time, enter or select the starting date and time in the Start Time controls (Outlook initially sets these controls to the date and time when you opened the form).

Then enter the event duration into the Duration text box or select a duration from the drop-down list. Or click the Start Timer button when the event starts (for example, when you initiate a phone call) and then click the Pause Timer button when the event has completed (for example, when you hang up the phone), and Outlook will display the time that has expired, in one-minute increments, in the Duration box.

■ To enter one or more contacts who are associated with the journal entry (perhaps the person you're speaking to on the phone), click the Contacts button and select one or more items from your Contacts folder (or from another folder you've created for storing Contact items). Outlook will then display the contact(s) in the adjoining text box. Entering a contact here links the journal entry to the contact; as a result, the Activities tab of the form for that contact will list the journal

1080

entry as well as other linked Outlook items. You can double-click a contact name in the Contacts box to open the contact.

■ To assign one or more categories to the journal entry, click the Categories button and in the Categories dialog box (shown in Figure 39-3, on page 1062), check any of the predefined categories you want to assign in the Available Categories list. To add a custom category to the list (and check it), type it into the Item(s) Belong To These Categories text box and click the Add To List button. You can use categories for finding, sorting, filtering, or grouping Outlook items.

For more information on using categories for finding, sorting, filtering, or grouping Outlook items, see "Finding Outlook Items or Disk Files," on page 1010, and "Sorting, Filtering, and Grouping Items in Folders," on page 1005.

For important information on creating custom categories, see the sidebar "Trouble with Custom Categories," on page 1044.

■ To mark the journal entry as private, check the Private option. (The journal entry will then be hidden if you share your Contacts folder with others.)

3 Click the Save And Close button on the form's Standard toolbar.

tip **Dial and Record a Call Using a Single Command**

You can telephone one of your contacts and create a journal entry to time and record the call, using a single command. To do this, select the contact in your Contacts folder, click the Dial button on the Standard toolbar, and before placing your call, check the Create New Journal Entry When Starting New Call option in the New Call dialog box (shown in Figure 39-16).

Dial

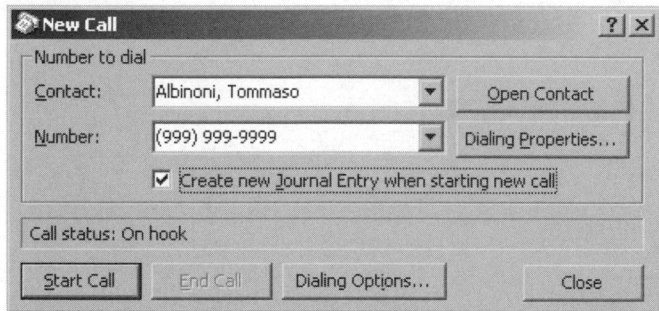

Figure 39-16. The New Call dialog box allows you to automatically create a record of every call you make.

> **tip** Navigate Quickly Through a Journal Timeline
>
> If you switch to the By Type, By Contact, or By Category view of the Journal folder, Outlook will display your journal entries in a timeline, grouping the items differently with each view. In a timeline view of the Journal folder, you can go to a particular time period by clicking the gray banner at the top of the Information Viewer and choosing a date from the calendar that drops down. Or, you can choose View, Go To, Go To Date or press Ctrl+G to display the Go To Date dialog box. To go to the time period displaying the current date, you can click the Today button on the Standard toolbar. You can change the range of days shown in the window by clicking the Day, Week, or Month button on the Standard toolbar.
>
> Today

Storing Miscellaneous Information in the Notes Folder

You can use the Notes folder—or any folder you've created to hold Note items—to quickly jot down free-form information on any topic. An individual note in the Notes folder is an electronic equivalent of a "sticky note."

To enter a new note, complete the following steps:

1 Open a blank Note form (shown in Figure 39-17) using one of the following methods:

New Note

- Open the Notes folder and choose Actions, New Note, click the New button on the Standard toolbar, press Ctrl+N, or double-click a blank spot in the Notes folder.

- With any folder open, choose Note from the New drop-down list on the Standard toolbar or press Ctrl+Shift+N.

Menu   Close

2/1/2001, 2:28 PM

Date and time when Outlook last saved the note

Figure 39-17. This figure shows a blank Note form for entering miscellaneous information.

2 Type any text you want into the note form, which consists of a single text box.

3 To set options for the note, click the Menu button to open the note's drop-down menu, as shown here:

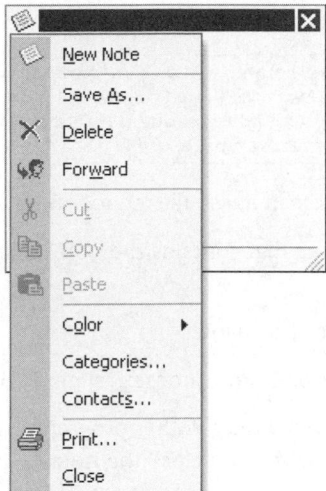

Then choose a command as follows:

- To change the background color of the note, choose a color from the Color submenu.

- To enter one or more contacts who are associated with the note (perhaps the person you're speaking to on the telephone while you're jotting down information), choose Contacts, click the Contacts button in the Contacts For Note dialog box (shown in Figure 39-18) and select one or more items from your Contacts folder (or from another folder you've created to contain Contact items). Outlook will then display the contact(s) in the adjoining text box. Entering a contact here links the note to the contact; as a result, the Activities tab of the form for that contact will list the note as well as other linked Outlook items. You can double-click a contact name in the Contacts box in the Contacts For Note dialog box to open the contact.

Figure 39-18. You use the Contacts For Note dialog box to enter contacts associated with a note.

- To assign one or more categories to the note, choose Categories and in the Categories dialog box (see Figure 39-3, on page 1062) check any of the predefined categories you want to assign in the Available Categories list. To add a custom category to the list (and check it), type it into the Item(s) Belong To These Categories text box and click the Add To List button. You can use categories for finding, sorting, filtering, or grouping Outlook items.

> For information on using categories for finding, sorting, filtering, or grouping Outlook items, see "Finding Outlook Items or Disk Files," on page 1010, and "Sorting, Filtering, and Grouping Items in Folders," on page 1005. For important information on creating custom categories, see the sidebar "Trouble with Custom Categories," on page 1044.

- ■ To save the contents of the note in a disk file, choose Save As.

- ■ To create a new e-mail message that contains the note as an attachment, choose Forward.

- ■ To create another note, choose New Note.

- ■ To delete, print, or close the Note form, choose Delete, Print, or Close.

4 You can leave the note open while you work in other programs, so that you can quickly add more information. Or you can close the note by clicking the Close button or pressing Esc; the note will then be displayed only as an item in the Notes folder. In either case, Outlook will automatically save the text you add; you don't have to issue a save command (as you do with other Outlook items or in a note editor like Microsoft Notepad).

tip **Organize Your Notes Using Colors**

To organize your notes into topics, you can assign the notes on each topic a different color. You can assign any of five colors from the menu in the Notes form, as described under step 3, or you can right-click the note in the Information Viewer and choose a color from the Color submenu on the shortcut menu. Once you've marked your notes using different colors, you can have Outlook group the notes by color; just switch to the By Color view.

note To change the default note color or size applied to the new notes you create, or to change the font used in all existing and new notes, choose Tools, Options, click the Note Options button in the Preferences tab of the Options dialog box, and choose the settings you want in the Note Options dialog box (see Figure 39-19). To remove the date and time stamp from the bottom of your notes, open the Other tab in the Options dialog box, click the Advanced Options button, and clear the When Viewing Notes Show Time And Date option.

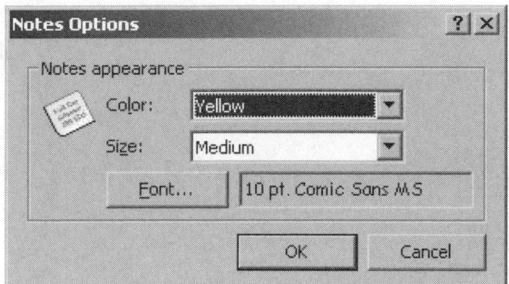

Figure 39-19. You can change the appearance of notes by using the Note Options dialog box.

Opening Web Sites

You can use Outlook for exploring the Web. You can view Web sites right within the Outlook window (as shown in Figure 39-20), or you can select a Web site in Outlook but have it opened in your Web browser (as shown in Figure 39-21).

Web page title   Folder Banner

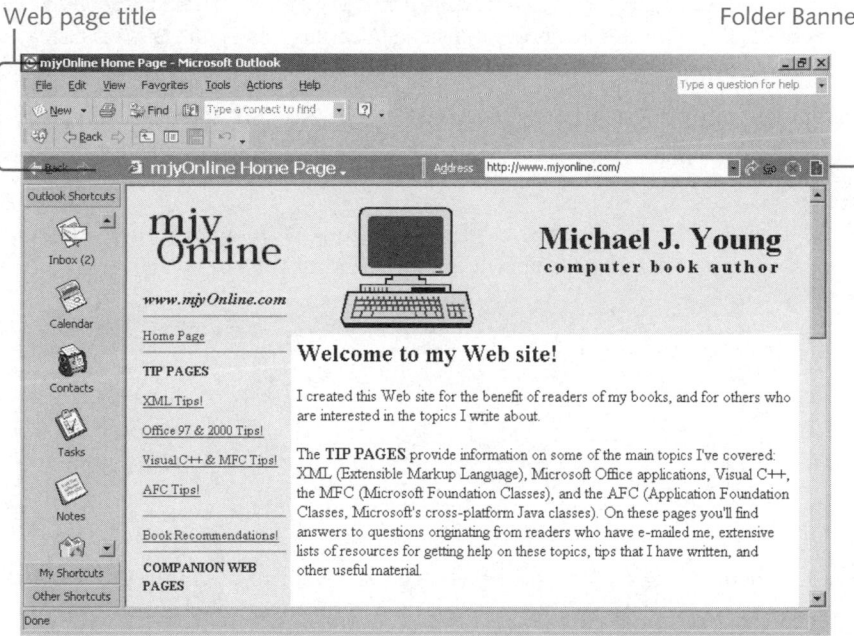

Figure 39-20. This figure shows a Web page displayed in the Outlook window.

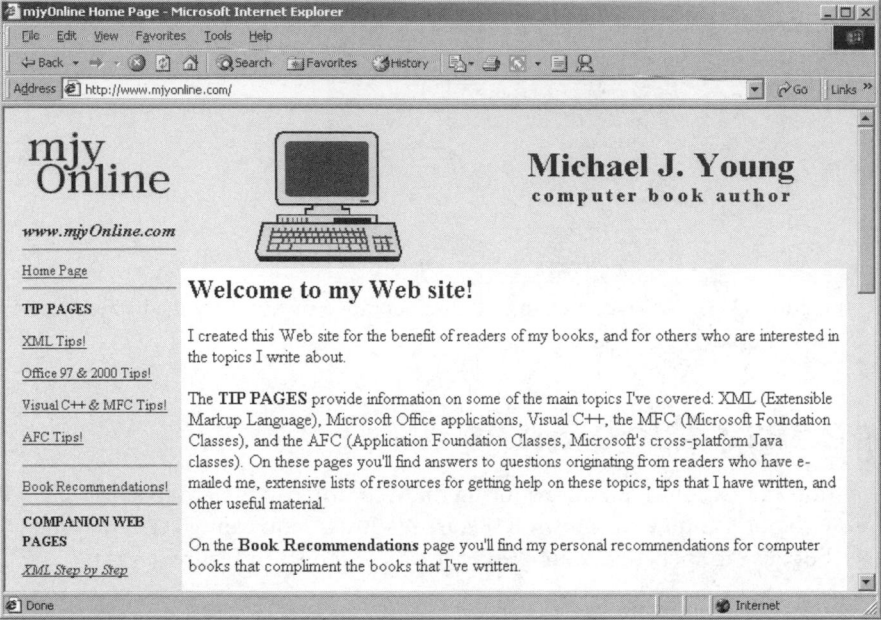

Figure 39-21. This figure shows the same Web page as Figure 39-20, displayed in Microsoft Internet Explorer.

You can use any of the following methods to view a Web page within the Information Viewer of the main Outlook window:

newfeature!

● Display the new Address bar in the Outlook window by double-clicking or dragging the Address label at the right end of the Folder Banner:

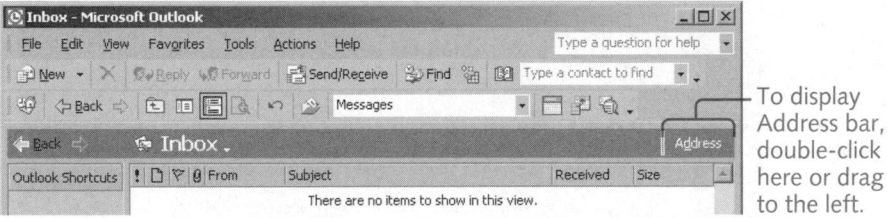

To display Address bar, double-click here or drag to the left.

Then enter the URL of the Web page you want to view into the Address text box, and press Enter or click the Go button. Or, select a formerly entered URL from the Address drop-down list.

1086

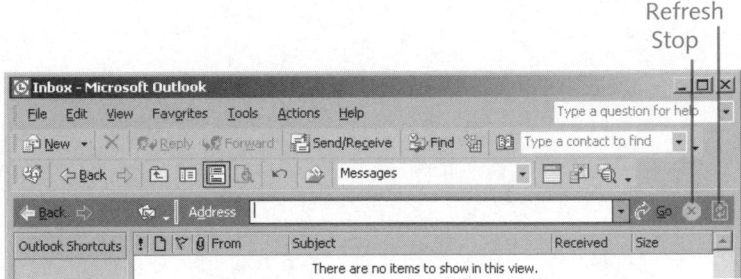

- Choose View, Toolbars, Web to display the Web toolbar, enter the URL of the Web page you want to open into the Address box, and press Enter. Or select a formerly entered URL from the Address drop-down list.

- Choose a Web page from the Favorites menu in Outlook. This menu directly accesses your Favorites file folder, which stores shortcuts to Web sites (the shortcuts that Microsoft has supplied as well as any you've added using Internet Explorer). To add a Web page shortcut, open the page in Outlook and choose Favorites, Add To Favorites. To work with the folders and shortcuts in your Favorites folder, choose Favorites, Organize Favorites.

- Click a shortcut to a Web page in the Outlook Bar.

> For instructions on adding Web page shortcuts to your Outlook Bar, see "Customizing the Outlook Bar," on page 1089.

You can use any of the following techniques in Outlook to open a Web page and display it in your default browser:

- In your Contacts folder, select a contact for which you've entered a Web page address and click the Explore Web Page button on the Advanced toolbar or press Ctrl+Shift+X.

- Click a hyperlink inserted into the large text box of an Outlook item. See the tip "Include Hyperlinks in Your Outlook Items," on page 993.

- In the Outlook window, open your Favorites file folder, one of its sub-folders, or any file folder that contains a shortcut to a Web site. Then double-click the shortcut to the Web page that you want to open.

> For more information on opening folders in Outlook, see "Accessing File Folders," on page 975.

- Choose View, Go To, Web Browser to run your default Web browser. Then enter the URL of the page you want to open into the browser.

Customizing Outlook

Customizing the Outlook Bar

The Outlook Bar contains shortcuts that you can click to open a Microsoft Outlook folder, a file folder, a file, or a Web page. The shortcuts are stored in separate groups; you open a particular group by clicking the group button at the top or bottom of the bar. Figure 40-1 shows the Outlook Bar as it appears after you've just installed Microsoft Outlook 2002.

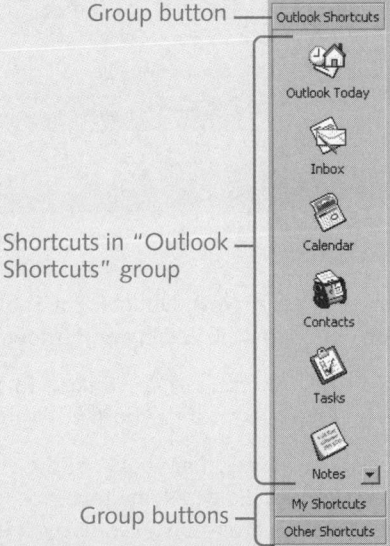

Group button ——

Shortcuts in "Outlook Shortcuts" group ——

Group buttons ——

Figure 40-1. This figure shows the initial Outlook Bar.

For information on using Outlook Bar shortcuts to open Outlook folders or file folders, see "Viewing Information in Outlook," on page 972. For information on using Outlook bar shortcuts to open Web pages, see "Opening Web Sites," on page 1085.

The following sections explain how to customize the Outlook Bar by adding, removing, renaming, moving, or copying Outlook Bar shortcuts or by adding, removing, or renaming shortcut groups. You can use these techniques to organize the folders, files, and pages that you work with; to make it faster to access the folders or other objects you use most frequently; and to update your set of shortcuts when you add or remove folders.

Working with Outlook Bar Shortcuts

To add an Outlook Bar shortcut that opens an Outlook folder or a file folder, complete the following steps:

1 If the shortcut group to which you want to add the new shortcut isn't currently displayed, open it by clicking its group button.

2 Right-click within the group—but *not* on a shortcut—and choose Outlook Bar Shortcut from the shortcut menu:

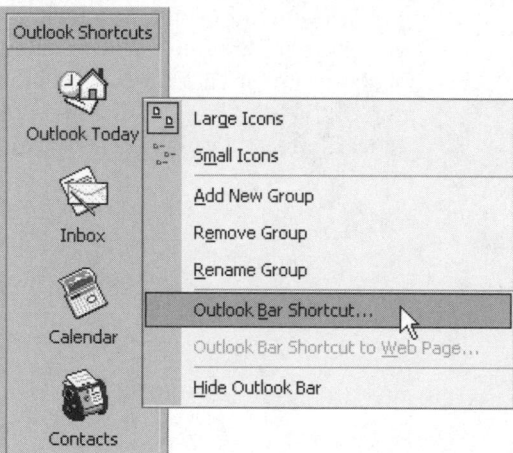

Or choose File, New, Outlook Bar Shortcut. Outlook will then display the Add To Outlook Bar dialog box (shown in Figure 40-2).

3 To create a shortcut to an Outlook folder, select Outlook in the Look In drop-down list, or to create a shortcut to a file folder, select File System.

4 Specify the folder that you want the shortcut to open by typing the folder name into the Folder Name text box, or by selecting the folder from the Folder Name drop-down list, or by selecting the folder in the hierarchical folder list.

5 Click the OK button.

Outlook will add the new shortcut to the bottom of the currently opened group. When you click the new shortcut, Outlook will open the folder and display its contents in the Information Viewer.

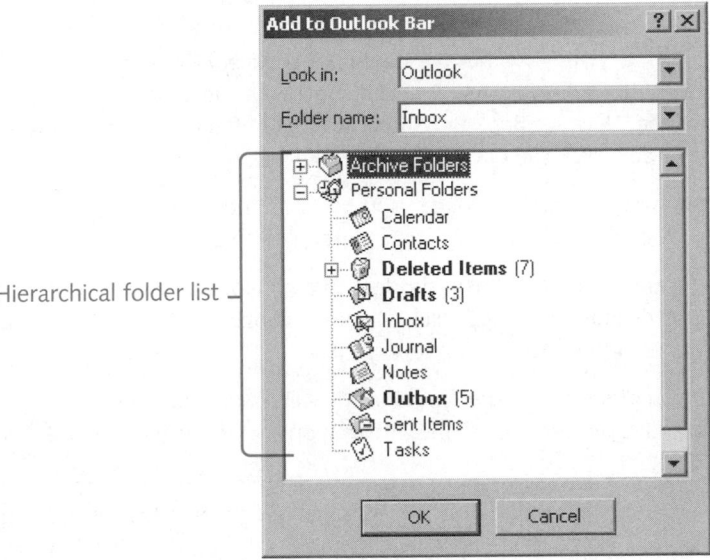

Hierarchical folder list ─

Figure 40-2. You use the Add To Outlook Bar dialog box to add a new shortcut to the Outlook Bar.

---

tip **Use the Folder List to Add a Shortcut**

If you have a permanent Folder List displayed, an easy way to add a shortcut that opens an Outlook folder or a file folder is to drag the folder name from the Folder List to the desired position in the Outlook Bar. For information on using the Folder List, see "Using Other Methods to Open Folders," on page 978.

To add a shortcut that opens a file, drag the file from its file folder and drop it at the desired position within the Outlook Bar. (You can drag a file from a folder displayed in Outlook, in Microsoft Windows Explorer, or in a folder window.) If the Outlook window is hidden when you start dragging the file, hold the pointer over the Outlook button in the Windows Taskbar until the Outlook window appears, and then complete the drag operation. If the Outlook Bar position where you want to add the shortcut isn't visible, while you drag you can hold the pointer over a group button to open that group or you can hold the pointer over the top or bottom of a group to scroll through the shortcuts. When you click the new shortcut, the file will be opened in the application that's registered to open the file type.

To add a shortcut that opens a Web page, complete the following steps:

1 Open the Web page in the Outlook window (*not* in your browser) by using the Address bar, the Web toolbar, or the Favorites menu, and then, if necessary, navigating to the specific page you want.

For information on displaying Web pages in the Outlook window, see "Opening Web Sites," on page 1085.

2 Right-click anywhere within the Outlook Bar *except* on a shortcut and choose Outlook Bar Shortcut To Web Page from the shortcut menu. Or choose File, New, Outlook Bar Shortcut To Web Page. If Outlook displays a message box, click the OK button.

Outlook will add the Web page shortcut to the bottom of the My Shortcuts group (regardless of which group is currently displayed).

3 If you want to move the new shortcut to a new position in the My Shortcuts group or in another group, follow the instructions for moving a shortcut given later in this section.

When you click the new shortcut, Outlook will connect to the Internet if necessary and display the page in the Information Viewer of the Outlook window.

note If want to add a shortcut that opens a Web page located on a local or network drive, you can drag the Web page file from its file folder and drop it on the exact position in the Outlook Bar where you want to add the shortcut, as explained in the instructions given previously in this section for adding a shortcut that opens a disk file.

To remove or rename an Outlook Bar shortcut, right-click the shortcut and from the shortcut menu, choose Remove From Outlook Bar or Rename Shortcut:

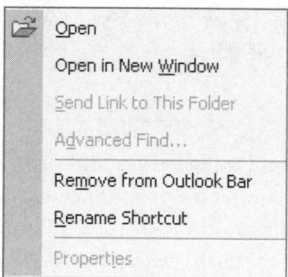

note If you delete a folder, file, or page, it's a good idea to remove any shortcut that opens that object. (You can leave the shortcut, but clicking it will only display an error message.) Keep in mind that removing or renaming a shortcut doesn't remove or rename the shortcut's target folder, file, or page.

To move a shortcut to another position within the same group or within another group, simply drag it to the new position. To make a copy of the shortcut, press Ctrl while you drag. If the target position isn't visible in the Outlook Bar, while you drag you can hold the pointer over a group button to open that group, or you can hold the pointer over the top or bottom of a group to scroll through the shortcuts.

Working with Groups

To remove or rename an Outlook Bar shortcut group, right-click the group button (or, for the currently displayed group, right-click anywhere within the group except on a shortcut) and choose Remove Group or Rename Group from the shortcut menu:

To add a new group, right-click anywhere in the Outlook Bar except on a shortcut and choose Add New Group from the shortcut menu. Then type a name for the group on the new group button.

> **note** To control the size of the shortcuts, you can choose Large Icons or Small Icons from the shortcut menu. Choosing the Small Icons option will reduce the amount of scrolling needed to access your shortcuts if you've added a large number of them to a group.

newfeature!

Adding, Modifying, and Removing Outlook Accounts

"Setting Up Outlook," on page 968, discussed setting up an e-mail account the first time you run Outlook. The Outlook setup program gets you started using Outlook by creating a single e-mail account either by importing settings (as well as messages and addresses) from an e-mail program already installed on your computer or by defining a new e-mail account. This section explains how to add one or more additional e-mail accounts and how to modify or remove e-mail accounts. (You would need two accounts, for example, if you have one e-mail service provided by your company for business use and another that your family uses for personal messages.)

You can also add (or modify or remove) directory accounts or address book accounts. A *directory account* lets you access an Internet directory service, such as Yahoo! People Search or Bigfoot Internet Directory Service, for looking up people's names and e-mail addresses. (An Internet directory service is also known as an LDAP [Lightweight Directory Access Protocol] server.) Once you install a directory account, you can look up e-mail addresses by choosing Tools, Address Book or by pressing Ctrl+Shift+B and

1093

then selecting the name of the directory account in the Show Names From The drop-down list (shown in Figure 40-3). Outlook will also use the directory account to look up the e-mail address of a name you type into the To (or Cc or Bcc) text box in a Message form (as well as looking them up in your Contacts folder), or you can use the directory account to look up e-mail addresses in the Select Names dialog box that appears when you click the To, Cc, Bcc, or Address Book button on the form. Finally, you can use the directory account to look up a contact's e-mail address in the Select Name dialog box that appears when you click the button to the right of the E-Mail text box in the Contact form.

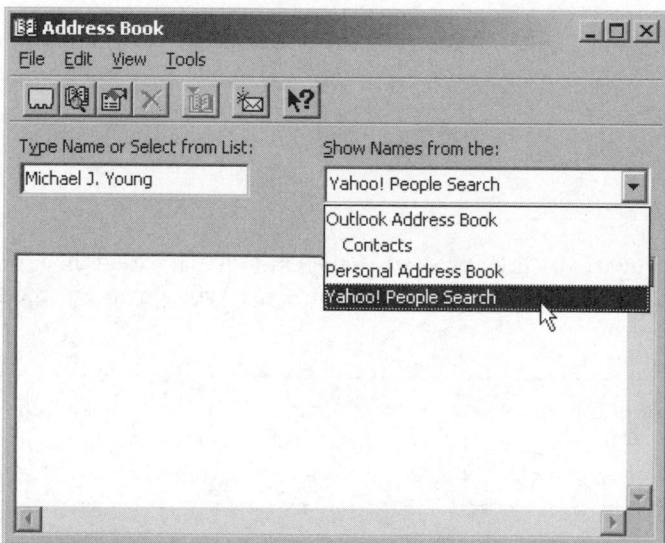

Figure 40-3. You can look up a name using a directory service in the Address Book dialog box.

note Outlook automatically looks up names you type into the To, Cc, or Bcc text boxes in a message header if the Automatic Name Checking option is checked. (If this option isn't checked, you can look up the addresses of names you've typed by clicking the Check Names button on the message header or on the Standard toolbar.) To access the Automatic Name Checking option, choose Tools, Options, click the E-mail Options button in the Preferences tab, click the Advanced E-Mail Options button, and look in the When Sending A Message area of the Advanced E-Mail Options dialog box (see Figure 38-2, on page 1022).

Check Names

Troubleshooting

Address Lookups Too Slow

You added a directory account for an LDAP server on the Internet. It now takes a long time for Outlook to look up names you type into a message header.

Having Outlook look up names you enter into your outgoing messages using a directory account can be quite useful if that account connects to a small, fast LDAP server on your company's intranet. But if the directory account connects to an LDAP server on the Internet, it will probably be too slow (especially if you have a slow Internet connection) and it will come up with too many "hits" for it to be practical for looking up names you type into message headers.

Fortunately, you can prevent Outlook from using a directory account for looking up names in the Message form, while still keeping the account available on your system (so that you can use it to look up names through the Address Book or Select Names dialog box, as discussed earlier in this section) and having Outlook automatically look up addresses in your Contacts folder. To do that, complete the following steps:

1 Choose Tools, Address Book or press Ctrl+Shift+B to open the Address Book dialog box (shown in Figure 40-3).

2 In the dialog box, choose Tools, Options to open the Addressing dialog box.

3 Select the directory account in the When Sending Mail... list at the bottom of the dialog box and click the Remove button (as shown in Figure 40-4).

  Alternatively, you can select the account and click the down arrow to move it down in the list. Outlook uses any address books and directory accounts in the order they're listed. If it finds a name in an address book, it won't go on to search the directory service.

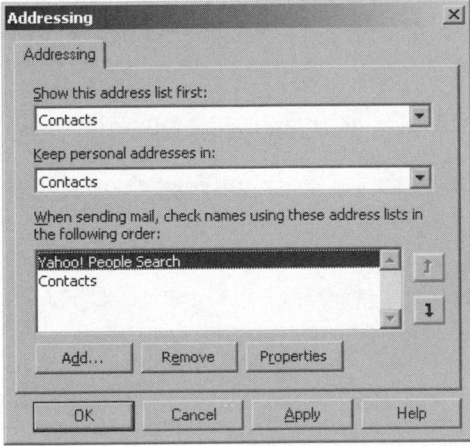

Figure 40-4. The Addressing dialog box lets you control the way Outlook handles addresses in the Address Book and e-mail messages.

1095

An *address book account* lets you use the Address Book or Select Names dialog box to look up names in your Contacts folder or in a Personal Address Book, and it also allows Outlook to automatically look up names you type into the To, Cc, or Bcc text boxes in a Message form. The Outlook setup program adds an address book account called Outlook Address Book that lets you look up names in your default Contacts folder. If you add one or more new Contacts-type folders, the Outlook Address Book account will let you look up names in any of these folders, as well as in the default Contacts folder.

> **note** To be able to access your Contacts folder or another Contacts-type folder through the Outlook Address Book account, the folder's Show This Folder As An E-mail Address Book property must be checked. This property is checked by default. If you want to access it, right-click the folder's icon in the Outlook Bar, choose Properties from the shortcut menu, and open the Outlook Address Book tab.

You can create one additional address book account for looking up names in a Personal Address Book. You can use an existing Personal Address Book or create a new empty one. (Note that rather than being stored in your Outlook data file, as your Contacts folder is, a Personal Address Book is stored in a separate file with the .pab extension.) Unless you already have addresses stored in a Personal Address Book that you want to use, you don't need to create a Personal Address Book account; you'll find it much simpler and more convenient to store all your addresses in your Contacts folder and use the address book account that Outlook has already set up.

InsideOut

With former versions of Outlook, using a Personal Address Book was an attractive alternative because it let you define groups of addresses called *personal distribution lists*, and the Contacts folder didn't have this feature. However, now that the Contacts folder provides distribution lists, there's little reason to start using a Personal Address Book.

To add, modify, or remove an e-mail account, complete the following steps:

1 Choose Tools, E-Mail Accounts to display the first dialog box of the E-Mail Accounts wizard (see Figure 40-5).

> **note** Another way to start the E-mail Accounts wizard is to choose Tools, Options, click the Mail Setup tab, and click the E-Mail Accounts button. Or, you can double-click the Mail item in the Windows Control Panel and click the E-Mail Accounts button in the Mail Setup–Outlook dialog box.

Chapter 40

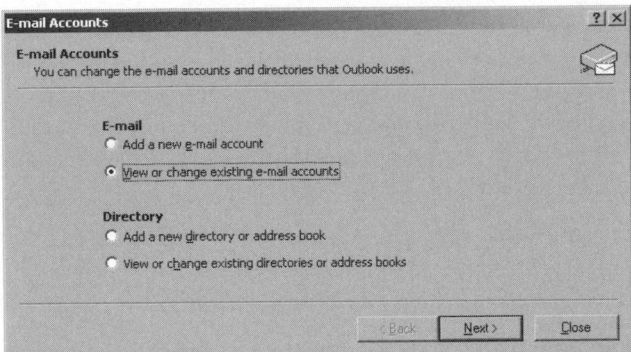

Figure 40-5. This figure shows the first dialog box of the E-Mail Accounts wizard.

2 Select the View Or Change Existing E-Mail Accounts option and click the Next button. (This option lets you add accounts as well as view, modify, or remove them. If you want only to add an account, you can choose Add A New E-Mail Account instead.) Outlook will display the second dialog box of the E-Mail Accounts wizard (shown in Figure 40-6).

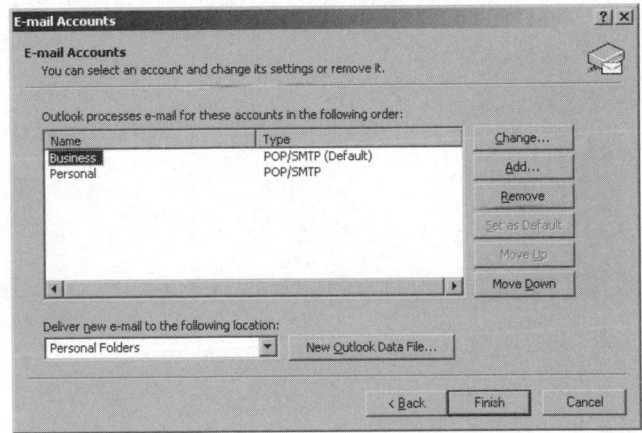

Figure 40-6. This is the second dialog box that the E-Mail Accounts wizard displays when you work with e-mail accounts.

3 In the second wizard dialog box, do one or more of the following:

- To add a new account, click the Add button and in the dialog boxes the wizard displays, select the e-mail account type and fill in the account details. (For more information, see "Setting Up Outlook," on page 968.)

- To modify or remove an account, select it in the list and click the Change or the Remove button.

◼ To mark an account as your default e-mail account, select it and click the Set As Default button. When you send an outgoing e-mail message, Outlook uses your default e-mail account unless you choose a different account from the Accounts drop-down menu on the message header or Standard toolbar. (This option doesn't affect the accounts used for receiving e-mail.)

◼ To change the order in which accounts are used for receiving e-mail (when you use multiple accounts for a send and receive operation), select an account and click the Move Up or Move Down button.

◼ To specify the Outlook data file to which incoming e-mail messages will be delivered (if more than one data file is opened) choose the name of the data file in the Deliver New E-Mail To The Following Location drop-down list. Data files are discussed in the next section.

4 Click the Finish button.

---

tip   **Import E-Mail Settings**

Another way to create an e-mail account is to import the settings from an e-mail program that's already installed on your computer. You can also import the e-mail messages and addresses you've stored using the previously installed e-mail program. The e-mail programs from which Outlook can import settings, messages, and addresses include Microsoft Outlook Express, Eudora Pro and Light, and Netscape Mail and Messenger. To import, choose File, Import And Export. Then, in the first Import And Export Wizard dialog box (shown in Figure 40-7), select Import Internet Mail Account Settings or select Import Internet Mail And Addresses, click the Next button, and fill in the requested information.

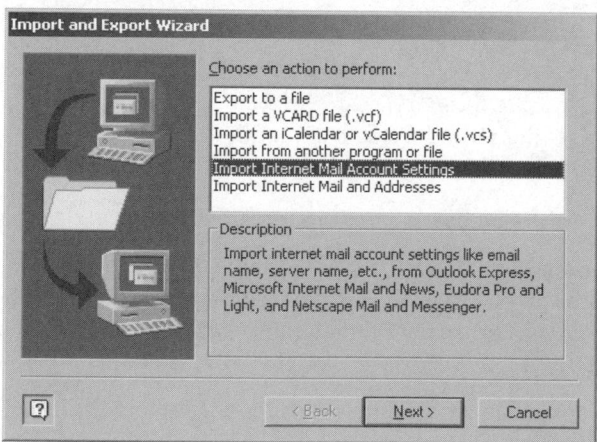

Figure 40-7.   This figure shows the first dialog box of the Import And Export Wizard.

To add, modify, or remove a directory service or address book account, follow these steps:

1 Choose Tools, E-Mail Accounts to display the first dialog box of the E-Mail Accounts wizard (see Figure 40-5, on page 1097).

2 Select the View Or Change Existing Directories Or Address Books option and click the Next button. (This option lets you add accounts as well as view, modify, or remove them. If you want only to add an account, you can instead select Add A New Directory Or Address Book.) Outlook will display the second dialog box of the E-Mail Accounts wizard (shown in Figure 40-8).

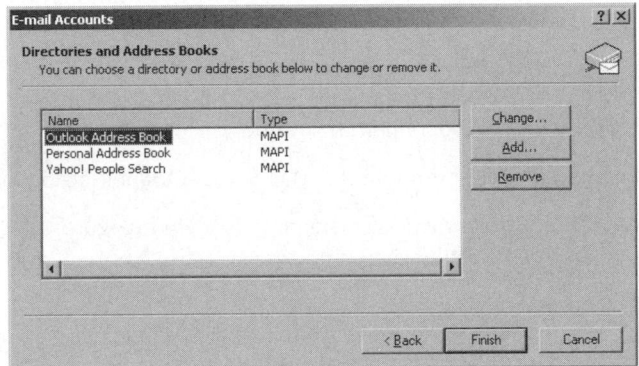

Figure 40-8. This is the second dialog box that the E-Mail Accounts wizard displays when you work with directories or address books.

3 To define a new account, click the Add button. In the dialog boxes the wizard displays, select an account type and fill in the account details. If you're adding an address book account, keep in mind that you can have only one Outlook Address Book account and one Personal Address Book account.

---

tip   **Find Information on Internet Directory Services**

Some installations of Windows have a set of Internet directory services installed, which you can use in Windows to look up people on the Internet. Although these services aren't initially accessible to Outlook, you can look up the properties of any of the services and use that information to define an Outlook directory account to access the same service. To do this, in Windows choose Start, Search, For People (or Start, Search, People, in some versions of Windows), right-click any directory service listed in the Look In drop-down list in the Find People dialog box, and choose Properties from the shortcut menu. Windows will display a Properties dialog box listing the directory service's properties. You can copy or write down these property settings and use the same values to set up that service in Outlook.

Using Separate Profiles

The accounts and the Outlook data file that the Outlook setup program creates, as well as any that you define as described in this chapter, are all part of the current Outlook *profile*. The Outlook setup program creates a single profile. If, however, you want to create one or more distinct Outlook setups, including different e-mail and other types of accounts as well as different Outlook data files (each of which would contain different folders and items), you can create one or more new profiles. You can then have Outlook load any profile when it starts. If, for example, two or more people used Outlook on the same computer and wanted separate accounts, folders, and items, each person could create and use a separate profile.

To create a new profile, perform the following steps:

1 Double-click the Mail program in the Windows Control Panel.

2 Click the Show Profiles button in the Mail Setup–Outlook dialog box.

3 Click the Add button in the Mail dialog box (shown in Figure 40-9), and type a name for the new profile when prompted.

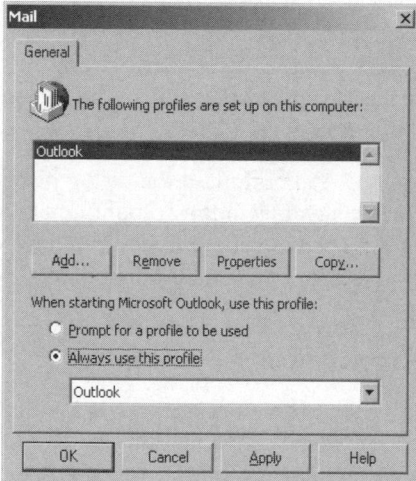

Figure 40-9. You use the Mail dialog box of the Mail program in the Control Panel to work with profiles.

4 Define accounts for the profile using the E-Mail Accounts wizard, as explained previously in this chapter (the wizard will automatically create a new data file for the profile).

When you've finished defining the new profile, you'll be returned to the Mail dialog box. As you can see in Figure 40-9, this dialog box lets you copy or remove a profile, change its properties (the accounts or data file), and control which profile Outlook uses. If you want to be able to switch profiles easily, select Prompt For A Profile To Be Used so that you can choose a profile each time you start Outlook.

newfeature!
Managing Outlook Data Files

Your Outlook information—consisting of your Outlook folders plus all items and item attachments contained in these folders—is stored in an *Outlook data file* on your computer. An Outlook data file is also known as a *personal folders file*, and it is assigned the .pst extension. The personal folders file format was also used in Outlook versions 97, 98, and 2000. You can therefore freely share your Outlook 2002 data file with users of previous Outlook versions.

The Outlook setup program creates a single personal folders file named Outlook.pst, adds the default Outlook folders to it, and adds the data file to the current profile so that it's opened whenever you start Outlook. Although this is the only Outlook data file you need, in some cases you might want to create one or more additional data files, as explained in the following section.

> **note** Like the accounts that are set up in Outlook (which are discussed in the previous sections) the Outlook data file or files that are opened in Outlook are part of your current Outlook profile. For information on creating and using more than one profile, see the sidebar "Using Separate Profiles," on the previous page.

> **tip** **Back Up Your Outlook Data File!**
>
> Because your Outlook data file contains all the information you've entered into Outlook and because it could become corrupted or be deleted accidentally, it's important to back it up regularly. You can probably use your current backup system (you do have one, right?), provided that your backup medium has sufficient capacity (Outlook data files can become quite large).
>
> You can also use the Outlook Personal Folders Backup utility, which is designed specifically for backing up your Outlook data file on a regular schedule. You can obtain this utility from the download page of the Microsoft Office Update Web site. You can connect to this site in Outlook by choosing Help, Office On The Web.
>
> If backing up your Outlook data file starts taking too much time and too much space on your backup medium, it's time to archive your folders. Archiving copies older items into a different Outlook data file, which you can back up separately if you want. For information on archiving, see "Archiving Items," on page 997.

Chapter 40

Do You Know Where Your Outlook Data File Is?

It's important to know your Outlook data file's name and location so that you can back it up regularly. (See the tip "Back Up Your Outlook Data File!" on page 1101.) You might also need to know the location of your Outlook data file so that you can copy it to another computer that has Outlook installed, allowing you to access your Outlook information on that computer. For example, you might want to copy your data file from your desktop computer to your notebook computer before leaving on a trip (and then copy it back when you return). Note that you need to quit Outlook before you can copy an opened data file.

To find the name and full file path of your Outlook data file, choose File, Data File Management and look in the list in the Outlook Data Files dialog box (see Figure 40-10). To see the full file path of the data file, you'll probably need to widen the Filename column by dragging the right border of the column heading and then scroll the list.

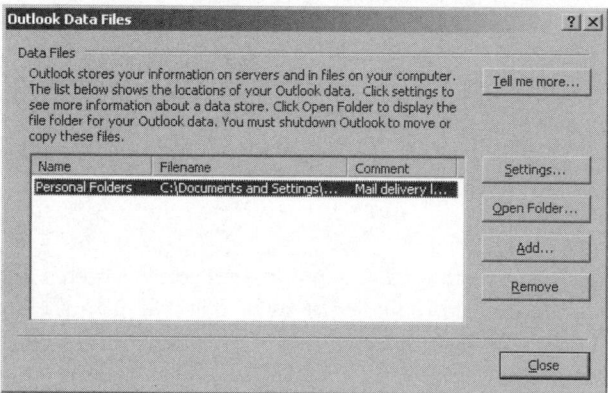

Figure 40-10.   The Outlook Data Files dialog box lets you work with the file or files storing your Outlook data.

You can even view the entire contents of the folder containing your Outlook data file by clicking the Open Folder button in the Outlook Data Files dialog box.

Note that if you've used the Outlook archiving feature, you might find an additional Outlook data file, which is used to store your archived items, listed in the Outlook Data Files dialog box. You specify the name and location of this file when you set up the archiving feature, as explained in "Archiving Items," on page 997. (The archiving data file appears in the Outlook Data Files dialog box only if the Show Archive In Folder List option is checked in the AutoArchive dialog box, which causes Outlook to open that data file permanently.)

Creating and Modifying Outlook Data Files

You can create one or more Outlook data files in addition to the one added by the Outlook setup program (or by the archive feature). You might, for example, want to create a new Outlook data file and copy some of your Outlook items into that file so that you can keep them safe, use them on a different computer, or share them with a co-worker.

To create or modify Outlook data files, complete the following steps:

1 Choose File, Data File Management to open the Outlook Data Files dialog box (shown in Figure 40-10).

2 In the Outlook Data Files dialog box, do one or more of the following:

- To create a new Outlook data file and open it in Outlook, click the Add button. Then, when prompted, specify a filename and location, type a name for the data file that will be used in Outlook (Outlook will display this name in the Outlook Data Files dialog box and in the Folder List), and select the data file options that you want. The new Outlook data file will initially have only the default Deleted Items folder; you can later add additional Outlook folders of any type.

- To compact an Outlook data file, to change its name in Outlook, or to add or change a password, select the file in the list and click the Settings button.

> **note** Initially, Outlook delivers your incoming e-mail to the Inbox of the Outlook data file created by the Outlook setup program. To have Outlook deliver your incoming e-mail to the Inbox of a different Outlook data file, choose Tools, E-Mail Accounts, select View Or Change Existing E-Mail Accounts, click the Next button, and select the name of the Outlook data file in the Deliver E-Mail To The Following Location drop-down list. The next time you start Outlook, your change will take effect. Outlook will then create a complete set of default Outlook folders (Calendar, Contacts, Journal, and so on) within the newly designated e-mail destination data file and it will offer to recreate your Outlook Bar shortcuts so that they work with the new default folders. Note that the Outlook data file where Outlook delivers your e-mail is also known as the *default* Outlook data file.

- To close an Outlook data file, select it in the list and click the Remove button. This doesn't delete the Outlook data file but merely closes it in Outlook, so you'll be able to reopen it later. (You can't close the Outlook data file designated as your e-mail delivery location.) Opening and closing Outlook data files is discussed in the next section.

3 Click the Close button in the Outlook Data Files dialog box.

Opening, Closing, and Working with Outlook Data Files

The Outlook data file where Outlook delivers your incoming e-mail (that is, the *default* Outlook data file) is always opened in Outlook. You can open one or more additional Outlook data files to work with the folders and items they contain or to copy or move folders or items between Outlook data files. For example, if a co-worker sent you an Outlook data file containing a set of items you need, such as contacts or appointments, you would have to open that data file to access those items. Or, to recover archived items, you would need to open the Outlook data file to which you archived your folders (if it isn't already open).

To open an Outlook data file, choose File, Open, Outlook Data File and select the file in the Open Outlook Data File dialog box. As mentioned in the previous section, when you create a new Outlook data file, it's automatically opened in Outlook.

When an Outlook data file is opened in Outlook, it appears in the Folder List along with the other opened data file or files. You can use the Folder List to open the data file's folders and to view its items (see Figure 40-11). You can also move either an Outlook folder (together with all its items and subfolders) or an individual item from one data file to another by dragging it in a permanently displayed Folder List. (To copy the folder or item, press Ctrl while dragging.)

Additional opened Outlook data file —

Default Outlook data file —

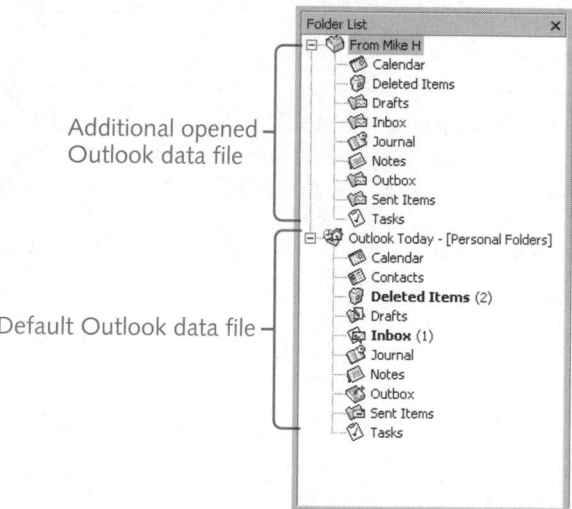

Figure 40-11. In this figure, the Folder List displays the default Outlook data file, plus an additionally opened data file.

note When an Outlook data file is opened in Outlook, it's also listed in the Outlook Data Files dialog box (shown in Figure 40-10, on page 1102), which was discussed in the previous section.

Chapter 40

For information on using the Folder List, see "Using Other Methods to Open Folders," on page 978.

To close an additional Outlook data file that's been opened (you can't close the default one), right-click the name of the data file in a permanently displayed Folder List, and choose Close *data file name* from the shortcut menu, as shown here:

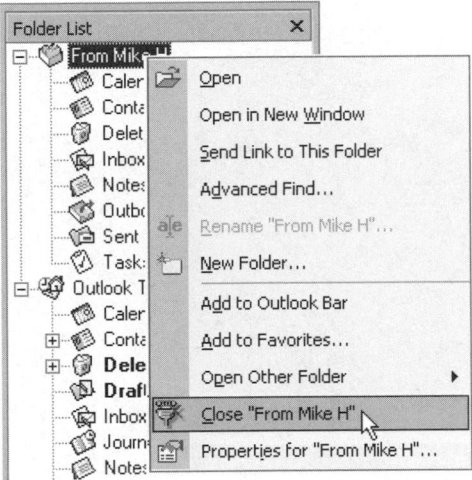

You can also close an Outlook data file by selecting it in the Outlook Data Files dialog box and clicking the Remove button, as explained in the previous section.

Part 7

FrontPage

Chapter 41

FrontPage Fundamentals

A Rundown on FrontPage

Although most of the Microsoft Office XP applications allow you to create Web pages and publish documents on the Web, the ultimate Office tool for Web publishing is Microsoft FrontPage 2002. FrontPage provides a set of site management tools that let you create, manage, and publish Web sites. It also includes a full-featured, integrated Web page editor. Here are some of the things you can do with the FrontPage site management tools:

● Quickly create an entire Web site using a template or wizard. Each template or wizard creates a collection of Web pages suitable for a particular purpose, such as establishing a corporate presence, conducting an online discussion, displaying personal information, managing a group project, or collaborating with your workgroup on a SharePoint team Web site. The template or wizard formats the pages consistently and adds shared borders, link bars, images, text, and other initial elements to get you started.

● Manage the folders and files in your Web site using an interface similar to Microsoft Windows Explorer.

● View the status of all files, Web pages, hyperlinks, components, and other elements in your Web site, and review the usage of a team Web site, using the Reports view.

- Use graphic views of your Web site to visualize, modify, and verify the hyperlinks that tie the pages together and let users navigate through your site and explore other sites.

- Apply stylistic themes to your Web site. Each theme instantly applies consistent styling to the background, text, lists, page banners, link bars, and other elements within every page in your site.

- Manage your Web site projects by keeping a list of the tasks that each team member needs to perform. Assign files, categorize files, control the site's source files, and use other workgroup techniques.

- Open and edit a Web site directly on the Web server. Or, work offline on a copy of your site stored on a local or network disk, and then publish your site to a Web server.

The FrontPage site management tools are discussed primarily in this chapter and in Chapter 42, "Managing Your Web Site with FrontPage."

Here's a sample of how you can use FrontPage to create and edit Web pages:

- Modify and add content to the pages in your Web site or create new pages. You can get a head start in creating a new page by using a template or wizard that adds an initial set of elements to the page and formats these elements consistently. Some templates or wizards create pages suitable for specific uses, such as a bibliography, a feedback form, or a table of contents. Others generate pages that have particular arrangements of columns (created using tables)—for example, one narrow left-aligned column, one column with two sidebars, or two columns.

- Add document libraries, lists, or surveys to a team Web site.

- Add and format text, symbols, images, video clips, horizontal dividing lines, hyperlinks, tables, forms, frames, and other standard Web page elements.

- Precisely format Web page elements by modifying, creating, and using Cascading Style Sheet styles.

- Add Web components such as date and time stamps, comments, dynamic effects (such as animated *hover buttons* that are activated when the pointer passes over them), forms for searching the site, spreadsheets or charts, hit counters, photo galleries, included files, link bars, tables of contents, site usage statistics, views of information stored on a team Web site, and controls that display information from Web sites such as MSN.

- Add Java Applets, ActiveX controls, and other advanced Web page controls.

- Check the spelling in your pages and consult a thesaurus.

Chapter 41: FrontPage Fundamentals

- Find or replace text.

- Preview your pages in a browser or print them.

Using FrontPage to create and edit Web pages is covered mainly in Chapter 43 through Chapter 45.

For a list of the new features included in FrontPage 2002, see "New FrontPage Features," on page 15.

Creating and Opening Webs

When you first run FrontPage (for example, by choosing Start, Programs, Microsoft FrontPage in Microsoft Windows), it displays a new, empty Web page, as shown in Figure 41-1.

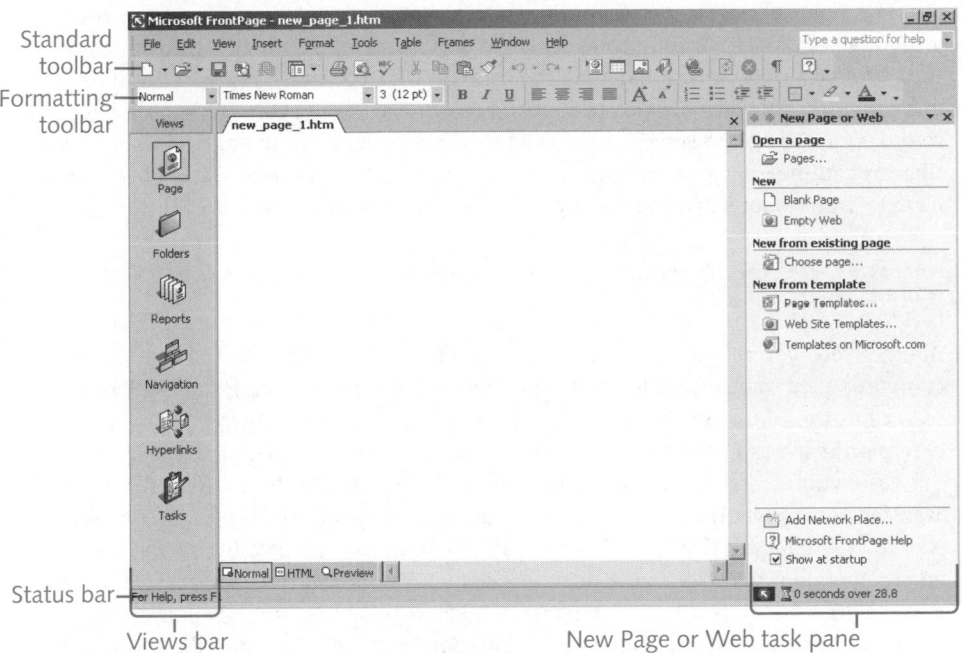

Figure 41-1. This figure shows the FrontPage window as it appears when you first start running the program.

---

note A *Web page* is a file in HTML (Hypertext Markup Language) format. A *Web browser* program, such as Microsoft Internet Explorer, downloads and displays a Web page from a *Web server* program installed on a computer attached to the World Wide Web or to your company's intranet. A Web page usually has the .htm or .html file extension.

Although you can use FrontPage to create and edit individual Web pages, to take advantage of many of the FrontPage features, you must first create a web or open a web you created previously. The term *web* (with a lowercase *w*) refers to a Web site that is created and managed using FrontPage. A web consists of a home page (stored in a file named Index.htm or Default.htm); other Web pages that are accessed from the home page; as well as image, multimedia, document, and other types of files that are displayed by the Web pages. A web also includes support folders and files that FrontPage uses for managing the web.

Creating a Web Offline or Online

You can create or open a web that's stored on a local or network disk location. In this case, you access the web using its file path. When your site is ready to view, you can use FrontPage's web publishing feature to copy the web to the Web server that will be used to deliver your site to the World Wide Web or to your company's intranet. This is the best way to create a web if your server is maintained by a separate Internet service provider or Web hosting company, or if you connect to it using a dial-up connection. Working on a web stored on a disk location is faster, saves you connect time, and provides you with a complete backup copy of the web in case something happens to the web files on the server. Also, while you modify an existing page, visitors to your site can continue to view the original version of the page on the server, and you won't have to worry about them seeing a page that's "under construction."

FrontPage's web publishing feature is discussed in Chapter 42, "Managing Your Web Site with FrontPage."

Alternatively, you can create or open a web that's stored directly on the Web server computer used to deliver your site to the Web or intranet, provided that the Web server has the Microsoft FrontPage Server Extensions, or other Microsoft server extensions such as Office 2000 Web Server Extensions or SharePoint Team Services. In this case, you access the web using the web's URL and the HTTP protocol (Hypertext Transfer Protocol, normally used for delivering Web pages to browsers). This is a good way to create a Web site if you have a fast, fulltime connection to the server, and you're confident that the web is being backed up routinely on the server. This method also makes it fast to test Web components, such as hit counters, that function only when the web is delivered from a Web server (and not just opened in the browser from a disk). Finally, this approach lets you easily use FrontPage's workgroup features to collaborate on building the site with your co-workers.

Workgroup features are covered in "Managing Your Web Projects," on page 1149.

Creating a Web Offline or Online *(continued)*   Whether it's on a disk or server location, a web is stored in a specially marked folder that contains—in addition to the web pages and other files you create—a set of subfolders (such as _vti_cnf and _vti_pvt) and files that FrontPage creates to allow it to manage the web. In Windows Explorer, a folder used to store a web is marked with a globe icon (see Figure 41-2).

Folder marked as a FrontPage web

- Corporate Presence
  - _borders
  - _derived
  - _fpclass
  - _overlay
  - _private
  - _themes
  - _vti_cnf
  - _vti_pvt
  - images

Figure 41-2.   This figure shows a folder on a local disk that stores a web named Corporate Presence, as viewed in Windows Explorer.

To create a new web, perform the following steps:

1 Click the down-arrow on the Create A New Normal Page button at the left end of the Standard toolbar and choose Web from the drop-down menu, as shown here:

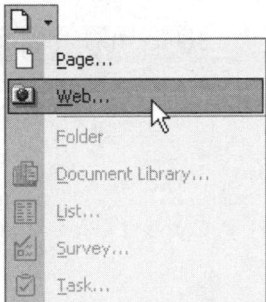

Alternatively, you can click the Web Site Templates command in the New Page Or Web task pane, which is shown in Figure 41-1, on page 1111. (If this task pane isn't displayed, open it by choosing File, New, Page Or Web.)

Chapter 41

1113

FrontPage will display the Web Site Templates dialog box (shown in Figure 41-3).

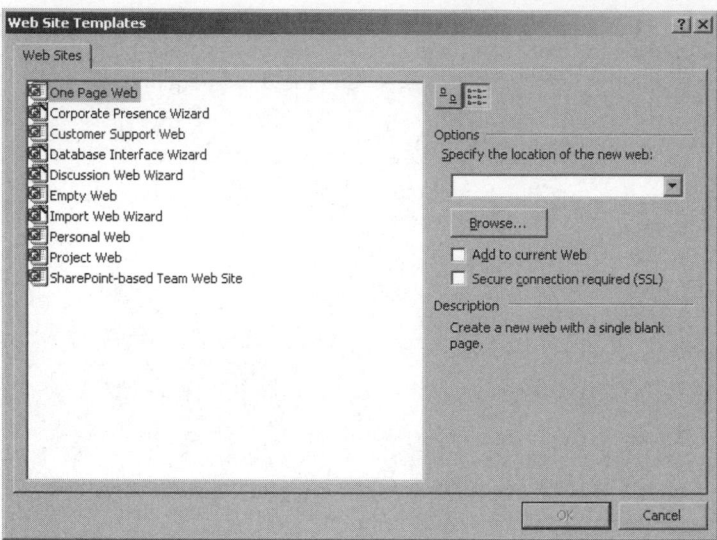

Figure 41-3. The Web Site Templates dialog box allows you to create a web based on a template.

2 Select a Web Site template or wizard from the list in the Web Site Templates dialog box, as described in Table 41-1.

Table 41-1. Creating a New Web by Selecting a Template in the Web Site Templates Dialog Box

To Create This Type of Web Site	Select This Template or Wizard
A Web site consisting initially of a single, blank page. You can later add content to this page and create additional pages as described in the following chapters.	One Page Web
A general-purpose corporate Web site, including a table of contents, forms for searching the site or providing feedback, and pages for presenting news and describing products and services.	Corporate Presence Wizard
A Web site that provides information and services for your customers, including pages for describing products, catalogs, or manuals, or for presenting frequently asked questions (FAQs); pages that allow customers to request service or leave suggestions; and a support forum. This template is designed primarily for software companies.	Customer Support Web

Chapter 41: FrontPage Fundamentals

Table 41-1. *(continued)*

To Create This Type of Web Site	Select This Template or Wizard
A Web site that allows visitors to view and update data in a database on the Web server.	Database Interface Wizard
A Web site for managing an online discussion group, including a table of contents, threads, and a search feature.	Discussion Web Wizard
A Web site that initially contains no pages, so that you can create your own pages (using the page templates of your choice) as described in the following chapters.	Empty Web
A Web site that consists of a set of Web pages or other files that you already have, located on a local or network disk or on a Web site.	Import Web Wizard
A Web site for yourself, including pages for providing information about yourself and your interests, for listing links to your favorite Web sites, for displaying photos, and for obtaining feedback from visitors (using a form).	Personal Web
A Web site for managing a group project, including pages containing a membership roster, a schedule, a file archive, a site search feature, a discussion forum, and contact information.	Project Web
A custom team Web site on a server running SharePoint Team Services. (See "Customizing and Creating SharePoint Team Web Sites," on page 1121.)	SharePoint-Based Team Web Site

tip **Look for Additional Templates**

To look for additional FrontPage templates that you can download, click the Templates On Microsoft.com command in the New Page Or Web task pane to connect with the Microsoft Office Template Gallery site on the Web.

3 Type the location where you want to create your new web into the Specify The Location Of The New Web text box in the Web Site Templates dialog box.

> **note** If you enter into the Specify The Location Of The New Web text box a folder that is already a FrontPage web, when you click the OK button, FrontPage will display an error message and won't let you overwrite the existing web.
>
> If you want to add the content supplied by a template or wizard to an existing web (you will be asked whether you want to overwrite any existing file that has the same name as a file supplied by the template or wizard), open that web before displaying the Web Site Templates dialog box. Then, in the Web Site Templates dialog box, check the Add To Current Web option rather than entering a location into the Specify The Location Of The New Web text box.

To store your web on a local or network disk location, enter the full path of the folder where you want to save it. To store your web directly on a Web server (one that has appropriate Microsoft server extensions), enter the full URL of the folder where you want to publish your web. Keep in mind that when you create a new web, you specify only the *folder* where the web is stored, *not* a specific file. If the folder you enter doesn't exist, FrontPage will create it.

> **note** If you enter into the Specify The Location Of The New Web text box the URL of a secure site that uses the SSL (Secure Sockets Layer) protocol, check the Secure Connection Required (SSL) option. (When connecting to this type of site, your URL will begin with *https://* rather than *http://*.)

You can click the Browse button to open an *existing* folder in the New Web Location dialog box, which is similar to the standard Open dialog box and lets you navigate to and open a folder on a disk or Web site. When you click the Open button in the New Web Location dialog box, you'll be returned to the Web Site Templates dialog box and the folder you opened will be entered into the Specify The Location Of The New Web text box. If you want FrontPage to create a new subfolder within that folder for storing your new web, you need to type the folder name at the end of the path or URL in the text box.

4 Click the OK button in the Web Site Templates dialog box.

Selecting a template or wizard other than One Page Web or Empty Web will create a new web that includes an initial set of pages. These pages will be given consistent formatting (by applying a theme, as explained later) and will include hyperlinks that let visitors navigate through the pages, as well as page banners, headings, tables, text, horizontal dividing lines, lists, and other initial elements that are appropriate for the particular type of web that the wizard or template creates. A wizard, such as the Corporate

Presence Wizard, asks a series of questions and customizes the web according to your choices. A template immediately generates the web without customization.

---

tip   **How to Use Subwebs**

If you create a new web in a subfolder of a folder that is already designated as a FrontPage web, your new web is termed a *subweb*.

Another way to create a subweb is to right-click the name of an existing subfolder within a web folder (in the FrontPage Folder List or in Folders view, described later in this chapter) and choose Convert To Web from the shortcut menu. FrontPage will then convert the subfolder to a web by adding the special folders and files that it uses to manage the web. It will also mark the subfolder with a globe icon to indicate that it's a web folder and not just a regular file folder.

Rather than creating a single huge web, it might be better to place some of the web's content into one or more subwebs. You can separately open each subweb, which will be small and fast to work with. If you publish the main web (as described in Chapter 42), you can publish any subwebs it contains at the same time. If you've opened a web that contains a subweb, you can open the subweb in a separate FrontPage window by simply double-clicking the subweb folder in FrontPage.

After you close the Web Site Templates dialog box, and after the wizard has finished (if you chose one), your new web will be opened in FrontPage. If you create a new web while an existing web is open, the new web will be displayed in a separate top-level FrontPage window. You can now modify the initial pages in the web, add or delete pages, and customize your web in other ways using the techniques given in the following sections and chapters. Figure 41-4 shows the home page (index.htm) of a new web created using the Personal Web template, ready for your customizations.

---

tip   **Change a Web's Name**

The name of a web is actually the name of the folder that contains the web files and subfolders. You can change the web name by choosing Tools, Web Settings, and entering a new name into the Web Name text box in the General tab of the Web Settings dialog box. Note that this will change the name of the folder in which the web is stored as well as the web name displayed in FrontPage. The FrontPage title bar, as well as many of the FrontPage views, identifies the web by displaying the full file path (such as C:\My Documents\My Webs\Personal) or the full Web address (such as *http://myserver/myweb*) of the folder where the web files are stored.) Note, however, that you can't change the name of a web that contains a subweb.

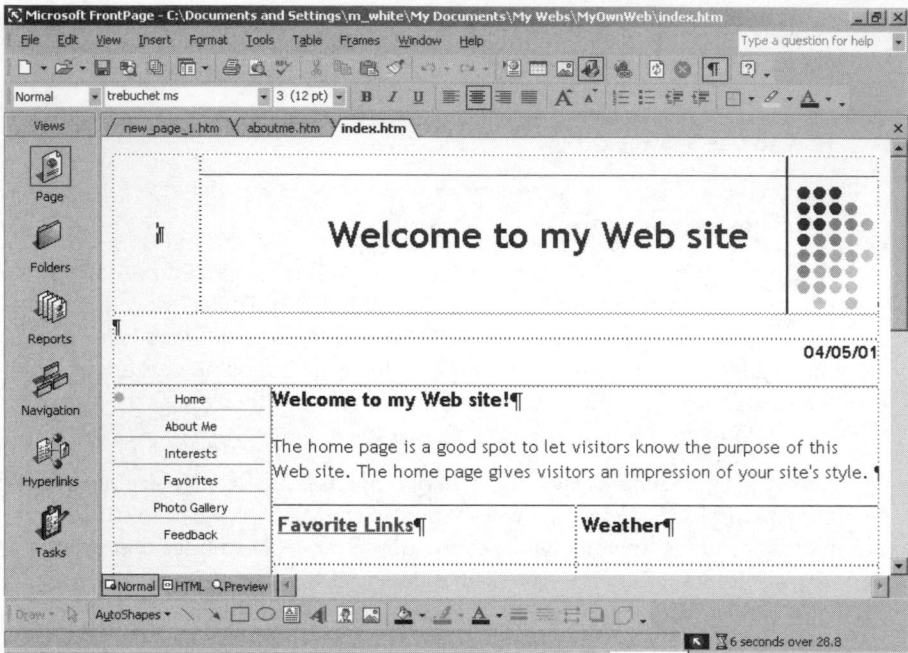

Figure 41-4. This figure shows the home page of a new web created using the Personal Web template.

---

tip **Delete a Web with Caution**

If you want to delete the current web, choose View, Folder List to open the Folder List (see Figure 41-5). (You can also open the Folders view, as discussed later in the chapter.) Then, in the Folder List, right-click the top-level folder (in Figure 42-5, that would be C:\My Documents\My Webs\Personal), and select Delete from the shortcut menu. FrontPage will then display a Confirm Delete dialog box that lets you choose whether to delete all the files belonging to the web, to delete only the files that FrontPage uses to maintain the web (leaving the pages, graphics files, and other files that contain the actual web content), or to cancel the deletion. Keep in mind that whichever choice you make, the change is permanent, and you won't be able to restore the deleted files or folders (unless you have made backup copies, which is always a good idea). FrontPage doesn't place these files and folders in the Recycle Bin folder.

Chapter 41: FrontPage Fundamentals

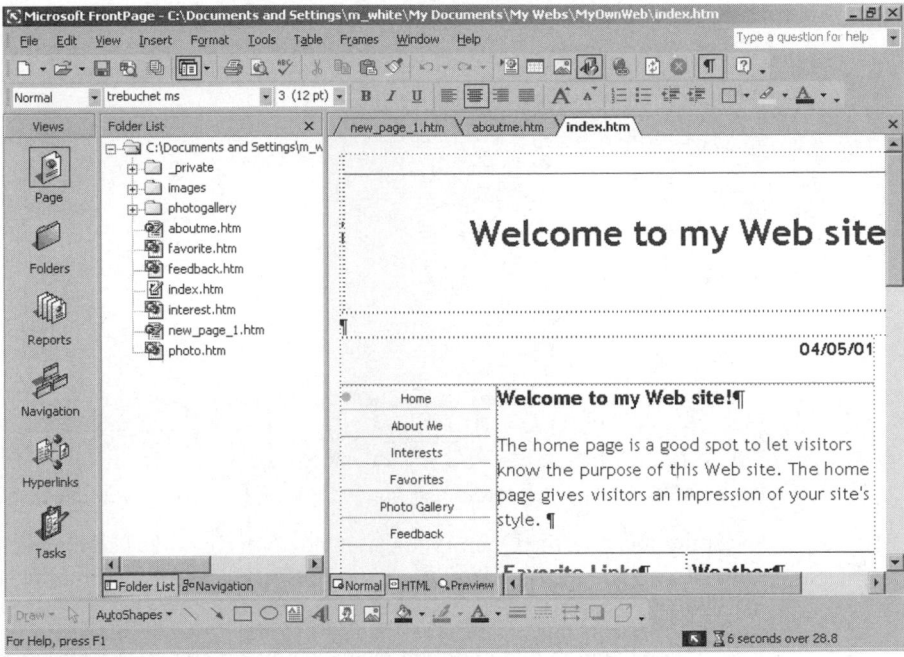

Figure 41-5. Here, the Folder List is displayed in Page view.

If you want to open a web in FrontPage—either one you created previously or a FrontPage web from another source that you want to modify—perform the following steps:

1 Choose File, Open Web. (Resist the temptation to choose the Open command, which will open an individual file, not a web.) Or, click the down-arrow on the Open button on the Standard toolbar and choose Open Web from the drop-down menu, shown here:

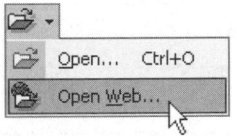

Either method displays the Open Web dialog box, shown in Figure 41-6.

note To modify a Web page or Web site that wasn't created in FrontPage, rather than opening the site directly in FrontPage, you need to use the Import Web Wizard in the Web Site Templates dialog box, as explained previously in this section.

Part 7: FrontPage

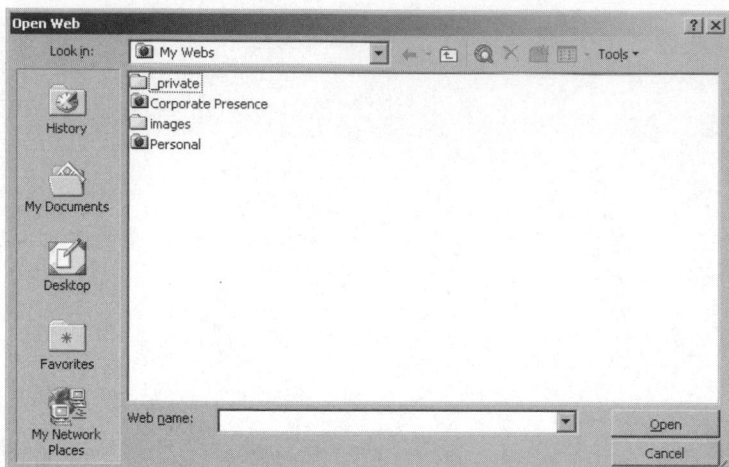

Figure 41-6. You can open an existing web using the Open Web dialog box.

2 Select the folder in the Open Web dialog box (which works like the standard Open dialog box displayed in Office applications) using one of the following methods:

- Open the web folder in the Open Web dialog box so that its contents are displayed.

- Open the folder that contains the web folder and then click the web folder in the dialog box to select it.

- Enter the full path or URL of the web folder into the Web Name text box.

You can select a folder on a local or network disk or on a Web site or intranet site.

3 Click the Open button.

> **tip** You can quickly reopen a web that you recently had open by choosing the web's name from the Recent Webs submenu of the File menu.

> **note** When you start FrontPage, it will reopen the web that was opened when you last quit the program, if any, if the Open Last Web Automatically When FrontPage Starts option is checked. You can find this option by choosing Tools, Options, clicking the General tab, and looking in the Startup area (see Figure 41-7).

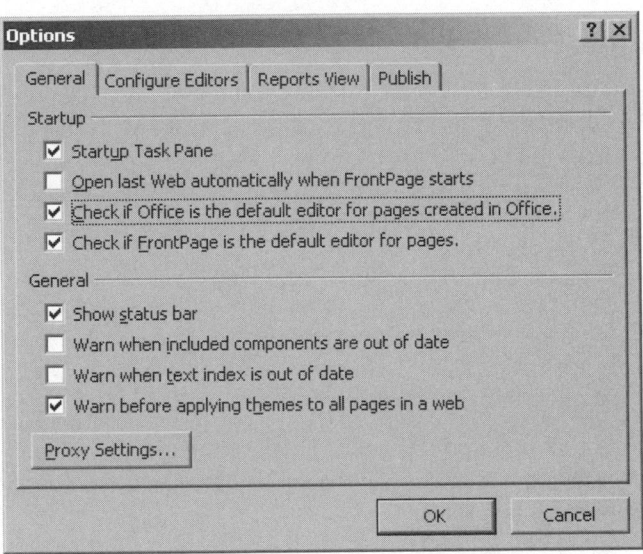

Figure 41-7. The General tab of the Options dialog box lets you select startup and general FrontPage options.

Customizing and Creating SharePoint Team Web Sites

A Web server on which the SharePoint Team Services server extensions are installed can host one or more *team Web sites*. A team Web site provides collaboration features that allow workgroups to share documents, exchange information, and work together on projects. These features include the following:

- Document libraries for storing and sharing Office documents.

- Survey questions and answers, summaries of tasks that need to be performed, discussion items that allow members to communicate, announcements, contact descriptions, event notices, and Internet links. Each of these types of information is stored in a collection known as a *list*.

- Custom lists for storing any type of information.

> Chapter 8, "Using SharePoint Team Services in Professional Workgroups," explains how to access a team Web site from Office applications or from a browser. It also describes how to make routine modifications to the site when accessing it in a browser.

Because a team Web site is actually a FrontPage web, you can modify it extensively using FrontPage.

Chapter 41

To modify a team Web site in FrontPage, perform the following main steps.

1 Follow the general steps given in the previous section for opening a web. In the Open Web dialog box, type the site's full URL into the Web Name text box and click the Open button. Alternatively, if you have created a shortcut to the site in your My Network Places (or Web Folders) folder, you can select that shortcut in the Open Web dialog box and click the Open button.

2 Manage the site, apply a theme, modify the Web pages in other ways, or create new Web pages using any of the general FrontPage techniques given in this part of the book. In addition, you can use the following FrontPage features, which are available only when you work on a web that resides on a server running SharePoint Team Services:

- You can add new custom document libraries, surveys, and other types of lists (including custom lists) to the site, or you can customize the properties of existing lists.

- You can view usage reports in FrontPage's Reports view. These reports indicate the total number of site visitors; the total number of bytes that visitors have downloaded; visitors' browsers, domains, and operating systems; and other statistics.

- You can add a Document Library View or List View Web component to a page, which allows visitors to view the contents of a SharePoint document library or list.

- You can create a custom form for adding, editing, or displaying items in a document library or other type of list by choosing Insert, Form, List Form from the Insert menu. You can also add a field to the form by choosing Insert, Form, List Field.

> The techniques for customizing libraries, lists, and other items are explained in "Adding Document Libraries, Lists, and Surveys to a SharePoint Team Web Site," on page 1131. For information on using the Reports view, see "Viewing Web Reports," on page 1151. For information on adding Web components, see "Adding Dynamic Content with Web Components," on page 1246. For general information on working with forms, see "Creating Interactive Forms to Collect Information," on page 1235.

You can also create a new team Web site on a server running SharePoint Team Services as a subweb of an existing team Web site. To do this, follow the general instructions for creating a new web given in the previous section. However, in the Web Site Templates dialog box, do the following:

1 Select the SharePoint-Based Team Web Site template in the list. This template will create all the basic components of a team Web site.

Chapter 41: FrontPage Fundamentals

2 In the Specify The Location Of The New Web box, type the full URL of an existing team Web site, followed by the name of the folder where you want to store the new subweb you're creating. For example, if a team Web site is set up at *http://OurCompany^.com* and you want to create a subweb that's stored in a folder named *Research*, you would type **http://OurCompany^.com/Research.** FrontPage would then create the new subfolder and make it a subweb of the existing web without overwriting or disturbing the existing web.

note When you create a new team Web site, you must create it directly on the Web server via the server's URL. You can't create it at a disk location and later publish it to the server.

3 Customize your site, as explained in step 2 of the previous procedure (see Figure 41-8).

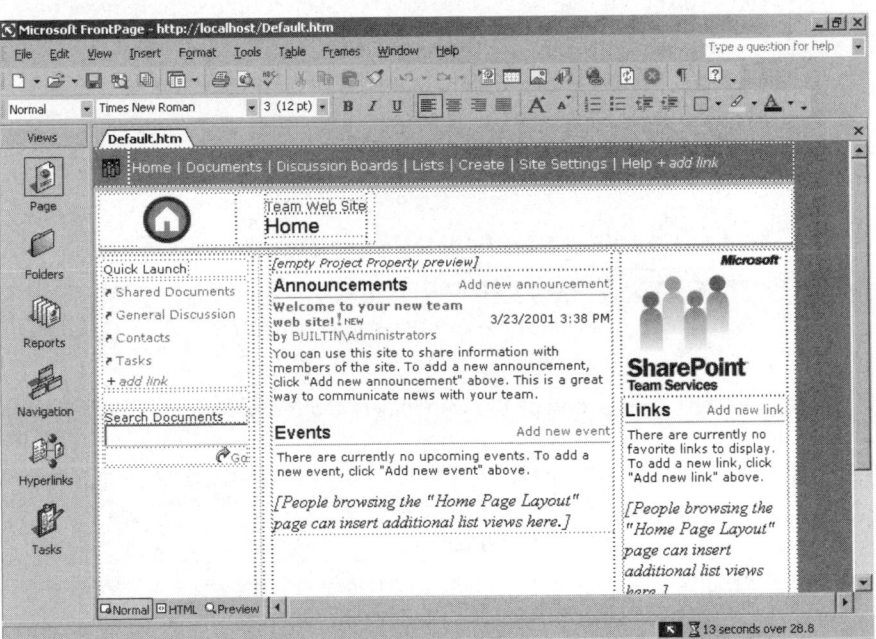

Figure 41-8. This figure shows the home page of a newly created team Web site opened in FrontPage.

Using FrontPage Views

FrontPage provides six views, each of which allows you to look at and work on a web in a different way. To work on a particular aspect of your web, first activate the appropriate view by clicking one of the icons on the Views bar, shown in Figure 41-5, on page 1119. (If the Views bar isn't visible, you can show it by choosing View, Views Bar.) You can also activate a view by choosing one of the view names from the View menu. (To open Reports view from the View menu, you have to choose a specific report name from the Reports submenu.) Note that the available toolbar buttons and menu items change according to the currently active view, so that you can choose only the commands appropriate for each view.

> **note** You can change the size of the icons on the Views bar by right-clicking anywhere on the bar and choosing either Small Icons or Large Icons from the shortcut menu. You can also choose Hide View Bar from this shortcut menu to remove the Views bar.

Table 41-2 briefly describes the purpose of each view. These views are discussed in greater detail in the chapters that follow. Note that in Folders, Reports, Navigation, or Hyperlinks view, you can double-click the name of a page to activate Page view, which lets you modify and add content to the page.

Table 41-2. **The Six FrontPage Views**

View	Description and Purpose	Discussed in
Page	Activates the FrontPage integrated Web page editor.	Chapters 43, 44, and 45
Folders	Shows all the web folders and the web files contained in these folders. This view lets you work with the folders and files using commands similar to those of Windows Explorer.	"Working with Your Web's Folders and Files," on page 1127
Reports	Displays a variety of different reports, which show the status of the files, Web pages, hyperlinks, components, and other elements in the current web, as well as usage statistics for a web on a server running SharePoint Team Services. This view helps you quickly locate problems in your Web site or evaluate its usage.	"Viewing Web Reports," on page 1151
Navigation	Graphically displays and allows you to modify the hierarchical navigation structure used by the link bars in your Web pages. Link bars allow visitors to move from page to page.	"Using Navigation View," on page 1142

Table 41-2. *(continued)*

View	Description and Purpose	Discussed in
Hyperlinks	Graphically displays information about all the hyperlinks in your Web pages and lets you check the integrity of those hyperlinks.	"Using Hyperlinks View," on page 1147
Tasks	Lets you manage tasks that you and other members of your workgroup need to perform to complete the current web.	"Managing Your Web Projects," on page 1149

Chapter 41

Chapter 42

Managing Your Web Site with FrontPage

Working with Your Web's Folders and Files

To work with the files that make up the current web, as well as the folders that contain these files, click the Folders icon on the Views bar to activate Folders view. These files include Web pages HTML (Hypertext Markup Language) files as well as the graphics, multimedia, documents, and other types of files displayed by the Web pages.

> **tip** **Use FrontPage, Not Windows Explorer, to Manage Your Web Files**
>
> You *could* use Windows Explorer to manage your web files and folders. However, it's much better to use FrontPage to perform all file management tasks, such as moving, renaming, or importing folders and files, because FrontPage maintains information on the current contents of the web and performs automatic tasks to keep your web files synchronized. For example, if you use Windows Explorer to move or rename a file that's the target of a hyperlink, the hyperlink will no longer work. In contrast, if you work with files and folders using FrontPage's Folders view, FrontPage will automatically modify hyperlinks as necessary so that they continue to function.

Folders view is shown in Figure 42-1. The left pane contains the Folder List, which displays a hierarchical list of the web folders. You can expand or collapse a branch of the folder hierarchy by clicking the box that has the plus (+) or minus (–) symbol. Also, you can select the next folder up in the hierarchy—if any—by right-clicking a blank spot in the right pane and choosing Up One Level from the shortcut menu. (FrontPage doesn't let you view the contents of folders that are higher than the web folder in your file system hierarchy.) Open a folder by clicking it in the Folder List; the right pane will then display the files and folders that are contained in that folder. Notice that the Folders view interface is quite similar to that of Windows Explorer when the Details view option is selected.

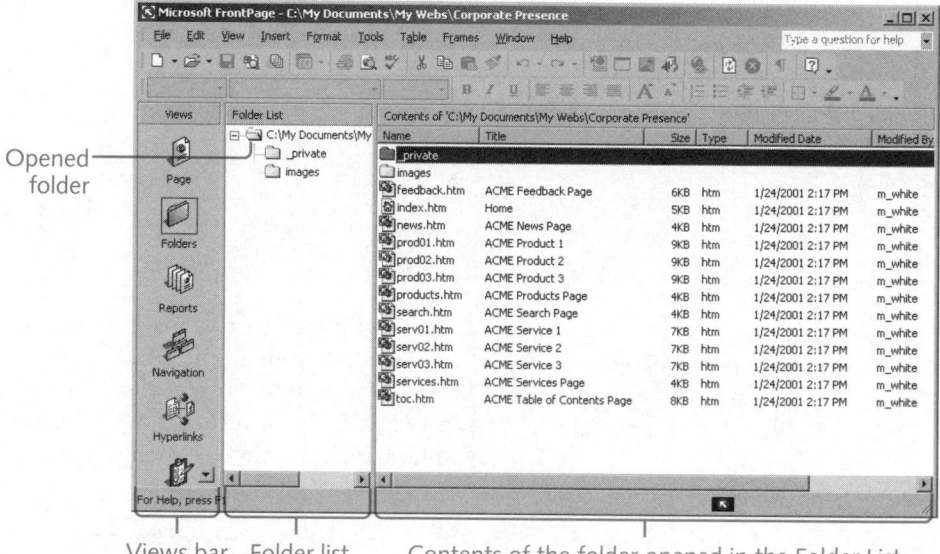

Opened folder

Views bar   Folder list   Contents of the folder opened in the Folder List

Figure 42-1. This figure shows Folders view, displaying the files in a web created using the Corporate Presence Wizard.

In the right pane of Folders view, you can sort the file list using the values in a particular column by clicking the button-like heading at the top of that column. Each click toggles between an ascending and a descending sort. (You can use this same technique to sort the task list in Tasks view.)

Troubleshooting

Some Web Folders Aren't Listed

Quite a few of the web folders that you can see in Windows Explorer, such as _borders and _vti_cnf, aren't shown in Folders view.

If the Show Hidden Files And Folders option isn't checked, in Folders view and in the Folder List FrontPage shows only the web folders containing the files that you directly work with in creating and modifying your web. It hides the folders containing the files that it uses internally for managing the web. The folders it hides are marked as hidden folders in the file system. Therefore, you can see them in Windows Explorer only if you've chosen to view hidden files and folders in Windows.

If, however, the Show Hidden Files And Folders option is checked, FrontPage shows most of the hidden folders and the files they contain in Folders view and in the Folder List. (Some folders are still hidden; for example, the _derived, _vti_cnf, and _vti_pvt hidden folders.) To access the Show Hidden Files And Folders option, choose Tools, Web Settings and click the Advanced tab.

Working with Folders

In Folders view, you can create, delete, rename, move, or copy folders using the same basic methods as in Windows Explorer. The commands for performing these operations are summarized in Table 42-1. The bulleted items in the right column represent alternative methods—use whichever one you prefer. You'll need to select a specific folder before using some of these commands. Note that you can also use any of these commands in the Folder List that you can display in Page, Navigation, or Hyperlinks view.

Table 42-1. Techniques for Working with Web Folders in FrontPage's Folders View or in the Folder List Displayed in Other Views

To Do This with Web Folders	Perform This Action
Create a new folder	Select the folder in which you want to create the new folder, and then do one of the following: ● Choose File, New, Folder. ● Click the down arrow on the Create A New Normal Page button at the left end of the Standard toolbar, and choose Folder from the drop-down menu, shown here: Page... Web... Folder Document Library... List... Survey... Task... ● Right-click a blank area in the Folder List or in the right pane of Folders view and choose New, Folder from the shortcut menu.
Delete a folder	● Right-click the folder and choose Delete from the shortcut menu. ● Select the folder and press Delete.
Rename a folder	● Right-click the folder and choose Rename from the shortcut menu. ● Select the folder and press F2.
Move (or copy) a folder	● Select the folder, choose Edit, Cut (or Copy), and then select the new location and choose Edit, Paste. ● Use the Cut (or Copy) and Paste toolbar buttons in the same way. ● Use the Cut (or Copy) and Paste commands on the right-click shortcut menu in the same way. ● Use the Ctrl+X (Cut) or Ctrl+C (Copy) and the Ctrl+V (Paste) shortcut keys in the same way. ● Use the mouse to drag the folder to a new location. (To copy the folder, press Ctrl while you drag.)

InsideOut

Use caution when deleting a web, a web folder, or a file in FrontPage. Although FrontPage asks for confirmation before deleting one of these items, for some reason, it deletes the item permanently and *doesn't* put it in your Recycle Bin. You therefore won't be able to recover a deleted web, folder, or file (unless you've made a backup copy, which is always a good idea!).

newfeature!
Adding Document Libraries, Lists, and Surveys to a SharePoint Team Web Site

If you are using FrontPage to modify a team Web site on a server running SharePoint Team Services from Microsoft—or if you've created a new team Web site—you can add new lists to the web. The types of lists you can add are document libraries; surveys; discussion boards; and links, announcements, contacts, events, tasks, or custom lists. Adding a list creates a new folder in your web that contains a set of default web pages used to display, create, and modify the information items stored in the list.

For general information on SharePoint Team Services and a description of the different types of SharePoint lists, see Chapter 8, "Using SharePoint Team Services in Professional Workgroups." For an overview of the techniques for customizing and creating SharePoint team Web sites in FrontPage, see "Customizing and Creating SharePoint Team Web Sites," on page 1121.

To create a new document library, survey, or any of the other types of lists mentioned, perform these basic steps:

1 In the Folder List, select the folder in which you want to create your new document library or the folder for storing the survey or other type of list. The folder created will be a subfolder of the folder you select.

2 On the File menu, open the New submenu, shown here:

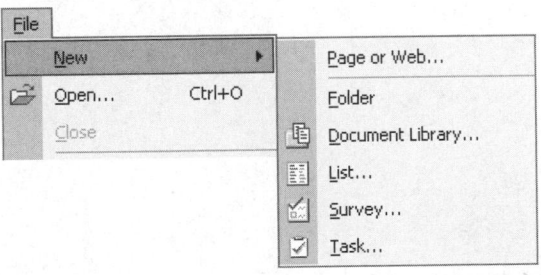

Then, choose the command for the type of list you want to create:

■ To create a document library, choose Document Library. FrontPage then opens the New Document Library dialog box, shown in Figure 42-2.

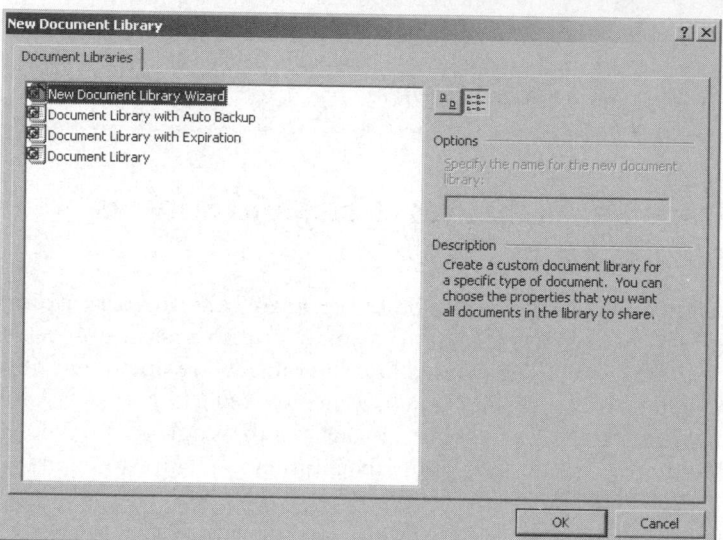

Figure 42-2. You create a new document library using the New Document Library dialog box.

■ To create a survey, choose Survey. FrontPage then opens the New Survey dialog box, shown in Figure 42-3.

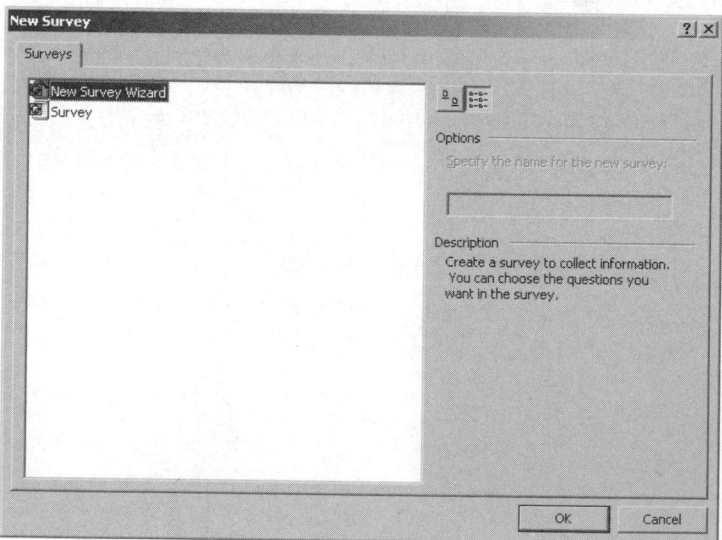

Figure 42-3. The New Survey dialog box presents options for creating a new survey.

Chapter 42: Managing Your Web Site with FrontPage

- To create a discussion board, links, announcements, contacts, events, tasks, or a custom list, choose List. FrontPage then opens the New List dialog box, shown in Figure 42-4.

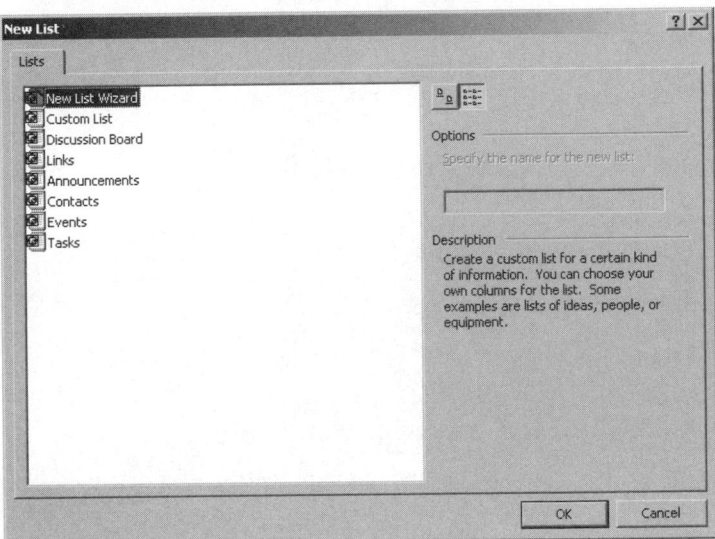

Figure 42-4. The New List dialog box provides options for creating a new list.

3 In the New Document Library, New Survey, or New List dialog box, do one of the following:

- To use a wizard to create a customized list, select the wizard at the top of the list—New Document Library Wizard, New Survey Wizard, or New List Wizard.

- To immediately create a particular type of list, choose one of the templates listed below the wizard. Notice that the dialog box displays a description of the selected template or wizard. Then, type a name for your list into the text box on the right (which is labeled according to the type of list you're creating, for example, Specify The Name For The New Document Library).

4 Click the OK button.

You can then modify the supporting Web pages contained in the folder for your new list using the techniques given in this part of the book.

You can also change many of the features of the list by right-clicking the folder used to store the list and choosing Properties from the shortcut menu to open the Properties dialog box (as shown in Figure 42-5). Keep in mind that you can also modify an existing document library or other type of list on a SharePoint team Web site by changing its properties in the same way. The specific properties you can view or set depend on the type of the list. The following are some of the most common.

Chapter 42

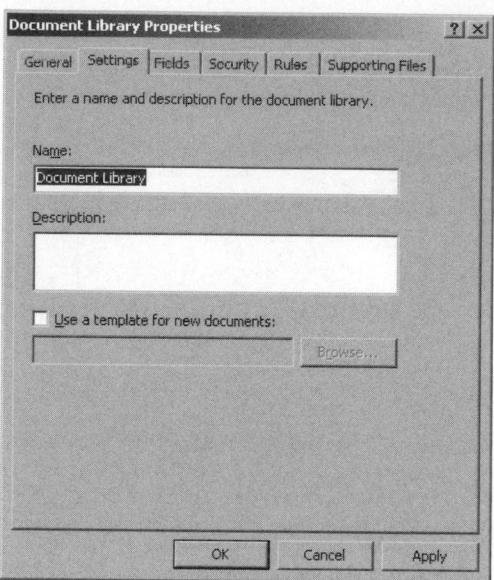

Figure 42-5. You can view or modify the properties of a document library by using the Document Library Properties dialog box.

- The folder permissions (for example, whether scripts can be run or files can be browsed) in the General tab

- The name and description of the list in the Settings tab

- The "fields"—that is, properties—that all items in the list will have (for example, ID, Last Modified, and Created Date) in the Fields tab

- The list's security settings (for example, who can read items, edit items, or change list settings) in the Security tab

- The names and locations of the list's supporting Web pages (for example, the default page used to view the list, and the Web pages containing the forms for displaying, creating, or modifying items) in the Supporting Files tab

> **note** You can create a custom form for adding, editing, or displaying items in a document library or other type of list by choosing Insert, Form, List Form. You can add a field to the form by choosing Insert, Form, List Field. For general information on working with forms, see "Creating Interactive Forms to Collect Information," on page 1235.

Working with Files

You can also use Windows Explorer methods in Folders view to select, delete, rename, move, copy, or open web files. Table 42-2 summarizes the commands for performing these operations. The bulleted items in the right column represent alternative methods—use whichever one you prefer. You will need to select a specific file before using some of these commands. Note that you can also use any of these commands (except those in the second table item for selecting files) in the Folder List that you can display in Page, Navigation, or Hyperlinks view.

Table 42-2. Techniques for Working with Web Files in FrontPage's Folders View or in the Folder List Displayed in Other Views

To Do This with Web Files	Perform This Action
Create a new web page	Select the folder in which you want to store the new page and then do one of the following: ● To create the page using a specific template, click the Page Templates command in the New Page Or Web task pane. Or, click the down arrow on the Create A New Normal Page button on the Standard toolbar and choose Page from the drop-down menu. ● To immediately create an empty page, right-click a blank spot in the Folder List or in the right pane of Folders view, and choose New Page from the shortcut menu. Or, press Ctrl+N. For details on creating new web pages, see "Creating a New Web Page," on page 1163.
Select all files in the currently opened folder	● Choose Edit, Select All. ● Press Ctrl+A. These commands are available in Folders view only.
Delete a file	● Right-click the file and choose Delete from the shortcut menu. ● Select the file and press Delete.
Rename a file	● Right-click the file and choose Rename from the shortcut menu. ● Select the file and press F2.
Move (or copy) a file	● Select the file, choose Edit, Cut (or Copy), and then select the target folder and choose Edit, Paste. ● Use the Cut (or Copy) and Paste toolbar buttons in the same way. ● Use the Cut (or Copy) and Paste commands on the right-click shortcut menu in the same way. ● Use the Ctrl+X (Cut) or Ctrl+C (Copy) and the Ctrl+V (Paste) shortcut keys in the same way. ● Use the mouse to drag the file to the new location. (To copy the file, press Ctrl while you drag.)

(continued)

Table 42-2. *(continued)*

To Do This with Web Files	Perform This Action
Open a file	● Double-click the file. ● Right-click the file and choose Open from the shortcut menu. ● Select the file and press Enter.

If you move a file that is the target of one or more hyperlinks in the web pages, FrontPage updates the hyperlinks so that they point to the correct location. Likewise, if you move a graphics file, FrontPage updates all image elements in the web pages that display the image.

When you open a web file using any of the commands shown in the last row of Table 42-2, it's opened in the editor program that FrontPage has been configured to use for the file's type. For example, a Web page (a file with an .htm, .html, or other Web page file extension) is opened in the Page view of FrontPage, and an XML (Extensible Markup Language) file (a file with the .xml extension) is opened in the Windows Notepad text editor. If no editor is configured in FrontPage for opening a particular file type, it is opened using the program (if any) that's registered to open the file type within Windows. For example, if you've installed Microsoft Photo Editor, a graphics file with the .gif or .jpg extension is opened in that program.

> **tip** **Configure FrontPage Editors**
>
> To specify the default editor program that FrontPage uses to open a web file with a particular extension (such as .gif or .jpg), choose Tools, Options and in the Options dialog box, click the Configure Editors tab (see Figure 42-6). If the Open Web Pages In The Office Application That Created Them option is checked in this dialog box, FrontPage opens web pages that are marked as being created in a Microsoft Office application other than FrontPage using that Office application; if the option isn't checked, FrontPage opens all web pages itself. (See "Saving a Document as a Web Page," on page 78.)
>
> To override the default editor, and open a web file in a particular editor, right-click the filename, choose Open With from the shortcut menu, and select an editor in the Open With Editor dialog box. Note, however, that this dialog box lists only the editors that have been configured to open one or more file types in the Configure Editors tab of the Options dialog box.

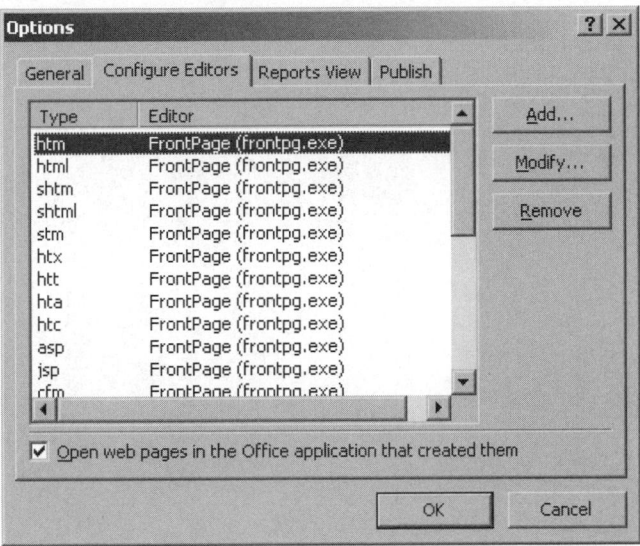

Figure 42-6. In the Configure Editors tab of the Options dialog box you can designate which programs open different types of web files.

> **tip** **Hide a Web File**
>
> You can hide a web page, graphics file, or other web file by moving it to the _private folder in your web. Visitors to your site won't be able to open or view the contents of any file in this folder. For example, you might temporarily store in _private a web page that you're working on and don't want visitors to view. To organize your private files, you can create subfolders within _private. All files within these subfolders are also hidden from browsers.

Importing Web Files and Folders

In addition to creating web files and folders within FrontPage, you can also import them from local or network disks or from the Internet. Importing files is especially important if you've been using another program to create Web pages, graphics files, or other web files and you now want to make those files part of a FrontPage web. Be sure to use one of the importing techniques discussed here rather than using Windows Explorer to copy files into one of your web's folders so that FrontPage is properly apprised of the files you're adding to the web.

To import one or more files, or folders together with the files they contain, into the currently opened web, perform the following steps:

1 In the Folder List, select the folder in which you want to store the file(s) or folder(s) you're importing.

2 Choose File, Import to open the Import dialog box (shown in Figure 42-7). You can choose this command when any view is active except the Reports and Tasks views.

Figure 42-7. The Import dialog box allows you to import files or folders into a web.

> **note** If a web isn't open when you choose File, Import, FrontPage opens the Web Site Templates dialog box and selects the Import Web Wizard, which lets you create a new web using a set of existing web pages or other files that are located on a local or network disk or on a Web site.

3 In the Import dialog box, do one of the following:

- To import one or more files or folders (plus all files in the folders) from local or network disk locations, add each of them to list. To add a file, click the Add File button; to add a folder, click the Add Folder button. When all files or folders you want to import are displayed in the list, click the OK button.

- To import a folder together with all of the web pages or other web files it contains (plus optionally all subfolders and their files), either from a disk location or from the Web, click the From Web button to run the Import Web Wizard.

With either technique, FrontPage will make a *copy* of the imported folders or files, leaving the originals intact.

InsideOut

The Import Web Wizard that runs when you click the From Web button in the Import dialog box is the same wizard that runs if you select the Import Web Wizard in the Web Site Templates dialog box when you are creating a new web (see "Creating and Opening Webs," on page 1111).

Be careful, however, when you run this wizard by clicking From Web in the Import dialog box. Although the opening wizard dialog box states that the wizard will create a new web, in reality it inserts the imported folders and files into the currently opened web, rather than inserting them into a newly created web. Be sure this is what you want to do before proceeding.

---

tip   **Use Dragging to Import**

Another way to import a file or folder into your web is to drag it from Windows Explorer or a folder window, and then drop it on the destination folder displayed in the FrontPage Folder List. The file will be *copied* into the web folder. (Unlike copying a file to a folder displayed in Microsoft Internet Explorer, you don't need to press Ctrl to make a copy.) If the FrontPage window is hidden when you start dragging the file or folder, hold the pointer over the FrontPage button in the Windows Taskbar until the FrontPage window appears, and then complete the drag operation.

Importing a Web Page and Its Graphics Files

To import a web page into the current web, including all or most of the graphics files that are displayed in the page, from a disk location or Internet address, perform the following steps.

1   Choose File, Open and in the Open File dialog box, select the web page you want to import and click the Open button. You can select a web page on a local or network disk or on a web site or other Internet location. FrontPage will now open the page in Page view.

---

note   If the Web page you open was created in an Office application other than FrontPage, it might be opened in the creating application. To open it in FrontPage, choose Tools, Options and in the Options dialog box, click the Configure Editors tab and clear the Open Web Pages In The Office Application That Created Them option (see Figure 42-6).

2   Choose File, Save As and in the Save As dialog box, save the page within the current web folder or in one of its subfolders. (If you save the file outside of the web folder, it won't become part of the current web.) Click the Change Title button if you want to give the imported copy of the page a different title.

Chapter 42

When you click the Save button in the Save As dialog box, if the imported page contains embedded images, FrontPage will display the Save Embedded Files dialog box (see Figure 42-8). For each of the graphics files displayed by the page, this dialog box lets you choose whether or not to save a local copy of the file within one of the folders in your web. (If you choose not to save a local copy, the page will reference the original copy of the graphics file, which must be accessible for the image to be displayed.) FrontPage will adjust the image references in the page according to your choices in the Save Embedded Files dialog box.

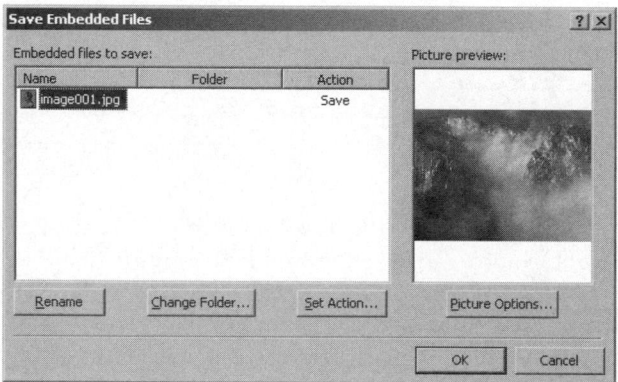

Figure 42-8. The Save Embedded Files dialog box lets you choose whether to save local copies of the files for embedded images.

This procedure makes a *copy* of imported page and graphics files, leaving the originals intact.

Troubleshooting

Graphics Files Not Saved

You used the technique presented in this section to import a web page. However, FrontPage didn't save copies of all the graphics files within your web.

When you use this technique, FrontPage saves only graphics files that are located within the same domain and that are referenced using relative paths. An image is displayed using the HTML IMG element, and the location of the graphics file is assigned to the SRC attribute of this element. FrontPage, for example, saves a graphics file for an IMG element where SRC is set to */library/images/curve.gif*, but it doesn't save a graphics file for an IMG element where SRC is set to *http://www.microsoft.com/library/images/arrow.gif*.

You can manually save any graphics file by opening the page in Internet Explorer, right-clicking the image, choosing Save Picture As, and selecting a folder within your web. (Other browsers should have similar commands.)

Working with Imported Web Files

After you import a Web page, you can modify it in FrontPage using the techniques given in the chapters in this part of the book. You can provide hyperlinks to the imported page to make it an integral part of the web and to allow visitors to access the page. (You can provide hyperlinks to the imported page either by manually inserting hyperlinks into other pages in the web or by adding the imported page to the navigation structure maintained in Navigation view, as explained later in this chapter.) To make the imported page look like other pages in your web, you'll need to explicitly apply the web's theme (if any) to that page. And if the web uses shared borders and you want them to appear in the imported page, you'll need to explicitly include the default shared borders by choosing Format, Shared Borders.

If you import an image file, you can display the image within any of your web pages.

For details on applying web themes, see "Using Themes to Quickly Change the Overall Page Format," on page 1226. For information on shared borders, see "Working With Shared Borders," on page 1189. For details on importing and using graphics, see "Inserting Images," on page 1179.

InsideOut

You can export a file from a web to a location outside the web by selecting the file in the right pane of Folders view or in the Folder List in another view, choosing the new File, Export command, and selecting a target folder in the Export Selected As dialog box. This will make a copy of the file in the target directory, leaving the file in your web intact. (You can export only a single file at a time using this method.) If, however, the page contains embedded images, FrontPage exports only the page itself and not the graphics files referenced by the image elements.

A better way to export a page that contains images is to open the page in Page view. Then choose File, Save As and select the target location in the Save As dialog box. When you click the Save button, FrontPage will display the Save Embedded Files dialog box, which lets you export any or all of the graphics files referenced by the page, in addition to the page itself. Keep in mind, however, that if you then edit the page and use the normal Save command, your changes will be saved to the *exported copy* of the page, *not* the copy of the page within the web. To open the web's copy, close the current page and then reopen the page from the file within the web.

Setting Up Your Web's Navigation Structure

FrontPage provides two views that let you work with the hyperlinks in the Web pages of your FrontPage web: Navigation and Hyperlinks. The following sections explain how to use each of these views to examine and modify hyperlinks.

"Viewing, Verifying, and Repairing Hyperlinks," on page 1156, shows how to work with hyperlinks using the Broken Hyperlinks report that you can display in FrontPage's Reports view. For information on manually adding hyperlinks to a Web page, see "Including Internal and External Hyperlinks," on page 1184.

note A hyperlink can be either internal or external. An *internal* hyperlink links to a location within the current web—either to a different location within the current page, or to a different page or file stored in the web. An *external* hyperlink links to a location outside the current web—for example, to a page on the World Wide Web.

Note that FrontPage sometimes uses the word *hyperlink* to refer to an *embedded image* (an HTML IMG element) in a Web page, which displays the contents of a graphics file within the page. In this book, however, *hyperlink* refers only to a true hyperlink element, which opens and displays a different file or a different part of the current page, unless otherwise stated.

Using Navigation View

Navigation view lets you visualize and modify the web's *navigation structure* (see Figure 42-9).

The navigation structure is a hierarchical arrangement of the pages in the web that controls the way *link bars* within the web's pages work. Specifically, it controls the functioning of link bars that have the "Bar based on navigation structure" type. A link bar of this type contains a set of automatically generated hyperlinks that let the visitor navigate to other pages in the web. In this type of link bar, you don't have to manually add links and specify their target locations. Rather, you simply assign the link bar a property such as Same Level or Back And Next (as described later in this section and shown in Figure 42-11), and FrontPage automatically generates the links required to navigate to other pages according to the web's navigation structure. For example, the Favorites page generated by the Personal Web template contains a link bar with the Same Level property. Using the navigation structure (shown in Figure 42-9) as a map, FrontPage generates links to the About Me, Interests, Favorites, Photo Gallery, and Feedback pages. (It also adds a link to the Welcome To My Web Site home page because the link bar's Home Page property is checked.)

Chapter 42: Managing Your Web Site with FrontPage

Navigation toolbar

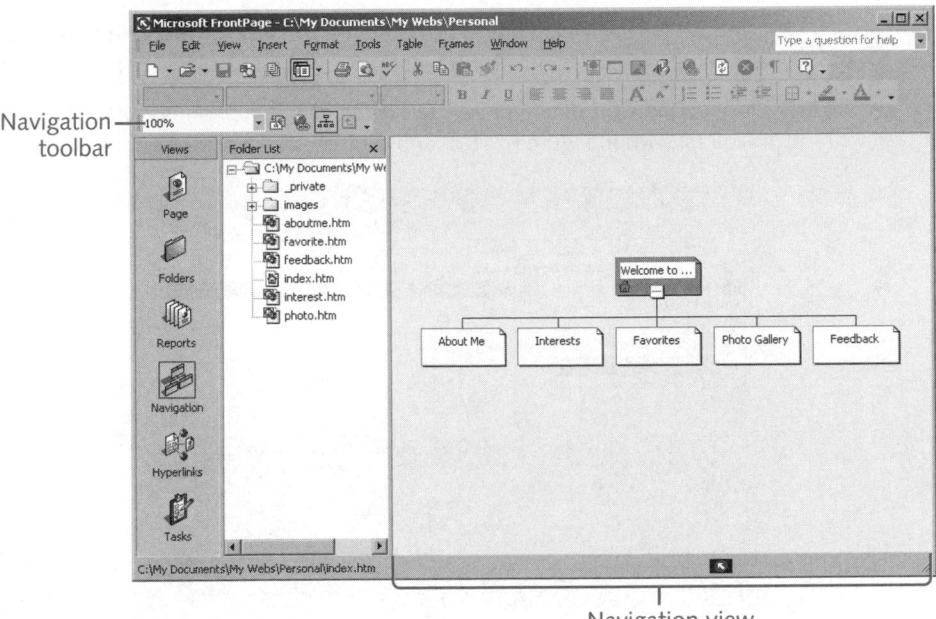

Navigation view

Figure 42-9. Here, Navigation view shows the navigation structure of a web created by using the Personal Web template.

note You can also create link bars with the "Bar with custom links" type or the "Bar with back and next links" type. These types aren't affected by the navigation structure. Rather, you have to add links manually, specifying the target locations of each.

In this section, the term *link bar* is used to refer specifically to the "Bar based on navigation structure" type.

The pages created by a web wizard or template, such as Corporate Presence Wizard or Personal Web, typically contain link bars that are based on the navigation structure, and the web's pages are added to the navigation structure. By changing the web's navigation structure, you can immediately change the targets of all link bars in the pages without having to edit each page and adjust individual hyperlinks.

You can add a link bar based on the navigation structure to any page by performing the following steps.

1 Open the page in Page view and place the insertion point at the position in the page where you want to insert the link bar.

Opening pages is discussed in "Opening an Existing Web Page," on page 1168.

Chapter 42

2 Choose Insert, Navigation. This will open the Insert Web Component dialog box and select the Link Bars component in the Component Type list.

3 In the Choose A Bar Type list, select the Bar Based On Navigation Structure type (shown in Figure 42-10), and click the Next button.

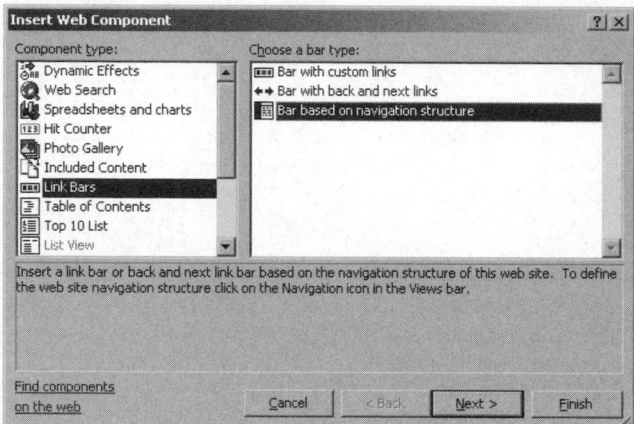

Figure 42-10. This figure shows the selections for inserting a link bar that's based on the navigation structure.

4 In the next two Insert Web Component dialog boxes that are displayed, select the link bar's style and orientation, and then click the Finish button. FrontPage will now display the General tab of the Link Bar Properties dialog box, which lets you set properties that specify the part of the navigation structure that FrontPage uses to generate the links on the link bar (see Figure 42-11).

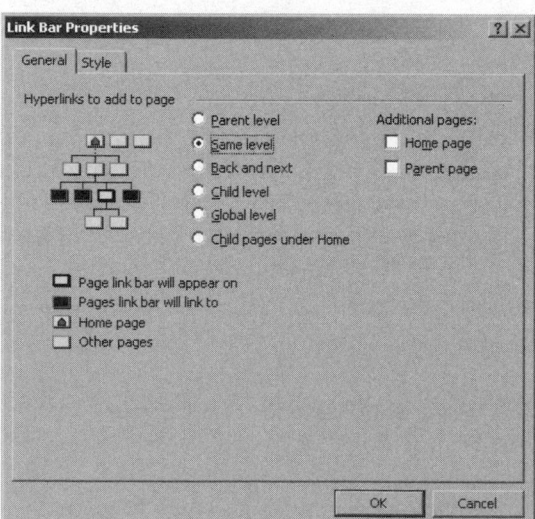

Figure 42-11. The General tab of the Link Bar Properties dialog box lets you select the portion of the web's navigation structure that the link bar will link to.

Chapter 42: Managing Your Web Site with FrontPage

For general information on inserting Web components, see "Adding Dynamic Content with Web Components," on page 1246.

5 Add the page to the web's navigation structure, if the page isn't already shown in Navigation view, as explained in the remainder of this section.

note   You can have FrontPage add link bars to the top, left, or right shared border when you set up shared borders, as explained in "Working with Shared Borders," on page 1189.

tip   **Customize Link Bar Labels**

You can modify the default labels that appear in link bars for links that navigate to the home page, the parent page, the previous page, or the next page. To do this, choose Tools, Web Settings and click the Navigation tab.

You can collapse or expand a branch of the navigation hierarchy displayed in Navigation view by clicking the box that has the (+) or (–) symbol at the top of that branch. You can also adjust the display by right-clicking a blank spot in Navigation view and choosing Zoom, Portrait/Landscape, or Expand All from the shortcut menu shown here.

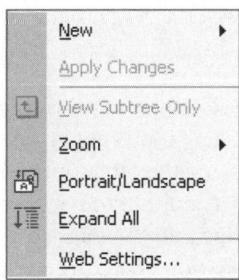

Or, you can right-click a page and choose View Subtree Only from the shortcut menu to display only the pages that are on the same level as that page. You can also perform these actions—except Expand All—by clicking equivalent buttons on the Navigation toolbar, shown in Figure 42-12.

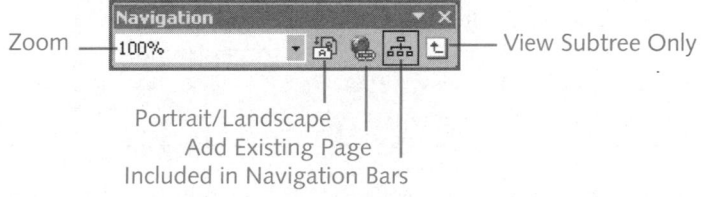

Figure 42-12.   The Navigation toolbar allows you to perform many of the same actions as the Navigation view shortcut menu.

Chapter 42

1145

> **note** Many of the web templates and wizards also add to each page a FrontPage compo-
> nent known as a *page banner*. A page banner displays the page's title in a decorative
> box at the top of the page, but only if the page is included in the navigation structure
> shown in Navigation view. (Page banners are discussed in "Adding Dynamic Content
> with Web Components," on page 1246.)

To change the position of a particular page in the navigation structure, simply drag
it to the new position. You can add a page to the structure (perhaps a new page you
added to the web) by dragging it from the Folder List to the desired position in the
structure. (If the Folder List isn't visible, choose View, Folder List or click the Toggle
Pane button on the Standard toolbar.) As you drag a page, temporary lines show the
effect of dropping it at each position.

Toggle
Pane

> **caution** Make sure that the Included In Navigation Bars property is enabled for all pages
> in the navigation hierarchy. If this option is disabled, both link bars and page banners
> are hidden on the page. (The option is enabled by default for all of the pages that a
> web template or wizard adds to a new web.) You can enable or disable this option by
> selecting a page in Navigation view and then clicking the Included In Navigation Bars
> button on the Navigation toolbar. Alternatively, you can right-click a page and choose
> Included In Navigation Bars from the shortcut menu. (The name of this property
> derives from the former name for a link bar, which was *navigation bar*.)

To remove a page from the navigation structure, click it to select it and press Delete, or
right-click it and choose Delete from the shortcut menu. Then, if prompted, select Remove
This Page From The Navigation Structure. (Note that selecting the other option, Delete
This Page From The Web, deletes the actual Web page file in addition to removing the page
from the hierarchy. Also, if you previously removed a page and then added it back,
FrontPage immediately removes the page from the navigation structure without
prompting you.) Once you remove a page from the navigation structure, it will no
longer be the target of link bars in other pages, and any link bar or page banner that it
contains will be hidden.

> **tip** **Apply Your Navigation Structure Changes**
>
> FrontPage might not immediately implement a change that you make to the nav-
> igation structure. To force it to immediately apply your change or changes to all
> affected pages in the web, right-click a blank spot in Navigation view and choose
> Apply Changes from the shortcut menu.

In Navigation view, you can also change a page's title by selecting the page and pressing
F2, or by right-clicking it and choosing Rename from the shortcut menu. (The title is
displayed on the browser's title bar, on the page banner—if the page has one—and in
various views in FrontPage.) You can open a page in Page view by double-clicking it or

Chapter 42: Managing Your Web Site with FrontPage

by using any of the other file-opening methods listed in Table 42-2. Finally, you can undo or redo many actions that you performed in Navigation view by choosing Edit, Undo or Edit, Redo.

---

tip newfeature! **View the Navigation Structure in Page View**

You can also view the web's navigation folder structure in Page view by opening the new Navigation pane, which is displayed to the right of the Views bar, replacing the Folder List if it's shown. Although this pane doesn't provide as many features for working with the navigation structure as Navigation view, you can modify the view or change certain features of the navigation structure by right-clicking a file or a blank area in the pane, or by using the Navigation toolbar (to display it, choose View, Toolbars, Navigation).

Using Hyperlinks View

Hyperlinks view graphically displays all the hyperlinks in your Web pages: those contained within link bars, as well as individual hyperlinks that a template or wizard included in your pages or that you added yourself (see Figure 42-13).

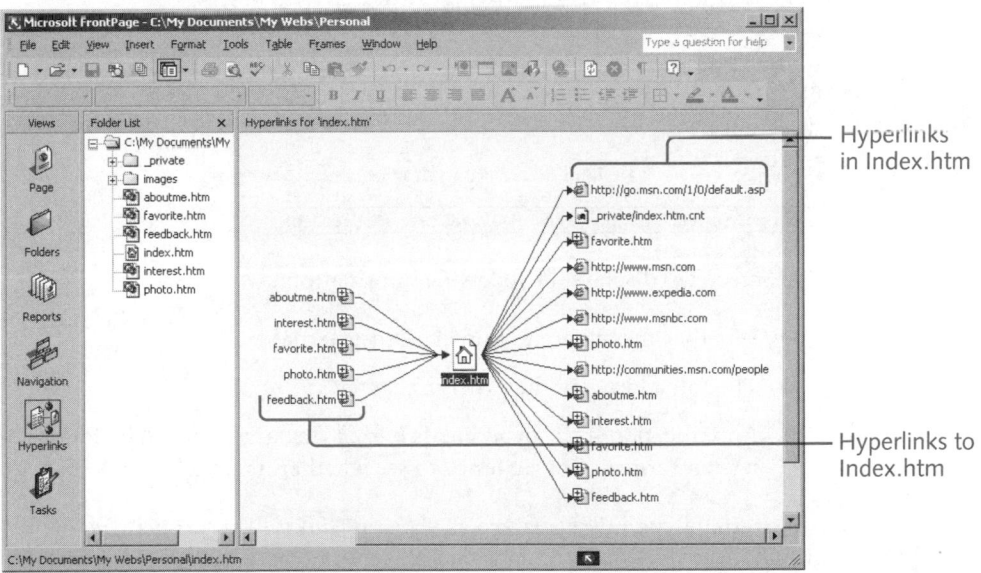

Figure 42-13. Here, Hyperlinks view shows the initial hyperlinks contained in a web created using the Personal Web template.

When you click a web file in the Folder List to select it, it's displayed in the center of Hyperlinks view. (You can also display a file in the center by right-clicking its name in Hyperlinks view and choosing Move To Center from the shortcut menu.) Hyperlinks

Chapter 42

view graphically shows all files containing hyperlinks *to* the central page (to the left of that page) and the targets of all hyperlinks *in* the page (to the right of that page). You can display more or less information in the Folder List or in Hyperlinks view by clicking the plus (+) or minus (–) box next to folder or file.

To modify the way hyperlinks are displayed, right-click a blank spot in Hyperlinks view to display the following shortcut menu.

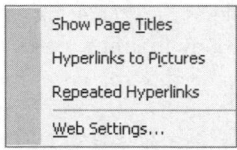

Then choose a command to select or deselect an option, as follows:

- To display the title of each page rather than its filename, select Show Page Titles.

- To show the graphics files referenced by embedded images (IMG elements), as well as true hyperlinks, select Hyperlinks To Pictures.

- If a page contains more than one hyperlink to a single target, to show all these hyperlinks, select Repeated Hyperlinks.

If you use the mouse to point to a file or target site to the left or right of the central file, FrontPage displays additional information about the hyperlink in a ScreenTip, as shown here:

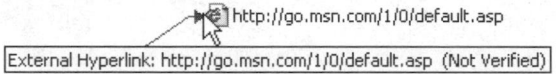

The ScreenTip displays the following information:

- Whether the hyperlink is internal or external

- The full address of the hyperlink target

- An indication if the hyperlink is *broken* (its target cannot be found) or if it's *not verified* (not yet tested to see whether its target exists)

An external hyperlink is marked as *not verified* until you explicitly verify it. (FrontPage automatically verifies internal hyperlinks, but not external ones because doing so can take a long time.) To verify an unverified hyperlink, or to retest a *broken* or verified hyperlink, right-click the file or site to the left or right of the central file in Hyperlinks view, and choose Verify Hyperlink from the shortcut menu. FrontPage will then attempt to open the target file. If it finds the target, it removes the *not verified* tag from the ScreenTip. If it doesn't find the target, it tags the hyperlink as *broken* in the ScreenTip and also adds a break to the line that extends to the hyperlink target in Hyperlinks view.

---

tip **Halt a Long Process**

Stop

Verifying external hyperlinks or embedded images can take a long time because it requires connecting with one or more other Web servers. If you want to halt the process, click the Stop button on the Standard toolbar. You can also click the Stop button to halt other potentially lengthy operations, such as importing files into your web.

You can repair a broken hyperlink by opening the page that contains it in Page view and then editing the hyperlink. Also, you can quickly repair all broken hyperlinks in the web by using the Broken Hyperlinks report.

For information on editing hyperlinks, see "Including Internal and External Hyperlinks," on page 1184. For details on using the Broken Hyperlinks report, see "Viewing, Verifying, and Repairing Hyperlinks," on page 1156.

Managing Your Web Projects

You can use Tasks view to manage tasks that you or your co-workers must complete to finish or to maintain a web (see Figure 42-14).

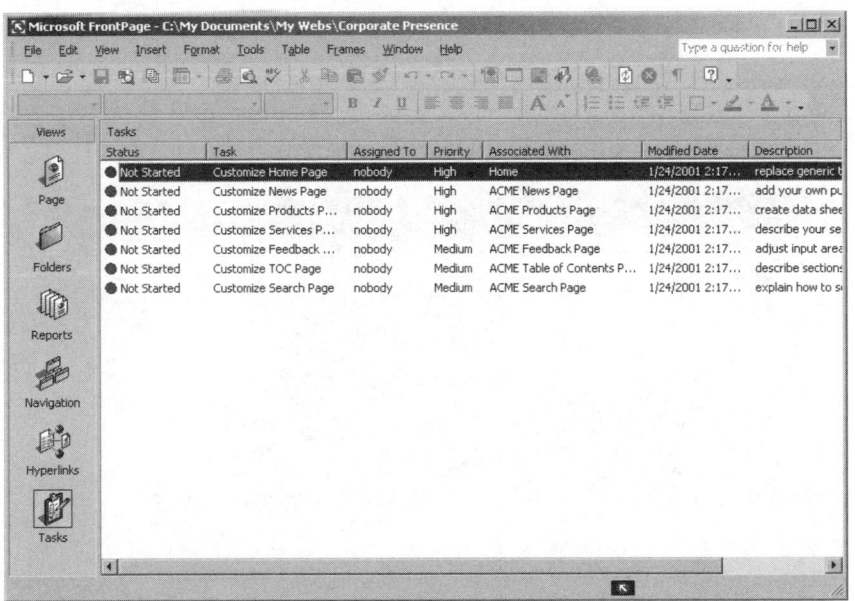

Figure 42-14. Here, Tasks view shows the tasks that the Corporate Presence Wizard adds to a new web.

Sometimes FrontPage automatically adds tasks to the list in Tasks view to inform you of unfinished jobs you need to complete. For example, if you create a new web using the Corporate Presence Wizard, FrontPage adds tasks to show you where you need to customize the web or add information for your own company. Also, if you use FrontPage to find or replace text or to check the spelling in your pages, you can have it add a task for each page that contains matching text or misspellings.

> For information on finding and replacing text, see "Finding and Replacing Text in Your Web Pages," on page 1173. For information on checking your spelling, see "Proofing Text in Your Web Pages," on page 1175.

In any FrontPage view, you can manually add a task to the list in Tasks view by choosing File, New, Task, or by clicking the down arrow next to the Create A New Normal Page button at the left end of the Standard toolbar and choosing Task from the drop-down menu shown here:

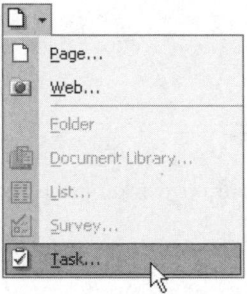

(In Tasks view, you can also create a new task by right-clicking a blank area in the view and choosing Add Task from the shortcut menu.) Then, define the new task by filling in the New Task dialog box that FrontPage displays (see Figure 42-15).

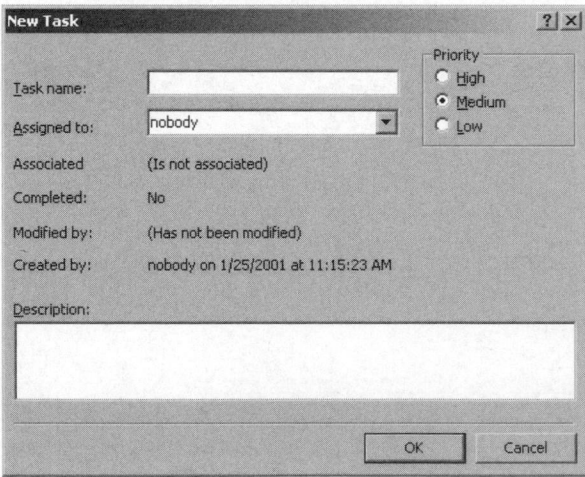

Figure 42-15. You can manually add a new task by defining it in the New Task dialog box.

If completing a task requires you to work with a particular file in your web, you can create a new task that is associated with that file. You can do this by selecting the file's name (in any view that lists files or in the Folder List) before opening the New Task dialog box using either of the two general methods given previously. The name of the associated file will be displayed in the New Task dialog box, as well as in Tasks view in the Associated With column. (In Figure 42-14, notice that all of the tasks added by the wizard are associated with files.)

When a task is associated with a file, you can open that file by selecting the task in Tasks view and then choosing Edit, Tasks, Start Task. Alternately, you can right-click the task and choose Start Task from the shortcut menu. If the file is a Web page, it will be opened in Page view; if it's a different type of file, it will be opened in the editor FrontPage is configured to use for that file type.

> Editor configurations are explained in "Working with Files," on page 1134, and the tip "Configuring FrontPage Editors," on page 1136.

To modify a task, double-click it in Tasks view, or right-click it and choose Edit Task from the shortcut menu, or select it and press Enter. FrontPage will open it in the Task Details dialog box, which has the same layout as the New Task dialog box shown in Figure 42-15. You can then change the task name, the person who is assigned the task, the task's priority, and its description. Also, clicking the Start Task button in the Task Details dialog box provides another way to open the file associated with the task, if there is one.

When you have finished a task, you can change its status from Not Started to Completed (and change the dot to the left of the task from red to green) by selecting the task in Tasks view and then choosing Edit, Tasks, Mark Complete. Or, you can right-click the task and choose Mark Complete from the shortcut menu.

To delete a task, right-click it and choose Delete Task, or select it and press Delete. To display all tasks that you haven't deleted, choose Edit, Tasks, Show History. Or, right-click a blank spot in Tasks view and select the Show History option on the shortcut menu. Unless this option is selected, completed tasks will be hidden (although not until you close and reopen the web or press F5).

Viewing Web Reports

Reports view allows you to display a variety of different reports that provide detailed information on the files, problems, and workflow status of your web, and—if the web is on a SharePoint team Web site—statistics on the web's usage. You can use this information to get an overview of the contents of your web; to spot potential problems, such as pages that load slowly, broken hyperlinks, and malfunctioning FrontPage components; and to ascertain the number of visitors your web is receiving and which pages are most popular.

To display a particular report, activate Reports view by clicking its icon on the Views bar, and then select the report you want from the Report list box on the Reporting toolbar, shown in Figure 42-16. This toolbar is normally displayed automatically when you activate Reports view. If it isn't visible, choose Views, Toolbars, Reporting.

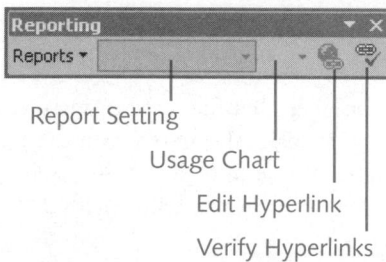

Report Setting

Usage Chart

Edit Hyperlink

Verify Hyperlinks

Figure 42-16. The Reporting toolbar allows you to select a specific report to view.

Alternatively, in any view you can choose the particular report you want to see from the Reports submenu on the View menu. This will activate Reports view and show the selected report. The available reports are briefly described in Table 42-3.

Table 42-3. **The Reports You Can Display in Reports View**

Report	Description
Site Summary	Displays the total numbers (and total sizes, where applicable) of files, pictures (embedded images), unlinked files, linked files, slow pages, older files, recently added files, hyperlinks, and other elements in your web.
Files Category	
All Files	Lists all the pages, graphics files, and other types of files contained in your web. For each file, it gives the name, title, folder location, size, type, modification date, author, comments, and—if available—the total number of page hits.
Recently Added Files	Lists the web files that have been created within the number of days currently selected in the Report Setting drop-down list on the Reporting toolbar (ranging from 1 to 365 days).
Recently Changed Files	Lists the web files that have been modified within the number of days currently selected in the Report Setting drop-down list on the Reporting toolbar (ranging from 1 to 365 days).
Older Files	Lists the web files that have not been modified within the number of days currently selected in the Report Setting drop-down list on the Reporting toolbar (ranging from 0 to 365 days).

Table 42-3. *(continued)*

Report	Description
Problems Category	
Unlinked Files	Lists the web files that cannot be opened by starting from the home page and following hyperlinks.
Slow Pages	Lists the pages in the web that have an estimated download time (at 28.8 Kbps) greater than the time selected in the Report Setting drop-down list on the Reporting toolbar (ranging from 0 to 600 seconds).
Broken Hyperlinks	Lists all individual hyperlinks in your web, or optionally just the external and broken internal hyperlinks, indicating the status of each. For more information, see the next section.
Component Errors	Lists all web files that contain Web components that are reporting errors. (If your web is stored on a disk location, this list will include Web components, such as hit counters, that won't function until your web is published to a Web server.) Web components are discussed in "Adding Dynamic Content with Web Components," on page 1246.
Workflow Category	
Review Status	Displays the current review status of each file in the web, indicating whether the file has been reviewed, and if so the result of that review. You can assign a review status to a file by selecting the filename, choosing File, Properties, clicking the Workgroup tab, and selecting an item in the Review Status drop-down list box. (The default statuses are Approved, Denied, and Pending Review.)
Assigned To	Displays, for each file in your web, the name of the person in your workgroup who has been assigned the responsibility for completing the file. You can assign a file to a person by selecting the filename, choosing File, Properties, clicking the Workgroup tab, and typing or selecting the person's name in the Assigned To box.
Categories	Displays the category of each file in your web. You can assign one or more categories to a file by selecting the filename, choosing File, Properties, clicking the Workgroup tab, and checking one or more standard categories in the Available Categories list or by clicking the Categories button to add one or more custom categories.

(continued)

Chapter 42

1153

Table 42-3. *(continued)*

Report	Description
Publish Status	Displays the publishing status of each file in your web. The publishing status of a file is set to either Publish or Don't Publish, indicating whether or not that particular file will be included when you publish your web. You can change the publishing status of a file by selecting the filename, choosing File, Properties, clicking the Workgroup tab, and either checking or clearing the Exclude This File When Publishing The Rest Of The Web option. You can also right-click the file in FrontPage and choose Don't Publish from the shortcut menu.
Checkout Status	If you've enabled the document check-in and check-out feature, you can display this report to view version control information on each file: the person—if any—who has checked out the file (that is, opened it), the file version number, and the date the file was locked if it is has been locked. The document check-in and check-out feature provides basic version control for files in a web, in environments where the web is stored on a shared network disk or Web site and several people are working on it. To enable check-in and check-out, choose Tools, Web Settings and check the Use Document Check-In And Check-Out option on the General tab.
newfeature! Usage Category	If your web is published on a SharePoint team Web site and if usage reporting has been enabled for the site, you can select from a large number of reports in this category. These reports provide usage summaries and page hit counts for various time periods; list the operating systems, browsers, and referring domains and URLs (Uniform Resource Locators) of site visitors; and display other statistics. You can enable usage reporting for a SharePoint team Web site through the site's Site Settings page, as described in "Customizing SharePoint," on page 200.

When you display certain reports, you can modify the information given by selecting options in the Report Setting drop-down list on the Reporting toolbar. For example, in the Recently Added Files report, you can select the number of previous days for which files are shown; and in the Slow Pages report, you can select the minimum download time for the files that are listed.

Also, if you double-click an item in a report (or single-click an underlined item), FrontPage performs a related action, if appropriate. The particular action depends on the type of item. For example, if you click the All Files item in the Site Summary report, it displays the All Files report. If you click the Uncompleted Tasks item in this same report, it activates Tasks view. And if you double-click the name of a page in the All Files report, it opens the page in Page view.

note You can modify features of Reports view in the Reports View tab of the Options dialog box (shown in Figure 42-17), which you open by choosing Tools, Options.

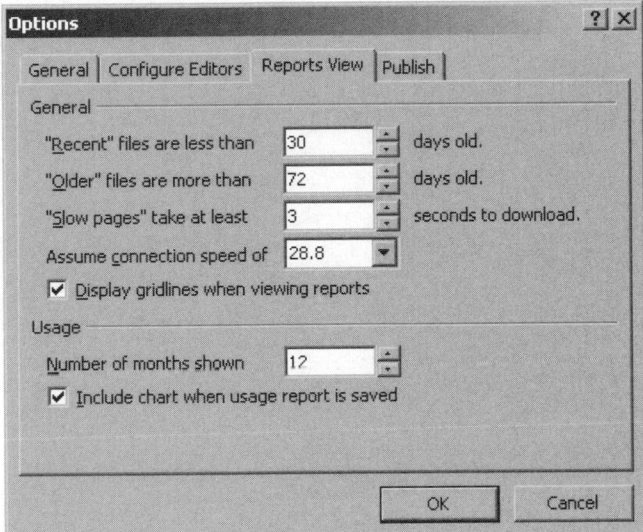

Figure 42-17. You can modify the features of the Reports view using the Reports View tab of the Options dialog box.

tip **Publish a Report**

You can publish a report by displaying it in a page in your web. To do this, open the report, right-click anywhere within the report, and choose Copy Report from the shortcut menu. Then, place the insertion point within the page in which you want to display the report and choose Edit, Paste. FrontPage will insert a copy of the report, displayed within a table. Note, however, that for some reason FrontPage doesn't provide a shortcut menu in the Site Summary page, so you can't use this method to publish that particular report.

Viewing, Verifying, and Repairing Hyperlinks

This chapter has described two FrontPage views that let you work with hyperlinks: Navigation and Hyperlinks. The Broken Hyperlinks report, shown in Figure 42-18, provides yet another way to view the hyperlinks in your web, as well as to verify hyperlinks and to repair broken ones.

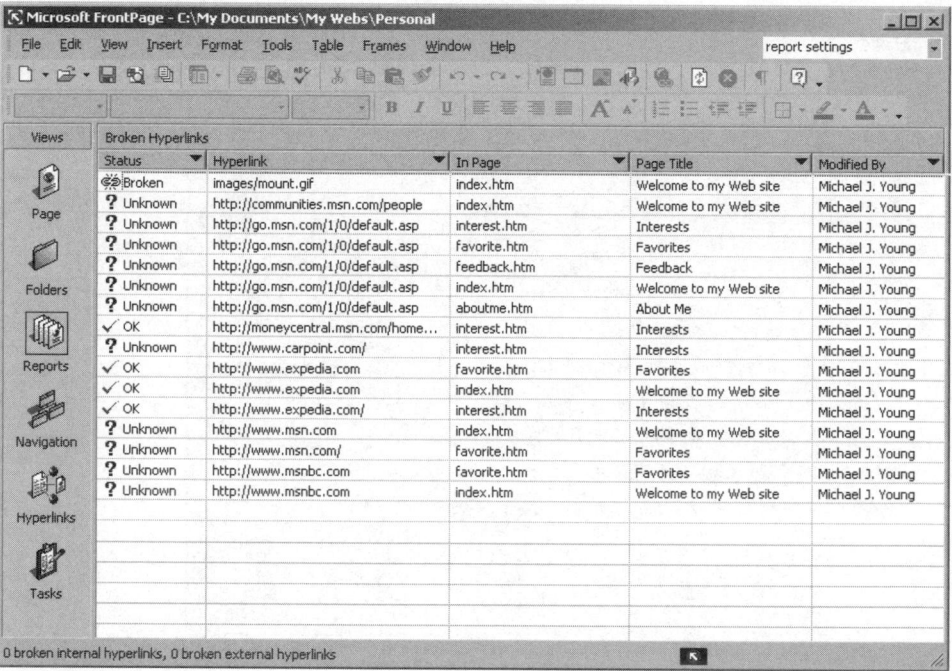

Figure 42-18. The Broken Hyperlinks report provides another way to work with the hyperlinks in your web.

caution If you have one or more Web pages opened in Page view with unsaved changes, you should save your changes before showing the Broken Hyperlinks report or checking hyperlinks, because FrontPage looks for hyperlinks within the disk files for the pages, not within unsaved versions of pages opened in Page view.

The first column of the Broken Hyperlinks report displays the status of each hyperlink. The following are the most common possible statuses.

● **OK** The hyperlink has been *verified*—that is, tested to see whether the target exists—and the target has been found.

● **Broken** Verification was attempted on the hyperlink, but the hyperlink target couldn't be found. (This doesn't necessarily mean the target doesn't exist—a bad Internet connection or a Web server problem or a cancelled verifying operation could be at fault.)

● **Unknown** The hyperlink hasn't yet been verified. This status is equivalent to the *not verified* tag displayed in Hyperlinks view. It applies to external hyperlinks only, because FrontPage automatically verifies all internal hyperlinks when it first compiles the report. An external hyperlink is marked as Unknown until you explicitly verify it.

> **note** The Broken Hyperlinks report lists embedded images in addition to actual hyperlinks, and the comments in this section apply to embedded images as well as hyperlinks.

Unlike the Navigation and Hyperlinks views, the Broken Hyperlinks report shows only the individual hyperlinks in your web pages—that is, the hyperlinks that *aren't* part of link bars. If the Show All Hyperlinks option is enabled, it shows all such hyperlinks; otherwise, it shows only external hyperlinks (with any status) and broken internal hyperlinks. You can enable or disable this option by right-clicking anywhere in the report and choosing Show All Hyperlinks from the shortcut menu.

> When you first display the Broken Hyperlinks report, FrontPage may display a message box asking whether you want it to verify the hyperlinks in your web. If you click Yes in this message box, FrontPage will verify all unknown external hyperlinks in your web.

You can verify or reverify an external hyperlink—OK, broken, or unknown—by right-clicking it and choosing Verify Hyperlink from the shortcut menu.

You can also verify all external hyperlinks with any status, or all unknown external hyperlinks, by clicking the Verify Hyperlinks button on the Reporting toolbar (shown in Figure 42-16) and then selecting the Verify All Hyperlinks option or the Verify Only Unknown Hyperlinks option in the Verify Hyperlinks dialog box (shown in Figure 42-19). You can also use the Verify Hyperlinks dialog box to verify just the selected hyperlink or hyperlinks. In addition, you can use it to resume a previous hyperlink verification that you interrupted by clicking the Stop button on the Standard toolbar.

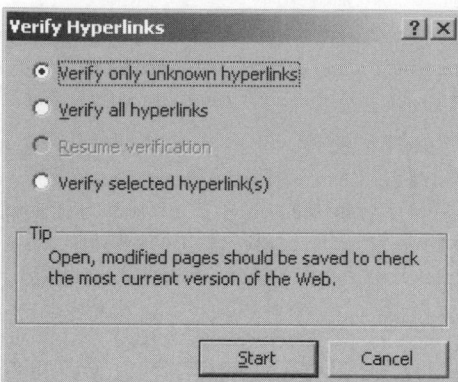

Figure 42-19. You can verify or resume verification of hyperlinks with the Verify Hyperlinks dialog box.

You can fix a broken hyperlink by double-clicking it in the Broken Hyperlinks report, by right-clicking it and choosing Edit Hyperlink from the shortcut menu, or by selecting it and clicking the Edit Hyperlink button on the Reporting toolbar. FrontPage then displays the Edit Hyperlink dialog box (shown in Figure 42-20), which lets you quickly fix the hyperlink without having to open and edit the page that contains it. The Edit Hyperlink dialog box lets you change a broken hyperlink in all pages where it occurs or in just one or more selected pages. You can either type the new hyperlink address or run your browser to locate the target.

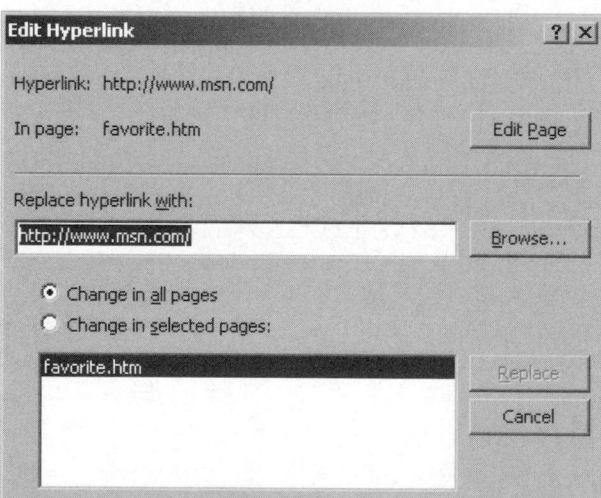

Figure 42-20. You can use the Edit Hyperlink dialog box to repair a broken hyperlink in any of the pages where it occurs.

newfeature! Publishing Your Web

Publishing your FrontPage web makes a *copy* of the entire web—all folders, pages, graphics files, other supporting files, and folders and files used internally by FrontPage—to a specified location on a Web server or on a local or network disk.

If your web is already located on the Web server that will deliver your pages to the World Wide Web or to your company's intranet, you don't need to publish it. If, however, your web isn't already stored on your Web server, you'll need to publish it in order to copy the entire web onto the server. For example, you might need to copy your web to your company's intranet server so that other people in your company can access it. Or, you might need to copy your web to the Web server maintained by your Internet service provider or Web hosting company to make your web available on the World Wide Web.

For information on places where you can store your web, see the sidebar "Creating a Web Offline or Online," on page 1112.

Another reason for publishing your web is simply to make a separate copy of it. For example, you might want to create a modified version of a web while leaving the original version intact.

To publish your web in any FrontPage view, perform the following steps:

1 Choose File, Publish Web. FrontPage will display the Publish Destination dialog box, shown in Figure 42-21.

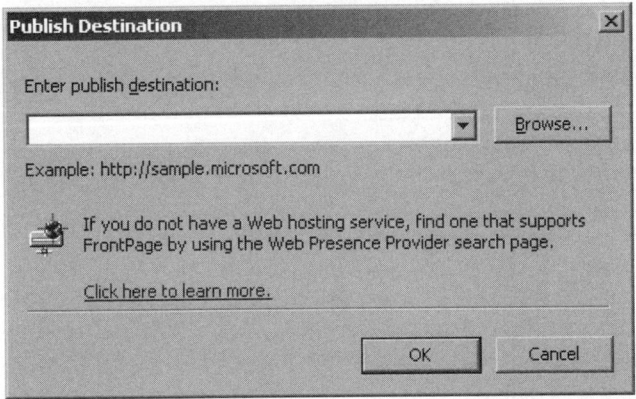

Figure 42-21. The Publish Destination dialog box prompts you for the destination location for your web.

---

tip   **Find a Hosting Service with FrontPage Server Extensions**

To take advantage of FrontPage's features it's important to publish your web to a Web server that has the Microsoft FrontPage Server Extensions, or other Microsoft server extensions such as Office 2000 Web Server Extensions or SharePoint Team Services. Fortunately, many Web hosting services now provide FrontPage Server Extensions, including services using Windows NT, Windows 2000, and Unix. In the Publish Destination dialog box (shown in Figure 42-21), you can click the Click Here To Learn More link to connect to a Microsoft site that helps you find a registered "Web presence provider" (that is, Web hosting service) that provides FrontPage Server Extensions. You can also find a wealth of comparisons, ratings, reviews, and additional information on a large number of Web hosts by consulting other Web host directories on the Web, computer magazines, and Internet newsgroups where webmasters congregate. Because of the great differences in the terms, services, and ratings of various hosts, it pays to shop carefully.

---

2 In the Enter Publish Destination text box, type the full URL or file path of the location where you want to publish your web, select a previously entered location in the drop-down list, or click the Browse button to select the location in the New Publish Location dialog box (which works just like the Open Web dialog box, shown in Figure 41-6 on page 1120). When you click the OK button, FrontPage will dial your Internet connection if necessary and then display the Publish Web dialog box (shown in Figure 42-22), which lists all of your web folders and files. A check to the left of a filename indicates that the file will be published during the current publishing session.

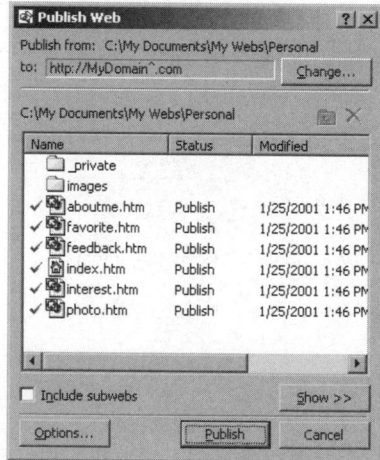

Figure 42-22.   The Publish Web dialog box provides many ways to control the publishing of your web.

Chapter 42: Managing Your Web Site with FrontPage

> **note** If you've previously published the current web, FrontPage will immediately show the Publish Web dialog box, skipping the Publish Destination dialog box. You can, however, modify your publishing destination by clicking the Change button in the Publish Web dialog box.

3 In the Publish Web dialog box, do one or more of the following:

■ To omit one or more files from the set of web files you publish, select them, right-click the selection, and choose Don't Publish from the shortcut menu shown here.

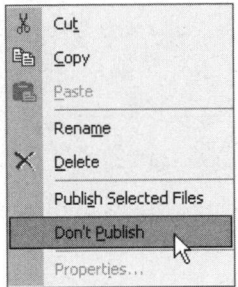

■ To immediately publish one or more specific files, select them, right-click the selection, and choose Publish Selected Files from the shortcut menu.

> **note** You can also publish one or more specific files by right-clicking them in the Folder List or in Folders view and choosing Publish Selected Files from the shortcut menu.

■ To perform other standard file operations—cut, copy, paste, rename, delete, or set properties—select one or more files and choose the corresponding command from the shortcut menu.

■ To view and work with the files and folders (if any) on the publishing destination location, click the Show >> button. This will open up an additional pane on the right that displays the contents of the publishing destination. You can work with these files and folders using the same shortcut menu that was described for files on the source web. When both panes are displayed, you can copy files in either direction between the source web and the publishing destination by dragging the filenames from one pane to the other.

■ To publish any subwebs within the web, check Include Subwebs.

■ To change publishing settings, click the Options button to open the Publish tab of the Options dialog box (see Figure 42-23).

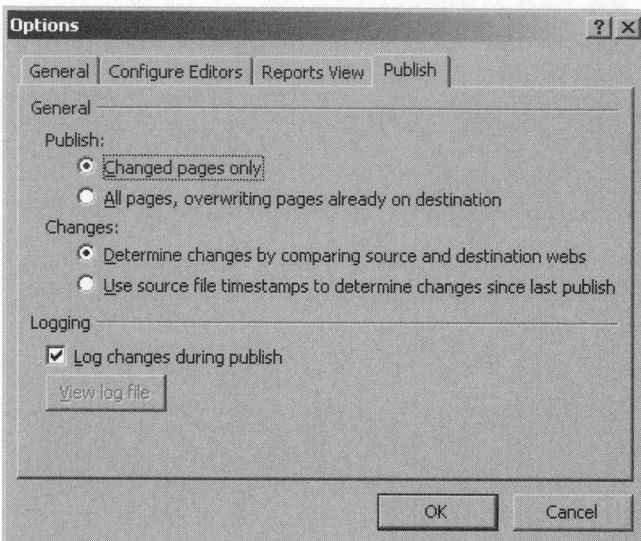

Figure 42-23. You can change publishing settings using the Publish tab of the Options dialog box.

4 Click the Publish button.

FrontPage will publish the web in the background. When all files have been published, FrontPage will notify you and let you view either the newly published site or a log listing the files that were published.

---

caution If you've previously published your web, clicking the Publish Web button on the Standard toolbar *doesn't* have the same effect as choosing File, Publish Web. Rather than giving you the opportunity to change the publishing location or set publishing options, it immediately publishes your web using the location and options you set previously.

Publish Web

Chapter 43

Creating and Editing Web Pages

Creating a New Web Page

You can create a new Web page to add to the Microsoft FrontPage 2002 web you're currently working on. You can also use FrontPage as a general-purpose HTML (Hypertext Markup Language) editor and create a Web page that isn't part of a web. FrontPage lets you create a new page whether or not a web is currently opened.

> **note** Keep in mind that if you haven't opened a web, many FrontPage features won't be available—for example, publishing, reports, hyperlink management, tasks, shared borders, and many of the FrontPage Web components.

To create a new blank page, use any of the following techniques:

- Click the Create A New Normal Page button at the left end of the Standard toolbar, shown here:

- Choose File, New, Page Or Web to open the New Page Or Web task pane (shown in Figure 43-1). Then click the Blank Page command in the New area of the task pane.

Chapter 43

Recently opened Web pages ─

Recently used Web page templates ─

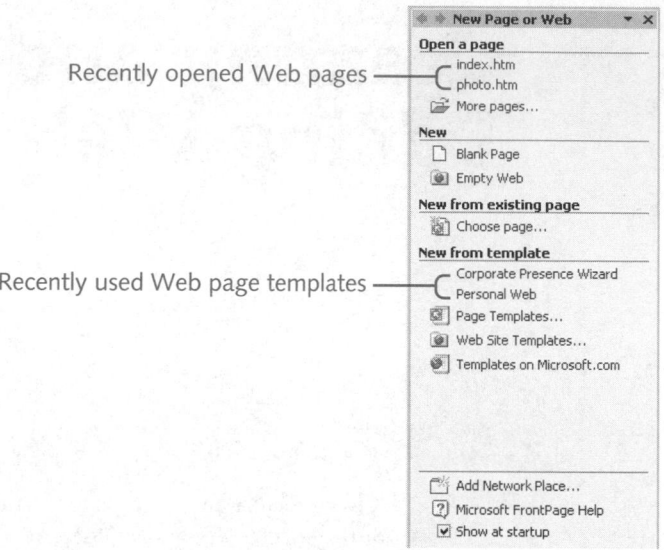

Figure 43-1. The New Page Or Web task pane provides a variety of ways to create or open Web pages.

● Press Ctrl+N.

---

new feature!

tip **Designate a Home Page**

When a visitor navigates to the root folder of your web without specifying a particular file in the URL (Uniform Resource Locator), the visitor's browser opens the page designated as your home page. In a FrontPage web, the page stored in the file Index.htm, in the root web folder, is designated as your home page. (FrontPage lists the Index.htm file with a home icon to indicate its home page status.) If you want to designate a different page as your home page, you can right-click that page in the Folder List or in Folders view and choose Set As Home Page from the shortcut menu. FrontPage will rename your former Index.htm file to Index-old.htm and then rename the file you clicked Index.htm. Note that if you create a new web that is stored directly on a Web server rather than on a local or network disk, FrontPage will name the home page Default.htm rather than Index.htm.

To get a head start in creating a particular type of Web page, you can create it using one of FrontPage's Web page templates, by performing the following steps:

1 Open the Page Templates dialog box using one of the following techniques:

■ Click the down arrow on the Create A New Normal Page button on the Standard toolbar, and choose Page from the drop-down menu, as shown on the next page.

Chapter 43: Creating and Editing Web Pages

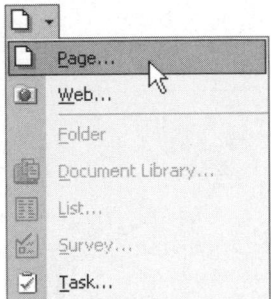

■ Choose File, New, Page Or Web to open the New Page Or Web task pane (shown in Figure 43-1). Then, click the Page Templates command in the New From Template area.

2 In the General tab of the Page Templates dialog box (shown in Figure 43-2), select the template or wizard you want to use as the basis for your new Web page. To help you choose a template, the dialog box shows a description and—for some templates—a preview image of the page that will be created using the selected template.

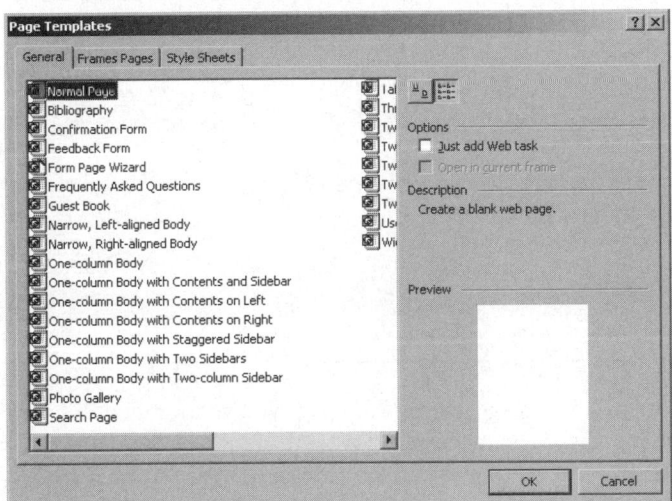

Figure 43-2. The General tab of the Page Templates dialog box presents a list of wizards and templates you can use as the basis for a new page.

> **note** If you don't want to work on the new page immediately, you can check the Just Add Web Task option. FrontPage will create the page, prompt you to save it, and add a task to Tasks view for finishing the page. To open the page, you can right-click the task and choose Start Task from the shortcut menu. Tasks are discussed in "Managing Your Web Projects," on page 1149.

> The Frames Pages tab is discussed in "Using Frames to Display Multiple Pages," on page 1240. The Style Sheets tab is explained in "Modifying, Creating, and Using Cascading Style Sheet Styles," on page 1230.

3 Click the OK button.

new feature!

note You can quickly create a Web page based on a recently used Web page template by clicking the template name at the top of the New From Template area of the New Page Or Web task pane (shown in Figure 43-1).

You can also use an existing Web page to create a new one by clicking the Choose Page command in the New From Existing Page area of the New Page Or Web task pane. The new page will be an exact copy of the existing page, but will have a new name (a default name that FrontPage assigns when it opens the page in Page view, and a permanent name you assign the first time you save the page).

FrontPage will then open your new page in Page view so that you can start adding content and customizing the page. The page will contain all of the content supplied by the template or wizard you chose. Also, if a web is currently opened, any theme assigned to the web will be applied to the new page, and any shared borders used in the web—plus the shared border contents—will be added to the page (see Figure 43-3).

> Shared borders are discussed in "Working with Shared Borders," on page 1189.

new feature!

tip Look for Additional Templates

To look for additional FrontPage templates that you can download, click the Templates On Microsoft.com command in the New Page Or Web task pane to connect with the Microsoft Office Template Gallery site on the Web.

Save

To save your new Web page, or any Web page you've modified in Page view, choose File, Save. Alternatively, you can click the Save button on the Standard toolbar or press Ctrl+S. Then, select a filename and location in the Save As dialog box. Although the Save As dialog box lets you save a Web page anywhere, if a web is opened and you want the page to be part of that web, be sure to save it in the web folder or one of its subfolders. If you want to change the title of the page, click the Change Title button in the Save As dialog box and type a new title before you click the Save button.

Chapter 43: Creating and Editing Web Pages

Top and left shared borders applied to web

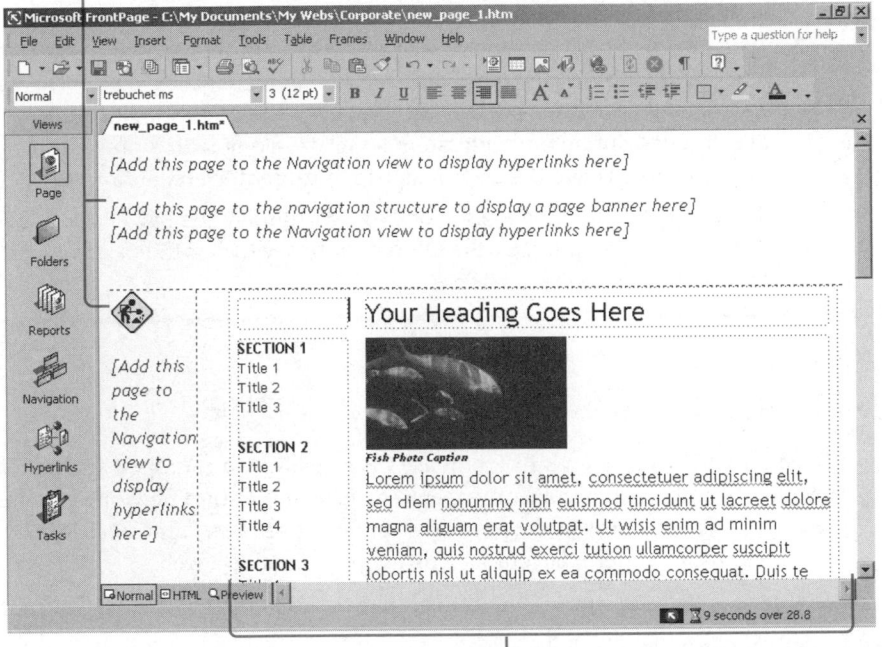

Content from Web page template

Figure 43-3. This figure shows a new page created using the One-Column Body With Contents On Left template.

Create Your Own Template

If you have created a Web page that you would like to use as the basis for creating additional pages, you can save the page as a custom FrontPage template. Your custom template will then appear in the General tab of the Page Templates dialog box so that you can use it to create new pages in the same way you can use one of the built-in templates supplied with FrontPage. To save a page as a FrontPage template, perform the following steps:

1 Choose File, Save As.

2 Select FrontPage Template (*.tem) in the Save As Type drop-down list in the Save As dialog box.

3 Click the Save button. You don't need to specify either a filename or a location for saving the template. FrontPage will later prompt you for the filename and it will automatically save the template in the required location.

(continued)

Create Your Own Template *(continued)*

4 Type new text or accept the default text when FrontPage prompts you for a title, name, and description in the Save As Template dialog box. (When you later open the Page Templates dialog box to create a new page, you'll see the title and description of your custom template, along with a preview image of the template.) Leave the Save Template In Current Web option clear.

5 If your page contains images, FrontPage will display the Save Embedded Files dialog box. Here, just click the OK button to save all of the page's graphics files along with the template.

Opening an Existing Web Page

To edit a Web page, open it in FrontPage's Page view. You can open and edit a page whether or not a web is currently open. The page might be a new one you created following the instructions in the previous section, a page you want to customize that was generated by a web template, or an existing page outside a web.

> **note** Opening a page outside of the current web and then saving it in the web is a convenient way to import into your web both the page and the graphics files for all images displayed in the page. See "Importing a Web Page and Its Graphics Files," on page 1139.

To open any Web page, perform the following steps:

1 Use any of the following methods to display the Open File dialog box:

- Choose File, Open.

- Click the down arrow on the Open button on the Standard toolbar and choose Open from the drop-down menu, as shown here:

- Press Ctrl+O.

- Choose File, New, Page Or Web and click the More Pages command in the Open A Page area of the New Page Or Web task pane (shown in Figure 43-1, on page 1164).

2 Select the page's filename and location in the Open File dialog box, which works just like the standard Open Office Document dialog box or Open dialog box in Microsoft Office applications.

> The Open Office Document and Open dialog boxes are explained in "Opening Existing Office Documents," on page 61.

You can also open a Web page that's part of the current web by double-clicking the filename in the Folder List or in a view that lists web files (Folders, Reports, Navigation, or Hyperlinks).

newfeature!

If you have several pages opened at once in Page view, you can activate a particular page by clicking the page's tab at the top of Page view, as shown here:

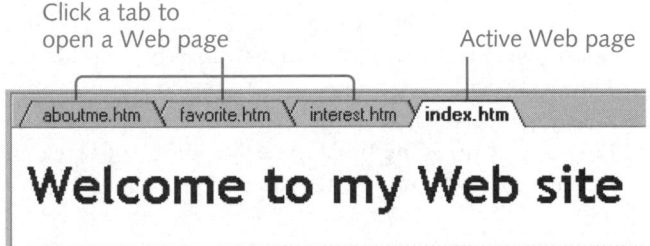

Click a tab to open a Web page

Active Web page

| aboutme.htm | favorite.htm | interest.htm | **index.htm** |

Welcome to my Web site

Or, you can use the old method of choosing a page's name from the Window menu.

> **note** You can reopen a recently opened page by clicking the filename at the top of the Open A Page area of the New Page Or Web task pane (shown in Figure 43-1) or by choosing the filename from the Recent Files submenu of the File menu.

Common Editing Tasks

You can use the editing techniques described in the following sections when you work with any of the basic page elements discussed in this chapter, as well as the more advanced elements covered in Chapter 45, "Adding Advanced Features to Your Web Pages." Most of these techniques are described briefly because they're quite similar to those used in Microsoft Word 2002 and other Microsoft Office XP applications.

Selecting

You can select blocks of text—including any embedded images, horizontal dividing lines, or other elements—by holding down the Shift key while you press an arrow key, or by dragging over the area with the mouse.

> You can also use almost any of the Word selection methods discussed in "Selecting the Text," on page 270.

You can select individual nontext elements, such as images, horizontal dividing lines, or Web components, by simply clicking them. Choosing Edit, Select All, or pressing

Ctrl+A, selects all text and other elements in the main body of the page (but not in shared borders).

Shared borders are discussed in "Working with Shared Borders," on page 1189.

Moving, Copying, and Deleting

You can move or copy selected blocks of text or other elements (such as images, horizontal dividing lines, and Web components) using the same basic methods that are used in Word. Namely, you can move the selected item by dragging it with the mouse or copy it by pressing Ctrl while you drag. You can also use the Clipboard to move or copy it by means of the standard Cut, Copy, and Paste commands. You can move or copy within a single page, between separate pages, or between documents. For example, you could use any of these methods to copy a block of text or an image from a document in Word to a page in FrontPage.

For details on copying and moving methods, see "Moving and Copying Text Using the Mouse," on page 275, and "Moving and Copying Text Using the Clipboard," on page 277. Keep in mind that these methods can be used with other selected page elements besides text.

newfeature!

When you paste text into a page, FrontPage chooses a default formatting option, but displays the Paste Options button so that you can select a different option. The available formatting options depend on the source and formatting of the text. For example, if you paste several paragraphs copied from a Word document, the Paste Options button gives you the choices shown here:

This is text copied and pasted from a Word document...

Paste Options

- ◉ Use Destination Styles
- ○ Keep Source Formatting
- ○ Keep Text Only

You can switch between choices to see which creates the effect you want.

newfeature!

note FrontPage displays the Paste Options button only if the Show Paste Options Buttons option is checked. You'll find this option by choosing Tools, Page Options and looking in the General tab.

You can select from a greater number of formatting options by using the Paste Special dialog box, rather than the standard Paste command and the Paste Options button. To paste, choose Edit, Paste Special to open the Convert Text dialog box, shown at the top of the next page.

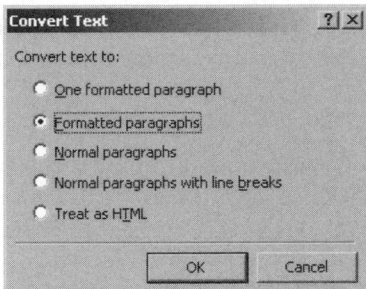

Then, select one of the following options:

- To insert the text as a single paragraph assigned the Formatted style, converting each paragraph break in the original text to a line break (and preserving all line breaks in the original text), select One Formatted Paragraph.

- To assign the inserted text the Formatted paragraph style, preserving the paragraph breaks in the original text (and converting line breaks to paragraph breaks), select Formatted Paragraphs.

note The Formatted style displays the text in a monospace font, without wrapping the lines, and preserving all space characters and line breaks in the original text. (FrontPage embeds the text assigned this style in an HTML PRE element.) For general information on FrontPage styles, see "Formatting Paragraphs," on page 1198.

- To apply the current formatting at the position in the page where you insert the text, preserving the paragraph breaks in the original text (and converting line breaks to paragraph breaks), select Normal Paragraphs or Normal Paragraphs With Line Breaks.

- To render any HTML elements in the pasted text (rather than displaying the tags as literal text), removing all paragraph and line breaks, select Treat As HTML. For example, if the text contained *important*, FrontPage would display the word *important* in bold and wouldn't display the ** and ** tags.

Finally, you can delete the selected block of text, image, horizontal dividing line, Web component, or other element by choosing Edit, Delete or by pressing the Delete key.

Undoing and Redoing Editing Actions

Undo

You can undo or redo your recent editing actions by choosing the usual Undo or Redo commands from the Edit menu, or by clicking the Undo or Redo buttons on the Standard toolbar. FrontPage also provides the following unique way to undo *all* editing

Redo

changes you have made since the page was last opened or saved. Make sure that you really want to discard all your changes, because you won't be able to restore them.

1 Choose View, Refresh or press F5.

2 Click the Yes button when FrontPage displays a message box asking whether you want to revert to the saved version of the page. (It will display this message only if you've made changes since the page was last opened or saved.)

The page will now be restored to its most recent saved version, removing your changes.

Adding the Text Content

Enter, edit, and navigate through text in Page view using the same basic methods as in Word, which are described in Chapter 11, "Efficient Editing in Word."

As in Word, you should let the text wrap automatically as you type a paragraph and press Enter only to create a new paragraph. (The position where each line in a paragraph wraps will ultimately be determined by the width of the browser window used to view the page.) You can insert a line break *within* a paragraph by pressing Shift+Enter. Most browsers insert extra vertical space between separate paragraphs, but not between lines separated by line breaks, so you can use a line break rather than a paragraph break to space separate lines more closely.

As explained in "Modifying Image Properties" on page 1214, when you assign left or right alignment to an image, the adjoining lines of text are placed to one side of the image. You can insert a special type of line break in one of these lines that forces the following line to be placed below the image rather than to one side of it (even if there is plenty of room for the line to the side of the image). To do this, choose Insert, Break to display the Break dialog box, shown here:

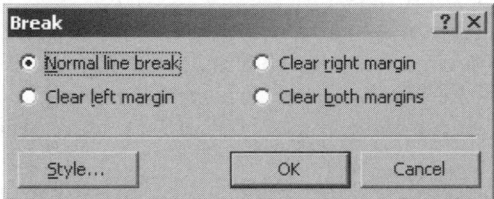

Then, select one of the options other than Normal Line Break, as follows:

● To move the following line below a left-aligned image only, select Clear Left Margin.

● To move the following line below a right-aligned image only, select Clear Right Margin.

Chapter 43: Creating and Editing Web Pages

● To move the following line below either a left-aligned or a right-aligned image, select Clear Both Margins.

> **tip** **Show or Hide Breaks**
>
> ¶
>
> Show All Click the Show All button on the Standard toolbar to show or hide the symbols that indicate the position of paragraph marks (¶) and line breaks (↵).

You can insert one of a selection of symbol characters not found on the keyboard by choosing Insert, Symbol. Then, in the Symbol dialog box, select the symbol you want and click the Insert button.

> For complete instructions on using the Symbol dialog box, see "Inserting Symbols and Foreign Characters," on page 246.

You can also insert the contents of an entire file by choosing Insert, File and then selecting the filename in the Select File dialog box, as seen here:

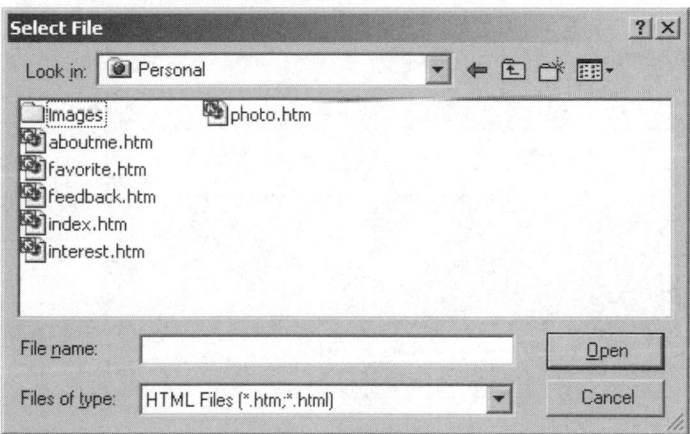

The Files Of Type list box displays the different file types you can insert, which include HTML files, Rich Text Format (RTF) files, text files, Word documents, and Microsoft Excel workbooks. When you insert the file, FrontPage converts it to HTML format and makes it an integral part of your page.

Finding and Replacing Text in Your Web Pages

In Page view, you can search for text within the active page by choosing Edit, Find or by pressing Ctrl+F, and then using the Find tab of the Find And Replace dialog box (be sure to leave the Current Page option selected), as shown on the next page.

Chapter 43

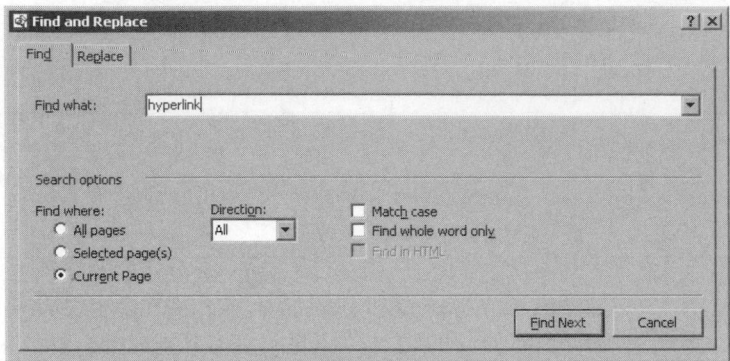

Each time you click the Find Next button, FrontPage will highlight the next occurrence of your search text within the active page.

In Page view, you can also replace text within the active page by choosing Edit, Replace or by pressing Ctrl+H, and then carrying out the operation using the Replace tab of the Find And Replace dialog box (again, be sure to leave the Current Page option selected), as shown here:

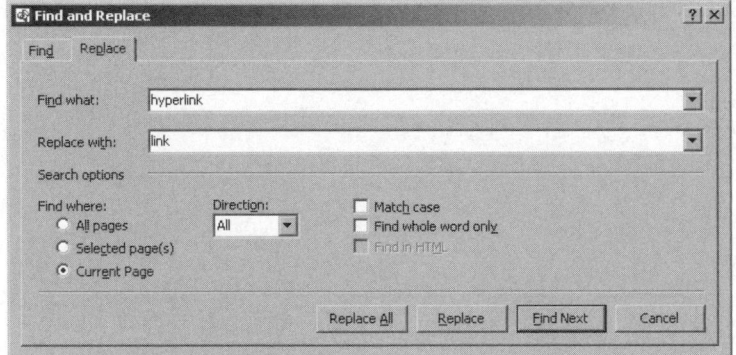

You can leave the Find And Replace dialog box open while you work on the page.

> **note** If the page contains one or more shared borders (discussed in "Working with Shared Borders," on page 1189), you can search for or replace text within all shared borders (omitting the main part of the page) by placing the insertion point within one of the shared border areas prior to using the Find or Replace command. (If the insertion point or selection is in the main part of the page, FrontPage will search or replace only within the main part.)

Chapter 43: Creating and Editing Web Pages

Alternatively, to use FrontPage to find or replace text in one or more pages belonging to the current web, in a single operation, in any view, perform the following steps:

1 If you want to find or replace text in one or more specific pages, select the file or files in the Folder List or in a FrontPage view that lists web files (Folders, Reports, Navigation, or Hyperlinks). If you want to search all pages in the web, you can skip this step.

2 To *find* text, choose Edit, Find or press Ctrl+F to display the Find tab of the Find And Replace dialog box. To *replace* text, choose Edit, Replace or press Ctrl+H to display the Replace tab.

3 Carry out the operation in the Find or Replace tab. If you selected files in step 1, you can find or replace text just within those pages by selecting the Selected Page(s) option. To find or replace text within *all* pages in your web, select the All Pages option.

4 The Find or Replace tab will list all pages that contain text matching your criteria (see Figure 43-4). You can now open the pages one at a time in the editor and complete your find or replace operation. To open a page, double-click it in the list.

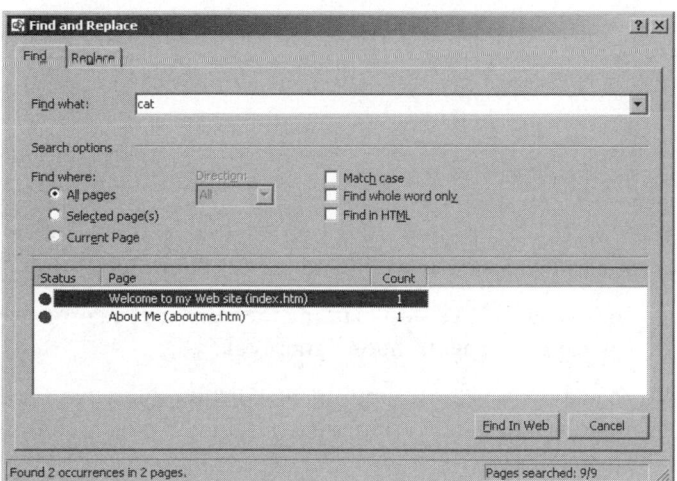

Figure 43-4.   In this figure, the Find command is used to search for text in all pages in the current web.

Proofing Text in Your Web Pages

FrontPage provides tools for checking your spelling and looking up synonyms. You can check your spelling or look up synonyms for words in the active page in the FrontPage editor, or you can check the spelling in an entire group of pages in your web.

note If your page contains text in a foreign language, you can set the language of a block of text so that FrontPage uses the correct dictionary for checking its spelling and looking up synonyms. To do this, select the text and, choose Tools, Set Language. For information on setting the language of text, see "Marking the Language," on page 504.

The easiest way to check your spelling in pages opened in the editor is to use the as-you-type spelling checker. If this feature isn't already enabled, you can turn it on by choosing Tools, Page Options and checking the Check Spelling As You Type option in the General tab. If this feature is enabled and you type a word in a page that the spelling checker doesn't recognize, FrontPage will mark the word with a red, wavy underline. You can then do one of the following:

- Ignore the word.

- Correct the word manually.

- Right-click the word and choose an option from the shortcut menu, as shown here:

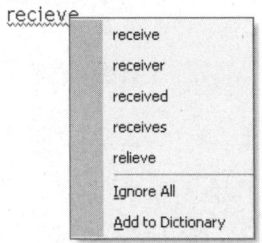

- If the correct spelling is displayed on the top section of the menu, you can choose that spelling to correct the word.

- To have FrontPage stop marking the word in the current page (until you close the page), choose Ignore All.

- To add the word to a supplemental dictionary so that FrontPage will stop marking the work permanently in all pages, choose Add To Dictionary.

If you clear the Check Spelling As You Type option in the General tab of the Page Options dialog box, FrontPage will stop marking newly typed misspellings, and any existing wavy underlines will be removed. You can hide the wavy underlines on all pages by checking the Hide Spelling Errors In All Documents option in this same tab.

If you would rather not deal with misspellings as you type text, you can check the spelling of a block of text or an entire page in Page view *after* you have entered it. If you're planning to use this method, you'll probably want to turn off the as-you-type spelling checker so you won't be bothered with the wavy underlines while you type. To check the spelling of text within the active page, perform the following steps:

Chapter 43: Creating and Editing Web Pages

1 To check spelling within a specific block of text, select the block. To check all text in the main text area, place the insertion point anywhere in the text.

note To check spelling within a shared border, you must select the text you want to check. FrontPage won't check spelling within any shared border if the insertion point or selection is in the main part of the page, or if you haven't selected text in a shared border. Shared borders are discussed in "Working with Shared Borders," on page 1189.

Spelling

2 Choose Tools, Spelling; click the Spelling button on the Standard toolbar; or press F7.

3 For each word it doesn't recognize, the spelling checker will display the Spelling dialog box, which you can use to change the spelling or to ignore the word and proceed with the check. This dialog box works very much like the Spelling And Grammar dialog box in Word.

You can also look up a synonym for a word or expression by selecting it—or by just placing the insertion point within a single word— and choosing Tools, Thesaurus or pressing Shift+F7. The FrontPage thesaurus is quite similar to the one in Word.

For details on Word's Spelling And Grammar dialog box, see "Checking the Spelling of Existing Text," on page 479. For details on Word's thesaurus feature, see "Finding Synonyms with the Thesaurus," on page 494.

To check the spelling in an entire group of pages in FrontPage, perform the following steps:

1 If you want to check spelling in one or more specific pages, select the file or files in the Folder List or in a FrontPage view that lists web files (Folders, Reports, Navigation, or Hyperlinks). If you want to check all pages in the web, you can be in any view; however, if you're in Page view, make sure the insertion point or selection isn't in a page (either close all pages or click in the Folder List)—otherwise, you'll check just the spelling in that page.

2 Choose Tools, Spelling; or click the Spelling toolbar button; or press F7. FrontPage will display the Spelling dialog box.

3 If you selected files in step 1, you can check spelling in just those pages by selecting the Selected Page(s) option in the Spelling dialog box. To check spelling within all pages in your web, select the Entire Web option. You can select the Add A Task For Each Page With Misspellings option to create a task in the Tasks view for every page that contains misspellings so that you can correct all misspellings later. Click the Start button to begin the check.

4 The Spelling dialog box will list all pages containing misspellings (see Figure 43-5). You can now open the pages one at a time in Page view and correct your misspellings. To open a page, double-click it in the list in the Spelling dialog box.

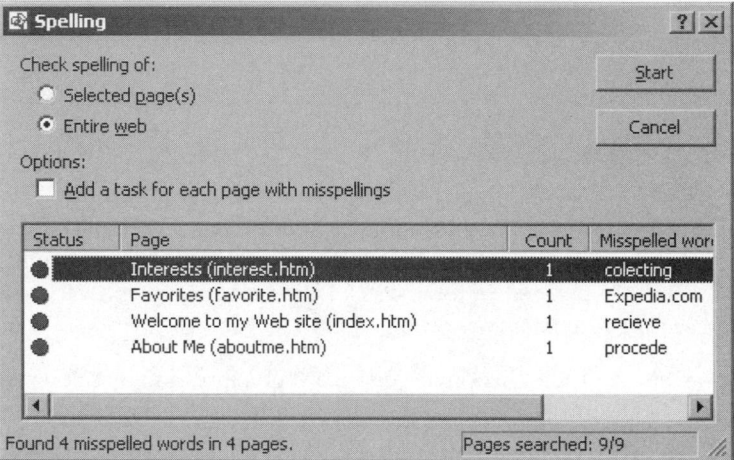

Figure 43-5. You can check spelling in all pages in the current web using the Spelling dialog box.

InsideOut

If a shared border contains a misspelling, FrontPage flags that misspelling for each page that displays the shared border. However, if you double-click one of these pages to correct the misspelling, FrontPage ignores the shared border and bypasses the misspelled word.

To work with misspellings in a shared border, you can later open any page that displays that shared border, select the shared border's text, and run another spelling check.

Alternatively, if you check the spelling in all pages in the web, you can open the actual page containing the shared border content from the Spelling dialog box and correct its spelling. The contents of the shared borders are stored in separate page files, named Left.htm, Top.htm, Right.htm, and Bottom.htm, which are stored in the _borders subfolder of your web. Shared borders are discussed in "Working with Shared Borders," on page 1189. Note, however, that the Spelling dialog box shows shared border pages only if the Show Hidden Files And Folders option is checked. You can access this option by choosing Tools, Web settings and clicking the Advanced tab.

Inserting Images

FrontPage provides more ways than ever to insert embedded images into your pages. The following are the different ways to add an image to a page:

- To add an image (or a movie or sound clip) from the collection of media files maintained by the Microsoft Clip Organizer program, choose Insert, Picture, Clip Art or click the Insert Clip Art button on the Drawing toolbar.

> **note**   If the Drawing Toolbar isn't displayed, you can show it by clicking the Drawing button on the Standard toolbar.

Insert
Picture
From File

- To insert an image from a graphics file, choose Insert, Picture, From File, or click the Insert Picture From File button on the Standard toolbar or on the Drawing toolbar.

- To add an image that's displayed in another program, copy the graphics into the Clipboard and paste the graphic data into the page in FrontPage.

newfeature!

- To add and arrange a collection of images quickly, choose Insert, Picture, New Photo Gallery.

newfeature!

- To create a drawing within FrontPage's Page view by adding one or more AutoShapes, choose Insert, Picture, AutoShapes, or use the Drawing toolbar.

newfeature!

Insert
WordArt

- To add decorative text, choose Insert, Picture, WordArt, or click the Insert WordArt button on the Drawing toolbar.

- To add a video clip, choose Insert, Picture, Video.

For information on inserting a file from the Clip Organizer, see "Inserting Pictures with the Clip Organizer," on page 115. For details on using the Clipboard to copy graphics, see "Importing Pictures," on page 125. For information on inserting a photo gallery, see "Adding a Photo Gallery," on page 1182. For complete information on creating drawings, see "Using AutoShapes to Create Drawings," on page 132. For instructions on adding decorative text, see "Using WordArt to Produce Special Text Effects," on page 141. For details on working with video clips, see "Inserting a Video Clip," on page 1183.

For each embedded image you insert, FrontPage normally adds an HTML image element (an IMG element) to the page. An image element doesn't store the actual data for the image; rather, it stores the URL of a separate graphics file, which the browser loads and displays when it processes the image element.

If you insert one or more images from the Clip Organizer, from graphics or video files located outside of the current web, or from the Clipboard, the next time you save the page, FrontPage will display the Save Embedded Files dialog box (see Figure 43-6), which lets you control the way FrontPage saves the graphics file for each embedded image. In this dialog box, you can perform one or more of the following actions:

- To control whether FrontPage saves a copy of the selected file within the web, click the Set Action button to open the Set Action dialog box. If you choose not to save the file, FrontPage will use a reference to the original file rather than creating a copy of the file within the web.

- To rename the selected file, click the Rename button.

- To change the location of the selected file within the web, click the Change Folder button.

- To select the format of the selected file, click the Picture Options button and in the Picture Options dialog box, select the JPEG or GIF format, as well as the options you want for the selected format. You can insert into a page an image in almost any format—for example, GIF, JPEG, bitmap, TIFF, Windows metafile, Postscript, and PCX. However, if FrontPage saves a copy of the file in the web, it will convert the graphics to either GIF or JPEG format (a .gif or .jpg file).

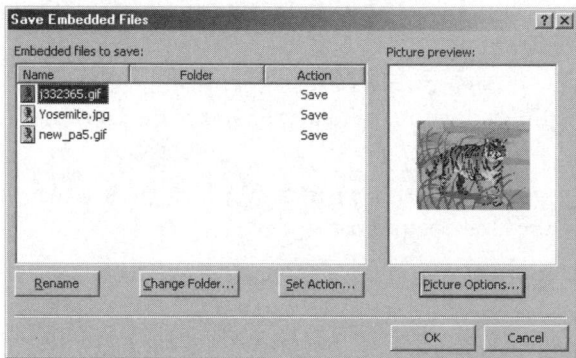

Figure 43-6. The Save Embedded Files dialog box lets you control the way FrontPage saves graphics files.

> **note** GIF (Graphics Interchange Format) and JPEG (Joint Photographic Experts Group) are the two most common graphics formats used on the Internet. GIF is ideal for efficiently storing an image that contains a moderate number of colors (typically 256 or less), while JPEG is best for storing an image based on a photograph that has many colors (more than 256).

If you insert an image from a graphics file that's already stored in your web (perhaps one supplied by the web template that you used to create the web or one that you imported into the web), FrontPage won't display the file in the Save Embedded Files dialog box. Nor will FrontPage display in this dialog box a file for an

Chapter 43: Creating and Editing Web Pages

AutoShape or a WordArt object that you insert; rather, it will automatically save the graphics within the web.

---

newfeature!

note If the VML Graphics option is enabled, FrontPage will save an AutoShape or WordArt image directly within the Web page in VML (Vector Markup Language) format, which is a plain-text description of a drawn image. If the Downlevel Image File option is checked, FrontPage will also include a regular IMG element that refers to a .gif file stored within the web as an alternative format for browsers that don't support VML. The automatically saved .gif file is stored in a subfolder within the web, which FrontPage hides but which you can view in Microsoft Windows Explorer. (The folder is given the same name as the page that contains the image.)

You can set the VML Graphics and Downlevel Image File options by choosing Tools, Page Options and clicking the Compatibility tab. See the tip "Ensure Compatibility" and Figure 43-15, on page 1195.

You can edit an image if you have installed a graphic editor program that supports the format of the image (GIF or JPEG) and if you have configured FrontPage to use that editor to open an image that is stored in a .gif or .jpg file. If these two conditions are met, you can open an embedded image in the designated editor by right-clicking it and choosing Edit Picture from the shortcut menu.

For instructions on configuring FrontPage to use an editor for a particular file type, see the tip "Configure FrontPage Editors," on page 1136. For information on changing the properties of an image, as well as modifying an image using the Pictures toolbar, see "Formatting Images," on page 1214.

Creating a Thumbnail Image

A large image can take up a lot of space in a page and can also require an undue amount of time to download. To solve this problem, you can have FrontPage replace the full image with a *thumbnail image*, which is a smaller version of the image. A thumbnail image is assigned a hyperlink to the full image so that when you view the page in a browser, you can click the thumbnail image to display the full image by itself in the browser window.

Auto Thumbnail

To convert an image to a thumbnail image, select it in FrontPage by clicking it, and then click the Auto Thumbnail button on the Pictures toolbar, or choose Auto Thumbnail from the Tools menu or from the shortcut menu that appears when you right-click the image, or press Ctrl+T. FrontPage will replace the image with a smaller version of the same image and it will assign the small image a hyperlink to the full image.

You can modify the appearance—the size, border, and edge treatment—of the thumbnail images you create by choosing Tools, Page Options and clicking the AutoThumbnail tab (see Figure 43-7). (The changes you make here will affect only the thumbnail images you subsequently generate, not those that have already been created.) In this tab, you can change the size and border thickness of a thumbnail image and you can add a beveled edge.

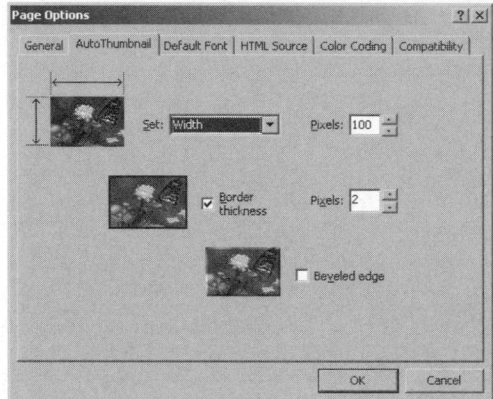

Figure 43-7. The AutoThumbnail tab of the Page Options dialog box allows you to set options for thumbnail images.

newfeature!

Adding a Photo Gallery

If you want to display a collection of images—derived from graphics files, a scanner, or a digital camera—you can quickly insert and arrange the images and create thumbnail images by adding a Photo Gallery component to your page (see Figure 43-8).

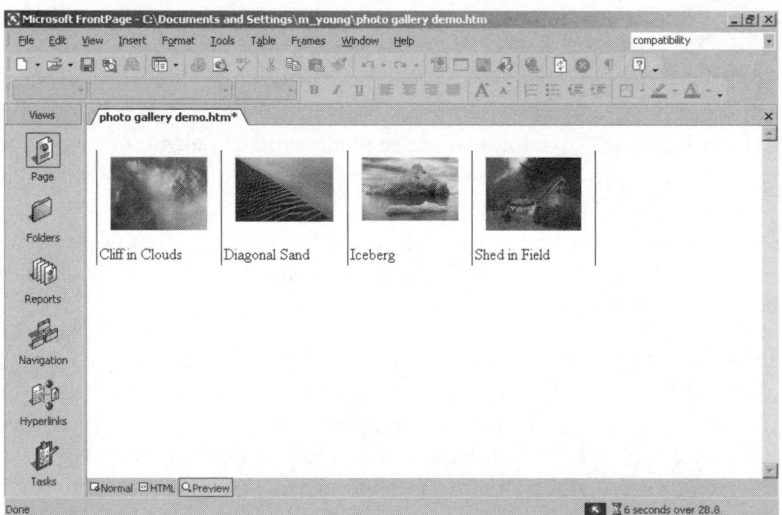

Figure 43-8. This Web page contains a single Photo Gallery component displaying the thumbnail versions of four images in FrontPage's Preview pane.

Chapter 43: Creating and Editing Web Pages

To insert a Photo Gallery component, perform the following steps:

1 Choose Insert, Picture, New Photo Gallery to open the Photo Gallery Properties dialog box.

2 To add the images, use the Pictures tab of the Photo Gallery Properties dialog box. To add each image, click the Add button and choose an image source from the drop-down menu. To work with each added image, select it in the list and use the controls in the Pictures tab (see Figure 43-9).

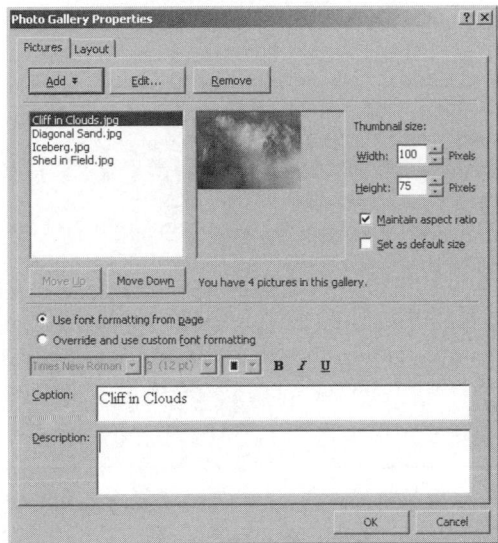

Figure 43-9.   The Pictures tab of the Photo Gallery dialog box is shown as it was completed to create the Photo Gallery shown in Figure 43-8.

3 Use the Layout tab to select the general arrangement of the images in the Photo Gallery.

> A Photo Gallery is a type of FrontPage Web component. For general information on inserting and working with Web components, see "Adding Dynamic Content with Web Components," on page 1246.

Inserting a Video Clip

You can insert a video clip into a Web page at the position of the insertion point by choosing Insert, Picture, Video and selecting a video file in the Video dialog box, which works just like the standard Open dialog box.

You can also add a video clip from the Clip Organizer by inserting a *movie*-type clip. See "Inserting Pictures with the Clip Organizer," on page 115. The video sequence is normally played when the page is first opened in a browser. However, "Modifying a Video Clip," on page 1221, explains how to modify the behavior of a video clip.

Separating Content with Horizontal Dividing Lines

A horizontal dividing line is an attractive element you can use to separate different parts of your page. If the page has a theme, horizontal dividing lines are given a style that blends with the overall look of the page. To insert a horizontal dividing line, place the insertion point at the position where you want to divide the page content and choose Insert, Horizontal Line. The line will occupy an entire row on the page.

> For information on modifying a horizontal dividing line, see "Formatting Other Page Elements," on page 1223.

Including Internal and External Hyperlinks

You can assign a hyperlink to a block of text, an image, a video clip, or a Web component. When the page is displayed in a browser, clicking an element that has been assigned a hyperlink causes the browser to display a different page, a different location within the same page, or a file such as an Office document or an image file. The file and the location that's displayed is known as the *target* of the hyperlink. If the target is a file other than a Web page, the browser might open it in a different application or let you save it in a disk file.

> **note** This section explains how to add individual hyperlinks to a page. Another way to add hyperlinks is to insert a link bar Web component, which contains a set of hyperlinks for navigating to other pages in the web. With link bars that are based on the web's navigation structure, FrontPage automatically creates and maintains the hyperlinks contained in the bar. For more information, see "Using Navigation View," on page 1142.

Hyperlink

To add a hyperlink or to modify a hyperlink you have already assigned to an element, select the text, image, or other element. Then choose Insert, Hyperlink; or click the Hyperlink button on the Standard toolbar; or press Ctrl+K. (The command won't be available if you've selected an element that can't be assigned a hyperlink, such as a horizontal dividing line.) Then, specify the target of the hyperlink in the Insert Hyperlink dialog box (which is labeled Edit Hyperlink if you're modifying an existing hyperlink; see Figure 43-10). Follow the instructions for using Word's Insert Hyperlink dialog box given in "Adding and Using Hyperlinks," on page 583. The Insert Hyperlink dialog box in FrontPage is the same as that in Word, except that it has a Parameters button that you can click to add information for querying a database, and a Style button you can click to modify the style of the hyperlink.

Chapter 43: Creating and Editing Web Pages

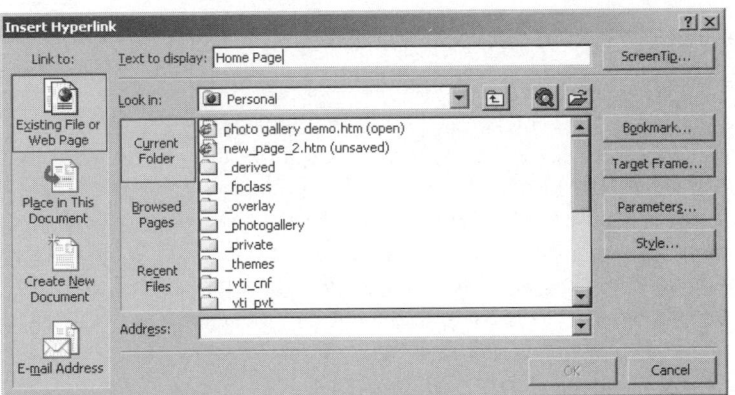

Figure 43-10. The Insert Hyperlink dialog box lets you add a hyperlink to a page.

caution If you specify a hyperlink to a local or network file using a full file path specification (such as c:\Documents\Summary.htm or file:///c:/Documents/Summary.htm), the hyperlink won't work if the page is viewed on a different computer (unless the same file happens to exist in the same folder on that computer). To make your hyperlinks portable, you should use a Web address—either a relative address to another file within the web, such as *images/sunset.htm*, or a full Web address such as *http://MyDomain^.com/mypage.htm.*

Normally when a hyperlink is clicked, the browser displays the beginning of the target file. If, however, the target of your hyperlink is a Web page—either the same page that contains the hyperlink or a different one—you can have the browser display a particular location within that page by doing the following actions:

1 Open the target page in Page view.

2 Select text at the target location within the page.

3 Assign a bookmark to that text by choosing Insert, Bookmark or pressing Ctrl+G and typing a bookmark name. (You can include spaces in the name.) The text will be marked with a dashed underline.

4 When you define the hyperlink (in the same page or in a different one), select the target page in the Insert Hyperlink dialog box, click the Bookmark button, and in the Select Place In Document dialog box, select the bookmark you just defined.

> **tip** **Open a Hyperlink Target in a Separate Window**
>
> You can force browsers to open the hyperlink target in a separate browser window, rather than replacing the contents of the current window. This can be a useful way to let visitors to your web view another Web site without closing your page, which would encourage them to leave your site. To do this, click the Target Frame button in the Insert Hyperlink (or Edit Hyperlink) dialog box (shown in Figure 43-10), and select the New Window item in the Common Targets list of the Target Frame dialog box. (The other options in this dialog box—other than Page Default (None), which causes the browser to open the target using its default method—apply only if the hyperlink is contained in a page that's displayed within a frame. For more information, see "Using Frames to Display Multiple Pages," on page 1240.)

To remove a hyperlink from a block of text or other element, select the element (or just place the insertion point anywhere within a block of text), open the Edit Hyperlink dialog box, and click the Remove Link button.

> **note** If the target of a hyperlink is a page or file within your web, and you later use FrontPage to move or rename the target, FrontPage automatically updates the hyperlink so you don't need to edit it manually.

In FrontPage's Page view, you can follow a hyperlink in a page by clicking it while pressing the Ctrl key or by right-clicking it and choosing Follow Hyperlink from the shortcut menu. (The Follow Hyperlink command isn't available for a hyperlink in a link bar.) Following a hyperlink opens the file that is the target of the hyperlink. If the target is a page (within the web, on a disk or network, or on the Web), it is opened and displayed in Page view so you can view and edit it. If it's a different type of file (such as an image file or Office document), it is opened in the associated editor program.

> For information on using the Hyperlinks or Reports view to work with the hyperlinks in the pages in your web, see "Using Hyperlinks View," on page 1147, or "Viewing, Verifying, and Repairing Hyperlinks," on page 1156. For information on assigning hyperlinks to specific areas within an image to create an image map, see "Enhancing Images Using the Pictures Toolbar," on page 1217. For information on setting colors for text hyperlinks, see "Modifying Page Properties," on page 1224.

Using Tables Effectively

You can arrange text, images, and other page elements in rows and columns using tables, which are almost identical to tables in Word documents. Tables are a very effective way to organize information and enhance the appearance of a Web page. They are potentially more important in Web pages than in Word documents because Web pages

Chapter 43

lack some of the other formatting features that are available for Word documents, such as multiple columns and tab characters for aligning text (the Tab key just inserts spaces). Fortunately, when creating Web pages in FrontPage, you can use tables to accomplish many of the same effects.

In FrontPage, you can insert a table by clicking the Insert Table button on the Standard toolbar and dragging to select the number of rows and columns, as shown here:

You can also insert and work with tables using the commands on the Table menu shown here:

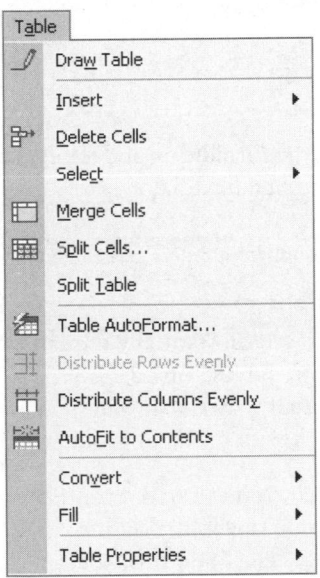

You can also use the newly expanded Tables toolbar seen on the next page.

Part 7: FrontPage

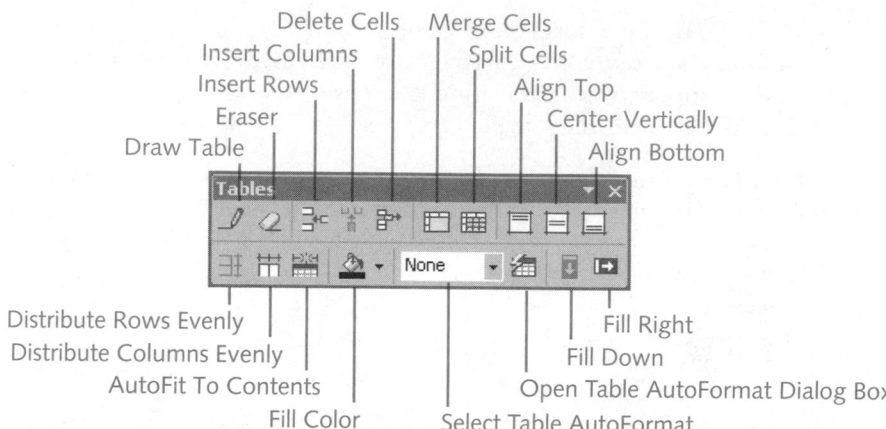

And you can apply or remove borders from a table using the new Border button on the Formatting toolbar shown here:

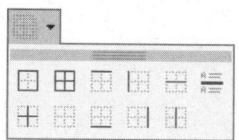

You can apply borders with greater control over the formatting and apply a background color or picture by using the Borders And Shading dialog box.

> The Borders And Shading dialog box is discussed in "Applying Borders and Shading," on page 1204.

The techniques for creating and modifying tables are substantially the same as those used in Word. For details, see "Arranging Text with Tables," on page 339, and "Adding Borders and Shading," on page 356. As you read that material, however, keep in mind the following differences in the way that you work with tables in FrontPage:

newfeature!

- In FrontPage, if you've added text to one cell, you can have FrontPage automatically copy that text to all cells in the same row to the right of that cell, or to all cells in the same column below that cell. To do this, select the cell with the content you want to duplicate, plus all cells to the right or below to which you want to copy the content. Then choose Table, Fill, Right or choose Table, Fill, Down; or, click the Fill Right or Fill Down button on the Tables toolbar.

- In FrontPage, you can't adjust the width of individual cells in a column. You can adjust the width of only the entire column.

- In FrontPage, you can't select a entire cell by clicking on its left edge. To select a cell, you need to choose Table, Select, Cell. (You can select several entire cells by dragging over them.)

- FrontPage doesn't display end-of-cell or end-of-row marks. To insert a column at the right end of the table, select the right column and choose Table, Insert, Rows Or Columns. Then select the Right Of Selection option in the Insert Rows Or Columns dialog box and click the OK button.

- In FrontPage, you can't change the orientation of text in table cells; that is, you can't make it read from bottom to top or from top to bottom.

- In FrontPage, you can't designate a row as a heading. (If a page break occurs within a table, Word repeats the heading row(s) at the top of the next page.) You can, however, display a caption above or below the table by choosing Table, Insert, Caption. You can modify the caption position (top or bottom of table), as well as its style, by choosing Table, Table Properties, Caption.

  You can also designate one or more cells as a table *header*, which normally centers the cell's text and displays it in bold. To do this, select the cell(s) and choose Table, Table Properties, Cell. Then check the Header Cell option in the Cell Properties dialog box.

- FrontPage offers only a single AutoFit option (AutoFit To Contents, on the Table menu). It doesn't offer the AutoFit To Window or Fixed Column options available in Word.

- The Table menu in FrontPage doesn't provide Sort, Formula, or Show Gridlines commands. (Gridlines are always visible in FrontPage when borders aren't applied.)

Working with Shared Borders

A page in a FrontPage web can display one or more shared borders. For example, the page shown in Figure 43-3, on page 1167, displays shared borders on the top and on the left. The contents of a shared border are identical in all web pages that display that shared border. If you add or edit an element in a shared border in one page, your modification affects the content of that shared border in all pages in the web that display it.

Often, when you create a new web using a wizard or template (such as the Corporate Presence Wizard), all pages in your web will display a top, left, and possibly a bottom shared border. Typically, the top shared border will contain a page banner and a link bar, the left shared border another link bar, and the bottom shared border—if any—an e-mail address, modification date, copyright notice, or other information.

A web has a *default* arrangement of shared borders; for instance, the default might be for all pages to display a top and a left shared border. A particular page can also have *individual* shared border settings, which override the default web settings.

To set the default shared borders, perform the following steps:

1 In any view, choose Format, Shared Borders.

2 In the Shared Borders dialog box, select the All Pages option (see Figure 43-11).

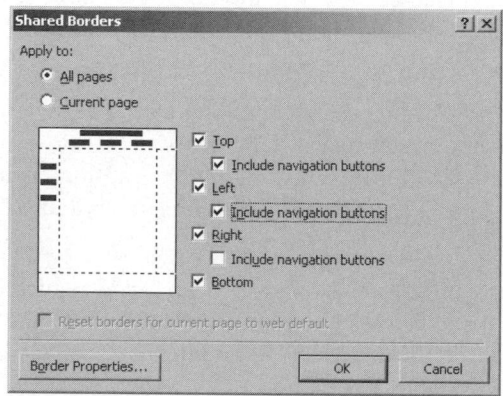

Figure 43-11. The Shared Borders dialog box provides options for working with shared borders.

3 Check the options for the particular shared borders you want to include. If you select a top, left, or right shared border, you can also check the adjoining Include Navigation Buttons option to have FrontPage automatically add a link bar (formerly known as a *navigation bar*) that is based on the web's navigation structure to the shared border.

newfeature!

4 To assign a background color or picture to any of the shared borders you selected in step 3, click the Border Properties button.

To assign individual shared border settings to one or more pages, perform the following steps:

1 Select the page(s) you want to modify in the Folder List or in any view that lists pages. Alternatively, for a single page, you can open it in Page view.

2 Choose Format, Shared Borders and in the Shared Borders dialog box, select the Selected Page(s) option. (If you opened a page in Page view in step 1, the option will be Current Page rather than Selected Page(s).) Then check the options for the shared borders you want to apply.

---

note When you're applying individual shared border settings, you can't check the Include Navigation Buttons options.

Chapter 43: Creating and Editing Web Pages

Troubleshooting

Shared Borders Command Is Unavailable

You want to apply shared borders to a set of pages you're creating, but the command is grayed on the Format menu and you can't choose it.

The shared borders command is one of the Web page features that is unavailable if you haven't opened a web in FrontPage but are using Page view to edit individual pages. Other unavailable features include publishing (the Publish Web command on the File menu); link bars, tables of contents, and several other Web components; and the features provided by the FrontPage views other than Page view.

newfeature!

3 To assign a background color or picture to any of the shared borders you selected in step 2, click the Border Properties button.

4 To remove the individual shared border settings and use the default settings for the selected pages, check the Reset Borders For Current Page To Web Default option.

When you work in the main area of the page, the shared border areas are marked with dotted lines. To add or edit elements in a shared border, click anywhere within it; the dotted lines will become solid lines. You can then work within the shared border the same way you work within the main area of the page.

note FrontPage stores the shared border content in Web page files named Bottom.htm, Left.htm, Right.htm, and Top.htm, which are kept in the hidden _borders subfolder within your web. If you wish, you can open and directly edit any of these pages.

Troubleshooting

Shared Borders Offer Little Control

You've added shared borders to the pages in your web to display common content that you want to appear in every page, but you have little control over the width, height, and text alignment of the shared border areas and you can't add visible borders to define these areas.

Shared borders are better in FrontPage 2002 than in earlier versions because they let you assign a separate background color or picture to any of the shared borders and to

(continued)

Shared Borders Offer Little Control *(continued)* the main area of the page. (In previous versions of FrontPage, the page background was applied to all shared borders as well as to the main area of the page.) However, you still have little control over the size of the shared borders or the alignment of text within them. The following alternative method lets you create border areas that contain shared content, but provide all the sizing, alignment, and visible border choices offered by FrontPage tables:

1 For each page in your web, add a table that fills the whole page, with the arrangement shown in Figure 43-12.

Table cell used for left border area   Table cell used for top border area

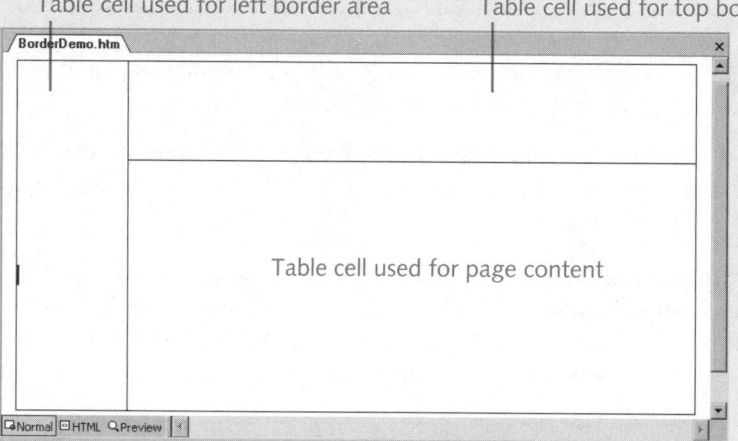

Figure 43-12. A table can be used to create page borders with shared content.

2 Format the size, text alignment, visible borders, background, and other features any way you wish for the left and top cells, which are used as your page border areas.

3 To include shared content in the left cell or in the top cell, create a separate page that contains the content that is to be displayed in the border area in all pages (perhaps a title and logo for the top border and a list of hyperlinks for the left border). Save the page within the web.

4 In each page, place the insertion point in the left or top cell, choose Insert, Web Component, and in the Insert Web Component dialog box, select Included Content in the Component Type list and select Page in the Choose A Type Of Content list. (See Figure 43-13.) Then, click the Finish button and type the name of the page you created in step 3 into the Include Page Properties dialog box.

Shared Borders Offer Little Control *(continued)*

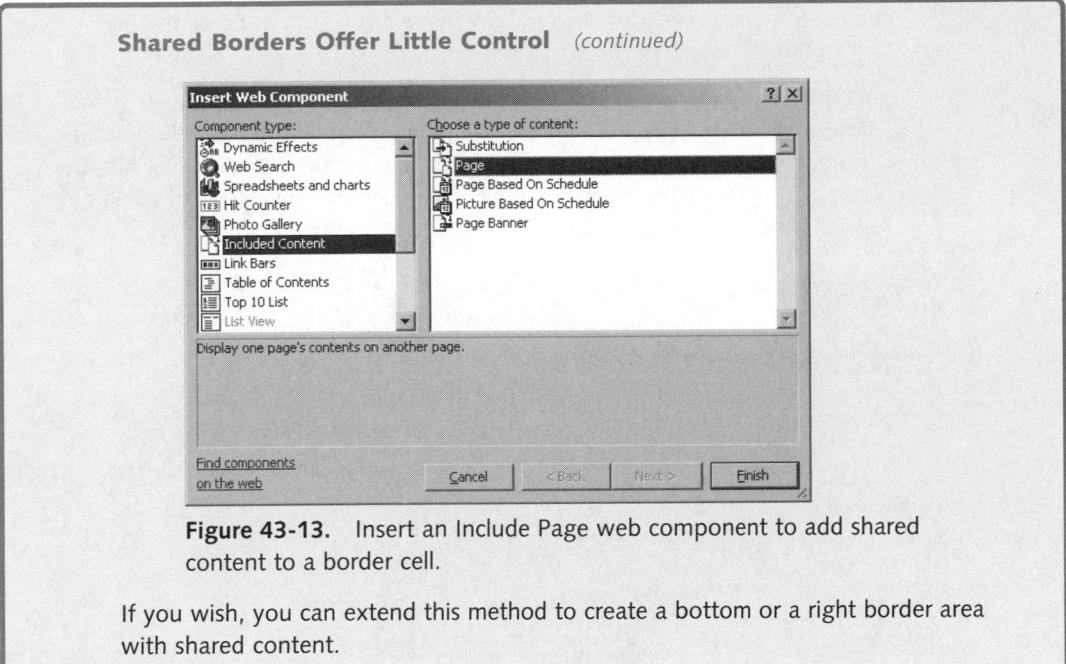

Figure 43-13. Insert an Include Page web component to add shared content to a border cell.

If you wish, you can extend this method to create a bottom or a right border area with shared content.

Previewing and Printing Your Page

You can quickly preview the way the page opened in Page view will appear in your browser by clicking the Preview button at the bottom of the Page view window. This will display the page within the Preview pane, which will render the page almost as if it were opened in your browser. To resume editing the page, click the Normal button to reopen the Normal pane.

You can also preview a page by opening it within any browser installed on your computer. To do this, perform the following steps:

1 If the page has unsaved changes, be sure to save it so that you'll see the latest version when you preview it.

2 Open the page in Page view, or select it in the Folder List or in a view that lists files.

3 Choose File, Preview In Browser. Then, in the Preview In Browser dialog box (shown in Figure 43-14), select the browser you want to use (if you have

Part 7: FrontPage

more than one), select the desired browser window size, and click the Preview button.

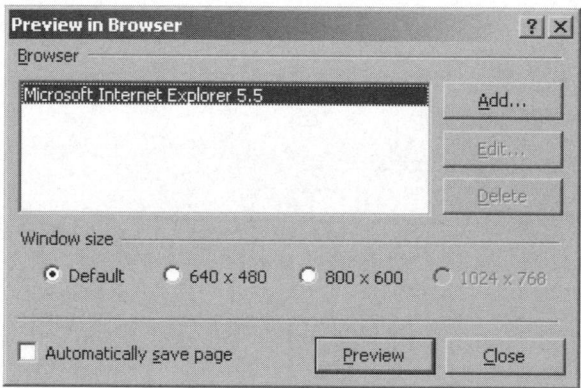

Preview in Browser

Alternatively, you can quickly open the page in your default Windows browser without displaying the Preview In Browser dialog box by clicking the Preview In Browser button on the Standard toolbar; by pressing Ctrl+Shift+B; or by right-clicking the filename in the Folder List or in a view that lists files and choosing Preview In Browser from the shortcut menu.

Figure 43-14.   You can preview a web page using the Preview In Browser dialog box.

You might want to use the Preview In Browser command rather than FrontPage's Preview pane if you've installed several different browsers on your computer and you want to verify that your page appears properly in all of them. For example, if you were preparing a page for an intranet in a company where employees use either Internet Explorer or Navigator, you might want to install both browsers and test your pages in both of them. Also, some web components—such as a table of contents—are displayed correctly only in a browser and not in the Preview pane.

You can print a hard copy of the page opened in the Normal or HTML pane of Page view by choosing commands from the File menu, as follows:

- To set a header, footer, or margins for the printed page, or to select the printer and printer settings, choose Page Setup.

- To preview the printed appearance of the page, choose Print Preview.

- To display the Print dialog box, which lets you select the printer and printing options, choose Print or press Ctrl+P.

Print

- To print the page immediately using your default printer and printing options, click the Print button on the Standard toolbar.

Chapter 43

---

tip   **Ensure Compatibility**

If you know the features of the Web server on which your page is published, or if you know the type or types of browsers that will be used to view your pages, you can have FrontPage allow you to add only those page elements and features that are supported by the available server and browser technologies. To do this, choose Tools, Page Options and click the Compatibility tab (see Figure 43-15). Then do either of the following:

● In the drop-down lists, select the specific browsers, browser versions, and servers that your visitors will use. FrontPage will automatically check or clear the check boxes for the appropriate technologies.

   or

● Check just the check boxes for the specific Web technologies available to your prospective site visitors and clear all the others.

After you do this, FrontPage will dim and disable the commands and options for adding features that rely on technologies that are cleared in the Compatibility tab.

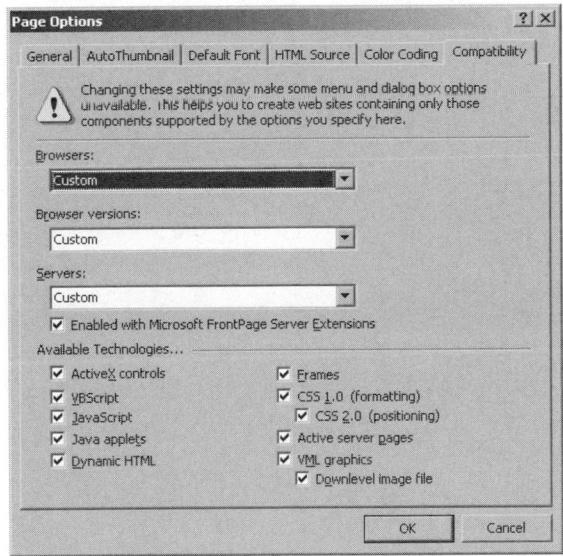

Figure 43-15.   The Compatibility tab of the Page Options dialog box lets you specify which browsers or servers will be used to view your web pages, or which technologies will be available.

Formatting Your Web Pages

A Page Formatting Overview

The previous chapter explained how to use Microsoft FrontPage 2002 to add the most basic elements to your Web pages. This chapter explains how to use Page view to format many of these elements, as well as the entire page and the more advanced elements discussed in Chapter 45, "Adding Advanced Features to Your Web Pages." In this chapter, to *format* means to modify the appearance, behavior, or other characteristics of the element or page.

The most common way to format an element is by opening its *properties* dialog box. For example, you can format text in the Font dialog box, a paragraph in the Paragraph dialog box, an image in the Picture Properties dialog box, and the entire page in the Page Properties dialog box. The methods for opening the properties dialog box depend on the particular element.

You can also format certain elements using special-purpose toolbars provided by FrontPage: the Formatting toolbar for formatting paragraphs, tables, and characters; the Positioning toolbar for positioning paragraphs; the DHTML Effects toolbar for applying animation and formatting effects to paragraphs; and the Pictures toolbar for formatting images. If the toolbar you want to use isn't currently displayed, you can show it by choosing its name from the Toolbars submenu of the View menu.

Finally, you can apply additional formatting features by using various menu commands (in addition to those that open properties dialog boxes or display toolbars). For example, you can use the Format, Borders And Shading command to add borders or background colors or images to paragraphs, and the Format, Page Transition command to assign transition effects to the entire page.

1197

> **note** If a theme has been applied to your page, FrontPage won't let you directly change some of the formatting defined by the theme. For instance, in a page that has a theme, you can't use the techniques presented in this chapter to directly modify the page background, the dimensions or color of a horizontal dividing line, or the default font displayed in Page view. You can, however, indirectly modify these formatting features by customizing the theme. (See "Using Themes to Quickly Change the Overall Page Format" on page 1226.)

Formatting Paragraphs

Applying paragraph formatting changes the appearance of one or more entire paragraphs of text. This section describes the following essential paragraph formatting techniques:

- Changing the paragraph style or format using the Formatting toolbar

- Changing the paragraph format using the Paragraph dialog box

- Applying bullets or numbering using the Bullets And Numbering dialog box

- Removing paragraph formatting

The following sections explain how to modify the format of a paragraph by adding borders or shading, positioning the paragraph text, or applying dynamic HTML (Hypertext Markup Language) effects.

To change the paragraph style or alignment, or to apply bullets, numbering, or borders using the Formatting toolbar, perform the following steps.

1 Select the paragraph or paragraphs you want to format. Or, to format a single paragraph, simply place the insertion point anywhere within it.

2 Use the controls on the Formatting toolbar (shown in Figure 44-1) as follows:

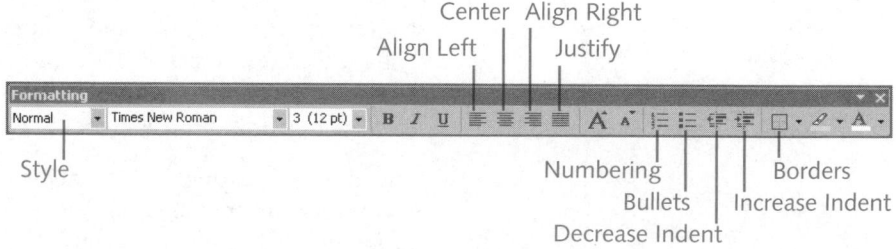

Figure 44-1. This labels the controls on the Formatting toolbar that can be used for formatting paragraphs.

Chapter 44: Formatting Your Web Pages

■ To change the paragraph style, choose an item in the Style drop-down list (other than Default Character Style), as shown here:

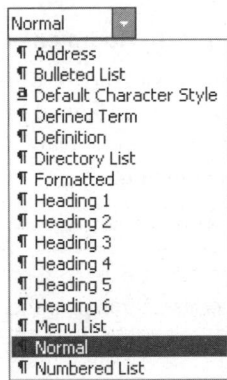

■ The best way to begin formatting a paragraph is to select the style from the Style drop-down list that most closely matches the function of the paragraph. For example, if the paragraph serves as body text, you should select the Normal style. (This style is applied by default to the text in a new, blank page.) Or, if the paragraph serves as a top-level heading, you should select the Heading 1 style. Applying a style converts the paragraph to the appropriate HTML element (see Table 44-1). Then, even if you apply no further paragraph or character formatting, the browser will display the paragraph using appropriate formatting features. (For instance, it might format a Heading 1 paragraph using a 24-point Times New Roman font, and a Normal paragraph using a 12-point Times New Roman font.)

Table 44-1. The Built-In FrontPage Styles

Built-In FrontPage Style	HTML Element(s) Applied to the Text	Description/Comment
Address	ADDRESS	For formatting a name, initials, an address, an author list, or other identifying information, typically at the bottom of a page.
Bulleted List	UL and LI	You can create a bulleted list by applying this style to each item. For greater control over the list's formatting, use the Bullets And Numbering dialog box, described later in this section.
Default Character Style	None	This style *doesn't* apply an HTML element. Rather, it is used to remove a custom character style as explained in "Modifying, Creating, and Using Cascading Style Sheet Styles," on page 1230.

(continued)

Table 44-1. *(continued)*

Built-In FrontPage Style	HTML Element(s) Applied to the Text	Description/Comment
Defined Term	DL and DT	To create a glossary or other list of term and description pairs, format each term using Defined Term and each following definition or description using Definition.
Definition	DL and DD	See the previous item.
Directory List	DIR and LI	For formatting a list of short items. Most browsers, however, treat this style the same as Bulleted List.
Formatted	PRE	Displays the text in a monospace font, preserving space characters and line breaks, without wrapping the lines. This style is often used to display program code.
Heading 1 through Heading 6	H1 through H6	For formatting top-level through level 6 headings.
Menu List	MENU and LI	For formatting a list of short menu items in a compact format. Most browsers, however, treat this style the same as Bulleted List.
Normal	P	For formatting a normal paragraph of body text.
Numbered List	OL and LI	You can create an automatically numbered list by applying this style to each item. For greater control control over the list's formatting, use the Bullets And Numbering dialog box, described later in this section.

note Formatting a paragraph by applying the appropriate style—rather than assigning individual paragraph and character formatting features—saves you time (you may not need to apply any further formatting), promotes formatting consistency throughout your document (for example, all headings with the Heading 1 style will look the same), and gives the browser greater latitude in applying formatting that's appropriate and that conforms to the user's preferences.

If you wish, you can then refine the formatting of the paragraph by applying specific paragraph or character formatting features, which will override the features of the style, using the techniques given in the remainder of this section and in the following sections. You can also refine the formatting of the paragraphs in your page by globally modifying the formatting of specific page elements or by creating and applying custom character or paragraph styles.

> Custom character and paragraph styles are explained in "Modifying, Creating, and Using Cascading Style Sheet Styles," on page 1230.

- To quickly convert the selected paragraphs to a bulleted or numbered list (or to remove existing bullets or numbers), click the Bullets or Numbering button. But for greater control over the list's formatting, use the Bullets And Numbering dialog box as described later in this section.

- To adjust the left indent of the selected paragraph, click the Increase Indent or Decrease Indent button. If you select an item within a bulleted or numbered list and click the Increase Indent button, the paragraph will be indented and will become a *nested* list item. Each click on Increase Indent will increase the level of nesting, and each click on Decrease Indent will decrease it. In a bulleted list, nested items will display different bullet characters, and in a numbered list, they will start a new numbering sequence. (After the first click, the bullet or number will disappear; it will reappear after subsequent clicks. So keep clicking!)

- To adjust the alignment of the selected paragraph or paragraphs, click the Align Left, Center, Align Right, or Justify button. If you click one of these buttons when it's already selected (displayed with a box around it), the alignment style will be removed and the paragraph will be assigned the Default alignment style, meaning that the browser will display it using the alignment style set in the browser.

- To quickly apply (or remove) one or more borders around the selected paragraph or paragraphs, or cell(s) in a table, click the down arrow on the Border button and choose a border style from the palette shown here:

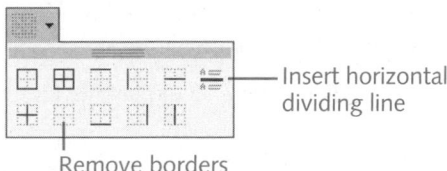

Insert horizontal dividing line

Remove borders

- To apply borders with more formatting options, or to apply a background color or picture, use the Borders And Shading dialog box, explained in "Applying Borders and Shading," on page 1204.

To modify the paragraph alignment, indentation, or spacing using the Paragraph dialog box, perform the following steps:

1 Select the paragraph or paragraphs you want to format. Or, to format a single paragraph, simply place the insertion point anywhere within it.

2 Choose Format, Paragraph or right-click the selection or paragraph you want to format and choose Paragraph from the shortcut menu. This will open the Paragraph dialog box (shown in Figure 44-2).

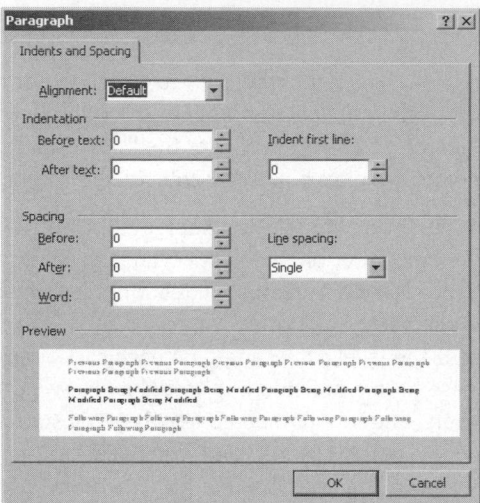

Figure 44-2. The Paragraph dialog box allows you to change the alignment, indentation, and spacing of a paragraph.

3 Select options in the dialog box until the sample paragraph in the Preview area has the look you want.

To convert paragraphs into a bulleted or numbered list using the Bullets And Numbering dialog box, perform the following steps:

1 Select the paragraphs containing the list items. (Or, to convert a single paragraph to a bulleted or numbered item, place the insertion point anywhere within it. When you press Enter at the end of a list paragraph, the next paragraph maintains the same list formatting.)

2 Choose Format, Bullets And Numbering to display the Bullets And Numbering dialog box.

3 Select options in the tabs of the Bullets And Numbering dialog box, as follows:

- To apply bullets consisting of an image from a graphics file, use the Picture Bullets tab (shown in Figure 44-3).

Chapter 44: Formatting Your Web Pages

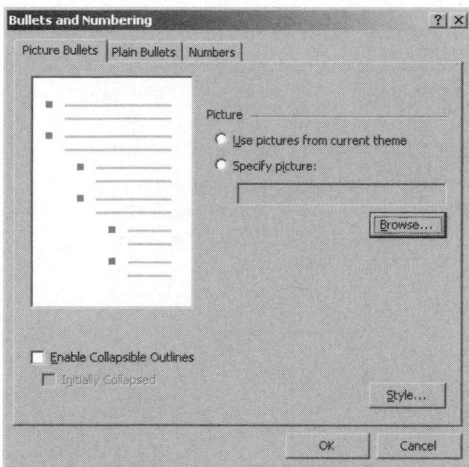

Figure 44-3. The Picture Bullets tab of the Bullets And Numbering dialog box allows you to apply bullets consisting of an image from a graphics file.

■ To apply one of the standard bullet styles that are built into browsers, use the Plain Bullets tab (shown in Figure 44-4).

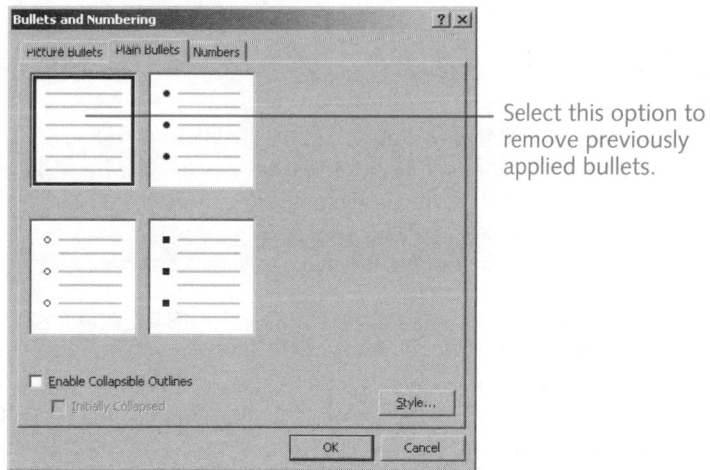

Select this option to remove previously applied bullets.

Figure 44-4. The Plain Bullets tab of the Bullets And Numbering dialog box is displayed only if the page has no theme.

note If a theme is applied to the current page, the Bullets And Numbering dialog box won't include the Plain Bullets tab, and you'll be able to apply only graphics bullets.

■ To create an automatically numbered list, use the Numbers tab to select a numbering style and to specify the starting number (as shown in
Figure 44-5).

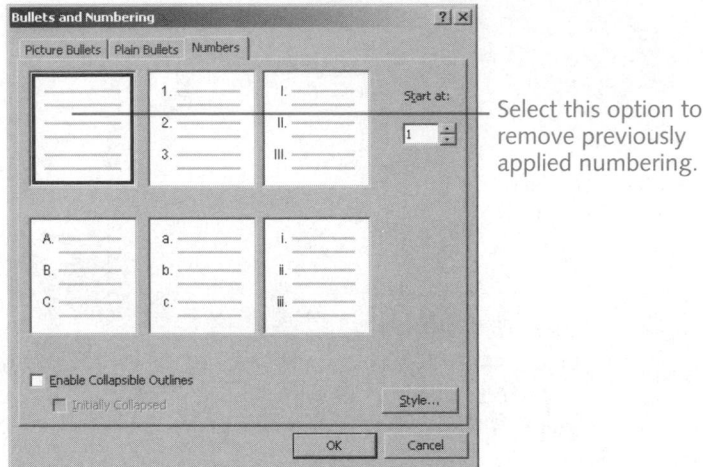

Select this option to
remove previously
applied numbering.

Figure 44-5.   The Numbers tab of the Bullets And Numbering dialog
box allows you to select a numbering style and a starting number.

newfeature!

note   As explained earlier in this section, you can use the Increase Indent and Decrease
Indent buttons on the Formatting toolbar to adjust the level of indentation of different list items, thereby converting a simple list into a multilevel outline. If you want the
page visitor to be able to collapse or expand the outline by clicking on it in a browser,
check the Enable Collapsible Outlines option in the Bullets And Numbering dialog box.
To start with a collapsed outline, also check the Initially Collapsed option.

To remove most of the formatting features discussed in this section that you've applied
to a paragraph, select the paragraph and choose Format, Remove Formatting or press
the Ctrl+Shift+Z or Ctrl+Spacebar shortcut key. The paragraph will revert to the Normal style, with no bullets or numbering, no indentation, the Default alignment style,
single line spacing with no extra spacing, and no shading. Keep in mind that this command will also remove character formatting. This command, however, won't remove
borders.

Applying Borders and Shading

You can emphasize one or more paragraphs or cells within a table by applying borders
or shading using the Borders And Shading dialog box. Perform the following steps:

1   Select the paragraph(s) or table cell(s). (To select a single table cell, place the
insertion point within it and choose Table, Select, Cell. If the entire cell isn't

Chapter 44: Formatting Your Web Pages

selected, you'll apply borders or shading to the paragraph within the cell, rather than to the cell itself.)

---

note If you select several paragraphs prior to applying borders, a single set of borders will be drawn around the entire group of paragraphs. To draw separate borders around each paragraph, select and apply borders to each paragraph individually, or use the Border button on the Formatting toolbar, described in the previous section, to apply all the borders at once.

---

2 Choose Format, Borders And Shading to open the Borders And Shading dialog box.

3 Select options in the tabs of the Borders And Shading dialog box until the sample paragraph in the Preview area has the look you want. (The Preview area on either tab shows the effects of the options selected on both tabs.) See Figures 44-6 and 44-7.

A foreground color you select on the Shading tab is applied to the text characters, while a background color fills the paragraph's background. Clicking the down arrow on the Background Color or Foreground Color control displays the same color palette shown by the Highlight and Font Color buttons on the Formatting toolbar.

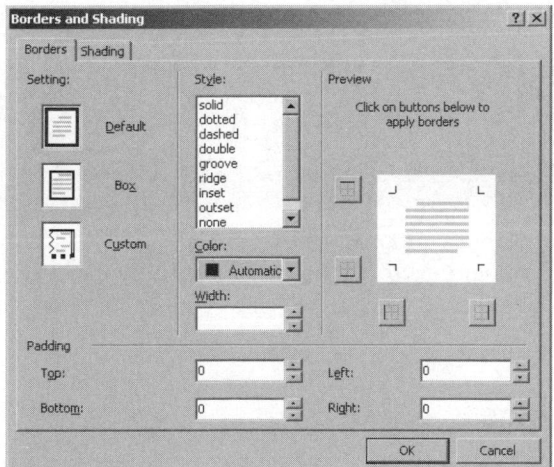

Figure 44-6. Apply borders using the Borders tab of the Borders And Shading dialog box.

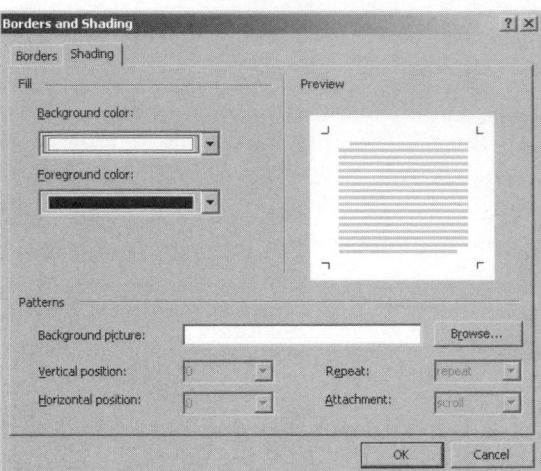

Figure 44-7. Apply shading using the Shading tab of the Borders And Shading dialog box.

> For more information on choosing a color from a color palette, see "Formatting Characters," on page 1210.

After you have applied a border or shading, you can adjust the size of the area enclosed by the border or shaded by clicking on the paragraph and then dragging one of the sizing handles that appear, as shown here:

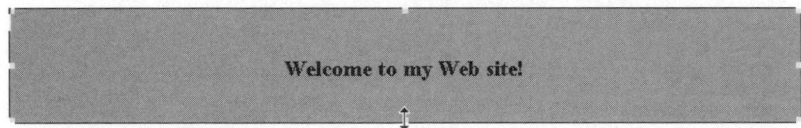

You can remove shading, but not borders, from a paragraph by selecting it and choosing Format, Remove Formatting, or pressing the Ctrl+Shift+Z or Ctrl+Spacebar shortcut key. Keep in mind that this command will also remove other paragraph as well as character formatting.

Positioning Paragraphs

Normally, all the text on a Web page is contained in a single stream of characters that flows from line to line and from paragraph to paragraph. In FrontPage, however, you can *position* a paragraph—that is, you can place it anywhere on the page, outside the normal flow of characters. A positioned paragraph can occupy the same area as a regular text paragraph or image, or as another positioned paragraph; and you can control the order in which the different elements overlap. Figure 44-8 shows a positioned paragraph used to create a margin note on a page.

Figure 44-8. You can use a positioned paragraph on a page to create a margin note.

The following is the fastest way to position a paragraph:

1 Choose View, Toolbars, Positioning to display the Positioning toolbar, shown here:

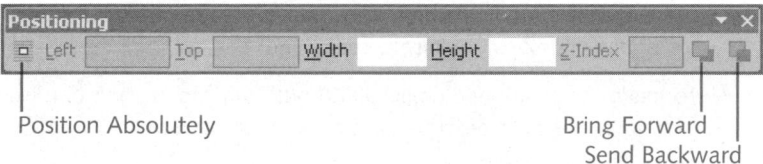

Position Absolutely   Bring Forward
                                       Send Backward

2 Place the insertion point anywhere within the paragraph you want to position.

3 Click the Position Absolutely button on the Positioning toolbar so that the button is selected. FrontPage will now draw sizing handles around the paragraph. (These handles will reappear whenever you click the paragraph.)

4 If you want to change the dimensions of the positioned paragraph, drag the appropriate sizing handle, as shown here:

Drag a sizing handle to change the dimensions of the positioned paragraph.

Alternatively, you can change the dimensions of the positioned paragraph by entering values into the Width and Height text boxes on the Positioning toolbar.

1207

5 If you want to move the positioned paragraph, make sure the paragraph is still selected so the sizing handles are visible, place the mouse pointer over one of the edges of the paragraph area, and when the pointer turns into a four-headed arrow, drag the paragraph to the desired location on the page, as shown here:

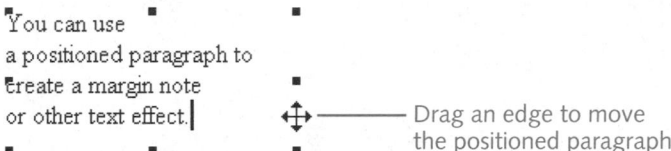

Drag an edge to move the positioned paragraph.

Alternatively, you can assign the positioned paragraph a precise position by typing the coordinates of the position into the Left and Top text boxes on the Positioning toolbar.

6 If you want to change the overlapping order for the positioned paragraph, click the Bring Forward or Send Backward button on the Positioning toolbar.

Alternatively, you can set the overlapping order by typing a value into the Z-Index text box on the Positioning toolbar. A positioned paragraph that has a higher index will be displayed on top of any positioned paragraph that has a lower index. And a positioned paragraph that has an index greater than or equal to 0 will be displayed on top of nonpositioned text, while one that has a negative index will be displayed behind nonpositioned text.

7 To make the positioned object stand out, you can apply a border or background shading, as described in the previous section.

---

newfeature!

tip **Position Text Using a Text Box**

You can also use a *text box* to position text, to draw a border around the text, to add shading, or to apply a wrapping or positioning style. Add a text box by clicking the Text Box button on the Drawing toolbar and then clicking on the position within the page where you want to insert the text box. Set a text box's properties by clicking on it and choosing Format, Text Box. For details on working with text boxes, see "Using Text Boxes to Create Precise Page Layouts," on page 510.

Creating Dynamic HTML Effects

You can use the DHTML Effects toolbar to animate a paragraph. The animation is known as a *dynamic HTML effect*, and it can consist of the paragraph's "flying" off the page in a particular direction, an instant change in the paragraph's format (the font, border, or shading), or another effect. You can have the animation occur when the page is first loaded into a browser, when you click the paragraph, when you double-click it, or when you place the mouse pointer over it.

> **note** Dynamic HTML effects won't work unless the browser used to view the page supports DHTML (dynamic HTML). Also, FrontPage won't let you add DHTML effects unless the Dynamic HTML option is checked. To access this option, choose Tools, Page Options and click the Compatibility tab in the Page Options dialog box. See the tip "Ensure Compatibility" and Figure 43-15 on page 1195.

To animate a paragraph, perform the following steps:

1 Display the DHTML Effects toolbar, shown here, by choosing View, Toolbars, DHTML Effects or by choosing Format, Dynamic HTML Effects.

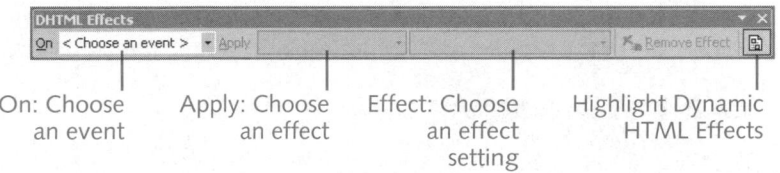

On: Choose   Apply: Choose   Effect: Choose   Highlight Dynamic
an event   an effect   an effect   HTML Effects
                                      setting

2 Place the insertion point anywhere within the paragraph you want to animate (or select several paragraphs).

3 To specify when the animation occurs, select an item in the On drop-down list on the DHTML Effects toolbar: Click, Double Click, Mouse Over, or Page Load.

4 To specify the general type of animation that occurs, select an item in the Apply drop-down list: Fly Out (to have the paragraph "fly" off the page) or Formatting (to have the formatting change). If you selected Mouse Over in step 3, only Formatting is available. If you selected Page Load, a variety of additional effects are available (Drop In By Word, Elastic, Fly In, and others).

5 To further specify the type of animation that occurs, select an item in the Effect drop-down list. The available items depend on your previous choices. For example, if you selected Fly Out in the Choose An Effect drop-down list, you can select To Left, To Top, To Bottom-Left, or another value, to specify the direction of the animation.

If the Highlight Dynamic HTML Effects button is selected on the DHTML Effects toolbar, any paragraph that has been assigned an effect will be highlighted in Page view (but not in the Preview pane or in a browser). You can test an effect by clicking the Preview button at the bottom of the Page view window to switch to the Preview pane, or by displaying the page in a browser. (The animation won't be displayed in Page view.) If you want to remove an effect from a paragraph, click the paragraph, and then click the Remove Effect button.

Formatting Characters

You can apply character formatting to change the appearance of one or more individual characters within your page. To format characters, either select a block of existing characters or place the insertion point at the position where you want to insert new characters. Then, choose either Format, Font or Format, Properties, or press Alt+Enter. (As a general rule, choosing the Properties command displays the properties dialog box for the currently selected element. If you have selected a block of characters, it will display the properties dialog box for characters, which is labeled Font.) Or, you can right-click the selected characters or insertion position and choose Font from the shortcut menu. FrontPage will then display the Font dialog box, shown in Figures 44-9 and 44-10. Select options in the Font and Character Spacing tabs of this dialog box until the text sample in the Preview area has the look you want, and then click the OK button.

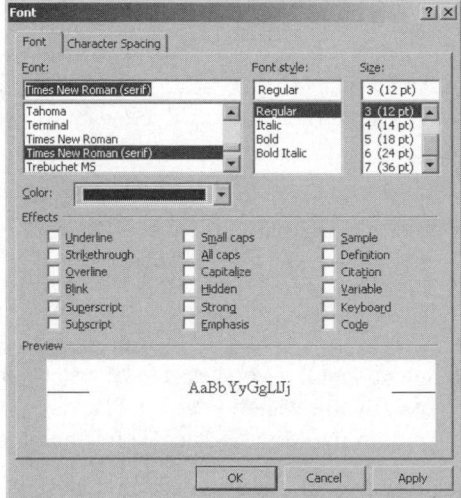

Figure 44-9. The Font tab of the Font dialog box is used to set the text font, style, size, color, and effects.

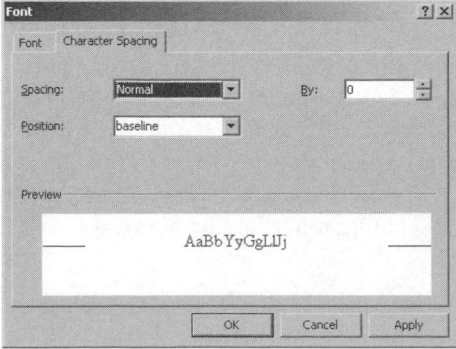

Figure 44-10. The Character Spacing tab of the Font dialog box is used to set the text spacing and position.

You can also quickly apply some of the available character formats to the selected text—or to the characters you will type at the current position of the insertion point—by using the Formatting toolbar shown here:

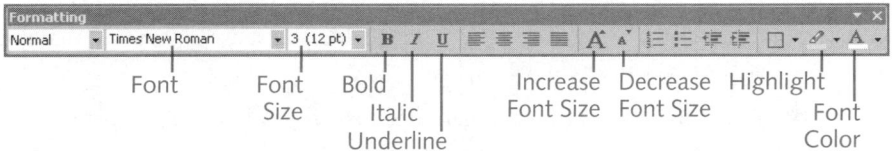

The buttons not labeled in this graphic are used for formatting paragraphs or tables, and are explained in "Formatting Paragraphs," on page 1198.

The Font Color button (as well as the Color drop-down list in the Font dialog box) sets the color of the text characters themselves, while the Highlight button sets the color of the background surrounding the characters. To apply a specific text or background color, click the Font Color button (or the equivalent Color drop-down list in the Font dialog box) or the Highlight button to display the color palette shown here:

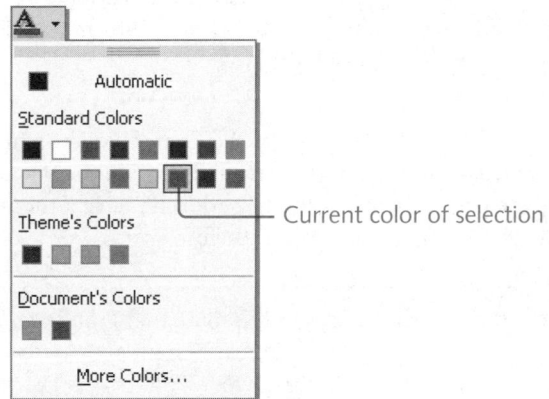

Current color of selection

Then, select an item on the palette as follows:

● To display the text using the default color defined by the theme, choose Automatic. If the page doesn't have a theme, this option will display the text using the text or background color defined in the Background tab of the Page Properties dialog box for the page.

The Background tab of the Page Properties dialog box is explained in "Modifying Page Properties," on page 1224.

● To apply a commonly used color, select a color in the Standard Colors area.

● To apply one of the colors defined by the page's theme, select a color in the Theme's Colors area (which appears only if the page has a theme). Using one of these colors instead of selecting a new one can help ensure that your text blends with the theme's overall color scheme.

- If you've previously applied specific colors to elements in the current page, you can reapply one of these colors by choosing a color in the Document's Colors area. This area of the palette helps you reuse colors and maintain a consistent color scheme.

- To choose from a much larger selection of standard colors, or to define a custom color, choose More Colors.

To reapply the previously applied text or background color, you can just click the Font Color or Highlight button rather than opening the palette.

tip **Match a Color**

If you see a color you like anywhere on your screen (perhaps in a Web page that you've opened in your browser), you can apply that exact color to an element in FrontPage by clicking the More Colors option on the color palette (for example, on the palette displayed by the Font Color or Highlight button on the Formatting toolbar). Then, in the More Colors dialog box, click the Select button and then click the color you want to use wherever it's displayed on your screen.

If you select the (Default Font) item in the Font list of the Font dialog box or in the Font drop-down list on the Formatting toolbar, the selected text will be displayed using the default font specified by the page's theme. If the page doesn't have a theme, then each browser will display the text using the font set in the browser.

note For a page that doesn't have a theme, you can select the fonts that FrontPage uses to display all text assigned the (Default Font) formatting. To select FrontPage's fonts, choose Tools, Page Options and click the Default Font tab (shown in Figure 44-11). You can then select a font for proportional text and one for fixed-width text. You can also choose fonts for each language that FrontPage displays. Keep in mind that your choices affect only the way the page appears in Page view, not the way it's displayed in a browser.

Also, if you select the Normal item in the Size list of the Font dialog box or in the Font Size drop-down list on the Formatting toolbar, the browser will display the text using the font size set in the browser for the style assigned to the paragraph containing the text. The font size for the Normal paragraph style (a P HTML element) is typically 12 points, and the font size for the Heading 1 paragraph style (an H1 element) is typically 24 points. (The exact size depends on the particular browser and the settings made in that browser.)

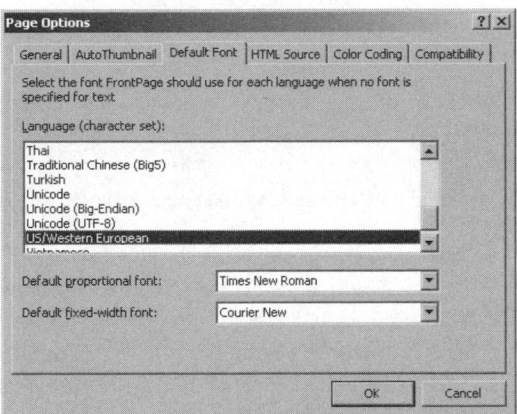

Figure 44-11. The Default Font tab of the Page Options dialog box allows you to select default fonts that FrontPage uses for displaying text.

Paragraph styles are discussed in "Formatting Paragraphs," on page 1198.

To remove any character formatting that has been applied to a block of text (by you or by the template used to create the page), select the characters and choose Format, Remove Formatting or press the Ctrl+Shift+Z or Ctrl+Spacebar shortcut key. The character format will revert to the (Default Font) font, the Regular font style, the Normal size, and the Automatic font and highlight colors, and any effects will be removed. Keep in mind that this command will also remove most types of paragraph formatting.

You can also format characters by defining and applying user-defined character styles, as explained in "Modifying, Creating, and Using Cascading Style Sheet Styles," on page 1230.

Troubleshooting

Kerning Isn't Available

You would like apply kerning to your characters as you can in Microsoft Word, but the feature isn't available in FrontPage.

Although FrontPage won't automatically kern your text, you can manually kern a specific letter pair (such as *Ta*) by selecting the characters and choosing Format, Font. Then, click the Character Spacing tab, select Condensed in the Spacing drop-down list, and in the By box enter the amount (in points) by which you want the intercharacter spacing to be reduced.

Formatting Images

The following sections describe how to modify images using the Picture Properties dialog box and the Pictures toolbar.

> "Inserting Images," on page 1179, explains how to insert an image in a page and how to convert an image element to a thumbnail image.

The first step is always to select the image, which you do by clicking it. FrontPage will display a set of sizing handles around the selected image. (You can also select an image by selecting one or more adjoining text characters and extending the selection highlight across the image. In this case, FrontPage will reverse the image colors rather than displaying sizing handles. However, using this method for selecting an image won't let you perform many of the formatting operations discussed in the next two sections.)

Modifying Image Properties

To modify an image's properties, perform the following steps.

1 Click the image to select it.

2 Choose Format, Properties; press Alt+Enter; or right-click the image and choose Picture Properties from the shortcut menu. This will open the Picture Properties dialog box.

3 To modify the size and position of the image, set options as follows in the Appearance tab (shown in Figure 44-12):

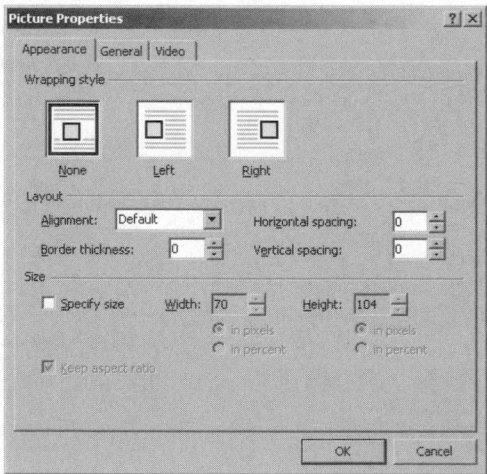

Figure 44-12. You can modify the size and position of an image in the Appearance tab of the Picture Properties dialog box.

- To change the displayed size of the image from its original size specified in the image file, check the Specify Size option and enter the size and size options using the controls in the Size area.

   Changing the size here *scales* the image—that is, it makes everything in the image larger or smaller. In the next section, you'll learn how to reduce the overall dimensions of an image by cropping it, which discards parts of the image rather than making all parts of the image smaller. You can also quickly scale an image by clicking it and dragging a sizing handle; if you drag a corner handle, the image proportions will be preserved. To restore an image to its original size, just clear the Specify Size option in the Appearance tab.

---

tip   Resample a Reduced Image

When you reduce the size of an image in the Picture Properties dialog box, you reduce its *displayed* size, but not the size of the image file. (The file still stores the complete data for the full image.) To reduce the size of the file to match the displayed image size, you can *resample* the image using the Resample button on the Pictures toolbar, described in "Enhancing Images Using the Pictures Toolbar," on page 1217. Resampling will produce an image file that is smaller and faster to download. However, because graphic data is permanently removed from the file, you won't be able to scale the image back to its original size without loss of image quality. (For this reason, before you resample an image, it's a good idea to make a backup copy of the image file.)

- To adjust the alignment of the image with respect to the adjoining text, select an option in the Alignment drop-down list. If you select the Left or the Right alignment option—or if you select the Left or Right wrapping style, which has the same effect—the image will be aligned with the left or right page margin, and the adjoining lines of text will wrap around the image. If you select any of the other alignment options, the image will be placed within a line of text and will be treated like a single text character; the particular option you select will affect the vertical alignment of the image with respect to the line of text that contains it. (The Default option is the same as Baseline.) The next section explains how to position an image anywhere on a page rather than aligning it with text.

- To display a border around the image, enter a thickness greater than 0 into the Border Thickness text box.

- To adjust the spacing between the image and the surrounding elements, enter a value into the Horizontal Spacing or Vertical Spacing text box.

Part 7: FrontPage

4 To change other image settings, use the General tab (shown in Figure 44-13) as follows:

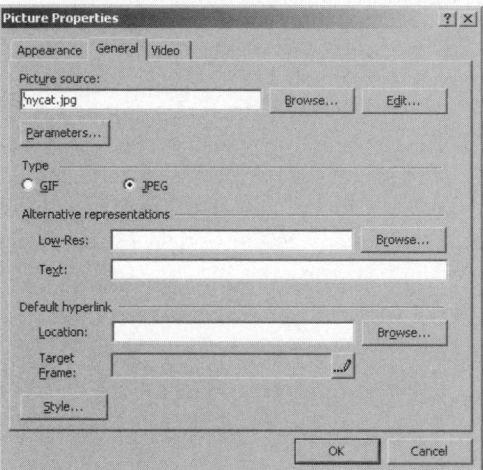

Figure 44-13. The General tab of the Picture Properties dialog box allows you to change other image settings.

■ To change the image file, type a new file path into the Picture Source text box or click the Browse button to select the file.

■ If you've installed an image editor and have configured FrontPage to use that editor, you can click the Edit button to edit the image.

> For information on configuring FrontPage to use a specific graphics editor that you have installed for editing a particular type of graphics file, see the tip "Configure FrontPage Editors," on page 1136.

■ To change the image format, select either the GIF or JPEG option.

■ To specify the location of a low-resolution version of the image file, which the browser can quickly download and display while the full image file is downloading, enter the file path into the Low-Res text box or click the Browse button to select the file. (In FrontPage, you can create a low-resolution version of an image file by using either the Auto Thumbnail feature or the Resample command, both described later in this chapter.)

■ To specify alternative text, type it into the Text text box. Some browsers will display this text while the image file is downloading, when the pointer is held over the image (the text will appear in a ScreenTip), or if images are disabled in the browser.

■ To assign a hyperlink to the image, use the controls in the Default Hyperlink area.

Chapter 44: Formatting Your Web Pages

> For information on assigning hyperlinks to an image, see "Working with Image Maps," on page 1221. Use the Video tab for formatting video clips, as explained in "Modifying a Video Clip," on page 1221.

> **tip** **Use the Formatting Toolbar to Align an Image Quickly**
>
> You can assign the selected image the Left or Right alignment style by clicking the Align Left or Align Right button on the Formatting toolbar. (When an image is selected, these two buttons don't have their usual effect of aligning a paragraph. The Center button, however, will affect the paragraph alignment, as usual.)

Enhancing Images Using the Pictures Toolbar

The Pictures toolbar lets you modify an image in a variety of unique ways not available through other FrontPage commands. To use this toolbar, first click the image to select it. If the Pictures toolbar doesn't appear automatically, choose View, Toolbars, Pictures to display it. The toolbar is shown in Figure 44-14, and its buttons are described in Table 44-2.

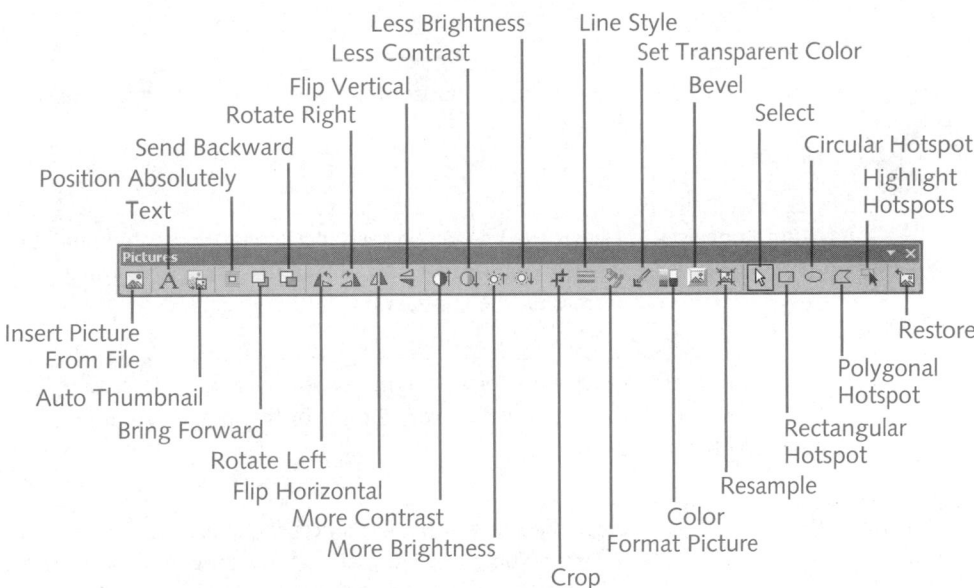

Figure 44-14. The Pictures toolbar provides many tools for working with images.

Table 44-2. **The Buttons on the Pictures Toolbar**

Button	Button Name	Description
	Insert Picture From File	Displays the Picture dialog box for inserting an image. (See "Inserting Images," on page 1179.)
A	Text	Adds a text label to the image. If you want, you can assign a hyperlink to a text label so that it functions as a hotspot.
	Auto Thumbnail	Converts the image to a thumbnail image. See "Creating a Thumbnail Image," on page 1181.
	Position Absolutely	Position Absolutely converts the image to a positioned image that you can move anywhere on the page.
	Bring Forward	Bring Forward and Send Backward change the overlapping order for a positioned image. A positioned image works just like a positioned paragraph. For details, see "Positioning Paragraphs," on page 1206.
	Send Backward	
	Rotate Left	Rotates the image counterclockwise or clockwise by 90 degrees.
	Rotate Right	
	Flip Horizontal	Flips the image horizontally or vertically, creating a mirror image.
	Flip Vertical	
	More Contrast	Adjusts the image contrast. Increasing the contrast makes the dark parts darker and the light parts lighter, while decreasing the contrast does the opposite.
	Less Contrast	
	More Brightness	Adjusts the image brightness. Increasing or decreasing the brightness makes all parts of the image lighter or darker.
	Less Brightness	
	Crop	Crops the image—that is, reduces the overall dimensions of the image by discarding parts of the image (in contrast to scaling the image to make it smaller, as discussed in the previous section). See the next section, "Cropping an Image."
	Line Style	Lets you change the style of the lines used to draw an AutoShape or the border around a text box. (This button isn't available for an image.)

Table 44-2. *(continued)*

Button	Button Name	Description
	Format Picture	Opens the Format dialog box for formatting an AutoShape, text box, or WordArt object. (This button isn't available for an image.)
	Set Transparent Color	Makes one of the colors in an image transparent, so that the page background colors show through wherever the image has the transparent color. See "Controlling Transparency," on page 1220.
	Color	Converts the color format of the image to Automatic, Grayscale, Black & White, or Wash Out.
	Bevel	Creates a beveled effect around the edges of the image to give it a three-dimensional look.
	Resample	Rewrites the image file based on the current displayed size of the image. When you *scale* an image (not crop it), its displayed size becomes different from the size defined in the image file. Resampling makes both sizes the same. If you've scaled an image down, resampling will make the image file smaller and faster to download and display.
	Select	When this button is enabled, you can click a hotspot to select it, and then you can use the mouse to resize or move the hotspot, or press Delete to delete it. (See "Working with Image Maps," on page 1221.)
	Rectangular Hotspot Circular Hotspot Polygonal Hotspot	Draws a rectangular, circular, or polygonal hotspot within the image. After you've drawn the hotspot, the Create Hyperlink dialog box will appear, where you can enter the hyperlink target. You can later edit the hyperlink by selecting the Select button and double-clicking the hotspot. (See "Working with Image Maps," on page 1221.)
	Highlight Hotspots	Displays the hotspots only, without the image, making it easier to locate hotspots within a busy image. (See Working with Image Maps," on page 1221.)
	Restore	Reverses any scaling you have done, or any changes you have made to the image using the Pictures toolbar since the image was inserted or last saved.

Chapter 44

Cropping an Image

To crop an image, perform the following steps:

1 Click the image to select it.

2 Click the Crop button on the Pictures toolbar (see Figure 44-14). FrontPage will then display cropping borders and handles on the image, as shown here:

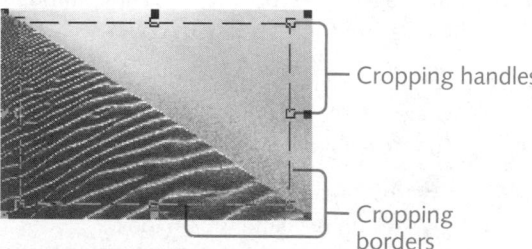

Cropping handles

Cropping borders

3 Drag one or more of the cropping handles to define the new image size.

4 Click the Crop button again or press Enter.

Note that you can't restore the discarded parts of a cropped image after you save the page. (Before you save the page, you can restore it by clicking the Restore button on the Pictures toolbar, as described in Table 44-2.) Therefore, before cropping, you might want to make a backup copy of the image.

Controlling Transparency

You can make a color in an image transparent by clicking the Set Transparent Color button on the Pictures toolbar (see Figure 44-14) and then clicking that color within the image. To make an image nontransparent and restore the transparent color to its original value, click the Set Transparent Color button and then click the color again. (Or click the Restore button on the Pictures toolbar to reverse *all* formatting changes you made since you inserted the image or last saved the page.)

---

tip Modify a Background Image

If the page doesn't have a theme and if you assigned it a background image (as discussed in "Modifying Page Properties," on page 1224), you can modify the background image by using one of the following buttons on the Pictures toolbar when no image is selected: Rotate Left, Rotate Right, Flip Horizontal, Flip Vertical, More Contrast, Less Contrast, More Brightness, Less Brightness, Color, Bevel, or Restore.

Working with Image Maps

As you can see in Figure 44-14 and Table 44-2, the Pictures toolbar includes a set of buttons that let you create and work with *image maps*: Select, Rectangular Hotspot, Circular Hotspot, Polygonal Hotspot, and Highlight Hotspots. An image map is an image that contains *hotspots*. A hotspot is a rectangular, circular, or polygonal area that is assigned a hyperlink. When you click a hotspot within the image, the browser opens the hyperlink target. An image map is commonly used as a graphical alternative to a set of text hyperlinks. For example, a Web page giving instructions on using a computer program could display an image of the program window with hotspots on various window features (menus, buttons, the status bar, and so on). Clicking a hotspot could display a page that describes the feature.

A hotspot is invisible in the browser. However, the mouse pointer changes—typically to a hand—when it's moved over a hotspot. You can define a hotspot by using the Rectangular Hotspot, Circular Hotspot, or Polygonal Hotspot button. The Polygonal Hotspot button is especially useful for creating a hotspot covering an irregular-shaped area of the image. Instructions on using these buttons are given in Table 44-2.

In an image map, you can also assign a *default* hyperlink to the entire image (as you can with an image that isn't an image map), using the standard techniques used to assign a hyperlink to text or other elements. Or you can assign a default hyperlink in the Default Hyperlink area in the General tab of the Picture Properties dialog box. A default hyperlink is activated by clicking anywhere within the image outside of a hotspot.

> Standard techniques for assigning hyperlinks are explained in "Including Internal and External Hyperlinks," on page 1184. The General tab of the Picture Properties dialog box is described in "Modifying Image Properties," on page 1214 and shown in Figure 44-13.

Modifying a Video Clip

"Inserting a Video Clip," on page 1183, explained how to add a video clip to a page, either from a video file or from the Clip Organizer. After you have inserted a video clip, you can modify its appearance and behavior using the Image Properties dialog box.

To modify a video clip, perform the following steps:

1 Select the video clip by clicking it and then choose Format, Properties or press Alt+Enter. Or, right-click the clip and choose Picture Properties from the shortcut menu. This will open the Video tab of the Picture Properties dialog box (shown in Figure 44-15).

Part 7: FrontPage

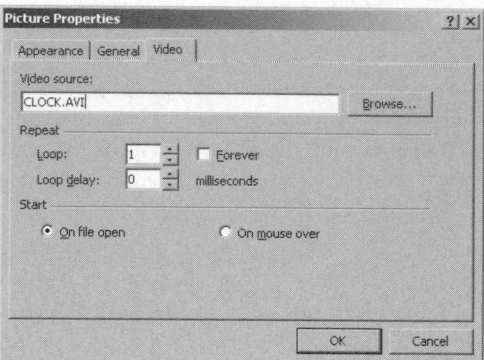

Figure 44-15. You can modify video clip settings using the Video tab of the Picture Properties dialog box.

2 Enter settings into the Video tab, as follows:

■ To display a different video file or to repair the reference to the current file, type the file path into the Video Source text box or click the Browse button to select the video file.

■ To specify *when* the video is played, select On File Open or On Mouse Over.

■ To specify *how many times* the video plays once it starts, use the controls in the Repeat area. Enter the desired pause, in milliseconds, between each repetition in the Loop Delay text box.

3 You can set any of the options in the General or Appearance tab of the Picture Properties dialog box. Note, however, that entering a source file or selecting a Type option (GIF or JPEG) on the General tab will have no effect on a video clip.

The General and Appearance tabs of the Picture Properties dialog box are explained in "Modifying Image Properties," on page 1214.

Another way to scale a video clip is by dragging a sizing handle, as explained for an image in "Modifying Image Properties," on page 1214.

You can also position a video clip by using the Position Absolutely, Bring Forward, and Send Backward buttons on the Pictures toolbar. The buttons are shown in Figure 44-14, on page 1217, and explained in Table 44-2, on page 1218.

Formatting Other Page Elements

You can format several additional types of page elements by opening the properties dialog box for the element. To open the properties dialog box for any of the elements mentioned in this section, click the element to select it and choose Format, Properties or press Alt+Enter. Or, you can right-click the element and choose *X* Properties from the shortcut menu, where *X* is a description of the element (for example, Horizontal Line, Form Field, Link Bar, or ActiveX Control).

You can format a horizontal dividing line in the Horizontal Line Properties dialog box, shown here:

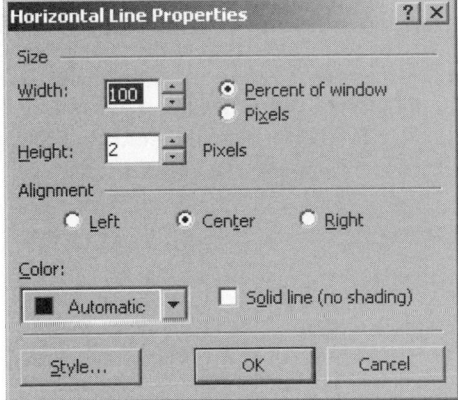

Note, however, that if the page is assigned a theme, you can modify only the horizontal alignment of the line (within the browser window) by selecting an option in the Alignment area, or the line's style by clicking the Style button.

You can also modify the properties of any of the following types of page elements, which are discussed in Chapter 45, "Adding Advanced Features to Your Web Pages:"

- Form fields, such as text boxes, check boxes, and push buttons.
- Web components, such as link bars, page banners, and hit counters.
- Advanced elements, such as Java applets, plug-ins, and ActiveX controls.

Form fields are discussed in detail in "Creating Interactive Forms to Collect Information," on page 1235. A general explanation of Web components is given in "Adding Dynamic Content with Web Components," on page 1246. Advanced elements are described in "Inserting Advanced Controls," on page 1250.

Formatting the Whole Page

In the following sections, you'll learn various ways to modify the appearance, behavior, and other characteristics of the entire page. All these changes affect the active page— that is, the one currently displayed in Page view.

Modifying Page Properties

To modify the properties of the active page displayed in Page view, do the following:

1 Make sure you're viewing the page in the Normal pane (not in the HTML or Preview pane) and choose File, Properties or right-click anywhere on the page and choose Page Properties from the shortcut menu. This will display the Page Properties dialog box.

2 To change the page's title, to modify the effect of clicking hyperlinks in the page, to add a background sound, or to make other changes, use the General tab (see Figure 44-16).

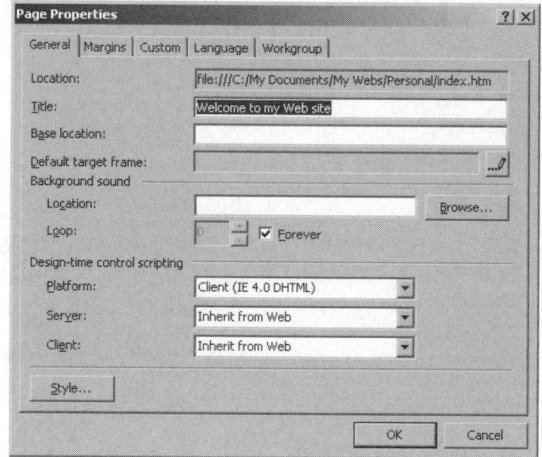

Figure 44-16. The General tab of the Page Properties dialog box allows you to add a background sound or to modify a page's title, hyperlinks, and other features.

3 To add a background picture to the page, to specify a solid background color, or to define text colors, use the Background tab (shown in Figure 44-17), taking note of the following points:

Chapter 44: Formatting Your Web Pages

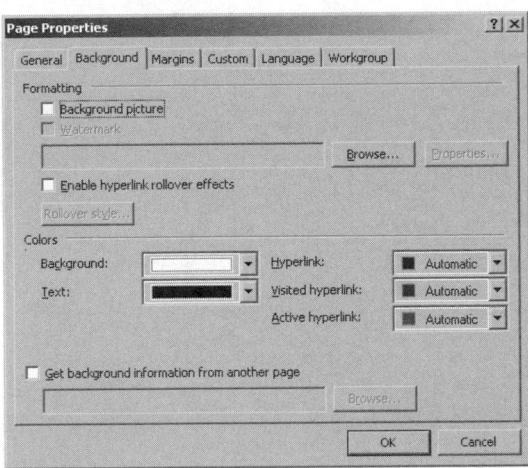

Figure 44-17. The Background tab of the Page Properties dialog box is available only if the page has no theme.

- The Background tab is displayed *only* if the page doesn't have a theme. If there's no theme, you can also open the Background tab by choosing Format, Background. (For a page with a theme, the Background tab isn't displayed because the properties set in this tab are defined by the theme and cannot be overridden.)

- For a page without a theme, the color selected in the Text drop-down list in the Background tab is applied to all text in the page that is assigned the Automatic text color. And if the Automatic color is selected in the Text list, each browser will display text with the Automatic color using the text color set in the browser.

- The hyperlink colors selected in the Background tab are applied to all hyperlinks on the page when it's viewed in a browser. The browser assigns the Hyperlink color to a hyperlink whose target hasn't yet been opened. It assigns the Visited Hyperlink color to a hyperlink whose target has already been opened, and it assigns the Active Hyperlink color to a hyperlink that is selected. (In Microsoft Internet Explorer, you can select a hyperlink by pressing the Tab key; it will then be marked with a dotted outline and you can open its target by pressing Enter.) Selecting the Automatic color value causes the browser to use the hyperlink color set in the browser.

4 To add a top or left margin to the page, use the Margins tab (shown in Figure 44-18).

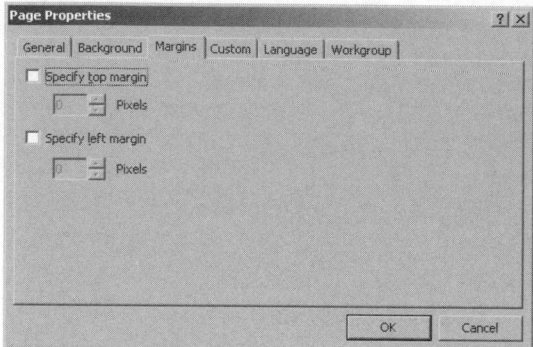

Figure 44-18. Use the Margins tab of the Page Properties dialog box to add a top or left margin to a page.

> **note** The top and left margins that you specify in the Margins tab are added to the outside of the top and left shared borders if they are displayed on the page. (The browser generates the margins in response to instructions inserted into the HTML file, while FrontPage generates shared borders using tables.)

5 To add custom information to the page's header (its HEAD element), use the Custom tab. Adding information to the header can be useful, for example, to list key words that Web search engines can use to index the page.

6 To set the page language and HTML encoding, use the Language tab.

7 To assign one or more categories or a review status to the page, to assign the page to a person in your workgroup, or to exclude the page when you publish the web, use the Workgroup tab.

> For information on categories and other workgroup features, see the "Workflow" category in Table 42-3, on page 1153.

Using Themes to Quickly Change the Overall Page Format

Applying a theme to a Web page assigns a set of consistent formatting features to all elements in that page, and applying the same theme to all pages in a web gives the entire web a consistent look.

FrontPage supplies more than 60 different themes. The following are just a few examples:

● Blueprint, which applies an architectural drawing motif

● Nature, for a bucolic look

● Topo, which makes your web resemble a topographical map

A theme affects the following characteristics of a web page:

- The page background color or image.

- The colors and fonts used for text with various paragraph styles (Normal and Heading 1 through Heading 6). The color or font is used only if the text is assigned the Automatic color setting or the (Default Font) font setting.

- The colors of text hyperlinks (regular, visited, and active).

- The images used for the bullets in bulleted lists.

- The image used for horizontal dividing lines.

- The text color, text font, and images used in page banners and link bars.

- The color of borders in tables.

> **note** Applying a theme to a page is the only way to format certain FrontPage components, such as page banners and link bars. Without a theme, these elements are displayed in plain text, and you have no way to enhance their appearance.

Every web has default theme settings: It is assigned either a specific theme or no theme. Also, a page within a web can have individual theme settings (a particular theme or no theme). The default theme settings are applied only to those pages in the web that don't have individual theme settings.

With most of the templates or wizards you can use to create a web (for example, the Personal Web template or the Corporate Presence Wizard), your new web is assigned a default theme that is applied to all pages. (Initially, none of the pages has individual theme settings.) You can later change the default theme settings—removing the theme, applying a new one, or changing the theme options—and you can assign individual theme settings to one or more of the pages in the web.

To change the default theme settings for the current web, perform the following steps:

1 Choose Format, Theme to open the Themes dialog box (shown in Figure 44-19). You can be in any FrontPage view when you do this.

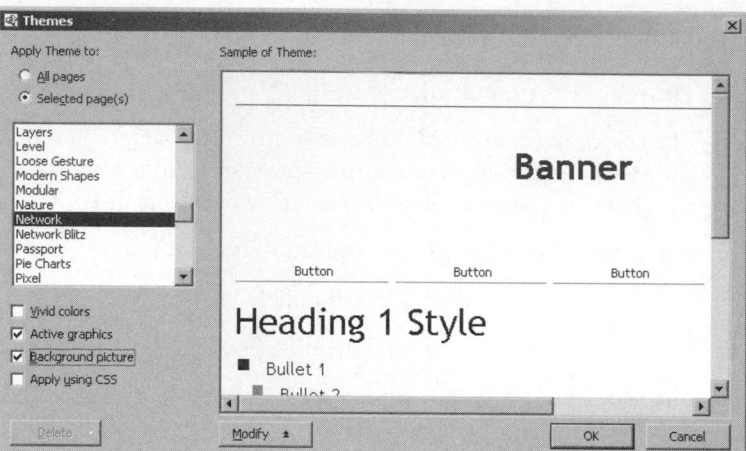

Figure 44-19. The Themes dialog box allows you to work with themes.

2 Select the All Pages option.

> **note** The All Pages option applies the theme settings to all pages that don't have individual theme settings, not necessarily to all pages in the web.

3 Select a theme in the list—or select (No Theme) to remove the theme—and check the theme options you want. The look of the selected theme, as well as the effects of the options you've checked, are shown in the Sample Of Theme area.

> **tip** **Create a Custom Theme**
>
> If none of the themes supplied with Microsoft Office XP precisely matches your needs or your sense of aesthetics, you can create a custom theme. To do this, in the Themes dialog box, select the theme that is the closest to the one you want to create and click the Modify button. A new set of buttons will appear, allowing you to customize various aspects of the selected theme and to save the modified theme under a new name. Your custom theme will then be displayed in the list of themes, and you can assign it to the current web or to other webs or web pages.

To assign individual theme settings to one or more pages in your web, perform the following steps:

1 Open the page in Page view, or select one or more pages in any FrontPage view that lists filenames (Folders, Reports, Navigation, or Hyperlinks) or in the Folder List.

2 Choose Format, Theme to open the Themes dialog box.

3 In the Themes dialog box, select the Selected Page(s) option.

4 Select a theme in the list—or select (No Theme) to remove the theme—and check the theme options you want. The look of the selected theme, as well as the effects of the options you've checked, are shown in the Sample Of Theme area.

Applying Dynamic Page Transition Effects

A final formatting touch is to add one or more *transition effects* to a page. A transition effect is an animated action that occurs when the page is either opened or closed in a browser.

> **note** Page transition effects won't work unless the browser used to view the page supports DHTML (dynamic HTML). Also, FrontPage won't let you add page transition effects unless the Dynamic HTML option is checked. To access this option, choose Tools, Page Options and click the Compatibility tab in the Page Options dialog box. See the tip "Ensure Compatibility" and Figure 43-15 on page 1195.

To add transition effects to the active page in FrontPage, perform the following steps:

1 Choose Format, Page Transition to open the Page Transitions dialog box (shown in Figure 44-20).

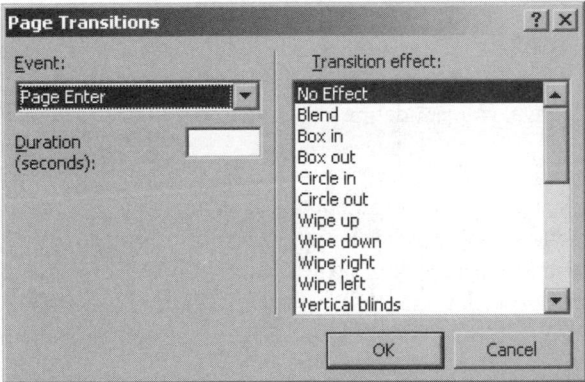

Figure 44-20. The Page Transitions dialog box lets you apply various page transition effects.

2 You can define up to four transition effects. To define each one, select an event in the Event drop-down list (see later descriptions), enter an effect duration in seconds into the Duration text box (see the following Note), and in the Transition Effect list select the effect you want to take place when the event occurs.

> **note** If you don't enter a value into the Duration text box, the effect duration will default to 1 second.

You can select any of the following events in the Event drop-down list:

- Page Enter, to have the effect occur when the user navigates *to* the page from any other page

- Page Exit, to have the effect occur when the user navigates *away from* the page to any other page

- Site Enter, to have the effect occur when the user navigates to the page from a page at a different Web site

- Site Exit, to have the effect occur when the user navigates away from the page to a page at a different Web site

To preview the transition effects you assigned to the page, open the page in a browser (for example, by choosing File, Preview In Browser), and then navigate back and forth between that page and another page or site. (It's normally difficult to navigate back and forth in the Preview pane in Page view because the pane doesn't provide navigation commands.)

Modifying, Creating, and Using Cascading Style Sheet Styles

This section gives a brief introduction to cascading style sheet (CSS) styles, which provide the ultimate tool for precisely formatting the elements in one or more pages in your web. In FrontPage, you can define CSS style settings at the following three levels:

- **Inline**   An inline CSS style setting is applied to an individual page element, such as a paragraph, heading, table, or image. FrontPage will use an inline CSS style setting when you apply certain formats to an element. For example, if you assign a block of text the Small Caps character style or if you assign a paragraph a left margin, FrontPage will implement the format by applying an inline CSS style setting to the block of text or to the paragraph.

> **note** An inline CSS style setting is added directly to the element's start-tag. For example, if you assign a paragraph a left indent of 10, FrontPage will generate the following start-tag for that paragraph:
>
> ```
> <p style="margin-left: 10">
> ```
>
> And if you assign the Small Caps character style, FrontPage will embed the characters in a SPAN element with the following start-tag:
>
> ```
> <span style="font-variant: small-caps">
> ```

FrontPage also generates one or more inline CSS style settings whenever you click the Style button in the Properties dialog box for an element and apply one or more formatting features in the Modify Style dialog box. For example, you'll see a Style button in the Table Properties dialog box, the Picture Properties dialog box, and the General tab of the Page Properties dialog box. The settings you make in the Modify Style dialog box will affect only the specific element whose Properties dialog box you've opened.

● **Embedded** An embedded CSS style setting is stored in a style sheet located in the page's header (the HEAD element) rather than in a particular element. You can create embedded CSS style settings that customize the formatting of a particular element—such as a top-level heading (an H1 element)—everywhere it occurs in the document, by performing the following steps:

1 Choose Format, Style to open the Style dialog box (shown in Figure 44-21).

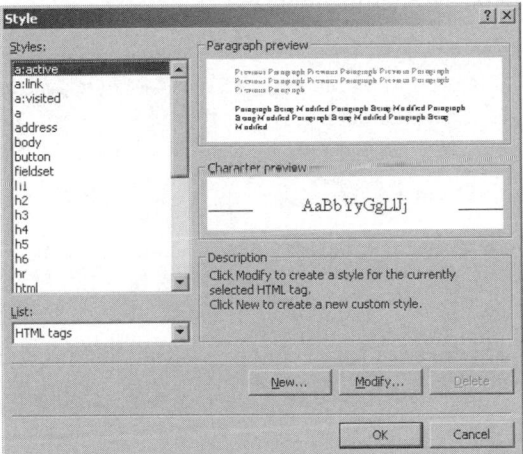

Figure 44-21. The Style dialog box allows you to create and modify embedded CSS styles.

2 Select HTML Tags in the List drop-down list to display HTML elements, and in the Styles list, select the particular element you want to customize. For example, you would select H1 to customize the formatting of all top-level headings (H1 elements) in the document.

3 Click the Modify button and select the desired formatting features in the Modify Style dialog box.

You can also add embedded CSS style settings that create a user-defined style that you can apply to any paragraph or block of characters in the document (much like a user-defined style in Word), by performing the steps listed at the top of the next page.

1231

1 Choose Format, Style to open the Style dialog box (see Figure 44-21).

2 Click the New button to open the New Style dialog box.

3 In the New Style dialog box, enter a name (also known as a *selector*) for your style, select Paragraph or Character to indicate the type of element the style will be applied to, and choose the desired formatting features.

Your new user-defined style will subsequently appear in the Styles drop-down list on the Formatting toolbar and you can use it just like one of the built-in FrontPage styles (such as Normal or Heading 1). Also, if you click the Style button in an element's Properties dialog box, you can format that element by selecting or typing the user-defined style name in the Class box in the Modify Style dialog box.

To remove a user-defined character style from text you've assigned it to, select the text and then select Default Character Style in the Style drop-down list on the Formatting toolbar.

> **note** Embedded CSS style settings are added to a STYLE element within the page's HEAD element. For example, if you create a style that modifies H1 elements by adding italic formatting, FrontPage will insert the following declaration into the STYLE element:
>
> ```
> h1 {font-style: italic}
> ```
>
> And if you create a user-defined paragraph style named CenteredDouble, which applies centered alignment and double spacing to a paragraph, FrontPage will add the following declaration to the STYLE element:
>
> ```
> .CenteredDouble {text-align: center; line-height: 200%}
> ```
>
> If you assign this user-defined style to a paragraph in the page, FrontPage will set the P element's CLASS attribute to the name of the style, as in this example:
>
> ```
> <p class="CenteredDouble">
> ```

● **External** An external CSS style setting is stored in a separate CSS file (with the .css extension) that is linked to one or more Web pages. Like an embedded CSS, an external CSS can contain styles that globally modify an HTML element, as well as user-defined styles that you can apply to individual elements in the page. The advantage of using an external CSS is that by attaching the same CSS to several pages (perhaps all the pages in a web) you can easily give them uniform formatting. To create an external CSS and attach it to a web page, perform the following basic steps:

1 Choose File, New, Page Or Web and then click Page Templates in the task pane.

2 Click the Style Sheets tab in the Page Templates dialog box, select a template for your new CSS, and click the OK button.

3 If you wish, you can customize the style sheet by creating styles that modify HTML elements or by adding user-defined styles, as explained under the description of embedded styles earlier in this section.

4 Save the CSS file within the current web.

5 To attach the CSS to a page, open the page and choose Format, Style Sheet Links. In the Link Style Sheet dialog box, click the Add button, and in the Select Style Sheet dialog box, select the new CSS file you created. Click the OK button, and then click the OK button in the Link Style Sheet dialog box.

Once you link an external CSS to a page, the styles in the CSS that modify elements will globally alter the formatting of basic elements throughout your page. Also, any user-defined styles defined in the linked CSS will be listed in the Style drop-down list on the Formatting menu so you can apply them to elements in the page. And, if you click the Style button in an element's Properties dialog box, you can format that element by typing the name of a user-defined style in the attached style sheet into the Class box in the Modify Style dialog box.

The term *cascading* in cascading style sheet derives from the fact that you can define style settings at various levels. If conflicting style settings are defined at different levels, an inline style setting takes precedence over an embedded style setting, and an embedded style setting takes precedence over an external style setting.

Troubleshooting

Formatting Features Are Unavailable

When you format your document, quite a few formatting features are disabled, such as Small Caps and several other character format settings, most paragraph formatting features, and the Borders And Shading and Position commands on the Format menu. Also, you can't use any of the CSS methods described in "Modifying, Creating, and Using Cascading Style Sheet Styles," on page 1230.

None of these features will be available if the CSS 1.0 option isn't checked in the Compatibility tab of the Page Options dialog box. To open this dialog box, choose Tools, Page Options. These features all use CSS styles. If some of your page visitors will be using older browsers without support for CSS, then you should clear the CSS 1.0 compatibility option so that all features that rely on CSS will be disabled in FrontPage and you won't inadvertently use them. If, however, your visitors will be

(continued)

Formatting Features Are Unavailable *(continued)* using browsers with CSS support, you should definitely check this option so that you can take full advantage of FrontPage's formatting capabilities. Furthermore, paragraph positioning (as discussed in "Positioning Paragraphs," on page 1206) requires support for CSS version 2.0. Therefore, if your target browsers support CSS 2.0, you should also make sure that the CSS 2.0 option is checked in the Compatibility tab so you can position paragraphs. Note that Microsoft Internet Explorer began supporting CSS 1.0 with version 3.0 of the browser, and CSS 2.0 with version 4.0.

For more information on the Compatibility tab of the Page Options dialog box, see the tip "Ensure Compatibility" and Figure 43-15 on page 1195.

Chapter 45

Adding Advanced Features to Your Web Pages

Creating Interactive Forms to Collect Information

A form consists of a collection of *fields* (sometimes known as *controls*)—such as text boxes, check boxes, and push buttons—that are used to collect information from visitors to your Web page. Each form normally includes a Submit button that the user clicks after filling in the fields to transmit the information, plus a Reset button that the user can click to clear all fields prior to entering new information. Figure 45-1 shows an example form as it appears in Microsoft FrontPage 2002, and Figure 45-2 shows the same form displayed in Microsoft Internet Explorer.

Part 7: FrontPage

Picture   Regular text

Textbox

Label

Text Area

Drop-Down
Box

Option Button

Checkbox

Push Button

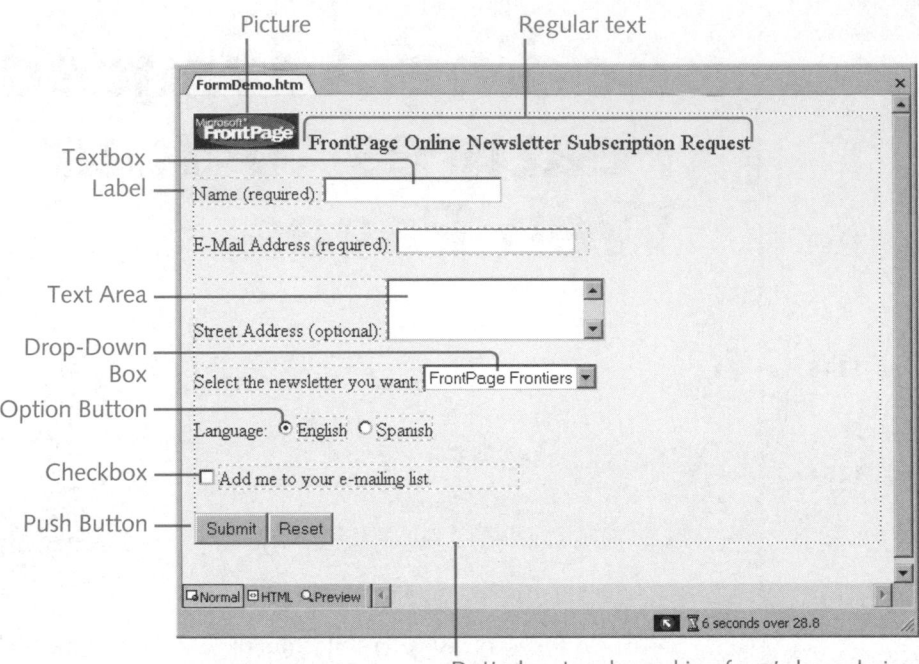

Dotted rectangle marking form's boundaries

Figure 45-1.   This figure shows a simple form displayed in FrontPage, in Page view.

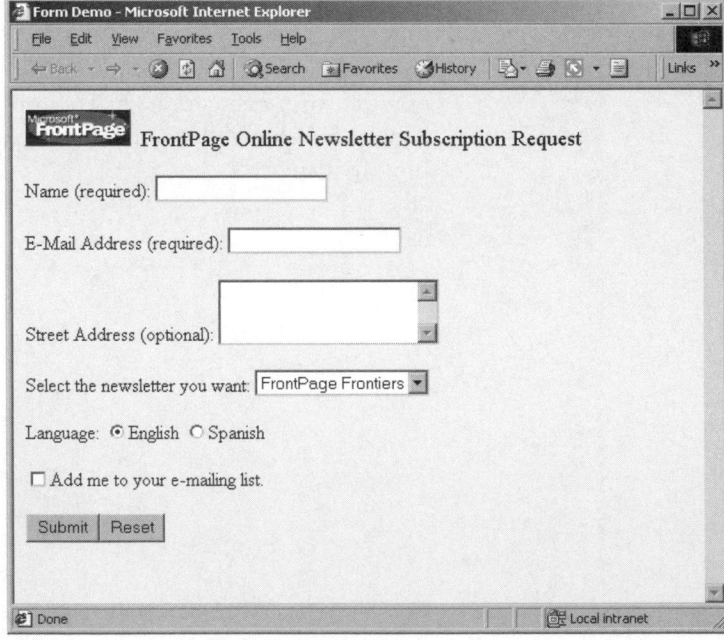

Figure 45-2.   Here, the form shown in Figure 45-1 is displayed in Internet Explorer.

To create a form in Page view, perform the following steps:

1 Place the insertion point at the position in your page where you want to add the form.

2 Insert the first form field by choosing the appropriate command from the Form submenu of the Insert menu, shown here:

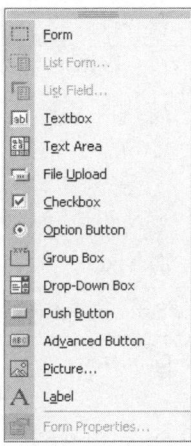

Table 45-1 briefly explains how to use the commands on the Form submenu and describes the different fields you can insert. When you insert the first field, FrontPage draws a dotted rectangle defining the boundaries of the form (browsers don't display this line) and automatically adds a Submit button and a Reset button to the form.

note FrontPage adds form boundaries and Submit and Reset buttons when you insert a field only if the Automatically Enclose Form Fields Within A Form option is checked. You'll find this option by choosing Tools, Page Options and clicking the General tab.

Table 45-1. **Using the Commands on the Form Submenu of the Insert Menu**

To Do This with Forms	Choose This Command
Insert the form boundaries, a Submit button, and a Reset button for a regular Web form	Form
Create a *list form*, which is a special-purpose form for adding, editing, or displaying items in a document library or list on a SharePoint team Web site	List Form This command is available only if you've opened a web on a SharePoint team Web site.

(continued)

Chapter 45

Table 45-1. *(continued)*

To Do This with Forms	Choose This Command
Insert a field into a list form	List Field This command is available only if you've opened a web on a SharePoint team Web site.
Insert a one-line text box	Textbox
Insert a multiline, scrolling text box	Text Area
Insert a one-line text box, plus a Browse button that opens the Choose File dialog box, so that the user can either type in a filename or select a file in the dialog box	File Upload
Insert a check box	Checkbox
Insert an option button	Option Button
Insert a box for grouping and labeling a set of fields	Group Box
Insert a drop-down list	Drop-Down Box
Insert a button	Push Button
Insert a button that allows you to type the label directly on the button and customize the button's width and height	Advanced Button
Insert an image	Picture
Link the selected text label and control (explained later in this section)	Label
Open the Form Properties dialog box for viewing or setting the properties of the form	Form Properties

3 Use the Form submenu to insert any additional fields that you want. Be sure to insert each additional field *within* the dotted rectangle marking the form. Otherwise, the new field will belong to a separate form and its information won't be submitted when the user clicks the Submit button. (Clicking a Submit button sends only the information within the same form as the button.)

You can arrange the fields as you like. Fields are a part of the normal flow of text and you can move or copy them just like text characters.

4 Add any text or other elements that you want in the form.

You can type in text to create a title, a label, instructions for completing the form, or other information. If you type a label next to a field (for example, if you type *Add me to your mailing list* following a check box), be sure to link the label and the associated field. Doing this makes the label and the field function as a unit when the form is displayed in a browser; for example, users will be able to check or clear a check box by clicking on the linked label as well as on the box itself. To link a label and a field, select both of them and then choose Insert, Form, Label. FrontPage draws a dotted rectangle around each linked label.

You can also insert tables, images, and almost any other element that can be inserted into a page.

5 Set the table properties.

You can change the properties of an individual field by selecting it and then choosing Format, Properties or pressing Alt+Enter to open the Properties dialog box. Or you can right-click the field and choose Form Field Properties from the shortcut menu. The properties you can set in the Properties dialog box depend on the type of the field. For example, for a drop-down list, you can enter the values that will be displayed in the list. And for a push button, you can change the button's label or designate the button as a Submit or Reset button.

To set the properties of the entire form, open the Form Properties dialog box (shown in Figure 45-3) by placing the insertion point anywhere within the form and choosing Insert, Form, Form Properties. Or you can right-click anywhere on the form and choose Form Properties from the shortcut menu. To control where the information from the form fields is sent when a user clicks the Submit button, choose an option in the Where To Store Results area and type in the required information. You can click the Options button to control the way the information is saved and to specify a confirmation page that the browser will display after the user clicks the Submit button.

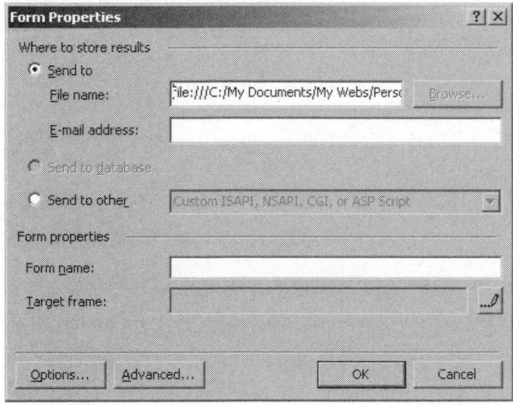

Figure 45-3. You can set the properties of the entire form in the Form Properties dialog box.

> **tip** **Use a Template to Create a Form**
>
> To get a head start in designing a form, you can create a new page using the Feed-back Form template, which adds a complete feedback form that you can customize, or the Form Page Wizard, which generates a custom form, laying out all the fields for you based on the choices you enter. For information on creating new pages using templates and wizards, see "Creating a New Web Page," on page 1163.

Using Frames to Display Multiple Pages

You can show several pages simultaneously in the browser window by displaying each page in a separate *frame*. Figure 45-4 shows an example of a set of frames, viewed in Internet Explorer. The frame on the left serves as a table of contents. When the user clicks one of the hyperlinks on the link bar contained in the left frame, the target page is displayed in the right frame.

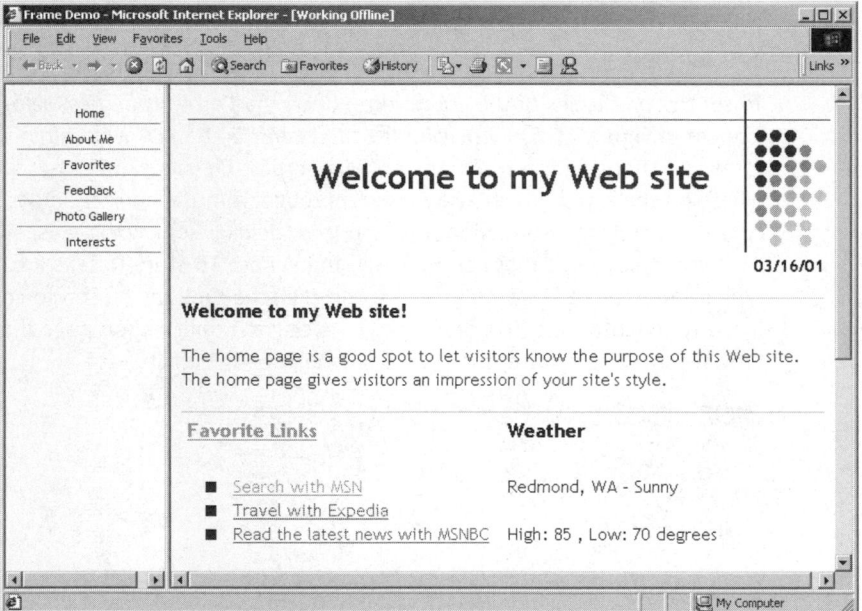

Figure 45-4. In this figure, frames are used to display two pages at once.

> **note** FrontPage won't let you create frames unless the Frames option is checked in the Compatibility tab of the Page Options dialog box (which you can open by choosing Tools, Page Options). See the tip "Ensure Compatibility" and Figure 43-15, on page 1195.

Chapter 45: Adding Advanced Features to Your Web Pages

To use frames, you must create a *frames page*, which defines the number and layout of the frames and optionally specifies the initial page to be displayed within each frame. When the user opens the frames page, the frames appear within the browser window, and each frame displays its initial page (if one has been specified for it). To create a frames page, perform the following steps:

1 Activate Page view.

2 Choose File, New, Page Or Web and then click Page Templates in the task pane to open the Page Templates dialog box.

3 Click the Frames Pages tab in the Page Templates dialog box (shown in Figure 45-5), select the template that defines the number and layout of frames that you want, and click the OK button. (Keep in mind that you'll be able to change the number or layout of the frames later.)

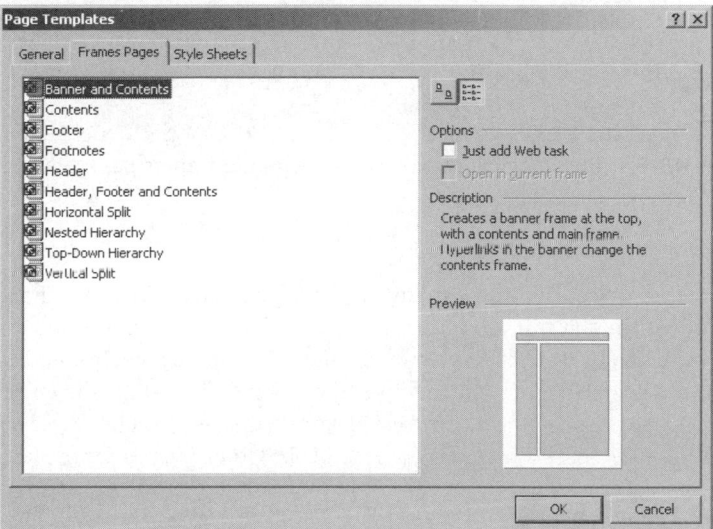

Figure 45-5. Select a template for creating a frames page in the Frames Pages tab of the Page Templates dialog box.

After you perform these steps, FrontPage will open the new frames page. An example is shown in Figure 45-6.

> **note** If you create a new web in FrontPage using the Discussion Wizard, the home page will be a frames page that is set up to display the other pages in the web.

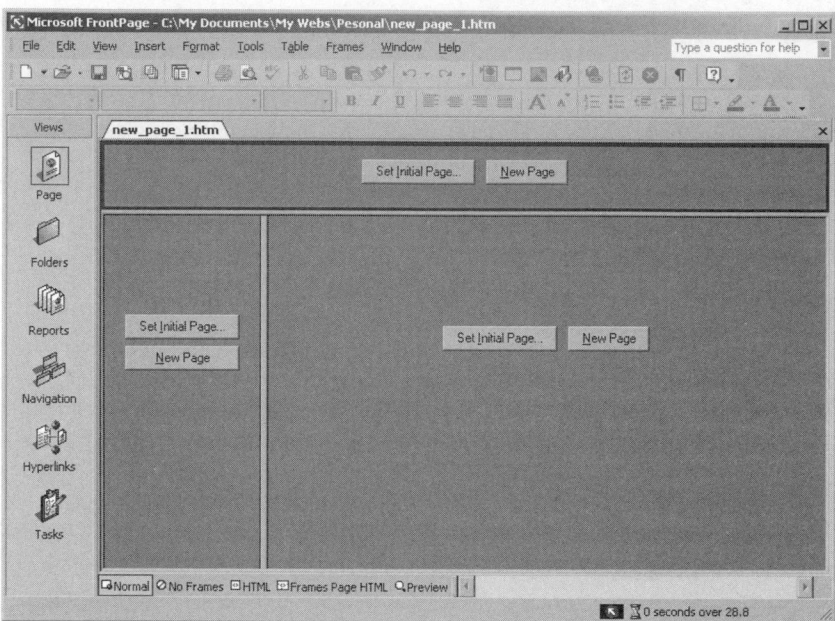

Figure 45-6. This example shows a newly created frames page based on the Banner And Contents template.

To have a particular frame initially display an existing page, click the Set Initial Page button within that frame, and then select the page. To have a frame initially display a newly created page, click the New Page button in the frame. If you don't add an existing or new page to a particular frame, that frame will initially be empty when the frames page is opened in a browser; however, a page could be displayed in that frame when the user clicks a hyperlink in one of the other frames (as explained shortly).

A page you add to a frame will be displayed within that frame in Page view, where you can use FrontPage commands to edit it. (If you want, you can also open and edit the page in a separate Page view window by right-clicking in the frame and choosing Open Page In New Window from the shortcut menu.) When you issue the Save command (by choosing File, Save, by clicking the Save button on the Standard toolbar, or by pressing Ctrl+S), FrontPage saves the frames page itself, plus all new or modified pages displayed in the individual frames. (The Save As dialog box displays a model of the frames page and highlights the frame FrontPage is about to save. When no frame is highlighted, FrontPage is about to save the frames page itself.)

You can modify a particular frame by clicking it to activate it (FrontPage will highlight its border) and then choosing a command from the Frames menu as shown at the top of the next page.

Chapter 45: Adding Advanced Features to Your Web Pages

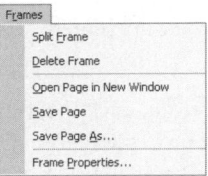

- To divide the frame horizontally or vertically into two frames, choose Split Frame.

- To remove the frame, choose Delete Frame.

- To edit the page contained in the frame within a full, separate window in Page view, choose Open Page In New Window.

- To save only the page displayed in the frame, choose Save Page or Save Page As.

- To change the frame's properties, choose Frame Properties to open the Frame Properties dialog box (shown in Figure 45-7).

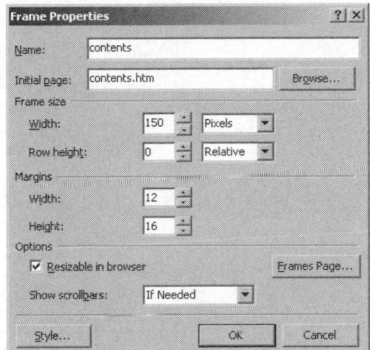

Figure 45-7. You can use the Frame Properties dialog box to change the properties of the selected frame within a frames page.

You can also change the initial size of a frame by simply dragging a border in the FrontPage editor. And you can split a frame by holding down Ctrl while you drag.

You can change the properties of the frames page itself by choosing Frames, Frame Properties and then clicking the Frames Page button at the bottom of the Frame Properties dialog box to open the Page Properties dialog box. This dialog box includes the usual tabs for setting page properties (described in "Modifying Page Properties," on page 1224), plus a Frames tab that allows you to adjust the spacing between frames and to show or hide the borders around the frames.

If you include a hyperlink on a page displayed within a frame, you can specify the particular frame in which the target is to be opened. For example, on a frames page that has two frames, the frame on the left could contain a page that has a list of hyperlinks and serves as a table of contents. The target of each hyperlink could be opened in the frame on the right. This way, the table of contents is always immediately accessible while the user views various pages in the right frame.

To specify a target frame when you create (or edit) a hyperlink, click the Target Frame button in the Insert Hyperlink (or Edit Hyperlink) dialog box (see Figure 43-10, on page 1185), and then select the target frame in the Target Frame dialog box. This dialog box displays a diagram of the frames; to select a frame, just click on it in the diagram. Also, in the General tab of the Page Properties dialog box for a page displayed in one of the frames, you can specify a default target frame for all hyperlinks on the page.

> For further details, see "Including Internal and External Hyperlinks," on page 1184. For more information on specifying a default target frame for hyperlinks, see "Modifying Page Properties" and Figure 44-16, on page 1224.

---

tip **Provide an Alternative for Browsers That Don't Support Frames**

When you create a frames page, FrontPage also creates an accompanying "no frames" page. If you attempt to open the frames page in a browser that doesn't support frames, the browser will display the "no frames" page instead. The "no frames" page can furnish an explanatory note or provide alternative content that doesn't rely on frames. To view or edit this page, click the No Frames button at the bottom of the Page view window. FrontPage will then display the "no frames" page within the No Frames pane of Page view.

---

newfeature!

Adding Inline Frames

In FrontPage, as an alternative to creating a frames page to view multiple pages, you can simply insert an *inline frame* into any page. An inline frame is a rectangular element in a page that displays another page and lets you scroll through it (see Figure 45-8).

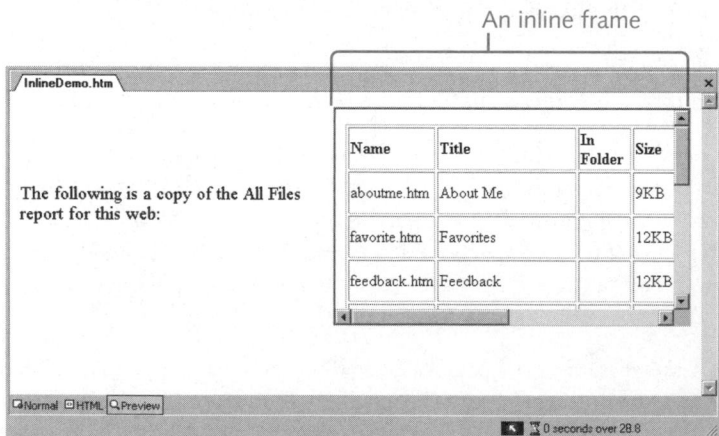

Figure 45-8. A Web page can contain an inline frame showing the contents of another page, as seen here in the Preview pane.

Chapter 45: Adding Advanced Features to Your Web Pages

To add an inline frame to a Web page, perform the following steps:

1 Place the insertion point at the position in the page where you want to display the inline frame and choose Insert, Inline Frame. FrontPage will then insert a blank inline frame, as shown here:

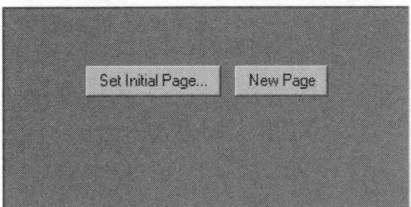

2 To select an existing page or to create a new page to display in the inline frame, click the Set Initial Page button or the New Page button in the blank inline frame.

3 To customize the inline frame, click a border (not the inside of the frame), so that sizing handles appear around the frame. Then you can change the size of the inline frame by dragging a sizing handle, and you can set the inline frame's properties by choosing Format, Properties or by pressing Alt+Enter, and then entering settings into the Inline Frame Properties dialog box (shown in Figure 45-9).

In the Inline Frame Properties dialog box, notice that the inline frame has an identifying name (I1 in Figure 45-9). You can make the inline frame the target of a hyperlink in the main page by clicking the Target Frame button in the Insert Hyperlink (or Edit Hyperlink) dialog box and then selecting that name in the Target Frame dialog box.

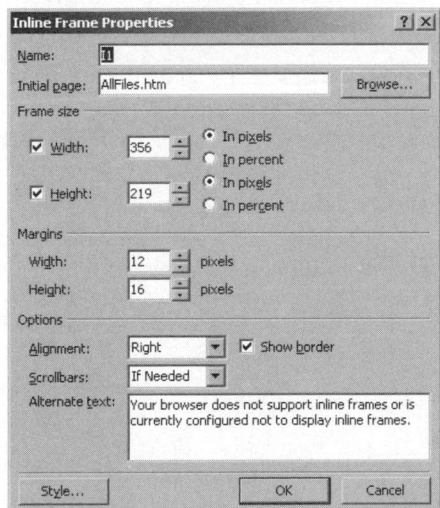

Figure 45-9. You can edit the properties of an inline frame in the Inline Frame Properties dialog box.

For general information on defining hyperlinks, see "Including Internal and External Hyperlinks," on page 1184.

Adding Dynamic Content with Web Components

A FrontPage *Web component* is an element that you can quickly insert into a Web page to automatically generate and display information or to add a feature. Many of these ready-to-run components let you add sophisticated capabilities to your Web pages and require little effort. The different types of Web components are described in Table 45-2.

Table 45-2. Web Components You Can Add to a Page

FrontPage Component Type	Description of Component(s)
Advanced Controls	● These components are described in the next section, "Inserting Advanced Controls."
Comment	● Comment: Lets you add text commentary that you can see when the page is opened in Page view, but that is hidden when the page is displayed in a browser.
Date And Time	● Date And Time: Displays the date and time when you last edited the page, or when the page was last automatically updated (for example, when FrontPage updates a hyperlink).
Document Library View	● Document Library View: Displays the contents of a document library on a SharePoint team Web site. You can insert this component only if you've opened a web stored on a Web server running SharePoint Team Services.
Dynamic Effects	● Hover Button: Displays a visual effect or plays a sound when you move the pointer over the button, or (for a sound) when you click the button. You can also assign a hyperlink to the button so that clicking it will open the hyperlink target. ● Marquee: Displays text that scrolls horizontally across the page. ● Banner Ad Manager: Runs a "slide show" displaying a series of images. You can control the amount of time each image is shown and select a transition effect that occurs when images are switched.

Table 45-2. *(continued)*

FrontPage Component Type	Description of Component(s)
Hit Counter	● Hit Counter: Keeps track of and displays the number of times someone has opened the page.
Included Content	● Page: Displays the contents of another page. If you want to display a block of text or other elements in several locations in your web, you can add the content to a single page and then use this Web component to insert that page in all the locations. With this method, you need to maintain only a single copy of the repeated content. See the Troubleshooting sidebar "Shared Borders Offer Little Control," on page 1191. ● Page Banner: Displays the page title. The banner's style is controlled by the page theme, and the page must be included in the web's navigation structure shown in Navigation view (otherwise, the banner will be hidden). ● Page Based On Schedule: Displays a specified page for a specified time period. This component is like a Page component, except that after the specified period, the included page is no longer displayed. It's useful for showing textual information that will expire on a certain date. ● Picture Based On Schedule: Displays a specified image for a specified time period, after which the image is hidden. This component is useful for showing graphical information that will expire on a certain date. ● Substitution: Displays the current value of a standard or user-defined web variable. The standard variables are Author (the person who created the page), Modified By (the person who most recently changed the page), Description (a description of the page), and Page URL (the full Web address or file path of the page). You can create user-defined variables for the web by choosing Tools, Web Settings and then clicking the Parameters tab in the Web Settings dialog box.

(continued)

---

tip   **Obtain Additional Web Components**

To look for additional Web components that you can download and add to your Web pages, click the Find Components On The Web link at the bottom of the Insert Web Component dialog box. This command will connect you to a Microsoft Office site on the Web.

Table 45-2. (continued)

FrontPage Component Type	Description of Component(s)
Link Bars	● Bar Based On Navigation Structure: Displays a set of hyperlinks that FrontPage automatically generates based on the current web navigation structure shown in Navigation view. (For more information, see "Using Navigation View," on page 1142.) The component's style is controlled by the page theme. ● Bar With Back And Next Links: Displays "Back" and "Next" custom hyperlinks. ● Bar With Custom Links: Displays a collection of custom hyperlinks. For a Bar With Back And Next Links component or a Bar With Custom Links component you must specify each of the custom hyperlinks. You do this in the Link Bar Properties dialog box that's displayed when you insert the link bar. You can add links later by clicking the Add Link command that appears to the right of the link bar in Page view. Also, FrontPage will display an item for the custom link bar in Navigation view; you can add or remove links by working with that item in Navigation view.
List View	● List View: Displays the contents of a list on a SharePoint team Web site. You can insert this component only if you've opened a web stored on a Webserver running SharePoint Team Services.
MSN Components	● Look Up A Stock Quote: Obtains and displays stock quotes from the MoneyCentral Web site. ● Search The Web With MSN: Lets the visitor perform a Web search using Microsoft Network.
MSNBC Components	● A set of components that obtain and display news and weather information from the MSNBC Web site.
Photo Gallery	● Photo Gallery: Displays a collection of images, automatically generating thumbnail images for each. For more information, see "Adding a Photo Gallery," on page 1182.
Spreadsheets And Charts	● Office Chart: Charts data that you enter or data obtained from a database in a column, bar, line, pie, or other type of chart. ● Office Pivot Table: Displays data from a database in an interactive pivot table. (For information on pivot tables, see Chapter 28, "Power Database Techniques: Lists, Filters, and Pivot Tables.") ● Office Spreadsheet: Displays the data you enter in a spreadsheet that the visitor can view or edit.

Chapter 45: Adding Advanced Features to Your Web Pages

Table 45-2. *(continued)*

FrontPage Component Type	Description of Component(s)
Table Of Contents	● Based On Page Category: Generates and automatically updates a list of hyperlinks to other pages in the web that belong to the category or categories you specify. (You assign categories to a page by selecting or opening the page, choosing Properties from the File menu, and clicking the Workgroup tab.) ● For This Web Site: Generates and automatically updates a list of hyperlinks to all other pages in the web.
Top 10 List	● Components that display web usage statistics in the form of top-10 lists: the 10 most visited pages in the web, the 10 most common referring visitor domains, the 10 most common visitor browsers, and so on.
Web Search	● Current Web: Generates a form that lets the user search through all the text on the pages of your web. The search results are displayed as a list of hyperlinks to the pages that contain matching text.

To add a Web component to a page, perform the following steps:

1 Place the insertion point at the position in the page where you want to display the Web component.

2 Insert the Web component as follows:

    ■ To insert a Date And Time or Comment component, choose Insert, Date And Time or Insert, Comment.

    ■ To insert any of the other types of components listed in Table 45-2, choose Insert, Web Component. Then, in the Insert Web Component dialog box (shown in Figure 45-10), select the component type in the Component Type list and then select a specific component or component style in the list to the right (the label on the right list depends on the component type you've selected; for example, Choose An Effect, Choose A Control, or Choose A Counter Style).

Then, click the Finish button. Or, with components that allow you to make additional settings (such as Link Bars), you can click the Next button to select settings or—if the button is enabled—click the Finish button to accept the default settings. In any case, FrontPage might now display one or more additional dialog boxes to gather required information for creating the Web component.

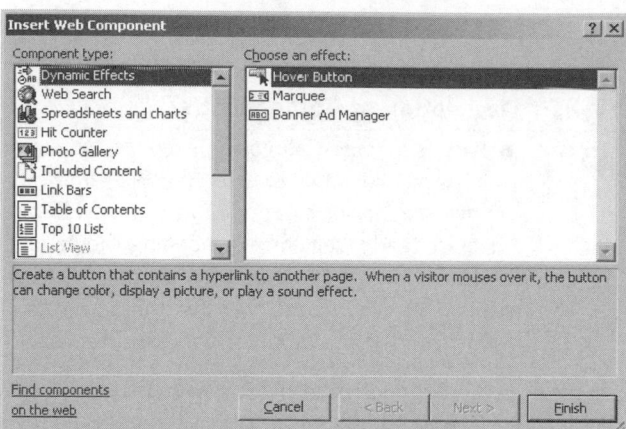

Figure 45-10. You insert most types of Web components using the Insert Web Component dialog box.

3 After the component is installed, you can change its properties by clicking the component and choosing Format, Properties or pressing Alt+Enter. Or, you can double-click the component. FrontPage will then display the Properties dialog box for the component, which lets you view and adjust properties (see Figure 45-11).

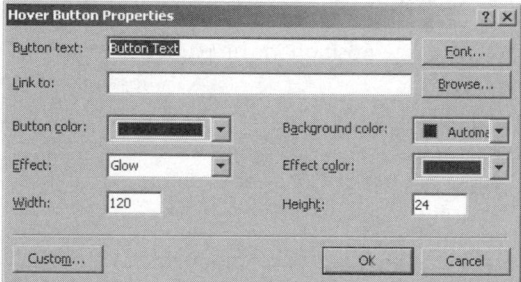

Figure 45-11. The Hover Button Properties dialog box is typical of the Properties dialog boxes that let you view and change the properties of Web components.

Inserting Advanced Controls

You can add several additional Web components to your page that FrontPage classifies as *advanced controls*. These components don't necessarily provide more advanced features than the Web components discussed in the previous section and shown in Table 45-2. Instead, they are considered advanced because they require you either to write program code or to obtain software from a third party. These controls are summarized in Table 45-3.

Table 45-3. **The Advanced Controls You Can Add to a Page**

Advanced Control	Description
ActiveX Control	A portable software module that you can insert in a Web page to perform a specific task or set of tasks. For example, an ActiveX control might display a calendar, run a multimedia presentation, or generate a chart. Before you can add an ActiveX control to a page, you must install the control on your computer.
Confirmation Field	Displays the contents of a specific field in a form that the visitor has submitted to the Web server. This component must be placed on the form's *confirmation page*, which is displayed when a visitor successfully submits the form. You can use a custom confirmation page for a form by clicking the Options button in the Form Properties dialog box (shown in Figure 45-3, on page 1239), clicking the Confirmation Page tab, and entering the name and location of the custom page (or clicking the Browse button to select the page).
Design-Time Control	An ActiveX control that you use while designing or editing a page. If you haven't installed any design-time controls on your computer, the Design-Time Control item will be unavailable in the Choose A Control list.
HTML	A block of HTML (Hypertext Markup Language) source that you type, which FrontPage inserts directly to the page file. This component lets you add features not supported by FrontPage. You must enter the code carefully because FrontPage doesn't check or modify it. (For more information, see "Working Directly with the HTML Source," on page 1254.)
Java Applet	A portable software module that you can insert in a Web page to perform a specific task or set of tasks. A Java applet is similar to an ActiveX control, except that it offers greater portability and security, and it doesn't have to be installed on your computer.
Plug-In	Another type of software module that extends the browser's capabilities. Plug-ins were originally designed for Netscape Navigator 2, but are also supported by Microsoft Internet Explorer version 3 and later.

To insert an advanced control, follow the general instructions for adding a Web component given in the previous section. In the Insert Web Component dialog box, select Advanced Controls in the Component Type list, and then select the specific control you want to insert in the Choose A Control list (shown in Figure 45-12).

Part 7: FrontPage

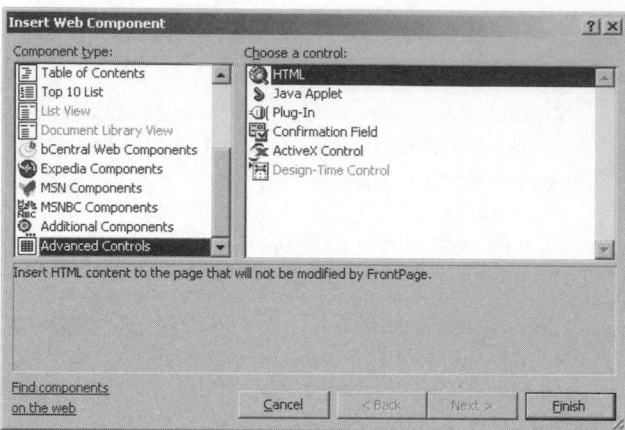

Figure 45-12. You insert advanced controls using the Insert Web Component dialog box.

note After you insert an HTML control, the results of the HTML source it contains won't be visible until you view the page in the Preview pane or open it in a browser.

Troubleshooting

Web Component Doesn't Work!

FrontPage lets you add Web Search, Hit Counter, and Top 10 List Web components to your page. However, when you save the page and view it in your browser, none of these components work.

Each of these Web components will work only if the page is delivered—over an intranet or on the World Wide Web—from a Web server that has the FrontPage Server Extensions installed. These components *won't* work if the page is opened in a browser from a local or network disk location.

If you've created your web on a disk location, these Web components will work correctly once you publish your web to a server that has the FrontPage Server Extensions.

For details, see the sidebar "Creating a Web Offline or Online," on page 1112, and the tip "Find a Hosting Service with FrontPage Server Extensions," on page 1160.

If your Web server doesn't have the FrontPage Server Extensions, it's best to disable these components so you don't inadvertently insert one of them. You can do this by choosing Tools, Page Options, clicking the Compatibility tab, and clearing the Enabled With Microsoft FrontPage Server Extensions option.

Troubleshooting

Can't Insert Web Component!

The Web component you want to add is dimmed in the Insert Web Component dialog box, so you can't insert it.

FrontPage doesn't let you insert a Web component if the required support isn't present. If a web isn't currently opened in FrontPage, you won't be able to insert any of the following types of Web components:

- Included Content, except Substitution
- Link Bars
- Table of Contents
- Top 10 List
- List View
- Document Library View
- Advanced Controls, Confirmation Field (You can insert the other types of Advanced Controls.)

You can't insert either of the following components unless you have opened a web that resides on a server running SharePoint Team Services from Microsoft:

- List View
- Document Library View

Each of the following Web components requires one or more of the Web technologies that you can have FrontPage enable or disable by choosing Tools, Page Options, clicking the Compatibility tab, and checking or clearing options. If a technology that a particular Web component requires is disabled in this tab, FrontPage won't let you insert it.

For details on browser compatibility, see the tip "Ensure Compatibility" and Figure 43-15, on page 1195.

- Dynamic Effects, except Marquee
- Web Search
- Spreadsheets And Charts
- Hit Counter
- Photo Gallery with the slide show layout (You can insert a Photo Gallery with any other layout.)
- Top 10 List
- List View
- Document Library View
- Advanced Controls, except HTML and Plug-In

Chapter 45

Working Directly with the HTML Source

If you're familiar with HTML, you can work directly with the HTML source for the active Web page using any of the following methods:

- To view or directly modify the HTML source for the entire Web page, click the HTML button at the bottom of the Page view window to activate the HTML pane, as shown here:

  Note, however, that the source you see in this pane might differ somewhat from the source in the HTML file that FrontPage saves on disk. For example, if the page displays a shared border, the table that creates the border won't be included in the source shown in the HTML pane. Also, a FrontPage component—such as a Date And Time component or an Include Page—will not yet be expanded into the actual content that will be added to the HTML file on disk.

- In the Normal pane of Page view, you can display the page's HTML tags by choosing View, Reveal Tags, or by pressing Ctrl+/. FrontPage will display the start-tag and the end-tag (if present) on either side of each page element. For example, the editor will display a <P> tag at the beginning of each paragraph, and a </P> tag at the end of each paragraph (assuming the paragraph has an end-tag). If you place the mouse pointer over a tag, a ScreenTip will display the complete content of the start-tag, including any attributes defined within that tag (for example, the target address for a hyperlink element). And if you click a start-tag or end-tag, FrontPage will highlight the matching tag and all content between the two tags. To hide the tags, choose Reveal Tags or press Ctrl+/ again.

- In the Normal pane of Page view, you can add a block of HTML source directly to the page at the position of the insertion point by inserting an HTML Web component.

> For more information on XML and XML syntax rules, see Michael J. Young, *XML Step by Step* (Redmond, Washington: Microsoft Press, 2000).

newfeature!

tip   **Make Your HTML Source Conform to XML Rules**

XML (Extensible Markup Language) doesn't define a specific set of elements, but it does enforce a fairly strict, consistent syntax to help eliminate incompatibilities. HTML, on the other hand, defines a specific set of elements so that browsers can universally interpret the language, but has relatively loose rules of syntax. You can create the best of both languages by having FrontPage convert the HTML source for your web page so that it conforms to the stricter syntax rules of XML. For example, if your page contains a start-tag for an element (such as <P> for a paragraph) but no matching end-tag (</P> for a paragraph), FrontPage will add the missing end-tag. (In XML, every element must have both a start-tag and an end-tag, or use an empty element tag, such as <HR/> for a horizontal dividing line.) Enforcing XML rules may eliminate ambiguities in your page's HTML source and reduce incompatibilities and differences in the way various browsers or other programs interpret and display the page.

To make your HTML source comply to XML rules, click the HTML button at the bottom of the Page view window to open the HTML pane, right-click anywhere within the page, and choose Apply XML Formatting Rules from the shortcut menu, as shown here:

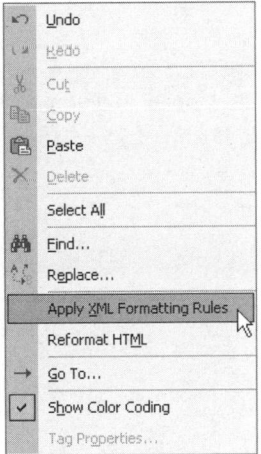

(Notice that this shortcut menu has some other useful commands for working in the HTML pane.)

> For information on inserting HTML Web components and other types of advanced controls, see "Inserting Advanced Controls," on page 1250.

You can change the colors that FrontPage applies to various components—such as tags, attribute names, or comments—in the HTML pane, or you can turn color coding off or on by choosing Tools, Page Options and clicking the Color Coding tab in the Page Options dialog box (shown in Figure 45-13). You can also change the way FrontPage formats the HTML source that it generates by clicking the HTML Source tab, also in the Page Options dialog box (as shown in Figure 45-14).

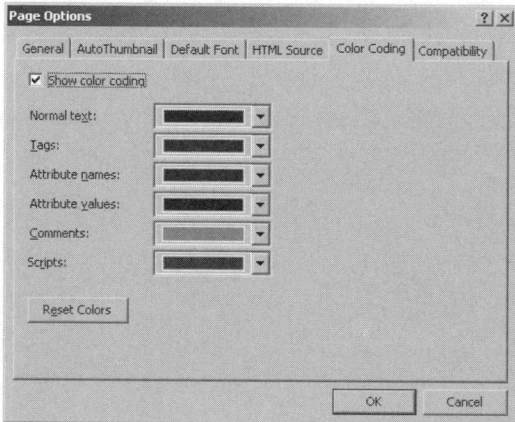

Figure 45-13. You can change the colors that FrontPage applies to components in the Color Coding tab of the Page Options dialog box.

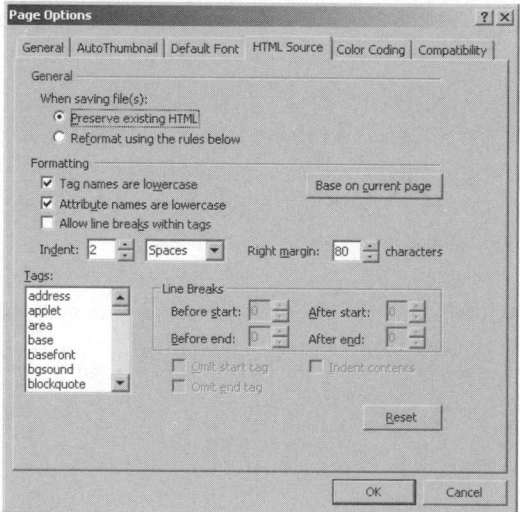

Figure 45-14. The HTML Source tab of the Page Options dialog box lets you control the way FrontPage formats HTML source.

Part 8

Access

Access Fundamentals

A Rundown on Access

Microsoft Access 2002 is the premier Microsoft Office XP application for managing data. Access, however, can also be fairly challenging to learn and might have more power than you really need. If the information you want to store is fairly simple—for example, an uncomplicated product inventory, a list of names and addresses, or a log of events—you might well be able to use an Office application that's more familiar to you.

For a description of the new features in Access 2002, see "New Access Features," on page 16.

For example, Microsoft Excel 2002 is ideal for storing basic lists of information. Each row in a worksheet can hold one record (for instance, the information on one product in your inventory), each cell in a row can hold one field (such as the description or price of a product), and the top row in the worksheet can display a label for each field. Excel lets you sort, find, filter, automatically fill, summarize, group, outline, subtotal, and work with the data in other ways. For more information, see Chapter 28, "Power Database Techniques: Lists, Filters, and Pivot Tables."

> **note** Database information is divided into *records*, and records are divided into *fields*. Each record stores the information on one of the individual items that the database tracks, such as a product, a client, or an expense. Each field stores an individual piece of information within a record (for example, the description or number of a product, the name or e-mail address of a client, or the amount or date of an expense). When database information is displayed in a tabular list, typically each row displays a single record and each column displays a particular field for all of the records.

Microsoft Outlook 2002 is superb for storing and sharing names and addresses, task descriptions, journal entries, appointments, and free-form notes, as well as messages. And, if you create custom forms and new folders in Outlook, you can use Outlook to store and share almost any type of information.

Microsoft Word 2002 is ideal for recording free-form information, such as research notes, especially when you use its outlining feature. And you can use Word tables to store and display reasonable amounts of numeric or textual data. Word even provides mathematical functions for working with numbers in tables, as well as database tools for working with data fields and records in tables.

However, if you want to store large amounts of information, if your data is fairly complex or interrelated, or if you spend much of your time working with information, you'll probably want to use Access. Access is a dedicated data management application. More than any other Office application, Access provides specialized data management tools, options for connecting to external databases, customization features, and facilities for publishing live data on the Web or on a company intranet.

One feature in particular sets Access apart from the other Office applications in storing data: Access lets you create a *relational database*. In contrast, information stored in an Excel worksheet, an Outlook folder, or a Word table, is stored as a *flat-file database*. A flat-file database consists basically of a single list of records, where each record stores *all* of the information on a particular item. For example, Figure 46-1 shows an inventory of books stored in a flat-file organization, where each record (row) stores all the information on a particular book. (Although this list was actually created in Access, it's similar to an Excel list or a Word table and *doesn't* take advantage of the Access relational database capabilities.)

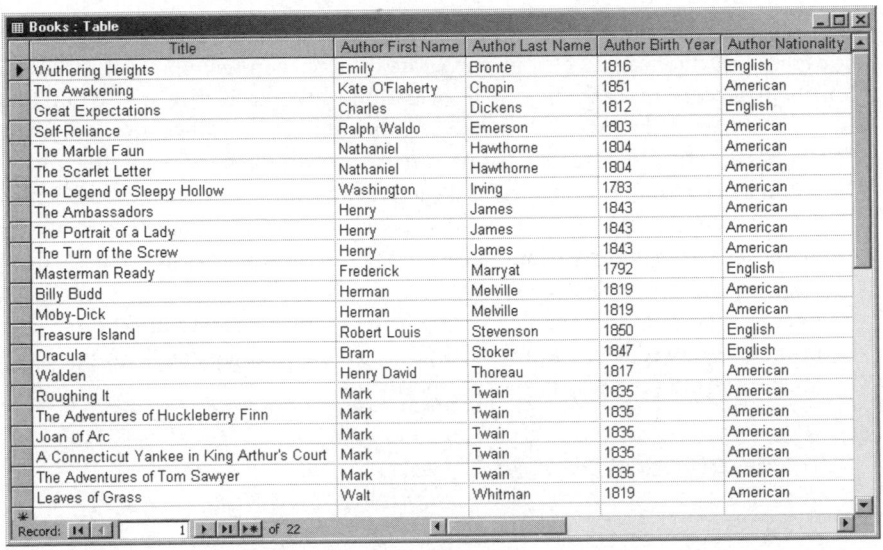

Figure 46-1. In a flat-file database, each record in a list stores all the information on a particular item. The data shown here belongs to the Book Inventory01 example database.

(Many of the examples in the Access chapters are based on various versions of the Book Inventory example database. These versions are named Book Inventory01, Book Inventory02, and so on. You'll find copies of these databases on the companion CD provided with this book under the filenames Book Inventory01.mdb, Book Inventory02.mdb, and so on.)

One major problem with a flat-file database organization is that information is usually duplicated in separate records. For example, in the list shown in Figure 46-1, wherever one author has written more than one book, all of that author's information—first name, last name, birth year, and nationality—is duplicated in the record for each book. Not only does this arrangement waste storage space, but also it requires unnecessary data entry, it increases the likelihood of errors (the more times you need to enter "1835" the more likely it is you'll make a typo), and it makes the data more difficult to maintain (for example, if you discover that an author's birth year is incorrect, you'll need to fix it in every record where it occurs).

note In Access an individual list of records is known as a *table*. The number of records entered into a table is limited only by storage capabilities, but each record has a fixed number of fields.

Chapter 46

A relational database solves the problem of duplicated data by storing a *single* copy of each set of duplicated fields in a separate list and then using identifiers to *relate* the lists. In Access, for example, the information shown in Figure 46-1 could be stored more efficiently by using two related Access tables, one table containing a list of book records and the other table a list of author records. Each record in the author table would have a unique identifier, and each record in the book table would include the unique identifier of the record for the book's author. The matching identifiers allow you to locate the information on each book's author and form the basis of the relationship between the tables (see Figure 46-2). You can then pull the separated data back together again in very flexible ways by using queries, reports, and other Access database objects (discussed later in the chapter), which can display data belonging to several tables according to the criteria you specify.

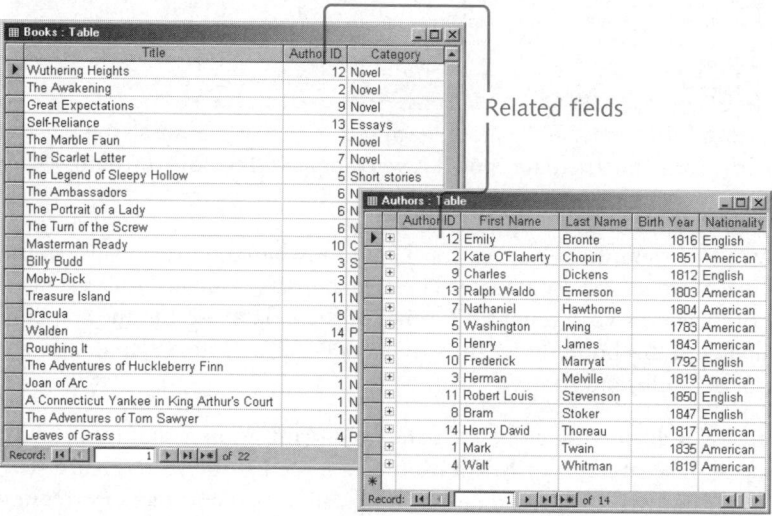

Figure 46-2. In Access you can eliminate duplicated information by storing data in two related tables, rather than in a single flat-file list. The tables shown here belong to the Book Inventory02 example database.

Furthermore, if a field stores the unique identifier of a record in a related table (as does the Author ID field in the Books table shown in Figure 46-2), rather than having to look up and type in the correct identifier (as was done in the Books table), Access lets you define a field so that it displays a drop-down list of the records in the related table. A field that displays a drop-down list of choices is known as a *lookup field*. For example, in the Books table you could convert the Author ID field to a lookup field that lists all author names, so that rather than typing the unique identifier for an author, the user would simply select the author's name from the list, as shown on the next page.

(Even though the field displays a value from another table, internally it still stores only a numeric identifier.)

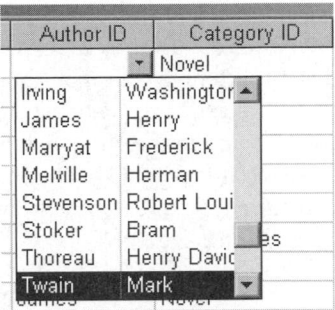

The next steps in consolidating the information displayed in the example Books table would be, first, to create a separate related table for storing the values displayed in the Category field (Novel, Essays, Short Stories, and so on), because these values are also repeated in many records, and, second, to convert Category to a lookup field. Using a related table and a lookup field is especially valuable for storing an information item such as a category, because the lookup field permits users to enter only a value contained in the drop-down list and prevents them from misspelling a category name or making up a new category on the fly. (Unofficial or misspelled categories would pose serious problems if you use the Category field to sort, filter, group, or work with the data in other ways.)

A relational database system such as Access provides the solution to yet another problem that you might encounter with a flat-file database. To illustrate this problem, consider the flat-file list of books shown in Figure 46-1 and imagine that some of the books have several authors. To store multiple authors in the flat-file database, you would have to add an arbitrary number of extra fields to store additional author information (wasting a great deal of space for the majority of books that have only a single author and possibly still not having room to store the authors for a book with many authors). In a relational database system, you can solve this problem by creating a separate related table of authors, plus an intermediate related table that stores book-author pairs. For information on this topic, see the Troubleshooting sidebar "Need a Many-to-Many Relationship," on page 1295.

Designing and Planning an Access Database

The previous section should have helped you decide whether Access is the appropriate application to use for managing your information and should have given you an understanding of some of the unique benefits that Access offers, primarily its relational database capabilities. If you've decided to use Access to store and manage your data, the following are the basic steps you need to follow. The details are given in the remainder of this chapter and in the following chapters in this part of the book.

1 Create a new database. An Access database stores a body of related information—for example, an inventory of assets, a set of customer descriptions, a product inventory, a ledger, a time and billing system, a collection catalog, a membership roster, an investment portfolio, or a set of class enrollment records. You can start with a blank database and design the entire database yourself. Or, you can use one of the database wizards provided with Access, which will build the basic structure for a particular type of database for you. Details are given in "Creating a New Database," on page 1267.

note Using the various types of Access wizards can eliminate many of the steps in this list. However, it's important to understand these steps so that you can modify the designs created by wizards or build your own designs when you can't find an appropriate wizard.

2 Add tables to the database. A table is a *database object* that stores data. (The other types of database objects, described later, are used to view, enter, edit, retrieve, and summarize the data contained in tables and to work with that information in other ways.) Each table contains a list of records storing information on one of the types of items that are tracked in your database. For example, in a book inventory database, you might add tables for listing books, authors, book categories, and binding types. You can create a blank table and then manually define the table's fields and specify the types of information stored in each field (such as Text, Number, Date/Time, or Currency). Or you can use the Table Wizard to create a table with predefined fields and then customize that table. Be sure to design your tables and their fields in a way that minimizes duplicated information, for all the reasons discussed in the previous section. Tables are covered in Chapter 47, "Setting Up Tables and Relationships."

tip   **Let Access Perform Your Calculations**

If you need to display values that Access can derive by performing math on information stored in your tables, *don't* include these values as table fields. Instead, in your queries, forms, and reports you can add fields that display the results of calculations based on existing table fields, without permanently storing these values in tables. Using calculated fields allows Access (rather than the person entering the data) to perform the calculation and eliminates storing unnecessary information. For example, if you want to display an inventory of office supplies, your table needs only two fields: Units On Hand (for example, number of boxes of pencils) and Measure Of Unit (for example, the number of pencils in a box). Access can do the multiplication and display the total number of each item in a query, form, or report.

3 Define or modify table relationships. Having your data optimally divided into separate, related tables isn't enough. Before Access can work with related data, the relationships between tables must be explicitly defined. In some cases Access will automatically define relationships for you. Sometimes, however, you'll need to use the Relationships window to explicitly define the relationships between tables or to modify the properties of the relationships that Access has set up. (Instructions for doing this are given in "Setting Up Table Relationships," on page 1291.) Figure 46-2 shows two related Word tables, which are displayed in Datasheet view.

4 Create other database objects for working with the data stored in the database tables. The following are brief descriptions of the main types of database objects, other than tables, that you can add to your database:

- **Query**   A tool for extracting, combining, and displaying data from one or more tables, according to criteria you specify. For example, in a book inventory database you could create a query to view a list of all hard-cover books with more than 500 pages that you purchased in the last five months. In a query you can sort information, summarize data (display totals, averages, counts, and so on), display the results of calculations on data, and choose exactly which fields are shown. You can view the results of a query in a tabular format (that is, Datasheet view, as shown in Figure 46-3) or you can view the query's data through a form or on a report. You can even use a query to update data automatically in one or more tables. The techniques for creating, modifying, and using queries are covered in Chapter 48, "Using Queries to Select and Combine Information."

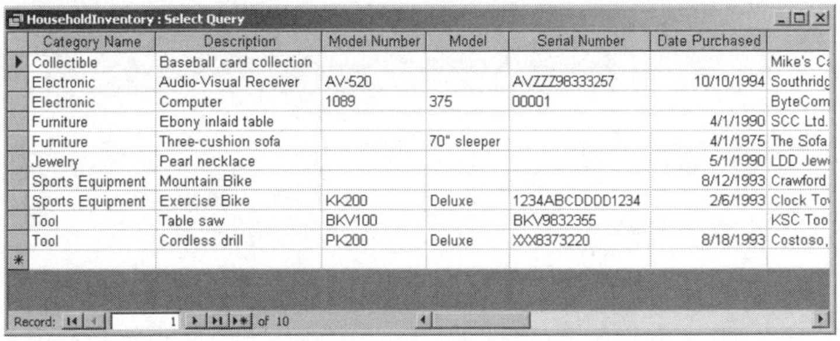

Category Name	Description	Model Number	Model	Serial Number	Date Purchased	
Collectible	Baseball card collection					Mike's Ca
Electronic	Audio-Visual Receiver	AV-520		AVZZZ98333257	10/10/1994	Southridg
Electronic	Computer	1089	375	00001		ByteCom
Furniture	Ebony inlaid table				4/1/1990	SCC Ltd.
Furniture	Three-cushion sofa		70" sleeper		4/1/1975	The Sofa
Jewelry	Pearl necklace				5/1/1990	LDD Jewe
Sports Equipment	Mountain Bike				8/12/1993	Crawford
Sports Equipment	Exercise Bike	KK200	Deluxe	1234ABCDDDD1234	2/6/1993	Clock Tov
Tool	Table saw	BKV100		BKV9832355		KSC Too
Tool	Cordless drill	PK200	Deluxe	XXX8373220	8/18/1993	Costoso,

Figure 46-3.   This query, displayed in Datasheet view, shows fields from four different database tables.

- **Form**   A window, similar to a dialog box, that contains a set of controls (such as labels, text boxes, and check boxes) that allow you to view, enter, or edit database information, typically one record at a time, as shown in Figure 46-4. In a form you can display data obtained directly from one or more tables or data that has been extracted using a query. Although it's possible to directly enter and edit the information in tables in Datasheet view, a database usually includes a set of forms, which can make entering and editing data considerably easier

1265

and can limit the fields that can be viewed or modified. The methods for creating, modifying, and using forms are described in Chapter 49, "Creating Forms and Data Access Pages for Working with Data."

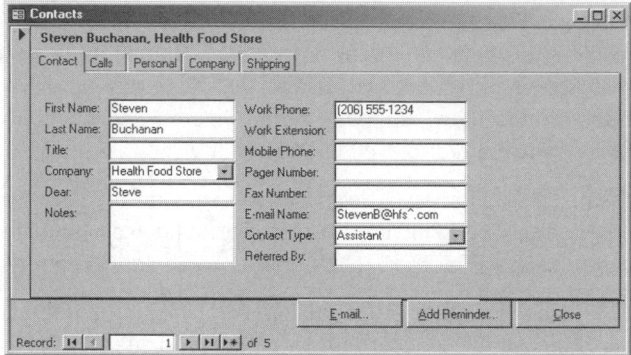

Figure 46-4. This form, displayed in Form view, lets you view and enter data belonging to two different tables one record at a time.

- **Data access page** A Web page, similar in appearance to a form, that you can publish on the Web or on a company intranet (see Figure 46-5). Users can open a data access page in their browsers and use it to view and update data from one or more tables in the database. Unlike other database objects, a data access page is stored in a set of separate files rather than incorporated into the database file. You'll find an introduction to creating data access pages in "Creating a Data Access Page," on page 1357.

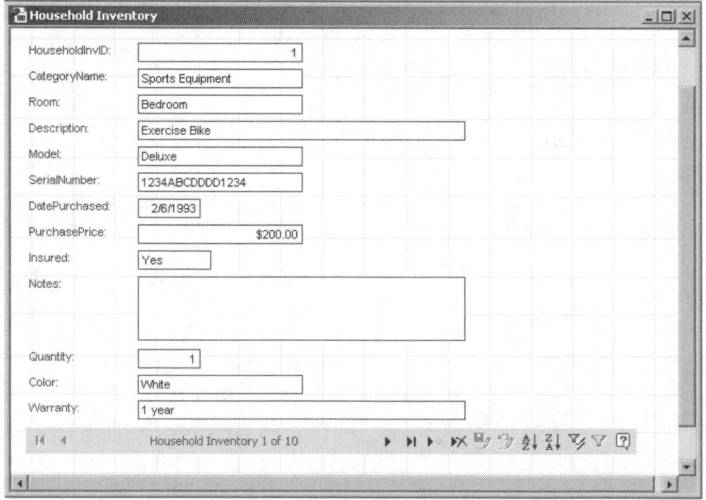

Figure 46-5. This data access page lets you view and modify the records belonging to a single table. It's displayed in Access in Page view.

> **note** Like a database or table, you can build a query, form, data access page, or report from scratch. Or you can use an Access wizard to create a fully functional database object that you can later customize.

■ **Report** Used primarily for printing selected database information. A report lets you label, group, sort, or summarize the data it presents (see Figure 46-6). And, like a form, a report can display data directly from one or more tables or it can display the results of a query. Access provides a variety of attractive, easy-to-read formats that you can apply to your reports.

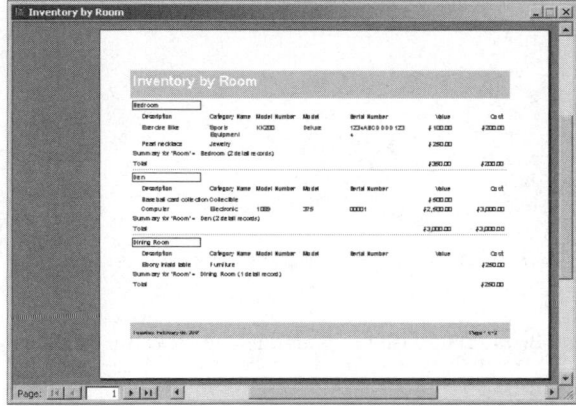

Figure 46-6. This report labels, groups, and summarizes (in total lines) data from an Access table. It's displayed in Access in Print Preview view.

5 Enter data into the database.

> **note** Keep in mind that queries, forms, data access pages, and reports provide tools for viewing, adding, modifying, selecting, combining, summarizing, sorting, and printing database information and working with that data in other ways. None of these objects actually stores data. In a database, all data is stored in one or more tables.

Creating a New Database

If you want to build a database from scratch, you can create a blank database and then manually add tables and other database objects one at a time. To create a blank database, follow these steps:

New

1 If the New File task pane (shown in Figure 46-7) isn't visible, show it by clicking the New toolbar button, choosing File, New, or pressing Ctrl+N.

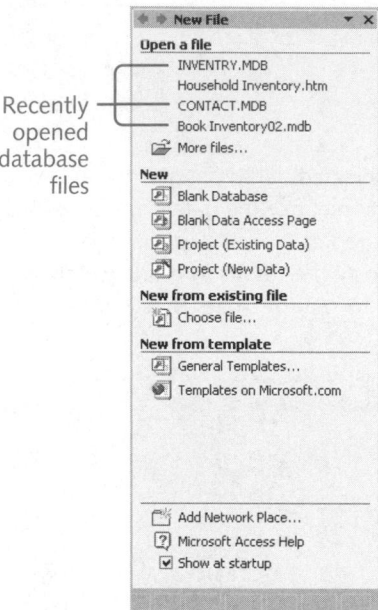

Recently opened database files

Figure 46-7. This figure shows the New File task pane that's displayed in Access.

2 Click the Blank Database command in the New area of the New File task pane.

3 Select a location and enter a name for your database file in the File New Database dialog box, which works just like the standard Save As dialog box.

Access will then save the new, blank database in the specified database file (which will have the .mdb extension), and it will open the Database window within the main Access window.

4 Add database objects as explained in the chapters in this part of the book.

If you can find an appropriate database wizard, you can gain a significant head start by using that wizard to create your database. To use a database wizard, follow these steps:

1 If the New File task pane isn't visible, show it by clicking the New toolbar button, choosing File, New, or pressing Ctrl+N.

New

2 Click the General Templates command in the New From Template area of the New File task pane.

3 Click the Databases tab of the Templates dialog box (shown in Figure 46-8), select a database wizard in the list, and click the OK button.

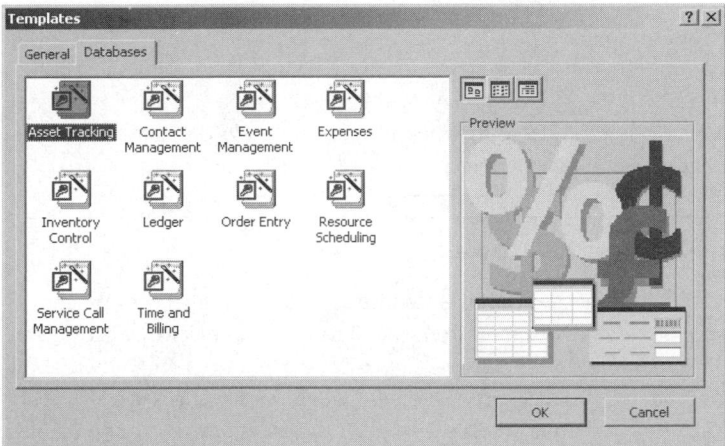

Figure 46-8. The Databases tab of the Templates dialog box lets you select a database wizard for creating a new Access database.

---

newfeature!

tip   Look for Additional Wizards

To look for additional Access wizards that you can download, click the Templates On Microsoft.com command in the New File task pane to connect to the Microsoft Office Template Gallery site on the Web.

---

4 Select a location and enter a name for your database file in the File New Database dialog box, which works just like the standard Save As dialog box. The database wizard will then display a series of dialog boxes.

5 In the wizard dialog boxes, select the features you want for your new database. Typically, you'll get to select one or more optional fields for each table that the wizard generates, the style of the forms and reports, and the database title. You can click the Finish button at any time to create the database using default settings for any options you haven't set.

Access will then generate the new database, adding a complete set of tables. Depending on the database design, it may also add queries, forms, and reports. It will automatically save the database in the database file you specified in step 4 (the file will have the .mdb extension), and it will open the Database window. Usually, the wizard will also create and open a Switchboard window, which provides a friendly interface that lets you open various database objects or close the database.

6 Modify the database objects using the techniques explained in the chapters in this part of the book.

> **note** You can use an existing Access database to create a new one by clicking the Choose File command in the New From Existing File area of the New File task pane. The new database will be an exact copy of the existing one but will have a new name that Access automatically assigns when it opens the new database. You can modify the filename in Windows Explorer.

> **tip** **Create a Database in Windows**
>
> You can create a new database without first running Access by choosing the New Office Document command from the Start menu in Microsoft Windows. To create a blank database, double-click the Blank Database item in the General tab of the New Office Document dialog box. To create a database using a wizard, click the Databases tab. For more information, see "Creating a Document Using the New Office Document Dialog Box," on page 53.

Access Projects vs. Access Databases

The New File task pane (shown in Figure 46-7) includes commands for creating a new *Access project file*—Project (Existing Data) and Project (New Data). You'll also find similarly named items for creating Access projects in the General tab of the Templates dialog box (shown, but not opened, in Figure 46-8).

Creating an Access project file, rather than an Access database, is an alternative way to set up database access. Rather than containing the actual data, an Access project file (which has the .adp file extension) stores settings for connecting to an external Microsoft SQL Server database. It's typically used to create a client-server application.

In contrast, an Access database (which has the .mdb file extension) contains the actual data, as well as definitions of database objects such as tables and queries. This data is managed by the Microsoft Jet database engine, which is included with the Access application.

The information in this book pertains to Access databases, *not* Access projects.

Using the Database Window and Object Views

Whenever a database is open, Access displays the Database window (shown in Figure 46-9), which serves as the central program location for working with the database objects (tables, queries, forms, and so on) in the opened database.

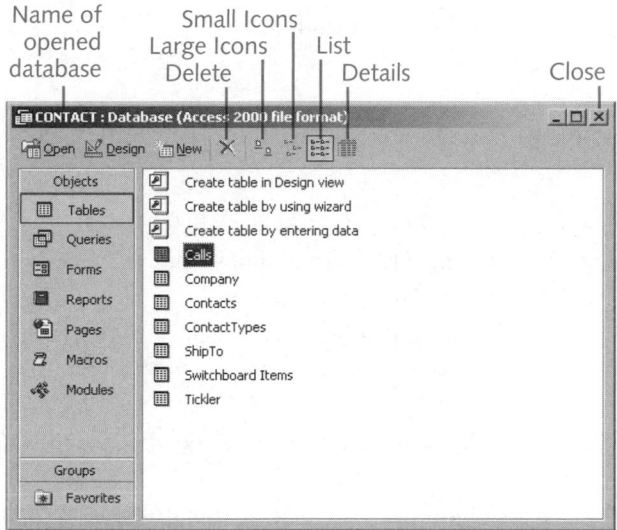

Figure 46-9. In the Database window, you can view, open, create, copy, move, rename, delete, organize, and perform other operations on the database objects in the opened database.

If the Database window is hidden by another window or is minimized, you can display it using one of the following methods:

● Click the button for the Database window on the Windows taskbar. This button will be labeled with the name of the database that you're working with, followed by a colon and the word *Database*. For example, if you're working with the CONTACT database, the label would be *CONTACT: Database*.

> **note** The Windows Taskbar displays a button for the Database window *only* if the Windows In Taskbar option is checked. You can find this option by choosing Tools, Options and looking in the View tab of the Options dialog box.

- Choose the item for opening the Database window from the Window menu in Access. The item is labeled the same way as the button on the Windows taskbar.

- Click the Database Window toolbar button.

Database Window

- Press F11.

The following are among the important ways you can work with database objects using the Database window:

- To work with a particular type of database object, click the corresponding button in the left column of the Database window—Tables, Queries, Forms, Reports, Pages, and so on.

- To view a database object, click it to select it and then click the Open button in the Database window, or just double-click the object. (This button will be labeled Preview for a report.)

- To change the design of a database object, select it and click the Design button.

- To create a new database object of the type currently displayed in the Database window, click the New button to open the New *Object* dialog box (New Table, New Query, New Form, New Report, or New Data Access page). The New *Object* dialog box will display a list of all the ways to create a new database object (the list varies according to the type of object you're creating). The remaining chapters in this part of the book give details on using each of the New *Object* dialog boxes.

- To make a copy of a database object, right-click it and choose Copy from the shortcut menu. Then right-click a blank spot in the Database window and choose Paste from the shortcut menu. You can also copy (or move) a database object to another database opened in a separate Access window by choosing the Copy (or Cut) command, and then choosing the Paste command in the Database window for the target database.

- To rename a database object, select it and press F2.

- To delete a database object, select it and press the Delete key or click the Delete button in the Database window.

- You can perform several additional operations on a database object by right-clicking it and choosing a command from the shortcut menu. For example, you can choose commands from the following shortcut menu when you right-click a table listed in the Database window:

Chapter 46

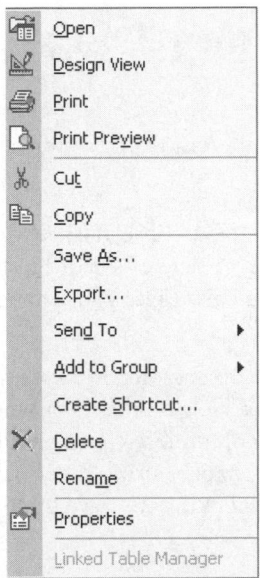

You can perform many of these same operations by selecting the object and choosing a command from the File or Edit menu.

● To close the current database, together with the Database window, click the Close button in the upper-right corner of the window.

Access provides several different *views* for working with database objects. When you select a database object in the Database window and click the Open button (or the Preview button for a report) or when you double-click an object, Access opens the object in a view that's appropriate for examining and modifying the object's data—Datasheet view for a table or query, Form view for a form, Page view for a data access page, and Print Preview view for a report. If you click the Design button, Access will open the object in Design view, where you can modify the object's design (for instance, the fields and their data types for a table).

Once you've opened a database object in any view, you can switch to any other available view by choosing a different view from the View menu or by clicking the down arrow on the View toolbar button and choosing a different view from the drop-down menu. The available views depend upon the type of the database object. With a table, for example, you can choose any of the following views:

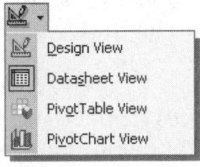

The following chapters explain the details of the commonly used views.

Saving, Closing, and Opening Databases in Access

The way an Access database is saved on disk is different from the way a typical Office document is saved, in the following respects:

- When you modify the *data* stored in the database in Datasheet or Form view—for example, when you add, change, or delete a record in the Datasheet view of a table—Access automatically saves your changes in the database file.

- When you modify the *design* of a database object—for instance, when you add, remove, or modify fields in the Design view of a table or when you change the columns in the Datasheet view of a query—you have to manually save your changes. You can save these changes using the usual commands—that is, by choosing File, Save, by clicking the Save toolbar button, or by pressing Ctrl+S.

Save

InsideOut

Preventing Data Loss

The automatic saving of data in Datasheet or Form view can help safeguard against the loss of information you've added. Keep in mind, however, that because of this feature you *can't* reverse changes you've made by simply abandoning the database without saving, as you can with a Word document or an Excel workbook. For example, if you accidentally delete a large group of records or fields, you can't reverse that change by simply closing the database without saving, because the change will already have been written to the database disk file. Nor can you reverse the deletion of one or more records or fields by issuing the Undo command. Although Access generally warns you before you it deletes the data, such deletions are permanent. And Access has commands that are capable of quickly deleting large amounts of data!

The best way to safeguard against loss of data in Access is to make frequent, regular backups of the database file and to always create a backup copy of the database before you make any significant changes to the data or design. That way you can revert to the previous state of the database if necessary.

- Because of the automatic data-saving feature of Access, when you create a new database, Access saves it to a disk file *before* it lets you start working on the database, as explained previously in this chapter.

To close the current database (and leave Access running), activate the Database window and either click the Close button in the upper-right corner of that window, or choose Close from the File menu. Creating a new database, or opening an existing one, also causes Access to close the current database.

new feature!

tip   **Select the Best Database Format**

When you create either a blank database or one based on a wizard, Access 2002 stores the database in an Access database file (an .mdb file) that has the same format that was used by Access 2000. This format works fine for smaller databases and offers the advantage of letting you easily share your database file with Access 2000 users.

If, however, you're creating a relatively large database, you may be able to obtain better performance by converting your database to the new Access 2002 format. To do this, choose Tools, Database Utilities, Convert Database, To Access 2002 File Format. Access will create a separate database file in the new format, leaving your original database file intact. Although you won't be able to immediately share an Access 2002 format database with users of former Access versions, you can convert it back to an earlier format by choosing Tools, Database Utilities, Convert Database, To Access 2000 File Format or by choosing Tools, Database Utilities, Convert Database, To Access 97 File Format.

Opening a Database

To open an existing database, use one of the standard techniques for opening an Office document:

Open

- In Access, choose Open from the File menu, click the Open toolbar button, or press Ctrl+O. Or in Windows, choose Open Office Document from the Start menu. Then, select the database file in the Open or in the Open Office Document dialog box.

   or

- Choose a recently opened database file from the bottom of the File menu or click the name of a recently opened database file in the Open A File area at the top of the New File task pane, which you can open by choosing New from the File menu (see Figure 46-7).

For details on these as well as other ways to open Office documents, see "Opening Existing Office Documents," on page 61.

Unlike most other Office applications, however, if you open a database from within Access, it will close any database that's already opened. To have more than one database open at the same time, you can open an additional database outside of Access (for example, by choosing Open Office Document from the Start menu in Windows or by double-clicking a database file in Windows Explorer). Or, you can start another Access instance by choosing Programs, Microsoft Access from the Start menu in Windows, and then open the database from within Access.

Chapter 46

Chapter 47

Setting Up Tables and Relationships

Creating a Table

To create a new table in Microsoft Access 2002, open the New Table dialog box (shown in Figure 47-1) as explained in "Using the Database Window and Object Views," on page 1271, and then select an option in the list, as follows, and click OK:

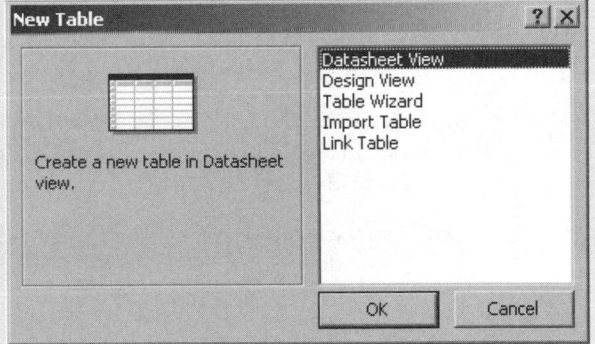

Figure 47-1. In the New Table dialog box you can select one of five ways to create a new table.

- To create a table containing a basic set of fields and to open that table in Datasheet view so you can begin adding data immediately, select the Datasheet View option. The table will initially have 10 fields (named Field1 through Field10), as shown in Figure 47-2. You'll need to save the table design before you close the table or switch to another view (Access will prompt you if you forget). When you first save the table, Access will assign a data type to each field according to the type of information you entered into that field (such as Text, Number, Date/Time, or Currency) and it will discard any of the initial fields in which you haven't entered data.

> For information on adding data and performing limited customizations to the table design in Datasheet view, see "Working in Datasheet View," on page 1296. For instructions on extensively modifying the table using Design view, see "Customizing a Table in Design View," on page 1280.

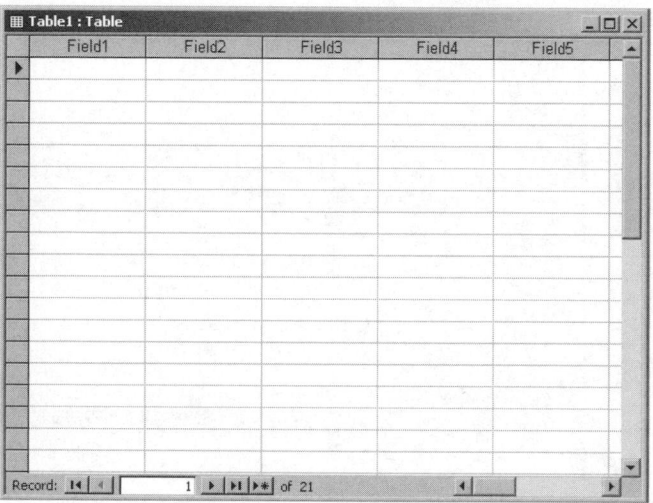

Figure 47-2. The Datasheet View option creates a new table containing 10 initial fields in which you can immediately start entering data. Only some of the fields are shown here.

● To open a new, blank table in Design view, where you can add fields and define their properties, select the Design View option. For more information, see "Customizing a Table in Design View," on page 1280.

● To create a new table using the Table Wizard, which will greatly assist you in adding fields to your new table and in assigning appropriate properties to these fields, select the Table Wizard option (see Figure 47-3). Once the wizard has generated your new table, you can open it in Datasheet view to immediately begin adding data or to perform limited modifications to the table design, as explained in "Working in Datasheet View," on page 1296. Or, you can open it first in Design view to customize the table design more extensively, as described in "Customizing a Table in Design View," on page 1280. Or you can enter data into the table using a form the Table Wizard creates.

> **note** You can have the Table Wizard automatically designate a *primary key* for the new table. See "Designating a Primary Key," on page 1290. If your database contains other tables, the wizard may also allow you to define relationships between your new table and existing tables. See "Setting Up Table Relationships," on page 1291.

Chapter 47

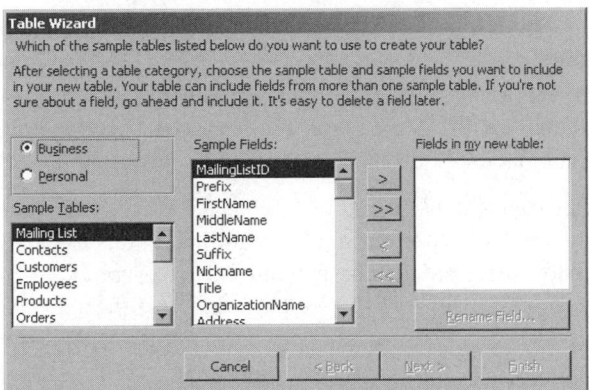

Figure 47-3. The Table Wizard helps you quickly add fields to a new table. It assigns an appropriate data type and other properties to each field it adds.

tip newfeature! **Export Access Data to XML or Other Formats**

You can export a table or other database object to an external file by selecting the object in the Database window and choosing File, Export. You can export a database object to an Access, Lotus 1-2-3, Paradox, or dBASE database; to an Excel workbook; to an XML document or an HTML or ASP (Active Server Page) Web page; to a text or RTF (Rich Text Format) file; or to an ODBC data source.

You can also export a table, query, form, or report to another Microsoft Office XP application by selecting the object in the Database window and then choosing a command from the Office Links submenu on the Tools menu:

The Merge It With Microsoft Word command is available only for a table or query. It runs a mail merge operation in Microsoft Word 2002, using the table or query as the recipient list. See Chapter 19, "Using Word to Automate Mailings."

- To create a new table in your Access database by importing data from an external database or other data source, select the Import Table option. You can import data from an Access, Lotus 1-2-3, Paradox, or dBASE database; from a Microsoft Excel workbook; from a Microsoft Outlook or Microsoft Exchange folder; from an XML (Extensible Markup Language) document or an HTML (Hypertext Markup Language) Web page; from a text file; or from an ODBC (open database connectivity) data source. The new table and its data will become an integral part of your Access database, just as if you had entered it within Access, and the data won't be affected by subsequent changes made to the data source after you import it.

● To create a new table that's linked to an external database or other data source, select the Link Table option. You can link a table to data in an Access, Paradox, or dBASE database; in an Excel workbook; in an Outlook or Exchange folder; in an HTML Web page; in a text file; or in an ODBC data source. Rather that storing the data itself, a linked table stores only a connection to the data source, and you can use the table to view or modify the data within that source. You should use linking rather than importing if the data is maintained by a separate application and you want to use Access to tap into the current data.

Customizing a Table in Design View

You can use Design view to define the design of a new, blank table you've created using the Design View option in the New Table dialog box. You can use it to customize the design of a new table you've created using one of the other options in the New Table dialog box. And you can use it to modify an existing table that already contains data. Design view allows you to add, remove, or rearrange fields; to define the name, the data type, and other properties of each field; and to designate a primary key for the table.

To open a table in Design view, follow the instructions given in "Using the Database Window and Object Views," on page 1271. Figure 47-4 shows the Books table in the Book Inventory03 example database, opened in Design view. The top portion of the Design view window lists the fields in the table, one per row, and gives the name, data type, and an optional description for each field. (These are three of the field's *properties*, which are explained in "Setting the Field Properties," on page 1284.) If you're using Design view to create a new table, this list will initially be empty.

The tabs in the bottom portion of the window show all the other properties for the current field. (The *current field* is the one that's selected in the field list—it's marked with an arrow in the box at the left end of the row.) Each property is displayed in a separate box within the grid.

Save

To save the changes you make in Design view choose File, Save; or click the Save toolbar button; or press Ctrl+S.

Chapter 47

Row selectors   A property box   Field list

The current field

Properties for the current field are displayed on these tabs.

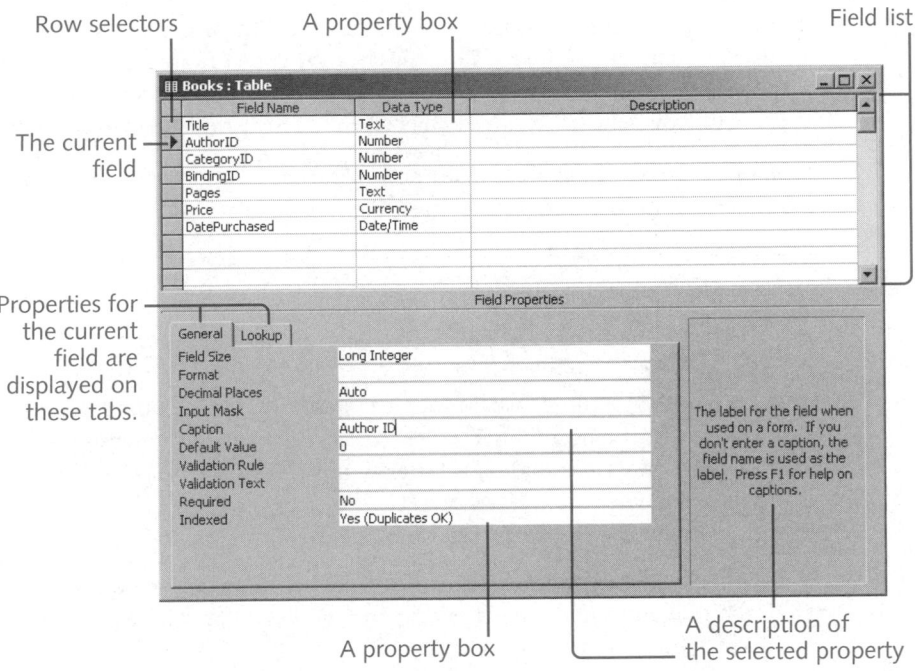

A property box   A description of the selected property

Figure 47-4. The Design view of a table lets you modify the table's fields and their properties. This table belongs to the Book Inventory03 example database.

Adding, Removing, and Rearranging Fields

Using Design view, you can add new fields to a table, remove fields, or move or copy fields from one position in the field list to another.

Adding a Field

To add a new field to a table at the end of the list, click in the Field Name column of the first blank row in the field list in the top portion of the Design view window and enter a field name. You can type up to 64 characters for the field name, including spaces. Ideally, however, you should make the name short and descriptive of the field's contents. It's also best to avoid including spaces in field names if you want to be able to easily access those fields from VBA (Visual Basic for Applications) code (in VBA names aren't allowed to contain spaces). If you want the field to be labeled with a "friendlier" name in Datasheet view, including spaces if you wish (for example, Type Of Binding rather than BindingID), you can assign that name to the field's Caption property (as described later in the chapter). If the Caption property has a value, Access will use it to label the field's column in Datasheet view; if the Caption property is blank, Access will label the column using the field name.

Insert
Rows

To insert a new field between two existing fields in the list, click the lower of the two fields, and then choose Insert, Rows or click the Insert Rows toolbar button. Another way to insert a field is to select the entire row below the desired insertion position by clicking the row selector (the box at the left end of the row), and then press the Insert key.

Don't be too concerned about your new field's initial position— you can easily move it (as described in "Moving or Copying a Field," on page 1283).

---

tip   **Use the Shortcut Menu**

As you work in Access, keep in mind that you can often display a shortcut menu of useful commands by right-clicking a field, title bar, column or row heading, or other object. The shortcut menu will provide commands that are appropriate for working with the particular object that you clicked. For example, you can insert a new field into a table by right-clicking the row below the desired insertion position and then choosing Insert Rows from the shortcut menu.

You should then proceed to set any of the field properties that you want to change from their default values, following the instructions that will be given in "Setting the Field Properties," on page 1284.

---

tip   **Have Access Build Your Field**

When you add a field, you may be able to save time by using the Field Builder, which lets you select and insert a predefined field suitable for a particular purpose (such as a telephone number in a table of contacts or a serial number in a table of products). The primary advantage of using the Field Builder is that a field you insert will have all its properties set to appropriate values. (The field builder offers the same list of pre-defined fields as the Table Wizard.)

Build

To use the Field Builder, click the row in the field list below the position where you want to insert the new field and click the Build toolbar button.

Removing a Field

Delete
Rows

To remove a field from the table, click anywhere in the field's row in the field list and choose Edit, Delete Rows or click the Delete Rows toolbar button. Another way to delete a field is to select its entire row by clicking the row selector (the box at the left end of the row) and then press the Delete key. You won't be able to delete a field that's used to create a relationship with another table; you must first remove the relationship.

> **caution** If a particular field already contains data, be aware that deleting the field will delete its data for every record in the table.
>
> Access now lets you undo multiple actions in Design view. (To undo an action, choose Edit, Undo; or click the Undo toolbar button; or press Ctrl+Z.) However, once you save the table design (which you must do before changing views), you won't be able to undo your deletion and the data will be permanently deleted.
>
> Undo

Moving or Copying a Field

Access uses the order in which the fields are listed in Design view as the default order of the fields in Datasheet view or in a form or report that you generate from the table. Therefore, you should arrange the fields in a logical order. Keep in mind, however, that in Datasheet view or in a form or report you can override the default field order and arrange the fields any way you want (without affecting their order in the Design view of the table).

To move a field to a different position in the field list, first select its entire row by clicking the row selector (the box at the left of the row). Then perform either of the following actions:

● Use the mouse to drag the row selector up or down to the new position:

Drag the row selector to move the selected field up or down in the list.

Field Name	Data Type	Description
Title	Text	
AuthorID	Number	
CategoryID	Number	
BindingID	Number	
Pages	Text	
Price	Currency	
DatePurchased	Date/Time	

● Choose Edit, Cut (or press Ctrl+X). Then click in the row below the desired new position of the field and choose Edit, Paste (or press Ctrl+V). Be sure to just click in the row below the desired insert position so that it contains the insertion point; if you select this entire row, it will be deleted when you paste. (Note that this method won't work if the field is currently part of one or more relationships. Also, if the field already contains data, that data will be lost.)

> **note** If you want to make a copy of a field, use the second method for moving a field, but choose the Copy command (or press Ctrl+C) rather than choosing the Cut command (or pressing Ctrl+X). After the field is copied, click the field name and type in a different, unique name. (You won't be able to save your modifications if two fields have the same name.) Note that although the original field's properties will be duplicated in the copy of the field, any data contained in the original field will *not* be transferred to the copy.

Setting the Field Properties

Each of the fields in a table is described by a set of *properties*. The field's properties determine how the field's data is stored, handled, or displayed. The properties include the field name, the data type, the description, and other features such as the field size, format, and caption. You can view and set a field's properties within the boxes in the Table Design view window (both in the field list at the top of the window and on the tabs in the bottom portion). (See Figure 47-4 on page 1281, for example.) Note that when the insertion point is within a property box, Access displays information about that property in the lower-right corner of the window, and you can get detailed information by pressing F1.

When you add a new field, you must enter a name for it. Access will assign all of the field's other properties a default setting. (For some fields the default setting is no value; that is, the property box will initially be blank.) You can modify any of these properties, or you can simply accept the default setting.

Renaming a Field

To change a field's name property, click in the Field Name column for that field and type in the name you want. Follow the naming instructions given at the beginning of "Adding a Field," on page 1281. Changing the field name won't affect any of the table's relationships.

Setting the Data Type

Every field is assigned a specific data type, which determines the kind of data that can be entered into the field. The default data type of a new field is Text. To change a field's data type, click in the Data Type column for that field, and select a new data type from the drop-down list:

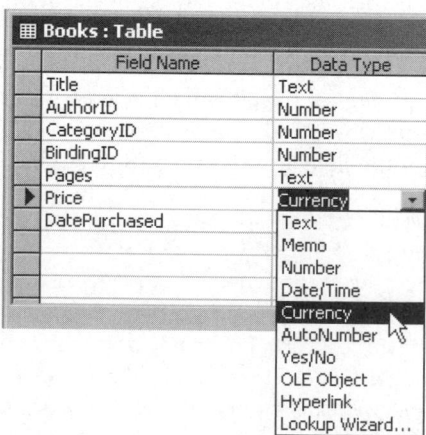

The available data types are described in Table 47-1.

Table 47-1. Data Types You Can Assign to Table Fields

Data Type	Usage
Text (default)	Holds any type of characters, either letters or numbers. The number of characters that can be stored depends on the value (0 to 255) assigned to the Field Size property (described later). Note that even if you set Field Size to 255, Access will use only the amount of memory required by each entry.
Memo	Similar to Text, but holds up to 64,000 characters.
Number	Holds a numeric value that you can use to perform calculations or comparisons. The size and type of number you can store is determined by the current setting of the Field Size property (described later).
Date/Time	Holds valid calendar dates for the years 100 through 9999 and clock times in either 12-hour or 24-hour format. This data type lets you sort and calculate data chronologically.
Currency	Accurately stores monetary values for use in financial calculations and comparisons.
AutoNumber	Stores a unique number that Access assigns as each new record is added. Access either increments the number by one with each new record, or it assigns a unique random number, according to the setting of the New Values property. These numbers aren't reused when you delete records, and you can't change the value of an AutoNumber field.
Yes/No	Efficiently stores one of two values: true or false, yes or no, on or off (according to the setting of the Format property). You can set the field using a check box in Datasheet view or on a form.
OLE Object	Holds an OLE (object linking and embedding) object (such as an Excel spreadsheet, a Word document, or a picture, sound, animation, or video clip) that you insert by using the Insert, Object command. See Chapter 7, "Sharing Data Among Office XP Applications," for information on OLE objects.
Hyperlink	Holds a hyperlink—that is, the location of another database object, an Office document, or a page on the Web. You insert the hyperlink into the field by choosing Insert, Hyperlink. You can then open the target object, document, or Web page by clicking the hyperlink in the field.

(continued)

Chapter 47

Table 47-1. *(continued)*

Data Type	Usage
Lookup Wizard	Selecting this item runs the Lookup Wizard, which assists you in converting the field to a lookup field, which is described in "A Rundown on Access," on page 1259. Before you select this item, you should *first* set the field's data type by selecting Text, Number or Yes/No from the list. (A field must have one of these three data types before you can convert it to a lookup field.) In Datasheet view a lookup field displays a drop-down list that contains values from another table or query or a fixed list of values that you specify when you use the Lookup Wizard. You can later modify the properties of a lookup field's list by changing values in the Lookup tab at the bottom of the Table Design view window.

caution   If a field already stores data, changing its data type can result in loss of information. For instance, if you change a field's data type from Text to Number, Access will permanently delete the contents of any field that doesn't contain a valid numeric value, and it may alter the values of numbers according to the field's Field Size property (for instance, if Field Size is set to Long Integer, Access will convert 29.95 to 30).

Troubleshooting

Items in Lookup Field Displayed Randomly

You used the Lookup Wizard to create a lookup field. In Datasheet view the field's drop-down list displays the correct fields from the related table, but the fields are listed in random order.

The Lookup Wizard doesn't let you apply a sorting order to the items displayed in the drop-down list of a lookup field. To have Access sort these items, click the lookup field in the field list in the Design view window, open the Lookup tab at the bottom of the window, click in the Row Source property box, and click the ellipsis (...) button that appears at the right of the box. Then, in the SQL Statement:Query Builder window, select Ascending or Descending in the Sort row, under the field you want to sort by. Close the SQL Statement:Query Builder window by clicking the X on the top right-hand corner of the window. If you wish to save the changes you made, answer Yes to the dialog box asking, "Do you want to save the changes made to the SQL statement and update the property?" For more information on applying a sort using a grid such as the one displayed in the SQL Statement:Query Builder window, see "Modifying a Query," on page 1316.

Adding a Description

If you wish, you can assign a description to a field by entering it into the Description column for that field. When a field is selected in Datasheet view, Access displays the field's description, if any, in the status bar. You might therefore want to create a description containing instructions or other information that would be useful to the person entering data into the table.

Setting Other Field Properties

You set the remaining field properties using the General and Lookup tabs in the bottom portion of the Table Design view window. To set additional properties for a field, complete the following steps:

1 Click anywhere within the field's row in the upper part of the Table Design view window or select the row. (It will then become the current field and will be marked with an arrow in the row selector.)

2 Click the General tab in the lower half of the window to set general-purpose properties or click the Lookup tab to modify the properties that apply specifically to a lookup field (as described in the last item in Table 47-1).

3 Click in the box for any property that you want to modify and enter a new value or select it from the drop-down list, if available. Consult the property description displayed in the help area on the right or press F1 for detailed information about the current property.

> **note** When you click in certain property boxes, an ellipsis (…) button appears to the right of the box. You can click this button to display a dialog box that will assist you in entering a value into the field. Which dialog box Access displays depends on the particular field. For example, it might show the Expression Builder dialog box, the Input Mask Wizard, or the SQL Statement:Query Builder window.

The set of additional properties that are available for a field depends on the field's data type. In general, these properties control the way data is entered, stored, and displayed in the field. The following sections describe some of the important properties.

Field Size Property

The Field Size property controls the amount of space that is allocated for a particular field. It's available only for a field that has the Text or Number data type. For a Text field, the Field Size specifies the maximum number of characters that can be stored in the field; you can enter a value between 0 and 255. (The default value is 50.) For a

Number field, you can select a value from the drop-down list that determines the size and type of number that the field can store:

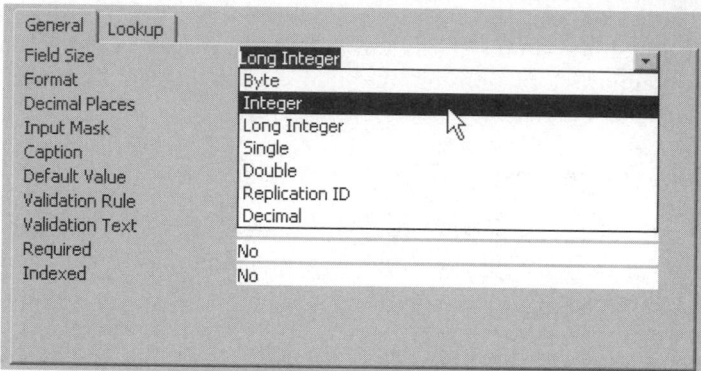

For example, you can use the Long Integer value (the default) to store whole numbers ranging from approximately –2 billion to +2 billion, or you can select the Double value to store numbers with decimal components (such as 3.14).

Format Property

The Format property determines how the data is displayed on the screen or how it's printed. Choose the format that you want from the drop-down list. For example, for a field that has the Date/Time data type, you can choose to display the date as a Long Date (for example, Saturday, December 1, 2001), as a Short Date (for example, 12/1/2001), or using other date and time formats.

Decimal Places Property

The Decimal Places property lets you choose the number of decimal places that Access displays for a field that has the Number or Currency data type. (It affects only the way the number is displayed, not the precision of the value that's stored internally.) Choose a specific number of decimal places from the drop-down list or choose Auto (the default value) to display the default number of decimal places for the field's Format property setting.

Input Mask Property

Most data types also give you the option to define an *input mask*. (By default, there is no input mask.) An input mask assists you in entering valid data into a field. It displays placeholder characters showing you the number of characters you need to enter (usually _ characters, which are replaced by the characters you type); it includes separator characters so you don't have to type them (such as the parentheses and dash in a telephone number); and it prevents you from typing an inappropriate character (for example, a letter when you're entering a phone number). Figure 47-5 shows an input mask applied to a field with the Date/Time data type, as it's displayed in Datasheet view.

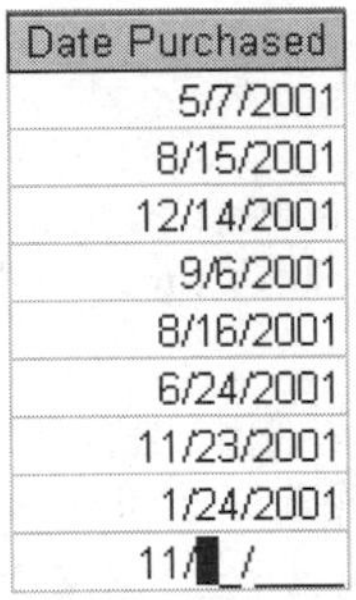

Date Purchased
5/7/2001
8/15/2001
12/14/2001
9/6/2001
8/16/2001
6/24/2001
11/23/2001
1/24/2001
11/ /

Figure 47-5. This input mask makes it easier to enter a valid date in the mm/dd/yyyy format.

The fastest way to define an input mask is to run the Input Mask Wizard by clicking the ellipsis (…) button that appears at the right end of the Input Mask property box when you click in it.

Caption Property

If you enter text into the box for the Caption property, Access will use this text to label the field in Datasheet view, at the top of the field's column. If you leave the Caption box empty (the default value), Access labels the field using the field name. This property gives you flexibility in the way your fields are labeled in Datasheet view, without your having to change the actual field name.

Default Value Property

If you're creating a database in which a field usually contains the same value—for example, the City field in an address database in which most of the addresses are in the same city—you can assign that value to the Default Value property. (By default, this property is blank.) Then, whenever Access creates a new record, it will insert the value into the field for you (for example, *New Orleans*). You can then change the value if necessary.

Required Property

If you select Yes in the Required property box, Access will require that a value be entered into the field when the record is created or modified. If you choose No (the default value), the field can be left empty.

Indexed Property

This property controls whether a field is *indexed*—that is, whether Access builds an index for the field. Indexing a field significantly speeds up searching, sorting, or running queries on that field, but it requires more space for storing the information and can make adding, deleting, or updating records slower. The primary key for a table (discussed in the next section) is automatically indexed. The choices in the drop-down list in the Indexed property box are listed on the next page.

- **Yes (Duplicates OK)** The field will be indexed, and you'll be able to enter the same value into more than one record.

- **Yes (No Duplicates)** The field will be indexed, and you must enter a unique value into the field for each record. (This is the default for a field that's designated as the primary key, discussed next.)

- **No** The field won't be indexed, and you'll be able to enter the same value into more than one record. (This is the default for all fields except one designated as the primary key.)

Designating a Primary Key

The primary key consists of one or more fields that Access can use to uniquely identify the records contained within the table. A table must have a primary key if it's on the "one" side of a one-to-many relationship, as explained in "Setting Up Table Relationships," on page 1291.

When you designate a single field as the primary key, the field's Indexed property is automatically set to Yes (No Duplicates) and you won't be able to change this setting. Thus, you can quickly sort or retrieve the records using the primary key field, and you'll be barred from entering duplicate values into this field. Also, when you enter or modify the data in a record, Access won't let you leave a primary key field blank.

In most cases a single field is used as the primary key, although in situations where the data in a single field can't be unique for each record, two or more fields can be designated. In this case the data in all the primary key fields combined must be unique for each record. (For example, an inventory table might contain a part number field and a subpart number field, where neither field is unique by itself but when taken together, they form a unique combination.) When multiple fields are used to create a primary key, the Indexed property for each component of the primary key will not be changed and remains editable, unlike a single field that is designated as the primary key.

Primary
Key

To designate a field, or a group of fields, as the primary key, select the field or fields in the field list and choose Edit, Primary Key or click the Primary Key toolbar button. (To select several fields, click the row selector for the first one, and then click the row selector for each additional one while holding down the Ctrl key.) Access will mark the primary key field(s) with a key icon, as shown here:

Books : Table	
Field Name	Data Type
BookID	AutoNumber
Title	Text
CategoryID	Number

Field designated as the primary key

To remove the primary key designation from a field, select it and choose the Primary Key command or click the Primary Key toolbar button again.

Setting Up Table Relationships

Before Access can work with related data, the relationships between related tables must be explicitly defined. When you create a database using a database wizard or when you add a table using the Table Wizard, Access will define relationships for you.

If the required relationships between tables aren't defined, in some cases Access will define them for you as they're needed—for instance, when you add a lookup field or when you insert a subdatasheet (discussed later in this chapter). In other cases, you must explicitly define the required relationships before Access can combine the related data—for example, when you use a wizard to create a query that displays data from two or more related tables. Explicitly defining a relationship also allows Access to maintain integrity of the related data.

> **note** Although this section focuses on tables, you can also define relationships for queries, and you may need to do so if you use a query as the basis for a report or for another query.

To view existing relationships, to define new ones, or to change relationship properties, follow these steps:

1 Close any tables that are opened. (You won't be able to make certain changes to a relationship if one of the related tables is open.)

Relationships

2 Open the Relationships window by choosing Tools, Relationships or—if the Database window is active—by clicking the Relationships toolbar button. Figure 47-6 shows the relationships that are defined in the Book Inventory03 example database.

> **note** If no relationships have yet been defined in your database, when you open the Relationships window, Access will first display the Show Table dialog box, explained in step 4 in this procedure.

The lines between the field lists in the Relationships window indicate relationships between specific fields. In a typical relationship, the field in one of the two tables has a unique value. Two types of fields store unique values: a primary key field and a field whose Indexed property is set to the value Yes (No Duplicates). The other table's field in a typical relationship has a non-unique value; that is, its Indexed property is set to No or to Yes (Duplicates OK). The table containing the unique field is commonly known as the *primary* table, and the table containing the non-unique field is commonly known as the *related* table. Because a field in a second record in the primary table can match the same field (data types must match, not necessarily field names) for several fields in the related table, the relationship between these fields is called a *one-to-many* relationship. The *one* side of a relationship line is marked with a "1" and the *many* side is marked with an infinity symbol (∞), but *only* if you've chosen to enforce referential integrity, as explained in the sidebar "Enforcing Referential Integrity," on page 1294.

A relationship

A field list

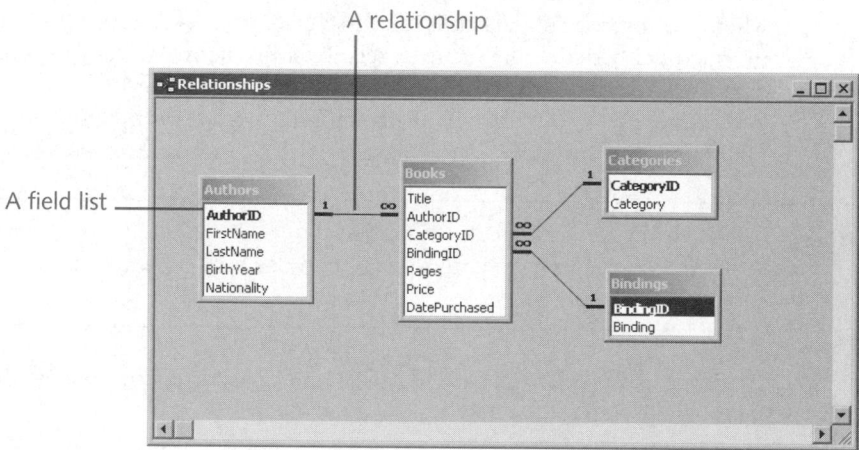

Figure 47-6. The Relationships window shows the relationships that have been defined between tables and queries in the database. These relationships belong to the Book Inventory03 example database.

note In the one-to-many relationship between the Authors and Books tables in the Book Inventory03 example database (shown in Figure 47-6), the field containing unique data is in the Authors table, which is therefore the primary table. The field containing non-unique, related data is in the Books table, which is therefore the related table.

Like the author descriptions, the book categories and binding types are also stored in related primary tables in the Book Inventory03 database, so that categories and binding types aren't duplicated in the Books table. Placing the categories and binding types in separate related tables also allows the user to select categories and binding types from lookup fields, rather than having to type in the values. See the discussion on the advantages of storing data in separate, related tables in "A Rundown on Access," on page 1311.

3 If necessary, arrange the field lists shown in the Relationships window so that you can see the relationship lines clearly. You can move a field list by using the mouse to drag its title bar.

> **note** If *both* fields in a relationship are unique, the relationship is known as *one-to-one*. For instance, in an employee database, if employee descriptions were stored in one table and their social security numbers were stored in a related table, the relationship would be one-to-one (each employee record would match a single social security record and vice versa). Breaking apart information like this is uncommon because it doesn't prevent duplicated data, and it would be more efficient to simply place all the data in a single table. One possible reason for doing it, however, would be to keep some information (such as a social security number, password, or birth date) confidential by placing it in a separate one-to-one related table that has limited access.

Show
Table

4 If one or more tables whose relationships you want to view or work with aren't shown in the Relationships window, choose Relationships, Show Table or click the Show Table toolbar button and select the table or tables in the Tables tab of the Show Table dialog box.

Show All
Relationships

> **note** You can hide a field list by clicking it and pressing Delete or choosing Relationships, Hide Table. Doing so won't remove any relationships that are associated with this table but will merely hide the field list and its relationships from view. You can show the lists for all tables involved in relationships by choosing Relationships, Show All or by clicking the Show All Relationships toolbar button.

5 To define a new relationship, drag the related field from the field list for one of the tables, drop it on the related field in the field list for the other table, and click the Create button in the Edit Relationships dialog box that Access shows (see Figure 47-7). Note that related fields don't need to have the same name, only the same data type (although they're often given the same name to clarify the relationship).

Notice that the Edit Relationships dialog box displays the type of the relationship, which is based on the related fields: One-To-Many or One-To-One, or Indeterminate. Access uses Indeterminate when it can't explicitly determine the relationship. For information on the Enforce Referential Integrity and related options, see the sidebar "Enforcing Referential Integrity," on page 1294. For a brief explanation of the options you can select by clicking the Join Type button, see the sidebar "Modify Table Relationships for a Query," on page 1319.

If you later want to change the features of a relationship, you can reopen the Edit Relationships dialog box for that relationship by double-clicking the relationship's line in the Relationships window.

6 To delete a relationship, click the line to select it and then press the Delete key.

Chapter 47

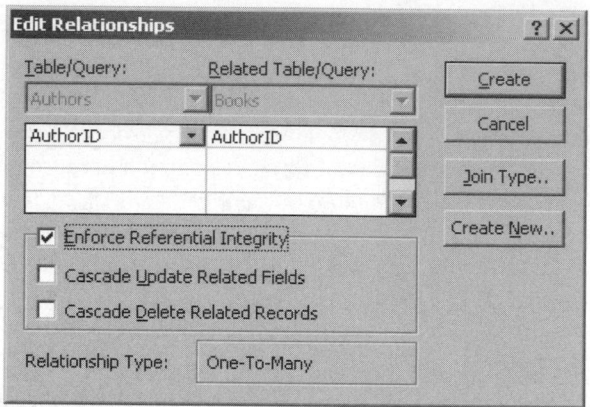

Figure 47-7. The Edit Relationships dialog box lets you add or change a relationship's features.

7 When you've finished working with relationships, close the Relationships window. If you've modified the layout of the window (that is, the tables that are included and their arrangement), Access will ask if you want to save the layout. (Rest assured that the relationships themselves have already been saved.) Be sure to click the Yes button if you want to reuse this same layout.

Enforcing Referential Integrity

When you define a relationship, you can check the Enforce Referential Integrity option in the Edit Relationships window to have Access make sure that the correspondence between the tables is maintained as you enter data and work with the database. Specifically, this option ensures that each record in the related table will properly match a record in the primary table. To select this option, the data types of the related fields must be the same, and the relationship can't be *indeterminate* (an invalid relationship for enforcing referential integrity in which neither related field can be explicitly determined to be unique). If the option is enabled, Access will control changes you attempt to make to the related fields in the following ways:

- Access won't allow you to enter a value into the related table field that lacks a matching value in the primary table field. You can, however, leave the related table field blank (indicating that it doesn't refer to any record).

- Access won't permit you to change the value in the primary table field if matching records are already in the related table field. For instance, in the Book Inventory03 example database (shown in Figure 47-6 and other figures), you wouldn't be able to change the value of the AuthorID field in any of the records in the Authors table because each of the AuthorID values is already used in the Books table. (Actually, in this example you couldn't change this field anyway because it has been assigned the AutoNumber data type.)

Enforcing Referential Integrity *(continued)*   However, if you check the Cascade Update Related Fields option in the Edit Relationships dialog box, Access will let you change the primary table field and will automatically update all the matching values in the related table field so that referential integrity is maintained between the two tables.

● Access won't let you delete a record in the primary table if matching records are in the related table. For instance, in the Book Inventory03 example database, you couldn't delete any of the Authors records because each one has matching records in the Books table. However, if you check the Cascade Delete Related Records option in the Edit Relationships dialog box, Access will enforce referential integrity by deleting all the matching records in the related table for each record you delete in the primary table.

Troubleshooting

Need a Many-to-Many Relationship

You need to connect two tables with a many-to-many relationship, but Access doesn't provide this type of relationship.

In Access you can indirectly set up a many-to-many relationship by creating an intermediate table. Consider, for instance, the Book Inventory03 example database (shown in Figure 47-6 and other figures in this part of the book). If some of the books have more than one author, and you want to be able to link a book to all the book's authors and to link an author to all the author's books, you need to set up a many-to-many relationship. You could set up this relationship, thereby allowing the book inventory database to support more than one author for each book, by performing the following steps:

1 Add a unique identifying field to the Books table, so that each record in the intermediate table can reference a specific book record (and make this field the primary key while you're at it). Also, eliminate the AuthorID field in the Books table because it's no longer needed.

2 Create an intermediate table (perhaps named BookAuthors) in which each record contains the unique identifier of a book record plus the unique identifier of an author record, thereby linking a book to one of its authors and an author to one of his or her books.

3 Define a relationship between the Books and BookAuthors tables and a relationship between the BookAuthors and Authors tables, as shown in Figure 47-8. Both these relationships will be one-to-many, but the overall result will be to connect Authors and Books in an indirect many-to-many relationship.

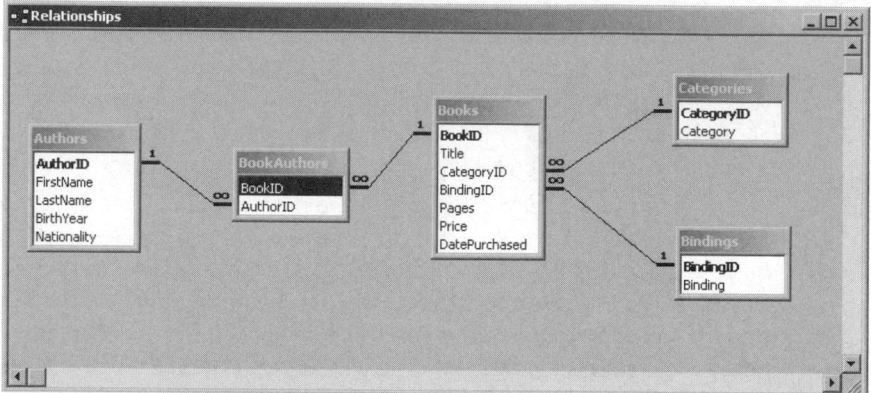

Figure 47-8. The BookAuthors table effectively creates a many-to-many relationship between the Books table and the Authors table. These relationships and tables belong to the Book Inventory04 example database.

Working in Datasheet View

Using Datasheet view is the most common way of viewing a table or a query. You can also view a form in Datasheet view, although you almost always work with forms in Form view. Figure 47-9 shows the Books table in the Book Inventory03 example database displayed in Datasheet view. In this view each column represents a single field in the database, and each row represents a record. To open a table (or a query or form) in Datasheet view, follow the instructions given in "Using the Database Window and Object Views," on page 1271.

Text here	Author ID	Category ID	Binding ID	Pages	Price
Wuthering Heights	Bronte	Novel	hardcover	424	$12.95
The Awakening	Chopin	Novel	mass market paperback	195	$4.95
Great Expectations	Dickens	Novel	mass market paperback	639	$6.95
Self-Reliance	Emerson	Essays	hardcover	249	$8.79
The Marble Faun	Hawthorne	Novel	trade paperback	473	$10.95
The Scarlet Letter	Hawthorne	Novel	trade paperback	253	$4.25
The Legend of Sleepy Hollow	Irving	Short stories	mass market paperback	98	$2.95
The Ambassadors	James	Novel	mass market paperback	305	$5.95
The Portrait of a Lady	James	Novel	mass market paperback	256	$4.95
The Turn of the Screw	James	Novel	trade paperback	384	$3.35
Masterman Ready	Marryat	Children's book	trade paperback	425	$12.89
Billy Budd	Melville	Short stories	mass market paperback	195	$4.49
Moby-Dick	Melville	Novel	hardcover	724	$9.95
Treasure Island	Stevenson	Novel	trade paperback	283	$11.85
Dracula	Stoker	Novel	hardcover	395	$17.95
Walden	Thoreau	Philosophy	mass market paperback	523	$6.95
Roughing It	Twain	Novel	mass market paperback	324	$5.25
The Adventures of Huckleberry Finn	Twain	Novel	mass market paperback	298	$5.49
Joan of Arc	Twain	Novel	trade paperback	465	$6.95
A Connecticut Yankee in King Arthur's Court	Twain	Novel	mass market paperback	385	$5.49
The Adventures of Tom Sawyer	Twain	Novel	mass market paperback	205	$4.75
Leaves of Grass	Whitman	Poetry	hardcover	462	$7.75
					$0.00

Record: 1 of 22

Figure 47-9. Datasheets provide an easy way to work with the data stored in your database. This table belongs to the Book Inventory03 example database.

Chapter 47

Entering and Editing Data in Datasheet View

New
Record

The last row in Datasheet view is available for adding new records and is marked with an asterisk (*) in the row selector (the box at the left end of the row) to indicate where the new record goes (as shown in Figure 47-9). You can quickly move to the last row by clicking the New Record toolbar button.

To enter data into a new record or to modify an existing record in the table, click the field that you want to fill in or modify. If you prefer using the keyboard, you can press the Enter or Tab key to move from left to right through the columns in a record. To move back a column, press Shift+Tab. You can enter or modify text in a field using the standard editing methods that all Office applications provide.

As soon as you begin entering or changing information in a record, the row selector to the left of the row displays a pencil icon, indicating that the record contains unsaved changes, as shown in Figure 47-10. Access will automatically save your changes (and remove the pencil icon) when you move to a different record. You can save your changes before then by pressing Shift+Enter. (The Save command on the File menu, the Save toolbar button, and the Ctrl+S shortcut key save any changes you've made to the layout of Datasheet view, *not* changes you've made to the current record.) You can abandon any unsaved changes you've made to a record, restoring it to its original state, by pressing Esc. When you first enter data into a new record in the last row, Access immediately creates a new blank row below the one that you're editing.

Record with unsaved changes

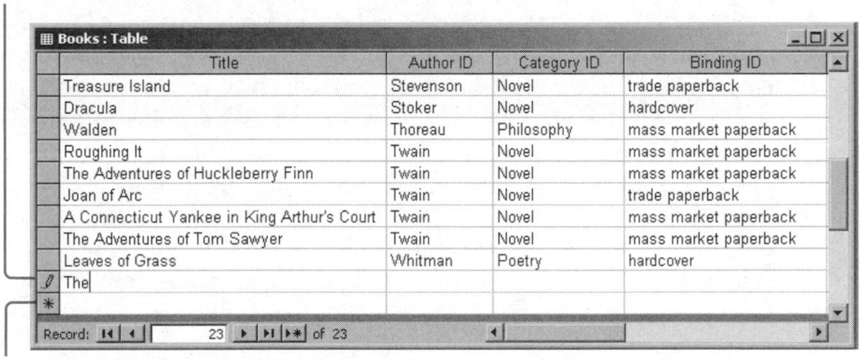

Title	Author ID	Category ID	Binding ID
Treasure Island	Stevenson	Novel	trade paperback
Dracula	Stoker	Novel	hardcover
Walden	Thoreau	Philosophy	mass market paperback
Roughing It	Twain	Novel	mass market paperback
The Adventures of Huckleberry Finn	Twain	Novel	mass market paperback
Joan of Arc	Twain	Novel	trade paperback
A Connecticut Yankee in King Arthur's Court	Twain	Novel	mass market paperback
The Adventures of Tom Sawyer	Twain	Novel	mass market paperback
Leaves of Grass	Whitman	Poetry	hardcover
The			

Record: 23 of 23

Empty row for adding a new record

Figure 47-10. Access uses a pencil icon to mark a record containing unsaved changes, and it uses an asterisk to mark the empty row at the end of the table where you enter the next new record.

To enter a value into a lookup field, select a value from the drop-down list, as shown on the next page.

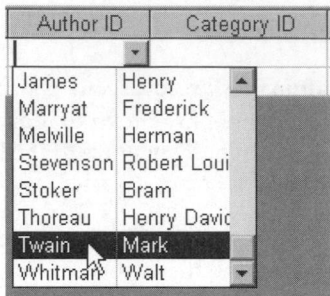

(If the Limit To List property has been set to Yes for the lookup field, if you type a value, it must match one of the items in the list. One of the purposes of a lookup field is to limit the values you can enter.)

If a field's Format property has been assigned a specific format, all you have to do is enter the value that goes into that field, in any convenient form, and move to another field. Access will then properly format the entry for you. For example, if a numeric field is formatted for currency, when you type **2.1** and move out of the field, Access displays the information in the field as $2.10.

A field that has an input mask, such as a date field, will display a template for you to fill in with the actual values, as shown in Figure 47-5.

---

tip   **Zoom a Field**

If you find entering data into a cell in Datasheet view a bit confining, or if the font is a little too small to see clearly, press Shift+F2 to open the Zoom dialog box, which lets you enter the field's data into a spacious, scrollable list box, and to select any font. (The font you select will be used only in the Zoom dialog box; it won't affect the text in the Datasheet view.) Zooming is especially useful for entering a large amount of text into a field with the Memo data type (which can hold up to 64,000 characters!). The Zoom dialog box will allow you to enter more data than is allowed for the field; however, when you click the OK button in the Zoom dialog box, Access will warn you that it's going to truncate the data. Also, the Zoom dialog box is not available for fields with the Date/Time data type.

Deleting Records

Delete
Record

To delete a record, select it by clicking its row selector, and then choose Edit, Delete Record; or click the Delete Record toolbar button; or press the Delete key. (If you use the menu command or toolbar button, you can just click anywhere in the record; you don't need to select the entire record.)

To delete an entire group of adjoining records, first select all of the records by clicking the row selector of one record and dragging the highlight up or down over the other records, and then issue the Delete command.

The record or records are removed from view and a dialog box appears, telling you exactly what you're deleting. If you realize that you're deleting something by mistake, click the No button to stop the deletion process. To proceed with the deletion, click the Yes button.

---

caution Once you delete a record and click the Yes button to confirm your action, you won't be able to restore the record. You *can't* undo a record deletion using the Undo command. If you ever want to restore a deleted record, you'll have to reenter it from scratch.

---

tip **Find or Replace Text Quickly**

Find

You can quickly find specified text in Datasheet view by choosing Edit, Find; or by clicking the Find toolbar button; or by pressing Ctrl+F. Then enter your search criteria into the Find tab of the Find And Replace dialog box (see Figure 47-11). To replace text, choose Edit, Replace or press Ctrl+H to open the Replace tab of the Find And Replace dialog box.

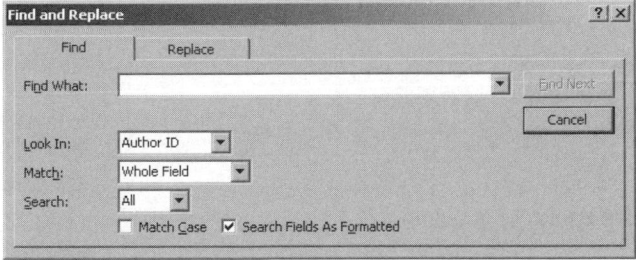

Figure 47-11. The Find And Replace dialog box lets you search for text in a single field or in an entire table.

Customizing Datasheet View

This section explains several ways to modify the design of the Datasheet view of the currently displayed table, query, or form. Some of the changes you can make affect only the layout of the Datasheet view and don't alter other views or the underlying structure of the table, query, or form. These changes include adjusting the column width or row height and rearranging the order of the columns. Other changes affect a table's underlying structure and alter the way the table appears in other views, such as Design view. These changes include renaming, adding, and deleting fields. (You can make these changes only to a table viewed in Datasheet view, not to a query or form.) Note that many of the techniques for modifying the design of the Datasheet view resemble techniques used in Excel worksheets.

You can change the width of a column in Datasheet view by dragging the right border of the column heading, as shown below:

Dragging a column border to a new position

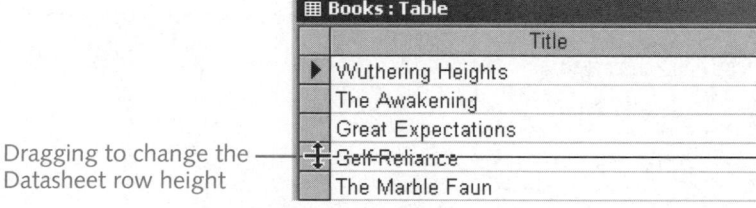

Original column border

You can change the height of *all* rows by dragging the bottom border of any row selector (one of the buttons to the left of the rows). You *can't* change the height of individual rows.

Dragging to change the
Datasheet row height

---

tip **Let Access Adjust the Width of a Column**

You can have Access determine the most appropriate width for a column by double-clicking the right border of the column heading. Access will then adjust the column width to the smallest possible size that can display all the information contained within that column (including the caption in the column heading).

The columns in Datasheet view are initially arranged in the order in which the corresponding fields are listed in Design view. However, you can rearrange the columns in Datasheet view any way you want. To move a particular column, select the column by clicking the column heading. Be sure to release the mouse button. Then drag the column heading right or left to the new location. (If you don't release the button after you first click the column heading, dragging will simply select multiple columns.) Note that changing the order of columns in Datasheet view doesn't change the underlying order of the fields as displayed in Design view or other views.

In Datasheet view, each column heading displays the Caption property of the field shown in that column, unless the Caption property is blank. In that case the heading displays the name of the field (the Field Name property). No matter which property is displayed in the heading, you can change the *field name* by double-clicking the column heading, typing a new name, and pressing Enter. The Caption property will be set to blank (if it wasn't already blank), and the heading will display the field name. (You can't assign a new value to the Caption property in Datasheet view.)

You can also add or delete columns in the Datasheet view of a table, thereby adding fields to or removing fields from the table. To add a column, click anywhere in the column to the right of the position where you want the new column, and then choose Insert, Column. Access will create a new column and will assign it an initial name; it will name the first column you add Field1, the second column Field2, and so on. You can then change the field name as described previously.

To delete a column, click anywhere in the column and choose Edit, Delete Column. You'll have the opportunity to confirm your action.

InsideOut

Keep in mind that when you delete a column, you're permanently removing a field—together with all its data—from the table. You *can't* issue the Undo command to reverse this action. If you delete a column and then realize later that you should have left that information where it was, you'll have to recreate the field and reenter that field's information for every record in the database, perhaps thousands! In short, be careful about deleting a column, and always make a backup copy of your database before making any major changes.

---

tip **Temporarily Hide Columns**

You can also temporarily hide one or more columns by selecting them and choosing Format, Hide Columns. To select a single column, click its heading. To include additional columns, keep the mouse button pressed and drag left or right (if you release the button after clicking, you'll move the initial column rather than extending the selection).

You can later make one or more hidden columns visible again by choosing Format, Unhide Columns and checking all the columns that you want to reappear.

Save

Access automatically saves any changes that affect a table's underlying structure (renaming, adding, or deleting a field, as well as edits to each record). If, however, you adjust the Datasheet view *layout* (the column width, row height, or column arrangement), you must save your changes by choosing File, Save; or clicking the Save toolbar button; or pressing Ctrl+S. If you haven't saved your layout changes, you'll be asked whether you want to do so when you close the table. If the changes aren't necessary, click No and the next time you open the table in Datasheet view, it will be displayed in its original layout.

Adding and Using Subdatasheets

If the table displayed in Datasheet view is the primary table in a one-to-many relationship, you can display the matching records in the related table by using a *subdatasheet*. For instance, if a subdatasheet were added to the Datasheet view of the Authors table in the Book Inventory03 example database, you could display a list of all books written by a particular author by clicking the plus (+) symbol in the first column to open the subdatasheet for that record, as shown in Figure 47-12.

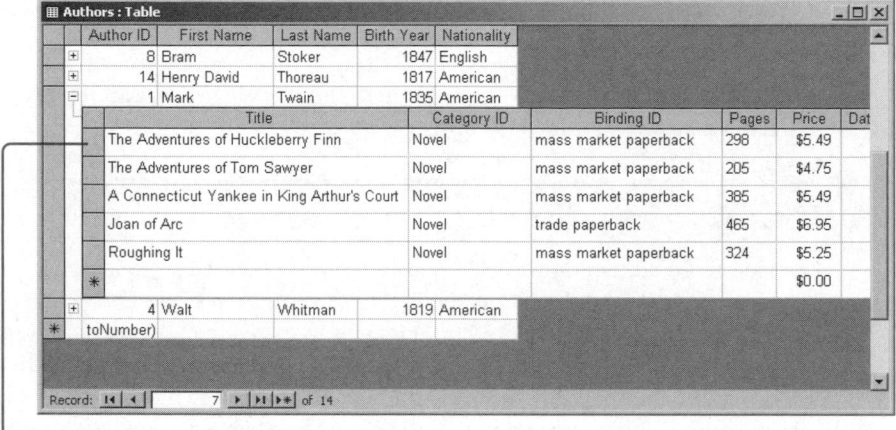

Subdatasheet displaying records in the Books
table that match author "Mark Twain"

Figure 47-12. You can display or hide the subdatasheet for a particular record by clicking the + or – in the first column. This table belongs to the Book Inventory03 example database.

If a table displayed in Datasheet view is the primary table in a *single* relationship, Access automatically adds a subdatasheet that displays the related table. If, however, the table is the primary table in more than one relationship, you must explicitly add the subdatasheet and specify the particular relationship you want to use by performing the following steps. (Before beginning this procedure, you might open the Relationships window so that you can see which fields and tables are related.)

1 Choose Insert, Subdatasheet. Access will open the Insert Subdatasheet dialog box (shown in Figure 47-13).

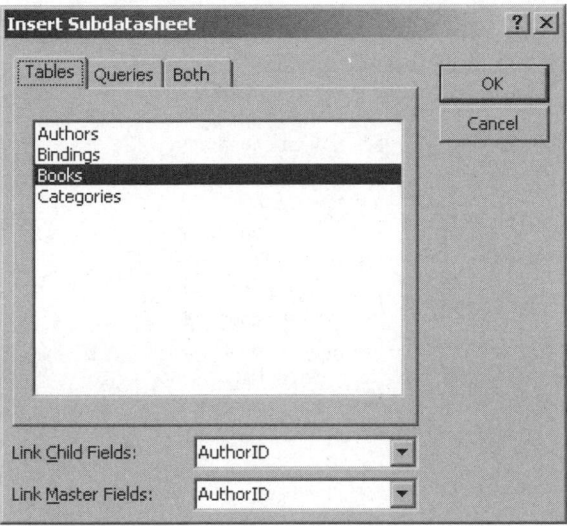

Figure 47-13. You can add or modify a subdatasheet using the Insert Subdatasheet dialog box.

2 In the list within the appropriate tab of the Insert Subdatasheet dialog box, select the related table (or query) you want to display in the subdatasheet.

3 In the Link Child Fields drop-down list, select the name of the related field in the related table (the table you want to display in the subdatasheet), if it isn't already selected.

4 In the Link Master Fields drop-down list, select the name of the related field in the primary table (the table currently displayed in Datasheet view), if it isn't already selected.

5 Click the OK button.

You can use this same procedure to modify an existing subdatasheet.

Sorting and Filtering in Datasheet View

The fastest way to sort the records in Datasheet view is to right-click the heading of the column you want to use as the sort key, and then choose Sort Ascending or Sort Descending from the shortcut menu, as shown at the top of the next page.

Chapter 47

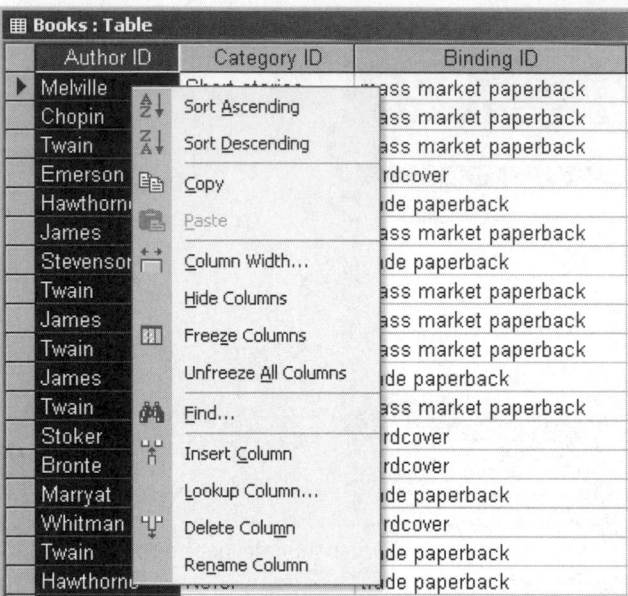

An ascending sort arranges number fields from smallest to largest (for example, –3, 0, 1, 2, 10), date fields from earliest to most recent (for example, 1/19/1948, 6/15/1994, 3/15/2001), and text fields in alphabetical order. A descending sort arranges fields in the opposite order.

You also *filter* the records in a table to display only those records that match your criteria, rather than displaying all the records in the table. You can apply a filter by selection or by using a form.

Applying a Filter by Selection

The fastest way to filter records is by finding a field in a record that contains the information you want to use as a filter criterion and then having Access list only those records that contain the same entry in that field. For example, in the Books table (in the Book Inventory03 example database), you might want to list all the hardcover books in stock. To do so, you first locate a record containing the entry that you want to use to select your records—in this case, a record that has the entry *hardcover* in the Binding ID field, as shown in Figure 47-14.

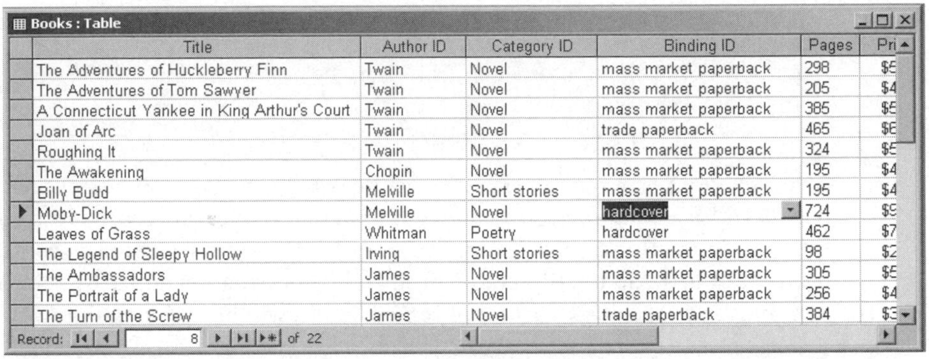

Books : Table					_□×
Title	Author ID	Category ID	Binding ID	Pages	Pri▲
The Adventures of Huckleberry Finn	Twain	Novel	mass market paperback	298	$5
The Adventures of Tom Sawyer	Twain	Novel	mass market paperback	205	$4
A Connecticut Yankee in King Arthur's Court	Twain	Novel	mass market paperback	385	$5
Joan of Arc	Twain	Novel	trade paperback	465	$6
Roughing It	Twain	Novel	mass market paperback	324	$5
The Awakening	Chopin	Novel	mass market paperback	195	$4
Billy Budd	Melville	Short stories	mass market paperback	195	$4
▶ Moby-Dick	Melville	Novel	hardcover ▾	724	$9
Leaves of Grass	Whitman	Poetry	hardcover	462	$7
The Legend of Sleepy Hollow	Irving	Short stories	mass market paperback	98	$2
The Ambassadors	James	Novel	mass market paperback	305	$5
The Portrait of a Lady	James	Novel	mass market paperback	256	$4
The Turn of the Screw	James	Novel	trade paperback	384	$3 ▾
Record: ⏮ ◀ [8] ▶ ⏭ ▶* of 22	◀			▶	

Figure 47-14. To start a Filter By Selection, you must first select the information you want to use as the filter criterion. This table belongs to the Book Inventory03 example database.

Filter By Selection

Either click anywhere within the field or select the whole entry to tell Access to match the field's entire contents. Then choose Records, Filter, Filter By Selection. Or, click the Filter By Selection toolbar button. Access will then show only the records that meet the filter criterion—that is, records that have the same value in the selected field. The Datasheet view of the Books table shown in Figure 47-14 would then appear as shown in Figure 47-15, where only hardcover books are displayed.

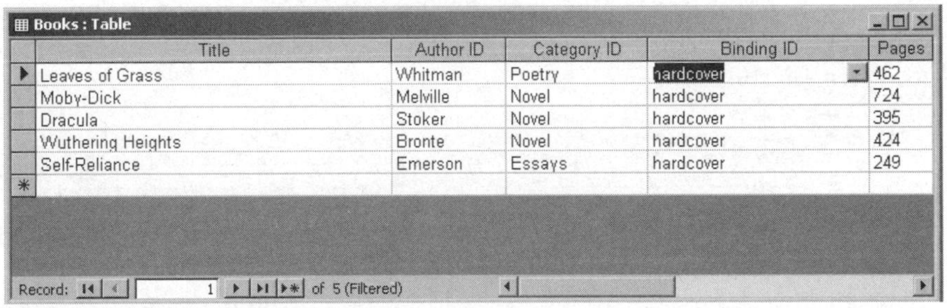

Books : Table				_□×
Title	Author ID	Category ID	Binding ID	Pages
▶ Leaves of Grass	Whitman	Poetry	hardcover ▾	462
Moby-Dick	Melville	Novel	hardcover	724
Dracula	Stoker	Novel	hardcover	395
Wuthering Heights	Bronte	Novel	hardcover	424
Self-Reliance	Emerson	Essays	hardcover	249
*				
Record: ⏮ ◀ [1] ▶ ⏭ ▶* of 5 (Filtered)	◀		▶	

Figure 47-15. This figure shows the same table as Figure 47-14 after applying a filter to show only hardcover books.

note To show all records *except* those that have the value of the field you selected, choose Records, Filter, Filter Excluding Selection.

Remove/
Apply
Filter

To return to viewing all your records, choose Records, Remove Filter/Sort or click the Remove/Apply Filter toolbar button. You can later reapply your most recently defined filter by simply choosing Records, Apply Filter/Sort or by clicking the Remove/Apply Filter toolbar button. (When a filter is applied, this button is selected, its ScreenTip label is Remove Filter, and clicking it removes the filter. After the filter has been removed, the button is deselected, its label is Apply Filter, and clicking it reapplies the previous filter.)

> **note** When a filter is currently applied, Access displays "(Filtered)" at the bottom of the Datasheet window, and it displays "FLTR" on the Access status bar. These indicators warn you that not all of the table's records are displayed.

If you select a portion of a field entry before issuing the Filter By Selection command, Access will use only the selected text in determining which records to display. For example, in the Books table shown in Figure 47-14, if you select the word *paperback* in one of the entries in the Binding ID field and you then apply Filter By Selection, both *mass market paperback* and *trade paperback* books will be included in the list.

Note, however, that if your selection includes the first letter in an entry, Access will match only fields that *start* with the selected text. For example, if you select the *M* in the Author ID field of the *Moby-Dick* record, Access will display only books with author names that start with *M*.

You can also filter records using the entries from several fields in a record. In this case Access will display only records that match *all* the selected entries. To do this, first be sure that the fields that have the values you want to use are next to each other. (You can move columns in the Datasheet window if necessary.) Then select all the entries to be used for the match and issue the Filter By Selection command. To select several adjoining field entries in a record, click the left end of one entry to select it (click when the pointer becomes a large plus sign) and without releasing the mouse button drag the highlight left or right over the other entry or entries. For example, if you made the following selection:

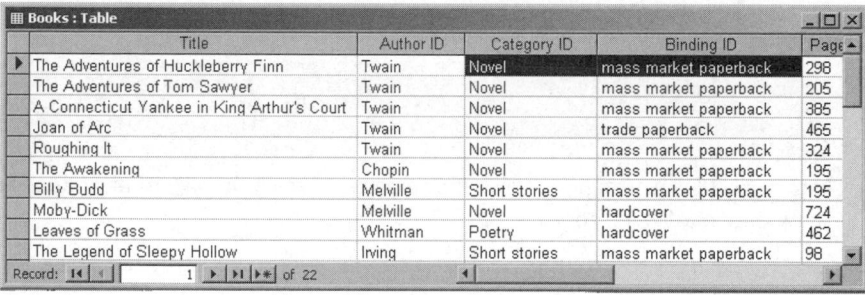

Access would display only the books that are mass market paperback novels.

Finally, you can select entries across adjoining records, rather than fields, and then use the Filter By Selection command. In this case Access will list records that match *any* of the selected field values. For instance, if you made the following selection:

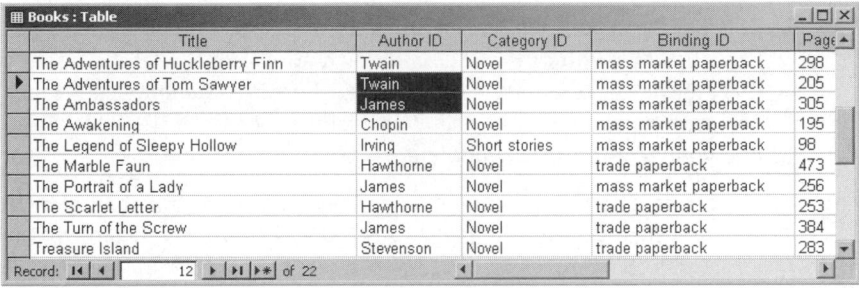

Access would display all of Mark Twain's books, all of Henry James's books, and no others. If the values you want to select don't happen to be in adjoining fields, you'll have to use one of the filtering methods described next.

Applying a Filter by Form

When you want to use more than one value to filter records, a more versatile approach is to use Filter By Form. The following are the steps of this procedure:

Filter By
Form

1 Choose Records, Filter, Filter By Form. Or, click the Filter By Form toolbar button. The records will be hidden and the Datasheet window will be converted to the Filter By Form window, which is shown in Figure 47-16.

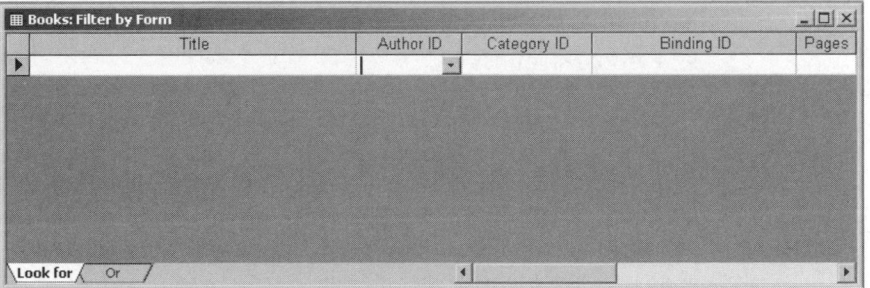

Figure 47-16. The Filter By Form window replaces the Datasheet window when you issue the Filter By Form command. (The Books table belongs to the Book Inventory03 example database.)

The Filter By Form window displays a single blank row in the same format as one of your records. (Note, however, that if you previously applied a filter to the table, in the Filter By Form window the fields used in the previous filter will initially contain the values you had assigned them.) The information in the Filter By Form window is divided into separate tabs: the Look For tab (the one that's displayed initially), plus one or more Or tabs. You display a particular tab by clicking a tab label at the bottom of the window.

2 Begin defining your filter by choosing entries in the fields shown in the Look For tab. When you click in a field, a down arrow appears at the right end. Click this arrow to display a drop-down list of the different values that are currently contained in that field within all the records of the table. Select the one you want to use for your filter.

You can select a value in more than one field to *reduce* the number of records shown. When you apply the filter, Access will display the records that match *all* the selected entries. For instance, in the Books example table, if you wanted to display all trade paperback novels, you would select *Novel* in the Category ID field and *trade paperback* in the Binding ID field, as shown here:

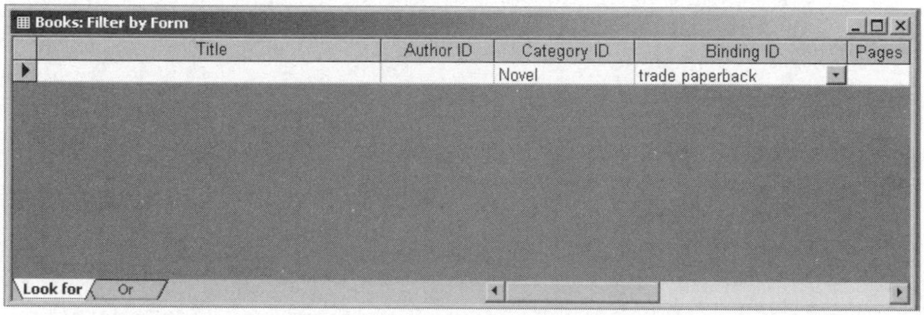

3 After you've selected all the values you want from the Look For tab, you can define alternative filter criteria to *expand* the number of records shown. You do this by displaying the first Or tab, which will show another row of fields. Select one or more values in these fields the same way you did in the Look For tab. When you apply the filter, Access will display all records that match *either* the values in the Look For tab *or* the values in the Or tab. For instance, in the Books example table, you could list all hardcover novels as well as all trade paperback novels by first selecting the values shown above on the Look For tab, and then on the first Or tab, selecting *Novel* in the Category ID field and *hardcover* in the Binding ID field:

You can expand the number of listed records even further by selecting values from additional Or tabs. Each time you select one or more values from an Or tab, another Or tab becomes available for you to display.

Rather than selecting a value in a field, you can specify a filter criterion by typing an expression containing a comparison operator. Table 47-2 shows the six standard comparison operators.

Table 47-2. **The Standard Comparison Operators**

Operator	Definition
>	Greater than
<	Less than
=	Equal to
<=	Less than or equal to
>=	Greater than or equal to
<>	Not equal to

To use a comparison operator, enter the operator, followed by the comparison value, into the field that contains the value to be evaluated. For example, to find all books that cost more than $20, you would enter the greater-than operator and the value **20** (that is, **>20**) into the Price field. If you don't use an operator and you just select a value in a field, Access assumes that you're searching for exact matches.

> **note** When you use Filter By Form, you can't easily tell Access to look for matches between two values. For example, you can't find books that have prices above $20 but below $40. For that, you need to use a query as described in Chapter 48, "Using Queries to Select and Combine Information."

Clear Grid

Remove/
Apply Filter

If you select a value in a field or type in a comparison expression and then decide that you don't really want to use it, you can delete the entry, remove the entire tab, or clear the entire filter. To delete a single entry, select it and press the Delete key. To remove a tab that you've created, display it and then choose Edit, Delete Tab. You can clear all the entries in the filter by choosing Edit, Clear Grid or by clicking the Clear Grid toolbar button.

4 Once you have specified all the values for your filter, you can activate the filter by choosing Filter, Apply Filter/Sort or by clicking the Remove/Apply Filter toolbar button. Access will then return you to the standard Datasheet window, showing only those records that match your filter.

For instance, here's how the example Book table would appear after you choose the filter values from the Look For and Or tabs described and shown in the preceding instructions:

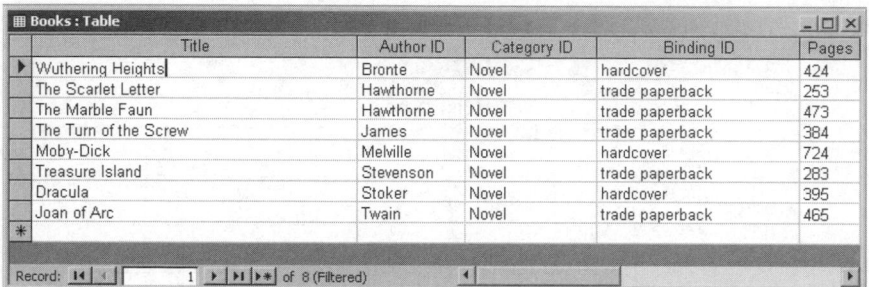

Remove/
Apply
Filter

To remove the filter and display all records, choose Records, Remove Filter/Sort or click the Remove Filter toolbar button. You can later reapply your most recently defined filter by simply choosing Records, Apply Filter/Sort or by clicking the Remove/Apply Filter button. (When a filter is applied, this button is selected, its ScreenTip label is Remove Filter, and clicking it removes the filter. After the filter has been removed, the button is deselected, its label is Apply Filter, and clicking it reapplies the previous filter.)

Other Ways to Sort and Filter

If you want to filter *and* sort the records in a table rather than perform the two-step process of first applying a filter and then sorting the records, you can use the Advanced Filter/Sort command on the Filter submenu of the Records menu. This command opens a window that's quite similar to Design view window of a query, except that it allows you to work with fields within the current table only. In the Advanced Filter/ Sort window, you can define criteria for sorting and filtering the records in the table, using one or more fields.

Better yet, you can create a query, which allows you to use fields from several tables for sorting and filtering and to control exactly which fields are displayed. The next chapter explains the techniques for creating, modifying, and using queries.

Using Queries to Select and Combine Information

Creating a Query

Queries and other database objects are described in "Designing and Planning an Access Database," on page 1263. To create a new query, open the New Query dialog box (shown in Figure 48-1) as explained in "Using the Database Window and Object Views," on page 1271, and then select an option in the list, as follows:

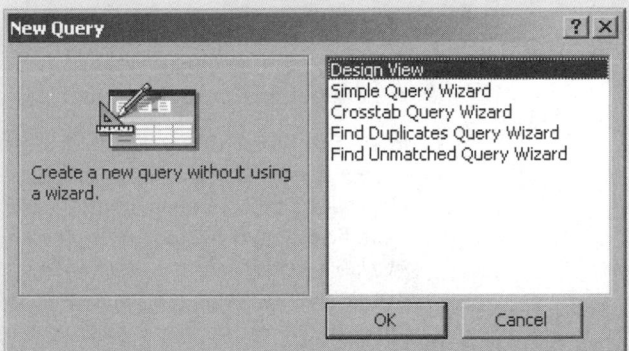

Figure 48-1. In the New Query dialog box you can select one of five ways to create a new query.

- To create your query from scratch in Design view, choose the Design View option. For information on designing the query in Design view, see "Modifying a Query," on page 1316.

- To have Microsoft Access 2002 assist you in designing the query, choose the Simple Query Wizard option. Using this wizard is the easiest way to create a new, general-purpose query, and it's discussed in the next section.

- To create a special-purpose query, known as a *crosstab query*, for comparing different subsets of the information in the database, choose the Crosstab Query Wizard option. See "Creating a Crosstab Query," on page 1328.

- To create a special-purpose query that can help you maintain your data, choose the Find Duplicates Query Wizard option or the Find Unmatched Query Wizard option. These two options are discussed in "Creating a Maintenance Query," on page 1315.

Once you have selected the option you want, click the OK button.

note Keep in mind that a query database object stores only the query definition—field names, data selection criteria, sorting orders, grouping information, and so on. It *doesn't* store the actual data that it displays; that data is stored only in the database tables. Consequently, every time you run a particular query, it shows the *current* state of the data stored in the database tables.

Creating a Basic Query with the Simple Query Wizard

The following is the procedure for creating a general-purpose query using the Simple Query Wizard. (The figures show the steps for creating a query that lists all the books written by each author in the Book Inventory03 example database. The query lists the author's first and last names and each book's title, price, and category. The query draws information from the Authors, Books, and Categories tables. If you want to see the final result as you read these steps, look ahead to Figure 48-5, on page 1315.)

1 Select the Simple Query Wizard option in the New Query dialog box and click the OK button. The Simple Query Wizard will start running.

2 In the first Simple Query Wizard dialog box, select all the fields you want to include in your query. You can select fields from one or more tables or other queries. To begin, select a table or query in the Tables/Queries drop-down list that has one or more fields you'd like to include. Then move all the fields that you want from the Available Fields list to the Selected Fields list, using the four buttons located between the lists. Repeat this operation to include fields from one or more additional tables or queries. (In Figure 48-2, on page 1313, we chose the First Name and Last Name fields from Authors, the Title and Price fields from Books, and the Category Field from Categories.) When you finish selecting fields, click the Next button to open the second wizard dialog box.

tip **Include All Needed Fields**

Be sure to include all the fields that you need—for displaying information in the query, for selecting the data that is displayed, or for sorting the results of the query.

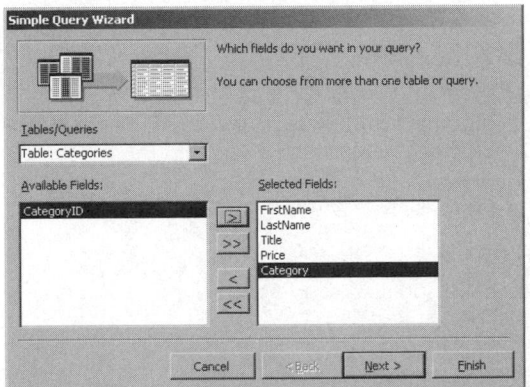

Figure 48-2. In the first Simple Query Wizard dialog box, you select all the fields that you need. The fields selected here are for creating the example query described in the text.

InsideOut

If you've selected fields belonging to two database objects (tables or queries) that don't have a formal relationship defined in the Relationships window, when you click the Next button Access will display a message box and will require you to explicitly define the relationship in the Relationships window and then to restart the wizard and reselect the fields you want. For some reason, Access won't simply create the necessary relationships for the current query, as it does when you add tables or queries without defined relationships to the query Design window (explained in "Modifying a Query," on page 1316). To avoid this problem, be sure to explicitly define relationships between all tables or queries that you want to use in your query, following the instructions given in "Setting Up Table Relationships," on page 1291.

3 If you selected one or more numeric fields in addition to the primary key (such as the book price in the example query), Access will display the second Simple Query Wizard dialog box shown in Figure 48-3, on page 1314. (If you *didn't* select a numeric field in the first dialog box, the wizard will immediately display the final dialog box, discussed in the next step.) In this dialog box, select the type of query, as follows:

  ■ To show the information on the query from *every* matching record, select Detail.

  ■ To display summary information from each *group* of matching records, rather than showing the information from all matching records, select Summary. Then click the Summary Options button, and in the Summary Options dialog box, select the type of summary value you want to be calculated—sum, average, minimum, or maximum. For example, if you selected the Summary option and the average summary value for the example query, the query would display a single line for each book category for each author. That line would show the author's first and last names, the category name, the name of the first book belonging to that category, and the average price of all of the author's books in that category. For more information, see "Summarizing Your Information," on page 1322.

When you're done, click the Next button.

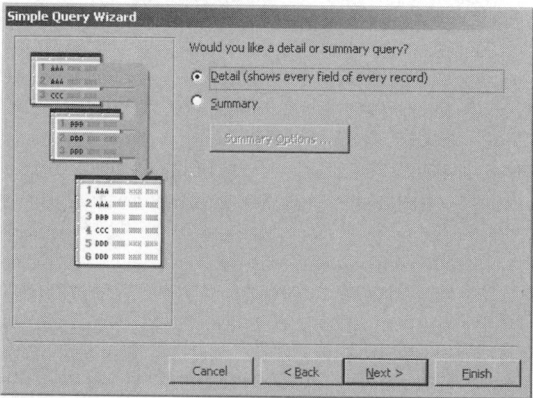

Figure 48-3. If you've selected a numeric field, the second Simple Query Wizard dialog box lets you choose the type of query you want. Here, the Detail option was selected for the example query.

4 In the final Simple Query Wizard dialog box, enter a new title for your query in the text box (as shown in Figure 48-4) or accept the default title. If you're ready to view your query immediately, select the Open The Query To View Information option to open the query in Datasheet view. If you want to examine and possibly modify the query design before you view the results, select the Modify The Query Design option to open the query in Design view, which is discussed in "Modifying a Query," on page 1316. Click the Finish button to proceed.

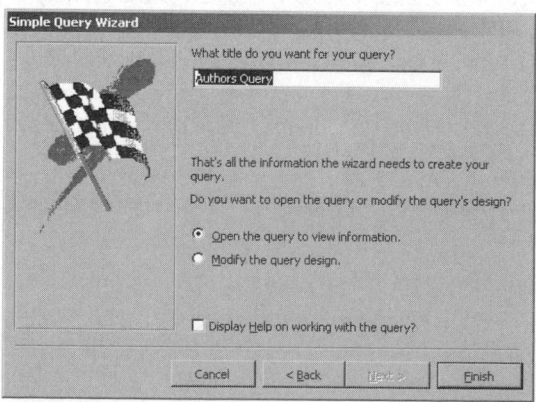

Figure 48-4. In the final Simple Query Wizard dialog box, you give the query a name and specify how it's to be opened. This figure shows the name given to the example query.

Figure 48-5 shows the example query displayed in Datasheet view. Notice that the rows aren't sorted in this query. (Because it lists the books written by each author, you would probably want the query to be sorted by the authors' last names.) For information on applying a sorting order or on making other customizations to a query, see "Modifying a Query," on page 1316.

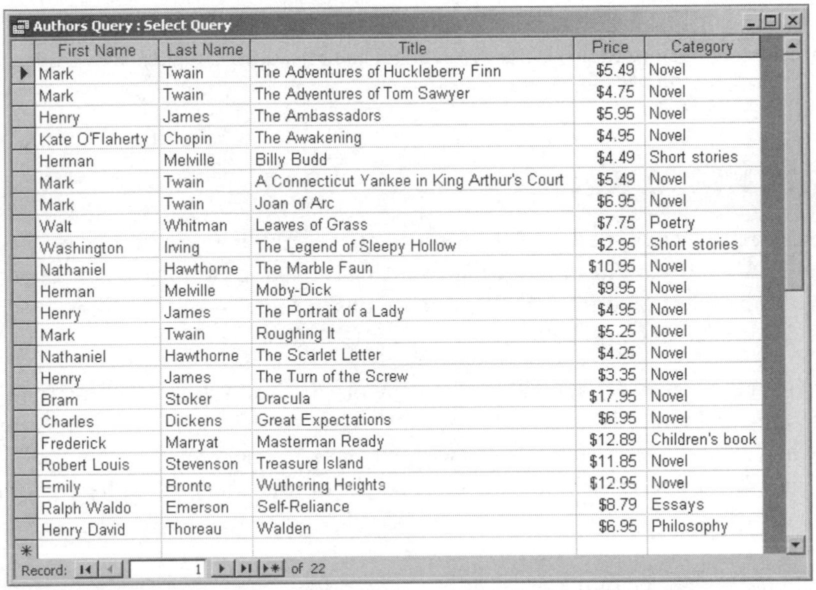

First Name	Last Name	Title	Price	Category
Mark	Twain	The Adventures of Huckleberry Finn	$5.49	Novel
Mark	Twain	The Adventures of Tom Sawyer	$4.75	Novel
Henry	James	The Ambassadors	$5.95	Novel
Kate O'Flaherty	Chopin	The Awakening	$4.95	Novel
Herman	Melville	Billy Budd	$4.49	Short stories
Mark	Twain	A Connecticut Yankee in King Arthur's Court	$5.49	Novel
Mark	Twain	Joan of Arc	$6.95	Novel
Walt	Whitman	Leaves of Grass	$7.75	Poetry
Washington	Irving	The Legend of Sleepy Hollow	$2.95	Short stories
Nathaniel	Hawthorne	The Marble Faun	$10.95	Novel
Herman	Melville	Moby-Dick	$9.95	Novel
Henry	James	The Portrait of a Lady	$4.95	Novel
Mark	Twain	Roughing It	$5.25	Novel
Nathaniel	Hawthorne	The Scarlet Letter	$4.25	Novel
Henry	James	The Turn of the Screw	$3.35	Novel
Bram	Stoker	Dracula	$17.95	Novel
Charles	Dickens	Great Expectations	$6.95	Novel
Frederick	Marryat	Masterman Ready	$12.89	Children's book
Robert Louis	Stevenson	Treasure Island	$11.85	Novel
Emily	Bronte	Wuthering Heights	$12.95	Novel
Ralph Waldo	Emerson	Self-Reliance	$8.79	Essays
Henry David	Thoreau	Walden	$6.95	Philosophy

Record: 1 of 22

Figure 48-5. This query is the result of the Simple Query Wizard choices shown in Figures 48-2 through 48-4.

Creating a Maintenance Query

In the New Query dialog box, Access provides two wizards you can select that create queries to help you maintain the integrity of the data in your tables.

The Find Duplicates Query Wizard creates a query that scans through a selected table or query and lists all records containing duplicate values for a given field. If you want to create a relationship between two tables, you can use this wizard to determine whether the related field in the primary table has duplicate values. (Recall from Chapter 47, "Setting Up Tables and Relationships," that the related field in the primary table in a relationship must have unique values.)

The Find Unmatched Query Wizard creates a query that compares two tables and locates any records in the first table that lack a related record in the second. This wizard can be useful for simply locating special cases within your data. (For instance, in the Book Inventory03 example database, you could find all authors for whom you have no books in your inventory. That is, you could obtain a list of all records in the Authors table that have no matching records in the Books table.) Also, if you're redesigning your database and want to define a one-to-many relationship between two existing tables, you can use this wizard to make sure that every record in the related table has a matching record in the primary table, which is required for maintaining referential integrity. (For instance, if you were just setting up the relationship between the Books and Authors tables in the Book Inventory03 example database, you could use this wizard to obtain a list of any records in the Books table that lack a matching record in the Authors table.)

> For information on relationships between tables and referential integrity, see "Setting Up Table Relationships," on page 1291.

Modifying a Query

You can use Design view to define a new query (one you created by selecting the Design View option in the New Query dialog box), to customize a new query (one you created by selecting one of the Wizard options in the New Query dialog box), or to modify an existing query of any type.

To open a query in Design view, follow the instructions given in "Using the Database Window and Object Views," on page 1271. Figure 48-6 shows the example query described in "Creating a Basic Query with the Simple Query Wizard," on page 1312, opened in Design view. You can see the results of this query in Figure 48-5, on page 1315.

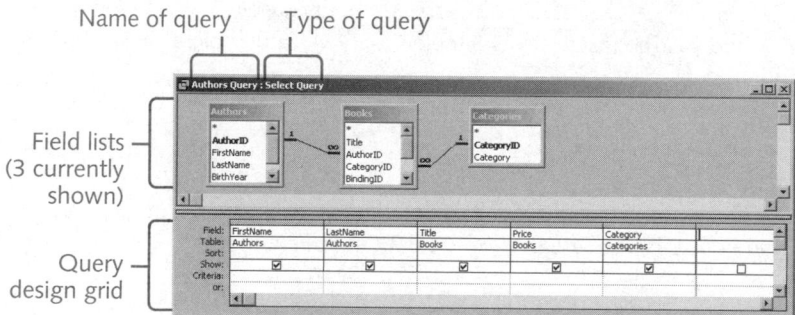

Figure 48-6. This query was created using the Simple Query Wizard with the choices shown in Figures 48-2 through 48-4 and was opened in Design view.

The top portion of the query Design view window displays field lists for one or more tables or other queries in the database and shows the relationships between these objects in the same way these relationships are shown in the Relationships window. (We rearranged the lists shown in Figure 48-6 to make the relationships easier to see.) You can use any of the listed fields in the query. The query is defined in the grid in the lower portion of the window. Each column in the query design grid defines a field that's displayed in the query, or is used to sort rows or select records, or is both displayed and used to sort or select.

In the query Design view window, you can perform one or more of the following actions to define or modify the query:

- If the table or query that contains a field you want to display or use in the query isn't shown in the top portion of the Design window, choose Show Table from the Query menu and select one or more tables or queries in the Show Table dialog box. Note that if you create a new query by selecting the Design View option in the New Query dialog box, Access automatically displays the Show Table dialog box before it opens the query Design window so that you can add the field lists you'll need. See the sidebar "Modify Table Relationships for a Query," on page 1319. To remove a field list, click it, and then either choose Query, Remove Table or press the Delete key.

- To add a field to a column, select it in the drop-down list in the Field row. Or, drag the field from the field list that displays it and drop it on the query design grid; this will insert a new column for that field to the left of the column where you dropped the field. To display on your query *all* fields belonging to a particular table or other query, select or drag the asterisk (*) item. For example, to display all fields contained in the Books table, select "Books.*" in the drop-down list, or drag the "*" from the top of the Books field list. When you add a field to the Field row in a column, Access automatically adds the field's table to the Table row in that column. (You can show or hide the Table row in the query design grid by selecting or deselecting the Table Names option on the View menu.)

> **note** The primary key field(s) for a table are formatted in **bold** in the field list.

- To sort the rows of the query by a particular field, select a sort type—Ascending or Descending—in the Sort row of the field's column. For instance, to sort the rows in the example query shown in Figure 48-6, on page 1316, by the authors' last names, you would select Ascending or Descending in the Sort row of the LastName column (see Figures 48-7 and 48-8, on page 1319). If you select a sort in more than one column, Access will apply the sorts in the order of the columns.

- To display a particular field in the query, check the box in the Show row of the field's column. If you want to use a field to sort rows or select records, but don't want the field to appear in the query, clear the box.

- To select the information displayed in the query, you can enter a value into the Criteria row of a particular field. For instance, to display only novels in the example query of Figure 48-6, on page 1316, you would type *Novel* in the Criteria row of the Category column. (Access will add quotation marks around the text when you save the query.) Also, with a numeric or date field, you can enter a comparison using the standard operators (>, <, >=, <=, and <>), as explained in Table 47-2 on page 1309). For instance, in the example query, to display only books that cost more than $10, you would type >**10** into the Criteria row of the Price column.

- To combine several selection criteria using *And* logic, enter them all into the Criteria row. For example, to show books that cost more than $10 *and* are novels, you would enter both of the criteria described in the previous item into the Criteria row. These criteria are shown in Figure 48-7, on page 1319, and the resulting query (listing the expensive novels) is shown in Figure 48-8, on page 1319.

- To add a selection criterion using *Or* logic, enter it into the Or row. For instance, to display books that either cost more than $10 dollars *or* are novels, you could enter **>10** into the Criteria row of the Price column and enter **Novel** into the Or row of the Category column. The query would list all of the novels, plus all of the books over $10. To add further *Or* criteria you can use additional rows at the bottom of the query design grid.

- To delete all your entries in a particular row or column, click in that row or column and choose Delete Rows or Delete Columns from the Edit menu. To delete all entries in the query design grid (make sure you want to!), choose Edit, Clear Grid.

Run

- To display the results of your query (that is, to *run* the query using the database's current contents), choose View, Datasheet View, choose Query, Run, or click the Run toolbar button.

View
Datasheet

View
Design

For information on working with a query (as well as a table or form) in Datasheet view, see "Working in Datasheet View," on page 1296.

Chapter 48

Save

● To save your query design, so that after you close the query you can later run or modify it from the Database window, choose File, Save, or click the Save toolbar button, or press Ctrl+S.

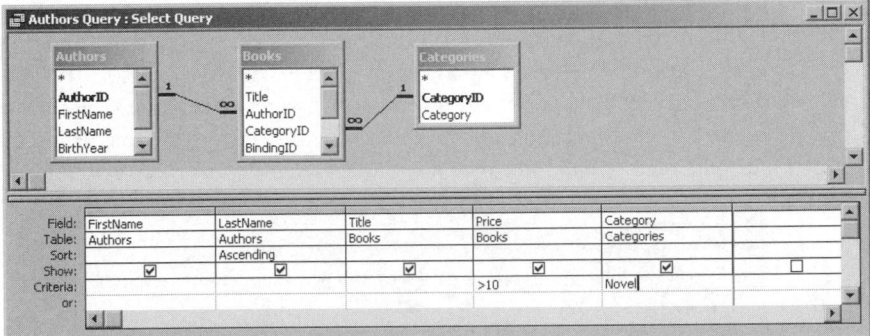

Figure 48-7. This query definition adds sorting and selection criteria to the example query in Figure 48-6. The results are shown in Figure 48-8.

Figure 48-8. These are the results of the query definition given in Figure 48-7.

Modify Table Relationships for a Query

When you create a new query, it acquires the default relationships and the properties of these relationships that are defined in the Relationships window, as explained in "Setting Up Table Relationships," on page 1291. These relationships are initially displayed in the top portion of the query Design window. (If two tables shown in the query Design window can be related, but *don't* have a relationship defined in the Relationships window, Access will add the relationship to the Design window. This relationship will be available only for the current query—it won't be added to the Relationships window.)

You can add, remove, or modify relationships within the query Design window using the methods described in "Setting Up Table Relationships" on page 1291. The changes you make here affect only the current query—they won't change the default relationships set up in the Relationships window and used elsewhere in the database.

(continued)

Chapter 48

Modify Table Relationships for a Query *(continued)*   In particular, in the query Design window you can double-click a relationship line to open the Join Properties dialog box (shown in Figure 48-9), which lets you change the *join type* of the relationship. A query always displays a row when it encounters a record in one table with a matching record in the other table (for instance, when the query finds a record in the Authors table with a matching record in the Books table). The join type controls whether or not the query will display a row when one of the tables has a record that *doesn't* have a matching record in the other table (for example, if the query finds an Authors record without a matching Books record).

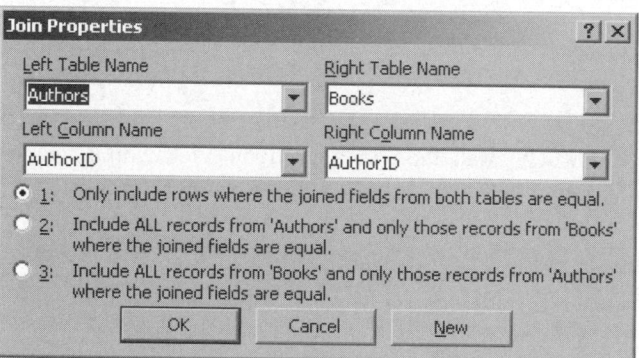

Figure 48-9.   The Join Properties dialog box lets you change the join type of a relationship, affecting the current query only.

Using Top-Value Queries

Access provides a useful enhancement to its sorting feature that allows you to look at the highest or lowest values for a field in a query. For instance, in the Authors Query example described in the previous section, you might be interested in looking at only the three least expensive titles. To look at the highest or lowest values, follow these steps:

1 Open the query in Design view.

2 Designate the field to be used for sorting the rows in the query. To look at the lowest values in the list, sort by selecting Ascending in the Sort row of the field's column. To look at the highest values in the list, sort by selecting Descending in the Sort row. (In the example, you would select an Ascending sort for the Price field.)

3 In the Top Values drop-down list on the toolbar, select the number of top or bottom values that you want to see. If the number you want isn't listed, type your own number into the box at the top of the list and press Enter. (In the example, you would need to type in **3**, as shown in Figure 48-10, on page 1321.)

> **tip** **View the Top or Bottom Percentage**
>
> The Top Values drop-down list also lets you select or type a percentage rather than an absolute number of values to be displayed. For example, in a query listing students and their test scores, you could select a Descending sort on the score field and enter **15%** into the Top Values list box to retrieve a list of students in the top 15 percent of the class (perhaps the ones who get A's).

4 To view the query results, use any method to switch to Datasheet view. (Figure 48-11 shows the results of the example query.)

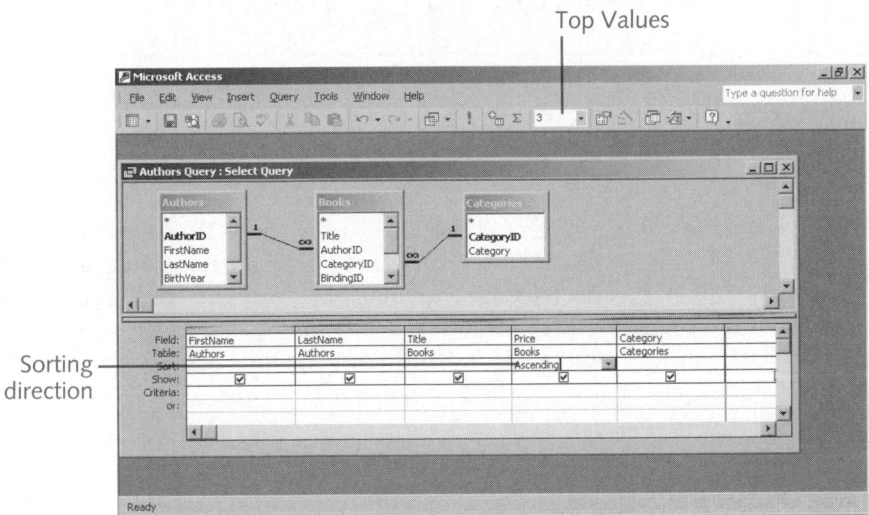

Figure 48-10. You can list just the top or bottom values in a sorted query by selecting a number or percentage in the Top Values drop-down list on the toolbar.

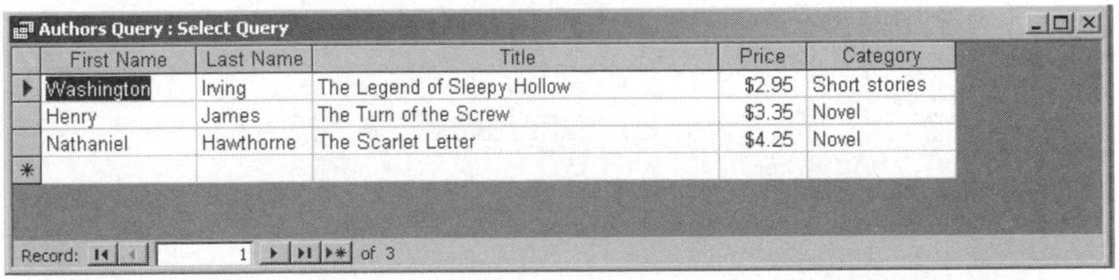

	First Name	Last Name	Title	Price	Category
▶	Washington	Irving	The Legend of Sleepy Hollow	$2.95	Short stories
	Henry	James	The Turn of the Screw	$3.35	Novel
	Nathaniel	Hawthorne	The Scarlet Letter	$4.25	Novel
*					

Record: ◄ ◄ 1 ► ►I ►* of 3

Figure 48-11. This figure shows the results of the query definition shown in Figure 48-10.

Summarizing Your Information

You can create a query that displays summary information for each group of matching records, rather than showing the information from all matching records. As explained in step 3 in the section "Creating a Basic Query with the Simple Query Wizard," on page 1312, if your query contains a numeric field, you can use the Simple Query Wizard to generate a query that displays summary information.

Totals

You can also use Design view to convert any *select query* to one that displays summary information. To do this, open the query in Design view and choose View, Totals or click the Totals toolbar button to display the Total row in the query design grid. (To remove the Total row, choose the command or click the button again.)

> **note** Most queries, and all of the queries described so far in this chapter, are *select queries*. A select query displays rows of information extracted from one or more tables or other queries. Other types of queries are described later in this chapter.

To summarize the values in a particular field, open the drop-down list in the Total row in the field's column (see Figure 48-12) and select one of the functions listed in Table 48-1, on page 1323. For a field that has the Number or Currency data type, you can select any of these functions. For a field that has a nonnumeric data type, such as text, you can select only the Count function (which displays the total number of matching records that have any value in that field) or First or Last (which displays the first or the last field value encountered).

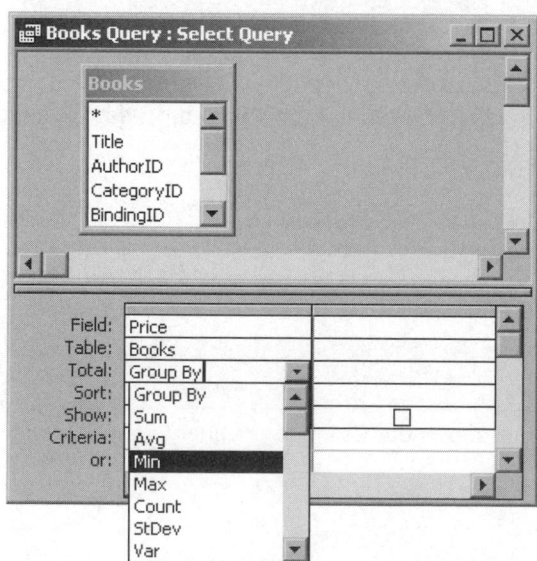

Figure 48-12. Adding the Total row lets you create a query that displays summary information. This query is included in the Book Inventory03 example database.

Chapter 48

Table 48-1. **The Functions You Can Select in the Total Row**

Function	Description
Sum	Adds up all the values within the group
Avg	Finds the average for all the values within the group
Min	Finds the lowest value within the group
Max	Finds the highest value within the group
Count	Determines the number of matching records within the group
StDev	Determines the standard deviation for the population defined by the group
Var	Determines the variance for the population defined by the group
First	Displays the first matching value in the group
Last	Displays the last matching value in the group

If you have only a single field in your design grid, and you select a summary function in the Total box (as shown in Figure 48-12, on page 1322), the resulting datasheet will display a single number that summarizes all matching values and will look similar to the one shown in Figure 48-13.

Figure 48-13. This figure shows the results of the query definition shown in Figure 48-12, with the Min function selected in the Total row of the Price column.

Notice that the query displayed in Datasheet view contains only an answer to your query and a column heading identifying the function and field that were used—in this case, MinOfPrice (the minimum value in the Price field).

More commonly, you use the Total row to perform calculations on *groups* of values within the matching records (as the function descriptions in Table 48-1 imply). To do this, you need to add a field to the grid that will be used to group the records, and then select the Group By option in that field's Total row. (This option is the default.) For instance, in the example query shown in Figure 48-12, on page 1322, you might want to determine the average price of each category of books (novels, essays, short stories, and so on). To do this, you would need to have two fields in your design grid: the CategoryID field, which is used for grouping the records, and the Price field, which is used for the calculation, as shown in Figure 48-14.

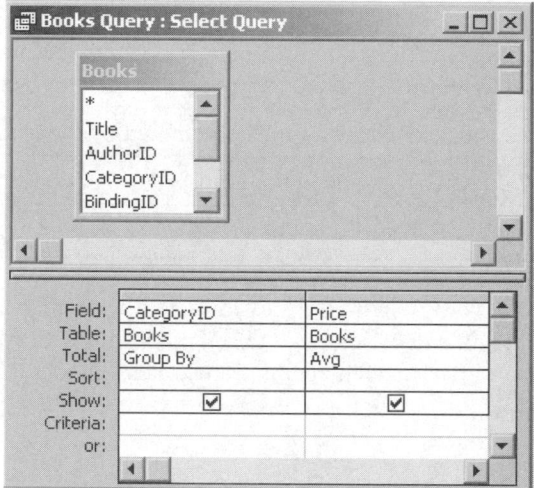

Figure 48-14. Adding a field and selecting Group By in the Total row provides a summary of each group of records.

When you run this type of query, Access lists each group together with the calculation result for the values within that group, as shown in Figure 48-15.

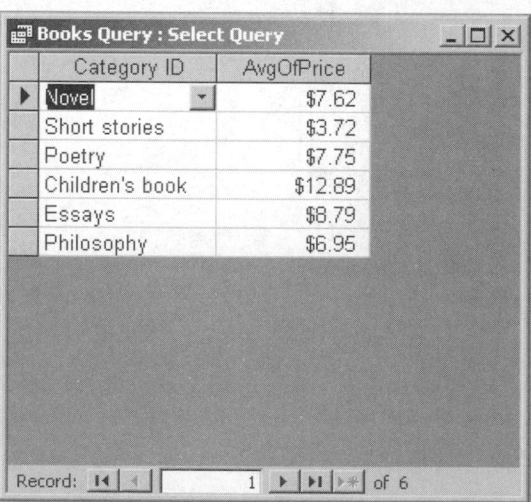

Figure 48-15. This figure shows the results of the query definition in Figure 48-14.

Keep in mind that you can control the order of the rows displayed in the query by using the Sort row, as explained in "Modifying a Query," on page 1316.

You can also use a field to select the specific records that are used in the summary calculation. You do this by choosing the Where option in the Total row in the field's column and then adding one or more selection criteria to that field's Criteria or Or rows. If you do this, the field will be used only to select records; it won't be used to group records and it won't be displayed in the query (Access won't allow you to check the Show box for the field).

Adding Calculated Fields

Sometimes you might want to display the result of a calculation, performed on information within the record or records displayed, within each row of a query, rather than summarizing values across records, as described in the previous section. To do this, the best approach is to create a calculated field. You can create such a field within a query, on a form, or within a report. For example, perhaps you'd like to see the purchase price of books if their prices were all increased by 15 percent. To include this information in a query, you would add a field to the query design grid that would perform this calculation. This new field is called a *calculated field* because it performs a computation rather than displaying the value of a field in a table.

To create a calculated field, click in the Field row in a blank column in the query design grid and enter the expression for calculating the value. Rather than typing the name of a field to be used in your calculation, you can click the down arrow to the right of the box and select the field name from the drop-down list; you would then type the remainder of the expression. Formulas for calculating fields are similar to formulas entered into cells in Microsoft Excel 2002 spreadsheets—the main difference is that rather than referring to cell addresses, you refer to field names. The formula will be calculated and its result displayed in every row of the query (or in every row of a report or on every record shown in a form).

Figure 48-16 shows an expression that calculates a 15 percent increase in the purchase price of each book (as the expression would appear immediately after you type it in, before you press Enter or run the query).

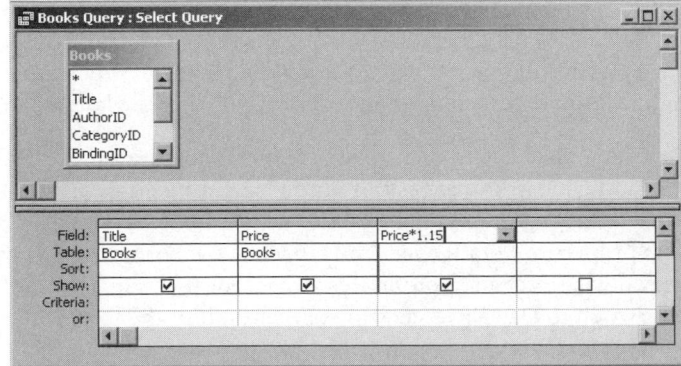

Figure 48-16. A calculated field contains an expression that computes a value based on other fields. This query is included in the Book Inventory03 example database.

When you run this query, you see the results shown in Figure 48-17. Notice that the field name consists of the letters *Expr* followed by a digit, indicating the sequence in which the calculated field was created, and that the results of the calculation aren't formatted. (When you display a field from a table, it acquires the field's formatting. But when you create a calculated field, it's initially unformatted.)

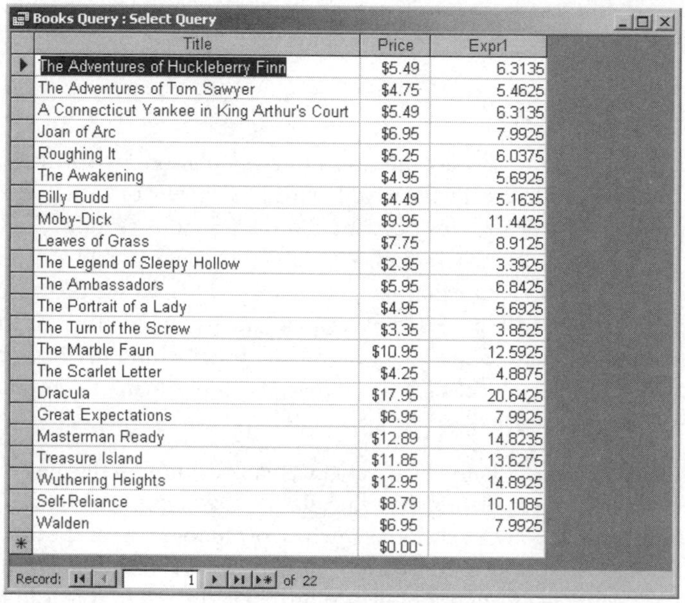

Title	Price	Expr1
The Adventures of Huckleberry Finn	$5.49	6.3135
The Adventures of Tom Sawyer	$4.75	5.4625
A Connecticut Yankee in King Arthur's Court	$5.49	6.3135
Joan of Arc	$6.95	7.9925
Roughing It	$5.25	6.0375
The Awakening	$4.95	5.6925
Billy Budd	$4.49	5.1635
Moby-Dick	$9.95	11.4425
Leaves of Grass	$7.75	8.9125
The Legend of Sleepy Hollow	$2.95	3.3925
The Ambassadors	$5.95	6.8425
The Portrait of a Lady	$4.95	5.6925
The Turn of the Screw	$3.35	3.8525
The Marble Faun	$10.95	12.5925
The Scarlet Letter	$4.25	4.8875
Dracula	$17.95	20.6425
Great Expectations	$6.95	7.9925
Masterman Ready	$12.89	14.8235
Treasure Island	$11.85	13.6275
Wuthering Heights	$12.95	14.8925
Self-Reliance	$8.79	10.1085
Walden	$6.95	7.9925
	$0.00	

Figure 48-17. This figure shows the results of the query design in Figure 48-16.

Fortunately, you're not stuck with the default format used by Access. It's quite easy to change both the name of the calculated field and its formatting. If you return to Design view, you'll notice that the expression you originally typed into the Field box for the calculated field (in the example, **Price*1.15**) has been reformatted to include a field name. In the example query the expression would now appear as follows:

```
Expr1: [Price]*1.15
```

To change the field name, just select the text before the colon and type the new name. For instance, in this example you could replace *Expr1* with *Expected Price*.

To format the calculated field, right-click anywhere in the column for the field in the query design grid, and choose Properties from the shortcut menu to display the field's *property sheet*. (A property sheet is a dialog box, usually tabbed, that lets you view or modify an object's properties.) On the General tab, click the Format property box, and from the drop-down list, select an appropriate format. For the example, you would choose Currency. Switch to Datasheet view to see the result of the formatting option you selected, as shown in Figure 48-18, on page 1327.

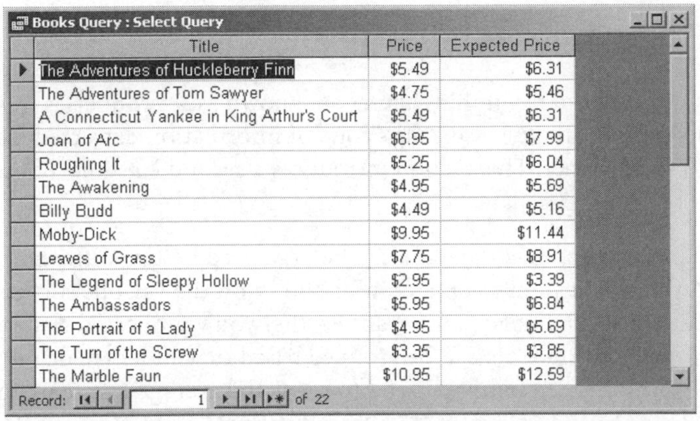

Figure 48-18. This figure shows the first part of the example query of Figures 48-16 and 48-17, after the calculated field was renamed and formatted.

Troubleshooting

Access Won't Run a Query with a Calculated Field

You created a query containing a calculated field, but whenever you try to switch to Datasheet view to see the query results, Access displays a mysterious dialog box titled Enter Parameter Value rather than running the query.

If you enter a name that *isn't* the name of one of the fields in the table(s) used in your query, Access will assume that the name is a *parameter* that must be entered each time the query is run. For instance, in the example query described in "Adding Calculated Fields," on page 1325, if you erroneously entered **Cost** rather than **Price** into the expression in the calculated field, Access would treat Cost as a parameter and prompt you for its value when you run the query, because the Books table used in this query doesn't contain a field named Cost.

Keep this behavior in mind for situations where you actually want to have Access prompt you for a parameter each time you run the query. For instance, in the Book Inventory03 example database, if you wanted to create a query that displays books that cost less than a specified amount, you could enter the expression **<[Cost]** into the Criteria row of the Price field. (The brackets are needed in this context to indicate that Cost is a name rather than a literal text value.) Because the Books table doesn't contain a field named Cost, Access will treat Cost as a parameter and will prompt you for its value each time you run the query.

Creating a Crosstab Query

All the queries discussed so far in this chapter are known as *select* queries. A select query is the most common type; it displays rows of information extracted from one or more tables or other queries. This section introduces a second category of query, the *crosstab query*.

Sometimes the information in a database can be organized by two different types of groupings, and you might want to extract information on the various subsets formed by the different groupings. Imagine, for example, that you've collected test results from a group of students. The students can be grouped based on gender (male or female) as well as age (15, 16, or 17). It might be useful to know the average test score for each of the possible subsets (15-year-old boys, 15-year-old girls, 16-year-old boys, 16-year-old girls, 17-year-old boys, and 17-year-old girls). You can accomplish this by using a statistical matrix called a *cross-tabulation*. In Access, you can generate a cross-tabulation by creating a crosstab query. The results of a crosstab query for the test score scenario just described are shown in Figure 48-19.

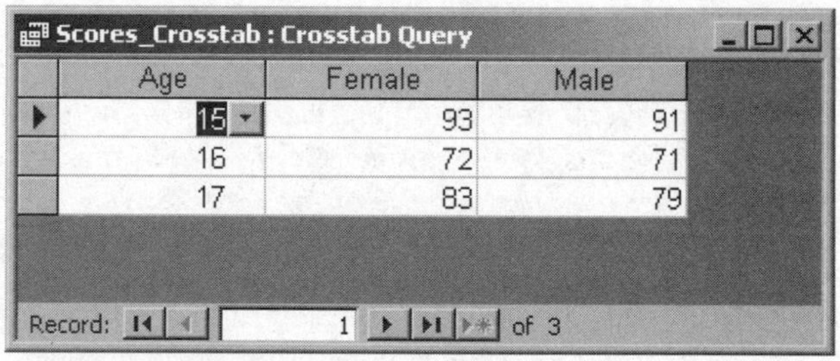

Age	Female	Male
15	93	91
16	72	71
17	83	79

Record: 1 of 3

Figure 48-19. This crosstab query is based on data from a table of test scores.

 The crosstab query used in this example is included in the Scores.mdb example database on the companion CD.

The following is a summary of the steps for creating a crosstab query using the Crosstab Query Wizard:

1 Open the New Query dialog box (shown in Figure 48-1, on page 1311) as explained in "Using the Database Window and Object Views," on page 1271.

2 In the New Query dialog box, select the Crosstab Query Wizard option and click OK.

3 In the first Crosstab Query Wizard dialog box, select the table or query containing the fields you want to include.

   For instance, to create the Scores_Crosstab example query shown in Figure 48-19, you would select the name of the table that stores the gender, age, and test score for each student. Here's how the table used by the example query appears in Design view:

▦ Scores : Table	
Field Name	**Data Type**
⚿▶ StudentID	AutoNumber
Name	Text
Gender	Text
Age	Number
Score	Number

4 In the second dialog box, select from one to three fields to be used for row headings. (For the example query, you would select just the Age field.)

5 In the third dialog box, select a single field to be used for the column headings. (For the example query, you would select the Gender field.)

6 In the fourth dialog box, select the field and the function you want to use to calculate the values displayed in the query for each subset—that is, for each column and row intersection. (For the example query, you would select the Score field and the Avg function to display the average test score for each subset.)

Also, check the Yes Include Row Sums option if you want to include an additional column that summarizes the values displayed in each row—the average of all values if you chose the Avg function, the sum of all values if you chose the Sum function, and so on. For instance, if you selected this option for the example query, the query would include a column that displays the average of the female value and the male value for each age. (To create the example query, you would clear this option.)

7 In the fifth and final dialog box, enter a name for the query (or accept the default name), and choose whether the new query should initially be opened in Datasheet view or in Design view. When you click the Finish button, the wizard will create the query.

---

tip **Convert a Query to a Crosstab**

You can also convert an existing query to a crosstab query. To do so, open it in Design view and choose Query, Crosstab Query. This command will add a Total and a Crosstab row to the query design grid and will convert the query to a crosstab query. In the Crosstab row, select Row Heading for one or more fields to designate the row headings, select Column Heading for one field to designate the column headings, and select Value for one field to designate the field you want to use to display the values in the row-column intersections. In the Total row, select Group By for the fields used for headings, and select a function (Sum, Avg, and so on) for the field used to display the values. The easiest way to learn how to set up a crosstab query in Design view is to study the design of a crosstab query generated by the Crosstab Query Wizard.

Chapter 48

Creating and Running Queries to Modify Data

So far, this chapter has described two major types of queries: the select query and the crosstab query. Four additional types of queries, which are known as *action queries*, can actually change your data: a make-table query, an append query, a delete query, and an update query.

> **caution**   Before running any of the queries discussed in the following sections, make a backup copy of your database. These queries can permanently modify your database, possibly removing a large amount of data. You can also back up the specific table(s) that will be modified by making copies of the table(s) using the Database window, as described in "Using the Database Window and Object Views," on page 1271.

The following are the general steps for creating and running an action query. The next sections discuss the particulars of each type of action query.

1 Open a new or an existing query in Design view, as described previously in this chapter.

2 Convert the query to an action query by choosing the query type—Make-Table Query, Update Query, Append Query, or Delete Query—from the Query menu. Or choose the query type from the Query Type drop-down list on the toolbar:

Query Type

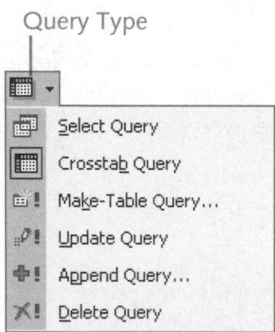

When you convert a query to an action query, the rows in the query design grid change according to the type of information that must be specified. For two of the query types (make-table and append), Access displays a dialog box to obtain more information before returning you to the Design window.

3 Fill in the query design grid. The particular rows that are available depend upon the type of query you're creating.

4 To preview the results of running the query, switch to Datasheet view by choosing Datasheet View from the View menu or from the View drop-down menu on the toolbar. (Do *not* choose the Run menu command or click the Run toolbar button at this stage.) The query will display a list of the records that it will append, delete, update, or add to a new table—without actually changing any data. (Unfortunately, however, when you preview an update query, it lists the records that it will modify but shows the current values, not the new values that the query will generate.)

> **note** With a select or crosstab query, the Run command on the Query menu and the Run toolbar button have the same effect as choosing Datasheet View from the View menu or from the View drop-down menu on the toolbar—that is, Access will simply switch to Datasheet view. With these types of queries, *running* a query is synonymous with *viewing a query in Datasheet view*.
>
> With an action query, however, the Run command and the Run toolbar button cause the query to perform its intended action—appending, deleting, updating, or inserting into a new table. In contrast, choosing Datasheet View from one of the View menus merely switches to Datasheet view so that you can preview the query's effect without actually changing data.

Run

5 Choose Query, Run or click the Run toolbar button to carry out the data modification.

Make-Table Query

The make-table query type creates a new table and adds to this table all of the information that the query selects. The new table can be in the current database or in a different one. A make-table query is especially useful for archiving information in a database. For instance, you could first use a make-table query to copy older records from the current table to an archive table. You could then convert the query to a Delete query, and use it to remove the older records from the current table.

Append Query

Like the make-table query type, the append query type adds the information it selects to another table, which can be either in the current database or in a different one. However, rather than creating and adding the information to a new table, it appends the information to an existing table, thereby adding new records at the end of the existing table. You often use this query to add a new batch of records to update an existing table; for instance, you might receive a database of new books published in the present year that you want to integrate with your existing books table.

Chapter 48

Delete Query

The most dangerous of these four queries is the delete query, which removes from your tables all records that match your conditions. This query can be useful for housekeeping—for example, you might use it to eliminate from your database all records with dates prior to January 1, 1999—but it can be dangerous if you make a mistake in defining your conditions. Be certain to back up your data and to preview the results in Datasheet view before clicking the Run button with this type of query!

Update Query

An update query provides a powerful way to change the value of any fields in your database for those records that match the conditions you specify. When you convert a query to an update query, Access adds an Update To row to the query design grid. You can use that row to specify a value or an expression that indicates how the value in a field should be changed.

You enter expressions using the same general guidelines that you follow when creating calculated fields. See "Adding Calculated Fields," on page 1325, for more information. The example query given in that section included a field that showed the result of increasing the purchase price by 15 percent. If you decided to actually raise the price of books by 15 percent, you could use an update query to change the value of the Price field in every record in the Books table to 115 percent of its previous value, permanently changing the data in your database.

Creating Forms and Data Access Pages for Working with Data

Creating a Form

Forms and other database objects in Microsoft Access 2002 are described in "Designing and Planning an Access Database," on page 1263. To create a new form, open the New Form dialog box (shown in Figure 49-1) as explained in "Using the Database Window and Object Views," on page 1271, and then select an option in the list, as follows:

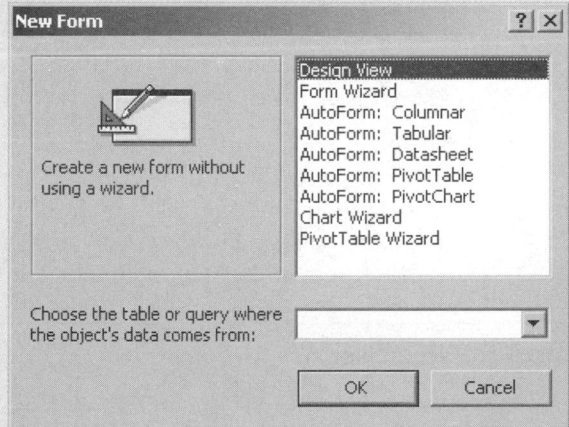

Figure 49-1. In the New Form dialog box, you can select one of nine ways to create a new form.

● To create the form yourself by adding controls one at a time in Design view, select the Design View option. For information on using Design view, see "Customizing a Form," on page 1339.

> **note** A form is usually associated with a specific table or query in the database, which is known as the *record source*. A typical form displays the records belonging to the record source one at a time and lets you add, modify, or delete these records.
>
> If you select any of the AutoForm options or the Chart Wizard option in the New Form dialog box, you *must* specify the table or query that will be the record source for the form by selecting that table or query in the drop-down list at the bottom of the dialog box, which displays all of the tables and queries in the database.
>
> If you select any of the other options, you can also specify a record source. Or, you can omit this step, leave the drop-down list blank, and then define the record source later in the process. (With the Design View option, you can even leave the form without a record source. You might do this to create a form that simply displays information and performs actions, such as the Switchboard form that some database wizards create as an alternative interface for accessing database objects.)

● To have Access create the form for you according to your specifications, select the Form Wizard option. The Form Wizard lets you choose the specific fields to include, which can belong to one or more tables or queries. See "Creating a Form Using the Form Wizard," on page 1335.

● To have Access quickly create a form that has a particular configuration (Columnar, Tabular, Datasheet, PivotTable, or PivotChart), based on the record source table or query you select in the drop-down list, select one of the five AutoForm options. Access will immediately create the form, including all fields from the record source and using default options without asking for your specifications.

● To use the Chart Wizard to create a form that contains a Microsoft Graph chart, select the Chart Wizard option. The chart will graph data from the data source that you select in the drop-down list. For information on charts generated by the Graph program, see "Constructing Charts Using Microsoft Graph," on page 144.

> **tip** **Insert a Chart into Any Form**
>
> No matter how you create a form, you can use the Chart Wizard to insert a chart into it by opening the form in Design view, choosing Insert, Chart, and dragging to mark the rectangular area on your form where you want to display the chart. The Chart Wizard will then start running and will guide you through the process of designing your chart.

● To have Access take information from one or more tables or queries and create a form containing a Microsoft Excel 2002 pivot table, select the PivotTable Wizard option. For information on Excel pivot tables, see Chapter 28, "Power Database Techniques: Lists, Filters, and Pivot Tables."

Once you have selected the option you want, click the OK button.

In general, it's easiest to use the Form Wizard or one of the AutoForm options to create at least a rough draft of your form. You can then customize the form, using the techniques described in "Customizing a Form," on page 1339.

Creating a Form Using the Form Wizard

The following is the procedure for generating a new form using the Form Wizard. (The figures show the steps for creating a form for viewing and editing a single table, Books, in the Book Inventory03 example database. If you want to see the final result as you read these steps, look ahead to Figure 49-6, on page 1338.)

1 In the New Form dialog box, select the Form Wizard option and click the OK button. (You *don't* need to select a record source in the drop-down list in the New Form dialog box.) The Form Wizard will start running.

2 In the first Form Wizard dialog box, shown in Figure 49-2 on page 1336, select all the fields you want to display on your form. The resulting form will contain a separate control for accessing each of the fields that you pick. To begin, in the Tables/Queries drop-down list, select the table or query that has the fields you want to include. This table or query will become the record source for the table, and all the fields that belong to it will be displayed in the Available Fields list. Then move all the fields that you want from the Available Fields list to the Selected Fields list, using the four buttons located between the lists. When the Selected Fields list has all the fields you want, click the Next button to display the second Form Wizard dialog box.

For information on selecting fields from more than one table or query, see the sidebar "Accessing Several Tables or Queries in a Form," on page 1338.

tip **Control the Field Order**

The order in which the fields are listed in the Selected Fields list is the order in which the wizard will arrange the fields in the form. Although you can't rearrange fields that have already been added to the Selected Fields list, you can control the position where the next field is added. To do this, first select the field in the Selected Fields list that is immediately above the position when you want to add the new field. Then add the new field; it will be placed just below the field you selected. If you don't like the position of a particular field in the Selected Fields list, select it, click the < button to remove it, and then add it back to the list at the desired position.

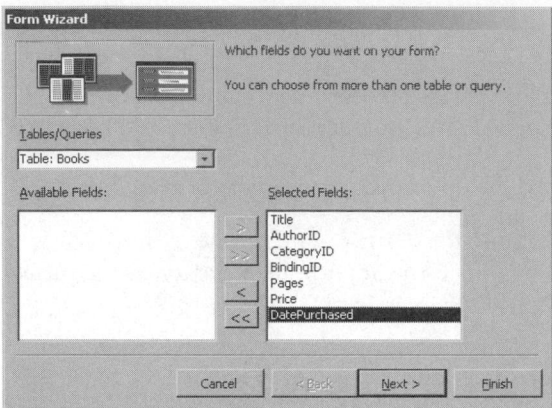

Figure 49-2. In the first Form Wizard dialog box, select all the fields you want to access from your new form. The fields selected here are for creating the example form.

3 In the second Form Wizard dialog box, shown in Figure 49-3, choose the basic arrangement of the controls on the form. To make your choice, select each option and observe the way the selected layout will look on your form, as shown in the dialog box. The Columnar layout is the most common and usually enables you to view a complete, single record at a time in Form view. The Tabular layout lets you view multiple records at the same time in Form view, while the Datasheet layout generates a form that's intended to be displayed in Datasheet view. The Justified layout arranges the form's objects to fill the form window. When you've selected the layout you want, click the Next button.

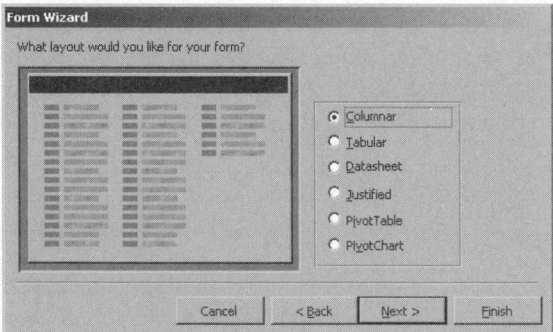

Figure 49-3. In the second Form Wizard dialog box, choose the form's layout. The layout selected here, Columnar, is used in the example form.

4 In the third Form Wizard dialog box, shown in Figure 49-4, choose the form's style, which affects the background color or pattern, the fonts, the look of the controls, and other features. Again, to help you make your choice, the dialog box shows how the form will look with each style option. (You can change the style later by displaying the form in Design view, clicking the AutoFormat button on the toolbar, and selecting a new style in the AutoFormat dialog box.) When you've made your choice, click the Next button to open the final wizard dialog box.

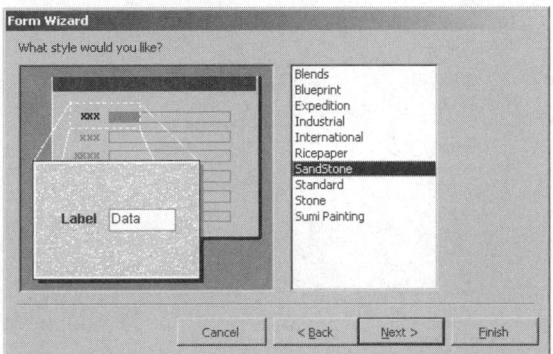

Figure 49-4. In the third Form Wizard dialog box, choose the form style. The style selected here, SandStone, is used in the example form.

5 In the final Form Wizard dialog box, shown in Figure 49-5, assign a name to the form and choose the way the form will initially be opened. If you select the first opening option, the form will be opened in Form view (or Datasheet view if you selected the Datasheet layout) so that you can immediately begin using the form to view or modify data, as discussed later in the chapter. If you select the second opening option, the form will be opened in Design view so that you can modify its design, as described in the next section, "Customizing a Form."

When you've made all your choices, click the Finish button to have Access create the form. (As you can with the other Access wizards, you can click the Finish button within any of the dialog boxes to create the form using the options you've set and the default choices for the options you haven't set.)

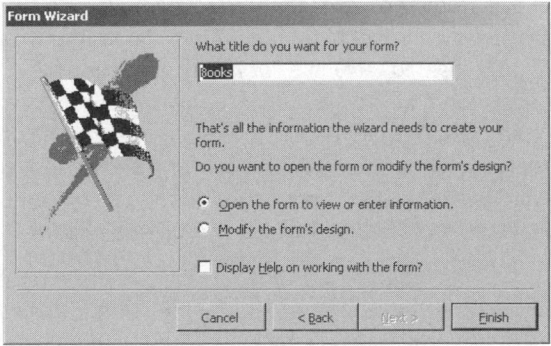

Figure 49-5. In the fourth Form Wizard dialog box, enter a name and select a form opening option. These are the options selected for the example form.

Figure 49-6 shows the example form, opened in Form view.

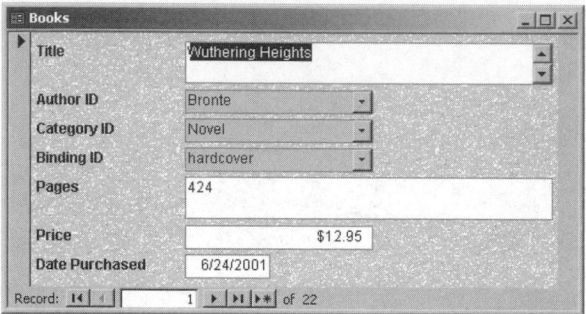

Figure 49-6. This form is the result of the Form Wizard choices shown in Figures 49-2 through 49-5. The form is included in the Book Inventory03 example database on the companion CD to this book.

Accessing Several Tables or Queries in a Form

When you select the fields for your form in the first Form Wizard dialog box, shown in Figure 49-2 on page 1336, you can add fields from several tables or queries. To add fields from each table or query, select it in the Tables/Queries drop-down list and then use the buttons to move the fields you want to the Selected Fields list.

If you add fields from several forms or queries, the wizard will display one or two additional dialog boxes that weren't shown in this section: one dialog box in which you specify the form or query by which you want to view your data (for example, if you selected fields from the Authors and the Books tables, you would choose to view your data either "by Authors" or "by Books") and possibly another dialog box in which you select a layout for a subform. The choices you make determine the form's record source.

If your form includes fields from two tables that are related in a one-to-many relation-ship and if you selected to view your data by the *primary* table, the wizard will let you display the records from the related table in a *subform* contained within the form. For instance, in the Book Inventory03 example database, if you chose to view your data by the Authors table (the primary table) and included one or more fields from the Books table (the related table), you could add the subform shown in Figure 49-7. As an alternative, the wizard will let you set up a *linked form*, which is an entirely sepa-rate form that displays the related data and which you open by clicking a button on the main form.

On the other hand, if you chose to view your data by the *related* table in the one-to-many relationship, when the form displays a record in the related table, it will simply display the unique matching fields from the primary table along with the fields from the current record in the related table. For instance, in the example described in the previous paragraph, if you chose to view your data by the Books table (the

Accessing Several Tables or Queries in a Form *(continued)*   related table), when the form displays a Books record, it would display the unique matching Author information along with the book title, as shown in Figure 49-8. (In this case the record source is actually an SQL (structured query language) query statement that selects fields from both tables.)

A form that accesses data from several tables or queries can be complex to design from scratch or to modify. However, if you create the form using the Form Wizard, almost everything is set up for you.

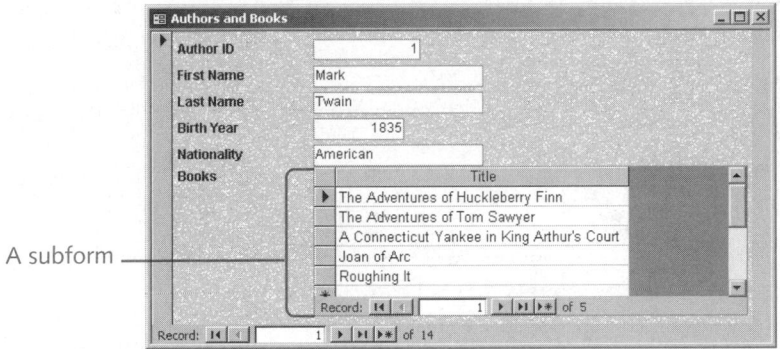

A subform

Figure 49-7.   This form shows the fields of the Authors primary table (the record source) and includes a subform for displaying the Title field of each matching record in the Books related table. The form is included in the Book Inventory03 example database.

Field from the current record in the Books table

Fields from the unique matching record in the Authors table

Figure 49-8.   This form shows the Title field of the Books related table, as well as the fields belonging to the unique matching record in the Authors primary table. The form is included in the Book Inventory03 example database.

Customizing a Form

You can use Design view to complete a new form that you created by selecting the Design View option in the New Form dialog box, to customize a new form that you created by selecting one of the Wizard options in the New Form dialog box, or to modify an existing form of any type. Design view lets you add, remove, or modify the controls that make up the form, as well as change the properties of the form itself.

To open a form in Design view, follow the instructions given in "Using the Database Window and Object Views," on page 1271. Figure 49-9 shows the example form described in the previous section, "Creating a Form Using the Form Wizard," opened in Design view. You can see the appearance of this form in Form view in Figure 49-6, on page 1338.

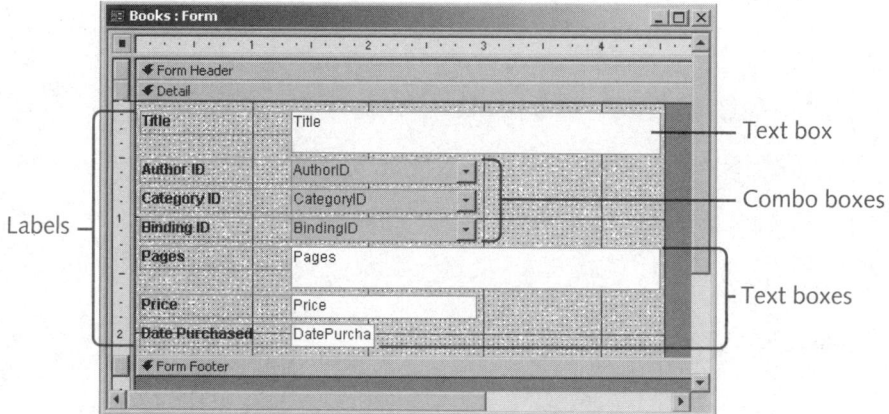

Figure 49-9. This form was created using the Form Wizard with the choices shown in Figures 49-2 through 49-5 and was opened in Design view.

In the form Design view window, you can perform one or more of the following actions to design or customize a form:

Field List

- To add a control that accesses a specific field in the form's record source, which is known as a *bound control*, drag the name of the field from the *field list* (see Figure 49-10), and drop it at the position on the form where you want to display the control. If the field list isn't visible, choose View, Field List or click the Field List toolbar button.

  Access will add a control that's appropriate for the type of the field, together with an attached text label. For example, if you drag a field with a text, numeric, or date data type, Access will add a text box. If you drag a field with the Yes/No data type, Access will add a check box. Or, if you drag a lookup field, Access will add a combo box that displays the lookup field values in its drop-down list.

For information on lookup fields, see Table 47-1, on page 1285.

Figure 49-10. This field list is displayed when the Books example form is opened in Design view.

Toolbox

● To add a bound control of a particular type, first click the button for the type of control you want in the Toolbox toolbar, and *then* drag the field from the field list. The Toolbox toolbar is shown in Figure 49-11 and its buttons are described in Table 49-1. If this toolbar isn't currently displayed, either choose View, Toolbars, Toolbox, or click the Toolbox toolbar button.

For example, if you would prefer to access a Yes/No field using a toggle button rather than a check box, you could click the Toggle Button button on the Toolbox toolbar and then drag the field from the field list to the form. Clicking a Toolbox button has an effect only if the type of control you click is appropriate for the data type of the field that you drag to the form. (For instance, clicking Command Button has no effect if you drag a text field, because you can't use a command button to access a text field.)

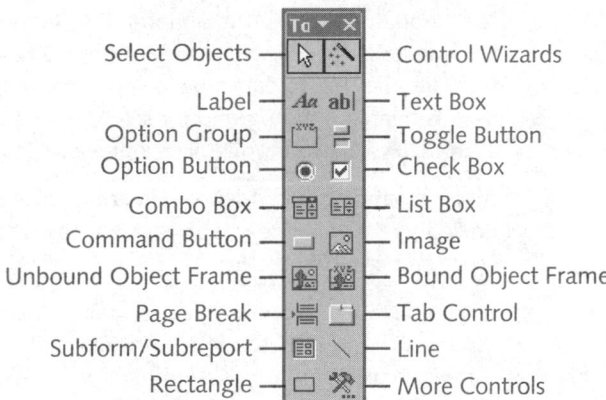

Figure 49-11. This figure shows the Toolbox toolbar buttons and their functions.

Table 49-1. **Toolbox Buttons for Modifying a Form's Design**

Button	Name	Description
	Select Objects	Lets you select a single control by clicking it or multiple controls by pressing Shift while clicking each one. When this button is selected, you can also select controls by dragging a selection rectangle around them.
	Label	Lets you display descriptive text for labeling a control or providing instructions. To add or edit the text in a label control, click the control once to select it and then click again to place the insertion point within the control. With most types of controls, when you add the control, Access automatically adds a text label that's attached to the control. (The behavior of attached controls is described in "Formatting a Form," on page 1345.)
	Option Group	Adds a set of option buttons, check boxes, or toggle buttons in which you can select only one control at a time. If an option group is bound to a field, a numeric value is stored in the field to indicate which control in the group is selected.
	Option Button	Adds a round button (also known as a *radio button*) that can be used to turn an option on or off. The button contains a black dot when the option is on. Although you can add an independent option button and bind it to a field with the Yes/No data type, an option button is usually used within an option group for selecting one of a set of mutually exclusive options (see previous table item).
	Combo Box	Adds a control that consists of a text box plus a drop-down list. You can either type text into the text box or select an item from the list.
	Command Button	Adds a rectangular button that you click to perform an action, such as going to the next record, printing the current record, or running a program. When you add a command button, you can use the Command Button Wizard to select the specific action that the button performs. (Control wizards are discussed under the "Control Wizards" item in this table.)
	Unbound Object Frame	Displays an OLE (object linking and embedding) object such as an Excel spreadsheet. The object is constant; it doesn't change with each record.

Table 49-1. *(continued)*

Button	Name	Description
	Page Break	Marks the position of a page break, which will cause the following text to be printed at the top of the next page if you print the form. The page break has no effect on viewing the form in Form view.
	Subform/ Subreport	Adds information from an additional table or query to a form or report so that you can view or modify its data. (See the sidebar "Accessing Several Tables or Queries in a Form," on page 1338.)
	Rectangle	Draws a rectangle on the form.
	Control Wizards	When this button is selected, Access will automatically run a wizard when you insert one of the following types of controls: an option group, a combo box, a list box, a command button, or a subform/subreport. The wizard will assist you in assigning the essential properties to the control or group of controls (such as the items displayed in a combo box, the action performed by clicking a command button, or the data shown in a subform/subreport). If you don't use a wizard, you'll probably need to assign appropriate properties manually using the control's property sheet, as discussed in "Formatting a Form," on page 1345.
	Text Box	Adds a box for displaying, entering, or modifying data.
	Toggle Button	Adds a rectangular push button that can be used to turn an option on or off. It appears pressed in when the option is on. A toggle button is suitable for binding to a field that has the Yes/No data type.
	Check Box	Adds a small square box that can be used to turn an option on or off. Contains a check mark when the option is on. When you drag a field with the Yes/No data type from the field list onto the form, by default Access adds a check box that is bound to the field.
	List Box	Adds a permanently displayed list of items (in contrast to a combo box, which displays a drop-down list). You set the control's value by selecting an item in the list.
	Image	Adds a constant picture to a form. (The picture doesn't change when you switch records.)

(continued)

Table 49-1. *(continued)*

Button	Name	Description
	Bound Object Frame	Displays OLE objects that are stored in the records of a table, such as employee photos. This control is intended to be bound to a field that has the OLE Object data type. The object will change as you view various records.
	Tab Control	Lets you divide the form into separate tabs. After you add and adjust the size of a tab control, you can add controls to any of its tabs. (For an example of a form that uses tabs, see Figure 46-4, on page 1266.)
	Line	Lets you draw a single straight line on a form.
	More Controls	Allows you to add an ActiveX control to your form. When you click this button, you can select from a menu listing the ActiveX controls that are installed on your computer.

- To add an unbound control, click the button for the control on the Toolbox toolbar, and then click the position on the form where you want to display the control. (Click the button and then click the form. Don't try to drag the button to the form as you do with fields in the field list!) An unbound control is one that *doesn't* access a field in the form's record source. Its value and appearance doesn't change as you display different records in the form, although you can alter the state of an unbound control, for example, by clicking a check box or typing in a text box.

  You can use unbound controls for a variety of purposes. For example, you can use an unbound label to label controls or display information or an unbound command button to perform an action. Also, you can use an unbound object frame, image, line, or rectangle to decorate the form or provide constant information that doesn't change from record to record.

- To delete a control, click it to select it and press the Delete key.

- To move, copy, or resize a control, or to modify its appearance or properties, follow the instructions given in the next section, "Formatting a Form."

For information on embedded OLE objects, see Chapter 7, "Sharing Data Among Office XP Applications."

Troubleshooting

Embedded OLE Object Isn't Displayed

You added an Unbound Object Frame control to display an embedded OLE object in your form. However, all you see is an icon for the program that created the object.

To display the content of the embedded object, rather than just an icon, click the control to select it, and choose Edit, *X* Object, Convert (where *X* is the object type, such as *Equation*). Then, in the Convert dialog box, clear the Display As Icon option.

Formatting a Form

The following is the general procedure for modifying the controls in a form or for changing the properties of a form section or of the form itself. You can also use these same steps for formatting a report, so if you're working with a report, substitute the word *report* for *form* as you read these instructions.

1 Open the form in Design view.

Toolbox

2 Make sure that the Select Objects button is selected on the Toolbox toolbar. (See Figure 49-11. If this toolbar isn't displayed, either choose View, Toolbars, Toolbox, or click the Toolbox toolbar button.)

3 Select the control or controls you want to modify, as follows:

    ■ To select a single control, click it. Access will display seven small sizing handles, plus one large moving handle around the selected control, as shown here:

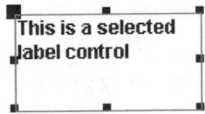

> **note** The first click on a text or combo box selects the control, and the second click places the insertion point within the control (if you want to select the control again at this point, you'll have to click on one of the control's borders).

    ■ To select several controls, click each one while pressing Shift. Or, you can select all the controls in a rectangular area by using the mouse to drag a selection rectangle around the controls, as shown here. (This will select all controls that are completely or partially contained within the rectangle.)

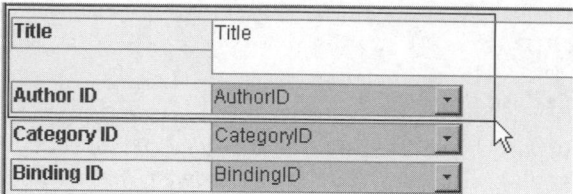

> **note** If you have selected several controls but want to exclude just one or two controls from the selection, hold down the Shift key and click each control you want to deselect.

- To select a specific form section—Form Header, Detail, or Form Footer—click the section's header, or click the button to the left of the header, or click on a blank spot within the section. This will deselect any selected controls. (Form sections are discussed later in this section.)

- To select the form (*not* all the controls in the form, but the form itself), click the form selection button in the upper-left corner of the form. This will deselect any selected control or form section, as shown here:

Form selection button

Section headers

> **note** If you know the name of a control, you can select it by choosing its name in the Object drop-down list at the left end of the Formatting toolbar. (The Formatting toolbar is explained later in this section.) You can also select a form section by choosing FormHeader, Detail, or FormFooter. Or, you can select the entire form by choosing Form.

4 Modify the selection according to the instructions in the following list:

- To change the size of a selected control, point to one of the seven sizing handles, and drag when the pointer becomes a two-headed arrow, as seen here:

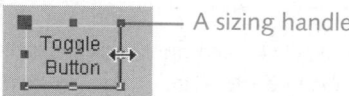

A sizing handle

Alternatively, to change the size of one or more selected controls, choose a command from the Size submenu on the Format menu, as shown here:

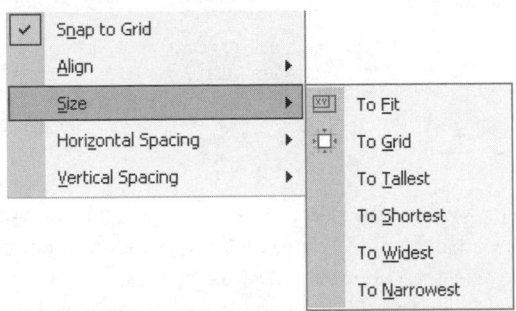

(If you've selected a single control, only the To Fit and To Grid commands are available.)

note Choosing To Grid from the Size submenu of the Format menu moves each of the boundaries of the selected control(s) to the nearest gridline on the form. If the Snap To Grid option on the Format menu is selected, resizing or moving a control always moves the control edge or edges that are repositioned to the nearest gridline. Gridlines are visible in Design view only if the Grid option is selected on the View menu (gridlines are active whether or not they're visible). In the figures in this section, gridlines were hidden for clarity.

- If a single control is selected, you can move it by pointing to either the moving handle or to one of the borders (but *not* to a sizing handle) and dragging when the pointer assumes the image of a hand, as seen here:

If several controls are selected, you can move all of them simultaneously by pointing to one of the borders on any of the controls (but *not* to a moving handle or to a sizing handle) and dragging when the pointer assumes the image of an open hand, as shown here:

If several controls are selected, you can move one of them independently of the others by pointing to its moving handle and dragging
when the pointer assumes the image of a hand with an extended index
finger, as shown here:

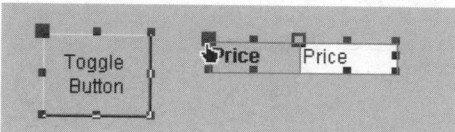

Recall that when you insert many types of controls, Access automatically
attaches a label to the control. When you click either the control or its
label to select it, the moving handle appears *both* on the control and on
the label (even though only one is selected). To move the control and the
label together, drag a border on the selected object; to move either the
control or the label independently, drag its moving handle.

> **note** You can move a control (or add a new one) to any position within the three sections
> of a form: Form Header, Detail, or Form Footer. Controls that you place in the Detail
> section appear in the main part of the form in Form view. Controls placed in the Form
> Header or Form Footer section appear in the Form Header or Form Footer section at
> the top or bottom of the form in Form view. (See Figure 49-12.) If the Form view win-
> dow is made too small to show all the controls, scroll bars appear that scroll the Detail
> section but not the Form Header or Form Footer sections. Note that the Form Header
> and Form Footer sections appear in Design view only if the View, Form Header/Footer
> menu option is selected.

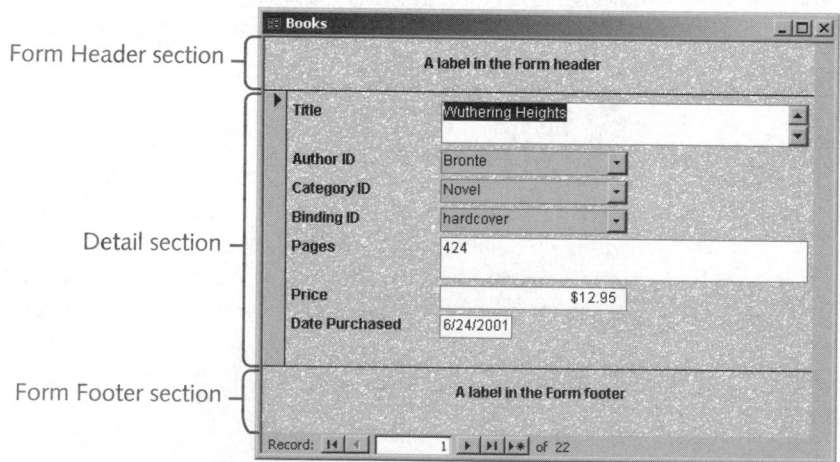

Figure 49-12. You can place controls in any of the three form sections that are
displayed in Form view.

■ To make a copy of the selected control or controls, choose Edit, Copy, and then choose Edit, Paste (or use the equivalent toolbar buttons or shortcut keys).

■ To align a group of selected controls, you can choose a command from the Align submenu of the Format menu, as shown here:

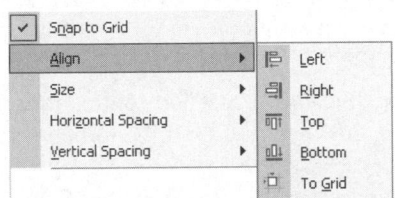

■ To adjust the spacing of a group of selected controls, open the Format menu and choose a command from the Horizontal Spacing submenu:

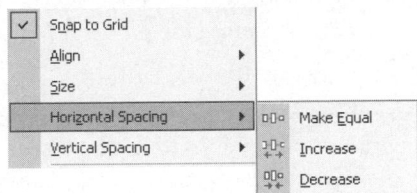

or from the Vertical Spacing submenu:

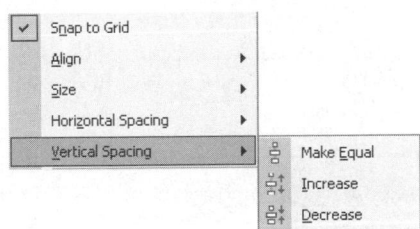

■ To alter the text formatting, background color, text color, border color or width, or visual effects (such as Raised or Shadowed) of the selected control(s), form section, or form, use the controls on the Formatting toolbar shown in Figure 49-13.

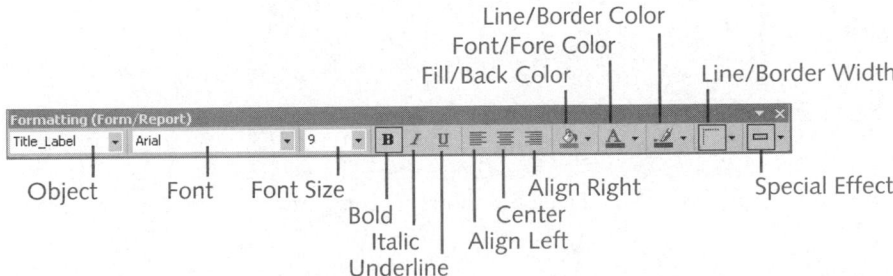

Figure 49-13. The Formatting toolbar lets you change the appearance of controls and any text they contain.

> **tip** **Use Separate Controls to Vary Text Formatting**
>
> Sometimes you might want to have a label that has two different text formats—for example, a label reading "*Full* Address." You can't apply multiple text formats to a control, although you can achieve the same result in a label by creating two label controls that are lined up to appear as if they were only one. Because each portion of the label is in a separate control, you can assign different formats to each.

Properties

■ To change the properties of the selected control or controls, the selected form section, or the form itself if the form is selected, choose View, Properties, or click the Properties toolbar button, or press F4 to display the *property sheet* for the selected object. A property sheet is a dialog box that contains a set of tabs for the different categories of properties available for the currently selected object. (See Figure 49-14.) You can leave the property sheet open while you work in Design view, and it lets you view or modify the properties of whatever object is currently selected.

> **note** A control inherits certain properties from the field that it accesses, while other properties must be explicitly set for the control. For example, if the Required property of a field in a table is set to Yes, any control that accesses this field will require data input. In contrast, assigning an input mask to a field's Input Mask property doesn't affect controls that access the field; instead, you must assign an input mask to the Input Mask property of the control itself. (To assign an input mask, click the Input Mask property box in the Data tab of the property sheet, and then click the ellipsis [...] box to run the Input Mask Wizard.)

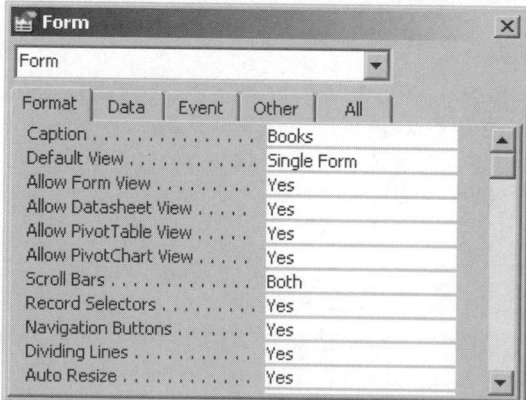

Figure 49-14. This figure shows the property sheet for the form itself.

tip   **Explore Properties**

To learn how the many properties listed in the property sheet affect different types of controls, select a control, open the property sheet, and click in any property box that you're curious about. Press F1 and Access's online Help system will take you directly to a complete explanation of the property. You can also choose Help, What's This?—the pointer will change to an arrow with a question mark—and then click the property box you're interested in.

tip   **Create a Calculated Control**

You can define the properties of a text box control so that it displays the result of a calculation performed on one or more of the fields in the record source, rather than simply displaying or setting the contents of a single field. To do this, display the text box's property sheet, click the Data tab, and enter the expression for the calculation you want to perform into the Control Source property box. (For a bound control, the Control Source property is normally set to the name of the field that the control is bound to.) For instance, in the Books example form shown in this chapter, if you wanted to display a text box control that shows the total book price including sales tax, you could enter the following expression (assuming the sales tax rate is 7 percent):

=[Price]*1.07

To properly format the calculated result, you could then select the Currency format in the Format property box in the property sheet's Format tab.

For help in entering a complex expression, you can click the ellipsis (...) button that appears at the right of the Control Source property box when it's active. This will run the Expression Builder.

A calculated control in a form is analogous to a calculated field in a query, which is discussed in "Adding Calculated Fields," on page 1325.

Viewing and Modifying Data in a Form

To use a form to view or modify the data that it accesses, open the form in Form view using any of the methods described in "Using the Database Window and Object Views," on page 1352. Figure 49-15 shows a form opened in Form view displaying an existing record.

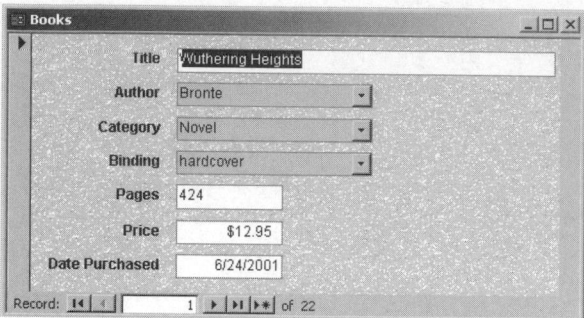

Figure 49-15. This form was generated using the Form Wizard and then customized in Design view. It accesses the records in the Books table of the Book Inventory03 example database.

The techniques you use in a form for entering information into a new record or for modifying an existing record are basically the same as the techniques you use in standard Microsoft Office XP dialog boxes. When entering or editing a record in a form, keep in mind the following points:

- When you add or modify data within the current record, Access displays a pencil icon on the vertical bar at the left of the form. This icon indicates that the record contains unsaved changes. When you move to a different record (using one of the methods described later in this section), Access automatically saves the original record's contents. You can also save the current record's contents at any time by choosing Records, Save Record or by pressing Shift+Enter.

Undo

- You can reverse changes you've made in the currently displayed record (or in the previously displayed record if you haven't yet changed the current record) by issuing the Undo command (choose Edit, Undo, or click the Undo toolbar button, or press Ctrl+Z) or by pressing Esc.

Spelling

- You can check the spelling of the text in *all* records by choosing Tools, Spelling, or clicking the Spelling toolbar button, or pressing F7. You can also have Access automatically replace specific text as you type by using the AutoCorrect feature; to set it up, choose Tools, AutoCorrect. The Spelling and AutoCorrect features work in essentially the same way they do in Microsoft Word 2002. For general instructions, see "Checking Spelling," on page 475, and "Automatically Fixing Your Text with AutoCorrect," on page 258.

newfeature!

note In Access 2002, you can modify the way the spelling checker works by choosing Tools, Options and opening the Spelling tab in the Options dialog box.

In a form, you can view any of the records belonging to the record source, and you can add new records to the record source or delete records from it. Access provides a small toolbar permanently positioned in the lower-left corner of the form (see Figure 49-16). You can use this toolbar to navigate through the existing records or to add new records.

Figure 49-16. This toolbar, displayed at the bottom of a form, displays the current record number and lets you navigate to any record or add a new record.

If you prefer to use the keyboard rather than the mouse, press Page Down to move forward a single record or Page Up to move back a single record. To jump to the start of the first record, press Ctrl+Home, and to jump to the end of the last record, press Ctrl+End. (If pressing Ctrl+Home or Ctrl+End moves the insertion point within a control instead of moving between records, press the Tab key once and try again.)

The Current Record text box displays the number of the currently displayed record. To open a specific record, you can type the record number into this box and press Enter.

---

tip **Find or Replace Text Quickly**

Find

You can quickly find specified text in any of the records by choosing Edit, Find, or by clicking the Find toolbar button, or by pressing Ctrl+F, and then entering your search criteria into the Find tab of the Find And Replace dialog box (see Figure 47-11, on page 1299). To replace text, choose Edit, Replace, or press Ctrl+H to open the Replace tab of the Find And Replace dialog box.

New Record

To create a new record, click the New Record button on the toolbar at the bottom of the form (see Figure 49-16) or click the New Record button on the main Access toolbar. The new record will be added to the form's record source and will be displayed in the form so that you can enter information into it.

Rather than entering mostly repetitive information for a new record, you can copy the data from another, similar record into the new record and then just modify the data as necessary. You can also copy information from one record over another record's data, replacing the original contents of the target record. To copy a record, complete the following steps:

1 Select the record that's the source of the information by displaying that record in the form and clicking the vertical bar at the left of the form to select the record. (This bar is equivalent to the row selector you see in Datasheet view, and it's highlighted when you click it.)

Click anywhere in this bar to select the entire record.

2 Choose Edit, Copy or press Ctrl+C. (If you want to move the source record's contents, choose Cut or press Ctrl+X instead.)

3 Display the target record in the form. (This record can be an existing one or a newly created one.) Make sure the vertical bar at the left is still highlighted, indicating that the entire record is selected.

4 Choose Edit, Paste or press Ctrl+V. The value of every control in the source record will be copied into the same control in the target record, except for any control that accesses a primary key field or other field that must have a unique value.

Delete Record

To permanently delete a record, display the record in the form, and then choose Edit, Delete Record, or click the Delete Record toolbar button. Access will require you to confirm the deletion before it removes the record. If the deletion will result in additional cascading deletions in related tables, a dialog box will inform you of that and give you an opportunity to stop. Just as when you delete a record in Datasheet view, once you confirm a deletion, the data is permanently lost—you can't restore it using the Undo button, and you'll have to manually reenter it if you want to restore it later.

---

tip **Sort or Filter Records Viewed in a Form**

You can sort or filter the records you view in a form in the same way that you sort or filter records when you view a table, query, or form in Datasheet view. For general instructions, see "Sorting and Filtering in Datasheet View," on page 1303.

Note that you can also display a form in Datasheet view. Each row in the Datasheet view of a form displays the controls for a particular record, one per column. Although Datasheet view is generally much less convenient for working with a form than Form view, it has the advantage of allowing you to view multiple records at a time.

Troubleshooting

All Records Have Disappeared

While viewing a form in Form view, you chose the Data Entry command from the Records menu to see what it does. Now all your records seem to be missing, and you can't get them back.

The Data Entry command switches on a special mode that allows you to enter new records but hides existing records in the data source. The confusing thing about the command is that you can't toggle it off by choosing the same menu option that turns it on (as you can with most commands that turn on special modes). Although the Data Entry command doesn't actually apply a filter (you don't see the Filtered message on the form or the FLTR message on the Access status bar), the way you turn data entry mode off is to choose Records, Remove Filter/Sort. Once you choose Remove Filter/Sort, you'll see all your records again.

Publishing Data on an Intranet Using a Data Access Page

A data access page is similar to a form. Like a form, it displays a collection of controls and allows you to access fields in one or more tables or queries in a database. Unlike a form, however, it's stored in a separate file rather than within the database. Because this file is in HTML (Hypertext Markup Language) format, it can be opened in a Web browser as well as in Access. And when it's opened in a browser, it doesn't merely display static information but rather allows you to navigate through the records in the record source table or query and to add, modify, or remove information, just as you can in Access. If you place the data access page and its supplemental files on a Web server on your organization's intranet and if you store the Access database on a shared network drive, other users in your organization can work with the database by opening the page in their Web browsers. Figure 49-17 shows a data access page viewed in Access, and Figure 49-18 shows the same page viewed in the Microsoft Internet Explorer Web browser. Both figures are on page 1356.

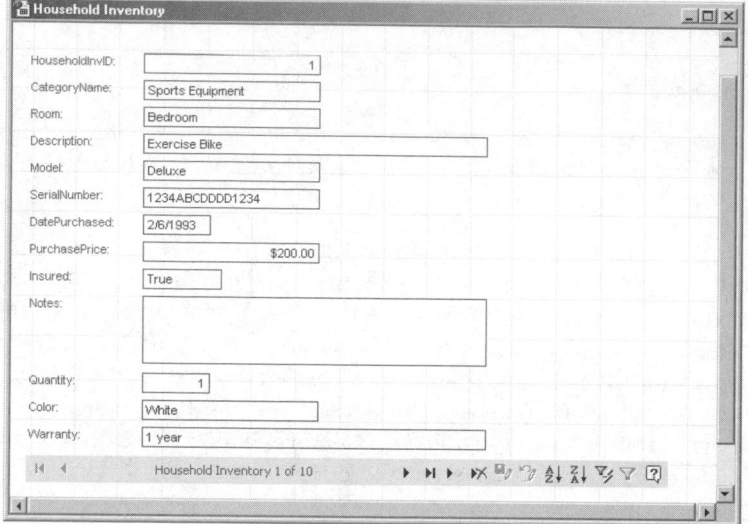

Figure 49-17. In Access a data access page functions like a form. This page is part of the Inventry.mdb example database.

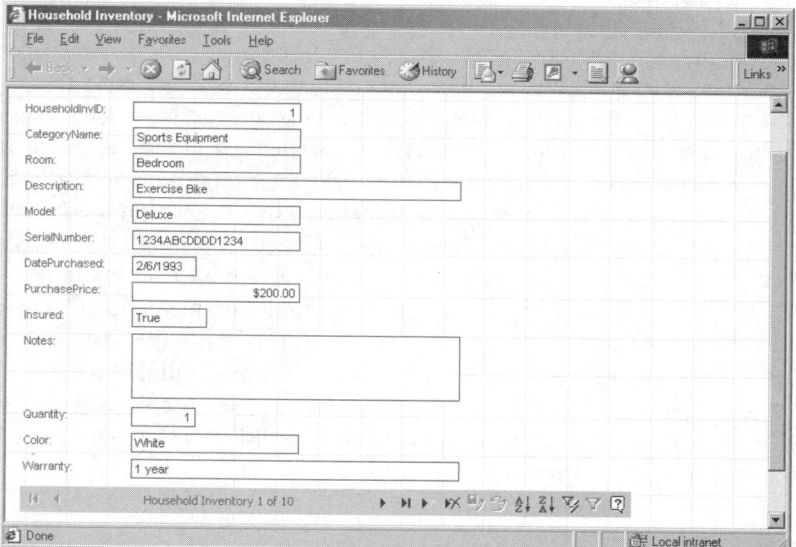

Figure 49-18. You can also open a data access page in a Web browser.

To use a particular data access page in Access, open the page using the instructions given in "Using the Database Window and Object Views," on page 1271. This will open the page in Page view (as shown in Figure 49-17), which is analogous to Form view for using a form. To open a data access page in a Web browser, you'll need to run your browser and enter the file path or URL where the page is stored on a local disk, shared network drive, or intranet Web server. (If you've already opened a data access page in

1356

Access, you can preview its appearance in your browser by choosing File, Web Page
Preview.)

For more information on opening a data access page from an intranet location, see "Publishing a Data Access Page," on page 1359.

To view or modify records in a data access page, you use the same basic techniques that
were described for forms in "Viewing and Modifying Data in a Form," on page 1351.
Notice, however, that a data access page typically contains a more complete toolbar
than a form, as shown in Figure 49-19.

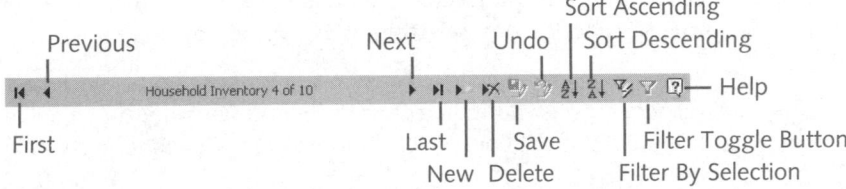

Figure 49-19. This is the toolbar displayed at the bottom of a data access page when
it's viewed in Page View in Access or when it's opened in a Web browser.

Creating a Data Access Page

To create a new data access page that connects to the currently opened Access database,
follow these steps:

1 Open the New Data Access Page dialog box (shown in Figure 49-20)
as explained in "Using the Database Window and Object Views," on
page 1271.

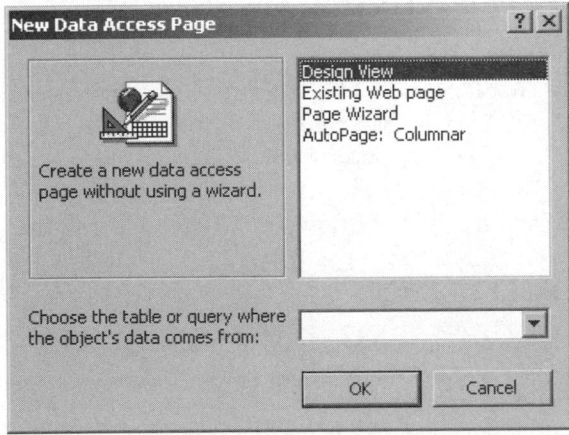

Figure 49-20. In the New Data Access Page dialog box, you can select one
of four ways to create a new data access page.

2 In the drop-down list near the bottom of the New Data Access Page dialog box, select the table or query that you want to use as the record source.

3 Select an option in the list to specify the way the new page will be created, and click the OK button. The options, listed below, are similar to those you can select in the New Form dialog box when you create a new form:

- To create a data access page from scratch in Design view, select the Design View option.

- To create a new data access page based on a Web page you already have, select the Existing Web Page option.

- To run a wizard that creates a new data access page for you, according to your specifications, select the Page Wizard option.

- To quickly generate a new data access page based on the selected record source, where the controls are arranged in a single column, using default options, select the AutoPage: Columnar option.

newfeature!

note You can also create a data access page from scratch in Design view by clicking the Blank Data Access Page command in the New File task pane. (You can open this task pane by choosing File, New.)

In general, the easiest way to create a new data access page is to select the Page Wizard option. Using the Page Wizard is simple yet flexible. It works much like the Form Wizard, which was discussed in "Creating a Form Using the Form Wizard," on page 1335. You might be able to use it to create your final page—or at least a preliminary version of your page that you can then customize, as discussed next.

newfeature!

tip   Convert Another Database Object to a Data Access Page

You can create a data access page by saving a copy of a table, query, form, or report as a data access page. To do this, select the database object in the Database window and choose File, Save As. Then, in the Save As dialog box, select Data Access Page in the As drop-down list, and enter a name for the data access page into the Save text box at the top.

Modifying a Data Access Page

To modify a data access page, open it in Design view using any of the methods explained in "Using the Database Window and Object Views," on page 1271.

Figure 49-21 shows the same form shown in Figures 49-17 and 49-18, opened in Design view. Design view lets you add, remove, resize, or rearrange the controls that make up the page. You can also modify the properties of any of the controls or of the page itself. The techniques for using Design view to modify a data access page are similar to those for customizing a form in Design view, which were described in "Customizing a Form," on page 1339.

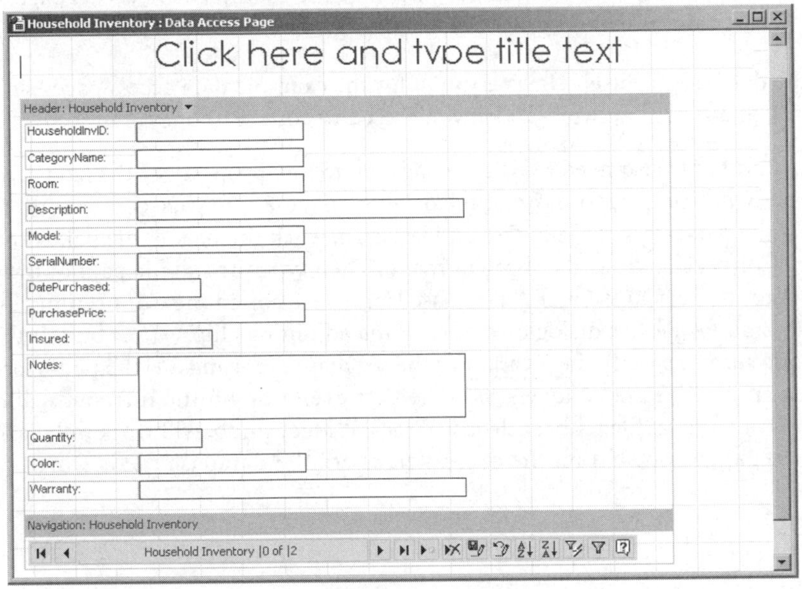

Figure 49-21. Design view provides an extensive set of tools for customizing a data access page.

Publishing a Data Access Page

The typical way to share a data access page with others in your organization is to store the data access page—together with its supplemental files—on a Web server on your intranet, and to store the Access database file on a shared network drive.

note Often, all files—the data access page, its supplemental files, and the database file—are stored in the *same* folder. This works if the folder can be accessed by the intranet's Web server *and* has been set up as a shared network folder.

If your data access page and its supplemental files aren't already stored on your intranet's Web server, you'll need to copy the files to the appropriate folder on the server. (If you're uncertain about where you need to post these files or how to transfer them to the server, contact your company Webmaster or network administrator.) Be sure to copy all of the following files to the server:

● **The HTML file containing the data access page.** (For the example data access page shown in Figures 49-17 and 49-18, this is Household Inventory.htm.)

● **The graphics and other supplemental files used by the data access page.** These files are stored in a subfolder bearing the same name as the data access page, followed by _files_. (For the example data access page, this subfolder is named Household Inventory_files.)

If the database file itself (Inventry.mdb for the example data access page) isn't already stored in a shared network folder, you'll need to copy it to one.

You'll probably also need to edit the *page connection* property of the data access page to properly indicate the location of the database file that the page connects to. To do this, open the data access page in Design view, right-click the page's title bar, and choose Page Connection from the shortcut menu. Then type the full file path of the database file into the Select Or Enter A Database Name text box in the Connection tab of the Data Link Properties dialog box, or click the adjoining ellipsis (…) button to select the file. Be sure to specify the location of the database file using a UNC path (for example, \\Inventory\C\Stock\Widgets.mdb) so that everyone on the intranet will be able to access it. (A local file path, such as C:\Stock\Widgets.mdb, will work only if the data access page is opened on the computer where the database file is stored.)

Generating Reports to Present Information

Creating a Report

Reports and other database objects are described in "Designing and Planning an Access Database," on page 1263. To create a new report, open the New Report dialog box (shown in Figure 50-1) as explained in "Using the Database Window and Object Views," on page 1271, and then select an option in the list, as follows, and click OK:

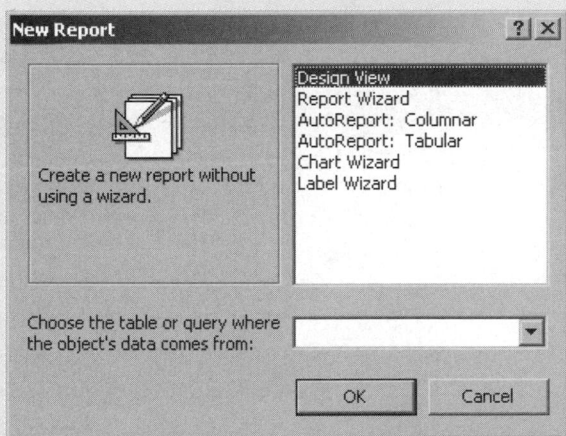

Figure 50-1. In the New Report dialog box you can select one of six ways to create a new report.

- To create a report from scratch using Design view, select the Design View option. Design view is discussed in "Modifying a Report," on page 1370.

- To have Microsoft Access 2002 help you design the report, select the Report Wizard option.

1361

Instructions for using the Report Wizard are given in "Using the Report Wizard," on page 1363.

● To use default settings to quickly create a report based on a single table or query, with a columnar or tabular layout, select the AutoReport: Columnar or the AutoReport: Tabular option. Either report will include all the fields belonging to the record source table or query that you select in the drop-down list at the bottom of the New Report dialog box.

In a *columnar report*, each field is presented in a separate row that has the field name on the left and the contents of the field on the right. Depending on the number of fields in your database, each record might fit on a single sheet of paper or might extend onto several sheets; you might even be able to fit several records on one page.

A *tabular report* organizes the information in rows and columns, where each record is displayed in a separate row, with each of its fields in a separate column. (To see an example of a tabular report generated by the Report Wizard, look ahead to Figure 50-11.)

note If you select the AutoReport option, the Chart Wizard option, or the Label Wizard option, you must also select a table or query in the drop-down list at the bottom of the New Report dialog box. This list shows all the tables and queries in the database. The report will display the fields belonging to the table or query you select, which is known as the report's *record source*.

If, however, you select the Design View or Report Wizard option, you can leave the drop-down list blank and specify the record source later in the process. With either of these options, you can display fields belonging to *several* related tables or queries. If the report displays records from several tables or queries, the record source is actually an SQL query statement that selects the desired information. If you use the wizard, will create this statement for you. If you create the report in Design view, you must assign the statement to the report's Record Source property (the easiest way to do this is to click the ellipsis button next to the Record Source property box to run the SQL Statement: Query Builder). Properties are discussed in "Modifying a Report," on page 1370.

● To use the Chart Wizard to create a report that contains a Microsoft Graph chart, select the Chart Wizard option. The chart will graph data from the data source that you select in the drop-down list. For information on charts generated by the Graph program, see "Constructing Charts Using Microsoft Graph," on page 144.

> **tip** **Insert a Chart into Any Report**
>
> No matter how you create your report, you can use the Chart Wizard to insert a chart into it by opening the report in Design view, choosing Insert, Chart, and dragging to mark the rectangular area on your report where you want to display the chart. The Chart Wizard will then start running and will guide you through the process of designing your chart.

- To use the Label Wizard to create mailing labels or other types of labels, select the Label Wizard option. The labels will display the information from the data source that you select in the drop-down list.

> **tip** **Use Word to Print Labels**
>
> Microsoft Word lets you print labels, form letters, envelopes, and other types of mail-merge output documents directly using an Access database as the recipient list (that is, as the data source). For printing labels, Word offers more features, greater flexibility, and perhaps a more familiar interface than the Access Label Wizard. If you've already opened the Access database you want to use for printing merge documents, a quick way to run Word's Mail Merge Wizard is to select the table you want to use as the recipient list in the Database window and then choose Tools, Office Links, Merge It With Microsoft Word. For information on using Word's mail-merge feature, see "Using the Mail Merge Wizard to Automate Large Mailings," on page 553.

Using the Report Wizard is the easiest way to design a report, and yet the wizard is quite flexible. Although selecting one of the AutoReport options is a faster way to create a columnar or tabular report based on the fields in a single table or query, you can use the Report Wizard to create these same types of reports and have much greater flexibility in the choice of fields and in the report design.

Using the Report Wizard

The following is the procedure for creating a report using the Report Wizard. (The figures show the steps for creating a report that displays a list of books, organized by binding type and author, in the Book Inventory03 example database. If you want to see the final result as you read these steps, look ahead to Figure 50-10.)

1 Select the Report Wizard option in the New Report dialog box and click the OK button. (You don't need to select a record source in the drop-down list in the New Report dialog box.)

2 In the first Report Wizard dialog box, shown in Figure 50-2 on page 1364, select the fields to be included in the report. You have the option of selecting from several related tables or queries, as you do when you use other Access wizards. Be sure to include all the fields that have any relevance to your report, whether the field values are to be displayed in each detail line, summarized, or used for grouping the records.

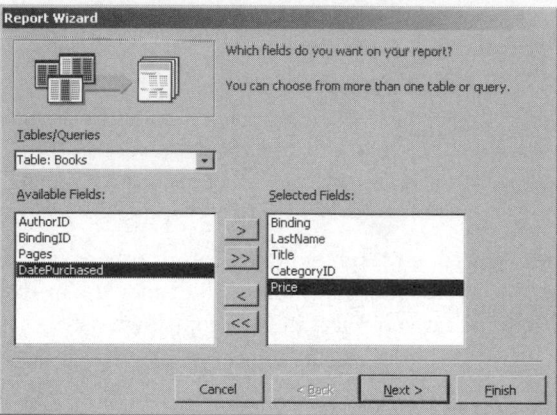

Figure 50-2. In the first Report Wizard dialog box, you select all the fields to be used in the report. These are the fields selected for the example report (they're from the Bindings-, Authors-, and Books-related tables).

Move the fields you want from the Available Fields list into the Selected Fields list by using, as necessary, the four buttons between the lists. To access fields from different tables or queries, select each one in the Tables/Queries drop-down list, and then move the fields you want. This list includes all the tables and queries defined in your database. When you've finished selecting fields, click the Next button to open the next Report Wizard dialog box.

3 If you selected fields from more than one table or query in the previous step, the second Report Wizard dialog box, shown in Figure 50-3, asks you to choose one table or query that will be used for grouping the information in the report, if possible. (You'll be able to select further grouping levels, based on individual fields, in the next Report Wizard dialog box.) After you've selected a grouping table, click the Next button.

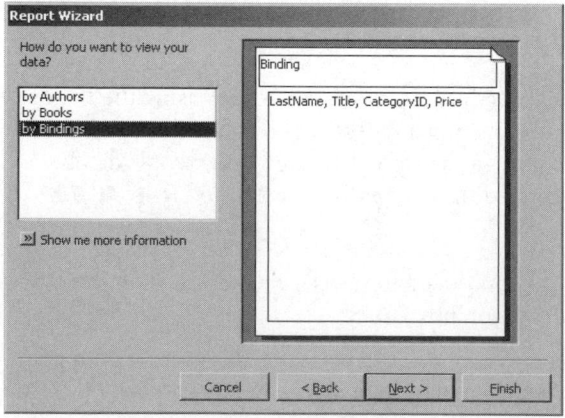

Figure 50-3. In the second Report Wizard dialog box (which appears only if you selected fields from more than one table or query), select a table or query to be used for grouping. This is the selection for the example report, in which the top-level grouping is by binding types.

> **note** In the Book Inventory03 example database, Bindings and Authors are both *primary tables* in one-to-many relationships with the Books table. Therefore, each record in the Bindings or Authors table can match many records in the Books table, and thus you can easily use the Bindings or Authors table for grouping records in the Books table. This isn't true for the Books table, however, because it constitutes the *related table* in both the relationships. Accordingly, if you selected the Books table, the Report Wizard wouldn't attempt to group your records for you. In the next Report Wizard dialog box, however, you would have the opportunity to specify grouping on the basis of individual fields. For information on relationships and the differences between primary and related tables, see "Setting Up Table Relationships," on page 1291.

4 In the third Report Wizard dialog box, shown in Figure 50-4, you can add grouping levels to your report by selecting one or more fields to be used to group the records.

In the example shown in Figure 50-4, because the Bindings table was selected in the second wizard dialog box, the field from this table, Binding, is already selected as the main grouping field in the third dialog box. (If the Books table had been selected in the previous dialog box, no grouping field would be defined yet.) In this example you could now add one or more fields to create *additional* grouping levels.

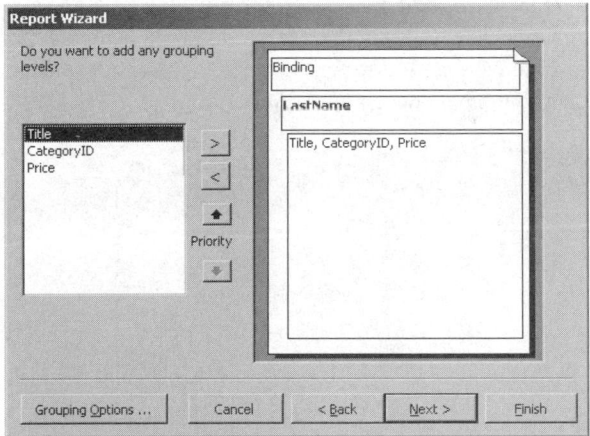

Figure 50-4. In the third Report Wizard dialog box, you can add grouping levels to your report. In the example report the LastName field was added as the second grouping level, as shown in this figure.

To add a grouping field, select it in the list at the left, and click the > button to move it into the report model at the right. To remove the field that's selected on the right, click the < button to move it back to the left. You can add up to three fields, which—when combined with an initially selected grouping field—would generate up to four grouping levels in your report. You can change the priority level of a grouping field that you've chosen by clicking the field name in the report model and then clicking the up arrow or down arrow Priority button. When you've finished defining the grouping of your records, click the Next button to move to the fourth Report Wizard dialog box.

---

tip **Use Grouping Levels to Summarize Information**

An important reason for including grouping levels is that they allow you to summarize numeric information within each group. For instance, including the Binding and LastName grouping levels in the example report would allow you to display the total cost of the books that have a particular binding type, as well as the total cost of all books by a particular author within a binding category. Instead of the sum, you could also display the average, minimum, or maximum book cost. Defining summary calculations is discussed in the sidebar "Setting Summary Options," on page 1367.

---

5 The fourth Report Wizard dialog box, shown in Figure 50-5, lets you choose the sorting order for the Detail section in the report. Note that the report groups are automatically sorted on the fields used for grouping. In this dialog box, however, you can choose one or more fields that will be used for sorting the detail lines falling within each group. Choose the primary sort field by selecting it from the top drop-down list (labeled 1). You can then choose one or more additional sort fields in the remaining drop-down lists. (Note that each list contains the names of only those report fields that aren't used for grouping.) For an explanation of the Summary Options button, see the sidebar "Setting Summary Options." When you're done with the fourth Report Wizard dialog box, click the Next button to move on to the next dialog box.

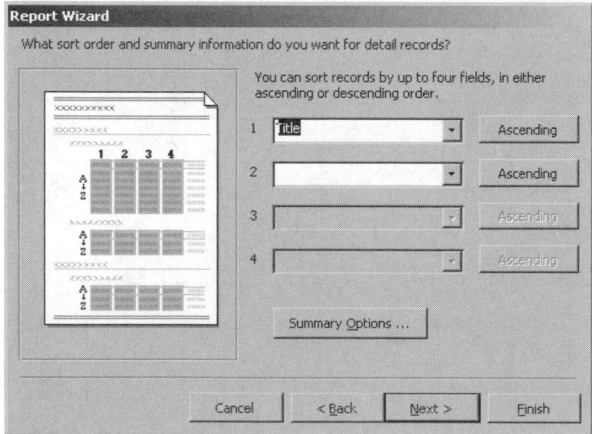

Figure 50-5. In the fourth Report Wizard dialog box you specify how to sort the detail lines in your report. In the example report Title is selected in the first list to sort the detail records by book title.

Setting Summary Options

One button in the fourth Report Wizard dialog box is crucial but easy to overlook: the Summary Options button. Click this button to open the Summary Options dialog box, shown in Figure 50-6. This dialog box lists each of the numeric or currency fields included in the your report's Detail section. As you can see in Figure 50-6, in the example report only the Price field (which has the Currency data type) qualifies as a summary field.

You can choose to have Access summarize the values in one or more of these fields for each group in the report. If you want a summary to appear in your report, simply check one of the summary value functions for the field that you want to summarize. Access can calculate the sum, average, minimum, or maximum value.

By selecting one of the Show options, you can specify whether the records within each group will be shown or only the summary information. In general, the first time you produce a report, you'll probably want to select Detail And Summary so that you can see clearly how Access is organizing the information. Later you might want to hide the detail information so that your report is more concise and contains fewer distractions. (You can do this by using Design view, described in "Modifying a Report," on page 1370.)

You can also select the Calculate Percent Of Total For Sums option to have Access calculate the percent of the grand total represented by each group total. In the example report you could determine what percentage of the total cost of the inventory was contributed by each group of books. When you've finished setting the summary options, click OK to return to the fourth Report Wizard dialog box.

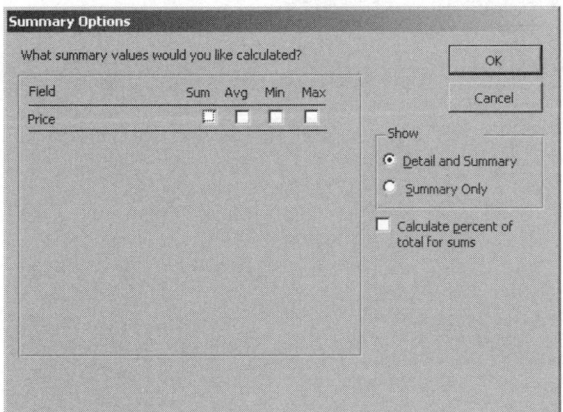

Figure 50-6. In the Summary Options dialog box you can have Access summarize numeric information for each group. For the example report, none of the summary functions are selected.

6 The fifth Report Wizard dialog box, shown in Figure 50-7 on page 1368, allows you to select your report's layout and orientation. Each layout option

Chapter 50

in this dialog box specifies how much of the database information is repeated at each level of the report. When you select an option, the model at the left of the dialog box gives you an idea of how your report will look:

■ The Stepped layout places each new group header in its own section of the report, putting no other information on the same line.

■ The Block layout compresses the information for the group header onto the same line as the information for the first detail listing in that group. This makes for a more vertically compact report, but often it's somewhat difficult to find the information you need.

■ The Outline 1 and Outline 2 layouts overlap the columns used for the grouping values but keep the text for each on a separate line. These layoutsa are useful when you have a report that's too wide to fit legibly on a single page. Alternatively, you can consider changing the page orientation from the Portrait option to the Landscape option, which gives you a wider page to work with.

■ The Align Left 1 and Align Left 2 layouts position the grouping fields flush with the left margin and repeat the detail headers at the top of each Detail section. These options provide the largest area across your page for your detail records, although they make distinguishing the different groups a bit more difficult.

When you're done setting options in the fifth Report Wizard dialog box, click the Next button to go to the sixth dialog box.

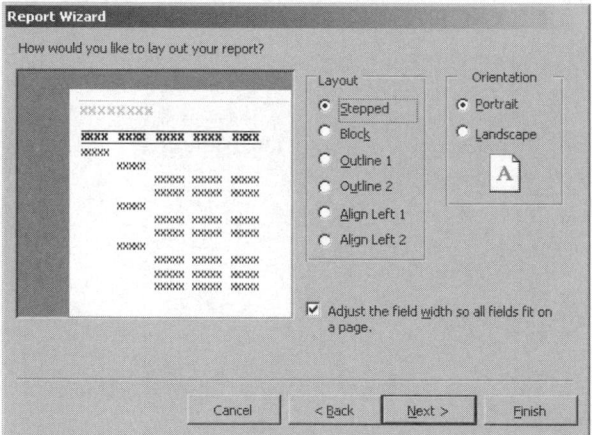

Figure 50-7. In the fifth Report Wizard dialog box, select your report's layout and orientation. These are the settings used for the example report.

7 The sixth dialog box of the Report Wizard, shown in Figure 50-8, lets you choose a formatting style for your report. These styles automatically apply fonts, borders, and spacing to your report design. In general, the simpler the design, the better your system's performance in producing the report. Complex designs involving a lot of graphics or shading might take significantly

1368

longer to create and, subsequently, to print out. When you're done selecting the style, click the Next button to move on to the seventh dialog box.

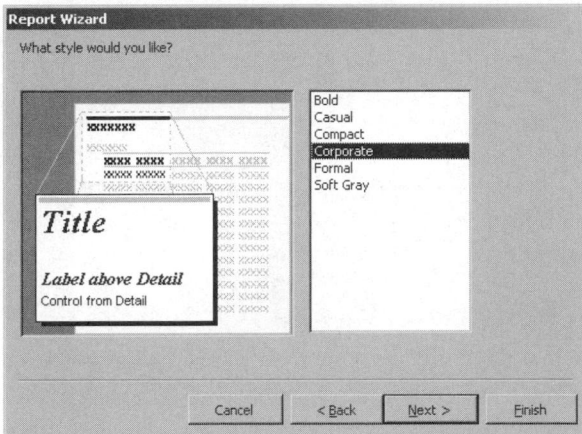

Figure 50-8. In the sixth Report Wizard dialog box, choose the style of the elements in your report. The example report uses the Corporate style.

8 In the seventh and final Report Wizard dialog box, shown in Figure 50-9, you can name your report and choose whether to immediately preview the report's printed appearance or open it in Design view so that you can modify its design, as explained next. Click the Finish button to generate and open your report.

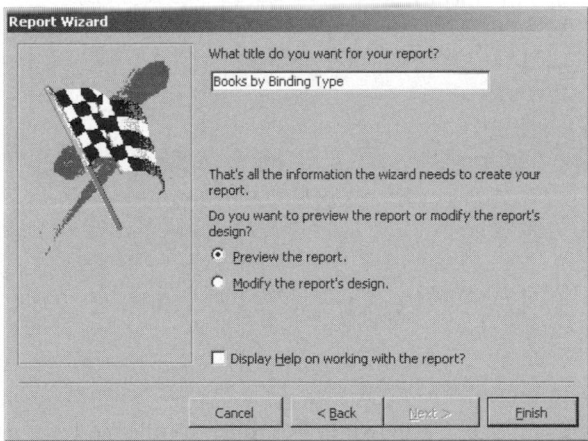

Figure 50-9. In the seventh (and last) Report Wizard dialog box, decide on a report name and choose how to open the report. The example report is named Books by Binding Type.

Figure 50-10, on page 1370, shows the example report, opened in Print Preview view. As is typical of a report generated by the Report Wizard, the field sizes and positions need some adjustment so that text isn't cut off and the column headings would benefit from friendlier names. Figure 50-11, also on page 1370, shows the same report after it has been modified slightly using report Design view, which is discussed in the next section.

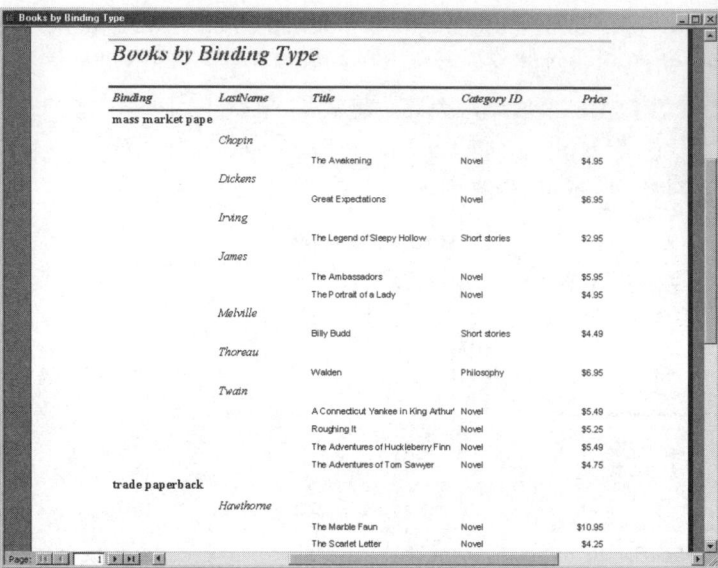

Figure 50-10. This report is the result of the Report Wizard choices shown in Figures 50-2 through 50-10.

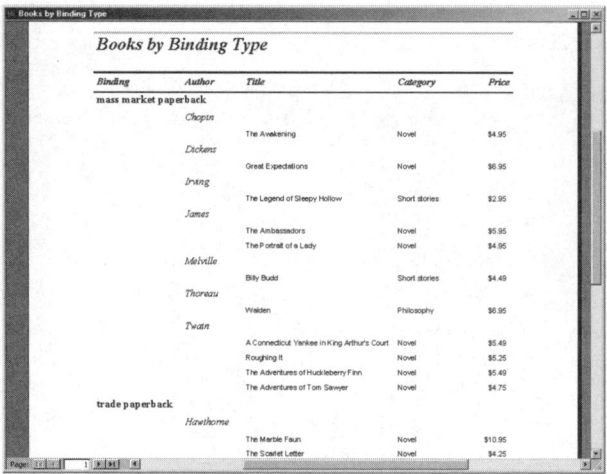

Figure 50-11. This is the report shown in Figure 50-10 after some minor customizations were made in Design view.

Modifying a Report

You can use Design view to design a new report that you created by selecting the Design View option in the New Report dialog box, to customize a new report that you created by selecting one of the Wizard or AutoReport options in the New Report dialog box, or to modify an existing report of any type. Design view lets you add, remove, or modify the controls that make up a report, work with report sections, and change the properties of the report itself.

To open a report in Design view, follow the instructions given in "Using the Database Window and Object Views," on page 1271. Figure 50-12 shows a report opened in Design view. In Figure 50-11 you can see how this report appears in Print Preview view.

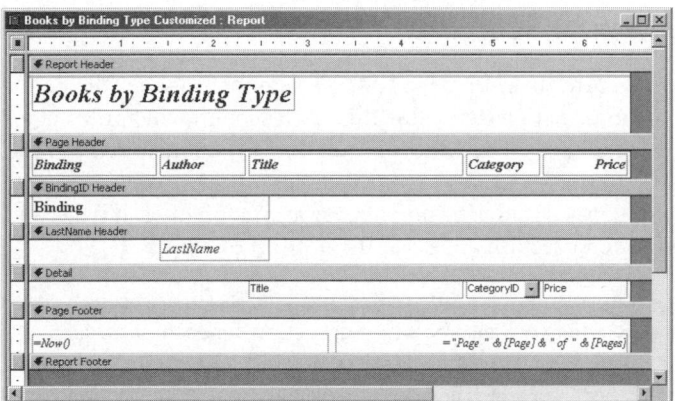

Figure 50-12. This report was created using the Report Wizard with the choices shown in Figures 50-2 through 50-10. It was then opened in Design view and slightly modified (headings were edited and control widths were adjusted).

As you can see in Figure 50-12 on page 1371, Design view for a report is essentially the same as Design view for a form. Like a form, a report consists of various controls added to different sections in Design view. In the example report the controls in the Report Header and Page Header sections are all labels, which display constant values wherever they appear on the report. The controls in all the other sections are text boxes (except CategoryID, as explained in the following note).

> **note** The CategoryID control in the example report's Detail section is a combo box control. The Report Wizard used a combo box rather than a text box because CategoryID in the Books table is a lookup field. When bound to a lookup field, a combo box displays the values from the related Categories table (Novel, Short Stories, and so on). A text box would display the field's actual contents, namely, the *identifiers* of the records in the related Categories table (1, 2, 3, and so on).

The controls in the BindingID Header, LastName Header, and Detail sections are bound to various fields in the report's record source, and they display the different values of the field when the report is printed. The two controls in the Page Footer section are calculated controls; that is, they display the results of the expressions that they contain. The left field displays the current day and date. The right field displays the current report page and the total number of pages in the report.

For information on creating calculated fields, see the tip "Create a Calculated Control," on page 1351.

In Design view for a report, you work with controls and format the report using the same basic techniques you use in Design view for a form. For a description of these techniques, see "Customizing a Form," on page 1339, and "Formatting a Form," on page 1345. The following sections cover several topics that apply specifically to reports.

Understanding Report Sections

As you can see in Figure 50-12 on page 1371, Design view divides the report into separate sections. The information defined within each section will appear at a specific position on the printed report. The Report Header information appears at the beginning of the first page, and the Report Footer information appears at the end of the last page. The contents of the Page Header section appear at the top of each page, and the contents of the Page Footer section appear at the bottom of each page.

If you chose to group your report using one or more fields (in the second and third Report Wizard dialog boxes), there will also be a header section for each of these fields. And if you chose to calculate summary values for one or more fields (using the Summary Options button in the fourth Report Wizard dialog box), there will be a footer section corresponding to each of the group header sections. The next section, "Controlling the Groupings," explains several ways to modify the group headers and footers in your report.

Finally, the information contained in the Detail section is displayed for each detail record printed on the report. You can study Figures 50-13 and 50-14 to see where the different sections displayed in Design view will appear on a printed report. These figures show the printed appearance of the report opened in Design view in Figure 50-12:

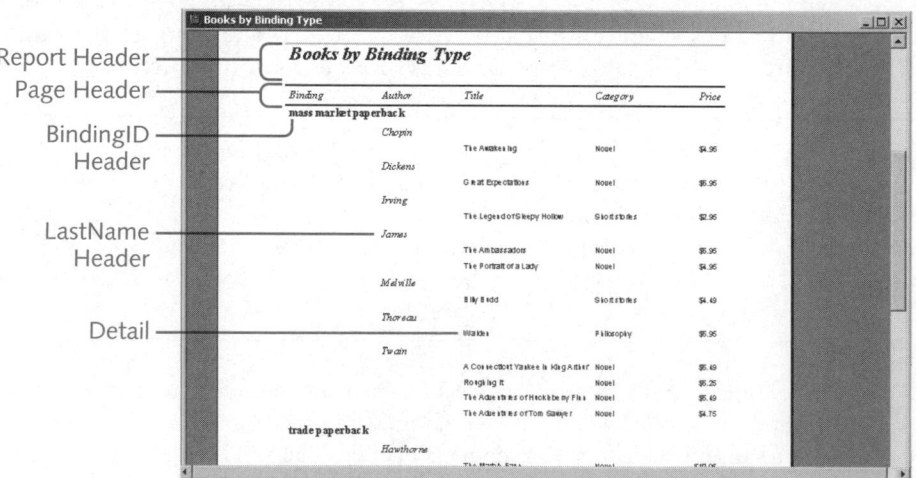

Figure 50-13. This is a report based on the design shown in Figure 50-12, showing the location of each of the report sections (except on the printed report).

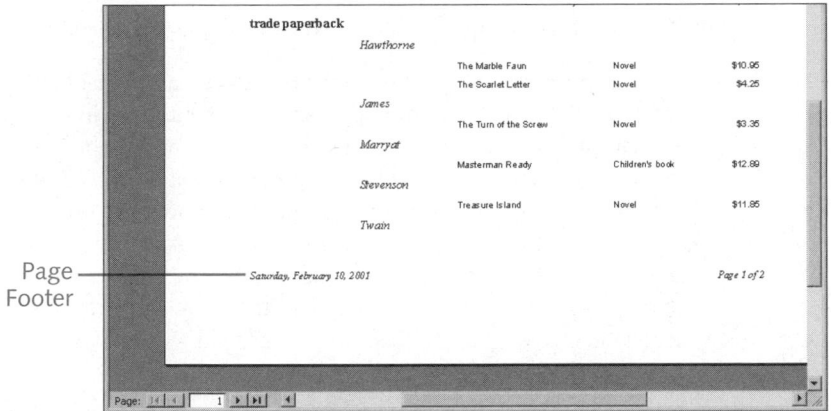

Figure 50-14. This is a report based on the design shown in Figure 50-12, showing the location of the Page Footer section on the printed report.

Controlling the Groupings

Sorting
And
Grouping

To control the way the records in your report are grouped and sorted, choose View, Sorting And Grouping or click the Sorting And Grouping toolbar button to open the Sorting And Grouping dialog box, shown in Figure 50-15.

Fields used
for grouping
records
(marked
with icons)

Field used
for sorting
detail records

Properties of
selected field
(BindingID)

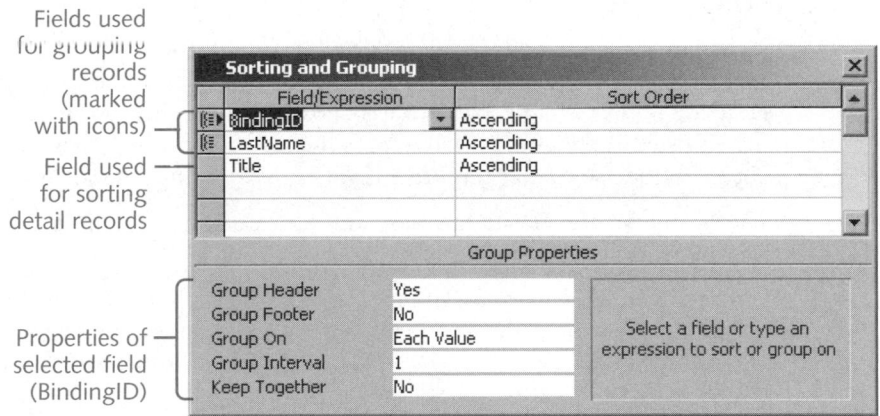

Figure 50-15. The Sorting And Grouping dialog box shown here contains the sorting and grouping settings for the example report.

---

note Figure 50-15 shows the sorting and grouping settings for the example report described in the previous sections. These options are the direct result of the choices that were made when the report was created using the Report Wizard—specifically, the choices made in the second, third, and fourth wizard dialog boxes, which are described in "Using the Report Wizard," on page 1363, and are shown in Figures 50-3 through 50-5.

In the Sorting And Grouping dialog box, you can do one or more of the following:

- To add another grouping level to the report, add a new field to an empty row in the Field/Expression column by selecting the field name in the drop-down list in that row. Then select a sorting order for the group in the Sort Order column. And, select Yes in the Group Header property box to display a header section for the group, or select Yes in the Group Footer property box to display a footer section for the group, or select Yes in both property boxes to display both a header and a footer section. The field will then be marked with a grouping icon. (If you don't select Yes in either of these two property boxes, the grouping icon won't appear next to the field and the field will be used for sorting detail records rather than for creating groupings.)

- To remove a grouping level from the report, click in the box to the left of the row containing the grouping field to select the entire row, and then press Delete. Note that this will remove the associated grouping section or sections from the report (header, footer, or both) *plus any fields contained in these sections.*

- The order in which the grouping fields are listed in the Sorting And Grouping dialog box is the order in which they are used to group records in your report. To change the grouping order, you can move a field in the list by clicking the box to the left of the field's row and then dragging the box up or down.

- To add or remove a field for sorting detail records in the report, use the same techniques, except be sure that No is selected in both the Group Header and the Group Footer property boxes. If more than one sorting field is listed, Access sorts detail records in the order in which these fields appear in the list; change this order if you want to change the sorting order.

- The Group On and Group Interval properties are important options that work together.

  For a grouping field, when the Group On property is set to Each Value (the most common setting), the report creates a new group for every distinct value of the grouping field. In this case the Group Interval setting has no effect. To change to a different grouping, select a new setting for the Group On property from the drop-down list. The available settings depend on the grouping field's data type. Then type a number into the Group Interval property box to quantify the Group On setting. For example, if the grouping field is numeric, you could select Interval in the Group On box and type 2 into the Group Interval box. As a result, the report would create a new group for every *other* distinct value, rather than for every distinct value.

  As another example, if the grouping field is text, you could select Prefix Characters in the Group On box and then type 1 into the Group Interval box. This would create a group for all records where the grouping field starts with *A*, another group for the *B*s, a third for the *C*s, and so on. To organize the information in smaller groups (*Aa, Ab, Ac*), you would type 2 into the Group Interval box.

- To ensure that a group—including the header, detail section, and footer—is always printed on the same page if possible, select the Whole Group setting in the Keep Together property box for the grouping field. Note that this setting tends to create blank space at the bottom of pages. By selecting the With First Detail setting, you can save paper and still ensure that the header is always printed together on the same page with at least one of the following detail records. This avoids having a new header appear at the bottom of a page with no data below it. For either of these settings, if there isn't room on a page to fit what's requested (a whole group, or a header plus at least one detail record), Access ignores the setting.

---

tip **Get Help on Properties**

For some group properties, you can obtain detailed information by placing the insertion point within the property box in the Sorting And Grouping dialog box and pressing F1.

You can also remove or add the Report Header and Report Footer sections, or the Page Header and Page Footer sections, by deselecting or selecting options on the View menu. To remove both the Page Header and the Page Footer sections, deselect the Page Header/Footer option on the View menu. Likewise, to remove both the Report Header and Report Footer, deselect the Report Header/Footer option. Note, however, that removing a header and footer in this way deletes any controls contained in them! (Access will ask for your confirmation first.) If you select one of these menu options again, the corresponding header and footer sections will reappear in Design view, but they will be empty of controls.

Previewing and Printing a Report

To preview your report's printed appearance, you can switch to either the Print Preview or Layout Preview view, using any of the methods discussed in "Using the Database Window and Object Views," on page 1271. To see the actual data that will print on the report, including all the report pages, switch to Print Preview view. To get a quick look at your report's general layout, you can switch to Layout Preview view, which shows only a sampling of the lines that will print. (Clicking the Preview button in the Database window opens the selected report in Print Preview view.)

---

note In addition to the general ways of switching to Print Preview view, if the report is open in Design view, you can open it in Print Preview by choosing File, Print Preview or by clicking the Print Preview toolbar button.

To set the margins, page orientation, paper source, column layout, and other page layout and printing settings, open the report in any view or select it in the Database window and choose File, Page Setup to open the Page Setup dialog box (see Figure 50-16).

(You can also open this dialog box by clicking the Setup button in the Print dialog box just before you print, as described next.)

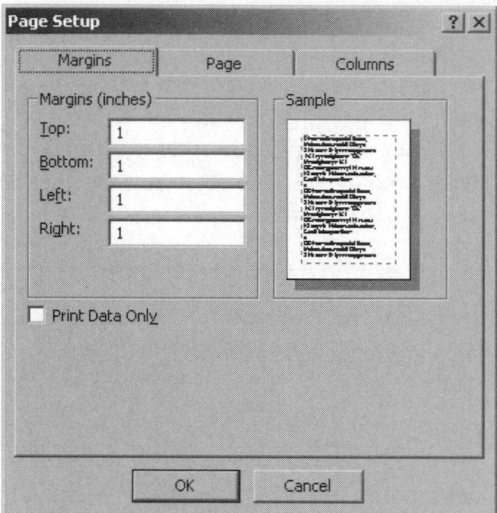

Figure 50-16. You can open the Page Setup dialog box for the selected or opened report by choosing File, Page Setup.

When you're ready to print your report, open it in any view or select it in the Database window, and then choose File, Print or press Ctrl+P to open the standard Print dialog box, which lets you select printer settings and print options. Or click the Print toolbar button to immediately print your report using default options.

Troubleshooting

Report Includes Blank Pages

When you print your report, unwanted blank pages are included.

If your report is too wide for the paper size specified in the Page tab of the Page Setup dialog box (shown in Figure 50-16), your printer might produce an unwanted blank page after every printed page. Try reducing the width of the margins in the Margins tab of the Page Setup dialog box or switching to the Landscape orientation in the Page Tab of the same dialog box. If neither remedy works, change your report's layout in Design view to reduce its width.

If you're getting an unwanted blank page at the end of your report and you don't have information in your report footer, make sure that the footer height is set to zero. To do this, open the report in Design view, right-click the band for the Report Footer section, choose Properties from the shortcut menu, and in the Format tab of the ReportFooter property sheet, set the Height property to 0".

1376

Part 9

Publisher

Chapter 51

Essential Publisher Techniques

Microsoft Publisher 2002 is desktop publishing software that's designed for people who aren't design professionals but who need to produce professional-looking publications. The typical Publisher user is routinely called upon to create publications quickly without the support of art directors, designers, or production studio staff who are experienced in page layout and digital prepress techniques.

To make it easy to move through a publication project, Publisher provides an assortment of automated tools, templates, and wizards. Many of these features—wizards, designs, and color schemes—have been redesigned for easy access in the Publisher task pane. Other enhancements to Publisher 2002 provide additional boosts to productivity, including the following:

- You can open more than one publication at a time, improving your ability to cut and paste between publications.

- After you've saved or published a brochure or newsletter as a Web page, you can convert the Web publication to print layout again in Publisher.

- You can format Microsoft Word documents with Publisher using the Word Import Wizard.

- Mail merge in Publisher 2002 functions more like the mail merge in Word, making it easier to use.

In this chapter you'll learn about

- The main features of the Publisher 2002 window

- Creating a simple publication quickly

- Entering and formatting text
- Creating a master page
- Creating layout and ruler guides
- Saving an object to the Design Gallery
- Using the Design Checker

When to Use Publisher

When should you choose Word to lay out a document, such as a business card or brochure, and when should you choose Publisher? Word processing applications, such as Word, include their own templates, often covering the same types of publications that Publisher contains. If you're comfortable using Word, and the number and style of templates suits your project, then use that application.

However, Publisher provides a wider variety of templates to choose from and gives you more control over your page's design. Publisher contains hundreds of sample layouts for publications, ranging from business cards to takeout menus to longer documents, such as newsletters or catalogs. Publisher also offers greater flexibility in page design because each object is inserted in a frame (or text box for text objects), which you can then resize, move, or format to create the desired layout for your publication. Word, on the other hand, primarily focuses on the page as a whole, offering less flexibility in page layout.

Publisher also supports full-color output—up to 12 spot colors in one publication—and offers the ability to combine process and spot colors in the same publication. Spot color refers to adding a second color besides black to a publication. Process color, often called four-color process printing, refers how the percentages of four component colors—cyan, magenta, yellow, and black (CMYK)—are combined or processed to make full-color images. In general, the improved support for commercial printing in Publisher 2002 makes it the only choice if you're taking your publication to a commercial printer, because Word doesn't offer this kind of support.

Exploring the Publisher Window

The easiest way to start Publisher is to click the Start button, point to Programs, and then choose the Microsoft Publisher menu option. When you first start Publisher, on the left side of the screen you see the task pane, which presents several options for creating new Publisher publications. On the right side of the screen is the Publication Gallery, which lists the publication templates available in the category currently selected in the task pane, as shown in Figure 51-1.

Chapter 51: Essential Publisher Techniques

Figure 51-1. The Publisher window opens with a Publication Gallery of Quick Publications and a task pane.

After you select a publication option, Publisher builds the publication according to your specifications and displays it in the Publisher window, as shown in Figure 51-2 after a business card is selected from the Publication Gallery.

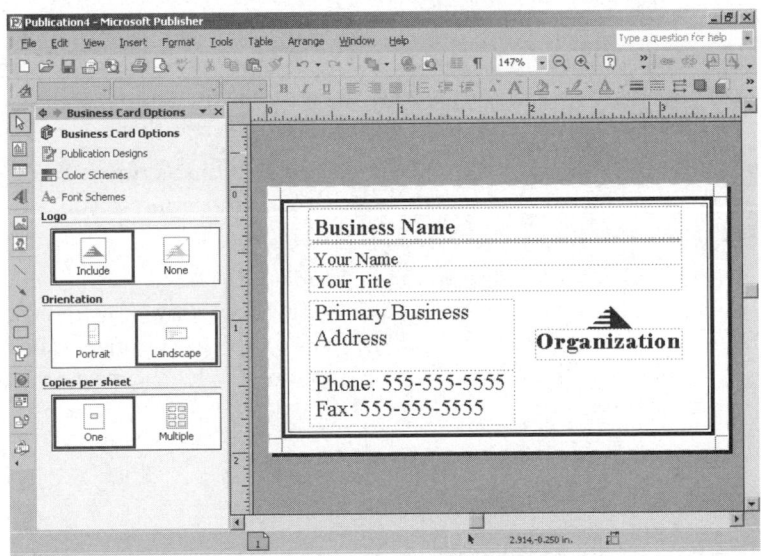

Figure 51-2. The Publisher window contains the tools you need to create publications.

You now have at your disposal the following user interface components, which share many features with the other programs in the Microsoft Office XP suite, including those listed on the next page.

Chapter 51

● The menu bar provides access to the commands and settings you use to create documents in Publisher. To choose a command from the Publisher menu, open the menu, point to the submenu (if there is one), and then click the command you want. For example, you can use the commands on the Zoom submenu of the View menu—Whole Page, Page Width, Selected Objects, or a percentage of the page—to gain perspective on your work.

● The toolbars give you quick access to often-used commands. By default, Publisher displays the Standard, Formatting, and Connect Frames toolbars below the menu bar. The Formatting toolbar changes depending on which tool or object is selected. The Objects toolbar, also a default toolbar, is located on the left side of the Publisher window, though it can be turned into a floating toolbar when dragged to any part of the application window.

● The task pane continues to appear on the left side of your screen and displays commands and options that you can choose depending on the task you're completing. In Publisher, the task pane presents commands for opening new publications, using the Office Clipboard, searching, selecting template options, controlling page content, choosing publication designs, setting color and font schemes, changing styles and formatting, and using mail merge. To open or close the task pane, click Task Pane on the View menu.

● Like the other Office application windows, the Publisher window contains sizing buttons that you can use to minimize, maximize, restore, and close it; a status bar that displays the mouse position and the selected object's size; and the Page Navigation button.

● When you click the scroll arrows at the top or bottom of the scroll bars, your publication scrolls up or down. (You can also drag the scroll box, using the mouse, to move your publication horizontally or vertically.)

● Lying along your layout's top and left side are Publisher's rulers. You use them to measure and align objects and position them in relation to your publication's margins.

● Below the Publisher title bar on the right side of the screen is the Online Help tool, which allows you to type a question using regular words (for example, "How do I use Print Preview?") whenever you need help using a feature. To use this tool, click the words "Type A Question For Help," type your question, and then press Enter.

Creating a Publication

If you want to start with a blank page in the workspace and hide the Publication Gallery of Quick Publications in that space, follow these steps:

1 Choose Tools, Options.

2 In the Options dialog box, in the General tab, clear the Use New Publication Task Pane At Startup check box, and then click OK.

Chapter 51: Essential Publisher Techniques

If you want to hide the task pane and simply start Publisher with a blank page, follow these additional steps:

1 Choose Tools, Options.

2 In the User Assistance tab in the Options dialog box, clear the Use Quick Publication Wizard For Blank Publications check box, and then click OK.

Publisher now opens with a blank page ready for the objects, text, formatting, and any additional pages you'll apply to create a publication.

However, the task pane provides the fastest mechanism for opening new publications or displaying existing publications. To create a new publication with a wizard or from a design set, complete the following steps:

1 Click the list box arrow at the top of the task pane to select By Publication Type or By Design Sets.

2 Click the publication or design category you want in the task pane.

3 Click a publication template in the Publication Gallery.

4 Publisher builds that selection and opens a task pane with options for changing the color scheme, font scheme, and publication design.

5 Replace the placeholder text and objects with your own material, and then click Save. The first time you save a publication, you're prompted to enter a name for your publication in the Save As dialog box, and your publication is saved, by default, as a Publisher or .pub file.

Figure 51-3 shows a wizard-based publication used to create a business card.

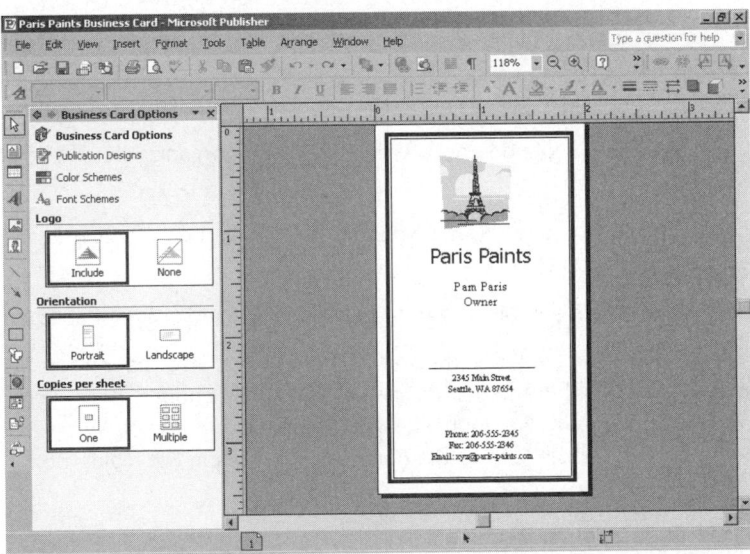

Figure 51-3. The Refined business card template lets you create a custom business card.

Creating a Personal Information Set

The first time you employ a Publisher wizard, you'll be prompted to fill in a personal information set so that the wizard can automate the flow of often-used data, such as your business name or address, throughout your publication. The entries in the personal information set operate like fields in a database: changes made to one field are reflected or synchronized in all the other instances of that field in your publication. To create a personal information set, follow these steps:

1 Choose Edit, Personal Information. The Personal Information dialog box appears, as shown here:

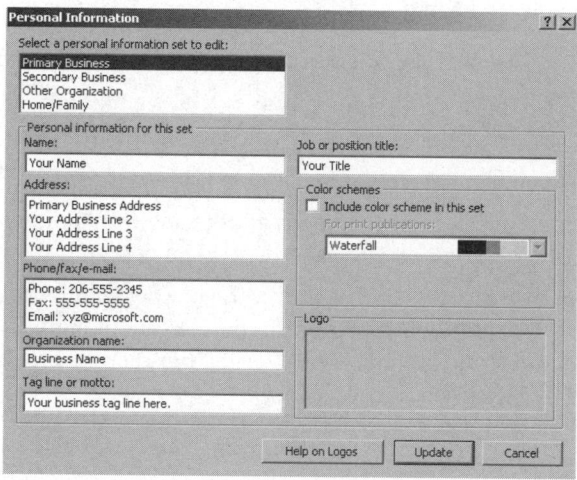

2 Click one of the four personal information sets that you want to associate with this publication.

3 Type your name, address, telephone and fax numbers, e-mail address, company name, title, and a descriptive phrase for your organization in the fields provided.

4 Click the check box under Color Schemes to include a color scheme with this personal information set.

5 Select a color scheme to be used from the list box under For Print Publications.

6 To insert a logo that will be attached to the personal information set, first close the Personal Information dialog box, and then choose Insert, Personal Information, Logo. Make your selections in the Logo Creation Wizard, save the publication, and return to the Personal Information Set dialog box.

7 Save the publication, and click Update.

If you've inserted a logo into this publication, it's now displayed under Logo, as shown in Figure 51-4.

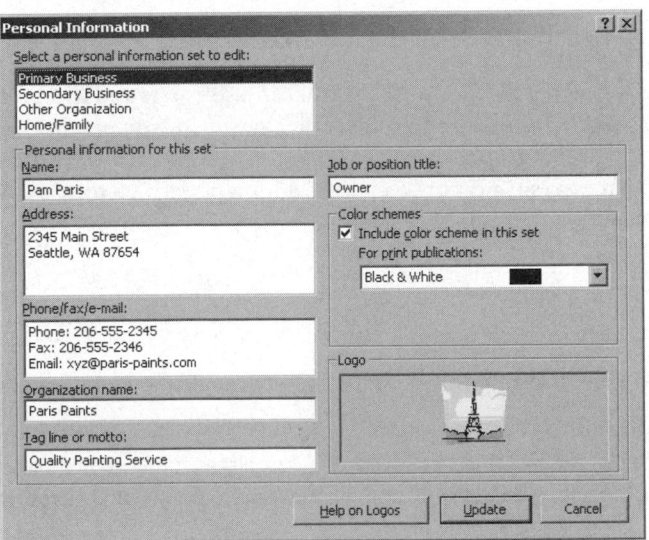

Figure 51-4. A clip art logo, inserted from the Clip Organizer, is stored with the personal information set.

When you want the information in a personal information set to be applied to all future publications, you should make your changes here, in the Personal Information dialog box. Or you can accomplish the same result by choosing Tools, Options and selecting the Update Personal Information When Saving check box in the User Assistance tab. When you make this selection, each time you change a field in the personal information set within a publication, it's automatically saved to the Personal Information dialog box when you save the document.

InsideOut

You can't delete a logo from the personal information set. You can delete the logo object from within the publication by right-clicking it and choosing Delete Object, but the change won't be reflected in the personal information set even if you try to update it. However, you can insert a new logo, which will replace the original listed in the Logo display box in the Personal Information Set dialog box.

You can also insert the personal information components individually into a publication. To do so, follow these steps:

1 Choose Insert, Personal Information.

2 Click the component you want to insert. Publisher inserts the component you selected into the page of your publication in a text box, which you can move, resize, and reformat.

Creating Your Own Publisher Templates

A template is a model publication that you can use as a foundation for building new publications. For example, when you create a postcard, you can have Publisher save the layout, particular graphic objects, and fonts to reuse in all your mailings. Reusing design elements saves time, cuts costs, and adds a pattern to your work that's unique and identifiable.

To save a publication as a template, follow these steps:

1 Choose File, Save As.

2 In the Save As dialog box, in the Save As Type list box, click Publisher Templates.

Your publication is saved in Publisher's Templates folder, which is stored in C:\Documents And Settings\User Name\Application Data\Microsoft\Templates.

> **note** If you've changed the default location for storing Word templates, your Publisher templates will also be stored in that new location.

3 To use a template as the basis for a new publication, simply choose From Template, select the file you want to use, and begin your new publication.

4 Save your publication as a Publisher file. The template remains unchanged in the Templates folder.

You can also start a new publication by selecting one of the other options under the New category in the task pane, or you can open an existing publication listed under the Open A Publication category.

When you choose to create a new publication based on an existing one, you can select either a Publisher document or a Word document as the basis for the new publication. Figure 51-5 shows the task pane after the selection of a Word document. The task pane now contains Word Import Options.

You'll follow these basic techniques whenever you open templates and wizards.

You can add your own graphics and text, and customize wizard-based publications using the options available in the task pane, as shown in the business card in Figure 51-3.

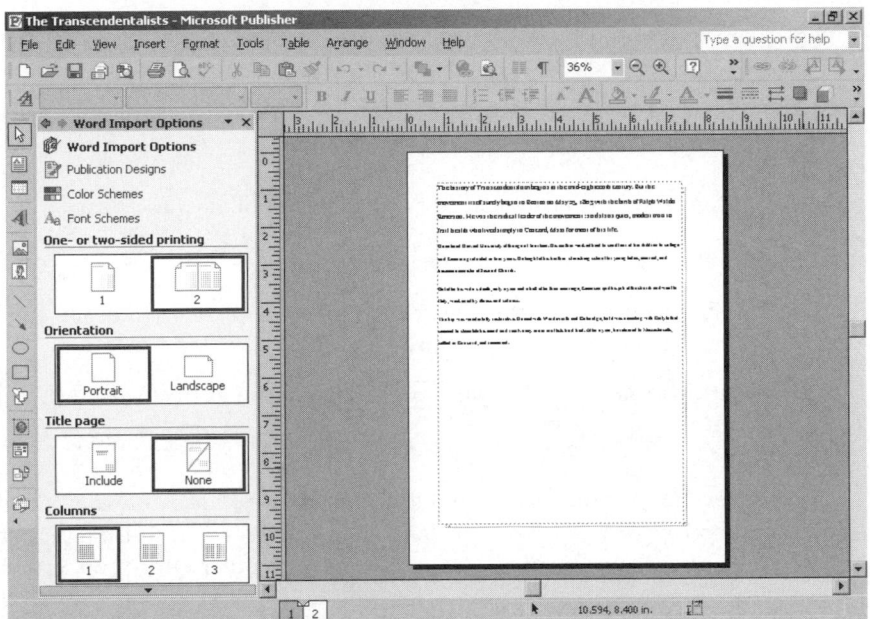

Figure 51-5. The Create New From Existing Publication dialog box lets you insert a Word document into Publisher.

Working with Text

In Publisher, unlike a word processing application, you must place all objects (such as text, graphics, pictures, or WordArt) inside a frame before you can manipulate them. Text is considered an object in Publisher and must be placed in a text box. After placing text in a text box, you can control the position, formatting, and flow of text in your publication.

Entering Text

To enter text, you can either replace text in Publisher placeholders with your own or enter text into a text box you've created. Then you can position the text box and, if necessary, resize, move, or format the text, as well as format the text box itself.

If you chose a Publisher wizard to organize your publication, your document contains text boxes filled with sample text, which you can replace by following these steps:

1 Select the text box you want to modify by clicking it, and select the text you want to replace.

2 Type your own text, which then replaces the selected text, or press Delete to clear the selected text and create empty text boxes for your text.

3 If you want to replace the text box as well as the text, right-click the edge of the text box, and then click Delete Object.

To create your own text boxes and add text to them, follow these steps:

1 Click the Text Box tool on the Objects toolbar.

2 Position the mouse pointer where you want your text box to begin, and then drag it diagonally to form the box.

3 Release the mouse button when the text box is the correct shape.

4 Type your text in the text box, and when you're finished, click outside the text box.

To move text, you simply select it and drag it to the new location when the pointer becomes the Drag icon, as shown below. You can also move text using the cut, copy, and paste options familiar to you from working with other Office applications.

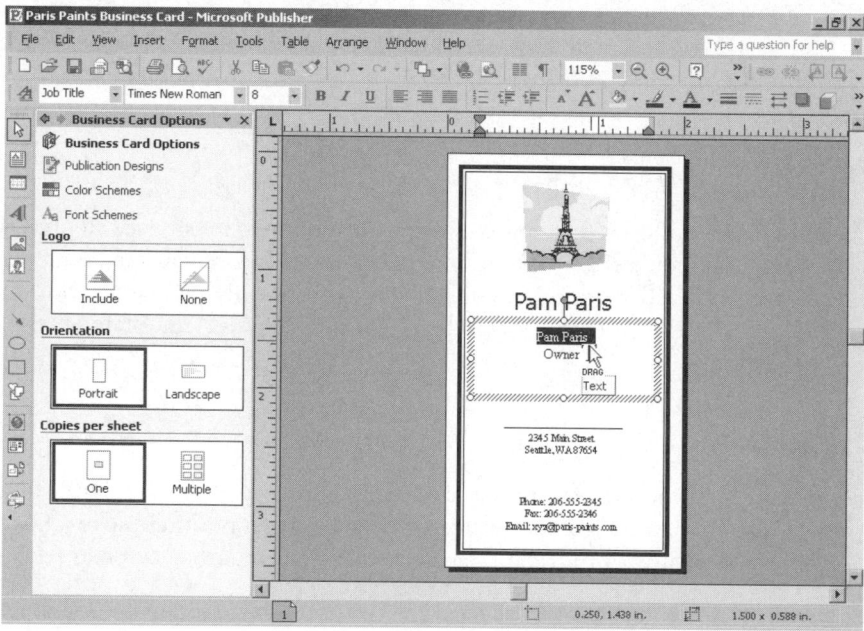

To move the text box, select it, and when the pointer becomes the Move icon, as seen on the next page, drag the text box to a new location.

Chapter 51: Essential Publisher Techniques

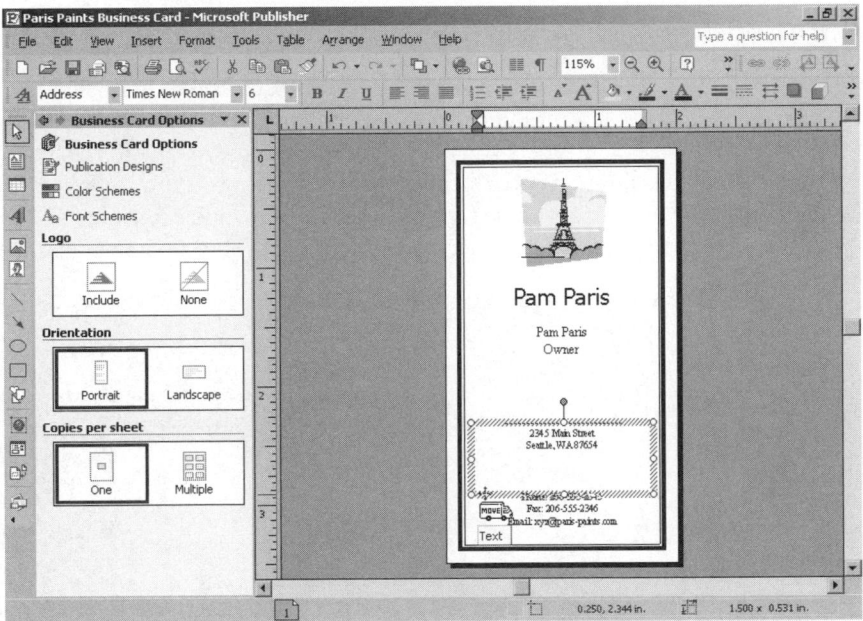

Importing Text

Often you can build a publication quickly by inserting text that you've created in another format, such as a letter created in Word or an expository piece stored in Rich Text Format (RTF). To import text created in another application, follow these steps:

1 In Publisher, select or create a text box for the text you want to insert.

2 Choose Insert, Text File.

3 In the Insert Text dialog box, enter the name of the file in the File Name box, and then click OK.

If the text you type doesn't fit into the text box, you can apply text autofitting to make the font size smaller by pointing to AutoFit Text on the Format menu, and clicking the option you prefer: None, Best Fit, or Shrink Text On Overflow.

> **note** You can edit text directly in Publisher or by using Word. Generally, the shorter the text, the easier it is to use Publisher as your word processor. But when you're editing a long document or one that runs over several pages or columns, it's easier to use Word. To edit Publisher text by using Word, you simply right-click the text box, point to Change Text, choose Edit Story In Microsoft Word, and make changes to your text. While you're editing in Word, the text box isn't visible, but by clicking Close & Return to *Your Publication* on the File menu in Word, you close the Word document and return to your publication, which is updated with your edits.

Working with Text in Overflow

When you've entered more text than your text box can hold, Publisher displays a message asking if you want Publisher to flow the text automatically or if you want to connect text boxes yourself. If you allow Publisher to flow text automatically, it will offer to create text boxes as needed and then flow the extra text into them. If you decide to connect the text boxes yourself, the Text in Overflow indicator (an "A" followed by an ellipses) appears in the lower-right corner of a text box, as shown here:

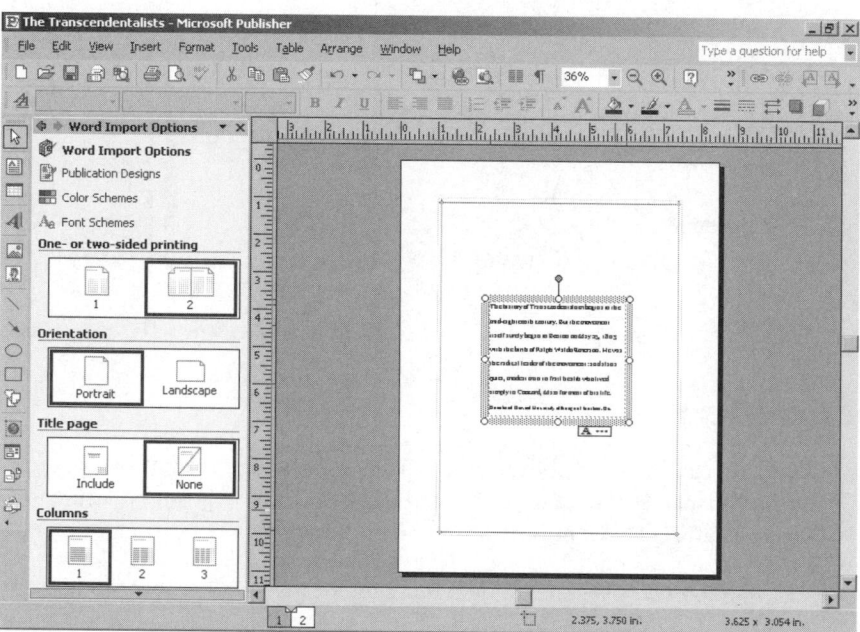

You can create room for the overflow in a variety of ways:

- Turn on copyfitting by choosing Format, AutoFit Text, and then clicking Best Fit or Shrink Text on Overflow. (Best Fit cannot shrink text smaller than one point.)

- Enlarge the text box by pointing to one of its sizing handles and dragging the handle when the mouse pointer becomes a Resize arrow.

- Create another text box by using the Text Box tool on the Objects toolbar.

- Insert another page by choosing Insert, Page and using the Insert Page dialog box to add a new text box on each additional page or to duplicate existing text boxes on the new page or pages, as seen on the next page.

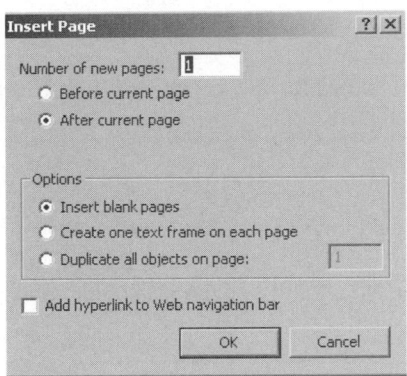

Connecting Text Boxes to Create a Story

You can connect text boxes in a series, which creates what Publisher 2002 refers to as a *story*. To create a chain of connected text boxes, follow these steps:

1 Create as many new text boxes as you want.

2 Select the text box you want to be first in the lineup. The Connect Frames toolbar becomes available.

3 On the Connect Frames toolbar, click Create Text Box Link. The pointer becomes an upright pitcher when you move it over the page.

4 Place the pointer over an empty text box and the pitcher tilts, as seen here:

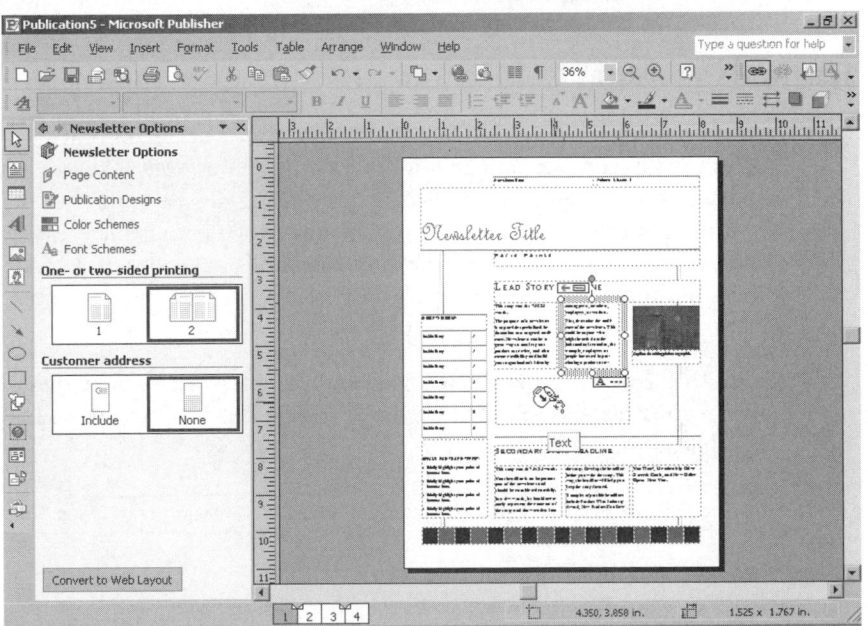

5 Click the empty text box to connect the two.

Any text in the overflow area of the first text box flows into the newly connected text box.

InsideOut

Publisher can't find text that's located in overflow when you use the Edit, Find command. Also, you must search for text in each text box individually by clicking each text box in a story and then clicking Find. Publisher can't search an entire chain of connected text boxes automatically.

To help your reader find these connected text boxes (or navigate through the story), you can add continued notices at the bottom of the text box. This is particularly useful when you're creating newsletters or long documents.

Adding Continued Notices

To add a continued notice to a text box, complete the following steps:

1 Right-click the text box where you want to place a continued notice, and then click Format Text Box.

2 Click the Text Box tab in the Format Text Box dialog box.

3 Under Text AutoFitting, click the Include Continued On Page check box, or click the Include Continued From Page check box, and then click OK.

Formatting Text

newfeature!

You can format text in ways familiar to you from working in other Office programs. Additionally, the task pane in Publisher contains new font schemes, which are sets of fonts that work well together. Because one of the most common errors inexperienced desktop publishers make is mixing fonts that don't complement each other, Publisher includes ready-made sets of major fonts for headings, titles, and headlines and minor fonts for body text and captions. Figure 51-6 shows how changing the font formatting can improve your text's readability.

newfeature!

Publisher 2002 contains a new Styles And Formatting task pane that contains options for creating text styles, which let you apply the same formatting to many paragraphs in a publication.

Instructions on how to create text styles are given in "Creating Text Styles," on page 1431.

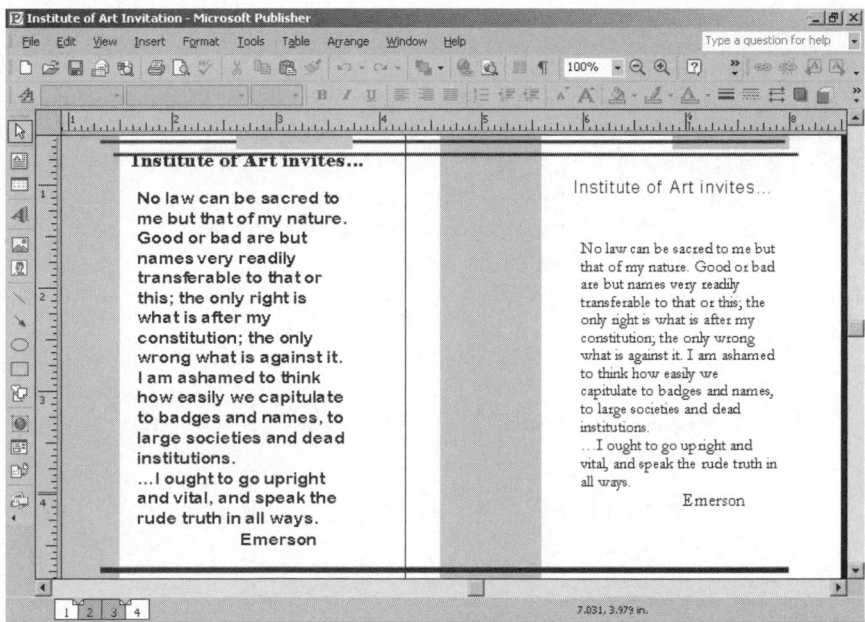

Figure 51-6. The image on the left is difficult to read compared to the one on the right, which contains body text in a more appropriate typeface for reading blocks of text.

Applying Font Schemes

When you want to change all the fonts in your publication, you can apply a new font scheme. To do so, follow these steps:

1 Click Font Schemes in the task pane of your open publication.

2 Rest your mouse pointer over a scheme to view a ScreenTip that lists the scheme's components.

3 Click the arrow in the right corner of the font scheme box for options to insert, modify, or delete the selected font scheme.

4 To further customize how your fonts are applied, click Font Scheme Options in the task pane. The Font Scheme Options dialog box appears, as seen here:

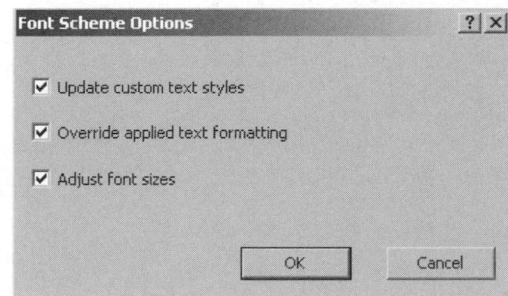

1393

InsideOut

When you're planning to take a publication to a commercial printer, plan ahead by choosing your fonts carefully. If your printer's system includes fonts that you used in your publication, you won't have to embed these fonts, which can significantly reduce the size of the file you're handing off. To promote a clean-looking publication, use the actual fonts installed on your computer, such as Arial Rounded MT Bold, rather than applying bold or italic formatting to a font such as Arial.

You can also make changes to individual text characters, using the Font, Font Size, and Font Color buttons on the Formatting toolbar, just as you can in the other Office applications. To make several changes to a font at a time, select the text, and then click Font on the Format menu.

You can also adjust the following formatting options from the Format menu:

- **Tracking**   The spacing between all selected text characters
- **Kerning**   The space between any two specific characters
- **Leading (pronounced *ledding*)**   The amount of white space between lines of text

To adjust tracking or kerning, follow these steps:

1 Select the text that you want to reformat.

2 Choose Format, Character Spacing. The Character Spacing dialog box appears, as shown here.

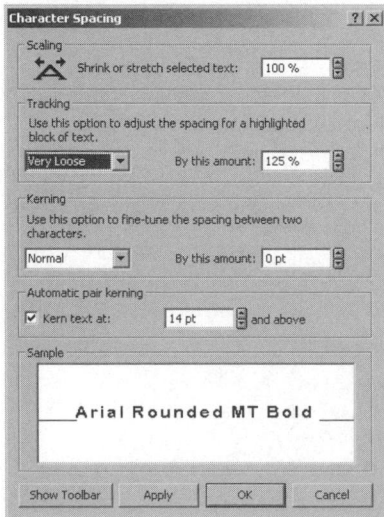

3 Under Tracking, choose the spacing you want to apply to the text you've selected. Six options are available. Choose Custom from the drop-down list to enter the exact percentage of tracking you want.

4 Under Kerning, select the options you want to define the space between any two characters. When you choose Expand or Condense, you can enter an amount in the By This Amount box.

You can also use the Character Spacing dialog box to apply scaling to characters. Scaling refers to stretching or shrinking letters horizontally to make them wider or narrower. You accomplish scaling by selecting the text to be scaled and entering a value for the effect in the Scaling box in the Character Spacing dialog box.

To change the space between lines, complete the following steps:

1 Select the text to reformat.

2 Choose Format, Line Spacing. The Line Spacing dialog box appears, as shown here:

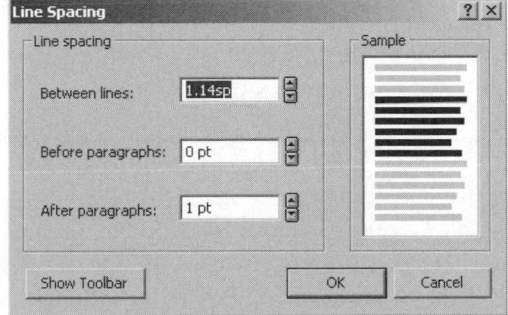

3 Type the amount of space in the Between Lines list box, followed by the unit of measurement you want to use. For inches, type **in**, for centimeters, **cm**, for points, **pt**, for picas, **pi**.

The amount of line spacing you specify here is added above each line or paragraph selected.

4 To set line spacing that varies to accommodate the largest font in the line of text, which is the default setting, type **sp** after the amount of spacing.

The amount you enter here is added below each line or paragraph of text.

5 To change spacing before or after paragraphs, type or select the amount you want in the appropriate boxes, and then click OK.

Creating Columns in a Text Box

You can quickly position the text in a text box into columns by following these steps:

1 Right-click the text box, and then click Format Text Box on the shortcut menu.

2 In the Format Text Box dialog box, click the Text Box tab, and then click Columns. The Columns dialog box appears, as seen here:

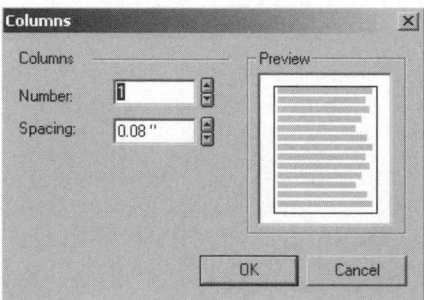

3 In the Columns dialog box, enter the number of columns and spacing between them, and then click OK.

The text in columns within a text box flows automatically into the next column.

InsideOut

Even if the current column isn't full, you can move text into the next column by forcing a column break. To do that, click at the beginning of the line or paragraph of text you want to move and hold down the Ctrl and Shift keys while pressing Enter. This action forces a column break.

Formatting Bulleted and Numbered Lists

Organizing text into lists helps emphasize important points in your publication and adds visual interest by breaking up dense blocks of text. You can create bulleted and numbered lists in text boxes.

To create bulleted or numbered lists, follow these steps:

1 Select the text in the text box that you want to format as a list.

2 Choose Format, Indents And Lists. The Indents And Lists dialog box appears.

3 Under Indent Settings, in the Indents And Lists dialog box, click Bulleted List or Numbered List. Figure 51-7 shows the changed options that result when you select Bulleted List.

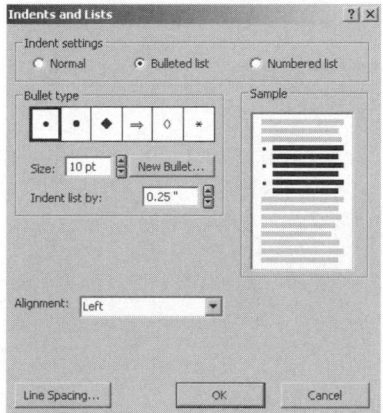

Figure 51-7. Clicking New Bullet lets you select a symbol to use as a bullet character.

4 Depending on your choice, options in the dialog box change to let you specify the bullet character or number format, as well as spacing and starting number options, respectively. Make your selections, and then click OK.

Formatting Text Boxes

In addition to changing the way the characters look in your text, you can also format the text box itself. You can apply a simple line border or a custom border to the box or use a Publisher-designed BorderArt element. In addition, you can apply color schemes, fill colors, and fill effects to text boxes. Publisher 2002 also contains the new Horizontal Rule feature, a particularly useful new feature that makes it easy to add a decorative rule under a line or to separate paragraphs. This feature is described in Chapter 52, "Creating Professional Brochures and Newsletters."

> For more information on using the color schemes, working with fill effects, and creating a horizontal rule, see Chapter 52, "Creating Professional Brochures and Newsletters."

Chapter 51

One of the simplest ways of drawing attention to a block of text is to emphasize the text box's border. To add a border to a text box, follow these steps:

1 Right-click the text box you want to format, and then click Format Text Box. The Format Text Box dialog box appears, as seen here:

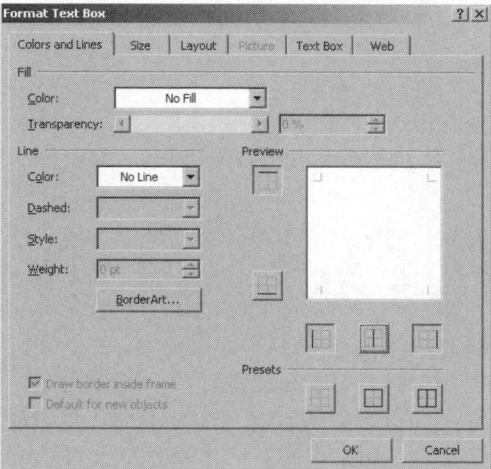

2 In the Colors And Lines tab, under Line, click the arrow in the Color box to select a color for the line border based on the color scheme for that publication, or more colors, or patterned lines.

3 Specify the type of line under Dashed, which includes decorative and broken lines, or under Style, which lets you select a point size for a standard line.

4 If you want, enter a custom value for the line border in the Weight box.

5 Click BorderArt to make selections in the BorderArt dialog box, and apply a custom border, if you've created one.

6 Click the sides of the border grid to apply your formatting to individual sides of the text box, if necessary, and then click OK. The text box now contains a decorative border, as is shown in Figure 51-8, which uses a Basic Black Squares border.

tip If you want the border to apply to the text box's outline, be sure to clear the Draw Border Inside Frame check box.

Chapter 51: Essential Publisher Techniques

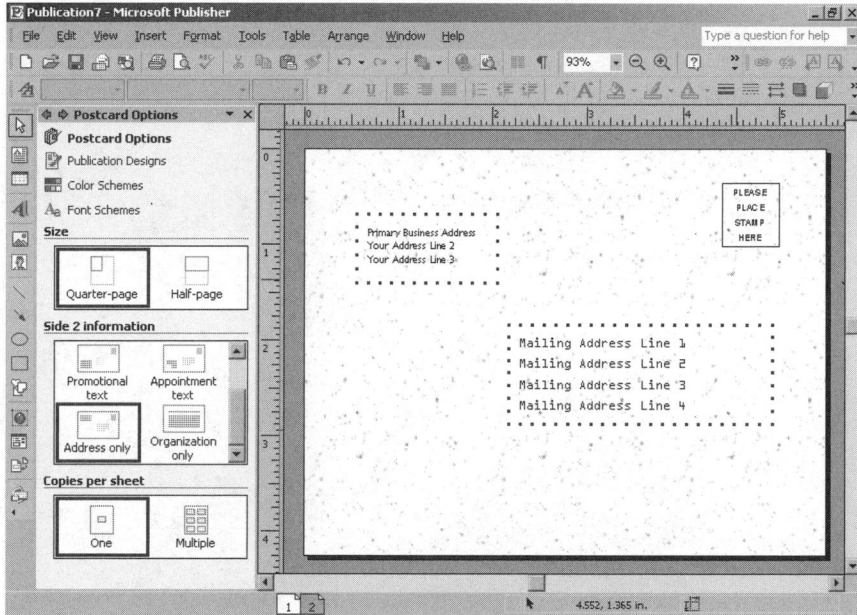

Figure 51-8. A border applied to this address field highlights it.

You can also add a color fill to the text box by selecting a color under Fill in the Format Text Box dialog box and use the sliding scroll bar in the Transparency box to set how transparent you want the color fill.

Working with Pages

Pages are the foundation of your publication. In Publisher, you can set options for adding or deleting pages, for adding and formatting page numbers, for creating oversized publications that print on several sheets of paper, or for tiling several copies of a small document that print on one sheet of paper.

newfeature!

In a page layout application, pages have a background and a foreground layer. In Publisher 2002, the new Master page manages the background layer. You can insert objects that will repeat on every page onto a Master page and move easily between the Master page and your publication's foreground page.

For instructions on creating Master pages, see "Creating Master Pages," on page 1402.

Page Setup

When planning page layout for a publication, consider page setup first. Publisher distinguishes between page size and paper size. This is an important element to consider, because when you're printing a publication from your desktop printer, it allows you to create publications that are smaller or larger than the paper inserted in your printer. To set up the pages, follow these steps:

1 Choose File, Page Setup. The Page Setup dialog box appears. Figure 51-9 shows a banner page setup.

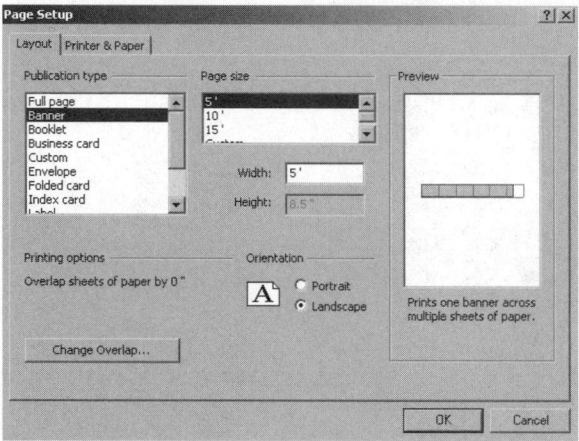

Figure 51-9. Under Page Size, you can specify the size of your publication.

2 In the Layout tab, specify the page options, including the orientation for the page.

3 In the Printer & Paper tab, specify the settings for your printer.

Printing Your Publication

If you want to print a small number of copies, using standard-sized paper (or a custom size supported by your printer) in low-resolution black and white or color, you can probably handle the printing process on a desktop printer. However, if you want your finished product to display high-resolution black-and-white, spot-color, or process-color printing and you have enough turnaround time, you'll want to take your publication to a commercial printing service, often called a service bureau. If you're planning to take your publication to a commercial printer, talk to the printer before deciding on font selection and color options. Also, there's a useful new item in Publisher Help called Checklist: Prepare A Publication For Commercial Print. Review the checklist before setting up your publication: it can help you to prepare files that will be compatible with the standards of your commercial print shop.

Troubleshooting

Your Publisher File Is Too Large to Fit on a Disk

You want to put your Publisher file on a disk to hand off to a commercial printer, but the file is too large.

A possible reason for the large file size is that you haven't compressed the file. To remedy this problem, use the Pack And Go Wizard to compress the file so it will fit on a disk. (If you compress your file using a compression tool, make sure that your commercial printer has the same version of the same tool so it can decompress your file.) You can also get around putting your file on a disk by sending it to the printer electronically.

Inserting and Deleting Pages

You can insert multiple pages at a time, but you can delete only one page at a time, which you do by moving to the page you want to delete and choosing Edit, Delete Page. To insert pages, follow these steps:

1 Move to the page before or after where you want to insert a new page.

2 Choose Insert, Page. The Insert Page dialog box appears, as shown here:

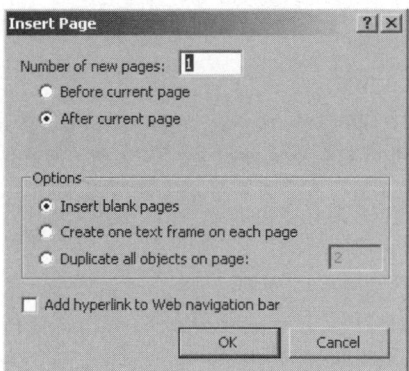

3 Type how many new pages you want, and specify options for them, including adding a hyperlink to the page if you're creating a Web page, and then click OK.

Creating Master Pages

All the pages in a publication have a foreground and a background layer. The foreground is different for every page in your publication—this is where you place the text and design elements that are unique to that page. The background is shared by all the pages, and the elements you place there appear on every page, which makes it a good place to position repeating elements such as page numbers, a business logo, or an organization's tag line. In Publisher 2002, the background is called the *Master page*.

To make changes to the Master page, follow these steps:

1 If you're working in the foreground, choose View, Master Page.

2 On the Master page, add, modify, or delete any objects you want reflected on the background.

> **note** You can't add or delete any pages while you're working on a Master page.

3 To return to the foreground, choose View, Master Page again.

You can turn off the Master page for selected pages in a publication. This technique is useful when you want to format a title page without a page number or a logo. To turn off a Master page, follow these steps:

1 Go to the foreground of the page whose Master page you want to suppress.

2 Choose View, Ignore Master Page.

3 If you're turning off the Master page for a two-page spread, the Ignore Background dialog box appears, and you can specify which background page you want to suppress.

Adding Page Numbers

You can add page numbers to the foreground or to the Master page. Publisher automatically numbers the pages and changes the numbering when you add or delete pages. To add page numbers to the Master page, follow these steps:

1 Choose View, Master Page.

2 Use the Text Box tool to create a text box for your page number.

If you don't create a text box to contain the numbers, Publisher gives you options to position them in a header or footer aligned left, center, or right, and the numbers appear without being framed by a text box.

3 Choose Insert, Page Numbers. The Page Number dialog box appears, as shown here:

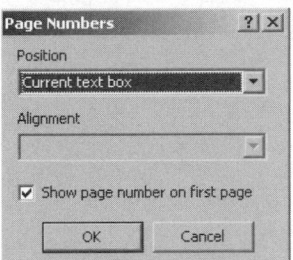

4 In the Page Number dialog box, specify the position and alignment for your page numbering system, as well as whether you want a page number to appear on the first page of your publication, and then click OK.

Publisher displays the number sign, which is automatically replaced by the correct page number on the foreground page.

5 To format the text box, right-click it, and then click Format Text Box on the shortcut menu.

You can change the attributes of the text box that contains the numbers and make the numbers a larger size, but you can't make changes to the number characters, such as changing them to Roman numerals.

Creating Layout Guides

If you're comfortable using Publisher's layout tools, you can maintain control of your publication's overall design whether you're customizing a wizard-based publication template or creating your own from scratch. The layout guides create a framework or grid for the text, columns, graphics, and headings that you repeat on every page.

When you're working in a wizard-based publication, you can see the layout guides: they're the pink and blue dotted lines that you can view if you have Boundaries And Guides turned on. The pink lines are the page divisions, and the blue lines create a safety zone for the margins, which are called *gutters*. If necessary, to view the layout guides, on the View menu, click Boundaries And Guides. You'll see guides similar to the ones shown in Figure 51-10, on page 1400. (Both layout and ruler guides are nonprinting.)

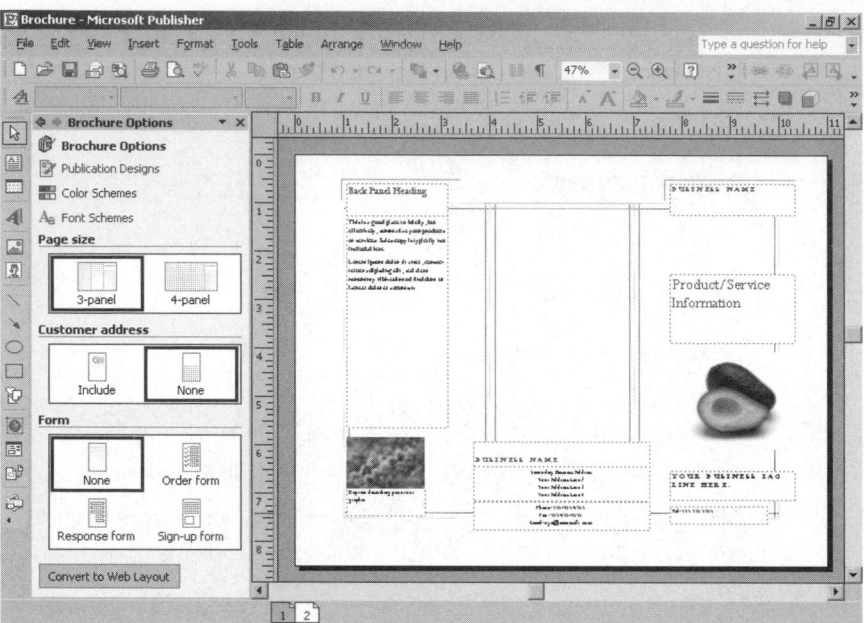

Figure 51-10. Layout guides for a brochure show the gutters reserved for the fold in the publication.

To specify how you want objects laid out in your publication, follow these steps:

1 On the Arrange menu, click Layout Guides.

2 In the Layout Guides dialog box (shown here), enter the requirements you want for margins, columns, and rows.

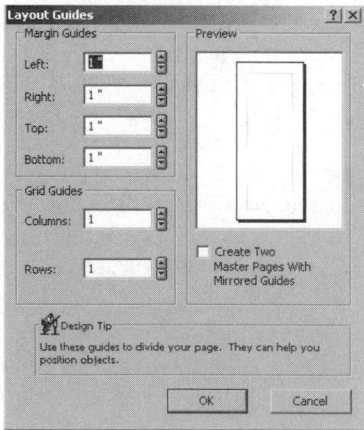

3 To create mirrored layouts when setting up your grid, select the Create Two Master Pages With Mirrored Guides check box, and click OK.

To move a layout guide, follow these steps:

1 Choose View, Master Page.

2 Hold down the Shift key, and drag the layout guide to reposition it.

3 To return to your publication's foreground page, choose View, Master Page again.

To hide layout guides, choose View, Boundaries And Guides to remove the check, or press Ctrl+Shift+O.

Mirrored layouts for pages that face each other are particularly useful when you're creating a booklet, newsletter, or catalog that's printed on both sides of the paper and bound. The mirrored guide lets you adjust the inner margins or gutters, creating an area to place the staple or spiral binding. Mirrored-page layout also means that objects (such as page numbers, graphics, or headers) are positioned on the Master page of the left page so that they mirror those on the Master page of the right page. This kind of symmetrical layout can help your reader navigate easily through your publication.

Using Rulers and Ruler Guides

Rulers lie along the top and left-hand side of the Publisher workspace. You can turn them off to see more of your publication by right-clicking anywhere in the window (except on a toolbar) and then clicking Rulers. You can move the rulers to measure or align design elements in your publication by placing the mouse pointer on the ruler you want to move, holding down the mouse button, and dragging it to a new location. If you want to move both rulers at once, point to the box where the two rulers meet, and drag from there.

Ruler guides are useful when you want to align several objects on a specific page. To add ruler marks to a page, follow these steps:

1 Hold down Shift, and when you see the Adjust handle, drag the pointer out from the rulers to create a new position for the guide.

2 Release the mouse button, and the ruler guide is displayed as a green dotted line, as illustrated in Figure 51-11, on page 1402.

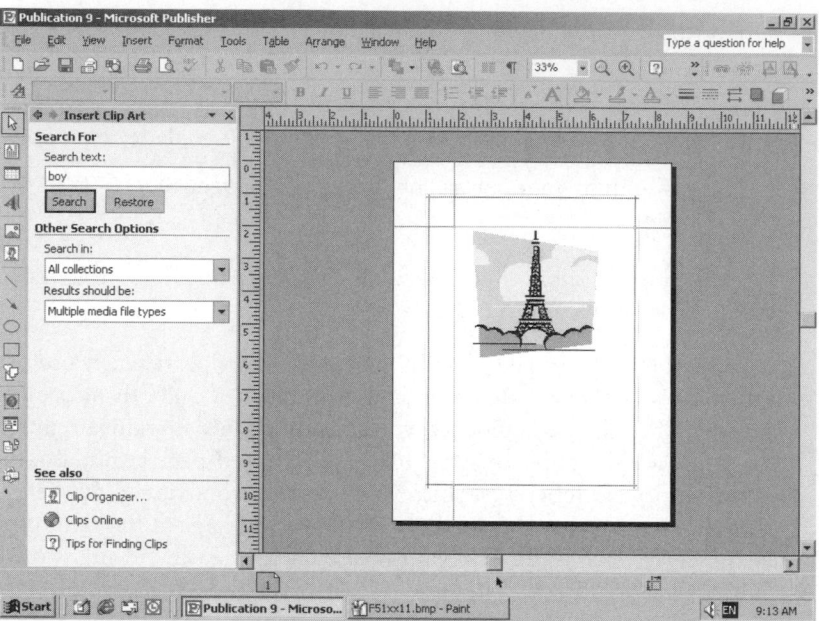

Figure 51-11. Ruler guides are useful when you want to measure or align an object.

You apply ruler guides on a page-by-page basis—they don't automatically apply to the entire publication as layout guides do, unless you apply them to the Master page.

To delete a ruler guide, do the following:

- Right-click the ruler guide, and then choose Undo Move Guide.

  or

- Hold down Shift while positioning the pointer over the ruler guide, and when the pointer becomes the Adjust icon, drag the ruler guide back to the ruler.

To delete all ruler guides in a publication, choose Arrange, Ruler Guides, and then click Clear All Ruler Guides.

Using Snap To Guides

Publisher's Snap To commands make objects on the page align with the rulers, guides, or other objects. Using this feature, you can position objects exactly where you want them, adding a professional look to your publications. To use Snap To guides, complete the following steps:

1 Choose Arrange, Snap, and then select the command you want to use. A check mark indicates that a command is active.

2 If your objects aren't snapping to each other, try placing them closer together.

3 If you've selected Snap To Ruler Marks or Snap To Guides, you should clear them to enhance Snap To Objects.

Using the Design Gallery

The Design Gallery contains a wide variety of Publisher-designed objects to enhance your publications, including professionally designed logos, headlines, calendars, mastheads, and other design elements that add polish to your work. These objects are called *smart objects*—preformatted design elements that have a wizard associated with them. You can use the elements in the Design Gallery to customize your publications. To insert a Design Gallery object into a publication, follow these steps:

1 Choose Insert, Design Gallery Object. (You don't have to choose a frame for the insertion. Design Gallery objects are inserted directly into your publication.)

The Microsoft Publisher Design Gallery appears, as seen here:

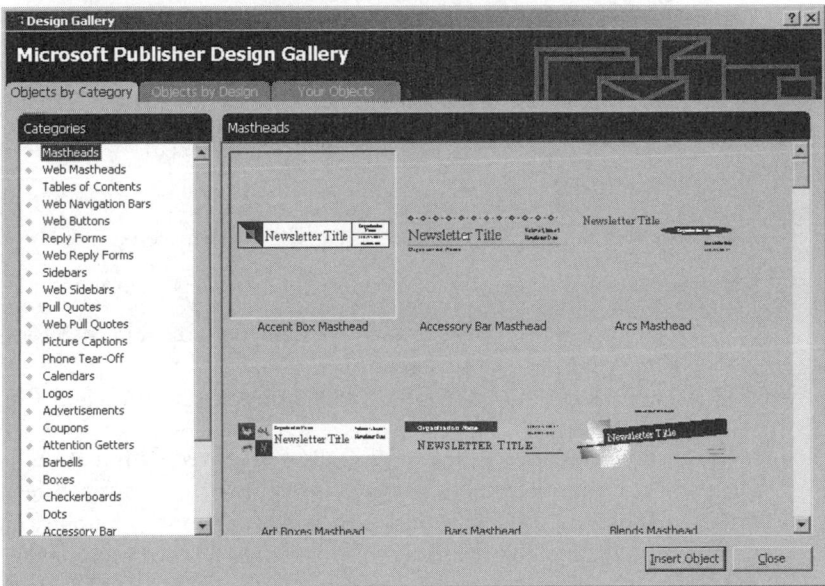

2 Select the category of design you want to use from the Objects By Category tab. The available objects are illustrated in the window to the right.

3 If you want to choose an object based on its design style, click the Objects By Design tab, and make your selection from the styles illustrated in that window.

4 When you've made your choice, click Insert Object.

Part 9: Publisher

Now you can move, resize, and format this object, using the wizard that's associated with it.

You can also create your own custom designs and store them in the Design Gallery so you can easily find and reuse them in other publications. To add your own designs to the Design Gallery, follow these steps:

1 Click the object that you've created that you want to add to the Design Gallery.

2 On the Objects toolbar, click Design Gallery Objects. The Design Gallery appears.

3 In the Your Objects tab, click Options, and then click Add Selection To Design Gallery. The Add Object dialog box appears, as shown here:

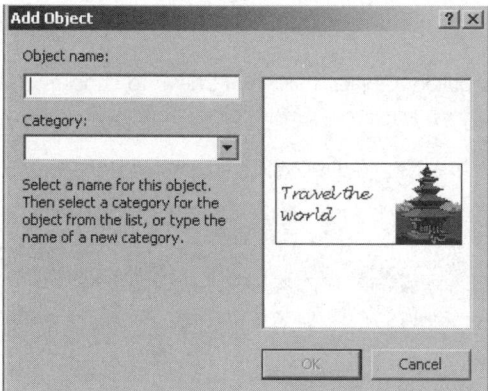

4 Type the name for your object in the Object Name box.

5 Type or select a category for the object in the Category box, and then click OK.

Type a category for the object in the Category box, and then click OK. After you have added a new category, it will appear in the drop-down list. If you want to assign the category to another object, you can select it from the list.

Selections that you add to the Design Gallery are saved with that publication. However, when you open another publication, you won't find the custom objects you stored in the original publication. To import them for use in another publication, you can simply open the original publication and copy and paste the custom element into the current publication. Because you can open multiple publications at one time in Publisher 2002, you don't have to go through the Design Gallery to locate saved custom objects.

Chapter 51: Essential Publisher Techniques

Using Design Checker

When you're satisfied with your publication's contents, Publisher's Design Checker can help guarantee that you don't print it with any embarrassing errors, such as an empty frame or text left in the overflow area.

To use the Design Checker, complete the following steps:

1 Choose Tools, Design Checker. The Design Checker dialog box appears. Publisher checks the pages you specify and can also check background pages.

2 Click Options to see which specific design elements Publisher can check for you. The Options dialog box appears, as shown here:

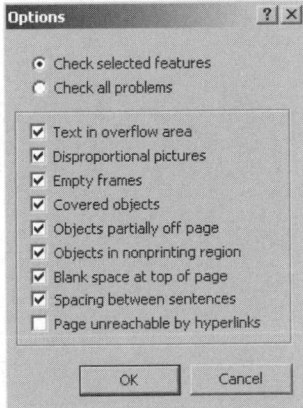

3 Make your selections, and then click OK in the Options dialog box and OK in the Design Checker dialog box to start the Design Checker. Publisher checks all the pages of your publication and notifies you of its findings by displaying a dialog box like this:

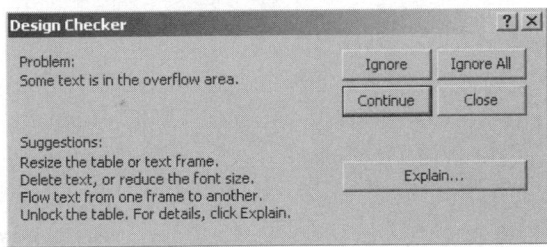

4 Click Explain, and Publisher provides advice to help solve each problem. It's up to you to decide if you want to follow Publisher's suggestions.

Chapter 52

Creating Professional Brochures and Newsletters

Brochures and newsletters can be highly effective ways to give information to your clients or constituents. To produce them quickly, you can use the wizard-based publication templates in Microsoft Publisher 2002 as a basis for your own documents, or you can create them from scratch by using a blank publication. In many cases, unless your organization provides a particular template, it's simpler to take the wizard-based layout and modify it by replacing the placeholder text and graphics with your own.

Brochures and newsletters contain opposite challenges. In a brochure, you need to format information in a small space so that it gets attention. In a newsletter, you need to flow long blocks of text to fill columns in a document. In this chapter, you'll learn techniques that will help you handle both challenges. To format information in a brochure, you'll need to learn the following skills:

- Working with color and fill effects
- Inserting and manipulating pictures
- Controlling layers, grouping, and alignment
- Formatting a drop cap
- Creating horizontal rules
- Adding typographic symbols
- Working with line breaks and hyphenation

To create a newsletter, you'll need to learn the following skills:

● Creating a text style

● Working with text wrapping

● Formatting headers and footers

● Creating a watermark

Creating an Effective Brochure

A brochure is a small, pamphlet-sized publication—typically an 8½-by-11-inch page folded into thirds to create three panels on each side of the paper. You can produce a three-fold brochure using Publisher and a desktop printer, as shown in Figure 52-1.

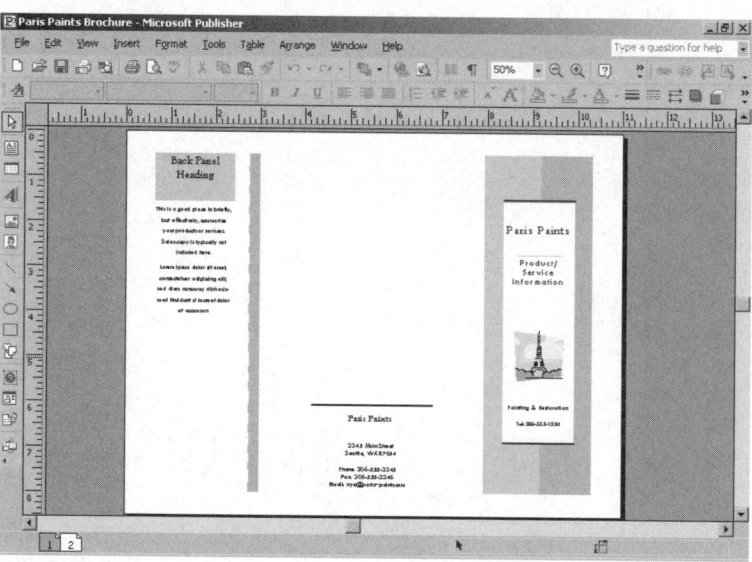

Figure 52-1. This informational brochure is based on the Straight Edge publication template.

Before you select a brochure from the Publication Gallery or start to lay one out as a blank publication, spend a few minutes planning your brochure. In a publication this small, every element counts. Good design practice suggests that you do the following:

● Break up text using headings, bulleted lists, or horizontal rules

● Use graphics and pictures that don't require lengthy captions

● Arrange the panels so they stand alone

● Use lots of white space

Chapter 52: Creating Professional Brochures and Newsletters

White space is the blank space on the page that doesn't contain text or graphics. It provides a place for your reader's eye to rest and assimilate the information contained in the other design elements.

Creating a Brochure from Scratch

If you decide to create your brochure from scratch, you set up the page by completing the following steps:

1 In the task pane, choose New, Blank Publication.

2 Choose File, Page Setup. The Page Setup dialog box appears.

3 Click Landscape to specify the page orientation.

4 Click OK to close the Page Setup dialog box.

5 Choose Arrange, Layout Guides.

6 In the Layout Guides dialog box, set the margin guides to specify the amount of white space you want on the external edges of the pages. (.05" on all sides provides an appealing amount of white space) and under Grid Guides, specify three columns and one row.

7 Choose Insert, Page, and specify one blank page after the current page.

8 Create ruler guides that make the internal margins larger. Adding at least an additional ³/₈ inch on each side of the internal pink layout guides prevents you from inserting objects too close to the fold line.

Now you can add text and graphics, and when you're ready to print on your desktop printer, you have three options:

● You can print on both sides of the paper if your printer supports duplex printing.

● You can print on both sides of the paper by manually feeding the paper through the printer a second time after printing it on one side.

● You can print the brochure on one side, and then photocopy the other side onto the back.

Working with Color Schemes

By default, Publisher applies color schemes to blank publications as well as to wizard-based ones. Publisher color schemes are predefined sets of six colors (in addition to the default colors assigned to hyperlinks and followed hyperlinks) which appear when you choose Format, Color Scheme. You can modify these sets and create your own custom color schemes, which helps maintain a consistent look within a publication. You can also reuse your custom color schemes in other publications.

To modify a color scheme, follow these steps:

1 Choose Format, Color Schemes. The Color Schemes task pane appears, as shown here:

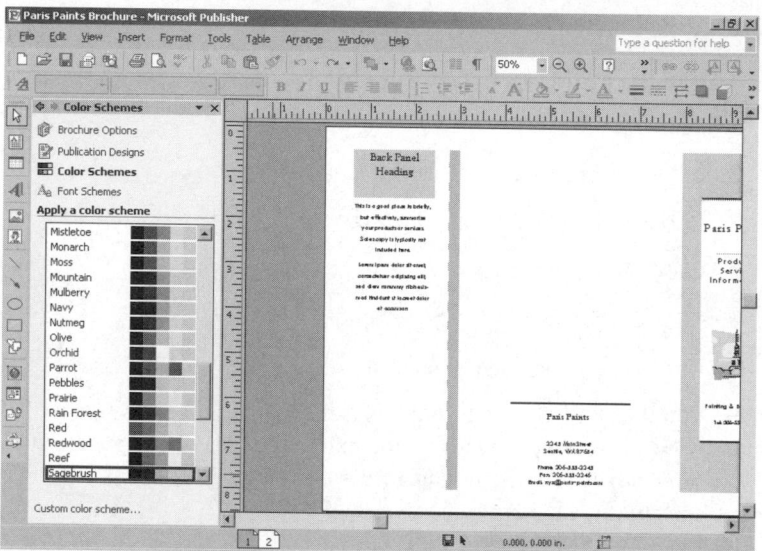

2 Click Custom Color Scheme in the lower-left corner of the task pane. The Color Schemes dialog box appears, as seen here:

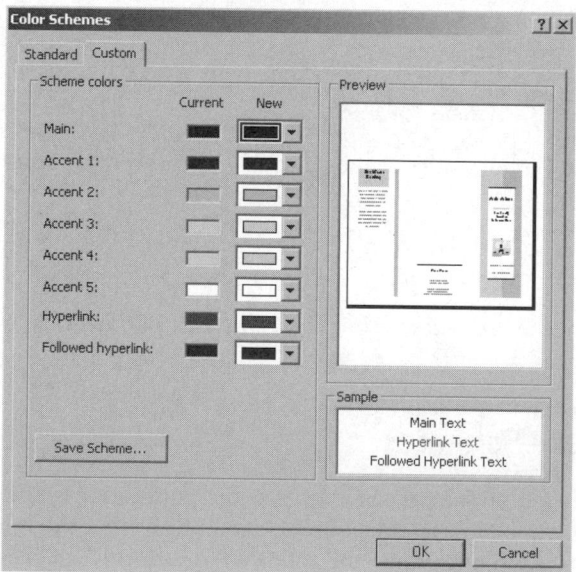

3 In the Custom tab of the Color Schemes dialog box, select the colors you want to use from the six drop-down palettes.

Chapter 52: Creating Professional Brochures and Newsletters

4 Click Save Scheme, and type a name for it in the Save Scheme dialog box.

After you assign a name to the custom color scheme, it appears (in alphabetical order) in the list of color schemes in the Color Schemes task pane.

Applying Color Fill Effects

You can add a solid color fill to frames or shapes. If you want to, you can apply a standard color fill or a custom color, or you can fill the frame or shape with a color chosen from one of the accent colors in a Publisher color scheme. To apply a color fill that isn't part of a Publisher color scheme, follow these steps:

1 Select the frame, text box, or shape you want to fill.

2 On the Formatting toolbar, click the down arrow in the Fill Color button, and then click More Fill Colors. The Colors dialog box appears, as shown here:

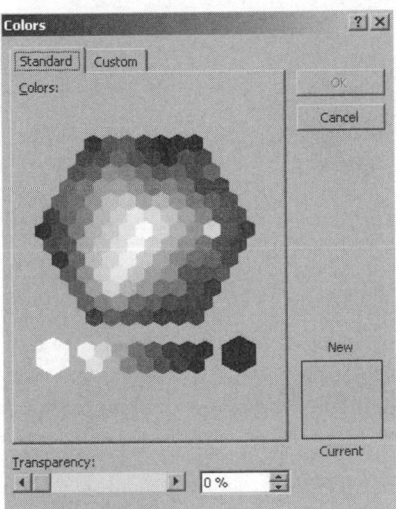

3 In the Standard tab, click to select one of the standard colors, and then click OK to apply it.

For more information on applying color fills to text boxes, see Chapter 51, "Essential Publisher Techniques."

When you want to define custom colors for your fills and fill effects, you can use one of the four standard color models (models provide different ways to mix color) that Publisher supports: the red, green, blue model (RGB), which is the standard model for on-screen color; the hue, saturation, and luminance model (HSL), which closely replicates perceived color; the cyan, magenta, yellow, black model (CMYK), which is the basis for four-color printing; or the Pantone model, a color-matching system for spot colors.

To define a CMYK, RGB, HSL, or Pantone color, follow these steps:

1 Select the frame or shape to which you want to apply a color, and then click the down arrow in the Fill Color button on the Formatting toolbar.

2 Click More Fill Colors, and then click the Custom tab of the Colors dialog box:

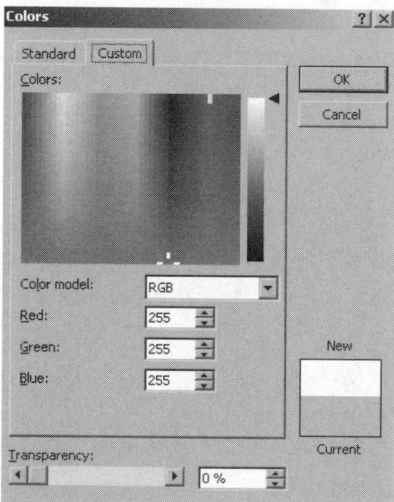

Figure 52-2. You create custom color schemes by using the appropriate color model permitted by your printing options.

3 In the Color Model box, select the color model you want to use.

4 Either select a color in the Colors palette, which automatically determines its numerical value, or type the appropriate values for the colors you want to use in the boxes supplied by that color model. (Pantone colors are selected from the Pantone Colors dialog box.)

5 Drag the arrow next to the color palette to adjust how much white or black to add to a color, as shown in Figure 52-2.

6 Drag the scroll bar in the Transparency box to determine how opaque or transparent to make the fill.

7 Click OK to apply your color choices.

If you want to further enhance a color fill, you can apply fill effects, which include tints, shades, patterns, and gradients. To create a custom fill effect for a frame or shape, follow these steps:

1 Select the frame or shape to which you want to apply a fill effect.

2 Click the down arrow in the Fill color button on the Formatting toolbar.

3 Click Fill Effects. The Fill Effects dialog box appears, as shown here:

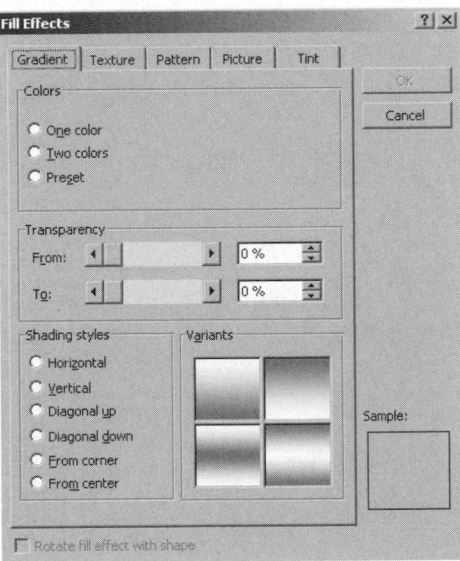

4 Pick the settings you want for the effect you're creating. Style options include effects using tints and shades of a color, different background patterns, a gradient fill that provides increasing shading using a tint or shade of one color, or inserting a picture to use as a background fill. (See Figure 52-3.)

Figure 52-3. You can use a picture as a background.

5 To change the color of a fill effect, select a new base color from within the Fill Effects dialog box.

6 Click OK to apply the effect.

> **tip** A *tint* is a color mixed with white. A *shade* is a color mixed with black. Using different tints of one spot color in a publication can give the impression that you're using a wider swathe of the color spectrum than is actually the case. You create a monochromatic color scheme by adding tints and shades of one base color found in a standard color scheme.

If you're taking your publication to a commercial printer, steer clear of the pattern effects. Patterns will increase your bill at the printer because it takes the service much longer to image this type of file to film.

Inserting Pictures

You can enhance your brochure's visual appeal by choosing graphics that support your message. To insert a picture into a publication, place the insertion point where you want to position the picture, and then follow these steps:

1 Choose Insert, Picture, and then choose From File. The Insert Picture dialog box appears.

2 In the File name box, select or type the file location for the picture you want to insert. If available, a preview of the picture appears in the dialog box to the right.

3 Click the Insert button, or double-click the image from the list. This embeds the image in your publication.

Linking to Picture Files

You typically follow the procedure outlined above to embed graphics into your publications when you're printing the publication on a desktop printer. However, if you're taking a publication to a commercial printer, you should determine if they want you to link to the graphics files or embed them directly into your publication. If the commercial printer will make individual color separations for your graphics files, they will request that you submit them as separate, linked files. To insert linked graphics files into a publication, follow the procedure above, but instead of step 3, click the down arrow next to the Insert button, and then click Link To File.

When you deliver your publication files to your commercial printing service, make sure that you include the linked image files on the disks you bring in or in the files you send electronically.

If the link becomes broken and you need to update it before bringing the files in, check the Graphics Manager by choosing Tools, Commercial Printing Tools and then clicking

Chapter 52: Creating Professional Brochures and Newsletters

Graphics Manager. You can create a new link using the Graphics Manager dialog box, shown here:

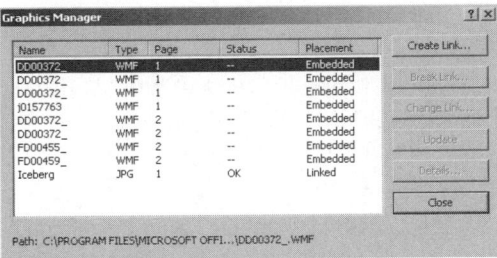

Moving and Resizing Pictures

You can move or resize inserted pictures to integrate them more gracefully into your publication. If you want to move a picture, do either of the following:

- Point the mouse pointer at a border of the picture frame, and when the pointer becomes the Move icon, drag the frame to a new location.

  or

- Select the picture frame, and on the Arrange menu, point to Nudge and click one of the arrows to move the object one pixel at a time.

In Publisher 2002, the Nudge toolbar is much easier to use. You can make it a floating toolbar, drag it to any location in the Publisher workspace, and leave it open while you arrange as many objects as you like. To do that, point to the bar at the top of the submenu, and then drag it to a new location, as shown in Figure 52-4.

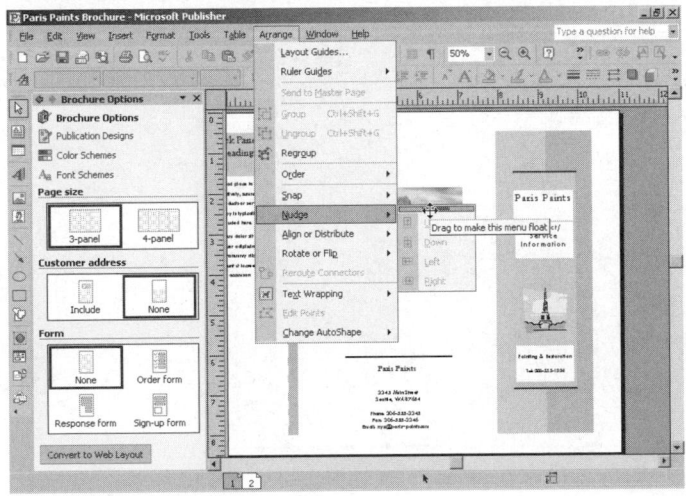

Figure 52-4. Use the arrows on the Nudge menu to move objects one pixel at a time.

Chapter 52

Depending on the file format your picture is stored in, you can more or less success-fully resize it by dragging the sizing handles. Image files are stored in two major file types: *bitmap* and *vector* graphics formats.

- A bitmapped image consists of a pattern of pixels or dots, such as you see in newspaper photos. If you enlarge a bitmap image to more than 100 per-cent, you'll lose a great deal in resolution, and the image will appear grainy. Photographs are often stored as bitmaps. The filemane extension for bitmaps is .bmp.

- A vector graphic consists of separate objects, such as lines or curves, which are defined by mathematical equations. An advantage of this mathematical description is that you can enlarge or reduce vector images, and the image remains crisp at any size. Clip art and drawn shapes are often stored as vector images. Common filename extensions for vector graphics include .wmf (Windows Metafile Format) and .eps (Encapsulated Postscript).

> For more information on importing graphics files into Microsoft Office documents and install-ing appropriate graphics filters, see Chapter 6, "Adding Professional Graphics and Special Effects to Office XP Documents.")

To resize a picture, use the sizing handles:

- To resize a picture by dragging, select the picture frame, position the pointer over a sizing handle, and drag out or in to resize.

- To resize a picture and maintain its original proportions, select the picture frame, hold down Shift, and drag a corner sizing handle.

- To resize by a specific amount, select the object, choose Format, Picture, and set proportions in the Size tab in the Format dialog box.

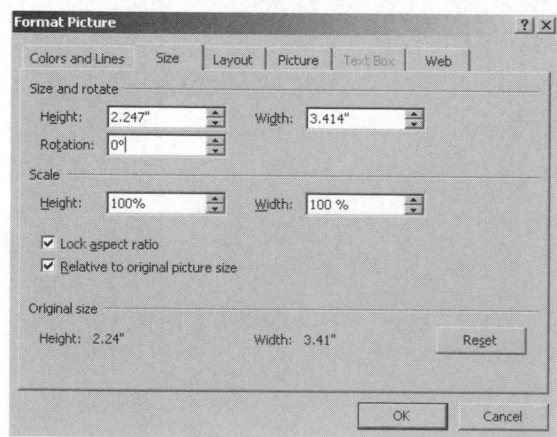

Chapter 52: Creating Professional Brochures and Newsletters

To use only part of a picture, you can crop elements that you want to hide using the Crop button on the Picture toolbar. To do that, complete the following steps:

1 Select the picture frame, and click the Crop button on the Picture toolbar. If the Picture toolbar isn't displayed, choose View, Toolbars, and then click Picture. See Figure 52-5.

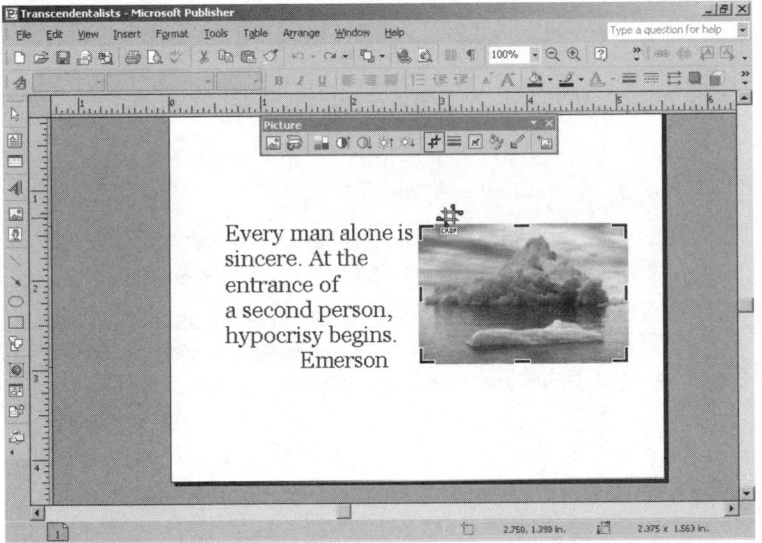

Figure 52-5. Cropping a picture can focus attention on part of the image.

2 Place the pointer, which is now the cropping pointer, on one of the cropping handles and drag the handle inward until just the portion of the picture you want to see remains by doing one of the following:

- Crop one side by dragging a center cropping handle on that side.

- Crop two sides evenly at one time by holding down Ctrl as you drag a center cropping handle.

- Crop all four sides evenly by holding down Ctrl while dragging a corner cropping handle.

3 To specify numerical cropping distances from the margins of the picture frame, choose Format, Picture, and then set values in the Picture tab under Crop From.

4 To turn off cropping, either click outside the picture frame, or click the Crop button again on the Picture toolbar.

Cropping an image doesn't erase parts of it—it simply hides the cropped portion. You can restore the cropped area by dragging the handle out from the center of the image.

Aligning Pictures and Other Objects

You can align objects to the ruler guides you've set for individual pages or to the layout guides that repeat on every page of your publication.

> For more information about ruler and layout guides, see Chapter 51, "Essential Publisher Techniques."

You can also align objects relative to each other. To do so, follow these steps:

1 Select the objects you want to align.

2 Choose Arrange, Align Or Distribute, and click the appropriate option on the Align Or Distribute drop-down list:

- If you want to align objects so they're centered on the page, click Relative To Margin Guides, and then click Align Center.

- To arrange objects so that they're an equal distance from one another, select the objects you want to arrange by clicking each one while holding down Shift, and then clicking Distribute Horizontally or Distribute Vertically.

Layering Frames

Brochures often use vertical design elements, such as blocks of color, to separate or emphasize text. You accomplish this look by creating a frame using the Rectangle tool (or another AutoShapes tool), adding a color fill, and then placing a text box or picture frame on top of it, as shown in Figure 52-6. How objects such as these are arranged on a page is referred to as the *stacking order*. Publisher automatically adds or stacks objects in the order in which you created them.

newfeature!

A new feature of Publisher 2002 is that text boxes are transparent by default. When you layer text boxes in a stack, the new frame doesn't cover the current one unless you make it opaque. You would employ this technique when you want to cover part of a design element or another text box. To make a text box opaque, complete the following steps:

1 Select the text box, and then press Ctrl+T.

2 To make the text box transparent again, press Ctrl+T again.

Chapter 52: Creating Professional Brochures and Newsletters

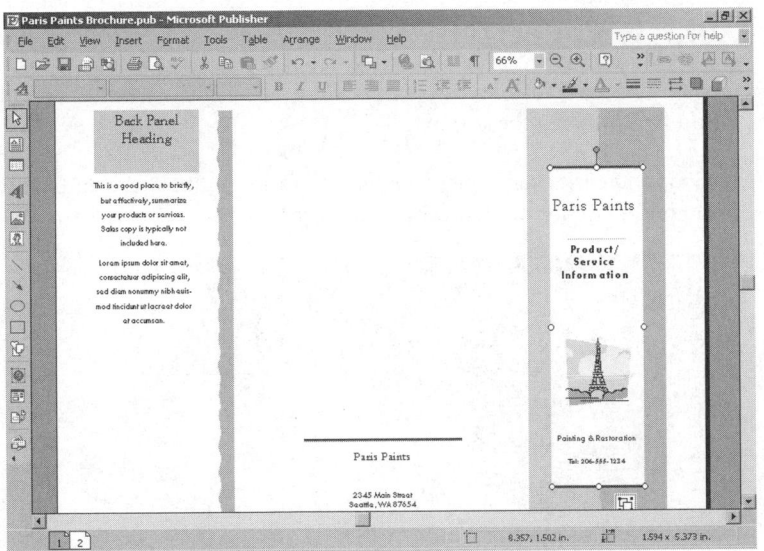

Figure 52-6. The first panel of this brochure layers five types of frames (AutoShapes, rectangle, text boxes, lines, and picture.

If you want to move an object that's hidden behind other frames, you can do so by following these steps:

1 Select the object that covers the one you want to move.

2 Press Tab to move forward through the group or Shift+Tab to move backward until you reach the object you want to move.

3 Select that object, choose Arrange, Order, and then click the appropriate command:

- Bring Forward brings the object one step closer to the front of the stack of objects.

- Bring To Front brings the object to the front of the stack.

- Send Backward sends the object one step backward.

- Send To Back sends the object to the bottom of the stack.

Grouping Multiple Objects

When you want to move, format, or rotate several objects at once, you can manipulate them as a unit by following these steps:

1 Press Shift and click every object you want in the group. A Group Objects button appears under the last object you select:

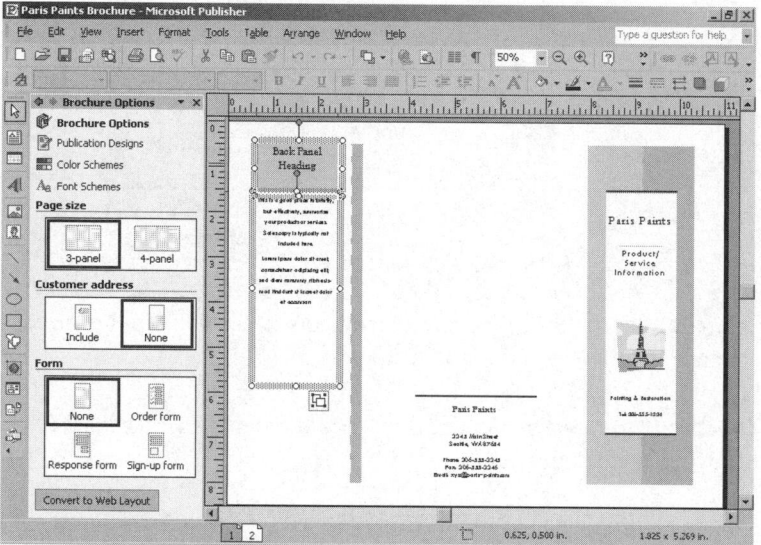

2 Click it to group the selected objects.

3 To ungroup the objects, click the grouped object to select it, and click the Ungroup Objects button.

Formatting a Drop Cap

Large or decorative letters placed at the beginning of a heading or paragraph in a brochure can quickly draw a reader into your publication. Using Publisher, you can format an initial capital letter in a variety of distinctive ways, which turns the letter into a graphic element in its own right.

> **note** *Initial caps* are first capital letters in text that align with the baseline of the first line of text. *Drop caps* are first capital letters that hang, or are dropped below, the first line of text.

Chapter 52: Creating Professional Brochures and Newsletters

You could manually create ornamental first letters by creating a text box for them using the Text Box tool and then formatting the individual letter. However, Publisher supplies many preformatted drop caps and initial caps for you to choose from, which you can then reuse in other publications. To insert a drop cap in your text, follow these steps:

1 Position the insertion point anywhere in the text whose first letter you want to format.

2 Choose Format, Drop Cap. The Drop Cap dialog box appears, as seen here:

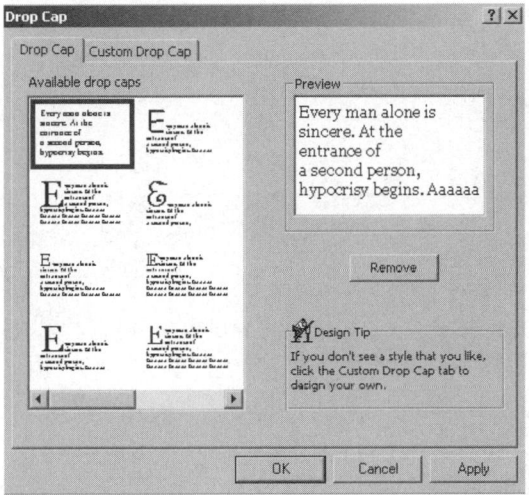

3 Click the Drop Cap tab to insert a preformatted drop or initial cap, and select a Drop Cap design under Available Drop Caps to preview the effect from within the dialog box.

4 Click OK to apply the formatting in your publication.

5 To create a custom drop or an initial cap, or if you want to format an entire first word or several letters at once, click the Custom Drop Cap tab.

6 Specify the number of letters you want to format as well as the custom letter size, position, and font, and then click OK. As shown in Figure 52-7 on page 1422, the initial letter displays the special formatting.

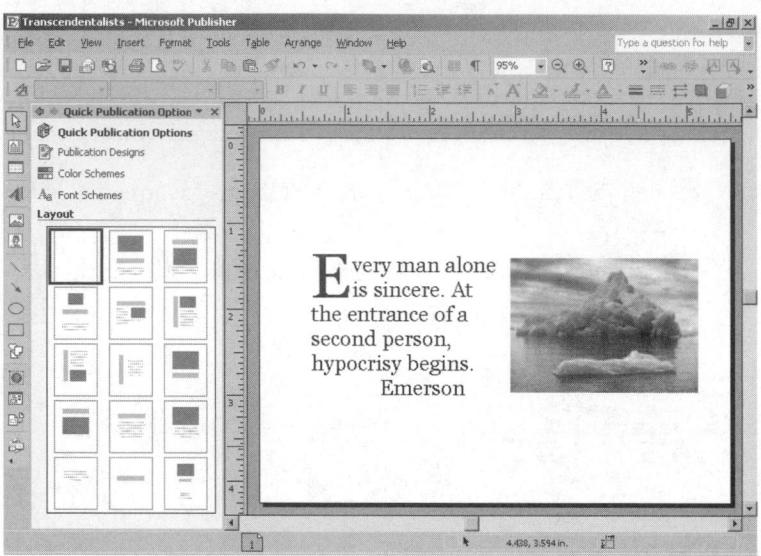

Figure 52-7. A letter becomes a graphical element with special formatting.

After you create a custom drop cap, that style is added to the list of available drop caps in the Drop Cap tab of the Drop Cap dialog box so that you can easily reuse it.

Adding Typographic Symbols

In the small space of a brochure, you want to be particularly careful about formatting text correctly. You also need to lead your reader logically through the folded publication. Applying correct typographic symbols can assist in both tasks.

A brochure often makes use of leading phrases or questions to move a reader to the next panel. The ellipsis character, the three dots that indicate that material has been left out of a sentence or that a sentence is trailing off, is different from three typed periods. In the brochure under construction in Figure 52-8, the ellipsis character is inserted from the Symbol dialog box.

To insert a true ellipsis, follow these steps:

1 Place the insertion point where you want to insert the ellipsis.

2 Choose Insert, Symbol, and the Symbol dialog box appears.

3 In the Special Characters tab, select the ellipsis character, and then click Insert.

4 Click the Close button to close the Symbol dialog box.

Chapter 52: Creating Professional Brochures and Newsletters

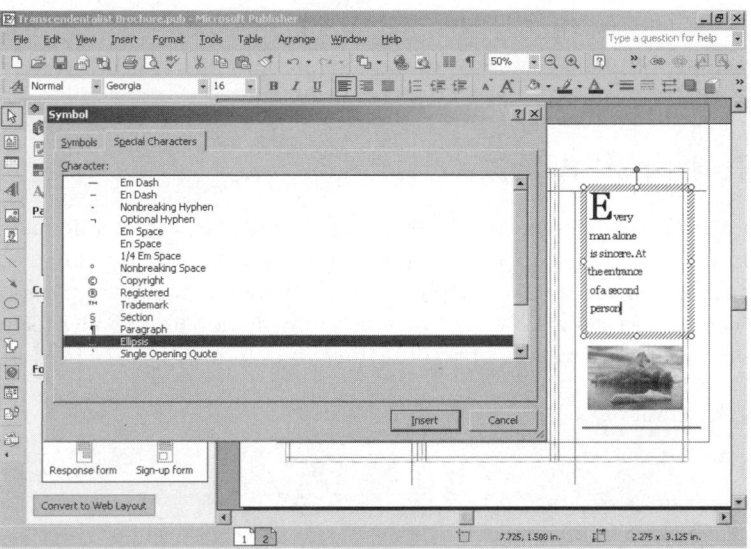

Figure 52-8. Use appropriate special typographic symbols.

The use of this character also makes the reader want to turn the page to see the next panel, as does the judicious use of the em dash. The em dash is also used to create a break in a sentence—in this case, it creates a more definite break than one set off by commas. One of the most glaring mistakes made by novice desktop publishers is to use the hyphen character instead of inserting a true em dash from the Symbol dialog box.

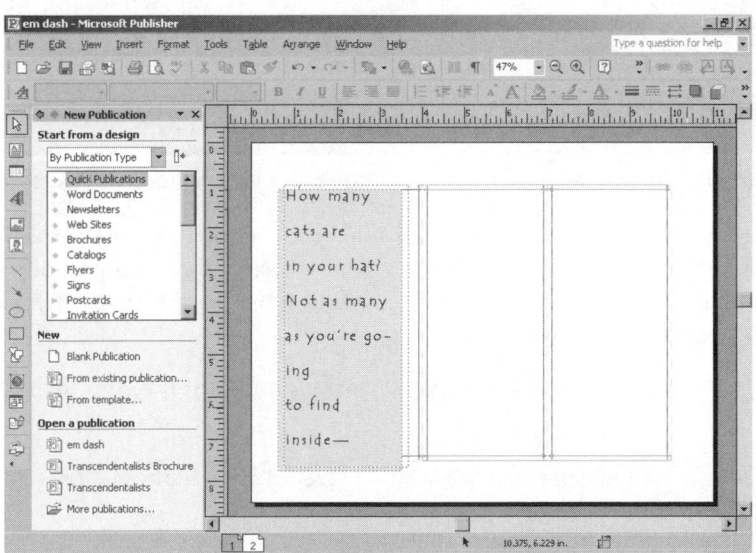

The en dash should also be used in your publications when necessary. The en dash is a slightly shorter dash than the em dash (it's the length of an *n* rather than an *m)* and is used to indicate a span or period of time. A good rule is that where you might use the

word "to," insert an en dash. For example: She reformatted pages 12–22. When inserting both em and en dashes, type them without inserting a space before or after the symbol.

newfeature!
Creating Horizontal Rules

Publisher 2002 contains a great new feature that lets you format a horizontal rule under text or between paragraphs without using the awkward underline character. Rules are lines that are used for emphasis or to separate elements from one another on a page. Figure 52-9 shows how clearly contact information listed on a brochure's back panel is delineated when a horizontal rule follows each item.

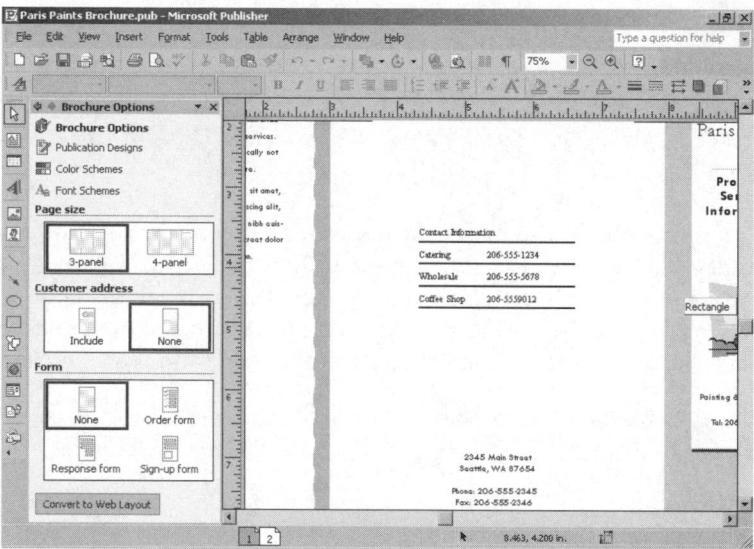

Figure 52-9.   Horizontal rules make it easy to read a list of phone numbers.

The disadvantage of using the Underline tool on the Formatting toolbar is that simply underlining text cuts off the descenders of fonts (such as the lower part of *g* or *p*) and places all underlines in the same position, giving you no control over their size, appearance, or position on the page.

To apply a horizontal rule, you must be working in a text box and then follow these steps:

1   Click within the paragraph to which you want to add horizontal rules.

2 Choose Format, Horizontal Rules. The Horizontal Rules dialog box appears, as shown here:

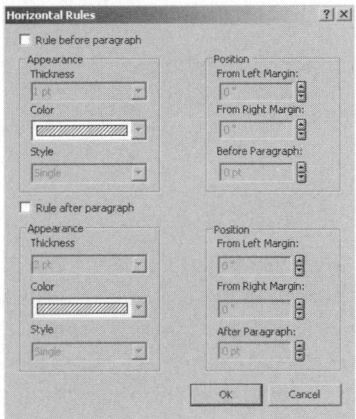

3 Specify whether you want to apply a rule before or after a paragraph, the appearance of the rule (thickness, color, and style), and its position in relation to the left and right margins and in relation to the text line above or below it.

4 When you've formatted the rules, click OK to apply them.

Working with Line Breaks and Hyphenation

A three-fold brochure affords limited space in which to type text. Avoid creating long lines of text that result in excessive hyphenation. In general, you should avoid lots of hyphenated words in all your publications: they break the flow of text and look unprofessional. Good design practice suggests that you allow no more than one hyphenated word in a row and preferably no more than one per paragraph. To accomplish this, you can force line breaks manually.

To force line breaks, place the insertion point before the character you want to wrap to the next line, and press Shift+Enter to force a break in the text there.

To change the frequency of hyphenation in the publication as a whole, follow these steps:

1 Choose Tools, Language, and then click Hyphenation. The Hyphenation dialog box appears, as shown here:

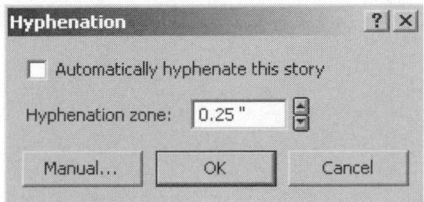

2 In the Hyphenation Zone box, specify the settings you want to apply. Making the zone smaller results in fewer white gaps in the text, which can be caused by reducing the number of hyphenations. Making the zone larger results in fewer hyphens in general and fewer hyphenations that leave syllables of one or two letters at the end of a line.

3 Click the Automatically Hyphenate This Story check box, and then click OK.

Creating a Newsletter

A newsletter can serve as a cost-effective promotional piece for a business or as a periodical for an organization and is often produced on a monthly or quarterly basis. If you're the editor of a periodic newsletter, you need to create a consistent, recognizable look for your publication, which you can accomplish by repeating elements on every page and in every issue of your publication. Spend time on designing your newsletter or customizing a Publisher-designed one so that you don't have to reinvent the layout.

Using the Tilt Newsletter Wizard (and inserting some clip art), you can create a small-business newsletter that looks like the one shown in Figure 52-10.

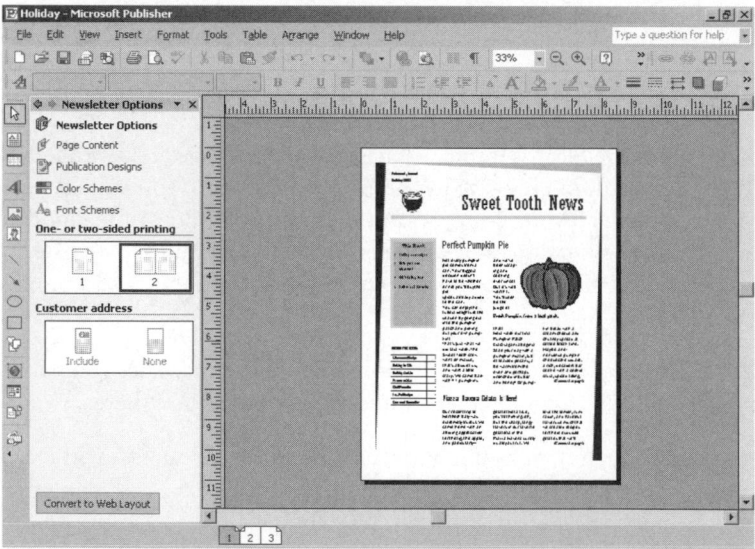

Figure 52-10. Newsletter Wizards include reusable elements such as the sidebar, table of contents, and masthead contained in this newsletter.

Creating Text Styles

newfeature!

In Publisher 2002, a new Styles And Formatting task pane contains options for working with text styles. A *text style* is a collection of formatting characteristics that you can format once and apply to paragraphs as many times as you want. Creating text styles is good design practice when working with a newsletter because it helps guarantee consistency in a long publication. And because newsletters tend to contain many different text styles for headlines, subheadings, pull quotes, body text, and footers, using text styles makes it easy to reuse formatting and shorten your production time.

In a text style, you can specify the font, font size, font color, indents, character and line spacing, tab stops, and bulleted and numbered list settings. You can quickly create a text style "by example," or you can manually enter the style characteristics using the Styles And Formatting task pane.

To create a text style by example, follow these steps:

1 Select the text that you want to use as a basis for the text style.

2 On the Formatting toolbar, click the Style box, and then type the name of your new text style over the name displayed in the box.

3 Press Enter. The Create Style By Example dialog box appears, as shown here:

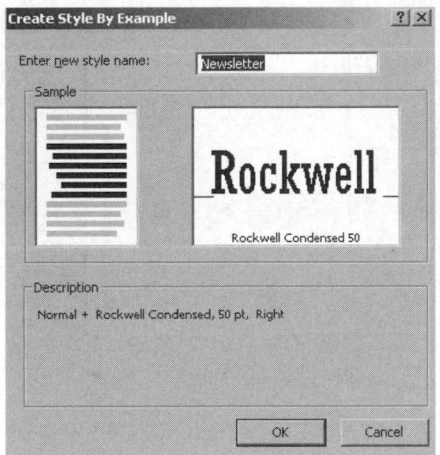

Chapter 52

4 Make sure that the name is correct in the Enter New Style Name box and that the formatting instructions are correct in the Sample and Description sections. Then click OK.

The new style is now included in the list of available styles in the task pane. If you made a change to the Normal style, it will show up in publications that you create from now on—the changes aren't retroactive.

To apply a text style to a new paragraph, click within the paragraph, and then click the style you want to apply in the Style box on the Formatting toolbar.

You can also create text styles from scratch by using the Styles And Formatting task pane. To create, modify, or import a text style, follow these steps:

1 Choose Format, Styles And Formatting, or click the down arrow in the task pane, and then click Styles And Formatting. The Styles And Formatting task pane appears, as shown here:

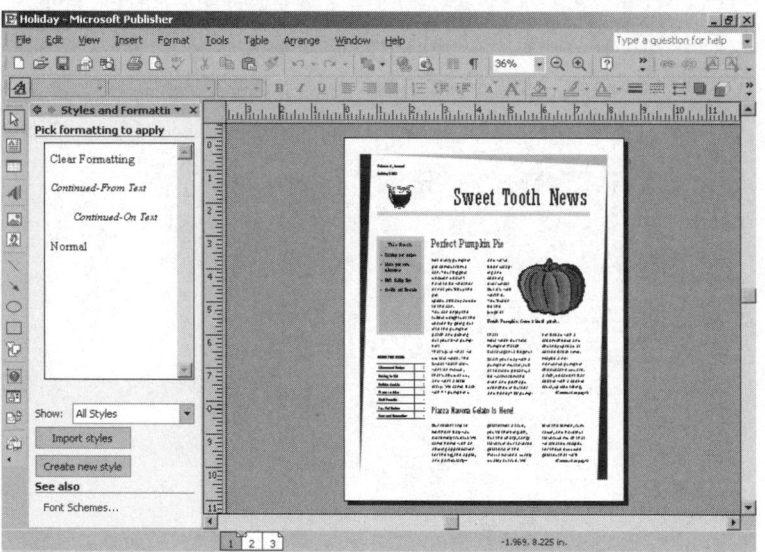

2 Click Create New Style, a button at the bottom of the task pane. The Create New Style dialog box appears, as shown here:

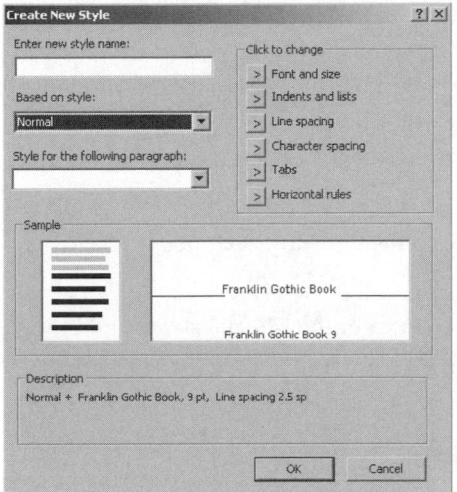

3 Type a new name for the style in the Enter New Style Name box.

4 Select one or more of the six options Publisher provides, and the appropriate dialog box appears.

5 Click OK to create the new style.

6 Repeat steps 2 through 5 to create more new styles.

Your new styles are now included in the task pane list of available styles and are also in the Style list box on the Formatting toolbar. To quickly apply one of these new styles, you click in the paragraph in which you want the style to apply and then click the name in the Style box on the Formatting toolbar.

You can also modify an existing text style by following these steps:

1 In the Styles and Formatting task pane, point to the style you want to modify.

2 When a down arrow appears next to the style name, click it, and then click Modify. The Change Style dialog box appears.

3 In the Change Style dialog box, select the style to change, make your changes to it, and then click OK to apply them.

You often need to import long articles or documents into a publication, particularly when you create a newsletter. If you want to also import the text styles those articles are based on, you can do so using the Styles And Formatting task pane. To import text styles, follow these steps:

1 In the Styles And Formatting task pane, click Import Styles at the bottom left of the task pane.

2 In the Import Styles dialog box, enter or select the file name of the document you want to import, and then click OK.

All the text styles from that document are now included in the list of available styles in the task pane.

You can also delete any text style except the Normal style by pointing to the style you want to remove in the Styles And Formatting task pane list, clicking the down arrow, and then clicking Delete.

Working with Text Wrapping

When you insert pictures into long columns of text, you often need to change how the picture interacts or *wraps* with surrounding text.

To create visual interest and maintain order on the page, it's good design practice to keep pictures at the end of a text frame, between columns of type, or at the bottom of a page when wrapping text around a graphic. By default, Publisher wraps the text around the entire picture frame, an option that's referred to as the Square wrapping style, as shown in Figure 52-11.

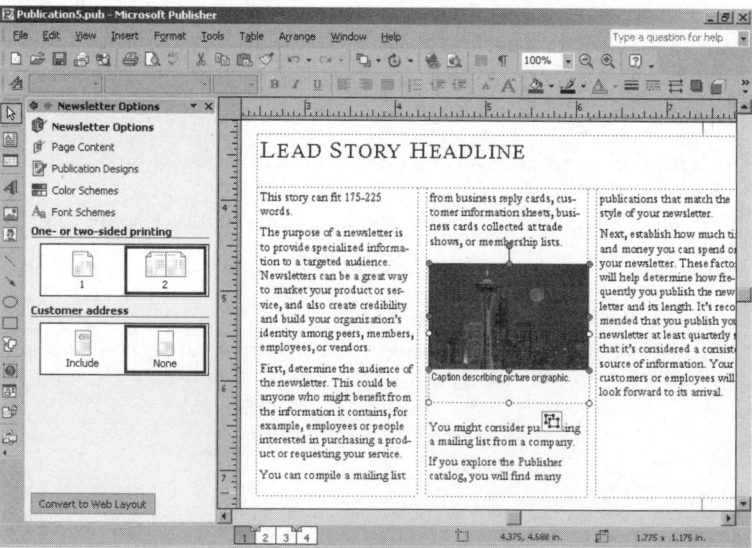

Figure 52-11. Moving this picture into a column of text causes the text to wrap around each side of the picture frame.

Chapter 52: Creating Professional Brochures and Newsletters

To edit text wrapping around a picture, follow these steps:

1 Select the picture, clip, or AutoShape, and then choose Format, Picture (or Object, or AutoShape). The Format Picture (or Object, or AutoShape) dialog box appears.

2 To wrap the text around the picture and not the picture frame, click the Layout tab.

3 Under Wrapping Style, select Square.

4 Under Wrap Text, click the option that specifies the side or sides you want the text to wrap around.

5 Under Distance From Text, clear the Automatic check box to enter the margins you want to set around your picture.

6 Position the picture precisely on the page by entering values in the boxes under Position On Page.

Wrapping text tightly around a graphic is a way of integrating the two elements. To manually create a tighter wrap around the picture, you can edit the individual wrap points by completing the following steps:

1 Select the picture you want to edit.

2 Choose Arrange, Text Wrapping, and then click Edit Wrap Points.

3 Position the mouse pointer over a sizing handle, and hold down the left mouse button. When it changes to an Adjust pointer, drag the handle to change the outline of the picture, as shown in Figure 52-12.

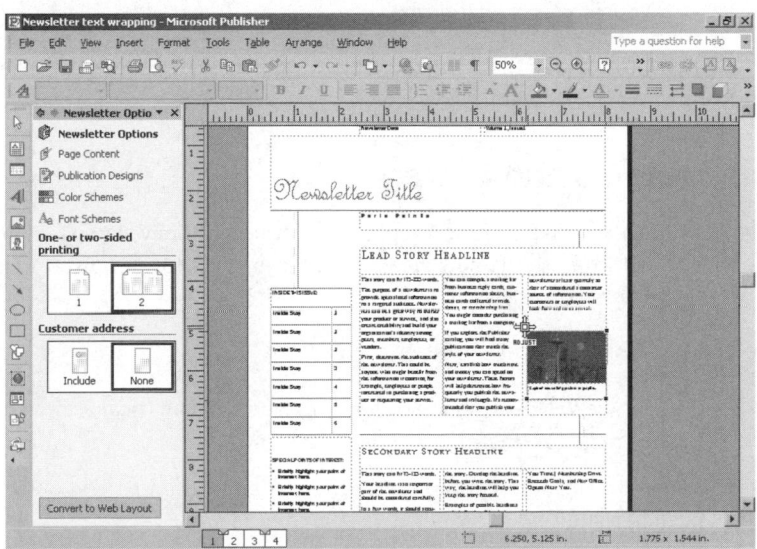

Figure 52-12. Dragging an edit wrap point creates an irregular wrap.

Chapter 52

4 To add another edit point, point to the border where you want the new handle, and when the pointer becomes the Add handle, press Ctrl, and click the border to create a new handle.

5 To delete a handle, press Ctrl+Shift, and then click the handle.

Moving Objects In Line with Text

newfeature!

Publisher 2002 includes a new feature that lets you move an object in line with text. The object is then treated as a text character and, as text is added or deleted, moves with the text. (An object that's formatted at an exact position on the page also moves when you add or delete text, but it never moves left or right from its formatted position.)

To insert an object that moves in line with text, follow these steps:

1 Select the text box to which you want to add the object, and then choose Insert, Object (or Picture, or AutoShape), and insert it into the text box.

2 Right-click the inserted object, click Format Object (or Picture, or AutoShape), and then click the Layout tab in the Format Object dialog box.

3 Under Object Position, click In-Line, and then click OK.

4 Under Horizontal Alignment, specify one of the following options:

 ■ Click Left for an object that stays next to the left margin.

 ■ Click Right for an object that stays next to the right margin.

 ■ Click Move Object With Text for an object that stays in the same position in a line of text.

If you want to remove the in line settings at any time, just click the Layout tab again, and under Object Position, click Exact.

Creating Headers and Footers

newfeature!

Headers or footers are common repeating elements in newsletters. In this version of Publisher, you can use the new Header And Footer feature to insert text or objects onto a Master page in your newsletter.

To create a header or footer, follow these steps:

1 Choose View, Header And Footer. Publisher automatically moves to the Master page for your publication.

2 Select the Header or Footer text box, and enter the text and objects you want repeated on every page, as shown in Figure 52-13.

Chapter 52: Creating Professional Brochures and Newsletters

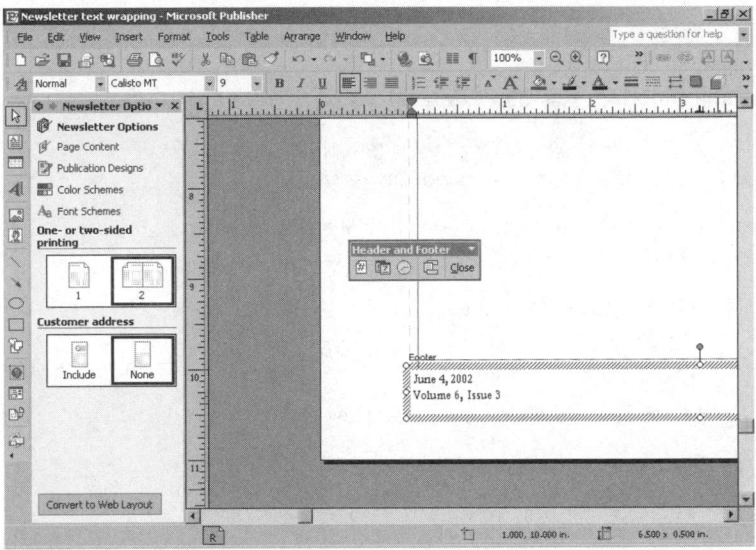

Figure 52-13. You can create a uniform header and footer for each page of a newsletter.

3 Click Close on the Header And Footer toolbar to return to your publication's foreground.

Creating a Watermark

When placing objects such as a logo on the Master page, it's useful to create a water-mark image so that the reader easily read the text that the image is positioned behind.

You can insert a picture onto the Master page of your publication and format it as a watermark, which is a faded image or text that shows through from the background, such as text that reads "Confidential" or "Draft."

To format a picture as a watermark, follow these steps:

1 Right-click the picture, and then click Format Picture.

2 In the Format Picture dialog box, click the Picture tab.

3 Under Image Control, click Washout in the Color list.

4 Click Recolor, and in the Recolor dialog box, select the color you want for the image. Click Apply and then click OK.

Troubleshooting

Troubleshooting: You Can't Convert a Text Item to a Watermark

You want to create a watermark from an AutoShape, WordArt object, or text item, but the Washout command is not available.

You can't convert these text items to a watermark unless they are first converted to a picture format.

To save an object as a picture, follow these steps:

1 Right-click the object, and then click Save As Picture from the shortcut menu.

2 In the Save As dialog box, select the picture format you want to use.

3 Specify where to save the file, and then click Save.

4 Delete the current version of the file in your publication.

5 If you want the watermark to appear on every page of your publication, move to the Master page, and choose Insert, Picture, From File to insert the new image file, which is now saved in a picture format.

6 Now follow the procedure given above for creating a watermark image.

Chapter 53

Advanced Web Publications

For ease of use and speedy transformation of content into Web content, Microsoft Publisher 2002 is a great tool. However, when it comes to Web site creation, it's not the most robust member of the Microsoft Office XP suite of applications. To create and maintain a complex business Web site, you'd probably choose Microsoft FrontPage, the Office application that contains more sophisticated tools for Web site management than Publisher. For bells and whistles, use FrontPage. When you need to create a basic Web site quickly, use Publisher.

Using Publisher, you can design electronic publications for the Web using the same elements that went into your print publications. Publisher 2002 now includes native support for HTML (Hypertext Markup Language) so that you can more easily make changes to a Publisher-designed Web site and no longer have to keep a separate copy of it in the Publisher file format. In addition to text and graphics, you can add multimedia elements to Web-based publications. The Office XP Clip Organizer contains photo images, video clips, sounds, and hundreds of small animation files, called GIFs (for Graphic Interchange Format), which can add impact to your site when used judiciously. You can also create interactive Web pages by including forms so that visitors to your site can order products or respond to surveys and questionnaires. And because color is free on the Web, you can brighten your pages by applying colorful backgrounds and vibrant graphics without incurring print costs.

Publisher wizards are available to guide you through the process, so when you want to reach a worldwide audience on the Web or connect with your colleagues on a company intranet, you can do so without having to become a Web master.

In this chapter you'll learn about

- Designing Web pages
- Inserting hyperlinks
- Creating a navigation bar
- Creating electronic forms
- Adding sounds and animations
- Selecting useful keywords and page titles for search engines
- Publishing Web pages to a Web server

Planning for the Web

Web publishing can be a far-reaching medium for your publishing efforts. You can use Publisher to create a personal Web page that lets your family and friends know what you're about or a corporate Web site that provides information about your products and services. When creating publications for the Web, you should engage in the same kind of planning that precedes any publishing activity: define your mission, your publication's goals, and your audience. However, a Web publication differs from a print publication in several key ways:

- Reading content on a computer screen is more difficult than reading it on a printed page. So you need to edit and edit again to create short pages, keeping your text concise and making every word count.

- Your Web pages are among millions of available pages, all just one click away. Your visitors quickly scan to find out if they're on the right page. If they don't find the core content they're looking for up front, they will visit another page. So write in small sentences, and put key words in bulleted lists or in headings so that visitors can immediately spot them.

- Until everyone has a fast Internet connection, keep graphics to a minimum. Web graphics often translate into lengthy download times, which prompt visitors to click to another site.

- Your visitors control the navigation on your site. Don't anticipate that they'll read your Web pages in sequential order, as they might in a print publication. Create Web pages that stand alone. Identify the site on each page, link back to the home page from every page, and make sure that the navigation bar indicates where the user is on the site and what links are available or have already been visited.

As you can see in Figure 53-1, a Web page created by Publisher displays the dynamic quality of electronic publishing.

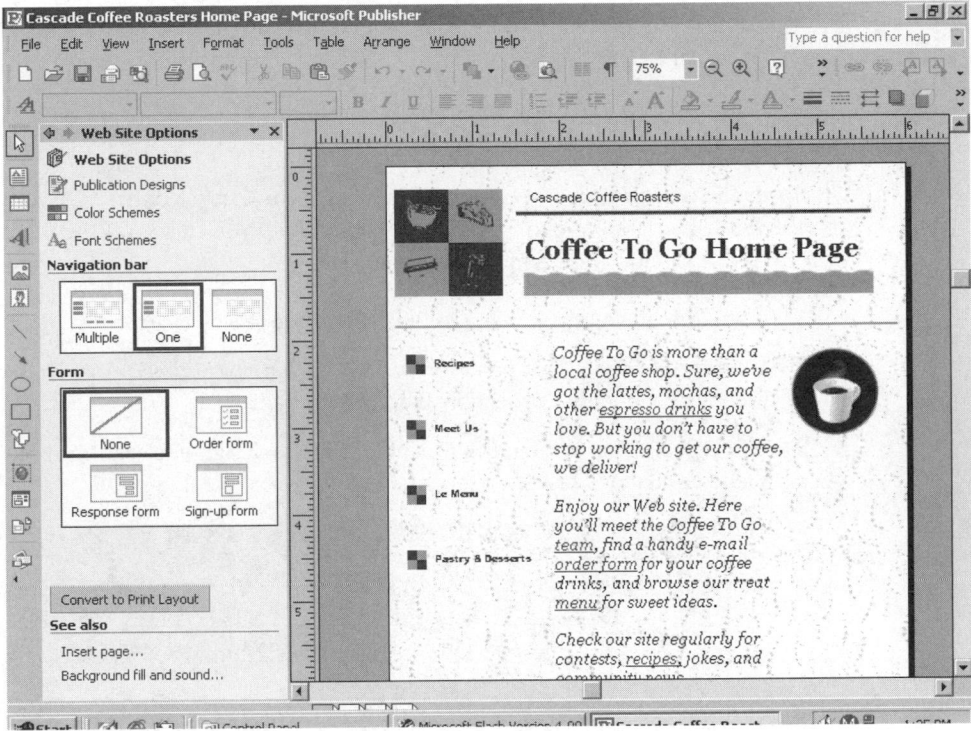

Figure 53-1. A small business home page uses the pages of its Web site to generate sales and foster community.

Creating Web Pages

Publisher 2002 offers a variety of ways to move into a Web project:

- The Web Site Options task pane is a wizard-based task pane that's by far the easiest approach to creating a Web publication. It works by providing options for you to choose from and then building a Web site around the choices you make.

- Creating a Web page using a blank publication provides an opportunity to try your wings as a Web designer, although this approach assumes that you can handle the design, layout, hyperlinks, and site navigation on your own.

- Convert To Web Layout (an option available in the Newsletter and Brochure Wizards) allows you to reuse the information in a Publisher-designed newsletter or brochure by converting the print publication to a Web site and opening the Web Options task pane.

- Save As Web Page (a command found on the File menu) begins the process of turning any publication into a Web site, whether you created it using a

Publisher wizard or built it from scratch by changing the file to an HTML document.

Using Publisher's Web Site Options

If this is the first time you've created a Web page, you can select the Web Site category in the Publisher task pane to employ a wizard to help you carry out the task. To open the Web Site Options task pane, follow these steps:

1   If you're not already working in Publisher, choose File, New.

2   Or, if the Publisher task pane for creating new publications is displayed, click Web Sites in the By Publication Type category list.

3   In the Publication Gallery (right pane), click the design you want to use. The Web Site Options task pane opens:

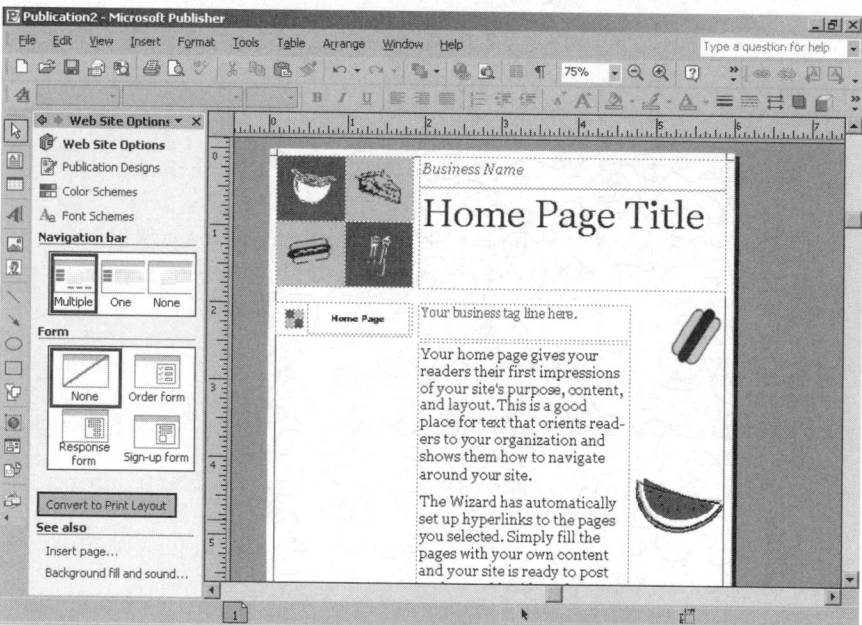

4   In the task pane, make the following selections to customize your page:

- **Navigation Bar**   If you're creating only one page, you don't need a navigation bar. If you're creating more than one page, choose between Multiple, which includes a horizontal and a vertical bar, and One, which includes just a vertical bar.

- **Form**   Choose from none, an order form, a response form, or a sign-up form to add electronic forms to your page.

- **Insert Page**   Clicking this option opens the Insert Page dialog box where you can select the Add Hyperlink To Web Navigation Bar check box to update the bars whenever you add a page.

- **Background Fill And Sound**   Clicking this option opens the Background task pane, which also includes color options.

- **Background Sound**   Clicking this option in the Background task pane opens the Web Options dialog box.

5 Edit the placeholder text and graphics as you do in other publications, by replacing it with your own, repositioning frames, and applying formatting.

Previewing Web Pages

To see how your publication looks as a Web page, you can preview it in a browser. To preview a Web page, complete the following steps:

1 Choose File, Web Page Preview.

2 If you have more than one page in your site, the Web Page Preview dialog box appears:

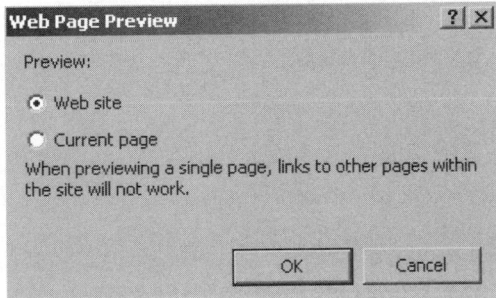

Click the options to choose to preview an entire site or just the current page. If you choose the current page, the links you've created to other pages in the site won't work.

3 Click OK, and your Web page or pages open in the default browser. Check to see if the overall page appearance works well and if the hyperlinks work correctly.

4 Click File, Close, to close the browser and return to Publisher.

As you build new pages, you should always preview your Web site. If possible, take the following precautions:

- Preview the site displayed on both a PC and a Macintosh computer.

- Use both of the most popular browsers (Microsoft Internet Explorer and Netscape Navigator) to test your pages.

● Test the pages after setting the display resolution of your monitor at both VGA (Video Graphics Adapter) and SVGA (Super Video Graphics Array).

● Vary the screen color settings from 16-bit color to 24-bit color to 256 colors.

Creating a Web Site from Scratch

When creating a Web page from scratch, you determine the page design—how to balance text, hyperlinks, and graphics for an Internet audience. To set up a Web page from a blank publication, follow these steps:

1 If you're not already working in Publisher, choose File, New.

2 Or, if the Publisher task pane for creating new publications is displayed, under New, click Blank Publication. Publisher displays a blank 8 1/2-by-11-inch page in portrait orientation.

3 Choose File, Page Setup. The Page Setup dialog box appears.

4 In the Page Setup dialog box, scroll to Web Page, as shown here:

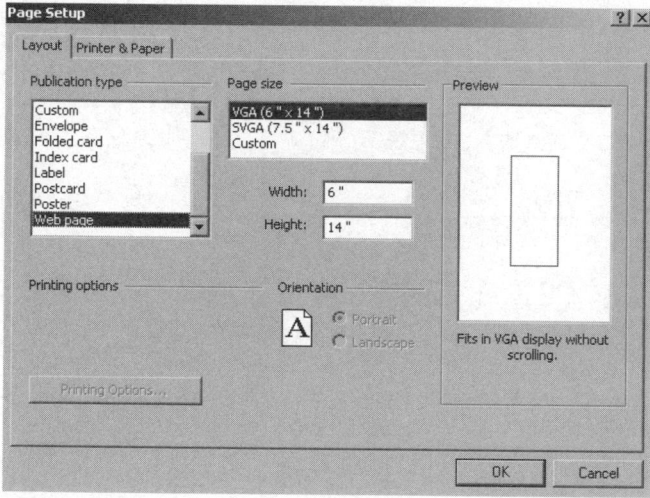

5 Under Page Size, select VGA, SVGA, or Custom, and then click OK.

tip **Set Page Dimensions**

The width of a Web page is determined by the display resolution of the monitors typically used by your audience. In academia and business, that's usually a 800-by-600 pixel screen. When you choose VGA, which is a 6-by-14-inch page or three and a half screens in a browser, you're choosing a standard size that permits most readers to view your pages without horizontal scrolling. Forcing visitors to scroll horizontally to view the pages on your Web site is definitely undesirable from a usability standpoint.

Part of the width of a Web page is used by the browser window in which it's displayed. So that readers can see the entire page, regardless of how many pixels are used by their browser window, set your page at 600 pixels wide rather than 640.

The height of a Web page is determined by the content of your Web publication. Long pages of text force readers to scroll vertically so that they lose sight of navigation elements, hyperlinks, the page title that identifies the particular page, and the site name at the top of the page. This kind of scrolling can be disorienting to readers. A good rule is to add a jump button—one that says Back To Top, for example—at the bottom of the page for every document longer than two vertical screens.

After you set up the page, you can format it. Establish a layout grid, using margins, columns, and rows, to provide continuity on each page of your site, as shown in the sample in Figure 53-2.

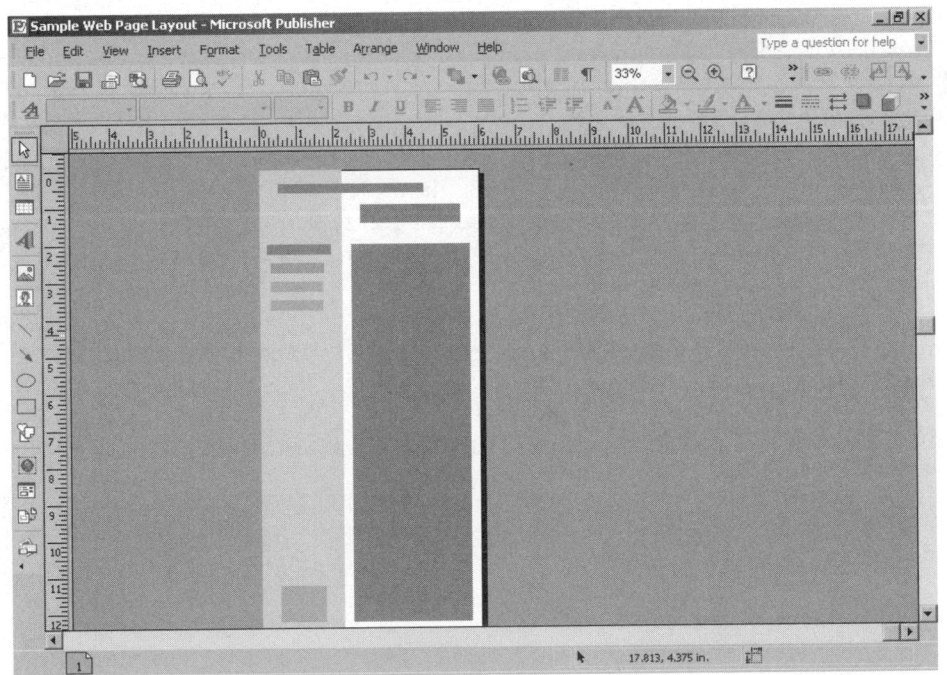

Figure 53-2. You can use a blank Web page in which to insert a basic Web page layout grid such as the one drawn here.

When Emerson wrote, "Consistency is the hobgoblin of little minds," he wasn't referring to Web design. Consider repeating the same graphics on each page: in addition to helping brand your site, repeating graphics also load faster because they're cached locally on your reader's system. (After you view a Web page, it's stored in the cache directory of your browser on your hard disk so that you don't have to download it again each time you want to look at it.)

Creating a Web Site from an Existing Publication

When you want to turn any publication into a Web site, whether a Publisher wizard created it or you built it from scratch, follow these steps:

1 Open the publication in Publisher, and choose File, Save As Web Page, type a new name for your publication, then click Save. A Publisher message box appears, telling you that it's exporting the publication to HTML file(s).

2 Choose Tools, Design Checker, and run it to see how the fonts, layout, and graphics work as a Web publication.

> For more information on Design Checker, see Chapter 51, "Essential Publisher Techniques."

3 Choose File, Web Page Preview.

You can convert a Publisher-designed newsletter or brochure to a Web page by simply clicking the Convert To Web Layout button in the lower-left corner of the Newsletter Or Brochure Options task pane.

Adding Hyperlinks

The ability to link content is one of the most exciting features of Web publishing. When you create a hyperlink, you connect text or graphics to another page on your site or to a Uniform Resource Locator (URL) of a different Web site or to an e-mail address, or to information you've saved in another Office program, such as a Microsoft Word document, a Microsoft Excel worksheet, or a Microsoft PowerPoint slide. Figure 53-3 shows hypertext links on a Web page. In this type of hyperlink, the underlined text forms the anchor for the link.

> For more information about using hyperlinks in other Office programs, see Chapter 34, "Adding Special Effects and Hyperlinks."

Chapter 53: Advanced Web Publications

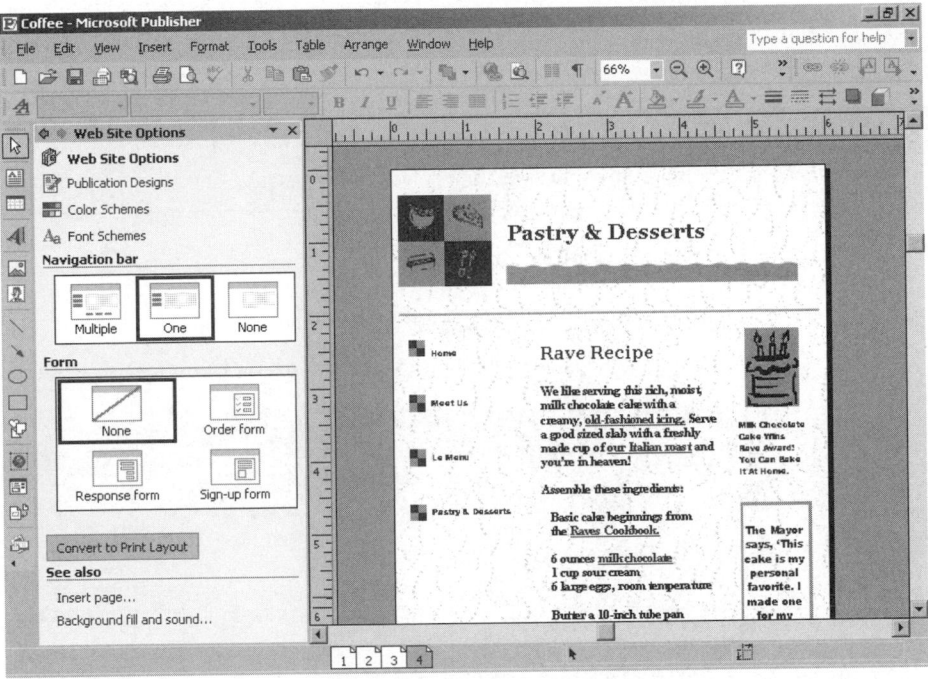

Figure 53-3. The reader clicks hypertext links, which are anchored in the text, to move to more information about the topics on your Web site.

When you create a hyperlink (or link), the text that the user clicks is displayed and underlined in a different color from the surrounding text. A followed link, one that the reader has already clicked, is displayed and underlined in another color. The standard colors are blue for links and purple for followed links. It's advisable to use the standard colors for links because your readers are already experienced in following them.

Hyperlinks can enrich your Web publication's content, but they can also distract your readers by providing an opportunity for them to leave your site. Place your links strategically. Good information design practice suggests the following:

- Point most links in your Web site to other pages within your site.

- If you link to another Web site, be sure to warn your readers that they're leaving your site.

- Don't place links too close to each other, because multiple hyperlinks in the same sentence make it difficult to read.

- Group related or "See Also" links at the end of a page or article.

- Create the hyperlink on well-chosen words in the sentence—use important words that describe the linked content to guide your reader.

Your home page is a logical place to start adding hyperlinks because this page leads visitors to other pages on your Web site.

> **tip** Don't create a link to the home page on the home page. It's annoying for your readers to click a hyperlink and find themselves in the same place.

To create a hyperlink, follow these steps:

1 Select the text for which you want to create a hyperlink.

2 Choose Insert, Hyperlink. The Insert Hyperlink dialog box appears, as seen here:

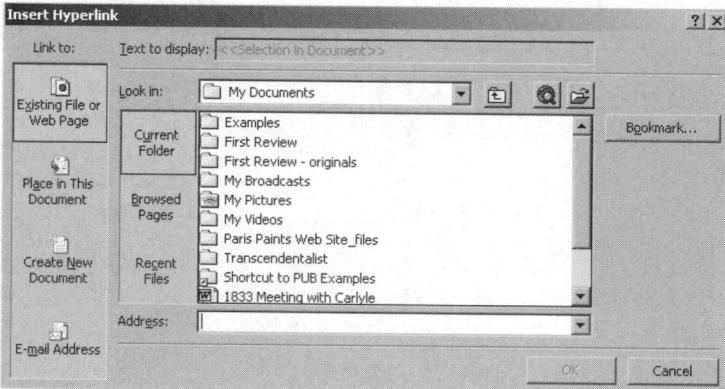

3 Select one of the four options in the Link To section to specify the hyperlink's target location.

4 Select or enter the location or address for the hyperlink, and then click OK.

The selected text is now underlined and displayed in blue, by default. The hyperlinks don't become active until you view these pages in a Web browser.

You can also link an object or graphic to another location. To insert a hyperlink into an object, follow the same steps as you did to insert a hyperlink into text, only this time select the object by clicking it. To delete a hyperlink, follow these steps:

1 Right-click the hyperlink, and click Hyperlink on the shortcut menu. The Edit Hyperlink dialog box appears.

2 In the Edit Hyperlink dialog box, click Remove Link. The text or object remains, but it's not a hyperlink anymore.

3 If necessary, delete the text, frame, or object using Publisher's tools.

You're responsible for maintaining the accuracy of your links. Because the Web constantly changes, you must regularly check the addresses of the hyperlinks in your file.

Creating a Hot Spot

A *hot spot* is the area on an object that's a hyperlink. When you create a hyperlink for an object using the Insert Hyperlink procedure, you're turning that object into one hot spot. In other instances—for example, when you have a large graphic that's segmented into parts or a company photo of several team members—you might want to create more than one hot spot or hyperlink on that object. Figure 53-4 shows how an image can be formatted with more than one hot spot. You can also group the hot spots with the picture so that they move when you reformat or move the image.

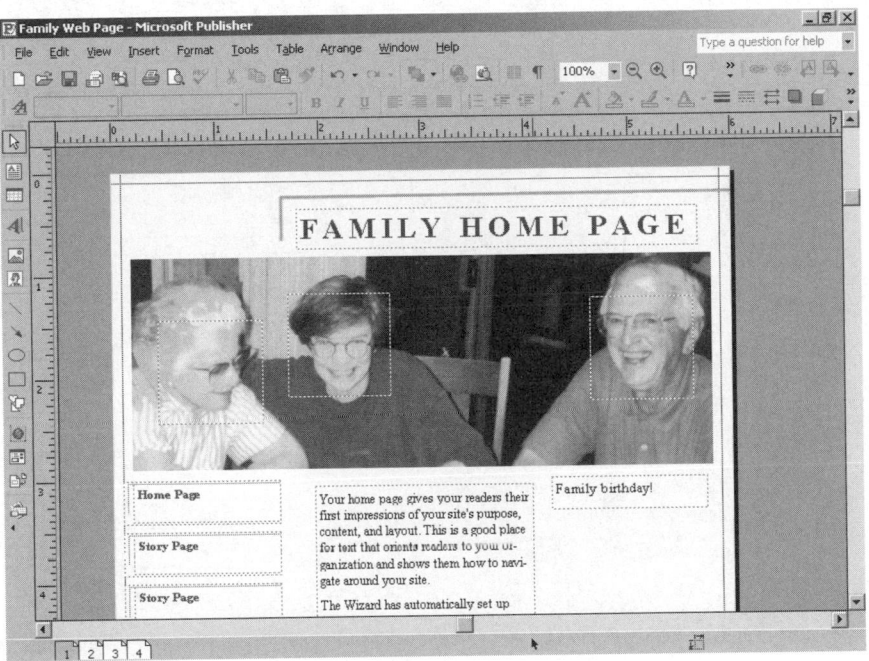

Figure 53-4. Hot spots insert a link in each section of this image and are displayed as transparent AutoShapes.

To create a hot spot, complete the following steps:

1 Click the Hot Spot tool on the Objects toolbar.

2 The Insert Hyperlink dialog box appears. Enter the appropriate information, and click OK to create the hot spot. The Insert Hyperlink dialog box closes.

3 A transparent AutoShape that contains the hyperlink you just specified is displayed on your Web page. Move it to the exact location you want to be the hot spot.

4 Repeat this procedure to create as many hot spots as you want, as shown in Figure 53-4.

To check the hot spots, open the Web pages in your browser by using Web Page Preview. The AutoShape outline is not visible when the page is viewed in a browser.

Creating Electronic Forms

Web publishing can be instantly interactive—you don't have to wait for your customer to receive a document in the mail and send a response form back to you. The wizards in this version of Publisher help you add electronic forms to your Web pages so visitors can communicate with you by e-mail. A business can take orders online, as a small espresso shop might do with an e-mail order for several coffee drinks. (See Figure 53-5.)

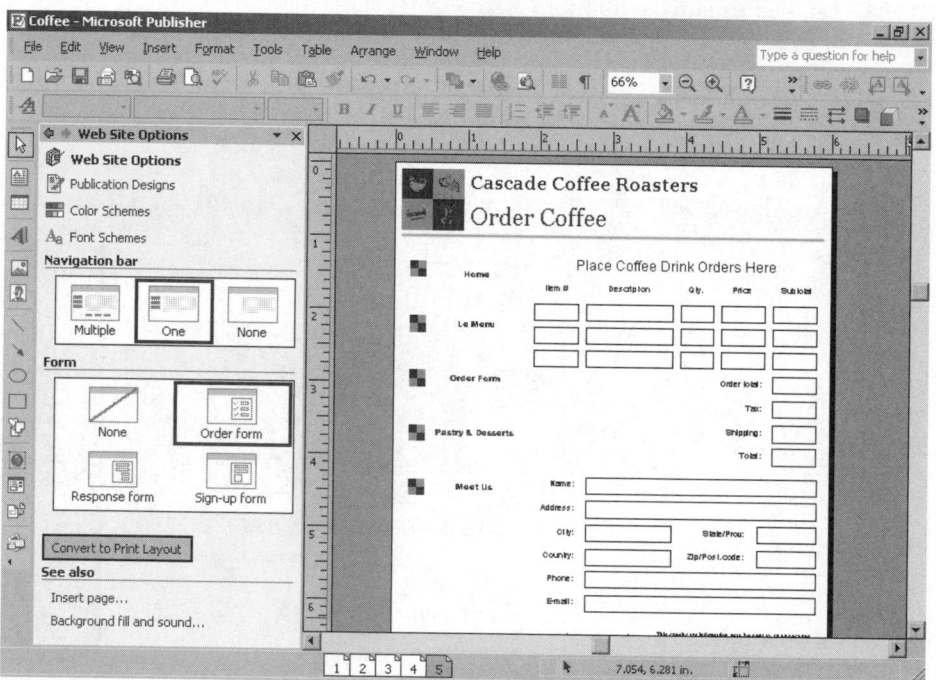

Figure 53-5. Forms are a convenient means of interacting with your customers or clients.

One caveat when offering response forms to your readers: Make sure to tell them what you're doing with the information they provide. Confirm that you don't sell or reveal their personal information to outside groups. Privacy issues continue to grow in importance as the Internet becomes more a part of people's lives.

You can create the type of form you want to include on your Web page in three ways:

● If you're creating a Publisher-designed Web page, select a form from the Web Site Options task pane. The wizard supplies a form template that you can customize with your own information.

● Insert a form from the Design Gallery by clicking Design Gallery Object on the Insert menu, clicking Web Reply Forms in the Categories list, and selecting the appropriate form.

● Create a form by using the Form Control tool on the Objects toolbar, shown on the next page. This tool provides a toolbar that supports six different form properties, which you can add to your form.

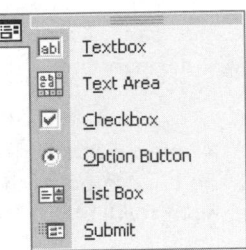

Before modifying the content in a Publisher-designed form, ungroup the items in the form. Then double-click the control you want to change, and make your changes in the appropriate dialog box.

Creating a Navigation Bar

Visitors move through your site by clicking navigation controls, which form a system of built-in hyperlinks holding the pages of your site together. Publisher contains two types of navigation bar: a vertical bar that's placed at the left side of the Web page, and a horizontal bar that's positioned at the bottom of the page and reflects the changes made to the vertical bar. You can reposition the vertical bar, but the horizontal one remains fixed. Figure 53-6 shows a wizard-based vertical navigation bar.

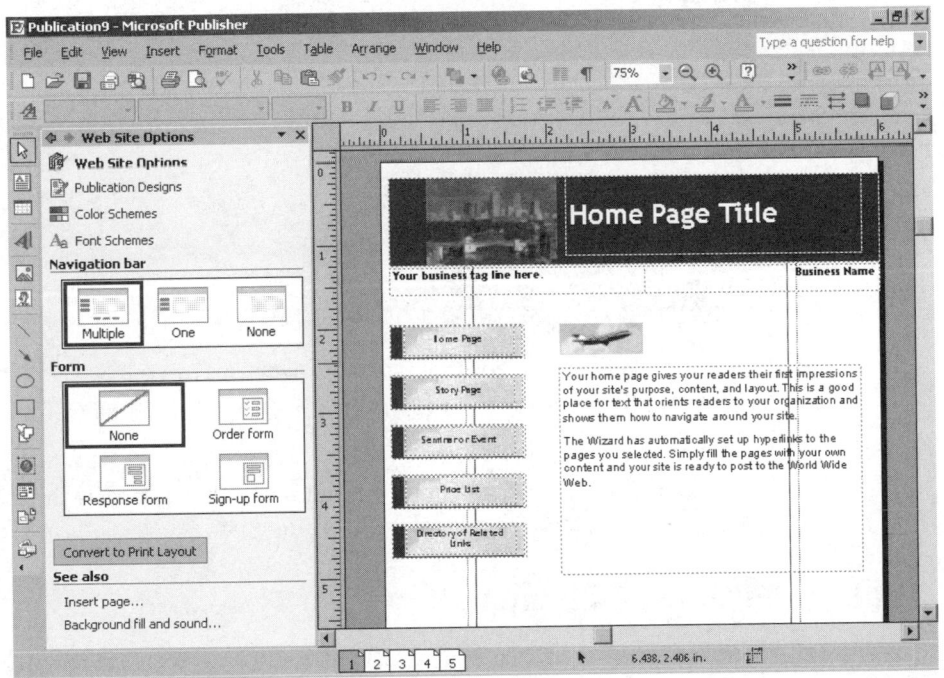

Figure 53-6. Publisher can automatically create a vertical navigation bar with hyperlinks to the other pages on your Web site.

If you're working in Publisher's Web Site Options task pane, select the navigation bar element you want to change, then select the type of navigation design you want to use from those listed in the task pane.

This option changes only the placement of the navigation element. To change its content, you must make standard formatting changes to the text boxes that make up the navigation bar or add new graphic elements from your media files.

You can also add predesigned navigation bars from Publisher's Design Gallery by choosing Insert, Design Gallery Object, Web Navigation Bars.

To automatically insert a Web navigation bar on every new page of your Web site that already has a navigation bar, take the following steps:

1 Choose Insert, Page. The Insert Page dialog box appears, as shown here:

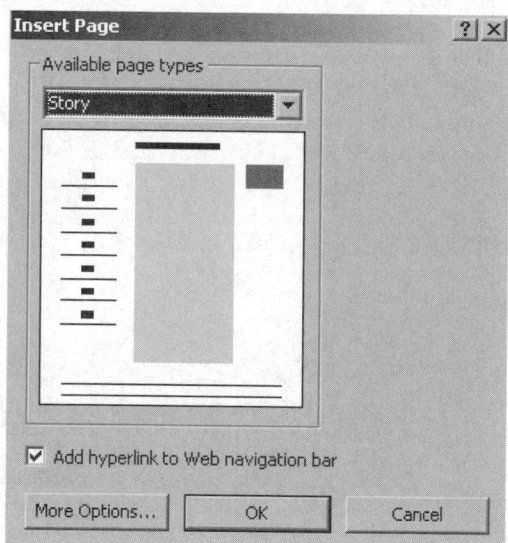

2 In the Insert Page dialog box, click the Add Hyperlink To Web Navigation Bar check box, specify the type of page you want to add, if necessary, and then click OK.

Now when you add or delete pages, Publisher automatically updates references to the titles and hyperlinks for those pages on the navigation bar.

Adding Multimedia Elements

Multimedia elements—audio, animated GIFs, three-dimensional animated graphics, and video clips—are commonly used on the Web, often on the home page or *splash screen* to introduce a Web site. (A splash screen, also known as a site cover, is a page that precedes the home page and functions as an entry way to your site. It often contains graphics or animation.) You can create your own animated files using software applications such as Macromedia Shockwave, Flash, or Director, or you can add media files you've imported into the Clip Organizer to your Web pages.

Inserting Sounds

Audio files that play in the background on your Web pages can add a mood, provide a sense of a speaker's personality, or supply pronunciation or other educational tips. Good quality sound files enhance the user experience while remaining small enough not to substantially add to download times.

You can easily add background sound to a Web page when you use the Web Site Options task pane. To do so, follow these steps:

1 In the Web Site Options task pane, click Background Fill And Sound. The Background task pane appears, as shown here:

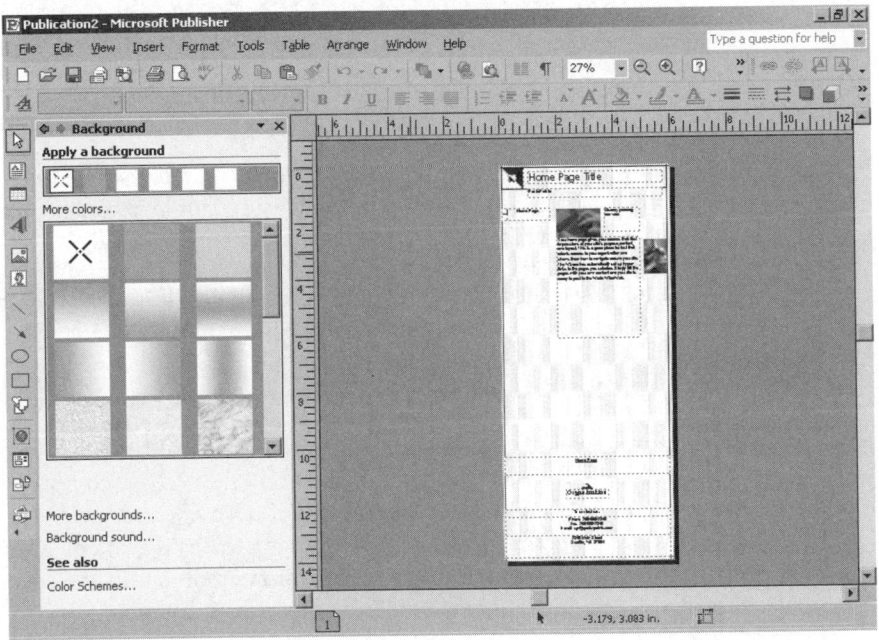

2 In the Background task pane, click Background Sound. The Web Options dialog box appears, as shown on the next page.

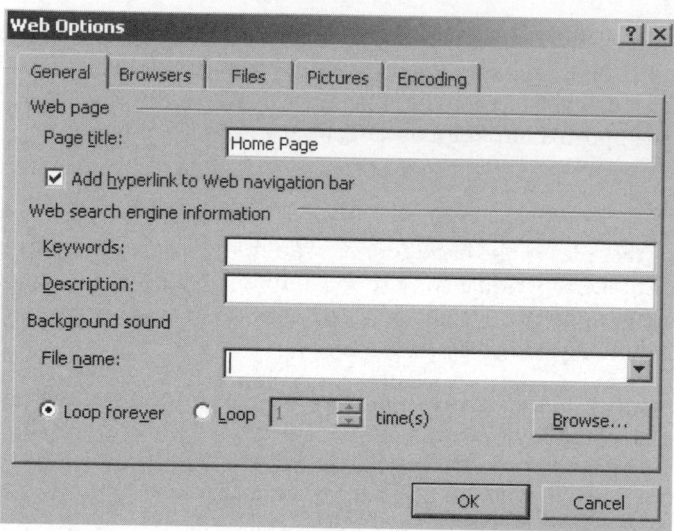

3 In the lower right corner, click Browse, and the Background Sound dialog box appears.

4 Locate the sound file you want to insert, and then double-click it to insert it onto your page.

5 Select whether you want the sound to loop continuously or play a specified number of times. (It's often best not to have sounds loop continuously because this can annoy visitors.) Then click OK in the Web Options dialog box.

You won't be able to hear the sound until you preview it in your browser, which you can do by using the File, Web Page Preview command.

Adding Web Animations

When you want to include dynamic graphics on your Web pages, visit the Clip Organizer, which contains hundreds of animated GIF files. These compressed image files download relatively quickly and can provide movement and variety on your Web pages. However, most readers agree that moving text is impossible to read, and any text is difficult to focus on when there is an animated object in the reader's peripheral vision. Use animation only when it adds to your message.

> **tip** Most multimedia files take longer to download than plain HTML pages. It's good design practice and common Web courtesy to let your readers know the size of the file they're about to download if it's over 50 KB in size, as well as the running time and file format of the file. You can supply this information in parentheses after the hyperlink, which alerts visitors to any potential problems they might have when downloading your multimedia files because they have older software or browser version, a low bandwidth connection, or lack the proper graphics filter.

Chapter 53: Advanced Web Publications

You can find the GIF files displayed here in the Clip Organizer's Web Elements/Animations category:

You can import JPEG (Joint Photographic Experts Group) files into the Clip Organizer from your own files or from the Web. JPEGs are most often used for photographs. You can also import video clips to add an interesting dimension to your site, but use them judiciously. Because they take a long time to download and can require users to install special software to play them, video clips are best used when you're sure your audience needs to see them.

Troubleshooting

Your Animations Won't Play

You've inserted animations from the Clip Organizer or your own files, but they won't run in Web Page Preview or after you publish your Web site.

The following are two possible reasons why your animations won't play:

- If you used the Copy and Paste technique to import the animation files, they often won't run. You must choose Insert, Picture instead.
- If you've rotated an animation, it will be disabled.

Chapter 53

Changing the Background of a Web Page

The Web Site Options task pane contains options for changing the background fill; adding fill effects such as gradients, texture, patterns, pictures, or tints; and modifying the color scheme.

> For more information on fill effects, see Chapter 52, "Creating Professional Brochures and Newsletters."

To modify the background of a Web page, follow these steps:

1 In the Web Site Options task pane, click Background Fill And Sound. The Background task pane appears.

2 Make changes here by pointing to the fill options and then clicking the down arrow on the selection box to apply the effect to one page or all the pages on your site.

3 If Publisher's preformatted backgrounds in the task pane aren't sufficient, click More Backgrounds. The Fill Effects dialog box appears, as seen here:

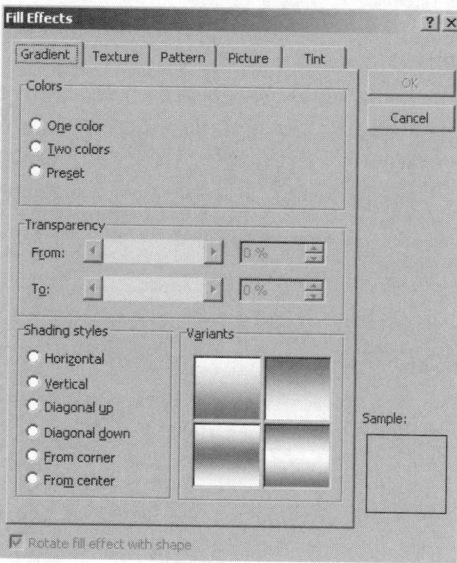

4 Use the options on the Gradient, Texture, Pattern, Picture, or Tint tabs to customize your background.

5 Make sure that you can read your text and hyperlinks against the new background before you apply it. Then click OK to apply it.

If you use large, bitmapped graphics as backgrounds, they take a long time to download. Stick with simple backgrounds, soft colors, and small images.

Writing Page Titles

When your Web pages are coded in HTML, every page is given a title in the page's header section, using a title tag. The title is a short, descriptive line of text that tells readers exactly what they'll find on your page. It's important to create meaningful titles because they are used by search indexes, are saved as bookmarks, and serve as navigational elements for readers moving within your site.

Here are some tips for writing good page titles and headlines:

- Put important words first in the title—recall that Web readers scan print quickly and click away if they don't see keywords early in the text.

- Don't use colons or backslashes in titles—not all operating systems can read these symbols if they're included in a file name.

- Create distinct titles for each page—identical or similar titles confuse readers, particularly when reviewing them in a bookmark or history list.

- Keep titles short so they are fully displayed in most browser windows at most display resolutions—aim for two to six words.

Create pages that can stand alone because those pages could be the only ones on your site that a visitor chooses to see. Place the site title in the upper-left corner of each page (your readers are accustomed to seeing one there), and create a title for each page that falls underneath the site title.

Selecting Keywords

Most people use search engines to find information on the Web. Before you publish your site to the Web, be sure to include searchable keywords that will lead readers to your site when they're searching for that topic. Visit the Web sites of several search engines for guidance on how to select useful keywords to describe the content available on your site. Tips for selecting keywords are the following:

- Use both plural and singular forms of words.

- Vary spelling; people can misspell or use acceptable variations on spelling.

- Combine words into phrases; studies show that people often search by phrases.

In HTML, keywords are contained in meta tags, which you can add to the Head section of your pages.

 **InsideOut**

Using Meta Tags

Often a search engine displays the first paragraph of your Web page in its search results. If you would like to write a short description of your site that appears instead, you can do so using meta tags. Meta tags contain the HTML code that describes specific attributes of your Web page. You can provide clear information to search engines by adding your own description and selection of keywords using the following types of meta tags.

● **Description meta tag**   After the first <HEAD> tag in the code at the top of your page, type <META NAME="description" CONTENT="[add description here]">

● **Keyword meta tag**   <META NAME="keywords" CONTENT="[add keywords here]">

Now search engines automatically display the description and keywords that you've selected to drive visitors to your site.

You can also assign keywords to each Web page by entering them in the Web Site Options dialog box. To do so, follow these steps:

1 Choose Tools, Options.

2 In the Options dialog box, click Web Options. The Web Options dialog box appears.

3 In the General tab of the Web Options dialog box, type keywords and a brief description of your site in the boxes provided.

If you know HTML, you can use the HTML Code Fragment tool on the Objects toolbar to add code. To add HTML code to your pages by using the HTML Code Fragment tool, follow these steps:

1 On the Objects toolbar, click the HTML Code Fragment tool. The HTML Code Fragment Properties dialog box appears, as shown here:

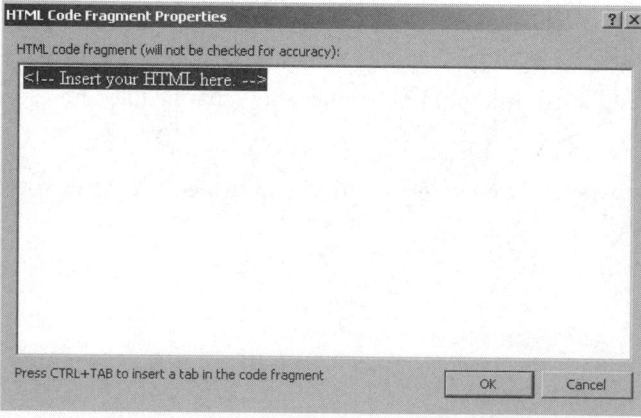

Chapter 53

2 Type your HTML code over the placeholder text.

3 Click OK to insert the code fragment, and then position the frame where you want the code to appear.

The HTML frame appears in Publisher, but when you view it in a Web browser, the code's function appears.

Publishing Web Pages

When you're ready to publish your Web pages, you can transfer the finished product to a Web server, which makes your site available on the Web or on a network that serves your company intranet. Publishing to the Web is accomplished by using a Web folder, a shortcut to place on a Web server where your Web site is available. Contact your Internet service provider or system administrator, and get the address or URL where your folder can be saved.

After you get the URL and any other specific requirements, such as how to name your home page or other file name conventions, you must add a Network Place for your Web site. To publish to a Web folder (if you're using the Microsoft Windows 2000 or Windows Me operating systems), follow these steps:

1 Choose File, Save As. Then click My Network Places, and double-click Add Network Place. The Add Network Place Wizard appears.

2 Click Create A Shortcut To An Existing Network Place, and then click Next.

3 Under Location, type the URL of the Web server or Exchange 2000 server you're using.

4 Under Shortcut Name, type a name for the network place, and then click Next.

5 Continue to follow the wizard's instructions to create the network place.

If you're using Windows 98 or Windows NT, select File, Save As and click Web Folders. Select the folder you want, or type the URL of the new Web Folder.

You can also publish your site to an FTP (File Transfer Protocol) site. You can obtain the necessary information on how to do this from your ISP (Internet Service Provider) or system administrator. To publish to an FTP site, you first have to create the site. You can do this by performing the following steps:

1 Choose File, Save As Web Page.

2 In the Save In box, click FTP Locations.

3 Double-click Add/Modify FTP Locations. The Add/Modify FTP Locations dialog box appears, as shown on the following page.

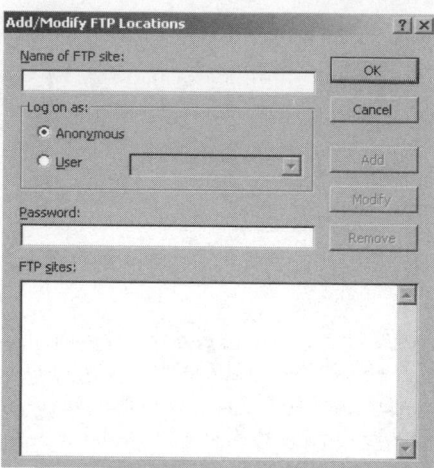

4 Type the information provided by your FTP host, and then click OK.

5 Click Cancel.

Now you can specify the FTP site where you will publish this Web site by following these steps:

1 Choose File, Save As Web Page.

2 In the Save In box, click FTP Locations.

3 Double-click the site you want to use from the list of available FTP sites.

4 Double-click the folder where you want to publish your Web site, and click Save.

You can also publish your Web site to a local folder on your computer. To do that, complete the following steps:

1 Choose File, Save As Web Page. The Save As dialog box appears.

2 Select the folder where you want to publish your Web site, and click OK.

Publishing your site to a Web server or an FTP server makes it available to viewers on the Web. When you save a publication as a Web page, Publisher saves all the text files as HTML files, converts the image files to GIF files, and copies hyperlinked files to the folder you specified. In the folder Publisher creates for your Web site, be sure to include any .exe or .zip files that you've provided for viewers to download.

Part 10

Supercharging Office XP with Macros and VBA

Building Your First Office XP Macro

If you're like most Microsoft Office XP users, much of the work that you do in Office applications can be repetitive. For example, you might always enter a series of headings in Microsoft Word 2002 documents, or routinely increase the width of the first few columns in your Microsoft Excel 2002 worksheets. If these actions take up much of your time, you might consider recording your commands as a macro and then running the macro whenever you need to do the work. A *macro* is a named set of instructions that tells Office XP to perform an action for you. In this chapter, you'll learn what Office macros look like and how you can use them to increase your productivity. You'll also learn how to record, run, and edit macros, and how to use the programming tools in the Microsoft Visual Basic development environment. The last section provides important information about configuring Office to minimize the threat posed by rogue computer viruses.

Carpe Datum: Knowing When to Build a Macro

Office's macro recording capabilities are impressive, but before you seize the data, you should make sure that Office doesn't already provide a built-in solution for your repetitive task. For example, if you routinely boldface your Excel column headings and increase their point size, you could record a macro that automatically formats the headings for you. However, it would actually be faster for you to Choose Format, Style to apply a heading style that accomplishes the same formatting effect. In other words, don't use macros unless the commands that you want to record are involved enough to require a macro.

This certainly doesn't mean that you shouldn't use macros to automate your Office documents. Actually, we're arguing just the opposite. Before you get started, though, it makes sense to take the time to become familiar with the majority of each Office application's features so that you know when Office offers a built-in solution and when to use macros to their greatest effect. The Visual Basic macro language in each Office application is sophisticated enough for many advanced tasks, such as communicating with other Microsoft Windows–based applications or controlling an entire inventory management system. However, the most useful macros are often the ones that automate just four or five simple commands.

Choosing an Office Application

In Office XP, you can record and run macros in three applications: Word, Excel, and PowerPoint. You can also create macros in Microsoft Access 2002, but the process is quite different, and we won't cover it in this book. (Rather than recording a macro, you build one in the Database window by clicking the Macros tab and specifying action arguments on a worksheet grid.)

In Word, Excel, and PowerPoint, you follow the same process to create macros. To record a new macro, choose Tools, Macro, Record New Macro. Run the commands you want to record, and then click Stop. To create a macro from scratch using Visual Basic, open the Visual Basic development environment by choosing Tools, Macro, Visual Basic Editor, and then type the text of the macro in a text editor window and save it to disk.

Because the macro creation process is identical in Word, Excel, and PowerPoint, it doesn't really matter which application you use to practice building Visual Basic macros. We've chosen to show the process in Word because word processing is the most popular activity in the corporate workplace and in many ways Word is the easiest application to understand conceptually. However, after you work through the tutorial sections in Part 10, you should feel free to create macros interchangeably in Word, Excel, and PowerPoint to suit your own needs and interests.

Recording a Macro

Let's start with a simple example. Imagine that you want to insert a standard mailing address for your company into a variety of Word documents. Rather than type the text from scratch each time, or use AutoText, you decide to create a macro that inserts the text automatically when you press the key combination Alt+A. Complete the following steps to record the macro by choosing Tools, Macro, Record New Macro:

1 Open the Word, Excel, or PowerPoint document in which you want to record the macro. If you want to follow these instructions exactly, open a blank Word document now.

2 Choose Tools, Macro, Record New Macro to open the Record Macro dialog box. Your screen should look like this one:

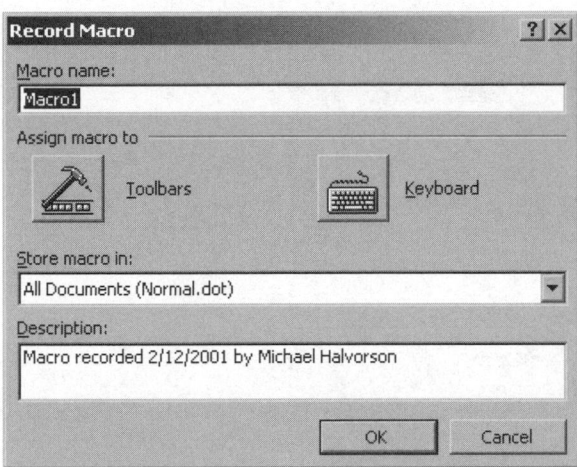

Notice the Store Macro In drop-down list, which prompts you for a place to save the macro. In Word, you can store your macro in the normal document template (Normal.dot), which allows you to run the macro in all Word documents, or you can store your macro in the current document by selecting the document name in the Store Macro In drop-down list. In Excel, you can store the macro in the Personal Macro Workbook (so it's available in all workbooks), or you can store it in the current workbook. In PowerPoint, you can save macros in any open presentation.

3 In the Macro Name text box, type **InsertAddress**, the name of your macro.

4 Click the Keyboard button in the Record Macro dialog box to display the Customize Keyboard dialog box, where you can specify the shortcut key that runs your macro. (In Excel and PowerPoint, you just specify the shortcut key in the Record Macro dialog box.)

note In Word, you can also create a toolbar button or menu command for the macro at this time. To do so, click the Toolbars button in the Record Macro dialog box and specify a custom menu command or toolbar button that will run the macro.

5 Press Alt+A to assign the shortcut key Alt+A to your macro, and then verify that the Save Changes In drop-down list is set to Normal.dot. Your dialog box should look similar to the one on the next page.

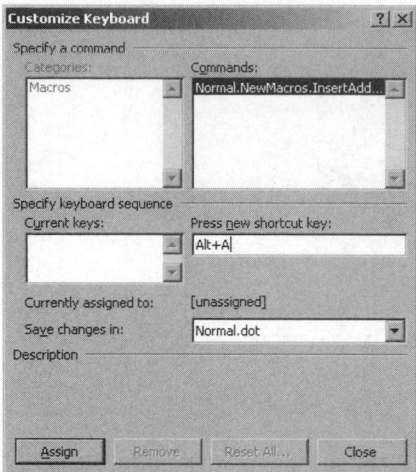

6 In the Customize Keyboard dialog box, click Assign, and then click Close to accept your keyboard shortcut and start recording the macro. Office displays the Stop Recording toolbar, shown here, and changes the mouse pointer to a recording icon:

From this point on, the macro recorder tapes any key you press or any command that you execute in Word.

InsideOut

Options for Macro Recording

The Stop Recording toolbar contains two useful toolbar buttons, Stop Recording and Pause/Resume Recording. When you're finished recording your macro, click the Stop Recording button, and Word stops saving your commands and closes the macro. If you want to pause the recording temporarily, click the Pause Recording button, modify your document as needed, and then click Resume Recorder when you're ready to continue.

7 Type the following address (or one of your own) in the active Word document, and then press Enter:

Outdoor Clothing Supply
1219 Hill Garden Drive
San Francisco, CA 94555
(415) 555-5555

8 Click Stop Recording to end your macro.

1466

That's all there is to it! Now that you have recorded your first macro, run it in your Word document to verify that it displays the address as you specified.

Running a Macro

To give you flexibility in automating your work, Office XP provides you with five methods for running your macros. You can do any of the following options:

● Choose Tools, Macro, Macros, and then double-click the macro name in the Macro dialog box.

● Press a macro shortcut key (if you have assigned one).

● Choose the macro from a menu (if you added the macro name to a menu).

● Click a custom macro button on a toolbar (if you assigned the macro to a toolbar button).

● Start the Visual Basic Editor, and run the macro inside the Visual Basic development environment.

Using the Macros Dialog Box

To run a macro using the Macros dialog box, follow these steps:

1 Press Enter to add a blank line to your document.

2 Choose Tools, Macro, and then click Macros. You'll see the following dialog box:

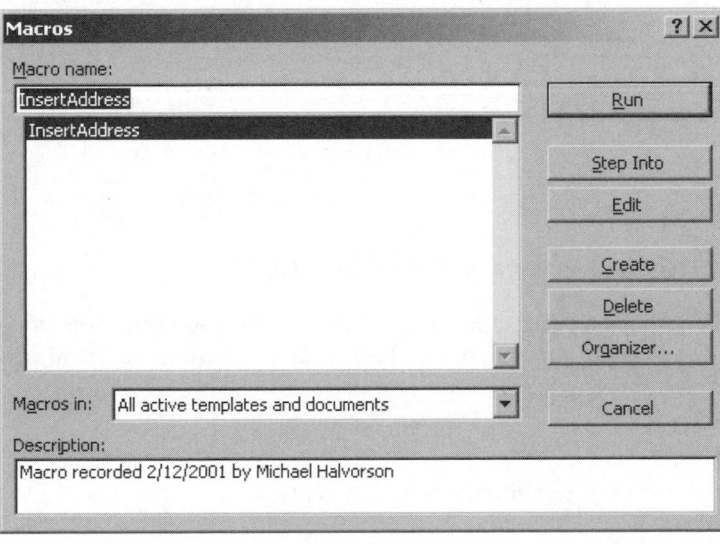

Chapter 54

The Macros dialog box is a comprehensive tool for managing macros. Using the Macros dialog box, you can run, debug (step into), edit, record (create), delete, and organize macros.

> **note** Because the Macros dialog box is so useful, you might want to memorize the keyboard shortcut for opening it (Alt+F8).

3 In the Macros In drop-down list, specify the location of the macro you want to run. By default, the macros in all your active (open) Word templates and documents are listed, but you can also list the macros in a specific template or document by picking a name from the Macros In list box.

4 Finally, in the Macro Name list box, double-click the macro you want to run. If you double-click the InsertAddress macro, your company address text is inserted into the current document, as shown here:

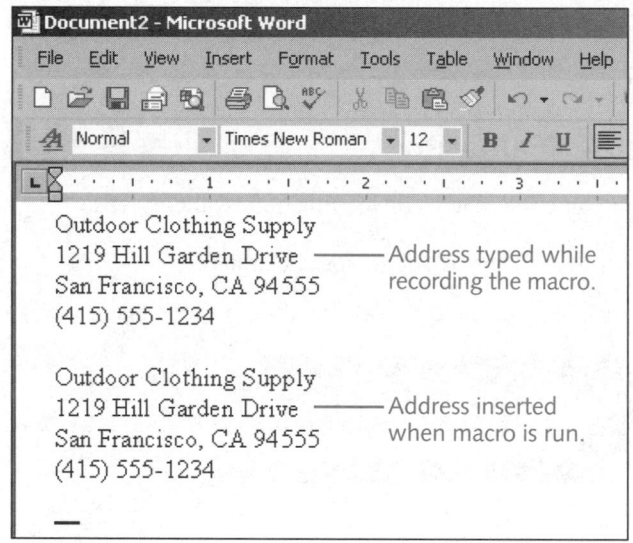

Using a Shortcut Key to Run Macros

If you assigned a shortcut key to your macro when you created it, you can also run it in Word by pressing the designated shortcut key. To run the InsertAddress macro using the Alt+A shortcut key, follow these steps:

1 Press Enter to add a blank line to your document.

2 Press Alt+A to run the InsertAddress macro.

Word runs the macro and inserts your company address in the current document. That's all there is to it!

Troubleshooting

Reversing the Effects of an Office Macro

You've run a macro in an Office application, but now you want to undo it.

When you run standard menu commands in Office applications, you can reverse them with the Edit menu's Undo command. But when you run an Office macro, you can't use Undo to reverse its effects in just one step. This creates a potential problem—how do you undo a macro that has produced unwanted results?

The solution is to use the Undo drop-down list on the Standard toolbar, which lets you undo more than one Office command at once. Office records each action a macro completes individually and displays them in the Undo drop-down list. You can reverse the effects of a macro by clicking the Undo drop-down list on the Standard toolbar and then selecting all the commands in the macro you want to undo. If you didn't create the macro yourself, you may need to study the commands in the Undo list box carefully—sometimes it can be difficult to determine which command was the first one in the macro.

Using Visual Basic to Edit a Macro

In Office XP, you can edit your recorded macros and create new macros from scratch by using the Visual Basic development environment, a special utility that has its own windows, menus, and programming tools. Word, Excel, PowerPoint, and Access all include this program, although in Access you can't use it to edit recorded macros. In this section, you'll learn how to use the Visual Basic development environment (also called the Visual Basic Editor) to edit the InsertAddress macro. Feel free to experiment a little in this section—the skills you learn will come in handy each time you work with macros.

To edit your InsertAddress macro using Visual Basic, perform the following steps:

1 Choose Tools, Macro, Macros. You'll see the Macros dialog box, which lists the InsertAddress macro in the Macro Name list box.

2 Click the InsertAddress macro, and then in the Macros dialog box click Edit. The Visual Basic development environment starts, as shown in Figure 54-1, on page 1470.

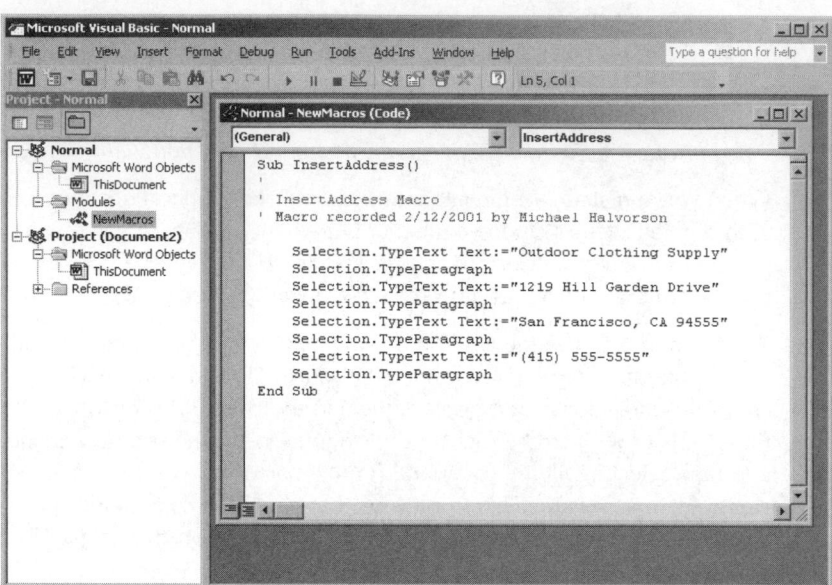

Figure 54-1. The Visual Basic development environment allows you to create new macros and modify existing ones.

The Visual Basic development environment (Visual Basic, for short) includes a variety of programming tools to help you write, edit, test, and manage your Word macros. The most important tools to identify now are the Project Explorer window, the Properties window, and the Code window. (We'll discuss each in this chapter.) You might see these tools in a slightly different arrangement on your screen if someone else has used your computer or if your setup options were different than ours.

The Code window is a large text-editing window that displays the contents of your Office macro in a programming language called Visual Basic. Each program statement in this macro follows a particular programming rule, and the trick to learning macro programming in Office is understanding the syntax principles and program logic behind each of the Visual Basic statements.

> **note** Another name for the exact spelling, order, and spacing of keywords in a macro is statement *syntax*.

The macro is stored in a special program code container called a *subroutine*, which is part of the more comprehensive container called a *module*. This particular subroutine is called InsertAddress, and it is delimited (or enclosed as a block of macro text) by the Sub and End Sub statements, respectively. Within the body of the subroutine, you'll see descriptive comments, which appear in green type, and the Visual Basic program statements that do the work of the macro, which appear in black type. In this macro, the Sub and End Sub statements appear in blue type, because they are special reserved words in the Visual Basic programming language called *keywords*.

To add a descriptive comment to the macro and edit the business phone number, perform the following steps:

1 Press the Down arrow key three times, and then press the Right arrow key once to move the insertion point after the fourth single quotation mark in the macro. (You can also use the mouse to move the insertion point if you prefer.)

2 Press Spacebar once, type **My first macro**, and press Enter.

Visual Basic inserts your new comment and displays it in green type. Comments are for documentation purposes only, and are not used by the macro when it runs. You should use comments as informal notes about how your macro works if you plan to share your macro with friends and work associates. (Comments are especially useful when you write complicated program statements.) Your Code window should look like this illustration:

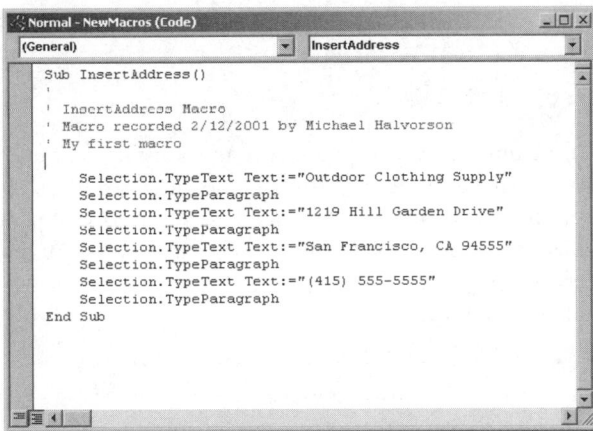

3 Now move the insertion point to the program statement containing the phone number you entered, and change the last four digits to **1234**. Your Code window should look like this:

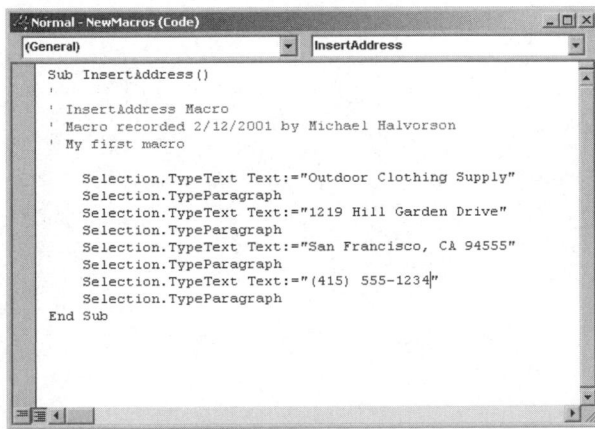

1471

This simple edit changes the content of your macro each time you run it. Although we're not focusing on the exact details of the Visual Basic program statements right now, you might find it interesting to know what the words *Selection* and *TypeText* are doing in the program code. Selection is an *object*, or a component of the current document or application that can be programmatically controlled. The Selection object designates a particular location in your document for action—either the text block that is highlighted or the current insertion point. TypeText is a *method*, or a command that can be executed using the specified object. When the TypeText method is used with the Selection object, Word inserts the text specified at the current insertion point—exactly what your InsertAddress macro does when you run it!

You're finished editing the InsertAddress macro for now. In the next section, you'll run the macro again and save your changes to disk.

Learning the Visual Basic Programming Tools

The Visual Basic development environment contains a number of useful programming tools to help you construct and manage your macros in Word, Excel, PowerPoint, and Access. In this section, you'll learn how to use the most important programming tools and how to organize them using a technique called *docking*. As you work through the remaining chapters of this part, you'll gain additional experience with the tools by constructing practical, working macros.

> **note** If you're not interested in all the details about programming tools right now, just skim this section and move on to the next chapter. You can use this information later as reference material.

The essential Visual Basic tools include:

- Menu bar
- Toolbars
- Project Explorer
- Properties window
- Online Help system

Using the Menu Bar

The menu bar in the Visual Basic development environment contains commands that are specifically designed to edit and manage your macros. These commands are identical in Word, Excel, PowerPoint, and Access. Table 54-1 describes the functionality of the menus.

Table 54-1. Menus in the Visual Basic Development Environment

Menu Name	Purpose
File	Saves macros, imports and exports useful routines, removes macros, and prints the contents of the Code window.
Edit	Edits and searches for text in the Code window, formats code, and displays information about available properties, methods, and constants.
View	Displays the various tools in the development environment.
Insert	Extends your macro by adding new objects and features. Specifies a new code procedure, a custom dialog box (UserForm), a module, or a supporting file.
Format	Formats the objects and text in a custom UserForm dialog box.
Debug	Detects and fixes bugs (defects) in your macros.
Run	Executes your macros. A special command, Break, is useful for debugging.
Tools	Customizes your macro by providing references to other object libraries and controls, text formatting options in the Code window, and property settings. The Macros command is identical to the Macros command on your Office application's Tools menu.
Add-Ins	Runs add-in commands and uses the Add-In Manager dialog box.
Window	Adjusts the size and orientation of windows in the development environment and switches between open documents.
Help	Displays online Help and connects to frequently used Visual Basic Web sites.

To run the InsertAddress macro using the Run Sub/UserForm command, perform the following steps:

1 Choose Run, Run Sub/UserForm. Word runs your macro again in the current document.

Because the InsertAddress macro has no visible user interface, you won't see it run in the Visual Basic development environment. You'll need to restore the document using the Windows taskbar to see the results.

2 Click the Microsoft Word program icon on the Windows taskbar. Windows restores Word and displays the current document.

3 Verify that the InsertAddress macro correctly displayed your address text. If you've followed all the examples in this chapter, you should see four addresses, and the last one should have a new phone number.

4 When you're ready to return to Visual Basic, click the Microsoft Visual Basic program icon on the Windows taskbar.

Run the macro again if you like, and take some time to experiment with other menus and commands.

Using the Visual Basic Toolbars

The Visual Basic toolbars provide rapid access to the most common commands and procedures in the Visual Basic development environment. By default, only the Standard toolbar appears, but you can add special-purpose Visual Basic toolbars by choosing View, Toolbars. Figure 54-2 shows the purpose of the buttons and controls on the Standard Visual Basic toolbar.

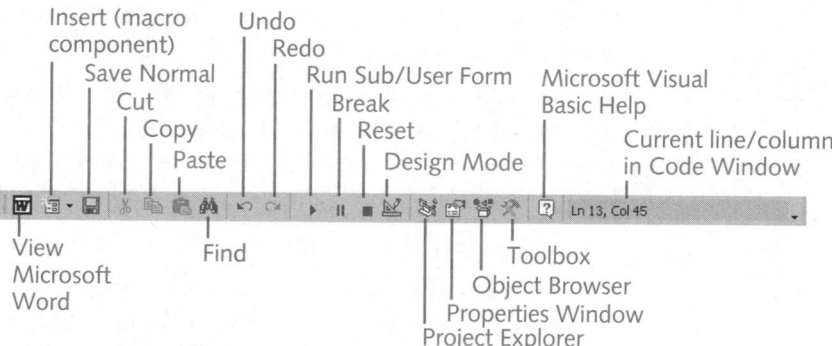

Figure 54-2. The Standard toolbar is the fastest way to issue commands in the Visual Basic development environment.

Using the Save Button to Save Your Changes

Save

After you modify a macro in the Visual Basic development environment, it makes good sense to save your changes to prevent accidental data loss because of a power failure or system crash. To save your macro, click the Save button on the Standard Visual Basic toolbar.

Visual Basic saves your macro to disk. If you have been following the instructions in this chapter, this action saves the InsertAddress macro to the Normal.dot template.

> **tip** **Save Macros by Using the Toolbar**
>
> The Save button on the Standard toolbar saves changes to the component that's currently highlighted in Project Explorer. To see the name of the file that Visual Basic will use when it saves, hold the mouse pointer over the Save button until a ScreenTip appears identifying the current filename.

Using Project Explorer

Project
Explorer

The Visual Basic Project Explorer is an organizational tool that displays a hierarchical list of the documents, or *projects*, currently open in your Office application, along with their supporting components. Using Project Explorer, you can add or delete components from a project, compare elements and reorganize them, and display items of interest. If the Project Explorer window isn't visible, you can display it by choosing View, Project Explorer, or by clicking the Project Explorer toolbar button.

When you first start using Project Explorer, you might find its assortment of folders and components a bit confusing, but stick with it. Project Explorer is a useful programming tool, and its secrets can be readily comprehended. Each project name corresponds to a document or template that's currently open in your application. In the Project Explorer window shown in Figure 54-3, the Normal.dot template and the Document2.doc document files are shown, along with their supporting component files. (If you've been following the examples to this point, these are the files you'll see.) You'll see additional projects in your Project Explorer window if you have other documents open, or if Microsoft Outlook is running and Word is your e-mail editor.

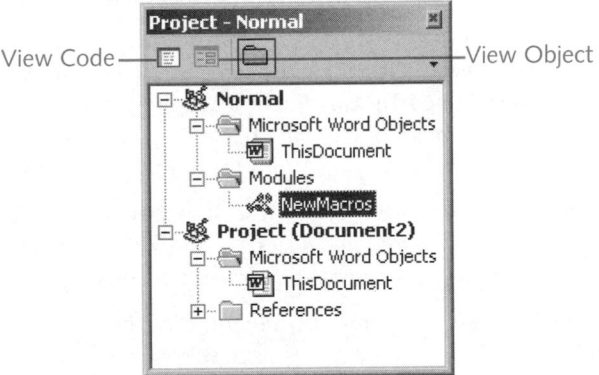

Figure 54-3. The Project Explorer window allows you to manage the components of a Visual Basic macro.

When you use Visual Basic, you can customize several different components of an Office document or template. As we demonstrated earlier in the chapter, you can

1475

record a macro and store it in a module that becomes part of the document or template. However, you can also add one or more of the following items to your project:

● Word objects, such as additional Word documents

● Standard modules, which contain macros and other useful program code

● Custom dialog boxes, called UserForms

● Class modules, which define objects and the methods and properties used to control them

● References to commands and objects in other Windows applications

Project Explorer keeps track of all these different components and provides access to them via two special buttons: View Code and View Object. To switch from one component to the next, click the project you want to work with, click the folder you want to open, and then click the component you want to view. If the component contains program code (such as a module or a UserForm), you can examine it by clicking the View Code button. If the component contains a user interface (such as a Word document or a UserForm), you can examine it by clicking the View Object button.

To use Project Explorer to examine the user interface for the sample document Document2.doc, perform the following steps:

1 Click the Project Explorer button on the toolbar.

The Project Explorer window is highlighted in the programming environment. If the window was not open, it appears now. You'll see a Project Explorer window.

2 Click the plus sign (+) next to your sample document, Project (Document2) in this example, to view all the project's components if they are not already visible. You'll see a folder named Microsoft Word Objects and a folder named References.

3 Double-click the Microsoft Word Objects folder to open it if it is not visible, and then select the object named ThisDocument. Each project you work with that is based on a Word document or template has a ThisDocument entry, which you can use to customize how your Word file opens and closes.

View
Object

4 To view the sample document's user interface, click the View Object button in the Project Explorer window. Word minimizes the Visual Basic development environment and displays the sample document (Document2).

5 When you're finished viewing the sample document, click the Microsoft Visual Basic icon on the Windows taskbar to return to Visual Basic.

6 Click the NewMacros module in the Normal project to switch back to the project that contains your InsertAddress macro.

7 Click the View Code button in the Project Explorer window to display the program code for your macro in the Code window, if it isn't visible.

  View Code

Using the Properties Window

The Properties window lets you change the characteristics, or *property settings*, of the Word objects, modules, and UserForms in your projects. A property setting is a quality of one of the components in your macro. For example, the Name property of the module in the Normal project that contains your InsertAddress macro is currently NewMacros. (Whenever you record a macro and place it in the Normal template, Word automatically places it in the NewMacros module.) If you'd like to change the name of this module to reflect its new contents, you can change it using the Properties window.

Inside the Properties window, you'll find an object drop-down list, which you can use to switch between objects in the active project component. This is especially useful when the component you're working with contains multiple objects, such as a UserForm dialog box.

The main part of the Properties window is a two-tabbed properties list with scroll bars, which contains property settings that you can modify while your macro is being built (a construction phase programmers call *design time*). In the Properties window, you can view property settings alphabetically or by category. As you'll learn in the next chapter, properties can also be set while your macro is running (at *run time*) if you modify property settings appropriately using program code.

Take a moment now to change the Name property setting for the NewMacros module in the Normal template. By changing this setting from NewMacros to InsertAddress, you can clearly identify the contents of your address macro later, and your NewMacros module won't become too unwieldy. (You can keep all your macros in the NewMacros module if you like, but we recommend that you save at least some of them in separate modules.) To change the Name property setting for the NewMacros module, perform the following steps:

1 Verify that the NewMacros module is selected in the Normal project.

2 Click the Properties Window button on the toolbar.

Properties Window

The Properties window is highlighted in the programming environment. (If the Properties window wasn't open, it appears now.) Your Properties window should look similar to this example:

The Properties window lists only one property for the NewMacros module, the Name property. Later you'll work with objects that contain dozens of property settings, but for now you can use this simpler form.

3 Double-click the NewMacros name in the Properties window, and press Delete to erase the current property setting.

4 Type **InsertAddress**, and then press Enter.

The setting of the Name property changes from NewMacros to InsertAddress, and the new name appears in the Properties window and in the Modules folder in Project Explorer.

Moving, Docking, and Resizing Tools

When you have the Project Explorer window, the Properties window, and several other programming tools to contend with on the screen, the Visual Basic development environment can become a pretty busy place. To give you complete control over the shape and size of the elements in the development environment, Office XP gives you the ability to move, dock, and resize each of the programming tools.

To move a window, the toolbox, or the toolbar, simply click the title bar and drag the object to a new location. If you align one window to the edge of another window, it attaches itself to the window, or *docks*. Dockable windows are advantageous because they always remain visible and they have similar characteristics to the toolbars and menus in Office applications. (They won't become hidden behind other windows.)

If you want to see more of a docked window, simply drag one of the borders to see more content. If you get tired of docking and want your tools to overlap each other, choose Tools, Options, click the Docking tab, and then clear the check mark from each tool you want to stand on its own.

As you work through the following chapters, practice moving, docking, and resizing the different tools in the Visual Basic development environment until you feel comfortable with them.

Using the Help System

The Visual Basic development environment comes with its own Help system that describes how to use the Visual Basic tools and how to write macros in each Office application. To access the complete Help system, you need to specify Visual Basic Help for each application when you run Setup because these files aren't included in the standard installation of Office XP. If you didn't specifically include these files, run Setup again now to install the necessary material.

You may also be able to install these files using Office's install-on-demand feature, which (if enabled) starts Setup automatically the first time you request Visual Basic Help and prompts you for the necessary Setup disc.

As you learned in Chapter 2, "Installing and Configuring Office XP," install-on-demand is a special Setup option that conserves hard disk space, but you can't tell if it is active until you try to run the command.

To use the Visual Basic Help resources, perform the following steps:

1 If the Visual Basic development environment is not already running, open it now by choosing Tools, Macros, Visual Basic Editor.

2 Choose Help, Microsoft Visual Basic Help.

3 If the Help files are missing, you'll have the opportunity to install them now by using the Office Setup program. Click Install Help Files and place the required disc (typically Office XP CD 1) in your CD-ROM drive.

4 In the Office Assistant dialog box, type the Visual Basic concept, task, or keyword that you would like additional information about. The Office Assistant presents you with one or more dialog boxes of information about the topic you requested.

Exiting Visual Basic

When you're finished working on a Visual Basic macro, you have two options: You can minimize the Visual Basic development environment and return to your Office application, or you can exit Visual Basic and return to your application. Unless you plan to edit another macro soon, you don't need to leave Visual Basic running. If you want to use it again, you can easily restart it using the Macros dialog box.

To minimize Visual Basic and return to Office, click the Minimize button on the Visual Basic title bar. Visual Basic appears as an icon on the Windows taskbar, and Word reappears in a window.

To exit Visual Basic and return to Office, click the Close button on the Visual Basic title bar. Visual Basic exits, and Word reappears in a window.

note The keyboard shortcut for exiting Visual Basic and returning to your Office application is Alt+Q.

Setting Macro Security

If you have been using computers for a while, you've probably heard about the potential threat created by computer viruses. A *virus* is a hidden macro or software program that works behind the scenes to annoy computer users and (in the most extreme circumstances) to destroy important data files and application software. Viruses don't just appear on computers—they are transmitted from one machine to another via computer networks, the Internet, diskettes, or other media. The transmission or infection

Chapter 54

process is usually silent and painless (at first): The nasty software developers who create viruses build the programs so that they attach themselves in hidden ways to files, folders, and application documents.

Because most of the applications in the Microsoft Office XP software suite have the ability to record and run macros, it is possible that a rogue software developer will try to pass along a hidden macro virus to you in an Office document such as an innocent-looking Word document or Excel workbook. Although you shouldn't lose sleep over this potential danger, you should be aware of the threat that viruses pose and practice safe computing by using only documents that come from authorized or known sources. To help simplify the process, Office XP provides a special Security command on the Macro submenu that works to detect macros originating from unsafe (or at least unrecognized) sources. If you are concerned about the threat posed to your data by computer viruses, you might want to use this command to further protect your system.

To use the Security command to seek protection from unsafe macros in Word, Excel, or PowerPoint, follow these steps:

1 Choose Tools, Macro, Security. The Security dialog box opens and contains two tabs, as shown here, Security Level and Trusted Sources:

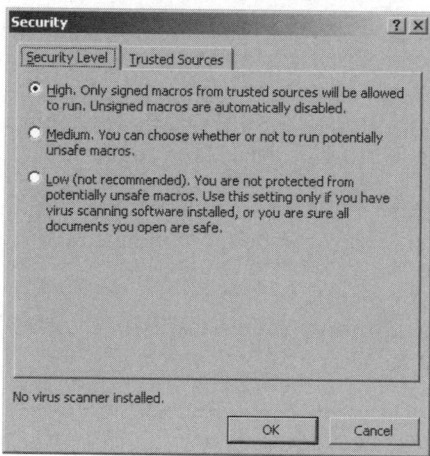

The Security Level tab is pretty self-explanatory. You are given three security options against macro viruses in documents you open in this application: High, Medium, and Low. The High option allows only signed macros to run in documents that you open, an indication that the software developer who developed the macro has created a digital signature that features his or her name and other pertinent information. This doesn't stop those macros from doing bad things to your computer, but the principle is that if a developer is fully known and registered, he won't develop malicious macros in the first place.

The Medium option asks this Office application to display a dialog box each time a document is opened that contains macros. You're then given the choice to enable those macros or not. This option is useful because it allows you to run macros that come from friends or trusted sources, but to disable mystery macros that you download in documents from the Internet. When you select the Medium option, a dialog box like the following appears when you open a document containing macros:

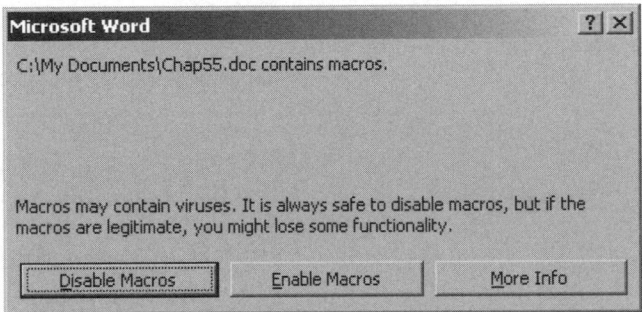

Finally, the Low option directs your application to run all macros in documents without warning you in any way. This option is fine if you know for certain that all of the documents you open will be okay, or if you are developing several Visual Basic macros and don't want to be bothered with warning messages from your own macro routines. However, be aware that some rogue macros have the ability to start themselves automatically, so don't think that you can safely open any document just because you don't run the macros. In a worst-case scenario, these macros could delete files on your hard disk, send out e-mail messages from your account, or subtly corrupt important business documents.

2 Click the Security Level option that you feel comfortable with. We recommend that you choose the Medium option.

3 Click the Trusted Sources tab to learn more about the macros on your system that are identified with digital signatures. This tab comes with a handy Remove button, so you can remove any vendor from the list that you don't trust.

In the Trusted Sources dialog box, you'll also see a new check box that has been designed to disable most of the dangerous macros that were written before June 2000. The feature is named Trust Access To Visual Basic Project, and except under very unusual configurations, this check box should be left empty at all times. Do not place a check mark in the Trust Access To Visual Basic Project dialog box unless you are instructed to do so by your system administrator or a trusted software publisher. This feature attempts to break the replication method of most Visual Basic macro viruses by limiting access to the VBProject and VBE objects—internal libraries in Office XP that rogue macros have used to corrupt system files in the past. In rare situations (for example, if an add-in you are using depends on VBProject or VBE), you may need to check this box, but don't do so unless you are told to by a "trusted" person. This new feature alone prevents many rogue macros from damaging your system, and you want to make sure that the default setting (no check mark) is selected.

4 When you're finished setting macro security, click OK to close the Security dialog box. Office XP enforces your security wishes in this application until you update this dialog box in the future.

Troubleshooting

You Want to Enable Macro Security in All Office Applications, Not Just One

When you choose Tools, Macro, Security, the macro security settings you select take effect only in the Office application you are currently using, but you want them to apply to all of your applications.

To make all of your applications safe from rogue viruses, configure macro security settings individually in Word, Excel, and PowerPoint. This will enforce security measures consistently across all three applications. If you like, you can set different security options for each application, too—you don't need just one setting. In addition, you'll find a more comprehensive database security system in Access, with several commands and options that you can set by choosing Tools, Security. The design of Office XP gives you the flexibility to set macro security differently for each application, but you need to remember to configure each one individually if you don't want to use the default security level.

Using Variables, Operators, and Functions to Manage Information

What are the mysterious commands that make Microsoft Office XP macros run? In this chapter, you'll learn about many of the Microsoft Visual Basic program statements that collectively constitute a macro. You'll learn how to use special values called constants to execute Office commands, and how to use storage containers called variables to store data temporarily in your macro. You'll also learn how to use Visual Basic functions to transfer information back and forth between Office documents, and how to use mathematical operators to perform tasks such as addition and multiplication. With this essential grounding in program syntax, you'll be ready to tackle more sophisticated Office management tasks.

Reading a Visual Basic Program Statement

As you learned in Chapter 54, "Building Your First Office XP Macro," the last chapter, a line of code in a Visual Basic program is called a *program statement*. A program statement is any combination of Visual Basic keywords, objects, properties, methods, functions, operators, and symbols that collectively create a valid instruction recognized by the Office macro interpreter. A complete program statement can be a simple keyword such as *Beep* that sounds a note from your computer's speaker, or it can be a combination of elements, such as the Microsoft Word 2002 program statement shown in Figure 55-1, which uses the TypeText method of the Selection object to insert the text *Outdoor Clothing Supply* into the current document.

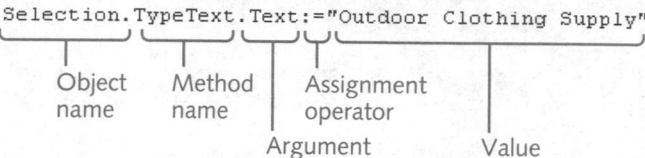

Figure 55-1. This figure shows an example of a typical Microsoft Word Visual Basic program statement.

The rules of construction that you must use when you build a program statement are called *statement syntax*. Office Visual Basic (also called Visual Basic for Applications, or VBA) shares many of its syntax rules with earlier versions of the Basic programming language and with other language compilers. The trick to writing good program statements is learning the syntax of the most useful language elements and then using those elements correctly, in conjunction with programming constructs called objects, properties, and methods, to manage Office's features.

What Is an Object?

Objects are the fundamental building blocks of Visual Basic; nearly everything you do in Visual Basic involves modifying objects. When you write Visual Basic macros for Office, your first task is to learn about the objects Office uses to represent its commands and features. For example, in Word the current, open document is stored in the Document object, and each document contains a Paragraph object corresponding to each paragraph.

A *collection* is an object that contains several other objects, usually of the same type. For example, the Documents object contains all the documents that are currently open in Word, and the Paragraphs object contains all the paragraphs in the current document or selection, as illustrated in Figure 55-2. By using properties and methods, you can modify a single object or an entire collection of objects.

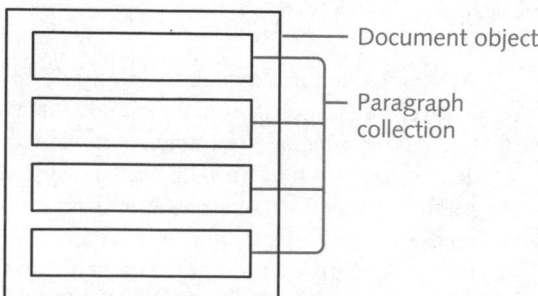

Figure 55-2. This illustration shows a Document object and its Paragraph collection.

What Are Properties and Methods?

Properties and *methods* are special keywords you use to manipulate Visual Basic objects. Using a bicycle metaphor, properties are attributes like the color or style of a bicycle (mountain bike, touring, or tandem), and methods are the actions a bicycle can perform (pedaling, jumping, or coasting). Some more specific examples follow.

Properties Are Attributes

A *property* is an attribute of an object or an aspect of its behavior. For example, the properties of a document include its name, its content, its save status, and which windows are currently open to view it. To change the characteristics of an object, you change the values of its properties.

Here's how it works. To set the value of a property, write a program statement that contains the following elements, in this order: a reference to one or more objects, each followed by a period; the property name; an equals sign; and the new property value. For example, this program statement uses the SplitSpecial property to open a separate pane in the active window to display all the footnotes in a document:

```
ActiveWindow.View.SplitSpecial = wdPaneFootnotes
```

In this case, both ActiveWindow and View are objects. (The View object is contained in the ActiveWindow object.) SplitSpecial is a property that can be assigned one of 18 values associated with split windows. In this example, the value we assigned to SplitSpecial is a constant named wdPaneFootnotes, a special value used to identify footnotes in Word's object library. (You'll learn more about properties and constants in the next section.)

Methods Perform Actions

A *method* is an action that an object can perform. For example, you can use the Save method to save all the open documents in Word by writing the following program statement:

```
Documents.Save
```

In most cases, methods are actions and properties are characteristics. Using a method causes something to happen to an object, whereas using a property returns information about the object or causes a quality of the object to change.

Learning More About the Office Object Model

Each chapter in Part 10 explores a new aspect of the Office object model, so you'll be getting lots of practice using objects, properties, and methods to streamline your document management tasks. However, you can also learn about the object model for each Office application on your own by using the features discussed in the following sections.

The Interactive Object Chart

If you use the Word Visual Basic Office Assistant to search for "Microsoft Word Objects" in the online Help (be sure you are in the Visual Basic editor), Word displays an interactive chart that you can use to explore the programmable objects in Word. When you click an object in the chart, Word displays an online Help file that describes how you use the object in Visual Basic code. (The process is similar for each Office application.)

Object Browser

The Visual Basic Editor includes a tool called the Object Browser that lets you display the properties and methods associated with all the objects in your system, including those supported by Office applications.

Microsoft Visual Basic Online Help

Office lists each object, property, and method in its online Visual Basic Help file for each application. You can access these Help topics by clicking the Office Assistant in the Visual Basic development environment. You can also press F1 while in the Object Browser or the Code window.

Code Window Auto List Feature

When you type the name of an Office application object and a period in the Code window, the Visual Basic Editor automatically lists all the properties and methods that you can use with the object. For example, if you type **ActiveDocument** and a period, a drop-down list of all the methods and properties associated with the ActiveDocument object appears. To specify one of the elements in your program code, simply click the desired method or property, and the element is appended to the statement.

In the following chapters, you'll learn more about using Office objects, properties, and methods in program statements. First, you'll learn how to assign values to properties by using Office constants.

Using Office Constants

A common characteristic of many Word macros is a program statement that changes the structure of a document or a command option in the word processor itself. For example, you might choose to change the line spacing in a particular paragraph to double space, or you might change Word's document view to Page Layout view. To make such a change in a Visual Basic macro, you need to use a *constant* in your program statement, a special value supplied by Office to adjust settings in each Office application.

True to its name, a constant is a named value that doesn't change while your macro runs. It replaces a number or word in your macro with a coded label that you can easily remember. You can create your own constants to store information, as you'll learn later in this chapter, but the most useful constants are special values called *intrinsic constants* that Office applications define in object libraries for your use.

For example, to change Word's document view to Print Layout, you could use the wdPrintView constant, as shown in the following program statement:

```
ActiveWindow.View.Type = wdPrintView
```

This example contains the following elements:

- The ActiveWindow object, which represents the current, open window in Word

- The View property, which returns an object representing the active view in the active window

- The Type property, which sets the document view type for the window (options include Normal, Online Layout, Page Layout, Master, or Outline)

- The wdPrintView Word constant, which sets the view to Print Layout view (other useful constants include wdNormalView, wdWebView, wdMasterView, wdPrintPreview and wdOutlineView)

InsideOut

Prefixes Identify the Object Library

The letters *wd* at the beginning of the wdPrintView constant identify it as an intrinsic constant in the Microsoft Word object library. The Word object library is a special file declaring objects, properties, methods, and constants that is automatically included in Word macros. Constants in the Word object library actually represent simple numbers; for example, wdPrintView contains the number 3. However, when you write Word macros, you'll find the constant names much easier to remember.

Other Office applications have their own constant prefixes and object libraries, including *xl* (Microsoft Excel object library), *ac* (Microsoft Access object library), and *vb* (VBA object library).

Using Constants to Create Custom Formatting

Take a moment now to try a simple example using Word constants. In this exercise, you'll create a macro, called CenterHeading, which uses Word constants to format selected text in a document with shading, border formatting, and center alignment.

You'll also learn how to type in a new macro from scratch using the Visual Basic Editor, a technique you'll return to often in Part 10.

 The CenterHeading macro is stored in the Chap55 document on the companion CD to this book.

To create the CenterHeading macro, follow these steps:

1 Start Word and open a new, blank document. In this exercise, you'll create the CenterHeading macro in a new document file, not in the Normal.dot template.

2 Choose Tools, Macro, Macros. Word opens the Macros dialog box, where you create and run Visual Basic macros.

3 Type **CenterHeading** in the Name text box, and then click the Macros In drop-down list and select your new, blank document in the list. (In this example, the new document is named Document2.)

4 Click Create.

Word starts the Visual Basic Editor and opens a new macro procedure named CenterHeading in the Code window. When you create a new macro from scratch, use the Code window to type in the program statements that make up the macro. You enter your code between the Sub and End Sub statements, which mark the beginning and ending of the macro, respectively.

5 Begin your macro now by typing the object name **Selection** followed by a period.

When you type a period after an object name that the Visual Basic Editor recognizes, a drop-down list appears containing a list of the objects, properties, and methods that are compatible with it, as shown here:

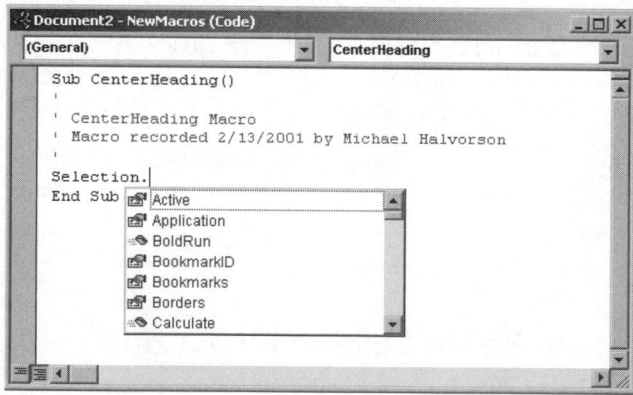

Each of the program statements in this macro begins with the Selection object, because you are formatting selected text in your Word document.

6 Scroll down the drop-down list and double-click the Shading property. Type a period to display a second drop-down list, as seen here:

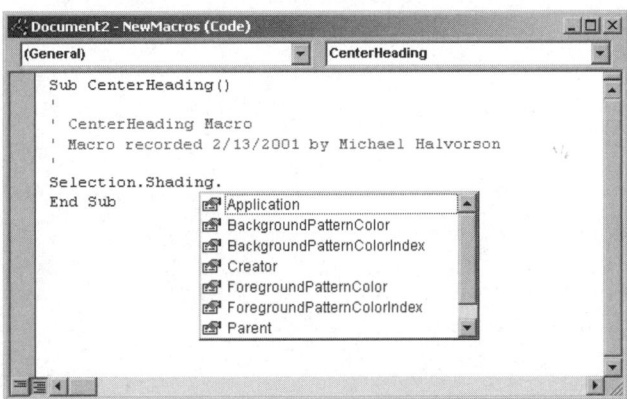

7 Double-click the Texture property in the list box to build a program statement that adjusts the shading formatting of the selected text in your document. The Visual Basic Editor displays the expression *Selection.Shading.Texture* in the Code window.

8 Finish your program statement by typing an equals sign (=), double-clicking the wdTexture10Percent constant in the drop-down list, and pressing Enter.

Congratulations! You have now completed your first program statement, a command that adds 10 percent background shading to the selected text in your Word document.

9 Complete your macro by entering the following three program statements. You can either use the drop-down lists to pick objects, properties, and constants (as you did earlier), or you can type the program statements directly into the Code window.

```
Selection.Borders(wdBorderBottom).LineStyle = wdLineStyleSingle
Selection.Borders(wdBorderBottom).LineWidth = wdLineWidth150pt
Selection.ParagraphFormat.Alignment = wdAlignParagraphCenter
```

The first two program statements, which use the Borders property, format the selected paragraph using a single underline border that is 1.5 points wide when you run the macro. Notice that two Word constants are used in each program statement, a constant that identifies which border is being formatted (wdBorderBottom), and a constant that selects the formatting options you have chosen (wdLineStyleSingle and wdLineWidth150pt). The final program statement uses the ParagraphFormat property to set the paragraph alignment of the selected paragraph to center alignment. The result is a window that looks like the following:

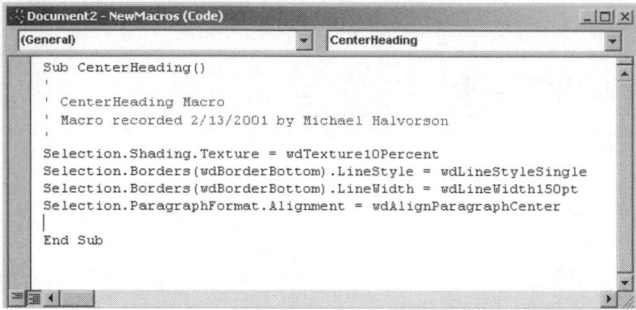

To run the CenterHeading macro in your Word document and create the custom formatting effect, follow these steps:

1 Click the View Microsoft Word button on the Visual Basic Editor toolbar. Word displays the blank document containing the CenterHeading macro.

2 Type **Table of Contents,** and press Enter to create some text that you can use to test your macro.

3 Select the entire line or paragraph that you typed, and change the point size to 16 points. (Your macro will function perfectly at any point size, but a medium-sized font looks best for a heading.)

> **note** The CenterHeading macro is designed for formatting paragraphs only, so you need to select everything you typed, including the end-of-paragraph mark. If you select only a few words or characters in a line, you'll get different results than those we show here.

4 Choose Tools, Macro, Macros.

5 Click the CenterHeading macro if it's not already selected, and then click Run.

Word runs your macro and formats the Table of Contents heading by using shading, border, and center alignment commands, as shown in Figure 55-3. If you want to save this macro, return to Word and save the file containing the macro by choosing File, Save As.

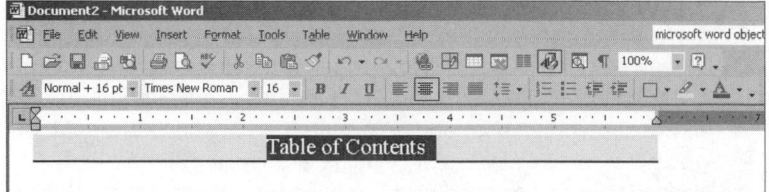

Figure 55-3. The CenterHeading macro demonstrates the formatting power of Word constants.

In the remaining chapters in Part 10 of this book, you might see line continuation characters at the end of some Visual Basic code lines. The line continuation character (_) is simply a device we're using to indicate line breaks for lines that are longer than 60 characters (for better readability). These breaks are acceptable to the Visual Basic interpreter. If you choose, you can type each of these long statements on one line if you don't include the continuation character. However, you might find the line continuation character useful if you want to see all your code at once. (The Code window can actually scroll to the right up to 1,024 characters.)

Troubleshooting

Breaking Strings in VBA Macro Code Causes Problems

You're in the middle of a Visual Basic macro and you decide to break one long line of code into two lines using the line continuation character (_). Unfortunately, the line of code contained a literal string value (text between quotation marks), and your edit has produced a compilation error and stopped the macro from running.

You cannot use a line continuation character to break a string that is enclosed in quotation marks. If you try to do this, Visual Basic will halt the execution of your macro and you'll need to fix it before you can continue. To troubleshoot the problem, find a way to place the entire quotation on one line, even if it extends well into the right margin of the VBA editor.

Declaring Variables

In the last section, you learned how to use unchanging values called constants to specify formatting options in your macros. In this section, you'll learn how to create temporary storage containers called *variables* to store information that is updated periodically as your macro runs. Variables are useful because they let you assign a short, easy-to-remember name to a piece of data you plan to work with. Variables can hold the following types of information:

- Numbers or words that you assign to your macro when you create it, such as an age or important date

- Special values that the user enters when the macro runs, such as a name or heading title

- Information from an Office document, such as words, paragraphs, cells, or slides

● The result of a specific calculation, such as the amount of sales tax that is due on a purchase

We cover the process of declaring and using variables in the next few sections.

Making Reservations for Variables: The Dim Statement

Before you use a variable, you need to make a reservation, or *dimension*, for it in your macro. You accomplish this by placing the Dim keyword and the name of the variable at the beginning of your macro. Such an action reserves room in memory for the variable when the macro runs, and it lets Visual Basic know what type of data it should expect to see later. For example, the statement Dim FullName creates space for a variable named FullName in a macro.

By default, Office creates variables in a general-purpose format, or *type*, called Variant. The Variant type can adapt itself to a variety of data formats, including numbers, words, dates, and so on. Although you can specifically declare your variables to be of an exact type to save memory, you'll rarely need to do so in Office macros.

Putting Variables to Work

After you declare a variable, you are free to assign information to it in your code. For example, the following program statement assigns the string *Clare of Assisi* to the FullName variable:

```
FullName = "Clare of Assisi"
```

After this assignment, you can use the FullName variable in place of Clare of Assisi in your code. For example, the assignment statement

```
Selection.TypeText Text:=FullName
```

would insert *Clare of Assisi* into the current document using the TypeText method of the Selection object.

Using Visual Basic Functions

An excellent use for a variable is to hold information in your macro that has been entered by the user. One way to manage this input is to use special Visual Basic keywords called *functions* that perform useful work and then return important values to the macro. In this section, you'll learn how to use the InputBox and MsgBox functions to manage input and output in an Office document, and how to use arguments to pass information to a function.

Using a Variable to Store Input

The InputBox function is designed as a simple way to receive input from the user and store it temporarily in a variable. In the following example, you'll enhance the CenterHeading macro by adding a dialog box that prompts the user for the name of a new heading. You'll also learn how to make a *procedure call* in a macro.

 The InsertHead macro is located in the Chap55 document on the companion CD to this book.

To add a dialog box that prompts a user for a new heading name, perform the following steps:

1 In Word, choose Tools, Macro, Macros.

Word opens the Macros dialog box. Because this macro uses the CenterHeading macro that you created earlier in the chapter, you should save the macro in the same document that CenterHeading is stored in.

2 Type **InsertHead** in the Name text box, and then click Create. Word starts the Visual Basic Editor and opens a new macro procedure named InsertHead in the Code window.

3 Type the following program statements to declare two variables and use the InputBox function:

```
Dim Prompt, Heading
Prompt = "Please enter your heading text."
Heading = InputBox$(Prompt)
Selection.Font.Size = 16
Selection.TypeText Text:=Heading
```

This time you're declaring two variables by using the Dim statement: Prompt and Heading. The second line in the event procedure assigns a group of characters, or a *text string,* to the Prompt variable. The macro then uses this message as a text argument for the InputBox function. (An *argument* is a value or expression passed to a subprocedure or a function.)

The next line *calls* (runs) the InputBox function and assigns the result of the execution—the text string the user enters—to the Heading variable. InputBox is a special Visual Basic function that displays a dialog box on the screen and prompts the user for input. In addition to supporting a prompt string, the InputBox function supports other arguments that you might want to use occasionally. Consult the Visual Basic online Help for details.

After InputBox has returned a text string to the macro, the fourth statement in the procedure changes the font size to 16 points (suitable for a heading), and the fifth statement inserts the text into your document using the TypeText method.

Now you'll use the commands in the CenterHeading macro to add some formatting interest to your new head. Rather than typing the CenterHeading statements again in your macro, you can accomplish the same effect by simply adding the name of the CenterHeading procedure to the bottom of your routine.

4 Below the Selection statement, type **CenterHeading,** and press Enter.

Adding the name of another procedure to your macro is known as *calling a procedure*. When the Visual Basic interpreter encounters this particular statement, it will run the CenterHeading macro in the InsertHead macro. Figure 55-4 shows the completed macro.

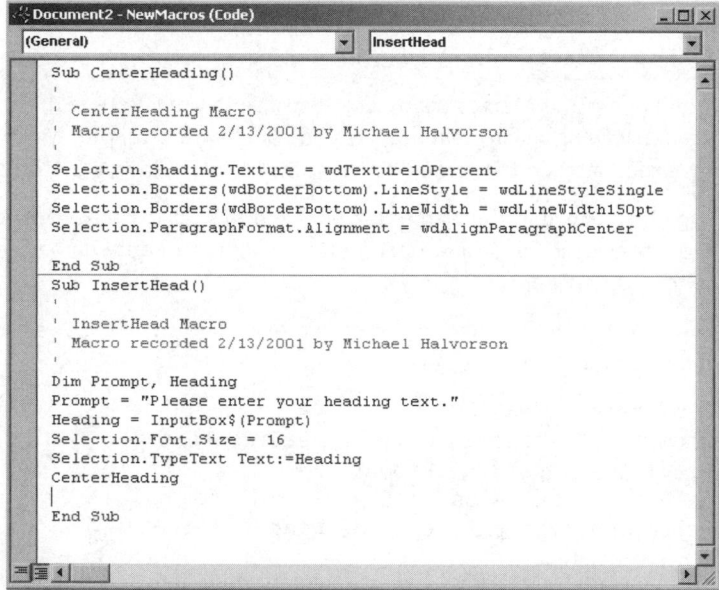

Figure 55-4. The InsertHead macro calls the CenterHeading macro.

InsideOut

Making Procedures Accessible

If you want to call one procedure from another procedure, you must place the procedures in the same module or declare the called procedure in a module that is in the current project or in the Normal.dot template. Otherwise, Visual Basic won't be able to find the procedure name you specify.

Now run the InsertHead macro in your Word document to try out the InputBox function and your two variables. To do so, follow these steps:

1 Click the View Microsoft Word button on the Visual Basic Editor toolbar. Word displays the document you created earlier in the chapter.

2 Move the insertion point to a blank line.

3 Choose Tools, Macro, Macros.

4 Click the InsertHead macro if it's not already selected, and then click Run. Word runs your macro and displays an InputBox using the prompt string you specified, as shown here:

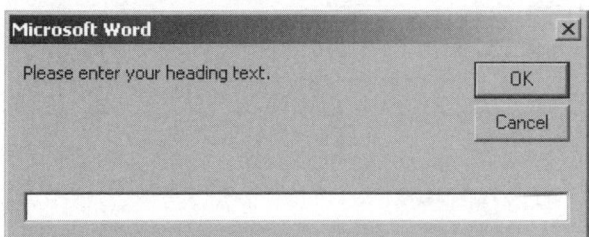

5 Type **Visual Basic is Fun!** and press Enter.

The InputBox function returns your heading to the macro and places it in the Heading variable. The program then uses the variable and the CenterHeading procedure to apply some custom formatting, as seen here:

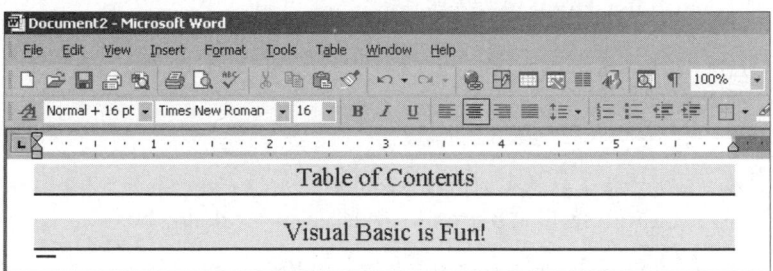

Any time you want to prompt the user for information in your programs, you can use the InputBox function. It provides a nice complement to the more sophisticated dialog boxes called UserForms. In the next example, you'll see how to use a similar function to display text in a dialog box.

You can find more information about UserForms in Chapter 57, "Using Toolbox Controls to Create a User Interface."

6 Click the Save button on Word's Standard toolbar to save the InsertHead macro to disk.

Chapter 55

InsideOut

What Are Arguments?

As you learned using InputBox, Visual Basic functions often use one or more arguments to define their activities. For example, the InputBox function used the Prompt variable as an argument to display dialog box instructions for the user. When a function uses one or more arguments, separate the arguments using commas and enclose the whole group of arguments in parentheses. The following example shows a function call that has two arguments:

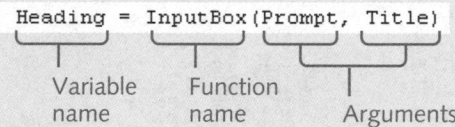

```
Heading = InputBox(Prompt, Title)
```
Variable name   Function name   Arguments

Using a Variable for Output

You can display the contents of a variable by assigning the variable to a method (such as the TypeText method of the Selection object) or by passing the variable as an argument to a dialog box function. One useful dialog box function for displaying output is the MsgBox function. Like InputBox, MsgBox takes one or more arguments as input, and you can assign the results of the function call to a variable.

The syntax for the MsgBox function is as follows:

```
ButtonClicked = MsgBox(Prompt, ButtonStyle, Title)
```

The following items are important:

- *ButtonClicked* represents a variable that receives the result of the function. It indicates which button was clicked in the dialog box.

- *Prompt* is the text to be displayed on the screen.

- *ButtonStyle* is a constant that determines the number and style of the buttons in the dialog box. Options include VbOKOnly, VbOKCancel, VbAbortRetryIgnore, VbYesNoCancel, VbYesNo, and VbRetryCancel.

- *Title* is the text displayed in the message box title bar.

note In Visual Basic syntax listings, items in italic type are placeholders for variables or other values in your program code. By convention, programmers use italics to highlight the parts of program syntax that you need to customize with your own instructions. (You'll also see this convention in the Visual Basic online Help.)

If you're just displaying a message in MsgBox, the assignment operator (=), the *ButtonClicked* variable, and the *ButtonStyle* argument are optional. You won't be using these in the following exercise; for more information about them, search for "MsgBox" in the Visual Basic online Help.

In the following exercise, you'll use a MsgBox function to display the user name associated with your copy of Word. This name is stored in the Options dialog box's User Information tab, and you can modify it in Word by choosing Tools, Options. Word places the registered user name in comments and revision annotations, so it's a good idea to check this setting periodically using a macro.

The DisplayUser macro is located in the Chap55 document on the companion CD to this book.

Using MsgBox to Display the Registered User

Often you'll find it handy to display a status message about a document by using a macro. To create a macro that displays information about the registered user, perform the following steps:

1 In Word, choose Tools, Macro, Macros.

2 Specify the document in which you want to store the macro using the Macros In list box.

3 Type **DisplayUser** in the Name text box, and then click Create. Word starts the Visual Basic Editor and opens a new macro procedure named DisplayUser in the Code window.

4 Type the following program statements to declare one variable and use the MsgBox function:

```
Dim DialogTitle
DialogTitle = "The current user name is"
MsgBox (Application.UserName), , DialogTitle
```

The first statement declares a variable to hold some descriptive text for the MsgBox function. The second statement assigns a text value to the variable. The third statement displays a message box on the screen and places the contents of the DialogTitle variable in the title bar. The UserName property of the Application object is then placed inside the message box. (When you don't use the ButtonClicked variable with MsgBox, the parentheses go around only the first argument.)

note You can also use the UserName property to set the user name in Word. For example, to change the user name to Michael Young, type Application.UserName = "Michael Young".

To run the DisplayUser macro in your Word document and try out the MsgBox function, follow these steps:

1 Click the View Microsoft Word button on the Visual Basic Editor toolbar. Word displays the active document.

2 Choose Tools, Macro, Macros.

3 Click the DisplayUser macro, and then click Run. Word loads the Visual Basic Editor, runs your macro, and displays the active user name for your copy of Word, as shown in this example:

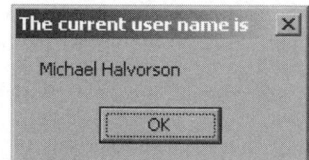

If the user name is incorrect, change it now by choosing Tools, Options, or write a macro to do it!

4 Click the Save button on Word's Standard toolbar to save the DisplayUser macro to disk.

Using Object Variables to Process Text

Another useful application for variables is holding portions of your document while your macro runs. For example, you might use a variable to hold a copy of a paragraph temporarily while you rearrange the paragraph's contents or move it to a new location. However, because documents and their contents are represented by objects in Visual Basic, you'll need to create a special container called an *object variable* when you want to reference an object in Office.

To declare an object variable in Visual Basic, use the following syntax:

```
Dim ObjectVar As Object
```

In the Dim statement, *ObjectVar* is the name of the variable you'll assign the object to later in your program code. For example, to create an object variable to hold text, you might use the following Dim statement:

```
Dim myText As Object
```

After you dimension an object variable, you can use it to reference an Office object by creating a Set statement, following this syntax:

```
Set ObjectVar = ObjectName
```

In the Set statement, *ObjectVar* is the name of your object variable, and *ObjectName* is an expression that returns an Office object. For example, to assign a Word Range object containing the text from the first paragraph in the active document to the myText object variable, you might use the following Set statement:

```
Set myText = ActiveDocument.Paragraphs(1).Range
```

After you assign an object to the object variable, you can use the variable just as you would the object. Thus, object variables save you typing time because the object variable names are usually shorter than the full object names. We'll use this method to work with Office objects regularly in Part 10 of this book.

 The CopyParagraph macro is located in the Chap55 document on the companion CD to this book.

Using an Object Variable to Copy Text

One practical use for an object variable is to hold a range reference when you copy text from one location to another. To create a macro that copies the first paragraph of the active document to a new document, perform the following steps:

1 In Word, choose Tools, Macro, Macros.

2 Specify the document in which you want to store the macro (Chap55.doc or other) using the Macros In list box.

3 Type **CopyParagraph** in the Name text box, and then click Create. Word starts the Visual Basic Editor and opens a new macro procedure named CopyParagraph in the Code window.

4 Type the following program statements:

```
Dim myText As Object
Set myText = ActiveDocument.Paragraphs(1).Range
Documents.Add
Selection.InsertAfter myText
```

The first statement declares a variable, myText, of type Object to hold the reference to a Range object. The second statement then assigns a Range object representing the first paragraph in the active document to myText. The object expression contains a collection index (1), which specifies the first paragraph in the Paragraphs collection. (The second paragraph has an index of 2, the third paragraph has an index of 3, and so on.)

> **note** The Range object contains only the text of the first paragraph, not the formatting. If you also want to copy the formatting of the paragraph, create a second object variable and use the Duplicate property of the Range object to copy the formatting.

Next the Add method adds a new document to the Documents collection, and the InsertAfter method inserts the current value of the myText object variable into the new Word document.

To run the CopyParagraph macro in your Word document, follow these steps:

1 Click the View Microsoft Word button on the Visual Basic Editor toolbar.

Word displays the active document. If you have been following the exercises so far in this chapter, your document contains two headings: Table of Contents and Visual Basic is Fun! The CopyParagraph macro should copy the first heading, Table of Contents, to a new document.

2 Choose Tools, Macro, Macros.

3 Select the CopyParagraph macro, and then click Run. Word runs your macro and creates a new document containing the Table of Contents paragraph (the text only, not the formatting), as shown here:

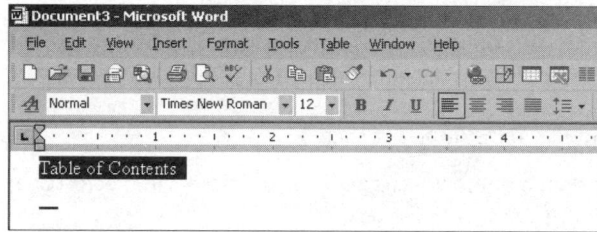

4 After you have verified the operation of your macro, close the new document and discard your changes. (You won't need to save the new document in this chapter.)

5 Display the Word document containing your new macro, and then click Save to save the CopyParagraph macro to disk.

Building Formulas

A *formula* is a statement that combines numbers, variables, operators, and keywords—or some of these elements—to create a new value. Visual Basic contains several language elements designed for use in formulas. In this section, you'll practice working with mathematical operators, the symbols used to tie together the parts of a formula. With a few exceptions, the mathematical symbols you'll use are the ones you use in everyday life, and their operations are fairly intuitive.

Visual Basic provides the mathematical operators shown in Table 55-1.

Table 55-1. **Visual Basic Mathematical Operators**

Operator	Mathematical Operation	Example
+	Addition	Sum = 15.95 + 22.50
–	Subtraction	Balance + 100 – 75
*	Multiplication	Product = 88 * 2
/	Division	Ratio = 6 / 5
\	Integer (whole number) division	FullDinners = 8 \ 3
Mod	Remainder division	Scraps = 8 Mod 3
^	Exponentiation (raising to a power)	AreaOfSquare = 5 ^ 2
&	String concatenation (joining words together)	FullName = "Bob" & "James"

Computing Formulas in Your Documents

Periodically, you might have to total numbers in an Office document or perform some sort of numeric calculation. The following exercise demonstrates how you can compute the sales tax for a number that is selected in the active document.

Word includes a formula feature that lets you total numbers in a table and perform other simple calculations. However, it doesn't contain a command that lets you make numeric computations on the fly using a selected number. Complete the following steps to build a macro that computes the total cost of an item including sales tax.

The SalesTax macro is located in the Chap55 document on the companion CD to this book.

1   In Word, choose Tools, Macro, Macros.

2   Specify the document in which you want to store the macro (Chap55.doc or other) using the Macros In list box.

3   Type **SalesTax** in the Name text box, and then click Create. Word starts the Visual Basic Editor and opens a new macro procedure named SalesTax in the Code window.

4   Type the following program statements:

```
Dim CostOfItem, TotalCost,
TaxRate = 1.091
CostOfItem = Selection.Text
TotalCost = CostOfItem * TaxRate
MsgBox Format(TotalCost, "$#,##0.00"), , "Total Cost with Tax"
```

InsideOut

Copying Macros to Word's Normal Template

This chapter contains five Word macros, each located in the NewMacros module in the Chap55 document on the companion CD to this book. If you'd like to copy one or more of these macros to the Normal.dot template (so that you can use them in Word without the Chap55.doc file open), perform the following steps:

1 Open the Macros dialog box, and click Organizer.

2 Verify that the Chap55 document is open in the left text box, and then select the NewMacros module in it.

3 Click Rename, and change the name of the NewMacros module to Chap55. (You can't copy one NewMacros module over another.)

4 Verify that the Normal template is open in the right text box, and then click Copy to copy the Chap55 module into the Normal template.

5 When you're finished copying macros, click Close.

The Dim statement declares three variables of the Variant type: CostOf Item, TotalCost, and TaxRate. Variant is a good choice in this case because the exact format of two numbers in your Word document is unknown: They could be large or small, integers or floating-point values, and so on. The third variable holds the current sales tax rate (in this example, 9.1 percent). Change this number to reflect your local sales tax rate, if any.

The third statement in the macro uses the Text property of the Selection object to return the currently selected text to the CostOf Item variable. The fourth statement then uses a formula and the multiplication operator to compute the total cost of the item plus sales tax. Finally, the MsgBox function displays the total with the help of the Format function, so the total appears with the proper currency formatting.

note The Format function can display the results of a calculation in a variety of formats, including percent, integer, date, string, and other custom formats. For more information, search for "Format function" in the Visual Basic online Help.

To run the SalesTax macro in your Word document, follow these steps:

1 Click the View Microsoft Word button on the Visual Basic Editor toolbar. Word displays the active document.

2 The SalesTax macro requires that you select a number in your document, so clear some room and type the following test values (one per line) so that you can evaluate the macro:

10
$1,000.00
five bucks

3 Select 10 as the first test number.

4 Run the SalesTax macro using the Macros dialog box. Word immediately displays a message box containing the total cost of a $10 item with 9.1 percent sales tax, as seen here:

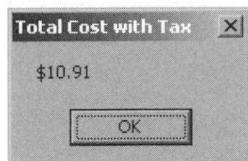

5 Click OK to close the dialog box, and then select $1,000.00 and run the macro again. (You should verify that the macro can handle currency formatting.)

Fortunately, you are using Variant variables in you macro, which can handle the switch between different types of numbers, resulting in the following display:

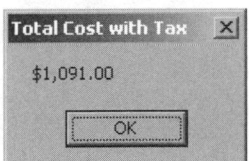

6 Click OK, and then select five bucks and run the macro.

This time, Visual Basic generates a run-time error that stops the macro and displays a dialog box explaining the problem, as shown here:

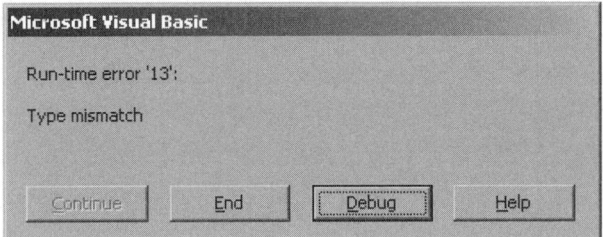

The words *type mismatch* mean that the value selected in the document (five bucks) cannot be multiplied by the value in the TaxRate constant (1.091). Unfortunately, this macro works only with numbers, not text.

7 Click Debug. Visual Basic highlights the program statement that caused the run-time error in the Code window.

8 Click the Reset button on the Visual Basic toolbar to stop the program.

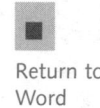

Return to Word

9 Click the Return To Word button on the Visual Basic toolbar to return to Word, and then click the Save button on Word's Standard toolbar to save the SalesTax macro to disk.

Adding Logic and Computing Power with Control Structures

Now it's time to make your macros sizzle with speed and power! In Chapter 55, "Using Variables, Operators, and Functions to Manage Information," you learned how to write Microsoft Office XP macros from scratch using several essential keywords in the Microsoft Visual Basic for Applications (VBA) programming language. In this chapter, you'll learn how to add logic and efficiency to your macros by writing conditional expressions, decision structures, and loops that manage the information in your documents. These skills allow you to write macros that rapidly format text elements, change settings in Office applications, manipulate collections, automate tables, and quickly open common documents.

Writing Conditional Expressions

One of the most useful tools for processing information in an event procedure is a conditional expression. A *conditional expression* is a part of a complete program statement that asks a true-or-false question about a property, a variable, or another piece of data in a macro. For example, the conditional expression

```
NumberOfWords < 100
```

evaluates to True if the NumberOfWords variable contains a value that is less than 100, and it evaluates to False if NumberOfWords contains a value that is greater than or equal to 100. Table 56-1 shows the comparison operators you can use in a conditional expression.

1505

Table 56-1. **The Heart of a Conditional Expression Is the Comparison Operator**

Comparison Operator	Meaning
=	Equal to
< >	Not equal to
>	Greater than
<	Less than
> =	Greater than or equal to
< =	Less than or equal to

> **note** Expressions that can be evaluated as true or false are also known as *Boolean expressions*, and the True or False result can be assigned to a Boolean variable or property.

Table 56-2 shows some conditional expressions and their results. You'll work with these expressions later in the chapter.

Table 56-2. **Sample Conditional Expressions and Their Results**

Conditional Expression	Result
10 < > 20	True (10 is not equal to 20)
Pages < 20	True if Pages is less than 20; otherwise, False
Application.UserName = "Hugh Victor"	True if the registered user name for your copy of Office is Hugh Victor; otherwise, False
Selection.Text = CityName	True if the selected text in your Word document matches the contents of the CityName variable; otherwise, False

Writing If...Then Decision Structures

Conditional expressions can control the order in which statements are executed when they are used in a special block of statements known as a *decision structure*. An If...Then decision structure lets you evaluate a condition in the program and control the flow of execution based on the result. In its simplest form, an If...Then decision structure is written on a single line, in the form "If condition Then statement," where the *condition* placeholder represents a conditional expression, and *statement* represents a valid VBA macro statement. For example,

```
If Application.UserName = "Hugh Victor" Then MsgBox "Welcome, Hugh!"
```

is an If...Then decision structure using the conditional expression Application. UserName = "Hugh Victor" to determine whether the macro should display the message "Welcome, Hugh!" in a message box on the screen. If the UserName property of the Application object contains a name that matches "Hugh Victor," Office displays the message box; otherwise, it skips the MsgBox statement and executes the next line in the macro. Conditional expressions always result in a True or False value, never in a maybe.

Testing Several Conditions in an If...Then Decision Structure

VBA also supports an If...Then decision structure that allows you to include several conditional expressions. This block of statements can be several lines long and contains the important keywords ElseIf, Else, and End If.

```
If condition1 Then
     statements executed if condition1 is True
ElseIf condition2 Then
     statements executed if condition2 is True
[Additional ElseIf clauses and statements can be placed here]
Else
     statements executed if none of the conditions is True
End If
```

In this structure, *condition1* is evaluated first. If this conditional expression is True, the block of statements below it is executed, one statement at a time. (You can include one or more program statements.) If the first condition is not True, the second conditional expression (*condition2*) is evaluated. If the second condition is True, the second block of statements is executed. (You can add additional ElseIf conditions and statements if you have more conditions to evaluate.) Finally, if none of the conditional expressions is True, the statements below the Else keyword are executed. The whole structure is closed at the bottom by the End If keywords.

In the next section, you'll use an If...Then decision structure to convert a selected heading style in Microsoft Word 2002 to formatted text in the Normal style. This macro is useful if you want to reduce the amount of space a Word document takes up or if you routinely convert one heading style to another.

 The ConvertStyles macro is located in the Chap56 document on the companion CD to this book.

Chapter 56

Using an If...Then Decision Structure to Convert Styles

Word's Normal template includes three default formatting styles for headings: Heading 1, Heading 2, and Heading 3. To convert these styles to all caps, underline, and italic formatting, perform the following steps:

1 Start Word and open a new, blank document.

2 Choose Tools, Macro, Macros. Word opens the Macros dialog box, where you create and run Visual Basic macros.

3 Type **ConvertStyles** in the Name text box, and then click the Macros In drop-down list and select your new, blank document in the list. (In this example, the new document is named Document1.)

4 Click Create. Word starts the Visual Basic Editor and opens a new macro procedure named ConvertStyles in the Code window.

5 Type the following program statements:

```
If Selection.Type = wdSelectionIP Then
    MsgBox "No text selected."
ElseIf Selection.FormattedText.Style = "Heading 1" Then
    Selection.FormattedText.Style = wdStyleNormal
    Selection.Font.AllCaps = True
ElseIf Selection.FormattedText.Style = "Heading 2" Then
    Selection.FormattedText.Style = wdStyleNormal
    Selection.Font.Underline = True
ElseIf Selection.FormattedText.Style = "Heading 3" Then
    Selection.FormattedText.Style = wdStyleNormal
    Selection.Font.Italic = True
End If
```

6 Click the Save button on the Visual Basic toolbar and then specify a filename for your document.

This macro consists entirely of an If...Then decision structure that contains one If statement and three ElseIf clauses. The first If statement uses the Selection object's Type property to see whether text is selected in the document that can be evaluated by the macro. If there is a text selection, the structure determines which heading style is active, converts the head back to the Normal style, and applies some simple text formatting to preserve the meaning of the heads. (Heading 1 becomes all caps, Heading 2 is underlined, and Heading 3 is formatted as italic.)

By changing the style and formatting constants used in this example, you could easily modify the Word macro to convert other styles or formatting options. Your screen should look like Figure 56-1.

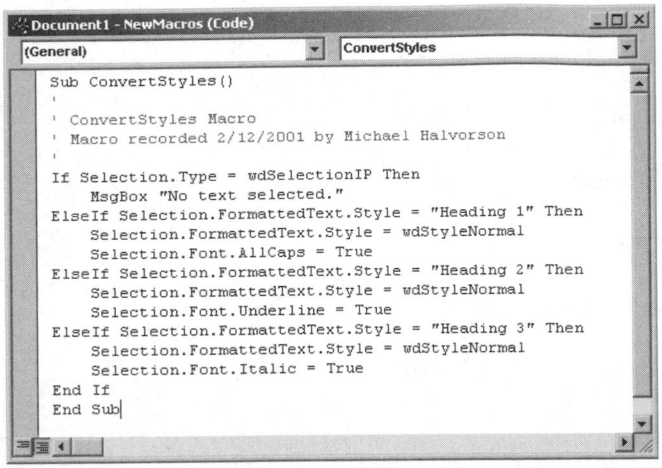

```
Document1 - NewMacros (Code)                              _ |□| ×|
(General)                        ▼    ConvertStyles              ▼

  Sub ConvertStyles()
  '
  ' ConvertStyles Macro
  ' Macro recorded 2/12/2001 by Michael Halvorson
  '
  If Selection.Type = wdSelectionIP Then
      MsgBox "No text selected."
  ElseIf Selection.FormattedText.Style = "Heading 1" Then
      Selection.FormattedText.Style = wdStyleNormal
      Selection.Font.AllCaps = True
  ElseIf Selection.FormattedText.Style = "Heading 2" Then
      Selection.FormattedText.Style = wdStyleNormal
      Selection.Font.Underline = True
  ElseIf Selection.FormattedText.Style = "Heading 3" Then
      Selection.FormattedText.Style = wdStyleNormal
      Selection.Font.Italic = True
  End If
  End Sub
```

Figure 56-1. The ConvertStyles macro is shown in the Visual Basic development environment.

Running the ConvertStyles Macro

To run the ConvertStyles macro to convert Word styles, follow these steps:

1 Click the View Microsoft Word button on the Visual Basic Editor toolbar.

2 At the top of the document, type **First Head, Second Head,** and **Third Head** on three lines. Place the heads on separate lines so you can test each level of formatting.

3 Select the first head, and apply the Heading 1 style by using the Style drop-down list on Word's Formatting toolbar.

4 Format the second head using the Heading 2 style and the third head using the Heading 3 style.

5 Now select First Head in your document, and run the ConvertStyles macro.

Be sure to select one head only and not multiple lines. When you run the macro, Word converts the selected head to all caps.

At this point, we assume you know how to start a macro. To review the five techniques you can use to run a macro in Office XP, see "Running a Macro," on page 1467.

6 Select Second Head, and run the macro. Word converts the second style to underlined type.

7 Select Third Head, and run the macro.

Word converts the third style to italic type. Figure 56-2 shows the three heads before and after the macro conversion.

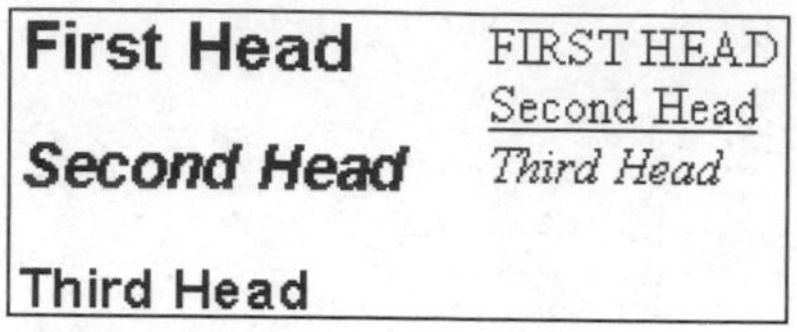

First Head

Second Head

Third Head

FIRST HEAD
Second Head
Third Head

Figure 56-2. The ConvertStyles macro converts Word headings from their default size to more compact styles.

8 Click Save to save the changes to your document.

InsideOut

Using Logical Operators in Conditional Expressions

Visual Basic lets you test more than one conditional expression in your If...Then and ElseIf clauses if you want to include more than one selection criterion in your decision structure. The extra conditions are linked together by using one or more of the logical operators shown in Table 56-3.

Table 56-3. Useful Logical Operators in VBA

Logical Operator	Meaning
And	If and only if both conditional expressions are True, then the result is True.
Or	If either conditional expression is True, then the result is True.
Not	If the conditional expression is False, then the result is True. If the conditional expression is True, then the result is False.
Xor	If one and only one of the conditional expressions is True, then the result is True. If both are True or both are False, then the result is False.

For example, the following decision structure uses the And logical operator to test an Office object:

```
If Application.UserName = "Michael Halvorson" _
     And Price < 300 Then
   MsgBox "Buy the product."
End If
```

You'll see an example of this operator later in the chapter.

Writing Select Case Decision Structures

Visual Basic also lets you control the execution of statements in your macros by using Select Case decision structures. A Select Case structure is similar to an If...Then...ElseIf structure, but it is more efficient when the branching depends on one key variable, or *test case*. In addition, Select Case structures make your macro code more readable for others and easier to update later. The syntax for a Select Case structure looks like this:

```
Select Case variable
Case value1
     program statements executed if value1 matches variable
Case value2
     program statements executed if value2 matches variable
Case value3
     program statements executed if value3 matches variable
.
.
.
End Select
```

A Select Case structure begins with the Select Case keywords and ends with the End Select keywords. You replace the *variable* placeholder with the variable, property, or other expression that is to be the key value, or test case, for the structure. You replace *value1*, *value2*, and *value3* with numbers, strings, or other values related to the test case being considered. If one of the values matches the variable, the statements below its Case clause are executed, and Visual Basic continues executing program code after the End Select statement.

You can include any number of Case clauses in a Select Case structure, and you can include more than one value in a Case clause. If you list multiple values after a case, separate them with commas. A Select Case structure also supports a Case Else clause that you can use to control how Visual Basic handles cases not captured by the preceding cases.

The following example shows how you can use a Select Case structure in an Office macro to display an appropriate message about a person's age. If the Age variable matches one of the Case values, an appropriate message is displayed by using a message box. If not, the Else clause is displayed.

```
Select Case Age
Case 16
     MsgBox "You can drive now!"
Case 18
     MsgBox "You can vote now!"
Case 21
     MsgBox "You can drink wine with your meals."
Case 65
     MsgBox "Time to retire and have fun!"
Case Else
     MsgBox "You're a great age! Enjoy it!"
End Select
```

A Select Case decision structure is usually much clearer than an If…Then structure and is more efficient when you're making three or more branching decisions based on one variable or property. However, when you're making two or fewer comparisons or when you're working with several different values, you'll probably want to use an If…Then decision structure.

Using Select Case to Determine a Document's Paper Size

The following exercise demonstrates how you can use a Select Case structure to display the current Word document's paper type. You can accomplish this task by using a macro to compare the PageSetup object's PaperSize property to three different Office constants associated with paper.

 The PaperSize macro is located in the Chap56 document on the companion CD to this book.

To write this macro, complete the following steps:

1 Choose Tools, Macro, Macros.

2 Select the document in which you want to store the macro using the Macros In drop-down list.

3 Type **PageSize** in the Name text box, and then click Create. Word starts the Visual Basic Editor and opens a new macro procedure named PageSize in the Code window.

4 Type the following program statements.

```
Dim PaperType
PaperType = ActiveDocument.PageSetup.PaperSize
Select Case PaperType
Case wdPaperLetter
    MsgBox "Document type is Letter (8 1/2 x 11)."
Case wdPaperLegal
    MsgBox "Document type is Legal (8 1/2 x 14)."
Case wdPaperEnvelope10
    MsgBox "Document type is Envelope 10 (4 1/8 x 9 1/2)."
Case Else
    MsgBox "Type unknown. Check File/Page Setup/Paper Size."
End Select
```

5 Click Save to save the macro to disk.

The PageSize macro requires no user input. It simply stores the current paper size in a Variant variable named PaperType and then uses a Select Case structure to determine which type of paper is in use. The results are then displayed in a message box for the user.

The default paper size in Word is Letter (8½-inch × 11-inch), but you can adjust this setting by choosing File, Page Setup. If you're ever uncertain about the page size, just run this macro.

Running the Macro

To run the PageSize macro and determine your document's paper size, perform the following steps:

1 Click the View Microsoft Word button on the Visual Basic Editor toolbar. Word displays the current document.

2 Run the PageSize macro. Word activates the Visual Basic Editor and displays a message box that describes the current document's paper type, as shown here:

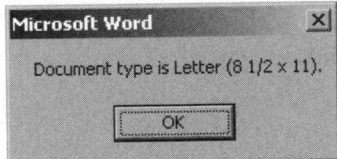

Before you print, you can use this information to make sure you have the right type of paper in your printer.

3 Experiment with the macro if you like by changing the paper type by choosing File, Page Setup. (The Paper Size tab controls the paper type.)

Troubleshooting

Your Macro Doesn't Account for Each Possibility in a Select Case Statement

You've written a useful macro that quickly reports the type of paper your document requires for a printout. But your document requires a paper type that you didn't plan for in your macro.

Select Case statements can supply dozens of Case arguments that test constants such as the ones you used in this paper-testing macro. You can add additional constants to this macro by searching for "PaperSize property" in the Word Visual Basic online Help and adding additional statements. However, all "open-ended" Select Case statements should end with an Else clause that handles possibilities your code doesn't specifically test for. In this macro, for example, we displayed the message "Type unknown. Check File/Page Setup/Paper Size." Use Else as a troubleshooting solution whenever there are document attributes, however unlikely, that you're not testing for.

Writing For...Next Loops

A For...Next loop lets you execute a specific group of program statements a set number of times in a macro. This control structure can be useful if you are performing several related calculations, working with collections of Office objects, or processing several pieces of user input. A For...Next loop is really just a shorthand way of writing out a long list of program statements. Because each group of statements in the list would perform essentially the same work, Visual Basic lets you define one group of statements and request that it be executed as many times as you want. The syntax for a For...Next loop looks like this:

```
For variable = start To end
    statements to be repeated
Next variable
```

In this syntax statement, For, To, and Next are required keywords, and the equals to (=) is a required operator. You replace the *variable* placeholder with the name of a numeric variable that keeps track of the current loop count, and you replace *start* and *end* with numeric values representing the starting and stopping points for the loop. The line or lines between the For and Next statements are the commands that are repeated each time the loop is executed.

For example, the following For...Next loop uses the TypeParagraph method to insert four carriage returns in a Word document:

```
For i = 1 To 4
    Selection.TypeParagraph
Next i
```

This loop is the functional equivalent of writing the Selection.TypeParagraph statement four times in a procedure. It looks the same to the Visual Basic interpreter as this:

```
Selection.TypeParagraph
Selection.TypeParagraph
Selection.TypeParagraph
Selection.TypeParagraph
```

The variable used in the loop is *i*, a single letter that, by convention, stands for the first integer counter in a For...Next loop. Each time the loop is executed, the counter variable is incremented by one. (The first time through the loop, the variable contains a value of 1, the value of *start*; the last time through, it contains a value of 4, the value of *end*.) As you'll see in the following sections, you can use this counter variable to great advantage in your loops.

Using a Loop to Manage Tables

For...Next loops work best when you're processing information that conforms to a particular pattern. For example, For...Next loops are handy when you want to add, remove, or modify information in tables. Each Word document and Microsoft PowerPoint 2002 presentation contains a Tables collection that holds each of the tables in a particular document. By using a combination of table methods and properties, you can create tables, insert information, remove information, format the entries, and so forth.

Creating a Macro That Automatically Builds Tables

The macro introduced here inserts a new table in the active Word document at the insertion point. The macro first prompts you for the number of rows and columns in the table and then creates the table if it's at least 2 × 2 in size. The macro uses a For...Next loop to add entries to each of the cells in the first column and then uses the AutoFormat command to format the entire table.

The AutoTable macro is located in the Chap56 document on the companion CD to this book.

To build the macro, follow these steps:

1 Choose Tools, Macro, Macros.

2 Select the document in which you want to store the macro using the Macros In drop-down list.

3 Type **AutoTable** in the Name text box, and then click Create. Word starts the Visual Basic Editor and opens a new macro procedure named AutoTable in the Code window.

4 Type the following program statements:

```
Dim iRows As Integer, iColumns As Integer
Dim myTable

iRows = InputBox("Number of Rows?")
iColumns = InputBox("Number of Columns?")

If iRows > 1 And iColumns > 1 Then '2x2 table required
    Set myTable = ActiveDocument.Tables.Add(Selection.Range, _
        iRows, iColumns)
    For i = 2 To iRows
        myTable.Cell(i, 1).Range.InsertAfter "Item " & i - 1
    Next i
    myTable.AutoFormat Format:=wdTableFormatColorful2
Else
    MsgBox "Sorry, minimum table size 2 rows and 2 columns."
End If
```

5 Click Save to save the macro to disk.

Chapter 56

This macro declares three important variables: iRows, an integer that contains the number of rows in the table; iColumns, an integer that contains the number of columns; and myTable, an object variable that represents the new table in the document. The main part of the macro is contained in an If...Then decision structure that uses the And logical operator to verify that the user has specified a large enough table. This bounds checking prevents the macro from crashing if the user enters a number that's too small to define a usable table.

Inside the If...Then decision structure, the For...Next loop uses a starting value of 2 so that text entry begins in the second row. (The first row is reserved for table headings.) The loop then uses the InsertAfter method to add text following the pattern Item 1, Item 2, Item 3, and so forth, until no more rows exist in the table.

Running the AutoTable Macro

To run the AutoTable macro you just created, follow these steps:

1 Click the View Microsoft Word button on the Visual Basic Editor toolbar.

2 Move the insertion point to a place where you'd like to create a table, and then run the AutoTable macro. Word displays an input box prompting you for the number of rows in your table, as seen here:

3 Type **9** and click OK. Word displays a second input box prompting you for the number of columns, as shown here:

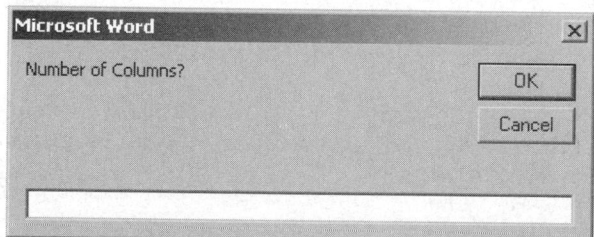

4 Type **4** and click OK. Word creates a 9-row by 4-column table in the current document, fills the first column with text entries, and applies automatic formatting (as shown in Figure 56-3).

Item 1			
Item 2			
Item 3			
Item 4			
Item 5			
Item 6			
Item 7			
Item 8			

Figure 56-3. The AutoTable macro instantly creates a preformatted table in your document.

5 If you plan to use this macro often, return to the Visual Basic Editor and customize the macro code to insert appropriate table headings and column text using the InsertAfter method, and specify your own preferences for table formatting using the AutoFormat method.

Using For...Each Loops

For...Next loops are useful if you know exactly how many times a particular group of statements should run, but what if you simply want to process each object in a collection? Fortunately, the designers of VBA included a special loop called For...Each that is specifically designed to march through each item in a collection. You'll find this especially useful when you're working with the Documents, Tables, Fields, Footnotes, Paragraphs, and Words collections.

The For...Each loop has the following syntax:

```
For Each element In collection
    statements to be repeated
Next element
```

The following items are important:

- The *element* placeholder represents a variable name that you enter of type Variant. When the loop runs, *element* stands for each item in the collection one by one.

- The *collection* placeholder represents the name of a valid collection in Office, such as Documents or Paragraphs.

Processing a Collection Using For...Each

The macro introduced here uses a For...Each loop to check each open Word document in the Documents collection for a file named MyLetter.doc. If the file is found in the collection, the macro makes it the active document in Word. If the file is not found, the macro loads the file from the root folder (C:\) on your hard disk.

> **note** This macro only runs correctly if you put a file named MyLetter.doc in the root folder on drive C (C:\). Because such a file doesn't exist in that location by default, you'll need to create a simple one there to get this example to work, or you'll need to specify a new path location in the macro.

on the CD The ShowLetter macro is located in the Chap56 document on the companion CD to this book. A sample MyLetter.doc file that you must place in C:\ to test the macro is also included on the CD.

To create the ShowLetter macro, perform the following steps:

1 Choose Tools, Macro, Macros.

2 Select the document in which you want to store the macro using the Macros In drop-down list.

3 Type **ShowLetter** in the Name text box, and then click Create. Word starts the Visual Basic Editor and opens a new macro procedure named ShowLetter in the Code window.

4 Type the following program statements:

```
Dim aDoc, docFound, docLocation
docLocation = "c:\MyLetter.doc"

For Each aDoc In Documents
    If InStr(1, aDoc.Name, "myletter.doc", 1) Then
        aDoc.Activate
        Exit For
    Else
        docFound = False
    End If
Next aDoc

If docFound = False Then Documents.Open FileName:=docLocation
```

5 Click Save to save the macro to disk.

The macro begins by declaring three variables, all of type Variant. The aDoc variable represents the current collection element in the For...Each loop, docFound is assigned a Boolean value of False if the document is not found in the Documents collection, and docLocation contains the file path of the MyLetter.doc file on disk.

The For...Each loop cycles through each document in the Documents collection, searching for the MyLetter file. If the file is detected by the InStr function (which detects one text string within another), the file is made the active document. If the file isn't found, the macro opens it by using the Documents object's Open method.

The InStr function's first argument (1) is an optional numeric start argument that sets the starting position for a search. The next two arguments, which are required, specify the text string being searched and the text string that you are looking for within the first string, respectively. The last argument, which is also optional, establishes the type of comparison. In this case, 1 represents a text comparison, which is the type of string you are looking for. If you want to see more information about the InStr function's arguments, search for InStr in Visual Basic's online Help.

Also note the Exit For statement, which we use to exit the For…Next loop when the MyLetter file has been found and activated. Introduced here for the first time, Exit For is a special program statement that you can use to exit a For…Next loop when continuing causes unwanted results. Periodically, you'll want to use Exit For in your own macros.

Running the ShowLetter Macro

To run the ShowLetter macro, perform the following steps:

1 Click the View Microsoft Word button on the Visual Basic Editor toolbar.

2 Click the New button twice to open two more Word documents. You should add a few documents to the Documents collection to test the macro properly.

3 Click the Word Window menu, and then click the document in which you saved the ShowLetter macro.

4 Run the ShowLetter macro to load the MyLetter.doc file.

Word opens MyLetter from the root folder when the macro doesn't locate the file in the Documents collection. Figure 56-4 shows our MyLetter.doc file, a short essay about the Italian Renaissance.

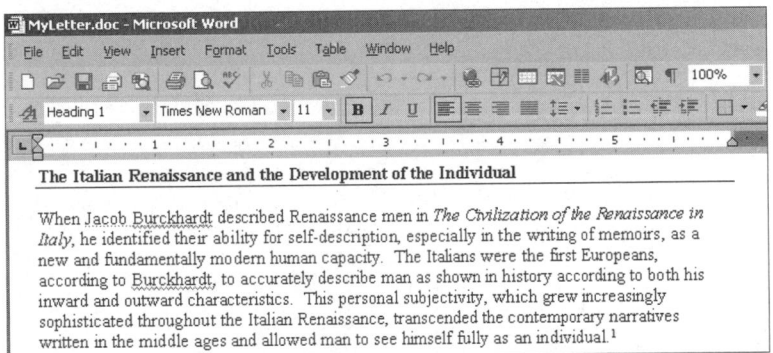

Figure 56-4. The ShowLetter macro opens the MyLetter.doc file if it's not in the current Documents collection.

5 Click the Window menu and display the document containing your macros again, and then run the ShowLetter macro. This time Word finds the MyLetter document in the Documents collection and displays it using the Activate method.

6 Close the MyLetter document and the two empty Word documents, and then click Save to save any changes you've made to disk.

Chapter 56

Using Toolbox Controls to Create a User Interface

Can macros have their own sharp-looking user interfaces? Something more than the Microsoft Office XP dialog boxes you've been using so far in Part 10? The answer is yes! In this chapter, you'll learn how custom macro interfaces, or *UserForms,* are designed and how they run in the Microsoft Visual Basic development environment. You'll also learn how to build UserForms, create programmable objects on them, configure UserForms using property settings, and customize UserForms using event procedures. The toolbox controls you'll use to accomplish this work include Label, CommandButton, Image, and TextBox. When you're finished, you'll have all the tools you need to build the ultimate user interface for any Office macro.

Getting Started with UserForms

The best way to get started with UserForms is to create a simple macro that opens a custom dialog box and uses it to display information. In this section, you'll create a music trivia macro that asks the user a simple question about a popular rock and roll instrument. Along the way, you'll learn the three fundamental steps of creating a Visual Basic UserForm: designing the user interface, setting properties, and writing event procedures.

> **note**   The process used to create UserForms is identical in this version of Microsoft Word, Excel, and PowerPoint. You'll find the same toolbox controls and property settings in each application.

Designing the User Interface

A UserForm is simply a custom dialog box that you create in the Visual Basic Editor by using programmable interface objects called *toolbox controls*. To open a UserForm in the Visual Basic Editor, choose Insert, UserForm. Each UserForm appears in a separate Project window in the Visual Basic Editor, and it's also listed in the Forms folder in Project Explorer. The first UserForm is named UserForm1, and subsequent UserForms are named UserForm2, UserForm3, and so on.

Whenever a UserForm is active in the Visual Basic Editor, a palette of toolbox controls also appears in a window, which allows you to add programmable interface objects to your UserForm (as shown in Figure 57-1). If you have used a drawing program such as Paint, you have many of the skills you need to use toolbox controls. To build the interface objects, click a control in the toolbox, and then draw the interface object by dragging with the mouse. This task is usually a simple matter of clicking to position one corner of the object and then dragging to create a rectangle that's exactly the size that you want. After you create the object—a text label, for example—you can resize it using the selection handles or you can relocate it by dragging. You can also resize or move the UserForm itself to create a dialog box in exactly the size and location you want.

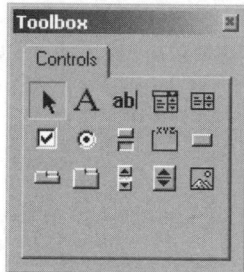

Figure 57-1. You create interface objects on your form using toolbox controls.

Building a Custom Dialog Box

To create a UserForm using the Label, Image, and CommandButton controls, perform the following steps:

1 Start Word. If Word is already running, open a new, blank document.

The MusicTrivia macro is located in the Chap57 document on the companion CD to this book. The Guitar.bmp file (a supporting bitmapped graphic) is also included on the CD.

2 Choose Tools, Macro, Macros. Word opens the Macros dialog box, where you create and run Visual Basic macros.

3 Type **MusicTrivia** in the Name text box, and then click the Macros In drop-down list and select your new, blank document in the list. (In this example, the new document is named Document1.)

4 Click Create. Word starts the Visual Basic Editor and opens a new macro procedure named MusicTrivia in the Code window.

5 Type the following program statements to load and open the UserForm:

```
Load UserForm1
UserForm1.Show
```

Every macro that opens a UserForm needs these two program statements to bring the UserForm into memory and display it. In this simple macro, you'll type only two lines in the macro. You'll type the remaining program statements into event procedures associated with the objects on the UserForm. (Event procedures are discussed in greater detail in "Writing Event Procedures," on page 1528.)

6 Choose Insert, UserForm.

The Visual Basic Editor opens a new UserForm in a window and displays the toolbox controls. The UserForm is named UserForm1, as seen here:

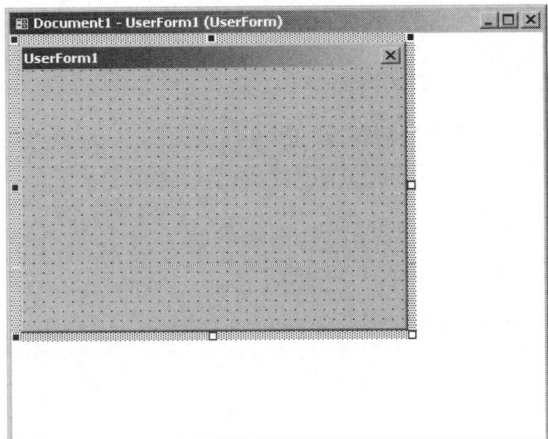

7 Click the Label control in the toolbox, shown here, and then place the mouse pointer over the UserForm.

The mouse pointer changes to crosshairs when it rests on the form. The crosshairs are designed to help you draw the rectangular shape of a label. When you hold down the left mouse button and drag, the label object takes shape and snaps to the grid formed by the intersection of dots on the form.

> **tip** To learn the name of a control in the toolbox, hold the mouse pointer over the control until its ToolTip appears.

Chapter 57

8 Move the mouse pointer to the middle of the UserForm (near the left edge), hold down the left mouse button, and then drag down and to the right. Stop dragging and release the mouse button when your label object looks like the one shown here:

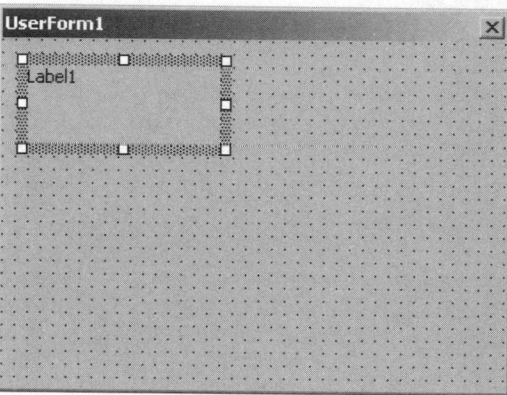

The purpose of a label object is to display formatted text on a UserForm. The first label object on a form is named Label1, and subsequent labels are named Label2, Label3, and so forth. You'll add text to the label object later.

9 Click the Label control in the toolbox again, and then create a second, smaller label object below the first one.

Each label object on a UserForm maintains its own set of properties and methods. By creating two separate label objects, you'll be able to manipulate them individually using program code.

10 Click the Image control in the toolbox, shown here:

Next, create a large, square image object on the right side of the form, as shown here:

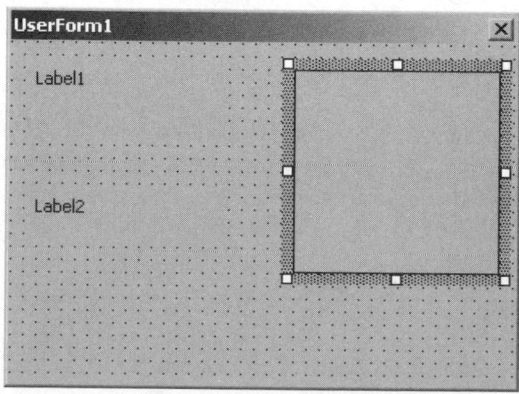

The purpose of an image object is to display clip art, photographs, bitmaps, and other electronic artwork on a UserForm. Specifically, an image object can display .ico, .wmf, .bmp, .cur, .jpg, and .gif files. You'll use this image object to display a photograph of the musical instrument that demonstrates the answer to the musical trivia question.

11 Click the CommandButton control in the toolbox, shown here:

Create a command button object at the bottom of your UserForm on the left side.

The purpose of a command button object is to create dialog box buttons on a UserForm. Typical command buttons include OK and Cancel, but you can also create your own button types.

12 Click the CommandButton control again, and then create a second command button object at the bottom of your UserForm on the right side.

You're finished creating objects on your UserForm. If the final dialog box doesn't look like the one shown in Figure 57-2, use the mouse to fine-tune the size and location of your objects.

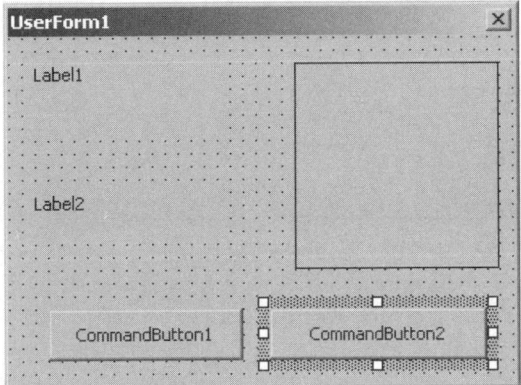

Figure 57-2. This UserForm includes five objects.

13 Click the Save button on the Visual Basic toolbar, and then specify a filename for your new document.

Setting Properties

After you create objects on your UserForm using toolbox controls, your next step is customizing the objects using property settings. As you learned in Chapter 54, "Building Your First Office XP Macro," a property setting is a quality or characteristic of an object that can change as your macro runs. You can change the property settings for objects on a UserForm by using the Properties window at design time (when your macro is being built), or by using program code at run time (while your macro is executing).

To set properties in the MusicTrivia macro's UserForm, follow these steps:

1 Click the first label object on the UserForm.

Before you can set a property for an object, you must select the object on the UserForm. When you select the first label object, its name (Label1) appears at the top of the Properties window in the Object drop-down list, as seen here:

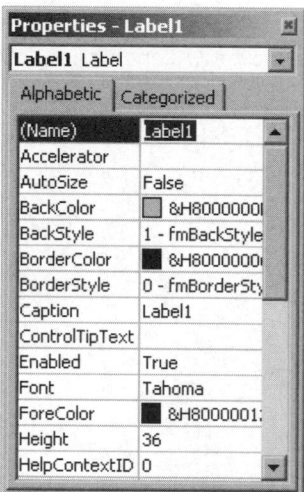

> **tip** To see more of the Properties window, double-click its title bar to display the window in its "floating" position in the Visual Basic Editor, a view that will reveal more property settings than if the Properties window were docked in a collapsed position. (If the Properties window still isn't big enough to suit your tastes, you can enlarge it by resizing it with the mouse.) To return the Properties window to a docked position, double-click the title bar again.

2 In the Properties window, double-click the text (Label1) to the right of the Caption property to select it, and press Delete.

The default text setting for the Caption property is deleted. Now enter a new caption.

3 Type **What rock and roll instrument is often played with sharp, slapping thumb movements?** and press Enter.

The contents of the Label1 object on the form change to match your trivia question. Because the label object's WordWrap property is set to True by default, the text wraps inside the label object.

4 Click the Label2 object on the UserForm, and follow the same steps to change its Caption property to **The Bass Guitar**.

5 With the Label2 object still selected, click the Visible property, and change its setting to False. That will keep the answer hidden until the first command button is pressed.

6 Click the Image1 object on the form. Now you'll set the PictureSizeMode, Picture, and Visible properties of the image object to display a photograph of a bass guitar when the user clicks a command button.

7 Click the PictureSizeMode property, and select 1-fmPictureSizeModeStretch in the drop-down list. This property setting resizes artwork in an image box so that it fits exactly.

8 Click the Picture property, and then click the button containing three dots in the setting field. A dialog box appears, as shown here, prompting you to select a piece of artwork for the image box.

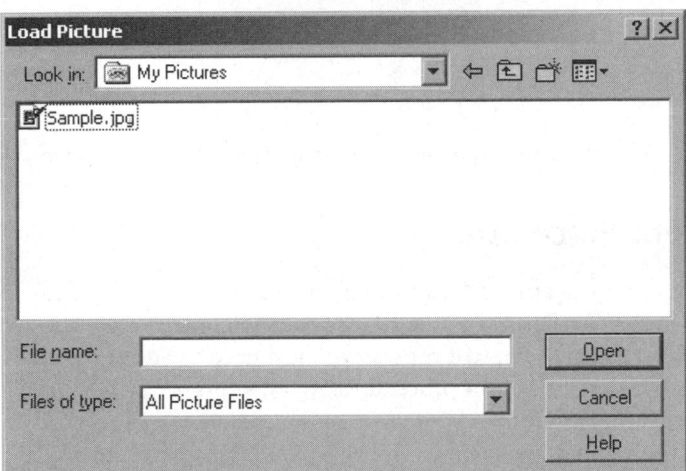

9 Browse to find a picture file on your system, and then click Open.

10 We recommend that you use the Guitar.bmp graphic located on this book's companion CD, but you can also select a piece of artwork from your own computer. (You'll find several in the \Windows folder.)

If you select the Guitar.bmp file, you'll see the photograph of a hip Seattle bass player now in the image box. (Look closely—he's currently demonstrating the slap-bass technique.)

11 Click the Visible property for the image object, and set it to False. You'll keep the photograph hidden until the user clicks the first command button.

12 Now select the first command button object on the form, and change its Caption property to **Answer**.

13 Change the Caption property of the second command button to **Quit**.

14 Click the UserForm itself (not an object), and then set the Caption property of the UserForm to **Music Trivia**.

You're finished setting properties for the macro, and your UserForm should look similar to the one shown in Figure 57-3.

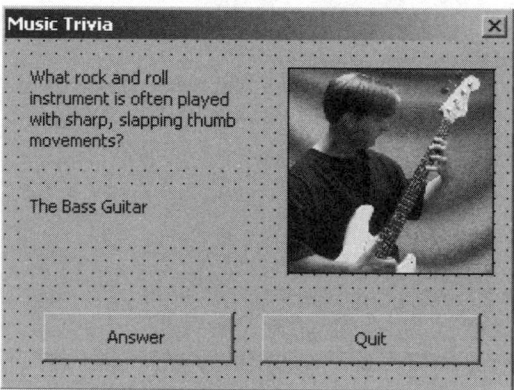

Figure 57-3. This is the completed user interface of the MusicTrivia UserForm.

Writing Event Procedures

The final step in creating a UserForm is writing the program code for the interface objects on the UserForm. Fortunately, most of the objects on a UserForm already know how to work when the macro runs, so you just need to add the final touches using a few carefully designed event procedures. An *event procedure* is a special routine that runs when an object on your form is manipulated at run time. (Technically, event procedures run when a specific *event* is triggered in the macro, such as a click, a double-click, or a drag-and-drop operation.) UserForm event procedures use the same Visual Basic macro language that you're familiar with, so you'll have little trouble figuring out what to do. Like Office macros, the trick to learning the ropes is understanding what the most important properties and methods do and then executing them in the proper sequence using program code.

Using the Code Window to Write Event Procedures

To write click event procedures for the two command button objects on the UserForm, CommandButton1 and CommandButton2, perform the following steps:

1 Double-click the CommandButton1 object (the button that has the Answer caption). The Visual Basic Editor opens the click event procedure for the CommandButton1 object in the Code window, as seen here:

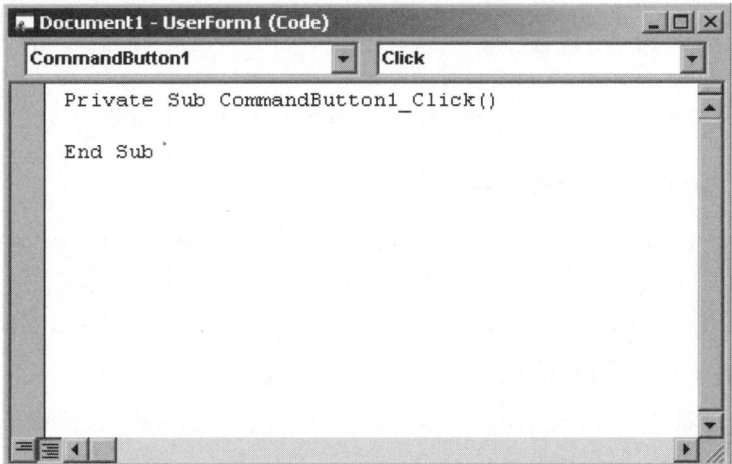

2 Type the following code between the Private Sub and End Sub statements:

```
Image1.Visible = True
Label2.Visible = True
```

These program statements make the Image1 and Label2 objects visible on the UserForm when the user clicks Answer.

3 Click the Object drop-down list in the Code window and select the CommandButton2 object.

4 Type **Unload UserForm1** between Private Sub and End Sub, as shown here:

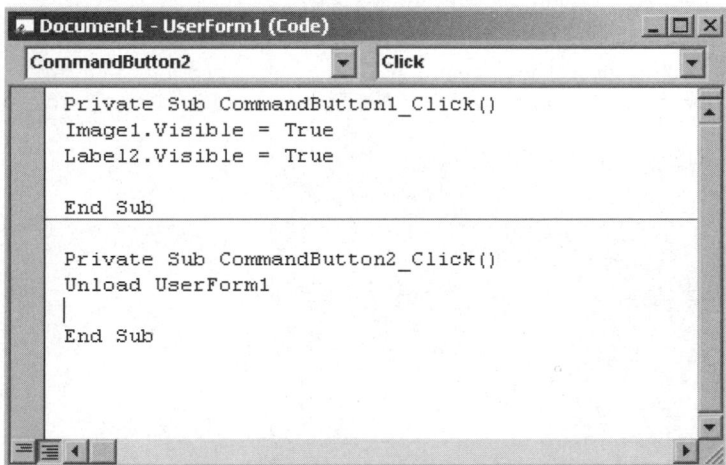

This line unloads the Music Trivia UserForm and closes the macro when the user clicks Quit.

> **note** Use the Unload statement whenever you want to close a UserForm and return to the Word macro that opened it.

5 Now click Save to save your UserForm and macro to disk.

Running the MusicTrivia Macro

Congratulations! You have built your first UserForm. Now return to Word and run the macro. To do so, follow these steps:

1 Click the View Microsoft Word button on the Visual Basic Editor toolbar.

2 Press Alt+F8, and double-click MusicTrivia.

Alt+F8 is the keyboard shortcut to display the Macros dialog box. After you double-click the macro name, Office starts the macro and displays the UserForm on the screen, as seen here (pretend you don't know the answer to our little puzzler):

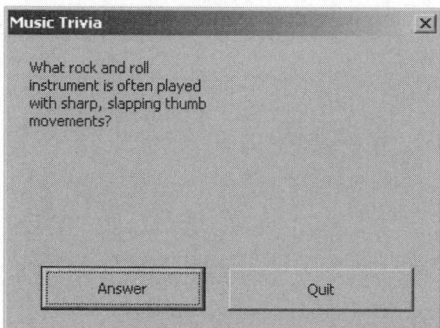

3 Click Answer. The answer and photograph appear on the form, as shown here, just as you stipulated in the CommandButton1 event procedure.

4 Click Quit to close the macro. The UserForm unloads and the macro stops.

> ## Troubleshooting
>
> **Images Don't Disappear as You Requested**
>
> *If a macro you're writing displays images on a UserForm, how and when those images appear is probably very important to you. What do you do if an image or control you want hidden doesn't disappear when you run the macro?*
>
> UserForms provide VBA programmers with several exciting opportunities—you can create a user interface that makes objects appear and disappear at set times or when you get specific feedback from the user of your macro. In this example, if you forgot to set the Image1 and Label2 Visible properties to False when you created the macro, Visual Basic won't hide the picture of the bass guitar (the answer to your puzzler) when the macro starts—spoiling the whole point of the program. If this happened to you, change the Visible properties for those objects using the Properties window. To manage how objects appear and disappear on UserForms, check the Visible property for each object to be sure that you get the right results when the macro starts. You can then adjust the Visible settings programmatically as the macro runs to create interesting visual effects!

Using the TextBox Control to Process Paragraphs

The Label control is useful if you want to display a short sentence on a UserForm, but if you want to exhibit or solicit large amounts of text, you'll want to use the TextBox control. A TextBox is a rectangular storage container for words, sentences, and paragraphs—the basic stuff of Office documents. You can receive text via a TextBox control, and provide your macro with raw material for text processing, comparing, or printing. You can also display text using the TextBox control, which may be material from an existing document, or information from the operating system or the macro itself. Best of all, the TextBox control is designed with ease of use in mind—you can display it with or without scroll bars, and you can select, copy, and paste information to and from a TextBox just like an Office document.

You can configure a text box object to handle multiple lines by setting three properties in the Properties window. Before you set these properties, be sure the text box object is selected.

- Set Multiline to True (to display more than one line).

- Set ScrollBars to 2-fmScrollBarsVertical or 3-fmScrollBarsBoth (to provide scroll bar access to lines that are not visible in the TextBox).

● Set WordWrap to True (to force text wraps at the right margin and disable horizontal scroll bars).

Processing Text in a Word Document

Chap57.doc, located on the companion CD to this book, contains the two macros developed in this chapter: MusicTrivia (a trivia macro) and ParaScan (a Word paragraph formatting utility). If you haven't already downloaded this file, do it now so that you can run the ParaScan macro, which we don't provide detailed construction steps for because of its length. The Chap57 document also contains sample text for the ParaScan macro.

The ParaScan macro uses a text box object to display each paragraph in a Word document, one by one. The macro contains Next, Format, and Delete buttons so that you can quickly scan the document and make formatting adjustments or delete unwanted material quickly. As you practice using the utility, you'll learn more about using program code to manipulate the contents of an Office document. To run this macro, perform the following steps:

1 Start Word (if it isn't already running), and open the Chap57.doc sample file located on the companion CD.

2 Press Alt+F8 to open the Macros dialog box, and then double-click the ParaScan macro. Word runs the macro and displays the ParaScan UserForm, shown here:

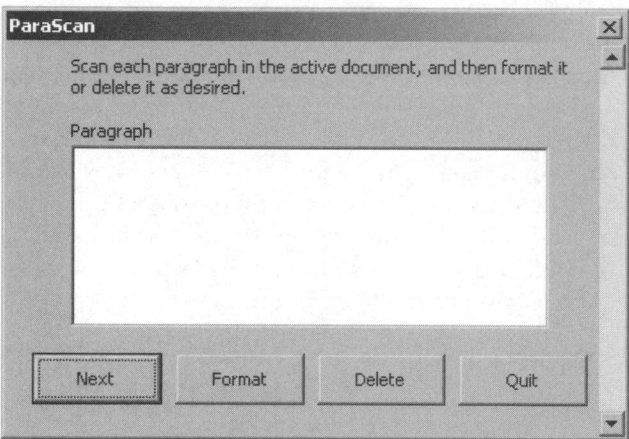

3 Start the macro by clicking Next in the UserForm. The macro selects the first paragraph in the Chap57 document and copies it to the text box object on the UserForm, as seen at the top of the next page.

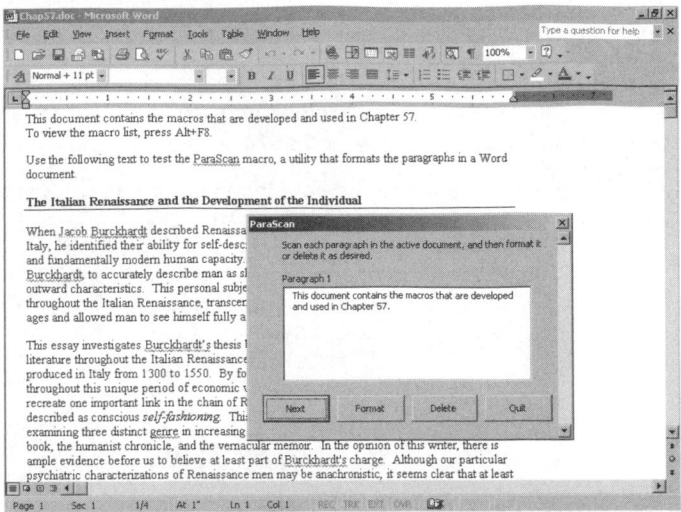

The four buttons at the bottom of the UserForm describe your options in this macro: You can scan the next paragraph by clicking Next; you can format the current paragraph by clicking Format; you can delete the current paragraph by clicking Delete; or you can close the macro by clicking Quit.

4 Click Next seven times to select the eighth paragraph in the document.

This paragraph is too long to fit entirely in the text box, but if you click the text box, a vertical scroll bar appears to let you view the hidden text.

5 Now click Format to change the font formatting in the paragraph. The macro opens the Font dialog box, as shown here, so that you can quickly make the formatting changes you want.

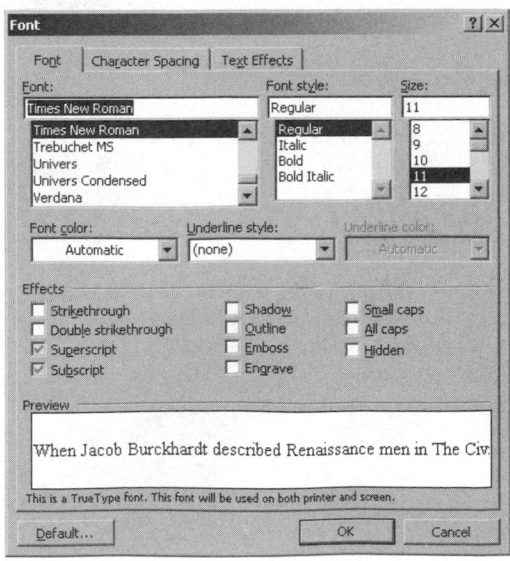

6 Change the font to 9 point, change the color to Blue, and then click OK. The macro formats the selected paragraph as you requested.

7 Click Next again, and then click Delete. The macro highlights a new paragraph and then deletes it when you click Delete.

8 Click Next a few more times to see how the ParaScan macro works, and then click Quit to close the macro.

> **note** We wrote the ParaScan macro primarily for demonstration purposes, but if you'd like to use it to manage your own documents, copy it to the Normal template now using the Organizer tool so that you can use it with all your documents. (Right now, it's available only in the Chap57 document.)

Reviewing the ParaScan Macro Code

ParaScan is a two-part macro. The first part is a simple two-line procedure named ParaScan that uses the Load statement and the Show method to open and display the UserForm2 dialog box on the screen. The real work of the macro happens in the second part, a custom UserForm containing an event procedure for each command button object in the user interface: Next, Format, Delete, and Quit.

Something new you'll see in this macro is a global, or *public*, variable named Num, which keeps track of the current paragraph in the document. A public variable is declared at the top of a module using the Public keyword, in a special section called Declarations. When you declare a public variable in a macro, the variable holds its value in all event procedures in the macro. By way of contrast, variables declared within an event procedure are *local* to the event procedure, meaning they are reset each time an event procedure is finished.

Loading Text in a Text Box Object

When the user clicks Next, the CommandButton1 Click event procedure is executed, as shown here:

```
Private Sub CommandButton1_Click()
Num = Num + 1
ActiveDocument.Paragraphs(num).Range.Select
TextBox1.Text = ActiveDocument.Paragraphs(Num).Range
Label1.Caption = "Paragraph " & Num
If Num = ActiveDocument.Paragraphs.Count Then
    CommandButton1.Enabled = False
End If
End Sub
```

This event procedure increments the Num variable, which tracks the current paragraph number in the document. Using the paragraph number, the routine then selects the current paragraph and copies it to the Text property of the TextBox1 object. The current paragraph is also displayed in the Label1 caption, and if the paragraph is the last one in the document, the Next button is disabled. (Clicking Next with no paragraphs left would cause a run-time error.)

Opening the Font Dialog Box

The second command button object (Format) opens Word's built-in Font dialog box so that the user can format the selected paragraph, using this syntax:

```
Private Sub CommandButton2_Click()
Dialogs(wdDialogFormatFont).Show
End Sub
```

A built-in dialog box is displayed when you use one of Word's dialog box constants with the Dialogs collection and the Show method.

InsideOut

The Dialogs Collection

The Dialogs collection contains a constant name for each dialog box that Word can display. To learn more about these constants, search for "built-in Word dialog boxes, displaying" in the Word Visual Basic online Help.

Deleting a Paragraph

The third command button (Delete) deletes the paragraph that is currently selected in the Word document and is visible in the TextBox1 object. Deleting the text is the easy part—a simple matter of using the Delete method and the active range, as the first line of the event procedure demonstrates:

```
Private Sub CommandButton3_Click()
ActiveDocument.Paragraphs(Num).Range.Delete
If Num >= 2 Then Num = Num - 1
ActiveDocument.Paragraphs(Num).Range.Select
TextBox1.Text = ActiveDocument.Paragraphs(Num).Range
Label1.Caption = "Paragraph " & Num
If Num = ActiveDocument.Paragraphs.Count Then
    CommandButton1.Enabled = False
End If
End Sub
```

```
Private Sub CommandButton4_Click()
Unload UserForm2
End Sub
```

536

Index of Troubleshooting Topics

Index to Troubleshooting Topics

Index to Troubleshooting Topics

Index

Note to the reader: **Italicized page numbers refer to figures, tables, and illustrations.**

margins
header and footer, 532
hiding, 547
marking, 541
mirror, 540
paragraph, 315
rulers for setting, 541–42
setting on pages, 536–42
workbook, 716–17
Margins tab, Page Setup dialog box, 536–40, *536*
Mark Index Entry dialog box, 436, *436*
marking
e-mail headers, 1028–30, *1029*
languages, 504–6
margins, 541
slides, 945–46, *945*
marquees, 592
master documents, 425
Master pages, 1402
master slides
editing, 892–95
formatting, 894–95
multiple masters, 857, 893
mathematical equations, 147–50
mathematical operators
Excel program, 616, 738, *738*, 739
Visual Basic, *1501*
MDI. *See* **multiple document interface**
measurement units
character formatting, 306–7
margins, 542
media clips. *See also* **movie clips; pictures; sounds**
defined, 115
importing into Clip Organizer, 124–25
inserting into documents, 119–20, 122
inserting into slides, 913–14
keywords assigned to, 125
managing, 123–24
searching for, 117–18, 121
Meeting form
Appointment tab, 1046–48, *1047*
Scheduling tab, 1051, *1051*
Tracking tab, 1050, *1050*
Meeting Minder tool, 946–47, *946*
meetings
converting appointments to, 1050
defined, 1040
online, 1042, 1067
planning, 1051–52, *1051*

meetings *(continued)*
proposing new times for, 1048, 1049, 1051
recurring, 1047
requesting of contacts, 1067
scheduling in Outlook, 1046–52
menu bar
adding menus to, 211
resetting, 215
menus. *See also* **shortcut menus**
adding to the menu bar, 211
changing icons on, 214–15
commands added to, 210–11
customizing, 205–6, 209–16
defined, 209
deleting, 211
items listed on, 209
macro command on, 1465
modifying items on, 212, *212–14*
removing items from, 211
restoring to default configuration, 215
usage data about, 222
Visual Basic, 1473–74, *1473*
voice command mode and, 96, 97
Merge Styles dialog box, 675–76, *675*
Merge Workbooks command, 704–5
merging. *See also* **mail merge feature**
documents, 455–56, 468
styles from workbooks, 674–75
workbooks, 704–5
Message form, 1023, *1024*
Message Options dialog box, *1035*
Messages view, Outlook program, 1023, *1023*
meta tags, 1458
methods, Visual Basic, 1485
Microphone Check window, 959
microphones, 90–91, 461, 941, 959
Microphone Wizard, 88–89, 99
Microsoft Access
action queries, 1330–32
automatic data-saving feature, 1274
calculated fields, 1325–27, *1327*
closing databases, 1274
comparing other Office applications to, 1259–60
converting Excel lists to, 794–95, *795*
creating databases, 1267–70
creating tables, 1277–80
crosstab queries, 1312, 1328–29, 1331
customizing forms, 1339–54

Microsoft Access *(continued)*
customizing tables, 1280–90
data access pages, 1266, *1266*, 1355–60, *1356*
Database window, 1271–73, *1271*
Datasheet view, 1273, 1277–78, *1278*, 1296–1310, *1296*
data types, 1284, *1285–86*
deleting records, 1298–99
designing and planning databases, 1263–67
enforcing referential integrity, 1294–95
entering and editing database data, 1297–98, *1297*
exporting data, 1279
Field Builder, 1282
field property settings, 1284–90
file formats, 1275
filtering records, 1304–10
finding and replacing text, 1299
forms, 1265–66, *1266*, 1333–55
modifying queries, 1316–27
modifying reports, 1370–75
new features, 16
opening databases, 1275
overview of, 1259–63
previewing reports, 1375
primary key designation, 1290
printing reports, 1376
project files, 1270
queries, 1265, *1265*, 1311–32
reports, 1267, *1267*, 1361–76
saving databases, 1274
sorting records, 1303–4, 1310
spelling checker, 1352
subdatasheets, 1302–3, *1302*
summary queries, 1322–25
table relationships, 1291–96
tasks performed by, 8
top-value queries, 1320–21
views available in, 1273
Microsoft Developer Network (MSDN), 39
Microsoft Download Center, 38
Microsoft Equation, 147–50
Microsoft Excel
adding rows and columns, 640
add-in utilities, 730–31, 810–18
aligning cell information, 650–54
analyzing lists, 791–94
animating elements, 923–25
arithmetic operators, 738, *738*
artwork used in, 618–19
AutoComplete feature, 612, 779

About the Authors

Michael Halvorson

is the author or co-author of over a dozen computer books, including *Running Microsoft Office 2000, Microsoft Visual Basic 6 Professional Step by Step, Learn Visual Basic Now, and Microsoft Word 97/Visual Basic Step by Step.* He worked at Microsoft Corporation from 1985 to 1993, where he was employed as a technical editor, acquisitions editor, and localization manager. He earned a B.A. in computer science from Pacific Lutheran University in Tacoma, Washington, and M.A. and Ph.D. degrees in history from the University of Washington in Seattle.

Michael has received awards from the Computer Press and Society for Technical Communication for his work as a technical writer, and the Thomas M. Power Award for excellence in historical writing. In 1998, he was a fellow at the Herzog August Bibliothek in Wolfenbüttel, Germany. He is currently a visiting assistant professor of history at Pacific Lutheran University.

Michael J. Young

has written books for computer users and developers since 1986. He has written more than two dozen computer books, including the best-selling *Running Microsoft Office* series (with Michael Halvorson) and *XML Step by Step*, both from Microsoft Press. He has used and written about Microsoft Office applications for more than a decade. He has also written extensively on MS-DOS, Windows, C, C++, Visual Basic, Java, XML, and animation, game, and graphics programming. Michael graduated from Stanford University with a degree in philosophy. He later studied computer science at several California colleges, completing coursework through the first year of graduate studies. Currently, he lives and works in Taos, New Mexico, where he is often seen frequenting the local coffeehouses or exploring the Sangre de Cristo Mountains.

You can contact Michael and find out more about what he does through his Web site at *www.mjyOnline.com*.

The manuscript for this book was prepared and galleyed using Microsoft Word 2000. Pages were composed by nSightWorks using Adobe PageMaker 6.52 for Windows, with text in Minion and display type in Syntax. Composed pages were delivered to the printer as electronic prepress files.

cover illustration
Daman Studio

cover designer
GIRVIN / Strategic Branding & Design

interior graphic designer
James D. Kramer

for nSight, Inc. *(www.nSightWorks.com)*

project manager
Susan H. McClung

technical editors
Don Lesser, Mannie White, Kitty Dougherty, Doug Slaughter, Kathleen Cinelli, Margaret Lampron, and Kate McLean

copy editors
Joseph Gustaitis and Teresa F. Horton

desktop specialists
Joanna Zito, Patty Fagan, Mary Beth McDaniel, Angela Montoya

proofreaders
Janet Cocker, Rebecca Merz, Katie Pickett

indexers
James Minkin and Rebecca Plunkett

Work smarter
as you experience
Office XP
inside out!

You know your way around the Office suite. Now dig into Microsoft Office XP applications and *really* put your PC to work! These supremely organized references pack hundreds of timesaving solutions, troubleshooting tips and tricks, and handy workarounds in concise, fast-answer format. All of this comprehensive information goes deep into the nooks and crannies of each Office application and accessory. Discover the best and fastest ways to perform everyday tasks, and challenge yourself to new levels of Office mastery with INSIDE OUT titles!

- MICROSOFT® OFFICE XP INSIDE OUT

- MICROSOFT WORD VERSION 2002 INSIDE OUT

- MICROSOFT EXCEL VERSION 2002 INSIDE OUT

- MICROSOFT OUTLOOK® VERSION 2002 INSIDE OUT

- MICROSOFT ACCESS VERSION 2002 INSIDE OUT

- MICROSOFT FRONTPAGE® VERSION 2002 INSIDE OUT

- MICROSOFT VISIO® VERSION 2002 INSIDE OUT

Microsoft®

mspress.microsoft.com

Target your
solution and fix it
yourself—fast!

When you're stuck with a computer problem, you need answers right now. *Troubleshooting* books can help. They'll guide you to the source of the problem and show you how to solve it right away. Use easy diagnostic flowcharts to identify problems. Get ready solutions with clear, step-by-step instructions. Go to quick-access charts with *Top 20 Problems* and *Prevention Tips*. Find even more solutions with handy *Tips* and *Quick Fixes.* Walk through the remedy with plenty of screen shots to keep you on track. Find what you need fast with the extensive, easy-reference index. And keep trouble at bay with the Troubleshooting Web site—updated every month with new FREE problem-solving information. Get the answers you need to get back to business fast with *Troubleshooting* books.

Self-paced
training
that works
as hard as you do!

Information-packed STEP BY STEP courses are the most effective way to teach yourself how to complete tasks with Microsoft® Office XP. Numbered steps and scenario-based lessons with practice files on CD-ROM make it easy to find your way while learning tasks and procedures. Work through every lesson or choose your own starting point—with STEP BY STEP modular design and straightforward writing style, *you* drive the instruction. And the books are constructed with lay-flat binding so you can follow the text with both hands at the keyboard. Select STEP BY STEP titles also provide complete, cost-effective preparation for the Microsoft Office User Specialist (MOUS) credential. It's an excellent way for you or your organization to take a giant step toward workplace productivity.

- **Microsoft Office XP Step by Step**
  ISBN 0-7356-1294-3

- **Microsoft Word Version 2002 Step by Step**
  ISBN 0-7356-1295-1

- **Microsoft Excel Version 2002 Step by Step**
  ISBN 0-7356-1296-X

- **Microsoft PowerPoint® Version 2002 Step by Step**
  ISBN 0-7356-1297-8

- **Microsoft Outlook® Version 2002 Step by Step**
  ISBN 0-7356-1298-6

- **Microsoft FrontPage® Version 2002 Step by Step**
  ISBN 0-7356-1300-1

- **Microsoft Access Version 2002 Step by Step**
  ISBN 0-7356-1299-4

- **Microsoft Project Version 2002 Step by Step**
  ISBN 0-7356-1301-X

- **Microsoft Visio® Version 2002 Step by Step**
  ISBN 0-7356-1302-8

mspress.microsoft.com

Get a **Free**
e-mail newsletter, updates,
special offers, links to related books,
and more when you
register on line!

Register your Microsoft Press® title on our Web site and you'll get a FREE subscription to our e-mail newsletter, *Microsoft Press Book Connections.* You'll find out about newly released and upcoming books and learning tools, online events, software downloads, special offers and coupons for Microsoft Press customers, and information about major Microsoft® product releases. You can also read useful additional information about all the titles we publish, such as detailed book descriptions, tables of contents and indexes, sample chapters, links to related books and book series, author biographies, and reviews by other customers.

Registration is easy. Just visit this Web page and fill in your information:

http://mspress.microsoft.com/register

Microsoft®

- -

PRODUCT ("Support Services"). Use of Support Services is governed by the Microsoft policies and programs described in the user manual, in "on-line" documentation, and/or in other Microsoft-provided materials. Any supplemental software code provided to you as part of the Support Services shall be considered part of the SOFTWARE PRODUCT and subject to the terms and conditions of this EULA. With respect to technical information you provide to Microsoft as part of the Support Services, Microsoft may use such information for its business purposes, including for product support and development. Microsoft will not utilize such technical information in a form that personally identifies you.

- **EULA Rights Transfer.** You may permanently transfer all of your rights under this EULA, provided you retain no copies, you transfer all of the SOFTWARE PRODUCT (including all component parts, the media and printed materials, any upgrades, this EULA, and, if applicable, the Certificate of Authenticity), **and** the recipient agrees to the terms of this EULA.

- **Termination.** Without prejudice to any other rights, Microsoft may terminate this EULA if you fail to comply with the terms and conditions of this EULA. In such event, you must destroy all copies of the SOFTWARE PRODUCT and all of its component parts.

3. **COPYRIGHT.** All title and copyrights in and to the SOFTWARE PRODUCT (including but not limited to any images, photographs, animations, video, audio, music, text, SAMPLE CODE, REDISTRIBUTABLES, and "applets" incorporated into the SOFTWARE PRODUCT) and any copies of the SOFTWARE PRODUCT are owned by Microsoft or its suppliers. The SOFTWARE PRODUCT is protected by copyright laws and international treaty provisions. Therefore, you must treat the SOFTWARE PRODUCT like any other copyrighted material **except** that you may install the SOFTWARE PRODUCT on a single computer provided you keep the original solely for backup or archival purposes. You may not copy the printed materials accompanying the SOFTWARE PRODUCT.

4. **U.S. GOVERNMENT RESTRICTED RIGHTS.** The SOFTWARE PRODUCT and documentation are provided with RESTRICTED RIGHTS. Use, duplication, or disclosure by the Government is subject to restrictions as set forth in subparagraph (c)(1)(ii) of the Rights in Technical Data and Computer Software clause at DFARS 252.227-7013 or subparagraphs (c)(1) and (2) of the Commercial Computer Software—Restricted Rights at 48 CFR 52.227-19, as applicable. Manufacturer is Microsoft Corporation/One Microsoft Way/Redmond, WA 98052-6399.

5. **EXPORT RESTRICTIONS.** You agree that you will not export or re-export the SOFTWARE PRODUCT, any part thereof, or any process or service that is the direct product of the SOFTWARE PRODUCT (the foregoing collectively referred to as the "Restricted Components"), to any country, person, entity, or end user subject to U.S. export restrictions. You specifically agree not to export or re-export any of the Restricted Components (i) to any country to which the U.S. has embargoed or restricted the export of goods or services, which currently include, but are not necessarily limited to, Cuba, Iran, Iraq, Libya, North Korea, Sudan, and Syria, or to any national of any such country, wherever located, who intends to transmit or transport the Restricted Components back to such country; (ii) to any end user who you know or have reason to know will utilize the Restricted Components in the design, development, or production of nuclear, chemical, or biological weapons; or (iii) to any end user who has been prohibited from participating in U.S. export transactions by any federal agency of the U.S. government. You warrant and represent that neither the BXA nor any other U.S. federal agency has suspended, revoked, or denied your export privileges.

DISCLAIMER OF WARRANTY

NO WARRANTIES OR CONDITIONS. MICROSOFT EXPRESSLY DISCLAIMS ANY WARRANTY OR CONDITION FOR THE SOFTWARE PRODUCT. THE SOFTWARE PRODUCT AND ANY RELATED DOCUMENTATION IS PROVIDED "AS IS" WITHOUT WARRANTY OR CONDITION OF ANY KIND, EITHER EXPRESS OR IMPLIED, INCLUDING, WITHOUT LIMITATION, THE IMPLIED WARRANTIES OF MERCHANTABILITY, FITNESS FOR A PARTICULAR PURPOSE, OR NONINFRINGEMENT. THE ENTIRE RISK ARISING OUT OF USE OR PERFORMANCE OF THE SOFTWARE PRODUCT REMAINS WITH YOU.

LIMITATION OF LIABILITY. TO THE MAXIMUM EXTENT PERMITTED BY APPLICABLE LAW, IN NO EVENT SHALL MICROSOFT OR ITS SUPPLIERS BE LIABLE FOR ANY SPECIAL, INCIDENTAL, INDIRECT, OR CONSEQUENTIAL DAMAGES WHATSOEVER (INCLUDING, WITHOUT LIMITATION, DAMAGES FOR LOSS OF BUSINESS PROFITS, BUSINESS INTERRUPTION, LOSS OF BUSINESS INFORMATION, OR ANY OTHER PECUNIARY LOSS) ARISING OUT OF THE USE OF OR INABILITY TO USE THE SOFTWARE PRODUCT OR THE PROVISION OF OR FAILURE TO PROVIDE SUPPORT SERVICES, EVEN IF MICROSOFT HAS BEEN ADVISED OF THE POSSIBILITY OF SUCH DAMAGES. IN ANY CASE, MICROSOFT'S ENTIRE LIABILITY UNDER ANY PROVISION OF THIS EULA SHALL BE LIMITED TO THE GREATER OF THE AMOUNT ACTUALLY PAID BY YOU FOR THE SOFTWARE PRODUCT OR US$5.00; PROVIDED, HOWEVER, IF YOU HAVE ENTERED INTO A MICROSOFT SUPPORT SERVICES AGREEMENT, MICROSOFT'S ENTIRE LIABILITY REGARDING SUPPORT SERVICES SHALL BE GOVERNED BY THE TERMS OF THAT AGREEMENT. BECAUSE SOME STATES AND JURISDICTIONS DO NOT ALLOW THE EXCLUSION OR LIMITATION OF LIABILITY, THE ABOVE LIMITATION MAY NOT APPLY TO YOU.

MISCELLANEOUS

This EULA is governed by the laws of the State of Washington USA, except and only to the extent that applicable law mandates governing law of a different jurisdiction.

Should you have any questions concerning this EULA, or if you desire to contact Microsoft for any reason, please contact the Microsoft subsidiary serving your country, or write: Microsoft Sales Information Center/One Microsoft Way/Redmond, WA 98052-6399.

MICROSOFT LICENSE AGREEMENT

(Book Companion CD)

SOFTWARE PRODUCT LICENSE

The SOFTWARE PRODUCT is protected by United States copyright laws and international copyright treaties, as well as other intellectual property laws and treaties. The SOFTWARE PRODUCT is licensed, not sold.

1. GRANT OF LICENSE. This EULA grants you the following rights:

a. Software Product. You may install and use one copy of the SOFTWARE PRODUCT on a single computer. The primary user of the computer on which the SOFTWARE PRODUCT is installed may make a second copy for his or her exclusive use on a portable computer.

b. Storage/Network Use. You may also store or install a copy of the SOFTWARE PRODUCT on a storage device, such as a network server, used only to install or run the SOFTWARE PRODUCT on your other computers over an internal network; however, you must acquire and dedicate a license for each separate computer on which the SOFTWARE PRODUCT is installed or run from the storage device. A license for the SOFTWARE PRODUCT may not be shared or used concurrently on different computers.

c. License Pak. If you have acquired this EULA in a Microsoft License Pak, you may make the number of additional copies of the computer software portion of the SOFTWARE PRODUCT authorized on the printed copy of this EULA, and you may use each copy in the manner specified above. You are also entitled to make a corresponding number of secondary copies for portable computer use as specified above.

d. Sample Code. Solely with respect to portions, if any, of the SOFTWARE PRODUCT that are identified within the SOFTWARE PRODUCT as sample code (the "SAMPLE CODE"):

   i. Use and Modification. Microsoft grants you the right to use and modify the source code version of the SAMPLE CODE, *provided* you comply with subsection (d)(iii) below. You may not distribute the SAMPLE CODE, or any modified version of the SAMPLE CODE, in source code form.

   ii. Redistributable Files. Provided you comply with subsection (d)(iii) below, Microsoft grants you a nonexclusive, royalty-free right to reproduce and distribute the object code version of the SAMPLE CODE and of any modified SAMPLE CODE, other than SAMPLE CODE (or any modified version thereof) designated as not redistributable in the Readme file that forms a part of the SOFTWARE PRODUCT (the "Non-Redistributable Sample Code"). All SAMPLE CODE other than the Non-Redistributable Sample Code is collectively referred to as the "REDISTRIBUTABLES."

   iii. Redistribution Requirements. If you redistribute the REDISTRIBUTABLES, you agree to: (i) distribute the REDISTRIBUTABLES in object code form only in conjunction with and as a part of your software application product; (ii) not use Microsoft's name, logo, or trademarks to market your software application product; (iii) include a valid copyright notice on your software application product; (iv) indemnify, hold harmless, and defend Microsoft from and against any claims or lawsuits, including attorney's fees, that arise or result from the use or distribution of your software application product; and (v) not permit further distribution of the REDISTRIBUTABLES by your end user. Contact Microsoft for the applicable royalties due and other licensing terms for all other uses and/or distribution of the REDISTRIBUTABLES.

2. DESCRIPTION OF OTHER RIGHTS AND LIMITATIONS.

   • **Limitations on Reverse Engineering, Decompilation, and Disassembly.** You may not reverse engineer, decompile, or disassemble the SOFTWARE PRODUCT, except and only to the extent that such activity is expressly permitted by applicable law notwithstanding this limitation.

   • **Separation of Components.** The SOFTWARE PRODUCT is licensed as a single product. Its component parts may not be separated for use on more than one computer.

   • **Rental.** You may not rent, lease, or lend the SOFTWARE PRODUCT.

   • **Support Services.** Microsoft may, but is not obligated to, provide you with support services related to the SOFTWARE